THE ANNOTATED®

SHERLOCK HOLMES

SIR ARTHUR CONAN DOYLE

The creator of Sherlock Holmes and John H. Watson, M.D., from a pastel portrait by Henry Gates, 1933, after an oil painting by the same artist, 1927. The original hangs in the National Portrait Gallery, London, a presentation by Sir Arthur's daughter, Lady Bromet.

THE ANNOTATED®

SHERLOCK HOLMES

THE FOUR NOVELS AND FIFTY-SIX SHORT STORIES COMPLETE

Lavishly illustrated with maps, diagrams,
photographs and drawings.

SIR ARTHUR CONAN DOYLE

Edited, with an Introduction, Notes, and Bibliography by William S. Baring-Gould

WINGS BOOKS
NEW YORK • AVENEL, NEW JERSEY

This 1992 edition is published by Wings Books,
distributed by Outlet Book Company, Inc.,
a Random House Company,
40 Engelhard Avenue, Avenel, New Jersey 07001,
by arrangement with Clarkson N. Potter, Inc./Publisher.

Grateful acknowledgment is given for the following: The text of
the Sherlock Holmes stories is used by permission of the Estate of
Sir Arthur Conan Doyle, and by arrangement with Doubleday &
Company, Inc. Photographs by G. F. Allen used by permission.
Photograph entitled "Wicken Lodge, Wicken Fen," by J. Allen
Cash. Used by permission. Photographs from *In the Footsteps of
Sherlock Holmes*, copyright © 1960 by Michael Harrison. Used
by permission of the author. Illustrations from *Sherlock Holmes*,
edited and abridged by Charles Verral and illustrated by Tom
Gill, copyright © 1957 by Western Publishing Company, Inc.
Used by permission of the publisher. Illustrations on pages 251,
261, 429, and 436 in Volume I, and page 342 in Volume II,
by Joseph Camana, from *Cases of Sherlock Holmes* by William
Kottmeyer, copyright 1947 by McGraw Hill Book Co. Used by
permission of the publisher. Map entitled "Haslital," copyright
Arts Graphiques Brugger S. A. Used by permission of the
publisher. Photograph entitled "Farnham" by Reece Winston.
Used by permission of the photographer.

ANNOTATED is a registered trademark,
and CLARKSON N. POTTER, POTTER, and colophon
are trademarks of Clarkson N. Potter, Inc.

Printed and bound in the United States of America

Library of Congress Cataloging-in-Publication Data

Doyle, Arthur Conan, Sir, 1859–1930.
    The annotated® Sherlock Holmes : the four novels and fifty-
six short stories complete / by Sir Arthur Conan Doyle ; edited,
with an introduction, notes, and bibliography by William S.
Baring-Gould ; illustrated with maps, diagrams, coats-of-arms,
photographs, and drawings by Charles Doyle...and numerous
others.
    p.   cm.
    Includes bibliographical references.
    ISBN 0-517-48102-2 : $29.99
    1. Holmes, Sherlock (Fictitious character)—Fiction.
2. Detective and mystery stories, English.   I. Baring-Gould,
William Stuart, 1913–   II. Title.
[PR4620.A5B3   1992]
    823′.8—dc20
                                          92-14297
                                          CIP

8 7 6 5 4 3 2 1

THE ANNOTATED®

SHERLOCK HOLMES

VOLUME I

TABLE OF CONTENTS

I trust that the younger public may find these romances of interest, and that here and there one of the older generation may recapture an ancient thrill.

ARTHUR CONAN DOYLE

Written in June, 1929, for his Preface to
The Complete Sherlock Holmes Long Stories

The enthusiast likes to dream of the great omnibus volume in which the whole Sherlockian codex would be annotated from end to end for a new generation.

CHRISTOPHER MORLEY

Written circa *November, 1943, for his Introduction to* Sherlock Holmes and Dr. Watson:
A Textbook of Friendship

I. TWO DOCTORS AND A DETECTIVE:

SIR ARTHUR CONAN DOYLE,
JOHN H. WATSON, M.D., AND
MR. SHERLOCK HOLMES OF BAKER STREET

. . . the most famous and best beloved
physician in literature . . .—VINCENT STARRETT
Introduction to the Limited Edition Club's
The Adventures of Sherlock Holmes

. . . the most convincing, the most brilliant,
the most congenial and well-loved
of all detectives of fiction.—A. E. Murch,
The Development of the Detective Novel

STEEL TRUE
BLADE STRAIGHT
ARTHUR CONAN DOYLE
KNIGHT
PATRIOT, PHYSICIAN & MAN OF LETTERS

—His Epitaph

"I HEAR OF SHERLOCK EVERYWHERE SINCE YOU BECAME HIS CHRONICLER"

[Mycroft Holmes to John H. Watson, M.D., "The Greek Interpreter"]

"It is possible that there are some, who will read this, who have never read *The Valley of Fear*," said Mr. Anthony Boucher, introducing that last of the Sherlock Holmes novels to Limited Editions Club subscribers in 1952. "It is probable that there are others who have not read it recently and remember no details. . . . If you belong to either of these groups, . . . forego, at least for the time being, the rest of this introduction . . ."

We echo Mr. Boucher. If you have never read a Sherlock Holmes story, or if you have not read one for a long time—advance immediately to the opening story in this book and continue, perhaps, until you have reached the end of the volume. Then, if you have a mind to, kindly return to this introduction.

•   •   •

And now that we are both well acquainted with Mr. Sherlock Holmes and Dr. John H. Watson, let us settle down to a leisurely discussion of the detective, the doctor, and the man who created them both; the tributes that have been paid to all three; and some of the major problems raised by the "Sacred Writings," or Saga, or Canon.**1**

"Dr. Watson, Mr. Sherlock Holmes," said young Stamford, introducing them. And having performed his catalytic task, he disappeared from the Saga forever.**2**

Holmes had solved problems before his meeting with Watson; he was to handle, solo, at least one case ("The Adventure of the Lion's Mane") after the partnership was dissolved by his retirement in late 1903; but the adventures we remember best are those in which the detective and the doctor both played a part, and which Watson then recounted as part of his long series of reminiscences.

Watson's handwriting was the despair of typesetters. And it seems curious that this should have been so: as Professor Remsen Ten Eyck Schenck has pointed out ("Holmes, Cryptanalysis and the Dancing Men"), "A large part of Watson's professional activity . . . lay in writing and compounding prescriptions. In this connection, the importance of accuracy had been most thoroughly drilled into him: if he should confuse berberine and bebeerine, grams with grains, ounces with drachms (the symbols for these two differ only slightly), it could easily cost a patient's life."

1 Or Conan.

2 Unless, turned forger, he was also that Archie Stamford whom Holmes, in "The Adventure of the Solitary Cyclist," referred to as having been captured near Farnham, on the borders of Surrey.

3 Writing as he often did of events in the very recent past, Watson had to be exceedingly careful that he did not land himself, or Holmes, or both, in serious legal trouble. In a defense of Watson as a writer, Mr. Humfrey Michell has said that: "Actually, he was the most painstaking and accurate of chroniclers, whose elaborate notes and memoranda on each case were models of laborious compilation; in fact they constituted the official records of Holmes' professional practice, in which accuracy was necessarily beyond all other considerations. When he set out to tell the stories to the public, it was another matter, and, with considerable ingenuity by confusing dates and places, he was able to throw the inquisitive so completely off the scent that identification becomes impossible."

4 "We are thus forced to the conclusion, unwilling though we may be to admit it, that Watson did at least sometimes alter his data or embellish them, to strengthen the story in some way."—Nathan L. Bengis, "Take a Bow, Dr. Watson."

"Watson loved to dramatize and romanticize his reports; and if accuracy of facts suffered, so be it."—Hyman Parker, "Birdy Edwards and the Scowrers Reconsidered."

PICARDY PLACE, EDINBURGH

Where, on May 22, 1859, Sir Arthur Conan Doyle was born. Photograph by Morris Rosenblum, *The Baker Street Journal*, December, 1963.

He seems seldom to have checked proof against his original manuscript; a flagrant example is "The Adventure of Wisteria Lodge," in which Watson let "1892" stand as the year of the adventure (in 1892, Watson supposedly thought Holmes dead and buried beneath the waters of the Reichenbach Fall in Switzerland).

His memory was often faulty. To take but one instance: in "The Adventure of the Veiled Lodger," Holmes asks Watson, "Have you no recollection of the Abbas Parva tragedy?" "None, Holmes." "And yet you were with me then."

He had a disregard for time-sequence relationships and an apparently complete lack of "time-sense." "With one shining exception ["The Adventure of the Devil's Foot"]," the late Professor Jay Finley Christ wrote ("An Adventure in the Lower Criticism; Part I: Doctor Watson and the Calendar"), "whenever a reminiscence gives us (whether specifically or deducibly) the *year* of action, together with the *month*, the *day of the month*, and the *day of the week*, we are led into confusion, frustration and high glee (?)."

Too, Victorian discreetness—and his own native shrewdness**3**—frequently made it necessary for him to veil a name, a place, a date, the exact nature of an event. His writings are studded with phrases like "due suppression," "any details which would help the reader to identify the college or the criminal would be injudicious and offensive," "a carefully guarded account," "somewhat vague in certain details," "my reticence," "I am obliged to be particularly careful to avoid any indiscretion," "no confidence will be abused."

Add to this the fact that Watson was a master storyteller, and that no small part of his skill as a writer was his ability to communicate to the reader the full drama of a situation. To do so, as he himself admits, sometimes required "a little editing." How revealing is his statement in "The Adventure of the Illustrious Client": "Then [Holmes] told the story, which I would repeat in this way . . ."**4**

And we can all be thankful that Dr. Watson wrote as he did: half the fun in reading and rereading the Saga is that of catching him out—as generations of his admirers have been discovering for more than three-quarters of a century now.

Of course, the truth of the matter is that Watson wrote as he did because his creator—and the creator of Holmes and young Stamford—was also a master storyteller who was sometimes discourteous to his "facts" for the sake of his story.

"In short stories it has always seemed to me that so long as you produce your dramatic effect, accuracy of detail matters little," Conan Doyle once said. "I have never striven for it and have made some bad mistakes in consequence. What matter if I hold my readers?"

What matter indeed? And hold his readers he did.

Arthur Conan Doyle, the author of the Sherlock Holmes stories (and of many other writings, fictional and nonfictional, which he held to be far more important works) was born at Picardy Place, Edinburgh, on May 22, 1859. He was the son of Charles Doyle, a civil servant and spare-time painter of Irish descent, and his wife Mary Foley Doyle, also of Irish parentage.

On both sides, the line was distinguished: Mrs. Doyle could trace her ancestry back to the ancient house of Percy-Louvain, three times allied by marriage with princesses of the Plantagenet line.

As for the Doyles, they came originally from Pont d'Oilly near Rouen, in Normandy. They took part in the conquest of Ireland, and in 1333, Alexander d'Oilly was granted lands in County Wexford by King Edward III. A Roman Catholic family, the Doyles of the 17th and 18th centuries were gradually evicted from their lands. At the beginning of the last century, John, Sir Arthur's grandfather, left Ireland to settle in London. There, under the initials "HB," he soon became the leading political caricaturist of his day. He was the first but by no means the last of his family to enter the *Dictionary of National Biography*. Three of his sons won the same recognition: James, as a historian and genealogist; Henry, as an artist and Director of the National Gallery, Dublin; Richard, also an artist and a friend of men like Dickens and Thackeray (we shall have more to say of "Dicky" Doyle later).**5**

Conan Doyle's schooling began at the age of seven and continued, when he was nine, at Hodder, the preparatory school of Stonyhurst College, which he attended until he was sixteen. A year of schooling at Feldkirch in Austria was followed by his return to Edinburgh in the summer of 1876. Edinburgh University had a well-deserved reputation for the fine medical training available there, and it was soon decided that young Arthur should become a doctor. He entered the University in October, 1876, and commenced what he later called a "long weary grind at botany, chemistry, anatomy,

5 For the growing number of people who take an interest in heraldry, here is the blazoning of the Doyle family coat-of-arms: Quarterly, 1st grand quarter: argent, within a bordure counter-compony or and sable, 3 bucks' heads gules, erased, and attired or, arranged 2 & 1, for DOYLE. 2nd grand quarter: argent, a fess between 3 tre-foils sable, within a bordure of the last, for FOLEY. 3rd grand quarter: quarterly, sable and erminois; in the 1st quarter a sword in bend sinis-ter argent, pommel and hilt or, encircled by a wreath of the last; in the 4th a cinquefoil of the 3rd; in the center chief, pendent from a crimson ribbon, bordered blue, a representation of the golden cross and clasps presented to Maj.-Gen. Pack by H.M. George III, in testimony of his royal approbation of the signal valor displayed by the said Maj.-Gen. Pack in diverse actions with the enemy in the Peninsula of Spain, for PACK. 4th grand quarter: quarterly, 1st & 4th, or, a lion rampant azure between 3 trefoils vert; 2nd & 3rd, azure, 3 fusils in fess or between 2 silver trefoils in pale, all within a border compony gules and argent, for PERCY. Crest: out of a ducal coronet, a buck's head gules, attired or. Moto: *Fortitudine Vincit*.

"... DURING MY LAST YEARS AT THE UNIVERSITY ..."
(THE MUSGRAVE RITUAL)

Arthur Conan Doyle as a student at Edinburgh. From *Introducing Mr. Sherlock Holmes*.

"... OUR OWN BLAZONINGS AND CHARGES ..."
(THE MUSGRAVE RITUAL)

Sir Arthur Conan Doyle's bookplate, showing the family coat-of-arms. *The Baker Street Journal*, September, 1962.

EX LIBRIS

FORTITUDINE VINCIT

SIR ARTHUR CONAN DOYLE
D.L., L.L.D., M.D.

. . . PICKED UP A HOUSE CALLED BUSH VILLA . . .

From *Murder for Pleasure*, by Howard Haycraft.

6 In the period with which we are concerned, the British shilling was worth slightly less than a quarter in U.S. currency, making the British pound of twenty shillings worth approximately five American dollars. These figures will be convenient, if not strictly accurate, to use in our Introduction and Notes, but the reader need not remember them: we will translate pence, shillings, and pounds into pennies, quarters, and dollars as we go along.

7 There seems little doubt that "Dr. Cullingworth" in Conan Doyle's autobiographical novel, *The Stark Munro Letters*, represents the eccentric Dr. Budd.

8 When the income-tax paper arrived that year, Conan Doyle filled it up to show he was not liable. The authorities returned the form with the words, "Most unsatisfactory" scrawled across it. Conan Doyle wrote, "I entirely agree"—and sent the form back to the authorities.

9 One of which, published anonymously, was acclaimed by the critics as the work of Robert Louis Stevenson.

physiology, and a whole list of compulsory subjects, many of which have a very indirect bearing upon the art of curing."

Trying to help his family in vacation times (Charles Doyle fathered six other children), he worked as a medical assistant to doctors in Sheffield; Ruyton-of-the-eleven-towns, a tiny place in Shropshire; and Aston, Birmingham, where he was assistant to Dr. Reginald Ratcliffe Hoare at Clifton House, Aston Road North, a site now marked by a plaque (as is the birthplace of Sir Arthur Conan Doyle in Edinburgh).

It was here that Conan Doyle's first short story, "The Mystery of Sassassa Valley," was written and sold for £3 3s. ($15.75)**6** to *Chamber's Journal*, where it was published in the issue of October, 1879.

In February of 1880, Conan Doyle accepted a job as surgeon on a whaling ship, the *Hope*, and spent seven months in the Arctic. In the latter part of 1880 he returned to Aston where he remained until early in 1881 as assistant to Dr. Hoare, after which he resumed his studies for the degree of Bachelor of Medicine, which he took in August, 1881, as he said, "with fair but not notable distinction."

A voyage to Africa as medical officer on the ship *Mayumba* followed; then he went into partnership, at Plymouth, with an explosive friend he had made at Edinburgh, Dr. George Budd.**7** Through no fault of Conan Doyle's, there was friction between him and Budd, and he decided to leave. He arrived at Southsea, a suburb of Portsmouth, on an afternoon in July, 1882, picked up a house called Bush Villa (later renamed Doyle House by the owners; destroyed in the Blitz in 1941) at a rental of £40 ($200) a year plus another £10 ($50) in taxes, hung up his carefully burnished brass plate, and embarked on a practice that was neither very exacting nor very rewarding: he made £154 ($770) the first year,**8** £250 ($1,250) the second, never more than £300 ($1,500).

It may be asked here why a man who was born a patrician should have been so poor and without influence at the very outset of his professional career; the scion of a family which, though far from wealthy, could yet afford to entertain the Prime Minister, Sir Walter Scott, Cardinal Newman, and other celebrated men at their dinner table. The answer lies in the fact that Conan Doyle, who had left the Catholic faith, considered it dishonorable to use his letters of introduction to the Duke of Norfolk, the Bishop of Southsea, and other Catholic notables.

Soon young Arthur Conan Doyle was engaged to Louise Hawkins, the daughter of one of his patients; she became his first wife on August 6, 1885, a month after Conan Doyle had taken his doctorate.

Meantime, between 1878 and 1883, Conan Doyle had written and sold a few short stories**9** and had completed two novels, *The Narrative of John Smith*, lost in the post and never recovered, and *The Firm of Girdlestone*, which was then still making a dreary round of the publishers.

Now, in the March of 1886, with time on his hands and creditors at his door, young Dr. Conan Doyle—he was then only twenty-six—turned his mind to the writing of a detective story.

•   •   •

Our friend, Mr. Michael Harrison, thinks that the plot of *A Study in Scarlet* may have suggested itself to Conan Doyle by the real-life disappearance, in London, of a German baker, Urban Napoleon Stanger, whose name is echoed in the "Stangerson" of the story.**10** A private detective named Wendel Scherer had been called in to find the missing man, but he failed to do so, and the baker's manager, Franz Felix Stumm, was charged with the murder.

Conan Doyle set out to create a private detective who would *not* fail in such an assignment because he would have developed "habits of observation and inference into a system,"**11** and he thought at once of one of his former teachers at the University, Joseph Bell, M.D., F.R.C.S., consulting surgeon to the Royal Infirmary and Royal Hospital for Sick Children, member of University Court, Edinburgh University; born in Edinburgh in 1837, he died in 1911.

A "thin, wiry, dark" man, "with a high-nosed acute face, penetrating gray eyes, angular shoulders" and a "high discordant" voice, Dr. Bell "would sit in his receiving room with a face like a Red Indian, and diagnose the people as they came in, before they even opened their mouths. He would tell them their symptoms, and even give them details of their past life; and hardly ever would he make a mistake."

Of the many anecdotes told of Dr. Joseph Bell, here is one of the lesser-known (from the *Lancet*, issue of August 1, 1956):

> A woman with a small child was shown in. Joe Bell said good morning to her and she said good morning in reply. "What sort of a crossing di' ye have fra' Burntisland?" "It was guid." "And had ye a guid walk up Inverleith Row?" "Yes." "And what did ye do with th' other wain?" "I left him with my sister in Leith." "And would ye still be working at the linoleum factory?" "Yes, I am." "You see, gentlemen, when she said good morning to me I noted her Fife accent, and, as you know, the nearest town in Fife is Burntisland. You noticed the red clay on the edges of the soles of her shoes, and the only such clay within twenty miles of Edinburgh is in the Botanical Gardens. Inverleigh Row borders the gardens and is her nearest way here from Leith. You observed that the coat she carried over her arm is too big for the child who is with her, and therefore she set out from home with two children. Finally she has a dermatitis on the fingers of the right hand which is peculiar to workers in the linoleum factory at Burntisland."

Here is how Conan Doyle himself wrote about this period in his life, in his autobiography, *Memories and Adventures:***12**

> I felt now that I was capable of something fresher and crisper and more workmanlike [than many of the detective stories that had been written up to that time]. Gaboriau had rather attracted me by the neat dovetailing of his plots, and Poe's masterful detective, M. Dupin, had from boyhood been one of my heroes. But could I

10 See Mr. Harrison's *London by Gaslight* and his standard guide to the London (and England) of Holmes and Watson, *In the Footsteps of Sherlock Holmes*.

11 As Mr. J. L. Hitchings was one of the first to point out (in "Sherlock Holmes, the Logician"), Holmes throughout the Canon is wont to refer to his entire process of reasoning as "the science of deduction." His usual method, however, is to make brilliant inferences from minute details he has observed—and this, strictly speaking, is *induction*—that is, reasoning from the particular to the general—rather than *deduction*—reasoning from the general to the particular. In "The Adventure of the Six Napoleons," Holmes refers to his reasoning as *inductive*, but in fact it is perhaps more *deductive* in this adventure than in any other.

12 "How"—Ellery Queen asked in his Introduction to *The Misadventures of Sherlock Holmes*—"how could [he] have resisted the overwhelming temptation to call his autobiography *Adventures and Memoirs*"?

YOUNG DR. ARTHUR CONAN DOYLE

As he looked in the Southsea days, from *Murder for Pleasure*, by Howard Haycraft.

DR. JOSEPH BELL OF EDINBURGH

An early photograph of the "fabulous original" upon whom Conan Doyle based Sherlock Holmes. From *Murder for Pleasure*, by Howard Haycraft.

13 It is perhaps worth noting that Sherlock Holmes' resemblance to Dr. Joseph Bell did not go unremarked by at least one of Conan Doyle's avid readers. From Vailima, Apia, Samoa, Robert Louis Stevenson wrote to Conan Doyle on April 5, 1893: ". . . can this be *our old friend Joe Bell?*"

14 Professor Nordon, after almost a decade of research and writing, has now completed a definitive biography of Sir Arthur Conan Doyle. At this writing, it has already been published in France and England, and a U.S. edition is forthcoming.

bring an addition of my own? I thought of my old teacher Joe Bell, of his eagle face, of his curious ways, of his eerie trick of spotting details. If he were a detective he would surely reduce this fascinating business to something nearer an exact science. I would try if I could get this effect. It was surely possible in real life, so why should I not make it plausible in fiction? It is all very well to say that a man is clever, but the reader wants to see examples of it—such examples as Bell gave us every day in the wards.

Again, in a letter to Dr. Bell dated May 4, 1892, Conan Doyle wrote:

It is most certainly to you that I owe Sherlock Holmes, and though in the stories I have the advantage of being able to place [the detective] in all sorts of dramatic positions, I do not think that his analytical work is in the least an exaggeration of some effects which I have seen you produce in the out-patient ward. Round the centre of deduction and inference and observation which I have heard you inculcate I have tried to build up a man who pushed the thing as far as it would go—further occasionally—and I am so glad that the result has satisfied you, who are the critic with the most right to be severe.

Dr. Conan Doyle dedicated *The Adventures of Sherlock Holmes* to Dr. Joseph Bell, and Dr. Joseph Bell contributed a note on "Mr. Sherlock Holmes" (originally published in the *Bookman* of London) to the fourth English edition of *A Study in Scarlet* (London: Ward, Lock & Bowden, 1893).13

This, then, was the *inception*.

But here let us try to be quite clear:

Bell himself states that Conan Doyle has made a great deal out of very little and proceeds to give the credit for Sherlock Holmes' genius to Conan Doyle's own gifts and training.

"You are yourself Sherlock Holmes and well you know it," he wrote to Conan Doyle.

Bell, undoubtedly, was the model for the consulting detective, Sherlock Holmes. But Bell was *not* Sherlock Holmes as we best know him. Save for his remarkable gift of deduction, Bell was never once able, in real-life crime cases, to show that he possessed any Holmesian powers; Conan Doyle, on the other hand, as we shall see, played a part in the investigation of many real-life crimes; certainly he was consulted by Sir Bernard Spilsbury, H. Ashton-Wolfe, and other criminologists and police officials.

Let us compare the character of Holmes with the character of his creator:

Holmes, like Conan Doyle, was partial toward old dressing gowns, clay pipes, keeping documents and lacking the time to arrange them, a habit of working with a magnifying glass on his desk and a pistol in the drawer. "Holmes' ancestors, like Conan Doyle's, were country squires," Professor Pierre Weil Nordon of the University of Paris14 has written in *Sir Arthur Conan Doyle*, a handsome volume issued in 1959 as a centenary memorial to the author, "the author's grand-mother, Marianna Conan, was of French descent and Holmes' own grandmother was the sister of the French artist, Horace Vernet; Holmes' bank was the same as Conan Doyle's; he was offered a knighthood in the same year and in the same month as Conan Doyle was knighted;**15** both evince a special interest in Winwood Reade, or in the origin of the Cornish dialect; both loathe suffragettes; both wish with the same eagerness the establishment of a close alliance between all English-speaking countries. Finally . . . Conan Doyle, like Holmes, was treated by criminologists as one of their colleagues, and was honoured by them when they gave his name to police laboratories."

The story of Conan Doyle's ingenuity in transmitting news of the first World War to British prisoners in Germany is well known: this he did by sending books in which he had put needle-pricks under various printed letters so as to spell out the desired messages, but beginning always with the third chapter in the belief that the German censors would examine the earlier chapters more carefully.

We have said that Conan Doyle interested himself in many real-life crimes: he investigated the Mrs. Rome case (result unknown); he looked into the missing Dane case (solved); he went to the scene of the killing in the Thorne murder. A statement from a journalist, now in the Conan Doyle archives, attests that it was Conan Doyle who put the police on the trail of that infamous murderer Smith in the celebrated "Brides-in-the-Bath" case.

As examples of Conan Doyle's interest in fair play and justice, however, the best-known cases are those of George Edalji and Oscar Slater.**16**

That Conan Doyle had a gift of his own for making quick and accurate deductions has been demonstrated in "Some Recollections of Sir Arthur Conan Doyle." Here Dr. Harold Gordon tells how Conan Doyle once

> stopped at the crib of a young baby, about two and a half years old. The child's mother was watching at the lad's side. Almost without hesitation, Sir Arthur turned to the mother and said, kindly but with authority, "You must stop painting the child's crib." Sure enough, the child was in with lead poisoning. We were aware of the diagnosis, but asked how he had arrived at the right conclusion so quickly. He smiled as he answered, "The child looked pale but well-fed. He was listless and his wrist dropped as he tried to hold a toy. The mother was neatly dressed, but she had specks of white paint on the fingers of her right hand. Children like to sharpen their teeth on the rails of a crib—so lead poisoning seemed a likely diagnosis."

Now, the name "Sherlock Holmes" did not come to Conan Doyle's mind in a flash of inspiration; he had to labor over it.

In *Memories and Adventures* he wrote: "What should I call the fellow? . . . One rebelled against the elementary art which gives some inkling of character in the name, and creates Mr. Sharps or Mr. Ferrets. First it was Sher*ringford* Holmes [our italics] . . ."

DR. JOSEPH BELL IN LATER LIFE

From *The Private Life of Sherlock Holmes*, by Vincent Starrett.

15 "How ridiculous that the author should only have been Knighted," the late Christopher Morley once commented. "He should have been Sainted."

16 George Edalji was sentenced in 1903 to seven years' penal servitude for horse-maiming. In 1906 Conan Doyle heard of this rather obscure case and, after exhaustive investigations lasting nearly a year, began a series of newspaper articles analyzing the incredibly weak evidence of the prosecution and making public "this blot upon the record of English justice." In consequence of Conan Doyle's endeavor, Edalji was released but denied compensation. In 1909, Oscar Slater was sentenced to death in Edinburgh for a brutal murder in Glasgow. This sentence was commuted to penal servitude for life. An unceasing battle was fought to prove Slater's innocence. Approached by Slater's lawyer, Conan Doyle took up this case of miscarriage of justice. It was not, however, until 1927 that Conan Doyle finally secured the release of Slater. The reader interested in knowing more about these cases is recommended to the three excellent accounts given by John Dickson Carr (in *The Life of Sir Arthur Conan Doyle*); Michael and Mollie Hardwick (in *The Man Who Was Sherlock Holmes*); and Vincent Starrett (in *The Private Life of Sherlock Holmes*).

17 The name Sherlock, as Mr. Duncan Mac-Dougald, Jr., has reported in "Some Onomatological Notes on 'Sherlock Holmes' and Other Names in the Sacred Writings," comes from the Irish *scorlóz*—Shearlock or Sherloch, which is derived from *searlóz*—Scurloch, Shirlock, or Sherloch, which in turn is the Gaelic version of the Anglo-Saxon *scortlog*, literally "short-lock," that is, one with shorn locks. Mr. MacDougald also notes that, according to Patrick Woulfe, *Irish Names and Surnames*, Dublin, 1923, the Sherlock family, "which, to judge from the name, is of Anglo-Saxon origin, had settled in Ireland before the beginning of the thirteenth century, and soon became very widespread, being found in Dublin, Meath, Louth, Wexford, Waterford, Tipperary, etc."

Sherlockian scholars, on the other hand, have speculated that Holmes was perhaps named for the famous Bishop Thomas Sherlock, 1678–1761, or his father, William Sherlock, 1641–1707, who became dean of St. Paul's and the author of *A Practical Discourse Concerning Death*. "There can be little doubt," Christopher Morley once wrote, "that the detective's full name was either Thomas Sherlock Holmes or William Sherlock Holmes."

But was even this the detective's *full* name? We know that Holmes took "Escott"—S (for Sherlock) Scott?—as his alias in "The Adventure of Charles Augustus Milverton," and this has led to the suggestion that the detective's *full* name was Thomas (or William) Sherlock Scott Holmes.

18 Sherlockians owe much of their information about Dr. James Watson to the researches of Dr. Maurice Campbell and his report of those researches to the Sherlock Holmes Society of London at their "Bruce-Partington Night Dinner," held on January 4, 1956.

19 The "middle-sized" will not pass without comment by that eminent Irregular, Mr. Elliot Kimball. In "The Stature of John H. Watson" he has demonstrated that "the amiable doctor was *five feet* and *ten inches* tall . . ."

20 In "The Adventure of the Red Circle," Holmes himself describes Watson's moustache as "modest."

21 He later repurchased the rights to the *Study*. Adrian M. Conan Doyle's recollection is that he paid £5,000 for them—two hundred times what he had originally been paid for the *Study*.

But Mr. Vincent Starrett first published in this country—in *The Private Life of Sherlock Holmes*—a page from an old notebook of Conan Doyle's on which the name Sherr*inford* Holmes—no *g*—is clearly to be seen.

Let us delve a little more deeply into the sources of the ultimate name—*Sherlock Holmes*.

The Holmes: As a student, Conan Doyle had gone without lunches to buy Oliver Wendell Holmes' *Autocrat, Poet*, and *Professor at the Breakfast Table* (as well as many other books). And Holmes (Oliver Wendell, Senior) was very much in the news in that May of 1886—he was making a famous and much-publicized visit to England. "Never have I so known and loved a man whom I had never seen," Conan Doyle wrote later. "It was one of the ambitions of my lifetime to look into his face, but by the irony of Fate I arrived in his native city just in time to lay a wreath on his newly turned grave."

The Sherlock: Mr. John Dickson Carr in his brilliant *Life of Sir Arthur Conan Doyle* tells us that the author hit on the Irish name of Sherlock**17** "entirely at random." But the Sherlocks *were* landowners in the very part of Ireland where the Doyle family had once held its estates—County Wicklow—and Conan Doyle, a student of heraldry, may well have seen the name in family papers. Again, Conan Doyle in a newspaper interview unearthed by Mr. Vincent Starrett was once quoted as saying that "years ago I made thirty runs [at cricket] against a bowler by the name of Sherlock, and I always had a kindly feeling for the name." We may take this quip for the little it is worth.

Now young Dr. Doyle needed a narrator for his story—a man who, mentally and physically, would provide a contrast with Holmes. Originally designated "Ormond Sacker," a name Conan Doyle speedily, and rightly, dropped as sounding much too dandified, "John H. Watson, M.D., late of the Army Medical Department," owes his surname to Conan Doyle's friend and fellow-member of the Southsea Literary and Scientific Society, *James* Elmwood Watson, M.D., Edinburgh, 1863. House physician at the Edinburgh Royal, then a physician to the British Consulate at Newchwung, Manchuria, Dr. James Watson had come to practice in Southsea in 1883.**18**

But here again other influences seem to have helped in molding the character. Watson only once in his own reminiscences allows a physical description of himself to creep in—in "The Adventure of Charles Augustus Milverton" he is "a middle-sized,**19** strongly built man—square jaw, thick neck, moustache . . ."**20**—and this is a very accurate description of Alfred Wood, in World War I, Major Alfred Wood, an associate of Conan Doyle's since 1885 who later served as secretary to the author until the Major's retirement in 1927.

And just as Conan Doyle in so many ways resembled Sherlock Holmes, so there are some remarkable parallels to be found in the lives of Conan Doyle and Dr. John H. Watson, though Conan Doyle was seven years the younger. Both started their medicine when they were seventeen, both studied at Edinburgh University, both received their M.D. degree when they were twenty-six (Conan Doyle at Edinburgh, Watson at the University of London). Conan Doyle had considered joining the army just as Watson did, but chose to go as a ship's surgeon instead. Both arrived at Plymouth by sea, Watson on November 26, 1880, Conan Doyle after a shorter voyage in July, 1882. Conan Doyle married in 1885 and Watson (your editor believes) married for the first time in 1886; both married again, Conan Doyle once, Watson perhaps twice.

And so at last, with his characters firmly fixed in his mind, Conan Doyle set furiously to work on the story he called at first *A Tangled Skein*; a month later, on a Sunday in late April, 1886, Mrs. Doyle was able to write to her husband's sister Lottie: "Arthur has written another book, a little novel about 200 pages long, called *A Study in Scarlet* . . ."

After several rejections it arrived, in October, 1886, on the desk of the chief editor of Ward, Lock & Co., Professor G. T. Bettany, who gave the manuscript to his wife to judge. She herself was a writer, and she was enthusiastic about the *Study:* "This man is a born novelist. It will be a great success!" But Messrs. Ward, Lock & Co. could not publish the manuscript for at least a year and they could give Conan Doyle only £25 ($125) for the copyright. The author objected to both the delay and the offer, and wrote to ask for a percentage of the sales. This was rejected, and Conan Doyle at last accepted the £25.**21**

"DR. WATSON, I PRESUME?"

Major Alfred Wood, for forty years secretary to Sir Arthur Conan Doyle. From *Sir Arthur Conan Doyle 1959 Centenary Memorial Volume.*

CONAN DOYLE'S NOTES FOR A STUDY IN SCARLET

A photostat of this page hangs in the museum of the Sherlock Holmes Tavern in Northumberland Street, London. The original of the page is a part of the Doyle Archives, in the possession of Mr. Adrian M. Conan Doyle. From *The Private Life of Sherlock Holmes,* by Vincent Starrett.

FRONT WRAPPER OF THE RARE FIRST EDITION OF
A STUDY IN SCARLET

The illustration, by an unknown artist, may be the first pictorial representation of Sherlock Holmes, although the late James Montgomery, certainly one of the foremost authorities on the iconography of the Canon, wrote that he could not support this connection. From *The Private Life of Sherlock Holmes,* by Vincent Starrett.

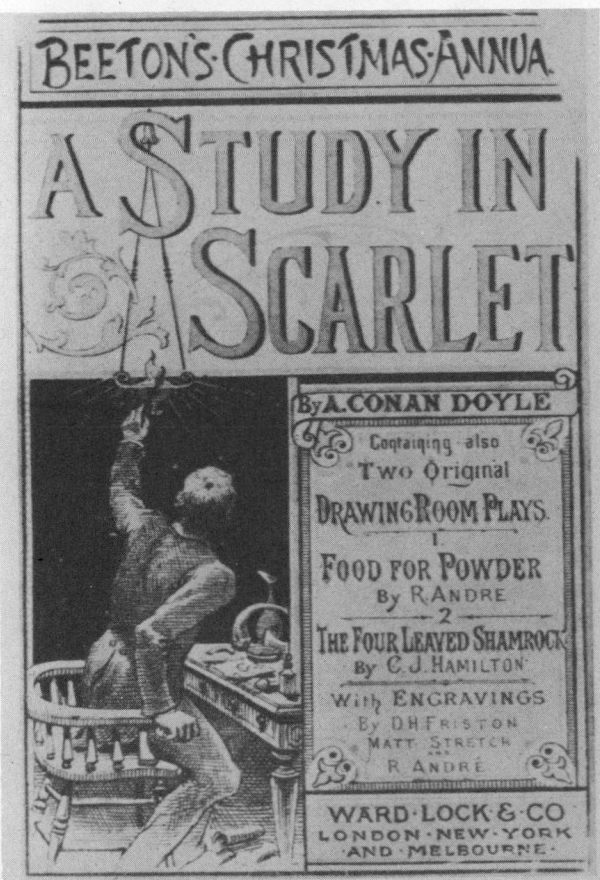

A STUDY IN SCARLET, THE INCREDIBLY RARE FIRST
SEPARATE PUBLICATION OF THE FIRST SHERLOCK
HOLMES STORY (1888)

From *The Baker Street Journal*, January, 1946

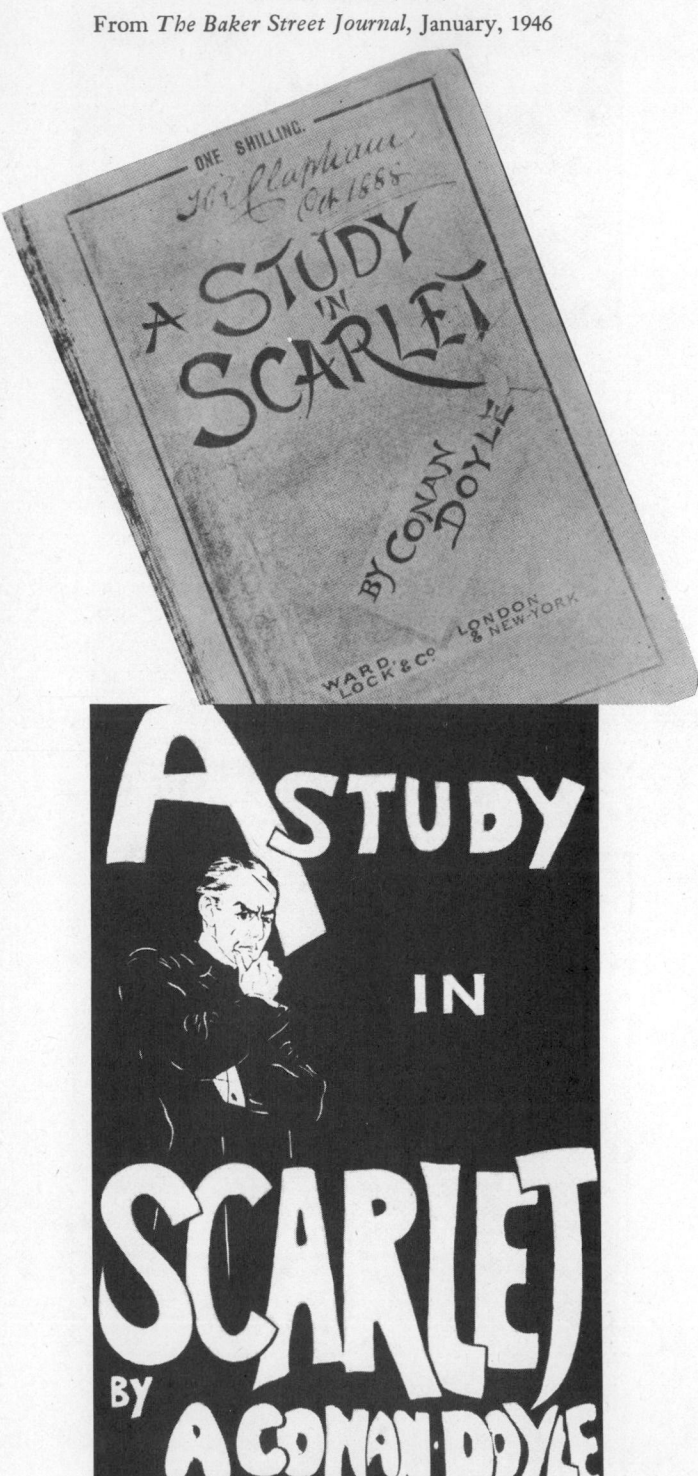

It was published, with four engravings, three of which show the initials D.H.F. (D. H. Friston),**22** in late November or early December, 1887, in the twenty-eighth issue of *Beeton's Christmas Annual*, a publication which had been founded in 1860 by Samuel Orchart Beeton and his wife Isabella Mary Beeton. The price: one shilling. "That lurid paperback," Mr. Vincent Starrett has written, "is today one of the rarest books of modern times—a keystone sought by discriminating collectors in every corner of the earth." A copy was last reported to have sold at more than $1,000— and it is noteworthy that, in spite of advertising and inquiries in the *London Times*, no copy of *Beeton's* could be found for the Sherlock Holmes Exhibition held during the Festival of Britain until a public-spirited citizen turned up with a copy he had acquired *for sixpence* at a London stall. Fortunately for collectors, the Baker Street Irregulars, Inc., and the Sherlock Holmes Society of London jointly published, in 1960, a complete and perfect facsimile edition of 168 pages —with multicolored cover, full contents including advertisements intact. Its price, then, to subscribers was $7, otherwise $10; today, it, too, is a collector's item.

The late Dorothy L. Sayers has said that *A Study in Scarlet* was "flung like a bombshell into the field of detective fiction,"**23** but Biographer Carr wrote: "And nothing happened. It was unlikely that any critic would trouble, at Christmas-time, to review an annual; and none did."

The indefatigable Vincent Starrett has nonetheless discovered one critic who *did* review the *Study*—in the *Graphic* for December 10, 1887:

It is not at all a bad imitation but it would never have been written but for Poe, Gaboriau and R. L. Stevenson. . . . Those who like detective stories and have not read the great originals will find the tale full of interest. It hangs together well and finishes ingeniously.

And the equally indefatigable Dr. Julian Wolff has discovered a September 1, 1888, review of the *Study* in its first book appearance—also in the *Graphic*, but the *Graphic* in a considerably kinder mood:

Nobody who cares for detective stories should pass over *A Study in Scarlet*. . . . The author has equalled the best of his predecessors. . . . He has actually succeeded in inventing a brand new detective. . . . The plot

JAMES GREIG'S COVER ILLUSTRATION FOR THE STUDY IN
SCARLET SUPPLEMENT TO THE WINDSOR MAGAZINE
FOR CHRISTMAS, 1895

is . . . daringly constructed. . . . There is no trace of vulgarity or slovenliness, too often characteristic of detective stories. . . . Besides being exceptionally ingenious, it may be read with pleasure by those [who] do not care for such things in a general way.

In any case, *Beeton's Christmas Annual* for Christmas, 1887, was a sellout. Early in 1888, Ward, Lock proposed a new edition in which the novel should appear by itself. "Though the author could [then] gain no penny out of it," Carr writes, "it was suggested that the new edition should be illustrated by his father, Charles Doyle. Ill and aged as he was, Charles Doyle produced six black-and-white drawings; and it must have brought tears to the old man's eyes when he learned his work was still wanted in London."

This edition of *A Study in Scarlet* in its original condition is by far the most difficult of all the Sherlock Holmes books for the collector to obtain; the location of only about four copies of each of the two printings is known.

The first American edition was published in Philadelphia by the J. B. Lippincott Company on March 1, 1890. An edition with a frontispiece and 39 other illustrations by George Hutchinson (11 of which were also included in the Lippincott edition of 1893) was published by Ward, Lock, Bowden & Co., London, in 1891. The previously mentioned note on "Mr. Sherlock Holmes" by Dr. Joseph Bell was included in the fourth English edition (London: Ward, Lock & Bowden, Ltd., 1893). And still another edition—this one with seven illustrations by James Greig—was issued as a supplement to the *Windsor Magazine* for Christmas, 1895.

Now, one reader of *A Study in Scarlet* was a Mr. Stoddard, the American editor of *Lippincott's Magazine*, which was published simultaneously in Philadelphia by J. B. Lippincott and in London by Ward, Lock. He wanted another Sherlock Holmes adventure to publish complete in a single issue, and he (or his representative: the record is not clear on this point) invited Conan Doyle and Oscar Wilde to dine at a London restaurant. Though Conan Doyle was then hard at work on his historical novel, *The White Company*, he promised *Lippincott's* another Sherlock Holmes adventure, and Wilde for his part agreed to write the short novel we know today as *The Picture of Dorian Gray*.

Conan Doyle paid a generous tribute to Wilde's artistry in *Memories and Adventures*. (Some critics, rather fancifully, have even thought that they could detect Wildean echoes in *The Sign of the Four*.) But Conan Doyle evidently did not recognize that Wilde, like Sherlock Holmes, could sometimes be guilty of a little leg-pulling. When Wilde urged Conan Doyle to see one of his plays—"Ah, you must go. It is wonderful. It is genius"—Conan Doyle rather heavily recorded in his diary that he thought Wilde must be mad.

The Sign of the Four; or, The Problem of the Sholtos, appeared in both the English and American *Lippincott's* for February, 1890, with a frontispiece by an unknown artist. Single copies of the issue, in either the London or the Philadelphia edition, are rarer than single copies of the *Strand Magazine* of 1891, but by no means as rare as *Beeton's*. (The

22 The fourth illustration is inscribed in very small letters W. M. H. Quick, "but available information has not yet determined conclusively whether that was the signature of the engraver or of a second artist," the late James Montgomery wrote in *A Study in Pictures*. "Certainly the illustration . . . is identical in style and execution with the three bearing the initials 'D.H.F.' "

23 Introduction to *Great Short Stories of Detection, Mystery and Horror*, titled, in the United States, *The Omnibus of Crime*.

THE COVER OF LIPPINCOTT'S MAGAZINE FOR
FEBRUARY, 1890

This was the first publication of the second Sherlock Holmes story, *The Sign of the Four*.

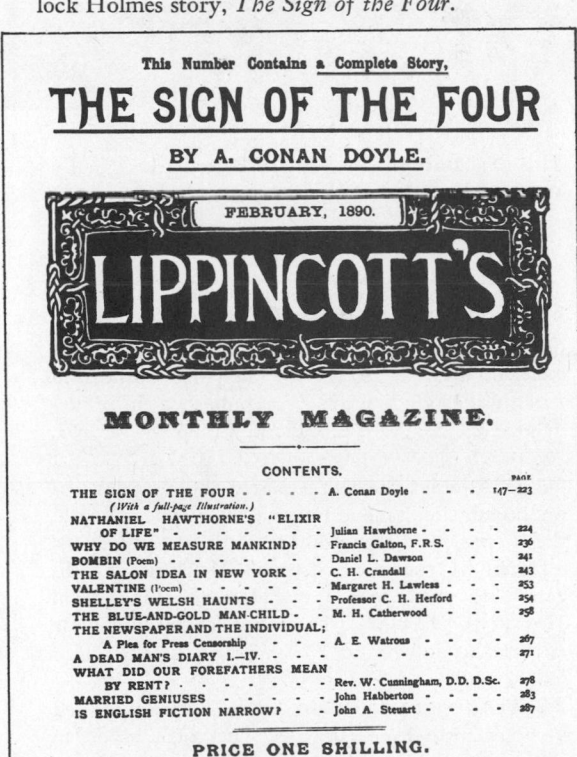

"WHAT HE HAD NOW WAS NO LONGER A PUPPET . . ."

This caricature by Sir Bernard Partridge originally appeared in *Punch* in 1926.

24 The earliest known book publication of *The Sign of the Four* in America was a piracy—by the *Once a Week Library* (New York: P. F. Collier), issue of March 15, 1891. The first authorized American book edition was published in Philadelphia by the J. B. Lippincott Company in 1893.

25 In America the first series of short stories was published, simultaneously with their appearance in the *Strand*, in a large number of daily newspapers, serviced by the newly formed McClure's Syndicate—"no small item," says Howard Haycraft in *Murder for Pleasure*, "in Holmes' early and wide American renown."

26 The first twelve short stories were published in book form by George Newnes of London in 1892, in an edition that included 104 illustrations drawn for the *Strand Magazine* by Sidney Paget. The first American edition of *The Adventures of Sherlock Holmes*, with a frontispiece and 15 other illustrations by Paget, was published by Harper & Brothers of New York that same year. In 1902 Newnes published a "Souvenir" edition that contained a frontispiece and 20 other illustrations by Paget, all from the 1892 edition, and in 1958 the Folio Society of London published a handsome edition with 12 illustrations by Paul Hogarth.

London issue is far harder to come by than the Philadelphia issue.) Just as bound *Strand*s are easier to find than single copies, so are bound *Lippincott's*.

When Spencer Blackett published the adventure in book form (with a frontispiece by Charles Kerr) in the spring of 1890—as *The Sign of Four*, which Conan Doyle always preferred to call it—"it faded away with scarcely more critical attention than had attended *A Study in Scarlet*."[24]

Said the critic of the London *Athenaeum* (December 6, 1890):

> A detective story is usually lively reading, but we cannot pretend to think that *The Sign of Four* is up to the level of the writer's best work. It is a curious medley, and full of horrors; and surely those who play at hide and seek with the fatal treasure are a curious company. The wooden-legged convict and his fiendish misshapen little mate, the ghastly twins, the genial prizefighters, the detectives wise and foolish, and the gentle girl whose lover tells the tale, twist in and out together in a mazy dance, culminating in that mad and terrible rush down the river which ends the mystery and the treasure. Dr. Doyle's admirers will read the little volume through eagerly enough, but they will hardly care to pick it up again.

No, the bombshell that was Holmes was not to explode until Conan Doyle conceived the then brand new (in England) idea of *writing a series of short stories around one central character*. His agent, A. P. Watt, sent the first of the series—"A Scandal in Bohemia"—to the acting editor of the *Strand Magazine*, "the shrewd, bespectacled, heavily moustached" Greenhough Smith, who liked the story and encouraged Conan Doyle to write a series of six, for which he agreed to pay an average of £35 ($175) each.

The speed with which Conan Doyle could work is shown by his diary: on Friday, April 10, 1891, a week after sending off "A Scandal in Bohemia," he noted: "Finished 'A Case of Identity.'" On Monday the 20th he sent off "The Red-Headed League." On the 27th he posted "The Boscombe Valley Mystery." After that he wrote "The Five Orange Pips," but it was not mailed until Monday, May 18th, because he was prostrated by an attack of influenza.

When "A Scandal in Bohemia" appeared in the July, 1891, issue of the *Strand*,[25] Holmes at last did blaze into popularity, and by October 14th of that year Conan Doyle could write to his mother that his publishers were "imploring him to continue Holmes."

He raised his price to £50 ($250) a story "irrespective of length" and a letter by return post agreed to his terms for six more adventures. He at once began work on the seventh in the series—"The Adventure of the Blue Carbuncle"—and by November 11th he was able to report to his mother that he had completed all but one of the additional half-dozen.[26]

"I think," Conan Doyle added casually, "of slaying Holmes in the last and winding him up for good. He takes my mind from better things."

"You won't!" his mother raged. "You can't. You *mustn't*."

So he ended the twelve adventures with that of "The Copper Beeches," based on an idea suggested to him by his mother. Sherlock Holmes' life—for the time being, at least—had been saved by "the Ma'am."

"They"—the editors of the *Strand*—"have been bothering me for more Sherlock Holmes tales," Conan Doyle wrote to his mother in February, 1892. "Under pressure I offered to do a dozen for a thousand pounds, but I sincerely hope they won't accept it now."

A thousand pounds—$5,000—was a very large payment in 1892, but accept it the *Strand* did, and "Silver Blaze," the first of the new series, duly appeared in the December, 1892, issue of the magazine.**27**

Early in the next year—but let Conan Doyle tell it himself: "I went with my wife for a short holiday in Switzerland, in the course of which we saw the wonderful falls of Reichenbach, a terrible place, and one that I thought would make a worthy tomb for Sherlock, even if I buried my banking account along with him . . ."**28**

Back home, Conan Doyle on April 6th again wrote to his mother: "I am in the middle of the last Holmes story, after which the gentleman vanishes, never to return. I am weary of his name."

"What he had now was no longer a puppet," John Dickson Carr wrote; "it was an Old Man of the Brain locked round him with a windpipe-grip."

And so, "with a happy sigh of relief," he sat down to write the story he had hopefully titled "The Final Problem."

"Killed Holmes," he noted laconically in his diary a short time later . . .

•   •   •

Sherlock Holmes dead?

The amazed readers of the *Strand Magazine* (and of *Mc-Clure's Magazine* in America) could scarcely believe their eyes. Conan Doyle heard of many who wept, of sober City men who even went to their work wearing mourning bands. He himself wrote:

> I was amazed at the concern expressed by the public. They say a man is never properly appreciated until he is dead, and the general protest against my summary execution of Holmes taught me how many and how numerous were his friends. "You Brute!" was the beginning of the letter of remonstrance which one lady sent me, and I expect she spoke for others beside herself. . . . I fear I was utterly callous myself, and only glad to have a chance of opening out into new fields of imagination, for the temptation of high prices made it difficult to get one's thoughts away from Holmes.

"There will be only a temporary interval in the Sherlock Holmes stories," the editors of the *Strand* rather hysterically hastened to assure their readers. "A new series will commence in an early number. Meanwhile, powerful detective stories will be contributed by other eminent writers."

"LIFE'S DARKEST MOMENT"

One of the late H. T. Webster's well-remembered cartoons.

27 In America, its first appearance was in the February 25, 1893, issue of *Harper's Weekly*. Eleven of the twelve short stories in this series (the exception is "The Cardboard Box") were first published in book form as *The Memoirs of Sherlock Holmes* by George Newnes of London in 1894. All twelve stories were included in the first American edition, published by Harper & Brothers of New York two months later in the year. At Conan Doyle's insistence, however, this edition was withdrawn from circulation and a second American edition, omitting "The Cardboard Box," was printed and distributed. Conan Doyle had grave thoughts about the propriety of "The Cardboard Box," with its outspoken—for those days—admission that there could be sex without marriage. With changing manners and morals, Conan Doyle relented and allowed the story to be printed in book form at last as part of his 1917 collection, *His Last Bow*.

28 Another result of the visit to Switzerland was Conan Doyle's poem, "An Alpine Walk," first published in the *Independent* for December 14, 1893; reprinted in the *Baker Street Journal*, Vol. XII, No. 3, New Series, July, 1962, p. 134.

29 Conan Doyle received, *for the American rights alone,* $5,000 a story for the thirteen stories that make up *The Return of Sherlock Holmes.* This is believed to be the highest price per story ever paid to an author up to that time.

"THE RE-APPEARANCE OF SHERLOCK HOLMES"

How the *Strand Magazine,* in its issue of October, 1901, promoted the public's reaction to the opening installments of *The Hound of the Baskervilles.*

But Dr. Conan Doyle stood firm—though "readers implored him, editors cajoled him, agents worried him, publishers tried to bribe him, some people even threatened him."

"I couldn't revive him if I would, at least not for years," Conan Doyle wrote to a friend, "for I have had such an overdose of him that I feel towards him as I do towards *pâté-de-foie-gras,* of which I once ate too much, so that the name of it gives me a sickly feeling to this day."

Not for eight years, not until 1901, would he publish a new Sherlock Holmes story, and then he was careful to date it *before* the Affair Reichenbach; *The Hound of the Baskervilles* was a *reminiscence,* not a *resurrection,* of Sherlock Holmes.

It was nonetheless a tremendous success.

The circulation of the *Strand* soared 30,000 copies an issue with the number in which the first installment of the *Hound* appeared (August, 1901); the magazine could not print enough copies fast enough to meet the demand; long queues formed in Southampton Street to buy them straight from the presses. George Newnes of London brought it out in book form in 1902, with 16 of Sidney Paget's 60 *Strand* illustrations, in the largest edition so far accorded a Sherlock Holmes book, and McClure, Phillips & Company of New York issued it in the same year in America, with eight of Paget's illustrations. On both sides of the Atlantic, Holmes enthusiasts greeted the volume with raptures.

Conan Doyle began to weaken somewhat in his decision never to resuscitate Holmes.

In an interview quoted in *Harper's Weekly* for August 31, 1901, he is reported to have said:

"I know that my friend Dr. Watson is a most trustworthy man, and I gave the utmost credit to his story of the dreadful affair in Switzerland. He may have been mistaken, of course. It may not have been Mr. Holmes who fell from the ledge at all, or the whole affair might be the result of hallucination . . ."

His final surrender came in October, 1903, with the publication of "The Adventure of the Empty House."**29**

The Return of Sherlock Holmes ended with "The Adventure of the Second Stain," published in the *Strand Magazine* for December, 1904, and *Collier's Magazine* for January 28, 1905. The thirteen stories that made up the series were first published in book form by George Newnes of London in 1905, with 16 illustrations by Sidney Paget. The first American edition, by McClure, Phillips & Company of New York, with a frontispiece and 12 interior illustrations by Charles Raymond Macauley, was published the same year. (The Newnes edition is now extremely hard to find—and it is growing less modestly priced with every passing year.)

"And yet," says Howard Haycraft . . .

And yet the reception of the new tales was not entirely unmixed. Doyle enjoyed relating a homely incident that expressed the popular mind neatly. "I think, sir," he quoted a Cornish boatman as saying to him, "when Holmes fell over that cliff he may not have killed himself, but he was never quite the same man afterwards."

The Return of Sherlock Holmes was followed by the novel, *The Valley of Fear,***30** and by two more collections of Sherlock Holmes short stories, *His Last Bow* (London: John Murray, 1917; New York: George H. Doran Company, 1917) and *The Case-Book of Sherlock Holmes* (London: John Murray, 1927; New York: George H. Doran Company, 1927).

The sixtieth, and last, of the Sherlock Holmes adventures, "Shoscombe Old Place," was published in March, 1927.

We should mention here, however, that Conan Doyle wrote two short stories in which Sherlock Holmes *may* be present, though offstage. The first, "The Man With the Watches," appeared in the *Strand Magazine* for July, 1898; here "a well-known criminal investigator" writes a letter to the press which purportedly appeared in the *Daily Gazette* in March of 1892. A month later, in its issue of August, 1898, the *Strand* published an account of "The Lost Special," in which Conan Doyle quoted a letter which appeared, it is said, on July 3, 1890, in the *London Times*, "over the signature of an amateur reasoner of some celebrity at that date." The extract begins: "It is one of the elementary principles of practical reasoning that when the impossible has been eliminated the residuum, *however improbable,* must contain the truth"—and this, as we shall see, was the favorite axiom of Mr. Sherlock Holmes.**31**

We should also mention that the August, 1948, issue of *Cosmopolitan Magazine* carried what was billed on the cover as "The Last Adventure of SHERLOCK HOLMES . . . A hitherto unpublished story by Sir Arthur Conan Doyle." This was the story titled "The Man Who Was Wanted," with two splendid illustrations by Robert Fawcett. In fact, the story was written by a retired English architect who had fallen upon hard times, Arthur Whitaker, who sent the story to Conan Doyle. "Create your own characters," Conan Doyle replied, but typically he sent Whitaker a check for £10 which was gratefully received. Conan Doyle then tossed "The Man Who was Wanted" into his wastebasket. Rescued by Lady Conan Doyle and filed among the author's papers, it was found years after the death of Lady and Sir Arthur Conan Doyle. The Doyle Estate, under the natural impression that it was indeed "a hitherto unpublished story by Sir Arthur Conan Doyle," sold it in good faith to the Hearst Magazines. It also appeared in three installments in the *Sunday Dispatch* of London, Manchester, and Edinburgh, issues of January 2, 9, and 16, 1949, with ten tiny illustrations about the size of a postage stamp and one larger illustration of Holmes the width of a column—no mention of the artist's name.

"And so, reader, Farewell to Sherlock Holmes," Conan Doyle wrote. "I thank you for your constancy and can but hope that some return has been made in the shape of that distraction from the worries of life and stimulating change of thought which can only be found in the fairy kingdom of romance."

Still, publishers continued to hope that Conan Doyle would write more about Sherlock Holmes. George Doran, in his *Chronicles of Barabbas* (1935) writes: "It occurred to me that since Doyle declined to write further Sherlock

30 *The Valley of Fear* was serialized in the United States in ten weekly installments from September 20, 1914, to November 22, 1914, inclusive, by the Associated Sunday Newspapers, Inc., a syndicated publication which formed a Sunday magazine supplement to various newspapers throughout the country. The series was illustrated by 12 drawings by Arthur I. Keller. This constitutes the first complete appearance of the story anywhere, since its monthly serialization in the *Strand Magazine* did not begin until the September, 1914, issue and did not end until May, 1915. There it was embellished with 31 illustrations by Frank Wiles. In book form also, the American edition, with seven illustrations by Arthur I. Keller, published by the George H. Doran Company of New York on March 1, 1915, constitutes the true first edition. The English edition, with a frontispiece by Frank Wiles, was first published by Smith, Elder & Co. of London on June 15, 1915 (dates taken from the *Publisher's Weekly* and the *Publisher's Circular*, respectively, by Professor David A. Randall for his article, "*The Valley of Fear* Bibliographically Considered").

31 The late Edgar W. Smith, in 1942, proposed that both these tales should be "subsumed" into the Holmesian Canon. It was pointed out at the time that the letter in the *Gazette* must have been the work of Mycroft Holmes, Sherlock being in Tibet at the time. It was also suggested that "The Lost Special" was material which Dr. Watson proposed to amplify into the case he once referred to as concerning "the papers of Ex-President Murillo."

32 After the death of a son in World War I, Conan Doyle had become deeply immersed in spiritualistic phenomena; indeed, he became a world leader in the movement.

"HIS GREATEST ADVENTURE"

Editorial comment on the death of Sir Arthur Conan Doyle, *New York World*, July 7, 1930.

Holmes adventures in anything like their old form, a biography of Dr. Watson . . . might provide him with a perfectly legitimate vehicle for further cases." Conan Doyle conceded that this was the best idea he had heard about for a revival of Holmes, but felt at the time "he could not take himself away from his psychic work."**32**

Early in 1930, Conan Doyle set forth on a lecture tour of the Continent from which he returned suffering from angina pectoris, the result of overstrain. "I am quite prepared to go or stay," he told a friend, "for I know that life and love go on forever."

At his home in Crowborough, Sussex, at half-past nine on the morning of July 7, 1930, Sir Arthur Conan Doyle died.

He lies today in the churchyard at Minstead in the heart of the New Forest—that same New Forest which provided the background for so many of the scenes in his book *The White Company*, that same New Forest for whose glades Watson yearned on a blazing hot day in August when Baker Street was "like an oven."

As this is written, a fitting memorial to Sir Arthur Conan Doyle is being prepared by his son Adrian. The eleventh-century Château de Lucens, Lucens, Switzerland, will house his papers, letters, documents, pressbooks, and other memorabilia—"probably the most complete biographical records of any literary figure in the past hundred years." Here, too, will be the third and finest of "the Sherlock Holmes Rooms" —a reproduction of the old sitting room where Holmes and Watson so often sat and talked while "the storm grew louder and louder, and the wind cried and sobbed like a child in the chimney."

CHÂTEAU DE LUCENS, LUCENS, SWITZERLAND

The new home of the Doyle Collection and the third and finest Sherlock Holmes Room. Photograph courtesy of Mr. Adrian M. Conan Doyle.

"HE IS NOW TRANSLATING MY SMALL WORKS INTO FRENCH"

[Sherlock Holmes to John H. Watson, M.D., The Sign of the Four]

It must not be thought that it was only in England and America that Sherlock Holmes was known and loved.

In France and Germany, the translated Canon enjoyed a great vogue.

Holland saw numerous translations of Holmes' exploits, many illustrated with the *Strand Magazine* drawings of Sidney Paget.

In prerevolutionary Russia, Sherlock Holmes had been a hero since individual stories from the Saga began to appear at the turn of the century; the works of Sir Arthur Conan Doyle, complete up to the time, were published in Russia in 1909.

In Spain and Latin America, the popularity of the great detective owed much to translations but even more to a lengthy series of pastiches called the *Memorias íntimes de Sherlock Holmes*.

One of the treasures of your editor's own collection is a copy of *The Hound of the Baskervilles* in Japanese.

That genial Sherlockian, Mr. Irving Fenton, has in fact devoted a good part of his long lifetime to collecting the adventures of Sherlock Holmes in foreign editions.

In short, as the late Elmer Davis wrote in "The Real Sherlock Holmes," "there can be few languages if any that do not know [Sherlock Holmes]. If you want to brush up on your Arabic, or your Swedish, or your Polish, or your Croatian, with the aid of a pony, you need go no farther than the New York Public Library to read the history of Sherlock Holmes in those tongues."

And Mr. Adrian M. Conan Doyle, the author's son, has stated in a letter which appeared in the *Daily Telegraph*, October 8, 1955, that in the previous year "our sales in all languages . . . totalled 500,000 copies. This has amounted to about 10 million copies over the past few years. The Russians owe us an equivalent of £500,000 in unpaid royalties. It should be added, however, that the Russian publishing figures include *The Lost World*, which seems to be as popular in Russia as Sherlock Holmes."

HOLMES IN RUSSIA, HOLMES IN HOLLAND

(*Above*) An edition of "The Adventure of the the Six Napoleons" published for the Little Library of the *Journal of the Red Army Soldier*. From *The Sherlock Holmes Journal*, Winter, 1956. (*Below*) A recent edition in Dutch of "The Adventure of the Naval Treaty" and "The Adventure of Charles Augustus Milverton." From *The Sherlock Holmes Journal*, Winter, 1961.

1 "The Adventure of the Two Collaborators" may be read in Ellery Queen's collection, *The Misadventures of Sherlock Holmes;* it was also reprinted in the *Baker Street Journal*, Vol. VII, No. 4, New Series, October, 1957, pp. 221B–24.

2 "The Field Bazaar" first appeared in the *Student*, Edinburgh, November 20, 1896. Its first separate appearance was in a private edition for the Sherlock Holmes Society's annual dinner, London, 1939, printed by Mr. A. G. Macdonell in an edition limited to 100 copies. Its first appearance in an anthology was in *221B: Studies in Sherlock Holmes*. Its second separate appearance, with an introduction by the late Edgar W. Smith, was by the Pamphlet House: Summit, N.J., 1947; limited to 250 copies.

3 "How Watson Learned the Trick" made its first appearance in the *Book of the Queen's Doll's House Library;* London: Methuen & Co., Ltd., Vol. II, pp. 92–94, edited by E. V. Lucas in 1924. Its first separate appearance was in a private edition by Robert J. Bayer and Vincent Starrett; Chicago: Camden House, 1947; limited to 60 copies. It made a magazine appearance in the *Baker Street Journal*, Vol. I, No. 2, New Series, April, 1951, with a special note by Edgar W. Smith. It was also included in Mr. Smith's anthology, the *Incunabular Sherlock Holmes*, in 1958.

In 1958, the Doyle Estate reported that it was drawing royalties in 72 currencies; and Mr. Adrian M. Conan Doyle has also stated (in a letter to *The New York Times*, reported on May 20, 1962), that the present translation of his father's works (Sherlock Holmes and others) "now can be met in forty-one languages, including Eskimo, Esperanto, Basuto, Afrikaans and shorthand. The works have been published in thirty-eight countries."

"It has been stated, and I think correctly, that the Sherlock Holmes books sales are second only to the Bible," Mr. Conan Doyle had written earlier.

"More significant of [Holmes'] stature than the translations" (we are again quoting Mr. Davis) "are the parodies, the burlesques, the apocryphal additions to his history. The best of the burlesques were by Bret Harte and John Kendrick Bangs, the indubitably worst by Mark Twain; Mr. Starrett lists many others, unfortunately omitting O. Henry's tale of the success of Shamrock Jolnes in finding the missing scrubwoman. Of the foreign imitations, some, such as [Maurice] Leblanc's *Arsène Lupin vs. Herlock Sholmes*, were apparently authorized, or at least condoned . . ."

Conan Doyle himself thought that by far the best of the parodies was "The Adventure of the Two Collaborators," written by Sir James M. Barrie after the play *Jane Annie*, on which he had collaborated with Conan Doyle in 1893, had proved a dismal failure.**1** But Holmes enthusiasts will perhaps prefer the two parodies of the Sherlock Holmes stories that were written by Conan Doyle himself. The first of these, "The Field Bazaar," takes the form of the familiar and well-loved Holmes-Watson breakfast scene.**2** The second, "How Watson Learned the Trick," written in the third person, again takes the form of a breakfast-table conversation.**3**

The pick of the short parodies and pastiches, written up to 1944, have been collected by Ellery Queen in the previously mentioned anthology, *The Misadventures of Sherlock Holmes*. Elsewhere (in his introduction to August Derleth's *The Memoirs of Solar Pons*) Ellery Queen has written:

> . . . more has been written about Sherlock Holmes than about any other character in fiction, and more has been written about Holmes *by others* than by [Conan Doyle] himself. The numerous pastiches, parodies, and burlesques of Sherlock Holmes have given birth to a whole mythogenesis of reasonable and unreasonable facsimiles, both of the character and the name. As a general rule, the writers of pastiches have retained the sacred and inviolate form—Sherlock Holmes—and rightfully, because a pastiche is a serious and sincere imitation in the exact manner of the original. But writers of parodies and burlesques, which are humorous or satirical take-offs, have had no such reverent scruples. They usually strive for the weirdest possible distortions, and it must be admitted that many highly ingenious travesties of the name have been conceived. Fortunately or unfortunately the name Sherlock Holmes is peculiarly susceptible to the twistings and misshapings of burlesque-minded idolators.

Here is a by-no-means complete list of these "twistings and misshapings":

Sherlock Abodes	Stately Homes
Fetlock Bones	(of England)
Haricot Bones	Purlock Hone
Thinlock Bones	Sheerluck Hums
Warlock Bones	Hemlock Jones
Oilcock Combs	Sherlaw Kombs
Herlock Domes	Sheerluck Ohms
Picklock Holes	Holmlock Shears
Hemlock Holmes	Kerlock Shomes
Loufork Holmes	Herlock Soames
Padlock Homes	Sheerluck Soames

And here is what "burlesque-minded idolators" have done to poor Watson:

Dawson	Whatsup
Potson	Whatson
Watsoname	Watts Ion
Goswell	Warsaw
Spotson	Watts
Watsis	

In science fiction, Sherlock Holmes even has a Martian counterpart in Syaloch, of the "Street of Those Who Prepare Nourishment in Ovens."[4]

Of the pastiches—the serious and sincere imitations in the manner of the original—Edgar W. Smith has written (in his introduction to August Derleth's *The Return of Solar Pons*):

> There is no Sherlockian worthy of his salt who has not, at least once in his life, taken Dr. Watson's pen in hand and given himself to the production of a veritable adventure. . . . The writing of a pastiche is compulsive and inevitable; it is, the psychologists would say, a wholesome manifestation of the urge that is in us all to return to the times and places we have loved and lost, an evidence, specifically, of our happily unrepressed desire to make ourselves at one with the Master of Baker Street and all his works—and to do this not only receptively, but creatively as well . . .

At the top of the list of the many pastiches that have been written by detective-story writers, famous literary figures, humorists, devotees, and others, we must certainly place Mr. Vincent Starrett's "The Adventure of the Unique Hamlet."[5]

Next on the list should go *The Exploits of Sherlock Holmes,* a series of twelve "simulacra" written by Adrian M. Conan Doyle and John Dickson Carr. Of these, six were written by Mr. Doyle, two by Mr. Carr, and four were collaborations. The first of the stories, "The Adventure of the Seven Clocks," appeared in *Life's* issue of December 29, 1952; the others began to appear in *Collier's Magazine* with its issue of May 23, 1953, superbly illustrated by the same Robert Fawcett who had provided two drawings for Arthur Whitaker's "The Man Who Was Wanted" in *Cosmopolitan.*

A word, too, should be said here about a remarkable series of parodies which has been appearing since February, 1960, with "The Adventure of the Ascot Tie," in *Ellery Queen's*

SHERLOCK HOLMES IN CARICATURE

A drawing by Peter Newell to illustrate John Kendrick Bangs' *The Pursuit of the House-Boat* (Harper & Brothers): *The stranger drew forth a bundle of business cards.*

4 See Poul Anderson's "The Martian Crown Jewels" in *The Science-Fictional Sherlock Holmes,* edited by Norman Metcalf. For an idea of how the far, far future may view Sherlock Holmes, see Anthony Boucher's "The Greatest Tertian" in the same volume.

5 The first edition, privately printed in 1920, was limited to 200 copies. It was originally planned that 100 copies were to be printed for Mr. Starrett and 100 copies for Mr. Walter M. Hill, with each man's name to appear on the title page of his respective copies in this format: "FOR THE FRIENDS OF [NAME INSERTED]." Due to an oversight on the part of the printer, only 10 copies with Mr. Starrett's name inserted were delivered, and 190 with Mr. Hill's name inserted. The volume is a great rarity, and those who would like to read "The Adventure of the Unique Hamlet" are advised that they may come by it easier in *The Misadventures of Sherlock Holmes; 221B;* or the revised and expanded edition of Mr. Starrett's *The Private Life of Sherlock Holmes.*

6 Two additional Solar Pons adventures, jointly agented by Mr. Derleth and Mr. Mack Reynolds, appear in *The Science-Fictional Sherlock Holmes:* "The Adventure of the Snitch in Time" and "The Adventure of the Ball of Nostradamus." The Solar Pons books have all been published by one of Mr. Derleth's own three publishing houses: Mycroft & Moran of Sauk City, Wisconsin. For the fourth volume the late Robert R. Pattrick prepared "A Chronology of Solar Pons"; for the fifth, Mr. Michael Harrison, author of *In the Footnotes of Sherlock Holmes*, contributed a monograph on Dr. Lyndon Parker, Pons' Watson.

Mystery Magazine. The author is Robert L. Fish, under his own name and a slightly disguised pseudonym the writer of a first-rate series of detective-intrigue-suspense-crime novels. We concur with Mr. Anthony Boucher, who has said that "It seems to me at least possible that Robert L. Fish is writing the very best Holmesian parodies in all the long history of the Misadventures." Mr. Fish's detective is Schlock Homes (of Bagle Street); his friend and companion in adventure is Dr. Watney.

Novel-length pastiches—beginning with *A Taste for Honey* (New York: Vanguard, 1941)—have been written by Mr. H. F. Heard; the name Sherlock Holmes is never mentioned, but they do concern a detective who calls himself "Mr. Mycroft" and keeps bees on the Sussex Downs.

In volume, however, the king of the pastiche writers is certainly Mr. August Derleth of Sauk City, Wisconsin. He wrote his first adventure of "Solar Pons"—"The Adventure of the Black Narcissus"—in the early autumn of 1928, when he was in his junior year at the University of Wisconsin, and it was published by Harold Hersey in the February, 1929, issue of *Dragnet Magazine*. In the September issue of the same magazine, Solar Pons appeared for a second time in "The Adventure of the Broken Chessman," and in 1945 he made his bow in his first book collection, *The Adventures of Solar Pons*. At this writing, there are four major collections of Solar Pons short stories—comprising, in all, 56 adventures from that of "The Frightened Baronet" to that of "The Innkeeper's Clerk"—*The Adventures, The Memoirs, The Return, The Reminiscences,* and *The Casebook of Solar Pons.***6**

As Mr. Vincent Starrett wrote in introducing the first Pontian collection, Pons is "a clever impersonator, with a twinkle in his eye, which tells us that he is not Sherlock Holmes, and knows that *we* know it, but that he hopes we will like him anyway for what he symbolizes"—and, Mr. Anthony Boucher has added, "for what he *is* as well."

Few admirers of Sherlock Holmes and Dr. John H. Watson could ask for anything more.

"I ... HAVE EVEN CONTRIBUTED TO THE LITERATURE OF THE SUBJECT"

[Sherlock Holmes, "The Red-Headed League"]

With the death of Sir Arthur Conan Doyle and the realization that no more Sherlock Holmes stories would come from his hand, the writings *about* Sherlock Holmes—"the Writings about the Writings"—began to take a somewhat more serious turn.

The reader has only to turn to the "References" listed at the end of this collection—a by-no-means complete list—to see how extensive this curious branch of literature has become.

One of the earliest of the critics, commentators, glossators, and chronologists was certainly "F. S.";[1] in an "open letter" to Dr. Watson, published in the *Cambridge Review* for January 23, 1902, he put many searching questions concerning the various dates mentioned in *The Hound of the Baskervilles.*

In that same year, 1902, Arthur Bartlett Maurice wrote two short pieces of editorial comment, "Some Inconsistencies of Sherlock Holmes" and "More Sherlock Holmes Theories" for the New York *Bookman* (also reprinted in *The Incunabular Sherlock Holmes*).

Two years later, in 1904, the English critic, essayist, historian, poet, and translator, Andrew Lang, 1844–1912, was reading "The Adventure of the Three Students" and subjecting it to careful analysis in *Longman's Magazine.*[2]

But a place of honor as the cornerstone work in any collection of Sherlockiana must certainly go to Father, later Monsignor, Ronald A. Knox for his "Studies in the Literature of Sherlock Holmes," a paper first read, in 1911, to the Gryphon Club of Trinity College, Oxford. "This new frolic in criticism was welcome at once," the late Christopher Morley recalled later; "those who were students at Oxford in that ancient day remember how Mr. Knox was invited round from college to college to re-read his agreeable lampoon; it was first printed [in 1912] in a journal of undergraduate highbrows (*The Blue Book*) then appropriately edited by W. H. L. Watson."

Before continuing our review of these critical landmarks, let us for a moment consider "the rule of the game," as the late Dorothy L. Sayers expressed it in *Unpopular Opinions:* "The rule of the game is that it must be played as solemnly as a county cricket match at Lord's; the slightest touch of extravagance or burlesque ruins the atmosphere."

We are dealing here, you see, with something entirely different from the parodies, burlesques, and pastiches about which we wrote in our preceding chapter: we are dealing with a highly specialized form of literary criticism.

1 "F. S." was Frank Sidgwick, 1879–1939, who later went into the book business (Sidgwick and Jackson) and published the poems of Rupert Brooke. His "open letter," with many other examples of early Sherlockiana, hard to come by elsewhere, has been reprinted in *The Incunabular Sherlock Holmes.*

2 See the interesting article by Mr. Roger Lancelyn Green, "Dr. Watson's First Critic," listed in our References.

And there is no denying that, in recent years, some of "the Writings about the Writings" have threatened to "ruin the atmosphere." Mr. S. C. Roberts (later Sir Sydney Roberts) in England and Mr. Vincent Starrett in America have both felt called upon to issue warnings to overzealous Sherlockians and Holmesians:**3** "One of the temptations that besets the investigator of the life and work of Sherlock Holmes," Roberts wrote in the first issue of *The Sherlock Holmes Journal*, "is the temptation to seek always after novelty. . . . Like the Athenians of the time of St. Paul, Holmesian enthusiasts are always eager for some new thing. Freshness of conjecture or of conclusion is of course attractive to all of us, but we have to remember that a straining after novelty for its own sake does not advance the purposes of sound scholarship. Still less does it accord with the principles and methods of Holmes himself, of the man who called always for data, and prescribed deduction in place of guess-work."

We have tried, in the Notes which accompany the stories that follow, to give ear to Sir Sydney's warning: the "scholarship" revealed in them, if fantastic at times, is, we hope, in most cases sound.

The publication of *Essays in Satire*, including "Studies in the Literature of Sherlock Holmes," in 1928 had two important results. First, the late Sir Desmond MacCarthy, 1877–1952, broadcast over the B.B.C. an important talk on Dr. Watson, one of the "Miniature Biographies" series, which was published in *The Listener*, December 11, 1929.

Second, Sir Sydney Roberts, then Mr. S. C. Roberts, composed "A Note on the Watson Problem" which was published by the University Press of Cambridge, England, in an edition limited to 100 copies.

This was followed, in 1931, by Roberts' *Doctor Watson: Prolegomena to a Biographical Problem*, described by the late Elmer Davis, in "The Real Sherlock Holmes," as "the fullest and best, but not yet definitive, biography of this enigmatic figure—perhaps the most typical of late-Victorian middleclass Englishmen, behind whose commonplace and stodgy front research reveals depths of psychological complexity still unplumbed."

In the following year, 1932, the late Harold Wilmerding Bell, 1885–1947, an American archeologist of note, produced the first attempt to date each of the Sherlock Holmes cases, recorded and unrecorded, in *Sherlock Holmes and Dr. Watson: The Chronology of Their Adventures*, a handsome, blue-green volume, published by Constable & Co., Ltd., of London, in a limited edition of 500 copies, priced at 15 shillings a copy. A copy of the original edition is very hard to find today, but twenty-one years after its first publication, a paperbound but page-by-page facsimile edition was printed from the original plates by the Baker Street Irregulars, Inc., 1953. Said the late Edgar W. Smith in his introduction to that volume: "[Bell] was a pioneer, working through a forest that had not, when he wrote, felt any but the most tentative of axes, and the trail he cut is all the more pleasant because it does, admittedly, have a few bad turnings."

October of that same year, 1932, saw the publication of *Sherlock Holmes: Fact or Fiction?* by the erudite and always delightful Mr. T. S. Blakeney. A chronology of sorts, it is also much more than that: its chapters on "Mr. Sherlock Holmes," "Holmes and Scotland Yard," and "The Literature of Sherlock Holmes" (plus its valuable appendices) throw a brilliant light on both Sherlock and the Saga. It, too, is a hard book to find in its original printing, and it, too, has been reproduced in page-by-page facsimile from the original plates by the Baker Street Irregulars, Inc. (1954).

Only two years later, in 1934, Bell edited the first of the Sherlockian anthologies, *Baker Street Studies*, "plumbing the depths of the Canon through eight different borings, with its list of collaborators chosen from among the foremost Sherlockian scholars of their—or any other—day." (The words are again those of Edgar Smith, in his introduction to the facsimile edition of *Baker Street Studies* published in 1955 by the Baker Street Irregulars.)

In that same year, 1934, The Macmillan Company published *The Private Life of Sherlock Holmes;* it is an authoritative, mellow, and wholly charming presentation of the life and times of the Master Detective by the greatest living Sherlockian, Mr. Vincent Starrett of Chicago.

Meantime, in 1930, Christopher Morley had written his enduring introduction to the Doubleday omnibus, *The Complete Sherlock Holmes;* ten years later, in 1940, came the first American anthology, edited by Vincent Starrett: *221B: Studies in Sherlock Holmes* was published originally by Macmillan; it too has been reprinted, in 1956, by the Baker Street Irregulars, Inc., in a paperbound facsimile edition.

March 31, 1944, was a particularly notable day in Sherlockian annals—it marked the publication of no less than three new books of Sherlockiana: Christopher Morley's *Sherlock Holmes and Dr. Watson: A Textbook of Friendship*, the first annotated collection (five stories); Ellery Queen's *The Misadventures of Sherlock Holmes*, the first collection of parodies and pastiches; and Edgar W. Smith's *Profile by Gaslight: An Irregular Reader About the Private Life of Sherlock Holmes*, an especially rich collection of verse, essays, and other commentaries.

Not until 1947 did the third Sherlockian chronology appear: *An Irregular Chronology of Sherlock Holmes of Baker Street*, by the late Professor (of the University of Chicago) Jay Finley Christ was published by the Fanlight House of Ann Arbor, Michigan, in an edition limited to 175 copies; it is one of the most scholarly and almost certainly the most daring of the (now) seven chronologies.

It was followed, in 1951, by the late Gavin Brend's *My Dear Holmes, A Study in Sherlock*, and, in 1953, by the late Dr. Ernest Bloomfield Zeisler's *Baker Street Chronology: Commentaries on the Sacred Writings of Dr. John H. Watson*. In 1955 came your editor's own attempt to date (by day of the week, date of the month and year) all of Holmes' cases, recorded and unrecorded, *The Chronological Holmes;* and the Reverend Henry T. Folsom has since (1964) produced a revised edition of his *Through the Years at Baker Street: A Chronology of Sherlock Holmes*, bringing to seven the number of full-length chronologies.[4]

Today, Sherlock Holmes is the only fictional character

[4] Other commentators—Mr. Svend Petersen, the late Robert R. Pattrick, the late Edgar W. Smith and others—have produced briefer chronological tables and listings, and these we will have cause to refer to in the Notes to the stories which follow.

5 *Sherlock Holmes of Baker Street: A Life of the World's First Consulting Detective*, by William S. Baring-Gould; New York: Clarkson N. Potter, Inc., 1962; as *Sherlock Holmes: A Biography* in England; London: Rupert Hart-Davis, Ltd., 1962; also published in French and German editions.

who has ever been the subject of a full-length "biography."**5** There is also a Sherlockian Concordance (by Professor Christ), a Sherlockian Repertory (by Mr. Smith), a Sherlockian Glossary (by Magistrate S. Tupper Bigelow of Toronto), two Sherlockian Encyclopedias (one by Michael and Mollie Hardwick, the other by Orlando Park), two Sherlockian Iconographies (one by the late James Montgomery, the other by Mr. Walter Klinefelter), a Baker Street Song Book (by the late Harvey Officer), a Sherlockian Almanac (by Mr. Svend Petersen), a Sherlockian Gazetteer (also by Mr. Smith), a Sherlockian Atlas (by Dr. Julian Wolff) and a Practical Handbook of Sherlockian Heraldry (also by Dr. Wolff).

One is reminded of the remark made by the late Christopher Morley as he once compared the list of contributors to *The Baker Street Journal* with the list of subscribers to that publication.

"Never," said Morley wryly, "never has so much been written by so many for so few."

"YOU WOULD HAVE MADE AN ACTOR,
AND A RARE ONE"

[*Inspector Athelney Jones to Mr. Sherlock Holmes*, The Sign of the Four]

On the night of October 23, 1899, Sherlock Holmes in the flesh—all six feet of him—stepped onto the stage of the Star Theatre in Buffalo, New York.**1**

Some skeptics have since claimed that Holmes was impersonated on that occasion—and for many nights thereafter—by a distinguished contemporary actor named William Gillette,**2** and there seems little doubt that Gillette *did* write the four-act drama called, simply and classically, *Sherlock Holmes*, "being a hitherto unpublished episode in the career of the great detective, and showing his connection with The Strange Case of Miss [Alice] Faulkner."

Mr. John Dickson Carr, in his *Life of Sir Arthur Conan Doyle*, tells us that Conan Doyle in 1897 wrote a play about Sherlock Holmes but was unable to get it accepted by any suitable actor-manager. Eventually the American producer Charles Frohman was granted permission to have Gillette rewrite the play; the actor is said to have done so in four weeks, working basically from three of Conan Doyle's stories, the two short stories, "A Scandal in Bohemia" and "The Final Problem" and the novel, *A Study in Scarlet*. Amazingly enough, Gillette up to that time had never read a Sherlock Holmes story.

Now he read them all—all that had been written up to that time—steeping himself in the great detective's character and achievements. One thing bothered him—what liberties might he take with Conan Doyle's famous character? At last he wrote to Conan Doyle: "May I marry Holmes?" "Marry him or murder him or do anything else you like with him," Conan Doyle is reported to have replied.

In the summer of 1899 Gillette visited England to submit the finished script to Conan Doyle, and it must have surprised the creator of Sherlock Holmes, attired, we may imagine, in a highly conservative top hat and frock coat, to see Gillette descend from the train: the actor had donned a deerstalker hat and a long caped overcoat as a suitable costume for that first meeting.

Sherlock Holmes opened in New York City two weeks after its premiere performance in Buffalo—at the Garrick Theatre on November 6, 1899.

"I can think of no more perfect realisation of a fictional character on the stage," the famous artist, Frederic Dorr Steele, who was later to illustrate so many of the Sherlock

1 Bruce McRae played Watson in the production, and the part of Professor Moriarty was taken by George Wessells.

2 William Hooker Gillette was born on July 23, 1853, the youngest of six children. He made his professional debut on September 13, 1875, at Boston's old Globe Theatre in a play called *Faint Heart*, and first appeared on the London stage at the Adelphi Theatre as Lewis Dumont in *Secret Service*.

WILLIAM GILLETTE AS SHERLOCK HOLMES

The dauntless figure that faced Professor James Moriarty in Gillette's melodrama of 1899, from *Catalogue of the Collection in The Sherlock Holmes Tavern*.

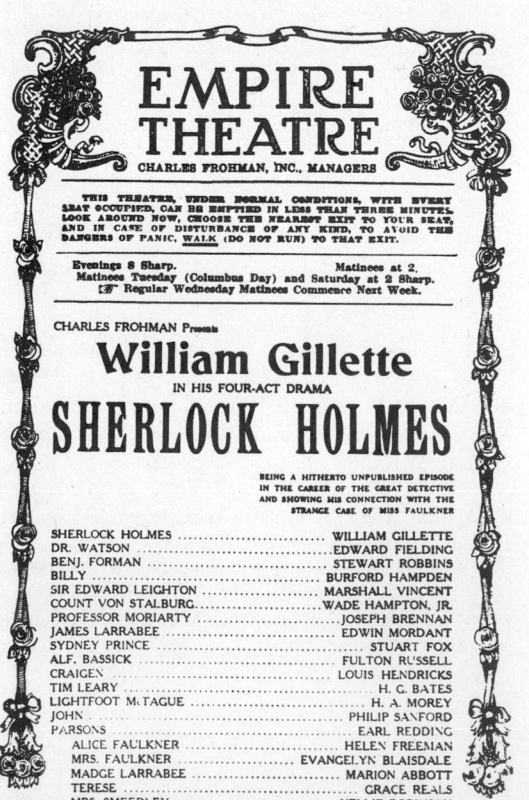

EMPIRE THEATRE
CHARLES FROHMAN, INC., MANAGERS

THIS THEATRE, UNDER NORMAL CONDITIONS, WITH EVERY SEAT OCCUPIED, CAN BE EMPTIED IN LESS THAN THREE MINUTES. LOOK AROUND NOW, CHOOSE THE NEAREST EXIT TO YOUR SEAT, AND IN CASE OF DISTURBANCE OF ANY KIND, TO AVOID THE DANGERS OF PANIC, WALK (DO NOT RUN) TO THAT EXIT.

Evenings 8 Sharp.   Matinees at 2.
Matinees Tuesday (Columbus Day) and Saturday at 2 Sharp.
☞ Regular Wednesday Matinees Commence Next Week.

CHARLES FROHMAN Presents

William Gillette
IN HIS FOUR-ACT DRAMA
SHERLOCK HOLMES

BEING A HITHERTO UNPUBLISHED EPISODE IN THE CAREER OF THE GREAT DETECTIVE AND SHOWING HIS CONNECTION WITH THE STRANGE CASE OF MISS FAULKNER

SHERLOCK HOLMES	WILLIAM GILLETTE
DR. WATSON	EDWARD FIELDING
BENJ. FORMAN	STEWART ROBBINS
BILLY	BURFORD HAMPDEN
SIR EDWARD LEIGHTON	MARSHALL VINCENT
COUNT VON STALBURG	WADE HAMPTON, JR.
PROFESSOR MORIARTY	JOSEPH BRENNAN
JAMES LARRABEE	EDWIN MORDANT
SYDNEY PRINCE	STUART FOX
ALF. BASSICK	FULTON RUSSELL
CRAIGEN	LOUIS HENDRICKS
TIM LEARY	H. G. BATES
LIGHTFOOT McTAGUE	H. A. MOREY
JOHN	PHILIP SANFORD
PARSONS	EARL REDDING
ALICE FAULKNER	HELEN FREEMAN
MRS. FAULKNER	EVANGELYN BLAISDALE
MADGE LARRABEE	MARION ABBOTT
TERESE	GRACE REALS
MRS. SMEEDLEY	NELLIE ROBINSON

Holmes short stories for *Collier's Magazine*, wrote many years later in "Sherlock Holmes in Pictures." "Gillette's quiet, but incisive, histrionic method exactly fitted such a part as Sherlock Holmes."

But the *New York Herald Tribune* declared that "the play has no lasting value whatever, unless it be the value of an occasional melodramatic incident; it is trivial at the beginning and feeble at the end"—a strange verdict indeed considering that the engagement at the Garrick continued until June 16, 1900, with capacity audiences at practically every performance.

After a series of performances at the Hollis Theatre in Boston starting on February 18, 1901, the play went on a most successful United States tour. It opened then in England at the Shakespeare Theatre in Liverpool on September 2, 1901, and played for the first time in London at the famous Lyceum Theatre (see *The Sign of the Four*), opening on September 9, 1901. There it scored a tremendous success, drawing capacity attendance until April 11, 1902. The play then toured the provinces as far north as Edinburgh.

Gillette in his time also wrote a sketch, "The Painful Predicament of Sherlock Holmes" (the "painful predicament" was that Holmes had a female client—played by Miss Ethel Barrymore—so voluble that the detective was unable to utter a single word during the entire length of the scene). "The Painful Predicament" was given as a benefit performance for Joseph Jefferson Holland at the Metropolitan Opera House in New York City on the afternoon of Friday, May 24, 1905. The parody was performed on at least three other occasions —in New York at the Criterion Theatre on April 14, 1905; in London at the Duke of York's Theatre on October 3, 1905; and as a curtain raiser to Gillette's play *Clarice* in Boston at the Colonial Theatre on Christmas Eve, 1905. Casting about in London for a Cockney boy who might act the part of Billy the Page, Gillette finally settled upon a little, frightened, underfed, sixteen-year-old named Charles Spencer Chaplin. (Charlie also played Billy for almost two years— well before 1905—when the English actor H. A. Saintsbury went on tour in Gillette's play, *Sherlock Holmes*.)

William Gillette was not the first actor to portray the great detective—that honor should apparently go to John Webb, who played Holmes in Glasgow, in a play by Charles Rogers, as early as May, 1894. But Gillette, after 1902, made almost a career in itself of playing Holmes. In 1916 he appeared as Holmes in a seven-reel motion picture produced by Essanay with Ernest Maupain as Professor Moriarty and Edward Fielding as Watson; this was Gillette's only venture within the medium of the screen.

Sherlock Holmes, the play, was revived or continued in 1904–05, 1910–11, 1915–16, 1929 (Springfield, Mass.) and 1931–32 (Boston). Gillette played the role for the last time in Princeton, New Jersey, on May 12, 1932; he died in Hartford, Connecticut, on April 29, 1937, at the age of eighty-

"CHARLES FROHMAN PRESENTS . . ."

The cast listing from the program of one of the later productions of Gillette's play, *Sherlock Holmes*, the Empire Theatre, New York City.

three, and today lies buried in the family plot at Farmington, Connecticut.

If William Gillette's *Sherlock Holmes* takes all honors as the most famous translation of Conan Doyle's most celebrated character to the medium of the stage, second place must certainly go to Conan Doyle's own dramatization of his famous short story, "The Adventure of the Speckled Band."

After his play, *The House of Temperley*, closed in May, 1910, Conan Doyle was left with the Royal Adelphi Theatre on his hands. Once more he turned to Holmes and wrote the play version of *The Speckled Band*, it is said, in two weeks. It opened on June 4, 1910, and the Sherlockian magic worked again: it was a box-office success from the start and ran for 169 continuous performances. The play, although keeping to the main plot of the story, has many variations,**3** some of the most interesting of which we will consider in our Notes to "The Adventure of the Speckled Band."

The previously mentioned H. A. Saintsbury played Holmes and the English actor Lyn Harding turned in a spectacular performance as the villainous "Dr. Rylott" (the Dr. *Roylott* of the story). A rock boa essayed the taxing role of "the speckled band." *The Speckled Band* was later filmed (in 1930–31) by the British and Dominion Film Company with Raymond Massey in the role of Holmes; Lyn Harding recreated his role as Rylott-Roylott; Harding also appeared as Holmes' archenemy, Professor James Moriarty, in two British-made motion pictures starring Arthur Wontner as Holmes.

Conan Doyle, in 1921, also wrote a one-act play about Holmes, "The Crown Diamond: An Evening with Sherlock Holmes," about which we shall have more to say later (see Chapter 73: ". . . It Is Undoubtedly Queer . . .").

To date, 21 serious plays have been based on the adventures of Sherlock Holmes: in 1903, for example, came the (unauthorized) drama, *Sherlock Holmes, Private Detective*, and 1905 saw a production called *The Bank of England: An Adventure in the Life of Sherlock Holmes*. Twenty-seven years later, in 1932, a somewhat startled London audience saw another Holmes play, *The Holmeses of Baker Street*, in which Sherlock appeared as a widower of over sixty—with a grown-up daughter named *Shirley*.

As Holmes was parodied in print, so was he satirized on the stage, and not only by Gillette in "The Painful Predicament": there was a burlesque called *Sheerluck Jones, or Why D'Gillette Him Off?*, with Clarence Blakiston in the title role; it appeared at Terry's Theatre in the Strand only a month after Gillette's *Sherlock Holmes* had opened at the Lyceum. This was followed, in January, 1902, by a turn in which "Sherlock Holmes" took the stage in many of London's music halls.**4**

Conan Doyle also authorized a play in four acts, *The Return of Sherlock Holmes*. Written originally by J. E. Harold Terry and Arthur Rose, *The Return* was later revised by Rose and Ernest Dudley and presented at the New Theatre, Bromley, on January 19, 1953. The original version, first produced at the Princess Theatre in 1923, ran for over 130 performances with the memorable Eille Norwood in the role of Holmes.**5**

LYN HARDING AS DR. GRIMESBY ROYLOTT, RAYMOND MASSEY AS SHERLOCK HOLMES

A scene from *The Speckled Band*, produced by the British and Dominion Film Company in 1931.

3 It has been published by Samuel French, London and New York, 1912.

4 A Holmes-Watson play in the interesting form of a puppet show—"The Case of the Elusive Train," by Charles Eames—was first presented by IBM at the New York World's Fair in the summer of 1964. The script has been published in the *Baker Street Journal*, Vol. XIV, No. 4, New Series, December, 1964, pp. 196–98.

5 Neither the original nor the revised version of *The Return of Sherlock Holmes* was ever published, but typed copies of the manuscript are held by a few lucky collectors.

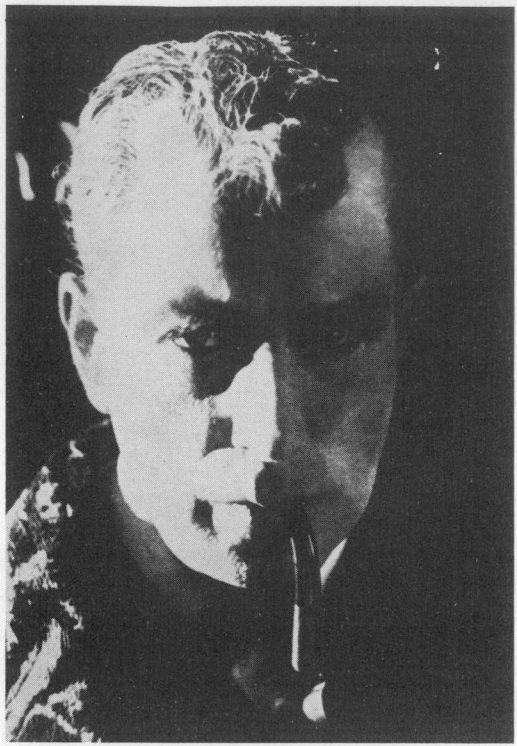

EILLE NORWOOD

This noted figure of the silent film in Britain as he appeared as Sherlock Holmes in *The Sign of the Four* for Stoll Productions, 1922.

Eille Norwood—his real name was Anthony Edward Brett; he chose his stage name because he once had a girl friend named Eille who lived in Norwood—was born October 11, 1861, at York, attended St. John's College, Cambridge, received an M.A. degree there, and married the actress Ruth Mackay. He played *Raffles* on tour and acted prior to his entry into films with such distinguished actors as H. B. Irving and Arthur Bourchier. He died in London on Christmas Eve, 1948, at the age of eighty-seven.

Norwood played Holmes not only in *The Return* but also on the screen in no less than 47 film adventures produced by the Stoll Film Company, starting as long ago as 1920. Conan Doyle had a very high opinion of Norwood's performances. In *Memories and Adventures,* the creator of Sherlock Holmes wrote: "Norwood has that rare quality which can only be described as glamour, which compels you to watch an actor eagerly even when he is doing nothing. He has the brooding eye which excites expectation and he has also a quite unrivaled power of disguise."

Still another English actor who made a name for himself in the role of Holmes was Arthur Wontner, 1875–1960. In the considered opinion of Mr. Vincent Starrett, "No better Sherlock Holmes than Arthur Wontner is likely to be seen and heard in pictures in our time. . . . His detective is the veritable fathomer of Baker Street in person."

Wontner was first chosen to play Holmes in December of 1930. With only an extremely limited budget, a modest film adaptation of "The Final Problem" and "The Adventure of the Empty House" was made in "a tin hut film studio" at Twickenham. The film was released in 1931 under the title of *The Sleeping Cardinal* (in England) and *Sherlock Holmes' Fatal Hour* (in America). It was an immediate success and, in America, made film history for the time by running for over a month on Broadway—then an almost unprecedented event for a British film.

The following year Mr. Wontner again impersonated Holmes in an adaptation of "The Adventure of Charles Augustus Milverton" called *The Missing Rembrandt.* Later in the same year, 1932, he appeared in *The Sign of the Four,*

ARTHUR WONTNER AS SHERLOCK HOLMES

(*Left*) In *The Missing Rembrandt* (1932) with Minnie Rayner as Mrs. Hudson, Ian Fleming as Dr. Watson. (*Right*) with Ian Fleming as Watson in *The Triumph of Sherlock Holmes* (1935).

and in 1935 he made an excellent version of *The Valley of Fear* under the title of *The Triumph of Sherlock Holmes*. Finally, in 1937, came his last bow as a screen Holmes in *Silver Blaze*. (In 1951, however, he again appeared as Holmes on television in connection with the Sherlock Holmes Exhibition at the Festival of Britain.)

Still another film Holmes (in Britain) was Peter Cushing, who turned in a notable performance in the Hammer production of *The Hound of the Baskervilles*, which opened at the London Pavilion on Friday, March 7, 1959. It was the seventh film *Hound* and the *121st* Holmes film. (In 1945 a copy of a German version of the *Hound* was found in Hitler's private film library at Berchtesgaden.)

Perhaps the earliest Holmes film of all was *Sherlock Holmes Baffled*, produced in 1903. Between 1908 and 1912 the Nordisk Film Company of Denmark made a long series of Holmes films, first with the Danish actor Holger Madsen, then with the German actor Alvin Neuss as Holmes. Italian, German, and French film companies were also quick to see the screen potentialities in Holmes.

In America, too, Holmes has had a long and distinguished film history, beginning in 1922 with his portrayal by John Barrymore, with Roland Young as Watson and Gustav von Seyffertitz as Moriarty. The most novel feature of the film —called *Sherlock Holmes* in the United States and *Moriarty* in England—was a prologue dealing with the youth and college career of Sherlock Holmes.

Clive Brook was another prominent film actor who played Holmes in America: in 1929, in the first talking Holmes film, made by Paramount, *The Return of Sherlock Holmes*, and again in 1933 in a sequel made for Fox Pictures. (A curious claim to distinction can be made by Reginald Owen, who is probably the only actor who has played both Holmes and Watson on the screen; in 1933 he was Watson to Clive Brook's Holmes, then, later in the same year, he was cast as Holmes in a film version of *A Study in Scarlet*.)

But there is little doubt that this country's best known Holmes today is Basil Rathbone, who first played the role in 1929 in 20th Century-Fox's *The Hound of the Baskervilles*. The late Nigel Bruce also made his debut as Dr. Watson in this same motion picture. Rathbone and Bruce were to repeat their portrayals in thirteen later films made for Universal between 1942 and 1946. The first three films rather unhappily showed a patriotic Holmes in World War II saving a secret bombsight from the Nazis, rescuing a vital document from a spy ring, and silencing a subversive radio station.

But this is not said to detract from Rathbone's characterization. As Mr. Anthony Howlett, the former Chairman of the Sherlock Holmes Society of London and an outstanding authority on the Holmes of stage and screen, has said: "The physical resemblance of Rathbone to the Sidney Paget illustrations [in the old *Strand Magazine*] was quite striking and, next to Arthur Wontner, probably no one has been so happily cast."

To turn to another medium, the radio adventures of Mr. Sherlock Holmes of Baker Street are still recalled with

GERMAN ACTOR ALWIN NEUSS AS THE GREAT DETECTIVE

From one of the early Holmes films between 1908 and 1912 by the Nordisk Film Company of Denmark, probably *The Murder in Baker Street*.

THE FILM HOLMES IN AMERICA

(*Above*) John Barrymore, with Gustav von Seyffertitz as Moriarty. (*Below*) Clive Brook as Sherlock Holmes.

"THE GAME IS AFOOT!"

Basil Rathbone as Sherlock Holmes and Nigel Bruce
as Dr. Watson in an ingeniously photographed
scene from Universal's *The House of Fear*.

MR. CARLETON HOBBS

The Sherlock Holmes of the British Broadcasting
Corporation.

pleasure by more than one generation of listeners. Basil Rathbone, Sir John Gielgud, and the late Sir Cedric Hardwicke are only three of the many fine actors who have appeared as Holmes on radio; in England there is also Mr. Carleton Hobbs, who has portrayed Holmes in a long series of radio plays (in one of which, "The Greek Interpreter," he played both Sherlock Holmes and Sherlock's brother Mycroft, in conversation together).

A series of 39 Holmes films for television, produced in Europe under the direction of Sheldon Reynolds, premiered in the New York City area on October 18, 1954. Ronald Howard, son of the late Leslie Howard, starred as Holmes, and H. Marion Crawford portrayed Watson as the sturdy fellow he really was.

On phonograph records also Holmes has left his mark: there is *Sherlock Holmes Explained by His Creator Sir Arthur Conan Doyle and Presented in Action by William Gillette* (issued in 1939 by the Gramophone Company, Limited, in Great Britain and by the National Vocarium in the United States; Conan Doyle's part was recorded in 1928, Gillette's in 1936). There is the Decca recording (No. K4164) which features Sir John Gielgud as Holmes, Sir Ralph Richardson as Watson and Orson Welles as Moriarty in dramatizations of "The Final Problem," the first meeting of Holmes and Watson and "The Adventure of Charles Augustus Milverton." And there are two series of "Talking Books" of Holmes adventures, issued by the Listening Library of New York City, the first narrated by John Brewster, the second by Basil Rathbone.

Sherlock Holmes—to the amusement (and distress) of some of his admirers—has even appeared in *ballet*. "The Great Detective," written by Margaret Dale to music by Richard Arnell, had its premiere performance at the Sadler Wells Ballet Theatre in London on January 21, 1953.

And there was more to come, as Fritz Weaver made his bow as Sherlock Holmes in the first musical comedy ever produced about the adventures of the world's greatest detective. *Baker Street*, with Inga Swenson as Irene Adler and Martin Gabel as Professor Moriarty, opened in Boston on Christmas Eve, 1964, and had its first New York performance on Tuesday, February 16, 1965.

FRITZ WEAVER AS SHERLOCK HOLMES

In the Alexander H. Cohen production of *Baker Street*, "a musical adventure of Sherlock Holmes," at the Brodway Theatre, New York City, 1965.

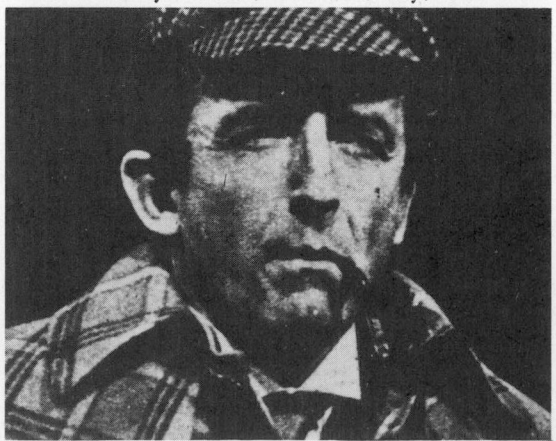

5

"YOUR PICTURES ARE NOT UNLIKE YOU, SIR, IF I MAY SAY SO"

["Killer" Evans, alias John Garrideb, to Mr. Sherlock Holmes, "The Adventure of the Three Garridebs"]

Conan Doyle—and Holmes enthusiasts everywhere—were fortunate that the editors of the *Strand Magazine* in England and *Collier's Magazine* in the United States were able to find two such superb artists as Sidney Paget and Frederic Dorr Steele to illustrate the great majority of the Sherlock Holmes stories.

Ironically, Sidney Paget was commissioned in error; the *Strand*'s editors were under the mistaken impression that they were writing to his artist-brother, Walter Paget, who had made the drawings for Sir H. Rider Haggard's *King Solomon's Mines* and *She*, but was perhaps best known for his illustrations for *Robinson Crusoe* and *Treasure Island*.**1**

Sidney Edward Paget was born on October 4, 1860, in London. He was the fifth son of the late Robert Paget, vestry clerk of Clerkenwell, was educated at a City school, and early developed a taste for drawing. On leaving school he studied from the antique at the British Museum for two years, after which he went to Heatherley's School of Art, in Norman Street, London, to study painting. Successful as an exhibitor (he showed two pictures at the Academy when he was only eighteen years old), he took a studio and began painting portraits and small pictures, at the same time illustrating books and papers, chiefly war subjects of Egypt and the Sudan. At twenty-one he entered the Royal Academy Schools for a term of six years, during which he carried off several important prizes.

Starting with "A Scandal in Bohemia" in the *Strand Magazine* for July, 1891, Paget produced a total of 357 drawings to illustrate *The Adventures*, *The Memoirs*, *The Hound of the Baskervilles*, and *The Return of Sherlock Holmes*, ending with "The Adventure of the Second Stain" in December, 1904.

Although brother "Wal" Paget had lost by misadventure the commission to illustrate the stories, he nonetheless made a major contribution to the picture many of us have of Holmes today: Walter Paget served as his brother Sidney's model for the great detective. So, too, did Paget take as his model for Dr. Watson another face familiar and convenient to him—that of his friend, Alfred Morris Butler, a well-known architect of the time.

1 After his brother Sidney's death, Walter Paget did illustrate a single Sherlock Holmes short story —"The Adventure of the Dying Detective" in the December, 1913, issue of the *Strand*.

"... WHAT PHIZ DID FOR PICKWICK, PAGET DID FOR
SHERLOCK HOLMES"

A *Strand Magazine* photograph of the English
artist who produced 357 Sherlock Holmes drawings.

2 Cuneo also illustrated the "Raffles" stories by
E. W. Hornung, Conan Doyle's brother-in-law,
when the Amateur Cracksman took over from the
Master Detective in the pages of *Collier's Magazine*,
whose editors had announced "The Second Stain"
as the "last" adventure of Sherlock Holmes. It was
Hornung who once said: "Though he might be
more humble, there's no police like Holmes."

3 "A curious and interesting point arises here,"
the artist's daughter, Winifred Paget, wrote in
"Full Circle." "If Holmes disappeared in April,
1891, and was not seen again until 1894, how did
he manage to send the cigarette case to my father
in 1893? Surely this is important evidence to support the theory that Holmes was not in Tibet or
Persia during those years but probably wandering
much nearer home in one of his many disguises
[see Chapter 46: "You May Have Heard of the
Remarkable Explorations of a Norwegian Named
Sigerson ..."]. The cigarette case could, I suppose, have been despatched by Mycroft Holmes
acting on his brother's instructions ..."

4 Steele himself always defended Paget: if his
earlier pictures seem imperfect to our eye, the
American artist pointed out, "it is partly because
of the crude woodcut reproductions." Those of
us who have seen the originals of Paget's illustrations heartily agree that his early work, at least,
lost much in the publishing.

Conan Doyle's own favorite illustrator was Cyrus Cuneo,
who never illustrated a Holmes adventure but did illustrate
many of Conan Doyle's other works;**2** Conan Doyle complained that Paget had made Holmes far handsomer than his
creator had ever intended him to be. But Conan Doyle was
honest enough to admit that this was probably a good thing:
it attracted a greater female readership to the stories in the
Strand.

Indeed, there is evidence that Conan Doyle was much impressed by Paget's work and considered him essential to the
success of each new venture; when the author wrote Greenhough Smith, the editor of the *Strand*, that he was contemplating putting Holmes into a real "creeper" to be called
The Hound of the Baskervilles, Conan Doyle specifically
asked for Paget as illustrator "in the event that Smith should
find the story acceptable."

With the disappearance of Holmes in "The Final Problem," the busy Paget apparently had time for the first time
to pursue the woman of his choice and eventually to marry
her on June 1, 1893. On the morning of his wedding day he
received a silver cigarette case bearing the inscription: "From
Sherlock Holmes 1893." The case became one of Paget's most
treasured possessions.**3**

Of Paget's work, the late James Montgomery has written
(*A Study in Pictures*):

It would be impossible to overestimate the influence
that he exerted upon the hearts and minds of the countless thousands who based their conception then—as they
still continue to do after sixty years—on his interpretation of Holmes, Watson, and the golden time "where it
is always 1895." From that day to this no characterization,
no other mood has been accepted by English readers,
and when his untimely death in 1908 necessarily shifted
his mantle to other shoulders, the artists who followed
him—several of greater skill and reputation—were compelled to subordinate themselves to the Paget style in all
essential particulars. It has been truly said that what
Phiz did for Pickwick, Paget did for Sherlock Holmes.

And now to America:

The late Elmer Davis wrote that Holmes in *The Return*
was "better than ever; for here in *Collier's* appeared, for the
first time in print, what has become the classic, final and
unalterable portrait of Sherlock Holmes. I say, for the first
time in print; it had long been familiar on the stage. For it
was William Gillette in a deerstalker cap who so unmistakably was Sherlock Holmes that, when Frederic Dorr Steele
[1874–1944] came to illustrate the stories in *The Return*, he
had to do no more than draw a picture of Gillette; and instantly all previous likenesses set down by Paget and Hyde
and Friston and the rest became merely collectors' items."

This is more than a little hard on Paget,**4** but many other
students of the Saga have certainly paid high tribute to
Steele's skill as an illustrator. Mr. Vincent Starrett has waxed
rhapsodic about Steele in his essay on Canonical illustrators
in *The Private Life of Sherlock Holmes;* "No one can touch
Steele in making you feel what is going on behind the door,"

the novelist Arthur Somers Roche once said; and the late Edmund Pearson went so far as to call Steele's drawings "the most interesting decorations of all time" in "Sherlock Holmes Among the Illustrators." "Countless other Americans," Montgomery wrote, "cannot possibly imagine any other portrayal of Holmes, Watson, and the adventures the two experienced, their whole love and enthusiasm for the tales being built on a recollection of and an association with the Steele illustrations . . ."**5**

Born in a lumber camp near Marquette, Michigan, but a New Yorker since boyhood, Frederic Dorr Steele studied at the National Academy of Design and the Art Students League, where he later taught drawing. He took his first job, on the old *Harper's Weekly*, for $15 a week "and glory," but soon graduated into free-lance work, illustrating the stories of such writers as Richard Harding Davis, Rudyard Kipling, O. Henry, and Mark Twain. Known primarily as an illustrator, Steele worked in nearly every medium except oil, and his drawings ranged from delicate pen work to bold poster designs in color. While vacationing at Monhegan, Maine, one summer, he developed an interest in cartography and a considerable skill as an etcher; he often asserted afterward that his "favorite drawing" was a large-scale map of Monhegan which, with characteristic patience, he spent twenty-four years perfecting.

Steele also had an enormous talent for caricature, which he exercised mercilessly upon fellow members of the Players Club, of which he was forty years a member. His membership in the Players acquainted him with most of the principal actors and actresses of the New York stage, many of whom—Katharine Cornell, Judith Anderson, Tallulah Bankhead, Helen Hayes, Maurice Evans, Josephine Hull, Walter Huston, Frank Craven, Bobby Clark, Ethel Waters, Paul Lukas, among others—he portrayed over fifteen years in the drama section of the *New York Herald Tribune*. He stood, according to one art critic, "in the first rank of American illustrators." Already represented in private collections and at the Carnegie Institute of Pittsburgh at the time of his death, Steele was also the first living illustrator to be exhibited at the Library of Congress.

"I did not need to be told to make my Sherlock look like Gillette," the artist wrote in "Sherlock Holmes in Pictures." "The thing was inevitable. I kept him in mind and even copied or adapted parts of a few of the stage photographs. At that time I had never seen the play, and it was not until 1929 that Mr. Gillette actually became my model in the flesh . . ."

Steele's original model for Sherlock Holmes was an Englishman named Robert King. Later, the artist "fell back on that standby of the studios, Frank B. Wilson," and his two sons. Later still, Steele's Sherlocks were drawn from "the fine frame and crag-like head" of a model named S. B. Doughty.

We have previously mentioned some of the many other artists who have illustrated the Canon in books and magazines; in Notes to come, we will have occasion to mention and to comment upon many others.

But no discussion of Holmes in art would be complete without some reference to the Holmes of the Sunday supplements and the daily "comic-strip" pages.

5 Montgomery himself, as we have seen, vastly preferred Paget as an illustrator to Steele; he deplored the American artist's frequent lack of accuracy in depicting scenes in *The Return* and many later adventures.

FREDERIC DORR STEELE

The artist shown at the first one-man show of his drawings, held at the Contemporary Arts Gallery in 1935. Photo by Steffen, *New York Herald Tribune*.

WILLIAM GILLETTE AS SKETCHED FROM LIFE BY FREDERIC DORR STEELE IN 1929

"MEANWHILE AT 221-B BAKER STREET . . ."

The Sherlock Holmes of the "comic strip" pages, as written by Edith Meiser and drawn by Frank Giacoia.

The late Sidney Smith, creator of "The Gumps," produced between 1911 and 1914 a series of color comics called "Sherlock Holmes, Jr." Years later, an adaptation of the stories by Edith Meiser, strikingly illustrated by Frank Giacoia, appeared in many United States newspapers. In this medium also Holmes was parodied—as "Hawkshaw, the Detective," for example, who appeared in the late 1910's and early 1920's in a comic strip drawn by Gus Mager, with a Dr. Watson who was called simply "Colonel."

All of us are familiar, too, with the Holmes who has appeared so often in newspaper and magazine advertising.

The late Judge Kenneth G. Brill, of St. Paul, Minnesota, made it his hobby to amass Holmesian advertisements; reviewing the collection after Judge Brill's death, Dean E. W. Zierbath of the University of Minnesota reported: "A spot check reveals some 67 references which I consider major, and 23 which might, because of the incomplete nature of the Holmesian reference, be regarded as minor. The majority of these are from the press or popular journals of the United States, but several Canadian and a few British examples are included."

Holmes seems to be every bit as popular in advertising today as he was at the turn of the century. Cocking an eye at such messages as that for Grand Cut Tobacco (see illustration) we feel he might well say—as he *did* say in "The Adventure of the Six Napoleons"—"The Press, Watson, is a most valuable institution, if you only know how to use it."

SHERLOCK HOLMES IN ADVERTISING

"The Press, Watson, is a most valuable institution, if you only know how to use it."

Now *there's* a tobacco you could smoke all day without burning your tongue.

Amazing, Holmes!

Elementary, my dear Watson—it's

Grand Cut

Never burns the tongue of old or young   2 oz 8/2

THE "THREE HOURS FOR LUNCH" CLUB IN SESSION

According to Mr. Robert Keith Leavitt, the historian of the Baker Street Irregulars, this drawing by George Ennis shows (*top row, left to right*) Franklin Abbot, Christ Cella, Frank V. Morley, "Torino" (a Cella waiter), Hulbert Footner, Mrs. Cella and (*front row*) Robert Keith Leavitt, Frank C. Henry, William S. Hall, Christopher Morley, Don Marquis, and Émile Gauvreau. From *The Baker Street Journal*, September, 1961.

6

"A SINGULAR SET OF PEOPLE, WATSON . . ."

[Sherlock Holmes, "The Adventure of Wisteria Lodge"]

The late Christopher Morley, 1890–1957, like the great Dr. Sam Johnson, had a flair for founding congenial clubs—among them a more or less stag affair called the Three Hours for Lunch Club and a slightly more coeducational dinner society, the *Grillparzer Sittenpolizei Verein*, or Grillparzer Morals-Police Association.

From these grew the Baker Street Irregulars.

The time was ripe for such a sodality—"even whisky-and-sodality," as Morley once said: William Gillette's recent revivals of his play *Sherlock Holmes* had met with great success, and the Doubleday omnibus, *The Complete Sherlock Holmes,* was enjoying wide circulation. Then came S. C. Roberts' brilliant little biography of *Doctor Watson* and Vincent Starrett's admirable *The Private Life of Sherlock Holmes*—the latter reviewed (December 2, 1933) in *The Saturday Review of Literature* (now the *Saturday Review*) by the late political commentator and essayist Elmer Davis, 1890–1958, in a stunning piece that Davis afterward revised into the form of an essay "On the Emotional Geology of Baker Street."

It was all but inevitable that the first meeting of what was to become the Baker Street Irregulars should be held. And held it was, on January 6, 1934, when a group of enthusiasts —drawn mostly from the members of the Three Hours for Lunch Club and GSV—met at the old Hotel Duane on Madison Avenue, New York City.

The name the Baker Street Irregulars, as an organization outside the pages of Sir Arthur Conan Doyle, seems to have appeared in print for the first time in Morley's "Bowling Green" column in the *SRL* for January 27, 1934. According to the "Bowling Green," the "secretary" of the BSI, William S. Hall, had allowed him—Morley—to "look over the minutes of the first meeting of the club." Among other business it appears that the matter of an official toast was discussed. It was agreed that the first health must always be drunk to "*The* Woman" (Irene Adler of "A Scandal in Bohemia"). Suggestions for succeeding sentiments were "Mrs. Hudson," "Mycroft," "The Second Mrs. Watson," "The Game Is Afoot!" and "The Second Most Dangerous Man in London."

By February 3, 1934, Morley was printing Holmesian correspondence under the heading of "The Baker Street Irregulars," and on February 17th he ran two significant items. The first was a letter from Mr. Vincent Starrett, a masterly presentation of the problem of the Moriarty brothers, both named James. The second was the document that constitutes

CROSSWORD 221 B (*Baker Street Irregular*)   *Mycroft Holmes*

ACROSS

1. A treatise on this, written at the age of twenty-one, had a European vogue and earned its author a professorship. (2 words, 8, 7)
8. It was of course to see these that Holmes enquired the way from Saxe-Coburg Square to the Strand (2 words, 10, 5)
11. How the pips were set (2)
13. Not an Eley's No. 2 (which is an excellent argument with a gentleman who can twist steel pokers into knots) but the weapon in the tragedy of Birlstone (3)
14. What was done on the opposite wall in bullet-pocks by the patriotic Holmes (2)
15. What Watson recognized when he put his hand on Bartholomew Sholto's leg (5)
18. Where Watson met young Stamford, who introduced him to Sherlock Holmes (3)
20. A kind of pet, over which Dr. Grimesby Roylott hurled the local blacksmith (4)
21. Holmes should have said this before being so sure of catching the murderers of John Openshaw (2)
22. The kind of Pedro whence came the tiger (3)
23. Though he knew the methods, Watson sometimes found it difficult to do this (3)
25. Patron saint of old Mr. Farquhar's affliction and perhaps of Abe Slaney's men (5)
27. Perhaps a measure of Holmes's chemicals (2)
28. In short, Watson (2)
29.   (2)
30. Curious that he did nothing in the nighttime (3)
31. This would obviously not describe the empty house opposite 221b Baker Street (3)
34. It seems likely that Watson's elder brother suffered from this disease (2)
35. Though you might have taken this at Lodge 29, Chicago, nevertheless, you had to pass a test as well at Lodge 341, Vermissa (4)
37. The *Star* of Savannah (4)
40. Mrs. Barclay's reproach (in The Crooked Man, of course) suggests the parable of this (3)
41. Scrawled in blood-red letters across the bare plaster at No. 3, Lauriston Gardens (5)
43. Holmes found this, because he was looking for it in the mud (5)
44. Suggests Jonathan Small's leg (3)
45. The brother who left Watson no choice but to relate The Final

Problem (2 words, 5, 8)

DOWN

1. A country district in the west of England where "Cooee" was a common signal (2 words, 8, 6)
2. Charles Augustus Milverton dealt with no niggard hand; therefore this would not describe him (4)
3. The kind of practice indulged by Mr. Williamson, the solitary cyclist's unfrocked clergyman—"there was a man of that name in orders, whose career has been a singularly dark one." (3)
4. There is comparatively as much sense in Hafiz. Indeed, it's a case of identity. (3 words, 2, 2, 6)
5. Caused the rift in the beryl coronet (3)
6. Many of Holmes's opponents had cause to (3)
7. Begins: 'Whose was it?' 'His who is gone.' 'Who shall have it?' 'He who will come.' (2 words, 8, 6)
9. of four (4)
10. The number of Napoleons plus the number of Randall gang (4)
12. One of the five sent 'S.H. for J.O.' (3)
16. To save the dying detective trouble, Mr. Culverton Smith was kind enough to give the signal by turning this up (3)
17. The blundering constable who failed to gain his sergeant's stripes in the Lauriston Gardens Mystery (5)
19. There was a giant one of Sumatra; yet it was unwritten (3)
23. How Watson felt after the Final Problem (3)
24. He was epollicate (8)
26. Initials of the second most dangerous man in London (2)
32. Though Miss Mary Sutherland's boots were not unlike, they were really odd ones; the one having this slightly decorated, and the other plain (3)
33. You may forgive the plural form of these tobaccos, since Holmes smoked so much of them (5)
36. Behind this Black Jack of Ballarat waited and smoked an Indian cigar, of the variety which are rolled in Rotterdam (4)
38 and 39. The best I can make of these is the Latin for the sufferers of the epidemic which pleased Holmes so extremely that he said 'A long shot, Watson, a very long shot,' and pinched the Doctor's arm (4)
42. One of the two in the cardboard box (3)
44. Initials of the street in which Mycroft lodged (2)

. . . THE CLOSEST THING THE BSI EVER HAD TO . . .
AN EXAMINATION

The crossword puzzle by Frank V. Morley, first published in *The Saturday Review of Literature*, May 3, 1934.

the Constitution and Buy—*Buy*, not *By*—Laws of the Baker Street Irregulars, the work of Elmer Davis.

It is worth quoting here in full:

CONSTITUTION
ARTICLE I

The name of this society shall be the Baker Street Irregulars.

ARTICLE II

Its purpose shall be the study of the Sacred Writings.

ARTICLE III

All persons shall be eligible for membership who pass an examination in the Sacred Writings set by officers of the society, and who are considered otherwise suitable.

ARTICLE IV

The officers shall be: a Gasogene, a Tantalus, and a Commissionaire.

The duties of the Gasogene shall be those commonly performed by a President.

The duties of the Tantalus shall be those commonly performed by a Secretary.

The duties of the Commissionaire shall be to telephone down for ice, White Rock, and whatever else may be required and available; to conduct all negotiations with waiters; and to assess the members pro rata for the cost of same.

BUY-LAWS

1. An annual meeting shall be held on January 6, at which the canonical toasts shall be drunk; after which the members shall drink at will.
2. The current round shall be bought by any member who fails to identify, by title of story and context, any quotation from the Sacred Writings submitted by any other member.

Qualification A. If two or more members fail so to identify, a round shall be bought by each of those so failing.

Qualification B. If the submitter of the quotation, upon challenge, fails to identify it correctly, he shall buy the round.

3. Special meetings may be called at any time or place by any one of three members, two of whom shall constitute a quorum.

Qualification A. If said two people are of opposite sexes, they shall use care in selecting the place of meeting, to avoid misinterpretation (or interpretation either, for that matter).

4. All other business shall be left for the monthly meeting.
5. There shall be no monthly meeting.

The Constitution refers to "an examination in the Sacred Writings" as a prerequisite for membership, but the closest thing the BSI ever had to such an examination was a crossword puzzle, concocted by a bored Frank V. Morley in the smokeroom of a Cunard liner during a dull Atlantic crossing. It was published—as by "Mycroft Holmes"—in the "Bowling Green" of May 3, 1934, with this challenge from Christopher

Morley: ". . . I will delay printing the solution of the cross-word for two weeks, to give our clients plenty of time to consider it. All those who send me correct solutions—but they must be correct in every detail—will automatically become members of the Baker Street Irregulars."

Fifteen perfect solutions were received, and Morley on May 29, 1934, wrote a letter to successful contestants of the male gender who had got their entries onto his desk before the deadline:**1**

"The first formal meeting of the Baker Street Irregulars will be at 144 East 45th Street [then the site of Christ Cella's Restaurant] on Tuesday, June 5th at 6:30 P.M. . . . The proprietor has set aside a room for us upstairs which we can use as permanent headquarters . . ."**2**

Of those invited, only eight were able to attend: in the order in which they were seated, they were Morley himself (the Gasogene), Malcolm Johnson, Allan Price, Harvey Officer, Earle Walbridge, Robert Keith Leavitt, Frank Henry, and William S. Hall.**3**

The next recorded meeting took place on Friday, December 7, 1934—"a sort of jump-the-gun Anniversary [of the birth of Sherlock Holmes] Dinner," Morley called it; the second Annual Dinner was held, less irregularly, on the night of January 6, 1936, a Monday. (Since then, however, the Annual Dinner of the Baker Street Irregulars has always been held on the Friday which falls closest to January 6th, unless that Friday is in too close conflict with the festivities attending the New Year.)

Records of the early Dinners are fragmentary, at best, but it seems that 18 or 20 Irregulars turned up for the 1934 Dinner, among them William Gillette, Frederic Dorr Steele, H. W. Bell, Gene Tunney, and Vincent Starrett. Also present was Alexander Woollcott; never a member of the BSI, Woollcott attended the first Dinner of the society as the guest of Vincent Starrett, whose hospitality he returned by writing a mocking piece about the Irregulars for the December 29, 1934, issue of *The New Yorker*.

1 The letter also went to certain of Morley's cronies in the Three Hours for Lunch Club who had made no attempt to solve the puzzle—the late Don Marquis, for example.

2 Morley later recalled that in addition to the meeting room there were "two retiring rooms, which we persuaded Christ Cella to label as Sherlock and Irene. This puzzled some customers, but was effective for segregation."

3 Until his death in 1961, Earle Walbridge was the only member of the BSI who had attended *every* meeting.

BYPLAY BEFORE THE 1947 DINNER OF THE BAKER STREET IRREGULARS

This dinner was held at the old Murray Hill Hotel in New York City on January 3rd. *Left to right:* Fred Dannay (one half of "Ellery Queen"), the late Elmer Davis, William S. Hall as Sherlock Holmes, the late Christopher Morley, and Rex Stout of Nero Wolfe and Archie Goodwin fame.

This is to certify that
having passed all of the tests prescribed by the
Constitution and Buy-Laws of the Society, is
hereby declared a full participating member of
THE BAKER STREET IRREGULARS
under the authentication Titular Investiture of

and is authorized, in the purlieus of the Sherlockian world, to "go everywhere, see everything, overhear everyone."
In witness whereof, and in recognition of distinguished services rendered in the Cause of
keeping green the Master's memory, there is
affixed hereto the Canonical Recompense of the
IRREGULAR SHILLING.

"It's the Baker Street Division of the
detective police force. . . . Here are
your wages." . . . He handed each of
them a shilling.—*A Study in Scarlet.*
"It is the unofficial force—the Baker
Street irregulars." . . . He handed
them a shilling each.—*The Sign of
the Four.*

FOR THE BAKER STREET IRREGULARS:

BUTTONS-CUM-COMMISSIONAIRE

THE CERTIFICATE OF INVESTITURE IN THE BAKER STREET
IRREGULARS

The name of the member, with the title of the
Sherlock Holmes adventure, recorded or unrecorded, which he will henceforth represent, is inserted at the top of the Certificate; at the lower
left is affixed a Victorian shilling.

"The happiest achievement of the BSI," Morley recalled
later, "was when it attracted the attention of our devoted
Edgar Smith. . . . He wrote in a vein of decorous modesty
asking if he could be put on the waiting list and offered to
undergo any sort of inquest of suitability. It was plain from
the first that here was *the* Man. . . . Mr. Edgar Smith's affectionate zeal, his delight in keeping orderly records and his
access to mimeographic, parchment-engrossing and secre-
tarial resources, all these were irresistible."

The late Edgar W. Smith, 1894–1960, joined the BSI in
1938—the same year in which he was made a Vice-President
of the General Motors Overseas Operations and Director of
that company's Institutional Relations. (He subsequently,
before his retirement, had responsibility for public and per-
sonnel relations as well as for research in international trade
and public affairs.)

It was Edgar Smith who launched the *Baker Street Journal*
as a quarterly publication in January, 1946, and it was Edgar
Smith who served as its editor until his death. "There were
those who were sure it could not possibly last for long," he
recalled in later years, "because practically everything that
might ever be said upon the subject of Sherlock Holmes had
already been said." But thirteen fat issues of the old *Journal*
were published, containing an aggregate of 1,700-odd closely
printed pages, all devoted exclusively to the life and times
of Sherlock Holmes. The *Journal* suspended publication for
a time (the last issue of the old *Journal* was dated January,
1949)4 but in January, 1951, a new series of *Journals* began
to issue, and the saga of the Saga continues to this day.

Although by the Certificate of Investiture, members of the
BSI are entitled to "go everywhere, see everything, overhear
everyone," they cannot do all these things in all places at
the same time. And so it was inevitable that Scion Societies
should spring up from Toronto, Ontario, to New Orleans,
Louisiana; from Boston, Massachusetts, to Los Angeles,
California.

The first to be formed was the Five Orange Pips of Westchester County. Founded in 1935 by Richard W. Clarke, its
membership grew to ten, but deaths in recent years have
reduced its present membership to the original number, five.
By far the most erudite of the Scion Societies, the Five
Orange Pips holds elaborate formal dinners at irregular intervals; its members have also written and published *The Best
of the Pips* (1955), by all odds one of the handsomest of the
many volumes of Sherlockian commentary sponsored by the
Scions.

The honor of being the first Scion Society to be formed
beyond the boundaries of the greater New York area goes
to the Speckled Band of Boston, founded April 26, 1940, by
the late James Keddie, Sr. It, too, has published handsome
volumes: *The Second Cab* (1957) and *The Third Cab*
(1960).

Indeed, there is today hardly a city of any size in the
United States where a member of the BSI cannot find a Scion
Society whose members share his interest in things Holmesian.

There are the Hounds of the Baskerville (*sic*) of Chicago,
founded 1943; the Scowrers of San Francisco, founded 1944,
the only Scion Society which can boast a female auxiliary,

---

4 Dr. Julian Wolff, who is now Commissionaire
of the BSI and editor of the *Journal*, has always
referred to the three issues unpublished in 1949 as
"The Missing Three-Quarters."

the Molly Maguires; the Greek Interpreters of East Lansing, Michigan, founded 1945; the Amateur Mendicant Society of Detroit, founded January, 1946; the Dancing Men of Providence and the Scandalous Bohemians of Akron, both founded February, 1946; the Six Napoleons of Baltimore, founded September, 1946; the Illustrious Clients of Indianapolis, founded October, 1946; the Creeping Men of Cleveland, founded April, 1947; the Sons of the Copper Beeches of Philadelphia, founded December, 1947; the Musgrave Ritualists of New York and the Norwegian Explorers of Minneapolis and St. Paul, both founded January, 1948; the Priory Scholars of Pittsburgh, founded October, 1948; the Red Circle of Washington, D.C., founded 1951; the Old Soldiers of Baker Street (the Old SOBs), founded 1952.

Affiliated with the BSI, and invading the bonds of Empire in one case at least, are the Red-Headed League of Sydney, Australia; the Baritsu Chapter of Tokyo, Japan; the Boulevard Assassins of Paris; the Sherlock Holmes Klubben i Danmark; and the Crew of the S.S. *Friesland* of Amsterdam, Holland.

To this far-from-complete list, yearly growing, should be added the William Gillette Memorial Luncheon and the Martha Hudson Breakfast, organized to take care of the other two meals of the day on which is annually held the BSI Dinner.

Meantime, as early as May 12, 1934, Christopher Morley was able to announce in the "Bowling Green" that "Mr. A. G. Macdonell writes that the English Sherlock Holmes Society has organized and sends greetings to our own Baker Street Irregulars. The SHS is to hold its first dinner on June 6th [1934] at a restaurant [Canuto's, since vanished] in Baker Street. 'June 6th being Derby Day,' says Mr. Macdonell, 'it was felt that "Silver Blaze" might well be discussed.' "

This Society would seem to have perished with the death of its first and only President, the Reverend Dick Sheppard; its Chairman was the late Ivar Gunn, whose widow, Margaret Gunn, is now the Honourable Co-Secretary of the reconstituted Sherlock Holmes Society of London.

Writing in the *Sherlock Holmes Journal* ("For a World Now Prepared"), Mr. Colin Prestige has stated that "the actual decision to form [this later] society was . . . taken on the evening of Tuesday, February 20, 1951. On that day Anthony D. Howlett, Professor (then Dr.) W. T. Williams and I had met [C. T.] Thorne at Marylebone to discuss certain ideas concerning the [Sherlock Holmes Exhibition at the Festival of Britain]. . . . As a result of this friendly evening, Jack Thorne convened a meeting for Friday, March 16, inviting a number of Holmesians to meet in the Marylebone Children's Library. . . . There were present R. Ivar Gunn, James E. Holroyd, Anthony D. Howlett, Owen T. C. Jones (of Toronto), Winifred Paget, Colin Prestige, C. T. Thorne, W. T. Williams and Patricia Coulson (Mrs. Wynne-Jones). Studying these careful minutes, it is instructive to note how faithfully the Society has kept to the tentative proposals then discussed: a *Journal*, preferably printed, was felt to be essential; it was thought meetings should be four times a year, spread over the winter months (in fact, there are usually five or six each year); it was agreed to exhibit old Holmes films;

and it was agreed that qualifications for membership should be interest rather than learning. Finally, it was determined to call a full-scale meeting for Wednesday, April 17, to decide whether or not to form a society."

So far as Mr. Prestige's excellent memory serves, the following were present at this historic meeting (prewar members are denoted with asterisks): *Ivor Black, *Maurice Campbell, *R. Ivar Gunn, Michael Hall, James E. Holroyd, Anthony D. Howlett, *Sir Gerald Kelly, Ian M. Leslie, Ed Lewis, Winifred Paget, Freda Pearce, Colin Prestige, C. T. Thorne, Guy Warrack, Michael Weight, W. T. Williams, and Patricia Wynne-Jones.

Today, the Society lists 290 members, exclusive of its ten officers.

Like the BSI, the Sherlock Holmes Society of London has its Scion Societies, among them the Reigate Squires, the Inner Brotherhood of the Four, the Abbey Grangers of Chislehurst, and the very active Milvertonians of Hampstead. Affiliated with the Society is at least one Continental Scion, the King of Scandinavia's Own Sherlockians (there is also the Society of the Solitary Cyclists of Sweden, founded January 9, 1964).

And, like the BSI, the Sherlock Holmes Society of London publishes a *Journal*, first issued in May, 1952, with James Edward Holroyd and Philip Dalton as coeditors. It was then a mimeographed, staple-bound little publication of 40 pages —a far cry from the printed, handsomely illustrated *Journal* of today, now under the editorship of the Marquess of Donegall, which is currently mailed twice a year to its subscribers.

"There have been, of course, occasional hard-minded observors who thought it silly for a group of grown men to dally so intently over a literature of entertainment for which even its own author had only moderate regard," Christopher Morley once wrote. "Let me repeat what I have said before, that no printed body of modern social history . . . either by purpose or accident contains a richer pandect of the efficient impulses of its age. It has shown itself keen forecast in many ways, and some of its allusions may yet again be painfully timely. I wouldn't be surprised at any moment to see Afghanistan, or the *Orontes*, or the Coptic Patriarchs, or the dynamics of an asteroid, reappear in the news."

7

"YOUR MERITS SHOULD BE PUBLICLY RECOGNIZED"

[John H. Watson, M.D., to Mr. Sherlock Holmes, A Study in Scarlet]

We have mentioned the Sherlock Holmes Exhibition which was held at Abbey House on Baker Street, London, N.W. 1, May 22nd to September 22nd in 1951 as part of the Festival of Britain. The conception was first debated by the Councillors of the Borough of Marylebone as long ago as October, 1950, as a fitting tribute to "their most distinguished resident." Approved, a sum running to several thousand pounds was appropriated, and the project was triumphantly carried out, to the great delight of the thousands of enthusiasts who flocked to the Exhibition.

Certainly the most heartwarming and ingenious display of this entire Exhibition was the reproduction of the sitting room at 221B. The experts who did the exhaustive research were headed by Mr. C. T. Thorne, then a librarian of the St. Marylebone Borough; Professor W. T. Williams was the chief scientific adviser; and the room itself was the work of Michael Weight, a talented stage designer.

Fifty-four thousand people had seen the Exhibition when it closed in London; it then opened a six-and-a-half-weeks run at the Plaza Art Galleries in New York City on July 2, 1952, on the first leg of what was to be an international tour. The original room was almost entirely broken up on its return from New York, but Mrs. Adrian M. Conan Doyle reconstructed it for the Sherlock Holmes Inn from exhibits and material supplied by her husband. The reconstructed room was moved to the Inn on December 12, 1957, where it may be seen today; many other items from the Exhibition are on display in the ground-floor barrooms. **1**

1 The first public Sherlockian room in the United States, the Irregulars' Room in Sage's Restaurant, Chicago, was opened on February 26, 1964.

SITTING ROOM, 221B BAKER STREET, RECONSTRUCTED FOR THE 1951 SHERLOCK HOLMES EXHIBITION BY MICHAEL WEIGHT

The drawing is by Ronald Searle and originally appeared in *Punch*.

CATALOGUE COVER OF SHERLOCK HOLMES EXHIBITION, 1951

Drawing of Holmes by Bruce Angrave.

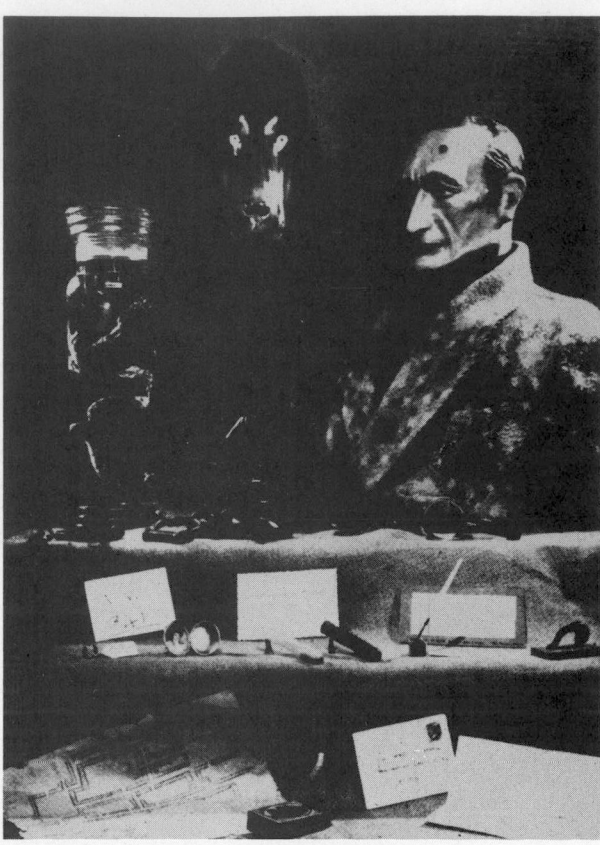

RELICS OF FAMOUS HOLMES CASES IN THE COLLECTION
OF THE SHERLOCK HOLMES TAVERN

But the best and most accurate reconstruction of Mr. Sherlock Holmes' sitting room rests at this writing in the vaults of the castle of Lucens. Mrs. Adrian M. Conan Doyle, actively assisted by Mr. Thorne, has worked for months past to create the Room; Thorne pronounces it the best of the three.

No more impressive tribute to Sherlock Holmes has ever been paid than this remarkable Exhibition. But we may note many others:

Item: The late President of the United States, Franklin Delano Roosevelt, chose to call the cabins at his weekend retreat where the Secret Service men sheltered "221B Baker Street."[2]

Item: The London County Council in recent years has renamed the street once called York Mews South; it is now *Sherlock* Mews.

Item: The Diorama Room at Madame Tussaud's famous wax museum now features a remarkable reconstruction of the chase on the moor in *The Hound of the Baskervilles;* that it should do so was first suggested by Mr. Humphrey Morton of the Milvertonians of Hampstead.

Item: As part of the celebration of the Conan Doyle Centenary in May, 1959, a handsome bookcase was placed on permanent loan to the St. Marylebone Council to encourage the building up of a comprehensive collection of Holmesian texts and higher criticism.

Item: No. 8, one of a group of twenty electric locomotives of the Metropolitan Railway named for Great Britain's Great Men from John Lyon (No. 1) to Christopher Wren (No. 20) was designated "The Sherlock Holmes." The nameplate, unhappily, had to be melted down for scrap metal during the dark days of World War II, but on Monday, October 5, 1953, the name was restored to one of the Metropolitan Line electric locomotives hauling passenger trains on the Aylesbury line between Baker Street and Rickmansworth. (It was returned to the Sherlock Holmes Society, its donor, however, on November 14, 1962, when the Metropolitan Line was modernized and the locomotive put out to pension; London Transport then arranged an impressive luncheon ceremony.)

Item: It was Old Irregular Tom Stix who conceived the idea of inaugurating the Silver Blaze Purse as a regular feature of the Eastern racing season. His conception saw realization in 1952, on the 18th of April, when the Silver Blaze Purse was run for the first time as the sixth (feature) race at Jamaica, Long Island, with a $5,000 purse for three-year-olds which had never won three races other than maiden or claiming 122 pounds; the distance was one mile and a sixteenth; there were eight entries of whom Quick Step was the winner. Today, Silver Blaze Handicaps or similarly named races are more or less annual features of the racing season not only in New York but also in Toronto, Ontario (where the Sherlockian Plate was first run at Woodbine in 1961); in Chicago (first run at Arlington Park on August 5, 1960); in San Francisco (first run at the Bay Meadows Track in San Mateo on October 20, 1961); and at Aalborg in Denmark (first run on September 29, 1963).

Still, first place after the Sherlock Holmes Exhibition should probably go to the series of memorials which have been installed at sites of Holmesian interest by devoted mem-

2 Only the Baker Street Irregulars knew, while he lived, that President Roosevelt was a free and accepted member of their order. After his death a collection of his letters to Edgar Smith, commenting shrewdly on many aspects of the Canon, was published by the society.

bers of the BSI and the Sherlock Holmes Society of London.

The first of these memorials was the inspiration of Mr. W. T. Rabe, organizer during World War II of the Old Soldiers of Baker Street. Mr. Rabe was instrumental in securing the erection of a plaque at the Rosslei Inn, in Meiringen, Switzerland, in the immediate vicinity of the Reichenbach Falls. The plaque was erected in November, 1952, and reads as follows:

> TO THIS VALLEY IN MAY, 1891, CAME DR. WATSON AND SHERLOCK HOLMES AND HERE HOLMES BESTED THE INFAMOUS PROF. MORIARTY IN MORTAL COMBAT: THOUGH HOLMES WAS THOUGHT TO HAVE PERISHED, HE ESCAPED AND RETURNED TO LONDON IN 1894. HE HAS SINCE RETIRED TO SUSSEX AND BEE-KEEPING.

On January 3, 1953, a second plaque—a circular bronze with white enamel lettering—was erected in Piccadilly on the north wall of the Criterion building. It reads:

> THIS PLAQUE
> COMMEMORATES THE
> HISTORIC MEETING EARLY
> IN 1881 AT THE ORIGINAL
> CRITERION LONG BAR
> OF DR. STAMFORD AND
> DR. JOHN H. WATSON
> WHICH LED TO THE INTRODUCTION
> OF DR. WATSON TO
> MR. SHERLOCK HOLMES

Beneath it is a small plaque inscribed:

> ERECTED BY THE BARITSU CHAPTER
> OF THE
> BAKER STREET IRREGULARS, TOKYO

A third plaque of handsome bronze was erected on January 21, 1954, at St. Bartholomew's Hospital, in the curator's room adjoining the pathological laboratory, facing the door and above the fireplace:

> AT THIS PLACE NEW YEAR'S DAY, 1881
> WERE SPOKEN THESE DEATHLESS WORDS
> "YOU HAVE BEEN
> IN AFGHANISTAN, I PERCEIVE"
> BY
> MR. SHERLOCK HOLMES
> IN GREETING TO
> JOHN H. WATSON, M.D.
> AT THEIR FIRST MEETING
> THE BAKER STREET IRREGULARS—1953
> BY THE AMATEUR MENDICANTS AT THE CAUCUS CLUB.

Still a fourth plaque was erected in June, 1957, at the Reichenbach Falls itself.**3**

SHERLOCK MEWS, LONDON, W. 1—FORMERLY YORK MEWS SOUTH

3 Since complete agreement cannot yet be reached on the true site of No. 221B, there is still no plaque on any house in Baker Street. We recall a meeting of the BSI at which two opposing groups argued hotly for their respective sites. Growing weary of the bickering, the late Earle Walbridge stalked to the bar with a muttered, "A plaque on both your houses."

ACROSS THIS "DREADFUL CAULDRON" OCCURRED
THE CULMINATING EVENT IN THE CAREER OF
SHERLOCK HOLMES, THE WORLD'S GREATEST
DETECTIVE, WHEN ON MAY 4, 1891 HE
VANQUISHED PROF. MORIARTY
THE NAPOLEON OF CRIME
ERECTED BY THE NORWEGIAN EXPLORERS
OF MINNESOTA AND THE SHERLOCK HOLMES
SOCIETY OF LONDON 25 JUNE 1957

Regrettably, there has not yet been erected on Baker Street the great statue of Holmes mentioned by Opal, Lady Portsock, writing in the year 1988, as described by Monsignor Ronald A. Knox in his *Memories of the Future*. When it *is* erected, its sponsors might well consider a life-sized duplication of the statuette, some 17 inches tall, commissioned by Mr. Luther Leon Norris of Culver City, California, and executed by the well-known sculptor, Luques Whitmore, a student of the great George Stanley, creator of the Hollywood Oscar.

Until that statue is one of London's noted landmarks, we present an illustration of the Norris-Whitmore Holmes.

THE NORRIS-WHITMORE HOLMES

The friends of Mr. Sherlock Holmes hope that a life-size reproduction of this statuette will someday stand in Portman Square, looking north up Baker Street.

TWO PLAQUES THAT HONOR HOLMES

(*Left*) The plaque at St. Bartholomew's Hospital, erected January 21, 1954, by the Amateur Mendicants Society of Detroit. (*Right*) The plaque at the Reichenbach Falls, erected June 25, 1947, by the Norwegian Explorers of Minneapolis and St. Paul and the Sherlock Holmes Society of London.

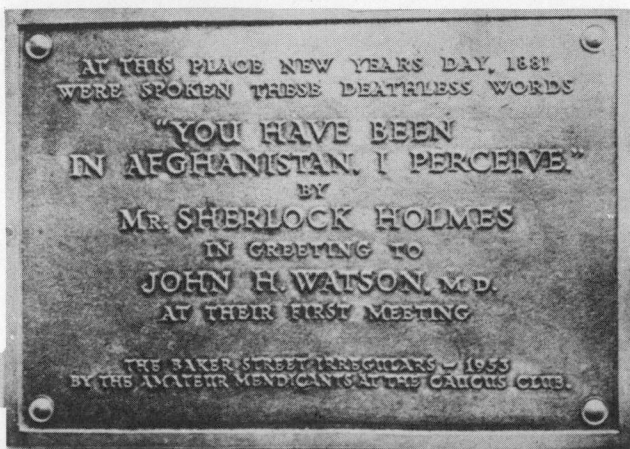

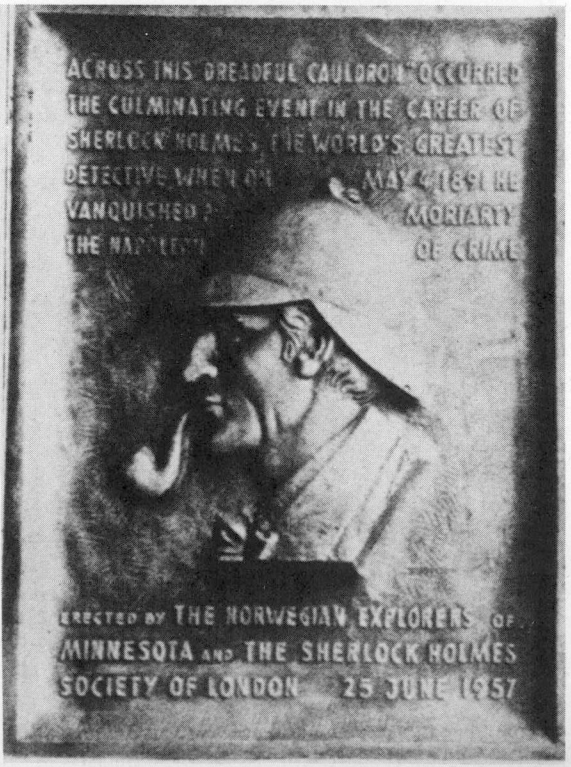

8

"THE BEST AND THE WISEST MAN
WHOM I HAVE EVER KNOWN"

[John H. Watson, M.D., of Sherlock Holmes, "The Final Problem"]

And now let us turn from the Sherlock Holmes of fiction to the Sherlock Holmes so many of us would like to think of as *fact:*

William (or Thomas) Sherlock Scott Holmes was born on the 6th of January, 1854, at the farmstead of Mycroft, near Sigerside, in the North Riding1 of Yorkshire.

Every one of these statements will be disputed by your editor's fellow Sherlockians and Holmesians, and this is no doubt how it should be.

The year of Holmes' birth, for example:

The speculations of scholars have placed this important event variously in the years 1852, 1853, 1854, 1855, 1857–58, and even in 1867.

The last year above is that given by Mr. Douglas M. Hoffecker in "Forgive Us, Oh Lord!" Mr. Hoffecker holds that when Holmes, in "The *Gloria Scott*," visited Donnithrope on "the fixed date" of 1885 he was eighteen years old, and was therefore born in 1867.

It is true that eighteen is the average age of students entering either Oxford or Cambridge, so most Sherlockians base their conclusions as to the year of Holmes' birth on (1) the date they assign to the adventure of "The *Gloria Scott*"; (2) the college year in which they believe this adventure to have taken place (that is, was Holmes at the time a first- or a second-year man?).

But there is a difficulty in this line of reasoning: Holmes must certainly have been a precocious youngster. He may even have been a child prodigy. Are we justified, then, in assuming that he was indeed eighteen, and not two or even three years younger, when he first entered a university?

There are, however, two other Canonical clues to the Master's age:

First, Holmes described himself as a "middle-aged" man in June, 1889 ("The Boscombe Valley Mystery"). ". . . while many are reluctant to admit it," the late A. Carson Simpson wrote in "It Must Have Been Two Other Fellows," "[thirty-five] has been accepted as middle age for many centuries. It is the halfway point of the Biblical 'threescore years and ten'; [Holmes] would have passed 'the middle of the pathway of our life,' as Dante puts it in the first line of the *Inferno*." If Holmes was, indeed, thirty-five in 1889, it follows that he was born in the year 1854.

1 Yorkshire folk will tell you that a *riding* measured the distance that a Saxon overlord could go riding in a day, but the true meaning is not so picturesque. A riding is only a thriding, or thirding, a division into three parts. There is, of course, no *South* Riding of Yorkshire. The three are the North, the East, and the West.

SHERLOCK HOLMES OF BAKER STREET

A portrait by Sidney Paget. The late James Montgomery wrote (*A Study in Pictures*): "Possibly the most satisfactory Paget portrait of Holmes is one that never appeared with any of the stories, but is reputed to have been rescued from a scrap basket by the artist's wife after he had torn it in half and discarded it." This wonderful character study of the Master in contemplative mood was first published in the *Cornhill Magazine* for Summer, 1951, reprinted in *The Baker Street Journal* for October, 1953, and distributed as a Christmas card in 1953 by the Sherlock Holmes Society of London. The original was on display at the Exhibitions in London (1951) and New York (1952).

Second, we are told that Holmes appeared to be a man of sixty in 1914 in his character of Altamont ("His Last Bow"). Again we reach 1854—but here we must register a violent dissent by the late Dr. Ernest Bloomfield Zeisler. Dr. Zeisler has pointed out that part of Holmes' disguise in this role was a goatee that might have made him look older than he actually was. "In *The Sign of the Four*," Dr. Zeisler wrote in *Baker Street Chronology*, "[Holmes] appears as an 'aged' man, clad in seafaring garb. In 'A Scandal in Bohemia' he appears once as a 'drunken-looking groom, ill-kempt and side-whiskered, with an inflamed face and disreputable clothes' and another time as an 'amiable and simpleminded Nonconformist clergyman.' In 'The Adventure of the Beryl Coronet' he is 'a loafer,' in 'The Adventure of the Empty House' he is 'an elderly deformed man carrying books,' and in 'The Adventure of Charles Augustus Milverton' [he appears as] a 'rakish young workman with a goatee.' It has not occurred to anyone to conclude from these descriptions that the Master actually was an aged man, a groom, a clergyman, a loafer, an elderly deformed man, or a young workman."

We see now why there is so much disagreement as to the year of Holmes' birth.

"We reach 1852 as the year . . . ," Mr. T. S. Blakeney wrote. "We are probably safe in thinking that an earlier date is inadmissible; but, on the other hand, 1853 is possible."

"While his birth certificate cannot be traced, it is generally accepted by commentators that Sherlock Holmes was born either late in 1852 or early in 1853," Mr. O. F. Grazebrook wrote in his *Studies in Sherlock Holmes, I.*

"1853 (late 1852 or early 1854): Birth of Sherlock Holmes," the late Dorothy L. Sayers stated in "Holmes' College Career."

"It would seem that the most likely year for [Holmes'] birth would be 1853," was the verdict of the late Gavin Brend.

Dr. Rufus S. Tucker also favored 1853 in his "Genealogical Notes on Holmes," and made an "Ancestory of Sherlock Holmes, of London," in which he said: "Born January 6, 1853."

In "Oxford or Cambridge or Both?" Mr. N. P. Metcalfe concurred with Dr. Tucker.

"We may deduce by the normal methods of arithmetic that [Holmes] was born in 1854, though arguments have been advanced in favor of 1852 or 1853," Mr. S. C. Roberts wrote in "The Personality of Sherlock Holmes."

"[Holmes] was probably born in 1855, or late in 1854," the late H. W. Bell decided.

"There is not enough evidence on which to date the Master's birth any more accurately than the interval 1857–59, with the probabilities favoring 1857 or 1858," was Dr. Zeisler's final verdict.

It would appear that Holmes could not have been born much before 1853 or much later than 1857; the Baker Street Irregulars have discussed the problem at length and have decided that they prefer 1854. Let us leave it at that.

For the "January 6th" we have the evidence of *The Valley of Fear*. That interesting case began on January 7th (1888) and we are told that Holmes on the morning of that day

2 Miss Revill had something to say about Watson also: his Sun is badly menaced, and the Grand Tine shows that he had a very susceptible heart and a tendency for burying wives because Saturn and Uranus in Taurus tangle with the Moon Wife.

"leaned upon his hand, with his untasted breakfast before him . . ." "Surely it is clear," Mr. Nathan L. Bengis wrote in "What Was the Month?", "that there had been some small jollification the night before in celebration of the Master's birthday, and that his lack of appetite was the result of a hangover?"

Again, Holmes quotes Shakespeare often, but *Twelfth Night* is the only such play that Holmes quotes *twice*. Twelfth Night is January 6th; Holmes, then, was especially fond of that play because January 6th was his own birthdate.

The ancient art of astrology provides a further clue: In the March, 1964, issue of the British astrology magazine *Prediction*, Miss Joan Revill has noted that in the early hours of January 6, 1854, Scorpio had just reached the ascendant. "Scorpio fits [Holmes] like a glove . . . impassive features . . . relentless, courageous prober of mysteries, dabbler in poisons and chemicals . . ." It seems that the Master got a bit of Virgo, too: "painstaking attention to details, finer shades of analysis and deduction, man of concentrated habits." Uranus came in also and made Holmes something of an eccentric, but *not* slovenly. Watching the agony column is a Third House activity, and Venus in Pisces would explain why he was so much attracted to Irene Adler, *the* woman.2

Opposed to the January school of thought, however, is the June school, represented by Messrs. Russell McLauchlin and Rolfe Boswell, who base their case on the emerald tiepin presented to Holmes by Queen Victoria for his successful solution to the theft of the Bruce-Partington submarine plans.

"If the Widow of Windsor took it into her dear, old head to give somebody a precious stone," Mr. McLauchlin wrote ("On the Dating of the Master's Birth"), "there is only one plan of selection that would have occurred to her. She would, of course, choose his birthstone. There is some question about birthstones, to be sure. There are ancient and modern theories. According to the former, the emerald is the birthstone for May. By more modern reckoning, it is the birthstone for June. Which system, so to speak, did Queen Victoria play?"

To this, Mr. Boswell has responded ("A Rare Day in June") that "the Queen, as her subjects well knew, was a stickler for the proprieties. In her day, the agate was first choice for May's birthstone, while the emerald held pride of place for June. . . . On balancing probabilities, it is apparent that the Master was born in June. Can that Rare Day be pinpointed? The reply is in the positive. . . . Sherlock Holmes was born on Saturday, June 17, 1854 [June 17th is Mr. Boswell's date for "The Red-Headed League"]."

But Mr. Bengis has struck a telling counterblow for the January school in "What Was the Month?": ". . . the only thing we can be sure of . . . is not that the gem was an emerald, but that it was green. Now the first choice for January . . . was the garnet. Further research has revealed that there is a somewhat rare variety of garnet, emerald green in color, called uvarovite. If the gem in the tiepin was uvarovite, it was still a garnet and therefore still a January stone, even though it looked like an emerald [to Watson]."

Mr. Michael Harrison has recently expressed the view that

Holmes may have been connected with the peerage of both Ireland and Great Britain (in his monograph, "The Blue Blood of the Holmeses"). The Irish peerage in question was that of Holmes of Kilmallock, an Irish barony created in the first year of King George III. This became extinct when Thomas, first Baron Holmes, died on July 21, 1764, leaving no male heirs. It was revived, however, on March 4, 1798, when his nephew Leonard Troughear (who had assumed the name of Holmes by Royal License) became Baron Holmes by a King's Letter of October 25, 1797. He died about May, 1804, again without leaving a male heir. But his elder daughter Elizabeth by her second husband, Sir Henry Worsley, did leave a son and heir who adopted the additional patronymic of Holmes, becoming Sir Henry Worsley Holmes, Baronet.

Sherlock Holmes himself, however, tells us only that his ancestors were "country squires, who appear to have led much the same life as is natural to their class" ("The Greek Interpreter").

"Clearly Holmes must have belonged to an old county family," Mr. S. C. Roberts wrote in "The Personality of Sherlock Holmes." "But whether it was the Shropshire Holmses or the Lincolnshire branch we do not know."

On the other hand, we have the authority of Conan Doyle himself that Holmes may have come from Surrey: in the Holmes-Watson parody, "How Watson Learned the Trick," Holmes, reading the cricket page of his newspaper, gives "a loud exclamation of interest" on finding that "Surrey was holding its own against Kent."

"Although a man may have only 'small experience of cricket clubs' (as Holmes admits in [Conan Doyle's other Holmes-Watson parody] 'The Field Bazaar') it is not unusual for him to follow his home county side with interest, even enthusiasm," Mr. Peter Richard wrote in "Completing the Canon." "It therefore would seem probable that Holmes' birthplace was in Surrey—possible, in fact, that his ancestors, being country squires and Reigate being in Surrey, that they were indeed the original Reigate Squires!"

This view has received enthusiastic endorsement from Mr.

THREE COATS OF ARMS OF MR. SHERLOCK HOLMES

The Holmes arms according to Mr. Rolfe Boswell ("A Connecticut Yankee in Support of Sir Arthur"): Argent a fess sable with three caltrops in the chief proper. A small crescent, symbol of a second son, is charged upon the fess to distinguish Sherlock from his elder brother Mycroft. Crest: a sinister hand proper encrusted with icicles grasping a banner gules, thereon a golden bee and the watchword EXCELSIOR in silver letters. Motto: We can but try.

The Holmes arms according to Mr. Belden Wigglesworth ("The Coat of Arms of Sherlock Holmes"): Quarterly, sable first and fourth, a cat-a-mountain argent, salient, armed and langued. Second party per bend sinister; first argent, a beehive with bees, diversely volant, sable; second azure, three millstones argent. Argent third, three fleurs-de-lis sable, their tips or. Crest: a fox proper passant-regardant. Motto: *Je pense, alors je suis* ("I think, therefore I am").

The Holmes arms according to Mr. William S. Hall ("The True and Proper Coat of Arms"): Argent, three buglehorns, sable. Crest: a lion rampant. Motto: *Justim et tenacem propositi* ("Just and firm of purpose").

MYCROFT, SIGERSIDE, NORTH RIDING

The lonely farm on the Yorkshire moors where Sherlock Holmes was born on January 6, 1854. From *Sherlock Holmes: A Biography*, by William S. Baring-Gould.

3 Against this view, however, we must in all fairness point out that Holmes *twice* (once in "The *Gloria Scott*" and again in "The Adventure of the Priory School") displays an ignorance of the North of England that would seem to have come only from a Southerner.

4 Mr. O. F. Grazebrook noted in "Oxford or Cambridge" that "a French strain . . . was also to be found in Lord Peter Wimsey's pedigree. It is perhaps the special advantage of French blood to give logic to the mind, and provide careers for private investigators."

We may also note here that Sir Arthur Conan Doyle was an ardent Francophile, and that his son, Adrian M. Conan Doyle, tells us that there is little doubt that Holmes' Vernet connection may be traced to a painting by Vernet given to Conan Doyle some time before he wrote *A Study in Scarlet* by his uncle Henry Doyle, Director of the National Gallery in Dublin. "With the painting are two letters from Richard Doyle, Henry's brother, on the subject of Vernet's artistic merit."

C. O. Merriman of the Sherlock Holmes Society of London. In "Birthplace of Holmes," Mr. Merriman noted, first, that Reigate is in the Vale of Holmesdale; second, that at least six of Holmes' cases were directly connected with Surrey and still more were in neighboring counties; third, that Holmes after his exertions against the machinations of Baron Maupertuis ("The Reigate Squires") would be likely to seek a rest cure in the pleasant countryside and soothing quiet of his own hometown.

Still a third view, to which your editor subscribes, holds that Holmes was a Yorkshire man, born in the North Riding.**3**

As the erudite Dr. Tucker wrote in his "Genealogical Notes on Holmes": "It has, I believe, not previously been pointed out that the name [of Holmes' brother] Mycroft is a clue to the origin of the family. Could any parent have inflicted so ugly a name on a helpless infant except for the strongest of family reasons? Obviously as the oldest son he was doomed to bear the name of the family estate. The North Riding of Yorkshire contains several manors by the name of 'Croft' or some compound of 'croft,' an old Saxon word that means an enclosed field. The founder of the Holmes line, in order to distinguish *his* 'croft' from the others, called it Mycroft, and Sherlock's older brother suffered the consequences . . ."

Christopher Morley was another strong supporter of the Yorkshire school of thought. "A study of the place-names of the Holdernesse region [in Yorkshire, between the North Sea and the Humber] assures me that the . . . squirearchy from which Sherlock . . . descended was certainly in this neighborhood," he wrote. "There, more than anywhere in England, one finds all possible variations of the ancient word *holm* [meaning an islet in a river or lake or near the mainland]."

Elsewhere Mr. Morley pinpointed his choice of Holmes' birthplace, declaring that it is still marked on the map as the Holmes Hall, "about 2½ miles east of the village of Croft on Tees, in the North Riding of Yorkshire. Lat. 54.29 N., Long. 1.30 W. . . ."

But of course we must not forget that there was also a *French* strain in Holmes' ancestry; he tells us, again in "The Greek Interpreter," that his grandmother was "the sister of Vernet, the French artist."**4**

In his scholarly essay, "Zero Wolf Meets Sherlock Holmes," Mr. Ben Wolf has traced the history of the Vernets for us:

The founder of the House of Vernet was named Antoine. He was born at Avignon, in 1689, and he died there in 1753. As he sired 22 children, one assumes that he did not have much free time for travel. Apparently, he did not have much leisure for painting, either, as Bryant's *Dictionary of Painters and Engravers* records only a single study, "Flowers and Birds," in the possession of the Musée Calvet, in Avignon.

Of his 22 offspring, four were to become painters. . . . Obviously, the distracted father of this enormous brood ran out of names at a point. Two of his four painting sons shared the name of Antoine. The other two, however, were named Claude Joseph and François Gabriel. . . .

Of the four painter sons, Claude Joseph, who was born also in Avignon in 1714, appears to have had the most active career. At the age of 17, a patron sent him to Rome to study. On the voyage he witnessed a violent storm and, according to tradition, lashed himself to the mast of the ship in order that he might accurately observe the effects for future painting. Both the ship and Vernet survived the ordeal, and in Rome he began by depicting his memories of the stormy sea. During his sojourn in the Eternal City—and doubtless as a result of his studies—he turned to the ruins and landscapes and costumes of Rome, adopting a style reminiscent of Salvator Rosa. He fell in love with the daughter of the Pope's Naval Commandant and, in due course, they were married.

During Claude Joseph's stay in Rome he had been shipping canvases back to France. They were much admired—one of his admirers being no less than Mme. de Pompadour. At her behest, he settled in Paris. He was admitted to the Académie and was commissioned by Louis XV to paint a set of 20 pictures of French seaports. His career seems to have proceeded swimmingly, but his last years were embittered by the madness and death of his wife. Incidentally, his own death could not have been staged more brilliantly, insofar as its setting was concerned. He died in the Louvre on 3 December 1789. . . .

Issue of this union was Antoine Charles Horace, known as Carle, who was born at Bordeaux,**5** in 1758. We are told that he drew horses when quite a child and studied painting principally with his father. At 21 he received the Second Prize of the Academy of Painting, and three years later the Grand Prize of Rome.

While in Italy he apparently raised considerable hell in the oat-sowing field, was overcome by remorse and almost became a monk, but his father managed to get him back to France. Although during the French Revolution his sympathies were at first with the People's Cause, his feelings in their behalf were somewhat dimmed by the fact that he received a musket-ball . . . through his hand during an uprising in Paris.

His earlier works had been classic in style. This period was followed by military subjects, and his canvas, "Morning of Austerlitz," earned the Legion of Honour in 1808. He died in 1836.

Charles Horace (or Carle) had a son named Émile Jean Horace. . . . The son was an ardent Bonapartist and remained one, even after the Restoration, which displeased the Bourbons to an understandable degree. Émile, however, was apparently possessed of footwork the equal of his brushwork. He was restored to favour in France and managed, possibly by absenting himself during changes in administration (*via* short sojourns in other European courts), to adjust himself to a succession of regimes. Filled with patriotism and facility, his canvases can be seen in great quantity at Versailles . . .

Robert Lefèvre pinx.   Fremy del. et Sculp.

5 "Here we have an association with the south of France," Christopher Morley wrote in "Was Sherlock Holmes an American?" "which [Holmes] acknowledges by his interest in Montpellier ["The Adventure of the Empty House," "The Disappearance of Lady Frances Carfax"], where he probably had French kindred. . . . It is significant that though he declined a knighthood in Britain ["The Adventure of the Three Garridebs"] he was willing to accept the Legion of Honour in France ["The Adventure of the Golden Pince-Nez"]. . . ."

L'ATELIER OF HORACE VERNET

From *Oxford or Cambridge*, by O. F. Grazebrook.

The weight of Sherlockian authority holds that Holmes' grandmother was the daughter of Antoine Charles Horace, called Carle, and the sister of Émile Jean Horace, called Horace; she was presumably born about the year 1787.

Let us look a little more closely at Horace Vernet, Sherlock Holmes' greatuncle:

> . . . from the pen of Mendelssohn the musician [Mr. O. F. Grazebrook wrote in *Oxford or Cambridge*] . . . we learn that gifted with extensive powers of perception, and a most astonishing memory, [Horace] Vernet was of so methodical and orderly a character that his mind was like a well-stocked bureau. Vernet had but to open a drawer in it and find what he needed. ("A man should keep his little brain attic stocked with all the furniture that he is likely to use, and the rest he can put away in the lumber room of his library, where he can get it if he wants it."—Sherlock Holmes, "The Five Orange Pips").

It was related of Holmes' great uncle that a single glance at a model was sufficient to tell him all that was necessary for the most minute detail of appearance. It is obvious, therefore, that some of these traits, these excellencies of Horace Vernet, were passed on in the family genes and are in themselves sufficient to account for many, if not all, of Sherlock Holmes' distinctive abilities. . . .

Horace Vernet's first picture was exhibited in the Salon of 1812; amid a host of other masterpieces, there is one, painted in 1822, which has a special interest for all students of Holmes literature. In that picture, the artist has painted himself in his studio, surrounded by men *boxing* and *fencing* (is it remarkable that Holmes was expert in both?) in the midst of a medley of clients, visitors, horses, *dogs* and models, and an assembly as variegated and fascinating as the clients, yet unborn, who were to throng and to climb the immortal stairs of Baker Street.

But the question remains: was Mlle. Vernet Holmes' *paternal* or *maternal* grandmother? Did she marry a Holmes, and bear Sherlock's father? Or did she marry a man with another name, and so bear the child who was to become the mother of Sherlock Holmes?

Mr. Rolfe Boswell speaks for the paternal school of thought in "A Connecticut Yankee in Support of Sir Arthur": "Some time between 1806 and 1808, Dr. Lathrop Holmes [of Woodstock, Connecticut, U.S.A.] appears to have married a daughter of . . . Carle Vernet. By the former Mlle. Vernet, Dr. Holmes was the father of at least one child, a son. . . . Sherlock was Oliver [Wendell Holmes] Senior's first cousin once removed, since he was the grandson of Dr. Lathrop Holmes, [who was in fact] Oliver's uncle; and, thus, Mr. Justice Holmes' second cousin."

On the other hand, Mr. Vincent Starrett has written in his *Private Life of Sherlock Holmes*: "[Holmes'] grandmother—but on which side? The mother's, one suspects, since in general his ancestors were English country squires."

And Mr. Ian Mackay, in "Knowledge of Politics—Feeble?", has written that "there was a revolutionary strain on the distaff side in Holmes . . ."

Of his mother and father, Holmes tells us nothing—a fact that led the late President of the United States, Franklin Roosevelt, to speculate that Holmes was a foundling. In one of the letters in *A Baker Street Folio,* Mr. Roosevelt wrote (to Mr. Belden Wigglesworth of the Speckled Band of Boston): "Being a foundling his one great failure was his inability after long search to find his parents."[6]

Dr. Tucker, speaking guardedly of President Roosevelt's original surmise in his "Genealogical Notes," wrote: "A noted authority—in fact the ultimate personification of authority in every field but this—has recently expressed the opinion that Holmes was a foundling. We cannot reject such an opinion offhand, but it is not a bar against further inquiry. This same personage has been known to use words in a Pickwickian sense. Moreover, to the scion of eight generations of Hudson Valley patroons a man whose ancestors were merely English country squires would naturally appear to be, comparatively speaking, a foundling."

We may perhaps surmise that Holmes' mother's Christian name was Violet: it is noteworthy that this name belonged to five ladies[7] whom Holmes later treated with more than his ordinary courtesy.

What was her surname before she became a Holmes?

She was a Miss Sherlock, Rolfe Boswell surmised ("A Connecticut Yankee in Support of Sir Arthur"); but Dr. Tucker thought it far more likely that Sherlock was the maiden name of Holmes' *paternal* grandmother. Mr. Elliot Kimball, on the other hand, writing in "The First Man Who Beat Holmes," has stated unequivocally that Holmes' maternal grandfather, he who married Mlle. Vernet and fathered Holmes' mother, was Sir Edward Sherrinford, in September of 1860 seventy-two years old.

On still another hand, Professor Jacques Barzun has argued ("How Holmes Came to Play the Violin") that Holmes' *mother,* rather than his grandmother, was a Vernet, and unmarried: "Holmes was obviously brought up in a retired way by his mother *alone.*"

As for Holmes *père,* we may be reasonably sure that he was named Sigurd or Siger Holmes, since Sherlock later took as his alias the name *Sigerson,* a Norwegian form of Sigurdson.

Holmes had, as we know, at least one brother: Mycroft Holmes, seven years Sherlock's senior, and born, therefore, in 1847.

But if Mycroft and Sherlock came from a line of country squires, as Sherlock said they did, why did not Mycroft, as the elder brother, inherit the family estate?

One possible explanation has been put forward by Messrs. J. H. and Humfrey Michell in "Sherlock Holmes the Chemist." Here it is suggested that Holmes' father had perhaps "been speculating in stocks and had been ruined. . . . Mycroft . . . is forced to take a humble position in the Civil Service, and Sherlock, his brilliant career at Cambridge cut short, retires to Montague Street to earn his bread and butter as a consulting detective."

[6] In a later letter, however, addressed to the late Edgar W. Smith, Mr. Roosevelt recanted and said: "On further study I am inclined to revise my former estimate that Holmes was a foundling. Actually he was born an American and was brought up by his father or a foster father in the underground world, thus learning all the tricks of the trade in the highly developed American art of crime."

[7] Miss Hunter in "The Adventure of the Copper Beeches," Miss Smith in "The Adventure of the Solitary Cyclist," Miss de Merville in "The Adventure of the Illustrious Client," Miss Westbury in "The Adventure of the Bruce-Partington Plans" and Miss Stonor in the *play* version of "The Adventure of the Speckled Band."

Another possible explanation has been advanced by Mr. R. S. Colborne ("Orphans of the Storm?"): "In writings on the origin and early life of Holmes, it does not appear to have been realized that Mycroft and Sherlock must have been sons of a second marriage. In the stable Victorian era, the landed squirearchy, from which Holmes and his brother stemmed, must have had another heir, and the fact that Sherlock Holmes seemed to have retained no connection with his family clearly points to a second marriage. Holmes senior probably lost his first wife and remarried in the late 1840's. He himself apparently died about 1864, when Sherlock was 10 years old, and the assumption of the squirearchy by the eldest son of the first marriage was the main reason for Sherlock's mother taking him and Mycroft away to start a new home . . ."

A third possible explanation is that there was a *third* brother, senior to Mycroft. "Watson had known Holmes for . . . years before he learned that his friend had even one brother, so the existence of another is not impossible," Mr. Anthony Boucher pointed out in "Was the Later Holmes an Imposter?" Dr. Tucker thought that this brother might have been named Gerard, but there is also the distinct possibility that the first Holmes son was named Sherrinford; after all, we know that Sherrinford was, in one sense at least, an elder Holmes than Sherlock.

Professor Jacques Barzun has suggested ("How Holmes Came to Play the Violin") that the Dr. Verner to whom Holmes alluded as his cousin when he bought Watson's practice ("The Adventure of the Norwood Builder") was very possibly a third brother, and Christopher Morley held that Sherlock and Mycroft had a brother younger than either of them whose name was Raffles Holmes. More recently, Mr. Jerry Neal Williamson has put forth the alarming suggestion ("'There Was Something Very Strange'") that Professor James Moriarty, the Napoleon of Crime, was really a Holmes brother, in age between Sherlock and Mycroft.

Dr. Tucker wrote that "Holmes never mentioned . . . his . . . father . . . because he died when Sherlock was too young to have formed any impression of him," and Mr. Michael Harrison (*In the Footsteps of Sherlock Holmes*) has also made out a very good case for Sherlock and Mycroft having been orphaned at a fairly early age.

In any case, Holmes is as reticent about his boyhood and his early schooling as he is about his parentage. But Mr. Bernard Davies has written ("Was Holmes a Londoner?") that Holmes' "obvious lack of the normal public school background displayed by Watson and his all-round proficiency in the arts of self-defense rather than team sports strongly suggests an education by a tutor."

This is also the view of Mr. S. C. Roberts ("The Personality of Sherlock Holmes"): ". . . it is perhaps legitimate to conjecture that, being temperamentally unfitted for the normal activities of public school life, either [Holmes] was privately educated from early boyhood or after a short period at a public school he was so miserable that his parents removed him to the care of a private tutor."

Your editor's own researches have convinced him that travel on the Continent accounted for much of Holmes' early life (as it did for another well-known Victorian, a clergyman and author, who entered Cambridge speaking six languages although he had never had a day of the British schooling usual in those times for sons of the landed gentry).

In *Sherlock Holmes of Baker Street* we have reported on these travels:

> . . . Siger Holmes led his entire family aboard the steamship *Lerdo* on July 7, 1855. They were bound for Bordeaux, across the Bay of Biscay. From Bordeaux they traveled to Pau, and there they wintered, taking a flat in the Grande Place. . . .
>
> They stayed at Pau until the May of 1858, until Sherlock was four. Then the whole family removed to Montpellier . . .

After a brief return to England:

> In October, 1860, [the Holmes family] crossed to Rotterdam. Two months later this wandering family, these genteel gypsies, pitched tent in Cologne.
>
> The Rhine in that winter of 1860–61 was frozen over, and the whole family had several months of peace during which Siger Holmes continued his studies. But when the ice began to break and whirl down the stream, the restless Yorkshireman got out his carriage and was off again. . . .
>
> Darmstadt, Karlsruhe, Stuttgart, Mannheim, Munich, Heidelberg—the carriage covered thousands of kilometers over bad roads, in all weathers and temperatures, the baggage piled on top, the family jostling within.
>
> Heidelberg to Berne, Berne to Lucerne, Lucerne to Thun by October—on and on the rumbling carriage rolled, beyond the cities, into villages and towns and wild corners of Europe where few English families had ever been before, where few for many years were to follow. They visited Italy, they traveled to the Tyrol and to Salzburg, they went to Vienna and thence to Dresden. They arrived in Saxony, and later stayed for a long time at Mannheim.
>
> The journey lasted almost four long years, and had a lifelong influence on young Master Sherlock Holmes. He developed an enviably intimate knowledge of Europe. He became to some extent a European, that civilized being whom the Western world has not yet succeeded in turning out in quantity. Unaware of a boy's ordinary interests, always in the company of his brothers and his parents . . . the whole bent of his character was formed at this time.
>
> It was a highly unusual childhood, but Sherlock Holmes was a highly unusual boy, destined to become a highly unusual man. . . .

Again, in 1868, it was Pau again for the Holmes family:

> Siger, Violet, and Sherlock Holmes sailed in September, 1868, from Plymouth to St. Malo, taking a leisurely month over the rolling miles southward, resolutely halt-

ing wherever they chanced to be each Sunday to attend the church that meant so much in the life of Sherlock's mother.

They arrived at Pau in October, 1868, thus beginning the last Continental visit Sherlock Holmes was ever to make with his parents.

From it, Sherlock was to get two benefits that would stand him in good stead for many years to come. To "toughen" the boy, Siger Holmes himself volunteered to teach him boxing. The father also had the son enrolled in the most celebrated fencing school in Europe, the salon of Maître Alphonse Bencin. . . .

Watson's annals make one other fact about Holmes' childhood clear: whether with a parent or parents or perhaps with some solid, bourgeois relations, he almost certainly must have spent at least some years in South London, in one of those districts later engulfed in the giant boroughs of Lambeth, Wandsworth, and Camberwell.

The evidence is in Chapter III of *The Sign of the Four*, where Holmes, although displaying an intimate knowledge of South London, calls *two of the streets by names long out of date*.**8**

"Brixton, Kennington, Vauxhall, Stockwell," Mr. Davies wrote in "Was Holmes a Londoner?"—"somewhere in this region stood a house which Holmes called home; one of those solid, middle-class villas that abounded in these once pleasant suburbs of the 'sixties. If it still stands it will be a little faded now, perhaps, just a number in a long, dreary highway. But Holmes would have known it before it had a number . . ."

We come now to "The *Gloria Scott*" and "The Musgrave Ritual," and a consideration of Holmes, the university undergraduate.

How long was he a student? At what university or universities?

Let us marshal the evidence given to us in these two early adventures:

1. "The *Gloria Scott*" was the first case in which Holmes was ever engaged.**9** He had already formed "habits of observation and inference" "into a system, although I had not yet appreciated the part they were to play in my life." The senior Trevor's recommendation, he tells us, was "the very first thing which ever made me feel that a profession might be made out of what had up to that time been the merest hobby."

2. Holmes speaks of "the two years that I was at college" —and tells us that during these two years "the only friend I made" was young Victor Trevor. "I was never a very sociable fellow, Watson, always rather fond of moping in my rooms and working out my own little methods of thought, so that I never mixed much with the men of my year. Bar fencing and boxing I had few athletic tastes, and then my line of study was quite distinct from that of the other fellows, so that we had no points of contact at all. Trevor was the only man I knew, and that only through the accident of his bull-terrier freezing on to my ankle one morning as I went down to chapel." "Finally he [young Trevor] invited

8 He refers to Stockwell Place, which became Stockwell *Road* in 1872, and Robert Street, which was displaced by *Robsart* Street in 1880. The late Gavin Brend ("Was Sherlock Holmes at Westminster?") took this as evidence that Holmes had been a day boy at Westminster. But the editors of the *Sherlock Holmes Journal* pointed out that Mr. Brend's argument applied as well to "the Greycoat School, formerly in Artillery Row, or even the local school round the corner in Great Peter Street. If the latter, there would be special significance in [Holmes'] panegyric on Board Schools in 'The Naval Treaty.'"

9 It is a strange tale—so strange that the late H. W. Bell considered Holmes to be "the dupe of a terrified but astute man nearly forty years his senior."

me down to his father's place in Donnithorpe, in Norfolk, and I accepted his hospitality for a month of the long vacation."

3. During Holmes' "last years at the university there was a good deal of talk there about myself and my methods" ("The Musgrave Ritual").

4. After Holmes came up to London, he had rooms in Montague Street, just round the corner from the British Museum. "There I waited, filling in my too abundant leisure time by studying all those branches of science which might make me more efficient." "You can hardly realize how difficult I found it at first, and how long I had to wait before I succeeded in making any headway." There were "months of inaction."

5. At last "cases came in my way" now and again, "principally through the introduction of old fellow students."

6. "The third of these cases was that of the Musgrave Ritual and it is to the interest which was aroused by that singular chain of events, and the large issues which proved to be at stake, that I made my first stride toward the position which I now hold."

7. Reginald Musgrave had been in the same college as Holmes and Holmes had "some slight acquaintance with him." But Holmes had seen nothing of Musgrave "for four years" until he walked into Holmes' rooms in Montague Street one morning.

8. Holmes' early cases (other than "The Musgrave Ritual") were "not all successes" but there were "some pretty little problems among them."

9. By the time of his first meeting with Watson Holmes had "established a considerable, though not a very lucrative, connection."

It should be abundantly clear by now that Holmes in these two adventures is talking about *two entirely different academic experiences.***10**

For consider:

1. Holmes speaks of "the two years that I was at college" and his "last years at the university." In England, as Dr. Ernest Bloomfield Zeisler noted, "a college is part of a university, but not every university student is in a college, at least, not in all universities." This, by itself, then, could mean that Holmes was at a university for *at least three* years, *two* of which he had spent in a college of that university.

2. But Reginald Musgrave had been in the *same* college as Holmes, and Holmes had "some slight acquaintance with him." Thus the college attended by Holmes and Musgrave *cannot be* the college attended for two years by Holmes and young Trevor, for at the latter college Trevor was the "*only* friend I made" and the "*only* man I knew."

3. In addition, as Miss Dorothy L. Sayers shrewdly pointed out ("Holmes' College Career"), Holmes and Musgrave must have been men of the *same year* as well as men of the *same college,* for if Musgrave were senior to Holmes, his reserved and somewhat exclusive manner would have precluded him from associating with an underclassman; if he were junior to Holmes, it would have precluded him from "sucking up" to an upperclassman.**11** But at the college

10 The late Elmer Davis would seem to have been the first to suggest that Holmes may have been a student at *both* Oxford and Cambridge (in December, 1933, in "The Real Sherlock Holmes" in *The Saturday Review of Literature*). Your editor was to elaborate on this view in 1955, in his *Chronological Holmes;* in December, 1956, Mr. N. P. Metcalfe treated the whole question at length in his splendid essay, "Oxford or Cambridge or Both?" Other commentators unhappily seem loath to accept this perceptive view, insisting that Holmes attended *one* or *another* of the two universities. As Mr. Davis wrote (in his Introduction to *The Return of Sherlock Holmes*): ". . . the question which of [these] ancient institutions of learning had the honor of educating, or at least housing for some years, Sherlock Holmes [is] a question chiefly of interest because graduates of each seem to want to wish him on the other. Dorothy Sayers and Monsignor Knox, both of Oxford, hold that he must have been a Cambridge man. . . . But S. C. Roberts, who is not only of Cambridge but at this writing [1952] *is* Cambridge—the Vice-Chancellor, the active head, of that university—says that Holmes must have been an Oxford man."

11 Mr. Melcalfe bears this out: ". . . men up at [a] University strictly stick to their own year (a rule only relaxed during and after the two world wars when the age of entry was anything from 18 to about 26 years)."

attended by Holmes and young Trevor, Holmes "*never* mixed much with the men of my year."

4. Our conclusion that Holmes attended two universities is further borne out by the early cases that came his way "principally through the introduction of old fellow students." A man who has "*no points of contact at all*" with his fellow students is not likely to be recommended by them later.

5. Our conclusion is further borne out by Musgrave's statement that Holmes "used to amaze us" with his powers in college and Holmes' statement that during his "last years at the university there was a good deal of talk there about myself and my methods." These years can hardly have been a part of the "two years . . . at college" when Holmes "was *never* a very sociable fellow" and was "*always* rather fond of moping in my rooms."

Holmes, then, was at *one* university for *two* years, during *both* of which he was in a college of that university; he was at *another* university for *at least three* years, during *at least one* of which he was in a college of that university.

We can now be fairly sure that what Holmes *really* said to Watson in telling him about the adventure of "The *Gloria Scott*" was: "the two years that I was at *X* college," perhaps adding, "at *A* university."

It is not, of course, the normal procedure for a man to attend one university for two years and another for at least three.**12** We must ask ourselves why Holmes did this. The answer leaps to the eye: following his second year at University *A* he had had an experience that convinced him that the course of study he was able to follow at his present university was not sufficient to equip him for the career he had determined upon at that time, and that he consequently must transfer to a university with more suitable facilities. *This experience can only have been* the adventure of "The *Gloria Scott*," for Holmes makes it very clear that old Trevor's recommendation was "the *very first thing* which ever made me feel that a *profession* might be made out of what had up to then been the merest *hobby*."

Holmes, then, must have enrolled at University *B* in the Michaelmas term following the long vacation during which "The *Gloria Scott*" adventure took place. At University *B*, as we have seen, he lived a very different life than he had lived at University *A*—further evidence that "The *Gloria Scott*" was in every way a major turning point in his life.

Holmes, although changing universities, would still speak of himself as a man of such-and-such a year—and Reginald Musgrave, as we have seen, was a man of this same year at University *B*. He was therefore a *third-year* man at that university when Holmes first knew him. We have every reason to believe that Musgrave, unlike Holmes, spent the normal number of years at University *B*. Since, in the 1870's, a three-year rather than the present four-year course of study, was the norm, Musgrave must have gone down in the year following the Michaelmas term in which Holmes first met him.

"Four years later"—at the time of "The Musgrave Ritual" —Holmes saw Musgrave again for the first time since Musgrave went down.

Between "The Musgrave Ritual" and his meeting with Watson, Holmes had established his considerable but not

---

12 But Holmes was by no means *unique* in attending *both* universities: as Mr. Davis pointed out in "The Real Sherlock Holmes": ". . . it is at least possible that Holmes may have been one of that small but distinguished company, including King Edward VII and Charles Stuart Calverley, who were both Oxford and Cambridge men."

very lucrative connection. Certainly we must allow a year, and probably longer, for him to do this. *Three* years is too long a period, however; Holmes tells us that it was to "the interest aroused by that singular chain of events" (The Musgrave Ritual) . . . that I made my first stride toward the position which I now hold," and Holmes after *three* years of striding would certainly have been able to afford rooms on his own, without seeking for a Watson to share the expenses with him. Thus "The Musgrave Ritual" took place in 1879, or, possibly, late in 1878.

"The Musgrave Ritual" had come after "months of inaction." "You can hardly realize how long I had to wait." Holmes must have waited in Montague Street for at least a year, perhaps as long as two. Thus Holmes took the rooms in Montague Street no earlier than 1876, no later than 1877.

Since he had not seen Musgrave for "four years," we see that Musgrave must have gone down in 1874 or 1875.

Holmes was a man of the same year as Musgrave, so *his* normal year to go down would also have been 1874 or 1875 (we know, however, that he spent two additional years at University *B*). He must therefore have enrolled at University *B* after the long vacation of 1873 or 1874—the long vacation of "The *Gloria Scott*."

What can we learn from "The *Gloria Scott*" that will help us to date the case more exactly? Holmes says:

1. There was "excellent wild-duck shooting in the fens' at the time of his visit to Donnithorpe. Professor Christ was the first to note that under the Act of 1872, the duck season *did not open* until August 1st. Holmes' visit must therefore have included a period after that date.

2. "At last I became so convinced that I was causing [old Trevor] uneasiness that I drew my visit to a close." It is clear, then, that Holmes did not stay at Donnithorpe for the full month for which he was invited. Since he says "at last" it is probable that he left at the end of about three weeks.

3. He tells us that "All this occurred during the first month of the long vacation."

4. "I went up to my London rooms, where I spent seven weeks working out a few experiments in organic chemistry. One day, however, when the autumn was far advanced and the vacation was drawing to a close, I received a telegram from my friend imploring me to return to Donnithorpe . . ." Popularly, in Great Britain, "autumn" comprises the months of August, September, and October. Holmes must therefore have been called back to Donnithorpe late in September, which means, in turn, that he drew his first visit to a close in the first week of August. Since he had spent about three weeks there, he must have arrived at Donnithorpe around the middle of July.

In the 1870's, old Trevor, "a man of some wealth and consideration, a J. P., and a landed proprietor," would certainly not have sent his only son to one of the lesser universities; as Miss Sayers said, he would want young Trevor to have all the advantages he himself had missed.

Young Trevor and Holmes were therefore students at one of England's two great universities—Oxford or Cambridge.**13**

In the years under consideration, the long vacation fell as

13 We should note here, however, that the Reverend Stephen Adams has suggested ("Holmes: A Student of London?") King's College at the University of London; Mr. G. W. Welch has suggested ("Which University?") Manchester University; and Mr. O. F. Grazebrook (*Oxford or Cambridge*) speaks of "a body of Medical opinion in [Birmingham] . . . who claimed that Sherlock Holmes had been educated at Queen's College in the town of Birmingham." Mr. Grazebrook, however, would have none of this: "At [the time of "The *Gloria Scott*" and "The Musgrave Ritual"], any reference to a University implied without any reservation at all either Oxford or Cambridge. Today, the mention of Universities available to students would make any such reference somewhat vague, but there can be no doubt at all that any consideration of which University, must be confined to one of these two."

follows at each of these universities:

	Oxford	Cambridge
1873	July 5–October 10	June 20–October 1
1874	July 11–October 10	June 26–October 1

One quickly sees that the Cambridge vacations will not begin to fit Holmes' description:

1. Neither provides a legal period for duck-hunting "during the first month of the long vacation."

2. Holmes would have received young Trevor's wire *c.* August 31st (1873) or September 6th (1874). At neither time was the autumn "far advanced"—and the vacation could hardly be said to be "drawing to a close"; the beginning of the Michaelmas was still about a month away.

The Oxford vacation of 1874, on the other hand, fits Holmes' description exactly:

1. His invitation to Donnithorpe for the first month of the long vacation would be for the month July 12–August 11th approximately, an invitation that would provide almost two weeks of legal duck-shooting in the fens.

2. He would have left Donnithorpe close to August 4th.

3. "Seven weeks working out a few experiments in organic chemistry" would bring us to September 22nd—at which time the autumn *was* "far advanced" and the beginning of the Michaelmas term was only a little over two weeks away.

We may conclude that:

1. "The *Gloria Scott*" took place in the long vacation of 1874.

2. Holmes enrolled at University *B* at the beginning of the Michaelmas term of 1874.

3. Musgrave went down in 1875.**14**

4. Since, as we have shown, Holmes continued to study at University *B* for two more years, he went to London and took rooms in Montague Street in 1877.

5. Reginald Musgrave visited him there in 1879, "four years" after Holmes had last seen him.**15**

We see, then, that Holmes was a student at Oxford University from the autumn of 1872 to the start of the long vacation in 1874. We know, further, that Holmes was a student at another of England's great universities from the autumn of 1874 to late in 1877 (during at least one of which he was in a college of that university). As Mr. Brend pointed out in *My Dear Holmes,* Musgrave, he of the "grey archways and mullioned windows and all the venerable wreckage of a feudal keep," certainly does not sound like the sort of undergraduate "whom one would expect to find at one of the lesser Universities in the seventies," and we are fully justified in designating University *B* as Cambridge.**16**

We must now deal briefly with an argument that has been raised to show that the university of "The *Gloria Scott*" could not have been Oxford:

Holmes as a first-year man at Oxford in 1872 would live *in college,* since students at that university reside in college for two years, moving into lodgings in the town only at the beginning of their third year of residence. At Cambridge, on the other hand, first-year men and second-year men are usually accommodated with lodgings in town.

14 Miss Sayers suggested that the month was March or December—March if he were taking a classical or mathematical tripos, December if he were taking a tripos in law and history.

15 In our notes to "The Musgrave Ritual" we will show that the exact date in the year 1879 may be determined.

16 While Mr. Metcalfe and your editor are in full agreement that Holmes attended *both* universities, Mr. Metcalfe holds that Holmes attended, first, Cambridge (October, 1871, to late September, 1873 or 1874), then Oxford (October, 1873 or 1874 to 1875 or 1876).

Holmes, as we know, was bitten by Victor Trevor's bull-terrier on his way to chapel. Since dogs are not allowed within the grounds at either university, it has been said that Holmes was going *from* his lodgings *to* chapel when he was bitten by the dog; he was therefore bitten outside the university grounds; he was therefore going *from* his lodgings *to* the university; he was therefore a student at Cambridge, where first- and second-year men go *from* lodgings *to* chapel at their college.

But this argument has been hotly contested.

Mr. S. C. Roberts has pointed out that Holmes may have stepped into the street to buy a newspaper before going to chapel. Mr. Metcalfe has suggested that Holmes' college may have been one of those at Oxford which has buildings on both sides of the road. Mr. Brend has asked: "Could not the dog have been smuggled into the college for the purpose of some practical joke? Alternatively, from the standpoint of the dog, could not the event happen both outside and inside the college? Why should it not have been frightened or hurt out in the street with the result that before it could be stopped it ran through the gate and fastened on to the unfortunate Holmes?" Indeed, Trevor's dog may have broken loose from its tethering in the college porch—for, despite the rules, this seems to have been an Oxford custom. Mr. Max Beerbohm has indicated this in *Zuleika Dobson:* "In the porch of the College there were, as usual, some chained-up dogs." And Mr. Roger Lancelyn Green has added, in a letter to the *Sherlock Holmes Journal,* that there were certainly in-college dogs at least at University College, Oxford, in the 1870's.

Again, Holmes may well have been bitten *off* the university grounds on his way to a chapel *in town.* If this perhaps seems out of character, it must be remembered that Holmes in later days was far from being an irreligious man: he knew his Bible well, and drew much inspiration therefrom.

We see that the dog cannot be allowed to stand as evidence for or against either university.

"Common consent amongst those who favor Oxford points to Christ Church as the most likely [college for Holmes to have attended]," Mr. Metcalfe wrote in "Oxford or Cambridge or Both?", and your editor most heartily agrees. As to Cambridge, Christopher Morley thought it likely that Peterhouse was Holmes' college, but Miss Sayers opted for Sidney Sussex because she found a *T. S. Holmes* at that college in the appropriate years. (Unhappily for Miss Sayers' theory, *this* Holmes later became the Chancellor of Wells Cathedral, as Mr. S. C. Roberts pointed out.) Your editor's own view is that Holmes entered Gonville and Caius College, famous for its associations with medicine and with the natural sciences.

It is possible—indeed it is highly probable—that Holmes spent as much time as he could afford in these early years in travel on the Continent and perhaps in America. Mr. A. N. Griffith ("Some Observations on Sherlock Holmes

THE COATS OF ARMS OF HOLMES' UNIVERSITIES

(*Left*) Oxford: Azure, an open book proper, leathered gules, garnished and having on the dexter side seven seals or, between three open crowns of the last. (*Right*) Cambridge: Gules, a cross ermine between four lions passant gardant or, and upon the cross a closed book, gules, edged, clasped and garnished gold.

CHRIST CHURCH COLLEGE, OXFORD

As it looked when Sherlock Holmes was an undergraduate there in 1872.

and Dr. Watson at Bart's") has found reason to believe that Holmes was in Strasbourg during the Franco-Prussian War of 1870–1871, and Mr. A. Carson Simpson (*I'm Off for Philadelphia in the Morning*) has postulated a visit to the City of Brotherly Love in the fall of 1873. Miss Dorothy L. Sayers ("Holmes' College Career") suggested that Holmes "in all probability . . . passed the year 1875 at a German university, with vacation trips to France and Italy, returning to England in December to take his B.A. and then proceeding (perhaps after a short holiday at home) to London . . ."

Mr. Charles B. Stephens ("The Birlstone Hoax") has advanced the interesting speculation that Holmes in 1875 "was one of the participants in the drama just beginning to unfold in Vermissa Valley, Pennsylvania, U.S.A. [*The Valley of Fear*]. . . . He resolved to go to America to study the techniques of criminal detection then being so successfully applied by the Pinkertons. Their work would appeal to him, because they were and still are 'private' detectives in the professional sense in which Holmes wished to apply his talents. No doubt he contacted the great Allan Pinkerton himself, and sought employment as an operative in order to learn at first hand the secrets of successful detection. We can well imagine that the ability and enthusiasm of the pupil commended him favorably to the tutor, so that when Pinkerton came to plan his strategy for capturing the Scowrers, he chose young Holmes for the role of Captain Marvin."

"My own thought"—Christopher Morley wrote in "Was Sherlock Holmes an American?"—"is that the opening of the Johns Hopkins University in Baltimore in 1876, and the extraordinary and informal opportunities offered there for graduate study, tempted [Holmes] across the water. . . . The great Centennial Exposition in Philadelphia (1876) was surely worth a visit; there he observed the mark of the Pennsylvania Small Arms Company (*The Valley of Fear*). During his year or so in the States he traveled widely. He met Wilson Hargreave who later became important in the New York Police Department—('The Adventure of the Dancing Men'), perhaps in connection with the case of Vanderbilt and the Yeggman, a record of which he kept in his scrapbook ('The Adventure of the Sussex Vampire'). He went to Chicago, where he made his first acquaintance with organized gangsterism ('My knowledge of the crooks of Chicago,' *v*. 'The Adventure of the Dancing Men'). I suggest that perhaps he visited his kinsmen the Sherlocks in Iowa —e.g. in Des Moines, where a younger member of the family, Mr. C. C. Sherlock, has since written so ably on rural topics (C. C. Sherlock: *Care and Management of Rabbits*, 1920; *The Modern Hen*, 1922; *Bulb Gardening*, 1922; *v*. *Who's Who in America*). Iowa is a great apiarian state (undoubtedly from the Sherlock side came the interest in roses, beekeeping, etc.). He must have gone to Topeka (otherwise how could he know there was no such person as Dr. Lysander Starr—'The Adventure of the Three Garridebs'); and of course he made pilgrimage to Cambridge, Mass., to pay respect to the great doctor, poet, and essayist. From Oliver Wendell Holmes, Jr., then a rising lawyer in Boston, he heard firsthand stories of the Civil War, which fired his interest in 'that gallant struggle' ('The Cardboard Box')."**17**

17 Your editor's own researches have led him to believe that it was in November, 1879, that Holmes sailed for America, not as a student but as an actor with the Sasanoff Shakespearian Company. His eight-months-long tour of the United States ended in August, 1880, when he embarked for his trip back to England.

Our date for the beginning of Holmes' practice—July, 1877—is fully borne out by Watson's statement at the beginning of "The Adventure of the Veiled Lodger" that Holmes "was in active practice for twenty-three years . . ."

Holmes' last datable case while in active practice was "The Adventure of the Creeping Man," in which he was engaged in September, 1903, and we are told by Watson that this was "one of the very last cases handled by Holmes before he retired from practice."

Some considerable time before the publication of "The Adventure of the Second Stain" in December, 1904, he had definitely retired and was keeping bees on the Sussex Downs, so it is fair to assume that his withdrawal to private life occurred *circa* October, 1903.

As Mr. H. W. Bell wrote, dead reckoning would oblige us to place the beginning of Holmes' career twenty-three years earlier—that is, late in 1880. But we learn ("The Final Problem" and "The Adventure of the Empty House") that there was a hiatus of three years—the Great Hiatus of May, 1891, to April, 1894—during which Holmes was presumed dead. Three years, then, must be prefixed to the autumn of 1880; and thus the latter half of 1877 is established as the beginning of the practice.

"The Musgrave Ritual" was the third of the cases that came Holmes' way after he took up his practice in Montague Street, and earnest research has enabled two distinguished Sherlockian scholars to identify the two earlier cases.

"As the student will discover by reading the *Proceedings* of the [British] Rifle Association for 1877, 1880 and 1881," Mr. Robert Keith Leavitt wrote in "Annie Oakley in Baker Street," "there was a scandal in that organization in the years 1877 and 1878 concerning alleged cheating by collusion between shooters and scorers during the course of rifle matches, and it became so notorious that the Association went to the trouble and expense of retaining counsel and agents to collect 'voluminous evidence against persons suspected of fraud at the matches.' "

Consulting the *Proceedings* for 1879, Mr. Leavitt found, in the records of one of the biggest matches, the Alexander, of the preceding year, 1878, that ninth place with a prize of £10 was won by *Corporal Holmes of the 19th North Yorkshires*. In the same year, the same Holmes had taken forty-eighth place in the match called the St. George's for a prize of £6.

Note that Corporal Holmes' unit was the 19th North Yorkshires, recall that Sherlock Holmes was born in the North Riding of Yorkshire. Obviously, Sherlock Holmes was the agent retained to gather the evidence of fraud. Naturally, he would have gathered that evidence in the guise of a competitor.

"This scandal, known as 'The Mullineaux Case,' " Mr. Leavitt concluded triumphantly, "occupied Holmes over three months [according to the *Proceedings*] but was handled by him with such competence and discretion that [as in so many of his later cases] legal proceedings were avoided and the details never became public, though as late as 1880 members of the Association who were in the know were clamoring for information—and being shut up for their pains."

THE ONLY KNOWN PHOTOGRAPH OF
MR. SHERLOCK HOLMES

Taken in Cettigne (Cetinj), Montenegro, in June, 1891, this priceless memento is reproduced from William S. Baring-Gould's *Sherlock Holmes: A Biography*

If Holmes' first case, in the Montague Street days, was perhaps somewhat prosaic, his second case of the time was exotic enough to delight the most romantic writer.

We shall see that Holmes, in the spring of the year 1887, was able to be of service to one who called himself Wilhelm Gottsreich Sigismond von Ormstein, Grand-Duke of Cassel-Falstein and hereditary King of Bohemia.

But was 1887 Holmes' *first* meeting with this mysterious personage?

Not at all, the late Edgar W. Smith suggested in "A Scandal in Identity."

"I shall not lament the loss of my incognito, for it enables me to thank you with the more authority."

These words, Mr. Smith wrote, might well have been addressed to Sherlock Holmes by "the hereditary King of Bohemia" in that spring of 1887. But they were not. "They were . . . addressed in 1878 to a certain Brackenbury Rich, a dashing lieutenant in Her Majesty's forces who had greatly distinguished himself in one of the lesser Indian hill wars, by one who called himself Prince Florizel. And as authority for their utterance we have the testimony not of John H. Watson, M.D. . . . but of Robert Louis Stevenson, who chronicled in his *New Arabian Nights*, the doings of this royal blade.

"Yet we cannot doubt," Mr. Smith continued, "on the strength of the evidence available in the two accounts, that Gottsreich and Florizel were one being and the same. However carefully the two narrators may have tried to give their heroes individuality, the likeness of their propensities, their characters, their very persons, shines with the clarity of a beacon through the pages in which their deeds are told. . . .

"We know, of course, to whom the embattled Gottsreich turned when blackmail reared its ugly head and ruin loomed upon the horizon. . . . But we are not told who it was, [nine] years earlier, who had engineered the escape of Florizel from the equally imminent, but purely physical terrors of the Suicide Club. 'All has been managed by the simplest means,' the faithful Colonel Geraldine reported. 'I arranged this afternoon with a celebrated detective. Secrecy has been promised and paid for.' Who could have merited the trust of Florizel's entourage in this previous hour of royal need? Who could have been brought to share the sacred confidence of this differently dangerous escapade? Who, indeed, but that same Great Man who was to serve the smitten Gottsreich so discreetly and so well in [the year 1887]?"

It is probable that it was during the period between "The Musgrave Ritual" and Holmes' meeting with Watson that he solved the Tarleton murders, the case of Vamberry, the wine merchant, that of the old Russian woman, the singular affair of the aluminium crutch, and that of Ricoletti of the club foot and his abominable wife ("The Musgrave Ritual").

Not all of the "pretty little problems" that were presented to Holmes during these early years were successes, however, and it is likely that it was also during this period that he was beaten three times by men ("The Five Orange Pips").

But now, for the time being, let us leave Sherlock Holmes of Baker Street and meet the other half of the Great Partnership that was so shortly to begin . . .

9

"GOOD OLD WATSON!"

[Sherlock Holmes, "His Last Bow"]

His name, we know, was *John* H. Watson, although his first wife, on one occasion, at least ("The Man with the Twisted Lip"), *did* call him James.

It is a name which is particularly fitting—the commonest of all masculine names, not only in English, but also in many European languages. It is a contraction of Johannes, which is derived from the Hebrew Johanan, from *Jah*—God—plus *chaanach*—grace.

Watson is "the son of Watt," the last word being a diminutive of Walter, from the Old High German Waldhar, from *vald*—rule—and *harja*—folk. But here, regrettably, we must note that "there is some evidence for a Scots strain in Watson"[1]—and *wat*, in Scottish, means "given to drinking." One interpretation of the name Watson might therefore be "the son of one given to drinking." A brother of Watson's, as we learn in *The Sign of the Four*, was a drunkard, and Watson himself was drinking at the Criterion bar when he met young Stamford, who introduced him to Holmes (*A Study in Scarlet*).

But what, we may ask, does that *H*. stand for?

Mr. S. C. Roberts early suggested (*Doctor Watson*) that Watson's mother was "a devout woman with Tractarian leanings" and that she caused her child to be baptized John *Henry* after the great Cardinal Newman.

To this, the late H. W. Bell objected (*Sherlock Holmes and Dr. Watson: The Chronology of Their Adventures*) that "Newman had become a Catholic in 1845, seven years before the date which Mr. Roberts proposes for Watson's birth [1852]. If Mrs. Watson had indeed the 'Tractarian leanings' with which Mr. Roberts credits her, she would hardly have named her son after the illustrious convert."

"Might it not be possible, though, that the Watsons, father and mother, were Tractarians who followed Newman along the path to Rome?", Mr. Gordon Sewell wrote in "Holmes and Watson in the South Country." "I think of Watson senior as a High Church parson in a North Hampshire village. He, too, had ridden on horseback through the parishes dropping tracts about fasting and baptism in the doors of neighbouring rectories. And then came the great crisis of Newman's change of allegiance. The Reverend Mr. Watson and his wife also make their submission. In that case young John Henry—like Sir Arthur Conan Doyle—would have been brought up a Catholic."

---

1 "Sturdily and essentially English as [John H. Watson] was, he may well, like most English people, have had a Scottish ancestor in his family tree. The English are probably the only people in the world who actually make a boast of mongrel ancestry. The words 'hundred per cent English' are never heard on true English lips, for the English know well enough that their crossbreeding is their strength."—Dorothy L. Sayers, "Dr. Watson's Christian Name."

A PORTRAIT OF JOHN H. WATSON, M.D., IN HIS PRIME
(ABOUT 1887)

The drawing is by Harry Eckman of the Amateur
Mendicant Society of Detroit, a scion society of
the Baker Street Irregulars.

But the late Dorothy L. Sayers was as vehement as Mr. Bell in totally rejecting the Newman theory. "If there were, in Dr. Watson's character, the slightest trace of Tractarian sympathies, or even of strong anti-Tractarian sympathies, the suggestion might carry some weight, for no one could be brought up in an atmosphere of Tractarian fervour without reacting to it in one way or another. But Watson's religious views remain completely colourless."

Miss Sayers, as we have seen, held that there was a Scots strain in Watson: "It may not be mere coincidence that led Holmes (a shrewd student of national character) to select the adjective 'pawky' for the vein of humour which Watson displayed in the adventure of *The Valley of Fear* and which took his distinguished friend a little aback. Watson's mother may have been a Scot—not, I think, a Highland woman, but a native of Eastern Scotland. The true Highlander is a Celt—quick-tempered, poetical and humourless—everything that Watson was not. Dourness and pawkiness belong to the Aberdeen side of the country" ("Dr. Watson's Christian Name").

"There is only one plain conclusion to be drawn from the facts," Miss Sayers concluded. "Only one name will reconcile the appellation 'James' with the initial letter 'H.' The doctor's full name was 'John Hamish Watson.' "

Hamish, Miss Sayers pointed out, is the Scottish form of "James," and "it is [not] at all unusual for a wife to call her husband by his second name, in preference to his first. . . . 'Hamish' seemed to [Mrs. John H. Watson] perhaps a little highfalutin. By playfully re-Englishing it to 'James' she found for her husband a pet name which was his own name as well."

"This proposal," Mr. Bliss Austin wrote in "What Son Was Watson?", "though entitled to consideration, is nevertheless open to serious objection. . . . I am told that in *good* Gaelic the equivalent of James is Seumas, which hasn't an *H* in it; finally, the whole notion seems a bit too hamish."

The late Christopher Morley agreed that Watson's middle name was *Henry*—not for Cardinal Newman, he maintained, but for Henry Ward Beecher, whose unframed portrait stood on top of Watson's books in the old sitting room at 221B Baker Street ("The Cardboard Box").

But there have been many other suggestions:

1. *Holmes*. Watson "was the Master's first cousin," Mr. Will Oursler wrote in "His French Cousin."

2. *Hubert*. "As revealed by incontestably-sound research on the present writer's part," Mr. Elliot Kimsball wrote in "The Stature of John H. Watson."

3. *Hudson*. "Mrs. Hudson [the landlady at 221 Baker Street] was Watson's grand aunt. . . . And in fact it was he who really engineered [the meeting with Holmes], because he wanted to live in the chambers his aunty had to let, and he could not afford the price she asked. She was a business woman . . . and would give no discount because of being a relative," Mrs. Crighton Sellars wrote in "A Visit with Sherlock Holmes."

4. *Huffham*. "It is probable that [Watson's mother] was an admirer of [Charles John Huffham] Dickens. It is more probable that she desired to name her son after a popular

literary figure of the day who was an intimate friend of her husband's relations [*David Copperfield* was dedicated to the Watsons: the Honourable Richard and Mrs. Watson of Rockingham Castle]," Miss Jane Throckmorton wrote in "'H.' Stands for—?".

Sherlockian scholars are generally but not unanimously agreed that John H. Watson was born in the year 1852. They arrive at this date by reasoning backwards from 1878, the year in which he received his doctor's degree at the University of London.**2**

But here we must register an objection from Dr. Vernon Pennell ("A Résumé of the Medical Life of John H. Watson, M.D., Late of the Army Medical Department"). "S. C. Roberts has pointed out, with a thin veil of anonymity, that [1878] was the same year as the M.D. taken by the late Sir Charters Symonds, F.R.C.S.—with a considerable weight of probability that Watson was born in the same year. Against this, however, we must allow that there is nothing in Watson's after life to suggest undue brilliance. He was certainly *not* a Charters Symonds—a truly brilliant alumnus of London University—and it is not unjust to suspect that on one or two occasions, in some part of his curriculum, he failed to satisfy the examiners and that he was probably a few years older than Symonds rather than younger. We cannot more accurately assess the years of Watson's birth than mention it was, in all probability, in the early '50s."

Mr. William Smith, writing in "'You Have Been in Gettysburg, I Perceive,'" has advanced an even earlier date: Watson, he says, was born in 1842. "In 1861, aged nineteen, Watson is to be discovered in Philadelphia, having saved sufficient funds from several years labor at odd jobs (see Conan Doyle's astonishing 'J. Habakuk Jephson's Statement' for a full, though slightly inaccurately detailed, sketch of a disguised Watson in his American days, complete with the ubiquitous Murray)**3** to matriculate at the School of Medicine of the University of Pennsylvania. . . .

"One fine morning, strolling past the Customs House, he observed that one Colonel John J. Murphy was raising a three-year regiment, the Twenty-Ninth Pennsylvania Volunteers. To one with burning Abolishionist convictions, the appeal of the recruiting posters and the flights of Murphy's Irish oratory must have proved irresistible, for, on the rolls of Company I, we can find the name of John Watson, enlisted July 1, 1861. This regiment was mustered into the Army on July 10, 1861, and subsequently saw action against Jackson in the Valley campaign, at Antietam and at Fredricksburg in 1862, and at Chancellorsville and Gettysburg in 1863. Its history after that crucial battle, though gallant, is hardly of interest to Sherlockians, for it was at Gettysburg, on July 3, 1863, that John Watson was injured, lost track of, and presumed to be dead. . . . Private John Murray of Company C, Twenty-Ninth Pennsylvania Volunteers, must have seen Watson fall, and managed to get him to safety in the town of Gettysburg that afternoon during the confusion caused by Longstreet's artillery barrage . . ."

Watson's birthday has been placed on July 7th by some commentators, who note that in *The Sign of the Four* the good doctor celebrated, on the opening day of the case, by

ROSTER OF THE TWENTY-NINTH PENNSYLVANIA
VOLUNTEERS

Showing the names of John M. Murray as a member of C Company and John Watson as a member of I Company.

2 "1852 is generally accepted as John H. Watson's year of birth from the fact that he graduated in medicine in 1878 . . ."—Dr. W. S. Bristowe, "The Mystery of the Third Continent." "Mr. Roberts has plausibly suggested that Watson was probably born in 1852."—H. W. Bell, *Sherlock Holmes and Dr. Watson: The Chronology of Their Adventures.*

3 Murray, as we learn in *A Study in Scarlet,* was the orderly who saved Watson's life at the fatal battle of Maiwand. In "J. Habakuk Jephson's Statement," first published in the January, 1884, issue of the *Cornhill Magazine,* three years before *A Study in Scarlet,* it is also "Murray" who saves the life of the hero—this time at the battle of Antietam.

THE COAT OF ARMS OF JOHN H. WATSON, M.D.,
ACCORDING TO MR. WILLIAM S. HALL

Or, on a chief vert, an ermine passant, proper.
Crest: an ermine passant, proper, vulned on the
shoulder, gules. Motto: *Mea gloria fides* ("Fidelity
is my glory").

taking Beaune with his lunch. But most chronologists now
hold that the opening day of *The Sign of the Four* was not
July 7th but September 18th.

Watson's birthplace is unknown, but data can be found
in his reminiscences which have led to much controversy.

Mr. T. S. Blakeney, for example, has speculated somewhat
tentatively ("The Apocryphal Ancestry of Dr. Watson")
that Watson was born in the neighborhood of Abingdon,
Berkshire, in 1854 or 1855 (not later than 1858), the son of
John Fairford Watson, the second, M.D., and Henrietta
Rivers, whom Watson *père* married not later than 1852.

On the other hand, the "incontestably-sound research"
of Mr. Elliott Kimball has demonstrated ("The Watsons of
Northumberland") that Watson was the youngest son of
Hubert Anselm Watson, a Northumberland squire of the
last century resident at the ancestral Manor of Norham, four
miles west-northwest of Mitford, a village in the beautiful
valley of the Wansbeck west of Morpeth, some seventeen
miles due north of Newcastle-on-Tyne. Watson Senior's
first wife, Mr. Kimball has declared, was Guinevere Bowcliff
or Bowcliffe, a Northumberland lass, who bore him two
sons: Hubert Anselm Junior, born March 19, 1846, and a
brother Harold Hubert, born May 11, 1848. The first Mrs.
Watson died on December 14, 1849, and Hubert Watson
Senior remarried on June 2, 1851; his second wife was Janet
Anne Dexter, descendant of an old Sussex family. Janet
Anne became the mother of a boy, John Hubert, on July 7, 1852.
Her untimely and lamented death occurred on March 16,
1853. Hubert Anselm Watson Senior died on February 3,
1869.

Mr. S. C. Roberts would place Watson's birthplace in
Hampshire on somewhat slender evidence: Watson yearned
for the glades of the New Forest or the shingle of Southsea
on a sultry summer's day in Baker Street ("The Cardboard
Box"), and he expressed admiration for the beauty of the
countryside stretching toward Aldershot when he was traveling to Winchester with Holmes in "The Adventure of the
Copper Beeches." But his knowledge of Hampshire and his
admiration for this lovely county may well have been
acquired in several other ways.

As Dr. W. S. Bristowe has written ("The Mystery of the
Third Continent"): "If this kind of evidence in favour of
Hampshire is to be admitted, it should be pointed out that a
stronger case can be presented for considering Sussex as his
county. On one occasion Watson speaks almost like a guide
book about the early Saxon history of the Forest Row neighbourhood ["The Adventure of Black Peter"]. Whilst on another his knowledge of the villages and houses in the district
south of Horsham is so intimate as to suggest past residence
there ["The Adventure of the Sussex Vampire"]. . . . Even
here we should notice that he does not say 'I was born in that
country, Holmes,' as we might have expected if his birthplace
was in the district."

Although but little is known about John H. Watson's early
days or how he was brought up, certain facts stand out
clearly.

For example, it seems certain that he spent a portion of his
boyhood in Australia: as he and Miss Morstan stood, "her

hand in mine" like two children in the grounds of Pondi-cherry Lodge (*The Sign of the Four*) and surveyed the great rubbish heaps which cumbered those grounds, Watson said: "I have seen something of the sort on the side of a hill near Ballarat, where the prospectors had been at work." "Of the influence of this Australian upbringing on the character of Doctor Watson we have abundant evidence," Mr. Roberts wrote in *Doctor Watson;* "his sturdy common sense, his coolness, his adaptability to rough conditions on Dartmoor or elsewhere are marks of that tightening of moral and physical fibre which comes from the hard schooling of colonial life."**4**

The presumption is that Watson *père* was attracted to Australia by the discovery of gold at Ballarat in 1851. In Australia he married, and in Australia John H. Watson and his elder brother were born.**5**

On the other hand, Watson *père* may have been attracted to Australia, not for its goldfields, but for the railroading then going on there. In "A Chronometric Excogitation," the late A. Carson Simpson wrote:

It is true that the goldrush in and around Ballarat began in 1851 and rivalled in intensity the days of the '49ers in California, but three months was reckoned a speedy voyage for the fastest clipper-ships to the gold diggings, and the new and infrequent steam service of the Peninsular & Oriental Steam Navigation Co. saved little time. It is hardly likely that the younger Watson would have been taken on such a long journey before he was, say, three years old, which would be in 1855. By then, the goldrush had been going for four years, the fever had abated somewhat, and the rich claims had almost all been pre-empted. Despite the Doctor's known propensity for speculating on shares and taking an occasional flyer on the ponies, somehow Sir Sydney [Roberts'] suggestion about the father does not ring true....

[Watson's father] was just such a man as would be chosen by one of the Australian Colonies for an important post in its expanding railway empire. [He played an important part, no doubt, in the completion of the Sydney Railway, which opened on September 26, 1855. Not the first railway in Australia, it was the first of any length, running 22 miles southwestwardly from Sydney to Liverpool.] It seems likely that sometime—probably late, for it left him with a lasting impression—in the period between 1855 and 1865 (when John H. Watson returned to England for his further schooling), his father took him to Ballarat in the course of a construc-tion survey of the Melbourne-Adelaide line.

This hypothesis ... enables us to paint a picture of [Watson's father as] a boy born during the Napoleonic Wars, say in 1810. He went to work young, as was usual in those days. He was fifteen years old when real rail-roading began in 1825, with George Stephenson driving his own locomotive (the "No. 1") at the head of a train on the Stockton & Darlington Railway. The perspica-cious, up-and-coming lad saw his opportunity and got into this rapidly-growing business. He learned, as one

4 Still, if Watson spent his early boyhood in Aus-tralia, it is curious that he does not comment upon the fact on many occasions when he had a fitting opportunity to do so: with Holy Peters, "one of the most unscrupulous rascals that Australia has evolved . . ." ("The Disappearance of Lady Frances Carfax"); with the beautiful and unhap-pily married Mary Fraser of Adelaide ("The Ad-venture of the Abbey Grange"); with the call of "Cooee" and the dying reference to a (Balla)rat in "The Boscombe Valley Mystery"; and especially in the case of the convict Trevor, who made his fortune in the gold diggings ("The *Gloria Scott*").

5 There may well have been one or more brothers: Holmes in *The Sign of the Four* speaks once of Watson's *eldest* brother, implying that John may have been the third or even later child in the family.

had to do in those days, by experience, and profited by it to such an extent that, at the age of thirty (in 1840), he could afford to buy a fifty-guinea watch.**6** Undoubtedly he continued to rise in his chosen profession, and, by the time he was forty-five (in 1855) was a railroader of recognized ability and experience. . . . The father came back to England when the future Doctor returned for his schooling, or shortly thereafter, and was an important figure in the engineering department of the Great Western Railway until his death or retirement [which accounts for Watson's ability to get a number of patients from among the officials at Paddington Station so soon after his establishing his practice in Paddington; see "The Adventure of the Engineer's Thumb"].

Mrs. Jennifer Chorley ("Some Diggings Down Under") has given us a very different picture of Watson's father. Him she has identified with William Watson, that same William Watson who, in 1861, as a member of the Gardiner gang of bushrangers attacked the Brennan Station on the Billabong with Henry Keene and Michael Lawler. Watson, unhappily, was the chief villain, but all three were captured and sentenced to death at Goulburn. "I don't care if it's tomorrow," William Watson was reported to have said. "Well, goodbye."

"This dreadful tragedy," Mrs. Chorley wrote, "must have killed Mrs. Watson. The two little boys, one about ten and the other a few years older, must have been sent back to England as orphans to be brought up by an aged relative. . . . No doubt Watson's brother inherited his father's weaknesses, nor is it surprising that, with such a history, 'he threw away his chances.' "

Although it is probable that Watson's mother—whom he never mentions—did die when the boy was very young, we would prefer to think that Watson's father, then a well-to-do man, returned to England with young John, perhaps leaving his older boy or boys in Australia.**7**

However, Dr. W. S. Bristowe has noted the intense feelings which Henry Ward Beecher's life aroused "in Watson's usually stolid imagination" ("The Cardboard Box") and he has suggested that both Watson's father and elder or eldest brother became converts to Beecher's cause soon after their return to England from Australia. Did Beecher's amazing eloquence in behalf of the Northern cause during the Civil War "lead Watson's father to cross the Atlantic in 1863 with his elder son leaving Watson at school in England in the care of his mother (if she was still alive) or more probably of a guardian in Sussex?" Dr. Bristowe has asked. "If we suppose that Watson's father was a casualty . . . we can at once begin to see why Watson had such a deep personal interest in Beecher as to install his portrait in Baker Street.**8** He would feel 'passionate indignation' against those Englishmen who opposed his father's hero during his mission in 1863. The campaign on which his father and brother had embarked would have caused his eyes to shine and his hands to clench as he thought of it. And then, as his mind turned to the consequences on the Watson family his face would have saddened just as Holmes described."

6 The meager Canonical information that we have about Watson's father comes from the incident in *The Sign of the Four* in which Holmes makes certin deductions about Watson's brother from this watch, inherited by the brother from the father.

7 When he reached London after his service in the Second Afghan War, John H. Watson stated that he had neither kith nor kin *in England*.

8 Mr. Robert Keith Leavitt has presented a very different view of Watson's interest in Beecher in his essay on "The Preposterously Paired Performances of the Preacher's Portrait." When Holmes made his deductions from the "H. W." initials on the back of the watch, the detective, Mr. Leavitt contends, intentionally or unintentionally overlooked the traces of a third initial—a "B."—and deduced "in one blinding flash the true identity of Watson's father."

The school to which Watson was sent is never mentioned but it would seem that it must have been one of the better known public schools from the fact that Watson's friend "Tadpole" Phelps of "The Naval Treaty" was "extremely well-connected," a nephew of Lord Holdhurst, and that it prepared Phelps for a scholarship to Cambridge.

"Our choice is greatly narrowed," Dr. Bristowe wrote, "when we remember that Watson played [rugby] for Blackheath ["The Adventure of the Sussex Vampire"] in later years which provides us with the reasonable assumption that it was one of the few public schools where rugby football was played in those days. When we also find that [Watson] decided to pursue the profession of an army surgeon and was for a time attached to a Berkshire regiment [*A Study in Scarlet*] we may think it not unlikely that Wellington College was the school selected for him. Wellington fills our requirements in being a well-known public school in Berkshire not too far distant from his home where rugby football was played and where the strong army influence induced him to join the service."

But Mr. Frederick Bryan-Brown has written (in "Sherlockian Schools and Schoolmasters") that: "I am not convinced that [Watson's school] must have been one of the leading schools because of Percy Phelps and his uncle and his university scholarship. Lord Holdhurst still had many calls even when Phelps was a prospering civil servant, and in earlier years would not have been able to spend too much on the education of his nephew. On the balance of probability I feel that Watson was a doctor's son (medicine, like art, is often in the blood). Holdhurst's sister had presumably married beneath her and yet not to money. What would be more likely than a brilliant, overworked, underpaid medical practitioner for her husband? A school was founded in the 1850's to cater for the sons of doctors and its rugby club was established by 1870. So I submit as something to be shot at, the hypothesis that Epsom College was Watson's school. . . . If a circle is drawn . . . at a radius of ten-plus miles with Reigate as its centre we get the area of Watson's youth, near enough to London for him to be at home there and yet not so far that he would be prevented by loyalty from referring to its cesspool-like qualities."

In any case, Watson's old school number—presumably the number of his locker in the bootroom—was thirty-one ("The Adventure of the Retired Colourman").

Most of what we know about Watson's medical training and military career comes to us from the doctor himself, in the opening pages of his first published reminiscence, *A Study in Scarlet.*

He tells us, first, that in the year 1878 he took his degree of Doctor of Medicine of the University of London.

This, to begin with, is a specialist's degree, taken only by a select few either in "pure" medicine or, perhaps, in pathology, public health, psychology, or midwifery. To qualify for it, Watson would first have had to take a Bachelor's degree of M.B. or B.S. or a diploma of M.R.C.S. or L.R.C.P. "Watson *might* have qualified for the M.B. as late as '77 or as early as '72," Dr. Pennell wrote, "for there were three alternative methods of procedure for the acquisition of an M.D. and each of these modes of entry could be modified according to whether or not the candidate was placed in the 'First Division' at the Second Examination. The delay might be two, three or even five years."

Watson would also have to have taken a B.S.—a Baccalaureate of Surgery—which could not be taken until one year after taking the M.B. and attendance at a course of instruction in operative surgery. It is extremely unlikely that Watson omitted to take the B.S., for he *was* a surgeon: he must have been to have held the post of House Surgeon at St. Bartholomew's Hospital, because only a House Surgeon would have a "dresser" (a surgeon's assistant) under him, as was young Stamford to Watson. "It seems not unlikely," Dr. Pennell continued, "that Watson commenced his medical studies about the age of eighteen [that is, in 1870], took five or five and a half years at least to satisfy the examiners of his sufficient knowledge of Medicine and Surgery to acquire the M.B., B.S. (Lond.). A further period of two years in hospital after qualifications, during which time he held the post of House Surgeon, seems reasonable, for in the '70s and '80s it was not uncommon for the junior staff appointments of House Surgeon or House Physician to be held for a period of one or two years rather than the six months' tenure of the present day. Indeed, Dr. Mortimer of Grimpen, is shown in Dr. Watson's *Medical Directory* [*The Hound of the Baskervilles*] to have been H.S. at Charing Cross Hospital from '82 to '84."

Although Dr. Pennell assumes that Watson took his degree of Bachelor of Medicine and his Baccalaureate of Surgery at the University of London, the honor of awarding him with those degrees should go, we think, to the University of Edinburgh.**9**

The evidence for this is Conan Doyle himself, who wrote, in "The Field Bazaar" (it is Holmes speaking to Watson here): "I saw upon [the envelope] the same shield-shaped device which I have observed upon your old college cricket cap. It was clear, then, that the request came from Edinburgh University—or from some club connected with the University."

Doubts that Watson was, in fact, a *Doctor* of Medicine have been cast by many commentators—not the least of them Conan Doyle, in the very essay mentioned above; here he has Holmes say: ". . . I began by glancing at the address, and I could tell . . . that it was an unofficial communication. This I gathered from the use of the word 'Doctor' upon the address, to which as a Bachelor of Medicine, you have no legal claim."

Add to this the statement that Holmes, admittedly in a fretful mood, made to Watson in "The Adventure of the Dying Detective": "After all, you are only a general practitioner with very limited experience and mediocre qualifications," and we are led to the conclusion that Watson was *not* a Doctor of Medicine but a Bachelor of Medicine with a Baccalaureate of Surgery. He might nonetheless be called "Doctor," but by courtesy only. The aforementioned James Mortimer, a man of precise mind, punctiliously disclaimed the title on the grounds that he possessed only the humble (or, as Holmes would say, mediocre) qualifications of a

9 Mr. Elliot Kimball agrees ("The Admirable Murray"); "Watson was a student at Edinburgh from 1870 to 1872."

Member of the Royal College of Surgeons; nevertheless, he is known from start to finish as *Dr.* Mortimer.

Watson tells us, next, that after taking the degree of "Doctor" of Medicine of the University of London, he proceeded to Netley to go through the course prescribed for surgeons in the army.

In all scholarly earnestness, we must ask here why a rising young physician whose medical career had opened, most promisingly, with the appointment of House Surgeon at St. Bartholomew's Hospital, should a few years later have decided to become an Assistant Surgeon in the British Army.

The late Elmer Davis, writing "On the Emotional Geology of Baker Street," suggested that Watson must have fallen insanely in love with some actress or singer who presently tired of him. It was Watson's continued pursuit of her— "undissuadable, shameless, ridiculous, and above all unconcealed"—that cost the house man at Bart's his position and his career.

But perhaps we are maligning Watson. As Dr. Reginald Fitz has written in "A Belated Eulogy: To John H. Watson, M.D.," the newspapers at the time "were bitter over the indignities that were being heaped upon the British Lion along the Indian Frontier, and the Russian Bear seemed always to be snarling. A good deal of recruiting was being done in London with fine promise of adventure and excitement to anyone with spirit. Therefore, Dr. Watson, good sport that he was, naturally joined the Colours as soon as he could. . . ."

It is likely, however, that Watson had done some traveling before entering the service. Dr. Vernon Pennell has suggested that "It is not unlikely that this versatile, if rather pedestrian practitioner, may have spent a year or more as a ship's surgeon after taking his Qualifying Examinations (the M.B. and the B.S.) and in that capacity he visited Australia, for a second time, and India for the first." And Mr. Elliot Kimball has written (*Dr. John H. Watson at Netley*): "Watson left the University of London at the close of the academic year in late June of 1878. He was at the end of a long road of study which had extended from 1872 to 1878. . . . It was more or less in desperation that Dr. Watson turned to an army career, qualified as a candidate for Netley, and went abroad, again, for the summer of 1879. . . . The course he took began in October, 1879, and was terminated in March, 1880."

Netley is near Southampton, and it was in the Royal Victoria Military Hospital there that Watson would have taken his training. This would have consisted of courses in pathology, military surgery, medicine, and hygiene; his instructors, as Mr. Kimball demonstrated in *Dr. Watson at Netley*, would have been Surgeon-General Sir Thomas Longmore in surgery; Surgeon-General W. Campbell Maclean in medicine; Surgeon-Major F.S.B.F. de Chaumont in hygiene; and Sir William Aikens in pathology.

Whether Watson was Hampshire-born or Australian-born or neither, he would certainly have had an opportunity at this time to explore the southern parts of the county, and so, years later, to be able to think nostalgically of the cool glades of the New Forest and the shingle (beach) at Southsea.

Having passed his examination, Watson was duly attached to the Fifth Northumberland Fusiliers as Assistant Surgeon. This, Dr. Pennell has written, is "a somewl · · ambiguous reference to the Fifth Regiment of Foot. The Northumberland Fusiliers are rightly proud of their titles 'The Fighting Fifth' and 'The Fifth Fusiliers.' Watson's nomenclature might possibly lead one to suppose that there were five or more *battalions* to this illustrious regiment—a most unlikely cadre at the time of the Afghan Wars, and an early example of Watson's inexactitude." (We may notice in passing that Fusiliers are infantry soldiers who formerly carried a fusil, or flintlock, but the name is still borne by some of the British infantry.)

Watson tells us that the Northumberland Fusiliers were in India at this time (in fact, they were); he necessarily had to travel there to join his regiment. Before he could do so, he states, the Second Afghan War had broken out.

"The Second Afghan War began in November, 1868," Mr. Kimball wrote in *Dr. Watson at Netley*, "but consisted in little more than piddling skirmishes until the spring of 1880. Indeed, there were two protracted lulls, during each of which it was anticipated that a negotiated peace would be declared. It was in the spring of 1880 that Ayub Khan recruited and assembled a powerful force which he put in the field with the intent to drive the British from Afghanistan. Actually the *first* battle of the Second Afghan War was Maiwand (July 27, 1880). When Watson wrote of war having broken out, he meant that Ayub Khan was in the field with an army, and that hostilities of major proportions were about to develop."

In his study of Watson's military career, "Watson, Come Here; I Want You: in Afghanistan," Professor Richard D. Lesh has written:

On landing at Bombay, Watson learned that his corps had advanced over the passes and was deep in the enemy's country. It is safe to assume that he then took, with numerous other officers who found themselves in the same position, a coastal steamer and disembarked at Karachi, the northern port of supply for the War. Here there were three choices up the Indus Valley toward the southwest passes. Assistant Surgeon Watson most certainly took the troop train by Indus Valley Railway to Sukkur, as the river steamers and camel caravans were much too tedious and were reserved for heavy cargo. A new railway ran from the Indus through Jacobabad to Sibi, a distance of 159 miles. Here Watson was attached to one of the numerous camel and horse caravans supplying troops beyond the passes.

It is most certain that Watson travelled to Dadar, close by, and entered that rocky arid defile known as Bolan Pass on his way to Quetta, 88 miles away. Here for the first time the caravan undoubtedly met the enemy in the form of murderous Ghazi raiders who would strike swiftly the lightly guarded encampments, terrorising the native baggage escorts and stealing horses and camels. The main command of the western sector of the Afghan operations was at Quetta (where the British

Army in 1851 officially recorded temperatures of 140° F.), and it was here that Watson caught up with the Fifth Northumberland Fusiliers and began his duties. Dysentery and enteric fever (typhoid) were responsible for far more deaths among the troops than enemy action, and the temperatures were so unbearable that troop movements were almost impossible. The tents were like ovens all night. Heat exhaustion and dehydration were deadly. On one recorded patrol of 25 men travelling 40 miles in two days' journey, 14 men perished of the heat.

But to the north at [Kandahar—Watson's Candahar], if the temperatures were less severe, the situation was more critical, and for this reason Assistant Surgeon Watson was ordered to duty with the Berkshires . . . at the post hospital at Kandahar, some 155 miles into Afghan territory and under sporadic harassment by the fanatic Ghazis and Pathans. . . .

Watson himself tells us that he was "removed" from his brigade—a word which has caused raised eyebrows among some commentators. "In British usage," Christopher Morley wrote, "the verb *seconded*, meaning transfer of an officer from his own regiment to some other outfit—or possibly promoted to staff duty—is always pronounced as in French: se*conded* (like absconded). Then, methought, poor Watson was se*conded* . . . from his Northumberland Fusiliers. . . .**10** But when I look it up, it says 'I was removed from my brigade.' That *removed* has to me a somewhat sinister sound? It doesn't sound *pukka* military talk at all, and seems to suggest less than promotion."

"Presumably," the late Dr. Ernest Bloomfield Zeisler commented in *Baker Street Chronology,* "there was some reason for [Watson's] removal, and this reason may well have been why he was not honoured or promoted [during the Afghan campaign]. . . . What could the reason have been? He was not courtmartialed or jailed or expelled from the Army; hence he had not been guilty of insubordination, disloyalty or desertion. We know from his subsequent career that he was not a coward, a drunkard or a quarreler. There remains one possible explanation: Watson had contracted a venereal disease, either syphilis or gonorrhea, both of which were always common in and about military establishments in those days. What presumably occurred is that Watson was laid up with acute gonorrhea while his brigade moved on; after several weeks of discomfort he was ready to return to duty but had to join another outfit because his own had gone ahead. For this reason he was not honoured or promoted even after being wounded in battle."

Whatever one may think of this, we must acknowledge that Dr. Watson *was* "removed" from his brigade and attached to the Berkshires, or, to give them their full title, Princess Charlotte of Wales' Royal Berkshire Regiment, composed of the 49th and 66th Foot. It was the 66th Foot to which Dr. Watson was attached, for it was this unit, commanded by Brigadier-General Burrows, which fought at the Battle of Maiwand.

In tracing Dr. Watson's military career, we should note here that the Fifth Northumberland Fusiliers is an establishment of the *Bengal* Army, and the Berkshires is an estab-

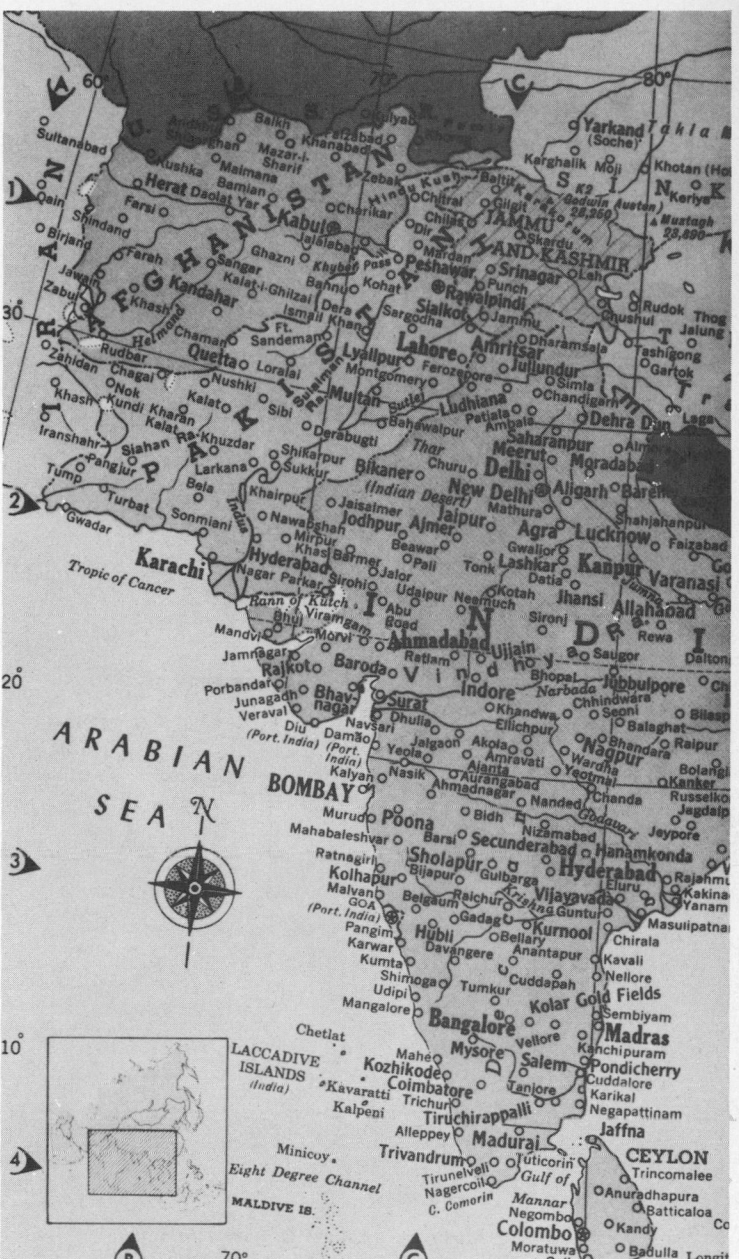

WATSON'S INDIA AND AFGHANISTAN

10 In "Dr. Watson and the British Army," Mrs. Crighton Sellars has observed that it is interesting to muse on the fact that had Watson "not been detached from the Fusiliers at Candahar . . . we might never have had the Sherlock Holmes stories; for the Fusiliers were not sent to Maiwand, and had Watson stayed with them he would not have acquired [the wound or wounds] which invalided him home and out of the service, and he would never have met Sherlock Holmes."

lishment of the *Bombay* Army. In neither case did Watson belong to the *Indian* Army, as he later wrote that he did in "The Problem of Thor Bridge."

On July 4, 1880, a British force of some 2,453 men and a large baggage escort left for the Helmand River near Girishk to take a stand against the advancing armies under Ayub Khan. The six companies of the Berkshires 66th Foot, Watson among them, were commanded by the valiant Lt.-Col. James Galbraith, who was to fall at Maiwand. Burrows' Berkshires were outflanked as Ayub Khan's main body of troops crossed the Helmand some thirty miles farther north than anticipated, at a point which is usually unfordable. Burrows was forced to retreat toward Kandahar and regroup for a stand in a desert valley just south of the village of Maiwand, which lies some fifty miles to the northwest of Kandahar.

On the morning of Tuesday, July 27, 1880, at nine o'clock, the "fatal battle of Maiwand" began. It was indeed a fatal battle, with an estimated 2,734 British soldiers engaged, of whom 934 were killed and 175 wounded. The 66th Foot lost ten officers and 275 men killed, two officers and 33 men wounded. When six o'clock came, a forlorn column of weary and dejected men were retreating to Kandahar, hopelessly beaten by an overwhelming enemy.

And the "murderous Ghazis,"**11** as Watson called them, poured a continuous fire on those retreating. The official report says that the majority of the casualties were caused by men falling from heat and exhaustion—the season was the hottest of the year; it was 105° F. in the shade—and the flight to Kandahar had to be undertaken after marching and fighting without food or water for twenty-four hours. Ayub Khan suffered severe casualties also, and could not pursue the remnants of the brigade more than five miles.

And what of Watson?

He was, he tells us, one of the wounded; he had been struck on the shoulder—we later learn, from Holmes, that it was his *left* shoulder—by a Jezail bullet,**12** which shattered the bone and grazed the subclavian artery.

Watson would have fallen into the hands of the murderous Ghazis had it not been for the devotion and courage shown by Murray, his orderly,**13** who threw him across a pack-horse and succeeded in bringing him safely to the British lines.

Watson was extremely fortunate—for, as Rudyard Kipling wrote, in "The Young British Soldier":

> When you're wounded and left on Afghanistan's plains,
> And the women come out to cut up what remains,
> Just roll to your rifle and blow out your brains
>   An' go to your Gawd like a soldier . . .

But Watson's "British lines" are a little mysterious: there *were no* British lines between Maiwand and Kandahar. Watson "must have been misinformed on this point," Mr. N. P. Metcalfe wrote in "The Date of the *Study in Scarlet*." ". . . he was in no fit state to act as a military correspondent and, anyway, probably relied on the information of his orderly, Murray. It was definitely a case of *sauve qui peut*."

11 Among Moslems, a Ghazi is a warrior champion, especially in the destruction of infidels.

12 "According to the best authorities, the rifle or musket from which this bullet is fired is long and heavy with a crooked stock and used with a forked rest. It is of native manufacture and is patterned after the British Lee-Enfield rifle. Bannerman's complete catalogue of military weapons does not list the Jezail rifle as such, although numerous India matchlock guns are featured. The bullets are often slugs made from nails or odd scraps of metal including silver, and may produce infected wounds."—Dr. Roland Hammond, "The Surgeon Probes Doctor Watson's Wound."

13 A noncommissioned officer or soldier who attends a superior officer to carry out his orders or to render other services.

There *were* two companies of the Berkshires under Major Ready who were stationed on detachment at Khelat-i-Ghilzai, some seventy miles northeast of Kandahar on the Kabul road. While these did not share in the defeat, they, like the man who took part in the battle, were cooped up in Kandahar from July 27th until General Roberts' relief force appeared before the town on August 31st, and General Phayre's from Quetta, 137 miles away, arrived on September 6th. The month's siege at Kandahar was rigorous and morale was low —yet Watson never mentions it.

It seems safe to conclude that he was never there. He tells us, certainly, that he was removed, with a great train of wounded sufferers, to the base hospital at Peshawar (which Watson spells Peshawur), the most distant command of the Afghan Operations in the extreme Northeast, a distance of some 480 miles.**14**

Whether Watson reached Peshawar via Kabul or via Quetta is a point debated by commentators; as is the route taken. In any case, Watson, we think, would have reached the base hospital at Peshawar by the end of August, 1880.

Here he rallied, and had already improved so far as to be able to walk about the wards, when he was struck down by "enteric fever, that curse of our Indian possessions."

"I am told by Dr. Louis A. Hauser, of the staff of the New York Hospital, that the term 'enteric fever,' which is now obsolete, was used at the time of the Afghan wars to describe intestinal fevers generally, including the fever now designated as typhoid," the late Edgar W. Smith wrote in "The Long Road from Maiwand." "The bacillus typhosus was not isolated by Eberth of Germany until the year 1880, but Dr. Hauser feels, despite the lack of facilities for accurate diagnosis available in India at the time, that Watson's malady was certainly typhoid, and he believes, from the references made, that it might have laid him low for three months."

But the length of Watson's bout with "enteric fever"—he tells us that his life was despaired of "for months"—is another matter of controversy.

As Mr. Metcalfe wrote, in "The Date of the *Study in Scarlet*," "With respect to Dr. Hauser, I feel that the opinion of a medical man who has himself experienced this disease [Dr. Maurice Campbell] is to be preferred. It is as follows: 'The duration of enteric fever (nowadays called typhoid) is three weeks—though, of course, the attack may vary from subject to subject and depend on the severity or mildness of the onset. After his hectic experiences . . . Watson's months of despair were probably only weeks; his remark that his life was despaired of for months should not be taken literally. That is not a reasonable statement about any ordinary complications of typhoid where the risk is generally over during a much shorter period. There is nothing so indeterminable as a long stay in a base hospital as anyone who has experienced it can vouch.'"

When at last Watson came to himself, he was so weak and emaciated that a medical board determined that not a day should be lost in sending him back to England.

He had, then, a rather long journey to take—by rail about a thousand miles from Peshawar to the port of Karachi, and then for about 600 miles by boat from Karachi to Bombay.

14 Mr. Samuel F. Howard has suggested ("More About Maiwand") that Watson would be sent, not to Peshawar, but to Multan, but Mr. T. S. Blakeney ("Some Disjecta Membra") doubts this: "Multan is a notoriously hot place and most unsuitable for wounded."

15 Named after the ancient name of Syria's principal river, now called El Asi or Nahr El-Ashy.

16 It was always Christopher Morley's belief that "the very day" was January 1, 1881—"a day when Watson would naturally be making resolutions for a more frugal life. . . . Also the fact of its being a Holiday would account for Holmes being *the only student working in the laboratory*."

JOHN H. WATSON, M.D., AT THE TIME OF HIS MEETING
WITH SHERLOCK HOLMES

From *Sherlock Holmes: A Biography*, by William S. Baring-Gould.

From Bombay he was dispatched in the troopship *Orontes***15** —and here, thanks to the researches of Mr. Metcalfe ("The Date of the *Study in Scarlet*"), we are able to determine the exact date. Mr. Metcalfe, scanning the Naval and Military Intelligence column of the *London Times* from July, 1880, to December, 1881, has revealed that "a ship called the *Orontes* was pressed into special service in July, 1880, and troops for Afghanistan and India were embarked on her on August 3rd. She sailed from Portsmouth to Queenstown, the Mediterranean and Bombay on August 4th. The journey was scheduled to take twenty-eight days, but she actually arrived in Bombay on September 1st. On October 31st, she left Bombay for Portsmouth, calling at Malta on November 16th, and arriving at Portsmouth on Friday afternoon, November 26th, *bringing home the first troops from Afghanistan, including eighteen invalids*."

This corresponds almost precisely with Watson's statement that he "landed a month later on Portsmouth jetty."

In Portsmouth "there are Sheer Jetty, Pitch House Jetty, South Jetty, etc.," Christopher Morley wrote, "but obviously where JHW landed was *Troopship Jetty* marked large as life on the map [in Muirhead's *Guide to England*]. . . . I can almost see the *Orontes* unloading . . . at the south end of the Royal Dock Yard, close to the Royal Naval College."

The wounded off the *Orontes* were sent to Netley, but Watson was not among them. Rather he "gravitated" to London, "that great cesspool into which all the loungers and idlers of the Empire are irresistibly drained."

"Gravitated" is a curious word for Watson to have used —by fast train, it takes only an hour and three-quarters to make the 74-mile run from Portsmouth to London—and we may perhaps assume that Watson at this time acquired some of that knowledge of Hampshire and Sussex which he displayed later.

In London Watson stayed for "some" time at a private hotel in the Strand. It was the Craven Hotel, Christopher Morley thought—and Mr. Michael Harrison has asked (*In the Footsteps of Sherlock Holmes*): "Could it have been Horrex's, at the corner of Norfolk Street, or Osmond's, at 87, Strand, or Scott's Private, at 13 Cecil Street?"

He led there, he tells us, "a comfortless, meaningless existence," and so alarming did the state of his finances become that he soon realized that he must make a complete alteration in his style of living. On the very day that he came to this conclusion, he was standing at the Criterion Bar, where he met young Stamford.**16**

Stamford, as we know, introduced Watson to Holmes. The two met "next day" and inspected the rooms at No. 221 Baker Street. "That very evening" Watson moved his things round from the hotel, and Sherlock Holmes followed him "on the following morning." The Great Partnership was about to begin.

10

"HE IS THE NAPOLEON OF CRIME, WATSON"

[Sherlock Holmes of Professor James Moriarty, "The Final Problem"]

Before considering the home of Holmes (and Watson)—its location, physical features and furnishings—we should look briefly at the most deep-dyed of all the villains with whom Mr. Sherlock Holmes of Baker Street ever had to contend.

He was a man extremely tall and thin, with rounded shoulders. He had gray hair above a forehead that domed out in a curve, and below that forehead his eyes, puckered and blinking, were deeply sunken into his pale, white head. He had a solemn way of talking, and the total impression he created was one of dignity and asceticism, somewhat marred by one unpleasant mannerism: his face, protruded forward, was forever oscillating from side to side in a curiously reptilian fashion.

"This man is a scholar," you and I would have said on meeting him, and we would have been right.

He was also the most dangerous man in the London of the 1880's, the greatest schemer of his time, the organizer of every devilry, the controlling brain of the underworld of what was then and still is one of the world's greatest cities.

He was Professor James Moriarty.

Note well the "James." We cannot doubt that "James" *was* his Christian name (if anything could be said to be Christian about so monstrous an individual), for we are given this on the authority of the man who knew him best and hated him most: Sherlock Holmes himself.

And yet, side by side with this, we have the authority of the man who knew *Holmes* best and loved him most, his companion and biographer, John H. Watson, M.D., that Professor Moriarty had a brother who followed a military career and rose to the rank of colonel. And the first name of this brother, we are told, *was James also.*

There was a third brother, less successful in life than Professor James and Colonel James: he was a stationmaster in the west of England. We are never told his name, but we must assume that it, too, was James—for, as Mr. Vincent Starrett long ago pointed out: "Two brothers named James would appear a trifle silly; but if there were three, one might well suppose some sort of sinister pattern . . ."

Mr. Elliot Kimball has written (in "The Watsons of Northumberland") that "There is nothing particularly extraordinary about the matter. Onomatologists (or nomenologists) have long been familiar with the fact that brothers of the

THE YOUTHFUL JAMES MORIARTY

(*Above*) At the age of eight. (*Below*) At the age of twenty-one. Photographs from *Sherlock Holmes: A Biography*, by William S. Baring-Gould.

1 As Mr. Duncan MacDougald, Jr., has shown ("Some Onomatological Notes on 'Sherlock Holmes' and Other Names in the Sacred Writings"), the name Moriarty comes from the Irish *o'muiriċerzaiz*—O Morierty, O Murtagh, Moriarty, from *muir*, "sea," plus the aspirated form of *ceart*, "right, true," plus the personal suffix *ach*.

2 Mr. Smith suggested 1846 for Moriarty's birth, and Professor H. W. Starr ("A Submersible Subterfuge or Proof Impositive") has opted for 1830: "Is it not likely that the portrait of Captain Nemo in [Jules Verne's] *Twenty Thousand Leagues Under the Sea* is a portrayal of a sinister figure well known to us—Professor James Moriarty?"

3 In "A Treatise on the Binomial Theorem," Mr. Poul Anderson has written: "The theorem itself is simply the expansion of the binomial $(a + b)$ raised to the nth power, where n is any number:

$$(a + b)^n = a^n + na^{n-1}b + \frac{n(n-1)}{1.2}a^{n-2}b^2$$

$$+ \frac{\ldots n(n-1)\ldots(n-r+1)}{r!}a^{n-r}b^r \ldots$$

$$b + \ldots + b^n$$

It vexed mathematicians for many centuries. The Hindus and the Arabs knew something of it. Newton discovered it about 1665, and an exposition is found in a letter dated 1676, but no real proof is given. Bernoulli and Euler sought the proof, but it remained for the Norwegian Niels Henrik Abel, 1802–1829, to demonstrate it rigorously for all n. This having been done before Moriarty's time, what remained for him? . . . It seems probable . . . that [he] was working on the basic idea of number itself, and that he developed a general binomial theorem applicable to other algebras than the one we know. If he could do this at the three-cornered age of 21, it is obvious that in his case, as in the Master's, genius flowered early."

same sibship not infrequently bore the same given name in earlier days. One staunch adherent of the Stuarts, who sired fourteen (14) sons named them all Charles; individuality in a cognominal sense, or with respect to the first given name, was not possible for the fourteen; but such identifications depended upon the second given name, *e.g.*, Charles Edward, Charles James, Charles Francis. Instances in which three or four brothers (or sisters) of the same sibship had the identical first given name are by no means uncommon. . . ."

Still, in the "sinister pattern" established by Moriarty *mère* and Moriarty *père* in the naming of their offspring, we like to think that we may have found the key to the aberrant personality that Professor Moriarty was later to become: he suffered psychologically as a child, we think, from a loss of identity in the Moriarty household, a loss that was to warp and twist what otherwise would have been a genius to admire, an intellect to esteem.

The Moriartys were of Irish extraction;[1] they were resident, we may suppose, in that part of the west of England where the youngest brother was later employed as a stationmaster. (The late Edgar W. Smith, in his "Prolegomena to a Memoir of Professor Moriarty," "suggested Liverpool on the basis that it "would qualify technically as the west of England" and "there are more Irishmen to the square foot [there] than in any other area on earth outside of Ireland, with the possible exception of Boston, Massachusetts.") We have reason to believe that Moriarty I, the later professor, was some ten years older than his archenemy Holmes. Holmes, we know, was born on January 6, 1854; Moriarty, then, was most probably born in 1844, although the latter part of 1843 is a distinct possibility.[2] He must have had an excellent education: in 1865, when he was only twenty-one, this remarkable youth wrote a treatise on the binomial theorem[3] which had a European vogue and won him the Chair of Mathematics at one of the lesser English universities at an annual salary of seven hundred pounds ($3,500).

One envies his students; Professor Moriarty must have been a marvelous instructor. Who can forget how, in *The Valley of Fear*, he was able to entrance Inspector MacDonald of Scotland Yard with such a lucid explanation of the nature of the eclipse, using as his props only a globe and a reflector lantern? (He "made it all clear in a minute," the Inspector exclaimed.)

But a treatise on the binomial theorem was child's play to the man who later wrote *The Dynamics of an Asteroid*. This *magnum opus* ascended to such rarefied heights of pure mathematics that it was all but incomprehensible to the scientific critics of the day. "The magnitude of his achievement," Mr. Anderson wrote ("A Treatise on the Binomial Theorem") "can be appreciated by reflecting that there are nine known major planets, all influencing the asteroid simultaneously, and that no general solution has yet been found even for the three-body problem. (Given the positions, masses, and velocities of three bodies acting under gravitation, find their orbits for all past time and all time to come.)" And the late Edgar Smith observed that Professor Einstein's Theory of Special Relativity, first published (*Ann. d. Physik*) in June, 1905, bore the "imitative title" *Zur Elektrodynamic Körper* (On the Electrodynamics of Moving Bodies).

Indeed, there seems little reason to doubt that Moriarty did anticipate Einstein in the construction of the formula $E = mc^2$. If, however, it was in fact Moriarty who first perceived the awful potentialities of atomic fission and fusion, and so paved the way for the atomic and the hydrogen bomb, we must also credit him with having laid much of the theoretical groundwork for man-made satellites and the space station now under consideration.

Despite his growing fame as one of the foremost abstract thinkers the world has ever known, dark rumors about Moriarty began to circulate through the little university town, and he was forced to resign his position. In the latter part of the 1870's or early in the 1880's he came to London, where he set himself up as an army coach. Not a very lucrative profession, one would have said. And yet he was somehow able to indulge his sincere love for and his vast appreciation of fine art: on his study wall there hung a painting by Jean-Baptiste Greuze; it showed a sweet young woman with her head on her hands, peeping at the observer sideways. Moriarty may have paid as much as £4,000 ($20,000) for it, for Holmes referred to another painting by Greuze, his *Jeune Fille à l'Agneau* which, in 1865, had fetched that magnificent sum.**4**

Too, as we later learn, Professor Moriarty was able to pay a stipend of £6,000 ($30,000) a year to his right-hand man, the *second* most dangerous man in London, the cheater at cards, the hunter of big game, and the authority on air guns as lethal weapons: the notorious Colonel Sebastian Moran.

The money—so much of it that Moriarty was compelled to keep at least six bank accounts—came, of course, from crime: from forgery cases, robberies, murders, and lesser atrocities. Not that there was ever anything to connect the ostensible "army coach" with a single illegal action. Dear me—Professor Moriarty's favorite expression—dear me, no.

Moriarty did little himself; he only planned. But his agents were numerous and splendidly organized. Was there a paper to be abstracted, a house to be rifled, a man to be removed —the word was passed to the Professor, and the matter was seen to. The agent might be caught. But the deep organizing power, which forever stood in the way of the law and threw a shield over the wrongdoer, was never caught—never so much as suspected. Moriarty pervaded London, and no one had ever heard of him.

PROFESSOR JAMES MORIARTY

As portrayed by Mr. Martin Gabel in Alexander H. Cohen's production of *Baker Street*, "a musical adventure of Sherlock Holmes."

4 In *The Private Life of Sherlock Holmes*, Mr. Vincent Starrett has suggested that Conan Doyle may have modeled Professor Moriarty on "Adam North, who stole the famous Gainsborough, in 1876, and hid it for a quarter of a century, but even that master criminal might have taken lessons from the Moriarty of Holmes and Watson, a figure of colossal resource and malevolence."

EX-PROFESSOR JAMES MORIARTY, SC.D.

As he looked at the time of his first meeting with Mr. Sherlock Holmes. From Edgar W. Smith, "Prolegomena to a Memoir of Professor Moriarty."

No one, that is, except Sherlock Holmes. Often it was only the smallest trace, the faintest indication, and yet it was enough to tell the master detective that the great malignant brain was there, as the gentlest tremors at the edge of the web remind one of the foul spider which lurks at its center. "Petty thefts, wanton assaults, purposeless outrage," Holmes once said, "—to the man who held the clue all could be worked into one connected whole."

The duel came to its climax in the early months of 1891. "You crossed my path on the 4th of January," Moriarty snarled at Holmes. "On the 23rd you incommoded me; by the middle of February I was seriously inconvenienced by you; at the end of March I was absolutely hampered in my plans; and now, at the close of April, I find myself placed in such a position through your continual persecution that I am in positive danger of losing my liberty. The situation is becoming an impossible one."

Little over a week later, it is said, Moriarty lay twisted and broken and dead at the foot of the Reichenbach Falls near the little village of Meiringen in Switzerland.

"London," Mr. Sherlock Holmes was to complain some years after, "has become a singularly uninteresting city since the death of the late lamented Professor Moriarty."

But was Moriarty in truth "the late lamented?"

For four long years, as we shall see, Watson and the world thought that Holmes also lay dead beneath the dark and swirling waters of the Reichenbach; but Holmes in 1894 was very much alive and once again "free to devote his life to examining those interesting little problems which the complex life of London so plentifully presents."

Why not Moriarty?

His body was never recovered; that much is certain. And the suspicion will not rest that Moriarty, like Holmes, survived and carried on.

He could hardly be alive today—after all, he would be at least 120 years of age. But anyone familiar with the history of evil in the world since 1894 has little difficulty in seeing that Professor Moriarty was taking advantage of a long period of social unrest to consolidate and expand his undisputed position as the Napoleon of crime . . .

11

"I HAVE MY EYE ON A SUITE IN BAKER STREET"

[*Sherlock Holmes*, A Study in Scarlet]

Early in this century a party of French schoolboys were visiting London. Asked what historic sight they chose to see first, they answered with one voice: "The house where Sherlock Holmes lives!"

221 Baker Street—it is one of the most famous addresses in all literature, and we have a right, as the late Christopher Morley once said, "to be interested in all details."

But we had better settle, first, the question of whether or not Conan Doyle had any particular house in mind as the home of Holmes and Watson. If he did, he declined to admit it: "But that is a point which for excellent reasons," he observed in his autobiography, "I will not decide."**1**

Indeed, Conan Doyle once went so far as to declare to an interviewer that, to the best of his memory, he had *never been* in Baker Street in his life, but here, almost certainly Conan Doyle was guilty of a bit of leg-pulling: there exists a photograph of the author taken by a photographer's studio, Messrs. Elliott and Fry, in Baker Street.

The "B" in 221B need not concern us long: it probably stood for *bis*, literally meaning *twice*, which was a frequent English identification for a subsidiary address. Christopher Morley cited Leonard Merrick's story *Conrad in Quest of His Youth* (1903) where one of his chorus girls gives her address as:

> Miss Tattic Lascelles
> c/o Madame Hermiance,
> 42 bis, Great Titchfield Street, W.

1 Years later, however, in his memoirs, *Back View*, Sir Harold Morris, Q.C., wrote that his father, Sir Malcolm, had suggested the Morris home on Baker Street to Conan Doyle as a suitable house for the detective and the doctor. Its *present* number is, not 221, but *21;* in Holmes' and Watson's day, its number was 77. Unhappily, it fails to answer a number of the qualifications we will outline for No. "221."

BAKER STREET ABOUT 1890

Portman Mansions, now Portman Street, is on the right. The picture shows the flat-fronted houses which were the standard type in Baker Street. Despite rebuilding, many of the old houses still remain. From The London Electrotype Agency, Ltd.

2 This house no longer exists. Along with its neighbors it was demolished to make room for the head offices of the Abbey National Building Society. It is now no more than a part of the site of Abbey House.

3 Baker Street was named for Sir Edward Baker, *c.* 1763–1825, a neighbor of the Portmans in Dorsetshire, who assisted Mr. Portman in developing his London estate. While Holmes was unquestionably its most famous resident, there were others: Mme. Tussaud at No. 59 (formerly No. 58); Edward Bulwer Lytton at No. 68 (formerly No. 31); William Pitt at No. 120 (formerly 14 York Place); Mrs. Sarah Siddons at No. 27 Upper Baker Street (a house that no longer exists); Arnold Bennett at Chiltern Court Mansions (over the Baker Street Station of the Underground).

4 This fact led Mr. Harrison to surmise that Watson, to get an imaginary number, divided the nonexistent 43 by 2 and got 21½. But both No. 21 and No. 21½ already existed. So Watson prefixed 21½ —or 21B—with his divisor, 2, and got 221B Baker Street.

BAKER STREET AS IT WAS IN 1881

From *The Baker Street Journal*, December, 1964.

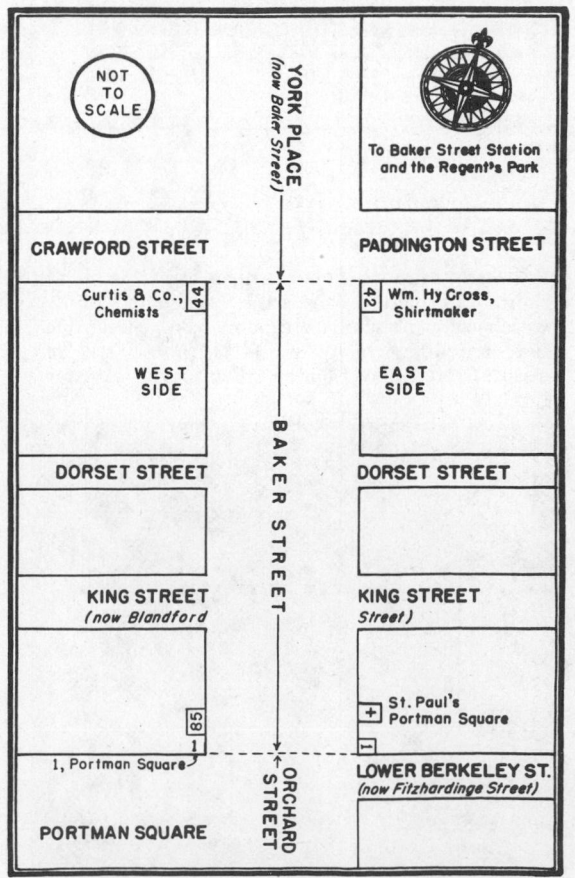

Mme. Hermiance ran a laundry on the ground floor, and Miss Tattie had rooms one flight up—on the English *first*, American *second* floor—just as Holmes and Watson did.

Let us begin our reexamination of the problem of the proper location of No. 221 by noting that the rooms shared for so many years by Holmes and Watson were positively *not* in the house which, until the 1930's, bore the number 221.**2**

Nor, in Holmes' and Watson's day, could *any* house in Baker Street proper have possibly been numbered 221.**3**

The facts are these:

1. Baker Street in 1881 was barely a quarter of a mile long. It consisted of some eighty generously proportioned, four-story buildings. At the southern end, the street passed along one side of Portman Square and continued to the south as Orchard Street, a name which it still bears. Northward, past the crossing of Crawford Street, on the west, and Paddington Street, on the east, it was called *York Place*, and beyond the crossing at Marylebone Road it was called *Upper Baker Street*. As Mr. Michael Harrison wrote, in "Why '221B'?", "The east side . . . ran from No. 1, at the corner of Lower Berkeley (now Fitzhardinge) Street, to No. 42. . . . The street numbers ran consecutively. On the opposite side of the road—the west side—the numbers ran, without a break, from No. 44 . . . at the corner of Crawford Street, to No. 85, which was the building immediately before the big Georgian house at the corner of Portman Square [No. 1, Portman Square]." The numbers in Baker Street proper ended, then, at 85, and there was no No. 43, Baker Street.**4**

2. On January 1, 1921, York Place was incorporated with Baker Street.

3. In 1930 Upper Baker Street was merged with Baker Street, and the entire street was renumbered on the west, or left going north, side—this, as we shall see, is the side that concerns us—from 185 to 247. *For the first time there was a No. 221 Baker Street.*

Had the quarters of 1881 been in the vicinity of the present Abbey House, then Holmes would have had to *anticipate* that Upper Baker Street, where he lived, would some day be merged with Baker Street proper, and that his house, after renumbering, would become 221—which is precisely what he *did* do, if we are to accept the suggestion put forward by Mr. A. L. Shearn in "The Street and the Detective": "It is the writer's considered opinion that notwithstanding other claims, Sherlock Holmes' real address was none other than this house which later became known as 221 Baker Street."

If, however, we choose to disregard this suggestion, we must ask what house in Baker Street proper, or beyond, Watson in 1881 masked as No. "221."

Our single most important piece of Canonical evidence here is the route followed by Holmes and Watson in "The Adventure of the Empty House"—from Cavendish Square into Manchester Street and so to Blandford Street, then down a narrow passage.

Now, *this narrow passage must be one of two:* Kendall Mews, leading south, or Blandford Mews, leading north.

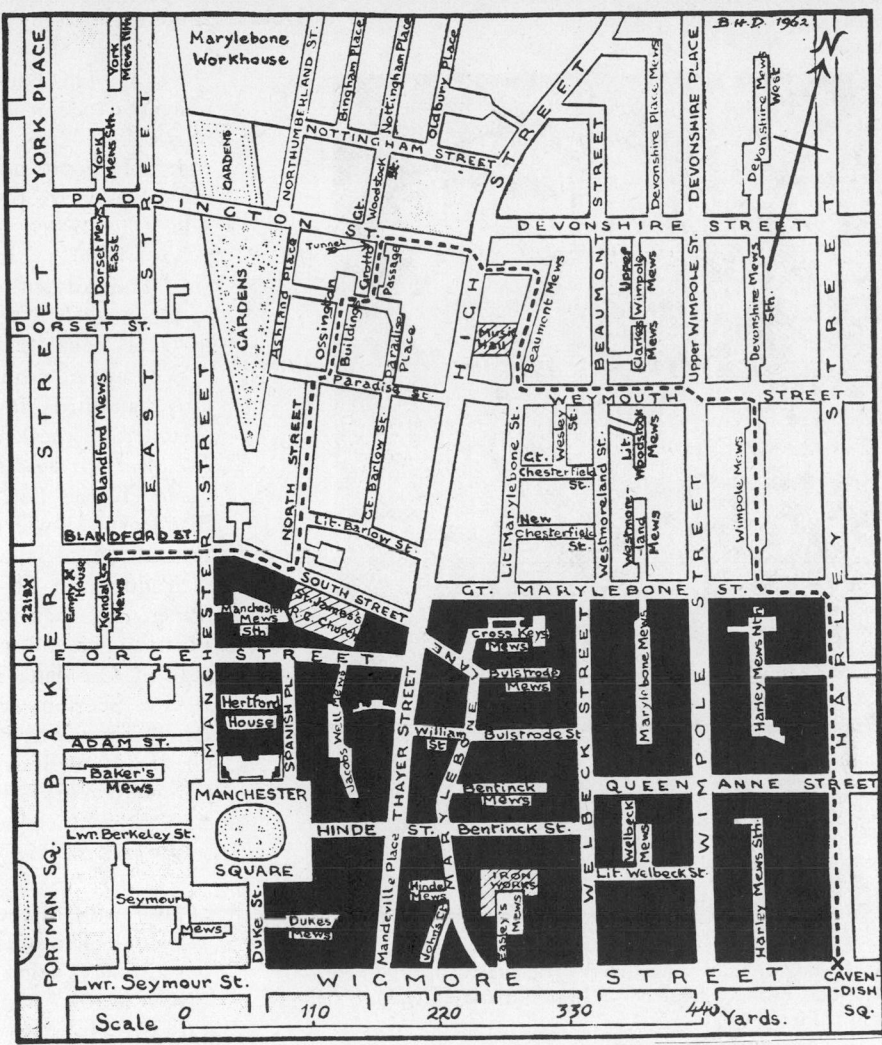

The text reads: "down a narrow passage." This would seem to indicate that Holmes and Watson turned *south* into Kendall Mews (had they gone north, Watson might better have said "up a narrow passage")—and this in turn would mean that 221 Baker Street, which stood opposite "Camden House"—"the empty house"—was on the *west* side of Baker Street, between George Street on the south and King (west)-Blandford (east) streets on the north, among the present Nos. 19–35.

Despite Watson's "down a narrow passage," let us for the moment, however, leave this segment of Baker Street proper and assume (as the late Gavin Brend, among others, did) that Holmes and Watson turned *north* into Blandford Mews. 221 Baker Street would then be on the *west* side of Baker Street, between King-Blandford streets on the south and Dorset Street on the north, among the present Nos. 37–67:

No. 49. "Reliable local authority has informed us that No. 49 is accepted in that district as being upon the site," Mr. T. S. Blakeney wrote in *Sherlock Holmes: Fact or Fiction?*

No. 61. "As between [the numbers 59, 61, and 63] there is little to choose and we are not justified in eliminating any of them, but if anything, the advantage is slightly in favor of No. 61," Mr. Brend wrote in *My Dear Holmes.***5**

"THE MEWS OF MARYLEBONE IN 1894"

On Mr. Bernard Davies' map, black-shaded blocks are those lying directly between Cavendish Square and Manchester Street, with *no* routes by ways of mews, etc. Unshaded blocks are those nearest to Cavendish Square which, in sequence, could have formed part of the journey taken by Holmes and Watson in "The Adventure of the Empty House." The suggested route from Cavendish Square to No. 34 Baker Street is shown by the bold dotted lines. From *The Sherlock Holmes Journal,* Winter, 1962.

5 Mr. Blakeney's No. 49 went down in the blitz, and Mr. Brend's No. 61 (which existed when he wrote his book) has now been demolished to make way for a large block of offices.

NO. 109 BAKER STREET

As photographed by Mr. D. Martin Dakin of The Sherlock Holmes Society of London; the original is in color.

No. 66. This house, we are told, once satisfied Mr. Vincent Starrett's "occult sense of rightness" as the dwelling place of Sherlock Holmes. But this number would be on the *east*, or right side going north, of Baker Street, and could therefore not have been opposite "Camden House," also on the east side.

Nos. 59–67A. "If one were to retrace the route followed [in "The Adventure of the Empty House"] one would be in the block of Nos. 59–67A," the late Paul McPharlin wrote in "221B Baker Street: Certain Physical Details."

We must now note that Holmes and Watson, turning north into Blandford Mews, *might* have continued along the route sketched by the late H. W. Bell in his *Sherlock Holmes and Dr. Watson: The Chronology of Their Adventures.* In this case "Holmes and Watson must have gone the length of Blandford Mews, crossed Dorset Street, kept on through Kenrick Place [then known as Dorchester Mews East], and at Paddington Street have turned to the right into East Street, and then to the left into Portman Mansions [now Portman Street], in order to reach York Mews North, in the rear of Camden House. (York Mews South—known since 1936 as Sherlock Mews, W. 1—which is entered from Paddington Street oposite the north end of Kenrick Place [Dorchester Mews East], is a blind alley, having no communication with York Mews South.)" 221 would then be on the *west* side of Baker Street, between Dorset Street on the south and the Marylebone Road on the north.

No. 109. "Necessarily one of half a dozen houses on the opposite side of the road [the western side] must be number 221B. . . . The present numbers 109 or 111 single themselves out as likely, being the central houses in the block. Our own choice is 109," Mr. Ernest H. Short wrote. And Mr. James Edward Holroyd is another who has proved to his own satisfaction that the present No. 109 was 221 Baker Street.

No. 111. "Spending a part of his summer vacation in London a few years ago, Dr. Gray Chandler Briggs of St. Louis, the well-known roentologist, mapped Baker Street from end to end. . . . Like Holmes himself, he had turned into a narrow alley and passed through a wooden gate into a yard, to find himself at the back door which admitted the detective. Looking in, he saw the long, straight hall extending through the house to a front door of solid wood, above which was a fan-shaped transom. Conclusive, all of it, for already over the door in front he had read the surviving placard—*Camden House.* . . . The deduction that followed this discovery was, obviously, elementary. Since Camden House stood opposite the famous lodgings, the rooms of Sherlock Holmes in Baker Street were, of necessity, those upon the second story of the building numbered 111." So wrote Mr. Vincent Starrett in his *Private Life of Sherlock Holmes.***6**

It now seems clear beyond all possible doubt that 221 was on the *west* side of Baker Street, despite Watson's statement in "The Cardboard Box" that the sunlight, which must have been *morning* sunlight, glared on the yellowed brickwork of the opposite house.

6 Dr. Briggs' identification of 221 Baker Street with the present No. 111 was first published in "Sherlock Holmes," by Frederic Dorr Steele, in *Sherlock Holmes Farewell Appearances of William Gillette, 1929–1930;* New York: Al. Greenstone, 1929, pp. 4–5, and illustrations, p. 7. No. 111 Baker Street was blitzed during World War II and was rebuilt as a block of offices.

But the question remains: was 221 (1) south of King-Blandford streets; (2) between King-Blandford streets and Dorset Street; or (3) north of Dorset Street?

A strong point in favor of the North-of-Dorset-Street school of thought is the fact, as noted by Dr. Briggs, that, until recent years, No. 118 Baker Street was indeed Camden House—Camden House School, a well-known preparatory school, now removed to neighboring Gloucester Place.

Against the North-of-Dorset-Street point of view, however, there is the fact, noted above, that, at the time of Holmes' adventures, the modern Nos. 109 and 111 *were not in Baker Street at all, but in York Place.*

Against the North-of-Dorset-Street view there is also the evidence of:

1. "The Red-Headed League." " 'You [Watson] walked briskly across [Hyde Park] from your home [in Kensington] to meet me [Holmes] at ten for that dramatic end to the plans of the Red-Headed League. You left on the stroke of 9:15, and I doubt if there is a man alive who could have reached No. 111 Baker Street on foot in that time."—James T. Hyslop, "The Master Adds a Postscript."

2. "The Adventure of the Blue Carbuncle." Assuming, as most commentators have, that Commissionaire Peterson lived at or very near 221 Baker Street,[7] identifying No. 221 as the modern No. 111 "would place us on the left-hand side [of Baker Street] going north, somewhere between York Street and Marylebone, or well towards the mainline railway station at Marylebone. But that theory becomes untenable when you consider the route which our good Commissionnaire Peterson took to get home after his Christmas jollification. . . . One glance at the map will convince you that no man in his right mind would try to reach 111 by such a route, but that it was, on the other hand, a natural direction for a man bound for any point in Baker Street between Blandford and the Oxford Street end."—James T. Hyslop, "The Master Adds a Postscript." In this same adventure, Watson tells us that his footfalls and Holmes' "rang out crisply and loudly as we swung through the doctors' quarter, Wimpole Street, Harley Street, and so through Wigmore Street into Oxford Street." "It is as clear as day," Mr. Hyslop continued, "that [the] path was that of men who lived in the southern part of Baker Street."

3. "The Adventure of the Beryl Coronet." "A further objection to . . . No. 111," Mr. Brend wrote in *My Dear Holmes*, "is that [it is] much too close to Baker Street Underground Station. . . . A passenger from the Underground [would not] take a cab to visit Holmes. He would no sooner have got into the cab then he would have to get out again."

Let us now summarize our evidence so far: the evidence of "The Adventure of the Empty House," "The Red-Headed League," "The Adventure of the Blue Carbuncle," and "The Adventure of the Beryl Coronet" would all seem to indicate that 221 Baker Street was a house on the west (or left going north) side of Baker Street, *below* Dorset Street.

NO. 111 BAKER STREET

The site of "221" according to Dr. Gray Chandler Briggs. No. 111 was demolished in the blitz.

7 "I am assuming that Peterson lived at 221B though I am not sure this is correct. Holmes gives him orders to carry out and he rushes into the room unannounced when his wife discovers the carbuncle. It looks as if he lived there . . ."—Gavin Brend, "The Route of the Blue Carbuncle." "The fact that Peterson was able to produce the Blue Carbuncle without leaving his post indicates clearly that Mrs. Peterson and the oven which was to receive the famous bird were very near at hand."—James T. Hyslop, "The Master Adds a Postscript."

"BAKER STREET IN 1894 FROM PORTMAN MANSIONS TO GEORGE STREET"

On Mr. Bernard Davies' map, small black triangles indicate front doors; black blobs with lines indicate street lamps. The map is based on Ordnance Survey 5-foot plans, sheet VII/51, 1st Edition, 1872 (east side only); resurveyed 1893–1894; 2nd edition, 1895. Modern numbering inserted. From *The Sherlock Holmes Journal*, Winter, 1959.

And now let us return to Kendall Mews and consider the situation if Holmes and Watson had turned *south* into it, as we believe they did. 221 Baker Street would then stand on the west side of Baker Street between George Street and King-Blandford streets, among the present Nos. 19–35.

Of *No. 19*, Mr. Hyslop has written: ". . . I think it is clear that our rooms were in South Baker Street, and yet if I can trust your estimate of distances we were at least 200 yards from the Oxford Street end. Personally, I would put it a little less than that. My estimate would be that our quarters were somewhere between George Street and Blandford Street on the left-hand (west) side going north . . . [probably] No. 19, first house after George Street, on the left-hand side going north."

Dr. Maurice Campbell in *Sherlock Holmes and Dr. Watson: A Medical Digression*, suggested *No. 27*, and Sir Harold Morris, as we have seen, has made a case for *No. 21* Baker Street.

And now let us consider *No. 31*.

This is the choice of Mr. Bernard Davies—a choice with which your editor most heartily concurs—and the evidence for it is to be found in Mr. Davies' remarkable study, "The Back Yards of Baker Street."

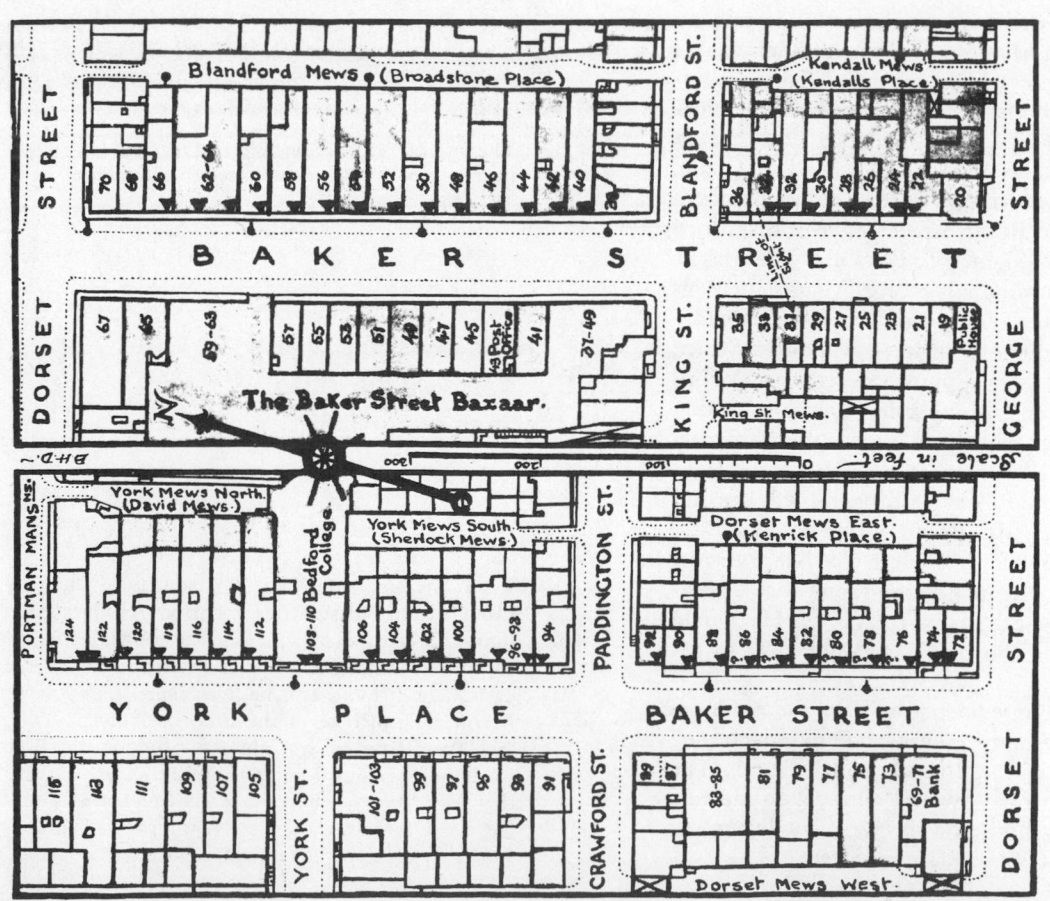

Mr. Davies searched first for "the Empty House," basing his hunt principally on the information contained in that adventure. The requirements are:

A. BACK

1. It must have had a mews or similar passage behind it giving access to the rear premises.

2. It must have possessed a backyard abutting on to the mews. As the back door opened into this yard the latter must have been *an open space in the rear*, and not a small enclosed court or air well within the building.

3. Holmes and Watson passed "through a wooden gate" from the mews into the yard; therefore there was no mews property intervening.

B. FRONT

4. Its front door and entrance hall must have been on the *south* side (that is, on the *right* side when viewed from the street), because "Holmes turned suddenly to the right" into the front room when approaching from the rear, impossible if the hall was on the north.

5. There was no streetlamp outside it in 1894. "There was no lamp near . . ."

Mr. Davies concluded that the house best answering these specifications was *the present No. 34, the former No. 15 Baker Street.*

Mr. Davies then searched for 221 itself, basing that search on these specifications:

A. BACK

1. It must have possessed a back yard large enough to contain a plane tree at the time of "The Problem of Thor Bridge" (1900). The tree may not have been very large, but the October wind "whirling the last remaining leaves" from its branches suggests that it was of reasonable height and foliage. The yard, therefore, was fairly spacious and open to the wind. Both factors, together with the phrase "behind our house," rule out a narrow well or court within the building.

B. FRONT

2. Here there are numerous points, but none of any practical use:

a. "Two large windows" in the sitting room (*A Study in Scarlet*). Very few Baker Street houses are only two window-widths across, but we cannot be certain how far across the frontage the room extended at that period.

b. One was a "bow window" ("The Adventure of the Beryl Coronet," "The Adventure of the Mazarin Stone"). "This is dubious," Mr. Davies wrote, "and may be a literary fancy."

c. At least three stories high, as Watson slept on the floor above the sitting room ("The Problem of Thor Bridge," "The Adventure of the Speckled Band" and many other references). All the original buildings have at least three floors, and most have four.

d. The front door possessed a semicircular fanlight ("The Adventure of the Blue Carbuncle"). This, in some form, was practically universal.

NO. 31 BAKER STREET TODAY

The site of "221," according to Mr. Bernard Davies. From *Sherlock Holmes: A Biography*, by William S. Baring-Gould.

8 Your editor is basing much of this description of No. 221 on a visit to No. 31 Baker Street which he had the pleasure of making in October, 1963, in company with Mr. Bernard Davies and Mr. Anthony Howlett, then Chairman of the Sherlock Holmes Society of London.

9 Holmes, in "The Naval Treaty," says: "Her cuisine is a little limited, but she has as good an idea of breakfast as a Scotchwoman."

e. The main staircase had seventeen steps up to the first landing ("A Scandal in Bohemia"). "My own researches," Mr. Davies wrote, "confirm those of Dr. W. S. Bristowe. All existing examples have about twenty, some more."

"a and b are so doubtful," Mr. Davies continued, "c and d so universal, while e is so in conflict with all the known facts that it is advisable to ignore the front elevation and rely solely on Point 1."

With "uncanny precision," this reliance led Mr. Davies to the identification of *the present No. 31, the former No. 72,* as No. "221."

"The clinching argument," Mr. Davies concluded, "is, of course, as plain as a pikestaff. No. 31 and No. 34 are opposite each other. Not dead opposite, it is true, but near enough for the sight-line to be no more than fifteen or twenty degrees off. . . . Here, and nowhere else, could that famous vigil have been kept opposite that bright window in the gloom on which 'the shadow of a man who was seated on a chair within was thrown in hard, black outline—a perfect reproduction of Holmes.' Our half-mile search of Baker Street could come to no more happy and reassuring end."

And now that we have found our way to No. 221 Baker Street, let us enter through the front door with its semicircular fanlight that Watson called so "well-remembered" ("A Scandal in Bohemia").**8**

Ahead of us, down a short and narrow passage, is a door leading to the stairs to the basement floor. In Mrs. Hudson's time, this floor was lighted, to some extent, by area windows, now paved over. It would accommodate the kitchen, a storeroom, a corner for the page boy, perhaps a waiting room for callers, although, for this last, we have only the doubtful authority of "The Adventure of the Mazarin Stone."

We picture it as a warm and cheerful place, even though it was underground and generally lit by artificial light. It would be furnished with deal tables and a dresser, chairs for meals, and perhaps a couple of Windsor armchairs for Mrs. Hudson's leisure moments with her "cronies." There would be a huge range fitted with ovens and boilers, and it would consume enormous quantities of coal, stored in a shed in the backyard. Batteries of iron or copper saucepans would reflect its flames, and with them would hang frying pans, skillets, skimmers, and sieves of varying finenesses. In the early days, Mrs. Hudson would have done all the cooking,**9** but we are told in "The Problem of Thor Bridge" that 221 Baker Street had a *new* cook, and a new cook implies that there must have been an *old* one, perhaps hired by Mrs. Hudson when Holmes' payments for her lodgings became "princely" in 1887 ("The Adventure of the Dying Detective"). She would expect to be supplied with numerous fancy molds for puddings, jellies, and aspics, as well as with preserving pans, bread tins, milk bowls, and many other utensils.

Returning to the ground floor passage, we would find, to our right on entering, a shop or office, the former dining room and pantry. The presence of Commissionaire Peterson, in "The Adventure of the Blue Carbuncle," suggests an office rather than a shop. To our left are two flights of steps, seventeen in all, leading to the first floor. At the head of the staircase we shall find (perhaps) two doors: the first we pass leads into Holmes' bedroom (if, again, we may trust "The Adventure of the Mazarin Stone"); the second is the door to the famous sitting room. At the west end of this passageway another flight of stairs climbs to the English *second*, American *third* floor.

Entering the sitting room, we see it as Watson first saw it on that day in late 1880 or early 1881: it is a "large airy" room, perhaps about thirty feet long, twenty-five feet wide, and ten feet high, "cheerfully furnished and illuminated by two broad [and, we can believe, low-silled] windows."

Mr. Michael Harrison has written (*In the Footsteps of Sherlock Holmes*) that "the reference to broad windows is curious: for all the windows of the Baker Street houses are of the same width: it is in their *height* that they vary."

And these windows are curious in more than their breadth; it is curious, for example, that Watson should speak of *two* windows, for Baker Street houses of this kind, as we have seen, almost uniformly boast *three* broad windows looking out into Baker Street (certainly No. 31 does).

Perhaps what Watson *meant* to say is that the sitting room had two broad windows flanking a third window, *a bow window*, for he mentions "the bow window" on more than one occasion.

And let us pause here for a moment to try to remove some of the confusion that exists in the minds of many of us between *bow* windows and *bay* windows, for they are two very different things. (No house in Baker Street had or has a *bay* window, but *bow* windows, in Holmes' and Watson's day, were rather plentiful.)

Mr. Ronald R. Weaver has made the distinction between these two "interesting details of the late Gothic school of architecture" remarkably clear in his essay, "Bow Window in Baker Street," in which he says: "The bay window is a structural affair, composed of plane or curved sections, projecting from the building elevation proper, with flat or curved glass conforming to the structural sections of the bay. But the bow window is merely a curved or rounded glass, set in a suitable frame. It can be incorporated in a bay, but it does not require such a structure. On the contrary, it is—or was—far more commonly installed in plane elevations, thereby affording an enlarged view. It was quite fashionable in the Victorian era, but its popularity waned because it was relatively fragile, and difficult and expensive to replace. The window in question, as appears by the Canon, was specifically a bow window. Therefore, no further time need be lost in looking for a bay, or evidence that such a device once existed, or has been removed, anywhere in Baker Street."

Mr. Weaver suggested that the bow window was shattered in the very first adventure shared by Holmes and Watson —*A Study in Scarlet*—during the frenzied efforts by which Mr. Jefferson Hope attempted to escape the clutches of Messrs. Holmes, Lestrade, Gregson, and Watson.

It was certainly replaced with another window of the bow type, for Holmes, at the time of *The Hound of the Baskervilles*, first spied Dr. Mortimer on his doorstep from "the recess of the window." Again, in "The Adventure of the

Beryl Coronet," Watson stood in the bow window and watched the unhappy Mr. Holder stagger down Baker Street.

It is probable that the bow window was shattered again by the firemen who put out the conflagration in 221B set off by the Moriarty gang in April, 1891—and it may have been shattered for a third time in April, 1894, by the expanding air gun bullet fired by Colonel Sebastian Moran ("The Adventure of the Empty House").**10**

Facing east, as they did, these windows would of course receive the morning sun ("Holmes held up the paper so that the sunlight shone full upon it"—"The Adventure of the Dancing Men"). They were equipped with blinds, and—although Watson does not mention it—they were probably hung with white Nottingham lace curtains between the blinds and the heavier serge, damask, or velvet drapes.

The floor of the room would be wide boards of good old English oak, painted or stained a dark brown, and covered, no doubt, with a well-worn carpet leaving bare only a foot or so around the edge of the room.

The wallpaper, like the carpet, would be heavily patterned in damask or floral designs. Dark reds, greens, and blues were the favorite colors, and these were repeated in the long thick drapes at the windows.

One wall would be marred, of course, by the patriotic "V. R." (Victoria Regina) punctured out by Holmes with a "hair-trigger revolver and a box of Boxer cartridges" ("The Musgrave Ritual"). This, as Mr. Robert Keith Leavitt has convincingly demonstrated in "Annie Oakley in Baker Street," would be the *script* V. R., with crown, and the wall that it disfigured, or adorned, would be the *south* wall, opposite the fireplace, which was centered in the north wall of the room.

We know, from "The Adventure of the Noble Bachelor" and later references, that a clock hung someplace on a wall.

Gas fixtures would be strategically placed on the walls to provide illumination ("Our gas was lit"—"The Adventure of the Copper Beeches"). But gas, in Holmes' and Watson's day, was not laid on casually; it was expensive, and was confined to the main rooms. Oil lamps would be used, both for economy and for additional lighting. These gave a soft, clear light, very restful to the eyes, but they involved a good deal of work in cleaning and filling. It is probable that a hanging lamp for mineral oil and candles was suspended from the center of the ceiling. At 221, as in most Victorian homes, a row of candlesticks would be placed on a hall table every night, and as each person retired, he would take one with him, and by its small light undress and go to bed.

There was, of course, no central heating at 221 Baker Street in Holmes' and Watson's day, so the fireplace with its cheery blaze of sea coals would be the sitting-room's only source of warmth and its chief attraction on a cold winter's day.**11** "Generally, . . . one thinks the life of the detective went on around the fireplace," Mr. Vincent Starrett wrote in *The Private Life of Sherlock Holmes*. "It follows that everything he might require would be within his reach; certainly it would be so by evening, on any day that he remained at home."

---

10 It is true that "The Adventure of the Mazarin Stone" would seem to indicate that the bow window was indeed a *bay* window, but this case, as we shall see, can hardly be taken as evidence for the true structural details of the 221B sitting room.

11 No fewer than 27 of the 60 adventures include mention of a fire.

THE ROOM'S FURNISHINGS, seen in picture at left, are itemized numerically above: **1**—The bust with which Holmes drew the fire of Colonel Sebastian Moran, "the second most dangerous man in London" (*The Adventure of the Empty House*). **2**—Holmes's "low-powered microscope" (*The Adventure of Shoscombe Old Place*). **3**—Bookshelf containing among other things Clark Russell's "fine sea stories" of which Watson was so fond. **4**—Portrait of Irene Adler, who was always "*the* woman" (*A Scandal in Bohemia*). **5**—Holmes's dark lantern (*The Red-Headed League*). **6**—The desk and chair Conan Doyle used in writing the Holmes stories. **7**—Tray with tea, half-eaten toast and boardinghouse china typical of the period. **8**—Watson's chair. **9**—Holmes's velvet-lined chair. **10**—The "acid-stained, deal-topped table" in "the chemical corner." **11**—The skin of the "swamp-adder" (*The Adventure of the Speckled Band*). **12**—Holmes's stick rack, on which is the cane he used to lash the Speckled Band. **13**—Watson's Afghanistan trophies. **14**—Code employed by Abe Slaney in *The Adventure of the Dancing Men*. **15**—The box containing Holmes's relics from *The Musgrave Ritual*. **16**—Holmes's "unanswered correspondence transfixed by a jack-knife into the very centre of his wooden mantelpiece." **17**—His tobacco, kept in the toe of a Persian slipper. **18**—The coal scuttle that held his cigars.

THE SITTING ROOM AT 221B BAKER STREET

With a key to the furnishings, from *Life*.

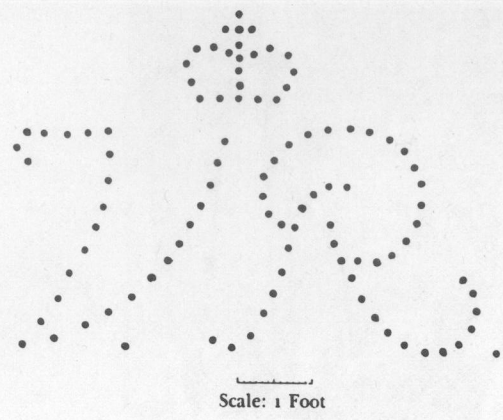

Scale: 1 Foot

THE SCRIPT V. R., WITH CROWN

This drawing, done to scale, of the script with which Holmes adorned the south wall of the sitting room at 221B Baker Street, was made by Mr. Robert Keith Leavitt to illustrate his essay, "Annie Oakley in Baker Street." From *Profile by Gaslight*, edited by Edgar W. Smith.

12 The cigars may have been Holmes', but the coal scuttle may well have been Watson's, if he was of Scots descent and a student, for a time, at the Medical College at the University of Edinburgh. As the late James Keddie, Sr., wrote in "Gasogene, Coal Box, Persian Slipper": "In Edinburgh the coal box was an ornament, and in it were stored such details of fireside comfort as slippers, unread magazines, and so forth. Why not cigars?" Scottish Sir James M. Barrie, in fact, kept both his cigars and his telephone in his coal scuttle. The scuttle is usually pictured as a metal vessel, but Mr. Frank A. Waters has suggested ("The Rooms in Baker Street") that it "was a square box made of wood."

13 The famous reconstruction of the Baker Street sitting room created for the Sherlock Holmes Exhibition during the Festival of Britain places Holmes' chemical corner, with its acid-stained, deal-topped table and its formidable array of bottles, retorts, and test tubes, in the northeast corner of the room. "Scientific charts" hung above it; one of them, surely, was a periodic table of the elements.

The fireplace was black marble, we think, with a mantel of wood. Holmes' unanswered correspondence was transfixed by a jackknife into the very center of this mantel; in one corner stood his cocaine bottle, and "all the plugs and dottles left from his smokes of the day before [were] carefully dried and collected on the corner of the mantlepiece" —"The Adventure of the Engineer's Thumb." A looking glass hung above it, as we know from "The Adventure of the Beryl Coronet."

Before the fireplace, we must place a bearskin hearthrug ("The Adventure of the Priory School"). The coal scuttle, containing Holmes' cigars,**12** stood to the right of the fireplace, we think, and the poker and the other fireplace instruments in their customary place to the left of the fire.

Handy, too, would be the Persian slipper stuffed with shag tobacco. It most probably hung by means of a ring to a hook on the wall to the right of the fireplace. This, too, was in all likelihood a custom introduced to Holmes by his good friend Watson via Edinburgh. Says Keddie Senior: "[In Edinburgh] even unto this day single Persian slippers may be purchased for the self-same purpose. . . . The slippers so far as I know were never sold in pairs. They were made of soft Persian leather and were without heels. The tobacco was stuffed into the forward, or toe part of the slipper." The Persian slipper could not have made a very good humidor, however; the tobacco would surely dry out and become covered with dust, in spite of the rate at which Holmes consumed it.

The bellpull, which Watson on one occasion at least, rang rather petulantly, would presumably hang in a convenient place, perhaps just to the right of the fireplace.

To each side of the fireplace stood an armchair—one Holmes', the other Watson's. We would prefer to give the *east* armchair, low and velvet-lined, to Holmes. This would allow him to sit adjacent to his coat-scuttle humidor and convenient to his chemicals.**13**

Watson in the west armchair would be well placed to "put the pearls in the safe and get out the papers of the Conk-Singleton forgery" ("The Adventure of the Six Napoleons"), as well as for maneuverings with the poker ("The Adventure of the Three Gables").

To the far right of the fireplace stood a breakfront bookcase ("The Adventure of the Noble Bachelor," "The Adventure of the Sussex Vampire"). (The safe was no doubt in the bottom of this bookcase.) Here Holmes kept his maps and his many reference books (*Whitaker's Almanack*, an American encyclopedia, the *Continental Gazetteer*, a *Crockford*, and a *Bradshaw*), his toxicology collection, soil analyses, chemistry texts, anatomical guides, factual writings about the misdeeds of criminals and fictional writings about the triumphs of detectives, volumes on singlestick playing, boxing and swordsmanship, law books. Here, too, we would find Hafiz and Horace, Tacitus, Flaubert and George Sand, Thoreau, Goethe, Carlyle, Meredith and Winwood Reade. Certainly a place of honor would be given to Holmes' own monographs. On the lowest, tallest shelves, we imagine, stood the commonplace books, all neatly lettered on their buckram backs in the precise and clerkly hand of Sherlock Holmes.

The major pieces furnishing the room—what Watson in "The Adventure of the Noble Bachelor" calls "our humble lodging-house mahogany"—would be for the most part heavily carved, highly polished early Victorian. Some of them, perhaps, were of rosewood.

Opposite the fireplace, against the south wall, beneath Holmes' patriotic "V. R.," would stand that piece of furniture variously referred to as a couch, sofa, or settee. It was done, we think, in a worn and faded green, and it was covered with several large cushions, which Holmes sometimes threw upon the floor to sit upon. Holmes' violin, when it did not stand in its accustomed place in the corner of the room, frequently lay carelessly upon the sofa. Handy to the sofa stood a small table (the "side-table" of "The Resident Patient"), marred, no doubt, by cigarette burns, and upon this table stood the pipe rack.

To one side of the sofa stood Holmes' desk, and, on the other side, Watson's. Holmes kept his desk locked (at least he did in 1883, as we know from "The Adventure of the Speckled Band"), and he kept his "small case-book" in one of its drawers. Sherlock's diary ("The Adventure of the Blanched Soldier") was probably kept in that same locked desk, although the "case-book" and the "diary" may be one and the same volume.

Another very important piece of furniture was the sideboard. The late Paul McPharlin ("221B Baker Street: Certain Physical Details") has placed it, correctly we think, against the west wall, relying on a quotation from J. C. Loudon's *Encyclopaedia of Architecture and Furniture* which says that a sideboard "is placed at the ends of drawing rooms. . . . The panels in the back are of looking glass; and the doors of the two pedestals have panels filled in with fluted silk. . . . The tops . . . are frequently formed of statuary marble, and the supports and the upper shelf of finest rosewood. . . . On the bottom board, in front of the lower glass, are placed vases for holding flowers, and a number of other ornaments."

Holmes and Watson kept their sideboard littered with tumblers, cigar boxes, odds and ends of cold food, and, of course, the spirit case and the gasogene.

The spirit case, or tantalus, was a metal stand with a rod rising from its center, to whose top were attached arms which embraced the necks of two or more decanters, locking about them with a small padlock.

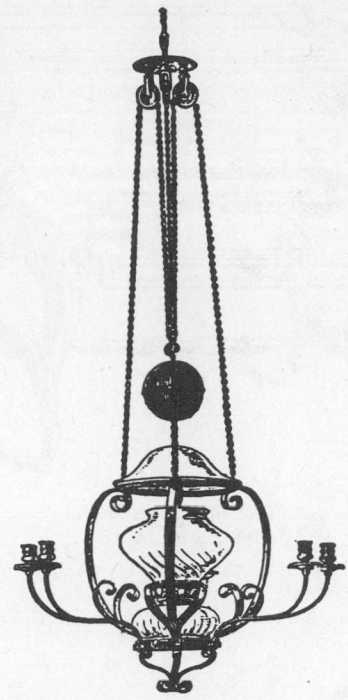

. . . A HANGING LAMP FOR MINERAL OIL AND CANDLES WAS SUSPENDED FROM THE CENTER OF THE CEILING

From *A History of Everyday Things in England*, Vol. IV.

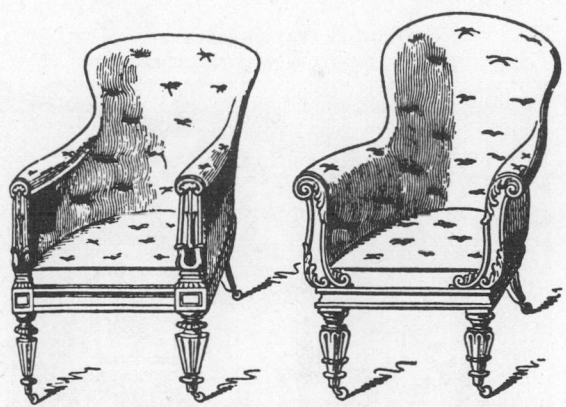

TO EACH SIDE OF THE FIREPLACE STOOD AN ARMCHAIR . . .

From *The Baker Street Journal*, April, 1947.

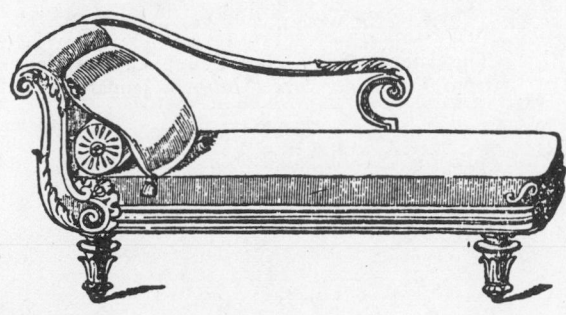

. . . THAT PIECE OF FURNITURE VARIOUSLY REFERRED TO AS A COUCH, SOFA, OR SETTEE

TO ONE SIDE OF THE SOFA
STOOD HOLMES' DESK . . .

THE GASOGENE

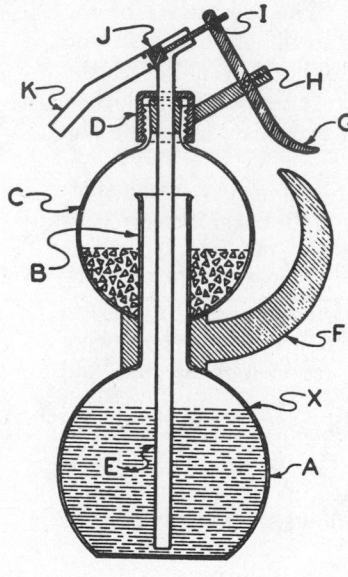

ANOTHER VERY IMPORTANT
PIECE OF FURNITURE WAS THE SIDEBOARD

Construction: This airtight system consists of a glass flask (A) with a long neck (B), and a small glass globe (C) mounted upon the flask. At the top of (C) is a removable screw-cap (D). Attached to the screw-cap are two tubes, (K) extending outside the globe and (E) extending nearly to the bottom of flask (A); also attached to the screw-cap is a valve (J) controlled by the lever-system (G), (H), and (I). A handle is provided in (F). (A) and (C) are usually enclosed in a stiff metal network, to prevent breakage, either by pressure or by accidental dropping or contact with other objects, should the "hand of the potter shake." *Operation*: Globe (A) is filled with beverage water. In (C) is deposited a small quantity of chemical tablets or salts. The screw-cap (D) is closed. The whole device is tipped so that water from (A) will run into (C) until (C) is about one-third full. The device is then brought back to a vertical position. The chemical action of the water upon the crystals in (C) produces carbonic acid gas (carbon dioxide) which builds up a pressure in (C) and is driven down through (B) into the water in (A). The operator grasps handle (F) and presses upon lever (G), holding some vessel under tube (K). The depression of (G) causes the levers (G) to pivot at (H) and pull at (I), thus opening the valve (J) and permitting water charged with gas to be ejected by pressure through the tube (E) into tube (K) and so into the vessel held below (K). Release of pressure upon (F) allows an internal spring to close (J) (not shown), closing the system.

THE WORKINGS OF THE GASOGENE

The late Professor Jay Finley Christ's drawing from *The Baker Street Journal*, January, 1946.

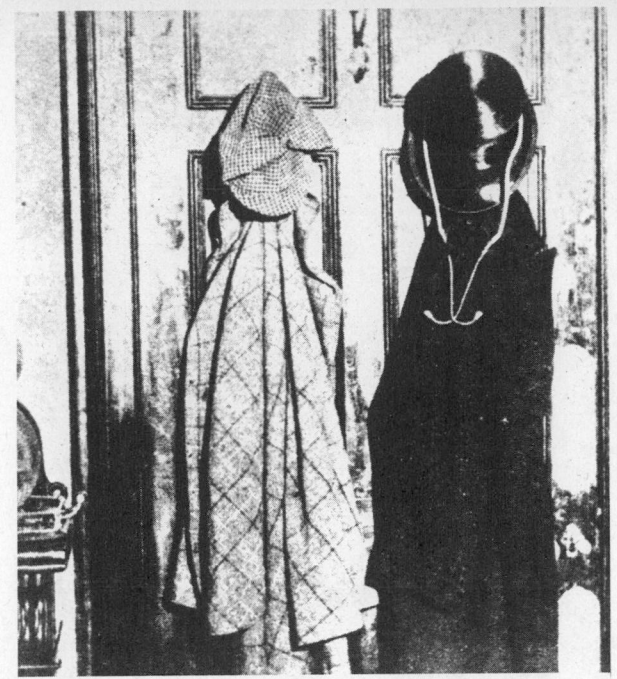

The stethoscope is perhaps a little out-of-period
(see notes to "A Scandal in Bohemia").

The gasogene, we are told by the late James Keddie, Sr.,
is "a glass vessel shaped like a figure 8—the upper part being
crowned with a handle and nozzle like a common, or beer-
garden, siphon for swizzling soda-water into your whisky.
The gasogene was loaded in its upper chamber with acid
crystals and sodas and whatnot to generate gas, which passed
into the lower chamber which was three parts filled with
water. The gas generated in the upper chamber aerated the
water in the lower chamber, and after a proper period had
elapsed the gasogene simply became the siphon of every
afternoon use. These contrivances had a habit of exploding,
and I well remember a room in my father's house in which
the wall paper was bejewelled with fine fragments of glass
which had been embedded in it by such an explosion. The
whole contrivance was enclosed in a wire netting, presumably
to hold the fragments together when the burst came, but the
smaller and more deadly pieces of glass shrapnel easily penetrated the mesh and anything within several feet of it."[14]

To the left of the sideboard, as we face it, is the door to
Holmes' bedroom; to *its* left is the door to the passageway.
Whether this hall door hinged to the left or to the right is
something of a problem, as Mr. James Edward Holroyd
pointed out in his delightful book, *Baker Street Byways:*
"Perhaps it achieves its greatest individuality in 'A Case of
Identity' in which it consecutively opened inwards, hinged
left; inwards, hinged right; outwards, hinged left!" On the
roomside of this door were the pegs for coats and hats. Here
hung Holmes' deerstalker and cape-backed overcoat, Watson's tophat and bowler, his stethoscope and his greatcoat.
Between the doors, we think, stood the cane rack, mentioned
in "The Red-Headed League."

In the center of the room was a table, the drop-leaf kind
to save room, we imagine, on the white cloth of which the
china and silver glimmered in the lamplight ("The Adventure of the Cooper Beeches"). On it stood a student
lamp which burned low until Holmes and Watson got back
from an adventure and turned it up ("The Adventure of
Charles Augustus Milverton").

We will have to scatter around the room one or more
wooden chairs, one of which was once used as a study rack
for a seedy hat ("The Adventure of the Blue Carbuncle").
There was also a basket chair, which Dr. Julian Wolff ("I
Have My Eye on a Suite in Baker Street") and Mr. Paul
McPharlin agreed should go to the east of the center table.[15]
We also must agree with this: Lady Hilda Trelawney Hope
had to "manoeuvre" to reach the basket chair and so place
the light at her back ("The Adventure of the Second Stain").

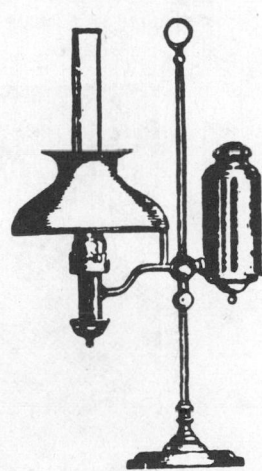

. . . A STUDENT LAMP WHICH BURNED LOW UNTIL
HOLMES AND WATSON GOT BACK FROM AN ADVENTURE
AND TURNED IT UP.

[14] A modern gasogene plays a key role in Mr.
John Dickson Carr's fine Dr. Gideon Fell short
story, "The Locked Room."

[15] "Few Americans," Christopher Morley wrote
in "The Blue Carbuncle, or, the Season of Forgiveness," "know what is a basket chair (Minty's Varsity Chair) invented (at Oxford?) to help students
fall asleep beside the fireplace." This suggests that
the basket chair may have been contributed to the
Baker Street menage by Holmes, as a relic of his
student days.

. . . A FRAMED PORTRAIT OF GENERAL GORDON AND AN
UNFRAMED PICTURE OF HENRY WARD BEECHER.

Mr. James Edward Holroyd has called attention to an article in the January, 1893, issue of the *Strand Magazine* in which it is stated that a Mr. Ed Clifford "was the only English artist General Gordon ever sat to." If Watson's "newly-framed picture" showed "Chinese" Gordon, then, it was most probably a reproduction of Mr. Clifford's painting.

The frequently mentioned visitor's chair—"the vacant chair upon which a newcomer must sit" ("The Five Orange Pips")—was probably a low, velvet-covered, brass-nail-edged, antimacassar-protected seat, calculated to ease the innocent and terrify the guilty; it faced the light, and must therefore have stood to the west of the center table.

We know that a stool stood at Holmes' chemical table, but we may be sure that at least one of the chairs was also equipped with a footstool, for Holmes "squatted down upon a stool" in the adventure of "The Musgrave Ritual."

We must also provide the room with a small bookcase for Watson's "medical shelf" (*The Hound of the Baskervilles*). Prominent on the shelf would be his own works: a small brochure with the somewhat fantastic title of *A Study in Scarlet* and that other volume called *The Sign of the Four* are specifically mentioned in the annals (*The Sign of the Four*, "The Cardboard Box"). Watson also kept a scrapbook into which he pasted clippings about Holmes' cases (*The Sign of the Four*) and a notebook in which he jotted his none-too-accurate observations ("The Adventure of Wisteria Lodge"). But the good doctor had other interests: on stormy evenings he liked to read one of Clark Russell's fine sea stories ("The Five Orange Pips"); at other times Henri Murger's *Vie de Bohème* attracted him (*A Study in Scarlet*), and he would often sit up late nodding over a yellow-backed novel ("The Boscombe Valley Mystery").

Watson's books, we are told in "The Cardboard Box," stood beneath a framed portrait of General Gordon and an unframed picture of Henry Ward Beecher. The framed portrait is generally accepted as having been a picture of Charles George ("Chinese") Gordon, the hero of Khartoum, 1833–1885, but Watson's thoughts when he looked at it soon turned to the Civil War, and this raises the question—might the picture have been that of John Brown Gordon, 1832–1904, Confederate general, senator, and Governor of Georgia?**16**

Finally it may be observed that a telephone had been installed by 1898 ("The Adventure of the Retired Colourman") although the use of it, particularly by Watson, seems to have been half-hearted and Holmes himself remained largely faithful to his telegrams.

"That the chamber was perennially untidy is one of the soundest of our certainties," Mr. Vincent Starrett wrote in "The Singular Adventures of Martha Hudson." "One fancies Watson as making shift to keep the place in order, but there is a clear record of his despair. The principal duties of the maid, then, upstairs, it may be ventured, was making up the beds." Mr. Starrett, as always, is quite correct: fresh editions of every paper were supplied by the news agent, we are told in "Silver Blaze," and Watson writes in "The Musgrave Ritual" that "month after month [Holmes'] papers accumulated, until every corner of the room was stacked with bundles of manuscript." Holmes' female clients, in the gowns of the 1880's and 1890's, must often have found it difficult to steer their way about the overcrowded room without knocking something over; fortunately for them, the art of graceful walking was included in the education of most young women.

We know, by many references, that Holmes' bedroom connected with the sitting room ("He went to his bedroom, from which he returned presently pulling a large tin box behind him"—"The Musgrave Ritual"; "Sherlock Holmes sprang to his feet . . . and rushed into his room"—*A Study in Scarlet;* "With a nod he vanished into the bedroom"— "A Scandal in Bohemia"; "he sprang to his feet and passed into his bedroom"—"The Adventure of Charles Augustus Milverton").

There are, however, two puzzling references in "The Adventure of the Beryl Coronet": here Holmes "hurried to his chamber and was down again in a few minutes" and later in the same afternoon "hastened upstairs" from the sitting room. "In spite of these apparently unambiguous statements," Mr. G. B. Newton wrote in "This Desirable Residence," "the theory that Holmes had even temporarily betaken himself to the top floor is I feel untenable. It is noticeable that while on other occasions Watson deliberately alluded to Holmes' 'bedroom' this time he refers to his 'chamber'—the word bedroom is not mentioned. It is also noticeable that Holmes used it for the purpose of getting into and out of one of his disguises. By this time he must have accumulated a considerable variety of disguises and other impedimenta and may well have used one of the [lumber] rooms upstairs as a kind of dressing room and store for this purpose. The use of the word 'chamber' may be a little odd but Watson who was pedantic enough to refer to one of his own works, *A Study in Scarlet,* as a 'brochure' was quite capable of applying the term chamber to almost any sort of apartment. We remain convinced that Holmes was firmly rooted to his first-floor bedroom throughout his years at Baker Street."

The bedroom, as we know, had two doors, one opening into the sitting room, the second into the first-floor passageway, but it is difficult, indeed impossible, to see how a door from the bedroom could possibly lead behind the curtain of the bow window, as we are told that it did in "The Adventure of the Marazin Stone." We must really regard this "adventure" as apocryphal.

Our best description of Holmes' bedroom comes to us in "The Adventure of the Dying Detective."**17** Here we learn that the bedroom, like the sitting room, had a fireplace, with a clock on the mantel and a litter of "pipes, tobacco pouches, penknives, revolver cartridges and other debris." Its "every wall" was adorned with the pictures of famous criminals. There was a "closet," more probably a wardrobe of oak or mahogany, out of which came many of Holmes' varied disguises. The bed was a large one, and had a high, solid head, for the portly Watson was able to squeeze behind it to later confront a chagrined Culverton Smith. There was a large tin box in the corner, which Holmes once dragged into the sitting room ("The Musgrave Ritual"). If we are to credit "The Adventure of the Mazarin Stone," it contained, in 1903, at least, a gramophone.

Its other furnishings were probably sparse. We would add a bedside table, complete with candlestick, a marble-topped washstand with a jug and basin of plain or flowered china, a chest of drawers and dressing mirror, a simple chair. These are the minimum requirements of an English bedroom.

. . . A WARDROBE OF OAK OR MAHOGANY, OUT OF WHICH CAME MANY OF HOLMES' VARIED DISGUISES.

. . . A MARBLE-TOPPED WASHSTAND WITH A JUG AND BASIN OF PLAIN OR FLOWERED CHINA . . .

17 Dr. Wolff disagrees; he believes the room described in "The Adventure of the Dying Detective" to be "the sitting-room converted to a sick room." Our view would seem to be borne out however, by Watson's statement that he heard "the opening and the closing of the bedroom door."

There has hitherto been some discussion as to whether or not a bathroom opened off Holmes' bedroom (or any other bedroom at 221 Baker Street). In "A Scandal in Bohemia" Watson tells us that Holmes returned to the Baker Street sitting room in the character of "a drunken groom, ill-kempt and side-whiskered with an inflamed face and disreputable clothes." "With a nod he vanished into the bedroom, whence he emerged in five minutes tweed-suited and respectable, as of old." But Holmes of course used his washstand to remove his makeup, not a bathroom: bathrooms, with hot water laid on, were not common until the very end of the nineteenth century. Where a room was reserved for bathing alone, it was usually an ordinary small room converted for the purpose, containing a fireplace, a wood-rimmed metal bath, and sometimes a shower bath of a sort. The water was heated by the kitchen fire. When Holmes or Watson took a bath (we know that Watson took one in *The Sign of the Four*) he would have done so in his bedroom, in a hip bath with a high back, or in a flat shallow pan of metal painted to look like wood. This was kept, when not in use, in the maid's closet or under the bed. When wanted it was set before the fire, with large towels spread under it to protect the carpet from splashes. It was filled with hot water brought up from the basement in metal cans, and in it the bather sat soaking and warming himself in comfort, without having to worry about keeping others waiting if he dallied too long. A screen, or covered towel horse, behind the bather protected him from draughts; and, when he was ready to get out, there were towels already warming before the fire in which to wrap himself. Other essential facilities for comfort and sanitation were provided by commodes, kept usually in the washstand.

And now let us climb the stairs to the English *second*, American *third*, floor of the house. Here we will find Watson's bedroom[18] (at the back) and Mrs. Hudson's bedroom (at the front). (The maid, we think, slept on the top floor, with the two lumber rooms.) It will be remembered that Watson in *A Study in Scarlet* heard both the landlady and the maid preceding him up to bed when he was awaiting Holmes' return one night in the sitting room.

Watson's bedroom has four ascertainable features: a view of a plane tree ("The Problem of Thor Bridge"), a shaving mirror ("The Boscombe Valley Mystery"), a clock on the mantel, and therefore a fireplace ("The Adventure of the Speckled Band") and, of course a bed ("The Adventure of the Speckled Band," "The Adventure of the Abbey Grange"). Surely it was always very neat and tidy, as became an ex-army officer.

Watson's bedroom was also the "spare" bedroom. It was available to Percy Phelps at the time of "The Naval Treaty," for Watson was not then living at 221 Baker Street. Some years later, however, when Watson was back in residence ("The Adventure of the Golden Pince-Nez"), Inspector Stanley Hopkins of Scotland Yard had to make do on the sofa in the sitting room, drawn up before the fire.

This, then, was 221 Baker Street. For Holmes and Watson, in every way, it was indeed "a most desirable residence."

WATSON'S BEDROOM

The only known illustration showing this room is the work of the Dutch draughtsman and cartoonist L. J. Jordaan, executed in 1909 for a Holmes-Watson pastiche.

18 By many references: "Sherlock Holmes was already at breakfast when I came down" ("The Five Orange Pips"); "I . . . was ready in a few minutes to accompany my friend down to the sitting-room" ("The Adventure of the Speckled Band"); "When I came down to breakfast in the morning" ("The Adventure of the Beryl Coronet"); "I descended to breakfast" ("The Problem of Thor Bridge").

12

WHAT IS IT THAT WE LOVE IN SHERLOCK HOLMES?

"What is it that we love in Sherlock Holmes?"

The late Edgar W. Smith asked, and answered, that question in an editorial first published in the *Baker Street Journal*'s second issue.

"We love the times in which he lived, of course," Edgar wrote, "the half-remembered, half-forgotten times of snug Victorian illusion, of gaslit comfort and contentment, of perfect dignity and grace. The world was poised precariously in balance, and rude disturbances were coming with the years; but those who moved upon the scene were very sure that all was well: that nothing ever would be any worse nor ever could be any better. There was no threat to righteousness and justice and the cause of peace on earth except from such as Moriarty and the lesser villains in his train. The cycle of events had come full turn, and the times were ripe for living—and for being lost. It is because their loss was suffered before they had been fully lived that they are times to which our hearts and longings cling.

"And we love the place in which the Master moved and had his being: the England of those times, fat with the fruits of her achievements, but strong and daring still with the spirit of imperial adventure. The seas were pounding, then as now, upon her coasts; the winds swept in across the moors, and fog came down on London. It was a stout and pleasant land, full of the flavor of the age; and it is small wonder that we who claim it in our thoughts should look to Baker Street as its epitome. For there the cabs rolled up before a certain door, and hurried steps were heard upon the stair, and England and her times had rendezvous within a hallowed room, at once familiar and mysterious. . . .

"But there is more than time and space and the yearning for things gone by to account for what we feel toward Sherlock Holmes. Not only there and then, but here and now, he stands before us as a symbol—a symbol, if you please, of all that we are not, but ever would be. His figure is sufficiently remote to make our secret aspirations for transference seem unshameful, yet close enough to give them plausibility. We see him as the fine expression of our urge to trample evil and to set aright the wrongs with which the world is plagued. He is Galahad and Socrates, bringing high adventure to our dull existences and calm, judicial logic to our biased minds. He is the success of all our failures; the bold escape from our imprisonment.

EDGAR W. SMITH, 1894–1960

From the Sherlockian Hall of Fame.

"Or, if this be too complex a psychological basis to account for our devotion, let it be said, more simply, that he is the personification of something in us that we have lost, or never had. For it is not Sherlock Holmes who sits in Baker Street, comfortable, competent and self-assured; it is ourselves who are there, full of a tremendous capacity for wisdom, complacent in the presence of our humble Watson, conscious of a warm well-being and a timeless, imperishable content. The easy chair in the room is drawn up to the hearthstone of our very hearts—it is *our* tobacco in the Persian slipper, and *our* violin lying so carelessly across the knees—it is *we* who hear the pounding on the stairs and the knock upon the door. The swirling fog without and the acrid smoke within bite deep indeed, for we taste them even now. And the time and place and all the great events are near and dear to us not because our memories call them forth in pure nostalgia, but because they are a part of us today.

"That is the Sherlock Holmes we love—the Holmes implicit and eternal in ourselves."

It is to the memory of Edgar Wadsworth Smith, April 1, 1894–September 17, 1960—one of "the best and the wisest" men it has ever been our great good fortune to know—that this edition of his favorite reading is dedicated.

WILLIAM S. BARING-GOULD

Stonycroft
East Woods Road
Pound Ridge, New York

II. THE EARLY HOLMES

[July and September, 1874, and Thursday, October 2, 1879]

"These are the records of your early work,
then?" I asked. "I have often wished
that I had notes of those cases."

"Yes, my boy; these were all done prematurely,
before my biographer had come to glorify me."

—*"The Musgrave Ritual"*

. . . IN THE COUNTRY OF THE BROADS

Photograph by J. Allan Cash, F.I.B.P., F.R.P.S., for *The Fens*, by
Alan Bloom, London: Robert Hale, Ltd., 1953.

13

THE *GLORIA SCOTT*

[Sunday, July 12, to Tuesday, August 4, and Tuesday, September 22, 1874]

"I HAVE some papers here," said my friend, Sherlock Holmes, as we sat one winter's night on **1** either side of the fire, "which I really think, Watson, it would be worth your while to glance over. These are the documents in the extraordinary case of the *Gloria Scott*, and this is the message which struck Justice of the Peace Trevor dead with horror when he read it."

He had picked from a drawer a little tarnished cylinder, and, undoing the tape, he handed me a short note scrawled upon a half sheet of slate-grey paper.

"The supply of game for London is going steadily up," it ran. "Head-keeper Hudson, we believe, has been now told to receive all orders for fly-paper, and for preservation of your hen pheasant's life."

As I glanced up from reading this enigmatical message I saw Holmes chuckling at the expression upon my face.

"You look a little bewildered," said he.

"I cannot see how such a message as this could inspire horror. It seems to me to be rather grotesque than otherwise."

"Very likely. Yet the fact remains that the reader, who was a fine, robust old man, was knocked clean down by it, as if it had been the butt-end of a pistol."

"You arouse my curiosity," said I. "But why did you say just now that there were very particular reasons why I should study this case?"

"Because it was the first in which I was ever engaged." **2**

I had often endeavoured to elicit from my companion what had first turned his mind in the direction of criminal research, but I had never caught him before in a communicative humour. Now he sat forward in his arm-chair, and spread out the documents upon his knees. Then he lit his pipe and sat for some time smoking and **3** turning them over.

"You never heard me talk of Victor Trevor?" he asked. "He was the only friend I made during the two years that I was at college. I was never a very sociable fellow, Watson, always rather fond of moping in my rooms and working out my own little methods of thought, so that I never mixed much with the men of my year. Bar

1 *one winter's night.* The winter of 1887–1888 suggests itself: after Watson's return to Baker Street, following the death of his first wife (see our Chapter 21, "Now, Watson, the Fair Sex Is Your Department"). It would be like Holmes to try to distract the doctor's mind from his grief by telling him about these early exploits—"The Musgrave Ritual" as well as "The *Gloria Scott*." The late H. W. Bell, on the other hand, cast his vote for the winter of 1886–1887, and Mr. George W. Welch concurred with Mr. Bell in his essay on "The Terai Planter."

2 *the first in which I was ever engaged."* Neither Holmes nor Watson dates the adventure of "The *Gloria Scott*" for us, but we suggest that it fell into two stages: *Sunday, July 12, to Tuesday, August 4, and Tuesday, September 22, 1874.* Sayers (with a leaning toward 1873) would date it in 1872. Blakeney, Brend, Davies, Folsom, and Harrison would date it 1873—as would Metcalfe (with a leaning toward 1874). Bell and Smith would date the adventure in 1875; Andrew, Christ, Pattrick, Petersen and Zeisler in 1876.

3 *Then he lit his pipe.* In his scholarly monograph on Holmes and tobacco ("No Fire Without Some Smoke"), Mr. John L. Hicks has written that: "No one can seriously doubt that the Master preferred a pipe to cigars and cigarettes. He smokes a pipe in thirty-five of the sixty cases in the Canon, probably does in three others, and in still another talks about his pipe without, as far as the reader knows, actually lighting it. He smokes nothing but a pipe in twenty-nine or, if one includes the doubtful instances, thirty-two. He indulges in cigars definitely in eight tales and probably in one other, and in cigarettes definitely in nine and probably in one other. In only ten cases does he smoke cigars and/or cigarettes but not a pipe. In eleven tales there is no mention of smoking by Holmes, but there is no reason to believe that the great man stopped the habit at any time, especially since these cases are scattered throughout his career. Holmes very likely smoked a pipe during the adventures recorded in the eleven tales in which there is no reference to smoking, as well as during those of the ten in which Watson names cigars and cigarettes. . . . Briar, clay and cherrywood pipes are . . . the only ones mentioned in the Sacred Writings. . . . Most admirers of Sherlock Holmes have believed that his favorite pipe was made of clay . . . but the evidence supports the theory that Holmes liked a briar pipe better than any other kind."

It will be noted that neither Holmes nor Watson ever mentioned a pipe with a *curved* stem; indeed, Mr. John Dickson Carr has stated that the curved pipe was unknown in England until the time of the Boer War (1889). Why, then has the curved pipe—a calabash or a meerschaum, for example—become a Holmesian trademark? Because Gillette, in playing the role of Holmes, found it difficult to speak his lines with a *straight* pipe between his lips; because Steele worked from photographs of Gillette as Holmes in drawing his famous illustrations for *Collier's Magazine*. (In Paget's illustrations for the *Strand*, all of Holmes' pipes had straight stems—as Professor Christ pointed out in his essay, "The Pipe and the Cap.")

Holmes must also have been a snuff-taker, else there would have been little reason for the King of Bohemia to present him with a snuffbox ("A Case of Identity").

4 *Bar fencing and boxing.* Conan Doyle himself never missed an opportunity to box with anyone who cared to take him on. He also played firstclass cricket, represented his county at football, reached the third round of the Amateur Billiards Championship, was a member of the British motorracing team in the Prince Henry Tour of 1911, and helped introduce skiing to Switzerland. In 1909, Conan Doyle received, but declined, an invitation to referee the forthcoming World Heavyweight Championship fight between Jim Jeffries and the Negro contender, Jack Johnson.

Those who believe, as your editor does, that the university of "The *Gloria Scott*" was Oxford have pointed to the fact that there was an excellent school of boxing there, according to Mr. E. B. Mitchell, the *Badminton Library*'s authority on boxing and sparring in 1889.

5 *Norfolk.* Norfolk—a land of fens and broad and swampy, lush meadowlands and flat, fertile farms —is said to be the richest county in England, and is certainly one that has changed the least since Holmes visited it in 1874 and again in 1898 ("The Adventure of the Dancing Men"). Norfolk is a maritime county in the *east* of England, yet Holmes later calls Norfolk "the north." Christopher Morley once commented that this was like calling Montreal "the west," and Mr. (later Sir) Paul H. Gore-Booth wrote in "The Journeys of Sherlock Holmes" that: "No normal Briton refers to Norfolk as 'the north.' " This is not an isolated

4 fencing and boxing I had few athletic tastes, and then my line of study was quite distinct from that of the other fellows, so that we had no points of contact at all. Trevor was the only man I knew, and that only through the accident of his bull-terrier freezing on to my ankle one morning as I went down to chapel.

" It was a prosaic way of forming a friendship, but it was effective. I was laid by the heels for ten days, and Trevor used to come in to inquire after me. At first it was only a minute's chat, but soon his visits lengthened, and before the end of the term we were close friends. He was a hearty, full-blooded fellow, full of spirit and energy, the very opposite to me in most respects ; but we found we had some subjects in common, and it was a bond of union when I learned that he was as friendless as I. Finally, he invited me down to his father's place at

5 Donnithorpe, in Norfolk, and I accepted his hospitality

6 for a month of the long vacation.

" Old Trevor was evidently a man of some wealth and

7 consideration, a J.P. and a landed proprietor. Donni-

8 thorpe is a little hamlet just to the north of Langmere, in

9 the country of the Broads. The house was an oldfashioned, wide-spread, oak-beamed, brick building, with a fine lime-lined avenue leading up to it. There was excellent wild-duck shooting in the fens, remarkably good

10-11 fishing, a small but select library, taken over, as I understood, from a former occupant, and a tolerable cook, so that it would be a fastidious man who could not put in a pleasant month there.

" Trevor senior was a widower, and my friend was his only son. There had been a daughter, I heard, but she

12 had died of diphtheria while on a visit to Birmingham. The father interested me extremely. He was a man of little culture, but with a considerable amount of rude strength both physically and mentally. He knew hardly any books, but he had travelled far, had seen much of the world, and had remembered all that he had learned. In person he was a thick-set, burly man, with a shock of grizzled hair, a brown, weather-beaten face, and blue eyes

". . . TREVOR USED TO COME IN TO INQUIRE AFTER ME."

Illustration by Sidney Paget for the *Strand Magazine*, April, 1893.

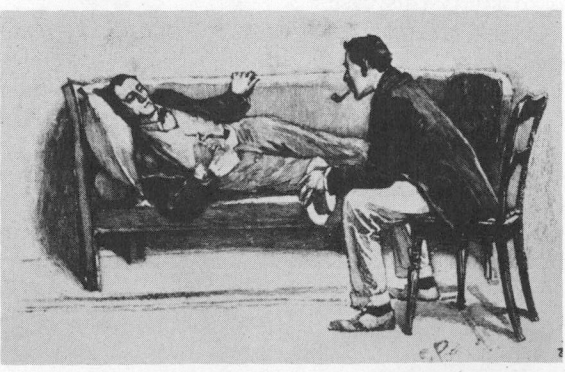

which were keen to the verge of fierceness.   Yet he had a reputation for kindness and charity on the country-side, and was noted for the leniency of his sentences from the bench.

" One evening, shortly after my arrival, we were sitting over a glass of port after dinner, when young Trevor **13** began to talk about those habits of observation and inference which I had already formed into a system, although I had not yet appreciated the part which they were to play in my life.   The old man evidently thought that his son was exaggerating in his description of one or two trivial feats which I had performed.

" ' Come now, Mr. Holmes,' said he, laughing good-humouredly, ' I'm an excellent subject, if you can deduce anything from me.'

" ' I fear there is not very much,' I answered. ' I might suggest that you have gone about in fear of some personal attack within the last twelve months.'

" The laugh faded from his lips, and he stared at me in great surprise.

" ' Well, that's true enough,' said he. ' You know, Victor,' turning to his son, ' when we broke up that poaching gang, they swore to knife us ; and Sir Edward **14** Hoby has actually been attacked.   I've always been on my guard since then, though I have no idea how you know it.'

" ' You have a very handsome stick,' I answered. ' By the inscription, I observed that you had not had it more than a year.   But you have taken some pains to bore the head of it and pour melted lead into the hole, so as to make it a formidable weapon.   I argued that you would not take such precautions unless you had some danger to fear.'

" ' Anything else ? ' he asked, smiling.

" ' You have boxed a good deal in your youth.'

" ' Right again.   How did you know it ?   Is my nose knocked a little out of the straight ? '

" ' No,' said I. ' It is your ears.   They have the peculiar flattening and thickening which marks the boxing **15** man.'

" ' Anything else ? '

" ' You have done a great deal of digging, by your callosities.' **16**

" ' Made all my money at the gold-fields.'

" ' You have been in New Zealand.'

" ' Right again.'

" ' You have visited Japan.'

" ' Quite true.'

" ' And you have been most intimately associated with someone whose initials were J. A., and whom you afterwards were eager to entirely forget.'

" Mr. Trevor stood slowly up, fixed his large blue eyes on me with a strange, wild stare, and then pitched forward on his face among the nutshells which strewed the cloth, in a dead faint.

" You can imagine, Watson, how shocked both his son and I were.   His attack did not last long, however, for when we undid his collar and sprinkled the water from one of the finger-glasses over his face, he gave a gasp or two and sat up.

instance (see "The Adventure of the Priory School"), and we can only conclude, with Sir Paul, that, for Holmes, "the north began some 120 miles from London in a generally northerly direction."

6 *the long vacation.* What we in America would call the summer vacation; in England, a period, roughly from July 1st to October 1st, during which a university is formally closed.

7 *a J.P.* Holmes has already told us that Trevor Senior was a Justice of the Peace—a subordinate magistrate appointed (first in 1327) to keep the peace in a specified district. In Great Britain and the United States his principal duties are to administer summary justice in minor cases, to commit for trial in a superior court on cause shown, and, in Great Britain, to grant licenses and act, if a county justice, as judge at quarter sessions.

8 *a little hamlet just to the north of Langmere.* Neither "Donnithorpe" nor "Langmere" is to be found on the map, but Mr. N. P. Metcalfe suggests (in "Oxford or Cambridge or Both?") that *Fordham,* later mentioned as the name of the doctor, "is also the name of a village near Downham Market in the fen country" and therefore may be helpful in identifying the true site of Squire Trevor's home.

9 *the Broads.* Generally, in England, broads are pieces of fresh water, formed by the broadening out of a river, or a marshy territory, with plentiful waterways.

10 *remarkably good fishing.* We see Holmes as a fisherman again in "The Adventure of Shoscombe Old Place."

11 *a small but select library.* An early example of Holmes' consuming interest in books. "I am an omnivorous reader," he tells us in "The Adventure of the Lion's Mane." In Baker Street he would spend many happy hours "buried among his old books" ("A Scandal in Bohemia"). This makes nonsense of Watson's early judgment, in *A Study in Scarlet,* that Holmes' knowledge of literature was "nil." It is of course possible to argue, as Mr. Bell pointed out in *Sherlock Holmes and Dr. Watson: The Chronology of Their Adventures,* "that Holmes' knowledge of literature in 1881 was in fact 'nil' [and that] it was Watson's influence and example that affected the change. But this is to take seriously Holmes' jocular reference to Watson as a man of letters ('The Adventure of Wisteria Lodge'); it is ascribing too much influence to a man whose preference ran to yellow-backed novels ('The Boscombe Valley Mystery') and the sea stories of Clark Russell ('The Five Orange Pips')." In fairness to Watson, however, it should be noted that it was he who tagged *A Study in Scarlet* with an apt quotation from Horace.

12 *but she had died of diptheria while on a visit to Birmingham.* "I should never marry myself, lest I bias my judgment," Holmes says in *The Sign of the Four*. But many distinguished commentators hold that Holmes *was* married, or at least had fallen deeply in love, at an early age:

Dr. Richard Asher in "Holmes and the Fair Sex": "From [Holmes' often later-expressed] attitude to women I think it is probable that early in his life he had an unfortunate love affair."

The late Elmer Davis in "The Real Sherlock Holmes": "Must we not suppose that in youth [Holmes] was strongly attracted to some blameless nitwit, perhaps the daughter of a neighboring country family; and that the discovery, happily not too belated, of her stupidity sickened him not only of her, but of an emotion which such a woman—even such a woman—could inspire?"

And Mr. S. C. Roberts, reflecting on the "curious sentence" given us here, has written ("Sherlock Holmes and the Fair Sex"): "Assuming, for the moment, that Trevor's sister was in fact alive at the time of [Holmes' meeting with Victor Trevor, and] assuming, further, that Holmes' specific, and yet wholly superfluous reference, conceals an indication of some closer interest than is conveyed in the bald sentence in the narrative . . . , are we not justified in the conjecture, to put it no higher, that Holmes was in fact attracted to Miss Trevor and that his hopes and affections were rudely shattered by the ravages of diptheria in Birmingham in the seventies?"

Miss Esther Longfellow ("The Distaff Side of Baker Street") scouts the conjecture that Holmes had any special interest in Miss Trevor, but she, too, believes that Holmes "was once married—at an early age—emerging shortly as a widower and that slightly cynical but undisillusioned man we know."

(See also "The Adventure of the Illustrious Client," Note 17.)

13 *a glass of port.* Holmes washed his supper down with a long draught of water in "The Five Orange Pips," but the attentive reader will have to look long and hard to find any other instance when he drank this liquid. "We may presume that Holmes used [water] for washing purposes, and perhaps, to a limited extent, for his chemical studies," Mr. Jørgen Cold wrote in "What Did Sherlock Holmes Drink?", but Holmes obviously preferred something a little stronger than water to drink whenever he could get it. Holmes, like many Englishmen, had a special fondness for port: he served it to his guests before the chase down the Thames in *The Sign of the Four* and he spoke highly (for Holmes) of the quality of the port served at the "Chequers" in "The Adventure of the Creeping Man."

14 *that poaching gang.* Under English law, it is unlawful to take game (poach), especially at night, on the lands of another; as a Justice of the Peace,

" ' Ah boys ! ' said he, forcing a smile. ' I hope I haven't frightened you. Strong as I look, there is a weak place in my heart, and it does not take much to knock me over. I don't know how you manage this, Mr. Holmes, but it seems to me that all the detectives of fact and of fancy would be children in your hands. That's your line of life, sir, and you may take the word of a man who has seen something of the world.'

" And that recommendation, with the exaggerated estimate of my ability with which he prefaced it, was, if you will believe me, Watson, the very first thing which ever made me feel that a profession might be made out of what had up to that time been the merest hobby. At the moment, however, I was too much concerned at the sudden illness of my host to think of anything else.

" ' I hope that I have said nothing to pain you, said I.

" ' Well, you certainly touched upon rather a tender point. Might I ask how you know and how much you know ? ' He spoke now in a half-jesting fashion, but a look of terror still lurked at the back of his eyes.

" ' It is simplicity itself,' said I. ' When you bared your arm to draw that fish into the boat, I saw that **17** " J. A." had been tattooed in the bend of the elbow. The letters were still legible, but it was perfectly clear from their blurred appearance, and from the staining of the skin round them, that efforts had been made to obliterate them. It was obvious, then, that those initials had once been very familiar to you, and that you had afterwards wished to forget them.'

" ' What an eye you have ! ' he cried, with a sigh of relief. ' It is just as you say. But we won't talk of it. Of all ghosts the ghosts of our old loves are the worst. Come into the billiard-room and have a quiet cigar.'

" From that day, amid all his cordiality, there was always a touch of suspicion in Mr. Trevor's manner towards me. Even his son remarked it. ' You've given the governor such a turn,' said he, ' that he'll never be sure again of what you know and what you don't know.' He did not mean to show it, I am sure, but it was so strongly in his mind that it peeped out at every action. At last I became so convinced that I was causing him uneasiness that I drew my visit to a close. On the very day, however, before I left, an incident occurred which proved in the sequel to be of importance.

" We were sitting out upon the lawn on garden chairs, the three of us, basking in the sun and admiring the view across the Broads, when the maid came out to say that there was a man at the door who wanted to see Mr. Trevor.

" ' What is his name ? ' asked my host.

" ' He would not give any.'

" ' What does he want, then ? '

" ' He says that you know him, and that he only wants a moment's conversation.'

" ' Show him round here.' An instant afterwards there appeared a little weazened fellow, with a cringing manner and a shambling style of walking. He wore an open jacket, with a splotch of tar on the sleeve, a red and

". . . FIXED HIS LARGE BLUE EYES ON ME WITH A STRANGE, WILD STARE . . ."

Illustration by William H. Hyde for *Harper's Weekly*, April 15, 1893. Of Hyde's illustrations, the late James Montgomery wrote (*A Study in Pictures*): "[They] are striking in their effect. Hyde chose to depict some of the most dramatic moments of the stories, but seemed to have a strange aversion to Holmes himself. In all his twenty-one pictures the Master is portrayed only five times, and in two of these he is seated in a chair with his back turned toward us. . . . Holmes [in this illustration] is shown as a mere stripling—almost too immature to make his amazingly deductive powers believable, and certainly far too young to be the college chum of the sophisticated Victor seated at his left. Of all recorded pictorial representations of the Master this is assuredly the earliest of his tender years."

black check shirt, dungaree trousers, and heavy boots badly worn. His face was thin and brown and crafty, with a perpetual smile upon it, which showed an irregular line of yellow teeth, and his crinkled hands were half closed in a way that is distinctive of sailors. As he came slouching across the lawn I heard Mr. Trevor make a sort of hiccoughing noise in his throat, and, jumping out of his chair, he ran into the house. He was back in a moment, and I smelt a strong reek of brandy as he passed me.

" ' Well, my man,' said he, ' what can I do for you ? '

" The sailor stood looking at him with puckered eyes, and with the same loose-lipped smile upon his face.

" ' You don't know me ? ' he asked.

" ' Why, dear me, it is surely Hudson ! ' said Mr. **18** Trevor, in a tone of surprise.

" ' Hudson it is, sir,' said the seaman. ' Why, it's thirty year and more since I saw you last. Here you are in your house, and me still picking my salt meat out of the harness cask.' **19**

" ' Tut, you will find that I have not forgotten old times,' cried Mr. Trevor, and, walking towards the sailor, he said something in a low voice. ' Go into the kitchen,' he continued out loud, ' and you will get food and drink. I have no doubt that I shall find you a situation.'

" ' Thank you, sir,' said the seaman, touching his forelock. ' I'm just off a two-yearer in an eight-knot tramp, **20** short handed at that, and I wants a rest. I thought I'd get it either with Mr. Beddoes or with you.'

Trevor senior would be bound to put down the practice within his jurisdiction. But as Mr. Welch, in "The Terai Planter," has asked: "Why should [Trevor senior's] treatment of 'poachers' lead to vows of vengeance? He was noted for the leniency of his sentences upon other wrongdoers."

15 *which marks the boxing man.*' But the late H. T. Webster pointed out ("Observations of Sherlock Holmes As an Athlete and Sportsman") that "in his early days, Holmes knew so little about wrestling that he was unaware that wrestlers as well as boxers have cauliflower ears . . ." Holmes was later to write two short monographs on the subject of the human ear ("The Cardboard Box").

16 *by your callosities.*' And Holmes was later to write "a curious little work" upon the influence of a trade upon the form of the hand (*The Sign of the Four*).

17 *tattooed in the bend of the elbow.* Holmes was later to write upon the subject of tattoo marks also ("The Red-Headed League").

18 *it is surely Hudson!*' "It has never been pointed out," Christopher Morley wrote in "Was Sherlock Holmes an American?", "that Holmes never admitted to Watson why he chose Mrs. Hudson's lodgings. She was the widow of the ruffian Hudson who blackmailed old Mr. Trevor—and so more than ever 'a long-suffering woman.'" And Mr. Manly Wade Wellman has added ("The Great Man's Great Son"): "It is the careless habit of many to consider [Mrs. Hudson] a widow, but Watson never says so. Yet Mr. Hudson was plainly not living at 221B Baker Street. This adds up to estrangement, and a good thing, too; for [he] was worthy of no woman, least of all of his wondrous wife. We know that once he lounged, a weazened, mocking, yellow-fanged blackmailer, around the beautiful home of Squire Trevor in Donnithorpe." (Mr. Wellman even went so far as to suggest that the Hudson of "The *Gloria Scott*" was also the Morse Hudson of "The Adventure of the Six Napoleons"—then an art dealer in the Kennington Road.) This view has been denied, however, and by Mrs. Hudson herself: "I never saw that bad Hudson and I certainly never wanted to. A convict indeed! My Hudson was a respectable tradesman, I'd have you know, in a very small way in Peckham, and he died when I was barely 25 years old" (Miss Zasu Pitts, in "Mrs. Hudson Speaks").

19 *the harness cask.*' A cask or tub with a rimmed cover used on board ship for keeping salt meats for current consumption.

20 *a two-yearer in an eight-knot tramp.* A two-year service on a freight-carrying vessel running on no regular line or timetable, with a maximum speed of eight knots.

" 'HUDSON IT IS, SIR,' SAID THE SEAMAN."

Illustration by Sidney Paget for the *Strand Magazine*, April, 1893. Note that Holmes seems to be wearing a *light blue* ribbon on his straw hat. This would indicate that he was, at the time of "The *Gloria Scott*," a student at Cambridge rather than Oxford—a point first noted by Christopher Morley in "Was Sherlock Holmes an American?"

21 *my London rooms*. There is nothing to prevent an undergraduate who has the means to do so from taking rooms in London in order to pursue a course of study during the long vacation, as the late Dorothy L. Sayers pointed out in "Holmes' College Career." It would take means: to maintain such a *pied-à-terre* in town, Holmes must have been fairly well off at this time, as the Messrs. J. H. and Humfrey Michell pointed out in "Sherlock Holmes the Chemist." It is very much to be doubted that these "London rooms" are the same as those in Montague Street which Holmes mentions in "The Musgrave Ritual." True, he speaks of the Montague Street rooms as those which he took when he "first" came up to London, but he undoubtedly meant the "first" in that case to be followed by "to establish myself in my career after I had completed my formal education."

22 *a few experiments in organic chemistry*. "What was Holmes' particular interest in chemical research?" the Michells asked in "Sherlock Holmes the Chemist." "It is not hard to answer that question, and we may say unhesitatingly—the coal tar derivatives [which Holmes studied in Montpellier during the period of the Great Hiatus; see "The Adventure of the Empty House"]." The Michells believe that Holmes went to London to be near the works recently established at Harrow by the brilliant chemist W. H. Perkin. Until 1856 nearly all dyes were made from plants or mosses, but in that year Perkin, only eighteen years old at the time, and an assistant at the Royal College of Chemistry in London, made a remarkable discovery. Experimenting with artificial quinine, he produced a dirty black powder that did not seem to be of any particular interest. He washed and liquefied it, however, and the totally unexpected result was a strong mauve dye. This was the beginning of aniline dyes, produced from coal tar. Perkin borrowed money from his father to set up

" 'Ah !' cried Mr. Trevor, ' you know where Mr. Beddoes is ? '

" ' Bless you, sir, I know where all my old friends are,' said the fellow, with a sinister smile, and slouched off after the maid to the kitchen. Mr. Trevor mumbled something to us about having been shipmates with the man when he was going back to the diggings, and then, leaving us on the lawn, he went indoors. An hour later, when we entered the house we found him stretched dead drunk upon the dining-room sofa. The whole incident left a most ugly impression upon my mind, and I was not sorry next day to leave Donnithorpe behind me, for I felt that my presence must be a source of embarrassment to my friend.

" All this occurred during the first month of the long **21** vacation. I went up to my London rooms, where I spent seven weeks working out a few experiments in organic **22** chemistry. One day, however, when the autumn was far advanced and the vacation drawing to a close, I received a telegram from my friend imploring me to return to Donnithorpe, and saying that he was in great need of my advice and assistance. Of course I dropped everything and set out for the north once more.

" He met me with the dog-cart at the station, and I **23** saw at a glance that the last two months had been very trying ones for him. He had grown thin and careworn, and had lost the loud, cheery manner for which he had been remarkable.

" ' The governor is dying,' were the first words he said.

" ' Impossible ! ' I cried. ' What is the matter ? '

" ' Apoplexy. Nervous shock. He's been on the verge all day. I doubt if we shall find him alive.'

" I was, as you may think, Watson, horrified at this unexpected news.

" ' What has caused it ? ' I asked.

" ' Ah, that is the point. Jump in, and we can talk it over while we drive. You remember that fellow who came upon the evening before you left us ? '

" ' Perfectly.'

" ' Do you know who it was that we let into the house that day ? '

" ' I have no idea.'

" ' It was the Devil, Holmes ! ' he cried.

" I stared at him in astonishment.

" ' Yes ; it was the Devil himself. We have not had a peaceful hour since—not one. The governor has never held up his head from that evening, and now the life has been crushed out of him, and his heart broken all through this accursed Hudson.'

" ' What power had he, then ? '

" ' Ah, that is what I would give so much to know. The kindly, charitable, good old governor ! How could he have fallen into the clutches of such a ruffian ? But I am so glad that you have come, Holmes. I trust very much to your judgment and discretion, and I know that you will advise me for the best.'

" We were dashing along the smooth, white country road, with the long stretch of Broads in front of us glimmering in the red light of the setting sun. From a grove upon our left I could already see the high chimneys and the flag-staff which marked the squire's dwelling.

" ' My father made the fellow gardener,' said my companion, ' and then, as that did not satisfy him, he was promoted to be butler. The house seemed to be at his mercy, and he wandered about and did what he chose in it. The maids complained of his drunken habits and his vile language. The dad raised their wages all round to recompense them for the annoyance. The fellow would take the boat and my father's best gun and treat himself to little shooting parties. And all this with such a sneering, leering, insolent face, that I would have knocked him down twenty times over if he had been a man of my own age. I tell you, Holmes, I have had to keep a tight hold upon myself all this time, and now I am asking myself whether, if I had let myself go a little more, I might not have been a wiser man.

" ' Well, matters went from bad to worse with us, and this animal, Hudson, became more and more intrusive, until at last, on his making some insolent reply to my father in my presence one day, I took him by the shoulder and turned him out of the room. He slunk away with a livid face, and two venomous eyes which uttered more threats than his tongue could do. I don't know what passed between the poor dad and him after that, but the dad came to me next day and asked me whether I would mind apologizing to Hudson. I refused, as you can imagine, and asked my father how he could allow such a wretch to take such liberties with himself and his household.

" ' " Ah, my boy," said he, " it is all very well to talk, but you don't know how I am placed. But you shall know, Victor. I'll see that you shall know, come what may ! You wouldn't believe harm of your poor old father, would you, lad ? " He was very much moved, and shut himself up in the study all day, where I could see through the window that he was writing busily.

" ' That evening there came what seemed to be a grand release, for Hudson told us that he was going to leave us. He walked into the dining-room as we sat after dinner and announced his intention in the thick voice of a half-drunken man.

" ' " I've had enough of Norfolk," said he, " I'll run down to Mr. Beddoes, in Hampshire. He'll be as glad **24** to see me as you were, I dare say."

" ' " You're not going away in an unkind spirit, Hudson, I hope ? " said my father, with a tameness which made my blood boil.

" ' " I've not had my 'pology," said he, sulkily, glancing in my direction.

his factory, and in a very short time the new purples became the rage. Gowns, gloves, hats, feathers, ribbons were all purple; one writer in 1859 declared that "We shall soon have purple omnibuses and purple houses." Later experiments produced greens, blues, magentas, and other shades, and the coal-tar industry was firmly established. At first the new shades were much harsher than those made from the old vegetable dyes, and, as a result, the fashionable Victorian lady went about in crude, startling colors that would be considered in very bad taste today.

23 *the last two months*. Holmes has already told us that *seven weeks* elapsed between his first and second visit to Donnithorpe. These seven weeks embraced the latter part of August and the early part of September—Holmes' "two months."

24 *Hampshire*. Or Hants, but officially Southampton since 1888. Hampshire is an undulating region in the South of England devoted to sheep raising and dairy farming, but it also has shipbuilding and a large maritime trade.

"HE MET ME WITH THE DOG-CART AT THE STATION."

The dog-cart shown above was not a cart drawn by a large dog, as some might think, but a sportsman's vehicle: a two-wheeled, one-horse cart with two seats back to back, the rear seat being so constructed that it could be shut to form a box for carrying a dog.

25 *bearing the Fordingbridge postmark.* Holmes' second visit to Donnithorpe could not have been made upon a Monday, because the letter to Trevor senior had been delivered—by post—on the preceding day.

"'"I'VE NOT HAD MY 'POLOGY," SAID HE, SULKILY.'"

Illustration by Sidney Paget for the *Strand Magazine*, April, 1893.

"'"Victor, you will acknowledge that you have used this worthy fellow rather roughly?"' said the dad, turning to me.

"'"On the contrary, I think that we have both shown extraordinary patience towards him," I answered.

"'"Oh, you do, do you?" he snarled. 'Very good, mate. We'll see about that!" He slouched out of the room, and half an hour afterwards left the house, leaving my father in a state of pitiable nervousness. Night after night I heard him pacing his room, and it was just as he was recovering his confidence that the blow did at last fall.'

"'And how?' I asked, eagerly.

"'In a most extraordinary fashion. A letter arrived for my father yesterday evening, bearing the Fording-**25** bridge postmark. My father read it, clapped both his hands to his head, and began running round the room in little circles like a man who has been driven out of his senses. When I at last drew him down on to the sofa, his mouth and eyelids were all puckered on one side, and I saw that he had a stroke. Dr. Fordham came over at once, and we put him to bed; but the paralysis has spread, he has shown no sign of returning consciousness, and I think that we shall hardly find him alive.'

"'You horrify me, Trevor!' I cried. 'What, then, could have been in this letter to cause so dreadful a result?'

"'Nothing. There lies the inexplicable part of it. The message was absurd and trivial. Ah, my God, it is as I feared!'

"As he spoke we came round the curve of the avenue, and saw in the fading light that every blind in the house had been drawn down. As we dashed up to the door, my friend's face convulsed with grief, a gentleman in black emerged from it.

"'When did it happen, doctor?' asked Trevor.

"'Almost immediately after you left.'

"'Did he recover consciousness?'

"'For an instant before the end.'

"'Any message for me?'

"'Only that the papers were in the back drawer of the Japanese cabinet.'

"My friend ascended with the doctor to the chamber of death, while I remained in the study, turning the whole matter over and over in my head, and feeling as sombre as ever I had done in my life. What was the past of this Trevor: pugilist, traveller, and gold-digger? and how had he placed himself in the power of this acid-faced seaman? Why, too, should he faint at an allusion to the half-effaced initials upon his arm, and die of fright when he had a letter from Fordingbridge? Then I remembered that Fordingbridge was in Hampshire, and that this Mr. Beddoes, whom the seaman had gone to visit, and presumably to blackmail, had also been mentioned as living in Hampshire. The letter, then, might either come from Hudson, the seaman, saying that he had betrayed the guilty secret which appeared to exist, or it might come from Beddoes, warning an old confederate that such a betrayal was imminent. So far it seemed clear enough.   But, then, how could the letter be trivial and grotesque as described by the son ? He must have mis-read it.   If so, it must have been one of those ingenious secret codes which mean one thing while they seem to mean another.   I must see this letter.   If there were a hidden meaning in it, I was confident that I could pluck it forth.   For an hour I sat pondering over it in the gloom, until at last a weeping maid brought in a lamp, and close at her heels came my friend Trevor, pale but composed, with these very papers which lie upon my knee held in his grasp.   He sat down opposite to me, drew the lamp to the edge of the table, and handed me a short note scribbled, as you see, upon a single sheet of grey paper. ' The supply of game for London is going steadily up,' it ran. ' Head-keeper Hudson, we believe, has been now told to receive all orders for fly-paper and for preservation of your hen pheasant's life.'

" I dare say my face looked as bewildered as yours did just now when first I read this message.   Then I re-read it very carefully.   It was evidently as I had thought, and some second meaning must be buried in this strange com-bination of words.   Or could it be that there was a pre-arranged significance to such phrases as ' fly-paper ' and ' hen pheasant '?   Such a meaning would be arbitrary, and could not be deduced in any way.   And yet I was loath to believe that this was the case, and the presence of the word ' Hudson ' seemed to show that the subject of the message was as I had guessed, and that it was from Bed-does rather than the sailor.   I tried it backwards, but the combination, ' Life pheasant's hen,' was not encouraging. Then I tried alternate words, but neither ' The of for ' nor ' supply game London ' promised to throw any light upon it.   Then in an instant the key of the riddle was in my hands, and I saw that every third word beginning with the first would give a message which might well drive old Trevor to despair.

" It was short and terse, the warning, as I now read it to my companion :

" ' The game is up. Hudson has told all. Fly for your life.'

" Victor Trevor sank his face into his shaking hands. ' It must be that, I suppose,' said he. ' This is worse than death, for it means disgrace as well.   But what is the meaning of these " head-keepers " and " hen pheasants "? '

' It means nothing to the message, but it might mean a good deal to us if we had no other means of discovering the sender.   You see that he has begun by writing, " The . . . game . . . is," and so on.   Afterwards he had, to fulfil the prearranged cipher, to fill in any two words in each space.   He would naturally use the first words which came to his mind, and if there were so many which referred to sport among them, you may be tolerably sure that he is either an ardent shot or interested in breeding. Do you know anything of this Beddoes ? '

" ' Why, now that you mention it,' said he, ' I remem-ber that my poor father used to have an invitation from him to shoot over his preserves every autumn.'

" ' Then it is undoubtedly from him that the note

26 *one of those ingenious secret codes.* Holmes was later to write "a trifling monograph" upon the subject of secret writings, in which he analyzed 160 separate ciphers ("The Adventure of the Danc-ing Men"). But we should point out here that Bed-does' message was more properly a *cipher* than a *code*, which is a form of secret writing in which one word is made to stand for another word (or phrase).

27 *the first words which came to his mind.* Holmes has here anticipated the word-association tests of modern psychology.

"THEN IN AN INSTANT THE KEY OF THE RIDDLE WAS IN MY HANDS . . ."

Illustration by Sidney Paget for the *Strand Maga-zine*, April, 1893.

THE BARQUE *Gloria Scott*

Actually, the barque *Macquarie*, built in 1875. The photograph, by Hughes & Son, Ltd., is from *Sailing Ships and Their Story*, by E. Keble Chatterton, London: Sidgwick & Jackson, Ltd., 1909. A barque is officially a three-masted vessel with the foremast and mainmast square-rigged, the mizzen-mast fore-and-aft rigged. Mr. Richard W. Clarke, in his extensive research "On the Nomenclature of Watson's Ships" was forced to conclude that the *Gloria Scott*, the *Norah Creina* of "The Resident Patient," and the *Sophy Anderson* of "The Five Orange Pips" were all "former childhood sweethearts whom Watson endeavored to honor in his sentimental way; hoping, no doubt, that their eyes would see the printed page where their names appeared."

28 *Falmouth*. The great port and fishing town in Cornwall.

comes,' said I. 'It only remains for us to find out what this secret was which the sailor Hudson seems to have held over the heads of these two wealthy and respected men.'

" ' Alas, Holmes, I fear that it is one of sin and shame ! ' cried my friend. ' But from you I shall have no secrets. Here is the statement which was drawn up by my father when he knew that the danger from Hudson had become imminent. I found it in the Japanese cabinet, as he told the doctor. Take it and read it to me, for I have neither the strength nor the courage to do it myself.'

" These are the very papers, Watson, which he handed to me, and I will read them to you as I read them in the old study that night to him. They are endorsed outside as you see : ' Some particulars of the voyage of the barque **28** *Gloria Scott*, from her leaving Falmouth on the 8th October, 1855, to her destruction in N. lat. 15° 20′, W. long. 25° 14′, on November 6th.' It is in the form of a letter, and runs in this way :

" My dear, dear son,—Now that approaching disgrace begins to darken the closing years of my life, I can write with all truth and honesty that it is not the terror of the law, it is not the loss of my position in the county, nor is it my fall in the eyes of all who have known me, which cuts me to the heart ; but it is the thought that you should come to blush for me—you who love me, and who have seldom, I hope, had reason to do other than respect me. But if the blow falls which is for ever hanging over me, then I should wish you to read this that you may know straight from me how far I have been to blame. On the other hand, if all should go well (which may kind God Almighty grant !), then if by any chance this paper should be still undestroyed, and should fall into your hands, I conjure you by all you hold sacred, by the memory of your dear mother, and by the love which has been between us, to hurl it into the fire, and to never **29** give one thought to it again.

" If, then, your eye goes on to read this line, I know that I shall already have been exposed and dragged from my home, or, as is more likely—for you know that my heart is weak—be lying with my tongue sealed for ever in death. In either case the time for suppression is past, and every word which I tell you is the naked truth ; and this I swear as I hope for mercy.

" My name, dear lad, is not Trevor. I was James Armitage in my younger days, and you can understand now the shock that it was to me a few weeks ago when your college friend addressed me in words which seemed to imply that he had surmised my secret. As Armitage it was that I entered a London banking house, and as Armitage I was convicted of breaking my country's laws, **30** and was sentenced to transportation. Do not think very harshly of me, laddie. It was a debt of honour, so-called, which I had to pay, and I used money which was not my own to do it, in the certainty that I could replace it before there could be any possibility of its being missed. But the most dreadful ill-luck pursued me. The money which I had reckoned upon never came to hand, and a premature examination of accounts exposed my deficit. The case might have been dealt leniently with, but the laws were more harshly administered thirty years ago than now, and on my twenty-third birthday I found myself chained as a felon with thirty-seven other convicts in the 'tween-decks of the barque *Gloria Scott*, bound for Australia.

" It was the year '55, when the Crimean War was at its height, and the old convict ships had been largely used as **31** transports in the Black Sea.   The Government was compelled therefore to use smaller and less suitable vessels for sending out their prisoners.   The *Gloria Scott* had been in the Chinese tea trade, but she was an old-fashioned, heavy-bowed, broad-beamed craft, and the new clippers **32** had cut her out.   She was a 500-ton boat, and besides her thirty-eight gaol-birds, she carried twenty-six of a crew, eighteen soldiers, a captain, three mates, a doctor, a chaplain, and four warders.   Nearly a hundred souls were in her, all told, when we set sail from Falmouth.

" The partitions between the cells of the convicts, instead of being of thick oak, as is usual in convict ships, were quite thin and frail.   The man next to me upon the aft side was one whom I had particularly noticed when we were led down to the quay.   He was a young man with a clear, hairless face, a long thin nose, and rather nutcracker jaws.   He carried his head very jauntily in the air, had a swaggering style of walking, and was above all else remarkable for his extraordinary height.   I don't think any of our heads would come up to his shoulder, and I am sure that he could not have measured less than six and a half feet.   It was strange among so many sad and weary faces to see one which was full of energy and resolution.   The sight of it was to me like a fire in a snowstorm. I was glad then to find that he was my neighbour, and gladder still when, in the dead of the night, I heard a whisper close to my ear, and found that he had managed to cut an opening in the board which separated us.

" ' Halloa, chummy ! ' said he, ' what's your name, and what are you here for ? '

" I answered him, and asked in turn who I was talking with.

" ' I'm Jack Prendergast,' said he, and, by God, you'll learn to bless my name before you've done with me ! '

" I remembered hearing of his case, for it was one which had made an immense sensation throughout the country, some time before my own arrest.   He was a man of good family and of great ability, but of incurably vicious habits, who had, by an ingenious system of fraud, obtained huge sums of money from the leading London merchants.

" ' Ah, ah ! You remember my case ? ' said he, proudly.

" ' Very well indeed.'

" ' Then maybe you remember something queer about it ? '

" ' What was that, then ? '

" ' I'd had nearly a quarter of a million, hadn't I ? '   **33**

" ' So it was said.'

" ' But none was recovered, eh ? '

" ' No.'

29 *and to never give one thought to it again.* As Mr. Welch has observed in "The Terai Planter," "The literary style is better than one would have expected from a man of little culture, who knew hardly any books."

30 *sentenced to transportation.* In criminal law, the sending away of a convict to a remote place to be held there as a measure of punishment.

31 *when the Crimean War was at its height.* The Crimean War began in 1854 and ended with the Treaty of Paris in February of 1856, and was actually at its height in 1855. But if 1855 was "thirty years ago" we should have to date "The *Gloria Scott*" in *1885*, and this, from what we know of Holmes' later history, is ridiculous. We must either: (1) discard "the year '55, when the Crimean War was at its height"; or (2) revise the "thirty years."

Most commentators prefer to do the former, and for three good reasons:

1. Hudson's "thirty year and more" (since he last saw Trevor senior) is in undesigned coincidence with Trevor's own "thirty years ago."

2. Trevor senior was "a fine, robust old man" at the time of his meeting with Holmes; he had completed his twenty-third year (he tells us) at the time of the sailing from Falmouth. This substantiates the passing of thirty years.

3. If we accept Trevor senior's "thirty years ago" we can believe that he had returned to England "more than twenty years" ago, married, and had a son who was a contemporary of Holmes (that is, born around 1854). If, on the other hand, we accept Trevor senior's "year '55," we must suppose, with the late Clifton R. Andrew ("Who Is Who, and When, in 'The *Gloria Scott*'") "that Victor Trevor was *not a natural son* of Old Man Trevor, but instead was a stepson . . .''

The complexities of dating this adventure have been cogently summed up by Mr. T. S. Blakeney in "More Disjecta Membra": "All sound critics, I think, agree that 1855 is impossible for [Holmes' adventure at Donnithorpe]; suggestions have been made, therefore, to put the date of the sailing back to 1845 and in this connection particular weight has attached to Professor Christ's note [in *An Irregular Chronology*] quoting the *Encyclopaedia Britannica* (11th edn.), that transportation of criminals [to Australia] was suspended in 1846. The most authoritative recent study of criminal transportation is Charles Bateson's *The Convict Ships: 1787–1868*, and it may be seen there that the *Britannica's* statement . . . is incorrect. Transportation to New South Wales, the main penal settlement, was abolished by Order-in-Council on May 22, 1840, but towards the end of 1844 it was proposed that 'exiles' (prisoners who had served a probationary period in England) might go out to the Port Philip district (which was only separated from N.S.W. on July 1, 1851). In 1848 Earl Grey revoked the Order-in-Council abolishing transportation to

N.S.W., but protests followed and in April, 1851, his revocation was rescinded. In 1853 transportation to Tasmania was abolished, but not until 1868 in Western Australia. It will thus be seen that 1846 did not see the end of the transportation system; although very few convicts reached N.S.W. after 1840, Trevor could have been going to Tasmania or W. Australia. It does not, to my thinking, in any way effect the need to alter old Trevor's sailing date from 1855 to 1845, but, since one's aim in all these matters is to emulate Holmes himself, in having a passion for exact knowledge, it is perhaps as well to draw attention to the true facts concerning the duration of the convict transportation system."

32 *the new clippers.* Fast sailing vessels—full-rigged ships of a type developed by American builders about 1840, characterized by fine lines, an overhanging bow, tall raking masts and a large sail area; ships, usually, of about 1,500 tons. Since Trevor senior calls the clippers "new" this is another indication that the *Gloria Scott* sailed from Falmouth in 1845 rather than 1855.

33 *nearly a quarter of a million.* Some $1,250,000 —a fantastic sum for 1845 (or 1855, either).

34 *the dibbs.* Correctly, *dibs*—slang for money.

" ' I'M JACK PRENDERGAST,' SAID HE."

Illustration by Sidney Paget for the *Strand Magazine*, April, 1893.

" ' Well, where d'ye suppose the balance is ? ' he asked.

" ' I have no idea,' said I.

" ' Right between my finger and thumb,' he cried. ' By God, I've got more pounds to my name than you have hairs on your head.   And if you've money, my son, and know how to handle it and spread it, you can do *anything* !   Now, you don't think it likely that a man who could do anything is going to wear his breeches out sitting in the stinking hold of a rat-gutted, beetle-ridden, mouldy old coffin of a China coaster ?   No, sir, such a man will look after himself, and will look after his chums. You may lay to that !   You hold on to him, and you may kiss the Book that he'll haul you through.'

" That was his style of talk, and at first I thought it meant nothing, but after a while, when he had tested me and sworn me in with all possible solemnity, he let me understand that there really was a plot to gain command of the vessel.   A dozen of the prisoners had hatched it before they came aboard ; Prendergast was the leader, and his money was the motive power.

" ' I'd a partner,' said he, ' a rare good man, as true as a **34** stock to a barrel.   He's got the dibbs, he has, and where do you think he is at this moment ?   Why, he's the chaplain of this ship—the chaplain, no less !   He came aboard with a black coat and his papers right, and money enough in his box to buy the thing right up from keel to main-truck.   The crew are his, body and soul.   He could buy 'em at so much a gross with a cash discount, and he did it before ever they signed on.   He's got two of the warders and Mercer the second mate, and he'd get the captain himself if he thought him worth it.'

" ' What are we to do, then ? ' I asked.

ONE OF "THE NEW CLIPPERS"

Shown here is the American clipper *Red Jacket,* internationally famous in her day for swift Atlantic crossings. In 1854, she did 413 miles in a day. This means that a sailing ship was driven for a day and a night at an average speed of about 18½ knots, a speed that steamers did not reach for another thirty years. The photo is from *The Sailing Ship: Six Thousand Years of History*, by Romola and R. C. Anderson, New York: Robert M. McBride & Company, 1947.

"'What do you think?' said he. 'We'll make the coats of some of these soldiers redder than ever the tailor did.'

"'But they are armed,' said I.

"'And so shall we be, my boy. There's a brace of pistols for every mother's son of us, and if we can't carry this ship, with the crew at our back, it's time we were all sent to a young Misses' boarding school. You speak to your mate on the left to-night, and see if he is to be trusted.'

"I did so, and found my other neighbour to be a young fellow in much the same position as myself, whose crime had been forgery. His name was Evans, but he afterwards changed it, like myself, and he is now a rich and prosperous man in the South of England. He was ready enough to join the conspiracy, as the only means of saving ourselves, and before we had crossed the Bay there were **35** only two of the prisoners who were not in the secret. One of these was of weak mind, and we did not dare to trust him, and the other was suffering from jaundice, and could not be of any use to us.

" From the beginning there was really nothing to prevent us taking possession of the ship. The crew were a set of ruffians, specially picked for the job. The sham chaplain came into our cells to exhort us, carrying a black bag, supposed to be full of tracts ; and so often did he come that by the third day we had each stowed away at the foot of our bed a file, a brace of pistols, a pound of powder, and twenty slugs. Two of the warders were agents of Prendergast, and the second mate was his right-hand man. The captain, the two mates, two warders, Lieutenant Martin, his eighteen soldiers, and the doctor were all that we had against us. Yet, safe as it was, we determined to neglect no precaution, and to make our attack suddenly at night. It came, however, more quickly than we expected, and in this way :

" One evening, about the third week after our start, the **36** doctor had come down to see one of the prisoners, who was ill, and, putting his hand down on the bottom of his bunk, he felt the outline of the pistols. If he had been silent he might have blown the whole thing ; but he was a nervous little chap, so he gave a cry of surprise and turned so pale, that the man knew what was up in an instant and seized him. He was gagged before he could give the alarm, and tied down upon the bed. He had unlocked the door that led to the deck, and we were through it in a rush. The two sentries were shot down, and so was a corporal who came running to see what was the matter. There were two more soldiers at the door of the state-room, and their muskets seemed not to be loaded, for they never fired upon us, and they were shot while trying to fix their bayonets. Then we rushed on into the captain's cabin, but as we pushed open the door there was an explosion from within, and there he lay with his head on the chart of the Atlantic, which was pinned upon the table, while the chaplain stood, with a smoking pistol in his hand, at his elbow. The two mates had both been seized by the crew, and the whole business seemed to be settled.

35 *the Bay*. The Bay of Biscay.

36 *about the third week after our start*. "This," Dr. Ernest Bloomfield Zeisler noted in his *Baker Street Chronology*, "would make it October 29th at the very latest, yet previously old Trevor wrote that the ship was destroyed on November 6th, which is the beginning of the *fifth* week after she sailed."

". . . WHILE THE CHAPLAIN STOOD, WITH A SMOKING PISTOL IN HIS HAND . . ."

Illustration by William H. Hyde for *Harper's Weekly*, April 15, 1893. Paget illustrated the same scene for the *Strand Magazine*, as did Arthur Twidle for the 1903 "Author's Edition" of *The Memoirs of Sherlock Holmes*, London: Smith, Elder.

"... WE PULLED HIM ABOARD THE BOAT ..."

Illustration by Sidney Paget for the *Strand Magazine*, April, 1893.

" The state-room was next the cabin, and we flocked in there and flopped down on the settees all speaking together, for we were just mad with the feeling that we were free once more.   There were lockers all round, and Wilson, the sham chaplain, knocked one of them in, and pulled out a dozen of brown sherry.   We cracked off the necks of the bottles, poured the stuff out into tumblers, and were just tossing them off, when in an instant, without warning, there came the roar of muskets in our ears, and the saloon was so full of smoke that we could not see across the table.   When it cleared away again the place was a shambles.   Wilson and eight others were wriggling on the top of each other on the floor, and the blood and brown sherry on that table turn me sick now when I think of it.   We were so cowed by the sight that I think we should have given the job up if it had not been for Prendergast.   He bellowed like a bull and rushed for the door with all that were left alive at his heels.   Out we ran, and there on the poop were the lieutenant and ten of his men.   The swing skylights above the saloon table had been a bit open, and they had fired on us through the slit.   We got on them before they could load, and they stood to it like men, but we had the upper hand of them, and in five minutes it was all over.   My God ! was there ever a slaughter-house like that ship ?   Prendergast was like a raging devil, and he picked the soldiers up as if they had been children and threw them overboard, alive or dead.   There was one sergeant that was horribly wounded, and yet kept on swimming for a surprising time, until someone in mercy blew out his brains.   When the fighting was over there was no one left of our enemies except just the warders, the mates, and the doctor.

" It was over them that the great quarrel arose.   There were many of us who were glad enough to win back our freedom, and yet who had no wish to have murder on our souls.   It was one thing to knock the soldiers over with their muskets in their hands, and it was another to stand by while men were being killed in cold blood.   Eight of us, five convicts and three sailors, said that we would not see it done.   But there was no moving Prendergast and those who were with him.   Our only chance of safety lay in making a clean job of it, said he, and he would not leave a tongue with power to wag in a witness-box.   It nearly came to our sharing the fate of the prisoners, but at last he said that if we wished we might take a boat and go   We jumped at the offer, for we were already sick of these bloodthirsty doings, and we saw that there would be worse before it was done.   We were given a suit of sailor's togs each, a barrel of water, two casks, one of **37** junk and one of biscuits, and a compass.   Prendergast threw us over a chart, told us that we were shipwrecked mariners whose ship had foundered in lat. $15°$ N. and long. $25°$ W., and then cut the painter and let us go.

" And now I come to the most surprising part of my story, my dear son.   The seamen had hauled the foreyard aback during the rising, but now as we left them they brought it square again, and, as there was a light wind from the north and east, the barque began to draw slowly away from us.   Our boat lay, rising and falling, upon the long, smooth rollers, and Evans and I, who were the most educated of the party, were sitting in the sheets working out our position and planning what coast we should make for. It was a nice question, for the Cape de Verds was about 500 miles to the north of us, and the African coast about 700 miles to the east. On the whole, as the wind **38** was coming round to north, we thought that Sierra Leone might be best, and turned our head in that direction, the barque being at that time nearly hull down on our starboard quarter. Suddenly as we looked at her we saw a dense black cloud of smoke shoot up from her, which hung like a monstrous tree upon the skyline. A few seconds later a roar like thunder burst upon our ears, and as the smoke thinned away there was no sign left of the *Gloria Scott*. In an instant we swept the boat's head round again, and pulled with all our strength for the place where the haze, still trailing over the water, marked the scene of this catastrophe.

" It was a long hour before we reached it, and at first we feared that we had come too late to save anyone. A splintered boat and a number of crates and fragments of spars rising and falling on the waves showed us where the vessel had foundered, but there was no sign of life, and we had turned away in despair when we heard a cry for help, and saw at some distance a piece of wreckage with a man lying stretched across it. When we pulled him aboard the boat he proved to be a young seaman of the name of Hudson, who was so burned and exhausted that he could give us no account of what had happened until the following morning.

" It seemed that after we had left, Prendergast and his gang had proceeded to put to death the five remaining prisoners : the two warders had been shot and thrown overboard, and so also had the third mate. Prendergast then descended into the 'tween-decks, and with his own hands cut the throat of the unfortunate surgeon. There only remained the first mate, who was a bold and active man. When he saw the convict approaching him with the bloody knife in his hand, he kicked off his bonds, which he had somehow contrived to loosen, and rushing down the deck he plunged into the afterhold.

" A dozen convicts who descended with their pistols in search of him found him with a match-box in his hand seated beside an open powder barrel, which was one of a hundred carried on board, and swearing that he would blow all hands up if he were in any way molested. An instant later the explosion occurred, though Hudson thought it was caused by the misdirected bullet of one of the convicts rather than the mate's match. Be the cause what it may, it was the end of the *Gloria Scott*, and of the rabble who held command of her.

" Such, in a few words, my dear boy, is the history of this terrible business in which I was involved. Next day we were picked up by the brig *Hotspur*, bound for Australia, whose captain found no difficulty in believing that we were the survivors of a passenger ship which had foundered. The transport ship, *Gloria Scott*, was set **39** down by the Admiralty as being lost at sea, and no word

38 *about 700 miles to the east.* Here Dr. Zeisler caught Trevor senior in another error: "The Cape Verde Islands lie between 14 degrees 47 minutes and 17 degrees 13 minutes North latitude, and are nowhere more than some 140 miles north of the position given for the shipwreck [N. Lat. 15° 20′, W. Long. 25° 14′]; and the westernmost point of the Cape Verde Islands is not more than 150 miles west of the African coast. Hence Trevor was mistaken in either his position or his distance."

39 *a passenger ship which had foundered.* ". . . is it conceivable that the captain of the *Hotspur* should not have closely questioned the nine castaways, in order to obtain a full account of the shipwreck, the name and destination of the ship, and all the many details which he would have had to embody in his report to the authorities?" the late H. W. Bell asked in *Sherlock Holmes and Dr. Watson: The Chronology of Their Adventures.* "It is certain that sooner or later he would have detected sufficient inconsistencies in their various accounts to arouse his suspicions, and to cause him to clap them all in irons until arrival at Sydney, where a full investigation would have had its inevitable sequel."

". . . THE BRIG *Hotspur* . . ."

Shown here is H.M.S. *Martin*, a training brig (a two-masted, square-rigged vessel) launched in 1836. The photo is from *Sailing Ships and Their Story*, by E. Keble Chatterton; London: Sidgwick & Jackson, Ltd., 1909.

40 *and we bought country estates.* "Another inconsistency," Mr. Bell continued, "is [Trevor senior's] statement that he, though an escaped convict, 'came back' to England, where he became a Justice of the Peace. This would have been to tempt Providence by needlessly multiplying the chances of discovery. It is far more probable that he was a colonial, that his misdeeds were committed in the Eastern seas (he admitted to Holmes an acquaintance with New Zealand and Japan) and that he fled to England in order to put the greatest possible distance between himself and the theatre of his crimes."

41 *Sweet Lord, have mercy on our souls!'* "The note at the end of the confession mentions the arrival of Beddoes' letter," Mr. Welch wrote in "The Terai Planter." "But the combined evidence of Victor and the doctor is that Mr. Trevor had a stroke immediately on reading this letter and never recovered consciousness, save for an instant before the end. It was *impossible* for him to have written the postscript and to have placed the papers in the Japanese cabinet." In Mr. Welch's view, Trevor senior was *not* dead but a living partner in a conspiracy that involved both Dr. Fordham and Victor Trevor. (See "A Scandal in Bohemia," Note 7.)

42 *"That was the narrative which I read that night.* "It is obvious," Mr. Bell concluded, "that Trevor's yarn is the fabric of his imagination . . . [and] we have now to consider the motive for this elaborate and mendacious history. A man does not confess, even posthumously, to a devoted son a false account of embezzlement, transportation and mutiny, unless he is trying desperately to conceal some far more heinous crime. What it was, we cannot, of course, know for certain; but it was sinister enough to induce him to submit to insolence and blackmail at Hudson's hands rather than let his son have any inkling of its true nature, and to lead him to invent a substitute account sufficiently lurid to prevent Victor from making further inquiries. Bearing in mind the fact that he was 'a man of little culture,' we are safe in assuming that he would not have departed from the circle of his own experiences in devising a false tale. Therefore, out of many engaging possibilities, the most probable is privacy, coupled with the murder of all on board and the scuttling of the ship —a theory which comes perilously close to his own story. If, then, we imagine Trevor, together with 'Beddoes' and Hudson, as the surviving criminals of such an enterprise, we may assume that the two friends marooned Hudson, or 'double-crossed' him in some way, and appropriated his share of the loot. The information, after so many years, that he was alive and out for revenge, would be ample reason for Trevor to have 'gone about in fear of some personal attack.' "

43 *the Terai.* A swampy lowland belt in India north of the Ganges River at the foot of the Himalayan Mountains.

has ever leaked out as to her true fate. After an excellent voyage the *Hotspur* landed us at Sydney, where Evans and I changed our names and made our way to the diggings, where among the crowds who were gathered from all nations, we had no difficulty in losing our former identities.

" The rest I need not relate. We prospered, we travelled, we came back as rich colonials to England, and **40** we bought country estates. For more than twenty years we have led peaceful and useful lives, and we hoped that our past was for ever buried. Imagine, then, my feelings when in the seaman who came to us I recognized instantly the man who had been picked off the wreck ! He had tracked us down somehow, and had set himself to live upon our fears. You will understand now how it was that I strove to keep peace with him, and you will in some measure sympathize with me in the fears which fill me, now that he has gone from me to his other victim with threats upon his tongue.

" Underneath is written, in a hand so shaky as to be hardly legible, ' Beddoes writes in cipher to say that H. **41** has told all. Sweet Lord, have mercy on our souls ! '

42 " That was the narrative which I read that night to young Trevor, and I think, Watson, that under the circumstances it was a dramatic one. The good fellow was **43** heartbroken at it, and went out to the Terai tea planting, where I hear that he is doing well. As to the sailor and Beddoes, neither of them was ever heard of again after that day on which the letter of warning was written. They both disappeared utterly and completely. No complaint had been lodged with the police, so that Beddoes had mistaken a threat for a deed. Hudson had been seen lurking about, and it was believed by the police that he had done away with Beddoes, and had fled. For myself, I believe that the truth was exactly the opposite. I think it is most probable that Beddoes, pushed to desperation, and believing himself to have been already betrayed, had revenged himself upon Hudson, and had fled from the country with as much money as he could lay his hands on. Those are the facts of the case, Doctor, and if they are of any use to your collection, I am sure that they are very heartily at your service."

14

THE MUSGRAVE RITUAL

[Thursday, October 2, 1879]

AN anomaly which often struck me in the character of my friend Sherlock Holmes was that, although in his methods of thought he was the neatest and most methodical of mankind, and although also he affected a certain quiet primness of dress, he was none the less in his personal habits one of the most untidy men that ever drove a fellow-lodger to distraction. Not that I am in the least conventional in that respect myself. The rough-and-tumble work in Afghanistan, coming on the top of a natural Bohemianism of disposition, has made me rather more lax than befits a medical man. But with me there is a limit, and when I find a man who keeps his cigars in the coal-scuttle, his tobacco in the toe-end of a Persian slipper, and his unanswered correspondence transfixed by a jack-knife into the very centre of his wooden mantelpiece, then I begin to give myself virtuous airs. I have always held, too, that pistol practice should distinctly be an open-air pastime ; and when Holmes in one of his queer humours would sit in an arm-chair, with his hair-trigger and a **1** hundred Boxer cartridges, and proceed to adorn the **2** opposite wall with a patriotic V.R. done in bullet-pocks, **3** I felt strongly that neither the atmosphere nor the appearance of our room was improved by it. **4**

"... WITH HIS HAIR-TRIGGER ..."

"The 'hair-trigger' pistol," Mr. Robert Keith Leavitt wrote in "Annie Oakley in Baker Street," "is an inherently dangerous weapon, prohibited in match shooting, impractical for sport and impractical in the extreme for detecting operations. Almost certainly this one was a single-shot 'salon' pistol of Continental make. [Captain Hugh B. C.] Pollard, the English authority [in his *The Book of the Pistol*, New York: Robert McBride & Co., 1917, from which the illustration above is taken] calls these 'wonderfully complicated . . . [but] so delicate . . . as to [be] practically worthless for ordinary use. . . . For trick work, like shooting the pips off the ace of clubs, they are invaluable.' No shooting with this weapon could conceivably improve practical proficiency in the use of the standard handgun."

1 *would sit in an arm-chair.* ". . . a position," Mr. Robert Keith Leavitt wrote in "Annie Oakley in Baker Street," "from which one may rarely or never expect to shoot with deadly intent. [Holmes] undertook a job of Spencerian nicety which almost certainly necessitated doubling his knees, resting his pistol hand on the right knee and supporting that hand by grasping its wrist with the left hand, the left forearm resting on the left knee. This position would be necessary for precision in explosive calligraphy but useful for little else." Mr. Leavitt's thesis, as we shall have several occasions to note, is that Holmes, a good shot with a rifle, was a poor shot at best with a handgun, and relied much more on Watson's marksmanship with such a weapon than he did on his own.

2 *Boxer cartridges.* ". . . the name Boxer," Leavitt wrote, "was used in England as a generic name for *any center-fire* cartridge—a form of ammunition perfected by Colonel Boxer, R.A., in 1867."

3 *a patriotic V.R.* For Victoria Regina, as previously noted. The late Christopher Morley held that Holmes shot the V.R. into the wall in 1887 to celebrate the Queen's Golden Jubilee on June 21st of that year ("Dr. Watson's Secret"), but other commentators are not agreed that Watson was sharing rooms with Holmes at that time.

4 *was improved by it.* Mr. Leavitt has written that of all Watson's understatements, this is the classic: ". . . center-fire cartridges cannot be made in small calibres or very low power. And in the nineteenth century the smallest center-fire—or Boxer—cartridge was cal. .310, slightly smaller than the modern .32, which packs 100 foot-pounds of muzzle energy. . . . Long before Holmes had finished, the room—*and the entire house*—would have been filled with gritty, white plaster-dust, and the end result after all hundred cartridges had been expended, would have been a vast area chipped away in a shallow concave and glowering out redly over a room littered ankle-deep in chunks of plaster and great ugly shards of what had once been good English brick." On the other hand, the authors of the *Catalogue of the Sherlock Holmes*

Exhibition held at Abbey House in 1951 felt that Dr. Watson applied the term "Boxer" loosely, and that the ammunition used by Holmes consisted of "rimfire" cartridges which would make little noise and accomplish little damage. Today the only survivor of the rimfire system is the .22 calibre cartridge.

5 *somewhere in these incoherent memoirs.* In *A Study in Scarlet.*

6 *his commonplace book.* Armine D. Mackenzie has suggested ("The Case of the Illustrious Predecessor") that Holmes "was perhaps the first special librarian of which there is record." It seems clear from the Canon that Holmes kept *three* permanent files. First in importance was his casebook, or diary, containing only the records of his own cases. Independent of these were the commonplace books and the index of biographies. Into the commonplace books Holmes pasted press cuttings about any incidents arresting his attention, including items from the agony column ("Bleat, unmitigated bleat!" he once called them, but they proved very useful to him in "The Adventure of the Red Circle.") Holmes' ceaseless gathering and filing of new cuttings would make the commonplace books awkward if not impossible to keep in alphabetical order, and this necessitated the index of biographies, an alphabetical cross-reference showing where to find items in the commonplace volumes. "Consequently," the late H. W. Bell wrote in *Sherlock Holmes and Dr. Watson: The Chronology of Their Adventures,* "when 'Morgan the poisoner, and Merridew of abominable memory' are quoted from the index ["The Adventure of the Empty House"], and when the long list of cases under the letter V ["The Adventure of the Sussex Vamprie"] are read out . . . , we cannot be sure if they refer to incidents in Holmes' own practice or not."

7 *Vamberry, the wine merchant.* A pastiche stemming from this reference of Holmes, Mr. A. Lloyd-Taylor's "The Wine Merchant," appeared in the *Sherlock Holmes Journal* in two parts—issues of Winter, 1959, and Spring, 1960.

8 *the singular affair of the aluminium crutch.* Or *crotch?* Why should a metal so rare and costly in those days have been used in making such a simple device as a crutch when wood would have done as well? It occurred to Mr. Rolfe Boswell that some other definition of the noun *crutch* might offer a more logical explanation. A dictionary published in England calls a crutch "a support . . . fork, crotch." And Mr. Boswell noted that "a 'support' worn at the 'crotch' sometimes *is* made of aluminium." A pastiche stemming from this reference of Holmes', "The Affair of the Aluminium Crutch," by H. Bedford-Jones, appeared originally in the *Palm Springs News,* February-March, 1936, and was reprinted in the *Baker Street Journal,* Vol. I, No. 1, Old Series, January, 1946.

Our chambers were always full of chemicals and of criminal relics, which had a way of wandering into unlikely positions, and of turning up in the butter-dish, or in even less desirable places. But his papers were my great crux. He had a horror of destroying documents, especially those which were connected with his past cases, and yet it was only once in every year or two that he would muster energy to docket and arrange them, for as I **5** have mentioned somewhere in these incoherent memoirs, the outbursts of passionate energy when he performed the remarkable feats with which his name is associated were followed by reactions of lethargy, during which he would lie about with his violin and his books, hardly moving, save from the sofa to the table. Thus month after month his papers accumulated, until every corner of the room was stacked with bundles of manuscript which were on no account to be burned, and which could not be put away save by their owner.

One winter's night, as we sat together by the fire, I ventured to suggest to him that as he had finished pasting **6** extracts into his commonplace book he might employ the next two hours in making our room a little more habitable. He could not deny the justice of my request, so with a rather rueful face he went off to his bedroom, from which he returned presently pulling a large tin box behind him. This he placed in the middle of the floor, and squatting down upon a stool in front of it he threw back the lid. I could see that it was already a third full of bundles of paper tied up with red tape into separate packages.

" There are cases enough here, Watson," said he, looking at me with mischievous eyes. " I think that if you knew all that I had in this box you would ask me to pull some out instead of putting others in."

" These are the records of your early work, then ? " I asked. " I have often wished that I had notes of those cases."

" Yes, my boy ; these were all done prematurely, before my biographer had come to glorify me." He lifted bundle after bundle in a tender, caressing sort of way. " They are not all successes, Watson," said he, " but there are some pretty little problems among them. Here's the record of the Tarleton murders, and the case of Vamberry, **7** the wine merchant, and the adventure of the old Russian **8** woman, and the singular affair of the aluminium crutch, as well as a full account of Ricoletti of the club foot and **9** his abominable wife. And here—ah, now ! this really is **10** something a little *recherché*."

He dived his arm down to the bottom of the chest, and brought up a small wooden box, with a sliding lid, such as children's toys are kept in. From within he produced a crumpled piece of paper, an old-fashioned brass key, a peg of wood with a ball of string attached to it, and three rusty old discs of metal.

" Well, my boy, what do you make of this lot ? " he asked, smiling at my expression.

" It is a curious collection."

" Very curious, and the story that hangs round it will strike you as being more curious still."

" These relics have a history, then ? "

"IT IS A CURIOUS COLLECTION."

Illustration by Sidney Paget for the *Strand Magazine*, May, 1893.

" So much so that they *are* history."

" What do you mean by that ? "

Sherlock Holmes picked them up one by one, and laid them along the edge of the table. Then he re-seated himself in his chair, and looked them over with a gleam of satisfaction in his eyes.

" These," said he, " are all that I have left to remind me of the episode of the Musgrave Ritual."

I had heard him mention the case more than once, though I had never been able to gather the details.

" I should be so glad," said I, " if you would give me an account of it."

" And leave the litter as it is ? " he cried, mischievously. " Your tidiness won't bear much strain, after all, Watson. But I should be glad that you should add this case to your annals, for there are points in it which make it quite unique in the criminal records of this or, I believe, of any other country. A collection of my trifling achievements would certainly be incomplete which contained no account of this very singular business.

" You may remember how the affair of the *Gloria Scott*, and my conversation with the unhappy man whose fate I told you of, first turned my attention in the direction of the profession which has become my life's work. You see me now when my name has become known far and wide, and when I am generally recognized both by the public and by the official force as being a final court of appeal in doubtful cases. Even when you knew me first, at the time of the affair which you have commemorated in ' A Study in Scarlet,' I had already established a **11** considerable, though not a very lucrative, connection. You can hardly realize, then, how difficult I found it at first, and how long I had to wait before I succeeded in **12** making any headway.

" When I first came up to London I had rooms in Montague Street, just round the corner from the British **13** Museum, and there I waited, filling in my too abundant **14** leisure time by studying all those branches of science

9 *Ricoletti of the club foot and his abominable wife.* "The truth may be—in part, at any rate—that Holmes' acid humor was responsible for many of the tantalizing references to cases still unrecorded by his Boswell," Mr. Vincent Starrett wrote in *The Private Life of Sherlock Holmes.* "His intentional mystification of that humble collaborator is frequently manifest in Watson's pages; what more likely than that the detective, in quizzical temper, whispered hints of extraordinary problems that actually had never come before him?"

10 *recherché.*" French: sought out with care; choice, hence of rare quality, elegance, or attractiveness, peculiar and refined in kind; also farfetched. When Holmes uses French words and phrases, as he so often does, we must remember that his grandmother was French.

11 *the affair which you have commemorated in 'A Study in Scarlet.'* Holmes has called Watson his "biographer"; and he has spoken of Watson's "annals" and "A collection of my trifling achievements"; now he says that Watson has "commemorated" the affair of *A Study in Scarlet.* It would seem that the "winter's night" on which Holmes told Watson the story of "The Musgrave Ritual" must therefore have been after December, 1887, when *A Study in Scarlet* was published in *Beeton's Christmas Annual.* This would seem to confirm our suggestion that the winter was that of 1887–1888 (see "The *Gloria Scott*," Note 1), although the winter of 1888–1889 is a distinct possibility. Mr. Bell, on the other hand, held that "Holmes had read [*A Study in Scarlet*] in manuscript."

12 *how long I had to wait.* Holmes, as we have seen, began his career as a consulting detective late in the year 1877. Most commentators and chronologists (Bell, Blakeney, Brend, Elie, Folsom, Hill, Harrison, Petersen, Roberts, Sayers, and Smith among them) believe that he waited a year for the adventure of "The Musgrave Ritual"; three (Baring-Gould, Pattrick, and Zeisler) believe that he waited two years; one (Christ) holds that he waited two and a half years, which (as the late Gavin Brend wrote in *My Dear Holmes*) may well be taken "as the extreme limit of [Holmes'] patience." We suggest that the adventure of "The Musgrave Ritual" took place on *Thursday, October 2, 1879.*

Holmes must have had some income upon which to live during this trying period, and Mr. Frederick Bryan-Brown has suggested (in "Sherlockian Schools and Schoolmasters") that Holmes perhaps in his Montague Street (see below) days may have augmented whatever family income he may have had by teaching: "The public schools were beginning to take Science masters as a novelty and I suggest that Holmes went round the corner to Gower Street where, free thinker that he was, he gained employment at University College School; here later (1890/91) went as a pupil another great medico-legal expert, Sir Bernard Spilsbury."

13 *Montague Street.* "Bedford House, a family seat of the Russell family, was demolished in 1800 and Montague Street was formed on the gardens of the mansion between 1803 and 1805," Mr. William H. Gill wrote in his essay on "Some Notable Sherlockian Buildings." "Holmes seems to have been attracted to the quiet and simple architecture of the late Georgian period for both [the rooms in Montague Street and 221B Baker Street] were in houses of this kind. Montague Street was not quite as fashionable as Baker Street, but the logical and unadorned houses must have appealed to Holmes' austere mind."

It is interesting to note here that Dr. Conan Doyle, when *he* first came up to London, had lodgings at 23 Montague *Place*, close to Baker Street, with a consulting room at 2 Devonshire Place. (Miss Violet Hunter, of "The Adventure of the Copper Beeches," also lived in Montague *Place*.)

"It is reasonable to suppose that, for a single room, with service—which included bringing up the hot-water and coals—but without meals, Sherlock Holmes paid between 10 s. [$2.50] and 15 s. [$3.75] a week," Mr. Michael Harrison wrote (*In the Footsteps of Sherlock Holmes*).

14 *the British Museum.* The British Museum, Augustus J. C. Hare wrote in his *Walks in London*, Vol. II, "was built on the site of Montague House, 1823–1847, from designs by Sir Robert Smirke, continued under his brother Sydney. Otherwise handsome, it is dwarfed and spoilt by having no suitable base. Its collections originated in the purchase of those of Sir Hans Sloane [of whom we shall hear in "The Adventure of the Three Garridebs"] in 1753. The most important gifts have been those of the Royal Library by George II, and of George III's library by George IV; the most important purchases those of Sir William Hamilton's collections, the Townley, Phigalian, and Elgin Marbles, Dr. Burney's MSS, and the Landsdowne and Arundel MSS."

These collections would have been invaluable to Holmes in preparing the monographs which many Sherlockian scholars believe that he wrote at this time:

"Those long hours in the rooms at Montague Street would have been admirable for literary enterprise, and it seems highly likely that many of them were thus employed" (Vincent Starrett: *The Private Life of Sherlock Holmes*).

"It cannot fail to be the earnest conviction of anyone who ponders deeply the problems presented by Holmes the author that not only were the technical writings the direct outgrowth of the special and out-of-the-ordinary studies which he undertook in preparation for his life's work while still at college, and which he continued after he came up to London, but that the composition of the major ones . . . was a *fait accompli* when the Baker Street menage became a reality" (Walter Klinefelter: "The Writings of Mr. Sherlock Holmes").

15 which might make me more efficient. Now and again cases came in my way, principally through the introduction of old fellow-students, for during my last years at the university there was a good deal of talk there about myself and my methods. The third of these cases was that of the Musgrave Ritual, and it is to the interest which was aroused by that singular chain of events, and the large issues which proved to be at stake, that I trace my first stride towards the position which I now hold.

" Reginald Musgrave had been in the same college as myself, and I had some slight acquaintance with him. He was not generally popular among the undergraduates, though it always seemed to me that what was set down as pride was really an attempt to cover extreme natural diffidence. In appearance he was a man of an exceedingly aristocratic type, thin, high-nosed, and large-eyed, with languid and yet courtly manners. He was indeed a scion of one of the very oldest families in the kingdom, though **16** his branch was a cadet one which had separated from the Northern Musgraves some time in the sixteenth century, **17** and had established itself in Western Sussex, where the manor house of Hurlstone is perhaps the oldest inhabited building in the county. Something of his birthplace seemed to cling to the man, and I never looked at his pale, keen face, or the poise of his head, without associating him with grey archways and mullioned windows and all the venerable wreckage of a feudal keep. Now and again we drifted into talk, and I can remember that more than once he expressed a keen interest in my methods of observation and inference.

" For four years I had seen nothing of him, until one morning he walked into my room in Montague Street. He had changed little, was dressed like a young man of fashion—he was always a bit of a dandy—and preserved the same quiet, suave manner which had formerly distinguished him.

" ' How has all gone with you, Musgrave ? ' I asked, after we had cordially shaken hands.

" ' You probably heard of my poor father's death,' said he. ' He was carried off about two years ago. Since then I have, of course, had the Hurlstone estates to manage, and as I am member for my district as well, my life has been a busy one ; but I understand, Holmes, that you are turning to practical ends those powers with which you used to amaze us.'

" ' Yes,' said I, ' I have taken to living by my wits.'

" ' I am delighted to hear it, for your advice at present would be exceedingly valuable to me. We have had some very strange doings at Hurlstone, and the police have been able to throw no light upon the matter. It is really the most extraordinary and inexplicable business.'

" You can imagine with what eagerness I listened to him, Watson, for the very chance for which I had been panting during all those months of inaction seemed to have come within my reach. In my inmost heart I believed that I could succeed where others failed, and now I had the opportunity to test myself.

" ' Pray let me have the details,' I cried.

" Reginald Musgrave sat down opposite to me, and lit the cigarette which I had pushed towards him.

"... I HAD ROOMS IN MONTAGUE STREET ..."

In which house did Sherlock Holmes lodge during his early days in London? "For years," Mr. James Edward Holroyd wrote, "I lived within five minutes' walk of [Montague Street]. In it there is a very pleasant private hotel called The Whitehall. I have always supposed that Sherlock chose this address for his first quarters since it would remind him of Brother Mycroft." Reliable local authority, however, states that Holmes' rooms were probably on the top floor having the fifth and sixth or ninth and tenth windows in the London County Council photograph shown above (from *Sherlock Holmes: A Biography*, by William S. Baring-Gould).

15 *all those branches of science which might make me more efficient.* Both Mrs. Winifred M. Christie ("Sherlock Holmes and Graphology") and Mr. Martin J. Swanson ("Graphologists in the Canon") have stated their conviction that graphology was one of those branches of science which Holmes studied at this time. Graphology, the study of hand-writing as a medium expressive of the writer's personality and character, was of more interest to the French than to the English in the nineteenth century, and one of its greatest exponents was Crépieux-Jamin, whose *magnum opus* was *L'Écriture et la Caractère*, published in 1888. By far the most concentrated graphological analysis in the Saga appears in "The Reigate Squires," which took place in 1887, a year *before* Crépieux-Jamin published *L'Écriture;* Holmes was a pioneer always.

16 *a cadet one.* A younger branch of the Musgrave family.

17 *Western Sussex.* Sussex, a maritime county in the South of England, is divided into Sussex East and Sussex West for administrative purposes. It is almost entirely an agricultural and pastoral region. Holmes adventured often in Sussex (*The Valley of Fear*, "The Adventure of Black Peter," "The Adventure of the Sussex Vampire") and chose its South Downs for his bee farm when the time came for retirement ("The Adventure of the Lion's Mane").

THE READING ROOM OF THE BRITISH MUSEUM

Where Holmes in 1877 studied the literature of crime and met Karl Marx (according to your editor's biography, *Sherlock Holmes of Baker Street*).

"... HE WAS A MAN OF AN EXCEEDINGLY ARISTOCRATIC TYPE, THIN, HIGH-NOSED, AND LARGE-EYED, WITH LANGUID AND YET COURTLY MANNERS."

Portrait of Reginald Musgrave by Sidney Paget for the *Strand Magazine*, May, 1893.

In fact, this is the manor house of *West Hoathly*, Sussex. The photograph, by Will F. Taylor of Reigate, is from *Sussex*, by Esther Meynell, London: Robert Hale, Limited, 1947.

"'... BEGAN TO STUDY IT WITH MINUTE ATTENTION.'"

Illustration by William H. Hyde for *Harper's Weekly*, May 13, 1893.

18 *I preserve*. To keep up and reserve for personal or special use; as, to preserve game or fish by raising and protecting it.

19 *a Don Juan*. Legendary hero of many literary works, supposedly based on the life of Don Juan Tehorio of Seville. Don Juan seduces a girl, then kills her father. He invites a statue of the father to a feast; it comes, seizes the libertine, and drags him to hell. Don Juan is the subject of Mozart's opera *Don Giovanni*, a ballet by Gluck, a poem by Byron; also used by Tellez (Tirso de Malina), T. Corneille, Goldini, Molière, Balzac, Robert Browning, and George Bernard Shaw.

"'You must know,' said he, 'that though I am a bachelor I have to keep up a considerable staff of servants at Hurlstone, for it is a rambling old place, and takes a **18** good deal of looking after. I preserve, too, and in the pheasant months I usually have a house-party, so that it would not do to be short-handed. Altogether there are eight maids, the cook, the butler, two footmen, and a boy. The garden and the stables, of course, have a separate staff.

"'Of these servants the one who had been longest in our service was Brunton, the butler. He was a young schoolmaster out of place when he was first taken up by my father, but he was a man of great energy and character, and he soon became quite invaluable in the household. He was a well-grown, handsome man, with a splendid forehead, and though he has been with us for twenty years he cannot be more than forty now. With his personal advantages and his extraordinary gifts, for he can speak several languages and play nearly every musical instrument, it is wonderful that he should have been satisfied so long in such a position, but I suppose that he was comfortable and lacked energy to make any change. The butler of Hurlstone is always a thing that is remembered by all who visit us.

"'But this paragon has one fault. He is a bit of a Don **19** Juan, and you can imagine that for a man like him it is not a very difficult part to play in a quiet country district.

"'When he was married it was all right, but since he has been a widower we have had no end of trouble with him. A few months ago we were in hopes that he was about to settle down again, for he became engaged to Rachel Howells, our second housemaid, but he has thrown her over since then and taken up with Janet Tregellis, the daughter of the head gamekeeper. Rachel, who is a very good girl, but of an excitable Welsh temperament, had a sharp touch of brain fever, and goes about the house now —or did until yesterday—like a black-eyed shadow of her former self. That was our first drama at Hurlstone, but a second one came to drive it from our minds, and it was prefaced by the disgrace and dismissal of butler Brunton.

" ' This is how it came about. I have said that the man was intelligent, and this very intelligence has caused his ruin, for it seems to have led to an insatiable curiosity about things which did not in the least concern him. I had no idea of the lengths to which this would carry him until the merest accident opened my eyes to it.

" ' I have said that the house is a rambling one. One night last week—on Thursday night, to be more exact—I found that I could not sleep, having foolishly taken a cup of strong *café noir* after my dinner. After struggling **20** against it until two in the morning I felt that it was quite hopeless, so I rose and lit the candle with the intention of continuing a novel which I was reading. The book, however, had been left in the billiard-room, so I pulled on my dressing-gown and started off to get it.

" ' In order to reach the billiard-room I had to descend a flight of stairs, and then to cross the head of the passage which led to the library and the gun-room. You can imagine my surprise when as I looked down this corridor I saw a glimmer of light coming from the open door of the library. I had myself extinguished the lamp and closed the door before coming to bed. Naturally, my first thought was of burglars. The corridors at Hurlstone have their walls largely decorated with trophies of old weapons. From one of these I picked a battle-axe, and then, leaving my candle behind me, I crept on tiptoe down the passage and peeped in at the open door.

" ' Brunton, the butler was in the library. He was sitting, fully dressed, in an easy chair, with a slip of paper, which looked like a map, upon his knee, and his forehead sunk forward upon his hand in deep thought. I stood, dumb with astonishment, watching him from the darkness. A small taper on the edge of the table shed a feeble light, which sufficed to show me that he was fully dressed. Suddenly, as I looked, he rose from his chair, and walking over to a bureau at the side, he unlocked it and drew out one of the drawers. From this he took a paper, and, returning to his seat, he flattened it out beside the taper on the edge of the table, and began to study it with minute attention. My indignation at this calm examination of our family documents overcame me so far that I took a step forward, and Brunton looking up saw me standing in the doorway. He sprang to his feet, his face turned livid with fear, and he thrust into his breast the chart-like paper which he had been originally studying.

" ' " So ! " said I, " this is how you repay the trust which we have reposed in you ! You will leave my service to-morrow."

" ' He bowed with the look of a man who is utterly crushed, and slunk past me without a word. The taper was still on the table, and by its light I glanced to see what the paper was which Brunton had taken from the

20 café noir. Black coffee—coffee without milk or cream.

" 'HE SPRANG TO HIS FEET, HIS FACE TURNED LIVID WITH FEAR . . .' "

Illustration by Sidney Paget for the *Strand Magazine*, May, 1893.

" '. . . OUR OWN BLAZONINGS AND CHARGES . . .' "

"The Musgraves," Dr. Julian Wolff wrote in his *Practical Handbook of Sherlockian Heraldry*, "are an ancient and loyal family. . . . Many prominent supporters of the Royalist side in the Civil Wars bore this honored name. [The arms are:] Azure, six annulets or, three, two and one."

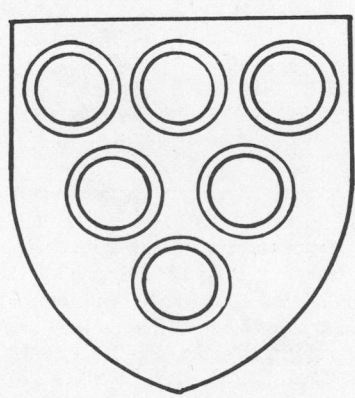

bureau. To my surprise it was nothing of any importance at all, but simply a copy of the questions and answers in the singular old observance called the Musgrave Ritual. It is a sort of ceremony peculiar to our family, which each Musgrave for centuries past has gone through upon his coming of age—a thing of private interest, and perhaps of some little importance to the archæologist, like our own blazonings and charges, but of no practical use whatever.

" ' " We had better come back to the paper afterwards," said I.

" ' " If you think it really necessary," he answered, with some hesitation.

" ' To continue my statement, however, I re-locked the bureau, using the key which Brunton had left, and I had turned to go, when I was surprised to find that the butler had returned and was standing before me.

" ' " Mr. Musgrave, sir," he cried, in a voice which was hoarse with emotion, " I can't bear disgrace, sir. I've always been proud above my station in life, and disgrace would kill me. My blood will be on your head, sir—it will, indeed—if you drive me to despair. If you cannot keep me after what has passed, then for God's sake let me give you notice and leave in a month, as if of my own free will. I could stand that, Mr. Musgrave, but not to be cast out before all the folk that I know so well."

" ' " You don't deserve much consideration, Brunton," I answered. " Your conduct has been most infamous. However, as you have been a long time in the family, I have no wish to bring public disgrace upon you. A month, however, is too long. Take yourself away in a week, and give what reason you like for going."

" ' " Only a week, sir ? " he cried in a despairing voice. " A fortnight—say at least a fortnight."

" ' " A week," I repeated, " and you may consider yourself to have been very leniently dealt with."

" ' He crept away, his face sunk upon his breast, like a broken man, while I put out the light and returned to my room.

" ' For two days after this Brunton was most assiduous in his attention to his duties. I made no allusion to what had passed, and waited with some curiosity to see how he would cover his disgrace. On the third morning, however, he did not appear, as was his custom, after breakfast to receive my instructions for the day. As I left the dining-room I happened to meet Rachel Howells, the maid. I have told you that she had only recently recovered from an illness, and was looking so wretchedly pale and wan that I remonstrated with her for being at work.

" ' " You should be in bed," I said. " Come back to your duties when you are stronger."

" ' She looked at me with so strange an expression that I began to suspect that her brain was affected.

" ' " I am strong enough, Mr. Musgrave," said she.

" ' " We will see what the doctor says," I answered. " You must stop work now, and when you go downstairs just say that I wish to see Brunton."

" ' " The butler is gone," said she.

" ' " Gone ! Gone where ? "

" ' " He is gone.   No one has seen him.   He is not in his room.   Oh, yes, he is gone—he is gone ! "   She fell back against the wall with shriek after shriek of laughter, while I, horrified at this sudden hysterical attack, rushed to the bell to summon help.   The girl was taken to her room, still screaming and sobbing, while I made inquiries about Brunton.   There was no doubt about it that he had disappeared.   His bed had not been slept in ; he had been seen by no one since he had retired to his room the night before ; and yet it was difficult to see how he could have left the house, as both windows and doors were found to be fastened in the morning.   His clothes, his watch, and even his money were in his room—but the black suit which he usually wore was missing.   His slippers, too, were gone, but his boots were left behind.   Where, then, could butler Brunton have gone in the night, and what could have become of him now ?

" ' Of course we searched the house from cellar to garret, but there was no trace of him.   It is as I have said a labyrinth of an old house, especially the original wing, which is now practically uninhabited, but we ransacked every room and attic without discovering the least sign of the missing man.   It was incredible to me that he could have gone away leaving all his property behind him, and yet where could he be ?   I called in the local police, but without success.   Rain had fallen on the night before, and we examined the lawn and the paths all round the house, but in vain.   Matters were in this state when a new development quite drew our attention away from the original mystery.

" ' For two days Rachel Howells had been so ill, sometimes delirious, sometimes hysterical, that a nurse had been employed to sit up with her at night.   On the third night after Brunton's disappearance, the nurse, finding her patient sleeping nicely, had dropped into a nap in the arm-chair, when she woke in the early morning to find the bed empty, the window open, and no signs of the invalid.   I was instantly aroused, and with the two footmen started off at once in search of the missing girl. It was not difficult to tell the direction which she had taken, for, starting from under her window, we could follow her footmarks easily across the lawn to the edge of the mere, where they vanished, close to the gravel path which leads out of the grounds.   The lake there is 8 feet deep, and you can imagine our feelings when we saw that the trail of the poor demented girl came to an end at the edge of it.

" ' Of course, we had the drags at once, and set to work to recover the remains ; but no trace of the body could we find.   On the other hand, we brought to the surface an object of a most unexpected kind.   It was a linen bag, which contained within it a mass of old rusted and discoloured metal and several dull-coloured pieces of pebble or glass.   This strange find was all that we could get from the mere, and although we made every possible search and inquiry yesterday, we know nothing of the fate either of Rachel Howells or Richard Brunton.   The county police are at their wits' end, and I have come up to you as a last resource.'

" You can imagine, Watson, with what eagerness I

21

21 *as a last resource.*' "When Musgrave comes to consult Holmes, he tells him that 'last week—on Thursday night' he discovered Brunton, the butler, in the library examining family documents. He dismissed the man from his service with a week's notice. 'For two days after this' [Friday and Saturday] he was 'most assiduous in his attention to his duties.' 'On the third morning [Sunday] he did not appear.' . . . Holmes, as appears from his narrative, was consulted on the following Thursday."
—H. W. Bell, *Sherlock Holmes and Dr. Watson: The Chronology of Their Adventures.*

22 " '*The sixth from the first.*' " It must be pointed out here that when "The Musgrave Ritual" was first published in the *Strand Magazine*, the Ritual consisted of *seven* couplets only—"What was the month?" "The sixth from the first"—was omitted. But when the story was included in the Newnes volume of *The Memoirs* in 1894, the eighth couplet was added. Somehow this suppressed time-clue—essential to anyone attempting to discover the whereabouts of the treasure by following the directions in the Ritual—had slipped back in, and all subsequent English editions retained it. Not so the American editions; perhaps their editors were worried that readers might not understand the complications of the month that was "The sixth from the first."

For, as Mr. Bell wrote, ". . . the chief problem in the dating of this case is to determine the season in which it happened. In the 'Ritual' of the Musgraves itself there is a fundamental ambiguity: the month specified . . . might have been reckoned either from March 25th, the legal beginning of the year in England from the fourteenth century until 1752, or from January 1st, as was common among historians during the period of the Stuarts."

We will now turn the matter over to Dr. Zeisler, who wrote (in *Baker Street Chronology*): "If January is counted as the first month, then the sixth month from this is . . . July, and if one reckons from March 25th then the sixth month from the first is the month from September 25th to October 24th. The Ritual, as we learn later, was written in the time of Charles II by one of his staunch adherents, who would probably date things not in the manner of the historians but in the usual legal manner of the time, so that there is, perhaps, a small probability in favor of the autumn date over the summer date, but too slight to be of much use. . . . But the Ritual was not written later than 1660. In 1752 the Gregorian calendar was adopted in England, and this entailed skipping eleven days, so that we must add eleven days to the above dates. Hence the intervals under consideration are July 12th to August 11th and October 6th to November 4th."

Dr. Zeisler further pointed out that Brunton, when told by Musgrave to leave in a week, begged for "a fortnight." "Thus at the time he was caught he must have calculated that six days later, namely the Thursday of the story, would be too early to satisfy the requirements of the Ritual, so that we can be sure that the day of the story was *not later than* July 12th or October 6th, respectively; or, if we allow the required day to be later in the month we conclude that the day of the story was not later than August 11th or November 4th, according to whether it was summer or autumn. Since two weeks would have satisfied Brunton we can likewise conclude that seven days after the story would have reached or passed the required day, so that the day of the story is *not before* July 5th or September 29th. Hence the day of the story is one of the intervals July 5th to August 11th and

listened to this extraordinary sequence of events, and endeavoured to piece them together, and to devise some common thread upon which they might all hang.

"The butler was gone. The maid was gone. The maid had loved the butler, but had afterwards had cause to hate him. She was of Welsh blood, fiery and passionate. She had been terribly excited immediately after his disappearance. She had flung into the lake a bag containing some curious contents. These were all factors which had to be taken into consideration, and yet none of them got quite to the heart of the matter. What was the starting-point of this chain of events? There lay the end of this tangled line.

" ' I must see that paper, Musgrave,' said I, ' which this butler of yours thought it worth his while to consult, even at the risk of the loss of his place.'

" ' It is rather an absurd business, this Ritual of ours,' he answered, ' but it has at least the saving grace of antiquity to excuse it. I have a copy of the questions and answers here, if you care to run your eye over them.'

"He handed me the very paper which I have here, Watson, and this is the strange catechism to which each Musgrave had to submit when he came to man's estate. I will read you the questions and answers as they stand :

" ' Whose was it ?
" ' His who is gone.
" ' Who shall have it ?
" ' He who will come.
" ' What was the month ?

22   " ' The sixth from the first.
" ' Where was the sun ?
" ' Over the oak.
" ' Where was the shadow ?
" ' Under the elm.
" ' How was it stepped ?
" ' North by ten and by ten, east by five and by five, south by two and by two, west by one and by one, and so under.
" ' What shall we give for it ?
" ' All that is ours.
" ' Why should we give it ?

23   " ' For the sake of the trust.
" ' The original has no date, but is in the spelling of the middle of the seventeenth century,' remarked Musgrave. ' I am afraid, however, that it can be of little help to you in solving this mystery.'

" ' At least,' said I, ' it gives us another mystery, and one which is even more interesting than the first. It may be that the solution of the one may prove to be the solution of the other. You will excuse me, Musgrave, if I say that your butler appears to me to have been a very clever man, and to have had a clearer insight than ten generations of his masters.'

" ' I hardly follow you,' said Musgrave. ' The paper seems to me of no practical importance.'

" ' But to me it seems immensely practical, and I fancy that Brunton took the same view. He had probably seen it before that night on which you caught him.'

" ' It is very possible. We took no pains to hide it.'

" ' He simply wished, I should imagine, to refresh his memory upon that last occasion. He had, as I understand, some sort of map or chart which he was comparing with the manuscript, and which he thrust into his pocket when you appeared ? '

" ' That is true. But what could he have to do with this old family custom of ours, and what does this rigmarole mean ? '

" ' I don't think that we should have much difficulty in determining that,' said I. ' With your permission we will take the first train down to Sussex and go a little more deeply into the matter upon the spot.'

" The same afternoon saw us both at Hurlstone. Possibly you have seen pictures and read descriptions of the famous old building, so I will confine my account of it to saying that it is built in the shape of an **L**, the long arm being the more modern portion, and the shorter the ancient nucleus from which the other has developed Over the low, heavy-lintelled door, in the centre of this old part, is chiselled the date 1607, but experts are agreed that the beams and stonework are really much older than this. The enormously thick walls and tiny windows **24** of this part had in the last century driven the family into building the new wing, and the old one was used now as a storehouse and a cellar when it was used at all. A splendid park, with fine old timber, surrounded the house, and the lake, to which my client had referred, lay close to the avenuc, about two hundred yards from the building.

" I was already firmly convinced, Watson, that there were not three separate mysteries here, but one only, and that if I could read the Musgrave Ritual aright, I should hold in my hand the clue which would lead me to the truth concerning both the butler Brunton, and the maid Howells. To that, then, I turned all my energies. Why should this servant be so anxious to master this old formula ? Evidently because he saw something in it which had escaped all those generations of country squires, and from which he expected some personal advantage. What was it, then, and how had it affected his fate ?

" It was perfectly obvious to me on reading the Ritual that the measurements must refer to some spot to which the rest of the document alluded, and that if we could find that spot we should be in a fair way towards knowing what the secret was which the old Musgraves had thought it necessary to embalm in so curious a fashion. There were two guides given us to start with, an oak and an elm. As to the oak, there could be no question at all. Right in front of the house, upon the left-hand side of the drive, there stood a patriarch among oaks, one of the most magnificent trees that I have ever seen.

" ' That was there when your Ritual was drawn up ? ' said I, as we drove past it.

" ' It was there at the Norman Conquest, in all probability,' he answered. ' It has a girth of 23 feet.'

" Here was one of my fixed points secured.

" ' Have you any old elms ? ' I asked.

" ' There used to be a very old one over yonder, but it was struck by lightning ten years ago, and we cut down the stump.'

September 29th to November 4th, and is most probably one of the intervals July 5th to July 12th and September 29th to October 6th."

23 " '*For the sake of the trust.*' The late T. S. Eliot's adaption of these lines in *Murder in the Cathedral* has led some commentators to speculate that Mr. Eliot and Dr. Conan Doyle were using a common source. This was not the case, as Mr. Eliot himself declared in a letter to Mr. Nathan L. Bengis quoted in the *Times Literary Supplement*, London, September 28, 1951: "My use of the Musgrave Ritual was deliberate and wholly conscious."

24 *The enormously thick walls.* "Walls six feet thick are common on rammed-earth cottages of the period; enormously thick walls might easily be ten feet or more through," Poul and Karen Anderson wrote in "The Curious Behavior of the Ritual in the Daytime."

" 'IT HAS A GIRTH OF 23 FEET.' "

Illustration by Sidney Paget for the *Strand Magazine*, May, 1893.

25 *It was 64 feet.*' "The Ritual had been prepared between the two Charleses—in the 1650s," the late Professor Jay Finley Christ wrote in "Musgrave Mathematics." "The oak was an enormous one which had stood at the time of the Conquest; and the elm was a sizeable tree in Musgrave's youth. It puts more than moderate strain upon my credulity, to consider that neither of these two trees grew a foot or so in height during two hundred years or more. Every foot of growth for either of them would have thrown the reckoning out by some eighteen inches!"

To this, Dr. Zeisler replied: "Professor Christ is mistaken as to the oak, for its growth would not have affected things since its only role was to give direction. But he is certainly correct as to the elm; its growth would have thrown things off very definitely. . . . The only possible explanation is that . . . the elm in this case had reached its maximum height before 1650, and the author of the Ritual had had an opportunity to learn that it was no longer growing in height."

26 *when the sun was just clear of the oak."* "What made it clear *where* the observer was to stand in order to see the sun over the oak?" Professor Christ asked in "Musgrave Mathematics." "Holmes seems to have stood just where the elm had been, but why? The compiler of the Ritual could not have stood there when the tree was in place."

27 *It was 9 feet in length.* If a rod of six feet threw a shadow of nine feet in Lat. 51° N. (for Sussex), then the sun was practically due west and 33.7° above the horizon and the time could not have been later than 4:20 P.M. But Professor Christ long ago demonstrated (*An Irregular Chronology*) that all these conditions are met with "during only about a week during the year. The week must run from just before to just after the summer solstice [June 21st]." But what does this make of the Ritual's "sixth month from the first"? And what of Holmes' remark (which must have been made not later than about 3:30 P.M.) that "It [the sun] was low in the heavens?" Dr. Zeisler, in his "elaborate analysis" of the problems engendered by this adventure concluded (*Baker Street Chronology*) that the sun *could* have been due west but "it could also have been either north or south of west . . ."

28 *almost to the wall of the house.* This, as we shall see, was the *west* wall of the "ancient nucleus."

29 *having first taken the cardinal points by my pocket compass.* "Now comes the strangest part of Holmes' exploit," Mr. A. D. Galbraith wrote in "The Real Moriarty." "The directions were taken with his pocket compass. But when the ancestral Musgrave buried the treasure, a perfect compass pointed almost true north, while when Holmes and Brunton found the hiding-place it pointed about 20° west of north. Thus the only way they could both come to the right spot would be to have com-

" ' You can see where it used to be ? '

" ' Oh, yes.'

" ' There are no other elms ? '

" ' No old ones, but plenty of beeches.'

" ' I should like to see where it grew.'

" We had driven up in a dog-cart, and my client led me away at once, without our entering the house, to the scar on the lawn where the elm had stood. It was nearly midway between the oak and the house. My investigation seemed to be progressing.

" ' I suppose it is impossible to find out how high the elm was ? ' I asked.

25 " ' I can give you it at once. It was 64 feet.'

" ' How do you come to know it ? ' I asked in surprise.

" ' When my old tutor used to give me an exercise in trigonometry it always took the shape of measuring heights. When I was a lad I worked out every tree and building on the estate.'

" This was an unexpected piece of luck. My data were coming more quickly than I could have reasonably hoped.

" ' Tell me,' I asked, ' did your butler ever ask you such a question ? '

" Reginald Musgrave looked at me in astonishment. ' Now that you call it to my mind,' he answered, ' Brunton *did* ask me about the height of the tree some months ago, in connection with some little argument with the groom.'

" This was excellent news, Watson, for it showed me that I was on the right road. I looked up at the sun. It was low in the heavens, and I calculated that in less than an hour it would lie just above the topmost branches of the old oak. One condition mentioned in the Ritual would then be fulfilled. And the shadow of the elm must mean the further end of the shadow, otherwise the trunk would have been chosen as the guide. I had then to find where the far end of the shadow would fall when the **26** sun was just clear of the oak."

" That must have been difficult, Holmes, when the elm was no longer there."

" Well, at least, I knew that if Brunton could do it, I could also. Besides, there was no real difficulty. I went with Musgrave to his study and whittled myself this peg, to which I tied this long string, with a knot at each yard. Then I took two lengths of a fishing-rod, which came to just 6 feet, and I went back with my client to where the elm had been. The sun was just grazing the top of the oak. I fastened the rod on end, marked out the direction of the shadow, and measured it. **27** It was 9 feet in length.

" Of course, the calculation was now a simple one. If a rod of 6 feet threw a shadow of 9 feet, a tree of 64 feet would throw one of 96 feet, and the line of one would of course be the line of the other. I measured out the distance, which brought me almost to the wall of the **28** house, and I thrust a peg into the spot. You can imagine my exultation, Watson, when within 2 inches of my peg I saw a conical depression in the ground. I knew that it was the mark made by Brunton in his measurements, and that I was still upon his trail.

" From this starting-point I proceeded to step, having first taken the cardinal points by my pocket compass. **29** Ten steps with each foot took me along parallel with the wall of the house, and again I marked my spot with a peg. Then I carefully paced off five to the east and two to the south. It brought me to the very threshold of the old door. Two steps to the west meant now that I was to go two paces down the stone-flagged passage, and this was the place indicated by the Ritual. ·

" Never have I felt such a cold chill of disappointment, Watson. For a moment it seemed to me that there must be some radical mistake in my calculations. The setting **30** sun shone full upon the passage floor, and I could see **31** that the old foot-worn grey stones, with which it was paved, were firmly cemented together, and had certainly not been moved for many a long year. Brunton had not been at work here. I tapped upon the floor, but it sounded the same all over, and there was no sign of any crack or crevice. But fortunately Musgrave, who had begun to appreciate the meaning of my proceedings, and who was now as excited as myself, took out his manuscript to check my calculations.

passes with the same error, which is hard to believe; and to have this error and the error in old Sir Ralph Musgrave's compass combine to compensate for the change of 20° in declination is incredible."

30 *some radical mistake in my calculations.* We may note here that the problem of "the emplacement of Hurlstone" is one that has long concerned Sherlockian scholars. Authoritative English references give the length of a pace as 30 inches (in quick time; double time is 33 inches). But was it a "pace" that Holmes used? Yes, for although he mentions the number of "steps" involved, and although the Ritual itself asks, "How was it stepped?", the fact remains that Holmes is precise in pointing out: "Then I carefully *paced* off . . ."

From the outside, it is possible to come to a threshold in the center of a wall from any one of three points of the compass. So, at first glance, there appear to be two possibilities here. First, that the old door might have been in the center of the *east* wall of the "ancient nucleus," thus:

Second, that the old door might have been in the center of the *north* wall, thus:

The apparent dilemma dissolves itself when one translates the pacings of the courses into linear distances, thus: 20 paces = 50 feet, 10 paces = 25 feet, 4 paces = 10 feet, 2 paces = 5 feet. Under the first drawing above, the width of the "ancient nucleus" could be little more than 30 feet at best. "A box sixty by thirty feet seems rather modest for 'one of the oldest families in the kingdom,'" Poul and Karen Anderson wrote in "The Curious Behavior of the Ritual in the Daytime." "When we consider one more fact, it becomes impossible. For the walls of this section are described as 'enormously thick.'"

Having eliminated the impossible, we must therefore conclude that Holmes was brought to the "very threshold" of a door in the center of the *north* wall of the older portion of the house.

The "emplacement of Hurlstone" must therefore have been this:

Or this:

The first plan clearly puts the oak too far to the west of Hurlstone—the old *or* the new portion —for the always precise Holmes to have said that it stood "right in front of the house."

We therefore suggest that the second plan represents the true emplacement—cramped as it still is, it is somewhat *less* cramped. There are, of course, other solutions, some of them involving plans in which the house must take the shape of an *inverted* L, which we do not feel is allowable. (Dr. Zeisler, indeed, was forced to conclude that the "stone-flagged passage" was *exterior* to the "ancient nucleus.") As Professor Christ justly concluded: "Certainly the place was not designed for the story . . ."

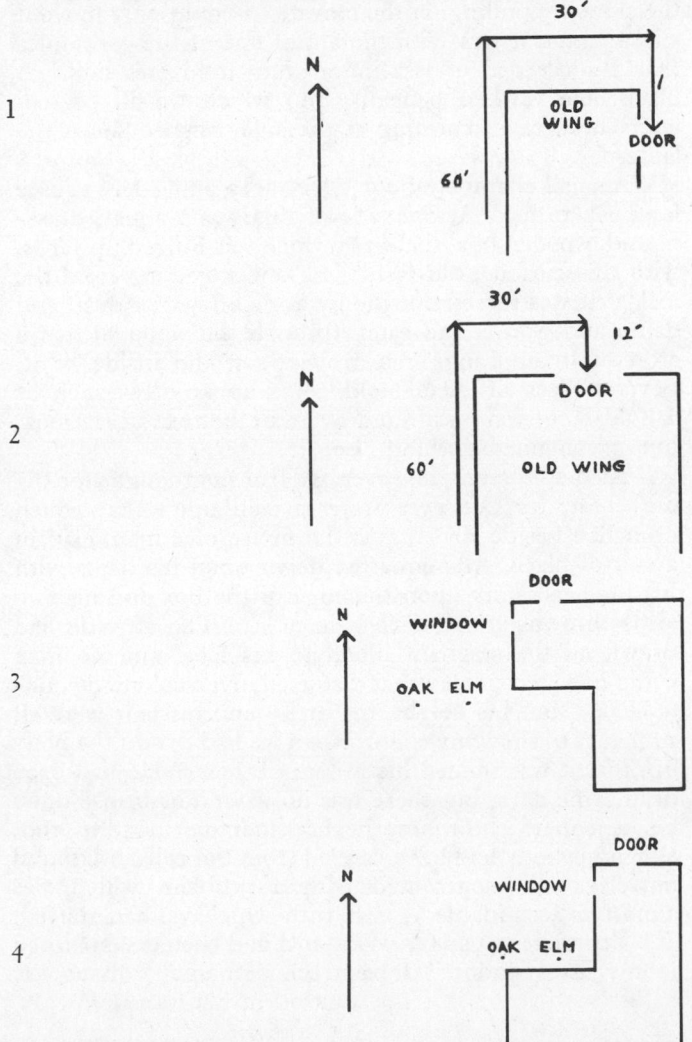

31 *The setting sun shone full upon the passage floor.* Since, as we have seen, the time must now be not later than about 4:30 P.M., Holmes' the *setting* sun must be modified to the *settling* sun, whatever the month of this adventure. But here is another indication that the sun of that day *was* shining from a direction practically due west. As Mr. Bell put it in *Sherlock Holmes and Dr. Watson: The Chronology of Their Adventures*: ". . . we are told that this old wing of the house had 'enormously thick walls and tiny windows'; therefore, unless the . . . sun had been shining straight through one such tiny window . . . in the west wall, its light could not possibly have reached the pavement. We have seen that the house faced the cardinal points; hence the sun must have been setting due west, and the season, consequently, was late September [or, in our view, early October]." And he added in a note: "In June, when the sun sets in the north-west, the light would have been lost in the deep window-embrasure, or would, at the farthest, have illuminated a small portion of the south wall of the passage."

". . . AND THIS WAS THE PLACE INDICATED BY THE
RITUAL"

Illustration by Sidney Paget for the *Strand Magazine*, May, 1893.

" ' And under,' he cried : ' you have omitted the " and under." ' "

" I had thought that it meant that we were to dig, but now, of course, I saw at once that I was wrong. ' There is a cellar under this, then ? ' I cried.

" ' Yes, and as old as the house. Down here, through this door.'

" We went down a winding stone stair, and my companion, striking a match, lit a large lantern which stood on **32** a barrel in the corner. In an instant it was obvious that we had at last come upon the true place, and that we had not been the only people to visit the spot recently.

" It had been used for the storage of wood, but the billets, which had evidently been littered over the floor, were now piled at the sides so as to leave a clear space in the middle. In this space lay a large and heavy flagstone, with a rusted iron ring in the centre, to which a thick shepherd's check muffler was attached.

" ' By Jove ! ' cried my client, ' that's Brunton's muffler. I have seen it on him, and could swear to it. What has the villain been doing here ? '

" At my suggestion a couple of the county police were summoned to be present, and I then endeavoured to raise the stone by pulling on the cravat. I could only move it slightly, and it was with the aid of one of the constables that I succeeded at last in carrying it to one side. A black hole yawned beneath, into which we all peered, while Musgrave, kneeling at the side, pushed down the lantern.

" A small chamber about 7 feet deep and 4 feet square lay open to us. At one side of this was a squat, brass-bound, wooden box, the lid of which was hinged upwards, with this curious, old-fashioned key projecting from the lock. It was furred outside by a thick layer of dust, and damp and worms had eaten through the wood so that a crop of living fungi was growing on the inside of it. Several discs of metal—old coins apparently—such as I hold here, were scattered over the bottom of the box, but it contained nothing else.

" At the moment, however, we had not thought for the old chest, for our eyes were riveted upon that which crouched beside it. It was the figure of a man, clad in a suit of black, who squatted down upon his hams with his forehead sunk upon the edge of the box and his two arms thrown out on each side of it. The attitude had drawn all the stagnant blood to his face, and no man could have recognized that distorted, liver-coloured countenance ; but his height, his dress, and his hair were all sufficient to show my client, when we had drawn the body up, that it was indeed his missing butler. He had been dead some days, but there was no wound or bruise upon his person to show how he had met his dreadful end. When his body had been carried from the cellar we found ourselves still confronted with a problem which was almost as formidable as that with which we had started.

" I confess that so far, Watson, I had been disappointed in my investigation. I had reckoned upon solving the matter when once I had found the place referred to in the Ritual ; but now I was there, and was apparently as far as ever from knowing what it was which the family had concealed with such elaborate precautions.   It is true that I had thrown a light upon the fate of Brunton, but now I had to ascertain how that fate had come upon him, and what part had been played in the matter by the woman who had disappeared.   I sat down upon a keg in the corner and thought the whole matter carefully over.

" You know my methods in such cases, Watson : I put myself in the man's place, and having first gauged his intelligence, I try to imagine how I should myself have proceeded under the same circumstances.   In this case the matter was simplified by Brunton's intelligence being quite first rate, so that it was unnecessary to make any allowance for personal equation, as the astronomers have dubbed it.   He knew that something valuable was concealed.   He had spotted the place.   He found that the stone which covered it was just too heavy for a man to move unaided.   What would he do next ?   He could not get help from outside, even if he had someone whom he could trust, without the unbarring of doors, and considerable risk of detection.   It was better, if he could, to have his helpmate inside the house.   But whom could he ask ?   This girl had been devoted to him.   A man always finds it hard to realize that he may have finally lost a woman's love, however badly he may have treated her. He would try by a few attentions to make his peace with the girl Howells, and then would engage her as his accomplice.   Together they would come at night to the cellar, and their united force would suffice to raise the stone. So far I could follow their actions as if I had actually seen them.

" But for two of them, and one a woman, it must have been heavy work, the raising of that stone.   A burly Sussex policeman and I had found it no light job.   What would they do to assist them ?   Probably what I should have done myself.   I rose and examined carefully the different billets of wood which were scattered round the floor.   Almost at once I came upon what I expected. One piece, about 3 feet in length, had a marked indentation at one end, while several were flattened at the sides as if they had been compressed by some considerable weight.   Evidently as they had dragged the stone up they had thrust the chunks of wood into the chink, until at last, when the opening was large enough to crawl through, they would hold it open by a billet placed lengthwise, which might very well become indented at the lower end, since the whole weight of the stone would press it down on to the edge of the other slab.   So far I was still on safe ground.

" And now, how was I to proceed to reconstruct this midnight drama ?   Clearly only one could get into the hole, and that one was Brunton.   The girl must have waited above.   Brunton then unlocked the box, handed up the contents, presumably—since they were not to be

32 *lit a large lantern which stood on a barrel in the corner.* But Musgrave earlier stated that the house had been thoroughly searched from cellar to garret. "If so," Mr. H. B. Williams asked in "Pleasure in Pictures," "why was this particular place missed? Musgrave knew it was there. He led Holmes to it and lit a match to light the lantern which he knew was standing on the barrel in the corner. Yet, familiar as he was with the cellar, the story would lead us to believe that it was missed in the search of the house. Incredible."

"IT WAS THE FIGURE OF A MAN . . ."

Illustration by Sidney Paget for the *Strand Magazine*, May, 1893.

found—and then—and then what happened ?

" What smouldering fire of vengeance had suddenly sprung into flame in this passionate Celtic woman's soul when she saw the man who had wronged her—wronged her perhaps far more than we suspected—in her power ? Was it a chance that the wood had slipped and that the stone had shut Brunton into what had become his sepulchre ? Had she only been guilty of silence as to his fate ? Or had some sudden blow from her hand dashed the support away and sent the slab crashing down into its place. Be that as it might, I seemed to see that woman's figure, still clutching at her treasure-trove, and flying wildly up the winding stair with her ears ringing perhaps with the muffled screams from behind her, and with the drumming of frenzied hands against the slab of stone which was choking her faithless lover's life out.

". . . STILL CLUTCHING AT HER TREASURE-TROVE . . ."

Illustration by William H. Hyde for *Harper's Weekly*, May 13, 1893.

" Here was the secret of her blanched face, her shaken nerves, her peals of hysterical laughter on the next morning. But what had been in the box ? What had she done with that ? Of course, it must have been the old metal and pebbles which my client had dragged from the mere. She had thrown them in there at the first opportunity, to remove the last trace of her crime.

" For twenty minutes I had sat motionless thinking the matter out. Musgrave still stood with a very pale face swinging his lantern and peering down into the hole.

" ' These are coins of Charles I,' said he, holding out the few which had been left in the box. ' You see we were right in fixing our date for the Ritual.'

" ' We may find something else of Charles I,' I cried, as the probable meaning of the first two questions of the Ritual broke suddenly upon me. ' Let me see the contents of the bag you fished from the mere.'

" We ascended to his study, and he laid the *débris* before me. I could understand his regarding it as of small importance when I looked at it, for the metal was almost black, and the stones lustreless and dull. I rubbed one of them on my sleeve, however, and it glowed afterwards like a spark, in the dark hollow of my hand. The metal-work was in the form of a double-ring, but it had been bent and twisted out of its original shape.

" ' You must bear in mind,' said I, ' that the Royal party made head in England even after the death of the King, and that when they at last fled they probably left many of their most precious possessions buried behind them, with the intention of returning for them in more peaceful times.'

" ' My ancestor, Sir Ralph Musgrave, was a prominent Cavalier, and the right-hand man of Charles II in his wanderings,' said my friend.

" ' Ah, indeed ! ' I answered. ' Well, now, I think that really should give us the last link that we wanted. I must congratulate you on coming into possession, though in rather a tragic manner, of a relic which is of great intrinsic value, but even of greater importance as an historical curiosity.'

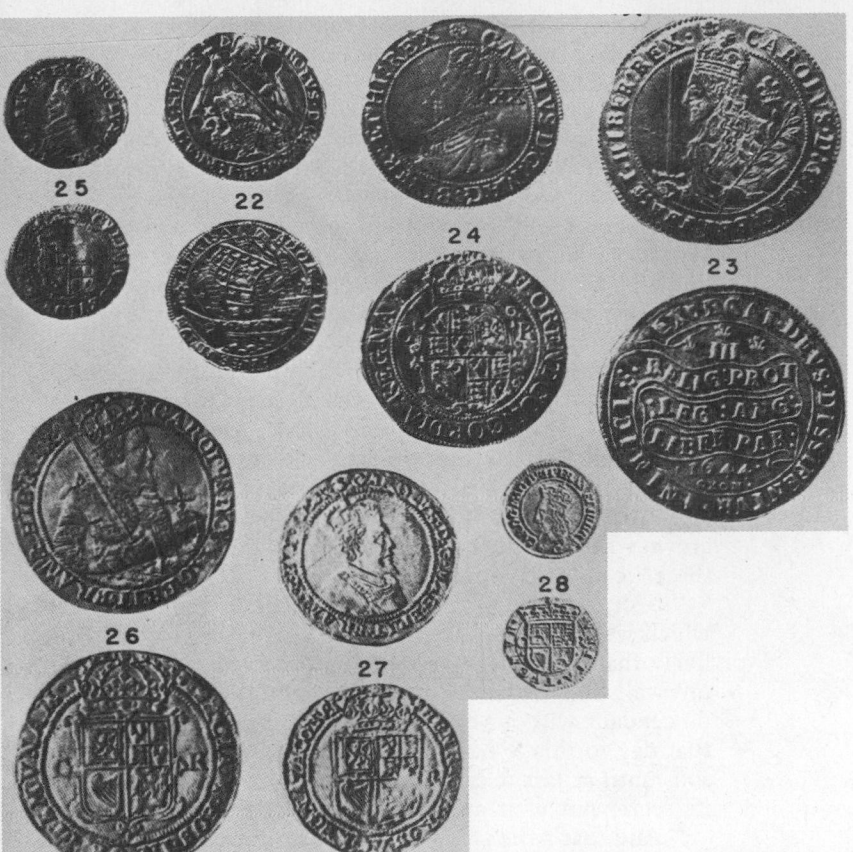

Charles I Gold of England: 22 n.d. angel, Tower mint. 23 1644 triple unite, Oxford mint. 24 n.d. unite, Truro mint. 25 n.d. crown, Tower mint. *Charles I Gold of Scotland:* 26 n.d. unit. 27 n.d. double-crown. 28 n.d. half-crown. The illustrations are from *Numismatics in the Canon*, Part II: "A Very Treasury of Coin of Divers Realms," by the late A. Carson Simpson. Mr. Simpson noted that Watson, "in describing the coins as 'rusty,' showed either a lamentable lack of precision or else a remarkable ability to forget the chemistry he had been compelled to study to get his M.D. Although laymen occasionally use the word 'rust' in its secondary sense of 'corrosion,' yet, at the time Watson was in the University of London and presumably received at least an elementary training in chemistry, usage confined it to hydrous ferric oxide. Despite the turbulent times in which Charles I lived, he had never been reduced to striking *iron* coins."

" 'THE CROWN!' "

The "battered and shapeless diadem," here shown restored, has been identified by Mr. Nathan L. Bengis ("Whose Was It? An Examination into the Crowning Lapse of Sherlockian Scholarship") as the ancient Crown of St. Edward, about which the few details that are known tally perfectly with those given in the story. "The 1649 inventory [of British regalia] described the crown of St. Edward (listed as King Alfred's Crown) as being of 'gould wyer worke, sett with slight stones.' This seems to signify a filigree frame, which could easily be bent out of shape, as was the crown found at Hurlstone. The 'gould' was probably a base metal gilded to resemble gold. . . . Such a metalwork, after defacement, would tarnish in over two centuries to the ugly 'almost black' described in the Canon. The 'slight stones' would be discolored in time, so that eventually they would lose their lustre and would have to be rubbed, as was done by Sherlock Holmes, for them to glow again. . . . It is now plain that when Sherlock Holmes spoke of the crown as having 'once encircled the brows of the royal Stuarts,' he was speaking the literal truth: the crown of St. Edward was indeed worn once, and once only, by James I and Charles I, on the occasion of their respective coronations."

33 *the moon was shining brightly in the sky.*
Professor Christ, who dated this case in June,
commented ("Musgrave Mathematics"): "Amazing, Holmes! In that latitude, there is no real night
at all for a month either way from the summer
solstice, twilight can hardly be said to close in,
and the nights are scarcely bright enough to permit the moon to shine brightly. She depends for
her apparent brightness largely upon contrast with
a dark sky."

Dr. Zeisler, who dated the case in October, concluded (*Baker Street Chronology*): "Hence we
know that on that day the moon set *after* the sun.
. . . [On Thursday, October 2, 1879—a date with
which your editor concurs] the sun was at altitude
33.7° at 1:05 P.M., the moon was only two days
past full and would have been shining brightly in
the sky at 6:00 P.M., although it would have risen
only eleven minutes before and twilight would
have begun only twenty-five minutes earlier."

34 *before they were allowed to retain it.* "The
most amazing feature of the whole story," Mr.
Bengis wrote in "Whose Was It?", "is not that
this relic survived, but that Reginald Musgrave
was allowed by the British Government to retain
it. . . . Whatever was paid could not have represented the minutest fraction of its worth as a
unique historic treasure. . . . The crown was a
public possession, and therefore no more negotiable than London Bridge."

Auctorial Note: For the March, 1927, issue of
the *Strand Magazine*, Sir Arthur Conan Doyle
was asked to draw up a list of his own favorite
Sherlock Holmes short stories, excluding those in
The Case-Book, which had not then been collected in book form. Sir Arthur chose twelve, of
which he ranked "The Musgrave Ritual" No. 11.

" ' What is it, then ? ' he gasped in astonishment.

" ' It is nothing less than the ancient crown of the
Kings of England.'

" ' The crown ! '

" ' Precisely. Consider what the Ritual says. How
does it run ? "Whose was it ?" "His who is gone."
That was after the execution of Charles. Then, " Who
shall have it ? " " He who will come." That was Charles
II, whose advent was already foreseen. There can, I
think, be no doubt that this battered and shapeless diadem
once encircled the brows of the Royal Stuarts.'

" ' And how came it in the pond ? '

" ' Ah, that is a question which will take some time to
answer,' and with that I sketched out the whole long
chain of surmise and of proof which I had constructed.
The twilight had closed in and the moon was shining
33 brightly in the sky before my narrative was finished.

" ' And how was it, then, that Charles did not get his
crown when he returned ? ' asked Musgrave, pushing back
the relic into its linen bag.

" ' Ah, there you lay your finger upon the one point
which we shall probably never be able to clear up. It is
likely that the Musgrave who held the secret died in the
interval, and by some oversight left this guide to his
descendant without explaining the meaning of it. From
that day to this it has been handed down from father to
son, until at last it came within reach of a man who tore
its secret out of it and lost his life in the venture.'

" And that's the story of the Musgrave Ritual, Watson.
They have the crown down at Hurlstone—though they
had some legal bother, and a considerable sum to pay
34 before they were allowed to retain it. I am sure that if
you mentioned my name they would be happy to show it
to you. Of the woman nothing was ever heard, and the
probability is that she got away out of England, and
carried herself, and the memory of her crime, to some
land beyond the seas."

III. THE PARTNERSHIP,
TO DR. WATSON'S FIRST MARRIAGE

[Early January, 1881, to November, 1886]

"Get your hat, said he.

"You wish me to come?"

"Yes, if you have nothing better to do."

—A Study in Scarlet

. . . TOOK MY DEGREE OF DOCTOR OF MEDICINE OF THE UNIVERSITY OF LONDON . . .

The University of London, in Watson's day housed in a new (1870) build-
ing which had been erected for the University at Burlington Gardens, was
chiefly founded by the exertions of Lord Brougham for the purpose of
providing education in literature, science, and the arts at moderate cost.
The foundation stone of the building now known as University College, in
Gower Street, shown here, was laid on April 30, 1827, by the Duke of
Sussex, and the building was opened on October 1, 1828. It was designed by
William Wilkins, R.A., the architect of the National Gallery, and built
under the direction of J. Gandy Deering, A.R.A. Today it has many affiliated colleges, institutions, and schools, such as the London School of Politics
and Political Science. Its medical colleges include St. Bartholomew's, Guy's
and Westminster hospitals. Watson, an admirer of General Charles George
Gordon ("The Cardboard Box"), would be pleased to know that among
the manuscripts owned by the library of the University of London is a
signed dispatch in Arabic sent by General Gordon from Khartoum on June
22, 1884. The engraving above is from a copy of T. H. Shepherd's *The
World's Metropolis*, 1857, in the Cambridge University Library.

15

A STUDY IN SCARLET

[Friday, March 4, to Monday, March 7, 1881]

(*Being a reprint from the Reminiscences of* JOHN H. WATSON, *M.D., Late of the Army Medical Department.*) **1**

◆
I ◆ MR SHERLOCK HOLMES
◆

In the year 1878 I took my degree of Doctor of Medicine of the University of London, and proceeded to Netley to go through the course prescribed for surgeons in the army. Having completed my studies there, I was duly attached to the Fifth Northumberland Fusiliers as Assistant Surgeon. The regiment was stationed in India at the time, and before I could join it, the second Afghan war had broken out. On landing at Bombay, I learned that my corps had advanced through the passes, and was already deep in the enemy's country. I followed, however, with many other officers who were in the same situation as myself, and succeeded in reaching Candahar in safety, where I found my regiment, and at once entered upon my new duties.

The campaign brought honours and promotion to many, but for me it had nothing but misfortune and disaster. I was removed from my brigade and attached to the Berkshires, with whom I served at the fatal battle of Maiwand. There I was struck on the shoulder by a Jezail bullet, which shattered the bone and grazed the subclavian artery. I should have fallen into the hands of the murderous Ghazis had it not been for the devotion and courage shown by Murray, my orderly, who threw me across a packhorse, and succeeded in bringing me safely to the British lines.

Worn with pain, and weak from the prolonged hardships which I had undergone, I was removed, with a great train of wounded sufferers, to the base hospital at Peshawur. Here I rallied, and had already improved so far as to be able to walk about the wards, and even to bask a little upon the verandah, when I was struck down by enteric fever, that curse of our Indian possessions. For months my life was despaired of, and when at last I came to myself and became convalescent, I was so weak and emaciated that a medical board determined that not a day should be lost in sending me back to England. I was despatched, accordingly, in the troopship *Orontes,* and landed a month later on Portsmouth jetty, with my health irretrievably ruined, but with permission from a paternal government to spend the next nine months in attempting to improve it.

1 (Being a reprint...) "Visualize, if you will, this volume for what it must be," the late Edgar W. Smith wrote in "A Bibliographical Note." "It is a fine, sturdy product, surely, nicely bound and neatly printed, and probably privately published along about the year 1885. Along with his account of the first adventure he shared with his roommate, we would find in it an assortment of the doctor's earlier writings: something, of course, about his experiences with women extending over many nations and three separate continents [*The Sign of the Four*], and a more detailed report of the things he saw in India, including, we must hope, a definitive account of how and where his wound-stripe or stripes came to be won. There was much he had to say: he was only 33 when he wrote, but, being the man he was, there was enough for him to call what he set down his 'Reminiscences.' "

Most students, however, feel that this edition of the "Reminiscences" never saw print: "In . . . recent years," Mr. John Ball, Jr., wrote in "The Second Collaboration," "intensive research has been put forth to locate every available edition [of Dr. Watson's published records], but no known copy of the *original* publication of the 'Reminiscences' referred to has ever been found. Since even a very limited edition would have left some traces for future researchers to uncover, the possibility presents itself that no such edition did, in fact, exist."

"How did Watson meet Dr. Doyle?" Mr. Bliss Austin asked in *A Baker Street Christmas Stocking* for 1962. He suggests that Conan Doyle himself may have shed some light on the question when he wrote in his autobiography: "My pleasant recollection of those days from 1880 to 1893 lay in my first introduction, as a more or less rising author, to the literary life of London." "He then goes on," Mr. Austin wrote, "to list a number of writers whom he met including 'Rudyard Kipling, James Stephen Phillips, Watson . . .' and a whole list of others. So he met Watson in literary circles! But what had Watson written to gain admission to such a select group? Obviously, his reminiscences of which *A Study in Scarlet* is an admitted reprint."

2 *an income of eleven shillings and sixpence a day.* Worth, in American currency in those days, about $2.87. It "may not seem a princely sum in this inflated era," Mr. L. S. Holstein wrote in "Bull Pups and Literary Agents," "but one should remember the time was the 1880's, when, in this country, the laboring day was twelve hours and the pay commonly one dollar, worth 100 cents."

"Eleven shillings sixpence a day was better than two hundred pounds a year and I am told that Hart's *Army List for the British Army* (1891) states that the full pay of an army surgeon was about two hundred pounds a year. Surely, then, this was no starvation income," Mr. Bliss Austin wrote in *A Baker Street Christmas Stocking* for 1962.

On the other hand, Mr. Michael Harrison has noted (*In the Footsteps of Sherlock Holmes*) that "for a man wishing to keep above the level of the working-class, the world of 1881 was not a cheap one." If Watson was staying at one of the smaller hotels off the Strand he would have had to pay probably 7/6 (about $1.87) for "bed and breakfast," which would leave him only four shillings ($1.00) a day for all other expenses. He might possibly get a single bedroom *en pension*, that is, at a boardinghouse rate, for 10/6 ($2.62) a day, but this would leave him only a shilling (25¢) a day for tobacco and extras.

It is very much to be doubted that Watson survived for long on his pension alone. From 1887 on, he would enjoy the proceeds of his accounts of the Sherlock Holmes cases, even if he shared those proceeds with his collaborator, Dr. Conan Doyle. Indeed, it has even been suggested that some of Watson's experiences before his meeting with Holmes may have furnished Dr. Conan Doyle with material for stories sold to the *Strand Magazine*, the *Cornhill Magazine*, and other English publications.

In addition, Mr. T. S. Blakeney has suggested (*Sherlock Holmes: Fact or Fiction?*) that Watson's father, "who could leave his eldest son a 50-guinea watch and (so Holmes deduced) probably other financial advantages, may not have overlooked the decidedly more respectable younger son. Watson may have inherited a bit of money, in addition to his 11/6 a day pension. He had to have *some* ready money to buy his practice after marrying Miss Morstan. Perhaps he got one of her pearls to sell. As these six splendid pearls (plus the remainder of the chaplet, which was in Thaddeus [Sholto's] possession) were Miss Morstan's property, I should think she might well have got a jeweler to reset the pearls in the chap-

... STAYED FOR SOME TIME AT A PRIVATE HOTEL IN THE STRAND ...

An ancient highway, the Strand: from the earliest days it connected London and Westminster; it is mentioned in documents that survive from pre-Norman Conquest times. Today it is a vast thoroughfare crowded with traffic—and so it was in Holmes' and Watson's day. But the name which the street bears reminds us that it began as little more than a country lane following the *strand*, the shore, of the Thames. In 1740 a Mr. Bathoe established London's first circulating library in the Strand, and about the same time it was the proper thing for ladies of fashion to visit Messrs. Twining's shop to sample a delicate china cup of that comparatively rare beverage, tea. Many of the taverns and coffeehouses in the Strand became meeting places for literary personalities; it followed that many publishers and booksellers set up their businesses there. The entertainment world also became centered there; in Holmes' and Watson's day most London theatres, including the Adelphi and the Gaiety, stood in or near the Strand. If we wish to know how it may have looked to Dr. Watson, we have the description by Augustus J. C. Hare in *Walks in London:* "If we could linger, as we might in the early morning, when there would be no great traffic to hinder us, we should see that, even now, the great street is far from unpicturesque. The houses, projecting, receding, still ornamented here and there with bow-windows, sometimes with a little sculpture or pargetting work, present a very broken outline to the sky; and, at the end, in the blue haze which is so beautiful on a fine day in London, rises the Flemish-looking steeple of St. Mary-le-Strand with the light streaming through its open pillars." The photograph, by London Transport Executive, is from Michael Harrison's *In the Footsteps of Sherlock Holmes*.

I had neither kith nor kin in England, and was therefore as free as air—or as free as an income of eleven shillings and sixpence a day will permit a man to be. Under such circum- **2** stances I naturally gravitated to London, that great cesspool into which all the loungers and idlers of the Empire are irresistibly drained. There I stayed for some time at a private hotel in the Strand, leading a comfortless, meaningless existence, and spending such money as I had, considerably more freely than I ought. So alarming did the state of my finances become, that I soon realized that I must either leave the metropolis and rusticate somewhere in the country, or that I must make a complete alteration in my style of living. Choos- **3** ing the latter alternative, I began by making up my mind to leave the hotel, and to take up my quarters in some less pretentious and less expensive domicile.

On the very day that I had come to this conclusion, I was standing at the Criterion Bar, when someone tapped me on the shoulder, and turning round I recognized young Stamford, who had been a dresser under me at Barts. The sight of a friendly face in the great wilderness of London is a pleasant thing indeed to a lonely man. In old days Stamford had never been a particular crony of mine, but now I hailed him with enthusiasm, and he, in his turn, appeared to be delighted to see me. In the exuberance of my joy, I asked him to lunch with me at the Holborn, and we started off together in a hansom.

let and sell the latter at Christie's. She'd have made some thousands for certain—perhaps five figures. I fancy Watson, by his marriage, made his financial condition a much easier one . . ."

The late Christopher Morley thought that Mary Morstan may have contributed to Watson's income after their marriage in another way: he suggested that Mary's skill with the needle enabled her to set up an expensive dressmaking shop ("Watson à la Mode").

3 *a complete alteration in my style of living.* Mr. John Ball, Jr., has suggested ("The Second Collaboration") that Watson and Conan Doyle prob-

. . . I WAS STANDING AT THE CRITERION BAR, WHEN SOMEONE TAPPED ME ON THE SHOULDER . . .

The Criterion Restaurant, designed by Thomas Verity, built in 1873 at a cost of £80,000, including the internal equipment, was then eight years old. Still with us, it "occupies about half the block lying within a rectangle formed by Haymarket, Jermyn Street, Piccadilly Circus, and Lower Regent Street. . . . Its white façade, capped by its two Second Empire truncated-pyramid roof towers [is] every bit as much of a landmark as aluminum Eros on his bronze fountain" (Michael Harrison, *In the Footsteps of Sherlock Holmes*). It stands on the site of the White Bear Inn, which was formerly one of the busiest coaching houses trading with the west and southwest of England. Dr. Watson frequented the establishment, we suppose, because the original proprietors were two Australians, Spiers and Pond. Or it may have been because the Criterion attracted the pretty society women of the period; it was also a great gathering place for racing men. It is regrettable to add that the site of the Criterion's original Long Bar is now occupied by one of the many *milk* bars in the great Forte chain. The illustration shown here was used by the Sherlock Holmes Society of London for its 1954 Christmas card.

... I ASKED HIM TO LUNCH WITH ME AT THE HOLBORN ...

The Holborn Restaurant, now demolished, stood at the west corner of Kingsway and High Holborn. Originally the Holborn Casino, it was the largest and best conducted dance hall in London during the seventies of the last century. "It was an example of Victorian classicism at its worst," Mr. William H. Gill wrote in "Some Notable Sherlockian Buildings," "with heavy Portland stone ashlar front, much superfluous ornament, and three floors covered with hideously proportioned windows. No doubt the fact that it had been recently patronised by Royalty [H.R.H. the Prince of Wales, later King Edward VII], impressed the young Watson and his companion." Dr. Watson took young Stamford to the Holborn, rather than lunching at the Criterion, because the Holborn was considerably cheaper. But despite the doctor's desire to economize, he generously stood Stamford to wine with his lunch. "There was a vintage Richebourg," Mr. Michael Harrison wrote (*In the Footsteps of Sherlock Holmes*), "on the wine list at 4s. 6d. [$1.12] a bottle—the Romanée, vintage 1865, at 10s. [$2.50] was a little past its prime; though the Nuits, vintage 1875, at 7s. 6d. [$1.87], was excellent. Let us assume that Watson compromised with his 'enthusiasm' and ordered a bottle at about five shillings [$1.25]. With what he would have called a 'pre-prandial' sherry, as well as coffee and cigars . . . he would have spent a pound [$5.00]." The Holborn described itself in an advertisement of 1880 as "one of the sights and one of the comforts of London." It combined, it said, the "attractions of the chief Parisian establishments with the quiet and order essential to English custom." Apart from luncheon it offered a *table d'hôte* dinner "at separate tables every evening from 5:30 to 8:30 in the Grand Salon, the Prince's Salon and the Duke's Salon." It included "two soups, two kinds of fish, two entrées, joints, sweets, cheese (in variety), salad, etc., with ices and dessert." The price was 3s. 6d. (about 87¢). "This favourite dinner is accompanied by a selection of high-class instrumental music." The woodcut shown here, from *The Builder*, reproduced in Michael Harrison's *In the Footsteps of Sherlock Holmes*, shows the restaurant before the addition of the wing at the corner of Little Queen Street, now Kingsway. The building on the right of the picture survives as a branch of Lloyd's Bank.

... HAD BEEN A DRESSER UNDER ME AT BARTS.

St. Bartholomew's Hospital—popularly known as Barts—lies within an irregular triangle formed by Newgate Street on the south, Giltspur Street on the west, and King Edward Street on the east. Tradition has it that the hospital was founded by Rahere, a sort of King's jester to Henry I. Rahere, on his deathbed, vowed that if he should by some miracle recover he would atone for his sins by dedicating a religious foundation. Rahere did recover, persuaded Henry to make him a grant of land, and there, in 1123, he built a hospital and a priory, both named for the saint who had appeared to him in a vision during his illness. Doctors other than John H. Watson who served Bart's in their time included Dr. Harvey, the personal physician to Charles I, who discovered the circulation of the blood; Percival Pott, who gave his name to the "Pott's fracture"; and John Abernethy, the brilliant surgeon whose lectures were so well attended that the lecture hall had to be enlarged to accommodate his listeners. Abernethy's brusqueness and independence were legendary; it is just as well that Watson did not call him in during "The Adventure of the Dying Detective" —he was adept at recognizing malingerers and treated them with withering scorn. Shown here is the Library and Museum of Bart's as it looked when Holmes was a research student and met Watson there. The etching, by Hulton, is from Michael Harrison's *In the Footsteps of Sherlock Holmes.*

... AND WE STARTED OFF TOGETHER IN A HANSOM.

"The gondolas of London" was the felicitous title conferred upon the hansom cabs by the great Benjamin Disraeli. Named for Joseph Aloysius Hansom, 1803–1882, redesigned by John Chapman, a rival carriage maker, made fashionable by Forder, whose luxurious hansom, constructed especially for the Prince of Wales, carried off first prize at the Carriage Exhibition of 1872, the hansom cab was in all probability the fastest vehicle devised up to that time for negotiating the narrow and congested streets of London at high speeds. The top-hatted driver sat high up at the back of the hansom, with the reins passing through a support on the front of the roof. The front of the hansom was open, except for two folding doors which came about halfway up and protected the traveler's feet and legs against the weather. To ride in this type of cab, with its brightly polished lamps and brasswork, its jingling harness and smartly trotting horse, was a highly pleasant experience, as both Holmes and Watson knew well. In their day there were more than 8,000 of the cabs circulating through London; in 1933, their centennial year, there were only three hansom cabs left in the entire city. The minimum hansom cab fare for one or two passengers was a shilling (25¢) for two miles and sixpence (12½¢) a mile over that, but a cabman was not obliged to drive over six miles even if he could charge more when he got beyond the "Four Mile Radius"—a circle drawn with Charing Cross as the center. As Kipling wrote in his poem, "Et Dona Ferentes":

> In extended observation of the ways and works of man
> From the Four Mile Radius roughly to the plains of
> Hindustan.

ably met at this time: "Despite the lack of immediate funds and the limitation of few friendships from which to draw strength and encouragement, Dr. Watson could not and did not fail to give some thought to the matter of setting up in practice. At about the same time, another physician, in closely parallel circumstances, found that he too had a need for gainful professional employment. It is not recorded at what time or under what circumstances the two young doctors met, but meet they unmistakably did. It may have been at a medical lecture, in the physicians' section of the public library, at a medical supply house where they had gone separately to ascertain the cost of the equipment needed to outfit a modest office. Wherever it was, a friendship and a collaboration was formed which was to enrich the world. For, great as was the association between Dr. Watson and Sherlock Holmes, of nearly equal importance to posterity was the second collaboration between Dr. Watson and the other physician who was also destined for immortal fame, Dr. Arthur Conan Doyle."

4 *looked rather strangely at me over his wine-glass.* "Had he some kind of intuition that he was to be one of the great liason-officers of literary history, that he was shortly to bring about a meeting comparable in its far-reaching influences with that other meeting arranged by Tom Davies in Russell Street, Covent Garden, more than a hundred years before?", Mr. S. C. Roberts asked in *Doctor Watson.* Mr. Roberts here refers to Thomas Davies, English actor and bookseller 1712–1785. Davies was a friend of Dr. Sam Johnson's; Johnson first met Boswell at Davies' home in 1763.

5 *well up in anatomy.* "Accurate, but unsystematic," was Watson's later judgment of Holmes' knowledge of anatomy.

'Whatever have you been doing with yourself, Watson?' he asked in undisguised wonder, as we rattled through the crowded London streets. 'You are as thin as a lath and as brown as a nut.'

I gave him a short sketch of my adventures, and had hardly concluded it by the time that we reached our destination.

'Poor devil!' he said commiseratingly, after he had listened to my misfortunes. 'What are you up to now?'

'Looking for lodgings,' I answered. 'Trying to solve the problem as to whether it is possible to get comfortable rooms at a reasonable price.'

'That's a strange thing,' remarked my companion, 'you are the second man today that has used that expression to me.'

'And who was the first?' I asked.

'A fellow who is working at the chemical laboratory up at the hospital. He was bemoaning himself this morning because he could not get someone to go halves with him in some nice rooms which he had found, and which were too much for his purse.'

'By Jove!' I cried; 'if he really wants someone to share the rooms and the expense, I am the very man for him. I should prefer having a partner to being alone.'

Young Stamford looked rather strangely at me over his **4** wine-glass. 'You don't know Sherlock Holmes yet,' he said; 'perhaps you would not care for him as a constant companion.'

'Why, what is there against him?'

'Oh, I didn't say there was anything against him. He is a little queer in his ideas—an enthusiast in some branches of science. As far as I know he is a decent fellow enough.'

'A medical student, I suppose?' said I.

'No—I have no idea what he intends to go in for. I believe **5** he is well up in anatomy, and he is a first-class chemist; but, as far as I know, he has never taken out any systematic medical classes. His studies are very desultory and eccentric,

"I'VE FOUND IT! I'VE FOUND IT," HE SHOUTED TO MY COMPANION . . .

Illustration by George Hutchinson for the London, 1891, Ward, Lock, Bowden & Co. edition of *A Study in Scarlet.* Hutchinson, the late James Montgomery wrote in *A Study in Pictures,* "taxes our romantic illusions to the utmost by his almost diabolically unattractive representations."

but he has amassed a lot of out-of-the-way knowledge which would astonish his professors.'

'Did you never ask him what he was going in for?' I asked.

'No; he is not a man that it is easy to draw out, though he can be communicative enough when the fancy seizes him.'

'I should like to meet him,' I said. 'If I am to lodge with anyone, I should prefer a man of studious and quiet habits. I am not strong enough yet to stand much noise or excitement. I had enough of both in Afghanistan to last me for the remainder of my natural existence. How could I meet this friend of yours?'

'He is sure to be at the laboratory,' returned my companion. 'He either avoids the place for weeks, or else he works there from morning till night. If you like, we will drive round together after luncheon.'

'Certainly,' I answered, and the conversation drifted away into other channels.

As we made our way to the hospital after leaving the Holborn, Stamford gave me a few more particulars about the gentleman whom I proposed to take as a fellow-lodger.

'You mustn't blame me if you don't get on with him,' he said; 'I know nothing more of him than I have learned from meeting him occasionally in the laboratory. You proposed this arrangement, so you must not hold me responsible.'

'If we don't get on it will be easy to part company,' I answered. 'It seems to me, Stamford,' I added, looking hard at my companion, 'that you have some reason for washing your hands of the matter. Is this fellow's temper so formidable, or what is it? Don't be mealy-mouthed about it.'

'It is not easy to express the inexpressible,' he answered with a laugh. 'Holmes is a little too scientific for my tastes—it approaches to cold-bloodedness. I could imagine his giving a friend a little pinch of the latest vegetable alkaloid, not out **6** of malevolence, you understand, but simply out of a spirit of inquiry in order to have an accurate idea of the effects. To do him justice, I think that he would take it himself with the same readiness. He appears to have a passion for definite and exact knowledge.'

'Very right too.'

'Yes, but it may be pushed to excess. When it comes to beating the subjects in the dissecting-rooms with a stick, it is certainly taking rather a bizarre shape.'

'Beating the subjects!'

'Yes, to verify how far bruises may be produced after death. I saw him at it with my own eyes.'

'And yet you say he is not a medical student?'

'No. Heaven knows what the objects of his studies are. But here we are, and you must form your own impressions about him.' As he spoke, we turned down a narrow lane and passed **7** through a small side-door, which opened into a wing of the great hospital. It was familiar ground to me, and I needed no guiding as we ascended the bleak stone staircase and made our way down the long corridor with its vista of whitewashed wall and dun-coloured doors. Near the farther end a low arched passage branched away from it and led to the chemical laboratory.

This was a lofty chamber, lined and littered with countless bottles. Broad, low tables were scattered about, which bristled with retorts, test-tubes, and little Bunsen lamps, with their **8**

6 *the latest vegetable alkaloid*. The first alkaloid, impure nicotine, was prepared by Derosne in 1803; by 1840 practically all the more important alkaloids (veratrine, strychnine, piperine, caffeine, quinine, bernerine, conine, stropine, codeine, aconite, and colchicene) had been isolated. Vegetable alkaloids are those which are obtained from plants, as distinguished from those that are extracted from viscera and stomach contents—the "animal" alkaloids. "The chemist," says the *Encyclopaedia Britannica*, "looks upon the alkaloids as fascinating problems for the exercise of his technique and imagination. He has devoted much attention to devising methods for their detection, isolation and purification; and he has displayed considerable ingenuity in splitting their intimate structures as will provide a basis for producing them at will in his laboratory."

7 *we turned down a narrow lane*. In entering Bart's, "Watson must have passed under the great Renaissance gateway designed by James Gibbs (the best of Wren's pupils) in 1702, whilst the bulk of the great hospital was built by the same architect in 1730," Mr. William H. Gill wrote in "Some Notable Sherlockian Buildings." "From the description given in *A Study in Scarlet* the simplicity of the laboratory points to it being a part of Gibbs' work, and it is pleasing to think that the two immortal friends first met in a room designed by one of Britain's greatest architects."

8 *little Bunsen lamps*. Named for their inventor, Robert Wilhelm Eberhard Bunsen (1811–1899), German chemist and discoverer, Professor of Heidelberg University. The Bunsen lamp consists typically of a straight tube, four or five inches long, with small holes for the entrance of air at the bottom. Illuminating gas being also admitted at the bottom, a mixture of gas and air is formed which burns at the top with a feebly luminous but intensely hot blue flame.

9 *There was only one student in the room.* Writing in the *St. Bartholomew's Hospital Journal*, Mr. A. N. Griffith noted ("Some Observations on Sherlock Holmes and Dr. Watson at Bart's") that "Augustus Mattiesson was the lecturer in chemistry at Bart's from 1870 onwards. Sir Norman Moore recalls that he had two private pupils; one was Moore himself, the other he does not name though he does give us some information about him. He had been in Strasbourg during the Franco-Prussian War, . . . when a shell passed through his house. Mattiesson was interested in opium and together they investigated its alkaloids. He was a constant and eager experimenter. The likeness between this student and Holmes becomes more and more apparent, and we may, in fact, conclude that they were the same person. If this be accepted, his position at Bart's is accounted for, his absence from Britain during the Franco-Prussian War explained [see "The Adventure of the Noble Bachelor," Note 28] as is his useful knowledge of German, for it will be remembered he was happy to quote Goethe quite glibly."

10 *The proportion of blood cannot be more than one in a million.* "Holmes . . . made a gross error in estimating to Watson . . . the concentration of his blood solution: one drop of blood in a litre of water . . . actually cannot be less than one in 30,000," Professor Remsen Ten Eyck Schenck wrote in "Baker Street Fables."

11 *a brownish dust was precipitated to the bottom of the glass jar.* "This can be neither of the known methods for the detection of blood, since the outmoded guaiac reaction gives a blue coloration and the usual benzedrine test a blue-green," Professor Schenck wrote. "Holmes' discovery would certainly be in universal use today were it valid, and it must therefore be concluded that his belief in its specificity for haemoglobin was unfounded. Presumably he discovered on further study that a similar result was obtained with other common substances, or else that it was not due to haemoglobin at all, but rather to some other ingredient present in the blood, but not peculiar to it."

". . . it is surely as valid to reason that this research finally resulted in the present-day haemochromogen test as it is to state that it is no test at all," Mr. L. S. Holstein reported in " '7. Knowledge of Chemistry—Profound.' " "Forensic chemistry has made great strides in the past two generations. That 'dull mahogany colour' that Watson observed may be the nineteenth century version of the pinkish cast of the haemochromogen crystals."

12 *The old guaiacum test.* "The guaiacum or lignum vitae tree is native to the West Indies and northern South America," Christopher Morley wrote in *Sherlock Holmes and Dr. Watson: A Textbook of Friendship*. "Both bark and resin

blue flickering flames. There was only one student in the **9** room, who was bending over a distant table absorbed in his work. At the sound of our steps he glanced round and sprang to his feet with a cry of pleasure. 'I've found it! I've found it,' he shouted to my companion, running towards us with a test-tube in his hand. 'I have found a reagent which is precipitated by hæmoglobin, and by nothing else.' Had he discovered a gold mine, greater delight could not have shone upon his features.

'Dr Watson, Mr Sherlock Holmes,' said Stamford, introducing us.

'How are you?' he said cordially, gripping my hand with a strength for which I should hardly have given him credit. 'You have been in Afghanistan, I perceive.'

'How on earth did you know that?' I asked in astonishment.

'Never mind,' said he, chuckling to himself. 'The question now is about hæmoglobin. No doubt you see the significance of this discovery of mine?'

'It is interesting, chemically, no doubt,' I answered, 'but practically——'

'Why, man, it is the most practical medico-legal discovery for years. Don't you see that it gives us an infallible test for blood stains. Come over here now!' He seized me by the coat-sleeve in his eagerness, and drew me over to the table at which he had been working. 'Let us have some fresh blood,' he said, digging a long bodkin into his finger, and drawing off the resulting drop of blood in a chemical pipette. 'Now, I add this small quantity of blood to a litre of water. You perceive that the resulting mixture has the appearance of pure water. The proportion of blood cannot be more than one in a **10** million. I have no doubt, however, that we shall be able to obtain the characteristic reaction.' As he spoke, he threw into the vessel a few white crystals, and then added some drops of a transparent fluid. In an instant the contents assumed a dull mahogany colour, and a brownish dust was precipitated to **11** the bottom of the glass jar.

'Ha! ha!' he cried, clapping his hands, and looking as delighted as a child with a new toy. 'What do you think of that?'

'It seems to be a very delicate test,' I remarked.

12 'Beautiful! beautiful! The old guaiacum test was very clumsy and uncertain. So is the microscopic examination for blood corpuscles. The latter is valueless if the stains are a few hours old. Now, this appears to act as well whether the blood is old or new. Had this test been invented, there are hundreds of men now walking the earth who would long ago have paid the penalty of their crimes.'

'Indeed!' I murmured.

'Criminal cases are continually hinging upon that one point. A man is suspected of a crime months perhaps after it has been committed. His linen or clothes are examined and brownish stains discovered upon them. Are they blood stains, or mud stains, or rust stains, or fruit stains, or what are they? That is a question which has puzzled many an expert, and why? Because there was no reliable test. Now we have the Sherlock Holmes test, and there will no longer be any difficulty.'

His eyes fairly glittered as he spoke, and he put his hand

over his heart and bowed as if to some applauding crowd conjured up by his imagination.

'You are to be congratulated,' I remarked, considerably surprised at his enthusiasm.

'There was the case of Von Bischoff at Frankfort last year. **13** He would certainly have been hung had this test been in existence. Then there was Mason of Bradford, and the notorious **14** Muller, and Lefevre of Montpellier, and Samson of New **15** Orleans. I could name a score of cases in which it would have been decisive.'

'You seem to be a walking calendar of crime,' said Stamford with a laugh. 'You might start a paper on those lines. Call it the "Police News of the Past."'

'Very interesting reading it might be made, too,' remarked Sherlock Holmes, sticking a small piece of plaster over the prick on his finger. 'I have to be careful,' he continued, turning to me with a smile, 'for I dabble with poisons a good deal.' He held out his hand as he spoke, and I noticed that it was all mottled over with similar pieces of plaster, and discoloured with strong acids.

'We came here on business,' said Stamford, sitting down on a high three-legged stool, and pushing another one in my direction with his foot. 'My friend here wants to take diggings; and as you were complaining that you could get no **16** one to go halves with you, I thought that I had better bring you together.'

Sherlock Holmes seemed delighted at the idea of sharing his rooms with me. 'I have my eye on a suite in Baker Street,' he said, 'which would suit us down to the ground. You don't mind the smell of strong tobacco, I hope?'

'I always smoke "ship's" myself,' I answered.   **17**

'That's good enough. I generally have chemicals about, and occasionally do experiments. Would that annoy you?'

'By no means.'

'Let me see—what are my other shortcomings. I get in the dumps at times, and don't open my mouth for days on end. You must not think I am sulky when I do that. Just let me alone, and I'll soon be right. What have you to confess now? It's just as well for two fellows to know the worst of one another before they begin to live together.'

I laughed at this cross-examination. 'I keep a bull pup,' I **18** said, 'and I object to row, because my nerves are shaken, and I get up at all sorts of ungodly hours, and I am extremely lazy. I have another set of vices when I'm well, but those are the **19** principal ones at present.'

'Do you include violin playing in your category of rows?' he asked, anxiously.

'It depends on the player,' I answered. 'A well-played violin is a treat for the gods—a badly-played one——'

'Oh, that's all right,' he cried, with a merry laugh. 'I think **20** we may consider the thing as settled—that is, if the rooms are agreeable to you.'

'When shall we see them?'

'Call for me here at noon tomorrow, and we'll go together and settle everything,' he answered.

'All right—noon exactly,' said I, shaking his hand.

We left him working among his chemicals, and we walked together towards my hotel.

have been much used in pharmacy. In testing for the presence of blood a tincture of 1 part resin to 6 parts alcohol was used. This was added to a smaller quantity of the liquid under examination, and shaken together with a few drops of hydrogen peroxide in ether. The ether dissolves the resin, and if haemoglobin is present the mixture turns bright blue."

In *The Shadow of the Wolf*, by the late R. Austin Freeman, we read this description of the process: ". . . He poured a quantity of the tincture [of guaiacum] on the middle of the stained area. The pool of liquid rapidly spread considerably beyond the limits of the stain, growing paler as it extended. Then Thorndyke cautiously dropped small quantities of ozonic ether at various points around the stained area, and watched closely as the two liquids mingled in the fabric of the sail. Gradually the ether spread towards the stain, and, first at one point and then at another, approached and finally crossed the wavy grey line; and at each point the same change occurred: first the faint grey line turned into a strong blue line, and then the colour extended to the enclosed space until the entire area of the stain stood out in a conspicuous blue patch. 'You understand the meaning of this,' said Thorndyke. 'This is a bloodstain.'"

According to Mr. P. M. Stone in his essay, "The Other Friendship: A Speculation," Holmes and Thorndyke knew each other well. "It seems a pity that they did not know each other's methods better," the late Edgar W. Smith once commented.

13 *last year*. This direct quotation from Holmes might be of great value to researchers in dating *A Study in Scarlet* once for all, but scholars have so far failed to determine the year in which Von Bischoff was tried and (presumably) acquitted.

14 *Bradford*. In Yorkshire—a center of the worsted-milling industry.

15 *Montpellier*. An indication of Holmes' lifelong interest in the south of France.

16 *diggings*. English slang for lodgings.

17 *'I always smoke "ship's" myself.'* Miss Sherry Keen ("Ship's or 'ship's'?") has noted that both *A Dictionary of Slang and Unconventional English* by Eric Partridge and *Soldier and Sailor, Words and Phrases* by Fraser and Gibbons refer to "ship's" as a "naval tobacco." "Ship's" with Watson was evidently a passing fancy, picked up from the sailors aboard the *Orontes*, for in "The Crooked Man" Holmes says to Watson: "Hum! you still smoke the Arcadia mixture of your bachelor days, then!"

18 *'I keep a bull pup.'* It is never heard of again. We must remember that Holmes in his college days had been bitten in the ankle by a bull terrier (Victor Trevor's) and Watson's bull pup may have found the same target irresistible. "Watson, that dog must go!" However, many Sherlockians —both dog-lovers and caniphobes—have pondered the problem of the bull pup, and other suggestions include these: 1) Mrs. Hudson objected to the animal, perhaps because she had an ancient terrier of her own; 2) The pup was accidentally killed by Watson, who stumbled while carrying the animal up the seventeen stairs to the sitting room; 3) The pup was a victim of one of Holmes' chemical experiments; 4) The dog, unable to stand the Baker Street menage, deserted. "The real mystery, it seems to me," Mr. L. S. Holstein wrote in "Bull Pups and Literary Agents," "is why Watson should have had a bull pup in the first place, no matter how great a dog-lover he may have been. He was a man without a home, up to the time of taking residence at 221B, and without means to feed an extra mouth even though that be only a dog's mouth. And can you imagine that the 'private hotel in the Strand' allowed him to keep a dog?"

19 *I have another set of vices when I'm well.* Watson perhaps refers here to his experience of women, his propensity for gambling, or his occasional intemperance.

20 *with a merry laugh.* "It is curious, and momentarily disconcerting, to find that Dr. Watson asserts in 'The Adventure of the Sussex Vampire,' that a dry chuckle was Mr. Holmes' 'nearest approach to a laugh,'" Dean Theodore C. Blegen wrote in "These Were Hidden Fires, Indeed!" (And in "The Adventure of the Mazarin Stone," Watson wrote of Holmes that he "seldom laughed.") "In case after case," Dean Blegen continued, "the doctor has reported roars and explosions and even paroxysms of laughter by Mr. Holmes. I think we must, unhappily, assume another little lapse of memory on Dr. Watson's part . . ."

Indeed, Mr. A. G. Cooper, in "Holmesian Humour," has uncovered 292 examples, and Messrs. Charles E. and Edward S. Lauterbach, in their extensive researches, have shown that "Holmes smiled 103 times, laughed 65 times, joked 58 times, chuckled 31 times, and expressed humor in other ways 59 times—a total of 316 responses to humorous situations or statements" ("The Man Who Seldom Laughed").

21 *"The proper study of mankind is man."* Watson quotes from *An Essay on Man,* Ep. ii, 1.2, by Alexander Pope, 1688–1744.

22 *so moderate did the terms seem.* "It is likely that Holmes and Watson shared an 'all-in' rent of between £3 [$15] and £4 [$20] a week—probably nearer the latter than the former," Mr. Michael Harrison wrote in *In the Footsteps of*

'By the way,' I asked suddenly, stopping and turning upon Stamford, 'how the deuce did he know that I had come from Afghanistan?'

My companion smiled an enigmatical smile. 'That's just his little peculiarity,' he said. 'A good many people have wanted to know how he finds things out.'

'Oh! a mystery is it?' I cried, rubbing my hands. 'This is very piquant. I am much obliged to you for bringing us to-**21** gether. "The proper study of mankind is man," you know.'

'You must study him, then,' Stamford said, as he bade me good-bye. 'You'll find him a knotty problem, though. I'll wager he learns more about you than you about him. Good-bye.'

'Good-bye,' I answered, and strolled on to my hotel, considerably interested in my new acquaintance.

◆

2 ◆ THE SCIENCE OF DEDUCTION

◆

We met next day as he had arranged, and inspected the rooms at No. 221B, Baker Street, of which he had spoken at our meeting. They consisted of a couple of comfortable bedrooms and a single large airy sitting-room, cheerfully furnished, and illuminated by two broad windows. So desirable in every way **22** were the apartments, and so moderate did the terms seem

UPON MY QUOTING THOMAS CARLYLE . . .

This is the portrait of Carlyle by Sir John Millais which hangs in the National Portrait Gallery, London.

when divided between us, that the bargain was concluded upon the spot, and we at once entered into possession. That very evening I moved my things round from the hotel, and on the following morning Sherlock Holmes followed me with several boxes and portmanteaus. For a day or two we were busily employed in unpacking and laying out our property to the best advantage. That done, we gradually began to settle down and to accommodate ourselves to our new surroundings.

Holmes was certainly not a difficult man to live with. He was quiet in his ways, and his habits were regular. It was rare for him to be up after ten at night, and he had invariably breakfasted and gone out before I rose in the morning. Some- **23** times he spent his day at the chemical laboratory, sometimes in the dissecting rooms, and occasionally in long walks, which appeared to take him into the lowest portions of the city. **24** Nothing could exceed his energy when the working fit was upon him; but now and again a reaction would seize him, and for days on end he would lie upon the sofa in the sitting-room, hardly uttering a word or moving a muscle from morning to night. On these occasions I have noticed such a dreamy, vacant expression in his eyes, that I might have suspected him of being addicted to the use of some narcotic, had not the temperance and cleanliness of his whole life forbidden such a notion. **25**

As the weeks went by, my interest in him and my curiosity **26** as to his aims in life gradually deepened and increased. His very person and appearance were such as to strike the attention of the most casual observer. In height he was rather over six feet, and so excessively lean that he seemed to be considerably taller. His eyes were sharp and piercing, save during **27** those intervals of torpor to which I have alluded; and his thin, hawk-like nose gave his whole expression an air of alertness and decision. His chin, too, had the prominence and squareness which mark the man of determination. His hands were **28** invariably blotted with ink and stained with chemicals, yet he was possessed of extraordinary delicacy of touch, as I frequently had occasion to observe when I watched him manipulating his fragile philosophical instruments.

The reader may set me down as a hopeless busybody, when I confess how much this man stimulated my curiosity, and how often I endeavoured to break through the reticence which he showed on all that concerned himself. Before pronouncing judgment, however, be it remembered how objectless was my life, and how little there was to engage my attention. My health forbade me from venturing out unless the weather was exceptionally genial, and I had no friends who would call upon me and break the monotony of my daily existence. Under these circumstances, I eagerly hailed the little mystery which hung around my companion, and spent much of my time in endeavouring to unravel it.

He was not studying medicine. He had himself, in reply to a question, confirmed Stamford's opinion upon that point. Neither did he appear to have pursued any course of reading which might fit him for a degree in science or any other recognized portal which would give him an entrance into the learned world. Yet his zeal for certain studies was remark- **29** able, and within eccentric limits his knowledge was so extra-

Sherlock Holmes. "Let us assume that Holmes and Watson were sharing a rent of some £200 [$1,000] a year, which might have included laundry, as well as food; but . . . it is unlikely that illuminating-gas was included in the 'all-in' terms, which may explain the references, frequent throughout Watson's writings, to the oil-lamps at 221B."

23 *before I rose in the morning.* Watson has already told us that he got up "at all sorts of ungodly hours." (Perhaps this is what he means when he writes, in "The Adventure of the Speckled Band," that "I was myself regular in my habits.") But he also tells us—again in "The Adventure of the Speckled Band"—that Holmes "was a late riser as a rule." And in *The Hound of the Baskervilles,* Watson tells us that Holmes "was usually very late in the mornings." Watson, then, must have been a slug-a-bed indeed—a view confirmed by the late breakfast he is having in "The Boscombe Valley Mystery."

24 *the lowest portions of the city.* Since Holmes was "a man who seldom took exercise for exercise's sake" ("The Yellow Face"), these "long walks" were obviously taken in connection with cases which Holmes was handling at the time.

25 *forbidden such a notion.* This is an amazingly shrewd observation on Watson's part. Holmes' tremendous exertions in the spring of 1887—six years after Watson made this statement—left him a very sick man. At that time, to Watson's deep distress, Holmes turned for solace to cocaine. Holmes tells us himself (*The Sign of the Four*) that he found its influence so transcendently stimulating and clarifying to the mind as to make him careless of the ravages inevitable upon his body and soul. By September, 1888, he was indulging in doses of 7 percent cocaine solution three times a day. It is pleasant to be able to record that Watson over the years was gradually able to cure Holmes completely of the habit. By the end of 1896 ("The Adventure of the Missing Three-Quarter") Holmes under ordinary conditions no longer craved this artificial stimulation.

We have stated here the majority view, but there are others: Dr. Charles Goodman, for example, believes that Holmes first took to cocaine neither from weakness nor from boredom but from toothache; he was, as Dr. Goodman has convincingly established ("The Dental Holmes") a chronic sufferer from pyorrhea.

Dr. George F. McCleary has examined the evidence and has arrived at the conclusion that Holmes was never a drug addict, but that he did succeed in deceiving the innocent Watson, and, in fact, took a certain delight in doing so: "All we know of Holmes' alleged addiction can be explained if we assume that he did not actually take the drug, but mystified Watson into believing that he did."

With this view Mr. Michael Harrison is in

strong disagreement (*In the Footsteps of Sherlock Holmes*): ". . . that Holmes had a serious addiction, all Watson's descriptions of Holmes' nervous activity makes clear: the restlessness, the ability to work for days without adequate sleep, and even without rest at all; the abrupt changes of mood; and the equally abrupt collapse into a somnolence not far (if at all) removed from a torpor bordering on coma: these, to those who have studied the effects of drug-addiction, are the unmistakable evidence of heavy and prolonged indulgence in some powerful narcotic."

A middle-road position has been expressed by Dr. Eugene F. Carey ("Holmes, Watson and Cocaine"), who has called Holmes "a judicious user" —a view shared by the late Edgar W. Smith ("Up from the Needle"): ". . . he was never a slave to the vice in the clinical sense of the term, for . . . he was always able to cast off the spell, and to find inspiration in the exhilaration of the chase."

26 *As the weeks went by.* Since the case described in *A Study in Scarlet* took place, as we shall see, in March, this is an indication that the partnership was formed early in the year or very late in the preceding year.

27 *His eyes were sharp and piercing.* They were gray eyes, as we are told later on numerous occasions.

28 *which mark the man of determination.* ". . . there seems little doubt that Holmes must have been enormously attractive to women," Dr. Richard Asher wrote in "Holmes and the Fair Sex." "His teeth may have detracted slightly from this impressive appearance for with his excessive consumption of shag they must have been heavily tobacco-stained and moreover we know that the left canine tooth had been knocked out by Mathews in the waiting-room at Charing Cross ["The Adventure of the Empty House"]; but perhaps he wore a denture."

29 *an entrance into the learned world.* We know to the contrary that Holmes was two years at Oxford and three years at Cambridge. But whether or not he was ever admitted to a degree or degrees is a point still debated by commentators.

30 *and what he had done.* "We do not know the circumstances in which this remark was made, but probably it was at a time when Holmes wanted to give his whole attention to a case as yet unsolved, and simply could not be bothered to be drawn into a discussion about Carlyle or anything else," the late Gavin Brend wrote in *My Dear Holmes*.

"The truth of the matter . . . is that Holmes was irritated by Watson's ill-concealed curiosity and took the occasion to cut him short, or that Holmes was guying his roommate . . .", Mr. Whitfield J. Bell, Jr., wrote in "Holmes and History."

ordinarily ample and minute that his observations have fairly astounded me. Surely no man would work so hard or attain such precise information unless he had some definite end in view. Desultory readers are seldom remarkable for the exactness of their learning. No man burdens his mind with small matters unless he has some very good reason for doing so.

His ignorance was as remarkable as his knowledge. Of contemporary literature, philosophy and politics he appeared to know next to nothing. Upon my quoting Thomas Carlyle, he inquired in the naïvest way who he might be and what he **30** had done. My surprise reached a climax, however, when I found incidentally that he was ignorant of the Copernican **31** Theory and of the composition of the Solar System. That any civilized human being in this nineteenth century should not be aware that the earth travelled round the sun appeared to be **32** to me such an extraordinary fact that I could hardly realize it.

'You appear to be astonished,' he said, smiling at my expression of surprise. 'Now that I do know it I shall do my best to forget it.'

'To forget it!'

'You see,' he explained, 'I consider that a man's brain originally is like a little empty attic, and you have to stock it with such furniture as you choose. A fool takes in all the lumber of every sort that he comes across, so that the knowledge which might be useful to him gets crowded out, or at best is jumbled up with a lot of other things, so that he has a difficulty in laying his hands upon it. Now the skilled workman is very careful indeed as to what he takes into his brainattic. He will have nothing but the tools which may help him in doing his work, but of these he has a large assortment, and all in the most perfect order. It is a mistake to think that that little room has elastic walls and can distend to any extent. Depend upon it there comes a time when for every addition of knowledge you forget something that you knew before. It is of the highest importance, therefore, not to have **33** useless facts elbowing out the useful ones.'

'But the Solar System!' I protested.

'What the deuce is it to me?' he interrupted impatiently: 'you say that we go round the sun. If we went round the moon it would not make a pennyworth of difference to me or to my work.'

(*continued on page 156*)

The latter is the more popular view among commentators: "Holmes was gently pulling Watson's leg," Christopher Morley wrote, "for shortly thereafter he glibly quotes Carlyle's most famous apothegm."

"I suspect that at that period Watson was far too ready to take Holmes' remarks *au pied de la lettre*," Mr. S. C. Roberts wrote in "The Personality of Sherlock Holmes."

Watson was later to learn that Holmes had, indeed, a very well-developed sense of mischief: in "The Problem of Thor Bridge," Holmes looked into Watson's eyes "with the peculiarly mischievous glance which was characteristic of his more imp-like moods," and on many other occasions Watson was sharply aware of Holmes' "mischievous twinkle."

But why, Christopher Morley asked, should Watson have raised the topic of Carlyle at all? "Because Carlyle died on February 4, 1881! Watson of course had read all the published obituaries, and they were undoubtedly still fresh in his mind, including the one referred to by George Gissing who wrote (in London, February 11, '81) that 'I have just risen from the memoir of Carlyle in the *Times*.' Obviously, Carlyle's recent death was the occasion for the mention Watson made of [the great Scottish author, historian and essayist, 1795–1881]."

31 *the Copernican Theory*. Nicholas Copernicus, Polish astronomer, 1473–1543, founded the system on which modern astronomy is based. In his famous treatise *De revolutionibus orbium coelestium*, published in 1543, he described the sun as the center of the solar system, with the earth revolving around it.

32 *I could hardly realize it*. More leg-pulling on Holmes' part. In "The Musgrave Ritual" he spoke of "any allowance for personal equation, as the astronomers have dubbed it." In "The Adventure of the Bruce-Partington Plans" he compares his brother Mycroft's visit to a planet leaving its orbit, and in "The Greek Interpreter" during a "desultory" chat "after tea on a summer evening" he discusses "the causes of the change in the obliquity of the ecliptic."

33 *useless facts elbowing out the useful ones*.' Holmes did not live up to his preaching here. He later extols "the oblique uses of knowledge" for their good results (*The Valley of Fear*), and of such knowledge he had more than the average stock, as he himself tells us in "The Adventure of the Lion's Mane."

34 SHERLOCK HOLMES—*his limits*. "A list of Watson's own points might, at this juncture, have been headed by the specification: 1. Knowledge of Sherlock Holmes.—Nil," said the late Edgar W. Smith.

35 *2. Knowledge of Philosophy.—Nil*. But in his preface to *His Last Bow*, Watson speaks of Holmes, in retirement, as dividing his time between philosophy and agriculture.

36 *4. Knowledge of Politics.—Feeble*. As Mr. T. S. Blakeney wrote in *Sherlock Holmes: Fact or Fiction?*, "it is hard to believe that Holmes, who had so close a grip on realities, could ever have taken much interest in the pettiness of party politics, nor could so strong an individualist have anything but contempt for the equalitarian ideals of much modern sociological theory."

But Mr. S. C. Roberts has written ("The Personality of Sherlock Holmes"): ". . . it is perfectly true that the clash of political opinions and of political parties does not seem to have aroused great interest in Holmes' mind. But, fundamentally, there can be no doubt that Holmes believed in democracy and progress. . . . It would be difficult to find a more concise expression of the confident aspirations of late Victorian liberalism [than Holmes' remarks on Board schools in "The Naval Treaty"]."

And Mr. Whitfield J. Bell, Jr., in "Holmes and History," has added that "Holmes' knowledge of politics was anything but weak or partial. Of the hurly-burly of the machines, the petty trade for office and advantage, it is perhaps true that Holmes knew little. But of politics on the highest level, in the grand manner, particularly international politics, no one was better informed . . .'"

I was on the point of asking him what that work might be, but something in his manner showed me that the question would be an unwelcome one. I pondered over our short conversation, however, and endeavoured to draw my deductions from it. He said that he would acquire no knowledge which did not bear upon his object. Therefore all the knowledge which he possessed was such as would be useful to him. I enumerated in my own mind all the various points upon which he had shown me that he was exceptionally well-informed. I even took a pencil and jotted them down. I could not help smiling at the document when I had completed it. It ran in this way:

34	SHERLOCK HOLMES—his limits.
	1. Knowledge of Literature.—Nil.
35	2. „ „ Philosophy.—Nil.
	3. „ „ Astronomy.—Nil.
36	4. „ „ Politics.—Feeble.
37	5. „ „ Botany.—Variable. Well up in belladonna, opium, and poisons generally. Knows nothing of practical gardening.
38	6. „ „ Geology.—Practical, but limited. Tells at a glance different soils from each other. After walks has shown me splashes upon his trousers, and told me by their colour and consistence in what part of London he had received them.
39	7. „ „ Chemistry.—Profound.
40	8. „ „ Anatomy.—Accurate, but unsystematic.
41	9. „ „ Sensational Literature.—Immense. He appears to know every detail of every horror perpetrated in the century.
	10. Plays the violin well.
42-43	11. Is an expert singlestick player, boxer, and swordsman.
44	12. Has a good practical knowledge of British law.

37 *and poisons generally*. "It is probably safe to assume, therefore, that Holmes . . . owned several important works in those fields," Miss Madeleine B. Stern wrote in her impressive study, "Sherlock Holmes: Rare Book Collector." "His toxicology collection probably included Santes Ardoyno's *Opus de Venenis*, though more likely in the Basle 1562 second edition than in the incunable first edition. To this he may well have added such fine volumes as Mercuriale's *De Venenis* (Frankfurt, 1584) and Codronchi's *De Morbis Veneficiia* (Milan, 1618). The nineteenth century produced many informative toxicologies which Holmes doubtless purchased from time to time. He was not likely to have passed up Sir Robert Christison's *Treatise on Poisons* (Edinburgh, 1829), since Christison had taught medical jurisprudence at Edinburgh and had performed the autopsy on one of the victims in the trial of Burke and Hare. Another treatise, published the same year, Morgan and Addison's *Essay on the Operation of Poisonous Agents upon the Living Body* was very possibly added to the Holmes collection, since it was the first book in English on the actions of poisons in the human body. Dragendorff, who introduced methods for the detection of poisons in the human body, was more likely represented on the Holmes shelf by his *Die Gerichtlichchemische Ermitter-*

ling von Giften (St. Petersburg, 1868). On the specific subject of opium, Holmes may have acquired Hartmann's *Discursis Qvidam de Opio* (London, 1753), and, of course, a first edition of De Quincey. It is likely that Holmes also owned a copy of the London, 1867, edition of De Quincey's *Confessions of an English Opium-Eater* —an edition to which are added Analects from John Paul Richter. Among the analects is one on 'The Grandeur of Man in His Littleness,' a concept to which Holmes referred during his work on *The Sign of the Four*. On the subject of belladonna, Holmes surely purchased Kilmer's treatise, *Belladonna: A Study of Its History, Action and Uses in Medicine*, when it appeared in 1894."

38 *Tells at a glance different soils from each other*. "Holmes' geological interest in soils . . . marks him out as a forerunner in this field," Miss Stern continued. "Most soil analyses appeared later than that date, except, for example, Bergman's *Specimen Academicum, Caussas Sterilitatis Agorum Exponens* (Upsala, 1754) which Holmes likely acquired. When the works of Sir John Bennett Lawes (*The Nitrogen as Nitric Acid in the Soils and Subsoils of . . . Rothamsted*, London, 1883) and Charles Barnard (*Talks About the Soil in Its Relation to Plants and Business*, New York, 1894) emerged . . . Holmes almost certainly added them to his library."

39 7. *Knowledge of Chemistry.—Profound.* Watson later misquoted himself as having said here "chemistry eccentric" ("The Five Orange Pips").

"Who can question, then," Miss Stern asked, "that . . . [Holmes] acquired Giovanni Batista della Porta's *De Distillatione* (Rome, 1608) with its splendid woodcuts of chemical apparatus, or Lavoisier's *Traité Élémentaire de Chimie* (Paris, 1789), *Lectures on the Elements of Chemistry* (Edinburgh, 1803) by Joseph Black, founder of quantitative analysis and pneumatic chemistry, or a first edition of Davy's *Elements of Chemical Philosophy* (London, 1812)."

40 8. *Knowledge of Anatomy.—Accurate, but unsystematic.* "It is difficult . . . to do more than suggest one or two titles that may have appeared on Holmes' shelf." (We are again quoting Miss Stern.) "Bidloo's *Anatomia* (Amsterdam, 1685) probably bore a Holmes *ex libris*, and it is even possible that the detector may have invested in one or two incunables, such as Mondino de' Luzzi's *Anothomia* (Pavia, 1478), the first book devoted solely to anatomy. It is difficult to be sure of this, however, though there is little doubt that Holmes acquired later works in the field, notably Sir Charles Bell's *System of Dissections* (Edinburgh, 1798–1803)."

41 9. *Knowledge of Sensational Literature.—Immense.* "This category comprises more or less factual writings about the misdeeds of real criminals," Professor Clarke Olney wrote in "The Literacy of Sherlock Holmes." "Sherlock makes frequent use of his unique knowledge of the classic cases in the annals of crime, from Jonathan Wild, to whom Holmes compares Professor Moriarty [*The Valley of Fear*], to Thomas Griffiths Wainewright, the poisoner ["The Adventure of the Illustrious Client"], and insists that such knowledge is invaluable to the practicing detective. It should surprise no one, therefore, that Holmes shows himself equally familiar with the exploits and methods of the fictional detectives M. Dupin of Poe and M. Lecoq of Gaboriau."

Miss Stern adds: "Though Holmes probably owned *The Newgate Calendar . . . from . . . 1700 to the Present Time* (London, 1773) as well as the later *Newgate Calendar: Containing the Lives . . . of . . . Housebreakers, Highwaymen, etc.,* by an Old-Bailey Barrister (London, 1840?), it must be admitted that his 'immense' knowledge of the field was based primarily upon his own commonplace books, in which, from time to time, he placed cuttings on crime, pasted extracts, and made out his ever useful indexes."

42 *singlestick player.* "A singlestick is about 34″ long," Mr. Ralph A. Ashton wrote in "The Secret Weapons of 221B Baker Street." "It is usually made of hickory or oak. . . . [It] has a basket guard to protect the user's hand from the onslaughts of his opponent. . . . The singlestick is essentially a slashing, whacking, battering, beating and clubbing sort

of weapon, designed to train sabre-fighters in the gentle art of carving the casques of men. The *coup d'honneur* in singlestick play is a broken head. . . . Singlestick play [should not be confused with] the French cane-fencing, which is specifically designed to teach one the art of self-defense with a walking-stick."

"It is doubtful if Holmes engaged in any singlestick competition after his early days in London," the late H. T. Webster wrote in "Observations of Sherlock Holmes as an Athlete and Sportsman," "but his youthful practice with it made the cane ["The Adventure of the Speckled Band"] or hunting crop an unusually formidable weapon in his hands. Watson declared that the latter was Holmes' favorite weapon ["The Adventure of the Six Napoleons"]. . . . Holmes therefore kept his hunting-crop in his rooms ["A Case of Identity"]. On one occasion, at least ["The Red-Headed League"], he found it effective protection against a man armed with a pistol."

43 *boxer, and swordsman.* We know that boxing and fencing were Holmes' only sports in his days at Oxford ("The *Gloria Scott*"). There is no Canonical report of Holmes with sword in hand, however, and it seems safe to assume that he seldom or never touched a foil or épée after his early acquaintanceship with Watson.

Miss Stern has added: "On singlestick and swordmanship [Holmes] may have owned the *Practise* (London, 1595) of Saviolo, L'Abbat's *Art of Fencing* (Dublin, 1734) and, more than likely, *Anti-Pugilism, or the Science of Defense Exemplified in Short and Easy Lessons, for the Practice of the Broad Sword and Single Stick . . . By a Highland Officer* (London, 1790) with four copperplates by Cruikshank. On boxing, he may well have purchased the Mercurialis, *De Arte Gymnastica* (Venice, 1573) with its boxing cuts, Whitehead's *Gymnasiad* (London, 1744), the first publication dealing exclusively with boxing in English, *The Art of Boxing* (1789) by the champion, Daniel Mendoza, and other lesser works on the Queensberry rules and *la boxe française*."

44 *a good practical knowledge of British law.* So much so that Mr. Albert P. Blaustein ("Sherlock Holmes as a Lawyer") holds that Holmes *was* a lawyer.

The late Fletcher Pratt added ("Very Little Murder") that "when the record of Mr. Holmes' cases is examined, we find that in every single case where an actual crime was committed . . . he obtained legal proof full enough to satisfy any jury; witness evidence plus circumstantial evidence, and in many cases . . . a confession in addition. . . . This demonstrates conclusively that Holmes' knowledge of the law was . . . profound."

Miss Stern has noted that "it is fairly safe . . . to suppose that [Holmes] owned Fitzherbert's *Great Abridgement of the Law* (London, 1516), the first serious attempt to systematize the law of England, as well as Littleton's *Tenures in English* (London, 1583) and a copy of the first edition of Blackstone's *Commentaries* (Oxford, 1765–1769)."

45 *Mendelssohn's Lieder*. The *Lieder ohne Wortes*, or "Songs Without Words," of Jakob Ludwig Felix Mendelssohn-Bartholdy, 1809–1847.

46 *fantastic and cheerful*. "I submit," the late Harvey Officer, composer of the *Baker Street Suite* for violin and piano, in five movements, wrote in "Sherlock Holmes and Music," "that you can do sonorous or melancholy chords or fantastic and cheerful chords on a piano with a certain degree of carelessness, but I defy any violinist to produce such chords on a violin that is lying carelessly across his knees. Chords on a violin are always a *tour de force*. They are not natural to the instrument. They can only be played when the violin is held strongly in its accustomed position, and even then they are not the violin's most expressive sounds. It is pre-eminently the instrument of melody, not of harmony."

"I suggest that Holmes, as he sat in his chair, placed the tail piece of the violin against his middle, holding his left arm under it and the fingers of that arm on the fingerboard in the usual way," William Braid White, Mus. Doc., wrote in "Sherlock Holmes and the Equal Temperament." "This would bring the violin to a position nearly at right angles to his body as he sat in the chair, leaving his right arm and hand free to use the bow, and the left arm and hand, as before remarked, equally free for the fingerboard."

Mr. Rolfe Boswell ("Quick, Watson, the Fiddle!") could not bring himself to agree with Dr. White's suggestion. Holmes' instrument, he thought, was not the violin at all but the "violin's darklinger congener"—the viola.

In any case, both Dr. White and Mr. Guy Warrack (*Sherlock Holmes and Music*) agree that when Holmes produced these chords he was reminding himself, and perhaps practicing, the famous *Chaconne* (at any rate, the introductory parts of it) from Johann Sebastian Bach's *D Minor Sonata* for violin alone.

47 *the trial upon my patience*. Mr. Emanuel Berg ("For It's Greatly to Their Credit") has taken Watson's wording here to indicate that the "series of favourite airs" were the work of William Schwenck Gilbert, 1836–1911, and Arthur Seymour Sullivan, 1842–1900, from *Trial by Jury* (produced March 25, 1875) to *Patience* (although *Patience* was not produced until April 23, 1881).

Mr. Warrack has suggested that Mendelssohn's *Auf Flugen des Gesanges* "might well have been [another] favourite with" Watson. "Only two versions were available [on the recordings of that time]," Mr. Anthony Boucher has noted in "The Records of Baker Street," "one by the soprano Irene Abendroth (7" black G & T, Dresden, 1902, 43181) and one by tenor Marian Alma (10" Berliner, Berlin, 1901, 42164 or 42167). But we can well imagine his satisfaction with the sturdy and popular English numbers—*Hearts of Oak, Robin Adair, The Lost Chord*—recorded by such native singers as Perceval Allen, Andrew Black, William

When I had got so far in my list I threw it into the fire in despair. 'If I can only find what the fellow is driving at by reconciling all these accomplishments, and discovering a calling which needs them all,' I said to myself, 'I may as well give up the attempt at once.'

I see that I have alluded above to his powers upon the violin. These were very remarkable, but as eccentric as all his other accomplishments. That he could play pieces, and difficult pieces, I knew well, because at my request he has played **45** me some of Mendelssohn's Lieder, and other favourites. When left to himself, however, he would seldom produce any music or attempt any recognized air. Leaning back in his arm-chair of an evening, he would close his eyes and scrape carelessly at the fiddle which was thrown across his knee. Sometimes the chords were sonorous and melancholy. Occasionally **46** they were fantastic and cheerful. Clearly they reflected the thoughts which possessed him, but whether the music aided those thoughts, or whether the playing was simply the result of a whim or fancy, was more than I could determine. I might have rebelled against these exasperating solos had it not been that he usually terminated them by playing in quick succession a whole series of my favourite airs as a slight compensa- **47** tion for the trial upon my patience.

During the first week or so we had no callers, and I had begun to think that my companion was as friendless a man as I was myself. Presently, however, I found that he had many acquaintances, and those in the most different classes of society. There was one little sallow, rat-faced, dark-eyed **48** fellow, who was introduced to me as Mr Lestrade, and who came three or four times in a single week. One morning a young girl called, fashionably dressed, and stayed for half an hour or more. The same afternoon brought a grey-headed, seedy visitor, looking like a Jew pedlar, who appeared to me to be much excited, and who was closely followed by a slipshod elderly woman. On another occasion an old white-haired

PRESENTLY, HOWEVER, I FOUND THAT HE HAD MANY ACQUAINTANCES . . .

Illustration by C. Coulston for *Stories of Sherlock Holmes*, Vol. I, New York and London: Harper & Brothers, 1904. Coulston, if we have correctly deciphered the name, is not mentioned in either of the two iconographies that have so far been published on Holmes.

gentleman had an interview with my companion; and on another, a railway porter in his velveteen uniform. When **49** any of these nondescript individuals put in an appearance, Sherlock Holmes used to beg for the use of the sitting-room, and I would retire to my bedroom. He always apologized to me for putting me to this inconvenience. 'I have to use this room as a place of business,' he said, 'and these people are my clients.' Again I had an opportunity of asking him a point-blank question, and again my delicacy prevented me from forcing another man to confide in me. I imagined at the time that he had some strong reason for not alluding to it, but he soon dispelled the idea by coming round to the subject of his own accord.

It was upon the 4th of March, as I have good reason to **50** remember, that I rose somewhat earlier than usual, and found that Sherlock Holmes had not yet finished his breakfast. The landlady had become so accustomed to my late habits that **51** my place had not been laid nor my coffee prepared. With the unreasonable petulance of mankind I rang the bell and gave a curt intimation that I was ready. Then I picked up a magazine from the table and attempted to while away the time **52** with it, while my companion munched silently at his toast. **53** One of the articles had a pencil mark at the heading, and I naturally began to run my eye through it.

Its somewhat ambitious title was *The Book of Life,* and it attempted to show how much an observant man might learn by an accurate and systematic examination of all that came in his way. It struck me as being a remarkable mixture of shrewdness and of absurdity. The reasoning was close and intense, but the deductions appeared to me to be far-fetched and exaggerated. The writer claimed by a momentary expression, a twitch of a muscle or a glance of an eye, to fathom a man's inmost thoughts. Deceit, according to him, was an impossibility in the case of one trained to observation and analysis. His conclusions were as infallible as so many propositions of Euclid. So startling would his results appear to the **54** uninitiated that until they learned the processes by which he had arrived at them they might well consider him as a necromancer.

'From a drop of water,' said the writer, 'a logician could infer the possibility of an Atlantic or a Niagara without having seen or heard of one or the other. So all life is a great chain, the nature of which is known whenever we are shown a single link of it. Like all other arts, the Science of Deduction and Analysis is one which can only be acquired by long and patient study, nor is life long enough to allow any mortal to attain the highest possible perfection in it. Before turning to those moral and mental aspects of the matter which present the greatest difficulties, let the inquirer begin by mastering more elementary problems. Let him on meeting a fellow-mortal, learn at a glance to distinguish the history of the man, and the trade or profession to which he belongs. Puerile as such an exercise may seem, it sharpens the faculties of observation, and teaches one where to look and what to look for. By a man's finger-nails, by his coat-sleeve, by his boot, by his trouser-knees, by the callosities of his forefinger and thumb, by his expression, by his shirt-cuffs—by each of these things a man's calling is plainly revealed. That all united should fail to enlighten the competent inquirer in any case is almost inconceivable.'

Green, John Harrison, Esther Palliser and William Paull—to say nothing of one Herbert Goddard, which was the psuedonym wisely chosen for such purposes by the suspiciously foreign-sounding Emilio do Gogorza (who also recorded for the Spanish as Carlos Francisco and for the French as M. Fernand)."

48 *one little sallow, rat-faced, dark-eyed fellow.* Mr. Lestrade—*Inspector* Lestrade, as we shortly learn, and Inspector *G.* Lestrade as he later signed himself in a letter to Holmes ("The Cardboard Box") had been, we are soon told, a Scotland Yard Inspector for twenty years and was to be a Scotland Yard Inspector twenty years later. As the late Gavin Brend wrote in "The Man from the Yard":

> A life of ease I am much afraid
> Was denied to Inspector G. Lestrade.
> With the *Study in Scarlet* in '81
> You'd think that his job had just begun.
> But nevertheless the fact appears
> He'd already put in some twenty years.
> And yet if the Garrideb case be true
> He was still at the Yard in 1902.
> I feel it must be exceedingly hard
> To spend forty years at Scotland Yard.

But it has never been clear just how this "little sallow, rat-faced, dark-eyed fellow"—clearly below the regulation height—ever got into the police in the first place. Watson mellowed in his attitude toward Lestrade as the years went on: in "The Adventure of the Second Stain" and "The Cardboard Box" he is using the terms "bulldog features" and "wiry, dapper and ferret-like" to describe Lestrade, and in *The Hound of the Baskervilles,* Lestrade is "a small, wiry, bulldog of a man." The outstanding study to date of Inspector G. Lestrade is that by Mr. L. S. Holstein. In "Inspector G. Lestrade" he has written: "We find [Lestrade] active in twelve of Dr. Watson's writings, as well as a reference to him in the text of 'The Adventure of the Three Garridebs.' . . . His Christian name is unknown to us. . . . One can speculate on the denotation of that tantalizing 'G.' from George to Gouverneur without success. There is no clue, and without a shred of evidence I lean toward Gustave as a name that fits the subject. [Sponsors of a French origin for Lestrade might identify G. also with Giles or Gracchus, as Mr. Eliot Kimball pointed out in his "Origin and Evolution of G. Lestrade: I—Onomatological Considerations."] If we make the generous assumption that he joined the Metropolitan Police at the age of twenty-one, he would have been on the high side of forty at the time of the Drebber affair, and we know he was still active in [1902]. We may draw the conclusion from all this that Lestrade was Holmes' senior by some ten or twelve years [born, that is, in 1844–1846], and served on the force more than forty years. At the outset, he may have pounded a beat . . . but because of his lack of stature, it is more likely that he came up through the records bureau, and not as a constable."

49 *a railway porter in his velveteen uniform.* As Mr. Robert Keith Leavitt observed in "Nummi in Arca or The Fiscal Holmes," ". . . Holmes very soon outgrew his dependence upon [clients like these], though he continued (be it said to his credit) to interest himself in such cases all through his years of affluence."

50 *the 4th of March.* A Friday in 1881. That it *was* 1881 has again been indicated by the late Christopher Morley. In "Was Sherlock Holmes an American?", he wrote: "Why . . . does Watson write, 'It was upon the 4th of March, as I have good reason to remember,' . . . And why was Holmes still at the breakfast table? It was the 4th of March, 1881, and Holmes was absorbed in reading the news dispatches about the inauguration, to take place that day, of President Garfield."

51 *The landlady.* This is the famous Mrs. Hudson, although we are not told her name in this adventure. She was Mrs. *Martha* Hudson if, as most commentators think, Mrs. Hudson and the housekeeper who served Holmes after his retirement to the Sussex Downs were one and the same. "A young widow, one imagines her to have been, who took up commercial housekeeping when the experiment of marriage was in some way tragically ended," Mr. Vincent Starrett wrote in his scholarly study of "The Singular Adventures of Martha Hudson." "But no whisper of her life before that day in 1881, when Holmes first called upon her, has ever been revealed. The notion persists that she had been unhappy; she kept so very still about it all." Some students take the fact that she had a "stately tread," as we soon learn, to mean that Mrs. Hudson was corpulent. "But stately, too, is the tread of many a queenly artist's model and showgirl," Mr. Manly Wade Wellman wrote in "The Great Man's Great Son." "Mrs. Hudson was opulently made, no more than five feet four inches tall, fair and rosy, with wide eyes of deepest blue. Connoisseurs of the eighties would, and probably did, call her a demm'd fine figure of a woman."

52 *a magazine.* It was the *Cornhill Magazine,* the late Edgar W. Smith thought. It was "unquestionably" the *Fortnightly,* in the late Christopher Morley's opinion.

53 *munched silently at his toast.* How Holmes accomplished this minor miracle is not known.

54 *Euclid.* The Greek mathematician often called "the father of geometry." He was born in and resided in Alexandria, Egypt, about 350–300 B.C. Euclid was famous for his *Elements,* a collection of theorems and problems which formed the basis of geometry until "modern mathematics" were introduced into the curricula.

55 *a third-class carriage.* Throughout the Canon, both Holmes and Watson travel first class, as did

'What ineffable twaddle!' I cried, slapping the magazine down on the table; 'I never read such rubbish in my life.'

'What is it?' asked Sherlock Holmes.

'Why, this article,' I said, pointing at it with my egg-spoon as I sat down to my breakfast. 'I see that you have read it since you have marked it. I don't deny that it is smartly written. It irritates me though. It is evidently the theory of some armchair lounger who evolves all these neat little paradoxes in the seclusion of his own study. It is not practical. I should **55** like to see him clapped down in a third-class carriage on the **56** Underground, and asked to give the trades of all his fellow-**57** travellers. I would lay a thousand to one against him.'

'You would lose your money,' Holmes remarked calmly. 'As for the article, I wrote it myself.'

'You!'

'Yes; I have a turn both for observation and for deduction. The theories which I have expressed there, and which appear to you to be so chimerical, are really extremely practical—so practical that I depend upon them for my bread and cheese.'

'And how?' I asked involuntarily.

'Well, I have a trade of my own. I suppose I am the only one in the world. I'm a consulting detective, if you can understand what that is. Here in London we have lots of Government detectives and lots of private ones. When these fellows are at fault, they come to me, and I manage to put them on the right scent. They lay all the evidence before me, and I am generally able, by the help of my knowledge of the history of crime, to set them straight. There is a strong family resem-**58** blance about misdeeds, and if you have all the details of a thousand at your finger ends, it is odd if you can't unravel **59** the thousand and first. Lestrade is a well-known detective. He got himself into a fog recently over a forgery case, and that was what brought him here.'

'And these other people?'

'They are mostly sent on by private inquiry agencies. They are all people who are in trouble about something, and want a little enlightening. I listen to their story, they listen to my comments, and then I pocket my fee.'

'But do you mean to say,' I said, 'that without leaving your room you can unravel some knot which other men can make nothing of, although they have seen every detail for themselves?'

'Quite so. I have a kind of intuition that way. Now and again a case turns up which is a little more complex. Then I have to bustle about and see things with my own eyes. You see I have a lot of special knowledge which I apply to the problem, and which facilitates matters wonderfully. Those rules of deduction laid down in that article which aroused your scorn are invaluable to me in practical work. Observation with me is second nature. You appeared to be surprised when I told you, on our first meeting, that you had come from Afghanistan.'

'You were told, no doubt.'

'Nothing of the sort. I *knew* you came from Afghanistan. From long habit the train of thoughts ran so swiftly through my mind that I arrived at the conclusion without being conscious of intermediate steps. There were such steps, however. The train of reasoning ran, "Here is a gentleman of a medical type, but with the air of a military man. Clearly an

NEW SCOTLAND YARD

The illustration is from *The Baker Street Journal*, Vol. III, No. 1, Old Series, January, 1948, p. 36.

BAKER STREET STATION ON THE DAY THE METROPOLITAN RAILWAY BEGAN OPERATIONS, JANUARY 9, 1863

Mr. Gladstone is seated in the truck in the foreground. The illustration is from G. M. Trevelyan's *Illustrated English Social History*, *Vol. IV, The Nineteenth Century*, London and New York: Longmans, Green and Co., Ltd., 1942 and 1944.

most men in their position in those days, and we know Watson's opinion of the Retired Colourman who insisted on traveling third class.

56 *on the Underground.* It was the City Solicitor, Charles Pearson, who first proposed to relieve the terrible congestion that made the narrow London streets all but impassable at times by encircling the metropolis with a tunnel-railroad, with frequent stations, which would connect with all the railway termini taking visitors in and out of the city. Despite long and bitter opposition to a "Sewer Railway" (*Punch*'s term), the first of London's "subways," the Metropolitan Railway Company, began operations, using coal-burning steam locomotives, on January 9, 1863, between Bishop's Road, Paddington, and Farringdon Street. On the opening day over 30,000 people traveled over the line, and from nine o'clock in the morning until past midday it was impossible to obtain a seat in the City-bound trains at any of the intermediate stations. The carriages were then mere open trucks (*see illustration*). In the evening the returning crowds from Farringdon Street were equally great. In the following year the number of passengers carried amounted to nearly 9.5 million, or more than three times the population of London at that time; as early as 1877 the Underground was carrying 56 million passengers a year. A second London Underground, the Metropolitan District Railway, followed the shallow design and used the steam locomotives of the first line, but the City and South London Railway, opened in 1890, was placed in tubes ranging from 48 to 105 feet beneath the surface, and began operations with electric locomotives that at least did away with the "fearsome mixture of coal smoke, sulphur, carbon dioxide and carbonic acid" that had formed the atmosphere of the Undergrounds up to that time.

57 *I would lay a thousand to one against him.'* An early indication that Watson was a man who relished gambling and betting.

58 *There is a strong family resemblance about misdeeds*. Later in *A Study in Scarlet*, Holmes says: "There is nothing new under the sun. It has all been done before." And in *The Valley of Fear* he says: "Everything comes in circles, even Professor Moriarty." "These remarks," Mr. T. S. Blakeney wrote in *Sherlock Holmes: Fact or Fiction?*, "suffice to show us why Holmes laid such stress on accumulating that knowledge of sensational literature . . . that so impressed Watson and Stamford. If you had all the details of a thousand cases at your fingerends, it was odd, said Holmes, if you could not unravel the thousand and first. Many times he impresses this point upon his listeners—to Lestrade, to Gregson, to Inspector MacDonald; and M. François le Villard was quick to acknowledge his indebtedness to the same faculty [*The Sign of the Four*]."

59 *Lestrade is a well-known detective*. Of the sixty cases recorded in the Canon, forty involve the official police. Of these, Lestrade, as we have seen, is mentioned or takes some part in thirteen. Gregson appears in four, Hopkins in four, Bradstreet in three, and others in seventeen.

60 *Clearly in Afghanistan."* ". . . for all Holmes knew, Watson could have been, not in Afghanistan, but in South Africa, where also the British Army had just concluded a sizeable colonial war, that of 1879–1880 against the Zulus," Mr. Samuel F. Howard wrote in "More About Maiwand." "Either Holmes had other data that he did not explain to Watson (or Watson did not pass on to us), or he was guilty of sheer guesswork. I prefer to believe he observed some other detail in Watson's appearance that he did not bother to repeat to Watson . . ."

61 *Dupin*. Ratiocinative hero of "The Murders in the Rue Morgue" (1841), "The Purloined Letter" (1845) and "The Mystery of Marie Rogêt" (1842). "Dupin, C. Auguste, poet and amateur of the arts and of deduction; b. *circa* 1820. Unmarried. Came of good family but suffered financial reverses. . . . Hobbies: Reading; living by candlelight during the day and wandering abroad at night. Residence: 33 Rue Donât, Faubourg St. Germain, Paris."—Kenneth Macgowan, *Sleuths: Twenty-three Great Detectives of Fiction and Their Best Stories*; New York: Harcourt, Brace & Company, 1931.

62 *Dupin was a very inferior fellow*. It is Holmes, not Conan Doyle, who is being less than gracious here. Conan Doyle once said that if he had to name the few books which had really influenced his own life, he would put Poe's stories second only to Macaulay's essays. He considered Poe to be "the supreme original short story writer," and he stressed the debt that all later writers of detective fiction owe to "those admirable stories of M. Dupin, so wonderful in their dramatic force, their reticence, their quick dramatic point" (*Through the Magic Door*). Speaking at a dinner sponsored

army doctor, then. He has just come from the tropics, for his face is dark, and that is not the natural tint of his skin, for his wrists are fair. He has undergone hardship and sickness, as his haggard face says clearly. His left arm has been injured. He holds it in a stiff and unnatural manner. Where in the tropics could an English army doctor have seen much hard- **60** ship and got his arm wounded? Clearly in Afghanistan." The whole train of thought did not occupy a second. I then remarked that you came from Afghanistan, and you were astonished.'

'It is simple enough as you explain it,' I said, smiling. 'You **61** remind me of Edgar Allen Poe's Dupin. I had no idea that such individuals did exist outside of stories.'

Sherlock Holmes rose and lit his pipe. 'No doubt you think that you are complimenting me in comparing me to Dupin,' he observed. 'Now, in my opinion, Dupin was **62** a very inferior fellow. That trick of his of breaking in on his friends' thoughts with an apropos remark after a quarter of an hour's silence is really very showy and superficial. He had some analytical genius, no doubt; but he was by no means such a phenomenon as Poe appeared to imagine.'

63   'Have you read Gaboriau's works?' I asked. 'Does Lecoq come up to your idea of a detective?'

Sherlock Holmes sniffed sardonically. 'Lecoq was a miserable bungler,' he said, in an angry voice; 'he had only one thing to recommend him, and that was his energy. That book made me positively ill. The question was how to identify an unknown prisoner. I could have done it in twenty-four hours. Lecoq took six months or so. It might be made a text-book for detectives to teach them what to avoid.'

I felt rather indignant at having two characters whom I had admired treated in this cavalier style. I walked over to the window, and stood looking out into the busy street. 'This fellow may be very clever,' I said to myself, 'but he is certainly very conceited.'

64   'There are no crimes and no criminals in these days,' he said, querulously. 'What is the use of having brains in our profession. I know well that I have it in me to make my name famous. No man lives or has ever lived who has brought the same amount of study and of natural talent to the detection of crime which I have done. And what is the result? There is no crime to detect, or, at most, some bungling villainy with a **65** motive so transparent that even a Scotland Yard official can see through it.'

I was still annoyed at his bumptious style of conversation. I thought it best to change the topic.

'I wonder what that fellow is looking for?' I asked, pointing to a stalwart, plainly-dressed individual who was walking slowly down the other side of the street, looking anxiously at the numbers. He had a large blue envelope in his hand, and was evidently the bearer of a message.

'You mean the retired sergeant of Marines,' said Sherlock Holmes.

'Brag and bounce!' thought I to myself. 'He knows that I cannot verify his guess.'

The thought had hardly passed through my mind when the man whom we were watching caught sight of the number on our door, and ran rapidly across the roadway. We heard a loud knock, a deep voice below, and heavy steps ascending the stair.

'For Mr Sherlock Holmes,' he said, stepping into the room and handing my friend the letter.

Here was an opportunity of taking the conceit out of him. He little thought of this when he made that random shot. 'May I ask, my lad,' I said, in the blandest voice, 'what your trade may be?'

'Commissionaire, sir,' he said, gruffly. 'Uniform away for **66** repairs.'

'And you were?' I asked, with a slightly malicious glance at my companion.

'A sergeant, sir, Royal Marine Light Infantry, sir. No **67** answer? Right, sir.'

He clicked his heels together, raised his hand in a salute, and was gone.

by the Authors' Club on March 1, 1909, to honor the centenary of Poe's birth, Conan Doyle said: ". . . his tales were one of the great landmarks and starting points in the literature of the last century for French as well as for English writers. For those tales have been so pregnant with suggestion, so stimulating to the minds of others, that it may be said of many of them that each is a root from which a whole literature has developed. . . . His original and inventive brain was always . . . opening up pioneer tracks for other men to explore. Where was the detective story until Poe breathed the breath of life into it?" Even Holmes seems to have changed his mind about Dupin later, if we take it for granted that he meant Dupin when he spoke to Watson about a "close reasoner" in Poe's passage to Watson and implies that Watson was the detractor—"inclined to treat the matter as a mere *tour-de-force* of the author" ("The Cardboard Box"). "Watson must have been a patient man to have endured this turn-about on Holmes' part," Mr. Morris Rosenblum commented in "Foreign Language Quotations in the Canon."

63 *Gaboriau's works?'* The works of the French novelist Émile Gaboriau, 1833–1873, whose detective stories about M. Lecoq include five books: *L'Affaire Lerouge* (1866), *Le Dossier 113* (1867), *Le Crime d'Orcival* (1868), *Monsieur Lecoq* (1869) and *Les Esclaves de Paris* (1869). "Through the jostling throng of *banquiers véreux*, Monsieur Lecoq, simple agent of the Sûreté, comes stepping, fresh as a bridegroom, *un beau gars, à l'oeil clair, à l'air resolu*, or, as casual visitors saw him in his careful disguise, a sober personage of distinguished appearance, with his gold spectacles, his white tie, his *mince redingote*. Against a canvas of tiresome puppets he stands out as a living figure."—Valentine Williams, "Gaboriau: Father of Detective Novels."

64 *'There are no crimes and no criminals in these days.'* Compare Holmes' observations in *The Sign*

of the Four and "The Adventure of Wisteria Lodge": "Crime is commonplace, existence is commonplace, and no qualities save those which are commonplace have any function upon earth"; "Life is commonplace, the papers are sterile; audacity and romance seem to have passed forever from the criminal world." "We clearly see from these observations," Mr. T. S. Blakeney wrote in *Sherlock Holmes: Fact or Fiction?*, "that the artist [in Holmes] has outstripped the social worker. Mr. Thomas Burke, we think, has been known to regret the good old, bad old days of Limehouse; so Holmes, too, could lament the lack of a first-class criminal. 'What we want,' he might have said with H. B. Irving, 'is a good bloody murder.' (Compare Holmes' almost bloodthirsty remarks to Watson at the opening of 'The Adventure of the Bruce-Partington Plans.') More than once we catch a wistful tone in his reference to the dear departed Professor Moriarty—see 'The Adventure of the Norwood Builder' and the tinge of hope that inspired his suggestion that Dr. Leslie Armstrong ["The Adventure of the Missing Three-Quarter"] might fill the gap left by the professor's death."

65 *Scotland Yard.* "Scotland Yard" is the popular name for the London Metropolitan Police force established in 1829 by Sir Robert Peel at No. 4 Whitehall Place—called "Scotland Yard" because the spot marked the site of a palace where, in Saxon times and later, the Kings of Scotland resided when they came to London to do homage to the Kings of England for fiefs held by them as vassals to the English crown—Cumberland, Huntingdon, and other places. Old Scotland Yard was housed in "a handsome building of three floors, of mellow London brick with Portland Stone dressings" (William H. Gill, "Some Notable Sherlockian Buildings"). "Former occupants, before the arrival of the police . . . , were the Royal Surveyors-General, including such illustrious names as Inigo Jones, Sir Christopher Wren, and Sir John Vanbrugh. The vast increase in population of the Outer Ring of the Metropolis between 1880 and 1900 made it imperative for the police to erect a new Headquarters. The architect selected was Norman Shaw who attempted to bring Scottish architecture to the English capital. The New Scotland Yard opened in 1891 [*see illustration*] was built on the actual foundations of a defunct National Opera House, designed by Francis Fowler in 1875. Its foundation stone was actually laid by the Duke of Edinburgh in 1878, but the new Opera House never climbed above its foundations. These may still be seen under New Scotland Yard, and Shaw erected his fierce Scottish baronial castle over them, built of dour granite, quarried by Dartmoor convicts." There is, at New Scotland Yard, a "Black Museum" which includes such exhibits as the false arm, dark spectacles and folding ladder of Holmes' "old friend," Charles Peace (see "The Adventure of the Illustrious Client").

66 '*Commissionaire.* A (normally) uniformed messenger employed by the Corps of Commissionaires founded in 1859 by Captain Sir Edward Walter for the employment of pensioned soldiers, sailors, and (now) airmen. Said the Langham Hotel's *Guide to London* in its 1881 edition: "Among the excellent features of London may be numbered the Corps of Commissionaires, composed of retired veterans, most of whom are decorated . . . who for a consideration will run a message, chaperone a young lady, attend an old one, fetch or carry a love-letter, tend the baby, and do a variety of things handily and surely, at the rate of sixpence an hour. . . . They are to be seen everywhere, in a uniform as gorgeous as a major-general's, and are always respectable and trustworthy."

67 *Royal Marine Light Infantry.* Unlike the Americans, who rate their Marines as part of the Navy, the British rate theirs as part of the Army. The British Marines grew out of the Trained Bands of London, and as, such they enjoy a unique privilege: they are allowed to march through London with drums beating and colors flying.

3 ❖ THE LAURISTON GARDENS MYSTERY

I confess that I was considerably startled by this fresh proof of the practical nature of my companion's theories. My respect for his powers of analysis increased wondrously. There still remained some lurking suspicion in my mind, however, that the whole thing was a prearranged episode, intended to dazzle me, though what earthly object he could have in taking me in was past my comprehension. When I looked at him, he had finished reading the note, and his eyes had assumed the vacant, lack-lustre expression which showed mental abstraction.

'How in the world did you deduce that?' I asked.

'Deduce what?' said he petulantly.

'Why, that he was a retired sergeant of Marines.'

'I have no time for trifles,' he answered, brusquely; then with a smile, 'Excuse my rudeness. You broke the thread of my thoughts; but perhaps it is as well. So you actually were not able to see that that man was a sergeant of Marines?'

'No, indeed.'

'It was easier to know it than to explain why I know it. If you were asked to prove that two and two made four, you might find some difficulty, and yet you are quite sure of the fact. Even across the street I could see a great blue anchor tattooed on the back of the fellow's hand. That smacked of the sea. He had a military carriage, however, and regulation side whiskers. There we have the marine. He was a man with some amount of self-importance and a certain air of command. You must have observed the way in which he held his head and swung his cane. A steady, respectable, middle-aged

man, too, on the face of him—all facts which led me to believe that he had been a sergeant.'

'Wonderful!' I ejaculated.

'Commonplace,' said Holmes, though I thought from his expression that he was pleased at my evident surprise and admiration. 'I said just now that there were no criminals. It appears that I am wrong—look at this!' He threw me over the note which the commissionaire had brought.

'Why,' I cried, as I cast my eye over it, 'this is terrible!'

'It does seem to be a little out of the common,' he remarked, calmly. 'Would you mind reading it to me aloud?'   **68**

This is the letter which I read to him:

MY DEAR MR SHERLOCK HOLMES,

There has been a bad business during the night at 3, Lauriston Gardens, off the Brixton Road. Our man on the beat saw a light there about two in the morning, and as the house was an empty one, suspected that something was amiss. He found the door open, and in the front room, which is bare of furniture, discovered the body of a gentleman, well dressed, and having cards in his pocket bearing the name of 'Enoch J. Drebber, Cleveland, Ohio, U.S.A.' There had been no robbery, nor is there any evidence as to how the man met his death. There are marks of blood in the room, but there is no wound upon his person. We are at a loss as to how he came into the empty house; indeed the whole affair is a puzzler. If you can come round to the house any time before twelve, you will find me there. I have left everything *in statu quo* until I hear from you. If you are unable to come, I shall **69** give you fuller details, and would esteem it a great kindness if you would favour me with your opinion.

Yours faithfully,
TOBIAS GREGSON.

'Gregson is the smartest of the Scotland Yarders,' my friend **70** remarked; 'he and Lestrade are the pick of a bad lot. They are both quick and energetic, but conventional—shockingly so. They have their knives into one another, too. They are as jealous as a pair of professional beauties. There will be some fun over this case if they are both put upon the scent.'   **71**

I was amazed at the calm way in which he rippled on. 'Surely there is not a moment to be lost,' I cried; 'shall I go and order you a cab?'   **72**

'I'm not sure about whether I shall go. I am the most incurably lazy devil that ever stood in shoe leather—that is, when the fit is on me, for I can be spry enough at times.'

'Why, it is just such a chance as you have been longing for.'

"... OFF THE BRIXTON ROAD."

The Brixton Road is, today, the Oxford Street of South London and contains some of the largest and finest shops to be found in that area. In Holmes' and Watson's day it was lined, on its east side, with shabby houses which have now been replaced with rows of quite handsome new buildings. (Mrs. Maggie Oakshott of "The Adventure of the Blue Carbuncle" bred geese in a garden back of No. 117 Brixton Road.) The photograph, from the Tate Central Library, is from Michael Harrison's *In the Footsteps of Sherlock Holmes*. It shows the Brixton Road in the winter of 1883, two years after the affair of *A Study in Scarlet*.

68 *'Would you mind reading it to me aloud?'* In *A Study in Scarlet* we see Holmes and Watson looking down from the second (American usage) story of their sitting room across wide Baker Street. Holmes pinpoints a stranger as a sergeant of Marines, partly from the tattoo of a blue anchor on the back of the fellow's hand. Now, says Mr. Jerry Neal Williamson, in "'And Especially Your Eyes,'" "only a man with tremendous 'long vision' could recognize at such a distance what might have been dirt, a scar, a birthmark, a shadow or a mole. Immediately after this remarkable evidence of Holmes' uncanny distance clarity the sleuth threw Watson a note brought him by the commissionaire, saying 'Would you mind reading it to me aloud?'" Holmes, Mr. Williamson deduces, was farsighted: "he suffered from hypermetropia. . . . The basic handicap of a hypermetropic individual can be quickly summed up. This person sees things at a distance with perception and clarity, while he finds it difficult to read clearly anything inches and sometimes feet from his eyes. It is the opposite of myopia; and it assuredly describes Sherlock Holmes." Mr. Williamson, we cannot help but feel, is correct; again and again, as we shall see, Holmes asks Watson (or another) "Would you read it to me aloud?"

69 in statu quo *until I hear from you.* Now this, as Mr. John Ball, Jr., has noted in "Early Days in Baker Street," is a remarkable deference to Holmes, the young amateur, by "the smartest of the Scotland Yarders," explicable only if Gregson recognized Holmes as his superior in both ability and rank. In Mr. Ball's view, Holmes from the start was a private agent in Her Majesty's Government, probably with the classification of a Queen's Messenger, "a unique and highly restricted office. Queen's (or King's) Messenger may go anywhere in the British Empire on official business, and have extraordinary authority in the field. They can, if necessary, command the services of a cruiser; they are diplomatic couriers *par excellence*, to whom are entrusted missions and specialized duties of the highest importance." (The King's Messengers of Charles II play an important role in Mr. John Dickson Carr's recent—1964—historical detective story, *Most Secret*.)

Mr. Robert Keith Leavitt has another view ("Nummi in Arca or The Fiscal Holmes"): "It is demonstrable that Holmes had no official commission from Scotland Yard to act in any of the affairs of record in the Canon. What, then, *was* the nature of Holmes' relation with the Inspectors from the Yard? Clearly this: he was a private detective engaged by each of them privately. For what purpose? For the enhancement of the Inspectors' professional reputations. And how was he paid? He was paid from the private pockets of his Inspector clients."

70 *the smartest of the Scotland Yarders.'* ". . . the only case that Gregson truly worked and collaborated with Holmes on was *A Study in Scarlet*," the late Clifton R. Andrew wrote in "That Scotland Yarder, Gregson—What a Help (?) He Was" (although Gregson appears or is mentioned in four other cases: *The Sign of the Four*, "The Greek Interpreter," "The Adventure of Wisteria Lodge," and "The Adventure of the Red Circle").

71 *if they are both put upon the scent.*' ". . . the experiment was never repeated," the late Gavin Brend wrote in *My Dear Holmes*. "Henceforward Lestrade and Gregson went their separate ways and we never again find them both appearing in the same case."

72 *'shall I go and order you a cab?'* Watson would not have had far to go: the cab rank in Baker Street was at the corner of Dorset Street, a trifle over a block, although a long block, away.

73 *an unofficial personage.*' ". . . on at least two occasions . . . Holmes disclaimed any official connections," Mr. John Ball, Jr., noted in "Early Days in Baker Street." "We must discount these claims to non-official status, for he believed firmly in saying, at all times, whatever was necessary to suit the purpose of the moment. He is certainly not the first confidential agent in history to deny the true source of his employment."

74 *a dun-coloured veil.* Here is another indication that the year of *A Study in Scarlet* was indeed 1881. Weather reports from the *Times* of London show that Friday, March 4, 1881 was "wet and unsettled," and the forecast was for "dull and cold, rain or snow." Saturday, March 4, 1882, on the other hand, was "cloudy" but "generally fine."

75 *the difference between a Stradivarius and an Amati.* The Amati of Cremona were a family of violin-makers which began with Andrew Amati, *fl.* 1535–1580, and reached its peak with Niccolo Amati, 1596–1684. Their pupil Antonio Stradivari or Antonius Stradivarius, 1644–1737, produced at least 1,116 instruments, including violas, cellos, viols, guitars and mandolins, between 1666 and 1737, the finest after 1700. Holmes' own violin, as we learn in "The Cardboard Box," was a Stradivarius. Mr. Guy Warrack in *Sherlock Holmes and Music* has asked why Holmes on this occasion did not mention the *third* great family of Cremonese luthiers—that of Giuseppe Antonio Guarneri (1683–1745).

76 *It biases the judgment.*' Compare: "It is a capital offense to theorize in advance of the facts" —"The Adventure of the Second Stain." "I make a point of never having any prejudices and of following docilely wherever fact may lead me"— "The Reigate Squires." "We approached the case with an absolutely blank mind, which is always an advantage"—"The Cardboard Box." "It is an error to argue in front of your data. You find yourself insensibly twisting them round to fit your theories" —"The Adventure of Wisteria Lodge." "One

'My dear fellow, what does it matter to me? Supposing I unravel the whole matter, you may be sure that Gregson, Lestrade, and Co. will pocket all the credit. That comes of **73** being an unofficial personage.'

'But he begs you to help him.'

'Yes. He knows that I am his superior, and acknowledges it to me; but he would cut his tongue out before he would own it to any third person. However, we may as well go and have a look. I shall work it out on my own hook. I may have a laugh at them, if I have nothing else. Come on!'

He hustled on his overcoat, and bustled about in a way that showed that an energetic fit had superseded the apathetic one.

'Get your hat,' he said.

'You wish me to come?'

'Yes, if you have nothing better to do.' A minute later we were both in a hansom, driving furiously for the Brixton Road.

74   It was a foggy, cloudy morning, and a dun-coloured veil hung over the house-tops, looking like the reflection of the mud-coloured streets beneath. My companion was in the best of spirits, and prattled away about Cremona fiddles, and the **75** difference between a Stradivarius and an Amati. As for myself, I was silent, for the dull weather and the melancholy business upon which we were engaged, depressed my spirits.

'You don't seem to give much thought to the matter in hand,' I said at last, interrupting Holmes' musical disquisition.

'No data yet,' he answered. 'It is a capital mistake to theor- **76** ize before you have all the evidence. It biases the judgment.'

'You will have your data soon,' I remarked, pointing with my finger; 'this is the Brixton Road, and that is the house, if I am not very much mistaken.'

'So it is. Stop, driver, stop!' We were still a hundred yards or so from it, but he insisted upon our alighting, and we finished our journey upon foot.

Number 3, Lauriston Gardens, wore an ill-omened and minatory look. It was one of four which stood back some little way from the street, two being occupied and two empty. The latter looked out with three tiers of vacant melancholy windows, which were blank and dreary, save that here and there a 'To Let' card had developed like a cataract upon the bleared panes. A small garden sprinkled over with a scattered eruption of sickly plants separated each of these houses from the street, and was traversed by a narrow pathway, yellowish in colour, and consisting apparently of a mixture of clay and of gravel. The whole place was very sloppy from the rain which had fallen through the night. The garden was bounded by a three-foot brick wall with a fringe of wood rails upon **77** the top and against this wall was leaning a stalwart police constable, surrounded by a small knot of loafers, who craned their necks and strained their eyes in the vain hope of catching some glimpse of the proceedings within.

I had imagined that Sherlock Holmes would at once have hurried into the house and plunged into a study of the mystery. Nothing appeared to be further from his intention. With an air of nonchalance which, under the circumstances, seemed to me to border upon affectation, he lounged up and down the pavement, and gazed vacantly at the ground, the sky, the opposite houses and the line of railings. Having finished his scrutiny, he proceeded slowly down the path, or rather down the fringe of grass which flanked the path, keeping his eyes riveted upon the ground. Twice he stopped, and once I saw him smile, and heard him utter an exclamation of satisfaction. There were many marks of footsteps upon the **78** wet clayey soil; but since the police had been coming and going over it, I was unable to see how my companion could hope to learn anything from it. Still I had had such extraordinary evidence of the quickness of his perceptive faculties, that I had no doubt that he could see a great deal which was hidden from me.

At the door of the house we were met by a tall, white-faced, flaxen-haired man, with a note-book in his hand, who rushed forward and wrung my companion's hand with effusion. 'It is indeed kind of you to come,' he said, 'I have had everything left untouched.'

'Except that!' my friend answered, pointing at the pathway. 'If a herd of buffaloes had passed along there could not **79** be a greater mess. No doubt, however, you had drawn your own conclusions, Gregson, before you permitted this.'

'I have had so much to do inside the house,' the detective said evasively. 'My colleague, Mr Lestrade, is here. I had relied upon him to look after this.'

Holmes glanced at me and raised his eyebrows sardonically. 'With two such men as yourself and Lestrade upon the ground there will not be much for a third party to find out,' he said.

Gregson rubbed his hands in a self-satisfied way. 'I think we have done all that can be done,' he answered; 'it's a queer case though, and I knew your taste for such things.'

'You did not come here in a cab?' asked Sherlock Holmes.

'No, sir.'

'Nor Lestrade?'

'No, sir.'

'Then let us go and look at the room.' With which inconsequent remark he strode on into the house, followed by Gregson, whose features expressed his astonishment.

A short passage, bare-planked and dusty, led to the kitchen and offices. Two doors opened out of it to the left and to the right. One of these had obviously been closed for many weeks. The other belonged to the dining-room, which was the apartment in which the mysterious affair had occurred. Holmes walked in, and I followed him with that subdued feeling at my heart which the presence of death inspires.

It was a large square room, looking all the larger from the absence of all furniture. A vulgar flaring paper adorned the walls, but it was blotched in places with mildew, and here and there great strips had become detached and hung down, exposing the yellow plaster beneath. Opposite the door was a showy fireplace, surmounted by a mantelpiece of imitation white marble. On one corner of this was stuck the stump of a red wax candle. The solitary window was so dirty that the light was hazy and uncertain, giving a dull grey tinge to everything, which was intensified by the thick layer of dust which coated the whole apartment.

All these details I observed afterwards. At present my attention was centred upon the single, grim, motionless figure which lay stretched upon the boards, with vacant, sightless eyes staring up at the discoloured ceiling. It was that of a

forms provisional theories and waits for time or fuller knowledge to explode them. A bad habit"— "The Adventure of the Sussex Vampire." "If I had not taken things for granted, if I had examined everything with the care which I would have shown had we approached the case *de novo* and had no cut-and-dried story to warp my mind, would I not then have found something more definite to go upon?"—"The Adventure of the Abbey Grange." "These abundant references," Mr. T. S. Blakeney wrote in *Sherlock Holmes: Fact or Fiction?*, ". . . show how keenly Holmes appreciated the liability to form one's suspicions on insufficient evidence. He was not, however, entirely immune from the tendency himself, for both in *The Sign of the Four* and 'The Adventure of the Missing Three-Quarter' he had to reform his theories, and in 'The Yellow Face' his conclusions were definitely wrong."

77 *with a fringe of wood rails upon the top*. Was "*Number 3, Lauriston Gardens*" *off* the Brixton Road, as Gregson said in his letter, or was it actually *in* the Brixton Road? Conflicting clues are to be found in *A Study in Scarlet*, and commentators are not agreed on their interpretation.

Both the late H. W. Bell ("Three Identifications") and Mr. Michael Harrison (*In the Footsteps of Sherlock Holmes*) have taken the view that the row of four houses was actually *in* the Brixton Road, and yet in a sense *off* it, being set back some distance from the pavement. "And in fact," Mr. Bell wrote, "there is no such group of four houses in any of the streets intersecting the Road. Furthermore, though there are in that thoroughfare several pairs of houses, a few groups of three and five, and many more extensive, there is only one which consists precisely of four. These four houses, it is pleasant to observe, correspond with almost perfect accuracy to Watson's description. They are three storeys in height, and are set back about thirty feet from the pavement, from which one mounts a few steps to the pathway leading to the front door. The gardens are bounded by a three-foot brick wall, upon which, however, the old wooden railing has been replaced by a more durable affair in iron. . . . They are numbered from 314 to 320. Since Watson specified No. 3, we may suppose that No. 318, the third in the row, was the scene of the death of Enoch J. Drebber."

"The nearest street bearing the name 'Lauriston,' is Lauriston Road, which leads off the South Side, Wimbledon Common;" Mr. Harrison wrote, "and not by any stretch of the topographical imagination can this be described as 'off the Brixton Road.' . . . 'Lauriston Gardens' was one of those small blocks of houses, set back from Brixton Road behind a wall, and with a small 'carriage drive,' which are still to be seen. . . . There is a block of five houses—numbered 152 to 160, Brixton Road, inclusive—which almost perfectly fit the description that Watson gives us of 'Lauriston Gardens.'"

On the other hand, Mr. Colin Prestige ("South London Adventures") is convinced that ". . . the area known as Myatt's Fields [*see sketch map*] immediately stands out as being the most probable location. . . . The streets which enclose the Fields vary in name; that on the east side is Knatchbull Road, and [a number of factors] would support the theory that No. 3, Lauriston Gardens was one of the houses along the northern stretch of Knatchbull Road. . . ."

78 *marks of footsteps.* Footprints—which Holmes and Watson always preferred to call "footsteps"— were clues of the utmost importance not only in *A Study in Scarlet* but also in *The Sign of the Four,* "The Resident Patient," *The Hound of the Baskervilles,* "The Adventure of the Beryl Coronet," and "The Adventure of the Golden Pince-Nez."

79 *a herd of buffaloes.* The late Christopher Morley always maintained that Holmes' use of this expression (he used it again in "The Boscombe Valley Mystery") was one of many indications that he had spent some time in America prior to his meeting with Watson.

80 *There is nothing new under the sun.* Holmes draws on Ecclesiastes, 1, 9: "There is no new thing under the sun." "But this generalization was not the glib and shallow schoolboy's 'History repeats itself,'" Mr. Whitfield J. Bell, Jr., wrote in "Holmes and History"; "nor was it dogma that nothing might contravene. Holmes had a feeling for the rhythms of human life, and he was always ready to admit the unusual and the unique. But history was serviceable to Holmes and had meaning to him because he saw that the wheel comes round, that power corrupts and tyranny must fail . . ."

man about forty-three or forty-four years of age, middle-sized, broad-shouldered, with crisp curling black hair, and a short, stubbly beard. He was dressed in a heavy broadcloth frock coat and waistcoat, with light-coloured trousers, and immaculate collar and cuffs. A top hat, well brushed and trim, was placed upon the floor beside him. His hands were clenched and his arms thrown abroad, while his lower limbs were interlocked, as though his death struggle had been a grievous one. On his rigid face there stood an expression of horror, and, as it seemed to me, of hatred, such as I have never seen upon human features. This malignant and terrible contortion, combined with the low forehead, blunt nose, and prognathous jaw, gave the dead man a singularly simous and ape-like appearance, which was increased by his writhing, unnatural posture. I have seen death in many forms, but never has it appeared to me in a more fearsome aspect than in that dark, grimy apartment, which looked out upon one of the main arteries of suburban London.

Lestrade, lean and ferret-like as ever, was standing by the doorway, and greeted my companion and myself.

'This case will make a stir, sir,' he remarked. 'It beats anything I have seen, and I am no chicken.'

'There is no clue?' said Gregson.

'None at all,' chimed in Lestrade.

Sherlock Holmes approached the body, and, kneeling down, examined it intently. 'You are sure that there is no wound?' he asked, pointing to numerous gouts and splashes of blood which lay all round.

'Positive!' cried both detectives.

'Then, of course, this blood belongs to a second individual —presumably the murderer, if murder has been committed. It reminds me of the circumstances attendant on the death of Van Jansen, in Utrecht, in the year '34. Do you remember the case, Gregson?'

'No, sir.'

'Read it up—you really should. There is nothing new
80 under the sun. It has all been done before.'

As he spoke, his nimble fingers were flying here, there, and everywhere, feeling, pressing, unbuttoning, examining, while his eyes wore the same far-away expression which I have already remarked upon. So swiftly was the examination made, that one would hardly have guessed the minuteness with which it was conducted. Finally, he sniffed the dead man's lips, and then glanced at the soles of his patent leather boots.

'He has not been moved at all?' he asked.

'No more than was necessary for the purposes of our examination.'

'You can take him to the mortuary now,' he said. 'There is nothing more to be learned.'

Gregson had a stretcher and four men at hand. At his call they entered the room, and the stranger was lifted and carried out. As they raised him, a ring tinkled down and rolled across the floor. Lestrade grabbed it up and stared at it with mystified eyes.

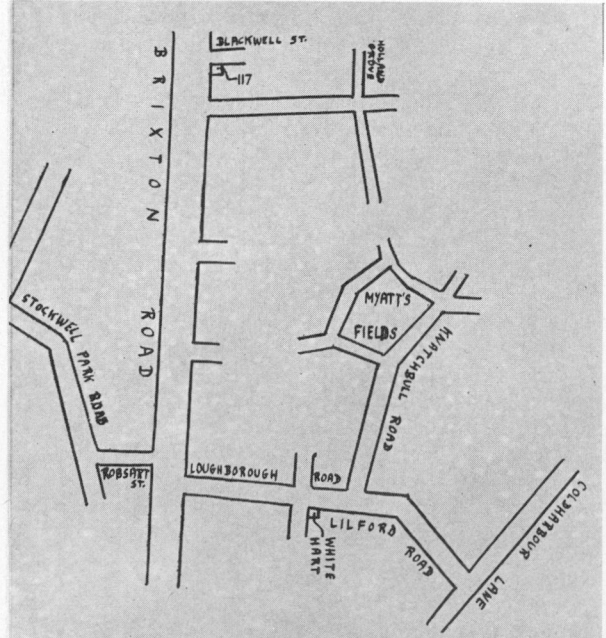

EAST OF THE BRIXTON ROAD

Mr. Colin Prestige's sketch map, from *The Sherlock Holmes Journal,* June, 1953, showing the White Hart, Holland Grove, Myatt's Fields and the Knatchbull Road. Also shown is No. 117 Brixton Road where Mrs. Maggie Oakshott bred geese ("The Adventure of the Blue Carbuncle").

'There's been a woman here,' he cried. 'It's a woman's wedding-ring.'

He held it out, as he spoke, upon the palm of his hand. We all gathered round him and gazed at it. There could be no doubt that that circlet of plain gold had once adorned the finger of a bride.

'This complicates matters,' said Gregson. 'Heaven knows, they were complicated enough before.'

'You're sure it doesn't simplify them?' observed Holmes. 'There's nothing to be learned by staring at it. What did you find in his pockets?'

'We have it all here,' said Gregson, pointing to a litter of objects upon one of the bottom steps of the stairs. 'A gold watch, No. 97163 by Barraud, of London. Gold Albert chain, **81** very heavy and solid. Gold ring, with masonic device. Gold pin—bull-dog's head, with rubies as eyes. Russian leather card-case, with cards of Enoch J. Drebber of Cleveland, corresponding with the E. J. D. upon the linen. No purse, but loose money to the extent of seven pounds thirteen. Pocket **82** edition of Boccaccio's *Decameron*, with name of Joseph **83** Stangerson upon the fly-leaf. Two letters—one addressed to E. J. Drebber and one to Joseph Stangerson.'

'At what address?'

'American Exchange, Strand—to be left till called for. They are both from the Guion Steamship Company, and refer to the sailing of their boats from Liverpool. It is clear that this unfortunate man was about to return to New York.'   **84**

81 *Gold Albert chain.* A watch chain made up of heavy links, named for Albert, Prince Consort of Queen Victoria, 1819–1861.

82 *seven pounds thirteen.* About $38.25.

83 *Boccaccio's* Decameron. Although the *Decameron* is the chief work of Giovanni Boccaccio, 1313–1375, he also wrote a biography of Dante, prose romances, and a verse satire on women, the *Corbaccio.*

84 *was about to return to New York.'* As Mr. N. P. Metcalfe pointed out ("The Date of the *Study in Scarlet*"), this again suggests 1881. Drebber's plan was to sail on the *Abyssinia* of the Guion Line, which in 1881 arrived at Queenstown from Liverpool en route to New York on March 6th.

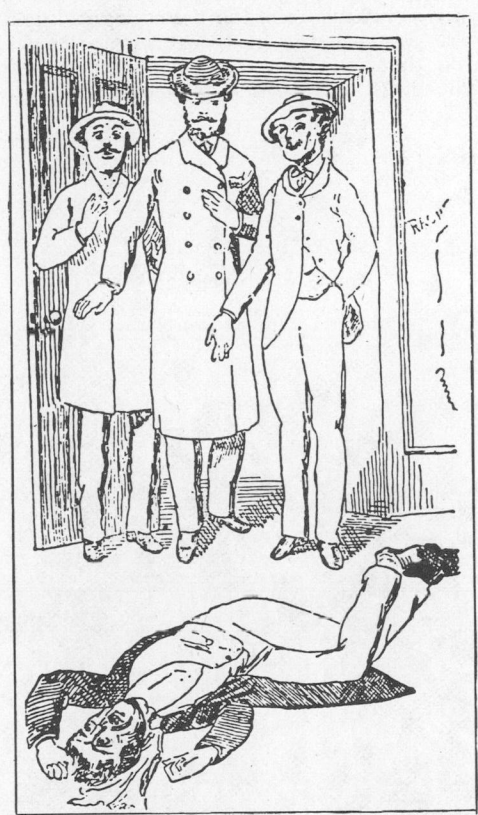

. . . THE SINGLE, GRIM, MOTIONLESS FIGURE . . . LAY STRETCHED UPON THE BOARDS . . .

One of the six drawings done by Charles Doyle, Conan Doyle's father, for *A Study in Scarlet*, London: Ward, Lock & Co., 1888. The late James Montgomery noted in *A Study in Pictures* that it shows a *bearded* Holmes and a Gregson with their coats buttoning from right to left instead of in the usual direction, although the letters of the word RACHE are in positive position.

AS HE SPOKE, HIS NIMBLE FINGERS WERE FLYING HERE, THERE, AND EVERYWHERE . . .

Illustration by D. H. Friston for *Beeton's Christmas Annual*, December, 1887. True to form, Lestrade and Gregson stand beside the body during this examination, but seemingly pay little heed to activities so far beyond their comprehension.

. . . FROM THE GUION STEAMSHIP COMPANY . . .

Named for an American, S. B. Guion, the company did a large transatlantic business from the 1860's to the 1880's. Their *Atlantic* was the first ship to cross the Atlantic in less than a week. ". . . to judge by its advertising cards, [one of which is shown at right] was the last word in transatlantic travel at the time," the late James Montgomery wrote in *Shots from the Canon*. "'The provisions supplied,' says a card, 'are abundant and excellent in quality, and are served and cooked by the company's stewards.' 'Bear in mind,' says another, 'that the Guion Line has not lost a single English, Welsh, Scotch or Irish passenger for the last 25 years.' These advantages evidently proved strong arguments to Drebber and Stangerson, who not only enjoyed the good things of life but also required a maximum degree of personal safety at all times to allay their constant jitters, brought on by an inward sense of guilt. They must have reasoned, not illogically, that if the steamship line had such a remarkable record in preserving its English, Welsh, Scotch and Irish passengers it was prepared to do the same thing for any Americans who might entrust themselves to its capable care."

'Have you made any inquiries as to this man Stangerson?'

'I did it at once, sir,' said Gregson. 'I have had advertisements sent to all the newspapers, and one of my men has gone to the American Exchange, but he has not returned yet.'

'Have you sent to Cleveland?'

'We telegraphed this morning.'

'How did you word your inquiries?'

'We simply detailed the circumstances, and said that we should be glad of any information which could help us.'

'You did not ask for particulars on any point which appeared to you to be crucial?'

'I asked about Stangerson.'

'Nothing else? Is there no circumstance on which this whole case appears to hinge? Will you not telegraph again?'

'I have said all I have to say,' said Gregson, in an offended voice.

Sherlock Holmes chuckled to himself, and appeared to be about to make some remark, when Lestrade, who had been in the front room while we were holding this conversation in the hall, reappeared upon the scene, rubbing his hands in a pompous and self-satisfied manner.

'Mr Gregson,' he said, 'I have just made a discovery of the highest importance, and one which would have been overlooked had I not made a careful examination of the walls.'

The little man's eyes sparkled as he spoke, and he was evidently in a state of suppressed exultation at having scored a point against his colleague.

'Come here,' he said, bustling back into the room, the atmosphere of which felt clearer since the removal of its ghastly inmate. 'Now, stand there!'

He struck a match on his boot and held it up against the wall.

'Look at that!' he said, triumphantly.

I have remarked that the paper had fallen away in parts. In this particular corner of the room a large piece had peeled off, leaving a yellow square of coarse plastering. Across this bare space there was scrawled in blood-red letters a single word—

RACHE.

HE STRUCK A MATCH ON HIS BOOT AND HELD IT UP AGAINST THE WALL.

Illustration by George Hutchinson for the London, 1891, Ward, Lock, Bowden & Co. edition of *A Study in Scarlet*.

'What do you think of that?' cried the detective, with the air of a showman exhibiting his show. 'This was overlooked because it was in the darkest corner of the room, and no one thought of looking there. The murderer has written it with his or her own blood. See this smear where it has trickled down the wall! That disposes of the idea of suicide anyhow. Why was that corner chosen to write it on? I will tell you. See that candle on the mantelpiece. It was lit at the time, and if it was lit this corner would be the brightest instead of the darkest portion of the wall.'

'And what does it mean now that you *have* found it?' asked Gregson in a depreciatory voice.

'Mean? Why, it means that the writer was going to put the female name Rachel, but was disturbed before he or she had time to finish. You mark my words, when this case comes to be cleared up, you will find that a woman named Rachel has something to do with it. It's all very well for you to laugh, Mr Sherlock Holmes. You may be very smart and clever, but the old hound is the best, when all is said and done.' **85**

'I really beg your pardon!' said my companion, who had ruffled the little man's temper by bursting into an explosion of laughter. 'You certainly have the credit of being the first of us to find this out and, as you say, it bears every mark of having been written by the other participant in last night's mystery. I have not had time to examine this room yet, but with your permission I shall do so now.'

As he spoke, he whipped a tape measure and a large round magnifying glass from his pocket. With these two implements **86** he trotted noiselessly about the room, sometimes stopping, occasionally kneeling, and once lying flat upon his face. So engrossed was he with his occupation that he appeared to have forgotten our presence, for he chattered away to himself under his breath the whole time, keeping up a running fire of exclamations, groans, whistles, and little cries suggestive of encouragement and of hope. As I watched him I was irresistibly reminded of a pure-blooded, well-trained foxhound as it dashes backwards and forwards through the covert, whining in its eagerness, until it comes across the lost scent. For twenty minutes or more he continued his researches, measuring with the most exact care the distance between marks which were entirely invisible to me, and occasionally applying his tape to the walls in an equally incomprehensible manner. In one place he gathered up very carefully a little pile of grey dust from the floor, and packed it away in an envelope. Finally he examined with his glass the word upon the wall, going over every letter of it with the most minute exactness. This done, he appeared to be satisfied, for he replaced his tape and his glass in his pocket.

'They say that genius is an infinite capacity for taking pains,' he remarked with a smile. 'It's a very bad definition, **87** but it does apply to detective work.'

Gregson and Lestrade had watched the manœuvres of their amateur companion with considerable curiosity and some contempt. They evidently failed to appreciate the fact, which I had begun to realize, that Sherlock Holmes' smallest actions were all directed towards some definite and practical end.

'What do you think of it, sir?' they both asked.

85 *the old hound is the best, when all is said and done.'* Less than a page later in Watson's account Lestrade changes his tune to "What do you think of it, sir?" "Watson failed to note this, as well as the liberties extended to Holmes which no responsible officer would give to an outsider, especially one who did not hold his complete respect," Mr. John Ball, Jr., wrote in "Early Days in Baker Street."

86 *a large round magnifying glass.* "The 'lens' is in use by Holmes in sixteen stories, with a full twenty-five references," Mr. Jerry Neal Williamson wrote in "Sherlock's Murder Bag."

87 *genius is an infinite capacity for taking pains.* This is the apothegm often attributed to Carlyle, in his *Life of Frederick the Great*, Book IV, Chapter 3: "Genius . . . which is the transcendent capacity for taking trouble first of all."

FINALLY HE EXAMINED WITH HIS GLASS THE WORD UPON THE WALL . . .

If we agree that the cover of *Beeton's Christmas Annual* for December, 1887, was not intended to be the first depiction of Mr. Sherlock Holmes, this frontispiece by D. H. Friston must be accorded that honor. It shows us Holmes as an unfamiliar figure in belted cape-coat and sideburns—and Watson as a walrus-mustached, doglike figure in a top hat. The other two grotesques are, of course, from left to right, Inspectors Lestrade and Gregson. Sometime between the first text illustration and this frontispiece, Gregson has seen fit to change his hat.

88 *Kennington Park Gate.'* Kennington Park, at the junction of Camberwell New Road, was originally a common, but was enclosed by iron railings in 1853 and converted into an ornamental park. About the same time the old Kennington turnpike gate, which stood near this spot, was removed. Audley Court, at "Kennington Park Gate," was presumably near the site of the old turnpike gate.

89 *'There has been murder done.* It is interesting to note, as an examination by the late Fletcher Pratt ("Very Little Murder") has shown, "that in the course of a long and brilliant career, Holmes was called upon to investigate only eight cases of murder. . . . In fifteen [of the sixty recorded cases], or one-quarter of the total, *no crime took place.*"

90 *a Trichinopoly cigar.* A cigar made from the dark tobacco grown near Trichinopoly in the Madras district of India. The Trichinopoly was usually a "pierced" cigar, open at both ends, and was often sold with a straw inserted through this opening to keep it clear until smoking.

91 *' "Rache" is the German for "revenge." "Rache* is [also] an old word meaning 'hunting dog,' and it could have been scribbled on the wall by Gregson (or Lestrade) to confuse his rival," the late Professor Jay Finley Christ pointed out in "Sherlock and the Canons."

92 *Parthian shot.* A concluding retort, so called because the ancient calvary of Parthia used to shoot backward as they fled.

'It would be robbing you of the credit of the case if I was to presume to help you,' remarked my friend. 'You are doing so well now that it would be a pity for anyone to interfere.' There was a world of sarcasm in his voice as he spoke. 'If you will let me know how your investigations go,' he continued, 'I shall be happy to give you any help I can. In the meantime I should like to speak to the constable who found the body. Can you give me his name and address?'

Lestrade glanced at his note-book. 'John Rance,' he said. 'He is off duty now. You will find him at 46, Audley Court,
88 Kennington Park Gate.'

Holmes took a note of the address.

'Come along, Doctor,' he said; 'we shall go and look him up. I'll tell you one thing which may help you in the case,' he continued, turning to the two detectives. 'There has been
89 murder done, and the murderer was a man. He was more than six feet high, was in the prime of life, had small feet for his height, wore coarse, square-toed boots and smoked a Trichi-
90 nopoly cigar. He came here with his victim in a four-wheeled cab, which was drawn by a horse with three old shoes and one new one on his off fore-leg. In all probability the murderer had a florid face, and the finger-nails of his right hand were remarkably long. These are only a few indications, but they may assist you.'

Lestrade and Gregson glanced at each other with an incredulous smile.

'If this man was murdered, how was it done?' asked the former.

'Poison,' said Sherlock Holmes curtly, and strode off. 'One other thing, Lestrade,' he added, turning round at the door:
91 ' "Rache" is the German for "revenge"; so don't lose your time looking for Miss Rachel.'

92   With which Parthian shot he walked away, leaving the two rivals open-mouthed behind him.

"HE CAME HERE WITH HIS VICTIM IN A FOUR-WHEELED CAB . . ."

Victorian cabs were of two kinds, the four-wheeler, or "growler," which carried four passengers but was slower than the other cab, the smart, two-wheeled hansom. It may have been called a "growler" because of its rumble and creak, or perhaps because of the cabby's habit of protesting an insufficient tip. The bowler, or billycock, hat was *de riguer* with the drivers of growlers. The photograph is from Michael Harrison's *In the Footsteps of Sherlock Holmes.*

4 ◆ WHAT JOHN RANCE HAD TO TELL

It was one o'clock when we left No. 3, Lauriston Gardens. Sherlock Holmes led me to the nearest telegraph office, **93** whence he dispatched a long telegram. He then hailed a cab, **94** and ordered the driver to take us to the address given us by Lestrade.

'There is nothing like first-hand evidence,' he remarked; **95** 'as a matter of fact, my mind is entirely made up upon the case, but still we may as well learn all that is to be learned.'

'You amaze me, Holmes,' said I. 'Surely you are not as sure as you pretend to be of all those particulars which you gave.'

'There's no room for a mistake,' he answered. 'The very first thing which I observed on arriving there was that a cab had made two ruts with its wheels close to the kerb. Now, up to last night, we have had no rain for a week, so that those **96** wheels which left such a deep impression must have been there during the night. There were the marks of the horse's hoofs, too, the outline of one of which was far more clearly cut than that of the other three, showing that that was a new shoe. Since the cab was there after the rain began, and was not there at any time during the morning—I have Gregson's word for that—it follows that it must have been there during the night, and, therefore, that it brought those two individuals to the house.'

'That seems simple enough,' said I; 'but how about the other man's height?'

'Why, the height of a man, in nine cases out of ten, can be told from the length of his stride. It is a simple calculation **97** enough, though there is no use my boring you with figures. I had this fellow's stride both on the clay outside and on the dust within. Then I had a way of checking my calculation. When a man writes on a wall, his instinct leads him to write about the level of his own eyes. Now that writing was just over six feet from the ground. It was child's play.'

'And his age?' I asked.

'Well, if a man can stride four and a half feet without the smallest effort, he can't be quite in the sere and yellow. That was the breadth of a puddle on the garden walk which he had evidently walked across. Patent-leather boots had gone round, and Square-toes had hopped over. There is no mystery about it at all. I am simply applying to ordinary life a few of those precepts of observation and deduction which I advocated in that article. Is there anything else that puzzles you?'

'The finger-nails and the Trichinopoly,' I suggested.

'The writing on the wall was done with a man's fore-finger dipped in blood. My glass allowed me to observe that the plaster was slightly scratched in doing it, which would not have been the case if the man's nail had been trimmed. I gathered up some scattered ash from the floor. It was dark in colour and flakey—such an ash as is only made by a Trichinopoly. I have made a special study of cigar ashes— in fact, I have written a monograph upon the subject. I flatter **98** myself that I can distinguish at a glance the ash of any known brand either of cigar or of tobacco. It is just in such details **99** that the skilled detective differs from the Gregson and Lestrade type.'

'And the florid face?' I asked.

93 *the nearest telegraph office*. In support of his identification of No. 318, Brixton Road, as "No. 3, Lauriston Gardens," the late H. W. Bell noted that about sixty yards up the road from No. 318, and on the same, or western side, there was a post-office, where, in England, telegrams may be dispatched, as late as 1896.

94 *dispatched a long telegram*. Despite its length, it would not have cost Holmes too much: in those days, a telegram could be sent for a shilling (25¢) anywhere in the United Kingdom for the first twenty words, not counting the names and addresses of the sender and the receiver. London and its suburbs had about 300 telegraph offices. The telegram, even after the introduction of the telephone, remained Holmes' favorite means of communication. He was no doubt mindful of the fact that, in the summer of 1846, it was the magnetic telegraph that made it possible to catch a thief who, running across the platform at Cambridge and leaping on a train, had been picked up by the police on reaching London. The *Daily News*, the first daily newspaper, edited by Charles Dickens, added the striking detail that the warning message from Cambridge had taken less than half a minute to speed to London.

95 *'There is nothing like first-hand evidence.'* "This truism was carefully borne in mind by Holmes—he was at all times prepared to hear the true facts of a case retold to him," Mr. T. S. Blakeney wrote in *Sherlock Holmes: Fact or Fiction?* "Equally he is found ready to relate the points of a problem to a listener, for, as he says, 'nothing clears up a case so much as stating it to another person ('Silver Blaze'). We find him adopting the same practice in 'The Adventure of the Abbey Grange,' 'The Man with the Twisted Lip' and 'The Adventure of Wisteria Lodge.'"

96 *we have had no rain for a week*. There was considerable rain in the week preceding Saturday, March 4, 1882—but in the week preceding Friday, March 4, 1881, it rained only once: a meager .01 inches fell on Sunday, February 27th—too little, surely, to discredit Holmes' statement. It seems safe to say, then, that his part in the case began on *Friday, March 4, 1881*, and not on Saturday, March 4, 1882, as has been contended by a number of commentators, notably the late Edgar W. Smith ("The Long Road from Maiwand").

97 *can be told from the length of his stride*. ". . . is not the length of a man's pace largely a matter of idiosyncracy—something which is not, at any rate materially, dependent upon stature?" Mr. J. B. Mackenzie asked in "Sherlock Holmes' Plots and Strategy." "Do not very many tall men take comparatively short steps, and a good number, of less inches, cover more ground with each? Have we not, besides, experience to testify that the upper and lower halves of the human body are often largely disproportioned?"

98 *I have written a monograph upon the subject.* Holmes probably drew on "Redi's *Esperienze intorno a Diverse Cose Naturali* (Florence 1686), containing the first scientific tests with nicotine, as well as the Philone de Conversationibus' *Venus Rebutee* (Cologne, 1722), an account of the various kinds of tobacco raised in Virginia and Germany with a description of the types of ash produced by each," Miss Madeleine B. Stern wrote in "Sherlock Holmes: Rare Book Collector." "His tobacco collection was not complete without Tiedmann's *Geschichte des Tabaka* (1856) dealing with various smoking mixtures and cake tobacco, cigars, cigarettes and snuff, nor—though it was not directly related to his studies—could Holmes have resisted the purchase of *Medical Reports, of the Effects of Tobacco* (1788) by Thomas Fowler, who wrote also on the effects of arsenic. It is interesting to note that Holmes' article, written by 1881, probably influenced Gaetano Casoria, whose treatise, *Sulla Combustibilitá alcune Varietá de Tobacchi,* with a chemical analysis of the ash of various tobaccos, appeared the following year."

Holmes did not at this time disclose the actual title of his monograph (*Upon the Distinction Between the Ashes of the Various Tobaccos: An Enumeration of 140 Forms of Cigar, Cigarette, and Pipe Tobacco, with Coloured Plates Illustrating the Difference in the Ash*). That remained unknown until his biographer gave to the world the story called *The Sign of the Four.* "Referred to again by its author . . . during his investigation of the murder of Charles McCarthy in Boscombe Valley," Mr. Walter Klinefelter wrote in "The Writings of Sherlock Holmes," the monograph "is the only one of Holmes' works which Watson quotes the detective as mentioning more than once in the Canon. Consequently, it may be inferred that he took more than a little pride in its authorship, probably considering it his most important contribution to what may be termed the minutiae of scientific detection. . . . It is known from Holmes' own statement (*The Sign of the Four*) that . . . François le Villard of the French detective service was [then] translating the work into his native language." Mr. Klinefelter added that a Philadelphia tobacconist once wrote to Conan Doyle to ask where he might obtain a copy of the monograph. "Rather funny, isn't it?" the author commented.

99 *I can distinguish at a glance the ash of any known brand.* "It is not generally considered possible, however, to distinguish one tobacco ash from another, particularly as ash varies according to the rate at which the tobacco is smoked," wrote the editors of the Catalogue of the Sherlock Holmes Exhibition.

100 *'My head is in a whirl.'* But let us note that having said this, Watson immediately comes out with a string of seven quite apposite questions.

'Ah, that was a more daring shot, though I have no doubt that I was right. You must not ask me that at the present state of the affair.'

100 I passed my hand over my brow. 'My head is in a whirl,' I remarked; 'the more one thinks of it the more mysterious it grows. How came these two men—if there were two men—into an empty house? What has become of the cabman who drove them? How could one man compel another to take poison? Where did the blood come from? What was the object of the murderer, since robbery had no part in it? How came the woman's ring there? Above all, why should the second man write up the German word RACHE before decamping? I confess that I cannot see any possible way of reconciling all these facts.'

My companion smiled approvingly.

'You sum up the difficulties of the situation succinctly and well,' he said. 'There is much that is still obscure, though I have quite made up my mind on the main facts. As to poor Lestrade's discovery, it was simply a blind intended to put the police upon a wrong track, by suggesting Socialism and **101** secret societies. It was not done by a German. The A, if you noticed, was printed somewhat after the German fashion. Now, a real German invariably prints in the Latin character, so that we may safely say that this was not written by one, but by a clumsy imitator who overdid his part. It was simply a ruse to divert inquiry into a wrong channel. I'm not going to tell you much more of the case, Doctor. You know a conjuror gets no credit when once he has explained his trick; and if I show you too much of my method of working, you will come to the conclusion that I am a very ordinary individual after all.'

'I shall never do that,' I answered; 'you have brought detection as near an exact science as it ever will be brought in this world.'

My companion flushed up with pleasure at my words, and the earnest way in which I uttered them. I had already observed that he was as sensitive to flattery on the score of his art as any girl could be of her beauty.

'I'll tell you one other thing,' he said. 'Patent-leathers and Square-toes came in the same cab, and they walked down the pathway together as friendly as possible—arm-in-arm, in all probability. When they got inside, they walked up and down the room—or rather, Patent-leathers stood still while Square-toes walked up and down. I could read all that in the dust; and I could read that as he walked he grew more and more excited. That is shown by the increased length of his strides. He was talking all the while, and working himself up, no doubt, into a fury. Then the tragedy occurred. I've told you all I know myself now, for the rest is mere surmise and conjecture. We have a good working basis, however, on which to **102** start. We must hurry up, for I want to go to Hallé's concert to **103-104** hear Norman Neruda this afternoon.'

This conversation had occurred while our cab had been threading its way through a long succession of dingy streets and dreary byways. In the dingiest and dreariest of them our driver suddenly came to a stand. 'That's Audley Court in there,' he said, pointing to a narrow slit in the line of dead-coloured brick. 'You'll find me here when you come back.'

 LADY HALLÉ.

ADY HALLÉ, whose maiden name was Wilhelmine Néruda, was born at Brünn, where her father was organist of the cathedral. She was a pupil of Jansa, and made her first appearance at Vienna at the age of six, and in London at the age of nine. After this she returned to the Continent, and in 1864 she married Ludwig Norman, a

Swedish musician. Since 1869 she has been in England every winter, playing especially at the concerts of Sir Charles Hallé, whom she married in 1888.

"HER ATTACK AND HER BOWING ARE SPLENDID."

Lady Hallé (the former Mme. Norman-Neruda) as she was depicted in the *Strand Magazine* in 1890 in "Celebrities Then and Now," a feature which appeared for many months in the pages of the *Strand*.

Audley Court was not an attractive locality. The narrow passage led us into a quadrangle paved with flags and lined by sordid dwellings. We picked our way among groups of dirty children, and through lines of discoloured linen, until we came to Number 46, the door of which was decorated with a small slip of brass on which the name Rance was engraved. On inquiry we found that the constable was in bed, and we were shown into a little front parlour to await his coming.

101 *Socialism and secret societies.* At this time, as the late Christopher Morley wrote in *Sherlock Holmes and Dr. Watson: A Textbook of Friendship*, "Socialists were sometimes (and perhaps unfairly) associated in the public mind with other groups who believed in violent action as a protest against the inequalities of civilization. There were a number of dynamite outrages in London in the eighties, which suggested the theme of Robert Louis Stevenson's humorous satire, *The Dynamiter*." An excellent account of the dynamite outrages will be found in Mr. Michael Harrison's *In the Footsteps of Sherlock Holmes*.

102 *Hallé's concert.* "During the last third of the nineteenth century," Mr. Paul S. Clarkson wrote in his stimulating essay, "'In the Beginning . . .'", "there was one annual series of London events as certain as the seasons or the months, viz., Charles Hallé's Popular Concerts. Beginning in 1861, they were repeated year after year during the late fall and winter with as much regularity and with as faithful a following, as the performances of the Boston Symphony and the New York Philharmonic Orchestras in this country and century. Born Karl Hallé in Westphalia, in 1819, this great pianist and director came to England in 1843. He began as a player and producer of chamber music recitals in London, but soon was conducting symphony orchestras and operatic performances, notably at Manchester, but also at Bristol, Liverpool, Edinburgh, Glasgow, Belfast, Dublin, and many other cities. It was Hallé who introduced Berlioz's instrumental and operatic compositions to England, as well as a great deal of Chopin. In recognition of his many contributions to the popularizing of fine music in the British Isles for nearly a half century, Hallé was knighted by Queen Victoria in 1888. The great symphony orchestra which he organized at Manchester in 1858 continued after his death in 1895, and to this day gives concerts and makes records of classical music in the grand tradition."

103 *to hear Norman Neruda.* "From the beginning," Mr. Clarkson continued, "Hallé procured the best instrumental soloists of the day, from the Continent as well as from England, to play for his concerts. Among these was the great violin virtuoso, 'the female Paganini' of her own—or perhaps of any—day—the brilliant, the beloved of the concert platform, the incomparable Mme. Norman-Neruda [unlike Watson, she always used the hyphen]. She was born in Brunn, in Moravia, in 1839, one of a long line and numerous family of fine musicians. Trained by the great Jansa, when seven years old she gave her first public recital, in Vienna. Even at that tender age, she excited as much amazement as admiration, in her rendering of a Bach sonata, for the strength of her bowing, the purity of her catilena, and the beauty of her execution, despite her small, childish hands. Holmes was far from being the first critic—or the last—to observe that 'her attack and her bowing are splendid.' She was christened Wilhelmina, which she shortened and Anglicized to Wilma for her engagements in London. She married a Swedish musician, Ludwig Norman, from whom she derived the first half of her hyphenated *nom de salle de concert*. Three years after his death, she married (in 1888) Hallé, with whom she had been closely associated on the concert stage for nearly twenty years, and was thenceforth, of course, usually referred to as Lady Hallé. In 1901, 'a certain gracious lady' conferred upon her the title 'Violinist to the Queen.' Beyond their love of great music, and their playing the violin, Mme. Norman-Neruda and Sherlock Holmes had another unusual and distinguished factor in common: each was the owner of a violin made by the great Cremonese, Antonio Stradivari. Norman-Neruda's was the famous 'Ernst Violin,' made in the master's 'Golden Period' (in 1709) which had had a most interesting and romantic history. It was purchased and presented to her, in 1876, by the Duke of Saxe-Coburg-Gotha (formerly the Duke of Edinburgh), and the Earls of Dudley and Hardwicke, as a token of their esteem. Thereafter, she played this great instrument with its 'ripe, woody, and yet sparkling quality' of tone, at all her concerts, including those on her American tour in 1899."

104 *this afternoon.*' The first of many indications that Watson, for one reason or another, is becoming hopelessly confused in the sequence of events he is recounting to us in *A Study in Scarlet*. By Watson's account, Holmes attended Hallé's concert on the afternoon of Friday, March 4, 1881. But this he could not possibly have done. As Mr. Clarkson pointed out: "Upon examining the actual records of the concert platform in London for this entire period, we shall find that the afternoon of *Saturday, March 5, 1881*, is the only date that historically meets all of [the] specifications. Hallé's 'Popular Concerts' were a biweekly feature of London's winter music season. They were given every year at St. James's Hall from about the first of December to the first of March—and always and only on Monday nights and on Saturday afternoons. Holmes' attendance 'this afternoon' fixes the day of the week to a Saturday, and no other possible day."

105 *the White Hart.* Identified by the late H. W. Bell as the Old White Horse on the Brixton Road. But Mr. Colin Prestige, in "South London Adventures," has written that there is only one White Hart in the district: '. . . although the present White Hart has only been in existence since 1938, it replaces an earlier 'pub' of the same name of considerable antiquity, which was on the same site until demolished for rebuilding in the 1930s." The site (*see sketch map*) is at the junction of Loughborough Road and Lilford Road.

106 *Holland Grove. See sketch map.* The "Henrietta Street" which follows is not now identifiable.

He appeared presently, looking a little irritable at being disturbed in his slumbers. 'I made my report at the office,' he said.

Holmes took a half-sovereign from his pocket and played with it pensively. 'We thought that we should like to hear it all from your own lips,' he said.

'I shall be most happy to tell you anything I can,' the constable answered, with his eyes upon the little golden disk.

'Just let us hear it all in your own way as it occurred.'

Rance sat down on the horsehair sofa, and knitted his brows as though determined not to omit anything in his narrative.

'I'll tell it ye from the beginning,' he said. 'My time is from ten at night to six in the morning. At eleven there was a fight
105 at the White Hart; but bar that all was quiet enough on the beat. At one o'clock it began to rain, and I met Harry Mur-
106 cher—him who has the Holland Grove beat—and we stood together at the corner of Henrietta Street a-talkin'. Presently —maybe about two or a little after—I thought I would take a look round and see that all was right down the Brixton Road. It was precious dirty and lonely. Not a soul did I meet all the way down, though a cab or two went past me. I was a-strollin' down, thinkin' between ourselves how uncommon
107 handy a four of gin hot would be, when suddenly the glint of a light caught me eye in the window of that same house. Now, I knew that them two houses in Lauriston Gardens was empty on account of him that owns them who won't have the drains seed to, though the very last tenant what lived in one of them died o' typhoid fever. I was knocked all in a heap, therefore, at seeing a light in the window, and I suspected as something was wrong. When I got to the door——'

'You stopped, and then walked back to the garden gate, my companion interrupted. 'What did you do that for?'

Rance gave a violent jump, and stared at Sherlock Holmes with the utmost amazement upon his features.

'Why, that's true, sir,' he said; 'though how you come to know it, Heaven only knows. Ye see when I got up to the door, it was so still and so lonesome, that I thought I'd be none the worse for someone with me. I ain't afeard of anything on this side o' the grave; but I thought that maybe it was him that died o' the typhoid inspecting the drains what killed him. The thought gave me a kind o' turn, and I walked back to the gate to see if I could see Murcher's lantern, but there wasn't no sign of him nor of anyone else.'

'There was no one in the street?'

'Not a livin' soul, sir, nor as much as a dog. Then I pulled myself together and went back and pushed the door open. All was quiet inside, so I went into the room where the light was a-burnin'. There was a candle flickerin' on the mantelpiece— a red wax one—and by its light I saw——'

'Yes, I know all that you saw. You walked round the room several times, and you knelt down by the body, and then you walked through and tried the kitchen door, and then——'

John Rance sprang to his feet with a frightened face and
108 suspicion in his eyes. 'Where was you hid to see all that?' he cried. 'It seems to me that you knows a deal more than you should.'

Holmes laughed and threw his card across the table to the constable. 'Don't get arresting me for the murder,' he said. 'I am one of the hounds and not the wolf; Mr Gregson or Mr Lestrade will answer for that. Go on, though. What did you do next?'

Rance resumed his seat, without, however, losing his mystified expression. 'I went back to the gate and sounded my whistle. That brought Murcher and two more to the spot.'

'Was the street empty then?'

'Well, it was, as far as anybody that could be of any good goes.'

'What do you mean?'

The constable's features broadened into a grin. 'I've seen many a drunk chap in my time,' he said, 'but never anyone so cryin' drunk as that cove. He was at the gate when I came out, a-leanin' up ag'in the railings, and a-singin' at the pitch o' his lungs about Columbine's New-fangled Banner, or some such stuff. He couldn't stand, far less help.'

'What sort of a man was he?' asked Sherlock Holmes.

John Rance appeared to be somewhat irritated at this digression. 'He was an uncommon drunk sort o' man,' he said. 'He'd ha' found hisself in the station if we hadn't been so took up.'

'His face—his dress—didn't you notice them?' Holmes broke in impatiently.

'I should think I did notice them, seeing that I had to prop him up—me and Murcher between us. He was a long chap, with a red face, the lower part muffled round——'

'That will do,' cried Holmes. 'What became of him?'

'We'd enough to do without lookin' after him,' the policeman said, in an aggrieved voice. 'I'll wager he found his way home all right.'

'How was he dressed?'

'A brown overcoat.'

'Had he a whip in his hand?'

'A whip—no.'

'He must have left it behind,' muttered my companion. 'You didn't happen to see or hear a cab after that?'

'No.'

'There's a half-sovereign for you,' my companion said, standing up and taking his hat. 'I am afraid, Rance, that you will never rise in the force. That head of yours should be for use as well as ornament. You might have gained your sergeant's stripes last night. The man whom you held in your hands is the man who holds the clue of this mystery, and whom we are seeking. There is no use of arguing about it now; I tell you that it is so. Come along, Doctor.'

We started off for the cab together, leaving our informant incredulous, but obviously uncomfortable.

'The blundering fool!' Holmes said, bitterly, as we drove back to our lodgings. 'Just to think of his having such an incomparable bit of good luck, and not taking advantage of it.'

'I am rather in the dark still. It is true that the description of this man tallies with your idea of the second party in this mystery. But why should he come back to the house after leaving it? That is not the way of criminals.'

'The ring, man, the ring: that was what he came back for. If we have no other way of catching him, we can always bait our line with the ring. I shall have him, Doctor—I'll lay you

HOLMES TOOK A HALF-SOVEREIGN FROM HIS POCKET . . .

The half-sovereign was valued at 10 shillings, or approximately \$2.50 in U.S. currency at that time. This piece, the late A. Carson Simpson wrote in *Numismatics in the Canon* (Part I: "Full Thirty Thousand Marks of English Coin"), "has many forerunners under varied names, including the rose-noble of Edward IV and the ryal of Henry VII. It was first named a half-sovereign by Henry VIII and a half-pound by Elizabeth I. The Stuarts and the Commonwealth called it a double-crown; the angel was also revalued at 10/–. It gave way to the half-guinea until George III's 1816 reform and was last struck regularly in London in 1915, but later in colonial mints. There are a number of Canonical references to the half-sovereign. . . . A characteristic one is Watson's: 'I took our mongrel accordingly and left him, together with a half-sovereign, at the old naturalist's in Pinchin Lane' (*The Sign of the Four*). Other references: 'A Scandal in Bohemia' (twice); *The Hound of the Baskervilles*; 'The Adventure of Black Peter' (twice)."

107 *a four of gin hot.* Fourpence (8¢) worth of gin with hot water and lemon.

108 '*Where was you hid to see all that?*' That Holmes was indeed on the spot at the time of the murder—disguised as the cab horse "with three old shoes and one new one on his off fore-leg"—was the astounding theory put forward by the late Robert S. Morgan in his volume *Spotlight on a Simple Case*, a *tour de force* that must be read to be believed.

109 *a little art jargon.* An early indication of Holmes' more than casual interest in art. In his day paintings were frequently called "A Study in Such and Such a Color." For instance, Whistler's "Nocturne in Green and Gold," or the Portrait of his Mother, often alluded to as "A Study in Black and Gray."

110 *Chopin's.* Frédéric François Chopin, 1810–1849, Polish composer and pianist. His highly romantic music, almost all for solo piano, includes piano concertos, mazurkas, polonaises, nocturnes, waltzes, preludes, etudes, scherzos, ballades, and sonatas.

111 *Tra-la-la-lira-lira-lay.'* "The principal, and for all practical purposes insuperable, difficulty [in identifying that little thing of Chopin's] lies in the fact . . . that Chopin *never composed one single piece for the solo violin,*" Mr. Paul S. Clarkson wrote in "In the Beginning. . . ." "Indeed, 'four times only did Chopin write for stringed instruments, and all four of the pieces contain parts for the cello. Only once did he add violin: in the (G minor) Trio . . .' Of course, any piano piece ever written can be 'arranged' for the violin, as everyone knows. But, as anyone also knows, concert violinists rarely, if ever, perform piano pieces. And no one will be surprised to hear that a search of all reported concert programs, for a period of several years prior to the occasion of Holmes'. . . question, discloses not one Chopin opus played by Mme. Norman-Neruda." Mr. Clarkson therefore suggested that Holmes, at a previous concert (June 4, 1880) heard Charles Hallé play Chopin's Nocturne in E (Op. 62, No. 2), and the Barcarolle in F sharp (Op. 60), also by Chopin, but also heard Mme. Norman-Neruda play her favorite Handel's D major sonata. It was the sonata he was thinking of, but he mistakenly attributed its composition to Chopin.

This is an ingenious suggestion, but it is only one of many ingenious suggestions put forward by Sherlockian scholars. As Dr. Julian Wolff wrote ("Just What Was That Little Thing of Chopin's?"): "The great interest in this question is evidenced by the amount of research that has been done and the number of papers published." Here is a list of the important literature on the subject and the conclusions reached by various authors, arranged in chronological order:

1) Warrack, Guy: *Sherlock Holmes and Music.* F minor Nocturne (Nocturne for piano, No. 15 in F minor).

2) Montgomery, James: "Chopin in Baker Street." Etude in E major, Opus 10 (Etude in E major for Piano, Op. 10, No. 3).

3) Zeisler, Dr. Ernest Bloomfield: "Tra-la-la-lira-lira-lay." Valse in E minor, No. 14 (Op. Posth.).

4) Thiman, Eric H., Mus. D.: "Tra-la-la-lira-lira-lay." Mazurka in E flat minor, Op. 6, No. 4.

5) Christie, Winifred M.: "Some Reflections on

two to one that I have him. I must thank you for it all. I might not have gone but for you, and so have missed the finest study I ever came across: a study in scarlet, eh? Why shouldn't we **109** use a little art jargon. There's the scarlet thread of murder running through the colourless skein of life, and our duty is to unravel it, and isolate it, and expose every inch of it. And now for lunch, and then for Norman Neruda. Her attack and **110** her bowing are splendid. What's that little thing of **Chopin's 111** she plays so magnificently: Tra-la-la-lira-lira-lay.'

Leaning back in the cab, this amateur bloodhound carolled away like a lark while I meditated upon the manysidedness of the human mind.

♦

5 ♦ OUR ADVERTISEMENT BRINGS A VISITOR

Our morning's exertions had been too much for my weak health, and I was tired out in the afternoon. After Holmes' departure for the concert, I lay down upon the sofa and endeavoured to get a couple of hours' sleep. It was a useless attempt. My mind had been too much excited by all that had occurred, and the strangest fancies and surmises crowded into it. Every time that I closed my eyes I saw before me the distorted, baboon-like countenance of the murdered man. So sinister was the impression which that face had produced upon me that I found it difficult to feel anything but gratitude for him who had removed its owner from the world. If ever human features bespoke vice of the most malignant type, they were certainly those of Enoch J. Drebber, of Cleveland. Still I recognized that justice must be done, and that the depravity of the victim was no condonement in the eyes of the law.

The more I thought of it the more extraordinary did my companion's hypothesis, that the man had been poisoned, appear. I remembered how he had sniffed his lips, and had no doubt that he had detected something which had given rise to the idea. Then, again, if not poison, what had caused the man's death, since there was neither wound nor marks of strangulation? But, on the other hand, whose blood was that which lay so thickly upon the floor? There were no signs of a struggle, nor had the victim any weapon with which he might have wounded an antagonist. As long as all these questions were unsolved, I felt that sleep would be no easy matter, either for Holmes or myself. His quiet, self-confident manner convinced me that he had already formed a theory which explained all the facts, though what it was I could not for an instant conjecture.

He was very late in returning—so late that I knew that the concert could not have detained him all the time. Dinner was on the table before he appeared.

'It was magnificent,' he said, as he took his seat. 'Do you remember what Darwin says about music? He claims that the power of producing and appreciating it existed among the **112** human race long before the power of speech was arrived at. Perhaps that is why we are so subtly influenced by it. There are vague memories in our souls of those misty centuries when the world was in its childhood.'

'That's rather a broad idea,' I remarked.

'One's ideas must be as broad as Nature if they are to interpret Nature,' he answered. 'What's the matter? You're **113** not looking quite yourself. This Brixton Road affair has upset you.'

'To tell the truth, it has,' I said. 'I ought to be more case-hardened after my Afghan experiences. I saw my own comrades hacked to pieces at Maiwand without losing my nerve.'

'I can understand. There is a mystery about this which stimulates the imagination; where there is no imagination there is no horror. Have you seen the evening paper?'   **114**

'No.'

'It gives a fairly good account of the affair. It does not mention the fact that when the man was raised up a woman's wedding ring fell upon the floor. It is just as well it does not.'

'Why?'

'Look at this advertisement,' he answered. 'I had one sent to every paper this morning immediately after the affair.'   **115**

He threw the paper across to me and I glanced at the place indicated. It was the first announcement in the 'Found' column. 'In Brixton Road, this morning,' it ran, 'a plain gold wedding ring, found in the roadway between the White Hart Tavern and Holland Grove. Apply Dr Watson, 221B, Baker Street, between eight and nine this evening.'

'Excuse my using your name,' he said. 'If I used my own, some of these dunderheads would recognize it, and want to meddle in the affair.'

'That is all right,' I answered. 'But supposing any one applies, I have no ring.'

'Oh yes, you have,' said he, handing me one. 'This will do very well. It is almost a facsimile.'

'And who do you expect will answer this advertisement?'

'Why, the man in the brown coat—our florid friend with the square toes. If he does not come himself, he will send an accomplice.'

'Would he not consider it as too dangerous?'

'Not at all. If my view of the case is correct, and I have every reason to believe that it is, this man would rather risk anything than lose the ring. According to my notion he dropped it while stooping over Drebber's body, and did not miss it at the time. After leaving the house he discovered his loss and hurried back, but found the police already in possession, owing to his own folly in leaving the candle burning. He had to pretend to be drunk in order to allay the suspicions which might have been aroused by his appearance at the gate. Now put yourself in that man's place. On thinking the matter over, it must have occurred to him that it was possible that he had lost the ring in the road after leaving the house. What would he do then? He would eagerly look out for the evening papers in the hope of seeing it among the articles found. His eye, of course, would light upon this. He would be overjoyed. Why should he fear a trap? There would be no reason in his eyes why the finding of the ring should be connected with the murder. He would come. He will come. You shall see him within an hour!'

'And then?' I asked.

'Oh, you can leave me to deal with him then. Have you any arms?'

'I have my old service revolver and a few cartridges.'   **116**

That Little Thing of Chopin's." Study in A minor, Op. 25, No. 11.

6) Harrison, Michael: *In the Footsteps of Sherlock Holmes.* The Impromptu in C sharp minor.

7) Smith, William: "That Little Thing of Chopin's." Fourth Polonaise, in C minor.

Dr. Wolff himself offered "the timid suggestion that . . . Watson was not quoting Holmes (or Chopin) at all, but was merely misquoting Tennyson (*The Lady of Shalott*): 'From the bank and from the river / He flash'd into the crystal mirror, / "Tirra lirra," by the river / Sang Sir Lancelot.' "

112 *long before the power of speech was arrived at.* Holmes is apparently referring to some comments made in *The Descent of Man* by Charles Robert Darwin, 1809–1882, the English naturalist, traveler, and philosopher who promulgated the theory of organic evolution by natural selection in his *Origin of Species* (1859).

113 *if they are to interpret Nature.'* "As an instance of an idea of Holmes' as broad as Nature, we may select his theory 'that the individual represents in his development the whole procession of his ancestors,' ["The Adventure of the Empty House"]," Mr. T. S. Blakeney commented in *Sherlock Holmes: Fact or Fiction?*

114 *Have you seen the evening paper?'* "Close at hand," Miss Madeleine B. Stern wrote in "Sherlock Holmes: Rare Book Collector," "—at 36 Baker Street—[Holmes] found the news-dealer, James Ellis Hawkins, who could dispatch the latest editions of the London papers to Holmes' rooms."

115 *immediately after the affair.'* But when? If Holmes sent the advertisement to the papers at the same time that he dispatched his "long telegram," it was then after one o'clock in the afternoon, and it would have been unusually smart of him to be able to send off a personal to the evening papers so late in the day and get it into that afternoon's editions. It would seem, certainly, that Watson has somehow lost a day, and that we have now arrived at the afternoon of Saturday, March 5, 1881, after Holmes' return from the concert.

116 *my old service revolver.* This weapon, Mr. Robert Keith Leavitt wrote in "Annie Oakley in Baker Street," "was the Adams 6-shot cal. .450 breech-loader, with a good honest 6″ barrel, standard in the British Army in the second Afghan War. Its somewhat scanted front sight (a decided advantage for carrying in the pocket but difficult to use in a dim light) was more than offset by the length of the barrel with ample sighting radius. It was precisely the weapon for such a shot as that at Tonga in *The Sign of the Four*."

The editors of the Catalogue of the Sherlock Holmes Exhibition thought it more likely that this revolver was "a .442/450 Solid Frame Webley

Double Action. While slower to load and reload than a modern self-ejecting revolver, these sturdy weapons were not superseded for many years. The self-ejector was not wholly adopted until 1885, and indeed the practice of quick ejection and quick reloading was only necessary in military-type weapons."

On at least ten occasions, Holmes asked Watson to take his revolver on a dangerous mission, or in the face of danger, to draw it, and Mr. Leavitt has concluded that "this fact in itself proves conclusively that Watson was much the better pistol shot of the two. There was every reason why he should have been. He put in a considerable stretch as an army surgeon—a post in which, as Miss Helen Simpson has pointed out ["Medical Career and Capacities of Dr. J. H. Watson"], his duties were light. In his leisure the methodical Watson obviously spent a great deal of time in pistol practice."

117 *I picked up at a stall yesterday.* "These are the words of a bibliophile," Mr. Whitfield J. Bell, Jr., wrote in "Holmes and History." "It was as a bibliophile, in fact, a collector of obscure volumes, that Holmes disguised himself on his return from France in 1894 ["The Adventure of the Empty House"]."

And Miss Madeleine B. Stern has added ("Sherlock Holmes: Rare Book Collector"): "It is supremely tempting . . . to ask ourselves where Holmes obtained his many fine books. . . . His favorite book dealer was almost undoubtedly Albert B. Clementson, who plied his trade at 73 Church Street, Kensington, and who suggested [the disguise used by Holmes in "The Adventure of the Empty House"]. . . . There were other dealers, scores of them, into whose musty shops Holmes surely ventured as he passed through the winding lanes and alleys of his London. The Strand was full of shops, where books towered to the ceiling and spilled over onto the floors as Holmes browsed among them, his expert's eye glancing at a calf or vellum back. Nevington Butts could always give him a field day, and who can doubt that he would walk through Camden passage without a visit to Mrs. Susannah Kettle, or through Church Street, Paddington, without a glance at Uriah Maggs' stock? For medical works, he could journey to Wardour Street, where Richard Kimpton plied a specialized trade, and everywhere—in Farringdon Street and New Oxford Street, on Praed Street and Drury Lane—he could, and did, wander through the dimly-lighted cellars and the intriguing anterooms of one bookseller after another. There was Framjee Feroza on Camberwell Road; there was William Wright on St. Martin's Lane; there was Mrs. Robenah Boyle on White Horse Street in Stepney—there were dozens upon dozens of dealers from whom he could buy the earliest on opium or the latest on belladonna. For a French treatise, he might patronize Madame Celine Subtil in Prince's Buildings, Coventry Street. . . . Some from whom he bought,

'You had better clean it and load it. He will be a desperate man; and though I shall take him unawares, it is as well to be ready for anything.'

I went to my bedroom and followed his advice. When I returned with the pistol, the table had been cleared, and Holmes was engaged in his favourite occupation of scraping upon his violin.

'The plot thickens,' he said, as I entered; 'I have just had an answer to my American telegram. My view of the case is the correct one.'

'And that is?' I asked eagerly.

'My fiddle would be the better for new strings,' he remarked. 'Put your pistol in your pocket. When the fellow comes, speak to him in an ordinary way. Leave the rest to me. Don't frighten him by looking at him too hard.'

'It is eight o'clock now,' I said, glancing at my watch.

'Yes. He will probably be here in a few minutes. Open the door slightly. That will do. Now put the key on the inside. Thank you! **117-118** This is a queer old book I picked up at a stall yesterday—*De Jure inter Gentes*—published in Latin at Liege in the Lowlands, in 1642. Charles's head was still firm on his shoulders when this little brown-backed volume was struck off.'

'Who is the printer?'

119 'Philippe de Croy, whoever he may have been. On the fly-leaf, in very faded ink, is written "Ex libris Gulielmi Whyte." I wonder who William Whyte was. Some pragmatical seventeenth-century lawyer, I suppose. His writing has a legal **120** twist about it. Here comes our man, I think.'

As he spoke there was a sharp ring at the bell. Sherlock Holmes rose softly and moved his chair in the direction of the **121** door. We heard the servant pass along the hall, and the sharp click of the latch as she opened it.

"MORE THAN ONCE . . . A GOOD FRIEND IN NEED"

So wrote Watson of his old service revolver in "The Problem of Thor Bridge." Identified by Mr. Robert Keith Leavitt as the Adams .450, shown above, Watson's old service revolver was standard in the British Army during the doctor's term of service. Though a good shot with this piece, Watson later replaced it with a more compact gun for pocket wear.

'Does Dr Watson live here?' asked a clear but rather harsh voice. We could not hear the servant's reply, but the door closed, and someone began to ascend the stairs. The footfall was an uncertain and shuffling one. A look of surprise passed over the face of my companion as he listened to it. It came slowly along the passage, and there was a feeble tap at the door.

'Come in,' I cried.

At my summons, instead of the man of violence whom we expected, a very old and wrinkled woman hobbled into the apartment. She appeared to be dazzled by the sudden blaze of light, and after dropping a curtsy, she stood blinking at us with her bleared eyes and fumbling in her pocket with nervous, shaky fingers. I glanced at my companion, and his face had assumed such a disconsolate expression that it was all I could do to keep my countenance.

The old crone drew out an evening paper, and pointed at our advertisement. 'It's this as has brought me, good gentlemen,' she said, dropping another curtsy; 'a gold wedding ring in the Brixton Road. It belongs to my girl Sally, as was married only this time twelve-month, which her husband is steward aboard a Union boat, and what he'd say if he come **122** 'ome and found her without her ring is more than I can think, he being short enough at the best o' times, but more especially when he has the drink. If it please you, she went to the circus **123** last night along with——'

'Is that her ring?' I asked.

'The Lord be thanked!' cried the old woman; 'Sally will be a glad woman this night. That's the ring.'

'And what may your address be?' I inquired, taking up a pencil.

'13, Duncan Street, Houndsditch. A weary way from here.' **124**

'The Brixton Road does not lie between any circus and Houndsditch,' said Sherlock Holmes sharply.

The old woman faced round and looked keenly at him from her little red-rimmed eyes. 'The gentleman asked me for *my* address,' she said. 'Sally lives in lodgings at 3, Mayfield Place, Peckham.' **125**

'And your name is——?'

'My name is Sawyer—hers is Dennis, which Tom Dennis married her—and a smart, clean lad, too, as long as he's at sea, and no steward in the company more thought of; but when on shore, what with the women and what with liquor shops——'

'Here is your ring, Mrs Sawyer,' I interrupted, in obedience to a sign from my companion; 'it clearly belongs to your daughter, and I am glad to be able to restore it to the rightful owner.'

With many mumbled blessings and protestations of gratitude the old crone packed it away in her pocket, and shuffled off down the stairs. Sherlock Holmes sprang to his feet the moment that she was gone and rushed into his room. He returned in a few seconds enveloped in an ulster and a cravat. 'I'll follow her,' he said, hurriedly; 'she must be an accomplice, and will lead me to him. Wait up for me.' The hall door had hardly slammed behind our visitor before Holmes had descended the stair. Looking through the window I could see her walking feebly along the other side, while her pursuer dogged her some little distance behind. 'Either his whole

or tried to buy, still flourish: George Harding, Henry Stevens & Son, Bumpus, Quaritch, Francis Edwards. Most of them have vanished, and with them have gone the records of Holmes' purchases."

118 De Jure inter Gentes. A volume titled *De Jure Naturae et Getium* was written in 1672 by Samuel Profendorf, born in Saxony in 1632. "Can this have been the work picked up by Holmes?" Mr. Morris Rosenblum asked in "Some Latin Byways in the Canon." "Could he or Watson's printer have been careless about the title and date?" (Mr. Rosenblum also suggested that the volume might have been "a curious edition of Hugo Grotius' celebrated *De Jure Belli et Pacis*, first printed in Paris in 1625 and based largely on the Roman *jus gentium*.)

On the other hand, Miss Madeleine B. Stern has suggested ("Sherlock Holmes: Rare Book Collector") that this volume was actually "one of the most extraordinary volumes in the Holmes treasure room!—a book unique both for its contents and its imprint. The *De Jure inter Gentes*, though published anonymously, was really written by Richard Zouche (1590–1661), the English civilian. Prior to Holmes' 'find,' the first edition was thought to have been printed in Oxford in 1650 under the title: *Juris et Judicii fecialis, sive Juris inter gentes*, and it was the second part of the title that suggested to Bentham the felicitous phrase, 'international law.' The anonymous edition, bearing the title *De Jure inter Gentes*, is rare enough when it carries the Leyden 1651 imprint. But Holmes' copy antedates even the so-called first edition of 1650, and hence is a find of extraordinary magnitude, one of the most desirable books in any legal collection."

119 *'Philippe de Croy, whoever he may have been.* "According to the *Grand Dictionnaire Universal, Larousse*, the name Cröuy, or Croy, belonged to one of the most ancient families of Europe, which claimed descent from the kings of Hungary," Mr. Morris Rosenblum wrote in "Some Latin Byways in the Canon." "A Philippe de Croy (1526–1595), the third Duke of Aerschot, went to Spain on military and diplomatic missions and attended the wedding of the son of Marguerite de Parme. Another Philippe de Croy, the first Duke of Solre, was sent to Madrid by the Estates-General to congratulate Philip II on the marriage of the Infanta in 1598, and made other missions later. These two Philippe de Croys were from the Lowlands and lived within about fifty years of the date mentioned by Holmes, but neither seems to have established a printing house. The De Croy family produced hundreds of notables, among whom were two cardinals, five bishops, many generals, scores of knights, artists and writers—but no printers!"

120 *His writing has a legal twist about it.* "As if he did not know that the copy had belonged to the English divine, William White, 1604–1678, who had fathered several interesting Latin works under the pseudonym of 'Gulielmus Phalerius.' " —Madeline B. Stern, "Sherlock Holmes: Rare Book Collector."

121 *the servant.* "Servants' wages were then very low, and almost everyone could afford to employ at least a maid," Marjorie and C. H. B. Quennell wrote in *A History of Everyday Things in England, Vol. IV, 1851 to 1914.* "In middle-class households there were usually two or three, and in larger houses many more, as well as men-servants. This made the work lighter for the individual but there was always a great deal to be done. Labour-saving devices were practically unknown, and houses were not designed to make the daily round easier. Much time was taken up in carrying coal and food upstairs; stone-paved halls and long passages, kitchens, sculleries and front-door steps needed continual scrubbing. The heavy furniture, often elaborately carved, required constant polishing, and two or three substantial meals had to be prepared and served every day."

"The morning after James Openshaw's visit to 221B in the matter of the Five Orange Pips, Watson comes down to find Holmes already at breakfast," the late Robert R. Pattrick wrote in "The

theory is incorrect,' I thought to myself, 'or else he will be led now to the heart of the mystery.' There was no need for him to ask me to wait up for him, for I felt that sleep was impossible until I heard the result of his adventure.

It was close upon nine when he set out. I had no idea how long he might be, but I sat stolidly puffing at my pipe and **126** skipping over the pages of Henri Murger's *Vie de Bohème.* Ten o'clock passed, and I heard the footsteps of the maid as they pattered off to bed. Eleven, and the more stately tread of the landlady passed my door, bound for the same destination. It was close upon twelve before I heard the sharp sound of his latch-key. The instant he entered I saw by his face that he had not been successful. Amusement and chagrin seemed to be struggling for the mastery, until the former suddenly carried the day, and he burst into a hearty laugh.

'I wouldn't have the Scotland Yarders know it for the world,' he cried, dropping into his chair; 'I have chaffed them so much that they would never have let me hear the end of it. I can afford to laugh, because I know that I will be even with them in the long run.'

'What is it then?' I asked.

'Oh, I don't mind telling a story against myself. That creature had gone a little way when she began to limp and show every sign of being footsore. Presently she came to a halt, and hailed a four-wheeler which was passing. I managed to be close to her so as to hear the address, but I need not

A VERY OLD AND WRINKLED WOMAN HOBBLED INTO THE APARTMENT . . . AND POINTED AT OUR ADVERTISEMENT.

How two different artists saw much the same scene: *left,* James Greig in an illustration for a supplement to the *Windsor Magazine,* Christmas, 1895. *right,* George Hutchinson in an illustration for the London, 1891, Ward, Lock, Bowden & Co. edition of *A Study in Scarlet.* (Charles Doyle, Conan Doyle's father, depicted the same situation in the 1888 Ward, Lock & Co. edition.) Of Greig's work, the late James Montgomery wrote (*A Study in Pictures*) that it was "possibly a little more urbane but still very much in the same undistinguished style as [the illustrations] of George Hutchinson . . ."

have been so anxious, for she sang it out loud enough to be heard at the other side of the street, "Drive to 13, Duncan Street, Houndsditch," she cried. This begins to look genuine, I thought, and having seen her safely inside, I perched myself behind. That's an art which every detective should be an expert at. Well, away we rattled, and never drew rein until we reached the street in question. I hopped off before we came to the door, and strolled down the street in an easy lounging way. I saw the cab pull up. The driver jumped down, and I saw him open the door and stand expectantly. Nothing came out though. When I reached him, he was groping about frantically in the empty cab, and giving vent to the finest assorted collection of oaths that ever I listened to. There was no sign or trace of his passenger, and I fear it will be some time before he gets his fare. On inquiring at Number 13 we found that the house belonged to a respectable paper-hanger, named Keswick, and that no one of the name either of Sawyer or Dennis had ever been heard of there.'

'You don't mean to say,' I cried, in amazement, 'that that tottering, feeble old woman was able to get out of the cab while it was in motion, without either you or the driver seeing her?'

'Old woman be damned!' said Sherlock Holmes, sharply. **127** 'We were the old women to be so taken in. It must have been a young man, and an active one, too, besides being an incomparable actor. The get-up was inimitable. He saw that he was **128** followed, no doubt, and used this means of giving me the slip. It shows that the man we are after is not as lonely as I imagined he was, but has friends who are ready to risk something for him. Now, Doctor, you are looking done-up. Take my advice and turn in.'

I was certainly feeling very weary, so I obeyed his injunction. I left Holmes seated in front of the smouldering fire, and long into the watches of the night, I heard the low, melancholy wailings of his violin, and knew that he was still ponder- **129** ing over the strange problem which he had set himself to unravel.

Case of the Superfluous Landlady." "'Just ring the bell,' says Holmes, 'and the maid will bring up your coffee.' The only other time Watson mentions the maid is in 1895, during the case of 'The Bruce-Partington Plans.'"

122 *a Union boat*. A steamer of the old Union line, which ran to South Africa. This company and the Castle Line were merged in 1900 to form the famous Union-Castle Line.

123 *the circus*. A favorite with Mid- and Late Victorians of all classes. The best-known circus

of the period was "Lord George" Sanger's. His Grand National Ampitheatre stood on the Westminster Bridge Road.

124 *Houndsditch*. The name derives from the old fosse which once encircled this quarter of the City and formed a depository for dead dogs.

125 *Peckham*. Formerly a village, Peckham increased greatly in population between 1820 and 1840 and has now become more or less joined to the metropolis as part of the borough of Camberwell.

126 Vie de Bohème. This 1848 collection of the sketches of Henri Murger, 1822–1861, onetime secretary to Count Aleksei Tolstoi, describes the fortunes and misfortunes, the loves, studies, amusements, and sufferings of a group of impecunious students, artists, and men of letters, of whom Rudolphe represents Murger himself. The sketches form the basis of Puccini's opera *La Bohème* (1898). The late Christopher Morley wrote (*Sherlock Holmes and Dr. Watson: A Textbook of Friendship*) that Watson was presumably "trying to improve his rather simple French by reading some of Holmes' books," but Mr. Benjamin Grosbayne ("Sherlock Holmes—Musician") thought "the not-so-sly implications" are that Watson "read wicked French books in the original so easily that he could skip about and . . . that he wants us to realize what a gay old dog he really is 'neath his respectable exterior."

127 '*Old woman be damned!*' Although we will read of many other occasions on which Holmes cursed, swore, or raved, this is the one instance on record on which we are told what he said.

128 *The get-up was inimitable*. "Much has been written on Sherlock Holmes' adeptness in the art of disguise," Mr. Nathan L. Bengis wrote in "Sherlock Stays After School." "It should be pointed out, however, that in at least two instances he was himself completely foiled by the disguise of others. . . . It almost staggers belief that Holmes would not have seen through the blatantly obvious disguise [employed here]."

129 *the low, melancholy wailings of his violin*. "This sounds as if the music might have been Bach's *Aria for the G String* or Paganini's '*Moses*' *Variations*, also for the fourth string," Mr. Benjamin Grosbayne wrote in "Sherlock Holmes—Musician." "It may also have been improvisation, just as Nicolò Paganini, whom Holmes so admired ["The Cardboard Box"], used to thrill audiences extemporaneously. . . . From the many descriptions of Holmes' style of violin playing . . . it is easy to see that Holmes consciously or subconsciously patterned his own style after that of [this] most glamorous violinist of all time."

130 *The papers next day.* Saturday, by Watson's account. If this is correct, it is still another blow at dating the case 1882: if it began on Saturday, March 4, 1882, papers would not have been published "next day," a Sunday. Nor, as we learn later, could the stable boy have seen Hope leaving Stangerson's room and thought it "early for a carpenter to be at work."

131 *leaders.* Editorials.

132 *The* Daily Telegraph. "The supposed comment by the three great newspapers is acute parody based on the style and predilections of each," the late Christopher Morley wrote in *Sherlock Holmes and Dr. Watson: A Textbook of Friendship.* "The *Telegraph*, then edited by the flamboyant G. A. Sala, was a popular journal of lively tone. The *Standard* was conservative and genteel. The *Daily News* was Liberal in sympathies." We may suppose that the *Times* (mentioned nine times in the Canon) was Holmes' favorite newspaper, and the *Telegraph* (seven mentions) was Watson's.

133 *the Vehmgericht.* A system of secret courts that grew up in Germany in the Middle Ages to execute punishment or revenge.

134 *aqua tofana.* A secret poison attributed to a Sicilian woman called Tofana.

135 *Carbonari.* A secret society of Italian patriots in the early nineteenth century, called Carbonari (charcoal burners) because its members met in the forests in the guise of woodcutters and charcoal burners.

136 *the Marchioness de Brinvilliers.* The French poisoner of the seventeenth century. Her gruesome career plays an extraordinary part in John Dickson Carr's brilliant detective story, *The Burning Court.*

137 *the principles of Malthus.* Thomas Robert Malthus, 1766–1834, English clergyman and writer on political economy. Malthus held "that population unchecked goes on doubling itself every twenty-five years—or increases in geometrical ratio. The rate according to which the productions of the earth increase must be totally of a different nature from the ratio of the increase in population. . . . Therefore, considering the present average state of the earth, the means of subsistence, under circumstances the most favorable to human industry, could not possibly be made to increase faster than in an arithmetical ratio. . . . The power of propagation being in every period so much superior, the increase of the human species can only be kept down to the level of the means of subsistence by the constant operation of the strong law of necessity, acting as a check upon the greater power" (*Essay on Population*).

138 *the Ratcliff Highway murders.* "These were the gruesome crimes described by De Quincey in

---

6 ⋮ **TOBIAS GREGSON SHOWS**
⋮ **WHAT HE CAN DO**

130 The papers next day were full of the 'Brixton Mystery,' as they termed it. Each had a long account of the affair, and **131** some had leaders upon it in addition. There was some information in them which was new to me. I still retain in my scrap-book numerous clippings and extracts upon the case. Here is a condensation of a few of them:

132 The *Daily Telegraph* remarked that in the history of crime there had seldom been a tragedy which presented stranger features. The German name of the victim, the absence of all other motive, and the sinister inscription on the wall, all pointed to its perpetration by political refugees and revolutionists. The Socialists had many branches in America, and the deceased had, no doubt, infringed their unwritten laws, and been tracked down by them. After alluding airily to the **133-134** Vehmgericht, aqua tofana, Carbonari, the Marchioness de **135 136** Brinvilliers, the Darwinian theory, the principles of Malthus, **137 138** and the Ratcliff Highway murders, the article concluded by admonishing the Government and advocating a closer watch over foreigners in England.

The *Standard* commented upon the fact that lawless outrages of the sort usually occurred under a Liberal Administra- **139** tion. They arose from the unsettling of the minds of the masses, and the consequent weakening of all authority. The deceased was an American gentleman who had been residing for some weeks in the Metropolis. He had stayed at the boarding-house of Madame Charpentier, in Torquay Ter- **140** race, Camberwell. He was accompanied in his travels by his private secretary, Mr Joseph Stangerson. The two bade adieu **141** to their landlady upon Tuesday, the 4th inst., and departed **142** to Euston Station with the avowed intention of catching the Liverpool express. They were afterwards seen together upon the platform. Nothing more is known of them until Mr Drebber's body was, as recorded, discovered in an empty house in the Brixton Road, many miles from Euston. How he came there, or how he met his fate, are questions which are still involved in mystery. Nothing is known of the whereabouts of Stangerson. We are glad to learn that Mr Lestrade and Mr Gregson, of Scotland Yard, are both engaged upon the case, and it is confidently anticipated that these well-known officers will speedily throw light upon the matter.

The *Daily News* observed that there was no doubt as to the crime being a political one. The despotism and hatred of Liberalism which animated the Continental Governments had had the effect of driving to our shores a number of men who might have made excellent citizens were they not soured by the recollection of all that they had undergone. Among these men there was a stringent code of honour, any infringement of which was punished by death. Every effort should be made to find the secretary, Stangerson, and to ascertain some particulars of the habits of the deceased. A great step had been gained by the discovery of the address of the house at which he had boarded—a result which was entirely due to the acuteness and energy of Mr Gregson of Scotland Yard.

Sherlock Holmes and I read these notices over together at breakfast, and they appeared to afford him considerable amusement.

'I told you that, whatever happened, Lestrade and Gregson would be sure to score.'

'That depends on how it turns out.'

'Oh, bless you, it doesn't matter in the least. If the man is caught, it will be *on account* of their exertions; if he escapes, is will be *in spite* of their exertions. It's heads I win and tails you lose. Whatever they do, they will have followers. "Un sot trouve toujours un plus sot qui l'admire." '   **143**

'What on earth is this?' I cried, for at this moment there came the pattering of many steps in the hall and on the stairs, accompanied by audible expressions of disgust upon the part of our landlady.

'It's the Baker Street division of the detective police force,' said my companion gravely; and as he spoke there rushed into the room half a dozen of the dirtiest and most ragged street arabs that ever I clapped eyes on.

' 'Tention!' cried Holmes, in a sharp tone, and the six dirty little scoundrels stood in a line like so many disreputable statuettes. 'In future you shall send up Wiggins alone to report, and the rest of you must wait in the street. Have you found it, Wiggins?'

'No, sir, we hain't,' said one of the youths.

'I hardly expected you would. You must keep on until you do. Here are your wages.' He handed each of them a shilling. 'Now, off you go, and come back with a better report next time.'   **144**

He waved his hand, and they scampered away downstairs like so many rats, and we heard their shrill voices next moment in the street.

'There's more work to be got out of one of those little beggars than out of a dozen of the force,' Holmes remarked. 'The mere sight of an official-looking person seals men's lips. These youngsters, however, go everywhere, and hear everything. They are as sharp as needles, too; all they want is organization.'

'Is it on this Brixton case that you are employing them?' I asked.

'Yes; there is a point which I wish to ascertain. It is merely a matter of time. Hullo! we are going to hear some news now with a vengeance! Here is Gregson coming down the road with beatitude written upon every feature of his face. Bound for us, I know. Yes, he is stopping. There he is!'

There was a violent peal at the bell, and in a few seconds the fair-haired detective came up the stairs, three steps at a time, and burst into our sitting-room.

'My dear fellow,' he cried, wringing Holmes' unresponsive hand, 'congratulate me! I have made the whole thing as clear as day.'

A shade of anxiety seemed to me to cross my companion's expressive face.

'Do you mean that you are on the right track?' he asked.

'The right track! Why, sir, we have the man under lock and key.'

'And his name is?'

'Arthur Charpentier, sub-lieutenant in Her Majesty's Navy,' cried Gregson pompously, rubbing his fat hands and inflating his chest.

Sherlock Holmes gave a sigh of relief and relaxed into a smile.

his masterpiece, 'Murder Considered As One of the Fine Arts,'" the late Christopher Morley wrote in *Sherlock Holmes and Dr. Watson: A Textbook in Friendship.* "The Ratcliff Highway, in the region of the docks, acquired such a sinister repute that its name was later changed to St. George's Street. As recently as 1910 a London guidebook said of it 'here is Jamrach's emporium of wild beasts, that have been known to escape into the streets, and of a Saturday night might not find themselves altogether without kindred society!'"

139 *a Liberal Administration.* The Liberal party in Britain (Lord John Russell is credited with the name) grew out of the Whig party. Its policies were free trade, religious liberty, abolition of slavery, and extension of the franchise.

140 *Camberwell.* "Camberwell, across the Thames in South London, was an unusual lodging place for well-to-do tourists—unless possibly they chose to be near the Crystal Palace, still very famous in those days [it was demolished about 1940 so that its great iron girders could be used for military material]," Christopher Morley wrote in *Sherlock Holmes and Dr. Watson: A Textbook of Friendship.* "Black's *London Guide* (1910) described Camberwell as 'an extremely prosaic suburb,' but it was always romantic to Dr. Watson, for reasons you will discover in *The Sign of the Four.* It has also a charming connotation in the name of a beautiful and rare butterfly, the Camberwell Beauty."

141 *Tuesday, the 4th inst.* The *Standard* was clearly wrong in calling the 4th, a Friday in 1881, a Tuesday, as virtually all commentators agree. The only Marches in this entire period in which the 4th fell on a Tuesday were 1879 (much too early) and 1884 (even more too late).

142 *Euston Station.* Originally designed as the terminus of the London and Birmingham Railway, now the principal terminus of the British Railways Midland Region, Euston was the first of the larger railroad stations to be erected in London (it occupies an area of twelve acres). Compared to the newer Waterloo and Victoria Stations, Euston today is shabby, inconvenient, and straggling. It was at Euston Station on November 1, 1848, that Messrs. W. H. Smith opened the first of the hundreds of bookstalls which have now made that firm a national institution.

143 *"Un sot trouve toujours un plus sot qui l'admire."* ' This is the end line (232) of Canto I of *L'Art Poétique* by Nicolas Boileau Despréaux, 1636–1711, and is translated as: "A fool can always find a greater fool to admire him." Mr. Dean W. Dickensheet, in his study of "Sherlock Holmes—Linguist," has shown that Holmes was fluent in English, idiomatic American, French, German, Italian, Norwegian, and Gaelic. He had some knowledge of Russian, Swedish, Dutch, and prob-

"IT'S THE BAKER STREET DIVISION OF THE DETECTIVE
POLICE FORCE."

Illustration by George Hutchinson for *A Study in
Scarlet;* London: Ward, Lock, Bowden & Co., 1891.

. . . THE SIX DIRTY LITTLE SCOUNDRELS STOOD IN A LINE
LIKE SO MANY DISREPUTABLE STATUETTES.

The first representation of the Baker Street Irregulars—one of the six drawings done by Charles
Doyle, Conan Doyle's father, for *A Study in Scarlet;* London: Ward, Lock & Co., 1888. It "has the
urchins saluting with their left hands, although the
quill pen is on the right of the writing block, as it
should be, and Holmes is gesturing with his right
forefinger," the late James Montgomery wrote in
A Study in Pictures. "Watson buttons his vest in
the wrong direction but one of the Irregulars
fastens his the other way, so nothing can be proved
there. And how one shudders at the figures of
Holmes and Watson—the former now clean shaven
and smiling vapidly in an ill-fitting toupee—the
latter bearded like a Saxon chieftain!"

'Take a seat, and try one of these cigars,' he said. 'We are
anxious to know how you managed it. Will you have some
145 whisky and water?'

'I don't mind if I do,' the detective answered. 'The tremendous exertions which I have gone through during the last day
146 or two have worn me out. Not so much bodily exertion, you
understand, as the strain upon the mind. You will appreciate
that, Mr Sherlock Holmes, for we are both brain-workers.'

'You do me too much honour,' said Holmes, gravely. 'Let
us hear how you arrived at this most gratifying result.'

The detective seated himself in the arm-chair, and puffed
complacently at his cigar. Then suddenly he slapped his thigh
in a paroxysm of amusement.

'The fun of it is,' he cried, 'that that fool Lestrade, who thinks himself so smart, has gone off upon the wrong track altogether. He is after the secretary Stangerson, who had no more to do with the crime than the babe unborn. I have no doubt that he has caught him by this time.'

The idea tickled Gregson so much that he laughed until he choked.

'And how did you get your clue?'

'Ah, I'll tell you all about it. Of course, Doctor Watson, this is strictly between ourselves. The first difficulty which we had to contend with was the finding of this American's antecedents. Some people would have waited until their advertisements were answered, or until parties came forward and volunteered information. That is not Tobias Gregson's way of going to work. You remember the hat beside the dead man?'

'Yes,' said Holmes; 'by John Underwood and Sons, 129, Camberwell Road.' **147**

Gregson looked quite crestfallen.

'I had no idea that you noticed that,' he said. 'Have you been there?'

'No.'

'Ha!' cried Gregson, in a relieved voice; 'you should never neglect a chance, however small it may seem.'

'To a great mind, nothing is little,' remarked Holmes, **148** sententiously.

'Well, I went to Underwood, and asked him if he had sold a hat of that size and description. He looked over his books, and came on it at once. He had sent the hat to a Mr Drebber, residing at Charpentier's Boarding Establishment, Torquay Terrace. Thus I got at his address.'

'Smart—very smart!' murmured Sherlock Holmes.

'I next called upon Madame Charpentier,' continued the detective. 'I found her very pale and distressed. Her daughter was in the room, too—an uncommonly fine girl she is, too; she was looking red about the eyes and her lips trembled as I spoke to her. That didn't escape my notice. I began to smell a rat. You know the feeling, Mr Sherlock Holmes, when you come upon the right scent—a kind of thrill in your nerves. "Have you heard of the mysterious death of your late boarder Mr Enoch J. Drebber, of Cleveland?" I asked.

'The mother nodded. She didn't seem able to get out a word. The daughter burst into tears. I felt more than ever that these people knew something of the matter.

' "At what o'clock did Mr Drebber leave your house for the train?" I asked.

' "At eight o'clock," she said, gulping in her throat to keep down her agitation. "His secretary, Mr Stangerson, said that there were two trains—one at 9.15 and one at 11. He was to catch the first."

' "And was that the last which you saw of him?"

'A terrible change came over the woman's face as I asked the question. Her features turned perfectly livid. It was some seconds before she could get out the single word "Yes"—and when it did come it was in a husky, unnatural tone.

'There was silence for a moment, and then the daughter spoke in a calm, clear voice.

' "No good can ever come of falsehood, mother," she said. "Let us be frank with this gentleman. We *did* see Mr Drebber again."

ably Chinese. His travels after Reichenbach required a knowledge of Arabic, but the languages of the Tibeto-Burman group, as well as any other Asian or African tongue, were spoken through interpreters. He had a superior knowledge of Latin and was capable of making comparative studies of ancient Cornish and Chaldean. He knew some Greek, some Persian, and had at least some knowledge of the philological antecedents of English, French, and German.

144 *come back with a better report next time.'* Holmes "loved children—how else could he have commanded the sworn services of Wiggins and those other invaluable urchins, the Baker Street Irregulars, or have kept the worship of Billy the page ["The Adventure of the Mazarin Stone"]?" —Manly Wade Wellman, "The Great Man's Great Son."

145 *whisky and water?'* Holmes and Watson drank plain water with their whisky in the early, less affluent days; the gasogene ("A Scandal in Bohemia") was a later sophistication. Mr. Michael Harrison has noted (*In the Footsteps of Sherlock Holmes*) that Irish whiskey was more widely drunk than Scotch whisky in Holmes' and Watson's day, and could be dearer. Watson does not seem to distinguish between Irish and Scotch, but he does invariably use the Scotch spelling *whisky*.

146 *during the last day or two.* If Gregson arrived at Baker Street on Saturday, as Watson tells us he did, he perhaps would not have referred to his exertions "during the last day or two." But the late Dr. Ernest Bloomfield Zeisler argued ("A Chronological Study in Scarlet") that Gregson "had been working on the case from about 3:00 A.M. of Friday until at least noon on Saturday; nine hours longer than a day and quite long enough to warrant calling it 'a day or so'; had it been a few hours more it should have been called 'two days' or 'almost two days.' "

147 *Camberwell Road.* Opened in 1820 from Kennington Common to Camberwell Green, the new road saved nearly two miles and a half in the distance from Westminster into Kent.

148 *'To a great mind, nothing is little.'* Compare: "It is of course a trifle, but there is nothing so important as trifles"—"The Man with the Twisted Lip." "It has long been a maxim of mine that the little things are infinitely the most important"—"A Case of Identity." "You know my method. It is founded upon the observance of trifles"—"The Boscombe Valley Mystery." "I dare call nothing trivial when I reflect that some of my most classic cases have had the least promising commencement"—"The Adventure of the Six Napoleons." "Holmes has, as Watson remarked, an extraordinary gift for minutiae [*The Sign of the Four*]," Mr. T. S. Blakeney commented in *Sherlock Holmes: Fact or Fiction?*

HE HANDED EACH OF THEM A SHILLING.

11 above is the 1824 shilling of George IV; *11a* the 1817 shilling of George III, reverse only; *11b* the 1821 shilling of George IV, reverse only; *11c* the 1893 shilling of Victoria, reverse only; *11d* the 1902 shilling of Edward VII, reverse only. The shilling, as we have seen, was worth slightly less than 25¢ in U.S. currency in Holmes' and Watson's day. As the late A. Carson Simpson wrote in *Numismatics in the Canon*, Part I: "The shilling of 12d. traces back to the testoon (the 'tester' of *A Midsummer Night's Dream*) of Henry VII (*circa* 1505), which derives its name from the Italian testone—literally a coin which bears the head (testa) of the ruler. It was, in fact, the first English silver coin which carried a true portrait—as distinct from the medieval conventional representation—of the monarch. Under Henry VIII, the name shilling (after the Anglo-Saxon money of account) began to come into use and was soon adopted generally. This denomination has been coined by all rulers since then except Mary Tudor, though, in the period of the silver bullion shortage during the reign of George III, there were several gaps over ten years in length. There are more Canonical references to the shilling than to any other coin. . . . Nine types of shilling were probably in circulation during the appropriate period."

149 *fourteen pounds a week.* About $70.

' "God forgive you!" cried Madame Charpentier, throwing up her hands, and sinking back in her chair. "You have murdered your brother."

' "Arthur would rather that we spoke the truth," the girl answered firmly.

' "You had best tell me all about it now," I said. "Half-confidences are worse than none. Besides, you do not know how much we know of it."

' "On your head be it, Alice!" cried her mother; and then, turning to me, "I will tell you all, sir. Do not imagine that my agitation on behalf of my son arises from any fear lest he should have had a hand in this terrible affair. He is utterly innocent of it. My dread is, however, that in your eyes and in the eyes of others he may appear to be compromised. That, however, is surely impossible. His high character, his profession, his antecedents would all forbid it."

' "Your best way is to make a clean breast of the facts," I answered. "Depend upon it, if your son is innocent he will be none the worse."

' "Perhaps, Alice, you had better leave us together," she said, and her daughter withdrew. "Now, sir," she continued, "I had no intention of telling you all this, but since my poor daughter has disclosed it I have no alternative. Having once decided to speak, I will tell you all without omitting any particular."

' "It is your wisest course," said I.

' "Mr Drebber has been with us nearly three weeks. He and his secretary, Mr Stangerson, had been travelling on the Continent. I noticed a 'Copenhagen' label upon each of their trunks, showing that that had been their last stopping-place. Stangerson was a quiet, reserved man, but his employer, I am sorry to say, was far otherwise. He was coarse in his habits and brutish in his ways. The very night of his arrival he became very much the worse for drink, and, indeed, after twelve o'clock in the day he could hardly ever be said to be sober. His manners towards the maid-servants were disgustingly free and familiar. Worst of all, he speedily assumed the same attitude towards my daughter, Alice, and spoke to her more than once in a way which, fortunately, she is too innocent to understand. On one occasion he actually seized her in his arms and embraced her—an outrage which caused his own secretary to reproach him for his unmanly conduct."

' "But why did you stand all this?" I asked. "I suppose that you can get rid of your boarders when you wish."

'Madame Charpentier blushed at my pertinent question. "Would to God that I had given him notice on the very day that he came," she said. "But it was a sore temptation. They **149** were paying a pound a day each—fourteen pounds a week, and this is the slack season. I am a widow, and my boy in the Navy has cost me much. I grudged to lose the money. I acted for the best. This last was too much, however, and I gave him notice to leave on account of it. That was the reason of his going."

' "Well?"

' "My heart grew light when I saw him drive away. My son is on leave just now, but I did not tell him anything of all this, for his temper is violent, and he is passionately fond of his sister. When I closed the door behind them a load seemed to be lifted from my mind. Alas, in less than an hour there was a ring at the bell, and I learned that Mr Drebber had returned. He was much excited, and evidently the worse for drink. He forced his way into the room, where I was sitting with my daughter, and made some incoherent remark about having missed his train. He then turned to Alice, and before my very face proposed to her that she should fly with him. 'You are of age,' he said, 'and there is no law to stop you. I have money enough and to spare. Never mind the old girl here, but come along with me now straight away. You shall live like a princess.' Poor Alice was so frightened that she shrank away from him, but he caught her by the wrist and endeavoured to draw her towards the door. I screamed, and at that moment my son Arthur came into the room. What happened then I do not know. I heard oaths and the confused sounds of a scuffle. I was too terrified to raise my head. When I did look up I saw Arthur standing in the doorway laughing, with a stick in his hand. 'I don't think that fine fellow will trouble us again,' he said. 'I will just go after him and see what he does with himself.' With those words he took his hat and started off down the street. The next morning we heard of Mr Drebber's mysterious death." **150**

'This statement came from Madame Charpentier's lips with many gasps and pauses. At times she spoke so low that I could hardly catch the words. I made shorthand notes of all that she **151** said, however, so that there should be no possibility of a mistake.'

'It's quite exciting,' said Sherlock Holmes, with a yawn. 'What happened next?'

'When Madame Charpentier paused,' the detective continued, 'I saw that the whole case hung upon one point. Fixing her with my eye in a way which I always found effective with women, I asked her at what hour her son returned.

' "I do not know," she answered.

' "Not know?"

' "No; he has a latch-key, and he let himself in."

' "After you went to bed?"

' "Yes."

' "When did you go to bed?"

' "About eleven."

' "So your son was gone at least two hours?"

' "Yes."

' "Possibly four or five?"

' "Yes."

' "What was he doing during that time?"

' "I do not know," she answered, turning white to her very lips.

'Of course after that there was nothing more to be done. I found out where Lieutenant Charpentier was, took two officers with me, and arrested him. When I touched him on the shoulder and warned him to come quietly with us, he answered us as bold as brass, "I suppose you are arresting me for being concerned in the death of that scoundrel Drebber," he said. We had said nothing to him about it, so that his alluding to it had a most suspicious aspect.'

'Very,' said Holmes.

'He still carried the heavy stick which the mother described him as having when he followed Drebber. It was a stout oak cudgel.'

'What is your theory, then?'

'Well, my theory is that he followed Drebber as far as the

150 *The next morning we heard of Mr. Drebber's mysterious death."* Mme. Charpentier would not, on the Friday afternoon, have referred to the morning of that day as 'the next morning," but as "this morning"—an indication that Gregson called on her, not on Friday, but on the following Saturday morning.

151 *I made shorthand notes.* Gregson (and later, Lestrade) probably followed the Pitman Method since the Gregg system did not come into vogue until about 1888. We may note here that an edition of *The Sign of the Four* was issued in Pitman's shorthand in 1898, and proved so popular that Gregg put the same book into shorthand in 1918.

Brixton Road. When there, a fresh altercation arose between them, in the course of which Drebber received a blow from the stick, in the pit of the stomach perhaps, which killed him without leaving any mark. The night was so wet that no one was about, so Charpentier dragged the body of his victim into the empty house. As to the candle, and the blood, and the writing on the wall, and the ring, they may all be so many tricks to throw the police on to the wrong scent.'

'Well done!' said Holmes in an encouraging voice. 'Really, Gregson, you are getting along. We shall make something of you yet.'

'I flatter myself that I have managed it rather neatly,' the detective answered proudly. 'The young man volunteered a statement, in which he said that after following Drebber some time, the latter perceived him, and took a cab in order to get away from him. On his way home he met an old shipmate, and took a long walk with him. On being asked where this old shipmate lived, he was unable to give any satisfactory reply. I think the whole case fits together uncommonly well. What amuses me is to think of Lestrade, who had started off upon the wrong scent. I am afraid he won't make much of it. Why, by Jove, here's the very man himself!'

It was indeed Lestrade, who had ascended the stairs while we were talking, and who now entered the room. The assurance and jauntiness which generally marked his demeanour and dress were, however, wanting. His face was disturbed and troubled, while his clothes were disarranged and untidy. He had evidently come with the intention of consulting with Sherlock Holmes, for on perceiving his colleague he appeared to be embarrassed and put out. He stood in the centre of the room, fumbling nervously with his hat and uncertain what to do. 'This is a most extraordinary case,' he said at last—'a most incomprehensible affair.'

'Ah, you find it so, Mr Lestrade!' cried Gregson, triumphantly. 'I thought you would come to that conclusion. Have you managed to land the secretary, Mr Joseph Stangerson?'

'The secretary, Mr Joseph Stangerson,' said Lestrade, gravely, 'was murdered at Halliday's Private Hotel about six o'clock this morning.'

7 ◆ LIGHT IN THE DARKNESS

The intelligence with which Lestrade greeted us was so momentous and so unexpected that we were all three fairly dumbfounded. Gregson sprang out of his chair and upset the remainder of his whisky and water. I stared in silence at Sherlock Holmes, whose lips were compressed and his brows drawn down over his eyes.

'Stangerson too!' he muttered. 'The plot thickens.'

'It was quite thick enough before,' grumbled Lestrade, taking a chair. 'I seem to have dropped into a sort of council of war.'

'Are you—are you sure of this piece of intelligence?' stammered Gregson.

'I have just come from his room,' said Lestrade. 'I was the first to discover what had occurred.'

'We have been hearing Gregson's view of the matter,' Holmes observed. 'Would you mind letting us know what you have seen and done?'

'I have no objection,' Lestrade answered, seating himself. 'I freely confess that I was of the opinion that Stangerson was concerned in the death of Drebber. This fresh development has shown me that I was completely mistaken. Full of the one idea, I set myself to find out what had become of the secretary. They had been seen together at Euston Station about half-past eight on the evening of the third. At two in the morning **152** Drebber had been found in the Brixton Road. The question which confronted me was to find out how Stangerson had been employed between 8.30 and the time of the crime, and what had become of him afterwards. I telegraphed to Liverpool, giving a description of the man, and warning them to keep a watch upon the American boats. I then set to work calling upon all the hotels and lodging-houses in the vicinity of Euston. You see, I argued that if Drebber and his companion had become separated, the natural course for the latter would be to put up somewhere in the vicinity for the night, and then to hang about the station again next morning.'

'They would be likely to agree on some meeting place beforehand,' remarked Holmes.

'So it proved. I spent the whole of yesterday evening in making inquiries entirely without avail. This morning I began very early, and at eight o'clock I reached Halliday's Private Hotel, in Little George Street. On my inquiry as to whether a Mr Stangerson was living there, they at once answered me in the affirmative.

' "No doubt you are the gentleman whom he was expecting," they said. "He has been waiting for a gentleman for two days."

' "Where is he now?" I asked.

' "He is upstairs in bed. He wished to be called at nine."

' "I will go up and see him at once," I said.

'It seemed to me that my sudden appearance might shake his nerves and lead him to say something unguarded. The Boots volunteered to show me the room: it was on the second **153** floor, and there was a small corridor leading up to it. The Boots pointed out the door to me, and was about to go downstairs again when I saw something that made me feel sickish, in spite of my twenty years' experience. From under the door there curled a little red ribbon of blood, which had meandered across the passage and formed a little pool along the skirting at the other side. I gave a cry, which brought the Boots back. He nearly fainted when he saw it. The door was locked on the inside, but we put our shoulders to it, and knocked it in. The window of the room was open, and beside the window, all huddled up, lay the body of a man in his nightdress. He was quite dead, and had been for some time, for his limbs were rigid and cold. When we turned him over, the Boots recognized him at once as being the same gentleman who had engaged the room under the name of Joseph Stangerson. The cause of death was a deep stab in the left

152 *on the evening of the third.* Corroborating Watson's statement that it was "upon the 4th of March" that Holmes was brought into the case.

153 *The Boots.* A servant at an inn or hotel who blackened boots and did minor offices for the guests.

154 *the mews.* Stableyard, or a back lane or alley leading to the stables.

155 *eighty odd pounds.* Some $400.

156 *a small chip ointment box.* A box made of thin wood.

side, which must have penetrated the heart. And now comes the strangest part of the affair. What do you suppose was above the murdered man?'

I felt a creeping of the flesh, and a presentiment of coming horror, even before Sherlock Holmes answered.

'The word RACHE, written in letters of blood,' he said.

'That was it,' said Lestrade, in an awestruck voice; and we were all silent for awhile.

There was something so methodical and so incomprehensible about the deeds of this unknown assassin, that it imparted a fresh ghastliness to his crimes. My nerves, which were steady enough on the field of battle, tingled as I thought of it.

'The man was seen,' continued Lestrade. 'A milk boy, passing on his way to the dairy, happened to walk down the lane **154** which leads from the mews at the back of the hotel. He noticed that a ladder, which usually lay there, was raised against one of the windows of the second floor, which was wide open. After passing, he looked back and saw a man descend the ladder. He came down so quietly and openly that the boy imagined him to be some carpenter or joiner at work in the hotel. He took no particular notice of him, beyond thinking in his own mind that it was early for him to be at work. He has an impression that the man was tall, had a reddish face, and was dressed in a long, brownish coat. He must have stayed in the room some little time after the murder, for we found blood-stained water in the basin, where he had washed his hands, and marks on the sheets where he had deliberately wiped his knife.'

I glanced at Holmes on hearing the description of the murderer which tallied so exactly with his own. There was, however, no trace of exultation or satisfaction upon his face.

'Did you find nothing in the room which could furnish a clue to the murderer?' he asked.

'Nothing. Stangerson had Drebber's purse in his pocket, but it seems that this was usual, as he did all the paying. There **155** was eighty odd pounds in it, but nothing had been taken. Whatever the motives of these extraordinary crimes, robbery is certainly not one of them. There were no papers or memoranda in the murdered man's pocket, except a single telegram, dated from Cleveland about a month ago, and containing the words, "J. H. is in Europe." There was no name appended to this message.'

'And there was nothing else?' Holmes asked.

'Nothing of any importance. The man's novel, with which he had read himself to sleep, was lying upon the bed, and his pipe was on a chair beside him. There was a glass of water on **156** the table, and on the window-sill a small chip ointment box containing a couple of pills.'

Sherlock Holmes sprang from his chair with an exclamation of delight.

'The last link,' he cried, exultantly. 'My case is complete.'

The two detectives stared at him in amazement.

'I have now in my hands,' my companion said, confidently, 'all the threads which have formed such a tangle. There are, of course, details to be filled in, but I am as certain of all the main facts, from the time that Drebber parted from Stangerson at the station, up to the discovery of the body of the latter, as if I had seen them with my own eyes. I will give you a proof of my knowledge. Could you lay your hand upon those pills?'

'I have them,' said Lestrade, producing a small white box; 'I took them and the purse and the telegram, intending to have them put in a place of safety at the Police Station. It was the merest chance my taking these pills, for I am bound to say that I do not attach any importance to them.'

'Give them here,' said Holmes. 'Now, Doctor,' turning to me, 'are those ordinary pills?'

They certainly were not. They were of a pearly grey colour, small, round, and almost transparent against the light. 'From their lightness and transparency, I should imagine that they are soluble in water,' I remarked.

'Precisely so,' answered Holmes. 'Now would you mind going down and fetching that poor little devil of a terrier which has been bad so long, and which the landlady wanted you to put out of its pain yesterday.'

I went downstairs and carried the dog upstairs in my arms. Its laboured breathing and glazing eye showed that it was not far from its end. Indeed, its snow-white muzzle proclaimed that it had already exceeded the usual term of canine existence. I placed it upon a cushion on the rug.

'I will now cut one of these pills in two,' said Holmes, and drawing his penknife he suited the action to the word. 'One half we return into the box for future purposes. The other half I will place in this wine glass, in which is a teaspoonful of water. You perceive that our friend, the Doctor, is right, and that it readily dissolves.'

'This may be very interesting,' said Lestrade, in the injured tone of one who suspects that he is being laughed at; 'I cannot see, however, what it has to do with the death of Mr Joseph Stangerson.'

'Patience, my friend, patience! You will find in time that it has everything to do with it. I shall now add a little milk to make the mixture palatable, and on presenting it to the dog we find that he laps it up readily enough.'

As he spoke he turned the contents of the wine glass into a saucer and placed it in front of the terrier, who speedily licked it dry. Sherlock Holmes' earnest demeanour had so far convinced us that we all sat in silence, watching the animal intently, and expecting some startling effect. None such appeared, however. The dog continued to lie stretched upon the cushion, breathing in a laboured way, but apparently neither the better nor the worse for its draught.

Holmes had taken out his watch, and as minute followed minute without result, an expression of the utmost chagrin and disappointment appeared upon his features. He gnawed his lip, drummed his fingers upon the table, and showed every other symptom of acute impatience. So great was his emotion that I felt sincerely sorry for him, while the two detectives smiled derisively, by no means displeased at this check which he had met.

'It can't be a coincidence,' he cried, at last springing from his chair and pacing wildly up and down the room; 'it is impossible that it should be a mere coincidence. The very pills which I suspected in the case of Drebber are actually found after the death of Stangerson. And yet they are inert. What can it mean? Surely my whole chain of reasoning cannot have

157 *proves to be capable of bearing some other interpretation.* Compare: "One should always look for a possible alternative and provide against it. It is the first rule of criminal investigation"—"The Adventure of Black Peter." "When you follow two separate trains of thought, you will find some point of intersection which should approximate to the truth"—"The Disappearance of Lady Frances Carfax." "One drawback of an active mind is that one can always conceive alternative explanations, which would make our scent a false one"—"The Problem of Thor Bridge."

158 *no new or special features from which deductions may be drawn.* Compare: "Singularity is almost invariably a clue. The more featureless and commonplace a crime is, the more difficult it is to bring home"—"The Boscombe Valley Mystery." "The more bizarre a thing is the less mysterious it proves to be"—"The Red-Headed League."

159 outré. French: exaggerated, excessive, unusual.

THE UNFORTUNATE CREATURE'S TONGUE SEEMED HARDLY TO HAVE BEEN MOISTENED IN IT BEFORE IT GAVE A CONVULSIVE SHUDDER IN EVERY LIMB, AND LAY AS RIGID AND LIFELESS AS IF IT HAD BEEN STRUCK BY LIGHTNING.

Illustration by George Hutchinson for *A Study in Scarlet;* London: Ward, Lock, Bowden & Co., 1891.

been false. It is impossible! And yet this wretched dog is none the worse. Ah, I have it! I have it!' With a perfect shriek of delight he rushed to the box, cut the other pill in two, dissolved it, added milk, and presented it to the terrier. The unfortunate creature's tongue seemed hardly to have been moistened in it before it gave a convulsive shiver in every limb, and lay as rigid and lifeless as if it had been struck by lightning.

Sherlock Holmes drew a long breath, and wiped the perspiration from his forehead. 'I should have more faith,' he said; 'I ought to know by this time that when a fact appears to be opposed to a long train of deductions it invariably **157** proves to be capable of bearing some other interpretation. Of the two pills in that box, one was of the most deadly poison, and the other was entirely harmless. I ought to have known that before ever I saw the box at all.'

This last statement appeared to me to be so startling that I could hardly believe that he was in his sober senses. There was the dead dog, however, to prove that his conjecture had been correct. It seemed to me that the mists in my own mind were gradually clearing away, and I began to have a dim, vague perception of the truth.

'All this seems strange to you,' continued Holmes, 'because you failed at the beginning of the inquiry to grasp the importance of the single real clue which was presented to you. I had the good fortune to seize upon that, and everything which has occurred since then has served to confirm my original supposition, and, indeed, was the logical sequence of it. Hence things which have perplexed you and made the case more obscure have served to enlighten me and to strengthen my conclusions. It is a mistake to confound strangeness with mystery. The most commonplace crime is often the most mysterious, because it presents no new or **158** special features from which deductions may be drawn. This murder would have been infinitely more difficult to unravel had the body of the victim been simply found lying in the **159** roadway without any of those *outré* and sensational accompaniments which have rendered it remarkable. These strange details, far from making the case more difficult, have really had the effect of making it less so.'

Mr Gregson, who had listened to this address with considerable impatience, could contain himself no longer. 'Look here, Mr Sherlock Holmes,' he said, 'we are all ready to acknowledge that you are a smart man, and that you have your own methods of working. We want something more than mere theory and preaching now, though. It is a case of taking the man. I have made my case out, and it seems I was wrong. Young Charpentier could not have been engaged in this second affair. Lestrade went after his man, Stangerson, and it appears that he was wrong too. You have thrown out hints here, and hints there, and seem to know more than we do, but the time has come when we feel that we have a right to ask you straight how much you do know of the business. Can you name the man who did it?'

'I cannot help feeling that Gregson is right, sir,' remarked Lestrade. 'We have both tried, and we have both failed. You have remarked more than once since I have been in the room that you had all the evidence which you require. Surely you will not withhold it any longer.'

'Any delay in arresting the assassin,' I observed, 'might give him time to perpetrate some fresh atrocity.'

Thus pressed by us all, Holmes showed signs of irresolution. He continued to walk up and down the room with his head sunk on his chest and his brows drawn down, as was his habit when lost in thought.

'There will be no more murders,' he said at last, stopping abruptly and facing us. 'You can put that consideration out of the question. You have asked me if I know the name of the assassin. I do. The mere knowing of his name is a small thing, however, compared with the power of laying our hands upon him. This I expect very shortly to do. I have good hopes of managing it through my own arrangements; but it is a thing which needs delicate handling, for we have a shrewd and desperate man to deal with, who is supported, as I have had occasion to prove, by another who is as clever as himself. As long as this man has no idea that anyone can have a clue there is some chance of securing him; but if he had the slightest suspicion, he would change his name, and vanish in an instant among the four million inhabitants of this great city. With- **160** out meaning to hurt either of your feelings, I am bound to say that I consider these men to be more than a match for the official force, and that is why I have not asked your assistance. If I fail, I shall, of course, incur all the blame due to this omission; but that I am prepared for. At present I am ready to promise that the instant that I can communicate with you without endangering my own combinations, I shall do so.'

Gregson and Lestrade seemed to be far from satisfied by this assurance, or by the depreciating allusion to the detective police. The former had flushed up to the roots of his flaxen hair, while the other's beady eyes glistened with curiosity and resentment. Neither of them had time to speak, however, before there was a tap at the door, and the spokesman of the street Arabs, young Wiggins, introduced his insignificant and unsavoury person.

'Please, sir,' he said, touching his forelock, 'I have the cab downstairs.'

'Good boy,' said Holmes, blandly. 'Why don't you introduce this pattern at Scotland Yard?' he continued, taking a pair of steel handcuffs from a drawer. 'See how beautifully the spring works. They fasten in an instant.'   **161**

'The old pattern is good enough,' remarked Lestrade, 'if we can only find the man to put them on.'

'Very good, very good,' said Holmes, smiling. 'The cabman may as well help me with my boxes. Just ask him to step up, Wiggins.'

I was surprised to find my companion speaking as though he were about to set out on a journey, since he had not said anything to me about it. There was a small portmanteau in the room, and this he pulled out and began to strap. He was busily engaged at it when the cabman entered the room.

'Just give me a help with this buckle, cabman,' he said, kneeling over his task, and never turning his head.

The fellow came forward with a somewhat sullen, defiant air, and put down his hands to assist. At that instant there was a sharp click, the jangling of metal, and Sherlock Holmes sprang to his feet again.

'Gentlemen,' he cried, with flashing eyes, 'let me introduce you to Mr Jefferson Hope, the murderer of Enoch Drebber and of Joseph Stangerson.'

160 *the four million inhabitants of this great city.* "In 1881, the Registrar-General's figures gave the population of London as close upon four millions, but even three years earlier, when the official population figure had been but 3,577,304, it was estimated that the people living within the Metropolitan Police district—the actual dwellers—totalled some four-and-a-half millions."—Michael Harrison, *In the Footsteps of Sherlock Holmes.*

161 *They fasten in an instant.*' "Cognoscenti will recall that Holmes advocated use of automatically-locking handcuffs as early as 1881 in the capture of Jefferson Hope. . . . A student of police methods has suggested that such handcuffs were not available prior to 1896. The issue is delegated to the specialist for resolution. Mr. Holmes may have pioneered in this field, and in that event the darbies used in 1881 represent the only mechanical invention by Holmes known to this writer."—Elliot Kimball, "Origin and Evolution of G. Lestrade: 2—A Matter of Mancinism."

. . . LESTRADE, AND HOLMES SPRANG UPON HIM LIKE SO
MANY STAGHOUNDS.

Illustration by George Hutchinson for *A Study in Scarlet*; London: Ward, Lock, Bowden & Co., 1891.

The whole thing occurred in a moment—so quickly that I had no time to realize it. I have a vivid recollection of that instant, of Holmes' triumphant expression and the ring of his voice, of the cabman's dazed, savage face, as he glared at the glittering handcuffs, which had appeared as if by magic upon his wrists. For a second or two we might have been a group of statues. Then with an inarticulate roar of fury, the prisoner wrenched himself free from Holmes' grasp, and hurled himself through the window. Woodwork and glass gave way before him; but before he got quite through, Gregson, Lestrade, and Holmes sprang upon him like so many staghounds. He was dragged back into the room, and then commenced a terrific conflict. So powerful and so fierce was he that the four of us were shaken off again and again. He appeared to have the convulsive strength of a man in an epileptic fit. His face and hands were terribly mangled by his passage through the glass, but the loss of blood had no effect in diminishing his resistance. It was not until Lestrade succeeded in getting his hand inside his neckcloth and half-strangling him that we made him realize that his struggles were of no avail; and even then we felt no security until we had pinioned his feet as well as his hands. That done, we rose to our feet breathless and panting.

'We have his cab,' said Sherlock Holmes. 'It will serve to take him to Scotland Yard. And now, gentlemen,' he continued, with a pleasant smile, 'we have reached the end of our little mystery. You are very welcome to put any questions that you like to me now, and there is no danger that I will refuse to answer them.'

PART II

The Country of the Saints

8 ❖ ON THE GREAT ALKALI PLAIN

In the central portion of the great North American Continent there lies an arid and repulsive desert, which for many a long year served as a barrier against the advance of civilization. From the Sierra Nevada to Nebraska, and from the Yellowstone River in the north to the Colorado upon the south, is a region of desolation and silence. Nor is Nature always in one mood throughout this grim district. It comprises snow-capped and lofty mountains, and dark and gloomy valleys. There are swift-flowing rivers which dash through jagged cañons; and there are enormous plains, which in winter are white with snow, and in summer are grey with the saline alkali dust. They all preserve, however, the common characteristics of barrenness, inhospitality and misery.

There are no inhabitants of this land of despair. A band of Pawnees or of Blackfeet may occasionally traverse it in order to reach other hunting-grounds, but the hardiest of the braves are glad to lose sight of those awesome plains, and to find themselves once more upon their prairies. The coyote skulks among the scrub, the buzzard flaps heavily through the air, and the clumsy grizzly bear lumbers through the dark ravines, and picks up such sustenance as it can amongst the rocks. These are the sole dwellers in the wilderness.

In the whole world there can be no more dreary view than that from the northern slope of the Sierra Blanco. As far as the eye can reach stretches the great flat plain-land, all dusted over with patches of alkali, and intersected by clumps of the dwarfish chaparral bushes. On the extreme verge of the horizon lie a long chain of mountain peaks with their rugged summits flecked with snow. In this great stretch of country there is no sign of life, nor of anything appertaining to life. There is no bird in the steel-blue heaven, no movement upon the dull, grey earth—above all, there is absolute silence. Listen as one may, there is no shadow of a sound in all that mighty wilderness; nothing but silence—complete and heart-subduing silence.

It has been said there is nothing appertaining to life upon the broad plain. That is hardly true. Looking down from the Sierra Blanco, one sees a pathway traced out across the desert, which winds away and is lost in the extreme distance. It is rutted with wheels and trodden down by the feet of many adventurers. Here and there there are scattered white objects which glisten in the sun, and stand out against the dull deposit of alkali. Approach, and examine them! They are bones: some large and coarse, others smaller and more delicate. The former have belonged to oxen, and the latter to men. For fifteen hundred miles one may trace this ghastly caravan route by these scattered remains of those who had fallen by the wayside.

Looking down on this very scene, there stood upon the fourth of May, eighteen hundred and forty-seven, a solitary traveller. His appearance was such that he might have been the very genius or demon of the region. An observer would have found it difficult to say whether he was nearer to forty or to sixty. His face was lean and haggard, and the brown parchment-like skin was drawn tightly over the projecting bones; his long, brown hair and beard were all flecked and dashed with white; his eyes were sunken in his head, and burned with an unnatural lustre; while the hand which grasped his rifle was hardly more fleshy than that of a skeleton. As he stood, he leaned upon his weapon for support, and yet his tall figure and the massive framework of his bones suggested a wiry and vigorous constitution. His gaunt face, however, and his clothes, which hung so baggily over his shrivelled limbs, proclaimed what it was that gave him that senile and decrepit appearance. The man was dying—dying from hunger and from thirst.

He had toiled painfully down the ravine, and on to this little elevation, in the vain hope of seeing some signs of water. Now the great salt plain stretched before his eyes, and the distant belt of savage mountains, without a sign anywhere of plant or tree, which might indicate the presence of moisture. In all that broad landscape there was no gleam of hope. North and east, and west he looked with wild, questioning eyes, and then he realized that his wanderings had come to an end, and that there, on that barren crag, he was about to die. 'Why not here, as well as in a feather bed, twenty years hence,' he muttered, as he seated himself in the shelter of a boulder.

Before sitting down, he had deposited upon the ground his useless rifle, and also a large bundle tied up in a grey shawl, which he had carried slung over his right shoulder. It appeared to be somewhat too heavy for his strength, for in lowering it, it came down on the ground with some little violence. Instantly there broke from the grey parcel a little moaning cry, and from it there protruded a small, scared face, with very bright brown eyes, and two little speckled, dimpled fists.

'You've hurt me!' said a childish voice reproachfully.

'Have I, though,' the man answered penitently; 'I didn't go for to do it.' As he spoke he unwrapped the grey shawl and extricated a pretty little girl of about five years of age, whose dainty shoes and smart, pink frock with its little linen apron, all bespoke a mother's care. The child was pale and wan, but her healthy arms and legs showed that she had suffered less than her companion.

'How is it now?' he answered anxiously, for she was still rubbing the towsy golden curls which covered the back of her head.

'Kiss it and make it well,' she said, with perfect gravity, showing the injured part up to him. 'That's what mother used to do. Where's mother?'

'Mother's gone. I guess you'll see her before long.'

'Gone, eh!' said the little girl. 'Funny, she didn't say goodbye; she 'most always did if she was just goin' over to auntie's for tea, and now she's been away three days. Say, it's awful dry, ain't it? Ain't there no water nor nothing to eat?'

'No, there ain't nothing, dearie. You'll just need to be patient awhile, and then you'll be all right. Put your head up ag'in me like that, and then you'll feel bullier. It ain't easy to talk when your lips is like leather, but I guess I'd best let you know how the cards lie. What's that you've got?'

'Pretty things! fine things!' cried the little girl enthusiastically, holding up two glittering fragments of mica. 'When we goes back to home I'll give them to brother Bob.'

'You'll see prettier things than them soon,' said the man confidently. 'You just wait a bit. I was going to tell you though —you remember when we left the river?'

'Oh, yes.'

'Well, we reckoned we'd strike another river soon, d'ye see. But there was somethin' wrong; compasses, or map, or somethin', and it didn't turn up. Water ran out. Just except a little drop for the likes of you, and—and——'

'And you couldn't wash yourself,' interrupted his companion gravely, staring up at his grimy visage.

'No, nor drink. And Mr Bender, he was the fust to go, and then Indian Pete, and then Mrs McGregor, and then Johnny Hones, and then, dearie, your mother.'

'Then mother's a deader too,' cried the little girl, dropping her face in her pinafore and sobbing bitterly.

'Yes, they all went except you and me. Then I thought there was some chance of water in this direction, so I heaved you over my shoulder and we tramped it together. It don't seem as though we've improved matters. There's an almighty small chance for us now!'

'Do you mean that we are going to die too?' asked the child, checking her sobs, and raising her tear-stained face.

'I guess that's about the size of it.'

'Why didn't you say so before?' she said, laughing gleefully. 'You gave me such a fright. Why, of course, now as long as we die we'll be with mother again.'

'Yes, you will, dearie.'

'And you too. I'll tell her how awful good you've been. I'll bet she meets us at the door of heaven with a big pitcher of water, and a lot of buckwheat cakes, hot, and toasted on both sides, like Bob and me was fond of. How long will it be first?'

'I don't know—not very long.' The man's eyes were fixed upon the northern horizon. In the blue vault of the heaven there had appeared three little specks which increased in size every moment, so rapidly did they approach. They speedily resolved themselves into three large brown birds, which circled over the heads of the two wanderers, and then settled upon some rocks which overlooked them. They were buzzards, the vultures of the west, whose coming is the forerunner of death.

'Cocks and hens,' cried the little girl gleefully, pointing at their ill-omened forms, and clapping her hands to make them rise. 'Say, did God make this country?'

'In course He did,' said her companion, rather startled by this unexpected question.

'He made the country down in Illinois, and He made the Missouri,' the little girl continued. 'I guess somebody else made the country in these parts. It's not nearly so well done. They forgot the water and the trees.'

'What would ye think of offering up prayer?' the man asked diffidently.

'It ain't night yet,' she answered.

'It don't matter. It ain't quite regular, but He won't mind that, you bet. You say over them ones that you used to say every night in the wagon when we was on the Plains.'

'Why don't you say some yourself?' the child asked with wondering eyes.

'I disremember them,' he answered. 'I hain't said none since I was half the height o' that gun. I guess it's never too late. You say them out, and I'll stand by and come in on the choruses.'

'Then you'll need to kneel down, and me too,' she said, laying the shawl out for that purpose. 'You've got to put your hands up like this. It makes you feel kind of good.'

It was a strange sight, had there been anything but the buzzards to see it. Side by side on the narrow shawl knelt the two wanderers, the little prattling child and the reckless, hardened adventurer. Her chubby face and his haggard, angular visage were both turned up to the cloudless heaven in heartfelt entreaty to that dread Being with whom they were face to face, while the two voices—the one thin and clear, the other deep and harsh—united in the entreaty for mercy and forgiveness. The prayer finished, they resumed their seat in the shadow of the boulder until the child fell asleep, nestling upon the broad breast of her protector. He watched over her slumber for some time, but Nature proved to be too strong for him. For three days and three nights he had allowed himself neither rest nor repose. Slowly the eyelids drooped over the tired eyes, and the head sunk lower and lower upon the breast, until the man's grizzled beard was mixed with the gold

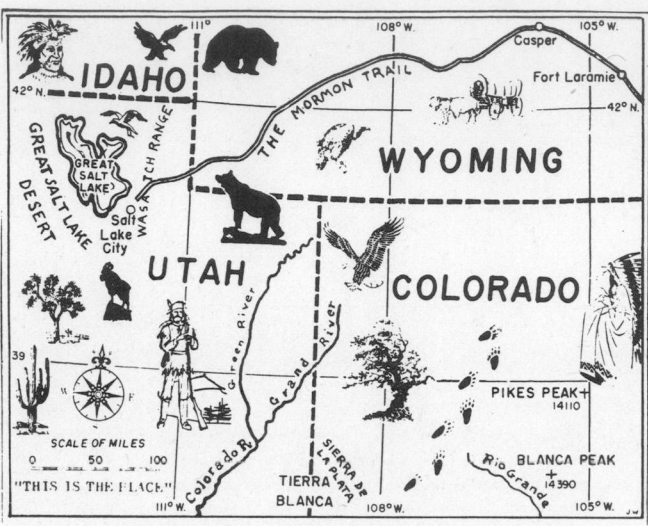

DR. JULIAN WOLFF'S MAP OF THE MORMON TRAIL

Dr. Wolff adds a word as the editor of *The Baker Street Journal:* "1. Present-day state boundaries are shown on the map. 2. There is a 'Sierra Blanca' but it is located in New Mexico, almost three hundred miles south of Blanca Peak in Colorado, shown here. 3. On older maps (*e.g.* 'Colton's Territories of New Mexico & Utah,' 1855) the Colorado River is shown as the Grand River above its junction with the Green River. 4. On Plate CXX ('Territory and Military Department of Utah, 1860') of the *Atlas to Accompany the Official Records of the Union and Confederate Armies*, Washington: Government Printing Office, 1891–1895, mountains called Sierra de la Plata are shown in the location indicated. Whether Plata (silver) could be confused with Blanco (white) is a point that might be discussed. Also, there is a locality labelled *Tierra Blanca*. However, all of these are far south of the Mormon Trail, and as far as our story is concerned, the Rio Grande and the Sierra Blanco must have been two other places. '. . . there was somethin' wrong; compasses, or map, or somethin'. . . .'"

tresses of his companion, and both slept the same deep and dreamless slumber.

Had the wanderer remained awake for another half-hour a strange sight would have met his eyes. Far away on the extreme verge of the alkali plain there rose up a little spray of dust, very slight at first, and hardly to be distinguished from the mists of the distance, but gradually growing higher and broader until it formed a solid, well-defined cloud. This cloud continued to increase in size until it became evident that it could only be raised by a great multitude of moving creatures. In more fertile spots the observer would have come to the conclusion that one of those great herds of bisons which graze upon the prairie land was approaching him. This was obviously impossible in these arid wilds. As the whirl of dust drew nearer to the solitary bluff upon which the two castaways were reposing, the canvas-covered tilts of wagons and the figures of armed horsemen began to show up through the haze, and the apparition revealed itself as being a great caravan upon its journey for the West. But what a caravan! When the head of it had reached the base of the mountains, the rear was not yet visible on the horizon. Right across the enormous plain stretched the straggling array, wagons and carts, men on horseback, and men on foot. Innumerable women who staggered along under burdens, and children who toddled beside the wagons or peeped out from under the white coverings. This was evidently no ordinary party of immigrants, but rather some nomad people who had been compelled from stress of circumstances to seek themselves a new country. There rose through the clear air a confused clattering and rumbling from this great mass of humanity, with the creaking of wheels and the neighing of horses. Loud as it was, it was not sufficient to rouse the two tired wayfarers above them.

At the head of the column there rode a score or more of grave, ironfaced men, clad in sombre, homespun garments and armed with rifles. On reaching the base of the bluff they halted, and held a short council among themselves.

'The wells are to the right, my brothers,' said one, a hard-lipped, clean-shaven man with grizzly hair.

'To the right of the Sierra Blanco—so we shall reach the Rio Grande,' said another.

'Fear not for water,' cried a third. 'He who could draw it from the rocks will not now abandon His chosen people.'

'Amen! amen!' responded the whole party.

They were about to resume their journey when one of the youngest and keenest-eyed uttered an exclamation and pointed up at the rugged crag above them. From its summit there fluttered a little wisp of pink, showing up hard and bright against the grey rocks behind. At the sight there was a general reining up of horses and unslinging of guns, while fresh horsemen came galloping up to reinforce the vanguard. The word 'Redskins' was on every lip.

'There can't be any number of Injuns here,' said the elderly man who appeared to be in command. 'We have passed the Pawnees, and there are no other tribes until we cross the great mountains.'

'Shall I go forward and see, Brother Stangerson,' asked one of the band.

'And I,' 'and I,' cried a dozen voices.

'Leave your horses below and we will await you here,' the

elder answered. In a moment the young fellows had dismounted, fastened their horses, and were ascending the precipitous slope which led up to the object which had excited their curiosity. They advanced rapidly and noiselessly, with the confidence and dexterity of practised scouts. The watchers from the plain below could see them flit from rock to rock until their figures stood out against the skyline. The young man who had first given the alarm was leading them. Suddenly his followers saw him throw up his hands, as though overcome with astonishment, and on joining him they were affected in the same way by the sight which met their eyes.

On the little plateau which crowned the barren hills there stood a single giant boulder, and against this boulder there lay a tall man, long-bearded and hard-featured, but of an excessive thinness. His placid face and regular breathing showed that he was fast asleep. Beside him lay a little child, with her round, white arms encircling his brown, sinewy neck, and her golden-haired head resting upon the breast of his velveteen tunic. Her rosy lips were parted, showing the regular line of snow-white teeth within, and a playful smile played over her infantile features. Her plump little white legs, terminating in white socks and neat shoes with shining buckles, offered a strange contrast to the long, shrivelled members of her companion. On the ledge of rock above this strange couple there stood three solemn buzzards, who, at the sight of the new-comers, uttered raucous screams of disappointment and flapped sullenly away.

The cries of the foul birds awoke the two sleepers, who stared about them in bewilderment. The man staggered to his feet and looked down upon the plain which had been so desolate when sleep had overtaken him, and which was now traversed by this enormous body of men and of beasts. His face assumed an expression of incredulity as he gazed, and he passed his bony hand over his eyes. 'This is what they call delirium, I guess,' he muttered. The child stood beside him, holding on to the skirt of his coat, and said nothing, but looked all around her with the wondering, questioning gaze of childhood.

The rescuing party were speedily able to convince the two castaways that their appearance was no delusion. One of them seized the little girl and hoisted her upon his shoulder, while two others supported her gaunt companion, and assisted him towards the wagons.

'My name is John Ferrier,' the wanderer explained; 'me and that little un are all that's left o' twenty-one people. The rest is all dead o' thirst and hunger away down in the south.'

'Is she your child?' asked someone.

'I guess she is now,' the other cried, defiantly; 'she's mine 'cause I saved her. No man will take her from me. She's Lucy Ferrier from this day on. Who are you, though?' he continued, glancing with curiosity at his stalwart, sunburned rescuers; 'there seems to be a powerful lot of ye.'

'Nigh upon ten thousand,' said one of the young men; 'we **162** are the persecuted children of God—the chosen of the Angel Merona.'

'I never heard tell on him,' said the wanderer. 'He appears to have chosen a fair crowd of ye.'

'Do not jest at that which is sacred,' said the other sternly.

162 *'Nigh upon ten thousand.'* "It is interesting to note that in Brigham Young's own record of the great journey to the Great Salt Lake Valley in 1847, he mentioned that he arrived with 143 men, 3 women and 2 children."—Rev. Otis R. Rice, "Clergymen in the Canon."

ONE OF THEM SEIZED THE LITTLE GIRL AND HOISTED HER
UPON HIS SHOULDER . . .

Illustration for *Beeton's Christmas Annual*, December, 1887. The picture is signed by W. M. R. Quick, but, as the late James Montgomery wrote (*A Study in Pictures*), "available informtaion has not yet determined conclusively whether that was the signature of the engraver or of a second artist. Certainly the illustration . . . is identical in style and execution with the three bearing the initials 'D. H. F.'"

163 *Joseph Smith*. It was in 1823, at Palmyra, New York, that a vision revealed the hiding place of the golden tablets to Joseph Smith, 1805–1844. Smith founded his first church in 1830, but the hostility of neighbors drove him to Kirtland, Ohio, and later to Nauvoo, Illinois. Trouble with non-Mormons led to his arrest on charges of treason. On July 27, 1844, he and his brother Hyrum were murdered by a mob at Carthage, Illinois.

164 *Brigham Young*. After Joseph Smith's assassination, Brigham Young, 1801–1877, became the dominant figure in Mormonism. He led the great migration west in 1846–1847, and directed the settlement at Salt Lake City. He seems to have been married in all to 27 wives, but he was a stern moralist as well as a brilliant leader.

'We are of those who believe in those sacred writings, drawn in Egyptian letters on plates of beaten gold, which were **163** handed unto the holy Joseph Smith at Palmyra. We have come from Nauvoo, in the State of Illinois, where we had founded our temple. We have come to seek a refuge from the violent man and from the godless, even though it be the heart of the desert.'

The name of Nauvoo evidently recalled recollections to John Ferrier. 'I see,' he said; 'you are the Mormons.'

'We are the Mormons,' answered his companions with one voice.

'And where are you going?'

'We do not know. The hand of God is leading us under the person of our Prophet. You must come before him. He shall say what is to be done with you.'

They had reached the base of the hill by this time, and were surrounded by crowds of the pilgrims—pale-faced, meek-looking women; strong, laughing children; and anxious, earnest-eyed men. Many were the cries of astonishment and of commiseration which arose from them when they perceived the youth of one of the strangers and the destitution of the other. Their escort did not halt, however, but pushed on, followed by a great crowd of Mormons, until they reached a wagon, which was conspicuous for its great size and for the gaudiness and smartness of its appearance. Six horses were yoked to it, whereas the others were furnished with two, or, at most, four apiece. Beside the driver there sat a man who could not have been more than thirty years of age, but whose massive head and resolute expression marked him as a leader. He was reading a brown-backed volume, but as the crowd approached he laid it aside, and listened attentively to an account of the episode. Then he turned to the two castaways.

'If we take you with us,' he said, in solemn words, 'it can only be as believers in our own creed. We shall have no wolves in our fold. Better far that your bones should bleach in this wilderness than that you should prove to be that little speck of decay which in time corrupts the whole fruit. Will you come with us on these terms?'

'Guess I'll come with you on any terms,' said Ferrier, with such emphasis that the grave Elders could not restrain a smile. The leader alone retained his stern, impressive expression.

'Take him, Brother Stangerson,' he said, 'give him food and drink, and the child likewise. Let it be your task also to teach him our holy creed. We have delayed long enough. Forward! On, on to Zion!'

'On, on to Zion!' cried the crowd of Mormons, and the words rippled down the long caravan, passing from mouth to mouth until they died away in a dull murmur in the far distance. With a cracking of whips and a creaking of wheels the great wagons got into motion, and soon the whole caravan was winding along once more. The Elder to whose care the two waifs had been committed led them to his wagon, where a meal was already awaiting them.

'You shall remain here,' he said. 'In a few days you will have recovered from your fatigues. In the meantime, remember **164** that now and for ever you are of our religion. Brigham Young has said it, and he has spoken with the voice of Joseph Smith, which is the voice of God.'

9 • THE FLOWER OF UTAH

This is not the place to commemorate the trials and privations endured by the immigrant Mormons before they came to their final haven. From the shores of the Mississippi to the western slopes of the Rocky Mountains they had struggled on with a constancy almost unparalleled in history. The savage man, and the savage beast, hunger, thirst, fatigue, and disease —every impediment which Nature could place in the way— had all been overcome with Anglo-Saxon tenacity. Yet the long journey and the accumulated terrors had shaken the hearts of the stoutest among them. There was not one who did not sink upon his knees in heartfelt prayer when they saw the broad valley of Utah bathed in the sunlight beneath them, and learned from the lips of their leader that this was the promised land, and that these virgin acres were to be theirs for evermore.

Young speedily proved himself to be a skilful administrator as well as a resolute chief. Maps were drawn and charts prepared, in which the future city was sketched out. All around farms were apportioned and allotted in proportion to the standing of each individual. The tradesman was put to his trade and the artisan to his calling. In the town streets and squares sprang up as if by magic. In the country there was draining and hedging, planting and clearing, until the next summer saw the whole country golden with the wheat crop. Everything prospered in the strange settlement. Above all, the great temple which they had erected in the centre of the city grew ever taller and larger. From the first blush of dawn until the closing of the twilight, the clatter of the hammer and the rasp of the saw were never absent from the monument which the immigrants erected to Him who had led them safe through many dangers.

The two castaways, John Ferrier and the little girl, who had shared his fortunes and had been adopted as his daughter, accompanied the Mormons to the end of their great pilgrimage. Little Lucy Ferrier was borne along pleasantly enough in Elder Stangerson's wagon, a retreat which she shared with the Mormon's three wives and with his son, a headstrong, forward boy of twelve. Having rallied, with the elasticity of childhood, from the shock caused by her mother's death, she soon became a pet with the women, and reconciled herself to this new life in her moving canvas-covered home. In the meantime Ferrier, having recovered from his privations, distinguished himself as a useful guide and an indefatigable hunter. So rapidly did he gain the esteem of his new companions, that when they reached the end of their wanderings, it was unanimously agreed that he should be provided with as large and as fertile a tract of land as any of the settlers, with the exception of Young himself, and of Stangerson, Kemball, Johnston, and Drebber, who were the four principal Elders.

On the farm thus acquired John Ferrier built himself a substantial log-house, which received so many additions in succeeding years that it grew into a roomy villa. He was a man of a practical turn of mind, keen in his dealings and skilful with his hands. His iron constitution enabled him to work morning and evening at improving and tilling his lands.

Hence it came about that his farm and all that belonged to him prospered exceedingly. In three years he was better off than his neighbours, in six he was well-to-do, in nine he was rich, and in twelve there were not half a dozen men in the whole of Salt Lake City who could compare with him. From the great inland sea to the distant Wahsatch Mountains there was no name better known than that of John Ferrier.

There was one way and only one in which he offended the susceptibilities of his co-religionists. No argument or persuasion could ever induce him to set up a female establishment after the manner of his companions. He never gave reasons for this persistent refusal, but contented himself by resolutely and inflexibly adhering to his determination. There were some who accused him of lukewarmness in his adopted religion, and others who put it down to greed of wealth and reluctance to incur expense. Others, again, spoke of some early love affair, and of a fair-haired girl who had pined away on the shores of the Atlantic. Whatever the reason, Ferrier remained strictly celibate. In every other respect he conformed to the religion of the young settlement, and gained the name of being an orthodox and straight-walking man.

Lucy Ferrier grew up within the log-house, and assisted her adopted father in all his undertakings. The keen air of the mountains and the balsamic odour of the pine trees took the place of nurse and mother to the young girl. As year succeeded to year she grew taller and stronger, her cheek more ruddy and her step more elastic. Many a wayfarer upon the high road which ran by Ferrier's farm felt long-forgotten thoughts revive in their minds as they watched her lithe, girlish figure tripping through the wheatfields, or met her mounted upon her father's mustang, and managing it with all the ease and grace of a true child of the West. So the bud blossomed into a flower, and the year which saw her father the richest of the farmers left her as fair a specimen of American girlhood as could be found in the whole Pacific slope.

It was not the father, however, who first discovered that the child had developed into the woman. It seldom is in such cases. That mysterious change is too subtle and too gradual to be measured by dates. Least of all does the maiden herself know it until the tone of a voice or the touch of a hand sets her heart thrilling within her, and she learns, with a mixture of pride and of fear, that a new and a larger nature has awoke within her. There are few who cannot recall that day and remember the one little incident which heralded the dawn of a new life. In the case of Lucy Ferrier the occasion was serious enough in itself, apart from its future influence on her destiny and that of many besides.

It was a warm June morning, and the Latter Day Saints were as busy as the bees whose hive they have chosen for their emblem. In the fields and in the streets rose the same hum of human industry. Down the dusty high roads defiled long streams of heavily laden mules, all heading to the west, for the gold fever had broken out in California, and the overland route lay through the city of the Elect. There, too, were droves of sheep and bullocks coming in from the outlying pasture lands, and trains of tired immigrants, men and horses equally weary of their interminable journey. Through all this motley assemblage, threading her way with the skill of an accomplished rider, there galloped Lucy Ferrier, her fair face flushed with the exercise and her long chestnut hair floating out behind her. She had a commission from her father in the city, and was dashing in as she had done many a time before, with all the fearlessness of youth, thinking only of her task and how it was to be performed. The travel-stained adventurers gazed after her in astonishment, and even the unemotional Indians, journeying in with their pelties, relaxed their accustomed stoicism as they marvelled at the beauty of the pale-faced maiden.

She had reached the outskirts of the city when she found the road blocked by a great drove of cattle, driven by a half-dozen wild-looking herdsmen from the plains. In her impatience she endeavoured to pass this obstacle by pushing her horse into what appeared to be a gap. Scarcely had she got fairly into it, however, before the beasts closed in behind her, and she found herself completely imbedded in the moving stream of fierce-eyed, long-horned bullocks. Accustomed as she was to deal with cattle, she was not alarmed at her situation, but took advantage of every opportunity to urge her horse on, in the hopes of pushing her way through the cavalcade. Unfortunately the horns of one of the creatures, either by accident or design, came in violent contact with the flank of the mustang, and excited it to madness. In an instant it reared up upon its hind legs with a snort of rage, and pranced and tossed in a way that would have unseated any but a skilful rider. The situation was full of peril. Every plunge of the excited horse brought it against the horns again, and goaded it to fresh madness. It was all that the girl could do to keep herself in the saddle, yet a slip would mean a terrible death under the hoofs of the unwieldy and terrified animals. Unaccustomed to sudden emergencies, her head began to swim, and her grip upon the bridle to relax. Choked by the rising cloud of dust and by the steam from the struggling creatures, she might have abandoned her efforts in despair, but for a kindly voice at her elbow which assured her of assistance. At the same moment a sinewy, brown hand caught the frightened horse by the curb, and forcing a way through the drove, soon brought her to the outskirts.

'You're not hurt, I hope, miss,' said her preserver respectfully.

She looked up at his dark, fierce face, and laughed saucily. 'I'm awful frightened,' she said, naïvely; 'whoever would have thought that Poncho would have been so scared by a lot of cows?'

'Thank God you kept your seat,' the other said earnestly. He was a tall, savage-looking young fellow, mounted on a powerful roan horse, and clad in the rough dress of a hunter, with a long rifle slung over his shoulders. 'I guess you are the daughter of John Ferrier,' he remarked; 'I saw you ride down from his house. When you see him, ask him if he remembers the Jefferson Hopes of St Louis. If he's the same Ferrier, my father and he were pretty thick.'

'Hadn't you better come and ask yourself?' she asked, demurely.

The young fellow seemed pleased at the suggestion, and his dark eyes sparkled with pleasure. 'I'll do so,' he said; 'we've been in the mountains for two months, and are not over and

. . . A SINEWY, BROWN HAND CAUGHT THE FRIGHTENED
HORSE BY THE CURB . . .

Illustration by George Hutchinson for *A Study in Scarlet*; London: Ward, Lock, Bowden & Co., 1891.

above in visiting condition. He must take us as he finds us.'

'He has a good deal to thank you for, and so have I,' she answered, 'he's awful fond of me. If those cows had jumped on me he'd have never got over it.'

'Neither would I,' said her companion.

'You! Well, I don't see that it would make much matter to you, anyhow. You ain't even a friend of ours.'

The young hunter's dark face grew so gloomy over this remark that Lucy Ferrier laughed aloud.

'There, I didn't mean that,' she said; 'of course, you are a friend now. You must come and see us. Now I must push along, or father won't trust me with his business any more. Good-bye!'

'Good-bye,' he answered, raising his broad sombrero, and bending over her little hand. She wheeled her mustang round, gave it a cut with her riding-whip, and darted away down the broad road in a rolling cloud of dust.

Young Jefferson Hope rode on with his companions, gloomy and taciturn. He and they had been among the Nevada Mountains prospecting for silver, and were returning to Salt Lake City in the hope of raising capital enough to work some lodes which they had discovered. He had been as keen as any of them upon the business until this sudden incident had drawn his thoughts into another channel. The sight of the fair young girl, as frank and wholesome as the Sierra breezes, had stirred his volcanic, untamed heart to its very depths. When she had vanished from his sight, he realized that a crisis had come in his life, and that neither silver speculations nor any other questions could ever be of such importance to him as this new and all-absorbing one. The love which had sprung up in his heart was not the sudden, changeable fancy of a boy, but rather the wild, fierce passion of a man of strong will and imperious temper. He had been accustomed to succeed in all that he undertook. He swore in his heart that he would not fail in this if human effort and human perseverance could render him successful.

He called on John Ferrier that night, and many times again, until his face was a familiar one at the farm-house. John, cooped up in the valley, and absorbed in his work, had had little chance of learning the news of the outside world during the last twelve years. All this Jefferson Hope was able to tell him, and in a style which interested Lucy as well as her father. He had been a pioneer in California, and could narrate many a strange tale of fortunes made and fortunes lost in those wild, halcyon days. He had been a scout, too, and a trapper, a silver explorer, and a ranchman. Wherever stirring adventures were to be had, Jefferson Hope had been there in search of them. He soon became a favourite with the old farmer, who spoke eloquently of his virtues. On such occasions, Lucy was silent, but her blushing cheek and her bright, happy eyes showed only too clearly that her young heart was no longer her own. Her honest father may not have observed these symptoms, but they were assuredly not thrown away upon the man who had won her affections.

One summer evening he came galloping down the road and pulled up at the gate. She was at the doorway, and came down to meet him. He threw the bridle over the fence and strode up the pathway.

'I am off, Lucy,' he said, taking her two hands in his, and

gazing tenderly down into her face; 'I won't ask you to come with me now, but will you be ready to come when I am here again?'

'And when will that be?' she asked, blushing and laughing.

'A couple of months at the outside. I will come and claim you then, my darling. There's no one who can stand between us.'

'And how about father?' she asked.

'He has given his consent, provided we get these mines working all right. I have no fear on that head.'

'Oh, well; of course, if you and father have arranged it all, there's no more to be said,' she whispered, with her cheek against his broad breast.

'Thank God!' he said hoarsely, stooping and kissing her. 'It is settled, then. The longer I stay, the harder it will be to go. They are waiting for me at the cañon. Good-bye, my own darling—good-bye. In two months you shall see me.'

He tore himself from her as he spoke, and, flinging himself upon his horse, galloped furiously away, never even looking round, as though afraid that his resolution might fail him if he took one glance at what he was leaving. She stood at the gate, gazing after him until he vanished from her sight. Then she walked back into the house, the happiest girl in all Utah.

IO · JOHN FERRIER TALKS WITH THE PROPHET

Three weeks had passed since Jefferson Hope and his comrades had departed from Salt Lake City. John Ferrier's heart was sore within him when he thought of the young man's return, and of the impending loss of his adopted child. Yet her bright and happy face reconciled him to the arrangement more than any argument could have done. He had always determined, deep down in his resolute heart, that nothing would ever induce him to allow his daughter to wed a Mormon. Such a marriage he regarded as no marriage at all, but as a shame and a disgrace. Whatever he might think of the Mormon doctrines, upon that one point he was inflexible. He had to seal his mouth on the subject, however, for to express an unorthodox opinion was a dangerous matter in those days in the Land of the Saints.

Yes, a dangerous matter—so dangerous that even the most saintly dared only whisper their religious opinions with bated breath, lest something which fell from their lips might be misconstrued, and bring down a swift retribution upon them. The victims of persecution had now turned persecutors on their own account, and persecutors of the most terrible description. Not the Inquisition of Seville, nor the German Vehmgericht, nor the Secret Societies of Italy, were ever able to put a more formidable machinery in motion than that which cast a cloud over the State of Utah.

Its invisibility, and the mystery which was attached to it, made this organization doubly terrible. It appeared to be

165 *a sinister and an ill-omened one.* As Mr. Michael Harrison has pointed out (*In the Footsteps of Sherlock Holmes*), the British reading public of 1887 was quite willing to believe these slanders on the Mormons. Mid-Victorian England was convinced that the Mormons "stole English servant-girls, to spirit them out of the country and to make them White Slaves in a Mormon harem." "There were riots over the Mormons," Mr. Harrison wrote, "especially when the servant-girls [compared] their lot below-stairs with the prospects offered of life in a state which has never known unemployment . . ."

omniscient and omnipotent, and yet was neither seen nor heard. The man who held out against the Church vanished away, and none knew whither he had gone or what had befallen him. His wife and his children awaited him at home, but no father ever returned to tell them how he had fared at the hands of his secret judges. A rash word or a hasty act was followed by annihilation, and yet none knew what the nature might be of this terrible power which was suspended over them. No wonder that men went about in fear and trembling, and that even in the heart of the wilderness they dared not whisper the doubts which oppressed them.

At first this vague and terrible power was exercised only upon the recalcitrants who, having embraced the Mormon faith, wished afterwards to pervert or to abandon it. Soon, however, it took a wider range. The supply of adult women was running short, and polygamy without a female population on which to draw was a barren doctrine indeed. Strange rumours began to be bandied about—rumours of murdered immigrants and rifled camps in regions where Indians had never been seen. Fresh women appeared in the harems of the Elders—women who pined and wept, and bore upon their faces the traces of an unextinguishable horror. Belated wanderers upon the mountains spoke of gangs of armed men, masked, stealthy, and noiseless, who flitted by them in the darkness. These tales and rumours took substance and shape, and were corroborated and re-corroborated, until they resolved themselves into a definite name. To this day, in the lonely ranches of the West, the name of the Danite Band, or **165** the Avenging Angels, is a sinister and an ill-omened one.

Fuller knowledge of the organization which produced such terrible results served to increase rather than to lessen the horror which it inspired in the minds of men. None knew who belonged to this ruthless society. The names of the participators in the deeds of blood and violence done under the name of religion were kept profoundly secret. The very friend to whom you communicated your misgivings as to the Prophet and his mission might be one of those who would come forth at night with fire and sword to exact a terrible reparation. Hence every man feared his neighbour, and none spoke of the things which were nearest his heart.

One fine morning John Ferrier was about to set out to his wheat-fields, when he heard the click of the latch, and, looking through the window, saw a stout, sandy-haired middle-aged man coming up the pathway. His heart leapt to his mouth, for this was none other than the great Brigham Young himself. Full of trepidation—for he knew that such a visit boded him little good—Ferrier ran to the door to greet the Mormon chief. The latter, however, received his salutations coldly, and followed him with a stern face into the sitting-room.

'Brother Ferrier,' he said, taking a seat, and eyeing the farmer keenly from under his light-coloured eyelashes, 'the true believers have been good friends to you. We picked you up when you were starving in the desert, we shared our food with you, led you safe to the Chosen Valley, gave you a goodly share of land, and allowed you to wax rich under our protection. Is not this so?'

'It is so,' answered John Ferrier.

'In return for all this we asked but one condition: that was, that you should embrace the true faith, and conform in every way to its usages. This you promised to do, and this, if common report says truly, you have neglected.'

'And how have I neglected it?' asked Ferrier, throwing out his hands in expostulation. 'Have I not given to the common fund? Have I not attended at the Temple? Have I not——?'

'Where are your wives?' asked Young, looking round him. 'Call them in, that I may greet them.'

'It is true that I have not married,' Ferrier answered. 'But women were few, and there were many who had better claims than I. I was not a lonely man: I had my daughter to attend to my wants.'

'It is of that daughter that I would speak to you,' said the leader of the Mormons. 'She has grown to be the flower of Utah, and has found favour in the eyes of many who are high in the land.'

John Ferrier groaned internally.

'There are stories of her which I would fain disbelieve— stories that she is sealed to some Gentile. This must be the gossip of idle tongues.

'What is the thirteenth rule in the code of the sainted Joseph Smith? "Let every maiden of the true faith marry one of the elect; for if she wed a Gentile, she commits a grievous sin." This being so, it is impossible that you, who profess the holy creed, should suffer your daughter to violate it.'

John Ferrier made no answer, but he played nervously with his riding-whip.

'Upon this one point your whole faith shall be tested—so it has been decided in the Sacred Council of Four. The girl is young, and we would not have her wed grey hairs, neither would we deprive her of all choice. We Elders have many heifers, but our children must also be provided. Stangerson **166** has a son, and Drebber has a son, and either of them would gladly welcome your daughter to their house. Let her choose between them. They are young and rich, and of the true faith. What say you to that?'

Ferrier remained silent for some little time with his brows knitted.

'You will give us time,' he said at last. 'My daughter is very young—she is scarce of an age to marry.'

'She shall have a month to choose,' said Young, rising from his seat. 'At the end of that time she shall give her answer.'

He was passing through the door, when he turned, with flushed face and flashing eyes. 'It were better for you, John Ferrier,' he thundered, 'that you and she were now lying blanched skeletons upon the Sierra Blanco, than that you should put your weak wills against the orders of the Holy Four!'

With a threatening gesture of his hand, he turned from the door, and Ferrier heard his heavy steps scrunching along the shingly path.

He was still sitting with his elbow upon his knee, consider-

166 *We Elders have many heifers.* "Heber C. Kemball, in one of his sermons, alludes to his hundred wives under this endearing epithet," Conan Doyle noted here.

ing how he should broach the matter to his daughter, when a soft hand was laid upon his, and looking up, he saw her standing beside him. One glance at her pale, frightened face showed him that she had heard what had passed.

'I could not help it,' she said, in answer to his look. 'His voice rang through the house. Oh, father, father, what shall we do?'

'Don't you scare yourself,' he answered, drawing her to him, and passing his broad, rough hand caressingly over her chestnut hair. 'We'll fix it up somehow or another. You don't find your fancy kind o' lessening for this chap, do you?'

A sob and a squeeze of his hand was her only answer.

'No; of course not. I shouldn't care to hear you say you did. He's a likely lad, and he's a Christian, which is more than these folk here, in spite o' all their praying and preaching. There's a party starting for Nevada tomorrow, and I'll manage to send him a message letting him know the hole we are in. If I know anything o' that young man, he'll be back here with a speed that would whip electro-telegraphs.'

Lucy laughed through her tears at her father's description.

'When he comes, he will advise us for the best. But it is for you that I am frightened, dear. One hears—one hears such dreadful stories about those who oppose the Prophet: something terrible always happens to them.'

'But we haven't opposed him yet,' her father answered. 'It will be time to look out for squalls when we do. We have a clear month before us; at the end of that, I guess we had best shin out of Utah.'

'Leave Utah!'

'That's about the size of it.'

'But the farm?'

'We will raise as much as we can in money, and let the rest go. To tell the truth, Lucy, it isn't the first time I have thought of doing it. I don't care about knuckling under to any man, as these folk do to their darned Prophet. I'm a free-born American, and it's all new to me. Guess I'm too old to learn. If he comes browsing about this farm, he might chance to run up against a charge of buck-shot travelling in the opposite direction.'

'But they won't let us leave,' his daughter objected.

'Wait till Jefferson comes, and we'll soon manage that. In the meantime, don't you fret yourself, my dearie, and don't get your eyes swelled up, else he'll be walking into me when he sees you. There's nothing to be afeard about, and there's no danger at all.'

John Ferrier uttered these consoling remarks in a very confident tone, but she could not help observing that he paid unusual care to the fastening of the doors that night, and that he carefully cleaned and loaded the rusty old shot-gun which hung upon the wall of his bedroom.

On the morning which followed his interview with the Mormon Prophet, John Ferrier went in to Salt Lake City, and having found his acquaintance, who was bound for the Nevada Mountains, he entrusted him with his message to Jefferson Hope. In it he told the young man of the imminent danger which threatened them, and how necessary it was that he should return. Having done thus he felt easier in his mind, and returned home with a lighter heart.

As he approached his farm, he was surprised to see a horse hitched to each of the posts of the gate. Still more surprised was he on entering to find two young men in possession of his sitting-room. One, with a long, pale face, was leaning back in the rocking-chair, with his feet cocked up upon the stove. The other, a bull-necked youth with coarse, bloated features, was standing in front of the window with his hands in his pockets whistling a popular hymn. Both of them nodded to Ferrier as he entered, and the one in the rocking-chair commenced the conversation.

'Maybe you don't know us,' he said. 'This here is the son of Elder Drebber, and I'm Joseph Stangerson, who travelled with you in the desert when the Lord stretched out His hand and gathered you into the true fold.'

'As He will all the nations in His own good time,' said the other in a nasal voice; 'He grindeth slowly but exceeding small.'

John Ferrier bowed coldly. He had guessed who his visitors were.

'We have come,' continued Stangerson, 'at the advice of our fathers to solicit the hand of your daughter for whichever of us may seem good to you and to her. As I have but four wives and Brother Drebber here has seven, it appears to me that my claim is the stronger one.'

'Nay, nay, Brother Stangerson,' cried the other; 'the question is not how many wives we have, but how many we can keep. My father has now given over his mills to me, and I am the richer man.'

'But my prospects are better,' said the other, warmly. 'When the Lord removes my father, I shall have his tanning yard and his leather factory. Then I am your elder, and am higher in the Church.'

'It will be for the maiden to decide,' rejoined young Drebber, smirking at his own reflection in the glass. 'We will leave it all to her decision.'

During this dialogue John Ferrier had stood fuming in the doorway, hardly able to keep his riding-whip from the backs of his two visitors.

'Look here,' he said at last, striding up to them, 'when my daughter summons you, you can come, but until then I don't want to see your faces again.'

The two young Mormons stared at him in amazement. In their eyes this competition between them for the maiden's hand was the highest of honours both to her and her father.

'There are two ways out of the room,' cried Ferrier; 'there is the door, and there is the window. Which do you care to use?'

His brown face looked so savage, and his gaunt hands so

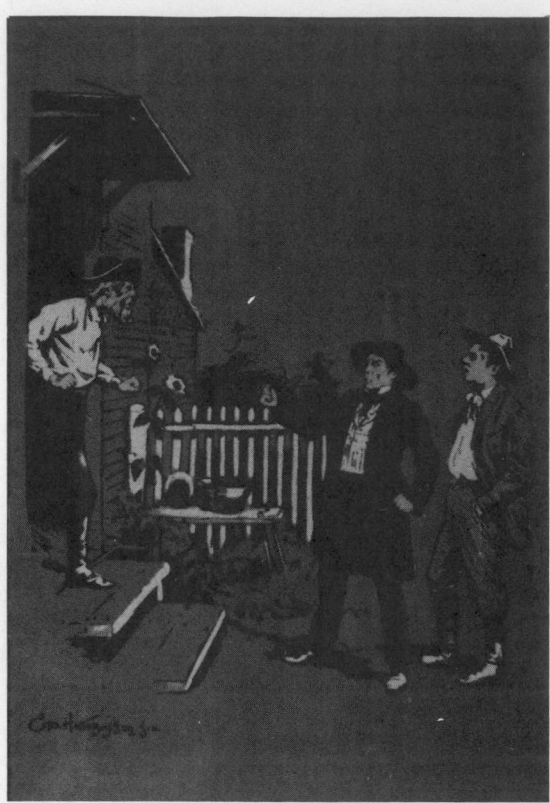

"YOU SHALL SMART FOR THIS!" STANGERSON CRIED,
WHITE WITH RAGE.

Illustration by George Hutchinson for *A Study in Scarlet*; London: Ward, Lock, Bowden & Co., 1891.

threatening, that his visitors sprang to their feet and beat a hurried retreat. The old farmer followed them to the door.

'Let me know when you have settled which it is to be,' he said, sardonically.

'You shall smart for this!' Stangerson cried, white with rage. 'You have defied the Prophet and the Council of Four. You shall rue it to the end of your days.'

'The hand of the Lord shall be heavy upon you,' cried young Drebber; 'He will arise and smite you!'

'Then I'll start the smiting,' exclaimed Ferrier, furiously, and would have rushed upstairs for his gun had not Lucy seized him by the arm and restrained him. Before he could escape from her, the clatter of horses' hoofs told him that they were beyond his reach.

'The young canting rascals!' he exclaimed, wiping the perspiration from his forehead; 'I would sooner see you in your grave, my girl, than the wife of either of them.'

'And so should I, father,' she answered, with spirit; 'but Jefferson will soon be here.'

'Yes. It will not be long before he comes. The sooner the better, for we do not know what their next move may be.'

It was, indeed, high time that someone capable of giving advice and help should come to the aid of the sturdy old farmer and his adopted daughter. In the whole history of the settlement there had never been such a case of rank disobedience to the authority of the Elders. If minor errors were punished so sternly, what would be the fate of this arch rebel. Ferrier knew that his wealth and position would be of no avail to him. Others as well known and as rich as himself had been spirited away before now, and their goods given over to the Church. He was a brave man, but he trembled at the vague, shadowy terrors which hung over him. Any known danger he could face with a firm lip, but this suspense was unnerving. He concealed his fears from his daughter, however, and affected to make light of the whole matter, though she, with the keen eye of love, saw plainly that he was ill at ease.

He expected that he would receive some message or remonstrance from Young as to his conduct, and he was not mistaken, though it came in an unlooked-for manner. Upon rising next morning he found, to his surprise, a small square of paper pinned on to the coverlet of his bed just over his chest. On it was printed in bold, straggling letters:

'Twenty-nine days are given you for amendment, and then——'

The dash was more fear-inspiring than any threat could have been. How this warning came into his room puzzled John Ferrier sorely, for his servants slept in an outhouse, and the doors and windows had all been secured. He crumpled the paper up and said nothing to his daughter, but the incident struck a chill into his heart. The twenty-nine days were evidently the balance of the month which Young had promised. What strength or courage could avail against an enemy armed with such mysterious powers? The hand which fastened that pin, might have struck him to the heart, and he could never have known who had slain him.

Still more shaken was he next morning. They had sat down to their breakfast, when Lucy with a cry of surprise pointed upwards. In the centre of the ceiling was scrawled, with a burned stick apparently, the number 28. To his daughter it was unintelligible, and he did not enlighten her. That night he sat up with his gun and kept watch and ward. He saw and he heard nothing, and yet in the morning a great 27 had been painted upon the outside of his door.

Thus day followed day; and as sure as morning came he found that his unseen enemies had kept their register, and had marked up in some conspicuous position how many days were still left to him out of the month of grace. Sometimes the fatal numbers appeared upon the walls, sometimes upon the floors, occasionally they were on small placards stuck upon the garden gate or the railings. With all his vigilance John Ferrier could not discover whence these daily warnings proceeded. A horror which was almost superstitious came upon him at the sight of them. He became haggard and restless, and his eyes had the troubled look of some hunted creature. He had but one hope in life now, and that was for the arrival of the young hunter from Nevada.

Twenty had changed to fifteen, and fifteen to ten, but there was no news of the absentee. One by one the numbers dwindled down, and still there came no sign of him. Whenever a horseman clattered down the road, or a driver shouted at his team, the old farmer hurried to the gate, thinking that help had arrived at last. At last, when he saw five give way to four and that again to three, he lost heart, and abandoned all hope of escape. Singlehanded, and with his limited knowledge of the mountains which surrounded the settlement, he knew that he was powerless. The more-frequented roads were strictly watched and guarded, and none could pass along them without an order from the Council. Turn which way he would, there appeared to be no avoiding the blow which hung over him. Yet the old man never wavered in his resolution to part with life itself before he consented to what he regarded as his daughter's dishonour.

He was sitting alone one evening pondering deeply over his troubles, and searching vainly for some way out of them. That morning had shown the figure 2 upon the wall of his house, and the next day would be the last of the allotted time. What was to happen then? All manner of vague and terrible fancies filled his imagination. And his daughter—what was to become of her after he was gone? Was there no escape from the invisible network which was drawn all round them? He sank his head upon the table and sobbed at the thought of his own impotence.

What was that? In the silence he heard a gentle scratching sound—low, but very distinct in the quiet of the night. It came from the door of the house. Ferrier crept out into the hall and listened intently. There was a pause for a few moments, and then the low, insidious sound was repeated. Someone was evidently tapping very gently upon one of the panels of the door. Was it some midnight assassin who had come to carry out the murderous orders of the secret tribunal? Or was it some agent who was marking up that the last day of grace had arrived. John Ferrier felt that instant death would be better than the suspense which shook his nerves and chilled his heart. Springing forward, he drew the bolt and threw the door open.

Outside all was calm and quiet. The night was fine, and the stars were twinkling brightly overhead. The little front

. . . AS HE WATCHED IT HE SAW IT WRITHE ALONG THE
GROUND AND INTO THE HALL . . .

Illustration by D. H. Friston for *Beeton's Christmas Annual*, December, 1887. George Hutchinson illustrated much the same scene for the London, 1891, Ward, Lock, Bowden & Co. edition of *A Study in Scarlet*, and J. Watson Davis for *Tales of Sherlock Holmes*, published by A. L. Burt Company, New York, in 1906.

167 '*Two thousand dollars in gold and five in notes.*' Mr. A. Carson Simpson, in his study of *Numismatics in the Canon* (Part II: "A Very Treasury of Coin of Divers Realms") has conjectured that part of this hoard was made up of privately issued gold pieces—really tokens—used at that time in the Far West—coins often referred to as "pioneer" or "territorial" gold. Most of these were probably produced in California. Some would be undated, but most would bear dates from 1849 to 1855. The denominations were generally $5, $10, $20; Ferrier may also have had some of the large, showy $50 pieces. Almost certainly his hoard also included gold pieces struck by the Mormons themselves; they were first issued in 1849 in denominations of $2.50, $5, $10, and $20.

garden lay before the farmer's eyes bounded by the fence and gate, but neither there nor on the road was any human being to be seen. With a sigh of relief Ferrier looked to right and to left, until, happening to glance straight down at his own feet, he saw to his astonishment a man lying flat upon his face upon the ground, with arms and legs all asprawl.

So unnerved was he at the sight that he leaned up against the wall with his hand to his throat to stifle his inclination to call out. His first thought was that the prostrate figure was that of some wounded or dying man, but as he watched it he saw it writhe along the ground and into the hall with the rapidity and noiselessness of a serpent. Once within the house the man sprang to his feet, closed the door, and revealed to the astonished farmer the fierce face and resolute expression of Jefferson Hope.

'Good God!' gasped John Ferrier. 'How you scared me. Whatever made you come in like that.'

'Give me food,' the other said, hoarsely. 'I have had no time for bit or sup for eight-and-forty hours.' He flung himself upon the cold meat and bread which were still lying upon the table from his host's supper, and devoured it voraciously. 'Does Lucy bear up well?' he asked, when he had satisfied his hunger.

'Yes. She does not know the danger,' her father answered.

'That is well. The house is watched on every side. That is why I crawled my way up to it. They may be darned sharp, but they're not quite sharp enough to catch a Washoe hunter.'

John Ferrier felt a different man now that he realized that he had a devoted ally. He seized the young man's leathery hand and wrung it cordially. 'You're a man to be proud of,' he said. 'There are not many who would come to share our danger and our troubles.'

'You've hit it there, pard,' the young hunter answered. 'I have a respect for you, but if you were alone in this business I'd think twice before I put my head into such a hornet's nest. It's Lucy that brings me here, and before harm comes on her I guess there will be one less o' the Hope family in Utah.'

'What are we to do?'

'Tomorrow is your last day, and unless you act tonight you are lost. I have a mule and two horses waiting in the Eagle Ravine. How much money have you?'

167 'Two thousand dollars in gold and five in notes.'

'That will do. I have as much more to add to it. We must push for Carson City through the mountains. You had best wake Lucy. It is as well that the servants do not sleep in the house.'

While Ferrier was absent, preparing his daughter for the approaching journey, Jefferson Hope packed all the eatables that he could find into a small parcel, and filled a stoneware jar with water, for he knew by experience that the mountain wells were few and far between. He had hardly completed his arrangements before the farmer returned with his daughter all dressed and ready for a start. The greeting between the lovers was warm, but brief, for minutes were precious, and there was much to be done.

'We must make our start at once,' said Jefferson Hope, speaking in a low but resolute voice, like one who realizes the greatness of the peril, but has steeled his heart to meet it. 'The front and back entrances are watched, but with caution we may get away through the side window and across the fields. Once on the road we are only two miles from the Ravine where the horses are waiting. By daybreak we should be half-way through the mountains.'

'What if we are stopped?' asked Ferrier.

Hope slapped the revolver butt which protruded from the front of his tunic. 'If they are too many for us, we shall take two or three of them with us,' he said with a sinister smile.

The lights inside the house had all been extinguished, and from the darkened window Ferrier peered over the fields which had been his own, and which he was now about to abandon for ever. He had long nerved himself to the sacrifice, however, and the thought of the honour and happiness of his daughter outweighed any regret at his ruined fortunes. All looked so peaceful and happy, the rustling trees and the broad, silent stretch of grainland, that it was difficult to realize that the spirit of murder lurked through it all. Yet the white face and set expression of the young hunter showed that in his approach to the house he had seen enough to satisfy him upon that head.

Ferrier carried the bag of gold and notes, Jefferson Hope had the scanty provisions and water, while Lucy had a small bundle containing a few of her more valued possessions. Opening the window very slowly and carefully, they waited until a dark cloud had somewhat obscured the night, and then one by one passed through into the little garden. With bated breath and crouching figures they stumbled across it, and gained the shelter of the hedge, which they skirted until they came to the gap which opened into the cornfield. They had just reached this point when the young man seized his two companions and dragged them down into the shadow, where they lay silent and trembling.

It was as well that his prairie training had given Jefferson Hope the ears of a lynx. He and his friends had hardly crouched down before the melancholy hooting of a mountain owl was heard within a few yards of them, which was immediately answered by another hoot at a small distance. At the same moment a vague, shadowy figure emerged from the gap for which they had been making, and uttered the plaintive signal cry again, on which a second man appeared out of the obscurity.

'Tomorrow at midnight,' said the first, who appeared to be in authority. 'When the whip-poor-will calls three times.'

'It is well,' returned the other. 'Shall I tell Brother Dreb-ber?'

'Pass it on to him, and from him to the others. Nine to seven!'

'Seven to five!' repeated the other; and the two figures flitted away in different directions. Their concluding words had evidently been some form of sign and countersign. The instant that their footsteps had died away in the distance, Jefferson Hope sprang to his feet, and helping his companions through the gap, led the way across the fields at the top of his speed, supporting and half-carrying the girl when her strength appeared to fail her.

'Hurry on! hurry on!' he gasped from time to time. 'We are through the line of sentinels. Everything depends on speed. Hurry on!'

Once on the high road, they made rapid progress. Only once did they meet anyone, and then they managed to slip into a field, and so avoid recognition. Before reaching the town the hunter branched away into a rugged and narrow footpath which led to the mountains. Two dark, jagged peaks loomed above them through the darkness, and the defile which led between them was the Eagle Cañon in which the horses were awaiting them. With unerring instinct Jefferson Hope picked his way among the great boulders and along the bed of a dried-up watercourse, until he came to the retired corner screened with rocks, where the faithful animals had been picketed. The girl was placed upon the mule, and old Ferrier upon one of the horses, with his money-bag, while Jefferson Hope led the other along the precipitous and dangerous path.

It was a bewildering route for anyone who was not accustomed to face Nature in her wildest moods. On the one side a great crag towered up a thousand feet or more, black, stern, and menacing, with long basaltic columns upon its rugged surface like the ribs of some petrified monster. On the other hand a wild chaos of boulders and debris made all advance impossible. Between the two ran the irregular track, so narrow in places that they had to travel in Indian file, and so rough that only practised riders could have traversed it at all. Yet, in spite of all dangers and difficulties, the hearts of the fugitives were light within them, for every step increased the distance between them and the terrible despotism from which they were flying.

They soon had a proof, however, that they were still within the jurisdiction of the Saints. They had reached the very wildest and most desolate portion of the pass when the girl gave a startled cry, and pointed upwards. On a rock which overlooked the track, showing out dark and plain against the sky, there stood a solitary sentinel. He saw them as soon as they perceived him, and his military challenge of 'Who goes there?' rang through the silent ravine.

'Travellers for Nevada,' said Jefferson Hope, with his hand upon the rifle which hung by his saddle.

They could see the lonely watcher fingering his gun, and peering down at them as if dissatisfied at their reply.

'By whose permission?' he asked.

'The Holy Four,' answered Ferrier. His Mormon experiences had taught him that that was the highest authority to which he could refer.

'Nine to seven,' cried the sentinel.

'Seven to five,' returned Jefferson Hope promptly, remembering the countersign which he had heard in the garden.

'Pass, and the Lord go with you,' said the voice from above. Beyond his post the path broadened out, and the horses were able to break into a trot. Looking back, they could see the solitary watcher leaning upon his gun, and knew that they had passed the outlying post of the Chosen People, and that freedom lay before them.

All night their course lay through intricate defiles and over irregular and rock-strewn paths. More than once they lost their way, but Hope's intimate knowledge of the mountains enabled them to regain the track once more. When morning broke, a scene of marvellous though savage beauty lay before them. In every direction the great snow-capped peaks hemmed them in, peeping over each other's shoulders to the far horizon. So steep were the rocky banks on either side of them that the larch and the pine seemed to be suspended over their heads, and to need only a gust of wind to come hurtling down upon them. Nor was the fear entirely an illusion, for the barren valley was thickly strewn with trees and boulders which had fallen in a similar manner. Even as they passed a great rock came thundering down with a hoarse rattle which woke the echoes in the silent gorges, and startled the weary horses into a gallop.

As the sun rose slowly above the eastern horizon the caps of the great mountains lit up one after the other, like lamps at a festival, until they were all ruddy and glowing. The magnificent spectacle cheered the hearts of the three fugitives and gave them fresh energy. At a wild torrent which swept out of a ravine they called a halt and watered their horses, while they partook of a hasty breakfast. Lucy and her father would fain have rested longer, but Jefferson Hope was inexorable. 'They will be upon our track by this time,' he said. 'Everything depends upon our speed. Once safe in Carson, we may rest for the remainder of our lives.'

During the whole of that day they struggled on through the defiles, and by evening they calculated that they were more than thirty miles from their enemies. At night-time they chose the base of a beetling crag, where the rocks offered some protection from the chill wind, and there, huddled together for warmth, they enjoyed a few hours' sleep. Before daybreak, however, they were up and on their way once more. They had seen no signs of any pursuers, and Jefferson Hope began to think that they were fairly out of the reach of the terrible organization whose enmity they had incurred. He little knew how far that iron grasp could reach, or how soon it was to close upon them and crush them.

About the middle of the second day of their flight their scanty store of provisions began to run out. This gave the hunter little uneasiness, however, for there was game to be had among the mountains, and he had frequently before had to depend upon his rifle for the needs of life. Choosing a sheltered nook, he piled together a few dried branches and made a blazing fire, at which his companions might warm themselves, for they were now nearly five thousand feet above the sea level, and the air was bitter and keen. Having tethered the horses, and bade Lucy adieu, he threw his gun over his shoulder, and set out in search of whatever chance might throw in his way. Looking back, he saw the old man and the young girl crouching over the blazing fire, while the three animals stood motionless in the background. Then the intervening rocks hid them from his view.

He walked for a couple of miles through one ravine after another without success, though, from the marks upon the

168 *the moon had not yet risen.* The night, we shortly learn, was that of August 4, 1860. Commenting on Dr. Watson's recurring difficulties with the moon ("An Adventure in the Lower Criticism, Part II: Dr. Watson and the Moon"), the late Professor Jay Finley Christ noted that "When Hope returned to his camp, it was 'dark,' because 'the moon had not yet risen.' The moon had been full on August 1st; on the 4th, the sun set at 7:41 and the moon rose at 8:21 P. M. Twilight ended officially at 9:00 P. M., according to the *American Almanac*. Perhaps it *was* dark in the canyons."

THE INSCRIPTION UPON THE PAPER WAS BRIEF, BUT TO THE POINT . . .

Illustration by George Hutchinson for *A Study in Scarlet*, London: Ward, Lock, Bowden & Co., 1891.

bark of the trees, and other indications, he judged that there were numerous bears in the vicinity. At last, after two or three hours' fruitless search, he was thinking of turning back in despair, when casting his eyes upwards he saw a sight which sent a thrill of pleasure through his heart. On the edge of a jutting pinnacle, three or four hundred feet above him, there stood a creature somewhat resembling a sheep in appearance, but armed with a pair of gigantic horns. The big-horn—for so it is called—was acting, probably, as a guardian over a flock which were invisible to the hunter; but fortunately it was heading in the opposite direction, and had not perceived him. Lying on his face, he rested his rifle upon a rock, and took a long and steady aim before drawing the trigger. The animal sprang into the air, tottered for a moment upon the edge of the precipice, and then came crashing down into the valley beneath.

The creature was too unwieldy to lift, so the hunter contented himself with cutting away one haunch and part of the flank. With this trophy over his shoulder, he hastened to retrace his steps, for the evening was already drawing in. He had hardly started, however, before he realized the difficulty which faced him. In his eagerness he had wandered far past the ravines which were known to him, and it was no easy matter to pick out the path which he had taken. The valley in which he found himself divided and subdivided into many gorges, which were so like each other that it was impossible to distinguish one from the other. He followed one for a mile or more until he came to a mountain torrent which he was sure that he had never seen before. Convinced that he had taken the wrong turn, he tried another, but with the same result. Night was coming on rapidly, and it was almost dark before he at last found himself in a defile which was familiar to him. Even then it was no easy matter to keep to the right track, for **168** the moon had not yet risen, and the high cliffs on either side made the obscurity more profound. Weighed down with his burden, and weary from his exertions, he stumbled along, keeping up his heart by the reflection that every step brought him nearer to Lucy, and that he carried with him enough to ensure them food for the remainder of their journey.

He had now come to the mouth of the very defile in which he had left them. Even in the darkness he could recognize the outline of the cliffs which bounded it. They must, he reflected, be awaiting him anxiously, for he had been absent nearly five hours. In the gladness of his heart he put his hands to his mouth and made the glen re-echo to a loud halloo as a signal that he was coming. He paused and listened for an answer. None came save his own cry, which clattered up the dreary, silent ravines, and was borne back to his ears in countless repetitions. Again he shouted, even louder than before, and again no whisper came back from the friends whom he had left such a short time ago. A vague, nameless dread came over him, and he hurried onwards frantically, dropping the precious food in his agitation.

When he turned the corner, he came full in sight of the spot where the fire had been lit. There was still a glowing pile of wood ashes there, but it had evidently not been tended since his departure. The same dead silence still reigned all round. With his fears all changed to convictions, he hurried on. There was no living creature near the remains of the fire:

animals, man, maiden, all were gone. It was only too clear that some sudden and terrible disaster had occurred during his absence—a disaster which had embraced them all, and yet had left no traces behind it.

Bewildered and stunned by this blow, Jefferson Hope felt his head spin round, and had to lean upon his rifle to save himself from falling. He was essentially a man of action, however, and speedily recovered from his temporary impotence. Seizing a half-consumed piece of wood from the smouldering fire, he blew it into a flame, and proceeded with its help to examine the little camp. The ground was all stamped down by the feet of horses, showing that a large party of mounted men had overtaken the fugitives, and the direction of their tracks proved that they had afterwards turned back to Salt Lake City. Had they carried back both of his companions with them? Jefferson Hope had almost persuaded himself that they must have done so, when his eye fell upon an object which made every nerve of his body tingle within him. A little way on one side of the camp was a low-lying heap of reddish soil, which had assuredly not been there before. There was no mistaking it for anything but a newly dug grave. As the young hunter approached it, he perceived that a stick had been planted on it, with a sheet of paper stuck in the cleft fork of it. The inscription upon the paper was brief, but to the point:

JOHN FERRIER,

FORMERLY OF SALT LAKE CITY.

Died August 4th, 1860.

The sturdy old man, whom he had left so short a time before, was gone, then, and this was all his epitaph. Jefferson Hope looked wildly round to see if there was a second grave, but there was no sign of one. Lucy had been carried back by their terrible pursuers to fulfil her original destiny, by becoming one of the harem of the Elder's son. As the young fellow realized the certainty of her fate, and his own powerlessness to prevent it, he wished that he, too, was lying with the old farmer in his last silent resting-place.

Again, however, his active spirit shook off the lethargy which springs from despair. If there was nothing else left to him, he could at least devote his life to revenge. With indomitable patience and perseverance, Jefferson Hope possessed also a power of sustained vindictiveness, which he may have learned from the Indians amongst whom he had lived. As he stood by the desolate fire, he felt that the only one thing which could assuage his grief would be thorough and complete retribution, brought by his own hand upon his enemies. His strong will and untiring energy should, he determined, be devoted to that one end. With a grim, white face, he retraced his steps to where he had dropped the food, and having stirred up the smouldering fire, he cooked enough to last him for a few days. This he made up into a bundle, and, tired as he was, he set himself to walk back through the mountains upon the track of the Avenging Angels.

For five days he toiled footsore and weary through the defiles which he had already traversed on horseback. At night he flung himself down among the rocks, and snatched a few hours of sleep; but before daybreak he was always well on his way. On the sixth day, he reached the Eagle Cañon, from which they had commenced their ill-fated flight. Thence he could look down upon the home of the Saints. Worn and exhausted, he leaned upon his rifle and shook his gaunt hand fiercely at the silent, widespread city beneath him. As he looked at it, he observed that there were flags in some of the principal streets, and other signs of festivity. He was still speculating as to what this might mean when he heard the clatter of horses' hoofs, and saw a mounted man riding towards him. As he approached, he recognized him as a Mormon named Cowper, to whom he had rendered services at different times. He therefore accosted him when he got up to him, with the object of finding out what Lucy Ferrier's fate had been.

'I am Jefferson Hope,' he said. 'You remember me.'

The Mormon looked at him with undisguised astonishment—indeed, it was difficult to recognize in this tattered, unkempt wanderer, with ghastly white face and fierce, wild eyes, the spruce young hunter of former days. Having, however, at last satisfied himself as to his identity, the man's surprise changed to consternation.

'You are mad to come here,' he cried. 'It is as much as my own life is worth to be seen talking with you. There is a warrant against you from the Holy Four for assisting the Ferriers away.'

'I don't fear them, or their warrant,' Hope said, earnestly. 'You must know something of this matter, Cowper. I conjure you by everything you hold dear to answer a few questions. We have always been friends. For God's sake, don't refuse to answer me.'

'What is it?' the Mormon asked uneasily. 'Be quick. The very rocks have ears and the trees eyes.'

'What has become of Lucy Ferrier?'

'She was married yesterday to young Drebber. Hold up, man, hold up; you have no life left in you.'

'Don't mind me,' said Hope faintly. He was white to the very lips, and had sunk down on the stone against which he had been leaning. 'Married you say?'

'Married yesterday—that's what those flags are for on the Endowment House. There was some words between young Drebber and young Stangerson as to which was to have her. They'd both been in the party that followed them, and Stangerson had shot her father, which seemed to give him the best claim; but when they argued it out in council, Drebber's party was the stronger, so the Prophet gave her over to him. No one won't have her very long though, for I saw death in her face yesterday. She is more like a ghost than a woman. Are you off, then?'

'Yes, I am off,' said Jefferson Hope, who had risen from his seat. His face might have been chiselled out of marble, so hard and set was its expression, while its eyes glowed with a baleful light.

'Where are you going?'

'Never mind,' he answered; and, slinging his weapon over his shoulder, strode off down the gorge and so away into the heart of the mountains to the haunts of the wild beasts. Amongst them all there was none so fierce and so dangerous as himself.

The prediction of the Mormon was only too well fulfilled.

Whether it was the terrible death of her father or the effects of the hateful marriage into which she had been forced, poor Lucy never held up her head again, but pined away and died within a month. Her sottish husband, who had married her principally for the sake of John Ferrier's property, did not affect any great grief at his bereavement; but his other wives mourned over her, and sat up with her the night before the burial, as is the Mormon custom. They were grouped round the bier in the early hours of the morning, when, to their inexpressible fear and astonishment, the door was flung open, and a savage-looking, weather-beaten man in tattered garments strode into the room. Without a glance or a word to the cowering women, he walked up to the white, silent figure which had once contained the pure soul of Lucy Ferrier. Stooping over her, he pressed his lips reverently to her cold forehead, and then, snatching up her hand, he took the wedding-ring from her finger. 'She shall not be buried in that,' he cried with a fierce snarl, and before an alarm could be raised sprang down the stairs and was gone. So strange and so brief was the episode that the watchers might have found it hard to believe it themselves or persuade other people of it, had it not been for the undeniable fact that the circlet of gold which marked her as having been a bride had disappeared.

For some months Jefferson Hope lingered among the mountains, leading a strange, wild life, and nursing in his heart the fierce desire for vengeance which possessed him. Tales were told in the city of the weird figure which was seen prowling about the suburbs, and which haunted the lonely mountain gorges. Once a bullet whistled through Stangerson's window and flattened itself upon the wall within a foot of him. On another occasion, as Drebber passed under a cliff a great boulder crashed down on him, and he only escaped a terrible death by throwing himself upon his face. The two young Mormons were not long in discovering the reason of these attempts upon their lives and led repeated expeditions into the mountains in the hope of capturing or killing their enemy, but always without success. Then they adopted the precaution of never going out alone or after nightfall, and of having their houses guarded. After a time they were able to relax these measures, for nothing was either heard or seen of their opponent, and they hoped that time had cooled his vindictiveness.

Far from doing so, it had, if anything, augmented it. The hunter's mind was of a hard, unyielding nature, and the predominant idea of revenge had taken such complete possession of it that there was no room for any other emotion. He was, however, above all things, practical. He soon realized that even his iron constitution could not stand the incessant strain which he was putting upon it. Exposure and want of wholesome food were wearing him out. If he died like a dog among the mountains, what was to become of his revenge then? And yet such a death was sure to overtake him if he persisted. He felt that that was to play his enemy's game, so he reluctantly returned to the old Nevada mines, there to recruit his health and to amass money enough to allow him to pursue his object without privation.

His intention had been to be absent a year at the most, but a combination of unforeseen circumstances prevented his leaving the mines for nearly five. At the end of that time, however, his memory of his wrongs and his craving for revenge were quite as keen as on that memorable night when he had stood by John Ferrier's grave. Disguised, and under an assumed name, he returned to Salt Lake City, careless what became of his own life as long as he obtained what he knew to be justice. There he found evil tidings awaiting him. There had been a schism among the Chosen People a few months before, some of the younger members of the Church having rebelled against the authority of the Elders, and the result had been the secession of a certain number of the malcontents, who had left Utah and become Gentiles. Among these had been Drebber and Stangerson; and no one knew whither they had gone. Rumour reported that Drebber had managed to convert a large part of his property into money, and that he had departed a wealthy man, while his companion, Stangerson, was comparatively poor. There was no clue at all, however, as to their whereabouts.

Many a man, however vindictive, would have abandoned all thought of revenge in the face of such a difficulty, but Jefferson Hope never faltered for a moment. With the small competence he possessed, eked out by such employment as he could pick up, he travelled from town to town through the United States in quest of his enemies. Year passed into year, his black hair turned grizzled, but still he wandered on, a human bloodhound, with his mind wholly set upon the one object to which he had devoted his life. At last his perseverance was rewarded. It was but a glance of a face in a window, but that one glance told him that Cleveland in Ohio possessed the men whom he was in pursuit of. He returned to his miserable lodgings with his plan of vengeance all arranged. It chanced, however, that Drebber, looking from his window, had recognized the vagrant in the street, and had read murder in his eyes. He hurried before a justice of the peace, accompanied by Stangerson, who had become his private secretary, and represented to him that they were in danger of their lives from the jealousy and hatred of an old rival. That evening Jefferson Hope was taken into custody, and not being able to find sureties, was detained for some weeks. When at last he was liberated it was only to find that Drebber's house was deserted, and that he and his secretary had departed for Europe.

Again the avenger had been foiled, and again his concentrated hatred urged him to continue the pursuit. Funds were wanting, however, and for some time he had to return to work, saving every dollar for his approaching journey. At last, having collected enough to keep life in him, he departed for Europe, and tracked his enemies from city to city, working his way in any menial capacity, but never overtaking the fugitives. When he reached St Petersburg, they had departed for Paris; and when he followed them there, he learned that they had just set off for Copenhagen. At the Danish capital he was again a few days late, for they had journeyed on to London, where he at last succeeded in running them to earth. As to what occurred there, we cannot do better than quote the old hunter's own account, as duly recorded in Dr Watson's Journal, to which we are already under such obligations.

13 ◆ A CONTINUATION OF THE
◆ REMINISCENCES OF JOHN WATSON, M.D.

Our prisoner's furious resistance did not apparently indicate
any ferocity in his disposition towards ourselves, for on finding himself powerless, he smiled in an affable manner, and
expressed his hopes that he had not hurt any of us in the
scuffle. 'I guess you're going to take me to the police station,'
he remarked to Sherlock Holmes. 'My cab's at the door. If
you'll loose my legs I'll walk down to it. I'm not so light to lift
as I used to be.'

Gregson and Lestrade exchanged glances, as if they thought
this proposition rather a bold one; but Holmes at once took
the prisoner at his word, and loosened the towel which we
had bound round his ankles. He rose and stretched his legs,
as though to assure himself that they were free once more. I
remember that I thought to myself, as I eyed him, that I had
seldom seen a more powerfully built man; and his dark, sunburned face bore an expression of determination and energy
which was as formidable as his personal strength.

'If there's a vacant place for a chief of the police, I reckon
you are the man for it,' he said, gazing with undisguised
admiration at my fellow-lodger. 'The way you kept on my
trail was a caution.'

'You had better come with me,' said Holmes to the two
detectives.

'I can drive you,' said Lestrade.

'Good! and Gregson can come inside with me. You, too,
Doctor. You have taken an interest in the case, and may as
well stick to us.'

I assented gladly, and we all descended together. Our
prisoner made no attempt at escape, but stepped calmly into
the cab which had been his, and we followed him. Lestrade
mounted the box, whipped up the horse, and brought us in
a very short time to our destination. We were ushered into a
small chamber, where a police inspector noted down our
prisoner's name and the names of the men with whose murder
he had been charged. The official was a white-faced, unemotional man, who went through his duties in a dull, mechanical
way. 'The prisoner will be put before the magistrates in the
course of the week,' he said; 'in the meantime, Mr Jefferson
Hope, have you anything that you wish to say? I must warn
you that your words will be taken down, and may be used
against you.'

'I've got a good deal to say,' our prisoner said slowly. 'I
want to tell you gentlemen all about it.'

'Hadn't you better reserve that for your trial?' asked the
inspector.

'I may never be tried,' he answered. 'You needn't look
startled. It isn't suicide I am thinking of. Are you a doctor?'
He turned his fierce, dark eyes upon me as he asked this last
question.

'Yes, I am,' I answered.

'Then put your hand here,' he said, with a smile, motioning
with his manacled wrists towards his chest.

I did so; and became at once conscious of an extraordinary
throbbing and commotion which was going on inside. The
walls of his chest seemed to thrill and quiver as a frail build-

169 *a dull humming and buzzing noise.* "Objections have been made to [Watson's] description of Jefferson Hope's aortic aneurism as being somewhat too sensational," Miss Helen Simpson wrote in "Medical Career and Capacities of Dr. J. H. Watson." "But it must be remembered that Watson was speaking as a doctor, to whom the implications of any considerable variation from the normal heartbeat were at once apparent; [his] phrases therefore must not be taken as his impression of actual sounds, but of sounds whose significance as danger signals he could only convey by some exaggeration in speech."

170 *over-exposure and under-feeding.* Watson's "discretion veils the fact that this kind of aneurism is generally a consequence of syphilis," Miss Simpson wrote. The late Dr. Ernest Bloomfield Zeisler concurred: "Though under-feeding had nothing to do with it, over-exposure most certainly did, namely over-exposure to the spirochete, though this is not what [Hope] meant to imply. Watson, however, was a well-trained physician and certainly knew what every junior medical student knew, namely that except in very rare cases when it is due to trauma—which was not involved here—aneurysm of the thoracic area is always due to syphilis."

ing would do inside when some powerful engine was at work. In the silence of the room I could hear a dull humming and **169** buzzing noise which proceeded from the same source.

'Why,' I cried, 'you have an aortic aneurism!'

'That's what they call it,' he said, placidly. 'I went to a doctor last week about it, and he told me that it is bound to burst before many days passed. It has been getting worse for **170** years. I got it from over-exposure and under-feeding among the Salt Lake Mountains. I've done my work now, and I don't care how soon I go, but I should like to leave some account of the business behind me. I don't want to be remembered as a common cut-throat.'

The inspector and the two detectives had a hurried discussion as to the advisability of allowing him to tell his story.

'Do you consider, Doctor, that there is immediate danger?' the former asked.

'Most certainly there is,' I answered.

'In that case it is clearly our duty, in the interests of justice, to take his statement,' said the inspector. 'You are at liberty, sir, to give your account, which I again warn you will be taken down.'

'I'll sit down, with your leave,' the prisoner said, suiting the action to the word. 'This aneurism of mine makes me easily tired, and the tussle we had half an hour ago has not mended matters. I'm on the brink of the grave, and I am not likely to lie to you. Every word I say is the absolute truth, and how you use it is a matter of no consequence to me.'

With these words, Jefferson Hope leaned back in his chair and began the following remarkable statement. He spoke in a calm and methodical manner, as though the events which he narrated were commonplace enough. I can vouch for the accuracy of the subjoined account, for I have had access to Lestrade's note-book, in which the prisoner's words were taken down exactly as they were uttered.

'It don't much matter to you why I hated these men,' he said; 'it's enough that they were guilty of the death of two human beings—a father and a daughter—and that they had, therefore, forfeited their own lives. After the lapse of time that has passed since their crime, it was impossible for me to secure a conviction against them in any court. I knew of their guilt, though, and I determined that I should be judge, jury and executioner all rolled into one. You'd have done the same, if you have any manhood in you, if you had been in my place.

'That girl that I spoke of was to have married me twenty years ago. She was forced into marrying that same Drebber, and broke her heart over it. I took the marriage ring from her dead finger, and I vowed that his dying eyes should rest upon that very ring, and that his last thoughts should be of the crime for which he was punished. I have carried it about with me, and have followed him and his accomplice over two continents until I caught them. They thought to tire me out, but they could not do it. If I die tomorrow, as is likely enough, I die knowing that my work in this world is done, and well done. They have perished, and by my hand. There is nothing left for me to hope for, or to desire.

'They were rich and I was poor, so that it was no easy matter for me to follow them. When I got to London my pocket was about empty, and I found that I must turn my hand to something for my living. Driving and riding are as natural to me as walking, so I applied at a cab-owner's office, and soon got employment. I was to bring a certain sum a week to the owner, and whatever was over that I might keep for myself. There was seldom much over, but I managed to scrape along somehow. The hardest job was to learn my way about, for I reckon that of all the mazes that ever were contrived, this city is the most confusing. I had a map beside me, though, and when once I had spotted the principal hotels and stations, I got on pretty well.

'It was some time before I found out where my two gentlemen were living; but I inquired and inquired until at last I dropped across them. They were at a boarding-house at Camberwell, over on the other side of the river. When once I found them out, I knew that I had them at my mercy. I had grown my beard, and there was no chance of their recognizing me. I would dog them and follow them until I saw my opportunity. I was determined that they should not escape me again.

'They were very near doing it for all that. Go where they would about London, I was always at their heels. Sometimes I followed them on my cab, and sometimes on foot, but the former was the best, for then they could not get away from me. It was only early in the morning or late at night that I could earn anything, so that I began to get behindhand with my employer. I did not mind that, however, as long as I could lay my hand upon the men I wanted.

'They were very cunning, though. They must have thought that there was some chance of their being followed, for they would never go out alone, and never after nightfall. During two weeks I drove behind them every day, and never once saw them separate. Drebber himself was drunk half the time, but Stangerson was not to be caught napping. I watched them late and early, but never saw the ghost of a chance; but I was not discouraged, for something told me that the hour had almost come. My only fear was that this thing in my chest might burst a little too soon and leave my work undone.

'At last, one evening I was driving up and down Torquay Terrace, as the street was called in which they boarded, when I saw a cab drive up to their door. Presently some luggage was brought out and after a time Drebber and Stangerson followed it, and drove off. I whipped up my horse and kept within sight of them, feeling very ill at ease, for I feared that they were going to shift their quarters. At Euston Station they got out, and I left a boy to hold my horse and followed them on to the platform. I heard them ask for the Liverpool train, and the guard answer that one had just gone, and there would not be another for some hours. Stangerson seemed to be put out at that, but Drebber was rather pleased than otherwise. I got so close to them in the bustle that I could hear every word that passed between them. Drebber said that he had a little business of his own to do, and that if the other would wait for him he would soon rejoin him. His companion remonstrated with him, and reminded him that they had resolved to stick together. Drebber answered that the matter was a delicate one, and that he must go alone. I could not catch what Stangerson said to that, but the other burst out swearing, and reminded him that he was nothing more than his paid servant, and that he must not presume to dictate to him.

171 *Waterloo Bridge.* Waterloo Bridge, first called Strand Bridge, was "the noble work of George Rennie, built 1811–1817 and opened on the second anniversary of the Battle of Waterloo," Augustus J. C. Hare wrote in *Walks in London*, Vol. I. "It is built of granite, and has nine arches, one hundred and twenty inches span and thirty-five high. Canova considered it 'the noblest bridge in the world—worth a visit from the remotest corners of the earth'; and Dupin describes it as 'a colossal monument worthy of Sesostris and the Caesars.' " The bridge of today is not the bridge that Holmes and Watson knew; in 1924, it was reported that one of the main arches had become weakened, and work on the present bridge began in 1937; on May 4, 1939, the cornerstone was laid.

172 *My mouth gets dry with the talking.'* Wrote Dr. Vernon Pennell in his "Resumé of the Medical Life of John H. Watson, M.D., Late of the Army Medical Department": "Although the criminal had just engaged in a battle royal with Holmes, Gregson, Lestrade and Watson himself, and had all but defeated them in his efforts to escape; though his wrists, hands and face were severely cut, the loss of blood heavy, and half strangled by Lestrade, he suffered no shortness of breath or other distress and only complained of a dryness of the throat after talking, which called for a glass of water. Indeed the only people short of breath were his captors who 'rose to their feet breathless and panting.' As Watson pronounced him *in extremis* and likely to die at any moment, one wonders why the violent struggle had not already precipitated the aneurismal burst which took place later in the comparative quietude of the prison cell, the night after his capture."

On that the secretary gave it up as a bad job, and simply bargained with him that if he missed the last train he should rejoin him at Halliday's Private Hotel; to which Drebber answered that he would be back on the platform before eleven, and made his way out of the station.

'The moment for which I had waited so long had at last come. I had my enemies within my power. Together they could protect each other, but singly they were at my mercy. I did not act, however, with undue precipitation. My plans were already formed. There is no satisfaction in vengeance unless the offender has time to realize who it is that strikes him, and why retribution has come upon him. I had my plans arranged by which I should have the opportunity of making the man who had wronged me understand that his old sin had found him out. It chanced that some days before a gentleman who had been engaged in looking over some houses in the Brixton Road had dropped the key of one of them in my carriage. It was claimed that same evening, and returned; but in the interval I had taken a moulding of it, and had a duplicate constructed. By means of this I had access to at least one spot in this great city where I could rely upon being free from interruption. How to get Drebber to that house was the difficult problem which I had now to solve.

'He walked down the road and went into one or two liquor shops, staying for nearly half an hour in the last of them. When he came out, he staggered in his walk, and was evidently pretty well on. There was a hansom just in front of me, and he hailed it. I followed it so close that the nose of my horse was within a yard of his driver the whole way. We rattled **171** across Waterloo Bridge and through miles of streets, until, to my astonishment, we found ourselves back in the terrace in which he had boarded. I could not imagine what his intention was in returning there; but I went on and pulled up my cab a hundred yards or so from the house. He entered it, and his hansom drove away. Give me a glass of water, if you **172** please. My mouth gets dry with the talking.

I handed him the glass, and he drank it down.

'That's better,' he said. 'Well, I waited for a quarter of an hour, or more, when suddenly there came a noise like people struggling inside the house. Next moment the door was flung open and two men appeared, one of whom was Drebber, and the other was a young chap whom I had never seen before. This fellow had Drebber by the collar, and when they came to the head of the steps he gave him a shove and a kick which sent him half across the road. "You hound!" he cried, shaking his stick at him; "I'll teach you to insult an honest girl!" He was so hot that I think he would have thrashed Drebber with his cudgel, only that the cur staggered away down the road as fast as his legs would carry him. He ran as far as the corner, and then, seeing my cab, he hailed me and jumped in. "Drive me to Halliday's Private Hotel," said he.

'When I had him fairly inside my cab, my heart jumped so with joy that I feared lest at this last moment my aneurism might go wrong. I drove along slowly, weighing in my own mind what it was best to do. I might take him right out into the country, and there in some deserted lane have my last interview with him. I had almost decided upon this, when he solved the problem for me. The craze for drink had seized him again, and he ordered me to pull up outside a gin palace. He went in, leaving word that I should wait for him. There he remained until closing time, and when he came out he was so far gone that I knew the game was in my own hands.

'Don't imagine that I intended to kill him in cold blood. It would only have been rigid justice if I had done so, but I could not bring myself to do it. I had long determined that he should have a show for his life if he chose to take advantage of it. Among the many billets which I have filled in America during my wandering life, I was once janitor and sweeper-out of the laboratory at York College. One day the professor was **173** lecturing on poisons, and he showed his students some alkaloid, as he called it, which he had extracted from some South American arrow poison, and which was so powerful that the **174** least grain meant instant death. I spotted the bottle in which this preparation was kept, and when they were all gone, I helped myself to a little of it. I was a fairly good dispenser, so I worked this alkaloid into small, soluble pills, and each pill I put in a box with a similar pill made without the poison. I determined at the time that when I had my chance my gentlemen should each have a draw out of one of these boxes, while I ate the pill that remained. It would be quite as deadly and a good deal less noisy than firing across a handkerchief. From that day I had always my pill boxes about with me, and the time had now come when I was to use them.

'It was nearer one than twelve, and a wild, bleak night, blowing hard and raining in torrents. Dismal as it was outside, I was glad within—so glad that I could have shouted out from pure exultation. If any of you gentlemen have ever pined for a thing, and longed for it during twenty long years, and then suddenly found it within your reach, you would understand my feelings. I lit a cigar, and puffed at it to steady my nerves, but my hands were trembling and my temples throbbing with excitement. As I drove, I could see old John Ferrier and sweet Lucy looking at me out of the darkness and smiling at me, just as plain as I see you all in this room. All the way they were ahead of me, one on each side of the horse, until I pulled up at the house in the Brixton Road.

'There was not a soul to be seen, nor a sound to be heard, except the dripping of the rain. When I looked in at the window, I found Drebber all huddled together in a drunken sleep. I shook him by the arm. "It's time to get out," I said.

' "All right, cabby," said he.

'I suppose he thought we had come to the hotel that he had mentioned, for he got out without another word, and followed me down the garden. I had to walk beside him to keep him steady, for he was still a little top-heavy. When we came to the door, I opened it, and led him into the front room. I give you my word that all the way, the father and the daughter were walking in front of us.

' "It's infernally dark," said he, stamping about.

' "We'll soon have a light," I said, striking a match and putting it to a wax candle which I had brought with me. "Now, Enoch Drebber," I continued, turning to him, and holding the light to my own face, "who am I?"

'He gazed at me with bleared, drunken eyes for a moment, and then I saw horror spring up in them, and convulse his whole features, which showed me that he knew me. He staggered back with a livid face, and I saw the perspiration break out upon his brow, while his teeth chattered in his head. At

173 *York College.* There is a York College in Nebraska, but it was not founded until 1890. Hope probably meant the old medical college of New York University.

174 *some South American arrow poison.* Hope presumably thought that he was using curare. But Mr. J. Raymond Hendrickson has written ("De Re Pharmaca") that "the alkaloid employed by Hope could have been what he believed it to be is denied by every detail of Drebber's *ante-mortem* and *post-mortem* appearance . . ." He suggests that the poison which killed Drebber was nicotine.

On the other hand, F. A. Allen, M.P.S., has written ("Devilish Drugs," Part I) that the poison "was evidently one of the erythrina alkaloids. . . . Let us suggest that an odorous and more potent alkaloid than . . . erythroidine, from the seeds of *E. corraloides*, awaits discovery by the explorer."

Again, Dr. George B. Koelle has written ("The Poisons of the Canon") that Hope must have confused a "South American arrow poison" with a "South African ordeal poison"—physostigmine or eserine. "This is highly potent, readily absorbed when taken by mouth, and the victim remains conscious nearly to the time of death; all these facts are consistent with Hope's account and Holmes' deductions."

HE COWERED AWAY WITH WILD CRIES AND PRAYERS
FOR MERCY . . .

Illustration by George Hutchinson for *A Study in Scarlet*, London: Ward, Lock, Bowden & Co., 1891. The scene is a favorite with Canonical artists: Arthur Twidle chose it for the single illustration he made for *A Study in Scarlet* for the "Author's Edition" published by John Murray, London, in 1903. Of Twidle's work the late James Montgomery wrote (*A Study in Pictures*): "Here at last one finds art work on a par with the story. . . . A superbly menacing Hope, with drawn dagger and pill box thrust forward toward the cringing Mormon, makes us fairly creep with horror at the awful retribution about to be exacted in the dilapidated room of the deserted house." J. Watson Davis later (1906) illustrated the same scene for the A. L. Burt Company's edition of *Tales of Sherlock Holmes*.

the sight I leaned my back against the door and laughed loud and long. I had always known that vengeance would be sweet, but I had never hoped for the contentment of soul which now possessed me.

' "You dog!" I said; "I have hunted you from Salt Lake City to St Petersburg, and you have always escaped me. Now, at last, your wanderings have come to an end, for either you or I shall never see tomorrow's sun rise." He shrank still farther away as I spoke, and I could see on his face that he thought I was mad. So I was for the time. The pulses in my temples beat like sledge-hammers, and I believe I would have had a fit of some sort if the blood had not gushed from my nose and relieved me.

' "What do you think of Lucy Ferrier now?" I cried, locking the door, and shaking the key in his face. "Punishment has been slow in coming, but it has overtaken you at last." I saw his coward lips tremble as I spoke. He would have begged for his life, but he knew well that it was useless.

' "Would you murder me?" he stammered.

' "There is no murder," I answered. "Who talks of murdering a mad dog? What mercy had you upon my poor darling, when you dragged her from her slaughtered father, and bore her away to your accursed and shameless harem."

' "It was not I who killed her father," he cried.

' "But it was you who broke her innocent heart," I shrieked, thrusting the box before him. "Let the high God judge between us. Choose and eat. There is death in one and life in the other. I shall take what you leave. Let us see if there is justice upon the earth, or if we are ruled by chance."

'He cowered away with wild cries and prayers for mercy, but I drew my knife and held it to his throat until he had obeyed me. Then I swallowed the other, and we stood facing one another in silence for a minute or more, waiting to see which was to live and which was to die. Shall I ever forget the look which came over his face when the first warning pangs told him that the poison was in his system? I laughed as I saw it, and held Lucy's marriage ring in front of his eyes. It was but for a moment, for the action of the alkaloid is rapid. A spasm of pain contorted his features; he threw his hands out in front of him, staggered, and then, with a hoarse cry, fell heavily upon the floor. I turned him over with my foot, and placed my hand upon his heart. There was no movement. He was dead!

'The blood had been streaming from my nose, but I had taken no notice of it. I don't know what it was that put it into my head to write upon the wall with it. Perhaps it was some mischievous idea of setting the police upon a wrong track, for I felt light-hearted and cheerful. I remembered a German being found in New York with RACHE written up above him, and it was argued at the time in the newspapers that the secret societies must have done it. I guessed that what puzzled the New Yorkers would puzzle the Londoners, so I dipped my finger in my own blood and printed it on a convenient place on the wall. Then I walked down to my cab and found that there was nobody about, and that the night was still very wild. I had driven some distance when I put my hand into the pocket in which I usually kept Lucy's ring, and found that it was not there. I was thunderstruck at this, for it was the only memento that I had of her. Thinking that I might have dropped it when I stooped over Drebber's body, I drove back, and leaving my cab in a side street, I went boldly up to the house—for I was ready to dare anything rather than lose the ring. When I arrived there, I walked right into the arms of a police-officer who was coming out, and only managed to disarm his suspicions by pretending to be hopelessly drunk.

'That was how Enoch Drebber came to his end. All I had to do then was to do as much for Stangerson, and so pay off John Ferrier's debt. I knew that he was staying at Halliday's Private Hotel, and I hung about all day, but he never came out. I fancy that he suspected something when Drebber failed to put in an appearance. He was cunning, was Stangerson, and always on his guard. If he thought he could keep me off by staying indoors he was very much mistaken. I soon found out which was the window of his bedroom, and early next morning I took advantage of some ladders which were lying **175** in the lane behind the hotel, and so made my way into his room in the grey of the dawn. I woke him up and told him that the hour had come when he was to answer for the life he had taken so long before. I described Drebber's death to him, and I gave him the same choice of the poisoned pills. Instead of grasping at the chance of safety which that offered him, he sprang from his bed and flew at my throat. In self-defence I stabbed him to the heart. It would have been the same in any case, for Providence would never have allowed his guilty hand to pick out anything but the poison.

'I have little more to say, and it's as well, for I am about done up. I went on cabbing it for a day or so intending to **176** keep at it until I could save enough to take me back to America. I was standing in the yard when a ragged youngster

175 *early next morning*. A curious phrase for Hope to use, if he confessed on the afternoon of the same day on which he had murdered Stangerson, as Watson tells us he did. It is suggested that while Hope must have murdered Stangerson on the morning of Saturday, March 5th, it was not until Sunday, March 6th, that his capture took place.

176 *I went on cabbing it for a day or so*. The late Professor Christ wrote: "That he could not possibly have done, for it was only on the same morning [Watson tells us] that Stangerson was done in."

In contrast, your editor has accepted Hope's statement as correct, and has inferred that it was made *after* Saturday, that is, on Sunday, March 6th: it will be recalled that Watson took down Hope's words "exactly as they were uttered from Lestrade's notebook."

To this, the late Dr. Zeisler replied: "Hope had not left his cab for forty-eight hours or so from the Thursday afternoon until his capture, except long enough to settle his accounts first with Drebber and then with Stangerson. He had been waiting nearly twenty-one years to wreak vengeance on these two, and had lately greatly feared that his aneurysm would rupture before he could be successful. His tremendous excitement, and the exaltation of the past few days, together with his lack of rest, could very easily account for his confusing one event with another, for he had in fact been cabbing it for a full thirty-six hours since Drebber's death. It was this same confusion which led him on the evening of his capture to refer to that very morning as 'next morning,' meaning the morning following the day on which he 'hung about' Stangerson's hotel; he would otherwise have called it 'this morning.'"

. . . I DIPPED MY FINGER IN MY OWN BLOOD AND PRINTED IT ON A CONVENIENT PLACE ON THE WALL.

Cover illustration by a unknown artist for a German-language edition of *A Study in Scarlet* published in Milwaukee, Wisconsin. Its discoverer, Mr. H. B. Williams, has stated that the publisher was the Milwaukee *Herold*, one of that city's old German-language newspapers.

177 *I went round suspecting no harm.* The late Clifton R. Andrew ("A Difficulty in *A Study in Scarlet*") and Mr. C. B. H. Vaill ("A Study in Intellects") have both called attention to this remarkable statement. Says Mr. Vaill: "Since Hope had by this time completed his second murder, it would be reasonable to suppose that his caution would be increased. But no; the fact that he was singled out of all the cabbies in London; by name, and directed to call at the very address which had proven to be a trap only a short time before, did not arouse even the 'slightest suspicion' which Holmes feared. Jefferson Hope waltzed right downtown into the new-style spring handcuffs, and that was that."

Mr. Larry Van Gelder has suggested one answer to the problem: Hope deliberately committed suicide. Aware, as he must have been, who Holmes was and where he lived, he knowingly walked into the "trap" and put up the struggle he did simply in order to "agitate his aneurism." "This theory," the late Edgar W. Smith commented, "seems much more plausible, it must be admitted, than the incredible system of events in which Watson would have us believe."

178 blasé. French: wearied or worn out by surfeit.

179 *My friend volunteered to go and see.* "Hope was a stranger in London and could have little, if any, knowledge of Sherlock Holmes or potential danger at 221B Baker Street," the late Robert R. Pattrick wrote in "Moriarty Was There." "He was, moreover, a murderer. Yet he claimed to have a friend sufficiently loyal to risk entering this possible police trap. And who, conveniently, was an expert in impersonation. Obviously, the true answer can only be—Moriarty. For a fee, of course. The agent escaped, and Hope would not give evidence. But the significance of the agent was not lost on Holmes. He had even warned Gregson and Lestrade: 'We have a shrewd and desperate man to deal with, who is supported, as I have had occasion to prove, by another who is as clever as himself. . . . I am bound to say that I consider these men to be more than a match for the official force.' "

asked if there was a cabby there called Jefferson Hope, and said that his cab was wanted by a gentleman at 221B, Baker **177** Street. I went round suspecting no harm, and the next thing I knew, this young man here had the bracelets on my wrists, and as neatly snackled as ever I saw in my life. That's the whole of my story, gentlemen. You may consider me to be a murderer; but I hold that I am just as much an officer of justice as you are.'

So thrilling had the man's narrative been and his manner was so impressive that we had sat silent and absorbed. Even **178** the professional detectives, *blasé* as they were in every detail of crime, appeared to be keenly interested in the man's story. When he finished, we sat for some minutes in a stillness which was only broken by the scratching of Lestrade's pencil as he gave the finishing touches to his shorthand account.

'There is only one point on which I should like a little more information,' Sherlock Holmes said at last. 'Who was your accomplice who came for the ring which I advertised?'

The prisoner winked at my friend jocosely. 'I can tell my own secrets,' he said, 'but I don't get other people into trouble. I saw your advertisement, and I thought it might be a plant, or it might be the ring which I wanted. My friend volunteered **179** to go and see. I think you'll own he did it smartly.'

'Not a doubt of that,' said Holmes, heartily.

'Now, gentlemen,' the inspector remarked, gravely, 'the forms of the law must be complied with. On Thursday the prisoner will be brought before the magistrates, and your attendance will be required. Until then I will be responsible for him.' He rang the bell as he spoke, and Jefferson Hope was led off by a couple of warders, while my friend and I made our way out of the station and took a cab back to Baker Street.

14 • THE CONCLUSION

We had all been warned to appear before the magistrates upon the Thursday; but when the Thursday came there was no occasion for our testimony. A higher Judge had taken the matter in hand, and Jefferson Hope had been summoned before a tribunal where strict justice would be meted out to him. On the very night after his capture the aneurism burst, and he was found in the morning stretched upon the floor of the cell, with a placid smile upon his face, as though he had been able in his dying moments to look back upon a useful life, and on work well done.

'Gregson and Lestrade will be wild about his death,' Holmes remarked, as we chatted it over next evening. 'Where will their grand advertisement be now?'

'I don't see that they had very much to do with his capture,' I answered.

'What you do in this world is a matter of no consequence,' returned my companion, bitterly. 'The question is, what can you make people believe that you have done. Never mind,' he continued, more brightly, after a pause. 'I would not have missed the investigation for anything. There has been no better case within my recollection. Simple as it was, there were several most instructive points about it.'

'Simple!' I ejaculated.

'Well, really, it can hardly be described as otherwise,' said Sherlock Holmes, smiling at my surprise. 'The proof of its intrinsic simplicity is, that without any help save a few very ordinary deductions I was able to lay my hand upon the criminal within three days.' **180**

'That is true,' said I.

'I have already explained to you that what is out of the common is usually a guide rather than a hindrance. In solving a problem of this sort, the grand thing is to be able to reason backwards. That is a very useful accomplishment, and a very easy one, but people do not practise it much. In the everyday affairs of life it is more useful to reason forwards, and so the other comes to be neglected. There are fifty who can reason synthetically for one who can reason analytically.'

'I confess,' said I, 'that I do not quite follow you.'

'I hardly expected that you would. Let me see if I can make it clearer. Most people, if you describe a train of events to them, will tell you what the result would be. They can put those events together in their minds, and argue from them that something will come to pass. There are few people, however, who, if you told them a result, would be able to evolve from their own inner consciousness what the steps were which led up to that result. This power is what I mean when I talk of reasoning backwards, or analytically.'

'I understand,' said I.

'Now this was a case in which you were given the result and had to find everything else for yourself. Now let me endeavour to show you the different steps in my reasoning. To begin at the beginning. I approached the house, as you know, on foot, and with my mind entirely free from all impressions. I naturally began by examining the roadway, and there, as I have already explained to you, I saw clearly the marks of a cab, which, I ascertained by inquiry, must have been there during the night. I satisfied myself that it was a cab and not a private carriage by the narrow gauge of the wheels. The ordinary London growler is considerably less wide than a gentleman's brougham.

180 *I was able to lay my hand upon the criminal within three days.'* As your editor has written elsewhere (*The Chronological Holmes*): "Surely Holmes would have made no such statement if he had in truth captured Hope within the two days allotted to him by Watson."

To this, Dr. Zeisler replied ("A Chronological Study in Scarlet:)" "It might be considered frivolous to point out that within two days actually is within three days. But it seems evident that the Master really said 'Within two days' and that the printed text is in error. This may have arisen in either of two ways: first, due to the fact that when Watson wrote his chronicle some six years after the events he himself was confused by the rapidity with which they had occurred; it is not strange if they seemed in retrospect to have occupied most of three days instead of two days; secondly, it is possible, of course, that Watson wrote '2' in his manuscript, and that the typesetter read '3'—for Watson's calligraphy was not quite perfect."

". . . A GENTLEMAN'S BROUGHAM."

The brougham, named for Henry, Lord Brougham, British lawyer, orator, writer, and statesman, 1778–1868, was a closed, four-wheeled vehicle with its two front wheels turning short on a pivot. The illustration, by John Leech, is from *A History of Everyday Things in England, Vol. IV, 1851 to 1914,* by Marjorie and C. H. B. Quennell.

181 *as the art of tracing footsteps.* Probably Holmes by this time had written his monograph "upon the tracing of footsteps, with some remarks upon the use of plaster of Paris as a preserver of impresses," of which he speaks in *The Sign of the Four.*

'This was the first point gained. I then walked slowly down the garden path, which happened to be composed of a clay soil, peculiarly suitable for taking impressions. No doubt it appeared to you to be a mere trampled line of slush, but to my trained eyes every mark upon its surface had a meaning. There is no branch of detective science which is so important **181** and so much neglected as the art of tracing footsteps. Happily, I have always laid great stress upon it, and much practice has made it second nature to me. I saw the heavy footmarks of the constables, but I saw also the track of the two men who had first passed through the garden. It was easy to tell that they had been before the others, because in places their marks had been entirely obliterated by the others coming upon the top of them. In this way my second link was formed, which told me that the nocturnal visitors were two in number, one remarkable for his height (as I calculated from the length of his stride) and the other fashionably dressed, to judge from the small and elegant impression left by his boots.

'On entering the house this last inference was confirmed. My well-booted man lay before me. The tall one, then, had done the murder, if murder there was. There was no wound upon the dead man's person, but the agitated expression upon his face assured me that he had foreseen his fate before it came upon him. Men who die from heart disease, or any sudden natural cause, never by any chance exhibit agitation upon their features. Having sniffed the dead man's lips, I detected a slightly sour smell, and I came to the conclusion that he had had poison forced upon him. Again, I argued that it had been forced upon him from the hatred and fear expressed upon his face. By the method of exclusion, I had arrived at this result, for no other hypothesis would meet the facts. Do not imagine that it was a very unheard-of idea. The forcible administration of poison is by no means a new thing in criminal annals. The cases of Dolsky in Odessa, and of Leturier in Montpellier, will occur at once to any toxicologist.

'And now came the great question as to the reason why. Robbery had not been the object of the murder, for nothing was taken. Was it politics, then, or was it a woman? That was the question which confronted me. I was inclined from the first to the latter supposition. Political assassins are only too glad to do their work and to fly. This murder had, on the contrary, been done most deliberately, and the perpetrator had left his tracks all over the room, showing that he had been there all the time. It must have been a private wrong, and not a political one, which called for such a methodical revenge. When the inscription was discovered upon the wall, I was more inclined than ever to my opinion. The thing was too evidently a blind. When the ring was found, however, it settled the question. Clearly the murderer had used it to remind his victim of some dead or absent woman. It was at this point that I asked Gregson whether he had inquired in his telegram to Cleveland as to any particular point in Mr Drebber's former career. He answered, you remember, in the negative.

'I then proceeded to make a careful examination of the room, which confirmed me in my opinion as to the murderer's height, and furnished me with the additional details as to the Trichinopoly cigar and the length of his nails. I had already come to the conclusion, since there were no signs of a struggle, that the blood which covered the floor had burst from the murderer's nose in his excitement. I could perceive that the track of blood coincided with the track of his feet. It is seldom that any man, unless he is very full-blooded, breaks out in this way through emotion, so I hazarded the opinion that the criminal was probably a robust and ruddy-faced man. Events proved that I had judged correctly.

'Having left the house, I proceeded to do what Gregson had neglected. I telegraphed to the head of the police at Cleveland, limiting my inquiry to the circumstances connected with the marriage of Enoch Drebber. The answer was conclusive. It told me that Drebber had already applied for the protection of the law against an old rival in love, named Jefferson Hope, and that this same Hope was at present in Europe. I knew now that I held the clue to the mystery in my hand, and all that remained was to secure the murderer.

'I had already determined in my own mind that the man who had walked into the house with Drebber was none other than the man who had driven the cab. The marks in the road showed me that the horse had wandered on in a way which would have been impossible had there been anyone in charge of it. Where, then, could the driver be, unless he were inside the house? Again, it is absurd to suppose that any sane man would carry out a deliberate crime under the very eyes, as it were, of a third person, who was sure to betray him. Lastly, supposing one man wished to dog another through London, what better means could he adopt than to turn cabdriver? All these considerations led me to the irresistible conclusion that Jefferson Hope was to be found among the jarveys of the **182** Metropolis.

'If he had been one, there was no reason to believe that he had ceased to be. On the contrary from his point of view, any sudden change would be likely to draw attention to himself. He would probably, for a time at least, continue to perform his duties. There was no reason to suppose that he was going under an assumed name. Why should he change his name in a country where no one knew his original one? I therefore organized my street arab detective corps, and sent them systematically to every cab proprietor in London until they ferreted out the man that I wanted. How well they succeeded, and how quickly I took advantage of it, are still fresh in your recollection. The murder of Stangerson was an incident which was entirely unexpected, but which could hardly, in any case, have been prevented. Through it, as you know, I came into possession of the pills, the existence of which I had already surmised. You see, the whole thing is a chain of logical sequences without a break or flaw.'

'It is wonderful!' I cried. 'Your merits should be publicly recognized. You should publish an account of the case. If you won't, I will for you.'

'You may do what you like, Doctor,' he answered. 'See here!' he continued, handing a paper over to me, 'look at this!'

It was the *Echo* for the day, and the paragraph to which **183** he pointed was devoted to the case in question.

'The public,' it said, 'have lost a sensational treat through the sudden death of the man Hope, who was suspected of the murder of Mr Enoch Drebber and of Mr Joseph Stangerson. The details of the case will probably be never known now,

"YOU MAY DO WHAT YOU LIKE, DOCTOR," HE ANSWERED.

"But this promise was long in its fulfillment," the late Edgar W. Smith wrote in "Dr. Watson and the Great Censorship." "The permission Holmes had so cavalierly given was withdrawn, we must believe, before Watson could act on it, and the facts, for all their drama and momentousness, were not revealed [until December, 1887]." The illustration, by George Hutchinson, is from *A Study in Scarlet*, London: Ward, Lock, Bowden & Co., 1891.

182 *the jarveys*. Cockney slang for coachmen or cabdrivers. The term perhaps comes from the name of Saint Gervase, whose emblem was the whip.

183 *It was the* Echo *for the day*. As your editor has written elsewhere (*The Chronological Holmes*): "Watson tells us that Hope died on the night of his capture, and that the next evening he and Holmes discussed the case. By Watson's account, this discussion would have come on the Sunday. This it could not have done, because Watson speaks of the *Echo* for the day."

Dr. Zeisler agreed that this discussion must have been on the Monday evening, "from which it follows that Hope died during the night of Sunday-

Monday." The difficulty here lies in the interpretation which one places upon Watson's statement that Hope died "on the very night after his capture." Your editor has taken this to mean that Hope was captured on Sunday, March 6, 1881, and died on that night; Dr. Zeisler took it to mean that Hope was captured on Saturday, March 5, 1881, and died on the night of the following day, Sunday, March 6—"the very night *after* [the day of] his capture."

"Clearly," your editor concluded, "what happened was this: Watson, eager to make his first account of a Holmes case as dramatic as possible, and to cast all possible credit on the Master and his methods, *telescoped the events of two days into one*."

This Dr. Zeisler considered "absolutely impossible, and for three reasons: 1) There was surely no need to make the case more dramatic than it was in any case, or to try to cast more credit on the Master and his methods than they would have deserved even if the case had lasted one day longer than it did; 2) if . . . Watson wished to make it appear that a three-day case had lasted only two days, would he, after elaborate distortions, have nullified his efforts by quoting the Master as saying that he had captured Hope 'within three days'? Surely, he would have been most careful at this very point to have altered it to 'two days.' 3) When Holmes glanced over Watson's chronicle—as he tells us he did in Chapter I of *The Sign of the Four*, he noticed the error but perhaps did not wish Watson to think that his criticisms were in any way dictated by vanity, and he considered a correction unnecessary inasmuch as careful reading would show that he had solved the case in two days."

184 *contemplar in arca."'* *Contemplar* is incorrect; the word should be *contemplor*. Watson here quotes a foreign author for the one and only time in the Saga; he draws upon the *First Satire* of the First Book (lines 66 and 67) of Horace, translated by Christopher Morely as "The Public hisses at me, but I'm pleased with myself in private when I look at the money in my box"; by Morris Rosenblum as "The People hiss at me but I applaud myself in my own home as I gaze fondly at the coins in my strongbox"; by Professor John B. Wolf as "People hiss at me, but I am satisfied with myself; I stay home and contemplate the money in my strongbox." Watson errs in calling the speaker "the Roman miser." As Mr. Rosenblum pointed out: "Every schoolboy knows . . . that Horace does not speak of a Roman miser but of a rich man in Athens."

Auctorial Note: In the competition conducted by the *Observer*, in which its readers were asked to vote on their favorite Sherlock Holmes stories, including both the short stories *and* the novels, *A Study in Scarlet* was given fourth place, falling just behind "The Adventure of the Speckled Band," *The Hound of the Baskervilles* and *The Sign of the Four*.

though we are informed upon good authority that the crime was the result of an old-standing and romantic feud, in which love and Mormonism bore a part. It seems that both the victims belonged, in their younger days, to the Latter Day Saints, and Hope, the deceased prisoner, hails also from Salt Lake City. If the case has had no other effect, it, at least, brings out in the most striking manner the efficiency of our detective police force, and will serve as a lesson to all foreigners that they will do wisely to settle their feuds at home, and not to carry them on to British soil. It is an open secret that the credit of this smart capture belongs entirely to the well-known Scotland Yard officials, Messrs Lestrade and Gregson. The man was apprehended, it appears, in the rooms of a certain Mr Sherlock Holmes, who has himself, as an amateur, shown some talent in the detective line, and who, with such instructors, may hope in time to attain to some degree of their skill. It is expected that a testimonial of some sort will be presented to the two officers as a fitting recognition of their services.'

'Didn't I tell you so when we started?' cried Sherlock Holmes with a laugh. 'That's the result of all our Study in Scarlet: to get them a testimonial!'

'Never mind,' I answered; 'I have all the facts in my journal, and the public shall know them. In the meantime you must make yourself contented by the consciousness of success, like the Roman miser—

184
    ' "Populus me sibilat, at mihi plaudo
    Ipse domi simul ac nummos contemplar in arca." '

16

"AS TO YOUR DATES, THAT IS THE BIGGEST MYSTIFICATION OF ALL"

[John H. Watson, M.D., to Sherlock Holmes,
"The Adventure of the Creeping Man"]

"Mr. Sherlock Holmes was in active practice for twenty-three years, and . . . during seventeen of these I was allowed to co-operate with him and to keep notes of his doings."

So Watson wrote in the opening lines of "The Adventure of the Veiled Lodger."

Ten of these seventeen years occupy the period from March, 1881 (*A Study in Scarlet*), to May, 1891 ("The Final Problem"). The partnership was reconstituted shortly after April, 1894 ("The Adventure of the Empty House"), and it came to an end with Holmes' retirement in the autumn of 1903—a period of nine years and six months, or a total of *nineteen and a half* years.

There were, then, two and a half years during the period of "the partnership" in which Watson did *not* "co-operate with" Holmes or "keep notes of his doings."

We know that Watson was living at Baker Street in late 1895 ("The Adventure of the Bruce-Partington Plans"); but he does *not* seem to be living there in October, 1896 ("The Adventure of the Veiled Lodger"). There is a presumption, amounting almost to a certainty, that late 1895–late 1896 is one of our "missing years."

Another possibility is the year May, 1901 ("The Adventure of the Priory School") to May, 1902 ("The Adventure of Shoscombe Old Place")—a period of twelve months during which there is no indication whatsoever that Watson was "allowed to co-operate with Holmes and to keep notes of his doings."

Even including this, however, would leave us with a period of *at least six months* to account for.

Here we may note a third remarkable fact: Watson recorded no Holmes case which took place between *A Study in Scarlet* (March, 1881) and "The Adventure of the Speckled Band" (April, 1883)—nor any case which took place between "The Adventure of the Speckled Band" and "The Resident Patient" (October, 1886)—*more than three years later.*

The Reverend Henry T. Folsom has suggested ("Seventeen Out of Twenty-Three") that Watson was on *sick leave* from the Army until shortly after March, 1881; he reported *back to duty* in the summer of 1881, serving his second hitch with the Army from summer, 1881, to spring, 1883.

Mr. S. C. Roberts, on the other hand, holds (*Doctor Watson*) that Watson spent a portion of the early days of the partnership in civilian travel. "In later years," Mr. Roberts wrote, "Watson refers to 'an experience of women which extends over many nations and three separate continents' [*The Sign of the Four*]. The three continents are clearly Europe, India, and Australia. In Australia he had been but a boy; in India he can have seen few women except the staff nurses at Peshawar. It is conceivable, though not likely, that he revisited Australia at this time. It is much more probable that Watson spent some time on the Continent and that, in particular, he visited such resorts as contained the additional attraction of a casino."

India, we may agree, is "clearly" one of Watson's "three separate continents." As the late Dr. Ernest Bloomfield Zeisler pointed out in *Baker Street Chronology:* "Throughout the Sacred Writings there are numerous evidences that Watson was inordinately susceptible to ladies and that in general he was successful with them; the Master says as much, and Watson's many palpitating descriptions of attractive young women and their silhouettes point in the same direction. It is quite likely that Watson found it physiologically impossible to be entirely deprived of women for as long as eighteen months of war."

Europe, also, we may clearly allow Mr. Roberts, remembering Watson's long residence in England during many, if not all, of the years between *A Study in Scarlet* and his boast of "three separate continents" in *The Sign of the Four*.

About *Australia*, however, even Mr. Roberts does not seem too happy; and Dr. W. S. Bristowe (in "The Mystery of the Third Continent") is really quite devastating: "The assumption is usually made that [the third continent] was Australia where [Watson] certainly spent some of his childhood days, but as he and 'Tadpole' Phelps were 'little boys' at school together in England, . . . I cannot believe that Watson was so precocious as to have had 'experience of women' in any man-of-the-world sense before leaving Australia at thirteen or younger to go to school in England."

Africa? Here Dr. Bristowe has written: ". . . it may be advisable to discount any claim which might be based on the hour or two [Watson] could have spent ashore at Port Said on his way to India. During the homeward journey, of course, he would have been too much of an invalid to take any interest."

And now let us consider the case for *America*.

Again, it is Dr. Bristowe who has summed up the case so cogently:

We know that Watson had notes of hundreds of cases from which only sixty were selected for publication, one by Holmes himself and others perhaps by Sir Arthur Conan Doyle. Of those selected by Watson it is remarkable to find about one in every five had some connection with America or Americans. Surely this is no coincidence. It shows a personal interest in America which is well illustrated by the special zest with which he describes the American scene in both *A Study in Scarlet* and *The Valley of Fear*. . . . My conclusion that America was the third continent to which Watson was referring now receives dramatic confirmation from a source whose authenticity can scarcely be doubted. It is well known that Sir Arthur Conan Doyle was closely associated with Watson and described him as his friend in 1908 [in the *Strand Magazine*] so anything from his pen must be treated with the highest respect. We have learned from Mr. J[ohn] Dickson Carr of some unpublished notes about Watson which were written by Sir Arthur Conan Doyle in 1889 under the title of *Angels of Darkness* (*The Life of Sir Arthur Conan Doyle*). Many details are withheld but we are allowed to know that Watson not only visited America but stayed on long enough in San Francisco to practice medicine there.

As we have seen, Dr. Bristowe has also held that both Watson's father and elder brother came to America to fight in the Civil War: it was to visit his dying brother that Watson came to America late in 1883 or early in 1884. His visit, Dr. Bristowe has suggested, "taxed" his resources beyond their limit with the result that he was forced to go into practice for a time in order to keep himself and to pay for the return passage to England."[1]

Other authorities, while agreeing that America was indeed the third continent, hold that Watson's visit there was made at a time other than 1884–1885.

Mr. William Smith, as we have already seem, has placed Watson in America in the 1860's, himself a participant in the American Civil War.

Mr. Robert Keith Leavitt, on the other hand, has held that Watson's visit to America was made in the year 1874, four years before Watson took his medical degree. "Obviously, the young man was making the Grand Tour." ("The Preposterously Paired Performances of the Preacher's Portrait.")

And Dr. Winthrop Weatherbee has written (in "The Third Continent"):

It will be recalled that, as a small boy, Watson attended an English school, where one of his classmates was "Tadpole" Phelps ["The Naval Treaty"]. Phelps, however, was in the fifth form when Watson was in the third, and it is not unreasonable to suppose that it was shortly after this time that the decline of the Watson family fortunes necessitated [an] emigration from England. When we recall Watson's old school-number [31 —see "The Adventure of the Retired Colourman"] everything falls into place. The only city in the northern part of the United States large enough at that time to support such an aggregation of schools was New York, where, to interpret what he said, Watson must have attended P.S. No. 31. . . .

If we are agreed that Watson, at some time prior to the adventure of *The Sign of the Four* (September, 1888) visited America, we have resolved the mystery of the three continents—but the mystery of the missing years that disrupted the partnership between 1881–1894 and 1894–1903 still calls for investigation.

[1] We shall have occasion to refer to this American visit again in Chapter 21, "Now, Watson, the Fair Sex Is Your Department," in which we shall consider the wives of Watson.

2 The late Dorothy L. Sayers, in "Dr. Watson, Widower," expressed her doubts that there was any break in the partnership at this time. She accounted for the missing years by suggesting an interruption between August, 1898, and July, 1900. "It was during this period (October, 1899) that the War broke out in the Transvaal, and it would be natural that Watson (that spirited old warhorse) should hear his country's call and hasten to place his services, in some capacity, at the disposal of his Government."

3 The reader must remember that it was not until September, 1903, with the first publication of "The Adventure of the Empty House," that Watson was allowed to reveal to the world that Holmes was not dead.

There is now general but by no means universal agreement that there were three breaks in the partnership, chronologically as follows:

1. A period between April, 1883 ("The Adventure of the Speckled Band"), and October, 1886 ("The Resident Patient"), during which Watson traveled, presumably to America.

2. A period between November, 1895 ("The Adventure of the Bruce-Partington Plans"), and October, 1896 ("The Adventure of the Veiled Lodger").**2**

3. A period between May, 1901 ("The Adventure of the Priory School"), and May, 1902 ("The Adventure of Shoscombe Old Place").

For an explanation of this third break, we cannot do better than to quote the words of the late Edgar W. Smith, in "Dr. Watson and the Great Censorship." After Holmes' Return in 1894

> the game was everywhere afoot. Great Sherlock strode the stage in majesty and dominance, and evil-doers cringed and slunk away. But for all the world might know, as far as John H. Watson was concerned, his friend lay crushed and broken still at the bottom of the Reichenbach Falls. **3**
>
> Back in 1890, before his disappearance, Holmes had told Watson quite bluntly that he had "degraded what should have been a course of lectures into a series of tales" ("The Adventure of the Copper Beeches"). . . . He accused him of recounting his stories "wrong end foremost" ("The Adventure of Wisteria Lodge"). And he said later, with even heavier sarcasm, "You slur over work of the utmost finesse and delicacy, in order to dwell upon sensational details which may excite, but cannot possibly instruct, the reader" ("The Adventure of the Abbey Grange"). No Wonder Watson felt impelled to hold his peace.
>
> We shall never learn what it was that broke the spell of silence—whether it was some new and urgent economic need, or an irresistible excess of enthusiasm, or sheer perverse defiance of the wishes of his friend—but the fact remains that in August, 1901, Watson threw caution to the winds and gave the world another tale of Sherlock Holmes. The *Strand Magazine* for that month carried the first instalment of an old and almost forgotten adventure, which was to run until April, 1902, under the title of *The Hound of the Baskervilles*. While this story was appearing, Watson was relegated arbitrarily to Holmes' outer limbo, for he shows no knowledge whatsoever of any of the Master's cases during the whole period in which the *Hound* was running.

About the cause of the 1895–1896 break, however, there is considerable difference of opinion.

The late H. W. Bell, as we shall see, when we come to consider "The Fair Sex" as Watson's department, suggested a quick marriage in 1896 lasting somewhat less than a year, but this suggestion has not survived careful examination.

Mr. Elliot Kimball, in "The Missing Year," has suggested a less legitimate liaison: in November of 1895, Mr. Kimball states, Watson met a blue-eyed blonde; an *affaire de cœur* persisted for a twelve-month. "Watson was no longer willing to temporize; hole-in-the-corner assignations were both distressing and ignoble; the Baker Street scene offered no scope for erotic exercises; wherefore, Watson cut the painter, took rooms, and departed from 221B, like a matured fledgling from the nest."

The late Gavin Brend advanced evidence pointing to a temporary estrangement between Holmes and Watson caused partly by Watson's excessive gambling on horses and partly by Watson's persistent nagging of Holmes about the drug habit, especially annoying to the detective because he knew he had permanently freed himself from the habit.

Mr. William D. Jenkins has recently (1964) put forward an extremely novel and interesting suggestion, for which the reader is referred to "The Adventure of the Solitary Cyclist," Note 3.

On the other hand, we may also recall here Holmes' marked reluctance to confide fully in Watson when he was engaged in matters of Government importance ("One has to be discreet when one talks of high matters of State").**4** We should also recall that Holmes' last recorded case in 1895 was "The Adventure of the Bruce-Partington Plans," at the conclusion of which he spent a day at Windsor and returned to Baker Street with a remarkably fine emerald tiepin. If "high matters of State" should call for investigation a short time later in the year 1895 or early in 1896, is it thinkable that those in high places in Britain would call on the services of any other investigator?

It is not, and we conclude that almost certainly Sherlock Holmes conducted a supremely important investigation for the British Crown in 1895–1896—and Watson, unfortunately for all of us, had to be left behind.

In this connection, we have two very interesting suggestions, the first of which has been put forward by Mr. L. A. Morrow in his essay, "A Diplomatic Secret": Mr. Morrow notes that in 1896 Guglielmo Marconi, the inventor of wireless, went to England armed with a letter to Sir William Preece, Engineer-in-Chief of the British Post Office, and a promise of help from his cousin Jameson Davis, a man "in considerable practice as an engineer in London." Mr. Davis afterward recalled how Marconi's "instruments were broken by the customs authorities, as they were not understood and were thought to be dangerous. New instruments had to be procured and these we ordered to Marconi's specifications." Finally, Marconi was ready to demonstrate his wireless in England and to try to get capital together for future expanded experimental work. Quoting *Marconi, the Man and His Wireless*, by Orrin E. Dunlap, Jr.; The Macmillan Company, New York, 1937, Mr. Morrow continues:

"Britain was interested in this thing called wireless and was anxious to get to the root of it." The British Government must have been more than a little annoyed at the customs authorities who had broken Marconi's instruments. We can imagine Mycroft, who occasionally *was*

4 See Dr. Felix Morley's illuminating remarks on this subject in "The Adventure of the Bruce-Partington Plans," Note 4.

5 It will be recalled that Holmes visited Poldhu in the March of 1897, at the time of "The Adventure of the Devil's Foot."

the British Government, saying decisively, "You must drop everything, Sherlock! Marconi must be protected not only from petty government officials but from crackpots who would interfere with his experiments. And you must find a good location on the coast for a high-powered transmitting station, too. Leave no stone unturned! This young Italian genius may be able to transmit clear across the Atlantic if he has a proper spot for his aerial." . . . Of course the assignment was carried out with Holmes' usual efficiency. There is no record of any more broken instruments nor of interference to experiments. On the contrary, successful tests were conducted at several locations . . . and in July of 1897 Marconi's company was incorporated with a capitalisation of £100,000. It is not difficult to guess the name of at least one of the original subscribers. . . .

Holmes' suggested site for the transmitting station was at Poldhu, in Cornwall:**5** In July of 1900 Marconi "went to the barren southwest tip of England and selected Poldhu . . . as the site for a pioneer transmitter, 199 times more powerful than any station ever built."

Our second suggestion concerning Holmes' activities in the missing year 1895–1896 comes from Dr. John D. Clark. In "A Chemist's View of Canonical Chemistry," Dr. Clark writes:

It has been remarked by many Sherlockian scholars that there is no record of Holmes' activities from the latter part of 1895 until October, 1896. Where the Canon offers no clue there is probably a good reason for the lack: " 'The dog did nothing in the night-time.' 'That was the curious incident' . . ." Under these circumstances, it is imperative that the student search somewhere else than in the field of criminology if he is to find traces of the activities of Mr. Sherlock Holmes.

The traces are there, and it is a remarkable fact that they have not already been pointed out. For in the year 1896 there appeared a series of papers which changed the history of the world—and may yet terminate it. And the *style* of the research they record is the style of Mr. Sherlock Holmes.

In 1895, M. Antoine Henri Becquerel (1852–1908), the third of a line of distinguished French scientists, was appointed to the chair of physics at the École Polytechnique in Paris. He immediately turned his attention to the fascinating question of the nature and properties of the X-rays, which had been discovered by W. K. Roentgen (1845–1923) less than a year previously. It is inconceivable that Holmes could have been unaware of this discovery. Nor is it unreasonable to believe that he, with his close connections with the scientific life of France, would have had any difficulty in obtaining entrance to the laboratories of the École Polytechnique, and to that of M. Becquerel. (After all, security and "need to know" had not yet been invented.) And it can hardly be doubted that once he had gained entrance to the laboratory, he would profoundly influence the course of the investigations conducted therein.

For consider what happened in the laboratory of M. Becquerel. It was known that X-rays were a peculiarly penetrating type of radiation, and that they produced a phosphorent effect when they impinged upon glass. Reasoning by analogy (frequently a dangerous procedure), several scientists thought that substances phosphorescent in ordinary light might themselves be emitting a penetrating radiation. M. Becquerel, testing this hypothesis, placed a certain phosphorescent material on top of an unexposed photographic plate wrapped in black paper, left it to its own devices for some days, and then developed the plate. Sure enough, the developed plate showed a faint image of the phosphorescent sample.

In the subsequent course of the investigation the methods of Holmes are so conspicuously present that it is impossible to conceive of his physical absence from the scene. For consider what happened next. Other phosphorescent materials were tried. Negative results. Conclusion: The phosphorescence of the original compound had nothing to do with its effect on the photographic plate. Then other, *non*-phosphorescent compounds containing the same elements as the original sample were tried. Positive results. Ergo—one particular element produced a penetrating radiation. Did others? The investigator (or more properly, and probably, investigators) tried compounds of every element they could lay their hands on. No results. "'. . . when all other contingencies fail, whatever remains, however, improbable, must be the truth.'" One element, and one element alone, of the dozens available to the investigators, spontaneously emitted a penetrating radiation, similar to X-rays.

The name of that element was uranium.

Holmes returned to London in October, 1896, when the papers reporting the discovery of radioactivity were either in print or in preparation. The basic discovery had been made, and he left its exploitation and development to others. Why he permitted no mention of his name in connection with the discovery is a fascinating question, but when, in 1903, M. Becquerel and M. Pierre Curie shared the Nobel Prize in chemistry, Holmes must have received the news with somewhat mixed feelings.

Perhaps he was just a little too far-sighted to wish his name to be associated with the most shattering discovery since the domestication of fire. If he could foresee even a little of the consequences, his early retirement to the Sussex Downs was not unreasonable. He wanted to enjoy them while they were still there.

Holmes was a distinguished forensic chemist. But it is only fair to remind the world that as a chemist he was something more. From Baker Street to the École Polytechnique to the Rutherford Laboratories at Cambridge, and on to Almagordo—the trace is there for anyone to see.

"REVERIES"

Wyndham Robinson pictures Holmes, in a nostalgic mood, meditating on some of the early Sidney Paget drawings.

17

THE ADVENTURE OF THE SPECKLED BAND

[*Friday, April 6, 1883*]

IN glancing over my notes of the seventy odd cases in which I have during the last eight years studied the **1** methods of my friend Sherlock Holmes, I find many tragic, some comic, a large number merely strange, but none commonplace ; for, working as he did rather for the love of his art than for the acquirement of wealth, he refused to associate himself with any investigation which did not tend towards the unusual, and even the fantastic. Of all these varied cases, however, I cannot recall any which presented more singular features than that which was associated with the well-known Surrey family of the **2** Roylotts of Stoke Moran. The events in question occurred in the early days of my association with Holmes, when we were sharing rooms as bachelors, in Baker Street. It is possible that I might have placed them upon record before, but a promise of secrecy was made at the time, from which I have only been freed during the last month by the untimely death of the lady to whom the pledge was given. It is perhaps as well that the facts should now come to light, for I have reasons to know there are widespread rumours as to the death of Dr. Grimesby Roylott which tend to make the matter even more terrible than the truth.

It was early in April, in the year '83, that I woke one **3** morning to find Sherlock Holmes standing, fully dressed, **4** by the side of my bed. He was a late riser as a rule, and, as the clock on the mantelpiece showed me that it was only a quarter past seven, I blinked up at him in some surprise, and perhaps just a little resentment, for I was myself regular in my habits.

" Very sorry to knock you up, Watson," said he, " but it's the common lot this morning. Mrs. Hudson has been knocked up, she retorted upon me, and I on you."

" What is it, then ? A fire ? "

" No, a client. It seems that a young lady has arrived in a considerable state of excitement, who insists upon seeing me. She is waiting now in the sitting-room. Now, when young ladies wander about the metropolis at this hour of the morning, and knock sleepy people up out of their beds, I presume that it is something very pressing which they have to communicate. Should it prove to be an interesting case, you would, I am sure, wish to follow it from the outset. I thought at any rate that I should call **5** you, and give you the chance."

1 *the last eight years.* The Reverend Henry T. Folsom has suggested ("Seventeen Out of Twenty-Three") that "The Adventure of the Speckled Band" must have been written after May, 1891, "because the wording of the first paragragh indicates that Holmes is thought to be *already* dead at the time of writing: '. . . for, working as he *did* . . . he *refused* to associate himself with any investigation . . .' Note the use of tenses—the simple and apparently tragic past tense." This interpretation would mean that Watson shared "seventy odd cases" with Holmes between 1883, the year of "The Adventure of the Speckled Band," and 1891. Mr. Frank A. Waters has estimated ("Upon the Probable Number of Cases of Mr. Sherlock Holmes") that the detective by the time of his retirement in late October, 1903, had handled some 1,700 cases.

2 *Surrey.* One of the "Home Counties" around London, Surrey is chiefly an agricultural county with some dairying and sheep raising. Here are Croyden (airport), Wimbledon (tennis matches), Epsom (horse racing) and Kew (botanical gardens). King John signed the Magna Carta at Runnymede in Surrey in the year 1215. Holmes found Surrey criminally fertile: it was the scene, not only of "The Adventure of the Speckled Band," but also of "The Reigate Squires," "The Naval Treaty," the adventures of the "Solitary Cyclist" and "Wisteria Lodge."

3 *It was early in April, in the year '83.* No Sherlockian chronologist in the long list that includes Baring-Gould, Bell, Blakeney, Brend, Christ, Folsom, Pattrick, Petersen, Smith, and Zeisler has so far disagreed with Dr. Watson, although your editor cannot agree with the consensus that the day of the adventure was Wednesday, April 4th.

4 *fully dressed.* "Holmes was fully dressed when he awakened Watson at 7:15 on a morning in April, '83," Mr. James Edward Holroyd commented in his column, "The Egg Spoon." "But if the visit of Miss Stoner was as urgent as he appeared to think, why waste valuable minutes getting into his own clothes before rousing Watson? Why not have slipped on one of his many dressing gowns? Or if

Masterly modesty forbade him to appear before a lady so scantily garbed, why not have asked Mrs. Hudson to call the doctor immediately?"

5 *you would, I am sure, wish to follow it.* We see that Watson in the past two years has firmly established himself as Holmes' comrade in detection.

6 *Leatherhead.* A small town on the river Mole with a narrow main street and several old inns, notably the Swan and the Running Horse. Its industries include tanning, brewing, and the manufacture of bricks and tiles.

7 *Waterloo.* The largest and finest railway terminal in Great Britain, Waterloo and its approaches cover the great part of the land enclosed by York Road, Waterloo Road, Lambeth Lower Marsh, and Westminster Bridge Road. The original terminus of the former London and South Western Railway was situated at Nine Elms, Vauxhall, at great inconvenience to London passengers who had to continue into the metropolis by bus, steamboat, or cab. In consequence, in 1848, the Railway extended their line to Waterloo at a cost of £800,000, most of it spent for the six bridges that had to be constructed along the two miles of new line. The present station, which was rebuilt between 1900 and 1921, covers two and a quarter acres, has twenty-one platforms and a normal service of 1,200 trains a day. It was formally opened by Queen Mary on March 21, 1922.

SHE RAISED HER VEIL AS SHE SPOKE, AND WE COULD SEE THAT SHE WAS INDEED IN A PITIABLE STATE OF AGITATION . . .

Illustration by Sidney Paget for the *Strand Magazine*, February, 1892.

"My dear fellow, I would not miss it for anything."

I had no keener pleasure than in following Holmes in his professional investigations, and in admiring the rapid deductions, as swift as intuitions, and yet always founded on a logical basis, with which he unravelled the problems which were submitted to him. I rapidly threw on my clothes, and was ready in a few minutes to accompany my friend down to the sitting-room. A lady dressed in black and heavily veiled, who had been sitting in the window, rose as we entered.

"Good morning, madam," said Holmes cheerily. "My name is Sherlock Holmes. This is my intimate friend and associate, Dr. Watson, before whom you can speak as freely as before myself. Ha, I am glad to see that Mrs. Hudson has had the good sense to light the fire. Pray draw up to it, and I shall order you a cup of hot coffee, for I observe that you are shivering."

"It is not cold which makes me shiver," said the woman in a low voice, changing her seat as requested.

"What then?"

"It is fear, Mr. Holmes. It is terror." She raised her veil as she spoke, and we could see that she was indeed in a pitiable state of agitation, her face all drawn and grey, with restless, frightened eyes, like those of some hunted animal. Her features and figure were those of a woman of thirty, but her hair was shot with premature grey, and her expression was weary and haggard. Sherlock Holmes ran her over with one of his quick, all-comprehensive glances.

"You must not fear," said he soothingly, bending forward and patting her forearm. "We shall soon set matters right, I have no doubt. You have come in by train this morning, I see."

"You know me, then?"

"No, but I observe the second half of a return ticket in the palm of your left glove. You must have started early, and yet you had a good drive in a dog-cart, along heavy roads, before you reached the station."

The lady gave a violent start, and stared in bewilderment at my companion.

"There is no mystery, my dear madam," said he, smiling. "The left arm of your jacket is spattered with mud in no less than seven places. The marks are perfectly fresh. There is no vehicle save a dog-cart which throws up mud in that way, and then only when you sit on the left-hand side of the driver."

"Whatever your reasons may be, you are perfectly correct," said she. "I started from home before six, **6** reached Leatherhead at twenty past, and came in by the **7** first train to Waterloo. Sir, I can stand this strain no longer, I shall go mad if it continues. I have no one to turn to—none, save only one, who cares for me, and he, poor fellow, can be of little aid. I have heard of you, Mr. Holmes; I have heard of you from Mrs. Farintosh, whom you helped in the hour of her sore need. It was from her that I had your address. Oh, sir, do you not think you could help me too, and at least throw a little light through the dense darkness which surrounds me? At present it is out of my power to reward you for your services, but in a month or two I shall be married, with the control of my own income, and then at least you shall not find me ungrateful."

Holmes turned to his desk, and unlocking it, drew out a small case-book which he consulted.

"Farintosh," said he. "Ah, yes, I recall the case ; it was concerned with an opal tiara. I think it was before your time, Watson. I can only say, madam, that I shall **8** be happy to devote the same care to your case as I did to that of your friend. As to reward, my profession is its reward ; but you are at liberty to defray whatever expenses I may be put to, at the time which suits you best. And **9** now I beg that you will lay before us everything that may help us in forming an opinion upon the matter."

"Alas !" replied our visitor. " The very horror of my situation lies in the fact that my fears are so vague, and my suspicions depend so entirely upon small points, which might seem trivial to another, that even he to whom of all others I have a right to look for help and advice looks upon all that I tell him about it as the fancies of a nervous woman. He does not say so, but I can read it from his soothing answers and averted eyes. But I have heard, Mr. Holmes, that you can see deeply into the manifold wickedness of the human heart. You may advise me how to walk amid the dangers which encompass me."

"I am all attention, madam."

" My name is Helen Stoner, and I am living with my stepfather, who is the last survivor of one of the oldest Saxon families in England, the Roylotts of Stoke Moran, on the western border of Surrey."   **10**

Holmes nodded his head. " The name is familiar to me," said he.

" The family was at one time among the richest in England, and the estate extended over the borders into Berkshire in the north, and Hampshire in the west. In **11-12** the last century, however, four successive heirs were of a dissolute and wasteful disposition, and the family ruin was eventually completed by a gambler, in the days of the Regency. Nothing was left save a few acres of ground **13** and the two-hundred-year-old house, which is itself crushed under a heavy mortgage. The last squire dragged out his existence there, living the horrible life of an aristocratic pauper ; but his only son, my stepfather, seeing that he must adapt himself to the new conditions, obtained an advance from a relative, which enabled him to take a medical degree, and went out to Calcutta, where, by his professional skill and his force of character, he established a large practice. In a fit of anger, however, caused by some robberies which had been perpetrated in the house, he beat his native butler to death, and narrowly escaped a capital sentence. As it was, he suffered a long term of imprisonment, and afterwards returned to England a morose and disappointed man.

" When Dr. Roylott was in India he married my mother, Mrs. Stoner, the young widow of Major-General Stoner, of the Bengal Artillery. My sister Julia and I were twins, **14** and we were only two years old at the time of my mother's re-marriage. She had a considerable sum of money, not less than a thousand a year, and this she bequeathed to

8 *I think it was before your time, Watson.* Mr. Howard Collins has asked ("Ex Libris Sherlock Holmes"): "But if [the case of Mrs. Farintosh] was before Watson's time, how did [Helen Stoner] get the Baker Street address?" And he has answered himself by saying: "Elementary! The case was begun before Holmes and Watson met, and the bill was rendered after the case was completed, by which time Holmes had moved to Baker Street." If Holmes rendered his bills on the first of the month, the case can thus be dated the first week in January, 1881.

9 *to defray whatever expenses I may be put to.* Holmes has come a long way in the two years which have passed since he depended for his bread and cheese on the clients to whose stories he listened, commented, and then pocketed his fee (*A Study in Scarlet*). As Mr. Thayer Cumings has noted ("Concerning Mr. Holmes' Fees"), Holmes "could afford to dine on 'oysters, a brace of grouse and something a little choice in white wine.' He could afford three shots of cocaine a day for many months at a time ('a seven per cent solution'). He could afford to go at will to the opera, or to Hallé's concert hall to hear Madame Norman-Neruda, and always to travel in the railway carriage first-class. He could afford to buy a Stradivarius. He could even afford a villa whenever he wanted one, or to travel abroad for as long as three years, and as far away as Tibet and Persia . . ." The fees which he must have collected to be able to afford these luxuries, Mr. Cumings thinks, "came from those cases for which we have not yet been prepared. . . . It must have been . . . [the] fascinating day-to-day *unrecorded* adventures which provided him with the wherewithal to live—and live to the hilt —the wonderful life he lived. *Lives*."

10 *on the western border of Surrey.* ". . . though no map, today or of 1883, will show the name 'Stoke Moran,' a little consideration of the clues will make it certain that Watson, under the name 'Stoke Moran,' has rather clumsily sought to conceal the identity of Stoke D'Abernon, a village some three miles (in a direct line) from the now populous town of Leatherhead," Mr. Michael Harrison wrote (*In the Footsteps of Sherlock Holmes*). The Roylott house—now demolished—Mr. Harrison has placed between the still-existing Slyfield House and Woodlands Park.

However: Miss Stoner has said that she "started from home before six, reached Leatherhead at twenty past, and came in by the first train to Waterloo." She reached Baker Street about seven, for Holmes, fully dressed, "knocked up" Watson at "only a quarter past seven." Reviewing this data Mr. Roger T. Clapp has pointed out (in "The Curious Problem of the Railway Timetables") that an examination of a Bradshaw of the period and the *A B C Railway Guide*, an equally reliable publication dating back to 1853, "discloses the singular fact that Helen Stoner could not have left Leatherhead in the morning in time to reach Baker Street by seven. The earliest train from Leatherhead to Waterloo left at 7:22, arriving at 8:11. Even if, allowing for a minor inaccuracy by Watson, she had actually taken the earlier train at 7:13 for London Bridge she still could not have arrived in the city before eight. . . . Helen Stoner undoubtedly did take a 6:20 train to London but not from Leatherhead since wherever Stoke Moran actually was it was not twenty minutes by dog-cart from Leatherhead. . . . If, for example, [Stoke Moran] was some twenty minutes by dog-cart from Clapham Junction then Helen Stoner could have easily caught the 6:25 to Waterloo arriving there at 6:39 and in ample time to get to Baker Street by seven."

11 *Berkshire*. Or Berks, an inland county in the Thames River basin. Largely agricultural, Berkshire has dairying and hog raising. At Windsor is the famous royal castle at which a certain gracious lady rewarded Holmes with an emerald tiepin. It was to Berkshire that Holmes and Watson went to solve the mystery of "Shoscombe Old Place."

12 *Hampshire*. In size the seventh of the English counties, Hampshire is packed with history. Romans, Saxons, Danes, and Normans landed there. Winchester was the first capital of a united England, and for a short period the capital, too, of a Scandinavian Empire. Many battles have been fought within its borders, and in the Puritan victory in Cheriton Wood which, so Clarendon recorded, "broke all the measures and altered the whole scheme of the king's counsels," the Civil War came to its end. It remains one of the most rural of the counties near London. Hampshire provided Holmes and Watson with two adventures, those of "The Copper Beeches" and "Thor Bridge."

13 *the Regency*. The last nine years, 1811–1820, of the reign of George III when, due to his periodic insanity, the government was conducted in the name of the Prince of Wales, later George IV. There was in truth a gay and dissolute group around the prince regent, of which the Roylott heir may well have been one.

14 *My sister Julia and I were twins*. It is interesting to note that in Conan Doyle's original manuscript, Helen Stoner is Helen Roylott, and Dr. Roylott is her father. In the 1910 play version, Helen and Julia appear as Enid and Violet Stonor (not Stoner). This last adds another bloom to the author's curious collection of Violets.

15 *Crewe*. An important railway junction in the county of Cheshire.

"LAST WEEK HE HURLED THE LOCAL BLACKSMITH OVER A PARAPET INTO A STREAM . . ."

Illustration by Sidney Paget for the *Strand Magazine*, February, 1892.

Dr. Roylott entirely whilst we resided with him, with a provision that a certain annual sum should be allowed to each of us in the event of our marriage. Shortly after our return to England my mother died—she was killed eight years ago in a railway accident near Crewe. Dr. Roylott then abandoned his attempts to establish himself in practice in London, and took us to live with him in the ancestral house at Stoke Moran. The money which my mother had left was enough for all our wants, and there seemed no obstacle to our happiness.

" But a terrible change came over our stepfather about this time. Instead of making friends and exchanging visits with our neighbours, who had at first been overjoyed to see a Roylott of Stoke Moran back in the old family seat, he shut himself up in his house, and seldom came out save to indulge in ferocious quarrels with whoever might cross his path. Violence of temper approaching to mania has been hereditary in the men of the family, and in my stepfather's case it had, I believe, been intensified by his long residence in the tropics. A series of disgraceful brawls took place, two of which ended in the police-court, until at last he became the terror of the village, and the folks would fly at his approach, for he is a man of immense strength, and absolutely uncontrollable in his anger.

" Last week he hurled the local blacksmith over a parapet into a stream and it was only by paying over all the money that I could gather together that I was able to avert another public exposure. He had no friends at all save the wandering gipsies, and he would give these vagabonds leave to encamp upon the few acres of bramble-covered land which represent the family estate, and would accept

in return the hospitality of their tents, wandering away with them sometimes for weeks on end.   He has a passion also for Indian animals, which are sent over to him by a correspondent, and he has at this moment a cheetah and a baboon, which wander freely over his grounds, and are **16** feared by the villagers almost as much as their master.

" You can imagine from what I say that my poor sister Julia and I had no great pleasure in our lives.   No servant would stay with us, and for a long time we did all the work of the house.   She was but thirty at the time of her death, and yet her hair had already begun to whiten, even as mine has."

" Your sister is dead, then ? "

" She died just two years ago, and it is of her death that I wish to speak to you.   You can understand that, living the life which I have described, we were little likely to see anyone of our own age and position.   We had, however, an aunt, my mother's maiden sister, Miss Honoria West- phail, who lives near Harrow, and we were occasionally **17** allowed to pay short visits at this lady's house.   Julia went there at Christmas two years ago, and met there a half-pay **18** Major of Marines, to whom she became engaged.   My stepfather learned of the engagement when my sister returned, and offered no objection to the marriage ; but within a fortnight of the day which had been fixed for the wedding, the terrible event occurred which has deprived me of my only companion."

Sherlock Holmes had been leaning back in his chair with his eyes closed, and his head sunk in a cushion, but he half opened his lids now, and glanced across at his visitor.

" Pray be precise as to details," said he.

" It is easy for me to be so, for every event of that dreadful time is seared into my memory.   The manor house is, as I have already said, very old, and only one wing is now inhabited.   The bedrooms in this wing are on the ground floor, the sitting-rooms being in the central block of the buildings.   Of these bedrooms, the first is Dr. Roylott's, the second my sister's, and the third my own. There is no communication between them, but they all open out into the same corridor.   Do I make myself plain ? "

" Perfectly so."

" The windows of the three rooms open out upon the lawn.   That fatal night Dr. Roylott had gone to his room early, though we knew that he had not retired to rest, for my sister was troubled by the smell of the strong Indian cigars which it was his custom to smoke.   She left her room, therefore, and came into mine, where she sat for some time, chatting about her approaching wedding.   At eleven o'clock she rose to leave me, but she paused at the door and looked back.

" ' Tell me, Helen,' said she, ' have you ever heard any- one whistle in the dead of the night ? '

" ' Never,' said I.

" ' I suppose that you could not possibly whistle your- self in your sleep ? '

" ' Certainly not.   But why ? '

" ' Because during the last few nights I have always, about three in the morning, heard a low clear whistle.   I

16 *a cheetah and a baboon.* "I don't know what kind of a watch-dog a baboon develops into," Mr. James Edward Holroyd wrote in "The Egg Spoon," "but to judge from this extract from *African Hunter* by J. A. Hunter (London: Hamish, Hamilton, 1954), Holmes and Watson had little to fear from the other half of the partnership: 'The cheetah is a long-legged cat, very gentle, and once much in demand among the Indian rajahs who domesticated them and kept them to hunt antelope, much as greyhounds are kept to course hares. Cheetahs are so good-natured that even an adult animal can easily be tamed. I do not believe that in the entire history of Africa there has been a single case of a cheetah attacking a human being.' It is of course possible that the Stoke Moran cheetah, having been sent from India, was a more intractable species than the one described above; just as, in reverse, the African elephant is less amenable to training than his Indian counterpart."

Despite Miss Stoner's "Indian animals," the pos- sibility exists that *both* the cheetah and the baboon came from Africa: apart from the small black baboon (*Cynopithecus niger* of the Celebes), as the editors of the Catalogue of the Sherlock Holmes Exhibition pointed out, baboons are confined to Africa and Arabia.

17 *Harrow.* In Middlesex, the home of the famous public school.

18 *half-pay.* The reduced pay of an army or navy officer when he is not on active service.

am a light sleeper, and it has awakened me. I cannot tell where it came from—perhaps from the next room, perhaps from the lawn. I thought that I would just ask you whether you had heard it.'

" ' No, I have not. It must be those wretched gipsies in the plantation.'

" ' Very likely. And yet if it were on the lawn I wonder that you did not hear it also.'

" ' Ah, but I sleep more heavily than you.'

" ' Well, it is of no great consequence, at any rate,' she smiled back at me, closed my door, and a few moments later I heard her key turn in the lock."

" Indeed," said Holmes. " Was it your custom always to lock yourselves in at night ? "

" Always."

" And why ? "

" I think that I mentioned to you that the Doctor kept a cheetah and a baboon. We had no feeling of security unless our doors were locked."

" Quite so. Pray proceed with your statement."

" I could not sleep that night. A vague feeling of impending misfortune impressed me. My sister and I, you will recollect, were twins, and you know how subtle are the links which bind two souls which are so closely allied. It was a wild night. The wind was howling outside, and the rain was beating and splashing against the windows. Suddenly, amidst all the hubbub of the gale, there burst forth the wild scream of a terrified woman. I knew that it was my sister's voice. I sprang from my bed, wrapped a shawl round me, and rushed into the corridor. As I opened my door I seemed to hear a low whistle, such as my sister described, and a few moments later a clanging sound, as if a mass of metal had fallen. As I ran down the passage my sister's door was unlocked, and revolved slowly upon its hinges. I stared at it horror-stricken, not knowing what was about to issue from it. By the light of the corridor lamp I saw my sister appear at the opening, her face blanched with terror, her hands groping for help, her whole figure swaying to and fro like that of a drunkard. I ran to her and threw my arms round her, but at that moment her knees seemed to give way and she fell to the ground. She writhed as one who is in terrible pain, and her limbs were dreadfully convulsed. At first I thought that she had not recognized me, but as I bent over her she suddenly shrieked out in a voice which I shall never forget, ' O, my God ! Helen ! It was the band ! The speckled band ! ' There was something else which she would fain have said, and she stabbed with her finger into the air in the direction of the Doctor's room, but a fresh convulsion seized her and choked her words. I rushed out, calling loudly for my stepfather, and I met him hastening from his room in his dressing-gown. When he reached my sister's side she was unconscious, and though he poured brandy down her throat, and sent for medical aid from the village, all efforts were in vain, for she slowly sank and died without having recovered her consciousness. Such was the dreadful end of my beloved sister."

" One moment," said Holmes ; " are you sure about this whistle and metallic sound ? Could you swear to it ? "

" That was what the county coroner asked me at the

" . . . I SAW MY SISTER APPEAR IN THE OPENING, HER FACE BLANCHED WITH TERROR . . ."

Illustration by Sidney Paget for the *Strand Magazine*, February, 1892.

inquiry.   It is my strong impression that I heard it, and yet among the crash of the gale, and the creaking of an old house, I may possibly have been deceived.”

“ Was your sister dressed ? ”

“ No, she was in her nightdress.   In her right hand was found the charred stump of a match, and in her left a matchbox.”

20

“ Showing that she had struck a light and looked about her when the alarm took place.   That is important.   And what conclusions did the coroner come to ? ”

“ He investigated the case with great care, for Dr. Roy-lott’s conduct had long been notorious in the county, but he was unable to find any satisfactory cause of death.   My evidence showed that the door had been fastened upon the inner side, and the windows were blocked by old-fashioned shutters with broad iron bars, which were secured every night.   The walls were carefully sounded, and were shown to be quite solid all round, and the flooring was also thoroughly examined, with the same result.   The chimney is wide, but is barred up by four large staples.   It is certain, therefore, that my sister was quite alone when she met her end.   Besides, there were no marks of any violence upon her.”

“ How about poison ? ”

“ The doctors examined her for it, but without success.”

“ What do you think that this unfortunate lady died of, then ? ”

“ It is my belief that she died of pure fear and nervous shock, though what it was which frightened her I cannot imagine.”

“ Were there gipsies in the plantation at the time ? ”

“ Yes, there are nearly always some there.”

“ Ah, and what did you gather from this allusion to a band—a speckled band ? ”

“ Sometimes I have thought that it was merely the wild talk of delirium, sometimes that it may have referred to some band of people, perhaps to these very gipsies in the plantation.   I do not know whether the spotted handkerchiefs which so many of them wear over their heads might have suggested the strange adjective which she used.”

Holmes shook his head like a man who is far from being satisfied.

“ These are very deep waters,” said he ; “ pray go on with your narrative.”

“ Two years have passed since then, and my life has been until lately lonelier than ever.   A month ago, however, a dear friend, whom I have known for many years, has done me the honour to ask my hand in marriage.   His name is Armitage—Percy Armitage—the second son of Mr. Armitage, of Crane Water, near Reading.   My step- **21** father has offered no opposition to the match, and we are to be married in the course of the spring.   Two days ago some repairs were started in the west wing of the building, **22** and my bedroom wall has been pierced, so that I have had to move into the chamber in which my sister died, and to sleep in the very bed in which she slept.   Imagine, then, my thrill of terror when last night, as I lay awake, thinking over her terrible fate, I suddenly heard in the silence of the night the low whistle which had been the herald of her own death.   I sprang up and lit the lamp, but nothing was to

19 *he poured brandy down her throat.* In many later cases, we shall see that Dr. Watson also uses brandy as his almost universal specific. “It is still held by many physicians and pharmacologists as well that brandy or whisky are useful therapeutic agents in emergencies,” Dr. Edward J. Van Liere wrote in “Dr. Watson’s Universal Specific.” “Dr. Torald Sellman, dean of American pharmacologists, in his textbook, *A Manual of Pharmacology,* W. B. Saunders Co., Philadelphia, 1946 6th ed., p. 704, writes: ‘Its temporary usefulness as a quickly acting stimulant can scarcely be doubted in the various forms of sudden circulatory collapse—syncope, exhaustion, hemorrhage, traumatic shock . . .’ He attributes its effect to reflex stimulation and on this account its action is brief. He writes further: ‘alcohol acts mainly as a temporary emergency remedy, to tide the patient over the immediate danger.’ He suggests a dose of 25 cc. of whisky or brandy (roughly an ounce) and that it should be repeated every 10 to 15 minutes according to effect.”

20 *and in her left a matchbox.”* Just how the unfortunate Julia Stoner’s hands could be “groping for help” with a match in her right hand and a matchbox in her left, we will leave to the reader to decide.

21 *Reading.* The county town of Berkshire, 36 miles southwest of London by Great Western Railway, a railway junction and agricultural center with famous nursery gardens. Oscar Wilde, who so much impressed Conan Doyle at their first meeting, wrote *The Ballad of Reading Gaol* while in prison there.

22 *some repairs were started in the west wing.* The repairs would not have been started on a Sunday, so the day on which Miss Stoner called on Holmes was not a Tuesday.

23 *as soon as it was daylight.* Miss Stoner has told us that she left Stoke Moran before 6:00 A.M. If it became daylight shortly before 6:00 A.M., the time of the year would have been early April, corroborating Watson.

24 *the crackling fire.* We will find several references in the Canon to "the crackling fire." (See, for example, "The Adventure of the Blue Carbuncle.") They are hard to understand. Holmes and Watson burned soft coal, surely, and soft coal may crack but seldom if ever crackles.

25 *upon some most important business.* The day was therefore a weekday.

be seen in the room.   I was too shaken to go to bed again,
23 however, so I dressed, and as soon as it was daylight I slipped down, got a dog-cart at the Crown Inn, which is opposite, and drove to Leatherhead, from whence I have come on this morning, with the one object of seeing you and asking your advice. '

" You have done wisely," said my friend.   " But have you told me all ? "

" Yes, all."

" Miss Stoner, you have not.   You are screening your stepfather."

" Why, what do you mean ? "

For answer Holmes pushed back the frill of black lace which fringed the hand that lay upon our visitor's knee. Five little livid spots, the marks of four fingers and a thumb, were printed upon the white wrist.

" You have been cruelly used," said Holmes.

The lady coloured deeply, and covered over her injured wrist.   " He is a hard man," she said, " and perhaps he hardly knows his own strength."

There was a long silence, during which Holmes leaned
24 his chin upon his hands and stared into the crackling fire.

" This is very deep business," he said at last.   " There are a thousand details which I should desire to know before I decide upon our course of action.   Yet we have not a moment to lose.   If we were to come to Stoke Moran to-day, would it be possible for us to see over these rooms without the knowledge of your stepfather ? "

" As it happens, he spoke of coming into town to-day
25 upon some most important business.   It is probable that he will be away all day, and that there would be nothing to disturb you.   We have a housekeeper now, but she is old and foolish, and I could easily get her out of the way."

" Excellent.   You are not averse to this trip, Watson ? "

" By no means."

" Then we shall both come.   What are you going to do yourself ? "

" I have one or two things which I would wish to do now that I am in town.   But I shall return by the twelve o'clock train, so as to be there in time for your coming."

" And you may expect us early in the afternoon.   I have myself some small business matters to attend to. Will you not wait and breakfast ? "

" No, I must go.   My heart is lightened already since I have confided my trouble to you.   I shall look forward to seeing you again this afternoon."   She dropped her thick black veil over her face, and glided from the room.

" And what do you think of it all, Watson ? " asked Sherlock Holmes, leaning back in his chair.

" It seems to me to be a most dark and sinister business."

" Dark enough and sinister enough."

" Yet if the lady is correct in saying that the flooring and walls are sound, and that the door, window, and chimney are impassable, then her sister must have been undoubtedly alone when she met her mysterious end."

" What becomes, then, of these nocturnal whistles, and what of the very peculiar words of the dying woman ? "

" I cannot think."

" When you combine the ideas of whistles at night, the

presence of a band of gipsies who are on intimate terms with this old doctor, the fact that we have every reason to believe that the doctor has an interest in preventing his stepdaughter's marriage, the dying allusion to a band, and finally, the fact that Miss Helen Stoner heard a metallic clang, which might have been caused by one of those metal bars which secured the shutters falling back into their place, I think there is good ground to think that the mystery may be cleared along those lines."

" But what, then, did the gipsies do ? "

" I cannot imagine."

" I see many objections to any such a theory."

" And so do I. It is precisely for that reason that we are going to Stoke Moran this day. I want to see whether the objections are fatal, or if they may be explained away. But what, in the name of the devil ! "

The ejaculation had been drawn from my companion by the fact that our door had been suddenly dashed open, and that a huge man framed himself in the aperture. His costume was a peculiar mixture of the professional and of the agricultural, having a black top-hat, a long frock-coat, and a pair of high gaiters, with a hunting-crop swinging in his hand. So tall was he that his hat actually brushed the cross-bar of the doorway, and his breadth seemed to span it across from side to side. A large face, seared with a thousand wrinkles, burned yellow with the sun, and marked with every evil passion, was turned from one to the other of us, while his deep-set, bile-shot eyes, and the high thin fleshless nose, gave him somewhat the resemblance to a fierce old bird of prey.

" Which of you is Holmes ? " asked this apparition.

" My name, sir, but you have the advantage of me," said my companion quietly.

" I am Dr. Grimesby Roylott, of Stoke Moran."

" Indeed, Doctor," said Holmes blandly. " Pray take a seat."

" I will do nothing of the kind. My stepdaughter has been here. I have traced her. What has she been saying to you ? "

" It is a little cold for the time of the year," said Holmes.

" What has she been saying to you ? " screamed the old man furiously.

" But I have heard that the crocuses promise well," continued my companion imperturbably.

" Ha ! You put me off, do you ? " said our new visitor, taking a step forward, and shaking his hunting-crop. " I know you, you scoundrel ! I have heard of you before. You are Holmes the meddler."

My friend smiled.

" Holmes the busybody ! "

His smile broadened.

" Holmes the Scotland Yard jack-in-office."

Holmes chuckled heartily. " Your conversation is most entertaining," said he. " When you go out close the door, for there is a decided draught."

" I will go when I have had my say. Don't you dare to meddle with my affairs. I know that Miss Stoner has been here—I traced her ! I am a dangerous man to fall foul of ! See here." He stepped swiftly forward, seized

. . . A HUGE MAN FRAMED HIMSELF IN THE APERTURE.

Illustration by Sidney Paget for the *Strand Magazine*, February, 1892.

HE STEPPED SWIFTLY FORWARD, SEIZED THE POKER, AND BENT IT INTO A CURVE WITH HIS HUGE BROWN HANDS.

Illustration by Joseph Camana for *Cases of Sherlock Holmes*, St. Louis: Webster Publishing Co., 1947.

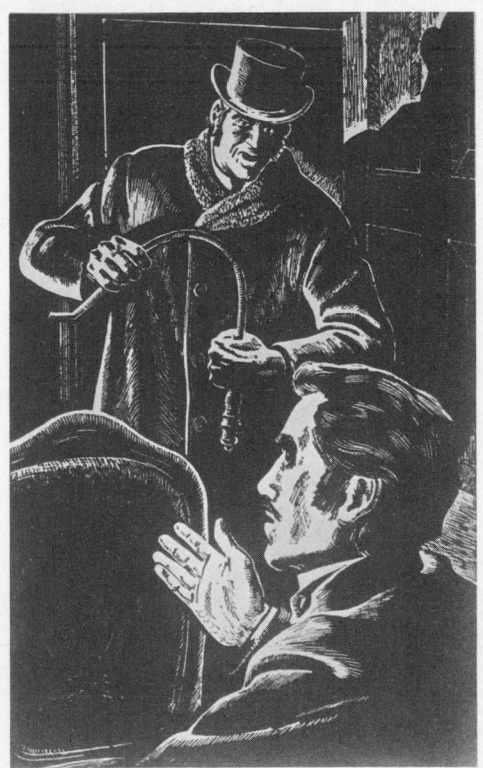

26 *Doctors' Commons.* Originally, the common table and dining hall of the Association or College of Doctors of Civil Law in London; later, the building near St. Paul's Churchyard, occupied by this corporation, in which there were ecclesiastical and admiralty courts and offices having jurisdiction over marriage licenses, divorces, registrations of wills, etc. The building was taken down in 1867; Holmes, in 1883, would have visited *Somerset House*, to which, in 1874, the wills previously registered at Doctors' Commons were transferred (a charge of one shilling is, and was, made for showing wills or registered copies thereof—an item for Holmes' expense account to Helen Stoner).

27 *an income of £250.* Worth, at the time, about $1,250 U.S. The total income, once amounting to about $5,000, had fallen to not more than $3,750.

28 *a trap.* Colloquial English for a one-horse, two-wheeled carriage on springs.

"... AN EXCELLENT ARGUMENT WITH GENTLEMEN WHO CAN TWIST STEEL POKERS INTO KNOTS."

This is not Watson's old service revolver, but a pistol acquired by him after his move to Baker Street. Actually, the gun was a *Webley's No. 2,* .320 bore, described in the Catalogue of the Sherlock Holmes Exhibition as "a small, heavy, but relatively effective weapon. . . . Essentially a pocket pistol it takes up little room but would be adequate for dealing with the most determined criminal. It was the smallest really practicable weapon of its time. . . . The Eley cartridges of the time were sold in boxes labeled to say which weapon they fitted; and [Holmes'] 'Eley No. 2' is probably a confusion arising out of a box marked in large letters 'Eley' and, in smaller letters, 'for the Webley Pistol, No. 2.' Moreover, some Webley pistols were marketed with 'Eley .320' on the barrel to prevent confusion with the Smith and Wesson .32, which was not the same as the British or Continental, .320, or the similar .32 Colt."

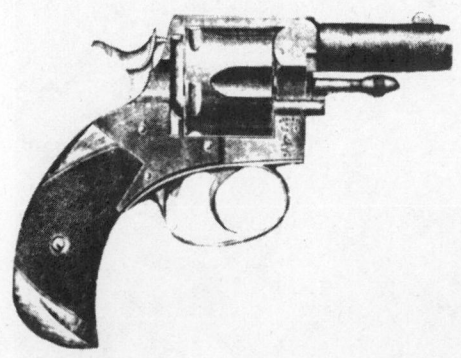

the poker, and bent it into a curve with his huge brown hands.

" See that you keep yourself out of my grip," he snarled, and hurling the twisted poker into the fireplace, he strode out of the room.

" He seems a very amiable person," said Holmes, laughing. " I am not quite so bulky, but if he had remained I might have shown him that my grip was not much more feeble than his own." As he spoke he picked up the steel poker, and with a sudden effort straightened it out again.

" Fancy his having the insolence to confound me with the official detective force ! This incident gives zest to our investigation, however, and I only trust that our little friend will not suffer from her imprudence in allowing this brute to trace her. And now, Watson, we shall order breakfast, and afterwards I shall walk down to Doctors'
26 Commons, where I hope to get some data which may help us in this matter."

It was nearly one o'clock when Sherlock Holmes returned from his excursion. He held in his hand a sheet of blue paper, scrawled over with notes and figures.

" I have seen the will of the deceased wife," said he. " To determine its exact meaning I have been obliged to work out the present prices of the investments with which it is concerned. The total income, which at the time of the wife's death was little short of £1,100, is now through the fall in agricultural prices not more than £750. Each
27 daughter can claim an income of £250, in case of marriage. It is evident, therefore, that if both girls had married this beauty would have had a mere pittance, while even one of them would cripple him to a serious extent. My morning's work has not been wasted, since it has proved that he has the very strongest motives for standing in the way of anything of the sort. And now, Watson, this is too serious for dawdling, especially as the old man is aware that we are interesting ourselves in his affairs, so if you are ready we shall call a cab and drive to Waterloo. I should be very much obliged if you would slip your revolver into your pocket. An Eley's No. 2 is an excellent argument with gentlemen who can twist steel pokers into knots. That and a tooth-brush are, I think, all that we need."

At Waterloo we were fortunate in catching a train for
28 Leatherhead, where we hired a trap at the station inn, and drove for four or five miles through the lovely Surrey
29 lanes. It was a perfect day, with a bright sun and a few fleecy clouds in the heavens. The trees and wayside hedges were just throwing out their first green shoots, and the air was full of the pleasant smell of the moist earth. To me at least there was a strange contrast between the sweet promise of the spring and this sinister quest upon which we were engaged. My companion sat in front of the trap, his arms folded, his hat pulled down over his eyes, and his chin sunk upon his breast, buried in the deepest thought. Suddenly, however, he started, tapped me on the shoulder, and pointed over the meadows.

" Look there ! " said he.

A heavily timbered park stretched up in a gentle slope, thickening into a grove at the highest point. From amidst the branches there jutted out the grey gables and high roof-tree of a very old mansion.

"Stoke Moran?" said he.

"Yes, sir, that be the house of Dr. Grimesby Roylott," remarked the driver.

"There is some building going on there," said Holmes; "that is where we are going."

"There's the village," said the driver, pointing to a cluster of roofs some distance to the left; "but if you want to get to the house, you'll find it shorter to go over this stile, and so by the footpath over the fields. There it is, where the lady is walking."

"And the lady, I fancy, is Miss Stoner," observed Holmes, shading his eyes. "Yes, I think we had better do as you suggest."

We got off, paid our fare, and the trap rattled back on its way to Leatherhead.

"I thought it as well," said Holmes, as we climbed the stile, "that this fellow should think we had come here as architects, or on some definite business. It may stop his gossip. Good afternoon, Miss Stoner. You see that we have been as good as our word."

Our client of the morning had hurried forward to meet us with a face which spoke her joy. "I have been waiting so eagerly for you," she cried, shaking hands with us warmly. "All has turned out splendidly. Dr. Roylott has gone to town, and it is unlikely that he will be back before evening."

"We have had the pleasure of making the Doctor's acquaintance," said Holmes, and in a few words he sketched out what had occurred. Miss Stoner turned white to the lips as she listened.

"Good heavens!" she cried, "he has followed me, then."

"So it appears."

"He is so cunning that I never know when I am safe from him. What will he say when he returns?"

"He must guard himself, for he may find that there is someone more cunning than himself upon his track. You must lock yourself from him to-night. If he is violent, we shall take you away to your aunt's at Harrow. Now, we must make the best use of our time, so kindly take us at once to the rooms which we are to examine."

The building was of grey, lichen-blotched stone, with a high central portion, and two curving wings, like the claws of a crab, thrown out on each side. In one of these wings the windows were broken, and blocked with wooden boards, while the roof was partly caved in, a picture of ruin. The central portion was in little better repair, but the right-hand block was comparatively modern, and the blinds in the windows, with the blue smoke curling up from the chimneys, showed that this was where the family resided. Some scaffolding had been erected against the end wall, and the stonework had been broken into, but there were no signs of any workmen at the moment of our visit. Holmes walked slowly up and down the ill-trimmed lawn, and examined with deep attention the outsides of the windows.

"This, I take it, belongs to the room in which you used

29 *It was a perfect day.* The day of the case was a bright, sunny day, and Wednesday, April 4, 1883, was a day on which the sun shone for only two hours and two minutes. The sun shone for nine hours and eight minutes on Monday, April 2, 1883, but we doubt that the repairs on the west wing would have been started on a Saturday. In your editor's opinion, the day was *Friday, April 6, 1883,* a day on which the sun shone for nine hours and two minutes. Early April is again corroborated by Watson's "first green shoots" and "sweet promise of the spring."

WE GOT OFF, PAID OUR FARE . . .

Illustration by Sidney Paget for the *Strand Magazine*, February, 1892.

30 *Wilton carpet.* A cut-pile Brussels carpet or rug first manufactured in the Wiltshire town of Wilton.

to sleep, the centre one to your sister's, and the one next to the main building to Dr. Roylott's chamber ? "

" Exactly so. But I am now sleeping in the middle one."

" Pending the alterations, as I understand. By the way, there does not seem to be any very pressing need for repairs at that end wall."

" There were none. I believe that it was an excuse to move me from my room."

" Ah ! that is suggestive. Now, on the other side of this narrow wing runs the corridor from which these three rooms open. There are windows in it, of course ? "

" Yes, but very small ones. Too narrow for anyone to pass through."

" As you both locked your doors at night, your rooms were unapproachable from that side. Now, would you have the kindness to go into your room, and to bar your shutters."

Miss Stoner did so, and Holmes, after a careful examination through the open window, endeavoured in every way to force the shutter open, but without success. There was no slit through which a knife could be passed to raise the bar. Then with his lens he tested the hinges, but they were of solid iron, built firmly into the massive masonry. " Hum ! " said he, scratching his chin in some perplexity, " my theory certainly presents some difficulties. No one could pass these shutters if they were bolted. Well, we shall see if the inside throws any light upon the matter."

A small side-door led into the whitewashed corridor from which the three bedrooms opened. Holmes refused to examine the third chamber, so we passed at once to the second, that in which Miss Stoner was now sleeping, and in which her sister had met her fate. It was a homely little room, with a low ceiling and a gaping fireplace, after the fashion of old country houses. A brown chest of drawers stood in one corner, a narrow white-counterpaned bed in another, and a dressing-table on the left-hand side of the window. These articles, with two small wicker-work chairs, made up all the furniture in the room, save **30** for a square of Wilton carpet in the centre. The boards round and the panelling of the walls were brown, worm-eaten oak, so old and discoloured that it may have dated from the original building of the house. Holmes drew one of the chairs into a corner and sat silent, while his eyes travelled round and round and up and down, taking in every detail of the apartment.

" Where does that bell communicate with ? " he asked at last, pointing to a thick bell-rope which hung down beside the bed, the tassel actually lying upon the pillow.

" It goes to the housekeeper's room."

" It looks newer than the other things ? "

" Yes, it was only put there a couple of years ago."

" Your sister asked for it, I suppose ? "

" No, I never heard of her using it. We used always to get what we wanted for ourselves."

" Indeed, it seemed unnecessary to put so nice a bell-pull there. You will excuse me for a few minutes while I satisfy myself as to this floor." He threw himself down upon his face with his lens in his hand, and crawled swiftly backwards and forwards, examining minutely the cracks between the boards. Then he did the same with the woodwork with which the chamber was panelled. Finally

"WHERE DOES THAT BELL COMMUNICATE WITH?" HE ASKED AT LAST . . .

A modern conception of Sherlock Holmes by Tom Gill, for the Simon and Schuster "Golden Picture Classic," *Sherlock Holmes*, 1957.

he walked over to the bed and spent some time in staring at it, and in running his eye up and down the wall.   Finally he took the bell-rope in his hand and gave it a brisk tug.

" Why, it's a dummy," said he.

" Won't it ring ? "

" No, it is not even attached to a wire.   This is very interesting.   You can see now that it is fastened to a hook just above where the little opening of the ventilator is."

" How very absurd !   I never noticed that before."

" Very strange ! " muttered Holmes, pulling at the rope. " There are one or two very singular points about this room.   For example, what a fool a builder must be to open a ventilator in another room, when, with the same trouble, he might have communicated with the outside air ! "

" That is also quite modern," said the lady.

" Done about the same time as the bell-rope," remarked Holmes.

" Yes, there were several little changes carried out about that time."

" They seem to have been of a most interesting character—dummy bell-ropes, and ventilators which do not ventilate.   With your permission, Miss Stoner, we shall now carry our researches into the inner apartment."

Dr. Grimesby Roylott's chamber was larger than that of his stepdaughter, but was as plainly furnished.   A camp bed, a small wooden shelf full of books, mostly of a technical character, an arm-chair beside the bed, a plain wooden chair against the wall, a round table, and a large iron safe were the principal things which met the eye. Holmes walked slowly round and examined each and all of them with the keenest interest.

" What's in here ? " he asked, tapping the safe.

" My stepfather's business papers."

" Oh ! you have seen inside, then ? "

" Only once, some years ago.   I remember that it was full of papers."

" There isn't a cat in it, for example ? "

" No.   What a strange idea ! "

" Well, look at this ! "   He took up a small saucer of milk which stood on the top of it.

" No ; we don't keep a cat.   But there is a cheetah and a baboon."

" Ah, yes, of course !   Well, a cheetah is just a big cat, and yet a saucer of milk does not go very far in satisfying its wants, I daresay.   There is one point which I should wish to determine."   He squatted down in front of the wooden chair, and examined the seat of it with the greatest attention.

" Thank you.   That is quite settled," said he, rising and putting his lens in his pocket.   " Hullo ! here is something interesting ! "

The object which had caught his eye was a small dog lash hung on one corner of the bed.   The lash, however, was curled upon itself, and tied so as to make a loop of whipcord.

" What do you make of that, Watson ? "

" It's a common enough lash.   But I don't know why it should be tied."

" That is not quite so common, is it ?   Ah, me ! it's a wicked world, and when a clever man turns his brain to

"WELL, LOOK AT THIS!" HE TOOK UP A SMALL SAUCER OF MILK . . .

Illustration by Sidney Paget for the *Strand Magazine*, February, 1892.

"GOOD-BYE, AND BE BRAVE . . ."

Illustration by Sidney Paget for the *Strand Magazine*, February, 1892.

crime it is the worst of all. I think that I have seen enough now, Miss Stoner, and, with your permission, we shall walk out upon the lawn."

I had never seen my friend's face so grim, or his brow so dark, as it was when we turned from the scene of this investigation. We had walked several times up and down the lawn, neither Miss Stoner nor myself liking to break in upon his thoughts before he roused himself from his reverie.

"It is very essential, Miss Stoner," said he, " that you should absolutely follow my advice in every respect."

"I shall most certainly do so."

"The matter is too serious for any hesitation. Your life may depend upon your compliance."

"I assure you that I am in your hands."

" In the first place, both my friend and I must spend the night in your room."

Both Miss Stoner and I gazed at him in astonishment.

"Yes, it must be so. Let me explain. I believe that that is the village inn over there ? "

"Yes, that is the ' Crown.' "

"Very good. Your windows would be visible from there ? "

"Certainly."

" You must confine yourself to your room, on pretence of a headache, when your stepfather comes back. Then when you hear him retire for the night, you must open the shutters of your window, undo the hasp, put your lamp there as a signal to us, and then withdraw with everything which you are likely to want into the room which you used to occupy. I have no doubt that, in spite of the repairs, you could manage there for one night."

"Oh, yes, easily."

"The rest you will leave in our hands."

"But what will you do ? "

"We shall spend the night in your room, and we shall investigate the cause of this noise which has disturbed you."

"I believe, Mr. Holmes, that you have already made up your mind," said Miss Stoner, laying her hand upon my companion's sleeve.

"Perhaps I have."

"Then for pity's sake tell me what was the cause of my sister's death."

"I should prefer to have clearer proofs before I speak."

"You can at least tell me whether my own thought is correct, and if she died from some sudden fright."

"No, I do not think so. I think that there was probably some more tangible cause. And now, Miss Stoner, we must leave you, for if Dr. Roylott returned and saw us, our journey would be in vain. Good-bye, and be brave, for if you will do what I have told you, you may rest assured that we shall soon drive away the dangers that threaten you."

Sherlock Holmes and I had no difficulty in engaging a bedroom and sitting-room at the Crown Inn. They were on the upper floor, and from our window we could command a view of the avenue gate, and of the inhabited wing of Stoke Moran Manor House. At dusk we saw Dr. Grimesby Roylott drive past, his huge form looming up beside the little figure of the lad who drove him. The boy had some slight difficulty in undoing the heavy iron gates, and we heard the hoarse roar of the Doctor's voice, and saw the fury with which he shook his clenched fists at him.   The trap drove on, and a few minutes later we saw a sudden light spring up among the trees as the lamp was lit in one of the sitting-rooms.

" Do you know, Watson," said Holmes, as we sat together in the gathering darkness, " I have really some scruples as to taking you to-night.   There is a distinct element of danger."

" Can I be of assistance ? "

" Your presence might be invaluable."

" Then I shall certainly come."

" It is very kind of you."

" You speak of danger.   You have evidently seen more in these rooms than was visible to me."

" No, but I fancy that I may have deduced a little more. I imagine that you saw all that I did."

" I saw nothing remarkable save the bell-rope, and what purpose that could answer I confess is more than I can imagine."

" You saw the ventilator, too ? "

" Yes, but I do not think that it is such a very unusual thing to have a small opening between two rooms.   It was so small that a rat could hardly pass through."

" I knew that we should find a ventilator before ever we came to Stoke Moran."

" My dear Holmes ! "

" Oh, yes, I did.   You remember in her statement she said that her sister could smell Dr. Roylott's cigar. Now, of course that suggests at once that there must be a communication between the two rooms.   It could only be a small one, or it would have been remarked upon at the coroner's inquiry.   I deduced a ventilator."

" But what harm can there be in that ? "

" Well, there is at least a curious coincidence of dates. A ventilator is made, a cord is hung, and a lady who sleeps in the bed dies.   Does not that strike you ? "

" I cannot as yet see any connection."

" Did you observe anything very peculiar about that bed ? "

" No."

" It was clamped to the floor.   Did you ever see a bed fastened like that before ? "

" I cannot say that I have."

" The lady could not move her bed.   It must always be in the same relative position to the ventilator and to the rope—for so we may call it, since it was clearly never meant for a bell-pull."

" Holmes," I cried, " I seem to see dimly what you are hitting at.   We are only just in time to prevent some subtle and horrible crime."

" Subtle enough and horrible enough.   When a doctor does go wrong he is the first of criminals.   He has nerve and he has knowledge. Palmer and Pritchard were among the heads of their profession.   This man strikes even deeper, but I think, Watson, that we shall be able to strike deeper still.   But we shall have horrors enough before the night is over : for goodness' sake let us have a quiet pipe, and turn our minds for a few hours to something more cheerful."

"WHEN A DOCTOR DOES GO WRONG HE IS THE FIRST OF CRIMINALS."

At left, William Palmer, executed in 1856 for the murder of a friend by poison. At right, that "benevolent monster," Edward William Pritchard, a Glasgow practitioner who was hanged in 1865 for poisoning his wife and mother-in-law. Excellent accounts of Palmer and Pritchard, both by Harold Eaton, will be found in *The Fifty Most Amazing Crimes of the Last 100 Years*, edited by J. M. Parrish and John R. Crossland, London: Odhams Press, Ltd., 1936, from which these sketches are taken.

31 *we were out on the dark road.* "This, too, checks with early April," the late Professor Jay Finley Christ wrote in *An Irregular Chronology,* "for in that month in 1883, the moon was not visible in the evening until the 13th."

About nine o'clock the light among the trees was extinguished, and all was dark in the direction of the Manor House. Two hours passed slowly away, and then, suddenly, just at the stroke of eleven, a single bright light shone out right in front of us.

"That is our signal," said Holmes, springing to his feet ; "it comes from the middle window."

As we passed out he exchanged a few words with the landlord, explaining that we were going on a late visit to an acquaintance, and that it was possible that we might spend the night there. A moment later we were out on **31** the dark road, a chill wind blowing in our faces, and one yellow light twinkling in front of us through the gloom to guide us on our sombre errand.

There was little difficulty in entering the grounds, for unrepaired breaches gaped in the old park wall. Making our way among the trees, we reached the lawn, crossed it, and were about to enter through the window, when out from a clump of laurel bushes there darted what seemed to be a hideous and distorted child, who threw itself on the grass with writhing limbs, and then ran swiftly across the lawn into the darkness.

"My God !" I whispered, ' did you see it ? '

Holmes was for the moment as startled as I. His hand closed like a vice upon my wrist in his agitation. Then he broke into a low laugh, and put his lips to my ear.

"It is a nice household," he murmured, "that is the baboon."

I had forgotten the strange pets which the Doctor affected. There was a cheetah, too ; perhaps we might find it upon our shoulders at any moment. I confess that I felt easier in my mind when, after following Holmes' example and slipping off my shoes, I found myself inside the bedroom. My companion noiselessly closed the shutters, moved the lamp on to the table, and cast his eyes round the room. All was as we had seen it in the day-time. Then creeping up to me and making a trumpet of his hand, he whispered into my ear again so gently that it was all that I could do to distinguish the words :

"The least sound would be fatal to our plans."

I nodded to show that I had heard.

"We must sit without a light. He would see it through the ventilator."

I nodded again.

"Do not go to sleep ; your very life may depend upon it. Have your pistol ready in case we should need it. I will sit on the side of the bed, and you in that chair."

I took out my revolver and laid it on the corner of the table.

Holmes had brought up a long thin cane, and this he placed upon the bed beside him. By it he laid the box of matches and the stump of a candle. Then he turned down the lamp and we were left in darkness.

How shall I ever forget that dreadful vigil ? I could not hear a sound, not even the drawing of a breath, and yet I knew that my companion sat open-eyed, within a few feet of me, in the same state of nervous tension in which I was myself. The shutters cut off the least ray of light, and we waited in absolute darkness. From outside came the occasional cry of a night-bird, and once at our very window a long drawn, cat-like whine, which told us that the cheetah was indeed at liberty. Far away we could hear the deep tones of the parish clock, which boomed out every quarter of an hour. How long they seemed, those quarters! Twelve o'clock, and one, and two, and three, and still we sat waiting silently for whatever might befall.

Suddenly there was the momentary gleam of a light up in the direction of the ventilator, which vanished immediately, but was succeeded by a strong smell of burning oil and heated metal. Someone in the next room had lit a dark lantern. I heard a gentle sound of movement, and then all was silent once more, though the smell grew stronger. For half an hour I sat with straining ears. Then suddenly another sound became audible—a very gentle, soothing sound, like that of a small jet of steam escaping continually from a kettle. The instant that we heard it, Holmes sprang from the bed, struck a match, and lashed furiously with his cane at the bell-pull.

"You see it, Watson?" he yelled. "You see it?"

But I saw nothing. At the moment when Holmes **32** struck the light I heard a low, clear whistle, but the sudden glare flashing into my weary eyes made it impossible for me to tell what it was at which my friend lashed so savagely. I could, however, see that his face was deadly pale, and filled with horror and loathing.

He had ceased to strike, and was gazing up at the ventilator, when suddenly there broke from the silence of the night the most horrible cry to which I have ever listened. It swelled up louder and louder, a hoarse yell of pain and fear and anger all mingled in the one dreadful shriek. They say that away down in the village, and even in the distant parsonage, that cry raised the sleepers from their beds. It struck cold to our hearts, and I stood gazing at Holmes, and he at me, until the last echoes of it had died away into the silence from which it rose.

32 *But I saw nothing.* We know that Watson's eyesight was phenomenally acute, for we are told in *The Hound of the Baskervilles* that he was able to discern a boy's figure at a distance of "several miles" with the naked eye. However, Dr. Vernon Pennell has deduced from Watson's statement here that Watson suffered as a minor defect a deficiency of Vitamin A that resulted in night blindness ("A Résumé of the Medical Life of John H. Watson, M.D., Late of the Army Medical Department").

HOLMES . . . LASHED FURIOUSLY WITH HIS CANE AT THE BELL-PULL.

Illustration by Sidney Paget for the *Strand Magazine*, February, 1892.

SOMEONE IN THE NEXT ROOM HAD LIT A DARK LANTERN.

The predecessor of the modern electric flashlight. "A dark lantern's principal use, and the way it differed from an ordinary hand lantern, was in respect that it could be darkened while lit, by a mechanism of its own," Mr. Melvin Cross wrote in "The Lantern of Sherlock Holmes." "The light could be shut off without extinguishing the flame, thereby rendering the user invisible at will to anyone foreign to his purpose. It was used in a crude form centuries ago for military purposes. Until within the past few years it was used to flash signals, a spring being attached to the shutter, and sold under the name of Boat Signal Lantern. . . . The construction of the various pieces used in the dark-lantern seems to be about the same in general principles; that is, the main body is cylindrical in form, with door and a pointed top, which latter is fluted and acts to let the heated air out. The door has a round projection extending directly away from the body, and here the lens is held. The door also gives access to the burner for lighting and adjustment. On the back are the carrying devices: generally near the bottom and in the front, is a small knob. This is pushed around in a slot to adjust the shade, which latter also acts as a reflector. When the light is on full, the reflector has been moved between the burner and the lens—a rather ingenious arrangement." Other references to dark lanterns and pocket lanterns—there are some twenty-two in all throughout the Canon—occur in *A Study in Scarlet, The Sign of the Four,* "The Greek Interpreter," "The Adventure of the Empty House," "The Adventure of Charles Augustus Milverton," "The Adventure of the Six Napoleons," "The Adventure of Wisteria Lodge," "The Adventure of the Red Circle," "The Adventure of the Bruce-Partington Plans" and "The Adventure of Shoscombe Old Place." Shown here, at top, are three small lanterns, compared in size with a pencil. The two right-hand pieces are pocket lanterns, complete with handles and vertical slides. At bottom, a lantern is shown with the shade open, half closed and closed. When the shutter is open (*left*) it is behind the burner and acts as a reflector. All lanterns are from the collection of Mr. Melvin Cross.

" What can it mean ? " I gasped.

" It means that it is all over," Holmes answered. " And perhaps, after all, it is for the best. Take your pistol, and we shall enter Dr. Roylott's room."

With a grave face he lit the lamp, and led the way down the corridor. Twice he struck at the chamber door without any reply from within. Then he turned the handle and entered, I at his heels, with the cocked pistol in my hand.

It was a singular sight which met our eyes. On the table stood a dark lantern with the shutter half open, throwing a brilliant beam of light upon the iron safe, the door of which was ajar. Beside this table, on the wooden chair, sat Dr. Grimesby Roylott, clad in a long grey dressing-gown, his bare ankles protruding beneath, and his feet thrust into red heelless Turkish slippers. Across his lap lay the short stock with the long lash which we had noticed during the day. His chin was cocked upwards, and his eyes were fixed in a dreadful rigid stare at the corner of the ceiling. Round his brow he had a peculiar yellow band, with brownish speckles, which seemed to be bound tightly round his head. As we entered he made neither sound nor motion.

" The band ! the speckled band ! " whispered Holmes.

I took a step forward. In an instant his strange headgear began to move, and there reared itself from among his hair the squat diamond-shaped head and puffed neck of a loathsome serpent.

" It is a swamp adder ! " cried Holmes—" the deadliest snake in India. He has died within ten seconds of being bitten. Violence does, in truth, recoil upon the violent, and the schemer falls into the pit which he digs for another. **33** Let us thrust this creature back into its den, and we can then remove Miss Stoner to some place of shelter, and let the county police know what has happened."

As he spoke he drew the dog whip swiftly from the dead man's lap, and throwing the noose round the reptile's neck, he drew it from its horrid perch, and, carrying it at arm's length, threw it into the iron safe, which he closed upon it.

Such are the true facts of the death of Dr. Grimesby Roylott, of Stoke Moran. It is not necessary that I should prolong a narrative which has already run to too great a length, by telling how we broke the sad news to the terrified girl, how we conveyed her by the morning train to the care of her good aunt at Harrow, of how the slow process of official inquiry came to the conclusion that the Doctor met his fate while indiscreetly playing with a dangerous pet. The little which I had yet to learn of the case was told me by Sherlock Holmes as we travelled back next day.

" I had," said he, " come to an entirely erroneous conclusion, which shows, my dear Watson, how dangerous it always is to reason from insufficient data. The presence of the gipsies, and the use of the word ' band,' which was used by the poor girl, no doubt, to explain the appearance which she had caught a horrid glimpse of by

ROUND HIS BROW HE HAD A PECULIAR YELLOW BAND, WITH BROWNISH SPECKLES, WHICH SEEMED TO BE BOUND TIGHTLY ROUND HIS HEAD.

Illustration by Joseph Camana for *Cases of Sherlock Holmes;* St. Louis: Webster Publishing Co., 1947. Sidney Paget illustrated the same scene for the *Strand Magazine,* February, 1892.

33 *the schemer falls into the pit which he digs for another.* Holmes again demonstrates his familiarity with Holy Writ: "He that diggeth a pit shall fall into it; and whoso breaketh an hedge, a serpent shall bite him" (Ecclesiastes, 1:2).

the light of her match, were sufficient to put me upon an entirely wrong scent. I can only claim the merit that I instantly reconsidered my position when, however, it became clear to me that whatever danger threatened an occupant of the room could not come either from the window or the door. My attention was speedily drawn, as I have already remarked to you, to this ventilator, and to the bell-rope which hung down to the bed. The discovery that this was a dummy, and that the bed was clamped to the floor, instantly gave rise to the suspicion that the rope was there as a bridge for something passing through the hole, and coming to the bed. The idea of a snake instantly occurred to me, and when I coupled it with my knowledge that the Doctor was furnished with a supply of creatures from India, I felt that I was probably on the right track. The idea of using a form of poison which could not possibly be discovered by any chemical test was just such a one as would occur to a clever and ruthless man who had had an Eastern training. The rapidity with which such a poison would take effect would also, from his point of view, be an advantage. It would be a sharp-eyed coroner indeed who could distinguish the two little dark punctures which would show where the poison fangs had done their work. Then I thought of the whistle. Of course, he must recall the snake before the morning light revealed it to the victim. He had trained it, probably by the use of the milk which we saw, to return to him when summoned. He would put it through the ventilator at the hour that he thought best, with the certainty that it would crawl down the rope, and land on the bed. It might or might not bite the occupant, perhaps she might escape every night for a week, but sooner or later she must fall a victim.

" I had come to these conclusions before ever I had entered his room. An inspection of his chair showed me that he had been in the habit of standing on it, which, of course, would be necessary in order that he should reach the ventilator. The sight of the safe, the saucer of milk, and the loop of whipcord were enough to finally dispel any doubts which may have remained. The metallic clang heard by Miss Stoner was obviously caused by her father hastily closing the door of his safe upon its terrible occupant. Having once made up my mind, you know the steps which I took in order to put the matter to the proof. I heard the creature hiss, as I have no doubt that you did also, and I instantly lit the light and attacked it."

" With the result of driving it through the ventilator."

" And also with the result of causing it to turn upon its master at the other side. Some of the blows of my cane came home, and roused its snakish temper, so that it flew upon the first person it saw. In this way I am no doubt indirectly responsible for Dr. Grimesby Roylott's death, and I cannot say that it is likely to weigh very heavily upon my conscience."

Auctorial and Bibliographical Note: There has been some discussion among the members of the Conan Doyle Literary Society that Sir Arthur's sister Connie (Mrs. E. W. Hornung) may have given him the idea upon which he based "The Adventure of the Speckled Band." In any case, of all the short stories (excluding those in the *Case-Book*), it was Sir Arthur's favorite: he placed it first on the "twelve best" list he drew up for the March, 1927, issue of the *Strand*. Of all the adventures, the short stories and the novels, it also ranked first with the readers of the *Observer*. The original manuscript, consisting of 33 folio pages, two in the hand of a secretary but containing corrections by Conan Doyle, was auctioned in London on March 26, 1934, bringing £82. It was later sold by Scribner's to a Chicago dealer. Its present location is unknown.

18

"IT IS ... THE DEADLIEST SNAKE IN INDIA"

[An Afterword to "The Adventure of the Speckled Band"]

Holmes called the speckled band "a swamp adder"—a name not now in common use, as the editors of the Catalogue of the Sherlock Holmes Exhibition noted: "It may be an obsolete vernacular name from some early work of natural history now forgotten; or it may be a purely local name, acquired by Holmes from one of his cosmopolitan acquaintances, in which case it is unlikely to appear in any standard work of reference. The identity of the snake must therefore be deduced from such information as we possess on its appearance and behaviour."

Let us therefore consider the data describing Dr. Roylott's messenger of death, as Watson has recorded it for us:

1. The snake, according to Holmes, was "Indian." "There is a wide-spread belief" (the editors of the Catalogue of the Exhibition continued) "that [the puff adder, *Bitis Arietans*] was the snake intended. The fact that it is African in origin does not disqualify it, since there is only circumstantial evidence that the snake was Indian. . . . However, the lethargic nature of this snake, its relatively slow-acting venom, and its striking markings (which could not reasonably be described, even by Julia Stoner immediately after being bitten, as speckled) seem to rule it out. Apart from the sea-snakes (*Hydrophiidae*) of the Indian coasts, whose flat oar-like tails would seem to preclude them from negotiating bell-ropes, there are no truly acquatic venomous snakes in India. Holmes' use of the term 'swamp adder' has caused some investigators to suggest the damp-loving river-jack vipers of the African rain-forests (*Bitis nasicornis* and *B. gabonica*); but these must be ruled out for precisely the same reasons as the puff adder."

2. Its fangs left "two little dark punctures" in its victims. "The only snakes that kill by poison fangs in India are divided . . . into two families—the *Elapidae* and the *Viperidie*," Mr. Douglas Lawson wrote in "The Speckled Band—What Was It?" "One of the major differences between these families is the difference in poison fangs. In *Elapidae* the relatively short fangs lie in the front of the jaw, and, on contact, eject poison into the victim—*but not in killing amounts*. After the ejection of the poison, the series of frontal teeth and four half-jaws pull the drugged victim closer to its attacker, and the poison fangs, embedded repeatedly, eject new quantities of poison at each contact. The result to an observer is that a victim of *Elapidae*'s poison has a series of marks where the poison fangs have embedded themselves again and again. In *Viperidie*, the poison fangs are much larger, and when not in use lie in the roof of the mouth at the back of the head. When the viper attacks, these poison fangs extend beyond the mouth and make the first contact with the victim; and only one contact. . . . Thus a victim poisoned by *Viperidie* has only two puncture marks, and this was what Holmes and Watson found when they examined the body of Dr. Roylott. We have therefore established that Dr. Roylott's messenger of death was an Indian viper."

3. *In color it was yellow with brown specks.* "Of the numerous viper families throughout the world," Mr. Lawson continued, "there are but two poisonous varieties in India . . . the Russell's Viper and *Echis Carinata* [the saw-scaled viper]. Of these two snakes, the most prolific and the most featured in Indian snake-lore is the Russell's Viper—consider the popularity of its names: Tic Polonga, Daboia Russelli, Daboia Elegans, Chain Viper, Ullo Borra, Siahchunder Amata —and Russell's Viper. In contrast, *Echis Carinata* has only one pseudonym." In Mr. Lawson's view, the death of Julia Stoner was caused by a young Russell's Viper, the death of Dr. Roylott by the *Echis Carinata*. Certainly the markings of the *Echis Carinata* would seem to correspond more closely than those of the Russell's Viper to the snake described by Watson: *Echis Carinata* has been described (by the late Dr. Raymond Lee Ditmars, in his *Snakes of the World;* New York: The Macmillan Company, 1931) as: "The body is browning-gray with three longitudinal series of whitish black-edged spots," whereas the Russell's Viper is described as a pale brown body, with three longitudinal series of black rings, centered with a chocolate brown and ringed in a frame of white and yellow.

4. *Its hiss was "gentle" and "soothing, like that of a small jet of steam escaping from a tea-kettle."* "The Russell's Viper is silent until thoroughly aroused," Mr. Lawson continued, "and then hisses violently on both the outgo and intake of its breath. The hissing of a Tic Polonga would have boomed on the Doctor's eardrums. Therefore, the Doctor did *not* hear the hissing of a Russell's Viper. However, the ophidologists agree on one snake that answers the description as though it were a tape recording: *Echis Carinata* probably does not hiss at all, but in any excitement, he emits a sibilant sound by the constant rubbing together of his scales as he coils and twists his lithe body, and the sound to the listener is 'that of steam escaping from a tea-kettle.' "

5. *It was perhaps three feet in length.* "The average length of a Russell's Viper is a strong four to five feet," Mr. Lawson continued. "Since the circumference of Dr. Roylott's head probably was not more than 27 inches, it would seem that a Russell's Viper must have encircled the head twice, still allowing room to park its neck in the Roylott scalp. Surely Dr. Watson would not have described such a voluminous headpiece as a 'speckled band.' What, then, could he have seen? The *Echis Carinata*, attaining a length of two to three feet, and a very much thinner snake than its bigger counterpart, would have answered photographically to Dr. Watson's description."

6. *Its bite caused death "within ten seconds" (in the case*

of Dr. Roylott). The bite of *no* snake would kill in so short a time as ten seconds; either Dr. Roylott was still alive when Holmes and Watson entered his room or the doctor had died of a heart attack and the snake embedded its fangs in a dead man (Mr. Lawson's theory). We may add here that both the Russell's Viper and *Echis Carinata* carry "haemotoxic" venom, which acts on the blood system—much slower to kill than "neurotoxic" venom, which acts on the nervous system.

7. *But Dr. Roylott's death "within ten seconds" is inconsistent with the death of Julia Stoner, who "slowly sank and died . . ."* "There had presumably been no change of snake," wrote the editors of the Catalogue of the Sherlock Holmes Exhibition, but both Mr. Lawson (as we have seen) and Mr. Rolfe Boswell ("Dr. Roylott's Wily Fillip") disagree with this verdict. In Mr. Boswell's view, Julia Stoner was bitten by a bamboo viper, Dr. Roylott by a Russell's Viper.

8. *It had a "squat, diamond-shaped head."* This is true to a greater or a lesser degree of practically all snakes.

9. *It had a "puffed neck."* This would seem to rule out both the Russell's Viper and *Echis Carinata;* the only snake that might answer to this description would be *Naja naja,* the cobra, which, indeed the editors of the Catalogue of the Sherlock Holmes Exhibition finally decided "the speckled band" to have been.

10. *The snake, we are told, is recalled to the doctor's room by a whistle.* But "how could this be when it is well known that snakes are quite deaf?", Mr. Laurence M. Klauber asked in "The Truth About the Speckled Band." "It is true that they are extraordinarily sensitive to vibrations of the substratum upon which they rest, so they often appear to hear sounds of sufficient magnitude to affect such a vibrator as a box in which they may be kept; but this could not be the case with a snake clinging tenuously to a flimsy bell-rope."

11. *"He had trained it, probably by the use of the milk which we saw."* Experts have said that no snake drinks milk from choice, though it may do so if it is thirsty enough and water is not available. "The creature lives on milk," Mr. Klauber wrote, "not a natural food of any snake and one that it will accept only rarely as a substitute for water, if the latter be unobtainable."

12. *The speckled band, we are told, "would crawl down the rope" "with . . . certainty."* Whether any snake would crawl down—and then up—a rope with certainty under these or similar conditions is another point debated by experts. Mr. Raymond Massey, who played the role of Holmes in a motion picture version of "The Adventure of the Speckled Band," stated in a letter to Mr. Nathan L. Bengis that the snake used "climbed down the bell-rope with a realism which I think satisfied the most rabid Holmes fan." On the other hand, Mr. Klauber has written: ". . . while admitting that a snake might slide down a bell-rope, it could certainly not climb up one, particularly with the lower end swinging loose above the fatal bed. For snakes do not climb as many think—by twining themselves around an object; they climb by wedging their bodies into any crannies and interstices, taking advantage of every irregularity or protusion upon which a loop of the body may be hooked. It is

by this method that they progress rapidly upon the rough bark of branching trees or the tangled skein of a vine."

It would seem, regretfully, that *no known species of snake fully satisfies all the requirements of "the speckled band."*

But if the "terrible occupant" of Dr. Roylott's safe was *not* a snake, what could it have been? In the opinion of Mr. Klauber, the creature was a horrible hybrid bred by Dr. Roylott—a sinister combination of the Mexican Gila monster (*Heloderma horridum*) and the spectacled or Indian cobra, now known as *Naja naja naja.* Such a creature would unite the intelligence and agility of the lizard with the inimical disposition of the snake. It would have fangs in the upper jaw inherited from one parent, and in the lower jaw from the other, and a venom incomparably strengthened by hybridization, "thus assuring the almost instant demise of any victim. Here we have an animal that would feed on the batter that was mistaken for milk, for so does its parent, the Gila monster; one with ears like any lizard, wherewith to hear a whistle; and one whose legs and claws permitted it to run up a bell-rope as easily as down. . . . Here was a reptile that would be handled with a noose on a dog switch; whereas any snake handler would have used a stick terminated with a hook. And, above all, when we combine the cobra and the heloderm the result is certain to assume the likeness of a speckled band."

.   .   .

FOR THREE HOURS WE STROLLED ABOUT TOGETHER . . .

Illustration by Sidney Paget for the *Strand Magazine*, August, 1893.

19

THE RESIDENT PATIENT

[Wednesday, October 6, to Thursday, October 7, 1886]

IN glancing over the somewhat incoherent series of memoirs with which I have endeavoured to illustrate a few of the mental peculiarities of my friend, Mr. Sherlock Holmes, I have been struck by the difficulty which I have experienced in picking out examples which shall in every way answer my purpose. For in those cases in which Holmes has performed some *tour-de-force* of **1** analytical reasoning, and has demonstrated the value of his peculiar methods of investigation, the facts themselves have often been so slight or so commonplace that I could not feel justified in laying them before the public. On the other hand, it has frequently happened that he has been concerned in some research where the facts have been of the most remarkable and dramatic character, but where the share which he has himself taken in determining their causes has been less pronounced than I, as his biographer, could wish. The small matter which I have chronicled under the heading of " A Study in Scarlet," and that other later one connected with the **2** loss of the *Gloria Scott*, may serve as examples of this Scylla and Charybdis which are for ever threatening his **3** historian. It may be that, in the business of which I am now about to write, the part which my friend played is not sufficiently accentuated ; and yet the whole train of circumstances is so remarkable that I cannot bring myself to omit it entirely from this series.

It had been a close, rainy day in October. " Unhealthy weather, Watson," said my friend. " But the evening has brought a breeze with it. What do you say to a ramble through London ? " **4**

I was weary of our little sitting-room, and gladly **5** acquiesced. For three hours we strolled about together, watching the ever-changing kaleidoscope of life as it ebbs and flows through Fleet Street and the Strand. Holmes' **6** characteristic talk, with its keen observance of detail and subtle power of inference, held me amused and enthralled.

It was ten o'clock before we reached Baker Street again. A brougham was waiting at our door.

" Hum ! A doctor's—general practitioner, I perceive," said Holmes. " Not been long in practice, but has had a good deal to do. Come to consult us, I fancy ! Lucky we came back ! "

I was sufficiently conversant with Holmes' methods to

1 tour-de-force. French: a feat of remarkable skill or strength.

2 *that other later one.* Watson is of course speaking in terms of the time of publication, not of occurrence.

3 *Scylla and Charybdis.* Scylla was a sea-monster with six heads, twelve feet, and a voice like the yelp of a dog. It lived in a cave by the sea, whence it thrust out its heads to snatch seamen from passing ships (Homer's *Odyssey*, Book XII, 1, 73). Opposite Scylla dwelt Charybdis, another sea monster. In later classical times these Homeric monsters were localized in the Gulf of Messina, Scylla as the rock on the Italian and Charybdis as a whirlpool on the Sicilian side.

4 *What do you say to a ramble through London?"* When "The Resident Patient" first saw publication in the *Strand Magazine* for August, 1893, this paragraph appeared as two paragraphs which read:

I cannot be sure of the exact date, for some of my memoranda upon the matter have been mislaid, but it must have been towards the end of the first year during which Holmes and I shared chambers in Baker Street. It was boisterous October weather, and we had both remained indoors all day, I because I feared with my shaken health to face the keen autumn wind, while he was deep in some of those abstruse chemical investigations which absorbed him utterly as long as he was engaged upon them. Towards evening, however, the breaking of a test-tube brought his research to a premature ending, and he sprang up from his chair with an exclamation of impatience and a clouded brow.

"A day's work ruined, Watson," said he, striding across to the window. "Ha! the stars are out and the wind has fallen. What do you say to a ramble through London?"

This, as we shall see, is a manifestly inaccurate version, which is why the two paragraphs became one when Watson's account of the case of "The Resident Patient" appeared in *Sherlock Holmes:*

The Complete Short Stories (London: John Murray, 1928).

Quite obviously, as the late Mr. H. W. Bell indicated in *Sherlock Holmes and Dr. Watson: The Chronology of Their Adventures,* the missing memoranda must eventually have been discovered; Watson undoubtedly consulted them before the publication of the first complete collection of his shorter chronicles, checked the fact that the month was indeed October, and removed from the text the paragraph about "the end of the first year during which Holmes and I shared chambers in Baker Street."

5 *I was weary of our little sitting-room.* Your editor believes that the adventure of "The Resident Patient" took place only a few weeks before Dr. Watson married for the first time. His approaching nuptials may well have accounted for the statement that he was "weary" of the sitting room at 221B at this time.

6 *Fleet Street.* "Fleet Street . . . takes its name from the once rapid and clear, but now fearfully polluted river Fleet, which has its source far away in the breezy heights of Hampstead, and flows through the valley where Farringdon Street now is, in which it once turned the mills which are still commemorated in Turnmill Street. . . . [Fleet Street has] always been considered as the chief approach to the City," Augustus J. C. Hare wrote in *Walks in London,* Vol. I. Fleet Street today is the center of the newspaper industry, and is equally famous for its many fine taverns.

7 *to be able to follow his reasoning.* Despite his constant self-disparagement, Watson made many deductions, some of them brilliant, on his own. Here he analyzes, in acceptable Sherlockian style, the physician with the unusual Resident Patient. In "A Scandal in Bohemia," Watson makes several pertinent deductions from the King's notepaper before the Master adds his own. Watson easily connects the Five Orange Pips with a seafaring man with no other indication than the postmarks. In *The Sign of the Four* he is able to deduce, with only a little prompting from the sleuth, that the murderer entered through the roof, *improbable as that was.* In *The Hound of the Baskervilles* his reconstruction of Dr. James Mortimer from his walking stick is shrewd if not altogther accurate. He later makes an accurate analysis of Mr. Mc-Carthy's fatal injuries at Boscombe Valley.

"Another instance is found in the opening pages of "The Adventure of Wisteria Lodge,' where Watson, from but one glance at Scott Eccles, gives us a string of accurate inferences worthy of Holmes himself," Mr. Nathan L. Bengis wrote in "Take a Bow, Dr. Watson." "So, too, Dr. Watson's interview with Mrs. Laura Lyons in *The Hound of the Baskervilles* is handled by him throughout with such admirable aplomb as to indicate that he would make an excellent prosecuting attorney if he had been inclined that way."

7 be able to follow his reasoning, and to see that the nature and state of the various medical instruments in the wicker basket which hung in the lamp-light inside the brougham had given him the data for his swift deduction. The light in our window above showed that this late visit was indeed intended for us. With some curiosity as to what could have sent a brother medico to us at such an hour, I followed Holmes into our sanctum.

A pale, taper-faced man with sandy whiskers rose up from a chair by the fire as we entered. His age may not have been more than three- or four-and-thirty, but his haggard expression and unhealthy hue told of a life which had sapped his strength and robbed him of his youth. His manner was nervous and shy, like that of a sensitive gentleman, and the thin white hand which he laid on the mantelpiece as he rose was that of an artist rather than of a surgeon. His dress was quiet and sombre, a black frock-coat, dark trousers, and a touch of colour about his neck-tie.

" Good evening, Doctor," said Holmes, cheerily ; " I am glad to see that you have only been waiting a very few minutes."

" You spoke to my coachman, then ? "

" No, it was the candle on the side-table that told me. Pray resume your seat and let me know how I can serve you."

" My name is Doctor Percy Trevelyan," said our visitor, **8** " and I live at 403 Brook Street."

" Are you not the author of a monograph upon obscure nervous lesions ? " I asked.

His pale cheeks flushed with pleasure at hearing that his work was known to me.

" I so seldom hear of the work that I thought it was **9** quite dead," said he. " My publishers give me a most discouraging account of its sale. You are yourself, I presume, a medical man ? "

" A retired Army surgeon."

" My own hobby has always been nervous disease. I should wish to make it an absolute speciality, but, of course, a man must take what he can get at first. This, however, is beside the question, Mr. Sherlock Holmes, and I quite appreciate how valuable your time is. The fact is that a very singular train of events has occurred recently at my house in Brook Street, and to-night they came to such a head that I felt it was quite impossible for me to wait another hour before asking for your advice and assistance."

Sherlock Holmes sat down and lit his pipe. " You are very welcome to both," said he. " Pray let me have a detailed account of what the circumstances are which have disturbed you."

" One or two of them are so trivial," said Dr. Trevelyan, " that really I am almost ashamed to mention them. But the matter is so inexplicable, and the recent turn which it has taken is so elaborate, that I shall lay it all before you, and you shall judge what is essential and what is not.

" I am compelled, to begin with, to say something of my own college career. I am a London University man, you know, and I am sure you will not think that I am unduly singing my own praises if I say that my student career was considered by my professors to be a very promising one.   After I had graduated I continued to devote myself to research, occupying a minor position in King's College Hospital, and I was fortunate enough to **10** excite considerable interest by my research into the pathology of catalepsy, and finally to win the Bruce Pinkerton prize and medal by the monograph on nervous **11** lesions to which your friend has just alluded.   I should not go too far if I were to say that there was a general impression at that time that a distinguished career lay before me.

"But the one great stumbling-block lay in my want of capital.   As you will readily understand, a specialist who aims high is compelled to start in one of a dozen streets in the Cavendish Square quarter, all of which entail **12** enormous rents and furnishing expenses.   Besides this preliminary outlay, he must be prepared to keep himself for some years, and to hire a presentable carriage and horse.   To do this was quite beyond my power, and I could only hope that by economy I might in ten years' time save enough to enable me to put up my plate.   Suddenly, however, an unexpected incident opened up quite a new prospect to me.

"This was a visit from a gentleman of the name of Blessington, who was a complete stranger to me.   He came up into my room one morning, and plunged into business in an instant.

"'You are the same Percy Trevelyan who has had so distinguished a career and won a great prize lately?' said he.   I bowed.

"'Answer me frankly,' he continued, 'for you will find it to your interest to do so.   You have all the cleverness which makes a successful man.   Have you the tact?'

"I could not help smiling at the abruptness of the question.

"'I trust that I have my share,' I said.

"'Any bad habits?   Not drawn towards drink, eh?'

"'Really, sir!' I cried.

"'Quite right!   That's all right!   But I was bound to ask.   With all these qualities why are you not in practice?'

"I shrugged my shoulders.

"'Come, come!' said he, in his bustling way.   It's the old story.   More in your brains than in your pocket, eh?   What would you say if I were to start you in Brook Street?'

"I stared at him in astonishment.

"'Oh, it's for my sake, not for yours,' he cried.   'I'll be perfectly frank with you, and if it suits you it will suit me very well.   I have a few thousands to invest, d'ye see, and I think I'll sink them in you.'

"'But why?' I gasped.

"'Well, it's just like any other speculation, and safer than most.'

"I STARED AT HIM IN ASTONISHMENT."

Illustration by Sidney Paget for the *Strand Magazine*, August, 1893.

"Indeed," Mr. Ed S. Woodhead concludes ("In Defense of Dr. Watson") "there is hardly a case that does not supply further evidence of Watson's perspicacity; but the best testimony of all is the fact that, although after each of his expeditions in search of details for Holmes he is taunted for his omissions, he is nevertheless sent out again on the same errands, time after time. And when Holmes in less sarcastic moods (when the evidence brought in by Watson is evaluated and the case grows less baffling?) he describes Watson's investigations as 'invaluable.' Probably Watson's best case was at Baskerville Hall where Holmes says, 'Our researches have evidently been running on parallel lines,' and his letters from that place of mystery are masterpieces."

8 *Brook Street.* ". . . so called from the Tye Bourne whose course it marks," Augustus J. C. Hare wrote in *Walks in London*, Vol. II. "No. 57, four doors from Bond Street, was the house of George Frederick Handel, the famous composer, who used to give rehearsals of his oratorios there." Brook Street today contains some elegant shops as well as the world-famous Claridge's Hotel, at the south corner of Davies Street; this hotel, formerly Mivart's, was opened in 1808.

9 *I thought it was quite dead.*" Your editor believes that Watson planned shortly to resume an active role in medicine. His knowledge of Dr. Trevelyan's obscure monograph would indicate that he was "boning up." Watson at this time perhaps thought of becoming a psychiatrist, since the work was on "nervous lesions." Watson in many later cases displays his keen interest in the treatment and cure of mental diseases.

10 *King's College Hospital.* Founded at Clare Market in 1839 in connection with King's College, King's College Hospital in Holmes' and Watson's day stood in Portugal Street, named in honor of Catherine of Braganza. The Hospital and its surroundings were built over the burial ground of St.

Clement Danes, where Nathaniel Lee, the bombastic dramatist, 1657–1692, author of *Sophonisba* and *Gloriana*, was buried, having been killed in a drunken street brawl. Here also was a monument to "Honest Joe Miller," the "Father of Jokes," 1684–1738.

11 *the Bruce Pinkerton prize*. "In spite of considerable research we have been unable to discover any connection between this gentleman and Bruce-Partington, the inventor of the submarine," the late Gavin Brend wrote in *My Dear Holmes*.

12 *the Cavendish Square quarter*. "Cavendish Square, laid out in 1717, takes its name (with the neighbouring Henrietta Street and Holles Street) from Lady Henrietta Cavendish Holles, who married, in 1713, Edward Harley, second Earl of Oxford. . . . At No. 24 lived and painted George Romney, always called by Sir Joshua Reynolds, whom he had the honour of rivalling, 'the man of Cavendish Square.' Princess Amelia, daughter of George II, lived in the large house at the corner of Harley Street. . . . There is little more worth noticing in the frightful district north of Oxford Street, which, with the exception of [Manchester Square and Cavendish Square] *generally* marks the limits of fashionable society."—Augustus J. C. Hare, *Walks in London*, Vol. II.

13 *Lady Day*. March 25th. Lady Day is a day observed in honor of the Virgin Mary, commemorating some occasion in her life; specifically, the Feast of the Annunciation.

14 *the West End*. The west side of London—basically the City of Westminster, as opposed to the east end of London, the business and financial district including the ancient City of London.

"'What am I to do, then?'

"'I'll tell you. I'll take the house, furnish it, pay the maids, and run the whole place. All you have to do is to wear out your chair in the consulting-room. I'll let you have pocket-money and everything. Then you hand over to me three-quarters of what you earn, and you keep the other quarter for yourself.'

"This was the strange proposal, Mr. Holmes, with which the man Blessington approached me. I won't weary you with the account of how we bargained and negotiated. It ended in my moving into the house next **13** Lady Day, and starting in practice on very much the same conditions as he had suggested. He came himself to live with me in the character of a resident patient. His heart was weak, it appears, and he needed constant medical supervision. He turned the two best rooms on the first floor into a sitting-room and bedroom for himself. He was a man of singular habits, shunning company and very seldom going out. His life was irregular, but in one respect he was regularity itself. Every evening at the same hour he walked into the consulting-room, examined the books, put down five and threepence for every guinea that I had earned, and carried the rest off to the strong box in his own room.

"I may say with confidence that he never had occasion to regret his speculation. From the first it was a success. A few good cases and the reputation which I had won in the hospital brought me rapidly to the front, and during the last year or two I have made him a rich man.

"So much, Mr. Holmes, for my past history and my relations with Mr. Blessington. It only remains for me now to tell you what has occurred to bring me here to-night.

"Some weeks ago Mr. Blessington came down to me in, as it seemed to me, a state of considerable agitation. He spoke of some burglary which, he said, had been com- **14** mitted in the West End, and he appeared, I remember, to be quite unnecessarily excited about it, declaring that a day should not pass before we should add stronger bolts to our windows and doors. For a week he continued to be in a peculiar state of restlessness, peering continually out of the windows, and ceasing to take the short walk which had usually been the prelude to his dinner. From his manner it struck me that he was in mortal dread of

"... PUT DOWN FIVE AND THREEPENCE FOR EVERY GUINEA THAT I HAD EARNED ..."

Five shillings and threepence meant that Blessington put down the then equivalent of approximately $1.31 for every $5.25 Trevelyan earned. The guinea, be it noted, equals 21 shillings. It is a unit of currency so aristocratic that there exists today no coin or banknote for it. (The guinea was last coined in 1813, and shown in the illustration above is an 1813 guinea of George III. The coin took its name from the Guinea Coast, later the Crown Colony of the Gold Coast of Africa, a very important source of gold exploited by the Royal African Company.) To this day, professional men in Britain state the fee for their services in guineas (see, in this connection, the "receipted bill for thirteen guineas, paid by Mr. Godfrey Staunton last month to Dr. Leslie Armstrong"—"The Adventure of the Missing Three-Quarter.") The guinea is also the usual unit used in pricing expensive luxuries (see, in this connection, "Silver Blaze," in which Mme. Lesurier of Bond Street charges 22 guineas for a costume). Shown below is a threepence of 1859.

something or somebody, but when I questioned him upon the point he became so offensive that I was compelled to drop the subject. Gradually as time passed his fears appeared to die away, and he had renewed his former habits, when a fresh event reduced him to the pitiable state of prostration in which he now lies.

"What happened was this. Two days ago I received the letter which I now read to you. Neither address nor **15** date is attached to it.

"'A Russian nobleman who is now resident in England,' it runs, 'would be glad to avail himself of the professional assistance of Dr. Percy Trevelyan. He has been for some years a victim to cataleptic attacks, on which, as is well known, Dr. Trevelyan is an authority. He proposes to call at about a quarter-past six to-morrow evening, if Dr. Trevelyan will make it convenient to be **16** at home.'

"This letter interested me deeply, because the chief difficulty in the study of catalepsy is the rareness of the disease. You may believe, then, that I was in my consulting-room when at the appointed hour, the page showed in the patient.

"He was an elderly man, thin, demure, and commonplace—by no means the conception one forms of a Russian nobleman. I was much more struck by the appearance of his companion. This was a tall young man, surprisingly handsome, with a dark, fierce face, and the limbs and chest of a Hercules. He had his hand under **17** the other's arm as they entered, and helped him to a chair with a tenderness which one would hardly have expected from his appearance.

"'You will excuse my coming in, Doctor,' said he to me, speaking English with a slight lisp. 'This is my father, and his health is a matter of the most overwhelming importance to me.'

"I was touched by this filial anxiety. 'You would, perhaps, care to remain during the consultation?' said I.

"'Not for the world,' he cried, with a gesture of horror. 'It is more painful to me than I can express. If I were to see my father in one of those dreadful seizures, I am convinced that I should never survive it. My own nervous system is an exceptionally sensitive one. With your permission I will remain in the waiting-room while you go into my father's case.'

"To this, of course, I assented, and the young man withdrew. The patient and I then plunged into a discussion of his case, of which I took exhaustive notes. He was not remarkable for intelligence, and his answers were frequently obscure, which I attributed to his limited acquaintance with our language. Suddenly, however, as I sat writing he ceased to give any answer at all to my inquiries, and on my turning towards him I was shocked to see that he was sitting bolt upright in his chair, staring at me with a perfectly blank and rigid face. He was again in the grip of his mysterious malady.

"My first feeling, as I have just said, was one of pity and horror. My second, I fear, was rather one of professional satisfaction. I made notes of my patient's pulse and temperature, tested the rigidity of his muscles, and

15 *Two days ago I received the letter.* The day on which the case began was therefore not a Tuesday.

16 *to-morrow evening.* The appointment would not have been made for a Sunday; the day on which the case began was therefore not a Monday.

17 *a Hercules.* Watson was later to compare the King of Bohemia to this most popular hero in the Greek and Roman legends, famous for his extraordinary strength and courage.

"HE HAD HIS HAND UNDER THE OTHER'S ARM AS THEY ENTERED, AND HELPED HIM TO A CHAIR . . ."

Illustration by Sidney Paget for the *Strand Magazine*, August, 1893.

". . . I WAS SHOCKED TO SEE THAT HE WAS SITTING BOLT UPRIGHT IN HIS CHAIR, STARING AT ME WITH A PERFECTLY BLANK AND RIGID FACE."

Illustration by William H. Hyde for *Harper's Weekly*, August 12, 1893.

18 *at the very same hour this evening.* The day on which the case began was therefore not a Sunday.

". . . HE BURST INTO MY CONSULTING-ROOM LIKE A MAN WHO IS MAD WITH PANIC."

Illustration by Sidney Paget for the *Strand Magazine*, August, 1893.

examined his reflexes. There was nothing markedly abnormal in any of these conditions, which harmonized with my former experiences. I had obtained good results in such cases by the inhalation of nitrite of amyl, and the present seemed an admirable opportunity of testing its virtues. The bottle was downstairs in my laboratory, so, leaving my patient seated in his chair, I ran down to get it. There was some little delay in finding it—five minutes, let us say—and then I returned. Imagine my amazement to find the room empty and the patient gone !

" Of course, my first act was to run into the waiting-room. The son had gone also. The hall door had been closed, but not shut. My page who admits patients is a new boy, and by no means quick. He waits downstairs, and runs up to show patients out when I ring the consulting-room bell. He had heard nothing, and the affair remained a complete mystery. Mr. Blessington came in from his walk shortly afterwards, but I did not say anything to him upon the subject, for to tell the truth, I have got in the way of late of holding as little communication with him as possible.

" Well, I never thought that I should see anything more of the Russian and his son, so you can imagine my **18** amazement when at the very same hour this evening they both came marching into my consulting-room, just as they had done before.

" ' I feel that I owe you a great many apologies for my abrupt departure yesterday, Doctor,' said my patient.

" ' I confess that I was very much surprised at it,' said I.

" ' Well, the fact is,' he remarked, ' that when I recover from these attacks my mind is always very clouded as to all that has gone before. I woke up in a strange room, as it seemed to me, and made my way out into the street in a sort of dazed way when you were absent.'

" ' And I,' said the son, ' seeing my father pass the door of the waiting-room, naturally thought that the consultation had come to an end. It was not until we had reached home that I began to realize the true state of affairs.'

" ' Well,' said I, laughing, ' there is no harm done, except that you puzzled me terribly ; so if you, sir, would kindly step into the waiting-room, I shall be happy to continue our consultation, which was brought to so abrupt an ending.'

" For half an hour or so I discussed the old gentleman's symptoms with him, and then, having prescribed for him, I saw him go off on the arm of his son.

" I have told you that Mr. Blessington generally chose this hour of the day for his exercise. He came in shortly afterwards and passed upstairs. An instant later I heard him running down, and he burst into my consulting-room like a man who is mad with panic.

" ' Who has been in my room ? ' he cried.

" ' No one,' said I.

" ' It's a lie ! ' he yelled. ' Come up and look.'

" I passed over the grossness of his language, as he seemed half out of his mind with fear. When I went upstairs with him he pointed to several footprints upon the light carpet.

" ' D'you mean to say those are mine ? ' he cried.

" They were certainly very much larger than any which he could have made, and were evidently quite fresh. It rained hard this afternoon, as you know, and my patients **19** were the only people who called. It must have been the case, then, that the man in the waiting-room had for some unknown reason, while I was busy with the other, ascended to the room of my resident patient. Nothing had been touched or taken, but there were the footprints to prove that the intrusion was an undoubted fact.

" Mr. Blessington seemed more excited over the matter than I should have thought possible, though, of course, it was enough to disturb anybody's peace of mind. He actually sat crying in an arm-chair, and I could hardly get him to speak coherently. It was his suggestion that I should come round to you, and of course I at once saw the propriety of it, for certainly the incident is a very singular one, though he appears to completely overrate its importance. If you would only come back with me in my brougham, you would at least be able to soothe him, though I can hardly hope that you will be able to explain this remarkable occurrence."

Sherlock Holmes had listened to this long narrative with an intentness which showed me that his interest was keenly aroused. His face was as impassive as ever, but his lids had drooped more heavily over his eyes, and his smoke had curled up more thickly from his pipe to emphasize each curious episode in the doctor's tale. As our visitor concluded Holmes sprang up without a word, handed me my hat, picked up his own from the table, and followed Dr. Trevelyan to the door. Within a quarter of an hour we had been dropped at the door of the physician's residence in Brook Street, one of those sombre, flat-faced houses which one associates with a West End practice. A small page admitted us, and we began at once to ascend the broad, well-carpeted stair.

But a singular interruption brought us to a standstill. The light at the top was suddenly whisked out, and from the darkness came a reedy, quavering voice.

" I have a pistol," it cried ; " I give you my word that I'll fire if you come any nearer."

" This really grows outrageous, Mr. Blessington," cried Dr. Trevelyan.

" Oh, then it is you, Doctor ? " said the voice, with a great heave of relief. " But those other gentlemen, are they what they pretend to be ? "

We were conscious of a long scrutiny out of the darkness.

" Yes, yes, it's all right," said the voice at last. " You can come up, and I am sorry if my precautions have annoyed you."

He re-lit the stair gas as he spoke, and we saw before us a singular-looking man, whose appearance, as well as his voice, testified to his jangled nerves. He was very fat, but had apparently at some time been much fatter, so that the skin hung about his face in loose pouches, like the cheeks of a bloodhound. He was of a sickly colour, and his thin, sandy hair seemed to bristle up with the

19 *It rained hard this afternoon.* In October, 1886, your editor's month and year for "The Resident Patient," the two rainiest days were the 12th, a Tuesday, and therefore not the day, and the 15th—a Friday. The 15th would be acceptable except for Watson's earlier adjective "close"—on Friday, the 15th of October, 1886, the wind achieved a pressure of 16.5 pounds. The *third* rainiest day in October, 1886, was Wednesday, October 6th—and the wind pressure on that day was only two pounds. We will attempt to justify our choice of the year 1886 later.

IN HIS HAND HE HELD A PISTOL . . .

Illustration by Sidney Paget for the *Strand Magazine*, August, 1893.

20 *Oxford Street.* Slightly over a mile in length, Oxford Street today is one of the finest thoroughfares in London and the most popular shopping street in the British Empire. In Holmes' and Watson's day, however, it was a rather shabby thoroughfare, lined with third-rate houses. Hare wrote of it: "Though Oxford Street was the high-road to the University, it derives its name from Edward Harley, Earl of Oxford, owner of the manor of Tyburn. It was formerly called the Tyburn Road, and, in 1729, was only enclosed by houses on its northern side. . . . Oxford Street leads to the north-eastern corner of Hyde Park, which is entered at Cumberland Gate by the Marble Arch —one of our national follies—a despicable caricature of the Arch of Constantine, originally erected by Nash at a cost of £75,000, as an approach to Buckingham Palace, and removed hither (when the palace was enlarged in 1851) at a cost of £4,340."

21 *Harley Street.* Then as now a street inhabited largely by consulting physicians and specialists. Hare wrote of it: "We may take Harley Street as a fair example of [its] dreary neighbourhood, with the grim rows of expressionless uniform houses, between which and 'unexceptionable society' Dickens draws such a vivid portrait in *Little Dorrit.* Taine shows it to us from a Frenchman's point of view. 'From Regent's Park to Piccadilly a funereal vista of broad interminable streets. The footway is macadamized and black. The monotonous rows of buildings are of blackened brick; the windowpanes flash in black shadows. Each house is divided from the street by its railings and area. Scarcely a shop, certainly not a pretty one: no plate-glass fronts, no prints. How sad we should find it! Nothing to catch or amuse the eye. Lounging is out of the question. One must work at home, or hurry by under an umbrella to one's office or club. (*Notes sur l'Angleterre.*)"

intensity of his emotion. In his hand he held a pistol, but he thrust it into his pocket as we advanced.

"Good evening, Mr. Holmes," said he ; "I am sure I am very much obliged to you for coming round. No one ever needed your advice more than I do. I suppose that Dr. Trevelyan has told you of this most unwarrantable intrusion into my rooms ? "

"Quite so," said Holmes. "Who are these two men, Mr. Blessington, and why do they wish to molest you ? "

"Well, well," said the resident patient, in a nervous fashion, "of course it is hard to say that. You can hardly expect me to answer that, Mr. Holmes."

"Do you mean that you don't know ? "

"Come in here, if you please. Just have the kindness to step in here."

He led the way into his bedroom, which was large and comfortably furnished.

"You see that ? " said he, pointing to a big black box at the end of his bed. "I have never been a very rich man, Mr. Holmes—never made but one investment in my life, as Dr. Trevelyan would tell you. But I don't believe in bankers. I would never trust a banker, Mr. Holmes. Between ourselves, what little I have is in that box, so you can understand what it means to me when unknown people force themselves into my rooms."

Holmes looked at Blessington in his questioning way, and shook his head.

"I cannot possibly advise you if you try to deceive me," said he.

"But I have told you everything."

Holmes turned on his heel with a gesture of disgust. "Good night, Dr. Trevelyan," said he.

"And no advice for me ? " cried Blessington, in a breaking voice.

"My advice to you, sir, is to speak the truth."

A minute later we were in the street and walking for **20** home. We had crossed Oxford Street, and were half-way **21** down Harley Street before I could get a word from my companion.

"Sorry to bring you out on such a fool's errand, Watson," he said, at last. "It is an interesting case, too, at the bottom of it."

"I can make little of it," I confessed.

"Well, it is quite evident that there are two men— more, perhaps, but at least two—who are determined for some reason to get at this fellow Blessington. I have no doubt in my mind that both on the first and on the second occasion that young man penetrated to Blessington's room, while his confederate, by an ingenious device, kept the doctor from interfering."

"And the catalepsy ! "

"A fraudulent imitation, Watson, though I should hardly dare to hint as much to our specialist. It is a very easy complaint to imitate. I have done it myself."

"And then ? "

"By the purest chance Blessington was out on each occasion. Their reason for choosing so unusual an hour for a consultation was obviously to ensure that there should be no other patient in the waiting-room. It just happened, however, that this hour coincided with Blessington's constitutional, which seems to show that they were not very well acquainted with his daily routine. Of course if they had been merely after plunder they would at least have made some attempt to search for it. Besides, I can read in a man's eye when it is his own skin that he is frightened for. It is inconceivable that this fellow could have made two such vindictive enemies as these appear to be without knowing of it. I hold it, therefore, to be certain that he does know who these men are, and that for reasons of his own he suppresses it. It is just possible that to-morrow may find him in a more communicative mood."

"Is there not one alternative," I suggested, "grotesquely improbable, no doubt, but still just conceivable? Might the whole story of the cataleptic Russian and his son be a concoction of Dr. Trevelyan's, who has, for his own purposes, been in Blessington's rooms?"

I saw in the gaslight that Holmes wore an amused smile at this brilliant departure of mine.

"My dear fellow," said he, "it was one of the first solutions which occurred to me, but I was soon able to corroborate the doctor's tale. This young man has left prints upon the stair carpet which made it quite superfluous for me to ask to see those which he had made in the room. When I tell you that his shoes were square-toed, instead of being pointed like Blessington's, and were quite an inch and a third longer than the doctor's, you will acknowledge that there can be no doubt as to his individuality. But we may sleep on it now, for I shall be surprised if we do not hear something further from Brook Street in the morning."

Sherlock Holmes' prophecy was soon fulfilled, and in a dramatic fashion. At half-past seven next morning, in the first dim glimmer of daylight, I found him standing **22** by my bedside in his dressing-gown.

"There's a brougham waiting for us, Watson," said he.

"What's the matter, then?"

"The Brook Street business."

"Any fresh news?"

"Tragic, but ambiguous," said he pulling up the blind. "Look at this—a sheet from a notebook with ' For God's sake, come at once—P. T.' scrawled upon it in pencil. Our friend the doctor was hard put to it when he wrote this. Come along, my dear fellow, for it's an urgent call."

In a quarter of an hour or so we were back at the physician's house. He came running out to meet us with a face of horror.

"Oh, such a business!" he cried, with his hands to his temples.

"What, then?"

"Blessington has committed suicide!"

Holmes whistled.

"Yes, he hanged himself during the night!"

We had entered, and the doctor had preceded us into what was evidently his waiting-room.

"I really hardly know what I am doing," he cried. "The police are already upstairs. It has shaken me most dreadfully."

22 *in the first dim glimmer of daylight.* Daybreak in England in October is shortly after 4:00 A.M. on the first of the month and about 5:00 A.M. on the thirty-first. "The first dim glimmer of daylight" must be discarded as a clue to the dating of "The Resident Patient," if the month is indeed October and the hour of Watson's awakening 7:30 A.M. "The morning might have been a cloudy one," the late Professor Jay Finley Christ wrote. ". . . Watson still had a slight nocturnal film over his eyes when he first woke up," was the verdict of the late Dr. Ernest Bloomfield Zeisler.

23 *When the maid entered about seven.* Trevelyan of course sent for Holmes at once. This confirms Watson's statement that Holmes awakened him "At half-past seven" in the morning.

HOLMES OPENED IT AND SMELLED THE SINGLE CIGAR
WHICH IT CONTAINED.

Illustration by Sidney Paget for the *Strand Magazine*, August, 1893.

" When did you find it out ? "

23 " He has a cup of tea taken in to him early every morning. When the maid entered about seven, there the unfortunate fellow was hanging in the middle of the room. He had tied his cord to the hook on which the heavy lamp used to hang, and he had jumped off from the top of the very box that he showed us yesterday."

Holmes stood for a moment in deep thought.

" With your permission," said he at last, " I should like to go upstairs and look into the matter." We both ascended, followed by the doctor.

It was a dreadful sight which met us as we entered the bedroom door. I have spoken of the impression of flabbiness which this man Blessington conveyed. As he dangled from the hook it was exaggerated and intensified until he was scarce human in his appearance. The neck was drawn out like a plucked chicken's, making the rest of him seem the more obese and unnatural by the contrast. He was clad only in his long night-dress, and his swollen ankles and ungainly feet protruded starkly from beneath it. Beside him stood a smart-looking police inspector, who was taking notes in a pocket-book.

" Ah, Mr. Holmes," said he, as my friend entered. " I am delighted to see you."

" Good morning, Lanner," answered Holmes. " You won't think me an intruder, I am sure. Have you heard of the events which led up to this affair ? "

" Yes, I heard something of them."

" Have you formed any opinion ? "

" As far as I can see, the man has been driven out of his senses by fright. The bed has been well slept in, you see. There's his impression deep enough. It's about five in the morning, you know, that suicides are most common. That would be about his time for hanging himself. It seems to have been a very deliberate affair."

" I should say that he has been dead about three hours, judging by the rigidity of the muscles," said I.

" Noticed anything peculiar about the room ? " asked Holmes.

" Found a screwdriver and some screws on the wash-hand stand. Seems to have smoked heavily during the night, too. Here are four cigar-ends that I picked out of the fire-place."

" Hum ! " said Holmes. " Have you got his cigar-holder ? "

" No, I have seen none."

" His cigar-case, then ? "

" Yes, it was in his coat pocket."

Holmes opened it and smelled the single cigar which it contained.

" Oh, this is a Havana, and these others are cigars of the peculiar sort which are imported by the Dutch from their East Indian colonies. They are usually wrapped in straw, you know, and are thinner for their length than any other brand." He picked up the four ends and examined them with his pocket lens.

" Two of these have been smoked from a holder and two without," said he. " Two have been cut by a not very sharp knife, and two have had the ends bitten off by a set of excellent teeth. This is no suicide, Mr. Lanner. It is a very deeply planned and cold-blooded murder."

" Impossible ! " cried the Inspector.

" And why ? "

" Why should anyone murder a man in so clumsy a fashion as by hanging him ? "

" That is what we have to find out."

" How could they get in ? "

" Through the front door."

" It was barred in the morning."

" Then it was barred after them."

" How do you know ? "

" I saw their traces. Excuse me a moment, and I may be able to give you some further information about it."

He went over to the door, and turning the lock he examined it in his methodical fashion. Then he took out the key, which was on the inside, and inspected that also. The bed, the carpet, the chairs, the mantelpiece, the dead body, and the rope were each in turn examined, until at last he professed himself satisfied, and with my aid and that of the Inspector cut down the wretched object, and **24** laid it reverently under a sheet.

" How about this rope ? " he asked.

" It is cut off this," said Dr. Trevelyan, drawing a large coil from under the bed. " He was morbidly nervous of fire, and always kept this beside him, so that he might escape by the window in case the stairs were burning."

" That must have saved them trouble," said Holmes, thoughtfully. " Yes, the actual facts are very plain, and I shall be surprised if by the afternoon I cannot give you the reasons for them as well. I will take this photograph of Blessington which I see upon the mantelpiece, as it may help me in my inquiries."

" But you have told us nothing," cried the doctor.

" Oh, there can be no doubt as to the sequence of events," said Holmes. " There were three of them in it : the young man, the old man, and a third to whose identity I have no clue. The first two, I need hardly remark, are the same who masqueraded as the Russian Count and his son, so we can give a very full description of them. They were admitted by a confederate inside the house. If I might offer you a word of advice, Inspector, it would be to arrest the page, who, as I understand has only recently come into your service, Doctor."

" The young imp cannot be found," said Dr. Trevelyan ; " the maid and the cook have just been searching for him."

Holmes shrugged his shoulders.

" He has played a not unimportant part in this drama," **25** said he. " The three men having ascended the stair, which they did on tiptoe, the elder man first, the younger man second, and the unknown man in the rear——"

" My dear Holmes ! " I ejaculated.

" Oh, there could be no question as to the superimposing of the footmarks. I had the advantage of learning which was which last night. They ascended then to Mr. Blessington's room, the door of which they found to be locked. With the help of a wire, however, they forced

24 *cut down the wretched object.* "Surely the first act of a doctor, or indeed of anyone else, would be to cut [Blessington] down and to endeavour immediately to restore his respiration before it was too late," the late Gavin Brend wrote in *My Dear Holmes.* "Instead the body is allowed to remain hanging while Holmes first questions Inspector Lanner and then examines the cigar-ends, the lock, the key, the bed, the carpet, the chairs, the mantelpiece, the body and the rope. Only after all this has been done is the body cut down."

25 *"He has played a not unimportant part in this drama."* The late Page Heldenbrand has written ("On an Obscure Nervous Page") that ". . . we must blow the whistle on Holmes when he insists that the page was [a confederate] because 1) he had not grown old and gray in Trevelyan's service, and 2) having heard of Blessington's . . . unnatural demise, he succumbed to youthful panic and vacated the premises. The very facts of the case eliminate the probability of the page's guilt. For if the 'Russian nobleman' and his 'son' had planted an ally inside the house, he would only have been needed to report on Blessington's movements. And Holmes himself pointed out that 'they were not very well acquainted with his daily routine'; indeed, their two calls upon Dr. Trevelyan coincided with Blessington's usual pre-dinner constitutional. Subsequently, of course, the door-opening confederate became necessary; but the page was no more qualified for the job than were the cook, the maid(s) and Dr. Percy Trevelyan. . . . [The] deduction that flight from the scene of the crime indicates guilt [is] one that is worthy of Lestrade."

round the key. Even without the lens, you will perceive, by the scratches on this ward, where the pressure was applied.

" On entering the room, their first proceeding must have been to gag Mr. Blessington. He may have been asleep, or he may have been so paralysed with terror as to have been unable to cry out. These walls are thick, and it is conceivable that his shriek, if he had time to utter one, was unheard.

" Having secured him, it is evident to me that a consultation of some sort was held. Probably it was something in the nature of a judicial proceeding. It must have lasted for some time, for it was then that these cigars were smoked. The older man sat in that wicker chair : it was he who used the cigar-holder. The younger man sat over yonder ; he knocked his ash off against the chest of drawers. The third fellow paced up and down. Blessington, I think, sat upright in the bed, but of that I cannot be absolutely certain.

" Well, it ended by their taking Blessington and hanging him. The matter was so pre-arranged that it is my belief that they brought with them some sort of block or pulley which might serve as a gallows. That screwdriver and those screws were, as I conceive, for fixing it up. Seeing the hook, however, they naturally saved themselves the trouble. Having finished their work they made off, and the door was barred behind them by their confederate."

We had all listened with the deepest interest to this sketch of the night's doings, which Holmes had deduced from signs so subtle and minute, that even when he had pointed them out to us, we could scarcely follow him in his reasonings. The Inspector hurried away on the instant to make inquiries about the page, while Holmes and I returned to Baker Street for breakfast.

" I'll be back by three," said he when we had finished our meal. " Both the Inspector and the doctor will meet me here at that hour, and I hope by that time to have cleared up any little obscurity which the case may still present."

"BLESSINGTON, I THINK, SAT UPRIGHT IN THE BED . . ."

Illustration by William H. Hyde for *Harper's Weekly*, August 12, 1893.

Our visitors arrived at the appointed time, but it was a quarter to four before my friend put in an appearance. From his expression as he entered, however, I could see that all had gone well with him.

" Any news, Inspector ? "

" We have got the boy, sir."

" Excellent, and I have got the men."

" You have got them ! " we cried all three.

" Well, at least I have got their identity. This so-called Blessington is, as I expected, well known at head-quarters, and so are his assailants. Their names are Biddle, Hayward, and Moffat."

" The Worthingdon bank gang," cried the Inspector.

" Precisely," said Holmes.

" Then Blessington must have been Sutton ? "

" Exactly," said Holmes.

" Why, that makes it as clear as crystal," said the Inspector.

But Trevelyan and I looked at each other in bewilderment.

" You must surely remember the great Worthingdon bank business," said Holmes ; " five men were in it, these four and a fifth called Cartwright. Tobin, the caretaker, was murdered, and the thieves got away with seven thousand pounds. This was in 1875. They were **26** all five arrested, but the evidence against them was by no means conclusive. This Blessington or Sutton, who was the worst of the gang, turned informer. On his evidence Cartwright was hanged, and the other three got fifteen years apiece. When they got out the other day, which was some years before their full term, they set **27** themselves, as you perceive, to hunt down the traitor and to avenge the death of their comrade upon him. Twice they tried to get at him and failed ; a third time, you see, it came off. Is there anything further which I can explain, Dr. Trevelyan ? "

" I think you have made it all remarkably clear," said the doctor. " No doubt the day on which he was so perturbed was the day when he read of their release in the newspapers."

26 *seven thousand pounds.* About $35,000.

27 *some years before their full term.* English justice in the seventies was no less swift than English justice today; we are justified in assuming that no time was lost in trying and sentencing the thieves who had "got away with seven thousand pounds." We do not know in what month the robbery occurred, but the men must have been sentenced in either 1875 or 1876. 1890, then, 1891 at the latest, would have been the year for their release had they served their full term. In those days, as the late Professor Jay Finley Christ pointed out in *An Irregular Chronology*, the penal laws of England provided a maximum remission of three years and 197 days from a sentence of fifteen years, for good behavior. We may be sure that Biddle, Hayward and Moffat, counting the days until they could petition for release and settle their score with Sutton, would comport themselves as model prisoners, in order to secure the maximum remission. The date of their release would therefore fall in the approximate period July, 1886, to June, 1887. The adventure of "The Resident Patient" took place, as we know, in the month of October; we may now with some confidence date it exactly to *Wednesday, October 6 and Thursday, October 7, 1886.*

"YOU HAVE GOT THEM !" WE CRIED ALL THREE.

Illustration by Sidney Paget for the *Strand Magazine,* August, 1893.

28 Norah Creina. "Creina" is an Irish term of endearment, and the phrase Watson employed is to be found in Thomas Moore's poem, "Lesbia Hath a Beaming Eye": "Beauty lies in many eyes; but love in yours, / my Nora creina."

29 *lost some years ago with all hands.* "Dr. Watson was in error," Professor Alan Lang Strout wrote in *The Saturday Review of Literature*, "for, only a year before [Watson wrote his account of "The Resident Patient"] the *Norah Creina* carried Mr. Dodd safely into Honolulu: see R. L. Stevenson's *The Wrecker*, which appeared serially in *Scribner's Magazine* in 1891 and as a book in 1892."

"Quite so. His talk about a burglary was the merest blind."

"But why could he not tell you this?"

"Well, my dear sir, knowing the vindictive character of his old associates, he was trying to hide his own identity from everybody as long as he could. His secret was a shameful one, and he could not bring himself to divulge it. However, wretch as he was, he was still living under the shield of British law, and I have no doubt, Inspector, that you will see that, though that shield may fail to guard, the sword of justice is still there to avenge."

Such were the singular circumstances in connection with the resident patient and the Brook Street doctor. From that night nothing has been seen of the three murderers by the police, and it is surmised at Scotland Yard that they were among the passengers of the ill-fated **28** steamer *Norah Creina*, which was lost some years ago **29** with all hands upon the Portuguese coast, some leagues to the north of Oporto. The proceedings against the page broke down for want of evidence, and the "Brook Street Mystery," as it was called, has never, until now, been fully dealt with in any public print.

. . .

"... ONE OF THOSE UNWELCOME SOCIAL SUMMONSES WHICH CALL UPON A MAN EITHER TO BE BORED OR TO LIE."

Holmes' remark, says Dr. Richard Asher in "Holmes and the Fair Sex," "sounds more like Oscar Wilde than Sherlock Holmes and shows not only that Holmes was much in demand at the highest social functions and attended them often enough to be bored." (See also "A Scandal in Bohemia," Note 5.) The illustration, by George du Maurier, is from a copy of *Society Pictures from Punch* (1891) in the British Museum.

20

THE ADVENTURE OF THE NOBLE BACHELOR

[Friday, October 8, 1886]

THE Lord St. Simon marriage, and its curious termination, have long since ceased to be a subject of interest in those exalted circles in which the unfortunate bridegroom moves. Fresh scandals have eclipsed it, and their more piquant details have drawn the gossips away from this four-year-old drama. **1** As I have reason to believe, however, that the full facts have never been revealed to the general public, and as my friend Sherlock Holmes had a considerable share in clearing the matter up, I feel that no memoir of him would be complete without some little sketch of this remarkable episode.

It was a few weeks before my own marriage, during **2** the days when I was still sharing rooms with Holmes in Baker Street, that he came home from an afternoon stroll to find a letter on the table waiting for him. I had remained indoors all day, for the weather had taken a sudden turn to rain, with high autumnal winds, and the jezail bullet which I had brought back in one of my limbs as a **3** relic of my Afghan campaign, throbbed with dull persistency. With my body in one easy chair and my legs upon another, I had surrounded myself with a cloud of newspapers, until at last, saturated with the news of the day, I **4** tossed them all aside and lay listless, watching the huge crest and monogram upon the envelope upon the table, and wondering lazily who my friend's noble correspondent could be.

"Here is a very fashionable epistle," I remarked as he entered. "Your morning letters, if I remember right, were from a fishmonger and a tide-waiter." **5**

"Yes, my correspondence has certainly the charm of variety," he answered, smiling, "and the humbler are usually the more interesting. This looks like one of those unwelcome social summonses which call upon a man either to be bored or to lie."

He broke the seal, and glanced over the contents.

"Oh, come, it may prove to be something of interest after all."

"Not social, then?"

"No, distinctly professional."

"And from a noble client?"

1 *this four-year-old drama.* Since Watson's account of the adventure appeared in the *Strand Magazine* for April, 1892, the case must have taken place before April, 1888, at the latest, and probably a good many months earlier, since Watson's "four-year-old drama" must be dated from the *writing* rather than the *publishing* of his account.

2 *a few weeks before my own marriage.* Generally accepted by other commentators to mean Watson's marriage to Mary Morstan, whom he met during the adventure of *The Sign of the Four*, and therefore dated by them to 1887 (Andrew, Bell, Brend, Harrison, Hoff, Morley, and Newton) or 1888 (Blakeney, Christ, Folsom, Knox, Pattrick, Petersen, Smith, White, and Zeisler). On the other hand, your editor holds that Watson here refers to the marriage he celebrated *circa* November 1, 1886—two-and-a-half years before his marriage, *circa* May 1, 1889, to Mary Morstan (see "Now, Watson, the Fair Sex Is Your Department").

HE BROKE THE SEAL, AND GLANCED OVER THE CONTENTS.

Illustration by Sidney Paget for the *Strand Magazine*, April, 1892.

3 *in one of my limbs.* A curious but perhaps a not-too-impossible way to refer to a shoulder wound which left Watson with a left arm which he held "in a stiff and unnatural manner" (see "Your Hand Stole Towards Your Old Wound . . .").

4 *saturated with the news of the day.* The day was not a Sunday, for papers would not have been published on a Sunday, nor would Holmes have received letters by the morning post on that day.

5 *a tide-waiter."* "All my life I have wondered just what was a 'tide-waiter'," the late Christopher Morley wrote. "Lo and behold the other day I was reading some of Robert Burns' letters (in *Autograph Poems and Letters of Robert Burns in the Collection of R. B. Adam,* privately printed, Buffalo, 1922). In August, 1795, he wrote to Mrs. Riddell discussing the possibilities of a protégé of hers getting a job as a tide-waiter. The context makes it abundantly plain that it meant a customs officer—one who waited for ships to come in with the tide. He wrote: 'I think there is little doubt but that your interest, if judicially directed, may procure a tide-waiter's place for your protégé, Shaw; but, alas, that is doing little for him! Fifteen pounds per an: is the salary; and the perquisites, in some lucky stations, may be ten more. . . . The appointment is not in the Excise; but in the Customs.'"

6 *the interest of his case.* Compare, from "The Adventure of the Copper Beeches": "To the man who loves art for its own sake, it is frequently in its least important and lowliest manifestations that the keenest pleasure is to be derived." Wrote Mr. T. S. Blakeney in *Sherlock Holmes: Fact or Fiction?:* "It is certainly true that Holmes, though no apostle of equality, and despite the fact that his services were sought by the rulers of many lands, was free from all taint of snobbishness, as evidenced by his epigrammatic comment on Lord St. Simon's fashionably-addressed letter."

7 *the agony column.* "Department of personal advertisements in newspapers, first made famous in the *Times* of London," the late Christopher Morley wrote in *Sherlock Holmes and Dr. Watson: A Textbook of Friendship.* "All such columns exhibit a weird or comic mixture of human perplexities, hence the appropriate nickname. An extraordinarily interesting and amusing little book is *The Agony Column of 'The Times,' 1800–1870,* edited by Alice Clay, London: Chatto & Windus, 1881. The late Earl Derr Biggers, creator of the detective Charlie Chan, said of this book, 'If I owned it I would never need to invent another plot.'"

8 *Lord St. Simon.* Holmes' repeated reference to "Lord St. Simon" is a curious solecism; as the *second* son of the Duke of Balmoral, the noble bachelor was "Lord Robert St. Simon," not "Lord St. Simon." In some editions of the Sacred Writ-

"One of the highest in England."

"My dear fellow, I congratulate you."

"I assure you, Watson, without affectation, that the status of my client is a matter of less moment to me than **6** the interest of his case. It is just possible, however, that that also may not be wanting in this new investigation. You have been reading the papers diligently of late, have you not?"

"It looks like it," said I ruefully, pointing to a huge bundle in the corner. "I have had nothing else to do."

"It is fortunate, for you will perhaps be able to post me up. I read nothing except the criminal news and the **7** agony column. The latter is always instructive. But if you have followed recent events so closely you must have **8** read about Lord St. Simon and his wedding?"

"Oh, yes, with the deepest interest."

"That is well. The letter which I hold in my hand is from Lord St. Simon. I will read it to you, and in return you must turn over these papers and let me have whatever bears upon the matter. This is what he says:

9   "'MY DEAR MR. SHERLOCK HOLMES,—Lord Backwater tells me that I may place implicit reliance upon your judgment and discretion. I have determined, therefore, to call upon you, and to consult you in reference to the very painful event which has occurred in connection with my wedding. Mr. Lestrade, of Scotland Yard, is acting already in the matter, but he assures me that he sees no objection to your co-operation, and that he even thinks that it might be of some assistance. I will call at four o'clock in the afternoon, and should you have any other engagement at that time, I hope you will postpone it, as this is a matter of paramount importance.—Yours faithfully,

'ROBERT ST. SIMON.'

10   It is dated from Grosvenor Mansions, written with a quill pen, and the noble lord has had the misfortune to get a smear of ink upon the outer side of his right little finger," remarked Holmes, as he folded up the epistle.

"He says four o'clock. It is three now. He will be here in an hour."

"Then I have just time, with your assistance, to get clear upon the subject. Turn over those papers, and arrange the extracts in their order of time, while I take a glance as to who our client is." He picked a red-covered **11** volume from a line of books of reference beside the mantelpiece. "Here he is," said he, sitting down and flattening it out upon his knee. "'Robert Walsingham de Vere St. Simon, second son of the Duke of Balmoral'—Hum! 'Arms: Azure, three caltrops in chief over a fess sable. **12** Born in 1846.' He's forty-one years of age, which is mature for marriage. Was Under-Secretary for the Colonies in a late Administration. The Duke, his father, was at one time Secretary for Foreign Affairs. They inherit Plantagenet blood by direct descent, and Tudor on the distaff side. Ha! Well, there is nothing very instructive in all this. I think I must turn to you, Watson, for something more solid."

" 'ARMS: AZURE, THREE CALTROPS IN CHIEF OVER A FESS SABLE.' "

Caltrops, we read in Mr. Rolfe Boswell's "A Connecticut Yankee in Support of Sir Arthur," "are four-spiked iron balls scattered on the ground in medieval warfare to impede the enemy's advance. 'I think they have strewn the highways with caltrops,' Beaumont and Fletcher recount in *Love's Pilgrimage*, 'no horse dares pass them.' The caltrop's four short, but strong, spikes, or gads, were conjoined in such a manner that, when thrown on the ground, one spike always would be erect. . . . The use of caltrops was revived by the New England colonists against the Indians."

The arms of the noble bachelor, as Watson has given them to us, commit a heraldic solecism. "It is a fundamental law of heraldry that metal should never be charged on metal, nor color on color," Mr. Boswell continued. "Caltrops normally would be depicted sable (black). Since the fess already has been blazoned as *sable*, therefore the field of the shield contains the falsity in blazonry. Since azure (blue) patently is in error, therefore the metal whose initial is also an *a* is the correct background for the . . . shield, namely argent (silver). In the preferred blazonry now used by twentieth-century heralds, the arms . . . become: 'Silver a fess sable with three caltrops in the chief proper.' That is, in their natural color, which would be iron-grey." (It is Mr. Boswell's theory that Holmes substituted *his own arms* for those of the noble bachelor in this description to Watson. He would add to the arms as described in the preferred blazonry "a small crescent, symbol of a second son . . . charged upon the fess to distinguish Sherlock from his elder brother, Mycroft.")

The heraldic use of color upon color or metal upon metal has been defended by Dr. Wolff in his *Practical Handbook of Sherlockian Heraldry*: ". . . not the best heraldry, but it is seen. The best example is found in the arms of the Kingdom of Jerusalem: argent a cross potent between four plain crosses or. Less known, but more spectacular, is the purple chief on a green field in the arms of Thackeray."

Dr. Wolff holds that Holmes substituted, not his own coat of arms, but that of James Boswell of Auchinleck, given by Robson as "az. on a fesse sa. three cinquefoils of the first.' Azure and a fess sable!" ("It is not an anti-climax," Dr. Wolff has added, "that the Boswell arms are really argent, not azure, with a fess sable. From what other work [than Robson] could [Holmes] have picked up his misinformation?")

Above, left: The coat of arms of Lord Robert St. Simon, according to Sherlock Holmes: Azure, three caltrops in chief over a fess sable. *Right:* The coat of arms substituted by Holmes for that of Lord Robert St. Simon, according to Dr. Julian Wolff. They are those of James Boswell of Auchinleck as they (mistakenly) appear in Robson: Azure on a fess sable three cinquefoils of the first.

ings he signs his note to Holmes (improperly) "St. Simon." In others, he signs himself (properly) "Robert St. Simon"—"just as the second son of the Duke of Denver signs himself 'Peter Wimsey,' and neither 'Wimsey' nor 'Lord Wimsey,' " Dr. William Braid White wrote in "Dr. Watson and the Peerage."

9 *Lord Backwater.* We hear of Lord Backwater again in 1890 (your editor's date): his horse, Desborough, ran against Silver Blaze in the Wessex Cup (or Plate). Other commentators have interpreted this reference to mean that "Silver Blaze" *preceded* "The Adventure of the Noble Bachelor." If it did not, however, there must have been another occasion on which Lord Backwater learned that one might place implicit reliance upon Holmes' judgment and discretion.

10 *Grosvenor Mansions.* On Victoria Street, at the corner of Palace Street. Begun in 1858, building operations were afterwards suspended, and the unfinished structure remained an eyesore for several years, after which it was purchased by the Freehold Investment Company and completed as a block of flats which were at first rented at £300 a year. The building, seven stories high, now consists principally of offices and shops.

11 *a red-covered volume.* Possibly a *Who's Who,* possibly a Burke's *Peerage,* possibly a Debrett, possibly a Doyle's *Official Baronage.* But Dr. Julian Wolff, in his *Practical Handbook of Sherlockian Heraldry,* has advanced a cogent reason for believing that it may also have been Thomas Robson's *The British Herald, or Cabinet of Armorial Bearings*—one of the three volumes of this work printed in Sunderland for the author in 1830.

12 *He's forty-one years of age.* Thus, on whatever day in 1846 Lord Robert may have been born —from January 1st to December 31st—he would have been closer to forty-one than to forty or forty-two between July 1, 1886, and June 30, 1888, and the case must fall within that period.

"THEY INHERIT PLANTAGENET BLOOD BY DIRECT DESCENT, AND TUDOR ON THE DISTAFF SIDE."

As Mr. Rolfe Boswell has pointed out ("A Connecticut Yankee in Support of Sir Arthur") "England's only ducal house which can fulfill this requirement is that of the Somersets, Dukes of Beaufort. . . . In quoting from his 'red-covered volume,' which Holmes takes care not to show Watson, 'flattening it out upon his knee,' the Master changes the surname Somerset to *St. Simon*, and makes his client 'second son of the *Duke of Balmoral*,' swiftly substituting a royal castle in Scotland . . . for the erstwhile royal castle in Anjou from which the Somersets take their title of Beaufort." Dr. Wolff has added: "The Duke of Beaufort . . . had an unmarried son who was born in 1847, not far from Watson's 1846—truly a noble bachelor! Those who choose to believe that Robert de Vere St. Simon was the son of the Duke of Beaufort may even derive some additional assurance from the coincidence that the present heir is H. Robert deVere Somerset." *Left:* the coat of arms of the Somersets, Dukes of Beaufort. It is blazoned: France and England quarterly within a bordure compony argent and azure. Crest: A portcullis or, nailed azure, chains gold. Supporters: Dexter, a panther argent, flames issuing from his mouth and ears proper, plain collared and chained or, and semé of torteaux, hurts and pomels alternately. Sinister, a wyvern vert, in the mouth a sinister hand couped at the wrist gules.

13 *Grosvenor Square*. Grosvenor Square, six acres in extent, takes its name from Sir Robert Grosvenor (d. 1732). Built between 1720 and 1730, it contained, in Holmes' and Watson's day, many large houses which have now given way to blocks of flats. Hare wrote of it: "For a century and a half . . . the most fashionable place of residence in London. . . . The old ironwork and flambeau extinguishers before many of the doors in Grosvenor Square deserve notice. In the [eighteenth] century the nobility were proud of their flambeau, and it is remarkable that the aristocratic Square refused to adopt the use of gas till compelled to do so by force of public opinion in 1842. . . . Grosvenor Square is crossed by the two great arteries Grosvenor Street and Brook Street."

The late Clifton R. Andrew's "The Little Problem of the Grosvenor Square Furniture Van," a pastische stemming from this reference of Holmes', appeared in the Freeport, Ohio, *Press* August 30-September 6, 1945.

14 *the Westbury House*. Today there is a Westbury Hotel in London, but the Westbury *House* is not now identifiable.

" I have very little difficulty in finding what I want," said I, " for the facts are quite recent, and the matter struck me as remarkable. I feared to refer them to you, however, as I knew that you had an inquiry on hand, and that you disliked the intrusion of other matters."

" Oh, you mean the little problem of the Grosvenor 13 Square furniture van. That is quite cleared up now—though, indeed, it was obvious from the first. Pray give me the results of your newspaper selections."

" Here is the first notice which I can find. It is in the personal column of the *Morning Post*, and dates, as you see, some weeks back. ' A marriage has been arranged,' it says, ' and will, if rumour is correct, very shortly take place, between Lord Robert St. Simon, second son of the Duke of Balmoral, and Miss Hatty Doran, the only daughter of Aloysius Doran, Esq., of San Francisco, Cal., U.S.A.' That is all."

" Terse and to the point," remarked Holmes, stretching his long, thin legs towards the fire.

" There was a paragraph amplifying this in one of the society papers of the same week. Ah, here it is. ' There will soon be a call for protection in the marriage market, for the present free-trade principle appears to tell heavily against our home product. One by one the management of the noble houses of Great Britain is passing into the hands of our fair cousins from across the Atlantic. An important addition has been made during the last week to the list of prizes which have been borne away by these charming invaders. Lord St. Simon, who has shown himself for over twenty years proof against the little god's arrows, has now definitely announced his approaching marriage with Miss Hatty Doran, the fascinating daughter of a Californian millionaire. Miss Doran, whose graceful figure and striking face attracted much attention at the 14 Westbury House festivities, is an only child, and it is currently reported that her dowry will run to considerably over the six figures, with expectancies for the future. As it is an open secret that the Duke of Balmoral has been compelled to sell his pictures within the last few years, and as Lord St. Simon has no property of his own, save the small estate of Birchmoor, it is obvious that the Californian heiress is not the only gainer by an alliance which will enable her to make the easy and common transition from a Republican lady to a British title.' "

" Anything else ? " asked Holmes, yawning.

" Oh yes ; plenty.   Then there is another note in the *Morning Post* to say that the marriage would be an absolutely quiet one, that it would be at St. George's, Hanover Square, that only half a dozen intimate friends would be **15** invited, and that the party would return to the furnished house at Lancaster Gate which has been taken by Mr. **16** Aloysius Doran.   Two days later—that is, on Wednesday last—there is a curt announcement that the wedding had taken place, and that the honeymoon would be passed at Lord Backwater's place, near Petersfield.   Those are all **17** the notices which appeared before the disappearance of the bride."

" Before the what ? " asked Holmes, with a start.

" The vanishing of the lady."

" When did she vanish, then ? "

" At the wedding breakfast."

" Indeed.   This is more interesting than it promised to be ; quite dramatic, in fact."

" Yes ; it struck me as being a little out of the common."   **18**

" They often vanish before the ceremony, and occasionally during the honeymoon ; but I cannot call to mind anything quite so prompt as this.   Pray let me have the details."

" I warn you that they are very incomplete."

" Perhaps we may make them less so."

" Such as they are, they are set forth in a single article of a morning newspaper of yesterday, which I will read to you.   It is headed ' Singular Occurrence at a Fashionable Wedding ' :

" ' The family of Lord Robert St. Simon has been thrown into the greatest consternation by the strange and painful episodes which have taken place in connection with his wedding.   The ceremony, as shortly announced in the papers of yesterday, occurred on the previous morning ; but it is only now that it has been possible to confirm **19** the strange rumours which have been so persistently floating about.   In spite of the attempts of the friends to hush the matter up, so much public attention has now been drawn to it that no good purpose can be served by affecting to disregard what is a common subject for conversation.

" ' The ceremony, which was performed at St. George's, Hanover Square, was a very quiet one, no one being present save the father of the bride, Mr. Aloysius Doran, the Duchess of Balmoral, Lord Backwater, Lord Eustace and Lady Clara St. Simon (the younger brother and sister of the bridegroom), and Lady Alicia Whittington.   The whole party proceeded afterwards to the house of Mr. Aloysius Doran, at Lancaster Gate, where breakfast had been prepared.   It appears that some little

15 *St. George's; Hanover Square.* This church did enjoy an almost complete monopoly on marriages in high life. Built by John James in 1724, named in honor of George I, its marriage registers were a perfect library of the autographs of illustrious persons, among which the bold signature of "Wellington" appeared frequently. At the beginning of the nineteenth century from 1,100 to 1,200 couples were sometimes united there in a year. Nelson's Lady Hamilton was married at St. George's on September 6, 1791. This being the case, it is astonishing, as the Reverend Otis R. Rice has pointed out in "Clergymen in the Canon," "that the solemnization of the marriage [in this adventure] was left to the vicar or even one of his curates. For one of his noble and social rank St. Simon could be expected to do better than that. Why not an Archbishop? Or at least the Bishop of London? Or some other bishop who was conveniently kicking about? Was there some strange or sinister reason (apart from the bride's lowly station) which necessitated calling upon a mere priest to officiate? Is there the sad possibility that, in the exigencies of life in a mining camp and later in the arduous work of clipping coupons, neither Hatty nor her father found time to have her baptized? Perish the thought! The fact remains, however, that the officiating 'clergyman' in the tale . . . did not have his name mentioned in the press notice; a *most* unusual omission. Nor was he invited to the wedding breakfast. Here is another example of a questionable cleric encountered in the pages of the Writings."

Hanover Square, Augustus J. C. Hare tells us, "received its name instead of that of Oxford Square, as was first intended, in the days of the early popularity of George I. The square was built about 1731, when the place for executions was removed from Tyburn, lest the inhabitants of 'the new square' should be annoyed by them."

16 *Lancaster Gate.* Then a long and impressive range of balconied buildings, completed in 1866, in a well-to-do residential quarter north of Hyde Park.

17 *Petersfield.* A market town in Hampshire.

18 *It struck me as being a little out of the common."* An excellent early example of Watson's "pawky" sense of humor (*The Valley of Fear*).

19 *occurred on the previous morning.* The case took a day of Holmes' time—a Friday. This is certain from the newspaper accounts: 1) On "Wednesday last" there had appeared "a curt announcement that the wedding had taken place"; 2) the morning paper of "yesterday" had reported that "the ceremony, as shortly announced in the papers of yesterday [the Wednesday], occurred on the previous morning . . ." (the Tuesday); 3) since the morning paper of "yesterday" was therefore the morning paper of Thursday, it follows that the case opened (and closed) on a Friday.

"'. . . SHE WAS EJECTED BY THE BUTLER AND THE
FOOTMAN.'"

Illustration by Sidney Paget for the *Strand Magazine*, April, 1892.

20 *a* danseuse. French: a female professional dancer; a ballet girl.

21 *our page-boy.* The Baker Street page boy is mentioned or makes an appearance in eight other adventures: "A Case of Identity" (October, 1887); *The Valley of Fear* (January, 1888); "The Yellow Face" (April, 1888); "The Greek Interpreter" (September, 1888); "The Naval Treaty" (August, 1889); "The Problem of Thor Bridge" (October, 1900); "The Adventure of Shoscombe Old Place" (May, 1902); and "The Adventure of the Mazarin Stone" (Summer, 1903).

In both *The Valley of Fear* and "The Adventure of the Mazarin Stone" we are told his given name—Billy. It is clear that a page boy was employed throughout most of the late eighties. But this cannot be the "young" page boy of the 1900–1903 period; either both boys were named Billy, or Billy was a generic name applied by Holmes and Watson to all the Baker Street page boys.

"It is possible," Mr. Vincent Starrett wrote in "The Singular Adventures of Martha Hudson,"

trouble had been caused by a woman, whose name has not been ascertained, who endeavoured to force her way into the house after the bridal party, alleging that she had some claim upon Lord St. Simon. It was only after a painful and prolonged scene that she was ejected by the butler and the footman. The bride, who had fortunately entered the house before this unpleasant interruption, had sat down to breakfast with the rest, when she complained of a sudden indisposition, and retired to her room. Her prolonged absence having caused some comment, her father followed her ; but learned from her maid that she had only come up to her chamber for an instant, caught up an ulster and bonnet, and hurried down to the passage. One of the footmen declared that he had seen a lady leave the house thus apparelled ; but had refused to credit that it was his mistress, believing her to be with the company. On ascertaining that his daughter had disappeared, Mr. Aloysius Doran, in conjunction with the bridegroom, instantly put themselves into communication with the police, and very energetic inquiries are being made, which will probably result in a speedy clearing up of this very singular business. Up to a late hour last night, however, nothing had transpired as to the whereabouts of the missing lady. There are rumours of foul play in the matter, and it is said that the police have caused the arrest of the woman who had caused the original disturbance, in the belief that, from jealousy or some other motive, she may have been concerned in the strange disappearance of the bride.' "

" And is that all ? "

" Only one little item in another of the morning papers, but it is a suggestive one."

" And it is ? "

" That Miss Flora Millar, the lady who had caused the disturbance, has actually been arrested. It appears that **20** she was formerly a *danseuse* at the Allegro, and that she had known the bridegroom for some years. There are no further particulars, and the whole case is in your hands now—so far as it has been set forth in the public press."

" And an exceedingly interesting case it appears to be. I would not have missed it for worlds. But there is a ring at the bell, Watson, and as the clock makes it a few minutes after four, I have no doubt that this will prove to be our noble client. Do not dream of going, Watson, for I very much prefer having a witness, if only as a check to my own memory."

21 " Lord Robert St. Simon," announced our page-boy, throwing open the door. A gentleman entered, with a pleasant, cultured face, high-nosed and pale, with something perhaps of petulance about the mouth, and with the steady, well-opened eye of a man whose pleasant lot it had ever been to command and to be obeyed. His manner was brisk, and yet his general appearance gave an undue impression of age, for he had a slight forward stoop, and a little bend of the knees as he walked. His hair, too, as he swept off his curly brimmed hat, was grizzled round the edges, and thin upon the top. As to his dress, it was careful to the verge of foppishness, with high collar, black frock-coat, white waistcoat, yellow gloves, patent-leather shoes, and light-coloured gaiters. **22** He advanced slowly into the room, turning his head from left to right, and swinging in his right hand the cord which held his golden eye-glasses.

"Good day, Lord St. Simon," said Holmes, rising and bowing. "Pray take the basket chair. This is my friend and colleague, Dr. Watson. Draw up a little to the fire, and we shall talk this matter over."

". . . SWINGING IN HIS RIGHT HAND THE CORD WHICH HELD HIS GOLDEN EYEGLASSES."

Portrait of Lord Robert St. Simon by Sidney Paget for the *Strand Magazine*, April, 1892.

"A most painful matter to me, as you can most readily imagine, Mr. Holmes. I have been cut to the quick. I understand you have already managed several delicate cases of this sort, sir, though I presume that they were hardly from the same class of society."

"No, I am descending."

"I beg pardon?"

"My last client of the sort was a king."

"Oh, really! I had no idea. And which king?"

"The King of Scandinavia." **23**

"What! Had he lost his wife?"

"You can understand," said Holmes suavely, "that I extend to the affairs of my other clients the same secrecy which I promise to you in yours."

"that [the page] was employed some months after the advent of the detective and the doctor, at a time when the increasing number of visitors, calling upon Mr. Sherlock Holmes, too frequently snatched the maid and Mrs. Hudson from their necessary household duties. Just conceivably he was a bit of swank on the part of Mrs. Hudson, who may well have looked forward to a time when she could afford a page, like other more prosperous landladies."

"If Billy's functions were confined to announcing visitors and running errands he must have had an extremely cushy time of it," Mr. G. B. Newton commented in "Billy the Page." "Even if he also valeted Holmes and Watson his duties would hardly have been onerous. On general grounds therefore it seems more likely that he was employed by Mrs. Hudson for general work in the house and that any references to 'our page-boy' were merely avuncular."

22 *gaiters.* Watson in later stories drops this old-fashioned word and modernizes his writing by calling these objects of male wearing apparel *spats.* Spats were one of the trademarks of the "Knut" of turn-of-the-century and later London —the well-to-do-young Englishmen who made a career out of their clubs. It was on the "Knuts" that P. G. Wodehouse based (and never changed) the characters of Bertie Wooster, Bingo Little, and all the other "Eggs, Beans and Crumpets" of that memorable institution, "the Drones Club."

23 *"The King of Scandinavia."* "Scandinavia is the peninsula on which Norway and Sweden are situated," Mr. Svend Petersen wrote in "When the Game Was Not Afoot." "At the time of the adventures in which the King of Scandinavia figures, that ruler was Oscar II, 1829–1907, who reigned over both nations from 1872 to 1905, Norway severing her personal connection with Sweden in the latter year."

It was to the second daughter of the King of Scandinavia, Clotilde Lothman von Saxe-Meningen, that the King of Bohemia was to be married ("A Scandal in Bohemia"), and commentators have surmised that it was perhaps to arrange this delicate business that Holmes was retained by the King of Scandinavia shortly before "The Adventure of the Noble Bachelor" (but, if so, the King of Bohemia certainly knew nothing about it).

Again, in late 1890 or early 1891, Holmes was to be of assistance to the Royal Family of Scandinavia ("The Final Problem").

In the light of the fact that Norway did not sever her connection with Sweden until 1905, it is quite possible that Holmes' visit to Norway in July, 1895 ("The Adventure of Black Peter") was also connected with a mission for Oscar II. It has been said that His Holiness, Pope Leo XIII, was the only client who *twice* commissioned Holmes (see *The Hound of the Baskervilles,* "The Adventure of Black Peter") but we learn here that this was not the case.

" Of course ! Very right ! very right ! I'm sure I beg pardon. As to my own case, I am ready to give you any information which may assist you in forming an opinion."

" Thank you. I have already learned all that is in the public prints, nothing more. I presume that I may take it as correct—this article, for example, as to the disappearance of the bride."

Lord St. Simon glanced over it. " Yes, it is correct, as far as it goes."

" But it needs a great deal of supplementing before anyone could offer an opinion. I think that I may arrive at my facts most directly by questioning you."

" Pray do so."

" When did you first meet Miss Hatty Doran ? "

" In San Francisco, a year ago."

" You were travelling in the States ? "

" Yes."

" Did you become engaged then ? "

" No."

" But you were on a friendly footing ? "

" I was amused by her society, and she could see that I was amused."

" Her father is very rich ? "

" He is said to be the richest man on the Pacific Slope."

" And how did he make his money ? "

" In mining. He had nothing a few years ago. Then he struck gold, invested it, and came up by leaps and bounds."

" Now, what is your own impression as to the young lady's—your wife's character ? "

The nobleman swung his glasses a little faster and stared down into the fire. " You see, Mr. Holmes," said he, " my wife was twenty before her father became a rich man. During that time she ran free in a mining camp, and wandered through woods or mountains, so that her education has come from nature rather than from the schoolmaster. She is what we call in England a tomboy, with a strong nature, wild and free, unfettered by any sort of traditions. She is impetuous—volcanic, I was about to say. She is swift in making up her mind, and fearless in carrying out her resolutions. On the other hand, I would not have given her the name which I have the honour to bear " (he gave a little stately cough) " had I not thought her to be at bottom a noble woman. I believe she is capable of heroic self-sacrifice, and that anything dishonourable would be repugnant to her."

" Have you her photograph ?

" I brought this with me." He opened a locket, and showed us the full face of a very lovely woman. It was not a photograph, but an ivory miniature, and the artist had brought out the full effect of the lustrous black hair, the large dark eyes, and the exquisite mouth. Holmes gazed long and earnestly at it. Then he closed the locket and handed it back to Lord St. Simon.

" The young lady came to London, then, and you renewed your acquaintance ? "

" Yes, her father brought her over for this last London season. I met her several times, became engaged to her, and have now married her."

" She brought, I understand, a considerable dowry."

" A fair dowry.   Not more than is usual in my family."

" And this, of course, remains to you, since the marriage is a *fait accompli* ? "   **24**

" I really have made no inquiries on the subject."

" Very naturally not.   Did you see Miss Doran on the day before the wedding ? "

" Yes."

" Was she in good spirits ? '

" Never better.   She kept talking of what we should do in our future lives."

" Indeed.   That is very interesting.   And on the morning of the wedding ? "

" She was as bright as possible—at least, until after the ceremony."

" And did you observe any change in her then ? "

" Well, to tell the truth, I saw then the first signs that I had ever seen that her temper was just a little sharp.   The incident, however, was too trivial to relate, and can have no possible bearing upon the case."

" Pray let us have it, for all that."

" Oh, it is childish.   She dropped her bouquet as we went towards the vestry.   She was passing the front pew at the time, and it fell over into the pew.   There was a moment's delay, but the gentleman in the pew handed it up to her again, and it did not appear to be the worse for the fall.   Yet, when I spoke to her of the matter, she answered me abruptly ; and in the carriage, on our way home, she seemed absurdly agitated over this trifling cause."

" Indeed.   You say that there was a gentleman in the pew.   Some of the general public were present, then ? "

" Oh, yes.   It is impossible to exclude them when the church is open."

" This gentleman was not one of your wife's friends ? "

" No, no ; I call him a gentleman by courtesy, but he was quite a common-looking person.   I hardly noticed his appearance.   But really I think that we are wandering rather far from the point."

" Lady St. Simon, then, returned from the wedding in a less cheerful frame of mind than she had gone to it. What did she do on re-entering her father's house ? "

" I saw her in conversation with her maid."

" And who is her maid ? "

" Alice is her name.   She is an American, and came from California with her."

" A confidential servant ? "

" A little too much so.   It seemed to me that her mistress allowed her to take great liberties.   Still, of course, in America they look upon these things in a different way."

" How long did she speak to this Alice ? "

" Oh, a few minutes.   I had something else to think of."

" You did not overhear what they said ? "

" Lady St. Simon said something about ' jumping a claim.'   She was accustomed to use slang of the kind.   I have no idea what she meant."

" American slang is very expressive sometimes.   And what did your wife do when she had finished speaking to her maid ? "

24 *a* fait accompli?" French: a thing accomplished and supposedly irrevocable.

". . . BUT THE GENTLEMAN IN THE PEW HANDED IT UP
TO HER AGAIN . . ."

Illustration by Sidney Paget for the *Strand Magazine*, April, 1892.

25 *"But this maid Alice, as I understand, de- poses.* Holmes' use of the word "deposes" is another example of his practical knowledge of the law.

". . . SHE WAS AFTERWARDS SEEN WALKING INTO HYDE PARK . . ."

"Hyde Park (open to carriages, not to cabs), the principal recreation ground of London, takes its name from the manor of Hyde, which belonged to the Abbey of Westminster," Augustus J. C. Hare wrote in *Walks in London*, Vol. II. "The first park was enclosed by Henry VIII, and the French Ambassador hunted there in 1550. In the time of Charles I, the park was thrown open to the public, but it was sold under the Common- wealth, when Evelyn complained that 'every coach was made to pay a shilling, and horse sixpence, by the sordid fellow who had purchas'd it of the State as they were call'd.' . . . Hyde Park has been much used of late years for radical meetings, and on Sundays numerous open-air congregations on the turf near the Marble Arch make the air re- sound with 'revival' melodies, and recall the days of Wesley and Whitefield." The photograph is from *The Baker Street Journal*, Vol. II, No. 1, Old Series, January, 1947.

" She walked into the breakfast-room."

" On your arm ? "

" No, alone. She was very independent in little matters like that. Then, after we had sat down for ten minutes or so, she rose hurriedly, muttered some words of apology, and left the room. She never came back."

25 " But this maid Alice, as I understand, deposes that she went to her room, covered her bride's dress with a long ulster, put on a bonnet, and went out."

" Quite so. And she was afterwards seen walking into Hyde Park in company with Flora Millar, a woman who is now in custody, and who had already made a disturb- ance at Mr. Doran's house that morning."

" Ah, yes. I should like a few particulars as to this young lady, and your relations to her."

Lord St. Simon shrugged his shoulders, and raised his eyebrows. " We have been on a friendly footing for some years—I may say on a *very* friendly footing. She used to be at the Allegro. I have not treated her un- generously, and she has no just cause of complaint against me, but you know what women are, Mr. Holmes. Flora was a dear little thing, but exceedingly hot-headed, and devotedly attached to me. She wrote me dreadful letters when she heard that I was to be married, and to tell the truth the reason why I had the marriage celebrated so quietly was that I feared lest there might be a scandal in the church. She came to Mr. Doran's door just after we returned, and she endeavoured to push her way in, utter- ing very abusive expressions towards my wife, and even threatening her, but I had foreseen the possibility of something of the sort, and I had given instructions to the servants, who soon pushed her out again. She was quiet when she saw that there was no good in making a row."

" Did your wife hear all this ? "

" No, thank goodness, she did not."

" And she was seen walking with this very woman afterwards ? "

" Yes. That is what Mr. Lestrade, of Scotland Yard, looks upon as so serious. It is thought that Flora decoyed my wife out, and laid some terrible trap for her."

" Well, it is a possible supposition."

" You think so, too ? "

" I did not say a probable one. But you do not yourself look upon this as likely ? "

" I do not think Flora would hurt a fly."

" Still, jealousy is a strange transformer of characters. Pray what is your own theory as to what took place ? "

" Well, really, I came to seek a theory, not to propound one. I have given you all the facts. Since you ask me, however, I may say that it has occurred to me as possible that the excitement of this affair, the consciousness that she had made so immense a social stride, had the effect of causing some little nervous disturbance in my wife."

" In short, that she had become suddenly deranged ? "

" Well, really, when I consider that she has turned her back—I will not say upon me, but upon so much that many have aspired to without success—I can hardly explain it in any other fashion."

" Well, certainly that is also a conceivable hypothesis," said Holmes, smiling. " And now, Lord St. Simon, I think that I have nearly all my data. May I ask whether you were seated at the breakfast-table so that you could see out of the window ? "

" We could see the other side of the road, and the Park."

" Quite so. Then I do not think that I need detain you any longer. I shall communicate with you."

" Should you be fortunate enough to solve this problem," said our client, rising.

" I have solved it."

" Eh ? What was that ? "

" I say that I have solved it."

" Where, then, is my wife ? "

" That is a detail which I shall speedily supply."

Lord St. Simon shook his head. " I am afraid that it will take wiser heads than yours or mine," he remarked, and bowing in a stately, old-fashioned manner, he departed.

" It is very good of Lord St. Simon to honour my head by putting it on a level with his own," said Sherlock Holmes, laughing. " I think that I shall have a whisky and soda and a cigar after all this cross-questioning. I had formed my conclusions as to the case before our client came into the room."

" My dear Holmes ! "

" I have notes of several similar cases, though none, as I remarked before, which were quite as prompt. My whole examination served to turn my conjecture into a certainty. Circumstantial evidence is occasionally very convincing, **26** as when you find a trout in the milk, to quote Thoreau's example." **27**

" But I have heard all that you have heard."

" Without, however, the knowledge of pre-existing cases which serves me so well. There was a parallel instance in Aberdeen some years back, and something on very much the same lines at Munich the year after the

26 *"Circumstantial evidence is occasionally very convincing*. Holmes had conflicting views on circumstantial evidence. In "The Boscombe Valley Mystery," he calls it "a very tricky thing." And in "The Problem of Thor Bridge," he says: "When once your point of view is changed, the very thing which was so damning becomes a clue to the truth."

27 *to quote Thoreau's example*. Holmes quotes Henry David Thoreau, 1817–1862, the American poet, naturalist, and essayist. As Miss Madeleine B. Stern wrote in "Sherlock Holmes: Rare Book Collector," this is "a clear enough sign that [Holmes] may have owned a copy of Thoreau's *Miscellanies* (Boston, 1863), to which Emerson has added a biographical sketch including sentences from the unpublished writings. Among the sentences was . . . the remark on circumstantial evidence, actually taken from the as yet unpublished *Journals* of Thoreau."

28 *the year after the Franco-Prussian War.* The war ended on January 28, 1871. Some commentators have surmised from Holmes' manner of speaking here that he may have had first-hand knowledge of one or both of these cases, attained, in the case of the affair at Munich, during a stay on the Continent in the years 1870–1871.

29 *a pea-jacket.* A short overcoat worn by sailors. *Pea* has nothing to do with its color; rather it comes from an old Dutch word, *pie* or *pij*, meaning coat. The pea-jacket was, on occasion, a favored garment with Holmes as well as Lestrade; the Master dons one in both "The Red-Headed League" and *The Sign of the Four*.

28 Franco-Prussian War. It is one of these cases—but hallo, here is Lestrade ! Good afternoon, Lestrade ! You will find an extra tumbler upon the sideboard, and there are cigars in the box."

29   The official detective was attired in a pea-jacket and cravat, which gave him a decidedly nautical appearance, and he carried a black canvas bag in his hand. With a short greeting he seated himself, and lit the cigar which had been offered to him.

" What's up, then ? " asked Holmes, with a twinkle in his eye. " You look dissatisfied."

" And I feel dissatisfied. It is this infernal St. Simon marriage case. I can make neither head nor tail of the business."

" Really ! You surprise me.

" Who ever heard of such a mixed affair ? Every clue seems to slip through my fingers. I have been at work upon it all day."

" And very wet it seems to have made you," said Holmes, laying his hand upon the arm of the pea-jacket.

" Yes, I have been dragging the Serpentine."

" In Heaven's name, what for ? "

" In search of the body of Lady St. Simon."

Sherlock Holmes leaned back in his chair and laughed heartily.

"... I HAVE BEEN DRAGGING THE SERPENTINE."

"A little to the north of Rotten Row [in Hyde Park]," Augustus J. C. Hare wrote in *Walks in London,* Vol. II, "is the Serpentine, an artificial lake of fifty acres, much frequented for bathing in summer and for skating in winter. There is a delightful drive along its northern bank. Near this are the oldest trees in the Park, some of them oaks said to have been planted by Charles II." The photograph, by J. Allen Cash, is from *The First Country Life Picture Book of London,* London: Country Life, Ltd., 1951.

" Have you dragged the basin of the Trafalgar Square fountain ? " he asked.

" Why ? What do you mean ? "

" Because you have just as good a chance of finding this lady in the one as in the other."

Lestrade shot an angry glance at my companion. " I suppose you know all about it," he snarled.

" Well, I have only just heard the facts, but my mind is made up."

" Oh, indeed ! Then you think that the Serpentine plays no part in the matter ? "

" I think it very unlikely."

" Then perhaps you will kindly explain how it is that we found this in it ? " He opened his bag as he spoke, and tumbled on to the floor a wedding dress of watered silk, a pair of white satin shoes, and a bride's wreath and veil, all discoloured and soaked in water. " There," said he, putting a new wedding-ring upon the top of the pile. " There is a little nut for you to crack, Master Holmes."

" Oh, indeed," said my friend, blowing blue rings into the air. " You dragged them from the Serpentine ? "

" No. They were found floating near the margin by a park-keeper. They were identified as her clothes, and it seemed to me that if the clothes were there the body would not be far off."

" By the same brilliant reasoning, every man's body is to be found in the neighbourhood of his wardrobe. And pray what did you hope to arrive at through this ? "

" At some evidence implicating Flora Millar in the disappearance."

" I am afraid you will find it difficult."

"THERE," HE SAID, PUTTING A NEW WEDDING-RING
UPON THE TOP OF THE PILE.

Illustration by Sidney Paget for the *Strand Magazine*, April, 1892.

"HAVE YOU DRAGGED THE BASIN OF THE TRAFALGAR
SQUARE FOUNTAIN?", . .

Augustus J. C. Hare, in his *Walks in London*, Vol. II, calls this famous square "a dreary expanse of granite with two granite fountains, intended to commemorate the last victory of Nelson. Its northern side is occupied by the miserable buildings of the National Gallery; its eastern and western sides by a hideous hotel and a frightful club. Where the noble Jacobian screen of Northumberland House . . . once drew the eye away from these abominations by its dignity and beauty, a view of the funnel-roof of Charing Cross Railway Station forms a poor substitute for the time-honoured palace of the Percy's! In the centre of the square is a Corinthian pillar of Devonshire granite, 145 feet in height, by W. Railton, erected in 1843. It supports a statue of Nelson by E. H. Bailey, R.A., a very poor work, which, however, does not much signify, as it can only be properly seen from the top of the Duke of York's column, which no one ascends. . . . On the east side of Trafalgar Square is its one ornament. Here, on a noble basement, approached by a broad flight of steps, rises the beautiful portico of the Church of St. Martin in the Fields." The photograph, by G. F. Allen, is from *The First Country Life Picture Book of London*, London: Country Life, Ltd., 1951.

30 "'*Oct. 4th.* There is no reason to doubt the month: Watson has earlier spoken of "high autumnal winds." More important, Holmes says, at the end of the case: "The only problem we have still to solve is now to while away these bleak autumnal evenings."

31 *glass sherry 8d.'* The room cost $2.00, the breakfast and lunch some 62½¢ each, the cocktail 25¢, the sherry, 16¢. We are later told that the bill was rendered by "one of the most expensive hotels" in London. *Eheu fugaces!*

32 *a couple of brace of cold woodcock.* "This admirable bird," Mr. Vincent Starrett wrote in "The Singular Adventures of Martha Hudson," "would appear to have been a favorite with Holmes. . . . [A] woodcock [was served] during the excitements of the detective's search for the Blue Carbuncle."

33 *a pheasant.* "The means of preparing woodcock and pheasant, when they are to be served cold, approach each other very closely, and the difference is only perceptible to a delicate palate," the late Fletcher Pratt wrote in "The Gastronomic Holmes." "Holmes was subtly flattering his guests by assuming that although they were Americans, they would know enough about the *haute cuisine* to be able to express an intelligent choice between the cold woodcock and the cold pheasant; that they would savor the fine distinction between the two and perhaps take a slice of each. . . . I think there can be little doubt about how the woodcock and the pheasant were served. At least one of them must have been *à la buloz* and the *chaud-froid.* There are only two possible recipes, the Bohemian, in which the bird appears in aspic in the center of a block of ice—which was impossible because the supper had to wait from 5:00 until after 9:00—and the recipe *à la croix de Berny,* which involves *pâté* and would therefore have been in conflict with the *pâté* already on the table in the pie. Therefore, the pheasant almost undoubtedly appeared in aspic, sliced and decorated with truffles coated with a sauce and served on a low bed of semolina. The woodcock would be gently poached, their skins removed, and the birds themselves coated with *chaud-froid* sauce and aspic, surrounded by cockscombs and mushrooms."

34 *a pâté-de-foie-gras pie.* "I have hunted through the works of culinary experts of Victoria's reign; I have found pigeon pies and pork pies and game pies, Christmas pies and venison pies and beef pies; nowhere a *pâté-de-foie-gras* pie," Miss Marie F. Rodell complained in "Living on Baker Street."

To this the erudite Morris Rosenblum replied: "Miss Rodell conjectures that Watson either used the words carelessly, or that the pie was a secret concoction of the trade, or finally that Watson himself was the inventor of the pie. It is time to call a halt to the constant practice of imputing a faulty memory to Watson, especially when a little

"Are you indeed, now?" cried Lestrade, with some bitterness. "I am afraid, Holmes, that you are not very practical with your deductions and your inferences. You have made two blunders in as many minutes. This dress does implicate Miss Flora Millar."

"And how?"

"In the dress is a pocket. In the pocket is a card-case. In the card-case is a note. And here is the very note." He slapped it down upon the table in front of him. "Listen to this. ' You will see me when all is ready. Come at once. F. H. M.' Now my theory all along has been that Lady St. Simon was decoyed away by Flora Millar, and that she, with confederates no doubt, was responsible for her disappearance. Here, signed with her initials, is the very note which was no doubt quietly slipped into her hand at the door, and which lured her within their reach."

"Very good, Lestrade," said Holmes, laughing. "You really are very fine indeed. Let me see it." He took up the paper in a listless way, but his attention instantly became riveted, and he gave a little cry of satisfaction. "This is indeed important," said he.

"Ha, you find it so?"

"Extremely so. I congratulate you warmly."

Lestrade rose in his triumph and bent his head to look. "Why," he shrieked, "you're looking on the wrong side."

"On the contrary, this is the right side."

"The right side? You're mad! Here is the note written in pencil over here."

"And over here is what appears to be a fragment of a hotel bill, which interests me deeply."

"There's nothing in it. I looked at it before," said **30** Lestrade. "' Oct. 4th, rooms 8*s.*, breakfast 2*s.* 6*d.*, **31** cocktail 1*s.*, lunch 2*s.* 6*d.*, glass sherry 8*d.*' I see nothing in that."

"Very likely not. It is most important all the same. As to the note, it is important also, or at least the initials are, so I congratulate you again."

"I've wasted time enough," said Lestrade, rising, "I believe in hard work, and not in sitting by the fire spinning fine theories. Good day, Mr Holmes, and we shall see which gets to the bottom of the matter first." He gathered up the garments, thrust them into the bag, and made for the door.

"Just one hint to you, Lestrade," drawled Holmes, before his rival vanished; "I will tell you the true solution of the matter. Lady St. Simon is a myth. There is not, and there never has been, any such person."

Lestrade looked sadly at my companion. Then he turned to me, tapped his forehead three times, shook his head solemnly, and hurried away.

He had hardly shut the door behind him, when Holmes rose and put on his overcoat. "There is something in what the fellow says about outdoor work," he remarked, "so I think, Watson, that I must leave you to your papers for a little."

It was after five o'clock when Sherlock Holmes left me, but I had no time to be lonely, for within an hour there arrived a confectioner's man with a very large flat box. This he unpacked with the help of a youth whom he had brought with him, and presently, to my very great astonishment, a quite epicurean little cold supper began to be laid out upon our humble lodging-house mahogany. There were a couple of brace of cold woodcock, a pheas- **32** ant, a *pâté-de-foie-gras* pie, with a group of ancient and **33-34** cobwebby bottles. Having laid out all these luxuries, **35** my two visitors vanished away, like the genii of the Arabian Nights, with no explanation save that the things had been paid for, and were ordered to this address.

Just before nine o'clock Sherlock Holmes stepped briskly into the room. His features were gravely set, but there was a light in his eye which made me think that he had not been disappointed in his conclusions.

" They have laid the supper, then," he said, rubbing his hands.

" You seem to expect company. They have laid for **36** five."

" Yes, I fancy we may have some company dropping in," said he. " I am surprised that Lord St. Simon has not already arrived. Ha ! I fancy that I hear his step now upon the stairs."

It was indeed our visitor of the morning who came bustling in, dangling his glasses more vigorously than ever, and with a very perturbed expression upon his aristocratic features.

" My messenger reached you, then ? " asked Holmes.

" Yes, and I must confess that the contents startled me beyond measure. Have you good authority for what you say ? "

" The best possible."

Lord St. Simon sank into a chair, and passed his hand over his forehead.

" What will the Duke say," he murmured, " when he hears that one of the family has been subjected to such a humiliation ? "

" It is the purest accident. I cannot allow that there is any humiliation."

" Ah, you look on these things from another standpoint."

" I fail to see that anyone is to blame. I can hardly see how the lady could have acted otherwise, though her abrupt method of doing it was undoubtedly to be regretted. Having no mother, she had no one to advise her at such a crisis."

" It was a slight, sir, a public slight," said Lord St. Simon, tapping his fingers upon the table.

" You must make allowance for this poor girl, placed in so unprecedented a position."

" I will make no allowance. I am very angry indeed, and I have been shamefully used."

" I think I heard a ring," said Holmes. " Yes, there are steps on the landing. If I cannot persuade you to take a lenient view of the matter, Lord St. Simon, I have brought an advocate here who may be more successful." He opened the door and ushered in a lady and gentleman.

" Lord St. Simon," said he, " allow me to introduce you to Mr. and Mrs. Francis Hay Moulton. The lady, I **37** think, you have already met."

At the sight of these new-comers our client had sprung from his seat, and stood very erect, with his eyes cast down and his hand thrust into the breast of his frock-coat,

additional research can clear his memory! The standard dictionaries reveal that the term '*pâté-de-foie-gras pie*' was used before Watson's time. Since *pâté-de-foie-gras* was the leading product of Strasburg in Alsace, the confection was also called a Strasburg pie. *The Oxford English Dictionary* has the following entries and illustrative quotations: '*Pâté-de-foie-gras*, pie or pasty of goose liver.' From Thackeray's *Yellowplush Papers* comes the quotation: 'He sent me out . . . for wot's called a Strasburg-pie—in French, a "patty defau graw." ' From H. S. Leigh's *Carols of Cockayne* (1869): 'Turtle and salmon and Strasbourg pie.' Culinary details about this pie can be found in Cassell's *Dictionary of Cookery* published in London and New York. No date of publication is given, but the copy which I consulted in the New York Public Library is stamped, 'Astor Library, September 30, 1864.' Copies were therefore available in the days of Holmes and Watson!"

35 *a group of ancient and cobwebby bottles.* "It is easy to presume that the dusty bottles were an aristocratic Burgundy matching the purpose and were no doubt a *Clos-Vougeot* or a similar brand," Mr. Jørgen Cold wrote in "What Did Sherlock Holmes Drink?"

If so, we may be sure it was a white *Clos-Vougeot* and not a red, for, as the late Fletcher Pratt wrote in "The Gastronomic Holmes": "Surely, with his fine taste in wines, Holmes would never have served reds beside pheasant and woodcock; and I am not aware of a white that could stand enough age to become cobwebby without also becoming vinegar. I can only suggest that he was once more exercising his delicate taste and immense knowledge by providing a Portugese rosé, which as a wired wine can stand much longer storage and, indeed, improves by it. The fact that there was not one, but a number of the ancient and cobwebby bottles, is very significant; quite clearly and very properly, Holmes expected to continue whatever drinking was done after the meal from the contents of these bottles. A Portugese rosé would serve this purpose admirably."

"It was definitely to the Bordeaux and the Burgundies that Holmes' natural tastes were inclined," the late Edgar W. Smith noted in "Up from the Needle." "Surprisingly, for an Englishman of his generation, he seems to have shunned the hocks completely. Nowhere are the vintages of the Moselle and the Rhineland given mention in the tales, and we are led to wonder if, forseeing the part he was to play in the Great War, he did not take it upon himself to set up a sort of individual boycott before the fact."

Holmes' wines probably came from the excellent wine-merchant's shop at No. 16 Baker Street, at the corner of Blandford Street. This shop, Mr. Michael Harrison tells us in *In the Footsteps of Sherlock Holmes*, belonged to the still-existing firm of H. Dolamore & Co.

"THE LADY, I THINK, YOU HAVE ALREADY MET."

Illustration by Sidney Paget for the *Strand Magazine*, April, 1892.

36 *They have laid for five.*" "There is food enough for four but not for five, although five places were laid," the late Fletcher Pratt noted in "The Gastronomic Holmes." "One woodcock or half a pheasant is exactly a portion, and since the *pâté* pie would be required as a garnish, it was evidently not intended to serve the fifth eater. That is, Holmes must have deduced that Lord St. Simon would not remain to share the repast; a point which Watson completely missed."

37 *Mr. and Mrs. Francis Hay Moulton.* Mr. Robert Keith Leavitt has suggested ("The Preposterously Paired Performances of the Preacher's Portrait") that Mr. Francis Hay Moulton is possibly identifiable with that Francis H. Moulton, a friend of Theodore Tilton, who acted as a go-between in Tilton's 1871 negotiations with Henry Ward Beecher and became a star witness at the Tilton-Beecher trial in 1874.

a picture of offended dignity. The lady had taken a quick step forward and had held out her hand to him, but he still refused to raise his eyes. It was as well for his resolution, perhaps, for her pleading face was one which it was hard to resist.

"You're angry, Robert," said she. "Well, I guess you have every cause to be."

"Pray make no apology to me," said Lord St. Simon bitterly.

"Oh, yes, I know that I treated you real bad, and that I should have spoken to you before I went; but I was kind of rattled, and from the time when I saw Frank here again, I just didn't know what I was doing or saying. I only wonder that I didn't fall down and do a faint right there before the altar."

"Perhaps, Mrs. Moulton, you would like my friend and me to leave the room while you explain this matter?"

"If I may give an opinion," remarked the strange gentleman, "we've had just a little too much secrecy over this business already. For my part, I should like all Europe and America to hear the rights of it." He was a small, wiry, sunburned man, with a sharp face and alert manner.

"Then I'll tell our story right away," said the lady. "Frank here and I met in '81, in McQuire's camp, near the Rockies, where Pa was working a claim. We were engaged to each other, Frank and I; but then one day father struck a rich pocket, and made a pile, while poor Frank here had a claim that petered out and came to nothing. The richer Pa grew, the poorer was Frank; so at last Pa wouldn't hear of our engagement lasting any longer, and he took me away to 'Frisco. Frank wouldn't throw up his hand, though; so he followed me there, and he saw me without Pa knowing anything about it. It would only have made him mad to know, so we just fixed it all up for ourselves. Frank said that he would go and make his pile, too, and never come back to claim me until he had as much as Pa. So then I promised to wait for him to the end of time, and pledged myself not to marry anyone else while he lived. 'Why shouldn't we be married right away, then,' said he, 'and then I will feel sure of you; and I won't claim to be your husband until I come back.' Well, we talked it over, and he had fixed it all up so nicely, with a clergyman all ready in waiting, that we just did it right there; and then Frank went off to seek his fortune and I went back to Pa.

"The next that I heard of Frank was that he was in Montana, and then he went prospecting into Arizona, and then I heard of him from New Mexico. After that came a long newspaper story about how a miners' camp had been attacked by Apache Indians, and there was my Frank's name among the killed. I fainted dead away, and I was very sick for months after. Pa thought I had a decline, and took me to half the doctors in 'Frisco. Not a word of news came for a year or more, so that I never doubted that Frank was really dead. Then Lord St. Simon came to 'Frisco, and we came to London, and a marriage was arranged, and Pa was very pleased, but I felt all the time that no man on this earth would ever take the place in my heart that had been given to my poor Frank.

" Still, if I had married Lord St. Simon, of course I'd have done my duty by him. We can't command our love, but we can our actions. I went to the altar with him with the intention that I would make him just as good a wife as it was in me to be. But you may imagine what I felt when, just as I came to the altar rails, I glanced back and saw Frank standing looking at me out of the first pew. I thought it was his ghost at first ; but, when I looked again, there he was still, with a kind of question in his eyes as if to ask me whether I were glad or sorry to see him. I wonder I didn't drop. I know that everything was turning round, and the words of the clergyman were just like the buzz of a bee in my ear. I didn't know what to do. Should I stop the service and make a scene in the church ? I glanced at him again, and he seemed to know what I was thinking, for he raised his fingers to his lips to tell me to be still. Then I saw him scribble on a piece of paper, and I knew he was writing me a note. As I passed his pew on the way out I dropped my bouquet over to him, and he slipped the note into my hand when he returned me the flowers. It was only a line asking me to join him when he made the sign to me to do so. Of course I never doubted for a moment that my first duty now was to him, and I determined to do just whatever he might direct.

" When I got back I told my maid, who had known him in California, and had always been his friend. I ordered her to say nothing, but to get a few things packed and my ulster ready. I know I ought to have spoken to Lord St. Simon, but it was dreadful hard before his mother and all those great people. I just made up my mind to run away, and explain afterwards. I hadn't been at the table ten minutes before I saw Frank out of the window at the other side of the road. He beckoned to me, and then began walking into the Park. I slipped out, put on my things, and followed him. Some woman came talking something or other about Lord St. Simon to me—seemed to me from the little I heard as if he had a little secret of his own before marriage also—but I managed to get away from her, and soon overtook Frank. We got into a cab together, and away we drove to some lodgings he had taken in Gordon Square, and that was my true **38** wedding after all those years of waiting. Frank had been a prisoner among the Apaches, had escaped, came on to 'Frisco, found that I had given him up for dead and had gone to England, followed me there, and had come upon me at last on the very morning of my second wedding."

" I saw it in a paper," explained the American. " It gave the name and the church, but not where the lady lived."

" Then we had a talk as to what we should do, and Frank was all for openness, but I was so ashamed of it all that I felt as if I would like to vanish away and never see any of them again, just sending a line to Pa, perhaps, to show him that I was alive. It was awful to me to think of all those lords and ladies sitting round that breakfast-table, and waiting for me to come back. So Frank took my wedding clothes and things, and made a bundle of

38 *Gordon Square*. "From the north-west angle of Bedford Square we may proceed, through Woburn Square, to Gordon Square, containing the modern Catholic Apostolic (Irvingite) Church, a handsome building in the early English style, by Brandon and Ritchie," Augustus J. C. Hare wrote in *Walks in London*, Vol. II.

"SOME WOMAN CAME TALKING SOMETHING OR OTHER ABOUT LORD ST. SIMON TO ME . . ."

Illustration by Sidney Paget for the *Strand Magazine*, April, 1892.

"I THINK THAT, WITH YOUR PERMISSION, I WILL NOW
WISH YOU ALL A VERY GOOD NIGHT."

Illustration by Sidney Paget for the *Strand Magazine*, April, 1892.

them so that I should not be traced, and dropped them
away somewhere where no one should find them.   It is
likely that we should have gone on to Paris to-morrow,
only that this good gentleman, Mr. Holmes, came round
to us this evening, though how he found us is more than I
can think, and he showed us very clearly and kindly that I
was wrong and that Frank was right, and that we should
put ourselves in the wrong if we were so secret.   Then he
offered to give us a chance of talking to Lord St. Simon
alone, and so we came right away round to his rooms at
once.   Now, Robert, you have heard all, and I am very
sorry if I have given you pain, and I hope that you do not
think very meanly of me."

Lord St. Simon had by no means relaxed his rigid attitude, but had listened with a frowning brow and a compressed lip to this long narrative.

"Excuse me," he said, "but it is not my custom to
discuss my most intimate personal affairs in this public
manner."

"Then you won't forgive me?   You won't shake
hands before I go?"

"Oh, certainly, if it would give you any pleasure."   He
put out his hand and coldly grasped that which she
extended to him.

"I had hoped," suggested Holmes, "that you would
have joined us in a friendly supper."

"I think that there you ask a little too much,"
responded his lordship.   "I may be forced to acquiesce
in these recent developments, but I can hardly be expected
to make merry over them.   I think that, with your permission, I will now wish you all a very good night."   He
included us all in a sweeping bow, and stalked out of the
room.

"Then I trust that you at least will honour me with
your company," said Sherlock Holmes.   "It is always a
joy to me to meet an American, Mr. Moulton, for I am
one of those who believe that the folly of a monarch and
the blundering of a Minister in fargone years will not
prevent our children from being some day citizens of the
same world-wide country under a flag which shall be a
quartering of the Union Jack with the Stars and Stripes."

". . . A FLAG WHICH SHALL BE A QUARTERING OF THE UNION JACK WITH
THE STARS AND STRIPES."

"Holmes was in advance of his time in holding these views, and
more recent historians of the War of Independence and its causes
tend to spread the responsibility and blame over others beside
George III and his Minister," Mr. T. S. Blakeney wrote in *Sherlock Holmes: Fact or Fiction?* "But the idea of an Anglo-American union has not been lost from view, and found favour in the
sight of the late Lord Fisher, among others."

"One may reasonably surmise," Dr. Felix Morley wrote in "The
Significance of the Second Stain," "that the two unfilled quarters
of this banner were in Holmes' mind dedicated to other important
democracies, probably France and the Netherlands, as the working basis of that federation of 'Union Now,' so persuasively urged
today by my good friend Clarence Streit."

But Dr. Julian Wolff (*Practical Handbook of Sherlockian Heraldry*) has suggested that "when Holmes expressed a hope to have
the two great nations live under this flag, as a loyal Englishman
he gave precedence to the Union Jack. However, it is assumed by
equally loyal Americans that there will be two forms of the flag.
The one for use in the United States ought to have the Stars and
Stripes in the first and fourth quarters and the Union Jack in the
second and third. There is a precedent for this in the Queen's
arms for Scotland: Quarterly, 1 and 4, Scotland; 2, England; 3,
Ireland."

"The case has been an interesting one," remarked Holmes, when our visitors had left, "because it serves to show very clearly how simple the explanation may be of an affair which at first sight seems to be almost inexplicable. Nothing could be more inexplicable. Nothing could be more natural than the sequence of events as narrated by this lady, and nothing stranger than the result when viewed, for instance, by Mr. Lestrade of Scotland Yard."

"You were not yourself at fault, then?"

"From the first, two facts were very obvious to me, the one that the lady had been quite willing to undergo the wedding ceremony, the other that she had repented of it within a few minutes of returning home. Obviously something had occurred during the morning, then, to cause her to change her mind. What could that something be? She could not have spoken to anyone when she was out, for she had been in the company of the bridegroom. Had she seen someone, then? If she had, it must be someone from America, because she had spent so short a time in this country that she could hardly have allowed anyone to acquire so deep an influence over her that the mere sight of him would induce her to change her plans so completely. You see we have already arrived, by a process of exclusion, at the idea that she might have seen an American. Then who could this American be, and why should he possess so much influence over her? It might be a lover; it might be a husband. Her young womanhood had, I knew, been spent in rough scenes, and under strange conditions. So far had I got before I ever heard Lord St. Simon's narrative. When he told us of a man in a pew, of the change in the bride's manner, of so transparent a device of obtaining a note as the dropping of a bouquet, of her resort to her confidential maid, and of her very significant allusion to claim-jumping, which in miners' parlance means taking possession of that which another person has a prior claim to, the whole situation became absolutely clear. She had gone off with a man, and the man was either a lover or was a previous husband, the chances being in favour of the latter."

"And how in the world did you find them?"

"It might have been difficult, but friend Lestrade held information in his hands the value of which he did not himself know. The initials were of course of the highest importance, but more valuable still was it to know that within a week he had settled his bill at one of the most **39** select London hotels."

"How did you deduce the select?"

"By the select prices. Eight shillings for a bed and eightpence for a glass of sherry, pointed to one of the most expensive hotels. There are not many in London which charge at that rate. In the second one which I visited in Northumberland Avenue, I learned by an inspection of the book that Francis H. Moulton, an American gentleman, had left only the day before, and on looking over the **40** entries against him, I came upon the very items which I had seen in the duplicate bill. His letters were to be forwarded to 226 Gordon Square, so thither I travelled, and being fortunate enough to find the loving couple at home,

39 *within a week he had settled his bill.* Dated, as we have seen, October 4th. Since Moulton had the receipted bill in his possession on Tuesday, the day of the wedding, he had obviously paid it that morning or earlier. It would seem clear that he paid it on the preceding day, Monday: the "curt announcement" on Wednesday that "the wedding had taken place" (on Tuesday) had appeared "two days later" than a note in the *Morning Post* (and no doubt in other newspapers) that the marriage was about to take place. These notes would therefore have appeared on Monday. Moulton saw an announcement of the wedding-to be that "gave the name of the church, but not where the lady lived." From the above, he must have seen this announcement on Monday (but not in the *Morning Post*, which told where the lady lived). A man of action, he would immediately pay his hotel bill and set out to find the lodgings in Gordon Square to which he took Hatty Doran after she had left her wedding breakfast so precipitously on the Tuesday. Moulton attended the wedding (on Tuesday), scribbled his note on the back of the duplicate of the hotel bill he had paid the day before, departed with Hatty to the lodgings in Gordon Square he had located the day before. October 4, 1886, *was* a Monday. We can now say with some confidence that "The Adventure of the Noble Bachelor" took place on *Friday, October 8, 1886.*

40 *had left only the day before.* Since Moulton had no place to go at the time of paying his hotel bill, he presumably left the bulk of the luggage he had brought from America in his hotel room, and therefore did not *check out* of the hotel; he simply settled his bill to that date. On Thursday, then, Moulton returned to the hotel, collected his luggage, and gave up his room.

I ventured to give them some paternal advice, and to point out to them that it would be better in every way that they should make their position a little clearer, both to the general public and to Lord St. Simon in particular. I invited them to meet him here, and, as you see, I made him keep the appointment."

" But with no very good results," I remarked. " His conduct was certainly not very gracious."

" Ah ! Watson," said Holmes, smiling, " perhaps you would not be very gracious either, if, after all the trouble of wooing and wedding, you found yourself deprived in an instant of wife and of fortune. I think that we may judge Lord St. Simon very mercifully, and thank our stars that we are never likely to find ourselves in the same position. Draw your chair up, and hand me my violin, for the only problem which we have still to solve is how to while away these bleak autumnal evenings."

Auctorial Note: Conan Doyle's own opinion of "The Adventure of the Noble Bachelor" was a low one. In a letter to a friend he put the story "about the bottom of the list."

"IN THE SECOND ONE WHICH I VISITED IN NORTHUMBERLAND AVENUE . . ."

This exceedingly handsome thoroughfare leads southeast of Charing Cross to the Embankment. Constructed across the grounds of Northumberland House at a total cost of £650,000, the avenue was opened to the public on March 18, 1876. It is rich in Sherlockian associations: the Turkish baths used by Holmes and Watson were in Northumberland Avenue, as was the hotel at which Sir Henry Baskerville was a guest (now the Sherlock Holmes Tavern). It is quite reasonable to suppose that this was the same hotel at which Mr. Francis Hay Moulton stayed. The hotels frequented by wealthy Orientals for whom Mr. Melas acted as guide ("The Greek Interpreter") were also located in Northumberland Avenue. The photograph below, from *Baker Street By-Ways*, by Mr. James Edward Holroyd, shows Northumberland Avenue looking toward Trafalgar Square. The Turkish baths used by Holmes and Watson were on the right-hand corner. The solitary hansom cab is stationed in front of what is now the Sherlock Holmes Tavern.

21

THE ADVENTURE OF THE SECOND STAIN

[Tuesday, October 12, to Friday, October 15, 1886]

I HAD intended the " Adventure of the Abbey Grange " to be the last of those exploits of my friend, Mr. Sherlock Holmes, which I should ever communicate to the public. This resolution of mine was not due to **1** any lack of material, since I have notes of many hundreds of cases to which I have never alluded, nor was it caused by any waning interest on the part of my readers in the singular personality and unique methods of this remarkable man. The real reason lay in the reluctance which Mr. Holmes has shown to the continued publication of his experiences. So long as he was in actual professional practice the records of his successes were of some practical value to him ; but since he has definitely retired from **2** London and betaken himself to study and bee-farming on the Sussex Downs, notoriety has become hateful to him, and he has peremptorily requested that his wishes in this matter should be strictly observed. It was only upon my **3** representing to him that I had given a promise that " The Adventure of the Second Stain " should be published when the time was ripe, and pointed out to him **4** that it was only appropriate that this long series of episodes should culminate in the most important international case which he has ever been called upon to handle, that I at last succeeded in obtaining his consent that a carefully guarded account of the incident should at last be laid before the public. If in telling the story I seem to be somewhat vague in certain details the public will readily understand that there is an excellent reason for my reticence.

It was, then, in a year, and even in a decade, that shall be nameless, that upon one Tuesday morning in autumn **5** we found two visitors of European fame within the walls of our humble room in Baker Street. The one, austere, **6** high-nosed, eagle-eyed, and dominant, was none other than the illustrious Lord Bellinger, twice Premier of Britain. The other, dark, clear-cut, and elegant, hardly yet of middle age, and endowed with every beauty of body and of mind, was the Right Honourable Trelawney Hope, Secretary for European Affairs, and the most **7**

1 *which I should ever communicate to the public.* "The Adventure of the Abbey Grange" was first published in the *Strand Magazine* for September, 1904. Three months later—in the *Strand* for December, 1904, our present adventure appeared for the first time. This was just two months after Holmes had retired from London and betaken himself to study and bee farming on the Sussex Downs.

2 *the records of his successes were of some practical value to him.* Mr. Roger T. Clapp has asked: "How . . . did Holmes secure the cases that were his meat and drink? . . . It was not the custom in those days for professional men to advertise, even to the limited extent modern professional ethics permit. So far as is known no newspapers or periodicals of the period carried Holmes' professional card. Further, in most, if not all, cases the press reports of the successful solution of a crime invariably gave all the credit to the professional police. In fact on many occasions Holmes deliberately permitted the police to take full credit —a shrewd business move this as it ensured continual reference of cases to him by his official friends. Pondering this problem he hit upon the idea . . . of having Watson advertise his abilities by publishing stories of his cases. That this was his underlying plan is quite clearly evidenced by his repeated—although subtle—suggestions that Watson select for his published stories those cases which best illustrated Holmes' deductive powers and resources, his constant references to his researches to indicate to prospective clients his unique technical equipment and his frequent complaints that Watson was sacrificing technical detail which would reflect Holmes' brilliance for the purely dramatic aspects of his cases. The next problem was to sell this idea to Watson. . . . Holmes utilized the since standard method of so subtly implanting the idea in Watson's mind that the Doctor would think it was his own. In the early days Holmes was careful to betray little interest in Watson's stories, even deprecating them at times. Essentially he gave the impression that if

The Premiers of Britain during the years when Holmes was in active practice were: Disraeli, 1874 (for the second time; he had succeeded Derby in 1867); Gladstone, 1880; Salisbury, 1885; Gladstone, 1886; Salisbury, 1886; Gladstone, 1892; Rosebery, 1894; Salisbury, 1895; Balfour, 1902. Since Watson was not with Holmes in 1874, when Disraeli was serving his second term as Premier, the Premier of "The Adventure of the Second Stain" must be either Gladstone or Salisbury. As the late Gavin Brend wrote in *My Dear Holmes:* "To decide between [Mr. Gladstone and Lord Salisbury] is no easy matter. Lord Bellinger is described as 'austere, high-nosed, eagle-eyed, and dominant.' This sounds far more like a description of [Gladstone] than of Lord Salisbury, but for this very reason we think we must choose the latter. Let us not forget Watson's statement that in certain details he is being deliberately vague. . . . He will . . . disguise his Prime Minister. The above pen-picture can hardly be described as a disguise of Gladstone. . . . We think . . . that the case occurred during Lord Salisbury's second period [as Prime Minister] from 1886 to 1892." Your editor is in complete agreement. Shown (*left*), then, is the coat of arms of "Lord Bellinger": Barry of ten, argent and azure, over all, six escutcheons, sable, three, two and one, each charged with a lion rampant of the first; a crescent for difference.

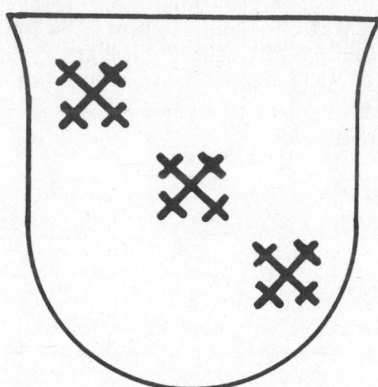

His arms, shown above, are blazoned: Argent, three cross crosslets in bend, sable.

Watson wanted to do that sort of thing it was all right with him. Later, possibly, when Watson's interest seemed to be flagging, Holmes would encourage him to write more, even suggesting cases . . ." We may add to Mr. Clapp's analysis the fact that Watson says (in *The Sign of the Four*) that *A Study in Scarlet* was written *especially to please* Holmes.

3 *should be strictly observed.* "The facts flatly contradict this assertion," the late Edgar W. Smith wrote in "Dr. Watson and the Great Censorship." "Actually, Holmes had scarcely had time to unpack his belongings in the comfort of his farmstead when the issue of the *Strand Magazine* for October, 1903, came out upon the stands with Watson's epochal 'Adventure of the Empty House,' in which he told an astounded, and no doubt bewildered world, that the Great Detective had not, after all, died in Switzerland in 1891, but that he had returned to his beloved London in 1894, and then and there had solved the murder

rising statesman in the country. They sat side by side upon our paper-littered settee, and it was easy to see from their worn and anxious faces that it was business of the most pressing importance which had brought them. The Premier's thin, blue-veined hands were clasped tightly over the ivory head of his umbrella, and his gaunt, ascetic face looked gloomily from Holmes to me. The European Secretary pulled nervously at his moustache and fidgeted with the seals of his watch-chain.

"When I discovered my loss, Mr. Holmes, which was at eight o'clock this morning, I at once informed the Prime Minister. It was at his suggestion that we have both come to you."

"Have you informed the police?"

"No, sir," said the Prime Minister, with the quick, decisive manner for which he was famous. "We have not done so, nor is it possible that we should do so. To inform the police must, in the long run, mean to inform the public. This is what we particularly desire to avoid."

"And why, sir?"

"Because the document in question is of such immense importance that its publication might very easily—I might almost say probably—lead to European complications of the utmost moment. It is not too much to say that peace or war may hang upon the issue. Unless its recovery can be attended with the utmost secrecy, then it may as well not be recovered at all, for all that is aimed at by those who have taken it is that its contents should be generally known."

" I understand.   Now, Mr. Trelawney Hope, 1 should be much obliged if you would tell me exactly the circumstances under which this document disappeared."

" That can be done in a very few words, Mr. Holmes. The letter—for it was a letter from a foreign potentate— **8** was received six days ago.   It was of such importance that I have never left it in my safe, but I have taken it across each evening to my house in Whitehall Terrace, **9** and kept it in my bedroom in a locked dispatch-box. It was there last night.   Of that I am certain.   I actually opened the box while I was dressing for dinner, and saw the document inside.   This morning it was gone.   The dispatch-box had stood beside the glass upon my dressing-table all night.   I am a light sleeper, and so is my wife. We are both prepared to swear that no one could have entered the room during the night.   And yet I repeat that the paper is gone."

" What time did you dine ? "

" Half-past seven."

" How long was it before you went to bed ? "

" My wife had gone to the theatre.   I waited up for her.   It was half-past eleven before we went to our room."

" Then for four hours the dispatch-box had lain unguarded ? "

" No one is ever permitted to enter that room save the housemaid in the morning, and my valet, or my wife's maid, during the rest of the day.   They are both trusty servants who have been with us for some time.   Besides, neither of them could possibly have known that there was anything more valuable than the ordinary departmental papers in my dispatch-box."

" Who did know of the existence of that letter ? "

" No one in the house."

" Surely your wife knew ? "

" No, sir ;   I had said nothing to my wife until I missed the paper this morning."

THEY SAT SIDE BY SIDE UPON OUR PAPER-LITTERED
SETTEE . . .

Illustration by Sidney Paget for the *Strand Magazine*, December, 1904.

of the Honourable Ronald Adair. It is difficult to believe that this was really news to the hundreds of people who had come in contact with the Master in the course of the dozens of cases he had handled since his tardily acknowledged resurrection, or to the many thousands of others who had heard of these cases, and, inevitably, of him. But the stolid and obediant Watson, after first repressing the story of his friend's demise for two years and eight months, had sought—operating under what he termed a 'positive prohibition'—to repress for nine years and six months the fact of his Return. And now, as Holmes himself looked on from the perspective of retirement, he gave the story to the world as news."

4 *when the time was ripe.* As we shall see, when we come to the adventure of "The Naval Treaty," Watson there refers to *an* "Adventure of the Second Stain" which he says took place in "the July which immediately succeeded my marriage." Of this adventure he wrote: "The new century will have come, however, before the story can be safely told." Whether or not this can be construed as "a promise" to publish the adventure "when the time was ripe" is a point debated by commentators.

5 *one Tuesday morning.* Note that this "Adventure of the Second Stain" began on a *Tuesday* morning.

6 *our humble room in Baker Street.* Chronologists who hold that this case and "The Adventure of the Second Stain" mentioned in "The Naval Treaty" are one and the same (as do Christ, Pattrick, Petersen and Zeisler) must explain: 1) Watson's "autumn" (instead of July); 2) the fact that he is apparently quite unmarried and living in Baker Street during the entire period of *this* adventure.

7 *Secretary for European Affairs.* Watson has said that the Right Honourable Trelawney Hope was "hardly of middle age," but *no* Foreign Secretary (Watson's "Secretary for European Affairs") throughout our period was that young a man. Still, as Mr. Brend wrote, "the case must . . . have occurred in the autumn of a year when the offices of Prime Minister and Foreign Secretary were held by two different men. But only the first year [of Lord Salisbury's second period as Prime Minister], 1886, meets this requirement. For Lord Iddesleigh, the first Foreign Secretary, died in January, 1887, and thereafter Lord Salisbury acted in both capacities. We can therefore decide that the case of 'The Second Stain' took place in the autumn of 1886." Again, your editor most heartily concurs.

To add to the "historicity" of Watson's account, we have the extremely valuable testimony of Dr. Felix Morley, who writes, in "The Significance of the Second Stain":

In the spring of 1886 Mr. Gladstone's Home Rule Bill was defeated and the subsequent general election swept Lord Salisbury, disguised by Watson as Lord Bellinger, into his second premiership. Salisbury promptly named Lord Iddesleigh, formerly Sir Stafford Northcote, as his Foreign Secretary. . . . Towards the close of that year—1886—occurred a series of startling Ministerial changes for which English historians have heretofore never been able fully to account. On Christmas Eve, Lord Randolph Churchill resigned, almost without explanation, as Chancellor of the Exchequer. Mr. W. H. Smith . . . followed suit by surrendering the War Office. Lord Iddesleigh was then literally ousted from the post of Foreign Secretary, which the Prime Minister himself assumed on January 4, 1887. Eight days later, as J. A. R. Marriot tells us (*England Since Waterloo*, p. 519) "the country was shocked to learn that he [Lord Iddesleigh] had died suddenly in the ante-room of the Premier's official residence at 10 Downing Street." Thus closed, "amid circumstances almost tragic, a life of high utility and complete blamelessness." How tragic the circumstances were the reader of "The Adventure of the Second Stain" can fully realize. While Holmes was able to restore the purloined letter he could not, evidently, prevent reports of Lord Iddesleigh's reckless carelessness with state papers from coming to the attention of the Cabinet. One recalls that Lady Hilda Trelawney Hope by her own admission "could not understand the consequences" in a matter of politics. I am on delicate ground, but it may be stated as a general rule that a lady who has twice been indiscreet is not unlikely to err a third time. Lady Hilda must have mentioned, perhaps before the butler, Jacobs, how Holmes had restored the letter which seemed to her so relatively unimportant. At any rate a new light is thrown on the unexplained resignation from Lord Salisbury's Cabinet and the sudden, "almost tragic" death of his Foreign Secretary.

8 *a foreign potentate.* Messrs. Bell, Blakeney, and Grazebrook have all suggested that the "foreign potentate" who sent the ill-advised letter must have been Kaiser Wilhelm II, and that "The Adventure of the Second Stain" must therefore be subsequent to June, 1888, when he ascended the throne. But Mr. Anthony Boucher has written: "The apparent reference to Wilhelm II which causes [these commentators] to date the published episode after his ascension to the throne in 1888 . . . is not to be taken too seriously in view of Watson's warning that this is a 'carefully guarded account . . . somewhat vague in certain details.' "

9 *Whitehall Terrace.* ". . . since there is not today —nor was sixty and more years ago—a 'Whitehall Terrace' to be found on a London map, it is evident that Watson means either 'Whitehall Gardens' or 'Richmond Terrace'—the latter, a block of 1791 houses being (though threatened) still standing," Mr. Michael Harrison wrote (*In the Footsteps of Sherlock Holmes*). "That 'Whitehall Terrace' is almost certainly meant for Richmond Terrace [is indicated by Trelawney Hope when

The Premier nodded approvingly.

"I have long known, sir, how high is your sense of public duty," said he. "I am convinced that in the case of a secret of this importance it would rise superior to the most intimate domestic ties."

The European Secretary bowed.

"You do me no more than justice, sir. Until this morning I have never breathed one word to my wife upon this matter."

"Could she have guessed?"

"No, Mr. Holmes, she could not have guessed—nor could anyone have guessed."

"Have you lost any documents before?"

"No, sir."

"Who is there in England who did know of the existence of this letter?"

"Each member of the Cabinet was informed of it yesterday; but the pledge of secrecy which attends every Cabinet meeting was increased by the solemn warning which was given by the Prime Minister. Good heavens, to think that within a few hours I should myself have lost it!" His handsome face was distorted with a spasm of despair, and his hands tore at his hair. For a moment we caught a glimpse of the natural man—impulsive, ardent, keenly sensitive. The next the aristocratic mask was replaced, and the gentle voice had returned. "Besides the members of the Cabinet there are two, or possibly three, departmental officials who know of the letter. No one else in England, Mr. Holmes, I assure you."

"But abroad?"

"I believe that no one abroad has seen it save the man who wrote it. I am well convinced that his ministers —that the usual official channels have not been employed."

Holmes considered for some little time.

"Now, sir, I must ask you more particularly what this document is, and why its disappearance should have such momentous consequences?"

The two statesmen exchanged a quick glance, and the Premier's shaggy eyebrows gathered in a frown.

"Mr. Holmes, the envelope is a long, thin one of pale blue colour. There is a seal of red wax stamped with a 10 crouching lion. It is addressed in large, bold handwriting to——"

"I fear," said Holmes, "that, interesting and indeed essential as these details are, my inquiries must go more to the root of things. What *was* the letter?"

"That is a State secret of the utmost importance, and I fear that I cannot tell you, nor do I see that it is necessary. If by the aid of the powers which you are said to possess you can find such an envelope as I describe with its enclosure, you will have deserved well of your country, and earned any reward which it lies in our power to bestow."

Sherlock Holmes rose with a smile.

"You are two of the most busy men in the country," said he, "and in my own small way I have also a good many calls upon me. I regret exceedingly that I cannot help you in this matter, and any continuation of this interview would be a waste of time."

The Premier sprang to his feet with that quick, fierce gleam of his deep-set eyes before which a Cabinet had cowered. "I am not accustomed——" he began, but mastered his anger and resumed his seat. For a minute or more we all sat in silence. Then the old statesman shrugged his shoulders.

"We must accept your terms, Mr. Holmes. No doubt you are right, and it is unreasonable for us to expect you to act unless we give you our entire confidence."

"I agree with you, sir," said the younger statesman.

"Then I will tell you, relying entirely upon your honour and that of your colleague, Dr. Watson. I may appeal to your patriotism also, for I could not imagine a greater misfortune for the country than that this affair should come out."

"You may safely trust us."

"The letter, then, is from a certain foreign potentate who has been ruffled by some recent colonial developments of this country. It has been written hurriedly and upon his own responsibility entirely. Inquiries have shown that his ministers know nothing of the matter. At the same time it is couched in so unfortunate a manner, and certain phrases in it are of so provocative a character, that its publication would undoubtedly lead to a most dangerous state of feeling in this country. There would be such a ferment, sir, that I do not hesitate to say that within a week of the publication of that letter this country would be involved in a great war."

Holmes wrote a name upon a slip of paper and handed it to the Premier.

"Exactly. It was he. And it is this letter—this letter which may well mean the expenditure of a thousand millions and the lives of a hundred thousand men—which has become lost in this unaccountable fashion."

"Have you informed the sender?"

"Yes, sir, a cipher telegram has been despatched."

"Perhaps he desires the publication of the letter."

"No, sir, we have strong reason to believe that he already understands that he has acted in an indiscreet and hot-headed manner. It would be a greater blow to him and to his country than to us if this letter were to come out."

"If this is so, whose interest is it that the letter should come out? Why should anyone desire to steal it or to publish it?"

"There, Mr. Holmes, you take me into regions of high international politics. But if you consider the European situation you will have no difficulty in perceiving the motive. The whole of Europe is an armed camp. There is a double league which makes a fair balance of military power. Great Britain holds the scales. If Britain were driven into war with one confederacy, it would assure the supremacy of the other confederacy, whether they joined in the war or not. Do you follow?"

he speaks of the letter he has "taken . . . across" each evening from the Foreign Office to his home]."

10 *stamped with a crouching lion.* This would have been a curious device for Kaiser Wilhelm II to have stamped in the red wax which sealed the letter. Had it been a double-headed eagle, on the other hand . . .

THE PREMIER SPRANG TO HIS FEET . . .

Illustration by Sidney Paget for the *Strand Magazine*, December, 1904.

" Very clearly. It is then the interest of the enemies of this potentate to secure and publish this letter, so as to make a breach between his country and ours ? "

" Yes, sir."

" And to whom would this document be sent if it fell into the hands of an enemy ? "

" To any of the great Chancelleries of Europe. It is probably speeding on its way thither at the present instant as fast as steam can take it."

Mr. Trelawney Hope dropped his head on his chest and groaned aloud. The Premier placed his hand kindly upon his shoulder.

" It is your misfortune, my dear fellow. No one can blame you. There is no precaution which you have neglected. Now, Mr. Holmes, you are in full possession of the facts. What course do you recommend ? "

Holmes shook his head mournfully.

" You think, sir, that unless this document is recovered there will be war ? "

" I think it is very probable."

" Then, sir, prepare for war."

" That is a hard saying, Mr. Holmes."

" Consider the facts, sir. It is inconceivable that it was taken after eleven-thirty at night, since I understand that Mr. Hope and his wife were both in the room from that hour until the loss was found out. It was taken, then, yesterday evening between seven-thirty and eleven-thirty, probably near the earlier hour, since whoever took it evidently knew that it was there, and would naturally secure it as early as possible. Now, sir, if a document of this importance were taken at that hour, where can it be now ? No one has any reason to retain it. It has been passed rapidly on to those who need it. What chance have we now to overtake or even to trace it ? It is beyond our reach."

The Prime Minister rose from the settee.

" What you say is perfectly logical, Mr. Holmes. I feel that the matter is indeed out of our hands."

" Let us presume, for argument's sake, that the document was taken by the maid or by the valet——"

" They are both old and tried servants."

" I understand you to say that your room is on the second floor, that there is no entrance from without, and that from within no one could go up unobserved. It must, then, be somebody in the house who has taken it. To whom would the thief take it ? To one of several international spies and secret agents, whose names are tolerably familiar to me. There are three who may be said to be the heads of their profession. I will begin my research by going round and finding if each of them is at his post. If one is missing—especially if he has disappeared since last night—we will have some indication as to where the document has gone."

" Why should he be missing ? " asked the European Secretary. " He would take the letter to an Embassy in London, as likely as not."

" I fancy not. These agents work independently, and their relations with the Embassies are often strained."

The Prime Minister nodded his acquiescence.

" I believe you are right, Mr. Holmes. He would take

"— IF IT MEANS ANOTHER PENNY ON THE INCOME TAX."

"The penny," the late A. Carson Simpson wrote (*Numismatics in the Canon*, Part I), "is the oldest British coin-denomination still in use. As its abbreviation 'd.' suggests, it is the lineal descendant of the Roman denarius, which, like the earlier British penny, was a silver coin. The silver penny survives only in Maundy Money. It became a copper coin in the late nineteenth century, and bronze in 1860. There are many Canonical references to the penny, which Holmes once referred to as a 'modest sum' (*The Valley of Fear*), but perhaps the most interesting one is that [given here] in which he threatened the happiness of every Englishman and which is, perhaps, his only statement lending itself to a Marxian interpretation."

so valuable a prize to headquarters with his own hands. I think that your course of action is an excellent one. Meanwhile, Hope, we cannot neglect our other duties on account of this one misfortune. Should there be any fresh developments during the day we shall communicate with you, and you will no doubt let us know the results of your own inquiries."

The two statesmen bowed and walked gravely from the room.

When our illustrious visitors had departed, Holmes lit his pipe in silence, and sat for some time lost in the deepest thought. I had opened the morning paper and was immersed in a sensational crime which had occurred in London the night before, when my friend gave an exclamation, sprang to his feet, and laid his pipe down upon the mantelpiece.

"Yes," said he, " there is no better way of approaching it. The situation is desperate, but not hopeless. Even now, if we could be sure which of them has taken it, it is just possible that it has not yet passed out of his hands. After all, it is a question of money with these fellows, and I have the British Treasury behind me. If it's on the market I'll buy it—if it means another penny on the income tax. It is conceivable that the fellow might hold it back to see what bids come from this side before he tries his luck on the other. There are only those three capable of playing so bold a game ; there are Oberstein, La Rothiere, and Eduardo Lucas. I will see each of **11** them."

I glanced at my morning paper.

"Is that Eduardo Lucas of Godolphin Street ? "   **12**

"Yes."

"You will not see him."

"Why not ? "

"He was murdered in his house last night."

My friend has so often astonished me in the course of our adventures that it was with a sense of exultation that I realized how completely I had astonished him. He stared in amazement, and then snatched the paper from my hands. This was the paragraph which I had been engaged in reading when he rose from his chair :

11 *Oberstein, La Rothiere, and Eduardo Lucas.* ". . . the first two reappear, with Oberstein as a principal character, in "The Adventure of the Bruce-Partington Plans," Dr. Felix Morley wrote in "The Significance of the Second Stain." "The date of [that] case is placed meticulously in the third week in November, 1895. . . . ["The Adventure of the Second Stain"], therefore, took place prior to November, 1895. We know it could not have been later because before the end of that month Oberstein was caught, with the missing Bruce-Partington submarine plans in his possession, and 'was safely engulfed for fifteen years in a British prison.' "

In consequence of the above line of reasoning, Messrs. Andrew, Bell, and Blakeney have all dated "The Adventure of the Second Stain" to 1894. It is curious, however, that the names of the spies in London were "tolerably familiar" to Holmes at the time of *this* adventure, whereas he had to get Brother Mycroft to jog his memory, at least as to their addresses, at the time of "The Bruce-Partington Plans." This is perhaps an indication that there was a lapse of some years, rather than a lapse of months, between the two adventures.

12 *Godolphin Street?*" We are shortly told that it was "one of the old-fashioned and secluded rows of eighteenth century houses which lie between the river and the Abbey, almost in the shadow of the great tower of the Houses of Parliament"— although it appears on no London map.

. . . BETWEEN THE RIVER AND THE ABBEY . . .

Westminster Abbey, here shown in a photograph by Acme, is a national shrine and one of England's finest Gothic buildings, the scene of the coronation of all English kings and queens since William I. It is the burial place of many kings and distinguished citizens, and a Poet's Corner in the south transept contains tombs of the great English poets. The present church was built mainly between the thirteenth and the fifteenth century.

13   MURDER IN WESTMINSTER.

A crime of a mysterious character was committed last night at 16 Godolphin Street, one of the old-fashioned and secluded rows of eighteenth-century houses which lie between the river and the Abbey, almost in the shadow of the great tower of the Houses of Parliament. This small but select mansion has been inhabited for some years by Mr. Eduardo Lucas, well known in society circles both on account of his charming personality and because he has the well-deserved reputation of being one of the best amateur tenors in the country. Mr. Lucas is an unmarried man, thirty-four years of age, and his establishment consists of Mrs. Pringle, an elderly housekeeper, and of Mitton, his valet. The former retires early and sleeps at the top of the house. The valet was out for the evening, visiting a friend at Hammersmith. From ten o'clock onwards Mr. Lucas had the house to himself. What occurred during that time has not yet transpired, but at a quarter to twelve Police-constable Barrett, passing along Godolphin Street, observed that the door of No. 16 was ajar. He knocked, but received no answer. Perceiving a light in the front room he advanced into the passage and again knocked, but without reply. He then pushed open the door and entered. The room was in a state of wild disorder, the furniture being all swept to one side, and one chair lying on its back in the centre. Beside this chair, and still grasping one of its legs, lay the unfortunate tenant of the house. He had been stabbed to the heart, and must have died instantly. The knife with which the crime had been committed was a curved Indian dagger, plucked down from a trophy of Oriental arms which adorned one of the walls. Robbery does not appear to have been the motive of the crime, for there had been no attempt to remove the valuable contents of the room. Mr. Eduardo Lucas was so well known and popular that his violent and mysterious fate will arouse painful interest and intense sympathy in a widespread circle of friends.

" Well, Watson, what do you make of this ? " asked Holmes, after a long pause.

" It is an amazing coincidence."

" A coincidence ! Here is one of three men whom we had named as possible actors in this drama, and he meets a violent death during the very hours when we know that that drama was being enacted. The odds are enormous against its being coincidence. No figures could express them. No, my dear Watson, the two events are connected—*must* be connected. It is for us to find the connection."

. . . ALMOST IN THE SHADOW OF THE GREAT TOWER OF THE HOUSES OF PARLIAMENT.

The present structure, shown left in a photograph by G. F. Allen for *The Second Country Life Picture Book of London*, London: Country Life, Ltd., 1953, was built in 1840–1859, from designs of Sir Charles Barry, R.A., in the Tudor style of Henry VIII. It is one of the largest Gothic buildings in the world. The "great tower of the Houses" is the Clock Tower, housing the world-famous "Big Ben." Three hundred and twenty feet high, the Clock Tower occupies nearly the same site as the ancient clock tower of Edward I, where the ancient Great Tom for four hundred years sounded the hours to the judges of England.

" But now the official police must know all."

" Not at all. They know all they see at Godolphin Street. They know—and shall know—nothing of Whitehall Terrace. Only *we* know of both events, and can trace the relation between them. There is one obvious point which would, in any case, have turned my suspicions against Lucas. Godolphin Street, Westminster, is only a few minutes' walk from Whitehall Terrace. The other secret agents whom I have named live in the extreme West End. It was easier, therefore, for Lucas than for the others to establish a connection or receive a message from the European Secretary's household—a small thing, and yet where events are compressed into a few hours it may prove essential. Halloa ! what have we here ? "

Mrs. Hudson had appeared with a lady's card upon her salver. Holmes glanced at it, raised his eyebrows, and handed it over to me.

" Ask Lady Hilda Trelawney Hope if she will be kind enough to step up," said he.

A moment later our modest apartment, already so distinguished that morning, was further honoured by the entrance of the most lovely woman in London. I had often heard of the beauty of the youngest daughter of the Duke of Belminster, but no description of it, and no contemplation of colourless photographs, had prepared me for the subtle, delicate charm and the beautiful colouring of that exquisite head. And yet as we saw it that autumn morning it was not its beauty which would be the first thing to impress the observer. The cheek was lovely, but it was paled with emotion ; the eyes were bright, but it was the brightness of fever ; the sensitive mouth was tight and drawn in an effort after self-command. Terror—not beauty—was what sprang first to **16** the eye as our fair visitor stood framed for an instant in the open door.

" Has my husband been here, Mr. Holmes ? "

" Yes, madam, he has been here."

" Mr. Holmes, I implore you not to tell him that I came here." Holmes bowed coldly and motioned the lady to a chair.

" Your ladyship places me in a very delicate position. I beg that you will sit down and tell me what you desire ; but I fear that I cannot make any unconditional promise."

She swept across the room and seated herself with her back to the window. It was a queenly presence—tall, graceful, and intensely womanly.

" Mr. Holmes," she said—and her white-gloved hands clasped and unclasped as she spoke—" I will speak frankly to you in the hope that it may induce you to speak frankly in return. There is complete confidence between my husband and me on all matters save one. That one is politics. On this his lips are sealed. He tells me nothing. Now, I am aware that there was a most deplorable occurrence in our house last night. I know that a paper has disappeared. But because the matter is political my husband refuses to take me into his complete confidence. Now it is essential—essential, I say—that I should thoroughly understand it. You are the only other person, save these politicians, who knows the true facts.

"NO, MY DEAR WATSON, THE TWO EVENTS ARE CONNECTED—*must* BE CONNECTED."

Illustration by Sidney Paget for the *Strand Magazine*, December, 1904.

13 *WESTMINSTER.* The borough of West London in which are located Westminster Abbey, the Houses of Parliament, Buckingham Palace, Saint James's Palace, and Downing Street with its famous No. 10.

14 *Hammersmith.* Borough of West London in which is located the home of St. Paul's School for boys, founded in 1509, attended by Milton and Pepys.

15 *It is for us to find the connection.*" "Holmes on more than one occasion warned against jumping to conclusions and theorizing without data," Mr. Nathan L. Bengis wrote in "Sherlock Stays After School." "Yet there are a number of occasions where he himself jumped at a conclusion which turned out to have no foundation in fact. In [the present] case, wonderful to relate, Watson was actually right, but allowed himself to be shouted down."

16 *in an effort after self-command.* "The doctor's pronounced susceptibility to . . . Lady Hilda Trelawney Hope is strongly indicative of the psychology of a man ripe and ready for marriage," Dr. Felix Morley wrote in "The Significance of the Second Stain." "It certainly does not suggest the reaction of one recently deprived of a very congenial mate. The authentic stamp of a bachelor ripe for the plucking is also evident in Watson's undisguised admiration for a comely female who is convicted by the facts of the story of being, to put it plainly, a perfect boob."

17 *"Now, Watson, the fair sex is your department."* "To a newly-married man," Dr. Felix Morley continued in "The Significance of the Second Stain," "even more to a recent widower, such a remark would have verged on ribaldry, and would therefore have been impossible to one of Holmes' innate delicacy of feeling."

SHE LOOKED BACK AT US FROM THE DOOR . . .

Illustration by Sidney Paget for the *Strand Magazine*, December, 1904.

I beg you, then, Mr. Holmes, to tell me exactly what has happened and what it will lead to. Tell me all, Mr. Holmes. Let no regard for your client's interests keep you silent, for I assure you that his interests, if he would only see it, would be best served by taking me into his complete confidence. What was this paper that was stolen?"

"Madam, what you ask me is really impossible."

She groaned and sank her face in her hands.

"You must see that this is so, madam. If your husband thinks fit to keep you in the dark over this matter, is it for me, who have only learned the true facts under the pledge of professional secrecy, to tell what he has withheld? It is not fair to ask it. It is him whom you must ask."

"I have asked him. I come to you as a last resource. But without your telling me anything definite, Mr. Holmes, you may do a great service if you would enlighten me on one point."

"What is it, madam?"

"Is my husband's political career likely to suffer through this incident?"

"Well, madam, unless it is set right it may certainly have a very unfortunate effect."

"Ah!" She drew in her breath sharply as one whose doubts are resolved.

"One more question, Mr. Holmes. From an expression which my husband dropped in the first shock of this disaster I understood that terrible public consequences might arise from the loss of this document."

"If he said so, I certainly cannot deny it."

"Of what nature are they?"

"Nay, madam, there again you ask me more than I can possibly answer."

"Then I will take up no more of your time. I cannot blame you, Mr. Holmes, for having refused to speak more freely, and you on your side will not, I am sure, think the worse of me because I desire, even against his will, to share my husband's anxieties. Once more I beg that you will say nothing of my visit." She looked back at us from the door, and I had a last impression of that beautiful, haunted face, the startled eyes, and the drawn mouth. Then she was gone.

17 "Now, Watson, the fair sex is your department," said Holmes, with a smile, when the dwindling *frou-frou* of skirts had ended in the slam of the door. "What was the fair lady's game? What did she really want?"

"Surely her own statement is clear and her anxiety very natural."

"Hum! Think of her appearance, Watson, her manner, her suppressed excitement, her restlessness, her tenacity in asking questions. Remember that she comes of a caste who do not lightly show emotion."

"She was certainly much moved."

"Remember also the curious earnestness with which she assured us that it was best for her husband that she should know all. What did she mean by that? And you must have observed, Watson, how she manœuvred to have the light at her back. She did not wish us to read her expression."

"Yes ; she chose the one chair in the room." **18**

"And yet the motives of women are so inscrutable. You remember the woman at Margate whom I suspected **19** for the same reason. No powder on her nose—that proved to be the correct solution. How can you build on such a quicksand ? Their most trivial action may mean volumes, or their most extraordinary conduct may depend upon a hairpin or a curling-tongs. Good morning, Watson."

"You are off ? "

"Yes ; I will while away the morning at Godolphin Street with our friends of the regular establishment. With Eduardo Lucas lies the solution of our problem, though I must admit that I have not an inkling as to what form it may take. It is a capital mistake to theorize in advance of the facts. Do you stay on guard, my good Watson, and receive any fresh visitors. I'll join you at lunch if I am able."

All that day and the next and the next Holmes was in a **20** mood which his friends would call taciturn, and others morose. He ran out and ran in, smoked incessantly, played snatches on his violin, sank into reveries, devoured sandwiches at irregular hours, and hardly answered the casual questions which I put to him. It was evident to me that things were not going well with him or his quest. He would say nothing of the case, and it was from the papers that I learned the particulars of the inquest, and the arrest with the subsequent release of John Mitton, the valet of the deceased. The coroner's jury brought in the obvious " Wilful murder," but the parties remained as unknown as ever. No motive was suggested. The room was full of articles of value, but none had been taken. The dead man's papers had not been tampered with. They were carefully examined, and showed that he was a keen student of international politics, an indefatigable gossip, a remarkable linguist, and an untiring letter-writer. He had been on intimate terms with the leading politicians of several countries. But nothing sensational was discovered among the documents which filled his drawers. As to his relations with women, they appeared to have been promiscuous but superficial. He had many acquaintances among them, but few friends, and no one whom he loved. His habits were regular, his conduct inoffensive. His death was an absolute mystery, and likely to remain so.

As to the arrest of John Mitton, the valet, it was a counsel of despair as an alternative to absolute inaction. But no case could be sustained against him. He had visited friends in Hammersmith that night. The *alibi* was complete. It is true that he started home at an hour which should have brought him to Westminster before the time when the crime was discovered, but his own explanation that he had walked part of the way seemed probable enough in view of the fineness of the night. He had **21** actually arrived at twelve o'clock, and appeared to be overwhelmed by the unexpected tragedy. He had always been on good terms with his master. Several of the

18 *the one chair in the room.*" Watson of course means the one chair in the room that would have put the light at her back. Thus Lady Hilda Trelawney Hope sat in *the basket chair*—the one chair in the sitting-room at 221B that, according to the highest authorities, would place a visitor's back to the light.

19 *Margate.* Municipal borough on the Isle of Thanet in Kent—a seaport and a popular summer resort.

20 *All that day and the next and the next.* Since (Watson has told us) "that day" was a Tuesday, "the next" was Wednesday and "the next" after that a Thursday. The case ended "Upon the fourth day"—and therefore upon a Friday.

21 *in view of the fineness of the night.* Watson, as we shall see, married for the first time *circa* November 1, 1886; "The Adventure of the Second Stain" must therefore have taken place late in September or during the month of October, 1886. The dates (as we have seen) were not Tuesday, October 5th to Friday, October 8th, however; in that period Holmes was solving both the adventure of "The Resident Patient" and "The Adventure of the Noble Bachelor." The possible dates would therefore seem to be: 1) Tuesday, September 28th, to Friday, October 1st; 2) Tuesday, October 12th, to Friday, October 15th; 3) Tuesday, October 19th, to Friday, October 22nd; 4) Tuesday, October 26th, to Friday, October 29th. The Monday night preceding the opening of the case had been a fine one. A meteorological examination of the four corresponding Mondays shows that *only one was without rain:* Monday, October 11th. We may therefore with some confidence date "The Adventure of the Second Stain" to *Tuesday, October 12 to Friday, October 15, 1886.*

dead man's possessions—notably a small case of razors—had been found in the valet's boxes, but he explained that they had been presents from the deceased, and the housekeeper was able to corroborate the story. Mitton had been in Lucas's employment for three years. It was noticeable that Lucas did not take Mitton on the Continent with him. Sometimes he visited Paris for three months on end, but Mitton was left in charge of the Godolphin Street house. As to the housekeeper, she had heard nothing on the night of the crime. If her master had a visitor, he had himself admitted him.

So for three mornings the mystery remained, so far as I could follow it in the papers. If Holmes knew more he kept his own counsel, but, as he told me that Inspector Lestrade had taken him into his confidence in the case. I knew that he was in close touch with every development. Upon the fourth day there appeared a long telegram from Paris which seemed to solve the whole question.

A discovery has just been made by the Parisian police (said the *Daily Telegraph*) which raises the veil which hung round the tragic fate of Mr. Eduardo Lucas, who met his death by violence last Monday night at Godolphin Street, Westminster. Our readers will remember that the deceased gentleman was found stabbed in his room, and that some suspicion attached to his valet, but that the case broke down on an *alibi*. Yesterday a lady, who has been known as Mme. Henri Fournaye, occupying a small villa in the Rue Austerlitz, was reported to the authorities by her servants as being insane. An examination showed that she had indeed developed mania of a dangerous and permanent form. On inquiry the police have discovered that Mme. Henri Fournaye only returned from a journey to London on Tuesday last, and there is evidence to connect her with the crime at Westminster. A comparison of photographs has proved conclusively that M. Henri Fournaye and Eduardo Lucas were really one and the same person, and that the deceased had for some reason lived a double life in London and Paris. Mme. Fournaye, who is of creole origin, is of an extremely excitable nature, and has suffered in the past from attacks of jealousy which have amounted to frenzy. It is conjectured that it was in one of these that she committed the terrible crime which has caused such a sensation in London. Her movements upon the Monday night have not yet been traced, but it is undoubted that a woman answering to her description attracted much attention at Charing Cross Station on Tuesday morning by the wildness of her appearance and the violence of her gestures. It is probable, therefore, that the crime was either committed when insane, or that its immediate effect was to drive the unhappy woman out of her mind. At present she is unable to give any coherent account of the past, and the doctors hold out no hopes of the re-establishment of her reason. There is evidence that a woman, who might have been Mme. Fournaye, was seen for some hours on Monday night watching the house in Godolphin Street.

"What do you think of that, Holmes?" I had read the account aloud to him, while he finished his breakfast.

"My dear Watson," said he, as he rose from the table and paced up and down the room, "you are most long-suffering, but if I have told you nothing in the last three days it is because there is nothing to tell. Even now this report from Paris does not help us much."

"Surely it is final as regards the man's death."

"The man's death is a mere incident—a trivial episode

". . . ATTRACTED MUCH ATTENTION AT CHARING CROSS STATION . . ."

The station was opened to the public on January 11, 1864, as the London terminus of the South-Eastern Railway. The etching, from the *Century Magazine*, December, 1888, is the work of Joseph Pennell.

—in comparison with our real task, which is to trace this document and save a European catastrophe. Only one important thing has happened in the last three days, and that is that nothing has happened. I get reports almost **22** hourly from the Government, and it is certain that nowhere in Europe is there any sign of trouble. Now, if this letter were loose—no, it *can't* be loose—but if it isn't loose, where can it be ? Who has it ? Why is it held back ? That's the question that beats in my brain like a hammer. Was it, indeed, a coincidence that Lucas should meet his death on the night when the letter disappeared ? Did the letter ever reach him ? If so, why is it not among his papers ? Did this mad wife of his carry it off with her ? If so, is it in her house in Paris ? How could I search for it without the French police having their suspicions aroused ? It is a case, my dear Watson, where the law is as dangerous to us as the criminals are. Every man's hand is against us, and yet the interests at stake are colossal. Should I bring it to a successful conclusion, it will certainly represent the crowning glory of my career. Ah, here is my latest from the front ! " He glanced hurriedly at the note which had been handed in. " Halloa ! Lestrade seems to have observed something of interest. Put on your hat, Watson, and we will stroll down together to Westminster."

It was my first visit to the scene of the crime—a high, dingy, narrow-chested house, prim, formal, and solid, like the century which gave it birth. Lestrade's bulldog features gazed out at us from the front window, and he greeted us warmly when a big constable had opened the door and let us in. The room into which we were shown was that in which the crime had been committed, but no trace of it now remained, save an ugly, irregular stain upon the carpet. This carpet was a small square drugget in the centre of the room, surrounded by a broad expanse of beautiful, old-fashioned, wood flooring in square blocks highly polished. Over the fireplace was a magnificent trophy of weapons, one of which had been used on that tragic night. In the window was a sumptuous writing-desk, and every detail of the apartment, the pictures, the rugs, and the hangings, all pointed to a taste which was luxurious to the verge of effeminacy.

" Seen the Paris news ? " asked Lestrade.

Holmes nodded.

" Our French friends seem to have touched the spot this time. No doubt it's just as they say. She knocked at the door—surprise visit, I guess, for he kept his life in watertight compartments. He let her in—couldn't keep her in the street. She told him how she had traced him, reproached him, one thing led to another, and then with that dagger so handy the end soon came. It wasn't all done in an instant, though, for these chairs were all swept over yonder, and he had one in his hand as if he had tried to hold her off with it. We've got it all as clear as if we had seen it."

Holmes raised his eyebrows.

" And yet you have sent for me ? "

" Ah, yes, that's another matter—a mere trifle, but the

22 *and that is that nothing has happened.* "As an illustration of the vital importance of negative evidence this is almost comparable with the classic and curious instance in 'Silver Blaze,' of the dog that 'did nothing in the night-time,' " Dr. Felix Morley wrote in "The Significance of the Second Stain." "In 'The Adventure of the Second Stain,' however, Holmes failed to make an equally brilliant—and obvious—deduction."

HE TOOK THE CORNER OF THE CARPET IN HIS HAND . . .

Illustration by Sidney Paget for the *Strand Magazine*, December, 1904.

"WHAT DO YOU MAKE OF THAT, MR. HOLMES?"

Illustration by Frederic Dorr Steele for the cover of *Collier's Magazine*, January 28, 1905.

sort of thing you take an interest in—queer, you know, and what you might call freakish. It has nothing to do with the main fact—can't have, on the face of it."

" What is it, then ? "

" Well, you know after a crime of this sort we are very careful to keep things in their position. Nothing has been moved. Officer in charge here day and night. This morning, as the man was buried and the investigation over—so far as this room is concerned—we thought we could tidy up a bit. This carpet. You see, it is not fastened down ; only just laid there. We had occasion to raise it. We found——"

" Yes ? You found——"

Holmes' face grew tense with anxiety.

" Well, I'm sure you would never guess in a hundred years what we did find. You see that stain on the carpet ? Well, a great deal must have soaked through, must it not ? "

" Undoubtedly it must."

" Well, you will be surprised to hear that there is no stain on the white woodwork to correspond."

" No stain ! But there must——"

" Yes ; so you would say. But the fact remains that there isn't."

He took the corner of the carpet in his hand and, turning it over, he showed that it was indeed as he said.

" But the under side is as stained as the upper. It must have left a mark."

Lestrade chuckled with delight at having puzzled the famous expert.

" Now I'll show you the explanation. There *is* a second stain, but it does not correspond with the other. See for yourself." As he spoke he turned over another portion of the carpet, and there, sure enough, was a great crimson spill upon the square white facing of the old-fashioned floor. " What do you make of that, Mr. Holmes ? "

" Why, it is simple enough. The two stains did correspond, but the carpet has been turned round. As it was square and unfastened, it was easily done."

" The official police don't need you, Mr. Holmes, to tell them that the carpet must have been turned round. That's clear enough, for the stains lie above each other —if you lay it over this way. But what I want to know is, who shifted the carpet, and why ? "

I could see from Holmes' rigid face that he was vibrating with inward excitement.

" Look here, Lestrade ! " said he. " Has that constable in the passage been in charge of the place all the time ? "

" Yes, he has."

" Well, take my advice. Examine him carefully. Don't do it before us. We'll wait here. You take him into the back room. You'll be more likely to get a confession out of him alone. Ask him how he dare to admit people and leave them alone in this room. Don't ask him if he has done it. Take it for granted. Tell him you *know* someone has been here. Press him. Tell him that a full confession is his only chance of forgiveness. Do exactly what I tell you ! ”

“ By George, if he knows I’ll have it out of him ! ” cried Lestrade. He darted into the hall, and a few moments later his bullying voice sounded from the back room.

“ Now, Watson, now ! ” cried Holmes, with frenzied eagerness. All the demoniacal force of the man masked behind that listless manner burst out in a paroxysm of energy. He tore the drugget from the floor, and in an instant was down on his hands and knees clawing at each of the squares of wood beneath it. One turned sideways as he dug his nails into the edge of it. It hinged back like the lid of a box. A small black cavity opened beneath it. Holmes plunged his eager hand into it, and drew it out with a bitter snarl of anger and disappointment. It was empty.

“ Quick, Watson, quick ! Get it back again ! ” The **23** wooden lid was replaced, and the drugget had only just been drawn straight, when Lestrade’s voice was heard in the passage. He found Holmes leaning languidly against the mantelpiece, resigned and patient, endeavouring to conceal his irrepressible yawns.

“ Sorry to keep you waiting, Mr. Holmes. I can see that you are bored to death with the whole affair. Well, he has confessed all right. Come in here, MacPherson. Let these gentlemen hear of your most inexcusable conduct.”

The big constable, very hot and penitent, sidled into the room.

“ I meant no harm, sir, I’m sure. The young woman came to the door last evening—mistook the house, she did. And then we got talking. It’s lonesome, when you’re on duty here all day.”

“ Well, what happened then ? ”

23 *“Quick, Watson, quick!* “Holmes was not addicated to the use of the word ‘Quick,’ ” Mr. C. B. H. Vaill wrote in “Quick, Watson, the Needle!” “He could never have said (and in the Canon never once does say), ‘Quick, Watson, the needle!’ ”

IT HINGED BACK LIKE THE LID OF A BOX

Illustration by Sidney Paget for the *Strand Magazine*, December, 1904.

HE FOUND HOLMES LEANING LANGUIDLY AGAINST THE MANTELPIECE . . .

Illustration by Charles Raymond Macauley for *The Return of Sherlock Holmes*, New York: McClure, Phillips and Company, 1905. This book, the late James Montgomery wrote in *A Study in Pictures*, “had an enormous vogue, and as a result Macauley’s illustrations were seen by millions, but in the light of Steele’s tremendous popularity they exerted no permanent influence upon the conception of American Sherlockians, and are now almost completely forgotten.”

24 *Queer Street.* An imaginary street or place of abode for queer people, especially for people who have become, or are likely to become, entangled in difficulties of any kind.

" She wanted to see where the crime was done—had read about it in the papers, she said. She was a very respectable, well-spoken young woman, sir, and I saw no harm in letting her have a peep. When she saw that mark on the carpet, down she dropped on the floor, and lay as if she were dead. I ran to the back and got some water, but I could not bring her to. Then I went round the corner to the ' Ivy Plant ' for some brandy, and by the time I had brought it back the young woman had recovered and was off—ashamed of herself, I dare say, and dared not face me."

" How about moving that drugget ? "

" Well, sir, it was a bit rumpled, certainly, when I came back. You see, she fell on it, and it lies on a polished floor with nothing to keep it in place. I straightened it out afterwards."

" It's a lesson to you that you can't deceive me, Constable MacPherson," said Lestrade, with dignity. " No doubt you thought that your breach of duty could never be discovered, and yet a mere glance at that drugget was enough to convince me that someone had been admitted to the room. It's lucky for you, my man, that nothing **24** is missing, or you would find yourself in Queer Street. I'm sorry to have to call you down over such a petty business, Mr. Holmes, but I thought the point of the second stain not corresponding with the first would interest you."

" Certainly it was most interesting. Has this woman only been here once, constable ? "

" Yes, sir, only once."

" Who was she ? "

" Don't know the name, sir. Was answering an advertisement about typewriting, and came to the wrong number—very pleasant, genteel young woman, sir."

" Tall ? Handsome ? "

" Yes, sir ; she was a well-grown young woman. I suppose you might say she was handsome. Perhaps some would say she was very handsome. ' Oh, officer, do let me have a peep ! ' says she. She had pretty, coaxing ways, as you might say, and I thought there was no harm in letting her just put her head through the door."

" How was she dressed ? "

" Quiet, sir—a long mantle down to her feet."

" What time was it ? "

" It was just growing dusk at the time. They were lighting the lamps as I came back with the brandy."

" Very good," said Holmes. " Come, Watson, I think that we have more important work elsewhere."

As we left the house Lestrade remained in the front room, while the repentant constable opened the door to let us out. Holmes turned on the step and held up something in his hand. The constable stared intently.

" Good Lord, sir ! " he cried, with amazement on his face. Holmes put his finger on his lips, replaced his hand in his breast-pocket, and burst out laughing as we turned down the street. " Excellent ! " said he. " Come, friend Watson, the curtain rings up for the last act. You will be relieved to hear that there will be no war, that the Right Honourable Trelawney Hope will suffer no set-back in his brilliant career, that the indiscreet Sovereign will receive no punishment for his indiscretion, that the Prime Minister will have no European complication to deal with, and that with a little tact and management upon our part nobody will be a penny the worse for what might have been a very ugly accident."

My mind filled with admiration for this extraordinary man.

"You have solved it!" I cried.

"Hardly that, Watson. There are some points which are as dark as ever. But we have so much that it will be our own fault if we cannot get the rest. We will go straight to Whitehall Terrace and bring the matter to a head."

When we arrived at the residence of the European Secretary it was for Lady Hilda Trelawney Hope that Sherlock Holmes inquired. We were shown into the morning-room.

"Mr. Holmes!" said the lady, and her face was pink with indignation, "this is surely most unfair and ungenerous upon your part. I desired, as I have explained, to keep my visit to you a secret, lest my husband should think that I was intruding into his affairs. And yet you compromise me by coming here, and so showing that there are business relations between us."

"Unfortunately, madam, I had no possible alternative. I have been commissioned to recover this immensely important paper. I must therefore ask you, madam, to be kind enough to place it in my hands."

The lady sprang to her feet, with the colour all dashed in an instant from her beautiful face. Her eyes glazed —she tottered—I thought that she would faint. Then with a grand effort she rallied from the shock, and a supreme astonishment and indignation chased every other expression from her features.

"You—you insult me, Mr. Holmes."

"Come, come, madam, it is useless. Give up the letter."

She darted to the bell.

"The butler shall show you out."

"Do not ring, Lady Hilda. If you do, then all my earnest efforts to avoid a scandal will be frustrated. Give up the letter, and all will be set right. If you will work with me, I can arrange everything. If you work against me, I must expose you."

She stood grandly defiant, a queenly figure, her eyes fixed upon his as if she would read his very soul. Her hand was on the bell, but she had forborne to ring it.

"You are trying to frighten me. It is not a very manly thing, Mr. Holmes, to come here and browbeat a woman. You say that you know something. What is it that you know?"

"Pray sit down, madam. You will hurt yourself there if you fall. I will not speak until you sit down. Thank you."

"I give you five minutes, Mr. Holmes."

"One is enough, Lady Hilda. I know of your visit to Eduardo Lucas, and of your giving him this document, of your ingenious return to the room last night, and of the

"YOU—YOU INSULT ME, MR. HOLMES."

Illustration by Sidney Paget for the *Strand Magazine*, December, 1904.

manner in which you took the letter from the hiding-place under the carpet."

She stared at him with an ashen face, and gulped twice before she could speak.

"You are mad, Mr. Holmes—you are mad!" she cried at last.

He drew a small piece of cardboard from his pocket. It was the face of a woman cut out of a portrait.

"I have carried this because I thought it might be useful," said he. "The policeman has recognized it."

She gave a gasp, and her head dropped back in her chair.

"Come, Lady Hilda. You have the letter. The matter may still be adjusted. I have no desire to bring trouble to you. My duty ends when I have returned the lost letter to your husband. Take my advice and be frank with me ; it is your only chance."

Her courage was admirable. Even now she would not own defeat.

"I tell you again, Mr. Holmes, that you are under some absurd illusion."

Holmes rose from his chair.

"I am sorry for you, Lady Hilda. I have done my best for you ; I can see that it is all in vain."

He rang the bell. The butler entered.

"Is Mr. Trelawney Hope at home ? "

"He will be home, sir, at a quarter to one."

Holmes glanced at his watch.

"Still a quarter of an hour," said he. "Very good, I shall wait."

The butler had hardly closed the door behind him when Lady Hilda was down on her knees at Holmes' feet, her hands outstretched, her beautiful face upturned and wet with her tears.

"Oh, spare me, Mr. Holmes! Spare me!" she pleaded, in a frenzy of supplication. "For Heaven's sake don't tell him! I love him so! I would not bring one shadow on his life, and this I know would break his noble heart."

Holmes raised the lady. "I am thankful, madam, that you have come to your senses even at this last moment! There is not an instant to lose. Where is the letter ? "

She darted across to a writing-desk, unlocked it, and drew out a long blue envelope.

"Here it is, Mr. Holmes. Would to Heaven I had never seen it ! "

"How can we return it ? " Holmes muttered. "Quick, quick, we must think of some way ! Where is the dispatch-box ? "

"Still in his bedroom."

"What a stroke of luck! Quick, madam, bring it here."

A moment later she had appeared with a red flat box in her hand.

"How did you open it before ? You have a duplicate key ? Yes, of course you have. Open it ! "

From out of her bosom Lady Hilda had drawn a small key. The box flew open. It was stuffed with papers. Holmes thrust the blue envelope deep down into the heart of them, between the leaves of some other document. The box was shut, locked, and returned to his bedroom.

" Now we are ready for him," said Holmes ; " we have still ten minutes. I am going far to screen you, Lady Hilda. In return you will spend the time in telling me frankly the real meaning of this extraordinary affair."

" Mr. Holmes, I will tell you everything," cried the lady. " Oh, Mr. Holmes, I would cut off my right hand before I gave him a moment of sorrow ! There is no woman in all London who loves her husband as I do, and yet if he knew how I have acted—how I have been compelled to act—he would never forgive me. For his own honour stands so high that he could not forget or pardon a lapse in another. Help me, Mr. Holmes ! My happiness, his happiness, our very lives are at stake ! "

" Quick, madam, the time grows short ! "

" It was a letter of mine, Mr. Holmes, an indiscreet letter written before my marriage—a foolish letter, a letter of an impulsive, loving girl. I meant no harm, and yet he would have thought it criminal. Had he read that letter his confidence would have been for ever destroyed. It is years since I wrote it. I had thought that the whole matter was forgotten. Then at last I heard from this man, Lucas, that it had passed into his hands, and that he would lay it before my husband. I implored his mercy. He said that he would return my letter if I would return him a certain document which he described in my husband's dispatch-box. He had some spy in the office who had told him of its existence. He assured me that no harm could come to my husband. Put yourself in my position, Mr. Holmes ! What was I to do ? "

" Take your husband into your confidence."

" I could not, Mr. Holmes, I could not ! On the one side seemed certain ruin ; on the other, terrible as it seemed to take my husband's papers, still in a matter of politics I could not understand the consequences, while in a matter of love and trust they were only too clear to me. I did it, Mr. Holmes ! I took an impression of his key ; this man Lucas furnished a duplicate. I opened his dispatch-box, took the paper, and conveyed it to Godolphin Street."

" What happened there, madam ? "

" I tapped at the door, as agreed. Lucas opened it. I followed him into his room, leaving the hall door ajar behind me, for I feared to be alone with the man. I remembered that there was a woman outside as I entered. Our business was soon done. He had my letter on his desk ; I handed him the document. He gave me the letter. At this instant there was a sound at the door. There were steps in the passage. Lucas quickly turned back the drugget, thrust the document into some hiding-place there, and covered it over.

" What happened after that is like some fearful dream. I have a vision of a dark, frantic face, of a woman's voice, which screamed in French, ' My waiting is not in vain. At last, at last I have found you with her ! ' There was a savage struggle. I saw him with a chair in his hand, a knife gleamed in hers. I rushed from the horrible scene, ran from the house, and only next morning in the paper did I learn the dreadful result. That night I was happy, for I had my letter, and I had not seen yet what the future would bring.

"It was next morning that I realized that I had only exchanged one trouble for another. My husband's anguish at the loss of his paper went to my heart. I could hardly prevent myself from there and then kneeling down at his feet and telling him what I had done. But that again would mean a confession of the past. I came to you that morning in order to understand the full enormity of my offence. From the instant that I grasped it my whole mind was turned to the one thought of getting back my husband's paper. It must still be where Lucas had placed it, for it was concealed before this dreadful woman entered the room. If it had not been for her coming, I should not have known where his hiding-place was. How was I to get into the room? For two days I watched the place, but the door was never left open. Last night I made a last attempt. What I did and how I succeeded, you have already learned. I brought the paper back with me, and thought of destroying it, since I could see no way of returning it without confessing my guilt to my husband. Heavens, I hear his step upon the stair!"

The European Secretary burst excitedly into the room.

"Any news, Mr. Holmes, any news?" he cried.

"I have some hopes."

"Ah, thank Heaven!" His face became radiant. "The Prime Minister is lunching with me. May he share your hopes? He has nerves of steel, and yet I know that he has hardly slept since this terrible event. Jacobs, will you ask the Prime Minister to come up? As to you, dear, I fear that this is a matter of politics. We will join you in a few minutes in the dining-room."

The Prime Minister's manner was subdued, but I could see by the gleam of his eyes and the twitchings of his bony hands that he shared the excitement of his young colleague.

"I understand that you have something to report, Mr. Holmes?"

"Purely negative as yet," my friend answered. "I have inquired at every point where it might be, and I am sure that there is no danger to be apprehended."

"But that is not enough, Mr. Holmes. We cannot live for ever on such a volcano. We must have something definite."

"I am in hopes of getting it. That is why I am here. The more I think of the matter the more convinced I am that the letter has never left this house."

"Mr. Holmes!"

"If it had it would certainly have been public by now."

"But why should anyone take it in order to keep it in this house?"

"I am not convinced that anyone did take it."

"Then how could it leave the dispatch-box?"

" I am not convinced that it ever did leave the dispatch-box."

" Mr. Holmes, this joking is very ill-timed. You have my assurance that it left the box."

" Have you examined the box since Tuesday morning ? "

" No ; it was not necessary."

" You may conceivably have overlooked it."

" Impossible, I say."

" But I am not convinced of it ; I have known such things happen. I presume there are other papers there. Well, it may have got mixed with them."

" It was on the top."

" Someone may have shaken the box and displaced it."

" No, no ; I had everything out."

" Surely it is easily decided, Hope ! " said the Premier. " Let us have the dispatch-box brought in."

The Secretary rang the bell.

" Jacobs, bring down my dispatch-box. This is a farcical waste of time, but still, if nothing else will satisfy you, it shall be done. Thank you, Jacobs ; put it here. I have always had the key on my watch-chain. Here are the papers, you see. Letter from Lord Merrow, report from Sir Charles Hardy, memorandum from Belgrade, note on the Russo-German grain taxes, letter from Madrid, note from Lord Flowers—good heavens ! what is this ? Lord Bellinger ! Lord Bellinger ! "

The Premier snatched the blue envelope from his hand.

" Yes, it is it—and the letter intact. Hope, I congratulate you ! "

" Thank you ! Thank you ! What a weight from my heart ! But this is inconceivable—impossible ! Mr. Holmes, you are a wizard, a sorcerer ! How did you know it was there ? "

" Because I knew it was nowhere else."

" I cannot believe my eyes ! " He ran wildly to the door. " Where is my wife ? I must tell her that all is well. Hilda ! Hilda ! " we heard his voice on the stairs.

The Premier looked at Holmes with twinkling eyes.

" Come, sir," said he. " There is more in this than meets the eye. How came the letter back in the box ? "

Holmes turned away smiling from the keen scrutiny of those wonderful eyes.

" We also have our diplomatic secrets," said he, and picking up his hat he turned to the door.

THE PREMIER SNATCHED THE BLUE ENVELOPE FROM HIS HAND.

Illustration by Sidney Paget for the *Strand Magazine*, December, 1904.

Auctorial and Bibliographical Note. Of the twelve short stories on his "best" list, excluding those in the *Case-Book*, Conan Doyle ranked "The Adventure of the Second Stain" eighth. The original manuscript, 31 small folio leaves (5½ in another hand), white vellum, was auctioned in New York City on January 26, 1922, bringing $170. It was later listed in Scribner's Sherlock Holmes Catalogue at $450. It is presently owned by Haverford College, Haverford, Pennsylvania, the gift of the late Christopher Morley.

EDITORIAL OFFICE OF "THE STRAND MAGAZINE."

nothing but strict business — a bookcase, desks, chairs, and many papers.

To the left, on the next floor, stands the editorial office of THE STRAND MAGAZINE, wherein, before the central writing-table, sits Mr. H. Greenhough Smith, in whose charge lies the selection and arrangement of the literary matter—the editing, in fact, of course under the supervision of Mr. Newnes—of this, by far the most widely-circulated monthly in the country.   This room also, with its bookcase, its cabinets for the reception of proofs and MSS., its telephones, and its many loose papers, is unmistakably a room for work.

Just so is the adjoining room, occupied by Mr. W. H. J. Boot, the Art Editor.   Like Mr. Greenhough Smith's room, it overlooks

EDITORIAL OFFICE OF THE "STRAND MAGAZINE"

Shown at his desk is the editor of the *Strand*, H. Greenhough Smith, friend of Conan Doyle. As the man responsible for the selection and arrangement of the *Strand*'s literary matter, he secured for his pages all the Sherlock Holmes short stories and the two later novels.

IV. FROM DR. WATSON'S FIRST MARRIAGE TO THE DEATH OF THE FIRST MRS. WATSON

[*circa* November 1, 1886 to late December, 1887, or early January, 1888]

"I should recommend you also to send a note . . .
to your wife to say that you have thrown in your lot with me."
—Sherlock Holmes to John H. Watson, M.D.,
"The Man with the Twisted Lip"

"A CERTAIN GRACIOUS LADY"

Victoria, Queen of Great Britain and Ireland (1837–1901) and Empress of India (1876–1901), she reigned over England during most of the Holmes-Watson period.

22

"NOW, WATSON, THE FAIR SEX IS YOUR DEPARTMENT"

[Sherlock Holmes, "The Adventure of the Second Stain"]

Much has been written on the subject of Dr. Watson's marriages and wives—so much, indeed, that the late Dorothy L. Sayers was moved to say: "There is a conspiracy afoot to provide Watson with as many wives as Henry VIII," and the late Gavin Brend was forced to remind his fellow Holmsesians that we are dealing, not with Bluebeard, but with Dr. John H. Watson.

And yet it is absolutely essential for the student who seeks to reconstruct, not only Watson's career, but also that of Holmes, to try to determine with as much exactitude as possible just how often Watson married, and whom he married, and when.

This is because the proper dating of so many of the cases hinges upon correctly interpreting a Watsonian reference to "my marriage." The good doctor tells us, for example, that "The Adventure of the Noble Bachelor" took place "a few weeks before my own marriage." "The Stockbroker's Clerk" was "shortly after my marriage." Three more adventures ("The Naval Treaty," a "Second Stain," and the unrecorded "Tired Captain") happened during "the July which immediately succeeded my marriage." Still another adventure, that of "The Dying Detective," occurred in "the second year of my married life."

Few students of the Canon question Watson's union with Mary Morstan, whom he wooed and won during the adventure of *The Sign of the Four*[1]—and most, but by no means all, students are now agreed that the proper year of *The Sign of the Four* is 1888 (whether the month was April, July or September is quite another matter). Our own date for the Morstan-Watson nuptials is *circa* May 1, 1889; other commentators have dated it June or November, 1887, and the late Christopher Morley, in "Dr. Watson's Secret," made a valiant effort to untangle some of "the infuriating inconsistencies of Watsonian chronology" by supposing that Watson had contracted a *secret* marriage with Mary some time before the adventure of *The Sign of the Four*.

When Holmes returned from the dead in April, 1894 ("The Adventure of the Empty House"), Watson spoke of his "sad bereavement," and most students have interpreted this to mean that Mary Morstan Watson died in 1891, 1892, 1893, or early 1894.[2]

At some time in 1902, between June 27th ("The Adventure of the Three Garridebs") and September 3rd ("The

[1] One student who did question it was the late A. Carson Simpson, who expressed the view that Watson married, not Mary Morstan of *The Sign of the Four*, but the widowed Mrs. Cecil Forrester of the same adventure. See "It Must Have Been Two Other Fellows."

[2] Dr. Ebbe Curtis Hoff, in "The Adventure of John and Mary," has suggseted the second half of 1892 on the basis of the fact that there is "a gap from June to December of that year in the otherwise monthly publications of Watson's accounts in the *Strand Magazine* which may be accounted for by her decease."

3 But Mr. D. Martin Dakin rejects this marriage entirely on the grounds that "The Adventure of the Blanched Soldier" is fictitious. "The whole reference is probably the mistake of a misguided writer who wanted to account for Holmes writing the story himself and had not the wit to realize that [the marriage referred to in it] belonged to an earlier period" ("The Problem of the *Case-Book*").

Adventure of the Illustrious Client"), Watson moved to rooms in Queen Anne Street. He was undoubtedly contemplating matrimony at that time, although his marriage may not have taken place until shortly before "The Adventure of the Blanched Soldier" (January, 1903), in which Holmes himself writes: "The good Watson had at that time deserted me for a wife . . ."**3**

We may date this marriage late (October, November, or December) 1902.

It is probable that Watson returned at once to the practice of medicine, for, in September, 1902 ("The Adventure of the Illustrious Client") he mentions "some pressing professional business of my own"; and by the summer of 1903 ("The Adventure of the Mazarin Stone") he bears "every sign of the busy medical man, with calls on his every hour."

The identity of this Mrs. Watson remains an enigma. Mr. S. C. Roberts has conjectured, somewhat playfully, that she was the young and beautiful Miss Violet de Merville of "The Adventure of the Illustrious Client." But the late Elmer Davis wrote ("The Real Sherlock Holmes") that ". . . the evidence adduced to support [this theory] is mere inference, and the probabilities are powerfully against it. Miss de Merville, with the 'ethereal otherworld beauty of a fanatic,' and 'a will of iron' was hardly the woman to attract a prudent middle-aged widower; if Dr. Watson had really that 'experience of women extending over many nations and three separate continents' of which he boasts in *The Sign of the Four* . . . he must have known that she was more dangerous than dynamite, supremely the sort of woman to avoid. Moreover, so solidly conventional a late Victorian as Watson would have been unlikely to marry a woman who had 'doted upon' and 'been obsessed by' the infamous Gruner; nor, possibly, would he have been drawn to one who had enlisted the interest, however chivalrous and paternal, of his sovereign."

Mr. Davis also made the valid point that Watson had left Baker Street for the Queen Anne Street rooms *before* he met Miss de Merville—if indeed he ever met her at all; there is no evidence that he did in the story.

It seems we must discard Miss Violet de Merville as the Mrs. Watson of 1902.

Who else, then, could she have been?

Mr. Stuart Palmer once speculated ("The Adventure of the Marked Man") that this Mrs. Watson was Signora Emilia Lucca of "The Adventure of the Red Circle"; Mr. Richard W. Clarke surmised ("On the Nomenclature of Watson's Ships") that she was a Miss Alicia Cutter of New York City, whom Watson had met during the problem of "The Disappearance of Lady Frances Carfax"; and the late Christopher Morley wrote: "In brooding on the problem of [Watson's 1902] marriage one could be tempted to wish that the superb Grace Dunbar of 'The Problem of Thor Bridge' might have been [that] Mrs. Watson. But knowing Senator Neil Gibson, it is unlikely." Morley on another occasion ventured the opinion that the Mrs. Watson of 1902 was Lady Frances Carfax herself, and this suggestion has received the enthusiastic support of Mr. George Haynes in "The Last Mrs. Watson."

Whoever this Mrs. Watson was, she behaved very differently from Mary Morstan Watson. "Can it be doubted," Elmer Davis wrote, "that [she] put her foot down well in advance of the ceremony, and made it a condition precedent on her acceptance that her husband should have no more to do with the sort of people he knew before he was married— i.e., conspicuously with Sherlock Holmes? The probability is supported by Holmes' own words in 'The Adventure of the Blanched Soldier'—'The good Watson had at that time deserted me for a wife, *the only selfish action which I can recall in our association*.' This clearly refers to the [1902] marriage because Mary Morstan Watson, from indifference or complaisance, never objected when her husband went off with Holmes. The [last] Mrs. Watson, obviously, was made of sterner stuff. Further, it may be inferred that she had known [Mary Morstan Watson], and had observed at first-hand the doctor's frequent darting away from the fireside. Not a relative, for Mary Morstan had no relatives in England; but, considering the difference in ages, she might well have been one of the daughters of Mrs. Cecil Forrester to whom Mary was once the governess. Some one, at any rate, who knew the circumstances well enough to tell the amorous doctor, 'I don't intend to go through what poor Mary suffered'; or (on the alternative hypothesis that it was Mary Watson rather than John Watson whose love grew cold): 'I care enough for you to want you to stay home.' "

Indeed, Christopher Morley thought that the Mrs. Watson of 1902 was so intent on keeping Watson away from Holmes and busy with his practice that she herself wrote at least one of the later adventures for him.

There is, however, another school of thought: one that holds that the "sad bereavement" to which Watson referred in "The Adventure of the Empty House" was not bereavement by death but the fact that Mary and John had separated: "Watson's so-called [1902] marriage was when he and Mary decided to resume mutual bed and board," Christopher Morley wrote in "Watson à la Mode," recanting on his previous opinions on the last Mrs. Watson.

This is also the view of Professor H. W. Starr ("Some New Light on Watson"): "Mary Morstan had not died at all; she is the wife—and the only wife—referred to throughout the entire Canon."[4]

Professor Starr, in collaboration with Mr. T. B. Hunt, elaborated on this view in "What Happened to Mary Morstan": "Mary Morstan . . . fought courageously—and with the Doctor's self-sacrificing help—against the inroads of insanity. Again and again his love and medical skill pulled her back from the shadow of the asylum; to her he gave the closing years of his life, attending her in seclusion, saving her from the final horror of an institution. This is the 'sad bereavement.' "

We must now consider briefly the suggestion put forward by the late H. W. Bell—that still another marriage by Watson accounts for the "missing year" late 1895 to late 1896. As noted in Chapter 16, this suggestion has not survived careful examination. Nonetheless, we most heartily concur with Mr. Bell that Watson *was* married three times—although we hold that his "third" marriage was *chronologically his first*.

[4] Others who have expressed a similar point of view include Mr. Daniel L. Moriarty in his "The Woman Who Beat Sherlock Holmes"; Mr. Wingate H. Bett in a letter to "Wigmore Street Post-Bag" in the *Sherlock Holmes Journal*; and Mr. Jerry Neal Williamson in "In Defense of Scotland Yard."

This view is based on researches which demonstrate (conclusively to us, at least) that Watson married for the first time *circa* November 1, 1886. His wife must have died very suddenly in late December, 1887, or early January, 1888; Watson was married and living in his house in Kensington when he called to wish Holmes the greetings of the season on the second day after Christmas, 1887 ("The Adventure of the Blue Carbuncle"), but he was back in Baker Street, where he was to remain for sixteen months, when the adventure of *The Valley of Fear* began on the morning of January 7, 1888.

Who was this Mrs. Watson?

There can be no certainty—but it is interesting to speculate that she may have been Miss Helen Stoner of "The Adventure of the Speckled Band."

In his remarkable exegesis, "A Scandal in Baker Street," Mr. Nathan L. Bengis has shown that Watson knew Helen well in India; she had been his nurse at Peshawar—and we know many patients eventually marry their nurses.

We also know that Helen met an *untimely* death. As Mr. Bengis wrote: "Note the telling effect of the italicized word, which, in a man as tight-lipped as Watson was, expresses more than a casual regret at the passing of a woman about thirty-nine."

We also know that her death occurred *before* Watson chronicled "The Adventure of the Speckled Band"—which could hardly have been earlier than March, 1889. This released him from his promise not to reveal the facts about the death of Dr. Grimesby Roylott; if Helen Stoner was indeed the first Mrs. Watson, it released him also from his marriage to her and made it possible for him to propose to Mary Morstan in September, 1888, and marry her *circa* May 1, 1889.

But there is another possibility, and a strong one.

We have already had cause to refer to the unfinished manuscript, *Angels of Darkness,* penned by Watson's friend Dr. Conan Doyle. There, it will be recalled, Conan Doyle revealed that Watson had for a time practiced medicine in San Francisco, California, U.S.A. But more than that was revealed: as Mr. John Dickson Carr wrote in his *Life of Sir Arthur Conan Doyle* (italics ours): "*Either* [*Watson*] *had a wife before he wedded Mary Morstan,* or else he heartlessly jilted the poor girl whom he holds in his arms as the curtain falls on *Angels of Darkness.*"

From what we already know of Watson's character, it is unthinkable that he should have "jilted the poor girl," and your editor is firm in his belief that the *first* Mrs. Watson was an American, a girl from San Francisco who was a patient of Watson's when he briefly practiced medicine there.

Now, at least four times in his chronicles, Watson attempts to imply that *The Sign of the Four* took place *earlier* than it actually did, or, alternatively, that certain cases in which he appears in the married state took place *after* September, 1888, leading the reader to suppose that the wife in these cases was Mary, when, in reality, she was (in our view) the girl from San Francisco.

In "A Scandal in Bohemia," for example, Watson speaks of the "well-remembered door" of No. 221 Baker Street—an address, he is careful to tell us, that he would always associate with his wooing. This was the first case published by Watson after the appearance of *The Sign of the Four*, in which he had described his wooing of Mary. The contemporary reader would naturally assume that the wife of "A Scandal in Bohemia" was Mary—and we really cannot blame him, for this was Watson's intention.

Again, in "The Red-Headed League," the police official, Jones, is made to say: "Once or twice, as in that business of the Sholto murder and the Agra treasure . . ." That Jones should remember, in October, 1887, an event that did not take place until September, 1888, is remarkable. It becomes even more remarkable when one notes that Police Official Jones of "The Red-Headed League" and Inspector Jones of *The Sign of the Four* were *two different men:* it was *Peter* Jones in "The Red-Headed League," but it was *Athelney* Jones in *The Sign of the Four* (Jones is not an unusual name, and it is possible that the two police officers were brothers).

Again, in "A Case of Identity," Watson tells us that he looked back to "the weird business of *The Sign of the Four*" —and in "The Five Orange Pips" Holmes *supposedly* mentions *The Sign of the Four* as a possibly more fantastic case. It is also in "The Five Orange Pips" that Watson says he was a dweller for a few days in Baker Street once more because his wife was on a visit to her *aunt's*. But it was her *mother* she was visiting in the first publication of Watson's chronicle in the *Strand Magazine* for November, 1891—and *Mary*, of course, was an orphan.[5]

Indeed, it is equally incredible that *Mary* should have been visiting an *aunt:* as Dr. Ebbe Curtis Hoff wrote in "The Adventure of John and Mary": "When Mary came home from India as a child to go to school in Edinburgh, her mother was already dead, and she had no relative in England. As a schoolgirl of seventeen, she had to face decisions arising out of the disappearance of her father and with no advice except that of the manager of the Langham Hotel and the police. If Mary had had an aunt, she would have come forward at [this] time of crisis and need. There is no mention of an aunt at that time because there was no aunt. Mary . . . had no relative in England."

It is apparent that the Mrs. Watson of "The Five Orange Pips" and Mary Morstan Watson, like Peter Jones and Athelney Jones, *were two different people*. Watson, who wished to conceal this fact, hastily changed "mother" to "aunt" when "The Five Orange Pips appeared in *The Adventures of Sherlock Holmes*, not realizing at the time that he was making the matter no better.

It is not impossible that Watson went even beyond this— that the "1890s" in his account of "The Red-Headed League," for example, were neither slips of the memory nor slips of the pen nor mistakes by the typesetter, but *insertions deliberately intended to confound the chronologically minded contemporary reader*, as they have certainly confused many later chronologists.[6]

Does all this seem out of character?

We will later have cause to note the extremely subtle way in which Watson attempted to confound the chronologically minded contemporary reader in "The Adventure of Charles Augustus Milverton" (although, in that chronicle, he did

[5] So was Helen Stoner—a point against the theory that she may have been the first Mrs. Watson.

[6] "Watson wove a tangled web in his chronology because he was deliberately trying to deceive," the late Christopher Morley wrote in "Dr. Watson's Secret."

7 Three times during 1890 Watson returned to Baker Street for longer or for shorter periods.

8 We may be sure that Mary *would* see Watson's published writings. As the late Dorothy L. Sayers wrote in "Dr. Watson's Christian Name," "Tenderly devoted as [Mary Watson] was to her husband, she could not have failed to read his stories attentively on publication. . . . On such dull matters as dates and historical facts, the dear woman would offer no comment, but on any details affecting her domestic life she would pounce like a tigress."

9 We should remember here that the first Mrs. Watson was Watson's *patient* before she was Watson's *wife*. She obviously suffered from poor health, and her very sudden death should not be unexpected.

warn the reader that he would make every effort to attempt to conceal the date).

Let us also remember that "in Watson's character underlies certainly a very marked streak, not only of pawky humor, but also of *cunning* and his friend Sherlock Holmes was every now and then brought up against it in a rather unexpected way. ('I never get your limits, Watson. There are unexplained possibilities about you,' Holmes would remark; or, again, 'Your native cunning . . .'). Holmes evidently spoke in a humorous vein on these occasions, but none the less . . ." (Cornelis Helling, "The True Story of the Dancing Men").

But *why* did Watson deliberately attempt to mislead the reader in at least four of his early chronicles?

The answer leaps to the eye when one considers these *publication dates:*

1. "A Scandal in Bohemia"—July, 1891.
2. "The Red-Headed League"—August, 1891.
3. "A Case of Identity"—September, 1891.
4. "The Five Orange Pips"—November, 1891.

In July to November, 1891, Watson was married to and living with Mary Morstan Watson. How would she feel with such a constant reminder *in the public prints* that in Watson's affections she was always second to "that other"? (See *The Sign of the Four*, Note 170).

The state of Mary's health made Watson's married life with her difficult enough, we know;**7** he had no intention of making it more difficult still by reminding her, in so many of the chronicles published in the *Strand Magazine* during their married life together, that she was not the first but the second Mrs. Watson.**8**

Let us now summarize Watson's marriages as we see them:

1. *Circa* November 1, 1886, Watson married the girl from San Francisco he had met while practicing medicine there, during the period when he was called to America to attend his ailing brother. He almost at once purchased a small and never very successful practice in Kensington. The first Mrs. Watson died, probably in late December, 1887, but very possibly early in January, 1888, and Watson returned to Baker Street.**9**

2. *Circa* May 1, 1889, Watson married Mary Morstan, whom he had met during the adventure of *The Sign of the Four* in September, 1888. He soon bought a connection in the Paddington district from old Mr. Farquhar ("The Stockbroker's Clerk"). Unlike his Kensington practice, his Paddington practice "increased steadily" ("The Engineer's Thumb"). (It is probable, as we have seen, that Mary Morstan Watson died in June, 1892, or shortly thereafter.)

3. In early October, 1902, Dr. John H. Watson married for the third time. Soon after that he returned to the practice of medicine, this time in Queen Anne Street. This, too, was a highly successful practice; Watson tells us (in "The Adventure of the Creeping Man") that it was "not inconsiderable" by September, 1903.

Truly, as Sherlock Holmes said, "the fair sex is your department," Watson.

23

THE REIGATE SQUIRES

[*Thursday, April 14, to Tuesday, April 26, 1887*]

IT was some time before the health of my friend, Mr. Sherlock Holmes, recovered from the strain caused by his immense exertions in the spring of '87. The whole question of the Netherland-Sumatra Company and of the colossal schemes of Baron Maupertuis is too recent in the minds of the public, and too intimately concerned with politics and finance, to be a fitting subject for this series of sketches. It led, however, in an indirect fashion to a singular and complex problem, which gave my friend an opportunity of demonstrating the value of a fresh weapon among the many with which he waged his lifelong battle against crime.

On referring to my notes, I see that it was on the 14th of April that I received a telegram from Lyons, which **1-2** informed me that Holmes was lying ill in the Hotel Dulong. Within twenty-four hours I was in his sick- **3** room, and was relieved to find that there was nothing **4** formidable in his symptoms. His iron constitution, however, had broken down under the strain of an investigation which had extended over two months, during which period he had never worked less than fifteen hours a day, and had more than once, as he assured me, kept to his task for five days at a stretch. The triumphant issue of his labours could not save him from reaction after so terrible an exertion, and at a time when Europe was ringing with his name, and when his room was literally ankle-deep with congratulatory telegrams, I found him a prey to the blackest depression. Even the knowledge that he had succeeded where the police of three countries had failed, and that he had outmanœuvred at every point the most accomplished swindler in Europe, was insufficient to rouse him from his nervous prostration.

Three days later we were back in Baker Street together, **5** but it was evident that my friend would be much the better for a change, and the thought of a week of springtime in the country was full of attractions to me also. My old friend Colonel Hayter, who had come under my **6** professional care in Afghanistan, had now taken a house **7** near Reigate, in Surrey, and had frequently asked me to come down to him upon a visit. On the last occasion he had remarked that if my friend would only come with me, he would be glad to extend his hospitality to him also. A little diplomacy was needed, but when Holmes understood that the establishment was a bachelor one, and that he would be allowed the fullest freedom, he fell in with my plans, and a week after our return from Lyons, we were

1 *the 14th of April.* The 14th of April, 1887, was a Thursday. Here, for the first time, all chronologists are in complete agreement with Watson. The case ended on Tuesday, April 26, 1887.

2 *I received a telegram.* Although your editor seems to stand alone in his contention that Watson was both married and in practice in April, 1887, he has stated his case for this view in *The Chronological Holmes:* "1) Had Holmes and Watson been sharing the Baker Street rooms together at this time, Holmes would almost certainly have invited his 'intimate friend and associate' to accompany him on as lengthy and trying an investigation as that of the Netherland-Sumatra Company. . . . 2) Watson says: 'Three days later we were back in Baker Street together.' Note the significant omission of the familiar '*our rooms* in Baker Street,' the stress on the '*together*.' 3) Watson seems to go out of his way to explain to us that 'a little diplomacy' was needed to get Holmes to Reigate, underlining that it was 'only when Holmes understood that *the establishment was a bachelor one*' that he consented to go. Here Watson is clearly explaining why he did not invite Holmes to convalesce at his—Watson's—home: *his* home was *not* a bachelor establishment; the Master would not want the first Mrs. Watson fussing over him when he was in good health, much less when he was ailing. 4) Watson says that 'all my professional caution' was destined to be wasted; later he says, 'Speaking professionally, it was admirably done.' In few other cases do we find Watson so playing the medical man; clearly 'The Reigate Squires' came at a time when he was in *active* practice. 5) Finally, we have Holmes' closing quotation: '*Our* quiet rest in the country has been a distinct success, and *I* shall certainly return, much invigorated, to Baker Street to-morrow.' Watson, then, was *not* to return to Baker Street on the morrow, but to his home and practice, which he had neglected only to care for his old and intimate friend."

3 *the Hotel Dulong.* There was a Hotel *Dubost* at 19 Place Carnot.

4 *Within twenty-four hours I was in his sickroom.* Watson therefore arrived in Lyons on Friday, April 15, 1887.

5 *Three days later we were back in Baker Street together.* Bringing us to Monday, April 18, 1887.

6 *who had come under my professional care in Afghanistan.* "He evidently was not the Colonel of the 66th [Foot of the Berkshires], who was Galbraith, killed at Maiwand; nor do I think that Hayter could have been the Colonel of the Northumberland Fusiliers, who kept the Khyber Line," Mrs. Crighton Sellars wrote in "Dr. Watson and the British Army." "In the year 1880, however, Hayter may have been of some lower rank, and he might have been in either regiment, or in some other organziation stationed at Candahar."

"It would seem fairly safe to identify him with the Major Charles Hayter who was director of Kabul Transport in the Second Afghan War (Hanna: *The Second Afghan War*, pp. 470, 525)," Mr. S. C. Roberts wrote in *Doctor Watson*.

7 *Reigate, in Surrey.* A residential suburb, 22 miles from London, in the Vale, be it noted, of *Holmesdale*.

8 *we were under the Colonel's roof.* Holmes and Watson therefore arrived at Reigate on Monday, April 25, 1887.

9 *an odd volume of Pope's 'Homer.'* Alexander Pope, 1688–1744, English poet, quoted by Watson in *A Study in Scarlet* (see Note 21). In 1720 appeared Pope's translation of the *Iliad* and in 1725–1726 the *Odyssey*, both tremendous literary and financial successes.

10 *next morning.* The morning of Tuesday, April 26, 1887.

BUT I HELD UP A WARNING FINGER.

Illustration by Sidney Paget for the *Strand Magazine*, June, 1893.

8 under the Colonel's roof. Hayter was a fine old soldier, who had seen much of the world, and he soon found, as I had expected, that Holmes and he had plenty in common.

On the evening of our arrival we were sitting in the Colonel's gun-room after dinner, Holmes stretched upon the sofa, while Hayter and I looked over his little armoury of firearms.

" By the way," said he, suddenly, " I'll take one of these pistols upstairs with me in case we have an alarm."

" An alarm ! " said I.

" Yes, we've had a scare in this part lately. Old Acton, who is one of our county magnates, had his house broken into last Monday. No great damage done, but the fellows are still at large."

" No clue ? " asked Holmes, cocking his eye at the Colonel.

" None as yet. But the affair is a petty one, one of our little country crimes, which must seem too small for your attention, Mr. Holmes, after this great international affair."

Holmes waved away the compliment, though his smile showed that it had pleased him.

" Was there any feature of interest ? "

" I fancy not. The thieves ransacked the library, and got very little for their pains. The whole place was turned upside down, drawers burst open and presses ransacked, **9** with the result that an odd volume of Pope's ' Homer,' two plated candlesticks, an ivory letter-weight, a small oak barometer, and a ball of twine are all that have vanished."

" What an extraordinary assortment ! " I exclaimed.

" Oh, the fellows evidently grabbed hold of anything they could get."

Holmes grunted from the sofa.

" The county police ought to make something of that," said he. " Why, it is surely obvious that——"

But I held up a warning finger.

" You are here for a rest, my dear fellow. For Heaven's sake, don't get started on a new problem when your nerves are all in shreds."

Holmes shrugged his shoulders with a glance of comic resignation towards the Colonel, and the talk drifted away into less dangerous channels.

It was destined, however, that all my professional **10** caution should be wasted, for next morning the problem obtruded itself upon us in such a way that it was impossible to ignore it, and our country visit took a turn which neither of us could have anticipated. We were at breakfast when the Colonel's butler rushed in with all his propriety shaken out of him.

" Have you heard the news, sir ? " he gasped. " At the Cunninghams', sir ! "

" Burglary ? " cried the Colonel, with his coffee-cup in mid-air.

" Murder ! "

The Colonel whistled. " By Jove ! " said he, " who's killed, then ? The J.P. or his son ? "

" Neither, sir. It was William, the coachman. Shot through the heart, sir, and never spoke again."

" Who shot him, then ? "

" The burglar, sir. He was off like a shot and got clean away. He'd just broke in at the pantry window when William came on him and met his end in saving his master's property."

" What time ? "

" It was last night, sir, somewhere about twelve."

" Ah, then, we'll step over presently," said the Colonel, coolly settling down to his breakfast again. " It's a baddish business," he added, when the butler had gone. " He's our leading squire about here, is old Cunningham, and a very decent fellow, too. He'll be cut up over this, for the man has been in his service for years, and was a good servant. It's evidently the same villains who broke into Acton's."

" And stole that very singular collection ? " said Holmes, thoughtfully.

" Precisely."

" Hum ! It may prove the simplest matter in the world ; but, all the same, at first glance this is just a little curious, is it not ? A gang of burglars acting in the country might be expected to vary the scene of their operations, and not to crack two cribs in the same district **11** within a few days. When you spoke last night of taking precautions, I remember that it passed through my mind that this was probably the last parish in England to which the thief or thieves would be likely to turn their attention ; which shows that I have still much to learn."

" I fancy it's some local practitioner," said the Colonel. " In that case, of course, Acton's and Cunningham's are just the places he would go for, since they are far the largest about here."

" And richest ? "

" Well, they ought to be ; but they've had a law-suit for some years which has sucked the blood out of both of them, I fancy. Old Acton has some claim on half Cunningham's estate, and the lawyers have been at it with both hands."

" If it's a local villain, there should not be much difficulty in running him down," said Holmes, with a yawn. " All right, Watson, I don't intend to meddle."

" Inspector Forrester, sir," said the butler, throwing open the door.

The official, a smart, keen-faced young fellow, stepped into the room. " Good morning, Colonel," said he. " I hope I don't intrude, but we hear that Mr. Holmes, of Baker Street, is here."

The Colonel waved his hand towards my friend, and the Inspector bowed.

" We thought that perhaps you would care to step across, Mr. Holmes."

" The Fates are against you, Watson," said he, laughing. " We were chatting about the matter when you came in, Inspector. Perhaps you can let us have a few details." As he leaned back in his chair in the familiar attitude, I knew that the case was hopeless.

" We had no clue in the Acton affair. But here we have plenty to go on, and there's no doubt it is the same party in each case. The man was seen."

" Ah ! "

" Yes, sir. But he was off like a deer after the shot

11 *to crack two cribs*. To "crack a crib" is thieves' slang—meaning to break into a house or store.

"INSPECTOR FORRESTER, SIR," SAID THE BUTLER, THROWING OPEN THE DOOR.

Illustration by Sidney Paget for the *Strand Magazine*, June, 1893.

that killed poor William Kirwan was fired.   Mr. Cunningham saw him from the bedroom window, and Mr. Alec Cunningham saw him from the back passage.   It was a quarter to twelve when the alarm broke out.   Mr. Cunningham had just got into bed, and Mister Alec was smoking a pipe in his dressing-gown.   They both heard William, the coachman, calling for help, and Mister Alec he ran down to see what was the matter.   The back door was open, and as he came to the foot of the stairs he saw two men wrestling together outside.   One of them fired a shot, the other dropped, and the murderer rushed across the garden and over the hedge.   Mr. Cunningham, looking out of his bedroom window, saw the fellow as he gained the road, but lost sight of him at once.   Mister Alec stopped to see if he could help the dying man, and so the villain got clean away.   Beyond the fact that he was a middle-sized man, and dressed in some dark stuff, we have no personal clue, but we are making energetic inquiries, and if he is a stranger we shall soon find him out."

" What was this William doing there ?   Did he say anything before he died ? "

" Not a word.   He lives at the lodge with his mother, and as he was a very faithful fellow, we imagine that he walked up to the house with the intention of seeing that all was right there.   Of course, this Acton business has put everyone on their guard.   The robber must have just burst open the door—the lock has been forced—when William came upon him."

" Did William say anything to his mother before going out ? "

" She is very old and deaf, and we can get no information from her.   The shock has made her half-witted, but I understand that she was never very bright.   There is one very important circumstance, however.   Look at this ! "

He took a small piece of torn paper from a notebook and spread it out upon his knee.

" This was found between the finger and thumb of the dead man.   It appears to be a fragment torn from a larger sheet.   You will observe that the hour mentioned upon it is the very time at which the poor fellow met his

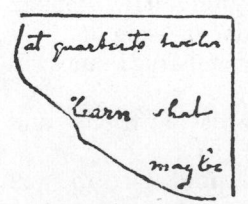

fate.   You see that his murderer might have torn the rest of the sheet from him or he might have taken this fragment from the murderer.   It reads almost as though it was an appointment."

Holmes took up the scrap of paper, a facsimile of which is here reproduced.

" Presuming that it is an appointment," continued the Inspector, " it is, of course, a conceivable theory that this William Kirwan, although he had the reputation of being an honest man, may have been in league with the thief.   He may have met him there, may even have helped him to break in the door, and then they may have fallen out between themselves."

" This writing is of extraordinary interest," said

Holmes, who had been examining it with intense concentration. " These are much deeper waters than I had thought." He sank his head upon his hands, while the Inspector smiled at the effect which his case had had upon the famous London specialist.

" Your last remark," said Holmes, presently, " as to the possibility of there being an understanding between the burglar and the servant, and this being a note of appointment from one to the other, is an ingenious and not entirely an impossible supposition. But this writing opens up——" He sank his head into his hands again and remained for some minutes in the deepest thought. When he raised his face I was surprised to see that his cheek was tinged with colour, and his eyes as bright as before his illness. He sprang to his feet with all his old energy.

" I'll tell you what ! " said he. " I should like to have a quiet little glance into the details of this case. There is something in it which fascinates me extremely. If you will permit me, Colonel, I will leave my friend, Watson, and you, and I will step round with the Inspector to test the truth of one or two little fancies of mine. I will be with you again in half an hour."

An hour and a half had elapsed before the Inspector returned alone.

" Mr. Holmes is walking up and down in the field outside," said he. " He wants us all four to go up to the house together."

" To Mr. Cunningham's ? "

" Yes, sir."

" What for ? "

The Inspector shrugged his shoulders. " I don't quite know, sir. Between ourselves, I think Mr. Holmes has not quite got over his illness yet. He's been behaving very queerly, and he is very much excited."

" I don't think you need alarm yourself," said I. " I have usually found that there was method in his madness."

" Some folk might say there was madness in his method," muttered the Inspector. " But he's all on fire to start, Colonel, so we had best go out, if you are ready."

We found Holmes pacing up and down in the field, his chin sunk upon his breast, and his hands thrust into his trouser pockets.

" The matter grows in interest," said he. " Watson, your country trip has been a distinct success. I have had a charming morning."

" You have been up to the scene of the crime, I understand ? " said the Colonel.

" Yes ; the Inspector and I have made quite a little reconnaissance together."

" Any success ? "

" Well, we have seen some very interesting things. I'll tell you what we did as we walk. First of all we saw the body of this unfortunate man. He certainly died from a revolver wound, as reported."

" Had you doubted it, then ? "

" Oh, it is as well to test everything. Our inspection was not wasted. We then had an interview with Mr. Cunningham and his son, who were able to point out the

. . . THE FINE OLD QUEEN ANNE HOUSE, WHICH BEARS THE DATE OF MALPLAQUET UPON THE LINTEL OF THE DOOR.

The reign of Queen Anne, first queen of Great Britain, last Stuart ruler, 1665–1714, was marked by the popularization of Palladian architecture (see "The Adventure of the Abbey Grange," Note 4). Malplaquet is the village in North France where, in 1709, Marlborough and Eugene of Savoy defeated the French. Gatton Hall, near Reigate, is one of several manorial houses in the district suspected of being "the fine old Queen Anne House." Mr. Charles O. Merriman has also noted that The Priory at Reigate (here illustrated, from *The Baker Street Journal*, June, 1963) is "a building of note . . . but does not bear the date of Malplaquet on the lintel of the door."

12 *"Throw the door open, officer."* Although there is an inspector present, Holmes gives direct orders to a constable, evidence of his increased stature with the official police, not only in London, but also in its suburbs.

exact spot where the murderer had broken through the garden hedge in his flight. That was of great interest."

" Naturally."

" Then we had a look at this poor fellow's mother. We could get no information from her, however, as she is very old and feeble."

" And what is the result of your investigations ? "

" The conviction that the crime is a very peculiar one. Perhaps our visit now may do something to make it less obscure. I think that we are both agreed, Inspector, that the fragment of paper in the dead man's hand, bearing, as it does, the very hour of his death written upon it, is of extreme importance."

" It should give a clue, Mr. Holmes."

" It *does* give a clue. Whoever wrote that note was the man who brought William Kirwan out of his bed at that hour. But where is the rest of that sheet of paper ? "

" I examined the ground carefully in the hope of finding it," said the Inspector.

" It was torn out of the dead man's hand. Why was someone so anxious to get possession of it ? Because it incriminated him. And what would he do with it ? Thrust it into his pocket most likely, never noticing that a corner of it had been left in the grip of the corpse. If we could get the rest of that sheet, it is obvious that we should have gone a long way towards solving the mystery."

" Yes, but how can we get at the criminal's pocket before we catch the criminal."

" Well, well, it was worth thinking over. Then there is another obvious point. The note was sent to William. The man who wrote it could not have taken it, otherwise of course he might have delivered his own message by word of mouth. Who brought the note, then ? Or did it come through the post ? "

" I have made inquiries," said the Inspector. " William received a letter by the afternoon post yesterday. The envelope was destroyed by him."

" Excellent ! " cried Holmes, clapping the Inspector on the back. " You've seen the postman. It is a pleasure to work with you. Well, here is the lodge, and if you will come up, Colonel, I will show you the scene of the crime."

We passed the pretty cottage where the murdered man had lived, and walked up an oak-lined avenue to the fine old Queen Anne house, which bears the date of Malplaquet upon the lintel of the door. Holmes and the Inspector led us round it until we came to the side gate, which is separated by a stretch of garden from the hedge which lines the road. A constable was standing at the kitchen door.

12 " Throw the door open, officer," said Holmes. " Now it was on those stairs that young Mr. Cunningham stood and saw the two men struggling just where we are. Old Mr. Cunningham was at that window—the second on the left—and he saw the fellow get away just to the left of that bush. So did the son. They are both sure of it on account of the bush. Then Mister Alec ran out and knelt beside the wounded man. The ground is very hard, you see, and there are no marks to guide us."

As he spoke two men came down the garden path, from round the angle of the house. The one was an elderly man, with a strong, deep-lined, heavy-eyed face; the other a dashing young fellow, whose bright, smiling expression and showy dress were in strange contrast with the business which had brought us there.

"Still at it, then?" said he to Holmes. "I thought you Londoners were never at fault. You don't seem to be so very quick after all."

"Ah! you must give us a little time," said Holmes, good-humouredly.

"You'll want it," said young Alec Cunningham. "Why, I don't see that we have any clue at all."

"There's only one," answered the Inspector. "We thought that if we could only find—— Good heavens! Mr. Holmes, what is the matter?"

My poor friend's face had suddenly assumed the most dreadful expression. His eyes rolled upwards, his features writhed in agony, and with a suppressed groan he dropped on his face upon the ground. Horrified at the suddenness and severity of the attack, we carried him into the kitchen, where he lay back in a large chair and breathed heavily for some minutes. Finally, with a shamefaced apology for his weakness, he rose once more.

"Watson would tell you that I have only just recovered from a severe illness," he explained. "I am liable to these sudden nervous attacks."

"Shall I send you home in my trap?" asked old Cunningham.

"Well, since I am here there is one point on which I should like to feel sure. We can very easily verify it."

"What is it?"

"Well, it seems to me that it is just possible that the arrival of this poor fellow William was not before but after the entrance of the burglar into the house. You appear to take it for granted that although the door was forced the robber never got in."

"I fancy that is quite obvious," said Mr. Cunningham, gravely. "Why, my son Alec had not yet gone to bed, and he would certainly have heard anyone moving about."

"Where was he sitting?"

"I was sitting smoking in my dressing-room."

"Which window is that?"

"The last on the left, next my father's."

"Both your lamps were lit, of course?"

"Undoubtedly."

"There are some very singular points here," said Holmes, smiling. "Is it not extraordinary that a burglar—and a burglar who had had some previous experience—should deliberately break into a house at a time when he could see from the lights that two of the family were still afoot?"

"He must have been a cool hand."

"Well, of course, if the case were not an odd one we should not have been driven to ask you for an explanation," said Mister Alec. "But as to your idea that the man had robbed the house before William tackled him, I think it a most absurd notion. Shouldn't we have

AS HE SPOKE TWO MEN CAME DOWN THE GARDEN PATH . . .

Illustration by William H. Hyde for *Harper's Weekly*, June 17, 1893.

"GOOD HEAVENS! MR. HOLMES, WHAT IS THE MATTER?"

Illustration by Sidney Paget for the *Strand Magazine*, June 1, 1893.

13 *Fifty pounds.* About $250.

14 *five hundred.*" About $2,500.

found the place disarranged and missed the things which he had taken ? "

" It depends on what the things were," said Holmes. " You must remember that we are dealing with a burglar who is a very peculiar fellow, and who appears to work on lines of his own.   Look, for example, at the queer lot of things which he took from Acton's—what was it ?—a ball of string, a letter-weight, and I don't know what other odds and ends ! "

" Well, we are quite in your hands, Mr. Holmes," said old Cunningham.   " Anything which you or the Inspector may suggest will most certainly be done."

" In the first place," said Holmes, " I should like you to offer a reward—coming from yourself, for the officials may take a little time before they would agree upon the sum, and these things cannot be done too promptly. I have jotted down the form here, if you would not mind **13** signing it.   Fifty pounds was quite enough, I thought."

14 " I would willingly give five hundred," said the J.P., taking the slip of paper and the pencil which Holmes handed to him.   " This is not quite correct, however," he added, glancing over the document.

" I wrote it rather hurriedly."

" You see you begin : ' Whereas, at about a quarter to one on Tuesday morning, an attempt was made '—and so on.   It was at a quarter to twelve, as a matter of fact."

I was pained at the mistake, for I knew how keenly Holmes would feel any slip of the kind.   It was his speciality to be accurate as to fact, but his recent illness had shaken him, and this one little incident was enough to show me that he was still far from being himself.   He was obviously embarrassed for an instant, while the Inspector raised his eyebrows and Alec Cunningham burst into a laugh.   The old gentleman corrected the mistake, however, and handed the paper back to Holmes.

" Get it printed as soon as possible," he said.   " I think your idea is an excellent one."

Holmes put the slip of paper carefully away in his pocket-book.

" And now," said he, " it would really be a good thing that we should all go over the house together, and make certain that this rather erratic burglar did not, after all, carry anything away with him."

Before entering, Holmes made an examination of the door which had been forced.   It was evident that a chisel or strong knife had been thrust in, and the lock forced back with it.   We could see the marks in the wood where it had been pushed in.

" You don't use bars, then ? " he asked.

" We have never found it necessary."

" You don't keep a dog ? "

" Yes ; but he is chained on the other side of the house."

" When do the servants go to bed ? '

" About ten."

" I understand that William was usually in bed also at that hour ? "

" Yes."

" It is singular that on this particular night he should

have been up.   Now, I should be very glad if you would have the kindness to show us over the house, Mr. Cunningham."

A stone-flagged passage, with the kitchens branching away from it, led by a wooden staircase directly to the first floor of the house.   It came out upon the landing opposite to a second more ornamental stair which led up from the front hall.   Out of this landing opened the drawing-room and several bedrooms, including those of Mr. Cunningham and his son.   Holmes walked slowly, taking keen note of the architecture of the house.   I could tell from his expression that he was on a hot scent, and yet I could not in the least imagine in what direction his inferences were leading him.

" My good sir," said Mr. Cunningham, with some impatience, " this is surely very unnecessary.   That is my room at the end of the stairs, and my son's is the one beyond it.   I leave it to your judgment whether it was possible for the thief to have come up here without disturbing us."

" You must try round and get on a fresh scent, I fancy," said the son, with a rather malicious smile.

" Still, I must ask you to humour me a little further.   I should like, for example, to see how far the windows of the bedrooms command the front.   This, I understand, is your son's room "—he pushed open the door—" and that, I presume, is the dressing-room in which he sat smoking when the alarm was given.   Where does the window of that look out to ? "   He stepped across the bedroom, pushed open the door, and glanced round the other chamber.

" I hope you are satisfied now ? " said Mr. Cunningham, testily.

" Thank you ; I think I have seen all that I wished."

" Then, if it is really necessary, we can go into my room."

" If it is not too much trouble."

The J.P. shrugged his shoulders, and led the way into his own chamber, which was a plainly furnished and commonplace room.   As we moved across it in the direction of the window, Holmes fell back until he and I were the last of the group.   Near the foot of the bed was a small square table, on which stood a dish of oranges and a carafe of water.   As we passed it, Holmes, to my unutterable astonishment, leaned over in front of me and deliberately knocked the whole thing over.   The glass smashed into a thousand pieces, and the fruit rolled about into every corner of the room.

" You've done it now, Watson," said he, coolly.   " A pretty mess you've made of the carpet."

I stooped in some confusion and began to pick up the fruit, understanding that for some reason my companion desired me to take the blame upon myself.   The others did the same, and set the table on its legs again.

" Holloa ! " cried the Inspector, " where's he got to ? " Holmes had disappeared.

" Wait here an instant," said young Alec Cunningham. " The fellow is off his head, in my opinion.   Come with me, father, and see where he has got to ! "

HOLMES . . . LEANED OVER IN FRONT OF ME AND DELIBERATELY KNOCKED THE WHOLE THING OVER.

Illustration by Sidney Paget for the *Strand Magazine*, June, 1893.

They rushed out of the room, leaving the Inspector, the Colonel, and me, staring at each other.

" 'Pon my word, I am inclined to agree with Mister Alec," said the official. " It may be the effect of this illness, but it seems to me that——"

His words were cut short by a sudden scream of " Help ! Help ! Murder ! " With a thrill I recognized the voice as that of my friend. I rushed madly from the room on to the landing. The cries, which had sunk down into a hoarse, inarticulate shouting, came from the room which we had first visited. I dashed in, and on into the dressing-room beyond. The two Cunninghams were bending over the prostrate figure of Sherlock Holmes, the younger clutching his throat with both hands, while the elder seemed to be twisting one of his wrists. In an instant the three of us had torn them away from him, and Holmes staggered to his feet, very pale, and evidently greatly exhausted.

" Arrest these men, Inspector ! " he gasped.

" On what charge ? "

" That of murdering their coachman, William Kirwan ! "

The Inspector stared about him in bewilderment. " Oh, come now, Mr. Holmes," said he at last ; " I am sure you don't really mean to——"

" Tut, man ; look at their faces ! " cried Holmes, curtly.

Never, certainly, have I seen a plainer confession of guilt upon human countenances. The older man seemed numbed and dazed, with a heavy, sullen expression upon his strongly marked face. The son, on the other hand, had dropped all that jaunty, dashing style which had characterized him, and the ferocity of a dangerous wild beast gleamed in his dark eyes and distorted his handsome features. The Inspector said nothing, but, stepping to the door, he blew his whistle. Two of his constables came at the call.

" I have no alternative, Mr. Cunningham," said he. " I trust that this may all prove to be an absurd mistake ; but you can see that—— Ah, would you ? Drop it ! " He struck out with his hand, and a revolver, which the younger man was in the act of cocking, clattered down upon the floor.

" Keep that," said Holmes, quickly putting his foot upon it. " You will find it useful at the trial. But this is what we really wanted." He held up a little crumpled piece of paper.

" The remainder of the sheet ? " cried the Inspector.

" Precisely."

" And where was it ? "

" Where I was sure it must be. I'll make the whole matter clear to you presently. I think, Colonel, that you and Watson might return now, and I will be with you again in an hour at the furthest. The Inspector and I must have a word with the prisoners ; but you will certainly see me back at luncheon-time."

Sherlock Holmes was as good as his word, for about one o'clock he rejoined us in the Colonel's smoking-room. He was accompanied by a little, elderly gentleman, who

THE TWO CUNNINGHAMS WERE BENDING OVER THE PROSTRATE FIGURE OF SHERLOCK HOLMES . . .

Illustration by Sidney Paget for the *Strand Magazine*, June, 1893.

was introduced to me as the Mr. Acton whose house had been the scene of the original burglary.

" I wished Mr. Acton to be present while I demonstrated this small matter to you," said Holmes, " for it is natural that he should take a keen interest in the details. I am afraid, my dear Colonel, that you must regret the hour that you took in such a stormy petrel as I am."

" On the contrary," answered the Colonel, warmly, " I consider it the greatest privilege to have been permitted to study your methods of working. I confess that they quite surpass my expectations, and that I am utterly unable to account for your result. I have not yet seen the vestige of a clue."

" I am afraid that my explanation may disillusionize you, but it has always been my habit to hide none of my methods, either from my friend Watson or from anyone who might take an intelligent interest in them. But first, as I am rather shaken by the knocking about which I had in the dressing-room, I think that I shall help myself to a dash of your brandy, Colonel. My strength has been rather tried of late."

" I trust you had no more of those nervous attacks."

Sherlock Holmes laughed heartily. " We will come to that in its turn," said he. " I will lay an account of the case before you in its due order, showing you the various points which guided me in my decision. Pray interrupt me if there is any inference which is not perfectly clear to you.

" It is of the highest importance in the art of detection to be able to recognize out of a number of facts which are incidental and which vital. Otherwise your energy and **15** attention must be dissipated instead of being concentrated. Now, in this case there was not the slightest doubt in my mind from the first that the key of the whole matter must be looked for in the scrap of paper in the dead man's hand.

" Before going into this I would draw your attention to the fact that if Alec Cunningham's narrative were correct, and if the assailant after shooting William Kirwan had *instantly* fled, then it obviously could not be he who tore the paper from the dead man's hand. But if it was not he, it must have been Alec Cunningham himself, for by the time the old man had descended several servants were upon the scene. The point is a simple one, but the Inspector had overlooked it because he had started with the supposition that these county magnates had had nothing to do with the matter. Now, I make a point of never having any prejudices and of following docilely wherever fact may lead me, and so in the very first stage **16** of the investigation I found myself looking a little askance at the part which had been played by Mr. Alec Cunningham.

" And now I made a very careful examination of the corner of paper which the Inspector had submitted to us. It was at once clear to me that it formed part of a very remarkable document. Here it is. Do you not now observe something very suggestive about it ? "

15 *which are incidental and which vital.* "No man, not even Holmes, could always be successful in this task," Mr. T. S. Blakeney wrote in *Sherlock Holmes: Fact or Fiction?*, "and he recognized the possibility of serious error, as in the remark: 'perhaps when a man has special knowledge and special powers like my own it rather encourages him to see a complex explanation when a simpler one is at hand' ["The Adventure of the Abbey Grange"]. Nevertheless, he was inclined to trust his intuitions rather than the surface impressions made by the data of a case—'there is nothing more deceptive than an obvious fact' ["The Boscombe Valley Mystery"]—and in a sarcastic phrase he observes, 'all my instincts are one way and all the facts are the other, and I much fear that British juries have not yet attained that pitch of intelligence when they will give the preference to my theories over Lestrade's facts' ["The Adventure of the Norwood Builder"]."

16 *wherever fact may lead me.* "Holmes keenly appreciated the great value of an open mind," Mr. George Simmons wrote in "Sherlock Holmes— The Inner Man," "and it seems that he was acquainted with [Thomas Henry] Huxley's ideas on the subject: 'Sit down before fact as a little child, be prepared to give up every preconceived notion, follow humbly and to whatever abysses nature leads, or you shall learn nothing.' "

"THE POINT IS A SIMPLE ONE . . ."

Illustration by Sidney Paget for the *Strand Magazine*, June, 1893.

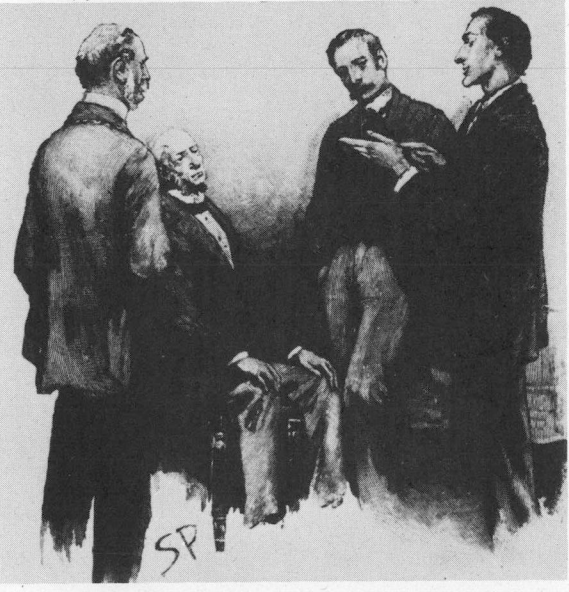

17 *with tolerable confidence.* "The deduction of a man's age from his handwriting is certainly a very doubtful matter," Mr. Vernon Rendall wrote in "The Limitations of Sherlock Holmes." "I do not believe that 'in normal cases one can place a man in his true decade with tolerable confidence.' This statement is not confirmed by my experience with a host of contributors writing for two papers for many years. . . . The period at which a hand becomes fixed varies widely, but, once settled, it remains unchanged for many years, though ill-health or excitement may introduce marked changes. See R. L. Stevenson's *The Wrong Box*, ch. VI."

"By modern standards Holmes was mistaken in thinking that you can tell the age of adult writers," Mrs. Winifred Christie wrote in "Sherlock Holmes and Graphology." "But he concluded perfectly rightly that you can deduce the state of health. What he called the broken-backed appearance of the older man's writing presents two symptoms: tremulousness shows debility, and the broken up-strokes heart disease. Heart weakness is confirmed by the presence of irrelevant dots."

"It has a very irregular look," said the Colonel.

"My dear sir," cried Holmes, "there cannot be the least doubt in the world that it has been written by two persons doing alternate words. When I draw your attention to the strong t's of ' at ' and ' to ' and ask you to compare them with the weak ones of ' quarter ' and ' twelve,' you will instantly recognize the fact. A very brief analysis of those four words would enable you to say with the utmost confidence that the ' learn ' and the ' maybe ' are written in the stronger hand, and the ' what ' in the weaker."

"By Jove, it's as clear as day!" cried the Colonel. "Why on earth should two men write a letter in such a fashion?"

"Obviously the business was a bad one, and one of the men who distrusted the other was determined that, whatever was done, each should have an equal hand in it. Now, of the two men it is clear that the one who wrote the ' at ' and ' to ' was the ringleader."

"How do you get at that?"

"We might deduce it from the mere character of the one hand as compared with the other. But we have more assured reasons than that for supposing it. If you examine this scrap with attention you will come to the conclusion that the man with the stronger hand wrote all his words first, leaving blanks for the other to fill up. These blanks were not always sufficient, and you can see that the second man had a squeeze to fit his ' quarter ' in between the ' at ' and the ' to,' showing that the latter were already written. The man who wrote all his words first is undoubtedly the man who planned this affair."

"Excellent!" cried Mr. Acton.

"But very superficial," said Holmes. We come now, however, to a point which is of importance. You may not be aware that the deduction of a man's age from his writing is one which has been brought to considerable accuracy by experts. In normal cases one can place a **17** man in his true decade with tolerable confidence. I say normal cases, because ill-health and physical weakness reproduce the signs of old age, even when the invalid is a youth. In this case, looking at the bold, strong hand of

"THERE CANNOT BE THE LEAST DOUBT IN THE WORLD THAT IT HAS BEEN WRITTEN BY TWO PERSONS . . ."

Illustration by William H. Hyde for *Harper's Weekly*, June 17, 1893.

the one, and the rather broken-backed appearance of the other, which still retains its legibility, although the t's have begun to lose their crossings, we can say that the one was a young man, and the other was advanced in years without being positively decrepit."

" Excellent ! " cried Mr. Acton again.

" There is a further point, however, which is subtler and of greater interest. There is something in common between these hands. They belong to men who are blood-relatives. It may be most obvious to you in the Greek e's, but to me there are many small points which indicate **18** the same thing. I have no doubt at all that a family mannerism can be traced in these two specimens of writing. I am only, of course, giving you the leading results now of my examination of the paper. There were twenty-three other deductions which would be of more interest to experts than to you. They all tended to **19** deepen the impression upon my mind that the Cunninghams, father and son, had written this letter.

" Having got so far, my next step was, of course, to examine into the details of the crime and to see how far they would help us. I went up to the house with the Inspector, and saw all that was to be seen. The wound upon the dead man was, as I was able to determine with absolute confidence, caused by a shot from a revolver fired at a distance of something over four yards. There was no powder-blackening on the clothes. Evidently, therefore, Alec Cunningham had lied when he said that the two men were struggling when the shot was fired. Again, both father and son agreed as to the place where the man escaped into the road. At that point, however, as it happens, there is a broadish ditch, moist at the bottom. As there were no indications of boot-marks about this ditch, I was absolutely sure not only that the Cunninghams had again lied, but that there had never been any unknown man upon the scene at all.

" And now I had to consider the motive of this singular crime. To get at this I endeavoured first of all to solve the reason of the original burglary at Mr. Acton's. I understood from something which the Colonel told us that a lawsuit had been going on between you, Mr. Acton,

18 *It may be most obvious to you in the Greek e's.* "Mr. Holmes was right in detecting family mannerisms in the Greek e's," Mrs. Christie continued. "There are family writings as there are family walks and voices."

19 *which would be of more interest to experts.* That Holmes was not exaggerating in any way has been shown by Mr. John Ball, Jr., in his essay, "The Twenty-Three Deductions": "Here, then, are the twenty-three points which Sherlock Holmes noted and from which he further strengthened his case against the Cunninghams and satisfied himself completely of their guilt: 1. The quality of the paper—costly, average, or cheap. 2. The rag content of the paper, if any. 3. The probable source of the paper (from the above). 4. The quality of the ink. 5. The chemical nature of the ink. 6. The probable source of the ink (from the above). 7. The age of the writing. 8. The presence, or absence, of folds in the paper. 9. Whether the fragment had been torn from the whole, or the whole from the fragment. 10. The direction of the tear—up or down. 11. Whether the first penman was right- or left-handed. 12. Whether the second penman was right or left-handed. 13. The type of pen used. 14. Whether or not both penmen used the same writing point. 15. Whether the fragment came from a corner of a standard sheet, or was otherwise cut from a larger piece of paper. 16. The original use of the paper—notepaper, wrapping paper, or other. 17. The presence or absence of erasures. 18. The evidence, or lack of evidence, that the writing had been blotted after the first writing. 19. The evidence, or lack of evidence, that the writing had been blotted after the second writing. 20. Whether or not both penmen had used the identical ink supply. 21. The presence, or absence, of fingernail marks made by the hand which tore the paper. 22. Any evidence of scent still clinging to the paper. 23. The presence, or absence, of extraneous marks or stains on the paper. This would also include evidence of pocket-rubbing had the whole document been carried on anyone's person for any length of time."

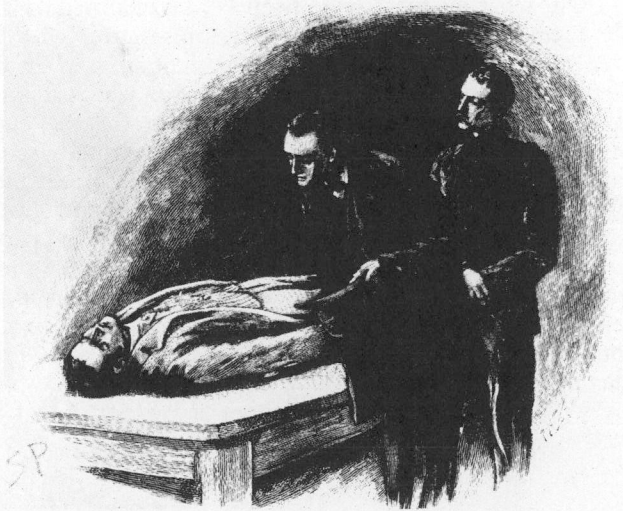

"THERE WAS NO POWDER-BLACKENING ON THE CLOTHES."

Illustration by Sidney Paget for the *Strand Magazine*, June, 1893.

and the Cunninghams. Of course, it instantly occurred to me that they had broken into your library with the intention of getting at some document which might be of importance in the case."

" Precisely so," said Mr. Acton ; " there can be no possible doubt as to their intentions. I have the clearest claim upon half their present estate, and if they could have found a single paper—which, fortunately, was in the strong box of my solicitors—they would undoubtedly have crippled our case."

" There you are ! " said Holmes, smiling. " It was a dangerous, reckless attempt, in which I seemed to trace the influence of young Alec. Having found nothing, they tried to divert suspicion by making it appear to be an ordinary burglary, to which end they carried off whatever they could lay their hands upon. That is all clear enough, but there was much that was still obscure. What I wanted above all was to get the missing part of that note. I was certain that Alec had torn it out of the dead man's hand, and almost certain that he must have thrust it into the pocket of his dressing-gown. Where else could he have put it ? The only question was whether it was still there. It was worth an effort to find out, and for that object we all went up to the house.

" The Cunninghams joined us, as you doubtless remember, outside the kitchen door. It was, of course, of the very first importance that they should not be reminded of the existence of this paper, otherwise they would naturally destroy it without delay. The Inspector was about to tell them the importance which was attached to it when, by the luckiest chance in the world, I tumbled down in a sort of fit and so changed the conversation."

" Good heavens ! " cried the Colonel, laughing. " Do you mean to say all our sympathy was wasted and your fit an imposture ? "

" Speaking professionally, it was admirably done," cried I, looking in amazement at this man who was for ever confounding me with some new phase of his astuteness.

" It is an art which is often useful," said he. " When I recovered I managed by a device, which had, perhaps, some little merit of ingenuity, to get old Cunningham to write the word ' twelve,' so that I might compare it with the ' twelve ' upon the paper."

" Oh, what an ass I have been ! " I exclaimed.

" I could see that you were commiserating with me over my weakness," said Holmes, laughing. " I was sorry to cause you the sympathetic pain which I know that you felt. We then went upstairs together, and having entered the room, and seen the dressing-gown hanging up behind the door, I contrived by upsetting a table to engage their attention for the moment and slipped back to examine the pockets. I had hardly got the paper, however, which was as I had expected, in one of them, when the two Cunninghams were on me, and would, I verily believe, have murdered me then and there but for your prompt and friendly aid. As it is, I feel that young man's grip on my throat now, and the father has twisted my wrist round in the effort to get the paper out of my hand.   They saw that I must know all about it, you see, and the sudden change from absolute security to complete despair made them perfectly desperate.

"I had a little talk with old Cunningham afterwards as to the motive of the crime.   He was tractable enough, though his son was a perfect demon, ready to blow out his own or anybody else's brains if he could have got to his revolver.   When Cunningham saw that the case against him was so strong he lost all heart, and made a clean breast of everything.   It seems that William had secretly followed his two masters on the night when they made their raid upon Mr. Acton's, and, having thus got them into his power, proceeded under threats of exposure to levy blackmail upon them.   Mister Alec, however, was a dangerous man to play games of that sort with.   It was a stroke of positive genius on his part to see in the burglary scare, which was convulsing the country-side, an opportunity of plausibly getting rid of the man whom he feared. William was decoyed up and shot ; and, had they only got the whole of the note, and paid a little more attention to detail in their accessories, it is very possible that suspicion might never have been aroused."

"And the note?" I asked.

Sherlock Holmes placed the subjoined paper before us.

"It is very much the sort of thing that I expected," said he.   "Of course, we do not yet know what the relations may have been between Alec Cunningham, William Kirwan, and Annie Morrison.   The result shows that the trap was skilfully baited.   I am sure that you cannot fail to be delighted with the traces of heredity shown in the p's and in the tails of the g's.   The absence of the i-dots in the old man's writing is also most characteristic.   Watson, I think our quiet rest in the country has been a distinct success, and I shall certainly return, much invigorated, to Baker Street to-morrow."

Auctorial and Bibliographical Note: Conan Doyle ranked "The Reigate Squires" twelfth on his list of the "twelve best" Sherlock Holmes short stories (excluding those in the *Case-Book*).

The adventure has had a curious titular history, outlined by the late Edgar W. Smith in the second issue of the old *Baker Street Journal:* "Of all the many corruptions which make the American text of the Saga so markedly inferior to the text of the John Murray (London) editions, there is none more striking than the deliberate change of the *title* of one of the tales. Originally called 'The Adventure of the Reigate Squire' in the *Strand Magazine* for June, 1893, this story became, more appropriately, 'The Reigate Squires' in both the Newnes *Memoirs* (1894) and the Murray short-story omnibus (1928). But when it first appeared in the United States, also in June, 1893, the editors of *Harper's Weekly*, evidently fearful that the term 'squires' might affront the robust American democracy of those days, mutated the title to 'The Reigate Puzzle'—and this senseless nomenclature has been perpetuated in both the Harper *Memoirs* (1894) and the . . . Doubleday omnibus (1930)."

A small fragment of the manuscript of "The Reigate Squires" is in the possession of Mr. Adrian Conan Doyle.

24

A SCANDAL IN BOHEMIA

[Friday, May 20, to Sunday, May 22, 1887]

1 the *woman*. Many students of Holmes' life hold that Irene Adler above all other women was the one he might have loved, even *did* love. This view has been hotly contested by other students of the Canon who maintain that what Holmes actually said to Watson on this occasion was something more on the order of "She is the woman who is mixed up in this case."

2 *but admirably balanced mind.* "The truth is that emotions, however abhorrent to [Holmes] in theory, are definitely a part of him in practice," Dean Theodore C. Blegen wrote in "These Were Hidden Fires, Indeed!" "They fill much of his life. They dictate many of his characteristic actions. He is a far cry from intellect frozen in unemotional ice. . . . He is flesh and blood. He is a man of moods. He is a man of emotions."

3 *save with a gibe and a sneer.* Watson, an incurable romantic, is being a little hard on Holmes in this early description of the detective as a frigid misogynist. In many later adventures, Holmes demonstrates that his was "a great heart as well as . . . a great brain."

4 *the late Irene Adler.* Watson must have written this before July, 1891, when "A Scandal in Bohemia" appeared in the *Strand Magazine*, and many commentators have since expressed doubts that Irene Adler was "the late" at that time. On the other hand, Mr. Jerry Neal Williamson has written ("A Scandal in 'A Scandal in Bohemia'"): "The solution of Watson's reference . . . is simple. [The King of Bohemia], not trusting to Holmes' ability, and using the detective for an alibi, murdered *the woman.*"

Mr. Manly Wade Wellman has concurred with this verdict ("A New Scandal in Bohemia"): "So young, so healthy, so much to live for—she could have died only by violence. Undoubtedly the ruffianly King of Bohemia, or his hired assassins, finally

I

1 TO Sherlock Holmes she is always *the* woman. I have seldom heard him mention her under any other name. In his eyes she eclipses and predominates the whole of her sex. It was not that he felt any emotion akin to love for Irene Adler. All emotions, and that one particularly, were abhorrent to his cold, **2** precise, but admirably balanced mind. He was, I take it, the most perfect reasoning and observing machine that the world has seen : but, as a lover, he would have placed himself in a false position. He never spoke of the softer **3** passions, save with a gibe and a sneer. They were admirable things for the observer—excellent for drawing the veil from men's motives and actions. But for the trained reasoner to admit such intrusions into his own delicate and finely adjusted temperament was to introduce a distracting factor which might throw a doubt upon all his mental results. Grit in a sensitive instrument, or a crack in one of his own high-power lenses, would not be more disturbing than a strong emotion in a nature such as his. And yet there was but one woman to him, and that woman **4** was the late Irene Adler, of dubious and questionable memory.

I had seen little of Holmes lately. My marriage had drifted us away from each other. My own complete happiness, and the home-centred interests which rise up around the man who first finds himself master of his own establishment, were sufficient to absorb all my attention ; **5** while Holmes, who loathed every form of society with his whole Bohemian soul, remained in our lodgings in Baker Street, buried among his old books, and alternating from week to week between cocaine and ambition, the drowsiness of the drug, and the fierce energy of his own keen nature. He was still, as ever, deeply attracted by the study of crime, and occupied his immense faculties and extraordinary powers of observation in following out those clues, and clearing up those mysteries, which had been abandoned as hopeless by the official police. From time to time I heard some vague account of his doings : of his

346

summons to Odessa in the case of the Trepoff murder, **6** of his clearing up of the singular tragedy of the Atkinson brothers at Trincomalee, and finally of the mission which **7** he had accomplished so delicately and successfully for the reigning family of Holland.   Beyond these signs of his **8** activity, however, which I merely shared with all the readers of the daily press, I knew little of my former friend and companion.

One night—it was on the 20th of March, 1888—I was **9** returning from a journey to a patient (for I had now returned to civil practice), when my way led me through **10** Baker Street.   As I passed the well-remembered door, which must always be associated in my mind with my wooing, and with the dark incidents of the Study in Scarlet, I was seized with a keen desire to see Holmes again, and to know how he was employing his extraordinary powers.   His rooms were brilliantly lit, and, even as I looked up, I saw his tall spare figure pass twice in a dark silhouette against the blind.   He was pacing the room swiftly, eagerly, with his head sunk upon his chest, and his hands clasped behind him.   To me, who knew his every mood and habit, his attitude and manner told their own story.   He was at work again.   He had risen out of his drug-created dreams, and was hot upon the scent of some new problem.   I rang the bell, and was shown up to the chamber which had formerly been in part my own.

AS I PASSED THE WELL-REMEMBERED DOOR . . .

Watson tells us here that it "must be associated in my mind with my wooing," and some students of the Saga who believe that Watson was wedded and widowered before his meeting with Mary Morstan take this as in indication that the Mrs. Watson of the "Scandal" must have been one of Holmes' early clients. As we have seen, in Chapter 22, Miss Helen Stoner of "The Adventure of the Speckled Band," has been suggested. The photograph shown below (of No. 31, Baker Street) is from *Sherlock Holmes: A Biography*, by William S. Baring-Gould.

found and killed her for that compromising picture. Sherlock Holmes must have heard the news shortly before he slipped away unseen from the Reichenbach Fall, and we who know him cannot doubt his immediate decision to do something about it."

Perhaps this in some part accounts for the seeming relish with which Holmes referred to "the late King of Bohemia" in August, 1914 ("His Last Bow").

5 *loathed every form of society.* "The word *society* is poorly chosen," Mr. Vincent Starrett wrote in *The Private Life of Sherlock Holmes*. "What Watson—a careless writer—intended to convey was that social life offended the Bohemian soul of his companion." This is consistent with Holmes' "one of those unwelcome social summonses" in "The Adventure of the Noble Bachelor."

6 *the Trepoff murder.* For an account of this case, the reader is referred to "The Adventure of the Seven Clocks" in *The Exploits of Sherlock Holmes*, by Adrian M. Conan Doyle and John Dickson Carr.

Mr. Rolfe Boswell, browsing in the *Musgorysky Reader*, once ran across a reference to one Fyodor Fyodorovich Trepoff, 1803–1899, who was military policemaster of St. Petersburg. "I wonder," Mr. Boswell wrote, "what connection he may have had with Mr. Holmes' 'summons to Odessa in the case of the Trepoff murder'? Since Fyodor was alive after [the time] when the 'Scandal in Bohemia' was called to the Master's notice, he could not, of course, have been the *victim*—but other interpretations are possible."

7 *the singular tragedy of the Atkinson brothers at Trincomalee.* It seems highly unlikely that Holmes found it necessary to visit Ceylon, where Trincomalee was an important naval base. It is perhaps more probable that British diplomats at The Hague placed the facts before Holmes at the same time that he was accomplishing his mission for the reigning family of Holland (see below), and that Holmes cleared up the matter long-distance, making this an "armchair" case.

On the other hand, Mrs. Winifred M. Christie has noted ("On the Remarkable Explorations of Sigerson"), that Holmes in September, 1888 (*The Sign of the Four*), was a master of the subject of Buddhism in Ceylon. "We may surmise that from then onwards he felt urgently impelled to make an equally exhaustive study of Buddhism in Tibet," an urge that led him, in the years of the Great Hiatus, to indulge in the remarkable explorations of Sigerson.

Mr. George W. Welch ("The Terai Planter") is another who is sure that Holmes visited Ceylon at this time. Mr. Welch's theory is that the "Atkinson brothers" were really young Trevor and Beddoes of "The *Gloria Scott*," and he explains many of the discrepancies in that adventure by suggesting that these two (with Trevor senior) were involved in a nefarious scheme. Holmes determined to bring the culprits to justice. "Having dealt with [the Trepoff murder at Odessa] Holmes moved East—perhaps by way of Bokhara and Samarkand—and so descended on the Terai district from the north. . . . [Young Trevor and Beddoes] eluded Holmes and fled south—throughout the length of India and then across the Palk Strait into Ceylon. . . . Holmes finally caught up with the Atkinson brothers at Trincomalee, and there settled the account between himself and two of the most cunning criminals of the nineteenth century."

8 *the reigning family of Holland.* The Dutch king was William III, 1817–1890. In 1879 he married Princess Emma of Waldeck-Pyrmont (born 1858). Wilhelmina, the only child of William and Emma, was born in 1880; ten years later she became queen on the death of her father. Emma died in 1934, forty-four years after her husband.

9 *the 20th of March 1888.* The 20th of March, 1888, was a Tuesday, and the case of "A Scandal in Bohemia," as we shall see, certainly did not open on a Tuesday. Watson's date is clearly in error, in whole or in part. Our own date for this case is *Friday, May 20, to Sunday, May 22, 1887.* However, Bell and many other commentators (Andrew, Heldenbrand, Hoff, Knox, Offord, Christopher Morley, and Wellman) accept Watson's 1888 as the year, while still others (Blakeney, Brend, Christ, Folsom, Harrison, Newton, Pattrick, Smith, and Zeisler) support 1889.

10 *I had now returned to civil practice.* How could Watson have "returned" to a type of practice which, by his own accounts, he had never engaged in before this time? His wording here is strong evidence for the San Francisco practice we have discussed earlier. The 1887 practice, as we learn in "The Red-Headed League," was in Kensington. But where in Kensington? The late Gavin Brend deduced from this adventure that it was within a two or three minutes' walk of South Kensington Station, and from "The Final Problem" he concluded that it was either 5, 6, or 8, Pelham Crescent. Miss Helen Simpson ("Medical Career and Capacities of Dr. J. H. Watson") thought that Watson would have paid "the usual price" for his Kensington practice—"three years' earnings, about £900 [$4,500] in all."

11 *threw across his case of cigars.* ". . . a smoker's act of desecration comparable with that of a wine drinker warming up his Château-Lafite in an aluminium saucepan," Colonel R. D. Sherbrooke-Walker, T.D., wrote in "Holmes, Watson and Tobacco."

12 *Just a trifle more, I fancy, Watson.* It is clear that some time has elapsed between Watson's marriage and the "Scandal." How long it takes a man to put on seven to eight pounds is a matter that varies tremendously with the individual. The change from living in Baker Street to being master of his own establishment must have been a considerable one for Watson, and it is possible that he added seven to eight pounds very quickly.

THEN HE STOOD BEFORE THE FIRE . . .

Sidney Paget's first illustration for a Sherlock Holmes story, from the *Strand Magazine,* July, 1891. Mr. Walter Klinefelter has written (*Sherlock Holmes in Portrait and Profile*) of Holmes as he appears here that "his chin is somewhat prominent; and his forehead is rather higher than the average, an effect that the artist no doubt found easy to reproduce because of the fact that the hair above Holmes' temples seems to have made a considerable recession by the time he was thirty-four, the age he had attained when he essayed to match his wits against those of *the* woman, Irene Adler. [In our view, Holmes was a year younger at the time—only thirty-three.] His cheekbones, too, are high, but his nose, though long and fairly large, has none of that beakiness which would suggest the Red Indian."

His manner was not effusive. It seldom was; but he was glad, I think, to see me. With hardly a word spoken, but with a kindly eye, he waved me to an arm-chair, threw **11** across his case of cigars, and indicated a spirit case and a gasogene in the corner. Then he stood before the fire, and looked me over in his singular introspective fashion.

"Wedlock suits you," he remarked. "I think, Watson, that you have put on seven and a half pounds since I saw you."

"Seven," I answered.

"Indeed, I should have thought a little more. Just a **12** trifle more, I fancy, Watson. And in practice again, I observe. You did not tell me that you intended to go into **13** harness."

'Then, how do you know?"

"I see it, I deduce it. How do I know that you have been getting yourself very wet lately, and that you have a most clumsy and careless servant girl?"

"My dear Holmes," said I, "this is too much. You would certainly have been burned had you lived a few centuries ago. It is true that I had a country walk on Thursday and came home in a dreadful mess; but, as I have changed my clothes, I can't imagine how you deduce **14** it. As to Mary Jane, she is incorrigible, and my wife has given her notice; but there again I fail to see how you work it out."

He chuckled to himself and rubbed his long nervous hands together.

"It is simplicity itself," said he ; "my eyes tell me that on the inside of your left shoe, just where the firelight strikes it, the leather is scored by six almost parallel cuts. Obviously they have been caused by some one who has very carelessly scraped round the edges of the sole in order to remove crusted mud from it. Hence, you see, my double deduction that you had been out in vile weather, and that you had a particularly malignant boot-slitting specimen of the London slavey. As to your practice, if a gentleman walks into my rooms smelling of iodoform, with a black mark of nitrate of silver upon his right forefinger, and a bulge on the side of his top hat to show where he has secreted his stethoscope, I must be dull indeed if I do not **15** pronounce him to be an active member of the medical profession."

I could not help laughing at the ease with which he explained his process of deduction. "When I hear you give your reasons," I remarked, "the thing always appears to me to be so ridiculously simple that I could easily do it myself, though at each successive instance of your reasoning I am baffled, until you explain your process. And yet I believe that my eyes are as good as yours."

"Quite so," he answered, lighting a cigarette, and throwing himself down into an arm-chair. "You see, but you do not observe. The distinction is clear. For example, you have frequently seen the steps which lead up from the hall to this room."

"Frequently."

"How often ? "

"Well, some hundreds of times."

"Then how many are there ? "

"How many ! I don't know."

"Quite so ! You have not observed. And yet you have seen. That is just my point. Now, I know that there are seventeen steps, because I have both seen and observed. By the way, since you are interested in these little problems, and since you are good enough to chronicle one or two of my trifling experiences, you may **16** be interested in this." He threw over a sheet of thick pink-tinted note-paper which had been lying open upon the table. "It came by the last post," said he. "Read **17** it aloud."

The note was undated, and without either signature or address.

"There will call upon you to-night, at a quarter to eight o'clock," it said, "a gentleman who desires to consult you upon a matter of the very deepest moment. Your recent services to one of the Royal Houses of Europe have shown that you are one who may safely be trusted with matters which are of an importance which can hardly be exaggerated. This account of you we have from all quarters received. Be in your chamber then at that hour, and do not take it amiss if your visitor wear a mask."

"This is indeed a mystery," I remarked. "What do you imagine that it means ? "

"I have no data yet. It is a capital mistake to theorise before one has data. Insensibly one begins to twist facts

13 *You did not tell me that you intended to go into harness.*" Holmes could not possibly have made this statement at this time if "A Scandal in Bohemia" followed closely on the heels of "The Reigate Squires," as we believe that it did. It must be remembered that the "Scandal" was written *before* and not after "The Reigate Squires." Watson, having hitherto chronicled only *A Study in Scarlet* and *The Sign of the Four* naturally found it necessary to prepare his public for the fact that he was a married man at the time of the "Scandal." Hence the "wedlock suits you . . . seven and a half pounds since I saw you . . . you did not tell me that you intended to go into harness" passages are descriptions almost certainly recorded on an earlier occasion—in our view, in April, 1887, at the time of "The Reigate Squires."

14 *Mary Jane.* The implication is that the newly established Watson household could support only one servant at this time. We have seen ("The Musgrave Ritual") that Hurlstone required the services of eight maids, a cook, a butler, two footmen, and a boy. "The gardens and the stables, of course, have a separate staff." As recently as October 18, 1960, the *Financial Times* reckoned that a well-appointed English household should enjoy the services of a butler, two footmen, an odd man, a head housemaid, two other housemaids, a cook, a kitchen maid, a lady's maid, a chauffeur, and three "daily helps" (quoted from Anthony Sampson's *The Anatomy of Britain*).

15 *to show where he has secreted his stethoscope.* We must not picture Dr. Watson going with a *modern* binaural instrument in his top hat. The stethoscope of his day was monaural—simply a hollow tube of hard rubber or some similar substance, belled at one end and flanged at the other, about six inches long and weighing little more than an ounce.

16 *to chronicle one or two of my trifling experiences.* Holmes later adds: "I am lost without my Boswell." By the time of the "Scandal," then, Watson had certainly begun to *write up* some of Holmes' cases. We cannot say, however, that this limits the "Scandal" to a time later than December, 1887, when *A Study in Scarlet* was published in *Beeton's Christmas Annual,* for Watson's chronicles were certainly in manuscript form, perhaps for many months, before they were printed.

17 *"It came by the last post."* In downtown London, in Holmes' and Watson's day, there were as many as *twelve* postal deliveries a day, and in Baker Street there were six. There were no Sunday deliveries, however—if one wanted to send a message on the Sabbath, he found it necessary to hire a Commissionaire or some other special messenger.

I CAREFULLY EXAMINED THE WRITING . . .

Illustration by Sidney Paget for the *Strand Maga-zine*, July, 1891.

to suit theories, instead of theories to suit facts.   But the note itself.   What do you deduce from it ? ''

I carefully examined the writing, and the paper upon which it was written.

" The man who wrote it was presumably well-to-do," I remarked, endeavouring to imitate my companion's processes.   " Such paper could not be bought under half a crown a packet.   It is peculiarly strong and stiff.''

" Peculiar—that is the very word," said Holmes.   " It is not an English paper at all.   Hold it up to the light.''

I did so, and saw a large *E* with a small *g*, a *P*, and a large *G* with a small *t* woven into the texture of the paper.

" What do you make of that ? '' asked Holmes.

" The name of the maker, no doubt ; or his monogram, rather.''

" Not at all.   The *G* with the small *t* stands for ' Gesellschaft,' which is the German for ' Company.'   It is a customary contraction like our ' Co.'   *P*, of course, stands for ' Papier.'   Now for the *Eg*.   Let us glance at our **18** Continental Gazetteer.''   He took down a heavy brown volume from his shelves.   " Eglow, Eglonitz—here we are, **19** Egria.   It is in a German-speaking country—in Bohemia, **20** not far from Carlsbad.   ' Remarkable as being the scene **21** of the death of Wallenstein, and for its numerous glass **22** factories and paper mills.'   Ha, ha, my boy, what do you make of that ? ''   His eyes sparkled, and he sent up a great blue triumphant cloud from his cigarette.

18 *our Continental Gazetteer.* Holmes used his Continental Gazetteer again when he checked the Andaman Islands in connection with *The Sign of the Four.* It was probably the *Gazetteer of the World,* first published in 1885, a standard reference work of the time.

19 *a German-speaking country.* In point of fact, the inhabitants of Bohemia were then only about 35 percent German.

20 *not far from Carlsbad.* While "Eglow" and "Eglonitz" are not to be identified in modern reference works, Egria, more correctly, *Eger,* is undoubtedly a town in Bohemia not far from Carlsbad. Bohemia itself, a former kingdom of Europe, later a crownland of Austria, is today a province of Czechoslovakia.

21 *the death of Wallenstein.* Properly, Albrecht Wenzel Eusebius von Waldstein, 1583–1634, Duke of Friedland, Sagan, and Mecklenburg. A Bohemian general in the Thirty Years' War, he was suspected of treason and assassinated. He is the subject of a tragedy by Schiller.

22 *paper mills.'* "It takes a deal of search to find references to paper mills [in Bohemia]," the late Professor Jay Finley Christ commented in "Problems in 'A Scandal in Bohemia.' " "Maybe the king used the whole of the national output for his correspondence and other purposes."

13

"SUCH PAPER COULD NOT BE BOUGHT UNDER HALF A CROWN A PACKET."

13 in the illustration is the 1817 George III "bull-head" half-crown; *13a* the 1826 George IV half-crown, reverse only; *13b* the 1836 William IV half-crown, reverse only; *13c* the 1887 Victoria half-crown, reverse only. A half-crown, worth two shillings sixpence, or approximately 60¢ in U.S. currency at the time, would have been a considerable expenditure for writing paper in Holmes' and Watson's day. The late A. Carson Simpson, in *Numismatics in the Canon,* Part I (from which the illustrations above and right were taken), tells us that this coin "began as a gold-piece" and descended "from the quarter rose-noble, . . . known as a half-crown under Henry VIII, . . . last struck in gold by James I. It became a silver coin in 1551, contemporaneously with the silver crown, and was coined by all subsequent monarchs except Mary I and Philip and Mary." It has more Canonical references than the crown, of which perhaps the most noteworthy is the Master's anxious query in "The Adventure of the Dying Detective": "How many half-crowns?" he asks when he directs Watson to put them in his watch pocket to keep him in better balance.

" The paper was made in Bohemia," I said.

" Precisely. And the man who wrote the note is a German. Do you note the peculiar construction of the sentence—' This account of you we have from all quarters received.' A Frenchman or Russian could not have written that. It is the German who is so uncourteous to his verbs. It only remains, therefore, to discover what is wanted by this German who writes upon Bohemian paper, and prefers wearing a mask to showing his face. And here he comes, if I am not mistaken, to resolve all our doubts."

As he spoke there was the sharp sound of horses' hoofs and grating wheels against the kerb, followed by a sharp pull at the bell. Holmes whistled.

" A pair by the sound," said he. " Yes," he continued, glancing out of the window. " A nice little brougham and a pair of beauties. A hundred and fifty guineas apiece. **23** There's money in this case, Watson, if there is nothing else."

" I think that I had better go, Holmes."

" Not a bit, Doctor. Stay where you are. I am lost without my Boswell. And this promises to be interesting. **24** It would be a pity to miss it."

" But your client——"

" Never mind him. I may want your help, and so may he. Here he comes. Sit down in that arm-chair, Doctor, and give us your best attention."

A slow and heavy step, which had been heard upon the stairs and in the passage, paused immediately outside the door. Then there was a loud and authoritative tap.

" Come in ! " said Holmes.

A man entered who could hardly have been less than six feet six inches in height, with the chest and limbs of a Hercules. His dress was rich with a richness which would, in England, be looked upon as akin to bad taste. Heavy bands of astrakhan were slashed across the sleeves and fronts of his double-breasted coat, while the deep blue cloak which was thrown over his shoulders was lined with flame-coloured silk, and secured at the neck with a brooch which consisted of a single flaming beryl. Boots which extended half-way up his calves, and which were trimmed at the tops with rich brown fur, completed the impression of barbaric opulence which was suggested by his whole appearance. He carried a broad-brimmed hat in his hand, while he wore across the upper part of his face, extending down past the cheek-bones, a black vizard mask, which he had apparently adjusted that very moment, for

A MAN ENTERED WHO COULD HARDLY HAVE BEEN LESS THAN SIX FEET SIX INCHES IN HEIGHT . . .

Illustration by Sidney Paget for the *Strand Magazine*, July, 1891.

23 *A hundred and fifty guineas apiece.* Say about $775 apiece in U.S. currency at the time.

24 *I am lost without my Boswell.* Holmes is of course being sarcastic at Watson's expense in this reference to James Boswell, 1740–1795, author of the *Life of Samuel Johnson*, one of the most celebrated biographies of all time. "You have degraded what should have been a course of lectures into a series of tales," Holmes complained to Watson in "The Adventure of the Copper Beeches." In "Mr. Sherlock Holmes and Dr. Samuel Johnson," Mr. Richard D. Altick has considered some of the many similarities between Johnson and Holmes, Boswell and Watson. He suggests that Watson read much in Boswell during the Afghan campaign.

13a   13b   13c

25 *"by binding you both to absolute secrecy for two years.* The case must have taken place before July, 1889, or Watson, a man of honor, could not have published his account of the "Scandal" in July, 1891.

. . . WITH A GESTURE OF DESPERATION, HE TORE THE MASK FROM HIS FACE . . .

Illustration by Sidney Paget for the *Strand Magazine*, July, 1891.

his hand was still raised to it as he entered. From the lower part of the face he appeared to be a man of strong character, with a thick, hanging lip, and a long straight chin, suggestive of resolution pushed to the length of obstinacy.

"You had my note?" he asked, with a deep, harsh voice and a strongly marked German accent. "I told you that I would call." He looked from one to the other of us, as if uncertain which to address.

"Pray take a seat," said Holmes. "This is my friend and colleague, Dr. Watson, who is occasionally good enough to help me in my cases. Whom have I the honour to address?"

"You may address me as the Count von Kramm, a Bohemian nobleman. I understand that this gentleman, your friend, is a man of honour and discretion, whom I may trust with a matter of the most extreme importance. If not, I should much prefer to communicate with you alone."

I rose to go, but Holmes caught me by the wrist and pushed me back into my chair. "It is both, or none," said he. "You may say before this gentleman anything which you may say to me."

The Count shrugged his broad shoulders. "Then I **25** must begin," said he, " by binding you both to absolute secrecy for two years, at the end of that time the matter will be of no importance. At present it is not too much to say that it is of such weight that it may have an influence upon European history."

"I promise," said Holmes.

"And I."

"You will excuse this mask," continued our strange visitor. "The august person who employs me wishes his agent to be unknown to you, and I may confess at once that the title by which I have just called myself is not exactly my own."

"I was aware of it," said Holmes dryly.

"The circumstances are of great delicacy, and every precaution has to be taken to quench what might grow to be an immense scandal and seriously compromise one of the reigning families of Europe. To speak plainly, the matter implicates the great House of Ormstein, hereditary kings of Bohemia."

"I was also aware of that," murmured Holmes, settling himself down in his arm-chair, and closing his eyes.

Our visitor glanced with some apparent surprise at the languid, lounging figure of the man who had been no doubt depicted to him as the most incisive reasoner, and most energetic agent in Europe. Holmes slowly re-opened his eyes, and looked impatiently at his gigantic client.

"If your Majesty would condescend to state your case," he remarked, "I should be better able to advise you."

The man sprang from his chair, and paced up and down the room in uncontrollable agitation. Then, with a gesture of desperation, he tore the mask from his face and hurled it upon the ground. "You are right," he cried, "I am the King. Why should I attempt to conceal it?"

"Why, indeed?" murmured Holmes. "Your Majesty had not spoken before I was aware that I was addressing

Wilhelm Gottsreich Sigismond von Ormstein, Grand Duke of Cassel-Falstein, and hereditary King of Bohemia."

"But you can understand," said our strange visitor, sitting down once more and passing his hand over his high, white forehead, "you can understand that I am not accustomed to doing such business in my own person. Yet the matter was so delicate that I could not confide it to an agent without putting myself in his power. I have come *incognito* from Prague for the purpose of consulting **26** you."

"Then, pray consult," said Holmes, shutting his eyes once more.

"The facts are briefly these : Some five years ago, during a lengthy visit to Warsaw, I made the acquaintance of the well-known adventuress Irene Adler. The name is no doubt familiar to you."

"Kindly look her up in my index, Doctor," murmured Holmes, without opening his eyes. For many years he had adopted a system of docketing all paragraphs concerning men and things, so that it was difficult to name a subject or a person on which he could not at once furnish information. In this case I found her biography sandwiched in between that of a Hebrew Rabbi and that of a **27** staff-commander who had written a monograph upon the deep-sea fishes.

26 incognito. Italian: unknown; under an assumed name, title, or character; not known or formally recognized, so as to avoid name and recognition; as a king traveling *incognito*.

27 *a Hebrew Rabbi.* Identified by Miss Ruth Berman ("On Docketing a Hebrew Rabbi") as Hermann Adler, Chief Rabbi of the United Congregations of the British Empire from 1891 to 1911, "a prominent figure in English public life."

"... AND HEREDITARY KING OF BOHEMIA."

His coat-of-arms, shown here, is blazoned: Gules, a lion rampant queue fourchée, and renownée, argent, crowned or. The real "King of Bohemia" at the time of the "Scandal" was Franz Josef von Hapsburg, "Emperor of Austria and Apostolic King of Hungary," but it could not have been the aging (born 1830) Franz Josef who called on Holmes in Baker Street. Possibly it was his only son and heir, the Grand Duke Rudolf (he who died so mysteriously in the hunting lodge at Mayerling on January 30, 1889); this was the late Professor Jay Finley Christ's view, as it is that of Dr. Julian Wolff. Mr. T. S. Blakeney ("A Case for Identification—in Bohemia") prefers to identify Holmes' visitor as the Archduke Franz Ferdinand; Professor John B. Wolf ("Another Incubus in the Saddle") has put forward Crown Prince Wilhelm von Hohenzollern of Prussia, soon to become Wilhelm II of the German Empire; and the late Edgar W. Smith, as we have seen in Chapter 8, once made a strong case ("A Scandal in Identity") for the then Prince of Wales, Albert Edward, later King Edward VII. If Mr. Smith was correct in his identification, it is possible that Sherlock Holmes was of service to Albert Edward on no less than five occasions—in the affair of the Suicide Club, in the case of "A Scandal in Bohemia," in "The Adventure of the Beryl Coronet," at the time of *The Hound of the Baskervilles* ("At the present time, one of the most revered names in England is being besmirched by a blackmailer, and only I can stop a disastrous scandal") and in "The Adventure of the Illustrious Client." It is small wonder that Edward VII offered Holmes a knighthood ("The Adventure of the Three Garridebs").

28 *Born in New Jersey in the year 1858.* And who was the woman Dr. Watson called "Irene Adler"? Professor John B. Wolf ("Another Incubus in the Saddle") has noted that "A rumor . . . so strong . . . it cannot be denied tells us of an affair between Prince Wilhelm and an American opera singer. Since the lady's name was subsequently emblazoned in lights over the Metropolitan in New York and she was hailed as one of the first great American opera stars, good taste encourages me to hide her name even now from those who might make something of youthful indiscretions."

On the other hand, Dr. Julian Wolff ("The Adventuress of Sherlock Holmes"), noting that a celebrated actress known as "the Jersey Lily" was born in 1852 and married in 1889 (*The Columbia Encyclopedia*) or 1899 (*the Enclyclopædia Britannica*), that her beauty "attracted the attention of the Prince of Wales," that she "had photographs of the Danish King and Queen" but that they had been lost or appropriated, has identified "Irene Adler" as the celebrated actress and noted beauty, Miss Lillie Langtry.

Many Sherlockians, however, would still prefer to believe that "Irene Adler" was the professional name taken by the late Clara Stephens of Trenton, New Jersey, the aunt of the late James Montgomery (for documentation, see his "Art in the Blood")":

> We never mention Aunt Clara,
> Her picture is turned to the wall,
> Though she lives on the French Riviera
> Mother says that she's dead to us all.

29 *this young person.* When one considers that Irene was at the most twenty-nine at this time, and that Holmes himself was a mere thirty-three, this superior attitude begins to look a trifle absurd.

30 *I am but thirty now."* The Grand Duke Rudolf was born in 1858; the Archduke Franz Ferdinand in 1863; Crown Prince Wilhelm von Hohenzollern in 1859; Albert Edward, the Prince of Wales, in 1841. By age alone, it should seem that the Grand Duke Rudolf comes closest to having been Holmes' visitor in May, 1887. (In fact, however, he had married in 1881.)

31 *Clotilde Lothman von Saxe-Meningen.* Professor Wolf, on his theory that the "King of Bohemia" was Crown Prince Wilhelm von Hohenzollern, points out that he was married to Princess Auguste-Victoria zu Schleswig-Holstein; Schleswig-Holstein being the *Danish* duchies of the second German reich.

"Let me see," said Holmes. "Hum! Born in New **28** Jersey in the year 1858. Contralto—hum! La Scala, hum! Prima donna Imperial Opera of Warsaw—Yes! Retired from operatic stage—ha! Living in London— quite so! Your Majesty, as I understand, became **29** entangled with this young person, wrote her some compromising letters, and is now desirous of getting those letters back."

"Precisely so. But how——"

"Was there a secret marriage?"

"None."

"No legal papers or certificates?"

"None."

"Then I fail to follow Your Majesty. If this young person should produce her letters for blackmailing or other purposes, how is she to prove their authenticity?"

"There is the writing."

"Pooh, pooh! Forgery."

"My private note-paper."

"Stolen."

"My own seal."

"Imitated."

"My photograph."

"Bought."

"We were both in the photograph."

"Oh, dear! That is very bad! Your Majesty has indeed committed an indiscretion."

"I was mad—insane."

"You have compromised yourself seriously."

"I was only Crown Prince then. I was young. I am **30** but thirty now."

"It must be recovered."

"We have tried and failed."

"Your Majesty must pay. It must be bought."

"She will not sell."

"Stolen, then."

"Five attempts have been made. Twice burglars in my pay ransacked her house. Once we diverted her luggage when she travelled. Twice she has been waylaid. There has been no result."

"No sign of it?"

"Absolutely none."

Holmes laughed. "It is quite a pretty little problem," said he.

"But a very serious one to me," returned the King, reproachfully.

"Very, indeed. And what does she propose to do with the photograph?"

"To ruin me."

"But how?"

"I am about to be married."

"So I have heard."

31 "To Clotilde Lothman von Saxe-Meningen, second daughter of the King of Scandinavia. You may know the strict principles of her family. She is herself the very soul of delicacy. A shadow of a doubt as to my conduct would bring the matter to an end."

"And Irene Adler?"

"Threatens to send them the photograph. And she will do it. I know that she will do it. You do not know her, but she has a soul of steel. She has the face of the most beautiful of women, and the mind of the most resolute of men. Rather than I should marry another woman, there are no lengths to which she would not go— none."

"You are sure that she has not sent it yet?"

"I am sure."

"And why?"

"Because she has said that she would send it on the day when the betrothal was publicly proclaimed. That will be next Monday."

"Oh, then, we have three days yet," said Holmes, with a yawn. "That is very fortunate, as I have one or two matters of importance to look into just at present. Your Majesty will, of course, stay in London for the present?"

"Certainly. You will find me at the Langham, under the name of the Count von Kramm."

"Then I shall drop you a line to let you know how we progress."

"Pray do so. I shall be all anxiety."

"Then, as to money?"

"You have *carte blanche*."

"Absolutely?"

"I tell you that I would give one of the provinces of my kingdom to have that photograph."

"And for present expenses?"

The King took a heavy chamois leather bag from under his cloak, and laid it on the table.

"There are three hundred pounds in gold, and seven hundred in notes," he said.

Holmes scribbled a receipt upon a sheet of his note-book, and handed it to him.

"And mademoiselle's address?" he asked.

"Is Briony Lodge, Serpentine Avenue, St. John's Wood."

Holmes took a note of it. "One other question," said he. "Was the photograph a cabinet?"

"It was."

"Then, good night, Your Majesty, and I trust that we

"...THREE HUNDRED POUNDS IN GOLD, AND SEVEN HUNDRED IN NOTES..."

A princely sum, equal to some $5,000 in U.S. currency at the time. The late A. Carson Simpson wrote that the "three hundred pounds in gold" may well have included the rarely seen five-pound piece (shown below)—"it would indeed have been a kingly gesture to tender sixty of these large, showy pieces."

32 *we have three days yet.*" Chronologists have found this sentence difficult to interpret: if Holmes excluded both Sunday and Monday as "working days," the interview with the King of Bohemia must have taken place on a Wednesday (Blakeney and Christ); if either, on a Thursday (Andrew, Bell, Folsom); if neither, on a Friday (Baring-Gould and Zeisler). In any case, it is difficult to see how Holmes could have made such a statement on a Tuesday (Watson and Christopher Morley). If the case began on a Wednesday or a Thursday, however, Watson's "country walk on Thursday" must have taken place as long as six or seven days before; certainly he would have "changed his clothes" in that time, and it would be far more natural for him to have said "last Thursday" or "a week ago." If, on the other hand, the case began on a Friday, Watson's walk must have taken place on the preceding day, and it would have been more natural for him to have said that he came home in a dreadful mess "yesterday." For the record, we note that Thursday, May 19, 1887, was a day on which the wind had increased "to a gale in almost all parts of our islands. . . . The weather is fine in Sweden and Germany, but squally and unsettled elsewhere. . . . Since yesterday morning rain has fallen generally. . . . Thunderstorms occurred . . . over the east of England. Temperature has fallen several degrees . . ." (weather report in the London *Times*).

33 *the Langham.* The Langham was the grandest of all London's hotels of the period: it had been visited by the Prince of Wales at its opening on June 12, 1865, and its foundation stone had been laid by the Earl of Shrewsbury on July 17, 1863. (It is now an office of the BBC.) ". . . the Langham . . . was designed by Messrs. Giles and Murray," Mr. William H. Gill wrote in "Some Notable Sherlockian Buildings." "It was built in a florid bastard Gothic and Renaissance mixture, and was by far the most magnificent hotel in the world. It covered an acre of ground, contained over 600 rooms, whilst the water supply came from an artesian well 300 feet below. Its huge dining room was packed with 2,000 diners on the day of its opening. Small wonder that it attracted the flashy King of Bohemia . . ." (It also attracted Captain Morstan, the father of Mary (*The Sign of the Four*) and the Honourable Philip Green ("The Disappearance of Lady Frances Carfax").)

34 *carte blanche.*" French: unconditional authority or permission to do what one pleases in any given matter. From a blank paper, especially a blank form or order duly signed by one person and given to another person to fill up at his own discretion.

35 *St. John's Wood.* Then a vast colony of second-rate villas. "St. John's Wood" Mr. A. L. Shearn wrote in "The Street and the Detective," "was the one place beyond all others where gentlemen of discretion provided for their mistresses in a proper manner, establishing them in quiet villas surrounded by sheltered gardens and high walls."

36 *a cabinet?*" A photograph 3⅞" × 5½" in size, larger than the *carte de visite* and smaller than *boudoir* size. "These fancy terms do not mean anything except photograph-sizes, which the professional photographers dreamed up," Magistrate S. Tupper Bigelow commented in his *Irregular Anglo-American Glossary of More or Less Unfamiliar Words, Terms and Phrases in the Sherlock Holmes Saga.*

37 *the two crimes which I have elsewhere recorded.* Watson refers to *A Study in Scarlet* and *The Sign of the Four;* it must be remembered that the "Scandal" was his third *published* Holmes adventure.

38 *a bijou villa.* A bijou is a jewel or a trinket, but the word is also used figuratively, as here.

39 *Chubb lock.* A patented lock of English manufacture, with tumblers, the invention of Charles Chubb. The date of Chubb's birth is not known, but he died May 16, 1845.

"... A DRUNKEN-LOOKING GROOM, ILL-KEMPT AND SIDE-WHISKERED WITH AN INFLAMED FACE AND DISREPUTABLE CLOTHES, ..."

Illustration by Sidney Paget for the *Strand Magazine*, July, 1891.

shall soon have some good news for you. And good night, Watson," he added, as the wheels of the Royal brougham rolled down the street. "If you will be good enough to call to-morrow afternoon, at three o'clock, I should like to chat this little matter over with you."

II

At three o'clock precisely I was at Baker Street, but Holmes had not yet returned. The landlady informed me that he had left the house shortly after eight o'clock in the morning. I sat down beside the fire, however, with the intention of awaiting him, however long he might be. I was already deeply interested in his inquiry, for, though it was surrounded by none of the grim and strange features which were associated with the two crimes which **37** I have elsewhere recorded, still, the nature of the case and the exalted station of his client gave it a character of its own. Indeed, apart from the nature of the investigation which my friend had on hand, there was something in his masterly grasp of a situation, and his keen, incisive reasoning, which made it a pleasure to me to study his system of work, and to follow the quick, subtle methods by which he disentangled the most inextricable mysteries. So accustomed was I to his invariable success that the very possibility of his failing had ceased to enter into my head.

It was close upon four before the door opened, and a drunken-looking groom, ill-kempt and side-whiskered with an inflamed face and disreputable clothes, walked into the room. Accustomed as I was to my friend's amazing powers in the use of disguises, I had to look three times before I was certain that it was indeed he. With a nod he vanished into the bedroom, whence he emerged in five minutes tweed-suited and respectable, as of old. Putting his hands into his pockets, he stretched out his legs in front of the fire, and laughed heartily for some minutes.

"Well, really!" he cried, and then he choked; and laughed again until he was obliged to lie back, limp and helpless, in the chair.

"What is it?"

"It's quite too funny. I am sure you could never guess how I employed my morning, or what I ended by doing."

"I can't imagine. I suppose that you have been watching the habits, and perhaps the house, of Miss Irene Adler."

"Quite so, but the sequel was rather unusual. I will tell you, however. I left the house a little after eight o'clock this morning, in the character of a groom out of work. There is a wonderful sympathy and freemasonry among horsey men. Be one of them, and you will know all that there is to know. I soon found Briony Lodge. **38** It is a bijou villa, with a garden at the back, but built out **39** in front right up to the road, two stories. Chubb lock to the door. Large sitting-room on the right side, well furnished, with long windows almost to the floor, and those preposterous English window fasteners which a child could open. Behind there was nothing remarkable, save that the passage window could be reached from the top of the coach-house. I walked round it and examined it closely from every point of view, but without noting anything else of interest.

"I then lounged down the street, and found, as I expected, that there was a mews in a lane which runs down by one wall of the garden. I lent the ostlers a hand in rubbing down their horses, and I received in exchange twopence, a glass of half-and-half, two fills of shag tobacco **40-41** and as much information as I could desire about Miss Adler, to say nothing of half a dozen other people in the neighbourhood in whom I was not in the least interested, but whose biographies I was compelled to listen to."

"And what of Irene Adler?" I asked.

"Oh, she has turned all the men's heads down in that part. She is the daintiest thing under a bonnet on this planet. So say the Serpentine Mews, to a man. She lives quietly, sings at concerts, drives out at five every day, and returns at seven sharp for dinner. Seldom goes out at other times, except when she sings. Has only one male

"SHE IS THE DAINTEST THING UNDER A BONNET ON THIS PLANET."

Bonnets and hats, 1848–1896, as drawn by Marjorie and C. H. B. Quennell for *A History of Everyday Things in England, Vol. IV, 1851 to 1914.*

40 *a glass of half-and-half.* A mixture of two malt liquors, usually porter and ale, but sometimes old and new ale. Holmes drank the glass of half-and-half in his character of "a drunken-looking groom," and again, in "The Adventure of the Blue Carbuncle," he drinks a glass of beer with the innkeeper Windigate; but he appears to have drunk malt liquors principally in the early years, and then only in situations which required it, not out of any special fondness.

41 *two fills of shag tobacco.* Says Joseph Fune in *A Paper: of Tobacco. Treating of the Rise, Progress, Pleasures, and Advantages of Smoking,* London: Chapman and Hall, 1839, p. 129: "Shag tobacco has obtained its distinctive name from its being so finely cut that the filaments appear like so much 'shag'—the old name for short and matted wool or hair. It is manufactured of the strongest and very worst kind of leaf, and is chiefly consumed by the poorer classes. Persons of a nervous temperament, who take little exercise, ought to particularly avoid smoking this kind of tobacco, as its frequent use is apt to induce paralytic afflictions. The present price of shag is fourpence [about 8¢ U.S. at the time of our adventure]."

Mr. John L. Hicks adds ("No Fire Without Some Smoke"): "It is reported that on one occasion when William Makepeace Thackeray visited his friend Alfred Tennyson, they smoked shag tobacco while praising Miss Barrett's poetry. . . . Great Victorians, both early and late, had a preference for shag as an aid to ratiocination." (It is thought by many Sherlockians that the detective acquired his lifelong liking for shag at this time.)

"... OF THE INNER TEMPLE."

The Inner and the Middle Temple (shown above in a photograph by G. F. Allen, from *The Second Country Life Picture Book of London;* London: Country Life, Ltd., 1953) belong respectively to legal societies of the same name and constitute two of the Inns of Court; they are buildings occupied by barristers and law students. Wrote the poet Spenser: "... Those bricky towers, / The which of Thames' broad aged back doe ride, / Where now the studious lawyers have their bowers, / There whilom went the Temple knights to ride, / Till they decayed through pride."

42 *'first to Gross and Hankey's.* Presumably a jewelry establishment, where Norton would buy the ring—although it is not listed in the directories of the day.

43 *the church of St. Monica in the Edgware Road.* A correspondent, Mr. T. L. A. Daintith of Coulsdon, Surrey, suggests that the marriage of Irene Adler to Godfrey Norton was a Catholic one: "To my mind, Holmes' whole description of the affair is that of an Anglican suddenly caught up in a nuptial Mass." He suggests that the ceremony took place in St. Agnes' Church, Cricklewood, just off the Edgware Road at the southern end:

visitor, but a good deal of him. He is dark, handsome, and dashing ; never calls less than once a day, and often twice. He is a Mr. Godfrey Norton, of the Inner Temple. See the advantages of a cabman as a confidant. They had driven him home a dozen times from Serpentine Mews, and knew all about him. When I had listened to all that they had to tell, I began to walk up and down near Briony Lodge once more, and to think over my plan of campaign.

"This Godfrey Norton was evidently an important factor in the matter. He was a lawyer. That sounded ominous. What was the relation between them, and what the object of his repeated visits ? Was she his client, his friend, or his mistress ? If the former, she had probably transferred the photograph to his keeping. If the latter, it was less likely. On the issue of this question depended whether I should continue my work at Briony Lodge, or turn my attention to the gentleman's chambers in the Temple. It was a delicate point, and it widened the field of my inquiry. I fear that I bore you with these details, but I have to let you see my little difficulties, if you are to understand the situation."

"I am following you closely," I answered.

"I was still balancing the matter in my mind when a hansom cab drove up to Briony Lodge, and a gentleman sprang out. He was a remarkably handsome man, dark, aquiline, and moustached—evidently the man of whom I had heard. He appeared to be in a great hurry, shouted to the cabman to wait, and brushed past the maid who opened the door with the air of a man who was thoroughly at home.

"He was in the house about half an hour, and I could catch glimpses of him, in the windows of the sitting-room, pacing up and down, talking excitedly and waving his arms. Of her I could see nothing. Presently he emerged, looking even more flurried than before. As he stepped up to the cab, he pulled a gold watch from his pocket and looked at it earnestly. ' Drive like the devil,'

42 he shouted, ' first to Gross and Hankey's in Regent Street, and then to the church of St. Monica in the Edgware

43 Road. Half a guinea if you do it in twenty minutes ! '

"Away they went, and I was just wondering whether I should not do well to follow them, when up the lane

44 came a neat little landau, the coachman with his coat only half buttoned, and his tie under his ear, while all the tags of his harness were sticking out of the buckles. It hadn't pulled up before she shot out of the hall door and into it. I only caught a glimpse of her at the moment, but she was a lovely woman, with a face that a man might die for.

" ' The Church of St. Monica, John,' she cried, 'and half a sovereign if you reach it in twenty minutes.'

"This was quite too good to lose, Watson. I was just balancing whether I should run for it, or whether I should perch behind her landau, when a cab came through the street. The driver looked twice at such a shabby fare ; but I jumped in before he could object. ' The Church of St. Monica,' said I, ' and half a sovereign if you reach it in twenty minutes.' It was twenty-five minutes to twelve,

45 and of course it was clear enough what was in the wind.

" My cabby drove fast. I don't think I ever drove faster, but the others were there before us. The cab and the landau with their steaming horses were in front of the door when I arrived. I paid the man and hurried into the church. There was not a soul there save the two whom I had followed, and a surpliced clergyman, who seemed to be expostulating with them. They were all three standing in a knot in front of the altar. I lounged up the side aisle like any other idler who has dropped into a church. Suddenly, to my surprise, the three at the altar faced round to me, and Godfrey Norton came running as hard as he could towards me.

" 'Thank God!' he cried. 'You'll do. Come! Come!'

" 'What then?' I asked.

"The only Catholic church actually *in* the Edgware Road is at the far end and no cab could possibly do the journey [to Regent Street and then to the far end of the Edgware Road] in twenty minutes. In any case the name St. Agnes is far more likely to be a disguise for St. Monica than is St. Anthony, the farther church."

The Edgware Road, embracing a part of the old Watling Street, runs diagonally from the Marble Arch to Cricklewood with scarcely a curve, and thence to Hendon, Edgware, and St. Albans. It is one of the broadest thoroughfares leading out of London, and has often been called "The Gateway to the Northwest."

44 *landau.* A two-seated, four-wheeled, covered vehicle with a top divided into two sections, the

" '. . . IN REGENT STREET . . .' "

Regent Street, nearly a mile in length, leads to the north from Pall Mall. Built by John Nash between 1816 and 1820, it takes its name from the Prince Regent, afterward George IV. It was on Regent Street that Holmes and Watson essayed in vain to trail the trailers of Sir Henry Baskerville. Here, too, Holmes was severely beaten by the minions of the lustful Gruner ("The Adventure of the Illustrious Client").

" 'HALF A GUINEA IF YOU DO IT IN TWENTY MINUTES!' "

Shown here is the 1787 gold half-guinea ("spade") of George III. The half-guinea, worth ten shillings sixpence, or some $2.62 in U.S. currency at the time, is worth sixpence (12¢) more than the half-sovereign Irene Adler (and Sherlock Holmes) were later to pay for the drive to St. Monica's. Norton's trip, however, involved *two* stops—the first at Gross and Hankey's.

back section of which could be let down or thrown back, while the front section could be removed or left stationary; named for the German town in which it was first manufactured.

45 *it was clear enough what was in the wind.* Clear to Holmes, perhaps, but the first of a series of very puzzling statements, nonetheless. By English law, a marriage once had to be solemnized before noon. But in May, 1886—almost two years before Watson's date for the "Scandal"—the legal period had been extended from 8:00 A.M. to 3:00 P.M. Surely Godfrey Norton, as a lawyer, should have known this.

46 *in search of a best man.* The facts are these: in English law, two witnesses are always required, and neither of these makes, much less mumbles, any responses; marriage ceremonies in a Catholic church or a church of the Church of England are not over with in an instant; no clergyman would marry a spinister and a bachelor if there were any "informality" about the license. In addition, as the Reverend Otis R. Rice has pointed out in "Clergymen in the Canon," "since the banns had obviously not been published, as required by canon law, the only legal procedure would be a special license from the Archbishop of Canterbury at Lambeth Palace." The opportunities for speculation are abundant here, and students of the Saga

" ' Come, man, come, only three minutes, or it won't be legal.'

" I was half dragged up to the altar, and before I knew where I was, I found myself mumbling responses which were whispered in my ear, and vouching for things of which I knew nothing, and generally assisting in the secure tying up of Irene Adler, spinster, to Godfrey Norton, bachelor. It was all done in an instant, and there was the gentleman thanking me on the one side and the lady on the other, while the clergyman beamed on me in front. It was the most preposterous position in which I ever found myself in my life, and it was the thought of it that started me laughing just now. It seems that there had been some informality about their licence, that the clergyman absolutely refused to marry them without a witness of some sort, and that my lucky appearance saved the bride-

46 groom from having to sally out into the streets in search of a best man. The bride gave me a sovereign, and I mean to wear it on my watch-chain in memory of the occasion."

" This is a very unexpected turn of affairs," said I ; " and what then ? "

" Well, I found my plans very seriously menaced. It looked as if the pair might take an immediate departure, and so necessitate very prompt and energetic measures on my part. At the church door, however, they separated, he driving back to the Temple, and she to her own house.

47 ' I shall drive out in the Park at five as usual,' she said as she left him. I heard no more. They drove away in

"... BEFORE I KNEW WHERE I WAS, I FOUND MYSELF MUMBLING RESPONSES ..."

Illustration by Sidney Paget for the *Strand Magazine*, July, 1891.

19   19a

"THE BRIDE GAVE ME A SOVEREIGN ..."

19 above is the 1871 sovereign of Victoria; *19a* the 1830 sovereign of George IV, reverse only. This standard gold coin of twenty shillings ($5.00) "had its origin as a large, thin hammered coin of Henry VII, which derived its name from the effigy of the enthroned ruler on its obverse. . . . It was struck by succeeding rulers until Charles I concentrated on the unit as his 20/–unit; the Commonwealth followed suit. Charles II introduced the guinea, the basic gold coin until George III's 1816 currency reform, which established the sovereign as the unit for as long as gold was regularly coined. The last sovereign regularly coined in London was in 1917, but colonial mints continued to strike them in later years. . . . Numismatists will all unite in the hope that [Holmes] neither had [the sovereign given to him by Irene] pierced nor had a loop soldered onto it . . . , but had a ring put around it with the loop attached to the ring, so as not to impair the coin."—A Carson Simpson, *Numismatics in the Canon*, Part I.

different directions, and I went off to make my own arrangements."

" Which are ? "

" Some cold beef and a glass of beer," he answered, ringing the bell. " I have been too busy to think of food, and I am likely to be busier still this evening. By the way, Doctor, I shall want your co-operation."

" I shall be delighted."

" You don't mind breaking the law ? "

" Not in the least."

" Nor running a chance of arrest ? "

" Not in a good cause."

" Oh, the cause is excellent ! "

" Then I am your man."

" I was sure that I might rely on you."

" But what is it you wish ? "

" When Mrs. Turner has brought in the tray I will make it clear to you. Now," he said, as he turned hungrily on the simple fare that our landlady had provided, " I must discuss it while I eat, for I have not much **48** time. It is nearly five now. In two hours we must be on the scene of action. Miss Irene, or Madame, rather, returns from her drive at seven. We must be at Briony Lodge to meet her."

" And what then ? "

" You must leave that to me. I have already arranged what is to occur. There is only one point on which I must insist. You must not interfere, come what may. You understand ? "

" I am to be neutral ? "

" To do nothing whatever. There will probably be some small unpleasantness. Do not join in it. It will end in my being conveyed into the house. Four or five minutes afterwards the sitting-room window will open. You are to station yourself close to that open window."

" Yes."

" You are to watch me, for I will be visible to you."

" Yes."

" And when I raise my hand—so—you will throw into the room what I give you to throw, and will, at the same time, raise the cry of fire. You quite follow me ? "

" Entirely."

" It is nothing very formidable," he said, taking a long cigar-shaped roll from his pocket. " It is an ordinary plumber's smoke rocket, fitted with a cap at either end to **49** make it self-lighting. Your task is confined to that. When you raise your cry of fire, it will be taken up by quite a number of people. You may then walk to the end of the street, and I will rejoin you in ten minutes. I hope that I have made myself clear ? "

" I am to remain neutral, to get near the window, to watch you, and, at the signal, to throw in this object, then to raise the cry of fire, and to await you at the corner of the street."

" Precisely."

" Then you may entirely rely on me."

" That is excellent. I think perhaps it is almost time that I prepared for the new rôle I have to play."

He disappeared into his bedroom, and returned in a

have taken full advantage of them. The late Page Heldenbrand, in "The Duplicity of Sherlock Holmes," has suggested that Norton was none other than Colonel Sebastian Moran, whom we shall meet in "The Adventure of the Empty House." And Dr. Ebbe C. and Mrs. Phoebe M. Hoff, in "The Affair at St. Monica's," have suggested that the "minister" was an imposter, as was "Godfrey Norton." The former was Shinwell Johnson, whom we shall meet in "The Adventure of the Illustrious Client," and the latter was an adventurer known in international circles as "Slick" or "The Gent." The entire affair had been arranged and paid for by the King of Bohemia's affianced, Clotilde.

47 *in the Park*. Possibly Hyde Park but more likely the nearer Regent's Park, on the road called the Outer Circle, surrounding the Inner Circle with its fine chestnut trees.

48 *the simple fare that our landlady had provided.* Another riddle for readers. In every other Holmes adventure, the name of the landlady, when it is given, is Mrs. *Hudson*. Did Mrs. Hudson, as landlady, provide the fare and Mrs. Turner the maid, perhaps, or a crony of Mrs. Hudson's, or her sister—merely serve it? Or is this simple absent-mindedness or forgetfulness on the part of Holmes (thinking, perhaps, of the principal in another case he was following at the time) or Watson (thinking, perhaps, of a patient waiting in his consulting room)? A short-lived marriage between Mrs. Hudson and a Mr. Turner has also been postulated. And there have been other explanations: Mrs. Turner "was only substituting for her cousin," the late Page Heldenbrand wrote in "Another Bohemian Scandal," "and was quickly to disappear from the Baker Street scene when Martha Hudson returned from a short visit and resumed her reign over the premises"; she was, it seems, that same Martha Turner who met Jack the Ripper on the night of August 7, 1888, in front of George Yard Buildings, a group of squalid tenements just off High Street in Whitechapel. Mr. Russell Mc-Lauchlin, on the other hand, has suggested ("What Price Baker Street?") that Mrs. Turner presided over a house in Baker Street used by Holmes as an "accommodation address"—perhaps one of those "five small refuges" he mentions in "The Adventure of Black Peter"—while Holmes and Watson actually lived in Mrs. Hudson's house in Gloucester Place; one street west of Baker Street, it, too, runs north from Portman Square to the Marylebone Road.

49 *an ordinary plumber's smoke rocket.* Once used by plumbers to test for leaks in drains.

50 *Mr. John Hare.* John Hare, 1844–1921, knighted in 1907, was an eminent English actor and manager of the day, and a close friend of W. S. Gilbert's. At the St. James's Theater between 1879 and 1888 he established his popularity in "character" and "men of the world" roles.

HE . . . RETURNED IN A FEW MINUTES IN THE CHARACTER OF AN AMIABLE AND SIMPLE-MINDED NONCONFORMIST CLERGYMAN.

Illustration by Sidney Paget for the *Strand Magazine*, July, 1891. "Holmes' calculated choice of the role of the *Nonconformist* rather than that of an *Anglican* divine was beneath [his] usual standard of courage and forthrightness," the Reverend Otis R. Rice wrote in "Clergymen in the Canon." "For he well knew that to impersonate a minister of the Established Church was a legal offense. In passing, it is interesting to note that the uniform of the Nonconformist padre of the day was as distinctive as was the dog-collar and black rabat of an Anglican. . . . All in all, this is not one of Mr. Holmes,' most ethical performances, no matter how important the ends may have seemed to him. . . . Holmes turns up again impersonating a man of the cloth in 'The Final Problem.' "

few minutes in the character of an amiable and simple-minded Nonconformist clergyman. His broad black hat, his baggy trousers, his white tie, his sympathetic smile, and general look of peering and benevolent curiosity, were **50** such as Mr. John Hare alone could have equalled. It was not merely that Holmes changed his costume. His expression, his manner, his very soul seemed to vary with every fresh part that he assumed. The stage lost a fine actor, even as science lost an acute reasoner, when he became a specialist in crime.

It was a quarter past six when we left Baker Street, and it still wanted ten minutes to the hour when we found **51** ourselves in Serpentine Avenue. It was already dusk, and the lamps were just being lighted as we paced up and down in front of Briony Lodge, waiting for the coming of its occupant. The house was just such as I had pictured it from Sherlock Holmes's succinct description, but the locality appeared to be less private than I expected. On the contrary, for a small street in a quiet neighbourhood, it was remarkably animated. There was a group of shabbily-dressed men smoking and laughing in a corner, a scissors-grinder with his wheel, two guardsmen who were flirting with a nurse-girl, and several well-dressed young men who were lounging up and down with cigars in their mouths.

"You see," remarked Holmes, as we paced to and fro in front of the house, "this marriage rather simplifies matters. The photograph becomes a double-edged weapon now. The chances are that she would be as averse to its being seen by Mr. Godfrey Norton, as our client is to its coming to the eyes of his Princess. Now the question is—Where are we to find the photograph?"

"Where, indeed?"

"It is most unlikely that she carries it about with her. It is cabinet size. Too large for easy concealment about a woman's dress. She knows that the King is capable of having her waylaid and searched. Two attempts of the sort have already been made. We may take it then that she does not carry it about with her."

"Where, then?"

"Her banker or her lawyer. There is that double possibility. But I am inclined to think neither. Women are naturally secretive, and they like to do their own secreting. Why should she hand it over to anyone else? She could trust her own guardianship, but she could not tell what indirect or political influence might be brought to bear upon a business man. Besides, remember that she had resolved to use it within a few days. It must be where she can lay her hands upon it. It must be in her own house."

"But it has twice been burgled."

"Pshaw! They did not know how to look."

"But how will you look?"

"I will not look."

"What then?"

"I will get her to show me."

"But she will refuse."

"She will not be able to. But I hear the rumble of wheels. It is her carriage. Now carry out my orders to the letter."

As he spoke, the gleam of the sidelights of a carriage came round the curve of the avenue. It was a smart little landau which rattled up to the door of Briony Lodge. As it pulled up, one of the loafing men at the corner dashed forward to open the door in the hope of earning a copper, but was elbowed away by another loafer who had rushed up with the same intention. A fierce quarrel broke out, which was increased by the two guardsmen, who took sides with one of the loungers, and by the scissors-grinder, who was equally hot upon the other side. A blow was struck, and in an instant the lady, who had stepped from her carriage, was the centre of a little knot of flushed and struggling men who struck savagely at each other with their fists and sticks. Holmes dashed into the crowd to protect the lady; but just as he reached her, he gave a cry and dropped to the ground, with the blood running freely down his face. At his fall the guardsmen took to their heels in one direction and the loungers in the other, while a number of better dressed people who had watched the scuffle without taking part in it, crowded in to help the lady and to attend to the injured man. Irene Adler, as I will still call her, had hurried up the steps; but she stood at the top with her superb figure outlined against the lights of the hall, looking back into the street.

"Is the poor gentleman much hurt?" she asked.

"He is dead," cried several voices.

"No, no, there's life in him," shouted another. "But he'll be gone before you can get him to hospital."

"He's a brave fellow," said a woman. "They would have had the lady's purse and watch if it hadn't been for him. They were a gang, and a rough one, too. Ah, he's breathing now."

"He can't lie in the street. May we bring him in, marm?"

"Surely. Bring him into the sitting-room. There is a comfortable sofa. This way, please!"

Slowly and solemnly he was borne into Briony Lodge, and laid out in the principal room, while I still observed the proceedings from my post by the window.. The lamps had been lit, but the blinds had not been drawn, so that I could see Holmes as he lay upon the couch. I do not know whether he was seized with compunction at that moment for the part he was playing, but I know that I never felt more heartily ashamed of myself in my life than when I saw the beautiful creature against whom I was conspiring, or the grace and kindliness with which she waited upon the injured man. And yet it would be the blackest treachery to Holmes to draw back now from the part which he had entrusted to me. I hardened my heart and took the smoke rocket from under my ulster. After all, I thought, we are not injuring her. We are but preventing her from injuring another.

Holmes had sat up upon the couch, and I saw him motion like a man who is in want of air. A maid rushed across and threw open the window. At the same instant I saw him raise his hand, and at the signal I tossed my rocket into the room with a cry of "Fire." The word was no sooner out of my mouth than the whole crowd of spectators, well dressed and ill—gentlemen, ostlers, and servant maids—joined in a general shriek of "Fire."

51 *It was already dusk.* In fairness to Watson's "March," this *does* sound like the latter part of that month, when sunset in London falls between 5:39 P.M. (on the 1st) and 6:30 P.M. (on the 31st). But the late Professor Jay Finley Christ long ago pointed out that this date, by Watson's account, would be March 21st, and that every March 21st on a weekday in any year falls within Lent, when the tradition of the Church frowns upon marriage, except in certain "emergencies, a subject upon which speculation is perilous." In our view, the adventure took place in *May;* in Watson's execrable handwriting, this word could easily be mistaken, by the typesetter, for "March."

. . . HE GAVE A CRY AND DROPPED TO THE GROUND . . .

Illustration by Sidney Paget for the *Strand Magazine,* July, 1891.

52 *Thick clouds of smoke curled through the room.* Despite Holmes' earlier gibes at Dupin in *A Study in Scarlet*, he was not above taking a leaf from the book of that "very inferior fellow" (see Edgar Allan Poe's "The Purloined Letter"). We have seen (*A Study in Scarlet*, Note 62) that Conan Doyle's own opinion of Poe was a high one. "As the creator I've praised to satiety / Poe's Monsieur Dupin, his skill and variety / . . . [Holmes], the created, would scoff and would sneer, / Where I, the creator, would bow and revere . . .", Conan Doyle once explained in a verse "To an Undiscerning Critic." "It is impossible to read [this passage in "A Scandal in Bohemia"], Mr. Vincent Starrett wrote in his *Private Life of Sherlock Holmes*, "without a bit of wonderment; what if the ingenious rocket had missed fire? Would not the whole planned sequence have gone agley? But Watson, although he may have faltered, never actually blundered. Holmes knew the qualities of his assistant. No case was ever lost by Watson's failure."

53 *They were all engaged for the evening.* It is apparent that even in these early days Holmes was able to summon up very quickly a large number of trained assistants. In our view, Holmes in this instance recruited his troupe from among his fellow-players in the days when he had been an actor in Shakespearean repertory.

54 *the Arnsworth Castle business.* For the account of a "Darlington Substitution Scandal," but hardly that mentioned by Holmes here, see "The Adventure of the Wax Gamblers," in *The Exploits of Sherlock Holmes*. For an account of "the Arnsworth Castle business," see "The Adventure of the Red Widow" in the same volume.

52 Thick clouds of smoke curled through the room, and out at the open window. I caught a glimpse of rushing figures, and a moment later the voice of Holmes from within, assuring them that it was a false alarm. Slipping through the shouting crowd I made my way to the corner of the street, and in ten minutes was rejoiced to find my friend's arm in mine, and to get away from the scene of the uproar. He walked swiftly and in silence for some few minutes, until we had turned down one of the quiet streets which lead towards the Edgware Road.

"You did it very nicely, Doctor," he remarked. "Nothing could have been better. It is all right."

"You have the photograph!"

"I know where it is."

"And how did you find out?"

"She showed me, as I told you that she would."

"I am still in the dark."

"I do not wish to make a mystery," said he, laughing. "The matter was perfectly simple. You, of course, saw that every one in the street was an accomplice. They were **53** all engaged for the evening."

"I guessed as much."

"Then, when the row broke out, I had a little moist red paint in the palm of my hand. I rushed forward, fell down, clapped my hand to my face, and became a piteous spectacle. It is an old trick."

"That also I could fathom."

"Then they carried me in. She was bound to have me in. What else could she do? And into her sitting-room which was the very room which I suspected. It lay between that and her bedroom, and I was determined to see which. They laid me on a couch, I motioned for air, they were compelled to open the window and you had your chance."

"How did that help you?"

"It was all-important. When a woman thinks that her house is on fire, her instinct is at once to rush to the thing which she values most. It is a perfectly overpowering impulse, and I have more than once taken advantage of it. In the case of the Darlington Substitution Scandal it was of use to me, and also in the Arnsworth Castle busi- **54** ness. A married woman grabs at her baby—an unmarried one reaches for her jewel box. Now it was clear to me that our lady of to-day had nothing in the house more precious to her than what we are in quest of. She would rush to secure it. The alarm of fire was admirably done. The smoke and shouting was enough to shake nerves of steel. She responded beautifully. The photograph is in a recess behind a sliding panel just above the right bell-pull. She was there in an instant, and I caught a glimpse of it as she half drew it out. When I cried out that it was a false alarm, she replaced it, glanced at the rocket, rushed from the room, and I have not seen her since. I rose, and, making my excuses, escaped from the house, I hesitated whether to attempt to secure the photograph at once; but the coachman had come in, and as he was watching me narrowly, it seemed safer to wait. A little over-precipitance may ruin all."

"And now?" I asked.

"Our quest is practically finished. I shall call with the King to-morrow, and with you, if you care to come with us. We will be shown into the sitting-room to wait for the lady, but it is probable that when she comes she may find neither us nor the photograph. It might be a satisfaction to His Majesty to regain it with his own hands."

"And when will you call?"

"At eight in the morning. She will not be up, so that we shall have a clear field. Besides, we must be prompt, for this marriage may mean a complete change in her life and habits. I must wire to the King without delay."

We had reached Baker Street, and had stopped at the door. He was searching his pockets for the key, when some one passing said:

"Good night, Mister Sherlock Holmes."

There were several people on the pavement at the time, but the greeting appeared to come from a slim youth in an ulster who had hurried by.

"I've heard that voice before," said Holmes, staring down the dimly lit street. "Now, I wonder who the deuce that could have been."

III

I slept at Baker Street that night, and we were engaged upon our toast and coffee when the King of Bohemia rushed into the room.

"You have really got it!" he cried, grasping Sherlock Holmes by either shoulder, and looking eagerly into his face.

"Not yet."

"But you have hopes?"

"I have hopes."

"Then, come. I am all impatience to be gone."

"We must have a cab."

"No, my brougham is waiting."

"Then that will simplify matters."

We descended, and started off once more for Briony Lodge.

"Irene Adler is married," remarked Holmes.

"Married! When?"

"Yesterday."

"But to whom?"

"To an English lawyer named Norton."

"But she could not love him?"

"I am in hopes that she does."

"And why in hopes?"

"Because it would spare Your Majesty all fear of future annoyance. If the lady loves her husband, she does not love Your Majesty. If she does not love Your Majesty there is no reason why she should interfere with Your Majesty's plan."

"It is true. And yet——! Well! I wish she had been of my own station! What a queen she would have made!" He relapsed into a moody silence which was not broken until we drew up in Serpentine Avenue.

The door of Briony Lodge was open, and an elderly woman stood upon the steps. She watched us with a sardonic eye as we stepped from the brougham.

"Mr. Sherlock Holmes, I believe?" said she.

"I am Mr. Holmes," answered my companion, looking

"GOOD NIGHT, MISTER SHERLOCK HOLMES."

Illustration by Sidney Paget for the *Strand Magazine*, July, 1891. Mr. James Edward Holroyd has noted that the drawing "gives additional support to the majority view that 221B was on the west side of Baker Street. We know that Irene was walking from north to south, because she had followed [Holmes and Watson] from St. John's Wood. The house is shown on her right, or west, side."

55 *Male costume is nothing new to me.* We know that Irene Adler was an operatic soprano, and Mr. Guy Warrack, in *Sherlock Holmes and Music*, has correctly concluded that "It is therefore to the male-impersonation contralto roles that we must look in trying to reconstruct Irene Adler's operatic career." He cites several such roles: Gluck's Orfeo, Arsace in Rossini's *Sermiramide*, Maffo Orsini in Donizetti's *Lucrezia Borgia* and "the page Urbain in Meyerbeer's *Les Hugenots*," an opera Holmes attended after he had successfully concluded the adventure of *The Hound of the Baskervilles*. Mr. Anthony Boucher had added the roles of Siébel in Gounod's *Faust*, Stéphano in his *Roméo et Juliette*, and Pieretto in Donizetti's *Linda di Chamounix* ("The Records of Baker Street").

at her with a questioning and rather startled gaze.

" Indeed ! My mistress told me that you were likely to call. She left this morning with her husband, by the 5.15 train from Charing Cross, for the Continent."

" What ! " Sherlock Holmes staggered back, white with chagrin and surprise. " Do you mean that she has left England ? "

" Never to return."

" And the papers ? " asked the King hoarsely. " All is lost."

" We shall see." He pushed past the servant, and rushed into the drawing-room, followed by the King and myself. The furniture was scattered about in every direction, with dismantled shelves, and open drawers, as if the lady had hurriedly ransacked them before her flight. Holmes rushed at the bell-pull, tore back a small sliding shutter, and, plunging in his hand, pulled out a photograph and a letter. The photograph was of Irene Adler herself in evening dress, the letter was superscribed to " Sherlock Holmes, Esq. To be left till called for." My friend tore it open and we all three read it together. It was dated at midnight of the preceding night, and ran in this way :—

" MY DEAR MR. SHERLOCK HOLMES,—You really did it very well. You took me in completely. Until after the alarm of fire, I had not a suspicion. But then, when I found how I had betrayed myself, I began to think. I had been warned against you months ago. I had been told that if the King employed an agent, it would certainly be you. And your address had been given me. Yet, with all this, you made me reveal what you wanted to know. Even after I became suspicious, I found it hard to think evil of such a dear, kind old clergyman. But, you know, I have been trained as an actress myself. Male **55** costume is nothing new to me. I often take advantage of the freedom which it gives. I sent John, the coachman, to watch you, ran upstairs, got into my walking clothes, as I call them, and came down just as you departed.

" Well, I followed you to your door, and so made sure that I was really an object of interest to the celebrated Mr. Sherlock Holmes. Then I, rather imprudently, wished you good night, and started for the Temple to see my husband.

" We both thought the best resource was flight when pursued by so formidable an antagonist ; so you will find the nest empty when you call to-morrow. As to the photograph, your client may rest in peace. I love and am loved by a better man than he. The King may do what he will without hindrance from one whom he has cruelly wronged. I keep it only to safeguard myself, and to preserve a weapon which will always secure me from any steps which he might take in the future. I leave a photograph which he might care to possess ; and I remain, dear Mr. Sherlock Holmes, very truly yours,

" IRENE NORTON, *née* ADLER."

" What a woman—oh, what a woman ! " cried the King

of Bohemia, when we had all three read this epistle. " Did I not tell you how quick and resolute she was ? Would she not have made an admirable queen ? Is it not a pity she was not on my level ? "

" From what I have seen of the lady, she seems, indeed, to be on a very different level to Your Majesty," said Holmes, coldly. " I am sorry that I have not been able to bring Your Majesty's business to a more successful conclusion."

" On the contrary, my dear sir," cried the King. " Nothing could be more successful. I know that her word is inviolate. The photograph is now as safe as if it were in the fire."

" I am glad to hear Your Majesty say so."

" I am immensely indebted to you. Pray tell me in what way I can reward you. This ring——" He slipped an emerald snake ring from his finger and held it out upon the palm of his hand.

56

" Your Majesty has something which I should value even more highly," said Holmes.

" You have but to name it."

" This photograph ! "

The King stared at him in amazement.

" Irene's photograph ! " he cried. " Certainly, if you wish it."

" I thank Your Majesty. Then there is no more to be done in the matter. I have the honour to wish you a very good morning." He bowed, and, turning away without observing the hand which the King had stretched out to him, he set off in my company for his chambers.

And that was how a great scandal threatened to affect the kingdom of Bohemia, and how the best plans of Mr. Sherlock Holmes were beaten by a woman's wit. He used to make merry over the cleverness of women, but I have not heard him do it of late. And when he speaks of Irene Adler, or when he refers to her photograph, it is always under the honourable title of *the* woman.

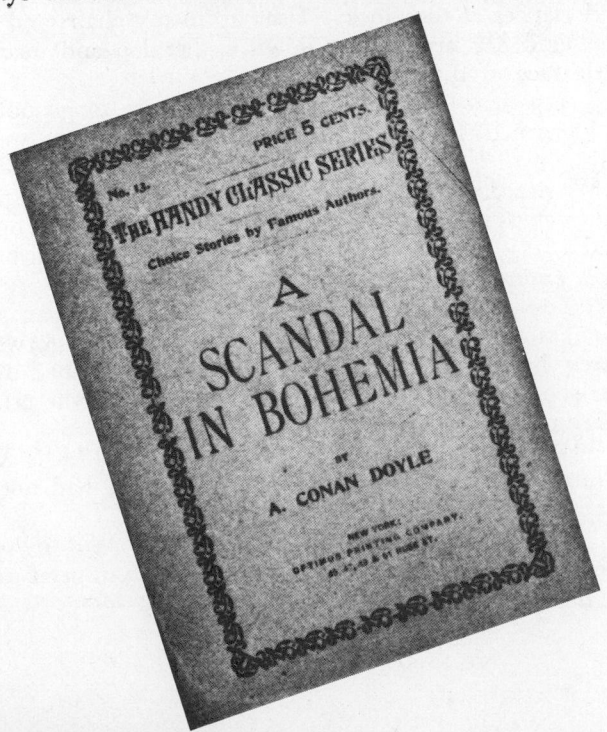

56 *held it out upon the palm of his hand.* Although the offer of the emerald snake ring met with a blunt refusal, Holmes later allowed himself to accept a snuff-box of old gold with a great amethyst in the center of the lid as a token of the King's appreciation ("A Case of Identity").

"THIS PHOTOGRAPH!"

Illustration by Sidney Paget for the *Strand Magazine*, July, 1891. "Those who are sentimentally inclined seize on the fact that Holmes asked the King of Bohemia for [Irene Adler's] photograph as evidence of attachment," Dr. Richard Asher wrote in "Holmes and the Fair Sex." "Is it not patently obvious that Holmes, having been deceived by her skill in disguising herself, wanted the photograph to add to his records to make sure that he would recognize her if she ever crossed his path again . . . ?"

Auctorial and Bibliographical Note: Conan Doyle ranked "A Scandal in Bohemia" fifth on his list of the "twelve best" short stories, excluding those in the *Case-Book;* the readers of the *Observer* ranked it sixth on their list of the best Sherlock Holmes short stories and novels. The original manuscript, consisting of thirty folio pages, the thirtieth of which is signed "A. Conan Doyle, 2 Upper Wimpole Street, London, W.", is now in the Library of the University of Texas at Austin, a presentation of Mr. Frederic A. Dannay. The first separate edition of this first of the short stories, a great rarity, is now thought to have been the small brochure illustrated here: No. 13 in the Handy Classic Series, published by the Optimus Printing Company of New York in 1895.

25

THE MAN WITH THE TWISTED LIP

[Saturday, June 18, to Sunday, June 19, 1887]

1 *the Theological College of St. George's.* Watson would naturally disguise the true name of a College whose principal had a brother "much addicted to opium." Could "St. George's" have been the Roman Catholic Missionary College of St. Joseph?

2 *De Quincey's.* Thomas de Quincey, 1785–1859, English essayist. The opium habit overcame him for a time and inspired his *Confessions of an English Opium-Eater*, first published in the *London Magazine* in 1821.

3 *June, '89.* Watson's "June" is accepted by all chronologists and commentators, his "'89" by all except your editor, who places the adventure in the June of 1887.

4 *like birds to a lighthouse.* Mr. John D. Beirle has pointed out ("The Curious Incident of the Drive Through Middlesex and Surrey") that this comment "surely does not agree with what we know to be the character of Mary Morstan Watson."

ISA WHITNEY, brother of the late Elias Whitney, D.D., Principal of the Theological College of St. George's, was much addicted to opium. The habit grew upon him, as I understand, from some foolish freak when he was at college, for having read De Quincey's description of his dreams and sensations, he had drenched his tobacco with laudanum in an attempt to produce the same effects. He found, as so many more have done, that the practice is easier to attain than to get rid of, and for many years he continued to be a slave to the drug, an object of mingled horror and pity to his friends and relatives. I can see him now, with yellow, pasty face, drooping lids and pin-point pupils, all huddled in a chair, the wreck and ruin of a noble man.

One night—it was in June, '89—there came a ring to my bell, about the hour when a man gives his first yawn, and glances at the clock. I sat up in my chair, and my wife laid her needlework down in her lap and made a little face of disappointment.

" A patient ! " said she. " You'll have to go out."

I groaned, for I was newly come back from a weary day.

We heard the door open, a few hurried words, and then quick steps upon the linoleum. Our own door flew open, and a lady, clad in some dark-coloured stuff with a black veil, entered the room.

" You will excuse my calling so late," she began, and then, suddenly losing her self-control, she ran forward, threw her arms about my wife's neck, and sobbed upon her shoulder. " Oh ! I'm in such trouble ! " she cried ; " I do so want a little help."

" Why," said my wife, pulling up her veil, " it is Kate Whitney. How you startled me, Kate ! I had not an idea who you were when you came in."

" I didn't know what to do, so I came straight to you." That was always the way. Folk who were in grief came to my wife like birds to a lighthouse.

" It was very sweet of you to come. Now, you must have some wine and water, and sit here comfortably and tell us all about it. Or should you rather that I sent James **5** off to bed ? "

" Oh, no, no. I want the Doctor's advice and help too. It's about Isa. He has not been home for two days. I am so frightened about him ! "

It was not the first time that she had spoken to us of her husband's trouble, to me as a doctor, to my wife as an old friend and school companion. We soothed and comforted her by such words as we could find. Did she know where her husband was ? Was it possible that we could bring him back to her ?

It seemed that it was. She had the surest information that of late he had, when the fit was on him, made use of an opium den in the furthest east of the City. Hitherto his orgies had always been confined to one day, and he had come back, twitching and shattered, in the evening. But now the spell had been upon him eight-and-forty hours, and he lay there, doubtless, among the dregs of the docks, breathing in the poison or sleeping off the effects. There he was to be found, she was sure of it, at the " Bar of Gold," in Upper Swandam Lane. But what was she to do ? How could she, a young and timid woman, make her way into such a place, and pluck her husband out from among the ruffians who surrounded him ?

There was the case, and of course there was but one way out of it. Might I not escort her to this place ? And, then, as a second thought, why should she come at all ? I was Isa Whitney's medical adviser, and as such I had influence over him. I could manage it better if I were alone. I promised her on my word that I would send him home in a cab within two hours if he were indeed at the address which she had given me. And so in ten minutes I had left my arm-chair and cheery sitting-room behind me, and was speeding eastward in a hansom on a strange errand, as it seemed to me at the time, though the future only could show how strange it was to be.

But there was no great difficulty in the first stage of my adventure. Upper Swandam Lane is a vile alley lurking behind the high wharves which line the north side of the river to the east of London Bridge. Between a slop shop **6-7** and a gin shop, approached by a steep flight of steps leading down to a black gap like the mouth of a cave, I found the den of which I was in search. Ordering my cab to wait, I passed down the steps, worn hollow in the centre by the ceaseless tread of drunken feet, and by the light of a flickering oil lamp above the door I found the latch and made my way into a long, low room, thick and heavy with the brown opium smoke, and terraced with wooden berths, like the forecastle of an emigrant ship.

Through the gloom one could dimly catch a glimpse of bodies lying in strange fantastic poses, bowed shoulders, bent knees, heads thrown back and chins pointing upwards, with here and there a dark, lack-lustre eye turned upon the new-comer. Out of the black shadows there glimmered little red circles of light, now bright, now faint, as the burning poison waxed or waned in the bowls of the metal pipes. The most lay silent, but some muttered to

5 *James.* We have previously noted one explanation for John Watson's wife calling him "James": that his middle name was Hamish, the Gaelic for James. The late H. W. Bell dismissed "James" as a mere typographical error. Mr. John Ball, Jr., has suggested that Watson's scribbled "John" could be misread as "James" by the typographer ("Early Days in Baker Street"). Christopher Morley ascribed the James to forgetfulness on the part of Mrs. Watson and even went so far as to suggest that this slip may eventually have led to a separation of the Watsons ("Was Sherlock Holmes an American?"). Mr. Giles Playfair argued that Watson deliberately falsified the records by having his wife refer to him as "James" (to avoid a possible libel action), but later threw in the cabby's name "John" as a clue to the true authorship of the story ("John and James"). Said Mr. T. S. Blakeney: "Composite authorship may generally be attributed to historical writings, irrespective of whether the original record was the work of the putative author or of another person of the same name; and the suggestion arises that the 'James' Watson spoken of [here] may be one of these editors" (*Sherlock Holmes: Fact or Fiction?*). The possibility that Watson's name was really James, whereas he chose for some unspecified reason to write as John H. has been advanced by Mr. J. S. Coltart in "The Watsons." James was the name of Watson's bull pup, says Mr. Ralph A. Ashton ("The Fourth Occupant, or The Room with the Twisted Tongue"); "James" was Watson's stepson, a view that depends on the doctor's marriage to Mrs. Forrester rather than to Mary Watson, as well as dating "The Man with the Twisted Lip." *after The Sign of the Four* (A. Carson Simpson, "It Must Have Been Two Other Fellows"); James was a playful reference to Watson's role as Holmes' Boswell—James Boswell (Dr. Ebbe Curtis Hoff, "The Adventure of John and Mary"); "There must have been a former husband—James by name" (Arthur K. Akers, "Who Was Mrs. Watson's First Husband?"). Finally, a new and startling hypotheses to account for the confusion—that there were *two* Watsons, John and James; that John died prematurely (shortly after the adventure of "The Reigate Squires"); and that James, seizing a good opportunity, thereupon masqueraded as his elder brother—has been provided by Mr. Bliss Austin in "What Son Was Watson?" (When we recall that Conan Doyle named Watson for his friend James Watson, the slip of the pen is understandable.)

6 *to the east of London Bridge.* The structure Holmes and Watson knew is the bridge on which work started in March, 1824. The first stone was laid on June 15, 1825, the tenth anniversary of the battle of Waterloo. On August 1, 1831, the completed work was opened to the public by William IV and Queen Adelaide.

There is, or was, no "Upper Swandam Lane" in the great city of London, and there is no "vile alley" on the north side of the river, east of London Bridge, which would be accessible to Watson's cab (almost the whole of the area is taken up by the Billingsgate Fish Market). Most commentators have selected Lower Thames Street, which stretches parallel to the Thames from London Bridge to All Hallows by the Tower of London. Mr. C. E. C. Townsend, on the other hand, concluded in his essay, "The Bar of Gold," that the opium den was "situated somewhere in the 200 yards of Wapping High Street that lie between Wapping Station and the bend where it joins Garnet Street." Mr. Alan Wilson ("Where Was the 'Bar of Gold'?") discarded Watson's "east of London Bridge" entirely and settled on No. 22 *Upper* Thames Street, to the *west* of London Bridge. The late H. W. Bell ("Three Identifications") was forced to resort to *crossing the river*. There, on the Surrey side, to the east of London Bridge, he found Stoney Lane, an alley leading into Tooley Street, with houses at the lower end overlooking the river; this he identified as "Upper Swandam Lane."

7 *a slop shop.* A small store selling clothing and other articles to sailors.

8 "*Of Friday, June 19.*" But June 19, 1889, was a *Wednesday* (as Isa Whitney thought it was), and the late Professor Jay Finley Christ accepted Wednesday, June 19, 1889, as the beginning of the case. Mr. Bell and Dr. Zeisler, however, both held that Watson's "Friday" was correct, and consequently were forced to discard his "19" (Bell for June 14th, Zeisler for June 21st). Another possible emendation would be to read "July" for "June," for in 1889 July 19th *did* fall on a Friday. Certainly Watson is in error about his "Friday": *or* his "June" *or* his "19" *or* his "'89." One or more of them *must* be wrong. In our view, the day was *Saturday, June 18, 1887.* Watson, in telling Whitney that it was "June 19" at "nearly eleven" on the Saturday night, made the not unnatural mistake of giving the next day's date.

themselves, and others talked together in a strange, low, monotonous voice, their conversation coming in gushes, and then suddenly tailing off into silence, each mumbling out his own thoughts, and paying little heed to the words of his neighbour. At the further end was a small brazier of burning charcoal, beside which on a three-legged wooden stool there sat a tall, thin old man, with his jaw resting upon his two fists, and his elbows upon his knees, staring into the fire.

As I entered, a sallow Malay attendant had hurried up with a pipe for me and a supply of the drug, beckoning me to an empty berth.

"Thank you, I have not come to stay," said I. "There is a friend of mine here, Mr. Isa Whitney, and I wish to speak with him."

There was a movement and an exclamation from my right, and, peering through the gloom, I saw Whitney, pale, haggard, and unkempt, staring out at me.

"My God! It's Watson," said he. He was in a pitiable state of reaction, with every nerve in a twitter. "I say, Watson, what o'clock is it?"

"Nearly eleven."

"Of what day?"

8   "Of Friday, June 19."

"Good heavens! I thought it was Wednesday. It *is* Wednesday. What d'you want to frighten a chap for?" He sank his face on to his arms, and began to sob in a high treble key.

"I tell you that it is Friday, man. Your wife has been waiting this two days for you. You should be ashamed of yourself!"

"So I am. But you've got mixed, Watson, for I have only been here a few hours, three pipes, four pipes—I forget how many. But I'll go home with you. I wouldn't frighten Kate—poor little Kate. Give me your hand! Have you a cab?"

"Yes, I have one waiting."

"Then I shall go in it. But I must owe something.

. . . THERE SAT A TALL, THIN OLD MAN, WITH HIS JAW RESTING UPON HIS TWO FISTS, AND HIS ELBOWS UPON HIS KNEES, STARING INTO THE FIRE.

Illustration by Sidney Paget for the *Strand Magazine*, December, 1891.

Find what I owe, Watson.   I am all off colour.   I can do nothing for myself."

I walked down the narrow passage between the double row of sleepers, holding my breath to keep out the vile, stupefying fumes of the drug, and looking about for the manager.   As I passed the tall man who sat by the brazier I felt a sudden pluck at my skirt, and a low voice whispered, " Walk past me, and then look back at me."   The words fell quite distinctly upon my ear.   I glanced down.   They could only have come from the old man at my side, and yet he sat now as absorbed as ever, very thin, very wrinkled, bent with age, an opium pipe dangling down from between his knees, as though it had dropped in sheer lassitude from his fingers.   I took two steps forward and looked back.   It took all my self-control to prevent me from breaking out into a cry of astonishment.   He had turned his back so that none could see him but I.   His form had filled out, his wrinkles were gone, the dull eyes had regained their fire, and there, sitting by the fire, and grinning at my surprise, was none other than Sherlock Holmes.   He made a slight motion to me to approach him, and instantly, as he turned his face half round to the company once more, subsided into a doddering, loose-lipped senility.

" Holmes ! " I whispered, " what on earth are you doing in this den ? "

" As low as you can," he answered, " I have excellent ears.   If you would have the great kindness to get rid of that sottish friend of yours, I should be exceedingly glad to have a little talk with you."

" I have a cab outside."

" Then pray send him home in it.   You may safely trust him, for he appears to be too limp to get into any mischief.   I should recommend you also to send a note by the cabman to your wife to say that you have thrown in your lot with me.   If you will wait outside, I shall be with **9** you in five minutes."

It was difficult to refuse any of Sherlock Holmes' requests, for they were always so exceedingly definite, and put forward with such an air of mastery.   I felt, however, that when Whitney was once confined in the cab, my mission was practically accomplished ; and for the rest, I could not wish anything better than to be associated with my friend in one of those singular adventures which were the normal condition of his existence.   In a few minutes I had written my note, paid Whitney's bill, led him out to the cab, and seen him driven through the darkness.   In a very short time a decrepit figure had emerged from the opium den, and I was walking down the street with Sherlock Holmes.   For two streets he shuffled along with a bent back and an uncertain foot.   Then, glancing quickly round, he straightened himself out and burst into a hearty fit of laughter.

" I suppose, Watson," said he, ' that you imagine that I have added opium-smoking to cocaine injections and all the other little weaknesses on which you have favoured me with your medical views."

" I was certainly surprised to find you there."

" But not more so than I to find you."

"HOLMES!" I WHISPERED, "WHAT ON EARTH ARE YOU DOING IN THIS DEN?"

Illustration by Sidney Paget for the *Strand Magazine*, December, 1891.

9 *to say that you have thrown in your lot with me.* In the view of the late Clifton R. Andrew ("What Happened to Watson's Married Life After June 14, 1889?"), Watson's marriage to the Mrs. Watson of "The Man with the Twisted Lip" was ended, not by her death, but by divorce. ". . . if the treatment accorded Mrs. Watson by the doctor in deference to Holmes' cajolery . . . wasn't the straw that broke the camel's back, I am most badly mistaken. Mrs. Watson's self-respect was given too stiff a jolt that time. When Watson finally did return home from his expedition, I am afraid there was a scene. I suppose it was something like this: 'Well, John (or James)—and my heart is breaking when I say this—I think we have reached the parting of our ways. It is all too evident that your friendship with Mr. Sherlock Holmes transcends your love for me and your home. Last night was the climax. How could you run off with Mr. Holmes and leave me to care for Kate Whitney, alone? Poor dear, she was so distraught, and we were waiting for your return and then that cabman gave me your note. Yes, this is the end—I have seen it coming this last year or so. I can't take the place of Mr. Holmes and his strange adventures. Let's face it, James (or John) and go our separate ways. Maybe we'll both be happier. I'm sure *you* will!' "

10 *"Near Lee, in Kent.* Lee is a residential suburb seven miles' drive from London—as Watson later states—along the Old Kent Road. Lee is no longer in Kent: in 1906 it became a part of the metropolitan borough of Lewisham. At Lee, in Popham House, lived Mr. John Scott Eccles, whom we will meet in "The Adventure of Wisteria Lodge."

"I came to find a friend."

"And I to find an enemy!"

"An enemy?"

"Yes, one of my natural enemies, or, shall I say, my natural prey. Briefly, Watson, I am in the midst of a very remarkable inquiry, and I have hoped to find a clue in the incoherent ramblings of these sots, as I have done before now. Had I been recognized in that den my life would not have been worth an hour's purchase, for I have used it before now for my own purposes, and the rascally Lascar who runs it has sworn vengeance upon me. There is a trap-door at the back of that building, near the corner of Paul's Wharf, which could tell some strange tales of what has passed through it upon the moonless nights."

"What! You do not mean bodies?"

"Aye, bodies, Watson. We should be rich men if we had a thousand pounds for every poor devil who has been done to death in that den. It is the vilest murder-trap on the whole river-side, and I fear Neville St. Clair has entered it never to leave it more. But our trap should be here!" He put his two forefingers between his teeth and whistled shrilly, a signal which was answered by a similar whistle from the distance, followed shortly by the rattle of wheels and the clink of horse's hoofs.

"Now, Watson," said Holmes, as a tall dog-cart dashed up through the gloom, throwing out two golden tunnels of yellow light from its side-lanterns, "you'll come with me, won't you?"

"If I can be of use."

"Oh, a trusty comrade is always of use. And a chronicler still more so. My room at the Cedars is a double-bedded one."

"The Cedars?"

"Yes; that is Mr. St. Clair's house. I am staying there while I conduct the inquiry."

"Where is it, then?"

10   "Near Lee, in Kent. We have a seven-mile drive before us."

"But I am all in the dark."

"IT IS THE VILEST MURDER-TRAP ON THE WHOLE RIVER-SIDE . . ."

There is, in fact, a Paul's Wharf (*shown at right*) which lies *west* of London Bridge on the north side of the Thames about midway between Blackfriars and Southwark Bridges, and is therefore discarded as a clue to the location of the "Bar of Gold" by all except Mr. Alan Wilson, who writes: "Halfway down Upper Thames Street is a small alley called Trig Lane. Farther on is another called Paul's Pier Wharf, and yet farther on another entitled Castle Barnard's Wharf. Behind these, on the river, are Paul's Wharf and East Paul's Wharf. It follows, then, that since the Bar of Gold backed on to the corner of Paul's Wharf, and Paul's Wharf is found behind Upper Thames Street (Upper Swandam Lane), we should be able to find the opium den lying between Trig Lane and Castle Barnard Wharf."

" Of course you are. You'll know all about it presently. Jump up here ! All right, John, we shall not need you. Here's half-a-crown. Look out for me tomorrow about eleven. Give her her head ! So long, then ! ' "

He flicked the horse with his whip, and we dashed away through the endless succession of sombre and deserted streets, which widened gradually, until we were flying across a broad balustraded bridge, with the murky river flowing sluggishly beneath us.   Beyond lay another broad wilderness of bricks and mortar, its silence broken only by the heavy, regular footfall of the policeman, or the songs and shouts of some belated party of revellers. A dull wrack was drifting slowly across the sky, and a star or two twinkled dimly here and there through the rifts of the clouds. Holmes drove in silence, with his head sunk upon his breast, and the air of a man who is lost in thought, whilst I sat beside him curious to learn what this new quest might be which seemed to tax his powers so sorely, and yet afraid to break in upon the current of his thoughts.   We had driven several miles, and were beginning to get to the fringe of the belt of suburban villas, when he shook himself, shrugged his shoulders, and lit up his pipe with the air of a man who has satisfied himself that he is acting for the best.

" You have a grand gift of silence, Watson," said he. " It makes you quite invaluable as a companion. 'Pon my word, it is a great thing for me to have someone to talk to, for my own thoughts are not over-pleasant. I was wondering what I should say to this dear little woman to-night when she meets me at the door."

" You forget that I know nothing about it."

" I shall just have time to tell you the facts of the case before we get to Lee. It seems absurdly simple, and yet, somehow, I can get nothing to go upon. There's plenty of thread, no doubt, but I can't get the end of it in my hand. Now, I'll state the case clearly and concisely to you, Watson, and maybe you may see a spark where all is dark to me."

" Proceed, then."

" Some years ago—to be definite, in May, 1884—there came to Lee a gentleman, Neville St. Clair by name, who appeared to have plenty of money. He took a large villa, laid out the grounds very nicely, and lived generally in good style. By degrees he made friends in the neighbourhood, and in 1887 he married the daughter of a local brewer, by whom he has now had two children. **11** He had no occupation, but was interested in several companies, and went into town as a rule in the morning, returning by the 5.14 from Cannon Street every night. Mr. St. Clair **12** is now 37 years of age, is a man of temperate habits, a good husband, a very affectionate father, and a man who is popular with all who know him. I may add that his whole debts at the present moment, as far as we have been able to ascertain, amount to £88 10s., while he has £220 standing to his credit in the Capital and Counties Bank. **13** There is no reason, therefore, to think that money troubles have been weighing upon his mind.

" Last Monday Mr. Neville St. Clair went into town

HE FLICKED THE HORSE WITH HIS WHIP . . .

Illustration by Sidney Paget for the *Strand Magazine*, December, 1891.

11 *by whom he has now had two children*. Here, admittedly, is a statement which, if allowed to stand, would date "The Man with the Twisted Lip" in 1889, as Watson said. As the late Dr. Ernest Bloomfield Zeisler pointed out, in his *Baker Street Chronology*, if the "boy had been conceived in accordance with the propriety of the Victorian times in which it occurred, and had also been born after the conventional period of gestation, he would have been about twenty and a half months old [in 1889], an age at which [a gift of small bricks—see below] would have been appropriate."

12 *Cannon Street*. Cannon Street Station, extending from Dowgate Hill nearly to Bush Lane, was constructed between 1864 and 1866, when the former South Eastern Railway extended its lines from London Bridge to Cannon Street and on to Charing Cross. The station was designed by Mr. John Hawkshaw, F.R.S., assisted by Sir J. W. Barry. No less than 27 million bricks were used in the erection of the arches under the station, the length of which is 687 feet, the width 202 feet, and the total height 120 feet.

13 *£88 10s., while he has £220 standing to his credit in the Capital and Counties Bank*. St. Clair owed the equivalent of $442.50, had $1,100 in the Capital and Counties Bank. This, as we learn in "The Adventure of the Priory School," was Holmes' own bank.

"... FRESNO STREET, WHICH BRANCHES OUT OF UPPER
SWANDAM LANE ..."

Fresno Street is another false name. But, if Mr.
Alan Wilson is correct in his identification of
"Upper Swandam Lane" as Upper Thames Street,
"Fresno Street . . . must lead off Upper Thames
Street at the Blackfriars end. It must also have
been on the north side of the street as a band of
policemen were coming down it on the way to
their beat [see above]. Between Blackfriars and
Paul's Pier Wharf (our farthest limit) there is,
however, *only one street*, and that is the small road
called Bennett's Hill, which leads from Queen Victoria Street to Upper Thames Street. This narrow
road enters Upper Thames Street at a point almost
exactly opposite No. 22 [Mr. Wilson's choice for
the building that housed the Bar of Gold, shown in
the photograph above]. . . . Mrs. St. Clair reached
the bottom of Bennett's Hill (Fresno Street) and
as she turned left into Upper Thames Street she
heard a cry and, looking up, saw her husband staring out of a second-floor window at No. 22 . . ."
Mr. Bell (still on the Surrey side of the Thames)
identified "Fresno Street" as Pickle Herring Street
and its continuation, Shad Thames.

rather earlier than usual, remarking before he started that
he had two important commissions to perform, and that
he would bring his little boy home a box of bricks. Now,
by the merest chance his wife received a telegram upon
this same Monday, very shortly after his departure, to the
effect that a small parcel of considerable value which she
had been expecting was waiting for her at the offices of
14 the Aberdeen Shipping Company. Now, if you are well
up in your London, you will know that the office of the
company is in Fresno Street, which branches out of Upper
Swandam Lane, where you found me to-night. Mrs. St.
Clair had her lunch, started for the City, did some shopping, proceeded to the company's office, got her packet,
and found herself exactly at 4.35 walking through Swandam Lane on her way back to the station. Have you
followed me so far ? "

" It is very clear."

" If you remember, Monday was an exceedingly hot
15 day, and Mrs. St. Clair walked slowly, glancing about
in the hope of seeing a cab, as she did not like the neighbourhood in which she found herself. While she walked
in this way down Swandam Lane she suddenly heard an
ejaculation or cry, and was struck cold to see her husband
looking down at her, and, as it seemed to her, beckoning
to her from a second-floor window. The window was
open, and she distinctly saw his face, which she describes
as being terribly agitated. He waved his hands frantically to her, and then vanished from the window so suddenly
that it seemed to her that he had been plucked back by
some irresistible force from behind. One singular point
which struck her quick feminine eye was that, although
he wore some dark coat, such as he had started to town
in, he had on neither collar nor necktie.

" Convinced that something was amiss with him, she
rushed down the steps—for the house was none other
than the opium den in which you found me to-night—
and, running through the front room, she attempted to
ascend the stairs which led to the first floor. At the foot
of the stairs, however, she met this Lascar scoundrel, of
whom I have spoken, who thrust her back, and, aided by
a Dane, who acts as assistant there, pushed her out into
the street. Filled with the most maddening doubts and
fears, she rushed down the lane, and, by rare good fortune,
met, in Fresno Street, a number of constables with an
inspector, all on their way to their beat. The inspector
and two men accompanied her back, and, in spite of the
continued resistance of the proprietor, they made their
way to the room in which Mr. St. Clair had last been seen.
There was no sign of him there. In fact, in the whole of
that floor there was no one to be found, save a crippled
wretch of hideous aspect, who, it seems, made his home
there. Both he and the Lascar stoutly swore that no one
else had been in the front room during that afternoon.
So determined was their denial that the inspector was
staggered, and had almost come to believe that Mrs. St.
Clair had been deluded when, with a cry, she sprang at a
small deal box which lay upon the table, and tore the lid
from it. Out there fell a cascade of children's bricks. It
was the toy which he had promised to bring home.

" This discovery, and the evident confusion which the cripple showed, made the inspector realize that the matter was serious. The rooms were carefully examined, and results all pointed to an abominable crime. The front room was plainly furnished as a sitting-room, and led into a small bedroom, which looked out upon the back of one of the wharves. Between the wharf and the bedroom window is a narrow strip, which is dry at low tide, but is covered at high tide with at least four and a half feet of water. The bedroom window was a broad one, and opened from below. On examination traces of blood were to be seen upon the window-sill, and several scattered drops were visible upon the wooden floor of the bedroom. Thrust away behind a curtain in the front room were all the clothes of Mr. Neville St. Clair, with the exception of his coat. His boots, his socks, his hat, and his watch—all were there. There were no signs of violence upon any of these garments, and there were no other traces of Mr. Neville St. Clair. Out of the window he must apparently have gone, for no other exit could be discovered, and the ominous blood-stains upon the sill gave little promise that he could save himself by swimming, for the tide was at its very highest at the moment of the tragedy.   **16**

" And now as to the villains who seemed to be immediately implicated in the matter. The Lascar was known to be a man of the vilest antecedents, but as by Mrs. St. Clair's story he was known to have been at the foot of the stair within a few seconds of her husband's appearance at the window, he could hardly have been more than an accessory to the crime. His defence was one of absolute ignorance, and he protested that he had no knowledge as to the doings of Hugh Boone, his lodger, and that he could not account in any way for the presence of the missing gentleman's clothes.

14 *the Aberdeen Shipping Company.* "There was an Aberdeen Steam Navigation Company, with offices at No. 102, Queen Victoria Street," the late H. W. Bell wrote in "Three Identifications." "But unless we are prepared to accept the equation: Cannon Street + East Cheap = Upper Swandam Lane, that 'vile alley,' and we are able to credit Neville St. Clair with the notable fear of hurling his jacket from East Cheap over the tops of the intervening houses into the Thames [see below], a distance of over 200 yards, we must recognize the presence of [a] coincidence."

15 *Monday was an exceedingly hot day.* There was *no* exceedingly hot Monday in the June of 1889. In 1887, on the other hand, Monday, June 13th *was* "an exceedingly hot day." The *Times'* evening weather report noted that "In London, where the sky has been almost cloudless, temperature has risen to a maximum of 81 deg. . . . The amount of bright sunshine registered today at Westminster has been about 13 hours 40 minutes."

16 *for the tide was at its very highest at the moment of the tragedy.* It must be admitted that the tide was *not* at its very highest just east of London Bridge shortly after 4:35 P.M. on Monday, June 13, 1887. Either the typesetter misread Watson's handwriting again or Mrs. St. Clair was mistaken about the "exact" time at which she was walking through Upper Swandam Lane. Your editor would vastly prefer either of these explanation to believing that Holmes did not know when the water just east of London Bridge was at its very highest.

"AT THE FOOT OF THE STAIRS, HOWEVER, SHE MET THIS LASCAR SCOUNDREL . . ."

Illustration by Sidney Paget for the *Strand Magazine,* December, 1891.

"HE IS A PROFESSIONAL BEGGAR . . ."

Illustration by Sidney Paget for the *Strand Magazine*, December, 1891.

17 *Threadneedle Street*. Originally Three-Needle Street, the home of London's Merchant Tailors. Here stands the Bank of England, sometimes referred to as "The Old Lady of Threadneedle Street." Here, too, Alexander Holder, of the responsible firm of Holder and Stevenson, had his office ("The Adventure of the Beryl Coronet").

18 *I have watched this fellow more than once.* ". . . had [Holmes] been as adept in seeing through the disguises of others as he was in fooling others with his own, [he] would have solved this case practically at the start. . . . He [describes] the beggar's appearance in such vivid detail as to leave no doubt that he had at least several times scrutinized the mendicant at close range. Yet apparently at no time during these close contacts did it occur to him that the 'shock of orange hair' and the 'pale face disfigured by a horrible scar' were—or even might be—a disguise. If he had come to the case with even the faintest surmise as to this fact, he would undoubtedly have solved it almost at once, without benefit of shag."
—Nathan L. Bengis, "Sherlock Stays After School."

19 *"Mrs. St. Clair had fainted at the sight of the blood upon the window.* Several pages later, however, Mrs. St. Clair notes that "I am not hysterical, nor given to fainting."

"So much for the Lascar manager. Now for the sinister cripple who lives upon the second floor of the opium den, and who was certainly the last human being whose eyes rested upon Neville St. Clair. His name is Hugh Boone, and his hideous face is one which is familiar to every man who goes much to the City. He is a professional beggar, though in order to avoid the police regulations he pretends to a small trade in wax vestas. Some **17** little distance down Threadneedle Street upon the left-hand side there is, as you may have remarked, a small angle in the wall. Here it is that the creature takes his daily seat, cross-legged, with his tiny stock of matches on his lap, and as he is a piteous spectacle a small rain of charity descends into the greasy leather cap which lies upon the pavement before him. I have watched this **18** fellow more than once, before ever I thought of making his professional acquaintance, and I have been surprised at the harvest which he has reaped in a short time. His appearance, you see, is so remarkable that no one can pass him without observing him. A shock of orange hair, a pale face disfigured by a horrible scar, which, by its contraction, has turned up the outer edge of his upper lip, a bull-dog chin, and a pair of very penetrating dark eyes, which present a singular contrast to the colour of his hair, all mark him out from amid the common crowd of mendicants, and so, too, does his wit, for he is ever ready with a reply to any piece of chaff which may be thrown at him by the passers-by. This is the man whom we now learn to have been the lodger at the opium den, and to have been the last man to see the gentleman of whom we are in quest."

"But a cripple!" said I. "What could he have done single-handed against a man in the prime of life?"

"He is a cripple in the sense that he walks with a limp; but, in other respects, he appears to be a powerful and well-nurtured man. Surely your medical experience would tell you, Watson, that weakness in one limb is often compensated for by exceptional strength in the others."

"Pray continue your narrative."

"Mrs. St. Clair had fainted at the sight of the blood **19** upon the window, and she was escorted home in a cab by the police, as her presence could be of no help to them in their investigations. Inspector Barton, who had charge of the case, made a very careful examination of the premises, but without finding anything which threw any light upon the matter. One mistake had been made in not arresting Boone instantly, as he was allowed some few minutes during which he might have communicated with his friend the Lascar, but this fault was soon remedied, and he was seized and searched, without anything being found which could incriminate him. There were, it is true, some bloodstains upon his right shirt-sleeve, but he pointed to his ring finger, which had been cut near the nail, and explained that the bleeding came from there, adding that he had been to the window not long before, and that the stains which had been observed there came doubtless from the same source. He denied strenuously having ever seen Mr. Neville St. Clair, and swore that the presence of the clothes in his room was as much a mystery to him as to the police. As to Mrs. St. Clair's assertion, that she had **actually seen her husband** at the window, he declared that she must have been either mad or dreaming. He was removed, loudly protesting, to the police station, while the inspector remained upon the premises in the hope that the ebbing tide might afford some fresh clue.

" And it did, though they hardly found upon the mud-bank what they had feared to find. It was Neville St. Clair's coat, and not Neville St. Clair, which lay un-covered as the tide receded. And what do you think they found in the pockets ? "

" I cannot imagine."

" No, I don't think you will guess. Every pocket stuffed with pennies and halfpennies—four hundred and twenty-one pennies, and two hundred and seventy half-pennies. It was no wonder that it had not been swept away by the tide. But a human body is a different matter. There is a fierce eddy between the wharf and the house. It seemed likely enough that the weighted coat had re-mained when the stripped body had been sucked away into the river."

" But I understand that all the other clothes were found in the room. Would the body be dressed in a coat alone ? "

" No, sir, but the facts might be met speciously enough. Suppose that this man Boone had thrust Neville St. Clair through the window, there is no human eye which could have seen the deed. What would he do then ? It would of course instantly strike him that he must get rid of the tell-tale garments. He would seize the coat then, and be in the act of throwing it out when it would occur to him that it would swim and not sink. He has little time, for he had heard the scuffle downstairs when the wife tried to force her way up, and perhaps he has already heard from his Lascar confederate that the police are hurrying up the street. There is not an instant to be lost. He rushes to some secret hoard, where he has accumulated the fruits of his beggary, and he stuffs all the coins upon which he can lay his hands into the pockets to make sure of the coat's sinking. He throws it out, and would have done the same with the other garments had not he heard the rush of steps below, and only just had time to close the window when the police appeared."

" It certainly sounds feasible."

" Well, we will take it as a working hypothesis for want of a better. Boone, as I have told you, was arrested and taken to the station, but it could not be shown that there had ever before been anything against him. He had for years been known as a professional beggar, but his life appeared to have been a very quiet and innocent one. There the matter stands at present, and the questions which have to be solved, what Neville St. Clair was doing in the opium den, what happened to him when there, where is he now, and what Hugh Boone had to do with his disappearance, are all as far from a solution as ever. I confess that I cannot recall any case within my experience which looked at the first glance so simple, and yet which presented such difficulties."

Whilst Sherlock Holmes had been detailing this singu-

"EVERY POCKET STUFFED WITH PENNIES AND HALF-PENNIES . . ."

"Before there was a distinct halfpenny coin, one (or rather two) could be made at home by anyone who possessed a pair of shears. The reverse of the penny of those days bore a *voided* cross, that is, one of which only the edges were raised. Since, like all hammered coins, these were quite thin, it was a simple matter to cut them in half, using the hol-low space between the raised edges of the cross as a guide. When Edward I struck a circular silver halfpenny, the voided cross on the penny was re-placed by a solid one: it extended to the edge, so that clipping could be easily detected."—A. Carson Simpson, *Numismatics in the Canon*, Part I. This is the only Canonical reference to the halfpenny (the 1863 bronze Victoria halfpenny is shown above). Mr. Simpson added that it is small wonder that the coat sunk, for the coins would have weighed about twelve pounds avoirdupois.

". . . AND HE STUFFS ALL THE COINS UPON WHICH HE CAN LAY HIS HANDS INTO THE POCKETS . . ."

Illustration by Sidney Paget for the *Strand Maga-zine*, December, 1891.

20 *and ending in Kent.* The reader who attempts to trace this route on a modern map should remember that it will show the county boundaries as they stand today. Before 1888 there was no County of London: north of the river London lay in Middlesex and south of the river in Surrey. The boundaries of these counties only withdrew to the suburbs when the County of London was created by Act of Parliament in 1888. "The correct conclusion from Holmes' statement," Mr. Michael Kaser once wrote to your editor, "is that the case took place, not in 1889, as Watson alleges, but at least a year earlier. . . . The present evidence supports the view that Watson mistook the year (or the typesetter misprinted it) in his account."

21 mousseline-de-soie. A soft thin silk fabric with a weave like that of muslin.

22 *a standing question.* "I fear she had designs on [Holmes]," Dr. Richard Asher wrote in "Holmes and the Fair Sex." ". . . she insisted on Holmes staying at her house in Kent, a seven-mile drive away [from London], far from the scene of his investigation. . . . When Watson drove down to her house she was not expecting Watson (it was only by chance that Holmes and Watson had met in an opium den). Was her attitude that of a bereaved wife or was she a designing woman? There she was, all decked out in . . . *mousseline-de-soie*, not to mention the pink chiffon. 'The door flew open and she stood with her figure outlined against the flood of light, one hand raised in eagerness, her body slightly bent, her head and face protruded, with eager eyes and parted lips, a standing question.' Surely as men of the world we can interpret that correctly. Watson goes on to record that when she saw there were two of them in the dog-cart she gave a cry which sank into a groan and Sherlock Holmes shook his head and shrugged his shoulders. . . . Is it not abundantly clear that Holmes had brought Watson with him as a chaperone? Anyway, that night Holmes got Watson to sleep in his room. Yet, even with his friend beside him, Holmes does not seem to have felt quite secure, for he sat up all night on a pile of cushions smoking shag and probably ruminating over his narrow escape."

lar series of events we had been whirling through the outskirts of the great town until the last straggling houses had been left behind, and we rattled along with a country hedge upon either side of us. Just as he finished, however, we drove through two scattered villages, where a few lights still glimmered in the windows.

"We are on the outskirts of Lee," said my companion. "We have touched on three English counties in our short drive, starting in Middlesex, passing over an angle of **20** Surrey, and ending in Kent. See that light among the trees? That is the Cedars, and beside that lamp sits a woman whose anxious ears have already, I have little doubt, caught the clink of our horse's feet."

"But why are you not conducting the case from Baker Street?" I asked.

"Because there are many inquiries which must be made out here. Mrs. St. Clair has most kindly put two rooms at my disposal, and you may rest assured that she will have nothing but a welcome for my friend and colleague. I hate to meet her, Watson, when I have no news of her husband. Here we are. Whoa, there, whoa!"

We had pulled up in front of a large villa which stood within its own grounds. A stable-boy had run out to the horse's head, and, springing down, I followed Holmes up the small, winding gravel drive which led to the house. As we approached the door flew open, and a little blonde woman stood in the opening, clad in some sort of light **21** *mousseline-de-soie*, with a touch of fluffy pink chiffon at her neck and wrists. She stood with her figure outlined against the flood of light, one hand upon the door, one half raised in eagerness, her body slightly bent, her head and face protruded, with eager eyes and parted lips, a **22** standing question.

"Well?" she cried, "well?" And then, seeing that there were two of us, she gave a cry of hope which sank into a groan as she saw that my companion shook his head and shrugged his shoulders.

"No good news?"

"None."

"No bad?"

"No."

"Thank God for that. But come in. You must be weary, for you have had a long day."

"This is my friend, Dr. Watson. He has been of most vital use to me in several of my cases, and a lucky chance has made it possible for me to bring him out and associate him with this investigation."

"I am delighted to see you," said she, pressing my hand warmly. "You will, I am sure, forgive anything which may be wanting in our arrangements, when you consider the blow which has come so suddenly upon us."

"My dear madam," said I, "I am an old campaigner, and if I were not, I can very well see that no apology is needed. If I can be of any assistance, either to you or to my friend here, I shall be indeed happy."

"Now, Mr. Sherlock Holmes," said the lady as we entered a well-lit dining-room, upon the table of which a cold supper had been laid out. "I should very much like to ask you one or two plain questions, to which I beg that you will give a plain answer."

" Certainly, madam."

" Do not trouble about my feelings. I am not hyster-ical, nor given to fainting. I simply wish to hear your real, real opinion."

" Upon what point ? "

" In your heart of hearts, do you think that Neville is alive ? "

Sherlock Holmes seemed to be embarrassed by the question. " Frankly now ! " she repeated, standing upon the rug, and looking keenly down at him, as he leaned back in a basket chair.

" Frankly, then, madam, I do not."

" You think that he is dead ? "

" I do."

" Murdered ? "

" I don't say that. Perhaps."

" And on what day did he meet his death ? "

" On Monday."

" Then perhaps, Mr. Holmes, you will be good enough to explain how it is that I have received this letter from him to-day ? "

Sherlock Holmes sprang out of his chair as if he had been galvanized.

" What ! " he roared.

" Yes, to-day." She stood smiling, holding up a little slip of paper in the air.

" May I see it ? "

" Certainly."

He snatched it from her in his eagerness, and smoothing it out upon the table, he drew over the lamp, and examined it intently. I had left my chair, and was gazing at it over his shoulder. The envelope was a very coarse one, and was stamped with the Gravesend postmark, and with the **23** date of that very day, or rather of the day before, for it **24** was considerably after midnight.

" Coarse writing ! " murmured Holmes. " Surely this is not your husband's writing, madam."

" No, but the enclosure is."

" I perceive also that whoever addressed the envelope had to go and inquire as to the address."

" How can you tell that ? "

" The name, you see, is in perfectly black ink, which has dried itself. The rest is of the greyish colour which shows that blotting-paper has been used. If it had been written straight off, and then blotted, none would be of a deep black shade. This man has written the name, and there has then been a pause before he wrote the address, which can only mean that he was not familiar with it. It is, of course, a trifle, but there is nothing so important as trifles. Let us now see the letter ! Ha ! there has been **25** an enclosure here ! "

" Yes, there was a ring. His signet ring."

" And you are sure that this is your husband's hand ? "

" One of his hands."

" One ? "

" His hand when he wrote hurriedly. It is very unlike his usual writing, and yet I know it well."

" ' Dearest, do not be frightened. All will come well.

"FRANKLY NOW!" SHE REPEATED . . .

Illustration by Sidney Paget for the *Strand Maga-zine*, December, 1891.

23 *Gravesend*. An ancient and busy river port in Kent where vessels on their way up the Thames change their sea pilots for river pilots. Pocohontas is buried at Gravesend.

24 *or rather the day before*. The morning could not have been a Monday morning, for the letter could not have been received on a Sunday.

25 *there is nothing so important as trifles*. "It was the opinion of Michelangelo that 'Trifles make perfection, but perfection is no trifle,'" Mr. George Simmons wrote in "Sherlock Holmes—The Inner Man." "Perhaps Holmes acquired some of that dilettante's knowledge of art, about which Watson [later] ragged him, from reading of the great Italian Master."

There is a huge error which it may take some little time to rectify. Wait in patience.—Neville.' Written in pencil upon a fly-leaf of a book, octavo size, no watermark. Posted to-day in Gravesend by a man with a dirty thumb. Ha ! And the flap has been gummed, if I am not very much in error, by a person who had been chewing tobacco. And you have no doubt that it is your husband's hand, madam ? "

" None. Neville wrote those words."

" And they were posted to-day at Gravesend. Well, Mrs. St. Clair, the clouds lighten, though I should not venture to say that the danger is over."

" But he must be alive, Mr. Holmes."

" Unless this is a clever forgery to put us on the wrong scent. The ring, after all, proves nothing. It may have been taken from him."

" No, no ; it is, it is, it is his very own writing ! "

" Very well. It may, however, have been written on Monday, and only posted to-day."

" That is possible."

" If so, much may have happened between."

" Oh, you must not discourage me, Mr. Holmes. I know that all is well with him. There is so keen a sympathy between us that I should know if evil came upon him. On the very day that I saw him last he cut himself in the bedroom, and yet I in the dining-room rushed upstairs instantly with the utmost certainty that something had happened. Do you think that I would respond to such a trifle, and yet be ignorant of his death ? "

" I have seen too much not to know that the impression of a woman may be more valuable than the conclusion of an analytical reasoner. And in this letter you certainly have a very strong piece of evidence to corroborate your view. But if your husband is alive and able to write letters, why should he remain away from you ? "

" I cannot imagine. It is unthinkable."

" And on Monday he made no remarks before leaving you ? "

" No."

" And you were surprised to see him in Swandam Lane ? "

" Very much so."

" Was the window open ? "

" Yes."

" Then he might have called to you ? "

" He might."

" He only, as I understand, gave an inarticulate cry ? "

" Yes."

" A call for help, you thought ? "

" Yes. He waved his hands."

" But it might have been a cry of surprise. Astonishment at the unexpected sight of you might cause him to throw up his hands."

" It is possible."

" And you thought he was pulled back."

" He disappeared so suddenly."

" He might have leaped back. You did not see anyone else in the room."

" No, but this horrible man confessed to having been there, and the Lascar was at the foot of the stairs."

" Quite so.   Your husband, as far as you could see, had his ordinary clothes on ? "

" But without his collar or tie.   I distinctly saw his bare throat."

" Had he ever spoken of Swandam Lane ? "

" Never."

" Had he ever shown any signs of having taken opium ? "

" Never."

" Thank you, Mrs. St. Clair.   Those are the principal points about which I wished to be absolutely clear.   We shall now have a little supper and then retire, for we may have a very busy day to-morrow."

A large and comfortable double-bedded room had been placed at our disposal, and I was quickly between the sheets, for I was weary after my night of adventure. Sherlock Holmes was a man, however, who when he had an unsolved problem upon his mind would go for days, and even for a week, without rest, turning it over, rearranging his facts, looking at it from every point of view, until he had either fathomed it, or convinced himself that his data were insufficient.   It was soon evident to me that he was now preparing for an all-night sitting.   He took off his coat and waistcoat, put on a large blue dressing-gown, and then wandered about the room collecting **26** pillows from his bed, and cushions from the sofa and arm-chairs.   With these he constructed a sort of Eastern divan, upon which he perched himself cross-legged, with an ounce of shag tobacco and a box of matches laid out in front of him.   In the dim light of the lamp I saw him sitting there, an old brier pipe between his lips, his eyes fixed vacantly upon the corner of the ceiling, the blue smoke curling up from him, silent, motionless, with the light shining upon his strong-set aquiline features.   So he sat as I dropped off to sleep, and so he sat when a sudden ejaculation caused me to wake up, and I found the summer sun shining into the apartment.   The pipe was still between his lips, the smoke still curled upwards, and the room was full of a dense tobacco haze, but nothing remained of the heap of shag which I had seen upon the previous night.

26 *a large blue dressing-gown.* In "The Adventure of the Blue Carbuncle," we are told that Holmes wore a purple dressing gown; in "the Adventure of the Empty House" that his dressing gown was mouse-colored (this gown reappears in "The Adventure of the Bruce-Partington Plans"). Three dressing gowns or one? "Elementary," Christopher Morley wrote in "Was Sherlock Holmes an American?" "This particular gown was blue when new. . . . It had gone purple by the time of 'The Blue Carbuncle.' During the long absence 1891–1894, when Mrs. Hudson faithfully aired and sunned it in the backyard, it faded to mouse." (Morley liked to wear, to dinners of the Baker Street Irregulars, a hideous tie striped in blue, purple, and mouse.) Elsewhere (as a footnote to Mr. Humfrey Michell's essay on "The Sartorial Sherlock Holmes"), the Old Gasogene wrote: "It has long been on my mind to mention the fact that our beloved Freddie Steele . . . misled us in the matter of [Holmes' dressing-gown]. Probably he himself took the notion from William Gillette, who wore as Sherlock one of those robes with satin cuffs and long satin lapels (perhaps even padded or quilted with a kind of diagonal stitch). Bathrobes of this type are definitely American; I don't believe they have ever been seen in Britain. . . . I'm sure Holmes' gown was not like that. It was of substantial wool or wool-flanelette, severely cut, with plenty of pockets, and large horn buttons. Rather than a twisted cord-girdle it was tied round with a strip of the same material . . ." On the other hand, Mr. S. B. Blake ("Sherlock Holmes' Dressing Gown(s)") suggested that Holmes had two gowns, one blue, one purple, that were burned in the fire set by Moriarty's minions in April, 1891, and that Holmes acquired a third gown in Italy which he took with him during his travels in Tibet and elsewhere.

THE PIPE WAS STILL BETWEEN HIS LIPS . . .

Illustration by Sidney Paget for the *Strand Magazine*, December, 1891.

27 *It was twenty-five minutes past four.* Watson tells us that he awoke on the second day of the case shortly before "twenty-five minutes past four" and found "the summer sun shining into the apartment"; soon thereafter he walked "out into the bright morning sunshine." In June in England the sun rises at 3:50 A.M. on the 1st, at 3:49 A.M. on the 30th. June is certainly the likeliest month of the year for the case, although, by the sun alone, the latter part of May and the early part of July are possibilities.

28 *Charing Cross.* "Dr. Johnson said, 'I think the full tide of existence is at Charing Cross.' . . . In 1266 a village on this site was spoken of as Cherringe, where William of Radnor, Bishop of Landaff, asked permission of Henry III to take up his abode in a hermitage during his visits to London. This earlier mention of the name unfortunately renders it impossible to derive it, as has often been done, from *La Chère Reine,* Eleanor, wife of Edward I. . . . to whom her husband erected here the last of the nine crosses which marked the resting-places of the beloved corpse in 1291 on its way from Lincoln to Westminster. More probably the name is derived from the Saxon word *Charan,* to turn, both the road and the river making a bend here."—Augustus J. C. Hare, *Walks in London,* Vol. I.

Here, at Charing Cross, stood the hospital which put the "C. C. H." on Dr. Mortimer's stick (*The Hound of the Baskervilles*); here, too, were the vaults of the bank of Cox & Co. which once contained a travel-worn, battered dispatch box with the name of John H. Watson, M.D., painted upon the lid ("The Problem of Thor Bridge").

29 *Gladstone bag.* A long, light, narrow leather traveling bag opening very wide; named for Britain's celebrated Prime Minister.

30 *Waterloo Bridge Road.* Constructed at the same time as Waterloo Bridge, about 1816.

31 *Wellington Street.* Constructed as an approach to Waterloo Bridge in 1829–1830, to run from the Thames to the Strand. Here stood the office of *Household Words* when Dickens edited it; here stands the Lyceum Theatre, of which we will read in *The Sign of the Four.*

32 *"Inspector Bradstreet, sir."* We will meet Bradstreet again in "The Adventure of the Blue Carbuncle" and "The Adventure of the Engineer's Thumb."

" Awake, Watson ? " he asked.

" Yes."

" Game for a morning drive ? "

" Certainly."

" Then dress. No one is stirring yet, but I know where the stable-boy sleeps, and we shall soon have the trap out." He chuckled to himself as he spoke, his eyes twinkled, and he seemed a different man to the sombre thinker of the previous night.

As I dressed I glanced at my watch. It was no wonder that no one was stirring. It was twenty-five minutes past **27** four. I had hardly finished when Holmes returned with the news that the boy was putting in the horse.

" I want to test a little theory of mine," said he, pulling on his boots. " I think, Watson, that you are now standing in the presence of one of the most absolute fools in Europe. I deserve to be kicked from here to Charing **28** Cross. But I think I have the key of the affair now."

" And where is it ? " I asked, smiling.

" In the bath-room," he answered. " Oh, yes, I am not joking," he continued, seeing my look of incredulity. " I have just been there, and I have taken it out, and I **29** have got it in this Gladstone bag. Come on, my boy, and we shall see whether it will not fit the lock."

We made our way downstairs as quickly as possible ; and out into the bright morning sunshine. In the road stood our horse and trap, with the half-clad stable-boy waiting at the head. We both sprang in, and away we dashed down the London road. A few country carts were stirring, bearing in vegetables to the metropolis, but the lines of villas on either side were as silent and lifeless as some city in a dream.

" It has been in some points a singular case," said Holmes, flicking the horse on into a gallop. " I confess that I have been as blind as a mole, but it is better to learn wisdom late, than never to learn it at all."

In town, the earliest risers were just beginning to look sleepily from their windows as we drove through the streets of the Surrey side. Passing down the Waterloo **30** Bridge Road we crossed over the river, and dashing up **31** Wellington Street wheeled sharply to the right, and found ourselves in Bow Street. Sherlock Holmes was well known to the Force, and the two constables at the door saluted him. One of them held the horse's head while the other led us in.

" Who is on duty ? " asked Holmes.

32 " Inspector Bradstreet, sir."

" Ah, Bradstreet, how are you ? " A tall, stout official had come down the stone-flagged passage, in a peaked cap and frogged jacket. " I wish to have a word with you, Bradstreet."

" Certainly, Mr. Holmes. Step into my room here."

It was a small office-like room, with a huge ledger upon the table, and a telephone projecting from the wall. The inspector sat down at his desk.

" What can I do for you, Mr. Holmes ? "

" I called about that beggar-man, Boone—the one who was charged with being concerned in the disappearance of Mr. Neville St. Clair, of Lee."

" Yes. He was brought up and remanded for further inquiries."

" So I heard. You have him here ? "

" In the cells."

" Is he quiet ? "

" Oh, he gives no trouble. But he is a dirty scoundrel."

" Dirty ? "

" Yes, it is all we can do to make him wash his hands, and his face is as black as a tinker's. Well, when once his case has been settled he will have a regular prison bath ; and I think, if you saw him, you would agree with me that he needed it."

" I should like to see him very much."

" Would you ? That is easily done. Come this way. You can leave your bag."

" No, I think I'll take it."

" Very good. Come this way, if you please." He led us down a passage, opened a barred door, passed down a winding stair, and brought us to a whitewashed corridor with a line of doors on each side.

" The third on the right is his," said the inspector. " Here it is ! " He quietly shot back a panel in the upper part of the door, and glanced through.

" He is asleep," said he. " You can see him very well."

We both put our eyes to the grating. The prisoner lay with his face towards us, in a very deep sleep, breathing slowly and heavily. He was a middle-sized man, coarsely clad as became his calling, with a coloured shirt protruding through the rent in his tattered coat. He was, as the inspector had said, extremely dirty, but the

. . . AND FOUND OURSELVES IN BOW STREET.

Bow Street, on the east of Covent Garden, has been associated with the principal police courts of London for several centuries, and gave its name to the Bow Street Runners, the predecessors of Lestrade and Gregson. Fielding lived in Bow Street while writing *Tom Jones;* it contained Will's, known as the "Wits' Coffee House"; and it was at No. 8 Bow Street that Boswell first saw Dr. Johnson. The photograph is from *Baker Street By-ways,* by James Edward Holroyd.

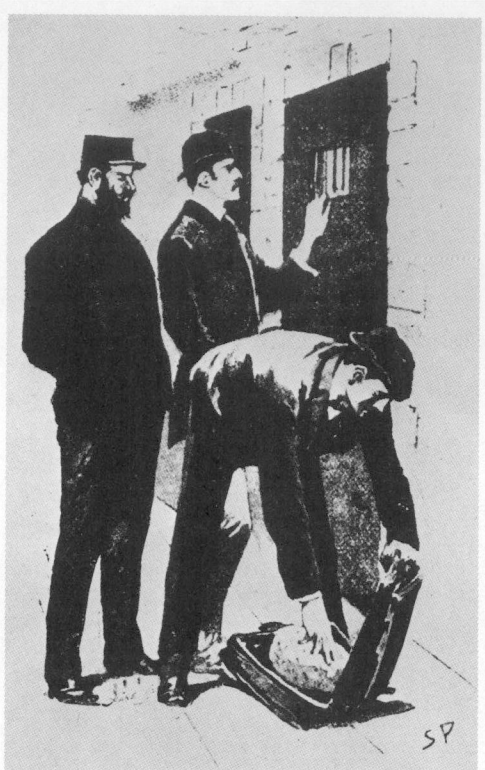

HE OPENED HIS GLADSTONE BAG AS HE SPOKE, AND TOOK
OUT, TO MY ASTONISHMENT, A VERY LARGE BATH SPONGE.

Illustration by Sidney Paget for the *Strand Magazine*, December, 1891.

. . . HE BROKE INTO A SCREAM . . .

Illustration by Sidney Paget for the *Strand Magazine*, December, 1891.

grime which covered his face could not conceal its repulsive ugliness. A broad weal from an old scar ran across it from eye to chin, and by its contraction had turned up one side of the upper lip, so that three teeth were exposed in a perpetual snarl. A shock of very bright red hair grew low over his eyes and forehead.

" He's a beauty, isn't he ? " said the inspector.

" He certainly needs a wash," remarked Holmes. ' I had an idea that he might, and I took the liberty of bringing the tools with me." He opened his Gladstone bag as he spoke, and took out, to my astonishment, a very large bath sponge.

" He ! he ! You are a funny one," chuckled the inspector.

" Now, if you will have the great goodness to open that door very quietly, we will soon make him cut a much more respectable figure."

" Well, I don't know why not," said the inspector. " He doesn't look a credit to the Bow Street cells, does he ? " He slipped his key into the lock, and we all very quietly entered the cell. The sleeper half turned, and then settled down once more into a deep slumber. Holmes stooped to the water jug, moistened his sponge, and then rubbed it twice vigorously across and down the prisoner's face.

" Let me introduce you," he shouted, " to Mr. Neville St. Clair, of Lee, in the county of Kent."

Never in my life have I seen such a sight. The man's face peeled off under the sponge like the bark from a tree. Gone was the coarse brown tint ! Gone, too, the horrid scar which had seamed it across, and the twisted lip which had given the repulsive sneer to the face ! A twitch brought away the tangled red hair, and there, sitting up in his bed, was a pale, sad-faced, refined-looking man, black-haired and smooth-skinned, rubbing his eyes, and staring about him with sleepy bewilderment. Then suddenly realizing the exposure, he broke into a scream, and threw himself down with his face to the pillow.

" Great heaven ! " cried the inspector, " it is, indeed, the missing man. I know him from the photograph."

The prisoner turned with the reckless air of a man who abandons himself to his destiny. " Be it so," said he. " And pray what am I charged with ? "

" With making away with Mr. Neville St.—— Oh, come, you can't be charged with that, unless they make a case of attempted suicide of it," said the inspector, with a grin. " Well, I have been twenty-seven years in the Force, but this really takes the cake."

" If I am Mr. Neville St. Clair, then it is obvious that no crime has been committed, and that, therefore, I am illegally detained."

" No crime, but a very great error has been committed," said Holmes. " You would have done better to have trusted your wife."

" It was not the wife, it was the children," groaned the prisoner. " God help me, I would not have them ashamed of their father. My God ! What an exposure ! What can I do ? "

Sherlock Holmes sat down beside him on the couch, and patted him kindly on the shoulder.

" If you leave it to a court of law to clear the matter up," said he, " of course you can hardly avoid publicity. On the other hand, if you convince the police authorities that there is no possible case against you, I do not know that there is any reason that the details should find their way into the papers. Inspector Bradstreet would, I am sure, make notes upon anything which you might tell us, and submit it to the proper authorities. The case would then never go into court at all."

" God bless you ! " cried the prisoner passionately. " I would have endured imprisonment, aye, even execution, rather than have left my miserable secret as a family blot to my children.

" You are the first who have ever heard my story. My father was a schoolmaster in Chesterfield, where I re- **33** ceived an excellent education. I travelled in my youth, took to the stage, and finally became a reporter on an evening paper in London. One day my editor wished to have a series of articles upon begging in the metropolis, and I volunteered to supply them. There was the point from which all my adventures started. It was only by trying begging as an amateur that I could get the facts upon which to base my articles. When an actor I had, of course, learned all the secrets of making up, and had been famous in the green-room for my skill. I took **34** advantage now of my attainments. I painted my face, and to make myself as pitiable as possible I made a good scar and fixed one side of my lip in a twist by the aid of a small slip of flesh-coloured plaster. Then with a red head of hair, and an appropriate dress, I took my station in the busiest part of the City, ostensibly as a match-seller, **35** but really as a beggar. For seven hours I plied my trade, and when I returned home in the evening I found, to my surprise, that I had received no less than twenty-six shillings and fourpence.   **36**

" I wrote my articles, and thought little more of the matter until, some time later, I backed a bill for a friend, and had a writ served upon me for £25. I was at my **37** wits' end where to get the money, but a sudden idea came to me. I begged a fortnight's grace from the creditor, asked for a holiday from my employers, and spent the time in begging in the City under my disguise. In ten days I had the money, and had paid the debt.

" Well, you can imagine how hard it was to settle down to arduous work at two pounds a week, when I knew that I could earn as much in a day by smearing my face with a little paint, laying my cap on the ground, and sitting still. It was a long fight between my pride and the money, but the dollars won at last, and I threw up reporting, and sat **38** day after day in the corner which I had first chosen, inspiring pity by my ghastly face and filling my pockets with coppers. Only one man knew my secret. He was the keeper of a low den in which I used to lodge in Swandam Lane, where I could every morning emerge as a squalid beggar, and in the evenings transform myself into a well-dressed man about town. This fellow, a Lascar,

33 *Chesterfield.* A manufacturing town in Derbyshire, not far from the Priory School and Holdernesse Hall ("The Adventure of the Priory School").

34 *the green-room.* The common waiting room for performers in a theatre, so called because it was originally decorated in green.

35 *the City.* The business and financial district in the East End of London—the City of London as opposed to the West End, the City of Westminster.

36 *twenty-six shillings and fourpence.* About $6.58.

37 *£25.* $125.

38 *but the dollars won at last.* The late A. Carson Simpson pointed out (*Numismatics in the Canon,* Part I) that "dollar" is British slang for the crown, or 5-shilling piece. We must read "crowns" when a Canonical character whose background is purely British speaks of "dollars" (as James Browner does in "The Cardboard Box": "All was as bright as a new dollar").

". . . YOU CAN IMAGINE HOW HARD IT WAS TO SETTLE DOWN TO ARDUOUS WORK AT TWO POUNDS A WEEK . . ."

This may be a reference to that little-used coin, the two-pound piece (the double-sovereign of George IV is shown below), for Neville St. Clair made this remark at a time when many businesses customarily paid their employees in coin rather than in notes or by cheque; some used the largest denominations available, to simplify the task of the paymasters.

39 *seven hundred pounds a year.* About $3,500.

was well paid by me for his rooms, so that I knew that my secret was safe in his possession.

" Well, very soon I found that I was saving considerable sums of money. I do not mean that any beggar in the **39** streets of London could earn seven hundred pounds a year—which is less than my average takings—but I had exceptional advantages in my power of making up, and also in a facility in repartee, which improved by practice, and made me quite a recognized character in the City. All day a stream of pennies, varied by silver, poured in upon me, and it was a very bad day upon which I failed to take two pounds.

" As I grew richer I grew more ambitious, took a house in the country, and eventually married, without anyone having a suspicion as to my real occupation. My dear wife knew that I had business in the City. She little knew what.

" Last Monday I had finished for the day, and was dressing in my room above the opium den, when I looked out of the window, and saw, to my horror and astonishment, that my wife was standing in the street, with her eyes fixed full upon me. I gave a cry of surprise, threw up my arms to cover my face, and rushing to my confidant, the Lascar, entreated him to prevent anyone from coming up to me. I heard her voice downstairs, but I knew that she could not ascend. Swiftly I threw off my clothes, pulled on those of a beggar, and put on my pigments and wig. Even a wife's eyes could not pierce so complete a disguise. But then it occurred to me that there might be a search in the room and that the clothes might betray me. I threw open the window, re-opening by my violence a small cut which I had inflicted upon myself in the bedroom that morning. Then I seized my coat, which was weighted by the coppers which I had just transferred to it from the leather bag in which I carried my takings. I hurled it out of the window, and it disappeared into the Thames. The other clothes would have followed, but at that moment there was a rush of constables up the stairs, and a few minutes after I found, rather, I confess, to my relief, that instead of being identified as Mr. Neville St. Clair, I was arrested as his murderer.

" I do not know that there is anything else for me to explain. I was determined to preserve my disguise as long as possible, and hence my preference for a dirty face. Knowing that my wife would be terribly anxious, I slipped off my ring, and confided it to the Lascar at a moment when no constable was watching me, together with a hurried scrawl, telling her that she had no cause to fear."

" That note only reached her yesterday," said Holmes.

" Good God ! What a week she must have spent."

" The police have watched this Lascar," said Inspector Bradstreet, " and I can quite understand that he might find it difficult to post a letter unobserved. Probably he handed it to some sailor customer of his, who forgot all about it for some days."

" That was it," said Holmes, nodding approvingly, " I

have no doubt of it.   But have you never been prosecuted for begging ? "

" Many times ; but what was a fine to me ? "

" It must stop here, however," said Bradstreet.   " If the police are to hush this thing up, there must be no more of Hugh Boone."

" I have sworn it by the most solemn oaths which a man can take."

" In that case I think that it is probable that no further steps may be taken.   But if you are found again, then all **40** must come out.   I am sure, Mr. Holmes, that we are very much indebted to you for having cleared the matter up. I wish I knew how you reach your results."

" I reached this one," said my friend, " by sitting upon five pillows and consuming an ounce of shag.   I think, Watson, that if we drive to Baker Street we shall just be in time for breakfast."

40 *no further steps may be taken.* "Imagine . . . a superintendent of police being complaisant enough to overlook a systematic robbery of the public by a fraudulent beggar, and undertaking without demur not to prosecute," Mr. J. B. Mackenzie wrote in "Sherlock Holmes' Plots and Strategy."

A Note on the "Canonicity" of "The Man with the Twisted Lip." "Viewed objectively," Mr. John D. Beirle wrote in "The Curious Incident of the Drive Through Middlesex and Surrey," " 'The Man with the Twisted Lip' gives evidence of hasty and even careless composition by someone not familiar with Dr. Watson's family life. . . . The unfortunate conclusion to which we are forced is that this 'adventure' is not by Dr. John H. Watson, nor is it, actually a recollection of facts. Rather, we must conclude that it is a work of pure fiction . . ."

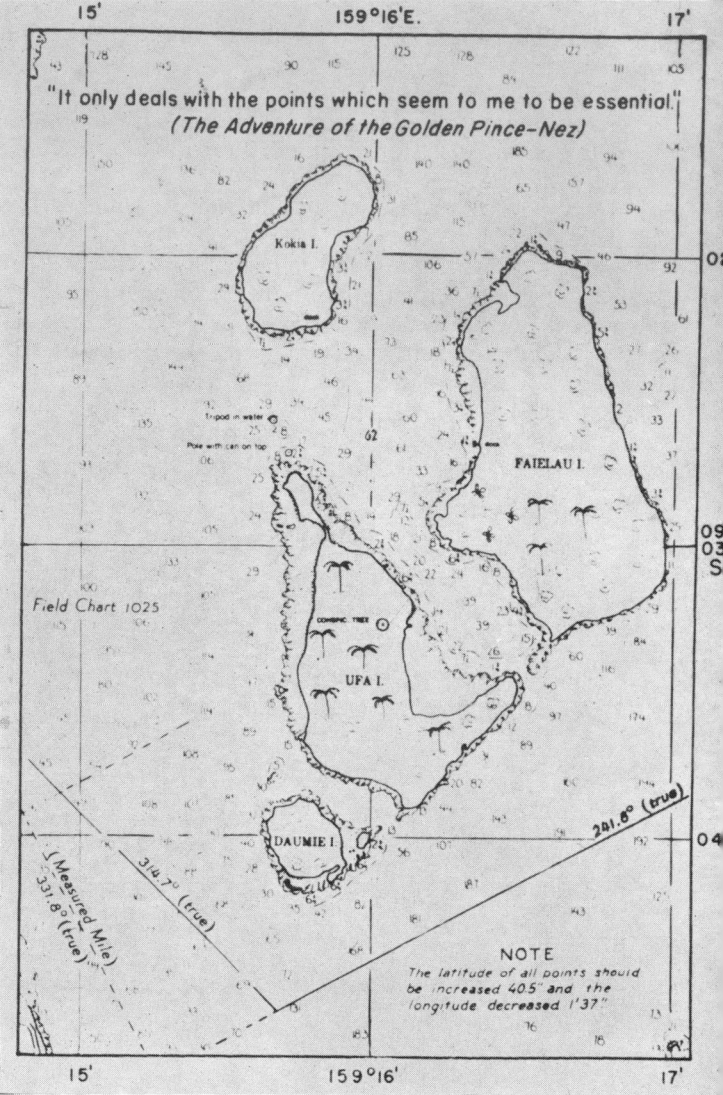

"It only deals with the points which seem to me to be essential."
(The Adventure of the Golden Pince-Nez)

NOTE
The latitude of all points should be increased 40.5' and the longitude decreased 1'37"

. . . THE SINGULAR ADVENTURES OF THE GRICE PATERSONS IN
THE ISLAND OF UFFA . . .

Mr. Page Heldenbrand, in his *Christmas Perennial*, has pointed out that "Paterson" should be read "Patteson"— "For in 1856, 'John Coleridge Patteson, afterwards bishop of Melanesia, had paid his first visit to the islands, and native teachers trained at the Melanesian mission college subsequently established themselves there' (*Encyclopædia Britannica*). So in 1887, then, we might expect to find missionary Grice Patteson carrying on his father's work in the Melanesia area . . ."

The arms of Patteson (*shown above*) are given by Dr. Wolff in his *Practical Handbook of Sherlockian Heraldry* as: Argent, on a fess indented between two mascles pale-wise sable, three fleurs-de-lys or. Crest: a pelican in her piety or, charged on the body with two fleurs-de-lys in fess sable between two roses gules barbed and seeded proper."

Dr. Wolff has also included in his *Sherlockian Atlas* a map of the island of Ufa ("Uffa") as charted by the U.S. Navy (H. O. Field Chart No. 1023, published December, 1943, on board U.S.S. *Pathfinder* under authority of the Secretary of the Navy; reprinted at the Hydrographic Office, February, 1944, showing a portion of the South Pacific Ocean, Solomon Islands, Russell Islands, Eastern Part, Sunlight Channel, and Renard Sound and Approaches)—reproduced above with embellishments by Dr. Wolff.

Mr. John Ball, Jr., in his "Practical Art of Baritsu," supports Dr. Wolff's identification, and suggests that solving the case called for Holmes to visit the South Pacific. It is probable, Mr. Ball thinks, that Holmes acquired his knowledge of baritsu ("The Adventure of the Empty House") at the Kodokan in Japan following this visit in the period April–December, 1887.

Needless to say, other commentators have held different views: Mr. Rolfe Boswell (" 'In Uffish Thought' ") has identified "the island of Uffa" with the great mound on which Norwich Castle stands, built by Uffa, King of the East Angles *circa* 580. The late Christopher Morley carried this idea of an "inland island" a step further by suggesting that any region in East Anglia rising above the fens or meadows is often known as an island, and said that he "would be inclined to think that Market Hill in Woodbridge was the Island of Uffa"; there, in old time, the Saxon serfs built their dwellings around the conspicuous burial ground of their departed chief, King Uffa.

The late Professor Jay Finley Christ, on the other hand, held ("James Boswell and the Island of Uffa") that "Uffa" was a Watsonian combination of Ulva and Staffa, two tiny islands just off the western coast of Scotland. To this, Mrs. Crighton Sellars added: "Please pass along to [Professor Christ] that I am sure there is an island of the name between South Uist and Staffa. It gets its name from the Gaelic word *Uibhir* which is pronounced Ui-ver or Uffa (the Gaelic BH is sounded as a V), a word meaning equivalent or equal quantity; in this instance clearly meaning equally distant from both Uist and Staffa."

Again, Mr. Edmund T. Price ("The Singular Adventures of the Grice Patersons in the Island of Uffa and the Loss of the British Barque *Sophy Anderson*") has suggested that "*Ophir* instead of *Uffa* opens an entirely new horizon for the singular adventures . . ."

THE FIVE ORANGE PIPS

[*Thursday, September 29, to Friday, September 30, 1887*]

WHEN I glance over my notes and records of the Sherlock Holmes cases between the years '82 and '90, I am faced by so many which present **1** strange and interesting features, that it is no easy matter to know which to choose and which to leave. Some, however, have already gained publicity through the papers, and others have not offered a field for those peculiar qualities which my friend possessed in so high a degree, and which it is the object of these papers to illustrate. Some, too, have baffled his analytical skill, and would be, as narratives, beginnings without an ending, while others have been but partially cleared up, and have their explanations founded rather upon conjecture and surmise than on that absolute logical proof which was so dear to him. There is, however, one of these last which was so remarkable in its details and so startling in its results, that I am tempted to give some account of it, in spite of the fact that there are points in connection with it which never have been, and probably never will be, entirely cleared up.

The year '87 furnished us with a long series of cases of **2** greater or less interest, of which I retain the records. Among my headings under this one twelve months, I find an account of the adventure of the Paradol Chamber, **3** of the Amateur Mendicant Society, who held a luxurious club in the lower vault of a furniture warehouse, of the facts connected with the loss of the British barque *Sophy Anderson*, of the singular adventures of the Grice Patersons in the island of Uffa, and finally of the Camberwell poisoning case. In the latter, as may be remembered, **4** Sherlock Holmes was able, by winding up the dead man's watch, to prove that it had been wound up two hours ago, and that therefore the deceased had gone to bed within that time—a deduction which was of the greatest importance in clearing up the case. All these I may sketch out at some future date, but none of them present such singular features as the strange train of circumstances which I have now taken up my pen to describe.

It was in the latter days of September, and the equinoctial gales had set in with exceptional violence. All day

1 *between the years '82 and '90.* Why is '81 omitted? "Clearly because *A Study in Scarlet* was the only case [in the year 1881] of which [Watson] had any record," the late Gavin Brend wrote in *My Dear Holmes.* "After this case it was no longer necessary for him to make a discreet withdrawal to his bedroom when a client arrived to see Holmes, as had been his custom during the first few weeks. . . . But he probably took no further part in the proceedings, and above all, he kept no notes. The idea of a permanent partnership had not yet occurred to either man." Returning to this theme in his essay, "From Maiwand to Marylebone," Mr. Brend wrote: [Holmes and Watson] "were complete strangers when they first appeared in Baker Street. Probably therefore some time would elapse before either of them thought of the possibility of a complete record of all the cases. I [visualize] 1881 as a year in which Watson spent most of his time in writing his account of the one case in which he had been allowed to participate, *A Study in Scarlet.* He would know little, if anything, of any other case which occurred during that year and above all he kept no records. It was only at the beginning of 1882 that systemized records of the cases came into existence."

2 *The year '87.* Although Watson nowhere tells us specifically that "The Five Orange Pips" was one of the cases that took place in the year 1887, the implication is strong that it did; there would otherwise be little reason for Watson to preface his account with an extended listing of some of the important cases of that year. Knox and Morley agree with your editor that the adventure *did* take place in 1887; Andrew, Bell, Brend, Harrison, Hoff, and Roberts have all dated it in 1888; Blakeney, Christ, Folsom, Pattrick, Petersen, Smith, and Zeisler in 1889.

3 *the adventure of the Paradol Chamber.* For a pastiche by Mr. Alan Wilson stemming from this reference of Dr. Watson's, see the *Sherlock Holmes Journal*, Vol. V., No. 2, Spring, 1961, pp. 45–50, and Vol. V, No. 3, Winter, 1961, pp. 78–82.

There is also a playlet by Mr. John Dickson Carr (first published in Vol. II, No. 3 of the *Unicorn News*, reprinted in the February, 1950, issue of *Ellery Queen's Mystery Magazine*); this Holmesian horseplay climaxed the 1948 Annual Dinner of the Mystery Writers of America, with Clayton Rawson as Sherlock Holmes, Lawrence G. Blochman as Dr. Watson, Audrey Roos as Lady Imogene Ferrers, and John Dickson Carr as the Marquis de Paradol.

4 *the Camberwell poisoning case.* For a pastiche stemming from this reference of Dr. Watson's, see "The Adventure of the Gold Hunter," by John Dickson Carr, in *The Exploits of Sherlock Holmes.*

5 *the wind cried and sobbed like a child in the chimney.* "It is high time," Mr. Bliss Austin remarked in "What Son Was Watson?", "that someone investigated this matter of how a child in a chimney sobs."

6 *Clark Russell's fine sea stories.* "Is it only coincidence," Christopher Morley once asked, "that in the [*Strand Magazine*'s] issue of October '91 there was a sea story ('Three in Charge') by Clark Russell; and lo, in the very next number, November '91, we find the good Watson reading Clark Russell by the fire . . . ?"

William Clark Russell, 1844–1911, was hailed by Sir Edwin Arnold as "the prose Homer of the great ocean" and by Algernon Charles Swinburne as "the greatest master of the sea, living or dead." Between 1867 and 1905 he published 65 titles of

the wind had screamed and the rain had beaten against the windows, so that even here in the heart of great, hand-made London we were forced to raise our minds for the instant from the routine of life, and to recognize the presence of those great elemental forces which shriek at mankind through the bars of his civilization, like untamed beasts in a cage. As evening drew in the storm grew louder and louder, and the wind cried and sobbed **5** like a child in the chimney. Sherlock Holmes sat moodily at one side of the fireplace cross-indexing his records of crime, whilst I at the other was deep in one of Clark Russell's **6** fine sea stories, until the howl of the gale from without seemed to blend with the text, and the splash of the rain to lengthen out into the long swash of the sea waves. My wife was on a visit to her aunt's, and for a few days I was a dweller once more in my old quarters at Baker Street.

" Why," said I, glancing up at my companion, " that was surely the bell ? Who could come to-night ? Some friend of yours, perhaps ? "

" Except yourself I have none," he answered. " I do not encourage visitors."

" A client, then ? "

" If so, it is a serious case. Nothing less would bring a man out on such a day, and at such an hour. But I take it that it is more likely to be some crony of the landlady's."

Sherlock Holmes was wrong in his conjecture, however, for there came a step in the passage, and a tapping at the door. He stretched out his long arm to turn the lamp away from himself and towards the vacant chair upon which a new-comer must sit. " Come in ! " said he.

The man who entered was young, some two-and-twenty **7** at the outside, well groomed and trimly clad, with something of refinement and delicacy in his bearing. The streaming umbrella which he held in his hand, and his long shining waterproof told of the fierce weather through which he had come. He looked about him anxiously in the glare of the lamp, and I could see that his face was pale and his eyes heavy, like those of a man who is weighed down with some great anxiety.

" I owe you an apology," he said, raising his golden pince-nez to his eyes. " I trust that I am not intruding. I fear that I have brought some traces of the storm and the rain into your snug chamber."

" Give me your coat and umbrella," said Holmes. " They may rest here on the hook, and will be dry presently. You have come up from the south-west, I see."

8 " Yes, from Horsham."

" That clay and chalk mixture which I see upon your **9** toe-caps is quite distinctive."

" I have come for advice."

" That is easily got."

" And help."

" That is not always so easy."

HE LOOKED ABOUT HIM ANXIOUSLY IN THE GLARE OF
THE LAMP . . .

Illustration by Sidney Paget for the *Strand Magazine*, November, 1891.

Portraits of Celebrities at Different Times of their Lives.

W. CLARK RUSSELL

BORN 1844.

MR. CLARK RUSSELL was born in New York of English parents. His literary taste is a natural gift, his mother being a niece of Charles Lloyd, the poet, and a cousin of Christopher Wordsworth, the late Bishop of Lincoln, and herself known as

From an]   AGE 17.   [Photograph.
As a Midshipman.

descriptions of sea-scenery, and his pictures of real-life sailors, are not likely soon to find a rival. Mr. Clark Russell's latest story, "List, Ye Landsmen," one of his very best is now appearing in *Tit-Bits.*

From an]   AGE 5.   [Oil Painting.

a poetess, and the authoress, among other things, of "The Wife's Dream." Mr. Clark Russell went to sea as a middy before he was fourteen, and during the next eight years picked up the thorough knowledge of seafaring life which he afterwards turned to such good use in his novels. His first book was "John Holdsworth," but it was his second story, "The Wreck of the Grosvenor," which he wrote in little more than two months and sold to a publisher for fifty pounds, which marked a new era in the evolution of the nautical novel. Since that time Mr. Clark Russell has had the sea to himself, and his

From a Photo. by   PRESENT DAY.   [Elliott & Fry.

. . . ONE OF CLARK RUSSELL'S FINE SEA-STORIES . . .

From "Portraits of Celebrities" in the *Strand Magazine,* issue of January, 1893.

fiction, most of them in three volumes, and 15 other titles as well. The book that Dr. Watson was reading, Christopher Morley suggested, was probably *Round the Galley Fire,* published in 1883: "This particular book had a special influence on [Conan Doyle]; so much so that he adapted its title for his own *Round the Red Lamp* some years later. Or I should like to think Watson's reading might have been that little masterpiece 'The Mystery of the Ocean Star'—first published in *Longman's Magazine* before '88 [and] included in a collection of stories imported to New York by Appleton in '88."

But Christopher Morley's brother Dr. Felix Morley thought it more likely that Watson was reading *A Sea Queen,* published by Harper's early in 1883 and containing the passage: ". . . and, above all, as I saw through the window, with masses of sulphur-colored scud sweeping along it, and the voices of the tempest, which shrieked like tortured children at the hall-door and the window-casements, and roared like the discharge of heavy ordnance in the chimneys" ("How the Child Got into the Chimney").

7 *some two-and-twenty at the outside.* Openshaw later says: "I was a youngster of twelve or so. That would be in 1878." The year cannot be later than 1888, and is more probably 1887.

8 *Horsham.* A town in Sussex, and one that Holmes and Watson were to visit in "The Adventure of the Sussex Vampire."

9 *quite distinctive.*" Said the editors of the Catalogue of the Sherlock Holmes Exhibition: "This conversation . . . seems to reveal a hiatus in Holmes' otherwise encyclopaedic knowledge . . . ; or it suggests either that Watson's notes were at fault when he mentions Horsham, or that Openshaw did not tell Holmes the whole truth about his movements. The (geological) map shows that Horsham stands on what are known as the Tunbridge Wells Sands (at the top of the Hastings Beds) and is closely surrounded on three sides by the Weald Clay. Apart from material deposited by builders or from some similar artificial source, it would have been quite impossible for Openshaw to get chalk on his toe-caps in or around Horsham. Sand and clay, perhaps; chalk and clay, no. . . . It will be observed, however, that somewhat to the north—on a line that passes through Dorking—there is a zone in which the traveller would pass rapidly through the Lower Greensand, Gault Clay, Upper Greensand (a very narrow strip) and the Chalk. . . . In this zone even a short walk could provide a mixture of chalk and clay. This condition is not confined to the southwest, but extends along a line to the southeast as far as Folkestone. Holmes' alleged statement that such a mixture implies a district to the southwest is simply not true; it seems more probable that Holmes said 'south,' and that Watson, with Horsham in mind, gratuitously improved on Holmes' statement when writing up his notes. However, the problem remains: how did Openshaw's boots come to bear traces of both clay and chalk? There seem to be three possibilities: 1) For 'Horsham' read, for example, 'Dorking'; Watson having through carelessness or from discretion altered the locale. 2) Openshaw had acquired the chalk on a previous journey and had simply omitted to clean his boots. This does not accord with the statement that he was 'well groomed and trimly clad.' 3) Openshaw broke his journey at Dorking to keep some appointment which he did not disclose to Holmes. Our preference is for solution 1), since Holmes would certainly have detected the deception implicit in 3)."

10 *He was wrongfully accused of cheating at cards.*" Major Prendergast was fortunate that Holmes was able to clear his name, for the Tankerville Club must have borne an evil reputation: a fellow member of the Major's was none other than the notorious Colonel Sebastian Moran ("The Adventure of the Empty House").

11 *three times by men and once by a woman.*" "That woman," the late H. W. Bell wrote in *Sherlock Holmes and Dr. Watson: The Chronology of Their Adventures*, "can only have been Irene Adler . . ." He, and many later commentators, consequently date "The Five Orange Pips" after "A Scandal in Bohemia." But the late Gavin Brend (*My Dear Holmes*) disagreed that the woman was Irene Adler: ". . . is there, in fact, any justification for this view? For a start, Holmes had a sincere respect and admiration for this attractive adventuress and was wont to eulogize her on the slightest provocation. To him she is always 'the woman.' But here we have not 'the woman' but 'a woman.' We should have expected something warmer—more appreciative. It might have been, for instance, 'a woman, but what a woman!' or 'a woman, the peerless Irene Adler!' As it stands it suggests some less exciting lady who defeated Holmes but failed to capture his imagination. As a candidate for this role we would like to advance the claims of Effie Munro of 'The Yellow Face.' This case . . . was one of Holmes' few failures. It was a problem set by a woman which defeated Holmes. Need we look any further?"

12 *Coventry.* A manufacturing town in Warwickshire, from which comes the phrase "sent to Coventry," meaning to ostracize socially. Coventry is also the home of Lady Godiva and Peeping Tom, whose legend, celebrated by Tennyson, was perpetuated until recently by pageants. Here, too, was the location of Cyril Morton's Midland Electric Company ("The Adventure of the Solitary Cyclist").

13 *Jackson's.* Thomas Jonathan Jackson, 1824–1863, next to Lee the Confederacy's greatest gen-

" I have heard of you, Mr. Holmes. I heard from Major Prendergast how you saved him in the Tankerville Club Scandal."

" Ah, of course. He was wrongfully accused of cheat-**10** ing at cards."

" He said that you could solve anything."

" He said too much."

" That you are never beaten."

" I have been beaten four times—three times by men **11** and once by a woman."

" But what is that compared with the number of your successes ? "

" It is true that I have been generally successful."

" Then you may be so with me."

" I beg that you will draw your chair up to the fire, and favour me with some details as to your case."

" It is no ordinary one."

" None of those which come to me are. I am the last court of appeal."

" And yet I question, sir, whether, in all your experience, you have ever listened to a more mysterious and inexplicable chain of events than those which have happened in my own family."

" You fill me with interest," said Holmes. " Pray give us the essential facts from the commencement, and I can afterwards question you as to those details which seem to me to be most important."

The young man pulled his chair up, and pushed his wet feet out towards the blaze.

" My name," said he, " is John Openshaw, but my own affairs have, so far as I can understand it, little to do with this awful business. It is a hereditary matter, so in order to give you an idea of the facts, I must go back to the commencement of the affair.

" You must know that my grandfather had two sons— my uncle Elias and my father Joseph. My father had a **12** small factory at Coventry, which he enlarged at the time of the invention of bicycling. He was the patentee of the Openshaw unbreakable tire, and his business met with such success that he was able to sell it, and to retire upon a handsome competence.

" My uncle Elias emigrated to America when he was a young man, and became a planter in Florida, where he was reported to have done very well. At the time of the war **13-14** he fought in Jackson's army, and afterwards under Hood, **15** where he rose to be a colonel. When Lee laid down his arms my uncle returned to his plantation, where he re-**16** mained for three or four years. About 1869 or 1870 he came back to Europe, and took a small estate in Sussex, near Horsham. He had made a very considerable fortune in the States, and his reason for leaving them was his aversion to the negroes, and his dislike of the Republican policy in extending the franchise to them. He was a singular man, fierce and quick-tempered, very foul-mouthed when he was angry, and of a most retiring disposition. During all the years that he lived at Horsham I doubt if ever he set foot in the town. He had a garden and two or three fields round his house, and there he would take his exercise, though very often for weeks on end he would never leave his room. He drank a great deal of brandy, and smoked very heavily, but he would see no society, and did not want any friends, not even his own brother.

"He didn't mind me, in fact he took a fancy to me, for at the time when he saw me first I was a youngster of twelve or so. That would be in the year 1878, after he had been eight or nine years in England. He begged my father to let me live with him, and he was very kind **17** to me in his way. When he was sober he used to be fond of playing backgammon and draughts with me, and he would make me his representative both with the servants and with the tradespeople, so that by the time that I was sixteen I was quite master of the house. I kept all the keys, and could go where I liked and do what I liked, so long as I did not disturb him in his privacy. There was one singular exception, however, for he had a single room, a lumber-room up among the attics, which was invariably locked, and which he would never permit either me or anyone else to enter. With a boy's curiosity I have peeped through the keyhole, but I was never able to see more than such a collection of old trunks and bundles as would be expected in such a room.

"One day—it was in March, 1883—a letter with a foreign stamp lay upon the table in front of the Colonel's plate. It was not a common thing for him to receive letters, for his bills were all paid in ready money, and he had no friends of any sort. ' From India ! ' said he, as he took it up, ' Pondicherry postmark ! What can this be ? ' Opening it hurriedly, out there jumped five little dried orange pips, which pattered down upon his plate. I began to laugh at this, but the laugh was struck from my lips at the sight of his face. His lip had fallen, his eyes were protruding, his skin the colour of putty, and he glared at the envelope which he still held in his trembling hand. ' K. K. K.,' he shrieked, and then : ' My God, my God, my sins have overtaken me.'

" ' What is it, uncle ? ' I cried.

" ' Death,' said he, and rising from the table he retired to his room, leaving me palpitating with horror. I took up the envelope, and saw scrawled in red ink upon the inner flap, just above the gum, the letter K three times repeated. There was nothing else save the five dried pips. What could be the reason of his overpowering terror ? I left the breakfast-table, and as I ascended the stairs I met him coming down with an old rusty key, which must have belonged to the attic, in one hand, and a small brass box, like a cash box, in the other.

" ' They may do what they like, but I'll checkmate them still,' said he, with an oath. ' Tell Mary that I shall want a fire in my room to-day, and send down to Fordham, the Horsham lawyer.'

"I did as he ordered, and when the lawyer arrived I was asked to step up to the room. The fire was burning brightly, and in the grate there was a mass of black, fluffy ashes, as of burned paper, while the brass box stood open and empty beside it. As I glanced at the box I noticed, with a start, that upon the lid were printed the treble K which I had read in the morning upon the envelope.

eral. At the first battle of Bull Run, he and his brigade won the sobriquet "Stonewall" by their stand. Jackson later won renown in the Shenandoah Valley campaign of 1862, and by his support of Lee in the Seven Days' Battles, by his generalship at the second battle of Bull Run and Fredericksburg. He was mortally wounded at Chancellorsville.

14 *Hood.* John Bell Hood, 1831–1879, Confederate general who commanded in the Atlanta campaign. His forces were virtually annhilated by G. H. Thomas at Nashville, and Hood resigned his command in January, 1865.

15 *Lee.* Robert Edward Lee, 1807–1870, general-in-chief of the Confederate armies in the Civil War; a great commander and a man of exalted character.

16 *where he remained for three or four years."* "One is tempted to identify . . . Openshaw with Captain F. M. Woodward, who commanded a scratch regiment of two Mississippi battalions under Hood at Nashville," Mr. Manly Wade Wellman wrote in "Two Southern Exposures of Sherlock Holmes"; "Woodward means a defended wood, and Openshaw an undefended one— wouldn't Watson handle the name problem just like that? Or Openshaw may be a sound-alike for the artillerist Bouanchaud, or for J. T. Holtzclaw, the infantry brigadier who was as savage as his surname. We cannot say for certain without more material."

17 *He begged my father to let me live with him.* "Elias led a solitary life in Horsham, so the desire for company in the house was understandable; but surely it was an oddly selfish request, calculated as it was to deprive a retired widower of his only child. (There is no mention of a Mrs. Openshaw, so presumably she was dead)," Mr. Benjamin Clark wrote in "The Horsham Fiasco." "Even odder, however, was the apparently ready acquiescence of the father to this arrangement. Joseph was a rich man so, as far as the present was concerned, the boy had nothing to gain materially by the change, which none the less he was perfectly willing to make without, apparently, any regrets. In short, all concerned, according to the record as we have it, saw nothing odd in this leaving of a solitary parent for an uncle who was a heavy drinker and who, from the account, had nothing better to offer his nephew in the way of education than an occasional game of backgammon or draughts (when he was sober), and the responsibilities incident to the running of a house. If—and this is the only probable explanation— Joseph consented to the arrangement to make sure of being Elias' heir, then his action for one already well off reveals a love of mammon that is almost indecent."

18 *and the lawyer took it away with him.* "I am not a lawyer," Mr. W. G. Daish wrote in "Ponderings and Pitfalls," "but I have sometimes wondered how far young Openshaw would have got with the will he witnessed . . . under which he was eventually to be a beneficiary and which, meanwhile, made his own father, his closest relative, the sole legatee."

19 *brought in a verdict of suicide.* ". . . surely an extraordinary verdict, under the circumstances, for who, drunk or sober, would ever attempt to end his life by lying face down in a two-feet-deep puddle?"—Benjamin Clark, "The Horsham Fiasco."

20 *some fourteen thousand pounds.* Some $70,000.

21 *March the 10th, 1883.* Openshaw tells us that his uncle came to England "about 1869 or 1870"— that by 1878 he had been "eight or nine years back"—that by the time he (John Openshaw) "was sixteen" he was "quite the master of the house"—and that it was shortly after this—to be precise, on "March the 10th, 1883" (a Saturday)— that his uncle was sent the pips. All of this is consistent with 1887 as the year of the case.

"WE FOUND HIM, WHEN WE WENT TO SEARCH FOR HIM, FACE DOWNWARDS IN A LITTLE GREEN-SCUMMED POOL . . ."

Illustration by Sidney Paget for the *Strand Magazine*, November, 1891.

" ' I wish you, John,' said my uncle, ' to witness my will. I leave my estate, with all its advantages and all its disadvantages to my brother, your father, whence it will, no doubt, descend to you. If you can enjoy it in peace, well and good ! If you find you cannot, take my advice, my boy, and leave it to your deadliest enemy. I am sorry to give you such a two-edged thing, but I can't say what turn things are going to take. Kindly sign the paper where Mr. Fordham shows you.'

" I signed the paper as directed, and the lawyer took it **18** away with him. The singular incident made, as you may think, the deepest impression upon me, and I pondered over it, and turned it every way in my mind without being able to make anything of it. Yet I could not shake off the vague feeling of dread which it left behind it, though the sensation grew less keen as the weeks passed, and nothing happened to disturb the usual routine of our lives. I could see a change in my uncle, however. He drank more than ever, and he was less inclined for any sort of society. Most of his time he would spend in his room, with the door locked upon the inside, but sometimes he would emerge in a sort of drunken frenzy and would burst out of the house and tear about the garden with a revolver in his hand, screaming out that he was afraid of no man, and that he was not to be cooped up, like a sheep in a pen, by man or devil. When these hot fits were over, however, he would rush tumultuously in at the door, and lock and bar it behind him, like a man who can brazen it out no longer against the terror which lies at the roots of his soul. At such times I have seen his face even on a cold day, glisten with moisture as though it were new raised from a basin.

" Well, to come to an end of the matter, Mr. Holmes, and not to abuse your patience, there came a night when he made one of those drunken sallies from which he never came back. We found him, when we went to search for him, face downwards in a little green-scummed pool, which lay at the foot of the garden. There was no sign of any violence, and the water was but two feet deep, so that the jury, having regard to his known eccentricity, **19** brought in a verdict of suicide. But I, who knew how he winced from the very thought of death, had much ado to persuade myself that he had gone out of his way to meet it. The matter passed, however, and my father entered into possession of the estate, and of some fourteen thou- **20** sand pounds, which lay to his credit at the bank."

" One moment," Holmes interposed. " Your statement is, I foresee, one of the most remarkable to which I have ever listened. Let me have the date of the reception by your uncle of the letter, and the date of his supposed suicide."

21 " The letter arrived on March the 10th, 1883. His death was seven weeks later, upon the night of the 2nd of May."

" Thank you. Pray proceed."

" When my father took over the Horsham property, he, at my request, made a careful examination of the attic, which had been always locked up. We found the brass box there, although its contents had been destroyed.

On the inside of the cover was a paper label, with the initials K. K. K. repeated upon it, and 'Letters, memoranda, receipts and a register' written beneath. These, we presume, indicated the nature of the papers which had been destroyed by Colonel Openshaw. For the rest, there was nothing of much importance in the attic, save a great many scattered papers and notebooks bearing upon my uncle's life in America. Some of them were of the war time, and showed that he had done his duty well, and had borne the repute of being a brave soldier. Others were of a date during the reconstruction of the Southern States, and were mostly concerned with politics, for he had evidently taken a strong part in opposing the carpet-bag politicians who had been sent down from the North. **22**

"Well, it was the beginning of '84, when my father came to live at Horsham, and all went as well as possible with us until the January of '85. On the fourth day after **23** the New Year I heard my father give a sharp cry of surprise as we sat together at the breakfast-table. There he was, sitting with a newly opened envelope in one hand and five dried orange pips in the outstretched palm of the other one. He had always laughed at what he called my cock-and-bull story about the Colonel, but he looked very puzzled and scared now that the same thing had come upon himself.

"'Why, what on earth does this mean, John?' he stammered.

"My heart had turned to lead. 'It is K. K. K.,' said I.

"He looked inside the envelope. 'So it is,' he cried. 'Here are the very letters. But what is this written above them?'

"'Put the papers on the sundial,' I read, peeping over his shoulder.

"'What papers? What sundial?' he asked.

"'The sundial in the garden. There is no other,' said I; 'but the papers must be those that are destroyed.'

"'Pooh!' said he, gripping hard at his courage. 'We are in a civilized land here, and we can't have tomfoolery of this kind. Where does the thing come from?'

"'From Dundee,' I answered, glancing at the postmark.

"'Some preposterous practical joke,' said he. 'What have I to do with sundials and papers? I shall take no notice of such nonsense.'

"'I should certainly speak to the police,' I said.

"'And be laughed at for my pains. Nothing of the sort.'

"'Then let me do so.'

"'No, I forbid you. I won't have a fuss made over such nonsense.'

"It was in vain to argue with him, for he was a very obstinate man. I went about, however, with a heart which was full of forebodings.

"On the third day after the coming of the letter my father went from home to visit an old friend of his, Major Freebody, who is in command of one of the forts upon Portsdown Hill. I was glad that he should go, for it seemed to me that he was farther from danger when he was away from home. In that, however, I was in error.

22 *the carpet-bag politicians.* Northern politicians who settled in the Southern states after the Civil War, so called from reckless speculating bankers of the West who often decamped with funds entrusted to them stowed in traveling bags made of carpeting.

23 *the January of '85.* ". . . it was almost two years later before the next Georgian expedition got under way. Surely a delay of that duration is all the more remarkable when one considers that while Colonel Openshaw was in possession of the papers he could not make public their contents without implicating himself, whereas his brother, if the records had still been in existence, ran no risk, and in fact might even, without being aware of their significance, have turned them over to the police, who in turn would have given them to the American authorities."—Benjamin Clark, "The Horsham Fiasco."

"'WHY, WHAT ON EARTH DOES THIS MEAN, JOHN?'"
HE STAMMERED.

Illustration by Sidney Paget for the *Strand Magazine*, November, 1891.

24 *Fareham.* Portsdown Hill is southwest of Fareham, a town in Hampshire northeast of Portsmouth and Southsea.

25 *two years and eight months have elapsed since then.* This statement would seem to prove conclusively that Openshaw visited Holmes in September, 1887.

26 *yesterday morning.* Since Openshaw's letter had been delivered "yesterday morning," the opening day of the case cannot have been a Monday.

27 *This is no time for despair.*" "Horace said it more tersely, 'Nil desperandum,' in *Odes*, Book I, 7," Morris Rosenblum wrote in "The Horatian Spirit in Holmes."

. . . HE SHOOK OUT . . . FIVE LITTLE DRIED ORANGE PIPS.

Illustration by Sidney Paget for the *Strand Magazine*, November, 1891.

Upon the second day of his absence I received a telegram from the Major, imploring me to come at once. My father had fallen over one of the deep chalk-pits which abound in the neighbourhood, and was lying senseless, with a shattered skull. I hurried to him, but he passed away without having ever recovered his consciousness.

24 He had, as it appears, been returning from Fareham in the twilight, and as the country was unknown to him, and the chalk-pit unfenced, the jury had no hesitation in bringing in a verdict of ' Death from accidental causes.' Carefully as I examined every fact connected with his death, I was unable to find anything which could suggest the idea of murder. There were no signs of violence, no footmarks, no robbery, no record of strangers having been seen upon the roads. And yet I need not tell you that my mind was far from at ease, and that I was wellnigh certain that some foul plot had been woven round him.

" In this sinister way I came into my inheritance. You will ask me why I did not dispose of it ? I answer because I was well convinced that our troubles were in some way dependent upon an incident in my uncle's life, and that the danger would be as pressing in one house as in another.

" It was in January, '85, that my poor father met his end, and two years and eight months have elapsed since

25 then. During that time I have lived happily at Horsham, and I had begun to hope that this curse had passed away from the family, and that it had ended with the last generation. I had begun to take comfort too soon, however ;

26 yesterday morning the blow fell in the very shape in which it had come upon my father."

The young man took from his waistcoat a crumpled envelope, and, turning to the table, he shook out upon it five little dried orange pips.

" This is the envelope," he continued. " The postmark is London—eastern division. Within are the very words which were upon my father's last message. ' K. K. K.' ; and then ' Put the papers on the sundial.' "

" What have you done ? " asked Holmes.

" Nothing."

" Nothing ? "

" To tell the truth "—he sank his face into his thin, white hands—" I have felt helpless. I have felt like one of those poor rabbits when the snake is writhing towards it. I seem to be in the grasp of some resistless, inexorable evil, which no foresight and no precautions can guard against."

" Tut ! Tut ! " cried Sherlock Holmes. " You must act, man, or you are lost. Nothing but energy can save

27 you. This is no time for despair."

" I have seen the police."

" Ah ? "

" But they listened to my story with a smile. I am

28 convinced that the inspector has formed the opinion that the letters are all practical jokes, and that the deaths of my relations were really accidents, as the jury stated, and were not to be connected with the warnings."

Holmes shook his clenched hands in the air. " Incredible imbecility ! ' he cried.

" They have, however, allowed me a policeman, who

may remain in the house with me."

" Has he come with you to-night ? "

" No. His orders were to stay in the house."

Again Holmes raved in the air.

" Why did you come to me ? " he said ; " and, above all, why did you not come at once ? "

" I did not know. It was only to-day that I spoke to Major Prendergast about my trouble, and was advised by him to come to you."

" It is really two days since you had the letter. We should have acted before this. You have no further evidence, I suppose, than that which you have placed before us—no suggestive detail which might help us."

" There is one thing," said John Openshaw. He rummaged in his coat pocket, and drawing out a piece of discoloured, blue-tinted paper, he laid it out upon the table. " I have some remembrance," said he, " that on the day when my uncle burned the papers I observed that the small, unburned margins which lay amid the ashes were of this particular colour. I found this single sheet upon the floor of his room, and I am inclined to think that it may be one of the papers which had, perhaps, fluttered out from among the others, and in that way have escaped destruction. Beyond the mention of pips, I do not see that it helps us much. I think myself that it is a page from some private diary. The writing is undoubtedly my uncle's."

Holmes moved the lamp, and we both bent over the sheet of paper, which showed by its ragged edge that it had indeed been torn from a book. It was headed " March, 1869," and beneath were the following enigmatical notices :

" 4th. Hudson came. Same old platform.

" 7th. Set the pips on McCauley, Paramore, and Swain of St. Augustine.

" 9th. McCauley cleared.

" 10th. John Swain cleared.

" 12th. Visited Paramore. All well."

" Thank you ! " said Holmes, folding up the paper and returning it to our visitor. " And now you must on no account lose another instant. We cannot spare time even to discuss what you have told me. You must get home instantly, and act."

" What shall I do ? "

" There is but one thing to do. It must be done at once. You must put this piece of paper which you have shown us into the brass box which you have described. You must also put in a note to say that all the other papers were burned by your uncle, and that this is the only one which remains. You must assert that in such words as will carry conviction with them. Having done this, you must at once put the box out upon the sundial, as directed. Do you understand ? "

" Entirely."

" Do not think of revenge, or anything of the sort, at present. I think that we may gain that by means of the law ; but we have our web to weave, while theirs is already woven. The first consideration is to remove the pressing danger which threatens you. The second

28 *the inspector.* "Incredible as this seems," Miss N. Currier Dorian wrote in " 'A Bad Lot,' " "the figures show that of the eight cases (*A Study in Scarlet, The Sign of the Four*, 'The Adventure of the Noble Bachelor,' 'The Boscombe Valley Mystery,' 'The Five Orange Pips,' 'The Adventure of the Empty House,' 'The Adventure of the Norwood Builder,' 'The Adventure of the Three Gables') in which Holmes collided with the authorities or criticized them severely, five are cases in which Lestrade represented the professionals (one—the *Study*—in company with Gregson), and one is Athelney Jones (*The Sign of the Four*); the other two are exceptions. 'The Five Orange Pips,' the first of these exceptions, does not name any officer in charge: in the face of the figures given, it is surely a reasonable guess that the man who brought down Holmes' charge of 'imbecility' was Lestrade. . . . The prevalent idea that Holmes had no use for Scotland Yard or any of the professional forces is not in keeping with the facts."

SHERLOCK HOLMES SAT FOR SOME TIME IN SILENCE WITH HIS HEAD SUNK FORWARD, AND HIS EYES BENT UPON THE RED GLOW OF THE FIRE.

Illustration by Sidney Paget for the *Strand Magazine*, November, 1891.

29 "*Save, perhaps, the Sign of the Four.*" See our remarks on this gratuitous insert of Watson's in our chapter, "Now, Watson, the Fair Sex Is Your Department."

30 *Cuvier*. Georges Léopold Chrétian Frédéric Dagobert, Baron Cuvier, 1769–1832, French naturalist, statesman, philosopher, founder of the science of comparative anatomy.

is to clear up the mystery, and to punish the guilty parties."

"I thank you," said the young man, rising, and pulling on his overcoat. "You have given me fresh life and hope. I shall certainly do as you advise."

"Do not lose an instant. And, above all, take care of yourself in the meanwhile, for I do not think that there can be a doubt that you are threatened by a very real and imminent danger. How do you go back?"

"By train from Waterloo."

"It is not yet nine. The streets will be crowded, so I trust that you may be in safety. And yet you cannot guard yourself too closely."

"I am armed."

"That is well. To-morrow I shall set to work upon your case."

"I shall see you at Horsham, then?"

"No, your secret lies in London. It is there that I shall seek it."

"Then I shall call upon you in a day, or in two days, with news as to the box and the papers. I shall take your advice in every particular." He shook hands with us, and took his leave. Outside the wind still screamed, and the rain splashed and pattered against the windows. This strange, wild story seemed to have come to us from amid the mad elements—blown in upon us like a sheet of seaweed in a gale—and now to have been reabsorbed by them once more.

Sherlock Holmes sat for some time in silence with his head sunk forward, and his eyes bent upon the red glow of the fire. Then he lit his pipe, and leaning back in his chair he watched the blue smoke rings as they chased each other up to the ceiling.

"I think, Watson," he remarked at last, "that of all our cases we have had none more fantastic than this."

29 "Save, perhaps, the Sign of Four."

"Well, yes. Save, perhaps, that. And yet this John Openshaw seems to me to be walking amid even greater perils than did the Sholtos."

"But have you," I asked, "formed any definite conception as to what these perils are?"

"There can be no question as to their nature," he answered.

"Then what are they? Who is this K. K. K., and why does he pursue this unhappy family?"

Sherlock Holmes closed his eyes, and placed his elbows upon the arms of his chair, with his finger-tips together. "The ideal reasoner," he remarked, "would, when he has once been shown a single fact in all its bearings, deduce from it not only all the chain of events which led up to it, but also all the results which would follow from it. As **30** Cuvier could correctly describe a whole animal by the contemplation of a single bone, so the observer who has thoroughly understood one link in a series of incidents, should be able accurately to state all the other ones, both before and after. We have not yet grasped the results which the reason alone can attain to. Problems may be solved in the study which have baffled all those who have sought a solution by the aid of their senses. To carry the art, however, to its highest pitch, it is necessary that the reasoner should be able to utilize all the facts which have come to his knowledge, and this in itself implies, as you will readily see, a possession of all knowledge, which, even in these days of free education and encyclopædias, is a somewhat rare accomplishment. It is not so impossible, however, that a man should possess all knowledge which is likely to be useful to him in his work, and this I have endeavoured in my case to do. If I remember rightly, you on one occasion, in the early days of our friendship, defined my limits in a very precise fashion."

"Yes," I answered, laughing. "It was a singular document. Philosophy, astronomy, and politics were marked at zero, I remember. Botany variable, geology profound as regards the mudstains from any region within fifty miles of town, chemistry eccentric, anatomy unsystematic, sensational literature and crime records unique, violin player, boxer, swordsman, lawyer, and self-poisoner by cocaine and tobacco. Those, I think, were the main points of my analysis."

Holmes grinned at the last item. "Well," he said, "I **31** say now, as I said then, that a man should keep his little brain attic stocked with all the furniture that he is likely to use, and the rest he can put away in the lumber-room of his library, where he can get it if he wants it. Now, for such a case as the one which has been submitted to us to-night, we need certainly to muster all our resources. Kindly hand me down the letter K of the American Encyclopædia which stands upon the shelf beside you. Thank **32** you. Now let us consider the situation, and see what may be deduced from it. In the first place, we may start with a strong presumption that Colonel Openshaw had some very strong reason for leaving America. Men at his time of life do not change all their habits, and exchange willingly the charming climate of Florida for the lonely life of an English provincial town. His extreme love of solitude in England suggests the idea that he was in fear of someone or something, so we may assume as a working hypothesis that it was fear of someone or something which drove him from America. As to what it was he feared, we can only deduce that by considering the formidable letters which were received by himself and his successors. Did you remark the postmarks of those letters?"

"The first was from Pondicherry, the second from Dundee, and the third from London."

"From East London. What do you deduce from that?"

"They are all seaports. That the writer was on board a ship."

"Excellent. We have already a clue. There can be no doubt that the probability—the strong probability—is that the writer was on board of a ship. And now let us consider another point. In the case of Pondicherry seven weeks elapsed between the threat and its fulfilment, in Dundee it was only some three or four days. Does that suggest anything?"

"A greater distance to travel."

"But the letter had also a greater distance to come."

"Then I do not see the point."

31 *Holmes grinned.* And small wonder. Watson in 1881 had made no reference to Holmes as a "self-poisoner by cocaine and tobacco," and he had called the detective's knowledge of chemistry "profound."

32 *the American Encyclopædia.* Miss Madeleine B. Stern suggests ("Sherlock Holmes: Rare Book Collector") that "the *International Encyclopædia* (New York, 1885), which contains an article on the Klan . . . was possibly the work in question."

33 *obviously of vital importance.* "Just how one or even three men were able to subdue the pistol-packing, drink-crazed [Elias] Openshaw and place him face down in a pool without leaving a sign of their presence will forever remain a mystery. . . . The murderer or murderers then returned to London *but without making any attempt to regain those records* we are told were the *sine qua non* of peaceful repose for some of the South's first men. . . . The circumstances attending the death of John's father verge even closer to the incredible. First by train to Horsham. . . . Then to Portsdown Hill. . . . And yet, after Joseph's death, nobody appeared in any of these places to testify to being questioned recently by a Southern-accented American. Once again there is no attempt to get the records, so presumably there is no end to insomnia in Dixieland."—Benjamin Clark, "The Horsham Fiasco."

" There is at least a presumption that the vessel in which the man or men are is a sailing ship. It looks as if they always sent their singular warning or token before them when starting upon their mission. You see how quickly the deed followed the sign when it came from Dundee. If they had come from Pondicherry in a steamer they would have arrived almost as soon as their letter. But as a matter of fact seven weeks elapsed. I think that those seven weeks represented the difference between the mail boat which brought the letter, and the sailing vessel which brought the writer."

" It is possible."

" More than that. It is probable. And now you see the deadly urgency of this new case, and why I urged young Openshaw to caution. The blow has always fallen at the end of the time which it would take the senders to travel the distance. But this one comes from London, and therefore we cannot count upon delay."

" Good God ! " I cried. " What can it mean, this relentless persecution ? "

33 " The papers which Openshaw carried are obviously of vital importance to the person or persons in the sailing ship. I think that it is quite clear that there must be more than one of them. A single man could not have carried out two deaths in such a way as to deceive a coroner's jury. There must have been several in it, and they must have been men of resource and determination. Their papers they mean to have, be the holder of them who it may. In this way you see K. K. K. ceases to be the initials of an individual, and becomes the badge of a society."

" But of what society ? "

" Have you never—" said Sherlock Holmes, bending forward and sinking his voice—" have you never heard of the Ku Klux Klan ? "

" I never have."

Holmes turned over the leaves of the book upon his knee. " Here it is," said he presently, " ' Ku Klux Klan. A name derived from a fanciful resemblance to the sound produced by cocking a rifle. This terrible secret society was formed by some ex-Confederate soldiers in the Southern States after the Civil War, and it rapidly formed local branches in different parts of the country, notably in Tennessee, Louisiana, the Carolinas, Georgia, and Florida. Its power was used for political purposes, principally for the terrorizing of the negro voters, and the murdering or driving from the country of those who were opposed to its views. Its outrages were usually preceded by a warning sent to the marked man in some fantastic but generally recognized shape—a sprig of oak leaves in some parts, melon seeds or orange pips in others. On receiving this the victim might either openly abjure his former ways, or might fly from the country. If he braved the matter out, death would unfailingly come upon him, and usually in some strange and unforeseen manner. So perfect was the organization of the society, and so systematic its methods, that there is hardly a case upon record where any man succeeded in braving it with impunity, or in which any of its outrages were traced home to the perpetrators. For some years the organization flourished, in spite of the efforts of the United States Government, and of the better classes of the community in the South. Eventually, in the year 1869, the movement rather suddenly collapsed, although there have been sporadic outbreaks of the same sort since that date.' **34**

"You will observe," said Holmes, laying down the volume, " that the sudden breaking up of the society was coincident with the disappearance of Openshaw from America with their papers. It may well have been cause and effect. It is no wonder that he and his family have some of the more implacable spirits upon their track. You can understand that this register and diary may implicate some of the first men in the South, and that there may be many who will not sleep easy at night until it is recovered."

"Then the page which we have seen——"

"Is such as we might expect. It ran, if I remember right, ' sent the pips to A, B, and C '—that is, sent the society's warning to them. Then there are successive entries that A and B cleared, or left the country, and finally that C was visited, with, I fear, a sinister result for C. Well, I think, Doctor, that we may let some light into this dark place, and I believe that the only chance young Openshaw has in the meantime is to do what I have told him. There is nothing more to be said or to be done to-night, so hand me over my violin and let us try to forget for half an hour the miserable weather, and the still more miserable ways of our fellow-men."

It had cleared in the morning, and the sun was shining with a subdued brightness through the dim veil which hangs over the great city. Sherlock Holmes was already at breakfast when I came down.

"You will excuse me for not waiting for you," said he ; " I have, I foresee, a very busy day before me in looking into this case of young Openshaw's."

"What steps will you take ? " I asked.

"It will very much depend upon the results of my first inquiries. I may have to go down to Horsham after all."

"You will not go there first ? "

"No, I shall commence with the City. Just ring the bell, and the maid will bring up your coffee."

As I waited, I lifted the unopened newspaper from the table and glanced my eye over it. It rested upon a heading which sent a chill to my heart. **35**

"Holmes," I cried, " you are too late."

"Ah ! " said he, laying down his cup, " I feared as much. How was it done ? " He spoke calmly, but I could see that he was deeply moved.

" My eye caught the name of Openshaw, and the heading ' Tragedy near Waterloo Bridge.' Here is the account : ' Between nine and ten last night Police-constable Cook, of the H Division, on duty near Waterloo Bridge, heard a cry for help and a splash in the water. The night, however, was extremely dark and stormy, so that, in spite of the help of several passers-by, it was quite impossible to effect a rescue. The alarm, however, was given, and, by the aid of the water police, the body was

34 *since that date*. Mr. Manly Wade Wellman has noted ("Two Southern Exposures of Sherlock Holmes") that the original Ku Klux Klan was "broken up and disbanded" by its Grand Wizard, Bedford Forrest, by the end of 1868. But the more disreputable element kept its masks, and even as in more recent years, pirated the K.K.K. label for the perpetration of outrages. Still, preservation of Klan secrets was hardly a matter for killing men in far countries: John C. Lister, one of the Klan's original six founders, published a revealing history of the order in 1884, and he was neither ambushed nor threatened nor even blamed by his former fellows.

35 *I lifted the unopened newspaper from the table*. Showing that the second day could not have been a Sunday.

"HOLMES," I CRIED, "YOU ARE TOO LATE."

Illustration by Sidney Paget for the *Strand Magazine*, November, 1891.

36 *I should send him away to his death——!"* "John Openshaw has the melancholy distinction of being one of the only two clients to be murdered after they had consulted Holmes, the other unfortunate being Hilton Cubitt of 'The Adventure of the Dancing Men,'" the late Gavin Brend wrote in *My Dear Holmes*.

37 *The Embankment*. This thoroughfare, extending from Blackfriars to Westminster Bridge, is one mile and a third in length and one hundred feet wide. It was formerly opened on July 13, 1870, by King Edward VII, then Prince of Wales, accompanied by Princess Louise. The first idea of embanking the Thames originated with Sir Christopher Wren upon the occasion of the rebuilding of London after the Great Fire of 1666.

38 *All day*. On the opening day of the case "the wind had screamed and the rain had beaten against the windows," according to Watson. The newspaper report of Openshaw's death called the night "extremely dark and stormy." The second day had "cleared in the morning and the sun was shining with a subdued brightness," again according to Watson. In the latter days of September, 1887, there are two days and two days only that answer this description: *Thursday the 29th and Friday the 30th*. In its Thursday morning report, the London *Times* noted rain falling "over the greater part of the British Islands . . . and the fall continues in many places. Thunderstorms have been prevalent." In its Thursday evening report, the *Times* noted "rain falling in London . . ." Said the *Times* in its report for the Friday morning: "Showers of rain have fallen very generally, and thunder and lightning have occurred in most places. The weather has since improved in many places." And in its evening report for the same day: "The weather is, on the whole, fair. . . . Thunder and lightning were again prevalent over our islands on Thursday night."

39 *Of these he took five*. The late Gavin Brend once wrote:

It takes me some time to get to grips
With this sinister business of orange pips.
So, kind Mr. Greengrocer, will you please wait
Whilst I get out a pencil and calculate?
There's five for McCauley and five for John Swain,
Five for Paramore, five again
For Uncle Elias and five for Dad
With five for young John though this makes me feel sad.
Then in case you should think I have ended too soon
Five more are required for Captain Calhoun.
So thirty-five pips, Mr. Greengrocer, please.
How many oranges needed for these?
Yes, I think at last I am coming to grips
With the mathematics of orange pips.

eventually recovered. It proved to be that of a young gentleman whose name, as it appears from an envelope which was found in his pocket, was John Openshaw, and whose residence is near Horsham. It is conjectured that he may have been hurrying down to catch the last train from Waterloo Station, and that in his haste and the extreme darkness, he missed his path, and walked over the edge of one of the small landing-places for river steamboats. The body exhibited no traces of violence, and there can be no doubt that the deceased had been the victim of an unfortunate accident, which should have the effect of calling the attention of the authorities to the condition of the riverside landing-stages.'"

We sat in silence for some minutes, Holmes more depressed and shaken than I had ever seen him.

" That hurts my pride, Watson," he said at last. " It is a petty feeling, no doubt, but it hurts my pride. It becomes a personal matter with me now, and, if God sends me health, I shall set my hand upon this gang. That he should come to me for help, and that I should send him **36** away to his death—— ! " He sprang from his chair, and paced about the room in uncontrollable agitation, with a flush upon his sallow cheeks, and a nervous clasping and unclasping of his long, thin hands.

" They must be cunning devils," he exclaimed at last. " How could they have decoyed him down there ? The **37** Embankment is not on the direct line to the station. The bridge, no doubt, was too crowded, even on such a night, for their purpose. Well, Watson, we shall see who will win in the long run. I am going out now ! "

" To the police ? "

" No ; I shall be my own police. When I have spun the web they may take the flies, but not before."

38 All day I was engaged in my professional work, and it was late in the evening before I returned to Baker Street. Sherlock Holmes had not come back yet. It was nearly ten o'clock before he entered, looking pale and worn. He walked up to the sideboard, and, tearing a piece from the loaf, he devoured it voraciously, washing it down with a long draught of water.

" You are hungry," I remarked.

" Starving. It had escaped my memory. I have had nothing since breakfast."

" Nothing ? "

" Not a bite. I had no time to think of it."

" And how have you succeeded ? "

" Well."

" You have a clue ? "

" I have them in the hollow of my hand. Young Openshaw shall not remain long unavenged. Why, Watson, let us put their own devilish trade-mark upon them. It is well thought of ! "

" What do you mean ? "

He took an orange from the cupboard, and tearing it to pieces, he squeezed out the pips upon the table. Of **39** these he took five, and thrust them into an envelope. On the inside of the flap he wrote, " S.H. for J.C." Then **40** he sealed it and addressed it to " Captain James Calhoun, Barque *Lone Star*, Savannah, Georgia."

" That will await him when he enters port," said he, chuckling. " It may give him a sleepless night. He will find it as sure a precursor of his fate as Openshaw did before him."

" And who is this Captain Calhoun ? "

" The leader of the gang. I shall have the others, but he first."

" How did you trace it, then ? "

He took a large sheet of paper from his pocket, all covered with dates and names.

" I have spent the whole day," said he, " over Lloyd's registers and the files of old papers, following the future **41** career of every vessel which touched at Pondicherry in January and in February in '83. There were thirty-six ships of fair tonnage which were reported there during those months. Of these, the *Lone Star* instantly attracted my attention, since, although it was reported as having cleared from London, the name is that which is given to one of the States of the Union."

" Texas, I think."

" I was not and am not sure which ; but I knew that the ship must have an American origin." **42**

" What then ? "

" I searched the Dundee records, and when I found that the barque *Lone Star* was there in January, '85, my suspicion became a certainty. I then inquired as to vessels which lay at present in the port of London."

" Yes ? "

" The *Lone Star* had arrived here last week. I went down to the Albert dock, and found that she had been **43** taken down the river by the early tide this morning, homeward bound to Savannah. I wired to Gravesend, and learned that she had passed some time ago, and as the wind is easterly, I have no doubt that she is now past the Goodwins, and not very far from the Isle of Wight." **44-45**

" What will you do, then ? "

" Oh, I have my hand upon him. He and the two mates are, as I learn, the only native-born Americans in the ship. The others are Finns and Germans. I also know that they were all three away from the ship last night. I had it from the stevedore, who has been loading their cargo. By the time their sailing ship reaches Savannah the mail boat will have carried this letter, and the cable will have informed the police of Savannah that these three gentlemen are badly wanted here upon a charge of murder."

There is ever a flaw, however, in the best laid of human plans, and the murderers of John Openshaw were never to receive the orange pips which would show them that another, as cunning and as resolute as themselves, was upon their track. Very long and severe were the equinoctial gales that year. We waited long for news of the *Lone Star* of Savannah, but none ever reached us. We did at last hear that somewhere far out in the Atlantic a shattered sternpost of a boat was seen swinging in the trough of a wave, with the letters " L. S." carved upon it, **46** and that is all which we shall ever know of the fate of the *Lone Star*.

40 "*Captain James Calhoun.* "All three murders . . . carry Moriarty's signature," Mr. James Buchholtz wrote in "A Tremor at the Edge of the Web." "Here are three homicides dismissed by the authorities as suicide or accident. . . . [Holmes' reference to the gang he would set his hand upon] is clearly to the gang he *did* eliminate within the next few years. . . . With Holmes in such a mood, there can be little doubt as to who the true recipient of orange pips which he sent was. . . . It is here that the death struggle above the Reichenbach Falls begins."

That Moriarty was behind the affair of the Pips is also the view of Mr. Benjamin Clark ("The Horsham Fiasco"): "If the smokescreen of Klan persecution were eliminated, attention would logically be turned to the question of who, after John's death, inherited Elias' considerable fortune and Joseph's handsome competence. We have at least *prima facie* evidence suggesting that the love of money ran strong in the Openshaws. . . . Also consider the propensity to violence apparent in the Colonel. Is the assumption improbable that these strains were to be found commingled in less diluted form in the blood of a relative whose name was never made known to us. Could that unknown, an individual of genius-like cleverness and fiendish greed, have engineered the whole scheme. By any chance could he have been—'Dear me, Mr. Holmes, dear me!' "

41 *Lloyd's registers.* Holmes refers to Lloyd's Register of Shipping, not to be confused with Lloyd's Bank or "Lloyd's of London."

42 *an American origin.*" It did, indeed. The barque *Lone Star*, a real ship, was "found in the Georgia register (owner—Johanssen Brothers of Savannah)," by Mr. Richard W. Clarke ("On the Nomenclature of Watson's Ships").

43 *the Albert dock.* See *The Sign of the Four*, Note 162.

44 *the Goodwins.* Dangerous shoals, about ten miles long, in the Straits of Dover, about five miles off the eastern coast of Kent.

45 *the Isle of Wight.*" An island off Hampshire, 23 by 13 miles; it has cement manufactures, is a summer resort, yachting center, and favorite place of residence.

46 *with the letters "L. S." carved upon it.* "A ship's stern-post ordinarily bears the craft's name, not her initials," Mr. Rolfe Boswell noted in "A Connecticut Yankee in Support of Sir Arthur."

Auctorial Note: Conan Doyle placed "The Five Orange Pips" seventh on his list of the "twelve best" Sherlock Holmes short stories, excluding those in the *Case-Book*.

27

A CASE OF IDENTITY

[Tuesday, October 18, to Wednesday, October 19, 1887]

1 *throughout three continents.* The two continents other than Europe in which Holmes was unofficial adviser and helper to everybody absolutely puzzled is an interesting subject for speculation.

2 *I picked up the morning paper.* The day was therefore not a Sunday.

"MY dear fellow, said Sherlock Holmes, as we sat on either side of the fire in his lodgings at Baker Street, " life is infinitely stranger than anything which the mind of man could invent. We would not dare to conceive the things which are really mere commonplaces of existence. If we could fly out of that window hand in hand, hover over this great city, gently remove the roofs, and peep in at the queer things which are going on, the strange coincidences, the plannings, the cross-purposes, the wonderful chains of events, working through generations, and leading to the most *outré* results, it would make all fiction with its conventionalities and foreseen conclusions most stale and unprofitable."

"And yet I am not convinced of it," I answered. " The cases which come to light in the papers are, as a rule, bald enough, and vulgar enough. We have in our police reports realism pushed to its extreme limits, and yet the result is, it must be confessed, neither fascinating nor artistic."

"A certain selection and discretion must be used in producing a realistic effect," remarked Holmes. " This is wanting in the police report, where more stress is laid perhaps upon the platitudes of the magistrate than upon the details, which to an observer contain the vital essence of the whole matter. Depend upon it there is nothing so unnatural as the commonplace."

I smiled and shook my head. " I can quite understand you thinking so," I said. " Of course, in your position of unofficial adviser and helper to everybody who is abso-

1 lutely puzzled, throughout three continents, you are brought in contact with all that is strange and bizarre.

2 But here "—I picked up the morning paper from the ground—" let us put it to a practical test. Here is the first heading upon which I come. ' A husband's cruelty to his wife.' There is half a column of print, but I know without reading it that it is all perfectly familiar to me. There is, of course, the other woman, the drink, the push, the blow, the bruise, the sympathetic sister or landlady. The crudest of writers could invent nothing more crude."

" Indeed, your example is an unfortunate one for your argument," said Holmes, taking the paper, and glancing his eye down it. " This is the Dundas separation case, and, as it happens, I was engaged in clearing up some small points in connection with it. The husband was a teetotaller, there was no other woman, and the conduct complained of was that he had drifted into the habit of winding up every meal by taking out his false teeth and hurling them at his wife, which you will allow is not an **3** action likely to occur to the imagination of the average story-teller. Take a pinch of snuff, Doctor, and acknowledge that I have scored over you in your example."

He held out his snuff-box of old gold, with a great amethyst in the centre of the lid. Its splendour was in such contrast to his homely ways and simple life that I could not help commenting upon it.

" Ah," said he, " I forgot that I had not seen you for some weeks. It is a little souvenir from the King of Bohemia in return for my assistance in the case of the Irene Adler papers." **4**

" And the ring ? " I asked, glancing at a remarkable brilliant which sparkled upon his finger. **5**

" It was from the reigning family of Holland, though **6** the matter in which I served them was of such delicacy that I cannot confide it even to you, who have been good enough to chronicle one or two of my little problems."

" And have you any on hand just now ? " I asked with interest.

" Some ten or twelve, but none which presents any feature of interest. They are important, you understand, **7** without being interesting. Indeed, I have found that it is usually in unimportant matters that there is a field for observation, and for the quick analysis of cause and effect which gives the charm to an investigation. The larger crimes are apt to be the simpler, for the bigger the crime, the more obvious, as a rule, is the motive. In these cases, save for one rather intricate matter which has been referred to me from Marseilles, there is nothing which presents any features of interest. It is possible, however, that I may have something better before very many minutes are over, for this is one of my clients, or I am much mistaken."

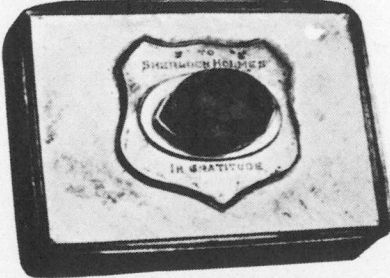

HE HELD OUT HIS SNUFF-BOX OF OLD GOLD, WITH A GREAT AMETHYST IN THE CENTRE OF THE LID.

The snuffbox, shown here, is now in the collection of the Sherlock Holmes Tavern. It was undoubtedly, we feel, the work of a gifted Bohemian craftsman and had been especially commissioned by the King. The work would take some time—say four or five months —but we are surely safe in saying that "A Scandal in Bohemia" and "A Case of Identity" probably fall within a six months' period and certainly fall with a twelve months' span.

3 *taking out his false teeth and hurling them at his wife.* "This interesting case . . . involved a bit of leg-pulling, I'm afraid, for . . . even today, with all the skill of modern dental science, we cannot construct a set of artificial teeth that would withstand such violent and frequent abuse," Dr. Charles Goodman wrote in "The Dental Holmes."

4 *the Irene Adler papers.*" The "papers" is a little mysterious. There were the letters written to Irene by the King of Bohemia, but, as Holmes himself pointed out, "How is she to prove their authenticity?" There were "No legal papers or certificates"; Holmes' concern was entirely with the photograph.

5 *a remarkable brilliant.* Perhaps a diamond, perhaps some other gem cut in the classic form of a brilliant: a form resembling two cones placed base to base, the upper being truncated comparatively near its base and the lower having the apex only cut off.

6 *the reigning family of Holland.* Another indication that "A Case of Identity" was not long after "A Scandal in Bohemia."

7 *none which presents any feature of interest.* Holmes at this period was evidently not yet so well off that he could afford to rid himself entirely of handling a number of small fry, similar to those who called upon his services in the early months of 1881 (*A Study in Scarlet*).

"THIS IS THE DUNDAS SEPARATION CASE . . ."

"Perhaps there may be some reason to believe that the arms are: argent, a lion rampant gules, as shown under 'Downdas of that ilk,' in the facsimile of an old heraldic manuscript," Dr. Julian Wolff wrote in his *Practical Handbook of Sherlockian Heraldry.*

. . . A BROAD-BRIMMED HAT WHICH WAS TILTED IN A
COQUETTISH DUCHESS-OF-DEVONSHIRE FASHION OVER HER
EAR.

This is Gainsborough's portrait of the Duchess of
Devonshire, Georgiana Cavendish, 1757–1806, a
celebrated beauty and setter of fashions.

SHERLOCK HOLMES WELCOMED HER WITH THE EASY
COURTESY FOR WHICH HE WAS REMARKABLE . . .

Illustration by Sidney Paget for the *Strand Magazine*, September, 1891.

He had risen from his chair, and was standing between the parted blinds, gazing down into the dull, neutral-tinted London street. Looking over his shoulder I saw that on the pavement opposite there stood a large woman with a heavy fur boa round her neck, and a large curling red feather in a broad-brimmed hat which was tilted in a coquettish Duchess-of-Devonshire fashion over her ear. From under this great panoply she peeped up in a nervous, hesitating fashion at our windows, while her body oscillated backwards and forwards, and her fingers fidgeted with her glove buttons. Suddenly, with a plunge, as of the swimmer who leaves the bank, she hurried across the road, and we heard the sharp clang of the bell.

" I have seen those symptoms before," said Holmes, throwing his cigarette into the fire. " Oscillation upon **8** the pavement always means an *affaire du cœur.* She would like advice, but is not sure that the matter is not too delicate for communication. And yet even here we may discriminate. When a woman has been seriously wronged by a man she no longer oscillates, and the usual symptom is a broken bell wire. Here we may take it that there is a love matter, but that the maiden is not so much angry as perplexed, or grieved. But here she comes in person to resolve our doubts."

As he spoke there was a tap at the door, and the boy in buttons entered to announce Miss Mary Sutherland, while the lady herself loomed behind his small black figure like a full-sailed merchantman behind a tiny pilot boat. Sherlock Holmes welcomed her with the easy courtesy for which he was remarkable, and having closed the door, and bowed her into an arm-chair, he looked over her in the minute and yet abstracted fashion which was peculiar to him.

" Do you not find," he said, " that with your short sight it is a little trying to do so much typewriting ? "

" I did at first," she answered, " but now I know where the letters are without looking." Then, suddenly realizing the full purport of his words, she gave a violent start, and looked up with fear and astonishment upon her broad, good-humoured face. " You've heard about me, Mr. Holmes," she cried, " else how could you know all that ? "

" Never mind," said Holmes, laughing, " it is my business to know things. Perhaps I have trained myself to see what others overlook. If not, why should you come to consult me ? "

" I came to you, sir, because I heard of you from Mrs. Etherege, whose husband you found so easy when the police and everyone had given him up for dead. Oh, Mr. Holmes, I wish you would do as much for me. I'm **9** not rich, but still I have a hundred a year in my own right, besides the little that I make by the machine, and I would give it all to know what has become of Mr. Hosmer Angel."

" Why did you come away to consult me in such a hurry ? " asked Sherlock Holmes, with his finger-tips together, and his eyes to the ceiling.

Again a startled look came over the somewhat vacuous face of Miss Mary Sutherland. " Yes, I did bang out of the house," she said, " for it made me angry to see the easy way in which Mr. Windibank—that is, my father—took it all.   He would not go to the police, and he would not go to you, and so at last, as he would do nothing, and kept on saying that there was no harm done, it made me mad, and I just on with my things and came right away to you."

"Your father ? " said Holmes. " Your stepfather, surely, since the name is different ? "

"Yes, my stepfather. I call him father, though it sounds funny, too, for he is only five years and two months older than myself."

"And your mother is alive ? "

"Oh, yes, mother is alive and well.   I wasn't best pleased, Mr. Holmes, when she married again so soon after father's death, and a man who was nearly fifteen years younger than herself.   Father was a plumber in the Tottenham Court Road, and he left a tidy business **10** behind him, which mother carried on with Mr. Hardy, the foreman, but when Mr. Windibank came he made her sell the business, for he was very superior, being a traveller in wines.   They got four thousand seven hundred for **11** the goodwill and interest, which wasn't near as much as father could have got if he had been alive."

I had expected to see Sherlock Holmes impatient under this rambling and inconsequential narrative, but, on the contrary, he had listened with the greatest concentration of attention.

"Your own little income," he asked, " does it come out of the business ? "

"Oh, no, sir, it is quite separate, and was left me by my Uncle Ned in Auckland.   It is in New Zealand Stock, paying $4\frac{1}{2}$ per cent.   Two thousand five hundred pounds was the amount, but I can only touch the interest." **12**

"You interest me extremely," said Holmes.   " And since you draw so large a sum as a hundred a year, with what you earn into the bargain, you no doubt travel a little and indulge yourself in every way.   I believe that a single lady can get on very nicely upon an income of about sixty pounds." **13**

"I could do with much less than that, Mr. Holmes, but you understand that as long as I live at home I don't wish to be a burden to them, and so they have the use of the money just while I am staying with them.   Of course that is only just for the time.   Mr. Windibank draws my interest every quarter, and pays it over to mother, and I find that I can do pretty well with what I earn at typewriting.   It brings me twopence a sheet, and I can often do from fifteen to twenty sheets in a day."

"IT BRINGS ME TWOPENCE A SHEET . . ."

"The twopence coin deserves some separate mention," the late A. Carson Simpson wrote in *Numismatics in the Canon*, Part I, "since it is the modern form of the old half-groat, a silver piece first struck by Edward III in 1351, when England finally found it needed a silver coin larger than the penny, and the groat and half-groat were added to the monetary system. It was struck regularly until it became an exclusively Maundy coin—even when the groat itself was dropped temporarily (from early in the reign of Elizabeth I through the Commonwealth) . . ." Shown here is the 1824 George IV Maundy twopence.

8 *an* affaire du cœur. French: a love affair.

9 *a hundred a year.* A hundred pounds; about $500 a year U.S. at the time.

10 *the Tottenham Court Road.* "The Tottenham Court Road," Mr. Harold P. Clunn wrote in *The Face of London*, "was a favourite resort of Londoners in the early part of the seventeenth century, because it led to the old Manor House of Totham Court. It was then a country road with hawthorn hedges and containing good pastures and meadows on both sides, but occasionally rowdiness and disorders occurred in this locality. Here booths were erected and gaming and prize-fighting were indulged in, which culminated in riots and other offences calculated to create a breach of the peace. Tottenham Court Road was mostly built between 1770 and 1800 and until the concluding years of the nineteenth century was a shabby street, but to-day it is the great centre of the London furnishing establishments and nearly the whole of the east side has been rebuilt in the past fifty years."

It was in Tottenham Court Road that Holmes found the broker who sold him a Stradivarius for only fifty-five shillings ("The Cardboard Box"). Here, too, was Morton and Waylight's, where the knocked-about Mr. Warren was timekeeper ("The Adventure of the Red Circle"). And it was at the corner of Tottenham Court Road and Goodge Street that a fracas occurred during which Mr. Henry Baker lost a goose ("The Adventure of the Blue Carbuncle").

11 *four thousand seven hundred.* About $23,500.

12 *Two thousand five hundred pounds.* About $12,500.

13 *about sixty pounds.* A highly revealing statement on the cost of living in Britain in the 1880's. A single lady could then get on very nicely upon an income of about sixty pounds—about $300—a year. Since Mary Sutherland had an income of one hundred pounds ($500) and an earned income of £37/18 (about $189.50—see below—assuming an average output of seventeen and a half sheets a day, a five-day week and no holidays) it is not surprising that she could dress in such finery.

"I MET HIM FIRST AT THE GASFITTERS' BALL . . ."

Illustration by Sidney Paget for the *Strand Magazine*, September, 1891.

"You have made your position very clear to me," said Holmes. "This is my friend, Dr. Watson, before whom you can speak as freely as before myself. Kindly tell us now all about your connection with Mr. Hosmer Angel."

A flush stole over Miss Sutherland's face, and she picked nervously at the fringe of her jacket. "I met him first at the gasfitters' ball," she said. "They used to send father tickets when he was alive, and then afterwards they remembered us, and sent them to mother. Mr. Windibank did not wish us to go. He never did wish us to go anywhere. He would get quite mad if I wanted so much as to join a Sunday school treat. But this time I was set on going, and I would go, for what right had he to prevent? He said the folk were not fit for us to know, when all father's friends were to be there. And he said that I had nothing fit to wear, when I had my purple plush that I had never so much as taken out of the drawer. At last, when nothing else would do, he went off to France upon the business of the firm, but we went, mother and I, with Mr. Hardy, who used to be our foreman, and it was there I met Mr. Hosmer Angel."

"I suppose," said Holmes, "that when Mr. Windibank came back from France, he was very annoyed at your having gone to the ball."

"Oh, well, he was very good about it. He laughed, I remembered, and shrugged his shoulders, and said there was no use denying anything to a woman, for she would have her way."

"I see. Then at the gasfitters' ball you met, as I understand, a gentleman called Mr. Hosmer Angel."

"Yes, sir. I met him that night, and he called next day to ask if we had got home all safe, and after that we met him—that is to say, Mr. Holmes, I met him twice for walks, but after that father came back again, and Mr. Hosmer Angel could not come to the house any more."

"No?"

"Well, you know, father didn't like anything of the sort. He wouldn't have any visitors if he could help it, and he used to say that a woman should be happy in her own family circle. But then, as I used to say to mother, a woman wants her own circle to begin with, and I had not got mine yet."

"But how about Mr. Hosmer Angel? Did he make no attempt to see you?"

"Well, father was going off to France again in a week, and Hosmer wrote and said that it would be safer and better not to see each other until he had gone. We could write in the meantime, and he used to write every day. I took the letters in in the morning so there was no need for father to know."

"Were you engaged to the gentleman at this time?"

"Oh yes, Mr. Holmes. We were engaged after the first walk that we took. Hosmer—Mr. Angel—was a **14** cashier in an office in Leadenhall Street—and——"

"What office?"

"That's the worst of it, Mr. Holmes, I don't know."

"Where did he live then?"

"He slept on the premises."

"And you don't know his address?"

"No—except that it was Leadenhall Street."

"Where did you address your letters, then?"

"To the Leadenhall Street Post Office, to be left till called for. He said that if they were sent to the office he would be chaffed by all the other clerks about having letters from a lady, so I offered to typewrite them, like he did his, but he wouldn't have that, for he said that when I wrote them they seemed to come from me but when they were typewritten he always felt that the machine had come between us. That will just show you how fond he was of me, Mr. Holmes, and the little things that he would think of."

"It was most suggestive," said Holmes. "It has long been an axiom of mine that the little things are infinitely the most important. Can you remember any other little things about Mr. Hosmer Angel?"

"He was a very shy man, Mr. Holmes. He would rather walk with me in the evening than in the daylight, for he said that he hated to be conspicuous. Very retiring and gentlemanly he was. Even his voice was gentle. He'd had the quinsy and swollen glands when he was young, he told me, and it had left him with a weak throat, and a hesitating, whispering fashion of speech. He was always well-dressed, very neat and plain, but his eyes were weak, just as mine are, and he wore tinted glasses against the glare."

"Well, and what happened when Mr. Windibank, your stepfather, returned to France?"

"Mr. Hosmer Angel came to the house again, and proposed that we should marry before father came back. He was in dreadful earnest, and made me swear, with my hands on the Testament, that whatever happened I would always be true to him. Mother said he was quite right to make me swear, and that it was a sign of his passion. Mother was all in his favour from the first, and was even fonder of him than I was. Then, when they talked of marrying within the week, I began to ask about father; but they both said never to mind about father, but just to tell him afterwards, and mother said she would make it all right with him. I didn't quite like that, Mr. Holmes. It seemed funny that I should ask his leave, as he was only a few years older than me; but I didn't want to do anything on the sly, so I wrote to father at Bordeaux, where the Company has its French offices, but the letter came back to me on the very morning of the wedding."

"It missed him then?"

"Yes, sir, for he had started to England just before it arrived."

"Ha! that was unfortunate. Your wedding was arranged, then, for the Friday. Was it to be in church?"

"Yes, sir, but very quietly. It was to be at St. Saviour's, near King's Cross, and we were to have break- **15** fast afterwards at the St. Pancras Hotel. Hosmer came **16** for us in a hansom, but as there were two of us, he put us both into it, and stepped himself into a four-wheeler which happened to be the only other cab in the street. We got to the church first, and when the four-wheeler drove up we waited for him to step out, but he never did, and when the cabman got down from the box and looked,

15 *King's Cross.* This neighborhood, Mr. Harold P. Clunn wrote in *The Face of London*, "was formerly known as Battlebridge and underwent a great transformation about 125 years ago. Before 1820 it had been a filthy and dangerous neighbourhood, and here the dustcarts of London used to be emptied. Afterwards all the mean hovels were removed and decent houses erected in their place. Battlebridge was renamed King's Cross after George IV and is supposed to have been the spot where King Alfred fought the Danes."

16 *St. Pancras Hotel.* St. Saviour's, or Southwark Cathedral, which stands at the south end of London Bridge, seems a most unlikely place for Miss Sutherland's wedding. Since she tells us that the wedding breakfast was to be celebrated at the St. Pancras Hotel, it is suggested that she confused St. Pancras Old Church, which *is* close to King's Cross, with the hotel at which the breakfast was to have been served.

". . . WHEN THE CABMAN GOT DOWN FROM THE BOX AND LOOKED, THERE WAS NO ONE THERE!"

Illustration by Sidney Paget for the *Strand Magazine*, September, 1891.

17 *That was last Friday*. Holmes says to Mary Sutherland: "Your wedding was arranged, then, for Friday . . ." and Mary answers: "That was last Friday, Mr. Holmes." The case therefore took place before the Friday of the following week, or Holmes and Mary would have said "a week ago today" rather than "the Friday" and "last Friday."

18 *last Saturday's* Chronicle." "Experience suggests that neither the bride nor the advertising department would proceed at this speed," the late Gavin Brend wrote in *My Dear Holmes*.

there was no one there ! The cabman said he could not imagine what had become of him, for he had seen him get **17** in with his own eyes. That was last Friday, Mr. Holmes, and I have never seen or heard anything since then to throw any light upon what became of him."

" It seems to me that you have been very shamefully treated," said Holmes.

" Oh no, sir ! He was too good and kind to leave me so. Why, all the morning he was saying to me that, whatever happened, I was to be true ; and that even if something quite unforeseen occurred to separate us, I was always to remember that I was pledged to him, and that he would claim his pledge sooner or later. It seemed strange talk for a wedding morning, but what has happened since gives a meaning to it."

" Most certainly it does. Your own opinion is, then, that some unforeseen catastrophe has occurred to him ? "

" Yes, sir. I believe that he foresaw some danger, or else he would not have talked so. And then I think that what he foresaw happened."

" But you have no notion as to what it could have been ? "

" None."

" One more question. How did your mother take the matter ? "

" She was angry, and said that I was never to speak of the matter again."

" And your father ? Did you tell him ? "

" Yes, and he seemed to think, with me, that something had happened, and that I should hear of Hosmer again. As he said, what interest could anyone have in bringing me to the doors of the church, and then leaving me ? Now, if he had borrowed my money, or if he had married me and got my money settled on him, there might be some reason ; but Hosmer was very independent about money, and never would look at a shilling of mine. And yet what could have happened ? And why could he not write ? Oh, it drives me half mad to think of it ! and I can't sleep a wink at night." She pulled a little handkerchief out of her muff, and began to sob heavily into it.

" I shall glance into the case for you," said Holmes, rising, " and I have no doubt that we shall reach some definite result. Let the weight of the matter rest upon me now, and do not let your mind dwell upon it further. Above all, try to let Mr. Hosmer Angel vanish from your memory, as he has done from your life."

" Then you don't think I'll see him again ? "

" I fear not."

" Then what has happened to him ? "

" You will leave that question in my hands. I should like an accurate description of him, and any letters of his which you can spare."

18 " I advertised for him in last Saturday's *Chronicle*," said she. " Here is the slip, and here are four letters from him."

" Thank you. And your address ? "

" 31 Lyon Place, Camberwell."

" Mr. Angel's address you never had, I understand. Where is your father's place of business ? "

" He travels for Westhouse & Marbank, the great claret

importers of Fenchurch Street."   **19**

"Thank you. You have made your statement very clearly. You will leave the papers here, and remember the advice which I have given you. Let the whole incident be a sealed book, and do not allow it to affect your life."

"You are very kind, Mr. Holmes, but I cannot do that. I shall be true to Hosmer. He shall find me ready when he comes back."

For all the preposterous hat and the vacuous face, there was something noble in the simple faith of our visitor which compelled our respect. She laid her little bundle of papers upon the table, and went her way, with a promise to come again whenever she might be summoned.

Sherlock Holmes sat silent for a few minutes with his finger-tips still pressed together, his legs stretched out in front of him, and his gaze directed upwards to the ceiling. Then he took down from the rack the old and oily clay pipe, which was to him as a counsellor, and, having lit it he leaned back in his chair, with the thick blue cloud-wreaths spinning up from him, and a look of infinite languor in his face.

"Quite an interesting study, that maiden," he observed. "I found her more interesting than her little problem, which, by the way, is rather a trite one. You will find parallel cases, if you consult my index, in Andover in '77, **20** and there was something of the sort at The Hague last year. Old as is the idea, however, there were one or two details which were new to me. But the maiden herself was most instructive."

"You appeared to read a good deal upon her which was quite invisible to me," I remarked.

"Not invisible, but unnoticed, Watson. You did not know where to look, and so you missed all that was important. I can never bring you to realize the importance of sleeves, the suggestiveness of thumb-nails, or the great issues that may hang from a bootlace. Now what did you gather from that woman's appearance? Describe it."

"Well, she had a slate-coloured, broad-brimmed straw hat, with a feather of a brickish red. Her jacket was black, with black beads sewn upon it, and a fringe of little black jet ornaments. Her dress was brown, rather darker than coffee colour, with a little purple plush at the neck and sleeves. Her gloves were greyish, and were worn through at the right forefinger. Her boots I didn't observe. She had small, round, hanging gold ear-rings, and a general air of being fairly well to do, in a vulgar, comfortable, easy-going way."

Sherlock Holmes clapped his hands softly together and chuckled.

"'Pon my word, Watson, you are coming along wonderfully. You have really done very well indeed. It is true that you have missed everything of importance, but you have hit upon the method, and you have a quick eye for colour. Never trust to general impressions, my boy, but concentrate yourself upon details. My first glance is always at a woman's sleeve. In a man it is perhaps better first to take the knee of the trouser. As you observe, this woman had plush upon her sleeves, which is a most use-

SHE LAID HER LITTLE BUNDLE OF PAPERS UPON THE TABLE . . .

Illustration by Sidney Paget for the *Strand Magazine*, September, 1891.

19 *Fenchurch Street.*" "From Lombard Street, Fenchurch Street leads to Aldgate, taking its name from the fenny ground caused by the overflowings of the Lang Bourne, a clear brook of sweet water which ran down Fen Church Street and Lombard Street as far as St. Mary Woolnoth, where it broke into several small rills which flowed southward to the Thames," Augustus J. C. Hare wrote in *Walks in London*, Vol. I. "Many of the buildings in this street bear a date immediately after the Great Fire, in which it was consumed. Pepys saw 'Fenchurch Street, Gracious Street, and Lombard Street all in dust.'"

20 *Andover.* A municipal borough in Hampshire.

21 *on the morning of the 14th*. Since Mr. Hosmer Angel disappeared on the day set for the wedding, and this day was "last Friday," we can now say with some assurance that "A Case of Identity" took place after a Friday the 14th and a Saturday the 15th and before a Friday the 21st. In what years between March, 1881, and August, 1890, can we find such a Friday and Saturday? We can find them in 1883 and 1888, when the 14th and 15th of *September* were a Friday and Saturday, and we can find them in 1881 and 1887, when the 14th and 15th of *October* were a Friday and Saturday. Evidence from *The Sign of the Four*, "A Scandal in Bohemia" and "The Red-Headed League" will eliminate for us 1881, 1883, and 1888. The Friday on which Hosmer Angel disappeared is clearly Friday, October 14, 1887, and the Saturday on which Mary's advertisement appeared Saturday, October 15, 1887.

22 *Balzac*. Honoré de Balzac, 1799–1850, French novelist, whose greatest work is his many-volumed *La Comédie humaine*.

ful material for showing traces. The double line a little above the wrist, where the typewritist presses against the table, was beautifully defined. The sewing-machine, of the hand type, leaves a similar mark, but only on the left arm, and on the side of it farthest from the thumb, instead of being right across the broadest part, as this was. I then glanced at her face, and observing the dint of a pince-nez at either side of her nose, I ventured a remark upon short sight and typewriting, which seemed to surprise her."

" It surprised me."

" But, surely, it was very obvious. I was then much surprised and interested on glancing down to observe that, though the boots which she was wearing were not unlike each other, they were really odd ones, the one having a slightly decorated toe-cap, and the other a plain one. One was buttoned only in the two lower buttons out of five, and the other at the first, third, and fifth. Now, when you see that a young lady, otherwise neatly dressed, has come away from home with odd boots, half buttoned, it is no great deduction to say that she came away in a hurry."

" And what else ? " I asked, keenly interested, as I always was, by my friend's incisive reasoning.

" I noted, in passing, that she had written a note before leaving home, but after being fully dressed. You observed that her right glove was torn at the forefinger, but you did not apparently see that both glove and finger were stained with violet ink. She had written in a hurry, and dipped her pen too deep. It must have been this morning, or the mark would not remain clear upon the finger. All this is amusing, though rather elementary, but I must go back to business, Watson. Would you mind reading me the advertised description of Mr. Hosmer Angel ? "

I held the little printed slip to the light. " Missing,"
21 it said, " on the morning of the 14th, a gentleman named Hosmer Angel. About 5ft. 7in. in height ; strongly built, sallow complexion, black hair, a little bald in the centre, bushy black side whiskers and moustache ; tinted glasses, slight infirmity of speech. Was dressed, when last seen, in black frock-coat faced with silk, black waistcoat, gold Albert chain, and grey Harris tweed trousers, with brown gaiters over elastic-sided boots. Known to have been employed in an office in Leadenhall Street. Anybody bringing," etc. etc.

" That will do," said Holmes. " As to the letters," he continued glancing over them, " they are very commonplace. Absolutely no clue in them to Mr. Angel,
22 save that he quotes Balzac once. There is one remarkable point, however, which will no doubt strike you."

" They are typewritten," I remarked.

" Not only that, but the signature is typewritten. Look at the neat little ' Hosmer Angel ' at the bottom. There is a date you see, but no superscription, except Leadenhall Street, which is rather vague. The point about the signature is very suggestive—in fact, we may call it conclusive."

" Of what ? "

" My dear fellow, is it possible you do not see how strongly it bears upon the case."

" I cannot say that I do, unless it were that he wished to be able to deny his signature if an action for breach of promise were instituted."

" No, that was not the point. However, I shall write two letters which should settle the matter. One is to a firm in the City, the other is to the young lady's stepfather, Mr. Windibank, asking him whether he could meet us here at six o'clock to-morrow evening. It is just as well that we should do business with the male relatives. And now, Doctor, we can do nothing until the answers to those letters come, so we may put our little problem upon the shelf for the interim."

I had had so many reasons to believe in my friend's subtle powers of reasoning, and extraordinary energy in action, that I felt that he must have some solid grounds for the assured and easy demeanour with which he treated the singular mystery which he had been called upon to fathom. Only once had I known him to fail, in the case of the King of Bohemia and of the Irene Adler photograph, but when I looked back to the weird business of the Sign of Four, and the extraordinary circumstances **23** connected with the Study in Scarlet, I felt that it would be a strange tangle indeed which he could not unravel.

I left him then, still puffing at his black clay pipe, with the conviction that when I came again on the next evening I would find that he held in his hands all the clues which would lead up to the identity of the disappearing bridegroom of Miss Mary Sutherland.

A professional case of great gravity was engaging my own attention at the time, and the whole of next day I was busy at the bedside of the sufferer. It was not until close upon six o'clock that I found myself free, and was able to spring into a hansom and drive to Baker Street, half afraid that I might be too late to assist at the *dénouement* of the little mystery. I found Sherlock Holmes **24** alone, however, half asleep, with his long, thin form curled up in the recesses of his arm-chair. A formidable array of bottles and test-tubes, with the pungent cleanly smell of hydrochloric acid, told me that he had spent his day in the chemical work which was so dear to him.

" Well, have you solved it ? " I asked as I entered.

" Yes. It was the bisulphate of baryta."   **25**

" No, no, the mystery ! " I cried.

" Oh, that ! I thought of the salt that I have been working upon. There was never any mystery in the matter, though, as I said yesterday, some of the details are of interest. The only drawback is that there is no law, I fear, that can touch the scoundrel."

" Who was he, then, and what was his object in deserting Miss Sutherland ? "

The question was hardly out of my mouth, and Holmes had not yet opened his lips to reply, when we heard a heavy footfall in the passage, and a tap at the door.

" This is the girl's stepfather, Mr. James Windibank," said Holmes. " He has written to me to say that he **26** would be here at six. Come in ! "

The man who entered was a sturdy middle-sized fellow, some thirty years of age, clean shaven, and sallow skinned, with a bland, insinuating manner, and a pair of wonder-

23 *when I looked back to the weird business of the Sign of Four.* See our remarks on this statement of Watson's in the chapter titled "Now, Watson the Fair Sex Is Your Department."

24 dénouement. French: the final revelation or occurrence which clarifies the nature and outcome of a plot.

25 *the bisulphate of baryta."* ". . . barium bisulfate does not exist . . . ," Professor Remsen Ten Eyck Schenck wrote in "Baker Street Fables."

But Mr. L. S. Holstein replied (" '7. Knowledge of Chemistry—Profound' "): "Although Dr. Schenck says barium bisulphate does not exist, a reference to Mellors' *Inorganic Chemistry* (Vol. III, p. 784) —a universally recognized authority—will elicit the information that the bisulphate does exist; and, in addition, Mellor states its known properties . . ."

The editors of the Catalogue of the Sherlock Holmes Exhibition wrote: "Barium Hydrogen Sulphate (Bisulphate of baryta) [is a] substance . . . first prepared by J. J. Berzelius in 1843. . . . It is decomposed by water. . . . Apart from some doubt as to its precise structure, the compound is of little interest, and has never been more than a chemical curiosity; it has certainly never been an article of commercial supply. The only source of such a compound would be from a private collection. It seems probable that a sealed tube of the substance which had lost its label was found by one of Holmes' friends in a University laboratory; and

I FOUND SHERLOCK HOLMES ALONE, . . . HALF ASLEEP, WITH HIS LONG, THIN FORM CURLED UP IN THE RECESSES OF HIS ARM-CHAIR.

Illustration by Sidney Paget for the *Strand Magazine*, September, 1891.

the finder, knowing that Holmes made something of a hobby of routine chemical analysis, asked him to identify it."

More recently, Mr. D. A. Redmond ("Some Chemical Problems in the Canon") has noted that the hexasulphide of barium, $BaS_6O_6.3H_2O$, may be precipitated by acetone. ("I had better postpone my analysis of the acetones."—Holmes in "The Adventure of the Copper Beeches.") Mr. Redmond suggests that this "points to a consistent pattern of investigation by the Master, lasting for an extended time. Stemming from his original investigation on blood, dating from his days at Bart's, he pursued a line of biochemical research singularly neglected by later workers."

26 "*He has written to me*. Holmes later tells us that he had also received a letter by the same post from Westhouse & Marbank. The second day of the adventure was therefore not a Sunday.

27 *dropped his gloves*. Mary Sutherland came to Baker Street with a large, heavy fur boa around her neck, with a broad-brimmed straw hat with a large, curling feather, with button gloves and with a jacket. The next afternoon Mr. Windibank came to Baker Street wearing a top hat with gloves, but there is no mention of an overcoat or an umbrella. We must therefore look for two warm, clear days in the period Monday, October 17, through Thursday, October 20, 1887: 1) Monday, October 17th, was "fair but cold and hazy." 2) On Tuesday, October 18th, the "weather was milder generally than of late" and "except in the North and Northwest" the weather was dry. 3) On Wednesday, October 19th, the weather was "fair on the whole." There were "light breezes from the west, with a

"WHAT! WHERE?" SHOUTED MR. WINDIBANK, TURNING WHITE TO THE LIPS, AND GLANCING ABOUT HIM LIKE A RAT IN A TRAP.

Illustration by Sidney Paget for the *Strand Magazine*, September, 1891.

fully sharp and penetrating grey eyes. He shot a questioning glance at each of us, placed his shiny top-hat upon the sideboard, and, with a slight bow, sidled down into the nearest chair.

" Good evening, Mr. James Windibank," said Holmes. " I think that this typewritten letter is from you, in which you made an appointment with me for six o'clock ! "

" Yes, sir. I am afraid that I am a little late, but I am not quite my own master, you know. I am sorry that Miss Sutherland has troubled you about this little matter, for I think it is far better not to wash linen of this sort in public. It was quite against my wishes that she came, but she is a very excitable, impulsive girl, as you may have noticed, and she is not easily controlled when she has made up her mind on a point. Of course, I do not mind you so much, as you are not connected with the official police, but it is not pleasant to have a family misfortune like this noised abroad. Besides, it is a useless expense, for how could you possibly find this Hosmer Angel ? "

" On the contrary," said Holmes quietly ; " I have every reason to believe that I will succeed in discovering Mr. Hosmer Angel."

Mr. Windibank gave a violent start, and dropped his **27** gloves. " I am delighted to hear it," he said.

" It is a curious thing," remarked Holmes, " that a typewriter has really quite as much individuality as a man's handwriting. Unless they are quite new, no two of them write exactly alike. Some letters get more worn than others, and some wear only on one side. Now, you remark in this note of yours, Mr. Windibank, that in every case there is some little slurring over of the ' e,' and a slight defect in the tail of the ' r.' There are fourteen other characteristics, but those are the more obvious."

" We do all our correspondence with this machine at the office, and no doubt it is a little worn," our visitor answered, glancing keenly at Holmes with his bright little eyes.

" And now I will show you what is really a very interesting study, Mr. Windibank," Holmes continued. " I think of writing another little monograph some of these **28** days on the typewriter and its relation to crime. It is a subject to which I have devoted some little attention. I have here four letters which purport to come from the missing man. They are all typewritten. In each case, not only are the ' e's ' slurred and the ' r's ' tailless, but you will observe, if you care to use my magnifying lens, that the fourteen other characteristics to which I have alluded are there as well."

Mr. Windibank sprang out of his chair, and picked up his hat. " I cannot waste time over this sort of fantastic talk, Mr. Holmes," he said. " If you can catch the man, catch him, and let me know when you have done it."

" Certainly," said Holmes, stepping over and turning the key in the door. " I let you know, then, that I have caught him ! "

" What ! where ? " shouted Mr. Windibank, turning white to his lips, and glancing about him like a rat in a trap.

"Oh, it won't do—really it won't," said Holmes suavely. "There is no possible getting out of it, Mr. Windibank. It is quite too transparent, and it was a very bad compliment when you said it was impossible for me to solve so simple a question. That's right! Sit down, and let us talk it over."

Our visitor collapsed into a chair with a ghastly face and a glitter of moisture on his brow. "It—it's not actionable," he stammered.

"I am very much afraid that it is not. But between ourselves, Windibank, it was as cruel, and selfish, and heartless a trick in a petty way as ever came before me. Now, let me just run over the course of events, and you will contradict me if I go wrong."

The man sat huddled up in his chair, with his head sunk upon his breast, like one who is utterly crushed. Holmes stuck his feet up on the corner of the mantelpiece, and leaning back with his hands in his pockets, began talking, rather to himself, as it seemed, than to us.

"The man married a woman very much older than himself for her money," said he, "and he enjoyed the use of the money of the daughter as long as she lived with them. It was a considerable sum for people in their position, and the loss of it would have made a serious difference. It was worth an effort to preserve it. The daughter was of a good, amiable disposition, but affectionate and warm-hearted in her ways, so that it was evident that with her fair personal advantages, and her little income, she would not be allowed to remain single long. Now her marriage would mean, of course, the loss of a hundred a year, so what does her stepfather do to prevent it? He takes the obvious course of keeping her at home, and forbidding her to seek the company of people of her own age. But soon he found that that would not answer for ever. She became restive, insisted upon her rights, and finally announced her positive intention of going to a certain ball. What does her clever stepfather do then? He conceives an idea more creditable to his head than to his heart. With the connivance and assistance of his wife he disguised himself, covered those keen eyes with tinted glasses, masked the face with a moustache and a pair of bushy whiskers, sunk that clear voice into an insinuating whisper, and, doubly secure on account of the girl's short sight, he appears as Mr. Hosmer Angel, and keeps off other lovers by making love himself."

"It was only a joke at first," groaned our visitor. "We never thought that she would have been so carried away."

"Very likely not. However that may be, the young lady was very decidedly carried away, and having quite made up her mind that her stepfather was in France, the suspicion of treachery never for an instant entered her mind. She was flattered by the gentleman's attentions, and the effect was increased by the loudly expressed admiration of her mother. Then Mr. Angel began to call, for it was obvious that the matter should be pushed as far as it would go, if a real effect were to be produced. There were meetings, and an engagement, which would finally secure the girl's affections from turning towards anyone else. But the deception could not be kept up for

clear or partially clear sky in many places." 4) On Thursday, October 20th, however, colder weather settled in "over the whole United Kingdom." It was foggy in the Southeast of England, with no sunshine whatever registered at Westminster. Clearly, Mary Sutherland visited Holmes on *Tuesday, October 18, 1887*; Mr. Windibank called, and the case ended, the next day—*Wednesday, October 19, 1887*.

28 *on the typewriter and its relation to crime.* "In . . . the *Journal of Criminal Law and Criminology* (November–December, 1947) there appears a review of an article in the *Police Journal*, the title of which is 'Identification of Typewriting,' reputedly by one George McLean," Mr. Archibald Hart wrote in "The Effects of Trades Upon Hands." "Is it not apparent that some hoarder of the only existent copies of all of Holmes' brochures is now releasing them one by one under false authorships? 'McLean' urges us to note the peculiarities of each typed character, the vertical and horizontal alignment, the side impressions of each character, and the shortening of the serifs in P, D, B, and H, and the diacritic in the letter T."

HE TOOK TWO SWIFT STEPS TO THE WHIP . . .

Illustration by Sidney Paget for the *Strand Magazine*, September, 1891.

ever. These pretended journeys to France were rather cumbrous. The thing to do was clearly to bring the business to an end in such a dramatic manner that it would leave a permanent impression upon the young lady's mind, and prevent her from looking upon any other suitor for some time to come. Hence those vows of fidelity exacted upon a Testament, and hence also the allusions to a possibility of something happening on the very morning of the wedding. James Windibank wished Miss Sutherland to be so bound to Hosmer Angel, and so uncertain as to his fate, that for ten years to come, at any rate, she would not listen to another man. As far as the church door he brought her, and then, as he could go no further, he conveniently vanished away by the old trick of stepping in at one door of a four-wheeler, and out at the other. I think that that was the chain of events, Mr. Windibank ! "

Our visitor had recovered something of his assurance while Holmes had been talking, and he rose from his chair now with a cold sneer upon his pale face.

" It may be so, or it may not, Mr. Holmes," said he, " but if you are so very sharp you ought to be sharp enough to know that it is you who are breaking the law now, and not me. I have done nothing actionable from the first, but as long as you keep that door locked you lay yourself open to an action for assault and illegal constraint."

" The law cannot, as you say, touch you," said Holmes, unlocking and throwing open the door, " yet there never was a man who deserved punishment more. If the young lady has a brother or a friend he ought to lay a whip across your shoulders. By Jove ! " he continued, flushing up at the sight of the bitter sneer upon the man's face, " it is not part of my duties to my client, but here's a hunting-crop handy, and I think I shall just treat myself to——" He took two swift steps to the whip, but before he could grasp it there was a wild clatter of steps upon the stairs, the heavy hall door banged, and from the window we could see Mr. James Windibank running at the top of his speed down the road.

" There's a cold-blooded scoundrel ! " said Holmes, laughing, as he threw himself down into his chair once more. " That fellow will rise from crime to crime until he does something very bad, and ends on a gallows. The case has, in some respects, been not entirely devoid of interest."

" I cannot now entirely see all the steps of your reasoning," I remarked.

" Well, of course it was obvious from the first that this Mr. Hosmer Angel must have some strong object for his curious conduct, and it was equally clear that the only man who really profited by the incident, as far as we could see, was the stepfather. Then the fact that the two men were never together, but that the one always appeared when the other was away, was suggestive. So were the tinted spectacles and the curious voice, which both hinted at a disguise, as did the bushy whiskers. My suspicions were all confirmed by his peculiar action in typewriting his signature, which of course inferred that his handwriting was so familiar to her that she would recognize even the smallest sample of it.   You see all these isolated facts, together with many minor ones, all pointed in the same direction."

" And how did you verify them ? "

" Having once spotted my man, it was easy to get corroboration.   I knew the firm for which this man worked.   Having taken the printed description, I eliminated everything from it which could be the result of a disguise—the whiskers, the glasses, the voice, and I sent it to the firm, with a request that they would inform me whether it answered the description of any of their travellers.   I had already noticed the peculiarities of the typewriter, and I wrote to the man himself at his business address, asking him if he would come here.   As I expected, his reply was typewritten, and revealed the same trivial but characteristic defects.   The same post brought me a letter from Westhouse & Marbank, of Fenchurch Street, to say that the description tallied in every respect with that of their employé, James Windibank.   *Voilà tout !* " **29**

" And Miss Sutherland ? "

" If I tell her she will not believe me.   You may remember the old Persian saying, ' There is danger for him who taketh the tiger cub, and danger also for whoso snatches a delusion from a woman.'   There is as much **30** sense in Hafiz as in Horace, and as much knowledge of the **31** world."

29 Voilà tout!" French: there, that is all; that is the whole of it.

30 *a delusion from a woman.*' "My own search through all accessible translations of Persian, Iranian, and other Oriental sayings has failed to turn up such a maxim," Mr. Morris Rosenblum wrote in "Foreign Language Quotations in the Canon." "In the very next sentence Holmes referred to Hafiz —but please note that very cleverly he did not say directly that Hafiz was the author of the expression. Nevertheless, I looked through the complete works of Hafiz in translation without coming across anything resembling the idea of the woman, tiger cubs, and delusions."

To this Mr. Bliss Austin added (*A Baker Street Christmas Stocking*, 1955) ". . . all efforts by a number of the Faithful to find this proverb in Hafiz have led to naught. . . . Among other sources, I consulted two authorities on Persia and its literature who were not only unacquainted with it but even expressed open doubt that it was genuine. . . . But apparently the stumbling block was the misleading reference to Hafiz. Thus I recently came across a book by Selwyn Garney Champion, M.D., entitled *Racial Proverbs, A Selection of the World's Proverbs, Arranged Linguistically* (New York: The Macmillan Company, 1938)—and there on page 469 as No. 216 of the Persian proverbs, I found: 'There is danger for whoso snatches a delusion from a woman.' So it seems that at least part of Holmes' quotation is authentic . . ."

31 *in Hafiz as in Horace.* Since the *Diwan* of the fourteenth century Persian poet Hafiz (the popular name for Shams ed-Din Mohammed), was not translated in its entirety into English prose until 1891, Miss Madeleine B. Stern has suggested ("Sherlock Holmes: Rare Book Collector") that "we must assume that Holmes' copy was either of the 1800 Hindley edition of the *Persian Lyrics* printed in Persian and English with verse and prose paraphrases and a catalogue of the Gazels, or of the fine 1875 edition containing a verse rendering of the principal poems by Bicknell." As to Holmes' copy of Horace, it was "doubtless, because of Holmes' interest in printing types, the Parma edition published by Bodoni . . ."

Bibliographical Note: The first separate edition of "A Case of Identity"—a great rarity—is now thought to have been the small brochure illustrated here, No. 10 in the Handy Classic Series, published by the Optimus Printing Company of New York in 1895.

THE RED-HEADED LEAGUE

[Saturday, October 29, to Sunday, October 30, 1887]

1 *one day.* Holmes thrice gives us the day on which the adventure of "The Red-Headed League" took place: "To-day is Saturday"; "To-day being Saturday rather complicates matters"; "Saturday would suit them better than any other day . . ." And Mr. Merryweather says: "It is the first Saturday night for seven-and-twenty years that I have not had my rubber."

2 *the autumn.* Both Mr. Rolfe Boswell ("A Rare Day in June") and Mr. Raymond A. de Groat ("The Guilty Pawnbroker, or The Lost Summer of 1890") insist that the month was not in "the autumn" but in June; Mr. Boswell dates the case June 17, 1890; Mr. de Groat June 21, 1890. But Watson's "autumn" would seem to be confirmed by the "October" of the sign and the fact that Mr. Jabez Wilson wore "a faded brown overcoat."

3 *last year.* Since "The Red-Headed League" was published in August, 1891, we might at first think that this indicated the autumn of 1890. But Watson's chronicles were in manuscript form long before they were published; his statement here means only that "The Red-Headed League" took place in the autumn before he chronicled the story.

4 *in the next room."* Watson presumably means Holmes' bedroom.

1-2-3 I HAD called upon my friend, Mr. Sherlock Holmes, one day in the autumn of last year, and found him in deep conversation with a very stout, florid-faced, elderly gentleman, with fiery red hair. With an apology for my intrusion, I was about to withdraw, when Holmes pulled me abruptly into the room, and closed the door behind me.

"You could not possibly have come at a better time, my dear Watson," he said cordially.

"I was afraid that you were engaged."

"So I am. Very much so."

4 "Then I can wait in the next room."

"Not at all. This gentleman, Mr. Wilson, has been my partner and helper in many of my most successful cases, and I have no doubt that he will be of the utmost use to me in yours also."

The stout gentleman half rose from his chair, and gave a bob of greeting, with a quick little questioning glance from his small, fat-encircled eyes.

"Try the settee," said Holmes, relapsing into his arm-chair, and putting his finger-tips together, as was his custom when in judicial moods. "I know, my dear Watson, that you share my love of all that is bizarre and outside the conventions and humdrum routine of every-day life. You have shown your relish for it by the enthusiasm which has prompted you to chronicle, and, if you will excuse my saying so, somewhat to embellish so many of my own little adventures."

"Your cases have indeed been of the greatest interest to me," I observed.

. . . A VERY STOUT, FLORID-FACED, ELDERLY GENTLEMAN, WITH FIERY RED HAIR.

Portrait of Jabez Wilson by Sidney Paget, for the *Strand Magazine*, August, 1891. "How old was Mr. Wilson?" Mr. Thomas L. Stix asked in "Concerning 'The Red-Headed League.' " Watson regarded him as "an elderly gentleman—which would mean 60, perhaps. At 60 one does not possess fiery red hair. Indeed, at 50 the pigmentation has changed."

" You will remember that I remarked the other day, just before we went into the very simple problem presented by Miss Mary Sutherland, that for strange effects **5** and extraordinary combinations we must go to life itself, which is always far more daring than any effort of the imagination."

" A proposition which I took the liberty of doubting."

" You did, Doctor, but none the less you must come round to my view, for otherwise I shall keep piling fact upon fact on you, until your reason breaks down under them and acknowledges me to be right. Now, Mr. Jabez Wilson here has been good enough to call upon me this morning, and to begin a narrative which promises to be one of the most singular which I have listened to for some time. You have heard me remark that the strangest and most unique things are very often connected not with the larger but with the smaller crimes, and occasionally, indeed, where there is room for doubt whether any positive crime has been committed. As far as I have heard, it is impossible for me to say whether the present case is an instance of crime or not, but the course of events is certainly among the most singular that I have ever listened to. Perhaps, Mr. Wilson, you would have the great kindness to recommence your narrative. I ask you not merely because my friend Dr. Watson has not heard the opening part, but also because the peculiar nature of the story makes me anxious to have every possible detail from your lips. As a rule, when I have heard some slight indication of the course of events I am able to guide myself by the thousands of other similar cases which occur to my memory. In the present instance I am forced to admit that the facts are, to the best of my belief, unique."

The portly client puffed out his chest with an appearance of some little pride, and pulled a dirty and wrinkled newspaper from the inside pocket of his greatcoat. As he glanced down the advertisement column, with his head thrust forward, and the paper flattened out upon his knee, I took a good look at the man, and endeavoured after the fashion of my companion to read the indications which might be presented by his dress or appearance.

I did not gain very much, however, by my inspection. Our visitor bore every mark of being an average commonplace British tradesman, obese, pompous, and slow. He wore rather baggy grey shepherds' check trousers, a not over-clean black frock-coat, unbuttoned in the front, and a drab waistcoat with a heavy brassy Albert chain, and a square pierced bit of metal dangling down as an ornament. A frayed top-hat, and a faded brown overcoat with a wrinkled velvet collar lay upon a chair beside him. Altogether, look as I would, there was nothing remarkable about the man save his blazing red head, and the expression of extreme chagrin and discontent upon his features.

Sherlock Holmes's quick eye took in my occupation and he shook his head with a smile as he noticed my questioning glances. " Beyond the obvious facts that he has at some time done manual labour, that he takes snuff, that he is a Freemason, that he has been in China, and that he **6** has done a considerable amount of writing lately, I can deduce nothing else."

5 *the very simple problem presented by Miss Mary Sutherland*. "The Red-Headed League" is later than "A Case of Identity," but only a little later, as shown by Holmes' "the other day."

6 *a Freemason*. A member of a widespread and celebrated secret society (called more fully the Free and Accepted Masons) consisting of persons who are united for fraternal purposes.

7 *"I won't insult your intelligence by telling you how I read that.* "As for us, gentlemen," Mr. Thomas L. Stix wrote in "Concerning 'The Red-Headed League,'" "we wish to have our intelligence insulted. How did Holmes know about the snuff? He didn't. But it sounded good, and he thought he could get away with it—and did . . ."

8 *and have even contributed to the literature of the subject.* Miss Madeleine B. Stern has noted ("Sherlock Holmes: Rare Book Collector") that "most of the works on tattooing, corporal marking and ethnic mutilation follow rather than precede Holmes." And Mr. Ernest C. Burnham, Jr., has added ("The Tattooed Fish in 'The Red-Headed League'") that "It is noteworthy that in our present enlightened age, there are only two major works (W. D. Hambly, *History of Tattooing*, Macmillan, 1927; H. Ebenstein, *Pierced Hearts and True Love*, D. Verschoyle, 1953) on the subject of tattooing . . ."

9 *quite peculiar to China.* Mr. Burnham has also pointed out that "China is conspicuous by its absence from the rolls of practitioners of tattooing, as the Chinese abhorred and condemned tattooing as barbarous, and they accordingly only used tattooing to mark criminals. . . . Furthermore, the usual designs used in all places were human figures and flowers, not fishes or animals . . ." Mr. Burnham has also noted that the right wrist is a most unusual part of the body to have tattooed, and that "staining" is a most peculiar way to refer to the technique of tattooing: "nothing is stained in tattoos . . . the colouring is introduced below the skin and not on the surface . . ." Mr. Burnham concluded that Jabez Wilson was tattooed in Japan and that Holmes mistook the coin worn by Mr. Wilson for a Chinese coin.

"WHEN, IN ADDITION, I SEE A CHINESE COIN HANGING FROM YOUR WATCH-CHAIN . . ."

Watson has called the coin "a square pierced bit of metal." Did he mean a "square, pierced, bit" or a "square-pierced bit"? Not the former, surely, for, as Mr. Martin J. Swanson has pointed out: "Nowhere can I find any mention of China having issued square coins at any time (the Chinese trademark was a round coin with a square hole), while Japan almost exclusively issued squared, pierced coins. We now see that Wilson surely received both tattoo and coin while in Japan, not China . . ."

The late A. Carson Simpson, on the other hand, has interpreted Watson's phrase to mean a "square-pierced bit." In his great work, *Numismatics in the Canon*, Part II, he pointed out that only one Chinese coin was "legal tender for all debts, public and private, irrespective of amount, until the end of the nineteenth century. It began in 618 A.D., when General Li Yüan became Emperor Kao Tsu, first of the T'ang Dynasty. He at once issued the new coin, known as 'current money of the newest beginning.' Called by the Chinese a 'tsien,' it was round, about an inch in diameter, with a square hole in the centre and a raised edge. It was generally a cast (not struck) coin and the material used ranged from high-grade brass to varying mixtures of copper, zinc, tin, lead and iron.

Mr. Jabez Wilson started up in his chair, with his forefinger upon the paper, but his eyes upon my companion.

"How, in the name of good fortune, did you know all that, Mr. Holmes?" he asked. "How did you know, for example, that I did manual labour? It's as true as gospel, and I began as a ship's carpenter."

"Your hands, my dear sir. Your right hand is quite a size larger than your left. You have worked with it, and the muscles are more developed."

"Well, the snuff, then, and the Freemasonry?"

7 "I won't insult your intelligence by telling you how I read that, especially as, rather against the strict rules of your order, you use an arc and compass breastpin."

"Ah, of course, I forgot that. But the writing?"

"What else can be indicated by that right cuff so very shiny for five inches, and the left one with the smooth patch near the elbow where you rest it upon the desk."

"Well, but China?"

"The fish which you have tattooed immediately above your right wrist could only have been done in China. I have made a small study of tattoo marks, and have even **8** contributed to the literature of the subject. That trick of staining the fishes' scales of a delicate pink is quite **9** peculiar to China. When, in addition, I see a Chinese coin hanging from your watch-chain, the matter becomes even more simple."

"The classic design was a simple one, bearing on one side ideographs representing the name of the reigning emperor, the date and the words 'precious circulating medium.' The reverse was generally blank, though some dynasties put the date there, in regnal years, and others the name of the mint. Some have simply a short arc at the top of the reverse, which has an interesting history. When a wax impression of the coin, with its revised legends (incorporating the new imperial name and date) was submitted to the Emperor Wen Teh for approval, one of his fashionably-long fingernails made a small curved gouge in the wax. The mintmasters, of course, realized that the approved design was that of the wax model in the condition in which it was handed back to them, and proceeded to strike the coin accordingly, nail-mark and all; one is shown on our plate.

"By now the reader will have realized that the coin in question is the one known to foreigners as the 'cash,' worth between $\frac{1}{8}$ and $\frac{1}{7}$ of a cent. It seems inconceivable that this very minor coin should have been the only legal tender of the vast Chinese Empire—the first country in the world to strike coins—for almost thirteen centuries, but such was the case, perhaps because the emperors, as 'sons of heaven,' felt themselves to be above giving even a thought to the meaner uses of trade. Whatever the reason, the humble brass 'cash' would go well with Jabez Wilson's 'brassy Albert chain' and we may fairly conclude that this was the coin which he wore."

Mr. Jabez Wilson laughed heavily. " Well, I never ! " said he. " I thought at first you had done something clever, but I see that there was nothing in it after all."

" I begin to think, Watson," said Holmes, " that I make a mistake in explaining. ' Omne ignotum pro magnifico,' you know, and my poor little reputation, such **10** as it is, will suffer shipwreck if I am so candid. Can you not find the advertisement, Mr. Wilson ? "

" Yes, I have got it now," he answered, with his thick, red finger planted half-way down the column. " Here it is. This is what began it all. You just read it for yourself, sir."

I took the paper from him and read as follows :—

" To the Red-Headed League.—On account of the bequest of the late Ezekiah Hopkins, of Lebanon, Penn., U.S.A., there is now another vacancy open which entitles a member of the League to a salary of four pounds a week **11** for purely nominal services. All red-headed men who are sound in body and mind, and above the age of twenty-one years, are eligible. Apply in person on Monday, at **12** eleven o'clock, to Duncan Ross, at the offices of the League, 7 Pope's Court, Fleet Street." **13**

" What on earth does this mean ? " I ejaculated, after I had twice read over the extraordinary announcement.

Holmes chuckled, and wriggled in his chair, as was his habit when in high spirits. " It is a little off the beaten track, isn't it ? " said he. " And now, Mr. Wilson, off you go at scratch, and tell us all about yourself, **14** your household, and the effect which this advertisement had upon your fortunes. You will first make a note, Doctor, of the paper and the date."

" It is *The Morning Chronicle*, of April 27, 1890. Just two months ago." **15**

10 '*Omne ignotum pro magnifico.*' "Although Holmes was no dilettante in Latin, he resorted to a full quotation from the Roman authors only [this] once," Mr. Morris Rosenblum noted in "Some Latin Byways in the Canon." Elsewhere ("Foreign Language Quotations in the Canon") Mr. Rosenblum wrote: "This is taken from the *Agricola* (*The Life and Character of Julius Agricola*), Chapter 30, Section 4, by Publius Cornelius Tacitus, written about 98 A.D. Translated as 'Everything unknown passes for something splendid,' this is one of the best known epigrams of Tacitus, and is often quoted to characterize the mystery and appeal of the unknown."

11 *four pounds a week*. About $20.

12 *Apply in person on Monday*. We shortly learn that Spaulding, Wilson's assistant, brought the paper to Wilson "*just this day* eight weeks" ago—and therefore on a Saturday. We shall see that Wilson was in error in saying "eight weeks" (*nine* weeks had passed), but there is no reason to believe that he was mistaken about the day of the week. But Wilson also says that he ordered Spaulding "to put up the shutters for the day, and to come right away with me." Watson, then, would appear to have misquoted the advertisement to us: it must have read "Apply in person *today*."

13 *Pope's Court*. "It is probable," the late H. W. Bell wrote in "Three Identifications," "that 'Pope's Court' is a transparent alias for Mitre Court, which connects Fleet Street with the Temple." But Mr. Michael Harrison wrote (*In the Footsteps of Sherlock Holmes*): "I had to go back to Rocque's map of London (1745) to find that [Pope's Court] was a court which lay between Bell Yard and Chancery Lane, being joined by two narrow alleys to each. It is shown (though not named) on Colonel Bayly's Ordnance Survey Map of 1874, and the Chancery Lane entrance to the eastern alley is still there: now closed by the door on the extreme left of the late eighteenth or early nineteenth century premises of Messrs. Jordan, the law-stationers. The alley now is merely a hall-way of the building—but it still exists."

14 *off you go at scratch*. The line from which contestants start a race. Holmes is saying, "Begin at the beginning."

15 *April 27, 1890. Just two months ago."* There is clearly something wrong here, since April 27, 1890, was a Sunday, a day on which newspapers would not have been published in Victorian London. "Just two months ago" would put the time of Wilson's interview with Holmes and Watson at about June 27th, making nonsense of Watson's "autumn." In addition, the *Morning Chronicle*, on which both Dickens and his father worked, had long been defunct. We suggest that the advertisement appeared on Saturday, August 27, 1887. Watson, we believe, was wrong about the year but perfectly correct about the date of the month—and it is easy to misread "August" as "April."

16 *a girl of fourteen.* She does not appear again —at least in "The Red-Headed League." But Magistrate S. Tupper Bigelow has suggested ("Two Canonical Problems Solved") that she was Patience Moran, whom we will meet in "The Boscombe Valley Mystery"—and a niece, he says, of Colonel Sebastian Moran of "The Adventure of the Empty House."

17 *a nice little crib.* In addition to beling thieves' cant for a house, store, shop, or the like ("to crack a crib"), *crib* is English slang for a berth or a job.

" Very good.   Now, Mr. Wilson ? "

" Well, it is just as I have been telling you, Mr. Sherlock Holmes," said Jabez Wilson, mopping his forehead, " I have a small pawnbroker's business at Coburg Square, near the City.   It's not a very large affair, and of late years it has not done more than just give me a living.   I used to be able to keep two assistants, but now I only keep one ; and I would have a job to pay him, but that he is willing to come for half wages, so as to learn the business."

" What is the name of this obliging youth ? " asked Sherlock Holmes.

" His name is Vincent Spaulding, and he's not such a youth either.   It's hard to say his age.   I should not wish a smarter assistant, Mr. Holmes ; and I know very well that he could better himself, and earn twice what I am able to give him.   But after all, if he is satisfied, why should I put ideas in his head ? "

" Why, indeed ?   You seem most fortunate in having an employé who comes under the full market price.   It is not a common experience among employers in this age. I don't know that your assistant is not as remarkable as your advertisement."

" Oh, he has his faults, too," said Mr. Wilson. " Never was such a fellow for photography.   Snapping away with a camera when he ought to be improving his mind, and then diving down into the cellar like a rabbit into its hole to develop his pictures.   That is his main fault ; but on the whole, he's a good worker.   There's no vice in him."

" He is still with you, I presume ? "

16 " Yes, sir.   He and a girl of fourteen, who does a bit of simple cooking, and keeps the place clean—that's all I have in the house, for I am a widower, and never had any family.   We live very quietly, sir, the three of us ; and we keep a roof over our heads, and pay our debts, if we do nothing more.

" The first thing that put us out was that advertisement. Spaulding, he came down into the office just this day eight weeks with this very paper in his hand, and he says :

" ' I wish to the Lord, Mr. Wilson, that I was a red-headed man.'

" ' Why that ? ' I asks.

" ' Why,' says he, ' here's another vacancy on the League of the Red-headed Men.   It's worth quite a little fortune to any man who gets it, and I understand that there are more vacancies than there are men, so that the trustees are at their wits' end what to do with the money. If my hair would only change colour, here's a nice little **17** crib all ready for me to step into.'

" ' Why, what is it, then ? ' I asked.   You see, Mr. Holmes, I am a very stay-at-home man, and, as my business came to me instead of my having to go to it, I was often weeks on end without putting my foot over the doormat.   In that way I didn't know much of what was going on outside, and I was always glad of a bit of news.

" ' Have you never heard of the League of the Red-headed Men ? ' he asked, with his eyes open.

" ' Never.'

" ' Why, I wonder at that, for you are eligible yourself for one of the vacancies.'

" ' And what are they worth ? ' I asked.

" ' Oh, merely a couple of hundred a year, but the work is slight, and it need not interfere much with one's other occupations.'

" Well, you can easily think that that made me prick up my ears, for the business has not been over good for some years, and an extra couple of hundred would have been very handy.

" ' Tell me all about it,' said I.

" ' Well,' said he, showing me the advertisement, ' you can see for yourself that the League has a vacancy, and there is the address where you should apply for particulars. As far as I can make out, the League was founded by an American millionaire, Ezekiah Hopkins, who was very peculiar in his ways. He was himself red-headed, and he had a great sympathy for all red-headed men ; so, when he died, it was found that he had left his enormous fortune in the hands of trustees, with instructions to apply the interest to the providing of easy berths to men whose hair is of that colour. From all I hear it is splendid pay, and very little to do.'

" ' But,' said I, ' there would be millions of red-headed men who would apply.'

" ' Not so many as you might think,' he answered. ' You see, it is really confined to Londoners, and to grown men. This American had started from London when he was young, and he wanted to do the old town a good turn. Then, again, I have heard it is no use your applying if your hair is light red, or dark red, or anything but real, bright, blazing, fiery red. Now, if you cared to apply, Mr. Wilson, you would just walk in ; but perhaps it would hardly be worth your while to put yourself out of the way for the sake of a few hundred pounds.'

" Now, it is a fact, gentlemen, as you may see for yourselves, that my hair is of a very full and rich tint, so that it seemed to me that, if there was to be any competition in the matter, I stood as good a chance as any man that I had ever met. Vincent Spaulding seemed to know so much about it that I thought he might prove useful, so I just ordered him to put up the shutters for the day, and to come right away with me. He was very willing to have a holiday, so we shut the business up, and started off for the address that was given us in the advertisement.

" I never hope to see such a sight as that again, Mr. Holmes. From north, south, east, and west every man who had a shade of red in his hair had tramped into the City to answer the advertisement. Fleet Street was choked with red-headed folk, and Pope's Court looked like **18** a coster's orange barrow. I should not have thought **19** there were so many in the whole country as were brought together by that single advertisement. Every shade of colour they were—straw, lemon, orange, brick, Irish-setter, liver, clay ; but, as Spaulding said, there were not many who had the real vivid flame-coloured tint. When I saw how many were waiting, I would have given it up in despair ; but Spaulding would not hear of it. How he did it I could not imagine, but he pushed and pulled and butted until he got me through the crowd, and right up to the steps which led to the office. There was a double stream upon the stair, some going up in hope, and some

... " 'YOU CAN SEE FOR YOURSELF THAT THE LEAGUE HAS A VACANCY . . .' "

Illustration by Sidney Paget for the *Strand Magazine*, August, 1891.

18 *Fleet Street was choked with red-headed folk.* Fleet Street, as we have seen, was the heart of London's newspaper industry, "yet no single newspaper reported this amazing spectacle. How came Fleet Street to miss this scoop right on its own doorstep?" (" 'The Red-Headed League' Reviewed").

19 *a coster's.* Short for costermonger: an apple seller; a hawker of fruit or vegetables from a street stand, barrow, or cart.

coming back dejected; but we wedged in as well as we could, and soon found ourselves in the office."

"Your experience has been a most entertaining one," remarked Holmes, as his client paused and refreshed his memory with a huge pinch of snuff. "Pray continue your very interesting statement."

"There was nothing in the office but a couple of wooden chairs and a deal table, behind which sat a small man, with a head that was even redder than mine. He said a few words to each candidate as he came up, and then he always managed to find some fault in them which would disqualify them. Getting a vacancy did not seem to be such a very easy matter after all. However, when our turn came, the little man was more favourable to me than to any of the others, and he closed the door as we entered, so that he might have a private word with us.

"'This is Mr. Jabez Wilson,' said my assistant, 'and he is willing to fill a vacancy in the League.'

"'And he is admirably suited for it,' the other answered. 'He has every requirement. I cannot recall when I have seen anything so fine.' He took a step backwards, cocked his head on one side, and gazed at my hair until I felt quite bashful. Then suddenly he plunged forward, wrung my hand, and congratulated me warmly on my success.

"'It would be injustice to hesitate,' said he. 'You will, however, I am sure, excuse me for taking an obvious precaution.' With that he seized my hair in both his hands, and tugged until I yelled with the pain. 'There is water in your eyes,' said he, as he released me. 'I perceive that all is as it should be. But we have to be careful, for we have twice been deceived by wigs and once by paint. I could tell you tales of cobbler's wax which would disgust you with human nature.' He stepped over to the window, and shouted through it at the top of his voice that the vacancy was filled. A groan of disappointment came up from below, and the folk all trooped away in different directions, until there was not a red head to be seen except my own and that of the manager.

"'My name,' said he, 'is Mr. Duncan Ross, and I am myself one of the pensioners upon the fund left by our noble benefactor. Are you a married man, Mr. Wilson? Have you a family?'

"I answered that I had not.

"His face fell immediately.

"'Dear me!' he said gravely, 'that is very serious indeed! I am sorry to hear you say that. The fund was, of course, for the propagation and spread of the red-heads as well as for their maintenance. It is exceedingly unfortunate that you should be a bachelor.'

"My face lengthened at this, Mr. Holmes, for I thought that I was not to have the vacancy after all; but after thinking it over for a few minutes, he said that it would be all right.

"'In the case of another,' said he, 'the objection might be fatal, but we must stretch a point in favour of a man with such a head of hair as yours. When shall you be able to enter upon your new duties?'

"THEN SUDDENLY HE PLUNGED FORWARD, WRUNG MY HAND, AND CONGRATULATED ME WARMLY ON MY SUCCESS."

Illustration by Sidney Paget for the *Strand Magazine*, August, 1891.

" ' Well, it is a little awkward, for I have a business already,' said I.

" ' Oh, never mind about that, Mr. Wilson ! ' said Vincent Spaulding. ' I shall be able to look after that for you.'

" ' What would be the hours ? ' I asked.

" ' Ten to two.'

" Now a pawnbroker's business is mostly done of an evening, Mr. Holmes, especially Thursday and Friday evening, which is just before pay-day ; so it would suit me very well to earn a little in the mornings. Besides, I knew that my assistant was a good man, and that he would see to anything that turned up.

" ' That would suit me very well,' said I. ' And the pay ? '

" ' Is four pounds a week.'

" ' And the work ? '

" ' Is purely nominal.'

" ' What do you call purely nominal ? '

" ' Well, you have to be in the office, or at least in the building, the whole time. If you leave, you forfeit your whole position for ever. The will is very clear upon that point. You don't comply with the conditions if you budge from the office during that time.'

" ' It's only four hours a day, and I should not think of leaving,' said I.

" ' No excuse will avail,' said Mr. Duncan Ross, ' neither sickness, nor business, nor anything else. There you must stay, or you lose your billet.'

" ' And the work ? '

" ' Is to copy out the *Encyclopædia Britannica*. There is the first volume of it in that press. You must find **20** your own ink, pens, and blotting-paper, but we provide **21** this table and chair. Will you be ready to-morrow ? ' **22**

" ' Certainly,' I answered.

" ' Then, good-bye, Mr. Jabez Wilson, and let me congratulate you once more on the important position which you have been fortunate enough to gain.' He bowed me out of the room, and I went home with my assistant, hardly knowing what to say or do, I was so pleased at my own good fortune.

" ' Well, I thought over the matter all day, and by evening I was in low spirits again ; for I had quite persuaded myself that the whole affair must be some great hoax or fraud, though what its object might be I could not imagine. It seemed altogether past belief that anyone could make such a will, or that they would pay such a sum for doing anything so simple as copying out the *Encyclopædia Britannica*. Vincent Spaulding did what he could to cheer me up, but by bedtime I had reasoned myself out of the whole thing. However, in the morning I determined to have a look at it anyhow, so I bought a penny bottle of ink, and with a quill pen, and seven sheets of foolscap **23** paper, I started off for Pope's Court.

" Well, to my surprise and delight everything was as right as possible. The table was set out ready for me, and Mr. Duncan Ross was there to see that I got fairly to work. He started me off upon the letter A, and then he left me ; but he would drop in from time to time to see that all was right with me. At two o'clock he bade me

20 *press*. An upright case or cupboard for the keeping of articles.

21 *You must find your own ink, pens, and blotting-*paper. "Is that a likely statement from the man who is the manager for the late Ezekiah Hopkins, philanthropist of Lebanon, Pennsylvania, U.S.A.? Would a man who paid four pounds a week for purely nominal services boggle at pen, ink, and blotting-paper?" Mr. Thomas L. Stix asked in "Concerning 'The Red-Headed League.' "

22 *Will you be ready to-morrow?* If the advertisement appeared on Saturday and was answered on Saturday, as we believe, Jabez Wilson was being asked to report for his first day's work on a Sunday. This is certainly highly unusual—and yet Wilson later tells us that "*Every* morning I was there at ten . . ." and Holmes himself speaks of Wilson's "absence *every* morning in the week . . ."

23 *foolscap*. Paper in sheets measuring approximately 13 by 16 or 17 inches—so called because the watermark of a fool's cap and bells was used by the old papermakers.

24 *might get on to the B's before very long.* As Mr. Thomas L. Stix has pointed out ("Concerning 'The Red-Headed League'"): "The *Encyclopædia Britannica*—the 1875 edition, which is the one that must have been used—has 928 pages in Volume One, and doesn't reach the article on Attica until page 794 of Volume Two. Now, the average page of the *Britannica* has 3,728 words. The calculation is simple. The pawnbroker says that he copied 6,419,616 words in eight weeks, working only four hours a day. That, gentlemen, is at the rate of 33,435 words per hour, or 557.25 words per minute. That is manifestly impossible. If he had copied at the rate of one page an hour—a prodigious amount to accomplish—Mr. Wilson would be just beginning to write about Ab-Ul-Mejid, 1823–1861—the Sultan of Turkey."

And the late Gavin Brend wrote:

> Archery, Abbots, Africa, Asia,
> Archimedes and Australasia,
> Alps, Architecture, Apes, Antiques:
> This could go on for weeks and weeks.
>
> How I look forward to the day
> That frees me from this monstrous "A"!
> "Copy out letter 'A,'" he said—
> And all because my hair is red!

25 *"THE RED-HEADED LEAGUE IS DIS-SOLVED.* Why did the League give notice to the unfortunate Mr. Wilson before it had accomplished its purpose? Why not pay him another four pounds? As Mr. Thomas L. Stix has observed ("Concerning 'The Red-Headed League'"), the posting of the notice "gave Mr. Wilson the opportunity—an opportunity that he seized brilliantly—to call in Mr. Sherlock Holmes."

good day, complimented me upon the amount that I had written, and locked the door of the office after me.

"This went on day after day, Mr. Holmes, and on Saturday the manager came in and planked down four golden sovereigns for my week's work. It was the same next week, and the same the week after. Every morning I was there at ten, and every afternoon I left at two. By degrees Mr. Duncan Ross took to coming in only once of a morning, and then, after a time, he did not come in at all. Still, of course, I never dared to leave the room for an instant, for I was not sure when he might come, and the billet was such a good one, and suited me so well, that I would not risk the loss of it.

"Eight weeks passed away like this, and I had written about Abbots, and Archery, and Armour, and Architecture, and Attica, and hoped with diligence that I might **24** get on to the B's before very long. It cost me something in foolscap, and I had pretty nearly filled a shelf with my writings. And then suddenly the whole business came to an end."

"To an end?"

"Yes, sir. And no later than this morning. I went to my work as usual at ten o'clock, but the door was shut and locked, with a little square of cardboard hammered on to the middle of the panel with a tack. Here it is, and you can read for yourself."

He held up a piece of white cardboard, about the size of a sheet of note-paper. It read in this fashion:—

25
26
"THE RED-HEADED LEAGUE IS DISSOLVED.
Oct. 9, 1890."

Sherlock Holmes and I surveyed this curt announcement and the rueful face behind it, until the comical side of the affair so completely over-topped every other consideration that we both burst out into a roar of laughter.

"I cannot see that there is anything very funny," cried our client, flushing up to the roots of his flaming head. "If you can do nothing better than laugh at me, I can go elsewhere."

"No, no," cried Holmes, shoving him back into the chair from which he had half risen. "I really wouldn't miss your case for the world. It is most refreshingly unusual. But there is, if you will excuse me saying so, something just a little funny about it. Pray what steps did you take when you found the card upon the door?"

"I was staggered, sir. I did not know what to do. Then I called at the offices round, but none of them seemed to know anything about it. Finally, I went to the landlord, who is an accountant living on the ground floor, and I asked him if he could tell me what had become of the Red-headed League. He said that he had never heard of any such body. Then I asked him who Mr. Duncan Ross was. He answered that the name was new to him.

". . . BUT THE DOOR WAS SHUT AND LOCKED . . ."

Illustration by Sidney Paget for the *Strand Magazine*, August, 1891.

" ' Well, said I, the gentleman at No. 4.'   **27**

" ' What, the red-headed man ? '

" ' Yes.'

" ' Oh,' said he, ' his name was William Morris. He was a solicitor, and was using my room as a temporary **28** convenience until his new premises were ready. He moved out yesterday.'

" ' Where could I find him ? '

" ' Oh, at his new offices. He did tell me the address. Yes, 17 King Edward Street, near St. Paul's.'   **29-30**

" I started off, Mr. Holmes, but when I got to that address it was a manufactory of artificial knee-caps, and no one in it had ever heard of either Mr. William Morris, or Mr. Duncan Ross."

" And what did you do then ? " asked Holmes.

" I went home to Saxe-Coburg Square, and I took the advice of my assistant. But he could not help me in any way. He could only say that if I waited I should hear by post. But that was not quite good enough, Mr. Holmes. I did not wish to lose such a place without a struggle, so, as I had heard that you were good enough to give advice to poor folk who were in need of it, I came right away to you."

" And you did very wisely," said Holmes. " Your case is an exceedingly remarkable one, and I shall be happy to look into it. From what you have told me I think that it is possible that graver issues hang from it than might at first sight appear."

" Grave enough ! " said Mr. Jabez Wilson. " Why, I have lost four pounds a week."

" As far as you are personally concerned," remarked Holmes, " I do not see that you have any grievance against this extraordinary league. On the contrary, you are, as I understand, richer by some thirty pounds, to say nothing of the minute knowledge which you have gained on every subject which comes under the letter A. You have lost nothing by them."

" No, sir. But I want to find out about them, and who they are, and what their object was in playing this prank —if it was a prank—upon me. It was a pretty expensive joke for them, for it cost them two-and-thirty pounds," **31**

" We shall endeavour to clear up these points for you. And, first, one or two questions, Mr. Wilson. This assistant of yours who first called your attention to the advertisement—how long had he been with you ? "

" About a month then."

" How did he come ? "

" In answer to an advertisement."

" Was he the only applicant ? "

" No, I had a dozen."

" Why did you pick him ? "

" Because he was handy, and would come cheap."

" At half wages, in fact."

" Yes."

" What is he like, this Vincent Spaulding ? "

" Small, stout-built, very quick in his ways, no hair on his face, though he's not short of thirty. Has a white splash of acid upon his forehead."

Holmes sat up in his chair in considerable excitement.

26 *Oct. 9, 1890.*" Here, too, something seems to be wrong: October 9, 1890, was not a Saturday but a *Thursday*. Still, as the late Gavin Brend wrote in *My Dear Holmes:* "There is no reason why the notice should bear the same date on which it was read by Wilson." The late Robert R. Pattrick agreed: "I see no reason to doubt that the sign was dated 'Oct. 9, 1890,' and was intended —deliberately and confusingly—to refer to Thursday [October 9, 1890]." In our view, the case opened on *Saturday, October 29, 1887.* (Holmes was thus perfectly correct in saying that he went into the problem of Miss Mary Sutherland just "the other day"; less than two weeks had elapsed between the two cases.) Watson was wrong on the year, but he was right on the month, and it is again charitable to believe that his "29" was misread by the typesetter as "9." It must be admitted that this is not a popular view: virtually all commentators date "The Red-Headed League" 1890. Three others who do not are Knox (1888), Folsom, and Zeisler (1889).

27 *'the gentleman at No. 4.'* As Mr. Colin Prestige seems to have been the first to point out: "From the advertisement in *The Morning Chronicle* of April 27, 1890, we read: "Apply . . . at the offices of the League, 7 Pope's Court.' But Jabez Wilson, on being told . . . that the name Duncan Ross was new to the landlord, quotes himself as saying, 'Well, the gentleman at No. 4.' "

28 *a solicitor.* One who represents a client in a court of justice; an attorney; formerly, in England, a practitioner in chancery only. In England solicitors prepare causes for the barristers, but have not the right to appear as advocates before the higher courts.

29 *King Edward Street.* Once called Stinking Lane because of the filth which used to accumulate there from the neighboring Newgate and Smithfield markets.

30 *St. Paul's.'* The great cathedral built by Christopher Wren, begun June 21, 1675, and finished thirty-five years later at a cost of £747,954 2s. 9d., all of which was raised by imposing a tax on every cauldron of coal brought into the port of London. Augustus J. C. Hare (*Walks in London*, Vol. I) wrote of St. Paul's: "When you are near it, the mighty dome is lost, but you have always an inward all-pervading impression of its existence, as you have seen it a thousand times rising in dark majesty over the city; or, as lighted up by the sun, it is sometimes visible from the river, when all minor objects are obliterated in mist. And, apart from the dome, the noble proportions of every pillar and cornice of the great church cannot fail to strike those who linger to look at them, while even the soot-begrimed garlands, which would be offensive were they clean, have here an indescribable stateliness."

HE CURLED HIMSELF UP IN HIS CHAIR . . .

Illustration by Sidney Paget for the *Strand Magazine*, August, 1891.

31 *it cost them two-and-thirty pounds."* About $160. Since Wilson was *not* paid on the Saturday on which he called on Holmes, it follows that he had been paid on the eight preceding Saturdays. Thus he is incorrect in saying: "Spaulding . . . came down to the office just this day *eight weeks* with this very paper in his hand," but he is correct in saying that "the manager . . . planked down four golden sovereigns" as pay for his first week's work and that "eight weeks passed away *like this."*

32 *for fifty minutes."* "Three pipes of shag in fifty minutes!" Colonel R. D. Sherbrooke-Walker, T.D., wrote in "Holmes, Watson and Tobacco." "It was not a feat—it was a monstrous abuse of the membrane of the nose and throat!"

33 *more to my taste than Italian or French.* "This is not to be taken too literally," Mr. Benjamin Grosbayne wrote in "Sherlock Holmes—Musician," "for in *The Hound of the Baskervilles* [Holmes invites Watson to hear *Les Huguenots*]. Surely, if he chose an opera by Meyerbeer, he must have liked French music also, though he may have gone only to hear the lyric cast of the evening regardless of the musical fare. And he may have felt that, after all, Meyerbeer was German born."

34 *Aldersgate.* Presumably, then, this station of the Metropolitan Line was the nearest to the mysterious Saxe-Coburg Square, and an important clue to its true location. The street in which the station

"I thought as much," said he. "Have you ever observed that his ears are pierced for ear-rings?"

"Yes, sir. He told me that a gipsy had done it for him when he was a lad."

"Hum!" said Holmes, sinking back in deep thought. "He is still with you?"

"Oh, yes, sir; I have only just left him."

"And has your business been attended to in your absence?"

"Nothing to complain of, sir. There's never very much to do of a morning."

"That will do, Mr. Wilson. I shall be happy to give you an opinion upon the subject in the course of a day or two. To-day is Saturday, and I hope that by Monday we may come to a conclusion."

"Well, Watson," said Holmes, when our visitor had left us, "what do you make of it all?"

"I make nothing of it," I answered, frankly. "It is a most mysterious business."

"As a rule," said Holmes, "the more bizarre a thing is the less mysterious it proves to be. It is your commonplace, featureless crimes which are really puzzling, just as a commonplace face is the most difficult to identify. But I must be prompt over this matter."

"What are you going to do then?" I asked.

"To smoke," he answered. "It is quite a three-pipe problem, and I beg that you won't speak to me for fifty **32** minutes." He curled himself up in his chair, with his thin knees drawn up to his hawk-like nose, and there he sat with his eyes closed and his black clay pipe thrusting out like the bill of some strange bird. I had come to the conclusion that he had dropped asleep, and indeed was nodding myself, when he suddenly sprang out of his chair with the gesture of a man who had made up his mind, and put his pipe down upon the mantelpiece.

"Sarasate plays at the St. James's Hall this afternoon," he remarked. "What do you think, Watson? Could your patients spare you for a few hours?"

"I have nothing to do to-day. My practice is never very absorbing."

"Then put on your hat, and come. I am going through the City first, and we can have some lunch on the way. I observe that there is a good deal of German music on the programme, which is rather more to my taste **33** than Italian or French. It is introspective, and I want to introspect. Come along!"

34   We travelled by the Underground as far as Aldersgate; and a short walk took us to Saxe-Coburg Square, the scene of the singular story which we had listened to in the morning. It was a pokey, little, shabby-genteel place, where four lines of dingy two-storied brick houses looked **35** out into a small railed-in enclosure, where a lawn of weedy grass and a few clumps of faded laurel bushes made a hard fight against a smoke-laden and uncongenial atmo- **36** sphere. Three gilt balls and a brown board with " JABEZ WILSON " in white letters, upon a corner house, announced the place where our red-headed client carried on his business. Sherlock Holmes stopped in front of it

"SARASATE PLAYS AT THE ST. JAMES'S HALL THIS AFTERNOON"...

Pablo Martín Melitón Sarasate y Navascues was born at Pamplona, Spain, on March 10, 1844, and died at Biarritz on September 20, 1908. Sarasate studied in France, entering the Paris Conservatoire in 1856, and playing all over Europe before making his first London appearance at the Crystal Palace in 1861. In the same year, he made his first appearance at the St. James's Hall, with which he was to be associated for the rest of his life. Mr. Benjamin Grosbayne wrote of him (in "Sherlock Holmes—Musician"): "His beauty of tone, aristocracy of style, grace of delivery, subtlety of rhythm and amazing dexterity with both hands made him a supreme favorite in every musical center of the world. With what delight Holmes must have heard the Iberian play his own *Gypsy Airs*, *Caprice Basque*, *Zapateado* and Bruch's *Scottish Fantasy*, still war-horses on present-day programs; and MacKenzie's *Pibroch Suite*, the last two dedicated to Sarasate himself. A record of the *Gypsy Airs* by the violinist-composer, made near the turn of the century when recording was in its infancy, is occasionally found in collectors' hands." From the chronological point of view, it is interesting to note that Sarasate did *not* play in London in October, 1890. As Mr. Rolfe Boswell wrote in "Sarasate, Sherlock and Shaw": "early that month Sarasate was giving a series of five brilliant concerts at Barcelona, before returning to England to play no fewer than twenty-eight times in London and the provinces, then going on to Germany for December." The St. James's Hall, we may add, no longer exists: it was demolished in 1905, and the Piccadilly Hotel now stands on its site. It opened in 1858, at a cost of £60,000. Charles Dickens gave readings there, and it also housed the early Moore and Burgess "Christy Minstrel" shows. There were three separate halls, one large, two small. As Mr. William H. Gill wrote in "Some Notable Sherlockian Buildings": "Our friends, who enjoyed its concerts, may not have appreciated its Moorish-style elevation designed by Owen Jones . . . nor its lofty Large Hall, flanked by two smaller music rooms. One can imagine Holmes and Watson in the front row of the Large Hall, and they must have supped in the spacious dining rooms added in 1875, before taking a hansom cab back to Baker Street."

stands was named for the northern gate of the City, the name of which (some say) is derived from the personal name "Ealdred" or "Aldred" and (others say) from the alder-trees which once grew around the gate. In Holmes' and Watson's day, Aldersgate was a shabby thoroughfare indeed, but during our own century it has greatly increased in importance.

35 *looked out into a small railed-in enclosure.* The late H. W. Bell long ago pointed out ("Three Identifications") that there are only two squares in the neighborhood of Aldersgate, one of which, Charterhouse Square, he eliminated by its extent, shape, and lack of seclusion. He found that the other—Bridgewater Square—satisfied "almost all the requirements . . ." Since Jabez Wilson's was a corner house, Mr. Bell cast his vote for No. 5, Bridgewater Square. On the other hand, Mr. W. J. Barnes, banking on Watson's later clue of Farringdon Street, has written ("Saxe-Coburg Square—A New Identification") that he prefers Northampton Square "with four wedge-shaped blocks adjacent. Two of these blocks each has a side on a main artery of sufficient length to include the five business establishments mentioned. . . . We reject the western block on St. John's Street in favour of the easterly block on Goswell Road. . . . Upper Ashby Street forms the north side of this block and Sebastian Street (formerly Upper Charles Street) the south side." And there are other views: Mr. N. P. Metcalfe at a meeting of the Sherlock Holmes

. . . A SHORT WALK TOOK US TO SAXE-COBURG SQUARE . . .

Illustration by Joseph Camana from *Cases of Sherlock Holmes*, St. Louis: Webster Publishing Company, 1947.

Society of London once favored a site backing on to Farringdon Street just north of the Holborn Viaduct, while the late Mr. Bill McGowan at the same meeting preferred Brooke Market at the back of Gray's Inn Road. Still another candidate—Charles Square—has been proposed by Mr. Michael Harrison in his book, *In the Footsteps of Sherlock Holmes*.

36 *Three gilt balls.* The ancient sign of a pawnbroker, originally the arms of the Medici family of Lombardy, the Lombards being widely known as moneylenders.

37 *thumped vigorously upon the pavement with his stick.* This is one of the two Canonical adventures in which Holmes carries a walking stick; the other is "The Adventure of the Illustrious Client," in which Holmes carries a stick to enable him to ward off the blows of his assailants in an anticipated attack.

38 *"Third right, fourth left."* These directions do not lead into the Strand from any square in London, the late H. W. Bell noted in "Three Identifications." "We do not know whether Spaulding made the first answer that came into his head, in order to save time and return to his excavating, or whether Watson has inadvertently misquoted him in his notes. But it is a fact that, if we alter the phrase to 'third left, fourth right,' we do obtain a route by which anyone not wholly deficient in a sense of direction could readily get to the Strand . . ."

39 *I have known something of him before."* "Would not the fourth smartest man in London have known what Sherlock Holmes looked like? He was famous enough even then," Mr. Thomas L. Stix commented in "Concerning 'The Red-Headed League.'"

And the late Robert R. Pattrick wrote ("Moriarty Was There"): "The 'fourth smartest man in London' would not be a freelance. It is even possible that the scheme of 'The Red-Headed League' was originated by Moriarty himself. . . . The capture of Clay ["Spaulding"] . . . was probably Holmes' greatest triumph in the long war. Clay, ranking just below Moriarty in cleverness, and second only to Colonel Moran in daring, would be a key man in the organization . . ."

with his head on one side and looked it all over, with his eyes shining brightly between puckered lids. Then he walked slowly up the street and then down again to the corner, still looking keenly at the houses. Finally he returned to the pawnbroker's, and, having thumped **37** vigorously upon the pavement with his stick two or three times, he went up to the door and knocked. It was instantly opened by a bright-looking, clean-shaven young fellow, who asked him to step in.

" Thank you," said Holmes, " I only wished to ask you how you would go from here to the Strand."

38 " Third right, fourth left," answered the assistant promptly, closing the door.

" Smart fellow, that," observed Holmes as we walked away. " He is, in my judgment, the fourth smartest man in London, and for daring I am not sure that he has not a claim to be third. I have known something of him be-**39** fore."

" Evidently," said I, " Mr. Wilson's assistant counts for a good deal in this mystery of the Red-headed League. I am sure that you inquired your way merely in order that you might see him."

" Not him."

" What then ? "

" The knees of his trousers."

" And what did you see ? "

" What I expected to see."

" Why did you beat the pavement ? "

" My dear Doctor, this is a time for observation, not for talk. We are spies in an enemy's country. We know something of Saxe-Coburg Square. Let us now explore the paths which lie behind it."

The road in which we found ourselves as we turned round the corner from the retired Saxe-Coburg Square presented as great a contrast to it as the front of a picture **40** does to the back. It was one of the main arteries which convey the traffic of the City to the north and west. The roadway was blocked with the immense stream of com-

IT WAS INSTANTLY OPENED BY A BRIGHT-LOOKING, CLEAN-SHAVEN YOUNG FELLOW . . .

Illustration by Sidney Paget for the *Strand Magazine*, August, 1891.

merce flowing in a double tide inwards and outwards, while the footpaths were black with the hurrying swarm of pedestrians. It was difficult to realize as we looked at the line of fine shops and stately business premises that they really abutted on the other side upon the faded and stagnant square which we had just quitted.

"Let me see," said Holmes, standing at the corner, and glancing along the line, "I should like just to remember the order of the houses here. It is a hobby of mine to have an exact knowledge of London. There is Mortimer's, the tobacconist, the little newspaper shop, the Coburg branch of the City and Suburban Bank, the Vegetarian Restaurant, and McFarlane's carriage-building depôt. That carries us right on to the other block. And now, Doctor, we've done our work, so it's time we had some play. A sandwich, and a cup of coffee, and then off to violin land, where all is sweetness, and delicacy, and harmony, and there are no red-headed clients to vex us with their conundrums."

My friend was an enthusiastic musician, being himself not only a very capable performer, but a composer of no ordinary merit. All the afternoon he sat in the stalls wrapped in the most perfect happiness, gently waving his long thin fingers in time to the music, while his gently smiling face and his languid, dreamy eyes were as unlike those of Holmes the sleuth-hound, Holmes the relentless, keen-witted, ready-handed criminal agent, as it was possible to conceive. In his singular character the dual **11** nature alternately asserted itself, and his extreme exactness and astuteness represented, as I have often thought, the reaction against the poetic and contemplative mood which occasionally predominated in him. The swing of his nature took him from extreme languor to devouring energy ; and, as I knew well, he was never so truly formidable as when, for days on end, he had been lounging in his arm-chair amid his improvisations and his black-letter editions. Then it was that the lust of the chase would suddenly come upon him, and that his brilliant reasoning power would rise to the level of intuition, until those who were unacquainted with his methods would look askance at him as on a man whose knowledge was not that of other mortals. When I saw him that afternoon so enwrapped in the music at St. James's Hall I felt that an evil time might be coming upon those whom he had set himself to hunt down.

"You want to go home, no doubt, Doctor," he remarked, as we emerged.

"Yes, it would be as well."

"And I have some business to do which will take some hours. This business at Coburg Square is serious."

"Why serious ?"

"A considerable crime is in contemplation. I have every reason to believe that we shall be in time to stop it. But to-day being Saturday rather complicates matters. I shall want your help to-night."

"At what time ?"

"Ten will be early enough."

"I shall be at Baker Street at ten."

"Very well. And, I say, Doctor ! there may be some little danger, so kindly put your army revolver in your

40 *It was one of the main arteries.* This was Aldersgate Street, presumably, or perhaps its continuation, Goswell Road. But Mr. Frank V. Morley has pointed out ("I Am puzzled About Saxe-Coburg Square") that the Goswell Road "is more Pickwick than the sort of Oxford Street described by Watson."

41 *as it was possible to conceive.* ". . . observe another great detective, Lord Peter Wimsey, in a similar situation: 'He was wrapped in the motionless austerity with which all genuine musicians listen to genuine music. Harriet was musican enough to respect this aloofness; she knew well enough that the ecstatic rapture on the face of the man opposite meant only that he was hoping to be thought musical, and that the elderly lady over the way, waving her fingers to the beat, was a musical moron (Dorothy L. Sayers, *Gaudy Night*, New York: Harcourt, Brace & Co., 1936, p. 467)."—Professor Remsen Ten Eyck Schenck, "Baker Street Fables."

ALL THE AFTERNOON HE SAT IN THE STALLS WRAPPED IN THE MOST PERFECT HAPPINESS . . .

Illustration by Sidney Paget for the *Strand Magazine*, August, 1891.

42 *Kensington.* A metropolitan borough distinguished as the "Royal Borough" by grant of Edward VII in 1901. It extends from the northwest part of the county boundary, where it adjoins the Middlesex borough of Willesden, for nearly four miles to Chelsea on its southeast, and it has an average breadth, northeast to southwest, of about one and a half miles. The borough includes about half of Kensington Gardens, including Kensington Palace. Kensington has long been a haunt of literary and artistic people. Kensington is also famous for its museums.

43 *as in that business of the Sholto murder and the Agra treasure.* See our remarks in "Now, Watson, the Fair Sex Is Your Department."

44 *some thirty thousand pounds.* Some $1,500,000.

pocket." He waved his hand, turned on his heel, and disappeared in an instant among the crowd.

I trust that I am not more dense than my neighbours, but I was always oppressed with a sense of my own stupidity in my dealings with Sherlock Holmes. Here I had heard what he had heard, I had seen what he had seen, and yet from his words it was evident that he saw clearly not only what had happened, but what was about to happen, while to me the whole business was still confused and **42** grotesque. As I drove home to my house in Kensington I thought over it all, from the extraordinary story of the red-headed copier of the *Encyclopædia* down to the visit to Saxe-Coburg Square, and the ominous words with which he had parted from me. What was this nocturnal expedition, and why should I go armed ? Where were we going, and what were we to do ? I had the hint from Holmes that this smooth-faced pawnbroker's assistant was a formidable man—a man who might play a deep game. I tried to puzzle it out, but gave it up in despair, and set the matter aside until night should bring an explanation.

It was a quarter past nine when I started from home and made my way across the Park, and so through Oxford Street to Baker Street. Two hansoms were standing at the door, and, as I entered the passage, I heard the sound of voices from above. On entering his room, I found Holmes in animated conversation with two men, one of whom I recognized as Peter Jones, the official police agent ; while the other was a long, thin, sad-faced man, with a very shiny hat and oppressively respectable frock-coat.

"Ha ! our party is complete," said Holmes, buttoning up his pea-jacket, and taking his heavy hunting-crop from the rack. "Watson, I think you know Mr. Jones, of Scotland Yard ? Let me introduce you to Mr. Merryweather, who is to be our companion in to-night's adventure."

"We're hunting in couples again, Doctor, you see," said Jones in his consequential way. "Our friend here is a wonderful man for starting a chase. All he wants is an old dog to help him to do the running down."

"I hope a wild goose may not prove to be the end of our chase," observed Mr. Merryweather gloomily.

"You may place considerable confidence in Mr. Holmes, sir," said the police agent loftily. "He has his own little methods, which are, if he won't mind my saying so, just a little too theoretical and fantastic, but he has the makings of a detective in him. It is not too much to say that once or twice, as in that business of the Sholto **43** murder and the Agra treasure, he has been more nearly correct than the official force."

"Oh, if you say so, Mr. Jones, it is all right ! " said the stranger, with deference. "Still, I confess that I miss my rubber. It is the first Saturday night for seven-and-twenty years that I have not had my rubber."

" I think you will find," said Sherlock Holmes, " that you will play for a higher stake to-night than you have ever done yet, and that the play will be more exciting. For you, Mr. Merryweather, the stake will be some **44** thirty thousand pounds ; and for you, Jones, it will be the man upon whom you wish to lay your hands."

" John Clay, the murderer, thief, smasher, and forger. He's a young man, Mr. Merryweather, but he is at the head of his profession, and I would rather have my bracelets on him than on any criminal in London. He's a remarkable man, is young John Clay. His grandfather was a Royal Duke, and he himself has been to Eton and **45** Oxford. His brain is as cunning as his fingers, and though we meet signs of him at every turn, we never know where to find the man himself. He'll crack a crib in Scotland one week, and be raising money to build an orphanage in Cornwall the next. I've been on his track **46** for years, and have never set eyes on him yet."

" I hope that I may have the pleasure of introducing you to-night. I've had one or two little turns also with Mr. John Clay, and I agree with you that he is at the head of his profession. It is past ten, however, and quite time that we started. If you two will take the first hansom, Watson and I will follow in the second."

Sherlock Holmes was not very communicative during the long drive, and lay back in the cab humming the tunes which he had heard in the afternoon. We rattled through an endless labyrinth of gas-lit streets until we emerged into Farringdon Street. **47**

" We are close there now," my friend remarked. " This fellow Merryweather is a bank director and personally interested in the matter. I thought it as well to have Jones with us also. He is not a bad fellow, though an absolute imbecile in his profession. He has one positive virtue. He is as brave as a bulldog, and as tenacious as a lobster if he gets his claws upon anyone. Here we are, and they are waiting for us."

We had reached the same crowded thoroughfare in which we had found ourselves in the morning. Our cabs were dismissed, and, following the guidance of Mr. Merryweather, we passed down a narrow passage, and through a side door, which he opened for us. Within there was a small corridor, which ended in a very massive iron gate. This also was opened, and led down a flight of winding stone steps, which terminated at another formidable gate. Mr. Merryweather stopped to light a lantern, and then conducted us down a dark, earth-smelling passage, and so, after opening a third door, into a huge vault or cellar, which was piled all round with crates and massive boxes.

" You are not very vulnerable from above," Holmes remarked, as he held up the lantern and gazed about him.

" Nor from below," said Mr. Merryweather, striking his stick upon the flags which lined the floor. " Why, dear me, it sounds quite hollow ! " he remarked, looking up in surprise.

" I must really ask you to be a little more quiet," said Holmes severely. " You have already imperilled the whole success of our expedition. Might I beg that you would have the goodness to sit down upon one of those boxes, and not to interfere ? "

The solemn Mr. Merryweather perched himself upon a crate, with a very injured expression upon his face, while Holmes fell upon his knees upon the floor, and, with the lantern and a magnifying lens, began to examine minutely the cracks between the stones. A few seconds sufficed

45 *His grandfather was a Royal Duke.* "It is generally agreed that John Clay's grandfather was one of the seven sons of George III because they were the Royal Dukes who were in action during the epoch that his link with royalty was forged," Dr. Julian Wolff wrote in *Practical Handbook of Sherlockian Heraldry.* Mr. Carl T. Erickson has made a case ("Royal Blood and Feet of Clay") for the third son, the Duke of Clarence, who later became William IV, and Mr. N. P. Metcalfe, at a meeting of the Sherlock Holmes Society of London, once eliminated six of the sons until only the Duke of Sussex remained. However, as Dr. Wolff concluded: "The truth is that there are too many suspects, none of them impossible—or even improbable."

46 *Cornwall.* A maritime county in the southwest of England, a peninsula ending in the promontory called Land's End. Cornwall is a county of low-lying plateaus with market and dairy farms in fertile valleys. It is a great fishing center, and its climate and picturesque coast towns make it popular with tourists.

47 *Farringdon Street.* The late H. W. Bell dismissed Farringdon *Street* as a slip of the pen, believing that Watson intended to refer to Farringdon *Road.* On the other hand, Mr. Barnes, as we have seen, found this clue "quite acceptable." The question remains: with Aldersgate Station only "a short walk" from Saxe-Coburg Square, why did Holmes and party endure a "long drive" through "an endless labyrinth of gas-lit streets"?

MR. MERRYWEATHER STOPPED TO LIGHT A LANTERN . . .

Illustration by Sidney Paget for the *Strand Magazine,* August, 1891.

38

38a   38b

39a   39

40

40a

41

42

to satisfy him, for he sprang to his feet again, and put his glass in his pocket.

"We have at least an hour before us," he remarked, "for they can hardly take any steps until the good pawnbroker is safely in bed. Then they will not lose a minute, for the sooner they do their work the longer time they will have for their escape. We are at present, Doctor— as no doubt you have divined—in the cellar of the City branch of one of the principal London banks. Mr. Merryweather is the chairman of directors, and he will explain to you that there are reasons why the more daring criminals of London should take a considerable interest in this cellar at present."

"It is our French gold," whispered the director. "We have had several warnings that an attempt might be made upon it."

"Your French gold?"

"Yes. We had occasion some months ago to strengthen our resources, and borrowed, for that purpose, thirty thousand napoleons from the Bank of France. It has become known that we have never had occasion to unpack the money, and that it is still lying in our cellar. The crate upon which I sit contains two thousand napoleons packed between layers of lead foil. Our reserve of bullion is much larger at present than is usually kept in a single branch office, and the directors have had mis- **48** givings upon the subject."

"... THIRTY THOUSAND NAPOLEONS FROM THE BANK OF FRANCE."

The late A. Carson Simpson, our specialist in the numismatics of the Canon, tells us in "A Very Treasury of Divers Realms" that "there can be no doubt that a 'napoleon' is a French 20-franc goldpiece." It is true that Holmes is said to have valued the shipment at "some £30,000." The 20-franc piece being worth about $3.86 and the pound close to $5.00, the value of 30,000 of the former would be closer to £20,000. This is almost certainly another of Watson's errors. The French gold napoleons shown above include: *38*, Louis XVIII, uniformed bust; *38a*, Bonaparte, First Consul, obverse only; *38b*, Napoleon I, obverse only; *39*, Louis XVIII, bare head, Perpignan mint; *39a*, Charles X, obverse only; *40*, Louis-Philippe; *40a*, Second Republic, Ceres head, obverse only; *41*, Napoleon III, Strasbourg mint; *42*, Third Republic, angel type.

" Which were very well justified," observed Holmes. " And now it is time that we arranged our little plans. I expect that within an hour matters will come to a head. In the meantime, Mr. Merryweather, we must put the screen over that dark lantern."

" And sit in the dark ? "

" I am afraid so. I had brought a pack of cards in my pocket, and I thought that, as we were a *partie carrée*, you **49-50** might have your rubber after all. But I see that the enemy's preparations have gone so far that we cannot risk the presence of a light. And, first of all, we must choose our positions. These are daring men, and, though we shall take them at a disadvantage they may do us some harm, unless we are careful. I shall stand behind this crate, and do you conceal yourself behind those. Then, when I flash a light upon them, close in swiftly. If they fire, Watson, have no compunction about shooting them down."

I placed my revolver, cocked, upon the top of the wooden case behind which I crouched. Holmes shot the slide across the front of his lantern, and left us in pitch darkness—such an absolute darkness as I have never before experienced. The smell of hot metal remained **51** to assure us that the light was still there, ready to flash out at a moment's notice. To me, with my nerves worked up to a pitch of expectancy, there was something depressing and subduing in the sudden gloom, and in the cold, dank air of the vault.

" They have but one retreat," whispered Holmes. " That is back through the house into Saxe-Coburg Square. I hope that you have done what I asked you, Jones ? "

" I have an inspector and two officers waiting at the front door."

" Then we have stopped all the holes. And now we must be silent and wait."

What a time it seemed ! From comparing notes afterwards it was but an hour and a quarter, yet it appeared to me that the night must have almost gone, and the dawn be breaking above us. My limbs were weary and stiff, for I feared to change my position, yet my nerves were worked up to the highest pitch of tension, and my hearing was so acute that I could not only hear the gentle breathing of my companions, but I could distinguish the deeper, heavier in-breath of the bulky Jones from the thin sighing note of the bank director. From my position I could look over the case in the direction of the floor. Suddenly my eyes caught the glint of a light.

At first it was but a lurid spark upon the stone pavement. Then it lengthened out until it became a yellow line, and then, without any warning or sound, a gash seemed to open and a hand appeared, a white, almost womanly hand, which felt about in the centre of the little area of light. For a minute or more the hand, with its writhing fingers, protruded out of the floor. Then it was withdrawn as suddenly as it appeared, and all was dark again save the single lurid spark, which marked a chink between the stones.

Its disappearance, however, was but momentary.

48 *the directors have had misgivings upon the subject.*" "Mr. [G. B.] Newton, who is a retired bank manager, confessed to astonishment at the singular way in which the directors of the City and Suburban Bank conducted their business. The 30,000 napoleons (not, incidentally, a very substantial sum with which to allay the possible anxieties of depositors) had been stored, not at the Bank of England, as would have been the normal procedure, nor even at the C. & S. Bank's own head office strong room, but in an apparently not very impregnable cellar below its Coburg branch. It had moreover 'become known' that the bullion was unpacked and lying in the cellar—a most reprehensible leakage of top-secret information for which no-one in particular seems to have been responsible. No wonder the directors had 'misgivings.' Yet, notwithstanding that 'they had had several warnings that an attempt might be made upon it,' they took no special precautions but apparently just hoped for the best. The keys giving access to this rather doubtful stronghold were apparently in the sole possession of Mr. Merryweather and Clay could have saved himself a good deal of trouble if he had knocked him on the head and stolen them."—" 'The Red-Headed League' Reviewed."

49 *I had brought a pack of cards in my pocket.* "Without a doubt," Mr. L. A. Morrow wrote in "The Game Is . . .", "Holmes' game was whist . . ." Whist was the famous card game from which modern bridge developed. The name is said to be derived from "Whist!" meaning to be silent, a reproach still applicable to those who are talkative at the card table. The game of whist was famous as far back as the eighteenth century, and Edmond Hoyle's *Treatise on Whist*, published in 1742, codified the rules. This book became the classic of card lore, hence the phrase "According to Hoyle."

Holmes' devotion to whist must have been exceedingly great; "taking a deck of cards instead of a gun when going after a desperate bank robber is hardly the action of one whose interest in cards is casual," as Mr. Morrow wrote. As Mr. Morrow and others have shown, Holmes studded his conversation with terms taken from the lexicon of a card enthusiast: "At present it must be admitted that the odd trick is in his possession, and, as you are aware, Watson, it is not my habit to leave the game in that condition," Holmes said in "The Adventure of the Missing Three-Quarter." "You see that we hold all the cards . . . ," he said in "The Greek Interpreter." "He will hold a card back for years in order to play it at the moment when the stake is best worth winning," Holmes said of Charles Augustus Milverton. "We have added one card to our hand, Watson, but it needs careful playing all the same," he said in "The Adventure of Shoscombe Old Place," and, in that same adventure: "We are getting some cards in our hands. . . . It's not an easy one to play . . ." "Now, Count, you are a card-player. When the other fellow has all the trumps, it saves time to throw down your hand,"

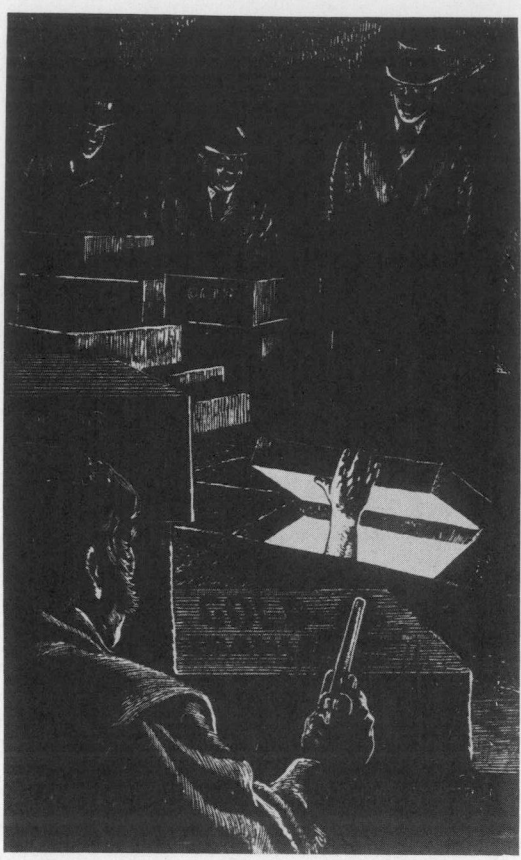

. . . A HAND APPEARED, A WHITE, ALMOST WOMANLY HAND, WHICH FELT ABOUT IN THE CENTRE OF THE LITTLE AREA OF LIGHT.

Illustration by Joseph Camana for *Cases of Sherlock Holmes*, St. Louis: Webster Publishing Company, 1947.

he warned in "The Adventure of the Mazarin Stone." "I see the fall of the cards," he said in "The Adventure of the Bruce-Partington Plans." And in *The Hound of the Baskervilles*, Holmes said: "We must see what further cards we have in our hands, and play them with decision."

50 *a partie carrée.* French: a party of four, more usually applied to a party of two men and two women.

51 *The smell of hot metal.* "Mr. Guy Warrack: 'How was it that Clay, who probably had a very sensitive nose, was not warned of the presence of Holmes and his party in the vault by the smell of their oil lamp?'"—"'The Red-Headed League' Reviewed."

52 *Jump, Archie, jump.* Mr. Jerry Neal Williamson has speculated ("The Sad Case of Young Stamford") that this Archie was the same Archie Stamford, the forger, later taken by Holmes and Watson near Farnham, on the borders of Surrey ("The Adventure of the Solitary Cyclist").

With a rending, tearing sound, one of the broad, white stones turned over upon its side, and left a square, gaping hole, through which streamed the light of a lantern. Over the edge there peeped a clean-cut, boyish face, which looked keenly about it, and then, with a hand on either side of the aperture, drew itself shoulder high and waist high, until one knee rested upon the edge. In another instant he stood at the side of the hole, and was hauling after him a companion, lithe and small like himself, with a pale face and a shock of very red hair.

"It's all clear," he whispered. "Have you the chisel, **52** and the bags. Great Scott! Jump, Archie, jump, and **53** I'll swing for it!"

Sherlock Holmes had sprung out and seized the intruder by the collar. The other dived down the hole, and I heard the sound of rending cloth as Jones clutched at his skirts. The light flashed upon the barrel of a revolver, but Holmes's hunting-crop came down on the **54** man's wrist, and the pistol clinked upon the stone floor.

"It's no use, John Clay," said Holmes blandly; "you have no chance at all."

"So I see," the other answered with the utmost coolness. "I fancy that my pal is all right, though I see you have got his coat-tails."

"There are three men waiting for him at the door," said Holmes.

"Oh, indeed. You seem to have done the thing very completely. I must compliment you."

"And I you," Holmes answered. "Your red-headed idea was very new and effective."

"You'll see your pal again presently," said Jones. "He's quicker at climbing down holes than I am. Just **55** hold out while I fix the derbies."

"I beg that you will not touch me with your filthy hands," remarked our prisoner, as the handcuffs clattered upon his wrists. "You may not be aware that I have royal blood in my veins. Have the goodness also when you address me always to say 'sir' and 'please.'"

"All right," said Jones, with a stare and a snigger. "Well, would you please, sir, march upstairs, where we can get a cab to carry your highness to the police station."

"That is better," said John Clay serenely. He made a sweeping bow to the three of us, and walked quietly off in the custody of the detective.

"Really, Mr. Holmes," said Mr. Merryweather, as we followed them from the cellar, "I do not know how the bank can thank you or repay you. There is no doubt that you have detected and defeated in the most complete manner one of the most determined attempts at bank robbery that have ever come within my experience."

"I have had one or two little scores of my own to settle with Mr. John Clay," said Holmes. "I have been at some small expense over this matter, which I shall expect the bank to refund, but beyond that I am amply repaid by having had an experience which is in many ways unique, and by hearing the very remarkable narrative of the Red-headed League."

"You see, Watson," he explained in the early hours

of the morning, as we sat over a glass of whisky-and-soda in Baker Street, " it was perfectly obvious from the first that the only possible object of this rather fantastic business of the advertisement of the League, and the copying of the *Encyclopædia*, must be to get this not over-bright pawnbroker out of the way for a number of hours every day. It was a curious way of managing it, but really it would be difficult to suggest a better. The method was no doubt suggested to Clay's ingenious mind by the colour of his accomplice's hair. The four pounds a week was a lure which must draw him, and what was it to them, who were playing for thousands ? They put in the advertisement ; one rogue has the temporary office, the other rogue incites the man to apply for it, and together they manage to secure his absence every morning in the week. From the time that I heard of the assistant having come for half-wages, it was obvious to me that he had some strong motive for securing the situation.''

" But how could you guess what the motive was ? ''

" Had there been women in the house, I should have suspected a mere vulgar intrigue. That, however, was out of the question. The man's business was a small one, and there was nothing in his house which could account for such elaborate preparations and such an expenditure as they were at. It must then be something out of the house. What could it be ? I thought of the assistant's fondness for photography, and his trick of vanishing into the cellar. The cellar ! There was the end of this tangled clue. Then I made inquiries as to this mysterious assistant, and found that I had to deal with one of the coolest and most daring criminals in London. He was doing something in the cellar—something which took many hours a day for months on end. What could it be, once more ? I could think of nothing save that he was running a tunnel to some other building.

" So far I had got when we went to visit the scene of action. I surprised you by beating upon the pavement with my stick. I was ascertaining whether the cellar stretched out in front or behind. It was not in front. Then I rang the bell, and, as I hoped, the assistant answered it. We have had some skirmishes, but we had never set eyes on each other before. I hardly looked at his face. His knees were what I wished to see. You must yourself have remarked how worn, wrinkled and stained they were. They spoke of those hours of burrowing. The only remaining point was what they were burrowing for. I walked round the corner, saw that the **56** City and Suburban Bank abutted on our friend's premises, and felt that I had solved my problem. When you drove home after the concert I called upon Scotland Yard, and upon the chairman of the bank directors, with the result that you have seen.''

" And how could you tell that they would make their attempt to-night ? '' I asked.

" Well, when they closed their League offices that was a sign that they cared no longer about Mr. Jabez Wilson's presence ; in other words, that they had completed their tunnel. But it was essential that they should use it soon, as it might be discovered, or the bullion might be removed.

53 *and I'll swing for it!*'' Did this merely mean that Clay would swing back through the trapdoor or was he anticipating that he would be hanged? "This must have been thieves' jargon," Magistrate S. Tupper Bigelow wrote in "Two Canonical Problems Solved," "or Dr. Watson didn't hear . . . correctly, because John Clay knew as well as anyone that in England of those days, only traitors (like Sir Roger Casement) and murderers were hanged . . .''

54 *Holmes' hunting-crop came down on the man's wrist.* "This adventure, if I am not mistaken, is the only one in which Holmes used his famous hunting-crop as a weapon. . . . Watson tells us in after years that a hunting-crop was Holmes' favorite weapon but I can't find any other instance of its use in offence or defence."—The late Clifton R. Andrew in a footnote to " 'The Red-Headed League' Reviewed.''

55 *the derbies.*'' The handcuffs.

56 *The only remaining point was what they were burrowing for.* Another remaining point is: What was done with the excavated earth? "How could it possibly have been disposed of?" Mr. Nathan L. Bengis wrote in "Sherlock Stays After School." "The amount of earth excavated in the digging of the tunnel . . . must have been prodigious. The dirt could not have been allowed to accumulate in the cellar, even if conceivably the

"IT'S NO USE, JOHN CLAY," SAID HOLMES BLANDLY . . .

Illustration by Sidney Paget for the *Strand Magazine*, August, 1891.

cellar was large enough to receive it, as a gigantic pile would have been too conspicuous to avoid detection should Wilson ever have taken it into his head to descend into the basement for a minute. The debris could not have been taken out into the street, as the risk of detection would have been too great between the hours of ten and two, when Wilson was away from his shop. Altogether, it is a neat puzzle . . ."

"The area underlying the footpath was the repository of the dirt," Mr. W. J. Barnes suggested. "John Clay had merely transported the excavated earth from one side of the cellar to the other . . ."

And Magistrate S. Tupper Bigelow suggested ("Two Canonical Problems Solved") that the earth was loaded into large empty cardboard boxes which were then taken away by a dray which delivered more cardboard boxes.

Also: how did the criminals hope to remove the bullion, the weight of which must have been enormous? "The task of lowering 15 crates into the tunnel, along it and up again would have been a herculean one for two men. And if this were achieved what were they going to do next? Loading it into a cart outside a pawnbroker's shop on a Sunday morning might well provoke some awkward questions and you cannot just go gadding about the countryside with large quantities of bullion in tow without attracting some attention" ("'The Red-Headed League' Reviewed").

To this question Mr. Charles Scholefield suggested that the criminals would use a carriage from McFarlane's Depot; probably the tunnel connected not only Wilson's but also McFarlane's with the bank.

57 *as it would give them two days for their escape.* But "two days" the robbers could *not* have had unless the Monday following the robbery on Sunday morning was a Bank Holiday, and no Bank Holiday falls during the autumn of the year.

58 *as Gustave Flaubert wrote to George Sand.* "The correct wording," Mr. Morris Rosenblum wrote in "Foreign Language Quotations in the Canon," "is 'L'homme n'est rien, l'œuvre tout.' . . . The quotation occurs in the letter dated December, 1875, pages 272–3 of *Lettres de Gustave Flaubert à George Sand*, Charpentier, Paris, 188?. The translation, 'The man is nothing, the work is everything,' is found on page 348, Letter CCCI of the English edition, *The George Sand-Gustave Flaubert Letters,* by Aimee L. McKenzie, Boni and Liveright, New York, 1921."

Saturday would suit them better than any other day, as it **57** would give them two days for their escape. For all these reasons I expected them to come to-night."

"You reasoned it out beautifully," I exclaimed in unfeigned admiration. "It is so long a chain, and yet every link rings true."

"It saved me from ennui," he answered, yawning. "Alas, I already feel it closing in upon me! My life is spent in one long effort to escape from the commonplaces of existence. These little problems help me to do so."

"And you are a benefactor of the race," said I.

He shrugged his shoulders. "Well, perhaps, after all, it is of some little use," he remarked. "'L'homme c'est rien—l'œuvre c'est tout,' as Gustave Flaubert wrote to **58** George Sand."

Auctorial and Bibliographical Note: Conan Doyle's own opinion of "The Red-Headed League" was a high one: he rated it in second position in his "twelve best" list of the short stories (excluding those in the *Case-Book*). It also rated high —No. 5—with the readers of the *Observer*, who considered both the short stories and the novels.

According to Mr. David A. Randall, "The Red-Headed League" was first published in book form in an unauthorized edition of Conan Doyle's short stories titled *The Doings of Raffles Haw*; New York: Lovell, Coryell and Company, August, 1892, as "Number Five in the Belmore Series."

29

THE ADVENTURE OF THE DYING DETECTIVE

[Saturday, November 19, 1887]

MRS. HUDSON, the landlady of Sherlock Holmes, was a long-suffering woman. Not only was her first-floor flat invaded at all hours by **1** throngs of singular and often undesirable characters, but her remarkable lodger showed an eccentricity and irregularity in his life which must have sorely tried her patience. His incredible untidiness, his addiction to music at strange hours, his occasional revolver practice within doors, his weird and often malodorous scientific experiments, and the atmosphere of violence and danger which hung around him made him the very worst tenant in London. On the other hand, his payments were princely. I have no doubt that **2** the house might have been purchased at the price which Holmes paid for his rooms during the years that I was with him.

The landlady stood in the deepest awe of him, and never dared to interfere with him, however outrageous his proceedings might seem. She was fond of him, too, for he had a remarkable gentleness and courtesy in his dealings with women. He disliked and distrusted the sex, but he was always a chivalrous opponent. Knowing how genuine was her regard for him, I listened earnestly to her story when she came to my rooms in the second year of my **3** married life and told me of the sad condition to which my poor friend was reduced.

" He's dying, Dr. Watson," said she. " For three days he has been sinking, and I doubt if he will last the day. **4** He would not let me get a doctor. This morning when I saw his bones sticking out of his face and his great bright eyes looking at me I could stand no more of it. ' With your leave or without it, Mr. Holmes, I am going for a doctor this very hour,' said I. ' Let it be Watson, then,' said he. I wouldn't waste an hour in coming to him, sir, or you may not see him alive."

I was horrified, for I had heard nothing of his illness. I need not say that I rushed for my coat and my hat. As we drove back I asked for the details.

" There is little I can tell you, sir. He has been working at a case down at Rotherhithe, in an alley near the **5** river, and he has brought this illness back with him. He took to his bed on Wednesday afternoon and has never

1 *her first-floor flat.* Watson of course uses "first-floor" in the English sense; an American would say "second-floor."

2 *his payments were princely.* There can be no doubt that Holmes by this time could easily afford the rent of the Baker Street suite without assistance—but "the impecunious Watson was no judge of what was princely," as Mr. Vincent Starrett wrote in "The Singular Adventures of Martha Hudson."

3 *in the second year of my married life.* Although Watson certainly married for a second (or a third) time in late 1902, most commentators are agreed that Holmes retired in 1903. It is therefore generally conceded that "The Adventure of the Dying Detective" did not take place in the November (*see below*) of that year. The date assigned to the adventure by the various commentators thus hinges on the date that each assigns to Watson's first marriage, and the consensus (Blakeney, Christ, Folsom, Pattrick, Petersen, Smith, and Zeisler) favors 1890. Messrs. Bell, Boucher, and Starrett chose 1888, Messrs. Andrew, Brend, and Harrison 1889. Your editor would again seem to stand alone in his selection of *1887*.

4 *"For three days he has been sinking.* The late Dr. Ernest Bloomfield Zeisler (*Baker Street Chronology*) well summed up the case for dating this adventure on a *Saturday:* "Mrs. Hudson says that the Master took to his bed on Wednesday afternoon, that 'for three days he has been sinking' and that 'for these three days neither food nor drink has passed his lips.' Watson tells Culverton Smith that the Master had been ill 'about three days.' Smith recalls to the Master that the poisoned box 'came on Wednesday.' Watson goes to the Master at once, and shortly after his arrival it is four o'clock. Since Wednesday afternoon to Saturday afternoon is three days there is no doubt that the story begins on a Saturday . . .'"

5 *Rotherhithe.* A section of London, long popularly known as Redriff, which includes the Surrey docks and is mainly inhabited by dock and waterside workers. The name may come from *rethra*, a mariner, and *hythe*, a haven.

6 *a foggy November day.* Our choice of the Saturday in November of 1887 on which this adventure took place is dictated by the weather reports in the London *Times*. In the Saturday–Sunday reports published in the Monday editions of that newspaper for November, 1887, fog is mentioned only once: in the report for *Saturday, November 19, 1887*.

. . . BUT IT WAS THAT GAUNT, WASTED FACE STARING AT ME FROM THE BED WHICH SENT A CHILL TO MY HEART.

Illustration by Frederic Dorr Steele for *Collier's Magazine*, November 22, 1913.

moved since.   For these three days neither food nor drink has passed his lips."

" Good God ! Why did you not call in a doctor ? "

" He wouldn't have it, sir. You know how masterful he is. I didn't dare to disobey him. But he's not long for this world, as you'll see for yourself the moment that you set eyes on him."

He was indeed a deplorable spectacle.   In the dim light **6** of a foggy November day the sick-room was a gloomy spot, but it was that gaunt, wasted face staring at me from the bed which sent a chill to my heart. His eyes had the brightness of fever, there was a hectic flush upon either cheek, and dark crusts clung to his lips ; the thin hands upon the coverlet twitched incessantly, his voice was croaking and spasmodic. He lay listlessly as I entered the room, but the sight of me brought a gleam of recognition to his eyes.

" Well, Watson, we seem to have fallen upon evil days," said he, in a feeble voice, but with something of his old carelessness of manner.

" My dear fellow ! " I cried, approaching him.

" Stand back ! Stand right back ! " said he, with the sharp imperiousness which I had associated only with moments of crisis. " If you approach me, Watson, I shall order you out of the house."

" But why ? "

" Because it is my desire. Is that not enough ? "

Yes, Mrs. Hudson was right. He was more masterful than ever. It was pitiful, however, to see his exhaustion.

" I only wished to help," I explained.

" Exactly ! You will help best by doing what you are told."

" Certainly, Holmes."

He relaxed the austerity of his manner.

" You are not angry ? " he asked, gasping for breath.

Poor devil, how could I be angry when I saw him lying in such a plight before me ?

" It's for your own sake, Watson," he croaked.

" For *my* sake ? "

" I know what is the matter with me. It is a coolie disease from Sumatra—a thing that the Dutch know more about than we, though they have made little of it up to date. One thing only is certain. It is infallibly deadly, and it is horribly contagious."

He spoke now with a feverish energy, the long hands twitching and jerking as he motioned me away.

" Contagious by touch, Watson—that's it, by touch. Keep your distance and all is well."

" Good heavens, Holmes ! Do you suppose that such a consideration weighs with me for an instant ? It would not affect me in the case of a stranger. Do you imagine it would prevent me from doing my duty to so old a friend ? "

Again I advanced, but he repulsed me with a look of furious anger.

" If you will stand there I will talk. If you do not you must leave the room."

I have so deep a respect for the extraordinary qualities

of Holmes that I have always deferred to his wishes, even when I least understood them. But now all my professional instincts were aroused. Let him be my master elsewhere, I at least was his in a sick-room.

"Holmes," said I, "you are not yourself. A sick man is but a child, and so I will treat you. Whether you like it or not, I will examine your symptoms and treat you for them."

He looked at me with venomous eyes.

"If I am to have a doctor whether I will or not, let me at least have someone in whom I have confidence," said he.

"Then you have none in me?"

"In your friendship, certainly. But facts are facts, Watson, and after all you are only a general practitioner with very limited experience and mediocre qualifications. It is painful to have to say these things, but you leave me no choice."

I was bitterly hurt.

"Such a remark is unworthy of you, Holmes. It shows me very clearly the state of your own nerves. But if you have no confidence in me I would not intrude my services. Let me bring Sir Jasper Meek or Penrose Fisher, or any of the best men in London. But someone you *must* have, and that is final. If you think that I am going to stand here and see you die without either helping you myself or bringing anyone else to help you, then you have mistaken your man."

"You mean well, Watson," said the sick man, with something between a sob and a groan. "Shall I demonstrate your own ignorance? What do you know, pray, of Tapanuli fever? What do you know of the black Formosa corruption?" **7**

"I have never heard of either."

"There are many problems of disease, many strange pathological possibilities, in the East, Watson." He paused after each sentence to collect his failing strength. "I have learned so much during some recent researches which have a medico-criminal aspect. It was in the **8** course of them that I contracted this complaint. You can do nothing."

"Possibly not. But I happen to know that Dr. Ainstree, the greatest living authority upon tropical disease, is now in London. All remonstrance is useless, Holmes. I am going this instant to fetch him." I turned resolutely to the door.

Never have I had such a shock! In an instant, with a tiger-spring, the dying man had intercepted me. I heard the sharp snap of a twisted key. The next moment he had staggered back to his bed, exhausted and panting after his one tremendous outflame of energy.

"You won't take the key from me by force, Watson. I've got you, my friend. Here you are, and here you will stay until I will otherwise. But I'll humour you." (All this in little gasps, with terrible struggles for breath between.) "You've only my own good at heart. Of course I know that very well. You shall have your way, but give me time to get my strength. Not now, Watson, not now. It's four o'clock. At six you can go."

I HEARD THE SHARP SNAP OF A TWISTED KEY.

Illustration by Walter Paget for the *Strand Magazine*, December, 1913.

7 *the black Formosa corruption?"* It has long been supposed that "Tapanuli fever" and "the black Formosa corruption" were nonexistent diseases, but research by Mr. Hugh L'Etang suggests that they exist and that they are in fact one and the same disease: tsutsugamushi fever, or scrub typhus. "This is an infectious disease transmitted by mites and found, among other places, in Japan, Formosa, the Pescadores, Sumatra, New Guinea, Northern Australia and the Philippines. . . . Tsutsugamushi disease is characterized in its early stages by the skin lesion where the mite has bitten the surface. First there is a red area, then an ulcer with a striking black crust. The commonest sites for this black ulcer are the neck, armpit, upper arm, groin, calf and ankle. The neighbouring lymph glands are enlarged. At the same time there is headache, chilliness, fever, weakness and generalized aches and pains. From the fifth to the eighth day a rash appears mainly on the trunk. The rash is dull red in colour, and when it fades leaves a brownish stain. During the second week the illness reaches a peak, the patient becomes apathetic and even delirious, and involvement of lungs and heart may be found. In some types of typhus, the face develops a blue-brown colour. However, I suggest that it is due to the characteristic black scar, rather than from the dark rash on the skin, that [the] name, the 'black Formosa corruption' may have been derived. The mortality in Formosa is 12%. . . . If . . . the existence of Formosa cannot be denied, the name Tapanuli sounds decidedly spurious. Yet, there is a place called Tapanuli. . . . It is a residency of 15,084 square miles on the North West Coast of Sumatra, and the population is just over one million. Tapanuli is a mountainous area with many peaks above 6,000 feet. In the northeast, there is a lake called Toba, the largest of the mountain lakes of Sumatra. Cultivation is confined to the valleys and flat coastal strips where maize, rice, coconuts, coffee, nutmegs and rubber are grown. . . ." ("Some Observations on the Black Formosa Corruption and Tapanuli Fever").

8 *some recent researches which have a medico-criminal aspect.* "Can there be any doubt," Miss Madeleine B. Stern wrote in "Sherlock Holmes: Rare Book Collector," "that those 'researches' included visits to the rare and secondhand bookshops of London? There was a wealth of related material from which Holmes could choose, all the way from Codronchi's *Methodus Testificandi* (Frankfurt, 1597), the first important work on

"This is insanity, Holmes."

"Only two hours, Watson. I promise you will go at six. Are you content to wait?"

"I seem to have no choice."

"None in the world, Watson. Thank you, I need no help in arranging the clothes. You will please keep your distance. Now, Watson, there is one other condition that I would make. You will seek help, not from the man you mention, but from the one that I choose."

"By all means."

"The first three sensible words that you have uttered since you entered this room, Watson. You will find some books over there. I am somewhat exhausted; I wonder how a battery feels when it pours electricity into a non-conductor? At six, Watson, we resume our conversation."

But it was destined to be resumed long before that hour, and in circumstances which gave me a shock hardly second to that caused by his spring to the door. I had stood for some minutes looking at the silent figure in the bed. His face was almost covered by the clothes and he appeared to be asleep. Then, unable to settle down to reading, I walked slowly round the room, examining the pictures of celebrated criminals with which every wall was adorned. Finally, in my aimless perambulation, I came to the mantelpiece. A litter of pipes, tobacco-pouches, syringes, pen-knives, revolver cartridges, and other *débris* was scattered over it. In the midst of these was a small black and white ivory box with a sliding lid. It was a neat little thing, and I had stretched out my hand to examine it more closely, when——

It was a dreadful cry that he gave—a yell which might have been heard down the street. My skin went cold and my hair bristled at that horrible scream. As I turned I caught a glimpse of a convulsed face and frantic eyes. I stood paralysed, with the little box in my hand.

"Put it down! Down, this instant, Watson—this instant, I say!" His head sank back upon the pillow and he gave a deep sigh of relief as I replaced the box upon the mantelpiece. "I hate to have my things touched, Wat-

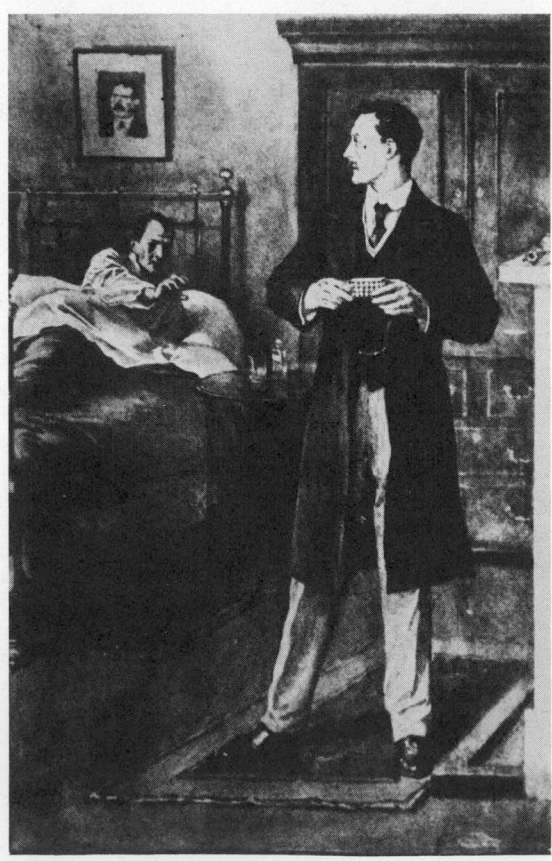

"PUT IT DOWN! DOWN, THIS INSTANT, WATSON—THIS INSTANT, I SAY!"

How two artists illustrated the same scene: *right*, Frederic Dorr Steele for *Collier's Magazine*, November 22, 1913; *left*, Walter Paget for the *Strand Magazine*, December, 1913.

son. You know that I hate it. You fidget me beyond endurance. You, a doctor—you are enough to drive a patient into an asylum. Sit down, man, and let me have my rest ! ' "

The incident left a most unpleasant impression upon my mind. The violent and causeless excitement, followed by this brutality of speech, so far removed from his usual suavity, showed me how deep was the disorganization of his mind. Of all ruins, that of a noble mind is the most deplorable. I sat in silent dejection until the stipulated time had passed. He seemed to have been watching the clock as well as I, for it was hardly six before he began to talk with the same feverish animation as before.

" Now, Watson," said he. " Have you any change in your pocket ? "

" Yes."

" Any silver ? "

" A good deal."

" How many half-crowns ? "

" I have five."

" Ah, too few ! Too few ! How very unfortunate, Watson ! However, such as they are you can put them in your watch-pocket. And all the rest of your money in your left trouser-pocket. Thank you. It will balance you so much better like that."

This was raving insanity. He shuddered, and again made a sound between a cough and a sob.

" You will now light the gas, Watson, but you will be very careful that not for one instant shall it be more than half on. I implore you to be careful. Watson. Thank you, that is excellent. No, you need not draw the blind. Now you will have the kindness to place some letters and papers upon this table within my reach. Thank you. Now some of that litter from the mantelpiece. Excellent, Watson ! There is a sugar-tongs there. Kindly raise that small ivory box with its assistance. Place it here among the papers. Good ! You can now go and fetch Mr. Culverton Smith, of 13 Lower Burke Street."

To tell the truth, my desire to fetch a doctor had somewhat weakened, for poor Holmes was so obviously delirious that it seemed dangerous to leave him. However, he was as eager now to consult the person named as he had been obstinate in refusing.

" I never heard the name," said I.

" Possibly not, my good Watson. It may surprise you to know that the man upon earth who is best versed in this disease is not a medical man, but a planter. Mr. Culverton Smith is a well-known resident of Sumatra, now visiting London. An outbreak of the disease upon his plantation, which was distant from medical aid, caused him to study it himself, with some rather far-reaching consequences. He is a very methodical person, and I did not desire you to start before six because I was well aware that you would not find him in his study. If you could persuade him to come here and give us the benefit of his unique experience of this disease, the investigation of which has been his dearest hobby, I cannot doubt that he could help me."

I give Holmes's remarks as a consecutive whole, and will not attempt to indicate how they were interrupted by

forensic medicine, to the latest researches in that delectable field. Holmes never could have resisted Antoine Louis' *Mémoire sur une Question Anatomique relative à la Jurisprudence* (Paris, 1763) in which the author weighed the differential signs of murder and suicide in cases of hanging. The articles of Hunter 'On the Uncertainty of the Signs of Murder, in the Case of Bastard Children' (London, 1784) and of Gross 'On Manual Strangulation' (Cincinnati, 1836) must have made an immediate appeal, while Bertillion's great work *Les Signalments Anthropométriques* (Paris, 1886), which introduced to the world the 'Bertillonage' method of identifying persons by selected measurements, must surely have been added to the medico-criminal bookshelf of Sherlock Holmes."

gaspings for breath and those clutchings of his hands which indicated the pain from which he was suffering. His appearance had changed for the worse during the few hours that I had been with him. Those hectic spots were more pronounced, the eyes shone more brightly out of darker hollows, and a cold sweat glimmered upon his brow. He still retained, however, the jaunty gallantry of his speech. To the last gasp he would always be the master.

" You will tell him exactly how you have left me," said he. " You will convey the very impression which is in your own mind—a dying man—a dying and delirious man. Indeed, I cannot think why the whole bed of the ocean is not one solid mass of oysters, so prolific the creatures seem. Ah, I am wandering ! Strange how the brain controls the brain. What was I saying, Watson ? "

" My directions for Mr. Culverton Smith."

" Ah, yes, I remember. My life depends upon it. Plead with him, Watson. There is no good feeling between us. His nephew, Watson—I had suspicions of foul play and I allowed him to see it. The boy died horribly. He has a grudge against me. You will soften him, Watson. Beg him, pray him, get him here by any means. He can save me—only he ! "

" I will bring him in a cab, if I have to carry him down to it."

" You will do nothing of the sort. You will persuade him to come. And then you will return in front of him. Make any excuse so as not to come with him. Don't forget, Watson. You won't fail me. You never did fail me. No doubt there are natural enemies which limit the increase of the creatures. You and I, Watson, we have done our part. Shall the world, then, be overrun by oysters ? No, no ; horrible ! You'll convey all that is in your mind."

I left him, full of the image of this magnificent intellect babbling like a foolish child. He had handed me the key, and with a happy thought I took it with me lest he should lock himself in. Mrs. Hudson was waiting, trembling and weeping, in the passage. Behind me as I passed from the flat I heard Holmes's high, thin voice in some delirious chant. Below, as I stood whistling for a cab, a man came on me through the fog.

" How is Mr. Holmes, sir ? " he asked.

It was an old acquaintance, Inspector Morton, of Scotland Yard, dressed in unofficial tweeds.

" He is very ill," I answered.

He looked at me in a most singular fashion. Had it not been too fiendish, I could have imagined that the gleam of the fanlight showed exultation in his face.

" I heard some rumour of it," said he.

The cab had driven up, and I left him.

Lower Burke Street proved to be a line of fine houses **9** lying in the vague borderland between Notting Hill and Kensington. The particular one at which my cabman pulled up had an air of smug and demure respectability in its old-fashioned iron railings, its massive folding-door, and its shining brasswork. All was in keeping with a solemn butler who appeared framed in the pink radiance **10** of a tinted electric light behind him.

9 *Notting Hill*. Notting Hill, or Kensington Park, as it is sometimes called, is a handsome quarter of the Royal Borough of Kensington, filled with broad streets, squares and crescents.

10 *a tinted electric light*. Since this is Watson's first mention of electric lighting, the reader may have some interest in the position in regard to electricity in England at that time. In a letter to your editor, the late Gavin Brend wrote: "It would have been theoretically possible [to find a private building lighted by electricity] at any time after 1880 but in practice it was most unlikely, for the original legislation was most restrictive and the first supply companies found it practically impossible to function. Only later in the eighties were the restrictions removed."

" Yes, Mr. Culverton Smith is in.   Dr. Watson !   Very good, sir, I will take up your card."

My humble name and title did not appear to impress Mr. Culverton Smith.   Through the half-open door I heard a high, petulant, penetrating voice.

" Who is this person ?   What does he want ?   Dear me, Staples, how often have I said that I am not to be disturbed in my hours of study ? "

There came a gentle flow of soothing explanation from the butler.

" Well, I won't see him, Staples.   I can't have my work interrupted like this.   I am not at home.   Say so. Tell him to come in the morning if he really must see me."

Again the gentle murmur.

" Well, well, give him that message.   He can come in the morning, or he can stay away.   My work must not be hindered."

I thought of Holmes tossing upon his bed of sickness, and counting the minutes, perhaps, until I could bring help to him.   It was not a time to stand upon ceremony. His life depended upon my promptness.   Before the apologetic butler had delivered his message I had pushed past him and was in the room.

With a shrill cry of anger a man rose from a reclining chair beside the fire.   I saw a great yellow face, coarse-grained and greasy, with heavy double-chin, and two sullen, menacing grey eyes which glared at me from under tufted and sandy brows.   A high bald head had a small velvet smoking-cap poised coquettishly upon one side of its pink curve.   The skull was of enormous capacity, and yet, as I looked down I saw to my amazement that the figure of the man was small and frail, twisted in the shoulders and back like one who has suffered from rickets in his childhood.

" What's this ? " he cried, in a high, screaming voice. " What is the meaning of this intrusion ?   Didn't I send you word that I would see you to-morrow morning ? "

" I am sorry," said I, " but the matter cannot be delayed. Mr. Sherlock Holmes———"

The mention of my friend's name had an extraordinary effect upon the little man.   The look of anger passed in an instant from his face.   His features became tense and alert.

" Have you come from Holmes ? " he asked.

" I have just left him."

" What about Holmes ?   How is he ? "

" He is desperately ill.   That is why I have come."

The man motioned me to a chair, and turned to resume his own.   As he did so I caught a glimpse of his face in the mirror over the mantelpiece.   I could have sworn that it was set in a malicious and abominable smile.   Yet I persuaded myself that it must have been some nervous contraction which I had surprised, for he turned to me an instant later with genuine concern upon his features.

" I am sorry to hear this," said he.   " I only know Mr. Holmes through some business dealings which we have had, but I have every respect for his talents and his character.   He is an amateur of crime, as I am of disease. For him the villain, for me the microbe.   There are my

"WHAT'S THIS?" HE CRIED, IN A HIGH, SCREAMING VOICE. "WHAT IS THE MEANING OF THIS INTRUSION?"

Illustration by Walter Paget for the *Strand Magazine*, December, 1913.

prisons," he continued, pointing to a row of bottles and jars which stood upon a side table. " Among those gelatine cultivations some of the very worst offenders in the world are now doing time."

" It was on account of your special knowledge that Mr. Holmes desired to see you. He has a high opinion of you, and thought that you were the one man in London who could help him."

The little man started, and the jaunty smoking-cap slid to the floor.

" Why ? " he asked. " Why should Mr. Holmes think that I could help him in his trouble ? "

" Because of your knowledge of Eastern diseases."

" But why should he think that this disease which he has contracted is Eastern ? "

" Because, in some professional inquiry, he has been working among Chinese sailors down in the docks."

Mr. Culverton Smith smiled pleasantly and picked up his smoking-cap.

" Oh, that's it—is it ? " said he. " I trust the matter is not so grave as you suppose. How long has he been ill ? "

" About three days."

" Is he delirious ? "

" Occasionally."

" Tut, tut ! This sounds serious. It would be inhuman not to answer his call. I very much resent any interruption to my work, Dr. Watson, but this case is certainly exceptional. I will come with you at once."

I remembered Holmes's injunction.

" I have another appointment," said I.

" Very good. I will go alone. I have a note of Mr. Holmes's address. You can rely upon my being there within half an hour at most."

It was with a sinking heart that I re-entered Holmes's bedroom. For all that I knew the worst might have happened in my absence. To my enormous relief, he had improved greatly in the interval. His appearance was as ghastly as ever, but all trace of delirium had left him and he spoke in a feeble voice, it is true, but with even more than his usual crispness and lucidity.

" Well, did you see him, Watson ? "

" Yes ; he is coming."

" Admirable, Watson ! Admirable ! You are the best of messengers."

" He wished to return with me."

" That would never do, Watson. That would be obviously impossible. Did he ask what ailed me ? "

" I told him about the Chinese in the East End."

" Exactly ! Well, Watson, you have done all that a good friend could. You can now disappear from the scene."

" I must wait and hear his opinion, Holmes."

" Of course you must. But I have reasons to suppose that this opinion would be very much more frank and valuable if he imagines that we are alone. There is just room behind the head of my bed, Watson."

" My dear Holmes ! "

" I fear there is no alternative, Watson. The room does not lend itself to concealment, which is as well, as it is the less likely to arouse suspicion.   But just there, Watson, I fancy that it could be done." Suddenly he sat up with a rigid intentness upon his haggard face. " There are the wheels, Watson. Quick, man, if you love me ! And don't budge, whatever happens—whatever happens, do you hear ? Don't speak ! Don't move ! Just listen with all your ears." Then in an instant his sudden access of strength departed, and his masterful, purposeful talk droned away into the low, vague murmurings of a semi-delirious man.

From the hiding-place into which I had been so swiftly hustled I heard the footfalls upon the stair, with the opening and the closing of the bedroom door. Then, to my surprise, there came a long silence, broken only by the heavy breathings and gaspings of the sick man. I could imagine that our visitor was standing by the bedside and looking down at the sufferer. At last that strange hush was broken.

" Holmes ! " he cried. ' Holmes ! " in the insistent tone of one who awakens a sleeper. " Can't you hear me, Holmes ? " There was a rustling, as if he had shaken the sick man roughly by the shoulder.

" Is that you, Mr. Smith ? " Holmes whispered. " I hardly dared hope that you would come."

The other laughed.

" I should imagine not," he said. " And yet, you see, I am here. Coals of fire, Holmes—coals of fire ! "

" It is very good of you—very noble of you. I appreciate your special knowledge."

Our visitor sniggered.

" You do. You are, fortunately, the only man in London who does. Do you know what is the matter with you ? "

" The same," said Holmes.

" Ah ! You recognize the symptoms ? "

" Only too well."

" Well, I shouldn't be surprised, Holmes. I shouldn't be surprised if it *were* the same. A bad look-out for you if it is. Poor Victor was a dead man on the fourth day— a strong, hearty young fellow. It was certainly, as you said, very surprising that he should have contracted an out-of-the-way Asiatic disease in the heart of London—a disease, too, of which I had made such a very special study. Singular coincidence, Holmes. Very smart of you to notice it, but rather uncharitable to suggest that it was cause and effect."

" I knew that you did it."

" Oh, you did, did you ? Well, you couldn't prove it, anyhow. But what do you think of yourself spreading reports about me like that, and then crawling to me for help the moment you are in trouble ? What sort of a game is that—eh ? "

I heard the rasping, laboured breathing of the sick man. " Give me the water ! " he gasped.

" You're precious near your end, my friend, but I don't want you to go till I have had a word with you. That's why I give you water. There, don't slop it about ! That's right. Can you understand what I say ? "

Holmes groaned.

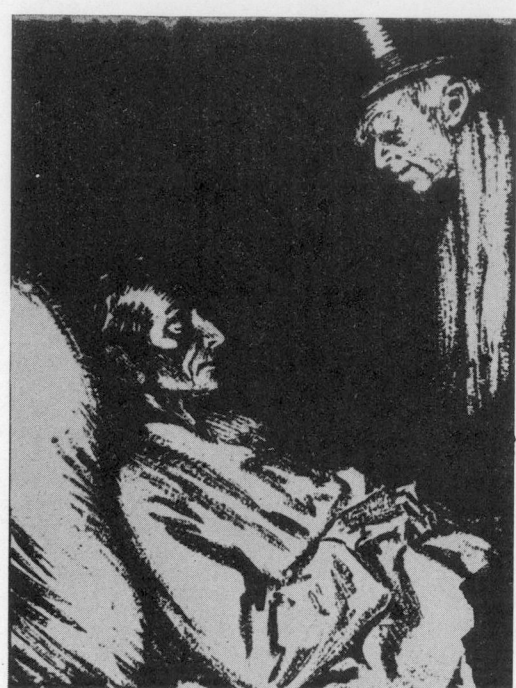

"I DON'T SEE YOU IN THE WITNESS-BOX. QUITE ANOTHER SHAPED BOX, MY GOOD HOLMES, I ASSURE YOU."

Illustration by Frederic Dorr Steele for *Collier's Magazine*, November 22, 1913.

11 *It drew blood*. Dr. George B. Koelle has suggested ("The Poisons of the Canon") that Culverton Smith's weapon was in fact the plague bacillus. "It is of considerable interest to note that the first account of the isolation of the etiologic agent of oriental plague, *Pastuerella pestis*, was [not] published [until] 1894. . . . Thus, Smith's unpublished studies, performed at his Sumatran plantation, preceded the recognized work by several years, but his pioneering efforts have escaped notice outside the Canon. . . . It will be recalled that Leora Arrowsmith, a character of fiction, was fatally infected by a cigarette which she inadvertently allowed to come into contact with a spilled culture of plague bacilli."

On the other hand, Mr. Hugh L'Etang ("Some Observations on the Black Formosa Corruption and Tapanuli Fever") holds that: ". . . snake venom would be a most convenient poison with which to load the box. The fang may well have been modelled on a snake's fang and hollowed, or grooved, to transmit the poison. . . . It seems likely that Victor Savage was killed by a neurotoxic or nerve poison. This could certainly be produced by the King Cobra of Malaya and the East Indies."

" Do what you can for me.   Let bygones be bygones," he whispered.   " I'll put the words out of my head—I swear I will.   Only cure me, and I'll forget it."

" Forget what ? "

" Well, about Victor Savage's death.   You as good as admitted just now that you had done it.   I'll forget it."

" You can forget it or remember it, just as you like.   I don't see you in the witness-box.   Quite another shaped box, my good Holmes, I assure you.   It matters nothing to me that you should know how my nephew died.   It's not him we are talking about.   It's you."

" Yes, yes."

" The fellow who came for me—I've forgotten his name —said that you contracted it down in the East End among the sailors."

" I could only account for it so."

" You are proud of your brains, Holmes, are you not ?   Think yourself smart, don't you ?   You came across someone who was smarter this time.   Now cast your mind back, Holmes.   Can you think of no other way you could have got this thing ? "

" I can't think.   My mind is gone.   For Heaven's sake help me ! "

" Yes, I will help you.   I'll help you to understand just where you are and how you got there.   I'd like you to know before you die."

" Give me something to ease my pain."

" Painful, is it ?   Yes, the coolies used to do some squealing towards the end.   Takes you as cramp, I fancy."

" Yes, yes ; it is cramp."

" Well, you can hear what I say, anyhow.   Listen now ! Can you remember any unusual incident in your life just about the time your symptoms began ? "

" No, no ; nothing."

" Think again."

" I'm too ill to think."

" Well, then, I'll help you.   Did anything come by post ? "

" By post ? "

" A box by chance ? "

" I'm fainting—I'm gone ! "

" Listen, Holmes ! "   There was a sound as if he was shaking the dying man, and it was all that I could do to hold myself quiet in my hiding-place.   " You must hear me.   You *shall* hear me.   Do you remember a box—an ivory box ?   It came on Wednesday.   You opened it—do you remember ? "

" Yes, yes, I opened it.   There was a sharp spring inside it.   Some joke——"

" It was no joke, as you will find to your cost.   You fool, you would have it and you have got it.   Who asked you to cross my path ?   If you had left me alone I would not have hurt you."

" I remember," Holmes gasped.   " The spring !   It **11** drew blood.   This box—this on the table."

" The very one, by George !   And it may as well leave the room in my pocket.   There goes your last shred of evidence.   But you have the truth now, Holmes, and you can die with the knowledge that I killed you.   You knew too much of the fate of Victor Savage, so I have sent you to share it. You are very near your end, Holmes. I will sit here and I will watch you die."

Holmes's voice had sunk to an almost inaudible whisper.

" What is that ? " said Smith. " Turn up the gas ? Ah, the shadows begin to fall, do they ? Yes, I will turn it up, that I may see you the better." He crossed the room and the light suddenly brightened. " Is there any other little service that I can do you, my friend ? "

" A match and a cigarette."

I nearly called out in my joy and my amazement. He was speaking in his natural voice—a little weak, perhaps, but the very voice I knew. There was a long pause, and I felt that Culverton Smith was standing in silent amazement looking down at his companion.

" What's the meaning of this ? " I heard him say at last, in a dry, rasping tone.

" The best way of successfully acting a part is to be it," said Holmes. " I give you my word that for three days I have tasted neither food nor drink until you were good enough to pour me out that glass of water. But it is the tobacco which I find most irksome. Ah, here *are* some cigarettes." I heard the striking of a match. " That is very much better. Halloa ! halloa ! Do I hear the step of a friend ? "

There were footfalls outside, the door opened, and Inspector Morton appeared.

" All is in order and this is your man," said Holmes. The officer gave the usual cautions. **12**

" I arrest you on the charge of the murder of one Victor Savage," he concluded.

" And you might add the attempted murder of one Sherlock Holmes," remarked my friend with a chuckle. " To save an invalid trouble, inspector, Mr. Culverton Smith was good enough to give our signal by turning up the gas. By the way, the prisoner has a small box in the right-hand pocket of his coat which it would be as well to remove. Thank you. I would handle it gingerly if I were you. Put it down here. It may play its part in the trial."

There was a sudden rush and a scuffle, followed by the clash of iron and a cry of pain.

" You'll only get yourself hurt," said the inspector. " Stand still, will you ? " There was the click of the closing handcuffs.

" A nice trap ! " cried the high, snarling voice. " It will bring *you* into the dock, Holmes, not me. He asked me to come here to cure him. I was sorry for him and I came. Now he will pretend, no doubt, that I have said anything which he may invent which will corroborate his insane suspicions. You can lie as you like, Holmes. My word is always as good as yours."

" Good heavens ! " cried Holmes. " I had totally forgotten him. My dear Watson, I owe you a thousand apologies. To think that I should have overlooked you ! I need not introduce you to Mr. Culverton Smith, since I understand that you met somewhat earlier in the evening Have you the cab below ? I will follow you when I am dressed, for I may be of some use at the station."

12 *The officer gave the usual cautions.* Under the law it is the duty of a police officer making an arrest to warn the person taken into custody that anything he says may be taken down and used as evidence.

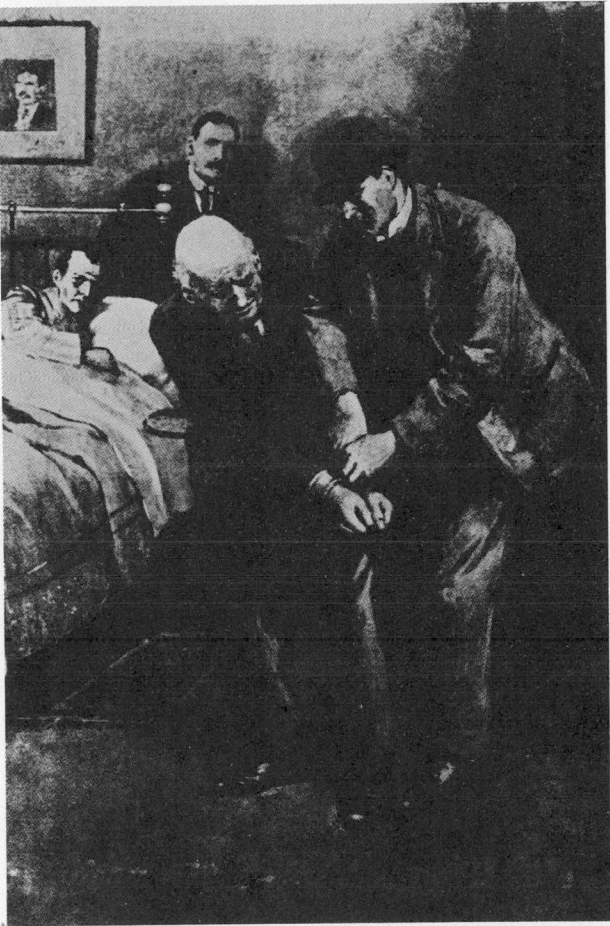

"YOU'LL ONLY GET YOURSELF HURT," SAID THE INSPECTOR. "STAND STILL, WILL YOU?"

Illustration by Walter Paget for the *Strand Magazine*, December, 1913.

13 *vaseline*. Your editor once insisted that Holmes, at the time of this adventure, would have used the term "petroleum jelly." He has since been corrected by that erudite scholar, Mr. Morris Rosenblum, who accurately pointed out that the word "vaseline" was introduced as a proprietary term by R. A. Chesebrough as long ago as 1872. "It is found in British publications in 1874 and 1876."

14 *upon which I have sometimes thought of writing a monograph*. It is doubtful that this projected work was ever undertaken, although the subject may have been intended to form a chapter in Holmes' contemplated textbook on the whole art of detection ("The Adventure of the Abbey Grange").

15 *a reversion*. In law, the returning of an estate to the grantor or his heirs, by operation of law, after the grant has terminated; hence, the residue of an estate left in the proprietor or owner thereof, to take effect in possession, by operation of law, after the termination of a limited or less estate carved out of it and conveyed to him. Holmes' use of the precise term is another indication of his practical knowledge of British law.

Bibliographical Note:
This is the cover of the *Strand* magazine for December, 1913, in which "The Adventure of the Dying Detective" made its first English appearance (it had previously appeared in the November 22, 1913, issue of *Collier's Magazine* in America). The story made its first appearance in book form in 1913 in a little (4″ by 5½″) volume published by the P. F. Collier Company of New York. The original manuscript of "The Adventure of the Dying Detective," with eighteen pages signed by Sir Arthur Conan Doyle at Crowborough, Sussex, July 27, 1923, was loaned by the late Denis P. S. Conan Doyle to the Sherlock Holmes Exhibition of 1951. In a letter to your editor dated January 20, 1966, Mr. Adrian M. Conan Doyle does not include it in the list of original manuscripts now in his possession.

" I never needed it more," said Holmes, as he refreshed himself with a glass of claret and some biscuits in the intervals of his toilet. " However, as you know, my habits are irregular, and such a feat means less to me than to most men. It was very essential that I should impress Mrs. Hudson with the reality of my condition, since she was to convey it to you, and you in turn to him. You won't be offended, Watson ? You will realize that among your many talents dissimulation finds no place, and that if you had shared my secret you would never have been able to impress Smith with the urgent necessity of his presence, which was the vital point of the whole scheme. Knowing his vindictive nature, I was perfectly certain that he would come to look upon his handiwork."

" But your appearance, Holmes—your ghastly face ? "

" Three days of absolute fast does not improve one's beauty, Watson. For the rest, there is nothing which a **13** sponge may not cure. With vaseline upon one's forehead, belladonna in one's eyes, rouge over the cheek-bones, and crusts of beeswax round one's lips, a very satisfying effect can be produced. Malingering is a subject upon which I **14** have sometimes thought of writing a monograph. A little occasional talk about half-crowns, oysters, or any other extraneous subject produces a pleasing effect of delirium."

" But why would you not let me near you, since there was in truth no infection ? "

" Can you ask, my dear Watson ? Do you imagine that I have no respect for your medical talents ? Could I fancy that your astute judgment would pass a dying man who, however weak, had no rise of pulse or temperature ? At four yards, I could deceive you. If I failed to do so, who would bring my Smith within my grasp ? No, Watson, I would not touch that box. You can just see if you look at it sideways where the sharp spring like a viper's tooth emerges as you open it. I dare say it was by some such device that poor Savage, who stood between this monster **15** and a reversion, was done to death. My correspondence, however, is, as you know, a varied one, and I am somewhat upon my guard against any packages which reach me. It was clear to me, however, that by pretending that he had really succeeded in his design I might surprise a confession. That pretence I have carried out with the thoroughness of the true artist. Thank you, Watson, you must help me on with my coat. When we have finished at the police-station I think that something nutritious at Simpson's would not be out of place."

"... I THINK THAT SOMETHING NUTRITIOUS AT SIMPSON'S WOULD NOT BE OUT OF PLACE."

Simpson's Tavern and Divan, as it looked before it was rebuilt in 1903–1904 when the Strand was widened at this point. Wrote Mr. Michael Harrison, from whose book, *In the Footsteps of Sherlock Holmes*, this photograph was taken: "A dinner from the joint was to be had for 2s. 6d. [about 61¢], and a fish dinner of 2s. 9d. [about 67¢] was served from 12:30 P.M. to 8:30 P.M." Simpson's-in-the-Strand was evidently one of Holmes' favorite London restaurants: he and Watson dined there *twice* during "The Adventure of the Illustrious Client."

30

THE ADVENTURE OF THE BLUE CARBUNCLE

[Tuesday, December 27, 1887]

I HAD called upon my friend Sherlock Holmes upon the second morning after Christmas, with the intention of wishing him the compliments of the season. He was lounging upon the sofa in a purple dressing-gown, a pipe-rack within his reach upon the right, and a pile of crumpled morning papers, evidently newly studied, near **2** at hand. Beside the couch was a wooden chair, and on the angle of the back hung a very seedy and disreputable hard felt hat, much the worse for wear, and cracked in several places. A lens and a forceps lying upon the seat of the chair suggested that the hat had been suspended in this manner for the purpose of examination.

" You are engaged," said I ; " perhaps I interrupt you."

" Not at all. I am glad to have a friend with whom I can discuss my results. The matter is a perfectly trivial one " (he jerked his thumb in the direction of the old hat), " but there are points in connection with it which are not entirely devoid of interest, and even of instruction."

I seated myself in his arm-chair, and warmed my hands before his crackling fire, for a sharp frost had set in, and the windows were thick with the ice crystals. " I suppose," I remarked, " that, homely as it looks, this thing has some deadly story linked on to it—that it is the clue which will guide you in the solution of some mystery, and the punishment of some crime."

" No, no. No crime," said Sherlock Holmes, laughing. " Only one of those whimsical little incidents which will happen when you have four million human beings all jostling each other within the space of a few square miles. Amid the action and reaction of so dense a swarm of humanity, every possible combination of events may be expected to take place, and many a little problem will be presented which may be striking and bizarre without being criminal. We have already had experience of such."

" So much so," I remarked, " that, of the last six cases which I have added to my notes, three have been entirely free of any legal crime." **3**

" Precisely. You allude to my attempt to recover the Irene Adler papers, to the singular case of Miss Mary

1 *upon the second morning after Christmas.* Watson's belatedness was most probably caused by the serious illness of his first wife; by January 7th of the following year, 1888, he was back in Baker Street. While 1889 is the favored year for this adventure (Andrew, Bell, Blakeney, Brend, Folsom, Knox, Pattrick, Smith, and Zeisler), a hardy minority (Christ, Kimball, Morley, and Petersen) has chosen 1890. Your editor would seem to stand alone once more in dating the adventure 1887.

2 *crumpled morning papers, evidently newly studied.* The day was obviously not a Sunday.

. . . ON THE ANGLE OF THE BACK HUNG A VERY SEEDY AND DISREPUTABLE HARD FELT HAT . . .

Illustration by Sidney Paget for the *Strand Magazine,* January, 1892.

3 *three have been entirely free of any legal crime."* "In fifteen [of Holmes' recorded cases]," the late Fletcher Pratt wrote in "Very Little Murder," "or one quarter of the total, *no crime took place.* In nine of these cases, there was no legal crime. . . . In six . . . no crime took place because Holmes prevented the felonious act. These cases in which there was no legal crime outnumber all other classifications. There are also four cases of acts within the purview of the law, although non-criminal: the three cases of justifiable homicide and the one of death by misadventure."

4 *the man with the twisted lip.* "The Adventure of the Blue Carbuncle was therefore later, but not much later, than "A Scandal in Bohemia," "A Case of Identity," and "The Man with the Twisted Lip." Lawyer Irving M. Fenton, with Watson's phrasing "entirely free of legal crime" in mind, wrote ("An Analysis of the Crimes and Near-Crimes at Appledore Towers in the Light of the English Criminal Law"): "Apparently [Watson] considered throwing a smoke-bomb into a house and creating a near-riot, just as a prank. A magistrate would call it disorderly conduct. So, too, to wash a man's face against his will is a technical assault."

5 *billycock.* Usually, a round, low-crowned soft felt hat, but sometimes a stiff felt hat, or bowler.

6 *Goodge Street.* A London street that retains much of its original appearance (shabby) and has so far been little invaded by modern buildings.

7 *a row broke out.* The late Gavin Brend, who traced "The Route of the Blue Carbuncle," felt sure that it was the south corner on which the row took place. The tallish man, he wrote, "is clearly proceeding northwards along Tottenham Court Road. Now, if the roughs are coming out of Goodge Street on the south side, neither party will see the other until they run into each other on the south side corner. On the other hand if the collision occurs on the north corner, no matter what direction the roughs approach each party is visible to the other and has no opportunity of avoiding the other if so desired. It is possible that both parties were in a belligerent mood and that neither made any attempt to avoid the crash. Yet I would like to think that the original cause was accidental. After all it was 'the season of forgiveness' and I would like to reduce all unpleasantness to a minimum . . ."

8 *the initials 'H. B.' are legible upon the lining of this hat.* Sherlockian commentators have been harsh on Holmes for his deductions from this hat. Magistrate S. Tupper Bigelow wrote ("The Blue Enigma"): "Holmes deduced . . . that the owner of the hat was Henry Baker and that the owner of the hat and the intended recipient of the bird were husband and wife. Such deductions are pure

Sutherland, and to the adventure of the man with the **4** twisted lip. Well, I have no doubt that this small matter will fall into the same innocent category. You know Peterson, the commissionaire ? "

" Yes. '

' It is to him that this trophy belongs."

" It is his hat."

" No, no ; he found it. Its owner is unknown. I beg **5** that you will look upon it, not as a battered billycock, but as an intellectual problem. And, first as to how it came here. It arrived upon Christmas morning, in company with a good fat goose, which is, I have no doubt, roasting at this moment in front of Peterson's fire. The facts are these. About four o'clock on Christmas morning, Peterson, who, as you know, is a very honest fellow, was returning from some small jollification, and was making his way homewards down Tottenham Court Road. In front of him he saw, in the gaslight, a tallish man, walking with a slight stagger, and carrying a white goose slung over his **6** shoulder. As he reached the corner of Goodge Street a **7** row broke out between this stranger and a little knot of roughs. One of the latter knocked off the man's hat, on which he raised his stick to defend himself, and, swinging it over his head, smashed the shop window behind him. Peterson had rushed forward to protect the stranger from his assailants, but the man, shocked at having broken the window and seeing an official-looking person in uniform rushing towards him, dropped his goose, took to his heels, and vanished amid the labyrinth of small streets which lie at the back of Tottenham Court Road. The roughs had also fled at the appearance of Peterson, so that he was left in possession of the field of battle, and also of the spoils of victory in the shape of this battered hat and a most unimpeachable Christmas goose."

" Which surely he restored to their owner ? "

" My dear fellow, there lies the problem. It is true that ' For Mrs. Henry Baker ' was printed upon a small card which was tied to the bird's left leg, and it is also true that the initials ' H. B.' are legible upon the lining of **8** this hat ; but, as there are some thousands of Bakers, and **9** some hundreds of Henry Bakers in this city of ours, it is not easy to restore lost property to any one of them."

THE ROUGHS HAD ALSO FLED AT THE APPEARANCE OF PETERSON . . .

Illustration by Sidney Paget for the *Strand Magazine*, January, 1892.

" What, then, did Peterson do ? "

" He brought round both hat and goose to me on Christmas morning, knowing that even the smallest problems are of interest to me. The goose we retained until this morning, when there were signs that, in spite of the slight frost, it would be well that it should be eaten without unnecessary delay. Its finder has carried it off therefore to fulfil the ultimate destiny of a goose, while I continue to retain the hat of the unknown gentleman who lost his Christmas dinner."

" Did he not advertise ? "

" No."

" Then, what clue could you have as to his identity ? "

" Only as much as we can deduce.'

" From his hat ? "

" Precisely."

" But you are joking. What can you gather from this old battered felt ? "

" Here is my lens. You know my methods. What can you gather yourself as to the individuality of the man who has worn this article ? "

I took the tattered object in my hands, and turned it over rather ruefully. It was a very ordinary black hat of the usual round shape, hard and much the worse for wear. The lining had been of red silk, but was a good deal discoloured. There was no maker's name ; but, as Holmes had remarked, the initials " H. B." were scrawled upon one side. It was pierced in the brim for a hat-securer, but the elastic was missing. For the rest, it was cracked, exceedingly dusty, and spotted in several places, although there seemed to have been some attempt to hide the discoloured patches by smearing them with ink.

" I can see nothing," said I, handing it back to my friend.

" On the contrary, Watson, you can see everything. You fail, however, to reason from what you see. You are too timid in drawing your inferences."

" Then, pray tell me what it is that you can infer from this hat ? "

He picked it up, and gazed at it in the peculiar introspective fashion which was characteristic of him. " It is perhaps less suggestive than it might have been," he remarked, " and yet there are a few inferences which are very distinct, and a few others which represent at least a strong balance of probability. That the man was highly intellectual is of course obvious upon the face of it, and also that he was fairly well-to-do within the last three years, although he has now fallen upon evil days. He had foresight, but has less now than formerly, pointing to a moral retrogression, which, when taken with the decline of his fortunes, seems to indicate some evil influence, probably drink, at work upon him. This may account also for the obvious fact that his wife has ceased to love him."

" My dear Holmes ! "

" He has, however, retained some degree of self-respect," he continued, disregarding my remonstrance. " He is a man who leads a sedentary life, goes out little, is out of training entirely, is middle-aged, has grizzled hair which he has had cut within the last few days, and

assumption. If 'H. B.' stood for 'Henry Baker,' which is by no means conclusive, it is just as logical to assume that Mrs. Henry Baker and Henry Baker were mother and son or daughter-in-law and father as husband and wife; Watson, indeed, suggested that the owner of the hat might have been a bachelor, and why not? The bird might have been intended for Mrs. Henry Baker, but 'H. B.' could stand for anything."

And Mr. Thomas L. Stix wrote ("Un-Christmas-like Thoughts on 'The Blue Carbuncle'"): "If we are to quibble, and we will, we should suggest the possibility that 'H. B.' in the hat and the card on the goose, 'For Mrs. Henry Baker,' do not necessarily prove that the 'H. B.' in the hat indicated Henry Baker. Even the casual student of the Sacred Writings will follow my meaning. The tobacco pouch found in the cabin of Black Peter Carey with the initials 'P. C.' did not belong to Peter Carey at all, but to Patrick Cairns. And again, in 'The Adventure of the Noble Bachelor,' the note which confused Lestrade . . . was from Francis Moulton, not Flora Miller . . ."

9 *some hundreds of Henry Bakers.* "A search of the Los Angeles County telephone books reveals but 16 Henry Bakers in a population of more than four million," the late Robert R. Pattrick once wrote. "Greater London [at this time] had a population of somewhat over five million. This would indicate that there could have been only about 20 Henry Bakers. Holmes, I fear, was guilty of gross exaggeration . . ."

The late Mr. Pattrick was correct: Magistrate S. Tupper Bigelow, in "The Blue Enigma," has noted that the London Post Office Directory of 1890 listed a paltry seven Henry Bakers; only 139 Bakers were listed altogether.

10 *"a man with so large a brain must have something in it."* "The 'big head, big brain; big brain, great mind' syllogism had many believers [in the nineteenth century], and the phrenologists were always weighing the brains of deceased murderers and madmen and comparing them in size with those of statesmen and writers . . .", Mr. Thomas M. McDade wrote in "Heads and Holmes."

But modern experts "do not believe that a large head necessarily indicates unusual brainpower," as Mr. Vernon Rendall wrote in "The Limitations of Sherlock Holmes." "I remember an old friend who had an abnormally big hat, and a big brain underneath it, saying that the biggest head he knew belonged to a singularly stupid man."

11 *then he has assuredly gone down in the world."* "Admitting the hat was three years old and that it was of the best quality, what justification is there for assuming that Baker could not still afford to buy an expensive hat or that it was the only one he had?" Magistrate S. Tupper Bigelow asked in "The Blue Enigma." "Men are notoriously fond of old hats. . . . On the basis of these data, Baker might well have had a battery of expensive hats at home, and chose to wear the billycock on that particular evening. So there is no evidence whatever that he had assuredly gone down in the world."

12 *which is a distinct proof of a weakening nature.* "By what kind of ratiocination Holmes concluded that moral rather than mental retrogression, whether from undue addiction to alcohol or otherwise, causes foresight to deteriorate is obscure. One is foresighted or one is not. As for reading foresight into the purchase of a hat-securer, it is equally attributable to the efficiency of a high-pressure salesman who sold Baker the hat; if the shop stocked hat-securers, the salesman, selling an expensive hat to a customer, would certainly make an effort to sell him one, and that he succeeded has nothing whatever to do with Baker's foresight but perhaps something to do with his susceptibility to suggestion. And why would Baker replace it, anyhow? They are not very practical gadgets, for one thing; they are a nuisance to wear, for another . . ."—Magistrate S. Tupper Bigelow, "The Blue Enigma."

13 *hardly be in the best of training.* "This, of course, is 'ineffable twaddle' and 'unmitigated bleat' at their best. There cannot be a three-year-old hat in the world, now or then, whether worn by the finest Olympic athlete or a skid-row bum, that does not have evidence of perspiration on its inside or on its inner band. Everybody perspires in given circumstances."—Magistrate S. Tupper Bigelow, "The Blue Enigma."

which he anoints with lime-cream. These are the more patent facts which are to be deduced from his hat. Also, by the way, that it is extremely improbable that he has gas laid on in his house."

"You are certainly joking, Holmes."

"Not in the least. Is it possible that even now when I give you these results you are unable to see how they are attained ? "

"I have no doubt that I am very stupid ; but I must confess that I am unable to follow you. For example, how did you deduce that this man was intellectual ? "

For answer Holmes clapped the hat upon his head. It came right over the forehead and settled upon the bridge of his nose. " It is a question of cubic capacity," said he : " **10** a man with so large a brain must have something in it."

"The decline of his fortunes, then ? "

"This hat is three years old. These flat brims curled at the edge came in then. It is a hat of the very best quality. Look at the band of ribbed silk, and the excellent lining. If this man could afford to buy so expensive a hat three years ago, and has had no hat since, then he **11** has assuredly gone down in the world."

"Well, that is clear enough, certainly. But how about the foresight, and the moral retrogression ? "

Sherlock Holmes laughed. " Here is the foresight," said he, putting his finger upon the little disc and loop of the hat-securer. " They are never sold upon hats. If this man ordered one, it is a sign of a certain amount of foresight, since he went out of his way to take this precaution against the wind. But since we see that he has broken the elastic, and has not troubled to replace it, it is obvious that he has less foresight now than formerly, **12** which is a distinct proof of a weakening nature. On the other hand, he has endeavoured to conceal some of these stains upon the felt by daubing them with ink, which is a sign that he has not entirely lost his self-respect."

"Your reasoning is certainly plausible."

" The further points, that he is middle-aged, that his hair is grizzled, that it has been recently cut, and that he uses lime-cream, are all to be gathered from a close examination of the lower part of the lining. The lens discloses a large number of hair-ends, clean cut by the scissors of the barber. They all appear to be adhesive, and there is a distinct odour of lime-cream. This dust, you will observe, is not the gritty, grey dust of the street, but the fluffy brown dust of the house, showing that it has been hung up indoors most of the time ; while the marks of moisture upon the inside are proof positive that the wearer perspired very freely, and could, therefore, **13** hardly be in the best of training."

"But his wife—you said that she had ceased to love him."

" This hat has not been brushed for weeks. When I see you, my dear Watson, with a week's accumulation of dust upon your hat, and when your wife allows you to go out in such a state, I shall fear that you also have been **14** unfortunate enough to lose your wife's affection."

"But he might be a bachelor."

" Nay, he was bringing home the goose as a peace-offering to his wife.   Remember the card upon the bird's leg."

" You have an answer to everything.   But how on earth do you deduce that the gas is not laid on in the house ? "

" One tallow stain, or even two, might come by chance ; but, when I see no less than five, I think that there can be little doubt that the individual must be brought into frequent contact with burning tallow—walks upstairs at night probably with his hat in one hand and a guttering candle in the other.   Anyhow, he never got tallow stains **15** from a gas jet.   Are you satisfied ? "

" Well, it is very ingenious," said I, laughing ; " but since, as you said just now, there has been no crime committed, and no harm done save the loss of a goose, all this seems to be rather a waste of energy."

Sherlock Holmes had opened his mouth to reply, when the door flew open, and Peterson the commissionaire rushed into the compartment with flushed cheeks and the face of a man who is dazed with astonishment.

" The goose, Mr. Holmes !   The goose, sir ! " he gasped.

" Eh !   What of it, then ?   Has it returned to life, and flapped off through the kitchen window ? " Holmes twisted himself round upon the sofa to get a fairer view of the man's excited face.

" See here, sir !   See what my wife found in its crop ! " He held out his hand, and displayed upon the centre of the palm a brilliantly scintillating blue stone, rather smaller than a bean in size, but of such purity and radiance that it twinkled like an electric point in the dark hollow of his hand.

Sherlock Holmes sat up with a whistle.   " By Jove, Peterson," said he, " this is treasure-trove indeed !   I suppose you know what you have got ? "

" A diamond, sir !   A precious stone !   It cuts into glass as though it were putty."   **16**

" It's more than a precious stone.   It's *the* precious stone."

" Not the Countess of Morcar's blue carbuncle ? " I **17** ejaculated.

"SEE WHAT MY WIFE FOUND IN ITS CROP !"

Illustration by Sidney Paget for the *Strand Magazine*, January, 1892.

But: ". . . a goose has no crop," Miss Mildred Sammons wrote in a letter to the "Line o'Type or Two" column of the *Chicago Tribune*, December 26, 1946.

Her letter started a controversy which has not died down to this day. The late Professor Jay Finley Christ wrote that Sherlock Holmes had made "an alimentary error . . ."

Dr. Rupert Coles, Chief Poultry Adviser of Britain's Ministry of Agriculture and Fish, as well as members of the Department of Ornithology at the Natural History Museum of Chicago later confirmed the statement.

But the Goose-Does-So-Have-a-Crop School has stout defenders, one of the stoutest of which was the late Dr. Ernest Bloomfield Zeisler, who called on experts in the poultry department of the Agricultural School of the University of New Hampshire to support his statement that "the crop of a goose is not as prominent or as easily seen as in a turkey but apparently all barnyard fowl possess crops" ("A Pigment of the Imagination").

14 *you also have been unfortunate enough to lose your wife's affection."* "Englishmen, or so I have heard it said, do not ask their wives for permission to go out until the wives have carefully inspected them and their hats, and many wives, English and others, don't know anything at all about their husbands' hats or even care; they may even be abed when the master leaves for work in the morning; or possibly they dawdle over another cup of coffee while their beloveds rush for the 7:35. They may, indeed, even be slatterns, so that dusty hats on their husbands would be the last thing in the world they would notice; and all such may nevertheless be deeply in love with their husbands."—Magistrate S. Tupper Bigelow, "The Blue Enigma."

15 *and a guttering candle in the other.* "But why take his hat upstairs at all," Mr. J. B. Mackenzie asked in "Sherlock Holmes' Plots and Strategy," "or—if he were in the habit of performing this out-of-the-way detail—why put it elsewhere than upon his head? Then, how would grease from the candle, held in one hand, fall on the hat, carried in the other?"

16 *It cuts into glass as though it were putty."* "This is a most unreliable method of testing gem stones," Mr. Philip Kasson wrote in "The True Blue: A Case of Identification." "Glass is relatively soft compared to most gems. Hardness means scratching ability, and a stone can be scratched by another of equal or greater hardness. Diamonds, rubies, sapphires, garnets, aquamarines, beryls, etc., etc., are all harder and will cut glass. Even glass will cut glass. Peterson's test proved nothing."

17 *the Countess of Morcar's blue carbuncle?"* "A carbuncle is a garnet, cut *en cabochon* (with a domed top). . . . Garnets come in many colours: white, yellow, green, red, orange, brown, purple, and black, but no blue garnet has ever been found."—Philip Kasson, "The True Blue."

18 *not within a twentieth part of the market price.*" "This would put the value of the blue stone at about £20,000, or $100,000, which is almost the amount Henry Hope spent for the [famous Hope diamond]."—Philip Kasson, "The True Blue."

19 *the Hotel Cosmopolitan.*" "I take the Cosmopolitan to be Claridge's," the late Gavin Brend wrote in "The Route of the Blue Carbuncle." "There are, no doubt, some other possible selections, but I believe they are fewer than might be supposed. The Ritz, the Carlton, the Berkeley and the Cecil all came into existence after 1889 though some of them were built on the sites of earlier hotels. The Savoy opened in October of that year but it is unlikely (I hope) that within a couple of months a bedroom grate would already be in need of repair."

20 *the Assizes.* The periodical sessions of the judges of the superior courts in every county of England for the purpose of administering justice in the trial and determination of civil and criminal cases.

21 *solder the second bar of the grate.* Aside from the fact that grates are not normally soldered, we may point to the fact that the 22nd of December could not have been a Sunday, or Horner would not have been at work. December 22, 1889, *was* a Sunday, which would seem to us to eliminate that year from consideration.

" Precisely so. I ought to know its size and shape, seeing that I have read the advertisement about it in *The Times* every day lately. It is absolutely unique, and its value can only be conjectured, but the reward offered of a thousand pounds is certainly not within a twentieth part **18** of the market price."

" A thousand pounds ! Great Lord of mercy ! " The commissionaire plumped down into a chair, and stared from one to the other of us.

" That is the reward, and I have reason to know that there are sentimental considerations in the background which would induce the Countess to part with half of her fortune if she could but recover the gem."

" It was lost, if I remember aright, at the Hotel Cos- **19** mopolitan," I remarked.

" Precisely so, on the twenty-second of December, just five days ago. John Horner, a plumber, was accused of having abstracted it from the lady's jewel-case. The evidence against him was so strong that the case has been **20** referred to the Assizes. I have some account of the matter here, I believe." He rummaged amid his newspapers, glancing over the dates, until at last he smoothed one out, doubled it over, and read the following paragraph :

" Hotel Cosmopolitan Jewel Robbery. John Horner, 26, plumber, was brought up upon the charge of having upon the 22nd inst., abstracted from the jewel-case of the Countess of Morcar the valuable gem known as the blue carbuncle. James Ryder, upper-attendant at the hotel, gave his evidence to the effect that he had shown Horner up to the dressing-room of the Countess of Morcar upon the day of the robbery, in order that he might solder the **21** second bar of the grate, which was loose. He had remained with Horner some little time but had finally been called away. On returning he found that Horner had disappeared, that the bureau had been forced open, and that the small morocco casket in which, as it afterwards transpired, the Countess was accustomed to keep her jewel, was lying empty upon the dressing-table. Ryder instantly gave the alarm, and Horner was arrested the same evening ; but the stone could not be found either upon his person or in his rooms. Catherine Cusack, maid to the Countess, deposed to having heard Ryder's cry of dismay on discovering the robbery, and to having rushed into the room, where she found matters were as described by the last witness. Inspector Bradstreet, B Division, gave evidence as to the arrest of Horner, who struggled frantically, and protested his innocence in the strongest terms. Evidence of a previous conviction for robbery having been given against the prisoner, the magistrate refused to deal summarily with the offence, but referred it to the Assizes. Horner, who had shown signs of intense emotion during the proceedings, fainted away at the conclusion, and was carried out of court."

" Hum ! So much for the police-court," said Holmes thoughtfully, tossing aside his paper. " The question for us now to solve is the sequence of events leading from a rifled jewel-case at one end to the crop of a goose in Tottenham Court Road at the other. You see, Watson, our little deductions have suddenly assumed a much more important and less innocent aspect.   Here is the stone ; the stone came from the goose, and the goose came from Mr. Henry Baker, the gentleman with the bad hat and all the other characteristics with which I have bored you. So now we must set ourselves very seriously to finding this gentleman, and ascertaining what part he has played in this little mystery.   To do this, we must try the simplest means first, and these lie undoubtedly in an advertisement in all the evening papers.   If this fail, I shall **22** have recourse to other methods.”

“ What will you say ? ”

“ Give me a pencil, and that slip of paper.   Now, then : ‘ Found at the corner of Goodge Street, a goose and a black felt hat.   Mr. Henry Baker can have the same by applying at 6.30 this evening at 221B Baker Street.’ That is clear and concise.”

“ Very.   But will he see it ? ”

“ Well, he is sure to keep an eye on the papers, since, to a poor man, the loss was a heavy one.   He was clearly so scared by his mischance in breaking the window, and by the approach of Peterson, that he thought of nothing but flight ; but since then he must have bitterly regretted the impulse which caused him to drop his bird.   Then, again, the introduction of his name will cause him to see it, for every one who knows him will direct his attention to it.   Here you are, Peterson, run down to the advertising agency, and have this put in the evening papers.” **23**

“ In which, sir ? ”

“ Oh, in the *Globe, Star, Pall Mall, St. James's Gazette, Evening News, Standard, Echo*, and any others that occur to you.” **24**

“ Very well, sir.   And this stone ? ”

“ Ah, yes, I shall keep the stone.   Thank you.   And, I say, Peterson, just buy a goose on your way back, and leave it here with me, for we must have one to give to this gentleman in place of the one which your family is now devouring.”

When the commissionaire had gone, Holmes took up the stone and held it against the light.   “ It's a bonny thing,” said he.   “ Just see how it glints and sparkles. Of course it is a nucleus and focus of crime.   Every good stone is.   They are the devil's pet baits.   In the larger and older jewels every facet may stand for a bloody deed. This stone is not yet twenty years old.   It was found in the banks of the Amoy River in Southern China, and is **25** remarkable in having every characteristic of the carbuncle, save that it is blue in shade, instead of ruby red.   In spite of its youth, it has already a sinister history.   There have been two murders, a vitriol-throwing, a suicide, and several robberies brought about for the sake of this forty-grain weight of crystallized charcoal.   Who would think **26-27** that so pretty a toy would be a purveyor to the gallows and the prison ?   I'll lock it up in my strong-box now, and drop a line to the Countess to say that we have it.”

“ Do you think this man Horner is innocent ? ”

“ I cannot tell.”

“ Well, then, do you imagine that this other one, Henry Baker, had anything to do with the matter ? ”

22 *an advertisement in all the evening papers.* Additional evidence that this day was not a Sunday. But how did Holmes get advertisements into all the evening papers when it was already midmorning?

23 *run down to the advertising agency.* A persistent rumor has it that when the first *Strand*s containing “The Adventure of the Blue Carbuncle” appeared on the stalls, the story here read: “run down to Willing's . . .” The *Strand*'s editors, catching the fact that Willing's Advertising Agency was being given a free advertisement, quietly changed the line to read “run down to the advertising agency.” If issues of the *Strand* containing the original wording do exist, they are certainly a collector's item—and one which no collector to our knowledge admits having.

24 *and any others that occur to you.*” Holmes “was not really allowing the commissionaire a very free hand,” Mr. James Edward Holroyd wrote. “In Dickens' *Dictionary of London*, 1889, I find that there were only three other evenings and all were specialized. The *Evening Corn Trade List* (£5 15s per annum) and the *Shipping and Mercantile Gazette* (5d. against the ½d. and 1d. charge of [the seven papers Holmes named]) were both commercial and probably prohibitive; while the remaining paper, the *Evening Post and Daily Recorder*, was a financial journal. None of the three would be likely to occur to the commissionaire, nor were they the kind of paper that a poor man like H. B. would be ‘sure to keep an eye on.’”

25 *the Amoy River in Southern China.* “. . . no garnet has ever been found in China, let alone on the banks of the Amoy River for the very good reason that there is no Amoy River in China, nor ever was,” Magistrate S. Tupper Bigelow wrote in “The Blue Enigma.” “Amoy is a city in southern China, but the Kiulung River, not the Amoy, flows into Amoy.”

26 *this forty-grain weight.* Holmes “did not seem to know that gems are weighed in carats, not just in England, but everywhere, then and now. It is true that the precise weight of a carat in grains differed from country to country, but an English carat of [that time] was 3.163 troy grains, which would make the weight of the blue carbuncle 12.62 English carats. Such a gem would not be ‘rather smaller than a bean in size’; it would be the size of a well-nourished lima bean, if we must use beans as a comparative basis.”—Magistrate S. Tupper Bigelow, “The Blue Enigma.”

27 *of crystallized charcoal.* Charcoal is a rather pure form of carbon, and crystallized carbon is a diamond, not a carbuncle. The chemical composition of the carbuncle is “a combination of the elements of magnesium, calcium, manganese or ferrous iron, together with any of the elements of aluminum, ferric iron, or chromium . . ."—Philip Kasson, "The True Blue."

Mr. Doyle W. Beckmeyer has suggested in "Valuable Sherlockian Hunting-Ground" that the blue "carbuncle" was in fact a star sapphire, but a sapphire is chemically aluminum oxide.

In Mr. Kasson's view, however, "the blue carbuncle" was a blue diamond—a view stoutly supported by Mr. D. A. Redmond in "Some Chemical Problems in the Canon." Here Mr. Redmond made the interesting suggestion that: "one name for massive black diamond is 'carbonado.' A gemstone discovered in a mass of carbonado, which would be a rare occurrence, might well have originally been called the 'Blue Carbonado.' In the course of the extensive travels . . . of the stone, this would readily be corrupted to a more familiar word: the 'Blue Carbuncle.' "

But perhaps Magistrate S. Tupper Bigelow sized up the situation most cogently when he wrote in "The Blue Enigma" that ". . . no gem discovered up to now can possibly satisfy the 'blue carbuncle' on all accounts."

28 *a Scotch bonnet.* A tam-o'-shanter; a soft woolen bonnet or cap with a flat circular crown, the circumference of which is about twice that of the head.

29 *It is a cold night.* December 27, 1887, was a Tuesday and a cold one. Said the *Times'* morning report: "Temperature has fallen generally. . . . Some frost prevails. . . . Over the greater part of England and Ireland . . . very cold, dry weather seems likely." And in its report for the evening of the same day: "Cold weather is reported generally, the maximum readings of the thermometer over England today being only . . . 33 deg. . . . in London."

"It is, I think, much more likely that Henry Baker is an absolutely innocent man, who had no idea that the bird which he was carrying was of considerably more value than if it were made of solid gold. That, however, I shall determine by a very simple test, if we have an answer to our advertisement."

"And you can do nothing until then?"

"Nothing."

"In that case I shall continue my professional round. But I shall come back in the evening at the hour you have mentioned, for I should like to see the solution of so tangled a business."

"Very glad to see you. I dine at seven. There is a woodcock, I believe. By the way, in view of recent occurrences, perhaps I ought to ask Mrs. Hudson to examine its crop."

I had been delayed at a case, and it was a little after half-past six when I found myself in Baker Street once more. As I approached the house I saw a tall man in a **28** Scotch bonnet, with a coat which was buttoned up to his chin, waiting outside in the bright semicircle which was thrown from the fanlight. Just as I arrived, the door was opened, and we were shown up together to Holmes' room.

"Mr. Henry Baker, I believe," said he, rising from his arm-chair, and greeting his visitor with the easy air of geniality which he could so readily assume. "Pray take **29** this chair by the fire, Mr. Baker. It is a cold night, and I observe that your circulation is more adapted for summer than for winter. Ah, Watson, you have just come at the right time. Is that your hat, Mr. Baker?"

"Yes, sir, that is undoubtedly my hat."

He was a large man, with rounded shoulders, a massive head, and a broad, intelligent face, sloping down to a pointed beard of grizzled brown. A touch of red in nose and cheeks, with a slight tremor of his extended hand, recalled Holmes' surmise as to his habits. His rusty black frock-coat was buttoned right up in front, with the collar turned up, and his lank wrists protruded from his sleeves without a sign of cuff or shirt. He spoke in a low staccato fashion, choosing his words with care, and gave the impression generally of a man of learning and letters who had had ill-usage at the hands of fortune.

"We have retained these things for some days," said Holmes, "because we expected to see an advertisement from you giving your address. I am at a loss to know now why you did not advertise."

Our visitor gave a rather shamefaced laugh. "Shillings have not been so plentiful with me as they once were," he remarked. I had no doubt that the gang of roughs who assaulted me had carried off both my hat and the bird. I did not care to spend more money in a hopeless attempt at recovering them."

"Very naturally. By the way, about the bird—we were compelled to eat it."

"To eat it!" Our visitor half rose from his chair in his excitement.

"Yes; it would have been no use to anyone had we not done so. But I presume that this other goose upon the sideboard, which is about the same weight and perfectly fresh, will answer your purpose equally well?"

" Oh, certainly, certainly ! " answered Mr. Baker, with a sigh of relief.

" Of course, we still have the feathers, legs, crop, and so on of your own bird, if you so wish——"

The man burst into a hearty laugh. " They might be useful to me as relics of my adventure," said he, " but beyond that I can hardly see what use the *disjecta membra* **30** of my late acquaintance are going to be to me.   No, sir, I think that, with your permission, I will confine my attentions to the excellent bird which I perceive upon the sideboard."

Sherlock Holmes glanced sharply across at me with a slight shrug of his shoulders.

" There is your hat, then, and there your bird," said he. " By the way, would it bore you to tell me where you got the other one from ?   I am somewhat of a fowl fancier, and I have seldom seen a better-grown goose."

" Certainly, sir," said Baker, who had risen and tucked his newly gained property under his arm.   " There are a few of us who frequent the Alpha Inn near the Museum— we are to be found in the Museum itself during the day, you understand.   This year our good host, Windigate by name, instituted a goose-club, by which, on consideration of some few pence every week, we were to receive a bird at Christmas.   My pence were duly paid, and the rest is **31** familiar to you.   I am much indebted to you, sir, for a Scotch bonnet is fitted neither to my years nor my gravity."   With a comical pomposity of manner he bowed solemnly to both of us, and strode off upon his way.

" So much for Mr. Henry Baker," said Holmes, when he had closed the door behind him.   " It is quite certain that he knows nothing whatever about the matter.   Are you hungry, Watson ? "

" Not particularly."

" Then I suggest that we turn our dinner into a supper, and follow up this clue while it is still hot."

" By all means."

It was a bitter night, so we drew on our ulsters and wrapped cravats about our throats.   Outside, the stars were shining coldly in a cloudless sky, and the breath of the passers-by blew out into smoke like so many pistol shots.   Our footfalls rang out crisply and loudly as we swung through the doctors' quarter, Wimpole Street, **32** Harley Street, and so through Wigmore Street into Oxford **33** Street.   In a quarter of an hour we were in Bloomsbury **34-35** at the Alpha Inn, which is a small public-house at the corner of one of the streets which runs down into Holborn. Holmes pushed open the door of the private bar, and ordered two glasses of beer from the ruddy-faced, white-aproned landlord.

" Your beer should be excellent if it is as good as your geese," he said.

" My geese ! "   The man seemed surprised.

" Yes.   I was speaking only half an hour ago to Mr. Henry Baker, who was a member of your goose-club."

" Ah ! yes, I see.   But you see, sir, them's not *our* geese."

" Indeed !   Whose, then ? "

" Well, I get the two dozen from a salesman in Covent Garden."   **36**

30 *the* disjecta membra. "The *disjecta membra* [scattered limbs] are an adaptation of a phrase in one of Horace's *Satires* (I, 4, line 62): 'Invenias disjecti membra poetae' ('You would still find the limbs of the dismembered poet'). Horace referred to the discernible traces of the poet whose works had been stripped of their original qualities by a transliteration or paraphrase."—Morris Rosenblum, "Some Latin Byways in the Canon."

31 *we were to receive a bird at Christmas.* The pleasant custom of an Alpha Inn Christmas Goose Club was revived by the Sherlock Holmes Society of London in 1959. Tickets were printed in "a deliciously Victorian style," and the draw was held at the Sherlock Holmes Tavern on December 23, 1959.

32 *Wimpole Street.* So named after Wimpole on the borders of Hertfordshire and Cambridgeshire, originally the country seat of the Harleys, Earls of Oxford. Wimpole Street and Harley Street (see "The Resident Patient," Note 21) run parallel.

33 *Wigmore Street.* Wigmore Street, now a smart shopping thoroughfare, extends from Cavendish Square to Portman Square. Like Wimpole Street, it derives its name from a country estate, Wigmore in Hertfordshire, whence Robert Harley took his title as Earl of Oxford, Earl Mortimer, and Lord Harley of Wigmore Castle.

34 *In a quarter of an hour.* The late H. W. Bell pointed out in "A Note on Dr. Watson's Wound" that, "Since the distance covered was about one mile and five-eighths, the rate was a mile in less than 9½ minutes."

WITH A COMICAL POMPOSITY OF MANNER HE BOWED SOLEMNLY TO BOTH OF US . . .

Illustration by Sidney Paget for the *Strand Magazine*, January, 1892.

... AT THE ALPHA INN, WHICH IS A SMALL PUBLIC-HOUSE AT THE CORNER OF ONE OF THE STREETS WHICH RUNS DOWN INTO HOLBORN.

The late Christopher Morley once expressed the view that "the Alpha Inn" was the Museum Tavern. "This fulfills all the necessary conditions," the late Gavin Brend wrote in "A Sherlock Holmes Anniversary," "but so too does the Plough, a corner [Little Russell Street] building in Museum Street, and my vote is for this house on the grounds that the stars in the constellation Plough are named after the Greek letters and Alpha is the biggest and brightest of them all." Holborn was originally called after the "Hole-Bourne," as the upper course of the Fleet River was known, from its running through a deep hollow. Holborn is known for its diamond trade. It is the smallest of the metropolitan boroughs; Bloomsbury is a part of it.

35 *Bloomsbury.* Bloomsbury is the district bounded by New Oxford Street and High Holborn on the south, Tottenham Court Road on the west, Euston Road on the north, and Southampton Row on the east. A district of wide streets and spacious squares, it is an excellent example of early town planning. It is today a region largely made up of boardinghouses and hotels, but it also, today, has many publishers' offices.

36 *Covent Garden.*" Covent Garden Market is meant. But Covent Garden Market was never a poultry market; it was—and is—a flower, fruit, and vegetable market. "How, then, did Watson come to confuse Covent Garden with what clearly must have been Leadenhall Market, some two miles away in the heart of the City of London?" Mr. Ian M. Leslie asked in "Dr. Watson's Christmas Party of 1889."

37 *Endell Street.* A northward continuation of Bow Street, leading to New Oxford Street. It was opened in 1845.

38 *to-morrow morning.*" The 28th of December in the year in which this adventure took place was therefore not a Sunday (as it was in 1890).

" Indeed ! I know some of them. Which was it ? "
" Breckinridge is his name."
" Ah ! I don't know him. Well, here's your good health, landlord, and prosperity to your house. Good night."
" Now for Mr. Breckinridge," he continued, buttoning up his coat, as we came out into the frosty air. " Remember, Watson, that though we have so homely a thing as a goose at one end of this chain, we have at the other a man who will certainly get seven years' penal servitude, unless we can establish his innocence. It is possible that our inquiry may but confirm his guilt ; but, in any case, we have a line of investigation which has been missed by the police, and which a singular chance has placed in our hands. Let us follow it out to the bitter end. Faces to the south, then, and quick march ! "

37 We passed across Holborn, down Endell Street, and so through a zigzag of slums to Covent Garden Market. One of the largest stalls bore the name of Breckinridge upon it, and the proprietor, a horsy-looking man, with a sharp face and trim side-whiskers, was helping a boy to put up the shutters.

" Good evening. It's a cold night," said Holmes.
The salesman nodded, and shot a questioning glance at my companion.

" Sold out of geese, I see," continued Holmes, pointing at the bare slabs of marble.

38 " Let you have five hundred to-morrow morning."
" That's no good."
" Well, there are some on the stall with the gas flare."
" Ah, but I was recommended to you."
" Who by ? "
" The landlord of the ' Alpha.' "
" Ah, yes ; I sent him a couple of dozen."
" Fine birds they were, too. Now where did you get them from ? "

To my surprise the question provoked a burst of anger from the salesman.

" Now then, mister," said he, with his head cocked and his arms akimbo, " what are you driving at ?   Let's have it straight, now."

" It is straight enough.   I should like to know who sold you the geese which you supplied to the ' Alpha.' "

" Well, then, I shan't tell you.   So now ! "

" Oh, it is a matter of no importance ; but I don't know why you should be so warm over such a trifle."

" Warm !   You'd be as warm, maybe, if you were as pestered as I am.   When I pay good money for a good article there should be an end of the business ; but it's ' Where are the geese ? ' and ' Who did you sell the geese to ? ' and ' What will you take for the geese ? '   One would think they were the only geese in the world, to hear the fuss that is made over them."

" Well, I have no connection with any other people who have been making inquiries," said Holmes carelessly. " If you won't tell us the bet is off, that is all.   But I'm always ready to back my opinion on a matter of fowls, and I have a fiver on it that the bird I ate is country bred."

" Well, then, you've lost your fiver, for it's town bred," snapped the salesman.

" It's nothing of the kind."

" I say it is."

" I don't believe you."

" D'you think you know more about fowls than I, who have handled them ever since I was a nipper ?   I tell you, all those birds that went to the ' Alpha ' were town bred."

" You'll never persuade me to believe that."

" Will you bet, then ? "

" It's merely taking your money, for I know that I am right.   But I'll have a sovereign on with you, just to teach you not to be obstinate."

The salesman chuckled grimly.   " Bring me the books, Bill," said he.

The small boy brought round a small thin volume and a great greasy-backed one, laying them out together beneath the hanging lamp.

" Now then, Mr. Cocksure," said the salesman, " I thought that I was out of geese, but before I finish you'll find that there is still one left in my shop.   You see this little book ? "

" Well ? "

" That's the list of the folk from whom I buy.   D'you see ?   Well, then, here on this page are the country folk, and the numbers after their names are where their accounts are in the big ledger.   Now, then !   You see this other page in red ink ?   Well, that is a list of my town suppliers. Now, look at that third name.   Just read it out to me."

" Mrs. Oakshott, 117 Brixton Road—249," read Holmes.

" Quite so.   Now turn that up in the ledger."

Holmes turned to the page indicated.   " Here you are, ' Mrs. Oakshott, 117 Brixton Road, egg and poultry supplier.' "

" Now, then, what's the last entry ? "

" ' December 22.   Twenty-four geese at 7s. 6d."   **39**

" Quite so.   There you are.   And underneath ? "

39 7s. 6d.' " About $1.87.

"JUST READ IT OUT TO ME."

Illustration by Sidney Paget for the *Strand Magazine*, January, 1892.

40 *12s.*' " $3.00

41 *the 'Pink 'Un'* A sporting journal, printed on pink paper, not unlike the American *Police Gazette*.

"WELL, YOU CAN ASK THE KING OF PROOSIA, FOR ALL I CARE."

"The King of Proosia" was Wilhelm II, 1859–1941, by all chronologies except your editor's; Wilhelm I, 1797–1888, by his. In either case, the coat of arms of "the King of Proosia" is shown here, from Dr. Julian Wolff's *Practical Handbook of Sherlockian Heraldry*.

40   " ' Sold to Mr. Windigate of the " Alpha " at 12s.' "

"What have you to say now ? "

Sherlock Holmes looked deeply chagrined. He drew a sovereign from his pocket and threw it down upon the slab, turning away with the air of a man whose disgust is too deep for words. A few yards off he stopped under a lamp-post, and laughed in the hearty, noiseless fashion which was peculiar to him.

" When you see a man with whiskers of that cut and the **41** ' Pink 'Un ' protruding out of his pocket, you can always draw him by a bet," said he. " I dare say that if I had put a hundred pounds down in front of him that man would not have given me such complete information as was drawn from him by the idea that he was doing me on a wager. Well, Watson, we are, I fancy, nearing the end of our quest, and the only point which remains to be determined is whether we should go on to this Mrs. Oakshott to-night, or whether we should reserve it for to-morrow. It is clear from what that surly fellow said that there are others besides ourselves who are anxious about the matter, and I should——"

His remarks were suddenly cut short by a loud hubbub which broke out from the stall which we had just left. Turning round we saw a little rat-faced fellow standing in the centre of the circle of yellow light which was thrown by the swinging lamp, while Breckinridge the salesman, framed in the door of his stall, was shaking his fists fiercely at the cringing figure.

" I've had enough of you and your geese," he shouted. " I wish you were all at the devil together. If you come pestering me any more with your silly talk I'll set the dog at you. You bring Mrs. Oakshott here and I'll answer her, but what have you to do with it ? Did I buy the geese off you ? "

" No ; but one of them was mine all the same," whined the little man.

" Well, then, ask Mrs. Oakshott for it."

" She told me to ask you."

" Well, you can ask the King of Proosia, for all I care. I've had enough of it. Get out of this ! " He rushed fiercely forward, and the inquirer flitted away into the darkness.

" Ha, this may save us a visit to Brixton Road," whispered Holmes. " Come with me, and we will see what is to be made of this fellow." Striding through the scattered knots of people who lounged round the flaring stalls, my companion speedily overtook the little man and touched him upon the shoulder. He sprang round, and I could see in the gaslight that every vestige of colour had been driven from his face.

" Who are you, then ? What do you want ? " he asked in a quavering voice.

" You will excuse me," said Holmes blandly, " but I could not help overhearing the questions which you put to the salesman just now. I think that I could be of assistance to you."

" You ? Who are you ? How could you know anything of the matter ? "

" My name is Sherlock Holmes. It is my business to know what other people don't know."

" But you can know nothing of this ? "

" Excuse me, I know everything of it.   You are endeavouring to trace some geese which were sold by Mrs. Oakshott, of Brixton Road, to a salesman named Breckinridge, by him in turn to Mr. Windigate, of the ' Alpha,' and by him to his club, of which Mr. Henry Baker is a member."

" Oh, sir, you are the very man whom I have longed to meet," cried the little fellow, with outstretched hands and quivering fingers. " I can hardly explain to you how interested I am in this matter."

Sherlock Holmes hailed a four-wheeler which was passing. " In that case we had better discuss it in a cosy room rather than in this wind-swept market-place," said he. " But pray tell me, before we go further, who it is that I have the pleasure of assisting."

The man hesitated for an instant. " My name is John Robinson," he answered, with a sidelong glance.

" No, no ; the real name," said Holmes sweetly. " It is always awkward doing business with an *alias*."

A flush sprang to the white cheeks of the stranger. " Well, then," said he, " my real name is James Ryder."

" Precisely so. Head attendant at the Hotel Cosmopolitan. Pray step into the cab, and I shall soon be able to tell you everything which you would wish to know."

The little man stood glancing from one to the other of us with half-frightened, half-hopeful eyes, as one who is not sure whether he is on the verge of a windfall or of a catastrophe. Then he stepped into the cab, and in half an hour we were back in the sitting-room at Baker Street. Nothing had been said during our drive, but the high, thin breathings of our new companion, and the claspings and unclaspings of his hands, spoke of the nervous tension within him.

" Here we are ! " said Holmes cheerily, as we filed into the room. " The fire looks very seasonable in this weather. You look cold, Mr. Ryder. Pray take the basket chair. I will just put on my slippers before we settle this little matter of yours. Now, then ! You want to know what became of those geese ? "

" Yes, sir."

" Or rather, I fancy, of that goose. It was one bird, I imagine, in which you were interested—white, with a black bar across the tail." **42**

Ryder quivered with emotion. " Oh, sir," he cried, " can you tell me where it went to ? "

" It came here."

" Here ? "

" Yes, and a most remarkable bird it proved. I don't wonder that you should take an interest in it. It laid an egg after it was dead—the bonniest, brightest little blue egg that ever was seen. I have it here in my museum."

Our visitor staggered to his feet, and clutched the mantelpiece with his right hand. Holmes unlocked his strong-box, and held up the blue carbuncle, which shone out like a star, with a cold, brilliant, many-pointed radiance. Ryder stood glaring with a drawn face, uncertain whether to claim or to disown it.

" The game's up, Ryder," said Holmes quietly. " Hold up, man, or you'll be into the fire. Give him an arm back into his chair, Watson. He's not got blood enough to go

"OH, SIR, YOU ARE THE VERY MAN WHOM I HAVE LONGED TO MEET."

Illustration by Sidney Paget for the *Strand Magazine*, January, 1892.

42 *white, with a black bar across the tail*." As Magistrate S. Tupper Bigelow has pointed out in his essay, "Barred-Tail Geese," there is no such thing as a *white* barred-tail goose, although the Pinkfooted Goose, which breeds in Greenland and Iceland, produces a barred-tail gosling "in the proportion of about one in 10,000."

"FOR GOD'S SAKE HAVE MERCY!" HE SHRIEKED.

Illustration by Sidney Paget for the *Strand Magazine*, January, 1892.

in for felony with impunity.   Give him a dash of brandy. So !   Now he looks a little more human.   What a shrimp it is, to be sure ! "

For a moment he had staggered and nearly fallen, but the brandy brought a tinge of colour into his cheeks, and he sat staring with frightened eyes at his accuser.

" I have almost every link in my hands, and all the proofs which I could possibly need, so there is little which you need tell me.   Still, that little may as well be cleared up to make the case complete.   You had heard, Ryder, of this blue stone of the Countess of Morcar's ? "

" It was Catherine Cusack who told me of it," said he, in a crackling voice.

" I see.   Her ladyship's waiting-maid.   Well, the temptation of sudden wealth so easily acquired was too much for you, as it has been for better men before you ; but you were not very scrupulous in the means you used.   It seems to me, Ryder, that there is the making of a very pretty villain in you.   You knew that this man Horner, the plumber, had been concerned in some such matter before, and that suspicion would rest the more readily upon him. What did you do, then ?   You made some small job in my lady's room—you and your confederate Cusack—and you managed that he should be the man sent for.   Then, when he had left, you rifled the jewel-case, raised the alarm, and had this unfortunate man arrested.   You then——"

Ryder threw himself down suddenly upon the rug, and clutched at my companion's knees.   " For God's sake, have mercy ! " he shrieked.   " Think of my father ! Of my mother !   It would break their hearts.   I never went wrong before !   I never will again.   I swear it.   I'll swear it on a Bible.   Oh, don't bring it into court !   For Christ's sake, don't ! "

" Get back into your chair ! " said Holmes sternly.   " It is very well to cringe and crawl now, but you thought little enough of this poor Horner in the dock for a crime of which he knew nothing."

" I will fly, Mr. Holmes.   I will leave the country, sir. Then the charge against him will break down."

" Hum !   We will talk about that.   And now let us hear a true account of the next act.   How came the stone into the goose, and how came the goose into the open market ? Tell us the truth, for there lies your only hope of safety."

Ryder passed his tongue over his parched lips.   " I will tell you it just as it happened, sir," said he.   " When Horner had been arrested, it seemed to me that it would be best for me to get away with the stone at once, for I did not know at what moment the police might not take it into their heads to search me and my room.   There was no place about the hotel where it would be safe.   I went out, as if on some commission, and I made for my sister's house. She had married a man named Oakshott, and lived in Brixton Road, where she fattened fowls for the market. All the way there every man I met seemed to me to be a policeman or a detective, and for all that it was a cold **43** night, the sweat was pouring down my face before I came to the Brixton Road.   My sister asked me what was the matter, and why I was so pale ; but I told her that I had been upset by the jewel robbery at the hotel.   Then I went into the back-yard, and smoked a pipe, and wondered what it would be best to do.

" I had a friend once called Maudsley, who went to the bad, and has just been serving his time in Pentonville. **44** One day he had met me, and fell into talk about the ways of thieves and how they could get rid of what they stole. I knew that he would be true to me, for I knew one or two things about him, so I made up my mind to go right on to Kilburn, where he lived, and take him into my confidence. **45** He would show me how to turn the stone into money. But how to get to him in safety ?   I thought of the agonies I had gone through in coming from the hotel.   I might at any moment be seized and searched, and there would be the stone in my waistcoat pocket.   I was leaning against the wall at the time, and looking at the geese which were waddling about round my feet, and suddenly an idea came into my head which showed me how I could beat the best detective that ever lived.

" My sister had told me some weeks before that I might have the pick of her geese for a Christmas present, and I knew that she was always as good as her word.   I would take my goose now, and in it I would carry my stone to Kilburn.   There was a little shed in the yard, and behind **46** this I drove one of the birds, a fine big one, white, with a barred tail.   I caught it and, prising its bill open, I thrust the stone down its throat as far as my finger could reach. The bird gave a gulp, and I felt the stone pass along its gullet and down into its crop.   But the creature flapped **47** and struggled, and out came my sister to know what was the matter.   As I turned to speak to her the brute broke loose, and fluttered off among the others.

44 *Pentonville.* Pentonville Prison, on Caledonian Road, was erected 1840–1842, on the "separate and silent system." It was called "a model prison," and was the one satirically treated by Dickens in the closing pages of *David Copperfield.* It occupies an area of 6¾ acres.

45 *Kilburn.* The district to the north of Maida Vale, once famous for a spring of mineral water belonging to a drinking house called Kilbourn Wells. Kilburn today is one of the most lively shopping centers of semisuburban London.

46 *carry my stone to Kilburn.* "An interesting parallel . . . has come to my notice while reading *Studies in Social History,* edited by Dr. J. H. Plumb," Mr. T. S. Blakeney wrote in "Some Disjecta Membra." "On page 193 one learns that Sir Robert Walpole's steward, John Wrott, used to secrete the rents he collected and sent to his master, inside geese, in order to hoodwink highwaymen, who in those days (early eighteenth century) infested the roads from Norfolk to London."

47 *I felt the stone pass along its gullet.* "The gem which was seen was small as a bean, / Yet hark to the quivering Ryder: / The jittery clown said he *felt* it pass down / As the bird took the jewel inside her."—Professor Jay Finley Christ, "Sherlock Backs a Turkey."

"BUT THE CREATURE FLAPPED AND STRUGGLED . . ."

"Let us pause for a minute at Mrs. Oakshott's residence," the late Gavin Brend wrote in "The Route of the Blue Carbuncle." "Suppose in its efforts to escape Ryder the goose had scrambled over the north garden wall of No. 117, where do you imagine that it would be? The answer is—believe it or not—that it would be in Baker Street! No. 117 [the photograph is by Mr. Alan Wilson of the Sherlock Holmes Society of London] stands at the corner of Brixton Road and a side street which since 1937 has been called Blackwell Street but which before that bore the name of Baker Street. If we were dealing with a work of fiction we might wonder whether this was a mere coincidence or whether the author selected 117 Brixton Road as a private joke of his own simply because he knew that it was adjacent to Baker Street, Brixton."

"The original No. 117 still stands, and is on a corner site, the side running along Blackwell Street," Mr. Colin Prestige wrote in "South London Adventures." "(As Gavin Brend recently pointed out, this Blackwell Street used to be known as Baker Street! The old name is still faintly visible, painted on the brickwork in washed-out colours.) The garden to No. 117 is very small. It is now covered with grass."

" ' Whatever were you doing with that bird, Jem ? ' says she.

" ' Well,' said I, ' you said you'd give me one for Christmas, and I was feeling which was the fattest.'

" ' Oh,' says she, ' we've set yours aside for you. Jem's bird, we call it. It's the big, white one over yonder. There's twenty-six of them, which makes one for you, and one for us, and two dozen for the market.'

" ' Thank you, Maggie,' says I ; ' but if it is all the same to you I'd rather have that one I was handling just now.'

" ' The other is a good three pound heavier,' she said, ' and we fattened it expressly for you.'

" ' Never mind. I'll have the other, and I'll take it now,' said I.

" ' Oh, just as you like,' said she, a little huffed. ' Which is it you want, then ? '

" ' That white one, with the barred tail, right in the middle of the flock.'

" ' Oh, very well. Kill it and take it with you.'

" Well, I did what she said, Mr. Holmes, and I carried the bird all the way to Kilburn. I told my pal what I had done, for he was a man that it was easy to tell a thing like that to. He laughed until he choked, and we got a knife and opened the goose. My heart turned to water, for there was no sign of the stone, and I knew that some terrible mistake had occurred. I left the bird, rushed back to my sister's, and hurried into the back-yard. There was not a bird to be seen there.

" ' Where are they all, Maggie ? ' I cried.

" ' Gone to the dealer's.'

" ' Which dealer's ? '

" ' Breckinridge, of Covent Garden.'

" ' But was there another with a barred tail ? ' I asked, ' the same as the one I chose ? '

" ' Yes, Jem, there were two barred-tailed ones, and I could never tell them apart.'

" Well, then, of course, I saw it all, and I ran off as hard as my feet would carry me to this man Breckinridge ; but he had sold the lot at once, and not one word would he tell me as to where they had gone. You heard him yourselves to-night. Well, he has always answered me like that. My sister thinks that I am going mad. Sometimes I think that I am myself. And now—and now I am myself a branded thief, without ever having touched the wealth for which I sold my character. God help me ! God help me ! " He burst into convulsive sobbing, with his face buried in his hands.

There was a long silence, broken only by his heavy breathing, and by the measured tapping of Sherlock Holmes' finger-tips upon the edge of the table. Then my friend rose, and threw open the door.

" Get out ! " said he.

" What, sir ! Oh, Heaven bless you ! "

" No more words. Get out ! "

And no more words were needed. There was a rush, a clatter upon the stairs, the bang of a door, and the crisp rattle of running footfalls from the street.

" After all, Watson," said Holmes, reaching up his hand for his clay pipe, " I am not retained by the police to supply their deficiencies.   If Horner were in danger it would be another thing, but this fellow will not appear against him, and the case must collapse.   I suppose that I am commuting a felony, but it is just possible that I am saving a soul. **48** This fellow will not go wrong again.   He is too terribly frightened.   Send him to gaol now, and you make him a gaolbird for life.   Besides, it is the season of forgiveness. **49** Chance has put in our way a most singular and whimsical problem, and its solution is its own reward.   If you will **50** have the goodness to touch the bell, Doctor, we will begin another investigation, in which also a bird will be the chief feature.''

HE BURST INTO CONVULSIVE SOBBING,
WITH HIS FACE BURIED IN HIS HANDS.

Illustration by Sidney Paget for the *Strand Magazine*, January, 1892.

48 *I suppose that I am commuting a felony*. In "The Adventure of the Priory School," Holmes accuses the Duke of Holdernesse of *condoning* a felony; in "The Adventure of the Mazarin Stone," Holmes agrees to *compound* a felony; and in "The Adventure of the Three Gables," he says: "Well, well, I suppose I shall have to *compound* a felony as usual." Is *commuting* here a confusion with *committing, condoning,* or *compounding*? Surely not: Holmes' knowledge of British law, as we have seen, was too profound for him to have made such an elementary mistake; nor was Holmes committing or compounding a felony in the strict legal sense of those words in England. He must therefore have meant *commute*, one meaning of which is "to exchange, especially one form of punishment for another, such as the exchanging of the death penalty for one of banishment." But this raises another question: as British Counsel E. J. C., writing in the *Baker Street Journal*, once pointed out, in England the power to commute an offense is *a prerogative of the Crown and may not be delegated to a mere subject.* Is Holmes by any chance hinting here that he—like John Clay—had royal blood in his veins? These are deep waters, indeed ...

49 *and you make him a gaolbird for life*. "Holmes' habit of letting off criminals is by now, of course, notorious," Mr. Robert Keith Leavitt wrote in "Nummi in Arca or The Fiscal Holmes." "In the 60 cases of record in the Writings, there are 37 definite felonies where the criminal was known to Mr. Sherlock Holmes. In no less than 14 of these cases did the celebrated detective take the law into his own hands and free the guilty person. In 23 cases the offender was taken by the police. In 7 cases justice was balked by suicide, by death at sea or by other acts of God. In 12 cases no crime was involved. And in 4 cases the criminal or criminals got away uncaught."

50 *its solution is its own reward*. "Yes—plus a little matter of a thousand pounds [reward], which [Holmes] quite evidently wasn't going to spilt with anyone," Mr. James C. Iraldi wrote in "The Other Geese."

Bibliographical Note: The first separate edition of "The Adventure of the Blue Carbuncle" was sponsored by the Baker Street Irregulars, Inc. It was published in New York in 1948, with an Introduction by the late Christopher Morley, a Bibliographical Note by the late Edgar W. Smith, and two of Sidney Paget's illustrations from the *Strand Magazine*.

A Day with Dr. Conan Doyle.

By Harry How.

ETECTIVISM up to date—that is what Dr. Conan Doyle has given us. We were fast becoming weary of the representative of the old school; he was, at his best, a very ordinary mortal, and, with the palpable clues placed in his path, the average individual could have easily cornered the "wanted" one without calling in the police or the private inquiry agent. Sherlock Holmes entered the criminal arena. He started on the track. A clever fellow; a cool, calculating fellow, this Holmes. He could see the clue to a murder in a ball of worsted, and certain conviction in a saucer of milk. The little things we regarded as nothings were all and everything to Holmes. He was an artful fellow, too; and though he knew "all about it" from the first, he ingeniously contrived to hold his secret until we got to the very last line in

CONAN DOYLE IN THE "STRAND"

"A Day with Dr. Conan Doyle," interview in the August, 1892, issue.

Strand readers were as interested in the creator as in his creations.

V. FROM DR. WATSON'S RETURN
TO BAKER STREET
TO HIS MARRIAGE TO MARY MORSTAN

[Late December, 1887, or early January, 1888, *circa* May 1, 1889]

"Don't go, doctor. I should prefer that you remain."
—Sherlock Holmes, *The Sign of the Four*.

According to the late H. W. Bell
(The Moated House at Brambletye,
from an 1890 etching)

"THE ANCIENT MANOR HOUSE OF BIRLSTONE,"
SCENE OF THE CRIME IN *THE VALLEY OF FEAR*

"It is evident," the late H. W. Bell wrote in "Three Identifications," "that Birlstone Manor must be sought for on or near the road connecting Tunbridge Wells, in Kent, with East Grinstead, in Sussex; and it is a fact that until some years ago there existed a house near Forest Row which fulfilled all the requirements of the story." (It may be noted that Conan Doyle himself lived for some years in the neighborhood of Forest Row.) "Forest Row," Mr. Bell continued, "lies twelve miles and six furlongs from Tunbridge Wells. Half a mile to the west are the remains of Brambletye House and Brambletye Manor . . ." It is Brambletye Manor, also called "The Moated House of Brambletye," that Mr. Bell would identify with "Birlstone Manor." Brambletye Manor, abandoned about 1631, was reoccupied before the end of the seventeenth century. An etching, dated 1809, shows that by the beginning of the nineteenth century the drawbridge had been abolished and replaced by a permanent construction in masonry. However, by 1892, at the latest, the original arrangement had been restored. After Douglas' death the drawbridge was once more replaced by a bridge of stone, which is, in fact, all that now remains of the building. Mr. Bell pointed out that the "ramping lion" on the ancient stone pillars at the entrance to the drive, which Watson attributed to "Capus of Birlstone" (*see p. 483*) was actually the crest of the last known occupant of the long-since ruined Brambletye *House*, Sir Richard James, Bart., in the reign of Charles II.

Indeed, Mr. Bell's identification of the Moated House of Brambletye as "Birlstone Manor" "does not bear cross-examination," as Mr. C. O. Merriman wrote in "A Case of Identity—No. 2." Mr. Merriman pointed out that: "1) the building certainly did not exist at the date when Holmes and Watson undertook the case of *The Valley of Fear*; 2) there is grave doubt about the double-moat and in addition many of the other means of identification in the Saga are not available; 3) the etching by Laetitia Byrne clearly shows no window was at a closer range than ten to twelve feet of the water in the moat . . ."

In a detailed examination, Mr. Merriman thereupon supported the late James Montgomery's identification of "Birlstone Manor" as Groombridge House (*A Case of Identity*).

According to the late
James Montgomery
and Mr. C. O. Merriman.

(Groombridge House,
Groombridge Kent.
Note door, right, giving facilities for umbrella-fishing by Sherlock Holmes.)

THE VALLEY OF FEAR

[Saturday, January 7, to Sunday, January 8, 1888]

PART I

The Tragedy of Birlstone

❖
I ❖ THE WARNING
❖

'I am inclined to think——' said I.   **1**

'I should do so,' Sherlock Holmes remarked, impatiently. **2**

I believe that I am one of the most long-suffering of mortals, but I admit that I was annoyed at the sardonic interruption.

'Really, Holmes,' said I, severely, 'you are a little trying at times.'

He was too much absorbed with his own thoughts to give any immediate answer to my remonstrance. He leaned upon his hand, with his untasted breakfast before him, and he stared at the slip of paper which he had just drawn from its envelope. Then he took the envelope itself, held it up to the light, and very carefully studied both the exterior and the flap.

'It is Porlock's writing,' said he, thoughtfully. 'I can hardly **3** doubt that it is Porlock's writing, though I have only seen it twice before. The Greek "e" with the peculiar top flourish is distinctive. But if it is from Porlock, then it must be something of the very first importance.'

He was speaking to himself rather than to me, but my vexation disappeared in the interest which the words awakened.

'Who, then, is Porlock?' I asked.

'Porlock, Watson, is a *nom de plume*, a mere identification **4** mark, but behind it lies a shifty and evasive personality. In **5** a former letter he frankly informed me that the name was not his own, and defied me ever to trace him among the teeming millions of this great city. Porlock is important, not for himself, but for the great man with whom he is in touch. Picture to yourself the pilot-fish with the shark, the jackal with the lion—anything that is insignificant in companionship with what is formidable. Not only formidable, Watson, but sinister—in the highest degree sinister. That is where he comes within my purview. You have heard me speak of Professor Moriarty?'

'The famous scientific criminal, as famous among crooks as——'

'My blushes, Watson,' Holmes murmured, in a deprecating voice.

'I was about to say "as he is unknown to the public." '

1 *'I am inclined to think—' said I.* Conan Doyle did not, at first, have any intention of making Dr. Watson the narrator of this adventure. The original manuscript (176 folio pages with many deletions, corrections, and additions in the author's hand) shows that such expressions as "said Dr. Watson" and "said he" are crossed out and the direct "said I" substituted. The manuscript was auctioned in New York City on January 30, 1923, bringing $275. It was later listed in Scribner's Sherlock Holmes Catalogue at $900. Except for its short "Epilogue" (which is lost or missing), it is owned today by old Irregular J. Bliss Austin of Pittsburgh.

2 *Sherlock Holmes remarked, impatiently.* Mr. Anthony Boucher has written, in his Introduction to *The Final Adventures of Sherlock Holmes*, Volume I, "This is a ripe, mature Holmes, free from external eccentricities, his hand unburdened by either the cocaine needle or the violin's bow. Here is Holmes as the perfect thinking mind, in cryptanalysis, in observation, in deduction. And here, more than in any other Canonical story that comes to mind, is Holmes at his most completely charming, whether playfully dangling the cryptically obvious before his colleagues (whom for once he respects) or ruefully admitting 'a distinct touch' from Watson's pawky humor. There is, in fact, more overt humor here than is usual in the Canon; there is a certain fey quality in this Holmes, 'his eyes sparkling with mischief.' Like the superb episodes from the memoirs of Etienne Gerard, the story manages at once to be deftly amusing and intensely exciting; and . . . we can only be deeply grateful to Dr. Watson for having served it up so magnificiently." For these and other reasons, as we shall shortly see, many commentators prefer to place *The Valley of Fear* late in Holmes' career.

3 *'It is Porlock's writing.'* "'A person on business from Porlock' interrupted forever the highest flight of the genius of Samuel Taylor Coleridge; a letter from Porlock provoked one of the greatest displays of the genius of Sherlock Holmes," Mr. Boucher continued in his Introduction. "I feel that some deeper meaning is latent here, but cannot define it—any more than I can understand how the comparison was omitted from the charming essay, 'Persons from Porlock,' by that noblest Holmesian of them all, Vincent Starrett [in *Bookman's Holiday*; New York: Random House, 1942]."

4 *a nom de plume.* French: a pen name; a writer's assumed name.

5 *a shifty and evasive personality.* "Although the thing cannot be proved, I am strongly of the opinion that Mycroft [Holmes, Sherlock's elder brother] was in fact the 'Fred Porlock' who acted as his brother's informer in *The Valley of Fear*," Monsignor Ronald A. Knox wrote in "The Mystery of Mycroft." There are, as shall see, many mysteries about Mycroft.

6 *libel in the eyes of the law.* "If we wonder why Watson forebore to publish *The Valley of Fear* at the time of the occurrence, the answer is found in the chronicle itself: 'In calling Moriarty a criminal you are uttering libel in the eyes of the law.' After Moriarty's death [in 1891] and when Holmes' return had released Watson from his vow of silence, the matter could finally be made public. And Watson, being Watson, waited a good long time."—Dr. John Dardess, "On the Dating of *The Valley of Fear*."

7 *solatium.* In law, compensation for injury to the feelings, as distinguished from compensation for pecuniary loss or physical injury. As always, when it is a question of the law, Holmes chooses the precise word.

8 *apocrypha.* From the Greek: hidden things; secrets.

'A touch—a distinct touch!' cried Holmes. 'You are developing a certain unexpected vein of pawky humour, Watson, against which I must learn to guard myself. But in calling Moriarty a criminal you are uttering libel in the eyes **6** of the law, and there lies the glory and the wonder of it. The greatest schemer of all time, the organizer of every devilry, the controlling brain of the underworld—a brain which might have made or marred the destiny of nations. That's the man. But so aloof is he from general suspicion—so immune from criticism—so admirable in his management and self-effacement, that for those very words that you have uttered he could hale you to a court and emerge with your year's **7** pension as a solatium for his wounded character. Is he not the celebrated author of *The Dynamics of an Asteroid*—a book which ascends to such rarefied heights of pure mathematics that it is said that there was no man in the scientific press capable of criticizing it? Is this a man to traduce? Foul-mouthed doctor and slandered professor—such would be your respective rôles. That's genius, Watson. But if I am spared by lesser men our day will surely come.'

'May I be there to see!' I exclaimed, devoutly. 'But you were speaking of this man Porlock.'

'Ah, yes—the so-called Porlock is a link in the chain some little way from its great attachment. Porlock is not quite a sound link, between ourselves. He is the only flaw in that chain so far as I have been able to test it.'

'But no chain is stronger than its weakest link.'

'Exactly, my dear Watson. Hence the extreme importance of Porlock. Led on by some rudimentary aspirations towards right, and encouraged by the judicious stimulation of an occasional ten-pound note sent to him by devious methods, he has once or twice given me advance information which has been of value—that highest value which anticipates and prevents rather than avenges crime. I cannot doubt that if we had the cipher we should find that this communication is of the nature that I indicate.'

Again Holmes flattened out the paper upon his unused plate. I rose and, leaning over him, stared down at the curious inscription, which ran as follows:

> 534 C2 13 127 36 31 4 17 21 41
> DOUGLAS 109 293 5 37 BIRLSTONE
> 26 BIRLSTONE 9 127 171

'What do you make of it, Holmes?'

'It is obviously an attempt to convey secret information.'

'But what is the use of a cipher message without the cipher?'

'In this instance, none at all.'

'Why do you say "in this instance"?'

'Because there are many ciphers which I would read as **8** easily as I do the apocrypha of the agony column. Such crude devices amuse the intelligence without fatiguing it. But this is different. It is clearly a reference to the words in a page of some book. Until I am told which page and which book I am powerless.'

'But why "Douglas" and "Birlstone"?'

'Clearly because those are words which were not contained in the page in question.'

'Then why has he not indicated the book?'

'Your native shrewdness, my dear Watson, that innate cunning which is the delight of your friends, would surely prevent you from enclosing cipher and message in the same envelope. Should it miscarry you are undone. As it is, both have to go wrong before any harm comes from it. Our second post is now overdue, and I shall be surprised if it does not bring us either a further letter of explanation or, as is more probable, the very volume to which these figures refer.'

Holmes's calculation was fulfilled within a very few minutes by the appearance of Billy, the page, with the very letter which we were expecting.

'The same writing,' remarked Holmes, as he opened the envelope, 'and actually signed,' he added, in an exultant voice, as he unfolded the epistle. 'Come, we are getting on, Watson.'

His brow clouded, however, as he glanced over the contents.

'Dear me, this is very disappointing! I fear, Watson, that all our expectations come to nothing. I trust that the man Porlock will come to no harm.

' "Dear Mr Holmes," he says, "I will go no further in this matter. It is too dangerous. He suspects me. I can see that he suspects me. He came to me quite unexpectedly after I had actually addressed this envelope with the intention of sending you the key to the cipher. I was able to cover it up. If he had seen it, it would have gone hard with me. But I read suspicion in his eyes. Please burn the cipher message, which can now be of no use to you.—FRED PORLOCK." '

Holmes sat for some little time twisting this letter between his fingers, and frowning, as he stared into the fire.

'After all,' he said at last, 'there may be nothing in it. It may be only his guilty conscience. Knowing himself to be a traitor, he may have read the accusation in the other's eyes.'

'The other being, I presume, Professor Moriarty?'

'No less. When any of that party talk about "he," you know whom they mean. There is one predominant "he" for all of them.'

'But what can he do?'

'Hum! That's a large question. When you have one of the first brains of Europe up against you and all the powers of darkness at his back, there are infinite possibilities. Anyhow, friend Porlock is evidently scared out of his senses. Kindly compare the writing in the note with that upon its envelope, which was done, he tells us, before this ill-omened visit. The one is clear and firm; the other hardly legible.'

'Why did he write at all? Why did he not simply drop it?'

'Because he feared I would make some inquiry after him in that case, and possibly bring trouble on him.'

'No doubt,' said I. 'Of course'—I had picked up the original cipher message and was bending my brows over it—'it's pretty maddening to think that an important secret may lie here on this slip of paper, and that it is beyond human power to penetrate it.'

Sherlock Holmes had pushed away his untasted breakfast and lit the unsavoury pipe which was the companion of his deepest meditations.

'I wonder!' said he, leaning back and staring at the ceiling. 'Perhaps there are points which have escaped your Machiavellian intellect. Let us consider the problem in the light of pure **9** reason. This man's reference is to a book. That is our point of departure.'

'A somewhat vague one.'

9 *Machiavellian.* Holmes refers to Niccolo Machiavelli, 1469–1527, Italian author and statesman. His most famous book, *The Prince*, was the first objective, scientific analysis of the methods by which political power is obtained and kept.

"WHAT DO YOU MAKE OF IT, HOLMES?"

This illustration by Frank Wiles, captioned "The Cipher—and the man who solved it," appeared as the frontispiece to the first installment of *The Valley of Fear* when it appeared in the *Strand Magazine*, September, 1914. Of this illustration, the late James Montgomery wrote (*A Study in Pictures*): "This striking close-up of the Master surely ranks with the best and most famous of all his portrayals, from Paget to Steele." And he added: "Wiles of course adheres to the accepted authentic mood, but without sacrificing any of that magic he develops a wealth of detail far exceeding any previous artist." And Walter Klinefelter has written of this frontispiece (*Sherlock Holmes in Portrait and Profile*): "If Wiles had not made another drawing for *The Valley of Fear*, he would still have to be given credit for a notable contribution to the portraiture of Sherlock Holmes."

10 *Even if I accepted the compliment for my-self.* "Surely . . . Holmes had a copy of the Bible—not of any inferior edition, either, but, aware as we are of his philological interest and his pre-occupation with 'Chaldee' ["The Adventure of the Devil's Foot"], of none other than the celebrated Complutensian Polyglot Bible edited under the auspices of Cardinal Ximenes between 1514 and 1517, and printed in Hebrew, Chaldee, Greek and Latin—the earliest, indeed, of the great Poly-glots. Yes, Holmes had probably acquired a treasure . . . [but a treasure which would] have proved of no aid in deciphering Porlock's message."—Madeleine B. Stern, "Sherlock Holmes: Rare Book Collector."

11 ' "*Bradshaw*"*!*' Bradshaw's, now, alas, no more, was the guide to British railways conceived by George Bradshaw, 1801–1853, an engraver of maps and plans of towns. The first issues of a northern and southern Bradshaw were published on Octo-ber 19, 1839, followed in January, 1840, by a unit-ing of the two. Of Bradshaw, R. J. Cruikshank wrote in *Roaring Century:* ". . . the creation of a Quaker who offered it as a piece of much-needed public service. For at least a hundred years it was to follow the Quaker custom of naming the months, First Month for January, Second Month for Feb-ruary and so on. At a time when scores of inde-pendent [railway] lines were sprouting, with great gaps between connections, the production of a guide was a miracle of patience. . . . The humorous journalists could not have taken greater delight in its obscurity of style and its esoteric allusiveness. . . . The hands, daggers and other printing devices in which Bradshaw indulged suggested the warn-ings of a secret society. . . . Comic Bradshaws were brought out to the further confusion of innocent minds. The gentle philanthropist must have been mildly puzzled at the Press he got—but Bradshaw survived to be an honoured British institution."

12 *inadmissible for the same reason.* Mr. Robert Winthrop Adams has suggested ("John H. Wat-son, M.D., Characterologist") that this "British Webster" was the *Comprehensive English Diction-ary;* London, Edinburgh, and Glasgow, 1868, by John Ogilvie, LL.D., Scottish lexicographer. But it is surprising, as Mr. Howard R. Schorin pointed out in his essay on "Cryptography in the Canon," that Holmes eliminated the dictionary: "it is pre-cisely this book which has been used for such mes-sages since the Revolutionary and Napoleonic wars, when the numbered-source code was most popular and in use. Fletcher Pratt, in *Secret and Urgent*, sums up the matter: 'Theoretically, any book will do, but as one must have access imme-diately to any word he wishes to use, only the dic-tionary will serve his purpose.' "

'Let us see, then, if we can narrow it down. As I focus my mind upon it, it seems rather less impenetrable. What indica-tions have we as to this book?'

'None.'

'Well, well, it is surely not quite so bad as that. The cipher message begins with a large 534, does it not? We may take it as a working hypothesis that 534 is the particular page to which the cipher refers. So our book has already become a *large* book, which is surely something gained. What other indications have we as to the nature of this large book? The next sign is C₂. What do you make of that, Watson?'

'Chapter the second, no doubt.'

'Hardly that, Watson. You will, I am sure, agree with me that if the page be given the number of the chapter is im-material. Also that if page 534 only finds us in the second chapter, the length of the first one must have been really intolerable.'

'Column!' I cried.

'Brilliant, Watson. You are scintillating this morning. If it is not column, then I am very much deceived. So now, you see, we begin to visualize a large book, printed in double columns, which are each of a considerable length, since one of the words is numbered in the document as the two hundred and ninety-third. Have we reached the limits of what reason can supply?'

'I fear that we have.'

'Surely you do yourself an injustice. One more coruscation, my dear Watson. Yet another brain-wave. Had the volume been an unusual one he would have sent it to me. Instead of that he had intended, before his plans were nipped, to send me the clue in this envelope. He says so in his note. This would seem to indicate that the book is one which he thought that I would have no difficulty in finding for myself. He had it, and he imagined that I would have it too. In short, Watson, it is a very common book.'

'What you say certainly sounds plausible.'

'So we have contracted our field of search to a large book, printed in double columns and in common use.'

'The Bible!' I cried, triumphantly.

'Good, Watson, good! But not, if I may say so, quite good **10** enough. Even if I accepted the compliment for myself, I could hardly name any volume which would be less likely to lie at the elbow of one of Moriarty's associates. Besides, the editions of Holy Writ are so numerous that he could hardly suppose that two copies would have the same pagination. This is clearly a book which is standardized. He knows for certain that his page 534 will exactly agree with my page 534.'

'But very few books would correspond with that.'

'Exactly. Therein lies our salvation. Our search is narrowed down to standardized books which anyone may be supposed to possess.'

11 ' "Bradshaw"!'

'There are difficulties, Watson. The vocabulary of "Brad-shaw" is nervous and terse, but limited. The selection of words would hardly lend itself to the sending of general messages. We will eliminate "Bradshaw." The dictionary is, **12** I fear, inadmissible for the same reason. What, then, is left?'

'An almanack.'

'Excellent, Watson! I am very much mistaken if you have not touched the spot. An almanack! Let us consider the claims of *Whitaker's Almanack*. It is in common use. It has the **13** requisite number of pages. It is in double column. Though reserved in its earlier vocabulary, it becomes, if I remember right, quite garrulous towards the end.' He picked the volume from his desk. 'Here is page 534, column two, a substantial block of print dealing, I perceive, with the trade and resources of British India. Jot down the words, Watson. Number thirteen is "Mahratta." Not, I fear, a very auspicious beginning. **14** Number one hundred and twenty-seven is "Government," which at least makes sense, though somewhat irrelevant to ourselves and Professor Moriarty. Now let us try again. What does the Mahratta Government do? Alas! the next word is "pigs'-bristles." We are undone, my good Watson! It is finished.'

He had spoken in jesting vein, but the twitching of his bushy eyebrows bespoke his disappointment and irritation. **15** I sat helpless and unhappy, staring into the fire. A long silence was broken by a sudden exclamation from Holmes, who dashed at a cupboard, from which he emerged with a second yellow-covered volume in his hand.

'We pay the price, Watson, for being too up-to-date,' he cried. 'We are before our time, and suffer the usual penalties. Being the seventh of January, we have very properly laid in **16** the new almanack. It is more than likely that Porlock took his message from the old one. No doubt he would have told us so had his letter of explanation been written. Now let us see what page 534 has in store for us. Number thirteen is "There," which is much more promising. Number one hundred and twenty-seven is "is"—"There is"'—Holmes's eyes were gleaming with excitement, and his thin, nervous fingers twitched as he counted the words—' "danger." Ha! ha! Capital! Put that down, Watson. "There is danger—may—come—very—soon—one." Then we have the name "Douglas"—"rich—country—now—at—Birlstone—House—Birlstone—confidence—is—pressing." There, Watson! what do you think of pure reason and its fruits? If the greengrocer had such a thing as a laurel-wreath I should send Billy round for it.'

I was staring at the strange message which I had scrawled, as he deciphered it, upon a sheet of foolscap on my knee.

'What a queer, scrambling way of expressing his meaning!' said I.

'On the contrary, he has done quite remarkably well,' said Holmes. 'When you search a single column for words with which to express your meaning, you can hardly expect to get everything you want. You are bound to leave something to the intelligence of your correspondent. The purport is perfectly clear. Some devilry is intended against one Douglas, whoever he may be, residing as stated, a rich country gentleman. He is sure—"confidence" was as near as he could get to "confident"—that it is pressing. There is our result, and a very workmanlike little bit of analysis it was.'

Holmes had the impersonal joy of the true artist in his better work, even as he mourned darkly when it fell below the high level to which he aspired. He was still chuckling over his success when Billy swung open the door and Inspector MacDonald of Scotland Yard was ushered into the room.

Those were the early days at the end of the 'eighties, when **17**

---

13 Whitaker's Almanack. Britain's best-known almanac, similar to the *World Almanac* in the United States, originally compiled by Joseph Whitaker, 1820–1895.

14 "*Mahratta.*" A confederation of chieftains in central India, broken up by the British in 1818.

15 *his bushy eyebrows*. A detail which adds to our picture of Holmes.

16 *the seventh of January*. A Saturday in 1888, our year for the adventure of *The Valley of Fear*.

17 *Those were the early days at the end of the 'eighties*. Eighteen-eighty-nine would appear to be the latest possible date for the adventure, if we are to credit Watson's statement. Of the chronologists who do accept it (and we shall see that there is a school which does not) Bell, Smith, and Starrett say 1887; Baring-Gould, Folsom, Pattrick, Stephens, and Zeisler say 1888; Christ and Morley say 1889.

18 *Aberdonian*. Relating to or characteristic of Aberdeen, Scotland.

19 *helped him to attain success*. It is a great pity that Watson did not see fit to chronicle either of these cases. Perhaps they included some of the unrecorded cases mentioned by Watson—the Camberwell poisoning case ("The Five Orange Pips"), for example; Porlock posted his cipher message to Holmes from Camberwell.

20 *this morning*.' Although Inspector MacDonald states that Douglas was murdered "this morning" (that is, on the morning of the seventh of January), we are told in the next chapter that the first alarm of murder went out "at eleven-forty-five" on the preceding night, the sixth.

Alec MacDonald was far from having attained the national fame which he has now achieved. He was a young but trusted member of the detective force, who had distinguished himself in several cases which had been entrusted to him. His tall, bony figure gave promise of exceptional physical strength, while his great cranium and deep-set, lustrous eyes spoke no less clearly of the keen intelligence which twinkled out from behind his bushy eyebrows. He was a silent, precise man, with
18 a dour nature and a hard Aberdonian accent. Twice already
19 in his career had Holmes helped him to attain success, his own sole reward being the intellectual joy of the problem. For this reason the affection and respect of the Scotchman for his amateur colleague were profound, and he showed them by the frankness with which he consulted Holmes in every difficulty. Mediocrity knows nothing higher than itself, but talent instantly recognizes genius, and MacDonald had talent enough for his profession to enable him to perceive that there was no humiliation in seeking the assistance of one who already stood alone in Europe, both in his gifts and in his experience. Holmes was not prone to friendship, but he was tolerant of the big Scotchman, and smiled at the sight of him.

'You are an early bird, Mr Mac,' said he. 'I wish you luck with your worm. I fear this means that there is some mischief afoot.'

'If you said "hope" instead of "fear" it would be nearer the truth, I'm thinking, Mr Holmes,' the inspector answered, with a knowing grin. 'Well, maybe a wee nip would keep out the raw morning chill. No, I won't smoke, I thank you. I'll have to be pushing on my way, for the early hours of a case are the precious ones, as no man knows better than your own self. But—but——'

The inspector had stopped suddenly, and was staring with a look of absolute amazement at a paper upon the table. It was the sheet upon which I had scrawled the enigmatic message.

'Douglas!' he stammered. 'Birlstone! What's this, Mr Holmes? Man, it's witchcraft! Where in the name of all that is wonderful did you get those names?'

'It is a cipher that Dr Watson and I have had occasion to solve. But why—what's amiss with the names?'

The inspector looked from one to the other of us in dazed astonishment.

'Just this,' said he, 'that Mr Douglas, of Birlstone Manor
20 House, was horribly murdered this morning.'

"WHAT'S THIS, MR. HOLMES? MAN, IT'S WITCHCRAFT!"

This is one of the twelve illustrations drawn by Arthur I. Keller for Associated Sunday Magazines, in which *The Valley of Fear* appeared in the United States between September 20 and November 22, 1914. Keller here exaggerates Watson's slowness of mentality (as compared to the swiftness of mentality of Holmes) into almost moronic proportions—aptly described by the late Edmund Pearson as "boobus Britannicus" ("Sherlock Holmes Among the Illustrators"). The late James Montgomery wrote of Keller (*A Study in Pictures*): His "pictures vary in quality, some being excellent, although none of the five depicting the English phase of the tale succeed in capturing the subtle Sherlockian mood. It is when the story shifts to America that he is most successful. There he is not hampered by the need for English flavor, and his portrayal of the rough men and primitive conditions in Vermissa Valley becomes very realistic indeed." Frank Wiles illustrated this same scene for the *Strand Magazine*, September, 1914.

2 ◆ MR SHERLOCK HOLMES DISCOURSES

It was one of those dramatic moments for which my friend existed. It would be an over-statement to say that he was shocked or even excited by the amazing announcement. Without having a tinge of cruelty in his singular composition, he was undoubtedly callous from long over-stimulation. Yet, if his emotions were dulled, his intellectual perceptions were exceedingly active. There was no trace then of the horror which I had myself felt at this curt declaration, but his face showed rather the quiet and interested composure of the chemist who sees the crystals falling into position from his over-saturated solution.

'Remarkable!' said he; 'remarkable!'

'You don't seem surprised.'

'Interested, Mr Mac, but hardly surprised. Why should I be surprised? I receive an anonymous communication from a quarter which I know to be important, warning me that danger threatens a certain person. Within an hour I learn that this danger has actually materialized, and that the person is dead. I am interested, but, as you observe, I am not surprised.'

In a few short sentences he explained to the inspector the facts about the letter and the cipher. MacDonald sat with his chin on his hands, and his great sandy eyebrows bunched into a yellow tangle.

'I was going down to Birlstone this morning,' said he. 'I had come to ask you if you cared to come with me—you and your friend here. But from what you say we might perhaps be doing better work in London.'

'I rather think not,' said Holmes.

'Hang it all, Mr Holmes!' cried the inspector. 'The papers will be full of the Birlstone Mystery in a day or two, but where's the mystery if there is a man in London who prophesied the crime before ever it occurred? We have only to lay our hands on that man and the rest will follow.'

'No doubt, Mr Mac. But how did you propose to lay your hands on the so-called Porlock?'

MacDonald turned over the letter which Holmes had handed him.

'Posted in Camberwell—that doesn't help us much. Name, you say, is assumed. Not much to go on, certainly. Didn't you say that you have sent him money?'

'Twice.'

'And how?'

'In notes to Camberwell post-office.'

'Did you never trouble to see who called for them?'

'No.'

The inspector looked surprised and a little shocked.

'Why not?'

'Because I always keep faith. I had promised when he first wrote that I would not try to trace him.'

'You think there is someone behind him?'

'I *know* there is.'

'This Professor that I have heard you mention?'

'Exactly.'

Inspector MacDonald smiled, and his eyelid quivered as he glanced towards me.

21 *the C.I.D.* The Criminal Investigation Department of Scotland Yard.

22 *Jean Baptiste Greuze.*' French genre and portrait painter, 1725–1805.

"YES, I SAW THE PICTURE—A YOUNG WOMAN WITH HER HEAD ON HER HANDS, PEEKING AT YOU SIDEWAYS."

This would seem to be the painting now in the National Galleries of Scotland (Catalogue No. NG437) described as *Girl with Arms Folded*.

'I won't conceal from you, Mr Holmes, that we think in the **21** C.I.D. that you have a wee bit of a bee in your bonnet over this Professor. I made some inquiries myself about the matter. He seems to be a very respectable, learned, and talented sort of man.'

'I'm glad you've got as far as to recognize the talent.'

'Man, you can't but recognize it. After I heard your view, I made it my business to see him. I had a chat with him on eclipses—how the talk got that way I canna think—but he had out a reflector lantern and a globe and made it all clear in a minute. He lent me a book, but I don't mind saying that it was a bit above my head, though I had a good Aberdeen upbringing. He'd have made a grand meenister, with his thin face and grey hair and solemn-like way of talking. When he put his hand on my shoulder as we were parting, it was like a father's blessing before you go out into the cold, cruel world.'

Holmes chuckled, and rubbed his hands.

'Great!' he said; 'great! Tell me, friend MacDonald; this pleasing and touching interview was, I suppose, in the Professor's study?'

'That's so.'

'A fine room, is it not?'

'Very fine—very handsome indeed, Mr Holmes.'

'You sat in front of his writing-desk?'

'Just so.'

'Sun in your eyes and his face in the shadow?'

'Well, it was evening, but I mind that the lamp was turned on my face.'

'It would be. Did you happen to observe a picture over the Professor's head?'

'I don't miss much, Mr Holmes. Maybe I learned that from you. Yes, I saw the picture—a young woman with her head on her hands, keeking at you sideways.'

'That painting was by Jean Baptiste Greuze.'

The inspector endeavoured to look interested.

22 'Jean Baptiste Greuze,' Holmes continued, joining his finger-tips and leaning well back in his chair, 'was a French artist who flourished between the years 1750 and 1800. I allude, of course, to his working career. Modern criticism has more than endorsed the high opinion formed of him by his contemporaries.'

The inspector's eyes grew abstracted.

'Hadn't we better——' he said.

'We are doing so,' Holmes interrupted. 'All that I am saying has a very direct and vital bearing upon what you have called the Birlstone Mystery. In fact, it may in a sense be called the very centre of it.'

MacDonald smiled feebly, and looked appealingly to me.

'Your thoughts move a bit too quick for me. Mr Holmes. You leave out a link or two, and I can't get over the gap. What in the whole wide world can be the connection between this dead painting man and the affair at Birlstone?'

'All knowledge comes useful to the detective,' remarked Holmes. 'Even the trivial fact that in the year 1865 a picture by Greuze, entitled "La Jeune Fille à l'agneau," fetched not **23** less than four thousand pounds—at the Portalis sale, may start a train of reflection in your mind.'

It was clear that it did. The inspector looked honestly interested.

'I may remind you,' Holmes continued, 'that the Professor's salary can be ascertained in several trustworthy books of reference. It is seven hundred a year.'   **24**

'Then how could he buy——'

'Quite so. How could he?'

'Aye, that's remarkable,' said the inspector, thoughtfully. 'Talk away, Mr Holmes. I'm just loving it. It's fine.'

Holmes smiled. He was always warmed by genuine admiration—the characteristic of the real artist.

'What about Birlstone?' he asked.

'We've time yet,' said the inspector, glancing at his watch. 'I've a cab at the door, and it won't take us twenty minutes to Victoria. But about this picture—I thought you **25** told me once, Mr Holmes, that you had never met Professor Moriarty.'

'No, I never have.'

'Then how do you know about his rooms?'

'Ah, that's another matter. I have been three times in his rooms, twice waiting for him under different pretexts and leaving before he came. Once—well, I can hardly tell about the once to an official detective. It was on the last occasion that I took the liberty of running over his papers, with the most unexpected results.'

'You found something compromising?'

'Absolutely nothing. That was what amazed me. However, you have now seen the point of the picture. It shows him to be a very wealthy man. How did he acquire wealth? He is unmarried. His younger brother is a station-master in the West of England. His chair is worth seven hundred a year. And he owns a Greuze.'

'Well?'

'Surely the inference is plain.'

'You mean that he has a great income, and that he must earn it in an illegal fashion?'

'Exactly. Of course, I have other reasons for thinking so—dozens of exiguous threads which lead vaguely up towards the centre of the web where the poisonous motionless creature is lurking. I only mention the Greuze because it brings the matter within the range of your own observation.'

'Well, Mr Holmes, I admit that what you say is interesting. It's more than interesting—it's just wonderful. But let us have it a little clearer if you can. Is it forgery, coining, burglary? Where does the money come from?'

'Have you ever read of Jonathan Wild?'   **26**

'Well, the name has a familiar sound. Someone in a novel, was he not? I don't take much stock of detectives in novels—chaps that do things and never let you see how they do them. That's just inspiration, not business.'

'Jonathan Wild wasn't a detective, and he wasn't in a novel. He was a master criminal, and he lived last century—1750 or thereabouts.'

'Then he's no use to me. I'm a practical man.'

'Mr Mac, the most practical thing that ever you did in your life would be to shut yourself up for three months and read twelve hours a day at the annals of crime. Everything comes in circles, even Professor Moriarty. Jonathan Wild was the hidden force of the London criminals, to whom he sold his brains and his organization on a fifteen per cent. commission. The old wheel turns and the same spoke comes up. It's all

23 *at the Portalis sale.* In the manuscript, the *Strand Magazine*, the first American edition of *The Valley of Fear* and the Doubleday omnibus, the painting fetched "one million and two hundred thousand francs—more than forty thousand pounds."

In fact, according to the *Times* of London (Literary Supplement, July 1, 1960) "the sale-room price of a Greuze has never exceeded the 129,000 francs given for *Les Oeufs Cassées* at the Demidoff sale in 1870."

Let us say that *La Jeune Fille à l'agneau* sold for some $20,000 U.S.

Greuze would seem to have painted at least five different pictures of a young girl with a lamb: 1) *L'Amitié* from the Marion Davis collection in the Los Angeles County Museum; 2) *L'Amitié* in the Mary Frick Jacobs collection of the Baltimore Art Museum; 3) a painting in the Wallace collection in London; 4) a painting in the National Art Gallery in London; 5) a painting in the Walters Art Gallery in Baltimore. According to Mr. Thomas L. Stix ("Who's Afraid of the Big Bad Moriarty") a picture, supposedly by Greuze, of a girl and a lamb was actually sold to Benjamin Disraeli for £1,800 at the Portalis sale of 1865. The picture proved to be a forgery; Portalis refunded the £1,800 to Disraeli and the picture "after Greuze" was subsequently sold "as is" for £45.

24 *seven hundred a year.'* About $3,500.

25 *Victoria.* The old Victoria Station of the London, Brighton and South Coast Railway and the London, Chatham and Dover Railway, first opened to the public on October 1, 1860. The original station cost £675,000 and covered eleven acres.

26 *Jonathan Wild?'* English artisan, fence, and informer. Holmes was mistaken in saying that Wild lived about 1750: he was hanged on May 24, 1725. Holmes was also mistaken in saying that Wild "wasn't in a novel": Wild was the subject of a satire by Fielding and a romance by Defoe.

27 *'Six thousand a year.* About $30,000.

been done before and will be again. I'll tell you one or two things about Moriarty which may interest you.'

'You'll interest me right enough.'

'I happen to know who is the first link in his chain—a chain with this Napoleon-gone-wrong at one end and a hundred broken fighting men, pickpockets, blackmailers, and card-sharpers at the other, with every sort of crime in between. His chief of the staff is Colonel Sebastian Moran, as aloof and guarded and inaccessible to the law as himself. What do you think he pays him?'

'I'd like to hear.'

27   'Six thousand a year. That's paying for brains, you see—the American business principle. I learned that detail quite by chance. It's more than the Prime Minister gets. That gives you an idea of Moriarty's gains and of the scale on which he works. Another point. I made it my business to hunt down some of Moriarty's cheques lately—just common innocent cheques that he pays his household bills with. They were drawn on six different banks. Does that make any impression on your mind?'

'Queer, certainly. But what do you gather from it?'

'That he wanted no gossip about his wealth. No single man should know what he had. I have no doubt that he has twenty banking accounts—the bulk of his fortune abroad in the Deutsche Bank or the Crédit Lyonnais as likely as not. Some time when you have a year or two to spare I commend to you the study of Professor Moriarty.'

Inspector MacDonald had grown steadily more impressed as the conversation proceeded. He had lost himself in his interest. Now his practical Scotch intelligence brought him back with a snap to the matter in hand.

'He can keep, anyhow,' said he. 'You've got us side-tracked with your interesting anecdotes, Mr Holmes. What really counts is your remark that there is some connection between the Professor and the crime. That you get from the warning received through the man Porlock. Can we for our present practical needs get any farther than that?'

'We may form some conception as to the motives of the crime. It is, as I gather from your original remarks, an inexplicable, or at least an unexplained, murder. Now, presuming that the source of the crime is as we suspect it to be, there might be two different motives. In the first place, I may tell you that Moriarty rules with a rod of iron over his people. His discipline is tremendous. There is only one punishment in his code. It is death. Now, we might suppose that this murdered man—this Douglas, whose approaching fate was known by one of the arch-criminal's subordinates—had in some way betrayed the chief. His punishment followed and would be known to all, if only to put the fear of death into them.'

'Well, that is one suggestion, Mr Holmes.'

'The other is that it has been engineered by Moriarty in the ordinary course of business. Was there any robbery?'

'I have not heard.'

'If so it would, of course, be against the first hypothesis and in favour of the second. Moriarty may have been engaged to engineer it on a promise of part spoils, or he may have been paid so much down to manage it. Either is possible. But, whichever it may be, or if it is some third combination, it is down at Birlstone that we must seek the solution. I know our man too well to suppose that he has left anything up here which may lead us to him.'

'Then to Birlstone we must go!' cried MacDonald, jumping from his chair. 'My word! it's later than I thought. I can give you gentlemen five minutes for preparation, and that is all.'

'And ample for us both,' said Holmes, as he sprang up and hastened to change from his dressing-gown to his coat. 'While we are on our way, Mr Mac, I will ask you to be good enough to tell me all about it.'

'All about it,' proved to be disappointingly little, and yet there was enough to assure us that the case before us might well be worthy of the expert's closest attention. He brightened and rubbed his thin hands together as he listened to the meagre but remarkable details. A long series of sterile weeks lay behind us, and here, at last, there was a fitting **28** object for those remarkable powers which, like all special gifts, become irksome to their owner when they are not in use. That razor brain blunted and rusted with inaction. Sherlock Holmes's eyes glistened, his pale cheeks took a warmer hue, and his whole eager face shone with an inward light when the call for work reached him. Leaning forward in the cab, he listened intently to MacDonald's short sketch of the problem which awaited us in Sussex. The inspector was himself dependent, as he explained to us, upon a scribbled account forwarded to him by the milk train in the early hours of the morning. White Mason, the local officer, was a personal friend, and hence MacDonald had been notified very much more promptly than is usual at Scotland Yard when provincials need their assistance. It is a very cold scent upon which the Metropolitan expert is generally asked to run.

'Dear Inspector MacDonald,' said the letter which he read to us, 'official requisition for your services is in separate envelope. This is for your private eye. Wire me what train in the morning you can get for Birlstone, and I will meet it—or have it met if I am too occupied. This case is a snorter. Don't waste a moment in getting started. If you can bring Mr Holmes, please do so, for he will find something after his own heart. You would think the whole thing had been fixed up for theatrical effect, if there wasn't a dead man in the middle of it. My word, it *is* a snorter!'

'Your friend seems to be no fool,' remarked Holmes.

'No, sir; White Mason is a very live man, if I am any judge.'

'Well, have you anything more?'

'Only that he will give us every detail when we meet.'

'Then how did you get at Mr Douglas and the fact that he had been horribly murdered?'

'That was in the enclosed official report. It didn't say "horrible." That's not a recognized official term. It gave the name John Douglas. It mentioned that his injuries had been in the head, from the discharge of a shot-gun. It also mentioned the hour of the alarm, which was close on to midnight last night. It added that the case was undoubtedly one of murder, but that no arrest had been made, and that the case was one which presented some very perplexing and extraordinary features. That's absolutely all we have at present, Mr Holmes.'

'Then, with your permission, we will leave it at that, Mr Mac. The temptation to form premature theories upon in-

LEANING FORWARD IN THE CAB, HE LISTENED INTENTLY TO MACDONALD'S SHORT SKETCH OF THE PROBLEM WHICH AWAITED US IN SUSSEX.

Illustration by Frank Wiles for the *Strand Magazine*, September, 1914.

29 *Weald.* A district in Kent, Sussex, and Surrey, extending along the coast from near Dover to Beachy Head, and reaching inward across the Downs to the east part of Hampshire.

30 *Tunbridge Wells.* A municipal borough in Kent. It became fashionable after chalybeate springs were discovered there in 1606.

31 *the time of the first Crusade.* 1095–1099.

32 *Hugo de Capus.* Mr. Bell found the mention of this name "the only really puzzling feature of the narrative." "The name," he wrote in "Three Identifications," "seems not to have existed in England, or, indeed anywhere nearer than the province of Carniola in the present kingdom of Yugoslavia."

To this Dr. Julian Wolff added (*Practical Handbook of Sherlockian Heraldry*): "Burke's *Visitations* mentions 'Hugo comes,' a nephew and companion of William the Conqueror. (Descent from Hugh Capet, King of France, may account for the de Capus.) Hugo's father, the half brother of William, was awarded seven hundred manors and it is not unlikely that the Red King, William Rufus, the Conqueror's son, granted Birlstone to Hugo who built a fortalice there. Eleventh-century heraldry is obscure, but Watson seemed to be familiar with the lion of de Capus—or perhaps he confused it with 'the rampant' lion of Des Champs, which came from France in 1746, not 1066."

sufficient data is the bane of our profession. I can only see two things for certain at present: a great brain in London and a dead man in Sussex. It's the chain between that we are going to trace.'

◆

3 ◆ THE TRAGEDY OF BIRLSTONE
◆

And now for a moment I will ask leave to remove my own insignificant personality and to describe events which occurred before we arrived upon the scene by the light of knowledge which came to us afterwards. Only in this way can I make the reader appreciate the people concerned and the strange setting in which their fate was cast.

The village of Birlstone is a small and very ancient cluster of half-timbered cottages on the northern border of the county of Sussex. For centuries it had remained unchanged, but within the last few years its picturesque appearance and situation have attracted a number of well-to-do residents, whose villas peep out from the woods around. These woods are locally supposed to be the extreme fringe of the great **29** Weald forest, which thins away until it reaches the northern chalk downs. A number of small shops have come into being to meet the wants of the increased population, so that there seems some prospect that Birlstone may soon grow from an ancient village into a modern town. It is the centre for a con-**30** siderable area of country, since Tunbridge Wells, the nearest place of importance, is ten or twelve miles to the eastward, over the borders of Kent.

About half a mile from the town, standing in an old park famous for its huge beech trees, is the ancient Manor House of Birlstone. Part of this venerable building dates back to the **31-32** time of the first Crusade, when Hugo de Capus built a fortalice in the centre of the estate, which had been granted to him by the Red King. This was destroyed by fire in 1543, and some of its smoke-blackened corner-stones were used when, in

THE LATE JAMES MONTGOMERY'S MAP OF GROOMBRIDGE PLACE

The late James Montgomery based his identification of "Birlstone Manor" as Groombridge House on a presentation copy of *The Valley of Fear* in which Conan Doyle wrote: "With all kind of remembrance from Arthur Conan Doyle who hopes you have pleasant memories of Groombridge House which is the old house herein described. June 22/21." Said Mr. Montgomery: "The village of Groombridge, situated on the northerly slopes of Ashdown Forest, once famous as a royal hunting ground, is only about three miles from Tunbridge Wells. . . . The village is located in two counties, the newer half (known today as the New Town) being in Sussex, and the older part (the Old Town), including Groombridge Place itself, lying in Kent. . . . We learn from the short account (*St. John the Evangelist, Groombridge, Kent,* by B. W. Shepherd-Walwyn) purchasable for sixpence . . . from the local tobacconist (now one L. V. Narramore) that a Saxon noble named Gromen built a castle here and surrounded it with a moat. . . . The castle was equipped with a drawbridge, which may have given rise to the name 'Groombridge.'"

Jacobean times, a brick country house rose upon the ruins **33**
of the feudal castle. The Manor House, with its many gables
and its small, diamond-paned windows, was still much as the
builder had left it in the early seventeenth century. Of the
double moats which had guarded its more warlike predecessor
the outer had been allowed to dry up, and served the humble
function of a kitchen garden. The inner one was still there,
and lay, forty feet in breadth, though now only a few feet
in depth, round the whole house. A small stream fed it and
continued beyond it, so that the sheet of water, though turbid, was never ditch-like or unhealthy. The ground-floor
windows were within a foot of the surface of the water. The
only approach to the house was over a drawbridge, the chains
and windlass of which had long been rusted and broken.
The latest tenants of the Manor House had, however, with
characteristic energy, set this right, and the drawbridge was
not only capable of being raised, but actually was raised every
evening and lowered every morning. By thus renewing the
custom of the old feudal days the Manor House was converted
into an island during the night—a fact which had a very
direct bearing upon the mystery which was soon to engage
the attention of all England.

The house had been untenanted for some years, and was
threatening to moulder into a picturesque decay when the
Douglases took possession of it. This family consisted of only
two individuals, John Douglas and his wife. Douglas was a
remarkable man both in character and in person; in age he
may have been about fifty, with a strong-jawed, rugged face,
a grizzling moustache, peculiarly keen grey eyes, and a wiry,
vigorous figure which had lost nothing of the strength and
activity of youth. He was cheery and genial to all, but somewhat offhand in his manners, giving the impression that he
had seen life in social strata on some far lower horizon than
the county society of Sussex. Yet, though looked at with some
curiosity and reserve by his more cultivated neighbours he
soon acquired a great popularity among the villagers, sub-
scribing handsomely to all local objects, and attending their
smoking concerts and other functions, where, having a remarkably rich tenor voice, he was always ready to oblige with
an excellent song. He appeared to have plenty of money,
which was said to have been gained in the Californian gold-

33 *in Jacobean times.* In the reign of James I of
England (1603–1625) and sometimes of James II
(1685–1688).

MAP OF
GROOMBRIDGE PLACE
(AFTER AN ORDNANCE SURVEY MAP)

1 MOAT	4 SUN DIAL
2 PRIEST'S HOUSE	5 JOHN PACKER'S
3 GHOSTLY OSTLER	CHURCH
DOORWAY	6 GATE

34 *Hampstead.* A metropolitan borough four miles northwest of the City. It stands upon one of the highest hills around London. The town occupies its southern slopes, the Heath its summit—it is 443 miles above sea level. The name is clearly derived from *ham or hame*, a home, and *steede*, a place, and has consequently the same meaning as "homestead." For a Holmes and Watson adventure that took place in Hampstead, see "Charles Augustus Milverton."

fields, and it was clear from his own talk and that of his wife that he had spent a part of his life in America. The good impression which had been produced by his generosity and by his democratic manners was increased by a reputation gained for utter indifference to danger. Though a wretched rider, he turned out at every meet, and took the most amazing falls in his determination to hold his own with the best. When the vicarage caught fire he distinguished himself also by the fearlessness with which he re-entered the building to save property, after the local fire brigade had given it up as impossible. Thus it came about that John Douglas, of the Manor House, had within five years won himself quite a reputation in Birlstone.

His wife, too, was popular with those who had made her acquaintance, though, after the English fashion, the callers upon a stranger who settled in the county without introductions were few and far between. This mattered the less to her as she was retiring by disposition and very much absorbed, to all appearance, in her husband and her domestic duties. It was known that she was an English lady who had met Mr Douglas in London, he being at that time a widower. She was a beautiful woman, tall, dark, and slender, some twenty years younger than her husband, a disparity which seemed in no wise to mar the contentment of their family life. It was remarked sometimes, however, by those who knew them best that the confidence between the two did not appear to be complete, since the wife was either very reticent about her husband's past life or else, as seemed more likely, was very imperfectly informed about it. It had also been noted and commented upon by a few observant people that there were signs sometimes of some nerve-strain upon the part of Mrs Douglas, and that she would display acute uneasiness if her absent husband should ever be particularly late in his return. On a quiet countryside, where all gossip is welcome, this weakness of the lady of the Manor House did not pass without remark, and it bulked larger upon people's memory when the events arose which gave it a very special significance.

There was yet another individual whose residence under that roof was, it is true, only an intermittent one, but whose presence at the time of the strange happenings which will now be narrated brought his name prominently before the public. This was Cecil James Barker, of Hales Lodge, Hampstead. Cecil Barker's tall, loose-jointed figure was a familiar one in the main street of Birlstone village, for he was a frequent and welcome visitor at the Manor House. He was the more noticed as being the only friend of the past unknown life of Mr Douglas who was ever seen in his new English surroundings. Barker was himself an undoubted Englishman, but by his remarks it was clear that he had first known Douglas in America, and had there lived on intimate terms with him. He appeared to be a man of considerable wealth, and was reputed to be a bachelor. In age he was rather younger than Douglas, forty-five at the most, a tall, straight, broad-chested fellow, with a clean-shaven prizefighter face, thick, strong, black eyebrows, and a pair of masterful black eyes which might, even without the aid of his very capable hands, clear a way for him through a hostile crowd. He neither rode nor shot, but spent his days in wandering round the old village with his pipe in his mouth, or in driving with his host, or in his absence with his hostess, over the beautiful countryside. 'An easy-going, free-handed gentleman,' said Ames, the butler. 'But, my word, I had rather not be the man that crossed him.' He was cordial and intimate with Douglas, and he was no less friendly with his wife, a friendship which more than once seemed to cause some irritation to the husband, so that even the servants were able to perceive his annoyance. Such was the third person who was one of the family when the catastrophe occurred. As to the other denizens of the old building, it will suffice out of a large household to mention the prim, respectable, and capable Ames and Mrs Allen, a buxom and cheerful person, who relieved the lady of some of her household cares. The other six servants in the house bear no relation to the events of the night of January 6th.

It was at eleven-forty-five that the first alarm reached the small local police-station in the charge of Sergeant Wilson, of the Sussex Constabulary. Mr Cecil Barker, much excited, had rushed up to the door and pealed furiously upon the bell. A terrible tragedy had occurred at the Manor House, and Mr John Douglas had been murdered. That was the breathless burden of his message. He had hurried back to the house, followed within a few minutes by the police-sergeant, who arrived at the scene of the crime a little past twelve o'clock, after taking prompt steps to warn the county authorities that something serious was afoot.

On reaching the Manor House the sergeant had found the drawbridge down, the windows lighted up, and the whole household in a state of wild confusion and alarm. The white-faced servants were huddling together in the hall, with the frightened butler wringing his hands in the doorway. Only Cecil Barker seemed to be master of himself and his emotions. He had opened the door which was nearest to the entrance, and had beckoned to the sergeant to follow him. At that moment there arrived Dr Wood, a brisk and capable general practitioner from the village. The three men entered the fatal room together, while the horror-stricken butler followed at their heels, closing the door behind him to shut out the terrible scene from the maid-servants.

The dead man lay upon his back, sprawling with outstretched limbs in the centre of the room. He was clad only in a pink dressing-gown, which covered his night clothes. There were carpet slippers upon his bare feet. The doctor knelt beside him, and held down the hand-lamp which had stood on the table. One glance at the victim was enough to show the healer that his presence could be dispensed with. The man had been horribly injured. Lying across his chest was a curious weapon, a shot-gun with the barrel sawn off a foot in front of the triggers. It was clear that this had been fired at close range, and that he had received the whole charge in the face, blowing his head almost to pieces. The triggers had been wired together, so as to make the simultaneous discharge more destructive.

The country policeman was unnerved and troubled by the tremendous responsibility which had come so suddenly upon him.

'We will touch nothing until my superiors arrive,' he said, in a hushed voice, staring in horror at the dreadful head.

'Nothing has been touched up to now,' said Cecil Barker. 'I'll answer for that. You see it all exactly as I found it.'

'When was that?' The sergeant had drawn out his notebook.

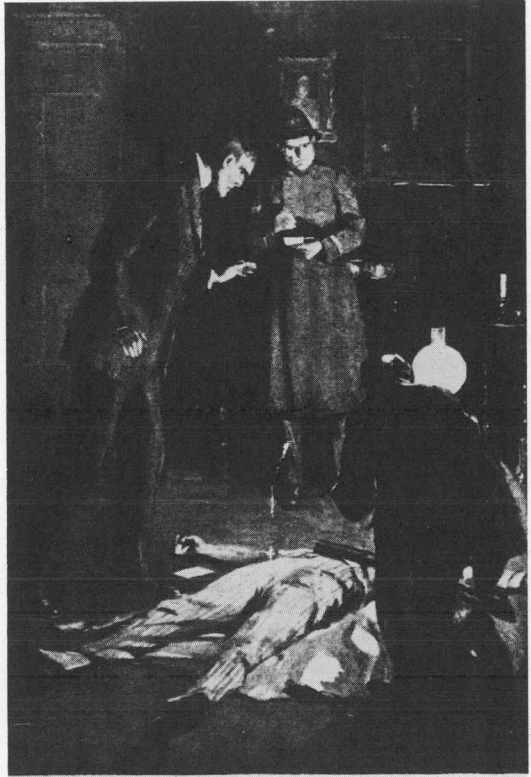

THE DOCTOR KNELT BESIDE HIM, AND HELD DOWN THE HAND-LAMP WHICH HAD STOOD ON THE TABLE.

Illustration by Frank Wiles for the *Strand Magazine*, October, 1914.

35 *nearer half-past four than six at this time of* *year.* "Sergeant Wilson says . . . that on the day of the tragedy sunset was nearer 4:30 than 6:00, and Inspector MacDonald says it was dusk by 4:30 P.M. Now sunset on January 6th is at 4:04 in London and is at most one minute earlier in Tunbridge Wells, and this fits very well with dusk at 4:40."—Dr. Ernest Bloomfield Zeisler, *Baker Street Chronology.*

'It was just half-past eleven. I had not begun to undress, and I was sitting by the fire in my bedroom, when I heard the report. It was not very loud—it seemed to be muffled. I rushed down. I don't suppose it was thirty seconds before I was in the room.'

'Was the door open?'

'Yes, it was open. Poor Douglas was lying as you see him. His bedroom candle was burning on the table. It was I who lit the lamp some minutes afterwards.'

'Did you see no one?'

'No. I heard Mrs Douglas coming down the stair behind me, and I rushed out to prevent her from seeing this dreadful sight. Mrs Allen, the housekeeper, came and took her away. Ames had arrived, and we ran back into the room once more.'

'But surely I have heard that the drawbridge is kept up all night.'

'Yes, it was up until I lowered it.'

'Then how could any murderer have got away? It is out of the question. Mr Douglas must have shot himself.'

'That was our first idea. But see.' Barker drew aside the curtain, and showed that the long, diamond-paned window was open to its full extent. 'And look at this!' He held the lamp down and illuminated a smudge of blood like the mark of a boot-sole upon the wooden sill. 'Someone has stood there in getting out.'

'You mean that someone waded across the moat?'

'Exactly.'

'Then, if you were in the room within half a minute of the crime, he must have been in the water at that very moment.'

'I have not a doubt of it. I wish to Heaven that I had rushed to the window. But the curtain screened it, as you can see, and so it never occurred to me. Then I heard the step of Mrs Douglas, and I could not let her enter the room. It would have been too horrible.'

'Horrible enough!' said the doctor, looking at the shattered head and the terrible marks which surrounded it. 'I've never seen such injuries since the Birlstone railway smash.'

'But, I say,' remarked the police-sergeant, whose slow, bucolic common sense was still pondering over the open window. 'It's all very well your saying that a man escaped by wading this moat, but what I ask you is—how did he ever get into the house at all if the bridge was up?'

'Ah, that's the question,' said Barker.

'At what o'clock was it raised?'

'It was nearly six o'clock,' said Ames, the butler.

'I've heard,' said the sergeant, 'that it was usually raised at sunset. That would be nearer half-past four than six at this **35** time of year.'

'Mrs Douglas had visitors to tea,' said Ames. 'I couldn't raise it until they went. Then I wound it up myself.'

'Then it comes to this,' said the sergeant. 'If anyone came from outside—*if* they did—they must have got in across the bridge before six and been in hiding ever since, until Mr Douglas came into the room after eleven.'

'That is so. Mr Douglas went round the house every night the last thing before he turned in to see that the lights were right. That brought him in here. The man was waiting, and shot him. Then he got away through the window and left his gun behind him. That's how I read it—for nothing else will fit the facts.'

The sergeant picked up a card which lay beside the dead man upon the floor. The initials V. V., and under it the number 341, were rudely scrawled in ink upon it.

'What's this?' he asked, holding it up.

Barker looked at it with curiosity.

'I never noticed it before,' he said. 'The murderer must have left it behind him.'

'V. V. 341. I can make no sense of that.'

'What's V. V.? Somebody's initials, maybe. What have you got there, Dr Wood?'

It was a good-sized hammer which had been lying upon the rug in front of the fireplace—a substantial, workmanlike hammer. Cecil Barker pointed to a box of brass-headed nails upon the mantelpiece.

'Mr Douglas was altering the pictures yesterday,' he said. 'I saw him myself standing upon that chair and fixing the big picture above it. That accounts for the hammer.'

'We'd best put it back on the rug where we found it,' said the sergeant, scratching his puzzled head in his perplexity. 'It will want the best brains in the force to get to the bottom of this thing. It will be a London job before it is finished.' He raised the hand-lamp and walked slowly round the room. 'Halloa!' he cried, excitedly, drawing the window curtain to one side. 'What o'clock were those curtains drawn?'

'When the lamps were lit,' said the butler. 'It would be shortly after four.'

'Someone has been hiding here, sure enough.' He held down the light, and the marks of muddy boots were very visible in the corner. 'I'm bound to say this bears out your theory, Mr Barker. It looks as if the man got into the house after four, when the curtains were drawn, and before six, when the bridge was raised. He slipped into this room because it was the first that he saw. There was no other place where he could hide, so he popped in behind this curtain. That all seems clear enough. It is likely that his main idea was to burgle the house, but Mr Douglas chanced to come upon him, so he murdered him and escaped.'

'That's how I read it,' said Barker. 'But, I say, aren't we wasting precious time? Couldn't we start out and scour the country before the fellow gets away?'

The sergeant considered for a moment.

'There are no trains before six in the morning, so he can't get away by rail. If he goes by road with his legs all dripping, it's odds that someone will notice him. Anyhow, I can't leave here myself until I am relieved. But I think none of you should go until we see more clearly how we all stand.'

The doctor had taken the lamp and was narrowly scrutinizing the body.

'What's this mark?' he asked. 'Could this have any connection with the crime?'

The dead man's right arm was thrust out from his dressing-gown and exposed as high as the elbow. About half-way up the forearm was a curious brown design, a triangle inside a circle, standing out in vivid relief upon the lard-coloured skin.

'It's not tattooed,' said the doctor, peering through his glasses. 'I never saw anything like it. The man has been branded at some time, as they brand cattle. What is the meaning of this?'

'I don't profess to know the meaning of it,' said Cecil Barker; 'but I've seen the mark on Douglas any time this last ten years.'

'And so have I,' said the butler. 'Many a time when the master has rolled up his sleeves I have noticed that very mark. I've often wondered what it could be.'

'Then it has nothing to do with the crime, anyhow,' said the sergeant. 'But it's a rum thing all the same. Everything about this case is rum. Well, what is it now?'

The butler had given an exclamation of astonishment, and was pointing at the dead man's outstretched hand.

'They've taken his wedding-ring!' he gasped.

'What!'

'Yes, indeed! Master always wore his plain gold wedding-ring on the little finger of his left hand. That ring with the rough nugget on it was above it, and the twisted snake-ring on the third finger. There's the nugget and there's the snake, but the wedding-ring is gone.'

'He's right,' said Barker.

'Do you tell me,' said the sergeant, 'that the wedding-ring was *below* the other?'

'Always!'

'Then the murderer, or whoever it was, first took off this ring you call the nugget-ring, then the wedding-ring, and afterwards put the nugget-ring back again.'

'That is so.'

The worthy country policeman shook his head.

'Seems to me the sooner we get London on to this case the better,' said he. 'White Mason is a smart man. No local job has ever been too much for White Mason. It won't be long now before he is here to help us. But I expect we'll have to look to London before we are through. Anyhow, I'm not ashamed to say that it is a deal too thick for the likes of me."

4 ⬩ DARKNESS

At three in the morning the chief Sussex detective, obeying the urgent call from Sergeant Wilson, of Birlstone, arrived from headquarters in a light dog-cart behind a breathless trotter. By the five-forty train in the morning he had sent his message to Scotland Yard, and he was at the Birlstone station at twelve o'clock to welcome us. Mr White Mason was a quiet, comfortable-looking person, in a loose tweed suit, with a clean-shaven, ruddy face, a stoutish body and powerful bandy legs adorned with gaiters, looking like a small farmer, a retired gamekeeper, or anything upon earth except a very favourable specimen of the provincial criminal officer.

'A real downright snorter, Mr MacDonald,' he kept repeat-**36** ing. 'We'll have the pressmen down like flies when they understand it. I'm hoping we will get our work done before they get poking their noses into it and messing up all the trails.

36 *pressmen*. Reporters.

There has been nothing like this that I can remember. There are some bits that will come home to you, Mr Holmes, or I am mistaken. And you also, Dr Watson, for the medicos will have a word to say before we finish. Your room is at the Westville Arms. There's no other place, but I hear that it is clean and good. The man will carry your bags. This way, gentlemen, if *you* please.'

He was a very bustling and genial person, this Sussex detective. In ten minutes we had all found our quarters. In ten more we were seated in the parlour of the inn and being treated to a rapid sketch of those events which have been outlined in the previous chapter. MacDonald made an occasional note, while Holmes sat absorbed with the expression of surprised and reverent admiration with which the botanist surveys the rare and precious bloom.

'Remarkable!' he said, when the story was unfolded. 'Most remarkable! I can hardly recall any case where the features have been more peculiar.'

'I thought you would say so, Mr Holmes,' said White Mason, in great delight. 'We're well up with the times in Sussex. I've told you now how matters were, up to the time when I took over from Sergeant Wilson between three and four this morning. My word, I made the old mare go! But I need not have been in such a hurry as it turned out, for there was nothing immediate that I could do. Sergeant Wilson had all the facts. I checked them and considered them, and maybe added a few on my own.'

'What were they?' asked Holmes, eagerly.

'Well, I first had the hammer examined. There was Dr Wood there to help me. We found no signs of violence upon it. I was hoping that, if Mr Douglas defended himself with the hammer, he might have left his mark upon the murderer before he dropped it on the mat. But there was no stain.'

'That, of course, proves nothing at all,' remarked Inspector MacDonald. 'There has been many a hammer murder and no trace on the hammer.'

'Quite so. It doesn't prove it wasn't used. But there might have been stains, and that would have helped us. As a matter of fact, there were none. Then I examined the gun. They were buck-shot cartridges, and, as Sergeant Wilson pointed out, the triggers were wired together so that if you pulled on the hinder one both barrels were discharged. Whoever fixed that up had made up his mind that he was going to take no chances of missing his man. The sawn gun was not more than two feet long; one could carry it easily under one's coat. There was no complete maker's name, but the printed letters "PEN" were on the fluting between the barrels, and the rest of the name had been cut off by the saw.'

'A big "P" with a flourish above it—"E" and "N" smaller?' asked Holmes.

'Exactly.'

'Pennsylvania Small Arm Company—well-known American firm,' said Holmes. **37**

White Mason gazed at my friend as the little village practitioner looks at the Harley Street specialist who by a word can solve the difficulties that perplex him.

'That is very helpful, Mr Holmes. No doubt you are right. Wonderful—wonderful! Do you carry the names of all the gunmakers in the world in your memory?'

37 *well-known American firm.'* Commentators have pointed to this remark, and to Holmes' earlier remark that "paying for brains" is "the American business principle" as evidence that Holmes was born in America or at least had spent some of his earlier years there.

38 *five years ago*. By our dating, then, Douglas would have taken the Manor House in 1883.

"TEN YEARS WITH SIR CHARLES CHANDOS—"

"Sir Charles does not play a prominent role in *The Valley of Fear*," Dr. Julian Wolff wrote in his *Practical Handbook of Sherlockian Heraldry*. "He is merely mentioned as the former employer of Ames, the butler . . . But Sir John Chandos, his ancestor, was the right-hand man of the Black Prince and appears prominently in chronicles of English chivalry. To all Canonical scholars, however, his greatest fame derives from the fact that his squire was a certain Nigel Loring.

"It is a surprise to find that there is any question about the arms of such a famous family. Yet in *The White Company* the arms are described as a scarlet wedge upon a silver field, while in *Sir Nigel* a red wedge upon a golden field is mentioned. Major T. G. Woolley's article, 'Three Interesting Seals' (*The Coat of Arms*, 3. no. 19, July, 1954) blazons them as 'Arg a pile gu.' In a letter to the editor of that magazine (3, no. 21, January, 1955) it is noted by George Walker that the modern Chandos families use a field of or. Robson's *British Herald* gives one with or, one argent and, to make the problem more complicated, another with ermine. In any event, the arms are as illustrated here and are blazoned: or (or argent, or ermine) a pile gules."

Holmes dismissed the subject with a wave.

'No doubt it is an American shot-gun,' White Mason continued. 'I seem to have read that a sawed-off shot-gun is a weapon used in some parts of America. Apart from the name upon the barrel, the idea had occurred to me. There is some evidence, then, that this man who entered the house and killed its master was an American.'

MacDonald shook his head. 'Man, you are surely travelling over-fast,' said he. 'I have heard no evidence yet that any stranger was ever in the house at all.'

'The open window, the blood on the sill, the queer card, marks of boots in the corner, the gun.'

'Nothing there that could not have been arranged. Mr Douglas was an American, or had lived long in America. So had Mr Barker. You don't need to import an American from outside in order to account for American doings.'

'Ames, the butler——'

'What about him? Is he reliable?'

'Ten years with Sir Charles Chandos—as solid as a rock. He has been with Douglas ever since he took the Manor **38** House five years ago. He has never seen a gun of this sort in the house.'

'The gun was made to conceal. That's why the barrels were sawn. It would fit into any box. How could he swear there was no such gun in the house?'

'Well, anyhow, he had never seen one.'

MacDonald shook his obstinate Scotch head. 'I'm not convinced yet that there was ever anyone in the house,' said he. 'I'm asking you to conseedar'—his accent became more Aberdonian as he lost himself in his argument. 'I'm asking you to conseedar what it involves if you suppose that this gun was ever brought into the house and that all these strange things were done by a person from outside. Oh, man, it's just inconceivable! It's clean aginst common sense. I put it to you, Mr Holmes, judging it by what we have heard.'

'Well, state your case, Mr Mac,' said Holmes, in his most judicial style.

'The man is not a burglar, supposing that he ever existed. The ring business and the card point to premeditated murder for some private reason. Very good. Here is a man who slips into a house with the deliberate intention of committing murder. He knows, if he knows anything, that he will have a deeficulty in making his escape, as the house is surrounded with water. What weapon would he choose? You would say the most silent in the world. Then he could hope, when the deed was done, to slip quickly from the window, to wade the moat, and to get away at his leisure. That's understandable. But is it understandable that he should go out of his way to bring with him the most noisy weapon he could select, knowing well that it will fetch every human being in the house to the spot as quick as they can run, and that it is all odds that he will be seen before he can get across the moat? Is that credible, Mr Holmes?'

'Well, you put the case strongly,' my friend replied, thoughtfully. 'It certainly needs a good deal of justification. May I ask, Mr White Mason, whether you examined the farther side of the moat at once, to see if there were any signs of the man having climbed out from the water?'

'There were no signs, Mr Holmes. But it is a stone ledge,

and one could hardly expect them.'

'No tracks or marks?'

'None.'

'Ha! Would there be any objection, Mr White Mason, to our going down to the house at once? There may possibly be some small point which might be suggestive.'

'I was going to propose it, Mr Holmes, but I thought it well to put you in touch with all the facts before we go. I suppose, if anything should strike you——' White Mason looked doubtfully at the amateur.

'I have worked with Mr Holmes before,' said Inspector MacDonald. 'He plays the game.'

'My own idea of the game, at any rate,' said Holmes, with a smile. 'I go into a case to help the ends of justice and the work of the police. If ever I have separated myself from the official force, it is because they have first separated themselves from me. I have no wish ever to score at their expense. At the same time, Mr White Mason, I claim the right to work in my own way and give my results at my own time—complete, rather than in stages.'

'I am sure we are honoured by your presence and to show you all we know,' said White Mason, cordially. 'Come along, Dr Watson, and when the time comes we'll all hope for a place in your book.' **39**

We walked down the quaint village street with a row of pollarded elms on either side of it. Just beyond were two **40** ancient stone pillars, weather-stained and lichen-blotched, bearing upon their summits a shapeless something which had once been the ramping lion of Capus of Birlstone. A short walk along the winding drive, with such sward and oaks around it as one only sees in rural England; then a sudden turn, and the long, low, Jacobean house of dingy, liver-coloured brick lay before us, with an old-fashioned garden of cut yews on either side of it. As we approached it there were the wooden drawbridge and the beautiful broad moat, as still and luminous as quicksilver in the cold winter sunshine. Three centuries had flowed past the old Manor House, centuries of births and of home-comings, of country dances and of the meetings of fox-hunters. Strange that now in its old age this dark business should have cast its shadow upon the venerable walls. And yet those strange peaked roofs and quaint over-hung gables were a fitting covering to grim and terrible intrigue. As I looked at the deep-set windows and the long sweep of the dull-coloured, water-lapped front I felt that no more fitting scene could be set for such a tragedy.

'That's the window,' said White Mason; 'that one on the immediate right of the drawbridge. It's open just as it was found last night.'

'It looks rather narrow for a man to pass.'

'Well, it wasn't a fat man, anyhow. We don't need your deductions, Mr Holmes, to tell us that. But you or I could squeeze through all right.'

Holmes walked to the edge of the moat and looked across. Then he examined the stone ledge and the grass border beyond it.

'I've had a good look, Mr Holmes,' said White Mason. 'There is nothing there; no sign that anyone has landed. But why should he leave any sign?'

'Exactly. Why should he? Is the water always turbid?'

. . . A SHAPELESS SOMETHING WHICH HAD ONCE BEEN THE RAMPING LION OF CAPUS OF BIRLSTONE.

The "ramping lion" as shown in Dr. Julian Wolff's *Practical Handbook of Sherlockian Heraldry.*

THEN HE EXAMINED THE STONE LEDGE AND THE GRASS BORDER BEYOND IT.

Illustration by Frank Wiles for the *Strand Magazine*, October, 1914.

39 *all hope for a place in your book.*' Since White Mason knows Watson as Holmes' biographer, it would seem to place the adventure of *The Valley of Fear* no earlier than January, 1888, after the appearance of *A Study in Scarlet* in *Beeton's Christmas Annual* in December, 1887.

40 *pollarded elms.* A pollarded tree is one that is shorn at the top so that it will produce a thick growth of slender shoots.

'Generally about this colour. The stream brings down the clay.'

'How deep is it?'

'About two feet at each side and three in the middle.'

'So we can put aside all idea of the man having been drowned in crossing?'

'No; a child could not be drowned in it.'

We walked across the drawbridge, and were admitted by a quaint, gnarled, dried-up person who was the butler—Ames. The poor old fellow was white and quivering from the shock. The village sergeant, a tall, formal, melancholy man, still held his vigil in the room of fate. The doctor had departed.

'Anything fresh, Sergeant Wilson?' asked White Mason.

'No, sir.'

'Then you can go home. You've had enough. We can send for you if we want you. The butler had better wait outside. Tell him to warn Mr Cecil Barker, Mrs Douglas, and the housekeeper that we may want a word with them presently. Now, gentlemen, perhaps you will allow me to give you the views I have formed first, and then you will be able to arrive at your own.'

He impressed me, this country specialist. He had a solid grip of fact and a cool, clear, common-sense brain, which should take him some way in his profession. Holmes listened to him intently, with no sign of that impatience which the official exponent too often produced.

'Is it suicide or is it murder—that's our first question, gentlemen, is it not? If it were suicide, then we have to believe that this man began by taking off his wedding-ring and concealing it; that he then came down here in his dressing-gown, trampled mud into a corner behind the curtain in order to give the idea someone had waited for him, opened the window, put blood on the——'

'We can surely dismiss that,' said MacDonald.

'So I think. Suicide is out of the question. Then a murder has been done. What we have to determine is whether it was done by someone outside or inside the house.'

'Well, let's hear the argument.'

'There are considerable difficulties both ways, and yet one or the other it must be. We will suppose first that some person or persons inside the house did the crime. They got this man down here at a time when everything was still, and yet no one was asleep. They then did the deed with the queerest and noisiest weapon in the world, so as to tell everyone what had happened—a weapon that was never seen in the house before. That does not seem a very likely start, does it?'

'No, it does not.'

'Well, then, everyone is agreed that after the alarm was given only a minute at the most had passed before the whole household—not Mr Cecil Barker alone, though he claims to have been the first, but Ames and all of them—were on the spot. Do you tell me that in that time the guilty person managed to make footmarks in the corner, open the window, mark the sill with blood, take the wedding-ring off the dead man's finger, and all the rest of it? It's impossible!'

'You put it very clearly,' said Holmes. 'I am inclined to agree with you.'

'Well, then, we are driven back to the theory that it was done by someone from outside. We are still faced with some big difficulties, but, anyhow, they have ceased to be impossibilities. The man got into the house between four-thirty and six—that is to say, between dusk and the time when the bridge was raised. There had been some visitors, and the door was open, so there was nothing to prevent him. He may have been a common burglar, or he may have had some private grudge against Mr Douglas. Since Mr Douglas has spent most of his life in America, and this shot-gun seems to be an American weapon, it would seem that the private grudge is the more likely theory. He slipped into this room because it was the first he came to, and he hid behind the curtain. There he remained until past eleven at night. At that time Mr Douglas entered the room. It was a short interview, if there were any interview at all, for Mrs Douglas declares that her husband had not left her more than a few minutes when she heard the shot.'

'The candle shows that,' said Holmes.

'Exactly. The candle, which was a new one, is not burned more than half an inch. He must have placed it on the table before he was attacked, otherwise, of course, it would have fallen when he fell. This shows that he was not attacked the instant that he entered the room. When Mr Barker arrived the lamp was lit and the candle put out.'

'That's all clear enough.'

'Well, now, we can reconstruct things on those lines. Mr Douglas enters the room. He puts down the candle. A man appears from behind the curtain. He is armed with this gun. He demands the wedding-ring—Heaven only knows why, but so it must have been. Mr Douglas gave it up. Then either in cold blood or in the course of a struggle—Douglas may have gripped the hammer that was found upon the mat—he shot Douglas in this horrible way. He dropped his gun and also, it would seem, this queer card, "V. V. 341," whatever that may mean, and he made his escape through the window and across the moat at the very moment when Cecil Barker was discovering the crime. How's that, Mr Holmes?'

'Very interesting, but just a little unconvincing.'

'Man, it would be absolute nonsense, if it wasn't that anything else is even worse,' cried MacDonald. 'Somebody killed the man, and whoever it was I could clearly prove to you that he should have done it some other way. What does he mean by allowing his retreat to be cut off like that? What does he mean by using a shot-gun when silence was his one chance of escape? Come, Mr Holmes, it's up to you to give us a lead, since you say Mr White Mason's theory is unconvincing.'

Holmes had sat intently observant during this long discussion, missing no word that was said, with his keen eyes darting to right and to left, and his forehead wrinkled with speculation.

'I should like a few more facts before I get so far as a theory, Mr Mac,' said he, kneeling down beside the body. 'Dear me! these injuries are really appalling. Can we have the butler in for a moment? . . . Ames, I understand that you have often seen this very unusual mark, a branded triangle inside a circle, upon Mr Douglas's forearm?'

'Frequently, sir.'

'You never heard any speculation as to what it meant?'

'No, sir.'

'It must have caused great pain when it was inflicted. It is undoubtedly a burn. Now, I observe, Ames, that there is a small piece of plaster at the angle of Mr Douglas's jaw. Did

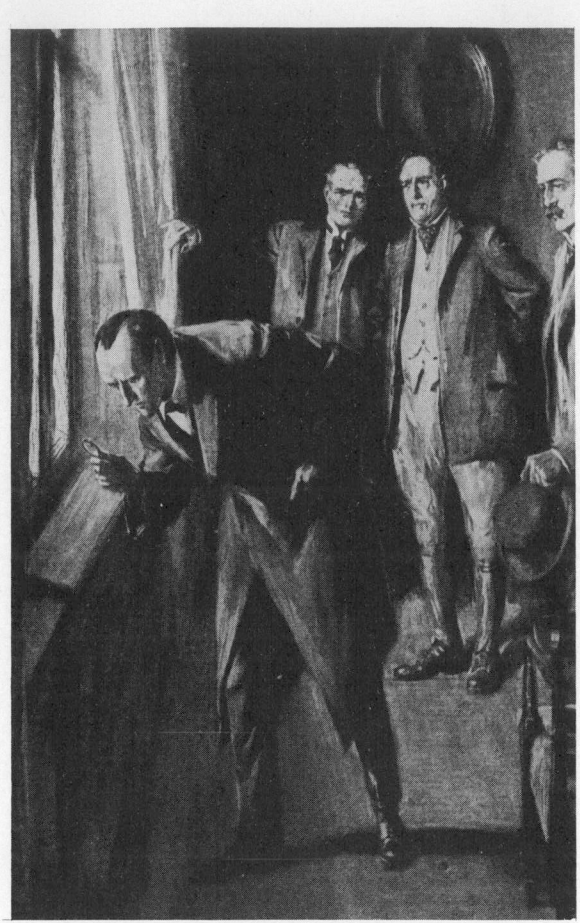

HOLMES HAD GONE TO THE WINDOW AND WAS
EXAMINING WITH HIS LENS THE BLOOD-MARK
UPON THE SILL.

Illustration by Frank Wiles for the *Strand Magazine*, October, 1914.

you observe that in life?'

'Yes, sir; he cut himself in shaving yesterday morning.'

'Did you ever know him cut himself in shaving before?'

'Not for a very long time, sir.'

'Suggestive!' said Holmes. 'It may, of course, be a mere coincidence, or it may point to some nervousness which would indicate that he had reason to apprehend danger. Had you noticed anything unusual in his conduct yesterday, Ames?'

'It struck me that he was a little restless and excited, sir.'

'Ha! The attack may not have been entirely unexpected. We do seem to make a little progress, do we not? Perhaps you would rather do the questioning, Mr Mac?'

'No, Mr Holmes; it's in better hands.'

'Well, then, we will pass to this card—"V. V. 341." It is rough cardboard. Have you any of the sort in the house?'

'I don't think so.'

Holmes walked across to the desk and dabbed a little ink from each bottle on to the blotting-paper. 'It has not been printed in this room,' he said; 'this is black ink, and the other purplish. It has been done by a thick pen, and these are fine. No, it has been done elsewhere, I should say. Can you make anything of the inscription, Ames?'

'No, sir, nothing.'

'What do you think, Mr Mac?'

'It gives me the impression of a secret society of some sort. The same with this badge upon the forearm.'

'That's my idea, too,' said White Mason.

'Well, we can adopt it as a working hypothesis, and then see how far our difficulties disappear. An agent from such a society makes his way into the house, waits for Mr Douglas, blows his head nearly off with this weapon, and escapes by wading the moat, after leaving a card beside the dead man which will, when mentioned in the papers, tell other members of the society that vengeance has been done. That all hangs together. But why this gun, of all weapons?'

'Exactly.'

'And why the missing ring?'

'Quite so.'

'And why no arrest? It's past two now. I take it for granted that since dawn every constable within forty miles has been looking out for a wet stranger?'

'That is so, Mr Holmes.'

'Well, unless he has a burrow close by, or a change of clothes ready, they can hardly miss him. And yet they *have* missed him up to now.' Holmes had gone to the window and was examining with his lens the blood-mark upon the sill. 'It is clearly the tread of a shoe. It is remarkably broad—a splay foot, one would say. Curious, because, so far as one can trace any footmark in this mud-stained corner, one would say it was a more shapely sole. However, they are certainly very indistinct. What's this under the side table?'

'Mr Douglas's dumb-bells,' said Ames.

'Dumb-bell—there's only one. Where's the other?'

'I don't know, Mr Holmes. There may have been only one. I have not noticed them for months.'

'One dumb-bell——' Holmes said, seriously, but his remarks were interrupted by a sharp knock at the door. A tall, sunburned, capable-looking, clean-shaven man looked in at us. I had no difficulty in guessing that it was the Cecil Barker of whom I had heard. His masterful eyes travelled quickly with a questioning glance from face to face.

'Sorry to interrupt your consultation,' said he, 'but you should hear the latest.'

'An arrest?'

'No such luck. But they've found his bicycle. The fellow left his bicycle behind him. Come and have a look. It is within a hundred yards of the hall door.'

We found three or four grooms and idlers standing in the drive inspecting a bicycle which had been drawn out from a clump of evergreens in which it had been concealed. It was a well-used Rudge-Whitworth, splashed as from a considerable journey. There was a saddle-bag with spanner and oil-can, but no clue as to the owner.

'It would be a grand help to the police,' said the inspector, 'if these things were numbered and registered. But we must be thankful for what we've got. If we can't find where he went to, at least we are likely to get where he came from. But what in the name of all that is wonderful made the fellow leave it behind? And how in the world has he got away without it? We don't seem to get a gleam of light in the case, Mr Holmes.'

'Don't we?' my friend answered, thoughtfully. 'I wonder!'

5 ❖ THE PEOPLE OF THE DRAMA

'Have you seen all you want of the study?' asked White Mason as we re-entered the house.

'For the time,' said the inspector; and Holmes nodded.

'Then perhaps you would now like to hear the evidence of some of the people in the house? We could use the dining-room, Ames. Please come yourself first and tell us what you know.'

The butler's account was a simple and a clear one, and he gave a convincing impression of sincerity. He had been engaged five years ago when Mr Douglas first came to Birlstone. He understood that Mr Douglas was a rich gentleman who had made his money in America. He had been a kind and considerate employer—not quite what Ames was used to, perhaps, but one can't have everything. He never saw any signs of apprehension in Mr Douglas—on the contrary, he was the most fearless man he had ever known. He ordered the drawbridge to be pulled up every night because it was the ancient custom of the old house, and he liked to keep the old ways up. Mr Douglas seldom went to London or left the village, but on the day before the crime he had been shopping at Tunbridge Wells. He, Ames, had observed some restlessness and excitement on the part of Mr Douglas upon that day, for he had seemed impatient and irritable, which was unusual with him. He had not gone to bed that night, but was in the pantry at the back of the house, putting away the silver, when he heard the bell ring violently. He heard no shot, but it was hardly possible he should, as the pantry and kitchens were at the very back of the house and there were several closed doors and a long passage between. The housekeeper had come out of her room, attracted by the violent ringing of the bell. They had gone to the front of the house together. As they reached the bottom of the stair he had seen Mrs Douglas coming down it. No, she was not hurrying—it did not seem to him that she was particularly agitated. Just as she reached the bottom of the stair Mr Barker had rushed out of the study. He had stopped Mrs Douglas and begged her to go back.

'For God's sake, go back to your room!' he cried. 'Poor Jack is dead. You can do nothing. For God's sake, go back!'

After some persuasion upon the stairs Mrs Douglas had gone back. She did not scream. She made no outcry whatever. Mrs Allen, the housekeeper, had taken her upstairs and stayed with her in the bedroom. Ames and Mr Barker had then returned to the study, where they had found everything exactly as the police had seen it. The candle was not lit at that time, but the lamp was burning. They had looked out of the window, but the night was very dark and nothing could be seen or heard. They had then rushed out into the hall, where Ames had turned the windlass which lowered the draw-bridge. Mr Barker had then hurried off to get the police.

Such, in its essentials, was the evidence of the butler.

The account of Mrs Allen, the housekeeper, was, so far as it went, a corroboration of that of her fellow-servant. The housekeeper's room was rather nearer to the front of the house than the pantry in which Ames had been working. She was preparing to go to bed when the loud ringing of the bell had attracted her attention. She was a little hard of hearing. Perhaps that was why she had not heard the sound of the shot, but in any case the study was a long way off. She remembered hearing some sound which she imagined to be the slamming of a door. That was a good deal earlier—half an hour at least before the ringing of the bell. When Mr Ames ran to the front she went with him. She saw Mr Barker, very pale and excited, come out of the study. He intercepted Mrs Douglas who was coming down the stairs. He entreated her to go back, and she answered him, but what she said could not be heard.

'Take her up. Stay with her!' he had said to Mrs Allen.

She had therefore taken her to the bedroom and endeavoured to soothe her. She was greatly excited, trembling all over, but made no other attempt to go downstairs. She just sat in her dressing-gown by her bedroom fire with her head sunk in her hands. Mrs Allen stayed with her most of the night. As to the other servants, they had all gone to bed, and the alarm did not reach them until just before the police arrived. They slept at the extreme back of the house, and could not possibly have heard anything.

So far the housekeeper—who could add nothing on cross-examination save lamentations and expressions of amazement.

Mr Cecil Barker succeeded Mrs Allen as a witness. As to the occurrences of the night before, he had very little to add to what he had already told the police. Personally, he was convinced that the murderer had escaped by the window. The blood-stain was conclusive, in his opinion, upon that point. Besides, as the bridge was up there was no other possible way of escaping. He could not explain what had become of the assassin, or why he had not taken his bicycle, if it were indeed his. He could not possibly have been drowned in the moat, which was at no place more than three feet deep.

In his own mind he had a very definite theory about the murder. Douglas was a reticent man, and there were some chapters in his life of which he never spoke. He had emigrated to America from Ireland when he was a very young man. He had prospered well, and Barker had first met him in California, where they had become partners in a successful mining claim at a place called Benito Canyon. They had done very well, but Douglas had suddenly sold out and started for England. He was a widower at that time. Barker had afterwards realized his money and come to live in London. Thus they had renewed their friendship. Douglas had given him the impression that some danger was hanging over his head, and he had always looked upon his sudden departure from California, and also his renting a house in so quiet a place in England, as being connected with this peril. He imagined that some secret society, some implacable organization, was on Douglas's track which would never rest until it killed him. Some remarks of his had given him this idea, though he had never told him what the society was, nor how he had come to offend it. He could only suppose that the legend upon the placard had some reference to this secret society.

'How long were you with Douglas in California?' asked Inspector MacDonald.

'Five years altogether.'

'He was a bachelor, you say?'

'A widower.'

'Have you ever heard where his first wife came from?'

'No; I remember his saying that she was of Swedish extraction, and I have seen her portrait. She was a very beautiful woman. She died of typhoid the year before I met him.'

'You don't associate his past with any particular part of America?'

'I have heard him talk of Chicago. He knew that city well and had worked there. I have heard him talk of the coal and iron districts. He had travelled a good deal in his time.'

'Was he a politician? Had this secret society to do with politics?'

'No; he cared nothing about politics.'

'You have no reason to think it was criminal?'

'On the contrary, I never met a straighter man in my life.'

'Was there anything curious about his life in California?'

'He liked best to stay and to work at our claim in the mountains. He would never go where other men were if he could help it. That's why I first thought that someone was after him. Then when he left so suddenly for Europe I made sure that it was so. I believe that he had a warning of some sort. Within a week of his leaving half a dozen men were inquiring for him.'

'What sort of men?'

'Well, they were a mighty hard-looking crowd. They came up to the claim and wanted to know where he was. I told them that he was gone to Europe and that I did not know where to find him. They meant him no good—it was easy to see that.'

'Were these men Americans—Californians?'

'Well, I don't know about Californians. They were Americans all right. But they were not miners. I don't know what they were, and was very glad to see their backs.'

'That was six years ago?'

41 *this business dates back not less than eleven years at the least?'* We later learn that the events at Vermissa Valley began on "the fourth of February in the year 1875." Douglas was there some three months, bringing us to May, 1875. Douglas married Ettie Shafter in Chicago and went to California after two attempts on his life. After Ettie's death, Douglas met Barker and they "were together five years in California." It is clear that the adventure of *The Valley of Fear* could not have taken place before January, 1886, and is probably some years after that.

'Nearer seven.'

'And then you were together five years in California, so that **41** this business dates back not less than eleven years at the least?'

'That is so.'

'It must be a very serious feud that would be kept up with such earnestness for as long as that. It would be no light thing that would give rise to it.'

'I think it shadowed his whole life. It was never quite out of his mind.'

'But if a man had a danger hanging over him, and knew what it was, don't you think he would turn to the police for protection?'

'Maybe it was some danger that he could not be protected against. There's one thing you should know. He always went about armed. His revolver was never out of his pocket. But, by bad luck, he was in his dressing-gown and had left it in the bedroom last night. Once the bridge was up I guess he thought he was safe.'

'I should like these dates a little clearer,' said MacDonald. 'It is quite six years since Douglas left California. You followed him next year, did you not?'

'That is so.'

'And he has been married five years. You must have returned about the time of his marriage.'

'About a month before. I was his best man.'

'Did you know Mrs Douglas before her marriage?'

'No, I did not. I had been away from England for ten years.'

'But you have seen a good deal of her since?'

Barker looked sternly at the detective.

'I have seen a good deal of *him* since,' he answered. 'If I have seen her, it is because you cannot visit a man without knowing his wife. If you imagine there is any connection——'

'I imagine nothing, Mr Barker. I am bound to make every inquiry which can bear upon the case. But I mean no offence.'

'Some inquiries are offensive,' Barker answered, angrily.

'It's only the facts that we want. It is in your interest and everyone's interests that they should be cleared up. Did Mr Douglas entirely approve your friendship with his wife?'

Barker grew paler, and his great strong hands were clasped convulsively together.

'You have no right to ask such questions!' he cried. 'What has this to do with the matter you are investigating?'

'I must repeat the question.'

'Well, I refuse to answer.'

'You can refuse to answer, but you must be aware that your refusal is in itself an answer, for you would not refuse if you had not something to conceal.'

Barker stood for a moment, with his face set grimly and his strong, black eyebrows drawn low in intense thought. Then he looked up with a smile.

'Well, I guess you gentlemen are only doing your clear duty, after all, and that I have no right to stand in the way of it. I'd only ask you not to worry Mrs Douglas over this matter, for she has enough upon her just now. I may tell you that poor Douglas had just one fault in the world, and that was his jealousy. He was fond of me—no man could be fonder of a friend. And he was devoted to his wife. He loved me to come here and was for ever sending for me. And yet if his wife and I talked together or there seemed any sympathy between us, a kind of wave of jealousy would pass over him and he would be off the handle and saying the wildest things in a moment. More than once I've sworn off coming for that reason, and then he would write me such penitent, imploring letters that I just had to. But you can take it from me, gentlemen, if it was my last word, that no man ever had a more loving, faithful wife—and I can say, also, no friend could be more loyal than I.'

It was spoken with fervour and feeling, and yet Inspector MacDonald could not dismiss the subject.

'You are aware,' said he, 'that the dead man's wedding-ring has been taken from his finger?'

'So it appears,' said Barker.

'What do you mean by "appears"? You know it as a fact.'

The man seemed confused and undecided.

'When I said "appears," I meant that it was conceivable that he had himself taken off the ring.'

'The mere fact that the ring should be absent, whoever may have removed it, would suggest to anyone's mind, would it not, that the marriage and the tragedy were connected?'

Barker shrugged his broad shoulders.

'I can't profess to say what it suggests,' he answered. 'But if you mean to hint that it could reflect in any way upon this lady's honour'—his eyes blazed for an instant, and then with an evident effort he got a grip upon his own emotions—'well, you are on the wrong track, that's all.'

'I don't know that I've anything else to ask you at present,' said MacDonald, coldly.

'There was one small point,' remarked Sherlock Holmes. 'When you entered the room there was only a candle lighted upon the table, was there not?'

'Yes, that was so.'

'By its light you saw that some terrible incident had occurred?'

'Exactly.'

'You at once rang for help?'

'Yes.'

'And it arrived very speedily?'

'Within a minute or so.'

'And yet when they arrived they found that the candle was out and that the lamp had been lighted. That seems very remarkable.'

Again Barker showed some signs of indecision.

'I don't see that it was remarkable, Mr Holmes,' he answered, after a pause. 'The candle threw a very bad light. My first thought was to get a better one. The lamp was on the table, so I lit it.'

'And blew out the candle?'

'Exactly.'

Holmes asked no further question, and Barker, with a deliberate look from one to the other of us, which had, as it seemed to me, something of defiance in it, turned and left the room.

Inspector MacDonald had sent up a note to the effect that he would wait upon Mrs Douglas in her room, but she had replied that she would meet us in the dining-room. She entered now, a tall and beautiful woman of thirty, reserved and self-possessed to a remarkable degree, very different from the tragic and distracted figure that I had pictured. It is true that her face was pale and drawn, like that of one who has endured a great shock, but her manner was composed, and the finely moulded hand which she rested upon the edge of the table was as steady as my own. Her sad, appealing eyes travelled from one to the other of us with a curiously inquisitive expression. That questioning gaze transformed itself suddenly into abrupt speech.

'Have you found out anything yet?' she asked.

Was it my imagination that there was an undertone of fear rather than of hope in the question?

'We have taken every possible step, Mrs Douglas,' said the inspector. 'You may rest assured that nothing will be neglected.'

'Spare no money,' she said, in a dead, even tone. 'It is my desire that every possible effort should be made.'

'Perhaps you can tell us something which may throw some light upon the matter.'

'I fear not, but all I know is at your service.'

'We have heard from Mr Cecil Barker that you did not actually see—that you were never in the room where the tragedy occurred?'

'No; he turned me back upon the stairs. He begged me to return to my room.'

'Quite so. You had heard the shot and you had at once come down.'

'I put on my dressing-gown and then came down.'

'How long was it after hearing the shot that you were stopped on the stair by Mr Barker?'

'It may have been a couple of minutes. It is so hard to reckon time at such a moment. He implored me not to go on. He assured me that I could do nothing. Then Mrs Allen, the housekeeper, led me upstairs again. It was all like some dreadful dream.'

'Can you give us any idea how long your husband had been downstairs before you heard the shot?'

'No, I cannot say. He went from his dressing-room and I did not hear him go. He did the round of the house every night, for he was nervous of fire. It is the only thing that I have ever known him nervous of.'

'That is just the point which I want to come to, Mrs Douglas. You have only known your husband in England, have you not?'

'Yes. We have been married five years.'

'Have you heard him speak of anything which occurred in America and which might bring some danger upon him?'

Mrs Douglas thought earnestly before she answered.

'Yes,' she said at last. 'I have always felt that there was a danger hanging over him. He refused to discuss it with me. It was not from want of confidence in me—there was the most complete love and confidence between us—but it was out of his desire to keep all alarm away from me. He thought I should brood over it if I knew all, and so he was silent.'

'How did you know it, then?'

Mrs Douglas's face lit with a quick smile.

'Can a husband ever carry about a secret all his life and a woman who loves him have no suspicion of it? I knew it in many ways. I knew it by his refusal to talk about some episodes in his American life. I knew it by certain precautions he took. I knew it by certain words he let fall. I knew it by the way he looked at unexpected strangers. I was perfectly certain that he had some powerful enemies, that he believed they were on his track and that he was always on his guard against them. I was so sure of it that for years I have been terrified if ever he came home later than was expected.'

'Might I ask,' said Holmes, 'what the words were which attracted your attention?'

' "The Valley of Fear," ' the lady answered. 'That was an expression he has used when I questioned him. "I have been in the Valley of Fear. I am not out of it yet." "Are we never to get out of the Valley of Fear?" I have asked him, when I have seen him more serious than usual. "Sometimes I think that we never shall," he has answered.'

'Surely you asked him what he meant by the Valley of Fear?'

'I did; but his face would become very grave and he would shake his head. "It is bad enough that one of us should have been in its shadow," he said. "Please God it shall never fall upon you." It was some real valley in which he had lived and in which something terrible had occurred to him—of that I am certain—but I can tell you no more.'

'And he never mentioned any names?'

'Yes; he was delirious with fever once when he had his hunting accident three years ago. Then I remember that there was a name that came continually to his lips. He spoke it with anger and a sort of horror. McGinty was the name—Bodymaster McGinty. I asked him, when he recovered, who Bodymaster McGinty was, and whose body he was master of. "Never of mine, thank God!" he answered, with a laugh and that was all I could get from him. But there is a connection between Bodymaster McGinty and the Valley of Fear.'

'There is one other point,' said Inspector MacDonald. 'You met Mr Douglas in a boarding-house in London, did you not, and became engaged to him there? Was there any romance, anything secret or mysterious, about the wedding?'

'There was romance. There is always romance. There was nothing mysterious.'

'He had no rival?'

'No; I was quite free.'

'You have heard, no doubt, that his wedding-ring has been taken. Does that suggest anything to you? Suppose that some enemy of his old life had tracked him down and committed this crime, what possible reason could he have for taking his wedding-ring?'

For an instant I could have sworn that the faintest shadow of a smile flickered over the woman's lips.

'I really cannot tell,' she answered. 'It is certainly a most extraordinary thing.'

'Well, we will not detain you any longer, and we are sorry to have put you to this trouble at such a time,' said the inspector. 'There are some other points, no doubt, but we can refer to you as they arise.'

She rose, and I was again conscious of that quick, questioning glance with which she had just surveyed us: 'What impression has my evidence made upon you?' The question might as well have been spoken. Then, with a bow, she swept from the room.

'She's a beautiful woman—a very beautiful woman,' said MacDonald, thoughtfully, after the door had closed behind her. 'This man Barker has certainly been down here a good deal. He is a man who might be attractive to a woman. He admits that the dead man was jealous, and maybe he knew best himself what cause he had for jealousy. Then there's that wedding-ring. You can't get past that. The man who tears a wedding-ring off a dead man's—— What do you say to it, Mr Holmes?'

My friend had sat with his head upon his hands, sunk in the deepest thought. Now he rose and rang the bell.

'Ames,' he said, when the butler entered, 'where is Mr Cecil Barker now?'

'I'll see, sir.'

He came back in a moment to say that Mr Barker was in the garden.

'Can you remember, Ames, what Mr Barker had upon his feet last night when you joined him in the study?'

'Yes, Mr Holmes. He had a pair of bedroom slippers. I brought him his boots when he went for the police.'

'Where are the slippers now?'

'They are still under the chair in the hall.'

'Very good, Ames. It is, of course, important for us to know which tracks may be Mr Barker's and which from outside.'

'Yes, sir. I may say that I noticed that the slippers were stained with blood, so, indeed, were my own.'

'That is natural enough, considering the condition of the room. Very good, Ames. We will ring if we want you.'

A few minutes later we were in the study. Holmes had brought with him the carpet slippers from the hall. As Ames had observed, the soles of both were dark with blood.

'Strange!' murmured Holmes, as he stood in the light of the window and examined them minutely. 'Very strange indeed!'

Stooping with one of his quick, feline pounces he placed the slipper upon the blood-mark on the sill. It exactly corresponded. He smiled in silence at his colleagues.

The inspector was transfigured with excitement. His native accent rattled like a stick upon railings.

'Man!' he cried, 'there's not a doubt of it! Barker has just marked the window himself. It's a good deal broader than any boot-mark. I mind that you said it was a splay foot, and here's the explanation. But what's the game, Mr Holmes—what's the game?'

'Aye, what's the game?' my friend repeated, thoughtfully.

White Mason chuckled and rubbed his fat hands together in his professional satisfaction.

'I said it was a snorter!' he cried. 'And a real snorter it is!'

... HE PLACED THE SLIPPER UPON THE BLOOD-MARK ON THE SILL.

Illustration by Frank Wiles for the *Strand Magazine*, November, 1914.

6 ❖ A DAWNING LIGHT

The three detectives had many matters of detail into which to inquire, so I returned alone to our modest quarters at the village inn; but before doing so I took a stroll in the curious, old-world garden which flanked the house. Rows of very ancient yew trees, cut into strange designs, girded it round. Inside was a beautiful stretch of lawn with an old sundial in the middle, the whole effect so soothing and restful that it was welcome to my somewhat jangled nerves. In that deeply peaceful atmosphere one could forget or remember only as some fantastic nightmare that darkened study with the sprawling, blood-stained figure upon the floor. And yet as I strolled round it and tried to steep my soul in its gentle balm, a strange incident occurred which brought me back to the tragedy and left a sinister impression in my mind.

I have said that a decoration of yew trees circled the garden. At the end which was farthest from the house they thickened into a continuous hedge. On the other side of this hedge, concealed from the eyes of anyone approaching from the direction of the house, there was a stone seat. As I approached the spot I was aware of voices, some remark in the deep tones of a man, answered by a little ripple of feminine laughter. An instant later I had come round the end of the hedge, and my eyes lit upon Mrs Douglas and the man Barker before they were aware of my presence. Her appearance gave me a shock. In the dining-room she had been demure and discreet. Now all pretence of grief had passed away from her. Her eyes shone with the joy of living, and her face still quivered with amusement at some remark of her companion. He sat forward, his hands clasped and his forearms on his knees, with an answering smile upon his bold, handsome face. In an instant—but it was just one instant too late—they resumed their solemn masks as my figure came into view. A hurried word or two passed between them, and then Barker rose and came towards me.

'Excuse me, sir,' said he, 'but am I addressing Dr Watson?'

I bowed with a coldness which showed, I dare say, very plainly the impression which had been produced upon my mind.

'We thought that it was probably you, as your friendship with Mr Sherlock Holmes is so well known. Would you mind coming over and speaking to Mrs Douglas for one instant?'

I followed him with a dour face. Very clearly I could see in my mind's eye that shattered figure upon the floor. Here within a few hours of the tragedy were his wife and his nearest friend laughing together behind a bush in the garden which had been his. I greeted the lady with reserve. I had grieved with her grief in the dining-room. Now I met her appealing gaze with an unresponsive eye.

'I fear that you think me callous and hard-hearted?' said she.

I shrugged my shoulders.

'It is no business of mine,' said I.

'Perhaps some day you will do me justice. If you only realized——'

'There is no need why Dr Watson should realize,' said Barker, quickly. 'As he has himself said, it is no possible business of his.'

'Exactly,' said I, 'and so I will beg leave to resume my walk.'

'One moment, Dr Watson,' cried the woman, in a pleading voice. 'There is one question which you can answer with more authority than anyone else in the world, and it may make a very great difference to me. You know Mr Holmes and his relations with the police better than anyone else can do. Supposing that a matter were brought confidentially to his knowledge, is it absolutely necessary that he should pass it on to the detectives?'

'Yes, that's it,' said Barker, eagerly. 'Is he on his own or is he entirely in with them?'

42 débonnaire. French: having affable or courteous bearing or manner; affable; complaisant; winsome; cheery.

43 *Shocking, Watson, shocking!'* Holmes, in a *débonnaire* frame of mind, "does not tell the whole story. The single dumb-bell which worried him could have been used alternately by the right and left arm and thus unilateral development prevented. Watson knew this, but like a good soldier he let Holmes have his fun and made no reply."—Dr. Edward J. Van Liere, "Sherlock Holmes and Doctor Watson, Perennial Athletes."

'I really don't know that I should be justified in discussing such a point.'

'I beg—I implore that you will, Dr Watson, I assure you that you will be helping us—helping me greatly if you will guide us on that point.'

There was such a ring of sincerity in the woman's voice that for the instant I forgot all about her levity and was moved only to do her will.

'Mr Holmes is an independent investigator,' I said. 'He is his own master, and would act as his own judgment directed. At the same time he would naturally feel loyalty towards the officials who were working on the same case, and he would not conceal from them anything which would help them in bringing a criminal to justice. Beyond this I can say nothing, and I would refer you to Mr Holmes himself if you want fuller information.'

So saying I raised my hat and went upon my way, leaving them still seated behind that concealing hedge. I looked back as I rounded the far end of it, and saw that they were still talking very earnestly together, and, as they were gazing after me, it was clear that it was our interview that was the subject of their debate.

'I wish none of their confidences,' said Holmes, when I reported to him what had occurred. He had spent the whole afternoon at the Manor House in consultation with his two colleagues, and returned about five with a ravenous appetite for a high tea which I had ordered for him. 'No confidences, Watson, for they are mighty awkward if it comes to an arrest for conspiracy and murder.'

'You think it will come to that?'

42 He was in his most cheerful and *débonnaire* humour.

'My dear Watson, when I have exterminated that fourth egg I will be ready to put you in touch with the whole situation. I don't say that we have fathomed it—far from it—but when we have traced the missing dumb-bell——'

'The dumb-bell!'

'Dear me, Watson, is it possible that you have not penetrated the fact that the case hangs upon the missing dumb-bell? Well, well, you need not be downcast, for, between ourselves, I don't think that either Inspector Mac or the excellent local practitioner has grasped the overwhelming importance of this incident. One dumb-bell, Watson! Consider an athlete with one dumb-bell. Picture to yourself the unilateral development—the imminent danger of a spinal **43** curvature. Shocking, Watson; shocking!'

He sat with his mouth full of toast and his eyes sparkling with mischief, watching my intellectual entanglement. The mere sight of his excellent appetite was an assurance of success, for I had very clear recollections of days and nights without a thought of food, when his baffled mind had chafed before some problem whilst his thin, eager features became more attenuated with the asceticism of complete mental concentration. Finally he lit his pipe, and, sitting in the inglenook of the old village inn, he talked slowly and at random about his case, rather as one who thinks aloud than as one who makes a considered statement.

'A lie, Watson—a great big, thumping, obtrusive, uncompromising lie—that's what meets us on the threshold. There is our starting-point. The whole story told by Barker is a lie.

But Barker's story is corroborated by Mrs Douglas. Therefore she is lying also. They are both lying and in a conspiracy. So now we have the clear problem—why are they lying, and what is the truth which they are trying so hard to conceal? Let us try, Watson, you and I, if we can get behind the lie and reconstruct the truth.

'How do I know that they are lying? Because it is a clumsy fabrication which simply *could* not be true. Consider! According to the story given to us the assassin had less than a minute after the murder had been committed to take that ring, which was under another ring, from the dead man's finger, to replace the other ring—a thing which he would surely never have done—and to put that singular card beside his victim. I say that this was obviously impossible. You may argue—but I have too much respect for your judgment, Watson, to think that you will do so—that the ring may have been taken before the man was killed. The fact that the candle had only been lit a short time shows that there had been no lengthy interview. Was Douglas, from what we hear of his fearless character, a man who would be likely to give up his wedding-ring at such short notice, or could we conceive of his giving it up at all? No, no, Watson, the assassin was alone with the dead man for some time with the lamp lit. Of that I have no doubt at all. But the gunshot was apparently the cause of death. Therefore the gunshot must have been fired some time earlier than we are told. But there could be no mistake about such a matter as that. We are in the presence, therefore, of a deliberate conspiracy upon the part of the two people who heard the gunshot—of the man Barker and of the woman Douglas. When on the top of this I am able to show that the blood-mark upon the window-sill was deliberately placed there by Barker in order to give a false clue to the police, you will admit that the case grows dark against him.

'Now we have to ask ourselves at what hour the murder actually did occur. Up to half-past ten the servants were moving about the house, so it was certainly not before that time. At a quarter to eleven they had all gone to their rooms with the exception of Ames, who was in the pantry. I have been trying some experiments after you left us this afternoon, and I find that no noise which MacDonald can make in the study can penetrate to me in the pantry when the doors are all shut. It is otherwise, however, from the housekeeper's room. It is not so far down the corridor, and from it I could vaguely hear a voice when it was very loudly raised. The sound from a shot-gun is to some extent muffled when the discharge is at very close range, as it undoubtedly was in this instance. It would not be very loud, and yet in the silence of the night it should have easily penetrated to Mrs Allen's room. She is, as she has told us, somewhat deaf, but none the less she mentioned in her evidence that she did hear something like a door slamming half an hour before the alarm was given. Half an hour before the alarm was given would be a quarter to eleven. I have no doubt that what she heard was the report of the gun, and that was the real instant of the murder. If this is so, we have now to determine what Mr Barker and Mrs Douglas, presuming that they are not the actual murderers, could have been doing from a quarter to eleven when the sound of the gun-shot brought them down, until a quarter-past eleven, when they rang the bell and summoned the servants. What were they doing, and why did they not instantly give the alarm? That is the question which faces us, and when it has been answered we will surely have gone some way to solve our problem.'

'I am convinced myself,' said I, 'that there is an understanding between those two people. She must be a heartless creature to sit laughing at some jest within a few hours of her husband's murder.'

'Exactly. She does not shine as a wife even in her own account of what occurred. I am not a whole-souled admirer of womankind, as you are aware, Watson, but my experience of life has taught me that there are few wives having any regard for their husbands who would let any man's spoken word stand between them and that husband's dead body. Should I ever marry, Watson, I should hope to inspire my wife with some feeling which would prevent her from being walked off by a housekeeper when my corpse was lying within a few yards of her. It was badly stage-managed, for even the rawest of investigators must be struck by the absence of the usual feminine ululation. If there had been nothing else, this incident alone would have suggested a pre-arranged conspiracy to my mind.'

'You think, then, definitely, that Barker and Mrs Douglas are guilty of the murder?'

'There is an appalling directness about your questions, Watson,' said Holmes, shaking his pipe at me. 'They come at me like bullets. If you put it that Mrs Douglas and Barker know the truth about the murder and are conspiring to conceal it, then I can give you a whole-souled answer. I am sure they do. But your more deadly proposition is not so clear. Let us for a moment consider the difficulties which stand in the way.

'We will suppose that this couple are united by the bonds of a guilty love and that they have determined to get rid of the man who stands between them. It is a large supposition, for discreet inquiry among servants and others has failed to corroborate it in any way. On the contrary, there is a good deal of evidence that the Douglases were very attached to each other.'

'That I am sure cannot be true,' said I, thinking of the beautiful, smiling face in the garden.

'Well, at least they gave that impression. However, we will suppose that they are an extraordinarily astute couple, who deceive everyone upon this point and who conspire to murder the husband. He happens to be a man over whose head some danger hangs——'

'We have only their word for that.'

Holmes looked thoughtful.

'I see, Watson. You are sketching out a theory by which everything they say from the beginning is false. According to your idea, there was never any hidden menace or secret society or Valley of Fear or Boss McSomebody or anything else. Well, that is a good, sweeping generalization. Let us see what that brings us to. They invent this theory to account for the crime. They then play up to the idea by leaving this bicycle in the park as a proof of the existence of some outsider. The stain on the window-sill conveys the same idea. So does the card upon the body, which might have been prepared in the house. That all fits into your hypothesis, Watson. But now we come on the nasty angular, uncompromising bits which won't slip into their places. Why a cut-off shot-gun of all weapons—and an American one at that? How could they be so sure that the sound of it would not bring someone on to them? It's a mere chance, as it is, that Mrs Allen did not start out to inquire for the slamming door. Why did your guilty couple do all this, Watson?'

'I confess that I can't explain it.'

'Then, again, if a woman and her lover conspire to murder a husband, are they going to advertise their guilt by ostentatiously removing his wedding-ring after his death? Does that strike you as very probable, Watson?'

'No, it does not.'

'And once again, if the thought of leaving a bicycle concealed had occurred to you, would it really have seemed worth doing when the dullest detective would naturally say this is an obvious blind, as the bicycle is the first thing which the fugitive needed in order to make his escape?'

'I can conceive of no explanation.'

'And yet there should be no combination of events for which the wit of man cannot conceive an explanation. Simply as a mental exercise, without any assertion that it is true, let me indicate a possible line of thought. It is, I admit, mere imagination, but how often is imagination the mother of truth? **44**

'We will suppose that there *was* a guilty secret, a really shameful secret, in the life of this man Douglas. This leads to his murder by someone who is, we will suppose, an avenger —someone from outside. This avenger, for some reason which I confess I am still at a loss to explain, took the dead man's wedding-ring. The vendetta might conceivably date back to the man's first marriage and the ring be taken for some such reason. Before this avenger got away Barker and the wife had reached the room. The assassin convinced them that any attempt to arrest him would lead to the publication of some hideous scandal. They were converted to this idea and preferred to let him go. For this purpose they probably lowered the bridge, which can be done quite noiselessly, and then raised it again. He made his escape, and for some reason thought that he could do so more safely on foot than on the bicycle. He therefore left his machine where it would not be discovered until he had got safely away. So far we are within the bounds of possibility, are we not?'

'Well, it is possible, no doubt,' said I, with some reserve.

'We have to remember, Watson, that whatever occurred is certainly something very extraordinary. Well now, to continue our supposititious case, the couple—not necessarily a guilty couple—realize after the murderer is gone that they have placed themselves in a position in which it may be difficult for them to prove that they did not themselves either do the deed or connive at it. They rapidly and rather clumsily met the situation. The mark was put by Barker's blood-stained slipper upon the window-sill to suggest how the fugitive got away. They obviously were the two who must have heard the sound of the gun, so they gave the alarm exactly as they would have done, but a good half-hour after the event.'

'And how do you propose to prove all this?'

'Well, if there were an outsider he may be traced and taken. That would be the most effective of all proofs. But if not— well, the resources of science are far from being exhausted.

44 *how often is imagination the mother of truth?* Joseph Conrad, 1857–1924, in *A Personal Record* (1912) called imagination "the supreme master of art as of life."

45 *the* genius loci. A beneficient spirit or demon thought by the ancient Romans to haunt a particular place.

I think that an evening alone in that study would help me much.'

'An evening alone!'

'I propose to go up there presently. I have arranged it with the estimable Ames, who is by no means whole-hearted about Barker. I shall sit in that room and see if its atmosphere brings **45** me inspiration. I'm a believer in the *genius loci*. You smile, friend Watson. Well, we shall see. By the way, you have that big umbrella of yours, have you not?'

'It is here.'

'Well, I'll borrow that, if I may.'

'Certainly—but what a wretched weapon! If there is danger——'

'Nothing serious, my dear Watson, or I should certainly ask for your assistance. But I'll take the umbrella. At present I am only awaiting the return of our colleagues from Tunbridge Wells, where they are at present engaged in trying for a likely owner to the bicycle.'

It was nightfall before Inspector MacDonald and White Mason came back from their expedition, and they arrived exultant, reporting a great advance in our investigation.

'Man, I'll admeet that I had my doubts if there was ever an outsider,' said MacDonald, 'but that's all past now. We've had the bicycle identified, and we have a description of our man, so that's a long step on our journey.'

'It sounds to me like the beginning of the end,' said Holmes; 'I'm sure I congratulate you both with all my heart.'

'Well, I started from the fact that Mr Douglas had seemed disturbed since the day before, when he had been at Tunbridge Wells. It was at Tunbridge Wells, then, that he had become conscious of some danger. It was clear, therefore, that if a man had come over with a bicycle it was from Tunbridge Wells that he might be expected to have come. We took the bicycle over with us and showed it at the hotels. It was identified at once by the manager of the Eagle Commercial as belonging to a man named Hargrave who had taken a room there two days before. This bicycle and a small valise were his whole belongings. He had registered his name as coming from London, but had given no address. The valise was London-made and the contents were British, but the man himself was undoubtedly an American.'

'Well, well,' said Holmes, gleefully, 'you have indeed done some solid work whilst I have been sitting spinning theories with my friend. It's a lesson in being practical, Mr Mac.'

'Aye, it's just that, Mr Holmes,' said the inspector with satisfaction.

'But this may all fit in with your theories,' I remarked.

'That may or may not be. But let us hear the end, Mr Mac. Was there nothing to identify this man?'

'So little that it was evident he had carefully guarded himself against identification. There were no papers or letters and no marking upon the clothes. A cycle-map of the county lay upon his bedroom table. He had left the hotel after breakfast yesterday morning upon his bicycle, and no more was heard of him until our inquiries.'

'That's what puzzles me, Mr Holmes,' said White Mason. 'If the fellow did not want the hue and cry raised over him, one would imagine that he would have returned and remained at the hotel as an inoffensive tourist. As it is, he must know that he will be reported to the police by the hotel manager, and that his disappearance will be connected with the murder.'

'So one would imagine. Still he has been justified of his wisdom up to date at any rate, since he has not been taken. But his description—what of that?'

MacDonald referred to his note-book.

'Here we have it so far as they could give it. They don't seem to have taken any very particular stock of him, but still the porter, the clerk, and the chambermaid are all agreed that this about covers the points. He was a man about five foot nine in height, fifty or so years of age, his hair slightly grizzled, a greyish moustache, a curved nose, and a face which all of them described as fierce and forbidding.'

'Well, bar the expression, that might almost be a description of Douglas himself,' said Holmes. 'He is just over fifty, with grizzled hair and moustache and about the same height. Did you get anything else?'

'He was dressed in a heavy grey suit with a reefer jacket, and he wore a short, yellow overcoat and a soft cap.'

'What about the shot-gun?'

'It is less than two feet long. It could very well have fitted into his valise. He could have carried it inside his overcoat without difficulty.'

'And how do you consider that all this bears upon the general case?'

'Well, Mr Holmes,' said MacDonald, 'when we have got our man—and you may be sure that I had his description on the wires within five minutes of hearing it—we shall be better able to judge. But even as it stands, we have surely gone a long way. We know that an American calling himself Hargrave came to Tunbridge Wells two days ago with bicycle and valise. In the latter was a sawn-off shot-gun, so he came with the deliberate purpose of crime. Yesterday morning he set off for this place upon his bicycle with his gun concealed in his overcoat. No one saw him arrive, so far as we can learn, but he need not pass through the village to reach the park gates, and there are many cyclists upon the road. Presumably he at once concealed his cycle among the laurels, where it was found, and possibly lurked there himself, with his eye on the house waiting for Mr Douglas to come out. The shot-gun is a strange weapon to use inside a house, but he had intended to use it outside, and then it has very obvious advantages, as it would be impossible to miss with it, and the sound of shots is so common in an English sporting neighbourhood that no particular notice would be taken.'

'That is all very clear!' said Holmes.

'Well, Mr Douglas did not appear. What was he to do next? He left his bicycle and approached the house in the twilight. He found the bridge down and no one about. He took his chance, intending, no doubt, to make some excuse if he met anyone. He met no one. He slipped into the first room that he saw and concealed himself behind the curtain. From thence he could see the drawbridge go up and he knew that his only escape was through the moat. He waited until a quarter-past eleven, when Mr Douglas, upon his usual nightly round, came into the room. He shot him and escaped, as arranged. He was aware that the bicycle would be described by the hotel people and be a clue against him, so he left it there and made

"I SAY, WATSON," HE WHISPERED, "WOULD YOU BE
AFRAID TO SLEEP IN THE SAME ROOM AS A
LUNATIC . . . ?"

Illustration by Arthur I. Keller for Associated
Sunday Magazines, 1914. Frank Wiles illustrated
the same scene (*Below*) for the *Strand Magazine*,
December, 1914.

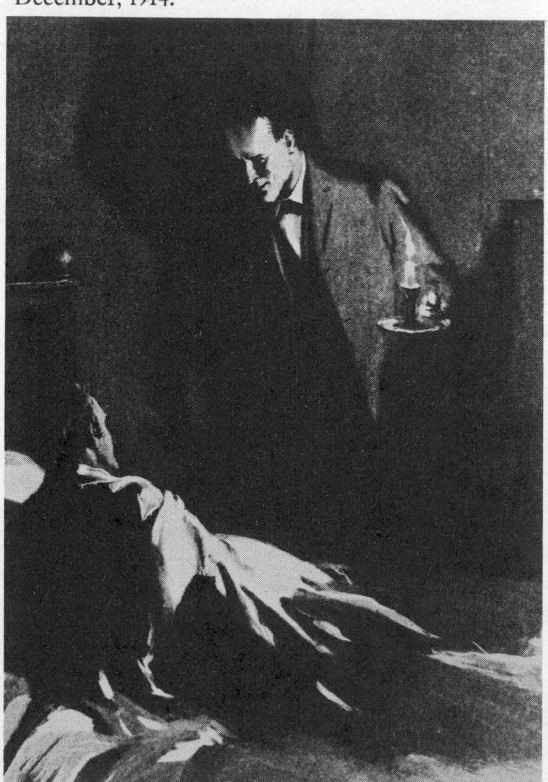

his way by some other means to London or to some safe
hiding-place which he had already arranged. How is that, Mr
Holmes?'

'Well, Mr Mac, it is very good and very clear so far as it
goes. That is your end of the story. My end is that the crime
was committed half an hour earlier than reported; that Mrs
Douglas and Mr Barker are both in a conspiracy to conceal
something; that they aided the murderer's escape—or at least,
that they reached the room before he escaped—and that
they fabricated evidence of his escape through the window,
whereas in all probability they had themselves let him
go by lowering the bridge. That's *my* reading of the first
half.'

The two detectives shook their heads.

'Well, Mr Holmes, if this is true we only tumble out of one
mystery into another,' said the London inspector.

'And in some ways a worse one,' added White Mason. 'The
lady has never been in America in her life. What possible
connection could she have with an American assassin which
would cause her to shelter him?'

'I freely admit the difficulties,' said Holmes. 'I propose to
make a little investigation of my own tonight, and it is just
possible that it may contribute something to the common
cause.'

'Can we help you, Mr Holmes?'

'No, no! Darkness and Dr Watson's umbrella. My wants are
simple. And Ames—the faithful Ames—no doubt he will
stretch a point for me. All my lines of thought lead me back
invariably to the one basic question—why should an athletic
man develop his frame upon so unnatural an instrument as
a single dumb-bell?'

It was late that night when Holmes returned from his
solitary excursion. We slept in a double-bedded room, which
was the best that the little country inn could do for us. I was
already asleep when I was partly awakened by his entrance.

'Well, Holmes,' I murmured, 'have you found out anything?'

He stood beside me in silence, his candle in his hand. Then
the tall, lean figure inclined towards me.

'I say, Watson,' he whispered, 'would you be afraid to sleep
in the same room as a lunatic, a man with softening of the
brain, an idiot whose mind has lost its grip?'

'Not in the least,' I answered in astonishment.

'Ah, that's lucky,' he said, and not another word would he
utter that night.

7 ❖ THE SOLUTION

Next morning, after breakfast, we found Inspector Mac-
Donald and Mr White Mason seated in close consultation in
the small parlour of the local police-sergeant. Upon the table

in front of them were piled a number of letters and telegrams, which they were carefully sorting and docketing. Three had been placed upon one side.

'Still on the track of the elusive bicyclist?' Holmes asked, cheerfully. 'What is the latest news of the ruffian?'

MacDonald pointed ruefully to his heap of correspondence.

'He is at present reported from Leicester, Nottingham, Southampton, Derby, East Ham, Richmond, and fourteen other places. In three of them—East Ham, Leicester, and Liverpool—there is a clear case against him and he has actually been arrested. The country seems to be full of fugitives with yellow coats.'

'Dear me!' said Holmes, sympathetically. 'Now, Mr Mac, and you, Mr White Mason, I wish to give you a very earnest piece of advice. When I went into this case with you I bargained, as you will no doubt remember, that I should not present you with half-proved theories, but that I should retain and work out my own ideas until I had satisfied myself that they were correct. For this reason I am not at the present moment telling you all that is in my mind. On the other hand, I said that I would play the game fairly by you, and I do not think it is a fair game to allow you for one unnecessary moment to waste your energies upon a profitless task. Therefore I am here to advise you this morning, and my advice to you is summed up in three words: Abandon the case.'

MacDonald and White Mason stared in amazement at their celebrated colleague.

'You consider it hopeless?' cried the inspector.

'I consider *your* case to be hopeless. I do not consider that it is hopeless to arrive at the truth.'

'But this cyclist. He is not an invention. We have his description, his valise, his bicycle. The fellow must be somewhere. Why should we not get him?'

'Yes, yes; no doubt he is somewhere, and no doubt we shall get him, but I would not have you waste your energies in East Ham or Liverpool. I am sure that we can find some shorter cut to a result.'

'You are holding something back. It's hardly fair of you, Mr Holmes.' The inspector was annoyed.

'You know my methods of work, Mr Mac. But I will hold it back for the shortest time possible. I only wish to verify my details in one way, which can very readily be done, and then I make my bow and return to London, leaving my results entirely at your service. I owe you too much to act otherwise, for in all my experience I cannot recall any more singular and interesting study.'

'This is clean beyond me, Mr Holmes. We saw you when we returned from Tunbridge Wells last night, and you were in general agreement with our results. What has happened since then to give you a completely new idea of the case?'

'Well, since you ask me, I spent, as I told you that I would, some hours last night at the Manor House.'

'Well, what happened?'

'Ah! I can only give you a very general answer to that for the moment. By the way, I have been reading a short, but clear and interesting, account of the old building, purchasable at the modest sum of one penny from the local tobacconist.' **46** Here Holmes drew a small tract, embellished with a rude engraving of the ancient Manor House, from his waistcoat

46 *a small tract*. Identified, as we have seen, by the late James Montgomery, as the account written by B. W. Shepherd-Walwyn.

47 *the second George*. George II, George Augustus, 1683–1760, was king 1726–1760. He was the last British king to lead troops in person, in the War of the Austrian Succession.

48 *often of extraordinary interest*. "We see in 'The Adventure of the Lion's Mane' an example of how Holmes could bring his out-of-the-way knowledge to bear on a problem, and he has a number of interesting remarks on this point in 'The Five Orange Pips,' " Mr. T. S. Blakeney wrote in *Sherlock Holmes: Fact or Fiction?*

pocket. 'It immensely adds to the zest of an investigation, my dear Mr Mac, when one is in conscious sympathy with the historical atmosphere of one's surroundings. Don't look so impatient, for I assure you that even so bald an account as this raises some sort of picture of the past in one's mind. Permit me to give you a sample. "Erected in the fifth year of the reign of James I., and standing upon the site of a much older building, the Manor House of Birlstone presents one of the finest surviving examples of the moated Jacobean residence——" '

'You are making fools of us, Mr Holmes.'

'Tut, tut, Mr Mac!—the first sign of temper I have detected in you. Well, I won't read it verbatim, since you feel so strongly upon the subject. But when I tell you that there is some account of the taking of the place by a Parliamentary colonel in 1644, of the concealment of Charles for several days in the course of the Civil War, and finally of a visit there **47** by the second George, you will admit that there are various associations of interest connected with this ancient house.'

'I don't doubt it, Mr Holmes, but that is no business of ours.'

'Is it not? Is it not? Breadth of view, my dear Mr Mac, is one of the essentials of our profession. The interplay of ideas and the oblique uses of knowledge are often of extraordinary **48** interest. You will excuse these remarks from one who, though a mere connoisseur of crime, is still rather older and perhaps more experienced than yourself.'

'I'm the first to admit that,' said the detective, heartily. 'You get to your point, I admit, but you have such a deuced round-the-corner way of doing it.'

'Well, well, I'll drop past history and get down to present-day facts. I called last night, as I have already said, at the Manor House. I did not see either Mr Barker or Mrs Douglas. I saw no necessity to disturb them, but I was pleased to hear that the lady was not visibly pining and that she had partaken of an excellent dinner. My visit was specially made to the good Mr Ames, with whom I exchanged some amiabilities which culminated in his allowing me, without reference to anyone else, to sit alone for a time in the study.'

'What! With that!' I ejaculated.

'No, no; everything is now in order. You gave permission for that, Mr Mac, as I am informed. The room was in its normal state, and in it I passed an instructive quarter of an hour.'

'What were you doing?'

'Well, not to make a mystery of so simple a matter, I was looking for the missing dumb-bell. It has always bulked rather large in my estimate of the case. I ended by finding it.'

'Where?'

'Ah! There we come to the edge of the unexplored. Let me go a little farther, a very little farther, and I will promise that you shall share everything that I know.'

'Well, we're bound to take you on your own terms,' said the inspector; 'but when it comes to telling us to abandon the case—— Why, in the name of goodness, should we abandon the case?'

'For the simple reason, my dear Mr Mac, that you have not got the first idea what it is that you are investigating.'

'We are investigating the murder of Mr John Douglas, of Birlstone Manor.'

'Yes, yes; so you are. But don't trouble to trace the mysterious gentleman upon the bicycle. I assure you that it won't help you.'

'Then what do you suggest that we do?'

'I will tell you exactly what to do, if you will do it.'

'Well, I'm bound to say I've always found you had reason behind all your queer ways. I'll do what you advise.'

'And you, Mr White Mason?'

The country detective looked helplessly from one to the other. Mr Holmes and his methods were new to him.

'Well, if it is good enough for the inspector it is good enough for me!' he said, at last.

'Capital' said Holmes. 'Well, then I should recommend a nice, cheery, country walk for both of you. They tell me that the views from Birlstone Ridge over the Weald are very remarkable. No doubt lunch could be got at some suitable hostelry, though my ignorance of the country prevents me from recommending one. In the evening, tired but happy——'

'Man, this is getting past a joke!' cried MacDonald, rising angrily from his chair.

'Well, well, spend the day as you like,' said Holmes, patting him cheerfully upon the shoulder. 'Do what you like and go where you will, but meet me here before dusk without fail—without fail, Mr Mac.'

'That sounds more like sanity.'

'All of it was excellent advice, but I don't insist, so long as you are here when I need you. But now, before we part, I want you to write a note to Mr Barker.'

'Well?'

'I'll dictate it, if you like. Ready?

'DEAR SIR,—It has struck me that it is our duty to drain the moat, in the hope that we may find some——'

'It's impossible,' said the inspector; 'I've made inquiry.'

'Tut, tut, my dear sir! Do, please, do what I ask you.'

'Well, go on.'

'——in the hope that we may find something which may bear upon our investigation. I have made arrangements, and the workmen will be at work early tomorrow morning diverting the **49** stream——'

'Impossible!'

'——diverting the stream, so I thought it best to explain matters beforehand.

Now sign that, and send it by hand about four o'clock. At that hour we shall meet again in this room. Until then we can each do what we like, for I can assure you that this inquiry has come to a definite pause.'

Evening was drawing in when we reassembled. Holmes was very serious in his manner, myself curious, and the detectives obviously critical and annoyed.

'Well, gentlemen,' said my friend, gravely, 'I am asking you now to put everything to the test with me, and you will judge for yourselves whether the observations which I have made justify the conclusions to which I have come. It is a chill evening, and I do not know how long our expedition may last, so I beg that you will wear your warmest coats. It is of the first importance that we should be in our places before it grows dark, so, with your permission, we will get started at once.'

49 *early tomorrow morning.* The third day of adventure (in fact, it ended on the second day) could not therefore have been a Sunday, and the first day, then, was not a Friday.

50 *'Possess our souls in patience.* "In your patience possess ye your souls."—Luke, 21:19. We shall see that this was a favorite expression of Holmes': "We can only possess our souls in patience," he says in "The Adventure of Wisteria Lodge," and "We can but possess our souls in patience" he says again in "The Adventure of the Three Garridebs."

51 *the pride and the justification of our life's work?* "This art was one of Holmes' strongest assets as a detective—he called it the scientific use of the imagination, 'the region where we balance probabilities and choose the most likely' (*The Hound of the Baskervilles*)," Mr. T. S. Blakeney wrote in *Sherlock Holmes: Fact or Fiction?*

We passed along the outer bounds of the Manor House park until we came to a place where there was a gap in the rails which fenced it. Through this we slipped, and then, in the gathering gloom, we followed Holmes until we had reached a shrubbery which lies nearly opposite to the main door and the drawbridge. The latter had not been raised. Holmes crouched down behind the screen of laurels, and we all three followed his example.

'Well, what are we to do now?' asked MacDonald, with some gruffness.

50 'Possess our souls in patience and make as little noise as possible,' Holmes answered.

'What are we here for at all? I really think that you might treat us with more frankness.'

Holmes laughed.

'Watson insists that I am the dramatist in real life,' said he. 'Some touch of the artist wells up within me and calls insistently for a well-staged performance. Surely our profession, Mr Mac, would be a drab and sordid one if we did not sometimes set the scene so as to glorify our results. The blunt accusation, the brutal tap upon the shoulder—what can one make of such a *dénouement*? But the quick inference, the subtle trap, the clever forecast of coming events, the triumphant vindication of bold theories—are these not the pride **51** and the justification of our life's work? At the present moment you thrill with the glamour of the situation and the anticipation of the hunter. Where would be that thrill if I had been as definite as a time-table? I only ask a little patience, Mr Mac, and all will be clear to you.'

'Well, I hope the pride and justification and the rest of it will come before we all get our death of cold,' said the London detective, with comic resignation.

We all had good reason to join in the aspiration, for our vigil was a long and bitter one. Slowly the shadows darkened over the long, sombre face of the old house. A cold, damp reek from the moat chilled us to the bones and set our teeth chattering. There was a single lamp over the gateway and a steady globe of light in the fatal study. Everything else was dark and still.

'How long is this to last?' asked the inspector, suddenly. 'And what is it we are watching for?'

'I have no more notion than you how long it is to last,' Holmes answered with some asperity. 'If criminals would always schedule their movements like railway trains it would certainly be more convenient for all of us. As to what it is we—— Well, *that's* what we are watching for.'

As he spoke the bright yellow light in the study was obscured by somebody passing to and fro before it. The laurels among which we lay were immediately opposite the window and not more than a hundred feet from it. Presently it was thrown open with a whining of hinges, and we could dimly see the dark outline of a man's head and shoulders looking out into the gloom. For some minutes he peered forth, in a furtive, stealthy fashion, as one who wishes to be assured that he is unobserved. Then he leaned forward, and in the intense silence we were aware of the soft lapping of agitated water. He seemed to be stirring up the moat with something which he held in his hand. Then suddenly he hauled something in as a fisherman lands a fish—some large, round object which obscured the light as it was dragged through the open casement.

'Now!' cried Holmes. 'Now!'

We were all upon our feet, staggering after him with our stiffened limbs, whilst he, with one of those outflames of nervous energy which could make him on occasion both the most active and the strongest man that I have ever known, ran swiftly across the bridge and rang violently at the bell. There was the rasping of bolts from the other side, and the amazed Ames stood in the entrance. Holmes brushed him aside without a word and, followed by all of us, rushed into the room which had been occupied by the man whom we had been watching.

The oil lamp on the table represented the glow which we had seen from outside. It was now in the hand of Cecil Barker, who held it towards us as we entered. Its light shone upon his strong, resolute, clean-shaven face and his menacing eyes.

'What the devil is the meaning of all this?' he cried. 'What are you after, anyhow?'

Holmes took a swift glance round and then pounced upon a sodden bundle tied together with cord which lay where it had been thrust under the writing-table.

'This is what we are after, Mr Barker. This bundle, weighted with a dumb-bell, which you have just raised from the bottom of the moat.'

Barker stared at Holmes with amazement in his face.

'How in thunder came you to know anything about it?' he asked.

'Simply that I put it there.'

'You put it there! You!'

'Perhaps I should have said "replaced it there," ' said Holmes. 'You will remember, Inspector MacDonald, that I was somewhat struck by the absence of a dumb-bell. I drew your attention to it, but with the pressure of other events you had hardly the time to give it the consideration which would have enabled you to draw deductions from it. When water is near and a weight is missing it is not a very far-fetched supposition that something has been sunk in the water. The idea was at least worth testing, so with the help of Ames, who admitted me to the room, and the crook of Dr Watson's umbrella, I was able last night to fish up and inspect this bundle. It was of the first importance, however, that we should be able to prove who placed it there. This we accomplished by the very obvious device of announcing that the moat would be dried tomorrow, which had, of course, the effect that whoever had hidden the bundle would most certainly withdraw it the moment that darkness enabled him to do so. We have no fewer than four witnesses as to who it was who took advantage of the opportunity, and so, Mr Barker, I think the word lies now with you.'

Sherlock Holmes put the sopping bundle upon the table beside the lamp and undid the cord which bound it. From within he extracted a dumb-bell, which he tossed down to its fellow in the corner. Next he drew forth a pair of boots. 'American, as you perceive,' he remarked, pointing to the toes. Then he laid upon the table a long, deadly, sheathed knife. Finally he unravelled a bundle of clothing, comprising a complete set of underclothes, socks, a grey tweed suit, and a short yellow overcoat.

'The clothes are commonplace,' remarked Holmes, 'save

THEN SUDDENLY HE HAULED SOMETHING IN AS A
FISHERMAN LANDS A FISH . . .

Illustration by Frank Wiles for the *Strand Magazine*, January, 1915. We should note here that— while cold weather is clearly indicated throughout the action of the adventure—the temperature was *not below freezing* on either the 8th or the 6th of January: on the 6th the bundle was lowered into the moat; on the 8th it was fished out. The late Dr. Ernest Bloomfield Zeisler has shown that 1889 will not answer this requirement: on January 6th of that year the temperature ranged from a low of 19.8 degrees to a high of 29.5 degrees. Dr. Zeisler also showed that a dark night was required on the 6th, for the tragedy, and the 8th, for the vigil. Eighteen-eighty-nine is ruled out once more: the moon was full on January 6th; it set at 9:53 P.M. on that day, but not until midnight on January 8th. Only 1888 meets the requirements: from the 6th to the 8th, according to the London *Times*, the minimum temperature reached was 38 degrees. As for the moon, it was at last quarter on the 6th, and did not rise before midnight on either the 6th or the 8th.

52 *Vermissa, U.S.A.* The town of "Vermissa," where Neale had his men's toggery, is most probably Pottsville, near the Schuykill anthracite region.

53 *Vermissa Valley.* Watsonese for the Shenandoah Valley.

54 peine forte et dure. French: heavy and harsh punishment.

only the overcoat, which is full of suggestive touches.' He held it tenderly towards the light, whilst his long, thin fingers flickered over it. 'Here, as you perceive, is the inner pocket prolonged into the lining in such a fashion as to give ample space for the truncated fowling-piece. The tailor's tab is on **52** the neck—Neale, Outfitter, Vermissa, U.S.A. I have spent an instructive afternoon in the rector's library, and have enlarged my knowledge by adding the fact that Vermissa is a flourishing little town at the head of one of the best-known coal and iron valleys in the United States. I have some recollection, Mr Barker, that you associated the coal districts with Mr Douglas's first wife, and it would surely not be too far-fetched an inference that the V. V. upon the card by the dead **53** body might stand for Vermissa Valley, or that this very valley, which sends forth emissaries of murder, may be that Valley of Fear of which we have heard. So much is fairly clear. And now, Mr Barker, I seem to be standing rather in the way of your explanation.'

It was a sight to see Cecil Barker's expressive face during this exposition of the great detective. Anger, amazement, consternation, and indecision swept over it in turn. Finally he took refuge in a somewhat acid irony.

'You know such a lot, Mr Holmes, perhaps you had better tell us some more,' he sneered.

'I have no doubt that I could tell you a great deal more, Mr Barker, but it would come with a better grace from you.'

'Oh, you think so, do you? Well, all I can say is that if there's any secret here it is not my secret, and I am not the man to give it away.'

'Well, if you take that line, Mr Barker,' said the inspector, quietly, 'we must just keep you in sight until we have the warrant and can hold you.'

'You can do what you damn please about that,' said Barker, defiantly.

The proceedings seemed to have come to a definite end so far as he was concerned, for one had only to look at that **54** granite face to realize that no *peine forte et dure* would ever force him to plead against his will. The deadlock was broken, however, by a woman's voice. Mrs Douglas had been standing listening at the half-opened door, and now she entered the room.

'You have done enough for us, Cecil,' said she. 'Whatever comes of it in the future, you have done enough.'

'Enough and more than enough,' remarked Sherlock Holmes, gravely. 'I have every sympathy with you, madam, and I should strongly urge you to have some confidence in the common sense of our jurisdiction and to take the police voluntarily into your complete confidence. It may be that I am myself at fault for not following up the hint which you conveyed to me through my friend, Dr Watson, but at that time I had every reason to believe that you were directly concerned in the crime. Now I am assured that this is not so. At the same time, there is much that is unexplained, and I should strongly recommend that you ask *Mr Douglas* to tell us his own story.'

Mrs Douglas gave a cry of astonishment at Holmes's words. The detectives and I must have echoed it, when we were aware of a man who seemed to have emerged from the wall, and who advanced now from the gloom of the corner in which he had appeared. Mrs Douglas turned, and in an instant her arms were round him. Barker had seized his outstretched hand.

'It's best this way, Jack,' his wife repeated. 'I am sure that it is best.'

'Indeed, yes, Mr Douglas,' said Sherlock Holmes. 'I am sure that you will find it best.'

The man stood blinking at us with the dazed look of one who comes from the dark into the light. It was a remarkable face—bold grey eyes, a strong, short-clipped, grizzled moustache, a square, projecting chin, and a humorous mouth. He took a good look at us all, and then, to my amazement, he advanced to me and handed me a bundle of paper.

'I've heard of you,' said he, in a voice which was not quite English and not quite American, but was altogether mellow and pleasing. 'You are the historian of this bunch. Well, Dr Watson, you've never had such a story as that pass through your hands before, and I'd lay my last dollar on that. Tell it your own way, but there are the facts, and you can't miss the public so long as you have those. I've been cooped up two days, and I've spent the daylight hours—as much daylight as I could get in that rat-trap—in putting the thing into words. You're welcome to them—you and your public. There's the story of the Valley of Fear.'

'That's the past, Mr Douglas,' said Sherlock Holmes, quietly. 'What we desire now is to hear your story of the present.'

'You'll have it, sir,' said Douglas. 'Can I smoke as I talk? Well, thank you, Mr Holmes; you're a smoker yourself, if I remember right, and you'll guess what it is to be sitting for two days with tobacco in your pocket and afraid that the smell will give you away.' He leaned against the mantelpiece and sucked at the cigar which Holmes had handed him. 'I've heard of you, Mr Holmes; I never guessed that I would meet you. But before you are through with that'—he nodded at my papers—'you will say I've brought you something fresh.'

Inspector MacDonald had been staring at the new-comer with the greatest amazement.

'Well, this fairly beats me!' he cried at last. 'If you are Mr John Douglas, of Birlstone Manor, then whose death have we been investigating for these two days, and where in the world have you sprung from now? You seemed to me to come out of the floor like a Jack-in-a-box.'

'Ah, Mr Mac,' said Holmes, shaking a reproving forefinger, 'you would not read that excellent local compilation which described the concealment of King Charles. People did not hide in those days without reliable hiding-places, and the hiding-place that has once been used may be again. I had persuaded myself that we should find Mr Douglas under this roof.'

'And how long have you been playing this trick upon us, Mr Holmes?' said the inspector angrily. 'How long have you allowed us to waste ourselves upon a search that you knew to be an absurd one?'

'Not one instant, my dear Mr Mac. Only last night did I form my views of the case. As they could not be put to the proof until this evening, I invited you and your colleague to take a holiday for the day. Pray, what more could I do? When I found the suit of clothes in the moat it at once became apparent to me that the body we had found could not have been the body of Mr John Douglas at all, but must be that of the bicyclist from Tunbridge Wells. No other conclusion was possible. Therefore I had to determine where Mr John Douglas himself could be, and the balance of probability was that, with the connivance of his wife and his friend, he was concealed in a house which had such conveniences for a fugitive, and awaiting quieter times, when he could make his final escape.'

'Well, you figured it out about right,' said Mr Douglas, approvingly. 'I thought I'd dodge your British law, for I was not sure how I stood under it, and also I saw my chance to throw these hounds once for all off my track. Mind you, from first to last I have done nothing to be ashamed of, and nothing that I would not do again, but you'll judge that for yourselves when I tell you my story. Never mind warning me, inspector; I'm ready to stand pat upon the truth.

'I'm not going to begin at the beginning. That's all there' —he indicated my bundle of papers—'and a mighty queer yarn you'll find it. It all comes down to this: that there are some men that have good cause to hate me and would give their last dollar to know that they had got me. So long as I am alive and they are alive, there is no safety in this world for me. They hunted me from Chicago to California; then they chased me out of America; but when I married and settled down in this quiet spot I thought my last years were going to be peaceable. I never explained to my wife how things were. Why should I pull her into it? She would never have a quiet moment again, but would be always imagining trouble. I fancy she knew something, for I may have dropped a word here or a word there—but until yesterday, after you gentlemen had seen her, she never knew the rights of the matter. She told you all she knew, and so did Barker here, for on the night when this thing happened there was mighty little time for explanations. She knows everything now, and I would have been a wiser man if I had told her sooner. But it was a hard question, dear'—he took her hand for an instant in his own—'and I acted for the best.

'Well, gentlemen, the day before these happenings I was over in Tunbridge Wells and I got a glimpse of a man in the street. It was only a glimpse, but I have a quick eye for these things, and I never doubted who it was. It was the worst enemy I had among them all—one who has been after me like a hungry wolf after a caribou all these years. I knew there was trouble coming, and I came home and made ready for it. I guessed I'd fight through it all right on my own. There was a time when my luck was the talk of the whole United States. I never doubted that it would be with me still.

'I was on my guard all that next day and never went out into the park. It's as well, or he'd have had the drop on me with that buckshot gun of his before ever I could draw on him. After the bridge was up—my mind was always more restful when that bridge was up in the evenings—I put the thing clear out of my head. I never figured on his getting into the house and waiting for me. But when I made my round in my dressing-gown, as my habit was, I had no sooner entered the study than I scented danger. I guess when a man has had dangers in his life—and I've had more than most in my time —there is a kind of sixth sense that waves the red flag. I saw the signal clear enough, and yet I couldn't tell you why. Next instant I spotted a boot under the window curtain, and then I saw why plain enough.

'I'd just the one candle that was in my hand, but there was a good light from the hall-lamp through the open door. I put down the candle and jumped for a hammer that I'd left on the mantel. At the same moment he sprang at me. I saw the glint of a knife and I lashed at him with the hammer. I got him somewhere, for the knife tinkled down on the floor. He dodged round the table as quick as an eel, and a moment later he'd got his gun from under his coat. I heard him cock it, but I had got hold of it before he could fire. I had it by the barrel, and we wrestled for it all ends up for a minute or more. It was death to the man that lost his grip. He never lost his grip, but he got it butt downwards for a moment too long. Maybe it was I that pulled the trigger. Maybe we just jolted it off between us. Anyhow, he got both barrels in the face, and there I was, staring down at all that was left of Ted Baldwin. I'd recognized him in the township and again when he sprang for me, but his own mother wouldn't recognize him as I saw him then. I'm used to rough work, but I fairly turned sick at the sight of him.

'I was hanging on to the side of the table when Barker came hurrying down. I heard my wife coming, and I ran to the door and stopped her. It was no sight for a woman. I promised I'd come to her soon. I said a word or two to Barker—he took it all in at a glance—and we waited for the rest to come along. But there was no sign of them. Then we understood that they could hear nothing, and that all that had happened was only known to ourselves.

'It was at that instant that the idea came to me. I was fairly dazzled by the brilliancy of it. The man's sleeve had slipped up and there was the branded mark of the Lodge upon his forearm. See here.'

The man whom we knew as Douglas turned up his own coat and cuff to show a brown triangle within a circle exactly like that which we had seen upon the dead man.

'It was the sight of that which started me on to it. I seemed to see it all clear at a glance. There was his height and hair and figure about the same as my own. No one could swear to his face, poor devil! I brought down this suit of clothes, and in a quarter of an hour Barker and I had put my dressing-gown on him and he lay as you found him. We tied all his things into a bundle, and I weighted them with the only weight I could find and slung them through the window. The card he had meant to lay upon my body was lying beside his own. My rings were put on his finger, but when it came to the wedding-ring'—he held out his muscular hand—'you can see for yourselves that I had struck my limit. I have not moved it since the day I was married, and it would have taken a file to get it off. I don't know, anyhow, that I would have cared to part with it, but if I had wanted to I couldn't. So we just had to leave that detail to take care of itself. On the other hand, I brought a bit of plaster down and put it where I am wearing one myself at this instant. You slipped up there, Mr Holmes, clever as you are, for if you had chanced to take off that plaster you would have found no cut underneath it.

'Well, that was the situation. If I could lie low for a while and then get away where I would be joined by my wife, we

I HEARD HIM COCK IT, BUT I HAD GOT HOLD OF IT
BEFORE HE COULD FIRE.

Illustration by Frank Wiles for the *Strand Magazine*, January, 1915.

55 *back some twenty years in time.* The story of "The Scowrers," which immediately follows, begins: "It was the fourth of February in the years 1875." If, as Watson says, this was a "journey back" of "some twenty years" it would seem that the adventure of *The Valley of Fear* took place *circa* 1895. There is a case, and a good case, for dating *The Valley of Fear* at the end of the *'nineties* rather than at the end of the 'eighties: 1) When Birdy Edwards, in February, 1875, traveled through the gorges of the Gilmerton Mountains from Stagville to Vermissa, he was "not far from his thirtieth year"; 2) he spent three months in the Valley, and at the end of that time he arrested the famous gang of Scowrers; 3) the date of the trial of the Scowrers may reasonably be assigned to the autumn of 1875; McGinty went to the scaffold and Ted Baldwin went to the penitentiary for ten years; 4) it was presumably in 1886, then, that Birdy Edwards was driven from Chicago to California, where he remained for five years; it could not have been, therefore, earlier than the end of 1892 that Edwards packed up and came to England; 5) this, we are told, was "nearer seven years than six" before the date of the killing at Birlstone; this would place the date of the killing not earlier than the January of 1899, and this would correspond both with Dr. Watson's estimate that Douglas (Edwards) "may have been about fifty" and his statement that the events at Birlstone were "some twenty years" after the events in the Vermissa Valley.

For these and other reasons, many commentators *have* dated *The Valley of Fear* at the end of the 'nineties; 1890.

But these commentators are faced with the embarrassing fact that Professor James Moriarty, who died, Watson tells us, on May 4, 1891, is very much alive at the time of *The Valley of Fear*. Thus the late Gavin Brend (*My Dear Holmes*) is driven to postulate a *second* Moriarty, arising phoenix-like out of the ashes of the first. And Mr. Anthony Boucher holds that "the case did take place some time shortly before Holmes' retirement . . . and did *not* involve Moriarty. Watson wrote it up as the two novelettes: a completely self-contained non-Moriarty story. Then he began brooding along these lines: 'The public likes Moriarty, but, hang it, the only really good case involving him was that Reichenbach business. Of course there was that stunning piece of work Holmes did in deciphering that letter from Porlock; but once he'd deciphered it, it led us into a very routine affair with no plot-value at all. And that time that he explained Moriarty to Inspector Mac, but that case was even worse . . . nothing but men in it. . . . *I know!* Let's use those two episodes as a prologue and blame the whole Birlstone business on Moriarty.'"

"The justification for . . . any date [at the end of the 'eighties] requires that Baldwin got out before his full term of ten years," Mr. T. S. Blakeney wrote in *Sherlock Holmes: Fact or Fiction?*, "and there is nothing unlikely about that. If such a murderous villain could escape the death penalty there would be nothing improbable in his managing to

would have a chance at last of living at peace for the rest of our lives. These devils would give me no rest so long as I was above ground, but if they saw in the papers that Baldwin had got his man there would be an end of all my troubles. I hadn't much time to make it clear to Barker and to my wife, but they understood enough to be able to help me. I knew all about this hiding-place, so did Ames, but it never entered his head to connect it with the matter. I retired into it, and it was up to Barker to do the rest.

'I guess you can fill in for yourselves what he did. He opened the window and made the mark on the sill to give an idea of how the murderer escaped. It was a tall order, that, but as the bridge was up there was no other way. Then, when everything was fixed, he rang the bell for all he was worth. What happened afterwards you know—and so, gentlemen, you can do what you please, but I've told you the truth and the whole truth, so help me, God! What I ask you now is, how do I stand by the English law?'

There was a silence, which was broken by Sherlock Holmes.

'The English law is, in the main, a just law. You will get no worse than your deserts from it. But I would ask you how did this man know that you lived here, or how to get into your house, or where to hide to get you?'

'I know nothing of this.'

Holmes's face was very white and grave.

'The story is not over yet, I fear,' said he. 'You may find worse dangers than the English law, or even than your enemies from America. I see trouble before you; Mr Douglas. You'll take my advice and still be on your guard.'

And now, my long-suffering readers, I will ask you to come away with me for a time, far from the Sussex Manor House of Birlstone, and far also from the year of grace in which we made our eventful journey which ended with the strange story of the man who had been known as John Douglas. I **55** wish you to journey back some twenty years in time, and westward some thousands of miles in space, that I may lay before you a singular and a terrible narrative—so singular and so terrible that you may find it hard to believe that, even as I tell it, even so did it occur. Do not think that I intrude one story before another is finished. As you read on you will find that this is not so. And when I have detailed those distant events and you have solved this mystery of the past we shall meet once more in those rooms in Baker Street where this, like so many other wonderful happenings, will find its end.

get out of prison before his time, whether by good conduct or by bribery."

More recent chronologist prefer to hold that it was *not* Baldwin who drove Douglas-Edwards from Chicago. As the late Dr. Ernest Bloomfield Zeisler wrote (in "Concerning *The Valley of Fear*"): 'it was most unlikely that the Scowrers would wait until Ted Baldwin's release from the penitentiary to make their attempt to drive Edwards from Chicago." We suggest that Dr. Watson sat down to chronicle the adventure of *The Valley of Fear* in the Missing Year 1895–1896; thus his "twenty years in time" dates, not from the tragedy at Birlstone, but from his *writing* of his chronicle.

PART II

The Scowrers   **56**

8 · THE MAN

It was the fourth of February in the year 1875. It had been a severe winter, and the snow lay deep in the gorges of the Gilmerton Mountains. The steam plough had, however, kept the rail-track open, and the evening train which connects the long line of coal-mining and iron-working settlements was slowly groaning its way up the steep gradients which lead from Stagville on the plain to Vermissa, the central township which lies at the head of the Vermissa Valley. From this point the track sweeps downwards to Barton's Crossing, Helmdale, and the purely agricultural county of Merton. It was a single-track railroad, but at every siding, and they were numerous, long lines of trucks piled with coal and with iron ore told of the hidden wealth which had brought a rude population and a bustling life to this most desolate corner of the United States of America.

For desolate it was. Little could the first pioneer who had traversed it have ever imagined that the fairest prairies and the most lush water-pastures were valueless compared with this gloomy land of black crag and tangled forest. Above the dark and often scarcely penetrable woods upon their sides, the high, bare crowns of the mountains, white snow and jagged rock, towered upon either flank, leaving a long, winding, tortuous valley in the centre. Up this the little train was slowly crawling.

The oil-lamps had just been lit in the leading passenger-car, a long, bare carriage in which some twenty or thirty people were seated. The greater number of these were work-men returning from their day's toil in the lower portion of the valley. At least a dozen, by their grimed faces and the safety lanterns which they carried, proclaimed themselves as miners. These sat smoking in a group, and conversed in low voices, glancing occasionally at two men on the opposite side of the car, whose uniform and badges showed them to be policemen. Several women of the labouring class, and one or two travellers who might have been small local storekeepers, made up the rest of the company, with the exception of one young man in a corner by himself. It is with this man that we are concerned. Take a good look at him, for he is worth it.

He is a fresh-complexioned, middle-sized young man, not far, one would guess, from his thirtieth year. He has large, shrewd, humorous grey eyes which twinkle inquiringly from time to time as he looks round through his spectacles at the people about him. It is easy to see that he is of a sociable and possibly simple disposition, anxious to be friendly to all men. Anyone could pick him at once as gregarious in his habits and communicative in his nature, with a quick wit and a ready smile. And yet the man who studied him more closely might discern a certain firmness of jaw and grim tightness about the lips which would warn him that there were depths beyond and that this pleasant, brown-haired young Irishman

56 *PART II The Scowrers.* Sir Arthur Conan Doyle never tried to keep it a secret that he had based Part II of *The Valley of Fear* on Allan J. Pinkerton's book, *The Molly Maguires and the Detectives,* published in 1877 in New York by G. W. Carleton and Company.

As Mr. Hyman Parker wrote in "Birdy Edwards and the Scowrers Reconsidered," "It is generally accepted that the Scowrers and the Molly Maguires were one and the same organization. It is submitted that the use of the true name was avoided by Watson because he knew that his distortion of some facts might subject him to civil and criminal prosecution for libel. Rather than risk this, Watson merely changed the names of people and places. Thus, the Molly Maguires became the Scowrers; the Shenandoah Valley became Vermissa Valley; Pottsville, Pennsylvania, became Vermissa; Commissioner Dormer became Councillor McGinty; the Ancient Order of Hibernians became the Ancient Order of Freemen [changed, in some American editions, to the Eminent Order of Freemen]; James McPharlan, a Pinkerton detective [aged twenty-nine when he began his investigations] became Birdy Edwards, and later John Douglas of Birlstone Manor; James McKenna (the assumed name of McPharlan) became Jack McMurdo (the assumed name of Edwards). However, the coffin notices and the Pinkerton Detective Agency remained unchanged."

We may add here that the Molly Maguires were also called the "White Boys" and "The Buckshots" after their (alleged) endearing habit of dressing in white sheets, sneaking up to a lighted window of an evening and letting fly with a double load of buckshot at whomever the Bodymaster happened to be annoyed.

Readers interested in learning more about the Molly Maguires are referred to two recent books: *Lament for the Molly Maguires,* by Arthur H. Lewis, and *The Molly Maguires,* by Wayne G. Broehl, Jr. Reviewing the latter in *The New York Times* (Book Review Section, November 15, 1964), Mr. William V. Shannon wrote: ". . . the Mollies have been the subject of considerable dispute in history and legend. They have been depicted as early labor martyrs and as victims of religious and ethnic prejudice. James McPharlan, the famous Pinkerton detective whose undercover work led to their conviction, has alternatively been pictured as a hero and a crafty *agent provocateur.* . . . [Mr. Broehl] confirms the prevailing consensus among historians, which is that most of the first 10 defendants were guilty of the crimes for which they were hanged, but that at least some of the others were not, or were punished too severely for their complicity."

might conceivably leave his mark for good or evil upon any society to which he was introduced.

Having made one or two tentative remarks to the nearest miner, and received only short gruff replies, the traveller resigned himself to uncongenial silence, staring moodily out of the window at the fading landscape. It was not a cheering prospect. Through the growing gloom there pulsed the red glow of the furnaces on the sides of the hills. Great heaps of slag and dumps of cinders loomed up on each side, with the high shafts of the collieries towering above them. Huddled groups of mean wooden houses, the windows of which were beginning to outline themselves in light, were scattered here and there along the line, and the frequent halting-places were crowded with their swarthy inhabitants. The iron and coal valleys of the Vermissa district were no resorts for the leisured or the cultured. Everywhere there were stern signs of the crudest battle of life, the rude work to be done, and the rude, strong workers who did it.

The young traveller gazed out into this dismal country with a face of mingled repulsion and interest, which showed that the scene was new to him. At intervals he drew from his pocket a bulky letter to which he referred, and on the margins of which he scribbled some notes. Once from the back of his waist he produced something which one would hardly have expected to find in the possession of so mild-mannered a man. It was a navy revolver of the largest size. As he turned it slantwise to the light, the glint upon the rims of the copper shells within the drum showed that it was fully loaded. He quickly restored it to his secret pocket, but not before it had been observed by a working man who had seated himself upon the adjoining bench.

'Halloa, mate!' said he. 'You seem heeled and ready.'

The young man smiled with an air of embarrassment.

'Yes,' said he; 'we need them sometimes in the place I come from.'

'And where may that be?'

'I'm last from Chicago.'

'A stranger in these parts?'

'Yes.'

'You may find you need it here,' said the workman.

'Ah! Is that so?' The young man seemed interested.

'Have you heard nothing of doings hereabouts?'

'Nothing out of the way.'

'Why, I thought the country was full of it. You'll hear quick enough. What made you come here?'

'I heard there was always work for a willing man.'

'Are you one of the Labour Union?'

'Sure.'

'Then you'll get your job, I guess. Have you any friends?'

'Not yet, but I have the means of making them.'

'How's that, then?'

'I am one of the Ancient Order of Freemen. There's no town without a lodge, and where there is a lodge I'll find my friends.'

The remark had a singular effect upon his companion. He glanced round suspiciously at the others in the car. The miners were still whispering among themselves. The two police officers were dozing. He came across, seated himself close to the young traveller, and held out his hand.

'Put it there,' he said.

A hand-grip passed between the two.

'I see you speak the truth. But it's well to make certain.'

He raised his right hand to his right eyebrow. The traveller at once raised his left hand to his left eyebrow.

'Dark nights are unpleasant,' said the workman.

'Yes, for strangers to travel,' the other answered.

'That's good enough. I'm Brother Scanlan, Lodge 341, Vermissa Valley. Glad to see you in these parts.'

'Thank you. I'm Brother John McMurdo, Lodge 29, Chicago. Bodymaster, J. H. Scott. But I am in luck to meet a brother so early.'

'Well, there are plenty of us about. You won't find the Order more flourishing anywhere in the States than right here in Vermissa Valley. But we could do with some lads like you. I can't understand a spry man of the Labour Union finding no work to do in Chicago.'

'I found plenty of work to do,' said McMurdo.

'Then why did you leave?'

McMurdo nodded towards the policemen and smiled.

'I guess those chaps would be glad to know,' he said.

Scanlan groaned sympathetically.

'In trouble?' he asked, in a whisper.

'Deep.'

'A penitentiary job?'

'And the rest.'

'Not a killing?'

'It's early days to talk of such things,' said McMurdo, with the air of a man who had been surprised into saying more than he intended. 'I've my own good reason for leaving Chicago, and let that be enough for you. Who are you that you should take it on yourself to ask such things?'

His grey eyes gleamed with sudden and dangerous anger from behind his glasses.

'All right, mate. No offence meant. The boys will think none the worse of you whatever you may have done. Where are you bound for now?'

'To Vermissa.'

'That's the third halt down the line. Where are you staying?'

McMurdo took out an envelope and held it close to the murky oil-lamp.

'Here is the address—Jacob Shafter, Sheridan Street. It's a boarding-house that was recommended by a man I knew in Chicago.'

'Well, I don't know it, but Vermissa is out of my beat. I live at Hobson's Patch, and that's here where we are drawing **57** up. But, say, there's one bit of advice I'll give you before we part. If you're in trouble in Vermissa, go straight to the Union House and see Boss McGinty. He is the bodymaster of Vermissa Lodge, and nothing can happen in these parts unless Black Jack McGinty wants it. So long, mate. Maybe we'll meet in Lodge one of these evenings. But mind my words; if you are in trouble go to Boss McGinty.'

Scanlan descended, and McMurdo was left once again to his thoughts. Night had now fallen, and the flames of the frequent furnaces were roaring and leaping in the darkness. Against their lurid background dark figures were bending and straining, twisting, and turning, with the motion of winch or of windlass, to the rhythm of an eternal clank and roar.

57 *Hobson's Patch*. "It does not require a very active imagination to identify Craig's Patch with the 'Hobson's Patch' of the Story," the late James Montgomery wrote in "Paging Birdy Edwards."

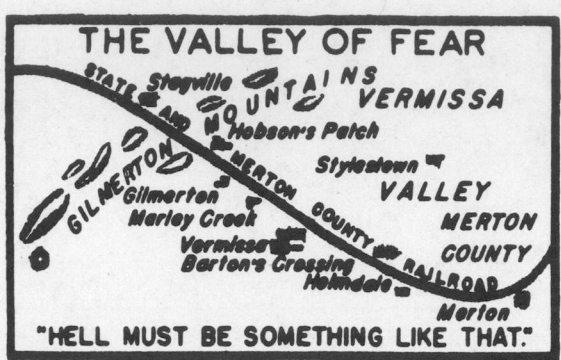

"I GUESS HELL MUST LOOK SOMETHING LIKE THAT . . ."

Dr. Julian Wolff's map of *The Valley of Fear.*

'I guess hell must look something like that,' said a voice. McMurdo turned and saw that one of the policemen had shifted in his seat and was staring out into the fiery waste.

'For that matter,' said the other policeman, 'I allow that hell must *be* something like that. If there are worse devils down yonder than some we could name, it's more than I'd expect. I guess you are new to this part, young man?'

'Well, what if I am?' McMurdo answered, in a surly voice.

'Just this, mister; that I should advise you to be careful in choosing your friends. I don't think I'd begin with Mike Scanlan or his gang if I were you.'

'What in thunder is it to you who are my friends?' roared McMurdo, in a voice which brought every head in the carriage round to witness the altercation. 'Did I ask you for your advice, or did you think me such a sucker that I couldn't move without it? You speak when you are spoken to, and by the Lord you'd have to wait a long time if it was me!'

He thrust out his face, and grinned at the patrolmen like a snarling dog.

The two policemen, heavy, good-natured men, were taken aback by the extraordinary vehemence with which their friendly advances had been rejected.

'No offence, stranger,' said one. 'It was a warning for your own good, seeing that you are, by your own showing, new to the place.'

'I'm new to the place, but I'm not new to you and your kind,' cried McMurdo, in a cold fury. 'I guess you're the same in all places, shoving your advice in when nobody asks for it.'

'Maybe we'll see more of you before very long,' said one of the patrolmen, with a grin. 'You're a real hand-picked one, if I am a judge.'

'I was thinking the same,' remarked the other. 'I guess we may meet again.'

'I'm not afraid of you, and don't you think it,' cried McMurdo. 'My name's Jack McMurdo—see? If you want me you'll find me at Jacob Shafter's, at Sheridan Street, Vermissa, so I'm not hiding from you, am I? Day or night I dare to look the like of you in the face. Don't make any mistake about that.'

There was a murmur of sympathy and admiration from the miners at the dauntless demeanour of the new-comer, while the two policemen shrugged their shoulders and renewed a conversation between themselves. A few minutes later the train ran into the ill-lit depot and there was a general clearing, for Vermissa was far the largest township on the line. McMurdo picked up his leather grip-sack, and was about to start off into the darkness when one of the miners accosted him.

'By gosh, mate, you know how to speak to the cops,' he said, in a voice of awe. 'It was grand to hear you. Let me carry your grip-sack and show you the road. I'm passing Shafter's on the way to my own shack.'

There was a chorus of friendly 'Good nights' from the other miners as they passed from the platform. Before ever he had set foot in it, McMurdo the turbulent had become a character in Vermissa.

The country had been a place of terror, but the township was in its way even more depressing. Down that long valley there was at least a certain gloomy grandeur in the huge fires and the clouds of drifting smoke, while the strength and industry of man found fitting monuments in the hills which he had spilled by the side of his monstrous excavations. But the town showed a dead level of mean ugliness and squalor. The broad street was churned up by the traffic into a horrible rutted paste of muddy snow. The sidewalks were narrow and uneven. The numerous gas-lamps served only to show more clearly a long line of wooden houses, each with its verandah facing the street, unkempt and dirty. As they approached the centre of the town the scene was brightened by a row of well-lit stores, and even more by a cluster of liquor saloons and gaming-houses, in which the miners spent their hard-earned but generous wages.

'That's the Union House,' said the guide, pointing to one saloon which rose almost to the dignity of being an hotel. 'Jack McGinty is the Boss there.'

'What sort of a man is he?' asked McMurdo.

'What! Have you never heard of the Boss?'

'How could I have heard of him when you know that I am a stranger in these parts?'

'Well, I thought his name was known right across the Union. It's been in the papers often enough.'

'What for?'

'Well'—the miner lowered his voice—'over the affairs.'

'What affairs?'

'Good Lord, mister, you are queer goods, if I may say it without offence. There's only one set of affairs that you'll hear of in these parts, and that's the affairs of the Scowrers.'

'Why, I seem to have read of the Scowrers in Chicago. A gang of murderers, are they not?'

'Hush, on your life!' cried the miner, standing still in his alarm, and gazing in amazement at his companion. 'Man, you won't live long in these parts if you speak in the open street like that. Many a man has had the life beaten out of him for less.'

'Well, I know nothing about them. It's only what I have read.'

'And I'm not saying that you have not read the truth.' The man looked nervously round him as he spoke, peering into the shadows as if he feared to see some lurking danger. 'If killing is murder, then God knows there is murder and to spare. But don't you dare to breathe the name of Jack McGinty in connection with it, stranger, for every whisper goes back to him, and he is not one that is likely to let it pass. Now, that's the house you're after—that one standing back from the street. You'll find old Jacob Shafter that runs it as honest a man as lives in this township.'

'I thank you,' said McMurdo, and shaking hands with his new acquaintance he plodded, his grip-sack in his hand, up the path which led to the dwelling-house, at the door of which he gave a resounding knock. It was opened at once by someone very different from what he had expected.

It was a woman, young and singularly beautiful. She was of the Swedish type, blonde and fair-haired, with the piquant **58** contrast of a pair of beautiful dark eyes, with which she surveyed the stranger with surprise and a pleasing embarrassment which brought a wave of colour over her pale face. Framed in the bright light of the open doorway, it seemed to McMurdo that he had never seen a more beautiful picture, the more attractive for its contrast with the sordid and gloomy

58 *of the Swedish type.* The Shafters, originally Germans, became Swedish in the English editions because it was impossible, in 1914–1915, to depict any German as a kindly character in an English publication.

"HUSH, ON YOUR LIFE!" CRIED THE MINER . . .

Illustration by Frank Wiles for the *Strand Magazine*, January, 1915.

surroundings. A lovely violet growing upon one of those black slagheaps of the mines would not have seemed more surprising. So entranced was he that he stood staring without a word, and it was she who broke the silence.

'I thought it was father,' said she, with a pleasing little touch of a Swedish accent. 'Did you come to see him? He is down town. I expect him back every minute.'

McMurdo continued to gaze at her in open admiration until her eyes dropped in confusion before this masterful visitor.

'No, miss,' he said at last; 'I'm in no hurry to see him. But your house was recommended to me for board. I thought it might suit me, and now I know it will.'

'You are quick to make up your mind,' said she, with a smile.

'Anyone but a blind man could do as much,' the other answered.

She laughed at the compliment.

'Come right in, sir,' she said. 'I'm Miss Ettie Shafter, Mr Shafter's daughter. My mother's dead, and I run the house. You can sit down by the stove in the front room until father comes along. Ah, here he is; so you can fix things with him right away.'

A heavy, elderly man came plodding up the path. In a few words McMurdo explained his business. A man of the name of Murphy had given him the address in Chicago. He in turn had had it from someone else. Old Shafter was quite ready. The stranger made no bones about terms, agreed at once to every condition, and was apparently fairly flush of money. For twelve dollars a week, paid in advance, he was to have board and lodging. So it was that McMurdo, the self-confessed fugitive from justice, took up his abode under the roof of the Shafters, the first step which was to lead to so long and dark a train of events, ending in a far-distant land.

9 ❖ THE BODYMASTER

McMurdo was a man who made his mark quickly. Wherever he was the folk around soon knew it. Within a week he had become infinitely the most important person at Shafter's. There were ten or a dozen boarders there, but they were honest foremen or commonplace clerks from the stores, of a very different calibre to the young Irishman. Of an evening when they gathered together his joke was always the readiest, his conversation the brightest, and his song the best. He was a born boon companion, with a magnetism which drew good humour from all around him.

And yet he showed again and again, as he had shown in the railway-carriage, a capacity for sudden, fierce anger which compelled the respect and even fear of those who met him. For the law, too, and all connected with it, he exhibited a bitter contempt which delighted some and alarmed others of his fellow-boarders.

From the first he made it evident, by his open admiration, that the daughter of the house had won his heart from the instant that he had set eyes upon her beauty and her grace. He was no backward suitor. On the second day he told her that he loved her, and from then onwards he repeated the same story with an absolute disregard of what she might say to discourage him.

'Someone else!' he would cry. 'Well, the worse luck for someone else! Let him look out for himself! Am I to lose my life's chance and all my heart's desire for someone else? You can keep on saying "No," Ettie! The day will come when you will say "Yes," and I'm young enough to wait.'

He was a dangerous suitor, with his glib Irish tongue and his pretty, coaxing ways. There was about him also that glamour of experience and of mystery which attracts a woman's interest and finally her love. He could talk of the sweet valleys of County Monaghan from which he came, of the lovely distant island, the low hills and green meadows of which seemed the more beautiful when imagination viewed them from this place of grime and snow. Then he was versed in the life of the cities of the North, of Detroit and the lumber-camps of Michigan, of Buffalo, and finally of Chicago, where he had worked in a saw-mill. And afterwards came the hint of romance, the feeling that strange things had happened to him in that great city, so strange and so intimate that they might not be spoken of. He spoke wistfully of a sudden leaving, a breaking of old ties, a flight into a strange world ending in this dreary valley, and Ettie listened, her dark eyes gleaming with pity and with sympathy—those two qualities which may turn so rapidly and so naturally to love.

McMurdo had obtained a temporary job as a book-keeper, for he was a well-educated man. This kept him out most of the day, and he had not found occasion yet to report himself to the head of the Lodge of the Ancient Order of Freemen. He was reminded of his omission, however, by a visit one evening from Mike Scanlan, the fellow-member whom he had met in the train. Scanlan, a small, sharp-faced, nervous, black-eyed man, seemed glad to see him once more. After a glass or two of whisky, he broached the object of his visit.

'Say, McMurdo,' said he, 'I remembered your address, so I made bold to call. I'm surprised that you've not reported to the bodymaster. What's amiss that you've not seen Boss McGinty yet?'

'Well, I had to find a job. I have been busy.'

'You must find time for him if you have none for anything else. Good Lord, man, you're mad not to have been down to the Union House and registered your name the first morning after you came here! If you fall foul of him—well, you *mustn't* —that's all.'

McMurdo showed mild surprise.

'I've been a member of Lodge for over two years, Scanlan, but I never heard that duties were so pressing as all that.'

'Maybe not in Chicago!'

'Well, it's the same society here.'

'Is it?' Scanlan looked at him long and fixedly. There was something sinister in his eyes.

'Is it not?'

'You'll tell me that in a month's time. I hear you had a talk with the patrolmen after I left the train.'

'How did you know that?'

'Oh, it got about—things do get about for good and for bad in this district.'

'Well, yes. I told the hounds what I thought of them.'

'By the Lord, you'll be a man after McGinty's heart!'

'What—does he hate the police, too?'

Scanlan burst out laughing.

'You go and see him, my lad,' said he, as he took his leave. 'It's not the police, but you, that he'll hate if you don't! Now, take a friend's advice and go at once!'

It chanced that on the same evening McMurdo had another more pressing interview which urged him in the same direction. It may have been that his attentions to Ettie had been more evident than before, or that they had gradually obtruded themselves into the slow mind of his good Swedish host; but, whatever the cause, the boarding-house keeper beckoned the young man into his private room and started on to the subject without any circumlocution.

'It seems to me, mister,' said he, 'dat you are gettin' set on my Ettie. Ain't dat so, or am I wrong?'

'Yes, that is so,' the young man answered.

'Well, I vant to tell you right now dat it ain't no manner of use. There's someone slipped in afore you.'

'She told me so.'

'Well, you can lay dat she told you truth! But did she tell you who it vas?'

'No; I asked her, but she would not tell.'

'I dare say not, the leetle baggage. Perhaps she did not vish to vrighten you avay.'

'Frighten!' McMurdo was on fire in a moment.

'Ah yes, my vriend! You need not be ashamed to be vrightened of him. It is Teddy Baldwin.'

'And who the devil is he?'

'He is a Boss of Scowrers.'

'Scowrers! I've heard of them before. It's Scowrers here and Scowrers there, and always in a whisper! What are you all afraid of? Who *are* the Scowrers?'

The boarding-house keeper instinctively sank his voice, as everyone did who talked about that terrible society.

'The Scowrers,' said he, 'are the Ancient Order of Freemen.'

The young man started.

'Why, I am a member of that Order myself.'

'You! I would never have had you in my house if I had known it—not if you vere to pay me a hundred dollar a veek.'

'What's amiss with the Order? It's for charity and good-fellowship. The rules say so.'

'Maybe in some places. Not here!'

'What is it here?'

'It's a murder society, dat's vat it is.'

McMurdo laughed incredulously.

'How do you prove that?' he asked.

'Prove it! Are there not vifty murders to prove it? Vat about Milman and Van Shorst, and the Nicholson vamily, and old Mr Hyam, and little Billy James, and the others? Prove it! Is dere a man or a voman in dis valley dat does not know it?'

'See here!' said McMurdo, earnestly. 'I want you to take back what you've said or else to make it good. One or the other you must do before I quit this room. Put yourself in my place. Here am I, a stranger in the town. I belong to a society that I know only as an innocent one. You'll find it through the length and breadth of the States, but always as an innocent one. Now, when I am counting upon joining it here, you tell me that it is the same as a murder society called the "Scowrers." I guess you owe me either an apology or else an explanation, Mr Shafter.'

'I can but tell you vat the whole vorld knows, mister. The bosses of the one are the bosses of the other. If you offend the one, it is the other dat vill strike you. We have proved it too often.'

'That's just gossip! I want proof!' said McMurdo.

'If you live here long you vill get your proof. But I vorget dat you are yourself one of dem. You vill soon be as bad as the rest. But you will find other lodgings, mister. I cannot have you here. Is it not bad enough dat one of these people come courting my Ettie, and dat I dare not turn him down, but dat I should have another for my boarder? Yes, indeed, you shall not sleep here after tonight!'

So McMurdo found himself under sentence of banishment both from his comfortable quarters and from the girl whom he loved. He found her alone in the sitting-room that same evening, and he poured his troubles into her ear.

'Sure, your father is after giving me notice,' he said. 'It's little I would care if it was just my room; but indeed, Ettie, though it's only a week that I've known you, you are the very breath of life to me, and I can't live without you.'

'Oh, hush, Mr McMurdo! Don't speak so!' said the girl. 'I have told you, have I not, that you are too late? There is another, and if I have not promised to marry him at once, at least I can promise no one else.'

'Suppose I had been first, Ettie, would I have had a chance?'

The girl sank her face into her hands.

'I wish to Heaven that you *had* been first,' she sobbed.

McMurdo was down on his knees before her in an instant.

'For God's sake, Ettie, let it stand at that!' he cried. 'Will you ruin your life and my own for the sake of this promise? Follow your heart, acushla! 'Tis a safer guide than any promise given before you knew what it was that you were saying.'

He had seized Ettie's white hand between his own strong brown ones.

'Say that you will be mine and we will face it out together.'

'Not here?'

'Yes, here.'

'No, no, Jack!' His arms were round her now. 'It could not be here. Could you take me away?'

A struggle passed for a moment over McMurdo's face, but it ended by setting like granite.

'No, here,' he said. 'I'll hold you against the world, Ettie, right here where we are!'

'Why should we not leave together?'

'No, Ettie, I can't leave here.'

'But why?'

'I'd never hold my head up again if I felt that I had been driven out. Besides, what is there to be afraid of? Are we not free folk in a free country? If you love me and I love you, who will dare to come between?'

'You don't know, Jack. You've been here too short a time. You don't know this Baldwin. You don't know McGinty and his Scowrers.'

'No, I don't know them, and I don't fear them, and I don't believe in them!' said McMurdo. 'I've lived among rough men, my darling, and instead of fearing them it has always ended that they have feared me—always, Ettie. It's mad on the face of it! If these men, as your father says, have done crime after crime, in the valley, and if everyone knows them by name, how comes it that none are brought to justice? You answer me that, Ettie!'

'Because no witness dares to appear against them. He would not live a month if he did. Also because they have always their own men to swear that the accused one was far from the scene of the crime. But surely, Jack, you must have read all this! I had understood that every paper in the States was writing about it.'

'Well, I have read something, it is true, but I had thought it was a story. Maybe these men have some reason in what they do. Maybe they are wronged and have no other way to help themselves.'

'Oh, Jack, don't let me hear you speak so! That is how he speaks—the other one!'

'Baldwin—he speaks like that, does he?'

'And that is why I loathe him so. Oh, Jack, now I can tell you the truth, I loathe him with all my heart; but I fear him also. I fear him for myself, but, above all, I fear him for father. I know that some great sorrow would come upon us if I dared to say what I really felt. That is why I have put him off with half-promises. It was in real truth our only hope. But if you would fly with me, Jack, we could take father with us and live for ever far from the power of these wicked men.'

Again there was the struggle upon McMurdo's face, and again it set like granite.

'No harm shall come to you, Ettie—nor to your father either. As to wicked men, I expect you may find that I am as bad as the worst of them before we're through.'

'No, no, Jack! I would trust you anywhere.'

McMurdo laughed bitterly.

'Good Lord, how little you know of me! Your innocent soul, my darling, could not even guess what is passing in mine. But, halloa, who's the visitor?'

The door had opened suddenly and a young fellow came swaggering in with the air of one who is the master. He was a handsome, dashing young man of about the same age and build as McMurdo himself. Under his broad-brimmed black felt hat, which he had not troubled to remove, a handsome face, with fierce, domineering eyes and a curved, hawkbill of a nose, looked savagely at the pair who sat by the stove.

Ettie had jumped to her feet, full of confusion and alarm.

'I'm glad to see you, Mr Baldwin,' said she. 'You're earlier than I had thought. Come and sit down.'

Baldwin stood with his hands on his hips looking at McMurdo.

'Who is this?' he asked, curtly.

'It's a friend of mine, Mr Baldwin—a new boarder here. Mr McMurdo, can I introduce you to Mr Baldwin?'

The young men nodded in a surly fashion to each other.

'Maybe Miss Ettie has told you how it is with us?' said Baldwin.

'I didn't understand that there was any relation between you.'

'Did you not? Well, you can understand it now. You can take it from me that this young lady is mine, and you'll find it a very fine evening for a walk.'

'Thank you, I am in no humour for a walk.'

'Are you not?' The man's savage eyes were blazing with anger. 'Maybe you are in a humour for a fight, Mr Boarder?'

'That I am,' cried McMurdo, springing to his feet. 'You never said a more welcome word.'

'For God's sake, Jack! Oh, for God's sake!' cried poor, distracted Ettie. 'Oh, Jack, Jack, he will do you a mischief!'

'Oh, it's "Jack," is it?' said Baldwin, with an oath. 'You've come to that already, have you?'

'Oh, Ted, be reasonable—be kind! For my sake, Ted, if ever you loved me, be great-hearted and forgiving!'

'I think, Ettie, that if you were to leave us alone we could get this thing settled,' said McMurdo, quietly. 'Or maybe, Mr Baldwin, you will take a turn down the street with me. It's a fine evening, and there's some open ground beyond the next block.'

'I'll get even with you without needing to dirty my hands,' said his enemy. 'You'll wish you had never set foot in this house before I am through with you.'

'No time like the present,' cried McMurdo.

'I'll choose my own time, mister. You can leave the time to me. See here!' He suddenly rolled up his sleeve and showed upon his forearm a peculiar sign which appeared to have been branded there. It was a circle with a triangle within it. 'D'you know what that means?'

'I neither know nor care!'

'Well, you will know. I'll promise you that. You won't be much older either. Perhaps Miss Ettie can tell you something about it. As to you, Ettie, you'll come back to me on your knees. D'ye hear, girl? On your knees! And then I'll tell you what your punishment may be. You've sowed—and, by the Lord, I'll see that you reap!' He glared at them both in fury. Then he turned upon his heel, and an instant later the outer door had banged behind him.

For a few moments McMurdo and the girl stood in silence. Then she threw her arms around him.

'Oh, Jack, how brave you were! But it is no use—you must fly! Tonight—Jack—tonight! It's your only hope. He will have your life. I read it in his horrible eyes. What chance have you against a dozen of them, with Boss McGinty and all the power of the Lodge behind them?'

McMurdo disengaged her hands, kissed her, and gently pushed her back into a chair.

'There, acushla, there! Don't be disturbed or fear for me. I'm a Freeman myself. I'm after telling your father about it. Maybe I am no better than the others, so don't make a saint of me. Perhaps you hate me, too, now that I've told you as much.'

'Hate you, Jack! While life lasts I could never do that. I've heard that there is no harm in being a Freeman anywhere but here, so why should I think the worse of you for that? But if you are a Freeman, Jack, why should you not go down and make a friend of Boss McGinty? Oh, hasten, Jack, hasten! Get your word in first, or the hounds will be on your trail.'

'I was thinking the same thing,' said McMurdo. 'I'll go right now and fix it. You can tell your father that I'll sleep here tonight and find some other quarters in the morning.'

The bar of McGinty's saloon was crowded as usual, for it was the favourite lounge of all the rougher elements of the town. The man was popular, for he had a rough, jovial disposition which formed a mask, covering a great deal which lay behind it. But, apart from this popularity, the fear in which he was held throughout the township, and, indeed, down the whole thirty miles of the valley and past the moun-tains upon either side of it, was enough in itself to fill his bar, for none could afford to neglect his goodwill.

Besides those secret powers which it was universally believed that he exercised in so pitiless a fashion, he was a high public official, a municipal councillor, and a commissioner for roads, elected to the office through the votes of the ruffians who in turn expected to receive favours at his hands. Rates and taxes were enormous, the public works were notoriously neglected, the accounts were slurred over by bribed auditors, and the decent citizen was terrorized into paying public blackmail, and holding his tongue lest some worse thing befall him. Thus it was that, year by year, Boss McGinty's diamond pins became more obtrusive, his gold chains more weighty across a more gorgeous vest, and his saloon stretched farther and farther, until it threatened to absorb one whole side of the Market Square.

McMurdo pushed open the swinging door of the saloon and made his way amid the crowd of men within, through an atmosphere which was blurred with tobacco smoke and heavy with the smell of spirits. The place was brilliantly lighted, and the huge, heavily gilt mirrors upon every wall reflected and multiplied the garish illumination. There were several bar-tenders in their shirt-sleeves hard at work, mix-ing drinks for the loungers who fringed the broad, heavily metalled counter. At the far end, with his body resting upon the bar, and a cigar stuck at an acute angle from the corner of his mouth, there stood a tall, strong, heavily built man, who could be none other than the famous McGinty himself. He was a black-maned giant, bearded to the cheek-bones, and with a shock of raven hair which fell to his collar. His com-plexion was as swarthy as that of an Italian, and his eyes were of a strange dead black, which, combined with a slight squint, gave them a particularly sinister appearance. All else in the man, his noble proportions, his fine features, and his frank bearing, fitted in with that jovial man-to-man manner which he affected. Here, one would say, is a bluff, honest fellow, whose heart would be sound, however rude his outspoken words might seem. It was only when those dead dark eyes, deep and remorseless, were turned upon a man that he shrank within himself, feeling that he was face to face with an infinite possibility of latent evil, with a strength and courage and cunning behind it which made it a thousand times more deadly.

Having had a good look at his man, McMurdo elbowed his way forward with his usual careless audacity, and pushed himself through the little group of courtiers who were fawn-ing upon the powerful Boss, laughing uproariously at the smallest of his jokes. The young stranger's bold grey eyes looked back fearlessly through their glasses at the deadly black ones which turned sharply upon him.

'Well, young man, I can't call your face to mind.'

'I'm new here, Mr McGinty.'

'You are not so new that you can't give a gentleman his proper title.'

"WELL, YOUNG MAN, I CAN'T CALL YOUR FACE TO MIND."

Illustration by Frank Wiles for the *Strand Maga-zine*, February, 1915.

'He's Councillor McGinty, young man,' said a voice from the group.

'I'm sorry, Councillor. I'm strange to the ways of the place. But I was advised to see you.'

'Well, you see me. This is all there is. What d'you think of me?'

'Well, it's early days. If your heart is as big as your body, and your soul as fine as your face, then I'd ask for nothing better,' said McMurdo.

'By gosh, you've got an Irish tongue in your head, anyhow,' cried the saloon-keeper, not quite certain whether to humour this audacious visitor or to stand upon his dignity. 'So you are good enough to pass my appearance?'

'Sure,' said McMurdo.

'And you were told to see me?'

'I was.'

'And who told you?'

'Brother Scanlan, of Lodge 341, Vermissa. I drink your health, Councillor, and to our better acquaintance.' He raised a glass with which he had been served to his lips and elevated his little finger as he drank it.

McGinty, who had been watching him narrowly, raised his thick black eyebrows.

'Oh, it's like that, is it?' said he. 'I'll have to look a bit closer into this, Mister——'

'McMurdo.'

'A bit closer, Mr McMurdo, for we don't take folk on trust in these parts, nor believe all we're told neither. Come in here for a moment, behind the bar.'

There was a small room there lined round with barrels. McGinty carefully closed the door, and then seated himself on one of them, biting thoughtfully on his cigar, and surveying his companion with those disquieting eyes. For a couple of minutes he sat in complete silence.

McMurdo bore the inspection cheerfully, one hand in his coat-pocket, the other twisting his brown moustache. Suddenly McGinty stooped and produced a wicked-looking revolver.

'See here, my joker,' said he; 'if I thought you were playing any game on us, it would be a short shrift for you.'

'This is a strange welcome,' McMurdo answered, with some dignity, 'for the bodymaster of a Lodge of Freemen to give to a stranger brother.'

'Aye, but it's just that same that you have to prove,' said McGinty, 'and God help you if you fail. Where were you made?'

'Lodge 29, Chicago.'

'When?'

'June 24th, 1872.'

'What bodymaster?'

'James H. Scott.'

'Who is your district ruler?'

'Bartholomew Wilson.'

'Hum! You seem glib enough in your tests. What are you doing here?'

'Working, the same as you, but a poorer job.'

'You have your back answer quick enough.'

'Yes, I was always quick of speech.'

'Are you quick of action?'

'I have had that name among those who knew me best.'

'Well, we may try you sooner than you think. Have you heard anything of the Lodge in these parts?'

'I've heard that it takes a man to be a brother.'

'True for you, Mr McMurdo. Why did you leave Chicago?'

'I'm hanged if I tell you that.'

McGinty opened his eyes. He was not used to being answered in such fashion, and it amused him.

'Why won't you tell me?'

'Because no brother may tell another a lie.'

'Then the truth is too bad to tell?'

'You can put it that way if you like.'

'See here, mister; you can't expect me, as bodymaster, to pass into the Lodge a man for whose past he can't answer.'

McMurdo looked puzzled. Then he took a worn newspaper-cutting from an inner pocket.

'You wouldn't squeal on a fellow?' said he.

'I'll wipe my hand across your face if you say such words to me,' cried McGinty, hotly.

'You are right, Councillor,' said McMurdo, meekly. 'I should apologize. I spoke without thought. Well, I know that I am safe in your hands. Look at that cutting.'

McGinty glanced his eyes over the account of the shooting of one Jonas Pinto, in the Lake Saloon, Market Street, Chicago, in the New Year week of '74.

'Your work?' he asked, as he handed back the paper.

McMurdo nodded.

'Why did you shoot him?'

'I was helping Uncle Sam to make dollars. Maybe mine were not as good gold as his, but they looked as well and were cheaper to make. This man Pinto helped me to shove the queer——'

'To do what?'

'Well, it means to pass the dollars out into circulation. Then he said he would split. Maybe he did split. I didn't wait to see. I just killed him and lighted out for the coal country.'

'Why the coal country?'

' 'Cause I'd read in the papers that they weren't too particular in those parts.'

McGinty laughed.

'You were first a coiner and then a murderer, and you came to these parts because you thought you'd be welcome?'

'That's about the size of it,' McMurdo answered.

'Well, I guess you'll go far. Say, can you make those dollars yet?'

McMurdo took half a dozen from his pocket. 'Those never passed the Washington mint,' said he.

'You don't say!' McGinty held them to the light in his enormous hand, which was as hairy as a gorilla's. 'I can see no difference! Gosh, you'll be a mighty useful brother, I'm thinking. We can do with a bad man or two amongst us, friend McMurdo, for there are times when we have to take our own part. We'd soon be against the wall if we didn't shove back at those that were pushing us.'

'Well, I guess I'll do my share of shoving with the rest of the boys.'

'You seem to have a good nerve. You didn't flinch when I put this pistol on you.'

'It was not me that was in danger.'

'Who, then?'

'It was you, Councillor.' McMurdo drew a cocked pistol from the side-pocket of his pea-jacket. 'I was covering you all the time. I guess my shot would have been as quick as yours.'

McGinty flushed an angry red and then burst into a roar of laughter.

'By gosh!' said he. 'Say, we've had no such holy terror come to hand this many a year. I reckon the Lodge will learn to be proud of you. Well, what the deuce do you want? And can't I speak alone with a gentleman for five minutes but you must butt in upon us?'

The bar-tender stood abashed.

'I'm sorry, Councillor, but it's Mr Ted Baldwin. He says he must see you this very minute.'

The message was unnecessary, for the set, cruel face of the man himself was looking over the servant's shoulder. He pushed the bar-tender out and closed the door on him.

'So,' said he, with a furious glance at McMurdo, 'you got here first, did you? I've a word to say to you, Councillor, about this man.'

'Then say it here and now, before my face,' cried McMurdo.

'I'll say it at my own time, in my own way.'

'Tut, tut!' said McGinty, getting off his barrel. 'This will never do. We have a new brother here, Baldwin, and it's not for us to greet him in such a fashion. Hold out your hand, man, and make it up.'

'Never!' cried Baldwin, in a fury.

'I've offered to fight him if he thinks I have wronged him,' said McMurdo. 'I'll fight him with fists, or, if that won't satisfy him, I'll fight him any other way he chooses. Now I'll leave it to you, Councillor, to judge between us as a bodymaster should.'

'What is it, then?'

'A young lady. She's free to choose for herself.'

'Is she?' cried Baldwin.

'As between two brothers of the Lodge, I should say that she was,' said the Boss.

'Oh, that's your ruling, is it?'

'Yes, it is, Ted Baldwin,' said McGinty, with a wicked stare. 'Is it you that would dispute it?'

'You would throw over one that has stood by you this five years in favour of a man that you never saw before in your life? You're not bodymaster for life, Jack McGinty, and, by God, when next it comes to a vote——'

The Councillor sprang at him like a tiger. His hand closed round the other's neck and he hurled him back across one of the barrels. In his mad fury he would have squeezed the life out of him if McMurdo had not interfered.

'Easy, Councillor! For Heaven's sake, go easy!' he cried, as he dragged him back.

McGinty released his hold, and Baldwin, cowed and shaken, gasping for breath, and shivering in every limb, as one who has looked over the very edge of death, sat up on the barrel over which he had been hurled.

'You've been asking for it this many a day, Ted Baldwin. Now you've got it,' cried McGinty, his huge chest rising and falling. 'Maybe you think if I were voted down from body-master you would find yourself in my shoes. It's for the Lodge to say that. But so long as I am the chief, I'll have no man lift his voice against me or my rulings.'

'I have nothing against you,' mumbled Baldwin, feeling his throat.

'Well, then,' cried the other, relapsing in a moment into a bluff joviality, 'we are all good friends again, and there's an end of the matter.'

He took a bottle of champagne down from the shelf and twisted out the cork.

'See now,' he continued, as he filled three high glasses, 'let us drink the quarrelling toast of the Lodge. After that, as you know, there can be no bad blood between us. Now, then, the left hand on the apple of my throat, I say to you, Ted Baldwin, what is the offence, sir?'

'The clouds are heavy,' answered Baldwin.

'But they will for ever brighten.'

'And this I swear.'

The men drank their wine, and the same ceremony was performed between Baldwin and McMurdo.

'There,' cried McGinty, rubbing his hands, 'that's the end of the black blood. You come under Lodge discipline if it goes farther, and that's a heavy hand in these parts, as Brother Baldwin knows, and as you will very soon find out, Brother McMurdo, if you ask for trouble.'

'Faith, I'd be slow to do that,' said McMurdo. He held out his hand to Baldwin. 'I'm quick to quarrel and quick to forgive. It's my hot Irish blood, they tell me. But it's over for me, and I bear no grudge.'

Baldwin had to take the proffered hand, for the baleful eye of the terrible Boss was upon him. But his sullen face showed how little the words of the other had moved him.

McGinty clapped them both on the shoulders.

'Tut! These girls, these girls!' he cried. 'To think that the same petticoats should come between two of my boys. It's the devil's own luck. Well, it's the colleen inside of them that must settle the question, for it's outside the jurisdiction of a bodymaster, and the Lord be praised for that. We have enough on us, without the women as well. You'll have to be affiliated to Lodge 341, Brother McMurdo. We have our own ways and methods, different to Chicago. Saturday night is our meeting, and if you come then we'll make you free for ever of the Vermissa Valley.'

10 ✦ LODGE 341, VERMISSA

On the day following the evening which had contained so many exciting events McMurdo moved his lodgings from old Jacob Shafter's and took up his quarters at the Widow Mac-Namara's, on the extreme outskirts of the town. Scanlan, his original acquaintance aboard the train, had occasion, shortly afterwards, to move into Vermissa, and the two lodged together. There was no other boarder, and the hostess was an easy-going old Irishwoman who left them to themselves, so that they had a freedom for speech and action welcome to men who had secrets in common. Shafter had relented to the extent of letting McMurdo come to his meals there when he liked, so that his intercourse with Ettie was by no means broken. On the contrary, it drew closer and more intimate as the weeks went by. In his bedroom at his new abode Mc-Murdo felt it to be safe to take out the coining moulds, and under many a pledge of secrecy a number of the brothers from the Lodge were allowed to come in and see them, each of them carrying away in his pocket some examples of the false money, so cunningly struck that there was never the slightest difficulty or danger in passing it. Why, with such a wonderful art at his command, McMurdo should condescend to work at all was a perpetual mystery to his companions, though he made it clear to anyone who asked him that if he lived without any visible means it would very quickly bring the police upon his track.

One policeman was, indeed, after him already, but the incident, as luck would have it, did the adventurer a great deal more good than harm. After the first introduction there were few evenings when he did not find his way to McGinty's saloon, there to make closer acquaintance with 'the boys,' which was the jovial title by which the dangerous gang who infested the place were known to each other. His dashing manner and fearlessness of speech made him a favourite with them all, while the rapid and scientific way in which he polished off his antagonist in an 'all in' bar-room scrap earned the respect of that rough community. Another incident, however, raised him even higher in their estimation.

Just at the crowded hour one night the door opened and a man entered with the quiet blue uniform and peaked cap of the Coal and Iron Police. This was a special body raised by the railways and colliery owners to supplement the efforts of the ordinary civil police, who were perfectly helpless in the face of the organized ruffianism which terrorized the district. There was a hush as he entered, and many a curious glance was cast at him, but the relations between policemen and criminals are peculiar in the States, and McGinty himself, standing behind the counter, showed no surprise when the inspector enrolled himself among his customers.

'A straight whisky, for the night is bitter,' said the police-officer. 'I don't think we have met before, Councillor?'

'You'll be the new captain?' said McGinty.

'That's so. We're looking to you, Councillor, and to the other leading citizens, to help us in upholding law and order in this township. Captain Marvin is my name—of the Coal and Iron.'

'We'd do better without you, Captain Marvin,' said Mc-Ginty, coldly. 'For we have our own police of the township, and no need for any imported goods. What are you but the paid tool of the men of capital, hired by them to club or to shoot your poorer fellow-citizens?'

'Well, well, we won't argue about that,' said the police-officer, good-humouredly. 'I expect we all do our duty same as we see it, but we can't all see it the same.' He had drunk off his glass and had turned to go, when his eyes fell upon the face of Jack McMurdo, who was scowling at his elbow. 'Halloa! halloa!' he cried, looking him up and down. 'Here's an old acquaintance.'

McMurdo shrank away from him.

'I was never a friend to you nor any other cursed copper in my life,' said he.

'An acquaintance isn't always a friend,' said the police-captain, grinning. 'You're Jack McMurdo of Chicago, right enough, and don't you deny it.'

McMurdo shrugged his shoulders.

'I'm not denying it,' said he. 'D'ye think I'm ashamed of my own name?'

'You've got good cause to be, anyhow.'

'What the devil d'you mean by that?' he roared, with his fists clenched.

'No, no, Jack; bluster won't do with me. I was an officer in Chicago before ever I came to this darned coal-bunker, and I know a Chicago crook when I see one.'

McMurdo's face fell.

'Don't tell me that you're Marvin of the Chicago Central!' he cried.

'Just that same old Teddy Marvin at your service. We haven't forgotten the shooting of Jonas Pinto up there.'

'I never shot him.'

'Did you not? That's good impartial evidence, ain't it? Well, his death came in uncommon handy for you, or they would have had you for shoving the queer. Well, we can let that be bygones, for, between you and me—and perhaps I'm going farther than my duty in saying it—they could get no clear case against you, and Chicago's open to you tomorrow.'

'I'm very well where I am.'

'Well, I've given you the office, and you're a sulky dog not to thank me for it.'

'Well, I suppose you mean well, and I do thank you,' said McMurdo, in no very gracious manner.

'It's mum with me so long as I see you living on the straight,' said the captain. 'But, by gum, if you get off on the cross after this it's another story! So good night to you—and good night, Councillor.'

He left the bar-room, but not before he had created a local hero. McMurdo's deeds in far Chicago had been whispered before. He had put off all questions with a smile as one who did not wish to have greatness thrust upon him. But now the thing was officially confirmed. The bar-loafers crowded round him and shook him heartily by the hand. He was free of the community from that time on. He could drink hard and show little trace of it, but that evening, had his mate Scanlan not been at hand to lead him home, the fêted hero would surely have spent his night under the bar.

On a Saturday night McMurdo was introduced to the Lodge. He had thought to pass in without ceremony as being an initiate of Chicago; but there were particular rites in Vermissa of which they were proud, and these had to be undergone by every postulant. The assembly met in a large room reserved for such purposes at the Union House. Some sixty members assembled at Vermissa, but that by no means represented the full strength of the organization, for there were several other lodges in the valley, and others across the mountains on either side, who exchanged members when any serious business was afoot, so that a crime might be done by men who were strangers to the locality. Altogether there were not fewer than five hundred scattered over the coal district.

In the bare assembly room the men were gathered round a long table. At the side was a second one laden with bottles and glasses, on which some members of the company were already turning their eyes. McGinty sat at the head with a flat black velvet cap upon his shock of tangled, black hair and a coloured, purple stole round his neck, so that he seemed to be a priest presiding over some diabolical ritual. To right and left of him were the higher Lodge officials, the cruel, handsome face of Ted Baldwin among them. Each of these wore some scarf or medallion as emblem of his office. They were, for the most part, men of mature age, but the rest of the company consisted of young fellows from eighteen to twenty-five, the ready and capable agents who carried out the commands of their seniors. Among the older men were many whose features showed the tigerish, lawless souls within, but looking at the rank and file it was difficult to believe that these eager and open-faced young fellows were in very truth a dangerous gang of murderers, whose minds had suffered such complete moral perversion that they took a horrible pride in their proficiency at the business, and looked with the deepest respect at the man who had the reputation for making what they called a 'clean job.' To their contorted natures it had become a spirited and chivalrous thing to volunteer for service against some man who had never injured them, and whom, in many cases, they had never seen in their lives. The crime committed, they quarrelled as to who had actually struck the fatal blow, and amused each other and the company by describing the cries and contortions of the murdered man. At first they had shown some secrecy in their arrangements, but at the time which this narrative describes their proceedings were extraordinarily open, for the repeated failures of the law had proved to them that, on the one hand, no one would dare to witness against them, and, on the other, they had an unlimited number of staunch witnesses upon whom they could call, and a well-filled treasure chest from which they could draw the funds to engage the best legal talent in the State. In ten long years of outrage there had been no single conviction, and the only danger that ever threatened the Scowrers lay in the victim himself, who, however out-numbered and taken by surprise, might, and occasionally did, leave his mark upon his assailants.

McMurdo had been warned that some ordeal lay before him, but no one would tell him in what it consisted. He was led now into an outer room by two solemn brothers. Through the plank partition he could hear the murmur of many voices from the assembly within. Once or twice he caught the sound of his own name, and he knew that they were discussing his candidature. Then there entered an inner guard, with a green and gold sash across his chest.

'The bodymaster orders that he shall be trussed, blinded, and entered,' said he. The three of them then removed his coat, turned up the sleeve of his right arm and finally passed a rope round above the elbows and made it fast. They next placed a thick, black cap right over his head and the upper part of his face, so that he could see nothing. He was then led into the assembly hall.

It was pitch-dark and very oppressive under his hood. He heard the rustle and murmur of the people round him, and then the voice of McGinty sounded, dull and distant, through the covering of his ears.

'John McMurdo,' said the voice, 'are you already a member of the Ancient Order of Freemen?'

He bowed in assent.

'Is your lodge No. 29, Chicago?'

He bowed again.

'Dark nights are unpleasant,' said the voice.

'Yes, for strangers to travel,' he answered.

'The clouds are heavy.'

'Yes; a storm is approaching.'

'Are the brethren satisfied?' asked the bodymaster.

There was a general murmur of assent.

'We know, brother, by your sign and by your countersign, that you are indeed one of us,' said McGinty. 'We would have you know, however, that in this county and in other counties of these parts we have certain rites, and also certain duties of our own, which call for good men. Are you ready to be tested?'

'I am.'

'Are you of stout heart?'

'I am.'

'Take a stride forward to prove it.'

As the words were said he felt two hard points in front of his eyes, pressing upon them so that it appeared as if he could not move forward without a danger of losing them. None the less, he nerved himself to step resolutely out, and as he did so the pressure melted away. There was a low murmur of applause.

'He is of stout heart,' said the voice. 'Can you bear pain?'

'As well as another,' he answered.

'Test him!'

It was all he could do to keep himself from screaming out, for an agonizing pain shot through his forearm. He nearly fainted at the sudden shock of it, but he bit his lip and clenched his hands to hide his agony.

'I can take more than that,' said he.

This time there was loud applause. A finer first appearance had never been made in the Lodge. Hands clapped him on the back, and the hood was plucked from his head. He stood blinking and smiling amid the congratulations of the brothers.

'One last word, Brother McMurdo,' said McGinty. 'You have already sworn the oath of secrecy and fidelity, and you are aware that the punishment for any breach of it is instant and inevitable death?'

'I am,' said McMurdo.

'And you accept the rule of the bodymaster for the time being under all circumstances?'

'I do.'

'Then, in the name of Lodge 341, Vermissa, I welcome you to its privileges and debates. You will put the liquor on the table, Brother Scanlan, and we will drink to our worthy brother.'

McMurdo's coat had been brought to him, but before putting it on he examined his right arm, which still smarted heavily. There, on the flesh of the forearm, was a clear-cut circle with a triangle within it, deep and red, as the branding-iron had left it. One or two of his neighbours pulled up their sleeves and showed their own Lodge marks.

'We've all had it,' said one, 'but not all as brave as you over it.'

'Tut! It was nothing,' said he; but it burned and ached all the same.

When the drinks which followed the ceremony of initiation had all been disposed of, the business of the Lodge proceeded.

IT WAS ALL HE COULD DO TO KEEP HIMSELF FROM
SCREAMING OUT . . .

Illustration by Arthur I. Keller for Associated Sunday Magazines, 1914. Frank Wiles illustrated the same scene for the *Strand Magazine*, March, 1915.

McMurdo, accustomed only to the prosaic performances of Chicago, listened with open ears, and more surprise than he ventured to show, to what followed.

'The first business on the agenda paper,' said McGinty, 'is to read the following letter from Division Master Windle, of Merton County, Lodge 249. He says:

DEAR SIR,

There is a job to be done on Andrew Rae, of Rae and Sturmash, coal-owners near this place. You will remember that your Lodge owes us a return, having had the services of two brethren in the matter of the patrolman last fall. If you will send two good men they will be taken charge of by Treasurer Higgins of this Lodge, whose address you know. He will show them when to act, and where.—Yours in freedom.

J. W. WINDLE, D.M.A.O.F.

'Windle has never refused us when we have had occasion to ask for the loan of a man or two, and it is not for us to refuse him.' McGinty paused and looked round the room with his dull, malevolent eyes. 'Who will volunteer for the job?'

Several young fellows held up their hands. The bodymaster looked at them with an approving smile.

'You'll do, Tiger Cormac. If you handle it as well as you did the last you won't be amiss. And you, Wilson.'

'I've no pistol,' said the volunteer, a mere boy in his teens.

'It's your first, is it not? Well, you have to be blooded some time. It will be a great start for you. As to the pistol, you'll find it waiting for you, or I'm mistaken. If you report yourselves on Monday it will be time enough. You'll get a great welcome when you return.'

'Any reward this time?' asked Cormac, a thick-set, dark-faced, brutal-looking young man, whose ferocity had earned him the nickname of 'Tiger.'

'Never mind the reward. You just do it for the honour of the thing. Maybe when it is done there will be a few odd dollars at the bottom of the box.'

'What has the man done?' asked young Wilson.

'Sure, it's not for the likes of you to ask what the man has done. He has been judged over there. That's no business of ours. All we have to do is to carry it out for them, same as they would for us. Speaking of that, two brothers from the Merton Lodge are coming over to us next week to do some business in this quarter.'

'Who are they?' asked someone.

'Faith, it is wiser not to ask. If you know nothing you can testify nothing, and no trouble can come of it. But they are men who will make a clean job when they are about it.'

'And time, too!' cried Ted Baldwin. 'Folk are getting out of hand in these parts. It was only last week that three of our men were turned off by Foreman Blaker. It's been owing him a long time, and he'll get it full and proper.'

'Get what?' McMurdo whispered to his neighbour.

'The business end of a buck-shot cartridge,' cried the man, with a loud laugh. 'What think you of our ways, brother?'

McMurdo's criminal soul seemed to have already absorbed the spirit of the vile association of which he was now a member.

'I like it well,' said he. ' 'Tis a proper place for a lad of mettle.'

Several of those who sat around heard his words and applauded them.

'What's that?' cried the black-maned bodymaster, from the end of the table.

' 'Tis our new brother, sir, who finds our ways to his taste.'

McMurdo rose to his feet for an instant.

'I would say, Worshipful Master, that if a man should be wanted I should take it as an honour to be chosen to help the Lodge.'

There was great applause at this. It was felt that a new sun was pushing its rim above the horizon. To some of the elders it seemed that the progress was a little too rapid.

'I would move,' said the secretary, Harraway, a vulture-faced old greybeard who sat near the chairman, 'that Brother McMurdo should wait until it is the good pleasure of the Lodge to employ him.'

'Sure, that was what I meant. I'm in your hands,' said McMurdo.

'Your time will come, brother,' said the chairman. 'We have marked you down as a willing man, and we believe that you will do good work in these parts. There is a small matter to-night in which you may take a hand, if it so please you.'

'I will wait for something that is worth while.'

'You can come tonight, anyhow, and it will help you to know what we stand for in this community. I will make the announcement later. Meanwhile'—he glanced at his agenda paper—'I have one or two more points to bring before the meeting. First of all, I will ask the treasurer as to our bank balance. There is the pension to Jim Carnaway's widow. He was struck down doing the work of the Lodge, and it is for us to see that she is not the loser.'

'Jim was shot last month when they tried to kill Chester Wilcox, of Marley Creek,' McMurdo's neighbour informed him.

'The funds are good at the moment,' said the treasurer, with the bank-book in front of him. 'The firms have been generous of late. Max Linder and Co. paid five hundred to be left alone. Walker Brothers sent in a hundred, but I took it on myself to return it and ask for five. If I do not hear by Wednesday their winding gear may get out of order. We had to burn their breaker last year before they became reasonable. Then the West Section Coaling Company has paid its annual contribution. We have enough in hand to meet any obligations.'

'What about Archie Swindon?' asked a brother.

'He has sold out and left the district. The old devil left a note for us to say that he had rather be a free crossing-sweeper in New York than a large mine-owner under the power of a ring of blackmailers. By gosh, it was as well that he made a break for it before the note reached us! I guess he dare not show his face in this valley again.'

An elderly, clean-shaven man, with a kindly face and a good brow, rose from the end of the table which faced the chairman.

'Mr Treasurer,' he asked, 'may I ask who has bought the property of this man that we have driven out of the district?'

'Yes, Brother Morris. It has been bought by the State and Merton County Railroad Company.'

'And who bought the mines of Todman and of Lee that came into the market in the same way last year?'

'The same company, Brother Morris.'

'And who bought the ironworks of Manson and of Shuman and of Van Deher and of Atwood, which have all been given up of late?'

'They were all bought by the West Wilmerton General Mining Company.'

'I don't see, Brother Morris,' said the chairman, 'that it matters a nickel to us who buys them, since they can't carry them out of the district.'

'With all respect to you, Worshipful Master, I think that it may matter very much to us. This process has been going on now for ten long years. We are gradually driving all the small men out of trade. What is the result? We find in their places great companies like the Railroad or the General Iron, who have their directors in New York or Philadelphia, and care nothing for our threats. We can take it out of their local bosses, but it only means that others will be sent in their stead. And we are making it dangerous for ourselves. The small men could not harm us. They had not the money nor the power. So long as we did not squeeze them too dry, they would stay on under our power. But if these big companies find that we stand between them and their profits, they will spare no pains and no expense to hunt us down and bring us to court.'

There was a hush at these ominous words, and every face darkened as gloomy looks were exchanged. So omnipotent and unchallenged had they been that the very thought that there was possible retribution in the background had been banished from their minds. And yet the idea struck a chill to the most reckless of them.

'It is my advice,' the speaker continued, 'that we bear less heavily upon the small men. On the day that they have all been driven out the power of this society will have been broken.'

Unwelcome truths are not popular. There were angry cries as the speaker resumed his seat. McGinty rose with gloom upon his brow.

'Brother Morris,' said he, 'you were always a croaker. So long as the members of the Lodge stand together there is no power in this United States that can touch them. Sure, have we not tried it often enough in the law courts? I expect the big companies will find it easier to pay than to fight, same as the little companies do. And now, brethren'—McGinty took off his black velvet cap and his stole as he spoke—'this Lodge has finished its business for the evening, save for one small matter which may be mentioned when we are parting. The time has now come for fraternal refreshment and for harmony.'

Strange indeed is human nature. Here were these men to whom murder was familiar, who again and again had struck down the father of the family, some man against whom they had no personal feeling, without one thought of compunction or of compassion for his weeping wife or helpless children, and yet the tender or pathetic in music could move them to tears. McMurdo had a fine tenor voice, and if he had failed to gain the goodwill of the Lodge before, it could no longer have been withheld after he had thrilled them with 'I'm Sitting on the Stile, Mary,' and 'On the Banks of Allan Water.' In his very first night the new recruit had made himself one of the most popular of the brethren, marked already for advancement and high office. There were other qualities needed, however, besides those of good fellowship, to make a worthy Freeman, and of these he was given an example before the evening was over. The whisky bottle had passed round many times, and the men were flushed and ripe for mischief, when their bodymaster rose once more to address them.

'Boys,' said he, 'there's one man in this town that wants trimming up, and it's for you to see that he gets it. I'm speaking of James Stanger, of the *Herald*. You've seen how he's been opening his mouth against us again?'

There was a murmur of assent, with many a muttered oath. McGinty took a slip of paper from his waistcoat pocket.

' "Law and Order!" That's how he heads it. "Reign of Terror in the Coal and Iron District. Twelve years have now elapsed since the first assassinations which proved the existence of a criminal organization in our midst. From that day these outrages have never ceased, until now they have reached a pitch which makes us the opprobrium of the civilized world. Is it for such results as this that our great country welcomes to its bosom the alien who flies from the despotisms of Europe? Is it that they shall themselves become tyrants over the very men who have given them shelter, and that a state of terrorism and lawlessness should be established under the very shadow of the sacred folds of the starry flag of freedom which would raise horror in our minds if we read of it as existing under the most effete monarchy of the East? The men are known. The organization is patent and public. How long are we to endure it? Can we for ever live——" Sure, I've read enough of the slush!' cried the chairman, tossing the paper down upon the table. 'That's what he says of us. The question I'm asking you is, What shall we say to him?'

'Kill him!' cried a dozen fierce voices.

'I protest against that,' said Brother Morris, the man of the good brow and shaven face. 'I tell you, brethren, that our hand is too heavy in this valley, and that there will come a point where, in self-defence, every man will unite to crush us out. James Stanger is an old man. He is respected in the township and the district. His paper stands for all that is solid in the valley. If that man is struck down, there will be a stir through this State that will only end with our destruction.'

'And how would they bring about our destruction, Mister Stand-back?' cried McGinty. 'Is it by the police? Sure, half of them are in our pay and half of them afraid of us. Or is it by the law courts and the judge? Haven't we tried that before now, and whatever came of it?'

'There is a Judge Lynch that might try the case,' said Brother Morris.

A general shout of anger greeted the suggestion.

'I have but to raise my finger,' cried McGinty, 'and I could put two hundred men into this town that would clear it out from end to end.' Then, suddenly raising his voice and bending his huge black brows into a terrible frown: 'See here, Brother Morris, I have my eye on you, and have had for some time. You've no heart yourself, and you try to take the heart out of others. It will be an ill day for you, Brother Morris, when your own name comes on our agenda paper, and I'm thinking that it's just there that I ought to place it.'

Morris had turned deadly pale and his knees seemed to give way under him as he fell back into his chair. He raised his glass in his trembling hand and drank before he could answer.

'I apologize, Worshipful Master, to you and to every brother in this Lodge if I have said more than I should. I am a faithful member—you all know that—and it is my fear lest evil come to the Lodge which makes me speak in anxious words. But I have greater trust in your judgment than in my own, Worshipful Master, and I promise you that I will not offend again.'

The bodymaster's scowl relaxed as he listened to the humble words.

'Very good, Brother Morris. It's myself that would be sorry if it were needful to give you a lesson. But so long as I am in this chair we shall be a united Lodge in word and in deed. And now, boys,' he continued, looking round at the company, 'I'll say this much—that if Stanger got his full deserts there would be more trouble than we need ask for. These editors hang together, and every journal in the State would be crying out for police and troops. But I guess you can give him a pretty severe warning. Will you fix it, Brother Baldwin?'

'Sure!' said the young man, eagerly.

'How many will you take?'

'Half a dozen, and two to guard the door. You'll come, Gower, and you, Mansel, and you, Scanlan, and the two Willabys.'

'I promised the new brother he should go,' said the chairman.

Ted Baldwin looked at McMurdo with eyes which showed that he had not forgotten nor forgiven.

'Well, he can come if he wants,' he said, in a surly voice. 'That's enough. The sooner we get to work the better.'

The company broke up with shouts and yells and snatches of drunken song. The bar was still crowded with revellers, and many of the brethren remained there. The little band who had been told off for duty passed out into the street, proceeding in twos and threes along the sidewalk so as not to provoke attention. It was a bitterly cold night, with a half-moon shining brilliantly in a frosty, star-spangled sky. The men stopped and gathered in a yard which faced a high building. The words 'Vermissa Herald' were printed in gold lettering between the brightly-lit windows. From within came the clanking of the printing-press.

'Here, you,' said Baldwin to McMurdo; 'you can stand below at the door and see that the road is kept open for us. Arthur Willaby can stay with you. You others come with me. Have no fear, boys, for we have a dozen witnesses that we are in the Union bar at this very moment.'

It was nearly midnight, and the street was deserted save for one or two revellers upon their way home. The party crossed the road and, pushing open the door of the newspaper office, Baldwin and his men rushed in and up the stair which faced them. McMurdo and another remained below. From the room above came a shout, a cry for help, and then the sound of trampling feet and of falling chairs. An instant later a grey-haired man rushed out on to the landing. He was seized before he could get farther, and his spectacles came tinkling down to McMurdo's feet. There was a thud and a groan. He was on his face and half a dozen sticks were clattering together as they fell upon him. He writhed, and his long, thin limbs quivered under the blows. The others ceased at last, but Baldwin, his cruel face set in an infernal smile, was hacking at the man's head, which he vainly endeavoured to defend with his arms. His white hair was dabbled with patches of blood. Baldwin was still stooping over his victim, putting in a short, vicious

"STAND BACK YOURSELF!" HE CRIED.

Illustration by Frank Wiles for the *Strand Magazine*, March, 1915.

blow whenever he could see a part exposed, when McMurdo dashed up the stair and pushed him back.

'You'll kill the man,' said he. 'Drop it!'

Baldwin looked at him in amazement.

'Curse you!' he cried. 'Who are you to interfere—you that are new to the Lodge? Stand back!' He raised his stick, but McMurdo had whipped his pistol out of his hip-pocket.

'Stand back yourself!' he cried. 'I'll blow your face in if you lay a hand on me. As to the Lodge, wasn't it the order of the bodymaster that the man was not to be killed, and what are you doing but killing him?'

'It's truth he says,' remarked one of the men.

'By gosh, you'd best hurry yourselves!' cried the man below. 'The windows are all lighting up and you'll have the whole township on your back inside of five minutes.'

There was indeed the sound of shouting in the street, and a little group of compositors and typesetters was forming in the hall below and nerving itself to action. Leaving the limp and motionless body of the editor at the head of the stair, the criminals rushed down and made their way swiftly along the street. Having reached the Union House, some of them mixed with the crowd in McGinty's saloon, whispering across the bar to the Boss that the job had been well carried through. Others, and among them McMurdo, broke away into side-streets, and so by devious paths to their own homes.

II · THE VALLEY OF FEAR

When McMurdo awoke next morning he had good reason to remember his initiation into the Lodge. His head ached with the effect of the drink, and his arm, where he had been branded, was hot and swollen. Having his own peculiar source of income, he was irregular in his attendance at his work, so he had a late breakfast and remained at home for the morning, writing a long letter to a friend. Afterwards he read the *Daily Herald*. In a special column, put in at the last moment, he read, 'Outrage at the *Herald* Office. Editor seriously injured.' It was a short account of the facts with which he was himself more familiar than the writer could have been. It ended with the statement:

> The matter is now in the hands of the police, but it can hardly be hoped that their exertions will be attended by any better results than in the past. Some of the men were recognized, and there is hope that a conviction may be obtained. The source of the outrage was, it need hardly be said, that infamous society which has held this community in bondage for so long a period, and against which the *Herald* has taken so uncompromising a stand. Mr Stanger's many friends will rejoice to hear that, though he has been cruelly and brutally beaten and has sustained severe injuries about the head, there is no immediate danger to his life.

Below, it stated that a guard of Coal and Iron Police, armed with Winchester rifles, had been requisitioned for the defence of the office.

McMurdo had laid down the paper, and was lighting his pipe with a hand which was shaky from the excesses of the previous evening, when there was a knock outside, and his landlady brought to him a note which had just been handed in by a lad. It was unsigned, and ran thus:

I should wish to speak to you, but had rather not do so in your house. You will find me beside the flagstaff upon Miller Hill. If you will come there now I have something which it is important for you to hear and for me to say.

McMurdo read the note twice with the utmost surprise, for he could not imagine what it meant or who was the author of it. Had it been in a feminine hand he might have imagined that it was the beginning of one of those adventures which had been familiar enough in his past life. But it was the writing of a man, and of a well-educated one, too. Finally, after some hesitation, he determined to see the matter through.

Miller Hill is an ill-kept public park in the very centre of the town. In summer it is a favourite resort of the people, but in winter it is desolate enough. From the top of it one has a view not only of the whole grimy, straggling town, but of the winding valley beneath, with its scattered mines and factories blackening the snow on either side of it, and of the wooded and white-capped ranges which flank it. McMurdo strolled up the winding path hedged in with evergreen until he reached the deserted restaurant which forms the centre of summer gaiety. Beside it was a bare flagstaff, and underneath it a man, his hat drawn down and the collar of his overcoat raised up. When he turned his face McMurdo saw that it was Brother Morris, he who had incurred the anger of the bodymaster the night before. The Lodge sign was given and exchanged as they met.

'I wanted to have a word with you, Mister McMurdo,' said the older man, speaking with a hesitation which showed that he was on delicate ground. 'It was kind of you to come.'

'Why did you not put your name to the note?'

'One has to be cautious, mister. One never knows in times like these how a thing may come back to one. One never knows either who to trust or who not to trust.'

'Surely one may trust brothers of the Lodge?'

'No, no; not always,' cried Morris, with vehemence. 'Whatever we say, even what we think, seems to go back to that man, McGinty.'

'Look here,' said McMurdo, sternly; 'it was only last night, as you know well, that I swore good faith to our bodymaster. Would you be asking me to break my oath?'

'If that is the view you take,' said Morris, sadly, 'I can only say that I am sorry I gave you the trouble to come to meet me. Things have come to a bad pass when two free citizens cannot speak their thoughts to each other.'

McMurdo, who had been watching his companion very narrowly, relaxed somewhat in his bearing.

'Sure, I spoke for myself only,' said he. 'I am a new-comer, as you know, and I am strange to it all. It is not for me to open my mouth, Mr Morris, and if you think well to say anything to me I am here to hear it.'

'And to take it back to Boss McGinty,' said Morris, bitterly.

'Indeed, then, you do me injustice there,' cried McMurdo. 'For myself I am loyal to the Lodge, and so I tell you straight, but I would be a poor creature if I were to repeat to any other what you might say to me in confidence. It will go no further than me, though I warn you that you may get neither help nor sympathy.'

'I have given up looking for either the one or the other,' said Morris. 'I may be putting my very life in your hands by what I say, but, bad as you are—and it seemed to me last night that you were shaping to be as bad as the worst—still you are new to it, and your conscience cannot yet be as hardened as theirs. That was why I thought to speak with you.'

'Well, what have you to say?'

'If you give me away, may a curse be on you!'

'Sure, I said I would not.'

'I would ask you, then, when you joined the Freemen's Society in Chicago, and swore vows of charity and fidelity, did ever it cross your mind that you might find it would lead you to crime?'

'If you call it crime,' McMurdo answered.

'Call it crime!' cried Morris, his voice vibrating with passion. 'You have seen little of it if you can call it anything else. Was it crime last night when a man, old enough to be your father, was beaten till the blood dripped from his white hairs? Was that crime—or what else would you call it?'

'There are some would say it was war,' said McMurdo. 'A war of two classes with all in, so that each struck as best it could.'

'Well, did you think of such a thing when you joined the Freemen's Society at Chicago?'

'No, I'm bound to say I did not.'

'Nor did I when I joined it at Philadelphia. It was just a benefit club and a meeting-place for one's fellows. Then I heard of this place—curse the hour that the name first fell upon my ears!—and I came to better myself. My God, to better myself! My wife and three children came with me. I started a dry goods store in Market Square, and I prospered well. The word had gone round that I was a Freeman, and I was forced to join the local Lodge, same as you did last night. I've the badge of shame on my forearm, and something worse branded on my heart. I found that I was under the orders of a black villain, and caught in a meshwork of crime. What could I do? Every word I said to make things better was taken as treason, same as it was last night. I can't get away, for all I have in the world is in my store. If I leave the society, I know well that it means murder to me, and God knows what to my wife and children. Oh, man, it is awful—awful!' He put his hands to his face, and his body shook with convulsive sobs.

McMurdo shrugged his shoulders.

'You were too soft for the job,' said he. 'You are the wrong sort for such work.'

'I had a conscience and a religion, but they made me a criminal among them. I was chosen for a job. If I backed down I knew well what would come to me. Maybe I'm a coward. Maybe it's the thought of my poor little woman and the children that makes me one. Anyhow, I went. I guess it will haunt me for ever. It was a lonely house, twenty miles from here, over the range yonder. I was told off for the door, same as you were last night. They could not trust me with the job. The others went in. When they came out their hands were crimson to the wrists. As we turned away a child was screaming out of the house behind us. It was a boy of five who had seen his father murdered. I nearly fainted with the horror of it, and yet I had to keep a bold and smiling face, for well I knew that if I did not it would be out of my house that they would come next with their bloody hands, and it would be my little Fred that would be screaming for his father. But I was a criminal then—part sharer in a murder, lost for ever in this world, and lost also in the next. I am a good Catholic, but the priest would have no word with me when he heard I was a Scowrer, and I am excommunicated from my faith. That's how it stands with me. And I see you going down the same road, and I ask you what the end is to be? Are you ready to be a cold-blooded murderer also, or can we do anything to stop it?'

'What would you do?' asked McMurdo abruptly. 'You would inform?'

'God forbid!' cried Morris. 'Sure, the very thought would cost me my life.'

'That's well,' said McMurdo. 'I'm thinking that you are a weak man, and that you make too much of the matter.'

'Too much! Wait till you have lived here longer. Look down the valley. See the cloud of a hundred chimneys that overshadows it. I tell you that the cloud of murder hangs thicker and lower than that over the heads of the people. It is the Valley of Fear—the Valley of Death. The terror is in the hearts of the people from the dusk to the dawn. Wait, young man, and you will learn for yourself.'

'Well, I'll let you know what I think when I have seen more,' said McMurdo, carelessly. 'What is very clear is that you are not the man for the place, and that the sooner you sell out—if you only get a dime a dollar for what the business is worth—the better it will be for you. What you have said is safe with me, but, by gosh! if I thought you were an informer——'

'No, no!' cried Morris, piteously.

'Well, let it rest at that. I'll bear what you have said in mind, and maybe some day I'll come back to it. I expect you meant kindly by speaking to me like this. Now I'll be getting home.'

'One word before you go,' said Morris. 'We may have been seen together. They may want to know what we have spoken about.'

'Ah, that's well thought of.'

'I offer you a clerkship in my store.'

'And I refuse it. That's our business. Well, so long, Brother Morris, and may you find things go better with you in the future.'

That same afternoon, as McMurdo sat smoking, lost in thought, beside the stove of his sitting-room, the door swung open, and its framework was filled with the huge figure of Boss McGinty. He passed the sign, and then, seating himself opposite to the young man, he looked at him steadily for some time, a look which was as steadily returned.

'I'm not much of a visitor, Brother McMurdo,' he said, at last. 'I guess I am too busy over the folk that visit me. But I thought I'd stretch a point and drop down to see you in your own house.'

'I'm proud to see you here, Councillor,' McMurdo answered, heartily, bringing his whisky bottle out of the cupboard. 'It's an honour that I had not expected.'

'How's the arm?' asked the Boss.

McMurdo made a wry face.

'Well, I'm not forgetting it,' he said. 'But it's worth it.'

'Yes, it's worth it,' the other answered, 'to those that are loyal, and go through with it, and are a help to the Lodge. What were you speaking to Brother Morris about on Miller Hill this morning?'

The question came so suddenly that it was well that he had his answer prepared. He burst into a hearty laugh.

'Morris didn't know I could earn a living here at home. He shan't know either, for he has got too much conscience for the likes of me. But he's a good-hearted old chap. It was his idea that I was at a loose end, and that he would do me a good turn by offering me a clerkship in a dry goods store.'

'Oh, that was it?'

'Yes, that was it.'

'And you refused it?'

'Sure. Couldn't I earn ten times as much in my own bedroom with four hours' work?'

'That's so. But I wouldn't get about too much with Morris.'

'Why not?'

'Well, I guess because I tell you not. That's enough for most folk in these parts.'

'It may be enough for most folks, but it ain't enough for me, Councillor,' said McMurdo, boldly. 'If you are a judge of men you'll know that.'

The swarthy giant glared at him, and his hairy paw closed for an instant round the glass as though he would hurl it at the head of his companion. Then he laughed in his loud, boisterous, insincere fashion.

'You're a queer card, for sure,' said he. 'Well, if you want reasons I'll give them. Did Morris say nothing to you against the Lodge?'

'No.'

'Nor against me?'

'No.'

'Well, that's because he daren't trust you. But in his heart he is not a loyal brother. We know that well, so we watch him, and we wait for the time to admonish him. I'm thinking that the time is drawing near. There's no room for scabby sheep in our pen. But if you keep company with a disloyal man, we might think that you were disloyal, too. See?'

'There's no chance of my keeping company with him, for I dislike the man,' McMurdo answered. 'As to being disloyal, if it was any man but you, he would not use the word to me twice.'

'Well, that's enough,' said McGinty, draining off his glass. 'I came down to give you a word in season, and you've had it.'

'I'd like to know,' said McMurdo, 'how you ever came to learn that I had spoken with Morris at all.'

McGinty laughed.

'It's my business to know what goes on in this township,' said he. 'I guess you'd best reckon on my hearing all that passes. Well, time's up, and I'll just say——'

But his leave-taking was cut short in a very unexpected fashion. With a sudden crash the door flew open, and three frowning, intent faces glared in at them from under the peaks of police caps. McMurdo sprang to his feet and half drew his revolver, but his arm stopped midway as he became conscious that two Winchester rifles were levelled at his head. A man in uniform advanced into the room, a six-shooter in his hand.

WITH A SUDDEN CRASH THE DOOR FLEW OPEN . . .

Illustration by Frank Wiles for the *Strand Magazine*, April, 1915.

It was Captain Marvin, once of Chicago, and now of the Coal and Iron Constabulary. He shook his head with a half smile at McMurdo.

'I thought you'd be getting into trouble, Mr Crooked McMurdo, of Chicago,' said he. 'Can't keep out of it, can you? Take your hat and come along with us.'

'I guess you'll pay for this, Captain Marvin,' said McGinty. 'Who are you, I'd like to know, to break into a house in this fashion, and molest honest, law-abiding men?'

'You're standing out in this deal, Councillor McGinty,' said the police-captain. 'We are not out after you, but after this man McMurdo. It is for you to help, not to hinder us in our duty.'

'He is a friend of mine, and I'll answer for his conduct,' said the Boss.

'By all accounts, Mr McGinty, you may have to answer for your own conduct some of these days,' the police captain answered. 'This man McMurdo was a crook before ever he came here, and he's a crook still. Cover him, patrolman, while I disarm him.'

'There's my pistol,' said McMurdo, coolly. 'Maybe, Captain Marvin, if you and I were alone and face to face, you would not take me so easily.'

'Where's your warrant?' asked McGinty. 'By gosh! a man might as well live in Russia as in Vermissa while folk like you are running the police. It's a capitalist outrage, and you'll hear more of it, I reckon.'

'You do what you think is your duty the best way you can, Councillor. We'll look after ours.'

'What am I accused of?' asked McMurdo.

'Of being concerned in the beating of old Editor Stanger at the *Herald* office. It wasn't your fault that it isn't a murder charge.'

'Well, if that's all you have against him,' cried McGinty, with a laugh, 'you can save yourself a deal of trouble by dropping it right now. This man was with me in my saloon playing poker up to midnight, and I can bring a dozen to prove it.'

'That's your affair, and I guess you can settle it in court tomorrow. Meanwhile, come on, McMurdo, and come quietly if you don't want a gun-butt across your head. You stand wide, Mr McGinty, for I warn you I will brook no resistance when I am on duty.'

So determined was the appearance of the captain that both McMurdo and his Boss were forced to accept the situation. The latter managed to have a few whispered words with the prisoner before they parted.

'What about——' he jerked his thumb upwards to signify the coining plant.

'All right,' whispered McMurdo, who had devised a safe hiding-place under the floor.

'I'll bid you good-bye,' said the Boss, shaking hands. 'I'll see Reilly, the lawyer, and take the defence upon myself. Take my word for it that they won't be able to hold you.'

'I wouldn't bet on that. Guard the prisoner, you two, and shoot him if he tries any games. I'll search the house before I leave.'

Marvin did so, but apparently found no trace of the concealed plant. When he had descended he and his men escorted McMurdo to the headquarters. Darkness had fallen and a keen blizzard was blowing, so that the streets were nearly deserted, but a few loiterers followed the group, and, emboldened by invisibility, shouted imprecations at the prisoner.

'Lynch the cursed Scowrer!' they cried. 'Lynch him!' They laughed and jeered as he was pushed into the police depot. After a short formal examination from the inspector-in-charge, he was handed on to the common cell. Here he found Baldwin and three other criminals of the night before, all arrested that afternoon, and waiting their trial next morning.

But even within this inner fortress of the law the long arm of the Freemen was able to extend. Late at night there came a jailer with a straw bundle for their bedding, out of which he extracted two bottles of whisky, some glasses, and a pack of cards. They spent an hilarious night without an anxious thought as to the ordeal of the morning.

Nor had they cause, as the result was to show. The magistrate could not possibly, on the evidence, have brought in the sentence which would have carried the matter to a higher court. On the one hand, the compositors and pressmen were forced to admit that the light was uncertain, that they were themselves much perturbed, and that it was difficult for them to absolutely swear to the identity of the assailants, although they believed that the accused were among them. Cross-examined by the clever attorney who had been engaged by McGinty, they were even more nebulous in their evidence. The injured man had already deposed that he was so taken by surprise by the suddenness of the attack that he could state nothing beyond the fact that the first man who struck him wore a moustache. He added that he knew them to be Scowrers, since no one else in the community could possibly have any enmity to him, and he had long been threatened on account of his outspoken editorials. On the other hand, it was clearly shown by the united and unfaltering evidence of six citizens, including that high municipal official, Councillor McGinty, that the men had been at a card party at the Union House until an hour very much later than the commission of the outrage. Needless to say that they were discharged with something very near to an apology from the Bench for the inconvenience to which they had been put, together with an implied censure of Captain Marvin and the police for their officious zeal.

The verdict was greeted with loud applause by a court in which McMurdo saw many familiar faces. Brothers of the Lodge smiled and waved. But there were others who sat with compressed lips and brooding eyes as the men filed out of the dock. One of them, a little, dark-bearded, resolute fellow, put the thoughts of himself and comrades into words as the ex-prisoners passed him.

'You damned murderers!' he said. 'We'll fix you yet.'

I2 ◆ THE DARKEST HOUR

If anything had been needed to give an impetus to Jack McMurdo's popularity among his fellows, it would have been his arrest and acquittal. That a man on the very night of joining the Lodge should have done something which brought him before the magistrate was a new record in the annals of the society. Already he had earned the reputation of a good boon companion, a cheery reveller, and withal a man of high temper, who would not take an insult even from the all-powerful Boss himself. But, in addition to this, he impressed his comrades with the idea that among them all there was not one whose brain was so ready to devise a bloodthirsty scheme, or whose hand would be more capable of carrying it out. 'He'll be the boy for the clean job,' said the oldsters to each other, and waited their time until they could set him to his work. McGinty had instruments enough already, but he recognized that this was a supremely able one. He felt like a man holding a fierce bloodhound in leash. There were curs to do the smaller work, but some day he would slip this creature upon its prey. A few members of the Lodge, Ted Baldwin among them, resented the rapid rise of the stranger, and hated him for it, but they kept clear of him, for he was as ready to fight as to laugh.

But if he gained favour with his fellows, there was another quarter, one which had become even more vital to him, in which he lost it. Ettie Shafter's father would have nothing more to do with him, nor would he allow him to enter the house. Ettie herself was too deeply in love to give him up altogether, and yet her own good sense warned her of what would come from a marriage with a man who was regarded as a criminal. One morning after a sleepless night she determined to see him, possibly for the last time, and make one strong endeavour to draw him from those evil influences which were sucking him down. She went to his house, as he had often begged her to do, and made her way into the room which he used as his sitting-room. He was seated at a table with his back turned and a letter in front of him. A sudden spirit of girlish mischief came over her—she was still only nineteen. He had not heard her when she pushed open the door. Now she tip-toed forward, and laid her hand lightly upon his bended shoulders.

If she had expected to startle him, she certainly succeeded, but only in turn to be startled herself. With a tiger spring he turned on her, and his right hand was feeling for her throat. At the same instant, with the other hand he crumpled up the paper that lay before him. For a moment he stood glaring. Then astonishment and joy took the place of the ferocity which had convulsed his features—a ferocity which had sent her shrinking back in horror as from something which had never before intruded into her gentle life.

'It's you!' said he, mopping his brow. 'And to think that you should come to me, heart of my hearts, and I should find nothing better to do than to want to strangle you! Come then, darling,' and he held out his arms. 'Let me make it up to you.'

But she had not recovered from that sudden glimpse of guilty fear which she had read in the man's face. All her woman's instinct told her that it was not the mere fright of a man who is startled. Guilt—that was it—guilt and fear.

'What's come over you, Jack?' she cried. 'Why were you so scared of me? Oh, Jack, if your conscience was at ease, you would not have looked at me like that.'

'Sure, I was thinking of other things, and when you came tripping so lightly on those fairy feet of yours——'

"GIVE IT UP, JACK! FOR MY SAKE—FOR GOD'S SAKE, GIVE IT UP!"

Illustration by Arthur I. Keller for Associated Sunday Magazines, 1914. Frank Wiles illustrated the same scene for the *Strand Magazine*, April, 1915.

'No, no; it was more than that, Jack.' Then a sudden suspicion seized her. 'Let me see that letter you were writing.'

'Ah, Ettie, I couldn't do that.'

Her suspicions became certainties.

'It's to another woman!' she cried. 'I know it. Why else should you hold it from me? Was it to your wife that you were writing? How am I to know that you are not a married man —you, a stranger, that nobody knows?'

'I am not married, Ettie. See now, I swear it. You're the only woman on earth to me. By the Cross of Christ, I swear it!'

He was so white with passionate earnestness that she could not but believe him.

'Well, then,' she cried, 'why will you not show me the letter?'

'I'll tell you, acushla,' said he. 'I'm under oath not to show it, and just as I wouldn't break my word to you, so I would keep it to those who hold my promise. It's the business of the Lodge, and even to you it's secret. And if I was scared when a hand fell on me, can't you understand it when it might have been the hand of a detective?'

She felt that he was telling the truth. He gathered her into his arms, and kissed away her fears and doubts.

'Sit here by me, then. It's a queer throne for such a queen, but it's the best your poor lover can find. He'll do better for you some of these days, I'm thinking. Now your mind is easy once again, is it not?'

'How can it ever be at ease, Jack, when I know that you are a criminal among criminals—when I never know the day that I may hear that you are in the dock for murder? McMurdo the Scowrer—that was what one of our boarders called you yesterday. It went through my heart like a knife.'

'Sure, hard words break no bones.'

'But they were true.'

'Well, dear, it's not as bad as you think. We are but poor men that are trying in our own way to get our rights.'

Ettie threw her arms round her lover's neck.

'Give it up, Jack! For my sake—for God's sake, give it up! It was to ask you that I came here today. Oh, Jack, see, I beg it of you on my bended knees. Kneeling here before you, I implore you to give it up.'

He raised her, and soothed her with her head against his breast.

'Sure, my darlin', you don't know what it is you are asking. How could I give it up when it would be to break my oath and to desert my comrades? If you could see how things stand with me, you could never ask it of me. Besides, if I wanted to, how could I do it? You don't suppose that the Lodge would let a man go free with all its secrets?'

'I've thought of that, Jack. I've planned it all. Father has saved some money. He is weary of this place, where the fear of these people darkens our lives. He is ready to go. We would fly together to Philadelphia or New York, where we should be safe from them.'

McMurdo laughed.

'The Lodge has a long arm. Do you think it could not stretch from here to Philadelphia or New York?'

'Well, then, to the West, or to England, or to Sweden, whence father came. Anywhere to get away from this Valley of Fear.'

McMurdo thought of old Brother Morris.

'Sure, it is the second time I have heard the valley so

named,' said he. 'The shadow does indeed seem to lie heavy on some of you.'

'It darkens every moment of our lives. Do you suppose that Ted Baldwin has ever forgiven us? If it were not that he fears you, what do you suppose that our chances would be? If you saw the look in those dark, hungry eyes of his when they fall on me!'

'By gosh! I'd teach him better manners if I caught him at it. But see here, little girl. I can't leave here. I can't. Take that from me once and for all. But if you will leave me to find my own way, I will try to prepare a way of getting honourably out of it.'

'There is no honour in such a matter.'

'Well, well, it's just how you look at it. But if you'll give me six months I'll work it so as I can leave without being ashamed to look others in the face.'

The girl laughed with joy.

'Six months!' she cried. 'Is it a promise?'

'Well, it may be seven or eight. But within a year at the farthest we will leave the valley behind us.'

It was most that Ettie could obtain, and yet it was something. There was this distant light to illuminate the gloom of the immediate future. She returned to her father's house more light-hearted than she had ever been since Jack McMurdo had come into her life.

It might be thought that as a member all the doings of the society would be told to him, but he was soon to discover that the organization was wider and more complex than the simple Lodge. Even Boss McGinty was ignorant as to many things, for there was an official named the county delegate living at Hobson's Patch, farther down the line, who had power over several different Lodges, which he wielded in a sudden and arbitrary way. Only once did McMurdo see him, a sly little grey-haired rat of a man with a slinking gait and a sidelong glance which was charged with malice. Evans Pott was his name, and even the great Boss of Vermissa felt towards him something of the repulsion and fear which the huge Danton may have felt for the puny but dangerous Robespierre. **59**

One day Scanlan, who was McMurdo's fellow-boarder, received a note from McGinty, enclosing one from Evans Pott, which informed him that he was sending over two good men, Lawler and Andrews, who had instructions to act in the neighbourhood, though it was best for the cause that no particulars as to their objects should be given. Would the bodymaster see to it that suitable arrangements be made for their lodgings and comfort until the time for action should arrive? McGinty added that it was impossible for anyone to remain secret at the Union House, and that, therefore, he would be obliged if McMurdo and Scanlan would put the strangers up for a few days in their boarding-house.

The same evening the two men arrived, each carrying his grip-sack. Lawler was an elderly man, shrewd, silent, and self-contained, clad in an old black frock-coat, which, with his soft felt hat and ragged, grizzled beard, gave him a general resemblance to an itinerant preacher. His companion, Andrews, was little more than a boy, frank-faced and cheerful, with the breezy manner of one who is out for a holiday, and means to enjoy every minute of it. Both of the men were total abstainers, and behaved in all ways as exemplary members of

59 *the huge Danton may have felt for the puny but dangerous Robespierre.* Georges Jacques Danton, 1759–1794, French revolutionist, was a lawyer who won immense popularity through his powerful oratory. As a leader of the Cordeliers, he championed the extreme left in the National Assembly and was instrumental in the overthrow of the monarchy in 1792. The rise of the extremists led by Maximillien Robespierre, 1758–1794, led Danton to seek a relatively moderate course. But Danton gradually lost his influence; early in 1794 he was arrested on a charge of conspiracy and, after a mock trial, guillotined.

society, with the one single exception that they were assassins who had often proved themselves to be most capable instruments for this Association of murder. Lawler had already carried out fourteen commissions of the kind, and Andrews three.

They were, as McMurdo found, quite ready to converse about their deeds in the past, which they recounted with the half-bashful pride of men who had done good and unselfish service for the community. They were reticent, however, as to the immediate job in hand.

'They chose us because neither I nor the boy here drink,' Lawler explained. 'They can count on us saying no more than we should. You must not take it amiss, but it is the orders of the county delegate that we obey.'

'Sure, we are all in it together,' said Scanlan, McMurdo's mate, as the four sat together at supper.

'That's true enough, and we'll talk till the cows come home of the killing of Charlie Williams, or of Simon Bird, or any other job in the past. But till the work is done we say nothing.'

'There are half a dozen about here that I have a word to say to,' said McMurdo, with an oath. 'I suppose it isn't Jack Knox, of Ironhill, that you are after? I'd go some way to see him get his deserts.'

'No; it's not him yet.'

'Or Herman Strauss?'

'No, nor him either.'

'Well, if you won't tell us, we can't make you, but I'd be glad to know.'

Lawler smiled, and shook his head. He was not to be drawn.

In spite of the reticence of their guests, Scanlan and McMurdo were quite determined to be present at what they called the 'fun.' When, therefore, at an early hour one morning McMurdo heard them creeping down the stairs, he awakened Scanlan, and the two hurried on their clothes. When they were dressed they found that the others had stolen out, leaving the door open behind them. It was not yet dawn, and by the light of the lamps they could see the two men some distance down the street. They followed them warily, treading noiselessly in the deep snow.

The boarding-house was near the edge of the township, and soon they were at the cross-roads which are beyond its boundary. Here three men were waiting, with whom Lawler and Andrews held a short, eager conversation. Then they all moved on together. It was clearly some notable job which needed numbers. At this point there are several trails which lead to various mines. The strangers took that which led to the Crow Hill, a huge business which was in strong hands, who had been able, thanks to their energetic and fearless New England manager, Josiah H. Dunn, to keep some order and discipline during the long reign of terror.

Day was breaking now, and a line of workmen were slowly making their way, singly and in groups, along the blackened path.

McMurdo and Scanlan strolled on with the others, keeping in sight of the men whom they followed. A thick mist lay over them, and from the heart of it there came the sudden scream of a steam whistle. It was the ten-minute signal before the cages descended and the day's labour began.

When they reached the open space round the mine-shaft there were a hundred miners waiting, stamping their feet and blowing on their fingers, for it was bitterly cold. The strangers stood in a little group under the shadow of the engine-house. Scanlan and McMurdo climbed a heap of slag, from which the whole scene lay before them. They saw the mine engineer, a great bearded Scotsman named Menzies, come out of the engine-house and blow his whistle for the cages to be lowered. At the same instant a tall, loose-framed young man, with a clean-shaven, earnest face, advanced eagerly towards the pit-head. As he came forward his eyes fell upon the group, silent and motionless, under the engine-house. The men had drawn down their hats and turned up their collars to screen their faces. For a moment the presentiment of death laid its cold hand upon the manager's heart. At the next he had shaken it off and saw only his duty towards intrusive strangers.

'Who are you?' he asked, as he advanced. 'What are you loitering there for?'

There was no answer, but the lad Andrews stepped forward and shot him in the stomach. The hundred waiting miners stood as motionless and helpless as if they were paralysed. The manager clapped his two hands to the wound and doubled himself up. Then he staggered away, but another of the assassins fired, and he went down sideways, kicking and clawing among a heap of clinkers. Menzies, the Scotsman, gave a roar of rage at the sight, and rushed with an iron spanner at the murderers, but was met by two balls in the face, which dropped him dead at their very feet. There was a surge forward of some of the miners, and an inarticulate cry of pity and of anger, but a couple of the strangers emptied their six-shooters over the heads of the crowd, and they broke and scattered, some of them rushing wildly back to their homes in Vermissa. When a few of the bravest had rallied, and there was a return to the mine, the murderous gang had vanished in the mists of the morning without a single witness being able to swear to the identity of these men who in front of a hundred spectators had wrought this double crime.

Scanlan and McMurdo made their way back, Scanlan somewhat subdued, for it was the first murder job that he had seen with his own eyes, and it appeared less funny than he had been led to believe. The horrible screams of the dead manager's wife pursued them as they hurried to the town. McMurdo was absorbed and silent, but he showed no sympathy for the weakening of his companion.

'Sure, it is like a war,' he repeated. 'What is it but a war between us and them, and we hit back where we best can?'

There was high revel in the Lodge room at the Union House that night, not only over the killing of the manager and engineer of the Crow Hill mine, which would bring this organization into line with the other blackmailed and terror-stricken companies of the district, but also over a distant triumph which had been wrought by the hands of the Lodge itself. It would appear that when the county delegate had sent over five good men to strike a blow in Vermissa, he had demanded that, in return, three Vermissa men should be secretly selected and sent across to kill William Hales, of Stake Royal, one of the best-known and most popular mine-owners in the Gilmerton district, a man who was believed not to have an enemy in the world, for he was in all ways a pattern employer. He had insisted, however, upon efficiency in the work, and had therefore paid off certain drunken and idle *employés* who were members of the all-powerful society.

60 contretemps. French: an unexpected embarrassing occurrence; an awkward incident.

Coffin notices hung outside his door had not weakened his resolution, and so in a free, civilized country he found himself condemned to death.

The execution had now been duly carried out. Ted Baldwin, who sprawled in the seat of honour beside the bodymaster, had been the chief of the party. His flushed face and glazed, bloodshot eyes told of sleeplessness and drink. He and his two comrades had spent the night before among the mountains. They were unkempt and weather-stained. But no heroes, returning from a forlorn hope, could have had a warmer welcome from their comrades. The story was told and retold amid cries of delight and shouts of laughter. They had waited for their man as he drove home at nightfall, taking their station at the top of a steep hill, where his horse must be at a walk. He was so furred to keep out the cold that he could not lay his hand on his pistol. They had pulled him out and shot him again and again.

None of them knew the man, but there is eternal drama in a killing, and they had shown the Scowrers of Gilmerton that the Vermissa men were to be relied upon. There had been one **60** *contretemps*, for a man and his wife had driven up while they were still emptying their revolvers into the silent body. It had been suggested that they should shoot them both, but they were harmless folk who were not connected with the mines, so they were sternly bidden to drive on and keep silent, lest a worse thing befall them. And so the blood-mottled figure had been left as a warning to all such hard-hearted employers, and the three noble avengers had hurried off into the mountains, where unbroken Nature comes down to the very edge of the furnaces and the slag-heaps.

It had been a great day for the Scowrers. The shadow had fallen even darker over the valley. But as the wise general chooses the moment of victory in which to redouble his efforts, so that his foes may have no time to steady themselves after disaster, so Boss McGinty, looking out upon the scene of his operations with brooding and malicious eyes, had devised a new attack upon those who opposed him. That very night, as the half-drunken company broke up, he touched McMurdo on the arm and led him aside into that inner room where they had their first interview.

'See here, my lad,' said he, 'I've got a job that's worthy of you at last. You'll have the doing of it in your own hands.'

'Proud I am to hear it,' McMurdo answered.

'You can take two men with you—Manders and Reilly. They have been warned for service. We'll never be right in this district until Chester Wilcox has been settled, and you'll have the thanks of every Lodge in the coalfields if you can down him.'

'I'll do my best, anyhow. Who is he, and where shall I find him?'

McGinty took his eternal half-chewed, half-smoked cigar from the corner of his mouth, and proceeded to draw a rough diagram on a page torn from his note-book.

'He's the chief foreman of the Iron Dyke Company. He's a hard citizen, an old colour-sergeant of the war, all scars and grizzle. We've had two tries at him, but had no luck, and Jim Carnaway lost his life over it. Now it's for you to take it over. That's the house, all alone at the Iron Dyke cross-road, same as you see here in the map, without another within earshot. It's no good by day. He's armed, and shoots quick and straight, with no questions asked. But at night—well, there he is, with his wife, three children, and a hired help. You can't pick or choose. It's all or none. If you could get a bag of blasting powder at the front door with a slow match to it——'

'What's the man done?'

'Didn't I tell you he shot Jim Carnaway?'

'Why did he shoot him?'

'What in thunder has that to do with you? Carnaway was about his house at night, and he shot him. That's enough for me and you. You've got to set the thing right.'

'There's these two women and the children. Do they go up, too?'

'They have to, else how can we get him?'

'It seems hard on them, for they've done nothing amiss.'

'What sort of talk is this? Do you stand back from it?'

'Easy, Councillor, easy. What have I ever said or done that you should think I would be after standing back from an order of the bodymaster of my own Lodge? If it's right or if it's wrong it's for you to decide.'

'You'll do it, then?'

'Of course I will do it.'

'When?'

'Well, you had best give me a night or two that I may see the house and make my plans. Then——'

'Very good,' said McGinty, shaking him by the hand. 'I leave it with you. It will be a great day when you bring us the news. It's just the last stroke that will bring them all to their knees.'

McMurdo thought long and deeply over the commission which had been so suddenly placed in his hands. The isolated house in which Chester Wilcox lived was about five miles off in an adjacent valley. That very night he started off all alone to prepare for the attempt. It was daylight before he returned from his reconnaissance. Next day he interviewed his two subordinates, Manders and Reilly, reckless youngsters, who were as elated as if it were a deer hunt. Two nights later they met outside the town, all three armed, and one of them carrying a sack stuffed with the powder which was used in the quarries. It was two in the morning before they came to the lonely house. The night was a windy one, with broken clouds drifting swiftly across the face of a three-quarter moon. They had been warned to be on their guard against bloodhounds, so they moved forward cautiously, with their pistols cocked in their hands. But there was no sound save the howling of the wind and no movement but the swaying branches above them. McMurdo listened at the door of the lonely house, but all was still within. Then he leaned the powder bag against it, ripped a hole in it with his knife, and attached the fuse. When it was well alight, he and his two companions took to their heels, and were some distance off, safe and snug in a sheltering ditch, before the shattering roar of the explosion, with the low, deep rumble of the collapsing building, told them that their work was done. No cleaner job had ever been carried out in the bloodstained annals of the society. But, alas that work so well organized and boldly conceived should all have gone for nothing! Warned by the fate of the various victims, and knowing that he was marked down for destruction, Chester Wilcox had moved himself and his family only the day before to some safer and less known quarters, where a guard of police should watch over them. It was an empty house which had been torn down by the gunpowder, and the grim old colour-sergeant of the war was still teaching discipline to the miners of Iron Dyke.

'Leave him to me,' said McMurdo. 'He's my man, and I'll get him sure, if I have to wait a year for him.'

A vote of thanks and confidence was passed in full Lodge, and so for the time the matter ended. When a few weeks later it was reported in the papers that Wilcox had been shot at from an ambuscade, it was an open secret that McMurdo was still at work upon his unfinished job.

Such were the methods of the Society of Freemen, and such were the deeds of the Scowrers by which they spread their rule of fear over the great and rich district which was for so long a period haunted by their terrible presence. Why should these pages be stained by further crimes? Have I not said enough to show the men and their methods? These deeds are written in history, and there are records wherein one may read the details of them. There one may learn of the shooting of Policemen Hunt and Evans because they had ventured to arrest two members of the society—a double outrage planned at the Vermissa Lodge, and carried out in cold blood upon two helpless and disarmed men. There also one may read of the shooting of Mrs Larbey whilst she was nursing her husband, who had been beaten almost to death by orders of Boss McGinty. The killing of the elder Jenkins, shortly followed by that of his brother, the mutilation of James Murdoch, the blowing-up of the Staphouse family, and the murder of the Stendals all followed hard upon each other in the same terrible winter. Darkly the shadow lay upon the Valley of Fear. The spring had come with running brooks and blossoming trees. There was hope for all Nature, bound so long in an iron grip; but nowhere was there any hope for the men and women who lived under the yoke of the terror. Never had the cloud above them been so dark and hopeless as in the early summer of the year '75.

13 ◆ DANGER

It was the height of the reign of terror. McMurdo, who had already been appointed inner Deacon, with every prospect of some day succeeding McGinty as bodymaster, was now so necessary to the councils of his comrades that nothing was done without his help and advice. The more popular he became, however, with the Freemen, the blacker were the scowls which greeted him as he passed along the streets of Vermissa. In spite of their terror the citizens were taking heart to bind themselves together against their oppressors. Rumours had reached the Lodge of secret gatherings in the *Herald* office and of distribution of firearms among the law-abiding people. But McGinty and his men were undisturbed by such reports. They were numerous, resolute, and well armed. Their opponents were scattered and powerless. It would all end, as it had done in the past, in aimless talk, and possibly in important arrests. So said McGinty, McMurdo, and all the bolder spirits.

It was a Saturday evening in May. Saturday was always the Lodge night, and McMurdo was leaving his house to attend it, when Morris, the weaker of the Order, came to see him. His brow was creased with care and his kindly face was drawn and haggard.

'Can I speak with you freely, Mr McMurdo?'

'Sure.'

'I can't forget that I spoke my heart to you once, and that you kept it to yourself, even though the Boss himself came to ask you about it.'

'What else could I do if you trusted me? It wasn't that I agreed with what you said.'

'I know that well. But you are the one that I can speak to and be safe. I've a secret here'—he put his hand to his breast —'and it is just burning the life out of me. I wish it had come to any one of you but me. If I tell it, it will mean murder, for sure. If I don't, it may bring the end of us all. God help me, but I am near out of my wits over it!'

McMurdo looked at the man earnestly. He was trembling in every limb. He poured some whisky into a glass and handed it to him.

'That's the physic for the likes of you,' said he. 'Now let me hear of it.'

Morris drank, and his white face took a tinge of colour.

'I can tell it you all in one sentence,' said he. 'There's a detective on our trail.'

McMurdo stared at him in astonishment.

'Why, man, you're crazy!' he said. 'Isn't the place full of police and detectives, and what harm did they ever do us?'

'No, no; it's no man of the district. As you say, we know them, and it is little that they can do. But you've heard of Pinkerton's?' **61**

'I've read of some folk of that name.'

'Well, you can take it from me you've no show when they are on your trail. It's not a take-it-or-miss-it Government concern. It's a dead earnest business proposition that's out for results, and keeps out till, by hook or by crook, it gets them. If a Pinkerton man is deep in this business we are all destroyed.'

'We must kill him.'

'Ah, it's the first thought that came to you! So it will be up at the Lodge. Didn't I say to you that it would end in murder?'

'Sure, what is murder? Isn't it common enough in these parts?'

'It is indeed, but it's not for me to point out the man that is to be murdered. I'd never rest easy again. And yet it's our own necks that may be at stake. In God's name what shall I do?' He rocked to and fro in his agony of indecision.

But his words had moved McMurdo deeply. It was easy to see that he shared the other's opinion as to the danger, and the need for meeting it. He gripped Morris's shoulder and shook him in his earnestness.

'See here, man,' he cried, and he almost screeched the words in his excitement, 'you won't gain anything by sitting keening like an old wife at a wake. Let's have the facts. Who is the fellow? Where is he? How did you hear of him? Why did you come to me?'

61 *Pinkerton's?*' The Pinkerton National Detective Agency, founded by Allan Pinkerton, 1819–1884. In addition to breaking up the Molly Maguires, Pinkerton's solved train robberies, acted as a Union spy service during the Civil War, and was active in the 1892 Homestead strike. As we have seen, its methods, particularly in the use of labor spies, were bitterly attacked by the trade unions.

'I came to you, for you are the one man that would advise me. I told you that I had a store in the East before I came here. I left good friends behind me, and one of them is in the telegraph service. Here's a letter that I had from him yesterday. It's this part from the top of the page. You can read it for yourself.'

This was what McMurdo read:

'How are the Scowrers getting on in your parts? We read plenty of them in the papers. Between you and me I expect to hear news from you before long. Five big corporations and the two railroads have taken the thing up in dead earnest. They mean it, and you can bet they'll get there. They are right deep down into it. Pinkerton has taken hold under their orders, and his best man, Birdy Edwards, is operating. The thing has got to be stopped right now.'

'Now read the postscript.'

'Of course, what I give you is what I learned in business, so it goes no further. It's a queer cipher that you handle by the yard every day and can get no meaning from.'

McMurdo sat in silence for some time with the letter in his restless hands. The mist had lifted for a moment, and there was the abyss before him.

'Does anyone else know of this?' he asked.

'I have told no one else.'

'But this man—your friend—has he any other person that he would be likely to write to?'

'Well, I dare say he knows one or two more.'

'Of the Lodge?'

'It's likely enough.'

'I was asking because it is likely that he may have given some description of this fellow, Birdy Edwards. Then we could get on his trail.'

'Well, it's possible. But I should not think he knew him. He is just telling me the news that came to him by way of business. How would he know this Pinkerton man?'

McMurdo gave a violent start.

'By gosh!' he cried, 'I've got him. What a fool I was not to know it! Lord, but we're in luck! We will fix him before he can do any harm. See here, Morris; will you leave this thing in my hands?'

'Sure, if you will only take it off mine!'

'I'll do that. You can stand right back and let me run it. Even your name need not be mentioned. I'll take it all on myself as if it were to me that this letter has come. Will that content you?'

'It's just what I would ask.'

'Then leave it at that and keep your head shut. Now I'll get down to the Lodge, and we'll soon make old man Pinkerton sorry for himself.'

'You wouldn't kill this man?'

'The less you know, friend Morris, the easier your conscience will be and the better you will sleep. Ask no questions, and let things settle themselves. I have hold of it now.'

Morris shook his head sadly as he left.

'I feel that his blood is on my hands,' he groaned.

'Self-protection is no murder, anyhow,' said McMurdo, smiling grimly. 'It's him or us. I guess this man would destroy us all if we left him long in the valley. Why, Brother Morris, we'll have to elect you bodymaster yet, for you've surely saved the Lodge.'

And yet it was clear from his actions that he thought more seriously of this new intrusion than his words would show. It may have been his guilty conscience; it may have been the reputation of the Pinkerton organization; it may have been the knowledge that great rich corporations had set themselves the task of clearing out the Scowrers; but, whatever his reason, his actions were those of a man who is preparing for the worst. Every paper which could incriminate him was destroyed before he left the house. After that he gave a long sigh of satisfaction, for it seemed to him that he was safe; and yet the danger must still have pressed somewhat upon him, for on his way to the Lodge he stopped at old Shafter's. The house was forbidden him, but when he tapped at the window Ettie came out to him. The dancing Irish devilry had gone from her lover's eyes. She read his danger in his earnest face.

'Something has happened!' she cried. 'Oh, Jack, you are in danger!'

'Sure, it is not very bad, my sweetheart. And yet it may be wise that we make a move before it is worse.'

'Make a move!'

'I promised you once that I would go some day. I think the time is coming. I had news tonight—bad news—and I see trouble coming.'

'The police?'

'Well, a Pinkerton. But, sure, you wouldn't know what that is, acushla, nor what it may mean to the likes of me. I'm too deep in this thing, and I may have to get out of it quick. You said you would come with me if I went.'

'Oh, Jack, it would be the saving of you.'

'I'm an honest man in some things, Ettie. I wouldn't hurt a hair of your bonnie head for all that the world can give, nor ever pull you down one inch from the golden throne above the clouds where I always see you. Would you trust me?'

She put her hand in his without a word.

'Well, then, listen to what I say and do as I order you, for indeed it's the only way for us. Things are going to happen in this valley. I feel it in my bones. There may be many of us that will have to look out for ourselves. I'm one, anyhow. If I go, by day or night, it's you that must come with me!'

'I'd come after you, Jack.'

'No, no; you shall come *with* me. If this valley is closed to me and I can never come back, how can I leave you behind, and me perhaps in hiding from the police with never a chance of a message? It's with me you must come. I know a good woman in the place I come from, and it's there I'd leave you till we can get married. Will you come?'

'Yes, Jack, I will come.'

'God bless you for your trust in me. It's a fiend out of hell that I should be if I abused it. Now, mark you, Ettie, it will be just a word to you, and when it reaches you you will drop everything and come right down to the waiting-hall at the depot and stay there till I come for you.'

'Day or night, I'll come at the word, Jack.'

Somewhat eased in mind now that his own preparations for escape had been begun, McMurdo went on to the Lodge. It had already assembled, and only by complicated signs and countersigns could he pass through the outer guard and inner guard who close-tiled it. A buzz of pleasure and welcome greeted him as he entered. The long room was crowded, and through the haze of tobacco smoke he saw the tangled black mane of the bodymaster, the cruel, unfriendly features of Baldwin, the vulture face of Harraway, the secretary, and a dozen more who were among the leaders of the Lodge. He rejoiced that they should all be there to take counsel over his news.

'Indeed, it's glad we are to see you, brother!' cried the chairman. 'There's business here that wants a Solomon in judgment to set it right.'

'It's Lander and Egan,' explained his neighbour, as he took his seat. 'They both claim the head-money given by the Lodge for the shooting of old man Crabbe over at Stylestown, and who's to say which fired the bullet?'

McMurdo rose in his place and raised his hand. The expression of his face froze the attention of the audience. There was a dead hush of expectation.

'Worshipful Master,' he said, in a solemn voice, 'I claim urgency.'

'Brother McMurdo claims urgency,' said McGinty. 'It's a claim that by the rules of this Lodge takes precedence. Now, brother, we attend you.'

McMurdo took the letter from his pocket.

'Worshipful Master and brethren,' he said, 'I am the bearer of ill news this day, but it is better that it should be known and discussed than that a blow should fall upon us without warning which would destroy us all. I have information that the most powerful and richest organizations in this State have bound themselves together for our destruction, and that at this very moment there is a Pinkerton detective, one Birdy Edwards, at work in the valley collecting the evidence which may put a rope round the neck of many of us, and send every man in this room into a felon's cell. That is the situation for the discussion of which I have made a claim of urgency.'

There was a dead silence in the room. It was broken by the chairman.

'What is your evidence for this, Brother McMurdo?' he asked.

'It is in this letter which has come into my hands,' said McMurdo. He read the passage aloud. 'It is a matter of honour with me that I can give no further particulars about the letter, nor put it into your hands, but I assure you that there is nothing else in it which can affect the interests of the Lodge. I put the case before you as it has reached me.'

'Let me say, Mr Chairman,' said one of the older brethren, 'that I have heard of Birdy Edwards, and that he has the name of being the best man in the Pinkerton service.'

'Does anyone know him by sight?' asked McGinty.

'Yes,' said McMurdo, 'I do.'

There was a murmur of astonishment through the hall.

'I believe we hold him in the hollow of our hands,' he continued, with an exulting smile upon his face. 'If we act quickly and wisely we can cut this thing short. If I have your confidence and your help it is little that we have to fear.'

'What have we to fear anyhow? What can he know of our affairs?'

'You might say so if all were as staunch as you, Councillor. But this man has all the millions of the capitalists at his back. Do you think there is no weaker brother among all our Lodges that could not be bought? He will get at our secrets—maybe has got them already. There's only one sure cure.'

'That he never leaves the valley,' said Baldwin.

McMurdo nodded.

'Good for you, Brother Baldwin,' he said. 'You and I have had our differences, but you have said the true word tonight.'

'Where is he, then? How shall we know him?'

'Worshipful Master,' said McMurdo, earnestly, 'I would put it to you that this is too vital a thing for us to discuss in open Lodge. God forbid that I should throw a doubt on anyone here, but if so much as a word of gossip got to the ears of this man there would be an end of any chance of our getting him. I would ask the Lodge to choose a trusty committee, Mr Chairman—yourself, if I might suggest it, and Brother Baldwin here, and five more. Then I can talk freely of what I know and of what I would advise should be done.'

The proposition was at once adopted and the committee chosen. Besides the chairman and Baldwin, there were the vulture-faced secretary, Harraway; Tiger Cormac, the brutal young assassin; Carter, the treasurer; and the brothers Willaby, who were fearless and desperate men who would stick at nothing.

The usual revelry of the Lodge was short and subdued, for there was a cloud upon the men's spirits, and many there for the first time began to see the cloud of avenging Law drifting up in that serene sky under which they had dwelt so long. The horrors which they had dealt out to others had been so much a part of their settled lives that the thought of retribution had become a remote one, and so seemed the more startling now that it came so closely upon them. They broke up early and left their leaders to their council.

'Now, McMurdo,' said McGinty, when they were alone. The seven men sat frozen in their seats.

'I said just now that I knew Birdy Edwards,' McMurdo explained. 'I need not tell you that he is not here under that name. He's a brave man, I dare bet, but not a crazy one. He passes under the name of Steve Wilson, and he is lodging at Hobson's Patch.'

'How do you know this?'

'Because I fell into talk with him. I thought little of it at the time, nor would have given it a second thought but for this letter, but now I'm sure it's the man. I met him on the cars when I went down the line on Wednesday—a hard case if ever there was one. He said he was a pressman. I believed it for the moment. Wanted to know all he could get about the Scowrers and what he called "the outrages" for the *New York Press*. Asked me every kind of question so as to get something for his paper. You bet I was giving nothing away. "I'd pay for it, and pay well," said he, "if I could get some stuff that would suit my editor." I said what I thought would please him best, and he handed me a twenty-dollar bill for my information. "There's ten times that for you," said he, "if you can find me all that I want." '

'What did you tell him, then?'

'Any stuff I could make up.'

'How do you know he wasn't a newspaper man?'

'I'll tell you. He got out at Hobson's Patch, and so did I. I chanced into the telegraph bureau, and he was leaving it.

' "See here," said the operator, after he'd gone out, "I guess we should charge double rates for this." "I guess you should," said I. He had filled the form with stuff that might have been Chinese for all we could make of it. "He fires a sheet of this off every day," said the clerk. "Yes," said I; "it's special news for his paper, and he's scared that the others should tap it." That was what the operator thought and what I thought at the time, but I think different now.'

'By gosh, I believe you are right!' said McGinty. 'But what do you allow that we should do about it?'

'Why not go right down now and fix him?' someone suggested.

'Aye, the sooner the better.'

'I'd start this next minute if I knew where we could find him,' said McMurdo. 'He's in Hobson's Patch, but I don't know the house. I've got a plan, though, if you'll only take my advice.'

'Well, what is it?'

'I'll go to the Patch tomorrow morning. I'll find him through the operator. He can locate him, I guess. Well, then, I'll tell him that I'm a Freeman myself. I'll offer him all the secrets of the Lodge for a price. You bet he'll tumble to it. I'll tell him the papers are at my house, and that it's as much as my life would be worth to let him come while folk were about. He'll see that that's horse sense. Let him come at ten o'clock at night, and he shall see everything. That will fetch him, sure.'

'Well?'

'You can plan the rest for yourselves. Widow MacNamara's is a lonely house. She's as true as steel and as deaf as a post. There's only Scanlan and me in the house. If I get his promise —and I'll let you know if I do—I'd have the whole seven of you come to me by nine o'clock. We'll get him in. If ever he gets out alive—well, he can talk of Birdy Edwards's luck for the rest of his days.'

'There's going to be a vacancy at Pinkerton's or I'm mistaken,' said McGinty. 'Leave it at that, McMurdo. At nine tomorrow we shall be with you. You once get the door shut behind him, and you can leave the rest with us.'

♦
14 ♦ THE TRAPPING OF BIRDY EDWARDS
♦

As McMurdo had said, the house in which he lived was a lonely one and very well suited for such a crime as they had planned. It was on the extreme fringe of the town, and stood well back from the road. In any other case the conspirators would have simply called out their man, as they had many a time before, and emptied their pistols into his body; but in this instance it was very necessary to find out how much he knew, how he knew it, and what had been passed on to his employers. It was possible that they were already too late and that the work had been done. If that were indeed so, they could at least have their revenge upon the man who had done it. But they were hopeful that nothing of great importance had yet come to the detective's knowledge, as otherwise, they argued, he would not have troubled to write down and forward such trivial information as McMurdo claimed to have given him. However, all this they would learn from his own lips. Once in their power they would find a way to make him speak. It was not the first time that they had handled an unwilling witness.

McMurdo went to Hobson's Patch as agreed. The police seemed to take a particular interest in him that morning, and Captain Marvin—he who had claimed the old acquaintance with him at Chicago—actually addressed him as he waited at the depot. McMurdo turned away and refused to speak with him. He was back from his mission in the afternoon, and saw McGinty at the Union House.

'He is coming,' he said.

'Good!' said McGinty. The giant was in his shirt-sleeves, with chains and seals gleaming athwart his ample waistcoat and a diamond twinkling through the fringe of his bristling beard. Drink and politics had made the Boss a very rich as well as powerful man. The more terrible, therefore, seemed that glimpse of the prison or the gallows which had risen before him the night before.

'Do you reckon he knows much?' he asked, anxiously.

McMurdo shook his head gloomily.

'He's been here some time—six weeks at the least. I guess he didn't come into these parts to look at the prospect. If he has been working among us all that time with the railroad money at his back, I should expect that he has got results, and that he has passed them on.'

'There's not a weak man in the Lodge,' cried McGinty. 'True as steel, every man of them. And yet, by the Lord, there is that skunk Morris. What about him? If any man gives us away it would be he. I've a mind to send a couple of the boys round before evening to give him a beating up and see what they can get from him.'

'Well, there would be no harm in that,' McMurdo answered. 'I won't deny that I have a liking for Morris and would be sorry to see him come to harm. He has spoken to me once or twice over Lodge matters, and though he may not see them the same as you or I, he never seemed the sort that squeals. But still, it is not for me to stand between him and you.'

'I'll fix the old devil,' said McGinty, with an oath. 'I've had my eye on him this year past.'

'Well, you know best about that,' McMurdo answered. 'But whatever you do must be tomorrow, for we must lie low until the Pinkerton affair is settled up. We can't afford to set the police buzzing today of all days.'

'True for you,' said McGinty. 'And we'll learn from Birdy Edwards himself where he got his news, if we have to cut his heart out first. Did he seem to scent a trap?'

McMurdo laughed.

'I guess I took him on his weak point,' he said. 'If he could get on a good trail of the Scowrers he's ready to follow it home. I took his money,' McMurdo grinned as he produced a wad of dollar notes, 'and as much more when he has seen all my papers.'

'What papers?'

'Well, there are no papers. But I filled him up about constitutions and books of rules and forms of membership. He expects to get right down to the end of everything before he leaves.'

'Faith, he's right there,' said McGinty, grimly. 'Didn't he ask you why you didn't bring him the papers?'

'As if I would carry such things, and me a suspected man, and Captain Marvin after speaking to me this very day at the depot!'

'Aye, I heard of that,' said McGinty. 'I guess the heavy end of this business is coming on to you. We could put him down an old shaft when we've done with him, but however we work it we can't get past the man living at Hobson's Patch and you being there today.'

McMurdo shrugged his shoulders.

'If we handle it right they can never prove the killing,' said he. 'No one can see him come to the house after dark, and I'll lay to it that no one will see him go. Now, see here, Councillor. I'll show you my plan, and I'll ask you to fit the others into it. You will all come in good time. Very well. He comes at ten. He is to tap three times, and me to open the door for him. Then I'll get behind him and shut it. He's our man then.'

'That's all easy and plain.'

'Yes, but the next step wants considering. He's a hard proposition. He's heavily armed. I've fooled him proper, and yet he is likely to be on his guard. Suppose I show him right into a room with seven men in it where he expected to find me alone. There is going to be shooting and somebody is going to be hurt.'

'That's so.'

'And the noise is going to bring every blamed copper in the township on to the top of us.'

'I guess you are right.'

'This is how I should work it. You will all be in the big room—same as you saw when you had a chat with me. I'll open the door for him, show him into the parlour beside the door, and leave him there while I get the papers. That will give me the chance of telling you how things are shaping. Then I will go back to him with some faked papers. As he is reading them I will jump for him and get my grip on his pistol arm. You'll hear me call, and in you will rush. The quicker the better, for he is as strong a man as I, and I may have more than I can manage. But I allow that I can hold him till you come.'

'It's a good plan,' said McGinty. 'The Lodge will owe you a debt for this. I guess when I move out of the chair I can put a name to the man that's coming after me.'

'Sure, Councillor, I am little more than a recruit,' said McMurdo, but his face showed what he thought of the great man's compliment.

When he had returned home he made his own preparations for the grim evening in front of him. First he cleaned, oiled and loaded his Smith and Wesson revolver. Then he surveyed the room in which the detective was to be trapped. It was a large apartment, with a long deal table in the centre and the big stove at one end. At each of the other sides were windows. There were no shutters to these—only light curtains which drew across. McMurdo examined these attentively. No doubt it must have struck him that the apartment was very exposed for so secret a matter. Yet its distance from the road made it of less consequence. Finally he discussed the matter with his fellow-lodger. Scanlan, though a Scowrer, was an inoffensive little man who was too weak to stand against the opinion of his comrades, but was secretly horrified by the deeds of blood at which he had sometimes been forced to assist. McMurdo told him shortly what was intended.

'And if I were you, Mike Scanlan, I would take a night off and keep clear of it. There will be bloody work here before morning.'

'Well, indeed, then, Mac,' Scanlan answered, 'it's not the will but the nerve that is wanting in me. When I saw Manager Dunn go down at the colliery yonder it was just more than I could stand. I'm not made for it, same as you or McGinty. If the Lodge will think none the worse of me, I'll just do as you advise, and leave you to yourselves for the evening.'

The men came in good time as arranged. They were outwardly respectable citizens, well-clad and cleanly, but a judge of faces would have read little hope for Birdy Edwards in those hard mouths and remorseless eyes. There was not a man in the room whose hands had not been reddened a dozen times before. They were as hardened to human murder as a butcher to sheep. Foremost, of course, both in appearance and in guilt, was the formidable Boss. Harraway, the secretary, was a lean, bitter man, with a long, scraggy neck and nervous jerky limbs—a man of incorruptible fidelity where the finances of the Order were concerned, and with no notion of justice or honesty to anyone beyond. The treasurer, Carter, was a middle-aged man with an impassive, rather sulky expression and a yellow parchment skin. He was a capable organizer, and the actual details of nearly every outrage had sprung from his plotting brain. The two Willabys were men of action, tall, lithe young fellows with determined faces, while their companion, Tiger Cormac, a heavy, dark youth, was feared even by his own comrades for the ferocity of his disposition. These were the men who assembled that night under the roof of McMurdo for the killing of the Pinkerton detective.

Their host had placed whisky upon the table, and they had hastened to prime themselves for the work before them. Baldwin and Cormac were already half drunk, and the liquor had brought out all their ferocity. Cormac placed his hands on the stove for an instant—it had been lighted, for the spring nights were still cold.

'That will do,' said he, with an oath.

'Aye,' said Baldwin, catching his meaning. 'If he is strapped to that we will have the truth out of him.'

'We'll have the truth out of him, never fear,' said McMurdo. He had nerves of steel, this man, for, though the whole weight of the affair was on him, his manner was as cool and unconcerned as ever. The others marked it and applauded.

'You are the one to handle him,' said the Boss, approvingly. 'Not a warning will he get till your hand is on his throat. It's a pity there are no shutters to your windows.'

McMurdo went from one to the other and drew the curtain tighter.

'Sure, no one can spy upon us now. It's close upon the hour.'

'Maybe he won't come. Maybe he'll get a sniff of danger,' said the secretary.

'He'll come, never fear,' McMurdo answered. 'He is as eager to come as you can be to see him. Hark to that!'

They all sat like wax figures, some with their glasses arrested half-way to their lips. Three loud knocks had sounded at the door.

'Hush!'

McMurdo raised his hand in caution. An exulting glance went round the circle and hands were laid upon hidden weapons.

'Not a sound for your lives!' McMurdo whispered, as he went from the room, closing the door carefully behind him.

With strained ears the murderers waited. They counted the steps of their comrade down the passage. Then they heard him open the outer door. There were a few words as of greeting. Then they were aware of a strange step inside and of an unfamiliar voice. An instant later came the slam of the door and the turning of the key in the lock. Their prey was safe within the trap. Tiger Cormac laughed horribly, and Boss McGinty clapped his great hand across his mouth.

'Be quiet, you fool!' he whispered. 'You'll be the undoing of us yet.'

There was a mutter of conversation from the next room. It seemed interminable. Then the door opened and McMurdo appeared, his finger upon his lip.

He came to the end of the table and looked round at them. A subtle change had come over him. His manner was as of one who has great work to do. His face had set into granite firmness. His eyes shone with a fierce excitement behind his spectacles. He had become a visible leader of men. They stared at him with eager interest, but he said nothing. Still with the same singular gaze, he looked from man to man.

'Well,' cried Boss McGinty at last, 'is he here? Is Birdy Edwards here?'

'Yes,' McMurdo answered slowly. 'Birdy Edwards is here. I am Birdy Edwards!'

There were ten seconds after that brief speech during which the room might have been empty, so profound was the silence. The hissing of a kettle upon the stove rose sharp

"NOT A SOUND FOR YOUR LIVES!" MCMURDO
WHISPERED . . .

Illustration by Arthur I. Keller for Associated Sunday Magazines, 1914.

and strident to the ear. Seven white faces, all turned upwards to this man who dominated them, were set motionless with utter terror. Then, with a sudden shivering of glass, a bristle of glistening rifle-barrels broke through each window, whilst the curtains were torn from their hangings. At the sight Boss McGinty gave the roar of a wounded bear and plunged for the half-opened door. A levelled revolver met him there, with the stern blue eyes of Captain Marvin of the Coal and Iron Police gleaming behind the sights. The Boss recoiled and fell back into his chair.

'You're safer there, Councillor,' said the man whom they had known as McMurdo. 'And you, Baldwin, if you don't take your hand off your gun you'll cheat the hangman yet. Pull it out, or, by the Lord that made me—— There, that will do. There are forty armed men round this house, and you can figure it out for yourselves what chance you have. Take their guns, Marvin!'

There was no possible resistance under the menace of those rifles. The men were disarmed. Sulky, sheepish, and very amazed, they still sat round the table.

'I'd like to say a word to you before we separate,' said the man who had trapped them. 'I guess we may not meet again until you see me on the stand in the court-house. I'll give you something to think over betwixt now and then. You know me now for what I am. At last I can put my cards on the table. I am Birdy Edwards, of Pinkerton's. I was chosen to break up your gang. I had a hard and a dangerous game to play. Not a soul, not one soul, not my nearest and dearest knew that I was playing it, except Captain Marvin here and my employers. But it's over tonight, thank God, and I am the winner!'

The seven pale, rigid faces looked up at him. There was an unappeasable hatred in their eyes. He read the relentless threat.

'Maybe you think that the game is not over yet. Well, I take my chance on that. Anyhow, some of you will take no further hand, and there are sixty more besides yourselves that will see a jail this night. I'll tell you this, that when I was put upon this job I never believed there was such a society as yours. I thought it was paper talk, and that I would prove it so. They told me it was to do with the Freemen, so I went to Chicago and was made one. Then I was surer than ever that it was just paper talk, for I found no harm in the society, but a deal of good. Still, I had to carry out my job, and I came for the coal valleys. When I reached this place I learned that I was wrong and that it wasn't a dime novel after all. So I stayed to look after it. I never killed a man in Chicago. I never minted a dollar in my life. Those I gave you were as good as any others, but I never spent money better. I knew the way into your good wishes, and so I pretended to you that the law was after me. It all worked just as I thought.

'So I joined your infernal Lodge and I took my share in your councils. Maybe they will say that I was as bad as you. They can say what they like, so long as I get you. But what is the truth? The night I joined you beat up old man Stanger. I could not warn him, for there was no time, but I held your hand, Baldwin, when you would have killed him. If ever I have suggested things, so as to keep my place among you, they were things which I knew that I could prevent. I could not save Dunn and Menzies, for I did not know enough, but I will see that their murderers are hanged. I gave Chester Wilcox warning, so that when I blew his house in he and his folk were in hiding. There was many a crime that I could not stop, but if you look back and think how often your man came home the other road, or was down in town when you went for him, or stayed indoors when you thought that he would come out, you'll see my work.'

'You blasted traitor!' hissed McGinty, through his closed teeth.

'Aye, John McGinty, you may call me that if it eases your smart. You and your like have been the enemy of God and man in these parts. It took a man to get between you and the poor devils of men and women that you held under your grip. There was just one way of doing it, and I did it. You call me a "traitor," but I guess there's many a thousand will call me a "deliverer" that went down into hell to save them. I've had three months of it. I wouldn't have three such months again if they let me loose in the Treasury at Washington for it. I had to stay till I had it all, every man and every secret, right here in this hand. I'd have waited a little longer if it hadn't come to my knowledge that my secret was coming out. A letter had come into the town that would have set you wise to it all. Then I had to act, and act quickly. I've nothing more to say to you, except that when my time comes I'll die easier when I think of the work I have done in this valley. Now, Marvin, I'll keep you no more. Have them in and get it over.'

There is little more to tell. Scanlan had been given a sealed note to be left at the address of Miss Ettie Shafter—a mission which he had accepted with a wink and a knowing smile. In the early hours of the morning a beautiful woman and a much-muffled man boarded a special train which had been sent by the railroad company, and made a swift, unbroken journey out of the land of danger. It was the last time that ever either Ettie or her lover set foot in the Valley of Fear. Ten days later they were married in Chicago, with old Jacob Shafter as witness of the wedding.

The trial of the Scowrers was held far from the place where their adherents might have terrified the guardians of the law. In vain they struggled. In vain the money of the Lodge— money squeezed by blackmail out of the whole country-side —was spent like water in the attempt to save them. That cold, clear, unimpassioned statement from one who knew every detail of their lives, their organization, and their crimes was unshaken by all the wiles of their defenders. At last, after so many years, they were broken and scattered. The cloud was lifted for ever from the valley. McGinty met his fate upon the scaffold, cringing and whining when the last hour came. Eight of his chief followers shared his fate. Fifty odd had various degrees of imprisonment. The work of Birdy Edwards was complete.

And yet, as he had guessed, the game was not over yet. There was another hand to be played, and yet another and another. Ted Baldwin, for one, had escaped the scaffold; so had the Willabys; so had several other of the fiercest spirits of the gang. For ten years they were out of the world, and then came a day when they were free once more—a day which Edwards, who knew his men, was very sure would be an end of his life of peace. They had sworn an oath on all that they thought holy to have his blood as a vengeance for their comrades. And well they strove to keep their vow. From Chicago he was chased, after two attempts so near to success that it was sure that the third would get him. From Chicago he went, under a changed name, to California, and it was there that the light went for a time out of his life when Ettie Edwards died. Once again he was nearly killed, and once again, under the name of Douglas, he worked in a lonely canyon, where, with an English partner named Barker, he amassed a fortune. At last there came a warning to him that the bloodhounds were on his track once more, and he cleared—only just in time—for England. And here came the John Douglas who for a second time married a worthy mate and lived for five years as a Sussex country gentleman—a life which ended with the strange happenings of which we have heard.

◆ EPILOGUE

The police-court proceedings had passed, in which the case of John Douglas was referred to a higher court. So had the Assizes, at which he was acquitted as having acted in self-defence. 'Get him out of England at any cost,' wrote Holmes to the wife. 'There are forces here which may be more dangerous than those he has escaped. There is no safety for your husband in England.'

Two months had gone by, and the case had to some extent passed from our minds. Then one morning there came an enigmatic note slipped into our letter-box. 'Dear me, Mr Holmes! Dear me!' said this singular epistle. There was neither superscription nor signature. I laughed at the quaint message, but Holmes showed an unwonted seriousness.

'Devilry, Watson!' he remarked, and sat long with a clouded brow.

Late that night Mrs Hudson, our landlady, brought up a message that a gentleman wished to see Holmes, and that the matter was of the utmost importance. Close at the heels of his messenger came Mr Cecil Barker, our friend of the moated Manor House. His face was drawn and haggard.

'I've had bad news—terrible news, Mr Holmes,' said he.

'I feared as much,' said Holmes.

'You have not had a cable, have you?'

'I have had a note from someone who has.'

'It's poor Douglas. They tell me his name is Edwards, but he will always be Jack Douglas of Benito Canyon to me. I told you that they started together for South Africa in the *Palmyra* three weeks ago.'

'Exactly.'

'The ship reached Cape Town last night. I received this cable from Mrs Douglas this morning:

'Jack has been lost overboard in gale off St Helena. No one knows how accident occurred—IVY DOUGLAS.'

'Ha! It came like that, did it?' said Holmes, thoughtfully. 'Well, I've no doubt it was well stage-managed.'

"I'VE HAD BAD NEWS—TERRIBLE NEWS, MR. HOLMES," SAID HE.

Illustration by Frank Wiles for the *Strand Magazine*, May, 1915.

'You mean that you think there was no accident?'

'None in the world.'

'He was murdered?'

'Surely!'

'So I think also. These infernal Scowrers, this cursed vindictive nest of criminals——'

'No, no, my good sir,' said Holmes. 'There is a master hand here. It is no case of sawed-off shot-guns and clumsy six-shooters. You can tell an old master by the sweep of his brush. I can tell a Moriarty when I see one. This crime is from London, not from America.'

'But for what motive?'

'Because it is done by a man who cannot afford to fail—one whose whole unique position depends upon the fact that all he does must succeed. A great brain and a huge organization have been turned to the extinction of one man. It is crushing the nut with the hammer—an absurd extravagance of energy—but the nut is very effectually crushed all the same.'

'How came this man to have anything to do with it?'

'I can only say that the first word that ever came to us of the business was from one of his lieutenants. These Americans were well advised. Having an English job to do, they took into partnership, as any foreign criminal could do, this great consultant in crime. From that moment their man was doomed. At first he would content himself by using his machinery in order to find their victim. Then he would indicate how the matter might be treated. Finally, when he read in the reports of the failure of this agent, he would step in himself with a master touch. You heard me warn this man at Birlstone Manor House that the coming danger was greater than the past. Was I right?'

Barker beat his head with his clenched fist in his impotent anger.

'Do you tell me that we have to sit down under this? Do you say that no one can ever get level with this king-devil?'

'No, I don't say that,' said Holmes, and his eyes seemed to be looking far into the future. 'I don't say that he can't be beat. But you must give me time—you must give me time!'

We all sat in silence for some minutes, while those fateful eyes still strained to pierce the veil.

32

THE YELLOW FACE

[Saturday, April 7, 1888]

IN publishing these short sketches, based upon the numerous cases which my companion's singular gifts have made me the listener to, and eventually the actor in some strange drama, it is only natural that I should dwell rather upon his successes than upon his failures. And this is not so much for the sake of his reputation, for indeed it was when he was at his wits' end that his energy and his versatility were most admirable, but because where he failed it happened so often that no one else succeeded, and that the tale was left for ever without a conclusion. Now and again, however, it chanced that even when he erred the truth was still discovered. I have notes of some half-dozen cases of the kind, of which the affair of the second stain, and that which I am now about **1** to recount are the two which present the strongest features of interest.

Sherlock Holmes was a man who seldom took exercise for exercise's sake. Few men were capable of greater muscular effort, and he was undoubtedly one of the finest boxers of his weight that I have ever seen ; but he looked **2** upon aimless bodily exertion as a waste of energy, and he seldom bestirred himself save where there was some professional object to be served. Then he was absolutely untiring and indefatigable. That he should have kept himself in training under such circumstances is remark- **3** able, but his diet was usually of the sparest, and his habits were simple to the verge of austerity. Save for the occasional use of cocaine he had no vices, and he only turned to the drug as a protest against the monotony of existence when cases were scanty and the papers uninteresting.

One day in early spring he had so far relaxed as to go for a walk with me in the Park, where the first faint shoots of green were breaking out upon the elms, and the sticky spearheads of the chestnuts were just beginning to burst into their five-fold leaves. For two hours we **4** rambled about together, in silence for the most part, as befits two men who know each other intimately. It was **5** nearly five before we were back in Baker Street once more.

" Beg pardon, sir," said our page-boy, as he opened the door ; " there's been a gentleman here asking for you, sir."

1 *the affair of the second stain.* Whether or not Holmes can be said to have "erred" in the adventure published as "The Second Stain" is a point still debated by commentators. Most hold that Holmes did *not* err in that adventure, and that Watson must therefore have kept notes of more than one adventure which he associated with a "second stain." A minority, however, holds that the adventure referred to here and the published adventure are one and the same. Thus Mr. Anthony Boucher has written that: "[It is true that Holmes erred] if one views the published adventure from the aspect of the murder of Eduardo Lucas, which was solved by chance, quite without the efforts of Holmes. By shifting the point of view to the recovery of the papers and making the murder irrelevant, Watson contrived, when he published the case, to make it appear a triumph." And Dr. Felix Morley has written ("The Significance of the Second Stain"): "Thinking he had completely solved the mystery [Holmes] says to Watson, 'You will be relieved to hear that there will be no war, that the Right Honourable Trelawney Hope will suffer no setback in his brilliant career . . . that the Prime Minister will have no European complication to deal with . . .' Can it be said, comparing that boast with the situation [that developed in England and on the Continent] that Holmes did not err, even though, in old Watson's truthful words, 'the truth was still discovered'?" The Doubleday omnibus refers here, not to "the second stain," but to "The Musgrave Ritual"—an emendation that scarcely helps matters, since "The Musgrave Ritual" was certainly not one of Holmes' failures.

2 *one of the finest boxers of his weight.* This was "a real compliment," Dr. Edward J. Van Liere wrote in "Sherlock Holmes and Doctor Watson, Perennial Athletes," "for Watson was a keen sportsman, who probably had had occasion to see many boxing matches and knew a good boxer when he saw one."

But what *was* Holmes' weight? "Presumably about the same as McMurdo [*The Sign of the*

Four].” the late H. T. Webster wrote in “Observations on Sherlock Holmes As an Athlete and Sportsman”; “and McMurdo, described as short and deep chested, sounds like a typical middleweight. Holmes was six feet tall, according to his own word [“The Adventure of the Three Students”], and probably weighed about 11 stone [154 pounds], which would make him resemble the celebrated Bob Fitzsimmons in build.”

3 *That he should have kept himself in training.* “How did Holmes and Watson keep themselves in good physical condition?” Dr. Van Liere asked. “This will always be a mystery. Search as we will, we can find no evidence that either Holmes or Watson kept themselves in training. This seems remarkable since there were times when they needed their strength and stamina in order to put their foes out of commission, and indeed there were occasions when their very lives depended upon it. . . . I, for one, am ready to believe that they did not lead such sedentary lives as Doctor Watson would have us think.”

4 *just beginning to burst into their five-fold leaves.* “From the description, the early part of April is indicated,” the late H. W. Bell wrote in *Sherlock Holmes and Dr. Watson: The Chronology of Their Adventures,* and he added in a note: “Mr. E. H. M. Cox, editor of the *New Flora and Silva,* writes me that in the average year the description of the text would indicate ‘about April 10th.’ ”

5 *two men who know each other intimately.* As early as April, 1883, Holmes referred to Watson as his “intimate friend and associate” (“The Adventure of the Speckled Band”), so by itself this statement means little in dating the case. At the least, however, it tends to indicate a later rather than an earlier relationship. Your editor and the Reverend Henry T. Folsom have settled on 1888, but many other years have their champions: 1882: Bell, Brend, Newton, Petersen, Starrett, Wellman; 1883: Christ and Smith; 1885 or 1886: Pattrick and Zeisler; 1887: Dr. Felix Morley. Holmes’ “occasional use of cocaine” and the presence of a page boy at Baker Street are other clues that point to the end of the ’eighties.

6 *I was badly in need of a case.* Even in the years when Holmes was most successful, there must have been stagnant periods in the practice. In any event, however, the adventure of “The Yellow Face” could not have taken place in a late March or early April when Holmes was demonstrably at work on a case.

7 *seven-and-sixpence.* About $1.87.

Holmes glanced reproachfully at me. “ So much for afternoon walks ! ” said he. “ Has this gentleman gone, then ? ”

“ Yes, sir.”

“ Didn’t you ask him in ? ”

“ Yes, sir ; he came in.”

“ How long did he wait ? ”

“ Half an hour, sir. He was a very restless gentleman, sir, a-walkin’ and a-stampin’ all the time he was here. I was waitin’ outside the door, sir, and I could hear him. At last he goes out into the passage and he cries : ‘ Is that man never goin’ to come ? ’ Those were his very words, sir. ‘ You’ll only need to wait a little longer,’ says I. ‘ Then I’ll wait in the open air, for I feel half choked,’ says he. ‘ I’ll be back before long,’ and with that he ups and he outs, and all I could say wouldn’t hold him back.”

“ Well, well, you did your best,” said Holmes, as we walked into our room. “ It’s very annoying though, **6** Watson. I was badly in need of a case, and this looks, from the man’s impatience, as if it were of importance. Halloa ! that’s not your pipe on the table ! He must have left his behind him. A nice old briar, with a good long stem of what the tobacconists call amber. I wonder how many real amber mouthpieces there are in London. Some people think a fly in it is a sign. Why, it is quite a branch of trade, the putting of sham flies into the sham amber. Well, he must have been disturbed in his mind to leave a pipe behind him which he evidently values highly.”

“ How do you know that he values it highly ? ” I asked.

“ Well, I should put the original cost of the pipe at **7** seven-and-sixpence. Now it has, you see, been twice mended : once in the wooden stem and once in the amber. Each of these mends, done, as you observe, with silver bands, must have cost more than the pipe did originally. The man must value the pipe highly when he prefers to patch it up rather than buy a new one with the same money.”

“ Anything else ? ” I asked, for Holmes was turning the pipe about in his hand and staring at it in his peculiar pensive way.

He held it up and tapped on it with his long, thin forefinger as a professor might who was lecturing on a bone.

“ Pipes are occasionally of extraordinary interest,” said he. “ Nothing has more individuality save, perhaps, watches and bootlaces. The indications here, however, are neither very marked nor very important. The owner is obviously a muscular man, left-handed, with an excellent set of teeth, careless in his habits, and with no need to practise economy.”

My friend threw out the information in a very off-hand way, but I saw that he cocked his eye at me to see if I had followed his reasoning.

" You think a man must be well-to-do if he smokes a seven-shilling pipe ? " said I.

" This is Grosvenor mixture at eightpence an ounce," **8** Holmes answered, knocking a little out on his palm. " As he might get an excellent smoke for half the price, he has no need to practise economy."

" And the other points ? "

" He has been in the habit of lighting his pipe at lamps and gas-jets. You can see that it is quite charred all **9** down one side. Of course, a match could not have done that. Why should a man hold a match to the side of his pipe ? But you cannot light it at a lamp without getting the bowl charred. And it is on the right side of the pipe. From that I gather that he is a left-handed man. You hold your own pipe to the lamp, and see how naturally you, being right-handed, hold the left side to the flame. You might do it once the other way, but not as a constancy. This has always been held so. Then he has bitten through his amber. It takes a muscular, energetic fellow, and one with a good set of teeth, to do that. But if I am not mistaken I hear him upon the stair, so we shall have something more interesting than his pipe to study."

An instant later our door opened, and a tall young man entered the room. He was well but quietly dressed in a dark-grey suit, and carried a brown wide-awake in his **10** hand. I should have put him at about thirty, though he was really some years older.

8 *eightpence.* About 16¢.

9 *"He has been in the habit of lighting his pipe at lamps and gas-jets.* A habit Holmes' client would seem to have shared with Holmes himself; see "The Adventure of Charles Augustus Milverton."

10 *a brown wide-awake.* A soft broad-brimmed felt hat.

"PIPES ARE OCCASIONALLY OF EXTRAORDINARY INTEREST," SAID HE.

How two artists imagined Sherlock Holmes in the same deductive moment. *Right,* William H. Hyde for *Harper's Weekly,* February 11, 1893. *Below,* Sidney Paget for the *Strand Magazine,* February, 1893.

" I beg your pardon," said he, with some embarrassment ; " I suppose I should have knocked. Yes, of course I should have knocked. The fact is that I am a little upset, and you must put it all down to that." He passed his hand over his forehead like a man who is half dazed, and then fell, rather than sat, down upon a chair.

" I can see that you have not slept for a night or two," said Holmes, in his easy, genial way. " That tries a man's nerves more than work, and more even than pleasure. May I ask how I can help you ? "

" I wanted your advice, sir. I don't know what to do, and my whole life seems to have gone to pieces."

" You wish to employ me as a consulting detective ? "

" Not that only. I want your opinion as a judicious man—as a man of the world. I want to know what I ought to do next. I hope to God you'll be able to tell me."

He spoke in little, sharp, jerky outbursts, and it seemed to me that to speak at all was very painful to him, and that his will all through was overriding his inclinations.

" It's a very delicate thing," said he. " One does not like to speak of one's domestic affairs to strangers. It seems dreadful to discuss the conduct of one's wife with two men whom I have never seen before. It's horrible to have to do it. But I've got to the end of my tether, and I must have advice."

" My dear Mr. Grant Munro——" began Holmes.

Our visitor sprang from his chair. " What ! " he cried. " You know my name ? "

" If you wish to preserve your *incognito*," said Holmes, smiling, " I should suggest that you cease to write your name upon the lining of your hat, or else that you turn the crown towards the person whom you are addressing. I was about to say that my friend and I have listened to many strange secrets in this room, and that we have had the good fortune to bring peace to many troubled souls. I trust that we may do as much for you. Might I beg you, as time may prove to be of importance, to furnish me with the facts of your case without further delay ? "

Our visitor again passed his hand over his forehead as if he found it bitterly hard. From every gesture and expression I could see that he was a reserved, self-contained man, with a dash of pride in his nature, more likely to hide his wounds than to expose them. Then suddenly, with a fierce gesture of his closed hand, like one who throws reserve to the winds, he began.

" The facts are these, Mr. Holmes," said he. " I am a married man, and have been so for three years. During that time my wife and I have loved each other as fondly, and lived as happily, as any two that ever were joined.

We have not had a difference, not one, in thought, or word, or deed. And now, since last Monday, there has suddenly sprung up a barrier between us, and I find that there is something in her life and in her thoughts of which I know as little as if she were the woman who brushes by me in the street. We are estranged, and I want to know why.

" Now there is one thing I want to impress upon you before I go any further, Mr. Holmes : Effie loves me. Don't let there be any mistake about that. She loves me with her whole heart and soul, and never more than now. I know it, I feel it. I don't want to argue about that. A man can tell easily enough when a woman loves him. But there's this secret between us, and we can never be the same until it is cleared."

" Kindly let me have the facts, Mr. Munro," said Holmes, with some impatience.

" I'll tell you what I know about Effie's history. She was a widow when I met her first, though quite young— only twenty-five. Her name then was Mrs. Hebron. She went out to America when she was young and lived in the town of Atlanta, where she married this Hebron, who was a lawyer with a good practice. They had one child, but the yellow fever broke out badly in the place, and both **11** husband and child died of it. I have seen his death cer- **12** tificate. This sickened her of America, and she came back to live with a maiden aunt at Pinner, in Middlesex. **13** I may mention that her husband had left her comfortably off, and that she had a capital of about four thousand five hundred pounds, which had been so well invested by him **14** that it returned an average of 7 per cent. She had only been six months at Pinner when I met her ; we fell in love with each other, and we married a few weeks after- wards.

" I am a hop merchant myself, and as I have an income of seven or eight hundred, we found ourselves comfortably off, and took a nice eighty-pound-a-year villa at Norbury. **15-16** Our little place was very countrified, considering that it is so close to town. We had an inn and two houses a little above us, and a single cottage at the other side of the field which faces us, and except those there were no houses until you get half-way to the station. My business took me into town at certain seasons, but in summer I had less to do, and then in our country home my wife and I were just as happy as could be wished. I tell you that there never was a shadow between us until this accursed affair began.

" There's one thing I ought to tell you before I go further. When we married, my wife made over all her property to me—rather against my will, for I saw how awkward it would be if my business affairs went wrong. However, she would have it so, and it was done. Well, about six weeks ago she came to me.

" ' Jack,' said she, ' when you took my money you said **17** that if ever I wanted any I was to ask you for it.'

" ' Certainly,' said I, ' it's all your own.'

" ' Well,' said she, ' I want a hundred pounds.' **18**

" I was a bit staggered at this, for I had imagined it was simply a new dress or something of the kind that she was after.

11 *the yellow fever broke out badly in the place.* Mr. Bell thought that John Hebron's death "un- doubtedly took place during an epidemic of al- most unprecedented malignity [which] visited a portion of the Southern states" in the summer and autumn of 1878 (according to Appleton's *Annual Cyclopaedia and Register of Important Events of the Year 1878*, New York, 1879, pp. 315 ff. "But now a very different problem arises," he wrote. "In the first place, there has never been, so far as we have been able to ascertain, any outbreak of yellow fever in Atlanta; and, as the city lies at an altitude of over 1,000 feet, and the climate is not of the damp, subtropical kind in which the disease flourishes, the occurrence of it there would be most unlikely. It is more probable that Hebron became infected elsewhere [New Orleans?], and returned to die in Atlanta."

12 *I have seen his death certificate.* But Mr. Stu- art C. Rand has pointed out ("What Sherlock Didn't Know") that neither the state of Georgia nor the city of Atlanta issued death certificates until they were provided for by an Act of 1914.

13 *Pinner.* Pinner gets its name from a small stream called the Pin, a tributary of the River Colne. The old village consists principally of one broad main street sloping down to the stream. Pinner is now joined to Harrow-on-the-Hill, two and three-quarter miles away, by a continuous line of houses and shops along the main London and Rickmansworth Road.

14 *four thousand five hundred pounds.* About $22,500. But to have such a sum return "an aver- age of 7 per cent" would be "an impossibility with any degree of safety," as Mr. R. M. McLaren pointed out in "Doctor Watson—Punter or Specu- lator?"

15 *eighty-pound-a-year villa.* Munro's annual in- come was at most $4,000, and he considered him- self "comfortably well off." He paid about $400 a year rental for a "nice" villa. This is another of the statements in the Canon that throws a reveal- ing light on the economics of the times in which Holmes and Watson lived.

16 *Norbury.* Now part of the County Borough of Croydon, Norbury in Holmes' and Watson's day was merely a hamlet on the fringe of London, with a railway station and a golf club.

17 " '*Jack,' said she.* Since Munro's Christian name, so far as we know, was *Grant,* we must presume "Jack" to be a nick- or pet-name used by his wife.

18 *a hundred pounds.*' About $500.

"' what may you be wantin'?' she asked . . ."

Illustration by Sidney Paget for the *Strand Magazine*, February, 1893.

"' What on earth for?' I asked.

"' Oh,' said she, in her playful way, ' you said that you were only my banker, and bankers never ask questions, you know.'

"' If you really mean it, of course you shall have the money,' said I.

"' Oh, yes, I really mean it.'

"' And you won't tell me what you want it for?'

"' Some day, perhaps, but not just at present, Jack.'

"So I had to be content with that, though it was the first time that there had ever been any secret between us. I gave her a cheque, and I never thought any more of the matter. It may have nothing to do with what came afterwards, but I thought it only right to mention it.

"Well, I told you just now that there is a cottage not far from our house. There is just a field between us, but to reach it you have to go along the road and then turn down a lane. Just beyond it is a nice little grove of Scotch firs, and I used to be very fond of strolling down there, for trees are always neighbourly kinds of things. The cottage had been standing empty this eight months, and it was a pity, for it was a pretty two-storied place, with an old-fashioned porch and honeysuckle about it. I have stood many a time and thought what a neat little homestead it would make.

"Well, last Monday evening I was taking a stroll down that way, when I met an empty van coming up the lane, and saw a pile of carpets and things lying about on the grass-plot beside the porch. It was clear that the cottage had at last been let. I walked past it, and then stopping, as an idle man might, I ran my eye over it, and wondered what sort of folk they were who had come to live so near us. And as I looked I suddenly became aware that a face was watching me out of one of the upper windows.

"I don't know what there was about that face, Mr. Holmes, but it seemed to send a chill right down my back. I was some little way off, so that I could not make out the features, but there was something unnatural and inhuman about the face. That was the impression I had, and I moved quickly forwards to get a nearer view of the person who was watching me. But as I did so the face suddenly disappeared, so suddenly that it seemed to have been plucked away into the darkness of the room. I stood for five minutes thinking the business over, and trying to analyse my impressions. I could not tell if the face was that of a man or a woman. But the colour was what impressed me most. It was of a livid dead yellow, and with something set and rigid about it, which was shockingly unnatural. So disturbed was I, that I determined to see a little more of the new inmates of the cottage. I approached and knocked at the door, which was instantly opened by a tall, gaunt woman, with a harsh, forbidding face.

"' What may you be wantin'?' she asked, in a northern accent.

"' I am your neighbour over yonder,' said I, nodding towards my house. ' I see that you have only just moved in, so I thought that if I could be of any help to you in any——'

" ' Aye, we'll just ask ye when we want ye,' said she, and shut the door in my face. Annoyed at the churlish rebuff, I turned my back and walked home. All the evening, though I tried to think of other things, my mind would still turn to the apparition at the window and the rudeness of the woman. I determined to say nothing about the former to my wife, for she is a nervous, highly strung woman, and I had no wish that she should share the unpleasant impression which had been produced upon myself. I remarked to her, however, before I fell asleep that the cottage was now occupied, to which she returned no reply.

" I am usually an extremely sound sleeper. It has been a standing jest in the family that nothing could ever wake me during the night; and yet somehow on that particular night, whether it may have been the slight excitement produced by my little adventure or not, I know not, but I slept much more lightly than usual. Half in my dreams I was dimly conscious that something was going on in the room, and gradually became aware that my wife had dressed herself and was slipping on her mantle and her bonnet. My lips were parted to murmur out some sleepy words of surprise or remonstrance at this untimely preparation, when suddenly my half-opened eyes fell upon her face, illuminated by the candle-light, and astonishment held me dumb. She wore an expression such as I had never seen before—such as I should have thought her incapable of assuming. She was deadly pale, and breathing fast, glancing furtively towards the bed, as she fastened her mantle, to see if she had disturbed me. Then, thinking that I was still asleep, she slipped noiselessly from the room, and an instant later I heard a sharp creaking, which could only come from the hinges of the front door. I sat up in bed and rapped my knuckles against the rail to make certain that I was truly awake. Then I took my watch from under the pillow. It was three in the morning. What on this earth could my wife be doing out on the country road at three in the morning?

" I had sat for about twenty minutes turning the thing over in my mind and trying to find some possible explanation. The more I thought the more extraordinary and inexplicable did it appear. I was still puzzling over it when I heard the door gently close again and her footsteps coming up the stairs.

" ' Where in the world have you been, Effie? ' I asked, as she entered.

" She gave a violent start and a kind of gasping cry when I spoke, and that cry and start troubled me more than all the rest, for there was something indescribably guilty about them. My wife had always been a woman of a frank, open nature, and it gave me a chill to see her slinking into her own room, and crying out and wincing when her own husband spoke to her.

" ' You awake, Jack? ' she cried, with a nervous laugh. ' Why, I thought that nothing could awaken you.'

" ' Where have you been? ' I asked, more sternly.

" ' I don't wonder that you are surprised,' said she, and I could see that her fingers were trembling as she undid

19 *that day.* That is, Tuesday, since Munro has told us that it was "last Monday evening" on which his troubles began.

20 *the Crystal Palace.* John Paxton, one of the owners of *Punch*, started life as gardener to the Duke of Devonshire. "In the supreme undertaking of his life," says R. J. Cruikshank in *Roaring Century*, "the building of the Crystal Palace for the Great Exhibition of 1851, Paxton displayed the originality and courage of genius. In an age bemused by bogus Gothic, he produced a design that was unlike anything else the Victorians had seen. Employing ideas of construction first worked out in building the conservatory at Chatsworth to house the giant Victoria Regina lily, Paxton gave this age the high temple of its pride. Rising in glittering bubbles of glass above the trees of Hyde Park, it looked as dream-like as the stately pleasure dome which Kubla Khan decreed in Xanadu. It seemed so frail that many people were sure the first hailstorm would shatter it. . . . The design of iron and glass, combining airy grace with massive strength, was so far ahead of its time that it was sixty years and more before architecture caught up with it." The Crystal Palace was removed from Hyde Park and re-erected at Sydenham (where Grant Munro walked to it) in 1854; it was torn down in 1941 because it served as a guide for enemy air raiders.

the fastenings of her mantle. 'Why, I never remember having done such a thing in my life before. The fact is, that I felt as though I were choking, and had a perfect longing for a breath of fresh air. I really think that I should have fainted if I had not gone out. I stood at the door for a few minutes, and now I am quite myself again.'

" All the time that she was telling me this story she never once looked in my direction, and her voice was quite unlike her usual tones. It was evident to me that she was saying what was false. I said nothing in reply, but turned my face to the wall, sick at heart, with my mind filled with a thousand venomous doubts and suspicions. What was it that my wife was concealing from me ? Where had she been during that strange expedition ? I felt that I should have no peace until I knew, and yet I shrank from asking her again after once she had told me what was false. All the rest of the night I tossed and tumbled, framing theory after theory, each more unlikely than the last.

19 " I should have gone to the City that day, but I was too perturbed in my mind to be able to pay attention to business matters. My wife seemed to be as upset as myself, and I could see from the little questioning glances which she kept shooting at me, that she understood that I disbelieved her statement, and that she was at her wits' ends what to do. We hardly exchanged a word during breakfast, and immediately afterwards I went out for a walk, that I might think the matter over in the fresh morning air.

20 " I went as far as the Crystal Palace, spent an hour in the grounds, and was back in Norbury by one o'clock. It happened that my way took me past the cottage, and I stopped for an instant to look at the windows and to see if I could catch a glimpse of the strange face which had stared out at me on the day before. As I stood there imagine my surprise, Mr. Holmes, when the door suddenly opened and my wife walked out !

" I was struck dumb with astonishment at the sight of her, but my emotions were nothing to those which showed themselves upon her face when our eyes met. She seemed for an instant to wish to shrink back inside the house again, and then, seeing how useless all concealment must be, she came forward with a very white face and frightened eyes which belied the smile upon her lips.

" ' Oh, Jack ! ' she said, ' I have just been in to see if I can be of any assistance to our new neighbours. Why do you look at me like that, Jack ? You are not angry with me ? '

" ' So,' said I, ' this is where you went during the night ? '

" ' What do you mean ? she cried.

" ' You came here. I am sure of it. Who are these people that you should visit them at such an hour ? '

" ' I have not been here before.'

" ' How can you tell me what you know is false ? ' I cried. ' Your very voice changes as you speak. When have I ever had a secret from you ? I shall enter that cottage, and I shall probe the matter to the bottom.'

" ' No, no, Jack, for God's sake ! ' she gasped, in incontrollable emotion.   Then as I approached the door, she seized my sleeve and pulled me back with convulsive strength.

"'I implore you not to do this, Jack,' she cried. 'I swear that I will tell you everything some day, but nothing but misery can come of it if you enter that cottage.'   Then, as I tried to shake her off, she clung to me in a frenzy of entreaty.

"'Trust me, Jack!' she cried. 'Trust me only this once.   You will never have cause to regret it.   You know that I would not have a secret from you if it were not for your own sake.   Our whole lives are at stake on this.   If you come home with me all will be well.   If you force your way into that cottage, all is over between us.'

"There was such earnestness, such despair, in her manner that her words arrested me, and I stood irresolute before the door.

"'I will trust you on one condition, and on one condition only,' said I at last.   'It is that this mystery comes to an end from now.   You are at liberty to preserve your secret, but you must promise me that there shall be no more nightly visits, no more doings which are kept from my knowledge.   I am willing to forget those which are passed if you will promise that there shall be no more in the future.'

"'I was sure that you would trust me,' she cried, with a great sigh of relief.   'It shall be just as you wish.   Come away, oh, come away up to the house!'   Still plucking at my sleeve she led me away from the cottage.   As we went I glanced back, and there was that yellow, livid face watching us out of the upper window.   What link could there be between that creature and my wife?   Or how could the coarse, rough woman whom I had seen the day before be connected with her?   It was a strange puzzle, and yet I knew that my mind could never know ease again until I had solved it.

"For two days after this I stayed at home, and my wife **21** appeared to abide loyally by our engagement, for, as far as I know, she never stirred out of the house.   On the third day, however, I had ample evidence that her solemn prom- **22** ise was not enough to hold her back from this secret influence which drew her away from her husband and her duty.

"I had gone into town on that day, but I returned by the 2.40 instead of the 3.36, which is my usual train.   As **23** I entered the house the maid ran into the hall with a startled face.

"'Where is your mistress?' I asked.

"'I think that she has gone out for a walk,' she answered.

"My mind was instantly filled with suspicion.   I rushed upstairs to make sure that she was not in the house.   As I did so I happened to glance out of one of the upper windows, and saw the maid with whom I had just been speaking running across the field in the direction of the cottage.   Then, of course, I saw exactly what it all meant.   My wife had gone over there and had asked the servant to call her if I should return.   Tingling with anger, I rushed down and strode across, determined to

. . . SHE SEIZED MY SLEEVE AND PULLED ME BACK
WITH CONVULSIVE STRENGTH.

Illustration by William H. Hyde for *Harper's Weekly*, February 11, 1893. Sidney Paget illustrated much the same scene for the *Strand Magazine*, February, 1893.

21 "*For two days after this*. That is, Wednesday and Thursday.

22 *On the third day*. That is, on Friday.

23 *the 2.40 instead of the 3.36*. Unfortunately, neither train appears to have existed in Holmes' and Watson's day.

24 *That was yesterday.* Mr. Grant Munro therefore called upon Mr. Sherlock Holmes on a Saturday.

" 'TELL ME EVERYTHING, THEN,' SAID I."

Illustration by Sidney Paget for the *Strand Magazine*, February, 1893.

end the matter once and for ever.   I saw my wife and the maid hurrying back together along the lane, but I did not stop to speak with them.   In the cottage lay the secret which was casting a shadow over my life.   I vowed that, come what might, it should be a secret no longer.   I did not even knock when I reached it, but turned the handle and rushed into the passage.

" It was all still and quiet upon the ground-floor.   In the kitchen a kettle was singing on the fire, and a large black cat lay coiled up in a basket, but there was no sign of the woman whom I had seen before.   I ran into the other room, but it was equally deserted.   Then I rushed up the stairs, but only to find two other rooms empty and deserted at the top.   There was no one at all in the whole house.   The furniture and pictures were of the most common and vulgar description, save in the one chamber at the window of which I had seen the strange face.   That was comfortable and elegant, and all my suspicions rose into a fierce, bitter blaze when I saw that on the mantelpiece stood a full-length photograph of my wife, which had been taken at my request only three months ago.

" I stayed long enough to make certain that the house was absolutely empty.   Then I left it, feeling a weight at my heart such as I had never had before.   My wife came out into the hall as I entered my house, but I was too hurt and angry to speak with her, and pushing past her I made my way into my study.   She followed me, however, before I could close the door.

" ' I am sorry that I broke my promise, Jack,' said she, ' but if you knew all the circumstances I am sure you would forgive me.'

" ' Tell me everything, then,' said I.

" ' I cannot, Jack, I cannot ! ' she cried.

" ' Until you tell me who it is that has been living in that cottage, and who it is to whom you have given that photograph, there can never be any confidence between us,' said I, and breaking away from her I left the house.

24 That was yesterday, Mr. Holmes, and I have not seen her since, nor do I know anything more about this strange business.   It is the first shadow that has come between us, and it has so shaken me that I do not know what I should do for the best.   Suddenly this morning it occurred to me that you were the man to advise me, so I have hurried to you now, and I place myself unreservedly in your hands.   If there is any point which I have not made clear, pray question me about it.   But above all tell me quickly what I have to do, for this misery is more than I can bear."

Holmes and I had listened with the utmost interest to this extraordinary statement, which had been delivered in the jerky, broken fashion of a man who is under the influence of extreme emotion.   My companion sat silent now for some time, with his chin upon his hand, lost in thought.

" Tell me," said he at last, " could you swear that this was a man's face which you saw at the window ? "

" Each time that I saw it I was some distance away from it, so that it is impossible for me to say."

" You appear, however, to have been disagreeably impressed by it."

"It seemed to be of an unnatural colour, and to have a strange rigidity about the features.   When I approached, it vanished with a jerk."

"How long is it since your wife asked you for a hundred pounds ? "

"Nearly two months."

"Have you ever seen a photograph of her first husband ? "

"No ; there was a great fire at Atlanta very shortly after his death, and all her papers were destroyed."   **25**

"And yet she had a certificate of death.   You say that you saw it ? "

"Yes, she got a duplicate after the fire."

"Did you ever meet anyone who knew her in America ? "

"No."

"Did she ever talk of revisiting the place ? '

"No."

"Or get letters from it ? "

"Not to my knowledge."

"Thank you.   I should like to think over the matter a little now.   If the cottage is permanently deserted we may have some difficulty ; if on the other hand, as I fancy is more likely, the inmates were warned of your coming, and left before you entered yesterday, then they may be back now, and we should clear it all up easily. Let me advise you, then, to return to Norbury and to examine the windows of the cottage again.   If you have reason to believe that it is inhabited do not force your way in, but send a wire to my friend and me.   We shall be with you within an hour of receiving it, and we shall then very soon get to the bottom of the business."

"And if it is still empty ? "

"In that case I shall come out to-morrow and talk it over with you.   Good-bye, and above all things do not fret until you know that you really have a cause for it."

"I am afraid that this is a bad business, Watson," said my companion, as he returned after accompanying Mr. Grant Munro to the door.   "What do you make of it ? "

"It had an ugly sound," I answered.

"Yes.   There's blackmail in it, or I am much mistaken."

"And who is the blackmailer ? "

"Well, it must be this creature who lives in the only comfortable room in the place, and has her photograph above his fireplace.   Upon my word, Watson, there is something very attractive about that livid face at the window, and I would not have missed the case for worlds."

"You have a theory ? "

"Yes, a provisional one.   But I shall be surprised if it does not turn out to be correct.   This woman's first husband is in that cottage."

"Why do you think so ? "

"How else can we explain her frenzied anxiety that her second one should not enter it ?   The facts, as I read them, are something like this : This woman was married in America.   Her husband developed some hateful qualities, or, shall we say, that he contracted some loathsome disease, and became a leper or an imbecile.   She fled

25 *there was a great fire at Atlanta very shortly after his death.* There has been no great fire in Atlanta since the time of William Tecumseh Sherman's visit to that city. For the record, however, the city of *Augusta*, Georgia, *has* suffered both a yellow fever epidemic and a great fire—but not in years that support any known Holmesian chronology.

from him at last, returned to England, changed her name, and started her life, as she thought, afresh. She had been married three years, and believed that her position was quite secure—having shown her husband the death certificate of some man whose name she had assumed—when suddenly her whereabouts was discovered by her first husband, or, we may suppose, by some unscrupulous woman who had attached herself to the invalid. They write to the wife and threaten to come and expose her. She asks for a hundred pounds and endeavours to buy them off. They come in spite of it, and when the husband mentions casually to the wife that there are new-comers in the cottage, she knows in some way that they are her pursuers. She waits until her husband is asleep, and then she rushes down to endeavour to persuade them to leave her in peace. Having no success, she goes again next morning, and her husband meets her, as he has told us, as she came out. She promises him then not to go there again, but two days afterwards, the hope of getting rid of those dreadful neighbours is too strong for her, and she makes another attempt, taking down with her the photograph which had probably been demanded from her. In the midst of this interview the maid rushes in to say that the master has come home, on which the wife, knowing that he would come straight down to the cottage, hurries the inmates out at the back door, into that grove of fir trees probably which was mentioned as standing near. In this way he finds the place deserted. I shall be very much surprised, however, if it is still so when he reconnoitres it this evening. What do you think of my theory ? ”

“ It is all surmise.”

“ But at least it covers all the facts. When new facts come to our knowledge which cannot be covered by it, it will be time enough to reconsider it. At present we can do nothing until we have a fresh message from our friend at Norbury.”

But we had not very long to wait. It came just as we had finished our tea. “ The cottage is still tenanted,” it said. “ Have seen the face again at the window. I’ll **26** meet the seven o’clock train, and take no steps until you arrive.”

He was waiting on the platform when we stepped out, and we could see in the light of the station lamps that he was very pale, and quivering with agitation.

“ They are still there, Mr. Holmes,” said he, laying his hand upon my friend’s sleeve. “ I saw lights in the cottage as I came down. We shall settle it now, once and for all.”

“ What is your plan, then ? ” asked Holmes, as we walked down the dark, tree-lined road.

“ I am going to force my way in and see for myself who is in the house. I wish you both to be there as witnesses.”

“ You are quite determined to do this, in spite of your wife’s warning that it is better that you should not solve the mystery ? ”

“ Yes, I am determined.”

“ Well, I think that you are in the right. Any truth

26 *the seven o’clock train*. Again, there was no such train.

is better than indefinite doubt. We had better go up at once. Of course, legally, we are putting ourselves hopelessly in the wrong, but I think that it is worth it."

It was a very dark night and a thin rain began to fall **27** as we turned from the high-road into a narrow lane, deeply rutted, with edges on either side. Mr. Grant Munro pushed impatiently forward, however, and we stumbled after him as best we could.

" There are the lights of my house," he murmured, pointing to a glimmer among the trees, " and here is the cottage which I am going to enter."

We turned a corner in the lane as he spoke, and there was the building close beside us. A yellow bar falling across the black foreground showed that the door was not quite closed, and one window in the upper story was brightly illuminated. As we looked we saw a dark blur moving across the blind.

" There is that creature," cried Grant Munro ; " you can see for yourselves that someone is there. Now follow me, and we shall soon know all."

We approached the door, but suddenly a woman appeared out of the shadow and stood in the golden track of the lamp-light. I could not see her face in the darkness, but her arms were thrown out in an attitude of entreaty.

" For God's sake, don't, Jack ! " she cried. " I had a presentiment that you would come this evening. Think better of it, dear ! Trust me again, and you will never have cause to regret it."

" I have trusted you too long, Effie ! " he cried, sternly. " Leave go of me ! I must pass you. My friends and I are going to settle this matter once and for ever." He pushed her to one side and we followed closely after him. As he threw the door open an elderly woman ran out in front of him and tried to bar his passage, but he thrust her back, and an instant afterwards we were all upon the stairs. Grant Munro rushed into the lighted room at the top, and we entered it at his heels.

It was a cosy, well-furnished apartment, with two candles burning upon the table and two upon the mantelpiece. In the corner, stooping over a desk, there sat what appeared to be a little girl. Her face was turned away as we entered, but we could see that she was dressed in a red frock, and that she had long white gloves on. As she whisked round to us I gave a cry of surprise and horror. The face which she turned towards us was of the strangest livid tint, and the features were absolutely devoid of any expression. An instant later the mystery was explained. Holmes, with a laugh, passed his hand behind the child's ear, a mask peeled off from her countenance, and there was a little coal-black negress with all her white teeth flashing in amusement at our amazed faces. I burst out laughing out of sympathy with her merriment, but Grant Munro stood staring, with his hand clutching at his throat.

" My God ! " he cried, " what can be the meaning of this ? "

" I will tell you the meaning of it," cried the lady, sweeping into the room with a proud, set face. " You

27 *It was a very dark night and a thin rain began to fall.* "Very dark" shortly after seven o'clock in Norbury and "a thin rain" would both seem to corroborate a date in early April.

. . . AND THERE WAS A LITTLE COAL-BLACK NEGRESS . . .

Illustration by Sidney Paget for the *Strand Magazine*, February, 1893.

But: "One glance at Lucy's coal-black complexion, after [Holmes] had literally unmasked her, should have told him that she could not be Effie Munro's child. Any anthropologist could have reminded him that the child of a mixed racial marriage has pigmentation approximately halfway between that of the parents."—Edward Quayle, "Suffer the Little Children . . ."

28 *I cut myself off from my race in order to wed him.* "The insuperable difficulty," the late H. W. Bell wrote in *Sherlock Holmes and Dr. Watson: The Chronology of Their Adventures,* "lies in the impossibility of any marriage between a coloured man and a white woman. According to the Constitution of the State of Georgia, adopted in 1865 [and retained in the revised Constitution adopted in 1878]: 'The marriage relation between white persons and persons of African descent is forever prohibited, and such marriages shall be null and void' (Art. 5, Sect. 1, par. 9). Moreover, further legislation provides that any officer issuing a license for marriage between two persons, one of whom is of African descent and the other white, shall be penalised by fine and imprisonment or both, while in the case of anyone performing such a marriage, the penalties are doubled. . . . Even on the theory that [Mrs. Munro and John Hebron] were married in some State in which such unions were permitted, their marriage upon their return to Atlanta, would have come to an abrupt and sanguinary end."

In reply to this, Mr. Manly Wade Wellman has written ("Two Southern Exposures of Sherlock Holmes"): "Laws against . . . mixed marriages, both in ante-bellum Georgia and in more modern times, have been cited with an air of settling the matter as mere romance. But other laws, that obtained here during the Reconstruction years when carpetbagger and scalawag leaders marshalled numerous Negro legislators and set up behaviors that have not obtained before or since, may . . . explain the seeming impossibility."

And Mr. Robert H. Schutz has written ("Some Problems in 'The Yellow Face'"): "Referring to one book on the subject of Negroes in the professional fields [C. G. Woodson, *The Negro Professional Man and the Community, with Special Emphasis on the Physician and Lawyer*], we find that as early as 1850 there were several Negro lawyers in New York City. Furthermore, there is an Atlanta in New York State (also in other northern states), and the New York State laws in 1880 did not prohibit inter-racial marriages."

29 *little Lucy is darker far than ever her father was.* Again, by the information given, this could not be anthropologically correct.

30 *what is to become of us, my child and me?"* "Seeing that every point in [Mrs. Munro's] story which we have been able to check is wholly false," Mr. Bell wrote, "we are driven to the conclusion that John Hebron was a white man; that in the course of a journey, perhaps in Alabama, in July, 1878, he became infected with yellow fever; that Mrs. Hebron had been engaged in a criminal intrigue with a Negro, whose name has not survived, and that her child's birth, following the death of her husband, was the reason for her flight. Her paramour was doubtless adequately dealt with.

have forced me against my own judgment to tell you, and now we must both make the best of it. My husband died at Atlanta. My child survived."

" Your child ! "

She drew a large silver locket from her bosom. " You have never seen this open."

" I understood that it did not open."

She touched a spring, and the front hinged back. There was a portrait within of a man, strikingly handsome and intelligent, but bearing unmistakable signs upon his features of his African descent.

" That is John Hebron, of Atlanta," said the lady, " and a nobler man never walked the earth. **28** I cut myself off from my race in order to wed him ; but never once while he lived did I for one instant regret it. It was our misfortune that our only child took after his people rather than mine. It is often so in such matches, and little Lucy **29** is darker far than ever her father was. But, dark or fair, she is my own dear little girlie, and her mother's pet." The little creature ran across at the words and nestled up against the lady's dress.

" When I left her in America," she continued, " it was only because her health was weak, and the change might have done her harm. She was given to the care of a faithful Scotchwoman who had once been our servant. Never for an instant did I dream of disowning her as my child. But when chance threw you in my way, Jack, and I learned to love you, I feared to tell you about my child. God forgive me, I feared that I should lose you, and I had not the courage to tell you. I had to choose between you, and in my weakness I turned away from my own little girl. For three years I have kept her existence a secret from you, but I heard from the nurse, and I knew that all was well with her. At last, however, there came an overwhelming desire to see the child once more. I struggled against it, but in vain. Though I knew the danger I determined to have the child over, if it were but for a few weeks. I sent a hundred pounds to the nurse, and I gave her instructions about this cottage, so that she might come as a neighbour without my appearing to be in any way connected with her. I pushed my precautions so far as to order her to keep the child in the house during the daytime, and to cover up her little face and hands, so that even those who might see her at the window should not gossip about there being a black child in the neighbourhood. If I had been less cautious I might have been more wise, but I was half crazy with fear lest you should learn the truth.

" It was you who told me first that the cottage was occupied. I should have waited for the morning, but I could not sleep for excitement, and so at last I slipped out, knowing how difficult it is to awaken you. But you saw me go, and that was the beginning of my troubles. Next day you had my secret at your mercy, but you nobly refrained from pursuing your advantage. Three days later, however, the nurse and child only just escaped from the back door as you rushed in at the front one. And now to-night you at last know all, and I ask you what is to **30** become of us, my child and me ? " She clasped her hands and waited for an answer.

It was a long two minutes before Grant Munro broke the silence, and when his answer came it was one of which I love to think. He lifted the little child, kissed her, and then, still carrying her, he held his other hand out to his wife, and turned towards the door.

"We can talk it over more comfortably at home," said he. "I am not a very good man, Effie, but I think that I am a better one than you have given me credit for being."

Holmes and I followed them down to the lane, and my friend plucked at my sleeve as we came out. "I think," said he, "that we shall be of more use in London than in Norbury."

Not another word did he say of the case until late that night when he was turning away, with his lighted candle, for his bedroom.

"Watson," said he, "if it should ever strike you that I am getting a little over-confident in my powers, or giving less pains to a case than it deserves, kindly whisper 'Norbury' in my ear, and I shall be infinitely obliged to you."

She preserved his portrait in her locket, and at last, when forced to give some sort of explanation to the infatuated Munro, carried the situation with a high hand and 'a proud, set face.' She was an actress of parts, and an accomplished liar; but her greatest distinction is that she deceived Sherlock Holmes."

HE LIFTED THE LITTLE CHILD . . .

Illustration by Sidney Paget for the *Strand Magazine*, February, 1893.

33

THE GREEK INTERPRETER

[Wednesday, September 12, 1888]

1 *my long and intimate acquaintance.* A later rather than an earlier year in the partnership is certainly indicated. Your editor favors 1888—as do Messrs. Christ, Folsom, Petersen, and Zeisler. Brend chose 1882, Newton 1883, Andrew 1886, Pattrick 1889, and Bell, Smith, and Sayers 1890.

2 *after tea.* Holmes would have been no true-born Englishman had he not wanted his tea occasionally. He accepts a 5:30 cup from Watson in *The Sign of the Four*, helps himself to a cup on another occasion ("The Adventure of the Beryl Coronet"), consumes hot tea before embarking on a journey to Kent ("The Adventure of the Abbey Grange"). At the Hereford arms in Ross, Holmes, Watson, and Lestrade sat over a cup of tea ("The Boscombe Valley Mystery"), and Holmes took his tea at an inn again in "The Naval Treaty."

3 *a summer evening.* We shortly learn that it was also a Wednesday evening.

4 *golf clubs.* That Holmes was then and is today a keen golfer is the theory held by Mr. Webster Evans, who notes (in "Sherlock Holmes and Sport") that in "The Adventure of Wisteria Lodge" Watson records the fact that Holmes "spent his days in long and often solitary walks" in the country. "Holmes murmured some excuse about it being very pleasant to see "the first green shoots upon the hedges and the catkins on the hazels.' But that word green—I wonder if he was really only walking. After all, golf is a game that would suit a man of Holmes' temperament. And as Professor Moriarty wrote *The Dynamics of an Asteroid*, why should not Holmes have written *The Dynamics of a Spheroid*—a book which, like Moriarty's, would certainly be likely to ascend to such rarefied heights of pure mathematics that there could be no man in the scientific press capable of criticising it!"

1 DURING my long and intimate acquaintance with Mr. Sherlock Holmes I had never heard him refer to his relations, and hardly ever to his own early life. This reticence upon his part had increased the somewhat inhuman effect which he produced upon me, until sometimes I found myself regarding him as an isolated phenomenon, a brain without a heart, as deficient in human sympathy as he was pre-eminent in intelligence. His aversion to women, and his disinclination to form new friendships, were both typical of his unemotional character, but not more so than his complete suppression of every reference to his own people. I had come to believe that he was an orphan with no relatives living, but one day, to my very great surprise, he began to talk to me about his brother.

2-3 It was after tea on a summer evening, and the conversation, which had roamed in a desultory, spasmodic **4** fashion from golf clubs to the causes of the change in the **5** obliquity of the ecliptic, came round at last to the question **6** of atavism and hereditary aptitudes. The point under discussion was how far any singular gift in an individual was due to his ancestry, and how far to his own early training.

"In your own case," said I, " from all that you have told me it seems obvious that your faculty of observation and your peculiar facility for deduction are due to your own systematic training."

"To some extent," he answered, thoughtfully. "My ancestors were country squires, who appear to have led much the same life as is natural to their class. But, none the less, my turn that way is in my veins, and may have come with my grandmother, who was the sister of Vernet, the French artist. Art in the blood is liable to take the strangest forms."

"But how do you know that it is hereditary?"

"Because my brother Mycroft possesses it in a larger degree than I do."

This was news to me, indeed. If there were another man with such singular powers in England, how was it that neither police nor public had heard of him? I put the question, with a hint that it was my companion's modesty which made him acknowledge his brother as his superior. Holmes laughed at my suggestion.

"My dear Watson," said he. "I cannot agree with those who rank modesty among the virtues. To the logician all things should be seen exactly as they are, and to under-estimate oneself is as much a departure from truth as to exaggerate one's own powers. When I say, therefore, that Mycroft has better powers of observation than I, you may take it that I am speaking the exact and literal truth."

"Is he your junior?"

"Seven years my senior."

"How comes it that he is unknown?"

"Oh, he is very well known in his own circle."

"Where, then?"

"Well, in the Diogenes Club, for example."

I had never heard of the institution, and my face must have proclaimed as much, for Sherlock Holmes pulled out his watch.

"The Diogenes Club is the queerest club in London, **7** and Mycroft one of the queerest men. He's always there **8** from a quarter to five till twenty to eight. It's six now, so if you care for a stroll this beautiful evening I shall be very happy to introduce you to two curiosities."

Five minutes later we were in the street, walking towards Regent Circus. **9**

"You wonder," said my companion, "why it is that Mycroft does not use his powers for detective work. He is incapable of it."

"But I thought you said——!"

"I said that he was my superior in observation and deduction. If the art of the detective began and ended in reasoning from an arm-chair, my brother would be the

. . . SHERLOCK HOLMES PULLED OUT HIS WATCH.

Illustration by Sidney Paget for the *Strand Maga-zine*, September, 1893.

5 *the change in the obliquity of the ecliptic.* The angle between the planes of the earth's equator and orbit (ecliptic) diminishes at the rate of $0''.47$ per year. Scientists say this rate of decrease will gradually slacken, and, after many thousands of years, the obliquity will be about $22\frac{1}{2}°$ and will begin to increase.

6 *atavism.* The recurrence, in a descendant, of characteristics of a remote ancestor, instead of those of an immediate ancestor—"reversion to the primitive."

7 *the queerest club in London.* Lord Donegall, the editor of the *Sherlock Holmes Journal*, has suggested that the Diogenes is "only an alias" for the Athenaeum. This famous London club was founded in 1824 ". . . for the association of individuals known for their scientific and literary attainments, artists of eminence in any class of the fine arts and noblemen and gentlemen distinguished as liberal patrons of science, literature, or the arts." Theodore Hook wrote of it:

> There's first the Athenaeum Club; so wise
> there's not a man of it
> That has not sense enough for six—in fact
> that is the plan of it;
> The very waiters answer you with eloquence
> Socratical,
> And always place the knives and forks in
> order mathematical.

The Athenaeum did not permit smoking until 1862, and it was one of the last clubs in London to install a bar.

8 *and Mycroft one of the queerest men.* As we have noted before, there are mysteries about Mycroft. Mr. Wilbur K. McKee has even gone so far as to suggest ("The Son of a Certain Gracious Lady") that "Mycroft Holmes was not actually the brother of Sherlock" at all but was really Albert Edward, Prince of Wales, later King Edward VII.

A less sensational suggestion has been made by Mr. J. Randolph Cox ("Mycroft Holmes: Private Detective"); in Mr. Cox's view, Mycroft Holmes, in earlier days, had himself been a consulting detective who chose to be known as *Martin Hewitt*. Shortly before the Bruce-Partington affair (November, 1895) Mycroft gave his old friend Brett, a journalist, permission to publish the reminiscences of his earlier exploits as *Martin Hewitt, Investigator,* as by Arthur Morrison; London: Ward, Lock & Bowden, 1894. This was followed, in 1895, by *Chronicles of Martin Hewitt;* in 1896 by *Adventures of Martin Hewitt;* in 1903 by *The Red Triangle.*

The late Monsignor Ronald A. Knox had a very different view of Mycroft ("The Mystery of Mycroft"): "Mycroft was, at this period of his life, in the service and in the pay of the ex-Professor [James Moriarty]."

9 *Regent Circus.* Possibly Oxford Circus, possibly Piccadilly Circus. As Mr. Michael Harrison explains (*In the Footsteps of Sherlock Holmes*): "When Nash was planning his new thoroughfare, to connect Langham Place with Pall Mall, he arranged for two 'piazzas,' one at the point where Oxford Street crossed the 'new'—'Regent'—Street, and the other at the junction of Coventry Street and Piccadilly. Yet both these piazzas were called, at the beginning, 'Regent Circus'; the one at the end of Piccadilly being known as 'the first Regent Circus,' and the one at Oxford Street being called 'the second Regent Circus.' It was not so very long before, in popular usage, 'the first Regent Circus' became 'Piccadilly Circus' [and the second "Oxford Circus"]; and it is somewhat extraordinary that Watson should have stuck to the old name, long before all but pedants and map-makers and officials of the Metropolitan Board of Works had given up the old, confusing name."

greatest criminal agent that ever lived. But he has no ambition and no energy. He would not even go out of his way to verify his own solutions, and would rather be considered wrong than take the trouble to prove himself right. Again and again I have taken a problem to him and have received an explanation which has afterwards proved to be the correct one. And yet he was absolutely incapable of working out the practical points which must be gone into before a case could be laid before a judge or jury."

" It is not his profession, then ? "

" By no means. What is to me a means of livelihood is to him the merest hobby of a dilettante. He has an extraordinary faculty for figures, and audits the books in **10** some of the Government departments. Mycroft lodges in Pall Mall, and he walks round the corner into White-**11** hall every morning and back every evening. From year's end to year's end he takes no other exercise, and is seen nowhere else, except only in the Diogenes Club, which is just opposite his rooms."

"MYCROFT LODGES IN PALL MALL . . ."

"From Trafalgar Square, Pall Mall, the handsomest street in London, leads to the west. Its name is a record of its having been the place where the game of Palle-malle was played—a game popular in the deserted streets of old sleepy Italian cities, and deriving its name from *Palla*, a ball, and *Maglia*, a mallet. It was introduced into England in the reign of James I, who . . . recommended his son Prince Henry to play it. Charles II, who was passionately fond of the game, removed the site for it to St. James's Park. . . . The street was not enclosed till about 1690, when it was at first called Catherine Street, in honour of Catherine of Braganza, and it still continued to be a fashionable promenade rather than a highway for carriage traffic. . . . Club-houses are the characteristic of the street, though none of the existing buildings dates beyond the [nineteenth] century. In the [eighteenth] century their place was filled by taverns where various literary and convivial societies held their meetings: Pepys in 1660 was frequently at one of these, 'Wood's at the Pell-Mell.' The first trial of street gas in London was made here in 1807, in a row of lamps, on the King's birthday, before the colonnade of Carlton House. Amid all the changes of the town, London-lovers have continued to give their best affections to Pall Mall, and how many there are who agree with the lines of Charles Morris—'In town let me live, then, in town let me die; / For in truth I can't relish the country, not I. / If one must have a villa in summer to dwell, / Oh! give me the sweet shady side of Pall Mall.' "—Augustus J. C. Hare, *Walks in London*, Vol. II. Our photograph, from James Edward Holroyd's *Baker Street By-ways*, shows Pall Mall, looking east, with a hansom cab turning into Lower Regent Street.

" I cannot recall the name."

" Very likely not. There are many men in London, you know, who, some from shyness, some from misanthropy have no wish for the company of their fellows. Yet they are not averse to comfortable chairs and the latest periodicals. It is for the convenience of these that the Diogenes Club was started, and it now contains the most unsociable and unclubbable men in town. No member is permitted to take the least notice of any other one. Save in the Strangers' Room, no talking is, under any circumstances, permitted, and three offences, if brought to the notice of the committee, render the talker liable to expulsion. My brother was one of the founders, and I have myself found it a very soothing atmosphere."

We had reached Pall Mall as we talked, and were walking down it from the St. James's end. Sherlock Holmes **12** stopped at a door some little distance from the Carlton, **13** and, cautioning me not to speak, he led the way into the hall. Through the glass panelling I caught a glimpse of a large and luxurious room in which a considerable number of men were sitting about and reading papers, each in his own little nook. Holmes showed me into a small chamber which looked out on to Pall Mall, and then, leaving me for a minute, he came back with a companion who I knew could only be his brother.

Mycroft Holmes was a much larger and stouter man than Sherlock. His body was absolutely corpulent, but his face, though massive, had preserved something of the

MYCROFT HOLMES WAS A MUCH LARGER AND STOUTER MAN THAN SHERLOCK.

Portrait of Mycroft Holmes by Sidney Paget for the *Strand Magazine*, September, 1893.

It is also extraordinary that Watson should mention "Regent Circus" here at all, for he tells us shortly that he and Holmes walked down Pall Mall "from the St. James's end." To approach Pall Mall from Baker Street, via St. James's, they would hardly go by way of "Regent Circus"— whether Watson meant Piccadilly Circus or Oxford Circus.

10 *audits the books in some of the Government departments.* "It is difficult to believe," Mr. S. C. Roberts has written, "that . . . Mycroft could have attained to such a position if he had not had an expensive public school and university education behind him."

And Mr. C. O. Merriman has added ("Unfair to Mycroft"): "I do not know if the rival claims of the Institute of Chartered Accountants of England and Wales and that of the Institute of Scottish Chartered Accountants have ever been registered on the score of Mycroft's early education but I think that perhaps I may take this opportunity of recording the fact that my first researches show clearly that Mycroft was a member of the English Institute. An examination of the Charter of Incorporation shows that a Mr. W. Holmes was an Associate Member. The upending of the 'M' can only be ascribed to a temperamental printer."

11 *Whitehall.* Running from Charing Cross to Parliament Street, Whitehall is the home of Britain's government offices and the Cenotaph (war memorial). Here was once the palace of the archbishops of York, in which Henry VIII and Cromwell died and outside which Charles I was executed.

12 *St. James's.* "From St. James's Palace, St. James's Street, built in 1670, and at first called Long Street, leads to Piccadilly. From its earliest days it has been popular. 'The Campus Martius of St. James's Street, / Where the beaux cavalry pace to and fro, / Before they take the field in Rotten Row.'—Sheridan."—Augustus J. C. Hare, *Walks in London*, Vol. II.

13 *the Carlton.* The Carlton *Hotel* was not erected until between 1897 and 1899; so Watson must refer here to the Carlton *Club* (then located in Pall Mall), founded at the Thatched House Tavern in 1832 to fight the supporters of the Reform Bill and to serve as a rallying point for the Tories after their wholesale defeat in the elections. Sir James Damery, of "The Adventure of the Illustrious Client," was a member of the Carlton.

14 "*I hear of Sherlock everywhere since you became his chronicler.* The adventure is therefore to be dated after the publication of *A Study in Scarlet* in December, 1887.

15 *that Manor House case.* If the adventure of "The Greek Interpreter" took place in September, 1888, as your editor believes that it did, it is curious that Sherlock and Mycroft on this occasion should not at least have mentioned the Jack the Ripper killings, the second of which took place on the night of August 7th, the third on August 31st, and the fourth on September 8th. The omission is especially curious in the light of the late Page Heldenbrand's comment in "Another Bohemian Scandal": "In view of the sensation caused by [Jack the] Ripper's contretemps, the utter despair of Scotland Yard, and the renown enjoyed by Holmes in 1888, we can be absolutely certain that he took a hand in attempting to discourage wayward Jack's cutting-up." This is also your editor's view, and he has attempted to reconstruct Holmes' part in the capture of Jack the Ripper in Chapter XV, "Jack the Harlot Killer," of *Sherlock Holmes of Baker Street*. We should also note here that Mr. Gordon Neitzke, in "Sherlock Holmes and Jack the Ripper," has voiced the alarming speculation that *Watson* was the Ripper.

16 *a sapper.* A member of a military engineer unit organized, trained, and equipped primarily for trench-digging and other field fortification work.

17 *He is in the artillery.*" "One could wish that they had gone a little further and told us whether the man belonged to the Royal Horse Artillery of the Field or Garrison branch," Mrs. Crighton Sellars wrote in "Dr. Watson and the British Army." "For my part, I deduce that the ex-Sergeant belonged to the Garrison Artillery, because he did not have the cavalry stride and because of his weight, which precluded too much riding and activity."

18 *there is another child to be thought of.*" Compare the above with a diagnosis once made by Dr. Joseph Bell: "Well, my man, you've served in the army." "Aye, sir." "Not long discharged?" "No, sir." "A Highland regiment?" "Aye, sir." "A non-com. officer?" "Aye, sir." "Stationed at Barbados?" "Aye, sir." "You see, gentlemen," Bell explained to his students, "the man was respectful but did not remove his hat. They do not in the army, but he would have learned civilian ways had he been long discharged. He has an air of authority and he is obviously Scottish. As to Barbados, his complaint is elephantiasis, which is West Indian and not British."

sharpness of expression which was so remarkable in that of his brother. His eyes, which were of a peculiarly light watery grey, seemed to always retain that far-away, introspective look which I had only observed in Sherlock's when he was exerting his full powers.

"I am glad to meet you, sir," said he, putting out a broad, flat hand, like the flipper of a seal. "I hear of **14** Sherlock everywhere since you became his chronicler. By the way, Sherlock, I expected to see you round last **15** week to consult me over that Manor House case. I thought you might be a little out of your depth."

"No, I solved it," said my friend, smiling.

"It was Adams, of course?"

"Yes, it was Adams."

"I was sure of it from the first." The two sat down together in the bow-window of the club. "To anyone who wishes to study mankind this is the spot," said Mycroft. "Look at the magnificent types! Look at these two men who are coming towards us, for example."

"The billiard-marker and the other?"

"Precisely. What do you make of the other?"

The two men had stopped opposite the window. Some chalk marks over the waistcoat pocket were the only signs of billiards which I could see in one of them. The other was a very small, dark fellow, with his hat pushed back and several packages under his arm.

"An old soldier, I perceive," said Sherlock.

"And very recently discharged," remarked the brother.

"Served in India, I see."

"And a non-commissioned officer."

"Royal Artillery, I fancy," said Sherlock.

"And a widower."

' But with a child."

'' Children, my dear boy, children."

"Come," said I, laughing, "this is a little too much."

"Surely," answered Holmes, "it is not hard to say that a man with that bearing, expression of authority, and sun-baked skin is a soldier, is more than a private, and is not long from India."

"That he has not left the service long is shown by his still wearing his 'ammunition boots,' as they are called," observed Mycroft.

"He has not the cavalry stride, yet he wore his hat on one side, as is shown by the lighter skin on that side of **16** his brow. His weight is against his being a sapper. He **17** is in the artillery."

"Then, of course, his complete mourning shows that he has lost someone very dear. The fact that he is doing his own shopping looks as though it were his wife. He has been buying things for children, you perceive. There is a rattle, which shows that one of them is very young. The wife probably died in child-bed. The fact that he has a picture-book under his arm shows that there is another **18** child to be thought of."

I began to understand what my friend meant when he said that his brother possessed even keener faculties than he did himself. He glanced across at me and smiled. Mycroft took snuff from a tortoiseshell box and brushed away the wandering grains from his coat with a large, red silk handkerchief.

" By the way, Sherlock," said he,   I have had something quite after your own heart—a most singular problem —submitted to my judgment. I really had not the energy to follow it up, save in a very incomplete fashion, but it gave me a basis for some very pleasing speculations. If you would care to hear the facts——"

" My dear Mycroft, I should be delighted."

The brother scribbled a note upon a leaf of his pocket-book, and, ringing the bell, he handed it to the waiter.

" I have asked Mr. Melas to step across," said he. " He lodges on the floor above me, and I have some slight acquaintance with him, which led him to come to me in his perplexity. Mr. Melas is a Greek by extraction, as I understand, and he is a remarkable linguist. He earns his living partly as interpreter in the law courts, partly by acting as guide to any wealthy Orientals who may visit the Northumberland Avenue hotels. I think I will leave him to tell his own very remarkable experience in his own fashion."

A few minutes later we were joined by a short, stout man, whose olive face and coal-black hair proclaimed his Southern origin, though his speech was that of an educated Englishman. He shook hands eagerly with Sherlock Holmes, and his dark eyes sparkled with pleasure when he understood that the specialist was anxious to hear his story.

" I do not believe that the police credit me—on my word I do not," said he, in a wailing voice. " Just because they have never heard of it before, they think that such a thing cannot be. But I know that I shall never be easy in my mind until I know what has become of my poor man with the sticking-plaster upon his face."

" I am all attention," said Sherlock Holmes.

" This is Wednesday evening," said Mr. Melas ; " well, then it was on Monday night—only two days ago, you understand—that all this happened. I am an interpreter, as, perhaps, my neighbour there has told you. I interpret all languages—or nearly all—but as I am a Greek by birth, and with a Grecian name, it is with that particular tongue that I am principally associated. For many years I have been the chief Greek interpreter in London, and my name is very well known in the hotels.

" It happens, not unfrequently, that I am sent for at strange hours, by foreigners who get into difficulties, or by travellers who arrive late and wish my services. I was not surprised, therefore on Monday night when a Mr. Latimer, a very fashionably dressed young man, came up to my rooms and asked me to accompany him in a cab, which was waiting at the door. A Greek friend had come to see him upon business, he said, and, as he could speak nothing but his own tongue, the services of an interpreter were indispensable. He gave me to understand that his house was some little distance off, in Kensington, and he seemed to be in a great hurry, bustling me rapidly into the cab when we had descended into the street.

" I say into the cab, but I soon became doubtful as to whether it was not a carriage in which I found myself.

19 *Shaftesbury Avenue.* The adventure must certainly have taken place after 1886, since Shaftesbury Avenue was not opened to traffic until that year. It was a widening of the former King and Dudley streets, except for the portion between Piccadilly Circus and Rupert Street. Today it is a street of theatres, dressmakers' and milliners' shops.

"... HE DREW UP THE WINDOWS ON EACH SIDE ..."

Illustration by Sidney Paget for the *Strand Magazine*, September, 1893.

It was certainly more roomy than the ordinary four-wheeled disgrace to London, and the fittings, though frayed, were of rich quality. Mr. Latimer seated himself opposite to me, and we started off through Charing Cross **19** and up the Shaftesbury Avenue. We had come out upon Oxford Street, and I had ventured some remark as to this being a roundabout way to Kensington, when my words were arrested by the extraordinary conduct of my companion.

"He began by drawing a most formidable-looking bludgeon loaded with lead from his pocket, and switched it backwards and forwards several times, as if to test its weight and strength. Then he placed it, without a word, upon the seat beside him. Having done this, he drew up the windows on each side, and I found to my astonishment that they were covered with paper so as to prevent my seeing through them.

"'I am sorry to cut off your view, Mr. Melas,' said he. 'The fact is that I have no intention that you should see what the place is to which we are driving. It might possibly be inconvenient to me if you could find your way there again.'

"As you can imagine, I was utterly taken aback by such an address. My companion was a powerful, broad-shouldered young fellow, and, apart from the weapon, I should not have had the slightest chance in a struggle with him.

"'This is very extraordinary conduct, Mr. Latimer,' I stammered. 'You must be aware that what you are doing is quite illegal.'

"'It is somewhat of a liberty, no doubt,' said he, 'but we'll make it up to you. But I must warn you, however, Mr. Melas, that if at any time to-night you attempt to raise an alarm or do anything which is against my interests, you will find it a very serious thing. I beg you to remember that no one knows where you are, and that whether you are in this carriage or in my house, you are equally in my power.'

"His words were quiet, but he had a rasping way of saying them which was very menacing. I sat in silence, wondering what on earth could be his reason for kidnapping me in this extraordinary fashion. Whatever it might be, it was perfectly clear that there was no possible use in my resisting, and that I could only wait to see what might befall.

"For nearly two hours we drove without my having the least clue as to where we were going. Sometimes the rattle of the stones told of a paved causeway, and at others our smooth, silent course suggested asphalt, but save this variation in sound there was nothing at all which could in the remotest way help me to form a guess as to where we were. The paper over each window was impenetrable to light, and a blue curtain was drawn across the glass-work in front. It was a quarter past seven when we left Pall Mall, and my watch showed me that it was ten minutes to nine when we at last came to a standstill. My companion let down the window and I caught a glimpse of a low, arched doorway with a lamp burning above it. As I was hurried from the carriage it swung open, and I found myself inside the house, with a vague impression of a lawn and trees on each side of me as I entered.   Whether these were private grounds, however, or *bona-fide* country **20** was more than I could possibly venture to say.

" There was a coloured gas-lamp inside, which was turned so low that I could see little save that the hall was of some size and hung with pictures.   In the dim light I could make out that the person who had opened the door was a small, mean-looking, middle-aged man with rounded shoulders.   As he turned towards us the glint of the light showed me that he was wearing glasses.

" ' Is this Mr. Melas, Harold ? ' said he.

" ' Yes.'

" ' Well done ! Well done ! No ill-will, Mr. Melas, I hope, but we could not get on without you.   If you deal fair with us you'll not regret it ; but if you try any tricks, God help you ! '

" He spoke in a jerky, nervous fashion, and with some giggling laughs in between, but somehow he impressed me with fear more than the other.

" ' What do you want with me ? ' I asked.

" ' Only to ask a few questions of a Greek gentleman who is visiting us, and to let us have the answers.   But say no more than you are told to say, or '—here came the nervous giggle again—' you had better never have been born.'

" As he spoke he opened a door and showed the way into a room which appeared to be very richly furnished— but again the only light was afforded by a single lamp half turned down.   The chamber was certainly large, and the way in which my feet sank into the carpet as I stepped across it told me of its richness.   I caught glimpses of velvet chairs, a high, white marble mantelpiece, and what seemed to be a suit of Japanese armour at one side of it. There was a chair just under the lamp, and the elderly man motioned that I should sit in it.   The younger had left us, but he suddenly returned through another door, leading with him a gentleman clad in some sort of loose dressing-gown, who moved slowly towards us.   As he came into the circle of dim light which enabled me to see him more clearly, I was thrilled with horror at his appearance.   He was deadly pale and terribly emaciated, with the protruding, brilliant eyes of a man whose spirit is greater than his strength.   But what shocked me more than any signs of physical weakness was that his face was grotesquely criss-crossed with sticking-plaster, and that one large pad of it was fastened over his mouth.

" ' Have you the slate, Harold ? ' cried the older man, as this strange being fell rather than sat down into a chair.   ' Are his hands loose ?   Now then, give him the pencil.   You are to ask the questions, Mr. Melas, and he will write the answers.   Ask him first of all whether he is prepared to sign the papers.'

" The man's eyes flashed fire.

" ' Never,' he wrote in Greek upon the slate.

" ' On no conditions ? ' I asked at the bidding of our tyrant.

" ' Only if I see her married in my presence by a Greek priest whom I know.'

" The man giggled in his venomous way.

". . . I WAS THRILLED BY HORROR AT HIS APPEARANCE."

Illustration by Sidney Paget for the *Strand Magazine*, September, 1893.

"'You know what awaits you, then?'

"'I care nothing for myself.'

"These are samples of the questions and answers which made up our strange, half-spoken, half-written conversation. Again and again I had to ask him whether he would give in and sign the document. Again and again I had the same indignant reply. But soon a happy thought came to me. I took to adding on little sentences of my own to each question—innocent ones at first, to test whether either of our companions knew anything of the matter, and then, as I found that they showed no sign, I played a more dangerous game. Our conversation ran something like this:

"'You can do no good by this obstinacy. *Who are you?*'

"'I care not. *I am a stranger in London.*'

"'Your fate will be on your own head. *How long have you been here?*'

"'Let it be so. *Three weeks.*'

"'The property can never be yours. *What ails you?*'

"'It shall not go to villains. *They are starving me.*'

"'You shall go free if you sign. *What house is this?*'

"'I will never sign. *I do not know.*'

"'You are not doing her any service. *What is your name?*'

"'Let me hear her say so. *Kratides.*'

"'You shall see her if you sign. *Where are you from?*'

"'Then I shall never see her. *Athens.*'

"Another five minutes, Mr. Holmes, and I should have wormed out the whole story under their very noses. My very next question might have cleared the matter up, but at that instant the door opened and a woman stepped into the room. I could not see her clearly enough to know more than that she was tall and graceful, with black hair, and clad in some sort of loose white gown.

"'Harold!' said she, speaking English with a broken, accent, 'I could not stay away longer. It is so lonely up there with only—oh, my God, it is Paul!'

"These last words were in Greek, and at the same instant the man, with a convulsive effort, tore the plaster from his lips, and screaming out 'Sophy! Sophy!'

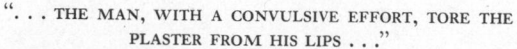

". . . THE MAN, WITH A CONVULSIVE EFFORT, TORE THE PLASTER FROM HIS LIPS . . ."

Illustration by William H. Hyde for *Harper's Weekly*, September 16, 1893. Sidney Paget illustrated the same scene for the *Strand Magazine*, September, 1893.

rushed into the woman's arms. Their embrace was but for an instant, however, for the younger man seized the woman and pushed her out of the room, while the elder easily overpowered his emaciated victim, and dragged him away through the other door. For a moment I was left alone in the room, and I sprang to my feet with some vague idea that I might in some way get a clue to what this house was in which I found myself. Fortunately, however, I took no steps, for, looking up, I saw that the older man was standing in the doorway, with his eyes fixed upon me.

" ' That will do, Mr. Melas,' said he. ' You perceive that we have taken you into our confidence over some very private business. We should not have troubled you only that our friend who speaks Greek and who began these negotiations has been forced to return to the East. It was quite necessary for us to find someone to take his place, and we were fortunate in hearing of your powers.'

" I bowed.

" ' There are five sovereigns here,' said he, walking up **21** to me, ' which will, I hope, be a sufficient fee. But remember,' he added, tapping me lightly on the chest and giggling, ' if you speak to a human soul about this —one human soul mind—well, may God have mercy upon your soul ! '

" I cannot tell you the loathing and horror with which this insignificant-looking man inspired me. I could see him better now as the lamp-light shone upon him. His features were peeky and sallow, and his little, pointed beard was thready and ill-nourished. He pushed his face forward as he spoke, and his lips and eyelids were continually twitching, like a man with St. Vitus's dance. **22** I could not help thinking that his strange, catchy little laugh was also a symptom of some nervous malady. The terror of his face lay in his eyes, however, steel grey, and glistening coldly, with a malignant, inexorable cruelty in their depths.

" ' We shall know if you speak of this,' said he. ' We have our own means of information. Now, you will find the carriage waiting, and my friend will see you on your way.'

" I was hurried through the hall, and into the vehicle, again obtaining that momentary glimpse of trees and a garden. Mr. Latimer followed closely at my heels, and took his place opposite to me without a word. In silence we again drove for an interminable distance, with the windows raised, until at last, just after midnight, the carriage pulled up.

" ' You will get down here, Mr. Melas,' said my companion. ' I am sorry to leave you so far from your house, but there is no alternative. Any attempt upon your part to follow the carriage can only end in injury to yourself.'

" He opened the door as he spoke, and I had hardly time to spring out when the coachman lashed the horse, and the carriage rattled away. I looked round me in astonishment. I was on some sort of a heathy common, mottled over with dark clumps of furze bushes. Far away stretched a line of houses, with a light here and there in the upper windows. On the other side I saw the red

21 *five sovereigns.* About $25.

22 *St. Vitus's dance.* "The term St. Vitus's dance is seldom used nowadays; it is presently called acute chorea," Dr. Edward J. Van Liere wrote in "Dr. Watson and Nervous Maladies." "This condition is characterized by irregular involuntary contractions of the muscles and is associated with a variable amount of psychic disturbance. The name 'St. Vitus's dance' has been handed down from the Middle Ages. Epidemics characterized by excitement, gesticulations, and dancing, brought about mainly by religious fervor, were in those days not uncommon. When these symptoms became excessive the people in the Rhenish provinces frequently made pilgrimages to the Chapel of St. Vitus in Zebern."

". . . I SAW SOMEONE COMING TOWARDS ME IN THE
DARKNESS."

Illustration by Sidney Paget for the *Strand Magazine*, September, 1893.

signal lamps of a railway.

"The carriage which had brought me was already out of sight. I stood gazing round and wondering where on earth I might be, when I saw someone coming towards me in the darkness. As he came up to me I made out that it was a railway porter.

"'Can you tell me what place this is?' I asked.

23 •"'Wandsworth Common,' said he.

"'Can I get a train into town?'

"'If you walk on a mile or so, to Clapham Junc-
24 tion,' said he, 'you'll just be in time for the last to Victoria.'

"So that was the end of my adventure, Mr. Holmes. I do not know where I was nor whom I spoke with, nor anything, save what I have told you. But I know that there is foul play going on, and I want to help that unhappy man if I can. I told the whole story to Mr. Mycroft Holmes next morning, and, subsequently, to the police."

We all sat in silence for some little time after listening to this extraordinary narrative. Then Sherlock looked across at his brother.

"Any steps?" he asked.

Mycroft picked up the *Daily News*, which was lying on a side-table.

"'Anybody supplying any information as to the where-abouts of a Greek gentleman named Paul Kratides, from Athens, who is unable to speak English, will be rewarded. A similar reward paid to anyone giving information about a Greek lady whose first name is Sophy. X 2473.' That was in all the dailies. No answer."

"How about the Greek Legation?"

"I have inquired. They know nothing."

"A wire to the head of the Athens police, then."

"Sherlock has all the energy of the family," said Mycroft, turning to me. "Well, you take up the case by all means, and let me know if you do any good."

"Certainly," answered my friend, rising from his chair. "I'll let you know, and Mr. Melas also. In the mean-time, Mr. Melas, I should certainly be on my guard if I were you, for, of course, they must know through these advertisements that you have betrayed them."

As we walked home together Holmes stopped at a telegraph office and sent off several wires.

"You see, Watson," he remarked, "our evening has been by no means wasted. Some of my most interesting cases have come to me in this way through Mycroft. The problem which we have just listened to, although it can admit of but one explanation, has still some distin-guishing features."

"You have hopes of solving it?"

"Well, knowing as much as we do, it will be singular indeed if we fail to discover the rest. You must yourself have formed some theory which will explain the facts to which we have listened."

"In a vague way, yes."

"What was your idea, then?"

"It seemed to me to be obvious that this Greek girl had been carried off by the young Englishman named Harold Latimer."

23   "'*Wandsworth Common.*' Wandsworth ("Wendel's farm") is the largest borough in the county of London, intersected by the small river Wandle. Its common, once the resort of gypsies, is today a beautiful pleasure ground well planted with trees, which contains a lake where fishing is allowed, a teahouse, and bowling greens.

24 *Clapham Junction.* An important railway junction about four miles from Central London.

" Carried off from where ? "

" Athens, perhaps."

Sherlock Holmes shook his head. " This young man could not talk a word of Greek. The lady could talk English fairly well. Inference, that she had been in England some little time, but he had not been in Greece."

" Well, then, we will presume that she had come on a visit to England, and that this Harold had persuaded her to fly with him."

" That is the more probable."

" Then the brother—for that, I fancy, must be the relationship—comes over from Greece to interfere. He imprudently puts himself into the power of the young man and his older associate. They seize him and use violence towards him in order to make him sign some papers to make over the girl's fortune—of which he may be trustee—to them. This he refuses to do. In order to negotiate with him, they have to get an interpreter, and they pitch upon this Mr. Melas, having used some other one before. The girl is not told of the arrival of her brother, and finds it out by the merest accident."

" Excellent, Watson," cried Holmes. " I really fancy that you are not far from the truth. You see that we hold all the cards, and we have only to fear some sudden act of violence on their part. If they give us time we must have them."

" But how can we find where this house lies ? "

" Well, if our conjecture is correct, and the girl's name is, or was, Sophy Kratides, we should have no difficulty in tracing her. That must be our main hope, for the brother, of course, is a complete stranger. It is clear that some time has elapsed since this Harold established these relations with the girl—some weeks at any rate—since the brother in Greece has had time to hear of it, and come across. If they have been living in the same place during this time, it is probable that we shall have some answer to Mycroft's advertisement."

We had reached our house in Baker Street whilst we had been talking, Holmes ascended the stairs first, and as he opened the door of our room he gave a start of surprise. Looking over his shoulder I was equally astonished. His brother Mycroft was sitting smoking in the arm-chair.

" Come in, Sherlock ! Come in, sir," said he, blandly, smiling at our surprised faces. " You don't expect such energy from me, do you, Sherlock ? But somehow this case attracts me."

" How did you get here ? "

" I passed you in a hansom."

" There has been some new development ? "

" I had an answer to my advertisement."

" Ah ! "

" Yes ; it came within a few minutes of your leaving."

" And to what effect ? "

Mycroft Holmes took out a sheet of paper.

" Here it is," said he, " written with a J pen on royal cream paper by a middle-aged man with a weak constitution. ' Sir,' he says, ' in answer to your advertisement of to-day's date, I beg to inform you that I know the young

"COME IN, SHERLOCK ! COME IN, SIR,"
SAID HE, BLANDLY . . .

Illustration by Sidney Paget for the *Strand Magazine*, September, 1893.

25 *Beckenham.* An urban district in Kent.

26 *Lower Brixton.*" A district of London now much favored by minor actors.

27 *It was almost dark.* Mycroft was always to be found at the Diogenes Club "from a quarter to five till twenty to eight," according to Holmes. On this Wednesday evening he took a hansom to Baker Street, passing Holmes and Watson on their walk home. After a brief conversation, the three ordered the four-wheeler and drove directly to Mr. Melas' lodgings in Pall Mall. "It was almost dark" at the time they arrived, according to Watson. Mycroft, leaving the Diogenes Club by hansom at 7:40 P.M., must have arrived at Baker Street shortly after 8:00 P.M., Holmes and Watson at about the same time. Their conversation would have taken a few minutes at most, their drive to Mr. Melas' lodgings (which we know were just opposite the Diogenes Club) no longer than Mycroft's drive from the Diogenes Club to Baker Street. The three would therefore have reached Mr. Melas' lodgings about 8:20 P.M. It cannot have been much earlier than that, as we have shown; it can hardly have been later; Mycroft, Sherlock, and Watson then drove from Pall Mall to Scotland Yard, waited "more than an hour" for Gregson, and reached London Bridge at "a quarter to ten." We must therefore find a Wednesday in the summer of 1888 when twilight ended at approximately 8:20 P.M. There can be only one choice: on Wednesday, September 5th, twilight ended at approximately 8:41 P.M.—too late for it to have been "almost dark" at 8:20 P.M.; on Wednesday, September 19th, twilight ended at approximately 8:04 P.M.—too early for it to have been "almost dark" at 8:20 P.M. The case therefore took place on *Wednesday, September 12, 1888* —a day on which twilight ended and darkness began at approximately 8:23 P.M. Holmes called the evening on which the case began a "beautiful evening," and he was perfectly correct in doing so: the London *Times'* report for Wednesday, September 12th, noted that "Fine weather . . . has become general over the British Isles. . . . with low night temperatures but mild days. The wind has been light or moderate in force."

lady in question very well. If you should care to call upon me, I could give you some particulars as to her painful history. She is living at present at The Myrtles, **25** Beckenham.—Yours faithfully, J. DAVENPORT.'

26   " He writes from Lower Brixton," said Mycroft Holmes. " Do you not think that we might drive to him now, Sherlock, and learn these particulars ? "

" My dear Mycroft, the brother's life is more valuable than the sister's story. I think we should call at Scotland Yard for Inspector Gregson, and go straight out to Beckenham. We know that a man is being done to death, and every hour may be vital."

" Better pick up Mr. Melas upon our way," I suggested ; " we may need an interpreter."

" Excellent ! " said Sherlock Holmes. " Send the boy for a four-wheeler, and we shall be off at once." He opened the table-drawer as he spoke, and I noticed that he slipped his revolver into his pocket. " Yes," said he, in answer to my glance, " I should say from what we have heard that we are dealing with a particularly dangerous gang."

27   It was almost dark before we found ourselves in Pall Mall, at the rooms of Mr. Melas. A gentleman had just called for him, and he was gone.

" Can you tell me where ? " asked Mycroft Holmes.

" I don't know, sir," answered the woman who had opened the door. " I only know that he drove away with the gentleman in a carriage."

" Did the gentleman give a name ? "

" No, sir."

" He wasn't a tall, handsome, dark young man ? "

" Oh, no, sir ; he was a little gentleman, with glasses, thin in the face, but very pleasant in his ways, for he was laughing all the time that he was talking."

" Come along ! " cried Sherlock Holmes, abruptly. " This grows serious ! " he observed, as we drove to Scotland Yard. " These men have got hold of Melas again.

. . . HE SLIPPED HIS REVOLVER INTO HIS POCKET.

"Holmes' revolver was unsuited in his hands to any other than muzzle-to-gizzard shooting," Mr. Robert Keith Leavitt wrote in "Annie Oakley in Baker Street." "It was the Webley Metropolitan Police Model—the same which Inspector Lestrade gaily said he carried whenever he had his pants on [*The Hound of the Baskervilles*]. This arm had the short 2½" barrel required for hip-pocket (or dressing-gown-pocket) wear, but on account of its short sight-radius, it was difficult for anybody but a past master to shoot with accuracy. It may be objected that two passages show Holmes *did* have confidence in this piece. In *The Sign of the Four* he loaded it with two and only two cartridges. This, however, indicated confidence rather in Tonga's than in his own accuracy. He knew he would have time for only two shots at best. In 'The Adventure of the Three Garridebs' he referred to his revolver as 'my old favourite,' but it must be obvious to the close student that he did so with a wry sneer."

He is a man of no physical courage, as they are well aware from their experience the other night. This villain was able to terrorize him the instant that he got into his presence. No doubt they want his professional services; but, having used him, they may be inclined to punish him for what they will regard as his treachery."

Our hope was that by taking train we might get to Beckenham as soon as, or sooner than, the carriage. On reaching Scotland Yard, however, it was more than an hour before we could get Inspector Gregson and comply with the legal formalities which would enable us to enter the house. It was a quarter to ten before we reached London Bridge, and half-past before the four of us alighted on the Beckenham platform. A drive of half a mile brought us to The Myrtles—a large, dark house, standing back from the road in its own grounds. Here we dismissed our cab, and made our way up the drive together.

" The windows are all dark," remarked the Inspector. " The house seems deserted."

" Our birds are flown and the nest empty," said Holmes.

" Why do you say so ? "

" A carriage heavily loaded with luggage has passed out during the last hour."

The Inspector laughed. " I saw the wheel-tracks in the light of the gate-lamp, but where does the luggage come in ? "

" You may have observed the same wheel-tracks going the other way. But the outward-bound ones were very much deeper—so much so that we can say for a certainty that there was a very considerable weight on the carriage."

" You get a trifle beyond me there," said the Inspector, shrugging his shoulders. " It will not be an easy door to force. But we will try if we cannot make someone hear us."

He hammered loudly at the knocker and pulled at the bell, but without any success. Holmes had slipped away, but he came back in a few minutes.

" I have a window open," said he.

" It is a mercy that you are on the side of the Force, and not against it, Mr. Holmes," remarked the Inspector, as he noted the clever way in which my friend had forced back the catch. " Well, I think that, under the circumstances, we may enter without waiting for an invitation."

One after the other we made our way into a large apartment, which was evidently that in which Mr. Melas had found himself. The Inspector had lit his lantern, and by its light we could see the two doors, the curtain, the lamp and the suit of Japanese mail as he had described them. On the table stood two glasses, an empty brandy bottle, and the remains of a meal.

" What is that ? " asked Holmes, suddenly.

We all stood still and listened. A low, moaning sound was coming from somewhere above our heads. Holmes rushed to the door and out into the hall. The dismal noise came from upstairs. He dashed up, the Inspector and I at his heels, while his brother, Mycroft, followed as quickly as his great bulk would permit.

"IT'S CHARCOAL!" HE CRIED.

Illustration by Sidney Paget for the *Strand Magazine*, September, 1893.

Three doors faced us upon the second floor, and it was from the central of these that the sinister sounds were issuing, sinking sometimes into a dull mumble and rising again into a shrill whine. It was locked, but the key was on the outside. Holmes flung open the door and rushed in, but he was out again in an instant with his hand to his throat.

" It's charcoal ! " he cried. " Give it time. It will clear."

Peering in, we could see that the only light in the room came from a dull, blue flame, which flickered from a small brass tripod in the centre. It threw a livid, unnatural circle upon the floor, while in the shadows beyond, we saw the vague loom of two figures, which crouched against the wall. From the open door there reeked a horrible, poisonous exhalation, which set us gasping and coughing. Holmes rushed to the top of the stairs to draw in the fresh air, and then, dashing into the room, he threw up the window and hurled the brazen tripod out into the garden.

" We can enter in a minute," he gasped, darting out again. " Where is a candle ? I doubt if we could strike a match in that atmosphere. Hold the light at the door and we shall get them out, Mycroft. Now ! "

With a rush we got to the poisoned men and dragged them out on to the landing. Both of them were blue-lipped and insensible, with swollen, congested faces and protruding eyes. Indeed, so distorted were their features that, save for his black beard and stout figure, we might have failed to recognize in one of them the Greek interpreter who had parted from us only a few hours before at the Diogenes Club. His hands and feet were securely strapped together and he bore over one eye the mark of a violent blow. The other, who was secured in a similar fashion, was a tall man in the last stage of emaciation, with several strips of sticking-plaster arranged in a grotesque pattern over his face. He had ceased to moan as we laid him down, and a glance showed me that for him, at least, our aid had come too late. Mr. Melas, however, still lived, and in less than an hour, with the aid of ammonia and brandy, I had the satisfaction of seeing him open his eyes, and of knowing that my hand had drawn him back from the dark valley in which all paths meet.

It was a simple story which he had to tell, and one which did but confirm our own deductions. His visitor **28** on entering his rooms had drawn a life-preserver from his sleeve, and had so impressed him with the fear of instant and inevitable death, that he had kidnapped him for the second time. Indeed, it was almost mesmeric the effect which this giggling ruffian had produced upon the unfortunate linguist, for he could not speak of him save with trembling hands and a blanched cheek. He had been taken swiftly to Beckenham, and had acted as interpreter in a second interview, even more dramatic than the first, in which the two Englishmen had menaced their prisoner with instant death if he did not comply with their demands. Finally, finding him proof against every threat, they had hurled him back into his prison, and after reproaching Melas with his treachery, which

28 *a life-preserver*. A short bludgeon, usually of flexible cane, whalebone, or the like, loaded with lead at one end.

appeared from the newspaper advertisements, they had stunned him with a blow from a stick, and he remembered nothing more until he found us bending over him.

And this was the singular case of the Grecian Interpreter, the explanation of which is still involved in some mystery. We were able to find out, by communicating with the gentleman who had answered the advertisement, that the unfortunate young lady came of a wealthy Grecian family, and that she had been on a visit to some friends in England. While there she had met a young man named Harold Latimer, who had acquired an ascendancy over her, and had eventually persuaded her to fly with him. Her friends, shocked at the event, had contented themselves with informing her brother at Athens, and had then washed their hands of the matter. The brother, on his arrival in England, had imprudently placed himself in the power of Latimer and of his associate, whose name was Wilson Kemp—a man of the foulest antecedents. These two, finding, that through his ignorance of the language, he was helpless in their hands, had kept him a prisoner, and had endeavoured, by cruelty and starvation, to make him sign away his own and his sister's property. They had kept him in the house without the girl's knowledge, and the plaster over the face had been for the purpose of making recognition difficult in case she should ever catch a glimpse of him. Her feminine perceptions, however, had instantly seen through the disguise when, on the occasion of the interpreter's first visit, she had seen him for the first time. The poor girl, however, was herself a prisoner, for there was no one about the house except the man who acted as coachman and his wife, both of whom were tools of the conspirators. Finding that their secret was out and that their prisoner was not to be coerced, the two villains, with the girl, had fled away at a few hours' notice from the furnished house which they had hired, having first, as they thought, taken vengeance both upon the man who had defied and the one who had betrayed them.

Months afterwards a curious newspaper cutting reached us from Buda-Pesth. It told how two Englishmen who had been travelling with a woman had met with a tragic end. They had each been stabbed, it seems, and the Hungarian police were of opinion that they had quarrelled and had inflicted mortal injuries upon each other. Holmes, however, is, I fancy, of a different way of thinking, and he holds to this day that if one could find the Grecian girl one might learn how the wrongs of herself and her brother came to be avenged.

IT THREW A LIVID, UNNATURAL CIRCLE UPON THE FLOOR . . .

Illustration by William H. Hyde for *Harper's Weekly*, September 16, 1893.

Bibliographical Note: On December 19, 1964, *The New York Times* reported from London that: "The manuscript of 'The Adventure of the Greek Interpreter'. . . was purchased today [December 18th] at auction for $12,600 by the author's son, Adrian Conan Doyle. . . . The manuscript . . . appears to be the only complete one from *The Memoirs* that has been sold on the open market. The 34-page manuscript was sold by a New York woman, according to Christie's. . . ." According to Mr. Lew D. Feldman of "The House of El Dieff," who exhibited the manuscript at the dinner of the Baker Street Irregulars on January 8, 1965, $12,600 is not only the highest price ever paid for a Sherlock Holmes manuscript or any other manuscript by Conan Doyle but also the highest price ever paid for a manuscript written in English by an author who lived during the twentieth century.

34

"YOUR HAND STOLE TOWARDS
YOUR OLD WOUND ..."

[Sherlock Holmes to John H. Watson, M.D., "The Cardboard Box"]

On the twenty-seventh day of July in the year 1880, John H. Watson, M.D., was doing his duty as Assistant Surgeon to the Berkshires (66th Foot) at the fatal battle of Maiwand when he was struck on the shoulder by a Jezail bullet, which shattered the bone and grazed the subclavian artery.

Few statements could be clearer or more circumstantial.

And yet, eight years later, in September, 1888, at the time of *The Sign of the Four*, Dr. Watson tells us that he sat nursing his wounded *leg*. "I had had a Jezail bullet through it some time before," he writes, "and though it did not prevent me from walking it ached wearily at every change in the weather."

"An army surgeon with a weak leg," was how he then described himself.

"Are you game for a six-mile trudge, Watson? . . . Your leg will stand it?" Holmes asks him solicitously—and later refers to "a six-mile limp for a half-pay officer with a damaged *tendo Achillis*."

Let us examine, first, the wound Dr. Watson tells us he suffered at the "fatal battle."

Expert medical testimony (the late Dr. Roland Hammond, in "The Surgeon Probes Doctor Watson's Wound") notes first that "the shoulder is broadly defined as that portion of the trunk between the upper portion of the arm and the base of the neck, especially the curved upper surfaces of this, and often including the part of the back between the two. It is the part of the body on which burdens are carried. On the other hand, the medical man in speaking of the shoulder, limits his definition to the articulation by which the arm is connected to the trunk." Watson's wound, Dr. Hammond thought, "may have been located nearer to the base of the neck than in the shoulder region."

The wound was on Watson's left side, we know, for Holmes in *A Study in Scarlet* says: "His [Watson's] left arm has been injured. He holds it in a stiff and unnatural manner."

The bullet shattered the bone, and Dr. Hammond—with Dr. John Dardess concurring ("The Maiwand-Criterion Hiatus")—held that this bone could only have been the clavicle or collarbone. Dr. J. W. Sovine ("The Singular Bullet") thought that it might have been one of three others—the left humerus, the left scapula, or the left rib—but Dr. Hammond was of the opinion that "an injury to the first rib . . . would have resulted in uncontrollable hemorrhage from the subclavian vein and artery and irreparable damage to the great nerve cable known as the brachial plexus lying directly behind the blood vessels."

The subclavian artery—which Watson tells us that the bullet "grazed" but not that it *severed*—ascends on the left side vertically from the arch of the aorta to the inner border of the scalenus anterior muscle. Passing behind this muscle, it curves over the first rib to its lower border where is passes beneath the clavicle and becomes the axillary artery. "It is evident," Dr. Hammond wrote, "that [this] artery could be grazed only where it lies on the first rib. . . . We must finally conclude that a bullet producing the damage described *might* avoid injury to important structures but it would be touch and go at best. The fracture of the clavicle must have been extensive with many loose chips of bone to knit into place. Although this bone repairs more readily than any other bone in the body, a compound fracture of the clavicle often leaves an unsightly deformity associated with pain and stiffness of the shoulder and arm. We are assured that Watson's recovery was complete, which is a tribute to a healthy constitution and skillful surgical care."

Here, then, is a healthy, young medico (Watson, according to the best authorities was twenty-eight at the time of the battle), who sustains a compound fracture of the clavicle from a bullet which grazes but *does not sever* the subclavian artery.

Why, then, was it necessary for Watson's orderly, Murray, to "throw him across a pack-horse" in order to bring him safely to "the British lines"?

Dr. Sovine suggests that "the Jezail bullet struck Dr. Watson just above and missing the left clavicle, while he was bent over a wounded patient; that it grazed the left subclavian artery and shattered the left scapula, then ricocheted, passing to the left and downward, describing a spiral curve deep under the skin of the chest and abdomen, thence downward into the left leg, coming to rest in the calf muscles. . . . The shoulder was still bothersome in 1881, but healed and forgotten by the fall of 1887; while the bullet in the leg would be forgotten most of the time, but quite painful during weather changes. . . . Apparently when the weather was decent [Watson's] leg was quite serviceable."

This is also the view of Mr. R. M. McLaren ("Doctor Watson—Punter or Speculator?"): "The wound sustained by Watson in Afghanistan was an extraordinary one, the bullet having entered his shoulder and emerged from his leg . . ."

The views expressed above may, perhaps, be summed up as the One Singular Wound at Maiwand School.

Other commentators are of the opinion that Watson was wounded *twice* at Maiwand, first in the shoulder, then in the leg. Dr. Reginald Fitz, for example, in his "A Belated Eulogy: to John H. Watson, M.D.", wrote: "Dr. Watson had a busy day at the front—until he copped two bullets, one in the leg and one in the shoulder." Dr. Dardess felt the same: "I think there can be little doubt . . . that Watson was wounded *twice* at Maiwand."

But, if this was the case, why did Watson, so precise about his shoulder wound, never mention a leg wound at Maiwand?

He did not mention it, still another school of commentators holds, because the wound was not properly in his "leg" at all, but in a part of his anatomy which his modesty and delicacy forbade his mentioning.

"A man 'thrown across a packhorse' ", the late James Keddie, Sr., mused in "The Mystery of the Second Wound," "presents a singularly enticing target. His head and arms hang down one side . . . his legs dangle on the other."

"Dr. Watson was painfully and honorably wounded on the left buttock while serving his country and comrades on the open field of battle," Mr. John Ball, Jr., wrote in "The Jezail Bullet." "He was, in all probability, bending over a fallen comrade, ministering to him when he was himself hit. He was serving with utter disregard for his own safety; any suggestion of cowardice in that he was not 'facing the foe' is an unwarranted slander. This is the one and only wound which he received. . . . He was never at any time shot in the shoulder, nor did he believe himself to have been so injured. He deliberately misrepresented his area of injury . . ."

That Watson's wound was indeed "of a fundamental nature" is also the opinion of Mr. G. W. Welch (" 'No Mention of That Local Hunt, Watson' ").

This Unmentionable Wound was what made it so difficult for Watson in later life to resist any female allurement, in the opinion of Mr. Belden Wigglesworth (" 'Many Nations and Three Separate Continents' "): "His extraordinary incontinence may really have been due to the continued irritation of the old scar in his perineum."

Dr. Julian Wolff, on the other hand, has cast aspersions on Watson's masculinity by suggesting ("That Was No Lady") that Watson's one wound at Maiwand was in the groin.

And Dr. Samuel R. Meaker, writing in "Watson Medicus," says: "I do not wish to be indelicate, but, after all, prudery has no place in scientific deliberations. So I would simply call attention to the fact that all three of Watson's marriages were childless."

Still another school of thought holds that Watson was wounded once at Maiwand (in the shoulder) and again, at some later date, in the leg.

"On the journey by pack-horse," Dr. Vernon Pennell wrote in "A Resumé of the Medical Life of John H. Watson, M.D., Late of the Army Medical Department," Watson "must have received one, or possibly two, more wounds, both by Jezail bullets."

And Lieutenant Colonel L. V. S. Blacker has suggested ("Dr. Watson's Wound(s)") that Watson "was taken up the Indus on the upper deck of [a] paddle steamer. After some days of voyaging upstream, the steamer would pass close under high banks where the frontier mountains close in upon it. In those days Wazir, Mahsud and other tribesmen ranged these mountains, rifle in fist. I suggest that one of these marauders took pot-shot at the steamer and his bullet struck the already wounded John Watson in the leg."

The Reverend Henry T. Folsom, on the other hand, holds that Watson acquired his second wound during a *second* hitch in the Army from the summer of 1881 to early 1883. "At that time, while apparently encountering some Ghazi guerrilla in a border incident, he caught a *second* Jezail, this time in the leg" ("Seventeen Out of Twenty-Three").

Still, Watson makes no mention whatsoever of a leg wound in any of the numerous 1887 cases, and it is somewhat difficult to believe that he received his second wound until sometime after early April, 1888 ("The Yellow Face").

Holmes' solicitude for Watson at the time of the adventure of *The Sign of the Four* suggests that Watson suffered his second wound while assisting Holmes on a case (compare Holmes' reaction to the wound received by Watson in 1902 during "The Adventure of the Three Garridebs").

Watson's second wound did not prevent him from walking, and we know that he walked for some distance in "The Greek Interpreter," which took place in the same month as *The Sign of the Four* (September, 1888), and just preceding that adventure.

Most probably, we think, Watson sustained his second wound in late April or early May, 1888, which would accord with his "some time before" in *The Sign of the Four*. It is of course curious that he was wounded for the second time by a Jezail bullet.

Happily, Watson seems to have made a swift and complete recovery. Only a month after *The Sign of the Four* he was able to say, in *The Hound of the Baskervilles*, "I am reckoned fleet of foot."

35

THE SIGN OF THE FOUR

[Tuesday, September 18, to Friday, September 21, 1888]

1 *hypodermic syringe.* Dr. Kohki Naganuma has questioned ("Sherlock Holmes and Cocaine") Holmes' use of cocaine by hypodermic injection at this time since "Karl Ludwig Schleich, of Berlin, [was] the first surgeon to use cocaine solution in hypodermic injection [in 1891]." But Dr. Julian Wolff has replied ("A Narcotic Monograph") that "although Schleich is usually given credit for priority in the use of cocaine by injection, actually the credit should go to a great American surgeon. The first such use of cocaine was not in 1891 by Schleich, as is generally supposed, but in 1884, by Dr. William S. Halsted. . . . 1884 was early enough so that it was no anachronism for Holmes to be taking cocaine injections when Watson said he was."

It should be pointed out that, at this time, there was no popular prejudice against drugs or drug-takers. As Mr. Michael Harrison has written (*In the Footsteps of Sherlock Holmes*): "In Holmes' day, not only was the purchase of most 'Schedule IV' drugs legal; Madeleine Smith and Mrs. Maybrick bought their arsenic; De Quincey and Dickens and Robert Louis Stevenson, their laudanum; with no more trouble than that with which they purchased their tooth-powder. No 'Dangerous Drug Act' had been passed, in its original form, when Holmes bought and took his cocaine in doses that Watson's description of the typical cocaine-addiction syndromes indicate to have been heavy ones. (Holmes probably purchased his supplies from either John Taylor, Chemist, at the corner of George Street and Baker Street—east side—or of Curtis and Company, No. 44, on the west side) . . ."

2 *the Beaune.* Beaune is a rather potent red wine from Burgundy, too strong a drink for lunch. The late Christopher Morley in "Dr. Watson's Secret" expressed his view that Watson was fortifying himself because, unknown to Holmes, he had married Mary Morstan some months before and knew that she would be calling on Holmes as a client that very afternoon.

3 *'morphine.* This is the only occasion in the entire Saga in which we find even the suggestion that Holmes ever took morphine.

1 Sherlock Holmes took his bottle from the corner of the mantelpiece, and his hypodermic syringe from its neat morocco case. With his long, white, nervous fingers he adjusted the delicate needle, and rolled back his left shirt-cuff. For some little time his eyes rested thoughtfully upon the sinewy forearm and wrist, all dotted and scarred with innumerable puncture-marks. Finally, he thrust the sharp point home, pressed down the tiny piston, and sank back into the velvet-lined arm-chair with a long sigh of satisfaction.

Three times a day for many months I had witnessed this performance, but custom had not reconciled my mind to it. On the contrary, from day to day I had become more irritable at the sight, and my conscience swelled nightly within me at the thought that I had lacked the courage to protest. Again and again I had registered a vow that I should deliver my soul upon the subject; but there was that in the cool, nonchalant air of my companion which made him the last man with whom one would care to take anything approaching to a liberty. His great powers, his masterly manner, and the experience which I had had of his many extraordinary qualities, all made me diffident and backward in crossing him.

2 Yet upon that afternoon, whether it was the Beaune which I had taken with my lunch, or the additional exasperation produced by the extreme deliberation of his manner, I suddenly felt that I could hold out no longer.

3 'Which is it today,' I asked, 'morphine or cocaine?'

He raised his eyes languidly from the old black-letter volume which he had opened.

4 'It is cocaine,' he said, 'a seven-per-cent. solution. Would you care to try it?'

'No, indeed,' I answered, brusquely. 'My constitution has not got over the Afghan campaign yet. I cannot afford to throw any extra strain upon it.'

He smiled at my vehemence. 'Perhaps you are right, Watson,' he said. 'I suppose that its influence is physically a bad one. I find it, however, so transcendently stimulating and clarifying to the mind that its secondary action is a matter of small moment.'

'But consider!' I said, earnestly. 'Count the cost! Your brain may, as you say, be roused and excited, but it is a pathological and morbid process, which involves increased tissue-change, and may at last leave a permanent weakness. You know, too, **5** what a black reaction comes upon you. Surely the game is hardly worth the candle. Why should you, for a mere passing pleasure, risk the loss of those great powers with which you have been endowed? Remember that I speak not only as one comrade to another, but as a medical man to one for whose constitution he is to some extent answerable.'

He did not seem offended. On the contrary, he put his finger-tips together, and leaned his elbows on the arms of his chair, like one who has a relish for conversation.

'My mind,' he said, 'rebels at stagnation. Give me problems, give me work, give me the most abstruse cryptogram, or the most intricate analysis, and I am in my own proper atmosphere. I can dispense then with artificial stimulants. But I abhor the dull routine of existence. I crave for mental exaltation. That is why I have chosen my own particular profession, or rather created it, for I am the only one in the world.'

'The only unofficial detective?' I said, raising my eyebrows.

'The only unofficial consulting detective,' he answered. 'I am the last and highest court of appeal in detection. When Gregson, or Lestrade, or Athelney Jones are out of their depths—which, by the way, is their normal state—the matter is laid before me. I examine the data, as an expert, and pronounce a specialist's opinion. I claim no credit in such cases. My name figures in no newspaper. The work itself, the pleasure of finding a field for my peculiar powers, is my highest reward. But you have yourself had some experience of my methods of work in the Jefferson Hope case.'

'Yes, indeed,' said I, cordially. 'I was never so struck by anything in my life. I even embodied it in a small brochure, with the somewhat fantastic title of "A Study in Scarlet." '   **6**

He shook his head sadly.

'I glanced over it,' said he. 'Honestly, I cannot congratulate you upon it. Detection is, or ought to be, an exact science, and should be treated in the same cold and unemotional manner. You have attempted to tinge it with romanticism, **7** which produces much the same effect as if you worked a love-story or an elopement into the fifth proposition of Euclid.' **8**

'But the romance was there,' I remonstrated. 'I could not tamper with the facts.'

'Some facts should be suppressed, or, at least, a just sense of proportion should be observed in treating them. The only point in the case which deserved mention was the curious analytical reasoning from effects to causes, by which I succeeded in unravelling it.'

I was annoyed at this criticism of a work which had been specially designed to please him. I confess, too, that I was irritated by the egotism which seemed to demand that every line of my pamphlet should be devoted to his own special doings. More than once during the years that I had lived with him in Baker Street I had observed that a small vanity underlay my companion's quiet and didactic manner. I made no remark, however, but sat nursing my wounded leg. I had had a Jezail bullet through it some time before, and, though it did not prevent me from walking, it ached wearily at every change of the weather.

4 '*a seven-per-cent. solution.* The fact that Holmes was resorting to cocaine injections "Three times a day" at this time is disturbing, but "a seven-per-cent. solution" is not in itself an extraordinarily heavy dose, according to F. A. Allen, M.P.S., in

his article "Devilish Drugs, Part I." "The strength of *injecto cocainae hypodermica*," he says, "became official in the B. P. in 1898 at ten per cent. May it not be presumed that, at least, Holmes was trying to 'cut down'? His occasional indiscretions, however, were still being recorded by Watson ten years later. One wonders, when they ceased, whether Holmes had found satisfactory treatment for his addictions in heroin, introduced from Germany about this time as a 'cure for the morphia habit,' and not condemned as such until a *B.M.J.* editorial in 1906 discussed the pharmacology of diamorphine."

5 *what a black reaction comes upon you.* " 'Cocaine is stuff that starts off making you feel just grand and with everything in the garden lovely. It peps you up and makes you feel you can do twice as much as you usually do. Take too much of it and you get violent mental excitement, delusions and delirium,' "—Agatha Christie, "The Case of the Drug Peddler" in *The Labors of Hercule.*

A more recent statement on the use of cocaine comes from Mr. Walter Modell of the Department of Pharmacology of Cornell University Medical College. In "Mass Drug Catastrophes and the Roles of Science and Technology," *Science*, 21 April, 1967, Vol. 156, No. 3773, Mr. Modell writes: "Although habit-forming, cocaine is not tenaciously so, and, since it is not physiologically addictive, strong personalities like Freud and Sherlock Holmes had no trouble in controlling the habit." However, he goes on to warn the reader that "Cocaine acts as a potent and sometimes unpredictable central stimulant, and rash and violent behavior have been attributed directly to its action; it is clearly anti-social. It is also highly toxic and, because of irregular and sometimes unanticipatedly rapid absorption, occasionally fatal."

6 *"A Study in Scarlet." '* Most commentators have taken this as a reference to *Beeton's Christmas Annual*, and have therefore insisted that *The Sign of the Four* must be dated after December, 1887—a view buttressed by Holmes' later remark that the criminal classes were coming to know him well, especially since Watson had taken to publishing "some" of his cases. On the other hand, Mr. H. B. Williams has suggested that it was the *original* publication of Watson's reminiscences (see *A Study in Scarlet*, Note 1) that Watson referred to here as "a small brochure" and "my pamphlet."

7 *to tinge it with romanticism.* It was probably the interlude with the Mormons that Holmes found tiresome.

8 *the fifth proposition of Euclid.' "*The Master here referred to the fifth proposition merely to illustrate his point," the late Dr. Ernest Bloomfield Zeisler wrote in "A Chronological *Study in Scarlet*," "for careful research has failed to reveal why any other proposition of Euclid would not have done as well."

9 *François le Villard*. "... a gentleman who may be identified as the son of Francisque Le Villard, author of works on the Paris theater," Miss Madeleine B. Stern wrote in "Sherlock Holmes: Rare Book Collector."

10 *this morning*. The chronologically minded reader will note that the day was therefore not a Sunday.

11 'coup-de-maîtres.' French: master strokes.

12 *'Oh, didn't you know?'* Of course Watson knew. Holmes had mentioned his monograph on cigar ashes in *A Study in Scarlet*.

13 *with coloured plates*. This phrase has suggested to Mr. Poul Anderson ("Art in the Blood") that Holmes "must certainly have been able to draw and even paint in fine detail, for ... surely he would not have entrusted the preparation of [these coloured plates] to anyone else. Likewise, in such adventures as 'The Norwood Builder,' he revealed considerable architectural acumen."

14 *lunkah*. Like the Trichonopoly, the lunkah is a thin cigar, open at both ends.

15 *bird's-eye*. A kind of pipe tobacco cut in small circular slices.

16 *as a preserver of impresses*. "Apropos of this monograph, it will be recalled that after his solution of the Priory School case in 1901 Holmes had material for an interesting note on the subject of faking the prints made by animals, with special reference to the devices employed by some of the robber Barons of Holdernesse during the Middle Ages to disguise the tracks of their horses," Mr. Walter Klinefelter wrote in "The Writings of Mr. Sherlock Holmes."

And Miss Madeleine B. Stern has added ("Sherlock Holmes: Rare Book Collector"): "Holmes' work . . . antedates most of the researches in this field. While much attention had been given before that time to fossil footprints, it was not until Holmes led the way that André Fréçon (*Des Empreintes en Général et de Leur Application dans . . . la Médecine Judiciare*, Lyons, 1889) in France and Anton Prant ('Ueber das Aufsuchen von Fuss-spuren und Handebrucken und ihre Identificrung,' *Arcgiv. f. Kriminal-Anthropologie*, Leipzig, 1899) in Germany could produce their works on the more modern variety of footprint. Some material on gypsum or plaster of Paris was, however, available to Holmes, who surely acquired for his work a copy of Richard Peters' *Agricultural Enquiries on Plaster of Paris* (Philadelphia, 1797) as well as Mathijsen's *De Bandage Platre* (Liège, 1654), a treatise which, incidentally, introduced the modern plaster-of-Paris bandage."

17 *upon the influence of a trade upon the form of the hand*. "For his study of the influence of a

'My practice has extended recently to the Continent,' said Holmes, after awhile, filling up his old briar-root pipe. 'I was **9** consulted last week by François le Villard, who, as you probably know, has come rather to the front lately in the French detective service. He has all the Celtic power of quick intuition, but he is deficient in the wide range of exact knowledge which is essential to the higher developments of his art. The case was concerned with a will, and possessed some features of interest. I was able to refer him to two parallel cases, the one at Riga in 1857, and the other at St Louis in 1871, which have suggested to him the true solution. Here is **10** the letter which I had this morning acknowledging my assistance.'

He tossed over, as he spoke, a crumpled sheet of foreign note-paper. I glanced my eyes down it, catching a profusion of notes of admiration, with stray *'magnifiques,' 'coup-de-*
11 *maîtres,'* and *'tours-de-force,'* all testifying to the ardent admiration of the Frenchman.

'He speaks as a pupil to his master,' said I.

'Oh, he rates my assistance too highly,' said Sherlock Holmes, lightly. 'He has considerable gifts himself. He possesses two out of the three qualities necessary for the ideal detective. He has the power of observation and that of deduction. He is only wanting in knowledge, and that may come in time. He is now translating my small works into French.'

'Your works?'

12 'Oh, didn't you know?' he cried, laughing. 'Yes, I have been guilty of several monographs. They are all upon technical subjects. Here, for example, is one "Upon the Distinction Between the Ashes of the Various Tobaccos." In it I enumerate a hundred and forty forms of cigar, cigarette, and pipe **13** tobacco, with coloured plates illustrating the difference in the ash. It is a point which is continually turning up in criminal trials, and which is sometimes of supreme importance as a clue. If you can say definitely, for example, that some murder had been done by a man who was smoking an Indian **14** lunkah, it obviously narrows your field of search. To the trained eye there is as much difference between the black ash **15** of a Trichinopoly and the white fluff of bird's-eye as there is between a cabbage and a potato.'

'You have an extraordinary genius for minutiæ,' I remarked.

'I appreciate their importance. Here is my monograph upon the tracing of footsteps, with some remarks upon the **16** uses of plaster of Paris as a preserver of impresses. Here, too, is a curious little work upon the influence of a trade upon **17-18** the form of the hand, with lithotypes of the hands of slaters, **19-20** sailors, cork-cutters, compositors, weavers, and diamond- **21-22** polishers. That is a matter of great practical interest to the **23** scientific detective—especially in cases of unclaimed bodies, **24** or in discovering the antecedents of criminals. But I weary you with my hobby.'

'Not at all,' I answered, earnestly. 'It is of the greatest interest to me, especially since I have had the opportunity of observing your practical application of it. But you spoke just now of observation and deduction. Surely the one to some extent implies the other.'

'Why, hardly,' he answered, leaning back luxuriously in his armchair, and sending up thick blue wreaths from his pipe.

"... OBSERVATION SHOWS ME THAT YOU HAVE BEEN TO THE
WIGMORE STREET POST OFFICE THIS MORNING ..."

At the time of this adventure, Wigmore Street was known as
Upper Seymour Street, and Holmes so refers to its Post Office in
early editions of *The Sign of the Four*. But why Watson went to
this Post Office at all is a small mystery: there was a Post Office
at No. 66 Baker Street, just across King Street from "No. 221,"
only six doors away.

'For example, observation shows me that you have been to
the Wigmore Street Post Office this morning, but deduction
lets me know that when there you dispatched a telegram.'

'Right!' said I. 'Right on both points! But I confess that I
don't see how you arrived at it. It was a sudden impulse upon
my part, and I have mentioned it to no one.'

'It is simplicity itself,' he remarked, chuckling at my surprise—'so absurdly simple that an explanation is superfluous;
and yet it may serve to define the limits of observation and
of deduction. Observation tells me that you have a little
reddish mould adhering to your instep. Just opposite the
Wigmore Street Office they have taken up the pavement and
thrown up some earth, which lies in such a way that it is
difficult to avoid treading in it in entering. The earth is of
this peculiar reddish tint which is found, as far as I know,
nowhere else in the neighbourhood. So much is observation.
The rest is deduction.'

'How, then, did you deduce the telegram?'

'Why, of course I knew that you had not written a letter,
since I sat opposite to you all morning. I see also in your open
desk there that you have a sheet of stamps and a thick bundle
of postcards. What could you go into the post office for, then,
but to send a wire? Eliminate all other factors, and the one **25**
which remains must be the truth.' **26**

'In this case it certainly is so,' I replied, after a little
thought. 'The thing, however, is, as you say, of the simplest.
Would you think me impertinent if I were to put your
theories to a more severe test?'

'On the contrary,' he answered; 'it would prevent me from
taking a second dose of cocaine. I should be delighted to look
into any problem which you might submit to me.'

'I have heard you say that it is difficult for a man to have
any object in daily use without leaving the impress of his individuality upon it in such a way that a trained observer might
read it. Now, I have here a watch which has recently come into

trade upon the form of the hand," Miss Stern
continued, Holmes "must have acquired, for his
medico-anatomical shelf, a copy of Ramazzini's
De Morbis Artificium Diatriba of 1670, the first
account of occupational diseases."

Mr. Archibald Hart has noted ("The Effects of
Trades Upon Hands") that "Gilbert Forbes (a
transparent alias) has reprinted Holmes' work
under the title of 'Some Observations on Occupational Markings.' This little article, brilliantly illustrated with twenty-five photographs and drawings (lithotypes) first appeared in the *Police
Journal*, London, England, October–December,
1946. It has been reprinted in the United States in
the *Journal of Criminal Law and Criminology*,
November–December, 1957."

And Professor Remsen Ten Eyck Schenck has
written ("The Effect of Trades Upon the Body"):
"A recent book of Rancesco Ronchese, M.D., entitled *Occupation Marks*, Grune & Stratton, New
York, 1948, will prove of interest to Irregulars.
Such a monograph might well have been developed
from Holmes' 'curious little work,' had only Watson's admiration for his colleague's methods been
sufficient to inspire closer to observation of his
patients, thus greatly extending the scope of the
study and permitting a collaboration which must
necessarily have constituted an advance in forensic
medicine."

18 *slaters*. "The marks probably included the fin-
gertips of the left hand worn smooth by handling
the stone, as seen also in masons and bricklayers
. . . , and calluses across the right palm from
gripping the hammer," Professor Schenck wrote.
"It is also reasonable that callosities of the knees
would be prominent . . . , since roofing is done
chiefly in a kneeling position."

19 *sailors*. "It is incredible that a sailor should
be thus distinguishable from a variety of other
possibilities," Professor Schenck continued. "A distinctive occupational mark arises from the perpetual
repetition of the same act in the same way, and
while a sailor's life is hard, it is extremely varied.
It would be at once apparent from a mariner's
hands that he did hard manual labor, and with
both hands instead of only with the right, but
there are surely a dozen trades to which this applies equally well."

20 *cork-cutters*. "The hand of the cork-cutter is
another phenomenon which has been banished from
the contemporary scene by modern machinery.
One can speculate that calluses were produced on
the thumb and first two fingers of the left hand by
grasping the cork, and similarly on the thumb and
across the inside of all four fingers of the right by
the handle of the knife . . ." (Schenck).

21 *compositors*. See "The Adventure of the Copper Beeches," Note 10.

22 *weavers.* "There is, unfortunately, no way at this date to establish just what constituted for Holmes the unmistakable manual stigma of the weaver," Professor Schenck continued. "A wide variety of calluses peculiar to the textile trades is described by [Rancesco Ronchese], but these differ with the particular assignment of the worker at the machine—the doffer, the quiller, the hooker, the mule spinner, etc.—and none of them could have been created by hand-looming. It is likely that the marks to which Holmes referred were calluses on the right hand from handling the shuttle, and perhaps on the left from the heddles . . ."

23 *diamond-polishers.* "Some clues [to the hand of the diamond-polisher] are available: jewelry polishers have nails worn smooth and stained red by the rouge . . . , lens polishers show certain nails worn down from picking the glass from its pitch bed . . . , and those who polish metal jewelry wear calluses from holding the metal parts against the wheel. . . . Since diamonds are polished in a pitch bed at the end of a 'dop stick' any or all of the three marks described might appear in a lapidary doing much hand work" (Schenck).

24 *the antecedents of criminals.* In four of his own cases—"A Case of Identity," "The Red-Headed League," "The Adventure of the Copper Beeches," and "The Adventure of the Solitary Cyclist"—Holmes demonstrates his personal proficiency in estimating the effects of various trades upon hands.

25 *but to send a wire?* "Equally well [Watson] might have gone for a money order or a postal order, to inquire the cost of sending a parcel to India or Australia, or to buy stamps of a different value to those contained in his sheet," Mr. Vernon Rendall commented in "The Limitations of Sherlock Holmes."

26 *the one which remains must be the truth.'* "This is the most famous maxim of Holmes, and it was a great favourite with him," Mr. T. S. Blakeney wrote in *Sherlock Holmes: Fact of Fiction?* "It is twice uttered in *The Sign of the Four* [". . . when you have eliminated the impossible, whatever remains, *however improbable*, must be the truth"], and we find it repeated almost identically in 'The Adventure of the Beryl Coronet,' 'The Adventure of the Bruce-Partington Plans' and 'The Adventure of the Blanched Soldier.' With it may be compared the remark to Watson in 'The Adventure of the Priory School': 'it *is* impossible as I state it, and therefore I must in some respect have stated it wrong.' "

my possession. Would you have the kindness to let me have an opinion upon the character or habits of the late owner?'

I handed him over the watch with some slight feeling of amusement in my heart, for the test was, as I thought, an impossible one, and I intended it as a lesson against the somewhat dogmatic tone which he occasionally assumed. He balanced the watch in his hand, gazed hard at the dial, opened the back, and examined the works, first with his naked eyes and then with a powerful convex lens. I could hardly keep from smiling at his crestfallen face when he finally snapped the case to and handed it back.

'There are hardly any data,' he remarked. 'The watch has been recently cleaned, which robs me of my most suggestive facts.'

'You are right,' I answered. 'It was cleaned before being sent to me.'

In my heart I accused my companion of putting forward a most lame and impotent excuse to cover his failure. What data could he expect from an uncleaned watch?

'Though unsatisfactory, my research has not been entirely barren,' he observed, staring up at the ceiling with dreamy, lack-lustre eyes. 'Subject to your correction, I should judge that the watch belonged to your elder brother, who inherited it from your father.'

'That you gather, no doubt, from the H. W. upon the back?'

'Quite so. The W. suggests your own name. The date of the watch is nearly fifty years back and the initials are as old as the watch; so it was made for the last generation. Jewellery usually descends to the eldest son, and he is most likely to have the same name as the father. Your father has, if I remember right, been dead many years. It has, therefore, been in the hands of your eldest brother.'

'Right, so far,' said I. 'Anything else?'

'He was a man of untidy habits—very untidy and careless. He was left with good prospects, but he threw away his chances, lived for some time in poverty with occasional short intervals of prosperity, and, finally, taking to drink, he died. That is all I can gather.'

I sprang from my chair and limped impatiently about the room with considerable bitterness in my heart.

'This is unworthy of you, Holmes,' I said. 'I could not have believed that you would have descended to this. You have made inquiries into the history of my unhappy brother, and you now pretend to deduce this knowledge in some fanciful way. You cannot expect me to believe that you have read all this from his old watch! It is unkind, and, to speak plainly, has a touch of charlatanism in it.'

'My dear Doctor,' said he, kindly, 'pray accept my apologies. Viewing the matter as an abstract problem, I had forgotten how personal and painful a thing it might be to you. I assure you, however, that I never even knew that you had a brother until you handed me the watch.'

'Then how in the name of all that is wonderful did you get these facts? They are absolutely correct in every particular.'

'Ah, that is good luck. I could only say what was the balance of probability. I did not at all expect to be accurate.'

'But it was not mere guesswork?'

'No, no: I never guess. It is a shocking habit—destructive to the logical faculty. What seems strange to you is only so because you do not follow my train of thought or observe the small facts upon which large inferences may depend. For example, I began by stating that your brother was careless. When you observe the lower part of that watch-case you notice that it is not only dinted in two places, but it is cut and marked all over from the habit of keeping other hard objects, such as coins or keys, in the same pocket. Surely it is no great feat to assume that a man who treats a fifty-guinea watch so cavalierly must be a careless man. Neither is it a **27** very far-fetched inference that a man who inherits one article of such value is pretty well provided for in other respects.'

I nodded, to show that I followed his reasoning.

'It is very customary for pawnbrokers in England, when they take a watch, to scratch the number of the ticket with a pin-point upon the inside of the case. It is more handy than a label, as there is no risk of the number being lost or transposed. There are no less than four such numbers visible to my lens on the inside of this case. Inference—that your brother was often at low water. Secondary inference—that he had occasional bursts of prosperity, or he could not have redeemed the pledge. Finally, I ask you to look at the inner plate, which contains the keyhole. Look at the thousands of **28** scratches all round the hole—marks where the key has slipped. What sober man's key could have scored those grooves? But you will never see a drunkard's watch without them. He winds it at night, and he leaves these traces of his unsteady hand. Where is the mystery in all this?'

'It is as clear as daylight,' I answered. 'I regret the injustice which I did you. I should have had more faith in your marvellous faculty. May I ask whether you have any professional inquiry on foot at present?'

'None. Hence the cocaine. I cannot live without brainwork. What else is there to live for? Stand at the window here. Was ever such a dreary, dismal, unprofitable world? See how the yellow fog swirls down the street and drifts across the dun-**29** coloured houses. What could be more hopelessly prosaic and material? What is the use of having powers, Doctor, when one has no field upon which to exert them? Crime is commonplace, existence is commonplace, and no qualities save those which are commonplace have any function upon earth.'

I had opened my mouth to reply to this tirade, when, with a crisp knock, our landlady entered, bearing a card upon the brass salver.

'A young lady for you, sir,' she said, addressing my companion.

'Miss Mary Morstan,' he read. 'Hum! I have no recollection of the name. Ask the young lady to step up, Mrs Hudson. Don't go, doctor. I should prefer that you remain.'

2 ❖ THE STATEMENT OF THE CASE

Miss Morstan entered the room with a firm step and an outward composure of manner. She was a blonde young lady,

27 *a fifty-guinea watch.* Holmes valued the watch at being worth the equivalent of about $262.50 U.S. at that time.

28 *the keyhole.* The stem-winding watch had been developed by 1840 but the key-wind was cheaper and more trouble-free. The owner of a key-winding watch usually kept the key on his watch chain; the Phi Beta Kappa key coveted by students was originally designed as a watch key.

29 *the yellow fog.* We are later told that "A dense drizzly fog lay low upon the great city," that "We plunged away at a furious pace through the foggy streets," and that "we had left the damp fog of the city behind us . . ." Although most commentators (Andrew, Ashton, Baring-Gould, Blakeney, Christ, Folsom, Knox, Pattrick, Petersen, Roberts, Smith, Starrett, and Zeisler) are today agreed that the adventure of *The Sign of the Four* took place in 1888, a strong minority (Austin, Bell, Brend, Bristowe, Harrison, Hoff, MacCarthy, McCleary, Montgomery, Christopher Morley, Offord, and Wellman) date the case 1887. But the month also is in dispute: April, June, July, and September all have their supporters. At this time, let us note only that fog would have been a phenomenon in June and July, at least.

MISS MORSTAN ENTERED THE ROOM WITH A FIRM STEP . . .

An illustration by an artist as yet unidentified. It comes from *Stories of Sherlock Holmes*, Vol. I, New York: Harper & Brothers, 1904.

30 *a little domestic complication.* Mr. Robert Keith Leavitt has suggested (in "Who Was Cecil Forrester?") that *Mr.* Cecil Forrester, Farintosh of "The Adventure of the Speckled Band," Woodhouse of "The Adventure of the Bruce-Partington Plans," and Colonel Upwood of *The Hound of the Baskervilles* were all one and the same man— "former friend of Captain Morstan and probably of the none-too-scrupulous Major Sholto, sometime husband of Mary Morstan's employer, party hanger-on, card-sharp and all-too-dubious hero of the strange adventure·of the politician, the lighthouse and the trained cormorant ["The Adventure of the Veiled Lodger"]."

And Mrs. Ruth Douglass, in "The Camberwell Poisoner," has advanced the speculation that the "little domestic complication" in Mrs. Forrester's household was the Camberwell Poisoning; that the poisoner was Mrs. Forrester; that she escaped justice and used Mary first as bait (for Watson) and then as a tool (in order to obtain poison, through Mary, from Watson's medical cabinet). She finally killed Mary.

31 *In the year 1878.* Mary Morstan was therefore born in 1861.

32 *a choking sob cut short the sentence.* "This is rather excessive emotion to be exhibited by an Englishwoman of the upper classes when speaking of an event which occurred ten years before and of a person she has long believed dead," Messrs. T. B. Hunt and H. W. Starr observed in "What Happened to Mary Morstan?" "She is subject to similar collapses whenever Captain Morstan's death is mentioned. How else can this be explained save by the existence of a marked Oedipus complex?"

small, dainty, well gloved, and dressed in the most perfect taste. There was, however, a plainness and simplicity about her costume which bore with it a suggestion of limited means. The dress was a sombre greyish beige, untrimmed and unbraided, and she wore a small turban of the same dull hue, relieved only by a suspicion of white feather in the side. Her face had neither regularity of feature nor beauty of complexion, but her expression was sweet and amiable, and her large blue eyes were singularly spiritual and sympathetic. In an experience of women which extends over many nations and three separate continents, I have never looked upon a face which gave a clearer promise of a refined and sensitive nature. I could not but observe that, as she took the seat which Sherlock Holmes placed for her, her lip trembled, her hand quivered, and she showed every sign of intense inward agitation.

'I have come to you, Mr Holmes,' she said, 'because you once enabled my employer, Mrs Cecil Forrester, to unravel

30 a little domestic complication. She was much impressed by your kindness and skill.'

'Mrs Cecil Forrester,' he repeated, thoughtfully. 'I believe that I was of some slight service to her. The case, however, as I remember it, was a very simple one.'

'She did not think so. But at least you cannot say the same of mine. I can hardly imagine anything more strange, more utterly inexplicable, than the situation in which I find myself.'

Holmes rubbed his hands, and his eyes glistened. He leaned forward in his chair with an expression of extraordinary concentration upon his clear-cut, hawk-like features.

'State your case,' said he, in brisk, business tones.

I felt that my position was an embarrassing one.

'You will, I am sure, excuse me,' I said, rising from my chair.

To my surprise, the young lady held up her gloved hand to detain me.

'If your friend,' she said, 'would be good enough to stop, he might be of inestimable service to me.'

I relapsed into my chair.

'Briefly,' she continued, 'the facts are these. My father was an officer in an Indian regiment, who sent me home when I was quite a child. My mother was dead, and I had no relative in England. I was placed, however, in a comfortable boarding establishment at Edinburgh, and there I remained until I was

31 seventeen years of age. In the year 1878 my father, who was senior captain of his regiment, obtained twelve months' leave and came home. He telegraphed to me from London that he had arrived all safe, and directed me to come down at once, giving the Langham Hotel as his address. His message, as I remember, was full of kindness and love. On reaching London I drove to the Langham, and was informed that Captain Morstan was staying there, but that he had gone out the night before and had not returned. I waited all day without news of him. That night, on the advice of the manager of the hotel, I communicated with the police, and next morning we advertised in all the papers. Our inquiries led to no result; and from that day to this no word has ever been heard of my unfortunate father. He came home with his heart full of hope, to find some peace, some comfort, and instead——'

She put her hand to her throat, and a choking sob cut short the sentence. **32**

'The date?' asked Holmes, opening his note-book.

'He disappeared upon the 3rd of December, 1878—nearly ten years ago.' **33**

'His luggage?'

'Remained at the hotel. There was nothing in it to suggest a clue—some clothes, some books, and a considerable number of curiosities from the Andaman Islands. He had been one **34** of the officers in charge of the convict guard there.'

'Had he any friends in town?'

'Only one that we know of—Major Sholto, of his own regiment, the 34th Bombay Infantry. The Major had retired **35** some little time before, and lived at Upper Norwood. We **36** communicated with him, of course, but he did not even know that his brother officer was in England.'

'A singular case,' remarked Holmes.

'I have not yet described to you the most singular part. About six years ago—to be exact, upon the 4th of May, 1882 **37** —an advertisement appeared in *The Times* asking for the address of Miss Mary Morstan, and stating that it would be to her advantage to come forward. There was no name or address appended. I had at that time just entered the family of Mrs Cecil Forrester in the capacity of governess. By her advice I published my address in the advertisement column. The same day there arrived through the post a small cardboard box addressed to me, which I found to contain a very large and lustrous pearl. No word of writing was enclosed. Since then every year upon the same date there has always appeared a similar box, containing a similar pearl, without any clue as to the sender. They have been pronounced by an expert to be of a rare variety and of considerable value. You can see for yourselves that they are very handsome.'

She opened a flat box as she spoke, and showed me six of the finest pearls that I had ever seen. **38**

'Your statement is most interesting,' said Sherlock Holmes. 'Has anything else occurred to you?'

'Yes, and no later than today. That is why I have come to you. This morning I received this letter, which you will per- **39** haps read for yourself.'

'Thank you,' said Holmes. 'The envelope, too, please. Post-mark, London, S.W. Date, July 7. Huml Man's thumb- **40–41** mark on corner—probably postman. Best quality paper. Envelopes at sixpence a packet. Particular man in his stationery.'

33 *nearly ten years ago.'* A statement that would seem to point to the period between June and early December, 1888, for the time of the adventure.

34 *the Andaman Islands.* In the Bay of Bengal, about 800 miles from the nearest part of India. They were occupied by the Japanese in 1942.

35 *the 34th Bombay Infantry.* "At the period of the Mutiny, when the events relating to Morstan and Sholto began, the regimental numbers of the Bombay Infantry of the Indian Army appear to have gone no higher than Thirty," Mrs. Crighton Sellars wrote in "Dr. Watson and the British Army." "I take it that this is one of the occasions on which Dr. Watson chose to create a fictional regiment in which to put his reprehensible characters. But there was a *Bengal 38th Infantry* known as 'The Agra Regiment' to which I make a guess that Captain Morstan and Major Sholto really belonged."

36 *Upper Norwood.* A suburb of London, part of the county borough of Croydon. Noted for its bracing air, it contained and still contains some good private hotels, such as the old-established Queen's Hotel in Church Road.

37 *the 4th of May, 1882.* A statement that would seem to point roughly to the period between early February and early August, 1888, for the time of the adventure.

38 *six of the finest pearls that I had ever seen.* The advertisement in the *Times* appeared on May 4, 1882. Miss Morstan's reply could not have appeared until the next day, and on that day she received the first pearl. The other pearls were received "every year upon the same date," that is, on May 5th, and she now has six pearls in all. Therefore her visit to Baker Street would seem to have been made after May 5, 1887, and before May 5, 1888. Students who argue for the June, July, or September of 1888 as the date of this adventure must therefore explain why Mary failed to produce *seven* pearls. It has been said that this was a note-taking error on Watson's part; that he wrote the two dates (1882 and 1888) and calculated

'. . . ENVELOPES AT SIXPENCE A PACKET . . .'

In U.S. currency at the time, the envelopes cost about 12¢ a packet. (We recall that the King of Bohemia paid about 60¢ U.S. for his writing paper.) "The sixpence," the late A. Carson Simpson wrote in *Numismatics in the Canon*, Part I, "was first struck in 1550 by Edward VI, omitted by Mary I, called a 'half-shilling' under William & Mary, then coined under its old name by all succeeding monarchs. The silver shortage caused George III to issue them in only one year (1787) between his accession and the 1816 currency reform." The sixpence is mentioned in the Canon three times.

' "BE AT THE THIRD PILLAR FROM THE LEFT OUTSIDE
THE LYCEUM THEATRE AT SEVEN O'CLOCK." '

The Lyceum Theatre was first built as an opera
house in 1794 by Dr. Samuel Arnold, the great-
grandfather of Edgar Allan Poe. It was destroyed
by fire and rebuilt in 1834. From 1878 to 1904 it
was managed by Sir Henry Irving and then became for a time a music hall. It still exists, as a
dance hall, at the corner of Exeter Street and
Wellington Street, the Strand.

the number of pearls he had seen by subtracting.
Mr. T. S. Blakeney has suggested that Mary "may
have had the first pearl she received made up into
a brooch or pendant, as she would not be expecting any more; but naturally, on finding pearls
came in every year, she would keep the remaining six together." And the late Professor Jay
Finley Christ thought that Mary might well have
sold the first pearl. The most probable explanation
on the whole would seem to be that Mary Morstan
produced seven pearls and seven box tops and
that Watson simply miscounted them; otherwise,
as the late Dr. Ernest Bloomfield Zeisler pointed
out, Holmes or his client would certainly have
commented on the situation.

39 *This morning*. We later learn that "This
morning" was a Tuesday morning.

40 *S.W*. South West—indicating the postal district of London from which the letter had been
mailed.

41 *July* 7. Thaddeus Sholto's letter to Mary Morstan had to arrive on the morning on which the
adventure began in order to arrange for the appointment for "tonight," but it might have been
mailed either late Monday night or early Tuesday
morning. Unfortunately for the 1887 School, July
7, 1887, was neither a Monday nor a Tuesday, but
a Saturday. What speaks for July, other than the
postmark on the letter? There is Thaddeus Sholto,
venturing forth "in a very long befrogged top-
coat" which "he buttoned tightly up in spite of
the closeness of the night." There is "a warm
wind" which "blew from the westward." There
are barefoot Irregulars, and there is Mary, late at
night, "seated by an open window, dressed in some
sort of white diaphanous material." All of these
might be interpreted as pointing towards July,
if it were not for the fact that we are later told
that it was "very hot *for the time of the year*."

No address. "Be at the third pillar from the left outside the
Lyceum Theatre tonight at seven o'clock. If you are distrust-
ful bring two friends. You are a wronged woman, and shall
have justice. Do not bring police. If you do, all will be in vain.
Your unknown friend." Well, really, this is a very pretty little
mystery! What do you intend to do, Miss Morstan?'
'That is exactly what I want to ask you.'
'Then we shall most certainly go—you and I and—yes, why,
Dr Watson is the very man. Your correspondent says two
friends. He and I have worked together before.'
'But would he come?' she asked, with something appealing
in her voice and expression.
'I shall be proud and happy,' said I, fervently, 'if I can be
of any service.'
'You are both very kind,' she answered. 'I have led a retired
life, and have no friends whom I could appeal to. If I am here
at six it will do, I suppose?'
'You must not be later,' said Holmes. 'There is one other
point, however. Is this handwriting the same as that upon
the pearl-box addresses?'
'I have them here,' she answered, producing half-a-dozen
pieces of paper.

'You are certainly a model client. You have the correct intuition. Let us see, now.' He spread out the papers upon the table, and gave little, darting glances from one to the other. 'They are disguised hands, except the letter,' he said, presently; 'but there can be no question as to the authorship. See how the irrepressible Greek *e* will break out, and see the twirl of the final *s*. They are undoubtedly by the same person. I should not like to suggest false hopes, Miss Morstan, but is there any resemblance between this hand and that of your father?'

'Nothing could be more unlike.'

'I expected to hear you say so. We shall look out for you, then, at six. Pray allow me to keep the papers. I may look into the matter before then. It is only half-past three. *Au revoir*, then.'

'*Au revoir*,' said our visitor; and with a bright, kindly glance from one to the other of us, she replaced her pearl-box in her bosom and hurried away.

Standing at the window, I watched her walking briskly down the street, until the grey turban and white feather were but a speck in the sombre crowd.

'What a very attractive woman!' I exclaimed, turning to my companion.

He had lit his pipe again, and was leaning back with drooping eyelids. 'Is she?' he said, languidly; 'I did not observe.' **42**

'You really are an automaton—a calculating machine,' I cried. 'There is something positively inhuman in you at times.'

He smiled gently.

'It is of the first importance,' he said, 'not to allow your judgment to be biased by personal qualities. A client is to me a mere unit, a factor in a problem. The emotional qualities are antagonistic to clear reasoning. I assure you that the most winning woman I ever knew was hanged for poisoning three little children for their insurance-money, and the most repel- **43** lent man of my acquaintance is a philanthropist who has spent nearly a quarter of a million upon the London poor.'

'In this case, however——'

'I never make exceptions. An exception disproves the rule. Have you ever had occasion to study character in handwriting? What do you make of this fellow's scribble?'

'It is legible and regular,' I answered. 'A man of business habits and some force of character.'

Holmes shook his head.

'Look at his long letters,' he said. 'They hardly rise above the common herd. That *d* might be an *a*, and that *l* an *e*. Men of character always differentiate their long letters, however illegibly they may write. There is vacillation in his *k*'s and self-esteem in his capitals. I am going out now. I have some few references to make. Let me recommend this book—one of the most remarkable ever penned. It is Winwood Reade's *Martyrdom of Man*. I shall be back in an hour.' **44**

I sat in the window with the volume in my hand, but my thoughts were far from the daring speculations of the writer. My mind ran upon our late visitor—her smiles, the deep, rich tones of her voice, the strange mystery which overhung her life. If she were seventeen at the time of her father's disappearance she must be seven-and-twenty now—a sweet **45**

In your editor's view, Thaddeus Sholto's letter was mailed late on *Monday, September 17, 1888*. Watson's no doubt carelessly written 'S 17' was misread, by himself or by the typesetter, as "Jl 7."

42 '*I did not observe*.' "It is possible that a man so observant that he would even notice the depth to which parsley had sunk into the butter on a hot day could fail to notice that Mary Morstan was attractive?" Dr. Richard Asher asked in "Holmes and the Fair Sex." "No; Holmes was aware of her charms and on guard against them. As he later said, 'A client is to me a mere unit, a factor in a problem. The emotional qualities are antagonistic to clear reasoning.' It seems that from this very point Holmes purposely did not allow any emotional feelings toward Miss Morstan to rise in himself. Not only because it would have been antagonistic to clear reasoning but because he saw that Watson, already deeply smitten, was musing upon her smiles and the deep rich tones of her voice until such dangerous thoughts came into his head that he plunged furiously into the latest treatise on pathology."

43 *three little children for their insurance-money*. "Who this woman was who attracted Holmes so strongly and came to such a dreadful end, we do not know," Dr. Asher continued. "She may have been Mrs. Morgan, for a poisoner called Morgan occupied a place of honour in his index among other distinguished M's ["The Adventure of the Empty House"]. Whoever she was, this woman seems to have left her mark upon Holmes."

44 *Winwood Reade's* Martyrdom of Man. William Winwood Reade, 1838–1875, traveler, novelist, and controversialist, was a nephew of Charles Reade. His *Martyrdom of Man* was published in London in 1872 by Trübner and Company of Paternoster Row. The book became so popular that by 1884 it had reached an eighth edition. Mr. S. C. Roberts ("The Personality of Sherlock Holmes") has written that the book was "one of the most popular monuments of nineteenth century rationalism. Holmes, with his social moodiness, his artistic temperament and his queer intellectual interests, had no doubt reacted against the conventional beliefs of his squirearchical family and Winwood Reade's book was exactly the work that would catch him on the rebound. It is a sad work and its conclusions may well have depressed a contemporary of Sherlock Holmes: 'A season of mental anguish is at hand and through this we must pass in order that our posterity may rise. The soul must be sacrificed; the hope in immortality must die.' "

45 *she must be seven-and-twenty now*. Since Captain Morstan came home in 1878, when Mary was seventeen, this is still another indication that 1888 was the year of the case.

46 *the 28th of April, 1882.'* Corroborating Mary's statement that the advertisement seeking her out appeared "upon the 4th of May, 1882"—"about six years ago."

47 *Four years later.* Corroborating Mary's statement that Captain Morstan returned to England and disappeared in 1878, which was "nearly ten years ago."

48 *rather than six years ago?* And Holmes later tells us that the Sholtos were six years searching for the treasure. As the date of Sholto's death cannot be in doubt, we again reach 1888 as the year of *The Sign of the Four.*

age, when youth has lost its self-consciousness and become a little sobered by experience. So I sat and mused, until such dangerous thoughts came into my head that I hurried away to my desk and plunged furiously into the latest treatise upon pathology. What was I, an Army surgeon with a weak leg and a weaker banking account, that I should dare to think of such things? She was a unit, a factor—nothing more. If my future were black, it was better surely to face it like a man than to attempt to brighten it by mere will-o'-the-wisps of the imagination.

3 ∙ IN QUEST OF A SOLUTION

It was half-past five before Holmes returned. He was bright, eager, and in excellent spirits, a mood which in his case alternated with fits of the blackest depression.

'There is no great mystery in this matter,' he said, taking the cup of tea which I had poured out for him; 'the facts appear to admit of only one explanation.'

'What! you have solved it already?'

'Well, that would be too much to say. I have discovered a suggestive fact, that is all. It is, however, *very* suggestive. The details are still to be added. I have just found, on consulting the back files of *The Times*, that Major Sholto, of Upper Norwood, late of the 34th Bombay Infantry, died upon the

46 28th of April, 1882.'

'I may be very obtuse, Holmes, but I fail to see what this suggests.'

'No? You surprise me. Look at it in this way, then. Captain Morstan disappears. The only person in London whom he could have visited is Major Sholto. Major Sholto denies

47 having heard that he was in London. Four years later Sholto dies. *Within a week of his death* Captain Morstan's daughter receives a valuable present, which is repeated from year to year, and now culminates in a letter which describes her as a wronged woman. What wrong can it refer to except this deprivation of her father? And why should the presents begin immediately after Sholto's death, unless it is that Sholto's heir knows something of the mystery and desires to make compensation? Have you any alternative theory which will meet the facts?'

'But what a strange compensation! And how strangely made! Why, too, should he write a letter now, rather than six

48 years ago? Again, the letter speaks of giving her justice. What justice can she have? It is too much to suppose that her father is still alive. There is no other injustice in her case that you know of.'

'There are difficulties; there are certainly difficulties,' said Sherlock Holmes, pensively; 'but your expedition of tonight will solve them all. Ah, here is a four-wheeler, and Miss Morstan inside. Are you all ready? Then we had better go down, for it is a little past the hour.'

I picked up my hat and my heaviest stick, but I observed that Holmes took his revolver from his drawer and slipped it into his pocket. It was clear that he thought that our night's work might be a serious one.

Miss Morstan was muffled in a dark cloak, and her sensitive face was composed, but pale. She must have been more than woman if she did not feel some uneasiness at the strange enterprise upon which we were embarking, yet her self-control was perfect, and she readily answered the few additional questions which Sherlock Holmes put to her.

'Major Sholto was a very particular friend of papa's,' she said. 'His letters were full of allusions to the Major. He and papa were in command of the troops at the Andaman Islands, so they were thrown a great deal together. By the way, a curious paper was found in papa's desk which no one could understand. I don't suppose that it is of the slightest importance, but I thought you might care to see it, so I brought it with me. It is here.'

Holmes unfolded the paper carefully and smoothed it out upon his knee. He then very methodically examined it all over with his double lens.

'It is paper of native Indian manufacture,' he remarked. 'It has at some time been pinned to a board. The diagram upon it appears to be a plan of part of a large building with numerous halls, corridors, and passages. At one point is a small cross done in red ink, and above it is "3.37 from left," in faded pencil-writing. In the left-hand corner is a curious hieroglyphic like four crosses in a line with their arms touching. Beside it is written, in very rough and coarse characters, "The sign of the four—Jonathan Small, Mahomet Singh, Abdullah Khan, Dost Akbar." No, I confess that I do not see how this bears upon the matter. Yet it is evidently a document of importance. It has been kept carefully in a pocket-book; for the one side is as clean as the other.'

'It was in his pocket-book that we found it.'

'Preserve it carefully, then, Miss Morstan, for it may prove to be of use to us. I begin to suspect that this matter may turn out to be much deeper and more subtle than I at first supposed. I must reconsider my ideas.'

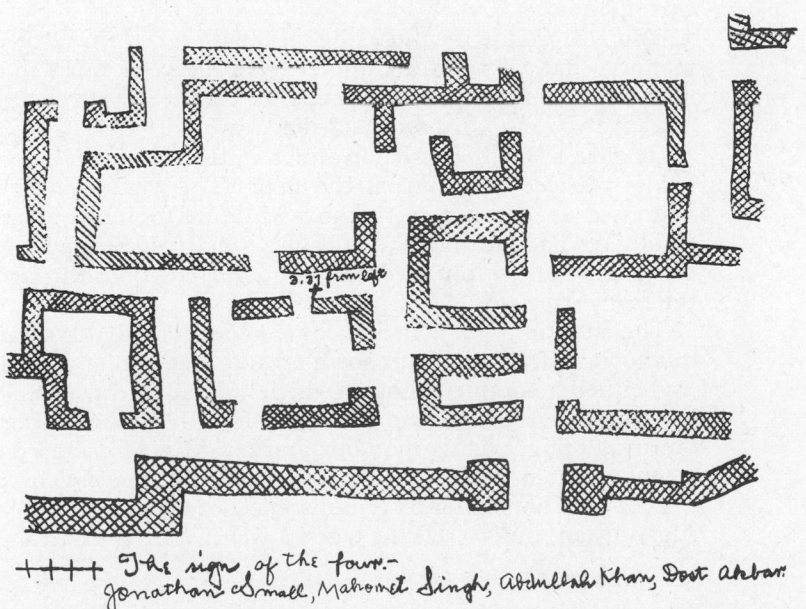

"YET IT IS EVIDENTLY A DOCUMENT OF IMPORTANCE."

Dr. Julian Wolff's reconstruction of the "plan of part of a large building with numerous halls, corridors, and passages."

49 *It was a September evening.* The late Clifton R. Andrew once wrote ("On the Dating of *The Sign of the Four*"): "Watson was speaking of the weather. . . . That evening in July, 1888, was so pleasantly cool and balmy—or perhaps blowing with such exceptional equinoctial violence—that it seemed to him not like an evening in July at all, but like an evening in September." The September School again points to the fog, which can only be otherwise explained by a combination of Beaune on the part of Watson and cocaine on the part of Holmes.

50 *a dense drizzly fog lay low upon the great city.* In fact, Tuesday, September 18, 1888, *was* a day on which the *Times* of London reported "fog and mist." No sunshine whatsoever was recorded on that day at Westminster.

51 *the crowds were already thick at the side-entrances.* "They were probably playing Shakespeare at the time of the rendezvous, which would account for the crowd of devotees," the late Christopher Morley wrote in *Sherlock Holmes and Dr. Watson: A Textbook of Friendship;* "though seven o'clock is surely too early for the carriage trade to be arriving. The 'side-entrances' would be to the gallery and the pit, where in the English custom seats are not reserved and the crowd 'queues up' to wait for the doors to open. By happy coincidence the play *Sherlock Holmes,* dramatized and starred by William Gillette, was first performed [in London] at the Lyceum Theatre, September 2, 1901."

He leaned back in the cab, and I could see by his drawn brow and his vacant eye that he was thinking intently. Miss Morstan and I chatted in an undertone about our present expedition and its possible outcome, but our companion maintained his impenetrable reserve until the end of our journey.

49   It was a September evening, and not yet seven o'clock, but the day had been a dreary one, and a dense drizzly fog lay

50 low upon the great city. Mud-coloured clouds drooped sadly over the muddy streets. Down the Strand the lamps were but misty splotches of diffused light, which threw a feeble circular glimmer upon the slimy pavement. The yellow glare from the shop-windows streamed out into the steamy, vaporous air, and threw a murky, shifting radiance across the crowded thoroughfare. There was, to my mind, something eerie and ghost-like in the endless procession of faces which flitted across these narrow bars of light—sad faces and glad, haggard and merry. Like all human kind, they flitted from the gloom into the light, and so back into the gloom once more. I am not subject to impressions, but the dull, heavy evening, with the strange business upon which we were engaged, combined to make me nervous and depressed. I could see from Miss Morstan's manner that she was suffering from the same feeling. Holmes alone could rise superior to petty influences. He held his open note-book upon his knee, and from time to time he jotted down figures and memoranda in the light of his pocket-lantern.

At the Lyceum Theatre the crowds were already thick at

51 the side-entrances. In front a continuous stream of hansoms and four-wheelers were rattling up, discharging their cargoes of shirt-fronted men and beshawled, bediamonded women. We had hardly reached the third pillar, which was our rendezvous, before a small, dark, brisk man in the dress of a coachman accosted us.

'Are you the parties who come with Miss Morstan?' he asked.

'I am Miss Morstan, and these two gentlemen are my friends,' said she.

He bent a pair of wonderfully penetrating and questioning eyes upon us.

'You will excuse me, miss,' he said, with a certain dogged manner, 'but I was to ask you to give me your word that neither of your companions is a police-officer.'

'I give you my word on that,' she answered.

He gave a shrill whistle, on which a street arab led across a four-wheeler and opened the door. The man who had addressed us mounted to the box, while we took our places inside. We had hardly done so before the driver whipped up his horse, and we plunged away at a furious pace through the foggy streets.

The situation was a curious one. We were driving to an unknown place, on an unknown errand. Yet our invitation was either a complete hoax—which was an inconceivable hypothesis—or else we had good reason to think that important issues might hang upon our journey. Miss Morstan's demeanour was as resolute and collected as ever. I endeavoured to cheer and amuse her by reminiscences of my adventures in Afghanistan; but, to tell the truth, I was myself so excited at our situation, and so curious as to our destination, that my stories were slightly involved. To this day she declares that I told her one moving anecdote as to how a musket looked into my tent at the dead of night, and how I fired a double-barrelled tiger cub at it. At first I had some idea as to the **52** direction in which we were driving; but soon, what with our pace, the fog, and my own limited knowledge of London, I lost my bearings, and knew nothing, save that we seemed to be going a very long way. Sherlock Holmes was never at fault, however, and he muttered the names as the cab rattled **53** through squares and in and out by tortuous by-streets.

'Rochester Row,' said he. 'Now Vincent Square. Now we **54–55** come out on the Vauxhall Bridge Road. We are making for **56** the Surrey side, apparently. Yes, I thought so. Now we are **57** on the bridge. You can catch glimpses of the river.' **58**

We did indeed get a fleeting view of a stretch of the Thames, with the lamps shining upon the broad, silent water; **59** but our cab dashed on, and was soon involved in a labyrinth of streets upon the other side.

'Wandsworth Road,' said my companion. 'Priory Road. **60–61** Larkhall Lane. Stockwell Place. Robert Street. Coldharbour **62–63** Lane. Our quest does not appear to take us to very fashionable **64–65** regions.'

We had indeed reached a questionable and forbidding neighbourhood. Long lines of dull brick houses were only relieved by the coarse glare and tawdry brilliancy of public-houses at the corners. Then came rows of two-storied villas, each with a fronting of miniature garden, and then again interminable lines of new, staring brick buildings—the mon-

"OUR QUEST DOES NOT APPEAR TO TAKE US TO VERY FASHIONABLE REGIONS."

This sketch map accompanied the late Robert R. Pattrick's article, "The Oasis in the Howling Desert," when it appeared in *The Sherlock Holmes Journal*, Spring, 1960.

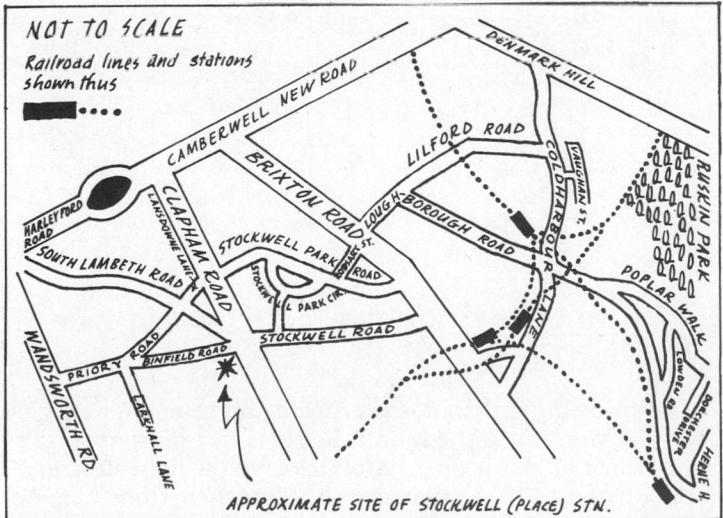

52 *a double-barrelled tiger cub.* "The celebrated 'double-barrelled' tiger cub must, I think, have been a snow leopard," Mr. T. S. Blakeney wrote in "Thoughts on *The Sign of the Four*." "According to Ellerman and Morrison-Scott, *Checklist of Palaearctic and Indian Mammals* (British Museum of Natural History, 1951), tigers do not inhabit the region of South Afghanistan or North West Frontier of India, so neither in the Kandahar/Maiwand region, nor in that of Peshawar, would Watson have found one."

53 *Sherlock Holmes was never at fault, however.* "It is a hobby of mine to have an exact knowledge of London," Holmes said in "The Red-Headed League." And in "The Adventure of the Empty House," Watson wrote: "Holmes' knowledge of the byways of London was extraordinary . . ."

54 *'Rochester Row.'* Rochester Row, leading to Horseferry Road, is about halfway along the Vauxhall Bridge Road on the east side. Its notable features include the Greycoat School, founded in 1698; St. Stephen's Church, founded in 1847; and the district police court, opened in 1846.

55 *Vincent Square.* Just south of Rochester Row is the old-fashioned Vincent Square, now used as a playground by the boys of the Westminster School.

56 *the Vauxhall Bridge Road.* Built about 1816, at the time of the erection of Vauxhall Bridge, the Vauxhall Bridge Road provides direct communication between Hyde Park Corner and Grosvenor Place and the south of London. It divides old Westminster from the quarter of Pimlico and South Belgravia.

57 *the Surrey side.* The south side of the Thames, which now forms the northern boundary of the county of Surrey.

58 *the bridge.* Holmes and Watson crossed on the bridge constructed in 1811–1816. The present span, an iron and steel structure 759 feet long and 80 feet wide, designed by Maurice Fitzmaurice, was not opened until 1906.

59 *the Thames.* The Thames, rising among the Cotswold Hills in Gloucestershire and running for 209 miles to the North Sea, is the principal river of England. The Thames flows through London and its suburbs for a distance of some 25 miles and attains a width of 750 feet at London Bridge.

60 *'Wandsworth Road.'* Which some editions of the Canon erroneously call "Wordsworth Road."

This has compounded confusion where confusion already exists, for there is a Wordsworth Road in London, miles away in another direction entirely. *Wandsworth* Road, on the other hand, is a right-handed turn at the south side of Vauxhall Bridge.

61 '*Priory Road*. There is, unhappily, no Priory Road in this part of London *today*. But, as the late Robert R. Pattrick pointed out in "The Oasis in the Howling Desert," "the street known today as 'Lansdowne Way' was then divided into two parts. The entire section between Wandsworth Road and Larkhall Lane was Priory Road."

62 *Larkhall Lane*. As Professor Stephen F. Crocker has said ("Louder, Holmes! and Stop Muttering!"): "They just came to it; of course they did not follow it. It would have taken them in the wrong direction and brought them out farther away on Wandsworth Road again."

63 *Stockwell Place*. There is, or was, no street of that name. But there was a Stockwell *Road*, a Stockwell *Park Road*, and a Stockwell *Park Circle* (*see sketch map*). Professor Crocker has logically suggested that "The word *place* can, of course, refer to a short street or court, a private residence terrace, or some similar variation from the ordinary street; but the word can also refer to a place, open space, or square, in a city or town. In this sense, the whole area could easily be referred to as 'Stockwell Place.'" Whether they proceeded north (via Stockwell Park Road) or south (via Binfield Road, Stockwell Road, and Stockwell Park Circle) they came next to Robert (Robsart) Street.

64 *Robert Street*. Then, and now, *Robsart* Street. But it had been *Robert* Street until April 30, 1880, when it was combined with Park Street to form the present Robsart Street.

65 *Coldharbour Lane*. The probable route was along Loughborough Road to Lilford Road and thence to Coldharbour Lane (*see map*).

66 *sahib*. Hindu term of courtesy for a European gentleman.

67 *khitmutgar*. Hindu for butler or manservant.

68 *like a mountain-peak from fir-trees*. "It is of interest to find that Sholto's noteworthy cranium had its parallel elsewhere," Mr. T. S. Blakeney wrote in "Thoughts on *The Sign of the Four*." "Compare the description by the late Sir Arthur

AT LAST THE CAB DREW UP AT THE THIRD HOUSE IN A NEW TERRACE.

This photograph of No. 3, Milkwood Road—S.E. 24—the possible residence of Thaddeus Sholto—was taken by Mr. Humphrey Morton of the Sherlock Holmes Society of London. On the other hand, the late Robert R. Pattrick suggested that the house might have stood on the street known today as Dorchester Drive.

ster tentacles which the giant city was throwing out into the country. At last the cab drew up at the third house in a new terrace. None of the other houses were inhabited, and that at which we stopped was as dark as its neighbours, save for a single glimmer in the kitchen-window. On our knocking, however, the door was instantly thrown open by a Hindu servant, clad in a yellow turban, white, loose-fitting clothes, and a yellow sash. There was something strangely incongruous in this Oriental figure framed in the commonplace doorway of a third-rate suburban dwelling-house.

66 'The sahib awaits you,' said he, and even as he spoke there came a high, piping voice from some inner room.

67 'Show them in to me, khitmutgar,' it cried. 'Show them straight in to me.'

4　◆　THE STORY OF THE BALD-HEADED MAN

We followed the Indian down a sordid and common passage, ill-lit and worse furnished, until he came to a door upon the right, which he threw open. A blaze of yellow light streamed out upon us, and in the centre of the glare there stood a small man with a very high head, a bristle of red hair all round the fringe of it, and a bald, shining scalp which shot out from

68 among it like a mountain-peak from fir-trees. He writhed his hands together as he stood, and his features were in a perpetual jerk—now smiling, now scowling, but never for an instant in repose. Nature had given him a pendulous lip, and a too visible line of yellow and irregular teeth, which he strove feebly to conceal by constantly passing his hand over the lower part of his face. In spite of his obtrusive baldness, he gave the impression of youth. In point of fact, he had just turned his thirtieth year.

'Your servant, Miss Morstan,' he kept repeating, in a thin, high voice. 'Your servant, gentlemen. Pray step into my little sanctum. A small place, Miss, but furnished to my own liking. An oasis of art in the howling desert of South London.'

We were all astonished by the appearance of the apartment into which he invited us. In that sorry house it looked as out-of-place as a diamond of the first water in a setting of brass. The richest and glossiest of curtains and tapestries draped the walls, looped back here and there to expose some richly-mounted painting or Oriental vase. The carpet was of amber and black, so soft and so thick that the foot sank pleasantly into it, as into a bed of moss. Two great tiger-skins thrown athwart it increased the suggestion of Eastern luxury, as did a huge hookah which stood upon a mat in the corner. A lamp **69** in the fashion of a silver dove was hung from an almost invisible golden wire in the centre of the room. As it burned it filled the air with a subtle and aromatic odour.

'Mr Thaddeus Sholto,' said the little man, still jerking and smiling. 'That is my name. You are Miss Morstan, of course. And these gentlemen——'

'This is Mr Sherlock Holmes, and this Dr Watson.'

'A doctor, eh?' cried he, much excited. 'Have you your stethoscope? Might I ask you—would you have the kindness? I have grave doubts as to my mitral valve, if you would be so **70** very good. The aortic I may rely upon, but I should value **71** your opinion upon the mitral.'

I listened to his heart, as requested, but was unable to find anything amiss, save, indeed, that he was in an ecstasy of fear, for he shivered from head to foot.

'It appears to be normal,' I said. 'You have no cause for uneasiness.'

Conan Doyle (*Conan Doyle Stories*, 'The Leather Funnel,' p. 466) of Lionel Dacre, who had a 'huge, dome-like skull, which curved upward from amongst his thinning locks, *like a snow-peak above its fringe of fir-trees*.' I draw no conclusion from this resemblance of heads—I merely call attention to it."

69 *hookah*. "Arabic word," the late Christopher Morley wrote in *Sherlock Holmes and Dr. Watson: A Textbook of Friendship*. "A tobacco pipe in which the smoke is inhaled through a long flexible tube which draws it through a bowl of perfumed water. Among Tenniel's famous illustrations in *Alice in Wonderland* (Chapter V) is a drawing of the Caterpillar smoking a hookah."

70 *mitral valve*. In the heart, the valve which guards the opening between the left auricle and the left ventricle, and prevents the blood in the ventricle from returning to the auricle.

71 *The aortic*. The valve which separates the left ventricle from the aorta, the great arterial trunk which carries blood from the heart to practically all parts of the body.

'MR. THADDEUS SHOLTO,' SAID THE LITTLE MAN . . .

Wrote Dr. Julian Wolff in his *Practical Handbook of Sherlockian Heraldry:* "In *The Private Life of Sherlock Holmes*, Vincent Starrett has a note that Watson's description of Thaddeus Sholto's house and conversation was the result of a meeting with Oscar Wilde. While no one will seriously state that Sholto was Wilde, himself, it does seem likely that he was very close to him. Students will immediately think of one Lord Alfred Douglas whose father was the eighth Marquess of Queensberry, John Sholto Douglas. It is not very difficult to deduce that Major John Sholto and his two sons may have been related to the Douglases and that they had similar arms, or the very same ones differenced.

"From *Burke's Peerage:* Quarterly: 1st and 4th, arg., a human heart, gu., imperially crowned, ppr.; on a chief, azure, three bullets of the field; 2nd and 3rd, az., a bend, between six cross-crosslets fitchée, or; all within a bordure, of the last, charged with the double tressure of Scotland. (The present illustration is taken from a facsimile of an old manuscript and shows a border engrailed gules instead of the one described—which pertains to the peerage, and would not be used by the major's family.)"

72 *I keep no other wines.* Chianti is a wine from the region of the Chianti Mountains in Tuscany, especially a dry red variety; Tokay is a moderately strong wine of a topaz color, produced in the vicinity of Tokay, in Hungary. The combination of the two is curious, as Mr. Cyrus Durgin pointed out in "The Speckled Band": "That, surely, is a strange combination of wines for household use, as occasional, social beverages. Chianti, which is a dry table wine, and does not keep well once the bottle is opened, is not likely to be found in Anglo-Saxon homes, up from the cellar and ready for drinking. . . . With Tokay, a sweeter and sometimes fortified wine, the matter is different. That could be a casual beverage for social amenity. I suppose the only conclusion is that a person who would keep only Tokay and Chianti—two wines very different in every respect—would necessarily be an eccentric person. I think we are entitled to assume, from the evidence of the narrative, that Mr. Thaddeus Sholto was indeed peculiar."

73 *a genuine Corot.* Jean Baptiste Camille Corot, 1796–1875, French landscape painter of the Barbizon School. Many of his paintings depict the misty hours before dawn, using mainly silvery grays and greens to create a very poetic effect.

74 *the Salvator Rosa.* Neapolitan painter, 1615–1673, famous for vigorous landscapes and spirited battle scenes.

75 *the Bourguereau.* Adolphe William Bouguereau, 1825–1905, French academic and sentimental painter. "This French painter was especially esteemed in the eighties and nineties," the late Christopher Morley wrote in *Sherlock Holmes and Dr. Watson: A Textbook of Friendship*. "His favorite subjects were religious and mythological; Mr. Sholto, as a man of refined tastes, would have been grieved to know that Bouguereau's *Nymphs and Faun* was for many years the most famous barroom painting in New York, at the old Hoffman House on Fifth Avenue."

76 *the modern French school.'* Sholto's statement, in terms of the artists he mentions, is somewhat questionable in the year 1888, fourteen years after the Impressionists had first shown in Paris. Mr. Ben Wolf ("Zero Wolf Meets Sherlock Holmes") has suggested that "Thaddeus would seem to have permitted his subscription to the *Gazette des Beaux Arts* to lapse some years earlier."

'You will excuse my anxiety, Miss Morstan,' he remarked, airily. 'I am a great sufferer, and I have long had suspicions as to that valve. I am delighted to hear that they are unwarranted. Had your father, Miss Morstan, refrained from throwing a strain upon his heart, he might have been alive now.'

I could have struck the man across the face, so hot was I at this callous and off-hand reference to so delicate a matter. Miss Morstan sat down, and her face grew white to the lips.

'I knew in my heart that he was dead,' said she.

'I can give you every information,' said he; 'and what is more, I can do you justice; and I will, too, whatever Brother Bartholomew may say. I am so glad to have your friends here, not only as an escort to you, but also as witnesses to what I am about to do and say. The three of us can show a bold front to Brother Bartholomew. But let us have no outsiders—no police or officials. We can settle everything satisfactorily among ourselves, without any interference. Nothing would annoy Brother Bartholomew more than any publicity.'

He sat down upon a low settee, and blinked at us inquiringly with his weak, watery blue eyes.

'For my part,' said Holmes, 'whatever you may choose to say will go no farther.'

I nodded to show my agreement.

'That is well! That is well!' said he. 'May I offer you a glass of Chianti, Miss Morstan? Or of Tokay? I keep no other **72** wines. Shall I open a flask? No? Well, then, I trust that you have no objection to tobacco smoke, to the balsamic odour of the Eastern tobacco. I am a little nervous, and I find my hookah an invaluable sedative.'

He applied a taper to the great bowl, and the smoke bubbled merrily through the rosewater. We sat all three in a semi-circle, with our heads advanced and our chins upon our hands, while the strange, jerky little fellow, with his high, shining head, puffed uneasily in the centre.

'When I first determined to make this communication to you,' said he, 'I might have given you my address; but I feared that you might disregard my request and bring unpleasant people with you. I took the liberty, therefore, of making an appointment in such a way that my man Williams might be able to see you first. I have complete confidence in his discretion, and he had orders, if he were dissatisfied, to proceed no further in the matter. You will excuse these precautions, but I am a man of somewhat retiring, and I might even say refined, tastes, and there is nothing more unæsthetic than a policeman. I have a natural shrinking from all forms of rough materialism. I seldom come in contact with the rough crowd. I live, as you see, with some little atmosphere of elegance around me. I may call myself a patron of the arts. **73** It is my weakness. The landscape is a genuine Corot, and, though a connoisseur might perhaps throw a doubt **74** upon that Salvator Rosa, there cannot be the least question **75** about the Bouguereau. I am partial to the modern French **76** school.'

'You will excuse me, Mr Sholto,' said Miss Morstan, 'but I am here at your request to learn something which you desire to tell me. It is very late, and I should desire the interview to be as short as possible.'

'At the best, it must take some time,' he answered; 'for we

shall certainly have to go to Norwood and see Brother Bartholomew. We shall all go and try if we can get the better of Brother Bartholomew. He is very angry with me for taking the course which has seemed right to me. I had quite high words with him last night. You cannot imagine what a terrible fellow he is when he is angry.'

'If we are to go to Norwood, it would perhaps be as well to start at once,' I ventured to remark.

He laughed until his ears were quite red.

'That would hardly do,' he cried. 'I don't know what he would say if I brought you in that sudden way. No, I must prepare you by showing you how we all stand to each other. In the first place, I must tell you that there are several points in the story of which I am myself ignorant. I can only lay the facts before you as far as I know them myself.

'My father was, as you may have guessed, Major John Sholto, once of the Indian Army. He retired some eleven years ago, and came to live at Pondicherry Lodge, in Upper Nor- **77** wood. He had prospered in India, and brought back with him a considerable sum of money, a large collection of valuable curiosities, and a staff of native servants. With these advantages he bought himself a house, and lived in great luxury. My twin-brother Bartholomew and I were the only children.

'I very well remember the sensation which was caused by the disappearance of Captain Morstan. We read the details in the papers, and knowing that he had been a friend of our father's, we discussed the case freely in his presence. He used to join in our speculations as to what could have happened. Never for an instant did we suspect that he had the whole secret hidden in his own breast, that of all men he alone knew the fate of Arthur Morstan.

'We did know, however, that some mystery, some positive danger, overhung our father. He was very fearful of going out alone, and he always employed two prize-fighters to act as porters at Pondicherry Lodge. Williams, who drove you to-night, was one of them. He was once light-weight champion of England. Our father would never tell us what it was he feared, but he had a most marked aversion to men with wooden legs. On one occasion he actually fired his revolver at a wooden-legged man, who proved to be a harmless tradesman canvassing for orders. We had to pay a large sum to hush the matter up. My brother and I used to think this a mere whim of my father's; but events have since led us to change our opinion.

'Early in 1882 my father received a letter from India which was a great shock to him. He nearly fainted at the breakfast-table when he opened it, and from that day he sickened to his death. What was in the letter we could never discover, but I could see as he held it that it was short and written in a scrawling hand. He had suffered for years from an enlarged spleen, but he now became rapidly worse, and towards the end of April we were informed that he was beyond all hope, **78** and that he wished to make a last communication to us.

'When we entered his room he was propped up with pillows and breathing heavily. He besought us to lock the door and to come upon either side of the bed. Then, grasping our hands, he made a remarkable statement to us, in a voice which was broken as much by emotion as by pain. I shall try and give it to you in his own very words.

77 *some eleven years ago.* Corroborating Mary's statement that Major Sholto "had retired some little time before" her father's death.

78 *towards the end of April.* Further evidence of the date of Sholto's decease.

79 *at this supreme moment.* "The standard of rectitude of the British (or Indian) Army officer in Holmes' day was regrettably low, judged by the types who flit across the screen," Mr. T. S. Blakeney wrote in "Thoughts on *The Sign of the Four*." Major Sholto "felt no compunction at being false to his charge as an officer commanding troops at Port Blair, though he had not only gambled himself to the verge of ruin, but had been ready to assist in the escape of four murderers in his care, only to double-cross them, and his confederate, Captain Morstan, in the end. Even his regrets about Miss Morstan were lip-service only—he urged his sons to do nothing for her in his lifetime. He must have had a hardened conscience indeed! He is fit to run Milverton close as being the worst man in London. Incidentally, one would like to know how Captain Morstan managed about his debts. He had had 'a nasty facer,' and he never, apparently, had a convenient uncle to leave him a fortune, as Sholto did. It is of interest to note, also, that neither Miss Morstan nor Watson were in the least troubled at the idea of taking the best part of a quarter of a million pounds' worth of jewels, though she had not the slightest right to them."

' "I have only one thing," he said, "which weighs upon my **79** mind at this supreme moment. It is my treatment of poor Morstan's orphan. The cursed greed which has been my besetting sin through life has withheld from her the treasure, half at least of which should have been hers. And yet I have made no use of it myself, so blind and foolish a thing is avarice. The mere feeling of possession has been so dear to me that I could not bear to share it with another. See that chaplet tipped with pearls beside the quinine-bottle? Even that I could not bear to part with, although I had got it out with the design of sending it to her. You, my sons, will give her a fair share of the Agra treasure. But send her nothing—not even the chaplet—until I am gone. After all, men have been as bad as this and have recovered.

' "I will tell you how Morstan died," he continued. "He had suffered for years from a weak heart, but he concealed it from everyone. I alone knew it. When in India, he and I, through a remarkable chain of circumstances, came into possession of a considerable treasure. I brought it over to England, and on the night of Morstan's arrival he came straight over here to claim his share. He walked over from the station, and was admitted by my faithful old Lal Chowdar, who is now dead. Morstan and I had a difference of opinion as to the division of the treasure, and we came to heated words. Morstan had sprung out of his chair in a paroxysm of anger, when he suddenly pressed his hand to his side, his face turned a dusky hue, and he fell backwards, cutting his head against the corner of the treasure-chest. When I stooped over him I found, to my horror, that he was dead.

' "For a long time I sat half distracted, wondering what I should do. My first impulse was, of course, to call for assistance; but I could not but recognize that there was every chance that I would be accused of his murder. His death at the moment of a quarrel, and the gash in his head, would be black against me. Again, an official inquiry could not be made without bringing out some facts about the treasure, which I was particularly anxious to keep secret. He had told me that no soul upon earth knew where he had gone. There seemed to be no necessity why any soul ever should know.

' "I was still pondering over the matter, when, looking up, I saw my servant, Lal Chowdar, in the doorway. He stole in and bolted the door behind him. 'Do not fear, sahib,' he said; 'no one need know that you have killed him. Let us hide him away, and who is the wiser?' 'I did not kill him,' said I. Lal Chowdar shook his head and smiled. 'I heard it all, sahib,' said he; 'I heard you quarrel, and I heard the blow. But my lips are sealed. All are asleep in the house. Let us put him away together.' That was enough to decide me. If my own servant could not believe my innocence, how could I hope to make it good before twelve foolish tradesmen in a jury-box? Lal Chowdar and I disposed of the body that night, and within a few days the London papers were full of the mysterious disappearance of Captain Morstan. You will see from what I say that I can hardly be blamed in the matter. My fault lies in the fact that we concealed not only the body, but also the treasure, and that I have clung to Morstan's share as well as to my own. I wish you, therefore, to make restitution. Put your ears down to my mouth. The treasure is hidden in——"

'At this instant a horrible change came over his expression; his eyes stared wildly, his jaw dropped, and he yelled, in a voice which I can never forget, "Keep him out! For Christ's sake, keep him out!" We both stared round at the window behind us upon which his gaze was fixed. A face was looking in at us out of the darkness. We could see the whitening of the nose where it was pressed against the glass. It was a bearded, hairy face, with wild, cruel eyes and an expression of concentrated malevolence. My brother and I rushed towards the window, but the man was gone. When we returned to my father, his head had dropped and his pulse had ceased to beat.

'We searched the garden that night, but found no sign of the intruder, save that just under the window a single footmark was visible in the flower-bed. But for that one trace, we might have thought that our imaginations had conjured up that wild, fierce face. We soon, however, had another and a more striking proof that there were secret agencies at work all round us. The window of my father's room was found open in the morning, his cupboards and boxes had been rifled, and upon his chest was fixed a torn piece of paper, with the words, "The sign of the four," scrawled across it. What the phrase meant, or who our secret visitor may have been, we never knew. As far as we can judge, none of my father's property had been actually stolen, though everything had been turned out. My brother and I naturally associated this peculiar incident with the fear which haunted my father during his life; but it is still a complete mystery to us.'

The little man stopped to relight his hookah, and puffed thoughtfully for a few moments. We had all sat absorbed, listening to his extraordinary narrative. At the short account of her father's death Miss Morstan had turned deadly white, and for a moment I feared that she was about to faint. She rallied, however, on drinking a glass of water which I quietly poured out for her from a Venetian carafe upon the side-table. Sherlock Holmes leaned back in his chair with an abstracted expression and the lids drawn low over his glittering eyes. As I glanced at him I could not but think how, on that very day, he had complained bitterly of the commonplaceness of life. Here at least was a problem which would tax his sagacity to the utmost. Mr Thaddeus Sholto looked from one to the other of us with an obvious pride at the effect which his story had produced, and then continued, between the puffs of his overgrown pipe.

'My brother and I,' said he, 'were, as you may imagine, much excited as to the treasure which my father had spoken of. For weeks and for months we dug and delved in every part of the garden without discovering its whereabouts. It was maddening to think that the hiding-place was on his very lips at the moment that he died. We could judge the splendour of the missing riches by the chaplet which he had taken out. Over this chaplet my Brother Bartholomew and I had some little discussion. The pearls were evidently of great value, and he was averse to part with them, for, between friends, my brother was himself a little inclined to my father's fault. He thought, too, that if we parted with the chaplet it might give rise to gossip, and finally bring us into trouble. It was all that I could do to persuade him to let me find out Miss Morstan's address and send her a detached pearl at fixed intervals, so that at least she might never feel destitute.'

80 "Le mauvais goût mène au crime." "Bad taste leads to crime." The expression was coined by Le Baron de Mareste but was immortalized by Stendal (Henri Beyle, 1783–1842).

81 *a valetudinarian*.' A person of feeble or delicate health or constitution; an invalid; one subject to frequent illness.

82 *half a million sterling*.' £500,000, or about $2,500,000. Sterling, as applied to money values, means of standard mint and fineness.

'It was a kindly thought,' said our companion, earnestly; 'it was extremely good of you.'

The little man waved his hand deprecatingly.

'We were your trustees,' he said; 'that was the view which I took of it, though Brother Bartholomew could not altogether see it in that light. We had plenty of money ourselves. I desired no more. Besides, it would have been such bad taste to have treated a young lady in so scurvy a fashion. *"Le mau-* **80** *vais goût mène au crime."* The French have a very neat way of putting these things. Our difference of opinion on this subject went so far that I thought it best to set up rooms for myself; so I left Pondicherry Lodge, taking the old khitmutgar and Williams with me. Yesterday, however, I learn that an event of extreme importance has occurred. The treasure has been discovered. I instantly communicated with Miss Morstan, and it only remains for us to drive out to Norwood and demand our share. I explained my views last night to Brother Bartholomew, so we shall be expected, if not welcome, visitors.'

Mr Thaddeus Sholto ceased, and sat twitching on his luxurious settee. We all remained silent, with our thoughts upon the new development which the mysterious business had taken. Holmes was the first to spring to his feet.

'You have done well, sir, from first to last,' said he. 'It is possible that we may be able to make you some small return by throwing some light upon that which is still dark to you. But, as Miss Morstan remarked just now, it is late, and we had best put the matter through without delay.'

Our new acquaintance very deliberately coiled up the tube of his hookah, and produced from behind a curtain a very long, befrogged top-coat with astrakhan collar and cuffs. This he buttoned tightly up, in spite of the extreme closeness of the night, and finished his attire by putting on a rabbit-skin cap with hanging lappets which covered the ears, so that no part of him was visible save his mobile and peaky face.

'My health is somewhat fragile,' he remarked, as he led the way down the passage. 'I am compelled to be a valetudi- **81** narian.'

Our cab was awaiting us outside, and our programme was evidently prearranged, for the driver started off at once at a rapid pace. Thaddeus Sholto talked incessantly, in a voice which rose high above the rattle of the wheels.

'Bartholomew is a clever fellow,' said he. 'How do you think he found out where the treasure was? He had come to the conclusion that it was somewhere indoors: so he worked out all the cubic space of the house, and made measurements everywhere, so that not one inch should be unaccounted for. Among other things, he found that the height of the building was seventy-four feet, but on adding together the heights of all the separate rooms, and making every allowance for the space between, which he ascertained by borings, he could not bring the total to more than seventy feet. There were four feet unaccounted for. These could only be at the top of the building. He knocked a hole, therefore, in the lath and plaster ceiling of the highest room, and there, sure enough, he came upon another little garret above it, which had been sealed up and was known to no one. In the centre stood the treasure-chest, resting upon two rafters. He lowered it through the hole, and there it lies. He computes the value of the jewels **82** at not less than half a million sterling.'

At the mention of this gigantic sum we all stared at one another open-eyed. Miss Morstan, could we secure her rights, would change from a needy governess to the richest heiress in England. Surely it was the place of a loyal friend to rejoice at such news; yet I am ashamed to say that selfishness took me by the soul, and that my heart turned as heavy as lead within me. I stammered out some few halting words of congratulation, and then sat downcast, with my head drooped, deaf to the babble of our new acquaintance. He was clearly a confirmed hypochondriac, and I was dreamily conscious that he was pouring forth interminable trains of symptoms, and imploring information as to the composition and action of innumerable quack nostrums, some of which he bore about in a leather case in his pocket. I trust that he may not remember any of the answers which I gave him that night. Holmes declares that he overheard me caution him against the great danger of taking more than two drops of castor-oil, while I recommended strychnine in large doses as a sedative. How- **83** ever that may be, I was certainly relieved when our cab pulled up with a jerk and the coachman sprang down to open the door.

'This, Miss Morstan, is Pondicherry Lodge,' said Mr Thaddeus Sholto, as he handed her out.

5 ♦ THE TRAGEDY OF PONDICHERRY LODGE

It was nearly eleven o'clock when we reached this final stage of our night's adventures. We had left the damp fog of the great city behind us, and the night was fairly fine. A warm wind blew from the westward, and heavy clouds moved slowly across the sky, with half a moon peeping occasionally through **84** the rifts. It was clear enough to see for some distance, but Thaddeus Sholto took down one of the side-lamps from the carriage to give us a better light upon our way.

Pondicherry Lodge stood in its own grounds, and was girt round with a very high stone wall topped with broken glass. A single narrow iron-clamped door formed the only means of entrance. On this our guide knocked with a peculiar postman-like rat-tat. **85**

'Who is there?' cried a gruff voice from within.

'It is I, McMurdo. You surely know my knock by this time.'

There was a grumbling sound and a clanking and jarring of keys. The door swung heavily back, and a short, deep-chested man stood in the opening, with the yellow light of the lantern shining upon his protruded face and twinkling, distrustful eyes.

'That you, Mr Thaddeus? But who are the others? I had no orders about them from the master.'

'No, McMurdo? You surprise me! I told my brother last night that I should bring some friends.'

'He hain't been out o' his room today, Mr Thaddeus, and I have no orders. You know very well that I must stick to regulations. I can let you in, but your friends they must just stop where they are.'

'THIS, MISS MORSTAN, IS PONDICHERRY LODGE' . . .

It must have been a house very similar to The Rookery, Streatham Common, shown here in an illustration from Michael Harrison's *In the Footsteps of Sherlock Holmes*.

83 *strychnine in large doses as a sedative.* Whether due to the Beaune or to the presence of Mary Morstan, it is quite clear that Watson on this Tuesday was far from his normal self.

84 *half a moon.* Further on, Watson says, "a moonbeam struck one corner and glimmered in a garret window," and Sholto says, "That is Bartholomew's window up there where the moonshine strikes." And later, when Watson is looking through the keyhole into the dead man's room, he says, "Moonlight was streaming into the room." A little later Watson says, "The moon still shone brightly on that angle of the house." There can, therefore, not be the least doubt that there was a moon visible in the London sky around 11:00 P.M. on the first night. But the words "streaming" and "brightly" make us doubt Watson's *half* a moon. For the record, the moon on Tuesday, September 18, 1888, was two days before the full; it rose at 5:55 P.M. and set at 3:12 A.M.

85 *postman-like rat-tat.* "The postman's double knock was traditional," the late Christopher Morley wrote in *Sherlock Holmes and Dr. Watson: A Textbook of Friendship:* "when the bells took the place of the old knocker it became a double ring. Hence James M. Cain's title, *The Postman Always Rings Twice.*"

86 *four-years back?'* "It is a little difficult to accept this date," Mr. T. S. Blakeney wrote in *Sherlock Holmes: Fact or Fiction?,* "for if McMurdo joined Major Sholto's household as one of his two pugilist protectors, it must have been earlier than 1882, the year of Sholto's death. Bartholomew Sholto would hardly have engaged him, as he had no need for a protector, though naturally he would take over his father's servants, which accounts for McMurdo's presence at Pondicherry Lodge in 1888. The latter's benefit night (presumably when he retired from the ring) would have been just prior to his being engaged by Major Sholto on the latter's retirement from the Army—about 1877."

This was an unexpected obstacle. Thaddeus Sholto looked about him in a perplexed and helpless manner.

'This is too bad of you, McMurdo!' he said. 'If I guarantee them, that is enough for you. There is the young lady, too. She cannot wait on the public road at this hour.'

'Very sorry, Mr Thaddeus,' said the porter, inexorably. 'Folk may be friends o' yours, and yet no friends o' the master's. He pays me well to do my duty, and my duty I'll do. I don't know none o' your friends.'

'Oh, yes, you do, McMurdo,' cried Sherlock Holmes, genially. 'I don't think you can have forgotten me. Don't you remember the amateur who fought three rounds with you at **86** Alison's rooms on the night of your benefit four years back?'

'Not Mr Sherlock Holmes!' roared the prizefighter. 'God's truth! how could I have mistook you? If instead o' standin' there so quiet you had just stepped up and given me that cross-hit of yours under the jaw, I'd ha' known you without a question. Ah, you're one that has wasted your gifts, you have! You might have aimed high, if you had joined the fancy.'

'You see, Watson, if all else fails me, I have still one of the scientific professions open to me,' said Holmes, laughing. 'Our friend won't keep us out in the cold now, I am sure.'

'In you come, sir, in you come—you and your friends,' he answered. 'Very sorry, Mr Thaddeus, but orders are very strict. Had to be certain of your friends before I let them in.'

Inside, a gravel path wound through desolate grounds to a huge clump of a house, square and prosaic, all plunged in shadow save where a moonbeam struck one corner and glimmered in a garret window. The vast size of the building, with

". . . THAT CROSS-HIT OF YOURS UNDER THE JAW . . ."

"The right cross," the late H. T. Webster wrote in "Observations on Sherlock Holmes as an Athlete and Sportsman," "is . . . the characteristic Sunday punch of the tall rangy type of boxer. . . . This punch, to the head or body, is delivered straight from the shoulder but with a slight pivoting motion of the body which gives it something of the character of a hook. It is called a cross, because it must cross either over or under the opponent's left arm to land. It is the natural counter to a left jab, and unskilled boxers commonly leave themselves open to it when they begin to carry their lefts too far forward to serve as an effective guard. The fact that McMurdo says nothing about Holmes' left does not indicate that it was not a good one, but simply that in three rounds it had not yet given him much trouble. Very few left jabs in the history of the ring have been powerful enough to conquer rugged and skilled opposition in a few rounds. On the other hand, Holmes' left proved sufficiently formidable when applied to the features of a mere slogging ruffian like Roaring Jack Woodley ["The Adventure of the Solitary Cyclist"], who . . . had to be carried home in a cart. In general, then, we can reconstruct Holmes' boxing style as somewhat like that of Jem Mace, Jim Corbett, and Mike Gibbons. . . . He stood up straight in the classic style, used his extraordinary speed of foot to avoid the infighting which is likely to be troublesome to a man with a lightly armored body, staggered his opponent with a straight left, which was punishing but not lethal, and finished him with that powerful right cross."

its gloom and its deathly silence, struck a chill to the heart. Even Thaddeus Sholto seemed ill at ease, and the lantern quivered and rattled in his hand.

'I cannot understand it,' he said. 'There must be some mistake. I distinctly told Bartholomew that we should be here, and yet there is no light in his window. I do not know what to make of it.'

'Does he always guard the premises in this way?' asked Holmes.

'Yes, he has followed my father's custom. He was the favourite son, you know, and I sometimes think that my father may have told him more than he ever told me. That is Bartholomew's window up there where the moonshine strikes. It is quite bright, but there is no light from within, I think.'

'None,' said Holmes. 'But I see the glint of a light in that little window beside the door.'

'Ah, that is the housekeeper's room. That is where old Mrs Bernstone sits. She can tell us all about it. But perhaps you would not mind waiting here for a minute or two, for if we all go in together, and she has had no word of our coming, she may be alarmed. But, hush! what is that?'

He held up the lantern, and his hand shook until the circles of light flickered and wavered all round us. Miss Morstan seized my wrist, and we all stood, with thumping hearts, straining our ears. From the great black house there sounded through the silent night the saddest and most pitiful of sounds —the shrill, broken whimpering of a frightened woman.

'It is Mrs Bernstone,' said Sholto. 'She is the only woman in the house. Wait here. I shall be back in a moment.'

He hurried for the door, and knocked in his peculiar way. We could see a tall old woman admit him, and sway with pleasure at the very sight of him.

'Oh, Mr Thaddeus, sir, I am so glad you have come! I am so glad you have come, Mr Thaddeus, sir!'

We heard her reiterated rejoicings until the door was closed and her voice died away into a muffled monotone.

Our guide had left us the lantern. Holmes swung it slowly round, and peered keenly at the house, and at the great rubbish-heaps which cumbered the grounds. Miss Morstan and I stood together, and her hand was in mine. A wondrous subtle thing is love, for here were we two, who had never seen each other before that day, between whom no word or even look of affection had ever passed, and yet now in an hour of trouble our hands instinctively sought for each other. I have marvelled at it since, but at the time it seemed the most natural thing that I should go out to her so, and, as she has often told me, there was in her also the instinct to turn to me for comfort and protection. So we stood hand-in-hand, like two children, and there was peace in our hearts for all the dark things that surrounded us.

'What a strange place!' she said, looking round.

'It looks as though all the moles in England had been let loose in it. I have seen something of the sort on the side of a hill near Ballarat, where the prospectors had been at work.'

'And from the same cause,' said Holmes. 'These are the traces of the treasure-seekers. You must remember that they were six years looking for it. No wonder that the grounds **87** look like a gravel-pit.'

87 *six years looking for it.* Additional evidence that the year of *The Sign of the Four* is 1888, since Thaddeus and Bartholomew had been looking for the Agra treasure since the death of their father in April, 1882.

At that moment the door of the house burst open, and Thaddeus Sholto came running out, with his hands thrown forward and terror in his eyes.

'There is something amiss with Bartholomew!' he cried. 'I am frightened! My nerves cannot stand it.'

He was, indeed, half blubbering with fear, and his twitching, feeble face peeping out from the great astrakhan collar had the helpless, appealing expression of a terrified child.

'Come into the house,' said Holmes, in his crisp, firm way.

'Yes, do!' pleaded Thaddeus Sholto. 'I really do not feel equal to giving directions.'

We all followed him into the housekeeper's room, which stood upon the left-hand side of the passage. The old woman was pacing up and down with a scared look and restless, picking fingers, but the sight of Miss Morstan appeared to have a soothing effect upon her.

'God bless your sweet, calm face!' she cried, with an hysterical sob. 'It does me good to see you. Oh, but I have been sorely tried this day!'

Our companion patted her thin, work-worn hand, and murmured some few words of kindly, womanly comfort, which brought the colour back into the other's bloodless cheeks.

'Master has locked himself in, and will not answer me,' she explained. 'All day I have waited to hear from him, for he often likes to be alone; but an hour ago I feared that something was amiss, so I went up and peeped through the keyhole. You must go up, Mr Thaddeus—you must go up and look for yourself. I have seen Mr Bartholomew Sholto, in joy and in sorrow for ten long years, but I never saw him with such a face on him as that.'

Sherlock Holmes took the lamp and led the way, for Thaddeus Sholto's teeth were chattering in his head. So shaken was he that I had to pass my hand under his arm as we went up the stairs, for his knees were trembling under him. Twice as we ascended Holmes whipped his lens out of his pocket and carefully examined marks which appeared to me to be mere shapeless smudges of dust upon the coco-nut-matting which served as a stair-carpet. He walked slowly from step to step, holding the lamp low, and shooting keen glances to right and left. Miss Morstan had remained behind with the frightened housekeeper.

The third flight of stairs ended in a straight passage of some length, with a great picture in Indian tapestry upon the right of it and three doors upon the left. Holmes advanced along it in the same slow and methodical way, while we kept close at his heels, with our long, black shadows streaming backwards down the corridor. The third door was that which we were seeking. Holmes knocked without receiving any answer, and then tried to turn the handle and force it open. It was locked on the inside, however, and by a broad and powerful bolt, as we could see when we set our lamp up against it. The key being turned, however, the hole was not entirely closed. Sherlock Holmes bent down to it, and instantly rose again with a sharp intaking of the breath.

'There is something devilish in this, Watson,' said he, more moved than I had ever before seen him. 'What do you make of it?'

I stooped to the hole, and recoiled in horror. Moonlight

was streaming into the room, and it was bright with a vague and shifty radiance. Looking straight at me, and suspended, as it were, in the air, for all beneath was in shadow, there hung a face—the very face of our companion Thaddeus. There was the same high, shining head, the same circular bristle of red hair, the same bloodless countenance. The features were set, **88** however, in a horrible smile, a fixed and unnatural grin, which in that still and moonlit room was more jarring to the nerves than any scowl or contortion. So like was the face to that of our little friend that I looked round at him to make sure that he was indeed with us. Then I recalled to mind that he had mentioned to us that his brother and he were twins.

'This is terrible!' I said to Holmes. 'What is to be done?'

'The door must come down,' he answered, and, springing against it, he put all his weight upon the lock.

It creaked and groaned, but did not yield. Together we flung ourselves upon it once more, and this time it gave way with a sudden snap, and we found ourselves within Bartholomew Sholto's chamber.

It appeared to have been fitted up as a chemical laboratory. A double line of glass-stoppered bottles was drawn up upon the wall opposite the door, and the table was littered over with Bunsen burners, test-tubes, and retorts. In the corners stood carboys of acid in wicker baskets. One of these appeared to leak or to have been broken, for a stream of dark-coloured liquid had trickled out from it, and the air was heavy with a peculiarly pungent, tar-like odour. A set of steps stood at one side of the room, in the midst of a litter of lath and plaster, and above them there was an opening in the ceiling large enough for a man to pass through. At the foot of the steps a long coil of rope was thrown carelessly together.

By the table, in a wooden arm-chair, the master of the house was seated all in a heap, with his head sunk upon his left shoulder, and that ghastly, inscrutable smile upon his face. He was stiff and cold, and had clearly been dead many hours. It seemed to me that not only his features, but all his limbs, were twisted and turned in the most fantastic fashion. By his hand upon the table there lay a peculiar instrument—a brown, close-grained stick, with a stone head like a hammer, rudely lashed on with coarse twine. Beside it was a torn sheet of note-paper with some words scrawled upon it. Holmes glanced at it, and then handed it to me.

'You see,' he said, with a significant raising of the eyebrows.

In the light of the lantern I read, with a thrill of horror, 'The sign of the four.'

'In God's name, what does it all mean?' I asked.

'It means murder,' said he, stooping over the dead man. 'Ah! I expected it. Look here!'

He pointed to what looked like a long, dark thorn stuck in the skin just above the ear.

'It looks like a thorn,' said I.

'It is a thorn. You may pick it out. But be careful, for it is poisoned.'

I took it up between my finger and thumb. It came away from the skin so readily that hardly any mark was left behind. One tiny speck of blood showed where the puncture had been.

'This is all an insoluble mystery to me,' said I. 'It grows darker instead of clearer.'

'On the contrary,' he answered, 'it clears every instant. I

88 *the same circular bristle of red hair.* "This was an amazing identification," the late Professor Jay Finley Christ wrote in *An Irregular Chronology.* "The reader is invited to try to distinguish red hair from brown or even from black, by the light of a half-moon, while the observer is peering through a partially stopped key-hole. Let him try it in the open, too, if he likes."

BY THE TABLE, IN A WOODEN ARM-CHAIR, THE MASTER OF THE HOUSE WAS SEATED . . .

Illustration by J. Watson Davis for *Tales of Sherlock Holmes*, New York: A. L. Burt Company, 1906.

IN THE LIGHT OF THE LANTERN I READ, WITH A THRILL OF HORROR,
THE SIGN OF THE FOUR.

(*Above*) This pen-and-ink drawing by an unknown artist illustrated the first Dutch translation of *The Sign of the Four*, published some seventy years ago. (*Below*) Frontispiece by Charles Kerr for *The Sign of the Four*, London: Spencer Blackett, 1890. Of this illustration, the late James Montgomery wrote (*A Study in Pictures*) that it "presents Holmes and Watson to us, but one wishes that it didn't. . . . Watson's terrified face rivals that of the corpse, while the black smudge of a mustache under Holmes' . . . nose completes our disillusionment." Of this illustration, Mr. Vincent Starrett wrote in *The Private Life of Sherlock Holmes*: ". . . a competent but uninspired interpretation of the episode. . . . Just possibly the blot upon our Sherlock's lip is intended to indicate the shade cast by his prodigious nose; it looks, however, like a touch of a moustache. For the rest, there is something statuelike and dauntless in the carriage of the famous head; the legs are statesmanlike in their determined stance; and all in all—what with the somewhat epileptic corpse, and Watson—the picture is a trifle comic."

only require a few missing links to have an entirely connected case.'

We had almost forgotten our companion's presence since we entered the chamber. He was still standing in the doorway, the very picture of terror, wringing his hands and moaning to himself. Suddenly, however, he broke out into a sharp, querulous cry.

'The treasure is gone!' he said. 'They have robbed him of the treasure! There is the hole through which we lowered it. I helped him to do it! I was the last person who saw him! I left him here last night, and I heard him lock the door as I came downstairs.'

'What time was that?'

'It was ten o'clock. And now he is dead, and the police will be called in, and I shall be suspected of having had a hand in it. Oh, yes, I am sure I shall. But you don't think so, gentlemen? Surely, you don't think that it was I? Is it likely that I would have brought you here if it were I? Oh, dear! oh, dear! I know that I shall go mad!'

He jerked his arms and stamped his feet in a kind of convulsive frenzy.

'You have no reason for fear, Mr Sholto,' said Holmes, kindly, putting his hand upon his shoulder; 'take my advice, and drive down to the station to report the matter to the police. Offer to assist them in every way. We shall wait here until your return.'

The little man obeyed in a half-stupefied fashion, and we heard him stumbling down the stairs in the dark.

6 : SHERLOCK HOLMES GIVES
  : A DEMONSTRATION

'Now, Watson,' said Holmes, rubbing his hands, 'we have half
an hour to ourselves. Let us make good use of it. My case is,
as I have told you, almost complete; but we must not err on
the side of over-confidence. Simple as the case seems now,
there may be something deeper underlying it.'

'Simple!' I ejaculated.

'Surely,' said he, with something of the air of a clinical
professor expounding to his class. 'Just sit in the corner there,
that your footprints may not complicate matters. Now to
work! In the first place, how did these folk come, and how
did they go? The door has not been opened since last night.
How of the window?' He carried the lamp across to it, muttering his observations aloud the while, but addressing them to
himself rather than to me. 'Window is snibbed on the inner **89**
side. Framework is solid. No hinges at the side. Let us open
it. No water-pipe near. Roof quite out of reach. Yet a man
has mounted by the window. It rained a little last night. Here
is the print of a foot in mould upon the sill. And here is a
circular muddy mark, and here again upon the floor, and here
again by the table. See here, Watson! This is really a very
pretty demonstration.'

I looked at the round, well-defined muddy disks.

'That is not a footmark,' said I.

'It is something much more valuable to us. It is the impression of a wooden stump. You see here on the sill is the
boot-mark, a heavy boot with a broad metal heel, and beside
it is the mark of the timber-toe.'

'It is the wooden-legged man.'

'Quite so. But there has been someone else—a very able and
efficient ally. Could you scale that wall, doctor?'

I looked out of the open window. The moon still shone
brightly on that angle of the house. We were a good sixty feet
from the ground, and, look where I would, I could see no
foothold, nor as much as a crevice in the brickwork.

'It is absolutely impossible,' I answered.

'Without aid it is so. But suppose you had a friend up here
who lowered you this good stout rope which I see in the
corner, securing one end of it to this great hook in the wall.
Then, I think, if you were an active man, you might swarm
up, wooden leg and all. You would depart, of course, in the
same fashion, and your ally would draw up the rope, untie
it from the hook, shut the window, snib it on the inside,
and get away in the way that he originally came. As a minor
point, it may be noted,' he continued, fingering the rope,
'that our wooden-legged friend, though a fair climber, was
not a professional sailor. His hands were far from horny.
My lens discloses more than one blood-mark, especially towards the end of the rope, from which I gather that he
slipped down with such velocity that he took the skin off
his hand.'

'This is all very well,' said I; 'but the thing becomes more
unintelligible than ever. How about this mysterious ally?
How came he into the room?'

'Yes, the ally!' repeated Holmes, pensively. 'There are
features of interest about this ally. He lifts the case from the
regions of the commonplace. I fancy that this ally breaks

89 *snibbed.* Fastened; bolted.

fresh ground in the annals of crime in this country—though parallel cases suggest themselves from India, and, if my memory serves me, from Senegambia.'

'How came he, then?' I reiterated. 'The door is locked; the window is inaccessible. Was it through the chimney?'

'The grate is much too small,' he answered. 'I had already considered that possibility.'

'How, then?' I persisted.

'You will not apply my precept,' he said, shaking his head. 'How often have I said to you that when you have eliminated the impossible, whatever remains, *however improbable,* must be the truth? We know that he did not come through the door, the window, or the chimney. We also know that he could not have been concealed in the room, as there is no concealment possible. Whence, then, did he come?'

'He came through the hole in the roof!' I cried.

'Of course he did. He must have done so. If you will have the kindness to hold the lamp for me, we shall now extend our researches to the room above—the secret room in which the treasure was found.'

He mounted the steps, and, seizing a rafter with either hand, he swung himself up into the garret. Then, lying on his face, he reached down for the lamp, and held it while I followed him.

The chamber in which we found ourselves was about ten feet one way and six the other. The floor was formed by the rafters, with thin lath and plaster between, so that in walking one had to step from beam to beam. The roof ran up to an apex, and was evidently the inner shell of the true roof to the house. There was no furniture of any sort, and the accumulated dust of years lay thick upon the floor.

'Here you are, you see,' said Sherlock Holmes, putting his hand against the sloping wall. 'This is a trap-door which leads out on to the roof. I can press it back, and here is the roof itself, sloping at a gentle angle. This, then, is the way by which Number One entered. Let us see if we can find some other traces of his individuality.'

He held down the lamp to the floor, and as he did so I saw for the second time that night a startled, surprised look come over his face. For myself, as I followed his gaze, my skin was cold under my clothes. The floor was covered thickly with the prints of a naked foot—clear, well-defined, perfectly formed, but scarce half the size of those of an ordinary man.

'Holmes,' I said, in a whisper, 'a child has done this horrid thing.'

He had recovered his self-possession in an instant.

'I was staggered for the moment,' he said, 'but the thing is quite natural. My memory failed me, or I should have been able to foretell it. There is nothing more to be learned here. Let us go down.'

'What is your theory, then, as to those footmarks?' I asked, eagerly, when we had regained the lower room once more.

'My dear Watson, try a little analysis yourself,' said he, with a touch of impatience. 'You know my methods. Apply them, and it will be instructive to compare results.'

'I cannot conceive anything which will cover the facts,' I answered.

'It will be clear enough to you soon,' he said, in an offhand way. 'I think that there is nothing else of importance here, but I will look.'

He whipped out his lens and a tape measure, and hurried about the room on his knees, measuring, comparing examining, with his long, thin nose only a few inches from the planks, and his beady eyes gleaming and deep-set like those of a bird. So swift, silent, and furtive were his movements, like those of a trained bloodhound picking out a scent, that I could not but think what a terrible criminal he would have made had he turned his energy and sagacity against the law instead of exerting them in its defence. As he hunted about he kept muttering to himself, and finally he broke out into a loud crow of delight.

'We are certainly in luck,' said he. 'We ought to have very little trouble now. Number One has had the misfortune to tread in the creosote. You can see the outline of the edge of his small foot here at the side of this evil-smelling mess. The carboy has been cracked, you see, and the stuff has leaked out.'

'What then?' I asked.

'Why, we have got him, that's all,' said he. 'I know a dog that would follow that scent to the world's end. If a pack can track a trailed herring across a shire, how far can a specially-trained hound follow so pungent a smell as this? It sounds like a sum in the rule of three. The answer should give us the **90** —— But, halloa! here are the accredited representatives of the law.'

Heavy steps and the clamour of loud voices were audible from below, and the hall door shut with a loud crash.

'Before they come,' said Holmes, 'just put your hand here on this poor fellow's arm, and here on his leg. What do you feel?'

'The muscles are as hard as a board,' I answered.

'Quite so. They are in a state of extreme contraction, far exceeding the usual *rigor mortis*. Coupled with this distortion of the face, this Hippocratic smile, or '*risus sardonicus*,' as the **91** old writers called it, what conclusion would it suggest to your mind?'

'Death from some powerful vegetable alkaloid,' I answered, 'some strychnine-like substance which would produce **92** tetanus.'

'That was the idea which occurred to me the instant I saw the drawn muscles of the face. On getting into the room I at once looked for the means by which the poison had entered the system. As you saw, I discovered a thorn which had been driven or shot with no great force into the scalp. You observe that the part struck was that which would be turned towards the hole in the ceiling if the man were erect in his chair. Now examine this thorn.'

I took it up gingerly and held it in the light of the lantern. It was long, sharp, and black, with a glazed look near the point as though some gummy substance had dried upon it. The blunt end had been trimmed and rounded off with a knife.

'Is that an English thorn?' he asked.

'No, it certainly is not.'

'With all these data you should be able to draw some just inference. But here are the regulars; so the auxiliary forces may beat a retreat.'

As he spoke, the steps which had been coming nearer sounded loudly on the passage, and a very stout, portly man in a grey suit strode heavily into the room. He was red-faced,

90 *the rule of three*. "I don't know whether the old name Rule of Three is still used in arithmetic," the late Christopher Morley wrote in *Sherlock Holmes and Dr. Watson: A Textbook of Friendship*. "It was applied to the principle that if three quantities of a proportion are known, the fourth can be determined; since the product of the means equals the product of the extremes. *Viz.*, if a:b::c:d, then ad = bc, and a = $\frac{bc}{d}$."

91 *Hippocratic smile*. From Hippocrates, ancient Greek physician, *c*. 460–*c*. 370 B.C., who made the earliest recorded notes of many symptoms of disease and death.

92 '*some strychnine-like substance*. A remarkable example of Dr. Watson's quick ability to make an accurate diagnosis. As Dr. George B. Koelle has written in "The Poisons of the Canon": "The possibilities which suggest themselves include stophanthin (a cardiac drug similar to digitalis) and two central nervous system stimulants, picrotoxin and strychnine. The last mentioned drug is the more reasonable choice. It is a highly potent agent which is obtained from the fruit of a tree indigenous to Australia. It would be rapidly absorbed from a wound. Following a series of violent convulsions, it produces death by tonic respiratory paralysis. One of its most striking features is the *risus sardonicus*, or sardonic grin, which may remain on the face of the victim. This was dramatically exhibited to our friends when they discovered the corpse of . . . Sholto."

93 *Bishopgate.* Properly, *Bishopsgate,* a district in the City of London. The name may have been due to the liability of the Bishop of London in medieval times, to make the hinges of Bishopsgate, in return for which he was allowed to receive one stick from every cart laden with wood as it entered the City through the gate.

burly, and plethoric, with a pair of very small, twinkling eyes, which looked keenly out from between swollen and puffy pouches. He was closely followed by an inspector in uniform, and by the still palpitating Thaddeus Sholto.

'Here's a business!' he said, in a muffled, husky voice. 'Here's a pretty business! But who are all these? Why, the house seems to be as full as a rabbit-warren!'

'I think you must recollect me, Mr Athelney Jones,' said Holmes, quietly.

'Why, of course I do!' he wheezed. 'It's Mr Sherlock Holmes, the theorist. Remember you! I'll never forget how you lectured us all on causes and inferences and effects in the Bishop-**93** gate jewel case. It's true you set us on the right track; but you'll own now that it was more by good luck than good guidance.'

'It was a piece of very simple reasoning.'

'Oh, come, now, come! Never be ashamed to own up. But what is all this? Bad business! Bad business! Stern facts here —no room for theories. How lucky that I happened to be out at Norwood over another case! I was at the station when the message arrived. What d'you think the man died of?'

'Oh, this is hardly a case for me to theorize over,' said Holmes, drily.

'No, no. Still, we can't deny that you hit the nail on the head sometimes. Dear me! Door locked, I understand. Jewels worth half a million missing. How was the window?'

'Fastened; but there are steps on the sill.'

'Well, well, if it was fastened the steps could have nothing to do with the matter. That's common-sense. Man might have died in a fit; but then the jewels are missing. Ha! I have a theory. These flashes come upon me at times. Just step outside, sergeant, and you, Mr Sholto. Your friend can remain. What do you think of this, Holmes? Sholto was, on his own confession, with his brother last night. The brother died in a fit, on which Sholto walked off with the treasure! How's that?'

'On which the dead man very considerately got up and locked the door on the inside.'

'Hum! There's a flaw there. Let us apply common-sense to the matter. This Thaddeus Sholto *was* with his brother; there *was* a quarrel: so much we know. The brother is dead and the jewels are gone. So much also we know. No one saw the brother from the time Thaddeus left him. His bed had not been slept in. Thaddeus is evidently in a most disturbed state of mind. His appearance is—well, not attractive. You see that I am weaving my web round Thaddeus. The net begins to close upon him.'

'You are not quite in possession of the facts yet,' said Holmes. 'This splinter of wood, which I have every reason to believe to be poisoned, was in the man's scalp where you still see the mark; this card, inscribed as you see it, was on the table, and beside it lay this rather curious stone-headed instrument. How does all that fit into your theory?'

'Confirms it in every respect,' said the fat detective, pompously. 'House is full of Indian curiosities. Thaddeus brought this up, and if this splinter be poisonous, Thaddeus may as well have made murderous use of it as any other man. The card is some hocus-pocus—a blind, as like as not. The only question is, how did he depart? Ah, of course, here is a hole in the roof.'

With great activity, considering his bulk, he sprang up the steps and squeezed through into the garret, and immediately afterwards we heard his exulting voice proclaiming that he had found the trap-door.

'He can find something,' remarked Holmes, shrugging his shoulders; 'he has occasional glimmerings of reason. *Il n'y a pas des sots si incommodes que ceux qui ont de l'esprit!*   **94**

'You see!' said Athelney Jones, reappearing down the steps again; 'facts are better than theories, after all. My view of the case is confirmed. There is a trap-door communicating with the roof, and it is partly open.'

'It was I who opened it.'

'Oh, indeed! You did notice it, then?' He seemed a little crestfallen at the discovery. 'Well, whoever noticed it, it shows how our gentleman got away. Inspector!'

'Yes, sir,' from the passage.

'Ask Mr Sholto to step this way.—Mr Sholto, it is my duty to inform you that anything which you may say will be used against you. I arrest you in the Queen's name as being concerned in the death of your brother.'

'There, now! Didn't I tell you?' cried the poor little man, throwing out his hands, and looking from one to the other of us.

'Don't trouble yourself about it, Mr Sholto,' said Holmes; 'I think that I can engage to clear you of the charge.'

'Don't promise too much, Mr Theorist, don't promise too much!' snapped the detective. 'You may find it a harder matter than you think.'

'Not only will I clear him, Mr Jones, but I will make you a free present of the name and description of one of the two people who were in this room last night. His name, I have every reason to believe, is Jonathan Small. He is a poorly educated man, small, active, with his right leg off, and wearing a wooden stump which is worn away upon the inner side. His left boot has a coarse, square-toed sole, with an iron band round the heel. He is a middle-aged man, much sunburned, and has been a convict. These few indications may be of some assistance to you, coupled with the fact that there is a good deal of skin missing from the palm of his hand. The other man——'

'Ah! the other man?' asked Athelney Jones, in a sneering voice, but impressed none the less, as I could easily see, by the precision of the other's manner.

'Is a rather curious person,' said Sherlock Holmes, turning upon his heel. 'I hope before very long to be able to introduce you to the pair of them. A word with you, Watson.'

He led me out to the head of the stair.

'This unexpected occurrence,' he said, 'has caused us rather to lose sight of the original purpose of our journey.'

'I have just been thinking so,' I answered; 'it is not right that Miss Morstan should remain in this stricken house.'

'No. You must escort her home. She lives with Mrs Cecil Forrester, in Lower Camberwell, so it is not very far. I will wait for you here if you will drive out again. Or perhaps you are too tired?'

'By no means. I don't think I could rest until I know more of this fantastic business. I have seen something of the rough side of life, but I give you my word that this quick succession of strange surprises tonight has shaken my nerve completely.

94 Il n'y a pas des sots si incommodes que ceux qui ont de l'esprit. "This is Number 451 of *Les Maximes* by François Duc de la Rochefoucauld, 1613–1680," Mr. Morris Rosenblum wrote in "Foreign Language Quotations in the Canon." "Holmes made one minor change which does not affect the meaning: the original has *point* instead of *pas*. The usual translation is, 'There are no fools so troublesome as those who have some wit.'"

95 *Lambeth*. "On crossing Westminster Bridge we are in Lambeth, originally a swamp, traversed by the great Roman road to Newhaven, now densely populated, and covered with a labyrinth of featureless streets and poverty-stricken courts," Augustus J. C. Hare wrote in *Walks in London*, Vol. II. "The name, by doubtful etymology, is derived from Lamb-hithe, a landing-place for sheep."

96 "Wir sind gewohnt dass die Menschen ver-höhnen was sie nicht verstehen." "Bayard Taylor's translation is, 'We are used to see that Man despises what he never comprehends,'" Mr. Morris Rosenblum wrote in "Foreign Language Quotations in the Canon." "The quotation is taken from *Faust, Part I*, and is found in the monologue by Faust when he addresses the Poodle in the Study-Room. Watson or his printers were at fault in not setting up the lines in their original poetic form:

Wir sind gewohnt, dass die Menschen verhöhnen
Was sie nicht verstehen."

97 *Goethe*. Johann Wolfgan von Goethe, 1749–1832, German poet, dramatist, novelist, scientist. "Is it not permissible to conclude that a set of Goethe's *Poetische and Prosaische Werke* (Stuttgart & Tübingen, 1836–1873) stood [on the Holmes bookshelf]?" Miss Madeleine B. Stern asked in "Sherlock Holmes: Rare Book Collector."

I should like, however, to see the matter through with you, now that I have got so far.'

'Your presence will be of great service to me,' he answered. 'We shall work the case out independently, and leave this fellow Jones to exult over any mare's-nest which he may choose to construct. When you have dropped Miss Morstan, I wish you to go to No. 3, Pinchin Lane, down near the water's edge at Lambeth. The third house on the right-hand side is a bird-stuffer's; Sherman is the name. You will see a weasel holding a young rabbit in the window. Knock old Sherman up, and tell him, with my compliments, that I want Toby at once. You will bring Toby back in the cab with you.'

'A dog, I suppose?'

'Yes, a queer mongrel, with a most amazing power of scent. I would rather have Toby's help than that of the whole detective force of London.'

'I shall bring him then,' said I. 'It is one now. I ought to be back before three, if I can get a fresh horse.'

'And I,' said Holmes, 'shall see what I can learn from Mrs Bernstone, and from the Indian servant, who, Mr Thaddeus tells me, sleeps in the next garret. Then I shall study the great Jones's methods and listen to his not too delicate sarcasms. *"Wir sind gewohnt dass die Menschen verhöhnen was sie nicht verstehen."* Goethe is always pithy.'

⁂

7 ⁜ THE EPISODE OF THE BARREL

The police had brought a cab with them, and in this I escorted Miss Morstan back to her home. After the angelic fashion of women, she had borne trouble with a calm face as long as there was someone weaker than herself to support, and I had found her bright and placid by the side of the frightened housekeeper. In the cab, however, she first turned faint, and then burst into a passion of weeping—so sorely had she been tried by the adventures of the night. She has told me since that she thought me cold and distant upon that journey. She little guessed the struggle within my breast, or the effort of self-restraint which held me back. My sympathies and my love went out to her, even as my hand had in the garden. I felt that years of the conventionalities of life could not teach me to know her sweet, brave nature as had this one day of strange experiences. Yet there were two thoughts which sealed the words of affection upon my lips. She was weak and helpless, shaken in mind and nerve. It was to take her at a disadvantage to obtrude love upon her at such a time. Worse still, she was rich. If Holmes's researches were successful, she would be an heiress. Was it fair, was it honourable, that a half-pay surgeon should take such advantage of an intimacy which chance had brought about? Might she not look upon me as a mere vulgar fortune-seeker? I could not bear to risk that such a thought should cross her mind. This Agra treasure intervened like an impassable barrier between us.

It was nearly two o'clock when we reached Mrs Cecil Forrester's. The servants had retired hours ago, but Mrs Forrester had been so interested by the strange message which Miss Morstan had received that she had sat up in the hope of her return. She opened the door herself, a middle-aged, graceful woman, and it gave me joy to see how tenderly her arm stole round the other's waist, and how motherly was the voice in which she greeted her. She was clearly no mere paid dependent, but an honoured friend. I was introduced, and Mrs Forrester earnestly begged me to step in and to tell her our adventures. I explained, however, the importance of my errand, and promised faithfully to call and report any progress which we might make with the case. As we drove away I stole a glance back, and I still seem to see that little group on the step—the two graceful, clinging figures, the half-opened door, the hall-light shining through stained glass, the barometer, and the bright stair-rods. It was soothing to **98** catch even that passing glimpse of a tranquil English home **99** in the midst of the wild, dark business which had absorbed us.

And the more I thought of what had happened, the wilder and darker it grew. I reviewed the whole extraordinary sequence of events as I rattled on through the silent, gas-lit streets. There was the original problem: that, at least, was pretty clear now. The death of Captain Morstan, the sending of the pearls, the advertisement, the letter—we had had light upon all those events. They had only led us, however, to a deeper and far more tragic mystery. The Indian treasure, the curious plan found among Morstan's baggage, the strange scene at Major Sholto's death, the rediscovery of the treasure immediately followed by the murder of the discoverer, the very singular accompaniments to the crime, the footsteps, the remarkable weapons, the words upon the card, corresponding with those upon Captain Morstan's chart—here was, indeed, a labyrinth in which a man less singularly endowed than my fellow-lodger might well despair of ever finding the clue.

Pinchin Lane was a row of shabby, two-storied brick houses in the lower quarter of Lambeth. I had to knock for some time at No. 3 before I could make any impression. At last, however, there was the glint of a candle behind the blind, and a face looked out at the upper window.

'Go on, you drunken vagabond,' said the face. 'If you kick up any more row, I'll open the kennels and let out forty-three dogs upon you.'

'If you'll let one out, it's just what I have come for,' said I.

'Go on!' yelled the voice. 'So help me gracious, I have a wiper in this bag, an' I'll drop it on your 'ead if you don't hook it!'

'But I want a dog,' I cried.

'I won't be argued with!' shouted Mr Sherman. 'Now, stand clear; for when I say "Three," down goes the wiper.'

'Mr Sherlock Holmes——' I began; but the words had a most magical effect, for the window instantly slammed down, and within a minute the door was unbarred and open. Mr Sherman was a lanky, lean old man, with stooping shoulders, a stringy neck, and blue-tinted glasses.

'A friend of Mr Sherlock is always welcome,' said he. 'Step **100** in, sir. Keep clear of the badger, for he bites. Ah, naughty, naughty! would you take a nip at the gentleman?' This to a

98 *the bright stair-rods*. These were not hand-rails, as some Americans might think, but the brass rods designed to hold the stair carpet in place; still found in many English homes.

99 *a tranquil English home*. "I like to think," the late Christopher Morley wrote in "Dr. Watson's Secret," "that Mrs. Forrester's 'tranquil English home,' with the stained glass in the front door, the barometer and the bright stair-rods, was in Knatchbull Road, Camberwell, for which Boucicault named the villain in *After Dark*."

100 '*A friend of Mr. Sherlock*. Mr. Sherman's "claim to our attention lies in the fact that, with the exception of brother Mycroft, he is the only person ever to refer to Holmes by his Christian name, albeit prefixed by the respectful 'Mister,'" Mr. Bernard Davies wrote in "Was Holmes a Londoner?" "In the eighties there was an animal dealer in Lower Kensington Lane, very close to the water's edge and within a stone's throw of Knight's Place, who might easily be the original of Mr. Sherman . . ." Your editor and other commentators have taken this as additional evidence that Sherlock Holmes spent at least a part of his boyhood in the South of London: "We can picture him now, a thin, eager youth helping the old man with the skinning, making impressions of bird and animal tracks in plaster of Paris, bursting with questions about the poisonous effects of vipers and swamp adders" (*Sherlock Holmes of Baker Street*). Clearly Charles Dickens also knew old Sherman well, for he used him as the basis for Mr. Venus in *Our Mutual Friend* which began to appear in serial form at just about this time.

101 *half spaniel and half lurcher.* "The lurcher being a cross between a collie and a greyhound, there are actually three 'halves' involved here," Mr. Stuart Palmer wrote in his "Notes on Certain Evidences of Caniphobia in Mr. Sherlock Holmes and His Associates." The lurcher is usually classified with the sporting group of dogs, whose forte is to lie in wait for and seize game, and not with the hounds, whose forte is tracking. "Toby's abilities are [therefore] very unusual, and must be attributed to the excellent training given him by his owner, Sherman, the bird-stuffer," Mrs. Eleanor S. Cole wrote in "Holmes, Watson and the K-9's."

102 *a lump of sugar.* "Surely proving that the good doctor (and the old naturalist, evidently) knew nothing of what sugar does to a dog's teeth and stomach," Mr. Palmer added.

103 *the Palace clock.* What Watson evidently thought he heard was the clock on the *Crystal* Palace, which, until it burned down, stood on Sydenham Hill. But Watson was in error, as Mr. Humfrey Michell pointed out in "The Palace Clock," "since there was no chiming clock at the 'Palace.' What he undoubtedly heard was the clock on the tower of the School for the Blind in Upper Norwood, which, for the benefit of those who could not see, struck the quarters, halves and hours in very resonant tones audible over a wide area."

104 *your bull's-eye.* Holmes is asking for the loan of the sergeant's lantern.

105 *this bit of card.* For "card" read "cord." This typographical error has persisted through many printings of the Saga.

stoat, which thrust its wicked head and red eyes between the bars of its cage. 'Don't mind that, sir; it's only a slow-worm. It hain't got no fangs, so I gives it the run o' the room, for it keeps the beetles down. You must not mind my bein' just a little short wi' you at first, for I'm guyed at by the children, and there's many a one just comes down this lane to knock me up. What was it that Mr Sherlock Holmes wanted, sir?'

'He wanted a dog of yours.'

'Ah! that would be Toby.'

'Yes, "Toby" was the name.'

'Toby lives at No. 7 on the left here.'

He moved slowly forward with his candle among the queer animal family which he had gathered round him. In the uncertain, shadowy light I could see dimly that there were glancing, glimmering eyes peeping down at us from every cranny and corner. Even the rafters above our heads were lined by solemn fowls, who lazily shifted their weight from one leg to the other as our voices disturbed their slumbers.

Toby proved to be an ugly, long-haired, lop-eared creature, **101** half spaniel and half lurcher, brown and white in colour, with a very clumsy, waddling gait. It accepted, after some **102** hesitation, a lump of sugar which the old naturalist handed to me, and, having thus sealed an alliance, it followed me to the cab, and made no difficulties about accompanying me. It **103** had just struck three on the Palace clock when I found myself back once more at Pondicherry Lodge. The ex-prizefighter McMurdo had, I found, been arrested as an accessory, and both he and Mr Sholto had been marched off to the station. Two constables guarded the narrow gate, but they allowed me to pass with the dog on my mentioning the detective's name.

Holmes was standing on the doorstep, with his hands in his pockets, smoking his pipe.

'Ah, you have him there!' said he. 'Good dog, then! Athelney Jones has gone. We have had an immense display of energy since you left. He has arrested not only friend Thaddeus, but the gatekeeper, the housekeeper, and the Indian servant. We have the place to ourselves, but for a sergeant upstairs. Leave the dog here and come up.'

We tied Toby to the hall table, and reascended the stairs. The room was as we had left it, save that a sheet had been draped over the central figure. A weary-looking police-sergeant reclined in the corner.

104 'Lend me your bull's-eye, sergeant,' said my companion.
105 'Now tie this bit of card round my neck, so as to hang it in front of me. Thank you. Now I must kick off my boots and stockings. Just you carry them down with you, Watson. I am going to do a little climbing. And dip my handkerchief into the creosote. That will do. Now come up into the garret with me for a moment.'

We clambered up through the hole. Holmes turned his light once more upon the footsteps in the dust.

'I wish you particularly to notice these footmarks,' he said. 'Do you observe anything noteworthy about them?'

'They belong,' I said, 'to a child or a small woman.'

'Apart from their size, though. Is there nothing else?'

'They appear to be much as other footmarks.'

'Not at all. Look here! This is the print of a right foot in the dust. Now I make one with my naked foot beside it. What is the chief difference?'

'Your toes are all cramped together. The other print has each toe distinctly divided.'

'Quite so. That is the point. Bear that in mind. Now, would you kindly step over to that flap-window and smell the edge of the wood-work? I shall stay over here, as I have this handkerchief in my hand.'

I did as he directed, and was instantly conscious of a strong tarry smell.

'That is where he put his foot in getting out. If *you* can trace him, I should think that Toby will have no difficulty. Now run downstairs, loose the dog, and look out for Blondin.' **106**

By the time that I got out into the grounds Sherlock Holmes was on the roof, and I could see him like an enormous glow-worm crawling very slowly along the ridge. I lost sight of him behind a stack of chimneys, but he presently reappeared, and then vanished once more upon the opposite side. When I made my way round there I found him seated at one of the corner eaves.

'That you, Watson?' he cried.

'Yes.'

'This is the place. What is that black thing down there?'

'A water-barrel.'

'Top on it?'

'Yes.'

'No sign of a ladder?'

'No.'

'Confound the fellow! It's a most breakneck place. I ought to be able to come down where he could climb up. The water-pipe feels pretty firm. Here goes, anyhow.'

There was a scuffling of feet, and the lantern began to come steadily down the side of the wall. Then with a light spring he came on to the barrel, and from there to the earth.

'It was easy to follow him,' he said, drawing on his stockings and boots. 'Tiles were loosened the whole way along, and in his hurry he had dropped this. It confirms my diagnosis, as you doctors express it.'

The object which he held up to me was a small pocket or pouch woven out of coloured grasses, and with a few tawdry beads strung round it. In shape and size it was not unlike a cigarette-case. Inside were half-a-dozen spines of dark wood, sharp at one end and rounded at the other, like that which had struck Bartholomew Sholto.

'They are hellish things,' said he. 'Look out that you don't prick yourself. I'm delighted to have them, for the chances are that they are all he has. There is the less fear of you or me finding one in our skin before long. I would sooner face a Martini bullet myself. Are you game for a six-mile trudge, **107** Watson?'

'Certainly,' I answered.

'Your leg will stand it?'

'Oh, yes.'

'Here you are, doggy! Good old Toby! Smell it, Toby, smell it!' He pushed the creosote handkerchief under the dog's nose, while the creature stood with its fluffy legs separated, and with a most comical cock to its head, like a connoisseur sniffing the *bouquet* of a famous vintage. Holmes then threw the handkerchief to a distance, fastened a stout cord to the mongrel's collar, and led him to the foot of the water-barrel.

106 *Blondin.'* Holmes compares himself to Charles Blondin, 1824–1897, the French acrobat who crossed Niagara Falls on a tightrope in 1855, 1859, and 1860. His real name was Jean François Gravelet.

107 *a Martini bullet.* A bullet from a type of rifle used at that time by the British Army.

108 *The east had been gradually whitening.* A statement of Watson's used by many chronologists to refute the "July" of the postmark on Thaddeus Sholto's letter to Mary Morstan. In July there is no real night in England until after the 20th of the month. In September, on the other hand, day breaks at 3:09 A.M. on the first, at approximately 3:37 A.M. on the fifteenth, and a few minutes after 4:00 A.M. on the thirtieth.

109 *eight-and-twenty hours' start.'* Jonathan Small had a wooden leg. He was "utterly unable to reach the lofty room of Bartholomew Sholto." But he was an active, healthy man of fifty or thereabouts who had led "a hard, open-air life." He scaled the wall bounding Pondicherry Lodge; he later "sprang" out of the *Aurora* when she buried her bow in a mudbank. A six-mile walk in two hours would have been well within the capabilities of such a man, desperately anxious to reach his destination. Small and his companion would therefore have left Pondicherry Lodge around one o'clock Tuesday morning, since we are later told that they reached their destination "about three." It is apparent, then, that they could not have left Pondicherry Lodge later than 1:00 A.M. on the Tuesday morning. Holmes and Watson therefore left Pondicherry Lodge around five o'clock on the Wednesday morning.

The creature instantly broke into a succession of high, tremulous yelps, and, with his nose on the ground, and his tail in the air, pattered off upon the trail at a pace which strained his leash and kept us at the top of our speed.

108 The east had been gradually whitening, and we could now see some distance in the cold, grey light. The square, massive house, with its black, empty windows and high, bare walls, towered up, sad and forlorn, behind us. Our course led right across the grounds, in and out among the trenches and pits with which they were scarred and intersected. The whole place, with its scattered dirt-heaps and ill-grown shrubs, had a blighted, ill-omened look which harmonized with the black tragedy which hung over it.

On reaching the boundary wall Toby ran along, whining eagerly, underneath its shadow, and stopped finally in a corner screened by a young beech. Where the two walls joined, several bricks had been loosened, and the crevices left were worn down and rounded upon the lower side, as though they had frequently been used as a ladder. Holmes clambered up, and, taking the dog from me, he dropped it over upon the other side.

'There's the print of wooden-leg's hand,' he remarked, as I mounted up beside him. 'You see the slight smudge of blood upon the white plaster. What a lucky thing it is that we have had no very heavy rain since yesterday! The scent will lie upon the road in spite of their eight-and-twenty hours' **109** start.'

I confess that I had my doubts myself when I reflected upon the great traffic which had passed along the London road in the interval. My fears were soon appeased, however. Toby never hesitated or swerved, but waddled on in his peculiar rolling fashion. Clearly, the pungent smell of the creosote rose high above all other contending scents.

'Do not imagine,' said Holmes, 'that I depend for my success in this case upon the mere chance of one of these fellows having put his foot in the chemical. I have knowledge now which would enable me to trace them in many different ways. This, however, is the readiest, and, since fortune has put it into our hands, I should be culpable if I neglected it. It has, however, prevented the case from becoming the pretty little intellectual problem which it at one time promised to be. There might have been some credit to be gained out of it, but for this too palpable clue.'

'There is credit, and to spare,' said I. 'I assure you, Holmes, that I marvel at the means by which you obtain your results in this case, even more than I did in the Jefferson Hope murder. The thing seems to me to be deeper and more inexplicable. How, for example, could you describe with such confidence the wooden-legged man?'

'Pshaw, my dear boy! it was simplicity itself. I don't wish to be theatrical. It is all patent and above-board. Two officers who are in command of a convict guard learn an important secret as to buried treasure. A map is drawn for them by an Englishman named Jonathan Small. You remember that we saw the name upon the chart in Captain Morstan's possession. He had signed it in behalf of himself and his associates—the sign of the four, as he somewhat dramatically called it. Aided by this chart, the officers—or one of them—gets the treasure and brings it to England, leaving, we will suppose, some condition under which he received it unfulfilled. Now, then, why did not Jonathan Small get the treasure himself? The answer is obvious. The chart is dated at a time when Morstan was brought into close association with convicts. Jonathan Small did not get the treasure because he and his associates were themselves convicts and could not get away.'

'But this is mere speculation,' said I.

'It is more than that. It is the only hypothesis which covers the facts. Let us see how it fits in with the sequel. Major Sholto remains at peace for some years, happy in the possession of his treasure. Then he receives a letter from India which gives him a great fright. What was that?'

'A letter to say that the men whom he had wronged had been set free.'

'Or had escaped. That is much more likely, for he would have known what their term of imprisonment was. It would not have been a surprise to him. What does he do then? He guards himself against a wooden-legged man—a white man, mark you, for he mistakes a white tradesman for him, and actually fires a pistol at him. Now, only one white man's name is on the chart. The others are Hindus or Mohammedans. There is no other white man. Therefore, we may say with confidence that the wooden-legged man is identical with Jonathan Small. Does the reasoning strike you as being faulty?'

'No: it is clear and concise.'

'Well, now, let us put ourselves in the place of Jonathan Small. Let us look at it from his point of view. He comes to England with the double idea of regaining what he would consider to be his rights, and of having his revenge upon the man who had wronged him. He found out where Sholto lived, and very possibly he established communications with someone inside the house. There is this butler, Lal Rao, whom we have not seen. Mrs Bernstone gives him far from a good character. Small could not find out, however, where the treasure was hid, for no one ever knew, save the major and one faithful servant who had died. Suddenly, Small learns that the major is on his death-bed. In a frenzy lest the secret of the treasure die with him, he runs the gauntlet of the guards, makes his way to the dying man's window, and is only deterred from entering by the presence of his two sons. Mad with hate, however, against the dead man, he enters the room that night, searches his private papers in the hope of discovering some memorandum relating to the treasure, and finally leaves a memento of his visit in the short inscription upon the card. He had doubtless planned beforehand that, should he slay the major, he would leave some such record upon the body as a sign that it was not a common murder, but, from the point of view of the four associates, something in the nature of an act of justice. Whimsical and bizarre conceits of this kind are common enough in the annals of crime, and usually afford valuable indications as to the criminal. Do you follow all this?'

'Very clearly.'

'Now, what could Jonathan Small do? He could only continue to keep a secret watch upon the efforts made to find the treasure. Possibly he leaves England and only comes back at intervals. Then comes the discovery of the garret, and he is instantly informed of it. We again trace the presence of some

110 *a damaged* tendo Achillis.' Or heel cord, lying immediately under the skin. As the late Dr. Roland Hammond pointed out in "The Attempted Mayhem of 'Silver Blaze,' " this tissue is formed by the conjoined tendons of the gastrocnemius and soleus muscles which form the calf of the leg.

111 *Now the red rim of the sun pushes itself over the London cloud-bank.* Holmes and Watson left Pondicherry Lodge around five o'clock on the Wednesday morning, as we have seen; within an hour at most of their leave-taking the sun rose. The sun on this Wednesday morning therefore rose between 5:30 and 6:00 A.M. The Wednesday we know was a fine, clear day, as evidenced by Holmes' "one little cloud floats like a pink feather . . ." On Wednesday, September 19, 1888, the weather, according to the London *Times*, was "fine generally. . . . Fair weather has prevailed today in all districts." Day broke at 3:45 A.M.; the sun rose at 5:44 A.M.

112 *Jean Paul?'* The pseudonym of J. P. F. Richter, 1763–1825, a German writer who had a great vogue in the early nineteenth century. The association with Carlyle is obvious: it was Carlyle who introduced Jean Paul's works to English readers. "Is it not permissible to conclude," Miss Madeleine B. Stern wrote in "Sherlock Holmes: Rare Book Collector," "that . . . Jean Paul's *Herbst-Blumine* (Tübingen, 1810–1820) [stood] on the Holmes' bookshelf? . . . It is likely that Holmes also owned a copy of the London 1867 edition of De Quincey's *Confessions of an English Opium-Eater*—an edition to which are added *Analects of Jean Paul Richter*. Among the analects is one on 'The Grandeur of Man in His Littleness,' a concept to which Holmes referred during his work on *The Sign of the Four*."

113 *having loaded two of the chambers.* "Thus it is demonstrable that [Holmes] fancies himself an obvious past-master with a handgun," Mr. Ralph A. Ashton wrote in "The Secret Weapons of 221B Baker Street." As we have already seen, Mr. Robert Keith Leavitt held that this "indicated confidence rather in Tonga's than in his own accuracy. He knew he would have time for only two shots at best."

confederate in the household. Jonathan, with his wooden leg, is utterly unable to reach the lofty room of Bartholomew Sholto. He takes with him, however, a rather curious associate, who gets over this difficulty, but dips his naked foot into creosote, whence come Toby, and a six-mile limp for a half-**110** pay officer with a damaged *tendo Achillis*.'

'But it was the associate, and not Jonathan, who committed the crime.'

'Quite so. And rather to Jonathan's disgust, to judge by the way he stamped about when he got into the room. He bore no grudge against Bartholomew Sholto, and would have preferred if he could have been simply bound and gagged. He did not wish to put his head in a halter. There was no help for it, however: the savage instincts of his companion had broken out, and the poison had done its work: so Jonathan Small left his record, lowered the treasure-box to the ground, and followed it himself. That was the train of events as far as I can decipher them. Of course, as to his personal appearance he must be middle-aged, and must be sunburned after serving his time in such an oven as the Andamans. His height is readily calculated from the length of his stride, and we know that he was bearded. His hairiness was the one point which impressed itself upon Thaddeus Sholto when he saw him at the window. I don't know that there is anything else.'

'The associate?'

'Ah, well, there is no great mystery in that. But you will know all about it soon enough. How sweet the morning air is! See how that one little cloud floats like a pink feather from some gigantic flamingo. Now the red rim of the sun pushes **111** itself over the London cloud-bank. It shines on a good many folk, but on none, I dare bet, who are on a stranger errand than you and I. How small we feel, with our petty ambitions and strivings, in the presence of the great elemental forces of **112** Nature! Are you well up in your Jean Paul?'

'Fairly so. I worked back to him through Carlyle.'

'That was like following the brook to the parent lake. He makes one curious but profound remark. It is that the chief proof of man's real greatness lies in his perception of his own smallness. It argues, you see, a power of comparison and of appreciation which is in itself a proof of nobility. There is much food for thought in Richter. You have not a pistol, have you?'

'I have my stick.'

'It is just possible that we may need something of the sort if we get to their lair. Jonathan I shall leave to you, but if the other turns nasty I shall shoot him dead.'

He took out his revolver as he spoke, and, having loaded **113** two of the chambers, he put it back into the right-hand pocket of his jacket.

We had during this time been following the guidance of Toby down the half-rural villa-lined roads which lead to the Metropolis. Now, however, we were beginning to come among continuous streets, where labourers and dockmen were already astir, and slatternly women were taking down shutters and brushing door-steps. At the square-topped corner public-houses business was just beginning, and rough-looking men were emerging, rubbing their sleeves across their beards after their morning wet. Strange dogs sauntered up and stared wonderingly at us as we passed, but our inimitable Toby looked neither to the right nor to the left, but trotted onwards with his nose to the ground and an occasional eager whine which spoke of a hot scent.

We had traversed Streatham, Brixton, Camberwell, and **114** now found ourselves in Kennington Lane, having borne away through the side-streets to the east of the Oval. The men **115** whom we pursued seemed to have taken a curiously zig-zag road, with the idea probably of escaping observation. They had never kept to the main road if a parallel side-street would serve their turn. At the foot of Kennington Lane they had edged away to the left through Bond Street and Miles Street. **116** Where the latter street turns into Knight's Place, Toby ceased **117** to advance, but began to run backwards and forwards with one ear cocked and the other drooping, the very picture of canine indecision. Then he waddled round in circles, looking up to us from time to time, as if to ask for sympathy in his embarrassment.

'What the deuce is the matter with the dog?' growled Holmes. 'They surely would not take a cab, or go off in a balloon.'

'Perhaps they stood here for some time,' I suggested.

'Ah! it's all right. He's off again,' said my companion, in a tone of relief.

He was indeed off, for after sniffing round again he suddenly made up his mind, and darted away with an energy and determination such as he had not yet shown. The scent appeared to be much hotter than before, for he had not even to put his nose on the ground, but tugged at his leash and tried to break into a run. I could see by the gleam in Holmes's eyes that he thought we were nearing the end of our journey.

Our course now ran down Nine Elms until we came to Broderick and Nelson's large timber-yard, just past the White Eagle tavern. Here the dog, frantic with excitement, turned **118** down through the side gate into the enclosure, where the sawyers were already at work. On the dog raced through sawdust and shavings, down an alley, round a passage, between two wood-piles, and finally, with a triumphant yelp, sprang upon a large barrel which still stood upon the hand-trolley on which it had been brought. With lolling tongue and blinking eyes, Toby stood upon the cask, looking from one to the other of us for some sign of appreciation. The staves of the barrel and the wheels of the trolley were smeared with a dark liquid, and the whole air was heavy with the smell of creosote.

Sherlock Holmes and I looked blankly at each other, and then burst simultaneously into an uncontrollable fit of laughter.

114 *Streatham.* Another London suburb now much favored by the minor lights of the acting profession. William Blake, poet and artist, 1757–1827, spent most of his life in this part of London, and Dr. Sam Johnson was almost domesticated at Streatham Park, the home of Henry Thrale.

115 *the Oval.* Kennington Oval, the ground of the Surrey County Cricket Club.

116 *Bond Street.* Now Bond Way.

117 *Knight's Place.* ". . . Knight's Place was . . . a terrace of houses in Wandsworth Road, on the left as one emerges from Miles Street, the crumbling remains of which may still be seen," Mr. Bernard Davies wrote in "Was Holmes a Londoner?"

118 *the White Eagle Tavern.* "I spent an afternoon and evening recently in attempt to find Mordecai Smith's landing-stage but without much success," Mr. Charles O. Merriman wrote in "Tar Derivatives Not Wanted." "I certainly passed the Southampton Arms, the Nine Elms Brewery and other hosteleries but of the White Eagle Tavern, there was no sign."

8 ❖ THE BAKER STREET IRREGULARS

'What now?' I asked. 'Toby has lost his character for infallibility.'

'He acted according to his lights,' said Holmes, lifting him

119 *Broad Street*. "... of Belmont Place, Prince's Street and Broad Street there was no trace," Mr. Merriman continued. Prince's Street, Mr. Davies explained in "Was Holmes a Londoner?" "survives as the eastern half of Black Prince Road, Lambeth, but Belmont Place is, alas, no more. It was, however, a similar row of buildings opposite Knight's Place at the corner of Nine Elms Lane, long since rebuilt. Obviously there is a typical Watsonian lacuna between Belmont Place, which the correct trail evidently passed, and 'Prince's Street,' involving the recrossing of Kennington Lane and then a detour, possibly via Tyers Street, until the riverside pier was reached 'at the end of Broad Street' (now Black Prince Road, West)."

down from the barrel and walking him out of the timber-yard. 'If you consider how much creosote is carted about London in one day, it is no great wonder that our trail should have been crossed. It is much used now, especially for the seasoning of wood. Poor Toby is not to blame.'

'We must get on the main scent again, I suppose.'

'Yes. And, fortunately, we have no distance to go. Evidently what puzzled the dog at the corner of Knight's Place was that there were two different trails running in opposite directions. We took the wrong one. It only remains to follow the other.'

There was no difficulty about this. On leading Toby to the place where he had committed his fault, he cast about in a wide circle and finally dashed off in a fresh direction.

'We must take care that he does not now bring us to the place where the creosote-barrel came from,' I observed.

'I had thought of that. But you notice that he keeps on the pavement, whereas the barrel passed down the roadway. No, we are on the true scent now.'

It tended down towards the river-side, running through
119 Belmont Place and Prince's Street. At the end of Broad Street it ran right down to the water's edge, where there was a small wooden wharf. Toby led us to the very edge of this, and there stood whining, looking out on the dark current beyond.

'We are out of luck,' said Holmes. 'They have taken to a boat here.'

Several small punts and skiffs were lying about in the water and on the edge of the wharf. We took Toby round to each in turn, but, though he sniffed earnestly, he made no sign.

Close to the rude landing-stage was a small brick house, with a wooden placard slung out through the second window. 'Mordecai Smith' was printed across it in large letters, and underneath, 'Boats to hire by the hour or day.' A second inscription above the door informed us that a steam launch was kept—a statement which was confirmed by a great pile of coke upon the jetty. Sherlock Holmes looked slowly round, and his face assumed an ominous expression.

'This looks bad,' said he. 'These fellows are sharper than I expected. They seem to have covered their tracks. There has, I fear, been preconcerted management here.'

He was approaching the door of the house, when it opened, and a little curly-headed lad of six came running out, followed by a stoutish, red-faced woman with a large sponge in her hand.

'You come back and be washed, Jack,' she shouted. 'Come back, you young imp; for if your father comes home and finds you like that, he'll let us hear of it.'

'Dear little chap!' cried Holmes, strategically. 'What a rosy-cheeked young rascal! Now, Jack, is there anything you would like?'

The youth pondered for a moment.

'I'd like a shillin',' said he.

'Nothing you would like better?'

'I'd like two shillin' better,' the prodigy answered, after some thought.

'Here you are, then! Catch!—A fine child, Mrs Smith!'

'Lor' bless you, sir, he is that, and forward. He gets a'most too much for me to manage, 'specially when my man is away days at a time.'

'Away, is he?' said Holmes, in a disappointed voice. 'I am sorry for that, for I wanted to speak to Mr Smith.'

'He's been away since yesterday mornin', sir, and, truth to tell, I am beginning to feel frightened about him. But if it was about a boat, sir, maybe I could serve as well.'

'I wanted to hire his steam launch.'

'Why, bless you, sir, it is in the steam launch that he has gone. That's what puzzles me; for I know there ain't more coals in her than would take her to about Woolwich and back. **120** If he'd been away in the barge I'd ha' thought nothin'; for many a time a job has taken him as far as Gravesend, and then if there was much doin' there he might ha' stayed over. But what good is a steam launch without coals?'

'He might have bought some at a wharf down the river.'

'He might, sir, but it weren't his way. Many a time I've heard him call out at the prices they charge for a few odd bags. Besides, I don't like that wooden-legged man, wi' his ugly face and outlandish talk. What did he want always knockin' about here for?'

'A wooden-legged man?' said Holmes, with bland surprise.

'Yes, sir, a brown, monkey-faced chap that's called more'n once for my old man. It was him that roused him up yester-night, and, what's more, my man knew he was comin', for he had steam up in the launch. I tell you straight, sir, I don't feel easy in my mind about it.'

'But, my dear Mrs Smith,' said Holmes, shrugging his shoulders, 'you are frightening yourself about nothing. How could you possibly tell that it was the wooden-legged man who came in the night? I don't quite understand how you can be so sure.'

'His voice, sir. I knew his voice, which is kind o' thick and foggy. He tapped at the winder—about three it would be. "Show a leg, matey," says he: "time to turn out guard." My old man woke up Jim—that's my eldest—and away they went, without so much as a word to me. I could hear the wooden leg clackin' on the stones.'

'And was this wooden-legged man alone?'

'Couldn't say, I am sure, sir. I didn't hear no one else.'

'I am sorry, Mrs Smith, for I wanted a steam launch, and I have heard good reports of the—— Let me see, what is her name?'

'The *Aurora*, sir.'

'Ah! She's not that old green launch with a yellow line, very broad in the beam?'

'No, indeed. She's as trim a little thing as any on the river. She's been fresh painted, black with two red streaks.'

'Thanks. I hope that you will hear soon from Mr Smith. I am going down the river, and if I should see anything of the *Aurora* I shall let him know that you are uneasy. A black funnel, you say?'

'No, sir. Black with a white band.'

'Ah, of course. It was the sides which were black. Good morning, Mrs Smith. There is a boatman here with a wherry, **121** Watson. We shall take it and cross the river.'

'The main thing with people of that sort,' said Holmes, as we sat in the sheets of the wherry, 'is never to let them think that their information can be of the slightest importance to you. If you do, they will instantly shut up like an oyster. If you listen to them under protest, as it were, you are very likely to get what you want.'

'Our course now seems pretty clear,' said I.

'What would you do, then?'

120 *Woolwich*. An unattractive garrison town and metropolitan borough, the site of Woolwich Dockyard and Woolwich Arsenal.

121 *a wherry*. A long, light rowboat, sharp at both ends.

122 *Greenwich*. A metropolitan borough lying on the south bank of the Thames, noted for its whitebait. Britain's Cabinet Ministers used to celebrate the close of the Parliamentary session with a "Whitebait Dinner" at Greenwich, but the custom was given up about 1880. Holmes surely had in his files a description of a ghastly murder that was committed at Greenwich on the night of February 7, 1818, when Mr. Bird, a retired tradesman, aged eighty-four, and Mary Symonds, his housekeeper, both had their skulls driven in by a large hammer. The house was plundered, and the discovery of the stolen property led to the conviction of the murderer, who was afterward executed on Pennenden Heath, near Maidstone.

123 *wharfingers?*' Wharf owners.

124 *Millbank Penitentiary*. A model prison built from designs of Jeremy Bentham (d. 1832). The prison was taken down in 1893, and the west part of the site is now covered by large blocks of workmen's dwellings, while the east portion, nearest the river, is occupied by the Tate Gallery, flanked on the north by Queen Alexandra's Military Hospital and on the south by the Royal Army Medical College.

'I would engage a launch and go down the river on the track of the *Aurora*.'

'My dear fellow, it would be a colossal task. She may have touched at any wharf on either side of the stream between **122** here and Greenwich. Below the bridge there is a perfect labyrinth of landing-places for miles. It would take you days and days to exhaust them, if you set about it alone.'

'Employ the police, then.'

'No. I shall probably call Athelney Jones in at the last moment. He is not a bad fellow, and I should not like to do anything which would injure him professionally. But I have a fancy for working it out myself, now that we have gone so far.'

'Could we advertise, then, asking for information from **123** wharfingers?'

'Worse and worse! Our men would know that the chase was hot at their heels, and they would be off out of the country. As it is, they are likely enough to leave, but as long as they think they are perfectly safe they will be in no hurry. Jones's energy will be of use to us there, for his view of the case is sure to push itself into the daily Press, and the runaways will think that everyone is off on the wrong scent.'

'What are we to do, then?' I asked, as we landed near Mill- **124** bank Penitentiary.

'Take this hansom, drive home, have some breakfast, and get an hour's sleep. It is quite on the cards that we may be afoot tonight again. Stop at a telegraph office, cabby! We will keep Toby, for he may be of use to us yet.'

We pulled up at the Great Peter Street post-office, and Holmes dispatched his wire.

'Whom do you think that is to?' he asked, as we resumed our journey.

'I am sure I don't know.'

'You remember the Baker Street division of the detective police force whom I employed in the Jefferson Hope case?'

'Well?' said I, laughing.

'This is just the case where they might be invaluable. If they fail, I have other resources; but I shall try them first. That wire was to my dirty little lieutenant, Wiggins, and I expect that he and his gang will be with us before we have finished our breakfast.'

It was between eight and nine o'clock now, and I was conscious of a strong reaction after the successive excitements of the night. I was limp and weary, befogged in mind and fatigued in body. I had not the professional enthusiasm which carried my companion on, nor could I look at the matter as a mere abstract intellectual problem. As far as the death of Bartholomew Sholto went, I had heard little good of him, and could feel no intense antipathy to his murderers. The treasure, however, was a different matter. That, or part of it, belonged rightfully to Miss Morstan. While there was a chance of recovering it I was ready to devote my life to the one object. True, if I found it, it would probably put her for ever beyond my reach. Yet it would be a petty and selfish love which would be influenced by such a thought as that. If Holmes could work to find the criminals, I had a tenfold stronger reason to urge me on to find the treasure.

A bath at Baker Street and a complete change freshened me up wonderfully. When I came down to our room I found the breakfast laid and Holmes pouring out the coffee.

'Here it is,' said he, laughing and pointing to an open newspaper. 'The energetic Jones and the ubiquitous reporter have fixed it up between them. But you have had enough of the case. Better have your ham and eggs first.'

I took the paper from him and read the short notice, which was headed, 'Mysterious Business at Upper Norwood.'

About twelve o'clock last night [said the *Standard*], Mr Bartholomew Sholto, of Pondicherry Lodge, Upper Norwood, was found dead in his room under circumstances which point to foul play. As far as we can learn, no actual traces of violence were found upon Mr Sholto's person, but a valuable collection of Indian gems which the deceased gentleman had inherited from his father has been carried off. The discovery was first made by Mr Sherlock Holmes and Dr Watson, who had called at the house with Mr Thaddeus Sholto, brother of the deceased. By a singular piece of good fortune, Mr Athelney Jones, the well-known member of the detective police force, happened to be at the Norwood Police Station, and was on the ground within half an hour of the first alarm. His trained and experienced faculties were at once directed towards the detection of the criminals, with the gratifying result that the brother, Thaddeus Sholto, has already been arrested, together with the housekeeper, Mrs Bernstone, an Indian butler named Lal Rao, and a porter, or gatekeeper, named McMurdo. It is quite certain that the thief or thieves were well acquainted with the house, for Mr Jones's well-known technical knowledge and his powers of minute observation have enabled him to prove conclusively that the miscreants could not have entered by the door or by the window, but must have made their way across the roof of the building, and so through a trap-door into a room which communicated with that in which the body was found. This fact, which has been very clearly made out, proves conclusively that it was no mere haphazard burglary. The prompt and energetic action of the officers of the law shows the great advantage of the presence on such occasions of a single vigorous and masterful mind. We cannot but think that it supplies an argument to those who would wish to see our detectives more decentralized, and so brought into closer and more effective touch with the cases which it is their duty to investigate.

'Isn't it gorgeous?' said Holmes, grinning over his coffee cup. 'What do you think of it?'

'I think that we have had a close shave ourselves of being arrested for the crime.'

'So do I. I wouldn't answer for our safety now, if he should happen to have another of his attacks of energy.'

At this moment there was a loud ring at the bell, and I could hear Mrs Hudson, our landlady, raising her voice in a wail of expostulation and dismay.

'By heavens, Holmes,' said I, half rising, 'I believe that they are really after us.'

'No, it's not quite so bad as that. It is the unofficial force—the Baker Street irregulars.'

As he spoke, there came a swift pattering of naked feet upon the stairs, a clatter of high voices, and in rushed a dozen dirty and ragged little street arabs. There was some show of discipline among them, despite their tumultuous entry, for they instantly drew up in line and stood facing us with expectant faces. One of their number, taller and older than the others, stood forward with an air of lounging superiority which was very funny in such a disreputable little scarecrow.

'Got your message, sir,' said he, 'and brought 'em on sharp. Three bob and a tanner for tickets.'

125

125 *Three bob and a tanner.* Slang for three shillings and sixpence (about 87¢). The boys had come from some distance if their tickets by bus or Underground cost threepence each.

'Here you are,' said Holmes, producing some silver. 'In future they can report to you, Wiggins, and you to me. I cannot have the house invaded in this way. However, it is just as well that you should all hear the instructions. I want to find the whereabouts of a steam launch called the *Aurora*, owner Mordecai Smith, black with two red streaks, funnel black with a white band. She is down the river somewhere. I want one boy to be at Mordecai Smith's landing-stage opposite Millbank to say if the boat comes back. You must divide it out among yourselves, and do both banks thoroughly. Let me know the moment you have news. Is that all clear?'

'Yes, guv'nor,' said Wiggins.

'The old scale of pay, and a guinea to the boy who finds the boat. Here's a day in advance. Now, off you go!'

He handed them a shilling each, and away they buzzed down the stairs, and I saw them a moment later streaming down the street.

'If the launch is above water they will find her,' said Holmes, as he rose from the table and lit his pipe. 'They can go everywhere, see everything, overhear everyone. I expect to hear before evening that they have spotted her. In the meanwhile, we can do nothing but await results. We cannot pick up the broken trail until we find either the *Aurora* or Mr Mordecai Smith.'

'Toby could eat these scraps, I dare say. Are you going to bed, Holmes?'

'No; I am not tired. I have a curious constitution. I never remember feeling tired by work, though idleness exhausts me completely. I am going to smoke and to think over this queer business to which my fair client has introduced us. If ever man had an easy task, this of ours ought to be. Wooden-legged men are not so common, but the other man must, I should think, be absolutely unique.'

'That other man again!'

'I have no wish to make a mystery of him to you, anyway. But you must have formed your own opinion. Now, do consider the data. Diminutive footmarks, toes never fettered by boots, naked feet, stone-headed wooden mace, great agility, small poisoned darts. What do you make of all this?'

'A savage!' I exclaimed. 'Perhaps one of those Indians who were the associates of Jonathan Small.'

'Hardly that,' said he. 'When first I saw signs of strange weapons, I was inclined to think so; but the remarkable character of the footmarks caused me to reconsider my views. Some of the inhabitants of the Indian Peninsula are small men, but none could have left such marks as that. The Hindu proper has long and thin feet. The sandal-wearing Mohammedan has the great toe well separated from the others, because the thong is commonly passed between. These little darts, too, could only be shot in one way. They are from a blowpipe. Now, then, where are we to find our savage?'

'South American,' I hazarded.

He stretched his hand up, and took down a bulky volume from the shelf.

'This is the first volume of a gazetteer which is now being published. It may be looked upon as the very latest authority. What have we here? "Andaman Islands, situated 340 miles to the north of Sumatra, in the Bay of Bengal." Hum! hum! What's all this? Moist climate, coral reefs, sharks, Port Blair, convict barracks, Rutland Island, cottonwoods—— Ah, here we are! "The aborigines of the Andaman Islands may perhaps claim the distinction of being the smallest race upon this earth, though some anthropologists prefer the Bushmen of Africa, the Digger Indians of America, and the Tierra del Fuegians. The average height is rather below four feet, although many full-grown adults may be found who are very much smaller than this. They are a fierce, morose, and intractable people, though capable of forming most devoted friendships when their confidence has once been gained." Mark that, Watson. Now, then, listen to this. "They are naturally hideous, having large, misshapen heads, small, fierce eyes, and distorted features. Their feet and hands, however, are remarkably small. So intractable and fierce are they, that all the efforts of the British officials have failed to win them over in any degree. They have always been a terror to shipwrecked crews, braining the survivors with their stone-headed clubs, or shooting them with their poisoned arrows. These massacres are invariably concluded by a cannibal feast." Nice, amiable people, Watson! If this fellow had **126** been left to his own unaided devices, this affair might have taken an even more ghastly turn. I fancy that, even as it is, Jonathan Small would give a good deal not to have employed him.'

'But how came he to have so singular a companion?'

'Ah, that is more than I can tell. Since, however, we had already determined that Small had come from the Andamans, it is not so very wonderful that this islander should be with him. No doubt we shall know all about it in time. Look here, Watson; you look regularly done. Lie down there on the sofa, and see if I can put you to sleep.'

He took up his violin from the corner, and as I stretched myself out he began to play some low, dreamy, melodious air —his own, no doubt, for he had a remarkable gift for improvisation. I have a vague remembrance of his gaunt limbs, his earnest face, and the rise and fall of his bow. Then I seemed to be floated peacefully away upon a soft sea of sound, until I found myself in dreamland, with the sweet face of Mary Morstan looking down upon me.

126 *Nice, amiable people, Watson!* As Mr. Roger Lancelyn Green pointed out in his article, "Dr. Watson's First Critic," Andrew Lang, writing in the *Quarterly Review*, July, 1904, was one of the earliest critics to catch Holmes out in this description of the Andaman Islanders. The Andamanese, Lang declared, "have neither the malignant qualities, nor the heads like mops, nor the customs, with which they are credited by Sherlock." In fact, they shave their heads, have an average height of four feet ten and a half inches, do not use blow-pipes or poisoned arrows, and show no traces of cannibalism. To this Mr. T. S. Blakeney added ("Thoughts on *The Sign of the Four*"): "What was the Gazetteer to which Holmes referred for information on the Andamanese? Not, one feels, a wholly reliable one, for the aborigines 1) are *not* cannibals—I was told in 1936, while on a visit to the Andaman Islands, by the Chief Commissioner, that when the aborigines had been questioned about this practice, they expressed horror at the idea; 2) are not naturally hideous (some of the Nicobarese Islanders have unpleasing features, particularly their mouths); 3) their average height is more like 4 ft. 9 in. to 5 ft. than under 4 ft. Holmes' gazetteer gave a very untrue picture of the Andamanese; they were rather attractive little people, whose treatment at the hands of the Government of India was nothing less than tragic."

9 ♦ A BREAK IN THE CHAIN

It was late in the afternoon before I woke, strengthened and refreshed. Sherlock Holmes still sat exactly as I had left him, save that he had laid aside his violin and was deep in a book. He looked across at me as I stirred, and I noticed that his face was dark and troubled.

'You have slept soundly,' he said. 'I feared that our talk would wake you.'

'I heard nothing,' I answered. 'Have you had fresh news, then?'

'Unfortunately, no. I confess that I am surprised and disappointed. I expected something definite by this time. Wiggins has just been up to report. He says that no trace can be found of the launch. It is a provoking check, for every hour is of importance.'

'Can I do anything? I am perfectly fresh now, and quite ready for another night's outing.'

'No; we can do nothing. We can only wait. If we go ourselves, the message might come in our absence, and delay be caused. You can do what you will, but I must remain on guard.'

'Then I shall run over to Camberwell and call upon Mrs Cecil Forrester. She asked me to, yesterday.'

'On Mrs Cecil Forrester?' asked Holmes with the twinkle of a smile in his eyes.

'Well, of course, on Miss Morstan too. They were anxious to hear what happened.'

'I would not tell them too much,' said Holmes. 'Women are never to be entirely trusted—not the best of them.'

I did not pause to argue over this atrocious sentiment.

'I shall be back in an hour or two,' I remarked.

'All right! Good luck! But, I say, if you are crossing the water you may as well return Toby, for I don't think it is at all likely that we shall have any use for him now.'

I took our mongrel accordingly, and left him, together with a half-sovereign, at the old naturalist's in Pinchin Lane. At Camberwell I found Miss Morstan a little weary after her night's adventures, but very eager to hear the news. Mrs Forrester, too, was full of curiosity. I told them all that we had done, suppressing, however, the more dreadful parts of the tragedy. Thus, although I spoke of Mr Sholto's death, I said nothing of the exact manner and method of it. With all my omissions, however, there was enough to startle and amaze them.

'It is a romance!' cried Mrs Forrester. 'An injured lady, half a million in treasure, a black cannibal, and a wooden-legged ruffian. They take the place of the conventional dragon or wicked earl.'

'And two knight-errants to the rescue,' added Miss Morstan, with a bright glance at me.

'Why, Mary, your fortune depends upon the issue of this search. I don't think that you are nearly excited enough. Just imagine what it must be to be so rich, and to have the world at your feet!'

It sent a little thrill of joy to my heart to notice that she showed no sign of elation at the prospect. On the contrary, she gave a toss of her proud head, as though the matter were one in which she took small interest.

'It is for Mr Thaddeus Sholto that I am anxious,' she said. 'Nothing else is of any consequence; but I think that he has behaved most kindly and honourably throughout. It is our duty to clear him of this dreadful and unfounded charge.'

It was evening before I left Camberwell, and quite dark by the time I reached home. My companion's book and pipe lay by his chair, but he had disappeared. I looked about in the hope of seeing a note, but there was none.

'I suppose that Mr Sherlock Holmes has gone out?' I said to Mrs Hudson as she came up to lower the blinds.

'No, sir. He has gone to his room, sir. Do you know, sir,'

sinking her voice into an impressive whisper, 'I am afraid for his health?'

'Why so, Mrs Hudson?'

'Well, he's that strange, sir. After you was gone he walked and he walked, up and down, and up and down, until I was weary of the sound of his footstep. Then I heard him talking to himself and muttering, and every time the bell rang out he came on the stair-head, with "What is that, Mrs Hudson?" And now he has slammed off to his room, but I can hear him walking away the same as ever. I hope he's not going to be ill, sir. I ventured to say something to him about cooling medicine, but he turned on me, sir, with such a look that I don't know however I got out of the room.'

'I don't think that you have any cause to be uneasy, Mrs Hudson,' I answered. 'I have seen him like this before. He has some small matter upon his mind which makes him restless.'

I tried to speak lightly to our worthy landlady, but I was myself somewhat uneasy when through the long night I still from time to time heard the dull sound of his tread, and knew how his keen spirit was chafing against this involuntary inaction.

At breakfast-time he looked worn and haggard, with a little **127** fleck of feverish colour upon either cheek.

'You are knocking yourself up, old man,' I remarked. 'I heard you marching about in the night.'

'No, I could not sleep,' he answered. 'This infernal problem is consuming me. It is too much to be baulked by so petty an obstacle, when all else had been overcome. I know the men, the launch, everything; and yet I can get no news. I have set other agencies at work, and used every means at my disposal. The whole river has been searched on either side, but there is no news, nor has Mrs Smith heard of her husband. I shall come to the conclusion soon that they have scuttled the craft. But there are objections to that.'

'Or that Mrs Smith has put us on a wrong scent.'

'No, I think that may be dismissed. I had inquiries made, and there is a launch of that description.'

'Could it have gone up the river?'

'I have considered that possibility too, and there is a search-party who will work up as far as Richmond. If no news comes **128** today, I shall start off myself tomorrow, and go for the men rather than the boat. But surely, surely, we shall hear something.'

We did not, however. Not a word came to us either from Wiggins or from the other agencies. There were articles in most of the papers upon the Norwood tragedy. They all appeared to be rather hostile to the unfortunate Thaddeus Sholto. No fresh details were to be found, however, in any of them, save that an inquest was to be held upon the following day. I walked over to Camberwell in the evening to report our ill-success to the ladies, and on my return I found Holmes dejected and somewhat morose. He would hardly reply to my questions, and busied himself all the evening in an abstruse chemical analysis which involved much heating of retorts and distilling of vapours, ending at last in a smell which fairly drove me out of the apartment. Up to the small hours of the morning I could hear the clinking of his test-tubes, which told me that he was still engaged in his malodorous experiment.

127 *At breakfast-time*. This would be Thursday morning, since the adventure began on a Tuesday (see Note 130).

128 *Richmond*. A municipal borough in Surrey, on the Thames. It is the site of the Palace of Sheen, where many sovereigns lived, a large deer park, and Kew Observatory. Here also was the Inn of the Star and Garter, which figures in Scott's works; it was torn down in 1919.

129 *In the early dawn.* Of the Friday morning.

130 *last Tuesday morning.* Of the four days covered by the action, the first is clearly Tuesday.

131 *the natural anxiety of a wife for her missing husband.* "What a pity," Mr. Charles B. Stephens wrote in "Holmes' Longest Shot?", "that Watson missed so completely this opportunity to applaud one of the longest shots his companion ever played. Consider the circumstances at the time when Holmes ordered this advertisement inserted, obviously no later than the preceding evening. The indefatigable Irregulars had drawn a blank in their search for the *Aurora*, and every lead seemed to run to a dead end. Holmes had only a slender, untested chain of reasoning on which to base his next move. He had to find the *Aurora* before he could spring his trap. With supreme confidence in his own reasoning and ability to succeed where others had failed, he deliberately inserted in the *Standard* the very advertisement that he felt reasonably certain would flush his quarry on the next evening. To make doubly certain of this effect on the fugitives, he added his Baker Street address to the copy. . . . The evidence seems clear and convincing that Holmes had this purpose in mind, and that he was looking to his own activities, not any possible answers to his advertisement, to turn up the missing *Aurora*. The reward was fantastic, the Baker Street address was wholly inconsistent with Watson's interpretation, and Holmes did nothing to prepare Watson for any possible visitors who might come in answer to the paragraph. It is true that had he not located the *Aurora* in time, Holmes could still have covered the flight of the criminals by alerting the police along the lower Thames. The fact remains that the gamble came off as he planned it . . ."

129 In the early dawn I woke with a start, and was surprised to find him standing by my bedside, clad in a rude sailor dress with a pea-jacket, and a coarse red scarf round his neck.

'I am off down the river, Watson,' said he. 'I have been turning it over in my mind, and I can see only one way out of it. It is worth trying, at all events.'

'Surely I can come with you, then?' said I.

'No; you can be much more useful if you will remain here as my representative. I am loth to go, for it is quite on the cards that some message may come during the day, though Wiggins was despondent about it last night. I want you to open all notes and telegrams, and to act on your own judgment if any news should come. Can I rely upon you?'

'Most certainly.'

'I am afraid that you will not be able to wire to me, for I can hardly tell yet where I may find myself. If I am in luck, however, I may not be gone so very long. I shall have news of some sort or other before I get back.'

I had heard nothing of him by breakfast-time. On opening the *Standard*, however, I found that there was a fresh allusion to the business.

> With reference to the Upper Norwood tragedy [it remarked], we have reason to believe that the matter promises to be even more complex and mysterious than was originally supposed. Fresh evidence has shown that it is quite impossible that Mr Thaddeus Sholto could have been in any way concerned in the matter. He and the housekeeper, Mrs Bernstone, were both released yesterday evening. It is believed, however, that the police have a clue as to the real culprits, and that it is being prosecuted by Mr Athelney Jones, of Scotland Yard, with all his well-known energy and sagacity. Further arrests may be expected at any moment.

'That is satisfactory so far as it goes,' thought I. 'Friend Sholto is safe, at any rate. I wonder what the fresh clue may be, though it seems to be a stereotyped form whenever the police have made a blunder.'

I tossed the paper down upon the table, but at that moment my eye caught an advertisement in the agony column. It ran in this way:

> **130** LOST.—Whereas Mordecai Smith, boatman, and his son Jim, left Smith's Wharf at or about three o'clock last Tuesday morning in the steam launch *Aurora*, black with two red stripes, funnel black with a white band, the sum of five pounds will be paid to anyone who can give information to Mrs Smith, at Smith's Wharf, or at 221*b*, Baker Street, as to the whereabouts of the said Mordecai Smith and the launch *Aurora*.

This was clearly Holmes's doing. The Baker Street address was enough to prove that. It struck me as rather ingenious, because it might be read by the fugitives without their seeing in it more than the natural anxiety of a wife for her missing **131** husband.

It was a long day. Every time that a knock came to the door, or a sharp step passed in the street, I imagined that it was either Holmes returning or an answer to his advertisement. I tried to read, but my thoughts would wander oft to our strange quest and to the ill-assorted and villainous pair whom we were pursuing. Could there be, I wondered, some radical flaw in my companion's reasoning? Might he not be suffering from some huge self-deception? Was it not possible that his nimble and speculative mind had built up this wild theory upon faulty premises? I had never known him to be wrong, and yet the keenest reasoner may occasionally be deceived. He was likely, I thought, to fall into error through the over-refinement of his logic—his preference for a subtle and bizarre explanation when a plainer and more commonplace one lay ready to his hand. Yet, on the other hand, I had myself seen the evidence, and I had heard the reasons for his deductions. When I looked back on the long chain of curious circumstances, many of them trivial in themselves, but all tending in the same direction, I could not disguise from myself that even if Holmes's explanation were incorrect the true theory must be equally *outré* and startling.

At three o'clock in the afternoon there was a loud peal at the bell, an authoritative voice in the hall, and, to my surprise, no less a person than Mr Athelney Jones was shown up to me. Very different was he, however, from the brusque and masterful professor of common-sense who had taken over the case so confidently at Upper Norwood. His expression was downcast, and his bearing meek and even apologetic.

'Good-day, sir; good-day,' said he. 'Mr Sherlock Holmes is out, I understand?'

'Yes, and I cannot be sure when he will be back. But perhaps you would care to wait. Take that chair and try one of these cigars.'

'Thank you; I don't mind if I do,' said he, mopping his face with a red bandanna handkerchief.

'And a whisky and soda?'

'Well, half a glass. It is very hot for the time of year; and **132** I have had a good deal to worry and try me. You know my theory about this Norwood case?'

'I remember that you expressed one.'

'Well, I have been obliged to reconsider it. I had my net drawn tightly round Mr Sholto, sir, when pop he went through a hole in the middle of it. He was able to prove an alibi which could not be shaken. From the time that he left his brother's room he was never out of sight of someone or other. So it could not be he who climbed over roofs and through trap-doors. It's a very dark case, and my professional credit is at stake. I should be very glad of a little assistance.'

'We all need help sometimes,' said I.

'Your friend Mr Sherlock Holmes is a wonderful man, sir,' said he, in a husky and confidential voice. 'He's a man who is not to be beat. I have known that young man go into a good many cases, but I never saw the case yet that he could not throw a light upon. He is irregular in his methods, and a little quick perhaps in jumping at theories; but, on the whole, I think he would have made a most promising officer and I don't care who knows it. I have had a wire from him this morning, by which I understand that he has got some clue to this Sholto business. Here is his message.'

He took the telegram out of his pocket, and handed it to me. It was dated from Poplar at twelve o'clock. 'Go to Baker **133** Street at once,' it said. 'If I have not returned, wait for me. I am close on the track of the Sholto gang. You can come with us tonight if you want to be in at the finish.'

'This sounds well. He has evidently picked up the scent again,' said I.

'Ah, then he has been at fault too,' exclaimed Jones, with

132 *It is very hot for the time of year.* "This is hardly a comment appropriate to July, when even a hot spell would be considered seasonable, but quite an acceptable comment in September, when drizzle, fog, close nights, warm west winds, or heat, may be expected to follow in close succession in London," Dr. Ebbe Curtis Hoff wrote in "The Adventure of John and Mary." For the record, the thermometer registered 65° in London at noon on Friday, September 21, 1888.

133 *Poplar.* A metropolitan borough in the East of London, taking its name from the trees which once flourished there.

134 *some of my cases*. It is possible that Holmes here confused the one *published* case with the number of cases Watson had undoubtedly *chronicled* by this time.

135 *I can step across the road and telephone.* "In September, 1879, there was an Exchange [in London] serving 10 subscribers," Colonel E. Ennalls Berl wrote in "Sherlock Holmes and the Telephone." "There was a company in Liverpool before 1883, and in 1883 the telephone was in operation in many cities. . . . In 1884 there was a public trunk line from London to Brighton, 40 or 50 miles, and as early as 1891 the Channel had been bridged, and Paris-London telephone service was inaugurated. . . . Naturally, as it was necessary for Jones to step across the road, it is clear that at that time there was no telephone at 221B Baker Street. But, according to Christopher Pulling, senior assistant secretary of Scotland Yard, there *was* one at the Yard, from 1887 on."

136 *I have oysters and a brace of grouse.* Grouse and oysters belong to September rather than to July, the first by law, the second by custom. The late Christopher Morley ("Was Sherlock Holmes an American?") always held that since Holmes had a liking for oysters he must have acquired his taste for them in their native habitat, otherwise Baltimore—additional evidence that he had traveled in America. This is borne out by the late Fletcher Pratt, writing in "The Gastronomic Holmes": "The English oysters, with their strong flavor of copper, are not the best preparation for a meal, but they were the best the market afforded and an excellent prelude to grouse. As for the grouse themselves, there is clearly no question as to how they were served. One brace of grouse would be insufficient for three men, one of whom was Watson, who did nothing to preserve his figure. Therefore there must have been three brace, one to each of the eaters; and if that is the case, they could only have been served in the classic manner prescribed by both Brillat-Savarin and Escoffier— roasted with the breasts only served, accompanied by a bread sauce, potato chips and a gravy made from the unused portions of the birds."

Readers who might like to serve a dinner *à la* Holmes are invited to try these recipes, prepared by Mr. Poul Ib Liebe ("Sherlock's Delights"), to which he has added an apricot pie: "Out of modesty—or possibly because of sheer forgetful-

evident satisfaction. 'Even the best of us are thrown off sometimes. Of course this may prove to be a false alarm; but it is my duty as an officer of the law to allow no chance to slip. But there is someone at the door. Perhaps this is he.'

A heavy step was heard ascending the stair, with a great wheezing and rattling as from a man who was sorely put to it for breath. Once or twice he stopped, as though the climb were too much for him, but at last he made his way to our door and entered. His appearance corresponded to the sounds which we had heard. He was an aged man, clad in seafaring garb, with an old pea-jacket buttoned up to his throat. His back was bowed, his knees were shaky, and his breathing was painfully asthmatic. As he leaned upon a thick oaken cudgel his shoulders heaved in the effort to draw the air into his lungs. He had a coloured scarf round his chin, and I could see little of his face save a pair of keen dark eyes, overhung by bushy white brows, and long grey side-whiskers. Altogether he gave me the impression of a respectable master mariner who had fallen into years and poverty.

'What is it, my man?' I asked.

He looked about him in the slow methodical fashion of old age.

'Is Mr Sherlock Holmes here?' said he.

'No; but I am acting for him. You can tell me any message you have for him.'

'It was to him himself I was to tell it,' said he.

'But I tell you I am acting for him. Was it about Mordecai Smith's boat?'

'Yes. I knows well where it is. An' I knows where the men he is after are. An' I knows where the treasure is. I knows all about it.'

'Then tell me, and I shall let him know.'

'It was to him I was to tell it,' he repeated, with the petulant obstinacy of a very old man.

'Well, you must wait for him.'

'No, no; I ain't goin' to lose a whole day to please no one. If Mr Holmes ain't here, then Mr Holmes must find it all out for himself. I don't care about the look of either of you, and I won't tell a word.'

He shuffled towards the door, but Athelney Jones got in front of him.

'Wait a bit, my friend,' said he. 'You have important information, and you must not walk off. We shall keep you, whether you like or not, until our friend returns.'

The old man made a little run towards the door, but, as Athelney Jones put his broad back up against it, he recognized the uselessness of resistance.

'Pretty sort o' treatment this!' he cried, stamping his stick. 'I come here to see a gentleman, and you two, who I never saw in my life, seize me and treat me in this fashion!'

'You will be none the worse,' I said. 'We shall recompense you for the loss of your time. Sit over here on the sofa, and you will not have long to wait.'

He came across sullenly enough, and seated himself with his face resting on his hands. Jones and I resumed our cigars and our talk. Suddenly, however, Holmes's voice broke in upon us.

'I think that you might offer me a cigar too,' he said.

We both started in our chairs. There was Holmes sitting close to us with an air of quiet amusement.

'Holmes!' I exclaimed. 'You here! But where is the old man?'

'Here is the old man,' said he, holding out a heap of white hair. 'Here he is—wig, whiskers, eyebrows, and all. I thought my disguise was pretty good, but I hardly expected that it would stand that test.'

'Ah, you rogue!' cried Jones, highly delighted. 'You would have made an actor, and a rare one. You had the proper work-house cough, and those weak legs of yours are worth ten pounds a week. I thought I knew the glint of your eye, though. You didn't get away from us so easily, you see.'

'I have been working in that get-up all day,' said he, lighting his cigar. 'You see, a good many of the criminal classes begin to know me—especially since our friend here took to publishing some of my cases: so I can only go on the war-path **134** under some simple disguise like this. You got my wire?'

'Yes; that was what brought me here.'

'How has your case prospered?'

'It has all come to nothing. I have had to release two of my prisoners, and there is no evidence against the other two.'

'Never mind. We shall give you two others in the place of them. But you must put yourself under my orders. You are welcome to all the official credit, but you must act on the lines that I point out. Is that agreed?'

'Entirely, if you will help me to the men.'

'Well, then, in the first place I shall want a fast police-boat —a steam launch—to be at the Westminster Stairs at seven o'clock.'

'That is easily managed. There is always one about there; but I can step across the road and telephone to make sure.' **135**

'Then I shall want two stanch men, in case of resistance.'

'There will be two or three in the boat. What else?'

'When we secure the men we shall get the treasure. I think that it would be a pleasure to my friend here to take the box round to the young lady to whom half of it rightfully belongs. Let her be the first to open it. Eh, Watson?'

'It would be a great pleasure to me.'

'Rather an irregular proceeding,' said Jones, shaking his head. 'However, the whole thing is irregular, and I suppose we must wink at it. The treasure must afterwards be handed over to the authorities until after the official investigation.'

'Certainly. That is easily managed. One other point. I should much like to have a few details about this matter from the lips of Jonathan Small himself. You know I like to work the details of my cases out. There is no objection to my having an unofficial interview with him, either here in my rooms or elsewhere, as long as he is efficiently guarded?'

'Well, you are master of the situation. I have had no proof yet of the existence of this Jonathan Small. However, if you can catch him, I don't see how I can refuse you an interview with him.'

'That is understood, then?'

'Perfectly. Is there anything else?'

'Only that I insist upon your dining with us. It will be ready in half an hour. I have oysters and a brace of grouse, **136** with something a little choice in white wines. Watson, you **137** have never yet recognized my merits as a housekeeper.'

ness—Holmes omits to inform us of the dessert, which might well have been apricot pie, a favorite Victorian sweet."

I. Oyster Special
  18 oysters
  1 lemon
  1 egg
  Flour
  Breadcrumbs
  ½ pound of lard.

  Each of the fresh oysters must be removed from the shells, soaked in lemon juice, rolled in flour, smeared with egg (slightly whipped), dipped into the crumbs, and finally boiled in the lard. A real delicacy!

II. Grouse *à la* Holmes
  3 grouse
  3 thin slices of bacon
  2 tsp. salt
  a little pepper

  Ingredients for frying:

  3 tsp. of butter
  2 cups of broth
  ½ cup of cream

  Sauce:

  2 cups of gravy (from the frying juice)
  ½ cup of cream
  a little salt
  1 tsp. of currant jelly

  Having skinned and cleansed the grouse, wings and legs are removed, the birds are rubbed with salt and pepper, and the breast-pieces are wrapped in bacon. The birds are then fried (first in the butter alone for a moment; then in the mixture of butter and broth) for about an hour, with occasional drippings of cream. Taste the gravy with salt, current jelly and cream *ad libitum*, and serve the ready dish with browned potatoes and mushrooms.

III. Apricot Pie
  1 pound of dried apricots
  6 eggs
  Sugar
  Vanilla

  The apricots are cooked and pressed through a sieve. The whites of the eggs are whipped (they must be quite stiff) to be mixed with the sweetened apricot mash and the whole mixture is then baked in the oven for about 20 minutes. The 6 egg yolks are whipped with sugar and vanilla to be served (cold) together with the (hot) pie.

  The recipes are intended for six persons.

137 *something a little choice in white wines.* Messrs. Morley and Pratt both suggested a Montrachet; Mr. Jorgen Cøld thought that it might have been a Steinberger Kabinett.

138 *on mediæval pottery.* Holmes' interest in many facets of the Middle Ages is suggested again in the adventures of "The Bruce-Partington Plans" and "The Three Students."

139 *on the Buddhism of Ceylon.* In his fascinating work, *Sherlock Holmes' Wanderjahre*, the late A. Carson Simpson demonstrated that Holmes during his stay in Tibet (1891–1893) "was assiduous in his study of Lamaistic Buddhism and eventually became an adept."

140 *bon vivant.* French: a lover of good living, especially of the table; a gourmet.

141 *filled up three glasses with port.* "It is to be noted," the late Fletcher Pratt wrote in "The Gastronomic Holmes," "that Holmes poured [the port] himself; another sign of the true gourmet, who would rather let a gorilla handle his sister than a waiter touch his port."

142 *a change of work is the best rest.* Holmes is referring to an aphorism usually credited to William Ewart Gladstone, 1809–1898, Prime Minister of England, 1868–1874, 1880–1885, 1886, 1892–1894. But, as Mr. T. S. Blakeney asked in "Thoughts on *The Sign of the Four,*" "can anyone say when and where he made this remark, and quote the authority for it?"

143 *succeeded in dissolving the hydrocarbon.* "It is inconceivable that dissolving a hydrocarbon should be a problem, even momentarily, to a chemist," Professor Remsen Ten Eyck Schenck wrote in "Baker Street Fables." "Holmes might as well have said 'when I had succeeded in tying my boot-lace,' with the air of having triumphed over great obstacles after days of heroic effort."

With this view, Dr. John D. Clark is in complete agreement ("A Chemist's View of Canonical Chemistry"): "There is rarely any difficulty in dissolving a hydrocarbon . . . All you have to do is apply a lighter liquid hydrocarbon, and *voilà!*, you have your solution. If you have ever removed a glob of tar from a fender with a gasoline-soaked rag, you know what I mean."

But Mr. Leon S. Holstein has written ("'7. Knowledge of Chemistry—Profound'"): ". . . it is my understanding, from those versed in the art, that one method of examining unknown organic compounds is to first determine physical properties, one of which is the solubility or insolubility

Our meal was a merry one. Holmes could talk exceedingly well when he chose, and that night he did choose. He appeared to be in a state of nervous exaltation. I have never known him so brilliant. He spoke on a quick succession **138** of subjects—on miracle plays, on mediæval pottery, on **139** Stradivarius violins, on the Buddhism of Ceylon, and on the warships of the future—handling each as though he had made a special study of it. His bright humour marked the reaction from his black depression of the preceding days. Athelney Jones proved to be a sociable soul in his hours of relaxation, **140** and faced his dinner with the air of a *bon vivant.* For myself, I felt elated at the thought that we were nearing the end of our task, and I caught something of Holmes's gaiety. None of us alluded during dinner to the cause which had brought us together.

When the cloth was cleared, Holmes glanced at his watch, **141** and filled up three glasses with port.

'One bumper,' said he, 'to the success of our little expedition. And now it is high time we were off. Have you a pistol, Watson?'

'I have my old service-revolver in my desk.'

'You had best take it, then. It is well to be prepared. I see that the cab is at the door. I ordered it for half-past six.'

It was a little past seven before we reached the Westminster Wharf, and found our launch awaiting us. Holmes eyed it critically.

'Is there anything to mark it as a police-boat?'

'Yes; that green lamp at the side.'

'Then take it off.'

The small change was made, we stepped on board, and the ropes were cast off. Jones, Holmes, and I sat in the stern. There was one man at the rudder, one to tend the engines, and two burly police-inspectors forward.

'Where to?' asked Jones.

'To the Tower. Tell them to stop opposite to Jacobson's Yard.'

Our craft was evidently a very fast one. We shot past the long lines of loaded barges as though they were stationary. Holmes smiled with satisfaction as we overhauled a river steamer and left her behind us.

'We ought to be able to catch anything on the river,' he said.

'Well, hardly that. But there are not many launches to beat us.'

'We shall have to catch the *Aurora*, and she has a name for being a clipper. I will tell you how the land lies, Watson. You recollect how annoyed I was at being baulked by so small a thing?'

'Yes.'

'Well, I gave my mind a thorough rest by plunging into a chemical analysis. One of our greatest statesmen has said that **142** a change of work is the best rest. So it is. When I had suc-**143** ceeded in dissolving the hydrocarbon which I was at work at, I came back to the problem of the Sholtos, and thought the whole matter out again. My boys had been up the river and down the river without result. The launch was not at any landing-stage or wharf, nor had it returned. Yet it could hardly have been scuttled to hide their traces, though that always remained as a possible hypothesis if all else failed. I knew that this man Small had a certain degree of low cunning, but I did not think him capable of anything in the nature of delicate finesse. That is usually a product of higher education. I then reflected that since he had certainly been in London some time—as we had evidence that he maintained a continual watch over Pondicherry Lodge—he could hardly leave at a moment's notice, but would need some little time, if it were only a day, to arrange his affairs. That was the balance of probability, at any rate.'

'It seems to me to be a little weak,' said I: 'it is more probable that he had arranged his affairs before ever he set out upon his expedition.'

'No, I hardly think so. This lair of his would be too valuable a retreat in case of need for him to give it up until he was sure that he could do without it. But a second consideration struck me. Jonathan Small must have felt that the peculiar appearance of his companion, however much he may have top-coated him, would give rise to gossip, and possibly be associated with this Norwood tragedy. He was quite sharp enough to see that. They had started from their head-quarters under cover of darkness, and he would wish to get back before it was broad light. Now, it was past three o'clock, according to Mrs Smith, when they got the boat. It would be quite bright, and people would be about in an hour or so. There-**144** fore, I argued, they did not go very far. They paid Smith well to hold his tongue, reserved his launch for the final escape, and hurried to their lodgings with the treasure-box. In a

in various reagents. The remark in question was merely to convey that whatever compound or admixture he was working on, Holmes had determined that it was soluble in some standard reagent."

144 *in an hour or so*. It would therefore be quite bright, and people would be about, a little past four o'clock on the Tuesday morning. Again, this is a meaningless statement in July. To sum up what we know about this Tuesday: there was fog, according to both Holmes and Watson, and it was a steamy, vaporous day, according to Watson. A half-moon (Watson says) rose well before 11:00 P.M. There was no rain on this day, according to Holmes, and it was a day on which it would have been "quite bright" shortly after 4:00 A.M. For the record, on Tuesday, September 18, 1888, "fog and mist" were "reported locally." No sunshine whatsoever was recorded at Westminster. The moon was two days before the full; it rose at 5:55 P.M. and set at 3:12 A.M. Day broke at 3:43 A.M., so it would certainly have been "quite bright" by 4:00 A.M.

"TO THE TOWER."

The Tower of London, from South Bank, as photographed by G. F. Allen for the *Second Country Life Picture Book of London*, London: Country Life, Ltd., 1953. The turreted and massive White Tower is the oldest part of the fortress. It was begun in the reign of William the Conquerer on a site that the Roman legionaries had used before him.

145 *the Downs*. The anchorage for ships inside the Goodwin Sands just south of the Thames Estuary.

couple of nights, when they had time to see what view the papers took, and whether there was any suspicion, they would make their way under cover of darkness to some ship at
145 Gravesend or in the Downs, where no doubt they had already arranged for passages to America or the Colonies.'

'But the launch? They could not have taken that to their lodgings.'

'Quite so. I argued that the launch must be no great way off, in spite of its invisibility. I then put myself in the place of Small, and looked at it as a man of his capacity would. He would probably consider that to send back the launch or to keep it at a wharf would make pursuit easy if the police did happen to get on his track. How, then, could he conceal the launch and yet have her at hand when wanted? I wondered what I should do myself if I were in his shoes. I could only think of one way of doing it. I might hand the launch over to some boat-builder or repairer, with directions to make a trifling change in her. She would then be removed to his shed or yard, and so be effectually concealed, while at the same time I could have her at a few hours' notice.'

'That seems simple enough.'

'It is just these very simple things which are extremely liable to be overlooked. However, I determined to act on the idea. I started at once in this harmless seaman's rig, and inquired at all the yards down the river. I drew blank at fifteen, but at the sixteenth—Jacobson's— I learned that the *Aurora* had been handed over to them two days ago by a wooden-legged man, with some trivial directions as to her rudder. "There ain't naught amiss with her rudder," said the foreman. "There she lies, with the red streaks." At that moment who should come down but Mordecai Smith, the missing owner! He was rather the worse for liquor. I should not, of course, have known him, but he bellowed out his name and the name of his launch. "I want her tonight at eight o'clock," said he—"eight o'clock sharp, mind, for I have two gentlemen who won't be kept waiting." They had evidently paid him well, for he was very flush of money, chucking shillings about to the men. I followed him some distance, but he subsided into an ale-house; so I went back to the yard, and, happening to pick up one of my boys on the way, I stationed him as a sentry over the launch. He is to stand at the water's edge and wave his handkerchief to us when they start. We shall be lying off in the stream, and it will be a strange thing if we do not take men, treasure and all.'

'You have planned it all very neatly, whether they are the right men or not,' said Jones; 'but if the affair were in my hands I should have had a body of police in Jacobson's Yard, and arrested them when they came down.'

'Which would have been never. This man Small is a pretty shrewd fellow. He would send a scout on ahead, and if anything made him suspicious he would lie snug for another week.'

'But you might have stuck to Mordecai Smith, and so been led to their hiding-place,' said I.

'In that case I should have wasted my day. I think that it is a hundred to one against Smith knowing where they live. As long as he has liquor and good pay, why should he ask questions? They send him messages what to do. No, I thought over every possible course, and this is the best.'

While this conversation had been proceeding, we had been

Our photograph, by G. F. Allen, is from the *Second Country Life Picture Book of London*, London: Country Life, Ltd., 1953. Watson's statement here is the one statement in the entire chronicle which casts any doubt whatsoever upon September: on the Friday that ended the case, sunset—Watson tells us—came a few minutes after seven. On September 1st, sunset would come at 6:44 P.M.; on September 15th it would come at 5:13 P.M.; on September 30th the time would be 5:38 P.M. No one can doubt that Holmes and Watson boarded the police launch "a little past seven" as Watson tells us they did: Holmes says he ordered the cab for half-past six and the launch "to be ready at the Westminster Stairs at seven o'clock." And Holmes tells us that Mordecai Smith ordered *his* launch to be ready "at eight o'clock sharp, mind . . ." In brief, we have only Watson's uncorroborated statement that sunset came shortly after seven o'clock, and not considerably earlier, on that Friday evening; such evidence cannot be allowed to outweigh the heavy Holmesian evidence that the sun rose sometime after five o'clock on the preceding Wednesday morning—before six, surely, and probably, from the conversation recorded by Watson, around 5:45.

shooting the long series of bridges which span the Thames. As we passed the City the last rays of the sun were gilding the cross upon the summit of St Paul's. It was twilight before we reached the Tower.

'That is Jacobson's Yard,' said Holmes, pointing to a bristle of masts and rigging on the Surrey side. 'Cruise gently up and down here under cover of this string of lighters.' He took a pair of night-glasses from his pocket and gazed some time at the shore. 'I see my sentry at his post,' he remarked, 'but no sign of a handkerchief.'

'Suppose we go downstream a short way and lie in wait for them,' said Jones, eagerly.

We were all eager by this time, even the policemen and stokers, who had a very vague idea of what was going forward.

'We have no right to take anything for granted,' Holmes answered. 'It is certainly ten to one that they go downstream, but we cannot be certain. From this point we can see the entrance of the yard, and they can hardly see us. It will be a clear night and plenty of light. We must stay where we are. 146 See how the folk swarm over yonder in the gaslight.'

'They are coming from work in the yard.'

'Dirty-looking rascals, but I suppose everyone has some little immortal spark concealed about him. You would not think it, to look at them. There is no *a priori* probability 147 about it. A strange enigma is man!'

146 *It will be a clear night and plenty of light.* Watson speaks later of the "moon glimmering on the marshland." For the record, the moon on the night of Friday, September 21, 1888, was one day past the full; it rose at 6:57 P.M.

147 a priori. Latin: from the first.

148 *So says the statistician.* "Now, for purposes of comparison, consider exactly what Reade did say," Professor Stephen F. Crocker wrote in "Sherlock Holmes Recommends Winwood Reade":

> All the events which occur upon the earth result from Law: even those actions which are entirely dependent on the caprices of the memory, or the impulse of the passions, are shown by statistics to be, when taken in the gross, entirely independent of the human will. As a single atom, man is an enigma; as a whole, he is a mathematical problem. As an individual, he is a free agent; as a species, the offspring of necessity.

"This passage is clearly the one Holmes had in mind because it is the only one in *The Martyrdom of Man* which resembles the one in *The Sign of the Four*. . . . But a comparison of the Holmes passage with that of Reade shows not only striking resemblances, but also significant differences."

149 *the Pool.* The name given to that part of the Thames between London Bridge and Cuckolds Point.

150 *the West India Docks.* The oldest enclosed docks in London, opened in 1802, the West India Docks lie between Limehouse and Blackwall, to the north of the Isle of Dogs. The three principal basins, the Import Dock, the Export Dock, and the South Dock, are stored principally with frozen mutton, rum, sugar, hops, grain, and hardwood timbers.

151 *the long Deptford Reach.* About a mile long, from the end of Limehouse Reach to Greenwich Ferry.

152 *the Isle of Dogs.* On the left bank of the Thames opposite Greenwich. "An uninviting title euphemistically derived from 'Isle of Ducks,' and applied to what was till lately about the best imitation on a small scale of the Great Dismal Swamp to be found in England. The place, it may be observed *en passant*, was not until late years an island at all, but simply a peninsula jutting out into the river between Limehouse and Blackwall. Just at the beginning of the [nineteenth] century, however, the Corporation, which had long been exercised by the demands of enterprising engineers for permission to cut the river straight and take possession of its old Scamandering bed for docks, took heart of grace, and cut a canal through the neck of the 'unlucky Isle of Doggs,' as Master Pepys hath it, and so opened a short cut for ships bound up and down the river. Apparently, however, the new road was not found satisfactory, for it has long since been closed and sold to the West India Dock Company, who now use it as a timber dock."—*Dickens' Dictionary of the Thames from Its Source to the Nore: An Unconventional Handbook.*

'Someone calls him a soul concealed in an animal,' I suggested.

'Winwood Reade is good upon the subject,' said Holmes. 'He remarks that, while the individual man is an insoluble puzzle, in the aggregate he becomes a mathematical certainty. You can, for example, never foretell what any one man will do, but you can say with precision what an average number will be up to. Individuals vary, but percentages remain constant. **148** So says the statistician. But do I see a handkerchief? Surely there is a white flutter over yonder.'

'Yes, it is your boy,' I cried. 'I can see him plainly.'

'And there is the *Aurora*,' exclaimed Holmes, 'and going like the devil! Full speed ahead, engineer. Make after that launch with the yellow light. By Heaven, I shall never forgive myself if she proves to have the heels of us!'

She had slipped unseen through the yard-entrance and passed behind two or three small craft, so that she had fairly got her speed up before we saw her. Now she was flying down the stream, near in to the shore, going at a tremendous rate. Jones looked gravely at her and shook his head.

'She is very fast,' he said. 'I doubt if we shall catch her.'

'We *must* catch her!' cried Holmes, between his teeth. 'Heap it on, stokers! Make her do all she can! If we burn the boat we must have them!'

We were fairly after her now. The furnaces roared, and the powerful engines whizzed and clanked, like a great metallic heart. Her sharp, steep prow cut through the still river-water and sent two rolling waves to right and to left of us. With every throb of the engines we sprang and quivered like a living thing. One great yellow lantern in our bows threw a long, flickering funnel of light in front of us. Right ahead a dark blur upon the water showed where the *Aurora* lay, and the swirl of white foam behind her spoke of the pace at which she was going. We flashed past barges, steamers, merchant-vessels, in and out, behind this one and round the other. Voices hailed us out of the darkness, but still the *Aurora* thundered on, and still we followed close upon her track.

'Pile it on, men, pile it on!' cried Holmes, looking down into the engine-room, while the fierce glow from below beat upon his eager, aquiline face. 'Get every pound of steam you can.'

'I think we gain a little,' said Jones, with his eyes on the *Aurora*.

'I am sure of it,' said I. 'We shall be up with her in a very few minutes.'

At that moment, however, as our evil fate would have it, a tug with three barges in tow blundered in between us. It was only by putting our helm hard down that we avoided a collision, and before we could round them and recover our way the *Aurora* had gained a good two hundred yards. She was still, however, well in view, and the murky, uncertain twilight was settling into a clear starlit night. Our boilers were strained to their utmost, and the frail shell vibrated and creaked with the fierce energy which was driving us along. **149–150** We had shot through the Pool, past the West India Docks, **151** down the long Deptford Reach, and up again after rounding **152** the Isle of Dogs. The dull blur in front of us resolved itself now clearly enough into the dainty *Aurora*. Jones turned our searchlight upon her, so that we could plainly see the figures upon her deck. One man sat by the stern, with something black between his knees, over which he stooped. Beside him lay a dark mass, which looked like a Newfoundland dog. The boy held the tiller, while against the red glare of the furnace I could see old Smith, stripped to the waist, and shovelling coals for dear life. They may have had some doubt at first as to whether we were really pursuing them, but now as we followed every winding and turning which they took there could no longer be any question about it. At Greenwich we were about three hundred paces behind them. At Blackwall **153** we could not have been more than two hundred and fifty. I have coursed many creatures in many countries during my **154** chequered career, but never did sport give me such a wild thrill as this mad, flying man-hunt down the Thames. Steadily we drew in upon them, yard by yard. In the silence of the night we could hear the panting and clanking of their machinery. The man in the stern still crouched upon the deck, and his arms were moving as though he were busy, while every now and then he would look up and measure with a glance the distance which still separated us. Nearer we came and nearer. Jones yelled to them to stop. We were not more than four boat's lengths behind them, both boats flying at a tremendous pace. It was a clear reach of the river, with Barking Level **155** upon one side and the melancholy Plumstead Marshes upon **156** the other. At our hail the man in the stern sprang up from the deck and shook his two clenched fists at us, cursing the while in a high, cracked voice. He was a good-sized, powerful man, and as he stood poising himself with legs astride, I could see that, from the thigh downwards, there was but a wooden stump upon the right side. At the sound of his strident, angry cries, there was a movement in the huddled bundle upon the deck. It straightened itself into a little black man—the smallest I have ever seen—with a great, misshapen head and a shock of tangled dishevelled hair. Holmes had already drawn his revolver, and I whipped out mine at the sight of this savage, distorted creature. He was wrapped in some sort of a dark ulster or blanket, which left only his face exposed; but that face was enough to give a man a sleepless night. Never have I seen features so deeply marked with all bestiality and cruelty. His small eyes glowed and burned with a sombre light, and his thick lips were writhed back from his teeth, which grinned and chattered at us with half-animal fury.

'Fire if he raises his hand,' said Holmes quietly.

We were within a boat's-length by this time, and almost within touch of our quarry. I can see the two of them now as they stood: the white man with his legs far apart, shrieking out curses, and the unhallowed dwarf with his hideous face, and his strong, yellow teeth gnashing at us in the light of our lantern.

It was well that we had so clear a view of him. Even as we looked he plucked out from under his covering a short, round piece of wood, like a school-ruler, and clapped it to his lips. Our pistols rang out together. He whirled round, threw up his arms, and, with a kind of choking cough, fell sideways into the stream. I caught one glimpse of his venomous, menacing eyes amid the white swirl of the waters. At the same moment the wooden-legged man threw himself upon the rudder and put it hard down, so that his boat made straight in for the southern bank, while we shot past her stern, only

153 *Blackwall.* On the left bank of the Thames from Orchard Wharf to the Isle of Dogs. "Here are the East India Docks, where the principal sailing ships trading with the port of London load and discharge. The visitor to these docks may still inspect some remaining few of the China tea-clippers—now [1892] almost run off the line by fast steamers—and the fine passenger ships trading to the Australasian ports. Adjoining the docks is the spacious ship-building yard of Messrs. Green, and farther down the river are the Trinity House head-quarters, beyond which again are the Royal Victoria and Albert Docks."—*Dickens' Dictionary of the Thames.*

154 *I have coursed many creatures in many countries.* One of the many passages in the Canon which show Watson's keen interest in hunting, as Mr. G. W. Welch has demonstrated in " 'No Mention of the Local Hunt, Watson.' "

155 *Barking Level.* On the left (Essex) bank of the Thames, at the northwest of Barking, more commonly called Tripcock Reach.

156 *Plumpstead Marshes.* Taking their name from the parish of Plumstead, a southeastern suburb of London. Until the middle of the nineteenth century the marshes formed a great alluvial deposit containing many thousands acres of land, five miles in length and one and a half miles wide, a hotbed of malaria.

clearing her by a few feet. We were round after her in an
instant, but she was already nearly at the bank. It was a wild
and desolate place, where the moon glimmered upon a wide
expanse of marsh-land, with pools of stagnant water and beds
of decaying vegetation. The launch, with a dull thud, ran up
upon the mud-bank, with her bow in the air and her stern
flush with the water. The fugitive sprang out, but his stump
instantly sank its whole length into the sodden soil. In vain
he struggled and writhed. Not one step could he possibly take
either forwards or backwards. He yelled in impotent rage, and
kicked frantically into the mud with his other foot; but his
struggles only bored his wooden pin the deeper into the sticky
bank. When we brought our launch alongside he was so
firmly anchored that it was only by throwing the end of a rope
over his shoulders that we were able to haul him out, and, to
drag him, like some evil fish over our side. The two Smiths,
father and son, sat sullenly in their launch, but came aboard
meekly enough when commanded. The *Aurora* herself we
hauled off and made fast to our stern. A solid iron chest of
Indian workmanship stood upon the deck. This, there could
be no question, was the same that had contained the ill-
omened treasure of the Sholtos. There was no key, but it was
of considerable weight, so we transferred it carefully to our
own little cabin. As we steamed slowly upstream again, we
flashed our searchlight in every direction, but there was
no sign of the Islander. Somewhere in the dark ooze at the
bottom of the Thames lie the bones of that strange visitor to
our shores.

'See here,' said Holmes, pointing to the wooden hatchway.
'We were hardly quick enough with our pistols.' There, sure
enough, just behind where we had been standing, stuck one
of those murderous darts which we knew so well. It must have
whizzed between us at the instant we fired. Holmes smiled at
it and shrugged his shoulders in his easy fashion, but I confess
that it turned me sick to think of the horrible death which
had passed so close to us that night.

11 ◆ THE GREAT AGRA TREASURE

Our captive sat in the cabin opposite to the iron box which
he had done so much and waited so long to gain. He was a
sunburned, reckless-eyed fellow, with a network of lines and
wrinkles all over his mahogany features, which told of a hard,
open-air life. There was a singular prominence about his
bearded chin which marked a man who was not to be easily
turned from his purpose. His age may have been fifty or thereabouts, for his black, curly hair was thickly shot with grey.
His face in repose was not an unpleasing one, though his
heavy brows and aggressive chin gave him, as I had lately seen,
a terrible expression when moved to anger. He sat now with
his handcuffed hands upon his lap, and his head sunk upon

his breast, while he looked with his keen, twinkling eyes at the box which had been the cause of his ill-doings. It seemed to me that there was more sorrow than anger in his rigid and contained countenance. Once he looked up at me with a gleam of something like humour in his eyes.

'Well, Jonathan Small,' said Holmes, lighting a cigar, 'I am sorry that it has come to this.'

'And so am I, sir,' he answered, frankly. 'I don't believe that I can swing over the job. I give you my word on the Book that I never raised hand against Mr Sholto. It was that little hell-hound Tonga who shot one of his cursed darts into him. I had no part in it, sir. I was as grieved as if it had been my blood-relation. I welted the little devil with the slack end of the rope for it, but it was done, and I could not undo it again.'

'Have a cigar,' said Holmes; 'and you had best take a pull out of my flask, for you are very wet. How could you expect so small and weak a man as this black fellow to overpower Mr Sholto and hold him while you were climbing the rope?'

'You seem to know as much about it as if you were there, sir. The truth is that I hoped to find the room clear. I knew the habits of the house pretty well, and it was the time when Mr Sholto usually went down to his supper. I shall make no secret of the business. The best defence that I can make is just the simple truth. Now, if it had been the old major I would have swung for him with a light heart. I would have thought no more of knifing him than of smoking this cigar. But it's cursed hard that I should be lagged over this young Sholto, with whom I had no quarrel whatever.'

'You are under the charge of Mr Athelney Jones, of Scotland Yard. He is going to bring you up to my rooms, and I shall ask you for a true account of the matter. You must make a clean breast of it, for if you do I hope that I may be of use to you. I think I can prove that the poison acts so quickly that the man was dead before ever you reached the room.'

'That he was, sir. I never got such a turn in my life as when I saw him grinning at me with his head on his shoulder as I climbed through the window. It fairly shook me, sir. I'd have half killed Tonga for it if he had not scrambled off. That was how he came to leave his club, and some of his darts, too, as he tells me, which I dare say helped to put you on our track; though how you kept on it is more than I can tell. I don't feel no malice against you for it. But it does seem a queer thing,' he added, with a bitter smile, 'that I, who have a fair claim to half a million of money, should spend the first half of my life building a breakwater in the Andamans, and am like to spend the other half digging drains at Dartmoor. It **157** was an evil day for me when first I clapped eyes upon the merchant Achmet and had to do with the Agra treasure, which never brought anything but a curse yet upon the man who owned it. To him, it brought murder, to Major Sholto it brought fear and guilt, to me it has meant slavery for life.'

At this moment Athelney Jones thrust his face and shoulders into the tiny cabin.

'Quite a family party,' he remarked. 'I think I shall have a pull at that flask, Holmes. Well, I think we may all congratulate each other. Pity we didn't take the other alive; but there was no choice. I say, Holmes, you must confess that you cut it rather fine. It was all we could do to overhaul her.'

"IT WAS THAT LITTLE HELL-HOUND TONGA WHO SHOT ONE OF HIS CURSED DARTS INTO HIM."

One of the eight superb pictures drawn by F. H. Townsend for the "Souvenir Edition" of *The Sign of the Four* published by George Newnes in 1903.

157 *Dartmoor*. That is, at Princetown Prison, in the wild upland country of South Devon. The prison was first built in 1809 to receive French prisoners captured in the Napoleonic Wars. (Conan Doyle has his Napoleonic D'Artagnan, the Brigadier Etienne Gerard, escape from Princetown Prison in the short story called "How the King Held the Brigadier" in *Exploits of Gerard*.) There are exciting allusions to Princetown Prison in our next adventure, *The Hound of the Baskervilles*.

158 *Vauxhall Bridge.* An iron structure of nine spans, built in 1811–1816 to connect Kennington with Pimlico.

159 *the obliging inspector.* "An obliging inspector indeed!," Mr. Ronald S. Bonn wrote in his prize-winning essay, "The Problem of the Postulated Doctor." "Would any inspector in London so have obliged any civilian in the world than this one—the one man alive whose conduct bore the imprimateur of Sherlock Holmes' friendship? And what must that obliging inspector's feelings have been, some time later—quite a long time later, Watson admits—when the doctor reappeared and cooly showed him an empty box?"

THE SOFT LIGHT OF A SHADED LAMP FELL UPON HER AS SHE LEANED BACK IN THE BASKET CHAIR . . .

One of the very few existing portraits of Miss Mary Morstan, by an as-yet-unidentified artist, from *Stories of Sherlock Holmes*, Vol. I, New York: Harper & Brothers, 1904.

'All is well that ends well,' said Holmes. 'But I certainly did not know that the *Aurora* was such a clipper.'

'Smith says she is one of the fastest launches on the river, and that if he had had another man to help him with the engines we should never have caught her. He swears he knew nothing of this Norwood business.'

'Neither he did,' cried our prisoner—'not a word. I chose his launch because I heard that she was a flier. We told him nothing; but we paid him well, and he was to get something handsome if we reached our vessel, the *Esmeralda*, at Gravesend, outward bound for the Brazils.'

'Well, if he has done no wrong we shall see that no wrong comes to him. If we are pretty quick in catching our men, we are not so quick in condemning them.' It was amusing to notice how the consequential Jones was already beginning to give himself airs on the strength of the capture. From the slight smile which played over Sherlock Holmes's face, I could see that the speech had not been lost upon him.

158 'We will be at Vauxhall Bridge presently,' said Jones, ' and shall land you, Dr Watson, with the treasure-box. I need hardly tell you that I am taking a very grave responsibility upon myself in doing this. It is most irregular; but of course an agreement is an agreement. I must, however, as a matter of duty, send an inspector with you, since you have so valuable a charge. You will drive, no doubt?'

'Yes, I shall drive.'

'It is a pity there is no key, that we may make an inventory first. You will have to break it open. Where is the key, my man?'

'At the bottom of the river,' said Small shortly.

'Hum! There was no use your giving this unnecessary trouble. We have had work enough already through you. However, doctor, I need not warn you to be careful. Bring the box back with you to the Baker Street rooms. You will find us there, on our way to the station.'

They landed me at Vauxhall, with my heavy iron box, and with a bluff, genial inspector as my companion. A quarter of an hour's drive brought us to Mrs Cecil Forrester's. The servant seemed surprised at so late a visitor. Mrs Cecil Forrester was out for the evening, she explained, and likely to be very late. Miss Morstan, however, was in the drawing-room; so to the drawing-room I went, box in hand, leaving the obliging

159 inspector in the cab.

She was seated by the open window, dressed in some sort of white diaphanous material, with a little touch of scarlet at the neck and waist. The soft light of a shaded lamp fell upon her as she leaned back in the basket chair, playing over her sweet, grave face, and tinting with a dull, metallic sparkle the rich coils of her luxuriant hair. One white arm and hand drooped over the side of the chair, and her whole pose and figure spoke of an absorbing melancholy. At the sound of my footfall she sprang to her feet, however, and a bright flush of surprise and of pleasure coloured her pale cheeks.

'I heard a cab drive up,' she said. 'I thought that Mrs Forrester had come back very early, but I never dreamed that it might be you. What news have you brought me?'

'I have brought something better than news,' said I, putting down the box upon the table and speaking jovially and boisterously, though my heart was heavy within me. 'I have brought you something which is worth all the news in the world. I have brought you a fortune.'

She glanced at the iron box.

'Is that the treasure, then?' she asked, coolly enough.

'Yes, this is the great Agra treasure. Half of it is yours and half is Thaddeus Sholto's. You will have a couple of hundred thousand each. Think of that! an annuity of ten thousand pounds. There will be few richer young ladies in England. Is it not glorious?'

I think that I must have been rather overacting my delight, and that she detected a hollow ring in my congratulations, for I saw her eyebrows rise a little, and she glanced at me curiously.

'If I have it,' said she, 'I owe it to you.'

'No, no,' I answered, 'not to me, but to my friend Sherlock Holmes. With all the will in the world, I could never have followed up a clue which has taxed even his analytical genius. As it was, we very nearly lost it at the last moment.'

'Pray sit down and tell me all about it, Dr Watson,' said she.

I narrated briefly what had occurred since I had seen her last. Holmes's new method of search, the discovery of the *Aurora*, the appearance of Athelney Jones, our expedition in the evening, and the wild chase down the Thames. She listened with parted lips and shining eyes to my recital of our adventures. When I spoke of the dart which had so narrowly missed us, she turned so white that I feared that she was about to faint.

'It is nothing,' she said, as I hastened to pour her out some water. 'I am all right again. It was a shock to me to hear that I had placed my friends in such horrible peril.'

'That is all over,' I answered. 'It was nothing. I will tell you no more gloomy details. Let us turn to something brighter. There is the treasure. What could be brighter than that? I got leave to bring it with me, thinking that it would interest you to be the first to see it.'

'It would be of the greatest interest to me,' she said. There was no eagerness in her voice, however. It had struck her, doubtless, that it might seem ungracious upon her part to be indifferent to a prize which had cost so much to win.

'What a pretty box!' she said, stooping over it. 'This is Indian work, I suppose?'

'Yes; it is Benares metal-work.'

'And so heavy!' she exclaimed, trying to raise it. 'The box alone must be of some value. Where is the key?'

'Small threw it into the Thames,' I answered. 'I must borrow Mrs Forrester's poker.'

There was in the front a thick and broad hasp, wrought in the image of a sitting Buddha. Under this I thrust the end of the poker and twisted it outward as a lever. The hasp sprang open with a loud snap. With trembling fingers I flung back the lid. We both stood gazing in astonishment. The box was empty!

No wonder that it was heavy. The iron-work was two-thirds of an inch thick all round. It was massive, well made, and solid, like a chest constructed to carry things of great price, but not one shred or crumb of metal or jewellery lay within it. It was absolutely and completely empty.

'The treasure is lost,' said Miss Morstan, calmly.

As I listened to the words and realized what they meant, a great shadow seemed to pass from my soul. I did not know

160 *as truly as ever a man loved a woman.* "Note the restraint of [this] avowal," Mr. Nathan L. Bengis wrote in "A Scandal in Baker Street." Watson "would not commit himself to say what we can easily imagine him to have declared to [an earlier love]: 'No man ever loved a woman as I love you.' . . . It is easy to see now that [Mary Morstan], jealous as she was, must have felt that in Watson's affections she was always second to 'that other.'"

'THERE ARE NO RUPEES FOR YOU THIS JOURNEY.'

From A. Carson Simpson's *Numismatics in the Canon,* Part II, we show the four types of rupee in circulation up to the time of *The Sign of the Four: 43* is the East India Company Surat mint sicca (no date); *44* is the East India Company William IV rupee of 1834; *44a* is the East India Company Victoria, bare head rupee of 1849, obverse only; *45* is the East India Company Victoria, crowned head rupee of 1862.

how this Agra treasure had weighed me down, until now that it was finally removed. It was selfish, no doubt, disloyal, wrong, but I could realize nothing save that the golden barrier was gone from between us.

'Thank God!' I ejaculated from my very heart.

She looked at me with a quick, questioning smile.

'Why do you say that?' she asked.

'Because you are within my reach again,' I said, taking her hand. She did not withdraw it. 'Because I love you, Mary, as **160** truly as ever a man loved a woman. Because this treasure, these riches, sealed my lips. Now that they are gone I can tell you how I love you. That is why I said, "Thank God."'

'Then I say "Thank God," too,' she whispered, as I drew her to my side.

Whoever had lost a treasure, I knew that night that I had gained one.

12   THE STRANGE STORY OF JONATHAN SMALL

A very patient man was that inspector in the cab, for it was a weary time before I rejoined him. His face clouded over when I showed him the empty box.

'There goes the reward!' said he, gloomily. 'Where there is no money there is no pay. This night's work would have been worth a tenner each to Sam Brown and me if the treasure had been there.'

'Mr Thaddeus Sholto is a rich man,' I said; 'he will see that you are rewarded, treasure or no.'

The inspector shook his head despondently, however.

'It's a bad job,' he repeated; 'and so Mr Athelney Jones will think.'

His forecast proved to be correct, for the detective looked blank enough when I got to Baker Street and showed him the empty box. They had only just arrived, Holmes, the prisoner, and he, for they had changed their plans so far as to report themselves at a station upon the way. My companion lounged in his arm-chair with his usual listless expression, while Small sat stolidly opposite to him with his wooden leg cocked over his sound one. As I exhibited the empty box he leaned back in his chair and laughed aloud.

'This is your doing, Small,' said Athelney Jones, angrily.

'Yes, I have put it away where you shall never lay hand on it,' he cried, exultantly. 'It is my treasure, and if I can't have the loot I'll take darned good care that no one else does. I tell you that no living man has any right to it, unless it is three men who are in the Andaman convict-barracks and myself. I know now that I cannot have the use of it, and I know that they cannot. I have acted all through for them as much as for myself. It's been the sign of four with us always. Well, I know that they would have had me do just what I have done, and throw the treasure into the Thames rather than let it go to kith or kin of Sholto or Morstan. It was not to make them rich that we did for Achmet. You'll find the treasure where the key is, and where little Tonga is. When I saw that your launch must catch us, I put the loot away in a safe place. There are no rupees for you this journey.'

'You are deceiving us, Small,' said Athelney Jones, sternly. 'If you had wished to throw the treasure into the Thames, it would have been easier for you to have thrown box and all.'

'Easier for me to throw, and easier for you to recover,' he answered, with a shrewd, side-long look. 'The man that was clever enough to hunt me down is clever enough to pick an iron box from the bottom of a river. Now that they are scattered over five miles or so, it may be a harder job. It went to my heart to do it, though. I was half mad when you came up with us. However, there's no good grieving over it. I've had ups in my life, and I've had downs, but I've learned not to cry over spilled milk.'

'This is a very serious matter, Small,' said the detective. 'If you had helped justice, instead of thwarting it in this way, you would have had a better chance at your trial.'

'Justice!' snarled the ex-convict. 'A pretty justice! Whose loot is this, if it is not ours? Where is the justice that I should give it up to those who have never earned it? Look how I have earned it! Twenty long years in that fever-ridden swamp, all **161** day at work under the mangrove-tree, all night chained up in the filthy convict-huts, bitten by mosquitoes, racked with ague, bullied by every cursed black-faced policeman who loved to take it out of a white man. That was how I earned the Agra treasure, and you talk to me of justice because I cannot bear to feel that I have paid this price only that another may enjoy it! I would rather swing a score of times, or have one of Tonga's darts in my hide, than live in a convict's cell and feel that another man is at his ease in a palace with the money that should be mine.'

Small had dropped his mask of stoicism, and all this came out in a wild whirl of words, while his eyes blazed and the handcuffs clanked together with the impassioned movement of his hands. I could understand, as I saw the fury and the passion of the man, that it was no groundless or unnatural terror which had possessed Major Sholto when he first learned that the injured convict was upon his track.

'You forget that we know nothing of all this,' said Holmes, quietly. 'We have not heard your story, and we cannot tell how far justice may originally have been on your side.'

'Well, sir, you have been very fair-spoken to me, though I can see that I have you to thank that I have these bracelets upon my wrists. Still, I bear no grudge for that. It is all fair and above-board. If you want to hear my story, I have no wish to hold it back. What I say to you is God's truth, every word of it. Thank you, you can put the glass beside me here, and I'll put my lips to it if I am dry.

'I am a Worcestershire man myself, born near Pershore. I **162** dare say you would find a heap of Smalls living there now if you were to look. I have often thought of taking a look round there, but the truth is that I was never much of a credit to the family, and I doubt if they would be so very glad to see me. They were all steady, chapel-going folk, small farmers, well known and respected over the country-side, while I was always a bit of a rover. At last, however, when I was about eighteen, I gave them no more trouble, for I got into a mess over a girl,

161 *Twenty long years in that fever-ridden swamp.* "The relief of Agra by Greathed was, as a matter of history, on 10th October, 1857, and as the Mutiny was virtually over before Small was arrested, his trial was certainly not much earlier than 1858," Mr. T. S. Blakeney wrote in *Sherlock Holmes: Fact or Fiction?* "He was in prison first in Agra, then Madras, before he proceeded to the Andamans, where he would arrive about 1860. Add his twenty years, plus the considerable time on his journey to England (as described), plus the time taken in locating Major Sholto, and we can see that the spring of 1882 as the date of the latter's death is just about right. It is true Small speaks of arriving in England 'some three or four years ago,' but he is not attempting chronological accuracy."

162 *Pershore.* Worcestershire is a county in West Central England; mostly hilly, it has famous orchards and much sheep pasturage. There are rich iron and coal deposits in the northern part. Its city of Worcester is the home of the world-famous "Worcestershire sauce." Pershore, Small's home town, is an ancient market village.

163 *taking the Queen's shilling*. The pay of Tommy Atkins at that time was a shilling a day:

> Jolly good pay
> Lucky to touch it
> A shilling a day.

164 *the 3rd Buffs*. "This is a real and very famous regiment," Mrs. Crighton Sellars wrote in "Dr. Watson and the British Army," "officially known as the Buffs (East Kent Regiment) consisting of the Third Foot. It is one of the oldest in the British Army, having its origin at the time of Queen Elizabeth [I]. . . . It is hard to believe that [Small] really belonged to this regiment, because it was sent to the Crimea in 1855—too late for Balaklava and Inkerman, but in time for the famous assault on the Redan—and stayed there until the Mutiny in India was over. The Buffs' previous service in India was under General Grey at Punniar against the Mahrattas in 1843, and I doubt if Small went there with them at that date, particularly as they had not been in England before that, but went to India from New South Wales."

165 *John Holder*. Mr. T. S. Blakeney, in "Thoughts on *The Sign of the Four*," suggests that John Holder "was a younger brother of Alexander Holder, the banker in 'The Adventure of the Beryl Coronet.' John Holder was, perhaps, the black sheep of a rather odd family, for not only was Alexander Holder temperamental till it could verge on madness . . . , but his son was a ne'er-do-well, and his niece's taste in men friends left a lot to be desired. I seem to see John Holder as the prototype of Kipling's Gentleman Ranker." And he added: "If this association between the cases of *The Sign of the Four* and 'The Beryl Coronet' is correct, it may not be the only one. I owe to our lamented friend, Gavin Brend, the excellent suggestion that the wooden-legged tradesman at whom Major Sholto once fired a revolver was none other than Francis Prosper, the fiancé of Lucy Parr, the maid at Fairbank, Streatham, the home of Alexander Holder. Streatham and Norwood are adjacent suburbs of London."

166 *the great mutiny*. "The Sepoy rebellion against British administration in India, 1857–1859," the late Christopher Morley wrote in *Sherlock Holmes and Dr. Watson: A Textbook of Friendship*. "Sepoys were native Indian troops. General McLeod Innes, V.C., in his history *The Sepoy Revolt* (1897) includes among immediate causes of the mutiny: 1) reduction of the British garrisons on account of the Crimean War; 2) an alleged prophecy, widely spread among superstitious natives, that British rule would come to an end in 100 years from Clive's conquest of Bengal in 1757; 3) equally superstitious dread of the railways and telegraphs being built; and 4) injudicious disregard of Hindu religious tenets. For instance,

163–164 and could only get out of it again by taking the Queen's shilling and joining the 3rd Buffs, which was just starting for India.

'I wasn't destined to do much soldiering, however. I had just got past the goose-step, and learned to handle my musket, when I was fool enough to go swimming in the Ganges. **165** Luckily for me, my company sergeant, John Holder, was in the water at the same time, and he was one of the finest swimmers in the Service. A crocodile took me, just as I was half-way across, and nipped off my right leg as clean as a surgeon could have done it, just above the knee. What with the shock and the loss of blood, I fainted, and should have been drowned if Holder had not caught hold of me and paddled for the bank. I was five months in hospital over it, and when at last I was able to limp out of it with this timber toe strapped to my stump I found myself invalided out of the army and unfitted for any active occupation.

'I was, as you can imagine, pretty down on my luck at this time, for I was a useless cripple, though not yet in my twentieth year. However, my misfortune soon proved to be a blessing in disguise. A man named Abel White, who had come out there as an indigo-planter, wanted an overseer to look after his coolies and keep them up to their work. He happened to be a friend of our colonel's who had taken an interest in me since the accident. To make a long story short, the colonel recommended me strongly for the post, and, as the work was mostly to be done on horseback, my leg was no great obstacle, for I had enough knee left to keep a good grip on the saddle. What I had to do was to ride over the plantation, to keep an eye on the men as they worked, and to report the idlers. The pay was fair, I had comfortable quarters, and altogether I was content to spend the remainder of my life in indigo-planting. Mr Abel White was a kind man, and he would often drop into my little shanty and smoke a pipe with me, for white folk out there feel their hearts warm to each other as they never do here at home.

'Well, I was never in luck's way long. Suddenly, without a **166** note of warning, the great mutiny broke upon us. One month India lay as still and peaceful, to all appearance, as Surrey or Kent; the next there were two hundred thousand black devils let loose, and the country was a perfect hell. Of course you know all about it, gentlemen—a deal more than I do, very like, since reading is not in my line. I only know what I saw with my own eyes. Our plantation was at a place called Muttra, near the border of the North-west Provinces. Night after night the whole sky was alight with the burning bungalows, and day after day we had small companies of Europeans passing through our estate with their wives and children, on their way to Agra, where were the nearest troops. Mr. Abel White was an obstinate man. He had it in his head that the affair had been exaggerated, and that it would blow over as suddenly as it had sprung up. There he sat on his **167** verandah, drinking whisky-pegs and smoking cheroots, while the country was in a blaze about him. Of course, we stuck by him, I and Dawson, who, with his wife, used to do the bookwork and the managing. Well, one fine day the crash came. I had been away on a distant plantation, and was riding slowly home in the evening, when my eye fell upon something **168** all huddled together at the bottom of a steep nullah. I rode down to see what it was, and the cold struck through my heart when I found it was Dawson's wife, all cut into ribbons and half-eaten by jackals and native dogs. A little farther up the road Dawson himself was lying on his face, quite dead, with an empty revolver in his hand, and four Sepoys lying across each other in front of him. I reined up my horse, wondering which way I should turn; but at that moment I saw thick smoke curling up from Abel White's bungalow, and the flames beginning to burst through the roof. I knew then that I could do my employer no good, but would only throw my own life away if I meddled in the matter. From where I stood I could see hundreds of the black fiends, with their red coats still on their backs dancing and howling round the burning house. Some of them pointed at me, and a couple of bullets sang past my head: so I broke away across the paddy-fields, **169** and found myself late at night safe within the walls at Agra.

'As it proved, however, there was no great safety here, either. The whole country was up like a swarm of bees. Wherever the English could collect in little bands, they held just the ground that their guns commanded. Everywhere else they were helpless fugitives. It was a fight of the millions against the hundreds; and the cruellest part of it was that these men that we fought against, foot, horse, and gunners, were our own picked troops, whom we had taught and trained, handling our own weapons and blowing our own bugle-calls. At Agra there were the 3rd Bengal Fusiliers, some **170** Sikhs, two troops of horse, and a battery of artillery. A volunteer corps of clerks and merchants had been formed, and this I joined, wooden leg and all. We went out to meet the rebels at Shahgunge early in July, and we beat them back for a time, but **171** our powder gave out, and we had to fall back upon the city.

'Nothing but the worst news came to us from every side—which is not to be wondered at, for if you look at the map you will see that we were right in the heart of it. Lucknow is rather better than a hundred miles to the east, and Cawnpore about as far to the south. From every point on the compass there was nothing but torture and murder and outrage.

'The city of Agra is a great place, swarming with fanatics and fierce devil-worshippers of all sorts. Our handful of men were lost among the narrow, winding streets. Our leader moved across the river, therefore, and took up his position in the old fort of Agra. I don't know if any of you gentlemen have ever read or heard anything of that old fort. It is a very queer place—the queerest that ever I was in, and I have been in some rum corners, too. First of all, it is enormous in size. I should think that the enclosure must be acres and acres. There is a modern part, which took all our garrison, women, children, stores, and everything else, with plenty of room over. But the modern part is nothing like the size of the old quarter, where nobody goes, and which is given over to the scorpions and the centipedes. It is all full of great, deserted halls, and winding passages, and long corridors twisting in and out, so that it is easy enough for folk to get lost in it. For this reason it was seldom that anyone went into it, though now and again a party with torches might go exploring.

'The river washes along the front of the old fort, and so protects it, but on the sides and behind there are many doors, and these had to be guarded, of course, in the old quarter as well as in that which was actually held by our troops. We were

a new rifle cartridge was introduced which was lubricated with animal grease; the cartridge cap had to be bitten off by the soldiers and this meant contamination to Hindus and Mohammedans. Also a new Enlistment Act was rumored to make it necessary for native troops to cross the ocean, which they called the Black Water and regarded with horror. The tragic massacre of European civilians at Cawnpore, the desperate defenses of Delhi and Lucknow, have become legendary. Most boys of my generation first read of them in the long series of historical juveniles written by good old G. A. Henty, 1832–1902."

167 *whisky-pegs*. Anglo-Indian slang for a highball; whisky or brandy with soda. The usual explanation for the name is that each drink is a peg in your coffin.

168 *nullah*. Hindu word for a ravine or valley.

169 *paddy-fields*. Rice-fields, from *padi*, a Malayan word for rice.

170 *the 3rd Bengal Fusiliers*. "By which," Mrs. Crighton Sellars wrote in "Dr. Watson and the British Army," Small "probably meant (or else Watson deliberately misquotes him) the Third Bengal Infantry—the famous *Guttrieka-pultan*—which stood firm and loyal during the Mutiny."

171 *Shahgunge*. Between Lucknow and Cawnpore.

172 *Punjaubees.* Small evidently used—and Watson accepted—"Punjaubee" (Punjabi) and "Sikh" as interchangeable terms, which of course they are not.

173 *Chilian Wallah.* This battle, fought January 13, 1849, won for Britain the territory of the Punjab.

174 *bhang.* Indian hemp, smoked or chewed as a narcotic.

short-handed, with hardly men enough to man the angles of the building and to serve the guns. It was impossible for us, therefore, to station a strong guard at every one of the innumerable gates. What we did was to organize a central guard-house in the middle of the fort, and to leave each gate under the charge of one white man and two or three natives. I was selected to take charge during certain hours of the night of a small isolated door upon the south-west side of the building. Two Sikh troopers were placed under my command, and I was instructed if anything went wrong to fire my musket, when I might rely upon help coming at once from the central guard. As the guard was a good two hundred paces away, however, and as the space between was cut up into a labyrinth of passages and corridors, I had great doubts as to whether they could arrive in time to be of any use in case of an actual attack.

'Well, I was pretty proud at having this small command given me, since I was a raw recruit, and a game-legged one at **172** that. For two nights I kept the watch with my Punjaubees. They were tall, fierce-looking chaps, Mahomet Singh and Abdullah Khan by name, both old fighting-men, who had **173** borne arms against us at Chilian Wallah. They could talk English pretty well, but I could get little out of them. They preferred to stand together and jabber all night in their queer Sikh lingo. For myself, I used to stand outside the gateway looking down on the broad, winding river and on the twinkling lights of the great city. The beating of drums, the rattle of tom-toms, and the yells and howls of the rebels, drunk with **174** opium and with bhang, were enough to remind us all night of our dangerous neighbours across the stream. Every two hours the officer of the night used to come round to all the posts, to make sure that all was well.

'The third night of my watch was dark and dirty, with a small, driving rain. It was dreary work standing in the gateway hour after hour in such weather. I tried again and again to make my Sikhs talk, but without much success. At two in the morning the rounds passed, and broke for a moment the weariness of the night. Finding that my companions would not be led into conversation, I took out my pipe, and laid down my musket to strike a match. In an instant the two Sikhs were upon me. One of them snatched my firelock up and levelled it at my head, while the other held a great knife to my throat and swore between his teeth that he would plunge it into me if I moved a step.

'My first thought was that these fellows were in league with the rebels, and that this was the beginning of an assault. If our door were in the hands of the Sepoys the place must fall, and the women and children be treated as they were in Cawnpore. Maybe you gentlemen think that I am just making out a case for myself, but I give you my word that when I thought of that, though I felt the point of the knife at my throat, I opened my mouth with the intention of giving a scream, if it was my last one, which might alarm the main guard. The man who held me seemed to know my thoughts; for, even as I braced myself to it, he whispered: "Don't make a noise. The fort is safe enough. There are no rebel dogs on this side of the river." There was the ring of truth in what he said, and I knew that if I raised my voice I was a dead man. I could read it in the fellow's brown eyes. I waited, therefore, in silence, to see what it was that they wanted from me.

' "Listen to me, sahib," said the taller and fiercer of the pair, the one whom they called Abdullah Khan. "You must either be with us now, or you must be silenced for ever. The thing is too great a one for us to hesitate. Either you are heart and soul with us on your oath on the cross of the Christians, or your body this night shall be thrown into the ditch, and we shall pass over to our brothers in the rebel army. There is no middle way. Which is it to be—death or life? We can only give you three minutes to decide, for the time is passing, and all must be done before the rounds come again."

' "How can I decide?" said I. "You have not told me what you want of me. But I tell you now that if it is anything against the safety of the fort I will have no truck with it, so you can drive home your knife, and welcome."

' "It is nothing against the fort," said he. "We only ask you to do that which your countrymen come to this land for. We ask you to be rich. If you will be one of us this night, we will swear to you upon the naked knife, and by the threefold oath, which no Sikh was ever known to break, that you shall have your fair share of the loot. A quarter of the treasure shall be yours. We can say no fairer."

' "But what is the treasure, then?" I asked. "I am as ready to be rich as you can be, if you will but show me how it can be done."

' "You will swear, then," said he, "by the bones of your father, by the honour of your mother, by the cross of your faith, to raise no hand and speak no word against us, either now or afterwards?"

' "I will swear it," I answered, "provided that the fort is not endangered."

' "Then, my comrade and I will swear that you shall have a quarter of the treasure, which shall be equally divided among the four of us."

' "There are but three," said I.

' "No; Dost Akbar must have his share. We can tell the **175** tale to you while we await them. Do you stand at the gate, Mahomet Singh, and give notice of their coming. The thing stands thus, sahib, and I tell it to you because I know that an oath is binding upon a Feringhee, and that we may trust you. **176** Had you been a lying Hindoo, though you had sworn by all the gods in their false temples, your blood would have been upon the knife and your body in the water. But the Sikh knows the Englishman, and the Englishman knows the Sikh. Hearken, then, to what I have to say.

' "There is a rajah in the northern provinces who has much wealth, though his lands are small. Much has come to him from his father, and more still he has set by himself, for he is of a low nature, and hoards his gold rather than spend it. When the troubles broke out he would be friends both with the lion and the tiger—with the Sepoy and with the Company's Raj. Soon, however, it seemed to him that the white men's day was come, for through all the land he could hear of nothing but of their death and their overthrow. Yet, being a careful man, he made such plans that, come what might, half at least of his treasure should be left to him. That which was in gold and silver he kept by him in the vaults of his palace; but the most precious stones and the choicest pearls that he had he put in an iron box, and sent it by a trusty servant, who, under the guise of a merchant, should take it to

175 *Dost Akbar.* "What sort of Sikhs were these . . . who rejoiced in such names as Mahomet Singh, Dost Akbar and Abdullah Khan?" Mr. T. S. Blakeney asked in "Thoughts on *The Sign of the Four*." "Do Sikhs sport such Mohammedan names? The name 'Singh' is the only admissable one of the lot. Moreover, just as we have seen a curious parallel between the heads of Thaddeus Sholto and a practitioner of black magic known to the late Sir Arthur Conan Doyle, so I may point to the odd fact that, just as these three Sikhs have names that Sikhs would not own, so in Conan Doyle's 'The Mystery of Cloomber' there are three Buddhists—Ram Singh, Lal Hoomi and Mowdar Khan—who have names that assuredly no Buddhist priests would possess."

And Dr. Andrew Boyd has added ("Dr. Watson's Dupe"): "Two Mohammedan names and one bizarre Mohammedan-Sikh hybrid. No educated man with years of service in the Indian Army could possibly have recorded them, even if he was recording another man's garbled narrative, without comment. For those who are not familiar with the way that Indian personal names are strictly related to religion, one may explain that Watson might as well have claimed a knowledge of Scotland and then set down a tale about three simple Highland soldiers named Venizelos, Vasco de Gama, and Voroshilov."

176 *Feringhee* Indian term for a European; said to be the native mispronunciation of the name "Frank."

"Undoubtedly it was . . . Brazilian moidores with which Small became familiar in India," the late A. Carson Simpson wrote in *Numismatics in the Canon*, Part II. Shown here are: *46*, the 1816 João, Prince Regent; *46a*, the 1822 João VI, reverse only; *47*, the 1826 Pedro I, Bahia mint; *47a*, the 1833 Pedro II, Rio de Janeiro mint, obverse only.

the fort at Agra, there to lie until the land is at peace. Thus, if the rebels won he would have his money; but if the Company conquered, his jewels would be saved to him. Having thus divided his hoard, he threw himself into the cause of the Sepoys, since they were strong upon his borders. By his doing this, mark you, sahib, his property becomes the due of those who have been true to their salt.

'"This pretended merchant, who travels under the name of Achmet, is now in the city of Agra, and desires to gain his way into the fort. He has with him as travelling-companion my foster-brother, Dost Akbar, who knows his secret. Dost Akbar has promised this night to lead him to a side-postern of the fort, and has chosen this one for his purpose. Here he will come presently and here he will find Mahomet Singh and myself awaiting him. The place is lonely, and none shall know of his coming. The world shall know of the merchant, Achmet, no more, but the great treasure of the rajah shall be divided among us. What say you to it, sahib?"

'In Worcestershire the life of a man seems a great and sacred thing; but it is very different when there is fire and blood all round you, and you have been used to meeting death at every turn. Whether Achmet, the merchant, lived or died was a thing as light as air to me, but at the talk about the treasure my heart turned to it, and I thought of what I might do in the old country with it, and how my folk would stare when they saw their ne'er-do-well coming back with his pockets full of gold moidores. I had, therefore, already made up my mind. Abdullah Khan, however, thinking that I hesitated, pressed the matter more closely.

'"Consider, sahib," said he, "that if this man is taken by the commandant he will be hung or shot, and his jewels taken by the Government, so that no man will be a rupee the better for them. Now, since we do the taking of him, why should we not do the rest as well? The jewels will be as well with us as in the Company's coffers. There will be enough to make every one of us rich men and great chiefs. No one can know about the matter, for here we are cut off from all men. What could be better for the purpose? Say again, then, sahib, whether you are with us, or if we must look upon you as an enemy."

'"I am with you heart and soul," said I.

'"It is well," he answered, handing me back my firelock. "You see that we trust you, for your word, like ours, is not to be broken. We have now only to wait for my brother and the merchant."

'"Does your brother know, then, of what you will do?" I asked.

'"The plan is his. He has devised it. We will go to the gate and share the watch with Mahomet Singh."

'The rain was still falling steadily, for it was just the beginning of the wet season. Brown, heavy clouds were drifting across the sky, and it was hard to see more than a stone-cast. A deep moat lay in front of our door, but the water was in places nearly dried up, and it could easily be crossed. It was strange to me to be standing there with those two wild Punjaubees waiting for the man who was coming to his death.

'Suddenly my eye caught the glint of a shaded lantern at the other side of the moat. It vanished among the mound-heaps, and then appeared again coming slowly in our direction.

' "Here they are!" I exclaimed.

' "You will challenge him, sahib, as usual," whispered Abdullah. "Give him no cause for fear. Send us in with him, and we shall do the rest while you stay here on guard. Have the lantern ready to uncover, that we may be sure that it is indeed the man."

'The light had flickered onwards, now stopping and now advancing, until I could see two dark figures upon the other side of the moat. I let them scramble down the sloping bank, splash through the mire, and climb half-way up to the gate, before I challenged them.

' "Who goes there?" said I, in a subdued voice.

' "Friends," came the answer. I uncovered my lantern and threw a flood of light upon them. The first was an enormous Sikh, with a black beard which swept nearly down to his cummerbund. Outside of a show I have never seen so tall a man. **177** The other was a little, fat, round fellow, with a great yellow turban, and a bundle in his hand, done up in a shawl. He seemed to be all in a quiver with fear, for his hands twitched as if he had the ague, and his head kept turning to left and right with two bright little twinkling eyes, like a mouse when he ventures out from his hole. It gave me the chills to think of killing him, but I thought of the treasure, and my heart set as hard as a flint within me. When he saw my white face he gave a little chirrup of joy, and came running up towards me.

' "Your protection, sahib," he panted; "your protection for the unhappy merchant Achmet. I have travelled across Rajpootana that I might seek the shelter of the fort at Agra. **178** I have been robbed and beaten and abused because I have been the friend of the Company. It is a blessed night this when I am once more in safety—I and my poor possessions."

' "What have you in the bundle?" I asked.

' "An iron box," he answered, "which contains one or two little family matters which are of no value to others, but which I should be sorry to lose. Yet I am not a beggar; and I shall reward you, young sahib, and your governor also, if he will give me the shelter I ask."

'I could not trust myself to speak longer with the man. The more I looked at his fat, frightened face, the harder did it seem that we should slay him in cold blood. It was best to get it over.

' "Take him to the main guard," said I. The two Sikhs closed in upon him on each side, and the giant walked behind, while they marched in through the dark gateway. Never was a man so compassed round with death. I remained at the gateway with the lantern.

'I could hear the measured tramp of their footsteps sounding through the lonely corridors. Suddenly it ceased, and I heard voices, and a scuffle, with the sound of blows. A moment later there came, to my horror, a rush of footsteps coming in my direction, with a loud breathing of a running man. I turned my lantern down the long, straight passage, and there was the fat man, running like the wind, with a smear of blood across his face, and close at his heels, bounding like a tiger, the great, black-bearded Sikh, with a knife flashing in his hand. I have never seen a man run so fast as that little merchant. He was gaining on the Sikh, and I could see that if he once passed me and got to the open air he would save himself yet. My heart softened to him, but again the thought of

177 *cummerbund*. Anglo-Indian form of the Hindu *kamar-band*, a loin cloth or sash worn around the waist.

178 *Rajpootana*. A region settled in the seventh century by the Rajputs, later an affiliation of 21 Indian states.

' ". . . I SHALL REWARD YOU, YOUNG SAHIB . . ." '

Frontispiece by "H.D." for *Lippincott's Monthly Magazine*, February, 1890.

his treasure turned me hard and bitter. I cast my firelock between his legs as he raced past, and he rolled twice over like
a shot rabbit. Ere he could stagger to his feet the Sikh was
upon him, and buried his knife twice in his side. The man
never uttered moan nor moved muscle, but lay where he had
fallen. I think myself that he may have broken his neck with
the fall. You see, gentlemen, that I am keeping my promise. I
am telling you every word of the business just exactly as it
happened, whether it is in my favour or not.'

He stopped, and held out his manacled hands for the
whisky-and-water which Holmes had brewed for him. For myself, I confess that I had now conceived the utmost horror of
the man, not only for this cold-blooded business in which he
had been concerned, but even more for the somewhat flippant
and careless way in which he narrated it. Whatever punishment was in store for him, I felt that he might expect no
sympathy from me. Sherlock Holmes and Jones sat with their
hands upon their knees, deeply interested in the story, but
with the same disgust written upon their faces. He may have
observed it, for there was a touch of defiance in his voice and
manner as he proceeded.

'It was all very bad, no doubt,' said he. 'I should like to
know how many fellows in my shoes would have refused a
share of this loot when they knew that they would have their
throats cut for their pains. Besides, it was my life or his when
once he was in the fort. If he had got out, the whole business
would come to light, and I should have been court-martialled
and shot as likely as not; for people were not very lenient at
a time like that.'

'Go on with your story,' said Holmes, shortly.

'Well, we carried him in, Abdullah, Akbar and I. A fine
weight he was, too, for all that he was so short. Mahomet
Singh was left to guard the door. We took him to a place
which the Sikhs had already prepared. It was some distance
off, where a winding passage leads to a great empty hall, the
brick walls of which were all crumbling to pieces. The earth
floor had sunk in at one place, making a natural grave, so we
left Achmet the merchant there, having first covered him
over with loose bricks. This done, we all went back to the
treasure.

'It lay where he had dropped it when he was first attacked.
The box was the same which now lies open upon your table.
A key was hung by a silken cord to that carved handle upon
the top. We opened it, and the light of the lantern gleamed
upon a collection of gems such as I have read of and thought
about when I was a little lad at Pershore. It was blinding to
look upon them. When we had feasted our eyes we took them
all out and made a list of them. There were one hundred and
forty-three diamonds of the first water, including one which
179 has been called, I believe, "the Great Mogul," and is said to
be the second largest stone in existence. Then there were
ninety-seven very fine emeralds, and one hundred and seventy
rubies, some of which, however, were small. There were forty
carbuncles, two hundred and ten sapphires, sixty-one agates,
and a great quantity of beryls, onyxes, cats'-eyes, turquoises,
and other stones, the very names of which I did not know at
the time, though I have become more familiar with them
since. Besides this, there were nearly three hundred very fine
pearls, twelve of which were set in a gold coronet. By the

179 *"the Great Mogul."* There is in fact a celebrated Golconda diamond called "The Great
Mogul," said to have weighed 787 carats before
cutting. It was found in 1650 or earlier, and belonged to the Great Mogul until the capture of
Delhi in 1739, since which time it has not been
traced. Does it lie at the bottom of the Thames?

way, these last had been taken out of the chest, and were not there when I recovered it.

'After we had counted our treasures we put them back into the chest and carried them to the gateway to show them to Mahomet Singh. Then we solemnly renewed our oath to stand by each other and be true to our secret. We agreed to conceal our loot in a safe place until the country should be at peace again, and then to divide it equally among ourselves. There was no use dividing it at present, for if gems of such value were found upon us it would cause suspicion, and there was no privacy in the fort nor any place where we could keep them. We carried the box, therefore, into the same hall where we had buried the body, and there, under certain bricks in the best-preserved wall, we made a hollow and put our treasure. We made careful note of the place, and next day I drew four plans, one for each of us, and put the sign of the four of us at the bottom, for we had sworn that we should each always act for all, so that none might take advantage. That is an oath that I can put my hand to my heart and swear that I have never broken.

'Well, there's no use my telling you gentlemen what came of the Indian Mutiny. After Wilson took Delhi and Sir Colin **180 – 181** relieved Lucknow the back of the business was broken. Fresh troops came pouring in, and Nana Sahib made himself scarce **182** over the frontier. A flying column under Colonel Greathed **183** came round to Agra and cleared the Pandies away from it. **184** Peace seemed to be settling upon the country, and we four were beginning to hope that the time was at hand when we might safely go off with our share of the plunder. In a moment, however, our hopes were shattered by our being arrested as the murderers of Achmet.

'It came about in this way. When the rajah put his jewels into the hands of Achmet, he did it because he knew that he was a trusty man. They are suspicious folk in the East, however; so what does this rajah do but take a second even more trusty servant and set him to play the spy upon the first? The second man was ordered never to let Achmet out of his sight, and he followed him like his shadow. He went after him that night, and saw him pass through the doorway. Of course, he thought he had taken refuge in the fort, and applied for admission there himself next day, but could find no trace of Achmet. This seemed to him so strange that he spoke about it to a sergeant of guides, who brought it to the ears of the commandant. A thorough search was quickly made and the body was discovered. Thus at the very moment that we thought that all was safe we were all four seized and brought to trial on a charge of murder—three of us because we had held the gate that night, and the fourth because he was known to have been in the company of the murdered man. Not a word about the jewels came out at the trial, for the rajah had been deposed and driven out of India; so no one had any particular interest in them. The murder, however, was clearly made out, and it was certain that we must all have been concerned in it. The three Sikhs got penal servitude for life, and I was condemned to death, though my sentence was afterwards commuted into the same as the others.

'It was rather a queer position that we found ourselves in then. There we were all four tied by the leg and with precious little chance of ever getting out again, while we each held a

180 *Wilson*. Brigadier-General Archdale Wilson, 1803–1874, commander of the Bengal artillery when the Mutiny broke out.

181 *Sir Colin*. Sir Colin Campbell, 1792–1863, one of the outstanding British leaders in the campaign.

182 *Nana Sahib*. One of the native leaders of the rebellion.

183 *Colonel Greathed*. Colonel William Wilberforce Harris Greathed, 1826–1878.

184 *Pandies*. Nickname for the mutineers, from the name of one Pande, a ringleader at the beginning of the trouble.

secret which might have put each of us in a palace if we could only have made use of it. It was enough to make a man eat his heart out to have to stand the kick and the cuff of every petty jack-in-office, to have rice to eat and water to drink, when that gorgeous fortune was ready for him outside, just waiting to be picked up. It might have driven me mad; but I was always a pretty stubborn one, so I just held on and bided my time.

'At last it seemed to me to have come. I was changed from Agra to Madras, and from there to Blair Island in the Andamans. There are very few white convicts at this settlement, and, as I had behaved well from the first, I soon found myself a sort of privileged person. I was given a hut in Hope Town, which is a small place, on the slopes of Mount Harriet, and I was left pretty much to myself. It is a dreary, fever-stricken place, and all beyond our little clearings was infested with wild cannibal natives, who were ready enough to blow a poisoned dart at us if they saw a chance. There was digging and ditching and yam-planting, and a dozen other things to be done, so we were busy enough all day; though in the evening we had a little time to ourselves. Among other things, I learned to dispense drugs for the surgeon, and picked up a smattering of his knowledge. All the time I was on the look-out for a chance of escape; but it is hundreds of miles from any other land, and there is little or no wind in those seas: so it was a terribly difficult job to get away.

'The surgeon, Dr Somerton, was a fast, sporting young chap, and the other young officers would meet in his rooms of an evening and play cards. The surgery, where I used to make up my drugs, was next to his sitting-room, with a small window between us. Often, if I felt lonesome, I used to turn out the lamp in the surgery, and then, standing there. I could hear their talk and watch their play. I am fond of a hand at cards myself, and it was almost as good as having one to watch the others. There was Major Sholto, Captain Morstan, and Lieutenant Bromley Brown, who were in command of the native troops, and there was the surgeon himself, and two or three prison-officials, crafty old hands who played a nice, sly, safe game. A very snug little party they used to make.

'Well, there was one thing which very soon struck me, and that was that the soldiers used always to lose and the civilians to win. Mind, I don't say there was anything unfair, but so it was. These prison-chaps had done little else than play cards ever since they had been at the Andamans, and they knew each other's game to a point, while the others just played to pass the time and threw their cards down anyhow. Night after night the soldiers got up poorer men, and the poorer they got the more keen they were to play. Major Sholto was the hardest hit. He used to pay in notes and gold at first, but soon it came to notes of hand and for big sums. He sometimes would win for a few deals, just to give him heart, and then the luck would set in against him worse than ever. All day he would wander about as black as thunder, and he took to drinking a deal more than was good for him.

'One night he lost even more heavily than usual. I was sitting in my hut when he and Captain Morstan came stumbling along on the way to their quarters. They were bosom friends, those two, and never far apart. The Major was raving about his losses.

' "It's all up, Morstan," he was saying, as they passed my hut. "I shall have to send in my papers. I am a ruined man."

' "Nonsense, old chap!" said the other, slapping him upon the shoulder. "I've had a nasty facer myself, but——" That was all I could hear, but it was enough to set me thinking.

'A couple of days later Major Sholto was strolling on the beach: so I took the chance of speaking to him.

' "I wish to have your advice, Major," said I.

' "Well, Small, what is it?" he asked, taking his cheroot from his lips.

' "I wanted to ask you, sir," said I, "who is the proper person to whom hidden treasure should be handed over. I know where half a million worth lies, and, as I cannot use it myself, I thought perhaps the best thing that I could do would be to hand it over to the proper authorities, and then perhaps they would get my sentence shortened for me."

' "Half a million, Small?" he gasped, looking hard at me to see if I was in earnest.

' "Quite that, sir—in jewels and pearls. It lies there ready for anyone. And the queer thing about it is that the real owner is outlawed and cannot hold property, so that it belongs to the first comer."

' "To Government, Small," he stammered, "to Government." But he said it in a halting fashion, and I knew in my heart that I had got him.

' "You think, then, sir, that I should give the information to the Governor-General?" said I, quietly.

' "Well, well, you must not do anything rash, or that you might repent. Let me hear all about it, Small. Give me the facts."

'I told him the whole story, with small changes, so that he could not identify the places. When I had finished he stood stock-still and full of thought. I could see by the twitch of his lip that there was a struggle going on within him.

' "This is a very important matter, Small," he said at last. "You must not say a word to anyone about it, and I shall see you again soon."

'Two nights later he and his friend, Captain Morstan, came to my hut in the dead of the night with a lantern.

' "I want you just to let Captain Morstan hear that story from your own lips, Small," said he.

'I repeated it as I had told it before.

' "It rings true, eh?" said he. "It's good enough to act upon?"

'Captain Morstan nodded.

' "Look here, Small," said the Major. 'We have been talking it over, my friend here and I, and we have come to the conclusion that this secret of yours is hardly a Government matter, after all, but is a private concern of your own, which, of course, you have the power of disposing of as you think best. Now the question is: What price would you ask for it? We might be inclined to take it up, and at least look into it, if we could agree as to terms." He tried to speak in a cool, careless way, but his eyes were shining with excitement and greed.

' "Why, as to that, gentlemen," I answered, trying also to be cool, but feeling as excited as he did, "there is only one bargain which a man in my position can make, I shall want you to help me to my freedom, and to help my three companions to theirs. We shall then take you into partnership, and give you a fifth share to divide between you."

' "Hum!" said he. "A fifth share! That is not very tempting."

' "It would come to fifty thousand apiece," said I.

' "But how can we gain your freedom? You know very well that you ask an impossibility."

' "Nothing of the sort," I answered. "I have thought it all out to the last detail. The only bar to our escape is that we can get no boat fit for the voyage, and no provisions to last us for so long a time. There are plenty of little yachts and yawls at Calcutta or Madras which would serve our turn well. Do you bring one over. We shall engage to get aboard her by night, and if you will drop us on any part of the Indian coast you will have done your part of the bargain."

' "If there were only one," he said.

' "None or all," I answered. "We have sworn it. The four of us must always act together."

' "You see, Morstan," said he, "Small is a man of his word. He does not flinch from his friends. I think we may very well trust him."

' "It's a dirty business," the other answered. "Yet, as you say, the money will save our commissions handsomely."

' "Well, Small," said the Major, "we must, I suppose, try and meet you. We must first, of course, test the truth of your story. Tell me where the box is hid, and I shall get leave of absence and go back to India in the monthly relief-boat to inquire into the affair."

' "Not so fast," said I, growing colder as he got hot. "I must have the consent of my three comrades. I tell you that it is four or none with us."

' "Nonsense!" he broke in. "What have three black fellows to do with our agreement?"

' "Black or blue," said I, "they are in with me, and we all go together."

'Well, the matter ended by a second meeting, at which Mahomet Singh, Abdullah Khan, and Dost Akbar were all present. We talked the matter over again, and at last we came to an arrangement. We were to provide both the officers with charts of the part of the Agra fort, and mark the place in the wall where the treasure was hid. Major Sholto was to go to India to test our story. If he found the box he was to leave it there, to send out a small yacht provisioned for a voyage, which was to lie off Rutland Island, and to which we were to make our way, and finally to return to his duties. Captain Morstan was then to apply for leave of absence, to meet us at Agra, and there we were to have a final division of the treasure, he taking the Major's share as well as his own. All this we sealed by the most solemn oaths that the mind could think or the lips utter. I sat up all night with paper and ink, and by the morning I had the two charts all ready, signed with the sign of four—that is, of Abdullah, Akbar, Mahomet, and myself.

'Well, gentlemen, I weary you with my long story, and I know that my friend Mr Jones is impatient to get me safely **185** stowed in chokey. I'll make it as short as I can. The villain Sholto went off to India, but he never came back again. Captain Morstan showed me his name among a list of passengers in one of the mail-boats very shortly afterwards. His uncle had died, leaving him a fortune, and he had left the army; yet he could stoop to treat five men as he had treated us. Morstan went over to Agra shortly afterwards, and found, as we expected, that the treasure was indeed gone. The scoundrel had

185 *chokey*. Anglo-Indian slang for jail or prison, from the Hindu *chauki*, meaning a four-sided place or building.

stolen it all, without carrying out one of the conditions on which we had sold him the secret. From that day I lived only for vengeance. I thought of it by day and I nursed it by night. It became an overpowering, absorbing passion with me. I cared nothing for the law—nothing for the gallows. To escape, to track down Sholto, to have my hand upon his throat—that was my one thought. Even the Agra treasure had come to be a smaller thing in my mind than the slaying of Sholto.

'Well, I have set my mind on many things in this life, and never one which I did not carry out. But it was weary years before my time came. I have told you that I had picked up something of medicine. One day when Dr Somerton was down with a fever a little Andaman Islander was picked up by a convict-gang in the woods. He was sick to death, and had gone to a lonely place to die. I took him in hand, though he was as venomous as a young snake, and after a couple of months I got him all right and able to walk. He took a kind of fancy to me then, and would hardly go back to his woods, but was always hanging about my hut. I learned a little of his lingo from him, and this made him all the fonder of me.

'Tonga—for that was his name—was a fine boatman, and owned a big, roomy canoe of his own. When I found that he was devoted to me and would do anything to serve me, I saw my chance of escape. I talked it over with him. He was to bring his boat round on a certain night to an old wharf which was never guarded, and there he was to pick me up. I gave him directions to have several gourds of water and a lot of yams, coco-nuts, and sweet potatoes.

'He was stanch and true, was little Tonga. No man ever had a more faithful mate. On the night named he had his boat at the wharf. As it chanced, however, there was one of the convict-guard down there—a vile Pathan who had never **186** missed a chance of insulting and injuring me. I had always vowed vengeance, and now I had my chance. It was as if fate had placed him in my way that I might pay my debt before I left the island. He stood on the bank with his back to me, and his carbine on his shoulder. I looked about for a stone to beat out his brains with, but none could I see.

'Then a queer thought came into my head, and showed me where I could lay my hand on a weapon. I sat down in the darkness and unstrapped my wooden leg. With three long hops I was on him. He put his carbine to his shoulder, but I struck him full, and knocked the whole front of his skull in. You can see the split in the wood now where I hit him. We both went down together, for I could not keep my balance; but when I got up I found him lying quiet enough. I made for the boat, and in an hour we were well out at sea. Tonga had brought all his earthly possessions with him, his arms and his gods. Among other things, he had a long bamboo spear, and some Andaman coco-nut matting, with which I made a sort of a sail. For ten days we were beating about, trusting to luck, and on the eleventh we were picked up by a trader which was going from Singapore to Jiddah with a cargo of Malay pilgrims. They were a rum crowd, and Tonga and I soon managed to settle down among them. They had one very good quality: they let you alone and asked no questions.

'Well, if I were to tell you all the adventures that my little chum and I went through, you would not thank me, for I

186 *Pathan*. A member of the principal race of Afghanistan. Many are still employed in the British Army, especially in the cavalry. They are counted among the bravest warriors in the East.

would have you here until the sun was shining. Here and there we drifted about the world, something always turning up to keep us from London. All the time, however, I never lost sight of my purpose. I would dream of Sholto at night. A hundred times I have killed him in my sleep. At last, however, some three or four years ago, we found ourselves in England. I had no great difficulty in finding where Sholto lived, and I set to work to discover whether he had realized the treasure, or if he still had it. I made friends with someone

187 who could help me—I name no names, for I don't want to get anyone else in a hole—and I soon found that he still had the jewels. Then I tried to get at him in many ways; but he was pretty sly, and had always two prizefighters, besides his sons and his khitmutgar on guard over him.

'One day, however, I got word that he was dying. I hurried at once to the garden, mad that he should slip out of my clutches like that, and, looking through the window, I saw him lying in his bed, with his sons on each side of him. I'd have come through and taken my chance with the three of them, only even as I looked at him his jaw dropped, and I knew that he was gone. I got into his room the same night, though, and I searched his papers to see if there was any record of where he had hidden our jewels. There was not a line, however, so I came away, bitter and savage as a man could be. Before I left I bethought me that if I ever met my Sikh friends again it would be a satisfaction to know that I had left some mark of our hatred; so I scrawled down the sign of the four of us, as it had been on the chart, and I pinned it on his bosom. It was too much that he should be taken to the grave without some token from the men whom he had robbed and befooled.

'We earned a living at this time by my exhibiting poor Tonga at fairs and other such places as the black cannibal. He would eat raw meat and dance his war-dance: so we always had a hatful of pennies after a day's work. I still heard all the news from Pondicherry Lodge, and for some years there was no news to hear, except that they were hunting for the treasure. At last, however, came what we had waited for so long. The treasure had been found. It was up at the top of the house, in Mr Bartholomew Sholto's chemical laboratory. I came at once and had a look at the place, but I could not see how, with my wooden leg, I was to make my way up to it. I learned, however, about a trap-door in the roof, and also about Mr Sholto's supper-hour. It seemed to me that I could manage the thing easily through Tonga. I brought him out with me with a long rope wound round his waist. He could climb like a cat, and he soon made his way through the roof, but, as ill-luck would have it, Bartholomew Sholto was still in the room, to his cost. Tonga thought he had done something very clever in killing him, for when I came up by the rope I found him strutting about as proud as a peacock. Very much surprised was he when I made at him with the rope's end and cursed him for a little, bloodthirsty imp. I took the treasure box and let it down, and then slid down myself, having first left the sign of the four upon the table, to show that the jewels had come back at last to those who had most right to them. Tonga then pulled up the rope, closed the window, and made off the way that he had come.

'I don't know that I have anything else to tell you. I had

187 *someone who could help me.* Professor James Moriarty, in the view of the late Robert R. Pattrick (*see below*).

188 *and was to give him a big sum.* "Queer strangers do not hire fast steam launches," the late Robert R. Pattrick wrote in "Moriarty Was There," "and have them stand in readiness for a day or two, on the basis of a promise. Something more tangible is required, and Small as yet had nothing to prove his story of 'a big sum.' . . . Moriarty, by means which we shall never know, apparently satisfied himself as to the truth of Small's story, made the plans, and advanced the money for the boat hire. Small, after obtaining the treasure, returned with it to the hideout which had been provided for him. The boat hire, and the additional 15% fee for Moriarty, was then paid from the treasure."

189 *the gentleman at the Andaman Isles.*' "Mr. Nathan Bengis has . . . stigmatized Small as a blackguard of the deepest dye," Mr. T. S. Blakeney wrote in "Thoughts on *The Sign of the Four*," "and we know that Holmes, Watson and Athelney Jones openly showed repugnance at Small's story. But I suggest that there is quite a lot to be said in defence of Small. It is not only that he took his defeat by Holmes in a very sporting fashion, though he might well have felt sore at missing by heard a waterman speak of the speed of Smith's launch, the *Aurora*, so I thought she would be a handy craft for our escape. I engaged with old Smith, and was to give him a big sum if he got us safe to our ship. He knew, no doubt, that **188** there was some screw loose, but he was not in our secrets. All this is the truth, and if I tell it to you, gentlemen, it is not to amuse you—for you have not done me a very good turn— but it is because I believe the best defence I can make is just to hold back nothing, but let all the world know how badly I have myself been served by Major Sholto, and how innocent I am of the death of his son.'

'A very remarkable account,' said Sherlock Holmes. 'A fitting wind-up to an extremely interesting case. There is nothing at all new to me in the latter part of your narrative, except that you brought your own rope. That I did not know. By the way, I had hoped that Tonga had lost all his darts; yet he managed to shoot one at us in the boat.'

'He had lost them all, sir, except the one which was in his blow-pipe at the time.'

'Ah, of course,' said Holmes. 'I had not thought of that.'

'Is there any other point which you would like to ask about?' asked the convict, affably.

'I think not, thank you,' my companion answered.

'Well, Holmes,' said Athelney Jones, 'you are a man to be humoured, and we all know that you are a connoisseur of crime; but duty is duty, and I have gone rather far in doing what you and your friend asked me. I shall feel more at ease when we have our story-teller here safe under lock and key. The cab still waits, and there are two inspectors downstairs. I am much obliged to you both for your assistance. Of course, you will be wanted at the trial. Good night to you.'

'Good night, gentlemen both,' said Jonathan Small.

'You first, Small,' remarked the wary Jones as they left the room. 'I'll take particular care that you don't club me with your wooden leg, whatever you may have done to the gentleman at the Andaman Isles.'   **189**

'Well, and there is the end of our little drama,' I remarked, after we had sat some time smoking in silence. 'I fear that it may be the last investigation in which I shall have the chance of studying your methods. Miss Morstan has done me the honour to accept me as a husband in prospective.'

He gave a most dismal groan.

'I feared as much,' said he. 'I really cannot congratulate you.'   **190**

I was a little hurt.

'Have you any reason to be dissatisfied with my choice?' I asked.

'Not at all. I think she is one of the most charming young ladies I ever met, and might have been most useful in such work as we have been doing. She had a decided genius that way; witness the way in which she preserved that Agra plan from all the other papers of her father. But love is an emotional thing, and whatever is emotional is opposed to that true, cold reason which I place above all things. I should **191** never marry myself, lest I bias my judgment.'   **192**

'I trust,' said I, laughing, 'that my judgment may survive the ordeal. But you look weary.'

'Yes, the reaction is already upon me. I shall be as limp as a rag for a week.'

so narrow a margin his escape with the loot. But there were, I think, many extenuating circumstances in the story of the killing of Achmet. . . . I urge, therefore, that Jonathan Small be judged with more leniency; he was placed in an impossible situation where whatever he did was likely to bring misfortune to someone."

190 *I really cannot congratulate you.*' "And why couldn't Holmes congratulate Watson?" Mr. Jerry Neal Williamson asked in "'The Latest Treatise Upon Pathology.'" "Because Holmes knew that Watson had shared an affair, and other things, with a certain well-known woman and had become entangled with her; and he feared that Watson would wound Mary, 'one of the most charming young ladies' Holmes had ever met. In Holmes' usual candid honesty, he could not express happiness over his companion's betrothal, for he did not feel it. Holmes was worried: for Watson, for Mary, and for Watson's mistress. . . . Dr. John H. Watson enjoyed a sporadic affair with none other than Irene Adler, during the years 1886 to 1888!"

There are, needless to say, other views: Dr. Ebbe Curtis Hoff, for example, in "The Adventure of John and Mary," has suggested that Holmes could not congratulate Watson because: 1) he lost a potential colleague in Mary; 2) he lost his Boswell; and 3) he saw ahead a tragic bereavement for his friend: when Mary first came to Baker Street "Holmes noticed . . . a thickening of the nails. . . . Holmes knew, of course, that this 'clubbing' of the fingers is pathognomic of a number of illnesses caused by faulty oxygenation of the blood, such as mitral stenosis or pulmonary tuberculosis."

191 *whatever is emotional is opposed to that true, cold reason which I place above all things.* "This is impressive enough," Dean Theodore C. Blegen wrote in "These Were Hidden Fires, Indeed!", "but we might remember that in 'The Adventure of the Abbey Grange' warm kindness rather than cold reason leads Mr. Holmes to play the role of judge, with Dr. Watson as jury, and Captain Crocker escapes the law. 'I had rather play tricks with the law of England than with my own conscience,' says Mr. Holmes, and we applaud him, for we want Crocker to go free and we sentimentally hope he will marry the lady in the case."

192 *I should never marry myself,* "There is no evidence . . . that Sherlock Holmes never had married," Miss Esther Longfellow wrote in "The Distaff Side of Baker Street." "He does not so say. He merely indicates that he never *should* . . . and that the state is distasteful to him because it would interfere with his work, to which he is now wedded. It is plain that Mr. Holmes knows exactly what effect marriage would have upon him. How would he know this if he had never married?"

193 *Shelman der Stoff.* "Credit is due to young Schiller also," Mr. Morris Rosenblum wrote in "Foreign Language Quotations in the Canon," "since the lines come from the *Xenian,* a collection written by Goethe and Schiller in 1796. . . . The use of *Mensch* is a departure from the original *Menschen.* The translation runs, 'Nature, alas, made only one being out of you although there was material for a good man and a rogue.' "

Mr. Bliss Austin has added ("Two Bibliographical Footnotes") that ". . . the Canonical version of this quotation omits the comma after *Schade.* This is clearly Watson's doing. Holmes, who—like Goethe—was always pithy, would hardly have recited this couplet complete with punctuation, and it probably never occurred to Watson that there should be a comma at this particular place."

Bibliographical Note: The readers of the *Observer* ranked *The Sign of the Four* No. 3 on their list of favorite Sherlock Holmes stories. The original manuscript, consisting of 160 leaves, folio, was auctioned in New York City on December 9, 1909, bringing $105. "Persistent rumor places this manuscript in Chicago, but diligent inquiry has failed to uncover its lucky possessor," Professor David A. Randall wrote in his scholarly bibliographical notes on *The Sign of the Four* in the *Baker Street Journal.* One folio sheet of the manuscript, about 220 words, the beginning of the story, with corrections in the author's hand as well as several printer's notations in ink, shown at right, was auctioned in New York City on November 22, 1929, bringing $50. In 1946 it was owned by Mr. Carroll A. Wilson; it was later (1954) in the possession of Mr. Ed Morris of Philadelphia. By far the most extensive and the most scholarly bibliography of *The Sign of the Four* is *The "Signs" of our Times* by Mr. Nathan L. Bengis; New York: Privately printed, June, 1956.

'Strange,' said I, 'how terms of what in another man I should call laziness alternate with your fits of splendid energy and vigour.'

'Yes,' he answered, 'there are in me the makings of a very fine loafer, and also of a pretty spry sort of a fellow. I often think of those lines of old Goethe:

193   Schade dass die Natur nur *einen* Mensch aus dir schuf,
Denn zum würdigen Mann war und zum Schelmen der Stoff.

By the way, apropos of this Norwood business, you see that they had, as I surmised, a confederate in the house, who could be none other than Lal Rao, the butler: so Jones actually has the undivided honour of having caught one fish in his great haul.'

'The division seems rather unfair,' I remarked. 'You have done all the work in this business. I get a wife out of it, Jones gets the credit; pray what remains for you?'

'For me,' said Sherlock Holmes, 'there still remains the cocaine-bottle.' And he stretched his long, white hand up for it.

The Sign of the Four.

Chapter I.
The Science of deduction.

Sherlock Holmes took his bottle from the corner of the mantelpiece and his hypodermic syringe from its neat morocco case. With his long, white, nervous fingers he adjusted the delicate needle, and rolled back his left shirt-cuff. For some little time his eyes rested thoughtfully upon the sinewy fore-arm and wrist all dotted and scarred with innumerable puncture-marks. Finally he thrust the sharp point home, pressed down the tiny piston, and sank back into the velvet-lined armchair with a long sigh of satisfaction.

Three times a day for many months I had witnessed this performance, but custom had not reconciled my mind to it. On the contrary, from day to day I had become more irritable at the sight, and my conscience swelled nightly within me at the thought that I had lacked the courage to protest. Again and again I had registered a vow that I should deliver my soul upon the subject, but there was that in the cool nonchalant air of my companion which made him the last man with whom one would care to take anything approaching to a liberty. His great powers, his masterly manner, and the experience which I had had of his many

5 · **4** · **3** · **2**

May Day

Bradford
Tarleton
LANCASHIRE
YO

New Brighton · Liverpool
THE PEAK
LOWER GILL MOOR
Mackleton · HALLAMSHIRE

Bangor

Crewe

Derby

53

Walsall
Aston
Birmingham
Co

W A L E S

WORCESTER-SHIRE

HEREFORDSHIRE · Pershore

Hereford
BOSCOMBE VALLEY
Ross

52

Gloucester
OXF
Abergavenny
STROUD VALLEY

RIVER SEVERN
Bristol
Swindon
E
S
Cren

ATLANTIC

Andove
Wilton
Winc
THOR MER

OCEAN

51

Fordingbridge

DEVONSHIRE
NEW FOR
Folkestone Court

Exeter

King's Pyland
GRIMPEN MIRE
Tavistock · THORSLEY PARISH
Grimpen
Princetown · Fernworthy
DART-
LONG DOWN · Coombe Tracey
MOOR
Plymouth
HIGH BARROW PARISH

PORTLAND

ENGLISH CHA

St. Ives · Redruth
Tredannick BEAUCHAMP ARRIANCE
Wollas
MOUNTS · Helston
POLDHU BAY · BAY

Gloria Scott

30

5 · **4** · **3** · **2**

0 5 10 15 20 25 30 35 40 45
MILES.

N

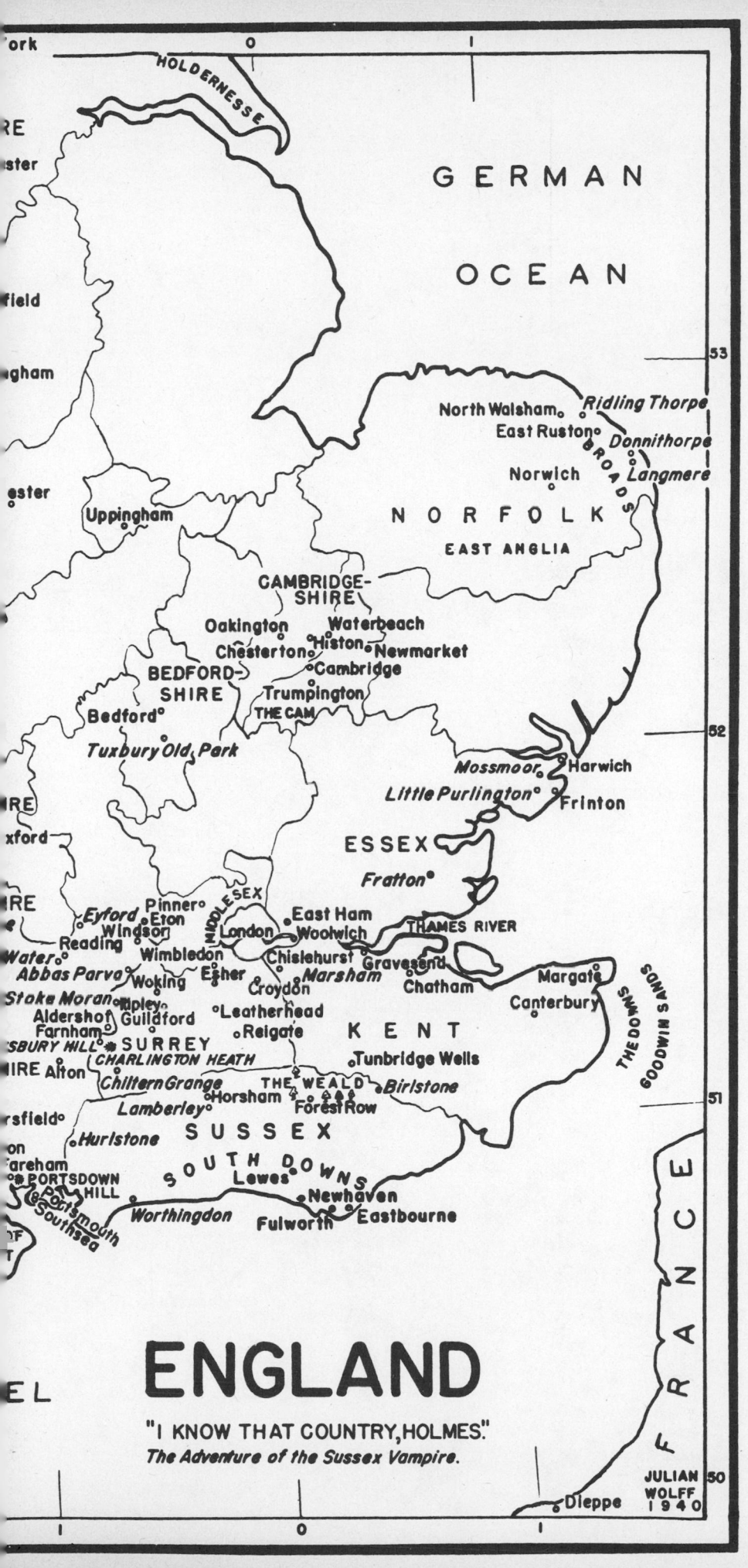

ENGLAND

"I KNOW THAT COUNTRY, HOLMES."
The Adventure of the Sussex Vampire.

JULIAN
WOLFF
1940

THE ANNOTATED®

SHERLOCK HOLMES

THE ANNOTATED®

SHERLOCK HOLMES

VOLUME II

V. FROM DR. WATSON'S RETURN TO BAKER STREET TO HIS MARRIAGE TO MARY MORSTAN

[late December, 1887, or early January, 1888, to *circa* May 1, 1889]

Continued from Vol. I

36

THE HOUND OF THE BASKERVILLES

[Tuesday, September 25, to Saturday, October 20, 1888]

I ♦ MR SHERLOCK HOLMES

Mr Sherlock Holmes, who was usually very late in the mornings, save upon those not infrequent occasions when he stayed **1** up all night, was seated at the breakfast-table. I stood upon the hearth-rug and picked up the stick which our visitor had left behind him the night before. It was a fine, thick piece of **2** wood, bulbous-headed, of the sort which is known as a 'Penang lawyer.' Just under the head was a broad silver band, nearly **3** an inch across. 'To James Mortimer, M.R.C.S., from his **4** friends of the C.C.H.,' was engraved upon it, with the date '1884.' It was just such a stick as the old-fashioned family prac- **5** titioner used to carry—dignified, solid, and reassuring.

'Well, Watson, what do you make of it?'

Holmes was sitting with his back to me, and I had given him no sign of my occupation.

'How did you know what I was doing? I believe you have eyes in the back of your head.'

'I have, at least, a well-polished, silver-plated coffee-pot in front of me,' said he. 'But, tell me, Watson, what do you make of our visitor's stick? Since we have been so unfortunate as to miss him and have no notion of his errand, this accidental souvenir becomes of importance. Let me hear you reconstruct the man by an examination of it.'

'I think,' said I, following so far as I could the methods of my companion, 'that Dr Mortimer is a successful elderly medical man, well-esteemed, since those who know him give him this mark of their appreciation.'

'Good!' said Holmes. 'Excellent!'

'I think also that the probability is in favour of his being a country practitioner who does a great deal of his visiting on foot.'

'Why so?'

'Because this stick, though originally a very handsome one, has been so knocked about that I can hardly imagine a town practitioner carrying it. The thick iron ferrule is worn down, so it is evident that he has done a great amount of walking with it.'

1 *who was usually very late in the mornings.* "Triumphant indeed must have been an occasion when Watson finished [breakfast] before Holmes," Mr. Vincent Starrett wrote in "The Singular Adventures of Martha Hudson"; "one such is recorded in the opening lines of *The Hound of the Baskervilles*. Sherlock Holmes, as we behold him, is still seated at the breakfast table, while Watson stands upon the hearth-rug, examining the handsome stick left by Dr. James Mortimer the night before. Obviously he has already finished, and in the warm glow of comfortable satiety he dares to venture some pregnant observations of his own."

2 *our visitor had left behind him the night before.* "It is curious," the late Gavin Brend observed in *My Dear Holmes*, "how frequently Holmes' clients . . . took insufficient care of their property. The result was always highly satisfactory, for Holmes invariably made a reconstruction of the missing client from the missing article."

3 *a 'Penang lawyer.'* A walking stick with a knobbed head, made from the stem of a small palm (*Licuala acutifida*) that grows in Penang, an island in the straits of Malacca.

4 *M.R.C.S.* Member of the Royal College of Surgeons.

5 *'1884.'* A date later corroborated by Watson's *Medical Directory*.

6 *in all the accounts which you have been so good as to give.* It has been said that the case must be after the Return (1894) because Holmes here speaks of "all the accounts" Watson has been "so good as to give of my own small achievements," and Watson later speaks of "the attempts which I had made to give publicity to [Holmes'] methods." The case is certainly after December, 1887, when *A Study in Scarlet* was published, because Stapleton, as we shall see, knew Watson as Holmes' biographer ("The records of your detective have reached us here, and you could not celebrate him without being known yourself"). But Watson began to *chronicle* Holmes' adventures as early as May, 1887 ("A Scandal in Bohemia"). More than a year later it would be quite proper for Holmes to speak of "all the accounts." And Watson, spurred by the appearance in print of *A Study in Scarlet*, would undoubtedly be making attempts to have other of his chronicles published.

7 *a remarkable power of stimulating it.* "Such double-edged testimony to Watson's assistance is only too typical," Mr. T. S. Blakeney wrote in *Sherlock Holmes: Fact or Fiction?*: "a long array of caustic comments on his friend's honest but scarcely brilliant qualities could be culled from Holmes' conversations. Indeed, the very last recorded for us, late at night on the second of August—'the most terrible August in the history of the world'—closed on just such a backhanded compliment. 'Good old Watson! You are the one fixed point in a changing age' ["His Last Bow"]. It was a securely-founded friendship which survived this withering frankness of expression."

'Perfectly sound!' said Holmes.

'And then again, there is the "friends of the C.C.H." I should guess that to be the Something Hunt, the local hunt to whose members he has possibly given some surgical assistance, and which has made him a small presentation in return.'

'Really, Watson, you excel yourself,' said Holmes, pushing back his chair and lighting a cigarette. 'I am bound to say that **6** in all the accounts which you have been so good as to give of my own small achievements you have habitually underrated your own abilities. It may be that you are not yourself luminous, but you are a conductor of light. Some people without possessing genius have a remarkable power of stimulating **7** it. I confess, my dear fellow, that I am very much in your debt.'

He had never said as much before, and I must admit that his words gave me keen pleasure, for I had often been piqued by his indifference to my admiration and to the attempts which I had made to give publicity to his methods. I was proud, too, to think that I had so far mastered his system as to apply it in a way which earned his approval. He now took the stick from my hands and examined it for a few minutes with his naked eyes. Then, with an expression of interest, he laid down his cigarette, and, carrying the cane to the window, he looked over it again with a convex lens.

'Interesting, though elementary,' said he, as he returned to his favourite corner of the settee. 'There are certainly one or two indications upon the stick. It gives us the basis for several deductions.'

'Has anything escaped me?' I asked, with some self-importance. 'I trust that there is nothing of consequence which I have overlooked?'

'I am afraid, my dear Watson, that most of your conclusions were erroneous. When I said that you stimulated me I meant, to be frank, that in noting your fallacies I was occasionally guided towards the truth. Not that you are entirely wrong in this instance. The man is certainly a country practitioner. And he walks a good deal.'

'Then I was right.'

'To that extent.'

. . . HE LOOKED OVER IT AGAIN WITH A CONVEX LENS.

Illustration by Sidney Paget for the *Strand Magazine*, August, 1901.

'But that was all.'

'No, no, my dear Watson, not all—by no means all. I would suggest, for example, that a presentation to a doctor is more likely to come from a hospital than from a hunt, and that when the initials "C.C." are placed before that hospital the words "Charing Cross" very naturally suggest themselves.'

'You may be right.'

'The probability lies in that direction. And if we take this as a working hypothesis we have a fresh basis from which to start our construction of this unknown visitor.'

'Well, then, supposing that "C.C.H." does stand for "Charing Cross Hospital," what further inferences may we draw?' **8**

'Do none suggest themselves? You know my methods. Apply them!'

'I can only think of the obvious conclusion that the man has practised in town before going to the country.'

'I think that we might venture a little farther than this. Look at it in this light. On what occasion would it be most probable that such a presentation would be made? When would his friends unite to give him a pledge of their good will? Obviously at the moment when Dr Mortimer withdrew from the service of the hospital in order to start in practice for himself. We know there has been a presentation. We believe there has been a change from a town hospital to a country practice. Is it, then, stretching our inference too far to say that the presentation was on the occasion of the change?'

'It certainly seems probable.'

'Now, you will observe that he could not have been on the *staff* of the hospital, since only a man well-established in a London practice could hold such a position, and such a one would not drift into the country. What was he, then? If he was in the hospital and yet not on the staff, he could only have been a house-surgeon or a house-physician—little more than a senior student. And he left five years ago—the date is on the stick. So your grave, middle-aged family practitioner vanishes into thin air, my dear Watson, and there emerges a young fellow under thirty, amiable, unambitious, absent-minded, and the possessor of a favourite dog, which I should describe roughly as being larger than a terrier and smaller than a mastiff.' **9** **10**

I laughed incredulously as Sherlock Holmes leaned back in his settee and blew little wavering rings of smoke up to the ceiling.

'As to the latter part, I have no means of checking you,' said I, 'but at least it is not difficult to find out a few particulars about the man's age and professional career.'

From my small medical shelf I took down the Medical Directory and turned up the name. There were several Mortimers, but only one who could be our visitor. I read his record aloud.

Mortimer, James, M.R.C.S., 1882, Grimpen, Dartmoor, Devon. House-surgeon, from 1882 to 1884, at Charing Cross Hospital. Winner of the Jackson Prize for Comparative Pathology, with essay entitled 'Is Disease a Reversion?' Corresponding member of the Swedish Pathological Society. Author of 'Some Freaks of Atavism' (*Lancet*, 1882), 'Do We Progress?' (*Journal of Psychology*, March, 1883). Medical Officer for the parishes of Grimpen, Thorsley, and High Barrow.

'No mention of that local hunt, Watson,' said Holmes, with

8 "*Charing Cross Hospital.*" This great hospital was founded in 1818, but the building which knew Dr. Mortimer was begun in 1829. "It has a pleasing reassuring frontage, in straight-forward Regency," Mr. William H. Gill wrote in "Some Notable Sherlockian Buildings."

9 *five years ago—the date is on the stick.* The earliest date so far assigned to this case is 1886 (Bell, followed by Heldenbrand and Randall); the latest is 1900 (Zeisler, followed by Folsom and Pattrick). Messrs. Blakeney, Frisbie, Hoff, Knox, Morley, Petersen, Sidgwick, and Smith all chose 1889; Howard and Welch picked 1894; Schonberg 1896; Christ 1897; and Brend and Jones both opted for 1899.

Watson appears to date the adventure quite definitely in 1889. We believe, however, that 1889 is impossible: Watson in 1889 was married and practicing medicine; here there is not a hint that he has either a wife or a consulting room. On the contrary, he is living in Baker Street, and when ordered off to Devonshire for an indefinite stay, he makes no reference to wife, patients, or an accommodating neighbor-doctor. Holmes, we feel, may not have meant *exactly* five years ago; after all, he was speaking informally, in a demonstration to Watson alone, and could have said "five years" if 1884 were somewhat less or somewhat more than five years ago. But he certainly meant closer to five than to four or six years; the case can hardly have taken place *before* July, 1888, or *after* June, 1890. As we shall shortly see, the case took place in late September and the first three weeks of October; the approximate date of the adventure is therefore September–October, 1888, or 1889, and there are, as we have said, good reasons for eliminating 1889.

10 *a young fellow under thirty.* If the date on the stick and in the *Medical Directory* is accepted, this is additional evidence that *The Hound of the Baskervilles* took place within a few years of 1884.

a mischievous smile, 'but a country doctor, as you very astutely observed. I think that I am fairly justified in my inferences. As to the adjectives, I said, if I remember right, amiable, unambitious, and absent-minded. It is my experience that it is only an amiable man in this world who receives testimonials, only an unambitious one who abandons a London career for the country and only an absent-minded one who leaves his stick and not his visiting-card after waiting an hour in your room.'

'And the dog?'

'Has been in the habit of carrying this stick behind his master. Being a heavy stick the dog has held it tightly by the middle, and the marks of his teeth are very plainly visible. The dog's jaw, as shown in the space between these marks, is too broad in my opinion for a terrier and not broad enough for a mastiff. It may have been—yes, by Jove, it *is* a curly-haired spaniel.'

He had risen and paced the room as he spoke. Now he halted in the recess of the window. There was such a ring of conviction in his voice that I glanced up in surprise.

'My dear fellow, how can you possibly be so sure of that?'

'For the very simple reason that I see the dog himself on our very doorstep, and there is the ring of its owner. Don't move, I beg you, Watson. He is a professional brother of yours, and your presence may be of assistance to me. Now is the dramatic moment of fate, Watson, when you hear a step upon the stair which is walking into your life, and you know not whether for good or ill. What does Dr James Mortimer, the man of science, ask of Sherlock Holmes, the specialist in crime? Come in!'

The appearance of our visitor was a surprise to me since I had expected a typical country practitioner. He was a very tall, thin man, with a long nose like a beak, which shot out between two keen, grey eyes, set closely together and sparkling brightly from behind a pair of gold-rimmed glasses. He was clad in a professional but rather slovenly fashion, for his frock-coat was dingy and his trousers frayed. Though young, his long back was already bowed, and he walked with a forward thrust of his head and a general air of peering benevolence. As he entered his eyes fell upon the stick in Holmes's hand, and he ran towards it with an exclamation of joy.

. . . HIS EYES FELL UPON THE STICK IN HOLMES' HAND . . .

Illustration by Sidney Paget for the *Strand Magazine*, August, 1901.

'I am so very glad,' said he. 'I was not sure whether I had left it here or in the Shipping Office. I would not lose that **11** stick for the world.'

'A presentation, I see,' said Holmes.

'Yes, sir.'

'From Charing Cross Hospital?'

'From one or two friends there on the occasion of my marriage.'

'Dear, dear, that's bad!' said Holmes, shaking his head.

Dr Mortimer blinked through his glasses in mild astonishment.

'Why was it bad?'

'Only that you have disarranged our little deductions. Your marriage, you say?'

'Yes, sir. I married, and so left the hospital, and with it all hopes of a consulting practice. It was necessary to make a home of my own.'

'Come, come, we are not so far wrong after all,' said Holmes. 'And now, Dr James Mortimer——'

'Mister, sir, Mister—a humble M.R.C.S.'

'And a man of precise mind, evidently.'

'A dabbler in science, Mr Holmes, a picker-up of shells on the shores of the great unknown ocean. I presume that it is Mr Sherlock Holmes whom I am addressing and not——'

'No, this is my friend Dr Watson.'

'Glad to meet you, sir. I have heard your name mentioned in connection with that of your friend. You interest me very much, Mr Holmes. I had hardly expected so dolichocephalic a skull or such well-marked supra-orbital development. Would you have any objection to my running my finger **12** along your parietal fissure? A cast of your skull, sir, until the **13** original is available, would be an ornament to any anthropological museum. It is not my intention to be fulsome, but I confess that I covet your skull.'   **14**

Sherlock Holmes waved our strange visitor into a chair.

'You are an enthusiast in your line of thought, I perceive, sir, as I am in mine,' said he. 'I observe from your forefinger that you make your own cigarettes. Have no hesitation in lighting one.'

The man drew out paper and tobacco and twirled the one up in the other with surprising dexterity. He had long, quivering fingers as agile and restless as the antennæ of an insect.

Holmes was silent, but his little darting glances showed me the interest which he took in our curious companion.

'I presume, sir,' said he at last, 'that it was not merely for the purpose of examining my skull that you have done me the honour to call here last night and again today?'

'No, sir, no; though I am happy to have had the opportunity of doing that as well. I came to you, Mr Holmes, because I recognize that I am myself an unpractical man, and because I am suddenly confronted with a most serious and extraordinary problem. Recognizing, as I do, that you are the second highest expert in Europe——'

'Indeed, sir! May I inquire who has the honour to be the first?' asked Holmes, with some asperity.

'To the man of precisely scientific mind the work of Monsieur Bertillon must always appeal strongly.'   **15**

'Then had you not better consult him?'

'I said, sir, to the precisely scientific mind. But as a practical

11 *the Shipping Office.* The first of many indications that the first day of the case was certainly not a Monday, since Dr. Mortimer could not have gone to the Shipping Office on a Sunday.

12 *supra-orbital development.* Dr. Mortimer is saying that he had not expected Holmes to have so long a skull or so much of his skull above the orbit of the eye.

13 *parietal fissure?* The parietal, or intraparietal fissure, is that in the upper portion of the convex surface of the parietal lobe of the brain.

14 *I confess that I covet your skull.* In "Dr. Mortimer Before the Bar," Mr. Benjamin Clark has suggested that Dr. James Mortimer, from the start of *The Hound of the Baskervilles*, was up to no good.

Mr. Jerry Neal Williamson has carried this one step further ("Dr. Mortimer-Moriarty") by alleging that "Dr. James Mortimer" was, in reality, Colonel James *Moriarty*, brother to the Napoleon of Crime, Professor James Moriarty.

15 *Monsieur Bertillon.* Alphonse Bertillon, 1853–1914, French anthropologist and the inventor of the system bearing his name. Under this system, records on anthropometric measurements and personal characteristics, such as the color of the eyes, the thumblines, fingerprints, scars, deformities, and the like (sometimes, also, photographs) are used as a means of identification, especially as applied to criminals. The measurements and characteristics are recorded on cards and classified according to the length of the head. The system was inaugurated in the United States in 1887; it was introduced in print in Bertillon's great work *Les Signalements Anthropométriques* (Paris, 1886). Though Holmes on this occasion was piqued, he later ("The Adventure of the Naval Treaty") "expressed his enthusiastic admiration of the French savant." To attempt to date either *The Hound of the Baskervilles* or "The Adventure of the Naval Treaty" by these remarks is, however, somewhat perilous, for Bertillon instituted his scientific classification as early as 1884, and Holmes and Mortimer, as men of precisely scientific minds, might both have known of him long before the publication of his theories.

16 *my little monograph upon the subject.* "From the fact that Holmes assumed Dr. James Mortimer may have read this paper, one deduces that it probably saw publication in some journal which enjoyed a wide circulation among men who followed the scientific professions," Mr. Walter Klinefelter wrote in "The Writings of Sherlock Holmes."

17 *the alternative use of the long* s *and the short.* If the thought was that the long *s* was used strictly in alternation or by chance, this was not so, as Mr. Arthur Godfrey pointed out in an issue of the *Baker Street Journal.* The long *s* was never used as the initial letter of a word if the capital *S* was used, nor was it used at the end of a word. It occurred only in the *body* of a word, and it was there used properly exclusively, except when it was doubled, and then the second *s* was a short one.

'IT APPEARS TO BE A STATEMENT OF SOME SORT.'

This reproduction of the Legend of the Baskervilles was the work of the late Owen F. Frisbie, of the Five Orange Pips of Westchester County, as a presentation to his friend Mr. Benjamin Clark, also of the Five Orange Pips. It now hangs on the wall of the barroom of the Sherlock Holmes Tavern in London.

man of affairs it is acknowledged that you stand alone. I trust, sir, that I have not inadvertently——'

'Just a little,' said Holmes. 'I think, Dr Mortimer, you would do wisely if without more ado you would kindly tell me plainly what the exact nature of the problem is in which you demand my assistance.'

2 • THE CURSE OF THE BASKERVILLES

'I have in my pocket a manuscript,' said Dr James Mortimer.

'I observed it as you entered the room,' said Holmes.

'It is an old manuscript.'

'Early eighteenth century, unless it is a forgery.'

'How can you say that, sir?'

'You have presented an inch or two of it to my examination all the time that you have been talking. It would be a poor expert who could not give the date of a document within a decade or so. You may possibly have read my little mono-

16 graph upon the subject. I put that at 1730.'

'The exact date is 1742.' Dr Mortimer drew it from his breast-pocket. 'This family paper was committed to my care by Sir Charles Baskerville, whose sudden and tragic death some three months ago created so much excitement in Devonshire. I may say that I was his personal friend as well as his medical attendant. He was a strong-minded man, sir, shrewd, practical, and as unimaginative as I am myself. Yet he took this document very seriously, and his mind was prepared for just such an end as did eventually overtake him.'

Holmes stretched out his hand for the manuscript, and flattened it upon his knee.

'You will observe, Watson, the alternative use of the long *s*

17 and the short. It is one of several indications which enabled me to fix the date.'

I looked over his shoulder at the yellow paper and the faded script. At the head was written: 'Baskerville Hall,' and below, in large scrawling figures: '1742.'

'It appears to be a statement of some sort.'

'Yes, it is a statement of a certain legend which runs in the Baskerville family.'

'But I understand that it is something more modern and practical upon which you wish to consult me?'

'Most modern. A most practical, pressing matter, which must be decided within twenty-four hours. But the manuscript is short and is intimately connected with the affair. With your permission I will read it to you.'

Holmes leaned back in his chair, placed his finger-tips together, and closed his eyes, with an air of resignation. Dr Mortimer turned the manuscript to the light, and read in a high, crackling voice the following curious, old-world narrative:

'Of the origin of the Hound of the Baskervilles there have been many statements, yet as I come in a direct line from Hugo Baskerville, and as I had the story from my father, who also had it from his, I have set it down with all belief that it occurred even as is here set forth. And I would have you believe, my sons, that the same Justice which punishes sin may also most graciously forgive it, and that no ban is so heavy but that by prayer and repentance it may be removed. Learn then from this story not to fear the fruits of the past, but rather to be circumspect in the future, that those foul passions whereby our family has suffered so grievously may not again be loosed to our undoing.

'Know then that in the time of the Great Rebellion (the history of which by the learned Lord Clarendon I most earnestly **18** commend to your attention) this Manor of Baskerville was held by Hugo of that name, nor can it be gainsaid that he was a most wild, profane, and godless man. This, in truth, his neighbours might have pardoned, seeing that saints have never flourished in those parts, but there was in him a certain wanton and cruel humour which made his name a by-word through the West. It chanced that this Hugo came to love (if, indeed, so dark a passion may be known under so bright a name) the daughter of a yeoman who held lands near the Baskerville estate. But the young maiden, being discreet and of good repute, would ever avoid him, for she feared his evil name. So it came to pass that one Michaelmas this Hugo, with five or six of his idle and wicked companions, stole down upon the farm and carried off the maiden, her father and brothers being from home, as he well knew. When they had brought her to the Hall the maiden was placed in an upper chamber, while Hugo and his friends sat down to a long carouse as was their nightly custom. Now, the poor lass upstairs was like to have her wits turned at the singing and shouting and terrible oaths which came up to her from below, for they say that the words used by Hugo Baskerville, when he was in wine, were such as might blast the man who said them. At last in the stress of her fear she did that which might have daunted the bravest or most active man, for by the aid of the growth of ivy which covered (and still covers) the south wall, she came down from under the eaves, and so homeward across the moor, there being three leagues betwixt the Hall and her father's farm.

'It chanced that some little time later Hugo left his guests to carry food and drink—with other worse things, perchance—to his captive, and so found the cage empty and the bird escaped. Then, as it would seem, he became as one that hath a devil, for rushing down the stairs into the dining-hall, he sprang upon the great table, flagons and trenchers flying before him, and he cried aloud before all the company that he would that very night render his body and soul to the Powers of Evil if he might but overtake the wench. And while the revellers stood aghast at the fury of the man, one more wicked or, it may be, more drunken than the rest, cried out that they should put the hounds upon her. Whereat Hugo ran from the house, crying to his grooms that they should saddle his mare and unkennel the pack, and giving the hounds a kerchief of the maid's, he swung them to the line, and so off full cry in the moonlight over the moor.

'Now, for some space the revellers stood agape, unable to understand all that had been done in such haste. But anon their bemused wits awoke to the nature of the deed which was like to be done upon the moorlands. Everything was now in an uproar, some calling for their pistols, some for their horses, and some for another flask of wine. But at length some sense came back to their crazed minds, and the whole of them, thirteen in number, took horse and started in pursuit. The moon shone clear above them, and they rode swiftly abreast, taking that course which the maid must needs have taken if she were to reach her own home.

'They had gone a mile or two when they passed one of the night shepherds upon the moorlands, and they cried to him to

18 *Lord Clarendon.* Edward Hyde, Earl of Clarendon, 1608–1674, English Royalist statesman, historian, Premier and Lord Chancellor; impeached and retired to France. The book referred to is his *History of the Great Rebellion*, 1702.

'" . . . SUCH A HOUND OF HELL AS GOD FORBID SHOULD
EVER BE AT MY HEELS." '

Illustration by Sidney Paget for the *Strand Magazine*, August, 1901.

19 *when the powers of evil are exalted.* As Mr. Bliss Austin has demonstrated in his monograph, "Dartmoor Revisited, or Discoveries in Devonshire," the "West-Country legend" Conan Doyle used as his point of departure for the legend of the Baskervilles would seem to have been that of Sir Richard Cabell, Lord of the Manor of Brooke, in the parish of Buckfastleigh. He was a gentleman of evil repute and on the night of his death, black hounds breathing fire and smoke raced over Dartmoor and howled around his manor house. According to the Reverend Sabine Baring-Gould, in his *Methuen's Little Guide to Devon*, Sir Richard's death took place in 1677. A pagoda-like building called the Sepulchre was erected over his grave to prevent his coming back to trouble the neighborhood again. It is still said that he will gnaw your finger if you venture to insert it in the keyhole of the locked door.

know if he had seen the hunt. And the man, as the story goes, was so crazed with fear that he could scarce speak, but at last he said that he had indeed seen the unhappy maiden, with the hounds upon her track. "But I have seen more than that," said he, "for Hugo Baskerville passed me upon his black mare, and there ran mute behind him such a hound of hell as God forbid should ever be at my heels."

'So the drunken squires cursed the shepherd and rode onwards. But soon their skins turned cold, for there came a sound of galloping across the moor, and the black mare, dabbled with white froth, went past with trailing bridle and empty saddle. Then the revellers rode close together, for a great fear was on them, but they still followed over the moor, though each, had he been alone, would have been right glad to have turned his horse's head. Riding slowly in this fashion, they came at last upon the hounds. These, though known for their valour and their breed, were whimpering in a cluster at the head of a deep dip or goyal, as we call it, upon the moor, some slinking away and some, with starting hackles and staring eyes, gazing down the narrow valley before them.

'The company had come to a halt, more sober men, as you may guess, than when they started. The most of them would by no means advance, but three of them, the boldest, or, it may be, the most drunken, rode forward down the goyal. Now it opened into a broad space in which stood two of those great stones, still to be seen there, which were set by certain forgotten peoples in the days of old. The moon was shining bright upon the clearing, and there in the centre lay the unhappy maid where she had fallen, dead of fear and of fatigue. But it was not the sight of her body, nor yet was it that of the body of Hugo Baskerville lying near her, which raised the hair upon the heads of these three dare-devil roysterers, but it was that, standing over Hugo, and plucking at his throat, there stood a foul thing, a great, black beast, shaped like a hound, yet larger than any hound that ever mortal eye has rested upon. And even as they looked the thing tore the throat out of Hugo Baskerville, on which, as it turned its blazing eyes and dripping jaws upon them, the three shrieked with fear and rode for dear life, still screaming, across the moor. One, it is said, died that very night of what he had seen, and the other twain were but broken men for the rest of their days.

'Such is the tale, my sons, of the coming of the hound which is said to have plagued the family so sorely ever since. If I have set it down it is because that which is clearly known hath less terror than that which is but hinted at and guessed. Nor can it be denied that many of the family have been unhappy in their deaths, which have been sudden, bloody, and mysterious. Yet may we shelter ourselves in the infinite goodness of Providence, which would not for ever punish the innocent beyond that third or fourth generation which is threatened in Holy Writ. To that Providence, my sons, I hereby commend you, and I counsel you by way of caution to forbear from crossing the moor in those **19** dark hours when the powers of evil are exalted.

'[This from Hugo Baskerville to his sons Rodger and John, with instructions that they say nothing thereof to their sister Elizabeth.]'

When Dr Mortimer had finished reading this singular narrative he pushed his spectacles up on his forehead and stared across at Mr Sherlock Holmes. The latter yawned and tossed the end of his cigarette into the fire.

'Well?' said he.

'Do you not find it interesting?'

'To a collector of fairy-tales.'

Dr Mortimer drew a folded newspaper out of his pocket. 'Now, Mr Holmes, we will give you something a little more recent. This is the *Devon County Chronicle* of June 14th of this year. It is a short account of the facts elicited at the death of Sir Charles Baskerville which occurred a few days before that date.'   **20**

My friend leaned a little forward and his expression became intent. Our visitor readjusted his glasses and began:

'The recent sudden death of Sir Charles Baskerville, whose name has been mentioned as the probable Liberal candidate for Mid-Devon at the next election, has cast a gloom over the county. Though Sir Charles had resided at Baskerville Hall for a comparatively short period his amiability of character and extreme generosity had won the affection and respect of all who had been brought into contact with him. In these days of *nouveaux riches* **21** it is refreshing to find a case where the scion of an old county family which has fallen upon evil days is able to make his own fortune and to bring it back with him to restore the fallen grandeur of his line. Sir Charles, as is well known, made large sums of money in South African speculation. More wise than those who go on until the wheel turns against them, he realized his gains and returned to England with them. It is only two years since he took up his residence at Baskerville Hall, and it is common talk how large were those schemes of reconstruction and improvement which have been interrupted by his death. Being himself childless, it was his openly-expressed desire that the whole countryside should, within his own lifetime, profit by his good fortune, and many will have personal reasons for bewailing his untimely end. His generous donations to local and county charities have been frequently chronicled in these columns.

'The circumstances connected with the death of Sir Charles cannot be said to have been entirely cleared up by the inquest, but at least enough has been done to dispose of those rumours to which local superstition has given rise. There is no reason whatever to suspect foul play, or to imagine that death could be from any but natural causes. Sir Charles was a widower, and a man who may be said to have been in some ways of an eccentric habit of mind. In spite of his considerable wealth he was simple in his personal tastes, and his indoor servants at Baskerville Hall consisted of a married couple named Barrymore, the husband acting as butler and the wife as housekeeper. Their evidence, corroborated by that of several friends, tends to show that Sir Charles's health has for some time been impaired, and points especially to some affection of the heart, manifesting itself in changes of colour, breathlessness, and acute attacks of nervous depression. Dr James Mortimer, the friend and medical attendant of the deceased, has given evidence to the same effect.

'The facts of the case are simple. Sir Charles Baskerville was in the habit every night before going to bed of walking down the famous Yew Alley of Baskerville Hall. The evidence of the Barrymores shows that this had been his custom. On the 4th of June Sir Charles had declared his intention of starting next day for London, and had ordered Barrymore to prepare his luggage. That night he went out as usual for his nocturnal walk, in the course of which he was in the habit of smoking a cigar. He never returned. At twelve o'clock Barrymore, finding the hall door still open, became alarmed and, lighting a lantern, went in search of his master. The day had been wet, and Sir Charles's footmarks were easily traced down the Alley. Half-way down this walk there is a gate which leads out on to the moor. There were indications that Sir Charles had stood for some little time here. He then proceeded down the Alley, and it was at the far end of it that his body was discovered. One fact which has not been explained is the statement of Barrymore that his master's footprints altered their character from the time that he passed the moor-gate, and that he appeared from thence onwards to

20 *a few days before that date.* We are shortly told that Sir Charles died "on the 4th of June." Since this was "some three months" before Dr. Mortimer's visit to Holmes, it would seem that the visit took place in the month of September. (In the original *Strand Magazine* version of the story, however, and in a number of subsequent book editions, the *Devon County Chronicle* of *May 14th* is referred to, and Sir Charles is said to have died "on the 4th of May.")

21 nouveaux riches. French: those who have recently become rich; parvenus.

22 *dyspnœa*. Labored breathing due to inadequate action of the heart and a consequent want of aeration of the blood.

23 *the Pope*. It was Pope Leo XIII, 1810–1903, whom Holmes obliged by solving the affair of the Vatican cameos. Holmes was later to investigate the sudden death of Cardinal Tosca at the express desire of this same Pope ("The Adventure of Black Peter").

have been walking upon his toes. One Murphy, a gipsy horse-dealer, was on the moor at no great distance at the time, but he appears by his own confession to have been the worse for drink. He declares that he heard cries, but is unable to state from what direction they came. No signs of violence were to be discovered upon Sir Charles's person and though the doctor's evidence pointed to an almost incredible facial distortion—so great that Dr Mortimer refused at first to believe that it was indeed his friend and patient who lay before him—it was explained that

22 that is a symptom which is not unusual in cases of dyspnœa and death from cardiac exhaustion. This explanation was borne out by the post-mortem examination, which showed long-standing organic disease, and the coroner's jury returned a verdict in accordance with the medical evidence. It is well that this is so, for it is obviously of the utmost importance that Sir Charles's heir should settle at the Hall, and continue the good work which has been so sadly interrupted. Had the prosaic finding of the coroner not finally put an end to the romantic stories which have been whispered in connection with the affair, it might have been difficult to find a tenant for Baskerville Hall. It is understood that the next-of-kin is Mr Henry Baskerville, if he be still alive, the son of Sir Charles Baskerville's younger brother. The young man, when last heard of, was in America, and inquiries are being instituted with a view to informing him of his good fortune.'

Dr Mortimer refolded his paper and replaced it in his pocket.

'Those are the public facts, Mr Holmes, in connection with the death of Sir Charles Baskerville.'

'I must thank you,' said Sherlock Holmes, 'for calling my attention to a case which certainly presents some features of interest. I had observed some newspaper comment at the time, but I was exceedingly preoccupied by that little affair of the

23 Vatican cameos, and in my anxiety to oblige the Pope I lost touch with several interesting English cases. This article, you say, contains all the public facts?'

'It does.'

'Then let me have the private ones.' He leaned back, put his finger-tips together, and assumed his most impassive and judicial expression.

'In doing so,' said Dr Mortimer, who had begun to show signs of some strong emotion, 'I am telling that which I have not confided to anyone. My motive for withholding it from the coroner's inquiry is that a man of science shrinks from placing himself in the public position of seeming to indorse a popular superstition. I had the further motive that Baskerville Hall, as the paper says, would certainly remain untenanted if anything were done to increase its already rather grim reputation. For both these reasons I thought that I was justified in telling rather less than I knew, since no practical good could result from it, but with you there is no reason why I should not be perfectly frank.

'The moor is very sparsely inhabited, and those who live near each other are thrown very much together. For this reason I saw a good deal of Sir Charles Baskerville. With the exception of Mr Frankland, of Lafter Hall, and Mr Stapleton, the naturalist, there are no other men of education within many miles. Sir Charles was a retiring man, but the chance of his illness brought us together, and a community of interests in science kept us so. He had brought back much scientific information from South Africa, and many a charming evening we have spent together discussing the comparative anatomy of the Bushman and the Hottentot.

'Within the last few months it became increasingly plain to me that Sir Charles's nervous system was strained to breaking point. He had taken this legend which I have read you exceedingly to heart—so much so that, although he would walk in his own grounds, nothing would induce him to go out upon the moor at night. Incredible as it may appear to you, Mr Holmes, he was honestly convinced that a dreadful fate overhung his family, and certainly the records which he was able to give of his ancestors were not encouraging. The idea of some ghastly presence constantly haunted him, and on more than one occasion he has asked me whether I had on my medical journeys at night ever seen any strange creature or heard the baying of a hound. The latter question he put to me several times, and always with a voice which vibrated with excitement.

'I can well remember driving up to his house in the evening, some three weeks before the fatal event. He chanced to be at his hall door. I had descended from my gig and was standing **24** in front of him, when I saw his eyes fix themselves over my shoulder, and stare past me with an expression of the most dreadful horror. I whisked round and had just time to catch a glimpse of something which I took to be a large black calf passing at the head of the drive. So excited and alarmed was he that I was compelled to go down to the spot where the animal had been and look around for it. It was gone, however, and the incident appeared to make the worst impression upon his mind. I stayed with him all the evening and it was on that occasion, to explain the emotion which he had shown, that he confided to my keeping that narrative which I read to you when first I came. I mention this small episode because it assumes some importance in view of the tragedy which followed, but I was convinced at the time that the matter was entirely trivial and that his excitement had no justification.

'It was at my advice that Sir Charles was about to go to London. His heart was, I knew, affected, and the constant anxiety in which he lived, however chimerical the cause of it might be, was evidently having a serious effect upon his health. I thought that a few months among the distractions of town would send him back a new man. Mr Stapleton, a mutual friend, who was much concerned at his state of health, was of the same opinion. At the last instant came this terrible catastrophe.

'On the night of Sir Charles's death Barrymore the butler, who made the discovery, sent Perkins the groom on horseback to me, and as I was sitting up late I was able to reach Baskerville Hall within an hour of the event. I checked and corroborated all the facts which were mentioned at the inquest. I followed the footsteps down the Yew Alley, I saw the spot at the moor-gate where he seemed to have waited, I remarked the change in the shape of the prints after that point, I noted that there were no other footsteps save those of Barrymore on the soft gravel, and finally I carefully examined the body, which had not been touched until my arrival. Sir Charles lay on his face, his arms out, his fingers dug into the ground, and his features convulsed with some strong emotion to such an extent that I could hardly have sworn to his identity. There was certainly no physical injury of any kind. But one false statement was made by Barrymore at the

24 *gig.* A light one-horse two-wheeled carriage.

25 *the footprints of a gigantic hound!'* "As any naturalist will assure you, it is not possible to identify the breed of a dog by his footprints," Professor Remsen Ten Eyck Schenck objected. "As Gertrude Stein might put it, when it comes to pawprints 'a dog is a dog is a dog.' One can eliminate some possibilities, of course, on the basis of size, and might even in some cases adduce further information as to whether the dog were smooth-coated or long-haired, since an excessively shaggy dog will have enough hair around his paws to blur the outlines of his tracks perceptibly. But to decide just like that whether a given set of prints were made by a Great Dane, a hound, a Newfoundland, a St. Bernard, or just plain dog? Never!"

To this Mr. Robert Clyne responded: "Technically [Professor Schenck] may be right—but he has not taken into consideration the psychological impact of the legend. Mortimer was acting quite normally in assuming that the dog was a hound."

inquest. He said that there were no traces upon the ground round the body. He did not observe any. But I did—some little distance off, but fresh and clear.'

'Footprints?'

'Footprints.'

'A man's or a woman's?'

Dr Mortimer looked strangely at us for an instant, and his voice sank almost to a whisper as he answered:

25   'Mr Holmes, they were the footprints of a gigantic hound!'

❖

3 ❖ THE PROBLEM
❖

I confess that at these words a shudder passed through me. There was a thrill in the doctor's voice which showed that he was himself deeply moved by that which he told us. Holmes leaned forward in his excitement, and his eyes had the hard, dry glitter which shot from them when he was keenly interested.

'You saw this?'

'As clearly as I see you.'

'And you said nothing?'

'What was the use?'

'How was it that no one else saw it?'

'The marks were some twenty yards from the body, and no one gave them a thought. I don't suppose I should have done so had I not known this legend.'

'There are many sheep-dogs on the moor?'

'No doubt, but this was no sheep-dog.'

'You say it was large?'

'Enormous.'

'But it had not approached the body?'

'No.'

'What sort of night was it?'

'Damp and raw.'

'But not actually raining?'

'No.'

'What is the alley like?'

'There are two lines of old yew hedge, twelve feet high and impenetrable. The walk in the centre is about eight feet across.'

'Is there anything between the hedges and the walk?'

'Yes, there is a strip of grass about six feet broad on either side.'

'I understand that the yew hedge is penetrated at one point by a gate?'

'Yes, the wicket-gate which leads on to the moor.'

'Is there any other opening?'

'None.'

'So that to reach the Yew Alley one either has to come down it from the house or else to enter it by the moor-gate?'

'There is an exit through a summer-house at the far end.'

'Had Sir Charles reached this?'

'No; he lay about fifty yards from it.'

'Now, tell me, Dr Mortimer—and this is important—the marks which you saw were on the path and not on the grass?'

'No marks could show on the grass.'

'Were they on the same side of the path as the moor-gate?'

'Yes; they were on the edge of the path on the same side as the moor-gate.'

'You interest me exceedingly. Another point. Was the wicket-gate closed?'

'Closed and padlocked.'

'How high was it?'

'About four feet high.'

'Then anyone could have got over it?'

'Yes.'

'And what marks did you see by the wicket-gate?'

'None in particular.'

'Good Heaven! Did no one examine?'

'Yes, I examined myself.'

'And found nothing?'

'It was all very confused. Sir Charles had evidently stood there for five or ten minutes.'

'How do you know that?'

'Because the ash had twice dropped from his cigar.'

'Excellent! This is a colleague, Watson, after our own heart. But the marks?'

'He had left his own marks all over that small patch of gravel. I could discern no others.'

Sherlock Holmes struck his hand against his knee with an impatient gesture.

'If I had only been there!' he cried. 'It is evidently a case of extraordinary interest, and one which presented immense opportunities to the scientific expert. That gravel page upon which I might have read so much has been long ere this smudged by the rain and defaced by the clogs of curious peasants. Oh, Dr Mortimer, Dr Mortimer, to think that you should not have called me in! You have indeed much to answer for.'

'I could not call you in, Mr Holmes, without disclosing these facts to the world and I have already given my reasons for not wishing to do so. Besides, besides——'

'Why do you hesitate?'

'There is a realm in which the most acute and most experienced of detectives is helpless.'

'You mean that the thing is supernatural?'

'I did not positively say so.'

'No, but you evidently think it.'

'Since the tragedy, Mr Holmes, there have come to my ears several incidents which are hard to reconcile with the settled order of Nature.'

'For example?'

'I find that before the terrible event occurred several people had seen a creature upon the moor which corresponds with this Baskerville demon, and which could not possibly be any animal known to science. They all agreed that it was a huge creature, luminous, ghastly and spectral. I have cross-examined these men, one of them a hard-headed countryman, one a farrier, and one a moorland farmer, who all tell the **26**

'YOU HAVE INDEED MUCH TO ANSWER FOR.'

Illustration by Sidney Paget for the *Strand Magazine*, September, 1901.

26 *a farrier.* One who shoes horses; a blacksmith.

same story of this dreadful apparition, exactly corresponding to the hell-hound of the legend. I assure you that there is a reign of terror in the district, and that it is a hardy man who will cross the moor at night.'

'And you, a trained man of science, believe it to be supernatural?'

'I do not know what to believe.'

Holmes shrugged his shoulders. 'I have hitherto confined my investigations to this world,' said he. 'In a modest way I have combated evil, but to take on the Father of Evil himself would, perhaps, be too ambitious a task. Yet you must admit that the footmark is material.'

'The original hound was material enough to tug a man's throat out, and yet he was diabolical as well.'

'I see that you have quite gone over to the supernaturalists. But now, Dr Mortimer, tell me this. If you hold these views, why have you come to consult me at all? You tell me in the same breath that it is useless to investigate Sir Charles's death, and that you desire me to do it.'

'I did not say that I desired you to do it.'

'Then how can I assist you?'

'By advising me as to what I should do with Sir Henry Baskerville, who arrives at Waterloo Station'—Dr Mortimer looked at his watch—'in exactly one hour and a quarter.'

'He being the heir?'

'Yes. On the death of Sir Charles we inquired for this young gentleman, and found that he had been farming in Canada. From the accounts which have reached us he is an excellent fellow in every way. I speak now not as a medical man but as a trustee and executor of Sir Charles's will.'

'There is no other claimant, I presume?'

'None. The only other kinsman whom we have been able to trace was Rodger Baskerville, the youngest of three brothers of whom poor Sir Charles was the elder. The second brother, who died young, is the father of this lad Henry. The third, Rodger, was the black sheep of the family. He came of the old masterful Baskerville strain, and was the very image, they tell me, of the family picture of old Hugo. He made England too hot to hold him, fled to Central America, and died there in 1876 of yellow fever. Henry is the last of the Baskervilles. In one hour and five minutes I meet him at Waterloo Station. I have had a wire that he arrived at Southampton this morning. Now, Mr Holmes, what would you advise me to do with him?'

'Why should he not go to the home of his fathers?'

'It seems natural, does it not? And yet, consider that every Baskerville who goes there meets with an evil fate. I feel sure that if Sir Charles could have spoken with me before his death he would have warned me against bringing this, the last of the old race, and the heir to great wealth, to that deadly place. And yet it cannot be denied that the prosperity of the whole poor, bleak countryside depends upon his presence. All the good work which has been done by Sir Charles will crash to the ground if there is no tenant of the Hall. I fear lest I should be swayed too much by my own obvious interest in the matter, and that is why I bring the case before you and ask for your advice.'

Holmes considered for a little time. 'Put into plain words, the matter is this,' said he. 'In your opinion there is a diabolical agency which makes Dartmoor an unsafe abode for a Baskerville—that is your opinion?'

'At least I might go the length of saying that there is some evidence that this may be so.'

'Exactly. But surely, if your supernatural theory be correct, it could work the young man evil in London as easily as in Devonshire. A devil with merely local powers like a parish vestry would be too inconceivable a thing.'

'You put the matter more flippantly, Mr Holmes, than you would probably do if you were brought into personal contact with these things. Your advice, then, as I understand it, is that the young man will be as safe in Devonshire as in London. He comes in fifty minutes. What would you recommend?'

'I recommend, sir, that you take a cab, call off your spaniel, who is scratching at my front door, and proceed to Waterloo to meet Sir Henry Baskerville.'

'And then?'

'And then you will say nothing to him at all until I have made up my mind about the matter.'

'How long will it take you to make up your mind?'

'Twenty-four hours. At ten o'clock tomorrow, Dr Mortimer, I will be much obliged to you if you will call upon me here, and it will be of help to me in my plans for the future if you will bring Sir Henry Baskerville with you.'

'I will do so, Mr Holmes.'

He scribbled the appointment on his shirt-cuff and hurried off in his strange, peering, absent-minded fashion. Holmes stopped him at the head of the stair.

'Only one more question, Dr Mortimer. You say that before Sir Charles Baskerville's death several people saw this apparition upon the moor?'

'Three people did.'

'Did any see it after?'

'I have not heard of any.'

'Thank you. Good morning.'

Holmes returned to his seat with that quiet look of inward satisfaction which meant that he had a congenial task before him.

'Going out, Watson?'

'Unless I can help you.'

'No, my dear fellow, it is at the hour of action that I turn to you for aid. But this is splendid, really unique from some points of view. When you pass Bradley's would you ask him to send up a pound of the strongest shag tobacco? Thank you. It would be as well if you could make it convenient not to return before evening. Then I should be very glad to compare impressions as to this most interesting problem which has been submitted to us this morning.'

I knew that seclusion and solitude were very necessary for my friend in those hours of intense mental concentration during which he weighed every particle of evidence, constructed alternative theories, balanced one against the other, and made up his mind as to which points were essential and which immaterial. I therefore spent the day at my club, and did not return to Baker Street until evening. It was nearly nine o'clock when I found myself in the sitting-room once more.

My first impression as I opened the door was that a fire had broken out, for the room was so filled with smoke that the

HE SCRIBBLED THE APPOINTMENT ON HIS SHIRT-CUFF . . .

Illustration by Sidney Paget for the *Strand Magazine*, September, 1901.

27 *a showery and miry day*. As we shall shortly see, the day was a Tuesday—in our view, Tuesday, September 25, 1888. On that day, according to the London *Times*, "Rain has fallen in the south and southeast. No bright sunshine has been registered at Westminster today."

28 *Stamford's*. This is clearly an error on Watson's part, for in the eighties, as today, London's leading map seller, and the sole agent for Ordnance and geological survey maps of England and Wales was Edward *Stanford* of 26 Cockspur Street, Charing Cross, now at 12 Long Acre.

29 *the hamlet of Grimpen*. No map of Dartmoor —not even a "very-large"-scale map—will show us Grimpen. If we look closely, however, we will have little difficulty in picking out a hamlet called *Widecombe-in-the-Moor*, which we suggest was "Grimpen." Widecombe was once famous for Widecombe Fair, celebrated in the English ballad of that title:

> Tom Pearse, Tom Pearse, lend me your grey
>   mare.
> All along, down along, out along lee.
> For I want to go to Widecombe Fair
>   Wi' Bill Brewer, Jan Stewer, Peter Gurney,
>   Peter Davy,
>   Dan'l Whiddon, Harry Hawk,
>   Old Uncle Tom Cobleigh and all.

30 *Here is Lafter Hall*. No Lafter Hall appears on our map, but there is a *Laughter* Tor, and it seems fair to assume that Laughter ("Lafter") Hall stood somewhere in its vicinity.

31 *High Tor*. Again, there is no "High Tor" on our map; Holmes perhaps referred to *Higher Tor* or to *Higher White Tor*, both shown.

32 *Foulmire*. This must, we think, be Watsonese for *Fox Tor Mire*, of which the Reverend Sabine Baring-Gould wrote in his *Book of Dartmoor*, first published in 1900 by Methuen & Co., Ltd., of London: it "once bore a very bad name. The only convict who really got away from Princetown [Prison] and was not recaptured was last seen making a bee-line for Fox Tor Mire."

33 *fourteen miles away*. Closer to *four* than to "fourteen"—to remain on the moor.

light of the lamp upon the table was blurred by it. As I entered, however, my fears were set at rest, for it was the acrid fumes of strong, coarse tobacco, which took me by the throat and set me coughing. Through the haze I had a vague vision of Holmes in his dressing-gown coiled up in an arm-chair with his black clay pipe between his lips. Several rolls of paper lay around him.

'Caught cold, Watson?' said he.

'No, it's this poisonous atmosphere.'

'I suppose it *is* pretty thick, now that you mention it.'

'Thick! It is intolerable.'

'Open the window, then! You have been at your club all day, I perceive.'

'My dear Holmes!'

'Am I right?'

'Certainly, but how——?'

He laughed at my bewildered expression.

'There is a delightful freshness about you, Watson, which makes it a pleasure to exercise any small powers which I possess at your expense. A gentleman goes forth on a showery **27** and miry day. He returns immaculate in the evening with the gloss still on his hat and his boots. He has been a fixture, therefore, all day. He is not a man with intimate friends. Where, then, could he have been? Is it not obvious?'

'Well, it is rather obvious.'

'The world is full of obvious things which nobody by any chance ever observes. Where do you think that I have been?'

'A fixture also.'

'On the contrary, I have been to Devonshire.'

'In spirit?'

'Exactly. My body has remained in this arm-chair; and has, I regret to observe, consumed in my absence two large pots of coffee and an incredible amount of tobacco. After you left **28** I sent down to Stamford's for the Ordnance map of this portion of the moor, and my spirit has hovered over it all day. I flatter myself that I could find my way about.'

'A large-scale map, I presume?'

'Very large.' He unrolled one section and held it over his knee. 'Here you have the particular district which concerns us. That is Baskerville Hall in the middle.'

'With a wood round it?'

'Exactly. I fancy the Yew Alley, though not marked under that name, must stretch along this line, with the moor, as you perceive, upon the right of it. This small clump of buildings **29** here is the hamlet of Grimpen, where our friend Dr Mortimer has his headquarters. Within a radius of five miles there are, as you see, only a very few scattered dwellings. Here is Lafter **30** Hall, which was mentioned in the narrative. There is a house indicated here which may be the residence of the naturalist —Stapleton, if I remember right, was his name. Here are two **31-32** moorland farm-houses, High Tor and Foulmire. Then four- **33** teen miles away the great convict prison of Princetown. Between and around these scattered points extends the desolate, lifeless moor. This, then, is the stage upon which tragedy has been played, and upon which we may help to play it again.'

'It must be a wild place.'

'Yes, the setting is a worthy one. If the devil did desire to have a hand in the affairs of men——'

'Then you are yourself inclining to the supernatural explanation.'

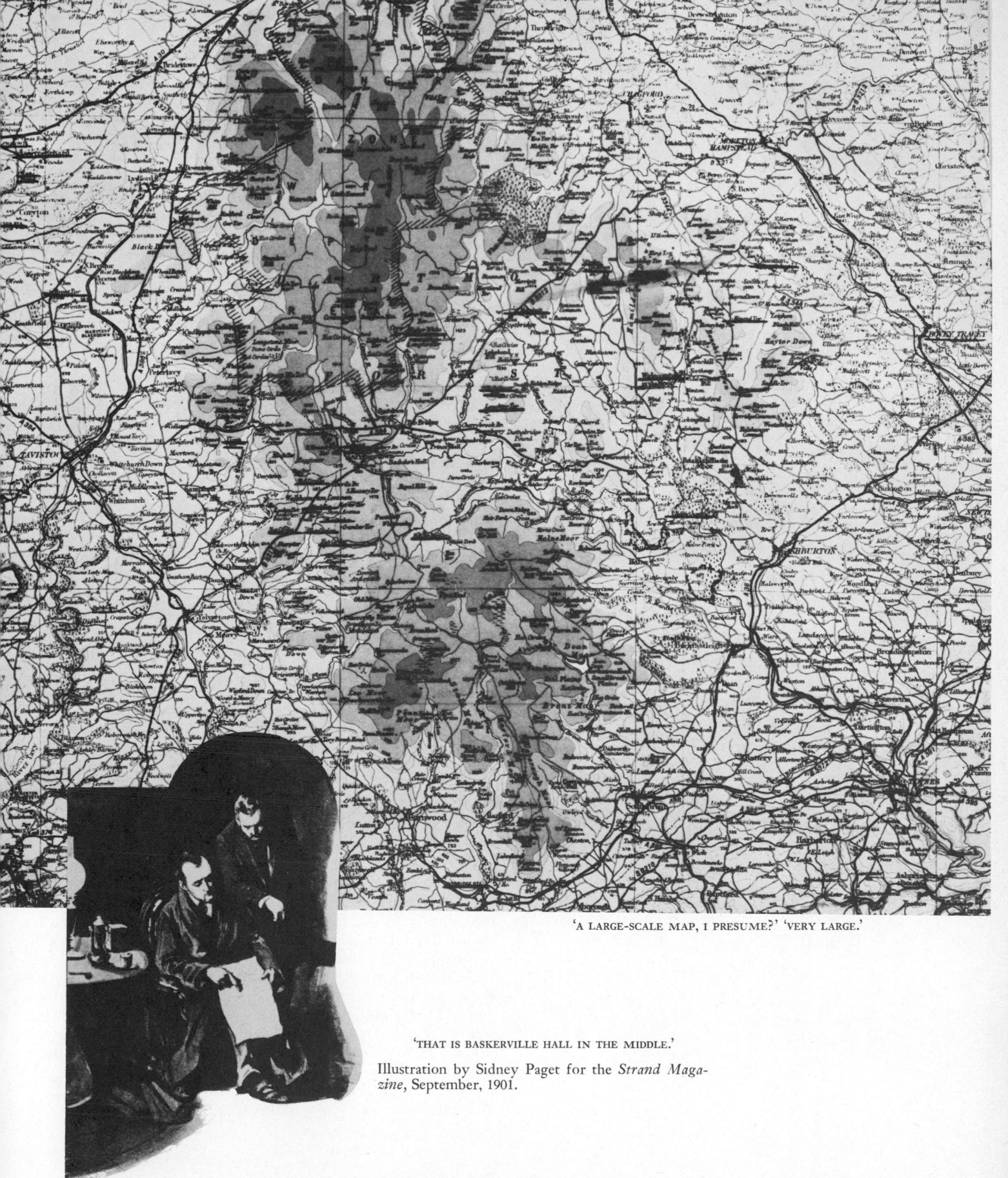

'A LARGE-SCALE MAP, I PRESUME?' 'VERY LARGE.'

'THAT IS BASKERVILLE HALL IN THE MIDDLE.'

Illustration by Sidney Paget for the *Strand Magazine*, September, 1901.

34 *a concentrated atmosphere helps a concentration of thought.* "If it is true that the English people enjoy a 'frowst' more than others," Mr. T. S. Blakeney wrote in *Sherlock Holmes: Fact or Fiction?*, "Holmes was, on unimpeachable testimony, English of the English. Watson awoke at The Cedars to find the room 'full of dense tobacco haze' ('The Man with the Twisted Lip'), and in *The Hound of the Baskervilles* found Holmes rejoicing in an atmosphere \so intolerable that he thought a fire had broken out.'"

'The devil's agents may be of flesh and blood, may they not? There are two questions waiting for us at the outset. The one is whether any crime has been committed at all; the second is, what is the crime and how was it committed? Of course, if Dr Mortimer's surmise should be correct, and we are dealing with forces outside the ordinary laws of Nature, there is an end of our investigation. But we are bound to exhaust all other hypotheses before falling back upon this one. I think we'll shut that window again, if you don't mind. It is a singular thing, but I find that a concentrated atmosphere helps a **34** concentration of thought. I have not pushed it to the length of getting into a box to think, but that is the logical outcome of my convictions. Have you turned the case over in your mind?'

'Yes, I have thought a good deal of it in the course of the day.'

'What do you make of it?'

'It is very bewildering.'

'It has certainly a character of its own. There are points of distinction about it. That change in the footprints, for example. What do you make of that?'

'Mortimer said that the man had walked on tiptoe down that portion of the alley.'

'He only repeated what some fool had said at the inquest. Why should a man walk on tiptoe down the alley?'

'What then?'

'He was running, Watson—running desperately, running for his life, running until he burst his heart and fell dead upon his face.'

'Running from what?'

'There lies our problem. There are indications that the man was crazed with fear before ever he began to run.'

'How can you say that?'

'I am presuming that the cause of his fears came to him across the moor. If that were so, and it seems most probable, only a man who had lost his wits would have run *from* the house instead of towards it. If the gipsy's evidence may be taken as true, he ran with cries for help in the direction where help was least likely to be. Then again, whom was he waiting for that night, and why was he waiting for him in the Yew Alley rather than in his own house?'

'You think that he was waiting for someone?'

'The man was elderly and infirm. We can understand his taking an evening stroll, but the ground was damp and the night inclement. Is it natural that he should stand for five or ten minutes, as Dr Mortimer, with more practical sense than I should have given him credit for, deduced from the cigar ash?'

'But he went out every evening.'

'I think it unlikely that he waited at the moor-gate every evening. On the contrary, the evidence is that he avoided the moor. That night he waited there. It was the night before he was to take his departure for London. The thing takes shape, Watson. It becomes coherent. Might I ask you to hand me my violin, and we will postpone all further thought upon this business until we have had the advantage of meeting Dr Mortimer and Sir Henry Baskerville in the morning.'

Our breakfast-table was cleared early, and Holmes waited in his dressing-gown for the promised interview. Our clients were punctual to their appointment, for the clock had just struck ten when Dr Mortimer was shown up, followed by the young baronet. The latter was a small, alert, dark-eyed man about thirty years of age, very sturdily built, with thick black eyebrows, and a strong, pugnacious face. He wore a ruddy-tinted tweed suit, and had the weather-beaten appearance of one who has spent most of his time in the open air, and yet there was something in his steady eye and the quiet assurance of his bearing which indicated the gentleman.

'This is Sir Henry Baskerville,' said Dr Mortimer.

'Why, yes,' said he, 'and the strange thing is, Mr Sherlock Holmes, that if my friend here had not proposed coming round to you this morning I should have come on my own. I understand that you think out little puzzles, and I've had one this morning which wants more thinking out than I am able to give to it.'

'Pray take a seat, Sir Henry. Do I understand you to say that you have yourself had some remarkable experience since you arrived in London?'

'Nothing of much importance, Mr Holmes. Only a joke, as like as not. It was this letter, if you can call it a letter, which reached me this morning.'

He laid an envelope upon the table, and we all bent over it. It was of common quality, greyish in colour. The address, 'Sir Henry Baskerville, Northumberland Hotel,' was printed in rough characters; the post-mark 'Charing Cross,' and the date of posting the preceding evening.

'Who knew that you were going to the Northumberland Hotel?' asked Holmes, glancing keenly across at our visitor.

'No one could have known. We only decided after I met Dr Mortimer.'

'But Dr Mortimer was, no doubt, already stopping there?'

'No, I had been staying with a friend,' said the doctor. 'There was no possible indication that we intended to go to this hotel.'

'Hum! Someone seems to be very deeply interested in your movements.' Out of the envelope he took a half-sheet of foolscap paper folded into four. This he opened and spread flat upon the table. Across the middle of it a single sentence had been formed by the expedient of pasting printed words upon it. It ran: 'As you value your life or your reason keep away from the moor.' The word 'moor' only was printed in ink.

'Now,' said Sir Henry Baskerville, 'perhaps you will tell me, Mr Holmes, what in thunder is the meaning of that, and who is it that takes so much interest in my affairs?'

'What do you make of it, Dr Mortimer? You must allow that there is nothing supernatural about this, at any rate?'

'No, sir, but it might very well come from someone who was convinced that the business is supernatural.'

'What business?' asked Sir Henry, sharply. 'It seems to me that all you gentlemen know a great deal more than I do about my own affairs.'

'You shall share our knowledge before you leave this room,

'THIS IS SIR HENRY BASKERVILLE . . .'

Portrait by Sidney Paget for the *Strand Magazine*, September, 1901.

HE GLANCED SWIFTLY OVER IT, RUNNING HIS EYES UP
AND DOWN THE COLUMNS.

Illustration by Sidney Paget for the *Strand Magazine*, September, 1901.

35 '*Capital article this on Free Trade*. The late Gavin Brend, in *My Dear Holmes*, expressed his opinion that an article on Free Trade would not have appeared in the *Times* until 1902 or 1903, but we do not feel that this can be allowed to stand; surely, since the days of Pitt, Free Trade has been a topic of discussion in England. It must be admitted, however, that the late Dr. Ernest Bloomfield Zeisler carefully examined the London *Times* for the last Tuesday in September for every year from 1884 to 1889 and 1894 to 1899 without finding the article in question.

36 *the special expert in crime*. "There is . . . little doubt," Miss Madeleine B. Stern wrote in "Sherlock Holmes: Rare Book Collector," "that specimens of Granjon's civilite, the Estienne, the Bodoni, Fournier Le Jeune, the great Enschede type specimen book with its exotic fonts, had all . . . found their way to Holmes' library . . ."

Sir Henry. I promise you that,' said Sherlock Holmes. 'We will confine ourselves for the present, with your permission, to this very interesting document, which must have been put together and posted yesterday evening. Have you yesterday's *Times*, Watson?'

'It is here in the corner.'

'Might I trouble you for it—the inside page, please, with the leading articles?' He glanced swiftly over it, running his eyes up and down the columns. 'Capital article this on Free **35** Trade. Permit me to give you an extract from it. "You may be cajoled into imagining that your own special trade or your own industry will be encouraged by a protective tariff, but it stands to reason that such legislation must in the long run keep away wealth from the country, diminish the value of our imports, and lower the general conditions of life in this island." What do you think of that, Watson?' cried Holmes, in high glee, rubbing his hands together with satisfaction. 'Don't you think that is an admirable sentiment?'

Dr Mortimer looked at Holmes with an air of professional interest, and Sir Henry Baskerville turned a pair of puzzled dark eyes upon me.

'I don't know much about the tariff and things of that kind,' said he; 'but it seems to me we've got a bit off the trail so far as that note is concerned.'

'On the contrary, I think we are particularly hot upon the trail, Sir Henry. Watson here knows more about my methods than you do, but I fear that even he has not quite grasped the significance of this sentence.'

'No, I confess that I see no connection.'

'And yet, my dear Watson, there is so very close a connection that the one is extracted out of the other. "You," "your," "your," "life," "reason," "value," "keep away," "from the." Don't you see now whence these words have been taken?'

'By thunder, you're right! Well, if that isn't smart!' cried Sir Henry.

'If any possible doubt remained it is settled by the fact that "keep away" and "from the" are cut out in one piece.'

'Well, now—so it is!'

'Really, Mr Holmes, this exceeds anything which I could have imagined,' said Dr Mortimer, gazing at my friend in amazement. 'I could understand anyone saying that the words were from a newspaper; but that you should name which, and add that it came from the leading article, is really one of the most remarkable things which I have ever known. How did you do it?'

'I presume, doctor, that you could tell the skull of a negro from that of an Esquimaux?'

'Most certainly.'

'But how?'

'Because that is my special hobby. The differences are obvious. The supra-orbital crest, the facial angle, the maxillary curve, the——'

'But this is my special hobby, and the differences are equally obvious. There is as much difference to my eyes between the leaded bourgeois type of a *Times* article and the slovenly print of an evening halfpenny paper as there could be between your negro and your Esquimaux. The detection of types is one of the most elementary branches of knowledge **36** to the special expert in crime, though I confess that once

From *The Times*, Aug. 18th, 1890

From *The Leeds Mercury*, Sept. 6th, 1890

LONDON, MONDAY, AUGUST 18, 1890.

THE SESSION.

The reproach of barrenness has been levelled at many recent Sessions, but in hardly any recorded case has it been as completely justified as in the present year. Party men may endlessly debate the question whether the larger share of responsibility for this disappointing result was due to the obstructive tactics of the Opposition or to the mismanagement of business by the Government, but an impartial judgment will not find much difficulty in assigning its proper weight to each of these influences.

'. . . THE LEADED BOURGEOIS TYPE OF A
TIMES ARTICLE . . .'

As Holmes remarked, a *Times* article is entirely distinctive. It is set in small Bourgeois, 9 pt., 2 pt. leaded, and is Miller and Richards "modern face."

The fatal accident to a lady at Starbeck by falling out of a railway carriage compartment owing to the door not having been fastened is, it should be understood, a form of accident entirely preventable if the method of shutting carriage-doors in use on one of the Scotch railways were adopted. On the Caledonian Railway, a compartment door only requires to be drawn inwards in order to shut itself. The lock has a double mechanism. Slamming the door to is practically an effectual closing of the door, and the turning of the door handle by hand, although an additional security, is not positively necessary, unless there is something defective in the lock. In this way a door cannot be open when it appears to be closed. Rights of patent, and refusal to allow other railways to make use of this ingenious method of fastening, probably explain why it is not in use on all other railways. If this be the explanation, it is regrettable, in the interests of public safety.

'. . . I CONFESS THAT ONCE WHEN I WAS VERY YOUNG
I CONFUSED THE LEEDS MERCURY WITH THE
WESTERN MORNING NEWS.'

The type used in the *Leeds Mercury* (now the *Yorkshire Post*) (*above*) at this period was Minion 7 pt., 1½ pt. leaded. That in the *Western Morning News* (*below*) was Old Style, Non-pareil (6 pt., 1½ pt. leaded).

when I was very young I confused the *Leeds Mercury* with the *Western Morning News*. But a *Times* leader is entirely distinctive, and these words could have been taken from nothing else. As it was done yesterday the strong probability was that we should find the words in yesterday's issue.'

'So far as I can follow you, then, Mr Holmes,' said Sir Henry Baskerville, 'someone cut out this message with a scissors——'

'Nail-scissors,' said Holmes. 'You can see that it was a very short-bladed scissors, since the cutter had to take two snips over "keep away."'

'That is so. Someone, then, cut out the message with a pair of short-bladed scissors, pasted it with paste——'

'Gum,' said Holmes.

'With gum on to the paper. But I want to know why the word "moor" should have been written?'

'Because he could not find it in print. The other words were all simple, and might be found in any issue, but "moor" would be less common.'

'Why, of course, that would explain it. Have you read anything else in this message, Mr Holmes?'

'There are one or two indications, and yet the utmost pains have been taken to remove all clues. The address, you observe, is printed in rough characters. But *The Times* is a paper which is seldom found in any hands but those of the highly educated. We may take it, therefore, that the letter was composed by an educated man who wished to pose as an uneducated one, and his effort to conceal his own writing suggests that that writing might be known, or come to be known by you. Again, you will observe, that the words are not gummed on in an accurate line, but that some are much

From *The Western Morning News*, 28th October, 1890

THE HAMPSTEAD MURDER.

PRISONER BEFORE THE MAGISTRATE.

EVIDENCE OF THE HUSBAND.

Mrs. Pearcy, who is charged with the murder of Mrs. Hogg, at Hampstead, was removed from Kentish Town to Marylebone Police Court at a quarter to eight yesterday morning. Since her arrest she has been very calm, making no reference to the crime, except remarking when charged :—"I know nothing about it." Her appearance would indicate her as being inferior in class to the deceased woman, but she certainly does not betray that vicious character which the police allege her to be endowed with. Her indifference, whether assumed or not, gave way during Sunday night, when she wept freely. When escorted from the cell to the prison van, which had been backed into the station-yard to avoid the assembled crowd, her eyes were blood-shot, and she looked dejected. The van was provided with additional officers, but as it passed through the crowd no feeling was expressed.

At the Marylebone Police Court yesterday Mary Eleanor Pearcy, 24, married, was brought up by Detective-Inspector Bannister, of the S Division, before Mr. Cooke, charged with the murder of Phœbe Hogg, at 2, Priory-street, on the 24th inst. She was further charged on suspicion with killing and slaying Phœbe Hanslope Hogg, aged 18 months. Mr. Freake Palmer, solicitor, defended.

Frank Samuel Hogg, of 141, Prince of Wales's-road, a furniture remover, said the deceased, Phœbe Hogg, was his wife. (The witness wept bitterly.) The child, Phœbe Hanslope Hogg, was his daughter. She was 18 months old. He last saw them on Friday morning, about nine o'clock. The witness then left to go to his work, and returned home at ten o'clock at night. He then found that his wife was not at home. His wife was 31 years of age last May. He went to the house of the prisoner, who had been friendly with his wife, to know if she had seen her. The prisoner's house was about six minutes' walk from his house. The prisoner was not at home, and he did not see her that night. He had not seen or spoken to her since the Wednesday before. To his knowledge there had not been any quarrel between his wife and the prisoner. He carried a latch-key of the prisoner's door, and had been in the habit of visiting her. He did not think his wife knew that he went there.

higher than others. "Life," for example, is quite out of its proper place. That may point to carelessness or it may point to agitation and hurry upon the part of the cutter. On the whole I incline to the latter view, since the matter was evidently important, and it is unlikely that the composer of such a letter would be careless. If he were in a hurry it opens up the interesting question why he should be in a hurry, since any letter posted up to early morning would reach Sir Henry before he would leave his hotel. Did the composer fear an interruption—and from whom?'

'We are coming now rather into the region of guess-work,' said Dr Mortimer.

'Say, rather, into the region where we balance probabilities and choose the most likely. It is the scientific use of the imagination, but we have always some material basis on which to start our speculations. Now, you would call it a guess, no doubt, but I am almost certain that this address has been written in an hotel.'

'How in the world can you say that?'

'If you examine it carefully you will see that both the pen and the ink have given the writer trouble. The pen has spluttered twice in a single word, and has run dry three times in a short address, showing that there was very little ink in the bottle. Now, a private pen or ink-bottle is seldom allowed to be in such a state, and the combination of the two must be quite rare. But you know the hotel ink and the hotel pen, where it is rare to get anything else. Yes, I have very little hesitation in saying that could we examine the wastepaper baskets of the hotels round Charing Cross until we found the remains of the mutilated *Times* leader we could lay our hands straight upon the person who sent this singular message. Halloa! Halloa! What's this?'

He was carefully examining the foolscap, upon which the words were pasted, holding it only an inch or two from his eyes.

'Well?'

'Nothing,' said he, throwing it down. 'It is a blank half-sheet of paper, without even a watermark upon it. I think we have drawn as much as we can from this curious letter; and now, Sir Henry, has anything else of interest happened to you since you have been in London?'

'Why, no, Mr Holmes. I think not.'

'You have not observed anyone follow or watch you?'

'I seem to have walked right into the thick of a dime novel,' said our visitor. 'Why in thunder should anyone follow or watch me?'

'We are coming to that. You have nothing else to report to us before we go into this matter?'

'Well, it depends upon what you think worth reporting.'

'I think anything out of the ordinary routine of life well worth reporting.'

Sir Henry smiled. 'I don't know much of British life yet, for I have spent nearly all my time in the States and in Canada. But I hope that to lose one of your boots is not part of the ordinary routine of life over here.'

'You have lost one of your boots?'

'My dear sir,' cried Dr Mortimer, 'it is only mislaid. You will find it when you return to the hotel. What is the use of troubling Mr Holmes with trifles of this kind?'

. . . HOLDING IT ONLY AN INCH OR TWO FROM HIS EYES.

Illustration by Sidney Paget for the *Strand Magazine*, September, 1901.

'Well, he asked me for anything outside the ordinary routine.'

'Exactly,' said Holmes, 'however foolish the incident may seem. You have lost one of your boots, you say?'

'Well, mislaid it, anyhow. I put them both outside my door last night, and there was only one in the morning. I could get no sense out of the chap who cleans them. The worst of it is that I only bought the pair last night in the Strand, and I have never had them on.'

'If you have never worn them, why did you put them out to be cleaned?'

'They were tan boots, and had never been varnished. That was why I put them out.'

'Then I understand that on your arrival in London yesterday you went out at once and bought a pair of boots?'

'I did a good deal of shopping. Dr Mortimer here went round with me. You see, if I am to be squire down there I must dress the part, and it may be that I have got a little careless in my ways out West. Among other things I bought these brown boots—gave six dollars for them—and had one stolen before ever I had them on my feet.'

'It seems a singularly useless thing to steal,' said Sherlock Holmes. 'I confess that I share Dr Mortimer's belief that it will not be long before the missing boot is found.'

'And now, gentlemen,' said the baronet, with decision, 'it seems to me that I have spoken quite enough about the little that I know. It is time that you kept your promise, and gave me a full account of what we are all driving at.'

'Your request is a very reasonable one,' Holmes answered. 'Dr Mortimer, I think you could not do better than to tell your story as you told it to us.'

Thus encouraged, our scientific friend drew his papers from his pocket, and presented the whole case as he had done upon the morning before. Sir Henry Baskerville listened with the deepest attention, and with an occasional exclamation of surprise.

'Well, I seem to have come into an inheritance with a vengeance,' said he, when the long narrative was finished. 'Of course, I've heard of the hound ever since I was in the nursery. It's the pet story of the family, though I never thought of taking it seriously before. But as to my uncle's death—well, it all seems boiling up in my head, and I can't get it clear yet. You don't seem quite to have made up your mind whether it's a case for a policeman or a clergyman.'

'Precisely.'

'And now there's this affair of the letter to me at the hotel. I suppose that fits into its place.'

'It seems to show that someone knows more than we do about what goes on upon the moor,' said Dr Mortimer.

'And also,' said Holmes, 'that someone is not ill-disposed towards you, since they warn you of danger.'

'Or it may be that they wish for their own purposes to scare me away.'

'Well, of course, that is possible also. I am very much indebted to you, Dr Mortimer, for introducing me to a problem which presents several interesting alternatives. But the practical point which we now have to decide, Sir Henry, is whether it is or is not advisable for you to go to Baskerville Hall.'

'Why should I not go?'

'. . . I ONLY BOUGHT THE PAIR LAST NIGHT
IN THE STRAND . . .'

G. H. Harris' bootshop in the Strand, at which Sir Henry Baskerville bought a pair of brown boots in 1888. The business, founded in 1865 by George Harris (who with his brother stands outside), has since been transferred to Savoy Buildings; The Bun Shop, though rebuilt, still survives. The photograph is from Michael Harrison's *In the Footsteps of Sherlock Holmes*.

37 *a very fine morning.* If this was the morning of Wednesday, September 26, 1888, as we believe, it was "a very fine morning." Said the *Times:* "In London the sheltered thermometer did not fall below 49 deg. . . . The rain noticed on Tuesday has ceased."

'THERE'S OUR MAN, WATSON! COME ALONG!'

Sidney Paget's famous "Regent Street" picture as he drew it for the *Strand Magazine*, September, 1901. In both the *Strand* and the Newnes book edition, however, the picture was printed *in reverse*, and many later editions have done the same thing.

'There seems to be danger.'

'Do you mean danger from this family fiend or do you mean danger from human beings?'

'Well, that is what we have to find out.'

'Whichever it is, my answer is fixed. There is no devil in hell, Mr Holmes, and there is no man upon earth who can prevent me from going to the home of my own people, and you may take that to be my final answer.' His dark brows knitted and his face flushed to a dusky red as he spoke. It was evident that the fiery temper of the Baskervilles was not extinct in this their last representative. 'Meanwhile,' said he, 'I have hardly had time to think over all that you have told me. It's a big thing for a man to have to understand and to decide at one sitting. I should like to have a quiet hour by myself to make up my mind. Now, look here, Mr Holmes, it's half-past eleven now, and I am going back right away to my hotel. Suppose you and your friend, Dr Watson, come round and lunch with us at two? I'll be able to tell you more clearly then how this thing strikes me.'

'Is that convenient to you, Watson?'

'Perfectly.'

'Then you may expect us. Shall I have a cab called?'

'I'd prefer to walk, for this affair has flurried me rather.'

'I'll join you in a walk, with pleasure,' said his companion.

'Then we meet again at two o'clock. Au revoir, and good morning!'

We heard the steps of our visitors descend the stair and the bang of the front door. In an instant Holmes had changed from the languid dreamer to the man of action.

'Your hat and boots, Watson, quick! Not a moment to lose!' He rushed into his room in his dressing-gown, and was back again in a few seconds in a frock-coat. We hurried together down the stairs and into the street. Dr Mortimer and Baskerville were still visible about two hundred yards ahead of us in the direction of Oxford Street.

'Shall I run on and stop them?'

'Not for the world, my dear Watson. I am perfectly satisfied with your company, if you will tolerate mine. Our friends **37** are wise, for it is certainly a very fine morning for a walk.'

He quickened his pace until we had decreased the distance which divided us by about half. Then, still keeping a hundred yards behind, we followed into Oxford Street and so down Regent Street. Once our friends stopped and stared into a shop window, upon which Holmes did the same. An instant afterwards he gave a little cry of satisfaction, and, following the direction of his eager eyes, I saw that a hansom cab with a man inside which had halted on the other side of the street was now walking slowly onwards again.

'There's our man, Watson! Come along! We'll have a good look at him, if we can do no more.'

At that instant I was aware of a bushy black beard and a pair of piercing eyes turned upon us through the side window of the cab. Instantly the trap-door at the top flew up, something was screamed to the driver, and the cab flew madly off down Regent Street. Holmes looked eagerly round for another, but no empty one was in sight. Then he dashed in wild pursuit amid the stream of the traffic, but the start was too great, and already the cab was out of sight.

'There now!' said Holmes, bitterly, as he emerged panting and white with vexation from the tide of vehicles. 'Was ever such bad luck and such bad management, too? Watson, Watson, if you are an honest man you will record this also and set it against my successes!'

'Who was the man?'

'I have not an idea.'

'A spy?'

'Well, it was evident from what we have heard that Baskerville has been very closely shadowed by someone since he has been in town. How else could it be known so quickly that it was the Northumberland Hotel which he had chosen? If they had followed him the first day, I argued that they would follow him also the second. You may have observed that I twice strolled over to the window while Dr Mortimer was reading his legend.'

'Yes, I remember.'

'I was looking out for loiterers in the street, but I saw none. We are dealing with a clever man, Watson. This matter cuts very deep, and though I have not finally made up my mind whether it is a benevolent or a malevolent agency which is in touch with us, I am conscious always of power and design. When our friends left I at once followed them in the hopes of marking down their invisible attendant. So wily was he that he had not trusted himself upon foot, but he had availed himself of a cab, so that he could loiter behind or dash past them and so escape their notice. His method had the additional advantage that if they were to take a cab he was all ready to follow them. It has, however, one obvious disadvantage.'

'It puts him in the power of the cabman.'

'Exactly.'

'What a pity we did not get the number!'

'My dear Watson, clumsy as I have been, you surely do not seriously imagine that I neglected to get the number? 2704 is our man. But that is no use to us for the moment.'

'I fail to see how you could have done more.'

'On observing the cab I should have instantly turned and walked in the other direction. I should then at my leisure have hired a second cab, and followed the first at a respectful distance, or, better still, have driven to the Northumberland Hotel and waited there. When our unknown had followed Baskerville home we should have had the opportunity of playing his own game upon himself, and seeing where he made for. As it is, by an indiscreet eagerness, which was taken advantage of with extraordinary quickness and energy by our opponent, we have betrayed ourselves and lost our man.'

We had been sauntering slowly down Regent Street during this conversation, and Dr Mortimer, with his companion, had long vanished in front of us.

'There is no object in our following them,' said Holmes. 'The shadow has departed and will not return. We must see what further cards we have in our hands, and play them with decision. Could you swear to that man's face within the cab?'

'I could swear only to the beard.'

'And so could I—from which I gather that in all probability it was a false one. A clever man upon so delicate an errand has no use for a beard save to conceal his features. Come in here, Watson!'

He turned into one of the district messenger offices, where he was warmly greeted by the manager.

'NOW, CARTWRIGHT, THERE ARE THE NAMES OF
TWENTY-THREE HOTELS HERE . . .'

Illustration by Sidney Paget for the *Strand Magazine*, September, 1901.

38 *Bond Street*. "Bond Street was built in 1686
by Sir Thomas Bond of Peckham, Comptroller of
the Household to Henrietta Maria, as Queen
Mother, who was created a baronet by Charles II,
and bought part of the Clarendon estate from
the Duke of Albemarle. The author of *Tristram
Shandy*, Laurence Sterne, died at 'the Silk Bag
Shop,' No. 41, March 18, 1768, without a friend
near him."—Augustus J. C. Hare, *Walks in London*, Vol. II.

It is possible that one of the picture galleries
Holmes and Watson visited was the Grosvenor
Gallery at No. 134. Opened May, 1877, by Sir
Coutts Lindsay, it had a doorway by Palladio,
brought from the Church of St. Lucia at Venice,
inserted in what Hare called "an inartistic front
of mountebank architecture."

'Ah, Wilson, I see you have not forgotten the little case in
which I had the good fortune to help you?'

'No, sir, indeed I have not. You saved my good name, and
perhaps my life.'

'My dear fellow, you exaggerate. I have some recollection,
Wilson, that you had among your boys a lad named Cartwright, who showed some ability during the investigation.'

'Yes, sir, he is still with us.'

'Could you ring him up? Thank you! And I should be glad
to have change of this five-pound note.'

A lad of fourteen, with a bright, keen face, had obeyed the
summons of the manager. He stood now gazing with great
reverence at the famous detective.

'Let me have the Hotel Directory,' said Holmes. 'Thank
you! Now, Cartwright, there are the names of twenty-three
hotels here, all in the immediate neighbourhood of Charing
Cross. Do you see?'

'Yes, sir.'

'You will visit each of these in turn.'

'Yes, sir.'

'You will begin in each case by giving the outside porter
one shilling. Here are twenty-three shillings.'

'Yes, sir.'

'You will tell him that you want to see the waste paper of
yesterday. You will say that an important telegram has mis-
carried, and that you are looking for it. You understand?'

'Yes, sir.'

'But what you are really looking for is the centre page of
The Times with some holes cut in it with scissors. Here is a
copy of *The Times*. It is this page. You could easily recognize
it, could you not?'

'Yes, sir.'

'In each case the outside porter will send for the hall porter,
to whom also you will give a shilling. Here are twenty-three
shillings. You will then learn in possibly twenty cases out of
the twenty-three that the waste of the day before has been
burned or removed. In the three other cases you will be shown
a heap of paper, and you will look for this page of *The Times*
among it. The odds are enormously against your finding it.
There are ten shillings over in case of emergencies. Let me
have a report by wire at Baker Street before evening. And
now, Watson, it only remains for us to find out by wire the
identity of the cabman, No. 2704, and then we will drop into
38 one of the Bond Street picture-galleries and fill in the time
until we are due at the hotel.'

5 ⋮ THREE BROKEN THREADS

Sherlock Holmes had, in a very remarkable degree, the power
of detaching his mind at will. For two hours the strange
business in which we had been involved appeared to be forgotten, and he was entirely absorbed in the pictures of the

modern Belgian masters. He would talk of nothing but art,
of which he had the crudest ideas, from our leaving the gallery
until we found ourselves at the Northumberland Hotel.

'Sir Henry Baskerville is upstairs expecting you,' said the
clerk. 'He asked me to show you up at once when you came.'

'Have you any objection to my looking at your register?'
said Holmes.

'Not in the least.'

The book showed that two names had been added after
that of Baskerville. One was Theophilus Johnson and family,
of Newcastle; the other Mrs Oldmore and maid, of High **39**
Lodge, Alton. **40**

'Surely that must be the same Johnson whom I used to
know,' said Holmes, to the porter. 'A lawyer, is he not, grey-
headed, and walks with a limp?'

'No, sir, this is Mr Johnson the coal-owner, a very active
gentleman, not older than yourself.'

'Surely you are mistaken about his trade?'

'No, sir; he has used this hotel for many years, and he is
very well known to us.'

'Ah, that settles it. Mrs Oldmore, too; I seem to remember
the name. Excuse my curiosity, but often in calling upon one
friend one finds another.'

'She is an invalid lady, sir. Her husband was once Mayor
of Gloucester. She always comes to us when she is in town.' **41**

'Thank you; I am afraid I cannot claim her acquaintance.
We have established a most important fact by these questions,
Watson,' he continued, in a low voice, as we went upstairs
together. 'We know now that the people who are so interested in our friend have not settled down in his own hotel.
That means that while they are, as we have seen, very anxious
to watch him, they are equally anxious that he should not
see them. Now, this is a most suggestive fact.'

'What does it suggest?'

'It suggests—halloa, my dear fellow, what on earth is the
matter?'

As we came round the top of the stairs we had run up
against Sir Henry Baskerville himself. His face was flushed
with anger, and he held an old and dusty boot in one of his
hands. So furious was he that he was hardly articulate, and

39 *Newcastle*. The county seat of Northumberland, on the River Tyne. Its great coal-shipping
industry gave rise to the popular expression "as
useless as carrying coals to Newcastle."

40 *Alton*. A market town in Hampshire.

41 *Gloucester*. The county seat of Gloucestershire, an industrial city on the Severn.

when he did speak it was in a much broader and more Western dialect than any which we had heard from him in the morning.

'Seems to me they are playing me for a sucker in this hotel,' he cried. 'They'll find they've started in to monkey with the wrong man unless they are careful. By thunder, if that chap can't find my missing boot there will be trouble. I can take a joke with the best, Mr Holmes, but they've got a bit over the mark this time.'

'Still looking for your boot?'

'Yes, sir, and mean to find it.'

'But surely, you said that it was a new brown boot?'

'So it was, sir. And now it's an old black one.'

'What! you don't mean to say——?'

'That's just what I do mean to say. I only had three pairs in the world—the new brown, the old black, and the patent leathers, which I am wearing. Last night they took one of my brown ones, and today they have sneaked one of the black. Well, have you got it? Speak out, man, and don't stand staring!'

An agitated German waiter had appeared upon the scene.

'No, sir; I have made inquiry all over the hotel, but I can hear no word of it.'

'Well, either that boot comes back before sundown, or I'll see the manager and tell him that I go right straight out of this hotel.'

'It shall be found, sir—I promise you that if you will have a little patience it will be found.'

'Mind it is, for it's the last thing of mine that I'll lose in this den of thieves. Well, well, Mr Holmes, you'll excuse my troubling you about such a trifle——'

'I think it's well worth troubling about.'

'Why, you look very serious over it.'

'How do you explain it?'

'I just don't attempt to explain it. It seems the very maddest, queerest thing that ever happened to me.'

'The queerest, perhaps,' said Holmes, thoughtfully.

'What do you make of it yourself?'

'Well, I don't profess to understand it yet. This case of yours is very complex, Sir Henry. When taken in conjunction with your uncle's death I am not sure that of all the five hun-
42 dred cases of capital importance which I have handled there is one which cuts so deep. But we hold several threads in our hands, and the odds are that one or other of them guides us to the truth. We may waste time in following the wrong one, but sooner or later, we must come upon the right.'

We had a pleasant luncheon in which little was said of the business which had brought us together. It was in the private sitting-room to which we afterwards repaired that Holmes asked Baskerville what were his intentions.

'To go to Baskerville Hall.'

'And when?'

'At the end of the week.'

'On the whole,' said Holmes, 'I think that your decision is a wise one. I have ample evidence that you are being dogged in London, and amid the millions of this great city it is difficult to discover who these people are or what their object can be. If their intentions are evil they might do you a mischief, and we should be powerless to prevent it. You did not know, Dr Mortimer, that you were followed this morning from my house?'

42 *the five hundred cases of capital importance which I have handled.* In "The Adventure of the Speckled Band," which Watson may have chronicled as late as 1891, he tells us that he has been glancing over his notes "of the seventy odd cases in which I have during the last eight years studied the methods of my friend Sherlock Holmes." Holmes himself in 1891 speaks of "over a thousand cases" ("The Final Problem"). It is therefore apparent that there were many cases in which Watson had no opportunity to share. If *The Hound of the Baskervilles* took place before 1891, as many commentators believe, it is also apparent that at least half of Holmes' "thousand cases" were "of capital importance."

Dr Mortimer started violently. 'Followed! By whom?'

'That, unfortunately, is what I cannot tell you. Have you among your neighbours or acquaintances on Dartmoor any man with a black, full beard?'

'No—or, let me see—why, yes. Barrymore, Sir Charles's butler, is a man with a full, black beard.'

'Ha! Where is Barrymore?'

'He is in charge of the Hall.'

'We had best ascertain if he is really there, or if by any possibility he might be in London.'

'How can you do that?'

'Give me a telegraph form. "Is all ready for Sir Henry?" That will do. Address to Mr Barrymore, Baskerville Hall. Which is the nearest telegraph-office? Grimpen. Very good, we will send a second wire to the postmaster, Grimpen: "Telegram to Mr Barrymore, to be delivered into his own hand. If absent, please return wire to Sir Henry Baskerville, Northumberland Hotel." That should let us know before evening whether Barrymore is at his post in Devonshire or not.'

'That's so,' said Baskerville. 'By the way, Dr Mortimer, who is this Barrymore, anyhow?'

'He is the son of the old caretaker, who is dead. They have looked after the Hall for four generations now. So far as I know, he and his wife are as respectable a couple as any in the county.'

'At the same time,' said Baskerville, 'it's clear enough that so long as there are none of the family at the Hall these people have a mighty fine home and nothing to do.'

'That is true.'

'Did Barrymore profit at all by Sir Charles's will?' asked Holmes.

'He and his wife had five hundred pounds each.'

'Ha! Did they know that they would receive this?'

'Yes; Sir Charles was very fond of talking about the provisions of his will.'

'That is very interesting.'

'I hope,' said Dr Mortimer, 'that you do not look with suspicious eyes upon everyone who received a legacy from Sir Charles, for I also had a thousand pounds left to me.'

'Indeed! And anyone else?'

'There were many insignificant sums to individuals and a large number of public charities. The residue all went to Sir Henry.'

'And how much was the residue?'

'Seven hundred and forty thousand pounds.' **43**

Holmes raised his eyebrows in surprise. 'I had no idea that so gigantic a sum was involved,' said he.

'Sir Charles had the reputation of being rich, but we did not know how very rich he was until we came to examine his securities. The total value of the estate was close on to a million.'

'Dear me! It is a stake for which a man might well play a desperate game. And one more question, Dr Mortimer. Supposing that anything happened to our young friend here—you will forgive the unpleasant hypothesis!—who would inherit the estate?'

'Since Rodger Baskerville, Sir Charles's younger brother, died unmarried, the estate would descend to the Desmonds, who are distant cousins. James Desmond is an elderly clergyman in Westmorland.' **44**

A scene from the 20th Century-Fox Film production of *The Hound of the Baskervilles:* Lionel Atwill as Dr. Mortimer, Basil Rathbone as Sherlock Holmes, Nigel Bruce as Dr. Watson. Sir Henry Baskerville was played by Richard Greene, best known today for his Robin Hood on the television screen.

43 '*Seven hundred and forty thousand pounds.*' After the five hundred pounds ($2,500) each to Mr. and Mrs. Barrymore and the thousand pounds ($5,000) to Dr. Mortimer, the estate amounted to some $3,700,000 in U. S. currency at the time.

44 *Westmorland.* A largely mountainous county in the north of England, the most sparsely populated county in England. Dairy farming and cattle raising are the chief occupations.

'Thank you. These details are all of great interest. Have you met Mr James Desmond?'

'Yes; he once came down to visit Sir Charles. He is a man of venerable appearance and of saintly life. I remember that he refused to accept any settlement from Sir Charles, though he pressed it upon him.'

'And this man of simple tastes would be the heir to Sir Charles's thousands?'

'He would be the heir to the estate, because that is entailed. He would also be the heir to the money unless it were willed otherwise by the present owner, who can, of course, do what he likes with it.'

'And have you made your will, Sir Henry?'

'No, Mr Holmes, I have not. I've had no time, for it was only yesterday that I learned how matters stood. But in any case I feel that the money should go with the title and estate. That was my poor uncle's idea. How is the owner going to restore the glories of the Baskervilles if he has not money enough to keep up the property? House, land, and dollars must go together.'

'Quite so. Well, Sir Henry, I am of one mind with you as to the advisability of your going down to Devonshire without delay. There is only one provision which I must make. You certainly must not go alone.'

'Dr Mortimer returns with me.'

'But Dr Mortimer has his practice to attend to, and his house is miles away from yours. With all the good will in the world, he may be unable to help you. No, Sir Henry, you must take with you someone, a trusty man, who will be always by your side.'

'Is it possible that you could come yourself, Mr Holmes?'

'If matters came to a crisis I should endeavour to be present in person; but you can understand that, with my extensive consulting practice and with the constant appeals which reach me from many quarters, it is impossible for me to be absent from London for an indefinite time. At the present instant one of the most revered names in England is being **45** besmirched by a blackmailer, and only I can stop a disastrous scandal. You will see how impossible it is for me to go to Dartmoor.'

'Whom would you recommend, then?'

Holmes laid his hand upon my arm.

'If my friend would undertake it there is no man who is better worth having at your side when you are in a tight place. No one can say so more confidently than I.'

The proposition took me completely by surprise, but before I had time to answer Baskerville seized me by the hand and wrung it heartily.

'Well, now, that is real kind of you, Dr Watson,' said he. 'You see how it is with me, and you know just as much about the matter as I do. If you will come down to Baskerville Hall and see me through I'll never forget it.'

The promise of adventure had always a fascination for me, and I was complimented by the words of Holmes and by the eagerness with which the baronet hailed me as a companion.

'I will come with pleasure,' said I. 'I do not know how I could employ my time better.'

'And you will report very carefully to me,' said Holmes. 'When a crisis comes, as it will do, I will direct how you shall act. I suppose that by Saturday all might be ready?'

45 *one of the most revered names in England is being besmirched by a blackmailer.* As we have seen, it has been suggested that this "most re-vered name" was that of Albert Edward, Prince of Wales. For a pastiche of this adventure, see "The Adventure of the Two Women," by Adrian M. Conan Doyle in *The Exploits of Sherlock Holmes.*

'Would that suit Dr Watson?'

'Perfectly.'

'Then on Saturday, unless you hear to the contrary, we shall meet at the 10.30 train from Paddington.' **46**

We had risen to depart when Baskerville gave a cry of triumph, and diving into one of the corners of the room he drew a brown boot from under a cabinet.

'My missing boot!' he cried.

'May all our difficulties vanish as easily!' said Sherlock Holmes.

'But it is a very singular thing,' Dr Mortimer remarked. 'I searched this room carefully before lunch.'

'And so did I,' said Baskerville. 'Every inch of it.'

'There was certainly no boot in it then.'

'In that case the waiter must have placed it there while we were lunching.'

The German was sent for, but professed to know nothing of the matter, nor could any inquiry clear it up. Another item had been added to that constant and apparently purposeless series of small mysteries which had succeeded each other so rapidly. Setting aside the whole grim story of Sir Charles's death, we had a line of inexplicable incidents all within the limits of two days, which included the receipt of the printed letter, the black-bearded spy in the hansom, the loss of the new brown boot, the loss of the old black boot, and now the return of the new brown boot. Holmes sat in silence in the cab as we drove back to Baker Street, and I knew from his drawn brows and keen face that his mind, like my own, was busy in endeavouring to frame some scheme into which all these strange and apparently disconnected episodes could be fitted. All afternoon and late into the evening he sat lost in tobacco and thought.

Just before dinner two telegrams were handed in. The first ran:

Have just heard that Barrymore is at the Hall.—BASKERVILLE.

The second:

Visited twenty-three hotels as directed, but sorry to report unable to trace cut sheet of *Times*.—CARTWRIGHT.

'There go two of my threads, Watson. There is nothing more stimulating than a case where everything goes against you. We must cast round for another scent.'

'We have still the cabman who drove the spy.'

'Exactly. I have wired to get his name and address from the Official Registry. I should not be surprised if this were an answer to my question.'

The ring at the bell proved to be something even more satisfactory than an answer, however, for the door opened and a rough-looking fellow entered who was evidently the man himself.

'I got a message from the head office that a gent at this address had been inquiring for 2704,' said he. 'I've driven my cab this seven years and never a word of complaint. I came here straight from the Yard to ask you to your face what you had against me.'

'I have nothing in the world against you, my good man,' said Holmes. 'On the contrary, I have half a sovereign for you if you will give me a clear answer to my questions.'

'Well, I've had a good day and no mistake,' said the cab-

46 *the 10.30 train from Paddington.*' The terminus of the Great Western Railway, now British Railways (Western Region). Its office buildings, partly destroyed in the blitz, are 580 feet long, and the platforms under the curved roof are 700 feet long. The roofing consists of three spans, each 50 feet in width. The center span is 54 feet high, and the side divisions 46 feet. Despite its age, Paddington still invites favorable comparison with more modern railway termini. There was a 10:30 Paddington to Plymouth train in Holmes' and Watson's day, but it seems to have run only on Sundays. On Saturdays, the best train left at 12:45 P.M.

47 *the Borough.* Clayton presumably means the borough of Marylebone, in which Baker Street is located. With its long straight streets and fine vistas, Marylebone has been called a "princely parish" (Thomas H. Shepherd, *London in the Nineteenth Century*, published in 1829).

48 *two guineas.* About $10.50 U.S.

man, with a grin. 'What was it you wanted to ask, sir?'

'First of all your name and address, in case I want you again.'

47   'John Clayton, 3, Turpey Street, the Borough. My cab is out of Shipley's Yard, near Waterloo Station.'

Sherlock Holmes made a note of it.

'Now, Clayton, tell me all about the fare who came and watched this house at ten o'clock this morning and afterwards followed the two gentlemen down Regent Street.'

The man looked surprised and a little embarrassed.

'Why, there's no good my telling you things, for you seem to know as much as I do already,' said he. 'The truth is that the gentleman told me that he was a detective, and that I was to say nothing about him to anyone.'

'My good fellow, this is a very serious business, and you may find yourself in a pretty bad position if you try to hide anything from me. You say that your fare told you that he was a detective?'

'Yes, he did.'

'When did he say this?'

'When he left me.'

'Did he say anything more?'

'He mentioned his name.'

Holmes cast a swift glance of triumph at me.

'Oh, he mentioned his name, did he? That was imprudent. What was the name that he mentioned?'

'His name,' said the cabman, 'was Mr Sherlock Holmes.'

Never have I seen my friend more completely taken aback than by the cabman's reply. For an instant he sat in silent amazement. Then he burst into a hearty laugh:

'A touch, Watson—an undeniable touch!' said he. 'I feel a foil as quick and supple as my own. He got home upon me very prettily that time. So his name was Sherlock Holmes, was it?'

'Yes, sir, that was the gentleman's name.'

'Excellent! Tell me where you picked him up, and all that occurred.'

'He hailed me at half-past nine in Trafalgar Square. He

48   said that he was a detective, and he offered me two guineas if I would do exactly what he wanted all day and ask no questions. I was glad enough to agree. First we drove down to the Northumberland Hotel, and waited there until two gentlemen came out and took a cab from the rank. We followed their cab until it pulled up somewhere near here.'

'This very door,' said Holmes.

'Well, I couldn't be sure of that, but I dare say my fare knew all about it. We pulled up half-way down the street and waited an hour and a half. Then the two gentlemen passed us, walking, and we followed down Baker Street and along——'

'I know,' said Holmes.

'Until we got three-quarters down Regent Street. Then my gentleman threw up the trap, and he cried that I should drive right away to Waterloo Station as hard as I could go. I whipped up the mare, and we were there under the ten minutes. Then he paid up his two guineas, like a good one, and away he went into the station. Only just as he was leaving he turned round and said: "It might interest you to know that you have been driving Mr Sherlock Holmes." That's how I came to know the name.'

'I see. And you saw no more of him?'

'Not after he went into the station.'

'And how would you describe Mr Sherlock Holmes?'

The cabman scratched his head. 'Well, he wasn't altogether such an easy gentleman to describe. I'd put him at forty years of age, and he was of a middle height, two or three inches shorter than you, sir. He was dressed like a toff, and he had **49** a black beard, cut square at the end, and a pale face. I don't know as I could say more than that.'

'Colour of his eyes?'

'No, I can't say that.'

'Nothing more that you can remember?'

'No, sir; nothing.'

'Well, then, here is your half-sovereign. There's another one waiting for you if you can bring any more information. Good night!'

'Good night, sir, and thank you!'

John Clayton departed chuckling, and Holmes turned to me with a shrug of the shoulders and a rueful smile.

'Snap goes our third thread, and we end where we began,' said he. 'The cunning rascal! He knew our number, knew that Sir Henry Baskerville had consulted me, spotted who I was in Regent Street, conjectured that I had got the number of the cab and would lay my hands on the driver, and so sent back this audacious message. I tell you, Watson, this time we have got a foeman who is worthy of our steel. I've been checkmated in London. I can only wish you better luck in Devon- **50** shire. But I'm not easy in my mind about it.'

'About what?'

'About sending you. It's an ugly business, Watson, an ugly, dangerous business, and the more I see of it the less I like it. Yes, my dear fellow, you may laugh, but I give you my word that I shall be very glad to have you back safe and sound in Baker Street once more.'

49 *a toff.* In old American slang, a dude; one who is stylishly dressed or who has a smart appearance.

50 *I've been checkmated in London.* In "The Adventure of the Retired Colourman," Holmes notes that Josiah Amberley excelled at chess—and comments, "One mark, Watson, of a scheming mind." While most Sherlockian students hold that Holmes was not himself a player, his talk is studded with terms that relate to the game. "I must plan some fresh opening move, for this gambit won't work," he says in "The Adventure of the Illustrious Client." "Check number one," he tells Watson on another occasion ("The Adventure of the Priory School") and "It is a provoking check," he says on another (*The Sign of the Four*). Most impressive of all is "The Adventure of the Blanched Soldier," which we are told *Holmes wrote himself.* Here he has Mr. Dodd say to Colonel Emsworth: "He looked up at last with the expression of one who has seen his adversary make a dangerous move at chess, and had decided how to meet it." We know that Simpson's-in-the-Strand was one of Holmes' favorite restaurants ("The Adventure of the Dying Detective," "The Adventure of the Illustrious Client") and it is worth noting here that Simpson's, in Holmes' and Watson's day, was not only a restaurant but also a chess divan, a principal gathering place in London for chessplayers, amateur and professional. It seems difficult to believe that Holmes did not indulge in an occasional game there.

6 ❖ BASKERVILLE HALL

Sir Henry Baskerville and Dr Mortimer were ready upon the appointed day, and we started as arranged for Devonshire. **51** Mr Sherlock Holmes drove with me to the station, and gave me his last parting injunction and advice.

'I will not bias your mind by suggesting theories or suspicions, Watson,' said he; 'I wish you simply to report facts in the fullest possible manner to me, and you can leave me to do the theorizing.'

'What sort of facts?' I asked.

'Anything which may seem to have a bearing, however indirect, upon the case, and especially the relations between young Baskerville and his neighbours, or any fresh particulars concerning the death of Sir Charles. I have made some inquiries myself in the last few days, but the results have, I fear,

51 *the appointed day.* Saturday, September 29, 1888, by our reckoning.

been negative. One thing only appears to be certain, and that is that Mr James Desmond, who is the next heir, is an elderly gentleman of a very amiable disposition, so that this persecution does not arise from him. I really think that we may eliminate him entirely from our calculations. There remain the people who will actually surround Sir Henry Baskerville upon the moor.'

'Would it not be well in the first place to get rid of this Barrymore couple?'

'By no means. You could not make a greater mistake. If they are innocent it would be a cruel injustice, and if they are guilty we should be giving up all chance of bringing it home to them. No, no, we will preserve them upon our list of suspects. Then there is a groom at the Hall, if I remember right. There are two moorland farmers. There is our friend Dr Mortimer, whom I believe to be entirely honest, and there is his wife, of whom we know nothing. There is this naturalist Stapleton, and there is his sister, who is said to be a young lady of attractions. There is Mr Frankland, of Lafter Hall, who is also an unknown factor, and there are one or two other neighbours. These are the folk who must be your very special study.'

'I will do my best.'

'You have arms, I suppose?'

'Yes, I thought it as well to take them.'

'Most certainly. Keep your revolver near you night and day, and never relax your precautions.'

Our friends had already secured a first-class carriage, and were waiting for us upon the platform.

'No, we have no news of any kind,' said Dr Mortimer, in answer to my friend's questions. 'I can swear to one thing, and that is that we have not been shadowed during the last **52** two days. We have never gone out without keeping a sharp watch, and no one could have escaped our notice.'

'You have always kept together, I presume?'

'Except yesterday afternoon. I usually give up one day to pure amusement when I come to town, so I spent it at the **53** Museum of the College of Surgeons.'

'And I went to look at the folk in the park,' said Baskerville. 'But we had no trouble of any kind.'

'It was imprudent, all the same,' said Holmes, shaking his head and looking very grave. 'I beg, Sir Henry, that you will not go about alone. Some great misfortune will befall you if you do. Did you get your other boot?'

'No, sir, it is gone for ever.'

'Indeed. That is very interesting. Well, good-bye,' he added, as the train began to glide down the platform. 'Bear in mind, Sir Henry, one of the phrases in that queer old legend which Dr Mortimer has read to us, and avoid the moor in those hours of darkness when the powers of evil are exalted.'

I looked back at the platform when we had left it far behind, and saw the tall, austere figure of Holmes standing motionless and gazing after us.

The journey was a swift and pleasant one, and I spent it in making the more intimate acquaintance of my two companions, and in playing with Dr Mortimer's spaniel. In a very few hours the brown earth had become ruddy, the brick had changed to granite, and red cows grazed in well-hedged fields where the lush grasses and more luxuriant vegetation spoke

52 *we have not been shadowed during the last two days.* As the late Dr. Ernest Bloomfield Zeisler wrote: "Sir Henry says he will leave at the end of the week; the Master instructs him to leave on Saturday, evidently the next following Saturday after the first day [of the adventure]. On the second day Sir Henry and Dr. Mortimer were shadowed. On the Saturday of departure the Master says he has made some inquiries 'in the last few days,' and Dr. Mortimer says they have 'not been shadowed during the last two days.' Since on Saturday morning they had not been shadowed the preceding two days but had been shadowed on the second day, it follows that the second day was Wednesday and the first day Tuesday.

53 *the Museum of the College of Surgeons.*' On the south side of Lincoln's Inn Fields, built in 1835. The Museum, which stood to the right of the College itself, was founded by John Hunter and "was intended to illustrate, as far as possible, the whole subject of life, by preparations of the bodies in which its phenomena are represented." One of the exhibits that might have attracted Dr. Mortimer was the skeleton of the elephant Chunee, brought to England in 1810; it stood 12 feet 4 inches high.

of a richer, if a damper climate. Young Baskerville stared eagerly out of the window, and cried aloud with delight as he recognized the familiar features of the Devon scenery.

'I've been over a good part of the world since I left it, Dr Watson,' said he; 'but I have never seen a place to compare with it.'

'I never saw a Devonshire man who did not swear by his county,' I remarked.

'It depends upon the breed of men quite as much as on the county,' said Dr Mortimer. 'A glance at our friend here reveals the rounded head of the Celt, which carries inside it the Celtic enthusiasm and power of attachment. Poor Sir Charles's head was of a very rare type, half Gaelic, half Ivernian in its characteristics. But you were very young when you last saw Baskerville Hall, were you not?'

'I was a boy in my teens at the time of my father's death, and had never seen the Hall, for he lived in a little cottage on the south coast. Thence I went straight to a friend in America I tell you it is all as new to me as it is to Dr Watson, and I'm as keen as possible to see the moor.'

'Are you? Then your wish is easily granted, for there is your first sight of the moor,' said Dr. Mortimer, pointing out of the carriage window.

Over the green squares of the fields and the low curve of a wood there rose in the distance a grey, melancholy hill, with a strange jagged summit, dim and vague in the distance, like some fantastic landscape in a dream. Baskerville sat for a long time, his eyes fixed upon it, and I read upon his eager face how much it meant to him, this first sight of that strange spot where the men of his blood had held sway so long and left their mark so deep. There he sat, with his tweed suit and his American accent, in the corner of a prosaic railway-carriage, and yet as I looked at his dark and expressive face I felt more than ever how true a descendant he was of that long line of high-blooded, fiery, and masterful men. There were pride, valour and strength in his thick brows, his sensitive nostrils, and his large hazel eyes. If on that forbidding moor a difficult and dangerous quest should lie before us, this was at least a comrade for whom one might venture to take a risk with the certainty that he would bravely share it.

. . . THERE ROSE IN THE DISTANCE A GREY, MELANCHOLY HILL, WITH A STRANGE JAGGED SUMMIT . . .

The "grey, melancholy hill" was, we think, what many hold to be the most impressive of all the Dartmoor hills—Brent Tor, shown left in a painting by E. A. Tozer from the Reverend Sabine Baring-Gould's *A Book of Dartmoor*. But Watson is slightly deceived by the distance when he writes of its "strange and jagged summit": what he saw crowning Brent Tor was the tower of its church, St. Michael of the Rock, shown close up in the photograph below.

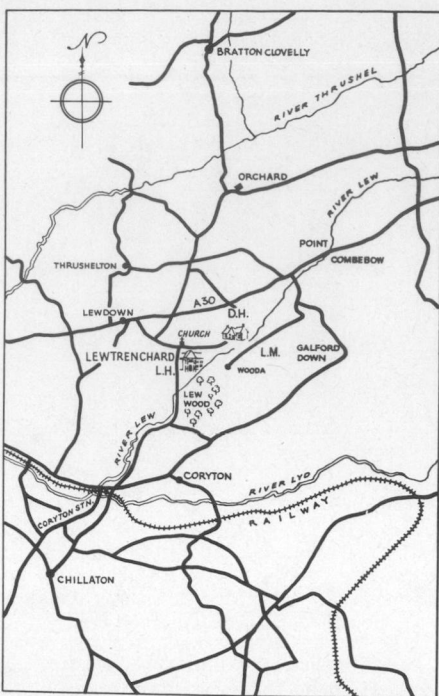

THE TRAIN PULLED UP AT A SMALL WAYSIDE STATION . . .

In his admirable article, "Always on Sunday, Watson!", Mr. William H. Gill has suggested that the station was either Brent or Ivy Bridge, both of which lie to the south of the moor (see our "very-large"-scale map of Dartmoor). Your editor would like to propose a third possibility: that Watson and his party continued along the line to Coryton Station (no longer in use, even as a "halt-on-demand"). Coryton Station, shown on the detail map above, lies on the north and west of the moor just ten miles as the crow flies from Princetown Prison.

54 *a wagonette with a pair of cobs.* A wagonette was a four-wheeled carriage, open, or made with a removable cover, furnished with a seat or bench at each side facing inward and with one or two seats or benches arranged laterally in front. The "cobs" which drew it were short-legged, strong horses, usually reserved for heavy carriage work.

55 *'There's a convict escaped from Princetown, sir.* No very unusual occurrence; even today, hardly a month passes when there is not an alarm out for an escaped prisoner on the moor.

56 *He's been out three days now.* The convict must therefore have escaped on the preceding Wednesday night or early on the Thursday morning.

The train pulled up at a small wayside station, and we all descended. Outside, beyond the low, white fence, a wagonette **54** with a pair of cobs was waiting. Our coming was evidently a great event, for station-master and porters clustered round us to carry out our luggage. It was a sweet, simple country spot, but I was surprised to observe that by the gate there stood two soldierly men in dark uniforms, who leaned upon their short rifles and glanced keenly at us as we passed. The coachman, a hard-faced, gnarled little fellow, saluted Sir Henry Baskerville, and in a few minutes we were flying swiftly down the broad white road. Rolling pasture lands curved upwards on either side of us, and old gabled houses peeped out from amid the thick green foliage, but behind the peaceful and sunlit countryside there rose ever, dark against the evening sky, the long, gloomy curve of the moor, broken by the jagged and sinister hills.

The wagonette swung round into a side road, and we curved upwards through deep lanes worn by centuries of wheels, high banks on either side, heavy with dripping moss and fleshy hart's-tongue ferns. Bronzing bracken and mottled bramble gleamed in the light of the sinking sun. Still steadily rising, we passed over a narrow granite bridge, and skirted a noisy stream, which gushed swiftly down, foaming and roaring amid the grey boulders. Both road and stream wound up through a valley dense with scrub oak and fir. At every turning Baskerville gave an exclamation of delight, looking eagerly about him and asking countless questions. To his eyes all seemed beautiful, but to me a tinge of melancholy lay upon the countryside, which bore so clearly the mark of the waning year. Yellow leaves carpeted the lanes and fluttered down upon us as we passed. The rattle of our wheels died away as we drove through drifts of rotting vegetation—sad gifts, as it seemed to me, for Nature to throw before the carriage of the returning heir of the Baskervilles.

'Halloa!' cried Dr Mortimer, 'what is this?'

A steep curve of heath-clad land, an outlying spur of the moor, lay in front of us. On the summit, hard and clear like an equestrian statue upon its pedestal, was a mounted soldier, dark and stern, his rifle poised ready over his forearm. He was watching the road along which we travelled.

'What is this, Perkins?' asked Dr Mortimer.

Our driver half turned in his seat.

55
56 'There's a convict escaped from Princetown, sir. He's been out three days now, and the warders watch every road and every station, but they've had no sight of him yet. The farmers about here don't like it, sir, and that's a fact.'

THE COACHMAN, A HARD-FACED, GNARLED LITTLE FELLOW, SALUTED SIR HENRY . . .

It is worth noting here that Conan Doyle dedicated *The Hound of the Baskervilles* to his friend Fletcher Robinson of Park Hill, Ipplepen, whose *coachman*, Harry M. Baskerville, shown left, provided the name used in the adventure.

'Well, I understand that they get five pounds if they can give information.'

'Yes, sir, but the chance of five pounds is but a poor thing compared to the chance of having your throat cut. You see, it isn't like any ordinary convict. This is a man that would stick at nothing.'

'Who is he, then?'

'It is Selden, the Notting Hill murderer.'

I remembered the case well, for it was one in which Holmes had taken an interest on account of the peculiar ferocity of the crime and the wanton brutality which had marked all the actions of the assassin. The commutation of his death sentence had been due to some doubts as to his complete sanity, so atrocious was his conduct. Our wagonette had topped a rise and in front of us rose the huge expanse of the moor, mottled with gnarled and craggy cairns and tors. A cold wind swept down from it and set us shivering. Somewhere there, on that desolate plain, was lurking this fiendish man, hiding in a burrow like a wild beast, his heart full of malignancy against the whole race which had cast him out. It needed but this to complete the grim suggestiveness of the barren waste, the chilling wind, and the darkling sky. Even Baskerville fell silent and pulled his overcoat more closely around him.

We had left the fertile country behind and beneath us. We looked back on it now, the slanting rays of a low sun turning the streams to threads of gold and glowing on the red earth new turned by the plough and the broad tangle of the woodlands. The road in front of us grew bleaker and wilder over huge russet and olive slopes, sprinkled with giant boulders. Now and then we passed a moorland cottage, walled and roofed with stone, with no creeper to break its harsh outline. Suddenly we looked down into a cup-like depression, patched with stunted oaks and firs which had been twisted and bent by the fury of years of storm. Two high, narrow towers rose over the trees. The driver pointed with his whip.

'Baskerville Hall,' said he.

Its master had risen, and was staring with flushed cheeks and shining eyes. A few minutes later we had reached the lodge gates, a maze of fantastic tracery in wrought iron, with weather-bitten pillars on either side, blotched with lichens, and surmounted by the boars' heads of the Baskervilles. The lodge was a ruin of black granite and bared ribs of rafters, but facing it was a new building, half constructed, the first-fruit of Sir Charles's South African gold.

Through the gateway we passed into the avenue, where the wheels were again hushed amid the leaves, and the old trees shot their branches in a sombre tunnel over our heads. Baskerville shuddered as he looked up the long, dark drive to where the house glimmered like a ghost at the farther end.

'Was it here?' he asked, in a low voice.

'No, no, the Yew Alley is on the other side.'

The young heir glanced round with a gloomy face.

'It's no wonder my uncle felt as if trouble were coming on him in such a place as this,' said he. 'It's enough to scare any man. I'll have a row of electric lamps up here inside of six months, and you won't know it again with a thousand-candle power Swan and Edison right here in front of the hall door.' **57**

'BASKERVILLE HALL,' SAID HE.

Illustration by Sidney Paget for the *Strand Magazine*, October, 1901.

57 *Swan and Edison.* Sir Joseph Wilson Swan, 1828–1914, an English inventor in photography and electricity, widely known for the incandescent lamp bearing his name, and Thomas Alva Edison, 1847–1913, one of the world's greatest inventors and the holder of more than a thousand important patents; he invented the incandescent lamp in 1879. Since the Swan and Edison lamps are of two different varieties, it must be presumed that Sir Henry actually said "Swan *or* Edison."

. . . AND THE HOUSE LAY BEFORE US.

A rather thorough investigation of the halls and houses in the vicinity of Coryton Station has unhappily, to date, revealed none that might be described as having "twin towers, ancient, crenellated, and pierced with many loopholes . . ."

Until a more fitting candidate presents itself, then, let us consider the claims of Lew House (or Hall), at Lew Trenchard, near Lew Down, Devon, shown above.

It has, to begin with, "lodge gates" which are "a maze of fantastic tracery in wrought iron, with weather-bitten pillars on either side, blotched with lichens . . ." It has, in addition, an avenue opening into a broad expanse of turf, and the house itself is "a heavy block of a building from which a porch" projects. "The whole front" is "draped in ivy, with a patch clipped bare here and there where a window or a coat-of-arms" breaks "through the dark veil." It also has "heavy mullioned windows," "high chimneys" and a "steep, high-angled roof."

Note now on our detail map (*see* p. 38) that between Lew House and the moor itself is a small stand of trees called Lew Wood. *Lew* Wood, we submit, is what Watson chose to call the *Yew* Alley.

Lew House has a notable collection of paintings, including both a Kneller and a Reynolds (*see* Notes 92 and 93); some of these hang in the Long Gallery (*shown below*), which looks out over Lew Wood and on to the moor—an ideal spot for the early-morning signaling of a butler named Barrymore.

Our identification of Lew House as "Baskerville Hall" is perhaps strengthened by the fact that the coat-of-arms of the family which has owned Lew House for many generations is charged—not with *boars*' heads—but with *bears*' heads proper, muzzled and ringed or.

On the basis of the boars' heads alone, Dr. Julian Wolff has identified "Baskerville Hall" as Mount Edgcumbe in Devonshire, the family seat of the Edgcumbes, whose coat-of-arms is blazoned: Gules, on a bend erminois, between two cottises or, three boars' heads couped, argent. It is also interesting to note that the Manor House, North Bovey, was used for Baskerville Hall in Gainsborough Pictures' 1932 motion-picture version of *The Hound of the Baskervilles*.

The avenue opened into a broad expanse of turf, and the house lay before us. In the fading light I could see that the centre was a heavy block of building from which a porch projected. The whole front was draped in ivy, with a patch clipped bare here and there where a window or a coat-of-arms broke through the dark veil. From this central block rose the twin towers, ancient, crenellated, and pierced with many loopholes. To right and left of the turrets were more modern wings of black granite. A dull light shone through heavy mullioned windows, and from the high chimneys which rose from the steep, high-angled roof there sprang a single black column of smoke.

'Welcome, Sir Henry! Welcome to Baskerville Hall!'

A tall man had stepped from the shadow of the porch to open the door of the wagonette. The figure of a woman was silhouetted against the yellow light of the hall. She came out and helped the man to hand down our bags.

'You don't mind my driving straight home, Sir Henry?' said Dr Mortimer. 'My wife is expecting me.'

'Surely you will stay and have some dinner?'

'No, I must go. I shall probably find some work awaiting me. I would stay to show you over the house, but Barrymore will be a better guide than I. Good-bye, and never hesitate night or day to send for me if I can be of service.'

The wheels died away down the drive while Sir Henry and I turned into the hall, and the door clanged heavily behind us. It was a fine apartment in which we found ourselves, large, lofty, and heavily raftered with huge balks of age-blackened oak. In the great old-fashioned fireplace behind the high iron dogs a log-fire crackled and snapped. Sir Henry and I held out our hands to it, for we were numb from our long drive. Then we gazed round us at the high, thin window of old stained glass, the oak panelling, the stags' heads, the coats-of-arms upon the walls, all dim and sombre in the subdued light of the central lamp.

'It's just as I imagined it,' said Sir Henry. 'Is it not the very picture of an old family home? To think that this should be the same hall in which for five hundred years my people have lived! It strikes me solemn to think of it.'

I saw his dark face lit up with a boyish enthusiasm as he gazed about him. The light beat upon him where he stood, but long shadows trailed down the walls and hung like a black canopy above him. Barrymore had returned from taking our luggage to our rooms. He stood in front of us now with the subdued manner of a well-trained servant. He was a remarkable-looking man, tall, handsome, with a square black beard and pale distinguished features.

'Would you wish dinner to be served at once, sir?'

'Is it ready?'

'In a very few minutes, sir. You will find hot water in your rooms. My wife and I will be happy, Sir Henry, to stay with you until you have made your fresh arrangements, but you will understand that under the new conditions this house will require a considerable staff.'

'What new conditions?'

'I only meant, sir, that Sir Charles led a very retired life, and we were able to look after his wants. You would, naturally, wish to have more company, and so you will need changes in your household.'

"WELCOME, SIR HENRY! WELCOME TO BASKERVILLE HALL!"

Illustration by Sidney Paget for the *Strand Magazine*, October, 1901.

'Do you mean that your wife and you wish to leave?'

'Only when it is quite convenient to you, sir.'

'But your family have been with us for several generations, have they not? I should be sorry to begin my life here by breaking an old family connection.'

I seemed to discern some signs of emotion upon the butler's white face.

'I feel that also, sir, and so does my wife. But to tell the truth, sir, we were both very much attached to Sir Charles, and his death gave us a shock and made these surroundings very painful to us. I fear that we shall never again be easy in our minds at Baskerville Hall.'

'But what do you intend to do?'

'I have no doubt, sir, that we shall succeed in establishing ourselves in some business. Sir Charles's generosity has given us the means to do so. And now, sir, perhaps I had best show you to your rooms.'

A square balustraded gallery ran round the top of the old hall, approached by a double stair. From this central point two long corridors extended the whole length of the building, from which all the bedrooms opened. My own was in the same wing as Baskerville's and almost next door to it. These rooms appeared to be much more modern than the central part of the house, and the bright paper and numerous candles did something to remove the sombre impression which our arrival had left upon my mind.

But the dining-room which opened out of the hall was a place of shadow and gloom. It was a long chamber with a step separating the daïs where the family sat from the lower portion reserved for their dependants. At one end a minstrels' gallery overlooked it. Black beams shot across above our heads, with a smoke-darkened ceiling beyond them. With rows of flaring torches to light it up, and the colour and rude hilarity of an old-time banquet, it might have softened; but now, when two black-clothed gentlemen sat in the little circle of light thrown by a shaded lamp, one's voice became hushed and one's spirit subdued. A dim line of ancestors, in every variety of dress, from the Elizabethan knight to the buck of the Regency, stared down upon us and daunted us by their silent company. We talked little, and I for one was glad when the meal was over and we were able to retire into the modern billiard-room and smoke a cigarette.

'My word, it isn't a very cheerful place,' said Sir Henry. 'I suppose one can tone down to it, but I feel a bit out of the picture at present. I don't wonder that my uncle got a little jumpy if he lived all alone in such a house as this. However, if it suits you, we will retire early tonight, and perhaps things may seem more cheerful in the morning.'

I drew aside my curtains before I went to bed and looked out from my window. It opened upon the grassy space which lay in front of the hall door. Beyond, two copses of trees moaned and swung in a rising wind. **58** A half moon broke through the rifts of racing clouds. In its cold light I saw beyond the trees a broken fringe of rocks and the long, low curve of the melancholy moor. I closed the curtain, feeling that my last impression was in keeping with the rest.

And yet it was not quite the last. I found myself weary and yet wakeful, tossing restlessly from side to side, seeking for the sleep which would not come. Far away a chiming clock

. . . THE DINING-ROOM WHICH OPENED OUT OF THE HALL WAS A PLACE OF SHADOW AND GLOOM.

Illustration by Sidney Paget for the *Strand Magazine*, October, 1901.

58 *A half moon.* Watson is quite correct: the moon on the night of Saturday, September 29, 1888, was just one day past the half. But Watson must have retired rather later than he recalled doing: the half-moon did not rise until 11:22 that night.

struck out the quarters of the hours, but otherwise a deathly silence lay upon the old house. And then suddenly, in the very dead of the night, there came a sound to my ears, clear, resonant, and unmistakable. It was the sob of a woman, the muffled, strangling gasp of one who is torn by an uncontrollable sorrow. I sat up in bed and listened intently. The noise could not have been far away, and was certainly in the house. For half an hour I waited with every nerve on the alert, but there came no other sound save the chiming clock and the rustle of the ivy on the wall.

7 ♦ THE STAPLETONS OF MERRIPIT HOUSE

The fresh beauty of the following morning did something to **59** efface from our minds the grim and grey impression which had been left upon both of us by our first experience of Baskerville Hall. As Sir Henry and I sat at breakfast the sunlight flooded in through the high mullioned windows, throwing watery patches of colour from the coats-of-arms which covered them. The dark panelling glowed like bronze in the golden rays, and it was hard to realize that this was indeed the chamber which had struck such a gloom into our souls upon the evening before.

'I guess it is ourselves and not the house that we have to blame!' said the baronet. 'We were tired with our journey and chilled by our drive, so we took a grey view of the place. Now we are fresh and well, so it is all cheerful once more.'

'And yet it was not entirely a question of imagination,' I answered. 'Did you, for example, happen to hear someone, a woman I think, sobbing in the night?'

'That is curious, for I did when I was half asleep fancy that I heard something of the sort. I waited quite a time, but there was no more of it, so I concluded that it was all a dream.'

'I heard it distinctly, and I am sure that it was really the sob of a woman.'

'We must ask about this right away.'

He rang the bell and asked Barrymore whether he could account for our experience. It seemed to me that the pallid features of the butler turned a shade paler still as he listened to his master's question.

'There are only two women in the house, Sir Henry,' he answered. 'One is the scullery-maid, who sleeps in the other wing. The other is my wife, and I can answer for it that the sound could not have come from her.'

And yet he lied as he said it, for it chanced that after breakfast I met Mrs Barrymore in the long corridor with the sun full upon her face. She was a large, impassive, heavy-featured woman with a stern, set expression of mouth. But her tell-tale eyes were red and glanced at me from between swollen lids. It was she, then, who wept in the night, and if she did so her husband must know it. Yet he had taken the obvious risk of discovery in declaring that it was not so. Why had he done

59 *The fresh beauty of the following morning.* Watson later tells us that the day (Sunday, September 30, 1888) was "sunlit" but "windy." The London *Times* reported that the weather on that day was "fine and bright at our southern, southwestern and central stations." The wind "blew strongly on some parts of our coasts."

This is Widecombe-in-the-Moor, which your editor believes to have been Dr. Watson's "Grimpen."

60 *The postmaster, who was also the village grocer.* Watson must have called upon the postmaster at his home rather than at his shop, since the day was a Sunday.

61 *the young baronet.* A baronet is a kind of hereditary knight, a title invented by King James I to pay for the settlement of Ulster. There are today about 1,500 of them.

this? And why did she weep so bitterly? Already round this pale-faced, handsome, black-bearded man there was gathering an atmosphere of mystery and of gloom. It was he who had been the first to discover the body of Sir Charles, and we had only his word for all the circumstances which led up to the old man's death. Was it possible that it was Barrymore, after all, whom we had seen in the cab in Regent Street? The beard might well have been the same. The cabman had described a somewhat shorter man, but such an impression might easily have been erroneous. How could I settle the point for ever? Obviously the first thing to do was to see the Grimpen postmaster, and find whether the test telegram had really been placed in Barrymore's own hands. Be the answer what it might, I should at least have something to report to Sherlock Holmes.

Sir Henry had numerous papers to examine after breakfast, so that the time was propitious for my excursion. It was a pleasant walk of four miles along the edge of the moor, leading me at last to a small grey hamlet, in which two larger buildings, which proved to be the inn and the house of Dr Mortimer, stood high above the rest. The postmaster, who **60** was also the village grocer, had a clear recollection of the telegram.

'Certainly, sir,' said he, 'I had the telegram delivered to Mr Barrymore exactly as directed.'

'Who delivered it?'

'My boy here. James, you delivered that telegram to Mr Barrymore at the Hall last week, did you not?'

'Yes, father, I delivered it.'

'Into his own hands?' I asked.

'Well, he was up in the loft at the time, so that I could not put it into his own hands, but I gave it into Mrs Barrymore's hands, and she promised to deliver it at once.'

'Did you see Mr Barrymore?'

'No, sir; I tell you he was in the loft.'

'If you didn't see him, how do you know he was in the loft?'

'Well, surely his own wife ought to know where he is,' said the postmaster, testily. 'Didn't he get the telegram? If there is any mistake it is for Mr Barrymore himself to complain.'

It seemed hopeless to pursue the inquiry any farther, but it was clear that in spite of Holmes's ruse we had no proof that Barrymore had not been in London all the time. Suppose that it were so—suppose that the same man had been the last who had seen Sir Charles alive, and the first to dog the new heir when he returned to England. What then? Was he the agent of others, or had he some sinister design of his own? What interest could he have in persecuting the Baskerville family? I thought of the strange warning clipped out of the leading article of *The Times*. Was that his work, or was it possibly the doing of someone who was bent upon counteracting his schemes? The only conceivable motive was that which had been suggested by Sir Henry, that if the family could be scared away a comfortable and permanent home would be secured for the Barrymores. But surely such an explanation as that would be quite inadequate to account for the deep and subtle scheming which seemed to be weaving an invisible net round **61** the young baronet. Holmes himself had said that no more complex case had come to him in all the long series of his sensational investigations. I prayed, as I walked back along the grey, lonely road, that my friend might soon be freed from his preoccupations and able to come down to take this heavy burden of responsibility from my shoulders.

Suddenly my thoughts were interrupted by the sound of running feet behind me and by a voice which called me by name. I turned, expecting to see Dr Mortimer, but to my surprise it was a stranger who was pursuing me. He was a small, slim, clean-shaven, prim-faced man, flaxen-haired and lean-jawed, between thirty and forty years of age, dressed in a grey suit and wearing a straw hat. A tin box for botanical specimens hung over his shoulder, and he carried a green butterfly-net in one of his hands.

'You will, I am sure, excuse my presumption, Dr Watson,' said he, as he came panting up to where I stood. 'Here on the moor we are homely folk, and do not wait for formal introductions. You may possibly have heard my name from our mutual friend, Mortimer. I am Stapleton, of Merripit House.' **62**

'Your net and box would have told me as much,' said I, 'for I knew that Mr Stapleton was a naturalist. But how did you know me?'

'I have been calling on Mortimer, and he pointed you out to me from the window of his surgery as you passed. As our road lay the same way, I thought that I would overtake you and introduce myself. I trust that Sir Henry is none the worse for his journey?'

'He is very well, thank you.'

'We were all rather afraid that after the sad death of Sir Charles the new baronet might refuse to live here. It is asking much of a wealthy man to come down and bury himself in a place of this kind, but I need not tell you that it means a very great deal to the countryside. Sir Henry has, I suppose, no superstitious fears in the matter?'

'I do not think that it is likely.'

'Of course you know the legend of the fiend dog which haunts the family?'

'I have heard it.'

'It is extraordinary how credulous the peasants are about here! Any number of them are ready to swear that they have seen such a creature upon the moor.' He spoke with a smile, but I seemed to read in his eyes that he took the matter more seriously. 'The story took a great hold upon the imagination of Sir Charles, and I have no doubt that it led to his tragic end.'

'But how?'

'His nerves were so worked up that the appearance of any dog might have had a fatal effect upon his diseased heart. I fancy that he really did see something of the kind upon that last night in the Yew Alley. I feared that some disaster might occur, for I was very fond of the old man, and I knew that his heart was weak.'

'How did you know that?'

'My friend Mortimer told me.'

'You think, then, that some dog pursued Sir Charles, and that he died of fright in consequence?'

'Have you any better explanation?'

'I have not come to any conclusion.'

'Has Mr Sherlock Holmes?'

The words took away my breath for an instant, but a glance at the placid face and steadfast eyes of my companion showed

62 *Merripit House*.' A glance at our "very-large"-scale map will show Merripit, in the heart of the moor.

63 *'The records of your detective have reached us here.* It would seem, as we have noted, that the adventure can have taken place no earlier than 1888, by reason of Stapleton's clear reference to Watson's published writings. But this view has been challenged by Mr. Peter A. Ruber, who writes ("On a Defense of H. W. Bell"): ". . . Stapleton does not refer to having read Watson's chronicles. Holmes' famous career would hardly have escaped the notice of the newspapers, no matter how many times he gave credit to Lestrade or Gregson and the rest of the minions of Scotland Yard. During these years Holmes surely would have been without problems had it not been for the . . . publicity that spread his fame world-wide."

that no surprise was intended.

'It is useless for us to pretend that we do not know you, Dr Watson,' said he. 'The records of your detective have **63** reached us here, and you could not celebrate him without being known yourself. When Mortimer told me your name he could not deny your identity. If you are here, then it follows that Mr Sherlock Holmes is interesting himself in the matter, and I am naturally curious to know what view he may take.'

'I am afraid that I cannot answer that question.'

'May I ask if he is going to honour us with a visit himself?'

'He cannot leave town at present. He has other cases which engage his attention.'

'What a pity! He might throw some light on that which is so dark to us. But as to your own researches, if there is any possible way in which I can be of service to you, I trust that you will command me. If I had any indication of the nature of your suspicions, or how you propose to investigate the case, I might perhaps even now give you some aid or advice.'

'I assure you that I am simply here upon a visit to my friend Sir Henry, and that I need no help of any kind.'

'Excellent!' said Stapleton. 'You are perfectly right to be wary and discreet. I am justly reproved for what I feel was an unjustifiable intrusion, and I promise you that I will not mention the matter again.'

We had come to a point where a narrow grassy path struck off from the road and wound away across the moor. A steep, boulder-sprinkled hill lay upon the right which had in bygone days been cut into a granite quarry. The face which was turned towards us formed a dark cliff, with ferns and brambles growing in its niches. From over a distant rise there floated a grey plume of smoke.

'A moderate walk along this moor-path brings us to Merripit House,' said he. 'Perhaps you will spare an hour that I may have the pleasure of introducing you to my sister.'

My first thought was that I should be by Sir Henry's side. But then I remembered the pile of papers and bills with which his study table was littered. It was certain that I could not help him with those. And Holmes had expressly said that I should study the neighbours upon the moor. I accepted Stapleton's invitation, and we turned together down the path.

'It is a wonderful place, the moor,' said he, looking round over the undulating downs, long green rollers, with crests of jagged granite foaming up into fantastic surges. 'You never tire of the moor. You cannot think the wonderful secrets which it contains. It is so vast, and so barren, and so mysterious.'

'You know it well, then?'

'I have only been here two years. The residents would call me a new-comer. We came shortly after Sir Charles settled. But my tastes led me to explore every part of the country round, and I should think that there are few men who know it better than I do.'

'Is it so hard to know?'

'Very hard. You see, for example, this great plain to the north here, with the queer hills breaking out of it. Do you observe anything remarkable about that?'

'It would be a rare place for a gallop.'

'You would naturally think so, and the thought has cost folk their lives before now. You notice those bright green spots scattered thickly over it?'

'Yes, they seem more fertile than the rest.'

Stapleton laughed. 'That is the great Grimpen Mire,' said he. 'A false step yonder means death to man or beast. Only yesterday I saw one of the moor ponies wander into it. He never came out. I saw his head for quite a long time craning out of the bog-hole, but it sucked him down at last. Even in dry seasons it is a danger to cross it, but after these autumn rains it is an awful place. And yet I can find my way to the very heart of it and return alive. By George, there is another of those miserable ponies!'

Something brown was rolling and tossing among the green sedges. Then a long, agonized, writhing neck shot upwards and a dreadful cry echoed over the moor. It turned me cold with horror, but my companion's nerves seemed to be stronger than mine.

'It's gone!' said he. 'The Mire has him. Two in two days, and many more, perhaps, for they get in the way of going there in the dry weather, and never know the difference until the Mire has them in its clutch. It's a bad place, the great Grimpen Mire.'

'And you say you can penetrate it?'

'Yes, there are one or two paths which a very active man can take. I have found them out.'

'But why should you wish to go into so horrible a place?'

'Well, you see the hills beyond? They are really islands cut off on all sides by the impassable Mire, which has crawled round them in the course of years. That is where the rare plants and the butterflies are, if you have the wit to reach them.'

'I shall try my luck some day.'

He looked at me with a surprised face. 'For God's sake put such an idea out of your mind,' said he. 'Your blood would be upon my head. I assure you that there would not be the least chance of your coming back alive. It is only by remembering certain complex landmarks that I am able to do it.'

'Halloa!' I cried. 'What is that?'

A long, low moan, indescribably sad, swept over the moor. It filled the whole air, and yet it was impossible to say whence it same. From a dull murmur it swelled into a deep roar and then sank back into a melancholy, throbbing murmur once again. Stapleton looked at me with a curious expression in his face.

'Queer place, the moor!' said he.

'But what is it?'

'The peasants say it is the Hound of the Baskervilles calling for its prey. I've heard it once or twice before, but never quite so loud.'

I looked round, with a chill of fear in my heart, at the huge swelling plain, mottled with the green patches of rushes. Nothing stirred over the vast expanse save a pair of ravens, which croaked loudly from a tor behind us.

'You are an educated man. You don't believe such nonsense as that?' said I. 'What do you think is the cause of so strange a sound?'

'Bogs make queer noises sometimes. It's the mud settling, or the water rising, or something.'

'THAT IS THE GREAT GRIMPEN MIRE,' SAID HE.

As is well known, Watson's "Great Grimpen Mire" is *Grimspound Bog*, three miles to the north and west of Widecombe-in-the-Moor, shown above in a photograph by C. E. Robinson from the Reverend Sabine Baring-Gould's *A Book of Dartmoor*. The trifling change of name here is a nice example of Watson's Victorian primness, for as Mr. Michael Harrison has reminded us (in *In the Footsteps of Sherlock Holmes*) the word "bog" is British schoolboy slang for "latrine."

64 *the last of the bitterns.*' "Stapleton ascribes the sound to a bittern—after having ascertained that Dr. Watson was not familiar with the bittern (*Botaurus stellaris*), as indeed he was not," Miss Lisa McGaw wrote in "Some Trifling Notes on Sherlock Holmes and Ornithology." "The bittern is a bird of the marsh, not the moor, and though all things are possible on the moor, the chance of a bittern booming in an alien locale at that precise moment is almost as negligible as was the bittern population in England at that time. Formerly abundant in Norfolk and Lincolnshire, the bittern nearly became extinct."

65 *Prehistoric man lived thickly on the moor.* This is quite true. Near Hound Tor, for example, not far from Grimspound, there is almost a metropolis of Neolithic huts which may be visited to this day.

66 *It is surely Cyclopides.*' Cyclopides, as the editors of the Catalogue of the Sherlock Holmes Exhibition have shown, is no longer valid as a generic name; it was created in 1819 by Hübner for five species, only one of which is British. This is the butterfly now known as the Chequered Skipper. "However, [Stapleton's] statement 'He is very rare' is, for Dartmoor, a considerable understatement; for it would have been the first and only record for that part of England. . . . It is nevertheless likely that the butterfly in question was one of the group (*Hesperiidae*) known as the Skippers. They all have a distinctive darting and rapid flight, and Watson's 'a small fly or moth' is very suggestive, since this group of butterflies is primitive and approaches the moths in a number of respects." Two Skippers which are known in Devon, but not on the moor, are the Lulworth Skipper and the Silver-spotted Skipper; of the remaining Skippers (the Dingy Skipper, the Grizzled Skipper, the Small Skipper and the Large Skipper), all are known on the moor, but none of them are "very rare" and it would be very seldom indeed that any of them would be found so late in the year.

'No, no, that was a living voice.'

'Well, perhaps it was. Did you ever hear a bittern booming?'

'No, I never did.'

'It's a very rare bird—practically extinct—in England now, but all things are possible upon the moor. Yes, I should not be surprised to learn that what we have heard is the cry of **64** the last of the bitterns.'

'It's the weirdest, strangest thing that ever I heard in my life.'

'Yes, it's rather an uncanny place altogether. Look at the hillside yonder. What do you make of those?'

The whole steep slope was covered with grey circular rings of stone, a score of them at least.

'What are they? Sheep-pens?'

'No, they are the homes of our worthy ancestors. Prehistoric **65** man lived thickly on the moor, and as no one in particular has lived there since, we find all his little arrangements exactly as he left them. These are his wigwams with the roofs off. You can even see his hearth and his couch if you have the curiosity to go inside.'

'But it is quite a town. When was it inhabited?'

'Neolithic man—no date.'

'What did he do?'

'He grazed his cattle on these slopes, and he learned to dig for tin when the bronze sword began to supersede the stone axe. Look at the great trench in the opposite hill. That is his mark. Yes, you will find some very singular points about the moor, Dr Watson. Oh, excuse me an instant. It is surely **66** Cyclopides.'

A small fly or moth had fluttered across our path, and in an instant Stapleton was rushing with extraordinary energy and speed in pursuit of it. To my dismay the creature flew straight for the great Mire, but my acquaintance never paused for an instant, bounding from tuft to tuft behind it, his green net waving in the air. His grey clothes and jerky, zigzag, irregular progress made him not unlike some huge moth himself. I was standing watching his pursuit with a mixture of admiration for his extraordinary activity and fear lest he should lose his footing in the treacherous Mire, when I heard the sound of steps, and, turning round, found a woman near me upon the path. She had come from the direction in which the plume of smoke indicated the position of Merripit House, but the dip of the moor had hid her until she was quite close.

I could not doubt that this was the Miss Stapleton of whom I had been told, since ladies of any sort must be few upon the moor, and I remembered that I had heard someone describe her as being a beauty. The woman who approached me was certainly that, and of a most uncommon type. There could not have been a greater contrast between brother and sister, for Stapleton was neutral-tinted, with light hair and grey eyes, while she was darker than any brunette whom I have seen in England—slim, elegant and tall. She had a proud, finely cut face, so regular that it might have seemed impassive were it not for the sensitive mouth and the beautiful dark, eager eyes. With her perfect figure and elegant dress she was, indeed, a strange apparition upon a lonely moorland path. Her eyes were on her brother as I turned, and then she quickened her pace towards me. I had raised my hat, and was about to make some explanatory remark, when her own words turned all my thoughts into a new channel.

'Go back!' she said. 'Go straight back to London, instantly.'

I could only stare at her in stupid surprise. Her eyes blazed at me, and she tapped the ground impatiently with her foot.

'Why should I go back?' I asked.

'I cannot explain.' She spoke in a low, eager voice, with a curious lisp in her utterance. 'But for God's sake do what I ask you. Go back, and never set foot upon the moor again.'

'But I have only just come.'

'Man, man!' she cried. 'Can you not tell when a warning is for your own good? Go back to London! Start tonight! Get away from this place at all costs! Hush, my brother is coming! Not a word of what I have said. Would you mind getting that orchid for me among the mare's-tails yonder? We are very **67** rich in orchids on the moor, though, of course, you are rather late to see the beauties of the place.'

Stapleton had abandoned the chase, and came back to us breathing hard and flushed with his exertions.

'Halloa, Beryl!' said he, and it seemed to me that the tone of his greeting was not altogether a cordial one.

'Well, Jack, you are very hot.'

'Yes, I was chasing a Cyclopides. He is very rare, and seldom found in the late autumn. What a pity that I should have missed him!'

He spoke unconcernedly, but his small light eyes glanced incessantly from the girl to me.

'You have introduced yourselves, I can see.'

'Yes. I was telling Sir Henry that it was rather late for him to see the true beauties of the moor.'

'Why, who do you think this is?'

'I imagine that it must be Sir Henry Baskerville.'

'No, no,' said I. 'Only a humble commoner, but his friend. My name is Dr Watson.'

A flush of vexation passed over her expressive face.

'We have been talking at cross purposes,' said she.

'Why, you had not very much time for talk,' her brother remarked, with the same questioning eyes.

'I talked as if Dr Watson were a resident instead of being merely a visitor,' said she. 'It cannot much matter to him whether it is early or late for the orchids. But you will come on, will you not, and see Merripit House?'

A short walk brought us to it, a bleak moorland house, once the farm of some grazier in the old prosperous days, but now put into repair and turned into a modern dwelling. An orchard surrounded it, but the trees, as is usual upon the moor, were stunted and nipped, and the effect of the whole place was mean and melancholy. We were admitted by a strange, wizened, rusty-coated old manservant, who seemed in keeping with the house. Inside, however, there were large rooms furnished with an elegance in which I seemed to recognize the taste of the lady. As I looked from their windows at the interminable granite-flecked moor rolling unbroken to the farthest horizon I could not but marvel at what could have brought this highly educated man and this beautiful woman to live in such a place.

'Queer spot to choose, is it not?' said he, as if in answer to my thought. 'And yet we manage to make ourselves fairly

67 *that orchid.* What was the orchid? The first difficulty is the lateness of the season, a time of year when few if any orchids would be in flower. The second difficulty is Miss Stapleton's statement that the orchid grew among mare's-tails (*Hippuris vulgaris* L.), which appear to be unknown on Dartmoor. It is probable that the plant referred to by Miss Stapleton was not the mare's-tail but the marsh horsetail (*Equisetum palustre*). Taking these difficulties into consideration, the editors of the Catalogue of the Sherlock Holmes Exhibition cast their vote for *Spiranthes spiralis* (L.) *Koch* (Ladies' tresses); it grows on Dartmoor, flowers from September to October, but would *not* be a plant of wet places that would be growing among either mare's-tail or horsetail. On the other hand, Mr. R. F. May, taking into consideration the same difficulties in his essay "*The Hound of the Baskervilles:* A Botanical Enquiry," felt that the orchid might well have been the Marsh Spotted Orchid (*Dacrylorchis maculata* subspecies *ericetorum*). "This orchid grows in damp acid peaty soil and in spongy marshes and is widely established in suitable places all over Britain. This plant has been seen in flower occasionally as late as the second half of September . . ."

68 *mechanical and uninteresting.* ". . . the . . . statement is nonsensical," Mr. Frederick Bryan-Brown wrote in "Sherlockian Schools and Schoolmasters," "as how, if he really felt it a privilege to mould the young minds, could he find the work mechanical and uninteresting? Frustrating? Yes. Exasperating? Often. Infuriating? Sometimes, but never mechanical and uninteresting."

happy, do we not, Beryl?'

'Quite happy,' said she, but there was no ring of conviction in her words.

68 'I had a school,' said Stapleton. 'It was in the North country. The work to a man of my temperament was mechanical and uninteresting, but the privilege of living with youth, of helping to mould those young minds and of impressing them with one's own character and ideals, was very dear to me. However, the fates were against us. A serious epidemic broke out in the school, and three of the boys died. It never recovered from the blow, and much of my capital was irretrievably swallowed up. And yet, if it were not for the loss of the charming companionship of the boys, I could rejoice over my own misfortune, for, with my strong tastes for botany and zoology, I find an unlimited field of work here, and my sister is as devoted to Nature as I am. All this, Dr Watson, has been brought upon your head by your expression as you surveyed the moor out of our window.'

'It certainly did cross my mind that it might be a little dull —less for you, perhaps, than for your sister.'

'No, no, I am never dull,' said she, quickly.

'We have books, we have our studies, and we have interesting neighbours. Dr Mortimer is a most learned man in his own line. Poor Sir Charles was also an admirable companion. We knew him well, and miss him more than I can tell. Do you think that I should intrude if I were to call this afternoon and make the acquaintance of Sir Henry?'

'I am sure that he would be delighted.'

'Then perhaps you would mention that I propose to do so. We may in our humble way do something to make things more easy for him until he becomes accustomed to his new surroundings. Will you come upstairs, Dr Watson, and inspect my collection of Lepidoptera? I think it is the most complete one in the south-west of England. By the time that you have looked through them lunch will be almost ready.'

But I was eager to get back to my charge. The melancholy of the moor, the death of the unfortunate pony, the weird sound which had been associated with the grim legend of the Baskervilles—all these things tinged my thoughts with sadness. Then on the top of these more or less vague impressions there had come the definite and distinct warning of Miss Stapleton, delivered with such intense earnestness that I could not doubt that some grave and deep reason lay behind it. I resisted all pressure to stay for lunch, and I set off at once upon my return journey, taking the grass-grown path by which we had come.

It seems, however, that there must have been some short cut for those who knew it, for before I had reached the road I was astounded to see Miss Stapleton sitting upon a rock by the side of the track. Her face was beautifully flushed with her exertions, and she held her hand to her side.

'I have run all the way in order to cut you off, Dr Watson,' said she. 'I had not even time to put on my hat. I must not stop, or my brother may miss me. I wanted to say to you how sorry I am about the stupid mistake I made in thinking that you were Sir Henry. Please forget the words I said, which have no application whatever to you.'

'But I can't forget them, Miss Stapleton,' said I. 'I am Sir Henry's friend, and his welfare is a very close concern of mine.

Tell me why it was that you were so eager that Sir Henry should return to London.'

'A woman's whim, Dr Watson. When you know me better you will understand that I cannot always give reasons for what I say or do.'

'No, no. I remember the thrill in your voice. I remember the look in your eyes. Please, please, be frank with me, Miss Stapleton, for ever since I have been here I have been conscious of shadows all round me. Life has become like that great Grimpen Mire, with little green patches everywhere into which one may sink and with no guide to point the track. Tell me, then, what it was that you meant, and I will promise to convey your warning to Sir Henry.'

An expression of irresolution passed for an instant over her face, but her eyes had hardened again when she answered me.

'You make too much of it, Dr Watson,' said she. 'My brother and I were very much shocked by the death of Sir Charles. We knew him very intimately, for his favourite walk was over the moor to our house. He was deeply impressed with the curse which hung over his family, and when this tragedy came I naturally felt that there must be some grounds for the fears he had expressed. I was distressed, therefore, when another member of the family came down to live here, and I felt that he should be warned of the danger which he will run. That was all which I intended to convey.'

'But what is the danger?'

'You know the story of the hound?'

'I do not believe in such nonsense.'

'But I do. If you have any influence with Sir Henry, take him away from a place which has always been fatal to his family. The world is wide. Why should he wish to live at the place of danger?'

'Because it *is* the place of danger. That is Sir Henry's nature. I fear that unless you can give me some more definite information than this it would be impossible to get him to move.'

'I cannot say anything definite, for I do not know anything definite.'

'I would ask you one more question, Miss Stapleton. If you meant no more than this when you first spoke to me, why should you not wish your brother to overhear what you said? There is nothing to which he, or anyone else, could object.'

'My brother is very anxious to have the Hall inhabited, for he thinks that it is for the good of the poor folk upon the moor. He would be very angry if he knew that I had said anything which might induce Sir Henry to go away. But I have done my duty now, and I will say no more. I must get back, or he will miss me and suspect that I have seen you. Good-bye!'

She turned, and had disappeared in a few minutes among the scattered boulders, while I, with my soul full of vague fears, pursued my way to Baskerville Hall.

'YOU KNOW THE STORY OF THE HOUND?'

Illustration by Sidney Paget for the *Strand Magazine*, November, 1901.

8 · FIRST REPORT OF DR WATSON

From this point onwards I will follow the course of events by transcribing my own letters to Mr Sherlock Holmes which **69** lie before me on the table. One page is missing, but otherwise they are exactly as written, and show my feelings and suspicions of the moment more accurately than my memory, clear as it is upon these tragic events, can possibly do.

70   BASKERVILLE HALL, *Oct. 13th.*

My dear Holmes,

My previous letters and telegrams have kept you pretty well up-to-date as to all that has occurred in this most God-forsaken corner of the world. The longer one stays here the more does the spirit of the moor sink into one's soul, its vastness, and also its grim charm. When you are once out upon its bosom you have left all traces of modern England behind you, but on the other hand you are conscious everywhere of the homes and the work of the prehistoric people. On all sides of you as you walk are the houses of these forgotten folk, with their graves and the huge monoliths which are supposed to have marked their temples. As you look at their grey stone huts against the scarred hillsides you leave your own age behind you, and if you were to see a skin-clad, hairy man crawl out from the low door, fitting a flint-tipped arrow on to the string of his bow, you would feel that his presence there was more natural than your own. The strange thing is that they should have lived so thickly on what must always have been most unfruitful soil. I am no antiquarian, but I could imagine that they were some unwarlike and harried race who were forced to accept that which none other would occupy.

All this, however, is foreign to the mission on which you sent me, and will probably be very uninteresting to your severely practical mind. I can still remember your complete indifference as to whether the sun moved round the earth or the earth round the sun. Let me, therefore, return to the facts concerning Sir Henry Baskerville.

If you have not had any report within the last few days it is because up till today there was nothing of importance to relate. Then a very surprising circumstance occurred, which I shall tell you in due course. But, first of all, I must keep you in touch with some of the other factors in the situation.

One of these, concerning which I have said little, is the escaped convict upon the moor. There is strong reason now to believe that he has got right away, which is a considerable relief to the lonely householders of this district. A fortnight **71** has passed since his flight, during which he has not been seen and nothing has been heard of him. It is surely inconceivable that he could have held out upon the moor during all that time. Of course, so far as his concealment goes there is no difficulty at all. Any one of these stone huts would give him a hiding-place. But there is nothing to eat unless he were to catch and slaughter one of the moor sheep. We think, therefore, that he has gone, and the outlying farmers sleep the better in consequence.

We are four able-bodied men in this household, so that we could take good care of ourselves, but I confess that I have

69 *One page is missing.* Why should a page be missing? Holmes was not careless with Watson's correspondence, we may be sure. The statement is particularly curious because the two letters, as reproduced, seem to be complete.

70 Oct. *13*th. A Saturday in our year, 1888.

71 *A fortnight has passed since his flight.* Since Selden escaped on the night of Wednesday, September 26th, or the morning of Thursday, September 27th, a fortnight had *not* passed since his flight. But Watson undoubtedly means that a fortnight had passed since he, Watson, *heard* on Saturday, September 29th, that Selden had escaped.

had uneasy moments when I have thought of the Stapletons. They live miles from any help. There are one maid, an old manservant, the sister and the brother, the latter not a very strong man. They would be helpless in the hands of a desperate fellow like this Notting Hill criminal, if he could once effect an entrance. Both Sir Henry and I were concerned at their situation, and it was suggested that Perkins the groom should go over to sleep there, but Stapleton would not hear of it.

The fact is that our friend the baronet begins to display a considerable interest in our fair neighbour. It is not to be wondered at, for time hangs heavily in this lonely spot to an active man like him, and she is a very fascinating and beautiful woman. There is something tropical and exotic about her which forms a singular contrast to her cool and unemotional brother. Yet he also gives the idea of hidden fires. He has certainly a very marked influence over her, for I have seen her continually glance at him as she talked as if seeking approbation for what she said. I trust that he is kind to her. There is a dry glitter in his eyes, and a firm set of his thin lips, which go with a positive and possibly a harsh nature. You would find him an interesting study.

He came over to call upon Baskerville on that first day, and the very next morning he took us both to show us the spot where the legend of the wicked Hugo is supposed to have had its origin. It was an excursion of some miles across the moor to a place which is so dismal that it might have suggested the story. We found a short valley between rugged tors which led to an open, grassy space flecked over with the white cotton grass. In the middle of it rose two great stones, worn and sharpened at the upper end, until they looked like the huge, corroding fangs of some monstrous beast. In every way it corresponded with the scene of the old tragedy. Sir Henry was much interested, and asked Stapleton more than once whether he did really believe in the possibility of the interference of the supernatural in the affairs of men. He spoke lightly, but it was evident that he was very much in earnest. Stapleton was guarded in his replies, but it was easy to see that he said less than he might, and that he would not express his whole opinion out of consideration for the feelings of the baronet. He told us of similar cases, where families had suffered from some evil influence, and he left us with the impression that he shared the popular view upon the matter.

On our way back we stayed for lunch at Merripit House, and it was there that Sir Henry made the acquaintance of Miss Stapleton. From the first moment that he saw her he appeared to be strongly attracted by her, and I am much mistaken if the feeling was not mutual. He referred to her again and again on our walk home, and since then hardly a day has passed that we have not seen something of the brother and sister. They dine here tonight, and there is some talk of our going to them next week. One would imagine that such a **72** match would be very welcome to Stapleton, and yet I have more than once caught a look of the strongest disapprobation in his face when Sir Henry has been paying some attention to his sister. He is much attached to her, no doubt, and would lead a lonely life without her, but it would seem the height of selfishness, if he were to stand in the way of her making

Hound Tor, as seen in a painting by E. A. Tozer, from the Reverend Sabine Baring-Gould's *A Book of Dartmoor*. In fact, there are *two* Hound Tors on the moor—not to mention a *Greathound* Tor.

72 *there is some talk of our going to them next week.* Watson later writes: "We are to dine at Merripit House next Friday" and his letters to Holmes and his diary datings make clear that this was Friday, the 19th. Between 1881 (when Holmes and Watson met) and 1901 (when *The Hound of the Baskervilles* was first published) there are only four years in which October 19th fell on a Friday: 1883 (too early), 1888, 1894, and 1900 (too late). Our choice therefore lies between 1888 and 1894, and your editor submits that the evidence is heavily in favor of 1888.

73 tête-à-tête. French: in private talk; face to face.

74 *Thursday, to be more exact.* Watson refers to Thursday, October 11th.

75 *the villagers of Fernworthy.* There is no *village* of Fernworthy on the map of Dartmoor, but there was, and is, a substantial *farming district* of that very name only three miles from Lew House.

so brilliant a marriage. Yet I am certain that he does not wish their intimacy to ripen into love, and I have several times observed that he has taken pains to prevent them from being **73** *tête-à-tête.* By the way, your instructions to me never to allow Sir Henry to go out alone will become very much more onerous if a love-affair were to be added to our other difficulties. My popularity would soon suffer if I were to carry out your orders to the letter.

74   The other day—Thursday, to be more exact—Dr Mortimer lunched with us. He has been excavating a barrow at Long Down, and has got a prehistoric skull which fills him with great joy. Never was there such a single-minded enthusiast as he! The Stapletons came in afterwards, and the good doctor took us all to the Yew Alley, at Sir Henry's request, to show us exactly how everything occurred upon that fatal night. It is a long, dismal walk, the Yew Alley, between two high walls of clipped hedge, with a narrow band of grass upon either side. At the far end is an old, tumble-down summer-house. Half-way down is the moor-gate where the old gentleman left his cigar-ash. It is a white wooden gate with a latch. Beyond it lies the wide moor. I remembered your theory of the affair and tried to picture all that had occurred. As the old man stood there he saw something coming across the moor, something which terrified him so that he lost his wits, and ran and ran until he died of sheer horror and exhaustion. There was the long, gloomy tunnel down which he fled. And from what? A sheep-dog of the moor? Or a spectral hound, black, silent, and monstrous? Was there a human agency in the matter? Did the pale, watchful Barrymore know more than he cared to say? It was all dim and vague, but always there is the dark shadow of crime behind it.

One other neighbour I have met since I wrote last. This is Mr Frankland, of Lafter Hall, who lives some four miles to the south of us. He is an elderly man, red-faced, white-haired, and choleric. His passion is for the British law, and he has spent a large fortune in litigation. He fights for the mere pleasure of fighting, and is equally ready to take up either side of a question, so that it is no wonder that he has found it a costly amusement. Sometimes he will shut up a right of way and defy the parish to make him open it. At others he will with his own hands tear down some other man's gate and declare that a path has existed there from time immemorial, defying the owner to prosecute him for trespass. He is learned in old manorial and communal rights, and he applies his knowledge sometimes in favour of the villagers **75** of Fernworthy and sometimes against them, so that he is periodically either carried in triumph down the village street or else burned in effigy, according to his latest exploit. He is said to have about seven law-suits upon his hands at present, which will probably swallow up the remainder of his fortune, and so draw his sting and leave him harmless for the future. Apart from the law he seems a kindly, good-natured person, and I only mention him because you were particular that I should send some description of the people who surround us. He is curiously employed at present, for, being an amateur astronomer, he has an excellent telescope, with which he lies upon the roof of his own house and sweeps the moor all day in the hope of catching a glimpse of the escaped convict. If he would confine his energies to this all would be well, but there are rumours that he intends to prosecute Dr Mortimer for opening a grave without the consent of the next-of-kin, because he dug up the neolithic skull in the barrow on Long Down. He helps to keep our lives from being monotonous, and gives a little comic relief where it is badly needed.

And now, having brought you up-to-date in the escaped convict, the Stapletons, Dr Mortimer, and Frankland, of Lafter Hall, let me end on that which is most important, and tell you more about the Barrymores, and especially about the surprising development of last night.

First of all about the test telegram, which you sent from London in order to make sure that Barrymore was really here. I have already explained that the testimony of the postmaster shows that the test was worthless and that we have no proof one way or the other. I told Sir Henry how the matter stood, and he at once, in his downright fashion, had Barrymore up and asked him whether he had received the telegram himself. Barrymore said that he had.

'Did the boy deliver it into your own hands?' asked Sir Henry.

Barrymore looked surprised, and considered for a little time.

'No,' said he, 'I was in the box-room at the time, and my wife brought it up to me.'

'Did you answer it yourself?'

'No; I told my wife what to answer, and she went down to write it.'

In the evening he recurred to the subject of his own accord.

'I could not quite understand the object of your questions this morning, Sir Henry,' said he. 'I trust that they do not mean that I have done anything to forfeit your confidence?'

Sir Henry had to assure him that it was not so and pacify him by giving him a considerable part of his old wardrobe, the London outfit having now all arrived.

Mrs Barrymore is of interest to me. She is a heavy, solid person, very limited, intensely respectable, and inclined to be puritanical. You could hardly conceive a less emotional subject. Yet I have told you how, on the first night here, I heard her sobbing bitterly, and since then I have more than once observed traces of tears upon her face. Some deep sorrow gnaws ever at her heart. Sometimes I wonder if she has a guilty memory which haunts her, and sometimes I suspect Barrymore of being a domestic tyrant. I have always felt that there was something singular and questionable in this man's character, but the adventure of last night brings all my suspicions to a head.

And yet it may seem a small matter in itself. You are aware that I am not a very sound sleeper, and since I have been on guard in this house my slumbers have been lighter than ever. Last night, about two in the morning, I was aroused by a stealthy step passing my room. I rose, opened my door, and peeped out. A long black shadow was trailing down the corridor. It was thrown by a man who walked softly down the passage with a candle held in his hand. He was in shirt and trousers, with no covering to his feet. I could merely see the outline, but his height told me that it was Barrymore. He walked very slowly and circumspectly, and there was something indescribably guilty and furtive in his whole appearance.

. . . HE STARED OUT INTO THE BLACKNESS OF THE MOOR.

Illustration by Sidney Paget for the *Strand Magazine*, November, 1901. Watson in speaking of the darkness of the night is again quite correct: the moon set at 10:40 P.M. on that Friday night, so it *would* have been very dark at two on the Saturday morning.

I have told you that the corridor is broken by the balcony which runs round the hall, but that it is resumed upon the farther side. I waited until he had passed out of sight, and then I followed him. When I came round the balcony he had reached the end of the farther corridor, and I could see from the glimmer of light through an open door that he had entered one of the rooms. Now, all these rooms are unfurnished and unoccupied, so that his expedition became more mysterious than ever. The light shone steadily, as if he were standing motionless. I crept down the passage as noiselessly as I could and peeped round the corner of the door.

Barrymore was crouching at the window with the candle held against the glass. His profile was half turned towards me, and his face seemed to be rigid with expectation as he stared out into the blackness of the moor. For some minutes he stood watching intently. Then he gave a deep groan, and with an impatient gesture he put out the light. Instantly, I made my way back to my room, and very shortly came the stealthy steps passing once more upon their return journey. Long afterwards when I had fallen into a light sleep I heard a key turn somewhere in a lock, but I could not tell whence the sound came. What it all means I cannot guess, but there is some secret business going on in this house of gloom which sooner or later we shall get to the bottom of. I do not trouble you with my theories, for you asked me to furnish you only with facts. I have had a long talk with Sir Henry this morning, and we have made a plan of campaign founded upon my observations of last night. I will not speak about it just now, but it should make my next report interesting reading.

9 ❖ SECOND REPORT OF DR WATSON

The Light upon the Moor

76   BASKERVILLE HALL, *Oct.* 15*th.*

My dear Holmes,

If I was compelled to leave you without much news during the early days of my mission you must acknowledge that I am making up for lost time, and that events are now crowding thick and fast upon us. In my last report I ended upon my top note with Barrymore at the window, and now I have quite a budget already which will, unless I am much mistaken, considerably surprise you. Things have taken a turn which I could not have anticipated. In some ways they have within the last forty-eight hours become much clearer and in some ways they have become more complicated. But I will tell you all, and you shall judge for yourself.

Before breakfast on the morning following my adventure I went down the corridor and examined the room in which Barrymore had been on the night before. The western window through which he had stared so intently has, I noticed, one peculiarity above all other windows in the house—it

76 Oct. *15*th. A Monday in our year, 1888.

commands the nearest outlook on to the moor. There is an opening between two trees which enables one from this point of view to look right down upon it, while from all the other windows it is only a distant glimpse which can be obtained. It follows, therefore, that Barrymore, since only this window would serve his purpose, must have been looking out for something or somebody upon the moor. The night was very dark, so that I can hardly imagine how he could have hoped to see anyone. It had struck me that it was possible that some love intrigue was on foot. That would have accounted for his stealthy movements and also for the uneasiness of his wife. The man is a striking-looking fellow, very well equipped to steal the heart of a country girl, so that this theory seemed to have something to support it. That opening of the door which I had heard after I had returned to my room might mean that he had gone out to keep some clandestine appointment. So I reasoned with myself in the morning, and I tell you the direction of my suspicions, however much the result may have shown that they were unfounded.

But whatever the true explanation of Barrymore's movements might be, I felt that the responsibility of keeping them to myself until I could explain them was more than I could bear. I had an interview with the baronet in his study after breakfast, and I told him all that I had seen. He was less surprised than I had expected.

'I knew that Barrymore walked about nights, and I had a mind to speak to him about it,' said he. 'Two or three times I have heard his steps in the passage, coming and going, just about the hour you name.'

'Perhaps, then, he pays a visit every night to that particular window,' I suggested.

'Perhaps he does. If so, we should be able to shadow him, and see what it is that he is after. I wonder what your friend Holmes would do if he were here?'

'I believe that he would do exactly what you now suggest,' said I. 'He would follow Barrymore and see what he did.'

'Then we shall do it together.'

'But surely he would hear us.'

'The man is rather deaf, and in any case we must take our chance of that. We'll sit up in my room tonight, and wait until he passes.' Sir Henry rubbed his hands with pleasure, and it was evident that he hailed the adventure as a relief to his somewhat quiet life upon the moor.

The baronet has been in communication with the architect who prepared the plans for Sir Charles, and with a contractor from London, so that we may expect great changes to begin here soon. There have been decorators and furnishers up from Plymouth, and it is evident that our friend has large **77** ideas, and means to spare no pains or expense to restore the grandeur of his family. When the house is renovated and refurnished, all that he will need will be a wife to make it complete. Between ourselves, there are pretty clear signs that this will not be wanting if the lady is willing, for I have seldom seen a man more infatuated with a woman than he is with our beautiful neighbour, Miss Stapleton. And yet the course of true love does not run quite as smoothly as one would under the circumstances expect. Today, for example, its surface was broken by a very unexpected ripple, which has caused our friend considerable perplexity and annoyance.

77 *Plymouth*. The nearest town of any great size to "Baskerville Hall." Plymouth was the rendezvous of the anti-Armada fleet; Drake, Hawkins, and Raleigh set out from Plymouth; and it was the last English port touched by the *Mayflower* on her voyage to the New World.

SIR HENRY PUT HIS HAND UPON MY SHOULDER . . .

Illustration by Sidney Paget for the *Strand Magazine*, December, 1901.

After the conversation which I have quoted about Barrymore, Sir Henry put on his hat and prepared to go out. As a matter of course, I did the same.

'What, are *you* coming, Watson?' he asked, looking at me in a curious way.

'That depends on whether you are going on the moor,' said I.

'Yes, I am.'

'Well, you know what my instructions are. I am sorry to intrude, but you heard how earnestly Holmes insisted that I should not leave you, and especially that you should not go alone upon the moor.'

Sir Henry put his hand upon my shoulder, with a pleasant smile.

'My dear fellow,' said he, 'Holmes, with all his wisdom, did not foresee some things which have happened since I have been on the moor. You understand me? I am sure that you are the last man in the world who would wish to be a spoil-sport. I must go out alone.'

It put me in a most awkward position. I was at a loss what to say or what to do, and before I had made up my mind he picked up his cane and was gone.

But when I came to think the matter over my conscience reproached me bitterly for having on any pretext allowed him to go out of my sight. I imagined what my feelings would be if I had to return to you and to confess that some misfortune had occurred through my disregard for your instructions. I assure you my cheeks flushed at the very thought. It might not even now be too late to overtake him, so I set off at once in the direction of Merripit House.

I hurried along the road at the top of my speed without seeing anything of Sir Henry, until I came to the point where the moor-path branches off. There, fearing that perhaps I had come in the wrong direction, after all, I mounted a hill from which I could command a view—the same hill which is cut into the dark quarry. Thence I saw him at once. He was on the moor-path, about a quarter of a mile off, and a lady was by his side who could only be Miss Stapleton. It was clear that there was already an understanding between them and that they had met by appointment. They were walking slowly along in deep conversation, and I saw her making quick little movements of her hands as if she were very earnest in what she was saying, while he listened intently, and once or twice shook his head in strong dissent. I stood among the rocks watching them, very much puzzled as to what I should do next. To follow them and break into their intimate conversation seemed to be an outrage, and yet my clear duty was never for an instant to let him out of my sight. To act the spy upon a friend was a hateful task. Still, I could see no better course than to observe him from the hill, and to clear my conscience by confessing to him afterwards what I had done. It is true that if any sudden danger had threatened him I was too far away to be of use, and yet I am sure that you will agree with me that the position was very difficult, and that there was nothing more which I could do.

Our friend, Sir Henry, and the lady had halted on the path, and were standing deeply absorbed in their conversation, when I was suddenly aware that I was not the only witness of their interview. A wisp of green floating in the air caught my eye, and another glance showed me that it was carried on a stick by a man who was moving among the broken ground. It was Stapleton with his butterfly-net. He was very much closer to the pair than I was, and he appeared to be moving in their direction. At this instant Sir Henry suddenly drew Miss Stapleton to his side. His arm was round her, but it seemed to me that she was straining away from him with her face averted. He stooped his head to hers, and she raised one hand as if in protest. Next moment I saw them spring apart and turn hurriedly round. Stapleton was the cause of the interruption. He was running wildly towards them, his absurd net dangling behind him. He gesticulated and almost danced with excitement in front of the lovers. What the scene meant I could not imagine, but it seemed to me that Stapleton was abusing Sir Henry, who offered explanations, which became more angry as the other refused to accept them. The lady stood by in haughty silence. Finally Stapleton turned upon his heel and beckoned in a peremptory way to his sister, who, after an irresolute glance at Sir Henry, walked off by the side of her brother. The naturalist's angry gestures showed that the lady was included in his displeasure. The baronet stood for a minute looking after them, and then he walked slowly back the way that he had come, his head hanging, the very picture of dejection.

What all this meant I could not imagine, but I was deeply ashamed to have witnessed so intimate a scene without my friend's knowledge. I ran down the hill, therefore, and met the baronet at the bottom. His face was flushed with anger and his brows were wrinkled, like one who is at his wits' ends what to do.

'Halloa, Watson! Where have you dropped from?' said he. 'You don't mean to say that you came after me in spite of all?'

I explained everything to him: how I had found it impossible to remain behind, how I had followed him and how I had witnessed all that had occurred. For an instant his eyes blazed at me, but my frankness disarmed his anger, and he broke at last into a rather rueful laugh.

'You would have thought the middle of that prairie a fairly safe place for a man to be private,' said he, 'but, by thunder, the whole countryside seems to have been out to see me do my wooing—and a mighty poor wooing at that! Where had you engaged a seat?'

'I was on that hill.'

'Quite in the back row, eh? But her brother was well up to the front. Did you see him come out on us?'

'Yes, I did.'

'Did he ever strike you as being crazy—this brother of hers?'

'I can't say that he ever did.'

'I dare say not. I always thought him sane enough until today, but you can take it from me that either he or I ought to be in a strait-jacket. What's the matter with me, anyhow? You've lived near me for some weeks, Watson. Tell me straight, now! Is there anything that would prevent me from making a good husband to a woman that I loved?'

'I should say not.'

'He can't object to my worldly position, so it must be myself that he has this down on. What has he against me? I never hurt man or woman in my life that I know of. And yet he would not so much as let me touch the tips of her fingers.'

. . . SIR HENRY SUDDENLY DREW MISS STAPLETON
TO HIS SIDE.

Illustration by Sidney Paget for the *Strand Magazine*, December, 1901.

'Did he say so?'

'That, and a deal more. I tell you, Watson, I've only known her these few weeks, but from the first I just felt that she was made for me, and she, too—she was happy when she was with me, and that I'll swear. There's a light in a woman's eyes that speaks louder than words. But he has never let us get together, and it was only today for the first time that I saw a chance of having a few words with her alone. She was glad to meet me, but when she did it was not love that she would talk about, and she wouldn't have let me talk about it either if she could have stopped it. She kept coming back to it that this was a place of danger, and that she would never be happy until I had left it. I told her that since I had seen her I was in no hurry to leave it, and that if she really wanted me to go, the only way to work it was for her to arrange to go with me. With that I offered in as many words to marry her, but before she could answer down came this brother of hers, running at us with a face on him like a madman. He was just white with rage, and those light eyes of his were blazing with fury. What was I doing with the lady? How dared I offer her attentions which were distasteful to her? Did I think that because I was a baronet I could do what I liked? If he had not been her brother I should have known better how to answer him. As it was I told him that my feelings towards his sister were such as I was not ashamed of, and that I hoped that she might honour me by becoming my wife. That seemed to make the matter no better, so then I lost my temper, too, and I answered him rather more hotly than I should, perhaps, considering that she was standing by. So it ended by his going off with her, as you saw, and here am I as badly puzzled a man as any in this country. Just tell me what it all means, Watson, and I'll owe you more than ever I can hope to pay.'

I tried one or two explanations, but, indeed, I was completely puzzled myself. Our friend's title, his fortune, his age, his character, and his appearance are all in his favour, and I know nothing against him, unless it be this dark fate which runs in his family. That his advances should be rejected so brusquely without any reference to the lady's own wishes, and that the lady should accept the situation without protest, is very amazing. However, our conjectures were set at rest by a visit from Stapleton himself that very afternoon. He had come to offer apologies for his rudeness of the morning, and after a long private interview with Sir Henry in his study the upshot of their conversation was that the breach is quite healed, and that we are to dine at Merripit House next Friday as a sign of it.

'I don't say now that he isn't a crazy man,' said Sir Henry; 'I can't forget the look in his eyes when he ran at me this morning, but I must allow that no man could make a more handsome apology than he has done.'

'Did he give any explanation of his conduct?'

'His sister is everything in his life, he says. That is natural enough, and I am glad that he should understand her value. They have always been together, and according to his account he has been a very lonely man with only her as a companion, so that the thought of losing her was really terrible to him. He had not understood, he said, that I was becoming attached to her, but when he saw with his own eyes that it was really so, and that she might be taken away from him, it gave him such a shock that for a time he was not responsible for what he said or did. He was very sorry for all that had passed, and he recognized how foolish and how selfish it was that he should imagine that he could hold a beautiful woman like his sister to himself for her whole life. If she had to leave him he had rather it was to a neighbour like myself than to anyone else. But in any case it was a blow to him, and it would take him some time before he could prepare himself to meet it. He would withdraw all opposition upon his part if I would promise for three months to let the matter rest, and to be content with cultivating the lady's friendship during that time without claiming her love. This I promised, and so the matter rests.'

So there is one of our small mysteries cleared up. It is something to have touched bottom anywhere in this bog in which we are floundering. We know now why Stapleton looked with disfavour upon his sister's suitor—even when that suitor was so eligible a one as Sir Henry. And now I pass on to another thread which I have extricated out of the tangled skein, the mystery of the sobs in the night, of the tear-stained face of Mrs Barrymore, of the secret journey of the butler to the western lattice-window. Congratulate me, my dear Holmes, and tell me that I have not disappointed you as an agent— that you do not regret the confidence which you showed in me when you sent me down. All these things have by one night's work been thoroughly cleared.

I have said 'by one night's work,' but, in truth, it was by two nights' work, for on the first we drew entirely blank. I **78** sat up with Sir Henry in his room until nearly three o'clock in the morning, but no sound of any sort did we hear except the chiming clock upon the stairs. It was a most melancholy vigil, and ended by each of us falling asleep in our chairs. Fortunately we were not discouraged, and we determined to try again. The next night we lowered the lamp and sat smoking cigarettes, without making the least sound. It was incredible how slowly the hours crawled by, and yet we were helped through it by the same sort of patient interest which the hunter must feel as he watches the trap into which he hopes the game may wander. One struck, and two, and we had almost for the second time given it up in despair, when in an instant we both sat bolt upright in our chairs, with all our weary senses keenly on the alert once more. We had heard the creak of a step in the passage.

Very stealthily we heard it pass along until it died away in the distance. Then the baronet gently opened his door, and we set out in pursuit. Already our man had gone round the gallery, and the corridor was all in darkness. Softly we stole along until we had come into the other wing. We were just in time to catch a glimpse of the tall, black-bearded figure, his shoulders rounded, as he tiptoed down the passage. Then he passed through the same door as before, and the light of the candle framed it in the darkness and shot one single yellow beam across the gloom of the corridor. We shuffled cautiously towards it, trying every plank before we dared to put our whole weight upon it. We had taken the precaution of leaving our boots behind us, but, even so, the old boards snapped and creaked beneath our tread. Sometimes it seemed impossible that he should fail to hear our approach. However, the man is fortunately rather deaf, and he was entirely

78 *by two nights' work.* That is, the night of Saturday to Sunday, October 13th to 14th, and the night of Sunday to Monday, October 14th to 15th.

'WHAT ARE YOU DOING HERE, BARRYMORE?'

Illustration by Sidney Paget for the *Strand Magazine*, December, 1901.

preoccupied in that which he was doing. When at last we reached the door and peeped through we found him crouching at the window, candle in hand, his white, intent face pressed against the pane, exactly as I had seen him two nights before.

We had arranged no plan of campaign, but the baronet is a man to whom the most direct way is always the most natural. He walked into the room, and as he did so Barrymore sprang up from the window with a sharp hiss of his breath, and stood, livid and trembling, before us. His dark eyes, glaring out of the white mask of his face, were full of horror and astonishment as he gazed from Sir Henry to me.

'What are you doing here, Barrymore?'

'Nothing, sir.' His agitation was so great that he could hardly speak, and the shadows sprang up and down from the shaking of his candle. 'It was the window, sir. I go round at night to see that they are fastened.'

'On the second floor?'

'Yes, sir, all the windows.'

'Look here, Barrymore,' said Sir Henry, sternly, 'we have made up our minds to have the truth out of you, so it will save you trouble to tell it sooner rather than later. Come now! No lies! What were you doing at that window?'

The fellow looked at us in a helpless way, and he wrung his hands together like one who is in the last extremity of doubt and misery.

'I was doing no harm, sir. I was holding a candle to the window.'

'And why were you holding a candle to the window?'

'Don't ask me, Sir Henry—don't ask me! I give you my word, sir, that it is not my secret, and that I cannot tell it. If it concerned no one but myself I would not try to keep it from you.'

A sudden idea occurred to me, and I took the candle from the window-sill, where the butler had placed it.

'He must have been holding it as a signal,' said I. 'Let us see if there is any answer'

I held it as he had done, and stared out into the darkness of the night. Vaguely I could discern the black bank of the trees and the lighter expanse of the moor, for the moon was behind the clouds. And then I gave a cry of exultation, for a tiny pin-point of yellow light had suddenly transfixed the dark veil, and glowed steadily in the centre of the black square framed by the window.

'There it is!' I cried.

'No, no, sir, it is nothing—nothing at all,' the butler broke in; 'I assure you, sir——'

'Move your light across the window, Watson!' cried the baronet. 'See, the other moves also! Now, you rascal, do you deny that it is a signal? Come, speak up! Who is your confederate out yonder, and what is this conspiracy that is going on?'

The man's face became openly defiant. 'It is my business, and not yours. I will not tell.'

'Then you leave my employment right away.'

'Very good, sir. If I must, I must.'

'And you go in disgrace. By thunder, you may well be ashamed of yourself. Your family has lived with mine for over a hundred years under this roof, and here I find you deep in some dark plot against me.'

'No, no, sir; no, not against you!'

It was a woman's voice, and Mrs Barrymore, paler and more horror-struck than her husband, was standing at the door. Her bulky figure in a shawl and skirt might have been comic were it not for the intensity of feeling upon her face.

'We have to go, Eliza. This is the end of it. You can pack our things,' said the butler.

'Oh, John, John, have I brought you to this? It is my doing, Sir Henry—all mine. He has done nothing except for my sake, and because I asked him.'

'Speak out, then! What does it mean?'

'My unhappy brother is starving on the moor. We cannot let him perish at our very gates. The light is a signal to him that food is ready for him, and his light out yonder is to show the spot to which to bring it.'

'Then your brother is——'

'The escaped convict, sir—Selden, the criminal.'

'That's the truth, sir,' said Barrymore. 'I said that it was not my secret, and that I could not tell it to you. But now you have heard it, and you will see that if there was a plot it was not against you.'

This, then, was the explanation of the stealthy expeditions at night and the light at the window. Sir Henry and I both stared at the woman in amazement. Was it possible that this stolidly respectable person was of the same blood as one of the most notorious criminals in the country?

'Yes, sir, my name was Selden, and he is my younger brother. We humoured him too much when he was a lad, and gave him his own way in everything, until he came to think that the world was made for his pleasure, and that he could do what he liked in it. Then, as he grew older, he met wicked companions, and the devil entered into him, until he broke my mother's heart and dragged our name in the dirt. From crime to crime he sank lower and lower, until it is only the mercy of God which has snatched him from the scaffold; but to me, sir, he was always the little curly-headed boy that I had nursed and played with, as an elder sister would. That was why he broke prison, sir. He knew that I was here, and that we could not refuse to help him. When he dragged himself here one night, weary and starving, with the warders hard at his heels, what could we do? We took him in and fed him and cared for him. Then you returned, sir, and my brother thought he would be safer on the moor than anywhere else until the hue and cry was over, so he lay in hiding there. But every second night we made sure if he was still there by putting a light in the window, and if there was an answer my husband took out some bread and meat to him. Every day we hoped that he was gone, but as long as he was there we could not desert him. That is the whole truth, as I am an honest Christian woman, and you will see that if there is blame in the matter it does not lie with my husband, but with me, for whose sake he has done all that he has.'

The woman's words came with an intense earnestness which carried conviction with them.

'Is this true, Barrymore?'

'Yes, Sir Henry. Every word of it.'

'Well, I cannot blame you for standing by your own wife. Forget what I have said. Go to your room, you two, and we shall talk further about this matter in the morning.'

When they were gone we looked out of the window again. Sir Henry had flung it open, and the cold night wind beat in

'THE ESCAPED CONVICT, SIR—SELDEN, THE CRIMINAL.'

Illustration by Sidney Paget for the *Strand Magazine*, December, 1901.

upon our faces. Far away in the black distance there still glowed that one tiny point of yellow light.

'I wonder he dares,' said Sir Henry.

'It may be so placed as to be only visible from here.'

'Very likely. How far do you think it is?'

'Out by the Cleft Tor, I think.'

'Not more than a mile or two off.'

'Hardly that.'

'Well, it cannot be far if Barrymore had to carry out the food to it. And he is waiting, this villain, beside that candle. By thunder, Watson, I am going out to take that man!'

The same thought had crossed my own mind. It was not as if the Barrymores had taken us into their confidence. Their secret had been forced from them. The man was a danger to the community, an unmitigated scoundrel for whom there was neither pity nor excuse. We were only doing our duty in taking this chance of putting him back where he could do no harm. With his brutal and violent nature, others would have to pay the price if we held our hands. Any night, for example, our neighbours, the Stapletons, might be attacked by him, and it may have been the thought of this which made Sir Henry so keen upon the adventure.

'I will come,' said I.

'Then get your revolver and put on your boots. The sooner we start the better, as the fellow may put out his light and be off.'

In five minutes we were outside the door, starting upon our expedition. We hurried through the dark shrubbery, amid the dull moaning of the autumn wind and the rustle of the falling leaves. The night-air was heavy with the smell of damp and decay. Now and again the moon peeped out for an **79** instant, but clouds were driving over the face of the sky, and **80** just as we came out on the moor a thin rain began to fall. The light still burned steadily in front.

'Are you armed?' I asked.

'I have a hunting-crop.'

'We must close in on him rapidly, for he is said to be a desperate fellow. We shall take him by surprise and have him at our mercy before he can resist.'

'I say, Watson,' said the baronet, 'what would Holmes say to this? How about that hour of darkness in which the power of evil is exalted?'

As if in answer to his words there rose suddenly out of the vast gloom of the moor that strange cry which I had already heard upon the borders of the great Grimpen Mire. It came with the wind through the silence of the night, a long, deep mutter, then a rising howl, and then the sad moan in which it died away. Again and again it sounded, the whole air throbbing with it, strident, wild, and menacing. The baronet caught my sleeve, and his face glimmered white through the darkness.

'Good heavens, what's that, Watson?'

'I don't know. It's a sound they have on the moor. I heard it once before.'

It died away, and an absolute silence closed in upon us. We stood straining our ears, but nothing came.

'Watson,' said the baronet, 'it was the cry of a hound.'

My blood ran cold in my veins, for there was a break in his voice which told of the sudden horror which had seized him.

'OUT BY THE CLEFT TOR, I THINK.'

The Cleft Tor can only be the famous *Cleft Rock*; it is not shown on our map, but it stands just above Holne Chase, which is shown; Cleft Rock is a tourist attraction today as surely as it was in 1888. Our photograph, by J. Amery, Esq., is from *A Book of Dartmoor* by the Reverend Sabine Baring-Gould.

79 *Now and again the moon peeped out for an instant*. Not for just an instant, surely, for Watson shortly hereafter sees the man on the moor "for a long time in the moonlight." According to Watson, "the moon was low upon the right"; later, Holmes says: "I was so imprudent as to allow the moon to rise behind me." There was a moon (three-quarters full) at this time, but it was rising in the afternoon, not in the early morning. Holmes must have said "shine" rather than "rise."

80 *a thin rain began to fall*. "Foggy or misty in the south and south-east of England," said the *Times* of London.

'What do they call this sound?' he asked.

'Who?'

'The folk on the countryside.'

'Oh, they are ignorant people. Why should you mind what they call it?'

'Tell me, Watson. What do they say of it?'

I hesitated, but could not escape the question.

'They say it is the cry of the Hound of the Baskervilles.'

He groaned, and was silent for a few moments.

'A hound it was,' he said at last, 'but it seemed to come from miles away over yonder, I think.'

'It was hard to say whence it came.'

'It rose and fell with the wind. Isn't that the direction of the great Grimpen Mire?'

'Yes, it is.'

'Well, it was up there. Come now, Watson, didn't you think yourself that it was the cry of a hound? I am not a child. You need not fear to speak the truth.'

'Stapleton was with me when I heard it last. He said that it might be the calling of a strange bird.'

'No, no, it was a hound. My God, can there be some truth in all these stories? Is it possible that I am really in danger from so dark a cause? You don't believe it, do you, Watson?'

'No, no.'

'And yet it was one thing to laugh about it in London, and it is another to stand out here in the darkness of the moor and to hear such a cry as that. And my uncle! There was the footprint of the hound beside him as he lay. It all fits together. I don't think that I am a coward, Watson, but that sound seemed to freeze my very blood. Feel my hand!'

It was as cold as a block of marble.

'You'll be all right tomorrow.'

'I don't think I'll get that cry out of my head. What do you advise that we do now?'

'Shall we turn back?'

'No, by thunder; we have come out to get our man, and we will do it. We are after the convict and a hell-hound, as likely as not, after us. Come on. We'll see it through if all the fiends of the pit were loose upon the moor.'

We stumbled slowly along in the darkness, with the black loom of the craggy hills around us, and the yellow speck of light burning steadily in front. There is nothing so deceptive as the distance of a light upon a pitch-dark night, and sometimes the glimmer seemed to be far away upon the horizon and sometimes it might have been within a few yards of us. But at last we could see whence it came, and then we knew that we were indeed very close. A guttering candle was stuck in a crevice of the rocks which flanked it on each side so as to keep the wind from it, and also to prevent it from being visible, save in the direction of Baskerville Hall. A boulder of granite concealed our approach, and crouching behind it we gazed over it at the signal light. It was strange to see this single candle burning there in the middle of the moor, with no sign of life near it—just the one straight, yellow flame and the gleam of the rock on each side of it.

'What shall we do now?' whispered Sir Henry.

'Wait here. He must be near his light. Let us see if we can get a glimpse of him.'

OVER THE ROCKS, IN THE CREVICE OF WHICH THE CANDLE
BURNED, THERE WAS THRUST OUT AN EVIL,
YELLOW FACE . . .

Illustration by Sidney Paget for the *Strand Magazine*, December, 1901.

The words were hardly out of my mouth when we both saw him. Over the rocks, in the crevice of which the candle burned, there was thrust out an evil, yellow face, a terrible animal face, all seamed and scored with vile passions. Foul with mire, with a bristling beard, and hung with matted hair, it might well have belonged to one of those old savages who dwelt in the burrows on the hillsides. The light beneath him was reflected in his small, cunning eyes, which peered fiercely to right and left through the darkness, like a crafty and savage animal who has heard the steps of the hunters.

Something had evidently aroused his suspicions. It may have been that Barrymore had some private signal which we had neglected to give, or the fellow may have had some other reason for thinking that all was not well, but I could read his fears upon his wicked face. Any instant he might dash out the light and vanish in the darkness. I sprang forward, therefore, and Sir Henry did the same. At the same moment the convict screamed out a curse at us and hurled a rock which splintered up against the boulder which had sheltered us. I caught one glimpse of his short, squat, strongly-built figure as he sprang to his feet and turned to run. At the same moment by a lucky chance the moon broke through the clouds. We rushed over the brow of the hill, and there was our man running with great speed down the other side, springing over the stones in his way with the activity of a mountain goat. A lucky long shot of my revolver might have crippled him, but I had brought it only to defend myself if attacked, and not to shoot an unarmed man who was running away.

We were both fair runners and in good condition, but we soon found that we had no chance of overtaking him. We saw him for a long time in the moonlight until he was only a small speck moving swiftly among the boulders upon the side of a distant hill. We ran and ran until we were completely blown, but the space between us grew ever wider. Finally we stopped and sat panting on two rocks, while we watched him disappearing in the distance.

And it was at this moment that there occurred a most strange and unexpected thing. We had risen from our rocks and were turning to go home, having abandoned the hopeless chase. The moon was low upon the right, and the jagged pinnacle of a granite tor stood up against the lower curve of its silver disc. There, outlined as black as an ebony statue on that shining background, I saw the figure of a man upon the tor. Do not think that it was a delusion, Holmes. I assure you that I have never in my life seen anything more clearly. As far as I could judge, the figure was that of a tall, thin man. He stood with his legs a little separated, his arms folded, his head bowed, as if he were brooding over that enormous wilderness of peat and granite which lay before him. He might have been the very spirit of that terrible place. It was not the convict. This man was far from the place where the latter had disappeared. Besides, he was a much taller man. With a cry of surprise I pointed him out to the baronet, but in the instant during which I had turned to grasp his arm the man was gone. There was the sharp pinnacle of granite still cutting the lower edge of the moon, but its peak bore no trace of that silent and motionless figure.

I wished to go in that direction and to search the tor, but it was some distance away. The baronet's nerves were still quivering from that cry, which recalled the dark story of his family, and he was not in the mood for fresh adventures. He had not seen this lonely man upon the tor, and could not feel the thrill which his strange presence and his commanding attitude had given to me. 'A warder, no doubt,' said he. 'The moor has been thick with them since this fellow escaped.' Well, perhaps his explanation may be the right one, but I should like to have some further proof of it. Today we mean to communicate to the Princetown people where they should look for their missing man, but it is hard lines that we have not actually had the triumph of bringing him back as our own prisoner. Such are the adventures of last night, and you must acknowledge, my dear Holmes, that I have done you very well in the matter of a report. Much of what I tell you is no doubt quite irrelevant, but still I feel that it is best that I should let you have all the facts and leave you to select for yourself those which will be of most service to you in helping you to your conclusions. We are certainly making some progress. So far as the Barrymores go, we have found the motive of their actions, and that has cleared up the situation very much. But the moor with its mysteries and its strange inhabitants remains as inscrutable as ever. Perhaps in my next I may be able to throw some light upon this also. Best of all would it be if you could come down to us. In any case you will hear from me again in the course of the next few days.

THERE, OUTLINED AS BLACK AS AN EBONY STATUE ON THAT SHINING BACKGROUND, I SAW THE FIGURE OF A MAN UPON THE TOR.

Illustration by Sidney Paget for the *Strand Magazine*, December, 1901.

10 ◆ EXTRACT FROM THE DIARY OF DR WATSON

So far I have been able to quote from the reports which I have forwarded during these early days to Sherlock Holmes. Now, however, I have arrived at a point in my narrative where I am compelled to abandon this method and to trust once more to my recollections, aided by the diary which I kept at the time. A few extracts from the latter will carry me on to those scenes which are indelibly fixed in every detail upon my memory. I proceed, then, from the morning which followed our abortive chase of the convict and our other strange experiences upon the moor.

October 16th.—A dull and foggy day, with a drizzle of rain. **81-82** The house is banked in with rolling clouds, which rise now and then to show the dreary curves of the moor, with thin, silver veins upon the sides of the hills, and the distant boulders gleaming where the light strikes upon their wet faces. It is melancholy outside and in. The baronet is in a black reaction after the excitements of the night. I am conscious myself of a weight at my heart and a feeling of impending danger—ever-present danger, which is the more terrible because I am unable to define it.

And have I not cause for such a feeling? Consider the long

81 October *16th*. Tuesday, October 16th, 1888, in our view. But there is a discrepancy here: Watson has told us that he will proceed "from the morning which followed our abortive chase of the convict and our other strange experiences on the moor," and this would have been the morning of Monday, October 15th. It seems clear that after the exhausting night on the moor and the composition of a lengthy letter to Holmes, Watson slept away most of Monday the 15th. Writing in his diary on Tuesday, October 16th, it would therefore seem to him that the abortive chase took place only the night before.

82 *A dull and foggy day, with a drizzle of rain.* Again, Watson was quite correct. The *Times* of London wrote of this day: "Dull, unsettled weather has set in at many of our . . . stations. In the central and south-eastern parts of England . . . a good deal of fog or mist has prevailed locally."

sequence of incidents which have all pointed to some sinister influence which is at work around us. There is the death of the last occupant of the Hall, fulfilling so exactly the conditions of the family legend, and there are the repeated reports from peasants of the appearance of a strange creature upon the moor. Twice I have with my own ears heard the sound which resembled the distant baying of a hound. It is incredible, impossible, that it should really be outside the ordinary laws of Nature. A spectral hound which leaves material footmarks and fills the air with its howling is surely not to be thought of. Stapleton may fall in with such a superstition, and Mortimer also; but if I have one quality upon earth it is common sense, and nothing will persuade me to believe in such a thing. To do so would be to descend to the level of these poor peasants who are not content with a mere fiend-dog, but must needs describe him with hell-fire shooting from his mouth and eyes. Holmes would not listen to such fancies, and I am his agent. But facts are facts, and I have twice heard this crying upon the moor. Suppose that there were really some huge hound loose upon it; that would go far to explain everything. But where could such a hound lie concealed, where did it get its food, where did it come from, how was it that no one saw it by day? It must be confessed that the natural explanation offers almost as many difficulties as the other. And always, apart from the hound, there was the fact of the human agency in London, the man in the cab, and the letter which warned Sir Henry against the moor. This at least was real, but it might have been the work of a protecting friend as easily as an enemy. Where was that friend or enemy now? Had he remained in London, or had he followed us down here? Could he—could he be the stranger whom I had seen upon the tor?

It is true that I have had only the one glance at him, and yet there are some things to which I am ready to swear. He is no one whom I have seen down here, and I have now met all the neighbours. The figure was far taller than that of Stapleton, far thinner than that of Frankland. Barrymore it might possibly have been, but we had left him behind us, and I am certain that he could not have followed us. A stranger, then, is still dogging us, just as a stranger had dogged us in London. We have never shaken him off. If I could lay my hands upon that man, then at last we might find ourselves at the end of all our difficulties. To this one purpose I must now devote all my energies.

My first impulse was to tell Sir Henry all my plans. My second and wisest one is to play my own game and speak as little as possible to anyone. He is silent and distrait. His nerves have been strangely shaken by that sound upon the moor. I will say nothing to add to his anxieties, but I will take my own steps to attain my own end.

We had a small scene this morning after breakfast. Barrymore asked leave to speak with Sir Henry, and they were closeted in his study some little time. Sitting in the billiard-room, I more than once heard the sound of voices raised, and I had a pretty good idea what the point was which was under discussion. After a time the baronet opened his door and called for me.

'Barrymore considers that he has a grievance,' he said. 'He thinks that it was unfair on our part to hunt his brother-in-law down when he, of his own free will, had told us the secret.'

The butler was standing, very pale but very collected, before us.

'I may have spoken too warmly, sir,' said he, 'and if I have I am sure that I beg your pardon. At the same time, I was very much surprised when I heard you two gentlemen come back this morning and learned that you had been chasing Selden. The poor fellow has enough to fight against without my putting more upon his track.'

'If you had told us of your own free will it would have been a different thing,' said the baronet. 'You only told us, or rather your wife only told us, when it was forced from you and you could not help yourself.'

'I didn't think you would have taken advantage of it, Sir Henry—indeed I didn't.'

'The man is a public danger. There are lonely houses scattered over the moor, and he is a fellow who would stick at nothing. You only want to get a glimpse of his face to see that. Look at Mr Stapleton's house, for example, with no one but himself to defend it. There's no safety for anyone until he is under lock and key.'

'He'll break into no house, sir. I give you my solemn word upon that. And he will never trouble anyone in this country again. I assure you, Sir Henry, that in a very few days the necessary arrangements will have been made and he will be on his way to South America. For God's sake, sir, I beg of you not to let the police know that he is still on the moor. They have given up the chase there, and he can lie quiet until the ship is ready for him. You can't tell on him without getting my wife and me into trouble. I beg you, sir, to say nothing to the police.'

'What do you say, Watson?'

I shrugged my shoulders. 'If he were safely out of the country it would relieve the taxpayer of a burden.'

'But how about the chance of his holding someone up before he goes?'

'He would not do anything so mad, sir. We have provided him with all that he can want. To commit a crime would be to show where he was hiding.'

'That is true,' said Sir Henry. 'Well, Barrymore——'

'God bless you, sir, and thank you from my heart! It would have killed my poor wife had he been taken again.'

'I guess we are aiding and abetting a felony, Watson? But, after what we have heard, I don't feel as if I could give the man up, so there is an end of it. All right, Barrymore, you can go.'

With a few broken words of gratitude the man turned, but he hesitated and then came back.

'You've been so kind to us, sir, that I should like to do the best I can for you in return. I know something, Sir Henry, and perhaps I should have said it before, but it was long after the inquest that I found it out. I've never breathed a word about it yet to mortal man. It's about poor Sir Charles's death.'

The baronet and I were both upon our feet.

'Do you know how he died?'

'No, sir, I don't know that.'

'What, then?'

'I know why he was at the gate at that hour. It was to meet

83 *Coombe Tracey.* A fair-sized town on the railroad is required, for it is at Coombe Tracey that Lestrade later springs from a first-class carriage of the London express to shake hands with Holmes and Watson. We find such a town— *Bovey* Tracey—on the east of the moor, and it seems unnecessary to look further for the original of Watson's "Coombe Tracey," an ingenious combination of Widecombe and Bovey Tracey.

a woman.'

'To meet a woman! He?'

'Yes, sir.'

'And the woman's name?'

'I can't give you the name, sir, but I can give you the initials. Her initials were L.L.'

'How do you know this, Barrymore?'

'Well, Sir Henry, your uncle had a letter that morning. He had usually a great many letters, for he was a public man and well known for his kind heart, so that everyone who was in trouble was glad to turn to him. But that morning, as it chanced, there was only this one letter, so I took the more **83** notice of it. It was from Coombe Tracey, and it was addressed in a woman's hand.'

'Well?'

'Well, sir, I thought no more of the matter, and never would have done had it not been for my wife. Only a few weeks ago she was cleaning out Sir Charles's study—it had never been touched since his death—and she found the ashes of a burned letter in the back of the grate. The greater part of it was charred to pieces, but one little slip, the end of a page, hung together, and the writing could still be read, though it was grey on a black ground. It seemed to us to be a postscript at the end of the letter, and it said: "Please, please, as you are a gentleman, burn this letter, and be at the gate by ten o'clock." Beneath it were signed the initials L.L.'

'Have you got that slip?'

'No, sir, it crumbled all to bits after we moved it.'

'Had Sir Charles received any other letters in the same writing?'

'Well, sir, I took no particular notice of his letters. I should not have noticed this one only it happened to come alone.'

'And you have no idea who L.L. is?'

'No, sir. No more than you have. But I expect if we could lay our hands upon that lady we should know more about Sir Charles's death.'

'I cannot understand, Barrymore, how you came to conceal this important information.'

'Well, sir, it was immediately after that our own trouble came to us. And then again, sir, we were both of us very fond of Sir Charles, as we well might be considering all that he has done for us. To rake this up couldn't help our poor master, and it's well to go carefully when there's a lady in the case. Even the best of us——'

'You thought it might injure his reputation?'

'Well, sir, I thought no good could come of it. But now you have been kind to us, and I feel as if it would be treating you unfairly not to tell you all that I know about the matter.'

'Very good, Barrymore; you can go.'

When the butler had left us, Sir Henry turned to me. 'Well, Watson, what do you think of this new light?'

'It seems to leave the darkness rather blacker than before.'

'So I think. But if we can only trace L.L. it should clear up the whole business. We have gained that much. We know that there is someone who has the facts if we can only find her. What do you think we should do?'

'Let Holmes know all about it at once. It will give him the clue for which he has been seeking. I am much mistaken if it does not bring him down.'

I went at once to my room and drew up my report of the morning's conversation for Holmes. It was evident to me that he had been very busy of late, for the notes which I had from Baker Street were few and short, with no comments upon the information which I had supplied, and hardly any reference to my mission. No doubt his blackmailing case is absorbing all his faculties. And yet this new factor must surely arrest his attention and renew his interest. I wish that he were here.

October 17th.—All day today the rain poured down, rust-**84** ling on the ivy and dripping from the eaves. I thought of the convict out upon the bleak, cold, shelterless moor. Poor fellow! Whatever his crimes, he has suffered something to atone for them. And then I thought of that other one—the face in the cab, the figure against the moon. Was he also out in that deluge—the unseen watcher, the man of darkness? In the evening I put on my waterproof and I walked far upon the sodden moor, full of dark imaginings, the rain beating upon my face and the wind whistling about my ears. God help those who wander into the Great Mire now, for even the firm uplands are becoming a morass. I found the Black Tor upon which I had seen the solitary watcher, and from its craggy summit I looked out myself across the melancholy downs. Rain squalls drifted across their russet face, and the heavy, slate-coloured clouds hung low over the landscape, trailing in grey wreaths down the sides of the fantastic hills. In the distant hollow on the left, half hidden by the mist, the two thin towers of Baskerville Hall rose above the trees. They were the only signs of human life which I could see, save only those prehistoric huts which lay thickly upon the slopes of the hills. Nowhere was there any trace of that lonely man whom I had seen on the same spot two nights before.

As I walked back I was overtaken by Dr Mortimer driving in his dog-cart over a rough moorland track, which led from the outlying farm-house of Foulmire. He has been very attentive to us, and hardly a day has passed that he has not called at the Hall to see how we were getting on. He insisted upon my climbing into his dog-cart and he gave me a lift homewards. I found him much troubled over the disappearance of his little spaniel. It had wandered on to the moor and had never come back. I gave him such consolation as I might, but I thought of the pony on the Grimpen Mire, and I do not fancy that he will see his little dog again.

'By the way, Mortimer,' said I, as we jolted along the rough road, 'I suppose there are few people living within driving distance of this whom you do not know?'

'Hardly any, I think.'

'Can you, then, tell me the name of any woman whose initials are L.L.?'

He thought for a few minutes. 'No,' said he. 'There are a few gipsies and labouring folk for whom I can't answer, but among the farmers or gentry there is no one whose initials are those. Wait a bit, though,' he added, after a pause. 'There is Laura Lyons—her initials are L.L.—but she lives in Coombe Tracey.'

'Who is she?' I asked.

'She is Frankland's daughter.'

'What? Old Frankland the crank?'

'Exactly. She married an artist named Lyons, who came sketching on the moor. He proved to be a blackguard and

I FOUND THE BLACK TOR UPON WHICH I HAD SEEN THE SOLITARY WATCHER . . .

The Black Tor, shown here in a drawing by A. B. Collier for the Reverend Sabine Baring-Gould's *A Book of Dartmoor*, exists to this day, and has on it a logan stone that can be rocked by means of a natural handle.

84 *All day today the rain poured down.* Although the *Times* did not report specifically on the weather at its southern stations in its remarks for Wednesday, October 17th, it noted "rain at Sumburgh Head," "thick local fogs" and "no bright sunshine at Westminster."

deserted her. The fault, from what I hear, may not have been entirely on one side. Her father refused to have anything to do with her, because she had married without his consent, and perhaps for one or two other reasons as well. So, between the old sinner and the young one the girl has had a pretty bad time.'

'How does she live?'

'I fancy old Frankland allows her a pittance, but it cannot be more, for his own affairs are considerably involved. Whatever she may have deserved, one could not allow her to go hopelessly to the bad. Her story got about, and several of the people here did something to enable her to earn an honest living. Stapleton did for one, and Sir Charles for another. I gave a trifle myself. It was to set her up in a typewriting business.'

He wanted to know the object of my inquiries, but I managed to satisfy his curiosity without telling him too much, for there is no reason why we should take anyone into our confidence. Tomorrow morning I shall find my way to Coombe Tracey, and if I can see this Mrs Laura Lyons, of equivocal reputation, a long step will have been made towards clearing one incident in this chain of mysteries. I am certainly developing the wisdom of the serpent, for when Mortimer pressed his questions to an inconvenient extent I asked him casually to what type Franklin's skull belonged, and so heard nothing but craniology for the rest of our drive. I have not lived for years with Sherlock Holmes for nothing.

I have only one other incident to record upon this tempestuous and melancholy day. This was my conversation with Barrymore just now, which gives me one more strong card which I can play in due time.

Mortimer had stayed to dinner, and he and the baronet played écarté afterwards. The butler brought me my coffee into the library, and I took the chance to ask him a few questions.

'Well,' said I, 'has this precious relation of yours departed, or is he still lurking out yonder?'

'I don't know, sir. I hope to Heaven that he has gone, for he has brought nothing but trouble here! I've not heard of him since I left out food for him last, and that was three days ago.'

'Did you see him then?'

'No, sir; but the food was gone when next I went that way.'

'Then he was certainly there?'

'So you would think, sir, unless it was the other man who took it.'

I sat with my coffee-cup half-way to my lips, and stared at Barrymore.

'You know that there is another man, then?'

'Yes, sir; there is another man upon the moor.'

'Have you seen him?'

'No, sir.'

'How do you know of him, then?'

'Selden told me of him, sir, a week ago or more. He's in hiding, too, but he's not a convict, so far as I can make out. I don't like it, Dr Watson—I tell you straight, sir, that I don't like it.' He spoke with a sudden passion of earnestness.

'Now, listen to me, Barrymore! I have no interest in this matter but that of your master. I have come here with no object except to help him. Tell me, frankly, what it is that you don't like.'

'YOU KNOW THAT THERE IS ANOTHER MAN, THEN?'

Illustration by Sidney Paget for the *Strand Magazine*, January, 1902.

Barrymore hesitated for a moment, as if he regretted his outburst, or found it difficult to express his own feelings in words.

'It's all these goings-on, sir,' he cried, at last, waving his hand towards the rain-lashed window which faced the moor. 'There's foul play somewhere, and there's black villainy brewing, to that I'll swear! Very glad I should be, sir, to see Sir Henry on his way back to London again!'

'But what is it that alarms you?'

'Look at Sir Charles's death! That was bad enough, for all that the coroner said. Look at the noises on the moor at night. There's not a man would cross it after sundown if he was paid for it. Look at this stranger hiding out yonder, and watching and waiting! What's he waiting for? What does it mean? It means no good to anyone of the name of Baskerville, and very glad I shall be to be quit of it all on the day that Sir Henry's new servants are ready to take over the Hall.'

'But about this stranger,' said I. 'Can you tell me anything about him? What did Selden say? Did he find out where he hid, or what he was doing?'

'He saw him once or twice, but he is a deep one, and gives nothing away. At first he thought that he was the police, but soon he found that he had some lay of his own. A kind of gentleman he was, as far as he could see, but what he was doing he could not make out.'

'And where did he say that he lived?'

'Among the old houses on the hillside—the stone huts where the old folk used to live.'

'But how about his food?'

'Selden found out that he has got a lad who works for him and brings him all he needs. I dare say he goes to Coombe Tracey for what he wants.'

'Very good, Barrymore. We may talk further of this some other time.'

When the butler had gone I walked over to the black window, and I looked through a blurred pane at the driving clouds and at the tossing outline of the wind-swept trees. It is a wild night indoors, and what must it be in a stone hut upon the moor? What passion of hatred can it be which leads a man to lurk in such a place at such a time? And what deep and earnest purpose can he have which calls for such a trial? There, in that hut upon the moor, seems to lie the very centre of that problem which has vexed me so sorely. I swear that another day shall not have passed before I have done all that man can do to reach the heart of the mystery.

11 ◆ THE MAN ON THE TOR

The extract from my private diary which forms the last chapter has brought my narrative up to the 18th of October, a time when these strange events began to move swiftly towards their terrible conclusion. The incidents of the next few days are indelibly graven upon my recollection, and I can tell them without reference to the notes made at the time. I start, then, from the day which succeeded that upon which I had established two facts of great importance, the one that Mrs Laura Lyons of Coombe Tracey had written to Sir Charles Baskerville and made an appointment with him at the very place and hour that he met his death, the other that the lurking man upon the moor was to be found among the stone huts upon the hillside. With these two facts in my possession I felt that either my intelligence or my courage must be deficient if I could not throw some further light upon these dark places.

I had no opportunity to tell the baronet what I had learned about Mrs Lyons upon the evening before, for Dr Mortimer remained with him at cards until it was very late. At breakfast, however, I informed him about my discovery, and asked him whether he would care to accompany me to Coombe Tracey. At first he was very eager to come, but on second thoughts it seemed to both of us that if I went alone the results might be better. The more formal we made the visit the less information we might obtain. I left Sir Henry behind, therefore, not without some prickings of conscience, and drove off upon my new quest.

When I reached Coombe Tracey I told Perkins to put up the horses, and I made inquiries for the lady whom I had come to interrogate. I had no difficulty in finding her rooms, which were central and well appointed. A maid showed me in without ceremony, and as I entered the sitting-room a lady who was sitting before a Remington typewriter, sprang up with a pleasant smile of welcome. Her face fell, however, when she saw that I was a stranger, and she sat down again and asked me the object of my visit.

The first impression left by Mrs Lyons was one of extreme beauty. Her eyes and hair were of the same rich hazel colour, and her cheeks, though considerably freckled, were flushed with the exquisite bloom of the brunette, the dainty pink which lurks at the heart of the sulphur rose. Admiration was, I repeat, the first impression. But the second was criticism. There was something subtly wrong with the face, some coarseness of expression, some hardness, perhaps, of eye, some looseness of lip which marred its perfect beauty. But these, of course, are afterthoughts. At the moment I was simply conscious that I was in the presence of a very handsome woman, and that she was asking me the reasons for my visit. I had not quite understood until that instant how delicate my mission was.

'I have the pleasure,' said I, 'of knowing your father.'

It was a clumsy introduction, and the lady made me feel it.

'There is nothing in common between my father and me,' she said. 'I owe him nothing, and his friends are not mine. If it were not for the late Sir Charles Baskerville and some other kind hearts I might have starved for all that my father cared.'

'It was about the late Sir Charles Baskerville that I have come here to see you.'

The freckles started out on the lady's face.

'What can I tell you about him?' she asked, and her fingers played nervously over the stops of her typewriter.

'You knew him, did you not?'

'I have already said that I owe a great deal to his kindness. If I am able to support myself it is largely due to the interest which he took in my unhappy situation.'

'Did you correspond with him?'

The lady looked quickly up, with an angry gleam in her hazel eyes.

'What is the object of these questions?' she asked, sharply.

'The object is to avoid a public scandal. It is better that I should ask them here than that the matter should pass outside our control.'

She was silent and her face was very pale. At last she looked up with something reckless and defiant in her manner.

'Well, I'll answer,' she said. 'What are your questions?'

'Did you correspond with Sir Charles?'

'I certainly wrote to him once or twice to acknowledge his delicacy and his generosity.'

'Have you the dates of those letters?'

'No.'

'Have you ever met him?'

'Yes, once or twice, when he came into Coombe Tracey. He was a very retiring man, and he preferred to do good by stealth.'

'But if you saw him so seldom and wrote so seldom, how did he know enough about your affairs to be able to help you, as you say that he has done?'

She met my difficulty with the utmost readiness.

'There were several gentlemen who knew my sad history and united to help me. One was Mr Stapleton, a neighbour and intimate friend of Sir Charles. He was exceedingly kind, and it was through him that Sir Charles learned about my affairs.'

I knew already that Sir Charles Baskerville had made Stapleton his almoner upon several occasions, so the lady's statement bore the impress of truth upon it.

'Did you ever write to Sir Charles asking him to meet you?' I continued.

Mrs Lyons flushed with anger again.

'Really, sir, this is a very extraordinary question.'

'I am sorry, madam, but I must repeat it.'

'Then I answer—certainly not.'

'Not on the very day of Sir Charles's death?'

The flush had faded in an instant, and a deathly face was before me. Her dry lips could not speak the 'No' which I saw rather than heard.

'Surely your memory deceives you,' said I. 'I could even quote a passage of your letter. It ran, "Please, please, as you are a gentleman, burn this letter, and be at the gate by ten o'clock."'

I thought that she had fainted, but she recovered herself by a supreme effort.

'Is there no such thing as a gentleman?' she gasped.

'You do Sir Charles an injustice. He *did* burn the letter. But sometimes a letter may be legible even when burned. You acknowledge now that you wrote it?'

'Yes, I did write it,' she cried, pouring out her soul in a torrent of words. 'I did write it. Why should I deny it? I have no reason to be ashamed of it. I wished him to help me. I believed that if I had an interview I could gain his help, so I asked him to meet me.'

'But why at such an hour?'

'Because I had only just learned that he was going to London next day and might be away for months. There were reasons why I could not get there earlier.'

'But why a rendezvous in the garden instead of a visit to the house?'

'Do you think a woman could go alone at that hour to a bachelor's house?'

'Well, what happened when you did get there?'

'I never went.'

'Mrs Lyons!'

'No, I swear it to you on all I hold sacred. I never went. Something intervened to prevent my going.'

'What was that?'

'That is a private matter. I cannot tell it.'

'You acknowledge, then, that you made an appointment with Sir Charles at the very hour and place at which he met his death, but you deny that you kept the appointment?'

'That is the truth.'

Again and again I cross-questioned her, but I could never get past that point.

'Mrs Lyons,' said I, as I rose from this long and inconclusive interview, 'you are taking a very great responsibility and putting yourself in a very false position by not making an absolutely clean breast of all that you know. If I have to call in the aid of the police you will find how seriously you are compromised. If your position is innocent, why did you in the first instance deny having written to Sir Charles upon that date?'

'Because I feared that some false conclusion might be drawn from it, and that I might find myself involved in a scandal.'

'And why were you so pressing that Sir Charles should destroy your letter?'

'If you have read the letter you will know.'

'I did not say that I had read all the letter.'

'You quoted some of it.'

'I quoted the postscript. The letter had, as I said, been burned, and it was not all legible. I ask you once again why it was that you were so pressing that Sir Charles should destroy this letter which he received on the day of his death.'

'The matter is a very private one.'

'The more reason why you should avoid a public investigation.'

'I will tell you, then. If you have heard anything of my unhappy history you will know that I made a rash marriage and had reason to regret it.'

'I have heard so much.'

'My life has been one incessant persecution from a husband whom I abhor. The law is upon his side, and every day I am faced by the possibility that he may force me to live with him. At the time that I wrote this letter to Sir Charles I had learned that there was a prospect of my regaining my freedom if certain expenses could be met. It meant everything to me— peace of mind, happiness, self-respect—everything. I knew Sir Charles's generosity, and I thought that if he heard the story from my own lips he would help me.'

'Then how is it that you did not go?'

'Because I received help in the interval from another source.'

'Why, then, did you not write to Sir Charles and explain this?'

'So I should have done had I not seen his death in the paper next morning.' **85**

The woman's story hung coherently together, and all my questions were unable to shake it. I could only check it by finding if she had, indeed, instituted divorce proceedings against her husband at or about the time of the tragedy.

It was unlikely that she would dare to say that she had not been to Baskerville Hall if she really had been, for a trap would be necessary to take her there, and could not have returned to Coombe Tracey until the early hours of the morning. Such an excursion could not be kept secret. The probability was, therefore, that she was telling the truth, or, at least, a part of the truth. I came away baffled and disheartened. Once again I had reached that dead wall which seemed to be built across every path by which I tried to get at the object of my mission. And yet the more I thought of the lady's face and of her manner the more I felt that something was being held back from me. Why should she turn so pale? Why should she fight against every admission until it was forced from her? Why should she have been so reticent at the time of the tragedy? Surely the explanation of all this could not be as innocent as she would have me believe. For the moment I could proceed no farther in that direction, but must turn back to that other clue which was to be sought for among the stone huts upon the moor.

And that was a most vague direction. I realized it as I drove back and noted how hill after hill showed traces of the ancient people. Barrymore's only indication had been that the stranger lived in one of these abandoned huts, and many hundreds of them are scattered throughout the length and breadth of the moor. But I had my own experience for a guide, since it had shown me the man himself standing upon the summit of the Black Tor. That, then, should be the centre of my search. From there I should explore every hut upon the moor until I lighted upon the right one. If this man were inside it I should find out from his own lips, at the point of my revolver if necessary, who he was and why he had dogged us so long. He might slip away from us in the crowd of Regent Street but it would puzzle him to do so upon the lonely moor. On the other hand, if I should find the hut, and its tenant should not be within it, I must remain there, however long the vigil, until he returned. Holmes had missed him in London. It would indeed be a triumph for me if I could run him to earth where my master had failed.

Luck had been against us again and again in this inquiry, but now at last it came to my aid. And the messenger of good fortune was none other than Mr Frankland, who was standing, grey-whiskered and red-faced, outside the gate of his garden, which opened on to the high road along which I travelled.

'Good day, Dr Watson,' cried he, with unwonted good humour, 'you must really give your horses a rest, and come in to have a glass of wine and to congratulate me.'

My feelings towards him were far from being friendly after what I had heard of his treatment of his daughter, but I was anxious to send Perkins and the wagonette home, and the opportunity was a good one. I alighted and sent a message to Sir Henry that I should walk over in time for dinner. Then

85 *had I not seen his death in the paper next morning*. This was quick work, as Sir Charles was not discovered until midnight.

I followed Frankland into his dining-room.

'It is a great day for me, sir—one of the red-letter days of my life,' he cried, with many chuckles. 'I have brought off a double event. I mean to teach them in these parts that law is law, and that there is a man here who does not fear to invoke it. I have established a right of way through the centre of old Middleton's park, slap across it, sir, within a hundred yards of his own front door. What do you think of that? We'll teach these magnates that they cannot ride rough-shod over the rights of the commoners, confound them! And I've closed the wood where the Fernworthy folk used to picnic. These infernal people seem to think that there are no rights of property, and that they can swarm where they like with their papers and their bottles. Both cases decided, Dr Watson, and both in my favour. I haven't had such a day since I had Sir John Morland for trespass, because he shot in his own warren.'

'How on earth did you do that?'

'Look it up in the books, sir. It will repay reading—Frankland v. Morland Court of Queen's Bench. It cost me £200, but I got my verdict.'

'Did it do you any good?'

'None, sir, none. I am proud to say that I had no interest in the matter. I act entirely from a sense of public duty. I have no doubt, for example, that the Fernworthy people will burn me in effigy tonight. I told the police last time they did it that they should stop these disgraceful exhibitions. The county constabulary is in a scandalous state, sir, and it has not afforded me the protection to which I am entitled. The case of Frankland v. Regina will bring the matter before the attention of the public. I told them that they would have occasion to regret their treatment of me, and already my words have come true.'

'How so?' I asked.

The old man put on a very knowing expression.

'Because I could tell them what they are dying to know; but nothing would induce me to help the rascals in any way.'

I had been casting round for some excuse by which I could get away from his gossip, but now I began to wish to hear more of it. I had seen enough of the contrary nature of the old sinner to understand that any strong sign of interest would be the surest way to stop his confidences.

'Some poaching case, no doubt?' said I, with an indifferent manner.

'Ha, ha, my boy, a very much more important matter than that! What about the convict on the moor?'

I started. 'You don't mean that you know where he is?' said I.

'I may not know exactly where he is, but I am quite sure that I could help the police to lay their hands on him. Has it never struck you that the way to catch that man was to find out where he got his food, and so trace it to him?'

He certainly seemed to be getting uncomfortably near the truth. 'No doubt,' said I; 'but how do you know that he is anywhere upon the moor?'

'I know it because I have seen with my own eyes the messenger who takes him his food.'

My heart sank for Barrymore. It was a serious thing to be in the power of this spiteful old busybody. But his next remark took a weight from my mind.

'You'll be surprised to hear that his food is taken to him

by a child. I see him every day through my telescope upon
the roof. He passes along the same path at the same hour, and
to whom should he be going except to the convict?'

Here was luck indeed! And yet I suppressed all appearance
of interest. A child! Barrymore had said that our unknown
was supplied by a boy. It was on his track, and not upon the
convict's, that Frankland had stumbled. If I could get his
knowledge it might save me a long and weary hunt. But incredulity and indifference were evidently my strongest cards.

'I should say that it was much more likely that it was the
son of one of the moorland shepherds taking out his father's
dinner.'

The least appearance of opposition struck fire out of the
old autocrat. His eyes looked malignantly at me, and his
grey whiskers bristled like those of any angry cat.

'Indeed, sir!' said he, pointing out over the wide-stretching
moor. 'Do you see that Black Tor over yonder? Well, do you
see the low hill beyond with the thorn-bush upon it? It is the
stoniest part of the whole moor. Is that a place where a shepherd would be likely to take his station? Your suggestion, sir,
is a most absurd one.'

I meekly answered that I had spoken without knowing all
the facts. My submission pleased him and led him to further
confidences.

'You may be sure, sir, that I have very good grounds before
I come to an opinion. I have seen the boy again and again
with his bundle. Every day, and sometimes twice a day, I have
been able—but wait a moment, Dr Watson. Do my eyes
deceive me, or is there at the present moment something
moving upon that hillside?'

It was several miles off, but I could distinctly see a small
dark dot against the dull green and grey.

'Come, sir, come!' cried Frankland, rushing upstairs. 'You
will see with your own eyes and judge for yourself.'

The telescope, a formidable instrument mounted upon a
tripod, stood upon the flat leads of the house. Frankland
clapped his eye to it and gave a cry of satisfaction.

'Quick, Dr Watson, quick, before he passes over the hill!'

There he was, sure enough, a small urchin with a little
bundle upon his shoulder, toiling slowly up the hill. When
he reached the crest I saw the ragged, uncouth figure outlined
for an instant against the cold blue sky. He looked round him,
with a furtive and stealthy air, as one who dreads pursuit.
Then he vanished over the hill.

'Well! Am I right?'

'Certainly, there is a boy who seems to have some secret
errand.'

'And what the errand is even a county constable could
guess. But not one word shall they have from me, and I bind
you to secrecy also, Dr Watson. Not a word! You understand?'

'Just as you wish.'

'They have treated me shamefully—shamefully. When the
facts come out in Frankland v. Regina I venture to think that
a thrill of indignation will run through the country. Nothing
would induce me to help the police in any way. For all they
cared it might have been me, instead of my effigy, which these
rascals burned at the stake. Surely you are not going! You
will help me to empty the decanter in honour of this great
occasion!'

But I resisted all his solicitations and succeeded in dissuad-

... THE FANTASTIC SHAPES OF BELLIVER AND VIXEN TOR.

Both of these are actual tors, and Watson has made no attempt to disguise their names, beyond changing BELL*EV*ER to BELL*IV*ER. Both will be found on our map, and Vixen Tor is shown above in a photograph by J. Shortridge for the Reverend Sabine Baring-Gould's *A Book of Dartmoor*. Both Belliver (Bellever) and Vixen Tor do have "fantastic shapes," and Watson might well have added that, viewed from one point, Vixen Tor and the Sphinx of Egypt bear a marked resemblance.

THIS MUST BE THE BURROW WHERE THE
STRANGER LURKED.

Reliable local authority assures us that this photograph by Stuart Black, F.R.P.S. (from *Sherlock Holmes: A Biography*, by William S. Baring-Gould) shows the veritable hut which housed for a time "The Man on the Tor."

ing him from his announced intention of walking home with me. I kept the road as long as his eye was on me, and then I struck off across the moor and made for the stony hill over which the boy had disappeared. Everything was working in my favour, and I swore that it should not be through lack of energy or perseverance that I should miss the chance which Fortune had thrown in my way.

The sun was already sinking when I reached the summit of the hill, and the long slopes beneath me were all golden-green on one side and grey shadow on the other. A haze lay low upon the farthest skyline, out of which jutted the fantastic shapes of Belliver and Vixen Tor. Over the wide expanse there was no sound and no movement. One great grey bird, a gull or curlew, soared aloft in the blue heaven. He and I seemed to be the only living things between the huge arch of the sky and the desert beneath it. The barren scene, the sense of loneliness, and the mystery and urgency of my task all struck a chill into my heart. The boy was nowhere to be seen. But down beneath me, in a cleft of the hills, there was a circle of the old stone huts, and in the middle of them there was one which retained sufficient roof to act as a screen against the weather. My heart leaped within me as I saw it. This must be the burrow where the stranger lurked. At last my foot was on the threshold of his hiding-place—his secret was within my grasp.

As I approached the hut, walking as warily as Stapleton would do when with poised net he drew near the settled butterfly, I satisfied myself that the place had indeed been used as a habitation. A vague pathway among the boulders led to the dilapidated opening which served as a door. All was silent within. The unknown might be lurking there, or he might be prowling on the moor. My nerves tingled with the sense of adventure. Throwing aside my cigarette, I closed my hand upon the butt of my revolver, and, walking swiftly up to the door, I looked in. The place was empty.

But there were ample signs that I had not come upon a false scent. This was certainly where the man lived. Some blankets rolled in a waterproof lay upon that very stone slab upon which neolithic man had once slumbered. The ashes of a fire were heaped in a rude grate. Beside it lay some cooking utensils and a bucket half-full of water. A litter of empty tins showed that the place had been occupied for some time, and I saw, as my eyes became accustomed to the chequered light,

a pannikin and a half-full bottle of spirits standing in the corner. In the middle of the hut a flat stone served the purpose of a table, and upon this stood a small cloth bundle—the same, no doubt, which I had seen through the telescope upon the shoulder of the boy. It contained a loaf of bread, a tinned tongue, and two tins of preserved peaches. As I set it down again, after having examined it, my heart leaped to see that beneath it there lay a sheet of paper with writing upon it. I raised it, and this was what I read, roughly scrawled in pencil:

'Dr Watson has gone to Coombe Tracey.'

For a minute I stood there with the paper in my hands thinking out the meaning of this curt message. It was I, then, and not Sir Henry, who was being dogged by this secret man. He had not followed me himself, but he had set an agent—the boy, perhaps—upon my track, and this was his report. Possibly I had taken no step since I had been upon the moor which had not been observed and repeated. Always there was this feeling of an unseen force, a fine net drawn round us with infinite skill and delicacy, holding us so lightly that it was only at some supreme moment that one realized that one was indeed entangled in its meshes.

If there was one report there might be others, so I looked round the hut in search of them. There was no trace, however, of anything of the kind, nor could I discover any sign which might indicate the character or intentions of the man who lived in this singular place, save that he must be of Spartan habits, and cared little for the comforts of life. When I thought of the heavy rains and looked at the gaping roof I understood how strong and immutable must be the purpose which had kept him in that inhospitable abode. Was he our malignant enemy, or was he by chance our guardian angel? I swore that I would not leave the hut until I knew.

Outside the sun was sinking low and the west was blazing with scarlet and gold. Its reflection was shot back in ruddy patches by the distant pools which lay amid the great Grimpen Mire. There were the two towers of Baskerville Hall, and there a distant blur of smoke which marked the village of Grimpen. Between the two, behind the hill, was the house of the Stapletons. All was sweet and mellow and peaceful in the golden evening light, and yet as I looked at them my soul shared none of the peace of Nature, but quivered at the vagueness and the terror of that interview which every instant was bringing nearer. With tingling nerves, but a fixed purpose, I sat in the dark recess of the hut and waited with sombre patience for the coming of its tenant.

And then at last I heard him. Far away came the sharp clink of a boot striking upon a stone. Then another and yet another, coming nearer and nearer. I shrank back into the darkest corner, and cocked the pistol in my pocket, determined not to discover myself until I had an opportunity of seeing something of the stranger. There was a long pause, which showed that he had stopped. Then once more the footsteps approached and a shadow fell across the opening of the hut.

'It is a lovely evening, my dear Watson,' said a well-known **86** voice. 'I really think that you will be more comfortable outside than in.'

. . . A SHADOW FELL ACROSS THE OPENING OF THE HUT.

Illustration by Sidney Paget for the *Strand Magazine*, January, 1902.

86 '*It is a lovely evening*. And Watson has previously told us that "All was sweet and mellow and peaceful in the golden evening light." Said the *Times* of London of this day: "The thick fogs which have lately prevailed over England have entirely disappeared. . . . Weather . . . was fine at most of the English and Continental stations."

For a moment or two I sat breathless, hardly able to believe my ears. Then my senses and my voice came back to me, while a crushing weight of responsibility seemed in an instant to be lifted from my soul. That cold, incisive, ironical voice could belong to but one man in all the world.

'Holmes!' I cried—'Holmes!'

'Come out,' said he, 'and please be careful with the revolver.'

I stooped under the rude lintel, and there he sat upon a stone outside, his grey eyes dancing with amusement as they fell upon my astonished features. He was thin and worn, but clear and alert, his keen face bronzed by the sun and rough-**87** ened by the wind. In his tweed suit and cloth cap he looked like any other tourist upon the moor, and he had contrived, with that cat-like love of personal cleanliness which was one of his characteristics, that his chin should be as smooth and **88** his linen as perfect as if he were in Baker Street.

'I never was more glad to see anyone in my life,' said I, as I wrung him by the hand.

'Or more astonished, eh?'

'Well, I must confess to it.'

'The surprise was not all on one side, I assure you. I had no idea that you had found my occasional retreat, still less that you were inside it, until I was within twenty paces of the door.'

'My footprint, I presume?'

'No, Watson; I fear that I could not undertake to recognize your footprint amid all the footprints of the world. If you seriously desire to deceive me you must change your tobacconist; for when I see the stub of a cigarette marked Bradley, **89** Oxford Street, I know that my friend Watson is in the neighbourhood. You will see it there beside the path. You threw it down, no doubt, at that supreme moment when you charged into the empty hut.'

'Exactly.'

'I thought as much—and knowing your admirable tenacity, I was convinced that you were sitting in ambush, a weapon within reach, waiting for the tenant to return. So you actually thought that I was the criminal?'

'I did not know who you were, but I was determined to find out.'

'Excellent, Watson! And how did you localize me? You saw me, perhaps, on the night of the convict hunt, when I was so imprudent as to allow the moon to rise behind me?'

'Yes, I saw you then.'

'And have, no doubt, searched all the huts until you came to this one?'

'No, your boy had been observed, and that gave me a guide where to look.'

'The old gentleman with the telescope, no doubt. I could not make it out when first I saw the light flashing upon the lens.' He rose and peeped into the hut, 'Ha, I see that Cartwright has brought up some supplies. What's this paper? So you have been to Coombe Tracey, have you?'

'Yes.'

'To see Mrs Laura Lyons?'

. . . THERE HE SAT UPON A STONE OUTSIDE . . .

Illustration by Sidney Paget for the *Strand Magazine*, February, 1902.

87 *cloth cap.* "In sixty adventures," the late Professor Jay Finley Christ wrote in "The Pipe and the Cap," "the fore-and-aft, or deerstalker, is noted only *three* times, and it never is called by either of these names. In 'The Boscombe Valley Mystery' . . . it is 'his close-fitting cloth cap'; in 'Silver Blaze' . . . it is 'an ear-flapped travelling cap,' and in *The Hound of the Baskervilles* . . . it says 'in his tweed suit and cloth cap, he looked like any other tourist.' Sidney Paget drew all of these *as* deer-stalkers, and in the same period (1891–1901) the *Strand Magazine* offered at least nine other illustrations of such caps. Some of the latter were done for stories by A. Conan Doyle ('The Club-Footed Grocer,' 1898), some by Paget for non-Doyle stories, some by other artists for other authors . . ."

To this the artist's daughter, Miss Winifred Paget, has added: "As a young man my father lived in the country, and it was during this time that he wore that surely now most famous of all hats—the deerstalker—and the fact that he liked it and found it comfortable inspired him to depict Holmes wearing it on so many occasions."

'Exactly.'

'Well done! Our researches have evidently been running on parallel lines, and when we unite our results I expect we shall have a fairly full knowledge of the case.'

'Well, I am glad from my heart that you are here, for indeed the responsibility and the mystery were both becoming too much for my nerves. But how in the name of wonder did you come here, and what have you been doing? I thought that you were in Baker Street working out that case of blackmailing.'

'That was what I wished you to think.'

'Then you use me, and yet do not trust me!' I cried, with some bitterness. 'I think that I have deserved better at your hands, Holmes.'

'My dear fellow, you have been invaluable to me in this as in many other cases, and I beg that you will forgive me if I have seemed to play a trick upon you. In truth, it was partly for your own sake that I did it, and it was my appreciation of the danger which you ran which led me to come down and examine the matter for myself. Had I been with Sir Henry and you it is evident that my point of view would have been the same as yours, and my presence would have warned our very formidable opponents to be on their guard. As it is, I have been able to get about as I could not possibly have done had I been living at the Hall, and I remain an unknown factor in the business, ready to throw in all my weight at a critical moment.'

'But why keep me in the dark?'

'For you to know could not have helped us, and might possibly have led to my discovery. You would have wished to tell me something, or in your kindness you would have brought me out some comfort or other, and so an unnecessary risk would be run. I brought Cartwright down with me—you remember the little chap at the Express office—and he has seen after my simple wants: a loaf of bread and a clean collar. What does man want more? He has given me an extra pair of eyes upon a very active pair of feet, and both have been invaluable.'

'Then my reports have all been wasted!' My voice trembled as I recalled the pains and the pride with which I had composed them.

Holmes took a bundle of papers from his pocket.

'Here are your reports, my dear fellow, and very well thumbed, I assure you. I made excellent arrangements, and they are only delayed one day upon their way. I must compliment you exceedingly upon the zeal and the intelligence which you have shown over an extraordinarily difficult case.'

I was still rather raw over the deception which had been practised upon me, but the warmth of Holmes's praise drove my anger from my mind. I felt also in my heart that he was right in what he said, and that it was really best for our purpose that I should not have known that he was upon the moor.

'That's better,' said he, seeing the shadow rise from my face. 'And now tell me the result of your visit to Mrs Laura Lyons—it was not difficult for me to guess that it was to see her that you had gone, for I am already aware that she is the one person in Coombe Tracey who might be of service to us in the matter. In fact, if you had not gone today it is exceedingly probable that I should have gone tomorrow.'

The sun had set and dusk was settling over the moor. The air had turned chill, and we withdrew into the hut for

88 *as perfect as if he were in Baker Street.* "This spruce appearance sounds so unlike the Holmes we know that one cannot help wondering if there was any feminine reason for it," Dr. Richard Asher wrote in "Holmes and the Fair Sex." "After all there was at Coombe Tracey, a few miles away, the redoubtable Mrs. Laura Lyons. . . . Or could it possibly have been Mrs. Barrymore, the butler's wife at Baskerville Hall?"

89 *Bradley, Oxford Street.* "In actual fact," Mr. J. C. Wimbush wrote in "Watson's Tobacconist," "there has always been a dearth of tobacconists in Oxford Street itself, that is, between Marble Arch and Oxford Circus. There is one, however, which was quite definitely . . . in existence . . . till 1890. It occupied what is now the southeast corner of the [D. H. Evans store], and its name is R. H. Hoar & Co., Ltd. . . . now situated at No. 6, Prince's Street, which runs north from Oxford Street just west of the Circus."

warmth. There, sitting together in the twilight, I told Holmes of my conversation with the lady. So interested was he that I had to repeat some of it twice before he was satisfied.

'This is most important,' said he, when I had concluded. 'It fills up a gap which I had been unable to bridge in this most complex affair. You are aware, perhaps, that a close intimacy exists between this lady and the man Stapleton?'

'I did not know of a close intimacy.'

'There can be no doubt about the matter. They meet, they write, there is a complete understanding between them. Now, this puts a very powerful weapon into our hands. If I could only use it to detach his wife——'

'His wife?'

'I am giving you some information now, in return for all that you have given me. The lady who has passed here as Miss Stapleton is in reality his wife.'

'Good heavens, Holmes! Are you sure of what you say? How could he have permitted Sir Henry to fall in love with her?'

'Sir Henry's falling in love could do no harm to anyone except Sir Henry. He took particular care that Sir Henry did not *make* love to her, as you have yourself observed. I repeat that the lady is his wife and not his sister.'

'But why this elaborate deception?'

'Because he foresaw that she would be very much more useful to him in the character of a free woman.'

All my unspoken instincts, my vague suspicions, suddenly took shape and centred upon the naturalist. In that impassive, colourless man, with his straw hat and his butterfly-net, I seemed to see something terrible—a creature of infinite patience and craft, with a smiling face and a murderous heart.

'It is he, then, who is our enemy—it is he who dogged us in London?'

'So I read the riddle.'

'And the warning—it must have come from her!'

'Exactly.'

The shape of some monstrous villainy, half seen, half guessed, loomed through the darkness which had girt me so long.

'But are you sure of this, Holmes? How do you know that the woman is his wife?'

'Because he so far forgot himself as to tell you a true piece of autobiography upon the occasion when he first met you, and I dare say he has many a time regretted it since. He *was* once a schoolmaster in the North of England. Now, there is no one more easy to trace than a schoolmaster. There are scholastic agencies by which one may identify any man who has been in the profession. A little investigation showed me that a school had come to grief under atrocious circumstances, and that the man who had owned it—the name was different —had disappeared with his wife. The descriptions agreed. When I learned that the missing man was devoted to entomology the identification was complete.'

The darkness was rising, but much was still hidden by the shadows.

'If this woman is in truth his wife, where does Mrs Laura Lyons come in?' I asked.

'That is one of the points upon which your own researches have shed a light. Your interview with the lady has cleared the situation very much. I did not know about a projected divorce between herself and her husband. In that case, regarding Stapleton as an unmarried man, she counted no doubt upon becoming his wife.'

'And when she is undeceived?'

'Why, then we may find the lady of service. It must be our first duty to see her—both of us—tomorrow. Don't you think, Watson, that you are away from your charge rather long? Your place should be at Baskerville Hall.'

The last red streaks had faded away in the west and night had settled upon the moor. A few faint stars were gleaming in a violet sky.

'One last question, Holmes,' I said, as I rose. 'Surely there is no need of secrecy between you and me. What is the meaning of it all? What is he after?'

Holmes's voice sank as he answered—'It is murder, Watson —refined, cold-blooded, deliberate murder. Do not ask me for particulars. My nets are closing upon him, even as his are upon Sir Henry, and with your help he is already almost at my mercy. There is but one danger which can threaten us. It is that he should strike before we are ready to do so. Another day—two at the most—and I have my case complete, but until then guard your charge as closely as ever a fond mother watched her ailing child. Your mission today has justified itself, and yet I could almost wish that you had not left his side—Hark!'

A terrible scream—a prolonged yell of horror and anguish burst out of the silence of the moor. That frightful cry turned the blood to ice in my veins.

'Oh, my God!' I gasped. 'What is it? What does it mean?'

Holmes had sprung to his feet, and I saw his dark, athletic outline at the door of the hut, his shoulders stooping, his head thrust forward, his face peering into the darkness.

'Hush!' he whispered. 'Hush!'

The cry had been loud on account of its vehemence, but it had pealed out from somewhere far off on the shadowy plain. Now it burst upon our ears, nearer, louder, more urgent than before.

'Where is it?' Holmes whispered; and I knew from the thrill of his voice that he, the man of iron, was shaken to the soul. 'Where is it, Watson?'

'There, I think.' I pointed into the darkness.

'No, there!'

Again the agonized cry swept through the silent night, louder and much nearer than ever. And a new sound mingled with it, a deep, muttered rumble, musical and yet menacing, rising and falling like the low, constant murmur of the sea.

'The hound!' cried Holmes. 'Come, Watson, come! Great heavens, if we are too late!'

He had started running swiftly over the moor, and I had followed at his heels. But now from somewhere among the broken ground immediately in front of us there came one last despairing yell, and then a dull, heavy thud. We halted and listened. Not another sound broke the heavy silence of the windless night.

I saw Holmes put his hand to his forehead, like a man distracted. He stamped his feet upon the ground.

'He has beaten us, Watson. We are too late.'

'No, no, surely not!'

'Fool that I was to hold my hand. And you, Watson, see what comes of abandoning your charge! But, by Heaven, if the worst has happened, we'll avenge him!'

Blindly we ran through the gloom, blundering against boulders, forcing our way through gorse bushes, panting up hills and rushing down slopes, heading always in the direction whence those dreadful sounds had come. At every rise Holmes looked eagerly round him, but the shadows were thick upon the moor and nothing moved upon its dreary face.

'Can you see anything?'

'Nothing.'

'But, hark, what is that?'

A low moan had fallen upon our ears. There it was again upon our left! On that side a ridge of rocks ended in a sheer cliff, which overlooked a stone-strewn slope. On its jagged face was spread-eagled some dark, irregular object. As we ran towards it the vague outline hardened into a definite shape. It was a prostrate man face downwards upon the ground, the head doubled under him at a horrible angle, the shoulders rounded and the body hunched together as if in the act of throwing a somersault. So grotesque was the attitude that I could not for the instant realize that that moan had been the passing of his soul. Not a whisper, not a rustle, rose now from the dark figure over which we stooped. Holmes laid his hand upon him, and held it up again, with an exclamation of horror. The gleam of the match which he struck shone upon his clotted fingers and upon the ghastly pool which widened slowly from the crushed skull of the victim. And it shone upon something else which turned our hearts sick and faint within us—the body of Sir Henry Baskerville!

There was no chance of either of us forgetting that peculiar ruddy tweed suit—the very one which he had worn on the first morning that we had seen him in Baker Street. We caught the one clear glimpse of it, and then the match flickered and went out, even as the hope had gone out of our souls. Holmes groaned, and his face glimmered white through the darkness.

'The brute! the brute!' I cried, with clenched hands. 'Oh, Holmes, I shall never forgive myself for having left him to his fate.'

'I am more to blame than you, Watson. In order to have my case well rounded and complete, I have thrown away the life of my client. It is the greatest blow which has befallen me in my career. But how could I know—how *could* I know —that he would risk his life alone upon the moor in the face of all my warnings?'

'That we should have heard his screams—my God, those screams!—and yet have been unable to save him! Where is this brute of a hound which drove him to his death? It may be lurking among these rocks at this instant. And Stapleton, where is he? He shall answer for this deed.'

'He shall. I will see to that. Uncle and nephew have been murdered—the one frightened to death by the very sight of a beast, which he thought to be supernatural, the other driven to his end in his wild flight to escape from it. But now we have to prove the connection between the man and the beast. Save from what we heard, we cannot even swear to the existence of the latter, since Sir Henry has evidently died from the fall. But, by heavens, cunning as he is, the fellow shall be in my

IT WAS A PROSTRATE MAN FACE DOWNWARDS
UPON THE GROUND . . .

Illustration by Sidney Paget for the *Strand Magazine*, February, 1902.

power before another day is past!'

We stood with bitter hearts on either side of the mangled body, overwhelmed by this sudden and irrevocable disaster which had brought all our long and weary labours to so piteous an end. Then, as the moon rose, we climbed to the **90** top of the rocks over which our poor friend had fallen, and from the summit we gazed out over the shadowy moor, half silver and half gloom. Far away, miles off, in the direction of Grimpen, a single steady, yellow light was shining. It could only come from the lonely abode of the Stapletons. With a bitter curse I shook my fist at it as I gazed.

'Why should we not seize him at once?'

'Our case is not complete. The fellow is wary and cunning to the last degree. It is not what we know, but what we can prove. If we make one false move the villain may escape us yet.'

'What can we do?'

'There will be plenty for us to do tomorrow. Tonight we can only perform the last offices to our poor friend.'

Together we made our way down the precipitous slope and approached the body, black and clear against the silvered stones. The agony of those contorted limbs struck me with a spasm of pain and blurred my eyes with tears.

'We must send for help, Holmes! We cannot carry him all the way to the Hall. Good heavens, are you mad?'

He had uttered a cry and bent over the body. Now he was dancing and laughing and wringing my hand. Could this be my stern, self-contained friend? These were hidden fires, indeed!

'A beard! A beard! The man has a beard!'

'A beard?'

'It is not the baronet—it is—why, it is my neighbour, the convict!'

With feverish haste we had turned the body over, and that dripping beard was pointing up to the cold, clear moon. There could be no doubt about the beetling forehead, the sunken animal eyes. It was, indeed, the same face which had glared upon me in the light of the candle from over the rock —the face of Selden, the criminal.

Then in an instant it was all clear to me. I remembered how the baronet had told me that he had handed his old wardrobe to Barrymore. Barrymore had passed it on in order to help Selden in his escape. Boots, shirt, cap—it was all Sir Henry's. The tragedy was still black enough, but this man had at least deserved death by the laws of his country. I told Holmes how the matter stood, my heart bubbling over with thankfulness and joy.

'Then the clothes have been the poor fellow's death,' said he. 'It is clear enough that the hound has been laid on from some article of Sir Henry's—the boot which was abstracted in the hotel, in all probability—and so ran this man down. There is one very singular thing, however: How came Selden, in the darkness, to know that the hound was on his trail?'

'He heard him.'

'To hear a hound upon the moor would not work a hard man like this convict into such a paroxysm of terror that he would risk recapture by screaming wildly for help. By his cries he must have run a long way after he knew the animal was on his track. How did he know?'

'A greater mystery to me is why this hound, presuming that

90 *Then, as the moon rose*. But the moon did not rise about nine o'clock on the evening of Thursday, October 18, 1888, as Watson tells us it did: it rose at 5:05 P.M. on that date.

IT WAS . . . THE FACE OF SELDEN, THE CRIMINAL.

Illustration by Sidney Paget for the *Strand Magazine*, February, 1902.

all our conjectures are correct——'

'I presume nothing.'

'Well, then, why this hound should be loose tonight. I suppose that it does not always run loose upon the moor. Stapleton would not let it go unless he had reason to think that Sir Henry would be there.'

'My difficulty is the more formidable of the two, for I think that we shall very shortly get an explanation of yours, while mine may remain for ever a mystery. The question now is, what shall we do with this poor wretch's body? We cannot leave it here to the foxes and the ravens.'

'I suggest that we put it in one of the huts until we can communicate with the police.'

'Exactly. I have no doubt that you and I could carry it so far. Halloa, Watson, what's this? It's the man himself, by all that's wonderful and audacious! Not a word to show your suspicions—not a word, or my plans crumble to the ground.'

A figure was approaching us over the moor, and I saw the dull red glow of a cigar. The moon shone upon him, and I could distinguish the dapper shape and jaunty walk of the naturalist. He stopped when he saw us, and then came on again.

'Why, Dr Watson, that's not you, is it? You are the last man that I should have expected to see out on the moor at this time of night. But, dear me, what's this? Somebody hurt? Not —don't tell me that it is our friend Sir Henry!'

He hurried past me and stooped over the dead man. I heard a sharp intake of his breath and the cigar fell from his fingers.

'Who—who's this?' he stammered.

'It is Selden, the man who escaped from Princetown.'

Stapleton turned a ghastly face upon us, but by a supreme effort he had overcome his amazement and his disappointment. He looked sharply from Holmes to me.

'Dear me! What a very shocking affair! How did he die?'

'He appears to have broken his neck by falling over these rocks. My friend and I were strolling on the moor when we heard a cry.'

'I heard a cry also. That was what brought me out. I was uneasy about Sir Henry.'

'Why about Sir Henry in particular?' I could not help asking.

'Because I had suggested that he should come over. When he did not come I was surprised, and I naturally became alarmed for his safety when I heard cries upon the moor. By the way'—his eyes darted again from my face to Holmes's— 'did you hear anything else besides a cry?'

'No,' said Holmes; 'did you?'

'No.'

'What do you mean, then?'

'Oh, you know the stories that the peasants tell about a phantom hound, and so on. It is said to be heard at night upon the moor. I was wondering if there were any evidence of such a sound tonight.'

'We heard nothing of the kind,' said I.

'And what is your theory of this poor fellow's death?'

'I have no doubt that anxiety and exposure have driven him off his head. He has rushed about the moor in a crazy state and eventually fallen over here and broken his neck.

'That seems the most reasonable theory,' said Stapleton,

'WHO—WHO'S THIS?' HE STAMMERED.

Illustration by Sidney Paget for the *Strand Magazine*, February, 1902.

and he gave a sigh which I took to indicate his relief. 'What do you think about it, Mr Sherlock Holmes?'

My friend bowed his compliments.

'You are quick at identification,' said he.

'We have been expecting you in these parts since Dr Watson came down. You are in time to see a tragedy.'

'Yes, indeed. I have no doubt that my friend's explanation will cover the facts. I will take an unpleasant remembrance back to London with me tomorrow.'

'Oh, you return tomorrow?'

'That is my intention.'

'I hope your visit has cast some light upon those occurrences which have puzzled us?'

Holmes shrugged his shoulders. 'One cannot always have the success for which one hopes. An investigator needs facts, and not legends or rumours. It has not been a satisfactory case.'

My friend spoke in his frankest and most unconcerned manner. Stapleton still looked hard at him. Then he turned to me.

'I would suggest carrying this poor fellow to my house, but it would give my sister such a fright that I do not feel justified in doing it. I think that if we put something over his face he will be safe until morning.'

And so it was arranged. Resisting Stapleton's offer of hospitality, Holmes and I set off to Baskerville Hall, leaving the naturalist to return alone. Looking back we saw the figure moving slowly away over the broad moor, and behind him that one black smudge on the silvered slope which showed where the man was lying who had come so horribly to his end.

'We're at close grips at last,' said Holmes, as we walked together across the moor. 'What a nerve the fellow has! How he pulled himself together in the face of what must have been a paralysing shock when he found that the wrong man had fallen a victim to his plot. I told you in London, Watson, and I tell you now again, that we have never had a foeman more worthy of our steel.'

'I am sorry that he has seen you.'

'And so was I at first. But there was no getting out of it.'

'What effect do you think it will have upon his plans, now that he knows you are here?'

'It may cause him to be more cautious, or it may drive him to desperate measures at once. Like most clever criminals, he may be too confident in his own cleverness and imagine that he has completely deceived us.'

'Why should we not arrest him at once?'

'My dear Watson, you were born to be a man of action. Your instinct is always to do something energetic. But supposing, for argument's sake, that we had him arrested tonight, what on earth the better off should we be for that? We could prove nothing against him. There's the devilish cunning of it! If he were acting through a human agent we could get some evidence, but if we were to drag this great dog to the light of day it would not help us in putting a rope round the neck of its master.'

'Surely we have a case.'

'Not a shadow of one—only surmise and conjecture. We should be laughed out of court if we came with such a story and such evidence.'

91 *Sufficient for tomorrow is the evil thereof.* Holmes again quotes Scripture: "Sufficient unto the day is the evil thereof," Matthew, 10:16.

'There is Sir Charles's death.'

'Found dead without a mark upon him. You and I know that he died of sheer fright, and we know also what frightened him; but how are we to get twelve stolid jurymen to know it? What signs are there of a hound? Where are the marks of its fangs. Of course, we know that a hound does not bite a dead body, and that Sir Charles was dead before ever the brute overtook him. But we have to *prove* all this, and we are not in a position to do it.'

'Well, then, tonight?'

'We are not much better off tonight. Again, there was no direct connection between the hound and the man's death. We never saw the hound. We heard it; but we could not prove that it was running upon this man's trail. There is a complete absence of motive. No, my dear fellow; we must reconcile ourselves to the fact that we have no case at present, and that it is worth our while to run any risk in order to establish one.'

'And how do you propose to do so?'

'I have great hopes of what Mrs Laura Lyons may do for us when the position of affairs is made clear to her. And I have my own plan as well. **91** Sufficient for tomorrow is the evil thereof; but I hope before the day is past to have the upper hand at last.'

I could draw nothing further from him, and he walked, lost in thought, as far as the Baskerville gates.

'Are you coming up?'

'Yes; I see no reason for further concealment. But one last word, Watson. Say nothing of the hound to Sir Henry. Let him think that Selden's death was as Stapleton would have us believe. He will have a better nerve for the ordeal which he will have to undergo tomorrow, when he is engaged, if I remember your report aright, to dine with these people.'

'And so am I.'

'Then you must excuse yourself, and he must go alone. That will be easily arranged. And now, if we are too late for dinner, I think that we are both ready for our suppers.'

13 ✦ FIXING THE NETS

Sir Henry was more pleased than surprised to see Sherlock Holmes, for he had for some days been expecting that recent events would bring him down from London. He did raise his eyebrows, however, when he found that my friend had neither any luggage nor any explanations for its absence. Between us we soon supplied his wants, and then over a belated supper we explained to the baronet as much of our experience as it seemed desirable that he should know. But first I had the unpleasant duty of breaking the news of Selden's death to Barrymore and his wife. To him it may have been an unmitigated relief, but she wept bitterly in her apron. To all the world he was the man of violence, half animal and half demon; but to her he always remained the little wilful boy of her own girlhood, the child who had clung to her hand. Evil indeed is the man who has not one woman to mourn him.

'I've been moping in the house all day since Watson went off in the morning,' said the baronet. 'I guess I should have some credit, for I have kept my promise. If I hadn't sworn not to go about alone I might have had a more lively evening, for I had a message from Stapleton asking me over there.'

'I have no doubt that you would have had a more lively evening,' said Holmes, dryly. 'By the way, I don't suppose you appreciate that we have been mourning over you as having broken your neck?'

Sir Henry opened his eyes. 'How was that?'

'This poor wretch was dressed in your clothes. I fear your servant who gave them to him may get into trouble with the police.'

'That is unlikely. There was no mark on any of them, so far as I know.'

'That's lucky for him—in fact, it's lucky for all of you, since you are all on the wrong side of the law in this matter. I am not sure that as a conscientious detective my first duty is not to arrest the whole household. Watson's reports are most incriminating documents.'

'But how about the case?' asked the baronet. 'Have you made anything out of the tangle? I don't know that Watson and I are much the wiser since we came down.'

'I think that I shall be in a position to make the situation rather more clear to you before long. It has been an exceedingly difficult and most complicated business. There are several points upon which we still want light—but it is coming, all the same.'

'We've had one experience, as Watson has no doubt told you. We heard the hound on the moor, so I can swear that it is not all empty superstition. I had something to do with dogs when I was out West, and I know one when I hear one. If you can muzzle that one and put him on a chain I'll be ready to swear you are the greatest detective of all time.'

'I think I will muzzle him and chain him all right if you will give me your help.'

'Whatever you tell me to do I will do.'

'Very good; and I will ask you also to do it blindly, without always asking the reason.'

'Just as you like.'

'If you will do this I think the chances are that our little problem will soon be solved. I have no doubt——'

He stopped suddenly and stared fixedly up over my head into the air. The lamp beat upon his face, and so intent was it and so still that it might have been that of a clear-cut classical statue, a personification of alertness and expectation.

'What is it?' we both cried.

I could see as he looked down that he was repressing some internal emotion. His features were still composed, but his eyes shone with amused exultation.

'Excuse the admiration of a connoisseur,' said he, as he waved his hand towards the line of portraits which covered the opposite wall. 'Watson won't allow that I know anything of art, but that is mere jealousy, because our views upon the subject differ. Now, these are a really very fine series of portraits.'

'Well, I'm glad to hear you say so,' said Sir Henry, glancing

HE STOPPED SUDDENLY AND STARED FIXEDLY UP OVER MY HEAD INTO THE AIR.

Illustration by Sidney Paget for the *Strand Magazine*, March, 1902.

92 *Kneller*. Sir Godfrey Kneller, 1646–1723. He succeeded Lely as court painter to Charles II, and many of his portraits hang at Hampton Court.

93 *Reynolds*. Sir Joshua Reynolds, 1723–1792. He and his assistants painted some 2,000 portraits and historical paintings, notable for their richness of color; in design he surpassed his rivals Gainsborough and Romney.

94 *Rodney*. George Brydges Rodney, first Baron Rodney, 1719–1792, British admiral. His defeat (1782) of a French fleet under De Grasse in the West Indies led to better peace terms with the French after the American Revolution.

95 *Pitt*. William Pitt, 1759–1806, Prime Minister (1783–1801) under George III.

'GOOD HEAVENS!' I CRIED, IN AMAZEMENT.

Illustration by Sidney Paget for the *Strand Magazine*, March, 1902.

with some surprise at my friend. 'I don't pretend to know much about these things, and I'd be a better judge of a horse or a steer than of a picture. I didn't know that you found time for such things.'

'I know what is good when I see it, and I see it now. That's **92** a Kneller, I'll swear, that lady in the blue silk over yonder, **93** and the stout gentleman with the wig ought to be a Reynolds. They are all family portraits, I presume?'

'Every one.'

'Do you know the names?'

'Barrymore has been coaching me in them, and I think I can say my lessons fairly well.'

'Who is the gentleman with the telescope?'

'That is Rear-Admiral Baskerville, who served under Rod- **94** ney in the West Indies. The man with the blue coat and the roll of paper is Sir William Baskerville, who was Chairman **95** of Committees of the House of Commons under Pitt.'

'And this Cavalier opposite to me—the one with the black velvet and the lace?'

'Ah, you have a right to know about him. That is the cause of all the mischief, the wicked Hugo, who started the Hound of the Baskervilles. We're not likely to forget him.'

96 I gazed with interest and some surprise upon the portrait.

'Dear me!' said Holmes, 'he seems a quiet, meek-mannered man enough, but I dare say that there was a lurking devil in his eyes. I had pictured him as a more robust and ruffianly person.'

'There's no doubt about the authenticity, for the name and the date, 1647, are on the back of the canvas.'

Holmes said little more, but the picture of the old roysterer seemed to have a fascination for him, and his eyes were continually fixed upon it during supper. It was not until later, when Sir Henry had gone to his room, that I was able to follow the trend of his thoughts. He led me back into the banqueting-hall, his bedroom candle in his hand, and he held it up against the time-stained portrait on the wall.

'Do you see anything there?'

I looked at the broad plumed hat, the curling love-locks, the white lace collar, and the straight, severe face which was framed between them. It was not a brutal countenance, but it was prim, hard and stern, with a firm-set, thin-lipped mouth, and a coldly intolerant eye.

'Is it like anyone you know?'

'There is something of Sir Henry about the jaw.'

'Just a suggestion, perhaps. But wait an instant!'

He stood upon a chair, and holding up the light in his left hand, he curved his right arm over the broad hat, and round the long ringlets.

'Good heavens!' I cried, in amazement.

The face of Stapleton had sprung out of the canvas.

'Ha, you see it now. My eyes have been trained to examine faces and not their trimmings. It is the first quality of a criminal investigator that he should see through a disguise.'

'But this is marvellous. It might be his portrait.'

97 'Yes, it is an interesting instance of a throw-back, which appears to be both physical and spiritual. A study of family portraits is enough to convert a man to the doctrine of reincarnation. The fellow is a Baskerville—that is evident.'

'With designs upon the succession.'

'Exactly. This chance of the picture has supplied us with one of our most obvious missing links. We have him, Watson, we have him, and I dare swear that before tomorrow night he will be fluttering in our net as helpless as one of his own butterflies. A pin, a cork, and a card, and we add him to the Baker Street collection!'

He burst into one of his rare fits of laughter as he turned away from the picture. I have not heard him laugh often, and it has always boded ill to somebody.

I was up betimes in the morning, but Holmes was afoot earlier still, for I saw him as I dressed coming up the drive.

'Yes, we should have a full day today,' he remarked, and he rubbed his hands with the joy of action. 'The nets are all in place, and the drag is about to begin. We'll know before the day is out whether we have caught our big, lean-jawed pike, or whether he has got through the meshes.'

'Have you been on the moor already?'

'I have sent a report from Grimpen to Princetown as to the death of Selden. I think I can promise that none of you will be troubled in the matter. And I have also communicated with my faithful Cartwright, who would certainly have pined away at the door of my hut as a dog does at his master's grave if I had not set his mind at rest about my safety.'

'What is the next move?'

'To see Sir Henry. Ah, here he is!'

'Good morning, Holmes,' said the baronet. 'You look like a general who is planning a battle with his chief of the staff.'

'That is the exact situation. Watson was asking for orders.'

'And so do I.'

'Very good. You are engaged, as I understand, to dine with our friends the Stapletons tonight.'

'I hope that you will come also. They are very hospitable people, and I am sure that they would be very glad to see you.'

'I fear that Watson and I must go to London.'

'To London?'

'Yes, I think that we should be more useful there at the present juncture.'

The baronet's face perceptibly lengthened. 'I hoped that you were going to see me through this business. The Hall and the moor are not very pleasant places when one is alone.'

'My dear fellow, you must trust me implicitly and do exactly what I tell you. You can tell your friends that we should have been happy to have come with you, but that urgent business required us to be in town. We hope very soon to return to Devonshire. Will you remember to give them that message?'

'If you insist upon it.'

'There is no alternative, I assure you.'

I saw by the baronet's clouded brow that he was deeply hurt by what he regarded as our desertion.

'When do you desire to go?' he asked, coldly.

'Immediately after breakfast. We will drive into Coombe Tracey, but Watson will leave his things as a pledge that he will come back to you. Watson, you will send a note to Stapleton to tell him that you regret that you cannot come.'

'I have a good mind to go to London with you,' said the baronet. 'Why should I stay here alone?'

'Because it is your post of duty. Because you gave me your

96 *I gazed with interest and some surprise upon the portrait.* "It is not known for certain who painted the portrait of Hugo Baskerville," Lord Donegall wrote in "Who Painted Hugo Baskerville?" "It is, however, fairly safe to deduce that, as the family portraits at Baskerville Hall included a Reynolds and a Kneller, it was the tradition of the Baskerville family to be painted by the best-known artist of the time. There is therefore little doubt that the portrait of Hugo Baskerville, painted in the 1640's, while he was serving the cause of Charles I, is the work of Franz Hals, the famous Dutch artist, one of whose best known works is the *Laughing Cavalier*."

97 *a throw-back.* But now a problem arises. What about Dr. Mortimer? "If he knew enough about atavism to write a book on the subject, he must have been well-versed in it indeed," Mr. Charles M. Pickard wrote in "The Reticence of Doctor Mortimer." "Then too, he had been in the Hall many times, visiting Sir Charles, and he had seen the portrait often. Surely he must have noticed the resemblance between Stapleton and Hugo. Besides, he tells Holmes that he has heard that Rodger Baskerville is the image of Hugo. Why, then, didn't he put two and two together and reason that 1) Stapleton was really a Baskerville; 2) that he was most likely Rodger's son; and 3) none of the trouble had arisen until Stapleton moved in. If he deduced the first two points, he must have come to the conclusion that Stapleton was up to no good."

word that you would do as you were told, and I tell you to stay.'

'All right, then, I'll stay.'

'One more direction! I wish you to drive to Merripit House. Send back your trap, however, and let them know that you intend to walk home.'

'To walk across the moor?'

'Yes.'

'But that is the very thing which you have so often cautioned me not to do.'

'This time you may do it with safety. If I had not every confidence in your nerve and courage I would not suggest it, but it is essential that you should do it.'

'Then I will do it.'

'And as you value your life, do not go across the moor in any direction save along the straight path which leads from Merripit House to the Grimpen Road, and is your natural way home.'

'I will do just what you say.'

'Very good. I should be glad to get away as soon after breakfast as possible, so as to reach London in the afternoon.'

I was much astounded by this programme, though I remembered that Holmes had said to Stapleton on the night before that his visit would terminate next day. It had not crossed my mind, however, that he would wish me to go with him, nor could I understand how we could both be absent at a moment which he himself declared to be critical. There was nothing for it, however, but implicit obedience; so we bade good-bye to our rueful friend, and a couple of hours afterwards we were at the station of Coombe Tracey and had dispatched the trap upon its return journey. A small boy was waiting upon the platform.

'Any orders, sir?'

'You will take this train to town, Cartwright. The moment you arrive you will send a wire to Sir Henry Baskerville, in my name, to say that if he finds the pocket-book which I have dropped he is to send it by registered post to Baker Street.'

'Yes, sir.'

'And ask at the station office if there is a message for me.'

The boy returned with a telegram, which Holmes handed to me. It ran—

'Wire received. Coming down with unsigned warrant. Arrive five-forty.—LESTRADE.'

'That is in answer to mine of this morning. He is the best of the professionals, I think, and we may need his assistance. Now, Watson, I think that we cannot employ our time better than by calling upon your acquaintance, Mrs Laura Lyons.'

His plan of campaign was beginning to be evident. He would use the baronet in order to convince the Stapletons that we were really gone, while we should actually return at the instant when we were likely to be needed. That telegram from London, if mentioned by Sir Henry to the Stapletons, must remove the last suspicions from their minds. Already I seemed to see our nets drawing closer round that lean-jawed pike.

Mrs Laura Lyons was in her office, and Sherlock Holmes opened his interview with a frankness and directness which considerably amazed her.

'I am investigating the circumstances which attended the

death of the late Sir Charles Baskerville,' said he. 'My friend here, Dr Watson, has informed me of what you have communicated, and also of what you have withheld in connection with that matter.'

'What have I withheld?' she asked defiantly.

'You have confessed that you asked Sir Charles to be at the gate at ten o'clock. We know that that was the place and hour of his death. You have withheld what the connection is between these events.'

'There is no connection.'

'In that case the coincidence must indeed be an extraordinary one. But I think that we shall succeed in establishing a connection after all. I wish to be perfectly frank with you, Mrs Lyons. We regard this case as one of murder, and the evidence may implicate not only your friend, Mr Stapleton, but his wife as well.'

The lady sprang from her chair. 'His wife!' she cried.

'The fact is no longer a secret. The person who has passed for his sister is really his wife.'

Mrs Lyons had resumed her seat. Her hands were grasping the arms of her chair, and I saw that the pink nails had turned white with the pressure of her grip.

'His wife!' she said again. 'His wife! He was not a married man.'

Sherlock Holmes shrugged his shoulders.

'Prove it to me! Prove it to me! And if you can do so——!' The fierce flash of her eyes said more than any words.

'I have come prepared to do so,' said Holmes, drawing several papers from his pocket. 'Here is a photograph of the couple taken in York four years ago. It is indorsed "Mr and **98** Mrs Vandeleur," but you will have no difficulty in recognizing him, and her also, if you know her by sight. Here are three written descriptions by trustworthy witnesses of Mr and Mrs Vandeleur, who at that time kept St Oliver's private school. Read them, and see if you can doubt the identity of these people.'

She glanced at them, and then looked up at us with the set, rigid face of a desperate woman.

'Mr Holmes,' she said, 'this man had offered me marriage on condition that I could get a divorce from my husband. He has lied to me, the villain, in every conceivable way. Not one word of truth has he ever told me. And why—why? I imagined that all was for my own sake. But now I see that I was never anything but a tool in his hands. Why should I preserve faith with him who never kept any with me? Why should I try to shield him from the consequences of his own wicked acts? Ask me what you like, and there is nothing which I shall hold back. One thing I swear to you, and that is, that when I wrote the letter I never dreamed of any harm to the old gentleman, who had been my kindest friend.'

'I entirely believe you, madam,' said Sherlock Holmes. 'The recital of these events must be very painful to you, and perhaps it will make it easier if I tell you what occurred, and you can check me if I make any material mistake. The sending of this letter was suggested to you by Stapleton?'

'He dictated it.'

'I presume that the reason he gave was that you would receive help from Sir Charles for the legal expenses connected with your divorce?'

THE LADY SPRANG FROM HER CHAIR.

Illustration by Sidney Paget for the *Strand Magazine*, March, 1902.

98 *York.* The great ecclesiastical and educational center of the North of England, second only to Canterbury in the Church of England.

'Exactly.'

'And then after you had sent the letter he dissuaded you from keeping the appointment?'

'He told me that it would hurt his self-respect that any other man should find the money for such an object, and that though he was a poor man himself he would devote his last penny to removing the obstacles which divided us.'

'He appears to be a very consistent character. And then you heard nothing until you read the reports of the death in the paper?'

'No.'

'And he made you swear to say nothing about your appointment with Sir Charles?'

'He did. He said that the death was a very mysterious one, and that I should certainly be suspected if the facts came out. He frightened me into remaining silent.'

'Quite so. But you had your suspicions?'

She hesitated and looked down. 'I knew him,' she said. 'But if he had kept faith with me I should always have done so with him.'

'I think that on the whole you have had a fortunate escape,' said Sherlock Holmes. 'You have had him in your power and he knew it, and yet you are alive. You have been walking for some months very near to the edge of a precipice. We must wish you good morning now, Mrs Lyons; and it is probable that you will very shortly hear from us again.'

'Our case becomes rounded off, and difficulty after difficulty thins away in front of us,' said Holmes, as we stood waiting for the arrival of the express from town. 'I shall soon be in the position of being able to put into a single connected narrative one of the most singular and sensational crimes of modern times. Students of criminology will remember the analogous incidents in Grodno, in Little Russia, in the year '66, and of course there are the Anderson murders in North Carolina, but this case possesses some features which are entirely its own. Even now we have no clear case against this very wily man. But I shall be very much surprised if it is not clear enough before we go to bed this night.'

The London express came roaring into the station, and a small, wiry bulldog of a man had sprung from a first-class carriage. We all three shook hands, and I saw at once from the reverential way in which Lestrade gazed at my companion that he had learned a good deal since the days when they had first worked together. I could well remember the scorn which the theories of the reasoner used then to excite in the practical man.

'Anything good?' he asked.

'The biggest thing for years,' said Holmes. 'We have two hours before we need think of starting. I think we might employ it in getting some dinner, and then, Lestrade, we will take the London fog out of your throat by giving you a breath of the pure night-air of Dartmoor. Never been there? Ah, well, I don't suppose you will forget your first visit.'

WE ALL THREE SHOOK HANDS . . .

Illustration by Sidney Paget for the *Strand Magazine*, March, 1902.

14 ❖ THE HOUND OF THE BASKERVILLES

One of Sherlock Holmes's defects—if, indeed, one may call it a defect—was that he was exceedingly loth to communicate his full plans to any other person until the instant of their fulfilment. Partly it came no doubt from his own masterful nature, which loved to dominate and surprise those who were around him. Partly also from his professional caution, which urged him never to take any chances. The result, however, was very trying for those who were acting as his agents and assistants. I had often suffered under it, but never more so than during that long drive in the darkness. The great ordeal was in front of us; at last we were about to make our final effort, and yet Holmes had said nothing, and I could only surmise what his course of action would be. My nerves thrilled with anticipation when at last the cold wind upon our faces and the dark, void spaces on either side of the narrow road told me that we were back upon the moor once again. Every stride of the horses and every turn of the wheels was taking us nearer to our supreme adventure.

Our conversation was hampered by the presence of the driver of the hired wagonette, so that we were forced to talk of trivial matters when our nerves were tense with emotion and anticipation. It was a relief to me, after that unnatural restraint, when we at last passed Frankland's house and knew that we were drawing near to the Hall and to the scene of action. We did not drive up to the door, but got down near the gate of the avenue. The wagonette was paid off and ordered to return to Coombe Tracey forthwith, while we started to walk to Merripit House.

'Are you armed, Lestrade?'

The little detective smiled. 'As long as I have my trousers, I have a hip-pocket, and as long as I have my hip-pocket I have something in it.'

'Good! My friend and I are also ready for emergencies.'

'You're mighty close about this affair, Mr Holmes. What's the game now?'

'A waiting game.'

'My word, it does not seem a very cheerful place,' said the detective, with a shiver, glancing round him at the gloomy slopes of the hill and at the huge lake of fog which lay over the Grimpen Mire. 'I see the lights of a house ahead of us.'

'That is Merripit House and the end of our journey. I must request you to walk on tiptoe and not to talk above a whisper.'

We moved cautiously along the track as if we were bound for the house, but Holmes halted us when we were about two hundred yards from it.

'This will do,' said he. 'These rocks upon the right make an admirable screen.'

'We are to wait here?'

'Yes, we shall make our little ambush here. Get into this hollow, Lestrade. You have been inside the house, have you not, Watson? Can you tell the position of the rooms? What are those latticed windows at this end?'

'I think they are the kitchen windows.'

'And the one beyond, which shines so brightly?'

'That is certainly the dining-room.'

'The blinds are up. You know the lie of the land best. Creep forward quietly and see what they are doing—but for Heaven's sake don't let them know that they are watched!'

I tiptoed down the path and stooped behind the low wall which surrounded the stunted orchard. Creeping in its shadow, I reached a point whence I could look straight through the uncurtained window.

There were only two men in the room, Sir Henry and Stapleton. They sat with their profiles towards me on either side of the round table. Both of them were smoking cigars, and coffee and wine were in front of them. Stapleton was talking with animation, but the baronet looked pale and distrait. Perhaps the thought of that lonely walk across the ill-omened moor was weighing heavily upon his mind.

As I watched them Stapleton rose and left the room, while Sir Henry filled his glass again and leaned back in his chair, puffing at his cigar. I heard the creak of a door and the crisp sound of boots upon gravel. The steps passed along the path on the other side of the wall under which I crouched. Looking over, I saw the naturalist pause at the door of an out-house in the corner of the orchard. A key turned in a lock, and as he passed in there was a curious scuffling noise from within. He was only a minute or so inside, and then I heard the key turn once more, and he passed me and re-entered the house. I saw him rejoin his guest and I crept quietly back to where my companions were waiting to tell them what I had seen.

'You say, Watson, that the lady is not there?' Holmes asked, when I had finished my report.

'No.'

'Where can she be, then, since there is no light in any other room except the kitchen?'

'I cannot think where she is.'

I have said that over the great Grimpen Mire there hung a dense, white fog. It was drifting slowly in our direction, and banked itself up like a wall on that side of us, low, but thick and well defined. The moon shone on it, and it looked like a great shimmering icefield, with the heads of the distant tors as rocks borne upon its surface. Holmes's face was turned towards it, and he muttered impatiently as he watched its sluggish drift.

'It's moving towards us, Watson.'

'Is that serious?'

'Very serious, indeed—the one thing upon earth which could have disarranged my plans. He can't be very long now. It is already ten o'clock. Our success and even his life may depend upon his coming out before the fog is over the path.'

99
100   The night was clear and fine above us. The stars shone cold and bright, while a half-moon bathed the whole scene in a soft, uncertain light. Before us lay the dark bulk of the house, its serrated roof and bristling chimneys hard outlined against the silver-spangled sky. Broad bars of golden light from the lower windows stretched across the orchard and the moor. One of them was suddenly shut off. The servants had left the kitchen. There only remained the lamp in the dining-room where the two men, the murderous host and the unconscious guest, still chatted over their cigars.

Every minute that white woolly plain which covered one-half of the moor was drifting closer and closer to the house. Already the first thin wisps of it were curling across the golden

99 *The night was clear and fine above us.* "Fair weather at all but our extreme western and northern stations," the London *Times* reported of the weather on Friday, October 19, 1888. "Fine weather is . . . likely to continue in most districts, with fog in many parts of England."

100 *a half-moon bathed the whole scene.* The moon may well have bathed the whole scene after ten o'clock (Holmes: "It is already ten o'clock"); it rose at 5:23 P.M., set at 5:37 A.M., but it was *not* a half-moon—it was full on that very day.

square of the lighted window. The farther wall of the orchard was already invisible, and the trees were standing out of a swirl of white vapour. As we watched it the fog-wreaths came crawling round both corners of the house and rolled slowly into one dense bank, on which the upper floor and the roof floated like a strange ship upon a shadowy sea. Holmes struck his hand passionately upon the rock in front of us, and stamped his feet in his impatience.

'If he isn't out in a quarter of an hour the path will be covered. In half an hour we won't be able to see our hands in front of us.'

'Shall we move farther back upon higher ground?'

'Yes, I think it would be as well.'

So as the fog-bank flowed onwards we fell back before it until we were half a mile from the house, and still that dense white sea, with the moon silvering its upper edge, swept slowly and inexorably on.

'We are going too far,' said Holmes. 'We dare not take the chance of his being overtaken before he can reach us. At all costs we must hold our ground where we are.' He dropped on his knees and clapped his ear to the ground. 'Thank heaven, I think that I hear him coming.'

A sound of quick steps broke the silence of the moor. Crouching among the stones, we stared intently at the silver-tipped bank in front of us. The steps grew louder, and through the fog, as through a curtain, there stepped the man whom we were awaiting. He looked round him in surprise as he emerged into the clear, starlit night. Then he came swiftly along the path, passed close to where we lay, and went on up the long slope behind us. As he walked he glanced continually over either shoulder, like a man who is ill at ease.

'Hist' cried Holmes, and I heard the sharp click of a cocking pistol. 'Look out! It's coming!'

HE LOOKED ROUND HIM IN SURPRISE AS HE EMERGED INTO THE CLEAR, STARLIT NIGHT.

Illustration by Sidney Paget for the *Strand Magazine*, March, 1902.

101 *threw himself face downwards upon the ground.* "Picayune and piddling derogators sneer at Lestrade who threw himself upon the ground in terror after beholding the horrendous hound—but sprang to his feet, immediately thereafter, and ran to the aid of Sir Henry Baskerville," Mr. Elliot Kimball wrote in "Watson's Neurosis." "At basis, courage has nothing in common with a positive manifestation, like the flow of gastric juice, or the twitch of a muscle fiber; it is, essentially, a subjective revelation of a NEGATION: the *repression* of a biological common denominator called FEAR. Confronted with the hideous unknown, Lestrade succumbed, momentarily, to dread (an entirely human reaction)—but rose above that devastating paralysis—and such behavior is *admirable* in the courageous little man. He who is too stupid to know fear is senseless, not brave; the man who knows fear, and finds it within him to subdue that fear is courageous, and deserves commendation for the feat."

. . . BUT NOT SUCH A HOUND AS MORTAL EYES
HAVE EVER SEEN.

Illustration by Sidney Paget for the *Strand Magazine*, March, 1902.

There was a thin, crisp, continuous patter from somewhere in the heart of that crawling bank. The cloud was within fifty yards of where we lay, and we glared at it, all three, uncertain what horror was about to break from the heart of it. I was at Holmes's elbow, and I glanced for an instant at his face. It was pale and exultant, his eyes shining brightly in the moonlight. But suddenly they started forward in a rigid, fixed stare, and his lips parted in amazement. At the same instant Lestrade gave a yell of terror and threw himself face downwards **101** upon the ground. I sprang to my feet, my inert hand grasping my pistol, my mind paralysed by the dreadful shape which had sprung out upon us from the shadows of the fog. A hound it was, an enormous coal-black hound, but not such a hound as mortal eyes have ever seen. Fire burst from its open mouth, its eyes glowed with a smouldering glare, its muzzle and hackles and dewlap were outlined in flickering flame. Never in the delirious dream of a disordered brain could anything more savage, more appalling, more hellish, be conceived than that dark form and savage face which broke upon us out of the wall of fog.

With long bounds the huge black creature was leaping down the track, following hard upon the footsteps of our friend. So paralysed were we by the apparition that we allowed him to pass before we had recovered our nerve. Then Holmes and I both fired together, and the creature gave a hideous howl, which showed that one at least had hit him. He did not pause, however, but bounded onwards. Far away on the path we saw Sir Henry looking back, his face white in the moonlight, his hands raised in horror, glaring helplessly at the frightful thing which was hunting him down.

But that cry of pain from the hound had blown all our fears to the winds. If he was vulnerable he was mortal, and if we could wound him we could kill him. Never have I seen a man run as Holmes ran that night. I am reckoned fleet of foot, but he outpaced me as much as I outpaced the little professional. In front of us as we flew up the track we heard

NEVER HAVE I SEEN A MAN RUN AS HOLMES RAN THAT NIGHT.

Miss Jane Jackson's diorama of the pursuit on the moor as displayed at Madame Tussaud's Wax Museum on the Marylebone Road, London. Dr. Edward J. Van Liere has written ("Sherlock Holmes and Doctor Watson, Perennial Athletes") that "Watson's statement . . . bespeaks high praise of Holmes as an exceptionally fast man. Watson, as a college student, had doubtless seen first-class track men perform, but nevertheless he distinctly implies that Holmes as a runner was in a class by himself."

scream after scream from Sir Henry and the deep roar of the hound. I was in time to see the beast spring upon its victim, hurl him to the ground and worry at his throat. But the next instant Holmes had emptied five barrels of his revolver into the creature's flank. With a last howl of agony and a vicious snap in the air it rolled upon its back, four feet pawing furiously, and then fell limp upon its side. I stooped, panting, and pressed my pistol to the dreadful, shimmering head, but it was useless to press the trigger. The giant hound was dead.

Sir Henry lay insensible where he had fallen. We tore away his collar, and Holmes breathed a prayer of gratitude when we saw that there was no sign of a wound and that the rescue had been in time. Already our friend's eyelids shivered and he made a feeble effort to move. Lestrade thrust his brandy-flask between the baronet's teeth, and two frightened eyes were looking up at us.

'My God!' he whispered. 'What was it? What, in Heaven's name, was it?'

'It's dead, whatever it is,' said Holmes. 'We've laid the family ghost once and for ever.'

In mere size and strength it was a terrible creature which was lying stretched before us. It was not a pure bloodhound and it was not a pure mastiff; but it appeared to be a combination of the two—gaunt, savage, and as large as a small lioness. Even now, in the stillness of death, the huge jaws seemed to be dripping with a bluish flame, and the small, deep-set, cruel eyes were ringed with fire. I placed my hand upon the glowing muzzle, and as I held them up my own fingers smouldered and gleamed in the darkness.

'Phosphorus,' I said.

'A cunning preparation of it,' said Holmes, sniffing at the dead animal. 'There is no smell which might have interfered with his power of scent. We owe you a deep apology, Sir Henry, for having exposed you to this fright. I was prepared for a hound, but not for such a creature as this. And the fog gave us little time to receive him.'

102

102 *it appeared to be a combination of the two.* "From its gigantic size I would hazard that there was more likely some Great Dane or Scottish Wolfhound mixture involved," Mr. Stuart Palmer wrote in "Notes on Certain Evidences of Caniphobia in Mr. Sherlock Holmes and His Associates."

And the late Owen Frisbie commented ("On the Origin of the Hound of the Baskervilles"): "Dr. Watson's statement that the Hound appeared to be a combination of bloodhound and mastiff does not hold up. . . . We conclude that we must look to the staghound for size and drive, and to the bloodhound for ability and will to take the line of a human."

. . . HOLMES HAD EMPTIED FIVE BARRELS OF HIS REVOLVER INTO THE CREATURE'S FLANK.

Illustration by Sidney Paget for the *Strand Magazine*, April, 1902. The flank, as Mr. Robert Keith Leavitt has commented in "Annie Oakley in Baker Street," is "A far from surely lethal portion of the beast, and one from which any reflected bullet, or any passing clear through the body, might have hit Sir Henry Baskerville with grievous or even fatal results." And surely Watson should have written "five *chambers*" rather than "five barrels" of Holmes' revolver?

'PHOSPHORUS,' I SAID.

Illustration by Sidney Paget for the *Strand Magazine*, April, 1902. But phosphorus is "a very deadly poison to dog and man," as Mr. Stuart Palmer pointed out in "Notes of Certain Evidences of Caniphobia in Mr. Sherlock Holmes and His Associates." Mr. D. A. Redmond has suggested ("Some Chemical Problems in the Canon") that the substance was not phosophorus but barium sulphide.

'You have saved my life.'

'Having first endangered it. Are you strong enough to stand?'

'Give me another mouthful of that brandy, and I shall be ready for anything. So! Now, if you will help me up. What do you propose to do?'

'To leave you here. You are not fit for further adventures tonight. If you will wait, one or other of us will go back with you to the Hall.'

He tried to stagger to his feet; but he was still ghastly pale and trembling in every limb. We helped him to a rock, where he sat shivering with his face buried in his hands.

'We must leave you now,' said Holmes. 'The rest of our work must be done, and every moment is of importance. We have our case, and now we only want our man.'

'It's a thousand to one against our finding him at the house,' he continued, as we retraced our steps swiftly down the path. 'Those shots must have told him that the game was up.'

'We were some distance off, and this fog may have deadened them.'

'He followed the hound to call him off—of that you may be certain. No, no, he's gone by this time! But we'll search the house and make sure.'

The front door was open, so we rushed in and hurried from room to room, to the amazement of a doddering old man-servant, who met us in the passage. There was no light save in the dining-room, but Holmes caught up the lamp, and left no corner of the house unexplored. No sign could we see of the man whom we were chasing. On the upper floor, however, one of the bedroom doors was locked.

'There's someone in here!' cried Lestrade. 'I can hear a movement. Open this door!'

A faint moaning and rustling came from within. Holmes struck the door just over the lock with the flat of his foot, and it flew open. Pistol in hand, we all three rushed into the room.

But there was no sign within it of that desperate and defiant villain whom we expected to see. Instead we were faced by an object so strange and so unexpected that we stood for a moment staring at it in amazement.

The room had been fashioned into a small museum, and the walls were lined by a number of glass-topped cases full of that collection of butterflies and moths the formation of which had been the relaxation of this complex and dangerous man. In the centre of this room there was an upright beam, which had been placed at some period as a support for the old worm-eaten balk of timber which spanned the roof. To this post a figure was tied, so swathed and muffled in the sheets which had been used to secure it that one could not for the moment tell whether it was that of a man or a woman. One towel passed round the throat, and was secured at the back of the pillar. Another covered the lower part of the face and over it two dark eyes—eyes full of grief and shame and a dreadful questioning—stared back at us. In a minute we had torn off the gag, unswathed the bonds, and Mrs Stapleton sank upon the floor in front of us. As her beautiful head fell upon her chest I saw the clear red weal of a whip-lash across her neck.

'The brute!' cried Holmes. 'Here, Lestrade, your brandy-bottle! Put her in the chair! She has fainted from ill-usage and exhaustion.'

She opened her eyes again. 'Is he safe?' she asked. 'Has he escaped?'

'He cannot escape us, madam.'

'No, no, I did not mean my husband. Sir Henry? Is he safe?'

'Yes.'

'And the hound?'

'It is dead.'

She gave a long sigh of satisfaction. 'Thank God! Thank God! Oh, this villain! See how he has treated me!' She shot her arms out from her sleeves, and we saw with horror that they were all mottled with bruises. 'But this is nothing—nothing! It is my mind and soul that he has tortured and defiled. I could endure it all, ill-usage, solitude, a life of deception, everything, as long as I could still cling to the hope that I had his love, but now I know that in this also I have been his dupe and his tool.' She broke into passionate sobbing as she spoke.

'You bear him no good-will, madam,' said Holmes. 'Tell us, then, where we shall find him. If you have ever aided him in evil, help us now and so atone.'

'There is but one place where he can have fled,' she answered. 'There is an old tin mine on an island in the heart of the Mire. It was there that he kept his hound, and there also he had made preparations so that he might have a refuge. That is where he would fly.'

The fog-bank lay like white wool against the window. Holmes held the lamp towards it.

'See,' said he. 'No one could find his way into the Grimpen Mire tonight.'

She laughed and clapped her hands. Her eyes and teeth gleamed with fierce merriment.

'He may find his way in, but never out,' she cried. 'How can he see the guiding wands tonight? We planted them together, he and I, to mark the pathway through the Mire. Oh, if I could only have plucked them out today! Then indeed you would have had him at your mercy.'

It was evident to us that all pursuit was in vain until the fog had lifted. Meanwhile we left Lestrade in possession of the house, while Holmes and I went back with the baronet to Baskerville Hall. The story of the Stapletons could no longer be withheld from him, but he took the blow bravely when he learned the truth about the woman whom he had loved. But the shock of the night's adventures had shattered his nerves, and before morning he lay delirious in a high fever, under the care of Dr Mortimer. The two of them were destined to travel together round the world before Sir Henry had become once more the hale, hearty man that he had been before he became master of that ill-omened estate.

And now I come rapidly to the conclusion of this singular narrative, in which I have tried to make the reader share those dark fears and vague surmises which clouded our lives so long, and ended in so tragic a manner. On the morning after the death of the hound the fog had lifted and we were guided by Mrs Stapleton to the point where they had found a pathway through the bog. It helped us to realize the horror of this

'THE BRUTE!' CRIED HOLMES. 'HERE, LESTRADE, YOUR BRANDY-BOTTLE!'

Illustration by Sidney Paget for the *Strand Magazine*, April, 1902.

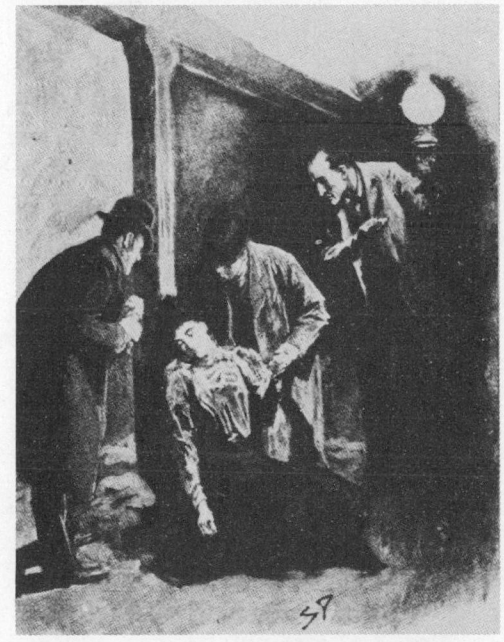

HE HELD AN OLD BLACK BOOT IN THE AIR.

Illustration by Sidney Paget for the *Strand Magazine*, April, 1902.

. . . A STAPLE AND CHAIN, WITH A QUANTITY OF GNAWED BONES, SHOWED WHERE THE ANIMAL HAD BEEN CONFINED.

Illustration by Sidney Paget for the *Strand Magazine*, April, 1902.

woman's life when we saw the eagerness and joy with which she laid us on her husband's track. We left her standing upon the thin peninsula of firm, peaty soil which tapered out into the widespread bog. From the end of it a small wand planted here and there showed where the path zigzagged from tuft to tuft of rushes among those green-scummed pits and foul quagmires which barred the way to the stranger. Rank reeds and lush, slimy water-plants sent an odour of decay and a heavy miasmatic vapour into our faces, while a false step plunged us more than once thigh-deep into the dark, quivering mire, which shook for yards in soft undulations around our feet. Its tenacious grip plucked at our heels as we walked, and when we sank into it it was as if some malignant hand was tugging us down into those obscene depths, so grim and purposeful was the clutch in which it held us. Once only we saw a trace that someone had passed that perilous way before us. From amid a tuft of cotton-grass which bore it up out of the slime some dark thing was projecting. Holmes sank to his waist as he stepped from the path to seize it, and had we not been there to drag him out he could never have set his foot upon firm land again. He held an old black boot in the air. 'Meyers, Toronto,' was printed on the leather inside.

'It is worth a mud bath,' said he. 'It is our friend Sir Henry's missing boot.'

'Thrown there by Stapleton in his flight.'

'Exactly. He retained it in his hand after using it to set the hound upon his track. He fled when he knew the game was up, still clutching it. And he hurled it away at this point of his flight. We know at least that he came so far in safety.'

But more than that we were never destined to know, though there was much which we might surmise. There was no chance of finding footsteps in the mire, for the rising mud oozed swiftly in upon them, but as we at last reached firmer ground beyond the morass we all looked eagerly for them. But no slightest sign of them ever met our eyes. If the earth told a true story, then Stapleton never reached that island of refuge towards which he struggled through the fog upon that last night. Somewhere in the heart of the great Grimpen Mire, down in the foul slime of the huge morass which had sucked him in, this cold and cruel-hearted man is for ever buried.

Many traces we found of him in the bog-girt island where he had hid his savage ally. A huge driving-wheel and a shaft half-filled with rubbish showed the position of an abandoned mine. Beside it were the crumbling remains of the cottages of the miners, driven away, no doubt, by the foul reek of the surrounding swamp. In one of these a staple and chain, with a quantity of gnawed bones, showed where the animal had been confined. A skeleton with a tangle of brown hair adhering to it lay among the *débris*.

'A dog!' said Holmes. 'By Jove, a curly-haired spaniel. Poor Mortimer will never see his pet again. Well, I do not know that this place contains any secret which we have not already fathomed. He could hide his hound, but he could not hush its voice, and hence came those cries which even in daylight were not pleasant to hear. On an emergency he could keep the hound in the out-house at Merripit, but it was always a risk, and it was only on the supreme day, which he regarded as the end of all his efforts, that he dared do it. This paste in the tin is no doubt the luminous mixture with which the creature was daubed. It was suggested, of course, by the story of the family hell-hound, and by the desire to frighten old Sir Charles to death. No wonder the poor devil of a convict ran and screamed, even as our friend did, and as we ourselves might have done, when he saw such a creature bounding through the darkness of the moor upon his track. It was a cunning device, for, apart from the chance of driving your victim to his death, what peasant would venture to inquire too closely into such a creature should he get sight of it, as many have done, upon the moor! I said it in London, Watson, and I say it again now, that never yet have we helped to hunt down a more dangerous man than he who is lying yonder'— he swept his long arm towards the huge mottled expanse of green-splotched bog which stretched away until it merged into the russet slopes of the moor.

15   ◆   A RETROSPECTION

It was the end of November, and Holmes and I sat, upon a raw and foggy night, on either side of a blazing fire in our sitting-room in Baker Street. Since the tragic upshot of our visit to Devonshire he had been engaged in two affairs of the utmost importance, in the first of which he had exposed the atrocious conduct of Colonel Upwood in connection with the **105** famous card scandal of the Nonpareil Club, while in the **106** second he had defended the unfortunate Mme Montpensier **107** from the charge of murder which hung over her in connection with the death of her step-daughter, Mlle Carère, the young lady who, as it will be remembered, was found six months later alive and married in New York. My friend was in excellent spirits over the success which had attended a succession of difficult and important cases, so that I was able to induce him to discuss the details of the Baskerville mystery. I had waited patiently for the opportunity, for I was aware that he would never permit cases to overlap, and that his clear and logical mind would not be drawn from its present work to dwell upon memories of the past. Sir Henry and Dr Mortimer were, however, in London, on their way to that long voyage which had been recommended for the restoration of his shattered nerves. They had called upon us that very afternoon, so that it was natural that the subject should come up for discussion.

'The whole course of events,' said Holmes, 'from the point of view of the man who called himself Stapleton, was simple and direct, although to us, who had no means in the beginning of knowing the motives of his actions and could only learn part of the facts, it all appeared exceedingly complex. I have had the advantage of two conversations with Mrs

103 *Beside it were the crumbling remains of the cottages of the miners.* It is pleasant to report that the Vitifer tin mines and the picturesquely named Golden Door Mine all do lie on a direct line between Grimpen-Grimspound and Merripit, the tiny village where Stapleton lived at Merripit House in the heart of the moor (see our "very-large"-scale map).

104 *'By Jove, a curly-haired spaniel.* "Sheer brilliance," Mr. Stuart Palmer commented in "Notes on Certain Evidences of Caniphobia in Mr. Sherlock Holmes and His Associates," "since the skeletal remains of a spaniel differ slightly if at all from any other small dog."

And Mr. Benjamin Clark wrote of this discovery ("Dr. Mortimer Before the Bar"): Watson "makes it clear that access to the island where the hound was chained was possible only to those who knew of and followed Stapleton's markers. That an animal could stray to the island, in such a miasmatic atmosphere, leaping from tuft to tuft, his power of scent useless, since 'rising mud oozed swiftly' over footsteps, is frankly incredible. It would be even more incredible to assume that if the hound was loose on the day of the spaniel's disappearance he had killed the small dog and carried him back to his lair as he was led thither by Stapleton. For it is obvious that the hound alone could not find his way through the bog without perishing like the moorland ponies. Moreover, meat, in those days, was not so hard to come by as to suggest that Stapleton would undertake the highly hazardous step of kidnaping a neighbor's dog to feed his brute. With all such impossible solutions removed, we are left with one which, improbable though it may appear at first, not only provides the only possible answer to explain the presence of the spaniel's remains on the island but opens the way to explaining certain otherwise baffling points in what Holmes told Lestrade was 'the biggest thing for years.' *The only way in the least degree likely that* the spaniel could have penetrated the bog was, of course, in the company of his master, Dr. James Mortimer. If this contention is valid, it necessarily follows that Dr. Mortimer must have been in league with Stapleton; for even if the doctor had come on the path to the island by chance he would, if he were an honest man, have immediately publicized his discovery of the hound."

105 *Colonel Upwood.* Dr. Julian Wolff, in his *Practical Handbook of Sherlockian Heraldry*, has identified Colonel Upwood with Sir William Gordon Cumming, at one time a lieutenant-colonel in the Scots Guards. In 1891 Sir William (according to the Literary Supplement of the London *Times*, February 28, 1948, and April 24, 1948) was accused of cheating at cards and the Prince of Wales himself was subpoenaed as a witness. Largely because of the Prince's evidence, Sir William lost the case. The Baccarat Case, as it was known, "aroused great interest and many people were convinced of Sir William's innocence."

106 *the Nonpareil Club.* In "Who Was Cecil Forrester?", Mr. Robert Keith Leavitt has noted that "Nonpareil is the English name for a type [size], corresponding to our six-point. Obviously the Nonpareil Club was a discreet, footnote kind of club composed of journalists." For a pastiche of this adventure by Adrian M. Conan Doyle, see "The Adventure of the Abbas Ruby" in *The Exploits of Sherlock Holmes.*

107 *the unfortunate Mme Montpensier.* For a pastiche of this adventure, by Adrian M. Conan Doyle and John Dickson Carr, see "The Adventure of the Black Baronet" in *The Exploits of Sherlock Holmes.*

108 *Yorkshire.* This largest of the English counties borders on the North Sea and extends almost to the Irish Sea. Besides having been, most probably, the county of Holmes' birth, it has many other literary associations: with Caedmon, Laurence Sterne, and the Brontë sisters.

'PERHAPS YOU WOULD KINDLY GIVE ME A SKETCH OF THE
COURSE OF EVENTS FROM MEMORY.'

Illustration by Sidney Paget for the *Strand Magazine*, April, 1902.

Stapleton, and the case has now been so entirely cleared up that I am not aware that there is anything which has remained a secret to us. You will find a few notes upon the matter under the heading B in my indexed list of cases.'

'Perhaps you would kindly give me a sketch of the course of events from memory.'

'Certainly, though I cannot guarantee that I carry all the facts in my mind. Intense mental concentration has a curious way of blotting out what has passed. The barrister who has his case at his fingers' end, and is able to argue with an expert upon his own subjects, finds that a week or two of the courts will drive it all out of his head once more. So each of my cases displaces the last, and Mlle Carère has blurred my recollection of Baskerville Hall. Tomorrow some other little problem may be submitted to my notice, which will in turn dispossess the fair French lady and the infamous Upwood. So far as the case of the Hound goes, however, I will give you the course of events as nearly as I can, and you will suggest anything which I may have forgotten.

'My inquiries show beyond all question that the family portrait did not lie, and that this fellow was indeed a Baskerville. He was a son of that Rodger Baskerville, the younger brother of Sir Charles, who fled with a sinister reputation to South America, where he was said to have died unmarried. He did, as a matter of fact, marry, and had one child, this fellow, whose real name is the same as his father. He married Beryl Garçia, one of the beauties of Costa Rica, and, having purloined a considerable sum of public money, he changed his name to Vandeleur and fled to England, where he established a school in the east of Yorkshire. His reason for attempting this special line of business was that he had struck up an acquaintance with a consumptive tutor upon the voyage home, and that he had used this man's ability to make the undertaking a success. Fraser, the tutor, died, however, and the school which had begun well, sank from disrepute into infamy. The Vandeleurs found it convenient to change their

name to Stapleton, and he brought the remains of his fortune, his schemes for the future, and his taste for entomology to the south of England. I learn at the British Museum that he was a recognized authority upon the subject, and that the name of Vandeleur has been permanently attached to a certain moth which he had, in his Yorkshire days, been the first to describe.

'We now come to that portion of his life which has proved to be of such intense interest to us. The fellow had evidently made inquiry, and found that only two lives intervened between him and a valuable estate. When he went to Devonshire his plans were, I believe, exceedingly hazy, but that he meant mischief from the first is evident from the way in which he took his wife with him in the character of his sister. The idea of using her as a decoy was clearly already in his mind, though he may not have been certain how the details of his plot were to be arranged. He meant in the end to have the estate, and he was ready to use any tool or run any risk for that end. His first act was to establish himself as near to his ancestral home as he could, and his second was to cultivate a friendship with Sir Charles Baskerville and with the neighbours.

'The baronet himself told him about the family hound, and so prepared the way for his own death. Stapleton, as I will continue to call him, knew that the old man's heart was weak, and that a shock would kill him. So much he had learned from Dr Mortimer. He had heard also that Sir Charles was superstitious, and had taken this grim legend very seriously. His ingenious mind instantly suggested a way by which the baronet could be done to death, and yet it would be hardly possible to bring home the guilt to the real murderer.

'Having conceived the idea, he proceeded to carry it out with considerable finesse. An ordinary schemer would have been content to work with a savage hound. The use of artificial means to make the creature diabolical was a flash of genius upon his part. The dog he bought in London from Ross and Mangles, the dealers in Fulham Road. It was the strongest and most savage in their possession. He brought it down by the North Devon line, and walked a great distance over the moor, so as to get it home without exciting any remarks. He had already on his insect hunts learned to penetrate the Grimpen Mire, and so had found a safe hiding-place for the creature. Here he kennelled it and waited his chance.

'But it was some time coming. The old gentleman could not be decoyed outside of his grounds at night. Several times Stapleton lurked about with his hound, but without avail. It was during these fruitless quests that he, or rather his ally, was seen by peasants, and that the legend of the demon dog received a new confirmation. He had hoped that his wife might lure Sir Charles to his ruin, but here she proved unexpectedly independent. She would not endeavour to entangle the old gentleman in a sentimental attachment which might deliver him over to his enemy. Threats and even, I am sorry to say, blows failed to move her. She would have nothing to do with it, and for a time Stapleton was at a deadlock.

'He found a way out of his difficulties through the chance that Sir Charles, who had conceived a friendship for him, made him the minister of his charity in the case of this unfortunate woman, Mrs Laura Lyons. By representing himself as a single man, he acquired complete influence over her, and he gave her to understand that in the event of her obtaining a divorce from her husband he would marry her. His plans were suddenly brought to a head by his knowledge that Sir Charles was about to leave the Hall on the advice of Dr Mortimer, with whose opinion he himself pretended to coincide. He must act at once, or his victim might get beyond his power. He therefore put pressure upon Mrs Lyons to write this letter, imploring the old man to give her an interview on the evening before his departure for London. He then, by a specious argument, prevented her from going, and so had the chance for which he had waited.

'Driving back in the evening from Coombe Tracey, he was in time to get his hound, to treat it with his infernal paint, and to bring the beast round to the gate at which he had reason to expect that he would find the old gentleman waiting. The dog, incited by its master, sprang over the wicket-gate and pursued the unfortunate baronet, who fled screaming down the Yew Alley. In that gloomy tunnel it must indeed have been a dreadful sight to seee that huge black creature, with its flaming jaws and blazing eyes, bounding after its victim. He fell dead at the end of the alley from heart disease and terror. The hound had kept upon the grassy border while the baronet had run down the path, so that no track but the man's was visible. On seeing him lying still the creature had probably approached to sniff at him, but, finding him dead, had turned away again. It was then that it left the print which was actually observed by Dr Mortimer. The hound was called off and hurried away to its lair in the Grimpen Mire, and a mystery was left which puzzled the authorities, alarmed the countryside, and finally brought the case within the scope of our observation.

'So much for the death of Sir Charles Baskerville. You perceive the devilish cunning of it, for really it would be almost impossible to make a case against the real murderer. His only accomplice was one who could never give him away, and the grotesque, inconceivable nature of the device only served to make it more effective. Both of the women concerned in the case, Mrs Stapleton and Mrs Laura Lyons, were left with a strong suspicion against Stapleton. Mrs Stapleton knew that he had designs upon the old man, and also of the existence of the hound. Mrs Lyons knew neither of these things, but had been impressed by the death occurring at the time of an uncancelled appointment which was only known to him. However, both of them were under his influence, and he had nothing to fear from them. The first half of his task was successfully accomplished, but the more difficult still remained.

'It is possible that Stapleton did not know of the existence of an heir in Canada. In any case he would very soon learn it from his friend Dr Mortimer, and he was told by the latter all details about the arrival of Henry Baskerville. Stapleton's first idea was that this young stranger from Canada might possibly be done to death in London without coming down to Devonshire at all. He distrusted his wife ever since she had refused to help him in laying a trap for the old man, and he dared not leave her long out of his sight for fear he should lose his influence over her. It was for this reason that he took her to London with him. They lodged, I find, at the Mex-

109 borough Private Hotel, in Craven Street, which was actually one of those called upon by my agent in search of evidence.

109 *Craven Street.* In Craven Street, leading from the Victoria Embankment to the Strand, there are several small hotels and restaurants which cater almost exclusively to short-term visitors to the metropolis.

Here he kept his wife imprisoned in her room while he, disguised in a beard, followed Dr Mortimer to Baker Street, and afterwards to the station and to the Northumberland Hotel. His wife had some inkling of his plans; but she had such a fear of her husband—a fear founded upon brutal ill-treatment—that she dare not write to warn the man whom she knew to be in danger. If the letter should fall into Stapleton's hands her own life would not be safe. Eventually, as we know, she adopted the expedient of cutting out the words which would form the message, and addressing the letter in a disguised hand. It reached the baronet, and gave him the first warning of his danger.

'It was very essential for Stapleton to get some article of Sir Henry's attire, so that, in case he was driven to use the dog, he might always have the means of setting him upon his track. With characteristic promptness and audacity he set about this at once, and we cannot doubt that the boots or chambermaid of the hotel was well bribed to help him in his design. By **110** chance, however, the first boot which was procured for him was a new one, and, therefore, useless for his purpose. He then had it returned and obtained another—a most instructive incident, since it proved conclusively to my mind that we were dealing with a real hound, as no other supposition could explain this anxiety to obtain an old boot and this indifference to a new one. The more *outré* and grotesque an incident is the more carefully it deserves to be examined, and the very point which appears to complicate a case is, when duly considered and scientifically handled, the one which is most likely to elucidate it.

'Then we had the visit from our friends next morning, shadowed always by Stapleton in the cab. From his knowledge **111** of our rooms and of my appearance, as well as from his general conduct, I am inclined to think that Stapleton's career of crime has been by no means limited to this single Baskerville affair. It is suggestive that during the last three years there have been four considerable burglaries in the West country, for none of which was any criminal ever arrested. The last of these, at Folkestone Court, in May, was remarkable for the cold-blooded pistolling of the page, who surprised the masked and solitary burglar. I cannot doubt that Stapleton recruited his waning resources in this fashion, and that for years he has been a desperate and dangerous man.

'We had an example of his readiness of resource that morning when he got away from us so successfully, and also of his audacity in sending back my own name to me through the cabman. From that moment he understood that I had taken over the case in London, and that therefore there was no chance for him there. He returned to Dartmoor and awaited the arrival of the baronet.'

'One moment!' said I. 'You have, no doubt, described the sequence of events correctly, but there is one point which you have left unexplained. What became of the hound when its master was in London?'

'I have given some attention to this matter, and it is undoubtedly of importance. There can be no question that Stapleton had a confidant, though it is unlikely that he ever placed himself in his power by sharing all his plans with him. There was an old manservant at Merripit House, whose name was Anthony. His connection with the Stapletons can be

110 *well bribed to help him in his design.* Mr. Benjamin S. Clark, pursuing his theory that Dr. James Mortimer was Stapleton's accomplice, wrote ("Dr. Mortimer Before the Bar"): "Now of course it is obvious that Mortimer stole the boot. The alternative explanation that one of the hotel employees had been bribed by Stapleton cannot bear the light of close scrutiny. In the first place, the risk to Stapleton, even disguised, was so great as to make it out of proportion to the gaining of a few days (for, as a visitor to Baskerville Hall, he could surely accomplish the same purpose more easily). Also, with no preliminaries (Stapleton had only just arrived in London) to walk into a strange hotel and find a bribable 'boots' to run the major risk of losing his job for a bribe that could not be suspiciously large, was a feat that could hardly be given better odds than a thousand to one."

111 *shadowed always by Stapleton in the cab.* "The simple question as to why Stapleton (taking the Holmesian explanation at face value) was following the two has apparently never been seriously examined," Mr. Clark continued. "We know that the entomologist had located Sir Henry's hotel (one boot had already been stolen) and he had spotted the visit to 221B Baker Street. Why, then, should he be running the risk of shadowing his victim *back* to his hotel? It will be recalled that Dr. Mortimer and Sir Henry were strolling along casually, looking in shop windows, and it was a fair guess that the hotel was then or later their destination, since Stapleton *knew* that they hadn't checked out. It goes beyond the bounds of credibility that Stapleton was following them in the fear that Holmes had advised the consulting of Scotland Yard. (If such had been the case Sir Henry and the doctor wouldn't have been walking.) No! Stapleton waited outside Holmes' office against the possibility that a diversion might be necessary, as indeed it was, since Holmes had just been told of the disappearance of the boot and was obviously suspicious. On leaving Baker Street, Dr. Mortimer presumably signaled to his confederate in the cab that (as anticipated) he was in need of some move to distract the detective, because—and this cannot be repeated too often—Mortimer had at all costs to be kept free from any taint of suspicion. Stapleton's dash in the cab was successful in accomplishing this purpose. Thenceforward he occupied all of Holmes' attention, and Dr. Mortimer, in the popular phrase, was 'as safe as a church.'"

112 *that a criminal expert should be able to distinguish.* The late Christopher Morley thought it probable that Holmes may even have written a monograph *Upon the Distinction Between the Various Perfumes: A Monograph on Natural and Synthetic Fragrances with Analyses of the 75 Primary Scents and a Memorandum by J. H. W. on the Types of Women Likely to Favour the Several Modes of Allure.*

traced for several years, as far back as the schoolmastering days, so that he must have been aware that his master and mistress were really husband and wife. This man has disappeared and has escaped from the country. It is suggestive that Anthony is not a common name in England, while Antonio is so in all Spanish or Spanish-American countries. The man, like Mrs Stapleton herself, spoke good English, but with a curious lisping accent. I have myself seen this old man cross the Grimpen Mire by the path which Stapleton had marked out. It is very probable, therefore, that in the absence of his master it was he who cared for the hound, though he may never have known the purpose for which the beast was used.

'The Stapletons then went down to Devonshire, whither they were soon followed by Sir Henry and you. One word now as to how I stood myself at that time. It may possibly recur to your memory that when I examined the paper upon which the printed words were fastened I made a close inspection for the watermark. In doing so I held it within a few inches of my eyes, and was conscious of a faint smell of the scent known as white jessamine. There are seventy-five perfumes, which it is very necessary that a criminal expert should be **112** able to distinguish from each other, and cases have more than once within my own experience depended upon their prompt recognition. The scent suggested the presence of a lady, and already my thoughts began to turn towards the Stapletons. Thus I had made certain of the hound, and had guessed at the criminal before ever we went to the West country.

'It was my game to watch Stapleton. It was evident, however, that I could not do this if I were with you, since he would be keenly on his guard. I deceived everybody, therefore, yourself included, and I came down secretly when I was supposed to be in London. My hardships were not so great as you imagine, though such trifling details must never interfere with the investigation of a case. I stayed for the most part at Coombe Tracey, and only used the hut upon the moor when it was necessary to be near the scene of action. Cartwright had come down with me, and in his disguise as a country boy he was of great assistance to me. I was dependent upon him for food and clean linen. When I was watching Stapleton, Cartwright was frequently watching you, so that I was able to keep my hand upon all the strings.

'I have already told you that your reports reached me rapidly, being forwarded instantly from Baker Street to Coombe Tracey. They were of great service to me, and especially that one incidentally truthful piece of biography of Stapleton's. I was able to establish the identity of the man and the woman, and knew at last exactly how I stood. The case had been considerably complicated through the incident of the escaped convict and the relations between him and the Barrymores. This also you cleared up in a very effective way, though I had already come to the same conclusions from my own observations.

'By the time that you discovered me upon the moor I had a complete knowledge of the whole business, but I had not a case which could go to a jury. Even Stapleton's attempt upon Sir Henry that night, which ended in the death of the unfortunate convict did not help us much in proving murder against our man. There seemed to be no alternative but to catch him red-handed, and to do so we had to use Sir Henry, alone and apparently unprotected, as a bait. We did so, and at the cost of a severe shock to our client we succeeded in completing our case and driving Stapleton to his destruction. That Sir Henry should have been exposed to this is, I must confess, a reproach to my management of the case, but we had no means of foreseeing the terrible and paralysing spectacle which the beast presented, nor could we predict the fog which enabled him to burst upon us at such short notice. We succeeded in our object at a cost which both the specialist and Dr Mortimer assure me will be a temporary one. A long journey may enable our friend to recover not only from his shattered nerves but also from his wounded feelings. His love for the lady was deep and sincere, and to him the saddest part of all this black business was that he should have been deceived by her.

'It only remains to indicate the part which she had played throughout. There can be no doubt that Stapleton exercised an influence over her which may have been love or may have been fear, or very possibly both, since they are by no means incompatible emotions. It was, at least, absolutely effective. At his command she consented to pass as his sister, though he found the limits of his power over her when he endeavoured to make her the direct accessory to murder. She was ready to warn Sir Henry so far as she could without implicating her husband, and again and again she tried to do so. Stapleton himself seems to have been capable of jealousy, and when he saw the baronet paying court to the lady, even though it was part of his own plan, still he could not help interrupting with a passionate outburst which revealed the fiery soul which his self-contained manner so cleverly concealed. By encouraging the intimacy he made it certain that Sir Henry would frequently come to Merripit House, and that he would sooner or later get the opportunity which he desired. On the day of the crisis, however, his wife turned suddenly against him. She had learned something of the death of the convict, and she knew that the hound was being kept in the out-house on the evening that Sir Henry was coming to dinner. She taxed her husband with his intended crime, and a furious scene followed, in which he showed her for the first time that she had a rival in his love. Her fidelity turned in an instant to bitter hatred, and he saw that she would betray him. He tied her up, therefore, that she might have no chance of warning Sir Henry, and he hoped, no doubt, that when the whole countryside put down the baronet's death to the curse of his family, as they certainly would do, he could win his wife back to accept an accomplished fact, and to keep silent upon what she knew. In this I fancy that in any case he made a miscalculation, and that, if we had not been there, his doom would none the less have been sealed. A woman of Spanish blood does not condone such an injury so lightly. And now, my dear Watson, without referring to my notes, I cannot give you a more detailed account of this curious case. I do not know that anything essential has been left unexplained.'

'He could not hope to frighten Sir Henry to death, as he had done the old uncle, with his bogy hound.'

'The beast was savage and half-starved. If its appearance did not frighten its victim to death, at least it would paralyse the resistance which might be offered.'

113 '*It is a formidable difficulty.* "Based on Holmes' interpretation of the case, the difficulty was not only formidable but well-nigh insuperable," Mr. Benjamin S. Clark wrote in "Dr. Mortimer Before the Bar." "The detective suggested that there were three possible courses Stapleton might pursue, two of which we can safely dismiss as ridiculous: namely, that Stapleton would appear in London in an 'elaborate disguise,' or furnish an accomplice with proofs and papers as an heir and retain a claim on part of the income. The third course proposed was that Stapleton claim the property from South America, establish his identity before the British authorities there, and so obtain the fortune without ever coming to England at all. The rather considerable 'rub' here, which seems to have been overlooked, is that not too many years earlier, after marrying the Costa Rican beauty, Beryl Garcia (presumably under the name of Baskerville, which as a claimant he would have to resume), Stapleton 'purloined a considerable sum of public money,' and, changing his name to Vandeleur, fled to England. However, if we meet this difficulty by shifting the locale to, say Australia, such a course of action, while it had infinitely more merit than the other two, was still not without serious risks. . . . But assume that, instead of the claim to the estate originating with Stapleton, a trusted friend of the family—lately executor of Sir Charles Baskerville's will—sees to it that documents or letters are found which indicate the possible existence of a hitherto unknown heir. Of course this friend will inform the court of his discovery, at the same time furnishing a clue to the whereabouts of the lucky individual . . ."

114 *the De Reszkes?* Jean de Reszke (1850–1925), Polish operatic tenor and teacher, was known for both lyric and Wagnerian roles. He was the leading tenor of the Metropolitan Opera, New York, from 1891 to 1901. His brother Edouard de Reszke (1855–1917) was a leading bass at the Metropolitan from 1891 to 1903.

According to Mr. Harold Schonberg, the music critic of *The New York Times*, "the only time the De Reszkes . . . ever sang together in *Les Huguenots* was at the Metropolitan Opera House, and the performance in question took place on November 25, 1896." On the other hand, Mr. Anthony Boucher, in correspondence with Dr. Charles Goodman, has stated that the De Reszkes sang the opera together 21 times from 1891 to 1901 at the Metropolitan alone, not counting touring engagement in London and elsewhere.

Elsewhere ("The Records of Baker Street") Mr. Boucher has asked: "Were the De Reszkes [Holmes'] real reason for wishing to hear *Les Huguenots?* How charmingly convincing a contralto may be in such roles [as the page Urbain] the modern audience may judge from the performances of Hertha Glaz; how brilliantly difficult is the music of Urbain's great entrance air, *Nobles seigneurs!* may be perceived from Victor's recent reissue of Louise Homer's 1905 recording

'No doubt. There only remains one difficulty. If Stapleton came into the succession, how could he explain the fact that he, the heir, had been living unannounced under another name so close to the property? How could he claim it without causing suspicion and inquiry?'

113 'It is a formidable difficulty, and I fear that you ask too much when you expect me to solve it. The past and the present are within the field of my inquiry, but what a man may do in the future is a hard question to answer. Mrs Stapleton has heard her husband discuss the problem on several occasions. There were three possible courses. He might claim the property from South America, establish his identity before the British authorities there, and so obtain the fortune without ever coming to England at all; or he might adopt an elaborate disguise during the short time that he need be in London; or, again, he might furnish an accomplice with the proofs and papers, putting him in as heir, and retaining a claim upon some proportion of his income. We cannot doubt, from what we know of him, that he would have found some way out of the difficulty. And now, my dear Watson, we have had some weeks of severe work, and for one evening, I think, we may turn our thoughts into more pleasant channels. I have a box for *Les Huguenots*. Have you

114 heard the De Reszkes? Might I trouble you then to be ready in half an hour, and we can stop at Marcini's for a little dinner on the way?'

'MIGHT I TROUBLE YOU THEN TO BE READY IN
HALF AN HOUR . . .'

Illustration by Sidney Paget for the *Strand Magazine*, April, 1902.

(Victor Heritage Series 15-1011). Irene Adler's spectacular entrance as Urbain must have been unforgettable; and it is more than understandable that a man might haunt later performances of *Les Huguenots,* half in vain hopes of finding a new portrayal to eclipse her memory, half to nurse the pleasant pain of recollection."

Auctorial and Bibliographical Note: In the March of 1901, Conan Doyle and his friend Fletcher Robinson (who later wrote *The Chronicles of Addington Peace;* London: Harper, 1905) were on a golfing holiday at the Royal Links Hotel at Cromer in Norfolk. "One raw Sunday afternoon when a wind rushed off the North Sea," while lounging in the comfort of their private sitting room, Robinson began telling legends of Dartmoor, one of which concerned a spectral hound. By the end of the month, Conan Doyle was at work on the story, which, at first, he had no intention of making an adventure of Sherlock Holmes. Then he thought to himself, "Why should I invent a character when I had him already in the form of Holmes?" It has been said that the novel is the only tale of Sherlock Holmes, long or short, in which the story dominates Holmes rather than Holmes dominating the story; in any case, critics are generally agreed that it is by far the best of the four Holmes novels, and many consider it Holmes' (and Watson's) finest hour. (The readers of the *Observer* placed *The Hound of the Baskervilles* second on their list of the favorite Holmes novels and short stories.) Conan Doyle had suggested that Robinson collaborate with him on the novel; although Robinson refused the offer, Conan Doyle acknowledged his debt by dedicating the novel to him. The dedication is curious in that three versions of it exist. The first is a footnote in the *Strand:*

> This story owes its inception to my friend, Mr. Fletcher Robinson, who has helped me both in the general plot and in the local details. —A. C. D.

In the first book edition, published by George Newnes, Ltd., London, in 1902, the dedication reads:

> My dear Robinson:
> It was to your account of a West-Country legend that this tale owes its inception. For this and for your help in detail all thanks
> Yours most truly,
> A. Conan Doyle
> Hindhead
> Haslemere

So it appears in all subsequent English, as opposed to the American, editions. But when, in the same year, 1902, McClure Phillips of New York published the first American edition, the dedication was slightly changed. It read:

> My dear Robinson:
> It was your account of a west country legend which first suggested the idea of this little tale to my mind.
> For this, and for the help which you have given me in its evolution, all thanks.
> Yours most truly,
> A. Conan Doyle

The apparent confusion here was at last clarified by Sir Arthur himself. In his Preface to *The Complete Sherlock Holmes,* he wrote:

> Then came the *Hound of the Baskervilles.* It arose from a remark by that fine fellow whose premature death was a loss to the world, Fletcher Robinson, that there was a spectral dog near his home on Dartmoor. That remark was the inception of the book, but I should add that the plot and every word of the actual narrative was my own.

When the complete manuscript of the novel was sent to McClure, Phillips in New York, they in turn handed the sheets, after they had served their purposes, to the American News Company for advertising purposes. Single sheets were sent to booksellers all over the country, where many of them were framed and used for window displays. Over the years, Mr. Lew D. Feldman of the House of El Dieff was able to obtain a number of these sheets for collectors. The only complete chapter known to have survived is XI ("The Man on the Tor"). It consists of 16 pages, folio. Auctioned in New York City on March 18, 1946, it brought $115. It is presently owned by the New York Public Library.

37

THE ADVENTURE OF THE COPPER BEECHES

[Friday, April 5, to Saturday, April 20, 1889]

1 *the* Daily Telegraph. The first day of the adventure was therefore not a Sunday.

2 *these little records of our cases.* Holmes later asks, "What do the public . . . care about the finer shades of analysis and deduction" displayed in them. This must mean that the case took place after December, 1887, when *A Study in Scarlet* was published in *Beeton's Christmas Annual*. Since the case, as we shall see, could not have taken place later than the spring of 1890, and Watson's second published case, *The Sign of the Four*, did not reach the public until the November of that year, Holmes must also have been thinking of Watsonian chronicles still in manuscript.

3 *causes célèbres,* French: celebrated cases.

4 *my friend's singular character.* "Watson was a keen student of human nature, however obtuse he may have pictured himself to be—for strategic reasons—in his stories," Mr. Robert Winthrop Adams wrote in "John H. Watson, M.D., Characterologist." "He well knew that, as Epictetus remarked, 'What a man sayeth of thee concerneth him that sayeth it more than it concerneth thee.' So he shrugged off Holmes' criticism with a mild disclaimer and kept right on putting 'colour and life' into his statements. In his very next [published] story ["Silver Blaze"] he polishes up the report of an almost routine investigation until it shines as one of the very best short stories in the Saga. What luck for us that Watson, with characteristic British obstinacy, refused to let the gleaming light of his story-telling genius be hidden under the bushel of his friend's dominant intellectuality!"

"YOU HAVE ERRED, PERHAPS," HE OBSERVED, TAKING UP A GLOWING CINDER WITH THE TONGS . . .

Illustration by Sidney Paget for the *Strand Magazine*, June, 1892.

"TO the man who loves art for its own sake," remarked Sherlock Holmes, tossing aside the advertisement sheet of the *Daily Telegraph*, " it is frequently in its least important and lowliest manifestations that the keenest pleasure is to be derived. It is pleasant to me to observe, Watson, that you have so far grasped this truth that in these little records of our cases which you have been good enough to draw up, and, I am bound to say, occasionally to embellish, you have given prominence not so much to the many *causes célèbres* and sensational trials in which I have figured, but rather to those incidents which may have been trivial in themselves, but which have given room for those faculties of deduction and of logical synthesis which I have made my special province."

" And yet," said I, smiling, " I cannot quite hold myself absolved from the charge of sensationalism which has been urged against my records."

" You have erred, perhaps," he observed, taking up a glowing cinder with the tongs, and lighting with it the long cherrywood pipe which was wont to replace his clay when he was in a disputatious rather than a meditative mood— " you have erred, perhaps, in attempting to put colour and life into each of your statements, instead of confining yourself to the task of placing upon record that severe reasoning from cause to effect which is really the only notable feature about the thing."

" It seems to me that I have done you full justice in the matter," I remarked with some coldness, for I was repelled by the egotism which I had more than once observed to be a strong factor in my friend's singular character.

" No, it is not selfishness or conceit," said he, answering, as was his wont, my thoughts rather than my words. " If I claim full justice for my art, it is because it is an impersonal thing—a thing beyond myself.   Crime is common.   Logic is rare.   Therefore it is upon the logic rather than upon the crime that you should dwell.   You have degraded what should have been a course of lectures into a series of tales." **5**

It was a cold morning of the early spring, and we sat **6** after breakfast on either side of a cheery fire in the old room in Baker Street.   A thick fog rolled down between **7** the lines of dun-coloured houses, and the opposing windows loomed like dark, shapeless blurs, through the heavy yellow wreaths.   Our gas was lit, and shone on the white cloth, and glimmer of china and metal, for the table had not been cleared yet.   Sherlock Holmes had been silent all the morning, dipping continuously into the advertisement columns of a succession of papers, until at last, having apparently given up his search, he had emerged in no very sweet temper to lecture me upon my literary shortcomings.

" At the same time," he remarked, after a pause, during which he had sat puffing at his long pipe and gazing down into the fire, " you can hardly be open to a charge of sensationalism, for out of these cases which you have been so kind as to interest yourself in, a fair proportion do not treat of crime, in its legal sense, at all.   The small matter in which I endeavoured to help the King of Bohemia, the singular experience of Miss Mary Sutherland, the problem connected with the man with the twisted lip, and the incident of the noble bachelor, were all matters which are outside the pale of the law.   But in avoiding the sensational, I **8** fear that you may have bordered on the trivial."

" The end may have been so," I answered, " but the methods I hold to have been novel and of interest."

" Pshaw, my dear fellow, what do the public, the great unobservant public, who could hardly tell a weaver by his tooth or a compositor by his left thumb, care about the **9-10** finer shades of analysis and deduction ! But, indeed, if you are trivial, I cannot blame you, for the days of the great cases are past.   Man, or at least criminal man, has lost all enterprise and originality.   As to my own little practice, it seems to be degenerating into an agency for recovering lost lead pencils and giving advice to young ladies from boarding-schools.   I think that I have touched bottom at last, however. This note I had this morning **11** marks my zero point, I fancy.   Read it ! "   He tossed a crumpled letter across to me.

It was dated from Montague Place upon the preceding **12** evening, and ran thus :

" DEAR MR. HOLMES,—I am very anxious to consult you as to whether I should or should not accept a situation which has been offered to me as governess.   I shall call at half-past ten to-morrow, if I do not inconvenience you.— Yours faithfully,

" VIOLET HUNTER." **13**

" Do you know the young lady ? " I asked.
" Not I."
" It is half-past ten now."

5 *a series of tales.*" Although Holmes allegedly did not approve of Watson's methods, he was sometimes pleased to fill out the record. In "The Adventure of the Norwood Builder," he says: "Well, well, I daresay that a couple of rabbits would account for both the blood and for the charred ashes. If you ever write an account, Watson, you can make rabbits serve your turn." And when Holmes applied himself to the task of writing up one of his adventures ("The Blanched Soldier") with no help from his Boswell, even he had to admit that "having taken my pen in my hand, I do begin to realize that the matter must be presented in such a way as may interest the reader."

6 *It was a cold morning of the early spring.* In your editor's view, it was *Friday, April 5, 1889,* a day on which the temperature fell to a low of 37.8°. Said the London *Times:* "Temperature . . . falling decidedly over England. . . . A very cold night is likely to occur over England tonight." Virtually all other commentators except Christ and Walter, who date the adventure 1891, believe that it took place in the spring of 1890.

7 *the old room in Baker Street.* All chronologists except your editor would seem to agree that Watson was married at the time of this adventure. This presents them with a difficulty, since Watson is here completely silent about a wife or professional duties and appears to be living in Baker Street, not for a few days only, but for the entire fortnight covered by the adventure. In our view, the adventure was the last shared by the doctor and the detective before Watson's marriage to Mary Morstan *circa* May 1, 1889.

8 *all matters which are outside the pale of the law.* "Leaving aside the question of whether Neville St. Clair had not been obtaining money under false pretences, there is as clear a case of bigamy in the incident of 'The Noble Bachelor' as one could wish for," Mr. S. T. L. Harbottle wrote in "Sherlock Holmes and the Law."

9 *a weaver by his tooth.* "Probably the best description [of a weaver's tooth] is given by Burket in *Oral Medicine*, Lippincott, Philadelphia, 1946, on page 573," Professor Remsen Ten Eyck Schenck wrote in "The Effect of Trades Upon the Body." " 'Tailors and seamstresses who are in the habit of cutting their thread with their teeth may show a characteristic tooth defect which consists of sharp V-shaped notches in the middle of the incisal edge of the incisors. The notching is most prominent in the upper incisors. When it is no longer possible to cut the thread because of loss of tooth structure, then the teeth on the opposite side are utilized.' "

10 *a compositor by his left thumb.* "A compositor's left thumb is often characterized by the formation of a callus on the tip, often with abrasion of the skin lower down, across the 'ball' of the digit," Professor Schenck continued. "In setting type, the 'stick' is held in the left hand and the type placed in it with the right. As each piece of type is dropped into the stick, the left thumb slides it into position against the last addition, and then holds the accumulated mass snugly in a corner."

11 *This note I had this morning.* Additional evidence that the opening day of the case was not a Sunday.

12 *Montague Place.* Not to be confused with Montague *Street*, where Holmes had rooms when he opened his practice in London. Montague Place runs at right angles to Montague Street, but like it, is a street which borders the British Museum.

13 "VIOLET. Holmes' hobby of collecting Violets has been noted by many commentators, many of whom suppose that women so named had some special importance to him. Miss Esther Longfellow, in "The Distaff Side of Baker Street" found the supposition "absurd when we face the probability that every tenth woman in England was, and still is, called Violet."

14 *the affair of the blue carbuncle.* Chronologically minded readers will of course have noted that this case must follow "A Scandal in Bohemia," "A Case of Identity," "The Man with the Twisted Lip," "The Adventure of the Noble Bachelor," and, now, "The Adventure of the Blue Carbuncle."

" 'THAT WILL DO,' SAID HE; 'I COULD NOT ASK FOR ANYTHING BETTER. CAPITAL! CAPITAL!' "

Illustration by Sidney Paget for the *Strand Magazine*, June, 1892.

" Yes, and I have no doubt that is her ring."

" It may turn out to be of more interest than you think. **14** You remember that the affair of the blue carbuncle, which appeared to be a mere whim at first, developed into a serious investigation.   It may be so in this case also."

" Well, let us hope so ! But our doubts will very soon be solved, for here, unless I am much mistaken, is the person in question."

As he spoke the door opened, and a young lady entered the room. She was plainly but neatly dressed, with a bright, quick face, freckled like a plover's egg, and with the brisk manner of a woman who has had her own way to make in the world.

" You will excuse my troubling you, I am sure," said she, as my companion rose to greet her ; " but I have had a very strange experience, and as I have no parents or relations of any sort from whom I could ask advice, I thought that perhaps you would be kind enough to tell me what I should do."

" Pray take a seat, Miss Hunter.   I shall be happy to do anything that I can to serve you."

I could see that Holmes was favourably impressed by the manner and speech of his new client.   He looked her over in his searching fashion, and then composed himself with his lids drooping and his finger-tips together to listen to her story.

" I have been a governess for five years," said she, " in the family of Colonel Spence Munro, but two months ago the Colonel received an appointment at Halifax, in Nova Scotia, and took his children over to America with him, so that I found myself without a situation.   I advertised and I answered advertisements, but without success.   At last the little money which I had saved began to run short, and I was at my wits' end as to what I should do.

" There is a well-known agency for governesses in the West End called Westaway's, and there I used to call about once a week in order to see whether anything had turned up which might suit me.   Westaway was the name of the founder of the business, but it is really managed by Miss Stoper.   She sits in her own little office, and the ladies who are seeking employment wait in an ante-room, and are then shown in one by one, when she consults her ledgers, and sees whether she has anything which would suit them.

" Well, when I called last week I was shown into the little office as usual, but I found that Miss Stoper was not alone.   A prodigiously stout man with a very smiling face, and a great heavy chin which rolled down in fold upon fold over his throat, sat at her elbow with a pair of glasses on his nose, looking very earnestly at the ladies who entered.   As I came in he gave quite a jump in his chair, and turned quickly to Miss Stoper :

" ' That will do,' said he ; ' I could not ask for anything better. Capital ! Capital !' He seemed quite enthusiastic and rubbed his hands together in the most genial fashion.   He was such a comfortable-looking man that it was quite a pleasure to look at him.

" ' You are looking for a situation, miss ? ' he asked.

" ' Yes, sir.'

" ' As governess ? '

" ' Yes, sir.'

" ' And what salary do you ask ? '

" ' I had four pounds a month in my last place with Colonel Spence Munro.'

" ' Oh, tut, tut ! sweating—rank sweating !' he cried, throwing his fat hands out into the air like a man who is in a boiling passion. ' How could anyone offer so pitiful a sum to a lady with such attractions and accomplishments ? '

" ' My accomplishments, sir, may be less than you imagine,' said I. ' A little French, a little German, music and drawing——' **15**

" ' Tut, tut !' he cried. This is all quite beside the question. The point is, have you or have you not the bearing and deportment of a lady ? There it is in a nut-shell. If you have not, you are not fitted for the rearing of a child who may some day play a considerable part in the history of the country. But if you have, why, then how could any gentleman ask you to condescend to accept anything under the three figures ? Your salary with me, madam, would commence at a hundred pounds a year.'

" You may imagine, Mr. Holmes, that to me, destitute as I was, such an offer seemed almost too good to be true. The gentleman, however, seeing perhaps the look of incredulity upon my face, opened a pocket-book and took out a note. **16**

" ' It is also my custom,' said he, smiling in the most pleasant fashion until his eyes were just two shining slits, amid the white creases of his face, ' to advance to my young ladies half their salary beforehand, so that they may meet any little expenses of their journey and their ward-robe.'

" It seemed to me that I had never met so fascinating and so thoughtful a man. As I was already in debt to my tradesmen, the advance was a great convenience, and yet there was something unnatural about the whole transac-tion which made me wish to know a little more before I quite committed myself.

" ' May I ask where you live, sir ? ' said I.

" ' Hampshire. Charming rural place. The Copper Beeches, five miles on the far side of Winchester. It is the most lovely country, my dear young lady, and the dearest old country house.'

" ' And my duties, sir ? I should be glad to know what they would be.'

" ' One child—one dear little romper just six years old. Oh, if you could see him killing cockroaches with a slipper ! Smack ! smack ! smack ! Three gone before you could wink !' He leaned back in his chair and laughed his eyes into his head again.

" I was a little startled at the nature of the child's amuse-ment, but the father's laughter made me think that perhaps he was joking.

" ' My sole duties, then,' I asked, ' are to take charge of a single child ? '

" ' No, no, not the sole, not the sole, my dear young lady,' he cried. ' Your duty would be, as I am sure your good sense would suggest, to obey any little commands which my wife might give, provided always that they were such commands as a lady might with propriety obey.

15 '*A little French, a little German, music and drawing* ——' "We may be sure [that Violet Hunter] knew of [Holmes'] French ancestry, of his knowledge of German, of his love for music, and that art was in his blood," Mr. Isaac S. George wrote in "Violet the Hunter." "She simply parades for Holmes' benefit the talents she feels he would appreciate in a woman as a companion; but she is careful not to overdo it. . . . She uses Rucastle's words to emphasize her qualities as a potential wife and mother."

16 *took out a note*. What note? Not a £50 note, surely: it would be unheard of to advance a full half year's salary. "Furthermore," the late A. Carson Simpson wrote in *Numismatics in the Canon*, Part II, "we know that he was thinking in terms of the more usual *quarterly* salary payments, rather than annual, for his second offer was of '£30 a quarter, or £120 a year.' On the basis of his original offer, her quarterly pay would have been £25 and half of that is £12-10-0; there were no single notes for either of these amounts, nor any combination of notes for the latter figure." Weighing the prob-abilities, Mr. Simpson voted for a £10 note, an approximation of £12-10-0.

" ' OH, IF YOU COULD SEE HIM KILLING COCKROACHES WITH A SLIPPER! SMACK! SMACK! SMACK!' "

Illustration by G. da Fonseca from *Premières Aven-tures de Sherlock Holmes;* Paris: Librarie Félix Juvier, n.d.

17 *It has been considered artistic.* Dr. Richard Asher is another commentator who believes that Miss Hunter had designs on Holmes. In "Holmes and the Fair Sex" he writes: "Throwing modesty to the winds, [Violet Hunter] pointed out her charms to [Holmes] in a singularly brazen fashion. . . . No doubt she wished to draw Holmes' attention to her best feature and keep his eyes off her face which Watson records was 'freckled like a plover's egg.'"

You see no difficulty, heh?'

"'I should be happy to make myself useful.'

"'Quite so. In dress now, for example! We are faddy people, you know—faddy, but kind-hearted. If you were asked to wear any dress which we might give you, you would not object to our little whim. Heh?'

"'No,' said I, considerably astonished at his words.

"'Or to sit here, or sit there, that would not be offensive, to you?'

"'Oh, no.'

"'Or to cut your hair quite short before you come to us?'

"I could hardly believe my ears. As you may observe, Mr. Holmes, my hair is somewhat luxuriant, and of a rather peculiar tint of chestnut. It has been considered **17** artistic. I could not dream of sacrificing it in this off-hand fashion.

"'I am afraid that that is quite impossible,' said I. He had been watching me eagerly out of his small eyes, and I could see a shadow pass over his face as I spoke.

"'I am afraid that it is quite essential,' said he. 'It is a little fancy of my wife's, and ladies' fancies, you know, madam, ladies' fancies must be consulted. And so you won't cut your hair?'

"'No, sir, I really could not,' I answered firmly.

"'Ah, very well; then that quite settles the matter. It is a pity, because in other respects you would really have done very nicely. In that case, Miss Stoper, I had best inspect a few more of your young ladies.'

"The manageress had sat all this while busy with her papers without a word to either of us, but she glanced at me now with so much annoyance upon her face that I could not help suspecting that she had lost a handsome commission through my refusal.

'Do you desire your name to be kept upon the books?' she asked.

"'If you please, Miss Stoper.'

"'Well, really, it seems rather useless, since you refuse the most excellent offers in this fashion,' said she sharply. 'You can hardly expect us to exert ourselves to find another such opening for you. Good day to you, Miss Hunter.' She struck a gong upon the table, and I was shown out by the page.

"Well, Mr. Holmes, when I got back to my lodgings and found little enough in the cupboard, and two or three bills upon the table, I began to ask myself whether I had not done a very foolish thing. After all, if these people had strange fads, and expected obedience on the most extraordinary matters, they were at least ready to pay for their eccentricity. Very few governesses in England are getting a hundred a year. Besides, what use was my hair to me? Many people are improved by wearing it short, and perhaps I should be among the number. Next day I was inclined to think that I had made a mistake, and by the day after I was sure of it. I had almost overcome my pride, so far as to go back to the agency and inquire whether the place was still open, when I received this letter from the gentleman himself. I have it here, and I will read it to you:

" THE COPPER BEECHES, NEAR WINCHESTER.

" DEAR MISS HUNTER,—Miss Stoper has very kindly given me your address, and I write from here to ask you whether you have reconsidered your decision.   My wife is very anxious that you should come, for she has been much attracted by my description of you.   We are willing to give thirty pounds a quarter, or £120 a year, so as to recompense you for any little inconvenience which our fads may cause you.   They are not very exacting after all. My wife is fond of a particular shade of electric blue, and would like you to wear such a dress indoors in the morning.   You need not, however, go to the expense of purchasing one, as we have one belonging to my dear daughter Alice (now in Philadelphia) which would, I should think, fit you very well.   Then, as to sitting here or there, or amusing yourself in any manner indicated, that need cause you no inconvenience.   As regards your hair, it is no doubt a pity, especially as I could not help remarking its beauty during our short interview, but I am afraid that I must remain firm upon this point, and I only hope that the increased salary may recompense you for the loss.   Your duties, as far as the child is concerned, are very light. Now do try to come, and I shall meet you with the dog-cart at Winchester.   Let me know your train.—Yours faithfully,

" JEPHRO RUCASTLE.

" That is the letter which I have just received, Mr. Holmes, and my mind is made up that I will accept it.   I **18** thought, however, that before taking the final step, I should like to submit the whole matter to your consideration."

" Well, Miss Hunter, if your mind is made up, that settles the question," said Holmes, smiling.

" But you would not advise me to refuse ? "

" I confess that it is not the situation which I should like to see a sister of mine apply for."   **19**

" What is the meaning of it all, Mr. Holmes ? "

" Ah, I have no data.   I cannot tell.   Perhaps you have yourself formed some opinion ? "

" Well, there seems to me to be only one possible solution.   Mr. Rucastle seemed to be a very kind, good-natured man.   Is it not possible that his wife is a lunatic, that he desires to keep the matter quiet for fear she should be taken to an asylum, and that he humours her fancies in every way in order to prevent an outbreak."

" That is a possible solution—in fact, as matters stand, it is the most probable one.   But in any case it does not seem to be a nice household for a young lady."

" But the money, Mr. Holmes, the money ! "

" Well, yes, of course, the pay is good—too good.   That is what makes me uneasy.   Why should they give you £120 a year, when they could have their pick for £40 ? There must be some strong reason behind."

" I thought that if I told you the circumstances you would understand afterwards if I wanted your help.   I should feel so much stronger if I felt that you were at the back of me."

18 *my mind is made up that I will accept it.* "It is just here that the lady gives herself away completely," Mr. Isaac S. George wrote in "Violet the Hunter." "As soon as she finishes reading the letter, without *asking or waiting* for advice; in fact before Holmes *has a chance to open his mouth*, she says flatly: "My mind is made up that I will accept it.' . . . Of *all* people, she consults a private detective for advice about accepting a position *after she has decided to take it.*"

19 *which I should like to see a sister of mine apply for.*" Commentators have taken this statement to mean that Holmes had a sister or sisters as well as a brother (or brothers): "May we venture on a very long shot and surmise, as Mr. Morley has also done, that Sherlock's remark . . . points to Holmes' sisters who, in the collapse of the family fortune, were perhaps forced to the genteel drudgery of governessing?" Messrs. J. H. and Humfrey Michell wrote in "Sherlock Holmes the Chemist."

Indeed, Mr. H. B. Williams has surmised that Violet Hunter was Holmes' (half) sister. "If the father of Mycroft and Sherlock had passed away and the mother had remarried a cousin, let us say (as was often the custom in those days) [Violet Hunter might well have been Holmes' half-sister]" ("Half-Sister; Half Mystery").

Mr. Robert Schutz is in full agreement with this view, as he states in "Half-Sister; No Mystery": "There is no direct evidence to contradict the assumption that Holmes' mother married a Mr. Hunter after the death of Sherlock's father, and gave birth to a daughter named Violet, twelve years after the birth of Sherlock."

HOLMES SHOOK HIS HEAD GRAVELY.

Illustration by Sidney Paget for the *Strand Magazine*, June, 1892.

20 *A fortnight went by.* Watson would seem, if he was speaking quite literally, to be saying that he is writing as of the fifteenth "case day."

21 *"I can't make bricks without clay."* In the adventure of "The Crooked Man" Holmes admits that his Biblical knowledge is a little rusty. But here he is probably not misquoting Exodus, 5:7: "Ye shall no more give the people straw to make bricks." Bricks *are* made from clay; Holmes was merely stating a fact.

22 *late one night.* The night of the fifteenth day —or perhaps a day or two later?

23 *Do come!* "And the phrase 'Do come!'," Mr. Isaac S. George wrote in "Violet the Hunter" "—is that a message from a person in trouble to a consulting detective? from a patient to a doctor? from a lawyer to a client or from one businessman to another? It most certainly is *not*. It is a cordial social message; a sugary, sentimental message often used by hospitable hostesses, ardent swains and romantically-inclined — yes, even designing — women."

24 *my analysis of the acetones.* "Acetone is a single chemical substance, not a category," Professor Remsen Ten Eyck Schenck wrote in "Baker Street Fables." "The term analysis could not meaningfully be employed here, either, since it implies the identification of the ingredients of a mixture. The statement is thus nonsensical from two standpoints."
To this Mr. Leon S. Holstein replied (" '7. Knowledge of Chemistry—Profound' "): "It is true that

" Oh, you may carry that feeling away with you. I assure you that your little problem promises to be the most interesting which has come my way for some months. There is something distinctly novel about some of the features. If you should find yourself in doubt or in danger——"

" Danger ! What danger do you foresee ? "

Holmes shook his head gravely. " It would cease to be a danger if we could define it," said he. '' But at any time, day or night, a telegram would bring me down to your help."

" That is enough." She rose briskly from her chair with the anxiety all swept from her face. " I shall go down to Hampshire quite easy in my mind now. I shall write to Mr. Rucastle at once, sacrifice my poor hair to-night, and start for Winchester to-morrow." With a few grateful words to Holmes she bade us both good night, and bustled off upon her way.

" At least," said I, as we heard her quick, firm step descending the stairs, " she seems to be a young lady who is very well able to take care of herself."

" And she would need to be," said Holmes gravely ; " I am much mistaken if we do not hear from her before many days are past."

20 It was not very long before my friend's prediction was fulfilled. A fortnight went by, during which I frequently found my thoughts turning in her direction, and wondering what strange side-alley of human experience this lonely woman had strayed into. The unusual salary, the curious conditions, the light duties, all pointed to something abnormal, though whether a fad or a plot, or whether the man were a philanthropist or a villain, it was quite beyond my powers to determine. As to Holmes, I observed that he sat frequently for half an hour on end, with knitted brows and an abstracted air, but he swept the matter away with a wave of his hand when I mentioned it. " Data ! data ! data ! " he cried impatiently. " I can't make bricks **21** without clay." And yet he would always wind up by muttering that no sister of his should ever have accepted such a situation.

The telegram which we eventually received came late **22** one night, just as I was thinking of turning in, and Holmes was settling down to one of those all-night researches which he frequently indulged in, when I would leave him stooping over a retort and a test-tube at night, and find him in the same position when I came down to breakfast in the morning. He opened the yellow envelope, and then, glancing at the message, threw it across to me.

" Just look up the trains in Bradshaw," said he, and turned back to his chemical studies.

The summons was a brief and urgent one.

" Please be at the Black Swan Hotel at Winchester at **23** midday to-morrow," it said. " Do come ! I am at my wits' end.

" HUNTER."

" Will you come with me ? " asked Holmes, glancing up.

" I should wish to."

" Just look it up, then."

" There is a train at half-past nine," said I, glancing over my Bradshaw. " It is due at Winchester at 11.30."

" That will do very nicely.   Then perhaps I had better postpone my analysis of the acetones, as we may need to be **24** at our best in the morning."

By eleven o'clock the next day we were well upon our **25** way to the old English capital.   Holmes had been buried in the morning papers all the way down, but after we had **26** passed the Hampshire border he threw them down, and began to admire the scenery.   It was an ideal spring day, **27** a light blue sky, flecked with little fleecy white clouds drifting across from west to east.   The sun was shining very brightly, and yet there was an exhilarating nip in the air, which set an edge to a man's energy.   All over the country-side, away to the rolling hills around Aldershot, **28** the little red and grey roofs of the farm-steadings peeped out from amidst the light green of the new foliage.

" Are they not fresh and beautiful ? " I cried, with all the enthusiasm of a man fresh from the fogs of Baker Street.

But Holmes shook his head gravely.

" Do you know, Watson," said he, " that it is one of the curses of a mind with a turn like mine that I must look at everything with reference to my own special subject.   You look at these scattered houses, and you are impressed by their beauty.   I look at them, and the only thought which comes to me is a feeling of their isolation, and of the impunity with which crime may be committed there."

acetone is acetone and is not a categorical designation; but the adverse critics should know that there is a series of products usually designated as the *ketone* or *acetone oils*, and in common parlance these are often referred to as *acetones*. It was the analysis of these materials that Violet Hunter's telegram caused to be put aside for more pressing matters."

And Mr. D. A. Redmond has suggested ("Some Chemical Problems in the Canon") that Holmes said, not "acetones" but "acetone bodies": "The adrenalin content of the blood, we know, rises suddenly during severe stresses of emotions, or intense muscular activity. The acetone or ketone bodies indicate this as well as certain metabolic conditions. For this reason the Master may have been investigating the *acetone bodies* in blood— we know his intense interest in blood [A *Study in Scarlet*]."

25 *the next day.* The sixteenth case day, at the earliest.

26 *the morning papers.* If this was indeed the sixteenth case day, as it appears to have been, it could not have been a Sunday, and the first day of the adventure was therefore not a Saturday.

27 *an ideal spring day.* In our view, the day was Saturday, April 20, 1889. *Whitaker's Almanack* tells us that no rain fell on that day and that there was a southwest wind. Since the *Times* of London of course published no Sunday edition, there was no report on the weather of the 20th in that paper, but the *Times* reported that the preceding day —Friday the 19th—was a day on which "conditions have been fair and genial, and temperature has risen."

"IT IS DUE AT WINCHESTER AT 11.30."

The relevant page in *Bradshaw's Guide*. "Naturally," Lord Dongegall once noted, "Watson does not record what Holmes said to him when they found themselves on a 9:30 A.M. train by which they could not reach Winchester until 52 minutes after they were supposed to meet Miss Hunter at the Black Swan. On the other hand, Watson may have had a second look at Bradshaw's, in time to get an un-breakfasted, infuriated Holmes on the 7:50, ariving at Winchester at 10:09 A.M. Had this been the case, however, Miss Hunter would hardly have been 'waiting for us.' "

28 *Aldershot.* Aldershot, to be visited by Holmes and Watson in the adventure of "The Crooked Man," is a military depot of long standing. "It lies to the west of the main road connecting Farnborough in the north with Farnham in the south," Mr. Michael Harrison wrote in *In the Footsteps of Sherlock Holmes*, "and is enclosed within a fairly regular rectangle formed by the main road, on the east, the Basingstroke Canal on the north, and the curving Blackwater River on the west and south. . . . Severely utilitarian in design, no less than in function, Aldershot was built and developed as a great camp; such town as there was existed merely to supply the needs of the barracks . . ."

29 *and none the wiser.* "Holmes' reaction was decidedly unEnglish," Professor Clarke Olney commented in "The Literacy of Sherlock Holmes"; "French, perhaps, even, one is tempted to say, Russian."

30 *the facts as far as we know them.* Compare Holmes' remark to Watson in "The Adventure of the Missing Three-Quarter": "I had seven different schemes for getting a glimpse of that telegram."

31 *an inn of repute. Baedeker's Guide to Britain* (1897 edition) does in fact recommend the Black Swan as a good place to stay when visiting historic Winchester.

" Good heavens ! " I cried. " Who would associate crime with these dear old homesteads ? "

" They always fill me with a certain horror. It is my belief, Watson, founded upon my experience, that the lowest and vilest alleys in London do not present a more dreadful record of sin than does the smiling and beautiful country-side."

" You horrify me ! "

" But the reason is very obvious. The pressure of public opinion can do in the town what the law cannot accomplish. There is no lane so vile that the scream of a tortured child, or the thud of a drunkard's blow, does not beget sympathy and indignation among the neighbours, and then the whole machinery of justice is ever so close that a word of complaint can set it going, and there is but a step between the crime and the dock. But look at these lonely houses, each in its own fields, filled for the most part with poor ignorant folk who know little of the law. Think of the deeds of hellish cruelty, the hidden wickedness which may go on, year in, year out, in such places, and **29** none the wiser. Had this lady who appeals to us for help gone to live in Winchester, I should never have had a fear for her. It is the five miles of country which makes the danger. Still, it is clear that she is not personally threatened."

" No. If she can come to Winchester to meet us she can get away."

" Quite so. She has her freedom."

" What *can* be the matter, then ? Can you suggest no explanation ? "

" I have devised seven separate explanations, each of **30** which would cover the facts as far as we know them. But which of these is correct can only be determined by the fresh information which we shall no doubt find waiting for us. Well, there is the tower of the Cathedral, and we shall soon learn all that Miss Hunter has to tell."

31 The " Black Swan " is an inn of repute in the High Street, at no distance from the station, and there we found the young lady waiting for us. She had engaged a sitting-room, and our lunch awaited us upon the table.

" I am so delighted that you have come," she said earnestly, " it is so kind of you both ; but indeed I do not know what I should do. Your advice will be altogether invaluable to me."

" Pray tell us what has happened to you."

" I will do so, and I must be quick, for I have promised Mr. Rucastle to be back before three. I got his leave to come into town this morning, though he little knew for what purpose."

" Let us have everything in its due order." Holmes thrust his long thin legs out towards the fire, and composed himself to listen.

" In the first place, I may say that I have met, on the whole, with no actual ill-treatment from Mr. and Mrs. Rucastle. It is only fair to them to say that. But I cannot understand them, and I am not easy in my mind about them."

" What can you not understand ? "

" Their reasons for their conduct. But you shall have

it all just as it occurred.   When I came down Mr. Rucastle
met me here, and drove me in his dog-cart to Copper
Beeches.   It is, as he said, beautifully situated, but it is
not beautiful in itself, for it is a large square block of a
house, whitewashed, but all stained and streaked with
damp and bad weather.   There are grounds round it,
woods on three sides, and on the fourth a field which slopes
down to the Southampton high-road, which curves past
about a hundred yards from the front door.   This ground
in front belongs to the house, but the woods all round are
part of Lord Southerton's preserves.   A clump of copper
beeches immediately in front of the hall door has given its
name to the place.

" I was driven over by my employer, who was as amiable
as ever, and was introduced by him that evening to his wife
and the child.   There was no truth, Mr. Holmes, in the
conjecture which seemed to us to be probable in your
rooms at Baker Street.   Mrs. Rucastle is not mad.   I
found her to be a silent, pale-faced woman, much younger
than her husband, not more than thirty, I should think,
while he can hardly be less than forty-five.   From their
conversation I have gathered that they have been married
about seven years, that he was a widower, and that his only
child by the first wife was the daughter who has gone to
Philadelphia.   Mr. Rucastle told me in private that the
reason why she had left them was that she had an unreasoning aversion to her stepmother.   As the daughter could
not have been less than twenty, I can quite imagine that
her position must have been uncomfortable with her
father's young wife.

" Mrs. Rucastle seemed to me to be colourless in mind
as well as in feature.   She impressed me neither favourably nor the reverse.   She was a nonentity.   It was easy
to see that she was passionately devoted both to her husband and to her little son.   Her light grey eyes wandered
continually from one to the other, noting every little want
and forestalling it if possible.   He was kind to her also in
his bluff boisterous fashion, and on the whole they seemed
to be a happy couple.   And yet she had some secret sorrow,
this woman.   She would often be lost in deep thought,
with the saddest look upon her face.   More than once I
have surprised her in tears.   I have thought sometimes
that it was the disposition of her child which weighed upon
her mind, for I have never met so utterly spoilt and so ill-
natured a little creature.   He is small for his age, with a
head which is quite disproportionately large.   His whole
life appears to be spent in an alternation between savage
fits of passion and gloomy intervals of sulking.   Giving
pain to any creature weaker than himself seems to be his
one idea of amusement, and he shows quite remarkable
talent in planning the capture of mice, little birds, and
insects.   But I would rather not talk about the creature,
Mr. Holmes, and, indeed, he has little to do with my
story."

" I am glad of all details," remarked my friend, " whether
they seem to you to be relevant or not."

" I shall try not to miss anything of importance.   The
one unpleasant thing about the house, which struck me at
once, was the appearance and conduct of the servants.

"I AM SO DELIGHTED THAT YOU HAVE COME,"
SHE SAID EARNESTLY . . .

Illustration by Sidney Paget for the *Strand Magazine*, June, 1892.

There are only two, a man and his wife.   Toller, for that's his name, is a rough, uncouth man, with grizzled hair and whiskers, and a perpetual smell of drink.   Twice since I have been with them he has been quite drunk, and yet Mr. Rucastle seemed to take no notice of it.   His wife is a very tall and strong woman with a sour face, as silent as Mrs. Rucastle, and much less amiable.   They are a most unpleasant couple, but fortunately I spend most of my time in the nursery and my own room, which are next to each other in one corner of the building.

" For two days after my arrival at the Copper Beeches my life was very quiet ; on the third, Mrs. Rucastle came down just after breakfast and whispered something to her husband.

" ' Oh yes,' said he, turning to me, ' we are very much obliged to you, Miss Hunter, for falling in with our whims so far as to cut your hair.   I assure you that it has not detracted in the tiniest iota from your appearance.   We shall now see how the electric blue dress will become you.   You will find it laid out upon the bed in your room and if you would be so good as to put it on we should both be extremely obliged.'

" The dress which I found waiting for me was of a peculiar shade of blue.   It was of excellent material, a sort of beige, but it bore unmistakable signs of having been worn before.   It could not have been a better fit if I had been measured for it.   Both Mr. and Mrs. Rucastle expressed a delight at the look of it which seemed quite exaggerated in its vehemence.   They were waiting for me in the drawing-room, which is a very large room, stretching along the entire front of the house, with three long windows reaching down to the floor.   A chair had been placed close to the central window, with its back turned towards it.   In this I was asked to sit, and then Mr. Rucastle, walking up and down on the other side of the room, began to tell me a series of the funniest stories that I have ever listened to.   You cannot imagine how comical he was, and I laughed until I was quite weary.   Mrs. Rucastle, however, who has evidently no sense of humour, never so much as smiled, but sat with her hands in her lap, and a sad, anxious look upon her face.   After an hour or so, Mr. Rucastle suddenly remarked that it was time to commence the duties of the day, and that I might change my dress, and go to little Edward in the nursery.

" Two days later this same performance was gone through under exactly similar circumstances.   Again I changed my dress, again I sat in the window, and again I laughed very heartily at the funny stories of which my employer had an immense repertoire, and which he told inimitably.   Then he handed me a yellow-backed novel, and, moving my chair a little sideways, that my own shadow might not fall upon the page, he begged me to read aloud to him.   I read for about ten minutes, beginning in the heart of a chapter, and then suddenly, in the middle of a sentence, he ordered me to cease and change my dress.

" You can easily imagine, Mr. Holmes, how curious I became as to what the meaning of this extraordinary performance could possibly be.   They were always very careful, I observed, to turn my face away from the window, so that I became consumed with the desire to see what was

"I READ FOR ABOUT TEN MINUTES . . ."

Illustration by Sidney Paget for the *Strand Magazine*, June, 1892.

going on behind my back. At first it seemed to be impossible, but I soon devised a means. My hand mirror had been broken, so a happy thought seized me, and I concealed a little of the glass in my handkerchief. On the next occasion, in the midst of my laughter, I put my handkerchief up to my eyes, and was able with a little management to see all that there was behind me. I confess that I was disappointed. There was nothing.

" At least, that was my first impression. At the second glance, however, I perceived that there was a man standing in the Southampton road, a small bearded man in a grey suit, who seemed to be looking in my direction. The road is an important highway, and there are usually people there. This man, however, was leaning against the railings which bordered our field, and was looking earnestly. I lowered my handkerchief, and glanced at Mrs. Rucastle to find her eyes fixed upon me with a most searching gaze. She said nothing, but I am convinced that she had divined that I had a mirror in my hand, and had seen what was behind me. She rose at once.

" ' Jephro,' said she, ' there is an impertinent fellow upon the road there who stares up at Miss Hunter.'

" ' No friend of yours, Miss Hunter ? ' he asked.

" ' No ; I know no one in these parts.'

" ' Dear me ! How very impertinent ! Kindly turn round, and motion him to go away.'

" ' Surely it would be better to take no notice ? '

" ' No, no, we should have him loitering here always. Kindly turn round, and wave him away like that.'

" I did as I was told, and at the same instant Mrs. Rucastle drew down the blind. That was a week ago, and from that time I have not sat again in the window, nor have I worn the blue dress, nor seen the man in the road."

" Pray continue," said Holmes. " Your narrative promises to be a most interesting one."

" You will find it rather disconnected, I fear, and there may prove to be little relation between the different incidents of which I speak. On the very first day that I was at Copper Beeches, Mr. Rucastle took me to a small outhouse which stands near the kitchen door. As we approached it I heard the sharp rattling of a chain, and the sound as of a large animal moving about.

" ' Look in here ! ' said Mr. Rucastle, showing me a slit between two planks. ' Is he not a beauty ? '

" I looked through, and was conscious of two glowing eyes, and of a vague figure huddled up in the darkness.

" ' Don't be frightened,' said my employer, laughing at the start which I had given. ' It's only Carlo, my mastiff. **32** I call him mine, but really old Toller, my groom, is the only man who can do anything with him. We feed him once a day, and not too much then, so that he is always as keen as mustard. Toller lets him loose every night, and God help the trespasser whom he lays his fangs upon. For goodness' sake don't you ever on any pretext set your foot over the threshold at night, for it is as much as your life is worth.'

" The warning was no idle one, for two nights later I **33** happened to look out of my bedroom window about two o'clock in the morning. It was a beautiful moonlight

32 *Carlo*. Evidently a popular name for a dog in the Holmes-Watson era: the spaniel in "The Adventure of the Sussex Vampire" was also named Carlo.

33 *two nights later*. Miss Hunter was to go to the Copper Beeches on the day after her visit to Holmes at 221B; "For two days" after this her life was very quiet; "on the third" day she caught her glimpse of the small bearded man in the grey suit; and "two nights later" would bring us to the fifth day.

34 *It was a beautiful moonlight night.* Tuesday, April 9, 1889—the day we believe this to have been —was a day on which the moon was one day past the half; it set at 2:37 in the morning, so that it would have been shining brightly about 2:00 A.M., as Miss Hunter said.

35 *"I am naturally observant, as you may have remarked, Mr. Holmes.* Another attempt of Violet's to ingratiate herself with Sherlock?

"I TOOK IT UP AND EXAMINED IT."

Illustration by Sidney Paget for the *Strand Magazine*, June, 1892.

34 night, and the lawn in front of the house was silvered over and almost as bright as day.   I was standing wrapt in the peaceful beauty of the scene, when I was aware that something was moving under the shadow of the copper beeches. As it emerged into the moonshine I saw what it was.   It was a giant dog, as large as a calf, tawny-tinted, with hanging jowl, black muzzle, and huge projecting bones.   It walked slowly across the lawn and vanished into the shadow upon the other side.   That dreadful silent sentinel sent a chill to my heart, which I do not think that any burglar could have done.

" And now I have a very strange experience to tell you. I had, as you know, cut off my hair in London, and I had placed it in a great coil at the bottom of my trunk.   One evening, after the child was in bed, I began to amuse myself by examining the furniture of my room, and by rearranging my own little things.   There was an old chest of drawers in the room, the two upper ones empty and open, the lower one locked.   I had filled the two first with my linen, and as I had still much to pack away, I was naturally annoyed at not having the use of the third drawer. It struck me that it might have been fastened by a mere oversight, so I took out my bunch of keys and tried to open it.   The very first key fitted to perfection, and I drew the drawer open.   There was only one thing in it, but I am sure that you would never guess what it was.   It was my coil of hair.

" I took it up and examined it.   It was of the same peculiar tint, and the same thickness.   But then the impossibility of the thing obtruded itself upon me.   How *could* my hair have been locked in the drawer ?   With trembling hands I undid my trunk, turned out the contents, and drew from the bottom my own hair.   I laid the two tresses together, and I assure you they were identical.   Was it not extraordinary ?   Puzzle as I would, I could make nothing at all of what it meant.   I returned the strange hair to the drawer, and I said nothing of the matter to the Rucastles, as I felt that I had put myself in the wrong by opening a drawer which they had locked.

" I am naturally observant as you may have remarked,
35 Mr. Holmes, and I soon had a pretty good plan of the whole house in my head.   There was one wing, however, which appeared not to be inhabited at all.   A door which faced that which led into the quarters of the Tollers opened into this suite, but it was invariably locked.   One day, however, as I ascended the stair, I met Mr. Rucastle coming out through this door, his keys in his hand, and a look on his face which made him a very different person to the round jovial man to whom I was accustomed.   His cheeks were red, his brow was all crinkled with anger, and the veins stood out at his temples with passion.   He locked the door, and hurried past me without a word or a look.

" This aroused my curiosity ; so when I went out for a walk in the grounds with my charge, I strolled round to the side from which I could see the windows of this part of the house.   There were four of them in a row, three of which were simply dirty, while the fourth was shuttered up.   They were evidently all deserted.   As I strolled up and down, glancing at them occasionally, Mr. Rucastle came out to me, looking as merry and jovial as ever.

" ' Ah ! ' said he, ' you must not think me rude if I passed you without a word, my dear young lady. I was preoccupied with business matters.'

" I assured him that I was not offended. ' By the way,' said I, ' you seem to have quite a suite of spare rooms up there, and one of them has the shutters up.'

" ' Photography is one of my hobbies,' said he. ' I have made my dark-room up there. But, dear me ! what an observant young lady we have come upon. Who would have believed it ? Who would have ever believed it ? " He spoke in a jesting tone, but there was no jest in his eyes as he looked at me. I read suspicion there, and annoyance, but no jest.

" Well, Mr. Holmes, from the moment that I understood that there was something about that suite of rooms which I was not to know, I was all on fire to go over them. It was not mere curiosity, though I have my share of that. It was more a feeling of duty—a feeling that some good might come from my penetrating to this place. They talk of woman's instinct ; perhaps it was woman's instinct which gave me that feeling. At any rate, it was there ; and I was keenly on the look-out for any chance to pass the forbidden door.

" It was only yesterday that the chance came. I may tell you that, besides Mr. Rucastle, both Toller and his wife find something to do in these deserted rooms, and I once saw him carrying a large black linen bag with him through the door. Recently he has been drinking hard, and yesterday evening he was very drunk ; and, when I came upstairs, there was the key in the door. I have no doubt at all that he had left it there. Mr. and Mrs. Rucastle were both downstairs, and the child was with them, so that I had an admirable opportunity. I turned the key gently in the lock, opened the door, and slipped through.

" There was a little passage in front of me, unpapered and uncarpeted, which turned at a right angle at the farther end. Round this corner were three doors in a line, the first and third of which were open. They each led into an empty room, dusty and cheerless, with two windows in the one, and one in the other, so thick with dirt that the evening light glimmered dimly through them. The centre door was closed, and across the outside of it had been fastened one of the broad bars of an iron bed, padlocked at one end to a ring in the wall, and fastened at the other with stout cord. The door itself was locked as well, and the key was not there. This barricaded door corresponded clearly with the shuttered window outside, and yet I could see by the glimmer from beneath it that the room was not in darkness. Evidently there was a skylight which let in light from above. As I stood in the passage gazing at this sinister door, and wondering what secret it might veil, I suddenly heard the sound of steps within the room, and saw a shadow pass backwards and forwards against the little slit of dim light which shone out from under the door. A mad, unreasoning terror rose up in me at the sight, Mr. Holmes. My overstrung nerves failed me suddenly, and I turned and ran—ran as though some dreadful hand were behind me, clutching at the skirt of my dress. I rushed down the passage, through the

" 'OH, I AM SO FRIGHTENED!' I PANTED."

Illustration by Sidney Paget for the *Strand Magazine*, June, 1892.

door, and straight into the arms of Mr. Rucastle, who was waiting outside.

" ' So,' said he, smiling, ' it was you, then. I thought it must be when I saw the door open.'

" ' Oh, I am so frightened ! ' I panted.

" ' My dear young lady ! my dear young lady ! '—you cannot think how caressing and soothing his manner was— ' and what has frightened you, my dear young lady ? '

" But his voice was just a little too coaxing. He overdid it. I was keenly on my guard against him.

" ' I was foolish enough to go into the empty wing,' I answered. ' But it is so lonely and eerie in this dim light that I was frightened and ran out again. Oh, it is so dreadfully still in there ! '

" ' Only that ? ' said he, looking at me keenly.

" ' Why, what do you think ? ' I asked.

" ' Why do you think that I lock this door ? '

" ' I am sure that I do not know.'

" ' It is to keep people out who have no business there. Do you see ? ' He was still smiling in the most amiable manner.

" ' I am sure if I had known——'

" ' Well, then, you know now. And if you ever put your foot over that threshold again——' here in an instant the smile hardened into a grin of rage, and he glared down at me with the face of a demon, ' I'll throw you to the mastiff.'

" I was so terrified that I do not know what I did. I suppose that I must have rushed past him into my room. I remember nothing until I found myself lying on my bed trembling all over. Then I thought of you, Mr. Holmes. I could not live there longer without some advice. I was frightened of the house, of the man, of the woman, of the servants, even of the child. They were all horrible to me. If I could only bring you down all would be well. Of course I might have fled from the house, but my curiosity was almost as strong as my fears. My mind was soon made up. I would send you a wire. I put on my hat and cloak, went down to the office, which is about half a mile from the house, and then returned, feeling very much easier. A horrible doubt came into my mind as I approached the door lest the dog might be loose, but I remembered that Toller had drunk himself into a state of insensibility that evening, and I knew that he was the only one in the household who had any influence with the savage creature, or who would venture to set him free. I slipped in in safety, and lay awake half the night in my joy at the thought of seeing you. I had no difficulty in getting leave to come into Winchester this morning, but I must be back before three o'clock, for Mr. and Mrs. Rucastle are going on a visit, and will be away all the evening, so that I must look after the child. Now I have told you all my adventures, Mr. Holmes, and I should be very glad if you could tell me what it all means, and, above all, what I should do."

Holmes and I had listened spellbound to this extraordinary story. My friend rose now, and paced up and down the room, his hands in his pockets, and an expression of the most profound gravity upon his face.

" Is Toller still drunk ? " he asked.

" Yes. I heard his wife tell Mrs. Rucastle that she could do nothing with him."

" That is well. And the Rucastles go out to-night ? "

" Yes."

" Is there a cellar with a good strong lock ? "

" Yes, the wine cellar."

" You seem to me to have acted all through this matter like a brave and sensible girl, Miss Hunter. Do you think that you could perform one more feat ? I should not ask it of you if I did not think you a quite exceptional woman."

" I will try. What is it ? "

" We shall be at the Copper Beeches by seven o'clock, my friend and I. The Rucastles will be gone by that time, and Toller will, we hope, be incapable. There only remains Mrs. Toller, who might give the alarm. If you could send her into the cellar, on some errand, and then turn the key upon her, you would facilitate matters immensely."

" I will do it."

" Excellent ! We shall then look thoroughly into the affair. Of course there is only one feasible explanation. You have been brought there to personate someone, and the real person is imprisoned in this chamber. That is obvious. As to who this prisoner is, I have no doubt that it is the daughter, Miss Alice Rucastle, if I remember right, who was said to have gone to America. You were chosen, doubtless, as resembling her in height, figure, and the colour of your hair. Hers had been cut off, very possibly in some illness through which she has passed, and so, of course, yours had to be sacrificed also. By a curious chance you came upon her tresses. The man in the road was, undoubtedly, some friend of hers—possibly her fiancé —and no doubt as you wore the girl's dress, and were so like her, he was convinced from your laughter, whenever he saw you, and afterwards from your gesture, that Miss Rucastle was perfectly happy, and that she no longer desired his attentions. The dog is let loose at night to prevent him from endeavouring to communicate with her. So much is fairly clear. The most serious point in the case is the disposition of the child."

" What on earth has that to do with it ? " I ejaculated.

" My dear Watson, you as a medical man are continually gaining light as to the tendencies of a child by the study of the parents. Don't you see that the converse is equally valid. I have frequently gained my first real insight into the character of parents by studying their children. This child's disposition is abnormally cruel, merely for cruelty's sake, and whether he derives this from his smiling father, as I should suspect, or from his mother, it bodes evil for the poor girl who is in their power."

" I am sure that you are right, Mr. Holmes," cried our client. " A thousand things come back to me which make me certain that you have hit it. Oh, let us lose not an instant in bringing help to this poor creature."

" We must be circumspect, for we are dealing with a very cunning man. We can do nothing until seven o'clock. At that hour we shall be with you, and it will not be long before we solve the mystery."

We were as good as our word, for it was just seven when

36 *in the light of the setting sun.* Saturday, April 20, 1889, was a day on which sunset was at 7:02 P.M.

37 *were sufficient to mark the house.* "You must have seen the house (it's still standing)," Mr. Gordon Sewell wrote in "Holmes and Watson in the South Country," "one of those square, stuccoed, late Georgian villas between Otterbourne and Chandler's Ford."

"YOU VILLAIN," SAID HE, "WHERE'S YOUR DAUGHTER?"

Illustration by Sidney Paget for the *Strand Magazine*, June, 1892.

we reached the Copper Beeches, having put up our trap at a wayside public-house. The group of trees, with their dark leaves shining like burnished metal in the light of the **36-37** setting sun, were sufficient to mark the house even had Miss Hunter not been standing smiling on the door-step.

"Have you managed it?" asked Holmes.

A loud thudding noise came from somewhere downstairs. "That is Mrs. Toller in the cellar," said she. "Her husband lies snoring on the kitchen rug. Here are his keys, which are the duplicates of Mr. Rucastle's."

"You have done well indeed!" cried Holmes, with enthusiasm. "Now lead the way, and we shall soon see the end of this black business."

We passed up the stair, unlocked the door, followed on down a passage, and found ourselves in front of the barricade which Miss Hunter had described. Holmes cut the cord and removed the transverse bar. Then he tried the various keys in the lock, but without success. No sound came from within, and at the silence Holmes' face clouded over.

"I trust that we are not too late," said he. "I think, Miss Hunter, that we had better go in without you. Now, Watson, put your shoulder to it, and we shall see whether we cannot make our way in."

It was an old rickety door and gave at once before our united strength. Together we rushed into the room. It was empty. There was no furniture save a little pallet bed, a small table, and a basketful of linen. The skylight above was open, and the prisoner gone.

"There has been some villainy here," said Holmes; "this beauty has guessed Miss Hunter's intentions, and has carried his victim off."

"But how?"

"Through the skylight. We shall soon see how he managed it." He swung himself up on to the roof. "Ah, yes," he cried, "here's the end of a long light ladder against the eaves. That is how he did it."

"But it is impossible," said Miss Hunter, "the ladder was not there when the Rucastles went away."

"He has come back and done it. I tell you that he is a clever and dangerous man. I should not be very much surprised if this were he whose step I hear now upon the stair. I think, Watson, that it would be as well for you to have your pistol ready."

The words were hardly out of his mouth before a man appeared at the door of the room, a very fat and burly man, with a heavy stick in his hand. Miss Hunter screamed and shrunk against the wall at the sight of him, but Sherlock Holmes sprang forward and confronted him.

"You villain," said he, "where's your daughter?"

The fat man cast his eyes round, and then up at the open skylight.

"It is for me to ask you that," he shrieked, "you thieves! Spies and thieves! I have caught you, have I? You are in my power. I'll serve you!" He turned and clattered down the stairs as hard as he could go.

"He's gone for the dog!" cried Miss Hunter.

"I have my revolver," said I.

"Better close the front door," cried Holmes, and we all

rushed down the stairs together. We had hardly reached the hall when we heard the baying of a hound, and then a **38** scream of agony, with a horrible worrying sound which it was dreadful to listen to. An elderly man with a red face and shaking limbs came staggering out at a side-door.

" My God ! " he cried. " Someone has loosed the dog. It's not been fed for two days. Quick, quick, or it'll be too late ! "

Holmes and I rushed out, and round the angle of the house, with Toller hurrying behind us. There was the huge famished brute, its black muzzle buried in Rucastle's throat, while he writhed and screamed upon the ground. Running up, I blew its brains out, and it fell over with its keen white teeth still meeting in the great creases of his neck. With much labour we separated them, and carried him, living but horribly mangled, into the house. We laid him upon the drawing-room sofa, and having despatched the sobered Toller to bear the news to his wife, I did what I could to relieve his pain. We were all assembled round him when the door opened, and a tall, gaunt woman entered the room.

" Mrs. Toller ! " cried Miss Hunter.

" Yes, miss. Mr. Rucastle let me out when he came back before he went up to you. Ah, miss, it is a pity you didn't let me know what you were planning, for I would have told you that your pains were wasted."

" Ha ! " said Holmes, looking keenly at her. " It is clear that Mrs. Toller knows more about this matter than anyone else."

" Yes, sir, I do, and I am ready enough to tell what I know."

" Then pray sit down, and let us hear it, for there are several points on which I must confess that I am still in the dark."

" I will soon make it clear to you," said she ; " and I'd have done so before now if I could ha' got out from the cellar. If there's police-court business over this, you'll remember that I was the one that stood your friend, and that I was Miss Alice's friend too.

" She was never happy at home, Miss Alice wasn't, from the time that her father married again. She was slighted like, and had no say in anything ; but it never really became bad for her until after she met Mr. Fowler at a friend's house. As well as I could learn, Miss Alice had rights of her own by will, but she was so quiet and patient, she was, that she never said a word about them, but just left everything in Mr. Rucastle's hands. He knew he was safe with her ; but when there was a chance of a husband coming forward, who would ask for all that the law could give him, then her father thought it time to put a stop on it. He wanted her to sign a paper so that whether she married or not, he could use her money. When she wouldn't do it, he kept on worrying her until she got brain fever, and for six weeks was at death's door. Then she got better at last, all worn to a shadow, and with her beautiful hair cut off ; but that didn't make no change in her young man, and he stuck to her as true as man could be."

" Ah," said Holmes, " I think that what you have been good enough to tell us makes the matter fairly clear, and that I can deduce all that remains. Mr. Rucastle, then, I

38 *the baying of a hound.* But Carlo, we know, was a mastiff, and "a mastiff might give a roar or a growl, but could not conceivably 'bay,' and furthermore, the hound belongs to an entirely different group of dogs, the largest of which are the Irish wolfhound and the Scottish deerhound, which both exceed the mastiff in height, but not in substance"—Mrs. Eleanor S. Cole, "Holmes, Watson and the K-9's."

RUNNING UP, I BLEW ITS BRAINS OUT . . .

Illustration by Sidney Paget for the *Strand Magazine*, June, 1892. Watson's statement here is perhaps another indication that he, not Holmes, was the better shot with a handgun. Holmes needed five shots to finish off the Hound of the Baskervilles, but Watson apparently needed only one shot to blow out the brains of the unpleasant mastiff Carlo.

39 locus standi. Latin: rightful position; a legal term and another indication of Holmes' knowledge of the law.

40 *manifested no further interest in her.* ". . . how delightful, the Doctor thought naively, if he and Holmes should both marry governesses—and alumnae of the same agency, for undoubtedly Mary, too, had been a client of Westaway's," the late Christopher Morley commented ("Dr. Watson's Secret").

41 *Walsall.* A town in Staffordshire.

Auctorial Note: It was Conan Doyle's mother, as we have seen—the Ma'am—who prevented, for a time, the "death" of Sherlock Holmes. Conan Doyle, ready at this time to rid himself of his creation "forever," would have done so had his mother not sent him an idea for a Holmes story that should concern a girl with "beautiful golden hair: who kidnapped and her hair shorn should be made to impersonate some other girl for a villainous purpose"; the golden-haired girl became the less spectacular chestnut-haired Violet Hunter of "The Adventure of the Copper Beeches"—and Holmes, for the time being, lived on.

presume, took to this system of imprisonment ? "

" Yes, sir."

" And brought Miss Hunter down from London in order to get rid of the disagreeable persistence of Mr. Fowler."

" That was it, sir."

" But Mr. Fowler, being a persevering man, as a good seaman should be, blockaded the house, and, having met you, succeeded by certain arguments, metallic or otherwise, in convincing you that your interests were the same as his."

" Mr. Fowler was a very kind-spoken, free-handed gentleman," said Mrs. Toller serenely.

" And in this way he managed that your good man should have no want of drink, and that a ladder should be ready at the moment when your master had gone out."

" You have it, sir, just as it happened."

" I am sure we owe you an apology, Mrs. Toller," said Holmes, " for you have certainly cleared up everything which puzzled us.   And here comes the country surgeon and Mrs. Rucastle, so I think, Watson, that we had best escort Miss Hunter back to Winchester, as it seems to me **39** that our *locus standi* now is rather a questionable one."

And thus was solved the mystery of the sinister house with the copper beeches in front of the door. Mr. Rucastle survived, but was always a broken man, kept alive solely through the care of his devoted wife. They still live with their old servants, who probably know so much of Rucastle's past life that he finds it difficult to part from them. Mr. Fowler and Miss Rucastle were married, by special licence, in Southampton the day after their flight, and he is now the holder of a Government appointment in the Island of Mauritius.   As to Miss Violet Hunter, my friend Holmes, rather to my disappointment, manifested no fur-**40** ther interest in her when once she had ceased to be the centre of one of his problems, and she is now the head of a **41** private school at Walsall, where I believe that she has met with considerable success.

VI. FROM DR. WATSON'S SECOND MARRIAGE TO THE DISAPPEARANCE OF SHERLOCK HOLMES

[Wednesday, May 1, 1889, to Monday, May 4, 1891]

"Miss Morstan has done me the honour to accept me as a husband in prospective."

He gave a most dismal groan.

"I feared as much," said he.

—*The Sign of the Four*

38

THE BOSCOMBE VALLEY MYSTERY

[Saturday, June 8, to Sunday, June 9, 1889]

1 *my wife.* While all chronologists are agreed that this wife was Mary Morstan, few are agreed on when Watson married her. For 1887: Bell and Brend (November); Morley (probably February or March). For 1888: Blakeney and Folsom (November). For 1889: Baring-Gould (*circa* May 1st); Christ (late February or early March); Zeisler (January). In your editor's view John and Mary were married some seven and a half months after their meeting at the time of *The Sign of the Four.* Both would have felt it proper that well over a year should elapse between the doctor's first and second marriage. Contributing to the delay were Watson's financial condition (he had to raise the price of a practice) and Mary's mental and physical condition—Holmes' "I trust Mrs. Watson has entirely recovered from all the little excitements connected with our adventure of The Sign of the Four" ("The Stockbroker's Clerk") indicates that her health would not permit a marriage soon after the climax of that case. Mr. S. C. Roberts has written (*Doctor Watson*) that the ceremony probably took place very quietly at St. Mark's or St. Hilda's, Camberwell. He adds that it is at least doubtful that Holmes could be induced to be best man, "since Watson would hardly be likely to omit a record of so personal a tribute . . ." But Mr. T. S. Blakeney (*Sherlock Holmes: Fact or Fiction?*) comments that since "Watson never even records his wedding, he could hardly mention what part in it Holmes may have played."

2 *I have a fairly long list at present."* We note that *this* practice, unlike the practice of 1887, which "was never very absorbing" ("The Red-Headed League"), was a busy one.

3 *Anstruther.* In "The Stockbroker's Clerk," Watson says to Holmes: "I do my neighbor's [practice] when he goes. He is always ready to work off the debt."

1 WE were seated at breakfast one morning, my wife and I, when the maid brought in a telegram. It was from Sherlock Holmes, and ran in this way :

" Have you a couple of days to spare ? Have just been wired for from the West of England in connection with Boscombe Valley tragedy. Shall be glad if you will come with me. Air and scenery perfect. Leave Paddington by the 11.15."

" What do you say, dear ? " said my wife, looking across at me. " Will you go ? "

" I really don't know what to say. I have a fairly **2** long list at present."

3 " Oh, Anstruther would do your work for you. You have been looking a little pale lately. I think that the change would do you good, and you are always so interested in Mr. Sherlock Holmes' cases."

" I should be ungrateful if I were not, seeing what I gained through one of them," I answered. " But if I **4** am to go I must pack at once, for I have only half an hour."

My experience of camp life in Afghanistan had at least had the effect of making me a prompt and ready traveller. My wants were few and simple, so that in less than the time stated I was in a cab with my valise, rattling away to Paddington Station. Sherlock Holmes was pacing up and down the platform, his tall, gaunt figure made even gaunter and taller by his long grey travelling-cloak and close-fitting cloth cap.

" It is really very good of you to come, Watson," said he. " It makes a considerable difference to me, having someone with me on whom I can thoroughly rely. Local aid is always either worthless or else biased. If you will keep the two corner seats I shall get the tickets."

We had the carriage to ourselves save for an immense **5** litter of papers which Holmes had brought with him. Among these he rummaged and read, with intervals of note-taking and of meditation, until we were past Reading. Then he suddenly rolled them all into a gigantic ball, and tossed them up on to the rack.

" Have you heard anything of the case ? " he asked.

" Not a word. I have not seen a paper for some days." **6**

" The London press has not had very full accounts. I have just been looking through all the recent papers in order to master the particulars. It seems, from what I gather, to be one of those simple cases which are so extremely difficult."

" That sounds a little paradoxical."

" But it is profoundly true. Singularity is almost invariably a clue. The more featureless and commonplace a crime is, the more difficult is it to bring it home. In this case, however, they have established a very serious case against the son of the murdered man."

" It is a murder, then ? "

" Well, it is conjectured to be so. I shall take nothing for granted until I have the opportunity of looking personally into it. I will explain the state of things to you, as far as I have been able to understand it, in a very few words.

" Boscombe Valley is a country district not very far from Ross, in Herefordshire. The largest landed pro- **7** prietor in that part is a Mr. John Turner, who made his money in Australia, and returned some years ago to the old country. One of the farms which he held, that of Hatherley, was let to Mr. Charles McCarthy, who was also an ex-Australian. The men had known each other in the Colonies, so that it was not unnatural that when they came to settle down they should do so as near each other as possible. Turner was apparently the richer man, so McCarthy became his tenant, but still remained, it seems, upon terms of perfect equality, as they were frequently together. McCarthy had one son, a lad of eighteen, and Turner had an only daughter of the same age, but neither of them had wives living. They appear to have avoided the society of the neighbouring English families, and to have led retired lives, though both the McCarthys were fond of sport, and were frequently seen at the race meetings of the neighbourhood. McCarthy kept two servants—a man and a girl. Turner had a considerable household, some half-dozen at the least. That is as much as I have been able to gather about the families. Now for the facts.

" On June 3—that is, on Monday last—McCarthy left **8** his house at Hatherley about three in the afternoon, and walked down to the Boscombe Pool, which is a small lake formed by the spreading out of the stream which runs down the Boscombe Valley. He had been out with his serving-man in the morning at Ross, and he had told the man that he must hurry, as he had an appointment of importance to keep at three. From that appointment he never came back alive.

" From Hatherley Farm-house to the Boscombe Pool is a quarter of a mile, and two people saw him as he passed over this ground. One was an old woman, whose name is not mentioned, and the other was William Crowder, a gamekeeper in the employ of Mr. Turner. Both these witnesses depose that Mr. McCarthy was walking alone. The gamekeeper adds that within a few minutes of his seeing Mr. McCarthy pass he had seen his son, Mr. James McCarthy, going the same way with a gun under

WE HAD THE CARRIAGE TO OURSELVES . . .

Illustration by Sidney Paget for the *Strand Magazine*, October, 1891.

4 *I have only half an hour."* Why was Watson, the busy medico, breakfasting at so late an hour as 10:45 A.M.?

5 *save for an immense litter of papers.* The day of the train ride *could* have been a Sunday and the papers those of the week before, but the presumption here is that Holmes and Watson traveled to Boscombe Valley on a weekday.

6 *I have not seen a paper for some days."* A further indication that Watson's practice at this time was an exceedingly busy one.

7 *Ross, in Herefordshire.* In fact, Boscombe is on the northern border of Somerset.

8 *"On June 3—that is, on Monday last.* In all the Canonical years before October, 1891, when "The Boscombe Valley Mystery" was published in the *Strand Magazine*, June 3rd fell on a Monday only once—in 1889. With Bigelow, Morley, Pattrick, and Zeisler dissenting—all of these vote for 1890— all other chronologists accept 1889 as the year of the adventure.

his arm. To the best of his belief, the father was actually in sight at the time, and the son was following him. He thought no more of the matter until he heard in the evening of the tragedy that had occurred.

"The two McCarthys were seen after the time when William Crowder, the gamekeeper, lost sight of them. The Boscombe Pool is thickly wooded round, with just a fringe of grass and of reeds round the edge. A girl of **9** fourteen, Patience Moran, who is the daughter of the lodgekeeper of the Boscombe Valley Estate, was in one of the woods picking flowers. She states that while she was there she saw, at the border of the wood and close by the lake, Mr. McCarthy and his son, and that they appeared to be having a violent quarrel. She heard Mr. McCarthy the elder using very strong language to his son, and she saw the latter raise up his hand as if to strike his father. She was so frightened by their violence that she ran away, and told her mother when she reached home that she had left the two McCarthys quarrelling near Boscombe Pool, and that she was afraid that they were going to fight. She had hardly said the words when young Mr. McCarthy came running up to the lodge to say that he had found his father dead in the wood, and to ask for the help of the lodge-keeper. He was much excited, without either his gun or his hat, and his right hand and sleeve were observed to be stained with fresh blood. On following him they found the dead body of his father stretched out upon the grass beside the Pool. The head had been beaten in by repeated blows of some heavy and blunt weapon. The injuries were such as might very well have been inflicted by the butt-end of his son's gun, which was found lying on the grass within a few paces of the body. Under these circumstances the young man was instantly arrested, and a verdict of ' Wilful Murder ' having been returned at the inquest on Tuesday, he was on Wednesday brought before the **10** magistrates at Ross, who have referred the case to the next assizes. Those are the main facts of the case as they came out before the coroner and at the police-court."

" I could hardly imagine a more damning case," I remarked. " If ever circumstantial evidence pointed to a criminal it does so here."

" Circumstantial evidence is a very tricky thing," answered Holmes thoughtfully ; " it may seem to point very straight to one thing, but if you shift your own point of view a little, you may find it pointing in an equally uncompromising manner to something entirely different. It must be confessed, however, that the case looks exceedingly grave against the young man, and it is very possible that he is indeed the culprit. There are several people in the neighbourhood, however, and among them Miss Turner, the daughter of the neighbouring landowner, who believe in his innocence, and who have retained **11** Lestrade, whom you may remember in connection with the Study in Scarlet, to work out the case in his interest. Lestrade, being rather puzzled, has referred the case to me, and hence it is that two middle-aged gentlemen are flying westward at fifty miles an hour, instead of quietly digesting their breakfasts at home."

"ON FOLLOWING HIM THEY FOUND THE DEAD BODY OF HIS FATHER . . ."

Illustration by Sidney Paget for the *Strand Magazine*, October, 1891.

9 *A girl of fourteen, Patience Moran.* As noted in "The Red-Headed League," Magistrate S. Tupper Bigelow has identified Patience Moran as a niece of Colonel Sebastian Moran and also as the "girl of fourteen" who did a bit of cooking for Jabez Wilson and kept his place clean. This of course assumes that "The Red-Headed League" and "The Boscombe Valley Mystery" both took place within one year's time.

" I am afraid," said I, " that the facts are so obvious that you will find little credit to be gained out of this case."

" There is nothing more deceptive than an obvious fact," he answered, laughing. " Besides, we may chance to hit upon some other obvious facts which may have been by no means obvious to Mr. Lestrade. You know me too well to think that I am boasting when I say that I shall either confirm or destroy his theory by means which he is quite incapable of employing, or even of understanding. To take the first example to hand, I very clearly perceive that in your bedroom the window is upon the right-hand side, and yet I question whether Mr. Lestrade would have noted even so self-evident a thing as that."

" How on earth—— ! "

" My dear fellow, I know you well. I know the military neatness which characterizes you. You shave every morning, and in this season you shave by the sunlight, but since your shaving is less and less complete as we get farther back on the left side, until it becomes positively slovenly as we get round the angle of the jaw, it is surely very clear that that side is less well illuminated than the other. I could not imagine a man of your habits looking **12** at himself in an equal light, and being satisfied with such a result. I only quote this as a trivial example of observation and inference. Therein lies my *métier*, and it is **13** just possible that it may be of some service in the investigation which lies before us. There are one or two minor points which were brought out in the inquest, and which are worth considering."

" What are they ? "

" It appears that his arrest did not take place at once, but after the return to Hatherley Farm. On the inspector of constabulary informing him that he was a prisoner, he remarked that he was not surprised to hear it, and that it was no more than his deserts. This observation of his had the natural effect of removing any traces of doubt which might have remained in the minds of the coroner's jury."

" It was a confession," I ejaculated.

" No, for it was followed by a protestation of innocence."

" Coming on the top of such a damning series of events, it was at least a most suspicious remark."

" On the contrary," said Holmes, " it is the brightest rift which I can at present see in the clouds. However innocent he might be, he could not be such an absolute imbecile as not to see that the circumstances were very black against him. Had he appeared surprised at his own arrest, or feigned indignation at it, I should have looked upon it as highly suspicious, because such surprise or anger would not be natural under the circumstances, and yet might appear to be the best policy to a scheming man. His frank acceptance of the situation marks him as either an innocent man, or else as a man of considerable self-restraint and firmness. As to his remark about his deserts, it was also not unnatural if you consider that he stood by the dead body of his father, and that there is no doubt that he had that very day so far forgotten his filial

10 *he was on Wednesday brought before the magistrates.* Had Holmes made this statement on Thursday, June 6th, he would surely have said that McCarthy was brought before the magistrates "yesterday." The case began, then, on Friday, June 7th; Saturday, June 8th; or Sunday, June 9th. Had it begun on Monday, June 10th, Holmes would probably have said earlier that Monday, June 3rd, was "a week ago today" rather than "Monday last," although this day is not impossible.

11 *retained Lestrade.* "Some have pounced on the word 'retained' as used by Holmes to conclude that Lestrade had gone into private practice for a period, but that judgment is not necessarily warranted, for it was not uncommon for Scotland Yarders to aid the provincial police, and Holmes' use of the word was purely conversational," Mr. L. S. Holstein wrote in "Inspector G. Lestrade."

12 *that side is less well illuminated than the other.* "Was not the calculator, to be able to draw this inference, required to impart a factor into the equation which may not have represented the fact, namely, that it was his friend's custom to face north when pursuing this routine, so that the light would strike on the right cheek?" Mr. J. B. Mackenzie asked in "Sherlock Holmes' Plots and Strategy."

13 *métier.* French: trade; profession.

14 *Bristol.* In Gloucestershire, on the Avon near the mouth of the Severn—a major world port as well as an industrial center.

"I DROPPED MY GUN, AND HELD HIM IN MY ARM ;··."

Illustration by Sidney Paget for the *Strand Magazine*, October, 1891.

duty as to bandy words with him, and even, according to the little girl whose evidence is so important, to raise his hand as if to strike him. The self-reproach and contrition which are displayed in his remark appear to me to be the signs of a healthy mind, rather than of a guilty one."

I shook my head. "Many men have been hanged on far slighter evidence," I remarked.

"So they have. And many men have been wrongfully hanged."

"What is the young man's own account of the matter?"

"It is, I am afraid, not very encouraging to his supporters, though there are one or two points in it which are suggestive. You will find it here, and may read it for yourself."

He picked out from his bundle a copy of the local Herefordshire paper, and having turned down the sheet, he pointed out the paragraph in which the unfortunate young man had given his own statement of what had occurred. I settled myself down in the corner of the carriage, and read it very carefully. It ran in this way:

"Mr. James McCarthy, the only son of the deceased, was then called, and gave evidence as follows: 'I had **14** been away from home for three days at Bristol, and had only just returned upon the morning of last Monday, the 3rd. My father was absent from home at the time of my arrival, and I was informed by the maid that he had driven over to Ross with John Cobb, the groom. Shortly after my return I heard the wheels of his trap in the yard, and, looking out of my window, I saw him get out and walk rapidly out of the yard, though I was not aware in which direction he was going. I then took my gun, and strolled out in the direction of the Boscombe Pool, with the intention of visiting the rabbit warren which is upon the other side. On my way I saw William Crowder, the gamekeeper, as he has stated in his evidence; but he is mistaken in thinking that I was following my father. I had no idea that he was in front of me. When about a hundred yards from the Pool I heard a cry of "Cooee!" which was a usual signal between my father and myself. I then hurried forward, and found him standing by the Pool. He appeared to be much surprised at seeing me, and asked me rather roughly what I was doing there. A conversation ensued, which led to high words, and almost to blows, for my father was a man of a very violent temper. Seeing that his passion was becoming ungovernable, I left him, and returned towards Hatherley Farm. I had not gone more than one hundred and fifty yards, however, when I heard a hideous outcry behind me, which caused me to run back again. I found my father expiring on the ground, with his head terribly injured. I dropped my gun, and held him in my arms, but he almost instantly expired. I knelt beside him for some minutes, and then made my way to Mr. Turner's lodge-keeper, his house being the nearest, to ask for assistance. I saw no one near my father when I returned, and I have no idea how he came by his injuries. He was not a popular man, being somewhat cold and forbidding in his manners; but he had, as far as I know, no active enemies. I know nothing further of the matter.'"

" The Coroner : Did your father make any statement to you before he died ?

" Witness : He mumbled a few words, but I could only catch some allusion to a rat.

" The Coroner : What did you understand by that ?

" Witness : It conveyed no meaning to me. I thought that he was delirious.

" The Coroner : What was the point upon which you and your father had this final quarrel ?

" Witness : I should prefer not to answer.

" The Coroner : I am afraid that I must press it.

" Witness : It is really impossible for me to tell you. I can assure you that it has nothing to do with the sad tragedy which followed.

" The Coroner : That is for the Court to decide. I need not point out to you that your refusal to answer will prejudice your case considerably in any future proceedings which may arise.

" Witness : I must still refuse.

" The Coroner : I understand that the cry of ' Cooee ' was a common signal between you and your father ?

" Witness : It was.

" The Coroner : How was it, then, that he uttered it before he saw you, and before he even knew that you had returned from Bristol ?

" Witness (with considerable confusion) : I do not know.

" A Juryman : Did you see nothing which aroused your suspicions when you returned on hearing the cry, and found your father fatally injured ?

" Witness : Nothing definite.

" The Coroner : What do you mean ?

" Witness : I was so disturbed and excited as I rushed out into the open, that I could think of nothing except my father. Yet I have a vague impression that as I ran forward something lay upon the ground to the left of me. It seemed to me to be something grey in colour, a coat of some sort, or a plaid perhaps. When I rose from my father I looked round for it, but it was gone.

" ' Do you mean that it disappeared before you went for help ? '

" ' Yes, it was gone.'

" ' You cannot say what it was ? '

" ' No, I had a feeling something was there.'

" ' How far from the body ? '

" ' A dozen yards or so.'

" ' And how far from the edge of the wood ?

" ' About the same.'

" ' Then if it was removed it was while you were within a dozen yards of it ? '

" ' Yes, but with my back towards it.'

" This concluded the examination of the witness."

" I see," said I, as I glanced down the column, " that the coroner in his concluding remarks was rather severe upon young McCarthy. He calls attention, and with reason, to the discrepancy about his father having signalled to him before seeing him, also to his refusal to give details of his conversation with his father, and his singular account of his father's dying words. They are all, as he remarks, very much against the son."

15 *my pocket Petrarch*. Petrarch, or Francesco Petrarca, 1304–1374, Italian poet, surpassed in Italian literature only by Dante.

"While it may excite some wonder that Holmes should have carried with him so delightful a little rarity, there can be no question that the volume to which he referred was any other than the charming *Il Petrarca* printed in italic letter at Lyons in 1550, ruled in red, and adorned with the delicate heart-shaped woodcut medallion showing portraits of Petrarch and Laura by Bernard Salomon," Miss Madeleine B. Stern wrote in "Sherlock Holmes: Rare Book Collector."

But Mr. S. F. Blake, in "Sherlock Holmes and the Italian Cipher," wrote that he hesitated to accept Miss Stern's confident selection "in view of the fact that in the *Catalogue of Printed Books in the British Museum* some 40 columns are devoted to listing their editions of Petrarch's works in Italian and other languages from 1468 or 1470 on. . . . Aside from the lack of any indication in the text pointing to this edition rather than to dozens of others, is it likely that any true bibliophile would carry in his pocket so rare an item as a 339-year-old volume of so noted a writer as Petrarch? Surely, if he indeed possessed this item, he would have left it safe at home with his other bibliographical treasures . . . , and contented himself on a railway journey with one of the more modern and less irreplaceable issues. At least 19 different 12mo, 16mo, or 32mo editions in Italian were published in the nineteenth century (up to 1886), but my own guess is that Holmes carried the Bohn 1859 edition in English."

Mr. H. B. Williams ("Then Falls Thy Shadow") points to the fact that in the sonnets of Petrarch are to be found the portrayal of perfect love which can never be consummated, and suggests that Holmes made Petrarch his pocket companion because the sonnets "mirrored a torture forever burning within the core of his [own] being"—his love "for a woman who never could be possessed," Irene Adler.

16 *We lunch at Swindon*. They *had* to lunch at Swindon; according to *Express Trains, English and Foreign*, by E. Foxwell and T. C. Farrar, London: Smith, Elder & Co., 1889: "Inclusive speed of trains on the Great Western is lessened by the obligation to pause ten minutes at Swindon, an obligation from which the refreshment proprietors will not free the company until the year 1940." In fact, however, the restriction was withdrawn in 1895.

17 *the broad gleaming Severn*. The river Severn runs through Western England and North Wales to the Bristol Channel, a distance of 210 miles; it is remarkable for having a bore that rises at times to nine feet.

18 *No wind, and not a cloud in the sky*. Later Holmes says: "It is of importance that it should

Holmes laughed softly to himself, and stretched himself out upon the cushioned seat. " Both you and the coroner have been at some pains," said he, " to single out the very strongest points in the young man's favour. Don't you see that you alternately give him credit for having too much imagination and too little ? Too little, if he could not invent a cause of quarrel which would give him the sympathy of the jury ; too much, if he evolved from his own inner consciousness anything so *outré* as a dying reference to a rat, and the incident of the vanishing cloth. No, sir, I shall approach this case from the point of view that what this young man says is true, and we shall see whither that hypothesis will lead us. And now here is

15 my pocket Petrarch, and not another word shall I say of this case until we are on the scene of action. We lunch

16 at Swindon, and I see that we shall be there in twenty minutes."

It was nearly four o'clock when we at last, after passing through the beautiful Stroud Valley and over the broad

17 gleaming Severn, found ourselves at the pretty little country town of Ross. A lean, ferret-like man, furtive and sly-looking, was waiting for us upon the platform. In spite of the light brown dust-coat and leather leggings which he wore in deference to his rustic surroundings, I had no difficulty in recognizing Lestrade, of Scotland Yard. With him we drove to the " Hereford Arms," where a room had already been engaged for us.

" I have ordered a carriage," said Lestrade, as we sat over a cup of tea. " I knew your energetic nature, and that you would not be happy until you had been on the scene of the crime."

" It was very nice and complimentary of you," Holmes answered. " It is entirely a question of barometric pressure."

Lestrade looked startled. " I do not quite follow," he said.

" How is the glass ? Twenty-nine, I see. No wind,

18 and not a cloud in the sky. I have a caseful of cigarettes here which need smoking, and the sofa is very much superior to the usual country hotel abomination. I do not think that it is probable that I shall use the carriage to-night."

Lestrade laughed indulgently. " You have, no doubt, already formed your conclusions from the newspapers," he said. " The case is as plain as a pikestaff, and the more one goes into it the plainer it becomes. Still, of course, one can't refuse a lady, and such a very positive one, too. She had heard of you, and would have your opinion, though I repeatedly told her that there was nothing which you could do which I had not already done. Why, bless my soul ! here is her carriage at the door."

He had hardly spoken before there rushed into the room one of the most lovely young women that I have ever seen in my life. Her violet eyes shining, her lips parted, a pink flush upon her cheeks, all thought of her natural reserve lost in her overpowering excitement and concern.

" Oh, Mr. Sherlock Holmes !" she cried, glancing from one to the other of us, and finally, with a woman's quick intuition, fastening upon my companion, " I am so glad that you have come. I have driven down to tell you so. I know that James didn't do it. I know it, and I want you to start upon your work knowing it, too. Never let yourself doubt upon that point. We have known each other since we were little children, and I know his faults as no one else does ; but he is too tender-hearted to hurt a fly. Such a charge is absurd to anyone who really knows him."

" I hope we may clear him, Miss Turner," said Sherlock Holmes. " You may rely upon my doing all that I can."

" But you have read the evidence. You have formed some conclusion ? Do you not see some loophole, some flaw ? Do you not yourself think that he is innocent ? "

" I think that it is very probable."

" There now ! " she cried, throwing back her head and looking defiantly at Lestrade. " You hear ! He gives me hope."

Lestrade shrugged his shoulders. " I am afraid that my colleague has been a little quick in forming his conclusions," he said.

" But he is right. Oh ! I know that he is right. James never did it. And about his quarrel with his father, I am sure that the reason why he would not speak about it to the coroner was because I was concerned in it."

" In what way ? " asked Holmes.

" It is no time for me to hide anything. James and his father had many disagreements about me. Mr. McCarthy was very anxious that there should be a marriage between us. James and I have always loved each other as brother and sister, but of course he is young and has seen very little of life yet, and—and—well, he naturally did not wish to do anything like that yet. So there were quarrels, and this, I am sure, was one of them."

" And your father ? " asked Holmes. " Was he in favour of such a union ? "

" No, he was averse to it also. No one but Mr. McCarthy was in favour of it." A quick blush passed over her fresh young face as Holmes shot one of his keen, questioning glances at her.

" Thank you for this information," said he. " May I see your father if I call to-morrow ? "

" I am afraid the doctor won't allow it."

" The doctor ? "

" Yes, have you not heard ? Poor father has never been strong for years back, but this has broken him down completely. He has taken to his bed, and Dr. Willows says that he is a wreck, and that his nervous system is shattered. Mr. McCarthy was the only man alive who had known dad in the old days in Victoria." **19**

" Ha ! In Victoria ! That is important."

" Yes, at the mines."

" Quite so ; at the gold mines, where, as I understand, Mr. Turner made his money."

" Yes, certainly."

" Thank you, Miss Turner. You have been of material assistance to me."

" You will tell me if you have any news to-morrow. No doubt you will go to the prison to see James. Oh,

not rain before we go over the ground," and Watson adds: "There was no rain as Holmes had foretold." And Watson tells us that the morning of the second—and closing—day of the case "broke bright and cloudless." In *Whitaker's Almanack* we read that 0.08 inches of rain fell on Friday, June 7, 1889, and that 1.37 inches fell on Monday, June 10, 1889. There was *no* rain, however, on either Saturday, June 8, 1889, or Sunday, June 9, 1889. On the Saturday, the barometer read 29.716 (on the Sunday, 29.489) and there was virtually *no wind* on the Saturday (the pressure was only 0.5 pounds). *Saturday, June 8, and Sunday, June 9, 1889*, fit Holmes' and Watson's descriptions exactly.

19 *Victoria*. The most densely populated and smallest state (except Tasmania) in Australia.

LESTRADE SHRUGGED HIS SHOULDERS.

Illustration by Sidney Paget for the *Strand Magazine*, October, 1891.

20 *Hereford.* Municipal borough on the Wye, birthplace of Nell Gwyn and David Garrick.

21 *yellow-backed novel.* A popular, cheap novel —so called from the former practice, especially in England, of binding such books in yellow board or paper covers.

. . . WHERE I LAY UPON THE SOFA AND TRIED TO INTEREST MYSELF IN A YELLOW-BACKED NOVEL.

Illustration by Sidney Paget for the *Strand Magazine*, October, 1891.

if you do, Mr. Holmes, do tell him that I know him to be innocent."

" I will, Miss Turner."

" I must go home now, for dad is very ill, and he misses me so if I leave him. Good-bye, and God help you in your undertaking." She hurried from the room as impulsively as she had entered, and we heard the wheels of her carriage rattle off down the street.

" I am ashamed of you, Holmes," said Lestrade with dignity, after a few minutes' silence. " Why should you raise up hopes which you are bound to disappoint ? I am not over-tender of heart, but I call it cruel."

" I think that I see my way to clearing James McCarthy," said Holmes. " Have you an order to see him in prison ? "

" Yes, but only for you and me."

20 " Then I shall reconsider my resolution about going out. We have still time to take a train to Hereford and see him to-night ? "

" Ample."

" Then let us do so. Watson, I fear that you will find it very slow, but I shall only be away a couple of hours."

I walked down to the station with them, and then wandered through the streets of the little town, finally returning to the hotel, where I lay upon the sofa and tried to **21** interest myself in a yellow-backed novel. The puny plot of the story was so thin, however, when compared to the deep mystery through which we were groping, and I found my attention wander so constantly from the fiction to the fact, that I at last flung it across the room, and gave myself up entirely to a consideration of the events of the day. Supposing that this unhappy young man's story was absolutely true, then what hellish thing, what absolutely unforeseen and extraordinary calamity, could have occurred between the time when he parted from his father and the moment when, drawn back by his screams, he rushed into the glade ? It was something terrible and deadly. What could it be ? Might not the nature of the injuries reveal something to my medical instincts ? I rang the bell, and called for the weekly county paper, which contained a verbatim account of the inquest. In the surgeon's deposition it was stated that the posterior third of the left parietal bone and the left half of the occipital bone had been shattered by a heavy blow from a blunt weapon. I marked the spot upon my own head. Clearly such a blow must have been struck from behind. That was to some extent in favour of the accused, as when seen quarrelling he was face to face with his father. Still, it did not go for very much, for the older man might have turned his back before the blow fell. Still, it might be worth while to call Holmes' attention to it. Then there was the peculiar dying reference to a rat. What could that mean ? It could not be delirium. A man dying from a sudden blow does not commonly become delirious. No, it was more likely to be an attempt to explain how he met his fate. But what could it indicate ? I cudgelled my brains to find some possible explanation. And then the incident of the grey cloth, seen by young McCarthy.

If that were true, the murderer must have dropped some part of his dress, presumably his overcoat, in his flight, and must have had the hardihood to return and carry it away at the instant when the son was kneeling with his back turned not a dozen paces off. What a tissue of mysteries and improbabilities the whole thing was ! I did not wonder at Lestrade's opinion, and yet I had so much faith in Sherlock Holmes' insight that I could not lose hope as long as every fresh fact seemed to strengthen his conviction of young McCarthy's innocence.

It was late before Sherlock Holmes returned. He came back alone, for Lestrade was staying in lodgings in the town.

" The glass still keeps very high," he remarked, as he **22** sat down. " It is of importance that it should not rain before we are able to go over the ground. On the other hand, a man should be at his very best and keenest for such nice work as that, and I did not wish to do it when fagged by a long journey. I have seen young McCarthy."

" And what did you learn from him ? "

" Nothing."

" Could he throw no light ? "

" None at all. I was inclined to think at one time that he knew who had done it, and was screening him or her, but I am convinced now that he is as puzzled as everyone else. He is not a very quick-witted youth, though comely to look at, and, I should think, sound at heart."

" I cannot admire his taste," I remarked, " if it is indeed a fact that he was averse to a marriage with so charming a young lady as this Miss Turner."

" Ah, thereby hangs a rather painful tale. This fellow is madly, insanely in love with her, but some two years ago, when he was only a lad, and before he really knew her, for she had been away five years at a boarding-school, what does the idiot do but get into the clutches of a barmaid in Bristol, and marry her at a registry office ! No one knows a word of the matter, but you can imagine how maddening it must be to him to be upbraided for not doing what he would give his very eyes to do, but what he knows to be absolutely impossible. It was sheer frenzy of this sort which made him throw his hands up into the air when his father, at their last interview, was goading him on to propose to Miss Turner. On the other hand, he had no means of supporting himself, and his father, who was by all accounts a very hard man, would have thrown him over utterly had he known the truth. It was with his barmaid wife that he had spent the last three days in Bristol, and his father did not know where he was. Mark that point. It is of importance. Good has come out of evil, however, for the barmaid, finding from the papers that he is in serious trouble, and likely to be hanged, has thrown him over utterly, and has written to him to say that she has a husband already in the Bermuda Dockyard, so that there is really no tie between them. I think that that bit of news has consoled young McCarthy for all that he has suffered."

" But if he is innocent, who has done it ? "

" Ah ! who ? I would call your attention very particularly to two points. One is that the murdered man had

22 *"The glass still keeps very high."* But 29 inches, Holmes' previous reading, "is a *low* barometer reading for London and Southern England—not 'very high' as Holmes appears to have supposed. The June normal is about 30 inches. Perhaps the great man's instrument was an aneroid out of proper adjustment."—Mr. E. L. Hawke of the Royal Meteorological Society, London, in a letter to your editor, July 31, 1955.

23 *George Meredith.* English novelist and poet, 1828–1909, whose writings are notable for their psychological insight and close inspection of the relationship between the individual and social events (we know that Conan Doyle, like Holmes, was attracted by Meredith: he remarked in *Through the Magic Door* that "his beloved *Richard Feveral* . . . lurks in yonder corner. What a great book it is, how wise and how witty!").

"May we not infer that Meredith's *Ordeal of Richard Feveral*, in the three-volume 1859 first edition . . . [was] among the choice items in the Holmes treasure-room?" Miss Madeleine B. Stern wrote in "Sherlock Holmes: Rare Book Collector."

And Mr. H. B. Williams ("Then Falls Thy Shadow") saw here "one more proof of the strong hold that the memory of Irene Adler had upon Holmes. As before, it is just a few words and here we must bow to the innate delicacy of John Watson, a delicacy which forbade him to set down the full conversation on this particular occasion. It is remarkable how this woman was able to break through the Master's iron guard and direct a portion of his conversational proclivities. . . . Irene Adler and George Meredith, what possible connection can they have? Yet one does not have too far to go into the life of Meredith before the key of Holmes' interest is found. George Meredith is also one of that suffering brotherhood who loves one who belongs to another, and thus, is forever lost. . . . Meredith and Janet Ross. The Master never did anything but what was buttressed by sound causes. Thus, in his desire to talk about George Meredith he found surcease from the strain of trying to keep *The* Woman locked within his breast."

an appointment with someone at the Pool, and that the someone could not have been his son, for his son was away, and he did not know when he would return. The second is that the murdered man was heard to cry 'Cooee!' before he knew that his son had returned. Those are the crucial points upon which the case depends. **23** And now let us talk about George Meredith, if you please, and we shall leave minor points until to-morrow."

There was no rain, as Holmes had foretold, and the morning broke bright and cloudless. At nine o'clock Lestrade called for us with the carriage, and we set off for Hatherley Farm and the Boscombe Pool.

"There is serious news this morning," Lestrade observed. "It is said that Mr. Turner, of the Hall, is so ill that his life is despaired of."

"An elderly man, I presume?" said Holmes.

"About sixty; but his constitution has been shattered by his life abroad, and he has been in failing health for some time. This business has had a very bad effect upon him. He was an old friend of McCarthy's, and, I may add, a great benefactor to him, for I have learned that he gave him Hatherley Farm rent free."

"Indeed! That is interesting," said Holmes.

"Oh, yes! In a hundred other ways he has helped him. Everybody about here speaks of his kindness to him."

"Really! Does it not strike you as a little singular that this McCarthy, who appears to have had little of his own, and to have been under such obligations to Turner, should still talk of marrying his son to Turner's daughter, who is, presumably, heiress to the estate, and that in such a very cocksure manner, as if it was merely a case of a proposal and all else would follow? It is the more strange since we know that Turner himself was averse to the idea. The daughter told us as much. Do you not deduce something from that?"

"We have got to the deductions and the inferences," said Lestrade, winking at me. "I find it hard enough to tackle facts, Holmes, without flying away after theories and fancies."

"You are right," said Holmes demurely; "you do find it very hard to tackle the facts."

"Anyhow, I have grasped one fact which you seem to find it difficult to get hold of," replied Lestrade with some warmth.

"And that is?"

"That McCarthy, senior, met his death from McCarthy, junior, and that all theories to the contrary are the merest moonshine."

"Well, moonshine is a brighter thing than fog," said Holmes, laughing. "But I am very much mistaken if this is not Hatherley Farm upon the left."

"Yes, that is it." It was a widespread, comfortable-looking building, two-storied, slate-roofed, with great yellow blotches of lichen upon the grey walls. The drawn blinds and the smokeless chimneys, however, gave it a stricken look, as though the weight of this horror still lay heavy upon it. We called at the door, when the maid, at Holmes' request, showed us the boots which her master

wore at the time of his death, and also a pair of the son's,
though not the pair which he had then had. Having
measured these very carefully from seven or eight different points, Holmes desired to be led to the courtyard,
from which we all followed the winding track which led
to Boscombe Pool.

Sherlock Holmes was transformed when he was hot
upon such a scent as this. Men who had only known the
quiet thinker and logician of Baker Street would have
failed to recognize him. His face flushed and darkened.
His brows were drawn into two hard, black lines, while
his eyes shone out from beneath them with a steely glitter.
His face was bent downwards, his shoulders bowed, his
lips compressed, and the veins stood out like whip-cord in
his long, sinewy neck. His nostrils seemed to dilate with
a purely animal lust for the chase, and his mind was so
absolutely concentrated upon the matter before him, that
a question or remark fell unheeded upon his ears, or at
the most only provoked a quick, impatient snarl in reply.
Swiftly and silently he made his way along the track
which ran through the meadows, and so by way of the
woods to the Boscombe Pool. It was damp, marshy
ground, as is all that district, and there were marks of
many feet, both upon the path and amid the short grass
which bounded it on either side. Sometimes Holmes
would hurry on, sometimes stop dead, and once he made
quite a little *détour* into the meadow. Lestrade and I
walked behind him, the detective indifferent and contemptuous, while I watched my friend with the interest
which sprang from the conviction that every one of his
actions was directed towards a definite end.

The Boscombe Pool, which is a little reed-girt sheet
of water some fifty yards across, is situated at the boundary
between the Hatherley Farm and the private park of the
wealthy Mr. Turner. Above the woods which lined it
upon the farther side we could see the red jutting pinnacles
which marked the site of the rich landowner's dwelling.
On the Hatherley side of the Pool the woods grew very
thick, and there was a narrow belt of sodden grass twenty
paces across between the edge of the trees and the reeds
which lined the lake. Lestrade showed us the exact spot
at which the body had been found, and indeed, so moist
was the ground, that I could plainly see the traces which
had been left by the fall of the stricken man. To Holmes,
as I could see by his eager face and peering eyes, very
many other things were to be read upon the trampled
grass. He ran round, like a dog who is picking up a
scent, and then turned upon my companion.

" What did you go into the Pool for ? " he asked.

" I fished about with a rake. I thought there might be
some weapon or other trace. But how on earth—— ? "

" Oh, tut, tut ! I have no time. That left foot of
yours with its inward twist is all over the place. A mole
could trace it, and there it vanishes among the reeds.
Oh, how simple it would all have been had I been here
before they came like a herd of buffalo, and wallowed all
over it. Here is where the party with the lodge-keeper
came, and they have covered all tracks for six or eight feet
round the body. But here are three separate tracks of the

. . . THE MAID, AT HOLMES' REQUEST, SHOWED US
THE BOOTS . . .

Illustration by Sidney Paget for the *Strand Magazine*, October, 1891.

same feet." He drew out a lens, and lay down upon his waterproof to have a better view, talking all the time rather to himself than to us. "These are young McCarthy's feet. Twice he was walking, and once he ran swiftly so that the soles are deeply marked, and the heels hardly visible. That bears out his story. He ran when he saw his father on the ground. Then here are the father's feet as he paced up and down. What is this, then? It is the butt end of the gun as the son stood listening. And this? Ha, ha! What have we here? Tip-toes, tip-toes! Square, too, quite unusual boots! They come, they go, they come again—of course that was for the cloak. Now where did they come from?" He ran up and down, sometimes losing, sometimes finding the track, until we were well within the edge of the wood and under the shadow of a great beech, the largest tree in the neighbourhood. Holmes traced his way to the farther side of this, and lay down once more upon his face with a little cry of satisfaction. For a long time he remained there, turning over the leaves and dried sticks, gathering up what seemed to me to be dust into an envelope, and examining with his lens not only the ground, but even the bark of the tree as far as he could reach. A jagged stone was lying among the moss, and this also he carefully examined and retained. Then he followed a pathway through the wood until he came to the high-road, where all traces were lost.

"It has been a case of considerable interest," he remarked, returning to his natural manner. "I fancy that this grey house on the right must be the lodge. I think that I will go in and have a word with Moran, and perhaps write a little note. Having done that, we may drive back to our luncheon. You may walk to the cab, and I shall be with you presently."

It was about ten minutes before we regained our cab, and drove back into Ross, Holmes still carrying with him the stone which he had picked up in the wood.

"This may interest you, Lestrade," he remarked, holding it out. "The murder was done with it."

"I see no marks."

"There are none."

"How do you know, then?"

"The grass was growing under it. It had only lain there a few days. There was no sign of a place whence it had been taken. It corresponds with the injuries. There is no sign of any other weapon."

"And the murderer?"

"Is a tall man, left-handed, limps with the right leg, wears thick-soled shooting-boots and a grey cloak, smokes Indian cigars, uses a cigar-holder, and carries a blunt penknife in his pocket. There are several other indications, but these may be enough to aid us in our search."

Lestrade laughed. "I am afraid that I am still a sceptic," he said. "Theories are all very well, but we have to deal with a hard-headed British jury."

24 "*Nous verrons*," answered Holmes calmly. "You work your own method, and I shall work mine. I shall

FOR A LONG TIME HE REMAINED THERE . . .

Illustration by Sidney Paget for the *Strand Magazine*, October, 1891.

24 "Nous verrons." French: "We shall see."

be busy this afternoon, and shall probably return to London by the evening train."

" And leave your case unfinished ? "

" No, finished."

" But the mystery ? "

" It is solved."

" Who was the criminal, then ? "

" The gentleman I describe."

" But who is he ? "

" Surely it would not be difficult to find out. This is not such a populous neighbourhood."

Lestrade shrugged his shoulders. " I am a practical man," he said, " and I really cannot undertake to go about the country looking for a left-handed gentleman with a game leg. I should become the laughing-stock of Scotland Yard."

" All right," said Holmes quietly. " I have given you the chance. Here arc your lodgings. Good-bye. I shall drop you a line before I leave."

Having left Lestrade at his rooms we drove to our hotel, where we found lunch upon the table. Holmes was silent and buried in thought, with a pained expression upon his face, as one who finds himself in a perplexing position.

" Look here, Watson," he said, when the cloth was cleared ; " just sit down in this chair and let me preach to you for a little. I don't quite know what to do, and I should value your advice. Light a cigar, and let me expound."

" Pray do so."

" Well, now, in considering this case there are two points about young McCarthy's narrative which struck us both instantly, although they impressed me in his favour and you against him. One was the fact that his father should, according to his account, cry ' Cooee ! ' before seeing him. The other was his singular dying reference to a rat. He mumbled several words, you understand, but that was all that caught the son's ear. Now from this double point our research must commence, and we will begin it by presuming that what the lad says is absolutely true."

" What of this ' Cooee ! ' then ? "

" Well, obviously it could not have been meant for the son. The son, as far as he knew, was in Bristol. It was mere chance that he was within earshot. The ' Cooee ! ' was meant to attract the attention of whoever it was that he had the appointment with. But ' Cooee ' is a distinctly Australian cry, and one which is used between Australians. There is a strong presumption that the person whom McCarthy expected him to meet at Boscombe Pool was someone who had been in Australia."

" What of the rat, then ? "

Sherlock Holmes took a folded paper from his pocket and flattened it out on the table. " This is a map of the Colony of Victoria," he said. " I wired to Bristol for it last night." He put his hand over part of the map. " What do you read ? " he asked.

" ARAT," I read.

25 *"It is wonderful!" I exclaimed.* But it might be pointed out that there are many other towns in Australia—Ararat, for example—to which "ARAT" would equally apply.

"HE HAD STOOD BEHIND THAT TREE . . ."

Illustration by Sidney Paget for the *Strand Magazine*, October, 1891.

" And now ? " He raised his hand.

" BALLARAT."

" Quite so. That was the word the man uttered, and of which his son only caught the last two syllables. He was trying to utter the name of his murderer. So-and-so of Ballarat."

25 " It is wonderful ! " I exclaimed.

" It is obvious. And now, you see, I had narrowed the field down considerably. The possession of a grey garment was a third point which, granting the son's statement to be correct, was a certainty. We have come now out of mere vagueness to the definite conception of an Australian from Ballarat with a grey cloak."

" Certainly."

" And one who was at home in the district, for the Pool can only be approached by the farm or by the estate, where strangers could hardly wander."

" Quite so."

" Then comes our expedition of to-day. By an examination of the ground I gained the trifling details which I gave to that imbecile Lestrade, as to the personality of the criminal."

" But how did you gain them ? "

" You know my method. It is founded upon the observance of trifles."

" His height I know that you might roughly judge from the length of his stride. His boots, too, might be told from their traces."

" Yes, they were peculiar boots."

" But his lameness ? "

" The impression of his right foot was always less distinct than his left. He put less weight upon it. Why ? Because he limped—he was lame."

" But his left-handedness ? "

" You were yourself struck by the nature of the injury as recorded by the surgeon at the inquest. The blow was struck from immediately behind, and yet was upon the left side. Now, how can that be unless it were by a left-handed man ? He had stood behind that tree during the interview between the father and son. He had even smoked there. I found the ash of a cigar, which my special knowledge of tobacco ashes enabled me to pronounce as an Indian cigar. I have, as you know, devoted some attention to this, and written a little monograph on the ashes of 140 different varieties of pipe, cigar, and cigarette tobacco. Having found the ash, I then looked round and discovered the stump among the moss where he had tossed it. It was an Indian cigar, of the variety which are rolled in Rotterdam."

" And the cigar-holder ? "

" I could see that the end had not been in his mouth. Therefore he used a holder. The tip had been cut off, not bitten off, but the cut was not a clean one, so I deduced a blunt penknife."

" Holmes," I said, " you have drawn a net round this man from which he cannot escape, and you have saved an innocent human life as truly as if you had cut the cord which was hanging him. I see the direction in which all this points. The culprit is——"

" Mr. John Turner," cried the hotel waiter, opening

the door of our sitting-room, and ushering in a visitor.

The man who entered was a strange and impressive figure. His slow, limping step and bowed shoulders gave the appearance of decrepitude, and yet his hard, deep-lined, craggy features, and his enormous limbs showed that he was possessed of unusual strength of body and of character. His tangled beard, grizzled hair, and out-standing, drooping eyebrows combined to give an air of dignity and power to his appearance, but his face was of an ashen white, while his lips and the corners of his nostrils were tinged with a shade of blue. It was clear to me at a glance that he was in the grip of some deadly and chronic disease.

" Pray sit down on the sofa," said Holmes gently. " You had my note ? "

" Yes, the lodge-keeper brought it up. You said that you wished to see me here to avoid scandal."

" I thought people would talk if I went to the Hall."

" And why did you wish to see me ? " He looked across at my companion with despair in his weary eyes, as though his question were already answered.

" Yes," said Holmes, answering the look rather than the words. " It is so. I know all about McCarthy."

The old man sank his face in his hands. " God help me ! " he cried. " But I would not have let the young man come to harm. I give you my word that I would have spoken out if it went against him at the Assizes."

" I am glad to hear you say so," said Holmes gravely.

" I would have spoken now had it not been for my dear girl. It would break her heart—it will break her heart when she hears that I am arrested."

" It may not come to that," said Holmes.

" What ! "

" I am no official agent. I understand that it was your daughter who required my presence here, and I am acting in her interests. Young McCarthy must be got off, however."

" I am a dying man," said old Turner. " I have had diabetes for years. My doctor says it is a question whether I shall live a month. Yet I would rather die under my own roof than in a gaol."

Holmes rose and sat down at the table with his pen in his hand and a bundle of paper before him. " Just tell us the truth," he said. " I shall jot down the facts. You will sign it, and Watson here can witness it. Then I could produce your confession at the last extremity to save young McCarthy. I promise you that I shall not use it unless it is absolutely needed."

" It's as well," said the old man ; " it's a question whether I shall live to the Assizes, so it matters little to me, but I should wish to spare Alice the shock. And now I will make the thing clear to you ; it has been a long time in the acting, but will not take me long to tell.

" You didn't know this dead man, McCarthy. He was a devil incarnate. I tell you that. God keep you out of the clutches of such a man as he. His grip has been upon me these twenty years, and he has blasted my life. I'll tell you first how I came to be in his power.

" It was in the early 'sixties at the diggings. I was a young chap then, hot-blooded and reckless, ready to turn

"MR. JOHN TURNER," CRIED THE HOTEL WAITER . . .

Illustration by Sidney Paget for the *Strand Magazine*, October, 1891.

26 *and made our way over to England.* In "Some Diggings Down Under," Mrs. Jennifer Chorley has written: "Black Jack's account of the gold robbery appears to be a condensed version of two famous bushranging exploits: 1) of 1853 (the Mc-Ivor Gold Robbery); and 2) of 1862 (the Eugowra Escort Robbery). The second raid was on the way to Sydney but both raids featured fights between six troopers and six bushrangers. In one, the driver was wounded and, in the other, killed. In both raids the bushrangers escaped, and though some were later caught and executed, some were never captured and the gold was never recovered. The raids, which included ambushes, seem to bear the mark of the same gang and a few weeks after Eugowra *'a man named Turner* was arrested at Yass.' No doubt he later escaped as his name is not among those executed later. All the bushrangers used a multitude of aliases."

my hand to anything ; I got among bad companions, took to drink, had no luck with my claim, took to the bush, and, in a word, became what you would call over here a highway robber. There were six of us, and we had a wild, free life of it, sticking up a station from time to time, or stopping the wagons on the road to the diggings. Black Jack of Ballarat was the name I went under, and our party is still remembered in the colony as the Ballarat Gang.

" One day a gold convoy came down from Ballarat to Melbourne, and we lay in wait for it and attacked it. There were six troopers and six of us, so it was a close thing, but we emptied four of their saddles at the first volley. Three of our boys were killed, however, before we got the swag. I put my pistol to the head of the wagon-driver, who was this very man McCarthy. I wish to the Lord that I had shot him then, but I spared him, though I saw his wicked little eyes fixed on my face, as though to remember every feature. We got away with the gold, became wealthy men, and made our way over **26** to England without being suspected. There I parted from my old pals, and determined to settle down to a quiet and respectable life. I bought this estate, which chanced to be in the market, and I set myself to do a little good with my money, to make up for the way in which I had earned it. I married, too, and though my wife died young, she left me my dear little Alice. Even when she was just a baby her wee hand seemed to lead me down the right path as nothing else had ever done. In a word, I turned over a new leaf, and did my best to make up for the past. All was going well when McCarthy laid his grip upon me.

" I had gone up to town about an investment, and I met him in Regent Street with hardly a coat to his back or a boot to his foot.

" ' Here we are, Jack,' says he, touching me on the arm ; ' we'll be as good as a family to you. There's two of us, me and my son, and you can have the keeping of us. If you don't—it's a fine, law-abiding country is England, and there's always a policeman within hail.'

" Well, down they came to the West Country, there was no shaking them off, and there they have lived rent free on my best land ever since. There was no rest for me, no peace, no forgetfulness ; turn where I would, there was his cunning, grinning face at my elbow. It grew worse as Alice grew up, for he soon saw I was more afraid of her knowing my past than of the police. Whatever he wanted he must have, and whatever it was I gave him without question, land, money, houses, until at last he asked for a thing which I could not give. He asked for Alice.

" His son, you see, had grown up, and so had my girl, and as I was known to be in weak health, it seemed a fine stroke to him that his lad should step into the whole property. But there I was firm. I would not have his cursed stock mixed with mine ; not that I had any dislike to the lad, but his blood was in him, and that was enough. I stood firm. McCarthy threatened. I braved him to do his worst. We were to meet at the Pool midway between our houses to talk it over.

"When I went down there I found him talking with his son, so I smoked a cigar, and waited behind a tree until he should be alone. But as I listened to his talk all that was black and bitter in me seemed to come uppermost. He was urging his son to marry my daughter with as little regard for what she might think as if she were a slut from off the streets. It drove me mad to think that I and all that I held most dear should be in the power of such a man as this. Could I not snap the bond? I was already a dying and a desperate man. Though clear of mind and fairly strong of limb, I knew that my own fate was sealed. But my memory and my girl! Both could be saved, if I could but silence that foul tongue. I did it, Mr. Holmes. I would do it again. Deeply as I have sinned, I have led a life of martyrdom to atone for it. But that my girl should be entangled in the same meshes which held me was more than I could suffer. I struck him down with no more compunction than if he had been some foul and venomous beast. His cry brought back his son; but I had gained the cover of the wood, though I was forced to go back to fetch the cloak which I had dropped in my flight. That is the true story, gentlemen, of all that occurred."

"Well, it is not for me to judge you," said Holmes, as the old man signed the statement which had been drawn out. "I pray that we may never be exposed to such a temptation."

"I pray not, sir. And what do you intend to do?"

"In view of your health, nothing. You are yourself **27** aware that you will soon have to answer for your deed at a higher court than the Assizes. I will keep your confession, and, if McCarthy is condemned, I shall be forced to use it. If not, it shall never be seen by mortal eye; and your secret, whether you be alive or dead, shall be safe with us."

"Farewell! then," said the old man solemnly. "Your own death-beds, when they come, will be the easier for the thought of the peace which you have given to mine." Tottering and shaking in all his giant frame, he stumbled slowly from the room.

27 *"In view of your health, nothing.* Mr. John Ball, Jr. ("Early Days in Baker Street") sees in this case another "revelation of Holmes' high official position" in the British government. "Consider this carefully: the crime was murder. Lestrade was on the case, and Lestrade was far from a fool. In a rural area, where prominent individuals are well known, Holmes supplied Lestrade with a detailed and unmistakable description of the murderer. A tall left-handed cripple would be easy for even Lestrade to find—and Lestrade, in fact, actually reported to Holmes the condition of this man's health. Yet Holmes in his own person pardoned the murderer, and Lestrade quietly dropped the case and did not make an arrest. It is inconceivable that a Scotland Yard inspector would let a known murderer off scot free unless he was under direct orders to do so."

"FAREWELL! THEN," SAID THE OLD MAN SOLEMNLY.

Illustration by Sidney Paget for the *Strand Magazine*, October, 1891.

28 *'There, but for the grace of God, goes Sherlock Holmes.'"* A paraphrase of the words uttered by John Bradford, 1510–1555, whenever he saw a criminal go by; wrongly credited by Holmes to the great English divine Richard Baxter, 1615–1691.

29 *submitted to the defending counsel.* "Since when," Mr. Albert P. Blaustein asked in "Sherlock Holmes As a Lawyer," "do laymen prepare objections for proceedings in a court of law? Have we convinced the skeptic [that Holmes was a lawyer]?"

Bibliographical Note: According to Professor David A. Randall, "The Boscombe Valley Mystery" was first published in book form in an unauthorized collection of Conan Doyle's short stories titled *The Doings of Raffles Haw*, New York: Lovell, Coryell & Co., August, 1892, as "Number Five in the Belmore Series."

" God help us ! " said Holmes, after a long silence. " Why does Fate play such tricks with poor helpless worms ?   I never hear of such a case as this that I do not think of Baxter's words, and say : ' There, but for the
28 grace of God, goes Sherlock Holmes.' "

James McCarthy was acquitted at the Assizes, on the strength of a number of objections which had been drawn
29 out by Holmes, and submitted to the defending counsel. Old Turner lived for seven months after our interview, but he is now dead ; and there is every prospect that the son and daughter may come to live happily together, in ignorance of the black cloud which rests upon their past.

39

THE STOCKBROKER'S CLERK

[Saturday, June 15, 1889]

SHORTLY after my marriage I had bought a con- **1**
nection in the Paddington district. Old Mr. **2**
Farquhar, from whom I purchased it, had at one
time an excellent general practice, but his age, and an
affliction of the nature of St. Vitus' dance from which he
suffered, had very much thinned it. The public, not
unnaturally, goes upon the principle that he who would
heal others must himself be whole, and looks askance at
the curative powers of the man whose own case is beyond
the reach of his drugs. Thus, as my predecessor weakened his practice declined, until when I purchased it
from him it had sunk from twelve hundred to little more
than three hundred a year. I had confidence, however, **3**
in my own youth and energy, and was convinced that in a **4**
very few years the concern would be as flourishing as ever.

For three months after taking over the practice I was
kept very closely at work, and saw little of my friend
Sherlock Holmes, for I was too busy to visit Baker Street,
and he seldom went anywhere himself save upon professional business. I was surprised, therefore, when one
morning in June, as I sat reading the *British Medical* **5**
Journal after breakfast, I heard a ring at the bell followed **6**
by the high, somewhat strident, tones of my old companion's voice.

" Ah, my dear Watson," said he, striding into the room,
" I am very delighted to see you. I trust that Mrs. Watson has entirely recovered from all the little excitements
connected with our adventure of the ' Sign of Four ' ? "

" Thank you, we are both very well," said I, shaking
him warmly by the hand.

" And I hope also," he continued, sitting down in the
rocking-chair, " that the cares of medical practice have not
entirely obliterated the interest which you used to take in
our little deductive problems."

" On the contrary," I answered ; " it was only last
night that I was looking over my old notes and classifying
some of our past results."

" I trust that you don't consider your collection
closed ? "

" Not at all. I should wish nothing better than to
have some more of such experiences."

" To-day, for example ? "

" Yes ; to-day, if you like."

" And as far off as Birmingham ? "

1 *Shortly after my marriage.* This is certainly
Watson's marriage to Mary Morstan, for Holmes
later says: "I trust that Mrs. Watson has entirely
recovered from all the little excitements connected
with our adventure of the 'Sign of the Four.'"
The year in which chronologists place this adventure consequently depends upon the date they
assign to Watson's marriage to Mary. The ranks
are fairly evenly divided between 1888 (Andrew,
Bell, Brend, Harrison, Heldenbrand, Hoff, Knox,
Morley, and Roberts) and 1889 (Baring-Gould,
Blakeney, Christ, Folsom, Pattrick, Petersen, Smith,
and Zeisler).

2 *the Paddington district.* In "The Adventure of
the Engineer's Thumb," Watson tells us that his
consulting room at this time was "no very great
distance from Paddington Station." "Watson [like
Holmes] seems to have been attracted by the quiet
appeal of Georgian architecture for he appears to
have practiced from houses of this period wherever
he lived," Mr. William H. Gill wrote in "Some
Notable Sherlockian Buildings." "His references
to Paddington Station seem to show that he lived
on the very last Estate to be laid out in London
in a gracious manner. The superb Paddington Estate, bounded by the Edgware Road, the Grand
Union Canal, Hyde Park and the Westbourne
Brook, contained some of the prettiest houses in
the fast-spreading metropolis, and there is no
doubt that Watson lived in the neighbourhood of
Norfolk Square. These tall, stucco-fronted profes-
sional-class houses would have suited a rising
young medical practitioner, and had none of the
flamboyance of the later period. The Paddington
Estate was laid out by George Gutch in 1838 and
coincided with the arrival of the Great Western
Railway, the favourite line of Holmes and Watson."

" It is impossible to say in which of Paddington's
many streets Watson lived," Mr. Michael Harrison wrote (*In the Footsteps of Sherlock Holmes*);
" he could have lived in Eastbourne Terrace, which
runs alongside the west wall of Paddington Station, and connects Praed Street with Bishop's
Bridge Road. It was a respectable street in his day
—though its degeneration into a 'red lamp' street
was inevitable—but it was noisy. It is far more

"HA! NOTHING COULD BE BETTER!" SAID HOLMES . . .

Illustration by Sidney Paget for the *Strand Maga-zine*, March, 1893.

likely that Watson lived across Praed Street, in Spring Street or London Street or even in Norfolk Square, which is separated from Praed Street only by a block of houses. He would thus be near enough to the Station to be known to the staff, while sufficiently removed from the traffic of Praed Street to enjoy a certain amount of quiet. His rent would have been (for a three-storeyed house in, say, Spring Street) about £60 [$300] per annum; a four-storeyed house in nearby Norfolk Square would have been about £80 [$400]; both figures exclusive of rates."

3 *from twelve hundred to little more than three hundred a year.* From $6,000 to little more than $1,500.

4 *my own youth and energy.* "Youth is, after all, a somewhat elastic term," the late Dr. Samuel R. Meaker wrote in "Watson Medicus," "but we would put Watson at a ripe 37 at this time. As to energy, he admitted frankly at his first meeting with Holmes that he was extremely lazy, and there is no evidence to show that he later reformed in this respect, except for brief periods."

5 *one morning in June.* It was a Saturday morning, as we learn later. Watson's statement that he "saw little" of Holmes for three months after taking over the practice has been interpreted by some commentators to mean that he bought the practice some three months *before* the adventure of "The Stockbroker's Clerk"—in March, let us say, and that he married Mary Morstan shortly before this, perhaps in January or February. But this is not necessarily the case: Watson says he saw "little," not "nothing," of Holmes during the first three months of his practice. In our view, Watson purchased his Paddington practice "shortly" after his marriage to Mary *circa* May 1, 1889.

7   " Certainly, if you wish it."

" And the practice ? "

" I do my neighbour's when he goes. He is always ready to work off the debt."

" Ha ! Nothing could be better ! " said Holmes, leaning back in his chair and looking keenly at me from under his half-closed lids. " I perceive that you have been unwell lately. Summer colds are always a little trying."

" I was confined to the house by a severe chill for three days last week. I thought, however, that I had cast off every trace of it."

" So you have. You look remarkably robust."

" How, then, did you know of it ? "

" My dear fellow, you know my methods."

" You deduced it, then ? "

" Certainly."

" And from what ? "

" From your slippers."

I glanced down at the new patent leathers which I was wearing. " How on earth—— ? " I began, but Holmes answered my question before it was asked.

" Your slippers are new," he said. " You could not have had them more than a few weeks. The soles which you are at this moment presenting to me are slightly scorched. For a moment I thought they might have got wet and been burned in the drying. But near the instep there is a small circular wafer of paper with the shopman's hieroglyphics upon it. Damp would of course have removed this. You had then been sitting with your feet outstretched to the fire, which a man would hardly do

8 even in so wet a June as this if he were in his full health."

Like all Holmes' reasoning, the thing seemed simplicity itself when it was once explained. He read the thought upon my features, and his smile had a tinge of bitterness.

" I am afraid that I rather give myself away when I explain," said he. " Results without causes are much more impressive. You are ready to come to Birmingham, then ? "

" Certainly. What is the case ? "

" You shall hear it all in the train. My client is outside in a four-wheeler. Can you come at once ? "

" In an instant." I scribbled a note to my neighbour, rushed upstairs to explain the matter to my wife, and joined Holmes upon the doorstep.

" Your neighbour is a doctor ? " said he, nodding at the brass plate.

" Yes. He bought a practice, as I did."

" An old-established one ? "

" Just the same as mine. Both have been ever since the houses were built."

" Ah, then you got hold of the better of the two."

" I think I did. But how do you know ? "

" By the steps, my boy. Yours are worn three inches deeper than his. But this gentleman in the cab is my client, Mr. Hall Pycroft. Allow me to introduce you to him. Whip your horse up, cabby, for we have only just time to catch our train."

The man whom I found myself facing was a well-built,

fresh-complexioned young fellow with a frank, honest face and a slight, crisp, yellow moustache. He wore a very shiny top-hat and a neat suit of sober black, which made him look what he was—a smart young City man, of the class who have been labelled Cockneys, but who give us our crack Volunteer regiments, and who turn out more fine athletes and sportsmen than any body of men in these islands. His round, ruddy face was naturally full of cheeriness, but the corners of his mouth seemed to me to be pulled down in a half-comical distress. It was not, however, until we were all in a first-class carriage and well started upon our journey to Birmingham, that I was able to learn what the trouble was which had driven him to Sherlock Holmes.

" We have a clear run here of seventy minutes," Holmes remarked. " I want you, Mr. Hall Pycroft, to tell my friend your very interesting experience exactly as you have told it to me, or with more detail if possible. It will be of use to me to hear the succession of events again. It is a case, Watson, which may prove to have something in it, or may prove to have nothing, but which at least presents those unusual and *outré* features which are as dear to you as they are to me. Now, Mr. Pycroft, I shall not interrupt you again."

Our young companion looked at me with a twinkle in his eye.

" The worst of the story is," said he, " that I show myself up as such a confounded fool. Of course, it may work out all right, and I don't see that I could have done otherwise ; but if I have lost my crib and get nothing in **9** exchange, I shall feel what a soft Johnny I have been. I'm not very good at telling a story, Dr. Watson, but it is like this with me.

" I used to have a billet at Coxon & Woodhouse, of Drapers' Gardens, but they were let in early in the spring **10** through the Venezuelan loan, as no doubt you remember, and came a nasty cropper. I had been with them five years, and old Coxon gave me a ripping good testimonial when the smash came ; but, of course, we clerks were all turned adrift, the twenty-seven of us. I tried here and tried there, but there were lots of other chaps on the same lay as myself, and it was a perfect frost for a long time. I had been taking three pounds a week at Coxon's, and I had saved about seventy of them, but I soon worked my way through that and out at the other end. I was fairly at the end of my tether at last, and could hardly find the stamps to answer the advertisements or the envelopes to stick them to. I had worn out my boots padding up office stairs, and I seemed just as far from getting a billet as ever.

" At last I saw a vacancy at Mawson & Williams', the great stockbroking firm in Lombard Street. I dare say E.C. is not much in your line, but I can tell you that this **11** is about the richest house in London. The advertisement was to be answered by letter only. I sent in my testimonial and application, but without the least hope of getting it. Back came an answer by return saying that if I would appear next Monday I might take over my new duties at once, provided that my appearance was

6 *as I sat reading the* British Medical Journal. Mr. S. C. Roberts has suggested ("A Note on the Watson Problem") that "it seems fair to deduce that the date was not later than 10 June" since "monthly Journals are normally read soon after their arrival at the beginning of the month."

7 *"Certainly, if you wish it."* "Watson jumped at the chance to go to Birmingham with Holmes," the late Christopher Morley wrote in "Dr. Watson's Secret." "He thought he might be able to persuade Sherlock to run out to Walsall (only eight miles away) to see Miss Hunter at the school where she was headmistress."

8 *so wet a June as this.* Baring-Gould, Christ, and Zeisler are agreed that the day was *Saturday, June 15, 1889.* As Dr. Zeisler wrote: "from the London *Times* we learn that there was some rain on the 1st and the 3rd, the 6th was a most foul day with immense rains all day, the 7th was hardly less wet than the 6th, there was rain all day long on the 10th, and there was rain on the 12th, 14th, and 15th. In the London *Times* for June 11, 1889, on page 3, we find that 'For more than three days there has not been one gleam of sunshine in London; the rainfall has amounted to more than half the average for the whole month.' . . . Whereas the 1st and the 8th were too early in the month to speak of a 'wet June,' this would have been entirely applicable on June 15th. Inasmuch as there was no rain at all after the 16th it is not likely that the Master would have called it a wet month on either the 22nd or the 29th . . ."

In our view, Watson must have caught his chill on the Monday afternoon following his return from Boscombe Valley, that is, on the 10th of June. No doubt, having been away from his practice for two days, he was out all day in the all-day rain. We believe that Watson was confined to his house on the Tuesday, Wednesday, and Thursday, the 11th to the 13th, recovering in time to join Holmes in the adventure of "The Stockbroker's Clerk" on Saturday, June 15th.

9 *lost my crib.* Cockney slang for "lost my job."

10 *Drapers' Gardens.* One of the many courts and narrow streets, leading nowhere in particular, which throng the home of the Stock Exchange brokers and their clerks—that quarter of the City which is enclosed by Moorgate on the west, London Wall on the north, Old Broad Street on the east, and Throgmorton Street on the south.

11 *E.C.* Eastern Central, the designation of the Post Office district in which most of the great London stockbrokering enterprises are to be found.

"... THE GREAT STOCKBROKING FIRM IN
LOMBARD STREET."

Lombard Street is "The street of bankers, which
derived its name from the Italian merchants who
frequented it before the reign of Edward II,"
Augustus J. C. Hare wrote in *Walks in London*,
Vol. I. "Jane Shore, the beloved of Edward IV,
was the wife of a goldsmith in this street; Guy, the
founder of Guy's Hospital, was a bookseller here;
and here, where his father was a linen-draper, the
poet Pope was born in 1688 amongst the merchants
and money-makers." Our photograph, by G. F.
Allen, is from the *Second County Life Picture
Book of London;* London: Country Life, 1953.

" 'MR. HALL PYCROFT, I BELIEVE?' SAID HE."

Illustration by William H. Hyde for *Harper's
Weekly*, March 11, 1893. Sidney Paget illustrated
the same scene for the *Strand Magazine*, March,
1893.

12 *The screw*. Cockney slang for "the salary."

satisfactory.   No one knows how these things are worked.
Some people say the manager just plunges his hand into
the heap and takes the first that comes.   Anyhow, it was
my innings that time, and I don't ever wish to feel better
12 pleased.   The screw was a pound a week rise, and the
duties just about the same as at Coxon's.

" And now I come to the queer part of the business.   I
was in diggings out Hampstead way—17 Potter's Terrace, was the address.   Well, I was sitting doing a smoke
that very evening after I had been promised the appointment, when up came my landlady with a card which had
' Arthur Pinner, financial agent,' printed upon it.   I had
never heard the name before, and could not imagine what
he wanted with me, but of course I asked her to show
him up.   In he walked—a middle-sized, dark-haired,
dark-eyed, black-bearded man, with a touch of the sheeny
about his nose.   He had a brisk kind of way with him
and spoke sharply, like a man that knew the value of
time.

" 'Mr. Hall Pycroft, I believe?' said he.

" 'Yes, sir,' I answered, and pushed a chair towards
him.

" 'Lately engaged at Coxon & Woodhouse's?'

" 'Yes, sir.'

" 'And now on the staff of Mawson's?'

" 'Quite so.'

" 'Well,' said he.   'The fact is that I have heard some
really extraordinary stories about your financial ability.
You remember Parker who used to be Coxon's manager?

He can never say enough about it.'

" Of course I was pleased to hear this. I had always been pretty smart in the office, but I had never dreamed that I was talked about in the City in this fashion.

" ' You have a good memory ? ' said he.

" ' Pretty fair,' I answered, modestly.

" ' Have you kept in touch with the market while you have been out of work ? ' he asked.

" ' Yes ; I read the Stock Exchange List every morning.'

" ' Now, that shows real application ! ' he cried. ' That is the way to prosper ! You won't mind my testing you, will you ? Let me see ! How are Ayrshires ? '

" ' One hundred and five, to one hundred and five and a quarter.'   **13**

" ' And New Zealand Consolidated ? '

" ' A hundred and four.'

" ' And British Broken Hills ? '

" ' Seven to seven and six.'

" ' Wonderful ! ' he cried, with his hands up. ' This   **14** quite fits in with all that I had heard. My boy, my boy, you are very much too good to be a clerk at Mawson's ! '

" **This** outburst rather astonished me, as you can think. ' Well,' said I, ' other people don't think quite so much of **me** as you seem to do, Mr. Pinner. I had a hard enough fight to get this berth, and I am very glad to have it.'

" ' Pooh, man, you should soar above it. You are not in your true sphere. Now I'll tell you how it stands with me. What I have to offer is little enough when measured by your ability, but when compared with Mawson's it is light to dark. Let me see ! When do you go to Mawson's ? '

" ' On Monday.'

" ' Ha ! ha ! I think I would risk a little sporting flutter that you don't go there at all.'

" ' Not go to Mawson's ? '

" ' No, sir. By that day you will be business manager of the Franco-Midland Hardware Company, Limited, with one hundred and thirty-four branches in the towns and villages of France, not counting one in Brussels and one in San Remo.'

" This took my breath away. ' I never heard of it,' said I.

" ' Very likely not. It has been kept very quiet, for the capital was all privately subscribed, and it is too good a thing to let the public into. My brother, Harry Pinner, is promoter, and joins the board after allotment as managing director. He knew that I was in the swim down here, and he asked me to pick up a good man cheap— a young, pushing man with plenty of snap about him. Parker spoke of you, and that brought me here to-night. We can only offer you a beggarly five hundred to start with——'

" ' Five hundred a year ! ' I shouted.

" ' Only that at the beginning, but you are to have an overriding commission of 1 per cent on all business done by your agents, and you may take my word for it that this will come to more than your salary.'

" ' But I know nothing about hardware.'

13 " '*One hundred and five, to one hundred and five and a quarter.*' In some American editions of the Canon, the bid and asked prices are given as "One hundred and six and a quarter to one hundred and five and seven-eights." Since bid and asked prices are given in that order, these figures incorrectly suggest that the bid was higher than the asking price.

14 " '*Wonderful!*' *he cried, with his hands up.* Writing in "Doctor Watson—Punter or Speculator?", Mr. R. M. McLaren has noted that "British Broken Hill was a mining company in Australia which was finally absorbed into North Broken Hill. New Zealand Consolidated went into liquidation in 1900. The third stock mentioned was 'Ayrshires.' . . . It is unlikely that this referred to an Ayr County Council loan since there would be no daily fluctuation in the price of such a stock. It is almost certain that this was a Stock Exchange nickname now forgotten. During their lifetime the stocks of the London, Midland and Scottish and the London and North Eastern Railway Companies were always referred to as 'Brum' and 'Berwick.' It is probable that, in a similar way at the time, the stocks of the former Glasgow and South Western Railway were known as 'Ayrshires.'"

" ' Tut, my boy, you know about figures.'

" My head buzzed, and I could hardly sit still in the chair. But suddenly a little chill of doubt came over me.

" ' I must be frank with you,' said I. ' Mawson only gives me two hundred, but Mawson is safe. Now, really, I know so little about your company that——'

" ' Ah, smart, smart ! ' he cried, in a kind of ecstasy of delight. ' You are the very man for us ! You are not to be talked over, and quite right too. Now here's a note for a hundred pounds ; and if you think that we can do business you may just slip it into your pocket as an advance upon your salary.'

" ' That is very handsome,' said I. ' When shall I take over my new duties ? '

" ' Be in Birmingham to-morrow at one,' said he. ' I have a note in my pocket here which you will take to my brother. You will find him at 126B Corporation Street, where the temporary offices of the company are situated. Of course he must confirm your engagement, but between ourselves it will be all right.'

" ' Really, I hardly know how to express my gratitude, Mr. Pinner,' said I.

" ' Not at all, my boy. You have only got your deserts. There are one or two small things—mere formalities— which I must arrange with you. You have a bit of paper beside you there. Kindly write upon it, " I am perfectly willing to act as business manager to the Franco-Midland Hardware Company, Limited, at a minimum salary of £500." '

" I did as he asked, and he put the paper in his pocket.

" ' There is one other detail,' said he. ' What do you intend to do about Mawson's ? '

" I had forgotten all about Mawson's in my joy.

" ' I'll write and resign,' said I.

" ' Precisely what I don't want you to do. I had a row over you with Mawson's manager. I had gone up to ask him about you, and he was very offensive—accused me of coaxing you away from the service of the firm, and that sort of thing. At last I fairly lost my temper. " If you want good men you should pay them a good price," said I. " He would rather have our small price than your big one," said he. " I'll lay you a fiver," said I, " that when he has my offer you will never so much as hear from him again." " Done ! " said he. " We picked him out of the gutter, and he won't leave us so easily." Those were his very words.'

" ' The impudent scoundrel ! ' I cried. ' I've never so much as seen him in my life. Why should I consider him in any way ? I shall certainly not write if you would rather that I didn't.'

" ' Good ! That's a promise ! ' said he, rising from his chair. ' Well, I am delighted to have got so good a man for my brother. Here is your advance of a hundred pounds, and here is the letter. Make a note of the address, 126B Corporation Street, and remember that one o'clock to-morrow is your appointment. Good night, and may you have all the fortune that you deserve.'

" That's just about all that passed between us as near as I can remember it. You can imagine, Dr. Watson, how pleased I was at such an extraordinary piece of good fortune. I sat up half the night hugging myself over it, and next day I was off to Birmingham in a train that would take me in plenty of time for my appointment. I took my things to an hotel in New Street, and then I made my way to the address which had been given me.

" It was a quarter of an hour before my time, but I thought that would make no difference. 126B was a passage between two large shops which led to a winding **15** stone stair, from which there were many flats, let as offices to companies or professional men. The names of the occupants were painted up at the bottom on the wall, but there was no such name as the Franco-Midland Hardware Company, Limited. I stood for a few minutes with my heart in my boots, wondering whether the whole thing was an elaborate hoax or not, when up came a man and addressed me. He was very like the chap that I had seen the night before, the same figure and voice, but he was clean shaven and his hair was lighter.

" ' Are you Mr. Hall Pycroft ? ' he asked.

" ' Yes,' said I.

" ' Ah ! I was expecting you, but you are a trifle before your time. I had a note from my brother this morning, in which he sang your praises very loudly.'

" ' I was just looking for the offices when you came.'

" ' We have not got our name up yet, for we only secured these temporary premises last week. Come up with me and we will talk the matter over.'

" I followed him to the top of a very lofty stair, and there right under the slates were a couple of empty and dusty little rooms, uncarpeted and uncurtained, into which he led me. I had thought of a great office with shining tables and rows of clerks such as I was used to, and I dare say I stared rather straight at the two deal chairs and one little table, which, with a ledger and a waste-paper basket, made up the whole furniture.

" ' Don't be disheartened, Mr. Pycroft,' said my new acquaintance, seeing the length of my face. ' Rome was not built in a day, and we have lots of money at our backs, though we don't cut much dash yet in offices. Pray sit down and let me have your letter.'

" I gave it to him, and he read it over very carefully.

" ' You seem to have made a vast impression upon my brother Arthur,' said he, ' and I know that he is a pretty shrewd judge. He swears by London, you know, and I by Birmingham, but this time I shall follow his advice. Pray consider yourself definitely engaged.'

" ' What are my duties ? ' I asked.

" ' You will eventually manage the great depôt in Paris, which will pour a flood of English crockery into the shops of one hundred and thirty-four agents in France. The purchase will be completed in a week, and meanwhile you will remain in Birmingham and make yourself useful.'

" ' How ? '

" For answer he took a big red book out of a drawer. ' This is a directory of Paris,' said he, ' with the trades after the names of the people. I want you to take it home with you, and to mark off all the hardware sellers with their addresses. It would be of the greatest use to me to have them.'

15 *126B was a passage between two large shops.* In "Browsings in Birmingham," Mr. Anthony G. Cooper has written that he investigated "126B Corporation Street" in the summer of 1959 and found that address to be part of a building called "Kings Hall," built in 1888.

". . . UP CAME A MAN AND ADDRESSED ME."

Illustration by Sidney Paget for the *Strand Magazine*, March, 1893.

16 *Friday—that is, yesterday.* Establishing the day of the adventure as a Saturday.

" ' Surely, there are classified lists ? ' I suggested.

" ' Not reliable ones. Their system is different to ours. Stick at it and let me have the lists by Monday, at twelve. Good day, Mr. Pycroft ; if you continue to show zeal and intelligence, you will find the company a good master.'

" I went back to the hotel with the big book under my arm, and with very conflicting feelings in my breast. On the one hand I was definitely engaged, and had a hundred pounds in my pocket. On the other, the look of the offices, the absence of name on the wall, and other of the points which would strike a business man, had left a bad impression as to the position of my employers. However, come what might, I had my money, so I settled down to my task. All Sunday I was kept hard at work, and yet by Monday I had only got as far as H. I went round to my employer, found him in the same dismantled kind of room, and was told to keep at it until Wednesday, and then come again. On Wednesday it was still unfinished, so I hammered away until Friday—that is, yester-**16** day. Then I brought it round to Mr. Harry Pinner.

" ' Thank you very much,' said he. ' I fear that I underrated the difficulty of the task. This list will be of very material assistance to me.'

" ' It took some time,' said I.

" ' And now,' said he, ' I want you to make a list of the furniture shops, for they all sell crockery.'

" ' Very good.'

" ' And you can come up to-morrow evening at seven, and let me know how you are getting on. Don't over-work yourself. A couple of hours at Day's Music-Hall in the evening would do you no harm after your labours.' He laughed as he spoke, and I saw with a thrill that his second tooth upon the left-hand side had been very badly stuffed with gold."

Sherlock Holmes rubbed his hands with delight, and I stared in astonishment at our client.

" You may well look surprised, Dr. Watson, but it is this way," said he. " When I was speaking to the other chap in London at the time that he laughed at my not going to Mawson's, I happened to notice that his tooth was stuffed in this very identical fashion. The glint of the gold in each case caught my eye, you see. When I put that with the voice and figure being the same, and only those things altered which might be changed by a razor or a wig, I could not doubt that it was the same man. Of course, you expect two brothers to be alike, but not that they should have the same tooth stuffed in the same way. He bowed me out and I found myself in the street, hardly knowing whether I was on my head or my heels. Back I went to my hotel, put my head in a basin of cold water, and tried to think it out. Why had he sent me from London to Birmingham ; why had he got there before me ; and why had he written a letter from himself to himself ? It was altogether too much for me, and I could make no sense of it. And then suddenly it struck me that what was dark to me might be very light to Mr. Sherlock Holmes. I had just time to get up to town by the night train, to see him this morning, and to bring you both back with me to Birmingham."

There was a pause after the stockbroker's clerk had concluded his surprising experience. Then Sherlock Holmes cocked his eye at me, leaning back on the cushions with a pleased and yet critical face, like a connoisseur who had just taken his first sip of a comet vintage.

" Rather fine, Watson, is it not ? " said he. " There are points in it which please me. I think you will agree with me that an interview with Mr. Arthur Harry Pinner in the temporary offices of the Franco-Midland Hardware Company, Limited, would be a rather interesting experience for both of us."

" But how can we do it ? " I asked.

" Oh, easily enough," said Hall Pycroft, cheerily. " You are two friends of mine who are in want of a billet, and what could be more natural than that I should bring you both round to the managing director ? "

" Quite so ! Of course ! " said Holmes. " I should like to have a look at the gentleman and see if I can make anything of his little game. What qualities have you, my friend, which would make your services so valuable ? or is it possible that——" He began biting his nails and staring blankly out of the window, and we hardly drew another word from him until we were in New Street.

At seven o'clock that evening we were walking, the three of us, down Corporation Street to the company's offices.

" It is of no use our being at all before our time," said our client. " He only comes there to see me apparently, for the place is deserted up to the very hour he names."

" That is suggestive," remarked Holmes.

" By Jove, I told you so ! " cried the clerk. " That's he walking ahead of us there."

He pointed to a smallish, blond, well-dressed man, who was bustling along the other side of the road. As we watched him he looked across at a boy who was bawling out the latest edition of the evening paper, and, running over among the cabs and 'buses, he bought one from him. Then clutching it in his hand he vanished through a doorway.

" There he goes ! " cried Hall Pycroft. " Those are the company's offices into which he has gone. Come with me and I'll fix it up as easily as possible."

Following his lead we ascended five stories, until we found ourselves outside a half-opened door, at which our client tapped. A voice within bade us " Come in," and we entered a bare, unfurnished room, such as Hall Pycroft had described. At the single table sat the man whom we had seen in the street, with his evening paper spread out in front of him, and as he looked up at us it seemed to me that I had never looked upon a face which bore such marks of grief, and of something beyond grief—of a horror such as comes to few men in a lifetime. His brow glistened with perspiration, his cheeks were of the dull dead white of a fish's belly, and his eyes were wild and staring. He looked at his clerk as though he failed to recognize him, and I could see, by the astonishment

. . . I HAD NEVER LOOKED UPON A FACE WHICH BORE SUCH MARKS OF GRIEF . . .

Illustration by William H. Hyde for *Harper's Weekly*, March 11, 1893. Sidney Paget illustrated the same scene for the *Strand Magazine*, March, 1893.

17 *Bermondsey*. A metropolitan borough on the right bank of the Thames below London Bridge. The name means "the island of Beormund" (a Saxon personal name) and indicates the formerly marshy character of the place. In Bermondsey is Rotherhithe, the scene of some of Holmes' investigations in "The Adventure of the Dying Detective."

depicted upon our conductor's face, that this was by no means the usual appearance of his employer.

" You look ill, Mr. Pinner," he exclaimed.

" Yes, I am not very well," answered the other, making obvious efforts to pull himself together, and licking his dry lips before he spoke. " Who are these gentlemen whom you have brought with you ? "

17 " One is Mr. Harris, of Bermondsey, and the other is Mr. Price, of this town," said our clerk, glibly. " They are friends of mine, and gentlemen of experience, but they have been out of a place for some little time, and they hoped that perhaps you might find an opening for them in the company's employment."

" Very possibly ! Very possibly ! " cried Mr. Pinner, with a ghastly smile. " Yes, I have no doubt that we shall be able to do something for you. What is your particular line, Mr. Harris ? "

" I am an accountant," said Holmes.

" Ah, yes, we shall want something of the sort. And you, Mr. Price ? "

" A clerk," said I.

" I have every hope that the company may accommodate you. I will let you know about it as soon as we come to any conclusion. And now I beg that you will go. For God's sake, leave me to myself ! "

These last words were shot out of him, as though the constraint which he was evidently setting upon himself had suddenly and utterly burst asunder. Holmes and I glanced at each other, and Hall Pycroft took a step towards the table.

" You forget, Mr. Pinner, that I am here by appointment to receive some directions from you," said he.

" Certainly, Mr. Pycroft, certainly," the other answered in a calmer tone. " You may wait here a moment, and there is no reason why your friends should not wait with you. I will be entirely at your service in three minutes, if I might trespass upon your patience so far." He rose with a very courteous air, and bowing to us he passed out through a door at the farther end of the room, which he closed behind him.

" What now ? " whispered Holmes. " Is he giving us the slip ? "

" Impossible," answered Pycroft.

" Why so ? "

" That door leads into an inner room."

" There is no exit ? "

" None."

" Is it furnished ? "

" It was empty yesterday."

" Then what on earth can he be doing ? There is something which I don't understand in this matter. If ever a man was three parts mad with terror, that man's name is Pinner. What can have put the shivers on him ? "

" He suspects that we are detectives," I suggested.

" That's it," said Pycroft.

Holmes shook his head. " He did not turn pale. He *was* pale when we entered the room," said he. " It is just possible that——"

His words were interrupted by a sharp rat-tat from the direction of the inner door.

" What the deuce is he knocking at his own door for ? " cried the clerk.

Again and much louder came the rat-tat-tat. We all gazed expectantly at the closed door. Glancing at Holmes I saw his face turn rigid, and he leaned forward in intense excitement. Then suddenly came a low gurgling, gargling sound and a brisk drumming upon woodwork. Holmes sprang frantically across the room and pushed at the door. It was fastened on the inner side. Following his example, we threw ourselves upon it with all our weight. One hinge snapped, then the other, and down came the door with a crash. Rushing over it, we found ourselves in the inner room.

It was empty.

But it was only for a moment that we were at fault. At one corner, the corner nearest the room which we had left, there was a second door. Holmes sprang to it and pulled it open. A coat and waistcoat were lying on the floor, and from a hook behind the door, with his own braces round his neck, was hanging the managing director of the Franco-Midland Hardware Company. His knees were drawn up, his head hung at a dreadful angle to his body, and the clatter of his heels against the door made the noise which had broken in upon our conversation. In an instant I had caught him round the waist and held him up, while Holmes and Pycroft untied the elastic bands which had disappeared between the livid creases of skin. Then we carried him into the other room, where he lay with a slate-coloured face, puffing his purple lips in and out with every breath—a dreadful wreck of all that he had been but five minutes before.

" What do you think of him, Watson ? " asked Holmes.

I stooped over him and examined him. His pulse was feeble and intermittent, but his breathing grew longer, and there was a little shivering of his eyelids which showed a thin white slit of ball beneath.

" It has been touch and go with him," said I, " but he'll live now. Just open that window and hand me the water carafe." I undid his collar, poured the cold water over his face, and raised and sank his arms until he drew a long natural breath.

" It's only a question of time now," said I, as I turned away from him.

Holmes stood by the table with his hands deep in his trousers pockets and his chin upon his breast.

" I suppose we ought to call the police in now," said he ; " and yet I confess that I like to give them a complete case when they come."

" It's a blessed mystery to me," cried Pycroft, scratching his head. " Whatever they wanted to bring me all the way up here for, and then——"

" Pooh ! All that is clear enough," said Holmes impatiently. " It is this last sudden move."

" You understand the rest, then ? "

" I think that is fairly obvious. What do you say, Watson ? "

I shrugged my shoulders.

" I must confess that I am out of my depths," said I.

" Oh, surely, if you consider the events at first they can

RUSHING OVER IT, WE FOUND OURSELVES IN THE INNER ROOM.

Illustration by Sidney Paget for the *Strand Magazine*, March, 1893.

HALL PYCROFT SHOOK HIS CLENCHED HANDS IN THE AIR.

Illustration by Sidney Paget for the *Strand Magazine*, March, 1893.

only point to one conclusion."

" What do you make of them ? "

" Well, the whole thing hinges upon two points. The first is the making of Pycroft write a declaration by which he entered the service of this preposterous company. Do you not see how very suggestive that is ? "

" I am afraid I miss the point."

" Well, why did they want him to do it ? Not as a business matter, for these arrangements are usually verbal, and there was no earthly business reason why this should be an exception. Don't you see, my young friend, that they were very anxious to obtain a specimen of your handwriting, and had no other way of doing it ? "

" And why ? "

" Quite so. Why ? When we answer that, we have made some progress with our little problem. Why ? There can be only one adequate reason. Someone wanted to learn to imitate your writing, and had to procure a specimen of it first. And now if we pass on to the second point, we find that each throws light upon the other. That point is the request made by Pinner that you should not resign your place, but should leave the manager of this important business in the full expectation that a Mr. Hall Pycroft, whom he had never seen, was about to enter the office upon the Monday morning."

" My God ! " cried our client, " what a blind beetle I have been ! "

" Now you see the point about the handwriting. Suppose that someone turned up in your place who wrote a completely different hand from that in which you had applied for the vacancy, of course the game would have been up. But in the interval the rogue learnt to imitate you, and his position was therefore secure, as I presume that nobody in the office had ever set eyes upon you ? "

" Not a soul," groaned Hall Pycroft.

" Very good. Of course, it was of the utmost importance to prevent you from thinking better of it, and also to keep you from coming into contact with anyone who might tell you that your double was at work in Mawson's office. Therefore they gave you a handsome advance on your salary, and ran you off to the Midlands, where they gave you enough work to do to prevent your going to London, where you might have burst their little game up. That is all plain enough."

" But why should this man pretend to be his own brother ? "

" Well, that is pretty clear also. There are evidently only two of them in it. The other is personating you at the office. This one acted as your engager, and then found that he could not find you an employer without admitting a third person into his plot. That he was most unwilling to do. He changed his appearance as far as he could, and trusted that the likeness, which you could not fail to observe, would be put down to a family resemblance. But for the happy chance of the gold stuffing your suspicions would probably have never been aroused."

Hall Pycroft shook his clenched hands in the air.

" Good Lord ! " he cried. " While I have been fooled in this way, what has this other Hall Pycroft been doing at Mawson's ? What should we do, Mr. Holmes ? Tell me what to do ! "

" We must wire to Mawson's."

" They shut at twelve on Saturdays."

" Never mind ; there may be some door-keeper or attendant——"

" Ah, yes ; they keep a permanent guard there on account of the value of the securities that they hold. I remember hearing it talked of in the City."

" Very good, we shall wire to him, and see if all is well, and if a clerk of your name is working there. That is clear enough, but what is not so clear is why at sight of us one of the rogues should instantly walk out of the room and hang himself."

" The paper ! " croaked a voice behind us. The man was sitting up, blanched and ghastly, with returning reason in his eyes, and hands which rubbed nervously at the broad red band which still encircled his throat.

" The paper ! Of course ! " yelled Holmes, in a paroxysm of excitement. " Idiot that I was ! I thought so much of our visit that the paper never entered my head for an instant. To be sure, the secret must lie there." He flattened it out on the table, and a cry of triumph burst from his lips.

" Look at this, Watson ! " he cried. " It is a London paper, an early edition of the *Evening Standard*. Here **18** is what we want. Look at the headlines—' Crime in the City. Murder at Mawson & Williams'. Gigantic Attempted Robbery ; Capture of the Criminal.' Here, Watson, we are all equally anxious to hear it, so kindly read it aloud to us."

It appeared from its position in the paper to have been the one event of importance in town, and the account of it ran in this way :

" A desperate attempt at robbery, culminating in the death of one man and the capture of the criminal, occurred this afternoon in the City. For some time back Mawson & Williams, the famous financial house, have been the guardians of securities which amount in the aggregate to a sum of considerably over a million sterling. So conscious was the manager of the responsibility which devolved upon him in consequence of the great interests at stake, that safes of the very latest construction have been employed, and an armed watchman has been left day and night in the building. It appears that last week a new clerk, named Hall Pycroft, was engaged by the firm. This person appears to have been none other than Beddington, the famous forger and cracksman, who, with his brother, has only recently emerged from a five years' spell of penal servitude. By some means, which are not yet clear, he succeeded in winning, under a false name, this official position in the office, which he utilized in order to obtain mouldings of various locks and a thorough knowledge of the position of the strong-room and the safes.

" It is customary at Mawson's for the clerks to leave at midday on Saturday. Sergeant Tuson, of the City Police, **19**

18 *an early edition of the* Evening Standard. "If everything went well it would have been just possible to get a few quire of that [issue of the *Evening Standard*] to Birmingham by 7 P.M.," Mr. John Hyslop wrote in "Sherlock Holmes and the Press." "But it would have been by no means an early edition. It would have been the very latest. And the Birmingham *Evening Despatch*, with a much fuller story, ought to have reached the fish and chip shops by the time that London paper arrived." Mr. Hyslop also pointed out that the headline, "Capture of the criminal," "is a gross breach of journalistic ethics: . . . the man is found guilty by the newspaper before he has even appeared before a magistrate."

19 *Sergeant Tuson.* Mr. Michael Harrison has suggested (*In the Footsteps of Sherlock Holmes*) that the name "Tuson may be an echo of Watson's impecunious days; it is the name of a well-known firm of pawnbrokers with branches in London and the provinces."

was somewhat surprised therefore to see a gentleman with a carpet bag come down the steps at twenty minutes past one. His suspicions being aroused, the sergeant followed the man, and with the aid of Constable Pollock succeeded, after a most desperate resistance, in arresting him. It was at once clear that a daring and gigantic robbery had been committed. Nearly a hundred thousand pounds' worth of American railway bonds, with a large amount of scrip in other mines and companies, were discovered in the bag. On examining the premises the body of the unfortunate watchman was found doubled up and thrust into the largest of the safes, where it would not have been discovered until Monday morning had it not been for the prompt action of Sergeant Tuson. The man's skull had been shattered by a blow from a poker, delivered from behind. There could be no doubt that Beddington had obtained entrance by pretending that he had left something behind him, and having murdered the watchman, rapidly rifled the large safe, and then made off with his booty. His brother, who usually works with him, has not appeared in this job, as far as can at present be ascertained, although the police are making energetic inquiries as to his whereabouts."

"Well, we may save the police some little trouble in that direction," said Holmes, glancing at the haggard figure huddled up by the window. "Human nature is a strange mixture, Watson. You see that even a villain and a murderer can inspire such affection that his brother turns to suicide when he learns that his neck is forfeited. However, we have no choice as to our action. The doctor and I will remain on guard, Mr. Pycroft, if you will have the kindness to step out for the police."

"WELL, WE MAY SAVE THE POLICE SOME LITTLE TROUBLE IN THAT DIRECTION," SAID HOLMES . . .

Illustration by Sidney Paget for the *Strand Magazine*, March, 1893.

40

THE NAVAL TREATY

[Tuesday, July 30, to Thursday, August 1, 1889]

THE July which immediately succeeded my marriage was made memorable by three cases of **1** interest in which I had the privilege of being associated with Sherlock Holmes, and of studying his methods. I find them recorded in my notes under the headings of "The Adventure of the Second Stain," **2** "The Adventure of the Naval Treaty," and "The Adventure of the Tired Captain." The first of these, **3** however, deals with interests of such importance, and implicates so many of the first families in the kingdom, that for many years it will be impossible to make it public. No case, however, in which Holmes was ever engaged has illustrated the value of his analytical methods so clearly or has impressed those who were associated with him so deeply. I still retain an almost verbatim report of the interview in which he demonstrated the true facts of the case to Monsieur Dubuque, of the Paris police, and Fritz von Waldbaum, the well-known specialist of Dantzig, both of whom had wasted their energies upon what proved to be side-issues. The new century will have come, however, before the story can be safely told. Meanwhile, I pass on to the second upon my list, which promised also, at one time, to be of national importance, and was marked by several incidents which give it a quite unique character.

During my school-days I had been intimately associated with a lad named Percy Phelps, who was of much the same age as myself, though he was two classes ahead of me. He was a very brilliant boy, and carried away every prize which the school had to offer, finishing his exploits by winning a scholarship, which sent him on to continue his triumphant career at Cambridge. He was, I remember, extremely well connected and even when we were all little boys together, we knew that his mother's brother was Lord Holdhurst, the great Conservative politician. This **4** gaudy relationship did him little good at school ; on the contrary, it seemed rather a piquant thing to us to chevy him about the playground and hit him over the shins with a wicket. But it was another thing when he came out **5** into the world. I heard vaguely that his abilities and the

1 *The July which immediately succeeded my marriage.* Watson's marriage to Mary Morstan, in the opinion of all chronologists. His "immediately" is taken by some as an indication that the marriage was in the spring of the year, rather than the preceding winter. The year, however, is again a matter of controversy, with supporters for 1887, 1888, and 1889.

2 *"The Adventure of the Second Stain."* Watson shortly tells us that in *this* "Adventure of the Second Stain" he retained in his notes "an almost verbatim report of the interview in which [Holmes] demonstrated the true facts of the case to Monsieur Dubuque, of the Paris police, and Fritz von Waldbaum, the well-known specialist of Dantzig, both of whom had wasted their energies in what proved to be side-issues." Now, this incident certainly did not take place in "The Adventure of the Second Stain" as recorded by Watson for the *Strand Magazine* (December, 1904) and *Collier's Weekly* (January 28, 1905). A number of distinguished commentators nevertheless maintain that the two adventures were one and the same. Mr. Anatole Chujoy, for example, in "The Only Second Stain," has written that "When Watson finally received permission from Holmes to relate 'The Adventure of the Second Stain,' he wrote it out in full, as he had promised his readers in 'The Adventure of the Naval Treaty.' He then showed the manuscript to Holmes, perhaps to check on some obscure detail. Reading the story, Holmes realized that some of the dramatis personae, or perhaps their progeny, were still alive and could be recognized. To avoid hurting them unnecessarily, after so many years or, perhaps, fearing libel action against Watson, Holmes cut the story short at the climactic moment of the return of the dangerous letter to the despatch-box and left out entirely the spy-hunt that followed it. Watson, of course, had not expected that Holmes would censor 'The Second Stain': he had never done so before. Hence the apparent discrepancy between the reference to the story in 'The Naval Treaty' and the story itself."

The late Gavin Brend, on the other hand, argued in *My Dear Holmes* that Watson's references in "The Yellow Face" and "The Adventure of the Naval Treaty" were part of a code. He noted that both were published in 1893, a year in which Holmes was believed dead by all but his brother Mycroft. To give Sherlock certain information, Mycroft Holmes drafted paragraphs which he asked Watson to incorporate in his accounts of the two cases. Sherlock, reading Watson's accounts, would then know that when the phrase "the second stain" appeared, the matter just preceding or following it was not to be taken literally.

These are ingenious explanations, indeed, but commentators who hold that the recorded adventure and "The Adventure of the Second Stain" referred to in "The Adventure of the Naval Treaty" are the same must still explain why the recorded adventure took place in the autumn, not in July, and in an autumn in which Watson was unmarried and living in Baker Street during the entire period of the adventure. Further, even Watson could hardly have forgotten that he had dated the "Second Stain" of "The Naval Treaty" quite precisely (for Watson); had that adventure and the published adventure been one and the same, it would have been pointless for him to go to such pains to conceal the date of the published adventure ("It was, then, in a year, and even in a decade, that shall be nameless . . .").

In our view, then, Watson retained notes of *three* adventures which he associated in one way or another with a "second strain": 1) the recorded adventure; 2) the "failure" mentioned in "The Yellow Face"; and 3) the adventure which took place in the July immediately following his marriage to Mary Morstan.

3 "*The Adventure of the Tired Captain.*" Mr. Alan Wilson has written a pastiche stemming from this reference of the doctor's which will be found in the *Sherlock Holmes Journal*, Vol. IV, No. 1, Winter, 1958, pp. 8–11, and Vol. IV, No. 2, Spring, 1959, pp. 48–51.

But Mr. Rolfe Boswell has held that Watson himself chronicled "The Adventure of the Tired Captain" as "The Adventure of the Missing Three-Quarter": "After all, Cyril Overton, 'the skipper of the Rugger team of Cambridge 'Varsity,' . . . *was* a captain. . . . That he was tired followed from Watson's description . . . 'haggard with anxiety.' "

4 *Lord Holdhurst, the great Conservative politician.* Mr. O. F. Grazebrook, in his *Studies in Sherlock Holmes, II: Politics and Premiers*, has identified Lord Holdhurst with Lord Salisbury, who was Prime Minister in 1888. But this ignores Watson's later comment: "The Cabinet Minister and *future* Prime Minister."

influence which he commanded had won him a good position at the Foreign Office, and then he passed completely out of my mind until the following letter recalled his existence :

6   " BRIARBRAE, WOKING.

" MY DEAR WATSON,—I have no doubt that you can remember ' Tadpole ' Phelps, who was in the fifth form when you were in the third. It is possible even that you may have heard that, through my uncle's influence, I obtained a good appointment at the Foreign Office, and that I was in a situation of trust and honour until a horrible misfortune came suddenly to blast my career.

" There is no use writing the details of that dreadful event. In the event of your acceding to my request, it is probable that I shall have to narrate them to you. I **7** have only just recovered from nine weeks of brain fever, and am still exceedingly weak. Do you think that you could bring your friend, Mr. Holmes, down to see me ? I should like to have his opinion of the case, though the authorities assure me that nothing more can be done. Do try to bring him down, and as soon as possible. Every minute seems an hour while I live in this horrible suspense. Assure him that, if I have not asked his advice sooner, it was not because I did not appreciate his talents, but because I have been off my head ever since the blow fell. Now I am clear again, though I dare not think of it too much for fear of a relapse. I am still so weak that I have to write, as you see, by dictating. Do try and bring him.

" Your old schoolfellow,
" PERCY PHELPS."

. . . WON HIM A GOOD POSITION AT THE FOREIGN OFFICE . . .

The Foreign Office, where Percy Phelps had a good position, as seen from St. James's Park. With the Home Office and the Colonial Office, it is housed in a fine quadrangle of buildings enclosed by Whitehall, Downing Street, St. James's Park, and King Charles Street. These were erected between 1868 and 1873 from the designs of Sir Gilbert Scott, in the Italian style, at a cost of £500,000.

There was something that touched me as I read this letter, something pitiable in the reiterated appeals to bring Holmes. So moved was I that, even if it had been a difficult matter, I should have tried it ; but, of course, I knew well that Holmes loved his art so, that he was ever as ready to bring his aid as his client could be to receive it. My wife agreed with me that not a moment should be lost in laying the matter before him, and so, within an hour of breakfast-time, I found myself back once more in the old rooms in Baker Street.

Holmes was seated at his side-table clad in his dressing-gown and working hard over a chemical investigation. A large curved retort was boiling furiously in the bluish flame of a Bunsen burner, and the distilled drops were condensing into a two-litre measure. My friend hardly glanced up as I entered, and I, seeing that his investigation must be of importance, seated myself in an arm-chair and waited. He dipped into this bottle or that, drawing out a few drops of each with his glass pipette, and finally brought a test-tube containing a solution over to the table. In his right hand he had a slip of litmus-paper.

"You come at a crisis, Watson," said he. " If this paper remains blue, all is well. If it turns red, it means a man's life." He dipped it into the test-tube, and it flushed at once into a dull, dirty crimson. " Hum ! I thought as much ! " he cried. " I shall be at your service in one instant, Watson. You will find tobacco in the Persian slipper." He turned to his desk and scribbled off several telegrams, which were handed over to the page-boy. Then he threw himself down in the chair opposite, and drew up his knees until his fingers clasped round his long, thin shins.

"A very commonplace little murder," said he. "You've got something better, I fancy. You are the stormy petrel of crime, Watson. What is it ?"

I handed him the letter, which he read with the most concentrated attention.

" It does not tell us very much, does it ? " he remarked, as he handed it back to me.

" Hardly anything."

" And yet the writing is of interest."

" But the writing is not his own."

" Precisely. It is a woman's."

" A man's surely ! " I cried.

" No, a woman's ; and a woman of rare character. You see, at the commencement of an investigation, it is something to know that your client is in close contact with someone who for good or evil has an exceptional nature. My interest is already awakened in the case. If you are ready, we will start at once for Woking and see this diplomatist who is in such evil case, and the lady to whom he dictates his letters."

We were fortunate enough to catch an early train at Waterloo, and in a little under an hour we found ourselves among the fir-woods and the heather of Woking. Briarbrae proved to be a large detached house standing in extensive grounds, within a few minutes' walk of the station. On sending in our cards we were shown into an elegantly appointed drawing-room, where we were joined in a few minutes by a rather stout man, who received us with much

5 *a wicket*. Watson in this sentence is guilty of two "colonialisms," pointing to his boyhood in Australia: "playground," to a youngster reared in England would be "playing field," and "wicket" would be "stump."

6 WOKING. Woking lies twelve miles northeast of Aldershot and due north of Guildford, in Surrey.

7 *nine weeks of brain fever*. Joseph Harrison later says that his sister Annie had nursed Phelps "these two months back." Phelps says the treaty was stolen "Nearly ten weeks ago—to be more accurate, on the 23rd of May . . ." "Here I have lain, Mr. Holmes, over nine weeks, unconscious, and raving with brain fever. . . . It is only during the last three days that my memory has quite returned." Forbes says that "The clerk, Gorot, has been shadowed all these nine weeks . . ." Holmes says, on the first day of the case, that "nearly ten weeks have elapsed . . ." Phelps later spoke of his "ten long weeks of agony." Percy Phelps' letter to Watson could not have been delivered until Saturday, July 27th, at the very earliest. But the first day of the case was not a Saturday: Holmes called on Lord Holdhurst at the Foreign Office late in the afternoon, which would not have been open late in the afternoon on a Saturday. Much less would it have been open on a Sunday; nor could Phelps' letter have been delivered on a Sunday; nor could Holmes have advertised in the evening papers. Thus the case must have opened on one of the three days Monday, July 29th; Tuesday, July 30th; or Wednesday, July 31st.

HOLMES WAS . . . WORKING HARD OVER A CHEMICAL INVESTIGATION.

Illustration by Sidney Paget for the *Strand Magazine*, October, 1893.

BRIARBRAE PROVED TO BE A LARGE DETACHED HOUSE
STANDING IN EXTENSIVE GROUNDS . . .

"It is tempting to identify 'Briarbrae' with an existing 'large detached house, standing in extensive grounds, within a few minutes' walk of the station'—Woodham Hall, which lies just off the cross-roads at Horsell Common," Mr. Michael Harrison wrote in *In the Footsteps of Sherlock Holmes*. But most commentators now consider 'Briarbrae' to have been Inchcape House (*shown above*), previously "Heatherside," Woking, now destroyed. "To enter the gate of Inchcape and Little Inchcape is to re-enter the enchanted world of 1887," Mrs. Jennifer Chorley wrote in "'Briarbrae' Revisited." "There stands the coach-house whose long-suffering horses awaited the summons to bear Holmes and Watson to the station (the journey on foot takes all of three minutes!) There, the 'side-entrance for tradespeople,' and, far off, one hears the church clock striking the quarters. . . . The 'extensive grounds' are still quite large although part of the gardens are now the site of a Presbyterian Church, and the huge clumps of rhododendrons (some 15–20 feet tall) and fir trees and a large conservatory evoke the Victorian era perfectly. The house is dated 1828 but its solid red dignity seems typically Victorian in spirit."

A YOUNG MAN, VERY PALE AND WORN, WAS LYING
UPON A SOFA NEAR THE OPEN WINDOW . . .

Illustration by William H. Hyde for *Harper's Weekly*, October 14, 1893.

hospitality. His age may have been nearer forty than thirty, but his cheeks were so ruddy and his eyes so merry, that he still conveyed the impression of a plump and mischievous boy.

" I am so glad that you have come," said he, shaking our hands with effusion. " Percy has been inquiring for you all the morning. Ah, poor old chap, he clings to any straw. His father and mother asked me to see you, for the mere mention of the subject is very painful to them."

" We have had no details yet," observed Holmes. " I perceive that you are not yourself a member of the family."

Our acquaintance looked surprised, and then glancing down he began to laugh.

" Of course you saw the ' J. H.' monogram on my locket," said he. " For a moment I thought you had done something clever. Joseph Harrison is my name, and as Percy is to marry my sister Annie, I shall at least be a relation by marriage. You will find my sister in his room, for she has nursed him hand-and-foot these two months back. Perhaps we had better go in at once, for I know how impatient he is."

The chamber into which we were shown was on the same floor as the drawing-room. It was furnished partly as a sitting- and partly as a bedroom, with flowers arranged daintily in every nook and corner. A young man, very pale and worn, was lying upon a sofa near the open window, through which came the rich scent of the garden and the balmy summer air. A woman was sitting beside him, and rose as we entered.

" Shall I leave, Percy ? " she asked.

He clutched her hand to detain her. " How are you, Watson ? " said he, cordially. " I should never have known you under that moustache, and I daresay you would not be prepared to swear to me. This, I presume, is your celebrated friend, Mr. Sherlock Holmes ? "

I introduced him in a few words, and we both sat down. The stout young man had left us, but his sister still remained, with her hand in that of the invalid. She was a striking-looking woman, a little short and thick for symmetry, but with a beautiful olive complexion, large, dark Italian eyes, and a wealth of deep black hair. Her rich tints made the white face of her companion the more worn and haggard by the contrast.

" I won't waste your time," said he, raising himself upon the sofa. " I'll plunge into the matter without further preamble. I was a happy and successful man, Mr. Holmes, and on the eve of being married, when a sudden and dreadful misfortune wrecked all my prospects in life.

" I was, as Watson may have told you, in the Foreign Office, and through the influence of my uncle, Lord Holdhurst, I rose rapidly to a responsible position. When my uncle became Foreign Minister in this Administration he gave me several missions of trust, and as I always brought them to a successful conclusion, he came at last to have the utmost confidence in my ability and tact.

" Nearly ten weeks ago—to be more accurate, on the 23rd of May—he called me into his private room and, after complimenting me upon the good work which I had done, informed me that he had a new commission of trust for me to execute.

" ' This,' said he, taking a grey roll of paper from his bureau, ' is the original of that secret treaty between England and Italy, of which, I regret to say, some rumours **8** have already got into the public Press.   It is of enormous importance that nothing further should leak out.   The French or Russian Embassies would pay an immense sum to learn the contents of these papers.   They should not leave my bureau were it not that it is absolutely necessary to have them copied.   You have a desk in your office ? '

" ' Yes, sir.'

" ' Then take the treaty and lock it up there.   I shall give directions that you may remain behind when the others go, so that you may copy it at your leisure, without **9** fear of being overlooked.   When you have finished, re-lock both the original and the draft in the desk, and hand them over to me personally to-morrow morning.'

"I WON'T WASTE YOUR TIME," SAID HE . . .

Illustration by Sidney Paget for the *Strand Magazine,* October, 1893.

" 'THEN TAKE THE TREATY AND LOCK IT UP THERE.' "

Illustration by Sidney Paget for the *Strand Magazine,* October, 1893.

8 *that secret treaty between England and Italy.* The late Fletcher Pratt, who dated "The Naval Treaty" in the July of 1887, based his case—and a good one—on the fact that there *was* a secret treaty between England and Italy in that year. "This document," he wrote in "Holmes and the Royal Navy," "was a secret understanding with the Italian government by which the latter was accorded a free hand in the seizure of Libya, in exchange for which Britain received a similar free hand in the Sudan and Upper Egypt, adjoining Ethiopia, then considered part of the Italian sphere of influence. We all know what the results of that free hand in the Sudan were: England was brought into direct conflict with French ambition in the same direction and the very brink of war with that nation. Is it necessary to rehearse the fact that at this time France was the second naval power of the world or that she herself had recently reached an agreement with Russia, the third naval power? That the two fleets together outnumbered that of Britain and made the Naval Defense Act [of 1888] a necessity? Need one remark there was precisely the sale of the 'Naval Treaty' to France and Russia that Holmes and the British Cabinet feared?"

9 *so that you may copy it at your leisure.* In an unpublished paper, "We Ask the Questions!", Mr. Thomas L. Stix has asked why should not the British Foreign Office have had duplicating machines. "True, the photostatic process had not been invented, but the railroad duplicator was in general use in 1880. It was not a cumbersome machine. It was moderately priced and it was used to insure accuracy and speed, certainly better by far than a hand-made copy by a sleepy subordinate. The French tissue copy was also available, but took more time. . . ."

10 *the Triple Alliance*. The secret Dual Alliance of Germany and Austria-Hungary, formed in 1879, was joined in 1882 by Italy and thus became the Triple Alliance.

" I took the papers and——"

" Excuse me an instant," said Holmes ; " were you alone during this conversation ? "

" Absolutely."

" In a large room ? "

" Thirty feet each way."

" In the centre ? "

" Yes, about it."

" And speaking low ? "

" My uncle's voice is always remarkably low.   I hardly spoke at all."

" Thank you," said Holmes, shutting his eyes ; " pray go on."

" I did exactly what he had indicated, and waited until the other clerks had departed.   One of them in my room, Charles Gorot, had some arrears of work to make up, so I left him there and went out to dine.   When I returned he was gone.   I was anxious to hurry my work, for I knew that Joseph, the Mr. Harrison whom you saw just now, was in town, and that he would travel down to Woking by the eleven o'clock train, and I wanted if possible to catch it.

" When I came to examine the treaty I saw at once that it was of such importance that my uncle had been guilty of no exaggeration in what he had said.   Without going into details, I may say that it defined the position **10** of Great Britain towards the Triple Alliance, and foreshadowed the policy which this country would pursue in the event of the French fleet gaining a complete ascendency over that of Italy in the Mediterranean.   The questions treated in it were purely naval.   At the end were the signatures of the high dignitaries who had signed it.   I glanced my eyes over it, and then settled down to my task of copying.

" It was a long document, written in the French language, and containing twenty-six separate articles.   I copied as quickly as I could, but at nine o'clock I had only done nine articles, and it seemed hopeless for me to attempt to catch my train.   I was feeling drowsy and stupid, partly from my dinner and also from the effects of a long day's work.   A cup of coffee would clear my brain.   A commissionaire remains all night in a little lodge at the foot of the stairs, and is in the habit of making coffee at his spirit-lamp for any of the officials who may be working overtime.   I rang the bell, therefore, to summon him.

" To my surprise, it was a woman who answered the summons, a large, coarse-faced, elderly woman, in an apron. She explained that she was the commissionaire's wife, who did the charing, and I gave her the order for the coffee.

" I wrote two more articles, and then, feeling more drowsy than ever, I rose and walked up and down the room to stretch my legs.   My coffee had not yet come, and I wondered what the cause of the delay could be. Opening the door, I started down the corridor to find out. There was a straight passage dimly lit which led from the room in which I had been working, and was the only exit from it.   It ended in a curving staircase, with the commissionaire's lodge in the passage at the bottom.   Halfway down this staircase is a small landing, with another passage running into it at right angles.   The second one leads, by means of a second small stair, to a side-door used by servants, and also as a short cut by clerks when coming from Charles Street.

" Here is a rough chart of the place."

" Thank you. I think that I quite follow you," said Sherlock Holmes.

" It is of the utmost importance that you should notice this point. I went down the stairs and into the hall, where I found the commissionaire fast asleep in his box, with the kettle boiling furiously upon the spirit-lamp, for the water was spurting over the floor. I had put out my hand and was about to shake the man, who was still sleeping soundly, when a bell over his head rang loudly, and he woke with a start.

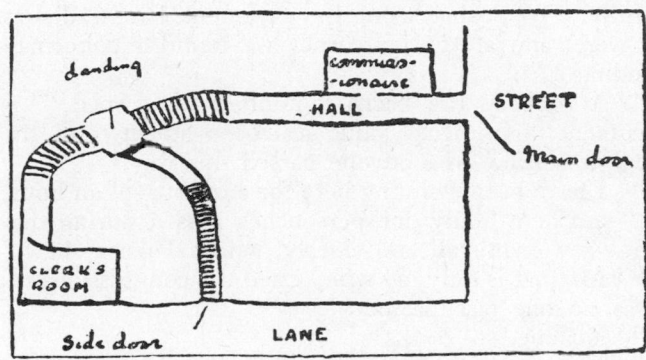

" HERE IS A ROUGH CHART OF THE PLACE."

" ' Mr. Phelps, sir ! ' said he, looking at me in bewilderment.

" ' I came down to see if my coffee was ready.'

" ' I was boiling the kettle when I fell asleep, sir.' He looked at me and then up at the still quivering bell, with an ever-growing astonishment upon his face.

" ' If you was here, sir, then who rang the bell ? ' he asked.

" ' The bell ! ' I said.   ' What bell is it ? '

" ' It's the bell of the room you were working in.'

" A cold hand seemed to close round my heart. Someone, then, was in that room where my precious treaty lay upon the table. I ran frantically up the stairs and along the passage. There was no one in the corridor, Mr. Holmes. There was no one in the room. All was exactly as I left it, save only that the papers committed to my care had been taken from the desk on which they lay. The copy was there and the original was gone."

Holmes sat up in his chair and rubbed his hands. I could see that the problem was entirely to his heart. " Pray, what did you do then ? " he murmured.

" I recognized in an instant that the thief must have come up the stairs from the side-door. Of course I must have met him if he had come the other way."

" You were satisfied that he could not have been concealed in the room all the time, or in the corridor which you have just described as dimly lighted ? "

" It is absolutely impossible. A rat could not conceal

" . . . I FOUND THE COMMISSIONAIRE FAST ASLEEP
IN HIS BOX . . ."

Illustration by Sidney Paget for the *Strand Magazine*, October, 1893.

" . . . THE PAPERS COMMITTED TO MY CARE HAD BEEN
TAKEN FROM THE DESK . . ."

Illustration by William H. Hyde for *Harper's Weekly*, October 14, 1893.

11 *"That is of enormous importance," said Holmes.* "What is of importance here," Mr. Michael Harrison wrote (*In the Footsteps of Sherlock Holmes*), "is that the nearest church to Charles Street, Whitehall, is St. Margaret's Westminster, adjoining Westminster Abbey. Both St. Margaret's and the Abbey's clock chime; but only a few yards away from the two is Big Ben, whose chime drowns all lesser chimes for a good half-mile around. It is extraordinary not only that Phelps should have mentioned the chiming of 'a neighbourhood church' when Big Ben was practically overhead, but that Holmes should not have remarked upon this."

12 *"The night was very dark, and a thin, warm rain was falling.* "'The July which immediately succeeded my marriage' was in 1889," the late Professor Jay Finley Christ wrote (*An Irregular Chronology*) "and the treaty was stolen on the rainy evening of May 23rd. The latter was a Tuesday, and a .19 inch rain fell on that date."

himself either in the room or the corridor. There is **no** cover at all."

"Thank you. Pray proceed."

"The commissionaire, seeing by my pale face that something was to be feared, had followed me upstairs. Now we both rushed along the corridor and down the steep steps which led to Charles Street. The door at the bottom was closed but unlocked. We flung it open and rushed out. I can distinctly remember that as we did so there came three chimes from a neighbouring church. It was a quarter to ten."

11   "That is of enormous importance," said Holmes, making a note upon his shirt cuff.

12   "The night was very dark, and a thin, warm rain was falling. There was no one in Charles Street, but a great traffic was going on, as usual, in Whitehall, at the extremity. We rushed along the pavement, bareheaded as we were, and at the far corner we found a policeman standing.

"'A robbery has been committed,' I gasped. 'A document of immense value has been stolen from the Foreign Office. Has anyone passed this way?'

"'I have been standing here for a quarter of an hour, sir,' said he; 'only one person has passed during that time—a woman, tall and elderly, with a Paisley shawl.'

"'Ah, that is only my wife,' cried the commissionaire. Has no one else passed?'

"'No one.'

"'Then it must be the other way that the thief took,' cried the fellow, tugging at my sleeve.

"But I was not satisfied, and the attempts which he made to draw me away increased my suspicions.

"'Which way did the woman go?' I cried.

"'I don't know, sir. I noticed her pass, but I had no special reason for watching her. She seemed to be in a hurry.'

"'How long ago was it?'

"'Oh, not very many minutes.'

"'Within the last five?'

"'Well, it could not be more than five.'

"'You're only wasting your time, sir, and every minute now is of importance,' cried the commissionaire. 'Take my word for it that my old woman has nothing to do with it, and come down to the other end of the street. Well, if you won't, I will,' and with that he rushed off in the other direction.

"But I was after him in an instant and caught him by the sleeve.

"'Where do you live?' said I.

"'No. 16 Ivy Lane, Brixton,' he answered; 'but don't let yourself be drawn away upon a false scent, Mr. Phelps. Come to the other end of the street, and let us see if we can hear of anything.'

"Nothing was to be lost by following his advice. With the policeman we both hurried down, but only to find the street full of traffic, many people coming and going, but all only too eager to get to a place of safety upon so wet a night. There was no lounger who could tell us who had passed.

" Then we returned to the office, and searched the stairs and the passage without result. The corridor which led to the room was laid down with a kind of creamy linoleum, which shows an impression very easily. We examined it very carefully, but found no outline of any footmark."

" Had it been raining all the evening ? "

" Since about seven."

" How is it, then, that the woman who came into the room about nine left no traces with her muddy boots ? "

" I am glad you raise the point. It occurred to me at the time. The charwomen are in the habit of taking off their boots at the commissionaire's office, and putting on list slippers." **13**

" That is very clear. There were no marks, then, though the night was a wet one ? The chain of events is certainly one of extraordinary interest. What did you do next ? "

" We examined the room also. There was no possibility of a secret door, and the windows are quite thirty feet from the ground. Both of them were fastened on the inside. The carpet prevents any possibility of a trap-door, and the ceiling is of the ordinary white-washed kind. I will pledge my life that whoever stole my papers could only have come through the door."

" How about the fireplace ? "

" They use none. There is a stove. The bell-rope hangs from the wire just to the right of my desk. Whoever rang it must have come right up to the desk to do it. But why should any criminal wish to ring the bell ? It is a most insoluble mystery."

" Certainly the incident was unusual. What were your next steps ? You examined the room, I presume, to see if the intruder had left any traces—any cigar-end, or dropped glove, or hairpin, or other trifle ? "

" There was nothing of the sort."

" No smell ? "

" Well, we never thought of that."

" Ah, a scent of tobacco would have been worth a great deal to us in such an investigation."

" I never smoke myself, so I think I should have observed it if there had been any smell of tobacco. There was absolutely no clue of any kind. The only tangible fact was that the commissionaire's wife—Mrs. Tangey was the name—had hurried out of the place. He could give no explanation save that it was about the time when the woman always went home. The policeman and I agreed that our best plan would be to seize the woman before she could get rid of the papers, presuming that she had them.

" The alarm had reached Scotland Yard by this time, and Mr. Forbes, the detective, came round at once and took up the case with a great deal of energy. We hired a hansom, and in half an hour we were at the address which had been given to us. A young woman opened the door, who proved to be Mrs. Tangey's eldest daughter. Her mother had not come back yet, and we were shown into the front room to wait.

" About ten minutes later a knock came at the door, and here we made the one serious mistake for which I

13 *list slippers*." Slippers made of list, a kind of textile.

14 *the brokers.*' Persons licensed to appraise and sell furniture distrained for nonpayment of rent; bailiffs.

" ' WHY, IF IT ISN'T MR. PHELPS, OF THE OFFICE ! "
SHE CRIED.

Illustration by Sidney Paget for the *Strand Magazine*, October, 1893.

blame myself. Instead of opening the door ourselves we allowed the girl to do so. We heard her say, ' Mother, there are two men in the house waiting to see you,' and an instant afterwards we heard the patter of feet rushing down the passage. Forbes flung open the door, and we both ran into the back room or kitchen, but the woman had got there before us. She stared at us with defiant eyes, and then suddenly recognizing me, an expression of absolute astonishment came over her face.

" ' Why, if it isn't Mr. Phelps, of the office ! ' she cried.

" ' Come, come, who did you think we were when you ran away from us ? ' asked my companion.

14   " ' I thought you were the brokers,' said she. ' We've had some trouble with a tradesman.'

" ' That's not quite good enough,' answered Forbes. ' We have reason to believe that you have taken a paper of importance from the Foreign Office, and that you ran in here to dispose of it. You must come back with us to Scotland Yard to be searched.'

" It was in vain that she protested and resisted. A four-wheeler was brought, and we all three drove back in it. We had first made an examination of the kitchen, and especially of the kitchen fire, to see whether she might have made away with the papers during the instant that she was alone. There were no signs, however, of any ashes or scraps. When we reached Scotland Yard she was handed over at once to the female searcher. I waited in an agony of suspense until she came back with her report. There were no signs of the papers.

" Then, for the first time, the horror of my situation came in its full force upon me. Hitherto I had been acting, and action had numbed thought. I had been so confident of regaining the treaty at once that I had not dared to think of what would be the consequence if I failed to do so. But now there was nothing more to be done, and I had leisure to realize my position. It was horrible ! Watson there would tell you that I was a nervous, sensitive boy at school. It is my nature. I thought of my uncle and of his colleagues in the Cabinet, of the shame which I had brought upon him, upon myself, upon everyone connected with me. What though I was the victim of an extraordinary accident ? No allowance is made for accidents where diplomatic interests are at stake. I was ruined ; shamefully, hopelessly ruined. I don't know what I did. I fancy I must have made a scene. I have a dim recollection of a group of officials who crowded round me endeavouring to soothe me. One of them drove down with me to Waterloo and saw me into the Woking train. I believe that he would have come all the way had it not been that Dr. Ferrier, who lives near me, was going down by that very train. The doctor most kindly took charge of me, and it was well he did so, for I had a fit in the station, and before we reached home I was practically a raving maniac.

" You can imagine the state of things here when they were roused from their beds by the doctor's ringing, and found me in this condition. Poor Annie here and my mother were broken-hearted. Dr. Ferrier had just heard enough from the detective at the station to be able to give an idea of what had happened, and his story did not mend matters. It was evident to all that I was in for a long illness, so Joseph was bundled out of this cheery bed-room, and it was turned into a sick-room for me. Here I have lain, Mr. Holmes, for over nine weeks, unconscious, and raving with brain fever. If it had not been for Miss Harrison here and for the doctor's care I should not be speaking to you now. She has nursed me by day, and a hired nurse has looked after me by night, for in my mad fits I was capable of anything. Slowly my reason has cleared, but it is only during the last three days that my memory has quite returned. Sometimes I wish that it never had. The first thing I did was to wire to Mr. Forbes, who had the case in hand. He came out and assured me that, though everything has been done, no trace of a clue has been discovered. The commissionaire and his wife have been examined in every way without any light being thrown upon the matter. The suspicions of the police then rested upon young Gorot, who, as you may remember, stayed overtime in the office that night. His remaining behind and his French name were really the only two points which could suggest suspicion ; but as a matter of fact, I did not begin work until he had gone, and his people are of Huguenot extrac- **15** tion, but as English in sympathy and tradition as you and I are. Nothing was found to implicate him in any way, and there the matter dropped. I turn to you, Mr. Holmes, as absolutely my last hope. If you fail me, then my honour as well as my position are for ever forfeited."

The invalid sank back upon his cushions, tired out by this long recital, while his nurse poured him out a glass of some stimulating medicine. Holmes sat silently with his head thrown back and his eyes closed in an attitude which might seem listless to a stranger, but which I knew betokened the most intense absorption.

" Your statement has been so explicit," said he at last, " that you have really left me very few questions to ask. There is one of the very utmost importance, however. Did you tell anyone that you had this special task to perform ? "

" No one."

" Not Miss Harrison here, for example ? "

" No. I had not been back to Woking between getting the order and executing the commission."

" And none of your people had by chance been to see you ? "

" None."

" Did any of them know their way about in the office ? "

" Oh, yes ; all of them had been shown over it."

" Still, of course, if you said nothing to anyone about the treaty, these inquiries are irrelevant."

" I said nothing."

" Do you know anything of the commissionaire ? "

" Nothing, except that he is an old soldier."

" What regiment ? "

" Oh, I have heard—Coldstream Guards." **16**

" Thank you. I have no doubt I can get details from Forbes. The authorities are excellent at amassing facts,

15 *Huguenot.* The Huguenots are the Calvinist Protestants of France. When the Edict of Nantes, which gave them complete toleration, was revoked in 1685, countless Huguenots fled to England (and to Holland, Germany, Switzerland, and America) where they contributed substantially to civic and industrial life.

16 *Coldstream Guards.*" "Watson, anxious to establish the good character of his man, assigns him to one of the most famous regiments in the whole British army," Mrs. Crighton Sellars wrote in "Dr. Watson and the British Army." "The Coldstreams ('Coalies'), now of the Household Brigade, were the fighting regiment of General Monk, which marched with him into London on February 2, 1660, to end the sway of the Roundheads and herald the return of the Monarchy."

17 *It is only goodness which gives extras.* Holmes "ignores the elementary fact, for students of natural history, that colour and scent are not 'extras' in blossoms," Mr. Vernon Rendall wrote in "The Limitations of Sherlock Holmes." "They are designed to attract the insects which fertilize them and so help produce the seed. Alone among great men, Ruskin adopted a similar standpoint when he noticed flowers—he was too pure to think of seed."

18 *we have much to hope from the flowers."* This is the only passage in the long Saga in which Holmes speaks forthrightly of religion. Compare Matthew 6:28, 29: "Consider the lilies of the field, how they grow; they toil not, neither do they spin. And yet I say unto you, That even Solomon in all his glory was not arrayed like one of these."

"WHAT A LOVELY THING A ROSE IS!"

Illustration by Sidney Paget for the *Strand Magazine*, October, 1893.

though they do not always use them to advantage. What a lovely thing a rose is!"

He walked past the couch to the open window, and held up the drooping stalk of a moss rose, looking down at the dainty blend of crimson and green. It was a new phase of his character to me, for I had never before seen him show any keen interest in natural objects.

"There is nothing in which deduction is so necessary as in religion," said he, leaning with his back against the shutters. "It can be built up as an exact science by the reasoner. Our highest assurance of the goodness of Providence seems to me to rest in the flowers. All other things, our powers, our desires, our food, are really necessary for our existence in the first instance. But this rose is an extra. Its smell and its colour are an embellishment of life, not a condition of it. It is only goodness which **17** gives extras, and so I say again that we have much to **18** hope from the flowers."

Percy Phelps and his nurse looked at Holmes during this demonstration with surprise and a good deal of disappointment written upon their faces. He had fallen into a reverie, with the moss rose between his fingers. It had lasted some minutes before the young lady broke in upon it.

"Do you see any prospect of solving this mystery, Mr. Holmes?" she asked, with a touch of asperity in her voice.

"Oh, the mystery!" he answered, coming back with a start to the realities of life. "Well, it would be absurd to deny that the case is a very abstruse and complicated one; but I can promise you that I will look into the matter and let you know any points which may strike me."

"Do you see any clue?"

"You have furnished me with seven, but of course I must test them before I can pronounce upon their value."

"You suspect someone?"

"I suspect myself——"

"What?"

"Of coming to conclusions too rapidly."

"Then go to London and test your conclusions."

"Your advice is very excellent, Miss Harrison," said Holmes, rising. "I think, Watson, we cannot do better. Do not allow yourself to indulge in false hopes, Mr. Phelps. The affair is a very tangled one."

"I shall be in a fever until I see you again," cried the diplomatist.

"Well, I'll come out by the same train to-morrow, though it's more than likely that my report will be a negative one."

"God bless you for promising to come," cried our client. "It gives me fresh life to know that something is being done. By the way, I have had a letter from Lord Holdhurst."

"Ha! What did he say?"

"He was cold, but not harsh. I dare say my severe illness prevented him from being that. He repeated that the matter was of the utmost importance, and added that no steps would be taken about my future—by which he means, of course, my dismissal—until my health was restored and I had an opportunity of repairing my misfortune."

"Well, that was reasonable and considerate," said Holmes. " Come, Watson, for we have a good day's work before us in town."

Mr. Joseph Harrison drove us down to the station, and we were soon whirling up in a Portsmouth train. Holmes was sunk in profound thought, and hardly opened his mouth until we had passed Clapham Junction.

"It's a very cheering thing to come into London by any of these lines which run high and allow you to look down upon the houses like this."

I thought he was joking, for the view was sordid enough, but he soon explained himself.

" Look at those big, isolated clumps of buildings rising up above the slates, like brick islands in a lead-coloured sea."

" The Board schools."

" Lighthouses, my boy! Beacons of the future! Capsules, with hundreds of bright little seeds in each, out of which will spring the wiser, better England of the future. I suppose that man Phelps does not drink?" **19**

" I should not think so."

" Nor should I. But we are bound to take every possibility into account. The poor devil has certainly got himself into very deep water, and it's a question whether we shall ever be able to get him ashore. What did you think of Miss Harrison?"

" A girl of strong character."

" Yes, but she is a good sort, or I am mistaken. She and her brother are the only children of an ironmaster somewhere up Northumberland way. Phelps got engaged to **20** her when travelling last winter, and she came down to be introduced to his people, with her brother as escort. Then came the smash, and she stayed on to nurse her lover, while brother Joseph, finding himself pretty snug, stayed on too. I've been making a few independent inquiries, you see. But to-day must be a day of inquiries." **21**

" My practice——" I began.

" Oh, if you find your own cases more interesting than mine——" said Holmes, with some asperity.

" I was going to say that my practice could get along very well for a day or two, since it is the slackest time in the year."

" Excellent," said he, recovering his good humour. " Then we'll look into this matter together. I think that we should begin by seeing Forbes. He can probably tell us all the details we want, until we know from what side the case is to be approached."

" You said you had a clue."

" Well, we have several, but we can only test their value by further inquiry. The most difficult crime to track is the one which is purposeless. Now, this is not purposeless. Who is it that profits by it? There is the **22** French Ambassador, there is the Russian, there is whoever might sell it to either of these, and there is Lord Holdhurst."

" Lord Holdhurst!"

" Well, it is just conceivable that a statesman might find himself in a position where he was not sorry to have such a document accidentally destroyed."

19 *the wiser, better England of the future.* "It would be difficult to find a more concise expression of the confident aspirations of late Victorian Liberalism," Mr. S. C. Roberts wrote in "The Personality of Sherlock Holmes." "Fundamentally, there can be no doubt that Holmes believed in democracy and progress."

20 *Northumberland.* A border county in the north of England—one with a rugged coastline, high moorlands, and fertile valleys in the interior.

21 *I've been making a few independent inquiries, you see.* But, as Mr. Guy Warrack rightly asked ("Passed to You, Admiralty Intelligence"), "from whom and, above all, *when?*"

22 *Who is it that profits by it?* "For many centuries," Mr. Morris Rosenblum wrote in "Some Latin Byways in the Canon," "the Latin original of that query ["*Cui bono?*"] has been a pitfall for those who had little Latin and those who had not a little. [They constantly translated it in the sense of 'What good is it?' "To what end does it serve?" —but its real meaning is "Who gains by it?" "To whom is it an advantage?"] . . . Holmes applied the phrase correctly, not only because of his thorough comprehension of ancient and medieval Latin, but also because of his encyclopedic knowledge of crime. He had met the phrase in the works of Cicero, especially in the oration *Pro Roscio Amerino*, a defense plea in a murder case of a type dear to the Holmesian heart."

. . . THE VIEW WAS SORDID ENOUGH . . .

Illustration by Sidney Paget for the *Strand Magazine*, October, 1893.

"I've heard of your methods before now, Mr. Holmes," said he tartly.

Illustration by Sidney Paget for the *Strand Magazine*, October, 1893.

" Not a statesman with the honourable record of Lord Holdhurst."

" It is a possibility, and we cannot afford to disregard it. We shall see the noble lord to-day, and find out if he can tell us anything.   Meanwhile, I have already set inquiries upon foot."

" Already ? "

" Yes, I sent wires from Woking station to every evening paper in London.   This advertisement will appear in each of them."

He handed over a sheet torn from the notebook.   On it was scribbled in pencil :

" £10 Reward.—The number of the cab which dropped a fare at or about the door of the Foreign Office in Charles Street, at a quarter to ten in the evening of May 23rd. Apply 221B Baker Street."

" You are confident that the thief came in a cab ? "

" If not, there is no harm done.   But if Mr. Phelps is correct in stating that there is no hiding-place either in the room or the corridors, then the person must have come from outside.   If he came from outside on so wet a night, and yet left no trace of damp upon the linoleum, which was examined within a few minutes of his passing, then it is exceedingly probable that he came in a cab. Yes, I think that we may safely deduce a cab."

" It sounds plausible."

" That is one of the clues of which I spoke.   It may lead us to something.   And then, of course, there is the bell—which is the most distinctive feature of the case. Why should the bell ring ?   Was it the thief that did it out of bravado ?   Or was it someone who was with the thief who did it in order to prevent the crime ?   Or was it an accident ?   Or was it——? "   He sank back into the state of intense and silent thought from which he had emerged, but it seemed to me, accustomed as I was to his every mood, that some new possibility had dawned suddenly upon him.

It was twenty-past three when we reached our terminus, and after a hasty luncheon at the buffet we pushed on at once to Scotland Yard.   Holmes had already wired to Forbes, and we found him waiting to receive us : a small, foxy man, with a sharp but by no means amiable expression.   He was decidedly frigid in his manner to us, especially when he heard the errand upon which we had come.

" I've heard of your methods before now, Mr. Holmes," said he, tartly.   " You are ready enough to use all the information that the police can lay at your disposal, and then you try to finish the case yourself and bring discredit upon them."

" On the contrary," said Holmes ;   " out of my last fifty-three cases my name has only appeared in four, and the police have had all the credit in forty-nine.   I don't blame you for not knowing this ;   for you are young and inexperienced ;   but if you wished to get on in your new duties you will work with me, and not against me."

" I'd be very glad of a hint or two," said the detective, changing his manner.   " I've certainly had no credit from the case so far."

" What steps have you taken ? "

" Tangey, the commissionaire, has been shadowed. He left the Guards with a good character, and we can find nothing against him.   His wife is a bad lot, though. I fancy she knows more about this than appears."

" Have you shadowed her ? "

" We have set one of our women on to her.   Mrs. Tangey drinks, and our woman has been with her twice when she was well on, but she could get nothing out of her."

" I understand that they have had brokers in the house ? "

" Yes, but they were paid off."

" Where did the money come from ? "

" That was all right.   His pension was due ; they have not shown any sign of being in funds."

" What explanation did she give of having answered the bell when Mr. Phelps rang for the coffee ? "

" She said that her husband was very tired and she wished to relieve him."

" Well, certainly that would agree with his being found, a little later, asleep in his chair.   There is nothing against them, then, but the woman's character.   Did you ask her why she hurried away that night ?   Her haste attracted the attention of the police-constable."

" She was later than usual, and wanted to get home."

" Did you point out to her that you and Mr. Phelps, who started at least twenty minutes after her, got there before her ? "

" She explains that by the difference between a 'bus and a hansom."

" Did she make it clear why, on reaching her house, she ran into the back kitchen ? "

" Because she had the money there with which to pay off the brokers."

" She has at least an answer for everything.   Did you ask her whether in leaving she met anyone or saw anyone loitering about Charles Street ? "

" She saw no one but the constable."

" Well, you seem to have cross-examined her pretty thoroughly.   What else have you done ? "

" The clerk, Gorot, has been shadowed all these nine weeks, but without result.   We can show nothing against him."

" Anything else ? "

" Well, we have nothing else to go upon—no evidence of any kind."

" Have you formed any theory about how that bell rang ? "

" Well, I must confess that it beats me.   It was a cool hand, whoever it was, to go and give the alarm like that."

" Yes, it was a queer thing to do.   Many thanks to you for what you have told me.   If I can put the man into your hands you shall hear from me. Come along, Watson ! "

" Where are we going to now ? " I asked, as we left the office.

" We are now going to interview Lord Holdhurst, the Cabinet Minister and future Premier of England."

23 *Downing Street.* "There is a fascination in the air of this little cul-de-sac," Theodore Hook wrote; "an hour's inhalation of its atmosphere affects some men with giddiness, others with blindness, and very frequently with the most obvious boastfulness." Named for Sir George Downing, Secretary of State in 1668, Downing Street is today known the world over for No. 10, the official residence of the British Prime Minister.

STANDING ON THE RUG BETWEEN US, . . . HE SEEMED
TO REPRESENT THAT NOT TOO COMMON TYPE,
A NOBLEMAN WHO IS IN TRUTH NOBLE.

Illustration by William H. Hyde for *Harper's Weekly*, October 21, 1893. Sidney Paget illustrated the same scene for the *Strand Magazine*, November, 1893.

We were fortunate in finding that Lord Holdhurst was **23** still in his chambers at Downing Street, and on Holmes sending in his card we were instantly shown up. The statesman received us with that old-fashioned courtesy for which he is remarkable, and seated us on the two luxurious easy chairs on either side of the fireplace. Standing on the rug between us, with his slight, tall figure, his sharp-featured, thoughtful face, and his curling hair prematurely tinged with grey, he seemed to represent that not too common type, a nobleman who is in truth noble.

"Your name is very familiar to me, Mr. Holmes," said he, smiling. "And, of course, I cannot pretend to be ignorant of the object of your visit. There has only been one occurrence in these offices which could call for your attention. In whose interest are you acting, may I ask?"

"In that of Mr. Percy Phelps," answered Holmes.

"Ah, my unfortunate nephew! You can understand that our kinship makes it the more impossible for me to screen him in any way. I fear that the incident must have a very prejudicial effect upon his career."

"But if the document is found?"

"Ah, that, of course, would be different."

"I had one or two questions which I wished to ask you, Lord Holdhurst."

"I shall be happy to give you any information in my power."

"Was it in this room that you gave your instructions as to the copying of the document?"

"It was."

"Then you could hardly have been overheard?"

"It is out of the question."

"Did you ever mention to anyone that it was your intention to give out the treaty to be copied?"

"Never."

"You are certain of that?"

"Absolutely."

"Well, since you never said so, and Mr. Phelps never said so, and nobody else knew anything of the matter, then the thief's presence in the room was purely accidental. He saw his chance and he took it."

The statesman smiled. "You take me out of my province there," said he.

Holmes considered for a moment. "There is another very important point which I wish to discuss with you," said he. "You feared, as I understand, that very grave results might follow from the details of this treaty becoming known?"

A shadow passed over the expressive face of the statesman. "Very grave results, indeed."

"And have they occurred?"

"Not yet."

"If the treaty had reached, let us say, the French or Russian Foreign Office, you would expect to hear of it?"

"I should," said Lord Holdhurst, with a wry face.

"Since nearly ten weeks have elapsed, then, and nothing has been heard, it is not unfair to suppose that for some reason the treaty has not reached them?"

Lord Holdhurst shrugged his shoulders.

" We can hardly suppose, Mr. Holmes, that the thief took the treaty in order to frame it and hang it up."

" Perhaps he is waiting for a better price."

" If he waits a little longer he will get no price at all. The treaty will cease to be a secret in a few months."

" That is most important," said Holmes. " Of course it is a possible supposition that the thief has had a sudden illness——"

" An attack of brain fever, for example ? " asked the statesman, flashing a swift glance at him.

" I did not say so," said Holmes, imperturbably. " And now, Lord Holdhurst, we have already taken up too much of your valuable time, and we shall wish you good day."

" Every success to your investigation, be the criminal who it may," answered the nobleman, as he bowed us out at the door.

" He's a fine fellow," said Holmes, as we came out into Whitehall. " But he has a struggle to keep up his position. He is far from rich, and has many calls. You noticed, of course, that his boots had been re-soled ? Now, Watson, I won't detain you from your legitimate work any longer. I shall do nothing more to-day, unless I have an answer to my cab advertisement. But I should be extremely obliged to you if you would come down with me to Woking to-morrow, by the same train which we took to-day."

I met him accordingly next morning, and we travelled down to Woking together. He had had no answer to his advertisement, he said, and no fresh light had been thrown upon the case. He had, when he so willed it, the utter immobility of countenance of a Red Indian, and I could not gather from his appearance whether he was satisfied or not with the position of the case. His conversation, I remember, was about the Bertillon system of measurements, and he expressed his enthusiastic admiration of the French savant.

We found our client still under the charge of his devoted nurse, but looking considerably better than before. He rose from the sofa and greeted us without difficulty when we entered.

" Any news ? " he asked, eagerly.

" My report, as I expected, is a negative one," said Holmes. " I have seen Forbes, and I have seen your uncle, and I have set one or two trains of inquiry upon foot which may lead to something."

" You have not lost heart, then ? "

" By no means."

" God bless you for saying that ! " cried Miss Harrison. " If we keep our courage and our patience, the truth must come out."

" We have more to tell you than you have for us," said Phelps, re-seating himself upon the couch.

" I hoped you might have something."

" Yes, we have had an adventure during the night, and one which might have proved to be a serious one." His expression grew very grave as he spoke, and a look of something akin to fear sprang up in his eyes. " Do you

"ANY NEWS?" HE ASKED, EAGERLY.

Illustration by Sidney Paget for the *Strand Magazine*, November, 1893.

know," said he, " that I begin to believe that I am the unconscious centre of some monstrous conspiracy, and that my life is aimed at as well as my honour ? "

" Ah ! " cried Holmes.

" It sounds incredible, for I have not, as far as I know, an enemy in the world.   Yet from last night's experience I can come to no other conclusion."

" Pray let me hear it."

" You must know that last night was the very first night that I have ever slept without a nurse in the room.   I was so much better that I thought I could dispense with one.   I had a night-light burning, however.   Well, about two in the morning I had sunk into a light sleep, when I was suddenly aroused by a slight noise.   It was like the sound which a mouse makes when it is gnawing a plank, and I lay listening to it for some time under the impression that it must come from that cause.   Then it grew louder, and suddenly there came from the window a sharp metallic snick.   I sat up in amazement.   There could be no doubt what the sounds were now.   The faint ones had been caused by someone forcing an instrument through the slit between the sashes, and the second by the catch being pressed back.

" There was a pause then for about ten minutes, as if the person were waiting to see whether the noise had awoken me.   Then I heard a gentle creaking as the window was very slowly opened.   I could stand it no longer, for my nerves are not what they used to be.   I sprang out of bed and flung open the shutters.   A man was crouching at the window.   I could see little of him, for he was gone like a flash.   He was wrapped in some sort of cloak, which came across the lower part of his face.   One thing only I am sure of, and that is that he had some weapon in his hand.   It looked to me like a long knife.   I distinctly saw the gleam of it as he turned to run."

" This is most interesting," said Holmes.   " Pray, what did you do then ? "

" I should have followed him through the open window if I had been stronger.   As it was, I rang the bell and roused the house.   It took me some little time, for the bell rings in the kitchen, and the servants all sleep upstairs. I shouted, however, and that brought Joseph down, and he roused the others.   Joseph and the groom found marks on the flower-bed outside the window, but the weather has been so dry lately that they found it hopeless to follow the trail across the grass.   There's a place, however, on the wooden fence which skirts the road which shows signs, they tell me, as if someone had got over and had snapped the top of the rail in doing so. I have said nothing to the local police yet, for I thought I had best have your opinion first."

This tale of our client's appeared to have an extraordinary effect upon Sherlock Holmes.   He rose from his chair and paced about the room in uncontrollable excitement.

" Misfortunes never come singly," said Phelps, smiling, though it was evident that his adventure had somewhat shaken him.

" You have certainly had your share," said Holmes.

" Do you think you could walk round the house with me ? "

" Oh, yes, I should like a little sunshine.   Joseph will **24** come too."

" And I also," said Miss Harrison.

" I am afraid not," said Holmes, shaking his head. " I think I must ask you to remain sitting exactly where you are."

The young lady resumed her seat with an air of displeasure.   Her brother, however, had joined us, and we set off all four together.   We passed round the lawn to the outside of the young diplomatist's window.   There were, as he had said, marks upon the flower-bed, but they were hopelessly blurred and vague.   Holmes stooped over them for an instant, and then rose, shrugging his shoulders.

" I don't think anyone could make much of this," said he.   " Let us go round the house and see why this particular room was chosen by the burglar.   I should have thought those larger windows of the drawing-room and dining-room would have had more attractions for him."

" They are more visible from the road," suggested Mr. Joseph Harrison.

" Ah, yes, of course.   There is a door here which he might have attempted.   What is it for ? "

" It is the side-entrance for tradespeople.   Of course, it is locked at night."

" Have you ever had an alarm like this before ? "

" Never," said our client.

" Do you keep plate in the house, or anything to attract burglars ? "

" Nothing of value."

Holmes strolled round the house with his hands in his pockets, and a negligent air which was unusual with him.

" By the way," said he to Joseph Harrison, " you found some place, I understand, where the fellow scaled the fence.   Let us have a look at that."

The young man led us to a spot where the top of one of the wooden rails had been cracked.   A small fragment of the wood was hanging down.   Holmes pulled it off and examined it critically.

" Do you think that was done last night ?   It looks rather old, does it not ? "

" Well, possibly so."

" There are no marks of anyone jumping down upon the other side.   No, I fancy we shall get no help here. Let us go back to the bedroom and talk the matter over."

Percy Phelps was walking very slowly, leaning upon the arm of his future brother-in-law.   Holmes walked swiftly across the lawn, and we were at the open window of the bedroom long before the others came up.

" Miss Harrison," said Holmes, speaking with the utmost intensity of manner, " you must stay where you are all day.   Let nothing prevent you from staying where you are all day.   It is of most vital importance."

" Certainly, if you wish it, Mr. Holmes," said the girl, in astonishment.

24 *I should like a little sunshine.* Joseph Harrison later said to his sister, "Why do you sit moping here, Annie? Come out into the sunshine!" The sun shone for only 3.1 hours on Tuesday, July 30th. On Wednesday, July 31st, on the other hand, the sun shone for 12.7 hours; this must be the second day. Your editor holds that the case began on *Tuesday, July 30th,* and ended on *Thursday, August 1, 1889.*

HOLMES PULLED IT OFF AND EXAMINED IT CRITICALLY.

Illustration by Sidney Paget for the *Strand Magazine*, November, 1893.

25 *the spare bedroom.* Watson's former bedroom, since he was no longer living at 221B Baker Street.

" When you go to bed lock the door of this room on the outside and keep the key. Promise to do this."

" But Percy ? "

" He will come to London with us."

" And I am to remain here ? "

" It is for his sake. You can serve him ! Quick ! Promise ! "

She gave a nod of assent just as the other two came up.

" Why do you sit moping there, Annie ? " cried her brother. " Come out into the sunshine ! "

" No, thank you, Joseph. I have a slight headache, and this room is deliciously cool and soothing."

" What do you propose now, Mr. Holmes ? " asked our client.

" Well, in investigating this minor affair we must not lose sight of our main inquiry. It would be a very great help to me if you could come up to London with us."

" At once ? "

" Well, as soon as you conveniently can. Say in an hour."

" I feel quite strong enough, if I can really be of any help."

" The greatest possible."

" Perhaps you would like me to stay there to-night."

" I was just going to propose it."

" Then if my friend of the night comes to revisit me, he will find the bird flown. We are all in your hands, Mr. Holmes, and you must tell us exactly what you would like done. Perhaps you would prefer that Joseph came with us, so as to look after me ? "

" Oh, no ; my friend Watson is a medical man, you know, and he'll look after you. We'll have our lunch here, if you will permit us, and then we shall all three set off for town together."

It was arranged as he suggested, though Miss Harrison excused herself from leaving the bedroom, in accordance with Holmes' suggestion. What the object of my friend's manœuvres was I could not conceive, unless it were to keep the lady away from Phelps, who, rejoiced by his returning health and by the prospect of action, lunched with us in the dining-room. Holmes had a still more startling surprise for us, however, for after accompanying us down to the station and seeing us into our carriage, he calmly announced that he had no intention of leaving Woking.

" There are one or two small points which I should desire to clear up before I go," said he. " Your absence, Mr. Phelps, will in some ways rather assist me. Watson, when you reach London you would oblige me by driving at once to Baker Street with our friend here, and remaining with him until I see you again. It is fortunate that you are old schoolfellows, as you must have much to talk **25** over. Mr. Phelps can have the spare bedroom to-night, and I shall be with you in time for breakfast, for there is a train which will take me into Waterloo at eight."

" But how about our investigation in London ? " asked Phelps, ruefully.

" We can do that to-morrow. I think that just at present I can be of more immediate use here."

"You might tell them at Briarbrae that I hope to be back to-morrow night," cried Phelps, as we began to move from the platform.

"I hardly expect to go back to Briarbrae," answered Holmes, and waved his hand to us cheerily as we shot out from the station.

Phelps and I talked it over on our journey, but neither of us could devise a satisfactory reason for this new development.

"I suppose he wants to find out some clue as to the burglary last night, if a burglar it was. For myself, I don't believe it was an ordinary thief."

"What is your idea, then?"

"Upon my word, you may put it down to my weak nerves or not, but I believe there is some deep political intrigue going on around me, and that, for some reason that passes my understanding, my life is aimed at by the conspirators. It sounds high-flown and absurd, but consider the facts! Why should a thief try to break in at a bedroom window, where there could be no hope of any plunder, and why should he come with a long knife in his hand?"

"You are sure it was not a housebreaker's jemmy?"

"Oh, no; it was a knife. I saw the flash of the blade quite distinctly."

"But why on earth should you be pursued with such animosity?"

"Ah! that is the question."

"Well, if Holmes takes the same view, that would account for his action, would it not? Presuming that your theory is correct, if he can lay his hands upon the man who threatened you last night, he will have gone a long way towards finding who took the naval treaty. It is absurd to suppose that you have two enemies, one of whom robs you while the other threatens your life."

"But Mr. Holmes said that he was not going to Briarbrae."

"I have known him for some time," said I, "but I never knew him do anything yet without a very good reason," and with that our conversation drifted off into other topics.

But it was a weary day for me. Phelps was still weak after his long illness, and his misfortunes made him querulous and nervous. In vain I endeavoured to interest him in Afghanistan, in India, in social questions, in anything which might take his mind out of the groove. He would always come back to his lost treaty; wondering, guessing, speculating, as to what Holmes was doing, what steps Lord Holdhurst was taking, what news we should have in the morning. As the evening wore on his excitement became quite painful.

"You have implicit faith in Holmes?" he asked.

"I have seen him do some remarkable things."

"But he never brought light into anything quite so dark as this?"

"Oh, yes; I have known him solve questions which presented fewer clues than yours."

"But not where such large interests are at stake?"

"I don't know that. To my certain knowledge he has

"I HARDLY EXPECT TO GO BACK TO BRIARBRAE," ANSWERED HOLMES . . .

Illustration by Sidney Paget for the *Strand Magazine*, November, 1893.

26 *three of the reigning Houses of Europe.* Watson presumably refers to Bohemia, Holland, and Scandinavia.

26 acted on behalf of three of the reigning Houses of Europe in very vital matters."

" But you know him well, Watson. He is such an inscrutable fellow, that I never quite know what to make of him. Do you think he is hopeful ? Do you think he expects to make a success of it ? "

" He has said nothing."

" That is a bad sign."

" On the contrary, I have noticed that when he is off the trail he generally says so. It is when he is on a scent, and is not quite absolutely sure yet that it is the right one, that he is most taciturn. Now, my dear fellow, we can't help matters by making ourselves nervous about them, so let me implore you to go to bed, and so be fresh for whatever may await us to-morrow."

I was able at last to persuade my companion to take my advice, though I knew from his excited manner that there was not much hope of sleep for him. Indeed, his mood was infectious, for I lay tossing half the night myself, brooding over this strange problem, and inventing a hundred theories, each of which was more impossible than the last. Why had Holmes remained at Woking ? Why had he asked Miss Harrison to stay in the sick-room all day ? Why had he been so careful not to inform the people at Briarbrae that he intended to remain near them ? I cudgelled my brains until I fell asleep in the endeavour to find some explanation which would cover all these facts.

It was seven o'clock when I awoke, and I set off at once for Phelps' room, to find him haggard and spent after a sleepless night. His first question was whether Holmes had arrived yet.

" He'll be here when he promised," said I, " and not an instant sooner or later."

And my words were true, for shortly after eight a hansom dashed up to the door and our friend got out of it. Standing in the window, we saw that his left hand was swathed in a bandage and that his face was very grim and pale. He entered the house, but it was some little time before he came upstairs.

" He looks like a beaten man," cried Phelps.

I was forced to confess that he was right. " After all," said I, " the clue of the matter lies probably here in town."

Phelps gave a groan.

" I don't know how it is," said he, " but I had hoped for so much from his return. But surely his hand was not tied up like that yesterday ? What can be the matter ? "

" You are not wounded, Holmes ? " I asked, as my friend entered the room.

" Tut, it is only a scratch through my own clumsiness," he answered, nodding his good morning to us. " This case of yours, Mr. Phelps, is certainly one of the darkest which I have ever investigated."

" I feared that you would find it beyond you."

" It has been a most remarkable experience."

" That bandage tells of adventures," said I. " Won't you tell us what has happened ? "

" After breakfast, my dear Watson.   Remember that I have breathed thirty miles of Surrey air this morning.   I suppose there has been no answer to my cabman advertisement ? Well, well, we cannot expect to score every time."

The table was all laid, and, just as I was about to ring, Mrs. Hudson entered with the tea and coffee. A few minutes later she brought in the covers, and we all drew up to the table, Holmes ravenous, I curious, and Phelps in the gloomiest state of depression.

" Mrs. Hudson has risen to the occasion," said Holmes, uncovering a dish of curried chicken. " Her cuisine is a little limited, but she has as good an idea of breakfast as a Scotchwoman. What have you there, Watson ? "

" Ham and eggs," I answered.

" Good ! What are you going to take, Mr. Phelps : curried fowl, eggs, or will you help yourself ? "

" Thank you, I can eat nothing," said Phelps.

" Oh, come ! Try the dish before you."

" Thank you, I would really rather not."

" Well, then," said Holmes, with a mischievous twinkle, " I suppose that you have no objection to helping me ? "

Phelps raised the cover, and as he did so he uttered a scream, and sat there staring with a face as white as the plate upon which he looked. Across the centre of it was lying a little cylinder of blue-grey paper. He caught it up, devoured it with his eyes, and then danced madly about the room, pressing it to his bosom and shrieking out in his delight. Then he fell back into an arm-chair, so limp and exhausted with his own emotions that we had to pour brandy down his throat to keep him from fainting.

" There ! there ! " said Holmes, soothingly, patting him upon the shoulder. " It was too bad to spring it on you like this ; but Watson here will tell you that I never can resist a touch of the dramatic."

Phelps seized his hand and kissed it. " God bless you ! " he cried ; " you have saved my honour."

" Well, my own was at stake, you know," said Holmes. " I assure you, it is just as hateful to me to fail in a case as it can be to you to blunder over a commission."

Phelps thrust away the precious document into the innermost pocket of his coat.

" I have not the heart to interrupt your breakfast any further, and yet I am dying to know how you got it and where it was."

Sherlock Holmes swallowed a cup of coffee and turned his attention to the ham and eggs. Then he rose, lit his pipe, and settled himself down into his chair.

" I'll tell you what I did first, and how I came to do it afterwards," said he. " After leaving you at the station I went for a charming walk through some admirable Surrey scenery to a pretty little village called Ripley, where I **27** had my tea at an inn, and took the precaution of filling **28** my flask and of putting a paper of sandwiches in my pocket. There I remained until evening, when I set off for Woking again and found myself in the high-road outside Briarbrae just after sunset.

" Well, I waited until the road was clear—it is never a

PHELPS RAISED THE COVER . . .

Illustration by William H. Hyde for *Harper's Weekly*, October 21, 1893. Sidney Paget illustrated the same scene for the *Strand Magazine*, November, 1893.

27 *a pretty little village called Ripley*. Ripley is some four miles from Woking by the road which winds its fantastically irregular course across the River Wey and Send Common.

28 *an inn.* "I can see no possible objection to identifying 'an inn' with the famous Talbot Inn, an old, red-brick, white-porched coaching house, which, in Holmes' day, was dozing through the 'recession' between the passing of the stagecoach and the coming of the cycle and motorcycle," Mr. Michael Harrison wrote (*In the Footsteps of Sherlock Holmes*).

"... MR. JOSEPH HARRISON STEPPED OUT
INTO THE MOONLIGHT."

Illustration by Sidney Paget for the *Strand Magazine*, November, 1893. Professor Christ and Dr.
Zeisler both noted that Watson must have mistaken
a "twilight" by Holmes for "moonlight," since the
moon was *not* shining at two o'clock in the morning on any of the possible days.

very frequented one at any time, I fancy—and then I
clambered over the fence into the grounds."

" Surely the gate was open ? " ejaculated Phelps.

" Yes ; but I have a peculiar taste in these matters.   I
chose the place where the three fir trees stand, and behind
their screen I got over without the least chance of anyone in the house being able to see me.   I crouched down
among the bushes on the other side, and crawled from one
to the other—witness the disreputable state of my trouser
knees—until I had reached the clump of rhododendrons
just opposite to your bedroom window.   There I squatted
down and awaited developments.

" The blind was not down in your room, and I could
see Miss Harrison sitting there reading by the table.   It
was a quarter past ten when she closed her book, fastened
the shutters, and retired.   I heard her shut the door, and
felt quite sure that she had turned the key in the lock."

" The key ? " ejaculated Phelps.

" Yes, I had given Miss Harrison instructions to lock
the door on the outside and take the key with her when
she went to bed.   She carried out every one of my
injunctions to the letter, and certainly without her co-operation you would not have that paper in your coat pocket.
She departed then, the lights went out, and I was left
squatting in the rhododendron bush.

" The night was fine, but still it was a very weary vigil.
Of course, it has the sort of excitement about it that the
sportsman feels when he lies beside the watercourse and
waits for the big game.   It was very long, though—
almost as long, Watson, as when you and I waited in that
deadly room when we looked into the little problem of the
' Speckled Band.'   There was a church clock down at
Woking which struck the quarters, and I thought more
than once that it had stopped.   At last, however, about
two in the morning, I suddenly heard the gentle sound of
a bolt being pushed back, and the creaking of a key.   A
moment later the servants' door was opened and Mr.
Joseph Harrison stepped out into the moonlight."

" Joseph ! " ejaculated Phelps.

" He was bare-headed, but he had a black cloak thrown
over his shoulder, so that he could conceal his face in an
instant if there were any alarm.   He walked on tiptoe
under the shadow of the wall, and when he reached the
window, he worked a long-bladed knife through the sash
and pushed back the catch.   Then he flung open the
window and, putting his knife through the crack in the
shutters, he thrust the bar up and swung them open.

" From where I lay I had a perfect view of the inside
of the room and of every one of his movements.   He lit
the two candles which stand upon the mantelpiece, and
then he proceeded to turn back the corner of the carpet
in the neighbourhood of the door.   Presently he stooped
and picked out a square piece of board, such as is usually
left to enable plumbers to get at the joints of the gas
pipes.   This one covered, as a matter of fact, the T-joint
which gives off the pipe which supplies the kitchen underneath.   Out of this hiding-place he drew that little
cylinder of paper, pushed down the board, rearranged
the carpet, blew out the candles, and walked straight

into my arms as I stood waiting for him outside the window.

" Well, he has rather more viciousness than I gave him credit for, has Master Joseph.   He flew at me with his knife, and I had to grass him twice, and got a cut over **29** the knuckles, before I had the upper hand of him.   He looked ' murder ' out of the only eye he could see with when we had finished, but he listened to reason and gave up the papers.   Having got them I let my man go, but I wired full particulars to Forbes this morning.   If he is quick enough to catch his bird, well and good !   But if, as I shrewdly suspect, he finds the nest empty before he gets there, why, all the better for the Government.   I fancy that Lord Holdhurst, for one, and Mr. Percy Phelps, for another would very much rather that the affair never got so far as a police-court."

" My God ! " gasped our client.   " Do you tell me that during these long ten weeks of agony, the stolen papers were within the very room with me all the time ? "

" So it was."

" And Joseph !   Joseph a villain and a thief ! "

" Hum !   I am afraid Joseph's character is a rather deeper and more dangerous one than one might judge from his appearance.   From what I have heard from him this morning, I gather that he has lost heavily in dabbling with stocks, and that he is ready to do anything on earth to better his fortunes.   Being an absolutely selfish man, when a chance presented itself he did not allow either his sister's happiness or your reputation to hold his hand."

Percy Phelps sank back in his chair.   " My head whirls," said he ; " your words have dazed me."

" The principal difficulty in your case," remarked Holmes, in his didactic fashion, " lay in the fact of there being too much evidence.   What was vital was overlaid and hidden by what was irrelevant.   Of all the facts which were presented to us, we had to pick just those which we deemed to be essential, and then piece them together in their order, so as to reconstruct this very remarkable chain of events.   I had already begun to suspect Joseph, from the fact that you had intended to travel home with him that night, and that therefore it was a likely enough thing that he should call for you—knowing the Foreign Office well—upon his way.   When I heard that someone had been so anxious to get into the bedroom, in which no one but Joseph could have concealed anything—you told us in your narrative how you had turned Joseph out when you arrived with the doctor—my suspicions all changed to certainties, especially as the attempt was made on the first night upon which the nurse was absent, showing that the intruder was well acquainted with the ways of the house."

" How blind I have been ! "

" The facts of the case, as far as I have worked them out, are these : This Joseph Harrison entered the office through the Charles Street door, and knowing his way he walked straight into your room the instant after you left it.   Finding no one there he promptly rang the bell, and at the instant that he did so his eyes caught the paper

29 *I had to grass him twice.* "Grass" in some of the American texts sometimes appears as "grasp." To "grass" is an old sporting term meaning to knock or bring down. "But to knock a man down twice may seem excessively rough treatment, even if he is armed with a long-bladed knife," Mr. James Edward Holroyd wrote. "I suggest that one has to go back to the earlier part of the story for the explanation. When Holmes and Watson first arrive at Briarbrae, Woking, they are greeted by this same J. H. with 'Percy has been enquiring for you all morning. Ah, poor chap, he clings to any straw.' Holmes would not like that. I think he remembered it and gave the prospective brother-in-law an extra one for luck when he got him alone!"

upon the table. A glance showed him that chance had put in his way a State document of immense value, and in a flash he had thrust it into his pocket and was gone. A few minutes elapsed, as you remember, before the sleepy commissionaire drew your attention to the bell, and those were just enough to give the thief time to make his escape.

"He made his way to Woking by the first train, and, having examined his booty and assured himself that it really was of immense value, he concealed it in what he thought was a very safe place, with the intention of taking it out again in a day or two, and carrying it to the French Embassy, or wherever he thought that a long price was to be had. Then came your sudden return. He, without a moment's warning, was bundled out of his room, and from that time onwards there were always at least two of you there to prevent him from regaining his treasure. The situation to him must have been a maddening one. But at last he thought he saw his chance. He tried to steal in, but was baffled by your wakefulness. You may remember that you did not take your usual draught that night."

"I remember."

"I fancy that he had taken steps to make that draught efficacious, and that he quite relied upon your being unconscious. Of course, I understood that he would repeat the attempt whenever it could be done with safety. Your leaving the room gave him the chance he wanted. I kept Miss Harrison in it all day, so that he might not anticipate us. Then, having given him the idea that the coast was clear, I kept guard as I have described. I already knew that the papers were probably in the room, but I had no desire to rip up all the planking and skirting in search of them. I let him take them, therefore, from the hiding-place, and so saved myself an infinity of trouble. Is there any other point which I can make clear?"

"Why did he try the window on the first occasion," I asked, "when he might have entered by the door?"

"In reaching the door he would have to pass seven bedrooms. On the other hand, he could get out on to the lawn with ease. Anything else?"

"You do not think," asked Phelps, "that he had any murderous intention? The knife was only meant as a tool."

"It may be so," answered Holmes, shrugging his shoulders. "I can only say for certain that Mr. Joseph Harrison is a gentleman to whose mercy I should be extremely unwilling to trust."

"IS THERE ANY OTHER POINT WHICH I CAN MAKE CLEAR?"

Illustration by Sidney Paget for the *Strand Magazine*, November, 1893.

41

THE CARDBOARD BOX

[*Saturday, August 31, to Monday, September 2, 1889*]

IN choosing a few typical cases which illustrate the remarkable mental qualities of my friend, Sherlock Holmes, I have endeavoured, so far as possible, to select those which presented the minimum of sensationalism, while offering a fair field for his talents. It is, however, unfortunately, impossible entirely to separate the sensational from the criminal, and a chronicler is left in the dilemma that he must either sacrifice details which are essential to his statement, and so give a false impression of the problem, or he must use matter which chance, and not choice, has provided him with. With this short preface I shall turn to my notes of what proved to be a strange, though a peculiarly terrible, chain of events.

It was a blazing hot day in August. Baker Street was **1** like an oven, and the glare of the sunlight upon the yellow brickwork of the house across the road was painful to the eye. It was hard to believe that these were the same walls which loomed so gloomily through the fogs of winter. Our blinds were half-drawn, and Holmes lay curled upon the sofa, reading and re-reading a letter which he had received by the morning post. For myself, my term of service in India had trained me to stand heat better than cold, and a thermometer at 90 was no hardship. But the morning paper was uninteresting. Parliament had risen. Everybody was out of town, and I yearned for **2** the glades of the New Forest or the shingle of Southsea. **3-4** A depleted bank account had caused me to postpone my holiday, and as to my companion, neither the country nor **5** the sea presented the slightest attraction to him. He loved to lie in the very centre of five millions of people, with his filaments stretching out and running through them, responsive to every little rumour or suspicion of unsolved crime. Appreciation of nature found no place among his many gifts, **6** and his only change was when he turned his mind from the evil-doer of the town to track down his brother of the country.

Finding that Holmes was too absorbed for conversation I had tossed aside the barren paper and, leaning back in my chair, I fell into a brown study. Suddenly my companion's voice broke in upon my thoughts.

1 *It was a blazing hot day in August.* The day, as we shall see, was a Saturday. The year must be 1889 or 1890: Holmes later mentions the case of *The Sign of the Four,* which we know took place in September, 1888; Watson's account of the adventure of "The Cardboard Box" was published in January, 1893; in the Augusts of 1891 and 1892 Holmes was believed to be dead by all except his brother Mycroft.

2 *Parliament had risen.* Such a report would appear in the morning paper on the day after the event. In the year under consideration, Parliament must therefore have risen on a Friday. In 1890, Parliament rose on August 18th, a Wednesday. In addition, there was no day in August, 1890, after the 18th when the temperature was higher than 69.6°. In 1889, on the other hand, Parliament rose on August 30th, a Friday. On the next day, the Saturday, the temperature hit 81.1°, making it an exceedingly hot day for England. We hold that the adventure began on *Saturday, August 31, 1889;* it closed two days later on *Monday, September 2, 1889.*

. . . I FELL INTO A BROWN STUDY.

Illustration by Sidney Paget for the *Strand Magazine,* January, 1893.

3 *the New Forest.* The 145 miles of the New Forest stretch from Southampton Water to the Wiltshire border. The New Forest was enclosed by that lover of the chase, William the Conqueror, and in it William Rufus, the inept son of a gifted father, was killed, perhaps accidentally, perhaps by design, by the arrow shot by William Tyrrell. There are few deer left today, and little other game in the Forest, which is Crown property, but it is still a sanctuary for birds, many of them rare in England, and its trees, birds, and quiet solitude make it a beauty spot of a kind hardly to be found anywhere else in England.

4 *the shingle of Southsea.* The beach at Southsea, the suburb of Portsmouth where, curiously enough, Dr. Arthur Conan Doyle early practiced medicine.

5 *A depleted bank account had caused me to postpone my holiday.* Watson in the August of 1889 was both married and in practice. Why, then, do we find him in this adventure living in Baker Street with Holmes? We believe the answer is clear when one properly interprets this statement. August, 1889, was less than a year after the excitements of *The Sign of the Four.* No doubt Mary Morstan Watson had not yet completely recovered from them. In such a heat wave as London was experiencing, Watson undoubtedly hoped that they might flee the metropolis together. When finances made this impossible, he gallantly gave up his own holiday and sent Mary off alone. To ease his loneliness, he moved for about a fortnight into Baker Street, bringing a few books and pictures with him. Mary—and Watson—returned to their own home shortly before September 7, 1889.

6 *Appreciation of nature found no place among his many gifts.* But this we cannot allow: see Holmes' comments on the beauty of the morning in *The Sign of the Four.* Read his little sermon on the rose in "The Naval Treaty." Our picture of Donnithorpe and the Norfolk countryside in "The *Gloria Scott*" comes only from Holmes, as does our picture of Hurlstone and West Surrey in "The Musgrave Ritual." "Of late I have been tempted to look into the problems of nature . . ." Holmes says in "The Final Problem." "Let us walk in these beautiful woods, Watson, and give a few hours to the birds and flowers," he says in "The Adventure of Black Peter." And in "The Adventure of the Lion's Mane," he writes: "On the morning of which I speak the wind had abated, and all nature was newly washed and fresh. It was impossible to work upon so delightful a day, and I strolled out before breakfast to enjoy the exquisite air."

7 *you expressed incredulity."* Holmes can hardly be referring here to the conversation recorded by Watson in *A Study in Scarlet.* We note, too, that Holmes apparently has changed his views: Dupin, "a very inferior fellow," has become "a close

" You are right, Watson," said he. " It does seem a most preposterous way of settling a dispute."

" Most preposterous ! " I exclaimed, and then suddenly realizing how he had echoed the inmost thought of my soul, I sat up in my chair and stared at him in blank amazement.

" What is this, Holmes ? " I cried. " This is beyond anything which I could have imagined."

He laughed heartily at my perplexity.

" You remember," said he, " that some little time ago when I read you the passage in one of Poe's sketches in which a close reasoner follows the unspoken thoughts of his companion, you were inclined to treat the matter as a mere *tour-de-force* of the author. On my remarking that I was constantly in the habit of doing the same thing you **7** expressed incredulity."

" Oh, no ! "

" Perhaps not with your tongue, my dear Watson, but certainly with your eyebrows. So when I saw you throw down your paper and enter upon a train of thought, I was very happy to have the opportunity of reading it off, and eventually of breaking into it, as a proof that I had been **8** *en rapport* with you."

But I was still far from satisfied. " In the example which you read to me," said I, " the reasoner drew his conclusions from the actions of the man whom he observed. If I remember right, he stumbled over a heap of stones, looked up at the stars, and so on. But I have been seated quietly in my chair, and what clues can I have given you ? "

" You do yourself an injustice. The features are given to man as the means by which he shall express his emotions, and yours are faithful servants."

" Do you mean to say that you read my train of thoughts from my features ? "

" Your features, and especially your eyes. Perhaps you cannot yourself recall how your reverie commenced ? "

" No, I cannot."

" Then I will tell you. After throwing down your paper, which was the action which drew my attention to you, you sat for half a minute with a vacant expression. Then your eyes fixed themselves upon your newly framed **9** picture of General Gordon, and I saw by the alteration in your face that a train of thought had been started. But it did not lead very far. Your eyes flashed across to the **10** unframed portrait of Henry Ward Beecher which stands upon the top of your books. Then you glanced up at the wall, and of course your meaning was obvious. You were thinking that if the portrait were framed, it would just cover that bare space and correspond with Gordon's picture over there."

" You have followed me wonderfully ! " I exclaimed.

" So far I could hardly have gone astray. But now your thoughts went back to Beecher, and you looked hard across as if you were studying the character in his features. Then your eyes ceased to pucker, but you continued to look across, and your face was thoughtful. You were recalling the incidents of Beecher's career. I was well aware that you could not do this without thinking of the mission which he undertook on behalf of the North at the time of the Civil War, for I remember your expressing your passionate indignation at the way in which he was received by the more turbulent of our people. You felt **11** so strongly about it, that I knew you could not think of Beecher without thinking of that also. When a moment later I saw your eyes wander away from the picture, I suspected that your mind had now turned to the Civil War, and when I observed that your lips set, your eyes sparkled, and your hands clenched, I was positive that you were indeed thinking of the gallantry which was shown by both sides in that desperate struggle. But then, again, your face grew sadder ; you shook your head. You were dwelling upon the sadness and horror and useless waste of life. Your hand stole towards your own old wound and a smile quivered on your lips, which showed me that the ridiculous side of this method of settling international questions had forced itself upon your mind. At this point I agreed with you that it was preposterous, and was glad to find that all my deductions had been correct."

" Absolutely ! " said I. " And now that you have explained it, I confess that I am as amazed as before."

" It was very superficial, my dear Watson, I assure you. I should not have intruded it upon your attention had you not shown some incredulity the other day. But I have in my hands here a little problem which may prove to be more difficult of solution than my small essay in thought-reading. Have you observed in the paper a short paragraph referring to the remarkable contents of a packet sent through the post to Miss Cushing, of Cross Street, Croydon ? "   **12**

" No, I saw nothing."

" Ah ! then you must have overlooked it. Just toss it over to me. Here it is, under the financial column. Perhaps you would be good enough to read it aloud."

I picked up the paper which he had thrown back to me, and read the paragraph indicated. It was headed, " A Gruesome Packet."

" Miss Susan Cushing, living at Cross Street, Croydon, has been made the victim of what must be regarded as a peculiarly revolting practical joke, unless some more sinister meaning should prove to be attached to the incident. At two o'clock yesterday afternoon a small packet, wrapped in brown paper, was handed in by the postman. A cardboard box was inside, which was filled with coarse salt. On emptying this, Miss Cushing was horrified to find two human ears, apparently quite freshly severed. The box had been sent by parcel post from Belfast upon the morning before. There is no indication as to the sender, and the matter is the more mysterious as Miss Cushing, who is a maiden lady of fifty, has led a most retired life, and has so few acquaintances or correspondents that it is a rare event for her to receive anything through the post. Some years ago, however, when she resided at Penge, she let apart- **13** ments in her house to three young medical students, whom she was obliged to get rid of on account of their noisy and irregular habits. The police are of opinion that this outrage may have been perpetrated upon Miss Cushing by these youths, who owed her a grudge, and who hoped to frighten her by sending her these relics of the dissecting-rooms. Some probability is lent to the theory by the fact that one of these students came from the North of Ireland, and, to the best of Miss Cushing's belief, from Belfast. In the meantime, the matter is being actively investigated, Mr. Lestrade, one of the very smartest of our detective officers, being in charge of the case."

reasoner." "It may therefore be assumed," Miss Madeleine B. Stern wrote in "Sherlock Holmes: Rare Book Collector," "that . . . probably between 1881 and [the time of "The Cardboard Box"], Holmes acquired a copy of the New York, Wiley and Putnam, 1845, edition of Poe's *Tales*, including both 'The Murders in the Rue Morgue,' which contained the passage in question [*see below*], and 'The Mystery of Marie Rogêt.' "

8 en rapport. French: harmony of relation; accordance; correspondence; agreement; sympathetic relation.

9 *General Gordon.* General Charles George Gordon ("Chinese Gordon"), 1833–1885, British soldier and administrator, Commander of the Chinese army that suppressed the Taiping Rebellion, Governor of the Egyptian Sudan, 1877–1880. Trying to crush the power of the Mahdi, he was killed at the siege of Khartoum. Popular indignation at his death helped to cause the fall of the Gladstone government in 1885.

10 *Henry Ward Beecher.* For Watson's possible interest or interests in Henry Ward Beecher, see Chapter 9, "Good Old Watson!"

11 *the more turbulent of our people.* "*Punch*'s reactions to the Beecher visit are worth looking at," Mr. Whitfield J. Bell, Jr., wrote in "Holmes and History"; "a brief account will be found in Carl Sandburg's *Lincoln: The War Years*, II, 515–7."

12 *Croydon?*" A suburb of London in Surrey, important since Holmes' and Watson's day for its airport, used by the military during World War II.

13 *Penge.* A district centering around the Sydenham-Crystal Palace Hill.

14 *honeydew tobacco.* A kind of smoking tobacco sweetened with molasses.

15 *Cross Street.* "The nearness of 'Cross Street'—it is, in reality, Cross *Road*—to the station . . . shows that the station in question was that known as 'East Croydon,' whose entrance is on George Street, Croydon's main thoroughfare," Mr. Michael Harrison wrote (*In the Footsteps of Sherlock Holmes*). "Coming out of East Croydon Station into George Street, the three men would have turned left, walked for a few yards along George Street, then turned left again, into Cherry Orchard Street, off which Cross Road branches. Watson's memory is a little at fault in describing Cross Road as a 'very long street'—it is, in fact, an exceedingly short one, but Watson's memory may be confusing Cross Road with St. James's Road, into which Cross Road leads, and which is, in truth, a very long road."

"WHAT IS THE USE OF ASKING ME QUESTIONS, WHEN I TELL YOU I KNOW NOTHING WHATEVER ABOUT IT?"

Illustration by Sidney Paget for the *Strand Magazine*, January, 1893.

"So much for the *Daily Chronicle*," said Holmes, as I finished reading. "Now for our friend Lestrade. I had a note from him this morning, in which he says : ' I think that this case is very much in your line. We have every hope of clearing the matter up, but we find a little difficulty in getting anything to work upon. We have, of course, wired to the Belfast post office, but a large number of parcels were handed in upon that day, and they have no means of identifying this particular one, or of remembering the sender. The box is a half-pound box of honeydew **14** tobacco, and does not help us in any way. The medical-student theory still appears to me to be the most feasible, but if you should have a few hours to spare, I should be very happy to see you out here. I shall be either at the house or in the police-station all day.' What say you, Watson ? Can you rise superior to the heat, and run down to Croydon with me on the off chance of a case for your annals ? "

" I was longing for something to do."

" You shall have it then. Ring for our boots, and tell them to order a cab. I'll be back in a moment, when I have changed my dressing-gown and filled my cigar-case."

A shower of rain fell while we were in the train, and the heat was far less oppressive in Croydon than in town. Holmes had sent on a wire, so that Lestrade, as wiry, as dapper, and as ferret-like as ever, was waiting for us at the station. A walk of five minutes took us to Cross **15** Street, where Miss Cushing resided.

It was a very long street of two-story brick houses, neat and prim, with whitened stone steps and little groups of aproned women gossiping at the doors. Half-way down, Lestrade stopped and tapped at a door, which was opened by a small servant girl. Miss Cushing was sitting in the front room, into which we were ushered. She was a placid-faced woman, with large, gentle eyes, and grizzled hair curving down over her temples on each side. A worked antimacassar lay upon her lap and a basket of coloured silks stood upon a stool beside her.

" They are in the outhouse, those dreadful things," said she, as Lestrade entered. " I wish that you would take them away altogether."

" So I shall, Miss Cushing. I only kept them here until my friend, Mr. Holmes, should have seen them in your presence."

" Why in my presence, sir ? "

" In case he wished to ask any questions."

" What is the use of asking me questions, when I tell you I know nothing whatever about it ? "

" Quite so, madam," said Holmes, in his soothing way. " I have no doubt that you have been annoyed more than enough already over this business."

" Indeed, I have, sir. I am a quiet woman and live a retired life. It is something new for me to see my name in the papers and to find the police in my house. I won't have those things in here, Mr. Lestrade. If you wish to see them you must go to the outhouse."

It was a small shed in the narrow garden which ran behind the house. Lestrade went in and brought out a yellow cardboard box, with a piece of brown paper and some string. There was a bench at the end of the path, and we all sat down while Holmes examined, one by one, the articles which Lestrade had handed to him.

" The string is exceedingly interesting," he remarked, holding it up to the light and sniffing at it. " What do you make of this string, Lestrade ? "

" It has been tarred."

" Precisely. It is a piece of tarred twine. You have also, no doubt, remarked that Miss Cushing has cut the cord with a scissors, as can be seen by the double fray on each side. This is of importance."

" I cannot see the importance," said Lestrade.

" The importance lies in the fact that the knot is left intact, and that this knot is of a peculiar character."

" It is very neatly tied. I had already made a note to that effect," said Lestrade, complacently.

" So much for the string, then," said Holmes, smiling ; " now for the box wrapper. Brown paper, with a distinct smell of coffee. What, did not observe it ? I think there can be no doubt of it. Address printed in rather straggling characters : ' Miss S. Cushing, Cross Street, Croydon.' Done with a broad-pointed pen, probably a J, and with very inferior ink. The word Croydon has been originally spelt with an *i*, which has been changed to *y*. The parcel was directed then by a man—the printing is distinctly masculine—of limited education and unacquainted with the town of Croydon. So far, so good ! The box is a yellow, half-pound honeydew box, with nothing distinctive save two thumb marks at the left bottom corner. It is filled with rough salt of the quality used for preserving hides and other of the coarser commercial purposes. And embedded in it are these very singular enclosures."

He took out the two ears as he spoke, and laying a board across his knee, he examined them minutely, while Lestrade and I, bending forward on each side of him, glanced alternately at these dreadful relics and at the thoughtful, eager face of our companion. Finally he returned them to the box once more, and sat for a while in deep meditation.

" You have observed, of course," said he at last, " that the ears are not a pair."

" Yes, I have noticed that. But if this were the practical joke of some students from the dissecting-rooms, it would be as easy for them to send two odd ears as a pair."

" Precisely. But this is not a practical joke."

" You are sure of it ? "

" The presumption is strongly against it. Bodies in the dissecting-rooms are injected with preservative fluid. These ears bear no signs of this. They are fresh too. They have been cut off with a blunt instrument, which would hardly happen if a student had done it. Again, carbolic or rectified spirits would be the preservatives which would suggest themselves to the medical mind, certainly not rough salt. I repeat that there is no practical joke here, but that we are investigating a serious crime."

A vague thrill ran through me as I listened to my companion's words and saw the stern gravity which had

... LAYING A BOARD ACROSS HIS KNEE, HE EXAMINED THEM MINUTELY ...

Illustration by Sidney Paget for the *Strand Magazine*, January, 1893.

16 *or earlier.* The *Daily Chronicle* of "today" reported that "at two o'clock yesterday afternoon a small packet . . . was handed in [at Croydon] by the postman. The box had been sent by parcel post from Belfast the morning before." "Two days" after the day on which the case opened, Holmes received "a bulky envelope" from Lestrade. A packet posted in Belfast in the morning could not possibly reach Croydon the same day; the newspaper must therefore have been correct in saying that it was posted one day and received the next. Holmes, having read the newspaper, should therefore have said either: "Today is Friday. The packet was posted on Wednesday morning. The tragedy, then, occurred on Tuesday or Monday, or earlier"; or, "Today is Saturday. The packet was posted on Thursday morning. The tragedy, then, occurred on Wednesday, or Tuesday, or earlier." We believe that the second alternative is the correct one, for two reasons: 1) If the case opened on a Friday, the bulky envelope received from Lestrade two days later must have arrived on a Sunday. If the case opened on a Saturday, on the other hand, it must have arrived on a Monday. It is far more likely that Lestrade used the regular post in the usual way than that he went to the expense of hiring a special messenger, as he would have had to do if the envelope were delivered on a Sunday. 2) In the first alternative, we would have to believe that Watson misquoted Holmes not once but thrice; in the second alternative, however, we need only change the "Friday" to "Saturday" to make the statement make sense. We hold that the murders were on Wednesday, that the packet was posted on Thursday and received on Friday, and that the case began on a Saturday and closed on the Monday two days later.

hardened his features. This brutal preliminary seemed to shadow forth some strange and inexplicable horror in the background. Lestrade, however, shook his head like a man who is only half convinced.

"There are objections to the joke theory, no doubt," said he ; " but there are much stronger reasons against the other. We know that this woman has led a most quiet and respectable life at Penge and here for the last twenty years. She has hardly been away from her home for a day during that time. Why on earth, then, should any criminal send her the proofs of his guilt, especially as, unless she is a most consummate actress, she understands quite as little of the matter as we do ? "

" That is the problem which we have to solve," Holmes answered, " and for my part I shall set about it by presuming that my reasoning is correct, and that a double murder has been committed. One of these ears is a woman's, small, finely formed, and pierced for an ear-ring. The other is a man's, sun-burned, discoloured, and also pierced for an ear-ring. These two people are presumably dead, or we should have heard their story before now. To-day is Friday. The packet was posted on Thursday morning. The tragedy, then, occurred on Wednesday or Tuesday, or **16** earlier. If the two people were murdered, who but their murderer would have sent this sign of his work to Miss Cushing ? We may take it that the sender of the packet is the man whom we want. But he must have some strong reason for sending Miss Cushing this packet. What reason then ? It must have been to tell her that the deed was done ; or to pain her, perhaps. But in that case she knows who it is. Does she know ? I doubt it. If she knew, why should she call the police in ? She might have buried the ears, and no one would have been the wiser. That is what she would have done if she had wished to shield the criminal. But if she does not wish to shield him she would give his name. There is a tangle here which needs straightening out." He had been talking in a high, quick voice, staring blankly up over the garden fence, but now he sprang briskly to his feet and walked towards the house.

" I have a few questions to ask Miss Cushing," said he.

" In that case I may leave you here," said Lestrade, " for I have another small business on hand. I think that I have nothing further to learn from Miss Cushing. You will find me at the police-station."

" We shall look in on our way to the train," answered Holmes. A moment later he and I were back in the front room, where the impassive lady was still quietly working away at her antimacassar. She put it down on her lap as we entered, and looked at us with her frank, searching blue eyes.

" I am convinced, sir," she said, " that this matter is a mistake, and that the parcel was never meant for me at all. I have said this several times to the gentleman from Scotland Yard, but he simply laughs at me. I have not an enemy in the world, as far as I know, so why should anyone play me such a trick ? "

" I am coming to be of the same opinion, Miss Cushing,"

said Holmes, taking a seat beside her. " I think that it is more than probable . . ." He paused, and I was surprised, on glancing round, to see that he was staring with singular intentness at the lady's profile. Surprise and satisfaction were both for an instant to be read upon his eager face, though when she glanced round to find out the cause of his silence he had become as demure as ever. I stared hard myself at her flat, grizzled hair, her trim cap, her little gilt ear-rings, her placid features ; but I could see nothing which could account for my companion's evident excitement.

" There were one or two questions——"

" Oh, I am weary of questions ! " cried Miss Cushing, impatiently.

" You have two sisters, I believe."

" How could you know that ? "

" I observed the very instant that I entered the room that you have a portrait group of three ladies upon the mantelpiece, one of whom is undoubtedly yourself, while the others are so exceedingly like you that there could be no doubt of the relationship."

" Yes, you are quite right. Those are my sisters, Sarah and Mary."

" And here at my elbow is another portrait, taken at Liverpool, of your younger sister, in the company of a man who appears to be a steward by his uniform. I observe that she was unmarried at the time."

" You are very quick at observing."

" That is my trade."

" Well, you are quite right. But she was married to Mr. Browner a few days afterwards. He was on the South American line when that was taken, but he was so fond of her that he couldn't abide to leave her for so long, and he got into the Liverpool and London boats."

" Ah, the *Conqueror*, perhaps ? "

" No, the *May Day*, when last I heard. Jim came down **17** here to see me once. That was before he broke the pledge ; but afterwards he would always take drink when he was ashore, and a little drink would send him stark, staring mad. Ah ! it was a bad day that ever he took a glass in his hand again. First he dropped me, then he quarrelled with Sarah, and now that Mary has stopped writing we don't know how things are going with them."

It was evident that Miss Cushing had come upon a subject on which she felt very deeply. Like most people who lead a lonely life, she was shy at first, but ended by becoming extremely communicative. She told us many details about her brother-in-law the steward, and then wandering off on to the subject of her former lodgers, the medical students, she gave us a long account of their delinquencies, with their names and those of their hospitals. Holmes listened attentively to everything, throwing in a question from time to time.

" About your second sister, Sarah," said he. " I wonder, since you are both maiden ladies, that you do not keep house together."

" Ah ! you don't know Sarah's temper, or you would wonder no more. I tried it when I came to Croydon, and we kept on until about two months ago, when we had to

17 *"No, the* May Day. The *Conqueror* and the *May Day*, real ships, were located by Mr. Richard W. Clarke ("On the Nomenclature of Watson's Ships") "in the Liverpool registry under ownership of the Liverpool, Dublin and London Steam Packet Co."

18 *New Street, Wallington?* Wallington is a residential district close to which many Roman remains have been found. With Beddington and Carshalton, it extends for a distance of about two and a half miles along the main road between Croydon and Sutton. "Where 'New Street' was, I cannot say," Mr. Michael Harrison wrote (*In the Footsteps of Sherlock Holmes*). "In Wallington there are Newminster Road, Newstead Walk and Newhouse Walk; but these are all streets of recent buildings."

19 *fifty-five shillings.* Holmes paid about $13.75 for a violin which was worth at least $2,500. Mr. Michael Harrison has remarked (*In the Footsteps of Sherlock Holmes*) that only an expert would have spotted that the violin was a Stradivarius, since "Antonio Stradivari put his small label right within the body of the instrument . . ."

"HOW FAR TO WALLINGTON?" HE SAID.

Illustration by Sidney Paget for the *Strand Magazine*, January, 1893.

part. I don't want to say a word against my own sister, but she was always meddlesome and hard to please, was Sarah."

"You say that she quarrelled with your Liverpool relations."

"Yes, and they were the best of friends at one time. Why, she went up there to live in order to be near them. And now she has no word hard enough for Jim Browner. The last six months that she was here she would speak of nothing but his drinking and his ways. He had caught her meddling, I suspect, and given her a bit of his mind, and that was the start of it."

"Thank you, Miss Cushing," said Holmes, rising and bowing. "Your sister Sarah lives, I think you said, at **18** New Street, Wallington? Good-bye, and I am very sorry that you should have been troubled over a case with which, as you say, you have nothing whatever to do."

There was a cab passing as we came out, and Holmes hailed it.

"How far to Wallington?" he asked.

"Only about a mile, sir."

"Very good. Jump in, Watson. We must strike while the iron is hot. Simple as the case is, there have been one or two very instructive details in connection with it. Just pull up at a telegraph office as you pass, cabby."

Holmes sent off a short wire, and for the rest of the drive lay back in the cab with his hat tilted over his nose to keep the sun from his face. Our driver pulled up at a house which was not unlike the one which we had just quitted. My companion ordered him to wait, and had his hand upon the knocker, when the door opened and a grave young gentleman in black, with a very shiny hat, appeared on the step.

"Is Miss Cushing at home?" asked Holmes.

"Miss Sarah Cushing is extremely ill," said he. "She has been suffering since yesterday from brain symptoms of great severity. As her medical adviser, I cannot possibly take the responsibility of allowing anyone to see her. I should recommend you to call again in ten days." He drew on his gloves, closed the door, and marched off down the street.

"Well, if we can't, we can't," said Holmes, cheerfully.

"Perhaps she could not, or would not have told you much."

"I did not wish her to tell me anything. I only wanted to look at her. However, I think that I have got all that I want. Drive us to some decent hotel, cabby, where we may have some lunch, and afterwards we shall drop down upon friend Lestrade at the police-station."

We had a pleasant little meal together, during which Holmes would talk about nothing but violins, narrating with great exultation how he had purchased his own Stradivarius, which was worth at least five hundred guineas, at a Jew broker's in Tottenham Court Road for **19** fifty-five shillings. This led him to Paganini, and we sat for an hour over a bottle of claret while he told me anecdote after anecdote of that extraordinary man. The afternoon was far advanced and the hot glare had softened into a mellow glow before we found ourselves at the police-station. Lestrade was waiting for us at the door.

" A telegram for you, Mr. Holmes," said he.

" Ha ! It is the answer !" He tore it open, glanced his eyes over it, and crumpled it into his pocket. " That's all right," said he.

" Have you found out anything ? "

" I have found out everything ! "

" What ! " Lestrade stared at him in amazement. " You are joking."

" I was never more serious in my life. A shocking crime has been committed, and I think I have now laid bare every detail of it."

" And the criminal ? "

Holmes scribbled a few words upon the back of one of his visiting-cards and threw it over to Lestrade.

" That is the name," he said. " You cannot effect an arrest until to-morrow night at the earliest. I should prefer that you do not mention my name at all in connection with the case, as I choose to be only associated with those crimes which present some difficulty in their solution. Come on, Watson." We strode off together to the station, leaving Lestrade still staring with a delighted face at the card which Holmes had thrown him.

" The case," said Sherlock Holmes, as we chatted over our cigars that night in our rooms at Baker Street, " is one where, as in the investigations which you have chronicled under the names of the ' Study in Scarlet ' and of the ' Sign of Four,' we have been compelled to reason back-**20** ward from effects to causes. I have written to Lestrade asking him to supply us with the details which are now wanting, and which he will only get after he has secured his man. That he may be safely trusted to do, for although he is absolutely devoid of reason, he is as tenacious as a bulldog when he once understands what he has to do, and indeed, it is just this tenacity which has brought him to the top at Scotland Yard."

" Your case is not complete, then ? " I asked.

" It is fairly complete in essentials. We know who the author of the revolting business is, although one of the victims still escapes us. Of course, you have formed your own conclusions."

" I presume that this Jim Browner, the steward of a Liverpool boat, is the man whom you suspect ? "

" Oh ! it is more than a suspicion."

" And yet I cannot see anything save very vague indications."

" On the contrary, to my mind nothing could be more clear. Let me run over the principal steps. We approached the case, you remember, with an absolutely blank mind, which is always an advantage. We had formed no theories. We were simply there to observe and to draw inferences from our observations. What did we see first ? A very placid and respectable lady, who seemed quite innocent of any secret, and a portrait which showed me that she had two younger sisters. It instantly flashed across my mind that the box might have been meant for one of these. I set the idea aside as one which could be disproved or confirmed at our leisure. Then we

. . . HE TOLD ME ANECDOTE AFTER ANECDOTE
OF THAT EXTRAORDINARY MAN.

A portrait of Niccolo Paganini attributed to Holmes' great uncle, Horace Vernet. Paganini, 1782–1840, "was lionized on reaching Paris," Mr. James C. Iraldi wrote in "That Extraordinary Man." "He moved in the highest circles, was invited everywhere, met everyone worth meeting—including Horace Vernet, the famous artist, for whom he sat for a portrait. Would it be so inconceivable as to imagine that, in the course of those sittings, Paganini met—and loved—Vernet's sister—the same lady who was destined to become—the grandmother of Sherlock Holmes?"

20 *the 'Sign of Four.' The Sign of the Four* was not to be *published* until November, 1890, but Holmes had quite obviously read Watson's *manuscript* of the adventure by this time.

21 *two short monographs from my pen upon the subject.* The "*Anthropological Journal*" is a carelessness on the part of Dr. Watson, as the late Earle F. Walbridge pointed out in "Jabez Wilson Reports"; Holmes referred to the *Journal of Anthropology*, later the *Journal of the Royal Anthropological Society.*

"It is interesting to note," the late Christopher Morley wrote in "Was Sherlock Holmes an American?", "that when Holmes spoke . . . of having written two monographs on Ears . . . the alert editor of the *Strand* at once took the hint. A few months later, in October and November, 1893, the *Strand* printed 'A Chapter on Ears,' with photos of the ears of famous people—including an ear of Dr. Oliver Wendell Holmes. Surely, from so retiring a philosopher, then eighty-four years old, this intimate permission could not have been had without the privileged intervention of Sherlock."

"There is no question," Miss Madeleine B. Stern added in "Sherlock Holmes: Rare Book Collector," "that for his aural researches [Holmes] obtained a copy of Falloppio's *Observationes anatomicae* (Venice, 1561), a work containing the first scientific account of the structure of the ear."

22 *the pinna.* The projecting portion of the exterior ear.

"... THIS STEWARD, AN IMPULSIVE MAN,
OF STRONG PASSIONS ..."

Portrait of Jim Browner by Sidney Paget for the *Strand Magazine*, January, 1893.

went to the garden, as you remember, and we saw the very singular contents of the little yellow box.

" The string was of the quality which is used by sailmakers aboard ship, and at once a whiff of the sea was perceptible in our investigation. When I observed that the knot was one which is popular with sailors, that the parcel had been posted at a port, and that the male ear was pierced for an ear-ring which is so much more common among sailors than landsmen, I was quite certain that all the actors in the tragedy were to be found among our seafaring classes.

" When I came to examine the address of the packet I observed that it was to Miss S. Cushing. Now, the oldest sister would, of course, be Miss Cushing, and although her initial was ' S ' it might belong to one of the others as well. In that case we should have to commence our investigation from a fresh basis altogether. I therefore went into the house with the intention of clearing up this point. I was about to assure Miss Cushing that I was convinced that a mistake had been made, when you may remember that I came suddenly to a stop. The fact was that I had just seen something which filled me with surprise, and at the same time narrowed the field of our inquiry immensely.

" As a medical man, you are aware, Watson, that there is no part of the body which varies so much as the human ear. Each ear is as a rule quite distinctive, and differs from all other ones. In last year's *Anthropological Journal* you will find two short monographs from my pen upon **21** the subject. I had, therefore, examined the ears in the box with the eyes of an expert, and had carefully noted their anatomical peculiarities. Imagine my surprise then, when, on looking at Miss Cushing, I perceived that her ear corresponded exactly with the female ear which I had just inspected. The matter was entirely beyond coincidence. **22** There was the same shortening of the pinna, the same broad curve of the upper lobe, the same convolution of the inner cartilage. In all essentials it was the same ear.

" Of course, I at once saw the enormous importance of the observation. It was evident that the victim was a blood relation, and probably a very close one. I began to talk to her about her family, and you remember that she at once gave us some exceedingly valuable details.

" In the first place, her sister's name was Sarah, and her address had, until recently, been the same, so that it was quite obvious how the mistake had occurred, and for whom the packet was meant. Then we heard of this steward, married to the third sister, and learned that he had at one time been so intimate with Miss Sarah that she had actually gone up to Liverpool to be near the Browners, but a quarrel had afterwards divided them. This quarrel had put a stop to all communications for some months, so that if Browner had occasion to address a packet to Miss Sarah, he would undoubtedly have done so to her old address.

" And now the matter had begun to straighten itself out wonderfully. We had learned of the existence of this steward, an impulsive man, of strong passions—you remember that he threw up what must have been a very superior berth, in order to be nearer to his wife—subject, too, to occasional fits of hard drinking.   We had reason to believe that his wife had been murdered, and that a man— presumably a seafaring man—had been murdered at the same time.   Jealousy, of course, at once suggests itself as the motive for the crime.   And why should these proofs of the deed be sent to Miss Sarah Cushing ?   Probably because during her residence in Liverpool she had some hand in bringing about the events which led to the tragedy. You will observe that this line of boats calls at Belfast, Dublin, and Waterford ; so that, presuming that Browner had committed the deed, and had embarked at once upon his steamer, the *May Day*, Belfast would be the first place at which he could post his terrible packet.

" A second solution was at this stage obviously possible, and although I thought it exceedingly unlikely, I was determined to elucidate it before going further.   An unsuccessful lover might have killed Mr. and Mrs. Browner, and the male car might have belonged to the husband. There were many grave objections to this theory, but it was conceivable.   I therefore sent off a telegram to my friend Algar, of the Liverpool Force, and asked him to find out if Mrs. Browner were at home, and if Browner had departed in the *May Day*.   Then we went on to Wallington to visit Miss Sarah.

" I was curious, in the first place, to see how far the family ear had been reproduced in her.   Then, of course, she might give us very important information, but I was not sanguine that she would.   She must have heard of the business the day before, since all Croydon was ringing with it, and she alone could have understood for whom the packet was meant.   If she had been willing to help justice she would probably have communicated with the police already.   However, it was clearly our duty to see her, so we went.   We found that the news of the arrival of the packet—for her illness dated from that time—had such an effect upon her as to bring on brain fever.   It was clearer than ever that she understood its full significance, but equally clear that we should have to wait some time for any assistance from her.

" However, we were really independent of her help. Our answers were waiting for us at the police-station, where I had directed Algar to send them.   Nothing could be more conclusive.   Mrs. Browner's house had been closed for more than three days, and the neighbours were of opinion that she had gone south to see her relatives.   It had been ascertained at the shipping offices that Browner had left aboard of the *May Day*, and I calculate that she is due in the Thames to-morrow night.   When he arrives he will be met by the obtuse but resolute Lestrade, and I have no doubt that we shall have all our details filled in."

Sherlock Holmes was not disappointed in his expectations.   Two days later he received a bulky envelope, which contained a short note from the detective, and a typewritten document, which covered several pages of foolscap.

" Lestrade has got him all right," said Holmes, glancing up at me.   " Perhaps it would interest you to hear what he says."

23 *Shadwell.* One of the poorest and most densely populated districts in East London.

". . . HE HELD OUT HIS HANDS QUIETLY ENOUGH
FOR THE DARBIES."

Illustration by Sidney Paget for the *Strand Magazine*, January, 1893.

" MY DEAR MR. HOLMES,—

" In accordance with the scheme which we had formed in order to test our theories "—" the ' we ' is rather fine, Watson, is it not ? "—" I went down to the Albert Dock yesterday at 6 p.m., and boarded the s.s. *May Day*, belonging to the Liverpool, Dublin, and London Steam Packet Company. On inquiry, I found that there was a steward on board of the name of James Browner and that he had acted during the voyage in such an extraordinary manner that the captain had been compelled to relieve him of his duties. On descending to his berth, I found him seated upon a chest with his head sunk upon his hands, rocking himself to and fro. He is a big, powerful chap, clean-shaven, and very swarthy—something like Aldridge, who helped us in the bogus laundry affair. He jumped up when he heard my business, and I had my whistle to my lips to call a couple of river police, who were round the corner, but he seemed to have no heart in him, and he held out his hands quietly enough for the darbies. We brought him along to the cells, and his box as well, for we thought there might be something incriminating ; but, bar a big sharp knife, such as most sailors have, we got nothing for our trouble. However, we find that we shall want no more evidence, for on being brought before the inspector at the station, he asked leave to make a statement, which was, of course, taken down, just as he made it, by our shorthand man. We had three copies typewritten, one of which I enclose. The affair proves, as I always thought it would, to be an extremely simple one, but I am obliged to you for assisting me in my investigation. With kind regards, yours very truly,   " G. LESTRADE."

Hum ! The investigation really was a very simple one," remarked Holmes ; " but I don't think it struck him in that light when he first called us in. However, let us see what Jim Browner has to say for himself. This is his statement, as made before Inspector Montgomery at the **23** Shadwell Police Station, and it has the advantage of being verbatim."

" Have I anything to say ? Yes, I have a deal to say. I have to make a clean breast of it all. You can hang me, or you can leave me alone. I don't care a plug which you do. I tell you I've not shut an eye in sleep since I did it, and I don't believe I ever will again until I get past all waking. Sometimes it's his face, but most generally it's hers. I'm never without one or the other before me. He looks frowning and black-like, but she has a kind o' surprise upon her face. Aye, the white lamb, she might well be surprised when she read death on a face that had seldom looked anything but love upon her before.

" But it was Sarah's fault, and may the curse of a broken man put a blight on her and set the blood rotting in her veins ! It's not that I want to clear myself. I know that I went back to drink, like the beast that I was. But she would have forgiven me ; she would have stuck as close to me as a rope to a block if that woman had never darkened our door. For Sarah Cushing loved me—that's the root of the business—she loved me, until all her love turned to poisonous hate when she knew that I thought more of my wife's foot-mark in the mud than I did of her whole body and soul.

"There were three sisters altogether. The old one was just a good woman, the second was a devil, and the third was an angel. Sarah was thirty-three, and Mary was twenty-nine when I married. We were just as happy as the day was long when we set up house together, and in all Liverpool there was no better woman than my Mary. And then we asked Sarah up for a week, and the week grew into a month, and one thing led to another, until she was just one of ourselves.

"I was blue ribbon at that time, and we were putting a **24** little money by, and all was as bright as a new dollar. My God, whoever would have thought that it could have come to this? Whoever would have dreamed it?

"I used to be home for the week-ends very often, and sometimes if the ship were held back for cargo I would have a whole week at a time, and in this way I saw a deal of my sister-in-law, Sarah. She was a fine tall woman, black and quick and fierce, with a proud way of carrying her head, and a glint from her eye like a spark from a flint. But when little Mary was there I had never a thought of her, and that I swear as I hope for God's mercy.

"It had seemed to me sometimes that she liked to be alone with me, or to coax me out for a walk with her, but I had never thought anything of that. But one evening my eyes were opened. I had come up from the ship and found my wife out, but Sarah at home. 'Where's Mary?' I asked. 'Oh, she has gone to pay some accounts.' I was impatient and paced up and down the room. 'Can't you be happy for five minutes without Mary, Jim?' says she. 'It's a bad compliment to me that you can't be contented with my society for so short a time.' 'That's all right, my lass,' said I, putting out my hand towards her in a kindly way, but she had it in both hers in an instant, and they burned as if they were in a fever. I looked into her eyes and I read it all there. There was no need for her to speak, nor for me either. I frowned and drew my hand away. Then she stood by my side in silence for a bit, and then put up her hand and patted me on the shoulder. 'Steady, old Jim!' said she; and with a kind o' mocking laugh, she ran out of the room.

"Well, from that time Sarah hated me with her whole heart and soul, and she is a woman who can hate too. I was a fool to let her go on biding with us—a besotted fool —but I never said a word to Mary, for I knew it would grieve her. Things went on much as before, but after a time I began to find that there was a bit of a change in Mary herself. She had always been so trusting and so innocent, but now she became queer and suspicious, wanting to know where I had been and what I had been doing, and whom my letters were from, and what I had in my pockets, and a thousand such follies. Day by day she grew queerer and more irritable, and we had causeless rows about nothing. I was fairly puzzled by it all. Sarah avoided me now, but she and Mary were just inseparable. I can see now how she was plotting and scheming and poisoning my wife's mind against me, but I was such a blind beetle

24 *blue ribbon.* On the wagon; not drinking; from a small strip of blue ribbon worn as a distinctive badge by an organization of teetotallers called the Blue Ribbon Army, founded in 1878.

"'THAT'S ALL RIGHT, MY LASS,' SAID I . . ."

Illustration by Sidney Paget for the *Strand Magazine*, January, 1893.

that I could not understand it at the time.   Then I broke my blue ribbon and began to drink again, but I think I should not have done it if Mary had been the same as ever. She had some reason to be disgusted with me now, and the gap between us began to be wider and wider.   And then this Alec Fairbairn chipped in, and things became a thousand times blacker.

" It was to see Sarah that he came to my house first, but soon it was to see us, for he was a man with winning ways, and he made friends wherever he went.   He was a dashing, swaggering chap, smart and curled, who had seen half the world, and could talk of what he had seen.   He was good company, I won't deny it, and he had wonderful polite ways with him for a sailor man, so that I think there must have been a time when he knew more of the poop than the forecastle.   For a month he was in and out of my house, and never once did it cross my mind that harm might come of his soft, tricky ways.   And then at last something made me suspect, and from that day my peace was gone for ever.

" It was only a little thing too.   I had come into the parlour unexpected, and as I walked in at the door I saw a light of welcome on my wife's face.   But as she saw who it was it faded again, and she turned away with a look of disappointment.   That was enough for me.   There was no one but Alec Fairbairn whose step she could have mistaken for mine.   If I could have seen him then I should have killed him, for I have always been like a madman when my temper gets loose.   Mary saw the devil's light in my eyes, and she ran forward with her hands on my sleeve. ' Don't, Jim, don't ! ' says she.   ' Where's Sarah ? ' I asked.   ' In the kitchen,' says she.   ' Sarah,' says I, as I went in, ' this man Fairbairn is never to darken my door again.'   ' Why not ? ' says she.   ' Because I order it.' ' Oh ! ' says she, ' if my friends are not good enough for this house then I am not good enough for it either.'   ' You can do what you like,' says I, ' but if Fairbairn shows his face here again, I'll send you one of his ears for a keepsake.' She was frightened by my face, I think, for she never answered a word, and the same evening she left my house.

" Well, I don't know now whether it was pure devilry on the part of this woman, or whether she thought that she could turn me against my wife by encouraging her to misbehave.   Anyway, she took a house just two streets off, and let lodgings to sailors.   Fairbairn used to stay there, and Mary would go round to have tea with her sister and him.   How often she went I don't know, but I followed her one day, and as I broke in at the door, Fairbairn got away over the back garden wall, like the cowardly skunk that he was.   I swore to my wife that I would kill her if I found her in his company again, and I led her back with me, sobbing and trembling, and as white as a piece of paper.   There was no trace of love between us any longer. I could see that she hated me and feared me, and when the thought of it drove me to drink then she despised me as well.

" Well, Sarah found that she could not make a living in Liverpool, so she went back, as I understand, to live with her sister in Croydon, and things jogged on much the same as ever at home.   And then came this last week and all the misery and ruin.

"It was in this way.   We had gone on the *May Day* for a round voyage of seven days, but a hogshead got loose and started one of our plates, so that we had to put back into port for twelve hours.   I left the ship and came home, thinking what a surprise it would be for my wife, and hoping that maybe she would be glad to see me so soon.   The thought was in my head as I turned into my own street, and at that moment a cab passed me, and there she was, sitting by the side of Fairbairn, the two chatting and laughing, with never a thought for me as I stood watching them from the footpath.

"I tell you, and I give you my word for it, that from that moment I was not my own master, and it is all like a dim dream when I look back on it.   I had been drinking hard of late, and the two things together fairly turned my brain.   There's something throbbing in my head now, like a docker's hammer, but that morning I seemed to have all Niagara whizzing and buzzing in my ears.

"Well, I took to my heels, and I ran after the cab.   I had a heavy oak stick in my hand, and I tell you I saw red from the first ; but as I ran I got cunning, too, and hung back a little to see them without being seen.   They pulled up soon at the railway station.   There was a good crowd round the booking-office, so I got quite close to them without being seen.   They took tickets for New Brighton. **25** So did I, but I got in three carriages behind them.   When we reached it they walked along the Parade, and I was never more than a hundred yards from them.   At last I saw them hire a boat and start for a row, for it was a very hot day, and they thought no doubt that it would be cooler on the water.

"It was just as if they had been given into my hands. There was a bit of a haze, and you could not see more than a few hundred yards.   I hired a boat for myself, and I pulled after them.   I could see the blur of their craft, but they were going nearly as fast as I, and they must have been a long mile from the shore before I caught them up. The haze was like a curtain all round us, and there were we three in the middle of it.   My God, shall I ever forget their faces when they saw who was in the boat that was closing in upon them ?   She screamed out.   He swore like a madman, and jabbed at me with an oar, for he must have seen death in my eyes.   I got past it and got one in with my stick, that crushed his head like an egg.   I would have spared her, perhaps, for all my madness, but she threw her arms round him, crying out to him, and calling him ' Alec.'   I struck again, and she lay stretched beside him.   I was like a wild beast then that had tasted blood. If Sarah had been there, by the Lord, she should have joined them.   I pulled out my knife, and—well, there ! I've said enough.   It gave me a kind of savage joy when I thought how Sarah would feel when she had such signs as these of what her meddling had brought about.   Then I tied the bodies into the boat, stove a plank, and stood by until they had sunk.   I knew very well that the owner would think that they had lost their bearings in the haze, and had drifted off out to sea.   I cleaned myself up, got

"I . . . GOT ONE IN WITH MY STICK, THAT CRUSHED
HIS HEAD LIKE AN EGG."

Illustration by Sidney Paget for the *Strand Magazine*, January, 1893.

back to land, and joined my ship without a soul having a suspicion of what had passed. That night I made up the packet for Sarah Cushing, and next day I sent it from Belfast.

" There you have the whole truth of it. You can hang me, or do what you like with me, but you cannot punish me as I have been punished already. I cannot shut my eyes but I see those two faces staring at me—staring at me as they stared when my boat broke through the haze. I killed them quick, but they are killing me slow ; and if I have another night of it I shall be either mad or dead before morning. You won't put me alone into a cell, sir ? For pity's sake don't, and may you be treated in your day of agony as you treat me now."

" What is the meaning of it, Watson ? " said Holmes, solemnly, as he laid down the paper. " What object is served by this circle of misery and violence and fear ? It must tend to some end, or else our universe is ruled by chance, which is unthinkable. But what end ? There is the great standing perennial problem to which human reason is as far from an answer as ever."

A PAGE FROM "A CHAPTER ON EARS" IN THE STRAND MAGAZINE, October, 1893.

The inspiration for Holmes' monograph on ears— or the monograph itself?

A CHAPTER ON EARS.

and also as a reservoir of sound before it passes into the drum of the ear. The smaller the concha, therefore, the more sensitive the

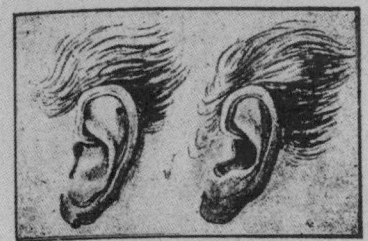

MOZART'S EAR.　　　NORMAL EAR.
From a Photograph by Warthle & Spinnhen of a Drawing in the Mozart Museum.

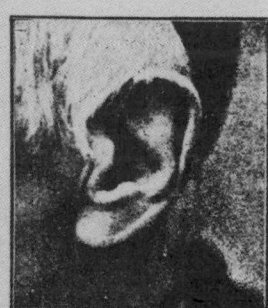

CARDINAL NEWMAN'S EAR.

organ to sound, as there is less medium to receive the current and distribute it.

The size of an ear is generally believed by many well-intentioned persons to be in inverse proportion to the size of the brain or amount of intellectual faculties. We see no reason to differ from this theory. The only eulogy of large ears most people have come across is that of Queen Titania, who praised the "fair, large ears" of Bottom, the weaver.

If the reader will accurately contemplate the ears of celebrities which appear in conjunction with these articles, they will become the possessors of some very curious facts. One of these facts is that to be great it is above all thing... to have an abridged h... man or woman

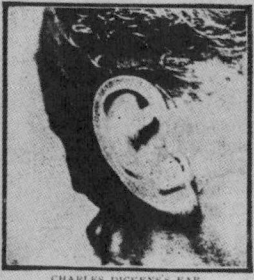

CHARLES DICKENS'S EAR.

cates. It is true that to inculcate this theory into the minds of youth might be, if not pernicious, at least undesirable. Knowing themselves to be equipped with the ægis of an abridged helix, children might possibly be tempted to neglect their studies in waiting for the flood which should drift them in the wake of Gladstone, and a score of his compeers.

But if a thin helix is a boon, a prominent anti-helix is just the reverse. Anyone who has, therefore, hitherto prided himself or herself upon a prominent anti-helix, or even exhibited it to his or her friends with some complacency, should make haste to bring about an alteration —not in their ears, for that might be embarrassing—but in their views. The police bureaus of the world teem

42

THE ADVENTURE OF THE ENGINEER'S THUMB

[Saturday, September 7, to Sunday, September 8, 1889]

OF all the problems which have been submitted to my friend Mr. Sherlock Holmes for solution during the years of our intimacy, there were only two which I was the means of introducing to his notice, that of Mr. Hatherley's thumb and that of Colonel Warburton's madness. Of these the latter may have [1] afforded a finer field for an acute and original observer, but the other was so strange in its inception and so dramatic in its details, that it may be the more worthy of being placed upon record, even if it gave my friend fewer openings for those deductive methods of reasoning by which he achieved such remarkable results. The story has, I believe, been told more than once in the newspapers, but, like all such narratives, its effect is much less striking when set forth *en bloc* in a single half-column of print than when the facts slowly evolve before your own eyes and the mystery clears gradually away as each new discovery furnishes a step which leads on to the complete truth. At the time the circumstances made a deep impression upon me, and the lapse of two years has hardly served to weaken the effect.

It was in the summer of '89, not long after my marriage, that the events occurred which I am now about to summarize. I had returned to civil practice, and had finally abandoned Holmes in his Baker Street rooms, although I continually visited him, and occasionally even persuaded him to forgo his Bohemian habits so far as to come and visit us. My practice had steadily increased, and as I happened to live at no very great distance from Paddington Station, I got a few patients from among the officials. One of these whom I had cured of a painful and lingering disease, was never weary of advertising my virtues, and of endeavouring to send me on every sufferer over whom he might have any influence.

One morning, at a little before seven o'clock, I was awakened by the maid tapping at the door, to announce that two men had come from Paddington, and were waiting in the consulting-room. I dressed hurriedly, for I knew by experience that railway cases were seldom trivial, and hastened downstairs. As I descended, my old ally, the guard, came out of the room, and closed the door tightly behind him.

1 *Colonel Warburton's madness.* A pastiche of this adventure by Rolfe Boswell appeared in the *Baker Street Journal*, Vol. XII, No. 2, New Series, June, 1962, pp. 85–98; another, by the late Norman W. Ward, appeared in *The Best of the Pips*, pp. 59–73; a third, titled "The Adventure of the Sealed Room," by Adrian M. Conan Doyle and John Dickson Carr, appeared in *The Exploits of Sherlock Holmes.*

2 *Victoria Street.* Victoria Street, opening into Broad Sanctuary and Parliament Square, was commenced in 1845 and was seven years in course of construction, being opened to the public on August 6, 1851. When first opened it was one of the sights of London. It opened up a magnificent new vista of Westminster Abbey and the new Houses of Parliament.

3 *the colour began to come back to his bloodless cheeks.* "In the patient's already excitable condition a hot drink rather than alcoholic stimulant might seem more appropriate," Miss Helen Simpson commented in "Medical Career and Capabilities of Dr. J. H. Watson."

HE UNWOUND THE HANDKERCHIEF AND HELD OUT HIS HAND.

Illustration by Sidney Paget for the *Strand Magazine*, March, 1892.

" I've got him here," he whispered, jerking his thumb over his shoulder ; " he's all right."

" What is it, then ? " I asked, for his manner suggested that it was some strange creature which he had caged up in my room.

" It's a new patient," he whispered. " I thought I'd bring him round myself ; then he couldn't slip away. There he is, all safe and sound. I must go now, Doctor, I have my dooties, just the same as you." And off he went, this trusty tout, without even giving me time to thank him.

I entered my consulting-room, and found a gentleman seated by the table. He was quietly dressed in a suit of heather tweed, with a soft cloth cap, which he had laid down upon my books. Round one of his hands he had a handkerchief wrapped, which was mottled all over with bloodstains. He was young, not more than five-and-twenty, I should say, with a strong masculine face ; but he was exceedingly pale, and gave me the impression of a man who was suffering from some strong agitation, which it took all his strength of mind to control.

" I am sorry to knock you up so early, Doctor," said he. " But I have had a very serious accident during the night. I came in by train this morning, and on inquiring at Paddington as to where I might find a doctor a worthy fellow very kindly escorted me here. I gave the maid a card, but I see that she has left it upon the side table."

I took it up and glanced at it. " Mr. Victor Hatherley, **2** hydraulic engineer, 16A Victoria Street (3rd floor)." That was the name, style, and abode of my morning visitor. " I regret that I have kept you waiting," said I, sitting down in my library chair. " You are fresh from a night journey, I understand, which is in itself a monotonous occupation."

" Oh, my night could not be called monotonous," said he, and laughed. He laughed very heartily, with a high ringing note, leaning back in his chair, and shaking his sides. All my medical instincts rose up against that laugh.

" Stop it ! " I cried. " Pull yourself together ! " and I poured out some water from a carafe.

It was useless, however. He was off in one of those hysterical outbursts which come upon a strong nature when some great crisis is over and gone. Presently he came to himself once more, very weary and blushing hotly.

" I have been making a fool of myself," he gasped.

" Not at all. Drink this ! " I dashed some brandy into the water, and the colour began to come back to his **3** bloodless cheeks.

" That's better ! " said he. " And now, Doctor, perhaps you would kindly attend to my thumb, or rather to the place where my thumb used to be."

He unwound the handkerchief and held out his hand. It gave even my hardened nerves a shudder to look at it. There were four protruding fingers and a horrid red spongy surface where the thumb should have been. It had been hacked or torn right out from the roots.

" Good heavens ! " I cried, " this is a terrible injury. It must have bled considerably."

" Yes, it did. I fainted when it was done ; and I think that I must have been senseless for a long time. When I came to, I found that it was still bleeding, so I tied one end of my handkerchief very tightly round the wrist, and braced it up with a twig."

" Excellent ! You should have been a surgeon."

" It is a question of hydraulics, you see, and came within my own province."

" This has been done," said I, examining the wound, by a very heavy and sharp instrument."

" A thing like a cleaver," said he.

" An accident, I presume ? "

" By no means."

" What, a murderous attack ! "

" Very murderous indeed."

" You horrify me."

I sponged the wound, cleaned it, dressed it ; and, finally, covered it over with cotton wadding and carbolized bandages. He lay back without wincing, though he bit his lip from time to time.

" How is that ? " I asked, when I had finished.

" Capital ! Between your brandy and your bandage, I feel a new man. I was very weak, but I have had a good deal to go through."

" Perhaps you had not better speak of the matter. It is evidently trying to your nerves."

" Oh, no ; not now. I shall have to tell my tale to the police ; but, between ourselves, if it were not for the convincing evidence of this wound of mine, I should be surprised if they believed my statement, for it is a very extraordinary one, and I have not much in the way of proof with which to back it up. And, even if they believe me, the clues which I can give them are so vague that it is a question whether justice will be done."

" Ha ! " cried I, " if it is anything in the nature of a problem which you desire to see solved, I should strongly recommend you to come to my friend Mr. Sherlock Holmes before you go to the official police."

" Oh, I have heard of that fellow," answered my visitor, " and I should be very glad if he would take the matter up, though of course I must use the official police as well. Would you give me an introduction to him ? "

" I'll do better. I'll take you round to him myself."

" I should be immensely obliged to you."

" We'll call a cab and go together. We shall just be in time to have a little breakfast with him. Do you feel equal to it ? "

" Yes. I shall not feel easy until I have told my story."

" Then my servant will call a cab, and I shall be with you in an instant." I rushed upstairs, explained the matter shortly to my wife, and in five minutes was inside a hansom, driving with my new acquaintance to Baker Street.

Sherlock Holmes was, as I expected, lounging about his sitting-room in his dressing-gown, reading the agony column of *The Times*, and smoking his before-breakfast **4** pipe, which was composed of all the plugs and dottles left from his smokes of the day before, all carefully dried and collected on the corner of the mantelpiece. He

4 *reading the agony column of* The Times. The day was therefore not a Sunday. Nor was it a Monday: Colonel Lysander Stark called on Mr. Hatherley "yesterday . . . just as I was leaving the office."

. . . HE SETTLED OUR NEW ACQUAINTANCE
UPON THE SOFA . . .

Illustration by Sidney Paget for the *Strand Magazine*, March, 1892.

. . . A MAN RATHER OVER THE MIDDLE SIZE
BUT OF AN EXCEEDING THINNESS.

Portrait of Colonel Lysander Stark by Sidney Paget for the *Strand Magazine*, March, 1892.

received us in his quietly genial fashion, ordered fresh rashers and eggs, and joined us in a hearty meal. When it was concluded he settled our new acquaintance upon the sofa, placed a pillow beneath his head, and laid a glass of brandy and water within his reach.

" It is easy to see that your experience has been no common one, Mr. Hatherley," said he. " Pray lie down there and make yourself absolutely at home. Tell us what you can, but stop when you are tired, and keep up your strength with a little stimulant."

" Thank you," said my patient, " but I have felt another man since the doctor bandaged me, and I think that your breakfast has completed the cure. I shall take up as little of your valuable time as possible, so I shall start at once upon my peculiar experiences."

Holmes sat in his big arm-chair, with the weary, heavy-lidded expression which veiled his keen and eager nature, while I sat opposite to him, and we listened in silence to the strange story which our visitor detailed to us.

" You must know," said he, " that I am an orphan and a bachelor, residing alone in lodgings in London. By profession I am a hydraulic engineer, and have had considerable experience of my work during the seven years that I was apprenticed to Venner & Matheson, the well-known firm of Greenwich. Two years ago, having served my time, and having also come into a fair sum of money through my poor father's death, I determined to start in business for myself, and took professional chambers in Victoria Street.

" I suppose that everyone finds his first independent start in business a dreary experience. To me it has been exceptionally so. During two years I have had three consultations and one small job, and that is absolutely all that my profession has brought me. My gross takings amount to twenty-seven pounds ten. Every day, from 5 nine in the morning until four in the afternoon, I waited in my little den, until at last my heart began to sink, and I came to believe that I should never have any practice at all.

" Yesterday, however, just as I was thinking of leaving the office, my clerk entered to say there was a gentleman waiting who wished to see me upon business. He brought up a card, too, with the name of ' Colonel Lysander Stark ' engraved upon it. Close at his heels 6 came the Colonel himself, a man rather over the middle size but of an exceeding thinness. I do not think that I have ever seen so thin a man. His whole face sharpened away into nose and chin, and the skin of his cheeks was drawn quite tense over his outstanding bones. Yet this emaciation seemed to be his natural habit, and due to no disease, for his eye was bright, his step brisk, and his bearing assured. He was plainly but neatly dressed, and his age, I should judge, would be nearer forty than thirty.

" ' Mr. Hatherley ? ' said he, with something of a German accent. ' You have been recommended to me, Mr. Hatherley, as being a man who is not only proficient in his profession, but is also discreet and capable of preserving a secret.'

" I bowed, feeling as flattered as any young man would at such an address. ' May I ask who it was who gave me so good a character?' I asked.

" ' Well, perhaps it is better that I should not tell you just at this moment. I have it from the same source that you are both an orphan and a bachelor, and are residing alone in London.'

" ' That is quite correct,' I answered, ' but you will excuse me if I say that I cannot see how all this bears upon my professional qualifications. I understood that it was on a professional matter that you wished to speak to me?'

" ' Undoubtedly so. But you will find that all I say is really to the point. I have a professional commission for you, but absolute secrecy is quite essential—*absolute* secrecy, you understand, and of course we may expect that more from a man who is alone than from one who lives in the bosom of his family.'

" ' If I promise to keep a secret,' said I, ' you may absolutely depend upon my doing so.'

" He looked very hard at me as I spoke, and it seemed to me that I had never seen so suspicious and questioning an eye.

" ' You do promise, then?' said he at last.

" ' Yes, I promise.'

" ' Absolute and complete silence, before, during, and after? No reference to the matter at all, either in word or writing?'

" ' I have already given you my word.'

" ' Very good.' He suddenly sprang up, and darting like lightning across the room he flung open the door. The passage outside was empty.

" ' That's all right,' said he, coming back. ' I know that clerks are sometimes curious as to their masters' affairs. Now we can talk in safety.' He drew up his chair very close to mine, and began to stare at me again with the same questioning and thoughtful look.

" A feeling of repulsion and of something akin to fear had begun to rise within me at the strange antics of this fleshless man. Even my dread of losing a client could not restrain me from showing my impatience.

" ' I beg that you will state your business, sir,' said I ; my time is of value.' Heaven forgive me for that last sentence, but the words came to my lips.

" ' How would fifty guineas for a night's work suit **7** you?' he asked.

" ' Most admirably.'

" ' I say a night's work, but an hour's would be nearer the mark. I simply want your opinion about a hydraulic stamping machine which has got out of gear. If you show us what is wrong we shall soon set it right ourselves. What do you think of such a commission as that?'

" ' The work appears to be light, and the pay munificent.'

" ' Precisely so. We shall want you to come to-night by the last train.'

" ' Where to?'

" ' To Eyford, in Berkshire. It is a little place near the **8** borders of Oxfordshire, and within seven miles of Reading. There is a train from Paddington which would bring you in there at about eleven fifteen.'

5 *twenty-seven pounds ten.* About $137.50 U.S. at the time.

6 '*Colonel Lysander Stark.*' This name was "almost certainly derived from Leander Starr Jameson who was such a notable, and at times notorious, figure in South African affairs during the nineties," Mr. Bliss Austin wrote in *A Baker Street Christmas Stocking* (1955). "Jameson was a native of Edinburgh and was educated for the medical profession at University College Hospital in London (M.D. 1877 or one year before Watson received his degree). Whether he was acquainted with either Dr. Watson or Dr. Conan Doyle is not clear. In 1878 he went to Kimberley where he came to know Cecil Rhodes. In 1891, Dr. Jim, as he was then called, was made Administrator of Rhodesia —and in November of that same year, Watson's report which first carried a variation of Jameson's name was submitted to the Editor of the *Strand*. One may well ask whether this was coincidence or osmosis; also, whether any significance attaches to the fact that Lysander was a highly questionable character. Later, in 1895, Dr. Jim became an international celebrity by leading an abortive raid into the Transvaal. But the other [Canonical] variation of his name [Lysander Starr in "The Adventure of the Three Garridebs"] did not appear in the *Strand* until 1925, some eight years after his death. In this case one suspects the further workings of osmosis. In any event, there seems ample grounds for Irregular speculation on this whole matter."

7 *fifty guineas.* About $262.50 U.S. at the time.

8 *Eyford, in Berkshire.* Research has so far failed to uncover an Eyford in Berkshire. There is one in Gloucestershire, but it is not on the railway.

9 *fuller's earth.* A sedimentary clay which has the property of absorbing basic colors. It is chiefly used in clarifying petroleum and refining edible oils.

" ' Very good.'

" ' I shall come down in a carriage to meet you.'

" ' There is a drive, then ? '

" ' Yes, our little place is quite out in the country. It is a good seven miles from Eyford station.'

" ' Then we can hardly get there before midnight. I suppose there would be no chance of a train back. I should be compelled to stop the night.'

" ' Yes, we could easily give you a shakedown.'

" ' That is very awkward. Could I not come at some more convenient hour ? '

" ' We have judged it best that you should come late. It is to recompense you for any inconvenience that we are paying you, a young and unknown man, a fee which would buy an opinion from the very heads of your profession. Still, of course, if you would like to draw out of the business, there is plenty of time to do so.'

" I thought of the fifty guineas, and of how very useful they would be to me. Not at all,' said I ; ' I shall be very happy to accommodate myself to your wishes. I should like, however, to understand a little more clearly what it is that you wish me to do.'

" ' Quite so. It is very natural that the pledge of secrecy which we have exacted from you should have aroused your curiosity. I have no wish to commit you to anything without your having it all laid before you. I suppose that we are absolutely safe from eavesdroppers ? '

" ' Entirely.'

" ' Then the matter stands thus. You are probably **9** aware that fuller's earth is a valuable product, and that it is only found in one or two places in England ? '

" ' I have heard so.'

" ' Some little time ago I bought a small place—a very small place—within ten miles of Reading. I was fortunate enough to discover that there was a deposit of fuller's earth in one of my fields. On examining it, however, I found that this deposit was a comparatively small one, and that it formed a link between two very much larger ones upon the right and the left—both of them, however, in the grounds of my neighbours. These good people were absolutely ignorant that their land contained that which was quite as valuable as a gold mine. Naturally, it was to my interest to buy their land before they discovered its true value ; but, unfortunately, I had no capital by which I could do this. I took a few of my friends into the secret, however, and they suggested that we should quietly and secretly work our own little deposit, and that in this way we should earn the money which would enable us to buy the neighbouring fields. This we have now been doing for some time, and in order to help us in our operations we erected a hydraulic press. This press, as I have already explained, has got out of order, and we wish your advice upon the subject. We guard our secret very jealously, however, and if it once became known that we had hydraulic engineers coming to our little house, it would soon rouse inquiry, and then, if the facts came out, it would be good-bye to any chance of getting these fields and carrying out our plans. That is why I have made you promise me that you will not tell a human being that you are going to Eyford to-night. I hope that I make it all plain ? '

" ' I quite follow you,' said I. ' The only point which I could not quite understand, was what use you could make of a hydraulic press in excavating fuller's earth, which, as I understand, is dug out like gravel from a pit.'

" ' Ah ! ' said he carelessly, ' we have our own process. We compress the earth into bricks, so as to remove them without revealing what they are. But that is a mere detail. I have taken you fully into my confidence now, Mr. Hatherley, and I have shown you how I trust you.' He rose as he spoke. ' I shall expect you, then, at Eyford, at 11.15.'

" ' I shall certainly be there.'

" ' And not a word to a soul.' He looked at me with a last long, questioning gaze, and then, pressing my hand in a cold, dank grasp, he hurried from the room.

" Well, when I came to think it all over in cool blood I was very much astonished, as you may both think, at this sudden commission which had been entrusted to me. On the one hand, of course, I was glad, for the fee was at least tenfold what I should have asked had I set a price upon my own services, and it was possible that this order might lead to other ones. On the other hand, the face and manner of my patron had made an unpleasant impression upon me, and I could not think that his explanation of the fuller's earth was sufficient to explain the necessity for my coming at midnight, and his extreme anxiety lest I should tell anyone of my errand. However, I threw all my fears to the winds, ate a hearty supper, drove to Paddington, and started off, having obeyed to the letter the injunction as to holding my tongue.

" At Reading I had to change not only my carriage but my station. However, I was in time for the last train to Eyford, and I reached the little dim-lit station after eleven o'clock. I was the only passenger who got out there, and there was no one upon the platform save a single sleepy porter with a lantern. As I passed out through the wicket-gate, however, I found my acquaintance of the morning waiting in the shadow upon the other side. Without a word he grasped my arm and hurried me into a carriage, the door of which was standing open. He drew up the windows on either side, tapped on the woodwork, and away we went as hard as the horse could go."

" One horse ? " interjected Holmes.

" Yes, only one."

" Did you observe the colour ? "

" Yes, I saw it by the sidelights when I was stepping into the carriage. It was a chestnut."

" Tired-looking or fresh ? "

" Oh, fresh and glossy."

" Thank you. I am sorry to have interrupted you. Pray continue your most interesting statement."

" Away we went then, and we drove for at least an hour. Colonel Lysander Stark had said that it was only seven miles, but I should think, from the rate that we seemed to go, and the time that we took, that it must have been nearer twelve. He sat at my side in silence all the time, and I was aware, more than once when I glanced in his direction, that he was looking at me with great intensity. The country roads seemed to be not very good in that part of the world, for we lurched and jolted terribly. I tried to look out of the windows to see something

Illustration by Sidney Paget for the *Strand Magazine*, March, 1892.

of where we were, but they were made of frosted glass, and I could make out nothing save an occasional blurr of a passing light.   Now and then I hazarded some remark to break the monotony of the journey, but the Colonel answered only in monosyllables, and the conversation soon flagged.   At last, however, the bumping of the road was exchanged for the crisp smoothness of a gravel drive and the carriage came to a stand.   Colonel Lysander Stark sprang out, and, as I followed after him, pulled me swiftly into a porch which gaped in front of us.   We stepped, as it were, right out of the carriage and into the hall, so that I failed to catch the most fleeting glance of the front of the house.   The instant that I had crossed the threshold the door slammed heavily behind us, and I heard faintly the rattle of the wheels as the carriage drove away.

" It was pitch dark inside the house, and the Colonel fumbled about looking for matches, and muttering under his breath.   Suddenly a door opened at the other end of the passage, and a long, golden bar of light shot out in our direction.   It grew broader, and a woman appeared with a lamp in her hand, which she held above her head, pushing her face forward and peering at us.   I could see that she was pretty, and from the gloss with which the light shone upon her dark dress I knew that it was a rich material.   She spoke a few words in a foreign tongue in a tone as though asking a question, and when my companion answered in a gruff monosyllable she gave such a start that the lamp nearly fell from her hand.   Colonel Stark went up to her, whispered something in her ear, and then, pushing her back into the room from whence she had come, he walked towards me again with the lamp in his hand.

" ' Perhaps you will have the kindness to wait in this room for a few minutes,' said he, throwing open another door.   It was a quiet little plainly furnished room, with a round table in the centre, on which several German books were scattered.   Colonel Stark laid down the lamp on the top of a harmonium beside the door.   ' I shall not keep you waiting an instant,' said he, and vanished into the darkness.

" I glanced at the books upon the table, and in spite of my ignorance of German, I could see that two of them were treatises on science, the others being volumes of poetry.   Then I walked across to the window, hoping that I might catch some glimpse of the country-side, but an oak shutter, heavily barred, was folded across it.   It was a wonderfully silent house.   There was an old clock ticking loudly somewhere in the passage, but otherwise everything was deadly still.   A vague feeling of uneasiness began to steal over me.   Who were these German people, and what were they doing, living in this strange, out-of-the-way place ?   And where was the place ?   I was ten miles or so from Eyford, that was all I knew, but whether north, south, east, or west, I had no idea.   For that matter, Reading, and possibly other large towns, were within that radius, so the place might not be so secluded after all.   Yet it was quite certain from the absolute stillness that we were in the country.   I paced up and down the room humming a tune under my breath to keep up my spirits, and feeling that I was thoroughly earning my fifty-guinea fee.

"Suddenly, without any preliminary sound in the midst of the utter stillness, the door of my room swung slowly open. The woman was standing in the aperture, the darkness of the hall behind her, the yellow light from my lamp beating upon her eager and beautiful face. I could see at a glance that she was sick with fear, and the sight sent a chill to my own heart. She held up one shaking finger to warn me to be silent, and she shot a few whispered words of broken English at me, her eyes glancing back, like those of a frightened horse, into the gloom behind her.

"'I would go,' said she, trying hard, as it seemed to me, to speak calmly; 'I would go. I should not stay here. There is no good for you to do.'

"'But, madam,' said I, 'I have not yet done what I came for. I cannot possibly leave until I have seen the machine.'

"'It is not worth your while to wait,' she went on. 'You can pass through the door; no one hinders.' And then, seeing that I smiled and shook my head, she suddenly threw aside her constraint, and made a step forward, with her hands wrung together. 'For the love of Heaven!' she whispered, 'get away from here before it is too late!'

"But I am somewhat headstrong by nature, and the more ready to engage in an affair when there is some obstacle in the way. I thought of my fifty-guinea fee, of my wearisome journey, and of the unpleasant night which seemed to be before me. Was it all to go for nothing? Why should I slink away without having carried out my commission, and without the payment which was my due? This woman might, for all I knew, be a monomaniac. With a stout bearing, therefore, though her manner had shaken me more than I cared to confess, I still shook my head, and declared my intention of remaining where I was. She was about to renew her entreaties when a door slammed overhead, and the sound of several footsteps were heard upon the stairs. She listened for an instant, threw up her hands with a despairing gesture, and vanished as suddenly and noiselessly as she had come.

"The new-comers were Colonel Lysander Stark, and a short thick man with a chinchilla beard growing out of the creases of his double chin, who was introduced to me as Mr. Ferguson.

"'This is my secretary and manager,' said the Colonel. 'By the way, I was under the impression that I left this door shut just now. I fear that you have felt the draught.'

"'On the contrary,' said I, 'I opened the door myself, because I felt the room to be a little close.'

"He shot one of his suspicious glances at me. 'Perhaps we had better proceed to business, then,' said he. 'Mr. Ferguson and I will take you up to see the machine.'

"'I had better put my hat on, I suppose.'

"'Oh no, it is in the house.' 10

"'What, do you dig fuller's earth in the house?'

"'No, no. This is only where we compress it. But never mind that! All we wish you to do is to examine

"'FOR THE LOVE OF HEAVEN!' SHE WHISPERED, 'GET AWAY FROM HERE BEFORE IT IS TOO LATE!'"

Illustration by Sidney Paget for the *Strand Magazine*, March, 1892.

10 "'*Oh no, it is in the house.*' Later events made it impossible for Mr. Hatherley to recover his headgear, so a puzzler is "the source of the tweed cap which Mr. Hatherley placed on Watson's books when he came to have his wound dressed," Mr. Bliss Austin wrote in "Thumbing His Way to Fame." "... since, the habits of British shopkeepers being what they are, it is most unlikely that he was able to replace it in the neighborhood of Paddington at a little after 6 in the morning, one can only conclude that Elise must have recovered it for him; though why she was so solicitous over a cap when his wound was left unattended, it is not easy to understand."

11 *it was indeed a gigantic one.* "Without going into technicalities it appears to have been of the duplex type invented by Sir Charles Davy in 1886—it was therefore quite new . . ." Mr. Ian McNeil wrote in "An Engineer's Thoughts on 'The Engineer's Thumb.'"

the machine and to let us know what is wrong with it.'

"We went upstairs together, the Colonel first with the lamp, the fat manager and I behind him. It was a labyrinth of an old house, with corridors, passages, narrow winding staircases, and little low doors, the thresholds of which were hollowed out by the generations who had crossed them. There were no carpets, and no signs of any furniture above the ground floor, while the plaster was peeling off the walls, and the damp was breaking through in green, unhealthy blotches. I tried to put on as unconcerned an air as possible, but I had not forgotten the warnings of the lady, even though I disregarded them, and I kept a keen eye upon my two companions. Ferguson appeared to be a morose and silent man, but I could see from the little that he said that he was at least a fellow-countryman.

"Colonel Lysander Stark stopped at last before a low door, which he unlocked. Within was a small square room, in which the three of us could hardly get at one time. Ferguson remained outside, and the Colonel ushered me in.

"'We are now,' said he, ' actually within the hydraulic press, and it would be a particularly unpleasant thing for us if anyone were to turn it on. The ceiling of this small chamber is really the end of the descending piston, and it comes down with the force of many tons upon this metal floor. There are small lateral columns of water outside which receive the force, and which transmit and multiply it in the manner which is familiar to you. The machine goes readily enough, but there is some stiffness in the working of it and it has lost a little of its force. Perhaps you will have the goodness to look it over, and to show us how we can set it right.'

"I took the lamp from him, and I examined the
11 machine very thoroughly. It was indeed a gigantic one, and capable of exercising enormous pressure. When I passed outside, however, and pressed down the levers which controlled it, I knew at once by the whishing sound that there was a slight leakage, which allowed a regurgitation of water through one of the side-cylinders. An examination showed that one of the india-rubber bands which was round the head of a driving-rod had shrunk so as not quite to fill the socket along which it worked. This was clearly the cause of the loss of power, and I pointed it out to my companions, who followed my remarks very carefully, and asked several practical questions as to how they should proceed to set it right. When I had made it clear to them, I returned to the main chamber of the machine, and took a good look at it to satisfy my own curiosity. It was obvious at a glance that the story of the fuller's earth was the merest fabrication, for it would be absurd to suppose that so powerful an engine could be designed for so inadequate a purpose. The walls were of wood, but the floor consisted of a large iron trough, and when I came to examine it I could see a crust of metallic deposit all over it. I had stooped and was scraping at this to see exactly what it was, when I heard a muttered exclamation in German, and saw the cadaverous face of the Colonel looking down at me.

" ' What are you doing there ? ' he asked.

" I felt angry at having been tricked by so elaborate a story as that which he had told me. ' I was admiring your fuller's earth,' said I ; ' I think that I should be better able to advise you as to your machine if I knew what the exact purpose was for which it was used.'

" The instant that I uttered the words I regretted the rashness of my speech. His face set hard, and a baleful light sprang up in his grey eyes.

" ' Very well,' said he, ' you shall know all about the machine.' He took a step backward, slammed the little door, and turned the key in the lock. I rushed towards it and pulled at the handle, but it was quite secure, and did not give in the least to my kicks and shoves. ' Hallo ! ' I yelled. ' Hallo ! Colonel ! Let me out ! '

" And then suddenly in the silence I heard a sound which sent my heart into my mouth. It was the clank of the levers, and the swish of the leaking cylinder. He had set the engine at work. The lamp still stood upon the floor where I had placed it when examining the trough. By its light I saw that the black ceiling was coming down upon me, slowly, jerkily, but, as none knew better than myself, with a force which must within a minute grind me to a shapeless pulp. I threw myself, screaming, against the door, and dragged with my nails at the lock. I implored the Colonel to let me out, but the remorseless clanking of the levers drowned my cries. The ceiling was only a foot or two above my head, and with my hand upraised I could feel its hard rough surface. Then it flashed through my mind that the pain of my death would depend very much upon the position in which I met it. If I lay on my face the weight would come upon my spine, and I shuddered to think of that dreadful snap. Easier the other way, perhaps, and yet had I the nerve to lie and look up at that deadly black shadow wavering down upon me ? Already I was unable to stand erect, when my eye caught something which brought a gush of hope back to my heart.

" I have said that though floor and ceiling were of iron, the walls were of wood. As I gave a last hurried glance around, I saw a thin line of yellow light between two of the boards, which broadened and broadened as a small panel was pushed backwards. For an instant I could hardly believe that here was indeed a door which led away from death. The next I threw myself through, and lay half fainting upon the other side. The panel had closed again behind me, but the crash of the lamp, and a few moments afterwards the clang of the two slabs of metal, told me how narrow had been my escape.

" I was recalled to myself by a frantic plucking at my wrist, and I found myself lying upon the stone floor of a narrow corridor, while a woman bent over me and tugged at me with her left hand, while she held a candle in her right. It was the same good friend whose warning I had so foolishly rejected.

" ' Come ! Come ! ' she cried breathlessly. ' They will be here in a moment. They will see that you are not there. Oh, do not waste the so precious time, but come ! '

" This time, at least, I did not scorn her advice. I

I RUSHED TOWARDS IT AND PULLED AT THE HANDLE . . .

Illustration by Sidney Paget for the *Strand Magazine*, March, 1892.

12 "*'Fritz! Fritz!' she cried in English*. "Was she also of German descent, and what was her relationship to the Colonel?" Mr. Richard W. Clarke asked in "Certain Ladies of Baker Street." "She called him 'Fritz' . . . [but] was she his wife, his mistress, his sister?'"

13 *my thumb had been cut off*. Was it indeed so? A man hanging as Hatherley was "could have had no more than two points of each finger above the edge of the sill, and his thumbs would have been some two or three inches below the edge on the outside of the sill," the late Professor Jay Finley Christ wrote in "Thumbs Up: Thumbs Down." "A strike from the cleaver could not have touched the thumbs unless it reached out so far that the heel of the implement was entirely beyond the edge of the sill; and even then it could not have cut off a thumb, because there was nothing below to serve as a chopping block. Moreover, even though Watson said that the blade had been sharp, he also said it appeared that the thumb 'had been hacked or torn right out from its roots,' which would have been highly unlikely under the circumstances. A sharp blade makes a clean cut!"

To this, Mr. Stanley MacKenzie responded ("The Engineer's Thumb"): "The explanation would appear to be contained in this part of Hatherley's statement: '. . . hanging with my

HE . . . CUT AT ME WITH HIS HEAVY WEAPON.

Illustration by Sidney Paget for the *Strand Magazine*, March, 1892.

staggered to my feet, and ran with her along the corridor and down a winding stair. The latter led to another broad passage, and, just as we reached it we heard the sound of running feet and the shouting of two voices—one answering the other—from the floor on which we were, and from the one beneath. My guide stopped, and looked about her like one who is at her wits' end. Then she threw open a door which led into a bedroom, through the window of which the moon was shining brightly.

"'It is your only chance,' said she. 'It is high, but it may be that you can jump it.'

"As she spoke a light sprang into view at the further end of the passage, and I saw the lean figure of Colonel Lysander Stark rushing forward with a lantern in one hand, and a weapon like a butcher's cleaver in the other. I rushed across the bedroom, flung open the window, and looked out. How quiet and sweet and wholesome the garden looked in the moonlight, and it could not be more than thirty feet down. I clambered out upon the sill, but I hesitated to jump, until I should have heard what passed between my saviour and the ruffian who pursued me. If she were ill-used, then at any risk I was determined to go back to her assistance. The thought had hardly flashed through my mind before he was at the door, pushing his way past her; but she threw her arms round him, and tried to hold him back.

12 "'Fritz! Fritz!' she cried in English, 'remember your promise after the last time. You said it should not be again. He will be silent! Oh, he will be silent!'

"'You are mad, Elise!' he shouted, struggling to break away from her. 'You will be the ruin of us. He has seen too much. Let me pass, I say!' He dashed her to one side, and, rushing to the window, cut at me with his heavy weapon. I had let myself go, and was hanging with my fingers in the window slot and my hands across the sill, when his blow fell. I was conscious of a dull pain, my grip loosened, and I fell into the garden below.

"I was shaken, but not hurt by the fall; so I picked myself up, and rushed off among the bushes as hard as I could run, for I understood that I was far from being out of danger yet. Suddenly, however, as I ran, a deadly dizziness and sickness came over me. I glanced down at my hand, which was throbbing painfully, and then, for **13** the first time, saw that my thumb had been cut off, and that the blood was pouring from my wound. I endeavoured to tie my handkerchief round it, but there came a sudden buzzing in my ears, and next moment I fell in a dead faint among the rose-bushes.

"How long I remained unconscious I cannot tell. It must have been a very long time, for the moon had sunk **14** and a bright morning was breaking when I came to myself. My clothes were all sodden with dew, and my coat-sleeve was drenched with blood from my wounded thumb. The smarting of it recalled in an instant all the particulars of my night's adventure, and I sprang to my feet with the feeling that I might hardly yet be safe from my pursuers. But, to my astonishment, when I came to look round me neither house nor garden were to be seen. I had been lying in an angle of the hedge close by the highroad, and just a little lower down was a long building, which proved, upon my approaching it, to be the very station at which I had arrived upon the previous night. Were it not for the ugly wound upon my hand, all that had passed during those dreadful hours might have been an evil dream.

" Half dazed, I went into the station, and asked about the morning train   There would be one to Reading in less than an hour.   The same porter was on duty, I found, as had been there when I arrived.   I inquired from him whether he had ever heard of Colonel Lysander Stark. The name was strange to him.   Had he observed a carriage the night before waiting for me ?   No, he had not. Was there a police station anywhere near ?   There was one about three miles off.

" It was too far for me to go, weak and ill as I was.   I determined to wait until I got back to town before telling my story to the police.   It was a little past six when I arrived, so I went first to have my wound dressed, and then the doctor was kind enough to bring me along here. I put the case into your hands, and shall do exactly what you advise."

We both sat in silence for some little time after listening to this extraordinary narrative. Then Sherlock Holmes pulled down from the shelf one of the ponderous commonplace books in which he placed his cuttings.

" Here is an advertisement which will interest you," said he. " It appeared in all the papers about a year ago.   Listen to this :—' Lost on the 9th inst., Mr. Jeremiah Hayling, aged 26, a hydraulic engineer. Left his lodgings at ten o'clock at night, and has not been heard of since. Was dressed in,' etc. etc.   Ha !   That represents the last time that the Colonel needed to have his machine overhauled, I fancy."

" Good heavens ! " cried my patient. " Then that explains what the girl said."

" Undoubtedly.   It is quite clear that the Colonel was a cool and desperate man, who was absolutely determined that nothing should stand in the way of his little game, like those out-and-out pirates who will leave no survivor from a captured ship.   Well, every moment now is precious, so, if you feel equal to it, we shall go down to Scotland Yard at once as a preliminary to starting for Eyford.

Some three hours or so afterwards we were all in the train together, bound from Reading to the little Berkshire village.   There were Sherlock Holmes, the hydraulic engineer, Inspector Bradstreet of Scotland Yard, a plain-clothes man, and myself.   Bradstreet had spread an ordnance map of the country out upon the seat, and was busy with his compasses drawing a circle with Eyford for its centre.

" There you are," said he.   " That circle is drawn at a radius of ten miles from the village.   The place we want must be somewhere near that line.   You said ten miles, I think, sir ? "

" It was an hour's good drive."

" And you think that they brought you back all that way when you were unconscious ? "

" They must have done so.   I have a confused memory, too, of having been lifted and conveyed somewhere."

fingers in the window *slot and my hands across the sill*, when his blow fell.' The *underlining* are mine. I imagine the 'slot' to have been a recess, flush with the sill into which the bottom of the window dropped. If the sill was, say, 5″ or more wide, and one's fingers were in the slot, the palm of the hand and thumb would be flat on top of the sill. The thumb would quite naturally, stick out sideways and be in a convenient position for amputation."

Those who hold that the thumb was indeed chopped off are still faced with a problem: which thumb? As Mr. Bliss Austin wrote ("Thumbing His Way to Fame"): "Dr. Julian Wolff, in the embellishments to his excellent map of London, shows the right thumb removed, yet I incline to the belief that it was his left thumb, though the evidence is far from conclusive. Assuming that Hatherley was right-handed, which is statistically probable, he could hardly have been so dextrous in tying tourniquets or eating hearty breakfasts had his right hand been injured. I have also discussed this matter with a noted experimental psychologist whose interest I have succeeded in arousing to the extent of undertaking some tests. His preliminary results, admittedly tentative, indicate that: 'a person in the state defined as stark madness, wielding a cleaver in his own right hand again the hands of an opponent placed opposite him on a window sill, will, approximately 99.44 times out of one hundred, attack the hand opposite his right, that is, the opponent's left hand.' "

14 *the moon had sunk and a bright morning was breaking*. By working forward and backward from the facts given us, we may determine that the moon on this night was shining brightly between 1:30 and 2:00 A.M., but that it had set no later than 3:30 A.M., and that daybreak was no later than that hour. In all the summer of 1889 there were two days and two days only which met these requirements: Saturday, September 7th, and Sunday, September 8th. Since the first day of the adventure was not a Sunday, it follows that Mr. Hatherley's adventure must have taken place on the night of Friday–Saturday, September 6–7, 1889; his visit to Holmes and Holmes' part in the action was on *Saturday–Sunday, September 7–8, 1889.*

15 *the amalgam which has taken the place of silver.*" It is to be doubted that Watson has correctly quoted Holmes, the chemist, in this sentence. "Had amalgamation really been carried out on a large scale," Mr. Bliss Austin wrote in "Thumbing His Way to Fame," "there should have been a considerable quantity of mercury about [since mercury is a necessary ingredient in any amalgam], yet the Canon states specifically that the firemen found only 'large masses of nickel and tin . . .' . . . Nor could the material used to make the spurious coins have been an amalgam of nickel or tin, because the former does not amalgamate with mercury at all, and the latter does so to such a limited extent that it would have been of little use for this purpose."

"A HOUSE ON FIRE?" ASKED BRADSTREET . . .

Illustration by Sidney Paget for the *Strand Magazine*, March, 1892.

"What I cannot understand," said I, "is why they should have spared you when they found you lying fainting in the garden. Perhaps the villain was softened by the woman's entreaties."

"I hardly think that likely. I never saw a more inexorable face in my life."

"Oh, we shall soon clear up all that," said Bradstreet. "Well, I have drawn my circle, and I only wish I knew at what point upon it the folk that we are in search of are to be found."

"I think I could lay my finger on it," said Holmes quietly.

"Really, now!" cried the inspector, "you have formed your opinion! Come now, we shall see who agrees with you. I say it is south, for the country is more deserted there."

"And I say east," said my patient.

"I am for west," remarked the plain-clothes man. "There are several quiet little villages up there."

"And I am for north," said I; "because there are no hills there, and our friend says that he did not notice the carriage go up any."

"Come," said the inspector, laughing; "it's a very pretty diversity of opinion. We have boxed the compass among us. Who do you give your casting vote to?"

"You are all wrong."

"But we can't *all* be."

"Oh, yes, you can. This is my point," he placed his finger on the centre of the circle. "This is where we shall find them."

"But the twelve-mile drive?" gasped Hatherley.

"Six out and six back. Nothing simpler. You say yourself that the horse was fresh and glossy when you got in. How could it be that, if it had gone twelve miles over heavy roads?"

"Indeed it is a likely ruse enough," observed Bradstreet thoughtfully. "Of course there can be no doubt as to the nature of this gang."

"None at all," said Holmes. "They are coiners on a large scale, and have used the machine to form the **15** amalgam which has taken the place of silver."

"We have known for some time that a clever gang was at work," said the inspector. "They have been turning out half-crowns by the thousand. We even traced them as far as Reading, but could get no further; for they had covered their traces in a way that showed that they were very old hands. But now, thanks to this lucky chance, I think that we have got them right enough."

But the inspector was mistaken, for those criminals were not destined to fall into the hands of justice. As we rolled in Eyford station we saw a gigantic column of smoke which streamed up from behind a small clump of trees in the neighbourhood, and hung like an immense ostrich feather over the landscape.

"A house on fire?" asked Bradstreet, as the train steamed off again on its way.

"Yes, sir," said the stationmaster.

"When did it break out?"

" I hear that it was during the night, sir, but it has got worse, and the whole place is in a blaze."

" Whose house is it ? "

" Dr. Becher's."

" Tell me," broke in the engineer, " is Dr. Becher a German, very thin, with a long sharp nose ? "

The stationmaster laughed heartily. " No, sir, Dr. Becher is an Englishman, and there isn't a man in the parish who has a better lined waistcoat. But he has a gentleman staying with him, a patient as I understand, who is a foreigner, and he looks as if a little good Berkshire beef would do him no harm."

The stationmaster had not finished his speech before we were all hastening in the direction of the fire. The road topped a low hill, and there was a great widespread whitewashed building in front of us, spouting fire at every chink and window, while in the garden in front three fire- **16** engines were vainly striving to keep the flames under.

" That's it ! " cried Hatherley, in intense excitement. " There is the gravel drive, and there are the rose-bushes where I lay. That second window is the one that I jumped from."

" Well, at least," said Holmes, " you have had your revenge upon them. There can be no question that it was your oil lamp which, when it was crushed in the press, set fire to the wooden walls, though no doubt they were **17** too excited in the chase after you to observe it at the time. Now keep your eyes open in this crowd for your friends of last night, though I very much fear that they are a good hundred miles off by now."

And Holmes' fears came to be realized, for from that day to this no word has ever been heard either of the beautiful woman, the sinister German, or the morose Englishman. Early that morning a peasant had met a cart, containing several people and some very bulky boxes, driving rapidly in the direction of Reading, but there all traces of the fugitives disappeared, and even Holmes' ingenuity failed to discover the least clue to their whereabouts.

The firemen had been much perturbed at the strange arrangements which they found within, and still more so by discovering a newly-severed human thumb upon a window-sill of the second floor. About sunset, however, their efforts were at last successful, and they subdued the flames, but not before the roof had fallen in, and the whole place reduced to such absolute ruin that, save some twisted cylinders and iron piping, not a trace remained of the machinery which had cost our unfortunate acquaintance so dearly. Large masses of nickel and of tin were discovered stored in an outhouse, but no coins were to be found, which may have explained the presence of those bulky boxes which have been already referred to.

How our hydraulic engineer had been conveyed from the garden to the spot where he recovered his senses might have remained for ever a mystery were it not for the soft mould, which told us a very plain tale. He had evidently been carried down by two persons, one of whom had remarkably small feet, and the other unusually large ones.

16 *spouting fire at every chink and window.* ". . . the fire . . . was noteworthy as an illustration of the fire-resistant quality of British buildings, and because it explains, in part, at least, much that happened during the great fire-blitzes to which this part of England was subjected more than fifty years later," Mr. Bliss Austin wrote in "Thumbing His Way to Fame." "The blaze started about 1:30 A.M. [and] . . . burned until sunset, which would have been about 8 P.M. What house in this country would have burned so blithely for twenty hours? As an example of slow-motion combustion it is exceeded only by the celebrated bush which burned but was not consumed."

17 *set fire to the wooden walls.* "Could igniting by any chance follow under the circumstances?" Mr. J. B. MacKenzie asked in "Sherlock Holmes' Plots and Strategy." "And, even if such were possible, would not the flame have been too momentary to allow of its extension to the walls? Where, too, would a draught sufficient to keep it alive come from?"

18 *"Experience," said Holmes, laughing.* The late Professor Jay Finley Christ was convinced that Hatherley was "a fraud who foiled Watson" (but not Holmes). ". . . one of my correspondents," he wrote in "Thumbs Up: Thumbs Down," "has suggested that this bird was in reality Mr. Jeremiah Hayling, an engineer who had disappeared a year earlier; that he had caught his hand in the press which he had been operating; that the fire (started in some manner unknown to us) offered him a chance to escape; and that he concocted the yarn about the cleaver to avoid explaining where he (Jeremiah) had been for a year. This is rather pleasing. It explains what puzzled Watson: why they 'spared you . . . fainting in the garden'; it tells us that the glib and wholly wrong description of Becher was a diversion, and that the finding of the thumb was evidence either of a plant or a Watsonian invention. As things were, a severed thumb (if there were any such) could neither drop upon the sill nor (likely) remain upon it; and it is rather hard to believe that the firemen found anything at all on a second-storey window, thirty feet above the ground, in the midst of a scene of 'absolute destruction.' "

On the whole, it was most probable that the silent Englishman, being less bold or less murderous than his companion, had assisted the woman to bear the unconscious man out of the way of danger.

" Well," said our engineer ruefully, as we took our seats to return to London, " it has been a pretty business for me ! I have lost my thumb, and I have lost a fifty-guinea fee, and what have I gained ? "

18 " Experience," said Holmes, laughing. " Indirectly it may be of value, you know ; you have only to put it into words to gain the reputation of being excellent company for the remainder of your existence."

"THANK YOU. I'LL FILL A VACANT PEG, THEN."

Illustration by Sidney Paget for the *Strand Magazine*, July, 1893.

43

THE CROOKED MAN

[Wednesday, September 11, to Thursday, September 12, 1889]

ONE summer night, a few months after my marriage, I was seated by my own hearth smoking 1 a last pipe and nodding over a novel, for my day's work had been an exhausting one. My wife had 2 already gone upstairs, and the sound of the locking of the hall door some time before told me that the servants 3 had also retired. I had risen from my seat and was knocking out the ashes of my pipe, when I suddenly heard the clang of the bell.

I looked at the clock. It was a quarter to twelve. This could not be a visitor at so late an hour. A patient, evidently, and possibly an all-night sitting. With a wry face I went out into the hall and opened the door. To my astonishment, it was Sherlock Holmes who stood upon my step.

"Ah, Watson," said he, "I hoped that I might not be too late to catch you."

"My dear fellow, pray come in."

"You look surprised, and no wonder! Relieved, too, I fancy! Hum! you still smoke the Arcadia mixture of your bachelor days, then! There's no mistaking that fluffy ash upon your coat. It's easy to tell that you've been accustomed to wear a uniform, Watson; you'll never pass as a pure-bred civilian as long as you keep that habit of carrying your handkerchief in your sleeve. 4 Could you put me up to-night?"

"With pleasure."

"You told me that you had bachelor quarters for one, and I see that you have no gentleman visitor at present. Your hat-stand proclaims as much."

"I shall be delighted if you will stay."

"Thank you. I'll fill a vacant peg, then. Sorry to see that you've had the British workman in the house. He's a token of evil. Not the drains, I hope?"

"No, the gas."

"Ah! He has left two nail marks from his boot upon your linoleum just where the light strikes it. No, thank you, I had some supper at Waterloo, but I'll smoke a pipe with you with pleasure."

I handed him my pouch, and he seated himself opposite to me, and smoked for some time in silence. I was well aware that nothing but business of importance could have

1 *a few months after my marriage.* Marriage I or Marriage II? Watson's "a few months" must mean at least three but not more than six. Reckoning from the approximate date of the first marriage would place the case in the period February–April, 1887, which is not "summer" in either the popular or the astronomical sense. Reckoning from the approximate date of the second marriage, on the other hand, would place the case in the period August–October, 1889, a period containing a month and three weeks of "summer" in the astronomical sense.

2 *had been an exhausting one.* Holmes later deduces that Watson is "professionally rather busy just now." There must have been busy periods even during the unsuccessful practice of Marriage I, but this is at least an indication that the case did indeed take place during the successful practice of Marriage II.

3 *the servants.* Further evidence of Watson's success: in the impecunious days of his first private practice, he could afford one servant only. "Watson's mention of 'the servants' seems, I feel, to imply that there were more than the bare minimum of two," Mr. Michael Harrison wrote (*In the Footsteps of Sherlock Holmes*). "What was the staff of Watson's house? Cook, housemaid and 'tweeney,' in all probability, for Watson did not keep his own carriage. . . . The total paid out in wages might have been as small as £52 [$260] per annum—or a pound a week [but] the probability is that the cook received £30 [$150] a year, the house-parlourmaid between £18 [$90] and £20 [$100], and the 'tweeney' anything from £10 [$50] to £15 [$75]."

4 *carrying your handkerchief in your sleeve.* A habit dating from Watson's army days, since the uniform tunic has no pocket for carrying a handkerchief.

5 *the position of these same readers.* Holmes certainly implies that Watson by this time had readers, indicating that the case took place after the publication of *A Study in Scarlet* in December, 1887. But Holmes must also be alluding to some of the chronicles *written* by Watson as early as May, 1887 ("A Scandal in Bohemia").

6 *Jackson.* But the accommodating neighbor-doctor of Marriage II was named Anstruther ("The Boscombe Valley Mystery"). While this speaks for Marriage I, it cannot be allowed to outweigh the considerably stronger evidence that the adventure of "The Crooked Man" took place during the period of Marriage II. Perhaps the neighbor-doctor's full name was Jackson Anstruther.

7 *the 11.10 from Waterloo."* There was no 11:10 from Waterloo to Aldershot, but Holmes and Watson could have taken an 11:50.

8 *the Royal Mallows.* In American editions *the Royal Munsters*, and this is a real regiment. Holmes later speaks of "The first battalion of the Royal Mallows (which is the old 117th) . . ." This is very odd, as Mr. D. Hinrich noted in "The Royal Mallows, 1854–1888." "None could have known better than Watson, an old Army man, that the highest number borne by a line regiment of the British Army before the Cardwell reforms was that of the 109th (later the second battalion, The Prince of Wales Leinster Regiment). . . . I submit . . . that . . . the first battalion, the Royal Mallows (the old 117th) is but a *nom de guerre* for the second battalion, the Royal Irish Fusiliers (the 89th Foot)."

If, on the other hand, we accept the evidence of the American editions that "the Royal Mallows" are the Royal Munsters, we must note, with Mrs. Crighton Sellars ("Dr. Watson and the British Army") that "The Royal Munster Fusiliers, at the time that Watson wrote of them, consisted of the 101st and 104th Regiments, both old regiments of the East India Company, raised by Clive. . . . Most [Royal Munster Fusiliers] were Irish, and it bears the Shamrock in addition to the Royal Tiger of Bengal, but it was not an Irish regiment in any sense. . . . I find no record of its having been in the Crimea, and it did not leave India until it came to England in 1871. . . . Aside from its Mutiny service, there seems to be nothing in the regimental history that corresponds with Watson's facts."

brought him to me at such an hour, so I waited patiently until he should come round to it.

" I see that you are professionally rather busy just now," said he, glancing very keenly across at me.

" Yes, I've had a busy day," I answered. " It may seem very foolish in your eyes," I added, " but really I don't know how you deduced it."

Holmes chuckled to himself.

" I have the advantage of knowing your habits, my dear Watson," said he. " When your round is a short one you walk, and when it is a long one you use a hansom. As I perceive that your boots, although used, are by no means dirty, I cannot doubt that you are at present busy enough to justify the hansom."

" Excellent ! " I cried.

" Elementary," said he. " It is one of those instances where the reasoner can produce an effect which seems remarkable to his neighbour, because the latter has missed the one little point which is the basis of the deduction. The same may be said, my dear fellow, for the effect of some of these little sketches of yours, which is entirely meretricious, depending as it does upon your retaining in your own hands some factors in the problem which are never imparted to the reader. Now, at present I am in **5** the position of these same readers, for I hold in this hand several threads of one of the strangest cases which ever perplexed a man's brain, and yet I lack the one or two which are needful to complete my theory. But I'll have them, Watson, I'll have them ! " His eyes kindled and a slight flush sprang into his thin cheeks. For an instant the veil had lifted upon his keen, intense nature, but for an instant only. When I glanced again his face had resumed that Red Indian composure which had made so many regard him as a machine rather than a man.

" The problem presents features of interest," said he ; " I may even say very exceptional features of interest. I have already looked into the matter, and have come, as I think, within sight of my solution. If you could accompany me in that last step, you might be of considerable service to me."

" I should be delighted."

" Could you go as far as Aldershot to-morrow ? "

6 " I have no doubt Jackson would take my practice."

" Very good. I want to start by the 11.10 from Water-
7 loo."

" That would give me time."

" Then, if you are not too sleepy, I will give you a sketch of what has happened and of what remains to be done."

" I was sleepy before you came. I am quite wakeful now."

" I will compress the story as far as may be done without omitting anything vital to the case. It is conceivable that you may even have read some account of the matter. It is the supposed murder of Colonel Barclay, of the Royal
8 Mallows, at Aldershot, which I am investigating."

" I have heard nothing of it."

" It has not excited much attention yet, except locally. The facts are only two days old. Briefly they are these :

" The Royal Mallows is, as you know, one of the

most famous Irish regiments in the British Army. It did wonders both in the Crimea and the Mutiny, and has since that time distinguished itself upon every possible occasion. It was commanded up to Monday night by James Barclay, a gallant veteran, who started as a full private, was raised to commissioned rank for his bravery at the time of the Mutiny, and so lived to command the regiment in which he had once carried a musket.

" Colonel Barclay had married at the time when he was a sergeant, and his wife, whose maiden name was Miss Nancy Devoy, was the daughter of a former colour-sergeant in the same corps. There was, therefore, as can be imagined, some little social friction when the young couple (for they were still young) found themselves in their new surroundings. They appear, however, to have quickly adapted themselves, and Mrs. Barclay has always, I understand, been as popular with the ladies of the regiment as her husband was with his brother officers. I may add that she was a woman of great beauty, and that even now, when she has been married for upwards of thirty years, she is still of a striking appearance. **9**

" Colonel Barclay's family life appears to have been a uniformly happy one. Major Murphy, to whom I owe most of my facts, assures me that he has never heard of any misunderstanding between the pair. On the whole, he thinks that Barclay's devotion to his wife was greater than his wife's to Barclay. He was acutely uneasy if he were absent from her for a day. She, on the other hand, though devoted and faithful, was less obtrusively affectionate. But they were regarded in the regiment as the very model of a middle-aged couple. There was absolutely nothing in their mutual relations to prepare people for the tragedy which was to follow.

" Colonel Barclay himself seems to have had some singular traits in his character. He was a dashing, jovial old soldier in his usual mood, but there were occasions on which he seemed to show himself capable of considerable violence and vindictiveness. This side of his nature, however, appears never to have been turned towards his wife. Another fact which had struck Major Murphy, and three out of five of the other officers with whom I conversed, was the singular sort of depression which came upon him at times. As the Major expressed it, the smile had often been struck from his mouth, as if by some invisible hand, when he has been joining in the gaieties and chaff of the mess table. For days on end, when the mood was on him, he had been sunk in the deepest gloom. This and a certain tinge of superstition were the only unusual traits in his character which his brother officers had observed. The latter peculiarity took the form of a dislike to being left alone, especially after dark. This puerile feature in a nature which was conspicuously manly had often given rise to comment and conjecture.

" The first battalion of the Royal Mallows (which is the old 117th) has been stationed at Aldershot for some years. The married officers live out of barracks, and the Colonel has during all this time occupied a villa called Lachine, about half a mile from the North Camp. The house stands in its own grounds, but the west side of it

9 *upwards of thirty years*. As Mr. T. S. Blakeney wrote in *Sherlock Holmes: Fact or Fiction?*: "The garrison at Bhurtee was relieved by Neill's column [*see below*], and his column we know from history was operating from May to September, 1857. . . . Barclay may have married in 1857, but more likely in '58, when things had quieted down in India. Holmes says that at the time of his death Barclay had been married for 'upwards of thirty years,' and this is checked by Mrs. Barclay's remark to Wild, that he was thought to have been dead 'this thirty years.' Add over thirty years to 1858, and we may fairly reach 1889 . . ."

10 *not more than thirty yards from the high-road.* "Colonel Barclay, then, lived to the east of Aldershot proper, beyond the Stanhope and the Wellington Lines, and most probably between the railway and the Blackwater River, in a district now known as 'North Town,'" Mr. Michael Harrison wrote (*In the Footsteps of Sherlock Holmes*).

. . . THE TWO WOMEN WITH THE COACHMAN CAME UP INTO THE HALL AND LISTENED TO THE DISPUTE . . .

Illustration by William H. Hyde for *Harper's Weekly*, July 8, 1893.

10 is not more than thirty yards from the high-road. A coachman and two maids form the staff of servants. These, with their master and mistress, were the sole occupants of Lachine, for the Barclays had no children, nor was it usual for them to have resident visitors.

" Now for the events at Lachine between nine and ten on the evening of last Monday.

" Mrs. Barclay was, it appears, a member of the Roman Catholic Church, and had interested herself very much in the establishment of the Guild of St. George, which was formed in connection with the Watt Street Chapel for the purpose of supplying the poor with cast-off clothing. A meeting of the Guild had been held that evening at eight, and Mrs. Barclay had hurried over her dinner in order to be present at it. When leaving the house, she was heard by the coachman to make some commonplace remark to her husband, and to assure him that she would be back before long. She then called for Miss Morrison, a young lady who lives in the next villa, and the two went off together to their meeting. It lasted forty minutes, and at a quarter-past nine Mrs. Barclay returned home, having left Miss Morrison at her door as she passed.

" There is a room which is used as a morning-room at Lachine. This faces the road, and opens by a large glass folding door on to the lawn. The lawn is thirty yards across, and is only divided from the highway by a low wall with an iron rail above it. It was into this room that Mrs. Barclay went upon her return. The blinds were not down, for the room was seldom used in the evening, but Mrs. Barclay herself lit the lamp and then rang the bell, asking Jane Stewart, the housemaid, to bring her a cup of tea, which was quite contrary to her usual habits. The Colonel had been sitting in the dining-room, but hearing that his wife had returned, he joined her in the morning-room. The coachman saw him cross the hall, and enter it. He was never seen again alive.

" The tea which had been ordered was brought up at the end of ten minutes, but the maid, as she approached the door, was surprised to hear the voices of her master and mistress in furious altercation. She knocked without receiving any answer, and even turned the handle, but only to find that the door was locked upon the inside. Naturally enough, she ran down to tell the cook, and the two women with the coachman came up into the hall and listened to the dispute which was still raging. They all agree that only two voices were to be heard, those of Barclay and his wife. Barclay's remarks were subdued and abrupt, so that none of them were audible to the listeners. The lady's, on the other hand, were most bitter, and when she raised her voice, could be plainly heard. ' You coward ! ' she repeated over and over again. ' What can be done now ? Give me back my life. I will never so much as breathe the same air as you again ! You coward ! You coward ! ' Those were scraps of her conversation, ending in a sudden dreadful cry in the man's voice, with a crash, and a piercing scream from the woman. Convinced that some tragedy had occurred, the coachman rushed to the door and strove to force it, while scream after scream issued from within. He was unable, how-

ever, to make his way in, and the maids were too distracted with fear to be of any assistance to him. A sudden
thought struck him, however, and he ran through the
hall door and round to the lawn, upon which the long
French windows opened. One side of the window was
open, which I understand was quite usual in the summer-
time, and he passed without difficulty into the room. His
mistress had ceased to scream, and was stretched insensible upon a couch, while with his feet tilted over the side
of an arm-chair, and his head upon the ground near the
corner of the fender, was lying the unfortunate soldier,
stone dead, in a pool of his own blood.

"Naturally the coachman's first thought, on finding
that he could do nothing for his master, was to open the
door. But here an unexpected and singular difficulty
presented itself. The key was not on the inner side of the
door, nor could he find it anywhere in the room. He
went out again, therefore, through the window, and having
obtained the help of a policeman and of a medical man,
he returned. The lady, against whom naturally the
strongest suspicion rested, was removed to her room, still
in a state of insensibility. The Colonel's body was then
placed upon the sofa, and a careful examination made of
the scene of the tragedy.

"The injury from which the unfortunate veteran was
suffering was found to be a ragged cut, some two inches
long, at the back part of his head, which had evidently
been caused by a violent blow from a blunt weapon. Nor
was it difficult to guess what that weapon may have been.
Upon the floor, close to the body, was lying a singular
club of hard carved wood with a bone handle. The
Colonel possessed a varied collection of weapons brought
from the different countries in which he had fought, and
it is conjectured by the police that this club was among
his trophies. The servants deny having seen it before,
but among the numerous curiosities in the house it is
possible that it may have been overlooked. Nothing else
of importance was discovered in the room by the police,
save the inexplicable fact that neither upon Mrs. Barclay's
person, nor upon that of the victim, nor in any part of the
room was the missing key to be found. The door had
eventually to be opened by a locksmith from Aldershot.

"That was the state of things, Watson, when upon the
Tuesday morning I, at the request of Major Murphy,
went down to Aldershot to supplement the efforts of the
police. I think you will acknowledge that the problem
was already one of interest, but my observations soon
made me realize that it was in truth much more extraordinary than would at first sight appear.

"Before examining the room I cross-questioned the
servants, but only succeeded in eliciting the facts which
I have already stated. One other detail of interest was
remembered by Jane Stewart, the housemaid. You will
remember that on hearing the sound of the quarrel she
descended and returned with the other servants. On
that first occasion, when she was alone, she says that the
voices of her master and mistress were sunk so low that
she could hear hardly anything, and judged by their tones,

. . . THE COACHMAN RUSHED TO THE DOOR . . .

Illustration by Sidney Paget for the *Strand Magazine*, July, 1893.

rather than their words, that they had fallen out. On my pressing her, however, she remembered that she heard the word ' David ' uttered twice by the lady. The point is of the utmost importance as guiding us towards the reason of the sudden quarrel. The Colonel's name, you remember, was James.

" There was one thing in the case which had made the deepest impression both upon the servants and the police. This was the contortion of the Colonel's face. It had set, according to their account, into the most dreadful expression of fear and horror which a human countenance is capable of assuming. More than one person fainted at the mere sight of him, so terrible was the effect. It was quite certain that he had foreseen his fate, and that it had caused him the utmost horror. This, of course, fitted in well enough with the police theory, if the Colonel could have seen his wife making a murderous attack upon him. Nor was the fact of the wound being on the back of his head a fatal objection to this, as he might have turned to avoid the blow. No information could be got from the lady herself, who was temporarily insane from an acute attack of brain fever.

" From the police I learned that Miss Morrison, who, you remember, went out that evening with Mrs. Barclay, denied having any knowledge of what it was which had caused the ill-humour in which her companion had returned.

" Having gathered these facts, Watson, I smoked several pipes over them, trying to separate those which were crucial from others which were merely incidental. There could be no question that the most distinctive and suggestive point in the case was the singular disappearance of the door-key. A most careful search had failed to discover it in the room. Therefore, it must have been taken from it. But neither the Colonel nor the Colonel's wife could have taken it. That was perfectly clear. Therefore a third person must have entered the room. And that third person could only have come in through the window. It seemed to me that a careful examination of the room and the lawn might possibly reveal some traces of this mysterious individual. You know my methods, Watson. There was not one of them which I did not apply to the inquiry. And it ended by my discovering traces, but very different ones from those which I had expected. There had been a man in the room, and he had crossed the lawn coming from the road. I was able to obtain five very clear impressions of his footmarks— one on the roadway itself, at the point where he had climbed the low wall, two on the lawn, and two very faint ones upon the stained boards near the window where he had entered. He had apparently rushed across the lawn, for his toe-marks were much deeper than his heels. But it was not the man who surprised me. It was his companion."

" His companion ! "

Holmes pulled a large sheet of tissue paper out of his pocket and carefully unfolded it upon his knee.

" What do you make of that ? " he asked.

The paper was covered with tracings of the footmarks

"WHAT DO YOU MAKE OF THAT?" HE ASKED.

Illustration by Sidney Paget for the *Strand Magazine*, July, 1893.

of some small animal.   It had five well-marked footpads,
an indication of long nails, and the whole print might be
nearly as large. as a dessert-spoon.

"It's a dog," said I.

"Did ever you hear of a dog running up a curtain?
I found distinct traces that this creature had done so."

"A monkey, then?"

"But it is not the print of a monkey."

"What can it be, then?"

"Neither dog, nor cat, nor monkey, nor any creature
that we are familiar with.   I have tried to reconstruct it
from the measurements.   Here are four prints where the
beast has been standing motionless.   You see that it is
no less than fifteen inches from forefoot to hind.   Add to
that the length of neck and head, and you get a creature
not much less than two feet long—probably more if there
is any tail.   But now observe this other measurement.
The animal has been moving, and we have the length of
its stride.   In each case it is only about three inches.
You have an indication, you see, of a long body with very
short legs attached to it.   It has not been considerate
enough to leave any of its hair behind it.   But its general
shape must be what I have indicated, and it can run up a
curtain and is carnivorous."

"How do you deduce that?"

"Because it ran up the curtain.   A canary's cage was
hanging in the window, and its aim seems to have been
to get at the bird."

"Then what was the beast?"

"Ah, if I could give it a name it might go a long way
towards solving the case.   On the whole it was probably
some creature of the weasel or stoat tribe—and yet it is
larger than any of these that I have seen."

"But what had it to do with the crime?"

"That also is still obscure.   But we have learned a
good deal, you perceive.   We know that a man stood in
the road looking at the quarrel between the Barclays—the
blinds were up and the room lighted.   We know also that
he ran across the lawn, entered the room, accompanied by
a strange animal, and that he either struck the Colonel,
or, as is equally possible, that the Colonel fell down from
sheer fright at the sight of him, and cut his head on the
corner of the fender.   Finally, we have the curious fact
that the intruder carried away the key with him when he
left."

"Your discoveries seem to have left the business more
obscure than it was before," said I.

"Quite so.   They undoubtedly showed that the affair
was much deeper than was at first conjectured.   I
thought the matter over, and I came to the conclusion
that I must approach the case from another aspect.   But
really, Watson, I am keeping you up, and I might just as
well tell you all this on our way to Aldershot to-morrow."

"Thank you, you've gone rather too far to stop."

"It was quite certain that when Mrs. Barclay left the
house at half-past seven she was on good terms with her
husband.   She was never, as I think I have said, ostentatiously affectionate, but she was heard by the coachman
chatting with the Colonel in a friendly fashion.   Now, it

was equally certain that immediately on her return she had gone to the room in which she was least likely to see her husband, had flown to tea, as an agitated woman will, and, finally, on his coming in to her, had broken into violent recriminations. Therefore, something had occurred between seven-thirty and nine o'clock which had completely altered her feelings towards him. But Miss Morrison had been with her during the whole of that hour and a half. It was absolutely certain, therefore, in spite of her denial, that she must know something of the matter.

" My first conjecture was that possibly there had been some passages between this young woman and the old soldier, which the former had now confessed to the wife. That would account for the angry return and also for the girl's denial that anything had occurred. Nor would it be entirely incompatible with most of the words overheard. But there was the reference to David, and there was the known affection of the Colonel for his wife to weigh against it, to say nothing of the tragic intrusion of this other man, which might, of course, be entirely disconnected with what had gone before. It was not easy to pick one's steps, but on the whole I was inclined to dismiss the idea that there had been anything between the Colonel and Miss Morrison, but more than ever convinced that the young lady held the clue as to what it was which had turned Mrs. Barclay to hatred of her husband. I took the obvious course, therefore, of calling upon Miss Morrison, of explaining to her that I was perfectly certain that she held the facts in her possession, and of assuring her that her friend, Mrs. Barclay, might find herself in the dock upon a capital charge unless the matter were cleared up.

" Miss Morrison is a little, ethereal slip of a girl, with timid eyes and blonde hair, but I found her by no means wanting in shrewdness and common sense. She sat thinking for some time after I had spoken, and then turning to me with a brisk air of resolution, she broke into a remarkable statement, which I will condense for your benefit.

" ' I promised my friend that I would say nothing of the matter, and a promise is a promise,' said she. ' But if I can really help her when so serious a charge is made against her, and when her own mouth, poor darling, is closed by illness, then I think I am absolved from my promise. I will tell you exactly what happened on Monday evening.

" ' We were returning from the Watt Street Mission, about a quarter to nine o'clock. On our way we had to pass through Hudson Street, which is a very quiet thoroughfare. There is only one lamp in it upon the left-hand side, and as we approached this lamp I saw a man coming towards us with his back very bent, and something like a box slung over one of his shoulders. He appeared to be deformed, for he carried his head low, and walked with his knees bent. We were passing him when he raised his face to look at us in the circle of light thrown by the lamp, and as he did so he stopped and screamed out in a dreadful voice, " My God, it's Nancy ! " Mrs.

"MY GOD, IT'S NANCY!"

Illustration by Sidney Paget for the *Strand Magazine*, July, 1893.

Barclay turned as white as death, and would have fallen down had the dreadful-looking creature not caught hold of her. I was going to call for the police, but she, to my surprise, spoke quite civilly to the fellow.

" ' "I thought you had been dead this thirty years, Henry," said she, in a shaking voice.

" ' "So I have,' said he, and it was awful to hear the tones that he said it in. He had a very dark, fearsome face, and a gleam in his eyes that comes back to me in my dreams. His hair and whiskers were shot with grey, and his face was all crinkled and puckered like a withered apple.

" ' "Just walk on a little way, dear," said Mrs. Barclay. " I want to have a word with this man. There is nothing to be afraid of." She tried to speak boldly, but she was still deadly pale, and could hardly get her words out for the trembling of her lips.

" ' I did as she asked me, and they talked together for a few minutes. Then she came down the street with her eyes blazing, and I saw the crippled wretch standing by the lamp-post and shaking his clenched fists in the air, as if he were mad with rage. She never said a word until we were at the door here, when she took me by the hand and begged me to tell no one what had happened. " It is an old acquaintance of mine who has come down in the world," said she. When I promised her that I would say nothing she kissed me, and I have never seen her since. I have told you now the whole truth, and if I withheld it from the police it is because I did not realize then the danger in which my dear friend stood. I know that it can only be to her advantage that everything should be known.'

" There was her statement, Watson, and to me, as you can imagine, it was like a light on a dark night. Everything which had been disconnected before began at once to assume its true place, and I had a shadowy presentiment of the whole sequence of events. My next step obviously was to find the man who had produced such a remarkable impression upon Mrs. Barclay. If he were still in Aldershot it should not be a very difficult matter. There are not such a very great number of civilians, and a deformed man was sure to have attracted attention. I spent a day in the search, and by evening—this very evening, Watson—I had run him down. The man's **11** name is Henry Wood, and he lives in lodgings in the same street in which the ladies met him. He has only been five days in the place. In the character of a registration agent I had a most interesting gossip with his landlady. The man is by trade a conjurer and performer, going round the canteens, after nightfall, and giving a little entertainment at each. He carries some creature about with him in his box, about which the landlady seemed to be in considerable trepidation, for she had never seen an animal like it. He uses it in some of his tricks, according to her account. So much the woman was able to tell me, and also that it was a wonder the man lived, seeing how twisted he was, and that he spoke in a strange tongue sometimes, and that for the last two nights she had heard him groaning and weeping in his bedroom. He was all right as far as money went, but in his deposit he had

11 *this very evening, Watson.* Holmes says: "The facts are only two days old." He tells us that the Royal Mallows "was commanded up to Monday night by James Barclay." He says: "Now for the events at Lachine between nine and ten on the evening of last Monday." He says: "Upon the Tuesday morning I . . . went down to Aldershot . . ." He "spent a day" (the Wednesday) in the search for the crooked man, and "by evening—this very evening, Watson—I had run him down." The case, then, began on a Wednesday; it ended the following day, Thursday.

. . . HE HAD GIVEN HER WHAT LOOKED LIKE
A BAD FLORIN.

"This 2/ piece," the late A. Carson Simpson wrote in *Numismatics in the Canon*, Part I, "bears an ancient name, that of the Florentine florino, which was at first a small silver coin, corresponding roughly to the penny; later it was a much more valuable gold coin. First coined in gold in 1252, it continued, with only minor changes in design, until the Florentine Republic became a Medici duchy in 1532. It circulated all over the Continent, enjoying a higher reputation there than the English silver penny. This being the case, it is not surprising that, when Edward III issued his first gold currency in 1344, its basic unit was a florin (worth exactly two of the Florentine ones) of a beautiful Gothic design inspired, perhaps, by some of the contemporary gold coins of Philippe VI de Valois. Like the earlier gold penny of Henry III, this florin contained more gold than its face value justified, and it lasted only a few months, to be replaced by the noble, later in the same year. The name was not revived until Victoria's time, when it became a silver coin. This denomination was the result of agitation for a decimal coinage, led by Sir John Bowring, the famous diplomat, Orientalist, poet and translator. Being worth 2/—, it is, of course, one-tenth of a pound sterling, and the first two types of the coin bore legends so stating. Although it is still coined, decimalization proceeded no further (except for the short-lived double-florin) probably because the traditional British system of currency, quite aside from considerations of prestige, is of such great international importance that it would be dangerous to change it." The illustration shows the florin of 1889, called the "Godless florin," because of the omission of the conventional DEI GRATIA.

12 *in spite of the warm weather*. We know that the case took place on a Wednesday and Thursday in the period of approximately August 1–September 22, 1889. The possible dates are: 1) July 31–August 1; 2) August 7–8; 3) August 14–15; 4) August 21–22; 5) August 28–29; 6) September 4–5; 7) September 11–12; 8) September 18–19. We know that Mrs. Watson was on holiday and Watson was living with Holmes in Baker Street at the time of "The Cardboard Box," which we have shown to have taken place in the period Saturday, August 31–Monday, September 2, 1889; by Saturday, September 7 ("The Engineer's Thumb") Mary and Watson himself had returned to their home in Paddington. It is extremely unlikely that Mary was on holiday for less than a fortnight; we can therefore eliminate August 21–22 and August 28–29 from our considerations. There are two clues to the proper period: 1) The Thursday on which Holmes concluded the case was a warm day; 2) the weather during the entire period Monday—Thursday inclusive appears to have been clear. Of the six remaining periods there was *one and one only* during which there was *no rain whatsoever*: Monday, September 9–Thursday, September 12. We hold that Holmes visited Watson on the evening of *Wednesday, September 11*, and solved the case the next day, *Thursday, September 12, 1889*. On that day the temperature rose to a high of 77.2°, so it was indeed "warm weather."

. . . HE WAS CROUCHING OVER A FIRE, AND THE LITTLE ROOM WAS LIKE AN OVEN.

Illustration by William H. Hyde for *Harper's Weekly*, July 8, 1893.

given her what looked like a bad florin. She showed it to me, Watson, and it was an Indian rupee.

" So now, my dear fellow, you see exactly how we stand and why it is I want you. It is perfectly plain that after the ladies parted from this man he followed them at a distance, that he saw the quarrel between husband and wife through the window, that he rushed in, and that the creature which he carried in his box got loose. That is all very certain. But he is the only person in this world who can tell us exactly what happened in that room."

" And you intend to ask him ? "

" Most certainly—but in the presence of a witness."

" And I am the witness ? "

" If you will be so good. If he can clear the matter up, well and good. If he refuses, we have no alternative but to apply for a warrant."

" But how do you know he will be there when we return ? "

" You may be sure that I took some precautions. I have one of my Baker Street boys mounting guard over him who would stick to him like a burr, go where he might. We shall find him in Hudson Street to-morrow, Watson ; and meanwhile I should be the criminal myself if I kept you out of bed any longer."

It was midday when we found ourselves at the scene of the tragedy, and, under my companion's guidance, we made our way at once to Hudson Street. In spite of his capacity for concealing his emotions I could easily see that Holmes was in a state of suppressed excitement, while I was myself tingling with that half-sporting, half-intellectual pleasure which I invariably experienced when I associated myself with him in his investigations.

" This is the street," said he, as he turned into a short thoroughfare lined with plain two-storied brick houses— " Ah ! here is Simpson to report."

" He's in all right, Mr. Holmes," cried a small street Arab, running up to us.

" Good, Simpson ! " said Holmes, patting him on the head. " Come along, Watson. This is the house." He sent in his card with a message that he had come on important business, and a moment later we were face to face with the man whom we had come to see. In spite of **12** the warm weather he was crouching over a fire, and the little room was like an oven. The man sat all twisted and huddled in his chair in a way which gave an indescribable impression of deformity, but the face which he turned towards us, though worn and swarthy, must at some time have been remarkable for its beauty. He looked suspiciously at us now out of yellow-shot bilious eyes, and, without speaking or rising, he waved towards two chairs.

" Mr. Henry Wood, late of India, I believe ? " said Holmes, affably. " I've come over this little matter of Colonel Barclay's death."

" What should I know about that ? "

" That's what I wanted to ascertain. You know, I suppose, that unless the matter is cleared up, Mrs. Barclay, who is an old friend of yours, will in all probability be tried for murder ? "

The man gave a violent start.

" I don't know who you are," he cried, " nor how you come to know what you do know, but will you swear that this is true that you tell me ? "

" Why, they are only waiting for her to come to her senses to arrest her."

" My God !   Are you in the police yourself ? "

" No."

" What business is it of yours, then ? "

" It's every man's business to see justice done."

" You can take my word that she is innocent."

" Then you are guilty ? "

" No, I am not."

" Who killed Colonel James Barclay, then ? "

" It was a just Providence that killed him.   But mind you this, that if I had knocked his brains out, as it was in my heart to do, he would have had no more than his due from my hands.   If his own guilty conscience had not struck him down, it is likely enough that I might have had his blood upon my soul.   You want me to tell the story ?   Well, I don't know why I shouldn't, for there's no cause for me to be ashamed of it.

" It was in this way, sir.   You see me now with my back like a camel and my ribs all awry, but there was a time when Corporal Henry Wood was the smartest man in the 117th Foot.   We were in India then, in cantonments, at a place we'll call Bhurtee.   Barclay, who died the other day, was sergeant in the same company as myself, and the belle of the regiment—aye, and the finest girl that ever had the breath of life between her lips—was Nancy Devoy, the daughter of the colour-sergeant.   There were two men who loved her, and one whom she loved ; and you'll smile when you look at this poor thing huddled before the fire, and hear me say that it was for my good looks that she loved me.

" Well, though I had her heart her father was set upon her marrying Barclay.   I was a harum-scarum, reckless lad, and he had had an education, and was already marked for the sword-belt.   But the girl held true to me, and it seemed that I would have had her, when the Mutiny broke out, and all Hell was loose in the country.

" We were shut up in Bhurtee, the regiment of us, with half a battery of artillery, a company of Sikhs, and a lot of civilians and women-folk.   There were ten thousand rebels round us, and they were as keen as a set of terriers round a rat cage.   About the second week of it our water gave out, and it was a question whether we could communicate with General Neill's column, which was moving up-country.   It was our only chance, for we could not hope to fight our way out with all the women and children, so I volunteered to go out and warn General Neill of our danger.   My offer was accepted, and I talked it over with Sergeant Barclay, who was supposed to know the ground better than any other man, and who drew up a route by which I might get through the rebel lines.   At ten o'clock the same night I started off upon my journey.   There were a thousand lives to save, but it was of only one that I was thinking when I dropped over the wall that night.

" My way ran down a dried-up water-course, which we

13

"MR. HENRY WOOD, LATE OF INDIA, I BELIEVE?"
SAID HOLMES, AFFABLY.

Illustration by Sidney Paget for the *Strand Magazine*, July, 1893.

13 *General Neill's column.* General James George Smith Neill, 1810–1857.

hoped would screen me from the enemy's sentries, but as I crept round the corner of it I walked right into six of them, who were crouching down in the dark, waiting for me. In an instant I was stunned with a blow, and bound hand and foot. But the real blow was to my heart and not to my head, for as I came to and listened to as much as I could understand of their talk, I heard enough to tell me that my comrade, the very man who had arranged the way I was to take, had betrayed me by means of a native servant into the hands of the enemy.

"Well, there's no need for me to dwell on that part of it. You know now what James Barclay was capable of. Bhurtee was relieved by Neill next day, but the rebels took me away with them in their retreat, and it was many a long year before I ever saw a white face again. I was tortured, and tried to get away, and was captured and tortured again. You can see for yourselves the state in which I was left. Some of them that fled into Nepaul took me with them, and then afterwards I was up past Darjeeling. The hill-folk up there murdered the rebels who had me, and I became their slave for a time until I escaped, but instead of going south I had to go north, until I found myself among the Afghans. There I wandered about for many a year, and at last came back to the Punjab, where I lived mostly among the natives, and picked up a living by the conjuring tricks that I had learned. What use was it for me, a wretched cripple, to go back to England, or to make myself known to my old comrades? Even my wish for revenge would not make me do that. I had rather that Nancy and my old pals should think of Harry Wood as having died with a straight back, than see him living and crawling with a stick like a chimpanzee. They never doubted that I was dead, and I meant that they never should. I heard that Barclay had married Nancy, and that he was rapidly rising in the regiment, but even that did not make me speak.

"But when one gets old, one has a longing for home. For years I've been dreaming of the bright green fields and the hedges of England. At last I determined to see them before I died. I saved enough to bring me across, and then I came here where the soldiers are, for I know their ways, and how to amuse them, and so earn enough to keep me."

"Your narrative is most interesting," said Sherlock Holmes. "I have already heard of your meeting with Mrs. Barclay and your mutual recognition. You then, as I understand, followed her home and saw through the window an altercation between her husband and her, in which she doubtless cast his conduct to you in his teeth. Your own feelings overcame you, and you ran across the lawn and broke in upon them."

"I did, sir, and at the sight of me he looked as I have never seen a man look before, and over he went with his head on the fender. But he was dead before he fell. I read death on his face as plain as I can read that text over the fire. The bare sight of me was like a bullet through his guilty heart."

"And then?"

". . . I WALKED RIGHT INTO SIX OF THEM . . ."

Illustration by Sidney Paget for the *Strand Magazine*, March, 1893.

"Then Nancy fainted, and I caught up the key of the door from her hand, intending to unlock it and get help. But as I was doing it it seemed to me better to leave it alone and get away, for the thing might look black against me, and anyway my secret would be out if I were taken. In my haste I thrust the key into my pocket, and dropped my stick while I was chasing Teddy, who had run up the curtain. When I got him into his box, from which he had slipped, I was off as fast as I could run."

"Who's Teddy ? " asked Holmes.

The man leaned over and pulled up the front of a kind of hutch in the corner. In an instant out there slipped a beautiful reddish-brown creature, thin, and lithe, with the legs of a stoat, a long thin nose, and a pair of the finest red eyes that ever I saw in an animal's head.

"It's a mongoose ! " I cried.

"Well, some call them that, and some call them ichneumon," said the man. "Snake-catcher is what I call them, and Teddy is amazing quick on cobras. I have one here without the fangs, and Teddy catches it every night to please the folk in the canteen. Any other point, sir ? "

"Well, we may have to apply to you again if Mrs. Barclay should prove to be in serious trouble."

"In that case, of course, I'd come forward."

"But if not, there is no object of raking up this scandal against a dead man, foully as he has acted. You have, at least, the satisfaction of knowing that for thirty years of his life his conscience bitterly reproached him for his wicked deed. Ah, there goes Major Murphy on the other side of the street. Good-bye, Wood ; I want to learn if anything has happened since yesterday."

We were in time to overtake the Major before he reached the corner.

"Ah, Holmes," he said, "I suppose you have heard that all this fuss has come to nothing ? "

"What, then ? "

"The inquest is just over. The medical evidence showed conclusively that death was due to apoplexy. You see, it was quite a simple case after all."

"Oh, remarkably superficial," said Holmes, smiling. "Come, Watson, I don't think we shall be wanted in Aldershot any more."

"There's one thing," said I, as we walked down to the station ; "if the husband's name was James, and the other was Henry, what was this talk about David ? "

"That one word, my dear Watson, should have told me the whole story had I been the ideal reasoner which you are so fond of depicting. It was evidently a term of reproach."

"Of reproach ? "

"Yes, David strayed a little now and then, you know, and on one occasion in the same direction as Sergeant James Barclay. You remember the small affair of Uriah and Bathsheba ? My Biblical knowledge is a trifle rusty, I fear, but you will find the story in the first or second of Samuel." **14**

". . . SOME CALL THEM ICHNEUMON . . ."

The illustration is from Bewick's *A General History of Quadrupeds*, 1807.

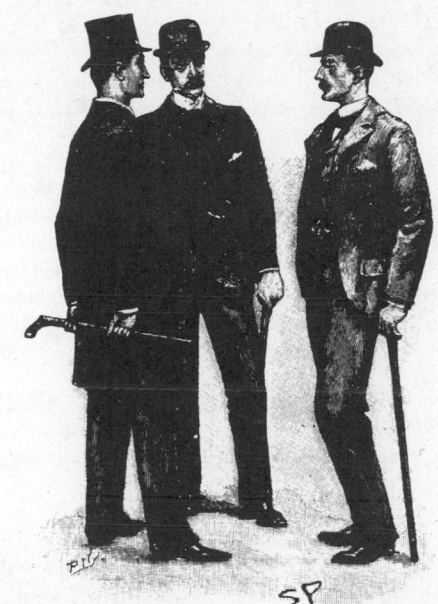

"YOU SEE, IT WAS QUITE A SIMPLE CASE AFTER ALL."

Illustration by Sidney Paget for the *Strand Magazine*, July, 1893.

14 *the first or second of Samuel.*" Watson would have found the story in the "second of Samuel," 11–13. In recent years some Sherlockians have speculated that Holmes by faith may have been a Roman Catholic. This view has been contested by the Reverend Henry Folsom. "If Holmes were a Roman," he says, "he would have referred here to "the first or second of *Kings*.'"

44

THE ADVENTURE OF WISTERIA LODGE

[*Monday, March 24, to Saturday, March 29, 1890*]

1 *a bleak and windy day towards the end of March in the year 1892.* We hope to show that "The Adventure of Wisteria Lodge" took place *Monday, March 24 to Saturday, March 29, 1890*. The Monday was indeed "a bleak and windy day" —"bleak" (a minimum temperature of 36.1°, against a fifty-year average of 42°) "with a fine rain" (0.27 inch)—and "windy" (a south wind, with a pressure of 2.5 pounds to the inch). The month was certainly March: "It is late in March," Mr. Scott Eccles tells us later; that night it was "a cold, dark March evening"; five days later, Watson speaks of "the shadows of the March evening." But Watson's "1892" is certainly a typographical error: Holmes in 1892 was thought to be dead and was in fact thousands of miles removed from Baker Street, traveling in Tibet (see "The Adventure of the Empty House").

2 *those narratives with which you have afflicted a long-suffering public.* The case must be after February, 1890, the month in which *The Sign of the Four* was published.

3 *the five orange pips.* But the fact that the affair of "The Red-Headed League" and that of "The Five Orange Pips" were fresh in Holmes' mind is perhaps an indication that "The Adventure of Wisteria Lodge" should be dated within a few years at most of 1887.

4 *Post Office, Charing Cross.*" The day-and-night post office in Charing Cross was one of the oldest of the London post offices; in Holmes' and Watson's day, it was tucked away on the ground floor of Morley's Hotel, but had its entrance on the south side of the Strand.

5 *Colonel Carruthers.* Not to be confused with the Mr. Robert Carruthers of "The Adventure of the Solitary Cyclist."

6 *not connected up with the work for which it was built.* Compare: "To let the brain work without sufficient material is like racing an engine. It racks itself to pieces." ("The Adventure of the

I—THE SINGULAR EXPERIENCE OF MR. JOHN SCOTT ECCLES

1 I FIND it recorded in my notebook that it was a bleak and windy day towards the end of March in the year 1892. Holmes had received a telegram whilst we sat at our lunch, and he had scribbled a reply. He made no remark, but the matter remained in his thoughts, for he stood in front of the fire afterwards with a thoughtful face, smoking his pipe, and casting an occasional glance at the message. Suddenly he turned upon me with a mischievous twinkle in his eyes.

" I suppose, Watson, we must look upon you as a man of letters," said he. " How do you define the word ' grotesque ' ? "

" Strange—remarkable," I suggested.

He shook his head at my definition.

" There is surely something more than that," said he ; " some underlying suggestion of the tragic and the terrible. If you cast your mind back to some of those narratives **2** with which you have afflicted a long-suffering public, you will recognize how often the grotesque has deepened into the criminal. Think of that little affair of the red-headed men. That was grotesque enough in the outset, and yet it ended in a desperate attempt at robbery. Or, again, **3** there was that most grotesque affair of the five orange pips, which led straight to a murderous conspiracy. The word puts me on the alert."

" Have you it there ? " I asked.

He read the telegram aloud.

" Have just had most incredible and grotesque experience. May I consult you ?—Scott Eccles, Post Office, **4** Charing Cross."

" Man or woman ? " I asked.

" Oh, man, of course. No woman would ever send a reply-paid telegram. She would have come."

" Will you see him ? "

" My dear Watson, you know how bored I have been **5** since we locked up Colonel Carruthers. My mind is like a racing engine, tearing itself to pieces because it is not **6** connected up with the work for which it was built. Life is commonplace, the papers are sterile ; audacity and romance seem to have passed for ever from the criminal world. Can you ask me, then, whether I am ready to look into any new problem, however trivial it may prove? But here, unless I am mistaken, is our client."

A measured step was heard upon the stairs, and a moment later a stout, tall, grey-whiskered and solemnly respectable person was ushered into the room. His life history was written in his heavy features and pompous manner. From his spats to his gold-rimmed spectacles he was a Conservative, a Churchman, a good citizen, orthodox and conventional to the last degree. But some **7** amazing experience had disturbed his native composure and left its traces in his bristling hair, his flushed, angry cheeks, and his flurried, excited manner. He plunged instantly into his business.

" I have had a most singular and unpleasant experience, Mr. Holmes," said he. " Never in my life have I been placed in such a situation. It is most improper—most outrageous. I must insist upon some explanation." He swelled and puffed in his anger.

" Pray sit down, Mr. Scott Eccles," said Holmes, in a soothing voice. " May I ask, in the first place, why you came to me at all ? "

" Well, sir, it did not appear to be a matter which concerned the police, and yet, when you have heard the facts, you must admit that I could not leave it where it was. Private detectives are a class with whom I have absolutely no sympathy, but none the less, having heard your name ——"

" Quite so. But, in the second place, why did you not come at once ? "

" What do you mean ? "

Holmes glanced at his watch.

" It is a quarter past two," he said. " Your telegram was dispatched about one. But no one can glance at your toilet and attire without seeing that your disturbance dates from the moment of your waking."

Our client smoothed down his unbrushed hair and felt his unshaven chin.

" You are right, Mr. Holmes. I never gave a thought to my toilet. I was only too glad to get out of such a house. But I have been running round making inquiries before I came to you. I went to the house agents, you know, and they said that Mr. Garcia's rent was paid up all right and that everything was in order at Wisteria Lodge."

" Come, come, sir," said Holmes, laughing. " You are like my friend Dr. Watson, who has a bad habit of telling his stories wrong end foremost. Please arrange your thoughts and let me know, in their due sequence, exactly what those events are which have sent you out unbrushed and unkempt, with dress-boots and waistcoat buttoned awry, in search of advice and assistance."

Our client looked down with a rueful face at his own unconventional appearance.

" I'm sure it must look very bad, Mr. Holmes, and I am not aware that in my whole life such a thing has ever happened before. But I will tell you the whole queer business, and when I have done so you will admit, I am sure, that there has been enough to excuse me."

But his narrative was nipped in the bud. There was a

Devil's Foot"). Mr. T. S. Blakeney feels that these remarks explain Holmes' occasional lapses into drug-taking.

7 *orthodox and conventional to the last degree.* ". . . from one glance at Scott Eccles, [Watson] gives us a string of accurate inferences worthy of Holmes himself," Mr. Nathan L. Bengis wrote in "Take a Bow, Dr. Watson."

"BUT I HAVE BEEN RUNNING AROUND AND MAKING INQUIRIES BEFORE I CAME TO YOU."

Illustration by Arthur Twidle for the *Strand Magazine*, September, 1908. ". . . the untimely death of Paget in 1908 made it necessary for other artists to assume the work of illustrating the *Strand*'s continuing series of Sherlock Holmes stories—at once an enviable and an unenviable assignment," the late James Montgomery wrote in *A Study in Pictures*. "The first illustrator to attempt this was Arthur Twidle. . . . He was selected by the *Strand* to draw ten pictures for . . . 'The Adventure of Wisteria Lodge' . . . They are splendid pictures, even though they lack a little of Paget's elusive charm, and indeed they give us considerably more detail in background than most of Paget's work. Holmes is perhaps a little taller, but possesses the same spare figure, receding temples and finely chiseled features. Watson is even more typically British than before, if such were possible. The other characters, and the settings in which all of them are placed, harmonize agreeably with the atmosphere of the times."

8 *Inspector Gregson of Scotland Yard.* This, too, is at least an indication that "The Adventure of Wisteria Lodge" is to be dated earlier rather than later, as Gregson seldom appears in the later adventures.

9 "*You traced him through the telegram, no doubt.*" Scott Eccles "was traced to Baker Street through the telegram, although in what way he was traced does not appear," Colonel E. Ennalls Berl commented in "Sherlock Holmes and the Telephone." "It will be recalled that Eccles, immediately upon his arrival from Esher, went to the Spanish Embassy, and from there to Mr. Melville's house, and thence to the Charing Cross Post Office. He could have gone to any other post office to send the wire. Whatever the system might have been for tracing Eccles through a telegram, it would seem that Gregson and Baynes had to know enough to look for him or his telegram at Charing Cross Post Office."

10 *Esher.* A village in Surrey.

OUR CLIENT HAD SAT UP WITH STARING EYES . . .

Illustration by Frederic Dorr Steele for *Collier's Magazine,* August 15, 1908. Arthur Twidle illustrated the same scene for the *Strand Magazine,* September, 1908.

bustle outside, and Mrs. Hudson opened the door to usher in two robust and official-looking individuals, one of whom **8** was well known to us as Inspector Gregson of Scotland Yard, an energetic, gallant, and, within his limitations, a capable officer. He shook hands with Holmes, and introduced his comrade as Inspector Baynes of the Surrey Constabulary.

" We are hunting together, Mr. Holmes, and our trail lay in this direction." He turned his bulldog eyes upon our visitor. " Are you Mr. John Scott Eccles, of Popham House, Lee ? "

" I am."

" We have been following you about all the morning."

9 " You traced him through the telegram, no doubt," said Holmes.

" Exactly, Mr. Holmes. We picked up the scent at Charing Cross Post Office and came on here."

" But why do you follow me ? What do you want ? "

" We wish a statement, Mr. Scott Eccles, as to the events which led up to the death last night of Mr. Aloysius **10** Garcia, of Wisteria Lodge, near Esher."

Our client had sat up with staring eyes and every tinge of colour struck from his astonished face.

" Dead ? Did you say he was dead ? "

" Yes, sir, he is dead."

" But how ? An accident ? "

" Murder, if ever there was one upon earth."

" Good God ! This is awful ! You don't mean—you don't mean that I am suspected ? "

" A letter of yours was found in the dead man's pocket, and we know by it that you had planned to pass last night at his house."

" So I did."

" Oh, you did, did you ? "

Out came the official notebook.

" Wait a bit, Gregson," said Sherlock Holmes. " All you desire is a plain statement, is it not ? "

" And it is my duty to warn Mr. Scott Eccles that it may be used against him."

" Mr. Eccles was going to tell us about it when you entered the room. I think, Watson, a brandy and soda would do him no harm. Now, sir, I suggest that you take no notice of this addition to your audience, and that you proceed with your narrative exactly as you would have done had you never been interrupted."

Our visitor had gulped off the brandy and the colour had returned to his face. With a dubious glance at the inspector's notebook, he plunged at once into his extraordinary statement.

" I am a bachelor," said he, " and, being of a sociable turn, I cultivate a large number of friends. Among these are the family of a retired brewer called Melville, living at Albemarle Mansion, Kensington. It was at his table that I met some weeks ago a young fellow named Garcia. He was, I understood, of Spanish descent and connected in some way with the Embassy. He spoke perfect English, was pleasing in his manners, and as good-looking a man as ever I saw in my life.

" In some way we struck up quite a friendship, this

young fellow and I. He seemed to take a fancy to me from the first, and within two days of our meeting he came to see me at Lee. One thing led to another, and it ended in his inviting me out to spend a few days at his house, Wisteria Lodge, between Esher and Oxshott. Yesterday **11** evening I went to Esher to fulfil this engagement.

" He had described his household to me before I went there. He lived with a faithful servant, a countryman of his own, who looked after all his needs. This fellow could speak English and did his housekeeping for him. Then there was a wonderful cook, he said, a half-breed whom he had picked up in his travels, who could serve an excellent dinner. I remember that he remarked what a queer household it was to find in the heart of Surrey, and that I agreed with him, though it has proved a good deal queerer than I thought.

" I drove to the place—about two miles on the south side of Esher. The house was a fair-sized one, standing back from the road, with a curving drive which was banked with high evergreen shrubs. It was an old, tumble-down building in a crazy state of disrepair. When the trap pulled up on the grass-grown drive in front of the blotched and weather-stained door, I had doubts as to my wisdom in visiting a man whom I knew so slightly. He opened the door himself, however, and greeted me with a great show of cordiality. I was handed over to the man-servant, a melancholy, swarthy individual, who led the way, my bag in his hand, to my bedroom. The whole place was depressing. Our dinner was *tête-à-tête*, and though my host did his best to be entertaining, his thoughts seemed to continually wander, and he talked so vaguely and wildly that I could hardly understand him. He continually drummed his fingers on the table, gnawed his nails, and gave other signs of nervous impatience. The dinner itself was neither well served nor well cooked, and the gloomy presence of the taciturn servant did not help to enliven us. I can assure you that many times in the course of the evening I wished that I could invent some excuse which would take me back to Lee.

" One thing comes back to my memory which may have a bearing upon the business that you two gentlemen are investigating. I thought nothing of it at the time. Near the end of dinner a note was handed in by the servant. I noticed that after my host had read it he seemed even more distrait and strange than before. He gave up all pretence at conversation and sat, smoking endless cigarettes, lost in his own thoughts, but he made no remark as to the contents. About eleven I was glad to go to bed. Some time later Garcia looked in at my door—the room was dark at the time—and asked me if I had rung. I said that I had not. He apologized for having disturbed me so late, saying that it was nearly one o'clock. I dropped off after this and slept soundly all night.

" And now I come to the amazing part of my tale. When I woke it was broad daylight. I glanced at my watch, and the time was nearly nine. I had particularly asked to be called at eight, so I was very much astonished at this forgetfulness. I sprang up and rang for the servant. There was no response. I rang again and again,

11 *Oxshott*. A town in Surrey.

12 *quarter-day is at hand*. Quarter days in England and Scotland mark a traditional division of the year: they are regarded as "beginning a quarter of the year when quarterly payments, as rent, become due, and various civic and business functions are carried out, such as election, payment of taxes, hiring of help, etc." English literature, especially in essays, fiction, and poetry, abounds in allusions to these days, which in England are Christmas, Lent, Midsummer (June 24th), and Michaelmas (September 29th):

> And when the tenants come to pay their quarter's rent,
> They bring some fowl at Midsummer, a dish of fish in Lent,
> At Christmas a capon, at Michaelmas a goose,
> And somewhat else at New-Year's tide, for fear their lease fly loose.

"IT WAS A DOG-GRATE, MR. HOLMES,
AND HE OVER-PITCHED IT."

Illustration by Arthur Twidle for the *Strand Magazine*, September, 1908. A dog-grate is a detached fire grate standing on supports called dogs.

with the same result. Then I came to the conclusion that the bell was out of order. I huddled on my clothes and hurried downstairs in an exceedingly bad temper to order some hot water. You can imagine my surprise when I found that there was no one there. I shouted in the hall. There was no answer. Then I ran from room to room. All were deserted. My host had shown me which was his bedroom the night before, so I knocked at the door. No reply. I turned the handle and walked in. The room was empty, and the bed had never been slept in. He had gone with the rest. The foreign host, the foreign footman, the foreign cook, all had vanished in the night! That was the end of my visit to Wisteria Lodge."

Sherlock Holmes was rubbing his hands and chuckling as he added this bizarre incident to his collection of strange episodes.

"Your experience is, so far as I know, perfectly unique," said he. "May I ask, sir, what you did then?"

"I was furious. My first idea was that I had been the victim of some absurd practical joke. I packed my things, banged the hall door behind me, and set off for Esher, with my bag in my hand. I called at Allan Brothers', the chief land agents in the village, and found that it was from this firm that the villa had been rented. It struck me that the whole proceeding could hardly be for the purpose of making a fool of me, and that the main object must be to get out of the rent. It is late in March, so quarter-day is **12** at hand. But this theory would not work. The agent was obliged to me for my warning, but told me that the rent had been paid in advance. Then I made my way to town and called at the Spanish Embassy. The man was unknown there. After this I went to see Melville, at whose house I had first met Garcia, but I found that he really knew rather less about him than I did. Finally, when I got your reply to my wire I came out to you, since I understand that you are a person who gives advice in difficult cases. But now, Mr. Inspector, I gather, from what you said when you entered the room, that you can carry the story on, and that some tragedy has occurred. I can assure you that every word I have said is the truth, and that, outside of what I have told you, I know absolutely nothing about the fate of this man. My only desire is to help the law in every possible way."

"I am sure of it, Mr. Scott Eccles—I am sure of it," said Inspector Gregson, in a very amiable tone. "I am bound to say that everything which you have said agrees very closely with the facts as they have come to our notice. For example, there was that note which arrived during dinner. Did you chance to observe what became of it?"

"Yes, I did. Garcia rolled it up and threw it into the fire."

"What do you say to that, Mr. Baynes?"

The country detective was a stout, puffy, red man, whose face was only redeemed from grossness by two extraordinarily bright eyes, almost hidden behind the heavy creases of cheek and brow. With a slow smile he drew a folded and discoloured scrap of paper from his pocket.

"It was a dog-grate, Mr. Holmes, and he over-pitched it. I picked this out unburned from the back of it."

Holmes smiled his appreciation.

" You must have examined the house very carefully to find a single pellet of paper."

" I did, Mr. Holmes. It's my way. Shall I read it, Mr. Gregson ? "

The Londoner nodded.

" The note is written upon ordinary cream-laid paper without watermark. It is a quarter-sheet. The paper is cut off in two snips with a short-bladed scissors. It has been folded over three times and sealed with purple wax, put on hurriedly and pressed down with some flat, oval object. It is addressed to Mr. Garcia, Wisteria Lodge. It says : ' Our own colours, green and white. Green **13** open, white shut. Main stair, first corridor, seventh right, green baize. God speed. D.' It is a woman's writing, done with a sharp-pointed pen, but the address is either done with another pen or by someone else. It is thicker and bolder, as you see."

" A very remarkable note," said Holmes, glancing it over. " I must compliment you, Mr. Baynes, upon your attention to detail in your examination of it. A few trifling points might perhaps be added. The oval seal is undoubtedly a plain sleeve-link—what else is of such a shape ? The scissors were bent nail-scissors. Short as the two snips are, you can distinctly see the same slight curve in each."

The country detective chuckled.

" I thought I had squeezed all the juice out of it, but I see there was a little over," he said. " I'm bound to say that I make nothing of the note except that there was something on hand, and that a woman, as usual, was at the bottom of it."

Mr. Scott Eccles had fidgeted in his seat during this conversation.

" I am glad you found the note, since it corroborates my story," said he. " But I beg to point out that I have not yet heard what has happened to Mr. Garcia, nor what has become of his household."

" As to Garcia," said Gregson, " that is easily answered. He was found dead this morning upon Oxshott Common, nearly a mile from his home. His head had been smashed **14** to pulp by heavy blows of a sand-bag or some such instrument, which had crushed rather than wounded. It is a lonely corner, and there is no house within a quarter of a mile of the spot. He had apparently been struck down first from behind, but his assailant had gone on beating him long after he was dead. It was a most furious assault. There are no footsteps nor any clue to the criminals."

" Robbed ? "

" No, there was no attempt at robbery."

" This is very painful—very painful and terrible," said Mr. Scott Eccles, in a querulous voice ; " but it is really uncommonly hard upon me. I had nothing to do with my host going off upon a nocturnal excursion and meeting so sad an end. How do I come to be mixed up with the case ? "

" Very simply, sir," Inspector Baynes answered. " The only document found in the pocket of the deceased was a letter from you saying that you would be with him on the night of his death. It was the envelope of this letter which

13 *'Our own colours, green and white.* "Green and white . . . are obviously false since they do not suit any Latin American country," Dr. Julian Wolff wrote in his *Practical Handbook of Sherlockian Heraldry.* "However, green and yellow are the colours of Brazil, and this fact furnishes a point of departure for further investigation. . . ."

14 *nearly a mile from his home.* There is Esher Common and Oxshott Heath, and Watson here seems to have combined the two. "Wisteria Lodge," it appears, lay between them, but somewhat nearer Esher than to Oxshott.

gave us the dead man's name and address. It was after nine this morning when we reached his house and found neither you nor anyone else inside it. I wired to Mr. Gregson to run you down in London while I examined Wisteria Lodge. Then I came into town, joined Mr. Gregson, and here we are."

" I think now," said Gregson, rising, " we had best put this matter into an official shape. You will come round with us to the station, Mr. Scott Eccles, and let us have your statement in writing."

" Certainly, I will come at once. But I retain your services, Mr. Holmes. I desire you to spare no expense and no pains to get at the truth."

My friend turned to the country inspector.

" I suppose that you have no objection to my collaborating with you, Mr. Baynes ? "

" Highly honoured, sir, I am sure."

" You appear to have been very prompt and business-like in all that you have done. Was there any clue, may I ask, as to the exact hour that the man met his death ? "

" He had been there since one o'clock. There was rain about that time, and his death had certainly been before the rain."

" But that is perfectly impossible, Mr. Baynes," cried our client. " His voice is unmistakable. I could swear to it that it was he who addressed me in my bedroom at that very hour."

" Remarkable, but by no means impossible," said Holmes, smiling.

" You have a clue ? " asked Gregson.

" On the face of it the case is not a very complex one, though it certainly presents some novel and interesting features. A further knowledge of facts is necessary before I would venture to give a final and definite opinion. By the way, Mr. Baynes, did you find anything remarkable besides this note in your examination of the house ? "

The detective looked at my friend in a singular way.

" There were," said he, " one or two *very* remarkable things. Perhaps when I have finished at the police-station you would care to come out and give me your opinion of them."

" I am entirely at your service," said Sherlock Holmes, ringing the bell. " You will show these gentlemen out, Mrs. Hudson, and kindly send the boy with this telegram. He is to pay a five-shilling reply."

We sat for some time in silence after our visitors had left. Holmes smoked hard, with his brows drawn down over his keen eyes, and his head thrust forward in the eager way characteristic of the man.

" Well, Watson," he asked, turning suddenly upon me, " what do you make of it ? "

" I can make nothing of this mystification of Scott Eccles."

" But the crime ? "

" Well, taken with the disappearance of the man's companions, I should say that they were in some way concerned in the murder and had fled from justice."

" That is certainly a possible point of view. On the face of it you must admit, however, that it is very strange that his two servants should have been in a conspiracy

"HE IS TO PAY A FIVE-SHILLING REPLY."

Although the crown, worth five shillings, is nowhere mentioned in the Canon, it is probable that the boy paid for the reply telegram with this coin (shown here is the Victorian "Gothic" crown.) The crown, the late A. Carson Simpson wrote in *Numismatics in the Canon*, Part I, "began as a goldpiece. Its original ancestor was the half rosenoble (or half ryal) of Edward IV's light coinage of 1464, which, however, was of short duration. It was first struck under its present name by Henry VIII as the 'crown of the double rose' in his second (Wolsey) coinage of 1526. Discontinued under Bloody Mary and William & Mary (when the angelet, or half-angel, was valued at 5/—), it was restored to the coinage by Elizabeth I and continued under the name of 'Britain crown' by James I and Charles I; it was last struck in gold under the Commonwealth. Meanwhile, Edward VI had established the *silver* crown, which has been struck by all subsequent rulers except Mary I, William & Mary and William IV. In recent times, its large size and weights have made it become unpopular, as happened also the U.S. silver dollar. It still circulated, however, in the period in which we are interested, which brings us through 1902; after that year, it was not struck again for a quarter of a century."

against him and should have attacked him on the one night when he had a guest. They had him alone at their mercy every other night in the week."

" Then why did they fly ? "

" Quite so. Why did they fly ? There is a big fact. Another big fact is the remarkable experience of our client, Scott Eccles. Now, my dear Watson, is it beyond the limits of human ingenuity to furnish an explanation which would cover both these big facts ? If it were one which would also admit of the mysterious note with its very curious phraseology, why, then it would be worth accepting as a temporary hypothesis. If the fresh facts which come to our knowledge all fit themselves into the scheme, then our hypothesis may gradually become a solution."

" But what is our hypothesis ? "

Holmes leaned back in his chair with half-closed eyes.

" You must admit, my dear Watson, that the idea of a joke is impossible. There were grave events afoot, as the sequel showed, and the coaxing of Scott Eccles to Wisteria Lodge had some connection with them."

" But what possible connection ? "

" Let us take it link by link. There is, on the face of it, something unnatural about this strange and sudden friendship between the young Spaniard and Scott Eccles. It was the former who forced the pace. He called upon Eccles at the other end of London on the very day after he first met him, and he kept in close touch with him until he got him down to Esher. Now, what did he want with Eccles ? What could Eccles supply ? I see no charm in the man. He is not particularly intelligent—not a man likely to be congenial to a quick-witted Latin. Why, then, was he picked out from all the other people whom Garcia met as particularly suited to his purpose ? Has he any one outstanding quality ? I say that he has. He is the very type of conventional British respectability, and the very man as a witness to impress another Briton. You saw yourself how neither of the inspectors dreamed of questioning his statement, extraordinary as it was."

" But what was he to witness ? "

" Nothing, as things turned out, but everything had they gone another way. That is how I read the matter."

" I see, he might have proved an alibi."

" Exactly, my dear Watson ; he might have proved an alibi. We will suppose, for argument's sake, that the household of Wisteria Lodge are confederates in some design. The attempt, whatever it may be, is to come off, we will say, before one o'clock. By some juggling of the clocks it is quite possible that they may have got Scott Eccles to bed earlier than he thought, but in any case it is likely that when Garcia went out of his way to tell him that it was one it was really not more than twelve. If Garcia could do whatever he had to do and be back by the hour mentioned he had evidently a powerful reply to any accusation. Here was this irreproachable Englishman ready to swear in any court of law that the accused was in his house all the time. It was an insurance against the worst."

" Yes, yes, I see that. But how about the disappearance of the others ? "

" I have not all my facts yet, but I do not think there

HE TOSSED IT ACROSS WITH A LAUGH.

Illustration by Arthur Twidle for the *Strand Magazine*, September, 1908.

15 *Rev. Joshua Stone, Nether Walsling*." "What is a parson doing in a 'large house' that is not his vicarage or rectory?" the Reverend Otis R. Rice asked in "Clergymen in the Canon." "You may say that the Reverend Mister Stone (or the Reverend Father Stone, if he had high church proclivities as is strongly to be suspected) had married a woman of large means and had graciously accepted the house at her hands or her family's. There is a remote possibility that he himself might have inherited the property upon the death of an older childless brother or brothers. But so rarely does this happen to a member of the clergy that one may justly be skeptical. Whatever the circumstances it is scarcely edifying to learn that one who preaches or should preach the virtues of simplicity and unostentation is himself living in a 'large house' classed by the local agents with those inhabited by a Lord, a Knight, a Justice of the Peace and two men of wealth . . ."

16 *the Bull*. The only fair-sized hotel in Esher is the *Bear*.

are any insuperable difficulties. Still, it is an error to argue in front of your data. You find yourself insensibly twisting them round to fit your theories."

" And the message ? "

" How did it run ? ' Our own colours, green and white.' Sounds like racing. ' Green open, white shut.' That is clearly a signal. ' Main stair, first corridor, seventh right, green baize.' This is an assignation. We may find a jealous husband at the bottom of it all. It was clearly a dangerous quest. She would not have said ' God speed ' had it not been so. ' D '—that should be a guide."

" The man was a Spaniard. I suggest that ' D ' stands for Dolores, a common female name in Spain."

" Good, Watson, very good—but quite inadmissible. A Spaniard would write to a Spaniard in Spanish. The writer of this note is certainly English. Well, we can only possess our souls in patience, until this excellent inspector comes back for us. Meanwhile we can thank our lucky fate which has rescued us for a few short hours from the insufferable fatigues of idleness."

An answer had arrived to Holmes' telegram before our Surrey officer had returned. Holmes read it, and was about to place it in his notebook when he caught a glimpse of my expectant face. He tossed it across with a laugh.

" We are moving in exalted circles," said he.

The telegram was a list of names and addresses : " Lord Harringby, The Dingle ; Sir George Folliott, Oxshott Towers ; Mr. Hynes Hynes, J.P., Purdey Place ; Mr. James Baker Williams, Forton Old Hall ; Mr. Henderson, 15 High Gable ; Rev. Joshua Stone, Nether Walsling."

" This is a very obvious way of limiting our field of operations," said Holmes. " No doubt Baynes, with his methodical mind, has already adopted some similar plan."

" I don't quite understand."

" Well, my dear fellow, we have already arrived at the conclusion that the message received by Garcia at dinner was an appointment or an assignation. Now, if the obvious reading of it is correct, and in order to keep this tryst one has to ascend a main stair and seek the seventh door in a corridor, it is perfectly clear that the house is a very large one. It is equally certain that this house cannot be more than a mile or two from Oxshott, since Garcia was walking in that direction, and hoped, according to my reading of the facts, to be back in Wisteria Lodge in time to avail himself of an alibi, which would only be valid up to one o'clock. As the number of large houses close to Oxshott must be limited, I adopted the obvious method of sending to the agents mentioned by Scott Eccles and obtaining a list of them. Here they are in this telegram, and the other end of our tangled skein must lie among them."

It was nearly six o'clock before we found ourselves in the pretty Surrey village of Esher, with Inspector Baynes as our companion.

Holmes and I had taken things for the night, and found 16 comfortable quarters at the Bull. Finally we set out in the company of the detective on our visit to Wisteria Lodge. It was a cold, dark March evening, with a sharp wind and a fine rain beating upon our faces, a fit setting for the wild common over which our road passed and the tragic goal to which it led us.

II—THE TIGER OF SAN PEDRO

A cold and melancholy walk of a couple of miles brought us to a high wooden gate, which opened into a gloomy avenue of chestnuts. The curved and shadowed drive led us to a low, dark house, pitch-black against a slate-coloured sky. From the front window upon the left of the door there peeped a glimmer of a feeble light.

" There's a constable in possession," said Baynes. " I'll knock at the window." He stepped across the grass plot and tapped with his hand on the pane. Through the fogged glass I dimly saw a man spring up from a chair beside the fire, and heard a sharp cry from within the room. An instant later a white-faced, hard-breathing policeman had opened the door, the candle wavering in his trembling hand.

" What's the matter, Walters ? " asked Baynes, sharply.

The man mopped his forehead with his handkerchief and gave a long sigh of relief.

" I am glad you have come, sir. It has been a long evening and I don't think my nerve is as good as it was."

" Your nerve, Walters ? I should not have thought you had a nerve in your body."

" Well, sir, it's this lonely, silent house and the queer thing in the kitchen. Then when you tapped at the window I thought it had come again."

" That what had come again ? "

" The devil, sir, for all I know. It was at the window."

" What was at the window, and when ? "

" It was just about two hours ago. The light was just fading. I was sitting reading in the chair. I don't know what made me look up, but there was a face looking in at me through the lower pane. Lord, sir, what a face it was ! I'll see it in my dreams."

" Tut, tut, Walters ! This is not talk for a police-constable."

" I know, sir, I know ; but it shook me, sir, and there's no use to deny it. It wasn't black, sir, nor was it white, nor any colour that I know, but a kind of queer shade like clay with a splash of milk in it. Then there was the size of it—it was twice yours, sir. And the look of it—the great staring goggle eyes, and the line of white teeth like a hungry beast. I tell you, sir, I couldn't move a finger, nor get my breath, till it whisked away and was gone. Out I ran and through the shrubbery, but thank God there was no one there."

" If I didn't know you were a good man, Walters, I should put a black mark against you for this. If it were the devil himself a constable on duty should never thank

". . . THERE WAS A FACE LOOKING IN AT ME THROUGH THE LOWER PANE."

Illustration by Arthur Twidle for the *Strand Magazine*, October, 1908.

God that he could not lay his hands upon him. I suppose the whole thing is not a vision and a touch of nerves?"

"That, at least, is very easily settled," said Holmes, lighting his little pocket lantern. "Yes," he reported, after a short examination of the grass bed, "a number twelve shoe, I should say. If he was all on the same scale as his foot he must certainly have been a giant."

"What became of him?"

"He seems to have broken through the shrubbery and made for the road."

"Well," said the inspector, with a grave and thoughtful face, "whoever he may have been, and whatever he may have wanted, he's gone for the present, and we have more immediate things to attend to. Now, Mr. Holmes, with your permission, I will show you round the house."

The various bedrooms and sitting-rooms had yielded nothing to a careful search. Apparently the tenants had brought little or nothing with them, and all the furniture down to the smallest details had been taken over with the house. A good deal of clothing with the stamp of Marx & Co., High Holborn, had been left behind. Telegraphic inquiries had been already made which showed that Marx knew nothing of his customer save that he was a good payer. Odds and ends, some pipes, a few novels, two of them in Spanish, an old-fashioned pinfire revolver, and a guitar were amongst the personal property.

"Nothing in all this," said Baynes, stalking, candle in hand, from room to room. "But now, Mr. Holmes, I invite your attention to the kitchen."

It was a gloomy, high-ceilinged room at the back of the house, with a straw litter in one corner, which served apparently as a bed for the cook. The table was piled with half-eaten dishes and dirty plates, the debris of last night's dinner.

"Look at this," said Baynes. "What do you make of it?"

He held up his candle before an extraordinary object which stood at the back of the dresser. It was so wrinkled

HE HELD UP HIS CANDLE BEFORE AN
EXTRAORDINARY OBJECT . . .

Illustration by Frederic Dorr Steele for *Collier's Magazine*, August 15, 1908. Arthur Twidle illustrated the same scene for the *Strand Magazine*, October, 1908.

and shrunken and withered that it was difficult to say what it might have been.   One could but say that it was black and leathery and that it bore some resemblance to a dwarfish human figure.   At first, as I examined it, I thought that it was a mummified negro baby, and then it seemed a very twisted and ancient monkey.   Finally I was left in doubt as to whether it was animal or human.   A double band of white shells was strung round the centre of it.

" Very interesting — very interesting indeed ! " said Holmes peering at this sinister relic.   " Anything more ? "

In silence Baynes led the way to the sink and held forward his candle.   The limbs and body of some large white bird, torn savagely to pieces with the feathers still on, were littered all over it.   Holmes pointed to the wattles on the severed head.

" A white cock," said he ;   " most interesting !   It is really a very curious case."

But Mr. Baynes had kept his most sinister exhibit to the last.   From under the sink he drew a zinc pail which contained a quantity of blood.   Then from the table he took a platter heaped with small pieces of charred bone.

" Something has been killed and something has been burned.   We raked all these out of the fire.   We had a doctor in this morning.   He says that they are not human."

Holmes smiled and rubbed his hands.

" I must congratulate you, inspector, on handling so distinctive and instructive a case.   Your powers, if I may say so without offence, seem superior to your opportunities."

Inspector Baynes' small eyes twinkled with pleasure.

" You're right, Mr. Holmes.   We stagnate in the provinces.   A case of this sort gives a man a chance, and I hope that I shall take it.   What do you make of these bones ? "

" A lamb, I should say, or a kid."

" And the white cock ? "

" Curious, Mr. Baynes, very curious.   I should say almost unique."

" Yes, sir, there must have been some very strange people with some very strange ways in this house.   One of them is dead.   Did his companions follow him and kill him ?   If they did we should have them, for every port is watched.   But my own views are different.   Yes, sir, my own views are very different."

" You have a theory, then ? "

" And I'll work it myself, Mr. Holmes.   It's only due to my own credit to do so.   Your name is made, but I have still to make mine.   I should be glad to be able to say afterwards that I had solved it without your help."

Holmes laughed good-humouredly.

" Well, well, inspector," said he.   " Do you follow your path and I will follow mine.   My results are always very much at your service if you care to apply to me for them.   I think that I have seen all that I wish in this house, and that my time may be more profitably employed elsewhere.   *Au revoir* and good luck ! "

I could tell by numerous subtle signs, which might have been lost upon anyone but myself, that Holmes was on a hot scent.   As impassive as ever to the casual observer,

FROM UNDER THE SINK HE DREW A ZINC PAIL . . .

Illustration by Arthur Twidle for the *Strand Magazine*, October, 1908.

17 *Day succeeded day*. A curious feature of this adventure is Watson's complete silence about his wife. We find him living at Baker Street once more, and not for a few days only: the case occupies almost a week. Neither does he mention his professional duties. His reticence about Mrs. Watson is not confined to this tale alone: in the story which follows, "Silver Blaze," and later, in "The Adventure of the Beryl Coronet," she is never once referred to. "Mr. S. C. Roberts has suggested that at about this period Mrs. Watson's health had begun to fail," the late H. W. Bell wrote in *Sherlock Holmes and Dr. Watson: The Chronology of Their Adventures*. "It may well be that her illness, which resulted fatally some three years later, had just been diagnosed, and that she had gone away to a sanatorium. What more natural, then, that Watson, in his loneliness and sorrow, should have returned for a while to Baker Street, leaving his patients, not for the first time, in the care of his neighbour, until he had recovered some measure of self-control."

18 *He prowled about with this equipment himself*. "It may be remarked that the only occasion Holmes ever noticed flowers was when he spoke of the beauty of a rose at the time of 'The Adventure of the Naval Treaty,'" Mr. Humfrey Michell wrote in "The Sartorial Sherlock Holmes," "and, as we well know, that remark was not prompted by a love of nature. Can we really believe that he would deceive a child when he prowled about with a spud, a tin box and an elementary book on botany during his singularly inept investigation of ['The Adventure of Wisteria Lodge']? Assuredly that strange story should be classed among the Apocrypha."

there were none the less a subdued eagerness and suggestion of tension in his brightened eyes and brisker manner which assured me that the game was afoot. After his habit he said nothing, and after mine I asked no questions. Sufficient for me to share the sport and lend my humble help to the capture without distracting that intent brain with needless interruption. All would come round to me in due time.

I waited, therefore—but, to my ever-deepening disappointment I waited in vain. **17** Day succeeded day, and my friend took no step forward. One morning he spent in town, and I learned from a casual reference that he had visited the British Museum. Save for this one excursion, he spent his days in long, and often solitary walks, or in chatting with a number of village gossips whose acquaintance he had cultivated.

"I'm sure, Watson, a week in the country will be invaluable to you," he remarked. "It is very pleasant to see the first green shoots upon the hedges and the catkins on the hazels once again. With a spud, a tin box, and an elementary book on botany, there are instructive days to be spent." He prowled about with this equipment himself, **18** but it was a poor show of plants which he would bring back of an evening.

Occasionally in our rambles we came across Inspector Baynes. His fat, red face wreathed itself in smiles and his small eyes glittered as he greeted my companion. He said little about the case, but from that little we gathered that he also was not dissatisfied at the course of events. I must admit, however, that I was somewhat surprised when, some five days after the crime, I opened my morning paper to find in large letters:

"THE OXSHOTT MYSTERY
A SOLUTION
ARREST OF SUPPOSED ASSASSIN."

Holmes sprang in his chair as if he had been stung when I read the head-lines.

"By Jove!" he cried. You don't mean that Baynes has got him?"

"Apparently," said I, as I read the following report:

"Great excitement was caused in Esher and the neighbouring district when it was learned late last night that an arrest had been effected in connection with the Oxshott murder. It will be remembered that Mr. Garcia, of Wisteria Lodge, was found dead on Oxshott Common, his body showing signs of extreme violence, and that on the same night his servant and his cook fled, which appeared to show their participation in the crime. It was suggested, but never proved, that the deceased gentleman may have had valuables in the house, and that their abstraction was the motive of the crime. Every effort was made by Inspector Baynes, who has the case in hand, to ascertain the hiding-place of the fugitives, and he had good reason to believe that they had not gone far, but were lurking in some retreat which had been already prepared. It was certain from the first, however, that they would eventually be detected, as the cook, from the evidence of one or two tradespeople who have caught a glimpse of him through the window, was a man of most remarkable appearance—being a huge and hideous mulatto, with yellowish features of a pronounced negroid type. This man has been seen since the crime, for he was detected and pursued by Constable Walters on the same evening, when he had the audacity to revisit Wisteria Lodge. Inspector Baynes, considering that such a visit must have some purpose in view, and was likely, therefore, to be repeated, abandoned the house, but left an ambuscade in the shrubbery. The man walked into the trap, and was captured last night after a struggle in which Constable Downing was badly bitten by the savage. We understand that when the prisoner is brought before the magistrates a remand will be applied for by the police, and **19** that great developments are hoped from his capture."

"Really we must see Baynes at once," cried Holmes, picking up his hat. "We will just catch him before he starts." We hurried down the village street and found, as we had expected, that the inspector was just leaving his lodgings.

"You've seen the paper, Mr. Holmes ? " he asked, holding one out to us.

"Yes, Baynes, I've seen it. Pray don't think it a liberty if I give you a word of friendly warning."

"Of warning, Mr. Holmes ? "

"I have looked into this case with some care, and I am not convinced that you are on the right lines. I don't want you to commit yourself too far, unless you are sure."

"You're very kind, Mr. Holmes."

"I assure you I speak for your good."

It seemed to me that something like a wink quivered for an instant over one of Mr. Baynes' tiny eyes.

"We agreed to work on our own lines, Mr. Holmes. That's what I am doing."

"Oh, very good," said Holmes. "Don't blame me."

"No, sir ; I believe you mean well by me. But we all have our own systems, Mr. Holmes. You have yours, and maybe I have mine."

"Let us say no more about it."

"You're welcome always to my news. This fellow is a perfect savage, as strong as a cart-horse and as fierce as the devil. He chewed Downing's thumb nearly off before they could master him. He hardly speaks a word of English, and we can get nothing out of him but grunts."

"And you think you have evidence that he murdered his late master ? "

"I didn't say so, Mr. Holmes ; I didn't say so. We all have our little ways. You try yours and I will try mine. That's the agreement."

Holmes shrugged his shoulders as we walked away together. "I can't make the man out. He seems to be riding for a fall. Well, as he says, we must each try our own way and see what comes of it. But there's something in Inspector Baynes which I can't quite understand."

"Just sit down in that chair, Watson," said Sherlock Holmes, when we had returned to our apartment at the Bull. "I want to put you in touch with the situation, as I may need your help to-night. Let me show you the evolution of this case, so far as I have been able to follow it. Simple as it has been in its leading features, it has none the less presented surprising difficulties in the way of an arrest. There are gaps in that direction which we have still to fill.

"We will go back to the note which was handed in to Garcia upon the evening of his death. We may put aside

19 *a remand.* A judicial order for recommittal.

"THE MAN WALKED INTO THE TRAP . . ."

Illustration by Arthur Twidle for the *Strand Magazine*, October, 1908.

this idea of Baynes' that Garcia's servants were concerned in the matter. The proof of this lies in the fact that it was *he* who had arranged for the presence of Scott Eccles, which could only have been done for the purpose of an alibi. It was Garcia, then, who had an enterprise, and apparently a criminal enterprise, in hand that night, in the course of which he met his death. I say criminal because only a man with a criminal enterprise desires to establish an alibi. Who, then, is most likely to have taken his life ? Surely the person against whom the criminal enterprise was directed. So far it seems to me that we are on safe ground.

"We can now see a reason for the disappearance of Garcia's household. They were *all* confederates in the same unknown crime. If it came off then Garcia returned, any possible suspicion would be warded off by the Englishman's evidence, and all would be well. But the attempt was a dangerous one, and if Garcia did *not* return by a certain hour it was probable that his own life had been sacrificed. It had been arranged, therefore, that in such a case his two subordinates were to make for some prearranged spot, where they could escape investigation and be in a position afterwards to renew their attempt. That would fully explain the facts, would it not ? "

The whole inexplicable tangle seemed to straighten out before me. I wondered, as I always did, how it had not been obvious to me before.

" But why should one servant return ? "

" We can imagine that, in the confusion of flight, something precious, something which he could not bear to part with, had been left behind. That would explain his persistence, would it not ? "

" Well, what is the next step ? "

" The next step is the note received by Garcia at the dinner. It indicates a confederate at the other end. Now, where was the other end ? I have already shown you that it could only lie in some large house, and that the number of large houses is limited. My first days in this village were devoted to a series of walks, in which in the intervals of my botanical researches I made a reconnaissance of all the large houses and an examination of the family history of the occupants. One house, and only one, riveted my attention. It is the famous old Jacobean grange of High Gable, one mile on the farther side of Oxshott, and less than half a mile from the scene of the tragedy. The other mansions belonged to prosaic and respectable people who live far aloof from romance. But Mr. Henderson, of High Gable, was by all accounts a curious man, to whom curious adventures might befall. I concentrated my attention, therefore, upon him and his household.

" A singular set of people, Watson—the man himself the most singular of them all. I managed to see him on a plausible pretext, but I seemed to read in his dark, deepset, brooding eyes that he was perfectly aware of my true business. He is a man of fifty, strong, active, with iron-grey hair, great bunched black eyebrows, the step of a deer, and the air of an emperor—a fierce, masterful man, with a red-hot spirit behind his parchment face. He is either a foreigner or has lived long in the Tropics, for he is yellow and sapless, but tough as whipcord.   His friend and secretary, Mr. Lucas, is undoubtedly a foreigner, chocolate brown, wily, suave and cat-like with a poisonous gentleness of speech.   You see, Watson, we have come already upon two sets of foreigners—one at Wisteria Lodge and one at High Gable—so our gaps are beginning to close.

" These two men, close and confidential friends, are the centre of the household ; but there is one other person, who for our immediate purpose may be even more important.   Henderson has two children—girls of eleven and thirteen.   Their governess is a Miss Burnet, an Englishwoman of forty or thereabouts.   There is also one confidential man-servant.   This little group forms the real family, for they travel about together, and Henderson is a great traveller, always on the move.   It is only within the last few weeks that he has returned, after a year's absence, to High Gable.   I may add that he is enormously rich, and whatever his whims may be he can very easily satisfy them.   For the rest, his house is full of butlers, footmen, maid-servants, and the usual overfed, underworked staff of a large English country-house.

" So much I learned partly from village gossip and partly from my own observation.   There are no better instruments than discharged servants with a grievance, and I was lucky enough to find one.   I call it luck, but it would not have come my way had I not been looking out for it.   As Baynes remarks, we all have our systems.   It was my system which enabled me to find John Warner, late gardener of High Gable, sacked in a moment of temper by his imperious employer.   He in turn had friends among the indoor servants, who unite in their fear and dislike of their master.   So I had my key to the secrets of the establishment.

" Curious people, Watson !   I don't pretend to understand it all yet, but very curious people anyway.   It's a double-winged house, and the servants live on one side, the family on the other.   There's no link between the two save for Henderson's own servant, who serves the family's meals.   Everything is carried to a certain door, which forms the one connection.   Governess and children hardly go out at all, except into the garden.   Henderson never by any chance walks alone.   His dark secretary is like his shadow.   The gossip among the servants is that their master is terribly afraid of something.   ' Sold his soul to the devil in exchange for money,' says Warner, ' and expects his creditor to come up and claim his own.'   Where they came from, or who they are, nobody has an idea.   They are very violent.   Twice Henderson has lashed at folk with his dog-whip, and only his long purse and heavy compensation have kept him out of the courts.

" Well, now, Watson, let us judge the situation by this new information.   We may take it that the letter came out of this strange household, and was an invitation to Garcia to carry out some attempt which had already been planned.   Who wrote the note ?   It was someone within the citadel, and it was a woman.   Who then, but Miss Burnet, the governess ?   All our reasoning seems to point that way.   At any rate, we may take it as a hypothesis, and see what consequences it would entail.   I may add that Miss

Burnet's age and character make it certain that my first idea that there might be a love interest in our story is out of the question.

"'If she wrote the note she was presumably the friend and confederate of Garcia. What, then, might she be expected to do if she heard of his death ? If he met it in some nefarious enterprise her lips might be sealed. Still, in her heart she must retain bitterness and hatred against those who had killed him, and would presumably help so far as she could to have revenge upon them. Could we see her, then, and try to use her ? That was my first thought. But now we come to a sinister fact. Miss Burnet has not been seen by any human eye since the night of the murder. From that evening she has utterly vanished. Is she alive ? Has she perhaps met her end on the same night as the friend whom she had summoned ? Or is she merely a prisoner ? There is the point which we still have to decide.

" You will appreciate the difficulty of the situation, Watson. There is nothing upon which we can apply for a warrant. Our whole scheme might seem fantastic if laid before a magistrate. The woman's disappearance counts for nothing, since in that extraordinary household any member of it might be invisible for a week. And yet she may at the present moment be in danger of her life. All I can do is to watch the house and leave my agent, Warner, on guard at the gates. We can't let such a situation continue. If the law can do nothing we must take the risk ourselves."

" What do you suggest ? "

" I know which is her room. It is accessible from the top of an outhouse. My suggestion is that you and I go to-night and see if we can strike at the very heart of the mystery."

It was not, I must confess, a very alluring prospect. The old house with its atmosphere of murder, the singular and formidable inhabitants, the unknown dangers of the approach, and the fact that we were putting ourselves legally in a false position, all combined to damp my ardour. But there was something in the ice-cold reasoning of Holmes which made it impossible to shrink from any adventure which he might recommend. One knew that thus, and only thus, could a solution be found. I clasped his hand in silence, and the die was cast.

But it was not destined that our investigation should have so adventurous an ending. It was about five o'clock, and the shadows of the March evening were beginning to fall, when an excited rustic rushed into our room.

" They've gone, Mr. Holmes. They went by the last train. The lady broke away, and I've got her in a cab downstairs."

" Excellent, Warner ! " cried Holmes, springing to his feet. " Watson, the gaps are closing rapidly."

In the cab was a woman, half-collapsed from nervous exhaustion. She bore upon her aquiline and emaciated face the traces of some recent tragedy. Her head hung listlessly upon her breast, but as she raised it and turned her dull eyes upon us, I saw that her pupils were dark dots in the centre of the broad grey iris. She was drugged with opium.

"I watched at the gate, same as you advised, Mr. Holmes," said our emissary, the discharged gardener. "When the carriage came out I followed it to the station. She was like one walking in her sleep ; but when they tried to get her into the train she came to life and struggled. They pushed her into the carriage. She fought her way out again. I took her part, got her into a cab, and here we are. I shan't forget the face at the carriage window as I led her away. I'd have a short life if he had his way—the black-eyed, scowling, yellow devil."

We carried her upstairs, laid her on the sofa, and a couple of cups of the strongest coffee soon cleared her brain from the mists of the drug. Baynes had been summoned by Holmes, and the situation rapidly explained to him.

"Why, sir, you've got me the very evidence I want," said the inspector, warmly, shaking my friend by the hand. "I was on the same scent as you from the first."

"What! You were after Henderson?"

"Why, Mr. Holmes, when you were crawling in the shrubbery at High Gable I was up one of the trees in the plantation and saw you down below. It was just who would get his evidence first."

"Then why did you arrest the mulatto?"

Baynes chuckled.

"I was sure Henderson, as he calls himself, felt that he was suspected, and that he would lie low and make no move so long as he thought he was in any danger. I arrested the wrong man to make him believe that our eyes were off him. I knew he would be likely to clear off then and give us a chance of getting at Miss Burnet."

Holmes laid his hand upon the inspector's shoulder.

"You will rise high in your profession. You have instinct and intuition," said he.

Baynes flushed with pleasure.

"I've had a plain-clothes man waiting at the station all the week. Wherever the High Gable folk go he will keep them in sight. But he must have been hard put to it when Miss Burnet broke away. However, your man picked her up, and it all ends well. We can't arrest without her evidence, that is clear, so the sooner we get a statement the better."

"Every minute she gets stronger," said Holmes, glancing at the governess. "But tell me, Baynes, who is this man Henderson?"

"Henderson," the inspector answered, "is Don Murillo, once called the Tiger of San Pedro."

The Tiger of San Pedro! The whole history of the man came back to me in a flash. He had made his name as the most lewd and bloodthirsty tyrant that had ever governed any country with a pretence to civilization. Strong, fearless, and energetic, he had sufficient virtue to enable him to impose his odious vices upon a cowering people for ten or twelve years. His name was a terror through all Central America. At the end of that time there was a universal rising against him. But he was as cunning as he was cruel, and at the first whisper of coming trouble he had secretly conveyed his treasures aboard a ship which was manned by devoted adherents. It was an empty palace which was stormed by the insurgents next day. The Dictator, his two children, his secretary, and

"SHE FOUGHT HER WAY OUT AGAIN."

Illustration by Arthur Twidle for the *Strand Magazine*, October, 1908.

20 *"Yes, sir; Don Murillo, the Tiger of San Pedro."* "The Emperor of Brazil was deposed in 1889 and spent the rest of his life in Europe, where he died [December 5, 1891]," Dr. Julian Wolff wrote in his *Practical Handbook of Sherlockian Heraldry.* "It is all so absurdly simple now. Don Murillo, the Tiger of San Pedro, was actually Dom Pedro II, the last Emperor of Brazil! One explanation has to be made, since Dom Pedro never was a tyrant. It must be remembered that Holmes and Watson received their information from a member of the opposition, Signora Victor Durando [*see below*]. Anyone who has read the opposition's opinions of our best and wisest men will easily understand."

21 *"They discovered him a year ago."* Don Murillo's ship had docked in Barcelona in 1886. His enemies had "been looking for him all the time for revenge, but it is only now that they have begun to find him out." "They discovered him a year ago." From this statement, the year cannot be earlier than 1887, and is probably several years after that.

"HE AND HIS MASTER DRAGGED ME TO MY ROOM . . ."

Illustration by Arthur Twidle for the *Strand Magazine*, October, 1908. Frederic Dorr Steele illustrated much the same scene for *Collier's Magazine*, August 15, 1908.

his wealth had all escaped them. From that moment he had vanished from the world, and his identity had been a frequent subject for comment in the European Press.

20 " Yes, sir ; Don Murillo, the Tiger of San Pedro," said Baynes. " If you look it up you will find that the San Pedro colours are green and white, same as in the note, Mr. Holmes. Henderson he called himself, but I traced him back, Paris and Rome and Madrid to Barcelona, where his ship came in in '86. They've been looking for him all the time for their revenge, but it is only now that they have begun to find him out."

21 " They discovered him a year ago," said Miss Burnet, who had sat up and was now intently following the conversation. " Once already his life has been attempted ; but some evil spirit shielded him. Now, again, it is the noble, chivalrous Garcia who has fallen, while the monster goes safe. But another will come, and yet another, until some day justice will be done ; that is as certain as the rise of to-morrow's sun." Her thin hands clenched, and her worn face blanched with the passion of her hatred.

" But how come you into this matter, Miss Burnet ? " asked Holmes. " How can an English lady join in such a murderous affair ? "

" I join in it because there is no other way in the world by which justice can be gained. What does the law of England care for the rivers of blood shed years ago in San Pedro, or for the ship-load of treasure which this man has stolen ? To you they are like crimes committed in some other planet. But *we* know. We have learned the truth in sorrow and in suffering. To us there is no fiend in hell like Juan Murillo, and no peace in life while his victims still cry for vengeance."

" No doubt," said Holmes, "he was as you say. I have heard that he was atrocious. But how are you affected ? "

" I will tell you it all. This villain's policy was to murder, on one pretext or another, every man who showed such promise that he might in time come to be a dangerous rival. My husband—yes, my real name is Signora Victor Durando—was the San Pedro Minister in London. He met me and married me there. A nobler man never lived upon earth. Unhappily, Murillo heard of his excellence, recalled him on some pretext, and had him shot. With a premonition of his fate he had refused to take me with him. His estates were confiscated, and I was left with a pittance and a broken heart.

" Then came the downfall of the tyrant. He escaped as you have just described. But the many whose lives he had ruined, whose nearest and dearest had suffered torture and death at his hands, would not let the matter rest. They banded themselves into a society which should never be dissolved until the work was done. It was my part after we had discovered in the transformed Henderson the fallen despot, to attach myself to his household and keep the others in touch with his movements. This I was able to do by securing the position of governess in his family. He little knew that the woman who faced him at every meal was the woman whose husband he had hurried at an hour's notice into eternity. I smiled on him, did my duty to his children, and bided my time. An attempt was made in Paris, and failed.   We zigzagged swiftly here and there over Europe, to throw off the pursuers, and finally returned to this house, which he had taken upon his first arrival in England.

" But here also the ministers of justice were waiting. Knowing that he would return there, Garcia, who is the son of the former highest dignitary in San Pedro, was waiting with two trusty companions of humble station, all three fired with the same reasons for revenge.   He could do little during the day, for Murillo took every precaution, and never went out save with his satellite Lucas, or Lopez as he was known in the days of his greatness.   At night, however, he slept alone, and the avenger might find him. On a certain evening, which had been prearranged, I sent my friend final instructions, for the man was for ever on the alert, and continually changed his room.   I was to see that the doors were open and the signal of a green or white light in a window which faced the drive was to give notice if all was safe, or if the attempt had better be postponed.

" But everything went wrong with us.   In some way I had excited the suspicion of Lopez, the secretary.   He crept up behind me, and sprang upon me just as I had finished the note.   He and his master dragged me to my room, and held judgment upon me as a convicted traitress. Then and there they would have plunged their knives into me, could they have seen how to escape the consequence of the deed.   Finally, after much debate, they concluded that my murder was too dangerous.   But they determined to get rid for ever of Garcia.   They had gagged me, and Murillo twisted my arm round until I gave him the address.   I swear that he might have twisted it off had I understood what it would mean to Garcia.   Lopez addressed the note which I had written, sealed it with his sleeve-link, and sent it by the hand of the servant, José. How they murdered him I do not know, save that it was Murillo's hand who struck him down, for Lopez had remained to guard me.   I believe he must have waited among the gorse bushes through which the path winds and struck him down as he passed.   At first they were of a mind to let him enter the house and to kill him as a detected burglar ; but they argued that if they were mixed up in an inquiry their own identity would at once be publicly disclosed and they would be open to further attacks.   With the death of Garcia the pursuit might cease, since such a death might frighten others from the task.

" All would now have been well for them had it not been for my knowledge of what they had done.   I have no doubt that there were times when my life hung in the balance.   I was confined to my room, terrorized by the most horrible threats, cruelly ill-used to break my spirit— see this stab on my shoulder and the bruises from end to end of my arms—and a gag was thrust into my mouth on the one occasion when I tried to call from the window. For five days this cruel imprisonment continued, with hardly enough food to hold body and soul together.   This afternoon a good lunch was brought me, but the moment **22** after I took it I knew that I had been drugged.   In a sort of dream I remember being half-led, half-carried to the carriage ; in the same state I was conveyed to the train.

22 *This afternoon a good lunch was brought me.* The first day of the case was not a Sunday: Mr. Scott Eccles "went to the house agents" before he called on Holmes. Nor was it a Tuesday: the crime took place shortly before one o'clock of the day on which Mr. Eccles called on Holmes; "five days after the crime," Watson "opened my morning paper." Watson's "five days" is corroborated by Holmes himself: the mulatto tried to recover his fetish, without success, on the night of the first day; "He waited three days longer, and then his piety or his superstitition drove him to try once more"; the mulatto's second attempt to recover his fetish was therefore on the fifth day of the story; he was taken on that occasion by Baynes, and Watson read an account of the capture in the morning newspaper of the sixth day—"five days after the [day of the] crime," as he tells us. The first day of the case and the sixth day of the case must fall within the same week, for Baynes says: "I've had a plain-clothes man at the station all week." Since the first day of the case was not Sunday or Tuesday, it must therefore have been Monday. More, Mr. Eccles said on the first day: "Quarter-day [March 25th] is at hand." The Monday on which the case began must therefore fall on March 24th or a very few days earlier.

We have seen (Note 2) that March, 1890, is the earliest possible date for "The Adventure of Wisteria Lodge." The latest possible date is the summer of 1895, for Watson tells us that one of the cases which enlivened the months between Holmes' Return (April 1894) and "The Adventure of the Norwood Builder" (August, 1895) was that of "the papers of ex-President Murillo." This case cannot *be* "The Adventure of Wisteria Lodge," which had nothing to do with "papers," a word stressed by Watson. Watson's statement must rather refer to a case arising from papers discovered after the murder of the Tiger of San Pedro, an event that took place at the Hotel Escurial in Madrid "some six months" after Holmes concluded his part in "The Adventure of Wisteria Lodge."

The month cannot be March, 1891, for in that month, as we shall see, Holmes and Watson shared no case. It cannot be March, 1892, or March, 1893, years of the Great Hiatus. Nor can it be March, 1894—Holmes did not return to England until April of that year. March, 1895, is also ruled out: Holmes, as we shall see, spent "some weeks"— from mid-March till after the first week in April— in a University town, studying English charters ("The Adventure of the Three Students"). The month must therefore have been *March, 1890*, and the Monday *the 24th*.

23 *our legal work begins.*" Perhaps another indication that Holmes was, in fact, a lawyer as well as a private investigator.

24 *Guildford.* A town in Surrey identified with the Astolat of Arthurian legend; the grave of Lewis Carroll is in Guildford.

"A CHAOTIC CASE, MY DEAR WATSON," SAID HOLMES, OVER AN EVENING PIPE.

Cover illustration by Frederic Dorr Steele for *Collier's Magazine*, August 15, 1908.

Only then, when the wheels were almost moving did I suddenly realize that my liberty lay in my own hands. I sprang out, they tried to drag me back, and had it not been for the help of this good man, who led me to the cab, I should never have broken away. Now, thank God, I am beyond their power for ever."

We had all listened intently to this remarkable statement. It was Holmes who broke the silence.

" Our difficulties are not over," he remarked, shaking his head. " Our police work ends, but our legal work **23** begins."

" Exactly," said I. " A plausible lawyer could make it out as an act of self-defence. There may be a hundred crimes in the background, but it is only on this one that they can be tried."

" Come, come," said Baynes, cheerily ; " I think better of the law than that. Self-defence is one thing. To entice a man in cold blood with the object of murdering him is another, whatever danger you may fear from him. No, no ; we shall all be justified when we see the tenants **24** of High Gable at the next Guildford Assizes."

It is a matter of history, however, that a little time was still to elapse before the Tiger of San Pedro should meet with his deserts. Wily and bold, he and his companion threw their pursuer off their track by entering a lodging-house in Edmonton Street and leaving by the back-gate into Curzon Square. From that day they were seen no more in England. Some six months afterwards the Marquess of Montalva and Signor Rulli, his secretary, were both murdered in their rooms at the Hotel Escurial at Madrid. The crime was ascribed to Nihilism, and the murderers were never arrested. Inspector Baynes visited us at Baker Street with a printed description of the dark face of the secretary, and of the masterful features, the magnetic black eyes, and the tufted brows of his master. We could not doubt that justice, if belated, had come at last.

" A chaotic case, my dear Watson," said Holmes, over an evening pipe. " It will not be possible for you to present it in that compact form which is dear to your heart. It covers two continents, concerns two groups of mysterious persons, and is further complicated by the highly respectable presence of our friend Scott Eccles, whose inclusion shows me that the deceased Garcia had a scheming mind and a well-developed instinct of self-preservation. It is remarkable only for the fact that amid a perfect jungle of possibilities we, with our worthy collaborator the inspector, have kept our close hold on the essentials and so been guided along the crooked and winding path. Is there any point which is not quite clear to you ? "

" The object of the mulatto cook's return ? "

" I think that the strange creature in the kitchen may account for it. The man was a primitive savage from the backwoods of San Pedro, and this was his fetish. When his companion and he had fled to some prearranged retreat —already occupied, no doubt, by a confederate—the companion had persuaded him to leave so compromising an article of furniture. But the mulatto's heart was with it, and he was driven back to it next day, when, on reconnoitring through the window, he found policeman Walters in possession. He waited three days longer, and then his piety or his superstition drove him to try once more. Inspector Baynes, who, with his usual astuteness, had minimized the incident before me, had really recognized its importance, and had left a trap into which the creature walked. Any other point, Watson ? ''

" The torn bird, the pail of blood, the charred bones, all the mystery of that weird kitchen ? ''

Holmes smiled as he turned up an entry in his notebook.

" I spent a morning in the British Museum reading up that and other points. Here is a quotation from Eckermann's *Voodooism and the Negroid Religions* :   **25**

" The true Voodoo-worshipper attempts nothing of importance without certain sacrifices which are intended to propitiate his unclean gods. In extreme cases these rites take the form of human sacrifices followed by cannibalism. The more usual victims are a white cock, which is plucked in pieces alive, or a black goat, whose throat is cut and body burned.

" So you see our savage friend was very orthodox in his ritual. It is grotesque, Watson,'' Holmes added, as he slowly fastened his notebook ; " but, as I have had occasion to remark, there is but one step from the grotesque to the horrible.''   **26**

25 *Eckermann's* Voodooism and the Negroid Religions. "This is a most intriguing title about which one would like to know more," Mr. Bliss Austin wrote in *A Baker Street Christmas Stocking* for 1955. "But, in spite of some considerable effort, I have never been able to find it, or even a reference to it, in any library in this country. . . . As a last resort, I decided to try the place where Holmes had seen it, or at least implied he had seen it. So last summer, during a visit to London, I followed his example by spending a morning in the British Museum. The results were completely negative. Eckermann on Voodooism is unknown there. Which leaves me with this question: Does anyone have any clew to the existence of this work, or are we to conclude that Holmes was once again pulling Watson's leg?"

26 *but one step from the grotesque to the horrible*." Holmes paraphrases Napoleon's saying: "There is but one step from the sublime to the ridiculous."

Bibliographical Note: "The Adventure of Wisteria Lodge" appeared as a title for this story only when book and omnibus editions were published: in *Collier's Magazine* for August 15, 1908, the whole story was entitled "The Singular Experience of Mr. J. Scott Eccles," and in England the *Strand* for September, 1908, called the first instalment "The Singular Experience of Mr. John Scott Eccles" and the second instalment, in October, "The Tiger of San Pedro."

". . . SACRIFICES WHICH ARE INTENDED TO PROPITIATE HIS UNCLEAN GODS."

Illustration by Arthur Twidle for the *Strand* magazine, October, 1908.

SHERLOCK HOLMES OF BAKER STREET

A painting in oils by Roy Hunt of the Council of Four, Denver, a Scion Society of the Baker Street Irregulars.

45

SILVER BLAZE

[Thursday, September 25, and Tuesday, September 30, 1890]

"I AM afraid, Watson, that I shall have to go," said Holmes, as we sat down together to our breakfast one morning.

" Go ! Where to ? "

" To Dartmoor—to King's Pyland." **1**

I was not surprised. Indeed, my only wonder was that he had not already been mixed up in this extraordinary case, which was the one topic of conversation through the length and breadth of England. For a whole day my companion had rambled about the room with his chin upon his chest and his brows knitted, charging and re-charging his pipe with the strongest black tobacco, and absolutely deaf to any of my questions or remarks. Fresh editions of every paper had been sent up by our newsagent only to be glanced over and tossed down into a corner. Yet, silent as he was, I knew perfectly well what it was over which he was brooding. There was but one problem before the public which could challenge his powers of analysis, and that was the singular disappearance of the favourite for the Wessex Cup, and **2** the tragic murder of its trainer. When, therefore, he suddenly announced his intention of setting out for the scene of the drama, it was only what I had both expected and hoped for.

" I should be most happy to go down with you if I should not be in the way," said I.

" My dear Watson, you would confer a great favour upon me by coming. And I think that your time will not be mis-spent, for there are points about this case which promise to make it an absolutely unique one. We have, I think, just time to catch our train at Paddington, and I will go further into the matter upon our journey. You would oblige me by bringing with you your very excellent field-glass."

And so it happened that an hour or so later I found myself in the corner of a first-class carriage, flying along, **3** *en route* for Exeter, while Sherlock Holmes, with his

1 *to King's Pyland.*" Mr. Michael Harrison, in *In the Footsteps of Sherlock Holmes*, has identified "King's Pyland" with Princetown, Devonshire.

2 *the Wessex Cup.* Watson later speaks of the same race as the Wessex *Plate*. He was not necessarily incorrect here, however: some dictionaries define *plate* as "a gold or silver cup or the like awarded as a prize in horse racing."

3 *flying along,* en route *for Exeter.* It would appear that Holmes and Watson did not travel on either of the crack trains from Paddington to Exeter, the Flying Dutchman or the Zulu, "since the Zulu left Paddington at 3:00 P.M., and the Dutchman departed at 11:45 A.M., half an hour after they were on their way," Mr. D. Marcus Hook wrote in "More on the Railway Journeys." "Yet it is difficult to believe that Holmes would have chosen to board a slower train at 11:15, even if there was one. . . . It seems reasonable to suppose, then, that they travelled on the Flying Dutchman . . . probably behind one of the 'Iron Duke' class of locomotives with eight-foot driving wheels. Perhaps it was the *Prometheus*? The only other alternative is that of the 'special.' But Holmes says across the breakfast table 'We have, I think, just time to catch our train at Paddington.' In that case they would hardly have left in a 'special' half an hour before the scheduled departure."

4 *fifty-three and a half miles an hour."* Some have doubted that the train could be traveling at such a speed, but Mr. Hook has pointed out that the speed "was not only possible, but necessary. Both the Flying Dutchman and the Zulu were allowed 87 minutes for the run from Paddington to Swindown. . . . This gives a start-to-stop average speed of $53\frac{1}{4}$ m.p.h., and it is obvious that top running speed, to maintain this average, would have to be made well above the $53\frac{1}{2}$ m.p.h. mark."

Mr. A. D. Galbraith, in "The Real Moriarty" has found this statement "completely inconsistent with Holmes' character. Again and again Holmes has been depicted as a man of precise mind, as a cold, pure reasoner. Then he must have meant that his calculation of the speed was in error by not more than a quarter of a mile an hour; that is, fifty-three and a half miles an hour was the nearest half mile an hour to the correct speed. But he timed the train with an ordinary watch, and over a fairly short interval—Watson's phrase is 'glancing at his watch,' and the speed could not be expected to be uniform for more than two minutes. He had to determine, from the second-hand of his watch, the time from the instant of passage of one telegraph post to that of another, probably a mile or more from it, and to count the posts between. Anyone who has tried this knows that an error of one second in the time is almost incredibly small; two seconds is good. An error of one second in a time interval of two minutes means an error of almost half a mile an hour, at this speed. Then the man of precise mind, even if confident of almost superhuman accuracy in his measurement of the time, would say 'between fifty-three and fifty-four miles an hour,' and a more reasonbale statement would be 'between fifty-two- and fifty-five.' Is Holmes trying to impress Watson, or is Watson trying to impress his readers?"

HOLMES . . . GAVE ME A SKETCH OF THE EVENTS . . .

Illustration by Sidney Paget for the *Strand Magazine,* December, 1892.

sharp, eager face framed in his ear-flapped travelling-cap, dipped rapidly into the bundle of fresh papers which he had procured at Paddington. We had left Reading far behind us before he thrust the last of them under the seat, and offered me his cigar-case.

" We are going well," said he, looking out of the window, and glancing at his watch. " Our rate at present is **4** fifty-three and a half miles an hour."

" I have not observed the quarter-mile posts," said I.

" Nor have I. But the telegraph posts upon this line are sixty yards apart, and the calculation is a simple one. I presume that you have already looked into this matter of the murder of John Straker and the disappearance of Silver Blaze ? "

" I have seen what the *Telegraph* and the *Chronicle* have to say."

" It is one of those cases where the art of the reasoner should be used rather for the sifting of details than for the acquiring of fresh evidence. The tragedy has been so uncommon, so complete, and of such personal importance to so many people that we are suffering from a plethora of surmise, conjecture, and hypothesis. The difficulty is to detach the framework of fact—of absolute, undeniable fact—from the embellishments of theorists and reporters. Then, having established ourselves upon this sound basis, it is our duty to see what inferences may be drawn, and which are the special points upon which the whole mystery turns. On Tuesday evening I received telegrams, both from Colonel Ross, the owner of the horse, and from Inspector Gregory, who is looking after the case, inviting my co-operation."

" Tuesday evening ! " I exclaimed. " And this is **5** Thursday morning. Why did you not go down yesterday ? "

" Because I made a blunder, my dear Watson—which is, I am afraid, a more common occurrence than anyone **6** would think who only knew me through your memoirs. The fact is that I could not believe it possible that the most remarkable horse in England could long remain concealed, especially in so sparsely inhabited a place as the north of Dartmoor. From hour to hour yesterday I expected to hear that he had been found, and that his abductor was the murderer of John Straker. When, however, another morning had come and I found that, beyond the arrest of young Fitzroy Simpson, nothing had been done, I felt that it was time for me to take action. Yet in some ways I feel that yesterday has not been wasted."

" You have formed a theory then ? "

" At least I have a grip of the essential facts of the case. I shall enumerate them to you, for nothing clears up a case so much as stating it to another person, and I can hardly expect your co-operation if I do not show you the position from which we start."

I lay back against the cushions, puffing at my cigar, while Holmes, leaning forward, with his long thin forefinger checking off the points upon the palm of his left hand, gave me a sketch of the events which had led to our journey.

". . . AND THE CALCULATION IS A SIMPLE ONE."

The late Professor Jay Finley Christ, in "Sherlock Pulls a Fast One," analyzed the problem and concluded that the calculation was *not* a simple one; Mr. Guy Warrack, in *Sherlock Holmes and Music*, also maintained that to arrive at this result Holmes would have been obliged to work out in his head an arithmetical sum of overwhelming complexity, and that it would have been impossible with a pocket watch to time the passage of the telegraph poles to the necessary tenth of a second. But Mr. S. C. Roberts, in "The Music of Baker Street," a review of Mr. Warrack's book, responded: "Mr. Warrack, if we may so express it, is making telegraph-poles out of fountain-pens. What happened, surely, was something like this: About half a minute before he addressed Watson, Holmes had looked at the second hand of his watch and then counted fifteen telegraph poles (he had, of course, *seen* the quarter-mile posts, but had not *observed* them, since they were not to be the basis of his calculation.) This would give him a distance of nine hundred yards, a fraction over half-a-mile. If a second glance at his watch had shown him that thirty seconds had passed, he would have known at once that the train was traveling at a good sixty miles an hour. Actually he noted that the train had taken approximately thirty-four seconds to cover the nine hundred yards; or, in other words, it was rather more than ten per cent (i.e., 6½ from sixty). The calculation, as he said, was a simple one; what made it simple was his knowledge, which of course Watson did not share, that the telegraph poles were sixty yards apart. Mr. Warrack's talk of 'sheer bluff' is manifestly irrelevant."

Mr. George W. Welch, in "The 'Silver Blaze' Formula," devised not one but two formulas said to be simple:

First Method:—Allow two seconds for every yard, and add another second for every 22 yards of the known interval. Then the number of objects passed in this time is the speed in miles an hour. Proof:—Let x = the speed in miles per hour, y = the interval between adjacent objects. 1 m.p.h. = 1,760 yards in 3,600 seconds = 1 yard in $\frac{3,600}{1,760}$ (= $\frac{45}{22}$ or 2.1/22 secs. = y yards in 2.1/22 y seconds x m.p.h. = xy yards in 2.1/22y seconds. Example:—Telegraph poles are set 60 yards apart. 60 × 2 = 120; 60 ÷ 22 = 3 (approx.); 120 + 3 = 123. Then, if after 123 seconds the observer is half-way between the 53rd and 54th poles, the speed is 53½ miles an hour.

Second Method:—When time or space will not permit the first method to be used, allow one second for every yard of the known interval, and multiply by 2.1/22 the number of objects passed in this time. The product is the speed in miles an hour. Example:—Telegraph poles are set 60 yards apart. After 60 seconds the observer is about 10 yards beyond the 26th pole. 26.1/6 × 2 = 52.1/3; 26.1/6 divided by 22 = 1.1/6 (approx.); 52.1/3 = 1.1/6 = 53½. Therefore the speed is 53½ miles an hour. The advantage of the first method is that the time to be used can be worked out in advance, leaving the observer nothing to do but count the objects against the second hand of his watch.

"Now," Dr. Julian Wolff wrote in "The Dynamics of the Binomial Theorem," "let us examine the problem in the light of pure reason. First of all, the speed in feet per second is easily found by determining the number of seconds taken to travel a known number of feet. Thus the speed when traveling 10 intervals between telegraph poles (1800 feet, since Holmes said that the posts were 60 yards apart) in T seconds is $\frac{1800}{T}$ feet per second. Multiplying this by 3600 gives the speed in feet per hour, and dividing the answer by 5280 gives the speed in miles per hour. Thus:

$$\text{miles per hour} = \frac{\frac{1800}{T} \times 3600}{5280} = \frac{1227.27}{T}$$

In other words, all that has to be done to determine the speed of the train in miles per hour is to divide 1227.27 (1227 is close enough for all ordinary purposes, such as puzzling Watson, for instance) by the number of seconds required to travel 1800 feet. And for those who do not care to perform even that calculation—and it is a simple one—a graph has been appended" (*see below.*)

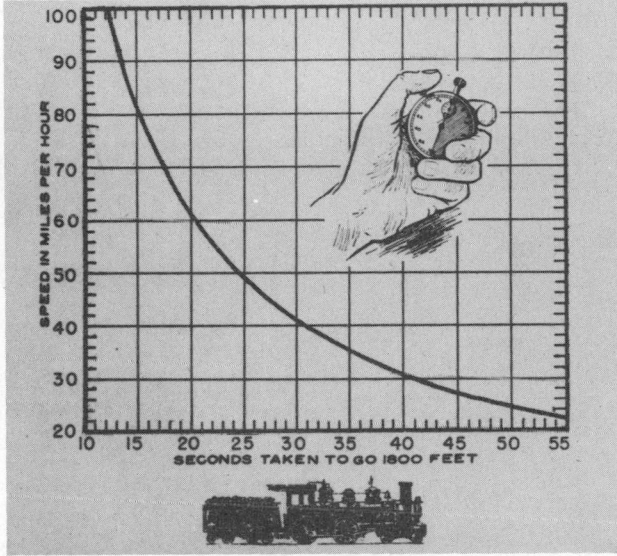

5 "*And this is Thursday morning*. Holmes tells us that he received telegrams inviting him to investigate the death of John Straker and the disappearance of Silver Blaze "on Tuesday evening." "From hour to hour yesterday [Wednesday] I expected to hear that he had been found. When, however, another morning [Thursday] had come . . ." This corroborates Watson's "And this is Thursday morning." The day, as we shall see, was a genial one: there is no mention of any rain and "the reds had all faded into greys" after the setting of the sun, indicating clear, bright weather.

6 *your memoirs*. The case must therefore be placed after the publication of *A Study in Scarlet* in December, 1887.

7 *Tavistock*. Largest of the moor towns in Devonshire.

8 *Capleton*. *Mapleton* in some American editions. Professor Christ thought they might have been the Falmouth House Stables of Mr. John Blundell Maple, Member of Parliament for Camberwell.

" Silver Blaze," said he, " is from the Isonomy stock, and holds as brilliant a record as his famous ancestor. He is now in his fifth year, and has brought in turn each of the prizes of the turf to Colonel Ross, his fortunate owner. Up to the time of the catastrophe he was first favourite for the Wessex Cup, the betting being three to one on. He has always, however, been a prime favourite with the racing public, and has never yet disappointed them, so that even at short odds enormous sums of money have been laid upon him. It is obvious, therefore, that there were many people who had the strongest interest in preventing Silver Blaze from being there at the fall of the flag next Tuesday.

" This fact was, of course, appreciated at King's Pyland, where the Colonel's training stable is situated. Every precaution was taken to guard the favourite. The trainer, John Straker, is a retired jockey, who rode in Colonel Ross's colours before he became too heavy for the weighing-chair. He has served the Colonel for five years as jockey, and for seven as trainer, and has always shown himself to be a zealous and honest servant. Under him were three lads, for the establishment was a small one, containing only four horses in all. One of these lads sat up each night in the stable, while the others slept in the loft. All three bore excellent characters. John Straker, who is a married man, lived in a small villa about two hundred yards from the stables. He has no children, keeps one maid-servant, and is comfortably off. The country round is very lonely, but about half a mile to the north there is a small cluster of villas which have **7** been built by a Tavistock contractor for the use of invalids and others who may wish to enjoy the pure Dartmoor air. Tavistock itself lies two miles to the west, while across the moor, also about two miles distant, is the larger **8** training establishment of Capleton, which belongs to Lord Backwater, and is managed by Silas Brown. In every

"SILVER BLAZE," SAID HE, IS FROM THE ISONOMY STOCK . . ."

Portrait of Silver Blaze by Sidney Paget for the *Strand Magazine*, December, 1892. "Isonomy" is misprinted "Somomy" in most American texts, which is unfortunate, because Isonomy was a real horse, and a remarkable one. He won the Cambridgeshire at Newmarket in 1878, the Manchester Plate and the Ascot Gold Cup in 1879, and the Ascot Gold Cup again in 1880. Isonomy first went to stud in 1881, and "Silver Blaze" was "in his fifth year": Silver Blaze could be said to be "in his fifth year" after his fourth birthday—but even if he were the first of Isonomy's many progeny, he could not have reached his fourth birthday until 1886; the case certainly took place *no* earlier than that year.

The late Professor Jay Finley Christ, in a notable speculation ("Silver Blaze: An Identification As of 1893 A.D."), has shown that "Down to the year 1892, when 'Silver Blaze' was published, there was one really outstanding horse of the Isonomy line. That horse was by some trick of fate called *Common*, but was far from acting other direction the moor is a complete wilderness, inhabited only by a few roaming gipsies. Such was the general situation last Monday night, when the catastrophe occurred.

" On that evening the horses had been exercised and watered as usual, and the stables were locked up at nine o'clock. Two of the lads walked up to the trainer's house, where they had supper in the kitchen, while the third, Ned Hunter, remained on guard. At a few minutes after nine the maid, Edith Baxter, carried down to the stables his supper, which consisted of a dish of curried mutton.

". . . THE MAID . . . CARRIED DOWN TO THE STABLES HIS SUPPER . . ."

Illustration by William H. Hyde for *Harper's Weekly*, February 25, 1893.

the part, as he turned out to be one of the truly great sons of Isonomy. . . . Sired by Isonomy and out of Thistle, Common was foaled in 1888. In '91, as a three-year-old, he was practically the horse of the year. Coming to the Two Thousand Guinea Stake as an 'outsider,' with no two-year-old performance to herald his greatness, Common won the Two Thousand 'very easily indeed' in April. In the Derby 'he again won casily'; and the St. James Place Stakes at Ascot he won 'in a canter.' . . . He completed the year (and his racing career) with the winning of the St. Leger at Doncaster in September of 1891, where the odds on him were 5 to 4. . . ."

Horses called Silvio and St. Blaise were both Derby winners, as the late Gavin Brend pointed out in "From the Horse's Mouth," Silvio in 1877, St. Blaise in 1883, but neither of these horses were of the Isonomy stock. "If we confine our attention to Isonomy's progeny the most hopeful claimant from the standpoint of phonetics would seem to be Seabreeze who won the Oaks and St. Leger in 1888 but who, I regret to say, was not a colt but a filly."

". . . A MAN APPEARED OUT OF THE DARKNESS . . ."

Illustration by Sidney Paget for the *Strand Magazine*, December, 1892.

9 *as it was very dark*. Most chronologists have followed Mr. Bell's inference from this that the season was early autumn. An exception was the late Dr. Ernest Bloomfield Zeisler, who held that the darkness must have been due to clouds, presaging the storm during the night, since "it was obviously not dark at well past nine" on the day Holmes and Watson visited Tavistock ("Some Observations Upon 'Silver Blaze'").

She took no liquid, as there was a water-tap in the stables, and it was the rule that the lad on duty should drink nothing else. The maid carried a lantern with her, as **9** it was very dark, and the path ran across the open moor.

"Edith Baxter was within thirty yards of the stables when a man appeared out of the darkness and called to her to stop. As he stepped into the circle of yellow light thrown by the lantern she saw that he was a person of gentlemanly bearing, dressed in a grey suit of tweed with a cloth cap. He wore gaiters, and carried a heavy stick with a knob to it. She was most impressed, however, by the extreme pallor of his face and by the nervousness of his manner. His age, she thought, would be rather over thirty than under it.

"'Can you tell me where I am?' he asked. 'I had almost made up my mind to sleep on the moor when I saw the light of your lantern.'

"'You are close to the King's Pyland training stables,' she said.

"'Oh, indeed! What a stroke of luck!' he cried. 'I understand that a stable boy sleeps there alone every night. Perhaps that is his supper which you are carrying to him. Now I am sure that you would not be too proud to earn the price of a new dress, would you?' He took a piece of white paper folded up out of his waistcoat pocket. 'See that the boy has this to-night, and you shall have the prettiest frock that money can buy.'

"She was frightened by the earnestness of his manner, and ran past him to the window through which she was accustomed to hand the meals. It was already open, and Hunter was seated at the small table inside. She had begun to tell him of what had happened, when the stranger came up again.

"'Good evening,' said he, looking through the window, 'I wanted to have a word with you.' The girl has sworn that as he spoke she noticed the corner of the little paper packet protruding from his closed hand.

"'What business have you here?' asked the lad.

"'It's business that may put something into your pocket,' said the other. 'You've two horses in for the Wessex Cup—Silver Blaze and Bayard. Let me have the straight tip, and you won't be a loser. Is it a fact that at the weights Bayard could give the other a hundred yards in five furlongs, and that the stable have put their money on him?'

"'So you're one of those damned touts,' cried the lad. 'I'll show you how we serve them in King's Pyland.' He sprang up and rushed across the stable to unloose the dog. The girl fled away to the house, but as she ran she looked back, and saw that the stranger was leaning through the window. A minute later, however, when Hunter rushed out with the hound he was gone, and though the lad ran all round the buildings he failed to find any trace of him."

"One moment!" I asked. "Did the stable boy, when he ran out with the dog, leave the door unlocked behind him?"

"Excellent, Watson; excellent!" murmured my companion. "The importance of the point struck me so forcibly, that I sent a special wire to Dartmoor yesterday to clear the matter up. The boy locked the door before he left it. The window, I may add, was not large enough for a man to get through.

"Hunter waited until his fellow-grooms had returned, when he sent a message up to the trainer and told him what had occurred. Straker was excited at hearing the account, although he does not seem to have quite realized its true significance. It left him, however, vaguely uneasy, and Mrs. Straker, waking at one in the morning, found that he was dressing. In reply to her inquiries, he said that he could not sleep on account of his anxiety about the horses, and that he intended to walk down to the stables to see that all was well. She begged him to remain at home, as she could hear the rain pattering against the windows, but in spite of her entreaties he pulled on his large mackintosh and left the house.

"Mrs. Straker awoke at seven in the morning, to find that her husband had not yet returned. She dressed herself hastily, called the maid, and set off for the stables. The door was open; inside, huddled together upon a chair, Hunter was sunk in a state of absolute stupor, the favourite's stall was empty, and there were no signs of his trainer.

"The two lads who slept in the chaff-cutting loft above the harness-room were quickly roused. They had heard nothing during the night, for they are both sound sleepers. Hunter was obviously under the influence of some powerful drug; and, as no sense could be got out of him, he was left to sleep it off while the two lads and the two women ran out in search of the absentees. They still had hopes that the trainer had for some reason taken out the horse for early exercise, but on ascending the knoll near the house, from which all the neighbouring moors were visible, they not only could see no signs of the favourite, but they perceived something which warned them that they were in the presence of a tragedy.

"About a quarter of a mile from the stables, John Straker's overcoat was flapping from a furze bush. Immediately beyond there was a bowl-shaped depression in the moor, and at the bottom of this was found the dead body of the unfortunate trainer. His head had been shattered by a savage blow from some heavy weapon, and he was wounded in the thigh, where there was a long, clean cut, inflicted evidently by some very sharp instrument. It was clear, however, that Straker had defended himself vigorously against his assailants, for in his right hand he held a small knife, which was clotted with blood up to the handle, while in his left he grasped a red and black silk cravat, which was recognized by the maid as having been worn on the preceding evening by the stranger who had visited the stables.

"Hunter, on recovering from his stupor, was also quite positive as to the ownership of the cravat. He was equally certain that the same stranger had, while standing at the window, drugged his curried mutton, and so deprived the stables of their watchman.

"As to the missing horse, there were abundant proofs in the mud which lay at the bottom of the fatal hollow, that he had been there at the time of the struggle. But

"HIS HEAD HAD BEEN SHATTERED BY A SAVAGE BLOW FROM SOME HEAVY WEAPON . . ."

Illustration by Sidney Paget for the *Strand Magazine*, December, 1892. William H. Hyde illustrated the same scene for *Harper's Weekly*, February 25, 1893.

from that morning he has disappeared; and although a large reward has been offered, and all the gipsies of Dartmoor are on the alert, no news has come of him. Finally an analysis has shown that the remains of his supper, left by the stable lad, contain an appreciable quantity of powdered opium, while the people of the house partook of the same dish on the same night without any ill effect.

"Those are the main facts of the case stripped of all surmise and stated as baldly as possible. I shall now recapitulate what the police have done in the matter.

"Inspector Gregory, to whom the case has been committed, is an extremely competent officer. Were he but gifted with imagination he might rise to great heights in his profession. On his arrival he promptly found and arrested the man upon whom suspicion naturally rested. There was little difficulty in finding him, for he was thoroughly well known in the neighbourhood. His name, it appears, was Fitzroy Simpson. He was a man of excellent birth and education, who had squandered a fortune upon the turf, and who lived now by doing a little quiet and genteel bookmaking in the sporting clubs of London. An examination of his betting-book shows that bets to the amount of five thousand pounds had been registered by him against the favourite.

"On being arrested he volunteered the statement that he had come down to Dartmoor in the hope of getting some information about the King's Pyland horses, and also about Desborough, the second favourite, which was in charge of Silas Brown, at the Capleton stables. He did not attempt to deny that he had acted as described upon the evening before, but declared that he had no sinister designs, and had simply wished to obtain first-hand information. When confronted with the cravat he turned very pale, and was utterly unable to account for its presence in the hand of the murdered man. His wet clothing showed that he had been out in the storm of the night before, and his stick, which was a Penang lawyer, weighted with lead, was just such a weapon as might, by repeated blows, have inflicted the terrible injuries to which the trainer had succumbed.

"On the other hand, there was no wound upon his person, while the state of Straker's knife would show that one, at least, of his assailants must bear his mark upon him. There you have it all in a nutshell, Watson, and if you can give me any light I shall be infinitely obliged to you."

I had listened with the greatest interest to the statement which Holmes, with characteristic clearness, had laid before me. Though most of the facts were familiar to me, I had not sufficiently appreciated their relative importance, nor their connection with each other.

"Is it not possible," I suggested, "that the incised wound upon Straker may have been caused by his own knife in the convulsive struggles which follow any brain injury?"

"It is more than possible; it is probable," said Holmes. "In that case, one of the main points in favour of the accused disappears."

"And yet," said I, "even now I fail to understand what the theory of the police can be."

"I am afraid that whatever theory we state has very grave objections to it," returned my companion. "The police imagine, I take it, that this Fitzroy Simpson, having drugged the lad, and having in some way obtained a duplicate key, opened the stable door, and took out the horse, with the intention, apparently, of kidnapping him altogether. His bridle is missing, so that Simpson must have put it on. Then, having left the door open behind him, he was leading the horse away over the moor, when he was either met or overtaken by the trainer. A row naturally ensued, Simpson beat out the trainer's brains with his heavy stick without receiving any injury from the small knife which Straker used in self-defence, and then the thief either led the horse on to some secret hiding-place, or else it may have bolted during the struggle, and be now wandering out on the moors. That is the case as it appears to the police, and improbable as it is, all other explanations are more improbable still. However, I shall very quickly test the matter when I am once upon the spot, and until then I really cannot see how we can get much further than our present position."

It was evening before we reached the little town of Tavistock, which lies, like the boss of a shield, in the middle of the huge circle of Dartmoor. Two gentlemen were awaiting us at the station; the one a tall fair man with lion-like hair and beard, and curiously penetrating light blue eyes, the other a small alert person, very neat and dapper, in a frock-coat and gaiters, with trim little side-whiskers and an eye-glass. The latter was Colonel Ross, the well-known sportsman, the other Inspector Gregory, a man who was rapidly making his name in the English detective service.

"I am delighted that you have come down, Mr. Holmes," said the Colonel. "The Inspector here has done all that could possibly be suggested; but I wish to leave no stone unturned in trying to avenge poor Straker, and in recovering my horse."

"Have there been any fresh developments?" asked Holmes.

"I am sorry to say that we have made very little progress," said the Inspector. "We have an open carriage outside, and as you would no doubt like to see the place before the light fails, we might talk it over as we **10** drive."

A minute later we were all seated in a comfortable landau and were rattling through the quaint old Devonshire town. Inspector Gregory was full of his case, and poured out a stream of remarks, while Holmes threw in an occasional question or interjection. Colonel Ross leaned back with his arms folded and his hat tilted over his eyes, while I listened with interest to the dialogue of the two detectives. Gregory was formulating his theory, which was almost exactly what Holmes had foretold in the train.

"The net is drawn pretty close round Fitzroy Simpson," he remarked, "and I believe myself that he is our man. At the same time, I recognize that the evidence is purely circumstantial, and that some new development may upset it."

"How about Straker's knife?"

"I AM DELIGHTED THAT YOU HAVE COME DOWN, MR. HOLMES," SAID THE COLONEL.

Illustration by Sidney Paget for the *Strand Magazine*, December, 1892.

10 *before the light fails.* It is not possible to reckon the time of sunset too accurately from the data given, but it is noteworthy that Holmes and Watson "completed a long agenda before dark," in the late Gavin Brend's phrase, although they arrived at Tavistock at "evening." We are no doubt safe in saying that sunset could not have been much before 5:30 P.M. This would indicate that the time of the year was late September.

11 *He has lodged twice at Tavistock in the summer.* Simpson may not have lodged there twice in the *same* summer, but since he was "well known" in Tavistock, the implication is strong that he had lodged there at least once in a summer just past; another indication that the season of the year is autumn.

" We have quite come to the conclusion that he wounded himself in his fall."

" My friend Dr. Watson made that suggestion to me as we came down. If so, it would tell against this man Simpson."

" Undoubtedly. He has neither a knife nor any sign of a wound. The evidence against him is certainly very strong. He had a great interest in the disappearance of the favourite, he lies under the suspicion of having poisoned the stable boy, he was undoubtedly out in the storm, he was armed with a heavy stick, and his cravat was found in the dead man's hand. I really think we have enough to go before a jury."

Holmes shook his head. " A clever counsel would tear it all to rags," said he. " Why should he take the horse out of the stable ? If he wished to injure it, why could he not do it there ? Has a duplicate key been found in his possession ? What chemist sold him the powdered opium ? Above all, where could he, a stranger to the district, hide a horse, and such a horse as this ? What is his own explanation as to the paper which he wished the maid to give to the stable boy ? "

" He says that it was a ten-pound note. One was found in his purse. But your other difficulties are not so formidable as they seem. He is not a stranger to the dis-

11 trict. He has twice lodged at Tavistock in the summer. The opium was probably brought from London. The key, having served its purpose, would be hurled away. The horse may lie at the bottom of one of the pits or old mines upon the moor."

" What does he say about the cravat ? "

" He acknowledges that it is his, and declares that he had lost it. But a new element has been introduced into the case which may account for his leading the horse from the stable."

Holmes pricked up his ears.

" We have found traces which show that a party of gipsies encamped on Monday night within a mile of the spot where the murder took place. On Tuesday they were gone. Now, presuming that there was some understanding between Simpson and these gipsies, might he not have been leading the horse to them when he was overtaken, and may they not have him now ? "

" It is certainly possible."

" The moor is being scoured for these gipsies. I have also examined every stable and outhouse in Tavistock, and for a radius of ten miles."

" There is another training stable quite close, I understand ? "

" Yes, and that is a factor which we must certainly not neglect. As Desborough, their horse, was second in the betting, they had an interest in the disappearance of the favourite. Silas Brown, the trainer, is known to have had large bets upon the event, and he was no friend to poor Straker. We have, however, examined the stables, and there is nothing to connect him with the affair."

" And nothing to connect this man Simpson with the interests of the Capleton stable ? "

" Nothing at all."

Holmes leaned back in the carriage and the conversation ceased. A few minutes later our driver pulled up at a neat little red-brick villa with overhanging eaves, which stood by the road. Some distance off, across a paddock, lay a long grey-tiled outbuilding. In every other direction the low curves of the moor, bronze-coloured from the fading ferns, stretched away to the skyline, broken only **12** by the steeples of Tavistock, and by a cluster of houses away to the westward, which marked the Capleton stables. We all sprang out with the exception of Holmes, who continued to lean back with his eyes fixed upon the sky in front of him, entirely absorbed in his own thoughts. It was only when I touched his arm that he roused himself with a violent start and stepped out of the carriage.

" Excuse me," said he, turning to Colonel Ross, who had looked at him in some surprise. " I was day-dreaming." There was a gleam in his eyes and a suppressed excitement in his manner which convinced me, used as I was to his ways, that his hand was upon a clue, though I could not imagine where he had found it.

" Perhaps you would prefer at once to go on to the scene of the crime, Mr. Holmes ? " said Gregory.

" I think that I should prefer to stay here a little and go into one or two questions of detail. Straker was brought back here, I presume ? "

" Yes, he lies upstairs. The inquest is to-morrow."

" He has been in your service some years, Colonel Ross ? "

" I have always found him an excellent servant."

" I presume that you made an inventory of what he had in his pockets at the time of his death, Inspector ? "

" I have the things themselves in the sitting-room, if you would care to see them."

" I should be very glad."

We all filed into the front room, and sat round the central table, while the Inspector unlocked a square tin box and laid a small heap of things before us. There was a box of vestas, two inches of tallow candle, an A.D.P. **13** briar-root pipe, a pouch of sealskin with half an ounce of **14** long-cut cavendish, a silver watch with a gold chain, five **15** sovereigns in gold, an aluminium pencil-case, a few papers, and an ivory-handled knife with a very delicate inflexible blade marked Weiss & Co., London. **16**

" This is a very singular knife," said Holmes, lifting it up and examining it minutely. " I presume, as I see blood-stains upon it, that it is the one which was found in the dead man's grasp. Watson, this knife is surely in your line."

" It is what we call a cataract knife," said I.

" I thought so. A very delicate blade devised for very delicate work. A strange thing for a man to carry with him upon a rough expedition, especially as it would not shut in his pocket."

" The tip was guarded by a disc of cork which we found beside his body," said the Inspector. " His wife tells us that the knife had lain for some days upon the dressing-

12 *bronze-coloured from the fading ferns.* Watson speaks later of "the faded ferns and brambles" which caught the evening light. Ferns on Dartmoor do not fade until the latter part of September or the first part of October—still another indication, to most chronologists, that this is an autumnal case. However, the late Dr. Ernest Bloomfield Zeisler wrote ("Some Observations Upon 'Silver Blaze'"): "First the ferns were 'fading'; several hours later they were 'faded.' This would be impossible unless these terms were descriptions of the *appearance* of the ferns in the evening light. Even green ferns would appear bronze-coloured and fading late in the day when the sun was low; and even green ferns would, several hours later, shortly before sunset, appear faded."

13 *vestas.* A vesta is a friction match, so named from the Roman goddess of the hearth and fire.

14 *an A.D.P. briar-root pipe.* "What is an A.D.P. pipe?" we asked Lord Donegall, editor of the *Sherlock Holmes Journal.* And Lord Donegall kindly replied (October 5, 1964): ". . . I went to Dunhill's and asked the oldest inhabitant, who has served me for 40 years . . . if he knew what an 'A.D.P.' pipe was. 'Indeed, yes, M'Lord,' said the Sage of Jermyn Street. 'In the old days A.D.P. stood for Alfred Dunhill Pipe!' . . . However, I have made further researches. During the courses of these, I discovered that there is a small factory outside Ancona, Italy, which specialises in roots for pipes from the *small* briar; as opposed to the Algerian *large* briar. Furthermore, that in the old days, . . . the late lamented Mr. Alfred D. bought his entire supply of briar roots from the Ancona factory. So, I now discount the too-easy glib answer of the Sage in favour of my own theory: I contend that A.D.P. meant 'Ancona Della Piccola.' The *sous-entendu* following 'Piccola' would, of course, be 'Pipa di Radice di Scopa.' "

15 *cavendish.* A kind of smoking tobacco softened and pressed into solid cakes; so called from the name of the maker.

16 *Weiss & Co., London.* "There is a London firm by this name which specializes in instruments used in eye surgery," the late Dr. Roland Hammond wrote in "The Attempted Mayhem of 'Silver Blaze.' "

17 *"Twenty-two guineas.* About $115.50 U.S. at
the time.

"HAVE YOU GOT THEM? HAVE YOU FOUND THEM?"
SHE PANTED.

Illustration by Sidney Paget for the *Strand Magazine*, December, 1892.

table, and that he had picked it up as he left the room.
It was a poor weapon, but perhaps the best that he could
lay his hand on at the moment."

"Very possible. How about these papers ? "

" Three of them are receipted hay-dealers' accounts.
One of them is a letter of instructions from Colonel Ross.
This other is a milliner's account for thirty-seven pounds
fifteen, made out by Madame Lesurier, of Bond Street, to
William Darbyshire. Mrs. Straker tells us that Darbyshire was a friend of her husband's, and that occasionally
his letters were addressed here."

" Madame Darbyshire had somewhat expensive tastes,"
remarked Holmes, glancing down the account. " Twenty-
17 two guineas is rather heavy for a single costume. However, there appears to be nothing more to learn, and we
may now go down to the scene of the crime."

As we emerged from the sitting-room a woman who had
been waiting in the passage took a step forward and laid
her hand upon the Inspector's sleeve. Her face was haggard, and thin, and eager ; stamped with the print of a
recent horror.

" Have you got them ? Have you found them ? " she
panted.

" No, Mrs. Straker ; but Mr. Holmes, here, has come
from London to help us, and we shall do all that is
possible."

" Surely I met you in Plymouth, at a garden-party,
some little time ago, Mrs. Straker," said Holmes.

" No, sir ; you are mistaken."

" Dear me ; why, I could have sworn to it. You wore a
costume of dove-coloured silk with ostrich feather trimming."

" I never had such a dress, sir," answered the lady.

" Ah ; that quite settles it," said Holmes ; and, with an
apology, he followed the Inspector outside. A short walk
across the moor took us to the hollow in which the body
had been found. At the brink of it was the furze bush
upon which the coat had been hung.

" There was no wind that night, I understand," said
Holmes.

" None ; but very heavy rain."

" In that case the overcoat was not blown against the
furze bushes, but placed there."

" Yes, it was laid across the bush."

" You fill me with interest. I perceive that the ground
has been trampled up a good deal. No doubt many feet
have been there since Monday night."

" A piece of matting has been laid here at the side, and
we have all stood upon that."

" Excellent."

" In this bag I have one of the boots which Straker
wore, one of Fitzroy Simpson's shoes, and a cast horseshoe
of Silver Blaze."

" My dear Inspector, you surpass yourself ! "

Holmes took the bag, and descending into the hollow
he pushed the matting into a more central position. Then
stretching himself upon his face and leaning his chin upon
his hands he made a careful study of the trampled mud
in front of him.

" Halloa ! " said he, suddenly, " what's this ? "

It was a wax vesta, half burned, which was so coated with mud that it looked at first like a little chip of wood.

" I cannot think how I came to overlook it," said the Inspector, with an expression of annoyance.

" It was invisible, buried in the mud. I only saw it because I was looking for it."

" What ! You expected to find it ? "

" I thought it not unlikely." He took the boots from the bag and compared the impressions of each of them with marks upon the ground. Then he clambered up to the rim of the hollow and crawled about among the ferns and bushes.

" I am afraid that there are no more tracks," said the Inspector. " I have examined the ground very carefully for a hundred yards in each direction."

" Indeed ! " said Holmes, rising, " I should not have the impertinence to do it again after what you say. But I should like to take a little walk over the moors before it grows dark, that I may know my ground to-morrow, and I think that I shall put this horseshoe into my pocket for luck."

Colonel Ross, who had shown some signs of impatience at my companion's quiet and systematic method of work, glanced at his watch.

" I wish you would come back with me, Inspector," said he. " There are several points on which I should like your advice, and especially as to whether we do not owe it to the public to remove our horse's name from the entries for the Cup."

" Certainly not," cried Holmes, with decision ; " I should let the name stand."

The Colonel bowed. " I am very glad to have had your opinion, sir," said he. " You will find us at poor Straker's house when you have finished your walk, and we can drive together into Tavistock."

He turned back with the Inspector, while Holmes and I walked slowly across the moor. The sun was beginning to sink behind the stables of Capleton, and the long sloping plain in front of us was tinged with gold, deepening into rich, ruddy brown where the faded ferns and brambles caught the evening light. But the glories of the landscape were all wasted upon my companion, who was sunk in the deepest thought.

" It's this way, Watson," he said, at last. " We may leave the question of who killed John Straker for the instant, and confine ourselves to finding out what has become of the horse. Now, supposing that he broke away during or after the tragedy, where could he have gone to ? The horse is a very gregarious creature. If left to himself, his instincts would have been either to return to King's Pyland or go over to Capleton. Why should he run wild upon the moor ? He would surely have been seen by now. And why should gipsies kidnap him ? These people always clear out when they hear of trouble, for they do not wish to be pestered by the police. They could not hope to sell such a horse. They would run a great risk and gain nothing by taking him. Surely that is clear."

" Where is he, then ? "

" I have already said that he must have gone to King's

Pyland or to Capleton.   He is not at King's Pyland, therefore he is at Capleton.   Let us take that as a working
hypothesis, and see what it leads us to.   This part of the
moor, as the Inspector remarked, is very hard and dry.
But it falls away towards Capleton, and you can see from
here that there is a long hollow over yonder, which must
have been very wet on Monday night.   If our supposition
is correct, then the horse must have crossed that, and
there is the point where we should look for his tracks."

We had been walking briskly during this conversation,
and a few more minutes brought us to the hollow in question.   At Holmes' request I walked down the bank to the
right, and he to the left, but I had not taken fifty paces
before I heard him give a shout, and saw him waving his
hand to me.   The track of a horse was plainly outlined
in the soft earth in front of him, and the shoe which he
took from his pocket exactly fitted the impression.

" See the value of imagination," said Holmes.   " It is
the one quality which Gregory lacks.   We imagined what
might have happened, acted upon the supposition, and find
ourselves justified.   Let us proceed."

We crossed the marshy bottom and passed over a
quarter of a mile of dry, hard turf.   Again the ground
sloped and again we came on the tracks.   Then we lost
them for half a mile, but only to pick them up once more
quite close to Capleton.   It was Holmes who saw them
first, and he stood pointing with a look of triumph upon
his face.   A man's track was visible beside the horse's.

" The horse was alone before," I cried.

" Quite so.   It was alone before.   Halloa ! what is this ?"

The double track turned sharp off and took the direction of King's Pyland.   Holmes whistled, and we both
followed along after it.   His eyes were on the trail, but I
happened to look a little to one side, and saw to my surprise the same tracks coming back again in the opposite
direction.

" One for you, Watson," said Holmes, when I pointed
it out ; " you have saved us a long walk which would
have brought us back on our own traces.   Let us follow
the return track."

We had not to go far.   It ended at the paving of
asphalt which led up to the gates of the Capleton stables.
As we approached a groom ran out from them.

" We don't want any loiterers about here," said he.

" I only wished to ask a question," said Holmes, with
his finger and thumb in his waistcoat pocket.   " Should I
be too early to see your master, Mr. Silas Brown, if I were
to call at five o'clock to-morrow morning ? "

" Bless you, sir, if anyone is about he will be, for he is
always the first stirring.   But here he is, sir, to answer
your questions for himself.   No, sir, no ; it's as much as
my place is worth to let him see me touch your money.
Afterwards, if you like."

As Sherlock Holmes replaced the half-crown which he
had drawn from his pocket, a fierce-looking elderly man
strode out from the gate with a hunting-crop swinging in
his hand.

" What's this, Dawson ? " he cried.   " No gossiping !
Go about your business !   And you—what the devil do
you want here ? "

"Ten minutes' talk with you, my good sir," said Holmes, in the sweetest of voices.

"I've no time to talk to every gadabout. We want no strangers here. Be off, or you may find a dog at your heels."

Holmes leaned forward and whispered something in the trainer's ear. He started violently and flushed to the temples.

"It's a lie!" he shouted. "An infernal lie!"

"Very good! Shall we argue about it here in public, or talk it over in your parlour?"

"Oh, come in if you wish to."

Holmes smiled. "I shall not keep you more than a few minutes, Watson," he said. "Now, Mr. Brown, I am quite at your disposal."

It was quite twenty minutes, and the reds had all faded into greys before Holmes and the trainer reappeared. Never have I seen such a change as had been brought about in Silas Brown in that short time. His face was ashy pale, beads of perspiration shone upon his brow, and his hands shook until the hunting-crop wagged like a branch in the wind. His bullying, overbearing manner was all gone too, and he cringed along at my companion's side like a dog with its master.

"Your instructions will be done. It shall be done," said he.

"There must be no mistake," said Holmes, looking round at him. The other winced as he read the menace in his eyes.

"Oh, no, there shall be no mistake. It shall be there. Should I change it first or not?"

Holmes thought a little and then burst out laughing. "No, don't," said he. "I shall write to you about it. No tricks now or——"

"Oh, you can trust me, you can trust me!"

"You must see to it on the day as if it were your own."

"You can rely upon me."

"Yes, I think I can. Well, you shall hear from me to-morrow." He turned upon his heel, disregarding the trembling hand which the other held out to him, and we set off for King's Pyland.

"A more perfect compound of the bully, coward and sneak than Master Silas Brown I have seldom met with," remarked Holmes, as we trudged along together.

"He has the horse, then?"

"He tried to bluster out of it, but I described to him so exactly what his actions had been upon that morning, that he is convinced that I was watching him. Of course, you observed the peculiarly square toes in the impressions, and that his own boots exactly corresponded to them. Again, of course, no subordinate would have dared to have done such a thing. I described to him how when, according to his custom, he was the first down, he perceived a strange horse wandering over the moor; how he went **18** out to it, and his astonishment at recognizing from the white forehead which has given the favourite its name that chance had put in his power the only horse which could beat the one upon which he had put his money. Then I described how his first impulse had been to lead him

"BE OFF, OR YOU SHALL FIND A DOG AT YOUR HEELS."

Illustration by Sidney Paget for the *Strand Magazine*, December, 1892.

18 *he perceived a strange horse wandering over the moor.* Holmes asked if he would find Silas Brown up and about if he called at Capleton at five o'clock in the morning, and was told by the stable boy that Brown was always "the first stirring." On the Tuesday morning, Brown had risen as early as usual, presumably, and had been able to perceive a strange horse on the moor. We can be sure that day must have broken between three and four in the morning on that occasion. All clues to the season, then, point to a journey to Devonshire in the last week of September and a race that must have been run *circa* October 1st, certainly within the first ten days of October.

back to King's Pyland, and how the devil had shown him how he could hide the horse until the race was over, and how he had led it back and concealed it at Capleton. When I told him every detail he gave it up, and thought only of saving his own skin."

" But his stables had been searched."

" Oh, an old horse-faker like him has many a dodge."

" But are you not afraid to leave the horse in his power now, since he has every interest in injuring it ? "

" My dear fellow, he will guard it as the apple of his eye. He knows that his only hope of mercy is to produce it safe."

" Colonel Ross did not impress me as a man who would be likely to show much mercy in any case."

" The matter does not rest with Colonel Ross. I follow my own methods, and tell as much or as little as I choose. That is the advantage of being unofficial. I don't know whether you observed it, Watson, but the Colonel's manner has been just a trifle cavalier to me. I am inclined now to have a little amusement at his expense. Say nothing to him about the horse."

" Certainly not, without your permission."

" And, of course, this is all quite a minor case compared with the question of who killed John Straker."

" And you will devote yourself to that ? "

" On the contrary, we both go back to London by the night train."

I was thunderstruck by my friend's words. We had only been a few hours in Devonshire, and that he should give up an investigation which he had begun so brilliantly was quite incomprehensible to me. Not a word more could I draw from him until we were back at the trainer's house. The Colonel and the Inspector were awaiting us in the parlour.

" My friend and I return to town by the midnight express," said Holmes. " We have had a charming little breath of your beautiful Dartmoor air."

The Inspector opened his eyes, and the Colonel's lips curled in a sneer.

" So you despair of arresting the murderer of poor Straker," said he.

Holmes shrugged his shoulders. " There are certainly grave difficulties in the way," said he. " I have every hope, however, that your horse will start upon Tuesday, and I beg that you will have your jockey in readiness. Might I ask for a photograph of Mr. John Straker ? "

The Inspector took one from an envelope in his pocket and handed it to him.

" My dear Gregory, you anticipate all my wants. If I might ask you to wait here for an instant, I have a question which I should like to put to the maid."

" I must say that I am rather disappointed in our London consultant," said Colonel Ross, bluntly, as my friend left the room. " I do not see that we are any further than when he came."

" At least, you have his assurance that your horse will run," said I.

19 *"That was the curious incident."* This is perhaps the most famous example of what the late Monsignor Ronald Knox felicitously termed the *Sherlockismus*.

20 *Four days later.* Since the race was on Tuesday, Watson is presumably counting from the Friday morning on which he and Holmes returned to London from Devonshire.

21 *Winchester.* We have seen that the adventure must have taken place in the autumn of a year later than 1887 (when *A Study in Scarlet* was published in *Beeton's Christmas Annual*) and before 1891 (in the April of which year Holmes was presumed dead). The possible years are therefore 1888, 1889, and 1890. Turning to the *Almanack*, we find six possible dates for the race: 1) Tuesday, October 2, 1888; 2) Tuesday, October 9, 1888; 3) Tuesday, October 1, 1889; 4) Tuesday, October 8, 1889; 5) Tuesday, September 30, 1890; and 6) Tuesday, October 7, 1890. We can at once eliminate the two dates in 1888 and the October 1st of 1889; *no* race meetings were

"Yes, I have his assurance," said the Colonel, with a shrug of his shoulders. "I should prefer to have the horse."

I was about to make some reply in defence of my friend, when he entered the room again.

"Now, gentlemen," said he, "I am quite ready for Tavistock."

As we stepped into the carriage one of the stable lads held the door open for us. A sudden idea seemed to occur to Holmes, for he leaned forward and touched the lad upon the sleeve.

"You have a few sheep in the paddock," he said. "Who attends to them?"

"I do, sir."

"Have you noticed anything amiss with them of late?"

"Well, sir, not of much account; but three of them have gone lame, sir."

I could see that Holmes was extremely pleased, for he chuckled and rubbed his hands together.

"A long shot, Watson; a very long shot!" said he, pinching my arm. "Gregory, let me recommend to your attention this singular epidemic among the sheep. Drive on, coachman!"

Colonel Ross still wore an expression which showed the poor opinion which he had formed of my companion's ability, but I saw by the Inspector's face that his attention had been keenly aroused.

"You consider that to be important?" he asked.

"Exceedingly so."

"Is there any other point to which you would wish to draw my attention?"

"To the curious incident of the dog in the night-time."

"The dog did nothing in the night-time."

'That was the curious incident," remarked Sherlock **19** Holmes.

Four days later Holmes and I were again in the train **20** bound for Winchester, to see the race for the Wessex Cup. **21** Colonel Ross met us, by appointment, outside the station, and we drove in his drag to the course beyond the town. His face was grave and his manner was cold in the extreme.

"I have seen nothing of my horse," said he.

"I suppose that you would know him when you saw him?" asked Holmes.

The Colonel was very angry. "I have been on the turf for twenty years, and never was asked such a question as that before," said he. "A child would know Silver Blaze with his white forehead and his mottled off foreleg."

"How is the betting?"

"Well, that is the curious part of it. You could have got fifteen to one yesterday, but the price has become shorter and shorter, until you can hardly get three to one now."

"Hum!" said Holmes. "Somebody knows something, that is clear!"

Illustration by Sidney Paget for the *Strand Magazine*, December, 1892.

held in Britain on those days. We must eliminate the October 8th of 1889 and the October 7th of 1890 because of the weather: in 1889, according to the London *Times*, there was "rain in almost all parts of the kingdom" on Thursday, October 3rd (which would have been the day of the journey to Devonshire); in 1890 there was no rain on either the 29th or the 30th of September (which would have been the night of Straker's murder and the disappearance of Silver Blaze). Only Tuesday, September 30, 1890, remains as the day of the race, but it is fitting that we check the corresponding dates for the murder and the journey to Devonshire with the weather columns of the *Times*. The night of the murder would have been the night of Monday, September 22nd to Tuesday, September 23rd. Said the *Times*' weather report for the Tuesday evening: "In the course of the past 24 hours the weather has been in a very . . . unsettled condition. . . . Thunder showers have been prevalent, especially in the south and southeast, and in many localities the rainfall has been large. The wind has . . . remained light in force." The day of the journey to Devonshire would have been Thursday, September 25th—a day on which the "weather was fine and bright in the east and south of England." We therefore hold that the adventure took place on *Thursday, September 25, and Tuesday, September 30, 1890*. It is true that the race meeting of September 30, 1890, was *not* at Winchester (indeed, Dr. Zeisler demonstrated that "in all the years between 1881 and 1903 there is no horse race scheduled at Winchester except on" July 17, 1888), but this need not worry us: as we shall see, Watson at this time was hardly a "Handy Guide to the Turf." He could have been as confused as to the *place* of the race as he was on other racing matters.

22 *drag.* A private stagecoach, with seats inside and on top.

23 (*purple cap, black sleeves*). "We are given what purports to be a copy of the race card," the late Gavin Brend wrote in *My Dear Holmes*, "but it in fact appears to have been compiled after the event, and from memory, by someone who was not accustomed to studying racing colours. Of the six starters only two, Silver Blaze and The Negro, appear to be sufficiently and adequately equipped. Pugilist has a pink cap and blue and black jacket. This might get by Messrs. Weatherby and Sons, who are responsible for the registration of racing colours, but we think it very doubtful. 'Blue and black jacket' is not sufficient. It should be 'blue and black stripes,' or 'blue and black hoops,' or 'blue and black quarters,' or possibly 'blue, black sleeves.' Iris seems to be short a cap, for his description is merely 'yellow and black stripes.' Desborough, 'yellow cap and sleeves,' appears to be even more exiguously clad, and Rasper, 'purple cap, black sleeves' is in the same precarious situation. Surely a racing man, accustomed to studying the colours on his race card, would realize that something else is required to connect the two sleeves?" We may add here that *no* races are reserved for four- and five-year-old horses, that any proper race card would state the age, weight, pedigree and trainer of each horse entered, as well as the time of the race.

24 *Fifteen to five against Desborough!* "There are a few examples of unreduced fractions sanctioned by long usage in racing odds, such as '6 to 4,' '100 to 8,' and '100 to 6,' but *not* we submit '15 to 5.' This we cannot accept in any circumstances whatsoever," Mr. Brend wrote.

25 *I stand to win a little on this next race.* On the *next race*—or on the race *just run?* Was Holmes in fact about to collect his winnings on Silver Blaze? "All facts point to the conclusion that Holmes with the connivance of Mr. Silas Brown, and probably with that of Lord Backwater, whose horse, Desborough, ran in the same race . . . deliberately framed the Wessex Plate," Mr. Robert Keith Leavitt wrote in "Nummi in Arca or The Fiscal Holmes."

". . . Leavitt's suggestion that Backwater's horse was pulled has the cogency almost of demonstrable fact," the late Elmer Davis seconded in his Introduction to *The Return of Sherlock Holmes.*

"Brown was to keep Silver Blaze in hiding as long as possible while Holmes, dashing down to London by the night train [on the Thursday preceding the race] was to place bets at as long odds as he could possibly get on Silver Blaze," Mr. Charles B. Stephens wrote in "Silas Brown, or, Who Shot Desborough's Bolt?" "To make doubly certain of the success of the coup, Brown was to instruct Desborough's jockey to run just the sort of race that Watson [later recorded] without

22 As the drag drew up in the enclosure near the grandstand, I glanced at the card to see the entries. It ran:

Wessex Plate. 50 sovs. each, h ft, with 1,000 sovs. added, for four- and five-year olds. Second £300. Third £200. New course (one mile and five furlongs).
1. Mr. Heath Newton's The Negro (red cap, cinnamon jacket).
2. Colonel Wardlaw's Pugilist (pink cap, blue and black jacket).
3. Lord Backwater's Desborough (yellow cap and sleeves).
4. Colonel Ross's Silver Blaze (black cap, red jacket).
5. Duke of Balmoral's Iris (yellow and black stripes).

23 6. Lord Singleford's Rasper (purple cap, black sleeves).

" We scratched our other one and put all hopes on your word," said the Colonel. " Why, what is that? Silver Blaze favourite ? "

" Five to four against Silver Blaze ! " roared the ring. " Five to four against Silver Blaze ! Fifteen to five

24 against Desborough ! Five to four on the field ! "

" There are the numbers up," I cried. " They are all six there."

" All six there ! Then my horse is running," cried the Colonel, in great agitation. " But I don't see him. My colours have not passed."

" Only five have passed. This must be he."

As I spoke a powerful bay horse swept out from the weighing enclosure and cantered past us, bearing on its back the well-known black and red of the Colonel.

" That's not my horse," cried the owner. " That beast has not a white hair upon its body. What is this that you have done, Mr. Holmes ? "

" Well, well, let us see how he gets on," said my friend, imperturbably. For a few minutes he gazed through my field-glass. " Capital ! An excellent start ! " he cried suddenly. " There they are, coming round the curve ! "

From our drag we had a superb view as they came up the straight. The six horses were so close together that a carpet could have covered them, but half-way up the yellow of the Capleton stable showed to the front. Before they reached us, however, Desborough's bolt was shot, and the Colonel's horse, coming away with a rush, passed the post a good six lengths before its rival, the Duke of Balmoral's Iris making a bad third.

" It's my race anyhow," gasped the Colonel, passing his hand over his eyes. " I confess that I can make neither head nor tail of it. Don't you think that you have kept up your mystery long enough, Mr. Holmes ? "

" Certainly, Colonel. You shall know everything. Let us all go round and have a look at the horse together. Here he is," he continued, as we made our way into the weighing enclosure where only owners and their friends find admittance. " You have only to wash his face and his leg in spirits of wine and you will find that he is the same old Silver Blaze as ever."

" You take my breath away ! "

" I found him in the hands of a faker, and took the liberty of running him just as he was sent over."

" My dear sir, you have done wonders. The horse looks very fit and well. It never went better in its life. I owe you a thousand apologies for having doubted your ability. You have done me a great service by recovering my horse. You would do me a greater still if you could lay your hands on the murderer of John Straker."

" I have done so," said Holmes, quietly.

The Colonel and I stared at him in amazement. " You have got him ! Where is he, then ? "

" He is here."

" Here ! Where ? "

" In my company at the present moment."

The Colonel flushed angrily. " I quite recognize that I am under obligations to you, Mr. Holmes," said he, " but I must regard what you have just said as either a very bad joke or an insult."

Sherlock Holmes laughed. " I assure you that I have not associated you with the crime, Colonel," said he ; " the real murderer is standing immediately behind you ! "

He stepped past and laid his hand upon the glossy neck of the thoroughbred.

" The horse ! " cried both the Colonel and myself.

" Yes, the horse. And it may lessen his guilt if I say that it was done in self-defence, and that John Straker was a man who was entirely unworthy of your confidence. But there goes the bell ; and as I stand to win a little on this next race, I shall defer a more lengthy explanation **25** until a more fitting time."

We had the corner of a Pullman car to ourselves that **26** evening as we whirled back to London, and I fancy that the journey was a short one to Colonel Ross as well as to myself, as we listened to our companion's narrative of the events which had occurred at the Dartmoor training stables upon that Monday night, and the means by which he had unravelled them.

" I confess," said he, " that any theories which I had formed from the newspaper reports were entirely erroneous. And yet there were indications there, had they not been overlaid by other details which concealed their true import. I went to Devonshire with the conviction that Fitzroy Simpson was the true culprit, although, of course, I saw that the evidence against him was by no means complete.

" It was while I was in the carriage, just as we reached the trainer's house, that the immense significance of the curried mutton occurred to me. You may remember that I was distrait, and remained sitting after you had all alighted. I was marvelling in my own mind how I could possibly have overlooked so obvious a clue."

" I confess," said the Colonel, " that even now I cannot see how it helps us."

" It was the first link in my chain of reasoning. Powdered opium is by no means tasteless. The flavour is not disagreeable, but it is perceptible. Were it mixed with any ordinary dish, the eater would undoubtedly detect it, and would probably eat no more. A curry was exactly the medium which would disguise this taste. By no possible supposition could this stranger, Fitzroy Simpson, have caused curry to be served in the trainer's family that night, and it is surely too monstrous a coincidence to suppose that he happened to come along with powdered opium upon the very night when a dish happened to be

HE STEPPED PAST AND LAID HIS HAND UPON THE GLOSSY NECK OF THE THOROUGHBRED.

Illustration by Sidney Paget for the *Strand Magazine*, December, 1892.

grasping its significance. . . . The evidence seems all too clear that it was Holmes, himself, who master-minded the manipulation of the betting odds to his own advantage, in derogation of his obligations to the man who had employed him for the investigation."

This same unhappy view is held by the famous sports columnist of the New York *Herald Tribune*, Mr. Red Smith; as is evident from a reading of his essay "The Nefarious Holmes" in *Views of Sport:* "Whenever Holmes' activities impinged upon the field of sports, he exhibited an ethical blind spot of shocking dimensions and it is common knowledge that he was the architect of an extraordinary piece of skullduggery in connection with a horse race." The essay further states that in 1891 Holmes said that his earnings from recent cases had left him free to live as he wished ("The Final Problem"); yet Holmes in "The Adventure of the Priory School" (1901) had to confess, "I am a poor man," and although Holmes received princely fees for his services he was practically always broke—"obviously because the bookies took everything he didn't have to lay out for happy dust." Mr. Smith then goes on to charge that: "It has been established that Mr. Sherlock Holmes was a horse player of degenerate principles who thought nothing of fixing a race, and when you bear in mind his first-hand knowledge of the use and effect of cocaine, he probably had his syringe in the veins of more than one thoroughbred."

Needless to say, this underhanded attack on Holmes in the public prints has met with spirited rebuttals, notably from Mr. Edward T. Buxton ("He Solved the Case and Won the Race"): Holmes "knew that at a word from him Silas Brown would have received a stiff jailing as well as being barred from his livelihood for the rest of his days, and that the 'bully and sneak' was well aware of it. Holmes also knew, however, that in spite of other faults the trainer for Lord Back-water's great Mapleton racing stables had to be thoroughly competent in his profession. With such a man under his thumb Holmes had the one man available who could train Silver Blaze to win the Wessex Cup. He had to, or go to jail. But it was also clear that . . . Colonel Ross would never have agreed to any such common-sense procedure, so Holmes very probably kept him in the dark . . ." There is still, of course, no reason why Holmes, under these circumstances, might not have placed a little something on Silver Blaze's nose. We are again in "deep waters."

26 *a Pullman car.* Some critics have doubted that Holmes and Watson and Colonel Ross would return to London from Winchester in "a Pullman car," but "this would be correct enough, as the L.S.W.R. (London & South Western Railway) did use Pullman cars on its Bournemouth service," as Mr. Edgar S. Rosenberger pointed out in "The Railway Journeys of Sherlock Holmes."

27 *so as to leave absolutely no trace.* The researches of the late Dr. Roland Hammond, reported in "The Attempted Mayhem of 'Silver Blaze,'" convinced him that "such an injury could not be inflicted to the tendons of a horse's ham with the instrument called for in the specifications."

served which would disguise the flavour. That is unthinkable. Therefore Simpson becomes eliminated from the case, and our attention centres upon Straker and his wife, the only two people who could have chosen curried mutton for supper that night. The opium was added after the dish was set aside for the stable boy, for the others had the same for supper with no ill effects. Which of them, then, had access to that dish without the maid seeing them ?

" Before deciding that question I had grasped the significance of the silence of the dog, for one true inference invariably suggests others. The Simpson incident had shown me that a dog was kept in the stables, and yet, though someone had been in and had fetched out a horse, he had not barked enough to arouse the two lads in the loft. Obviously the midnight visitor was someone whom the dog knew well.

" I was already convinced, or almost convinced, that John Straker went down to the stables in the dead of the night and took out Silver Blaze. For what purpose ? For a dishonest one, obviously, or why should he drug his own stable boy ? And yet I was at a loss to know why. There have been cases before now where trainers have made sure of great sums of money by laying against their own horses, through agents, and then prevented them from winning by fraud. Sometimes it is a pulling jockey. Sometimes it is some surer and subtler means. What was it here ? I hoped that the contents of his pockets might help me to form a conclusion.

" And they did so. You cannot have forgotten the singular knife which was found in the dead man's hand, a knife which certainly no sane man would choose for a weapon. It was, as Dr. Watson told us, a form of knife which is used for the most delicate operations known in surgery. And it was to be used for a delicate operation that night. You must know, with your wide experience of turf matters, Colonel Ross, that it is possible to make a slight nick upon the tendons of a horse's ham, and to do it subcutaneously so as to leave absolutely no **27** trace. A horse so treated would develop a slight lameness which would be put down to a strain in exercise or a touch of rheumatism, but never to foul play."

" Villain ! Scoundrel ! " cried the Colonel.

" We have here the explanation of why John Straker wished to take the horse out on to the moor. So spirited a creature would have certainly roused the soundest of sleepers when it felt the prick of the knife. It was absolutely necessary to do it in the open air."

" I have been blind ! " cried the Colonel. " Of course, that was why he needed the candle, and struck the match."

" Undoubtedly. But in examining his belongings, I was fortunate enough to discover, not only the method of the crime, but even its motives. As a man of the world, Colonel, you know that men do not carry other people's bills about in their pockets. We have most of us quite enough to do to settle our own. I at once concluded that

Straker was leading a double life, and keeping a second establishment. The nature of the bill showed that there was a lady in the case, and one who had expensive tastes. Liberal as you are with your servants, one hardly expects that they can buy twenty-guinea walking dresses for their women. I questioned Mrs. Straker as to the dress without her knowing it, and having satisfied myself that it had never reached her, I made a note of the milliner's address, and felt that by calling there with Straker's photograph, I could easily dispose of the mythical Darbyshire.

"From that time on all was plain. Straker had led out the horse to a hollow where his light would be invisible. Simpson, in his flight, had dropped his cravat, and Straker had picked it up with some idea, perhaps, that he might use it in securing the horse's leg. Once in the hollow he had got behind the horse, and had struck a light, but the creature, frightened at the sudden glare, and with the strange instinct of animals feeling that some mischief was intended, had lashed out, and the steel shoe had struck Straker full on the forehead. He had already, in spite of the rain, taken off his overcoat in order to do his delicate task, and so, as he fell, his knife gashed his thigh. Do I make it clear?"

"Wonderful!" cried the Colonel. "Wonderful! You might have been there."

"My final shot was, I confess, a very long one. It struck me that so astute a man as Straker would not undertake this delicate tendon-nicking without a little practice. What could he practise on? My eyes fell upon the sheep, and I asked a question which, rather to my surprise, showed that my surmise was correct."

"You have made it perfectly clear, Mr. Holmes."

"When I returned to London I called upon the milliner, who at once recognized Straker as an excellent customer, of the name of Darbyshire, who had a very dashing wife with a strong partiality for expensive dresses. I have no doubt that this woman had plunged him over head and ears in debt, and so led him into this miserable plot."

"You have explained all but one thing," cried the Colonel. "Where was the horse?"

"Ah, it bolted and was cared for by one of your neighbours. We must have an amnesty in that direction, I think. This is Clapham Junction, if I am not mistaken, and we shall be in Victoria in less than ten minutes. If **28** you care to smoke a cigar in our rooms, Colonel, I shall be happy to give you any other details which might interest you."

28 *Victoria.* But Holmes, traveling from Winchester, would be riding the London & South Western Railway, later the western division of the Southern Railway, and his London terminus would be, not Victoria, but Waterloo Station (nor would a train from Winchester to London pass through Clapham Junction). Is this perhaps another indication that Watson was wrong when he said that the race was at Winchester?

Auctorial Note: In his autobiography, *Memories and Adventures*, Sir Arthur Conan Doyle wrote:

Sometimes I have got upon dangerous ground where I have taken risks through my own want of knowledge of the correct atmosphere. I have, for example, never been a racing man, and yet I ventured to write "Silver Blaze" in which the mystery depends upon the laws of training and racing. The story is all right, and Holmes may have been at the top of his form, but my ignorance cries aloud to heaven. I read an excellent and very damaging criticism of the story in some sporting paper, written clearly by a man who *did* know, in which he explained the exact penalties which would come upon everyone concerned if they had acted as I described. Half would have been in jail, and the other half warned off the turf forever. However, I have never been nervous about details, and one must be masterful sometimes.

Although Conan Doyle omitted "Silver Blaze" from his "best" list (as did the readers of the *Observer*), it is clear that he thought highly of the story; indeed, he wagered his wife a shilling that she could not guess the name of the murderer. And critics generally have written that "Silver Blaze" gave Sherlock Holmes one of his finest hours. "In our estimation," Ellery Queen wrote in his anthology, *Sporting Blood*, "'Silver Blaze' belongs prominently to any list of the five leading Sherlockian short stories. It represents the great Holmes at his incisive, dynamic best; despite its author's biographical apology, it reveals no obvious turf errors—at least, to the lay reader; and we could find no finer yarn to head our parade of The Great Sports Detective Stories."

46

THE ADVENTURE OF THE BERYL CORONET

[Friday, December 19, to Saturday, December 20, 1890]

1 *the snow of the day before still lay deep upon the ground.* The adventure, as we shall see, opened on a Friday, as Watson says and infers it did, in the opinion of most chronologists, but Watson's "February" is demonstrably wrong: in all the possible years (the farther limit is set by the fact that Watson's account of the adventure appeared in the May, 1892, issue of the *Strand Magazine*) there appear to have been only two Februarys in which there was a substantial fall of snow. The first was in February, 1881, (six inches on the 20th–21st, four inches on the 23rd). But in February, 1881, Watson had yet to share a case with Holmes and professed to know nothing of his companion's unusual occupation. The second substantial fall of snow was in February, 1886. But this was on the 28th, a Sunday, an impossible day in view of other statements in Watson's account of the adventure. Can we find a Thursday in a month other than February in the years under consideration on which there was a heavy fall of snow in London? We can, thanks to Mr. E. L. Hawke of the Royal Meteorological Society. In a letter to your editor dated November 29, 1954, Mr. Hawke wrote:

A fairly careful search through the London weather archives of 1881–1890 has brought to light only two Thursday snowfalls of appreciable amount:

a. March 17, 1887. A light daytime fall, not exceeding half an inch in depth. But there was already snow left from a heavy storm two days earlier; this had covered the ground five or six inches deep in N. W. London. Sharp frost during the night of the 17th–18th. Over six hours' sunshine on the Friday (18th). Moon near last quarter.

b. December 18, 1890. A substantial and general fall throughout London. Average depth three to four inches. Hard frost at night. No sunshine on the Friday (19th). Moon near first quarter.

The information we have received from the adventure of "The Reigate Squires" (in March,

"HOLMES," said I, as I stood one morning in our bow-window looking down the street, " here is a madman coming along. It seems rather sad that his relatives should allow him to come out alone."

My friend rose lazily from his arm-chair, and stood with his hands in the pockets of his dressing-gown, looking over my shoulder. It was a bright, crisp February morning, and the snow of the day before still lay deep upon the **1** ground, shimmering brightly in the wintry sun. Down the centre of Baker Street it had been ploughed into a brown crumbly band by the traffic, but at either side and on the heaped-up edges of the footpaths it still lay as white as when it fell. The grey pavement had been cleaned and scraped, but was still dangerously slippery, so that there were fewer passengers than usual. Indeed, from the direction of the Metropolitan station no one was coming save the single gentleman whose eccentric conduct had drawn my attention.

He was a man of about fifty, tall, portly, and imposing, with a massive, strongly marked face and a commanding figure. He was dressed in a sombre yet rich style, in black frock-coat, shining hat, neat brown gaiters, and well-cut pearl-grey trousers. Yet his actions were in absurd contrast to the dignity of his dress and features, for he was running hard, with occasional little springs, such as a weary man gives who is little accustomed to set any tax upon his legs. As he ran he jerked his hands up and down, waggled his head, and writhed his face into the most extraordinary contortions.

" What on earth can be the matter with him ? " I asked.

" He is looking up at the numbers of the houses."

" I believe that he is coming here," said Holmes, rubbing his hands.

" Here ? "

" Yes ; I rather think he is coming to consult me professionally. I think that I recognize the symptoms. Ha ! did I not tell you ? " As he spoke, the man, puffing and blowing, rushed at our door, and pulled at our bell until the whole house resounded with the clanging.

A few moments later he was in our room, still puffing, still gesticulating, but with so fixed a look of grief and despair in his eyes that our smiles were turned in an instant to horror and pity. For a while he could not get his words out, but swayed his body and plucked at his hair like one who has been driven to the extreme limits of his reason. Then, suddenly springing to his feet, he beat his head against the wall with such force that we both rushed upon him, and tore him away to the centre of the room. Sherlock Holmes pushed him down into the easy chair, and, sitting beside him, patted his hand, and chatted with him in the easy, soothing tones which he knew so well how to employ.

" You have come to me to tell me your story, have you not ? " said he. " You are fatigued with your haste. Pray wait until you have recovered yourself, and then I shall be most happy to look into any little problem which you may submit to me."

The man sat for a minute or more with a heaving chest, fighting against his emotion. Then he passed his handkerchief over his brow, set his lips tight, and turned his face towards us.

" No doubt you think me mad ? " said he.

" I see that you have had some great trouble," responded Holmes.

" God knows I have !—a trouble which is enough to unseat my reason, so sudden and so terrible is it. Public disgrace I might have faced, although I am a man whose character has never yet borne a stain. Private affliction also is the lot of every man ; but the two coming together, and in so frightful a form, have been enough to shake my very soul. Besides, it is not I alone. The very noblest in the land may suffer, unless some way be found out of this horrible affair."

" Pray compose yourself, sir," said Holmes, " and let me have a clear account of who you are, and what it is that has befallen you."

" My name," answered our visitor, " is probably familiar to your ears. I am Alexander Holder, of the banking firm of Holder & Stevenson, of Threadneedle Street."

1887, Holmes was on the Continent, bringing to a successful conclusion the taxing affair of the Netherland-Sumatra Company) makes 1887 quite impossible. The case began, then, on *Friday, December 19, 1890;* it ended the next day, *Saturday, December 20, 1890.*

"THE MAN SAT FOR A MINUTE WITH A HEAVING CHEST, FIGHTING AGAINST HIS EMOTION. THEN HE PASSED HIS HANDKERCHIEF OVER HIS BROW. . ."

Illustration by Sidney Paget for the *Strand Magazine,* May, 1892.

THE NAME WAS INDEED WELL KNOWN TO US . . .

Dr. Julian Wolff has conjectured (*Practical Handbook of Sherlockian Heraldry*) that "This great banker, whose name was indeed well known to Holmes, may have been one of the Glyns. It is difficult to conceive of so precious a possession as the Beryl Coronet being entrusted to any other banker. This great family has gained many honours in banking and public life. Anyone bearing one of the highest, noblest, and most exalted names in England could hardly deal with any other in a matter so important and so confidential. Robson's has the arms: 'ar. an eagle displ. with two heads sa. guttee d'or.' "

2 *the police inspector.* Gregson or Lestrade or another?

3 *one of the highest, noblest, most exalted names in England.* The late Edgar W. Smith's identification of this illustrious client as His Royal Highness, Albert Edward, Prince of Wales ("A Scandal in Identity") was supported by the late A. Carson Simpson in his essay, "Whose Was It? Conjectures on a Coronet," which demonstrates that H.R.H. was also the Duke of Rothesay, the oldest duchy in Scotland, and therefore the legitimate wearer of a duke's coronet which was, at the same time, "a national possession" and one that the Prince could easily get his hands on.

The name was indeed well known to us, as belonging to the senior partner in the second largest private banking concern in the City of London. What could have happened, then, to bring one of the foremost citizens of London to this most pitiable pass ? We waited, all curiosity, until with another effort he braced himself to tell his story.

" I feel that time is of value," said he, " that is why I **2** hastened here when the police inspector suggested that I should secure your co-operation. I came to Baker Street by the Underground, and hurried from there on foot, for the cabs go slowly through this snow. That is why I was so out of breath, for I am a man who takes very little exercise. I feel better now, and I will put the facts before you as shortly and yet as clearly as I can.

" It is, of course, well known to you, that in a successful banking business as much depends upon our being able to find remunerative investments for our funds, as upon our increasing our connection and the number of our depositors. One of our most lucrative means of laying out money is in the shape of loans, where the security is unimpeachable. We have done a good deal in this direction during the last few years, and there are many noble families to whom we have advanced large sums upon the security of their pictures, libraries, or plate.

" Yesterday morning I was seated in my office at the Bank, when a card was brought in to me by one of the clerks. I started when I saw the name, for it was that of none other than—well, perhaps even to you I had better say no more than that it was a name which is a household word all over the earth—one of the highest, noblest, most **3** exalted names in England. I was overwhelmed by the honour, and attempted, when he entered, to say so, but he plunged at once into business with the air of a man who wishes to hurry quickly through a disagreeable task.

" ' Mr. Holder,' said he, ' I have been informed that you are in the habit of advancing money.'

" ' The firm do so when the security is good,' I answered.

" ' It is absolutely essential to me,' said he, ' that I should have fifty thousand pounds at once. I could of course borrow so trifling a sum ten times over from my friends, but I much prefer to make it a matter of business, and to carry out that business myself. In my position you can readily understand that it is unwise to place oneself under obligations.'

" ' For how long, may I ask, do you want this sum ? ' I asked.

" ' Next Monday I have a large sum due to me, and I shall then most certainly repay what you advance, with whatever interest you think it right to charge. But it is very essential to me that the money should be paid at once.'

" ' I should be happy to advance it without further parley from my own private purse,' said I, ' were it not that the strain would be rather more than it could bear. If, on the other hand, I am to do it in the name of the firm, then in justice to my partner I must insist that, even in your case, every business-like precaution should be taken.'

" ' I should much prefer to have it so,' said he, raising up a square, black morocco case which he had laid beside his chair. ' You have doubtless heard of the Beryl coronet ? '

" ' One of the most precious public possessions of the Empire,' said I.

" ' Precisely.' He opened the case, and there, embedded in soft, flesh-coloured velvet, lay the magnificent piece of jewellery which he had named. ' There are thirty-nine enormous beryls,' said he, ' and the price of the gold chasing is incalculable. The lowest estimate would put the worth of the coronet at double the sum which I have asked. I am prepared to leave it with you as my security.'

" I took the precious case into my hands and looked in some perplexity from it to my illustrious client.

"THERE . . . LAY THE MAGNIFICENT PIECE OF JEWELLERY . . ."

The coronet worn by a duke on state and official occasions, when he must appear in public so distinguished, and clad in his robes, is decorated on the circlet with engraving, and bears on the upper edge eight strawberry leaves. The cap, which is the same for all nobility, is of crimson velvet, turned up (or guarded) ermine. The coronet of a duke should not be confused with the ducal coronet so often blazoned in heraldic achievements. This is represented quite differently: first, the cap is absent; second, the circlet is generally plain, though it may be jewelled; and finally only three strawberry leaves decorate the upper edge; it is used in place of a wreath of the colors between helmet and crest, and for crowning or gorging animals.

"I TOOK THE PRECIOUS CASE INTO MY HANDS . . ."

Illustration by Sidney Paget for the *Strand Magazine*, May, 1892.

" ' You doubt its value ? ' he asked.

" ' Not at all. I only doubt——'

" ' The propriety of my leaving it. You may set your mind at rest about that. I should not dream of doing so were it not absolutely certain that I should be able in four days to reclaim it. It is a pure matter of form. Is the **4** security sufficient ? '

" ' Ample.'

" ' You understand, Mr. Holder, that I am giving you a strong proof of the confidence which I have in you, founded upon all that I have heard of you. I rely upon you not only to be discreet and to refrain from all gossip upon the matter, but, above all, to preserve this coronet with every possible precaution, because I need not say that a great public scandal would be caused if any harm were to befall it. Any injury to it would be almost as serious as its complete loss, for there are no beryls in the world to match these, and it would be impossible to replace them. I leave it with you, however, with every confidence, and I shall call for it in person on Monday morning.'

" Seeing that my client was anxious to leave, I said no more ; but, calling for my cashier, I ordered him to pay over fifty thousand-pound notes. When I was alone once more, however, with the precious case lying upon the table

4 *in four days.* Watson has quoted Holder as saying: "Yesterday morning I was seated in my office at the Bank." The illustrious client who came to him on that day said he would have a large sum due him "next Monday" and so "should be able in four days" to reclaim the coronet. "Yesterday" was therefore a Thursday and Holmes' part in the case began on a Friday.

in front of me, I could not but think with some misgivings of the immense responsibility which it entailed upon me. There could be no doubt that, as it was a national possession, a horrible scandal would ensue if any misfortune should occur to it. I already regretted having ever consented to take charge of it. However, it was too late to alter the matter now, so I locked it up in my private safe, and turned once more to my work.

"When evening came, I felt that it would be an imprudence to leave so precious a thing in the office behind me. Bankers' safes had been forced before now, and why should not mine be? If so, how terrible would be the position in which I should find myself! I determined, therefore, that for the next few days I would always carry the case backwards and forwards with me, so that it might never be really out of my reach. With this intention, I called a cab, and drove out to my house at Streatham, carrying the jewel with me. I did not breathe freely until I had taken it upstairs, and locked it in the bureau of my dressing-room.

"And now a word as to my household, Mr. Holmes, for I wish you to thoroughly understand the situation. My groom and my page sleep out of the house, and may be set aside altogether. I have three maid-servants who have been with me a number of years, and whose absolute reliability is quite above suspicion. Another, Lucy Parr, the second waiting-maid, has only been in my service a few months. She came with an excellent character, however, and has always given me satisfaction. She is a very pretty girl, and has attracted admirers who have occasionally hung about the place. That is the only drawback which we have found to her, but we believe her to be a thoroughly good girl in every way.

"So much for the servants. My family itself is so small that it will not take me long to describe it. I am a widower, and have an only son, Arthur. He has been a disappointment to me, Mr. Holmes, a grievous disappointment. I have no doubt that I am myself to blame. People tell me that I have spoiled him. Very likely I have. When my dear wife died I felt that he was all I had to love. I could not bear to see the smile fade even for a moment from his face. I have never denied him a wish. Perhaps it would have been better for both of us had I been sterner, but I meant it for the best.

"It was naturally my intention that he should succeed me in my business, but he was not of a business turn. He was wild, wayward, and, to speak the truth, I could not trust him in the handling of large sums of money. When he was young he became a member of an aristocratic club, and there, having charming manners, he was soon the intimate of a number of men with long purses and expensive habits. He learned to play heavily at cards and to squander money on the turf, until he had again and again to come to me and implore me to give him an advance upon his allowance, that he might settle his debts of honour. He tried more than once to break away from the dangerous company which he was keeping, but each time the influence of his friend Sir George Burnwell was enough to draw him back again.

" And, indeed, I could not wonder that such a man as Sir George Burnwell should gain an influence over him, for he has frequently brought him to my house, and I have found myself that I could hardly resist the fascination of his manner.   He is older than Arthur, a man of the world to his finger-tips, one who has been everywhere, seen everything, a brilliant talker, and a man of great personal beauty.   Yet when I think of him in cold blood, far away from the glamour of his presence, I am convinced from his cynical speech, and the look which I have caught in his eyes, that he is one who should be deeply distrusted. So I think, and so, too, thinks my little Mary, who has a woman's quick insight into character.

" And now there is only she to be described.   She is my niece ; but when my brother died five years ago and left her alone in the world I adopted her, and have looked upon her ever since as my daughter.   She is a sunbeam in my house—sweet, loving, beautiful, a wonderful manager and housekeeper, yet as tender and quiet and gentle as a woman could be.   She is my right hand.   I do not know what I could do without her.   In only one matter has she ever gone against my wishes.   Twice my boy has asked her to marry him, for he loves her devotedly, but each time she has refused him.   I think that if anyone could have drawn him into the right path it would have been she, and that his marriage might have changed his whole life ; but now, alas ! it is too late—for ever too late !

" Now, Mr. Holmes, you know the people who live under my roof, and I shall continue with my miserable story.

" When we were taking coffee in the drawing-room that night, after dinner, I told Arthur and Mary my experience, and of the precious treasure which we had under our roof, suppressing only the name of my client.   Lucy Parr, who had brought in the coffee, had, I am sure, left the room ; but I cannot swear that the door was closed.   Mary and Arthur were much interested, and wished to see the famous coronet, but I thought it better not to disturb it.

" ' Where have you put it ? ' asked Arthur.

" ' In my own bureau.'

" ' Well, I hope to goodness the house won't be burgled during the night,' said he.

" ' It is locked up,' I answered.

" ' Oh, any old key will fit that bureau.   When I was a youngster I have opened it myself with the key of the box-room cupboard.'

" He often had a wild way of talking, so that I thought little of what he said.   He followed me to my room, however, that night with a very grave face.

" ' Look here, dad,' said he, with his eyes cast down. ' Can you let me have two hundred pounds ? '

" ' No, I cannot ! ' I answered sharply.   ' I have been far too generous with you in money matters.'

" ' You have been very kind,' said he ; ' but I must have this money, or else I can never show my face inside the club again.'

" ' And a very good thing, too ! ' I cried.

" ' Yes, but you would not have me leave it a dishonoured man,' said he.   ' I could not bear the disgrace.   I must raise the money in some way, and if you will not let me have it, then I must try other means.'

5 *the third demand during the month.* Perhaps an indication that "The Adventure of the Beryl Coronet" took place later rather than earlier in the month under consideration.

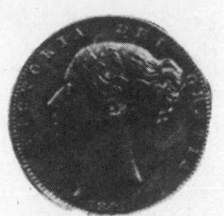 

" 'YOU SHALL NOT HAVE A FARTHING FROM ME . . .' "

Shown is the 1841 Victoria farthing. "The farthing (fourthing or quarter-penny)," the late A. Carson Simpson wrote in *Numismatics in the Canon: Part I*, "was originally made from the silver penny, as a home-workshop project, in the same way as the halfpenny; it required only an additional cut along the other arm of the voided cross. This type was also replaced by a circular silver farthing, one year earlier than the halfpenny." This is the only Canonical reference to the farthing.

" I was very angry, for this was the third demand dur-
5 ing the month. ' You shall not have a farthing from me,' I cried, on which he bowed and left the room without another word.

" When he was gone I unlocked my bureau, made sure that my treasure was safe, and locked it again.   Then I started to go round the house to see that all was secure—a duty which I usually leave to Mary, but which I thought it well to perform myself that night.   As I came down the stairs I saw Mary herself at the side-window of the hall, which she closed and fastened as I approached.

" ' Tell me, dad,' said she, looking, I thought, a little disturbed, ' did you give Lucy, the maid, leave to go out to-night ? '

" ' Certainly not.'

" ' She came in just now by the back door. I have no doubt that she has only been to the side-gate to see someone, but I think that it is hardly safe, and should be stopped.'

" ' You must speak to her in the morning, or I will, if you prefer it.   Are you sure that everything is fastened ? '

" ' Quite sure, dad.'

" ' Then, good night.'   I kissed her, and went to my bedroom, where I was soon asleep.

" I am endeavouring to tell you everything, Mr. Holmes, which may have any bearing upon the case, but I beg that you will question me upon any point which I do not make clear."

" On the contrary, your statement is singularly lucid."

" I come to a part of my story now in which I should wish to be particularly so.   I am not a very heavy sleeper, and the anxiety in my mind tended, no doubt, to make me even less so than usual.   About two in the morning, then, I was awakened by some sound in the house.   It had ceased ere I was wide awake, but it had left an impression behind it as though a window had gently closed somewhere. I lay listening with all my ears.   Suddenly, to my horror, there was a distinct sound of footsteps moving softly in the next room.   I slipped out of bed, all palpitating with fear, and peeped round the corner of my dressing-room door.

" ' Arthur ! ' I screamed, ' you villain ! you thief ! How dare you touch that coronet ? '

" The gas was half up, as I had left it, and my unhappy boy, dressed only in his shirt and trousers, was standing beside the light, holding the coronet in his hands.   He appeared to be wrenching at it, or bending it with all his strength.   At my cry he dropped it from his grasp, and turned as pale as death.   I snatched it up and examined it. One of the gold corners, with three of the beryls in it, was missing.

" ' You blackguard ! ' I shouted, beside myself with rage. ' You have destroyed it ! You have dishonoured me for ever !   Where are the jewels you have stolen ? '

" ' Stolen ! ' he cried.

" ' Yes, you thief ! ' I roared, shaking him by the shoulder.

" ' There are none missing.   There cannot be any missing,' said he.

" ' There are three missing.   And you know where they

are. Must I call you a liar as well as a thief ? Did I not see you trying to tear off another piece ? '

" ' You have called me names enough,' said he ; ' I will not stand it any longer. I shall not say another word about this business since you have chosen to insult me. I will leave your house in the morning, and make my own way in the world.'

" ' You shall leave it in the hands of the police ! ' I cried, half mad with grief and rage. ' I shall have this matter probed to the bottom.'

" ' You shall learn ñothing from me,' said he, with a passion such as I should not have thought was in his nature. ' If you choose to call the police, let them find what they can.'

" By this time the whole house was astir, for I had raised my voice in my anger. Mary was the first to rush into my room, and at the sight of the coronet and of Arthur's face, she read the whole story, and, with a scream, fell down senseless on the ground. I sent the housemaid for the police, and put the investigation into their hands at once. When the inspector and a constable entered the house, Arthur, who had stood sullenly with his arms folded, asked me whether it was my intention to charge him with theft. I answered that it had ceased to be a private matter, but had become a public one, since the ruined coronet was national property. I was determined that the law should have its way in everything.

" ' At least,' said he, ' you will not have me arrested at once. It would be to your advantage as well as mine if I might leave the house for five minutes.'

" ' That you may get away, or perhaps that you may conceal what you have stolen,' said I. And then realizing the dreadful position in which I was placed, I implored him to remember that not only my honour, but that of one who was far greater than I, was at stake ; and that he threatened to raise a scandal which would convulse the nation. He might avert it all if he would but tell me what he had done with the three missing stones.

" ' You may as well face the matter,' said I ; ' you have been caught in the act, and no confession could make your guilt more heinous. If you but make such reparation as is in your power, by telling us where the beryls are, all shall be forgiven and forgotten.'

" ' Keep your forgiveness for those who ask for it,' he answered, turning away from me with a sneer. I saw that he was too hardened for any words of mine to influence him. There was but one way for it. I called in the inspector, and gave him into custody. A search was made at once, not only of his person, but of his room, and of every portion of the house where he could possibly have concealed the gems ; but no trace of them could be found, nor would the wretched boy open his mouth for all our persuasions and our threats. This morning he was removed to a cell, and I, after going through all the police formalities, have hurried round to you, to implore you to use your skill in unravelling the matter. The police have openly confessed that they can at present make nothing of it. You may go to any expense which you think necessary. I have already offered a reward of a thousand pounds. My

"AT MY CRY HE DROPPED IT FROM HIS GRASP . . ."

Illustration by Sidney Paget for the *Strand Maga-zine*, May, 1892.

God, what shall I do! I have lost my honour, my gems, and my son in one night. Oh, what shall I do!"

He put a hand on either side of his head, and rocked himself to and fro, droning to himself like a child whose grief has got beyond words.

Sherlock Holmes sat silent for some few minutes, with his brows knitted and his eyes fixed upon the fire.

" Do you receive much company ? " he asked.

" None, save my partner with his family, and an occasional friend of Arthur's. Sir George Burnwell has been several times lately. No one else, I think."

" Do you go out much in society ? "

" Arthur does. Mary and I stay at home. We neither of us care for it."

" That is unusual in a young girl."

" She is of a quiet nature. Besides, she is not so very young. She is four-and-twenty."

" This matter, from what you say, seems to have been a shock to her also."

" Terrible ! She is even more affected than I."

" You have neither of you any doubt as to your son's guilt ? "

" How can we have, when I saw him with my own eyes with the coronet in his hands ? "

" I hardly consider that a conclusive proof. Was the remainder of the coronet at all injured ? "

" Yes, it was twisted."

" Do you not think, then, that he might have been trying to straighten it ? "

" God bless you ! You are doing what you can for him and for me. But it is too heavy a task. What was he doing there at all ? If his purpose were innocent, why did he not say so ? "

" Precisely. And if he were guilty, why did he not invent a lie ? His silence appears to me to cut both ways. There are several singular points about the case. What did the police think of the noise which awoke you from your sleep ? "

" They considered that it might be caused by Arthur's closing his bedroom door."

" A likely story ! As if a man bent on felony would slam the door so as to awake a household. What did they say, then, of the disappearance of these gems ? "

" They are still sounding the planking and probing the furniture in the hope of finding them."

" Have they thought of looking outside the house ? "

" Yes, they have shown extraordinary energy. The whole garden has already been minutely examined."

" Now, my dear sir," said Holmes, " is it not obvious to you now that this matter really strikes very much deeper than either you or the police were at first inclined to think ? It appeared to you to be a simple case ; to me it seems exceedingly complex. Consider what is involved by your theory. You suppose that your son came down from his bed, went, at great risk, to your dressing-room, opened your bureau, took out your coronet, broke off by main force a small portion of it, went off to some other place, concealed three gems out of the thirty-nine, with such skill that nobody can find them, and then returned with the other thirty-six into the room in which he exposed himself to the greatest danger of being discovered. I ask you now, is such a theory tenable ? "

" But what other is there ? " cried the banker with a gesture of despair. " If his motives were innocent, why does he not explain them ? "

" It is our task to find that out," replied Holmes, " so now, if you please, Mr. Holder, we will set off for Streatham together and devote an hour to glancing a little more closely into details."

My friend insisted upon my accompanying them in their expedition, which I was eager enough to do, for my curiosity and sympathy were deeply stirred by the story to which we had listened. I confess that the guilt of the banker's son appeared to me to be as obvious as it did to his unhappy father, but still I had such faith in Holmes' judgment that I felt that there must be some grounds for hope as long as he was dissatisfied with the accepted explanation. He hardly spoke a word the whole way out to the southern suburb, but sat with his chin upon his breast, and his hat drawn over his eyes, sunk in the deepest thought. Our client appeared to have taken fresh heart at the little glimpse of hope which had been presented to him, and he even broke into a desultory chat with me over his business affairs. A short railway journey, and a shorter walk, brought us to Fairbank, the modest residence of the great financier.

Fairbank was a good-sized square house of white stone, standing back a little from the road. A double carriage sweep, with a snow-clad lawn, stretched down in front to the two large iron gates which closed the entrance. On the right side was a small wooden thicket which led into a narrow path between two neat hedges stretching from the road to the kitchen door, and forming the tradesmen's entrance. On the left ran a lane which led to the stables, and was not itself within the grounds at all, being a public, though little used, thoroughfare. Holmes left us standing at the door, and walked slowly all round the house, across the front, down the tradesmen's path, and so round by the garden behind into the stable lane. So long was he that Mr. Holder and I went into the dining-room, and waited by the fire until he should return. We were sitting there in silence when the door opened, and a young lady came in. She was rather above the middle height, slim, with dark hair and eyes, which seemed the darker against the absolute pallor of her skin. I do not think that I have ever seen such deadly paleness in a woman's face. Her lips, too, were bloodless, but her eyes were flushed with crying. As she swept silently into the room she impressed me with a greater sense of her grief than the banker had done in the morning, and it was the more striking in her as she was evidently a woman of strong character, with immense capacity for self-restraint. Disregarding my presence, she went straight to her uncle, and passed her hand over his head with a sweet womanly caress.

" You have given orders that Arthur should be liberated, have you not, dad ? " she asked.

" No, no, my girl, the matter must be probed to the bottom."

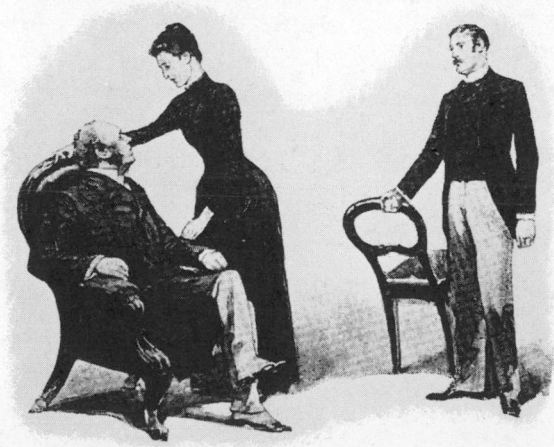

DISREGARDING MY PRESENCE, SHE WENT STRAIGHT TO HER UNCLE . . .

Illustration by Sidney Paget for the *Strand Magazine*, May, 1892.

" But I am so sure that he is innocent. You know what women's instincts are. I know that he has done no harm, and that you will be sorry for having acted so harshly."

" Why is he silent, then, if he is innocent ? "

" Who knows ? Perhaps because he was so angry that you should suspect him."

" How could I help suspecting him, when I actually saw him with the coronet in his hand ? "

" Oh, but he had only picked it up to look at it. Oh, do, do take my word for it that he is innocent. Let the matter drop, and say no more. It is so dreadful to think of our dear Arthur in prison ! "

" I shall never let it drop until the gems are found—never, Mary ! Your affection for Arthur blinds you as to the awful consequences to me. Far from hushing the thing up, I have brought a gentleman down from London to inquire more deeply into it."

" This gentleman ? " she asked, facing round to.me.

" No, his friend. He wished us to leave him alone. He is round in the stable lane now."

" The stable lane ? " She raised her dark eyebrows. " What can he hope to find there ? Ah, this, I suppose, is he. I trust, sir, that you will succeed in proving, what I feel sure is the truth, that my cousin Arthur is innocent of this crime."

" I fully share your opinion, and, I trust with you, that we may prove it," returned Holmes, going back to the mat to knock the snow from his shoes. " I believe I have the honour of addressing Miss Mary Holder. Might I ask you a question or two ? "

" Pray do, sir, if it may help to clear this horrible affair up."

" You heard nothing yourself last night ? "

" Nothing, until my uncle here began to speak loudly. I heard that, and I came down."

" You shut up the windows and doors the night before. Did you fasten all the windows ? "

" Yes."

" Were they all fastened this morning ? "

" Yes."

" You have a maid who has a sweetheart ? I think that you remarked to your uncle last night that she had been out to see him ? "

" Yes, and she was the girl who waited in the drawing-room, and who may have heard uncle's remarks about the coronet."

" I see. You infer that she may have gone out to tell her sweetheart, and that the two may have planned the robbery."

" But what is the good of all these vague theories," cried the banker impatiently, " when I have told you that I saw Arthur with the coronet in his hands ? "

" Wait a little, Mr. Holder. We must come back to that. About this girl, Miss Holder. You saw her return by the kitchen door, I presume ? "

" Yes ; when I went to see if the door was fastened for the night I met her slipping in. I saw the man, too, in the gloom."

" Do you know him ? "

"Oh, yes ; he is the greengrocer who brings our vegetables round.   His name is Francis Prosper."

"He stood," said Holmes, "to the left of the door—that is to say, farther up the path than is necessary to reach the door ? "

"Yes, he did."

"And he is a man with a wooden leg ? "

Something like fear sprang up in the young lady's expressive black eyes.   "Why, you are like a magician," said she.   "How do you know that ? "   She smiled, but there was no answering smile in Holmes' thin, eager face.

"I should be very glad now to go upstairs," said he. "I shall probably wish to go over the outside of the house again.   Perhaps I had better take a look at the lower windows before I go up."

He walked swiftly round from one to the other, pausing only at the large one which looked from the hall on to the stable lane.   This he opened, and made a very careful examination of the sill with his powerful magnifying lens. "Now we shall go upstairs," said he, at last.

The banker's dressing-room was a plainly furnished little chamber with a grey carpet, a large bureau, and a long mirror.   Holmes went to the bureau first, and looked hard at the lock.

"Which key was used to open it ? " he asked.

"That which my son himself indicated—that of the cupboard of the lumber-room."

"Have you it here ? "

"That is it on the dressing-table."

Sherlock Holmes took it up and opened the bureau.

"It is a noiseless lock," said he.   "It is no wonder that it did not wake you.   This case, I presume, contains the coronet.   We must have a look at it."   He opened the case, and, taking out the diadem, he laid it upon the table. It was a magnificent specimen of the jeweller's art, and the thirty-six stones were the finest that I have ever seen.   At one side of the coronet was a crooked cracked edge, where a corner holding three gems had been torn away.

"Now, Mr. Holder," said Holmes ; "here is the corner which corresponds to that which has been so unfortunately lost.   Might I beg that you will break it off."

The banker recoiled in horror.   "I should not dream of trying," said he.

"Then I will."   Holmes suddenly bent his strength upon it, but without result.   "I feel it give a little," said he ; "but, though I am exceptionally strong in the fingers, it would take me all my time to break it.   An ordinary man could not do it.   Now, what do you think would happen if I did break it, Mr. Holder ?   There would be a noise like a pistol shot.   Do you tell me that all this happened within a few yards of your bed, and that you heard nothing of it ? "

"I do not know what to think.   It is all dark to me."

"But perhaps it may grow lighter as we go.   What do you think, Miss Holder ? "

"I confess that I still share my uncle's perplexity."

"Your son had no shoes or slippers on when you saw him ? "

SOMETHING LIKE FEAR SPRANG UP IN THE YOUNG LADY'S EXPRESSIVE BLACK EYES.

Illustration by Sidney Paget for the *Strand Magazine*, May, 1892.

HE . . . WAS DOWN AGAIN IN A FEW MINUTES DRESSED
AS A COMMON LOAFER.

Illustration by Sidney Paget for the *Strand Magazine*, May, 1892.

" He had nothing on save only his trousers and shirt."

" Thank you. We have certainly been favoured with extraordinary luck during this inquiry, and it will be entirely our own fault if we do not succeed in clearing the matter up. With your permission, Mr. Holder, I shall now continue my investigations outside."

He went alone, at his own request, for he explained that any unnecessary footmarks might make his task more difficult. For an hour or more he was at work, returning at last with his feet heavy with snow and his features as inscrutable as ever.

" I think that I have seen now all that there is to see, Mr. Holder," said he ; " I can serve you best by returning to my rooms."

" But the gems, Mr. Holmes. Where are they ? "

" I cannot tell."

The banker wrung his hands. " I shall never see them again ! " he cried. " And my son ? You give me hopes ? "

" My opinion is in no way altered."

" Then for God's sake what was this dark business which was acted in my house last night ? "

" If you can call upon me at my Baker Street rooms to-morrow morning between nine and ten I shall be happy to do what I can to make it clearer. I understand that you give me *carte blanche* to act for you, provided only that I get back the gems, and that you place no limit on the sum I may draw."

" I would give my fortune to have them back."

" Very good. I shall look into the matter between this and then. Good-bye ; it is just possible that I may have to come over here again before evening."

It was obvious to me that my companion's mind was now made up about the case, although what his conclusions were was more than I could even dimly imagine. Several times during our homeward journey I endeavoured to sound him upon that point, but he always glided away to some other topic, until at last I gave it over in despair. It was not yet three when we found ourselves in our room once more. He hurried to his chamber, and was down again in a few minutes dressed as a common loafer. With his collar turned up, his shiny seedy coat, his red cravat, and his worn boots, he was a perfect sample of the class.

" I think that this should do," said he, glancing into the glass above the fireplace. " I only wish that you could come with me, Watson, but I fear that it won't do. I may be on the trail in this matter, or I may be following a will-o'-the-wisp, but I shall soon know which it is. I hope that I may be back in a few hours." He cut a slice of beef from the joint upon the sideboard, sandwiched it between two rounds of bread, and, thrusting this rude meal into his pocket, he started off upon his expedition.

I had just finished my tea when he returned, evidently in excellent spirits, swinging an old elastic-sided boot in his hand. He chucked it down into a corner and helped himself to a cup of tea.

" I only looked in as I passed," said he. " I am going right on."

" Where to ? "

" Oh, to the other side of the West End.   It may be some time before I get back.   Don't wait up for me in case I should be late."

" How are you getting on ? "

" Oh, so-so.   Nothing to complain of.   I have been out to Streatham since I saw you last, but I did not call at the house.   It is a very sweet little problem, and I would not have missed it for a good deal.   However, I must not sit gossiping here, but must get these disreputable clothes off and return to my highly respectable self."

I could see by his manner that he had stronger reasons for satisfaction than his words alone would imply.   His eyes twinkled, and there was even a touch of colour upon his sallow cheeks.   He hastened upstairs, and a few minutes later I heard the slam of the hall door, which told me that he was off once more upon his congenial hunt.

I waited until midnight, but there was no sign of his return, so I retired to my room.   It was no uncommon thing for him to be away for days and nights on end when he was hot upon a scent, so that his lateness caused me no surprise.   I do not know at what hour he came in, but when I came down to breakfast in the morning, there he was with a cup of coffee in one hand and the paper in the other, as fresh and trim as possible.

" You will excuse my beginning without you, Watson," said he ; " but you remember that our client has rather an early appointment this morning."

" Why, it is after nine now," I answered.   " I should not be surprised if that were he.   I thought I heard a ring."

It was, indeed, our friend the financier.   I was shocked by the change which had come over him, for his face, which was naturally of a broad and massive mould, was now pinched and fallen in, while his hair seemed to be at least a shade whiter.   He entered with a weariness and lethargy which was even more painful than his violence of the morning before, and he dropped heavily into the arm-chair which I pushed forward for him.

" I do not know what I have done to be so severely tried," said he.   " Only two days ago I was a happy and prosperous man, without a care in the world.   Now I am left to a lonely and dishonoured age.   One sorrow comes close upon the heels of another.   My niece Mary has deserted me."

" Deserted you ? "

" Yes.   Her bed this morning had not been slept in, her room was empty, and a note lay for me upon the hall table. I had said to her last night, in sorrow and not in anger, that if she had married my boy all might have been well with him.   Perhaps it was thoughtless of me to say so.   It is to that remark that she refers in this note : ' My dearest Uncle—I feel that I have brought this trouble upon you, and that if I had acted differently this terrible misfortune might never have occurred.   I cannot, with this thought in my mind, ever again be happy under your roof, and I feel that I must leave you for ever.   Do not worry about my future, for that is provided for ; and, above all, do not

6 *as I should be proud to see my own son do.*
Like Holmes' remark in "The Adventure of the
Copper Beeches" ("I confess that it is not the situation which I should like to see a sister of mine
apply for") this statement has furnished commentators with considerable grounds for speculation.

Mr. Rex Stout has suggested ("Watson Was a
Woman") that Lord Peter Death Bredon Wimsey
was a son of the Master Detective; Dr. John D.
Clark ("Some Notes Relating to a Preliminary Investigation Into the Paternity of Nero Wolfe")
and your editor (*Sherlock Holmes of Baker
Street*) have supported the theory that a better
case can be made for someone considerably closer
to Mr. Stout than Lord Peter; Mr. Marion Prince
has put in a claim ("Sherlock and Son") for Inspector Stanley Hopkins; the late A. Carson Simpson advanced the interesting theory ("I'm Off for
Philadelphia in the Morning") that Joseph Rou-
letabille, the young reporter-detective hero of
seven novels by Gaston Leroux, 1868–1927, distinguished French journalist and author, was a
son of Sherlock; and Mr. Manly Wade Wellman's
candidate for the honor ("The Great Man's Great
Son") is Bertie Wooster's bulging-browed valet,
Jeeves.

"The End of Sherlock Holmes," an unusual
pastiche signed A.E.P., would have us believe that
Holmes married Miss Alice Falkland (of William
Gillette's play, *Sherlock Holmes*) *circa* 1903–1905
and by her had a son. Mr. Ellery Queen, commenting on this in his *Misadventures of Sherlock
Holmes*, there added: "Other instances dealing
with the scion of Sherlock Holmes include John
Kendrick Bangs' Raffles Holmes, who was the
'son' of Sherlock and the 'grandson' of Raffles . . . ;
and Sherlock Holmes, Jr., the hero of a color-
comic series that appeared in the Sunday supplements of many American newspapers between
1911 and 1914, drawn by no less a person than
Sidney Smith, the creator of the famous 'Gumps.'
There is also Frederic Arnold Kummer's and Basil
Mitchell's Shirley Holmes, daughter of Sherlock,
assisted by Joan Watson, daughter of Dr. Watson . . ."

search for me, for it will be fruitless labour, and an ill
service to me.   In life or in death, I am ever your loving—
MARY.'   What could she mean by that note, Mr. Holmes ?
Do you think it points to suicide ? "

" No, no, nothing of the kind.   It is perhaps the best
possible solution.   I trust, Mr. Holder, that you are nearing the end of your troubles."

" Ha !   You say so !   You have heard something, Mr.
Holmes ; you have learned something !   Where are the
gems ? "

" You would not think a thousand pounds apiece an
excessive sum for them ? "

" I would pay ten."

" That would be unnecessary.   Three thousand will
cover the matter.   And there is a little reward, I fancy.
Have you your cheque-book ?   Here is a pen.   Better
make it out for four thousand pounds."

With a dazed face the banker made out the required
cheque.   Holmes walked over to his desk, took out a little
triangular piece of gold with three gems in it, and threw it
down upon the table.

With a shriek of joy our client clutched it up.

" You have it ! " he gasped.   " I am saved !   I am
saved ! "

The reaction of joy was as passionate as his grief had
been, and he hugged his recovered gems to his bosom.

" There is one other thing you owe, Mr. Holder," said
Sherlock Holmes, rather sternly.

" Owe ! "   He caught up a pen.   " Name the sum,
and I will pay it."

" No, the debt is not to me.   You owe a very humble
apology to that noble lad, your son, who has carried himself in this matter as I should be proud to see my own son
6 do, should I ever chance to have one."

" Then it was not Arthur who took them ? "

" I told you yesterday, and I repeat to-day, that it was
not."

" You are sure of it !   Then let us hurry to him at once,
to let him know that the truth is known."

" He knows it already.   When I had cleared it all up I
had an interview with him, and finding that he would not
tell me the story, I told it to him, on which he had to confess that I was right, and to add the very few details which
were not yet quite clear to me.   Your news of this morning, however, may open his lips."

" For Heaven's sake tell me, then, what is this extraordinary mystery ! "

" I will do so, and I will show you the steps by which
I reached it.   And let me say to you, first, what it is hardest
for me to say and for you to hear.   There has been an
understanding between Sir George Burnwell and your
niece, Mary.   They have now fled together."

" My Mary ?   Impossible ! "

" It is, unfortunately, more than possible ; it is certain.
Neither you nor your son knew the true character of this
man when you admitted him into your family circle.   He
is one of the most dangerous men in England—a ruined
gambler, an absolutely desperate villain ; a man without

heart or conscience. Your niece knew nothing of such **7** men. When he breathed his vows to her, as he had done to a hundred before her, she flattered herself that she alone had touched his heart. The devil knows best what he said, but at last she became his tool, and was in the habit of seeing him nearly every evening."

" I cannot, and I will not, believe it ! " cried the banker with an ashen face.

" I will tell you, then, what occurred in your house that night. Your niece, when you had, as she thought, gone to your room, slipped down and talked to her lover through the window which leads into the stable lane. His footmarks had pressed right through the snow, so long had he stood there. She told him of the coronet. His wicked lust for gold kindled at the news, and he bent her to his will. I have no doubt that she loved you, but there are women in whom the love of a lover extinguishes all other loves, and I think that she must have been one. She had hardly listened to his instructions when she saw you coming downstairs, on which she closed the window rapidly, and told you about one of the servants' escapade with her wooden-legged lover, which was all perfectly true.

" Your boy, Arthur, went to bed after his interview with you, but he slept badly on account of his uneasiness about his club debts. In the middle of the night he heard a soft tread pass his door, so he rose, and looking out, was surprised to see his cousin walking very stealthily along the passage, until she disappeared into your dressing-room. Petrified with astonishment the lad slipped on some clothes, and waited there in the dark to see what would come of this strange affair. Presently she emerged from the room again, and in the light of the passage lamp your son saw that she carried the precious coronet in her hands. She passed down the stairs, and he, thrilling with horror, ran along and slipped behind the curtain near your door whence he could see what passed in the hall beneath. He saw her stealthily open the window, hand out the coronet to someone in the gloom, and then closing it once more hurry back to her room, passing quite close to where he stood hid behind the curtain.

" As long as she was on the scene he could not take any action without a horrible exposure of the woman whom he loved. But the instant she was gone he realized how crushing a misfortune this would be for you, and how all-important it was to set it right. He rushed down, just as he was, in his bare feet, opened the window, sprang out into the snow, and ran down the lane, where he could see a dark figure in the moonlight. Sir George Burnwell tried **8** to get away, but Arthur caught him, and there was a struggle between them, your lad tugging at one side of the coronet, and his opponent at the other. In the scuffle, your son struck Sir George, and cut him over the eye. Then something suddenly snapped, and your son, finding that he had the coronet in his hands, rushed back, closed the window, ascended to your room, and had just observed that the coronet had been twisted in the struggle and was endeavouring to straighten it, when you appeared upon the scene."

7 *a man without heart or conscience.* The late Robert R. Pattrick maintained ("Moriarty Was There") that "the entire affair of the Beryl Coronet has sinister overtones which have never been properly examined. Burnwell's careful cultivation of the friendships of both Arthur and Mary smacks of a devious plot being brewed. Surely it was not entirely by chance he was lurking outside the house the very night the Coronet was brought there. It seems probable that [Burnwell] was a Moriarty agent assigned especially to confiscate the Coronet."

8 *a dark figure in the moonlight.* It must be admitted that the moon was wrong for both of the dates suggested by the snowfall (March 17, 1887, and December 18, 1890). The moon did not rise until 3:09 on the morning of Friday, March 18, 1887; it set at 11:46 on the night of Thursday, December 18, 1890, to rise again at 12:51 P.M. on Friday, December 19th.

... ARTHUR CAUGHT HIM ...

Illustration by Sidney Paget for the *Strand Magazine*, May, 1892.

" Is it possible ? " gasped the banker.

" You then roused his anger by calling him names at a moment when he felt that he had deserved your warmest thanks. He could not explain the true state of affairs without betraying one who certainly deserved little enough consideration at his hands. He took the more chivalrous view, however, and preserved her secret."

" And that was why she shrieked and fainted when she saw the coronet," cried Mr. Holder. " Oh, my God ! what a blind fool I have been. And his asking to be allowed to go out for five minutes ! The dear fellow wanted to see if the missing piece were at the scene of the struggle. How cruelly I have misjudged him ! "

" When I arrived at the house," continued Holmes, " I at once went very carefully round it to observe if there were any traces in the snow which might help me. I knew that none had fallen since the evening before, and also that there had been a strong frost to preserve impressions. I passed along the tradesmen's path, but found it all trampled down and indistinguishable. Just beyond it, however, at the far side of the kitchen door, a woman had stood and talked with a man, whose round impression on one side showed that he had a wooden leg. I could even tell that they had been disturbed, for the woman had run back swiftly to the door, as was shown by the deep toe and light heel-marks, while Wooden-leg had waited a little, and then had gone away. I thought at the time that this might be the maid and her sweetheart, of whom you had already spoken to me, and inquiry showed it was so. I passed round the garden without seeing anything more than random tracks, which I took to be the police ; but when I got into the stable lane a very long and complex story was written in the snow in front of me.

" There was a double line of tracks of a booted man, and a second double line which I saw with delight belonged to a man with naked feet. I was at once convinced from what you had told me that the latter was your son. The first had walked both ways, but the other had run swiftly, and, as his tread was marked in places over the depression of the boot, it was obvious that he had passed after the other. I followed them up, and found that they led to the hall window, where Boots had worn all the snow away while waiting. Then I walked to the other end, which was a hundred yards or more down the lane. I saw where Boots had faced round, where the snow was cut up, as though there had been a struggle, and, finally, where a few drops of blood had fallen, to show me that I was not mistaken. Boots had then run down the lane, and another little smudge of blood showed that it was he who had been hurt. When he came to the high-road at the other end, I found that the pavement had been cleared, so there was an end to that clue.

" On entering the house, however, I examined, as you remember, the sill and framework of the hall window with my lens, and I could at once see that someone had passed out. I could distinguish the outline of an instep where the wet foot had been placed in coming in. I was then beginning to be able to form an opinion as to what had occurred. A man had waited outside the window, some-one had brought him the gems ; the deed had been over-seen by your son, he had pursued the thief, had struggled with him, they had each tugged at the coronet, their united strength causing injuries which neither alone could have effected. He had returned with the prize, but had left a fragment in the grasp of his opponent. So far I was clear. The question now was, who was the man, and who was it brought him the coronet ?

" It is an old maxim of mine that when you have ex-cluded the impossible, whatever remains, however improb-able, must be the truth. Now, I knew that it was not you who had brought it down, so there only remained your niece and the maids. But if it were the maids, why should your son allow himself to be accused in their place ? There could be no possible reason. As he loved his cousin, however, there was an excellent explanation why he should retain her secret—the more so as the secret was a disgrace-ful one. When I remembered that you had seen her at that window, and how she had fainted on seeing the coro-net again, my conjecture became a certainty.

" And who could it be who was her confederate ? A lover evidently, for who else could outweigh the love and grati-tude which she must feel to you ? I knew that you went out little, and that your circle of friends was a very limited one. But among them was Sir George Burnwell. I had heard of him before as being a man of evil reputation among women. It must have been he who wore those boots, and retained the missing gems. Even though he knew that Arthur had discovered him, he might still flatter himself that he was safe, for the lad could not say a word without compromising his own family.

" Well, your own good sense will suggest what measures I took next. I went in the shape of a loafer to Sir George's house, managed to pick up an acquaintance with his valet, learned that his master had cut his head the night before, and finally, at the expense of six shillings, made all sure by buying a pair of his cast-off shoes. With these I journeyed down to Streatham, and saw that they exactly fitted the tracks."

" I saw an ill-dressed vagabond in the lane yesterday **9** evening," said Mr. Holder.

" Precisely. It was I. I found that I had my man, so I came home and changed my clothes. It was a delicate part which I had to play then, for I saw that a prosecution must be avoided to avert scandal, and I knew that so astute a villain would see that our hands were tied in the matter. I went and saw him. At first, of course, he denied every-thing. But when I gave him every particular that had occurred, he tried to bluster, and took down a life-preserver from the wall. I knew my man, however, and I clapped a pistol to his head before he could strike. Then he became a little more reasonable. I told him that we would give him a price for the stones he held—a thousand pounds apiece. That brought out the first signs of grief he had shown. ' Why, dash it all ! ' said he, ' I've let them go at

". . . I CLAPPED A PISTOL TO HIS HEAD . . ."

Illustration by Sidney Paget for the *Strand Maga-zine*, May, 1892. As Mr. Robert Keith Leavitt has observed ("Annie Oakley in Baker Street") "when-ever [Holmes] had occasion to pull a gun on a really desperate character, he got as near as pos-sible to his man before showing his weapon. His standard practice of clapping a pistol right against his captive's head [see also "The Adventure of the Dancing Men" and "The Adventure of the Maza-rin Stone"] is ample evidence of awareness of per-sonal fallability with the handgun."

9 *an ill-dressed vagabond.* "One might wonder if there was such a thing as a 'well-dressed vaga-bond' in those days," the late Page Heldenbrand commented in "Sherlock Holmes in Disguise."

10 *"A day which has saved England from a great public scandal."* "The injuries to the coronet pose a problem for which there seems to be no solution," the late A. Carson Simpson wrote in "Whose Was It? Conjectures on a Coronet." "We are told that 'any injury' to it would be almost as serious as its complete loss.' But it was in fact injured, being twisted out of shape and having a piece broken off. How did Alexander Holder expect to get it made as good as new between Saturday morning, when he got back the missing piece, and the following Monday, when the borrower would return to reclaim it? If this could not be done, how did he expect to placate the borrower on Monday, unless by a little genteel blackmail? Apparently he did not worry about these questions, for his first act, after getting back the missing piece, was to rush off—not to the nearest goldsmith, as one might expect, but—to make his peace with his son Arthur."

six hundred for the three !' I soon managed to get the address of the receiver who had them, on promising him that there would be no prosecution. Off I set to him, and after much chaffering I got our stones at a thousand apiece. Then I looked in upon your son, told him that all was right, and eventually got to my bed about two o'clock, after what I may call a really hard day's work."

"A day which has saved England from a great public **10** scandal," said the banker, rising. " Sir, I cannot find words to thank you, but you shall not find me ungrateful for what you have done. Your skill has indeed exceeded all that I have ever heard of it. And now I must fly to my dear boy to apologize to him for the wrong which I have done him. As to what you tell me of poor Mary, it goes to my heart. Not even your skill can inform me where she is now."

" I think that we may safely say," returned Holmes, " that she is wherever Sir George Burnwell is. It is equally certain, too, that whatever her sins are, they will soon receive a more than sufficient punishment."

47

THE FINAL PROBLEM

[Friday, April 24, to Monday, May 4, 1891]

IT is with a heavy heart that I take up my pen to write these the last words in which I shall ever record the singular gifts by which my friend Mr. Sherlock Holmes was distinguished. In an incoherent and, as I deeply feel, an entirely inadequate fashion, I have endeavoured to give some account of my strange experiences in his company from the chance which first brought us together at the period of the " Study in Scarlet," up to the time of his interference in the matter of the " Naval Treaty "—an interference which had the **1** unquestionable effect of preventing a serious international complication. It was my intention to have stopped there, and to have said nothing of that event which has created a void in my life which the lapse of two years has done little to fill. My hand has been forced, however, by the recent letters in which Colonel James Moriarty defends the memory of his brother, and I have no choice but to lay the facts before the public exactly as they occurred. I alone know the absolute truth of the matter, and I am satisfied that the time has come when no good purpose is to be served by its suppression. As far as I know, there have been only three accounts in the public Press : that in the *Journal de Genève* upon May 6th, 1891, the Reuter's despatch in the English papers upon May 7th, and finally the recent letters to which I have alluded. Of these the first and second were extremely condensed, while the last is, as I shall now show, an absolute perversion of the facts. It lies with me to tell for the first time what really took place between Professor Moriarty and Mr. Sherlock Holmes.

It may be remembered that after my marriage, and my subsequent start in private practice, the very intimate relations which had existed between Holmes and myself became to some extent modified. He still came to me from time to time when he desired a companion in his investigations, but these occasions grew more and more seldom, until I find that in the year 1890 there were only three cases of which I retain any record. During the **2** winter of that year and the early spring of 1891, I saw in the papers that he had been engaged by the French Government upon a matter of supreme importance, and I **3** received two notes from Holmes, dated from Narbonne **4** and from Nîmes, from which I gathered that his stay in France was likely to be a long one. It was with some **5**

1 *in the matter of the "Naval Treaty."* As the late Dr. Ernest Bloomfield Zeisler wrote (*Baker Street Chronology*): "Watson was obviously thinking of the dates of publication, as we see that 'The Naval Treaty' was the last case published before the publication of 'The Final Problem.'"

2 *there were only three cases of which I retain any record.* The three cases, as we have seen, were "The Adventure of Wisteria Lodge," "Silver Blaze" and "The Adventure of the Beryl Coronet."

3 *a matter of supreme importance.* In his prize-winning essay, "Study of an Untold Tale," Mr. Edward F. Clark, Jr., has shown that Holmes' service to the French Government was to recover a famous painting stolen from the Louvre by the English Napoleon of Crime, Professor James Moriarty, and his gang. The recovery was made in the south of France on or about February 15th—i.e., "the middle of February" in Moriarty's later complaint to Holmes.

4 *Narbonne.* Since Narbonne is famous for its honey, it has been suggested that Holmes may have got his first interest in beekeeping there.

5 *his stay in France was likely to be a long one.* Mrs. Winifred M. Christie has noted ("On the Remarkable Explorations of Sigerson") that Holmes "was necessarily much in France" in the early months of 1891. "On January 31, 1891, Monsieur Gabriel Bonvalot, Prince Henry of Orleans and Father Dedeken gave an illustrated talk on their work in Tibet to the French Geographical Society in Paris. Mr. Holmes may easily have heard their lecture." This, Mrs. Christie suggests, may have been one of the factors that led Holmes, during the years of the Great Hiatus, to travel for two years in Tibet.

6 *the 24th of April.* A Friday in 1891.

7 *"Of air-guns."* Not to be confused with the air rifles so dear to the heart of the American boy. As Mr. William Perceval wrote in "Sherlock Holmes and Air-Guns": "The first known example of an air-gun was a single shot model made by Güter of Nuremberg as long ago as 1530. Other German gunsmiths, such as Lobsinger (1550) and Mavin (1600), then developed a repeating air-gun. One maker at this period, Dumbler, even perfected a gun which could fire through a 1-inch plank, but was forbidden to market it on the ground that it was 'a murderous weapon with which a man might be killed and yet not know what hit him.' Indeed so unsporting was the weapon thought to be that gunmakers made air-guns resemble ordinary muskets as much as possible."

. . . I SAW IN THE LIGHT OF THE LAMP THAT TWO OF
HIS KNUCKLES WERE BURST AND BLEEDING.

Illustration by Sidney Paget for the *Strand Magazine*, December, 1893.

"AYE, THERE'S THE GENIUS AND THE WONDER OF THE
THING!" HE CRIED.

Illustration by Harry C. Edwards for *McClure's Magazine*, December, 1893.

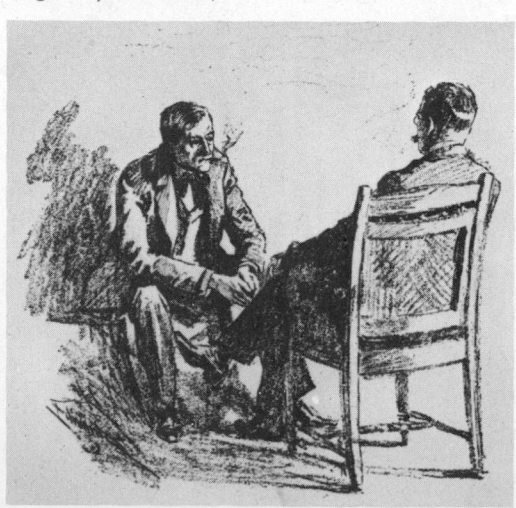

surprise, therefore, that I saw him walk into my consult-
6 ing-room upon the evening of the 24th of April. It struck me that he was looking even paler and thinner than usual.

"Yes, I have been using myself up rather too freely," he remarked, in answer to my look rather than to my words ; " I have been a little pressed of late. Have you any objection to my closing your shutters ? "

The only light in the room came from the lamp upon the table at which I had been reading. Holmes edged his way round the wall, and flinging the shutters together, he bolted them securely.

"You are afraid of something ? " I asked.

"Well, I am."

"Of what ? "

7   "Of air-guns."

"My dear Holmes, what do you mean ? "

" I think that you know me well enough, Watson, to understand that I am by no means a nervous man. At the same time, it is stupidity rather than courage to refuse to recognize danger when it is close upon you. Might I trouble you for a match ? " He drew in the smoke of his cigarette as if the soothing influence was grateful to him.

" I must apologize for calling so late," said he, " and I must further beg you to be so unconventional as to allow me to leave your house presently by scrambling over your back garden wall."

" But what does it all mean ? " I asked.

He held out his hand, and I saw in the light of the lamp that two of his knuckles were burst and bleeding.

" It's not an airy nothing, you see," said he, smiling. " On the contrary, it is solid enough for a man to break his hand over. Is Mrs. Watson in ? "

" She is away upon a visit."

" Indeed ! You are alone ? "

" Quite."

" Then it makes it the easier for me to propose that you should come away with me for a week on to the Continent."

" Where ? "

" Oh, anywhere. It's all the same to me."

There was something very strange in all this. It was not Holmes' nature to take an aimless holiday, and something about his pale, worn face told me that his nerves were at their highest tension. He saw the question in my eyes, and, putting his finger-tips together and his elbows upon his knees, he explained the situation.

" You have probably never heard of Professor Moriarty ? " said he.

8   " Never."

" Aye, there's the genius and the wonder of the thing ! " he cried. " The man pervades London, and no one has heard of him. That's what puts him on a pinnacle in the records of crime. I tell you, Watson, in all seriousness, that if I could beat that man, if I could free society of him, I should feel that my own career had reached its summit, and I should be prepared to turn to some more placid line in life. Between ourselves, the recent cases in which I have been of assistance to the Royal Family of Scandinavia, and to the French Republic, have left me in such a position that I could continue to live in the quiet fashion which is most congenial to me, and to concentrate my attention upon my chemical researches. But I could **9** not rest, Watson, I could not sit quiet in my chair, if I thought that such a man as Professor Moriarty were walking the streets of London unchallenged."

" What has he done, then ? "

" His career has been an extraordinary one. He is a man of good birth and excellent education, endowed by Nature with a phenomenal mathematical faculty. At the age of twenty-one he wrote a treatise upon the Binomial Theorem, which has had a European vogue. On the strength of it, he won the Mathematical Chair at one of our smaller Universities, and had, to all appearance, a most brilliant career before him. But the man had hereditary tendencies of the most diabolical kind. A criminal strain ran in his blood, which, instead of being modified, was increased and rendered infinitely more dangerous by his extraordinary mental powers. Dark rumours gathered round him in the University town, and eventually he was compelled to resign his Chair and to come down to London, where he set up as an Army coach. So much is known to the world, but what I am telling you now is what I have myself discovered.

" As you are aware, Watson, there is no one who knows the higher criminal world of London so well as I do. For years past I have continually been conscious of some power behind the malefactor, some deep organizing power which for ever stands in the way of the law, and throws its shield over the wrong-doer. Again and again in cases of the most varying sorts—forgery cases, robberies, murders—I have felt the presence of this force, and I have deduced its action in many of those undiscovered crimes in which I have not been personally consulted. For years I have endeavoured to break through the veil which shrouded it, and at last the time came when I seized my thread and followed it, until it led me, after a thousand cunning windings, to ex-Professor Moriarty of mathematical celebrity.

" He is the Napoleon of crime, Watson. He is the organizer of half that is evil and of nearly all that is undetected in this great city. He is a genius, a philosopher, an abstract thinker. He has a brain of the first order. He sits motionless, like a spider in the centre of its web, but that web has a thousand radiations, and he knows well every quiver of each of them. He does little himself. He only plans. But his agents are numerous and splendidly organized. Is there a crime to be done, a paper to be abstracted, we will say, a house to be rifled, a man to be removed—the word is passed to the Professor, the matter is organized and carried out. The agent may be caught. In that case money is found for his bail or his defence. But the central power which uses the agent is never caught—never so much as suspected. This was the organization which I deduced, Watson, and which I devoted my whole energy to exposing and breaking up.

8 *"Never."* It must be remembered that "The Final Problem" was written and published *before The Valley of Fear*. Therefore, as Dr. John Dardess long ago pointed out ("On the Dating of *The Valley of Fear*), Watson's negative here was "merely literary license, necessary for the properly dramatic introduction of Moriarty to the public: if Watson had replied in the affirmative to Holmes' question, there would be no reason for his ensuing description of the professor. Hence, the . . . passage may deal with something that never actually took place, both question and answer being purely rhetorical, and the interpolated description probably recorded on some earlier occasion."

This same view has been expressed by Mr. G. B. Newton ("The Date of *The Valley of Fear*") and by Mr. James Buchholtz ("A Tremor at the Edge of the Web"): "The description of Moriarty [Watson] puts into the mouth of Holmes had doubtless been made on an earlier occasion but its transposition becomes *artistically* necessary as Watson, the practiced story-teller, instantly and rightly recognized." "By professing to be ignorant of Moriarty's existence, Watson was able to sketch in the background for the dramatic Reichenbach Falls incident. He had only to alter the time of a well-remembered conversation which may have taken place any time prior to 1891 between Holmes and his Boswell."

9 *to concentrate my attention upon my chemical researches.* But let us note here that Holmes, when he did come to retire in the October of 1903, turned his attention, not to chemical researches, but to philosophy and agriculture.

"HE IS THE NAPOLEON OF CRIME, WATSON."

Portrait of Professor James Moriarty by Sidney Paget for the *Strand Magazine*, December, 1893.

". . . PROFESSOR MORIARTY STOOD BEFORE ME."

Illustration by Harry C. Edwards for *McClure's Magazine*, December, 1893.

"HE PEERED AT ME WITH GREAT CURIOSITY IN HIS PUCKERED EYES."

In "Chip Off the Old Block?" the late James Montgomery noted the extraordinary resemblance between Professor James Moriarty and Fernand De Brinon, Vichy representative to German-occupied France during World War II. The fact that there is, in New Orleans, a Moriarty Monument in Metairie Cemetery, led Mr. Montgomery to the conclusion that Moriarty had issue through a marriage with a French Creole lady, which would "account for a French traitor son, who carried on [the Professor's] reprehensible career under the thinly-disguised alias of De Brinon."

"But the Professor was fenced round with safeguards so cunningly devised that, do what I would, it seemed impossible to get evidence which could convict in a court of law. You know my powers, my dear Watson, and yet at the end of three months I was forced to confess that I had at last met an antagonist who was my intellectual equal. My horror at his crimes was lost in my admiration at his skill. But at last he made a trip—only a little, little trip—but it was more than he could afford, when I was so close upon him. I had my chance, and, starting from that point, I have woven my net round him until now it is all ready to close. In three days, that is to say on Monday next, matters will be ripe, and the Professor, with all the principal members of his gang, will be in the hands of the police. Then will come the greatest criminal trial of the century, the clearing up of over forty mysteries, and the rope for all of them—but if we move at all prematurely, you understand, they may slip out of our hands even at the last moment.

"Now, if I could have done this without the knowledge of Professor Moriarty, all would have been well. But he was too wily for that. He saw every step which I took to draw my toils round him. Again and again he strove to break away, but I as often headed him off. I tell you, my friend, that if a detailed account of that silent contest could be written, it would take its place as the most brilliant bit of thrust-and-parry work in the history of detection. Never have I risen to such a height, and never have I been so hard pressed by an opponent. He cut deep, and yet I just undercut him. This morning the last steps were taken, and three days only were wanted to complete the business. I was sitting in my room thinking the matter over, when the door opened and Professor Moriarty stood before me.

"My nerves are fairly proof, Watson, but I must confess to a start when I saw the very man who had been so much in my thoughts standing there on my threshold. His appearance was quite familiar to me. He is extremely tall and thin, his forehead domes out in a white curve, and his two eyes are deeply sunken in his head. He is clean-shaven, pale, and ascetic-looking, retaining something of the professor in his features. His shoulders are rounded from much study, and his face protrudes forward, and is for ever slowly oscillating from side to side in a curiously reptilian fashion. He peered at me with great curiosity in his puckered eyes.

"'You have less frontal development than I should have expected,' said he at last. 'It is a dangerous habit to finger loaded firearms in the pocket of one's dressing-gown.'

"The fact is that upon his entrance I had instantly recognized the extreme personal danger in which I lay. The only conceivable escape for him lay in silencing my tongue. In an instant I had slipped the revolver from the drawer into my pocket, and was covering him through the cloth. At his remark I drew the weapon out and laid it cocked upon the table. He still smiled and blinked, but there was something about his eyes which made me feel very glad that I had it there.

"'You evidently don't know me,' said he.

" 'On the contrary,' I answered, ' I think it is fairly evident that I do. Pray take a chair. I can spare you five minutes if you have anything to say.'

" ' All that I have to say has already crossed your mind,' said he.

" ' Then possibly my answer has crossed yours,' I replied.

" ' You stand fast ? '

" ' Absolutely.'

" He clapped his hand into his pocket, and I raised the pistol from the table. But he merely drew out a memorandum-book in which he had scribbled some dates.

" ' You crossed my path on the 4th of January,' said he. **10** ' On the 23rd you incommoded me ; by the middle of February I was seriously inconvenienced by you ; at the end of March I was absolutely hampered in my plans ; and now, at the close of April, I find myself placed in such a position through your continual persecution that I am in positive danger of losing my liberty. The situation is becoming an impossible one.'

" ' Have you any suggestion to make ? ' I asked.

" ' You must drop it, Mr. Holmes,' said he, swaying his face about. ' You really must, you know.'

" ' After Monday,' said I.

" ' Tut, tut ! ' said he. ' I am quite sure that a man of your intelligence will see that there can be but one outcome to this affair. It is necessary that you should withdraw. You have worked things in such a fashion that we have only one resource left. It has been an intellectual treat to me to see the way in which you have grappled with this affair, and I say, unaffectedly, that it would be a grief to me to be forced to take any extreme measure. You smile, sir, but I assure you that it really would.'

" ' Danger is part of my trade,' I remarked.

" ' This is not danger,' said he. ' It is inevitable destruction. You stand in the way not merely of an individual, but of a mighty organization, the full extent of which you, with all your cleverness, have been unable to realize. You must stand clear, Mr. Holmes, or be trodden under foot.'

" ' I am afraid,' said I, rising, ' that in the pleasure of this conversation I am neglecting business of importance which awaits me elsewhere.'

" He rose also and looked at me in silence, shaking his head sadly.

" ' Well, well,' said he at last. ' It seems a pity, but I have done what I could. I know every move of your game. You can do nothing before Monday. It has been a duel between you and me, Mr. Holmes. You hope to place me in the dock. I tell you that I will never stand in the dock. You hope to beat me. I tell you that you will never beat me. If you are clever enough to bring destruction upon me, rest assured that I shall do as much to you.'

" ' You have paid me several compliments, Mr. Moriarty,' said I. ' Let me pay you one in return when I say that if I were assured of the former eventuality I would, in the interests of the public, cheerfully accept the latter.'

"I CAN SPARE YOU FIVE MINUTES IF YOU HAVE ANYTHING TO SAY."

A flesh-and-blood Holmes, in the person of William Gillette, gets the drop on his archenemy, Professor James Moriarty, on the Garrick stage in 1899.

10 " ' *You crossed my path on the 4th of January.*' "There is not the slightest doubt in my mind that what Moriarty actually said was 'the 7th of January,' and that the '4' is but another example of Watson's careless handwriting," Mr. Nathan L. Bengis wrote in "What Was the Month?" "The two digits are easily confused in any case. I know that the chronological experts will be up in arms against me, but I cannot help feeling that here we have the best of all possible reasons for assigning The Valley of Fear [which, as we have seen, began on a 7th of January] to January, 1891."

This is tempting, as Mr. T. S. Blakeney earlier wrote (*Sherlock Holmes: Fact or Fiction?*), "but the objections . . . are considerable. Moriarty's phrase 'crossed my path' must be taken to mean that Holmes had in some degree, not perhaps very large, *hampered* the professor's activities, but he cannot be said to have done so in *The Valley of Fear*, since Douglas was 'removed' quite satisfactorily some little time later. Moriarty was bound to know of Holmes, as did most London criminals, long before the clash came, and on the latter's own showing in *The Valley of Fear* he knew all about Moriarty, and had warned Scotland Yard accordingly. What seems most plausible is that Holmes worked quietly and waited patiently for many months . . . before he was in a position to start his contest with Moriarty on 4th January, 1891."

"... AND SO HE TURNED HIS ROUNDED BACK UPON ME AND WENT PEERING AND BLINKING OUT OF THE ROOM."

Illustration by Sidney Paget for the *Strand Magazine*, December, 1893.

11 *a brick came down from the roof of one of the houses.* The building was perhaps the big department store, Marshall & Snelgrove, established in 1837; it fronts on Oxford Street.

12 *if you could come on to the Continent with me."* Holmes suggests—to Watson, at least—that his prime purpose in leaving for the Continent is to escape the unwelcome attentions of the Moriarty gang. As Mr. Walter P. Armstrong, Jr., has written ("The Truth About Sherlock Holmes"): "To those of us who know Holmes this is incredible. He was never one to shirk danger, as he had told Moriarty himself in no uncertain terms a short time before. The only possible conclusion is that . . . Sherlock Holmes was luring Professor Moriarty into a trap."

Mr. Jerry Neal Williamson, on the other hand, has come to the conclusion that Professor James "Moriarty" was in fact Professor James *Holmes*, an elder brother of Sherlock's, a younger brother of Mycroft's (" 'There Was Something Very Strange' "). "The flight from England must have been made to give James a chance to escape with his life. . . . Acting as a decoy, Sherlock Holmes 'fled,' vanished, and lived on the funds of his honest brother [Mycroft] until the gang was gone and James a free but broken man. Just as he found compassion for James Ryder ["The Adventure of the Blue Carbuncle"], the detective found compassion for his criminal brother."

" ' I can promise you the one but not the other,' he snarled, and so turned his rounded back upon me and went peering and blinking out of the room.

" That was my singular interview with Professor Moriarty. I confess that it left an unpleasant effect upon my mind. His soft, precise fashion of speech leaves a conviction of sincerity which a mere bully could not produce. Of course, you will say : ' Why not take police precautions against him ? ' The reason is that I am well convinced that it is from his agents the blow would fall. I have the best of proofs that it would be so."

" You have already been assaulted ? "

" My dear Watson, Professor Moriarty is not a man who lets the grass grow under his feet. I went out about midday to transact some business in Oxford Street. As I passed the corner which leads from Bentinck Street on to the Welbeck Street crossing a two-horse van furiously driven whizzed round and was on me like a flash. I sprang for the footpath and saved myself by the fraction of a second. The van dashed round from Marylebone Lane and was gone in an instant. I kept to the pavement after that, Watson, but as I walked down Vere Street a brick **11** came down from the roof of one of the houses, and was shattered to fragments at my feet. I called the police and had the place examined. There were slates and bricks piled upon the roof preparatory to some repairs, and they would have me believe that the wind had toppled over one of these. Of course I knew better, but I could prove nothing. I took a cab after that and reached my brother's rooms in Pall Mall, where I spent the day. Now I have come round to you, and on my way I was attacked by a rough with a bludgeon. I knocked him down, and the police have him in custody ; but I can tell you with the most absolute confidence that no possible connection will ever be traced between the gentleman upon whose front teeth I have barked my knuckles and the retiring mathematical coach, who is, I dare say, working out problems upon a blackboard ten miles away. You will not wonder, Watson, that my first act on entering your rooms was to close your shutters, and that I have been compelled to ask your permission to leave the house by some less conspicuous exit than the front door."

I had often admired my friend's courage, but never more than now, as he sat quietly checking off a series of incidents which must have combined to make up a day of horror.

" You will spend the night here ? " I said.

" No, my friend ; you might find me a dangerous guest. I have my plans laid, and all will be well. Matters have gone so far now that they can move without my help as far as the arrest goes, though my presence is necessary for a conviction. It is obvious, therefore, that I cannot do better than get away for the few days which remain before the police are at liberty to act. It would be a **12** great pleasure to me, therefore, if you could come on to the Continent with me."

" The practice is quiet," said I, " and I have an accommodating neighbour. I should be glad to come."

" And to start to-morrow morning ? "

" If necessary."

" Oh yes, it is most necessary. Then these are your instructions, and I beg, my dear Watson, that you will obey them to the letter, for you are now playing a double-handed game with me against the cleverest rogue and the most powerful syndicate of criminals in Europe. Now listen ! You will despatch whatever luggage you intend to take by a trusty messenger unaddressed to Victoria to-night. In the morning you will send for a hansom, desiring your man to take neither the first nor the second which may present itself. Into this hansom you will jump, and you will drive to the Strand end of the Low-ther Arcade, handing the address to the cabman upon a slip of paper, with a request that he will not throw it away. Have your fare ready, and the instant that your cab stops, dash through the Arcade, timing yourself to reach the other side at a quarter-past nine. You will find a small brougham waiting close to the kerb, driven by a fellow with a heavy black cloak tipped at the collar with red. Into this you will step, and you will reach Victoria in time for the Continental express."

" Where shall I meet you ? "

" At the station. The second first-class carriage from the front will be reserved for us."

" The carriage is our rendezvous, then ? "

" Yes."

It was in vain that I asked Holmes to remain for the evening. It was evident to me that he thought he might bring trouble to the roof he was under, and that that was the motive which impelled him to go. With a few hurried words as to our plans for the morrow he rose and came out with me into the garden, clambering over the wall which leads into Mortimer Street, and immediately **13** whistling for a hansom, in which I heard him drive away.

In the morning I obeyed Holmes' injunctions to the **14** letter. A hansom was procured with such precautions as would prevent its being one which was placed ready for us, and I drove immediately after breakfast to the Lowther Arcade, through which I hurried at the top of my speed. A brougham was waiting with a very massive driver wrapped in a dark cloak, who, the instant that I had stepped in, whipped up the horse and rattled off to Victoria Station. On my alighting there he turned the carriage, and dashed away without so much as a look in my direction.

So far all had gone admirably. My luggage was waiting for me, and I had no difficulty in finding the carriage in which Holmes had indicated, the less so as it was the only one in the train which was marked " Engaged." My only source of anxiety now was the non-appearance of Holmes. The station clock marked only seven minutes from the time when we were due to start. In vain I searched among the groups of travellers and leave-takers for the lithe figure of my friend. There was no sign of him. I spent a few minutes in assisting a venerable Italian priest, who was endeavouring to make a porter understand, in his broken English, that his luggage was to be booked through to Paris. Then, having taken

INTERIOR OF LOWTHER ARCADE, STRAND, LONDON.

". . . YOU WILL DRIVE TO THE STRAND END OF THE LOWTHER ARCADE . . ."

". . . the most historic, and rather dubious of reputation [of London's bazaars] was the Lowther Arcade—built 1830," Mr. Michael Harrison wrote (*In the Footsteps of Sherlock Holmes*). "The exiled Louis Philippe used to stroll through the Lowther Arcade, ogling the pretty assistants who were the famous principal attraction of this Victorian shopping-centre."

13 *Mortimer Street.* Mortimer Street runs parallel to Oxford Street, connecting Goodge Street on the east with the north side of Cavendish Square and Wigmore Street on the west. Its appearance here is a little mysterious, to say the least: it would not seem to fit in with either of Watson's practices, that in Kensington or that in the Paddington district.

14 *In the morning.* The morning of Saturday, April 25, 1891.

. . . MY DECREPIT ITALIAN FRIEND . . .

Illustration by Sidney Paget for the *Strand Magazine*, December, 1893.

15 *Holmes had gone as quickly as he had come.*
". . . for a second time," the Reverend Otis R. Rice wrote in "Clergymen in the Canon," "it was a little unchivalrous of Holmes to avoid legal culpability by impersonating a Roman Catholic priest, an act for which there was at the time the same immunity as in the previous impersonation of a Nonconformist minister ["A Scandal in Bohemia"]. Holmes, a consummate actor, seems to have played the part well. Yet he, who usually had such an eye for complete disguise, neglected to provide himself on this occasion with the breviary and beads, without which no venerable Italian priest would ever have traveled. Watson, as a Protestant and not recognizing the discrepancy, reports the only accoutrement as a 'black cassock and hat which had formed his disguise.' "

16 *"Every precaution is still necessary."* "It is a logical supposition," Mr. Walter P. Armstrong, Jr., wrote in "The Truth About Sherlock Holmes," "that by [this] date it was fairly well known that Watson and Holmes were closely associated, as Watson had published accounts of several of their joint adventures. Surely Moriarty must have known it. Then why did not Holmes go to the Continent alone? Why assume an elaborate disguise and have as his travelling companion a man who was himself a dead giveaway? Obviously because he *wanted* Moriarty to follow him. The disguise, the change of trains, the altered itinerary, simply served to keep the whole thing from being too transparent. Holmes never for a moment

another look round, I returned to my carriage, where I found that the porter, in spite of the ticket, had given me my decrepit Italian friend as a travelling companion. It was useless for me to explain to him that his presence was an intrusion, for my Italian was even more limited than his English, so I shrugged my shoulders resignedly and continued to look out anxiously for my friend. A chill of fear had come over me, as I thought that his absence might mean that some blow had fallen during the night. Already the doors had all been shut and the whistle blown, when——

" My dear Watson," said a voice, " you have not even condescended to say good morning."

I turned in incontrollable astonishment. The aged ecclesiastic had turned his face towards me. For an instant the wrinkles were smoothed away, the nose drew away from the chin, the lower lip ceased to protrude and the mouth to mumble, the dull eyes regained their fire, the drooping figure expanded. The next the whole frame

15 collapsed, and Holmes had gone as quickly as he had come.

" Good heavens ! " I cried. " How you startled me ! "

16 " Every precaution is still necessary," he whispered. " I have reason to think that they are hot upon our trail. Ah, there is Moriarty himself."

17 The train had already begun to move as Holmes spoke. Glancing back I saw a tall man pushing his way furiously through the crowd and waving his hand as if he desired to have the train stopped. It was too late, however, for we were rapidly gathering momentum, and an instant later had shot clear of the station.

" With all our precautions, you see that we have cut it rather fine," said Holmes, laughing. He rose, and throwing off the black cassock and hat which had formed his disguise, he packed them away in a hand-bag.

" Have you seen the morning paper, Watson ? "

" No."

" You haven't seen about Baker Street, then ? "

" Baker Street ? "

" They set fire to our rooms last night. No great harm was done."

" Good heavens, Holmes ! This is intolerable."

" They must have lost my track completely after their bludgeon-man was arrested. Otherwise they could not have imagined that I had returned to my rooms. They have evidently taken the precaution of watching you, however, and that is what has brought Moriarty to Victoria. You could not have made any slip in coming ? "

" I did exactly what you advised."

" Did you find your brougham ? "

" Yes, it was waiting."

" Did you recognize your coachman ? "

" No."

" It was my brother Mycroft. It is an advantage to get about in such a case without taking a mercenary into your confidence. But we must plan what we are to do about Moriarty now."

" As this is an express, and as the boat runs in connection with it, I should think we have shaken him off very effectively."

"My dear Watson, you evidently did not realize my meaning when I said that this man may be taken as being quite on the same intellectual plane as myself. You do not imagine that if I were the pursuer I should allow myself to be baffled by so slight an obstacle. Why, then, should you think so meanly of him?"

"What will he do?"

"What I should do."

"What would you do, then?"

"Engage a special."

"But it must be late."

"By no means. This train stops at Canterbury; and **18** there is always at least a quarter of an hour's delay at the boat. He will catch us there."

"One would think that we were the criminals. Let us have him arrested on his arrival."

"It would be to ruin the work of three months. We should get the big fish, but the smaller would dart right and left out of the net. On Monday we should have them all. No, an arrest is inadmissible."

"What then?"

"We shall get out at Canterbury."

"And then?"

"Well, then we must make a cross-country journey to Newhaven, and so over to Dieppe. Moriarty will again do what I should do. He will get on to Paris, mark down

thought that Moriarty would fail to see through them. Holmes was fully aware that the official police were incapable of dealing with such a man. The only solution was to give him his personal attention. And yet he could hardly shoot him down in cold blood in law-abiding England. So step by step he enticed him out of the country to as lonely a spot as could be found, and then he dèliberately offered himself as bait for the trap which he was about to spring."

17 *The train had already begun to move.* As the late Professor Jay Finley Christ pointed out in *Finch's Final Fling*, Von Neumann and Morgenstern, in *Theory of Games and Economic Behavior* (Princeton Press, 1944) analyze the mathematical probabilities in the business. They show that Holmes had a 60 percent chance of success if he stopped, while the professor had the same chance of winning if Holmes went on. A footnote, however, says that the mathematical odds were definitely in favor of the pursuer and that Holmes "is as good as 48 percent dead when his train pulls out."

18 *Canterbury.* Canterbury, the "Mother of England," is not elsewhere mentioned in the Chronicles.

"IT WAS MY BROTHER MYCROFT."

Illustration by Harry C. Edwards for *McClure's Magazine*, December, 1893.

"ENGAGE A SPECIAL."

"A purse deep enough for the suitably grand fare—usually five shillings [$1.25] a mile—could command a first-class carriage, a light engine, and a line cleared of slower traffic," Mr. Bernard Davies wrote in "Canonical Connections." But "Professor Moriarty's dramatic chase . . . must have been a superlative triumph of organization of the London, Chatham & Dover Railway Co.," as Mr. E. P. Greenwood wrote in "Some Random Thoughts on Railway Journeys by Holmes and Watson." "Think of the many signalmen between London and Dover who had to be informed at very short notice and the many train movements which had to be suspended; to say nothing of all the complicated signal and point operations which had to be made to let Moriarty's special through. Without a doubt the Traffic Superintendent was one of Moriarty's creatures and most of the railway company's servants concerned were part of his sinister and complex organisation; all the same, they must have been pretty hard put to it!" The photograph, from Mr. Michael Harrison's *In the Footsteps of Sherlock Holmes*, shows a "special" of the old South-Eastern Railway. In the background is a London Board School: what Holmes, in "The Naval Treaty," called "a beacon of the future."

"... AND MAKE OUR WAY AT OUR LEISURE INTO
SWITZERLAND ..."

Dr. Julian Wolff's map of "Operation Reichenbach," from his *Sherlockian Atlas*.

19 *At Canterbury, therefore, we alighted.* Although it has generally been assumed that Holmes and Watson were making for Paris via the Dover-Calais route, Mr. Bernard Davies has shown ("Can-

our luggage, and wait for two days at the depot. In the meantime we shall treat ourselves to a couple of carpet bags, encourage the manufactures of the countries through which we travel, and make our way at our leisure into Switzerland, via Luxembourg and Basle."

I am too old a traveller to allow myself to be seriously inconvenienced by the loss of my luggage, but I confess that I was annoyed at the idea of being forced to dodge and hide before a man whose record was black with unutterable infamies. It was evident, however, that Holmes understood the situation more clearly than I did. At **19** Canterbury, therefore, we alighted, only to find that we should have to wait an hour before we could get a train to Newhaven.

I was still looking rather ruefully after the rapidly disappearing luggage van which contained my wardrobe, when Holmes pulled my sleeve and pointed up the line.

"Already, you see," said he.

Far away from among the Kentish woods there arose a thin spray of smoke. A minute later a carriage and engine could be seen flying along the open curve which leads to the station. We had hardly time to take our places behind a pile of luggage when it passed with a rattle and a roar, beating a blast of hot air into our faces.

"There he goes," said Holmes, as we watched the carriage swing and rock over the points. "There are limits, you see, to our friend's intelligence. It would have been a *coup de maître* had he deduced what I would deduce and acted accordingly."

"And what would he have done had he overtaken us ?"

"There cannot be the least doubt that he would have made a murderous attack upon me. It is, however, a game at which two may play. The question now is whether we should take a premature lunch here, or run our chance of starving before we reach the buffet at **20** Newhaven."

We made our way to Brussels that night and spent two days there, moving on upon the third day as far as Stras-**21** burg. On the Monday morning Holmes had telegraphed

WE HAD HARDLY TIME TO TAKE OUR PLACES BEHIND A
PILE OF LUGGAGE WHEN IT PASSED WITH A RATTLE
AND A ROAR ...

Illustration by Sidney Paget for the *Strand Magazine*, December, 1893. Harry C. Edwards illustrated the same scene for *McClure's Magazine*, December, 1893.

to the London police, and in the evening we found a reply waiting for us at our hotel. Holmes tore it open, and then with a bitter curse hurled it into the grate.

" I might have known it," he groaned. " He has escaped ! "

" Moriarty ! "

" They have secured the whole gang with the exception of him. He has given them the slip. Of course, **22** when I had left the country there was no one to cope with him. But I did think that I had put the game in their hands. I think that you had better return to England, Watson."

" Why ? "

" Because you will find me a dangerous companion now. This man's occupation is gone. He is lost if he returns to London. If I read his character right he will devote his whole energies to revenging himself upon me. He said as much in our short interview, and I fancy that he meant it. I should certainly recommend you to return to your practice."

WE MADE OUR WAY TO BRUSSELS THAT NIGHT . . .

Could they have caught a boat that night? Mr. Davies continues: "In April, 1891, the L.B.S.C.R. ran only one boat a day to Dieppe. This left Newhaven at 11 P.M. following the arrival of the 9 P.M. express from London Bridge. It was the only boat they could have caught, so their three-and-a-half-hour journey from Canterbury could have been taken at a much more leisurely pace. The boat, one of the Brighton's fleet of four steel-built, electrically-lighted paddle-steamers:—*Normandy, Brittany, Paris* and *Rouen* [the *Paris* is shown above]—took almost five and a half hours on the crossing, docking in Dieppe at 4:23 in the morning. If they were lucky enough to secure unbooked cabins they could have snatched a few hours sleep. . . . The final problem . . . is:—How did they go from Dieppe to Brussels, avoiding Paris? This takes us on a Continental ramble and, at the same time, introduces us to a delightfully colourful work, *Bradshaw's Continental Railway, Steam Navigation and Conveyance Guide*. . . . There were several possible cross-country routes avoiding Paris, all of them via Arras, but none which would have got them to Brussels earlier than 6:05 that evening. No doubt they took the best of a bad lot by taking the Paris train as far as Rouen and alighting there at 5:41 A.M. From there they would catch the 6:30 to Amiens, via Serqueux, then another arriving at 11:02. An hour's wait and they could leave for Brussels by the 12:07 via Douai, Valenciennes and Mons. It was certainly gone six on the Sunday evening by the time they arrived in the Belgian capital."

onical Connections") that Holmes' intended destination must have been Ostend, regardless of where he sent their luggage: ". . . if we consult *Bradshaw's Monthly Railway Guide* for April, 1891, we find the following morning boat-trains: —an 8:30 and an 11 o'clock, both for Calais, and a 10 o'clock for Ostend, all first- and second-class only. As regards departure time the Ostend Boat Express is the only one that qualifies, but if any doubts remain as to which train Holmes and Watson travelled by, they are soon dispelled by a glance down the columns of Bradshaw. . . . The 10 A.M. Ostend train . . . had a two-hour timing, stopping at Herne Hill, Chatham, Canterbury and Dover Priory, five minutes before the Harbour, where it arrived at 12 noon. It was the only morning boat-express to do so, and therefore the only possible train on which Holmes and Watson could have commenced their cross-country wanderings."

20 *the buffet at Newhaven*." Could Holmes and Watson have made the cross-country journey satisfactorily to Newhaven? Again, Mr. Bernard Davies has shown that they could: "The boat-train stopped at Herne Hill at 10:12 and at Chatham at 10:51 and reached Canterbury at its appointed time at 11:29. . . . In actual fact the next train on the South Eastern branch to Ashford left in about forty minutes, at 12:08, but it probably seemed the best part of an hour [to Watson] in restrospect. It ran via Chatham, Chilham and Wye, arriving at Ashford Junction at 12:40. After a twenty-minute wait the South Eastern dispatched a slow Hastings train at 1:00 P.M. . . . Holmes and Watson trundled along in easy stages via Ham Street, Appledore, Rye and Winchelsea, arriving at Hastings at 2:03. Here there was a smart change to the London, Brighton and South Coast Railway train, with its mustard-yellow engine and crimson-ended brakevan, running as it did non-stop from Bexhill to Lewes where it pulled in at 3:05. At Lewes, where they changed once more, they had a wait of twenty-five minutes, as the local for Newhaven left at 3:30 and deposited them at the Harbour at 3:45."

21 *upon the third day as far as Strasburg*. Holmes and Watson presumably spent Monday, April 27th, and Tuesday, April 28th, in Brussels, moving to Strasburg on Wednesday, April 29th. ". . . intensive research of hotel registers shows that the great detective [stopped] at the very best hotel in Strasburg—the Maison Rouge," Mr. Thayer Cumings wrote in "Don't Write—Telegraph!"

22 " '*They have secured the whole gang with the exception of him*. We learn in "The Adventure of the Empty House" that this was not true, since the notorious Colonel Sebastian Moran, next to Moriarty the most dangerous man in London, was still very much at large, as was one other member of the gang. The London police, in 1891, evidently did not know these two as criminals—or, if they did, as members of the Moriarty gang.

23 *the Strasburg* salle-à-manger. "The dining room of their hotel," the late Christopher Morley wrote in *Sherlock Holmes and Dr. Watson: A Textbook of Friendship*. "Under less anxious circumstances Holmes, who enjoyed good food, would have taken time to enjoy Strasburg's world-famous goose-liver pie . . . , but it cannot be digested in haste."

24 *and were well on our way to Geneva.* "The keenness with which Holmes pursued Moriarty is clear from the fact that the departure to which Watson casually refers . . . was a departure in the small hours (3:55 A.M.), since there was no evening train on the 1890–91 winter timetable," Mr. Michael C. Kaser wrote in "Sherlock Holmes on the Continent." "They reached Geneva via Colmar, Basel, Biel and Lausanne, at 3:18 the following afternoon (the 30th), and we know they passed the night at Geneva, probably at the Hôtel de l'Écu, the most patronised by literary Englishmen at that time."

25 *For a charming week.* "The night that Holmes and Watson spent in Geneva can be dated as that of the 30th of April without shadow of doubt," Mr. Kaser continued. "The date is important, for the 'week' they spent in 'wandering up the valley of the Rhone' shrinks upon such investigation to be no more than Thursday, May 1st, since by the 3rd they had reached Meiringen. When Watson writes of a 'week wandering up the valley,' it is obviously a sarcastic reference to the easy pace of the train, for while from Geneva the slowest train of the day took eight and three-quarter hours, even the fastest took six hours to reach Leuk: today the journey is less than three hours."

26 *and so, by way of Interlaken, to Meiringen.* "The line to Leukerbad, at the foot of the Gemmi Pass, had not been built, and obviously they must have left Leuk on 2nd May," Mr. Kaser continued. "A study of the map Holmes must have used for his fateful journey—Blatt 17 of the *Topgraphische Karte der Schweiz*, in the revision of 1882—shows clearly the path from Leukerbad to the Gemmi and its bifurcation before the Daubensee. . . . It is obvious that Holmes followed the right bank, since the rock dislodged in a presumed attempt on his life came from the *right*, and fell thence into the lake behind him. Moreover, the right bank path is shown on the map as the better one. They would have reached Kandersteg very late; with no train on the Leuk side and no cable car on the Kandersteg side as there is today, it is a full day's walk. The railway from Kandersteg to Spiez was not built until much later, and the regular diligence service in that year did not operate until 1st June. They were perhaps able to hire a carriage and catch the 10:05 A.M. boat from Spiez, which, via Interlaken, connected with the train leaving Brienz at 1:00 P.M."

It was hardly an appeal to be successful with one who was an old campaigner as well as an old friend. We sat **23** in the Strasburg *salle-à-manger* arguing the question for half an hour, but the same night we had resumed our **24** journey and were well on our way to Geneva.

25 For a charming week we wandered up the Valley of the Rhone, and then, branching off at Leuk, we made our way over the Gemmi Pass, still deep in snow, and so, by way **26** of Interlaken, to Meiringen. It was a lovely trip, the dainty green of the spring below, the virgin white of the winter above ; but it was clear to me that never for one instant did Holmes forget the shadow which lay across him. In the homely Alpine villages or in the lonely mountain passes, I could still tell, by his quick glancing eyes and his sharp scrutiny of every face that passed us, that he was well convinced that, walk where we would, we could not walk ourselves clear of the danger which was dogging our footsteps.

Once, I remember, as we passed over the Gemmi, and walked along the border of the melancholy Daubensee, a large rock which had been dislodged from the ridge upon our right clattered down and roared into the lake behind us. In an instant Holmes had raced up on to the ridge, and, standing upon a lofty pinnacle, craned his neck in every direction. It was in vain that our guide assured him that a fall of stones was a common chance in the spring-time at that spot. He said nothing, but he smiled at me with the air of a man who sees the fulfilment of that which he had expected.

And yet for all his watchfulness he was never depressed. On the contrary, I can never recollect having seen him in such exuberant spirits. Again and again he recurred to the fact that if he could be assured that society was freed from Professor Moriarty, he would cheerfully bring his own career to a conclusion.

" I think that I may go so far as to say, Watson, that I have not lived wholly in vain," he remarked. " If my record were closed to-night I could still survey it with **27** equanimity. The air of London is the sweeter for my presence. In over a thousand cases I am not aware that I have ever used my powers upon the wrong side. Of late I have been tempted to look into the problems furnished by Nature rather than those more superficial ones for which our artificial state of society is responsible. Your memoirs will draw to an end, Watson, upon the day that I crown my career by the capture or extinction of the most dangerous and capable criminal in Europe."

I shall be brief, and yet exact, in the little which remains for me to tell. It is not a subject on which I would willingly dwell, and yet I am conscious that a duty devolves upon me to omit no detail.

It was upon the 3rd of May that we reached the little village of Meiringen, where we put up at the 'Englischer **28** Hof, then kept by Peter Steiler the elder. Our landlord was an intelligent man, and spoke excellent English, having served for three years as waiter at the Grosvenor **29** Hotel in London. At his advice, upon the afternoon of the 4th we set off together with the intention of crossing the hills and spending the night at the Hamlet of Rosen-

Reproduced from a contemporary steel engraving by the late James Montgomery.

A panoramic view of Meiringen and the Hasli Valley from a brochure distributed by Popularis Tours, Inc., of New York City. Copyright Brügger S.A., Ltd., Meiringen.

. . . WE MADE OUR WAY OVER TO THE GEMMI PASS . . .

Photograph by Lord Donegall, who writes: "Watson deserves credit for making the 2¾ hrs. up this path with his game leg. (Or perhaps his wound was in his shoulder on that day!)."

. . . A LARGE ROCK . . . CLATTERED DOWN AND ROARED INTO THE LAKE BEHIND US.

Illustration by Sidney Paget for the *Strand Magazine*, December, 1893. Harry C. Edwards illustrated the same scene for *McClure's Magazine*, December, 1893.

WE REACHED THE LITTLE VILLAGE OF MEIRINGEN . . .

The population of Meiringen was then under 3,000. "Prior to the great fire of 1891, which almost demolished the village, Meiringen was a little, old-world place consisting of quaint cottages round a little Swiss Church erected in the early pre-Reformation period," says the *Guide Through Europe*, published by the Hamburg-American Line in 1905. "The church escaped the flames; and, together with a few wooden structures and the Austrian Tower that stands out among the woods to the right of the Mühlbach, it still tells of the middle-age appearance worn by the hamlet within the last few years. At the present time, it possesses a number of fine hotels and boarding houses, which give it the character of a modern health-resort. It is the principal village in the narrow and fertile Hasli Valley, whose beauty has won for the spot the title of the 'Front Garden of the Bernese Oberland.' Through this valley flows the river Aare, flanked by wooded steeps. To the S., the river forms the Reichenbach Falls . . ."

"The destruction of Meiringen [by fire] so soon after the epic event that transpired nearby suggests its immolation at the hand of [a Moriarty henchman], enraged as he must have been at the death of his leader and the escape of his intended victim," the late James Montgomery wrote in "Meiringen Musings."

. . . WE SAW A SWISS LAD COME RUNNING ALONG IT
WITH A LETTER IN HIS HAND.

Illustration by Harry C. Edwards for *McClure's
Magazine*, December, 1893.

IT IS, INDEED, A FEARFUL PLACE.

". . . the Fall of Reichenbach is not actually a single fall, even though it is labeled as such," Messrs. Bryce Crawford, Jr., and R. C. Moore wrote in "The Final Problem—Where?" "Actually, it is three falls. . . From the beginning of the upper falls, the water plunges down into a pool not far above the viewing platform [that now exists on the west or right side of the falls as one faces it]. From this upper segment the water plunges, not in a single sheer drop but with several minor cascades caused by rocks in the path of the fall which have not completely washed away. The middle segment is by far the most spectacular, with its several interruptions, its roar of waters rushing against the containing cliffs, and its end in a pool of great depth and magnitude. . . . The first question therefore [is]: Did Holmes and Moriarty struggle at the upper segment and did Moriarty fall into the pool at the bottom of it; or was the struggle at the middle segment? . . . The middle segment fits the [Canonical] description perfectly. . . . But here again the question arises, exactly where? One must rule out the possibility of the struggle having taken place on the west side of the falls . . . For . . . in 1891 . . . [there was no] path up the right side of the mountain. The presumption therefore is that the struggle took place on the left side of the fall. There is indeed a path that leads up the left side of the mountain. It goes clear to the top and crosses over the upper segment via a foot bridge before taking off to Rosenlaui. . . . There is no . . . ledge there today, [but] there [was] one in 1891 . . . about two-thirds of the way up. Appearances strongly suggest that part of the cliff fell away . . . in March, 1944, [when] there was a substantial erosion and fall of rock at the middle segment."

laui. We had strict injunctions, however, on no account to pass the falls of Reichenbach, which are about half-way up the hill, without making a small detour to see them.

It is, indeed, a fearful place. The torrent, swollen by the melting snow, plunges into a tremendous abyss, from which the spray rolls up like the smoke from a burning house. The shaft into which the river hurls itself is an immense chasm, lined by glistening, coal-black rock, and narrowing into a creaming, boiling pit of incalculable depth, which brims over and shoots the stream onward over its jagged lip. The long sweep of green water roaring for ever down, and the thick flickering curtain of spray hissing for ever upwards, turn a man giddy with their constant whirl and clamour. We stood near the edge peering down at the gleam of the breaking water far below us against the black rocks, and listening to the half-human shout which came booming up with the spray out of the abyss.

The path has been cut half-way round the fall to afford a complete view, but it ends abruptly, and the traveller has to return as he came. We had turned to do so, when we saw a Swiss lad come running along it with a letter in his hand. It bore the mark of the hotel which we had just left, and was addressed to me by the landlord. It appeared that within a very few minutes of our leaving, an English lady had arrived who was in the last stage of consumption. She had wintered at Davos Platz, and was journeying now to join her friends at Lucerne, when a sudden hæmorrhage had overtaken her. It was thought that she could hardly live a few hours, but it would be a great consolation to her to see an English doctor, and, if I would only return, etc. etc. The good Steiler assured me in a postscript that he would himself look upon my

30-31

compliance as a very great favour, since the lady absolutely refused to see a Swiss physician, and he could not but feel that he was incurring a great responsibility.

The appeal was one which could not be ignored. It was impossible to refuse the request of a fellow-countrywoman dying in a strange land. Yet I had my scruples about leaving Holmes. It was finally agreed, however, that he should retain the young Swiss messenger with him as guide and companion while I returned to Meiringen. My friend would stay some little time at the fall, he said, and would then walk slowly over the hill to Rosenlaui, where I was to rejoin him in the evening. As I turned away I saw Holmes with his back against a rock and his arms folded, gazing down at the rush of the waters. It was the last that I was ever destined to see of him in this world.

When I was near the bottom of the descent I looked back. It was impossible, from that position, to see the fall, but I could see the curving path which winds over the shoulder of the hill and leads to it. Along this a man was, I remember, walking very rapidly. I could see his black figure clearly outlined against the green behind him. I noted him, and the energy with which he walked, but he passed from my mind again as I hurried on upon my errand.

It may have been a little over an hour before I reached Meiringen. Old Steiler was standing at the porch of his hotel.

" Well," said I, as I came hurrying up, " I trust that she is no worse ? "

A look of surprise passed over his face, and at the first quiver of his eyebrows my heart turned to lead in my breast.

" You did not write this ? " I said, pulling the letter from my pocket. " There is no sick Englishwoman in the hotel ? "

" Certainly not," he cried. " But it has the hotel mark upon it ! Ha ! it must have been written by that tall Englishman who came in after you had gone. He said——"

But I waited for none of the landlord's explanations. In a tingle of fear I was already running down the village street, and making for the path which I had so lately descended. It had taken me an hour to come down. For all my efforts, two more had passed before I found myself at the fall of Reichenbach once more. There was Holmes' alpenstock still leaning against the rock by which I had left him. But there was no sign of him, and it was in vain that I shouted. My only answer was my own voice reverberating in a rolling echo from the cliffs around me.

It was the sight of that alpenstock which turned me cold and sick. He had not gone to Rosenlaui, then. He had remained on that three-foot path, with sheer wall on one side and sheer drop upon the other, until his enemy had overtaken him. The young Swiss had gone too. He had probably been in the pay of Moriarty, and had left the two men together. And then what had happened ? Who was to tell us what had happened then ?

27 *survey it with equanimity.* Mr. Morris Rosenblum has suggested ("The Horatian Spirit in Holmes") that "Sherlock was obviously recalling appropriate lines from the *Odes* of Horace. The first passage that comes to mind is: *Aequam memento rebus in arduis / Servare mentem. . . . Odes,* 11, 3. 'Remember to keep your "equanimity" when you are in trouble.' "

28 *Peter Steiler the elder.* "No such hotel [as the Englischer Hoff] exists today," Mr. Michael C. Kaser wrote in "Sherlock Holmes on the Continent," "but there are Steiners (a slip of Watson's pen there) still tradesmen in Meiringen—one a tobacconist and another a haberdasher."

29 *the Grosvenor Hotel.* The Grosvenor Hotel, which was opened in 1861, shortly after the completion of Victoria Station, is a handsome building 300 feet long and 100 feet high, with its main frontage to the Buckingham Palace Road.

30 *the last stage of consumption.* If Mary Morstan Watson suffered from (and shortly died of) consumption, as many commentators believe, "the genius of Moriarty is here revealed that he chose the surest way of decoying Watson away from Holmes, knowing from his dossier on Watson that Mrs. Watson was herself a consumptive in an advanced stage."—Dr. Ebbe Curtis Hoff, "The Adventure of John and Mary."

31 *Davos Platz.* A town in the east of Switzerland. It is, in fact, a health resort for consumptives.

. . . I SAW HOLMES WITH HIS BACK AGAINST A ROCK AND HIS ARMS FOLDED, GAZING DOWN AT THE RUSH OF THE WATERS.

Illustration by Harry C. Edwards for *McClure's Magazine,* December, 1893. Sidney Paget illustrated the same scene for the *Strand Magazine,* December, 1893.

32 *Two lines of footmarks were clearly marked along the further end of the path, both leading away from me.* Mr. Pope R. Hill, Sr., has written (in "The Final Problem") that "The crowning absurdity in the published account is shown by the tracks. On the three-foot ledge, Holmes is supposed to have walked *with his back to Moriarty.* This would have meant certain death for Holmes, with absolutely no chance for him to bring about the death of Moriarty.... If Holmes had backed away from Moriarty, one set of tracks would be pointing forward and the other backward. Both sets were said to lead in the same direction toward the end of the path, which meant one man was walking in front of the other *with his back turned.* Neither man would have walked in front of the other like that, for it would have meant *his* certain death and the escape of his opponent."

But the late A. Carson Simpson wrote ("The Curious Incident of the Missing Corpse"): "The writer likes to think that the best traditions of British sportsmanship were observed by both sides in the epochal struggle. There are several indications of this. Holmes, an expert singlestick player and swordsman, no doubt had a useful knowledge of the quarter-staff; his six-foot alpenstock would have been perfect for such play, while the crook at its end offered some of the advantages of a medieval bill—yet he did not use it. Likewise, Moriarty allowed the note to Watson to be written and left under the cigarette case. Everything points to a mutual decision to fight it out on a man-to-man basis."

And Mr. Webster Evans has added ("Sherlock Holmes and Sport."): "Personally I have always thought that, considering his skill with the singlestick, Holmes was more than sporting in leaving his stick with the cigarette box. Moriarty, however, with equal nicety [as we learn later], 'drew no weapon.'"

I stood for a minute or two to collect myself, for I was dazed with the horror of the thing. Then I began to think of Holmes' own methods and to try to practise them in reading this tragedy. It was, alas! only too easy to do. During our conversation we had not gone to the end of the path, and the alpenstock marked the place where we had stood. The blackish soil is kept for ever soft by the incessant drift of spray, and a bird would leave its tread upon it. **32** Two lines of footmarks were clearly marked along the further end of the path, both leading away from me. There were none returning. A few yards from the end the soil was all ploughed up into a patch of mud, and the brambles and ferns which fringed the chasm were torn and bedraggled. I lay upon my face and peered over, with the spray spouting up all around me. It had darkened since I had left, and now I could only see here and there the glistening of moisture upon the black walls, and far away down at the end of the shaft the gleam of the broken water. I shouted; but only that same half-human cry of the fall was borne back to my ears.

But it was destined that I should after all have a last word of greeting from my friend and comrade. I have said that his alpenstock had been left leaning against a rock which jutted on to the path. From the top of this boulder the gleam of something bright caught my eye, and, raising my hand, I found that it came from the silver cigarette-case which he used to carry. As I took it up a small square of paper upon which it had lain fluttered down on to the ground. Unfolding it I found that it consisted of three pages torn from his notebook and addressed to me. It was characteristic of the man that the direction was as precise, and the writing as firm and clear, as though it had been written in his study.

"MY DEAR WATSON," he said, "I write these few lines through the courtesy of Mr. Moriarty, who awaits my convenience for the final discussion of those questions which lie between us. He has been giving me a sketch of the methods by which he avoided the English police and kept himself informed of our movements. They certainly confirm the very high opinion which I had formed of his abilities. I am pleased to think that I shall be able to free society from any further effects of his presence, though I fear that it is at a cost which will give pain to my friends, and especially, my dear Watson, to you. I have already explained to you, however, that my career had in any case reached its crisis, and that no possible conclusion to it could be more congenial to me than this. Indeed, if I may make a full confession to you, I was quite convinced that the letter from Meiringen

... A SMALL SQUARE OF PAPER ... FLUTTERED DOWN
ON TO THE GROUND.

Illustration by Sidney Paget for the *Strand Magazine*, December, 1893.

was a hoax, and I allowed you to depart on that errand under the persuasion that some development of this sort would follow. Tell Inspector Patterson that the papers which he needs to convict the gang are in pigeon-hole M., done up in a blue envelope and inscribed 'Moriarty.' I made every disposition of my property before leaving England, and handed it to my brother Mycroft. Pray give my greetings to Mrs. Watson, and believe me to be, my dear fellow,

                 "Very sincerely yours,
                      "SHERLOCK HOLMES."   **33**

A few words may suffice to tell the little that remains. An examination by experts leaves little doubt that a personal contest between the two men ended, as it could hardly fail to end in such a situation, in their reeling over, locked in each other's arms. Any attempt at recovering the bodies was absolutely hopeless, and there, **34** deep down in that dreadful cauldron of swirling water and seething foam, will lie for all time the most dangerous criminal and the foremost champion of the law of their generation. The Swiss youth was never found again, and there can be no doubt that he was one of the numerous agents whom Moriarty kept in his employ. As to the gang, it will be within the memory of the public how completely the evidence which Holmes had accumulated exposed their organization, and how heavily the hand of the dead man weighed upon them. Of their terrible chief few details came out during the proceeding, and if I have now been compelled to make a clear statement of his career, it is due to those injudicious champions who have endeavoured to clear his memory by attacks upon him whom I shall ever regard as the best and the wisest man whom I have ever known.   **35**

33 "*SHERLOCK HOLMES.*" Mr. Lorenzo J. Chieco, Certified Grapho-Analytical Psychologist, has reconstructed from Holmes' known traits of character and personality the signature reproduced here:

34 *Any attempt at recovering the bodies was absolutely hopeless.* Why? "The Reichenbach, it is true, is a brawling stream in its upper reaches, but, below the Falls, it settles down for its last short flow into the Aare at Meiringen," the late A. Carson Simpson wrote in "The Curious Incident of the Missing Corpse." "The Aare, in turn, travels fairly calmly for seven or eight miles until it empties into the Lake of Brienz. Moriarty's corpse should have been found floating in the lake or in one of the streams, but was not. This cannot have been for lack of searching, since, when the in-

"I MADE EVERY DISPOSITION OF MY PROPERTY BEFORE
LEAVING ENGLAND . . ."

In the *London Mystery Magazine* for June, 1955, a document purporting to be the last will and testament of Mr. Sherlock Holmes was reproduced in facsimile, with a prefatory note, unsigned, ascribing the discovery of the paper to Mr. Nathan L. Bengis, Keeper of the Crown of the Musgrave Ritualists of New York. Although strong doubts have been raised as to its genuineness, notably by Professor Jacques Barzun in "Sherlock Holmes' Will—A Forgery," Mr. Bengis has made a spirited rebuttal in "Where There's a Will, There's a Pay."

cident occurred, it was believed that there were two bodies to look for—Holmes' as well as the Professor's. Although the distraught Dr. Watson considered that 'any attempt at recovering the bodies was absolutely hopeless,' the Swiss, more experienced in such matters, and accustomed to seeing the corpse of a mountaineer emerge from a glacier some decades after he fell into a crevasse, would know better, and would not fail to make a thorough search."

In Mr. Simpson's view, the corpse of Professor Moriarty was not found because he had developed an Atomic Accelerator, a weapon more terrible than the atomic or hydrogen-bomb, which he turned upon himself as a last resort. But Mr. Poul Anderson ("A Treatise on the Binomial Theorem") has taken issue with Mr. Simpson: "the theory overlooks one basic item: that in order to accelerate mass, and so shrink it, energy must be applied. A shrinkage of one-half through velocity would require an energy equivalent to the original mass. Thus, to reduce, let us say, a 6-foot, 170-pound man to three feet, an energy of 170 pounds must be applied. Now a mass of one gram is equivalent to 9×10^{20} ergs, sufficient to raise a 30,000-ton ship more than 19 miles into the air. Mass-energy to the amount of 170 pounds, necessarily applied to Moriarty's body through the law of equal and opposite reaction, would not only have destroyed the Reichenbach Falls in one annihilating blow but probably would have left a large hole in place of the entire Republic of Switzerland. Mr. Simpson goes yet further: postulating that objects were shrunk to nearly zero size. In order to do this, Moriarty would have to convert the entire sidereal universe into energy, a project somewhat too large even for his ambitious nature."

35 *the best and the wisest man whom I have ever known.* "Watson's words," Mr. Morris Rosenblum wrote in "Foreign Language Quotations in the Canon," "are an echo of the final paragraph of [Plato's] *Phaedo*, describing the death of Socrates: 'Such was the end, Echecrates, of our friend, who was, as we may say, of all those of his time whom we have ever known, the best and wisest and most righteous man.'"

Auctorial and Bibliographical Note: Conan Doyle's own opinion of "The Final Problem" was a high one: he placed it No. 4 on his "twelve best" list of the short stories. Of the original manuscript, only "a noble fragment" is recorded, the "original autograph manuscript of Sherlock Holmes' letter to Dr. Watson, regarding his last meeting with Professor Moriarty." The fragment was auctioned in Philadelphia on December 8, 1915; its present location is unknown.

. . . A PERSONAL CONTEST BETWEEN THE TWO MEN ENDED . . . IN THEIR REELING OVER, LOCKED IN EACH OTHER'S ARMS

Illustration by Sidney Paget for the *Strand Magazine*, December, 1893. Harry C. Edwards illustrated the same sad scene for *McClure's Magazine*, December, 1893.

VII. FROM HOLMES' RETURN TO DR. WATSON'S THIRD MARRIAGE

[Thursday, April 5, 1894 to October, 1902]

"Once again Mr. Sherlock Holmes is free to devote his life to examining those interesting little problems which the complex life of London so plentifully presents."

—"The Adventure of the Empty House"

48

"YOU MAY HAVE READ OF THE REMARKABLE EXPLORATIONS OF A NORWEGIAN NAMED SIGERSON . . ."

We must here anticipate Holmes' Return to examine critically what has aptly been termed the Great Hiatus—the three years, May, 1891, to April, 1894, when all the world, except his brother Mycroft, thought Sherlock Holmes dead.

In "The Adventure of the Empty House," Holmes tells Watson (and us): "I travelled for two years in Tibet . . . , and amused myself by visiting Lhassa and spending some days with the head Llama. . . . I then passed through Persia, looked in at Mecca, and paid a short but interesting visit to the Khalifa at Khartoum. . . . Returning to France, I spent some months in a research into the coal-tar derivatives, which I conducted at a laboratory at Montpelier, in the south of France."

Now, "here . . . is a tale compounded of fallacy, anachronism and paradox," the late Edgar W. Smith wrote in "Sherlock Holmes and the Great Hiatus"; "an itinerary that starts from the realm of the merely improbable and carries us swiftly to the never-never land of the globally impossible; a fantasy that rivals the most befuddled denizen of Upper Swandam Lane. The doings at Reichenbach, we may all agree, are veiled in a mist of considerable doubt. But the Years of the Hiatus which lie beyond are enshrouded in a fog so thick that the streets of London itself have never known its like."

These are strong words, trebly strong in coming from one of the most distinguished of all Sherlockian scholars, past or present, and we must first of all see upon what grounds Mr. Smith (and many other commentators) have based their doubts about the Holmes itinerary as Watson has given it to us.

Let us look at the Master Detective's statements, one by one:

1. "*I travelled for two years in Tibet . . . and amused myself by visiting Lhassa and spending some days with the head Llama.*" As Mr. Ogden Nash has so delightfully pointed out in *Many Long Years Ago:*

> The one-l lama,
> He's a priest,
> The two-l llama,
> He's a beast . . .

and it is most unfortunate that our text here reads *Llama* and not *Lama*. Since it is highly unlikely that Holmes, confusing Tibet with Peru, spent some days with a high-ranking llama, he presumably passed his time with one of the dignitaries of

Tibetan Lamaism, probably not the Dalai Lama, then a youth who lived in much seclusion, but perhaps either the Pan-chen Rim-Poche (the Tashai or Teshai Lama) or the Regent, abbot of the great Ten-gye-ling Monastery in Lhassa, then one of the four major monasteries in Tibet. The late A. Carson Simpson, in Volume Two of his great work, *Sherlock Holmes' Wanderjahre*, voted for the Regent, who has been called "the head Lama" by no less an authority than Sir Charles Bell (*Tibet, Past and Present*, Oxford, 1924); although Mrs. Winifred M. Christie ("On the Remarkable Explorations of Sigerson") thought it more likely that Holmes' host was the Pan-chen Lama, who outranked the Dalai Lama spiritually although subordinate to him in worldly matters. But here Mr. Smith entered his first objection: *no* European, Norwegian or otherwise, he pointed out, "came anywhere near the forbidden city of Lhassa until 1903, when a military mission under Lt. Col. Younghusband battered its way into the Lama's presence by force of arms. Two Englishmen, Captain Bower and Dr. Thorold, crossed the borders of Tibet in 1891; and in 1892—by which time Holmes must have begun to tire of the amusement his visit was affording him—an Englishwoman, Miss Taylor, came within 150 miles of the holy of holies. The record for peaceful penetration—still as far from Lhassa itself as Philadelphia from New York—was established by a Mr. and Mrs. Littledale in 1895; but from that point on all foreigners, including the Scandinavian, seem to have given up the idea of carrying European culture to the innocent Tibetans until, nearly a decade later, the task was finally and successfully accomplished with benefit of Gatling gun and other light artillery. There can be no confusion in all of this: Holmes was neither a woman nor a soldier, and we must be constrained now to believe that he was not even a Norwegian. The first two years of his reputed itinerary we may, therefore, dismiss as a figment."

Dr. John D. Clark, in his paper, "Some Notes Relating to a Preliminary Investigation into the Paternity of Nero Wolfe," has expressed his agreement with this position: "Holmes' account of his travels in Tibet and through Persia are the purest invention on his part. . . . The mention of the 'Norwegian traveller Sigerson' is cleverly designed to lead to a degree of confusion in Watson's mind between the mythical Norwegian and the very real Sven Hedin who was at that time starting his Central Asian researches. . . ."

And Mr. H. B. Williams has added that Holmes "could have found no better method of informing the Moriarty organization of his whereabouts [than through his letters to the London newspapers, concerning the remarkable explorations of which Watson "may have read"]. Proof of this . . . is to be had in the consideration of the short biography of Colonel Moran included in Holmes' fine collection of *M*'s ["The Adventure of the Empty House"]. Colonel Moran is therein listed as the author of *Heavy Game of the Western Himalayas*. Any exploration of the Himalayas and Tibet would be of intense interest to him. Holmes having no time to build up [his] alter ego, [Sigerson], the exploits of this hereto unknown explorer meant that Moran would explore the background of this newcomer being chronicled in the daily press. It would not be long before Holmes' disguise would have been penetrated."[1]

[1] But the late A. Carson Simpson shortly afterwards pointed out that in Tibet at that time the postal system, such as it was, was strictly for government officials; there were no postage stamps until 1913, and then for internal use only. "Such being the case, there is little force in the suggestion that newspaper accounts of Sigerson's explorations would have alerted Col. Moran to investigate; these could not even have been started on their way to the papers until after Holmes was safely out of Tibet."

2. "*I then passed through Persia . . .*" "It is to be hoped" (Mr. Smith continued) "that this transit, if it really occurred, was both rapid and discreet, and that Holmes did not tarry long in search of a mate to the slipper which still, we may suppose, was hanging by the fireplace in the empty room at Baker Street. For Persia, in the year 1893, was seething with unrest, and all strangers, particularly Englishmen and Russians, whose governments were even then sparring for political advantage in this ancient land, were regarded with suspicion."

3. "*. . . looked in at Mecca . . .*" "There, too, if [Holmes] arrived early in the summer of 1893" (we are still quoting Mr. Smith), "he would have run into trouble in the form of a modest civil war. Mecca itself was probably sanctuary to all the faithful in common, but in nearby Mulaida a fierce battle had recently been waged between overzealous Mohammedan factions and, in crossing from 'the western borders of Persia to the ultimate shrine of Islam, Holmes would have had to pass through territory which was still witness to brisk if sporadic skirmishing. . . . It is to be earnestly doubted, in view of the excitements prevailing, that Holmes' 'look-in' at Mecca was from any very close point of vantage."

4. "*. . . paid a short but interesting visit to the Khalifa at Khartoum . . .*" The Khalifa, we may note to begin with, was the Mohammedan ruler of the Sudan south of Egypt and Libya, a region which was a storm center of British foreign policy in the 'eighties and 'nineties. And now let us return to Mr. Smith: ". . . the curious incident of the Khalifa at Khartoum, in the year 1893, is that the Khalifa was not at Khartoum. That historic city on the banks of the Nile had been leveled to the ground in 1885, and the Mahdist government had taken up its residence in nearby Omdurman, where the Calif ["Khalifa"] Abdullah held forth embattled until 1888, when Kitchener overthrew him and returned the seat of Sudanese affairs once more to Khartoum."

5. "*. . . spent some months in a research into the coal-tar derivatives, which I conducted in a laboratory at Montpelier, in the south of France.*" It is again to be deeply regretted that our text here reads *Montpelier*, for Montpelier—with one *l*—is 1) a city in Bear Lake County, Idaho; 2) a city in Blockford County, Indiana; 3) a village in Williams County, Ohio; 4) the county seat of Washington County, Vermont, and the capital of that state. We assume that Watson meant *Montpellier*, with two *l*'s, which, happily, *is* a city in the south of France. Aside from Watson's spelling, little exception can be taken to this statement, although—as Professor Remsen Ten Eyck Schenck pointed out in "Baker Street Fables"— "no chemist would be guilty of making it. At least 80% of all the research work in chemistry done by thousands of men in the last hundred years could be so described, since about that proportion of the known organic compounds are coal-tar derivatives. The remark is therefore windy, grandiose and so diffuse as to be practically devoid of meaning."

Despite these formidable objections, there exists a highly articulate group of Sherlockian commentators—the Apologistic, or Fundamentalist, School—which maintains that Holmes did almost exactly what he said he did at the time of the Great Hiatus: visited the head Lama in Lhassa, passed through Persia, looked in at Mecca, and interviewed the Khalifa (but not, perhaps, at Khartoum).

Let us briefly review the opinions of this school, starting with its views on Tibet.

1. *On Tibet.* Here our outstanding authority is certainly Mr. Simpson, who has traced virtually every step of Holmes' explorations in the Forbidden Land in his monumental study of *Sherlock Holmes' Wanderjahre*. Mr. Simpson demonstrates with considerable believeability that Holmes outfitted his expedition at Darjeeling, made the eighteen-mile trip by cart-road to the valley of the Teesta River, crossed the river by means of the Teesta Bridge, and started a sixty-mile trip over a narrow and crude pony-track to the Tibetan frontier. This was probably the most uncomfortable part of the trip because of the Himalayan leeches. Contending with leeches all the way, Holmes followed the pony-track through Kalimpong, gradually climbing along the river to Rangpo, where he left it and entered Native Sikkim. Here began the steep climb to the Tibetan frontier. The Master crossed the Jelep La (Pass) on the frontier and made the steep ascent to the Chumbi Valley. The beginning of the climb up the Chumbi Valley to the settlement of Chumbi was easy. From there the way climbed to Phari Dzong, forty miles from the Jelep La. Holmes had to cross several other passes before reaching Lhassa, over 210 miles away. "There [Holmes'] first act would be to call on the Head Lama and to present him with the traditional white scarf." It is Mr. Simpson's hypothesis that the "head Lama" (Regent, in his view) then commissioned Holmes to solve the mystery of the Abominable Snowman, then known only by his footprints in the snow. This would take Holmes into the Everest region. His interest in Buddhism would of course lead him to visit the Rocky Valley Inner Monastery (Rongbuk), sixteen miles from Mount Everest, and the Monastery of the Mount of Blessing—Ta-shi Lhun-po, at Shigaste. In the course of his Snowman researches he would investigate the whole vicinity of Everest, as well as the slopes of the mountain itself. "This made him the first European—and probably the first man—to set foot on the sacred ground of the highest mountain in the world. To the British Empire, therefore, belongs the credit for the first partial ascent, as well as for finishing the job on that memorable May 29, 1953, over sixty years later." It is at this time that Holmes would naturally visit the Kharta Valley, to the eastward (*see below*). His Snowman researches completed, Holmes moved westward to Ladakh, under British protection, to replenish his funds. "After travelling around Ladakh for a time, he no doubt headed east for his researches into the geology of Central Tibet,"**2** returning by a more northerly course to Toghral Ombo, where his homeward journey, via Persia, Mecca, Khartoum and the south of France began.

2. *On Persia.* Here a correspondent (and a considerable authority on both Persia and Mecca), Mr. Benson Murray, writes: "Persia in [1893] may have been 'seething with unrest,' but I doubt that this would have bothered a man of Holmes' accomplishments. Sykes makes mention of the cancellation of the tobacco *régie* in 1892 'after disturbances had broken out and intense hostility had been displayed towards

2 As mentioned by Mr. P. M. Stone in his "Sussex Interview" with Holmes.

3 Mr. Murray adds: "In spite of [very strict] restrictions [against the visits of non-Muslims to Mecca] a number of people have visited Mecca and left reports. The classic reports are probably those of Burckhardt (in Mecca 1814) and Burton (in Mecca 1853). Including Holmes . . . I am aware of 28 visitors, mostly of European origin, who have left accounts in European languages. These accounts range from that of Ludovico Varthema who visited the city in 1503 to H. B. St. J. Philby who made the pilgrimage in 1931. I question the veracity of the account of a visit made to Mecca by Arnold von Harff. If his account is true he would be the first western visitor —1496."

Mr. Murray also suggests an interesting *reason* for Holmes' visit: "In 1877 'an Englishman professing Mohammedanism' visited Mecca. He resided there for some six months, and his account (which appeared in 1881) is of considerable interest. . . . In this work he makes mention of an Englishwoman in Mecca. Upon his return from Mecca he attempted to make contact with her to see if she could be brought from Mecca to England. The material in the appendix of the book casts some doubt on whether she really was English although all reports indicate that her command of the language was very good. In 1877 she had been residing in Mecca since the Indian Mutiny of 1857. Shortly after 1877 she appears to have been taken back to India, and it was reported that she did not want 'rescue.' I know nothing of her subsequent history but it is possible that by 1893 she had been once again taken to Mecca and by that time she desired to spend her last years in England. At the time of Holmes' visit [presumably to affect her rescue] she would have been in her sixties. The book in question is (J.) T. F. Keane, *Six Months in Mecca*, London, 1881."

Europeans' (*History of Persia*, II, 373). Browne characterizes the period from 1890 to 1896 as 'notable for political fermentation which brought on revolution' (*Literary History of Persia*, IV, 156). Shuster (*The Strangling of Persia*) makes no particular mention of unrest. Certainly Gertrude Bell's *Persian Pictures* (trip made 1892; work first published with additional material 1894) shows no seething unrest."

3. *On Mecca.* "I do not remember" (we are again quoting our authority on the history of the Middle East, Mr. Benson Murray) "that either Hurgronje, who visited Mecca in 1885, or Gervais-Courtellement, who was there in 1894, mentions civil war. Neither of these accounts is presently at hand to me, but a check of de Gaury's *Rulers of Mecca* (London, 1951) and Hogarth's *History of Arabia* (Oxford, 1922) indicates nothing more than a struggle between the Ottoman administration and the Sherif. I would scarcely call this civil war."**3**

4. *On Khartoum.* "One would think," the late Dr. Ernest Bloomfield Zeisler wrote in *Baker Street Chronology*, "that Khartoum and Omdurman are at opposite poles of the earth. As a matter of fact they are only a mile or two apart, Khartoum being on the right bank of the Nile and Omdurman on the left bank directly opposite. It is true that the Khalifa's capital was at that time not Khartoum but Omdurman. The former had been besieged by the Mahdists and captured on January 26, 1885, the day they killed General Gordon. Almost every building in Khartoum was destroyed. On June 22, 1885, the Mahdi died and was succeeded by the Khalifa, whose capital was Omdurman. It was not until September of 1898 that Omdurman was captured by General Kitchener, and the capital was transferred back to Khartoum. The Master's visit to the Khalifa was probably late in 1893, at which time Khartoum had been partly rebuilt, and it is quite possible that the Khalifa actually was in Khartoum when the Master saw him, though it is more likely that it was in Omdurman rather than in Khartoum. It was probably either a slip of the tongue by the Master or a slip of the pen by Watson which led to this slight error in the account. But this cannot stamp the entire story as untrue. The two cities were joined by much history and by a bridge, and it would have been easy to mis-speak or mis-write one for the other. Indeed, this very slip speaks rather potently for the truth of the story, for if the Master had been trying to deceive the public he would have been careful to avoid so obvious an error."

And the late A. Carson Simpson added: "Indeed, the 'Khalifa-Khartoum' error, rightly understood, *confirms* the visit to Tibet. Service in Afghanistan would not familiarize Watson with the name of every region in the far end of Tibet, especially one not on a recognized trade-route. So when Holmes referred to passing through *Kharta*, the name was unknown to the Doctor, who confused it with Khartoum —a place only too well known to every Britisher at that time. He did not realize that the Master was referring to a district in south-eastern Tibet, just north of the eastern end of Nepal. Instead, Watson erroneously associated it with the Sudan, probably misled by the reference to the Khalifa, and misunderstood Kharta as Khartoum, which the Master undoubtedly never mentioned at all in speaking of his 'short but interesting visit to the Khalifa.' "

Opposed to the Apologistic, or Fundamentalist, School of Sherlockian Commentary, however, is a group we may call the Interpretive School. This group holds that Holmes, for one reason or another, was not being entirely frank with Watson in his brief description of his travels—or, alternatively, that Watson, for one reason or another, was not being entirely frank with his readers.

In this latter vein, for example, Mr. Walter P. Armstrong, Jr., writes (in "The Truth About Sherlock Holmes"): "Not only was Holmes in London [during the entire period 1891–1894], but he was living in the same house with Watson all the time. . . . So it becomes apparent that Watson never believed that Holmes lay at the bottom of the Reichenbach Fall; that on the contrary he helped him to lay a false trail and later published an account of his death which he knew to be false; that during the three years during which he was supposed to be traveling under the name of Sigerson, Holmes was in fact in London waiting for Colonel Moran to make a false move, and Watson knew it; that after the apprehension of Colonel Moran [Holmes] assumed his true character; and that Watson then, in order to conceal his lapse from the strictest veracity, composed a fictional account of his escape and return. . . . Watson has deceived us. But we cannot blame him, for the deception was necessary in order to trap the wily members of the Moriarty gang who remained."**4**

Mr. Edgar W. Smith, on the other hand, noting that Holmes in "The Adventure of the Dancing Men" "made reference in familiar terms to 'my friend Wilson Hargreave, of the New York Police Bureau'" and spoke confidently, in that same adventure, of "my knowledge of the crooks of Chicago," wrote that: "Such friendships and such knowledge are not credibly acquired, even by a man of Holmes' attainments, on a mail-order basis, and in both instances the statements as he made them have a ring of authority which speaks eloquently of first-hand acquaintance and information." In the Smith view, then, Holmes spent the years of the Great Hiatus, not in Tibet, Persia, Arabia, the Egyptian Sudan, and the south of France, but in the United States of America. Indeed, he concluded that: "It is obvious [in the murders of Andrew Jackson Borden and his wife, Abby Durfee Borden, at Fall River, Massachusetts, on the fourth of August in the year 1892] that some unseen hand was steadily at work in the weaving of [the] net [that caught and held Lizzie Borden, who was indicted on December 2, 1892], and it should be equally obvious to us whose hand that was. Confronted as they were by the bloodiest and most blood-curdling murder in the annals of crime, it is wholly reasonable to suppose that the police of Fall River . . . should have appealed to the closest thing there is in America to a Scotland Yard—the New York Police Bureau. And in rallying to meet that appeal it would be incredible that Wilson Hargreave should have failed to call in turn upon the aid and counsel of the greatest criminal investigator of all time, who sat beside him at the moment—or that Sherlock Holmes should have refused to heed that call."

A third view, popular with this school, holds that Holmes

4 The late Gavin Brend agreed with Mr. Armstrong that Holmes was in London all the time—but Mr. Brend went on to suggest (*My Dear Holmes*) that Colonel James Moriarty took over the gang after his brother's death and that Sherlock Holmes joined the gang in disguise in order to break it up; it was during this period, Mr. Brend held, that Mycroft communicated with Sherlock by the "second stain" code through Watson's reports of "The Yellow Face" and "The Naval Treaty."

5 But the late Elmer Davis commented (*Introducing Mr. Sherlock Holmes*): "If any such interlude of dalliance is admissible at all, which I doubt, it is more likely to have lasted three weeks than three years. What a three weeks! you may say. What, indeed." And Dean Theodore C. Blegen wrote ("These Were Hidden Fires, Indeed"): "The theory is engaging and cannot be dismissed lightly, but there is no documentation . . ."

6 In "The Truth About Moriarty," which has also appeared under the title of "Mr. Moriarty."

7 Moriarty not only survived, he reformed, in the view of Miss Ruth Berman. She has suggested that some evidence of this may be found in the Periodic Chart of the Elements, which shows that Element 67, one of the rare earths, was called *Holmium* by its discoverer, as a tribute to Holmes by the reformed Moriarty.

during the years of the Great Hiatus was acting as a secret agent for the Allies and was therefore circumspect with Watson about the areas he actually visited. "In the Far East he must have observed with sage foreboding Japan's preparations for the Chinese war of 1894 that would begin the march of Japanese imperialism," Mr. Manly Wade Wellman wrote in "Scoundrels in Bohemia." "His other activities concentrated on Persia, the East African Coast, and France—hot spots of international dispute then and later."

Nor should we forget here those who believe that the Great Hiatus was a period when Love at last Conquered All. Here is Mr. Stanley McComas, speaking for this group in his essay, "Love at Lhassa": ". . . after Reichenbach, Holmes met Irene Adler in Florence and married her without delay. He was in a hurry to get there, too. Can anyone believe that a man, torn and bleeding from a nasty adventure on a ledge over the Reichenbach Falls, would do 'ten miles over the mountains in the darkness' [see "The Adventure of the Empty House"] merely out of fear of an old man with an air gun?"**5**

And now we must consider the speculations of still a third group of commentators—the Sensationalist School—whose theories may be conveniently grouped under three major headings:

1. *Both Holmes and Moriarty survived Reichenbach.*

a. Holmes survived (said the late A. G. Macdonell**6**) because he was a pure invention of Holmes', part of an elaborate hoax. In Mr. Macdonell's view, "Holmes selected a perfectly ordinary ex-professor and fastened on to the unfortunate man the fearful reputation which has dogged him ever since." Holmes did this, we are told, because in the late 'eighties he found himself slipping. To explain his failures, he therefore invented a supercriminal. At Reichenbach, Holmes clung to one rock and Moriarty to another; Moriarty was then resuscitated in 1899 (Mr. Macdonell's date) to play his part in *The Valley of Fear.*

b. Or Moriarty survived because he and Holmes were one and the same man. In *Sherlock Holmes: Fact or Fiction?*, Mr. T. S. Blakeney reported this as the "very subtle suggestion . . . thrown out in private by a distinguished writer whose name cannot be divulged." The evidence for the hypothesis is: 1) Holmes' testimony that Moriarty existed is all we have; 2) Holmes was a master at disguise; 3) Holmes had someone impersonate Moriarty at Reichenbach. Mr. Blakeney then commented: "The more we reflect on this Holmes-Moriarty hypothesis the more we are convinced that it is adequately answered in Holmes' own words: 'it seems to have only one drawback, and that is that it is intrinsically impossible.' "

c. Or Moriarty survived because he used a double at Reichenbach. "Is it not logical," Mr. H. B. Williams wrote in "A Non-Canonical Clue," "that Moriarty would pit one of greater physical ability than he possessed to engage in a hand-to-hand struggle with Holmes? There must have been times in the pursuance of his nefarious doings that the employment of a double was mandatory. Why not at this time use one whose strength could cope with Holmes' bodily powers?"**7**

2. *Neither Holmes nor Moriarty survived Reichenbach.*

The late Monsignor Ronald A. Knox was forced to conclude his *Studies in the Literature of Sherlock Holmes* with the solemn thought that Holmes had indeed been killed at Reichenbach, and that—while "all the stories were written by Watson"—they consisted in part of a "genuine cycle [which] actually happened" and in part of "spurious adventures [which were] the lucubrations of his own unaided invention."

The late Page Heldenbrand was another who believed that Holmes perished at the Reichenbach. Some of the later-chronicled adventures, he contended in "The Adventures of the Dead Detective," took place before Holmes' demise ("The Adventure of Charles Augustus Milverton," "The Second Stain," "The Adventure of the Dying Detective," *The Valley of Fear*), while others were fictions concocted by Watson for his personal gain.

And Mr. Rolfe Boswell has agreed that a rock "carried both Holmes and Moriarty over the falls—a strike without a spare." The later Holmes, he holds ("Sarasate, Sherlock and Shaw"), was a fictive creature, "recreated from the chasm to line the pockets" of writers other than Watson.

Writing in "Who Killed Holmes?", Mr. Marvin Grasse has answered his own question by suggesting that it was Watson and Mycroft. This theory runs as follows: Watson had a long-smoldering hatred for Holmes, who had taunted him repeatedly, and finally had wrecked his marriage; Mycroft, too, was jealous of his younger brother and anxious to inherit his wealth. So Watson and Mycroft connived together, Mycroft being the tall Englishman hurrying to meet Sherlock. And Watson, after helping Mycroft to bash in Holmes' brains, not only scribbled the cunning alibi note that recalled him to the hotel, but composed Sherlock's death message as well.

And Mr. Anthony Boucher, writing in "Was the Later Holmes an Imposter?", has based his case that the later Holmes *was* an imposter on these four points:

a. "The protero-Holmes announced his intended retirement after the triumph over Moriarty. . . . The returned Holmes continues in practice for almost a decade after the complete annihilation of the Moriarty gang."

b. "The original Holmes plays the violin frequently. . . . The deutero-Holmes never once plays the violin.**8** . . . [He] is apparently more interested in vocal music . . ."

c. "Holmes I was addicted to the use of cocaine and morphine. Holmes II uses no stronger stimulant than shag."

d. ". . . the *ur*-Holmes knows off-hand [the names of] the three leading free-lance spies in London ["The Second Stain"] . . . Holmes [in 1895, in "The Adventure of the Bruce-Partington Plans"] is forced to appeal to Mycroft for their names . . ."

Other commentators, notably Mr. Eustace Portugal and Professor John B. Wolf, have added to Mr. Boucher's list:

e. Holmes I and II are inconsistent in respect to their attitudes to the law.**9**

f. In later cases, Holmes shows a tendency to gibe at his opponents; this would be like Moriarty, but unlike Holmes.

8 Mr. Boucher is not quite correct here. In "The Adventure of the Norwood Builder" (August, 1895), Watson wrote: "For two hours he [Holmes] droned away upon his violin . . ."

9 A point on which Magistrate S. Tupper Bigelow has expanded in his essay, "Sherlock Holmes Was No Burglar": ". . . what of Holmes' colossal ignorance of the law of burglary and unlawful entry after the Return? . . . It would appear . . . that this . . . provides powerful ammunition for those who espouse the theory of [a] deutero-Holmes. There is no instance in the Canon before the Return, for example, in which Holmes revealed his contempt for what he believed to be the law so far as burglary was concerned. Nor is there a case in which he thought he had committed burglary or even unlawful entry, before the Return. On the contrary, compare Holmes' respect for a search-warrant in 'The Greek Interpreter' with his utter disdain for such a scrap of paper in 'The Disappearance of Lady Frances Carfax.' Furthermore, it must be pointed out, Holmes' sublimated yearnings for a criminal career are made evident in the Canon only after the Return."

10 Mr. McDiarmid argues that Holmes actually did retire after vanquishing Moriarty and that the later cases are either 1) special cases, which Holmes felt he had to undertake (e.g., "His Last Bow"); or 2) reports of earlier cases issued by Watson, who for some reason wished to maintain the fiction that Holmes was in active practice until 1903.

g. Holmes I quotes both German and French several times; Holmes II never does.

h. Holmes I demonstrates a considerable knowledge of horse racing ("Silver Blaze"); Holmes II has to make Watson his "Handy Guide to the Turf" ("The Adventure of Shoscombe Old Place").

Mr. Boucher concluded that "Mycroft saw to it that there should be a Sherlock Holmes. He found a cousin, markedly similar to the lost brother and possessed of some of the intellectual attainments characteristic of the Vernet strain of blood. He would be capable of playing the role of Sherlock reasonably well on his own, and if need be, he could always call upon Mycroft. . . . The three *Wanderjahre*, 1891–1894, were doubtless spent, not in Tibet nor in the ruins of Khartoum, but in the Pall Mall lodgings opposite the Diogenes Club under the careful tutelage of Mycroft, with visits (no doubt in disguise) to the empty lodgings in Baker Street, where files and scrapbooks might be consulted and memorized. The Adair murder provided the perfect moment for the resurrection, and Sherlock Holmes once more walked the streets of London."

This is an ingenious theory, argued with much plausibility —but we must add that Mr. Boucher himself later abandoned it, in favor of the Armstrong Holmes-Never-Left-London Theory.

3. *Moriarty alone survived Reichenbach.* This is the view of Mr. Eustace Portugal, who, like Mr. Boucher, based his case largely on the changes in Holmes' nature after the Return. "It is my opinion," Mr. Portugal wrote in "The Holmes-Moriarty Duel," "that it is Professor Moriarty who keeps bees on the Sussex Downs, and that the body of Sherlock Holmes lies in the Reichenbach abyss."

But—as Mr. Boucher has written—Mr. Portugal's evidence "amounts to hardly more than the fact that the mathematician [like Holmes] was . . . tall and thin. This solution, though pleasantly outrageous, has little to recommend it."

Let us conclude our examination of the years of the Great Hiatus with this quotation from Mr. E. W. McDiarmid ("Reichenbach and Beyond"):

"No conclusive evidence has appeared to make one believe that Holmes lies buried in the chasm at Reichenbach. Nor is there conclusive evidence to suggest that the period of the Great Hiatus was not just that: the interlude between the early practice and some later events. And finally, we must agree that whether or not Holmes returned to active practice,**10** he *did* return—and, at least by 1903, had fulfilled his dream of retiring to a Sussex bee farm."

49

THE ADVENTURE OF THE EMPTY HOUSE

[Thursday, April 5, 1894]

IT was in the spring of the year 1894 that all London was interested, and the fashionable world dismayed, by the murder of the Honourable Ronald Adair, **1** under most unusual and inexplicable circumstances. The public has already learned those particulars of the crime which came out in the police investigation ; but a good deal was suppressed upon that occasion, since the case for the prosecution was so overwhelmingly strong that it was not necessary to bring forward all the facts. Only now, at the end of nearly ten years, am I allowed **2** to supply those missing links which make up the whole of that remarkable chain. The crime was of interest in itself, but that interest was as nothing to me compared to the inconceivable sequel, which afforded me the greatest shock and surprise of any event in my adventurous life. Even now, after this long interval, I find myself thrilling as I think of it, and feeling once more that sudden flood of joy, amazement, and incredulity which utterly submerged my mind. Let me say to that public which has shown some interest in those glimpses which I have occasionally given them of the thoughts and actions of a very remarkable man that they are not to blame me if I have not shared my knowledge with them, for I should have considered it my first duty to have done so had I not been barred by a positive prohibition from his own lips, which was only withdrawn upon the third of last month. **3**

It can be imagined that my close intimacy with Sherlock Holmes had interested me deeply in crime, and that after his disappearance I never failed to read with care the various problems which came before the public and I even attempted more than once for my own private satisfaction to employ his methods in their solution, though with indifferent success. There was none, however, which appealed to me like this tragedy of Ronald Adair. As I read the evidence at the inquest, which led up to a verdict of wilful murder against some person or persons unknown, I realized more clearly than I had ever done the loss which the community had sustained by the death of Sherlock Holmes. There were points about this strange business which would, I was sure, have specially appealed to him, and the efforts of the police would have been supplemented, or more probably anticipated, by the trained observation and the alert mind of the first criminal agent in Europe. All day as I drove

1 *the Honourable Ronald Adair.* "British conventions in regard to titles are sometimes puzzling to the American reader," the late Christopher Morley wrote in *Sherlock Holmes and Dr. Watson: A Textbook of Friendship.* "Young Ronald Adair has the courtesy prefix The Honourable because he is the child of a 'peer' (viz., a nobleman; there are five degrees of nobility: duke, marquis, earl, viscount, baron). Similarly his sister Hilda would be known as The Honourable Hilda Adair. The prefix Honourable is also given by courtesy to judges of the higher courts and some government officials, as is also done, though more casually, in the U.S. This attribution of honor is not acquired by marriage: if Ronald had married Miss Woodley they would have been announced by the butler as The Honourable Ronald Adair and Mrs. Adair. The most frequent error made by those unfamiliar with these traditional labels is to use the title of honor as a substitute for Mister. When Dr. Doyle was knighted and became Sir Arthur Conan Doyle it would be wrong to refer to him as 'Sir Doyle,' just as you would never call Sir Walter Scott 'Sir Scott.' Sir Walter Scott, Bart., means Sir Walter Scott, Baronet; the Baronet's title is hereditary and passes to his son. The order of simple knighthood, as in the case of Doyle, is personal and not hereditary. In these innocent old formalities are many entertaining distinctions. For instance the formal address for the Earl of Maynooth would be Right Honourable the Earl of Maynooth. His wife would be The Countess of Maynooth, but referred to informally as Lady Maynooth. Perhaps it was the complexity of all this that discouraged plain Miss Edith Woodley."

2 *at the end of nearly ten years.* "The Adventure of the Empty House" was published in the *Strand Magazine*, October, 1903, and in *Collier's Magazine*, September 26, 1903.

3 *the third of last month.* Allowing for magazine printing schedules, the time Watson would have needed to write his account of the adventure, and the time required by the artists to prepare illustrations, it is probable that "the third of last month" was no later than the third of June, 1903, some four months before Holmes' retirement.

ALL DAY AS I DROVE UPON MY ROUND . . .

Here Dr. Joseph Bell of Edinburgh, the prototype of Sherlock Holmes, makes *his* daily round.

4 *an operation for cataract.* "The Australian colonies were Victoria, New South Wales, South Australia, West Australia and Queensland; but they also included the 'two adjacent islands' of Tasmania and New Zealand," Mrs. Jennifer Chorley wrote in "Some Diggings Down Under." "Taking these seven, three (Victoria-Hopetown; South Australia-Kintore; New Zealand-Glasgow) were governed by earls. But Tasmania had Viscount Gormansion —not an earl but the only Irish peer. My mother is a Tasmanian by birth and judging from accounts of Tasmania at this time by my late grandmother, it is surprising that the Adairs could not enjoy this beautiful place in preference to Park Lane. I have a great-uncle, now in his 90's, still living in Melbourne, where he was practicing medicine, in 1893–4. I am sure he would agree that a cataract operation could have been performed in Melbourne or Sydney. But Tasmania might not have had the facilities so perhaps the Countess had some justification for returning to England."

5 *March 30, 1894.* A Friday. Watson has said that he would "recapitulate the facts as they were known to the public at the time of the inquest." The inquest cannot have been before, or long after, Monday, April 2, 1894.

6 *the Baldwin.* A "card-playing club, which . . . admits no strangers, is the Baldwin, in Pall Mall, which opens at two o'clock in the afternoon. The stakes here are very small," Mr. Ralph Nevill wrote in *London Clubs, Their History and Treasures,* London: Chatto & Windus, 1911.

7 *the Cavendish.* The Cavendish Club, on the north side of Piccadilly, between Down Street and Park Lane, was later taken over by the Cavalry Club.

upon my round I turned over the case in my mind, and found no explanation which appeared to me to be adequate. At the risk of telling a twice-told tale I will recapitulate the facts as they were known to the public at the conclusion of the inquest.

The Honourable Robert Adair was the second son of the Earl of Maynooth, at that time Governor of one of the Australian colonies. Adair's mother had returned from **4** Australia to undergo an operation for cataract, and she, her son Ronald, and her daughter Hilda were living together at 427 Park Lane. The youth moved in the best society, had, so far as was known, no enemies, and no particular vices. He had been engaged to Miss Edith Woodley, of Carstairs, but the engagement had been broken off by mutual consent some months before, and there was no sign that it had left any very profound feeling behind it. For the rest, the man's life moved in a narrow and conventional circle, for his habits were quiet and his nature unemotional. Yet it was upon this easygoing young aristocrat that death came in most strange and unexpected form between the hours of ten and eleven-**5** twenty on the night of March 30, 1894.

Ronald Adair was fond of cards, playing continually, but never for such stakes as would hurt him. He was a **6-7-8** member of the Baldwin, the Cavendish, and the Bagatelle Card Clubs. It was shown that after dinner on the day of his death he had played a rubber of whist at the latter club. He had also played there in the afternoon. The evidence of those who had played with him—Mr. Murray, Sir John Hardy, and Colonel Moran—showed that the game was whist, and that there was a fairly equal fall of the cards. Adair might have lost five pounds, but not more. His fortune was a considerable one, and such a loss could not in any way affect him. He had played nearly every day at one club or other, but he was a cautious player, and usually rose a winner. It came out in evidence that in partnership with Colonel Moran he had **9** actually won as much as £420 in a sitting some weeks before from Godfrey Milner and Lord Balmoral. So much for his recent history, as it came out at the inquest.

On the evening of the crime he returned from the club exactly at ten. His mother and sister were out spending the evening with a relation. The servant deposed that she heard him enter the front room on the second floor, generally used as his sitting-room. She had lit a fire there, and as it smoked she had opened the window. No sound was heard from the room until eleven-twenty, the hour of the return of Lady Maynooth and her daughter. Desiring to say good night, she had attempted to enter her son's room. The door was locked on the inside, and no answer could be got to their cries and knocking. Help was obtained, and the door forced. The unfortunate young man was found lying near the table. His head had been horribly mutilated by an expanded revolver bullet, but no weapon of any sort was to be found in the room. On the table lay two bank-notes for **10** £10 each and £17 10s. in silver and gold, the money arranged in little piles of varying amount. There were some figures also upon a sheet of paper with the names of some club friends opposite to them, from which it was conjectured that before his death he was endeavouring to make out his losses or winnings at cards.

A minute examination of the circumstances served only to make the case more complex.   In the first place, no reason could be given why the young man should have fastened the door upon the inside.   There was the possibility that the murderer had done this and had afterwards escaped by the window.   The drop was at least twenty feet, however, and a bed of crocuses in full bloom **11** lay beneath.   Neither the flowers nor the earth showed any sign of having been disturbed, nor were there any marks upon the narrow strip of grass which separated the house from the road.   Apparently, therefore, it was the young man himself who had fastened the door. But how did he come by his death ?   No one could have climbed up to the window without leaving traces.   Suppose a man had fired through the window, it would indeed be a remarkable shot who could with a revolver inflict so deadly a wound.   Again, Park Lane is a frequented thoroughfare, and there is a cab-stand within a hundred yards of the house.   No one had heard a shot. And yet there was the dead man, and there the revolver bullet, which had mushroomed out, as soft-nosed bullets will, and so inflicted a wound which must have caused instantaneous death.   Such were the circumstances of the Park Lane Mystery, which were further complicated by entire absence of motive, since, as I have said, young Adair was not known to have any enemy, and no attempt had been made to remove the money or valuables in the room.

All day I turned these facts over in my mind, endeavouring to hit upon some theory which could reconcile them all, and to find that line of least resistance which my poor friend had declared to be the starting-point of every investigation.   I confess that I made little progress.   In the evening I strolled across the Park, and found myself about six o'clock at the Oxford Street end of Park Lane. A group of loafers upon the pavements, all staring up at a particular window, directed me to the house which I had come to see.   A tall, thin man with coloured glasses, whom I strongly suspected of being a plain-clothes detective, was pointing out some theory of his own, while the others crowded round to listen to what he said. I got as near as I could, but his observations seemed to me to be absurd, so I withdrew again in some disgust. As I did so I struck against an elderly deformed man, who had been behind me, and I knocked down several books which he was carrying.   I remember that as I picked them up I observed the title of one of them, *The Origin of Tree Worship*, and it struck me that the fellow must be some **12** poor bibliophile who, either as a trade or as a hobby, was a collector of obscure volumes.   I endeavoured to apologize for the accident, but it was evident that these books which I had so unfortunately maltreated were very precious objects in the eyes of their owner.   With a snarl of contempt he turned upon his heel, and I saw his curved back and white side-whiskers disappear among the throng.

My observations of No. 427 Park Lane did little to clear up the problem in which I was interested.   The house

8 *the Bagatelle*. Watson has presumably masked the actual name of the club at which Adair played on the day of his death.

9 *£420*. About $2,100 U.S. at the time.

10 *£17 10s. in silver and gold*. About $187.50 in all.

11 *a bed of crocuses in full bloom*. Watson evidently confused crocuses with another flower, for, as the late Gavin Brend pointed out in *My Dear Holmes*, "the crocus is hardly likely to be blooming [in England] at the end of March, and it would seem that January 30th would be a more appropriate date."

12 The Origin of Tree Worship. "Everywhere and, before the world was laicized, at all times, trees have been worshipped," Mr. Aldous Huxley has written. "It is not to be wondered at. . . . Half hidden in the darkness, half displayed in the air of heaven, the tree stands there, magnificent, a manifest god. . . . Trees in the mass can be almost terrible."

. . . I KNOCKED DOWN SEVERAL BOOKS WHICH HE WAS CARRYING.

A popular scene with the Canonical artists: it has been depicted by Sidney Paget in the *Strand Magazine*, October, 1903; by Frederic Dorr Steele in *Collier's Magazine*, September 26, 1903; by Charles Raymond Macauley in *The Return of Sherlock Holmes*, New York: McClure, Phillips & Co., 1905.

Miss Madeleine B. Stern has written ("Sherlock Holmes: Rare Book Collector") that ". . . we may safely assume that what [Watson] called *The Origin of Tree Worship* was actually *Der Baumkultus*, written by Boetticher in 1856, a title to which Watson, for the sake of his English public, translated a bit too freely."

To this Magistrate S. Tupper Bigelow has added ("Those Five Volumes"): "Oddly enough, there is not a book ever written in the English language called *The Origin of Tree Worship*. About the closest we can get to it is *Tree and Serpent Worship*, James Ferguson, London, 1873, and *The Sacred Tree in Religion and Myth*, Philpot, London, 1897. The latter can be ruled out at once, of course, as it was published after 1894." But see also Note 17.

13 *I retraced my steps to Kensington.* But Watson's practice in the years 1889–1891 was in *Paddington.* Why has he now returned to Kensington, the scene of his earlier (1886–1887) practice? In our view, the answer is to be found in Watson's career as a writer. As the late Edgar W. Smith wrote in "Dr. Watson and the Great Censorship": "Watson returned to England [from Switzerland], heartbroken, weary, and mourning the death of the best and wisest man whom he had ever known. He sought to lose himself in work, apparently. . . . Almost immediately the stories that had been simmering in his brain for so long began to pour forth in a great flood. The world was electrified by the appearance in the *Strand Magazine* for July, 1891, not two months after Holmes' disappearance, of the first of these long-suppressed adventures, given under the fetching title of 'A Scandal in Bohemia.' From then until December, 1893, they came in a steady stream, two round dozen in all."

Now, how could a doctor with a successful practice ("The Boscombe Valley Mystery") which "steadily increased" ("The Engineer's Thumb") find the time and energy needed to pour forth "two round dozen" chronicles in "a great flood," "a steady stream"? *Some* of them we know had been written as early as May, 1887 ("A Scandal in Bohemia"), but many of the cases Watson related in the *Strand* during the period of the Great Hiatus occurred much later in the partnership; with Watson so busy with his Paddington practice from May, 1889, on, they simply could not have been committed to paper until shortly before publication. What Watson did now seems clear: he sold the Paddington practice and with the proceeds repurchased the "small Kensington practice" of his first marriage—a practice which was "never very absorbing" ("The Red-Headed League")—a

. . . SHERLOCK HOLMES WAS STANDING SMILING AT ME ACROSS MY STUDY TABLE.

Illustration by Frederic Dorr Steele for *Collier's Magazine*, September 26, 1903. Sidney Paget illustrated the same dramatic scene for the *Strand Magazine*, October, 1903.

was separated from the street by a low wall and railing, the whole not more than five feet high. It was perfectly easy, therefore, for anyone to get into the garden ; but the window was entirely inaccessible, since there was no water-pipe or anything which could help the most active man to climb it. More puzzled than ever, I retraced **13** my steps to Kensington. I had not been in my study five minutes when the maid entered to say that a person desired to see me. To my astonishment, it was none other than my strange old book-collector, his sharp, wizened face peering out from a frame of white hair, and his precious volumes, a dozen of them at least, wedged under his right arm.

" You're surprised to see me, sir," said he, in a strange, croaking voice.

I acknowledged that I was.

" Well, I've a conscience, sir, and when I chanced to see you go into this house, as I came hobbling after you, I thought to myself, I'll just step in and see that kind gentleman, and tell him that if I was a bit gruff in my manner there was not any harm meant, and that I am much obliged to him for picking up my books."

" You make too much of a trifle," said I. " May I ask how you knew who I was ? "

" Well, sir, if it isn't too great a liberty, I am a neighbour of yours, for you'll find my little bookshop at the **14** corner of Church Street, and very happy to see you, I am **15** sure. Maybe you collect yourself, sir ; here's *British* **16-17-18** *Birds*, and *Catullus*, and *The Holy War*—a bargain every one of them. With five volumes you could just fill that gap on that second shelf. It looks untidy, does it not, sir ? "

I moved my head to look at the cabinet behind me. When I turned again Sherlock Holmes was standing smiling at me across my study table. I rose to my feet,

stared at him for some seconds in utter amazement, and then it appears that I must have fainted for the first and the last time in my life. Certainly a grey mist swirled **19** before my eyes, and when it cleared I found my collar-ends undone and the tingling after-taste of brandy upon my lips. Holmes was bending over my chair, his flask **20** in his hand.

"My dear Watson," said the well-remembered voice, "I owe you a thousand apologies. I had no idea that you would be so affected."

I gripped him by the arm.

"Holmes!" I cried. "Is it really you? Can it indeed be that you are alive? Is it possible that you succeeded in climbing out of that awful abyss?"

"Wait a moment!" said he. "Are you sure that you are really fit to discuss things? I have given you a serious shock by my unnecessarily dramatic appearance."

"I am all right; but indeed, Holmes, I can hardly believe my eyes. Good heavens, to think that you—you of all men—should be standing in my study!" Again I gripped him by the sleeve and felt the thin, sinewy arm beneath it. "Well, you're not a spirit, anyhow," said I. "My dear chap, I am overjoyed to see you. Sit down, and tell me how you came alive out of that dreadful chasm."

He sat opposite to me and lit a cigarette in his old nonchalant manner. He was dressed in the seedy frock-coat of the book merchant, but the rest of that individual lay in a pile of white hair and old books upon the table. Holmes looked even thinner and keener than of old, but there was a dead-white tinge in his aquiline face which **21** told me that his life recently had not been a healthy one.

"I am glad to stretch myself, Watson," said he. "It is no joke when a tall man has to take a foot off his stature for several hours on end. Now, my dear fellow, in the matter of these explanations we have, if I may ask for your co-operation, a hard and dangerous night's work in front of us. Perhaps it would be better if I gave you an account of the whole situation when that work is finished."

"I am full of curiosity. I should much prefer to hear now."

"You'll come with me to-night?"

"When you like and where you like."

"This is indeed like the old days. We shall have time for a mouthful of dinner before we need go. Well, then, about that chasm. I had no serious difficulty in getting out of it, for the very simple reason that I never was in it."

"You never were in it?"

"No, Watson, I never was in it. My note to you was absolutely genuine. I had little doubt that I had come to the end of my career when I perceived the somewhat sinister figure of the late Professor Moriarty standing upon the narrow pathway which led to safety. I read an inexorable purpose in his grey eyes. I exchanged some remarks with him, therefore, and obtained his courteous permission to write the short note which you afterwards received. I left it with my cigarette-box and my stick, and I walked along the pathway, Moriarty still

practice he knew from experience would provide a livelihood and *still give him time* for his writing.

14 *at the corner of Church Street.* As Miss Madeleine B. Stern has shown ("Sherlock Holmes: Rare Book Collector"), Holmes on this occasion assumed the guise of his bookdealer, Alfred B. Clementson, who plied his trade at 73 Church Street, Kensington, W. (*London Post-Office Directory* for 1890). Church Street, we may add, leads north to Notting Hill, where Selden (*The Hound of the Baskervilles*) committed his brutal murder. The street takes its name from the Carmelite Church, an unfinished early Gothic building by E. W. Pugin, begun in 1865.

15 *Maybe you collect yourself, sir.* The old bookseller now mentions three titles. Then he says: "With five volumes you could just fill that gap on the second shelf." Obviously, two of the three titles must have been two-volume editions or one of the three titles must have been a three-volume edition—a point which seems to have been made for the first time by Magistrate S. Tupper Bigelow in "Those Five Volumes."

16 British Birds. ". . . not a minor nineteenth-century work, but the fine *History of British Birds* with the Bewick wood engravings printed in two volumes at Newcastle in 1797 and 1804," Miss Stern wrote.

To this, Miss Lisa McGaw added ("Some Trifling Notes on Sherlock Holmes and Ornithology"): "A perusal of Raymond Irwin's *British Bird Books: An Index to British Ornithology*, A.D. *1481* to A.D. *1948* (London: Grafton & Co., 1951) reveals no volume entitled simply *British Birds* prior to early 1894. There is, however, a six-volume work by Francis O. Morris entitled *A History of British Birds* (Groombridge, 1851–57) and bearing on its spine the label *Morris' British Birds*. Could that have been what Holmes was carrying? It seems likely, although it would have been nearly an armful in itself if he had all six volumes. To suggest that this work was obscure is misleading because, in its day, it was well known in its field. Three reissues of the first edition, four revised editions, and two cabinet editions attest to its popularity among persons interested in birds. Its 357 hand-colored plates, all rather good, greatly enhanced the work in an era when accurate bird drawings were rare, and that helped to counteract the fact that the information in the text was not too reliable. If this is the work referred to, Holmes undoubtedly possessed a first edition, which would have increased its value as a collector's item."

But to both these commentators, Magistrate Bigelow responded: "An equally good guess would be Robert Mudie's *The Feathered Tribes of the British Islands*, lettered on its spine *Mudie's British Birds*, the first edition of which appeared in London in 1853, and a fourth edition . . . , similarly spine-lettered, in 1878. . . . Furthermore, Bewick's two volumes were spine-lettered *History of British Birds,* so as between Bewick and Mudie, it would appear that Mudie has the slight advantage. . . . Both books are in two volumes. What we must have, obviously, is a book on British birds in three volumes. We are bound, therefore, to discard Morris' *History of British Birds,* 1878, in six volumes; and A. Thorburn's *British Birds,* 1915, in one volume. . . . We are not assisted, either, by the three-volume *British Birds and Their Nests* by Vesey B. Fitzgerald, London, 1953, nor the three-volume *British Birds, Trees and Wild Flowers* by Walter M. Gallichan, London, 1915. There seems, indeed, to be only one possible solution. William Yarrell's *A History of British Birds* was first published in London by John Van Voorst in 1843; a second edition appeared in 1845 and a third in 1846. Each edition was published in three volumes. On the spine of each volume of all editions is lettered *Yarrell's British Birds.*"

17 Catullus. "The first Aldine Catullus: *Catullus, Tibulius, Propertius,* printed in italic letter by Aldus at Venice in 1502, with the title-page in the first state, reading *Propetius* for *Propertius*—a rare edition though, of course, not under the circumstances, an incunable," Miss Stern wrote.

"Mr. Norman Dodge of Goodspeed's Bookshop in Boston believes the Catullus was the one printed by the noted typographer John Baskerville, 1706–1765," the late Christopher Morley added.

But Mr. Bliss Austin (in "Two Bibliographical Footnotes") held that "the Catullus and *The Origin of Tree Worship* were one and the same book! It is a work by Grant Allen, entitled *The Attis of Caius Valerius Catullus, Translated into English Verse, with Dissertations on the Myth of Attis, on the Origin of Tree-Worship, and on the Galliambic Metre.* It was published, in an edition limited to 550 copies, as Volume VI of the *Bibliotheque de Carabas* in London in 1892 by David Nutt."

18 The Holy War. To Miss Stern, this was ". . . obviously a copy of the 1639 first edition of Thomas Fuller's *History of the Holy Warre,* and not one of the numerous reprints of that popular work on the Crusades."

Mr. Austin wrote: ". . . I should like to suggest as a possible alternative John Bunyan's *The Holy War,* which bears the subtitle: 'Made by King Shaddai upon Diabolus for the Regaining of the Metropolis of the World; or the Losing and Taking Again of the Town of Mansoul.' This, the second most famous of Bunyan's works, was first published in 1682 in a small octavo volume which was quite handsome by the standards of the day. It was, within a few years, translated into Dutch, German, Gaelic, Portugese and Turkish. The first edition would, I am certain, have been an item worthy of Holmes' attention."

Magistrate Bigelow wrote: "*The Holy War* must surely have been some edition of Bunyan's famous work, first published in 1682. Sherlock Holmes' copy could scarcely have been a first edi-

at my heels. When I reached the end I stood at bay. He drew no weapon, but he rushed at me and threw his long arms around me. He knew that his own game was up, and was only anxious to revenge himself upon me. We tottered together upon the brink of the fall. I have some knowledge, however, of baritsu, or the Japanese **22** system of wrestling, which has more than once been very useful to me. I slipped through his grip, and he with a horrible scream kicked madly for a few seconds and clawed the air with both his hands. But for all his efforts he could not get his balance, and over he went. With my face over the brink I saw him fall for a long way. Then he struck a rock, bounded off, and splashed into the water."

I listened with amazement to this explanation, which Holmes delivered between the puffs of his cigarette.

" But the tracks ! " I cried. " I saw with my own eyes that two went down the path and none returned."

" It came about in this way. The instant that the professor had disappeared it struck me what a really extraordinarily lucky chance Fate had placed in my way. I knew that Moriarty was not the only man who had sworn my death. There were at least three others whose desire for vengeance upon me would only be increased by the **23** death of their leader. They were all most dangerous

WE TOTTERED TOGETHER UPON THE BRINK OF THE FALL.

"The death of Sherlock Holmes" as seen by two different artists (and compare with Paget's illustration of the same scene in "The Final Problem"). The first illustration shown here is by Arthur Twidle, from the 1903 "Author's Edition" of *The Memoirs of Sherlock Holmes;* the second is by John Nunney from *Look and Learn,* issue of June 23, 1962. It will be noted that the artists did not agree on which bank of the falls the struggle took place (Paget and Twidle, left bank; Nunney, right bank).

men. One or other would certainly get me. On the other hand, if all the world was convinced that I was dead they would take liberties, these men; they would lay themselves open, and sooner or later I could destroy them. Then it would be time for me to announce that I was still in the land of the living. So rapidly does the brain act that I believe I had thought this all out before Professor Moriarty had reached the bottom of the Reichenbach Fall.

" I stood up and examined the rocky wall behind me. In your picturesque account of the matter, which I read with great interest some months later, you assert that the wall was sheer. This was not literally true. A few small footholds presented themselves, and there was some indication of a ledge. The cliff is so high that to climb it all was an obvious impossibility, and it was equally impossible to make my way along the wet path without leaving some tracks. I might, it is true, have reversed my boots, as I have done on similar occasions, but the **24** sight of three sets of tracks in one direction would certainly have suggested a deception. On the whole, then, it was best that I should risk the climb. It was not a pleasant business, Watson. The fall roared beneath me. I am not a fanciful person, but I give you my word that I seemed to hear Moriarty's voice screaming at me out of the abyss. A mistake would have been fatal.

"WITH MY FACE OVER THE BRINK I SAW HIM FALL FOR A LONG WAY."

Cover illustration by Frederic Dorr Steele for *Collier's Magazine*, September 26, 1903. "The resultant print of [Holmes'] prone body in the moist earth should have betrayed his escape to the Swiss experts," Mr. Anthony Boucher wrote in "Was the Later Holmes an Imposter?", "but it is conceivable that Watson's similar print overlay his."

tion, as there is no first edition of this work in the United States . . . and the only first edition [the *Encyclopædia Britannica*'s Library Research Service] knows about is in the British Museum. . . . No known edition . . . was published in two volumes [although] there were no less than 44 editions of *The Holy War* published in England and the United States from 1682 to 1795 inclusive . . ."

To this Professor David A. Randall has added ("The Adventure of the Notorious Forger") that Holmes offered *British Birds* and *The Holy War* "out of all the millions [of volumes] he could have possessed" because his true reason for returning to England was to unmask Thomas James Wise, the great literary forger, and "he naturally had with him some volumes in which the forger also would be interested."

19 *for the first and the last time in my life.* "It is true that the manner of Holmes' return was sufficiently melodramtic to accelerate the most sluggish pulse," Mr. S. C. Roberts wrote in *Doctor Watson*, "but it is hardly enough to account for an old campaigner like Watson falling into a dead faint. Clearly, his constitution had not fully recovered from the ravages of recent grief and worry [caused by the final illness and subsequent death of Mary Morstan Watson]."

And Mr. Walter P. Armstrong, Jr., has written ("The Truth About Sherlock Holmes"): "This was such an uncharacteristic act that it has led to the wildest conjectures. It is a weakness to which old soldiers are seldom addicted; but it is one which is all too apparent to writers of fiction. A Watson who in real life had never fainted might easily in composing an imaginative account of an emotional scene which never happened depict Watson as fainting."

20 *his flask in his hand.* "Did Sherlock Holmes, as one of the properties in his character of an aged bibliophile, carry a hip flask?" Mr. Armstrong asked. "It does not seem likely."

21 *a dead-white tinge in his aquiline face.* "This is hardly what would be expected of a man who has been wandering in unknown portions of Tibet and under the burning sun of the Egyptian Sudan," Mr. Armstrong continued. "But it is exactly what we would expect of a man who has been spending much time indoors and venturing out only in a heavy disguise." (Mr. Armstrong, we will remember, holds that Holmes spent the entire period of the Great Hiatus in London.)

22 *baritsu, or the Japanese system of wrestling.* In his article, "The Mystery of Baritsu: A Sidelight Upon Sherlock Holmes' Accomplishments," Mr. Ralph Judson has shown that a Mr. E. W. Barton-Wright had published in *Pearson's Magazine* in the March and April, 1899, issues, an article called "The New Art of Self-Defence." He "described therein a few of the three hundred methods of attack and counter-attack that comprise the New

Art of Self-Defence, to which I have given the name of Bartisu . . ." (after Barton). "In giving the name Bartisu to a number of selected methods of Ju-Jutsu, adapted to European needs and costume, Mr. Barton-Wright followed a well-established precedent," Mr. Judson wrote. "Many of the exponents of this art in Japan founded their own schools and gave their own names to the methods they taught. . . . Dr. Watson must have read Mr. Barton-Wright's article in the *Pearson's Magazine* in 1899, got the word 'Bartisu' stuck in his mind, and, in describing, in 1903, the return of his friend, inadvertently written 'Baritsu' . . . instead of Ju-Jutsu"—the system of Japanese wrestling by which Holmes actually overcame Professor Moriarty. Since Holmes knew a Japanese system of wrestling in 1891, and since it takes roughly seven years to become proficient in this art and reach instinctive actions and reactions to every kind of attack, it is likely that he started his training around 1883–1884. When Holmes shortly tells us that he slipped through Moriarty's grip, this is what he is likely to have done: "In one fast and smooth movement, dropping on one knee, [Holmes] gripped with one hand Moriarty's heel, which was closer to the abyss, and lifting the heel and with it the foot, diagonally, away from himself, he pushed hard, at the same time, with his other hand, into the groin of the captured leg, applying terrific leverage."

23 *at least three others whose desire for vengeance upon me would only be increased by the death of their leader.* "The reasons given by Holmes . . . for his daring ascent of the rock-wall above the Reichenbach are unsatisfactory," Mr. T. S. Blakeney wrote in *Sherlock Holmes: Fact or Fiction?* "If he were believed dead, he affirmed, his enemies in Moriarty's gang would drop their caution, commit indiscretions, and leave themselves open to his attack. But at the time he was excogitating these considerations, he was unaware that any of Moriarty's followers were at large! On the contrary, he had recently had a wire from the London police saying (not quite accurately, as events were to prove) that they had secured the whole organization. Holmes did not become aware of Colonel Moran's presence [*see below*] till after he had acted upon his idea, and his statement of his thoughts, as given by Watson, must have been coloured by wisdom after the event."

24 *I might, it is true, have reversed my boots.* ". . . a trick that is common enough practice among horsethieves, but is somewhat impractical here in view of the shape of the human foot," Mr. Anthony Boucher wrote in "Was the Later Holmes an Imposter?"

"If Holmes could, or ever did, put his shoes on backwards, volumes could be written on the physiology of his foot," Mr. Walter P. Armstrong, Jr., commented in "The Truth About Sherlock Holmes." "It would never have occurred to Holmes, the detective; but it did to Watson, the writer of fiction."

More than once, as tufts of grass came out in my hand or my foot slipped in the wet notches of the rock, I thought that I was gone. But I struggled upwards, and at last I reached a ledge several feet deep and covered with soft green moss, where I could lie unseen in the most perfect comfort. There I was stretched when you, my dear Watson, and all your following were investigating in the most sympathetic and inefficient manner the circumstances of my death.

" At last, when you had all formed your inevitable and totally erroneous conclusions, you departed for the hotel, and I was left alone. I had imagined that I had reached the end of my adventures, but a very unexpected occurrence showed me that there were surprises still in store for me. A huge rock, falling from above, boomed past me, struck the path, and bounded over into the chasm. For an instant I thought that it was an accident ; but a moment later, looking up, I saw a man's head against the **25** darkening sky, and another stone struck the very ledge upon which I was stretched, within a foot of my head. Of course, the meaning of this was obvious. Moriarty had not been alone. A confederate—and even that one glance had told me how dangerous a man that confederate was—had kept guard while the professor had attacked me. From a distance, unseen by me, he had been a wit- **26** ness of his friend's death and of my escape. He had waited, and then, making his way round to the top of the cliff, he had endeavoured to succeed where his comrade had failed.

" I did not take long to think about it, Watson. Again I saw that grim face look over the cliff, and I knew that it was the precursor of another stone. I scrambled down on to the path. I don't think I could have done it in cold blood. It was a hundred times more difficult than getting up. But I had no time to think of the danger, for **27** another stone sang past me as I hung by my hands from the edge of the ledge. Half-way down I slipped, but by the blessing of God I landed, torn and bleeding, upon the path. I took to my heels, did ten miles over the mountains in the darkness, and a week later I found myself in Florence, with the certainty that no one in the world knew what had become of me.

" I had only one confidant—my brother Mycroft. I owe you many apologies, my dear Watson, but it was all-important that it should be thought I was dead, and it is quite certain that you would not have written so convincing an account of my unhappy end had you not yourself thought that it was true. Several times during the last three years I have taken up my pen to write to you, but always I feared lest your affectionate regard for me should tempt you to some indiscretion which would betray my secret. For that reason I turned away from you this evening when you upset my books, for I was in danger at the time, and any show of surprise and emotion upon your part might have drawn attention to my identity and led to **28** the most deplorable and irreparable results. As to Mycroft, I had to confide in him in order to obtain the money which I needed. The course of events in London did not run so well as I had hoped, for the trial of the Moriarty gang left two of its most dangerous members, my own most vindictive enemies, at liberty. I travelled for two **29** years in Tibet, therefore, and amused myself by visiting Lhassa and spending some days with the head Llama. You may have read of the remarkable explorations of a Norwegian named Sigerson, but I am sure that it never occurred to you that you were receiving news of your friend. I then passed through Persia, looked in at Mecca, and paid a short but interesting visit to the Khalifa at Khartoum, the results of which I have communicated to the Foreign Office. Returning to France, I spent some months in a research into the coal-tar derivatives, which I conducted in a laboratory at Montpelier, in the south of France. Having concluded this to my satisfaction, and learning that only one of my enemies was now left in London, I was about to return, when my movements were hastened by the news of this remarkable Park Lane Mystery, which not only appealed to me by its own merits, but which seemed to offer some most peculiar personal opportunities. I came over at once to London, called in my own person at Baker Street, threw Mrs. Hudson into violent hysterics, and found that Mycroft had preserved my rooms and my papers exactly as they had always been. So it was, my dear Watson, that at two **30** o'clock to-day I found myself in my old arm-chair in my own old room, and only wishing that I could have seen my old friend Watson in the other chair which he has so often adorned."

Such was the remarkable narrative to which I listened on that April evening—a narrative which would have been utterly incredible to me had it not been confirmed by the actual sight of the tall, spare figure and the keen, eager face which I had never thought to see again. In some manner he had learned of my own sad bereavement, and his sympathy was shown in his manner rather than in his words. "Work is the best antidote to sorrow, my dear Watson," said he, "and I have a piece of work for us both to-night which, if we can bring it to a successful conclusion, will in itself justify a man's life on this planet." In vain I begged him to tell me more. "You will hear and see enough before morning," he answered. "We have three years of the past to discuss. Let that suffice until half-past nine, when we start upon the notable adventure of the empty house."

It was indeed like old times when, at that hour, I found myself seated beside him in a hansom, my revolver in my pocket and the thrill of adventure in my heart. Holmes was cold and stern and silent. As the gleam of the street-lamps flashed upon his austere features, I saw that his brows were drawn down in thought and his thin lips compressed. I knew not what wild beast we were about to hunt down in the dark jungle of criminal London, but I was well assured from the bearing of this master huntsman that the adventure was a most grave one, while the sardonic smile which occasionally broke through his ascetic gloom boded little good for the object of our quest.

I had imagined that we were bound for Baker Street, but Holmes stopped the cab at the corner of Cavendish Square. I observed that as he stepped out he gave a **31** most searching glance to right and left, and at every

To comments like these the Fundamentalists have responded: "You can't easily put boots on backward, the uppers crumple and hamper; but *shoes* . . . are easily reversed and can be walked in, with care, far enough to leave a misleading spoor. You trample down the flanges of the shoe, and tie the laces over your ankle" (the late Christopher Morley). "It is very easy to put one's shoes on backwards to reverse the direction in which they point; it is merely necessary to cut the toe and part of the shoe directly back of this, and then to put the feet into the shoes from the toe end" (the late Dr. Ernest Bloomfield Zeisler).

25 *the darkening sky.* Watson's (and Holmes') time references in "The Final Problem" and "The Adventure of the Empty House" have been severely criticized by Mr. Anthony Boucher and Mr. Walter P. Armstrong, Jr.; as stoutly defended by the late Dr. Ernest Bloomfield Zeisler, the late A. Carson Simpson, and the late Professor Jay Finley Christ.

Let us first present the case *against* (Mr. Boucher in "Was the Later Holmes an Imposter?"):

"In 'The Final Problem,' we have Watson's statement that the trip from Meiringen to the Reichenbach Fall takes two hours uphill and one hour down. Holmes and Watson leave Meiringen 'in the afternoon,' which cannot mean earlier than one o'clock; we shall see . . . that it must have been closer to two. They arrived at the Fall, then, at four; and Watson leaves, allowing for his awed inspection of the Fall and his conversation with the bearer of the false message, around four fifteen. His trip to Meiringen and back adds another three hours so that he discovers the tragedy at a quarter past seven. In the latitude of Meiringen (46° 45′ N.), the sun sets on May 4th at about seven ten, with slight variations for local standard time. When Watson leans over the brim, 'it had darkened since I left, and now I could only see here and there the glistening of moisture upon the black walls, and far away down at the end of the shaft the gleam of broken water.' Watson makes a careful study of the scene and of Holmes' note and leaves at about seven-thirty. It is probably quite dark by then; night comes quickly in high mountains. Now it is highly unlikely that 'experts,' who, as Watson informs us, examined the ground, were on call in 'the little village of Meiringen,' on a May evening. But even granting the deutero-Holmes' assertion that this examination took place on the same day, the experts could not have reached the site in less than three hours after Watson left to summon them—in other words, at ten-thirty. It would take them at least half an hour to reach 'their inevitable and totally erroneous conclusions.' Holmes cannot have been left alone, then, before eleven o'clock, by which time he has been lying on the ledge for almost seven hours. It is therefore some time after eleven when Holmes recognizes Colonel Sebastian Moran as the rock-throwing confederate. Conceivably Moran's 'thin, projecting nose' and 'high bald forehead' might have been recognizable in silhouette at night, but Holmes describes 'a man's head against the darkening sky.'

In short, that sky had been darkening from seven-fifteen until some minutes after eleven—a meteorological phenomena surely deserving some Holmesian contribution to the literature of the subject."

But the late A. Carson Simpson replied (*Sherlock Holmes' Wanderjahre*, Vol. I) that Watson "says it took him an hour to get down to Meiringen and, 'for all his efforts,' two more hours to get back to the Fall. On the contrary, Baedeker, whose timing is always on the conservative side, says that it takes only three-quarters of an hour to walk up from Meiringen to the Upper Fall; the whole trip to Rosenlaui requires only three. . . . Actually, the good Doctor's trip downhill to Meiringen cannot have taken more than a half-hour at an ordinary pace, and we may be sure that, exerting 'all his efforts,' he got back up to the Fall in about the same length of time. After vainly seeking for Holmes, he would have walked or run down to Meiringen in some twenty minutes, to raise a search-party. A simple arithmetical calculation will demonstrate that the various trips to and fro could easily be made, with ample margins between trips, before sunset at 7:10 P.M."

And Dr. Zeisler has added (*Baker Street Chronology*): "There is not the slightest indication that Watson made the upward journey *three* times. When Watson learned from Steiler that the letter had been a hoax he rushed back up to the Fall, and there is no reason at all to think that he made another trip down to fetch the police; indeed, we can be certain that he did *not* do this. Watson told Steiler that he suspected foul play, and Steiler surely fetched the police and sent them up after Watson without delay, so that they probably arrived at the Fall shortly after Watson. It took Watson two hours to rush up to the top, so that we may allow a longer time for the trip up by the Master and Watson, who did not rush. If we allow two and a half hours for the first trip up, then it was about five and a half hours from the time they left the hotel together until Watson returned to the Fall. If they left the hotel at 2:00 P.M., . . . then Watson and the police would have made their investigations between 7:30 and 8:30 P.M. It is true that sunset was a few minutes past seven, but it is not true that it was dark at 8:30 P.M. Twilight at that season and place lasts a good two hours, so that it is not really dark until 9:00 P.M. or after. . . ."

Professor Christ agreed that there is not "the slightest suggestion or basis for an assumption that Watson made *three* trips to the Fall, nor that he brought experts 'later,' " and he presented the following suggested time schedule ("The Later Holmes an Imposter: A Sequel"):

2:00 Holmes and Watson left the inn.
4:00 Holmes and Watson reach the Fall.
4:15 The messenger reaches the Fall.
4:20 Watson leaves the Fall.
4:45 Holmes struggles with Moriarty.
5:20 Watson reaches the inn.
5:25 Watson leaves the inn, running, with guides following shortly thereafter.

subsequent street corner he took the utmost pains to assure that he was not followed. Our route was certainly a singular one. Holmes' knowledge of the by-ways of London was extraordinary, and on this occasion he passed rapidly, and with an assured step, through a network of mews and stables the very existence of which I had never known. We emerged at last into a small road, lined with old, gloomy houses, which led us into Manchester Street, and so to Blandford Street. Here he turned swiftly down a narrow passage, passed through a wooden gate into a deserted yard, and then opened with a key the back door of a house. We entered together, and he closed it behind us.

The place was pitch dark, but it was evident to me that it was an empty house. Our feet creaked and crackled over the bare planking, and my outstretched hand touched a wall from which the paper was hanging in ribbons. Holmes' cold, thin fingers closed round my wrist and led me forward down a long hall, until I dimly saw the murky fanlight over the door. Here Holmes turned suddenly to the right, and we found ourselves in a large, square, empty room, heavily shadowed in the corners, but faintly lit in the centre from the lights of the street beyond. There was no lamp near, and the window was thick with dust, so that we could only just discern each other's figures within. My companion put his hand upon my shoulder, and his lips close to my ear.

" Do you know where we are ? " he whispered.

" Surely that is Baker Street," I answered, staring through the dim window.

" Exactly. We are in Camden House, which stands opposite to our own old quarters."

" But why are we here ? "

"WE ARE IN CAMDEN HOUSE, WHICH STANDS OPPOSITE TO OUR OWN OLD QUARTERS."

"The empty house"—the present No. 32 Baker Street—as photographed for your editor's biography, *Sherlock Holmes*.

" Because it commands so excellent a view of that picturesque pile.   Might I trouble you, my dear Watson, to draw a little nearer to the window, taking every precaution not to show yourself, and then to look up at our old rooms—the starting-point of so many of our little adventures ? We will see if my three years of absence have entirely taken away my power to surprise you."

I crept forward and looked across at the familiar window. As my eyes fell upon it I gave a gasp and a cry of amazement.   The blind was down, and a strong light was burning in the room.   The shadow of a man who was seated in a chair within was thrown in hard, black outline upon the luminous screen of the window.   There was no mistaking the poise of the head, the squareness of the shoulders, the sharpness of the features.   The face was turned half-round, and the effect was that of one of those black silhouettes which our grandparents loved to frame. It was a perfect reproduction of Holmes.   So amazed was I that I threw out my hand to make sure that the man himself was standing beside me.   He was quivering with silent laughter.

" Well ? " said he.

" Good heavens ! " I cried.   " It's marvellous."

I CREPT FORWARD AND LOOKED ACROSS AT THE
FAMILIAR WINDOW.

Illustration by Sidney Paget for the *Strand Magazine*, October, 1903.

7:25   Watson reaches the Fall.
7:30   Guides reach the Fall. Sunset, moon about 30 degrees west of meridian.
8:00   Party left the Fall.
8:15   Holmes saw head against the darkening sky.
8:30   Holmes descended from the cliff.

26 *he had been a witness of his friend's death and of my escape.* "In other words," Mr. Stanley McComas wrote in "Love at Lhassa," "Moran *saw him alive,* so Moran will *believe he is dead.* Every underworld character in London must have known Holmes was alive. Watson's acceptance of this incongruous tale can only be put down to his shock at seeing Holmes again."

And Mr. Boucher wrote ("Was the Later Holmes an Imposter?") : "Holmes' purported motive in going underground and allowing Watson to believe him dead was to trap the remaining Moriartists. But his own account makes nonsense of that motive; the one person, aside from Mycroft, who knew that he was certainly not dead, and who had seen him alive after the destruction of Moriarty, was the new chief of the gang, Colonel Sebastian Moran."

27 *another stone sang past me.* "Why"—the late Edgar W. Smith asked in "The Old Shikari"— "why, when Moriarty had fallen to his death, and Holmes had scrambled up to the ledge again, did the best rifle shot in all India resort to hurling rocks at his intended victim? . . . We may be sure that it was not with a view to giving Holmes an even break. It is obvious that the plotters had forgotten to bring a suitable weapon with them, and that Moran found himself, in his extremity, reduced to only such expedients as nature could provide. There are those who have contended that this was not an oversight, but a matter of necessity, and that the pursuers went weaponless into battle because of the great difficulties, in those days, attendant upon importing firearms into law-abiding Switzerland. To them I say that the ingenuity which permitted a lethal air-gun to be disguised effectively as a walking-stick would not have boggled at the project of masking that same air-gun to even better advantage, in the guise of an alpenstock. No—both Moriarty and Moran were off their feed that day, and we, in common with Sherlock Holmes, must be ever grateful for it."

28 *led to the most deplorable and irreparable results.* "Will this explanation hold water?" Mr. Armstrong wrote. "I doubt it. In the first place, Holmes said he turned away in order that Watson should not recognize him and give the game away. And yet, hardly more than a few minutes later, he voluntarily came to Watson and revealed himself. True, he may have wished to avoid a scene in public; but if he had so little confidence in Watson's self-control, why did he come to him at all? . . . Above all, why did he turn aside? On numerous occasions when he knew Holmes to be alive

Watson had failed to penetrate his various disguises. In fact, Holmes delighted in trying them on him and made some very cutting remarks upon his failure to see through them. It is incredible that his confidence in his art of make-up had grown so weak that he was afraid Watson would recognize in the aged bookseller a man whom he thought long dead."

29 *left two of its most dangerous members, my own most vindictive enemies, at liberty.* "But Holmes could not have known that before the trial, and even before he had seen Colonel Moran against the darkening sky" (Boucher).

30 *exactly as they had always been.* "Yet in another place," Mr. Armstrong wrote, "[Holmes] makes the statement that Mycroft had only visited his rooms once, and a second visit is a cause for great excitement ("The Adventure of the Bruce-Partington Plans"). Mycroft could hardly have kept the rooms up without visiting them, especially as they had been burned shortly prior to Holmes' departure; for although the damage was slight, it was sufficient to deserve notice in the press. Nor could he restore them to their former state on the basis of a single visit, even though his powers of observation were admittedly great. Neither could Mrs. Hudson, unfamiliar with many of the esoteric devices which her distinguished lodger employed in his trade. In fact, only one man could have done it, and that man was Watson. Naturally he did not want his name to appear, because he is supposed to have thought that Holmes was dead."

31 *Cavendish Square.* Cavendish Square, laid out in 1717, takes its name from Lady Henrietta Cavendish Holles, as does the adjoining Henrietta Street and Holles Street. It stands directly opposite Hanover Square on the south side of Oxford Street.

32 *age doth nor wither nor custom stale my infinite variety."* Holmes paraphrases Shakespeare's *Antony and Cleopatra:* "Age cannot wither her, nor custom stale her infinite variety . . ."—Act II, Scene 2, lines 241–242.

33 *Grenoble.* "Presumably, in the intervals between sittings, the Master of Baker Street found much to interest him in that ancient town, not the least being the famous 'hanging bridges,' one over the Isère and the other over the Drac," Mr. Belden Wigglesworth wrote in "The French Background of Sherlock Holmes."

34 *They watched them continuously.* "Credat Judaeus Apella" the late Monsignor Ronald A. Knox wrote in "The Mystery of Mycroft"; "you do not really watch a house on the chance of its being revisited, for three years on end. No, Colonel Moran's information will have come, as usual, from Mycroft; Sherlock, as usual, conceals the equivocal

" I trust that age doth not wither nor custom stale **my**
32 infinite variety," said he, and I recognized in his voice the joy and pride which the artist takes in his own creation. " It really is rather like me, is it not ? "

" I should be prepared to swear that it was you."

" The credit of the execution is due to Monsieur Oscar
33 Meunier, of Grenoble, who spent some days in doing the moulding. It is a bust in wax. The rest I arranged myself during my visit to Baker Street this afternoon."

" But why ? "

" Because, my dear Watson, I had the strongest possible reason for wishing certain people to think that I was there when I was really elsewhere."

" And you thought the rooms were watched ? "

" I *knew* that they were watched."

" By whom ? "

" By my old enemies, Watson. By the charming society whose leader lies in the Reichenbach Fall. You must remember that they knew, and only they knew, that I was still alive. Sooner or later they believed that I should come back to my rooms. They watched them
34 continuously, and this morning they saw me arrive."

" How do you know ? "

" Because I recognized their sentinel when I glanced out of my window. He is a harmless enough fellow, Parker by name, a garrotter by trade, and a remarkable performer upon the jews' harp. I cared nothing for him. But I cared a great deal for the much more formidable person who was behind him, the bosom friend of Moriarty, the man who dropped the rocks over the cliff, the most cunning and dangerous criminal in London. That is the man who is after me to-night, Watson, and that is the man who is quite unaware that we are after *him.*"

My friend's plans were gradually revealing themselves. From this convenient retreat the watchers were being watched and the trackers tracked. That angular shadow up yonder was the bait, and we were the hunters. In silence we stood together in the darkness and watched the hurrying figures who passed and repassed in front of us. Holmes was silent and motionless ; but I could tell that he was keenly alert, and that his eyes were fixed intently upon the stream of passers-by. It was a bleak and
35 boisterous night, and the wind whistled shrilly down the long street. Many people were moving to and fro, most of them muffled in their coats and cravats. Once or twice it seemed to me that I had seen the same figure before, and I especially noticed two men who appeared to be sheltering themselves from the wind in the doorway of a house some distance up the street. I tried to draw my companion's attention to them, but he gave a little ejaculation of impatience, and continued to stare into the street. More than once he fidgeted with his feet and tapped rapidly with his fingers upon the wall. It was evident to me that he was becoming uneasy, and that his plans were not working out altogether as he had hoped. At last, as midnight approached and the street gradually cleared, he paced up and down the room in uncontrollable agitation. I was about to make some remark to him, when I raised my eyes to the lighted window, and again

experienced almost as great a surprise as before. I clutched Holmes' arm and pointed upwards.

" The shadow has moved ! " I cried.

It was, indeed, no longer the profile, but the back, which was turned towards us.

Three years had certainly not smoothed the asperities of his temper, or his impatience with a less active intelligence than his own.

" Of course it has moved," said he. " Am I such a farcical bungler, Watson, that I should erect an obvious dummy and expect that some of the sharpest men in Europe would be deceived by it ? We have been in this room two hours, and Mrs. Hudson has made some change in that figure eight times, or once every quarter of an hour. She works it from the front, so that her shadow may never be seen. Ah ! " He drew in his breath with a shrill, excited intake. In the dim light I saw his head thrown forward, his whole attitude rigid with attention. Those two men might still be crouching in the doorway, but I could no longer see them. All was still and dark, save only that brilliant yellow screen in front of us with the black figure outlined upon its centre. Again in the utter silence I heard that thin, sibilant note which spoke of intense suppressed excitement. An instant later he pulled me back into the blackest corner of the room, and I felt his warning hand upon my lips. The fingers which clutched me were quivering. Never had I known my friend more moved, and yet the dark street still stretched lonely and motionless before us.

But suddenly I was aware of that which his keener senses had already distinguished. A low, stealthy sound came to my ears, not from the direction of Baker Street, but from the back of the very house in which we lay concealed. A door opened and shut. An instant later steps crept down the passage—steps which were meant to be silent, but which reverberated harshly through the empty house. Holmes crouched back against the wall, and I did the same, my hand closing upon the handle of my revolver. Peering through the gloom, I saw the vague outline of a man a shade blacker than the blackness of the open door. He stood for an instant, and then he crept forward, crouching, menacing, into the room. He was within three yards of us, this sinister figure, and I had braced myself to meet his spring, before I realized that he had no idea of our presence. He passed close beside us, stole over to the window, and very softly and noiselessly raised it for half a foot. As he sank to the level of this opening the light of the street, no longer dimmed by the dusty glass, fell full upon his face. The man seemed to be beside himself with excitement. His two eyes shone like stars, and his features were working convulsively. He was an elderly man, with a thin projecting nose, a high, bald forehead, and a huge grizzled moustache. An opera-hat was pushed to the back of his head, and an evening dress shirt-front gleamed out through his open overcoat. His face was gaunt and swarthy, scored **36** with deep, savage lines. In his hand he carried what appeared to be a stick, but as he laid it down upon the floor it gave a metallic clang. Then from the pocket of his overcoat he drew a bulky object, and he busied

part his brother has been playing in the drama, and fobs off his credulous biographer with a manifest lie."

35 *It was a bleak and boisterous night.* The only day in early April, 1894, that could possibly be called both bleak and windy was Thursday, April 5th. On that day the temperature fell to a low of 36.7° (fifty-year average for the day, 45°) and the wind achieved a pressure of 4.7 pounds. (We must remember what Watson tells us in "The Cardboard Box": "For myself, my term of service in India had trained me to stand heat better than cold . . ." What might have been brisk, even bracing, to another may well have been bleak, even bitter, to Watson.) The inquest on the Honourable Ronald Adair must therefore have concluded on Wednesday, April 4, 1894.

36 *an evening dress shirt-front gleamed out through his open overcoat.* "But why was [Colonel Moran] thus attired for a sniping expedition in an empty house?" Colonel Ronald Sherbrooke-Walker asked in "Clothes Canonical." "Perhaps like Mr. Holmes and Dr. Watson in their foray on Appledore Towers ["The Adventure of Charles Augustus Milverton"] he thought he would fit better into the landscape than he would in battle-dress."

. . . THE LIGHT OF THE STREET . . . FELL FULL UPON HIS FACE.

Illustration by Sidney Paget for the *Strand Magazine*, October, 1903.

THEN HIS FINGER TIGHTENED ON THE TRIGGER.

Illustration by Joseph Camana from *Cases of Sher-lock Holmes*, St. Louis: Webster Publishing Company, 1947.

. . . WITH CONVULSIVE STRENGTH HE SEIZED HOLMES BY THE THROAT; BUT I STRUCK HIM ON THE HEAD WITH THE BUTT OF MY REVOLVER . . .

Illustration by Sidney Paget for the *Strand Magazine*, October, 1903.

himself in some task which ended with a loud, sharp click, as if a spring or bolt had fallen into its place. Still kneeling upon the floor, he bent forward and threw all his weight and strength upon some lever, with the result that there came a long, whirling, grinding noise, ending once more in a powerful click. He straightened himself then, and I saw that what he held in his hand was a sort of a gun, with a curiously misshapen butt. He opened it at the breech, put something in, and snapped the breech-block. Then, crouching down, he rested the end of the barrel upon the ledge of the open window, and I saw his long moustache droop over the stock and his eye gleam as it peered along the sights. I heard a little sigh of satisfaction as he cuddled the butt into his shoulder, and saw that amazing target, the black man on the yellow ground, standing clear at the end of his foresight. For an instant he was rigid and motionless. Then his finger tightened on the trigger. There was a strange, loud whiz and a **37** long, silvery tinkle of broken glass. At that instant Holmes sprang like a tiger on to the marksman's back and hurled him flat upon his face. He was up again at a moment, and with convulsive strength he seized Holmes by the throat ; but I struck him on the head with the butt of my revolver, and he dropped again upon the floor. I fell upon him, and as I held him my comrade blew a shrill call upon a whistle. There was the clatter of running feet upon the pavement, and two policemen in uniform, with one plain-clothes detective, rushed through the front entrance and into the room.

" That you, Lestrade ? " said Holmes.

" Yes, Mr. Holmes. I took the job myself. It's good to see you back in London, sir."

" I think you want a little unofficial help. Three unde-tected murders in one year won't do, Lestrade. But you handled the Molesey Mystery with less than your usual— that's to say, you handled it fairly well."

We had all risen to our feet, our prisoner breathing hard, with a stalwart constable on each side of him. Already a few loiterers had begun to collect in the street. Holmes stepped up to the window, closed it, and dropped the blinds. Lestrade had produced two candles, and the policemen had uncovered their lanterns. I was able at last to have a good look at our prisoner.

It was a tremendously virile and yet sinister face which was turned towards us. With the brow of a philosopher above and the jaw of a sensualist below, the man must have started with great capacities for good or for evil. But one could not look upon his cruel blue eyes, with their drooping, cynical lids, or upon the fierce, aggressive nose and the threatening, deep-lined brow, without reading Nature's plainest danger-signals. He took no heed of any of us, but his eyes were fixed upon Holmes' face with an expression in which hatred and amazement were equally blended. " You fiend ! " he kept on muttering —" you clever, clever fiend ! "

" Ah, colonel," said Holmes, arranging his rumpled collar, " ' journeys end in lovers' meetings,' as the old **38** play says. I don't think I have had the pleasure of seeing you since you favoured me with those attentions as I lay on the ledge above the Reichenbach Fall."

The colonel still stared at my friend like a man in a trance. "You cunning, cunning fiend!" was all that he could say.

"I have not introduced you yet," said Holmes. This, gentlemen, is Colonel Sebastian Moran, once of Her Majesty's Indian Army, and the best heavy game shot that our Eastern Empire has ever produced. I believe I am correct, colonel, in saying that your bag of tigers still remain unrivalled?"

The fierce old man said nothing, but still glared at my companion; with his savage eyes and bristling moustache, he was wonderfully like a tiger himself.

"I wonder that my very simple stratagem could deceive so old a shikari," said Holmes. "It must be **39** very familiar to you. Have you not tethered a young kid under a tree, lain above it with your rifle, and waited for the bait to bring up your tiger? This empty house is my tree, and you are my tiger. You have possibly had other guns in reserve in case there should be several tigers, or in the unlikely supposition of your own aim failing you. These," he pointed around, "are my other guns. The parallel is exact."

Colonel Moran sprang forward with a snarl of rage, but the constables dragged him back. The fury upon his face was terrible to look at.

"I confess that you had one small surprise for me," said Holmes. "I did not anticipate that you would yourself make use of this empty house and this convenient front window. I had imagined you as operating from the street, where my friend Lestrade and his merry men were awaiting you. With that exception, all has gone as I expected."

Colonel Moran turned to the official detective.

"You may or may not have just cause for arresting me," said he, "but at least there can be no reason why I should submit to the gibes of this person. If I am in the hands of the law, let things be done in a legal way."

"Well, that's reasonable enough," said Lestrade. "Nothing further you have to say, Mr. Holmes, before we go?"

Holmes had picked up the powerful air-gun from the floor, and was examining its mechanism.

"An admirable and unique weapon," said he, "noise-

37 *a long, silvery tinkle of broken glass.* "Does a revolver bullet, fired from an air-gun across a street through a window, cause a 'long, silvery tinkle of broken glass'?" Magistrate S. Tupper Bigelow asked in "Two Canonical Problems Solved." "All the ones I've ever seen or heard about drill a neat hole even through plate glass."

38 *as the old play says.* Holmes slightly misquotes *Twelfth Night*, Act II, Scene 3, line 46: "Journeys end in lovers meeting." As we have previously noted, *Twelfth Night* is the only one of Shakespeare's works which Holmes quotes twice (see "The Adventure of the Red Circle," Note 10).

39 *shikari.* Hindu word for a sportsman or hunter.

THE FIERCE OLD MAN SAID NOTHING, BUT STILL GLARED AT MY COMPANION . . .

Illustration by Frederic Dorr Steele for *Collier's Magazine*, September 26, 1903.

COLONEL MORAN SPRANG FORWARD WITH A SNARL OF RAGE . . .

Illustration by Sidney Paget for the *Strand Magazine*, October, 1903.

40 *Von Herder, the blind German mechanic.*
"How did a mechanic come to have a title of
nobility?" the late Elmer Davis asked in his introduction to *The Return of Sherlock Holmes.*
"Even big industrialists found them hard to come
by, in the Kaiserreich. Or, alternatively, how did
a nobleman happen to become a mechanic?"

Mr. Ralph A. Ashton has given us an answer
in his biography of Von Herder (from "Colonel
Moran's Infamous Air Rifle")" "Augustus Heinrich Friedrich Kartiffelschale von Herder was
born Vienna 1 April 1803. Mother: Fräulein
Schmutzi Liebelnhastic von Herder. Father: unknown. Knighted by Friedrich Wilhelm IV (date
unknown) for research into problems of using
dehydrated water as a propellant in place of gunpowder. (By removing all traces of moisture from
water, it could be concentrated into a very small
place; when reconstituted, it expanded and forced
the bullet from the barrel with explosive energy.)
Blinded by acid in 1839 while experimenting with
poisoned bullets. Died by gunshot wounds 1 April
1901, believed to have been inflicted by a jealous
husband.—Unpublished notes of Rudolf von
Esche."

less and of tremendous power. I knew Von Herder, the
40 blind German mechanic, who constructed it to the order
of the late Professor Moriarty. For years I have been
aware of its existence, though I have never before had
an opportunity of handling it. I commend it very
specially to your attention, Lestrade, and also the bullets
which fit it."

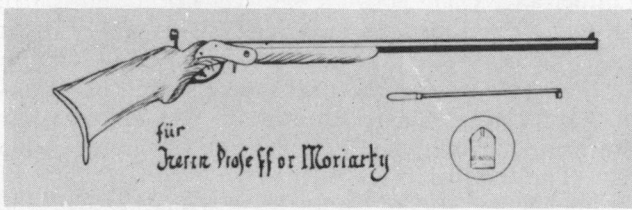

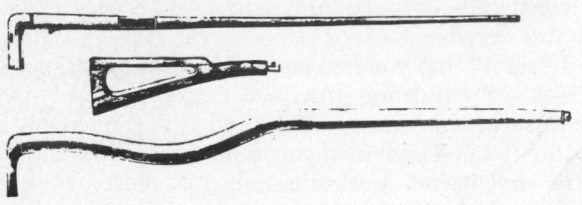

"I COMMEND IT VERY SPECIALLY TO YOUR ATTENTION . . ."

There existed, from the middle of the eighteenth century, a rare
arm, the Blozenbüchse, a breech-loading air-powered rifle designed
to shoot darts over a range of about 10 meters. It was unerringly
accurate; it was virtually noiseless. Mr. Ashton has suggested
("Colonel Moran's Infamous Air Rifle") that von Herder adapted
this gun to meet the two other specifications set up by Professor
Moriarty: first, he bored the Bolzenbüchse to carry a revolver
bullet of sufficient caliber to kill; second, to make the gun portable, and in a form unrecognizable as a gun, he redesigned the
one-piece Bolzenbüchse rifle into a two-piece take-down model.
"Von Herder didn't create anything. He merely adapted an existing type of firearm. It is interesting to note that this was not lost
on Holmes, who did not classify von Herder as a master gunsmith.
He called him a blind German mechanic."

On the other hand, Mr. William Percival has written ("Sherlock Holmes and Air-Guns") that "there can be little doubt that
[Colonel Moran's air-gun] was of the air chamber walking stick
air rifle type. The walking stick air rifle was an exclusively English invention, first made in the early 1840's. Messrs. Townsend
and Reilly were the most prolific makers. These guns ceased to
be made in the early 1900's and good examples are now both rare
and expensive. They closely resembled ordinary walking sticks

"You can trust us to look after that, Mr. Holmes," said Lestrade, as the whole party moved towards the door. "Anything further to say?"

"Only to ask what charge you intend to prefer?"

"What charge, sir? Why, of course, the attempted murder of Mr. Sherlock Holmes."

"Not so, Lestrade. I do not propose to appear in the matter at all. To you, and to you only, belongs the credit of the remarkable arrest which you have effected. Yes, Lestrade, I congratulate you! With your usual happy mixture of cunning and audacity you have got him."

"Got him! Got whom, Mr. Holmes?"

"The man whom the whole Force has been seeking in vain—Colonel Sebastian Moran, who shot the Honourable Ronald Adair with an expanding bullet from an air-gun through the open window of the second-floor front of No. 427 Park Lane, upon the 30th of last month. **41** That's the charge, Lestrade. And now, Watson, if you can endure the draught from a broken window, I think that half an hour in my study over a cigar may afford you some profitable amusement."

Our old chambers had been left unchanged, through the supervision of Mycroft Holmes and the immediate care of Mrs. Hudson. As I entered I saw, it is true, an unwonted tidiness, but the old landmarks were all in their places. There were the chemical corner and the acid-stained deal-topped table. There upon a shelf **42** was the row of formidable scrap-books and books of reference which many of our fellow-citizens would have been so glad to burn. The diagrams, the violin-case,

and would be murderous weapons in the wrong hands. As there was no recoil, the firing position was to hold the knob against the cheek and sight along the stick, but some sticks (such as that used by Colonel Moran) had a crooked handle and were fired from the shoulder. They operated at a pressure of 400–500 pounds per square inch or more, being pumped up manually by a separate pump. (It has been queried whether Watson's description of Moran's method of loading did not indicate a spring-operated air gun. The answer is probably that in the semi-darkness, Watson confused the loading of the gun with the operation of the air pump. No spring-operated air gun could have been of the requisite power.) One pumping sufficed for at least 20 shots and, by means of compensating valves, the power did not greatly diminish as the pressure fell. The extreme range was about 350 yards, and at 50 yards bullets (soft-nosed expanding revolver bullets, if desired) would easily penetrate a 1-inch wooden plank."

Shown here are, first, the Bolzenbüchse and, second, the von Herder adaptation according to Mr. Ashton (each with its ammunition, slightly reduced in size) and its lever or *Hebel*. The following illustration shows walking-stick guns from a catalogue of W. W. Greener, Birmingham and London, about 1900. The first is for .410 shotgun shells. The second is an air rifle to be used with a pump (not shown).

41 *through the open window of the second-floor front.* Since Park Lane fronts on Hyde Park for its entire length, the question arises: Where was the Colonel when he shot? As Mr. Russell McLauchlin wrote, in his "Ballade on a Daring Theme":

> Across the way the land is stark,
> Of building there is not a trace,
> Only the semi-rural Park
> Confronts the fatal mansion's face;
> The fence, the trees which interlace
> Their branches in that sightly spot,
> These occupy the total space.
> Where was the Colonel when he shot?

Mr. Percival Wilde, in "The Bust in the Window," wrote that "Colonel Moran must have fired from a spot near the Marble Arch entrance of Hyde Park, in the Park itself, and must have done so without attracting the least attention from the masses of humanity which are so much in evidence 'between the hours of ten and eleven-twenty' P.M. A comparable shot would be one fired into a third-story window of the Astor Hotel by a marksman standing on the east side of Broadway at an identical time of night."

The late Edgar W. Smith, writing in "The Old Shikari," thought that Moran must have "climbed a strategically-placed tree in the park to put himself on a level with the second-storey window at 427 Park Lane (two flights up, mind you), behind which young Adair was sitting."

And Magistrate S. Tupper Bigelow, in "Two Canonical Problems Solved," asked: "If Moran killed [Adair], where was Moran when he fired the shot—in a helicopter?"

42 *the acid-stained deal-topped table.* "Deal, in British usage, means simply lumber or timber," Mr. D. A. Redmond wrote in "Some Chemical Problems in the Canon." "Critics have suggested that a plain softwood table, or bench, would be unsuited for chemical use, and soon pitted by the Master's experiments [but] the description 'acid-stained' has been misinterpreted. A standard method of acid-proofing wooden laboratory bench tops is to coat them successively with potassium nitrate solution and with boiling aniline and hydrocholoric acid. This spectacular process produces a dense black stain. Here is our 'acid-stained deal-topped table'—a properly finished laboratory bench."

43 *Here it is!*" In *Design for Murder*, a detective novel by Percival Wilde, published by Random House, one Mary Ashton finds fault with "The Adventure of the Empty House." A bullet fired from the ground floor of a house on one side of the street, could not, she claims: 1) penetrate both the shadow and the bust of Sherlock Holmes which is casting it, since the bust must be at some distance from its shadow; or 2) if it struck both shadow and bust, it should strike the lamp which is in a straight line with them; and 3) it would, in any event, because of the elevation of the gun's muzzle, finally strike the ceiling and not the far wall of the room which is the starting point for so many of Dr. Watson's stories.

Mr. Robert S. Schultz, however, writing in "The Ballistics of the Empty House," refused to admit any of these claims: 1) "the distance of the bust from the window cannot have been great: in Watson's words, the shadow 'was thrown in hard, black outline upon the luminous screen of the window.' Consideration of the most elementary laws of optics shows that, had the bust been at any distance from the window, and particularly, had it been closer to the lamp than to the window, the shadow would have been large and fuzzy, with features indistinct. . . . The present writer concludes that the bust could not have been much more than one foot from the window." 2) "The four objects (lamp, bust, shadow and gun) could have been in a straight line relationship to each other only if Moran had fired from the first floor instead of from the ground floor. In this event, the lamp would obviously have been smashed. The point is, of course, inconsistent with Wilde's other two points. . . . Needless to say, all this talk about straight lines is misleading; one would think it was well known that the path of a bullet is a parabola, not a straight line." 3) After an elaborate analysis of the heights and distances involved, Mr. Schultz concluded that "We have only Mrs. Hudson's word that the bullet 'flattened itself against the wall,' and in the midst of the excitement she might not have observed correctly." The bullet, Mr. Schultz thought, more probably hit the ceiling.

To the first of these points, Mr. Wilde replied ("The Bust in the Window"): "With a large light source there would have been both umbra and penumbra, and the shadow would have been indistinct; with a point-source such as the lamp we know so well, there was no penumbra, and the shadow was sharp for all positions of the bust." To the second: "The height of the shadow above the muzzle of the gun was far more than [Mr. Schultz] admits, and while I rule that Mary Ashton . . . was liberal when she referred to 'thirty degrees,' I decline to find that the angle was so small that it was inconsequential." To the third: "One concludes that only in a room of the most palatial dimensions could this ungracious bullet have hit the ceiling; one descries that Martha Hudson's observations were also accurate."

and the pipe-rack—even the Persian slipper which contained the tobacco—all met my eye as I glanced round me. There were two occupants of the room—one Mrs. Hudson, who beamed upon us both as we entered ; the other, the strange dummy which had played so important a part in the evening's adventures. It was a wax-coloured model of my friend, so admirably done that it was a perfect facsimile. It stood on a small pedestal table with an old dressing-gown of Holmes' so draped round it that the illusion from the street was absolutely perfect.

" I hope you preserved all precautions, Mrs. Hudson ? " said Holmes.

" I went to it on my knees, sir, just as you told me."

" Excellent. You carried the thing out very well. Did you observe where the bullet went ? "

" Yes, sir. I'm afraid it has spoilt your beautiful bust, for it passed right through the head and flattened itself on the wall. I picked it up from the carpet. Here it **43** is ! "

Holmes held it out to me. " A soft revolver bullet, as you perceive, Watson. There's genius in that—for who would expect to find such a thing fired from an air-gun ? All right, Mrs. Hudson, I am much obliged for your assistance. And now, Watson, let me see you in your old seat once more, for there are several points which I should like to discuss with you."

He had thrown off the seedy frock-coat, and now he was the Holmes of old, in the mouse-coloured dressing-gown which he took from his effigy.

" The old shikari's nerves have not lost their steadiness nor his eyes their keenness," said he, with a laugh, as he inspected the shattered forehead of his bust.

" Plumb in the middle of the back of the head and smack through the brain. He was the best shot in India, and I expect that there are few better in London. Have you heard the name ? "

" No, I have not."

" Well, well, such is fame ! But then, if I remember aright, you had not heard the name of Professor James Moriarty, who had one of the great brains of the century. Just give me down my index of biographies from the shelf."

He turned over the pages lazily, leaning back in his chair and blowing great clouds of smoke from his cigar.

" My collection of M's is a fine one," said he. " Moriarty himself is enough to make any letter illustrious, and here is Morgan the poisoner, and Merridew of abominable memory, and Mathews, who knocked out **44** my left canine in the waiting-room at Charing Cross, and, finally, here is our friend of to-night."

He handed over the book, and I read : " *Moran, Sebastian, Colonel.* Unemployed. Formerly 1st Ben- **45** galore Pioneers. Born London, 1840. Son of Sir Augustus Moran, C.B., once British Minister to Persia. **46** Educated Eton and Oxford. Served in Jowaki Campaign, Afghan Campaign, Charasiab (dispatches), Sher- **47** pur, and Cabul. Author of *Heavy Game of the Western Himalayas*, 1881 ; *Three Months in the Jungle*, 1884.

"MY COLLECTION OF M'S IS A FINE ONE," SAID HE.

Illustration by Frederic Dorr Steele for *Collier's Magazine*, September 26, 1903. Sidney Paget illustrated the same scene for the *Strand Magazine*, October, 1903.

"SON OF SIR AUGUSTUS MORAN, C.B. . . ."

Companion of the Bath, a member of the Honorary Order of the Bath, founded in 1725; so called from the ceremonial cleansing performed by members before joining. As the onetime British Minister to Persia, Sir Augustus Moran would have received the Civil rather than the Military Order of the Bath; the badge of the Civil Order is shown above.

Address : Conduit Street. Clubs : The Anglo-Indian, **48** the Tankerville, the Bagatelle Card Club."

On the margin was written in Holmes' precise hand : " The second most dangerous man in London." **49**

" This is astonishing," said I, as I handed back the volume. " The man's career is that of an honourable soldier."

" It is true," Holmes answered. " Up to a certain point he did well. He was always a man of iron nerve, and the story is still told in India how he crawled down a drain after a wounded man-eating tiger. There are some trees, Watson, which grow to a certain height and then suddenly develop some unsightly eccentricity. You will see it often in humans. I have a theory that the individual represents in his development the whole procession of his ancestors, and that such a sudden turn to good or evil stands for some strong influence which came into the line of his pedigree. The person becomes, as it were, the epitome of the history of his own family."

" It is surely rather fanciful."

" Well, I don't insist upon it. Whatever the cause, Colonel Moran began to go wrong. Without any open scandal, he still made India too hot to hold him. He retired, came to London, and again acquired an evil name. It was at this time that he was sought out by Professor Moriarty, to whom for a time he was chief of the staff. Moriarty supplied him liberally with money, and used him only in one or two very high-class jobs which no ordinary criminal could have undertaken. You may have some recollection of the death of Mrs. Stewart, of Lauder, in 1887. Not ? Well, I am sure Moran **50** was at the bottom of it ; but nothing could be proved. So cleverly was the colonel concealed that even when the Moriarty gang was broken up we could not incriminate

But Mr. Schultz stuck to his air guns: "Moran sighted at the shadow thrown upon the screen, allowing for the fact that there was a distance of about one foot or so from the shadow to the actual target. . . . The angle of fire was somewhat over eleven degrees. The bullet rose, following a parabola. By the time it had passed through the wax bust its initial velocity was somewhat retarded, both because of the pull of gravity and because of the resistance of the wax. Nevertheless, the remaining velocity was adequate to carry the bullet above the lamp, which was not smashed, and on across the room."

44 *who knocked out my left canine.* "Of course, we in the dental profession know that under normal conditions [Holmes'] canine tooth could never have been easily 'knocked out,'" Dr. Charles Goodman wrote in "The Dental Holmes." "Even the dental surgeon, equipped with specially devised forceps, must exert unusual leverage and force to remove that type of tooth. I am advised by one of my colleagues, who is also an official examiner of the Royal Boxing Commission, that in all his wide experience he never saw a normal canine knocked out in a boxing match. Therefore I am sure that . . . Holmes had pyorrhea."

We may also note that Dr. Jay Weiss, in "Holmes As a Patient," came to this identical conclusion independently. In addition, research by the late Rudolph Elie ("The Battle of Charing Cross") has enabled him to pinpoint Holmes' encounter with Mathews to the night of November 12, 1878. On that night, according to the London *Times* of January 3, 1879, one *Thomas Mathews* took part in a riot in which a detective named James Hand attributed the saving of his life to the fortunate intervention of an unidentified person, unquestionably Holmes. Mathews, we are glad to learn, was sentenced to 15 months' imprisonment with hard labor.

45 *1st Bengalore Pioneers. Bangalore* Pioneers in some American editions. Neither the Bengalore nor the Bangalore Pioneers ever existed, but, as Mrs. Crighton Sellars has written in "Dr. Watson and the British Army," "there was a very famous Corps in the Indian Army called The Corps of Madras Sappers and Miners (The Queen's Own), which consisted of two separate bodies, the Engineers and the Pioneers, whose history, dating from capture of Seringapatam, closely parallels Moran's service during his time with it. Bangalor, near the eastern boundary of Mysore, is just next to the district of Madras, and this may account for the association of the districts in Watson's mind when he came to paraphrasing the name of the real regiment to which his knave belonged. The Madras Pioneers served in the Afghan Campaign, Sherpur and Cabul, and had detachments in the Jowaki Campaign; also at [Charasiab]."

46 *Educated Eton and Oxford.* "It has often been noticed," the late Christopher Morley wrote in *Sherlock Holmes and Dr. Watson: A Textbook of Friendship,* "that this education can produce some notable results. In Holmes' experience both [Colonel Moran], 'the second most dangerous man in London' and [John Clay of "The Red-Headed League"], 'the fourth smartest man in London' had studied at Eton and Oxford."

47 *Sherpur, and Cabul.* "The first of these [campaigns]," the late Edgar W. Smith wrote in "The Old Shikari," "was against the Jowaki Afridis in the northern fastnesses, where, under Colonel Mocatta, [Moran] was one of a force of 1,500 sent to punish these wild Pathan tribesmen for the recalcitrant attitude they were showing toward the British. The Afghan campaign itself came upon the heels of a contre-temps with Russia which has had familiar echoes since, and it was precipitated by the rough treatment given to a British diplomatic mission at the hands of the Amir of the tribes. When the armies marched to avenge these insults and to hold the gem of India secure in Victoria's crown, Moran found himself embroiled in the gruesome doings around Kabul. At Sherpur, he served under General Frederick S. L. Roberts, later Earl Roberts; and at [Charasiab, more properly Charasia or Charasiah], he found himself under the direct command of General T. D. Baker. In this last battle, as Holmes' index of biographies confirms, Moran's bravery was so exceptional that he was mentioned in the dispatches."

48 *Conduit Street.* One of the tributary thoroughfares leading out of Regent Street, and today perhaps the most imposing from a shopping point of view. It takes its name from Conduit Mead, an open field of 27 acres until 1713. In this street Charles James Fox was born on January 24, 1749.

him. You remember at that date, when I called upon you in your rooms, how I put up the shutters for fear of air-guns ? No doubt you thought me fanciful. I knew exactly what I was doing, for I knew of the existence of this remarkable gun, and I knew also that one of the best shots in the world would be behind it. When we were in Switzerland he followed us with Moriarty, and it was undoubtedly he who gave me that evil five minutes on the Reichenbach ledge.

"You may think that I read the papers with some attention during my sojourn in France, on the look-out for any chance of laying him by the heels. So long as he was free in London my life would really not have been worth living. Night and day the shadow would have been over me, and sooner or later his chance must have come. What could I do ? I could not shoot him at sight, or I should myself be in the dock. There was no use appealing to a magistrate. They cannot interfere on the strength of what would appear to them to be a wild suspicion. So I could do nothing. But I watched the criminal news, knowing that sooner or later I should get him. Then came the death of this Ronald Adair. My chance had come at last ! Knowing what I did, was it not certain that Colonel Moran had done it ? He had played cards with the lad ; he had followed him home from the club ; he had shot him through the open window. There was not a doubt of it. The bullets **51** alone are enough to put his head in a noose. I came over at once. I was seen by the sentinel, who would, I knew, direct the colonel's attention to my presence. He could not fail to connect my sudden return with his crime, and to be terribly alarmed. I was sure that he would make an attempt to get me out of the way *at once*, and would bring round his murderous weapon for that purpose. I left him an excellent mark in the window, and, having warned the police that they might be needed—by the way, Watson, you spotted their presence in that doorway with unerring accuracy—I took up what seemed to me to be a judicious post for observation, never dreaming that he would choose the same spot for his attack. Now, my dear Watson, does anything remain for me to explain ?"

"Yes," said I. "You have not made it clear what was Colonel Moran's motive in murdering the Honourable Ronald Adair."

"Ah ! my dear Watson, there we come into those realms of conjecture where the most logical mind may be at fault. Each may form his own hypothesis upon the present evidence, and yours is as likely to be correct as mine."

"You have formed one, then ? "

"I think that is not difficult to explain the facts. It came out in evidence that Colonel Moran and young Adair had between them won a considerable amount of money. Now, Moran undoubtedly played foul—of that I have long been aware. I believe that on the day of the murder, Adair had discovered that Moran was cheating. Very likely he had spoken to him privately, and had threatened to expose him unless he voluntarily resigned his membership of the club and promised not to play cards again. It is unlikely that a youngster like Adair would at once make a hideous scandal by exposing a well-known man so much older than himself. Probably he acted as I suggest. The exclusion from his clubs would mean ruin to Moran, who lived by his ill-gotten card gains. He therefore murdered Adair, who at the time was endeavouring to work out how much money he should himself return, since he could not profit by his partner's foul play. He locked the door, lest the ladies should surprise him and insist upon knowing what he was doing with these names and coins. Will it pass?"

"I have no doubt that you have hit upon the truth."

"It will be verified or disproved at the trial. Meanwhile, come what may, Colonel Moran will trouble us no more, the famous air-gun of Von Herder will embellish the **52** Scotland Yard Museum, and once again Mr. Sherlock Holmes is free to devote his life to examining those interesting little problems which the complex life of London so plentifully presents."

49 *"The second most dangerous man in London."* The most dangerous man in London had of course been Professor James Moriarty; the worst man in London we will meet in "The Adventure of Charles Augustus Milverton."

50 *Lauder.* A town in Berwickshire, Scotland.

51 *The bullets alone are enough to put his head in a noose.* Not so, as we shall see shortly. In making this statement, Holmes was anticipating by about fifteen years the part that ballistics would play in the investigation of crime. In 1894, ballistics was unknown at Scotland Yard, or, for that matter, at any police department in the world. The police became aware of its possibilities no earlier than 1909. By 1910 all modern police forces were using it in their investigation of crimes committed with the aid of firearms.

52 *Colonel Moran will trouble us no more.* The fact remains that Holmes referred to "the living Sebastian Moran" in 1902 ("The Adventure of the Illustrious Client") and implied that he was alive and at liberty as late as the outbreak of World War I ("His Last Bow"): "The old sweet song. It was a favorite ditty of the late lamented Professor Moriarty. Colonel Sebastian Moran *has* also been known to warble it." This is not at all as unlikely as it may sound. We have the opinion of Magistrate S. Tupper Bigelow ("Two Canonical Problems Solved") that the case against Moran "boils down to this: Adair was killed; the expanding revolver bullet that killed him was similar to one that was shot from Moran's air-gun; therefore Moran killed Adair." It is interesting in this connection to note that the villain of the play *The Crown Diamond*, from which Conan Doyle fashioned the Sherlock Holmes short story "The Adventure of the Mazarin Stone" was *Colonel Sebastian Moran*. "The Adventure of the Mazarin Stone," virtually all commentators are agreed, took place in the summer of 1903.

Auctorial Note: It has been said that Sir Arthur Conan Doyle's second wife supplied him with the idea for "The Adventure of the Empty House," and how Sherlock Holmes could safely and "logically" be brought back to life in the pages of *Collier's* and the *Strand*. In any case, the story ranked high with Sir Arthur himself, who placed it No. 6 on his list of the "twelve best" Sherlock Holmes short stories.

50

THE ADVENTURE OF THE GOLDEN PINCE-NEZ

[Wednesday, November 14, to Thursday, November 15, 1894]

1 *the red leech.* ". . . most leeches are not red, but olive-green to brown in colour," Mr. Paul H. Gore-Booth wrote in "The Journeys of Sherlock Holmes." "The inference may be that Watson was referring to one of the red-*blooded* leeches (e.g. *Hirudo medicinalis*, the medicinal leech or *Haemopsis* (*aulastomum*) *gulo*, the horseleech, both of which are common in the British Isles); alternatively he may have meant *Pontobdella muricata*, also green in colour but identified by Professor [F. E.] Beddard [of Oxford, England, a leading contemporary expert] also as a large red-coloured leech occasionally observed by fishermen on the basking shark."

The late A. Carson Simpson submitted (*Sherlock Holmes' Wanderjahre*, Vol. III) that Holmes' experience with Himalayan leeches during his stay in Tibet peculiarly qualified him to uncover the truth of this case. "If there are red leeches anywhere in the world, they must have at least a token representation in the Teesta Valley and Sikkim. Of course, many leeches, when engorged, have their skins so far distended that the color of their blood-meal shows through, giving them a reddish tone. Perhaps poor Crosby encountered a gigantic leech—a mutation or a 'sport,' if you will —that was able to drain *all* the blood from his system, leaving only a shrunken corpse."

Mr. Simpson did not, however, exclude the possibility that "the term 'leech' was used in its extended meaning of 'physician,' and that the 'red' refers to 1) the color of his hair (as Eric the Red); or 2) the color of his clothes (as Count Amadeo VII of Saxony—*il Conte Rosso*—who affected a red costume in tournaments); or 3) his association with blood-letting (as 'Red' or 'Bloody' Jeffreys); or 4) his political complexion, in which case he would naturally select the capitalist Crosby as his victim."

2 *the Addleton tragedy.* "The 'Addleton' tragedy is probably a misunderstanding for 'Addlestone,'" Mr. Paul H. Gore-Booth wrote, "a conjecture founded on no hypothesis save that, while Addleton does not, as far as I know, exist, Addlestone is in Surrey, which was the scene of many of Holmes' exploits. We may justifiably suspect a printer's error faithfully repeated in subsequent editions."

WHEN I look at the three massive manuscript volumes which contain our work for the year 1894 I confess that it is very difficult for me, out of such a wealth of material, to select the cases which are most interesting in themselves and at the same time most conducive to a display of those peculiar powers for which my friend was famous. As I turn over the pages I see my notes upon the repulsive story of the **1** red leech and the terrible death of Crosby the banker. **2** Here also I find an account of the Addleton tragedy and **3** the singular contents of the ancient British barrow. The famous Smith-Mortimer succession case comes also within this period, and so does the tracking and arrest of Huret, the Boulevard assassin—an exploit which won for Holmes **4** an autograph letter of thanks from the French President and the Order of the Legion of Honour. Each of these would furnish a narrative, but on the whole I am of opinion that none of them unite so many singular points **5** of interest as the episode of Yoxley Old Place, which includes, not only the lamentable death of young Willoughby Smith, but also those subsequent developments which threw so curious a light upon the causes of the crime.

It was a wild, tempestuous night towards the close of November. Holmes and I sat together in silence all the **6** evening, he engaged with a powerful lens deciphering the **7** remains of the original inscription upon a palimpsest, I **8** deep in a recent treatise upon surgery. Outside the wind howled down Baker Street, while the rain beat fiercely against the windows. It was strange there in the very depths of the town, with ten miles of man's handiwork on every side of us, to feel the iron grip of Nature, and to be conscious that to the huge elemental forces all London was no more than the molehills that dot the fields. I walked to the window and looked out on the deserted street.

. . . AN EXPLOIT WHICH WON FOR HOLMES . . . THE ORDER OF THE LEGION OF HONOUR.

The occasional lamps gleamed on the expanse of muddy road and shining pavement. A single cab was splashing its way from the Oxford Street end.   **9**

"Well, Watson, it's as well we have not to turn out tonight," said Holmes, laying aside his lens and rolling up the palimpsest. "I've done enough for one sitting. It is trying work for the eyes. So far as I can make out, it is nothing more exciting than an Abbey's accounts dating from the second half of the fifteenth century. Halloa ! halloa ! halloa ! What's this ? "

Amid the droning of the wind there had come the stamping of a horse's hoofs and the long grind of a wheel as it rasped against the kerb. The cab which I had seen had pulled up at our door.

"What can he want ? " I ejaculated, as a man stepped out of it.

"Want ! He wants us. And we, my poor Watson, want overcoats and cravats and goloshes, and every aid that man ever invented to fight the weather. Wait a bit, though ! There's the cab off again ! There's hope yet. He'd have kept it if he had wanted us to come. Run down, my dear fellow, and open the door, for all virtuous folk have been long in bed."

When the light of the hall lamp fell upon our midnight visitor, I had no difficulty in recognizing him. It was young Stanley Hopkins, a promising detective, in whose career Holmes had several times shown a very practical interest.

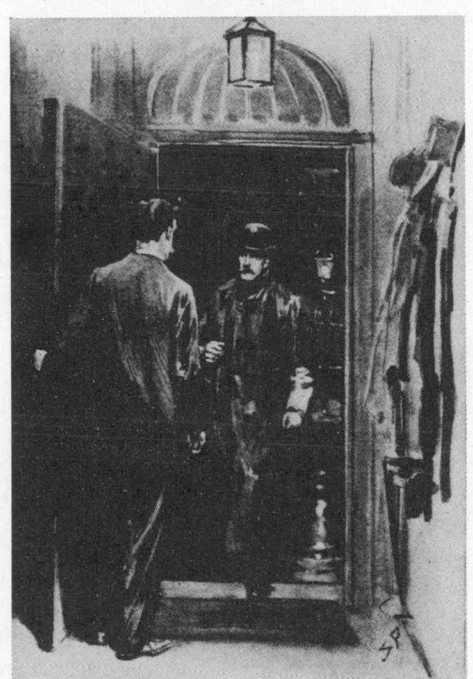

IT WAS YOUNG STANLEY HOPKINS, A PROMISING
DETECTIVE . . .

Illustration by Sidney Paget for the *Strand Magazine*, July, 1904. We shall meet Stanley Hopkins again—in "The Adventure of Black Peter," "The Adventure of the Missing Three-Quarter," and "The Adventure of the Abbey Grange." As we have previously noted, Mr. Marion Prince has advanced the theory that *Stanley Hopkins* was the son of *Sherlock Holmes*.

"The Adventure of the Foulkes Rath," a pastiche stemming from this reference of Dr. Watson's, by Adrian M. Conan Doyle, appears in *The Exploits of Sherlock Holmes*.

3 *the singular contents of the ancient British barrow.* "While no hint is vouchsafed us of its contents and circumstances, it is unlikely that anyone could open one of the ancient burial places of the original inhabitants of Britain without acquiring or having acquired a first-hand knowledge of Britain's pre-history," Mr. Whitfield J. Bell, Jr., noted in "Holmes and History."

We may also note that Watson's phrase has been enlarged upon by Mr. Poul Anderson in "Time Patrol," in which Holmes himself makes a brief anonymous appearance.

4 *the French President.* M. Jean-Paul-Pierre Casimir-Perier, 1847–1907, was the President of France in 1894. Mr. Svend Petersen has pointed out, in his *Sherlock Holmes Almanac*, that M. Casimer-Perier's predecessor, Marie François Sadi-Carnot, was assassinated, which may have accounted for the former's gratitude toward Sherlock Holmes.

5 *Yoxley Old Place.* We are shortly told that Yoxley Old Place was "down in Kent, seven miles from Chatham and three from the railway line." This may be, but Mr. Humfrey Michell has pointed out that there is a very real Yoxley Old *Hall* near Bury St. Edmunds in Suffolk.

6 *Holmes and I sat together in silence all the evening.* "I . . . sold my practice and returned to share the old quarters at Baker Street," Watson tells us in "The Adventure of the Norwood Builder," the second-*published* adventure in *The Return* series. "A young doctor named Verner . . . purchased my small Kensington practice, and [gave] with astonishingly little demur the highest price that I ventured to ask—an incident which only explained itself some years later, when I found that Verner was a distant relation of Holmes' and that it was my friend who had really found the money."

7 *the original inscription upon a palimpsest.* A parchment or other writing material, written upon twice, the original having been erased in whole or in part to make room for the second. Valuable fragments of ancient literature have been recovered in manuscripts by the use of chemical reagents, and Holmes was almost certainly making use of his chemical corner in this instance. Mr. Morris Rosenblum has noted ("Some Latin By-ways in the Canon") that Holmes "must have possessed an intimate knowledge of post-classical Latin to decipher 'the remains of the original inscription upon a palimpsest' and to pursue 'some laborious researches into early English charters ["The Adventure of the Three Students"], since these documents were undoubtedly written in late Latin, intelligible only to expert philologists."

8 *a recent treatise upon surgery.* "Doctor Watson has been rated somewhere between the extremes of merely a good First Aid man and a well trained surgeon," the late Dr. Roland Hammond wrote in "The Surgeon Probes Doctor Watson's Wound." "The proper level of his competence would probably be that of an average general practitioner of medicine. There is no evidence of any outstanding ability as a surgeon in spite of the fact that he was reading a recent treatise on surgery."

And Mr. A. S. Galbraith has added ("The Real Moriarty"): "It is clear from the stories that Watson can write, and write very well, and that he is reasonably well read. He is a capable physician, with the scientific knowledge appropriate to the general practitioner of his day, and he tries by reading to keep up to date in his work."

9 *splashing its way from the Oxford Street end.* Dr. Watson would not be able to see such a sight today: an experimental one-way traffic scheme in the Baker Street-Gloucester Place area has now been made permanent.

" Is he in ? " he asked eagerly.

" Come up, my dear sir," said Holmes' voice from above. " I hope you have no designs upon us on such a night as this."

The detective mounted the stairs, and our lamp gleamed upon his shining waterproof. I helped him out of it, while Holmes knocked a blaze out of the logs in the grate.

" Now, my dear Hopkins, draw up and warm your toes," said he. " Here's a cigar, and the doctor has a prescription containing hot water and a lemon which is good medicine on a night like this. It must be something important which has brought you out in such a gale."

" It is indeed, Mr. Holmes. I've had a bustling afternoon, I promise you. Did you see anything of the Yoxley case in the latest editions ? "

" I've seen nothing later than the fifteenth century to-day."

" Well, it was only a paragraph, and all wrong at that, so you have not missed anything. I haven't let the grass grow under my feet. It's down in Kent, seven miles from Chatham and three from the railway line. I was wired for at three-fifteen, reached Yoxley Old Place at five, conducted my investigation, was back at Charing Cross by the last train and straight to you by cab."

" Which means, I suppose, that you are not quite clear about your case ? "

" It means that I can make neither head nor tail of it. So far as I can see it is just as tangled a business as ever I handled, and yet at first it seemed so simple that one couldn't go wrong. There's no motive, Mr. Holmes. That's what bothers me—I can't put my hand on a motive. Here's a man dead—there's no denying that—but, so far as I can see, no reason on earth why anyone should wish him harm."

Holmes lit his cigar and leaned back in his chair.

" Let us hear about it," said he.

" I've got my facts pretty clear," said Stanley Hopkins. " All I want now is to know what they all mean. The story, so far as I can make it out, is like this. Some years ago this country house, Yoxley Old Place, was taken by an elderly man, who gave the name of Professor Coram. He was an invalid, keeping his bed half the time, and the other half hobbling round the house with a stick, or being pushed about the grounds by the gardener in a bath-chair. He was well liked by the few neighbours who called upon him, and he has the reputation down there of being a very learned man. His household used to consist of an elderly housekeeper, Mrs. Marker, and of a maid, Susan Tarlton. These have both been with him since his arrival, and they seem to be women of excellent character. The professor is writing a learned book, and he found it necessary about a year ago to engage a secretary. The first two that he tried were not successes ; but the third, Mr. Willoughby Smith, a very young man straight from the University, seems to have been just what his employer wanted. His work consisted in writing all the morning to the professor's dictation, and he usually spent the evening in hunting up references and passages which bore upon the next day's work. This Willoughby Smith has nothing against him either as a boy at Uppingham or as a young man at **10** Cambridge. I have seen his testimonials, and from the first he was a decent, quiet, hard-working fellow, with no weak spot in him at all. And yet this is the lad who has met his death this morning in the professor's study under circumstances which can point only to murder."

The wind howled and screamed at the windows. Holmes and I drew closer to the fire while the young inspector slowly and point by point developed his singular narrative.

" If you were to search all England," said he, " I don't suppose you could find a household more self-contained or free from outside influences. Whole weeks would pass and not one of them go past the garden gate. The professor was buried in his work, and existed for nothing else. Young Smith knew nobody in the neighbourhood, and lived very much as his employer did. The two women had nothing to take them from the house. Mortimer, the gardener, who wheels the bath-chair, is an Army pensioner—an old Crimean man of excellent character. He does not live in the house, but in a three-roomed cottage at the other end of the garden. Those are the only people that you would find within the grounds of Yoxley Old Place. At the same time, the gate of the garden is a hundred yards from the main London to Chatham road. It opens with a latch, and there is nothing to prevent anyone from walking in.

" Now I will give you the evidence of Susan Tarlton, who is the only person who can say anything positive about the matter. It was in the forenoon, between eleven and twelve. She was engaged at the moment in hanging some curtains in the upstairs front bedroom. Professor Coram was still in bed, for when the weather is bad he seldom rises before midday. The housekeeper was busied with some work in the back of the house. Willoughby Smith had been in his bedroom, which he uses as a sitting-room ; but the maid heard him at that moment pass along the passage and descend to the study immediately below her. She did not see him, but she says that she could not be mistaken in his quick, firm tread. She did not hear the study door close, but a minute or so later there was a dreadful cry in the room below. It was a wild, hoarse scream, so strange and unnatural that it might have come either from a man or a woman. At the same instant there was a heavy thud, which shook the whole house, and then all was silence. The maid stood petrified for a moment, and then, recovering her courage, she ran downstairs. The study door was shut, and she opened it. Inside young Mr. Willoughby Smith was stretched upon the floor. At first she could see no injury, but as she tried to raise him she saw that blood was pouring from the under side of his neck. It was pierced by a very small but very deep wound, which had divided the carotid artery. The instrument with which the injury had been inflicted lay upon the carpet beside him. It was one of those small sealing-wax knives to be found on old-fashioned writing-tables, with

10 *Uppingham*. An ancient public school in Rutlandshire.

an ivory handle and a stiff blade. It was part of the fittings of the professor's own desk.

" At first the maid thought that young Smith was already dead, but on pouring some water from the carafe over his forehead, he opened his eyes for an instant. ' The professor,' he murmured—' it was she.' The maid is prepared to swear that those were the exact words. He tried desperately to say something else, and he held his right hand up in the air. Then he fell back dead.

" In the meantime the housekeeper had also arrived upon the scene, but she was just too late to catch the young man's dying words. Leaving Susan with the body, she hurried to the professor's room. He was sitting up in bed, horribly agitated, for he had heard enough to convince him that something terrible had occurred. Mrs. Marker is prepared to swear that the professor was still in his night-clothes, and, indeed, it was impossible for him to dress without the help of Mortimer, whose orders were to come at twelve o'clock. The professor declares that he heard the distant cry, but that he knows nothing more. He can give no explanation of the young man's last words, ' The professor—it was she,' but imagines that they were the outcome of delirium. He believes that Willoughby Smith had not an enemy in the world, and can give no reason for the crime. His first action was to send Mortimer, the gardener, for the local police. A little later the chief constable sent for me. Nothing was moved before I got there, and strict orders were given that no one should walk upon the paths leading to the house. It was a splendid chance of putting your theories into practice, Mr. Sherlock Holmes. There was really nothing wanting."

" Except Mr. Sherlock Holmes ! " said my companion, with a somewhat bitter smile. " Well, let us hear about it. What sort of job did you make of it ? "

" I must ask you first, Mr. Holmes, to glance at this rough plan, which will give you a general idea of the

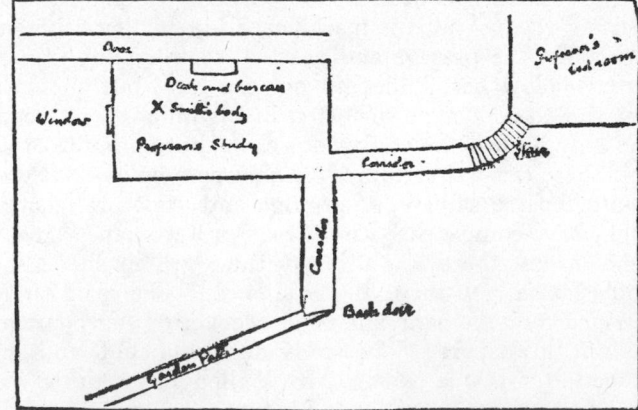

position of the professor's study and the various points of the case. It will help you in following my investigations."

He unfolded the rough chart, which I here reproduce, and he laid it across Holmes' knee. I rose, and, standing behind Holmes, I studied it over his shoulder.

" It is very rough, of course, and it only deals with the points which seem to me to be essential. All the rest you will see later for yourself. Now, first of all, presuming that the assassin entered the house, how did he or she come in ? Undoubtedly by the garden path and the back door, from which there is direct access to the study. Any other way would have been exceedingly complicated. The escape must also have been made along that line, for of the two other exits from the room one was blocked by Susan as she ran downstairs, and the other leads straight to the professor's bedroom. I therefore directed my attention at once to the garden path, which was saturated with recent rain and would certainly show any foot-marks.

" My examination showed me that I was dealing with a cautious and expert criminal. No footmarks were to be found on the path. There could be no question, how-ever, that someone had passed along the grass border which lines the path, and that he had done so in order to avoid leaving a track. I could not find anything in the nature of a distinct impression, but the grass was trodden down and someone had undoubtedly passed. It could only have been the murderer, since neither the gardener nor anyone else had been there that morning, and the rain had only begun during the night."

" One moment," said Holmes. " Where does this path lead to ? "

" To the road."

" How long is it ? "

" A hundred yards or so."

" At the point where the path passes through the gate you could surely pick up the tracks ? "

" Unfortunately the path was tiled at that point."

" Well, on the road itself ? "

" No ; it was all trodden into mire."

" Tut-tut ! Well, then, these tracks upon the grass— were they coming or going ? "

" It was impossible to say. There was never any outline."

" A large foot or a small ? "

" You could not distinguish."

Holmes gave an ejaculation of impatience. " It has been pouring rain and blowing a hurricane ever since," said he. " It will be harder to read now than that palimpsest. Well, well, it can't be helped. What did you do, Hopkins, after you had made certain that you had made certain of nothing ? "

" I think I made certain of a good deal, Mr. Holmes. I knew that someone had entered the house cautiously from without. I next examined the corridor. It is lined with coconut matting, and had taken no impression of any kind. This brought me into the study itself. It is a scantily furnished room. The main article is a large writing-table with a fixed bureau. This bureau consists of a double column of drawers with a central small cup-board between them. The drawers were open, the cup-board locked. The drawers, it seems, were always open, and nothing of value was kept in them. There were some papers of importance in the cupboard, but there

"IT WAS FOUND NEAR THE BUREAU, AND JUST TO THE LEFT OF IT, AS MARKED UPON THE CHART."

Illustration by Sidney Paget for the *Strand Maga-zine*, July, 1904.

HE HELD THEM ON HIS NOSE, ENDEAVOURED TO READ THROUGH THEM . . .

Cover illustration by Frederic Dorr Steele for *Col-lier's Magazine*, October 29, 1904. Sidney Paget il-lustrated the same scene for the *Strand Magazine*, July, 1904.

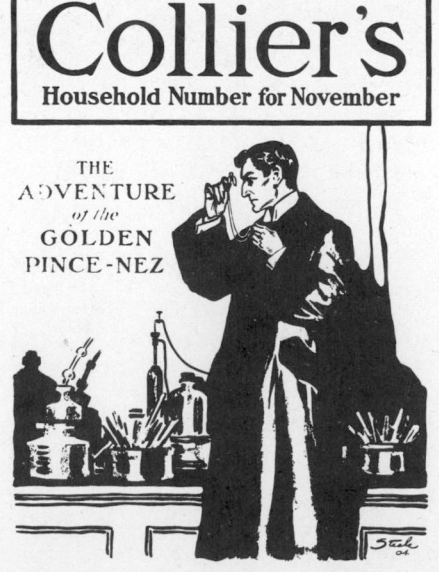

were no signs that this had been tampered with, and the professor assures me that nothing was missing. It is certain that no robbery had been committed.

"I come now to the body of the young man. It was found near the bureau, and just to the left of it, as marked upon that chart. The stab was on the right side of the neck and from behind forwards, so that it is almost impossible that it could have been self-inflicted."

"Unless he fell upon the knife," said Holmes.

"Exactly. The idea crossed my mind. But we found the knife some feet away from the body, so that seems impossible. Then, of course, there are the man's own dying words. And, finally, there was this very important piece of evidence which was found clasped in the dead man's right hand."

From his pocket Stanley Hopkins drew a small paper packet. He unfolded it, and disclosed a golden pince-nez, with two broken ends of black silk cord dangling from the end of it. "Willoughby Smith had excellent sight," he added. "There can be no question that this was snatched from the face or the person of the assassin."

Sherlock Holmes took the glasses into his hand and examined them with the utmost attention and interest. He held them on his nose, endeavoured to read through them, went to the window and stared up the street with them, looked at them most minutely in the full light of the lamp, and finally, with a chuckle, seated himself at the table and wrote a few lines upon a sheet of paper, which he tossed across to Stanley Hopkins.

"That's the best I can do for you," said he. "It may prove to be of some use."

The astonished detective read the note aloud. It ran as follows :

"Wanted, a woman of good address, attired like a lady. She has a remarkably thick nose, with eyes which are set close upon either side of it. She has a puckered forehead, a peering expression, and probably rounded shoulders. There are indications that she has had re-course to an optician at least twice during the last few months. As her glasses are of remarkable strength, and as opticians are not very numerous, there should be no difficulty in tracing her."

Holmes smiled at the astonishment of Hopkins, which must have been reflected upon my features.

"Surely my deductions are simplicity itself," said he. "It would be difficult to name any articles which afford a finer field for inference than a pair of glasses, especially so remarkable a pair as these. That they belong to a woman I infer from their delicacy, and also, of course, from the last words of the dying man. As to her being a person of refinement and well dressed, they are, as you perceive, handsomely mounted in solid gold, and it is inconceivable that anyone who wore such glasses could be slatternly in other respects. You will find that the clips are too wide for your nose, showing that the lady's nose was very broad at the base. This sort of nose is usually a short and coarse one, but there are a sufficient number of exceptions to prevent me from being dogmatic or from insisting upon this point in my description. My own face is a narrow one, and yet I find that I cannot get my eyes into the centre, or near the centre, of these glasses. Therefore, the lady's eyes are set very near to the sides of the nose. You will perceive, Watson, that the glasses are concave and of unusual strength. A lady whose vision has been so extremely contracted all her life is sure to have the physical characteristics of such vision, which are seen in the forehead, the eyelids, and the shoulders."

" Yes," I said, " I can follow each of your arguments. I confess, however, that I am unable to understand how you arrive at the double visit to the optician."

Holmes took the glasses into his hand.

" You will perceive," he said, " that the clips are lined with tiny bands of cork to soften the pressure upon the nose. One of these is discoloured and worn to some slight extent, but the other is new. Evidently one has fallen off and been replaced. I should judge that the older of them has not been there more than a few months. They exactly correspond, so I gather that the lady went back to the same establishment for the second."

" By George, it's marvellous ! " cried Hopkins, in an ecstasy of admiration. " To think that I had all that evidence in my hand and never knew it ! I had intended, however, to go the round of the London opticians."

" Of course you would. Meanwhile, have you anything more to tell us about the case ? "

" Nothing, Mr. Holmes. I think that you know as much as I do now—probably more. We have had inquiries made as to any stranger seen on the country roads or at the railway station. We have heard of none. What beats me is the utter want of all object in the crime. Not a ghost of a motive can anyone suggest."

" Ah ! there I am not in a position to help you. But I suppose you want us to come out to-morrow ? "

" If it is not asking too much, Mr. Holmes. There's a train from Charing Cross to Chatham at six in the morning, **12** and we should be at Yoxley Old Place between eight and nine."

" Then we shall take it. Your case has certainly some features of great interest, and I shall be delighted to look into it. Well, it's nearly one, and we had best get a few hours' sleep. I dare say you can manage all right on the sofa in front of the fire. I'll light my spirit-lamp and **13** give you a cup of coffee before we start."

The gale had blown itself out next day, but it was a bitter morning when we started upon our journey. We saw the cold winter sun rise over the dreary marshes of the Thames and the long, sullen reaches of the river, which I shall ever associate with our pursuit of the Andaman Islander in the earlier days of our career. **14** After a long and weary journey we alighted at a small station some miles from Chatham. While a horse was **15** being put into a trap at the local inn we snatched a hurried breakfast, and so we were all ready for business when we at last arrived at Yoxley Old Place. A constable

11 *could be slatternly in other respects.* "The conclusion that a woman who wears gold pince-nez must be well-dressed is unconvincing," Mr. Vernon Rendall wrote in "The Limitations of Sherlock Holmes." "People, when they first buy glasses, know nothing of the price, and the vendor naturally provides them with the most expensive form of eyewear. Vanity also induces them to have gold fittings, and they may insist on a detail which concerns their face, even if they cannot run to good clothes. Forty years ago, it must be remembered, horn spectacles had not come into fashion, and glasses, being regarded as a disfigurement, were not so often worn as they are to-day. Gold-rimmed glasses may have been bought during a period of prosperity which in later life the owner no longer enjoyed. . . . As I write, a notice appears in the papers of a woman with gold-rimmed glasses whose dull, if not slatternly clothing, as described, resembles that of a charwoman rather than what is prescribed by the 'dictates of fashion.' "

12 *at six in the morning.* There was, in fact, such a train at 6:12 A.M. They would have traveled by the old Southeastern and Chatham line.

13 *I'll light my spirit-lamp.* Why a spirit-lamp, when we know very well that the sitting room at 221B had gas laid on? And, as Mr. D. A. Redmond noted in "Some Chemical Problems in the Canon," "it is not likely that in a private lodging, for which he was paying 'princely' rentals, Holmes' gas supply would be equipped with a shilling-in-the-slot meter and his pockets empty of coins. Had he not paid his gas bill?"

14 *in the earlier days of our career.* Watson in this adventure must be speaking of the night of *November 14th,* a day on which the wind achieved a pressure of 29.5 pounds to the inch and there was 0.35 inch of rain, and the morning of *November 15th,* when the wind slackened to only 1.9 pounds and the temperature was 42.1 degrees. (We have already noted that Watson was unusually sensitive to drops in the temperature. In addition, as the late Professor Jay Finley Christ noted, "We are further entitled to doubt [Watson's impressions of bitter weather here] because he said that the streets were muddy and the pavement shiny as he looked out the window, and the men 'loitered the morning away in the garden,' at Coram's.") These two days were a Wednesday and Thursday. The late Dr. Ernest Bloomfield Zeisler chose to date this case October, 1894. He rightly said that November 14th–15th are not "towards the close of November." We, on the other hand, would sacrifice Watson's "towards the close" of November to preserve both his "November" and his "winter sun" (October is not "winter" in either the popular or the astronomical sense of the word). Dr. Zeisler also held that the month could not be November because: 1) Watson saw the sun rise after the start of their journey, which we know began at six; 2) the time of sunrise cannot be long after six because Watson, seeing the Thames, was reminded of the pursuit of the Islander and therefore could not have been long upon his journey. Certainly Watson saw the sun rise between the start of the journey and its close between eight and nine (on November 15, 1895, sunrise was at 7:20 A.M.); certainly he glimpsed the Thames and was reminded of the adventure of *The Sign of the Four*. But there is nothing in Watson's statement to lead us to believe that these incidents were *simultaneous*.

15 *a small station some miles from Chatham*. Mr. Michael Harrison has suggested (*In the Footsteps of Sherlock Holmes*) that the station was Higham. Of Yoxley Old Place, he writes: "It can only have been just off the main Gravesend-Chatham road, at the village of Shorne, only a few yards from Dickens' old house, Gadshill, and equally near to the famed Falstaff Inn, at the summit of Gadshill itself—that long slope which leads down to the Medway—at whose top Prince Hal, and Falstaff, and Nym and the rest, used to waylay travellers."

met us at the garden gate.

" Well, Wilson, any news ? "

" No, sir, nothing."

" No reports of any stranger seen ? "

" No, sir. Down at the station they are certain that no stranger either came or went yesterday."

" Have you had inquiries made at inns and lodgings ? "

" Yes, sir ; there is no one that we cannot account for."

" Well, it's only a reasonable walk to Chatham. Anyone might stay there, or take a train without being observed. This is the garden path of which I spoke, Mr. Holmes. I'll pledge my word there was no mark on it yesterday."

" On which side were the marks on the grass ? "

" This side, sir. This narrow margin of grass between the path and the flower-bed. I can't see the traces now, but they were clear to me then."

" Yes, yes ; someone has passed along," said Holmes, stooping over the grass border. " Our lady must have picked her steps carefully, must she not, since on the one side she would leave a track on the path, and on the other an even clearer one on the soft bed ? "

" Yes, sir, she must have been a cool hand."

I saw an intent look pass over Holmes' face.

" You say that she must have come back this way ? "

" Yes, sir ; there is no other."

" On this strip of grass ? "

" Certainly, Mr. Holmes."

" Hum ! It was a very remarkable performance— very remarkable. Well, I think we have exhausted the path. Let us go farther. This garden door is usually kept open, I suppose ? Then this visitor had nothing to do but to walk in. The idea of murder was not in her mind, or she would have provided herself with some sort of weapon, instead of having to pick this knife off the writing-table. She advanced along this corridor, leaving no traces upon the coconut matting. Then she found herself in this study. How long was she there ? We have no means of judging."

" Not more than a few minutes, sir. I forgot to tell you that Mrs. Marker, the housekeeper, had been in there tidying not very long before—about a quarter of an hour she says."

" Well, that gives us a limit. Our lady enters this room, and what does she do ? She goes over to the writing-table. What for ? Not for anything in the drawers. If there had been anything worth her taking it would scarcely have been locked up. No ; it was for something in that wooden bureau. Halloa ! what is that scratch upon the face of it ? Just hold a match, Watson. Why did you not tell me of this, Hopkins ? "

The mark which he was examining began upon the brasswork on the right-hand side of the keyhole, and extended for about four inches, where it had scratched the varnish from the surface.

" I noticed it, Mr. Holmes. But you'll always find scratches round a keyhole."

" This is recent—quite recent. See how the brass

shines where it is cut.   An old scratch would be the same
colour as the surface.   Look at it through my lens.
There's the varnish, too, like earth on each side of a
furrow.   Is Mrs. Marker there?"

A sad-faced, elderly woman came into the room.
" Did you dust this bureau yesterday morning?"
" Yes, sir."
" Did you notice this scratch?"
" No, sir, I did not."
" I am sure you did not, for a duster would have swept
away these shreds of varnish.   Who has the key of this
bureau?"
" The professor keeps it on his watch-chain."
" Is it a simple key?"
" No, sir; it is a Chubb's key."
" Very good.   Mrs. Marker, you can go.   Now we are
making a little progress.   Our lady enters the room,
advances to the bureau, and either opens it or tries to do so.
While she is thus engaged young Willoughby Smith
enters the room.   In her hurry to withdraw the key she
makes this scratch upon the door.   He seizes her, and she,
snatching up the nearest object, which happens to be this
knife, strikes at him in order to make him let go his hold.
The blow is a fatal one.   He falls and she escapes, either
with or without the object for which she has come.   Is
Susan the maid there?   Could anyone have got away
through that door after the time that you heard the cry,
Susan?"

" No, sir; it is impossible.   Before I got down the
stair I'd have seen anyone in the passage.   Besides, the
door never opened, for I would have heard it."

" That settles this exit.   Then no doubt the lady went
out the way she came.   I understand that this other
passage leads only to the professor's room.   There is no
exit that way?"

" No, sir."

" We shall go down it and make the acquaintance of
the professor.   Halloa, Hopkins! this is very important,
very important indeed.   The professor's corridor is also
lined with coconut matting."

" Well, sir, what of that?"

" Don't you see any bearing upon the case?   Well,
well, I don't insist upon it.   No doubt I am wrong.
And yet it seems to me to be suggestive.   Come with
me and introduce me."

We passed down the passage, which was of the same
length as that which led to the garden.   At the end was a
short flight of steps ending in a door.   Our guide knocked,
and then ushered us into the professor's bedroom.

It was a very large chamber, lined with innumerable
volumes, which had overflowed from the shelves and lay in
piles in the corners, or were stacked all round at the base
of the cases.   The bed was in the centre of the room, and
in it, propped up with pillows, was the owner of the house.
I have seldom seen a more remarkable-looking person.
It was a gaunt, aquiline face which was turned towards
us, with piercing dark eyes, which lurked in deep hollows
under overhung and tufted brows.   His hair and beard
were white, save that the latter was curiously stained with

"DID YOU DUST THIS BUREAU YESTERDAY MORNING?"

Illustration by Sidney Paget for the *Strand Magazine*, July, 1904.

"YES, SIR, IT IS A CRUSHING BLOW," SAID THE OLD MAN.

Illustration by Frederic Dorr Steele for *Collier's Magazine*, October 29, 1904.

yellow around his mouth. A cigarette glowed amid the tangle of white hair, and the air of the room was fetid with stale tobacco smoke. As he held out his hand to Holmes I perceived that it also was stained yellow with nicotine.

"A smoker, Mr. Holmes?" said he, speaking well-chosen English with a curious little mincing accent. "Pray take a cigarette. And you, sir? I can recommend them, for I have them especially prepared by Ionides of Alexandria. He sends me a thousand at a time, and I grieve to say that I have to arrange for a fresh supply every fortnight. Bad, sir, very bad; but an old man has few pleasures. Tobacco and my work—that is all that is left to me."

Holmes had lit a cigarette, and was shooting little darting glances all over the room.

"Tobacco and my work, but now only tobacco," the old man exclaimed. "Alas, what a fatal interruption! Who could have foreseen such a terrible catastrophe? So estimable a young man! I assure you that after a few months' training he was an admirable assistant. What do you think of the matter, Mr. Holmes?"

"I have not yet made up my mind."

"I shall indeed be indebted to you if you can throw a light where all is so dark to us. To a poor bookworm and invalid like myself such a blow is paralysing. I seem to have lost the faculty of thought. But you are a man of action—you are a man of affairs. It is part of the every-day routine of your life. You can preserve your balance in every emergency. We are fortunate indeed in having you at our side."

Holmes was pacing up and down on one side of the room whilst the old professor was talking. I observed that he was smoking with extraordinary rapidity. It was evident that he shared our host's liking for the fresh Alexandrian cigarettes.

"Yes, sir, it is a crushing blow," said the old man. "That is my *magnum opus*—the pile of papers on the side-table yonder. It is my analysis of the documents found in the Coptic monasteries of Syria and Egypt, a work which will cut deep at the very foundations of revealed religion. With my enfeebled health I do not know whether I shall ever be able to complete it now that my assistant has been taken from me. Dear me, Mr. Holmes; why, you are even a quicker smoker than I am myself."

Holmes smiled.

"I am a connoisseur," said he, taking another cigarette from the box—his fourth—and lighting it from the stub of that which he had finished. "I will not trouble you with any lengthy cross-examination, Professor Coram, since I gather that you were in bed at the time of the crime and could know nothing about it. I would only ask this—What do you imagine that this poor fellow meant by his last words: 'The professor—it was she'?"

The professor shook his head.

"Susan is a country girl," said he, "and you know the incredible stupidity of that class. I fancy that the poor fellow murmured some incoherent, delirious words, and that she twisted them into this meaningless message."

" I see. You have no explanation yourself of the tragedy ? "

" Possibly an accident ; possibly—I only breathe it among ourselves—a suicide. Young men have their hidden troubles—some affair of the heart, perhaps, which we have never known. It is a more probable supposition than murder."

" But the eyeglasses ? "

" Ah ! I am only a student—a man of dreams. I cannot explain the practical things of life. But still, we are aware, my friend, that love-gages may take strange shapes. By all means take another cigarette. It is a pleasure to see anyone appreciate them so. A fan, a glove, glasses—who knows what article may be carried as a token or treasured when a man puts an end to his life ? This gentleman speaks of footsteps on the grass ; but, after all, it is easy to be mistaken on such a point. As to the knife, it might well be thrown far from the unfortunate man as he fell. It is possible that I speak as a child, but to me it seems that Willoughby Smith has met his fate by his own hand."

Holmes seemed struck by the theory thus put forward, and he continued to walk up and down for some time, lost in thought and consuming cigarette after cigarette.

" Tell me, Professor Coram," he said at last, " what is in that cupboard in the bureau ? "

" Nothing that would help a thief. Family papers, letters from my poor wife, diplomas of Universities which have done me honour. Here is the key. You can look for yourself."

Holmes picked up the key and looked at it for an instant ; then he handed it back.

" No ; I hardly think that it would help me," said he. " I should prefer to go quietly down to your garden and turn the whole matter over in my head. There is something to be said for the theory of suicide which you have put forward. We must apologize for having intruded upon you, Professor Coram, and I promise that we won't disturb you until after lunch. At two o'clock we will come again and report to you anything which may have happened in the interval."

Holmes was curiously distrait, and we walked up and down the garden path for some time in silence.

" Have you a clue ? " I asked at last.

" It depends upon those cigarettes that I smoked," said he. " It is possible that I am utterly mistaken. The cigarettes will show me."

" My dear Holmes," I exclaimed, " how on earth——"

" Well, well, you may see for yourself. If not, there's no harm done. Of course, we always have the optician clue to fall back upon, but I take a short cut when I can get it. Ah, here is the good Mrs. Marker ! Let us **16** enjoy five minutes of instructive conversation with her."

I may have remarked before that Holmes had, when he liked, a peculiarly ingratiating way with women, and that he very readily established terms of confidence with them. In half the time which he had named he had captured the housekeeper's goodwill, and was chatting with her as if he had known her for years.

" Yes, Mr. Holmes, it is as you say, sir. He does smoke

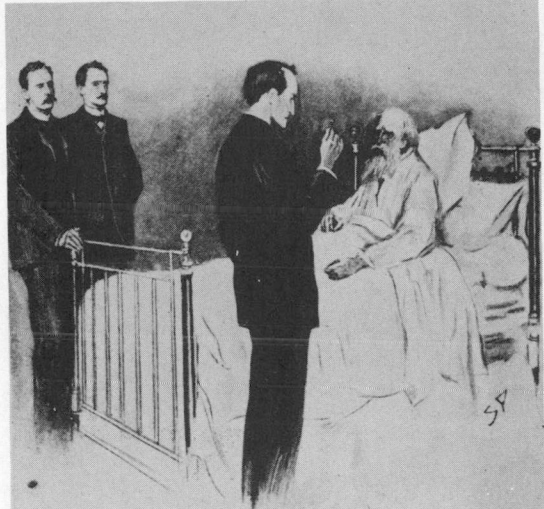

HOLMES PICKED UP THE KEY AND LOOKED AT IT FOR AN INSTANT . . .

Illustration by Sidney Paget for the *Strand Magazine*, July, 1904.

16 *I take a short cut when I can get it.* How truly the "short cut" Holmes used in this case was inspired may be seen by a comparison of "The Adventure of the Golden Pince-Nez" with the first episode in "The History of the Destruction of Bel and the Dragon" as recorded in the Old Testament Apocrypha. "Of course the stories are different, but the pivotal points are the same," Professor Stephen F. Crocker wrote in his "Pseudepigraphical Matter in the Holmesian Canon." Another commentator, Professor Clarke Olney, has suggested ("The Literacy of Sherlock Holmes") that the trick used by Holmes here was adapted from the artifice of Frocin, the evil-minded dwarf who sprinkled flour between the beds occupied by Tristram and Isolde.

something terrible. All day and sometimes all night, sir. I've seen that room of a morning—well, sir, you'd have thought it was a London fog. Poor young Mr. Smith, he was a smoker also, but not as bad as the professor. His health—well, I don't know that it's better nor worse for the smoking."

" Ah ! " said Holmes, " but it kills the appetite."

" Well, I don't know about that, sir."

" I suppose the professor eats hardly anything ? "

" Well, he is variable. I'll say that for him."

" I'll wager he took no breakfast this morning, and won't face his lunch after all the cigarettes I saw him consume."

" Well, you're out there, sir, as it happens, for he ate a remarkably big breakfast this morning. I don't know when I've known him make a better one, and he's ordered a good dish of cutlets for his lunch. I'm surprised myself, for since I came into that room yesterday and saw young Mr. Smith lying there on the floor I couldn't bear to look at food. Well, it takes all sorts to make a world, and the professor hasn't let it take his appetite away."

We loitered the morning away in the garden. Stanley Hopkins had gone down to the village to look into some rumours of a strange woman who had been seen by some children on the Chatham road the previous morning. As to my friend, all his usual energy seemed to have deserted him. I had never known him handle a case in such a half-hearted fashion. Even the news brought back by Hopkins that he had found the children and that they had undoubtedly seen a woman exactly corresponding with Holmes' description, and wearing either spectacles or eyeglasses, failed to rouse any sign of keen interest. He was more attentive when Susan, who waited upon us at lunch, volunteered the information that she believed Mr. Smith had been out for a walk yesterday morning, and that he had only returned half an hour before the tragedy occurred. I could not myself see the bearing of this incident, but I clearly perceived that Holmes was weaving it into the general scheme which he had formed in his brain. Suddenly he sprang from his chair, and glanced at his watch. " Two o'clock, gentlemen," said he. " We must go up and have it out with our friend the professor."

The old man had just finished his lunch, and certainly his empty dish bore evidence to the good appetite with which his housekeeper had credited him. He was, indeed, a weird figure as he turned his white mane and his glowing eyes towards us. The eternal cigarette smouldered in his mouth. He had been dressed and was seated in an arm-chair by the fire.

" Well, Mr. Holmes, have you solved this mystery yet ? " He shoved the large tin of cigarettes which stood on a table beside him towards my companion. Holmes stretched out his hand at the same moment, and between them they tipped the box over the edge. For a minute or two we were all on our knees retrieving stray cigarettes from impossible places. When we rose again I observed that Holmes' eyes were shining and his cheeks tinged with colour. Only at a crisis have I seen those battle-signals flying.

" Yes," said he, " I have solved it."

Stanley Hopkins and I stared in amazement. Something like a sneer quivered over the gaunt features of the old professor.

" Indeed ! In the garden ? "

" No, here."

" Here ! When ? "

" This instant."

" You are surely joking, Mr. Sherlock Holmes. You compel me to tell you that this is too serious a matter to be treated in such a fashion."

" I have forged and tested every link of my chain, Professor Coram, and I am sure that it is sound. What your motives are, or what exact part you play in this strange business, I am not yet able to say. In a few minutes I shall probably hear it from your own lips. Meanwhile, I will reconstruct what is past for your benefit, so that you may know the information which I still require.

" A lady yesterday entered your study. She came with the intention of possessing herself of certain documents which were in your bureau. She had a key of her own. I have had an opportunity of examining yours, and I do not find that slight discoloration which the scratch made upon the varnish would have produced. You were not an accessory, therefore, and she came, so far as I can read the evidence, without your knowledge to rob you."

The professor blew a cloud from his lips.

" This is most interesting and instructive," said he. " Have you no more to add ? Surely, having traced this lady so far, you can also say what has become of her."

" I will endeavour to do so. In the first place, she was seized by your secretary, and stabbed him in order to escape. This catastrophe I am inclined to regard as an unhappy accident, for I am convinced that the lady had no intention of inflicting so grievous an injury. An assassin does not come unarmed. Horrified by what she had done, she rushed wildly away from the scene of the tragedy. Unfortunately for her she had lost her glasses in the scuffle, and as she was extremely short-sighted she was really helpless without them. She ran down a corridor, which she imagined to be that by which she had come—both were lined with coconut matting—and it was only when it was too late that she understood that she had taken the wrong passage and that her retreat was cut off behind her. What was she to do ? She could not go back. She could not remain where she was. She must go on. She went on. She mounted a stair, pushed open a door, and found herself in your room."

The old man sat with his mouth open staring wildly at Holmes. Amazement and fear were stamped upon his expressive features. Now, with an effort, he shrugged his shoulders and burst into insincere laughter.

" All very fine, Mr. Holmes," said he. " But there is one little flaw in a splendid theory. I was myself in my room, and I never left it during the day."

" I am aware of that, Professor Coram."

" And you mean to say that I could lie upon that bed and not be aware that a woman had entered my room ? "

" I never said so. You *were* aware of it. You spoke

... A WOMAN RUSHED OUT INTO THE ROOM.

Illustration by Sidney Paget for the *Strand Magazine*, July, 1904.

with her. You recognized her. You aided her to escape."

Again the professor burst into high-keyed laughter. He had risen to his feet, and his eyes glowed like embers.

" You are mad!" he cried. " You are talking insanely. I helped her to escape? Where is she now? "

" She is there," said Holmes, and he pointed to a high bookcase in the corner of the room.

I saw the old man throw up his arms, a terrible convulsion passed over his grim face, and he fell back in his chair. At the same instant the bookcase at which Holmes pointed swung round upon a hinge, and a woman rushed out into the room.

" You are right," she cried, in a strange foreign voice. " You are right! I am here."

She was brown with the dust and draped with the cobwebs which had come from the walls of her hiding-place. Her face, too, was streaked with grime, and at the best she could have never been handsome, for she had the exact physical characteristics which Holmes had divined, with, in addition, a long and obstinate chin. What with her natural blindness, and what with the change from dark to light, she stood as one dazed, blinking about her to see where and who we were. And yet, in spite of all these disadvantages, there was a certain nobility in the woman's bearing, a gallantry in the defiant chin and in the upraised head, which compelled something of respect and admiration. Stanley Hopkins had laid his hand upon her arm and claimed her as his prisoner, but she waved him aside gently, and yet with an overmastering dignity which compelled obedience. The old man lay back in his chair, with a twitching face, and stared at her with brooding eyes.

" Yes, sir, I am your prisoner," she said. " From where I stood I could hear everything, and I know that you have learned the truth. I confess it all. It was I who killed the young man. But you are right, you who say that it was an accident. I did not even know that it was a knife which I held in my hand, for in my despair I snatched anything from the table and struck at him to make him let me go. It is the truth that I tell."

" Madame," said Holmes, " I am sure that it is the truth. I fear that you are far from well."

She had turned a dreadful colour, the more ghastly under the dark dust-streaks upon her face. She seated herself on the side of the bed ; then she resumed.

" I have only a little time here," she said, " but I would have you to know the whole truth. I am this man's wife. He is not an Englishman. He is a Russian. His name I will not tell."

For the first time the old man stirred. " God bless you, Anna!" he cried. " God bless you!"

She cast a look of the deepest disdain in his direction. " Why should you cling so hard to that wretched life of yours, Sergius? " said she. " It has done harm to many and good to none—not even to yourself. However, it is not for me to cause the frail thread to be snapped before God's time. I have enough already upon my soul since I crossed the threshold of this cursed house. But I must speak, or I shall be too late.

" I have said, gentlemen, that I am this man's wife. He was fifty and I a foolish girl of twenty when we married. It was in a city of Russia, a University—I will not name the place."

" God bless you, Anna ! " murmured the old man again.

" We were reformers—revolutionists—Nihilists, you understand. He and I and many more. Then there came a time of trouble, a police officer was killed, many **17** were arrested, evidence was wanted, and in order to save his own life and to earn a great reward my husband betrayed his own wife and his companions. Yes ; we were all arrested upon his confession. Some of us found our way to the gallows and some to Siberia. I was among these last but my term was not for life. My husband came to England with his ill-gotten gains, and has lived in quiet ever since, knowing well that if the Brotherhood knew where he was not a week would pass before justice would be done."

The old man reached out a trembling hand and helped himself to a cigarette. " I am in your hands, Anna," said he. " You were always good to me."

" I have not yet told you the height of his villainy ! " said she. " Among our comrades of the Order there was one who was the friend of my heart. He was noble, unselfish, loving—all that my husband was not. He hated violence. We were all guilty—if that is guilt—but he was not. He wrote for ever dissuading me from such a course. These letters would have saved him. So would my diary, in which from day to day I had entered both my feelings towards him and the view which each of us had taken. My husband found and kept both diary and letters. He hid them, and he tried hard to swear away the young man's life. In this he failed, but Alexis was sent a convict to Siberia, where now, at this moment, he works in a salt mine. Think of that, you villain, you villain ; now, now, at this very moment, Alexis, a man whose name you are not worthy to speak, works and lives like a slave, and yet I have your life in my hands and I let you go ! "

" You were always a noble woman, Anna," said the old man, puffing at his cigarette.

She had risen, but she fell back again with a little cry of pain.

" I must finish," she said. " When my term was over I set myself to get the diary and letters, which if sent to the Russian Government, would procure my friend's release. I knew that my husband had come to England. After months of searching I discovered where he was. I knew that he still had the diary, for when I was in Siberia I had a letter from him once reproaching me and quoting some passages from its pages. Yet I was sure that with his revengeful nature he would never give it to me of his own free will. I must get it for myself. With this object I engaged an agent from a private detective firm, who entered my husband's house as secretary—it was your second secretary, Sergius, the one who left you so hurriedly. He found that papers were kept in the cupboard, and he got an impression of

17 *Then there came a time of trouble.* See Job 38:23; Psalms 9:9, 27:5; Jeremiah 2:27. "Strange phrasing for a Russian revolutionist," Professor Crocker wrote, "but perhaps she had a Christian upbringing!"

"I AM IN YOUR HANDS, ANNA," SAID HE.

Illustration by Sidney Paget for the *Strand Magazine*, July, 1904.

the key. He would not go farther. He furnished me with a plan of the house, and he told me that in the forenoon the study was always empty, as the secretary was employed up here. So at last I took my courage in both hands and I came down to get the papers for myself. I succeeded, but at what a cost!

" I had just taken the papers and was locking the cupboard when the young man seized me. I had seen him already that morning. He had met me in the road, and I had asked him to tell me where Professor Coram lived, not knowing that he was in his employ."

" Exactly! exactly!" said Holmes. " The secretary came back and told his employer of the woman he had met. Then in his last breath he tried to send a message that it was she—the she whom he had just discussed with him."

" You must let me speak," said the woman, in an imperative voice, and her face contracted as if in pain. " When he had fallen I rushed from the room, chose the wrong door, and found myself in my husband's room. He spake of giving me up. I showed him that if he did so his life was in my hands. If he gave me to the law I could give him to the Brotherhood. It was not that I wished to live for my own sake, but it was that I desired to accomplish my purpose. He knew that I would do what I said—that his own fate was involved in mine. For that reason, and for no other, he shielded me. He thrust me into that dark hiding-place, a relic of old days, known only to himself. He took his meals in his own room, and so was able to give me part of his food. It was agreed that when the police left the house I should slip away by night and come back no more. But in some way you have read our plans." She tore from the bosom of her dress a small packet. " These are my last words," said she; " here is the packet which will save Alexis. I confide it to your honour and to your love of justice. Take it! You will deliver it at the Russian Embassy. Now I have done my duty, and——"

" Stop her!" cried Holmes. He had bounded across the room and had wrenched a small phial from her hand.

" Too late!" she said, sinking back on the bed. " Too **18** late! I took the poison before I left my hiding-place. My head swims! I am going! I charge you, sir, to remember the packet."

" A simple case, and yet in some ways an instructive one," Holmes remarked as we travelled back to town. " It hinged from the outset upon the pince-nez. But for the fortunate chance of the dying man having seized these I am not sure that we could ever have reached our solution. It was clear to me from the strength of the glasses that the wearer must have been very blind and helpless when deprived of them. When you asked me to believe that she walked along a narrow strip of grass without once making a false step I remarked, as you may remember, that it was a noteworthy performance. In my mind, I set it down as an impossible performance, save in the unlikely case that she had a second pair of glasses. I was forced, therefore, to seriously consider the hypothesis that she

HE HAD BOUNDED ACROSS THE ROOM AND HAD WRENCHED A SMALL PHIAL FROM HER HAND.

Illustration by Sidney Paget for the *Strand Magazine*, July, 1904.

18 *I took the poison.* "Tr. Aconite is believed to be the suicide weapon of Anna Coram," Dr. J. W. Sovine wrote in "The Toxicanon." "She swallowed the poison from a small phial, which suggests a potent liquid. She lived about fifteen minutes . . . and was conscious and able to talk correctly until nearly the end, which rules out hypnotics, opium derivatives and corrosive poisons. The poison was too slow for cyanide."

had remained within the house. On perceiving the similarity of the two corridors, it became clear that she might very easily have made such a mistake, and in that case it was evident that she must have entered the professor's room. I was keenly on the alert, therefore, for whatever would bear out this supposition, and I examined the room narrowly for anything in the shape of a hiding-place. The carpet seemed continuous and firmly nailed, so I dismissed the idea of a trap-door. There might well be a recess behind the books. As you are aware, such devices are common in old libraries. I observed that books were piled on the floor at all other points, but that one bookcase was left clear. This, then, might be the door. I could see no marks to guide me, but the carpet was of a dun colour, which lends itself very well to examination. I therefore smoked a great number of those excellent cigarettes, and I dropped the ash all over the space in front of the suspected bookcase. It was a simple trick, but exceedingly effective. I then went downstairs, and I ascertained in your presence, Watson, without your quite perceiving the drift of my remarks, that Professor Coram's consumption of food had increased— as one would expect when he is supplying a second person. We then ascended to the room again, when, by upsetting the cigarette-box, I obtained a very excellent view of the floor, and was able to see quite clearly, from the traces upon the cigarette ash, that the prisoner had, in our absence, come out from her retreat. Well, Hopkins, here we are at Charing Cross, and I congratulate you on having brought your case to a successful conclusion. You are going to headquarters, no doubt. I think, Watson, you and I will drive together to the Russian Embassy."

Bibliographical Note: Inscribed "Sherlock Holmes original manuscript from Arthur Conan Doyle to H. Greenhough Smith, a souvenir of 20 years of collaboration. Feb. 8/16," the original manuscript of this story, in 53 pages, 4to, is believed to be the only presentation by the author of one of his manuscript-writings. The manuscript was auctioned in London on March 26, 1934, bringing £120. Its present location is unknown.

51

THE ADVENTURE OF THE THREE STUDENTS

[Friday, April 5, to Saturday, April 6, 1895]

1 *one of our great University towns*. Oxford or Cambridge? The debate has been a prolonged one, and we shall try here to give the case for and against each university as fairly as we can. We may note, to begin with, that Watson's use of the word *town* speaks for Cambridge: Oxford in 1895 was a city, Cambridge still a town.

2 *some laborious researches in Early English charters*. "It is significant of [Holmes] and the quality of his historical knowledge and interest that [he] chose for his most original and serious work this very field of history which Charles Gross said was at the time 'so sadly neglected in England' (*Sources and Literature of English History, from the earliest times to about 1485*, London, 1900, p. 28)," Mr. Whitfield J. Bell, Jr., wrote in "Holmes and History."

And Mr. T. S. Blakeney has noted ("The Location of 'The Three Students'") that Holmes' study shows that he could read court hand, the Gothic or Saxon writing used in English public records. ". . . I submit," Mr. Blakeney continued, "that the probabilities are almost overwhelming that it would be to Oxford, not to Cambridge, that a student in 1895 would most naturally gravitate for the study of Early English charters. Bishop Stubbs had, as Regius Professor of History, established the Oxford historical school as predominant in England at that time. And Stubbs had given a particular impetus to medieval history studies, and had himself, in 1870, issued his 'Select Charters and other Illustrations of English Constitutional History from the Earliest Times to the Reign of Edward I.' Furthermore, in 1878, Mr. W. H. Turner had published his 'Calendar of Charters and Rolls' in the Bodleian Library, just the sort of volume that an amateur historian, as Holmes was, would find invaluable. Against this solidly enthroned tradition of the Oxford Medieval History School, what had Cambridge to offer? The Historical Tripos there was only established in 1875 (the Law and History Tripos had begun in 1870) and in Dr. G. P. Gooch's view (*Studies in Modern History*, p. 314) Seeley was the first scholar of the

IT was in the year '95 that a combination of events, into which I need not enter, caused Mr. Sherlock Holmes and myself to spend some weeks in one of **1** our great University towns, and it was during this time that the small but instructive adventure which I am about to relate befell us. It will be obvious that any details which would help the reader to exactly identify the college or the criminal would be injudicious and offensive. So painful a scandal may well be allowed to die out. With due discretion the incident itself may, however, be described, since it serves to illustrate some of those qualities for which my friend was remarkable. I will endeavour in my statement to avoid such terms as would serve to limit the events to any particular place, or give a clue as to the people concerned.

We were residing at the time in furnished lodgings close to a library where Sherlock Holmes was pursuing some **2** laborious researches in Early English charters—researches which led to results so striking that they may be the subject of one of my future narratives. Here it was that one evening we received a visit from an acquaintance, Mr. Hilton Soames, tutor and lecturer at the College of St. Luke's. Mr. Soames was a tall, spare man, of a nervous and excitable temperament. I had always known him to be restless in his manner, but on this particular occasion he was in such a state of uncontrollable agitation that it was clear something very unusual had occurred.

" I trust, Mr. Holmes, that you can spare me a few hours of your valuable time. We have had a very painful incident at St. Luke's, and really, but for the happy chance of your being in the town, I should have been at a loss what to do."

" I am very busy just now, and I desire no distractions,' my friend answered. " I should much prefer that you called in the aid of the police."

" No, no, my dear sir ; such a course is utterly impossible. When once the law is evoked it cannot be stayed again, and this is just one of those cases where, for the credit of the college, it is most essential to avoid scandal. Your discretion is as well known as your powers, and you

"I TRUST, MR. HOLMES, THAT YOU CAN SPARE ME A
FEW HOURS OF YOUR VALUABLE TIME."

Illustration by Frederic Dorr Steele for *Collier's
Magazine*, September 24, 1904.

are the one man in the world who can help me. I beg
you, Mr. Holmes, to do what you can."

My friend's temper had not improved since he had been
deprived of the congenial surroundings of Baker Street.
Without his scrap-books, his chemicals, and his homely
untidiness, he was an uncomfortable man. He shrugged
his shoulders in ungracious acquiescence, while our **3**
visitor in hurried words and with much excitable gesticu-
lation poured forth his story.

" I must explain to you, Mr. Holmes, that to-morrow is
the first day of the examination for the Fortescue Scholarship. I am one of the examiners. My subject is Greek,
and the first of the papers consists of a large passage of
Greek translation which the candidate has not seen.
This passage is printed on the examination paper, and it
would naturally be an immense advantage if the candidate
could prepare it in advance. For this reason great care
is taken to keep the paper secret.

" To-day about three o'clock the proofs of this paper
arrived from the printers. The exercise consists of half
a chapter of Thucydides. I had to read it over carefully, **4**
as the text must be absolutely correct. At four-thirty my
task was not yet completed. I had, however, promised
to take tea in a friend's rooms, so I left the proof upon my
desk. I was absent rather more than an hour. You are
aware, Mr. Holmes, that our college doors are double—a
green baize one within and a heavy oak one without. As **5**
I approached my outer door I was amazed to see a key in
it. For an instant I imagined that I had left my own
there, but on feeling in my pocket I found that it was all
right. The only duplicate which existed, so far as I
knew, was that which belonged to my servant, Bannister, **6**
a man who has looked after my room for ten years, and
whose honesty is absolutely above suspicion. I found that
the key was indeed his, that he had entered my room to
know if I wanted tea, and that he had very carelessly left
the key in the door when he came out. His visit to my
room must have been within a very few minutes of my

front rank to hold the Cambridge Chair of History. He was Regius Professor from 1869–95; but
it seems fair to say that medieval history was somewhat in abeyance during this period, as compared
with Oxford, and Maitland only made his great
influence felt from the 1890s onwards. There was
nothing comparable to Turner's 'Calendar,' nor
was the University Library at Cambridge so well
endowed with early charters as was the Bodleian.
If it be objected that Holmes might have studied
in a Cambridge College library, and not at the
University library, one must point out that the
late Dr. M. R. James only began to publish his
volumes of Catalogues of Western MSS in Cambridge college libraries in 1895—too late to be of
service to Holmes. even had they contained the
sort of material he needed. And that Holmes would
have required all such aids as could be given him
may be regarded as certain. . . . His real intellectual gifts were scientific rather than historical, and
Miss Dorothy Sayers (*Unpopular Opinions*, pp.
142, 899) has made out a good case for his having,
when at the University himself, taken the Natural
Sciences Tripos rather than any other. Medieval
history studies would be a learned hobby of his
and he would stand in need of any help that
scholars might have prepared to guide the inexpert
student. Beyond question, Oxford in the year 1895
would have been the most probable centre at which
to study early charters . . ."

The late Christopher Morley was in complete
agreement with Mr. Blakeney. In *Sherlock Holmes
and Dr. Watson: A Textbook of Friendship*, he
wrote: ". . . Holmes is (1895) visiting one of the
Universities to do research in Early English charters. My own theory is that he was at Oxford consulting the excellent Stubbs, Bishop of Oxford and
Regius Professor of History, who was in that year
preparing his 8th edition of the *Select Charters*, a
classic among historical students. Holmes' special
interest may have been the 10th section of the
famous Dialogue de Scaccario or Dialogue on the
Exchequer (c. 1200). This section deals with murder which it defines thus: *Murdrum proprie dicitur
mors alicujus occulta, cujus interfector ignoratur.*
(Murder, properly so-called, is the secret death
of anyone whose slayer is not known.) This is not
the same as the modern definition of murder, which
distinguishes it from manslaughter and homicide
by the element of 'malice aforethought.' "

On the other hand, Dr. W. S. Bristowe writes
("Oxford or Cambridge?") that Mr. Blakeney "is
entirely fair, as always, in his erudite review of
charters at each University, but the story he un-
folds is of a later development of historical research at Cambridge and of a growing recognition
of their neglected wealth of old documents. Indeed
at the very time of Holmes' visit to Cambridge in
1895, Mr. Blakeney tells us that the late Dr. M. R.
James was starting to publish his volumes of Catalogues of Western MSS in Cambridge college
libraries. This surely would be the very moment
when a man interested in research in the same field
would be eager to meet Dr. James and to examine
documents freshly coming to light."

To this the late A. Carson Simpson added: "I had always assumed that it was at Oxford that the Master pursued his study of Early English charters . . . perhaps because of the trail-blazing work in that field done by Canon Stubbs. While this volume (F. E. Harmer, *Anglo-Saxon Writs;* Manchester University Press, 1952) is on writs, rather than on charters, it is significant, that a large proportion of the material came from various libraries in Cambridge. The distinction between writs and charters has only been recognized quite recently, and it may be that the 'striking results' of Holmes' researches, to which Watson makes reference, were the beginning of the recognition of this distinction."

3 *He shrugged his shoulders in ungracious acquiescence.* "Scarcely had ["The Adventure of the Three Students"] appeared in the June number of the *Strand Magazine* of 1904," Mr. Roger Lancelyn Green wrote in "Dr. Watson's First Critic," "when Andrew Lang . . . subjected it to careful analysis in his monthly *causerie* 'At the Sign of the Ship' in *Longman's Magazine* (July, 1904), and put forward an interesting theory. . . . Lang's contention was that Holmes and Watson were, in this case, made victims of an elaborate hoax prepared, and brilliantly acted, by Mr. Hilton Soames the tutor, with the aid and connivance of Gilchrist, if not of Bannister the gyp. Playing on Holmes' complete ignorance of Greek literature, Soames of St. Luke's came to [Holmes] with a cock-and-bull story, which would not have taken in a Fifth Form boy.' "

Holmes was indeed the victim of an elaborate hoax, but Watson was not, in the view of Mr. Vernon Rendall (*The London Nights of Belsize*). As Mr. T. S. Blakeney wrote in *Sherlock Holmes: Fact or Fiction?*, Rendall "boldly claims that Watson deliberately hoodwinked Holmes . . . with the aid of Soames, Gilchrist and Bannister. Holmes, it is suggested, was worried over his charters, and to prevent his finding solace in drugs, Watson arranged a spoof job for him to investigate. . . . Mr. [S. C.] Roberts has characterized the theory of a put-up job as 'interesting, though not wholly convincing' ('A Note on the Watson Problem'). To Father Ronald Knox the solecisms in this adventure are one of three lines of evidence that the stories in the collection known as *The Return of Sherlock Holmes* are 'lucubrations of his [Watson's] own unaided invention' (*Essays in Satire*). . . . Upon the general theory of a spoof job, we may observe that Watson and his confederates would need to have been consummate actors to humbug Holmes. We have no special reason to think Watson was a good deceiver: on the contrary, Holmes told him that his features were very expressive ["The Cardboard Box"], and his strongly individual characteristics more than once betrayed him [*The Hound of the Baskervilles* (Watson's cigarette); "The Crooked Man" (habit of carrying his handkerchief in his sleeve); "The Disap-

leaving it. His forgetfulness about the key would have mattered little upon any other occasion, but on this one day it has produced the most deplorable consequences.

"The moment I looked at my table I was aware that some one had rummaged among my papers. The proof **7** was in three long slips. I had left them all together. Now I found that one of them was lying on the floor, one was on the side-table near the window, and the third was where I had left it."

Holmes stirred for the first time.

"The first page on the floor, the second in the window, and the third where you left it," said he.

"Exactly, Mr. Holmes. You amaze me. How could you possibly know that?"

"Pray continue your very interesting statement."

"For an instant I imagined that Bannister had taken the unpardonable liberty of examining my papers. He denied it, however, with the utmost earnestness, and I am convinced that he was speaking the truth. The alternative was that someone passing had observed the key in the door, had known that I was out, and had entered to look at the papers. A large sum of money is at stake, for the scholarship is a very valuable one, and an unscrupulous man might very well run a risk in order to gain advantage over his fellows.

"Bannister was very much upset by the incident. He had nearly fainted when we found that the papers had undoubtedly been tampered with. I gave him a little brandy and left him collapsed in a chair while I made a most careful examination of the room. I soon saw that the intruder had left other traces of his presence besides the rumpled papers. On the table in the window were

"HOW COULD YOU POSSIBLY KNOW THAT?"

Illustration by Sidney Paget for the *Strand Magazine*, June, 1904.

several shreds from a pencil which had been sharpened. A broken tip of lead was lying there also. Evidently the rascal had copied the paper in a great hurry, had broken **8** his pencil, and had been compelled to put a fresh point to it."

" Excellent ! " said Holmes, who was recovering his good humour as his attention became more engrossed by the case. " Fortune has been your friend."

" This was not all. I have a new writing-table with a fine surface of red leather. I am prepared to swear, and so is Bannister, that it was smooth and unstained. Now I found a clean cut in it about three inches long—not a mere scratch, but a positive cut. Not only this, but on the table I found a small ball of black dough, or clay, with specks of something which looks like sawdust in it. I am convinced that these marks were left by the man who rifled the papers. There were no footmarks and no other evidence as to his identity. I was at my wits' end, when suddenly the happy thought occurred to me that you were in the town, and I came straight round to put the matter into your hands. Do help me, Mr. Holmes ! You see my dilemma. Either I must find the man, or else the examination must be postponed until fresh papers are prepared, and since this cannot be done without explanation, there will ensue a hideous scandal, which will throw a cloud not only on the college but on the University. Above all things, I desire to settle the matter quietly and discreetly." **9**

" I shall be happy to look into it and to give you such advice as I can," said Holmes, rising and putting on his overcoat. " This case is not entirely devoid of interest. Had anyone visited you in your room after the papers came to you ? "

" Yes ; young Daulat Ras, an Indian student who lives on the same stair, came in to ask me some particulars about the examination."

" For which he was entered ? "

" Yes."

" And the papers were on your table ? "

" To the best of my belief they were rolled up."

" But might be recognized as proofs ? "

" Possibly."

" No one else in your room ? "

" No."

" Did anyone know that these proofs would be there ? "

" No one save the printer . "

" Did this man Bannister know ? "

" No, certainly not. No one knew."

" Where is Bannister now ? "

" He was very ill, poor fellow ! I left him collapsed in the chair. I was in such a hurry to come to you."

" You left your door open ? "

" I locked the papers up first."

" Then it amounts to this, Mr. Soames, that unless the Indian student recognized the roll as being proofs, the man who tampered with them came upon them accidentally without knowing that they were there."

" So it seems to me."

Holmes gave an enigmatic smile.

pearance of Lady Frances Carfax" (method of tying his bootlaces)]. Again, although Watson was not averse to 'taking a rise' out of Holmes if he had the chance [*The Valley of Fear*], his straightforward character and complete honesty do not fit him for any high degree of deception. Moreover, the need of such deception is not established; so far, indeed, from Holmes appearing to be worried over his charters, we are told he reached some striking results—evidence of success than otherwise."

4 *half a chapter of Thucydides.* One of the greatest of ancient historians, c. 460–400 B.C. His one work is his history of the Peloponnesian War to 411 B.C.

But "every man who went in [for the Fortescue Scholarship] (they were not schoolboys but senior men) had read the whole of Thucydides," Andrew Lang complained in his July, 1904, article in *Longman's Magazine*. To set Thucydides for an "unseen," Lang continued, "would be the act of an idiot."

"As the description indicates, an 'unseen' is a passage with which it should be reasonably certain that no candidate will be familiar," Lord Donegall added in "Lunatic Banker's Royal Client—Dr. Watson Tries Semi-Fiction." "But any candidate for the Fortescue Scholarship would know his Thucydides as well as an Honours Student in English Literature knows his *Hamlet*."

5 *a green baize one within and a heavy oak one without."* Dr. W. S. Bristowe has pointed out that "This system of doors is common to both [Oxford and Cambridge]. Furthermore, Watson remarked . . . that 'we received a visit from an acquaintance,' so it is not unlikely that they had both been to [Soames'] rooms during their stay of 'some weeks.' "

6 *my servant, Bannister.* If the University is Oxford, Bannister would be known as "the scout"; if Cambridge, as "the gyp."

7 *The proof was in three long slips.* But no "half a chapter" of Thucydides would take up three long "slips"—galley proofs. No whole chapter, even, is as long as that.

8 *Evidently the rascal had copied the paper in a great hurry.* "There had never been any need to copy the portion of Thucydides set for the examination," Mr. Richard S. Schwartz wrote in "Three Students in Search of a Scholar." "All serious editions of Thucydides have an index of proper names, and only a glance at the set piece is necessary to note the odd names in it. A glance at the index, in turn, and a check through the text, and the passage is located. The sense of the first and last sentence completes the location. Nothing could be more useless than copying the entire passage, since the text was either owned by the student or available in the college library. I have checked on the most important editions of Thucydides published in the nineteenth century before the year '95. All but one, a cheap German edition, had such an index. Even if this was the one owned by [the copier], he would have had easy access to one with an index."

9 *Above all things, I desire to settle the matter quietly and discreetly."* ". . . at Cambridge," Mr. N. P. Metcalfe wrote in "Oxford or Cambridge or Both?", "there are always duplicate papers for each examination which are only printed the night before, and Oxford would surely have a similar scheme; so it is difficult to understand why Soames did not quietly 'make the switch," after notifying his fellow examiners of the occurrence."

10 *It was already twilight.* It was "at four-thirty" that Hilton Soames says he "left the proof upon his desk" and "was absent for more than an hour." Thus he returned to his room after 5:30. He found a key in his door and the examination papers tampered with; he called and questioned Bannister, gave him brandy, and "made a most careful examination of the room." He then "came straight around to put the matter" into Holmes' hands, and "poured forth his story." All of this—especially the "most careful examination" of Soames' room—took time; he can hardly have concluded his story much before 6:30, after which Holmes and Watson went directly to St. Luke's, evidently a short walk from their lodgings. We conclude that twilight on that day must have fallen close to 6:40 P.M.; it can hardly have been much later, for Holmes said, "It is nearly nine" at the close of an investigation that included a careful examination of Soames' room, interviews with Bannister, Gilchrist and Daulat Ras, an attempt to visit McClaren, and calls on four stationers. The term, as we shall see, was the Lent term. This ended at Oxford on April 6th, at Cambridge on March 27th in the year 1895. March 27th is too early in the year for twilight at approximately 6:40 P.M., and therefore indicates to your editor that the University of "The Three Students" was *Oxford*, not Cambridge. Twilight close to 6:40 P.M. indicates the latest possible date in Oxford's Lent term. In addition, it is our opinion that the Fortescue examination would most probably be given on the closing day of the term —*Saturday, April 6, 1895.* We conclude that the case ended on that day and began on the preceding day, *Friday, April 5th*, a day on which the sun set (and twilight began) at 6:37 P.M.

. . . WITH HIS NECK CRANED, HE LOOKED INTO THE ROOM.

Illustration by Sidney Paget for the *Strand Magazine*, June, 1904.

"Well," said he, " let us go round. Not one of your cases, Watson—mental, not physical. All right ; come if you want to. Now, Mr. Soames—at your disposal ! "

The sitting-room of our client opened by a long, low, latticed window on to the ancient lichen-tinted court of the old college. A Gothic arched door led to a worn stone staircase. On the ground floor was the tutor's room. Above were three students, one on each story. **10** It was already twilight when we reached the scene of our problem. Holmes halted and looked earnestly at the window. Then he approached it, and, standing on tiptoe, with his neck craned, he looked into the room. " He must have entered through the door. There is no opening except the one pane," said our learned guide.

" Dear me ! " said Holmes, and he smiled in a singular way as he glanced at our companion. " Well, if there is nothing to be learned here we had best go inside."

The lecturer unlocked the outer door and ushered us into his room. We stood at the entrance while Holmes made an examination of the carpet.

" I am afraid there are no signs here," said he. " One could hardly hope for any upon so dry a day. Your servant seems to have quite recovered. You left him in a chair, you say ; which chair ? "

" By the window there."

" I see. Near this little table. You can come in now. I have finished with the carpet. Let us take the little table first. Of course, what has happened is very clear. The man entered and took the papers, sheet by sheet, from the central table. He carried them over to the window table, because from there he could see if you came across the courtyard, and so could effect an escape."

" As a matter of fact, he could not," said Soames, " for I entered by the side-door."

" Ah, that's good ! Well, anyhow, that was in his mind. Let me see the three strips. No finger impressions—no ! Well, he carried over this one first and he copied it. How long would it take him to do that, using every possible contraction ? A quarter of an hour, not less. Then he tossed it down and seized the next. He was in the midst of that when your return caused him to make a very hurried retreat—*very* hurried, since he had not time to replace the papers which would tell you that he had been there. You were not aware of any hurrying feet on the stair as you entered the outer door ? "

" No, I can't say I was."

" Well, he wrote so furiously that he broke his pencil, and had, as you observe, to sharpen it again. This is of interest, Watson. The pencil was not an ordinary one. It was about the usual size with a soft lead ; the outer colour was dark blue, the maker's name was printed in silver lettering, and the piece remaining is only about an inch and a half long. Look for such a pencil, Mr. Soames, and you have got your man. When I add that he possesses a large and very blunt knife, you have an additional aid."

Mr. Soames was somewhat overwhelmed by this flood of information. " I can follow the other points," said he, " but really in this matter of the length——"

Holmes held out a small chip with the letters NN and a space of clear wood after them.

" You see ? "

' No, I fear that even now——"

" Watson, I have always done you an injustice. There are others. What could this NN be ? It is at the end of a word. You are aware that Johann Faber is the most **11** common maker's name. Is it not clear that there is just as much of the pencil left as usually follows the Johann ? " He held the small table sideways to the electric light. " I **12** was hoping that if the paper on which he wrote was thin some trace of it might come through upon this polished surface. No, I see nothing. I don't think there is anything more to be learned here. Now for the central table. This small pellet is, I presume, the black doughy mass you spoke of. Roughly pyramidal in shape and hollowed out, I perceive. As you say, there appear to be grains of sawdust in it. Dear me, this is very interesting. And the cut—a positive tear, I see. It began with a thin scratch and ended in a jagged hole. I am much indebted to you for directing my attention to this case, Mr. Soames. Where does that door lead to ? "

" To my bedroom."

" Have you been in it since your adventure ? "

" No ; I came straight away for you."

" I should like to have a glance round. What a charming, old-fashioned room ! Perhaps you will kindly wait a minute until I have examined the floor. No, I see nothing. What about this curtain ? You hang your clothes behind it. If anyone were forced to conceal himself in this room he must do it there, since the bed is too low and the wardrobe too shallow. No one there, I suppose ? "

As Holmes drew the curtain I was aware, from some little rigidity and alertness of his attitude, that he was

11 *Johann Faber.* Johann Lothar von Faber, of Germany, 1817–1896.

12 *to the electric light.* The reader may wonder if colleges at Oxford (or Cambridge) were equipped with electric light in 1895. The answer is that most Oxford colleges were so equipped and so were at least some of the Cambridge colleges. Dr. Bristowe, who plumps for Cambridge as the University of "The Three Students," rather hoped that he might identify "St. Luke's" as Cambridge's St. John's— "the only college in Cambridge bearing the name of an apostle and to alter the name to that of another apostle represented a fairly obvious mental process when a change in name was under consideration by Watson." "But," he continued, "the insurmountable difficulty then arose that electric light was confined to the Hall, Chapel and lamps in First Court in 1895 and was not installed in rooms until 1911." Dr. Bristowe was nonetheless capable of throwing out a subtle hint about "St. Luke's" if that college were indeed at Cambridge: "Rooms in Caius had electric light by 1895 and it was to Caius that Watson's close friend, Mr. Conan Doyle, sent his sons through Watson's introduction, perhaps, to Hilton Soames." Those who hold that the University of "The Three Students" was Oxford will side with Mr. Metcalfe, who wrote that "St. Luke's" was perhaps "the most 'medical' of the Oxford colleges, for St. Paul (Colossians, 4.14) speaks of St. Luke as 'the beloved physician.' "

". . . THE THREE MEN WHO INHABIT THESE ROOMS."

Illustration by Frederic Dorr Steele for *Collier's Magazine*, September 24, 1904.

13 *got his Blue for the hurdles and the long jump.* At both Oxford and Cambridge, anyone who represented the University at sport was commonly referred to—but quite incorrectly—as a "Blue." There was no true Blue for the long jump at Cambridge in 1895, but at Oxford there was: he was the late Captain C. B. Fry who represented Oxford in this event throughout the period 1892 to 1895. If we can rely on Watson's data, Gilchrist must therefore have been either C. B. Fry's second string at Oxford or else his opponent from Cambridge. ". . . C. B. Fry's second string, W. J. Oaklet, was a Blue for both [the hurdles and the long jump] in 1895 and in fact got his Blue for them in 1894," Dr. Bristowe wrote. There seems little doubt that Gilchrist at this time (April 5th) would be training for the Amateur Athletic Championships and other important athletic events which took place in the summer.

prepared for an emergency. As a matter of fact the drawn curtain disclosed nothing but three or four suits of clothes hanging from a line of pegs. Holmes turned away, and stooped suddenly to the floor.

"Halloa ! What's this ? " said he.

It was a small pyramid of black, putty-like stuff, exactly like the one upon the table of the study. Holmes held it out on his open palm in the glare of the electric light.

" Your visitor seems to have left traces in your bedroom as well as in your sitting-room, Mr. Soames."

" What could he have wanted there ? "

" I think it is clear enough. You came back by an unexpected way, and so he had no warning until you were at the very door. What could he do ? He caught up everything which would betray him, and he rushed into your bedroom to conceal himself."

" Good gracious, Mr. Holmes, do you mean to tell me that all the time I was talking to Bannister in this room we had the man prisoner if we had only known it ? "

" So I read it."

" Surely there is another alternative, Mr. Holmes ? I don't know whether you observed my bedroom window."

" Lattice-paned, lead framework, three separate windows, one swinging on hinge and large enough to admit a man."

" Exactly. And it looks out on an angle of the courtyard so as to be partly invisible. The man might have effected his entrance there, left traces as he passed through the bedroom, and, finally, finding the door open, have escaped that way."

Holmes shook his head impatiently.

" Let us be practical," said he. " I understand you to say that there are three students who use this stair and are in the habit of passing your door ? "

" Yes, there are."

" And they are all in for this examination ? "

" Yes."

" Have you any reason to suspect any one of them more than the others ? "

Soames hesitated.

" It is a very delicate question," said he. " One hardly likes to throw suspicion where there are no proofs."

" Let us hear the suspicions. I will look after the proofs."

" I will tell you, then, in a few words, the character of the three men who inhabit these rooms. The lower of the three is Gilchrist, a fine scholar and athlete ; plays in the Rugby team and the cricket team for the college, and got **13** his Blue for the hurdles and the long jump. He is a fine, manly fellow. His father was the notorious Sir Jabez Gilchrist, who ruined himself on the Turf. My scholar has been left very poor, but he is hard-working and industrious. He will do well.

" The second floor is inhabited by Daulat Ras, the Indian. He is a quiet, inscrutable fellow, as most of those Indians are. He is well up in his work, though his Greek is his weak subject. He is steady and methodical.

" The top floor belongs to Miles McLaren. He is a brilliant fellow when he chooses to work—one of the brightest intellects of the University ; but he is wayward, dissipated, and unprincipled. He was nearly expelled over a card scandal in his first year. He has been idling all this term, and he must look forward with dread to the **14** examination."

" Then it is he whom you suspect ? "

" I dare not go so far as that. But of the three he is perhaps the least unlikely."

" Exactly. Now, Mr. Soames, let us have a look at your servant, Bannister."

He was a little, white-faced, clean-shaven, grizzly haired fellow of fifty. He was still suffering from this sudden disturbance of the quiet routine of his life. His plump face was twitching with his nervousness, and his fingers could not keep still.

" We are investigating this unhappy business, Bannister," said his master.

" Yes, sir."

" I understand," said Holmes, " that you left your key in the door ? "

" Yes, sir."

" Was it not very extraordinary that you should do this on the very day when there were these papers inside ? "

" It was most unfortunate, sir. But I have occasionally done the same thing at other times."

" When did you enter the room ? "

" It was about half-past four. That is Mr. Soames' tea-time."

" How long did you stay ? "

" When I saw that he was absent I withdrew at once."

" Did you look at these papers on the table ? "

" No, sir ; certainly not."

" How came you to leave the key in the door ? "

" I had the tea-tray in my hand. I thought I would come back for the key. Then I forgot."

" Has the outer door a spring lock ? "

" No, sir."

" Then it was open all the time ? "

" Yes, sir."

" Any one in the room could get out ? "

" Yes, sir."

" When Mr. Soames returned and called for you, you were very much disturbed ? "

" Yes, sir. Such a thing has never happened during the many years that I have been here. I nearly fainted, sir."

" So I understand. Where were you when you began to feel bad ? "

" Where was I, sir ? Why, here, near the door."

" That is singular, because you sat down in that chair over yonder near the corner. Why did you pass these other chairs ? "

" I don't know, sir. It didn't matter to me where I sat."

" I really don't think he knew much about it, Mr. Holmes. He was looking very bad—quite ghastly."

" You stayed here when your master left ? "

" Only for a minute or so. Then I locked the door and went to my room."

" Whom do you suspect ? "

" Oh, I would not venture to say, sir. I don't believe

14 *He has been idling all this term.* Another indication that "The Adventure of the Three Students" took place at the very end of a term—in our view, the Lent term.

"HOW CAME YOU TO LEAVE THE KEY IN THE DOOR?"

Illustration by Sidney Paget for the *Strand Magazine*, June, 1904.

15 *we will take a walk in the quadrangle.* At Oxford it is a "quadrangle," at Cambridge it is a "court," and it has been said that Holmes' use of the word "quadrangle" here is a powerful argument for Oxford. But both Watson and Soames, in this same adventure, use the word "court" or "courtyard" (Watson also uses "quadrangle"). In fact, Holmes himself also refers to the "quadrangle" as the "courtyard"—thus, as the Reverend Stephen Adams wrote in "Holmes: A Student of London?", "displaying a nice disregard for the better feelings of either University."

THREE YELLOW SQUARES OF LIGHT SHONE ABOVE US IN
THE GATHERING GLOOM.

Illustration by Charles Raymond Macauley for *The Return of Sherlock Holmes*, New York: McClure, Phillips & Co., 1905. Alert students will note that Mr. Macauley has placed two of the students on the same floor, whereas the text tells us that their rooms were on three separate floors, one above another.

. . . HE INSISTED ON DRAWING IT ON HIS NOTEBOOK . . .

Illustration by Sidney Paget for the *Strand Magazine*, June, 1904.

there is any gentleman in this University who is capable of profiting by such an action. No, sir, I'll not believe it."

"Thank you; that will do," said Holmes. "Oh, one more word. You have not mentioned to any of the three gentlemen whom you attend that anything is amiss?"

"No, sir; not a word."

"You haven't seen any of them?"

"No, sir."

"Very good. Now, Mr. Soames, we will take a walk **15** in the quadrangle, if you please."

Three yellow squares of light shone above us in the gathering gloom.

"Your three birds are all in their nests," said Holmes, looking up. "Halloa! What's that? One of them seems restless enough."

It was the Indian, whose dark silhouette appeared suddenly upon the blind. He was pacing swiftly up and down his room.

"I should like to have a peep at each of them," said Holmes. "Is it possible?"

"No difficulty in the world," Soames answered. "This set of rooms is quite the oldest in the college, and it is not unusual for visitors to go over them. Come along, and I will personally conduct you."

"No names, please!" said Holmes, as we knocked at Gilchrist's door. A tall, flaxen-haired, slim young fellow opened it, and made us welcome when he understood our errand. There were some really curious pieces of mediæval domestic architecture within. Holmes was so charmed with one of them that he insisted on drawing it on his notebook, broke his pencil, had to borrow one from our host, and finally borrowed a knife to sharpen his own. The same curious accident happened to him in the rooms of the Indian—a silent little hook-nosed fellow, who eyed us askance and was obviously glad when Holmes' architectural studies had come to an end. I could not see that in either case Holmes had come upon

the clue for which he was searching. Only at the third did our visit prove abortive. The outer door would not open to our knock, and nothing more substantial than a torrent of bad language came from behind it. "I don't care who you are. You can go to blazes!" roared the angry voice. "To-morrow's the exam., and I won't be drawn by anyone."

"A rude fellow," said our guide, flushing with anger as we withdrew down the stair. "Of course, he did not realize that it was I who was knocking, but none the less his conduct was very uncourteous, and, indeed, under the circumstances, rather suspicious."

Holmes' response was a curious one.

"Can you tell me his exact height?" he asked.

"Really, Mr. Holmes, I cannot undertake to say. He is taller than the Indian, not so tall as Gilchrist. I suppose five foot six would be about it."

"That is very important," said Holmes. "And now, Mr. Soames, I wish you good night."

Our guide cried aloud in his astonishment and dismay. "Good gracious, Mr. Holmes, you are surely not going to leave me in this abrupt fashion! You don't seem to realize the position. To-morrow is the examination. I must take some definite action to-night. I cannot allow the examination to be held if one of the papers has been tampered with. The situation must be faced."

"You must leave it as it is. I shall drop round early to-morrow morning and chat the matter over. It is possible that I may be in a position then to indicate some course of action. Meanwhile you change nothing—nothing at all."

"Very good, Mr. Holmes."

"You can be perfectly easy in your mind. We shall certainly find some way out of your difficulties. I will take the black clay with me, also the pencil cuttings. Good-bye."

When we were out in the darkness of the quadrangle we again looked up at the windows. The Indian still paced his room. The others were invisible.

"Well, Watson, what do you think of it?" Holmes asked as we came out into the main street. "Quite a little parlour game—sort of three-card trick, is it not? There are your three men. It must be one of them. You take your choice. Which is yours?"

"The foul-mouthed fellow at the top. He is the one with the worst record. And yet that Indian was a sly fellow also. Why should he be pacing his room all the time?"

"There is nothing in that. Many men do it when they are trying to learn anything by heart."

"He looked at us in a queer way."

"So would you if a flock of strangers came in on you when you were preparing for an examination next day, and every moment was of value. No, I see nothing in that. Pencils, too, and knives—all was satisfactory. But that fellow *does* puzzle me."

"Who?"

"Why, Bannister, the servant. What's his game in the matter?"

16 *There were only four stationers of any consequence in the town.* The late Gavin Brend felt that Holmes' knowledge of all four stationers was an indication that he himself had been a student at the University of "The Three Students." Since we know that Holmes was a student at *both* Oxford and Cambridge, it is of course only natural that he should have known his way about at either University.

17 *the landlady babbled of green peas.* ". . . surely an oblique allusion to Falstaff, who, it will be recalled, 'babbled of green fields' on his deathbed [*Henry V*]," Professor Clarke Olney wrote in "The Literacy of Sherlock Holmes."

There is, moreover, a chronological significance to the statement. In England, green peas are usually a June delicacy. How to reconcile this with a sunset appropriate to April, the need for Holmes to wear an overcoat and Gilchrist to wear gloves in the afternoon? "As for Holmes wearing an overcoat and Gilchrist gloves, we have to take changed fashions into account as well as the risk of April showers or the cold East wind for which Cambridge, at least, is notorious," Dr. Bristowe wrote. "Green peas [in April] are not so easy, but it is clear from their being the only item on the menu to be mentioned that they were a special delicacy and horticulturists tell me that limited quantities grown under glass can be supplied even in March."

18 *three little pyramids of black, doughy clay.* We soon learn that they came from the University jumping pit—another indication, Mr. Brend pointed out, that Holmes was well acquainted with the University of "The Three Students," since he found the jumping pit shortly after "the untimely hour of six"—an hour when there would certainly have been few people about from whom to ask directions.

Dr. Bristowe disagreed: the Iffley Road running track at Oxford, he pointed out, is only a mile from a central point like Carfax "so why did [Holmes] have to walk five miles if he is in his own University town of Oxford? Even allowing for some exaggeration in order to impress Watson, the discrepancy is too great. Fenners' at Cambridge is even closer to the center of town. It is just over three-quarters of a mile from the Market Place (close to the University Library) and it is not easy to find. Surely we are forced to conclude that Holmes got lost . . ."

That, your editor holds, could happen at either Oxford or Cambridge; let us remember that "bar boxing and fencing," neither of which is done in a jumping pit, Holmes in his University days indulged in no sports.

But there is even greater significance to those "three little pyramids of black, doughy clay": they provide the most powerful argument for those who hold that the University of the "Three Students" was Cambridge. The point is perhaps best made by Dr. Bristowe in his illuminating article, "The Three Students in Limelight, Electric Light and Daylight":

" He impressed me as being a perfectly honest man."

" So he did me. That's the puzzling part. Why should a perfectly honest man—well, well, here's a large stationer's. We shall begin our researches here."

16 There were only four stationers of any consequence in the town, and at each Holmes produced his pencil chips and bid high for a duplicate. All were agreed that one could be ordered, but that it was not a usual size of pencil, and that it was seldom kept in stock. My friend did not appear to be depressed by his failure, but shrugged his shoulders in half-humorous resignation.

" No good, my dear Watson. This, the best and only final clue, has run to nothing. But, indeed, I have little doubt that we can build up a sufficient case without it. By Jove ! my dear fellow, it is nearly nine, and the land- **17** lady babbled of green peas at seven-thirty. What with your eternal tobacco, Watson, and your irregularity at meals, I expect that you will get notice to quit, and that I shall share your downfall—not, however, before we have solved the problem of the nervous tutor, the careless servant, and the three enterprising students."

Holmes made no further allusion to the matter that day, though he sat lost in thought for a long time after our belated dinner. At eight in the morning he came into my room just as I finished my toilet.

" Well, Watson," said he, " it is time we went down to St. Luke's. Can you do without breakfast ? "

" Certainly."

" Soames will be in a dreadful fidget until we are able to tell him something positive."

" Have you anything positive to tell him ? "

" I think so."

" You have formed a conclusion ? "

" Yes, my dear Watson ; I have solved the mystery."

" But what fresh evidence could you have got ? "

" Aha ! It is not for nothing that I have turned myself out of bed at the untimely hour of six. I have put in two hours' hard work and covered at least five miles, with something to show for it. Look at that ! "

He held out his hand. On the palm were three little **18** pyramids of black, doughy clay.

" Why, Holmes, you had only two yesterday ! "

" And one more this morning. It is a fair argument, that wherever No. 3 came from is also the source of Nos. 1 and 2. Eh, Watson ? Well, come along and put friend Soames out of his pain."

The unfortunate tutor was certainly in a state of pitiable agitation when we found him in his chambers. In a few hours the examinations would commence and he was still in the dilemma between making the facts public and allowing the culprit to compete for the valuable scholarship. He could hardly stand still, so great was his mental agitation, and he ran towards Holmes with two eager hands outstretched.

" Thank Heaven that you have come ! I feared that you had given it up in despair. What am I to do ? Shall the examination proceed ? "

" Yes ; let it proceed, by all means."

" But this rascal—— ? "

" He shall not compete."

" You know him ? "

" I think so.   If this matter is not to become public we must give ourselves certain powers, and resolve ourselves into a small private court-martial.   You there, if you please, Soames !   Watson, you here !   I'll take the arm-chair in the middle.   I think that we are now sufficiently imposing to strike terror into a guilty breast.   Kindly ring the bell ! "

Bannister entered, and shrank back in evident surprise and fear at our judicial appearance.

" You will kindly close the door," said Holmes. " Now, Bannister, will you please tell us the truth about yesterday's incident ? "

The man turned white to the roots of his hair.

" I have told you everything, sir."

" Nothing to add ? "

" Nothing at all, sir."

" Well, then, I must make some suggestions to you. When you sat down on that chair yesterday, did you do so in order to conceal some object which would have shown who had been in the room ? "

Bannister's face was ghastly.

" No, sir ; certainly not."

" It is only a suggestion," said Holmes suavely.   " I frankly admit that I am unable to prove it.   But it seems probable enough, since the moment that Mr. Soames' back was turned you released the man who was hiding in that bedroom."

Bannister licked his dry lips.

" There was no man, sir."

" Ah, that's a pity, Bannister.   Up to now you may have spoken the truth, but now I know that you have lied."

The man's face set in sullen defiance.

" There was no man, sir."

" Come, come, Bannister."

" No, sir ; there was no one."

" In that case you can give us no further information. Would you please remain in the room ?   Stand over there near the bedroom door.   Now, Soames, I am going to ask you to have the great kindness to go up to the room of young Gilchrist, and to ask him to step down into yours."

An instant later the tutor returned, bringing with him the student.   He was a fine figure of a man, tall, lithe, and agile, with a springy step and a pleasant, open face. His troubled blue eyes glanced at each of us, and finally rested with an expression of blank dismay upon Bannister in the farther corner.

" Just close the door," said Holmes.   " Now, Mr. Gilchrist, we are all quite alone here, and no one need ever know one word of what passes between us.   We can be perfectly frank with each other.   We want to know, Mr. Gilchrist, how you, an honourable man, ever came to commit such an action as that of yesterday ? "

The unfortunate young man staggered back, and cast a look full of horror and reproach at Bannister.

" No, no, Mr. Gilchrist, sir ; I never said a word— never one word ! " cried the servant.

" No, but you have now," said Holmes.   " Now, sir,

"Remembering an article on athletics by C. B. Fry in the *Strand Magazine* in 1902, I found an interesting comment that 'a kind of clay [had been] invented by the groundsman at Fenners' and that this invention had just been imitated in 1902 by the Queen's Club, London, for their long jump pit.   I wrote to Captain Fry and in his reply of 21st December, 1955, he confirmed that throughout his time at Oxford he always had to jump into a soft sandy material. 'I saw no damped semi-clay soil in the Long Jump pit till at Queens in 1903,' he wrote. 'It was introduced there, I fancy, by Mr. Clement Jackson, the Hertford (Oxford) don ex-hurdle A. A. champion after I did the World Records 23 ft. 6½ in. in 1902, because the Americans did not make allowance for breakaway behind the heel mark. I really did 24 ft. 2½ in.' Here, I submit, we have positive proof from this distinguished contemporary of Gilchrist that the mud which led to his detection was invented by the Cambridge groundsman and was unique to Cambridge in 1895."

AN INSTANT LATER THE TUTOR RETURNED . . .

Illustration by Sidney Paget for the *Strand Magazine*, June, 1904.

"The Adventure of the Three Students"

"NO, BUT YOU HAVE NOW," SAID HOLMES.

Cover illustration by Frederic Dorr Steele for *Collier's Magazine*, September 24, 1904.

"COME, COME," SAID HOLMES KINDLY; "IT IS HUMAN
TO ERR . . ."

Illustration by Sidney Paget for the *Strand Magazine*, June, 1904.

you must see that after Bannister's words your position is hopeless, and that your only chance lies in a frank confession."

For a moment Gilchrist, with upraised hand, tried to control his writhing features. The next he had thrown himself on his knees beside the table, and, burying his face in his hands, he burst into a storm of passionate sobbing.

"Come, come," said Holmes kindly; "it is human to err, and at least no one can accuse you of being a callous criminal. Perhaps it would be easier for you if I were to tell Mr. Soames what occurred, and you can check me where I am wrong. Shall I do so? Well, well, don't trouble to answer. Listen, and see that I do you no injustice.

"From the moment, Mr. Soames, that you said to me that no one, not even Bannister, could have told that the papers were in your room, the case began to take a definite shape in my mind. The printer one could, of course, dismiss. He could examine the papers in his own office. The Indian I also thought nothing of. If the proofs were in roll he could not possibly know what they were. On the other hand, it seemed an unthinkable coincidence that a man should dare to enter the room, and that by chance on that very day the papers were on the table. I dismissed that. The man who entered knew that the papers were there. How did he know?

"When I approached your room I examined the window. You amused me by supposing that I was contemplating the possibility of someone having in broad daylight, under the eyes of all these opposite rooms, forced himself through it. Such an idea was absurd. I was measuring how tall a man would need to be in order to see as he passed what papers were on the central table. I am six feet high, and I could do it with an effort. No one less than that would have a chance. Already, you see, I had reason to think that if one of your three students was a man of unusual height he was the most worth watching of the three.

"I entered, and I took you into my confidence as to the suggestions of the side-table. Of the centre table I

could make nothing, until in your description of Gilchrist you mentioned that he was a long-distance jumper. Then the whole thing came to me in an instant, and I only needed certain corroborative proofs, which I speedily obtained.

"What happened was this. This young fellow had employed his afternoon at the athletic grounds, where he had been practising the jump. He returned carrying his jumping-shoes, which are provided, as you are aware, with several spikes. As he passed your window he saw, **19** by means of his great height, these proofs upon your table, and conjectured what they were. No harm would have been done had it not been that as he passed your door he perceived the key which had been left by the carelessness of your servant. A sudden impulse came over him to enter and see if they were indeed the proofs. It was not a dangerous exploit, for he could always pretend that he had simply looked in to ask a question.

"Well, when he saw that they were indeed the proofs, it was then that he yielded to temptation. He put his shoes on the table. What was it you put on that chair near the window?"

"Gloves," said the young man.

Holmes looked triumphantly at Bannister.

"He put his gloves on the chair, and he took the proofs, sheet by sheet, to copy them. He thought the tutor must return by the main gate, and that he would see him. As we know, he came back by the side-gate. Suddenly he heard him at the very door. There was no possible escape. He forgot his gloves, but he caught up his shoes and darted into the bedroom. You observe that the scratch on that table is slight at one side, but deepens in the direction of the bedroom door. That in itself is enough to show us that the shoes had been drawn in that direction, and that the culprit had taken refuge there. The earth round the spike had been left on the table, and a second sample was loosened and fell in the bedroom. I may add that I walked out to the athletic grounds this morning, saw that tenacious black clay is used in the jumping-pit, and carried away a specimen of it, together with some of the fine tan or sawdust which is strewn over it to prevent the athlete from slipping. Have I told the truth, Mr. Gilchrist?"

The student had drawn himself erect.

"Yes, sir, it is true," said he.

"Good heavens, have you nothing to add?" cried Soames.

"Yes, sir, I have, but the shock of this disgraceful exposure has bewildered me. I have a letter here, Mr. Soames, which I wrote to you early this morning in the middle of a restless night. It was before I knew that my sin had found me out. Here it is, sir. You will see that I have said, 'I have determined not to go in for the examination. I have been offered a commission in the Rhodesian Police, and I am going out to South Africa at once.'"

"I am indeed pleased to hear that you did not intend to profit by your unfair advantage," said Soames. "But why did you change your purpose?"

Gilchrist pointed to Bannister.

19 *which are provided, as you are aware, with several spikes.* Did track athletes in 1895 wear spiked shoes? They did, as Dr. Bristowe has shown. In "The Three Students in Limelight, Electric Light and Daylight," he has called attention to a book published in 1887 which advised "spikes of less than half an inch for cinder tracks at the universities but spikes up to three-quarters of an inch for use on grass." Dr. Bristowe also reported that Captain C. B. Fry recalled a detail of singular interest—those who went in for field sports at Oxford in 1895 got their spiked running shoes "from a small cobbler near Dorset Square, *Baker Street*."

"HERE IT IS, SIR."

Illustration by Sidney Paget for the *Strand Magazine*, June, 1904.

20 *Let us see in the future how high you can rise.*" "Since we have had no news of Gilchrist in South Africa," Dr. Bristowe wrote, "it may be worth mentioning that J. L. B. Smith (the discoverer of the coelocanth) writes in his book, *Old Fourlegs* (1956) that the most important collection of South African fishes up to 1930 was made by the late J. D. F. Gilchrist, who was a Professor and a man 'with a great heart and great mind.'"

Bibliographical Note: The original manuscript of "The Adventure of the Three Students," 224 to leaves, white vellum, is owned by the Houghton Library of Harvard University, the gift of Mr. Norton Perkins.

" There is the man who sent me in the right path," said he.

" Come now, Bannister," said Holmes. " It will be clear to you from what I have said that only you could have let this young man out, since you were left in the room and must have locked the door when you went out. As to his escaping by that window, it was incredible. Can you not clear up the last point in this mystery, and tell us the reason for your action ? "

" It was simple enough, sir, if you only had known ; but with all your cleverness it was impossible that you could know. Time was, sir, when I was butler to old Sir Jabez Gilchrist, this young gentleman's father. When he was ruined I come to the college as servant, but I never forgot my old employer because he was down in the world. I watched his son all I could for the sake of the old days. Well, sir, when I came into this room yesterday when the alarm was given, the first thing I saw was Mr. Gilchrist's tan gloves a-lying in that chair. I knew those gloves well, and I understood their message. If Mr. Soames saw them the game was up. I flopped down into that chair, and nothing would budge me until Mr. Soames he went for you. Then out came my poor young master, whom I had dandled on my knee, and confessed it all to me. Wasn't it natural, sir, that I should save him, and wasn't it natural also that I should try to speak to him as his dead father would have done, and make him understand that he could not profit by such a deed ? Could you blame me, sir ? "

" No, indeed ! " said Holmes heartily, springing to his feet. " Well, Soames, I think we have cleared your little problem up, and our breakfast awaits us at home. Come, Watson ! As to you, sir, I trust that a bright future awaits you in Rhodesia. For once you have fallen low. **20** Let us see in the future how high you can rise."

52

THE ADVENTURE OF THE SOLITARY CYCLIST

[Saturday, April 13, to Saturday, April 20, 1895]

FROM the years 1894 to 1901 inclusive, Mr. Sherlock Holmes was a very busy man. It is safe to say that there was no public case of any difficulty in which he was not consulted during those eight years, and there were hundreds of private cases, some of them of the most intricate and extraordinary character, in which he played a prominent part. Many startling successes and a few unavoidable failures were the outcome of this long period of continuous work. As I have preserved very full notes of all these cases, and was myself personally engaged in many of them, it may be imagined that it is no easy task to know which I should select to lay before the public. I shall, however, preserve my former rule, and give the preference to those cases which derive their interest not so much from the brutality of the crime as from the ingenuity and dramatic quality of the solution. For this reason I will now lay before the reader the facts connected with Miss Violet Smith, the solitary cyclist of Charlington, and the curious **1** sequel of our investigation, which culminated in unexpected tragedy. It is true that the circumstances did not permit of any striking illustration of those powers for which my friend was famous, but there were some points about the case which made it stand out in those long records of crime from which I gather the material for these little narratives.

On referring to my notebook for the year 1895, I find that it was upon Saturday, April 23, that we first heard of **2** Miss Violet Smith. Her visit was, I remember, extremely unwelcome to Holmes, for he was immersed at the moment in a very abstruse and complicated problem concerning the peculiar persecution to which John Vincent Harden, the well-known tobacco millionaire, had **3** been subjected. My friend, who loved above all things precision and concentration of thought, resented anything which distracted his attention from the matter in hand. And yet without harshness which was foreign to his nature it was impossible to refuse to listen to the story of the young and beautiful woman, tall, graceful, and queenly, who presented herself at Baker Street late in the evening and implored his assistance and advice.

1 *Charlington.* Near Farnham, in Surrey.

2 *Saturday, April 23.* Something is clearly wrong here, since April 23, 1895, was a *Tuesday*. Is Watson's "Saturday" wrong? Hardly. Miss Violet Smith came to town every Saturday forenoon and returned to Chiltern Grange on Monday; she says on the day of her visit to Holmes: "Again I had to cycle to the station. That was this morning." Is Watson's "April" wrong? Hardly. Miss Smith says her interview with Carruthers and Woodley took place "Last December—four months ago." Watson speaks of "golden patches of flowering gorse," "the bright spring sunshine," "the freshness of the spring," "the budding green of the woods." Is his "23" wrong? If so, the date must be April 6th, 13th, 20, or 27th. Of these, the 13th is certainly the most likely to be mistaken for his "23." Or is his "1895" wrong? If so, the date must be April 23, 1898, for 1898 is the only year from 1894 to 1901, the limits set by Watson, in which the 23rd of April fell on a Saturday. Holmes and Watson journeyed to Chiltern Grange on the Saturday following Miss Smith's visit, and Watson tells us that "A rainy night had been followed by a glorious morning." The possible dates are: 1) Friday, April 12–Saturday, April 13, 1895; 2) Friday, April 19–Saturday, April 20, 1895; 3) Friday, April 26–Saturday, April 27, 1895; 4) Friday, May 3–Saturday, May 4, 1895; 5) Friday, April 29–Saturday, April 30, 1898. Of these, only Friday, April 19–Saturday, April 20, 1895, answer Watson's description. Miss Violet Smith's call on Holmes must therefore have been on *Saturday, April 13, 1895*. This, as we have seen, was the date most likely to have been mistaken by the typesetter as "23."

3 *John Vincent Harden.* Properly, John Vincent *Hardin,* as Mr. William D. Jenkins has shown in his remarkable study, "A Peculiar Persecution." John Vincent Hardin was a cousin of John Wesley Hardin, "probably the most deadly gunman the American West ever produced," whose plan to visit England with the Buffalo Bill Wild West

Show subjected his socially ambitious cousin, the tobacco millionaire, to his peculiar persecution. Mr. Jenkins' essay also provides a new solution for the "Missing Year" late 1895–late 1896, a period during much of which (Mr. Jenkins suggests) Watson was in Texas preparing for publication the manuscript called *The Life of John Wesley Hardin, As Written by Himself* (reissued in 1961 by the University of Oklahoma Press).

4 *Archie Stamford, the forger.* Mr. Jerry Neal Williamson has speculated that he was the "Archie" of "The Red-Headed League" and also the young Stamford who introduced Holmes to Watson ("The Sad Case of Young Stamford").

MY FRIEND TOOK THE LADY'S UNGLOVED HAND . . .

Illustration by Sidney Paget for the *Strand Magazine*, January, 1904.

It was vain to urge that his time was already fully occupied, for the young lady had come with the determination to tell her story, and it was evident that nothing short of force could get her out of the room until she had done so. With a resigned air and a somewhat weary smile, Holmes begged the beautiful intruder to take a seat and to inform us what it was that was troubling her.

" At least it cannot be your health," said he, as his keen eyes darted over her ; " so ardent a bicyclist must be full of energy."

She glanced down in surprise at her own feet, and I observed the slight roughening of the side of the sole caused by the friction of the edge of the pedal.

" Yes, I bicycle a good deal, Mr. Holmes, and that has something to do with my visit to you to-day."

My friend took the lady's ungloved hand and examined it with as close an attention and as little sentiment as a scientist would show to a specimen.

" You will excuse me, I am sure. It is my business," said he, as he dropped it. " I nearly fell into the error of supposing that you were typewriting. Of course, it is obvious that it is music. You observe the spatulate finger-end, Watson, which is common to both professions ? There is a spirituality about the face, however " —he gently turned it towards the light—" which the typewriter does not generate. This lady is a musician."

" Yes, Mr. Holmes, I teach music."

" In the country, I presume, from your complexion."

" Yes, sir ; near Farnham, on the borders of Surrey."

" A beautiful neighbourhood, and full of the most interesting associations. You remember, Watson, that it was **4** near there that we took Archie Stamford, the forger. Now, Miss Violet, what has happened to you near Farnham, on the borders of Surrey ? "

The young lady, with great clearness and composure, made the following curious statement :

". . . NEAR FARNHAM, ON THE BORDERS OF SURREY."

Photograph by Reece Winston, A.P.P.S., of Bristol, from *Surrey*, by Eric Parker; London: Robert Hale, Ltd. Farnham lies to the extreme west of the county of Surrey, almost on the border of Hampshire, on the edge of the New Forest, for which Watson longed in "The Cardboard Box." It is ten miles southwest of Guildford, and but three miles to the south of the famous military center of Aldershot, well known to Holmes and Watson from the adventure of "The Crooked Man."

" My father is dead, Mr. Holmes. He was James Smith, who conducted the orchestra at the old Imperial Theatre. My mother and I were left without a relation **5** in the world except one uncle, Ralph Smith, who went to Africa twenty-five years ago, and we have never had a word from him since. When father died we were left very poor, but one day we were told that there was an advertisement in *The Times* inquiring for our whereabouts. You can imagine how excited we were, for we thought that someone had left us a fortune. We went at once to the lawyer whose name was given in the paper. There we met two gentlemen, Mr. Carruthers and Mr. Woodley, who were home on a visit from South Africa. They said that my uncle was a friend of theirs, that he died some months before in poverty in Johannesburg, and that he had asked them with his last breath to hunt up his relations and see that they were in no want. It seemed strange to us that Uncle Ralph, who took no notice of us when he was alive, should be so careful to look after us when he was dead ; but Mr. Carruthers explained that the reason was that my uncle had just heard of the death of his brother, and so felt responsible for our fate."

" Excuse me," said Holmes ; " when was this interview ? "

" Last December—four months ago."

" Pray proceed."

" Mr. Woodley seemed to me to be a most odious person. He was for ever making eyes at me—a coarse, puffy-faced, red-moustached young man, with his hair plastered down on each side of his forehead. I thought that he was perfectly hateful—and I was sure that Cyril would not wish me to know such a person."

" Oh, Cyril is his name ! " said Holmes, smiling.

The young lady blushed and laughed.

" Yes, Mr. Holmes ; Cyril Morton, an electrical engineer, and we hope to be married at the end of the summer. Dear me, how *did* I get talking about him ? What I wished to say was that Mr. Woodley was perfectly odious, but that Mr. Carruthers, who was a much older man, was more agreeable. He was a dark, sallow, clean-shaven, silent person ; but he had polite manners and a pleasant smile. He inquired how we were left, and on finding that we were very poor he suggested that I should come and teach music to his only daughter, aged ten. I said that I did not like to leave my mother, on which he suggested that I should go home to her every week-end, and he offered me a hundred a year, which was certainly splendid pay. So it ended by my accepting, and I went down to Chiltern Grange, about six miles from Farnham. Mr. Carruthers was a widower, but he had engaged a lady-housekeeper, a very respectable, elderly person, called Mrs. Dixon, to look after his establishment. The child was a dear, and everything promised well. Mr. Carruthers was very kind and very musical, and we had most pleasant evenings together. Every week-end I went home to my mother in town.

" The first flaw in my happiness was the arrival of the red-moustached Mr. Woodley. He came for a visit of a week, and oh, it seemed three months to me ! He was a

5 *the old Imperial Theatre*. Erected in 1875, it once covered (with the adjoining Westminster Aquarium) the site now occupied by the Wesleyan Central Hall on the north side of Tothill Street. The Imperial was leased during its later years to Mrs. Lily Langtry, and this brought it more popularity with the London public than had hitherto been the case.

6 *the 12.22 to town.* There was, unhappily, no such train.

7 *Crooksbury Hill.* ". . . only one district," Mr. Michael Harrison wrote (*In the Footsteps of Sherlock Holmes*) "can meet all [the] requirements of distance, direction, and having 'Crooksbury Hill' between it and Farnham: that is Charleshill, which lies on the north side of the main road from Farnham to Milford, and has its boundaries marked by the bend that the River Wey takes after it has crossed the main road at a point just slightly west of Elstead. 'Crooksbury Hill' may be either Crooksbury Heath, which could be called a hill, or it may be that part of Crooksbury Common known as Monk's Hill. I feel that the latter is more likely."

"I SLOWED DOWN MY MACHINE . . ."

Illustration by Sidney Paget for the *Strand Magazine*, January, 1904.

dreadful person, a bully to everyone else, but to me something infinitely worse. He made odious love to me, boasted of his wealth, said that if I married him I would have the finest diamonds in London, and finally, when I would have nothing to do with him, he seized me in his arms one day after dinner—he was hideously strong— and he swore that he would not let me go until I had kissed him. Mr. Carruthers came in, and tore him off from me, on which he turned upon his own host, knocking him down and cutting his face open. That was the end of his visit, as you can imagine. Mr. Carruthers apologized to me next day, and assured me that I should never be exposed to such an insult again. I have not seen Mr. Woodley since.

" And now, Mr. Holmes, I come at last to the special thing which has caused me to ask your advice to-day. You must know that every Saturday forenoon I ride on my bicycle to Farnham Station in order to get the 12.22 **6** to town. The road from Chiltern Grange is a lonely one, and at one spot it is particularly so, for it lies for over a mile between Charlington Heath upon one side and the woods which lie round Charlington Hall upon the other. You could not find a more lonely tract of road anywhere, and it is quite rare to meet so much as a cart, or a peasant, until you reach the high-road near Crooks- **7** bury Hill. Two weeks ago I was passing this place when I chanced to look back over my shoulder, and about two hundred yards behind me I saw a man, also on a bicycle. He seemed to be a middle-aged man, with a short, dark beard. I looked back before I reached Farnham, but the man was gone, so I thought no more about it. But you can imagine how surprised I was, Mr. Holmes, when on my return on the Monday I saw the same man on the same stretch of road. My astonishment was increased when the incident occurred again, exactly as before, on the following Saturday and Monday. He always kept his distance, and did not molest me in any way, but still it certainly was very odd. I mentioned it to Mr. Carruthers, who seemed interested in what I said, and told me that he had ordered a horse and trap, so that in future I should not pass over these lonely roads without some companion.

" The horse and trap were to have come this week, but for some reason they were not delivered, and again I had to cycle to the station. That was this morning. You can think that I looked out when I came to Charlington Heath, and there, sure enough, was the man, exactly as he had been the two weeks before. He always kept so far from me that I could not clearly see his face, but it was certainly someone whom I did not know. He was dressed in a dark suit with a cloth cap. The only thing about his face that I could clearly see was his dark beard. To-day I was not alarmed, but I was filled with curiosity, and I determined to find out who he was and what he wanted. I slowed down my machine, but he slowed down his. Then I stopped altogether, but he stopped also. Then I laid a trap for him. There is a sharp turning of the road, and I pedalled very quickly round this, and then I stopped and waited. I expected him to shoot round and pass me before he could stop. But he never appeared.   Then I went back and looked round the corner.   I could see a mile of road, but he was not on it. To make it the more extraordinary there was no side-road at this point down which he could have gone."

Holmes chuckled and rubbed his hands.

"This case certainly presents some features of its own," said he.   "How much time elapsed between your turning the corner and your discovery that the road was clear ? "

"Two or three minutes."

"Then he could not have retreated down the road, and you say that there are no side-roads ? "

"None."

"Then he certainly took a footpath on one side or the other."

"It could not have been on the side of the heath or I should have seen him."

"So by the process of exclusion we arrive at the fact that he made his way towards Charlington Hall, which, as I understand, is situated in its own grounds on one side of the road.   Anything else ? "

"Nothing, Mr. Holmes, save that I was so perplexed that I felt I should not be happy until I had seen you and had your advice."

Holmes sat in silence for some little time.

"Where is the gentleman to whom you are engaged ? " he asked at last.

"He is in the Midland Electric Company, at Coventry."

"He would not pay you a surprise visit ? "

"Oh, Mr. Holmes ! As if I should not know him ! "

"Have you had any other admirers ? "

"Several before I knew Cyril."

"And since ? "

"There was this dreadful man, Woodley, if you can call him an admirer."

"No one else ? "

Our fair client seemed a little confused.

"Who was he ? " asked Holmes.

"Oh, it may be a mere fancy of mine ; but it has seemed to me sometimes that my employer, Mr. Carruthers, takes a great deal of interest in me.   We are thrown rather together.   I play his accompaniments in the evening.   He has never said anything.   He is a perfect gentleman.   But a girl always knows."

"Ha ! " Holmes looked grave.   "What does he do for a living ? "

"He is a rich man."

"No carriages or horses ? "

"Well, at least he is fairly well-to-do.   But he goes into the city two or three times a week.   He is deeply interested in South African gold shares."

"You will let me know any fresh development, Miss Smith.   I am very busy just now, but I will find time to make some inquiries into your case.   In the meantime, take no step without letting me know.   Good-bye, and I trust that we shall have nothing but good news from you."

"It is part of the settled order of Nature that such a girl should have followers," said Holmes, as he pulled at his meditative pipe, " but for choice not on bicycles in

"IT IS PART OF THE SETTLED ORDER OF NATURE THAT SUCH A GIRL SHOULD HAVE FOLLOWERS," SAID HOLMES, AS HE PULLED AT HIS MEDITATIVE PIPE . . .

Cover illustration by Frederic Dorr Steele for *Collier's Magazine*, December 26, 1903.

8 ménage. French: the persons taken collectively who occupy one house; a household.

9 *so I started early and caught the 9.13.* There were 9:15 and 9:45 trains, but no trains at 9:13 or 9:50 Waterloo to Farnham.

lonely country roads. Some secretive lover, beyond all doubt. But there are curious and suggestive details about the case, Watson."

" That he should appear only at that point ? "

" Exactly. Our first effort must be to find who are the tenants of Charlington Hall. Then, again, how about the connection between Carruthers and Woodley, since they appear to be men of such different types ? How came they *both* to be so keen upon looking up Ralph Smith's relations ? One more point. What sort of a **8** *ménage* is it which pays double the market price for a governess, but does not keep a horse although six miles from the station ? Odd, Watson—very odd."

" You will go down ? "

" No, my dear fellow, *you* will go down. This may be some trifling intrigue, and I cannot break my other important research for the sake of it. On Monday you will arrive early at Farnham ; you will conceal yourself near Charlington Heath ; you will observe these facts for yourself, and act as your own judgment advises. Then, having inquired as to the occupants of the Hall, you will come back to me and report. And now, Watson, not another word of the matter until we have a few solid stepping-stones on which we may hope to get across to our solution."

We had ascertained from the lady that she went down upon the Monday by the train which leaves Waterloo at **9** 9.50, so I started early and caught the 9.13. At Farnham Station I had no difficulty in being directed to Charlington Heath. It was impossible to mistake the scene of the young lady's adventure, for the road runs between the open heath on one side, and an old yew hedge upon the other, surrounding a park which is studded with magnificent trees. There was a main gateway of lichen-studded stone, each side-pillar surmounted by mouldering heraldic emblems ; but besides this central carriage-drive I observed several points where there were gaps in the hedge and paths leading through them. The house was invisible from the road, but the surroundings all spoke of gloom and decay.

The heath was covered with golden patches of flowering gorse, gleaming magnificently in the light of the bright spring sunshine. Behind one of these clumps I took up my position, so as to command both the gateway of the Hall and a long stretch of the road upon either side. It had been deserted when I left it, but now I saw a cyclist riding down it from the opposite direction to that in which I had come. He was clad in a dark suit, and I saw that he had a black beard. On reaching the end of the Charlington grounds he sprang from his machine and led it through a gap in the hedge, disappearing from my view.

A quarter of an hour passed and then a second cyclist appeared. This time it was the young lady coming from the station. I saw her look about her as she came to the Charlington hedge. An instant later the man emerged from his hiding-place, sprang upon his bicycle, and followed her. In all the broad landscape those were the only moving figures, the graceful girl sitting very straight upon her machine, and the man behind her bending low over his handle-bar, with a curiously furtive suggestion in every movement. She looked back at him and slowed her pace. He slowed also. She stopped. He at once stopped, too, keeping two hundred yards behind her. Her next movement was as unexpected as it was spirited. She suddenly whisked her wheels round and dashed straight at him ! He was as quick as she, however, and darted off in desperate flight. Presently she came back up the road again, her head haughtily in the air, not deigning to take further notice of her silent attendant. He had turned also, and still kept his distance until the curve of the road hid them from my sight.

I remained in my hiding-place, and it was well that I did so, for presently the man reappeared cycling slowly back. He turned in at the Hall gates and dismounted from his machine. For some few minutes I could see him standing among the trees. His hands were raised, and he seemed to be settling his necktie. Then he mounted his bicycle and rode away from me down the drive towards the Hall. I ran across the heath and peered through the trees. Far away I could catch glimpses of the old grey building with its bristling Tudor chimneys, but the drive ran through a dense shrubbery, and I saw no more of my man.

However, it seemed to me that I had done a fairly good morning's work, and I walked back in high spirits to Farnham. The local house agent could tell me nothing about Charlington Hall, and referred me to a well-known firm in Pall Mall. There I halted on my way home, and met with courtesy from the representative. No, I could not have Charlington Hall for the summer. I was just too late. It had been let about a month ago. Mr. Williamson was the name of the tenant. He was a respectable elderly gentleman. The polite agent was afraid he could say no more, as the affairs of his clients were not matters which he could discuss.

Mr. Sherlock Holmes listened with attention to the long report which I was able to present to him that evening, but it did not elicit that word of curt praise which I had hoped for and should have valued. On the contrary, his austere face was even more severe than usual as he commented upon the things that I had done and the things that I had not.

" Your hiding-place, my dear Watson, was very faulty. You should have been behind the hedge ; then you would have had a close view of this interesting person. As it is you were some hundreds of yards away, and can tell me even less than Miss Smith. She thinks she does not know the man ; I am convinced she does. Why, otherwise, should he be so desperately anxious that she should not get so near him as to see his features ? You describe him as bending over the handle-bar. Concealment again, you see. You really have done remarkably badly. He returns to the house, and you want to find out who he is. You come to a London house agent ! "

" What should I have done ? " I cried, with some heat.

" Gone to the nearest public-house. That is the centre of country gossip. They would have told you every name, from the master to the scullery-maid. Williamson ! It conveys nothing to my mind. If he is an elderly man he is not this active cyclist who sprints away from that athletic young lady's pursuit. What have we gained by your expedition? The knowledge that the girl's story is true. I never doubted it. That there is a connection between the cyclist and the Hall. I never doubted that either. That the Hall is tenanted by Williamson. Who's the better for that? Well, well, my dear sir, don't look so depressed. We can do little more until next Saturday, and in the meantime I may make one or two inquiries myself."

Next morning we had a note from Miss Smith, recounting shortly and accurately the very incidents which I had seen, but the pith of the letter lay in the postscript:

" I am sure that you will respect my confidence, Mr. Holmes, when I tell you that my place here has become difficult owing to the fact that my employer has proposed marriage to me. I am convinced that his feelings are most deep and most honourable. At the same time my promise is, of course, given. He took my refusal very seriously, but also very gently. You can understand, however, that the situation is a little strained."

" Our young friend seems to be getting into deep waters," said Holmes thoughtfully, as he finished the letter. " The case certainly presents more features of interest and more possibility of development than I had originally thought. I should be none the worse for a quiet, peaceful day in the country, and I am inclined to run down this afternoon and test one or two theories which I have formed."

Holmes' quiet day in the country had a singular termination, for he arrived at Baker Street late in the evening with a cut lip and a discoloured lump upon his forehead, besides a general air of dissipation which would have made his own person the fitting object of a Scotland Yard investigation. He was immensely tickled by his own adventures, and laughed heartily as he recounted them.

" I get so little active exercise that it is always a treat," said he. " You are aware that I have some proficiency in the good old British sport of boxing. Occasionally it is of service. To-day, for example, I should have come to very ignominious grief without it."

I begged him to tell me what had occurred.

" I found that country pub which I had already recommended to your notice, and there I made my discreet inquiries. I was in the bar, and a garrulous landlord was giving me all that I wanted. Williamson is a white-bearded man, and he lives alone with a small staff of servants at the Hall. There is some rumour that he is or has been a clergyman; but one or two incidents of his short residence at the Hall struck me as peculiarly unecclesiastical. I have already made some inquiries at a clerical agency, and they tell me that there *was* a man of that name in orders whose career has been a singularly dark one. The landlord further informed me that there are usually week-end visitors—' a warm lot, sir '—at the Hall, and especially one gentleman with a red moustache, Mr. Woodley by name, who was always there. We had got as far as this when who should walk in but the gentleman himself, who had been drinking his beer in the tap-room, and had heard the whole conversation. Who was I? What did I want? What did I mean by asking questions? He had a fine flow of language, and his adjectives were very vigorous. He ended a string of abuse by a vicious back-hander, which I failed to entirely avoid. The next few minutes were delicious. It was a straight left against a slogging ruffian. I emerged as you see me. Mr. Woodley went home in a cart. So ended my country trip, and it must be confessed that, however enjoyable, my day on the Surrey border has not been much more profitable than your own."

The Thursday brought us another letter from our client.

"You will not be surprised, Mr. Holmes (said she), to hear that I am leaving Mr. Carruthers' employment. Even the high pay cannot reconcile me to the discomforts of my situation. On Saturday I come up to town, and I do not intend to return. Mr. Carruthers has got a trap, and so the dangers of the lonely road, if there ever were any dangers, are now over.

"As to the special cause of my leaving, it is not merely the strained situation with Mr. Carruthers, but it is the reappearance of that odious man, Mr. Woodley. He was always hideous, but he looks more awful than ever now, for he appears to have had an accident and he is much disfigured. I saw him out of the window, but I am glad to say I did not meet him. He had a long talk with Mr. Carruthers, who seemed much excited afterwards. Woodley must be staying in the neighbourhood, for he did not sleep here, and yet I caught a glimpse of him again this morning slinking about in the shrubbery. I would sooner have a savage wild animal loose about the place. I loathe and fear him more than I can say. How *can* Mr. Carruthers endure such a creature for a moment? However, all my troubles will be over on Saturday."

"So I trust, Watson, so I trust," said Holmes gravely. "There is some deep intrigue going on round that little woman, and it is our duty to see that no one molests her upon that last journey. I think, Watson, that we must spare time to run down together on Saturday morning, and make sure that this curious and inconclusive investigation has no untoward ending."

I confess that I had not up to now taken a very serious view of the case, which had seemed to me rather grotesque and bizarre than dangerous. That a man should lie in wait for and follow a very handsome woman is no un-heard-of thing, and if he had so little audacity that he not only dared not address her, but even fled from her approach, he was not a very formidable assailant. The ruffian Woodley was a very different person, but, except on the one occasion, he had not molested our client, and now he visited the house of Carruthers without intruding upon her presence. The man on the bicycle was doubt-less a member of those week-end parties at the Hall of which the publican had spoken; but who he was or what he wanted was as obscure as ever. It was the severity

"IT WAS A STRAIGHT LEFT AGAINST A SLOGGING RUFFIAN."
Illustration by Sidney Paget for the *Strand Magazine*, January, 1904.

"I EMERGED AS YOU SEE ME. MR. WOODLEY WENT HOME IN A CART."

Illustration by Frederic Dorr Steele for *Collier's Magazine*, December 26, 1903.

of Holmes' manner and the fact that he slipped a revolver into his pocket before leaving our rooms which impressed me with the feeling that tragedy might prove to lurk behind this curious train of events.

A rainy night had been followed by a glorious morning, and the heath-covered country-side, with the glowing clumps of flowering gorse, seemed all the more beautiful to eyes which were weary of the duns and drabs and slate-greys of London. Holmes and I walked along the broad, sandy road inhaling the fresh morning air, and rejoicing in the music of the birds and the fresh breath of the spring. From a rise of the road on the shoulder of Crooksbury Hill we could see the grim Hall bristling out from amidst the ancient oaks, which, old as they were, were still younger than the building which they surrounded. Holmes pointed down the long tract of road which wound, a reddish-yellow band, between the brown of the heath and the budding green of the woods. Far away, a black dot, we could see a vehicle moving in our direction. Holmes gave an exclamation of impatience.

" I had given a margin of half an hour," said he. " If that is her trap she must be making for the earlier train. I fear, Watson, that she will be past Charlington before we can possibly meet her."

From the instant that we passed the rise we could no longer see the vehicle, but we hastened onwards at such a pace that my sedentary life began to tell upon me, and I was compelled to fall behind. Holmes, however, was always in training, for he had inexhaustible stores of nervous energy upon which to draw. His springy step never slowed, until suddenly, when he was a hundred yards in front of me, he halted, and I saw him throw up his hand with a gesture of grief and despair. At the same instant an empty dog-cart, the horse cantering, the reins trailing, appeared round the curve of the road and rattled swiftly towards us.

" Too late, Watson ; too late ! " cried Holmes, as I ran panting to his side. " Fool that I was not to allow for the earlier train ! It's abduction, Watson—abduction ! Murder ! Heaven knows what ! Block the road ! Stop the horse ! That's right. Now jump in, and let us see if I can repair the consequences of my own blunder."

We had sprung into the dog-cart, and Holmes, after turning the horse, gave it a sharp cut with the whip, and we flew back along the road. As we turned the curve the whole stretch of road between the Hall and the heath was opened up. I grasped Holmes' arm.

" That's the man ! " I gasped.

A solitary cyclist was coming towards us. His head was down and his shoulders rounded as he put every ounce of energy that he possessed on to the pedals. He was flying like a racer. Suddenly he raised his bearded face, saw us close to him, and pulled up, springing from his machine. That coal-black beard was in singular contrast to the pallor of his face, and his eyes were as bright as if he had a fever. He stared at us and at the dog-cart. Then a look of amazement came over his face.

" Halloa ! Stop there ! " he shouted, holding his bicycle to block our road. " Where did you get that dog-cart ? Pull up, man ! " he yelled, drawing a pistol

"TOO LATE, WATSON; TOO LATE !" CRIED HOLMES . . .

Illustration by Sidney Paget for the *Strand Magazine*, January, 1904.

from his side-pocket. " Pull up, I say, or, by George, I'll put a bullet into your horse ! "

Holmes threw the reins into my lap and sprang down from the cart.

" You're the man we want to see. Where is Miss Violet Smith ? " he said in his quick, clear way.

" That's what I am asking you. You're in her dog-cart. You ought to know where she is."

" We met the dog-cart on the road. There was no one in it. We drove back to help the young lady."

" Good Lord ! Good Lord ! What shall I do ? " cried the stranger, in an ecstasy of despair. " They've got her, that hellhound Woodley and the blackguard parson. Come, man, come, if you really are her friend. Stand by me and we'll save her, if I have to leave my carcass in Charlington Wood."

He ran distractedly, his pistol in his hand, towards a gap in the hedge. Holmes followed him, and I, leaving the horse grazing beside the road, followed Holmes.

" This is where they came through," said he, pointing to the marks of several feet upon the muddy path. " Halloa ! Stop a minute ! Who's this in the bush ? "

It was a young fellow about seventeen, dressed like an ostler, with leather cords and gaiters. He lay upon his back, his knees drawn up, a terrible cut upon his head. He was insensible, but alive. A glance at his wound told me that it had not penetrated the bone.

" That's Peter, the groom," cried the stranger. " He drove her. The beasts have pulled him off and clubbed him. Let him lie ; we can't do him any good, but we may save her from the worst fate that can befall a woman."

We ran frantically down the path, which wound among the trees. We had reached the shrubbery which surrounded the house when Holmes pulled up.

" They didn't go to the house. Here are their marks on the left—here, beside the laurel bushes ! Ah, I said so ! "

As he spoke a woman's shrill scream—a scream which vibrated with a frenzy of horror—burst from the thick green clump of bushes in front of us. It ended suddenly on its highest note with a choke and a gurgle.

" This way ! This way ! They are in the bowling alley," cried the stranger, darting through the bushes. " Ah, the cowardly dogs ! Follow me, gentlemen ! Too late ! too late ! by the living Jingo ! "

We had broken suddenly into a lovely glade of greensward surrounded by ancient trees. On the farther side of it, under the shadow of a mighty oak, there stood a singular group of three people. One was a woman, our client, drooping and faint, a handkerchief round her mouth. Opposite her stood a brutal, heavy-faced, red-moustached young man, his gaitered legs parted wide, one arm akimbo, the other waving a riding-crop, his whole attitude suggestive of triumphant bravado. Between them an elderly, grey-bearded man, wearing a short surplice over a light tweed suit, had evidently just com- **10** pleted the wedding service, for he pocketed his Prayer Book as we appeared, and slapped the sinister bridegroom upon the back in jovial congratulation.

" They're married ! " I gasped.

10 *a short surplice.* "It appears that there are two patterns of short surplice in Dress Regulations— the Cotta, which has short sleeves, and the Roman Alb, with longer sleeves," Colonel Ronald D. Sherbrooke-Walker wrote in "Clothes Canonical." "We have no information as to which 'the old reprobate' was wearing."

AS WE APPROACHED, THE LADY STAGGERED AGAINST
THE TRUNK OF THE TREE FOR SUPPORT.

Illustration by Sidney Paget for the *Strand Magazine*, January, 1904.

HE SPUN ROUND WITH A SCREAM AND FELL UPON
HIS BACK . . .

Illustration by Sidney Paget for the *Strand Magazine*, January, 1904.

"Come on !" cried our guide; "come on !" He rushed across the glade, Holmes and I at his heels. As we approached, the lady staggered against the trunk of the tree for support. Williamson, the ex-clergyman, bowed to us with mock politeness, and the bully Woodley advanced with a shout of brutal and exultant laughter.

"You can take your beard off, Bob," said he. "I know you right enough. Well, you and your pals have just come in time for me to be able to introduce you to Mrs. Woodley."

Our guide's answer was a singular one. He snatched off the dark beard which had disguised him and threw it on the ground, disclosing a long, sallow, clean-shaven face below it. Then he raised his revolver and covered the young ruffian, who was advancing upon him with his dangerous riding-crop swinging in his hand.

"Yes," said our ally, " I *am* Bob Carruthers, and I'll see this woman righted if I have to swing for it. I told you what I'd do if you molested her, and, by the Lord, I'll be as good as my word !"

"You're too late. She's my wife !"

"No, she's your widow."

His revolver cracked, and I saw the blood spurt from the front of Woodley's waistcoat. He spun round with a scream and fell upon his back, his hideous red face turning suddenly to a dreadful mottled pallor. The old man, still clad in his surplice, burst into such a string of foul oaths as I have never heard, and pulled out a revolver of his own, but before he could raise it he was looking down the barrel of Holmes' weapon.

"Enough of this," said my friend coldly. "Drop that pistol ! Watson, pick it up ! Hold it to his head ! Thank you. You, Carruthers, give me that revolver. We'll have no more violence. Come, hand it over !"

"Who are you, then ?"

"My name is Sherlock Holmes."

"Good Lord !"

"You have heard of me, I see. I will represent the official police until their arrival. Here, you !" he shouted to the frightened groom, who had appeared at the edge of the glade. "Come here. Take this note as hard as you can ride to Farnham." He scribbled a few words upon a leaf from his notebook. "Give it to the super-intendent at the police-station. Until he comes, I must detain you all under my personal custody."

The strong, masterful personality of Holmes dominated the tragic scene, and all were equally puppets in his hands. Williamson and Carruthers found themselves carrying the wounded Woodley into the house, and I gave my arm to the frightened girl. The injured man was laid on his bed, and at Holmes' request I examined him. I carried my report to where he sat in the old tapestry-hung dining-room with his two prisoners before him.

"He will live," said I.

"What !" cried Carruthers, springing out of his chair. " I'll go upstairs and finish him first. Do you tell me that that girl, that angel, is to be tied to Roaring Jack Woodley for life ?"

"You need not concern yourself about that," said Holmes. "There are two very good reasons why she should under no circumstances be his wife. In the first place, we are very safe in questioning Mr. Williamson's right to solemnize a marriage."

" I have been ordained," cried the old rascal.

" And also unfrocked." **11**

" Once a clergyman, always a clergyman."

" I think not. How about the licence ? "

" We had a licence for the marriage. I have it here in my pocket."

" Then you got it by a trick. But in any case a forced marriage is no marriage, but it is a very serious felony, as **12** you will discover before you have finished. You'll have time to think the point out during the next ten years or so, unless I am mistaken. As to you, Carruthers, you would have done better to keep your pistol in your pocket."

" I begin to think so, Mr. Holmes ; but when I thought of all the precaution I had taken to shield this girl —for I loved her, Mr. Holmes, and it is the only time that ever I knew what love was—it fairly drove me mad to think that she was in the power of the greatest brute and bully in South Africa, a man whose name is a holy terror from Kimberley to Johannesburg. Why, Mr. Holmes, you'll hardly believe it, but ever since that girl has been in my employment I never once let her go past this house, where I knew these rascals were lurking, without following her on my bicycle just to see that she came to no harm. I kept my distance from her, and I wore a beard so that she should not recognize me, for she is a good and high-spirited girl, and she wouldn't have stayed in my employment long if she had thought that I was following her about the country roads."

" Why didn't you tell her of her danger ? "

" Because then, again, she would have left me, and I couldn't bear to face that. Even if she couldn't love me it was a great deal to me just to see her dainty form about the house, and to hear the sound of her voice."

" Well," said I, " you call that love, Mr. Carruthers, but I should call it selfishness."

" Maybe the two things go together. Anyhow, I couldn't let her go. Besides, with this crowd about, it was well that she should have someone near to look after her. Then when the cable came I knew they were bound to make a move."

" What cable ? "

Carruthers took a telegram from his pocket.

" That's it ! " said he. It was short and concise :

" The old man is dead."

" Hum ! " said Holmes. " I think I see how things worked, and I can understand how this message would, as you say, bring them to a head. But while we wait, you might tell me what you can."

The old reprobate with the surplice burst into a volley of bad language.

" By Heaven," said he, " if you squeal on us, Bob Carruthers, I'll serve you as you served Jack Woodley ! You can bleat about the girl to your heart's content, for that's your own affair, but if you round on your pals to this

11 *"And also unfrocked."* "What [Holmes] meant was 'deposed,'" the Reverend Otis R. Rice wrote in "Clergymen in the Canon." "This is the correct term of this form of ecclesiastical demise."

12 *a very serious felony.* Holmes was correct. As the Reverend Otis R. Rice continued: "The sacraments and sacramentals administered by a priest are valid whether he is inhibited, deposed, or not. In this respect Williamson's flippant remark, 'Once a clergyman, always a clergyman' was in a sense true. He was accountable for such an act and open to ecclesiastical and civil action for solemnizing any marriage after his deposition. Religiously, morally and legally, however, this mock ceremony was no marriage because of the lack of *intention* and *consent* upon the part of Violet Smith. The very fact that she was gagged was presumptive proof of her lack of 'free consent.' Unlike any other sacrament, the priest in solemnizing Holy Matrimony as practiced by the Church of England, is not the minister of the rite. The *bride and groom* themselves are its ministers. The officiating divine, in the name of the Church, blesses and attests the marriage, which the couple themselves perform. Without Miss Smith's *intention* and *willingness* to perform the marriage, it was in the eyes of the Church invalid. One wonders why Williamson did not know this. Possibly his theological education had been as fragmentary as had been his liturgical training. What informed Anglican clergyman would have believed he was 'solemnizing a marriage' while wearing 'a short surplice over a light tweed suit'?"

plain-clothes copper it will be the worst day's work that ever you did "

" Your reverence need not be excited," said Holmes, lighting a cigarette. " The case is clear enough against you, and all I ask is a few details for my private curiosity. However, if there's any difficulty in your telling me I'll do the talking, and then you will see how far you have a chance of holding back your secrets. In the first place, three of you came from South Africa on this game—you, Williamson, you, Carruthers, and Woodley."

" Lie number one," said the old man ; " I never saw either of them until two months ago, and I have never been in Africa in my life, so you can put that in your pipe and smoke it, Mr. Busybody Holmes ! "

" What he says is true," said Carruthers.

" Well, well, two of you came over. His reverence is our own home-made article. You had known Ralph Smith in South Africa. You had reason to believe he would not live long. You found out that his niece would inherit his fortune. How's that—eh ? "

Carruthers nodded, and Williamson swore.

" She was next-of-kin, no doubt, and you were aware that the old fellow would make no will."

" Couldn't read or write," said Carruthers.

" So you came over, the two of you, and hunted up the girl. The idea was that one of you was to marry her, and the other have a share of the plunder. For some reason Woodley was chosen as the husband. Why was that ? "

" We played cards for her on the voyage. He won."

" I see. You got the young lady into your service, and there Woodley was to do the courting. She recognized the drunken brute that he was, and would have nothing to do with him. Meanwhile, your arrangement was rather upset by the fact that you had yourself fallen in love with the lady. You could no longer bear the idea of this ruffian owning her."

" No, by George, I couldn't ! "

" There was a quarrel between you. He left you in a rage, and began to make his own plans independently of you."

" It strikes me, Williamson, there isn't very much that we can tell this gentleman," cried Carruthers, with a bitter laugh. " Yes, we quarrelled, and he knocked me down. I am level with him on that, anyhow. Then I lost sight of him. That was when he picked up with this cast padre here. I found that they had set up house-keeping together at this place on the line that she had to pass for the station. I kept my eye on her after that, for I knew there was some devilry in the wind. I saw them from time to time, for I was anxious to know what they were after. Two days ago Woodley came up to my house with this cable, which showed that Ralph Smith was dead. He asked me if I would stand by the bargain. I said I would not. He asked me if I would marry the girl myself and give him a share. I said I would willingly do so, but that she would not have me. He said, ' Let us get her married first, and after a week or two she may see things a bit different.' I said I would have nothing to do with violence. So he went off cursing, like the foul-mouthed blackguard that he was, and swearing that he would have her yet. She was leaving me this week-end, and I had got a trap to take her to the station, but I was so uneasy in my mind that I followed her on my bicycle. She had got a start, however, and before I could catch her the mischief was done. The first thing I knew about it was when I saw you two gentlemen driving back in her dog-cart."

Holmes rose and tossed the end of his cigarette into the grate. "I have been very obtuse, Watson," said he. "When in your report you said that you had seen the cyclist as you thought arrange his necktie in the shrubbery, that alone should have told me all. However, we may congratulate ourselves upon a curious and in some respects a unique case. I perceive three of the county constabu-lary in the drive, and I am glad to see that the little ostler is able to keep pace with them ; so it is likely that neither he nor the interesting bridegroom will be permanently damaged by their morning's adventures. I think, Wat-son, that in your medical capacity you might wait upon Miss Smith and tell her that if she is sufficiently recovered we shall be happy to escort her to her mother's home. If she is not quite convalescent you will find that a hint that we were about to telegraph to a young electrician in the Midlands would probably complete the cure. As to you, Mr. Carruthers, I think that you have done what you could to make amends for your share in an evil plot. There is my card, sir, and if my evidence can be of help to you in your trial it shall be at your disposal."

In the whirl of our incessant activity it has often been difficult for me, as the reader has probably observed, to round off my narratives, and to give those final details which the curious might expect. Each case has been the prelude to another, and the crisis once over, the actors have passed for ever out of our busy lives. I find, how-ever, a short note at the end of my manuscripts dealing with this case, in which I have put it upon record that Miss Violet Smith did indeed inherit a large fortune, and that she is now the wife of Cyril Morton, the senior partner of Morton and Kennedy, the famous Westmin-ster electricians. Williamson and Woodley were both tried for abduction and assault, the former getting seven years and the latter ten. Of the fate of Carruthers I have no record, but I am sure that his assault was not viewed very gravely by the Court, since Woodley had the reputation of being a most dangerous ruffian, and I think that a few months were sufficient to satisfy the demands of justice.

HOLMES ROSE AND TOSSED THE END OF HIS CIGARETTE INTO THE GRATE.

Illustration by Sidney Paget for the *Strand Maga-zine*, January, 1904.

Bibliographical Note: The manuscript of "The Adventure of the Solitary Cyclist," about 7,000 words, with cancellations and insertions in two exercise books, 8vo, vellum by Spealls, was auc-tioned in New York City on January 26, 1922, bringing $120. It was auctioned again in London on January 28, 1935; sold in one lot with "The Adventure of the Priory School" and "The Ad-venture of the Dancing Men" for £66. It was auc-tioned for a third time in New York City on April 26, 1927, ringing $160. Its present location is un-known.

53

THE ADVENTURE OF BLACK PETER

[Wednesday, July 3, to Friday, July 5, 1895]

1 *the Duke of Holdernesse.* Watson refers to "The Adventure of the Priory School." He must have written his account of "The Adventure of Black Peter" some years after the event, since "The Adventure of the Priory School" did not take place until May, 1901.

2 *In this memorable year '95.* There is no reason to doubt that the year *was* 1895: Inspector Stanley Hopkins tells us later that Captain Carey "was born in '45—fifty years of age."

3 *the sudden death of Cardinal Tosca.* Cardinal "Tosca" has been identified by Mr. Francis Albert Young ("Upon the Identification of Cardinal Tosca") as Cardinal Luigi Ruffo-Scilla, whose collapse and death, at the age of fifty-five, in Rome on May 29, 1895, came as a great surprise to many.

A pastiche stemming from this reference of Dr. Watson's, by Mr. Issac S. George, appeared in the *Baker Street Journal*, Vol. III, No. 1, Old Series, January, 1946, pp. 72-82.

4 *Wilson, the notorious canary-trainer.* At their 1949 dinner, The Speckled Band of Boston announced a prize competition for the best attempt at writing the story of "the arrest of Wilson." The winning entry, a playlet, was "The Yellow Birds," by Mr. Roger T. Clapp, published in *The Third Cab*, Boston: Privately printed, 1960, pp. 64-80.

Dr. Watson's reference also served to inspire a pastiche by Adrian M. Conan Doyle in *The Exploits of Sherlock Holmes;* it is titled "The Adventure of the Deptford Horror."

But: "How could a canary trainer become notorious if he stayed with canaries?" Mr. "Red" Smith asked in "The Nefarious Holmes." "There is absolutely nothing whatsoever in any way, shape, or form notorious about canaries. A bird trainer, however, can branch out, as Hirsch Jacobs has demonstrated in our day; Mr. Jacobs began with pigeons and went on to become America's leading

I HAVE never known my friend to be in better form, both mental and physical, than in the year '95. His increasing fame had brought with it an immense practice, and I should be guilty of an indiscretion if I were even to hint at the identity of some of the illustrious clients who crossed our humble threshold in Baker Street. Holmes, however, like all great artists, lived for his art's sake, and, save in the case of the Duke of **1** Holdernesse, I have seldom known him claim any large reward for his inestimable services. So unworldly was he—or so capricious—that he frequently refused his help to the powerful and wealthy where the problem made no appeal to his sympathies, while he would devote weeks of most intense application to the affairs of some humble client whose case presented those strange and dramatic qualities which appealed to his imagination and challenged his ingenuity.

2 In this memorable year '95 a curious and incongruous succession of cases had engaged his attention, ranging from his famous investigation of the sudden death of **3** Cardinal Tosca—an inquiry which was carried out by him at the express desire of his Holiness the Pope—down **4** to his arrest of Wilson, the notorious canary-trainer, which removed a plague-spot from the East End of London. Close on the heels of these two famous cases came **5** the tragedy of Woodman's Lee, and the very obscure circumstances which surrounded the death of Captain Peter Carey. No record of the doings of Mr. Sherlock Holmes would be complete which did not include some account of this very unusual affair.

During the first week of July my friend had been absent so often and so long from our lodgings that I knew he had something on hand. The fact that several rough-looking men called during that time and inquired for Captain Basil made me understand that Holmes was working somewhere under one of the numerous disguises and names with which he concealed his own formidable identity. He had at least five small refuges in different **6** parts of London in which he was able to change his personality. He said nothing of his business to me, and it was not my habit to force a confidence. The first positive sign which he gave me of the direction which his investigation was taking was an extraordinary one. He had gone out before breakfast, and I had sat down to mine, when he strode into the room, his hat upon his head, and a huge, barb-headed spear tucked like an umbrella under his arm.

" Good gracious, Holmes ! " I cried. " You don't mean to say that you have been walking about London with that thing ? "

" I drove to the butcher's and back."

" The butcher's ? "

" And I return with an excellent appetite. There can be no question, my dear Watson, of the value of exercise before breakfast. But I am prepared to bet that you will not guess the form that my exercise has taken."

" I will not attempt it."

He chuckled as he poured out the coffee.

" If you could have looked into Allardyce's back shop you would have seen a dead pig swung from a hook in the ceiling, and a gentleman in his shirt-sleeves furiously stabbing at it with this weapon. I was that energetic person, and I have satisfied myself that by no exertion of my strength can I transfix the pig with a single blow. Perhaps you would care to try ? "

" Not for worlds. But why were you doing this ? "

" Because it seemed to me to have an indirect bearing upon the mystery of Woodman's Lee. Ah, Hopkins, I got your wire last night, and I have been expecting you. Come and join us."

Our visitor was an exceedingly alert man, thirty years of age, dressed in a quiet tweed suit, but retaining the erect bearing of one who was accustomed to official uniform. I recognized him at once as Stanley Hopkins, a young police inspector for whose future Holmes had high hopes, while he in turn professed the admiration and respect of a pupil for the scientific methods of the famous amateur. Hopkins' brow was clouded and he sat down with an air of deep dejection.

" No, thank you, sir. I breakfasted before I came round. I spent the night in town, for I came up yesterday to report."

" And what had you to report ? "

" Failure, sir—absolute failure."

" You have made no progress ? "

" None."

" Dear me ! I must have a look at the matter."

" I wish to heavens that you would, Mr. Holmes. It's my first big chance, and I am at my wits' end. For goodness' sake come down and lend me a hand."

" Well, well, it happens that I have already read all the available evidence, including the report of the inquest, with some care. By the way, what do you make of that tobacco-pouch found on the scene of the crime ? Is there no clue there ? "

Hopkins looked surprised.

" It was the man's own pouch, sir. His initials were inside it. And it was of sealskin—and he an old sealer."

" But he had no pipe."

horse-trainer in eleven of twelve consecutive years. It stands to reason that Holmes' man, Wilson, followed a similar course . . ."

5 *Woodman's Lee.* Mr. Michael Harrison (*In the Footsteps of Sherlock Holmes*) has suggested that "Woodman's Lee" is Coleman's Hatch, near Forest Row in Sussex.

6 *He had at least five small refuges in different parts of London.* "The reference is tantalizing and obscure," Mr. Vincent Starrett wrote in *The Private Life of Sherlock Holmes*. "The rooms of Mycroft Holmes, opposite the Diogenes Club, would certainly be one of them; but it would be satisfying to know the others. . . . It may be assumed that in all of his five refuges he stored the materials of deception, as well as quantities of shag tobacco."

"YOU DON'T MEAN TO SAY THAT YOU HAVE BEEN WALKING ABOUT LONDON WITH THAT THING?"

Illustration by Sidney Paget for the *Strand Magazine*, March, 1904.

" No, sir, we could find no pipe ; indeed, he smoked very little. And yet he might have kept some tobacco for his friends."

" No doubt. I only mention it because if I had been handling the case I should have been inclined to make that the starting-point of my investigation. However, my friend Dr. Watson knows nothing of this matter, and I should be none the worse for hearing the sequence of events once more. Just give us some short sketch of the essentials."

Stanley Hopkins drew a slip of paper from his pocket.

" I have a few dates here which will give you the career of the dead man, Captain Peter Carey. He was born in '45—fifty years of age. He was a most daring and successful seal and whale fisher. In 1883 he commanded the steam sealer *Sea Unicorn*, of Dundee. He had then had several successful voyages in succession, and in the following year, 1884, he retired. After that he travelled for some years, and finally he bought a small place called Woodman's Lee, near Forest Row, in Sussex. There he has lived for six years, and there he died just a week ago to-day.

" There were some most singular points about the man. In ordinary life he was a strict Puritan—a silent, gloomy fellow. His household consisted of his wife, his daughter, aged twenty, and two female servants. These last were continually changing, for it was never a very cheery situation, and sometimes it became past all bearing. The man was an intermittent drunkard, and when he had the fit on him he was a perfect fiend. He has been known to drive his wife and his daughter out of doors in the middle of the night, and flog them through the park until the whole village outside the gates was aroused by their screams.

" He was summoned once for a savage assault upon the old vicar, who had called upon him to remonstrate with him upon his conduct. In short, Mr. Holmes, you would go far before you found a more dangerous man than Peter Carey, and I have heard that he bore the same character when he commanded his ship. He was known in the trade as Black Peter, and the name was given him, not only on account of his swarthy features and the colour of his huge beard, but for the humours which were the terror of all around him I need not say that he was loathed and avoided by every one of his neighbours, and that I have not heard one single word of sorrow about his terrible end.

" You must have read in the account of the inquest about the man's cabin, Mr. Holmes ; but perhaps your friend here has not heard of it. He had built himself a wooden outhouse—he always called it ' the cabin '—a few hundred yards from his house, and it was here that he slept every night. It was a little, single-roomed hut, sixteen feet by ten. He kept the key in his pocket, made his own bed, cleaned it himself, and allowed no other foot to cross the threshold. There are small windows on each side, which were covered by curtains, and never opened. One of these windows was turned towards the high-road, and when the light burned in it at night the folk used to point it out to each other, and wonder what Black Peter was doing in there. That's the window, Mr. Holmes, which gave us one of the few bits of positive evidence that came out at the inquest.

"You remember that a stonemason, named Slater, walking from Forest Row about one o'clock in the morning —two days before the murder—stopped as he passed the grounds and looked at the square of light still shining among the trees. He swears that the shadow of a man's head turned sideways was clearly visible on the blind, and that this shadow was certainly not that of Peter Carey, whom he knew well. It was that of a bearded man, but the beard was short, and bristled forwards in a way very different from that of the captain. So he says, but he had been two hours in the public-house, and it is some distance from the road to the window. Besides, this refers to the Monday, and the crime was done upon the Wednesday. **7**

"On the Tuesday Peter Carey was in one of his blackest moods, flushed with drink and as savage as a dangerous wild beast. He roamed about the house, and the women ran for it when they heard him coming. Late in the evening he went down to his own hut. About two o'clock the following morning his daughter, who slept with her window open, heard a most fearful yell from that direction, but it was no unusual thing for him to bawl and shout when he was in drink, so no notice was taken. On rising at seven one of the maids noticed that the door of the hut was open, but so great was the terror which the man caused that it was midday before anyone would venture down to see what had become of him. Peeping into the open door, they saw a sight which sent them flying with white faces into the village. Within an hour I was on the spot, and had taken over the case.

"Well, I have fairly steady nerves, as you know, Mr. Holmes, but I give you my word that I got a shake when I put my head into that little house. It was droning like a harmonium with the flies and bluebottles, and the floor and walls were like a slaughter-house. He had called it a cabin, and a cabin it was, sure enough, for you would have thought that you were in a ship. There was a bunk at one end, a sea-chest, maps and charts, a picture of the *Sea Unicorn*, a line of log-books on a shelf, all exactly as one would expect to find it in a captain's room. And there in the middle of it was the man himself, his face twisted like a lost soul in torment, and his great brindled beard stuck upwards in his agony. Right through his broad breast a steel harpoon had been driven, and it had sunk deep into the wood of the wall behind him. He was pinned like a beetle on a card. Of course, he was quite dead, and had been so from the instant that he uttered that last yell of agony.

"I know your methods, sir, and I applied them. Before I permitted anything to be moved I examined most carefully the ground outside, and also the floor of the room. There were no footmarks."

"Meaning that you saw none?"

"I assure you, sir, that there were none."

"My good Hopkins, I have investigated many crimes, but I have never yet seen one which was committed by a flying creature. As long as the criminal remains upon

7 *the crime was done upon the Wednesday*. Since Captain Peter Carey died "just a week ago to-day," and since we are in "the first week of July" "in the year '95," the opening day of the adventure must be *Wednesday, July 3, 1895*. It ended two days later—on the morning of *Friday, July 5, 1895*.

two legs so long must there be some indentation, some abrasion, some trifling displacement which can be detected by the scientific searcher. It is incredible that this blood-bespattered room contained no trace which could have aided us. I understand, however, from the inquest that there were some objects which you failed to overlook ? "

The young inspector winced at my companion's ironical comments.

" I was a fool not to call you in at the time, Mr. Holmes. However, that's past praying for now. Yes, there were several objects in the room which called for special attention. One was the harpoon with which the deed was committed. It had been snatched down from a rack on the wall. Two others remained there, and there was a vacant place for the third. On the stock was engraved ' S.s. *Sea Unicorn*, Dundee.' This seemed to establish that the crime had been done in a moment of fury, and that the murderer had seized the first weapon which came in his way. The fact that the crime was committed at two in the morning, and yet Peter Carey was fully dressed, suggested that he had an appointment with the murderer, which is borne out by the fact that a bottle of rum and two dirty glasses stood upon the table."

" Yes," said Holmes ; " I think that both inferences are permissible. Was there any other spirit but rum in the room ? "

" Yes ; there was a tantalus containing brandy and whisky on the sea-chest. It is of no importance to us, however, since the decanters were full and it had therefore not been used."

" For all that its presence has some significance," said Holmes. " However, let us hear some more about the objects which do seem to you to bear upon the case."

" There was this tobacco-pouch upon the table."

" What part of the table ? "

" It lay in the middle. It was of coarse sealskin—the straight-haired skin, with a leather thong to bind it. Inside was ' P. C.' on the flap. There was half an ounce of strong ship's tobacco in it."

" Excellent ! What more ? "

Stanley Hopkins drew from his pocket a drab-covered notebook. The outside was rough and worn, the leaves were discoloured. On the first page were written the initials " J. H. N." and the date " 1883." Holmes laid it on the table and examined it in his minute way, while Hopkins and I gazed over each shoulder. On the second page were printed the letters " C. P. R.," and then came several sheets of numbers. Another heading was Argentine, another Costa Rica, and another San Paulo, each with pages of signs and figures after it.

" What do you make of these ? " asked Holmes.

" They appear to be lists of Stock Exchange securities. I thought that ' J. H. N.' were the initials of a broker, and that ' C. P. R.' may have been his client."

" Try Canadian Pacific Railway," said Holmes.

Stanley Hopkins swore between his teeth, and struck his thigh with his clenched hand.

" What a fool I have been ! " he cried. " Of course

HOLMES LAID IT ON THE TABLE AND EXAMINED IT
IN HIS MINUTE WAY . . .

Illustration by Sidney Paget for the *Strand Magazine*, March, 1904.

it is as you say. Then ' J. H. N.' are the only initials we have to solve. I have already examined the old Stock Exchange lists, and I can find no one in 1883 either in the House or among the outside brokers whose initials **8** correspond with these. Yet I feel that the clue is the most important one that I hold. You will admit, Mr. Holmes, that there is a possibility that these initials are those of the second person who was present—in other words, of the murderer. I would also urge that the introduction into the case of a document relating to large masses of valuable securities gives us for the first time some indication of a motive for the crime."

Sherlock Holmes' face showed that he was thoroughly taken aback by this new development.

" I must admit both your points," said he. " I confess that the notebook, which did not appear at the inquest, modifies any views which I may have formed. I had come to a theory of the crime in which I can find no place for this. Have you endeavoured to trace any of the securities here mentioned ? "

" Inquiries are now being made at the offices, but I fear that the complete register of the stock-holders of these South American concerns is in South America, and that some weeks must elapse before we can trace the shares."

Holmes had been examining the cover of the notebook with his magnifying lens.

" Surely there is some discoloration here," said he.

" Yes, sir, it is a blood-stain. I told you that I picked the book off the floor."

" Was the blood-stain above or below ? "

" On the side next the boards."

" Which proves, of course, that the book was dropped after the crime was committed."

" Exactly, Mr. Holmes. I appreciated that point, and I conjectured that it was dropped by the murderer on his hurried flight. It lay near the door."

" I suppose that none of these securities have been found among the property of the dead man ? "

" No, sir."

" Have you any reason to suspect robbery ? "

" No, sir. Nothing seemed to have been touched."

" Dear me, it is certainly a very interesting case. Then there was a knife, was there not ? "

" A sheath-knife, still in its sheath. It lay at the feet of the dead man. Mrs. Carey has identified it as being her husband's property."

Holmes was lost in thought for some time.

" Well," said he at last, " I suppose I shall have to come out and have a look at it."

Stanley Hopkins gave a cry of joy.

" Thank you, sir. That will indeed be a weight off my mind."

Holmes shook his finger at the Inspector.

" It would have been an easier task a week ago," said he. " But even now my visit may not be entirely fruitless. Watson, if you can spare the time, I should be very glad of your company. If you will call a four-wheeler, Hopkins, we shall be ready to start for Forest Row in a quarter of an hour."

8 *the House.* Hopkins presumably refers to the London Stock Exchange, which had its first home in Jonathan's Coffee House in Change Alley.

Alighting at the small wayside station, we drove for some miles through the remains of widespread woods, which were once part of that great forest which for so long held the Saxon invaders at bay—the impenetrable " weald," for sixty years the bulwark of Britain. Vast sections of it have been cleared, for this is the seat of the first ironworks of the country, and the trees have been felled to smelt the ore. Now the richer fields of the North have absorbed the trade, and nothing save these ravaged groves and great scars in the earth show the work of the past. Here in a clearing upon the green slope of a hill stood a long, low stone house, approached by a curving drive running through the fields. Nearer the road, and surrounded on three sides by bushes, was a small outhouse, one window and the door facing in our direction. It was the scene of the murder.

Stanley Hopkins led us first to the house, where he introduced us to a haggard, grey-haired woman, the widow of the murdered man, whose gaunt and deep-lined face, with the furtive look of terror in the depths of her red-rimmed eyes, told of the years of hardship and ill-usage which she had endured. With her was her daughter, a pale, fair-haired girl, whose eyes blazed defiantly at us as she told us that she was glad that her father was dead, and that she blessed the hand which had struck him down. It was a terrible household that Black Peter Carey had made for himself, and it was with a sense of relief that we found ourselves in the sunlight again and making our way along the path which had been worn across the fields by the feet of the dead man.

The outhouse was the simplest of dwellings, wooden-walled, single-roofed, one window beside the door, and one on the farther side. Stanley Hopkins drew the key from his pocket, and had stooped to the lock, when he paused with a look of attention and surprise upon his face.

" Someone has been tampering with it," he said.

There could be no doubt of the fact. The woodwork was cut, and the scratches showed white through the paint, as if they had been that instant done. Holmes had been examining the window.

" Someone has tried to force this also. Whoever it was has failed to make his way in. He must have been a very poor burglar."

" This is a most extraordinary thing," said the Inspector ; " I could swear that these marks were not here yesterday evening."

" Some curious person from the village, perhaps," I suggested.

" Very unlikely. Few of them would dare to set foot in the grounds, far less try to force their way into the cabin. What do you think of it, Mr. Holmes ? "

" I think that fortune is very kind to us."

" You mean that the person will come again ? "

" It is very probable. He came expecting to find the door open. He tried to get in with the blade of a very small penknife. He could not manage it. What would he do ? "

" Come again next night with a more useful tool."

" So I should say. It will be our fault if we are not

"SOMEONE HAS BEEN TAMPERING WITH IT," HE SAID.

Illustration by Sidney Paget for the *Strand Magazine*, March, 1904.

there to receive him.   Meanwhile, let me see the inside of the cabin."

The traces of the tragedy had been removed, but the furniture of the little room still stood as it had been on the night of the crime.   For two hours, with the most intense concentration, Holmes examined every object in turn, but his face showed that his quest was not a successful one. Once only he paused in his patient investigation.

" Have you taken anything off this shelf, Hopkins ? "

" No ; I have moved nothing."

" Something has been taken.   There is less dust in this corner of the shelf than elsewhere.   It may have been a book lying on its side.   It may have been a box.   Well, well, I can do nothing more.   Let us walk in these beautiful woods, Watson, and give a few hours to the birds and the flowers.   We shall meet you here later, Hopkins, and see if we can come to closer quarters with the gentleman who has paid this visit in the night."

It was past eleven o'clock when we formed our little ambuscade.   Hopkins was for leaving the door of the hut open, but Holmes was of opinion that this would rouse the suspicions of the stranger.   The lock was a perfectly simple one, and only a strong blade was needed to push it back.   Holmes also suggested that we should wait, not inside the hut, but outside it among the bushes which grew round the farther window.   In this way we should be able to watch our man if he struck a light, and see what his object was in this stealthy nocturnal visit.

It was a long and melancholy vigil, and yet it brought with it something of the thrill which the hunter feels when he lies beside the water-pool and waits for the coming of the thirsty beast of prey.   What savage creature was it which might steal upon us out of the darkness ?   Was it a fierce tiger of crime, which could only be taken fighting hard with flashing fang and claw, or would it prove to be some skulking jackal, dangerous only to the weak and unguarded ?   In absolute silence we crouched amongst the bushes, waiting for whatever might come.   At first the steps of a few belated villagers, or the sound of voices from the village, lightened our vigil ; but one by one these interruptions died away, and an absolute stillness fell upon us, save for the chimes of the distant church, which told us of the progress of the night, and for the rustle and whisper of a fine rain falling amid the foliage which roofed us in.

Half-past two had chimed, and it was the darkest hour which precedes the dawn, when we all started as a low but sharp click came from the direction of the gate.   Someone had entered the drive.   Again there was a long silence, and I had begun to fear that it was a false alarm, when a stealthy step was heard upon the other side of the hut, and a moment later a metallic scraping and clicking. The man was trying to force the lock !   This time his skill was greater or his tool was better, for there was a sudden snap and the creak of the hinges.   Then a match was struck, and next instant the steady light from a candle filled the interior of the hut.   Through the gauze curtain our eyes were all riveted upon the scene within.

. . . HOLMES EXAMINED EVERY OBJECT IN TURN . . .

Cover illustration by Frederic Dorr Steele for *Collier's Magazine*, February 27, 1904.

HE SANK DOWN UPON THE SEA-CHEST . . .

Illustration by Sidney Paget for the *Strand Magazine*, March, 1904.

The nocturnal visitor was a young man, frail and thin, with black moustache which intensified the deadly pallor of his face. He could not have been much above twenty years of age. I have never seen any human being who appeared to be in such a pitiable fright, for his teeth were visibly chattering, and he was shaking in every limb. He was dressed like a gentleman, in Norfolk jacket and knickerbockers, with a cloth cap upon his head. We watched him staring round with frightened eyes. Then he laid the candle-end upon the table and disappeared from our view into one of the corners. He returned with a large book, one of the log-books which formed a line upon the shelves. Leaning on the table, he rapidly turned over the leaves of this volume until he came to the entry which he sought. Then, with an angry gesture of his clenched hand, he closed the book, replaced it in the corner, and put out the light. He had hardly turned to leave the hut when Hopkins' hand was on the fellow's collar, and I heard his loud gasp of terror as he understood that he was taken. The candle was relit, and there was our wretched captive shivering and cowering in the grasp of the detective. He sank down upon the sea-chest, and looked helplessly from one of us to the other.

" Now, my fine fellow," said Stanley Hopkins, " who are you, and what do you want here ? "

The man pulled himself together and faced us with an effort at self-composure.

" You are detectives, I suppose ? " said he. " You imagine I am connected with the death of Captain Peter Carey. I assure you that I am innocent."

" We'll see about that," said Hopkins. " First of all, what is your name ? "

" It is John Hopley Neligan."

I saw Holmes and Hopkins exchange a quick glance.

" What are you doing here ? "

" Can I speak confidentially ? "

" No, certainly not."

" Why should I tell you ? "

" If you have no answer it may go badly with you at the trial."

The young man winced.

" Well, I will tell you," he said. " Why should I not ? And yet I hate to think of this old scandal gaining a new lease of life. Did you ever hear of Dawson & Neligan ? "

I could see from Hopkins' face that he never had ; but Holmes was keenly interested.

" You mean the West Country bankers," said he. " They failed for a million, ruined half the county families of Cornwall, and Neligan disappeared."

" Exactly. Neligan was my father."

At last we were getting something positive, and yet it seemed a long gap between an absconding banker and Captain Peter Carey pinned against the wall with one of his own harpoons. We all listened intently to the young man's words.

" It was my father who was really concerned. Dawson had retired. I was only ten years of age at the time, but I was old enough to feel the shame and horror of it all. It has always been said that my father stole all the securities and fled. It is not true. It was his belief that if he were given time in which to realize them all would be well, and every creditor paid in full. He started in his little yacht **9** for Norway just before the warrant was issued for his arrest. I can remember that last night when he bade farewell to my mother. He left us a list of the securities he was taking, and he swore that he would come back with his honour cleared, and that none who had trusted him would suffer. Well, no word was ever heard from him again. Both the yacht and he vanished utterly. We believed, my mother and I, that he and it, with the securities that he had taken with him, were at the bottom of the sea. We had a faithful friend, however, who is a business man, and it was he who discovered some time ago that some of the securities which my father had with him have reappeared on the London market. You can imagine our amazement. I spent months in trying to trace them, and at last, after many doublings and difficulties, I discovered that the original seller had been Captain Peter Carey, the owner of this hut.

" Naturally I made some inquiries about the man. I found that he had been in command of a whaler which was due to return from the Arctic seas at the very time when my father was crossing to Norway. The autumn of that year was a stormy one, and there was a long succession of southerly gales. My father's yacht may well have been blown to the north, and there met by Captain Peter Carey's ship. If that were so, what had become of my father ? In any case, if I could prove from Peter Carey's evidence how these securities came on the market, it would be a proof that my father had not sold them, and that he had no view to personal profit when he took them.

" I came down to Sussex with the intention of seeing the captain, but it was at this moment that his terrible death occurred. I read at the inquest a description of his cabin, in which it stated that the old log-books of his vessel were preserved in it. It struck me that if I could see what occurred in the month of August, 1883, on board the *Sea Unicorn*, I might settle the mystery of my father's fate. I tried last night to get at these log-books, but was unable to open the door. To-night I tried again, and succeeded ; but I find that the pages which deal with that month have been torn from the book. It was at that moment I found myself a prisoner in your hands."

" Is that all ? " asked Hopkins.

" Yes, that is all." His eyes shifted as he said it.

" You have nothing else to tell us ? "

He hesitated.

" No ; there is nothing."

" You have not been here before last night ? "

" No."

" Then how do you account for *that* ? " cried Hopkins, as he held up the damning notebook, with the initials of our prisoner on the first leaf, and the blood-stain on the cover.

The wretched man collapsed. He sank his face in his hands and trembled all over.

9 *and every creditor paid in full*. "What I do not quite grasp is what the Receiver in Bankruptcy of the defunct banking firm of Dawson and Neligan had been doing all these years?" Mr. Humfrey Michell wrote in a "Letter to Baker Street." "It would have been a simple matter for him to obtain the record of the missing securities from the family and take the appropriate steps to obtain title to them for the benefit of the creditors. The only explanation I can think of, and I admit it is very improbable, is that young Neligan was a liar and was after something else than share certificates. If so, he was a very successful one, because he bamboozled Sherlock Holmes."

" Where did you get it ? " he groaned. " I did not know. I thought I had lost it at the hotel."

" That is enough," said Hopkins sternly. " Whatever else you have to say you must say in court. You will walk down with me now to the police-station. Well, Mr. Holmes, I am very much obliged to you and to your friend for coming down to help me. As it turns out your presence was unnecessary, and I would have brought the case to this successful issue without you ; but none the less I am very grateful. Rooms have been reserved for you at the Brambletye Hotel, so we can all walk down to the village together."

" Well, Watson, what do you think of it ? " askcd Holmes as we travelled back next morning.

" I can see that you are not satisfied."

" Oh, yes, my dear Watson, I am perfectly satisfied. At the same time Stanley Hopkins' methods do not commend themselves to me. I am disappointed in Stanley Hopkins. I had hoped for better things from him. One should always look for a possible alternative and provide against it. It is the first rule of criminal investigation."

" What, then, is the alternative ? "

" The line of investigation which I have myself been pursuing. It may give nothing. I cannot tell. But at least I shall follow it to the end."

Several letters were waiting for Holmes at Baker Street. He snatched one of them up, opened it, and burst out into a triumphant chuckle of laughter.

" Excellent, Watson. The alternative develops. Have you telegraph forms ? Just write a couple of messages for me : ' Sumner, Shipping Agent, Ratcliff Highway. Send three men on, to arrive ten to-morrow morning.— Basil.' That's my name in those parts. The other is ' Inspector Stanley Hopkins, 46 Lord Street, Brixton. Come breakfast to-morrow at nine-thirty. Important. Wire if unable to come.—Sherlock Holmes.' There, Watson, this infernal case had haunted me for ten days. I hereby banish it completely from my presence. To-morrow I trust that we shall hear the last of it for ever."

Sharp at the hour named Inspector Stanley Hopkins appeared, and we sat down together to the excellent breakfast which Mrs. Hudson had prepared. The young detective was in high spirits at his success.

" You really think that your solution must be correct ? " asked Holmes.

" I could not imagine a more complete case."

" It did not seem to me conclusive."

" You astonish me, Mr. Holmes. What more could one ask for ? "

" Does your explanation cover every point ? "

" Undoubtedly. I find that young Neligan arrived at the Brambletye Hotel on the very day of the crime. He came on the pretence of playing golf. His room was on the ground floor, and he could get out when he liked. That very night he went down to Woodman's Lee, saw Peter Carey at the hut, quarrelled with him, and killed him with the harpoon. Then, horrified by what he had done, he fled out of the hut, dropping the notebook which he had brought with him in order to question Peter Carey about these different securities. You may have observed that some of them were marked with ticks, and the others—the great majority—were not. Those which are ticked have been traced on the London market ; but the others presumably were still in the possession of Carey, and young Neligan, according to his own account, was anxious to recover them in order to do the right thing by his father's creditors. After his flight he did not dare to approach the hut again for some time ; but at last he forced himself to do so in order to obtain the information which he needed. Surely that is all simple and obvious ? "

Holmes smiled and shook his head.

" It seems to me to have only one drawback, Hopkins, and that is that it is intrinsically impossible. Have you tried to drive a harpoon through a body ? No ? Tut, tut, my dear sir, you must really pay attention to these details. My friend Watson could tell you that I spent a whole morning in that exercise. It is no easy matter, and requires a strong and practised arm. But this blow was delivered with such violence that the head of the weapon sank deep into the wall. Do you imagine that this anæmic youth was capable of so frightful an assault ? Is he the man who hob-nobbed in rum and water with Black Peter in the dead of the night ? Was it his profile that was seen on the blind two nights before ? No, no, Hopkins ; it is another and a more formidable person for whom we must seek."

The detective's face had grown longer and longer during Holmes' speech. His hopes and his ambitions were all crumbling about him. But he would not abandon his position without a struggle.

" You can't deny that Neligan was present that night, Mr. Holmes. The book will prove that. I fancy that I have evidence enough to satisfy a jury, even if you are able to pick a hole in it. Besides, Mr. Holmes, I have laid my hand upon *my* man. As to this terrible person of yours, where is he ? "

" I rather fancy that he is on the stair," said Holmes serenely. " I think, Watson, that you would do well to put that revolver where you can reach it." He rose, and laid a written paper upon a side-table. " Now we are ready," said he.

There had been some talking in gruff voices outside, and now Mrs. Hudson opened the door to say that there were three men inquiring for Captain Basil.

" Show them in one by one," said Holmes.

The first who entered was a little ribston-pippin of a man, with ruddy cheeks and fluffy white side-whiskers. Holmes had drawn a letter from his pocket.

" What name ? " he asked.

" James Lancaster."

" I am sorry, Lancaster, but the berth is full. Here is half a sovereign for your trouble. Just step into this room and wait there for a few minutes."

The second man was a long, dried-up creature, with lank hair and sallow cheeks. His name was Hugh

10 *ribston-pippin.* A variety of apple.

11 *this room.* Holmes' bedroom.

Pattins. He also received his dismissal, his half-sovereign, and the order to wait.

The third applicant was a man of remarkable appearance. A fierce, bull-dog face was framed in a tangle of hair and beard, and two bold dark eyes gleamed behind the cover of thick, tufted, overhung eyebrows. He saluted and stood sailor-fashion, turning his cap round in his hands.

" Your name ? " asked Holmes.

" Patrick Cairns."

" Harpooner ? "

" Yes, sir. Twenty-six voyages."

" Dundee, I suppose ? "

" Yes, sir."

" And ready to start with an exploring ship ? "

" Yes, sir."

" What wages ? "

" Eight pounds a month."

" Could you start at once ? "

" As soon as I get my kit."

" Have you your papers ? "

" Yes, sir." He took a sheaf of worn and greasy forms from his pocket. Holmes glanced over them and returned them.

" You are just the man I want," said he. " Here's the agreement on the side-table. If you sign it the whole matter will be settled."

The seaman lurched across the room and took up the pen.

" Shall I sign here ? " he asked, stooping over the table.

Holmes leaned over his shoulder and passed both hands over his neck.

" This will do," said he.

I heard a click of steel and a bellow like an enraged bull. The next instant Holmes and the seaman were rolling on the ground together. He was a man of such gigantic strength that, even with the handcuffs which Holmes had so deftly fastened upon his wrists, he would have quickly overpowered my friend had Hopkins and I not rushed to his rescue. Only when I pressed the cold muzzle of the revolver to his temple did he at last understand that resistance was vain. We lashed his ankles with cord and rose breathless from the struggle.

" I must really apologize, Hopkins," said Sherlock Holmes ; " I fear that the scrambled eggs are cold. However, you will enjoy the rest of your breakfast all the better, will you not, for the thought that you have brought your case to a triumphant conclusion ? "

Stanley Hopkins was speechless with amazement.

" I don't know what to say, Mr. Holmes," he blurted out at last, with a very red face. " It seems to me that I have been making a fool of myself from the beginning. I understand now, what I should never have forgotten, that I am the pupil and you are the master. Even now I see what you have done, but I don't know how you did it, or what it signifies."

" Well, well," said Holmes good-humouredly. " We all learn by experience, and your lesson this time is that you should never lose sight of the alternative. You were

"SHALL I SIGN HERE?" HE ASKED . . .

Illustration by Sidney Paget for the *Strand Magazine*, March, 1904.

so absorbed in young Neligan that you could not spare a thought to Patrick Cairns, the true murderer of Peter Carey.''

The hoarse voice of the seaman broke in on our conversation.

" See here, mister," said he, " I make no complaint of being man-handled in this fashion, but I would have you call things by their right names.   You say I murdered Peter Carey ; I say I *killed* Peter Carey, and there's all the difference.   Maybe you don't believe what I say.   Maybe you think I am just slinging you a yarn."

" Not at all," said Holmes.   " Let us hear what you have to say."

" It's soon told, and, by the Lord, every word of it is truth.   I knew Black Peter, and when he pulled out his knife I whipped a harpoon through him sharp, for I knew that it was him or me.   That's how he died.   You can call it murder.   Anyhow, I'd as soon die with a rope round my neck as with Black Peter's knife in my heart."

" How came you there ? " asked Holmes.

" I'll tell it you from the beginning.   Just sit me up a little so as I can speak easy.   It was in '83 that it happened—August of that year.   Peter Carey was master of the *Sea Unicorn*, and I was spare harpooner.   We were coming out of the ice-pack on our way home, with head winds and a week's southerly gale, when we picked up a little craft that had been blown north.   There was one man on her—a landsman.   The crew had thought she would founder, and had made for the Norwegian coast in the dinghy.   I guess they were all drowned.   Well, we took him on board, this man, and he and the skipper had some long talks in the cabin.   All the baggage we took off with him was one tin box.   So far as I know the man's name was never mentioned, and on the second night he disappeared as if he had never been.   It was given out that he had either thrown himself overboard or fallen overboard in the heavy weather that we were having.   Only one man knew what had happened to him, and that was me, for with my own eyes I saw the skipper tip up his heels and put him over the rail in the middle watch of a dark night, two days before we sighted the Shetland lights.

" Well, I kept my knowledge to myself and waited to see what would come of it.   When we got back to Scotland it was easily hushed up, and nobody asked any questions.   A stranger died by an accident, and it was nobody's business to inquire.   Shortly after Peter Carey gave up the sea, and it was long years before I could find where he was.   I guessed that he had done the deed for the sake of what was in that tin box, and that he could afford now to pay me well for keeping my mouth shut.

" I found out where he was through a sailor man that had met him in London, and down I went to squeeze him. The first night he was reasonable enough, and was ready to give me what would make me free of the sea for life. We were to fix it all two nights later.   When I came I found him three-parts drunk and in a vile temper.   We sat down and we drank and we yarned about old times, but the more he drank the less I liked the look on his face. I spotted that harpoon upon the wall, and I thought I

"WE SAT DOWN AND WE DRANK AND WE YARNED ABOUT OLD TIMES . . ."

Illustration by Sidney Paget for the *Strand Magazine*, March, 1904.

might need it before I was through. Then at last he broke out at me, spitting and cursing, with murder in his eyes and a great clasp-knife in his hand. He had not time to get it from the sheath before I had the harpoon through him. Heavens! what a yell he gave; and his face gets between me and my sleep! I stood there, with his blood splashing round me, and I waited for a bit; but all was quiet, so I took heart once more. I looked round, and there was the tin box on a shelf. I had as much right to it as Peter Carey, anyhow, so I took it with me and left the hut. Like a fool I left my baccy-pouch upon the table.

" Now I'll tell you the queerest part of the whole story. I had hardly got outside the hut when I heard someone coming, and I hid among the bushes. A man came slinking along, went into the hut, gave a cry as if he had seen a ghost, and legged it as hard as he could run until he was out of sight. Who he was or what he wanted is more than I can tell. For my part, I walked ten miles, got a train at Tunbridge Wells, and so reached London, and no one the wiser.

" Well, when I came to examine the box I found there was no money in it, and nothing but papers that I would not dare to sell. I had lost my hold on Black Peter, and was stranded in London without a shilling. There was only my trade left. I saw these advertisements about harpooners and high wages, so I went to the shipping agents, and they sent me here. That's all I know, and I say again that if I killed Black Peter the law should give me thanks, for I saved them the price of a hempen rope."

" A very clear statement," said Holmes, rising and lighting his pipe. " I think, Hopkins, that you should lose no time in conveying your prisoner to a place of safety. This room is not well adapted for a cell, and Mr. Patrick Cairns occupies too large a portion of our carpet."

" Mr. Holmes," said Hopkins, " I do not know how to express my gratitude. Even now I do not understand how you attained this result."

" Simply by having the good fortune to get the right clue from the beginning. It is very possible that if I had known about this notebook it might have led away my thoughts, as it did yours. But all I heard pointed in the one direction. The amazing strength, the skill in the use of the harpoon, the rum and water, the sealskin tobacco-pouch, with the coarse tobacco—all these pointed to a seaman, and one who had been a whaler. I was convinced that the initials ' P. C.' upon the pouch were a coincidence, and not those of Peter Carey, since he seldom smoked, and no pipe was found in his cabin. You remember that I asked whether whisky and brandy were in the cabin. You said they were. How many landsmen are there who would drink rum when they could get these other spirits? Yes, I was certain it was a seaman."

" And how did you find him? "

" My dear sir, the problem had become a very simple one. If it were a seaman, it could only be a seaman who had been with him on the *Sea Unicorn*.   So far as I could learn, he had sailed in no other ship.   I spent three days in wiring to Dundee, and at the end of that time I had **12** ascertained the names of the crew of the *Sea Unicorn* in 1883. When I found Patrick Cairns among the harpooners my research was nearing its end.   I argued that the man was probably in London, and that he would desire to leave the country for a time.   I therefore spent some days in the East End, devised an Arctic expedition, put forward tempting terms for harpooners who would serve under Captain Basil—and behold the result!"

"Wonderful!" cried Hopkins.   "Wonderful!"

"You must obtain the release of young Neligan as soon as possible," said Holmes.   "I confess that I think you owe him some apology.   The tin box must be returned to him, but, of course, the securities which Peter Carey has sold are lost for ever.   There's the cab, Hopkins, and you can remove your man.   If you want me for the trial, my address and that of Watson will be somewhere in Norway—I'll send particulars later."

12 *I spent three days in wiring to Dundee.* ". . . since there was a telephone across the road [*The Sign of the Four*], it would have been simpler to call Hopkins at the Brixton Police Station [rather than to telegraph him to come to breakfast], and should he have been absent, the police would have delivered the message and forwarded his reply at once," Colonel E. Ennalls Berl wrote in "Sherlock Holmes and the Telephone." "But, worst of all, Holmes 'spent three days in wiring to Dundee' to get crew lists of the *Sea Unicorn* when it seems almost certain that a much shorter telephone struggle through the Dundee police would have given him the information."

Or, as the late Fletcher Pratt suggested in "Holmes and the Royal Navy," "Admiralty records would have supplied the necessary information in the matter . . . without the necessity of Holmes spending three days in wiring to Dundee."

54

THE ADVENTURE OF THE NORWOOD BUILDER

[Tuesday, August 20, to Wednesday, August 21, 1895]

1 *some months.* We soon learn that the month was August (Holmes "crawled about the lawn with an August sun" on his back), the weather had been "very warm these past few days" and there had been no rain for some days: "This drought has made everything as hard as iron." Watson can not mean 1894: there was no period in the August of that year in which the weather was both dry and hot. In August, 1895, on the other hand, there was no rain from Wednesday, August 14 (when there was a meager 0.01 inches), to Tuesday, August 22. From Tuesday, August 13, when the maximum temperature was 64.8°, it rose steadily to a high of 82.2° on Monday, August 19th. But the case did not open on a Monday: Mr. John Hector McFarlane "was very surprised . . . when yesterday, about three o'clock in the afternoon" Mr. Jonas Oldacre "walked into my office in the City." We believe that the case took place on *Tuesday, August 20, and Wednesday, August 21, 1895.* The selection of 1895 over 1894 is strengthened by the fact that Watson did not include "The Adventure of the Norwood Builder" in his list of important cases of 1894 ("The Adventure of the Golden Pince-Nez").

2 *it was my friend who had really found the money.* "The connection between the younger doctor and that grandmother [of Holmes] who was the sister of Vernet is obvious," Mr. Vincent Starrett wrote in *The Private Life of Sherlock Holmes.* "Verner would be the English form of Vernet, or a corruption of the French name after a year or so in England. And Dr. Verner would be a cousin of the detective, twice or thrice removed."

"Since the money for the purchase was provided by Holmes who, unworldly as he was in the matter of payment for his services, could certainly at this period command high fees when he chose, we may assume that it was not less than Watson had given in the first place, i.e., about £1,000 [$5,000]," Miss Helen Simpson wrote in "Medical Career and Capacities of Dr. J. H. Watson."

"FROM the point of view of the criminal expert," said Mr. Sherlock Holmes, "London has become a singularly uninteresting city since the death of the late lamented Professor Moriarty."

"I can hardly think that you would find many decent citizens to agree with you," I answered.

"Well, well, I must not be selfish," said he, with a smile, as he pushed back his chair from the breakfast-table. "The community is certainly the gainer, and no one the loser, save the poor out-of-work specialist, whose occupation has gone. With that man in the field one's morning paper presented infinite possibilities. Often it was only the smallest trace, Watson, the faintest indication, and yet it was enough to tell me that the great malignant brain was there, as the gentlest tremors of the edges of the web remind one of the foul spider which lurks in the centre. Petty thefts, wanton assaults, purposeless outrage—to the man who held the clue all could be worked into one connected whole. To the scientific student of the higher criminal world no capital in Europe offered the advantages which London then possessed. But now——" He shrugged his shoulders in humorous deprecation of the state of things which he had himself done so much to produce.

At the time of which I speak, Holmes had been back for **1** some months, and I, at his request, had sold my practice and returned to share the old quarters in Baker Street. A young doctor, named Verner, had purchased my small Kensington practice, and given with astonishingly little demur the highest price that I ventured to ask—an incident which only explained itself some years later, when I found that Verner was a distant relation of Holmes', and that it was my friend who had really found the **2** money.

Our months of partnership had not been so uneventful as he had stated, for I find, on looking over my notes, that this period includes the case of the papers of ex-President Murillo, and also the shocking affair of the Dutch steamship, *Friesland,* which so nearly cost us both **3** our lives. His cold and proud nature was always averse, however, to anything in the shape of public applause, and he bound me in the most stringent terms to say no further word of himself, his methods, or his successes—a prohibition which, as I have explained, has only now been removed.

Mr. Sherlock Holmes was leaning back in his chair after his whimsical protest, and was unfolding his morning paper in a leisurely fashion, when our attention was arrested by a tremendous ring at the bell, followed immediately by a hollow drumming sound, as if someone were beating on the outer door with his fist. As it opened there came a tumultuous rush into the hall, rapid feet clattered up the stair, and an instant later a wild-eyed and frantic young man, pale, dishevelled, and palpitating, burst into the room. He looked from one to the other of us, and under our gaze of inquiry he became conscious that some apology was needed for this unceremonious entry.

" I'm sorry, Mr. Holmes," he cried. " You mustn't blame me. I am nearly mad. Mr. Holmes, I am the unhappy John Hector McFarlane."

He made the announcement as if the name alone would explain both his visit and its manner, but I could see by my companion's unresponsive face that it meant no more to him than to me.

" Have a cigarette, Mr. McFarlane," said he, pushing his case across. " I am sure that with your symptoms my friend Dr. Watson here would prescribe a sedative. The weather has been so very warm these last few days. Now, if you feel a little more composed, I should be glad if you would sit down in that chair and tell us very slowly and quietly who you are and what it is that you want. You mentioned your name as if I should recognize it, but I assure you that, beyond obvious facts that you are a bachelor, a solicitor, a Freemason, and an asthmatic, I know nothing whatever about you."

Familiar as I was with my friend's methods, it was not difficult for me to follow his deductions, and to observe the untidiness of attire, the sheaf of legal papers, the watch-charm, and the breathing which had prompted them. Our client, however, stared in amazement.

" Yes, I am all that, Mr. Holmes, and in addition I am the most unfortunate man at this moment in London. For Heaven's sake don't abandon me, Mr. Holmes! If they come to arrest me before I have finished my story, make them give me time, so that I may tell you the whole truth. I could go to gaol happy if I knew that you were working for me outside."

" Arrest you ! " said Holmes. " This is really most grati—most interesting. On what charge do you expect to be arrested ? "

" Upon the charge of murdering Mr. Jonas Oldacre, of Lower Norwood."

My companion's expressive face showed a sympathy which was not, I am afraid, unmixed with satisfaction.

. . . A WILD-EYED AND FRANTIC YOUNG MAN, PALE, DISHEVELLED, AND PALPITATING, BURST INTO THE ROOM.

Illustration by Sidney Paget for the *Strand Magazine*, November, 1903.

The reader interested in the later career of young Dr. Verner is recommended to Mr. Anthony Boucher's "The Anomoly of the Empty Man," in his collection *Far and Away* (New York: Ballantine Books, 1953).

3 *which so nearly cost us both our lives.* The *Friesland*, a real ship, was located by Mr. Richard W. Clarke ("On the Nomenclature of Watson's Ships") "under Belgian rather than French registry." The late Christopher Morley, who crossed in her on one of her later voyages, Philadelphia to Liverpool, September, 1910, described her as "a beauty, a smart little Red Star liner."

Mr. Ray Kierman, noting that it was "the SS *Friesland*, a Dutch-American liner," which sighted Professor Challenger's pterodactyl when it escaped from the Queen's Hall (*The Lost World*) suggested, in "A Shocking Affair," that Holmes and Watson, retained by Challenger, had chartered the steamship and "placed the vessel in the very path [Holmes'] matchless brain told him the beast would pursue [on its flight back to Maple White Land]. . . . There seems no doubt that Holmes lured the monster to the very decks of the vessel, and there . . . fought it out. . . . There seems little doubt, either, that Watson, in the nick of time, when the pterodactyl had Holmes down for the last prod of its vile and lethal beak, stepped forward and sent a bullet through the brainless skull of the creature . . ."

But Mr. T. S. Blakeney objected ("Some Disjecta Membra") that : "Unfortunately, the dates do not appear to agree. Holmes' affair on the *Friesland* was after The Return and before 'The Adventure of the Norwood Builder' [which Mr. Blakeney places in August, 1894], and this would give us Spring/Summer of 1894. This was not the time of year when Challenger's pterodactyl left England; Malone gives the date as November 7th/8th, though closer examination makes it clear that the month could not have been earlier than December. The year of *The Lost World* would seem to be 1906 . . ."

"Dear me !" said he; "it was only this moment at breakfast that I was saying to my friend, Dr. Watson, that sensational cases had disappeared out of our papers."

Our visitor stretched forward a quivering hand and picked up the *Daily Telegraph*, which still lay upon Holmes' knee.

"If you had looked at it, sir, you would have seen at a glance what the errand is on which I have come to you this morning. I feel as if my name and my misfortune must be in every man's mouth." He turned it over to expose the central page. "Here it is, and with your permission I will read it to you. Listen to this, Mr. Holmes. The headlines are : ' Mysterious affair at Lower Norwood. Disappearance of a Well-known Builder. Suspicion of Murder and Arson. A Clue to the Criminal.' That is the clue which they are already following, Mr. Holmes, and I know that it leads infallibly to me. I have been followed from London Bridge Station, and I am sure that they are only waiting for the warrant to arrest me. It will break my mother's heart—it will break her heart !" He wrung his hands in an agony of apprehension, and swayed backwards and forwards in his chair.

I looked with interest upon this man, who was accused of being the perpetrator of a crime of violence. He was flaxen-haired and handsome in a washed-out negative fashion, with frightened blue eyes and a clean-shaven face, with a weak, sensitive mouth. His age may have been about twenty-seven ; his dress and bearing, that of a gentleman. From the pocket of his light summer overcoat protruded the bundle of endorsed papers which proclaimed his profession.

"We must use what time we have," said Holmes. "Watson, would you have the kindness to take the paper and to read me the paragraph in question ?"

Underneath the vigorous headlines which our client had quoted I read the following suggestive narrative :

4   Late last night, or early this morning, an incident occurred at Lower Norwood which points, it is feared, to a serious crime. Mr. Jonas Oldacre is a well-known resident of that suburb, where he has carried on his business as a builder for many years. Mr. Oldacre is a bachelor, fifty-two years of age, and lives in Deep Dene House, at the Sydenham end of the road of that name. He has had the reputation of being a man of eccentric habits, secretive and retiring. For some years he has practically withdrawn from the business, in which he is said to have amassed considerable wealth. A small timber-yard still exists, however, at the back of the house, and last night, about twelve o'clock, an alarm was given that one of the stacks was on fire. The engines were soon upon the spot, but the dry wood burned with great fury, and it was impossible to arrest the conflagration until the stack had been entirely consumed. Up to this point the incident bore the appearance of an ordinary accident, but fresh indications seem to point to serious crime. Surprise was expressed at the absence of the master of the establishment from the scene of the fire, and an inquiry followed which showed that he had disappeared from the house. An examination of his room revealed that the bed had not been slept in, that a safe which stood in it was open, that a number of important papers were scattered about the room, and, finally, that there were signs of a murderous struggle, slight traces of blood being found within the room,

"I HAVE BEEN FOLLOWED FROM LONDON BRIDGE STATION . . ."

The approach to London Bridge Station, in a photograph taken about 1880. From Michael Harrison's *In the Footsteps of Sherlock Holmes*.

4 *Late last night, or early this morning.* "Now this really was swift work in the *Telegraph* office," Mr. John Hyslop wrote in "Sherlock Holmes and the Press." "The murder took place, said the newspaper, last night or in the early morning. Yet here was the *Telegraph* with a full story . . ."

and an oaken walking-stick which also showed stains of blood upon the handle. It is known that Mr. Jonas Oldacre had received a late visitor in his bedroom upon that night, and the stick found has been identified as the property of this person, who is a young London solicitor named John Hector McFarlane, junior partner of Graham & McFarlane, of 426 Gresham Buildings, E.C. The police believe that they have evidence in their possession which supplies a very convincing motive for the crime, and altogether it cannot be doubted that sensational developments will follow.

LATER.—It is rumoured as we go to press that Mr. John Hector McFarlane has actually been arrested on the charge of the murder of Mr. Jonas Oldacre. It is at least certain that a warrant has been issued. There have been further and sinister developments in the investigation at Norwood. Besides the signs of a struggle in the room of the unfortunate builder, it is now known that the French windows of his bedroom (which is on the ground floor) were found to be open, that there were marks as if some bulky object had been dragged across to the wood-pile, and, finally, it is asserted that charred remains have been found among the charcoal ashes of the fire The police theory is that a most sensational crime has been committed, that the victim was clubbed to death in his own bedroom, his papers rifled, and his dead body dragged across to the wood-stack, which was then ignited so as to hide all traces of the crime. The conduct of the criminal investigation has been left in the experienced hands of Inspector Lestrade, of Scotland Yard, who is following up the clues with his accustomed energy and sagacity.

Sherlock Holmes listened with closed eyes and finger-tips together to this remarkable account.

" The case has certainly some points of interest," said he, in his languid fashion. " May I ask, in the first place, Mr. McFarlane, how it is that you are still at liberty, since there appears to be enough evidence to justify your arrest ? "

" I live at Torrington Lodge, Blackheath, with my **5** parents, Mr. Holmes ; but last night, having to do business very late with Mr. Jonas Oldacre, I stayed at an hotel in Norwood, and came to my business from there. **6** I knew nothing of this affair until I was in the train, when I read what you have just heard. I at once saw the horrible danger of my position, and I hurried to put the case into your hands. I have no doubt that I should have been arrested either at my City office or at my home. A man followed me from London Bridge Station, and I have no doubt—— Great heaven, what is that ? "

It was a clang of the bell, followed instantly by heavy steps upon the stair. A moment later our old friend Lestrade appeared in the doorway. Over his shoulder I caught a glimpse of one or two uniformed policemen outside.

" Mr. John Hector McFarlane," said Lestrade.

Our unfortunate client rose with a ghastly face.

" I arrest you for the wilful murder of Mr. Jonas Oldacre, of Lower Norwood."

McFarlane turned to us with a gesture of despair, and sank into his chair once more like one who is crushed.

" One moment, Lestrade," said Holmes. " Half an hour more or less can make no difference to you, and the gentleman was about to give us an account of this very interesting affair, which might aid us in clearing it up."

" I think there will be no difficulty in clearing it up,"

5 *Blackheath*. In Lewisham, Blackheath is one of the most agreeable of the London suburbs. Blackheath Common, comprising 267 acres, is known as the place where Wat Tyler in 1381 and Jack Cade in 1450 marshaled their hosts; here, too, once took place many highway robberies; here, too, the game of golf was introduced to an unappreciative London public by James I.

6 *and came to my business from there*. "It has always bothered me," the late Christopher Morley wrote, "why could not the unhappy John Hector McFarlane get back from Lower Norwood to Blackheath that night? It was 'between eleven and twelve' when he and Jonas Oldacre finished their business. Young McFarlane said that it was so late he couldn't get back to Blackheath. . . . He could certainly have got back to Blackheath that night if he had really wanted to. It was only four miles if he wanted to walk."

"MR. JOHN HECTOR MCFARLANE," SAID LESTRADE.

Illustration by Frederic Dorr Steele for *Collier's Magazine*, October 31, 1903.

7 *are the rough draft.* ". . . an English will, to be valid, requires two witnesses," Mr. S. T. L. Harbottle wrote in "Sherlock Holmes and the Law." "If it be supposed that McFarlane himself was the second witness then this would have invalidated the bequest of almost all Oldacre's property to McFarlane (Wills Act of 1837). In either case the will's main object was defeated. . . . Either [McFarlane] was a most unreliable solicitor who had acted in error, or he intended to defraud his client. . . . I fear McFarlane deliberately planned that the will should be ineffective. The fact that it was written on blue paper (at that time universally used for drafts and not for final copies or engrossments) then assumes a sinister significance."

said Lestrade grimly.

" None the less, with your permission, I should be much interested to hear his account."

" Well, Mr. Holmes, it is difficult for me to refuse you anything, for you have been of use to the Force once or twice in the past, and we owe you a good turn at Scotland Yard," said Lestrade. " At the same time, I must remain with my prisoner, and I am bound to warn him that anything he may say will appear in evidence against him."

" I wish nothing better," said our client. " All I ask is that you should hear and recognize the absolute truth."

Lestrade looked at his watch. " I'll give you half an hour," said he.

" I must explain first," said McFarlane, " that I knew nothing of Mr. Jonas Oldacre. His name was familiar to me ; for many years ago my parents were acquainted with him, but they drifted apart. I was very much surprised, therefore, when yesterday, about three o'clock in the afternoon, he walked into my office in the City. But I was still more astonished when he told me the object of his visit. He had in his hand several sheets of a note-book, covered with scribbled writing—here they are—and he laid them on my table.

" ' Here is my will,' said he. ' I want you, Mr. McFarlane, to cast it into proper legal shape. I will sit here while you do so."

" I set myself to copy it, and you can imagine my astonishment when I found that, with some reservations, he had left all his property to me. He was a strange, little, ferret-like man, with white eyelashes, and when I looked up at him I found his keen grey eyes fixed upon me with an amused expression. I could hardly believe my own senses as I read the terms of the will ; but he explained that he was a bachelor with hardly any living relation, that he had known my parents in his youth, and that he had always heard of me as a very deserving young man, and was assured that his money would be in worthy hands. Of course, I could only stammer out my thanks. The will was duly finished, signed, and witnessed by my clerk. This is it on the blue paper, and

7 these slips, as I have explained, are the rough draft. Mr. Jonas Oldacre then informed me that there were a number of documents—building leases, title-deeds, mortgages, scrip, and so forth—which it was necessary that I should see and understand. He said that his mind would not be easy until the whole thing was settled, and he begged me to come out to his house at Norwood that night, bringing the will with me, and to arrange matters. ' Remember, my boy, not one word to your parents about the affair until everything is settled. We will keep it as a little surprise for them.' He was very insistent upon this point, and made me promise it faithfully.

" You can imagine, Mr. Holmes, that I was not in a humour to refuse him anything that he might ask. He was my benefactor, and all my desire was to carry out his wishes in every particular. I sent a telegram home, therefore, to say that I had important business on hand,

and that it was impossible for me to say how late I might be. Mr. Oldacre had told me that he would like me to have supper with him at nine, as he might not be home before that hour. I had some difficulty in finding his house, however, and it was nearly half-past before I reached it. I found him——"

" One moment ! " said Holmes. " Who opened the door ? "

" A middle-aged woman, who was, I suppose, his housekeeper."

" And it was she, I presume, who mentioned your name ? "

" Exactly," said McFarlane.

" Pray proceed."

Mr. McFarlane wiped his damp brow, and then continued his narrative :

" I was shown by this woman into a sitting-room, where a frugal supper was laid out. Afterwards Mr. Jonas Oldacre led me into his bedroom, in which there stood a heavy safe. This he opened and took out a mass of documents, which we went over together. It was between eleven and twelve when we finished. He remarked that we must not disturb the housekeeper. He showed me out through his own French window, which had been open all this time."

" Was the blind down ? " asked Holmes.

" I will not be sure, but I believe that it was only half down. Yes, I remember how he pulled it up in order to swing open the window. I could not find my stick, and he said, ' Never mind, my boy ; I shall see a good deal of you now, I hope, and I will keep your stick until you come back to claim it.' I left him there, the safe open, and the papers made up in packets upon the table. It was so late that I could not get back to Blackheath, so I spent the night at the ' Anerley Arms,' and I knew nothing more until I read of this horrible affair in the morning."

" Anything more that you would like to ask, Mr. Holmes ? " said Lestrade, whose eyebrows had gone up once or twice during this remarkable explanation.

" Not until I have been to Blackheath."

" You mean to Norwood," said Lestrade.

" Oh, yes ; no doubt that is what I must have meant," said Holmes, with his enigmatical smile. Lestrade had learned by more experiences than he would care to acknowledge that that razor-like brain could cut through that which was impenetrable to him. I saw him look curiously at my companion.

" I think I should like to have a word with you presently, Mr. Sherlock Holmes," said he. " Now, Mr. McFarlane, two of my constables are at the door, and there is a four-wheeler waiting." The wretched young man arose, and with a last beseeching glance at us he walked from the room. The officers conducted him to the cab, but Lestrade remained.

Holmes had picked up the pages which formed the rough draft of the will, and was looking at them with the keenest interest upon his face.

" There are some points about that document, Lestrade, are there not ? " said he pushing them over.

THE WRETCHED YOUNG MAN AROSE . . .

Illustration by Sidney Paget for the *Strand Magazine*, November, 1903.

The official looked at them with a puzzled expression.

" I can read the first few lines, and these in the middle of the second page, and one or two at the end. Those are as clear as print," said he ; " but the writing in between is very bad, and there are three places where I cannot read it at all."

" What do you make of that ? " said Holmes.

" Well, what do *you* make of it ? "

" That it was written in a train ; the good writing represents stations, the bad writing movement, and the very bad writing passing over points. A scientific expert would pronounce at once that this was drawn up on a suburban line, since nowhere save in the immediate vicinity of a great city could there be so quick a succession of points. Granting that his whole journey was occupied in drawing up the will, then the train was an express, only stopping once between Norwood and London Bridge."

Lestrade began to laugh.

" You are too many for me when you begin to get on your theories, Mr. Holmes," said he. " How does this bear on the case ? "

" Well, it corroborates the young man's story to the extent that the will was drawn up by Jonas Oldacre in his journey yesterday. It is curious—is it not ?—that a man should draw up so important a document in so haphazard a fashion. It suggests that he did not think it was going to be of much practical importance. If a man drew up a will which he did not intend ever to be effective he might do it so."

" Well, he drew up his own death-warrant at the same time," said Lestrade.

" Oh, you think so ? "

" Don't you ? "

" Well, it is quite possible ; but the case is not clear to me yet."

" Not clear ? Well, if that isn't clear, what *could* be clearer ? Here is a young man who learns suddenly that if a certain older man dies he will succeed to a fortune. What does he do ? He says nothing to anyone but he arranges that he shall go out on some pretext to see his client that night ; he waits until the only other person in the house is in bed, and then in the solitude of the man's room he murders him, burns his body in the wood-pile, and departs to a neighbouring hotel. The blood-stains in the room and also on the stick are very slight. It is probable that he imagined his crime to be a bloodless one, and hoped that if the body were consumed it would hide all traces of the method of his death—traces which for some reason must have pointed to him. Is all this not obvious ? "

" It strikes me, my good Lestrade, as being just a trifle too obvious," said Holmes. " You do not add imagination to your other great qualities ; but if you could for one moment put yourself in the place of this young man, would you choose the very night after the will had been made to commit your crime ? Would it not seem dangerous to you to make so very close a relation between the two incidents ? Again, would you choose an occasion when you are known to be in the house, when a servant has let you in ?   And, finally, would you take the great pains to conceal the body and yet leave your own stick as a sign that you were the criminal ?   Confess, Lestrade, that all this is very unlikely."

" As to the stick, Mr. Holmes, you know as well as I do that a criminal is often flurried and does things which a cool man would avoid.   He was very likely afraid to go back to the room.   Give me another theory that would fit the facts."

" I could very easily give you half a dozen," said Holmes.   " Here, for example, is a very possible and even probable one.   I make you a free present of it.   The older man is showing documents which are of evident value.   A passing tramp sees them through the window, the blind of which is only half down.   Exit the solicitor. Enter the tramp !   He seizes a stick, which he observes there, kills Oldacre, and departs after burning the body."

" Why should the tramp burn the body ? "

" For the matter of that, why should McFarlane ? "

" To hide some evidence."

" Possibly the tramp wanted to hide that any murder at all had been committed."

" And why did the tramp take nothing ? "

" Because they were papers that he could not negotiate."

Lestrade shook his head, though it seemed to me that his manner was less absolutely assured than before.

" Well, Mr. Sherlock Holmes, you may look for your tramp, and while you are finding him we will hold on to our man.   The future will show which is right.   Just notice this point, Mr. Holmes—that so far as we know none of the papers were removed, and that the prisoner is the one man in the world who had no reason for removing them since he was heir-at-law and would come into them in any case."

My friend seemed struck by this remark.

" I don't mean to deny that the evidence is in some ways very strongly in favour of your theory," said he.   " I only wish to point out that there are other theories possible. As you say, the future will decide.   Good morning !   I dare say that in the course of the day I shall drop in at Norwood and see how you are getting on."

When the detective departed my friend rose and made his preparations for the day's work with the alert air of a man who has a congenial task before him.

" My first movement, Watson," said he, as he bustled into his frock-coat, " must, as I said, be in the direction of Blackheath."

" And why not Norwood ? "

" Because we have in this case one singular incident coming close to the heels of another singular incident. The police are making the mistake of concentrating their attention upon the second because it happens to be the one which is actually criminal.   But it is evident to me that the logical way to approach the case is to begin by trying to throw some light upon the first incident—the curious will, so suddenly made, and to so unexpected an heir.   It may do something to simplify what followed. No, my dear fellow, I don't think you can help me.   There is no prospect of danger, or I should not dream of stir-

"MY FIRST MOVEMENT, WATSON, . . . MUST . . . BE IN THE DIRECTION OF BLACKHEATH."

Illustration by Sidney Paget for the *Strand Magazine*, November, 1903.

ring out without you. I trust that when I see you in the evening I will be able to report that I have been able to do something for this unfortunate youngster who has thrown himself upon my protection."

It was late when my friend returned, and I could see by a glance at his haggard and anxious face that the high hopes with which he had started had not been fulfilled. For an hour he droned away upon his violin, endeavouring to soothe his own ruffled spirits. At last he flung down the instrument and plunged into a detailed account of his misadventures.

"It's all going wrong, Watson—all as wrong as it can go. I kept a bold face before Lestrade, but, upon my soul, I believe that for once the fellow is on the right track and we are on the wrong. All my instincts are one way, and all the facts are the other, and I much fear that British juries have not yet attained that pitch of intelligence when they will give the preference to my theories over Lestrade's facts."

"Did you go to Blackheath?"

"Yes, Watson, I went there, and I found very quickly that the late lamented Oldacre was a pretty considerable blackguard. The father was away in search of his son. The mother was at home—a little, fluffy, blue-eyed person, in a tremor of fear and indignation. Of course, she would not admit even the possibility of his guilt. But she would not express either surprise or regret over the fate of Oldacre. On the contrary, she spoke of him with such bitterness that she was unconsciously considerably strengthening the case of the police ; for, of course, if her son had heard her speak of the man in that fashion it would predispose him towards hatred and violence. 'He was more like a malignant and cunning ape than a human being,' said she, 'and he always was, ever since he was a young man.'

" 'You knew him at the time?' said I.

" 'Yes, I knew him well ; in fact, he was an old suitor of mine. Thank Heaven that I had the sense to turn away from him and to marry a better, if a poorer, man. I was engaged to him, Mr. Holmes, when I heard a shocking story of how he had turned a cat loose in an aviary, and I was so horrified at his brutal cruelty that I would have nothing more to do with him.' She rummaged in a bureau, and presently she produced a photograph of a woman, shamefully defaced and mutilated with a knife. 'That is my own photograph,' said she. 'He sent it to me in that state, with his curse, upon my wedding morning.'

" 'Well,' said I, 'at least he has forgiven you now, since he has left all his property to your son.'

" 'Neither my son nor I want anything from Jonas Oldacre, dead or alive,' she cried, with a proper spirit. 'There is a God in heaven, Mr. Holmes, and that same God who has punished that wicked man will show in His own good time that my son's hands are guiltless of his blood.'

"Well, I tried one or two leads, but could get at nothing which would help our hypothesis, and several points which would make against it. I gave it up at last, and off I went to Norwood.

" 'HE SENT IT TO ME IN THAT STATE, WITH HIS CURSE, UPON MY WEDDING MORNING.' "

Illustration by Sidney Paget for the *Strand Magazine*, November, 1903.

" This place, Deep Dene House, is a big modern villa of staring brick, standing back in its own grounds, with a laurel-clumped lawn in front of it. To the right and some distance back from the road was the timber-yard which had been the scene of the fire. Here's a rough plan on a leaf of my notebook. This window on the left is the one which opens into Oldacre's room. You can look into it from the road, you see. That is about the only bit of consolation I have had to-day. Lestrade was not there, but his head constable did the honours. They had just made a great treasure-trove. They had spent the morning raking among the ashes of the burned wood-pile, and besides the charred organic remains they had secured several discoloured metal discs. I examined them with care, and there was no doubt that they were trouser buttons. I even distinguished that one of them was marked with the name of ' Hyams,' who was Old-acre's tailor. I then worked the lawn very carefully for signs and traces, but this drought has made every-thing as hard as iron. Nothing was to be seen save that somebody or a bundle had been dragged through a low privet hedge which is in a line with the wood-pile. All that, of course, fits in with the official theory. I crawled about the lawn with an August sun on my back. But I got up at the end of an hour no wiser than before.

" Well, after this fiasco I went into the bedroom and examined that also. The blood-stains were very slight, mere smears and discolorations, but undoubtedly fresh. The stick had been removed, but there also the marks were slight. There is no doubt about the stick belonging to our client. He admits it. Footmarks of both men could be made out on the carpet, but none of any third person, which again is a trick for the other side. They were piling up their score all the time, and we were at a stand-still.

" Only one little gleam of hope did I get—and yet it amounted to nothing. I examined the contents of the safe, most of which had been taken out and left on the table. The papers had been made up into sealed en-velopes, one or two of which had been opened by the police. They were not, so far as I could judge, of any great value, nor did the bank book show that Mr. Old-acre was in such very affluent circumstances. But it seemed to me that all the papers were not there. There were allusions to some deeds—possibly the more valuable —which I could not find. This, of course, if we could definitely prove it, would turn Lestrade's argument against himself, for who would steal a thing if he knew that he would shortly inherit it ?

" Finally, having drawn every other cover and picked up no scent, I tried my luck with the housekeeper. Mrs. Lexington is her name, a little, dark, silent person, with suspicious and sidelong eyes. She could tell us something if she would—I am convinced of it. But she was as close as wax. Yes, she had let Mr. McFar-lane in at half-past nine. She wished her hand had withered before she had done so. She had gone to bed at half-past ten. Her room was at the other end of the house, and she could hear nothing of what passed. Mr. McFarlane had left his hat, and to the best of her

8 *who wanted us to get him off in '87?* The late
H. W. Bell thought that Stevens was perhaps the
murderer in the Camberwell Poisoning Case, referred to in "The Five Orange Pips."

belief his stick, in the hall. She had been awakened by
the alarm of fire. Her poor, dear master had certainly
been murdered. Had he any enemies ? Well, every
man had enemies, but Mr. Oldacre kept himself very
much to himself, and only met people in the way of
business. She had seen the buttons, and was sure that
they belonged to the clothes which he had worn last
night. The wood-pile was very dry, for it had not rained
for a month. It burned like a tinder, and by the time
she reached the spot nothing could be seen but flames.
She and all the firemen smelled the burned flesh from
inside it. She knew nothing of the papers, nor of Mr.
Oldacre's private affairs.

" So, my dear Watson, there's my report of a failure.
And yet—and yet"—he clenched his thin hands in a paroxysm of conviction—" I *know* it's all wrong. I feel it in
my bones. There is something that has not come out,
and that housekeeper knows it. There was a sort of
sulky defiance in her eyes which only goes with guilty
knowledge. However, there's no good talking any more
about it, Watson ; but unless some lucky chance comes
our way I fear that the Norwood Disappearance Case
will not figure in that chronicle of our successes which
I foresee that a patient public will sooner or later have to
endure."

" Surely," said I, " the man's appearance would go
far with any jury ? "

" That is a dangerous argument, my dear Watson.
You remember that terrible murderer, Bert Stevens, who
8 wanted us to get him off in '87 ? Was there ever a
more mild-mannered, Sunday-school young man ? "

" It is true."

" Unless we succeed in establishing an alternative
theory, this man is lost. You can hardly find a flaw in
the case which can now be presented against him, and
all further investigation has served to strengthen it. By
the way, there is one curious little point about those
papers which may serve us as the starting-point for an
inquiry. On looking over the bank book I found that
the low state of the balance was principally due to large
cheques which have been made out during the last year
to Mr. Cornelius. I confess that I should be interested to know who this Mr. Cornelius may be with
whom a retired builder has such very large transactions.
Is it possible that he has had a hand in the affair ? Cornelius might be a broker, but we have found no scrip
to correspond with these large payments. Failing any
other indication, my researches must now take the
direction of an inquiry at the bank for the gentleman
who has cashed these cheques. But I fear, my dear
fellow, that our case will end ingloriously by Lestrade
hanging our client, which will certainly be a triumph for
Scotland Yard."

I do not know how far Sherlock Holmes took any sleep
that night, but when I came down to breakfast I found
him pale and harassed, his bright eyes the brighter for the
dark shadows round them. The carpet round his chair
was littered with cigarette ends, and with the early
editions of the morning papers. An open telegram lay
upon the table.

"What do you think of this, Watson?" he asked, tossing it across.

It was from Norwood, and ran as follows:

"Important fresh evidence to hand. McFarlane's guilt definitely established. Advise you to abandon case.—LESTRADE."

"This sounds serious," said I.

"It is Lestrade's little cock-a-doodle of victory," Holmes answered with a bitter smile. "And yet it may be premature to abandon the case. After all, important fresh evidence is a two-edged thing, and may possibly cut in a very different direction to that which Lestrade imagines. Take your breakfast, Watson, and we will go out together and see what we can do. I feel as if I shall need your company and your moral support to-day."

My friend had no breakfast himself, for it was one of his peculiarities that in his more intense moments he would permit himself no food, and I have known him presume upon his iron strength until he has fainted from pure inanition. "At present I cannot spare energy and nerve force for digestion," he would say, in answer to my medical remonstrances. I was not surprised, therefore, when this morning he left his untouched meal behind him and started with me for Norwood. A crowd of morbid sightseers were still gathered round Deep Dene House, which was just such a suburban villa as I had pictured. Within the gates Lestrade met us, his face flushed with victory, his manner grossly triumphant.

"Well, Mr. Holmes, have you proved us to be wrong yet? Have you found your tramp?" he cried.

"I have formed no conclusion whatever," my companion answered.

"But we formed ours yesterday, and now it proves to be correct; so you must acknowledge that we have been a little in front of you this time, Mr. Holmes."

"You certainly have the air of something unusual having occurred," said Holmes.

Lestrade laughed loudly.

"You don't like being beaten any more than the rest of us do," said he. "A man can't expect always to have it his own way—can he, Dr. Watson? Step this way, if you please, gentlemen, and I think I can convince you once for all that it was John McFarlane who did this crime."

He led us through the passage and out into a dark hall beyond.

"This is where young McFarlane must have come out to get his hat after the crime was done," said he. "Now look at this." With dramatic suddenness he struck a match, and by its light exposed a stain of blood upon the whitewashed wall. As he held the match nearer I saw that it was more than a stain. It was the well-marked print of a thumb.

"Look at that with your magnifying glass, Mr. Holmes."

"Yes, I am doing so."

"You are aware that no two thumb-marks are alike?"

"I have heard something of the kind."   **9**

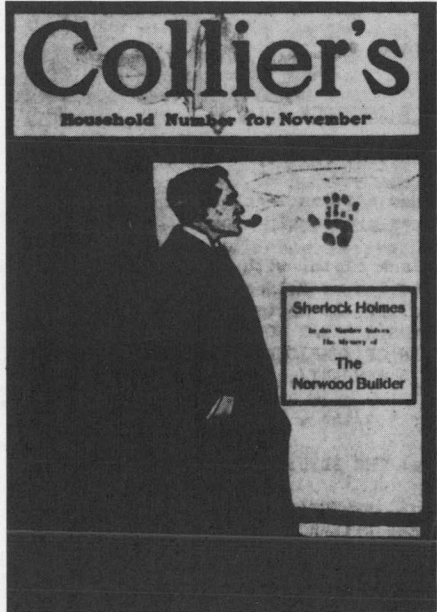

IT WAS THE WELL-MARKED PRINT OF A THUMB.

The cover of *Collier's Magazine* for October 31, 1903, showing Frederic Dorr Steele's illustration. We see that Holmes for some reason has chosen to wear his dressing gown to Deep Dene House. In addition, "the well-marked print of a thumb" has grown into the bloody print of an entire hand. Sidney Paget illustrated the same scene for the *Strand Magazine*, November, 1903.

9 *"I have heard something of the kind."* "It is odd," Mr. Vernon Rendall wrote in "The Limitations of Sherlock Holmes," "since [Holmes] admired the work of Bertillon ["The Naval Treaty"], that he did not discover the important paper which Galton gave to the British Association in 1899 on *Finger-prints and the Detection of Crime in India.* Galton's method was examined by a committee appointed by Asquith, in 1894. . . . Finger-prints as a means of detecting criminals were first used by Sir William Herschel of the I.C.S. in the district of Hooghli, in Bengal. They were recognized as superior to Bertillon's anthropometry, and were recommended for all India in a report of 1896. All one can suggest is that Holmes was not eager to take up other people's methods. With his vanity, he found it difficult to use another expert to help him."

But Mr. Rendall is clearly in error here. Since "The Adventure of the Norwood Builder" took place in 1895, it is hardly odd that Holmes had not read a paper given in 1899. On the contrary, the obviously sarcastic tone of Holmes' "I have heard something of the kind" clearly indicates that he had studied fingerprints and was aware of their importance in the detection of crime. It is more difficult to explain how Lestrade, in 1895, was aware that "no two thumb-prints are alike," since the system was not adopted by Scotland Yard until 1901.

" Well, then, will you please compare that print with this wax impression of young McFarlane's right thumb, taken by my orders this morning ? "

As he held the waxen print close to the blood-stain it did not take a magnifying glass to see that the two were undoubtedly from the same thumb. It was evident to me that our unfortunate client was lost.

" That is final," said Lestrade.

" Yes, that is final," I voluntarily echoed.

" It is final," said Holmes.

Something in his tone caught my ear, and I turned to look at him. An extraordinary change had come over his face. It was writhing with inward merriment.

His two eyes were shining like stars. It seemed to me that he was making desperate efforts to restrain a convulsive attack of laughter.

" Dear me ! Dear me ! " he said at last. " Well, now, who would have thought it ? And how deceptive appearances may be, to be sure ! Such a nice young man to look at ! It is a lesson to us not to trust our own judgment—is it not, Lestrade ? "

" Yes, some of us are a little too much inclined to be cocksure, Mr. Holmes," said Lestrade. The man's insolence was maddening, but we could not resent it.

" What a providential thing that this young man should press his right thumb against the wall in taking his hat from the peg ! Such a very natural action, too, if you come to think of it." Holmes was outwardly calm, but his whole body gave a wriggle of suppressed excitement as he spoke. " By the way, Lestrade, who made this remarkable discovery ? "

" It was the housekeeper, Mrs. Lexington, who drew the night constable's attention to it ? "

" Where was the night constable ? "

" He remained on guard in the bedroom where the crime was committed, so as to see that nothing was touched."

" But why didn't the police see this mark yesterday ? "

" Well, we had no particular reason to make a careful examination of the hall. Besides, it's not in a very prominent place, as you see."

" No, no, of course not. I suppose there is no doubt that the mark was there yesterday ? "

Lestrade looked at Holmes as if he thought he was going out of his mind. I confess that I was myself surprised both at his hilarious manner and at his rather wild observation.

" I don't know whether you think that McFarlane came out of gaol in the dead of the night in order to strengthen the evidence against himself," said Lestrade. " I leave it to any expert in the world whether that is not the mark of his thumb."

" It is unquestionably the mark of his thumb."

" There, that's enough," said Lestrade. " I am a practical man, Mr. Holmes, and when I have got my evidence I come to my conclusions. If you have anything to say you will find me writing my report in the sitting-room."

Holmes had recovered his equanimity, though I still seemed to detect gleams of amusement in his expression.

" Dear me, this is a very sad development, Watson, is it not ? " said he. " And yet there are singular points about it which hold out some hopes for our client."

" I am delighted to hear it," said I heartily. " I was afraid it was all up with him."

" I would hardly go so far as to say that, my dear Watson. The fact is that there is one really serious flaw in this evidence to which our friend attaches so much importance."

" Indeed, Holmes ! What is it ? "

" Only this—that I *know* that that mark was not there when I examined the hall yesterday. And now, Watson, let us have a little stroll round in the sunshine."

With a confused brain, but with a heart into which some warmth of hope was returning, I accompanied my friend in a walk round the garden. Holmes took each face of the house in turn and examined it with great interest. He then led the way inside, and went over the whole building from basement to attics. Most of the rooms were unfurnished, but none the less Holmes inspected them all minutely. Finally, on the top corridor, which ran outside three untenanted bedrooms, he again was seized with a spasm of merriment.

" There are really some very unique features about this case, Watson," said he. " I think it is time now that we took our friend Lestrade into our confidence. He has had his little smile at our expense, and perhaps we may do as much by him if my reading of this problem proves to be correct. Yes, yes ; I think I see how we should approach it."

The Scotland Yard inspector was still writing in the parlour when Holmes interrupted him.

" I understood that you were writing a report of this case," said he.

" So I am."

" Don't you think it may be a little premature ? I can't help thinking that your evidence is not complete."

Lestrade knew my friend too well to disregard his words. He laid down his pen and looked curiously at him.

" What do you mean, Mr. Holmes ? "

" Only that there is an important witness whom you have not seen."

" Can you produce him ? "

" I think I can."

" Then do so."

" I will do my best. How many constables have you ? "

" There are three within call."

" Excellent ! " said Holmes. " May I ask if they are all large, able-bodied men with powerful voices ? "

" I have no doubt they are, though I fail to see what their voices have to do with it."

" Perhaps I can help you to see that, and one or two other things as well," said Holmes. " Kindly summon your men, and I will try."

... A LITTLE WIZENED MAN DARTED OUT ...

Illustration by Sidney Paget for the *Strand Magazine*, November, 1903.

Five minutes later three policemen had assembled in the hall.

" In the outhouse you will find a considerable quantity of straw," said Holmes. " I will ask you to carry in two bundles of it. I think it will be of the greatest assistance in producing the witness whom I require. Thank you very much. I believe you have some matches in your pocket, Watson. Now, Mr. Lestrade, I will ask you all to accompany me to the top landing."

As I have said, there was a broad corridor there, which ran outside three empty bedrooms. At one end of the corridor we were all marshalled by Sherlock Holmes, the constables grinning, and Lestrade staring at my friend with amazement, expectation, and derision chasing each other across his features. Holmes stood before us with an air of a conjurer who is performing a trick.

" Would you kindly send one of your constables for two buckets of water ? Put the straw on the floor here, free from the wall on either side. Now I think that we are all ready."

Lestrade's face had begun to grow red and angry.

" I don't know whether you are playing a game with us, Mr. Sherlock Holmes," said he. " If you know anything, you can surely say it without all this tom-foolery."

" I assure you, my good Lestrade, that I have an excellent reason for everything that I do. You may possibly remember that you chaffed me a little some hours ago, when the sun seemed on your side of the hedge, so you must not grudge me a little pomp and ceremony now. Might I ask you, Watson, to open that window, and then to put a match to the edge of the straw ? "

I did so, and, driven by the draught, a coil of grey smoke swirled down the corridor, while the dry straw crackled and flamed.

" Now we must see if we can find this witness for you, Lestrade. Might I ask you all to join in the cry of ' Fire ' ? Now, then : one, two, three——"

" Fire ! " we all yelled.

" Thank you. I will trouble you once again."

" Fire ! "

" Just once more, gentlemen, and all together."

" Fire ! " The shout must have rung over Norwood.

It had hardly died away when an amazing thing happened. A door suddenly flew open out of what appeared to be solid wall at the end of the corridor, and a little wizened man darted out of it, like a rabbit out of its burrow.

" Capital ! " said Holmes calmly. " Watson, a bucket of water over the straw. That will do ! Lestrade, allow me to present you with your principal missing witness, Mr. Jonas Oldacre."

The detective stared at the new-comer with blank amazement. The latter was blinking in the bright light of the corridor, and peering at us and at the smouldering fire. It was an odious face—crafty, vicious, malignant, with shifty, light-grey eyes and white eyelashes.

" What's this, then ? " said Lestrade at last. " What have you been doing all this time, eh ? "

Oldacre gave an uneasy laugh, shrinking back from the furious red face of the angry detective.

" I have done no harm."

" No harm ? You have done your best to get an innocent man hanged. If it wasn't for this gentleman here, I am not sure that you would not have succeeded."

The wretched creature began to whimper.

" I am sure, sir, it was only my practical joke."

" Oh ! a joke, was it ? You won't find the laugh on your side, I promise you. Take him down and keep him in the sitting-room until I come. Mr. Holmes," he continued, when they had gone, " I could not speak before the constables, but I don't mind saying, in the presence of Dr. Watson, that this is the brightest thing that you have done yet, though it is a mystery to me how you did it. You have saved an innocent man's life, and you have prevented a very grave scandal, which would have ruined my reputation in the Force."

Holmes smiled and clapped Lestrade upon the shoulder.

" Instead of being ruined, my good sir, you will find that your reputation has been enormously enhanced. Just make a few alterations in that report which you were writing, and they will understand how hard it is to throw dust in the eyes of Inspector Lestrade."

" And you don't want your name to appear ? "

" Not at all. The work is its own reward. Perhaps I shall get the credit also at some distant day when I permit my zealous historian to lay out his foolscap once more —eh, Watson ? Well, now, let us see where this rat has been lurking."

A lath-and-plaster partition had been run across the passage six feet from the end, with a door cunningly concealed in it. It was lit within by slits under the eaves. A few articles of furniture and a supply of food and water were within, together with a number of books and papers.

" There's the advantage of being a builder," said Holmes as we came out. " He was able to fix up his own little hiding-place without any confederate—save, of course, that precious housekeeper of his, whom I should lose no time in adding to your bag, Lestrade."

" I will take your advice. But how did you know of this place, Mr. Holmes ? "

" I made up my mind that the fellow was in hiding in the house. When I paced one corridor and found it six feet shorter than the corresponding one below, it was pretty clear where he was. I thought he had not the nerve to lie quiet before an alarm of fire. We could, of course, have gone in and taken him, but it amused me to make him reveal himself ; besides, I owed you a little mystification, Lestrade, for your chaff in the morning."

" Well, sir, you certainly got equal with me on that. But how in the world did you know that he was in the house at all ? "

" The thumb-mark, Lestrade. You said it was final ; and so it was, in a very different sense. I knew it had not been there the day before. I pay a good deal of attention to matters of detail, as you may have observed, and I had examined the hall, and was sure that the wall was clear. Therefore, it had been put on during the night."

HOLMES SMILED AND CLAPPED LESTRADE
UPON THE SHOULDER.

Illustration by Sidney Paget for the *Strand Magazine*, November, 1903.

" But how ? "

" Very simply. When those packets were sealed up, Jonas Oldacre got McFarlane to secure one of the seals by putting his thumb upon the soft wax. It would be done so quickly and so naturally that I dare say the young man himself has no recollection of it. Very likely it just so happened, and Oldacre had himself no notion of the use he would put it to. Brooding over the case in that den of his, it suddenly struck him what absolutely damning evidence he could make against McFarlane by using that thumb-mark. It was the simplest thing in the world for him to take a wax impression from the seal, to moisten it in as much blood as he could get from a pin-prick, and to put the mark upon the wall during the night, either with his own hand or with that of his house-keeper. If you examine among these documents which he took with him into his retreat, I will lay you a wager that you find the seal with the thumb-mark upon it."

" Wonderful ! " said Lestrade. " Wonderful ! It's all as clear as crystal, as you put it. But what is the object of this deep deception, Mr. Holmes ? "

It was amusing to me to see how the detective's over-bearing manner had changed suddenly to that of a child asking questions of its teacher.

" Well, I don't think that is very hard to explain. A very deep, malicious, vindictive person is the gentleman who is now awaiting us downstairs. You know that he was once refused by McFarlane's mother ? You don't ! I told you that you should go to Blackheath first and Norwood afterwards. Well, this injury, as he would consider it, has rankled in his wicked, scheming brain, and all his life he has longed for vengeance, but never seen his chance. During the last year or two things have gone against him—secret speculation, I think—and he finds himself in a bad way. He determines to swindle his creditors, and for this purpose he pays large cheques to a certain Mr. Cornelius, who is, I imagine, himself under another name. I have not traced these cheques yet, but I have no doubt that they were banked under that name at some provincial town where Oldacre from time to time led a double existence. He intended to change his name altogether, draw this money, and vanish, starting life again elsewhere."

" Well, that's likely enough."

" It would strike him that in disappearing he might throw all pursuit off his track, and at the same time have an ample and crushing revenge upon his old sweetheart, if he could give the impression that he had been mur-dered by her only child. It was a masterpiece of vil-lainy, and he carried it out like a master. The idea of the will, which would give an obvious motive for the crime, the secret visit unknown to his own parents, the retention of the stick, the blood, and the animal remains and buttons in the wood-pile, all were admirable. It was a net from which it seemed to me a few hours ago that there was no possible escape. But he had not that supreme gift of the artist, the knowledge of when to stop. He wished to improve that which was already perfect—to draw the rope tighter yet round the neck of his unfortunate victim—and so he ruined all. Let us descend, Lestrade. There are just one or two questions that I would ask him."

The malignant creature was seated in his own parlour with a policeman upon each side of him.

" It was a joke, my good sir ; a practical joke, nothing more," he whined incessantly. " I assure you, sir, that I simply concealed myself in order to see the effect of my disappearance, and I am sure that you would not be so unjust as to imagine that I would have allowed any harm to befall poor young Mr. McFarlane."

" That's for the jury to decide," said Lestrade. " Anyhow, we shall have you on a charge of conspiracy, if not for attempted murder."

" And you'll probably find that your creditors will impound the banking account of Mr. Cornelius," said Holmes.

The little man started and turned his malignant eyes upon my friend.

" I have to thank you for a good deal," said he. " Perhaps I'll pay my debt some day."

Holmes smiled indulgently.

" I fancy that for some few years you will find your time very fully occupied," said he. " By the way, what was it you put into the wood-pile besides your old trousers ? A dead dog, or rabbits, or what ? You won't tell ? Dear me, how very unkind of you ! Well, well, I dare say that a couple of rabbits would account both for the blood and for the charred ashes. If ever you write an account, Watson, you can make rabbits serve your turn."

Bibliographical Note: The original manuscript of "The Adventure of the Norwood Builder," 50 pages, with numerous corrections, was donated by Sir Arthur Conan Doyle to a Red Cross Charity Sale and auctioned in London, April 22, 1918, bringing £12. It was auctioned again in New York City on February 13, 1923, bringing $100, and again in New York City, February 8, 1926, bringing only $60. It is presently owned by the New York Public Library.

55

THE ADVENTURE OF THE BRUCE-PARTINGTON PLANS

[Thursday, November 21, to Saturday, November 23, 1895]

1 *From the Monday to the Thursday.* Watson in this adventure is unusually precise in his dating, and there is no reason to doubt him: the meteorological reports for the period are quite compatible with his description of the weather. The case opened on *Thursday, November 21, 1895;* it closed on *Saturday, November 23, 1895.*

2 *the music of the Middle Ages.* ". . . it is strongly to be doubted that the word *recently* is accurate, for one does not suddenly become an authority in this field in a short time simply by adopting a hobby and with little or no technical study," Mr. Benjamin Grosbayne wrote in "Sherlock Holmes —Musician."

3 *an impending change of Government.* "There was indeed a 'revolution' (Turkey), 'a possible war' (troops left for Ashanti) and 'an impending change of Government' (Bechuanaland became part of Cape Colony)," Mrs. Jennifer Chorley wrote in "1896–1964, 'The Wheel Has Come Full Circle.'"

But the "impending change of Government" was probably much closer to Baker Street than Bechuanaland, as Mr. Owen F. Grazebrook pointed out in his essay on "Royalty" (in the Sherlockian Canon): "It was in July '95 that Lord Roseberry retired, after the country had thrown from office the remnants of the Liberal Party; it was the first among many of the Liberal debacles, and the corridors of Hatfield were full of rejoicing and bicycles. There can be no question that in November '95, 'an impending change of Government' in the ordinary sense of the words, would *not* be filling the columns of the Press. The only event of any importance in Court and political circles that Autumn was the substitution of the Duke of Cambridge by Lord Wolseley as Commander-in-Chief. An affair which needed a delicate hand, for it was Mr. Broderick's vote of censure, nominally on the supply of cordite, but in reality on the personality of the Commander-in-Chief, which had brought down the Government. Queen Victoria was not very fond of Wolseley, and very fond of the

IN the third week of November, in the year 1895, a dense yellow fog settled down upon London. From the Monday to the Thursday I doubt whether it was ever possible from our windows in Baker Street to see the loom of the opposite houses. The first day Holmes had spent in cross-indexing his huge book of references. The second and third had been patiently occupied upon a subject which he had recently made his hobby—the music of the Middle Ages. But when, for the fourth time, after pushing back our chairs from breakfast we saw the greasy, heavy brown swirl still drifting past us and condensing in oily drops upon the window-panes, my comrade's impatient and active nature could endure this drab existence no longer. He paced restlessly about our sitting-room in a fever of suppressed energy, biting his nails, tapping the furniture, and chafing against inaction.

" Nothing of interest in the paper, Watson ? " he said.

I was aware that by anything of interest, Holmes meant anything of criminal interest. There was the news of a revolution, of a possible war, and of an impending change of Government ; but these did not come within the horizon of my companion. I could see nothing recorded in the shape of crime which was not commonplace and futile. Holmes groaned and resumed his restless meanderings.

" The London criminal is certainly a dull fellow," said he, in the querulous voice of the sportsman whose game has failed him. " Look out of this window, Watson. See how the figures loom up, are dimly seen, and then blend once more into the cloud-bank. The thief or the murderer could roam London on such a day as the tiger does the jungle, unseen until he pounces, and then evident only to his victim."

" There have," said I, " been numerous petty thefts."

Holmes snorted his contempt.

" This great and sombre stage is set for something more worthy than that," said he. " It is fortunate for this community that I am not a criminal."

" It is, indeed ! " said I, heartily.

" Suppose that I were Brooks or Woodhouse, or any of the fifty men who have good reason for taking my life, how long could I survive against my own pursuit ? A summons, a bogus appointment, and all would be over.

It is well they don't have days of fog in the Latin countries —the countries of assassination. By Jove ! here comes something at last to break our dead monotony."

It was the maid with a telegram. Holmes tore it open and burst out laughing.

"Well, well ! What next ? " said he. " Brother Mycroft is coming round."

" Why not ? " I asked.

" Why not ? It is as if you met a tram-car coming down a country lane. Mycroft has his rails and he runs on them. His Pall Mall lodgings, the Diogenes Club, Whitehall—that is his cycle. Once, and only once, he has been here. What upheaval can possibly have derailed him ? "

" Does he not explain ? "

Holmes handed me his brother's telegram.

" Must see you over Cadogan West. Coming at once. MYCROFT."

" Cadogan West ? I have heard the name."

" It recalls nothing to my mind. But that Mycroft should break out in this erratic fashion ! A planet might as well leave its orbit. By the way, do you know what Mycroft is ? "

I had some vague recollection of an explanation at the time of the Adventure of the Greek Interpreter.

" You told me that he had some small office under the British Government."

Holmes chuckled.

" I did not know you quite so well in those days. One has to be discreet when one talks of high matters of state. **4** You are right in thinking that he is under the British Government. You would also be right in a sense if you said that occasionally he *is* the British Government."

" My dear Holmes ! "

" I thought I might surprise you. Mycroft draws four hundred and fifty pounds a year, remains a subordinate, **5** has no ambitions of any kind, will receive neither honour nor title, but remains the most indispensable man in the country."

" But how ? "

" Well, his position is unique. He has made it for himself. There has never been anything like it before, nor will be again. He has the tidiest and most orderly brain, with the greatest capacity for storing facts, of any man living. The same great powers which I have turned to the detection of crime he has used for this particular business. The conclusions of every department are passed to him, and he is the central exchange, the clearing-house, which makes out the balance. All other men are special- **6** ists, but his specialism is omniscience. We will suppose that a Minister needs information as to a point which involves the Navy, India, Canada and the bi-metallic ques- **7** tion ; he could get his separate advices from various departments upon each, but only Mycroft can focus them all, and say off-hand how each factor would affect the other. They began by using him as a short-cut, a convenience ; now he has made himself an essential. In that great brain of his everything is pigeon-holed, and can be

Duke. It may well be that in Dr. Watson's somewhat slipshod mind, *and being an old Army veteran*, the office of Commander-in-Chief *was* connected with the governance of the country, and that the substitution of the Duke by Wolseley meant, to him at any rate, 'an impending change of Government.' If this is so, November, 1895, may stand as being correct, for in November of that year the Queen graciously received Lord Wolseley and, to continue a military metaphor, 'buried the hatchet.' "

4 *One has to be discreet when one talks of high matters of state.* Dr. Felix Morley has written ("The Significance of the Second Stain") that "much can be read into Sherlock's tactful remark to Watson at this time." One can understand, Dr. Morley holds, that Watson's wound or wounds may have developed in him an isolationist attitude that could "stir a subconscious resentment whenever Holmes seemed inclined to endorse the principles of collective action. And we know that Holmes realized this idiosyncracy in his friend and as a result deliberately concealed many of the very important international undertakings to which his practice led. Thus Watson only knew from newspaper references that . . . Holmes was 'engaged by the French Government upon a matter of supreme importance' ["The Final Problem"]. The doctor was never told of the very delicate matter in which Holmes . . . had served the reigning family of Holland ["A Case of Identity"]. And more than five years passed after Watson's introduction to Mycroft Holmes before Sherlock thought it wise to give the doctor any indication of the enormous importance of his brother's governmental post."

5 *four hundred and fifty pounds a year.* About $2,250 in U.S. currency at the time.

6 *the clearing-house, which makes out the balance.* "Mycroft's curious position in the Government would seem to have points in common with that of his German contemporary, Holstein." Mr. T. S. Blakeney noted in *Sherlock Holmes: Fact or Fiction?*

7 *the bi-metallic question.* The ratio between gold and silver as legal tender. It was at that time an important political topic, particularly in the United States.

8 *and what is he to Mycroft?*" "... an instinctive paraphrase of Hamlet's 'What's Hecuba to him or he to Hecuba,'" Professor Clarke Olney wrote in "The Literacy of Sherlock Holmes."

9 *Woolwich Arsenal*." Woolwich, then part of Kent, has not changed much since Holmes *floruit*. Mr. Michael Harrison described it well (*In the Footsteps of Sherlock Holmes*): "Arsenal buildings, barracks, Georgian houses of senior officials, and miles of drab two-stories for the workers."

10 *Aldgate Station*. Not to be confused with Aldersgate, from which Holmes and Watson descended from the Underground during their reconnoitering mission at the time of "The Red-Headed League."

11 *wide of the metals upon the left hand of the track*. "The metals" is English for *rails*; in Britain, it should be remembered, all traffic moves on the left.

12 *Willesden*. A century ago Willesden, then called Wilsdon, was a retired village five miles from Oxford Street; today the borough of Willesden includes Brondesbury, Harlesden, Kensal Rise, and part of Cricklewood, and is an important railway junction of British Railways, Midland Region.

handed out in an instant. Again and again his word has decided the national policy. He lives in it. He thinks of nothing else save when, as an intellectual exercise, he unbends if I call upon him and ask him to advise me on one of my little problems. But Jupiter is descending to-day. What on earth can it mean ? Who is Cadogan **8** West, and what is he to Mycroft ? "

" I have it," I cried, and plunged among the litter of papers upon the sofa. " Yes, yes, here he is, sure enough ! Cadogan West was the young man who was found dead on the Underground on Tuesday morning."

Holmes sat up at attention, his pipe half-way to his lips.

" This must be serious, Watson. A death which has caused my brother to alter his habits can be no ordinary one. What in the world can he have to do with it ? The case was featureless as I remember it. The young man had apparently fallen out of the train and killed himself. He had not been robbed, and there was no particular reason to suspect violence. Is that not so ? "

" There has been an inquest," said I, " and a good many fresh facts have come out. Looked at more closely, I should certainly say that it was a curious case."

" Judging by its effect upon my brother, I should think it must be a most extraordinary one." He snuggled down in his arm-chair. " Now, Watson, let us have the facts."

" The man's name was Arthur Cadogan West. He was twenty-seven years of age, unmarried, and a clerk at **9** Woolwich Arsenal."

" Government employ. Behold the link with brother Mycroft ! "

" He left Woolwich suddenly on Monday night. Was last seen by his fiancée, Miss Violet Westbury, whom he left abruptly in the fog about 7.30 that evening. There was no quarrel between them and she can give no motive for his action. The next thing heard of him was when his dead body was discovered by a platelayer named Mason, **10** just outside Aldgate Station on the Underground system in London."

" When ? "

" The body was found at six on the Tuesday morning. It was lying wide of the metals upon the left hand of the **11** track as one goes eastward, at a point close to the station, where the line emerges from the tunnel in which it runs. The head was badly crushed—an injury which might well have been caused by a fall from the train. The body could only have come on the line in that way. Had it been carried down from any neighbouring street, it must have passed the station barriers, where a collector is always standing. This point seems absolutely certain."

" Very good. The case is definite enough. The man, dead or alive, either fell or was precipitated from a train. So much is clear to me. Continue."

" The trains which traverse the lines of rail beside which the body was found are those which run from west to east, **12** some being purely Metropolitan, and some from Willesden and outlying junctions. It can be stated for certain that this young man, when he met his death, was travelling in this direction at some late hour of the night, but at what point he entered the train it is impossible to state."

"His ticket, of course, would show that."

"There was no ticket in his pockets."

"No ticket! Dear me, Watson, this is really very singular. According to my experience it is not possible to reach the platform of a Metropolitan train without exhibiting one's ticket. Presumably, then, the young man had one. Was it taken from him in order to conceal the station from which he came? It is possible. Or did he drop it in the carriage? That also is possible. But the point is of curious interest. I understand that there was no sign of robbery?"

"Apparently not. There is a list here of his possessions. His purse contained two pounds fifteen. He had **13** also a cheque-book on the Woolwich branch of the Capital and Counties Bank. Through this his identity was established. There were also two dress-circle tickets for the Woolwich Theatre, dated for that very evening. Also a small packet of technical papers."

Holmes gave an exclamation of satisfaction.

"There we have it at last, Watson! British Government—Woolwich Arsenal—Technical papers—Brother Mycroft, the chain is complete. But here he comes, if I am not mistaken, to speak for himself."

A moment later the tall and portly form of Mycroft Holmes was ushered into the room. Heavily built and massive, there was a suggestion of uncouth physical inertia in the figure, but above this unwieldy frame there was perched a head so masterful in its brow, so alert in its steel-grey, deep-set eyes, so firm in its lips, and so subtle in its play of expression, that after the first glance one forgot the gross body and remembered only the dominant mind.

At his heels came our old friend Lestrade, of Scotland Yard—thin and austere. The gravity of both their faces foretold some weighty quest. The detective shook hands without a word. Mycroft Holmes struggled out of his overcoat and subsided into an arm-chair.

"A most annoying business, Sherlock," said he. "I extremely dislike altering my habits, but the powers that be would take no denial. In the present state of Siam it is most awkward that I should be away from the office. But it is a real crisis. I have never seen the Prime Minister so upset. As to the Admiralty—it is buzzing like an **14** overturned beehive. Have you read up the case?"

"We have just done so. What were the technical papers?"

"Ah, there's the point! Fortunately, it has not come out. The Press would be furious if it did. The papers which this wretched youth had in his pocket were the plans of the Bruce-Partington submarine."

Mycroft Holmes spoke with a solemnity which showed his sense of the importance of the subject. His brother and I sat expectant.

"Surely you have heard of it? I thought everyone had heard of it."

"Only as a name."

"Its importance can hardly be exaggerated. It has been the most jealously guarded of all Government secrets. **15** You may take it from me that naval warfare becomes impos-

13 *two pounds fifteen.* About $13.

14 *I have never seen the Prime Minister so upset.* The Prime Minister at the time was Lord Salisbury, and Mr. T. S. Blakeney has remarked (*Sherlock Holmes: Fact or Fiction?*) that "The seriousness of the theft may be realized less from the peculiar properties of a Bruce-Partington submarine than from the fact that even Lord Salisbury had been shaken out of his habitual imperturbability. The loss of a very secret report on the possibility of forcing the Dardanelles could leave him unmoved (*Secret and Confidential*, by Brigadier-General W. H.-H. Waters, pp. 53–4), but Mycroft had seldom seen [him] so upset as over the Cadogan West mystery."

15 *the most jealously guarded of all Government secrets.* How to reconcile this remark with Mycroft's previous "I thought everyone had heard of it" is something we will not attempt.

A MOMENT LATER THE TALL AND PORTLY FORM OF MYCROFT HOLMES WAS USHERED INTO THE ROOM.

Illustration by Arthur Twidle for the *Strand Magazine*, December, 1908.

16 *naval warfare becomes impossible within the radius of a Bruce-Partington's operation.* But there is not much doubt that Mycroft Holmes' hopes were completely disappointed, as the late Fletcher Pratt pointed out in "Holmes and the Royal Navy." "The date was 1895; and not for a decade and a half thereafter was any submarine produced which made the operations of surface ships even dangerous, to say nothing of impossible. As a matter of fact England herself built no submarines of any kind until 1903, eight years after the recovery of the plans of the wonder-working Bruce-Partington, and the submarines built by the Royal Navy at that time were from the designs of John Holland, the plans themselves being purchased in America." France, on the other hand, Mr. Pratt continued, only a year later, in 1896, laid down a new submarine of revolutionary design named the *Morse*. The *Morse* turned out to be a miserable failure and never made more than a couple of voyages at sea, but the suspicion will not rest that she was designed from the stolen Bruce-Partington plans. It should be noted here that Conan Doyle, in a story called "Danger!", written in 1913, predicted with great prophetic accuracy, even in small details, the consequences of a submarine blockade which would prevent any food-ship of any nationality from reaching the British Isles. When it appeared in the *Strand Magazine* for July, 1914, naval officialdom dismissed the threat as meaningless. Admiral Sir Compton Domville, K.C.B., in an extraordinary instance of unintentional and exact compliment, felt "compelled to say that I think it most improbable, and more like one of Jules Verne's stories than any other author I know."

17 *even he was forced to go to the Woolwich office.* Mrs. Crighton Sellars seems to have been the first to point out that "Woolwich . . . since 1869 has been an *Army* arsenal." Commenting on this in a letter to Mrs. Sellars, Captain P. C. W. Howe of the Royal Navy wrote: "As far as the Navy was concerned no [submarine plans were being made at Woolwich in 1895]. The Naval authorities were quite against the development and introduction of the submarine boat until they were practically forced into considering the question about 1900. . . . The only conceivable connection I can think of was that in the early days of torpedo development, the Royal Engineers had a torpedo of the Brennan type which could be directed from the shore and was used to protect the entrance to naval harbors, and these torpedos were dealt with at Woolwich Arsenal."

18 *"I play the game for the game's own sake."* As we know, Holmes accepted the Legion of Honor from France ("The Adventure of Wisteria Lodge") but was later to decline a knighthood from England ("The Adventure of the Three Garridebs").

16 sible within the radius of a Bruce-Partington's operation. Two years ago a very large sum was smuggled through the Estimates and was expended in acquiring a monopoly of the invention. Every effort has been made to keep the secret. The plans, which are exceedingly intricate, comprising some thirty separate patents, each essential to the working of the whole, are kept in an elaborate safe in a confidential office adjoining the Arsenal, with burglar-proof doors and windows. Under no conceivable circumstances were the plans to be taken from the office. If the Chief Constructor of the Navy desired to consult them, **17** even he was forced to go to the Woolwich office for the purpose. And yet here we find them in the pockets of a dead junior clerk in the heart of London. From an official point of view it's simply awful."

"But you have recovered them ? "

" No, Sherlock, no ! That's the pinch. We have not. Ten papers were taken from Woolwich. There were seven in the pockets of Cadogan West. The three most essential are gone—stolen, vanished. You must drop everything, Sherlock. Never mind your usual petty puzzles of the police-court. It's a vital international problem that you have to solve. Why did Cadogan West take the papers, where are the missing ones, how did he die, how came his body where it was found, how can the evil be set right ? Find an answer to all these questions, and you will have done good service for your country."

" Why do you not solve it yourself, Mycroft ? You can see as far as I."

" Possibly, Sherlock. But it is a question of getting details. Give me your details, and from an arm-chair I will return you an excellent expert opinion. But to run here and run there, to cross-question railway guards, and lie on my face with a lens to my eye—it is not my *métier*. No, you are the one man who can clear the matter up. If you have a fancy to see your name in the next honours list——"

My friend smiled and shook his head.

18 " I play the game for the game's own sake," said he. " But the problem certainly presents some points of interest, and I shall be very pleased to look into it. Some more facts, please."

" I have jotted down the more essential ones upon this sheet of paper, together with a few addresses which you will find of service. The actual official guardian of the papers is the famous Government expert, Sir James Walter, whose decorations and sub-titles fill two lines of a book of reference. He has grown grey in the service, is a gentleman, a favoured guest in the most exalted houses, and above all a man whose patriotism is beyond suspicion. He is one of two who have a key of the safe. I may add that the papers were undoubtedly in the office during working hours on Monday, and that Sir James left for London about three o'clock taking his key with him. He **19** was at the house of Admiral Sinclair at Barclay Square during the whole of the evening when this incident occurred."

" Has the fact been verified ? "

" Yes ; his brother, Colonel Valentine Walter, has testified to his departure from Woolwich, and Admiral Sinclair to his arrival in London ; so Sir James is no longer a direct factor in the problem."

" Who was the other man with a key ? "

" The senior clerk and draughtsman, Mr. Sidney Johnson. He is a man of forty, married, with five children. He is a silent, morose man, but he has, on the whole, an **20** excellent record in the public service. He is unpopular with his colleagues, but a hard worker. According to his own account, corroborated only by the word of his wife, he was at home the whole of Monday evening after office hours, and his key has never left the watch-chain upon which it hangs."

" Tell us about Cadogan West."

" He has been ten years in the Service, and has done good work. He has the reputation of being hot-headed and impetuous, but a straight, honest man. We have nothing against him. He was next Sidney Johnson in the office. His duties brought him into daily personal contact with the plans. No one else had the handling of them."

" Who locked the plans up that night ? "

" Mr. Sidney Johnson, the senior clerk."

" Well, it is surely perfectly clear who took them away. They are actually found upon the person of this junior clerk, Cadogan West. That seems final, does it not ? "

" It does, Sherlock, and yet it leaves so much unexplained. In the first place, why did he take them ? "

" I presume they were of value ? "

" He could have got several thousands for them very easily."

" Can you suggest any possible motive for taking the papers to London except to sell them ? "

" No, I cannot."

" Then we must take that as our working hypothesis. Young West took the papers. Now this could only be done by having a false key——"

" Several false keys. He had to open the building and the room."

" He had, then, several false keys. He took the papers to London to sell the secret, intending, no doubt, to have the plans themselves back in the safe next morning before they were missed. While in London on this treasonable mission he met his end."

" How ? "

" We will suppose that he was travelling back to Woolwich when he was killed and thrown out of the compartment."

" Aldgate, where the body was found, is considerably past the station for London Bridge, which would be his route to Woolwich."

" Many circumstances could be imagined under which he would pass London Bridge. There was someone in the carriage, for example, with whom he was having an absorbing interview. This interview led to a violent scene, in which he lost his life. Possibly he tried to leave the carriage, fell out on the line, and so met his end. The other closed the door. There was a thick fog, and nothing could be seen."

19 *Barclay Square.* Watson for some unspecified reason of his own seems to have chosen this phonetic spelling of London's famous Berkeley Square, built 1698, named from Berkeley House in Piccadilly. In Holmes' and Watson's day it had the best trees of any square in London: all planes (sycamores), "the only trees" (wrote Augustus J. C. Hare in his *Walks in London*, Vol. II), "which thoroughly enjoy a smoky atmosphere." It was in No. 11 Berkeley Square that Horace Walpole died in 1797. In No. 45 the great Lord Clive, founder of the British Empire in India, committed suicide, November 22, 1774. No. 50 had at this time a great notoriety as a haunted house, and was a source of many strange stories and surmises.

20 *He is a silent, morose man.* "The humorous effect of this rhetorical device (known as 'amphibology') was characteristic of the Holmes family," the late Christopher Morley noted in *Sherlock Holmes and Dr. Watson: A Textbook of Friendship,* and cited Sherlock Holmes' famous riposte in "Silver Blaze" *re* the curious incident of the dog in the nighttime.

"No better explanation can be given with our present knowledge; and yet consider, Sherlock, how much you leave untouched. We will suppose, for argument's sake, that young Cadogan West *had* determined to convey these papers to London. He would naturally have made an appointment with the foreign agent and kept his evening clear. Instead of that he took two tickets for the theatre, escorted his fiancée half-way there, and then suddenly disappeared."

"A blind," said Lestrade, who had sat listening with some impatience to the conversation.

"A very singular one. That is objection No. 1. Objection No. 2: We will suppose that he reaches London and sees the foreign agent. He must bring back the papers before morning or the loss will be discovered. He took away ten. Only seven were in his pocket. What had become of the other three? He certainly would not leave them of his own free will. Then, again, where is the price of his treason? One would have expected to find a large sum of money in his pocket."

"It seems to me perfectly clear," said Lestrade. "I have no doubt at all as to what occurred. He took the papers to sell them. He saw the agent. They could not agree as to price. He started home again, but the agent went with him. In the train the agent murdered him, took the more essential papers, and threw his body from the carriage. That would account for everything, would it not?"

"Why had he no ticket?"

"The ticket would have shown which station was nearest the agent's house. Therefore he took it from the murdered man's pocket."

"Good, Lestrade, very good," said Holmes. "Your theory holds together. But if this is true, then the case is at an end. On the one hand the traitor is dead. On the other the plans of the Bruce-Partington submarine are presumably already on the Continent. What is there for us to do?"

"To act, Sherlock—to act!" cried Mycroft, springing to his feet. "All my instincts are against this explanation. Use your powers! Go to the scene of the crime! See the people concerned! Leave no stone unturned! In all your career you have never had so great a chance of serving your country."

"Well, well!" said Holmes, shrugging his shoulders. "Come, Watson! And you, Lestrade, could you favour us with your company for an hour or two? We will begin our investigation by a visit to Aldgate Station. Good-bye, Mycroft. I shall let you have a report before evening, but I warn you in advance that you have little to expect."

An hour later, Holmes, Lestrade and I stood upon the underground railroad at the point where it emerges from the tunnel immediately before Aldgate Station. A courteous red-faced old gentleman represented the railway company.

"This is where the young man's body lay," said he, indicating a spot about three feet from the metals. "It

"THIS IS WHERE THE YOUNG MAN'S BODY LAY," SAID HE . . .

Illustration by Frederic Dorr Steele for *Collier's Magazine*, December 18, 1908.

could not have fallen from above, for these, as you see, are all blank walls.   Therefore, it could only have come from a train, and that train, so far as we can trace it, must have passed about midnight on Monday."

" Have the carriages been examined for any sign of violence ? "

" There are no such signs, and no ticket has been found."

" No record of a door being found open ? "

" None."

" We have had some fresh evidence this morning," said Lestrade.   " A passenger who passed Aldgate in an ordinary Metropolitan train about 11.40 on Monday night declares that he heard a heavy thud, as of a body striking the line, just before the train reached the station.   There was dense fog, however, and nothing could be seen.   He made no report of it at the time.   Why, whatever is the matter with Mr. Holmes ? "

My friend was standing with an expression of strained intensity upon his face, staring at the railway metals where they curved out of the tunnel.   Aldgate is a junction, and there was a network of points.   On these his eager, questioning eyes were fixed, and I saw on his keen, alert face that tightening of the lips, that quiver of the nostrils, and concentration of the heavy tufted brows which I knew so well.

" Points," he muttered ; " the points."

" What of it ? What do you mean ? "

" I suppose there are no great number of points on a system such as this ? "

" No ; there are very few."

" And a curve, too.   Points, and a curve.   By Jove ! if it were only so."

" What is it, Mr. Holmes ? Have you a clue ? "

" An idea—an indication, no more.   But the case certainly grows in interest.   Unique, perfectly unique, and yet why not ?   I do not see any indications of bleeding on the line."

" There were hardly any."

" But I understand that there was a considerable wound."

" The bone was crushed, but there was no great external injury."

" And yet one would have expected some bleeding. Would it be possible for me to inspect the train which contained the passenger who heard the thud of a fall in the fog ? "

" I fear not, Mr. Holmes.   The train has been broken up before now, and the carriages redistributed."

" I can assure you, Mr. Holmes," said Lestrade, " that every carriage has been carefully examined.   I saw to it myself."

It was one of my friend's most obvious weaknesses that he was impatient with less alert intelligences than his own.

" Very likely," said he, turning away.   " As it happens, it was not the carriages which I desired to examine.   Watson, we have done all we can here.   We need not trouble you any further, Mr. Lestrade.   I think our investigations must now carry us to Woolwich."

At London Bridge, Holmes wrote a telegram to his

MY FRIEND WAS STANDING WITH AN EXPRESSION OF STRAINED INTENSITY UPON HIS FACE . . .

Illustration by Arthur Twidle for the *Strand Magazine*, December, 1908.

21 *a complete list of all foreign spies or international agents known to be in England.* Much has been made of the point that Holmes, at the time of "The Adventure of the Second Stain," knew offhand the names of the principal foreign spies in London, but that here he had to call on brother Mycroft's help. If the former occasion was in 1886 and the latter not until 1895, however, a lapse of memory is understandable. But it is by no means clear that any such lapse of memory existed. As Mr. Walter P. Armstrong, Jr., wrote in "The Truth About Sherlock Holmes": "Even supposing that Holmes was fully aware of [the identities of important foreign spies or international agents] this poses three additional questions: Were they in England? What were their addresses? Were there any others who might undertake so ambitious a plot as that involved in the theft of the Bruce-Partington plans? Of course it was the addresses in which he was particularly interested, and it was certainly logical to assume that in [almost ten] years men in such an uncertain line of business might have moved. Mycroft understood all this, for in his reply he said, 'There are numerous small fry, but few who would handle so big an affair.' . . . No doubt Holmes could have acquired [his] information through his own resources, but it was easier to wire Mycroft and time was pressing."

22 *his body was on the* roof *of a carriage.*" Holmes' "recognition of the fact that West's body was on the roof of the carriage seems a very long shot in the dark," Mr. T. S. Blakeney wrote in *Sherlock Holmes: Fact or Fiction?*, "and one cannot but feel that this was Holmes' lucky day. 'A single blunder on the part of the guilty man would have thrown all Holmes' deductions out of joint'—Father Knox's rather sweeping generalization—certainly applies to 'The Bruce-Partington Plans.'"

brother, which he handed to me before dispatching it. It ran thus :

" See some light in the darkness, but it may possibly flicker out. Meanwhile, please send by messenger, to await return at Baker Street, a complete list of all foreign **21** spies or international agents known to be in England, with full address.—SHERLOCK."

" That should be helpful, Watson," he remarked, as we took our seats in the Woolwich train. " We certainly owe brother Mycroft a debt for having introduced us to what promises to be a really very remarkable case."

His eager face still wore that expression of intense and high-strung energy, which showed me that some novel and suggestive circumstance had opened up a stimulating line of thought. See the foxhound with hanging ears and drooping tail as it lolls about the kennels, and compare it with the same hound as, with gleaming eyes and straining muscles, it runs upon a breast-high scent—such was the change in Holmes since the morning. He was a different man to the limp and lounging figure in the mouse-coloured dressing-gown who had prowled so restlessly only a few hours before round the fog-girt room.

" There is material here. There is scope," said he. " I am dull indeed not to have understood its possibilities."

" Even now they are dark to me."

" The end is dark to me also, but I have hold of one idea which may lead us far. The man met his death elsewhere, **22** and his body was on the *roof* of a carriage."

" On the roof ! "

" Remarkable, is it not ? But consider the facts. Is it a coincidence that it is found at the very point where the train pitches and sways as it comes round on the points ? Is not that the place where an object upon the roof might be expected to fall off ? The points would affect no object inside the train. Either the body fell from the roof, or a very curious coincidence has occurred. But now consider the question of the blood. Of course, there was no bleeding on the line if the body had bled elsewhere. Each fact is suggestive in itself. Together they have a cumulative force."

" And the ticket, too ! " I cried.

" Exactly. We could not explain the absence of a ticket. This would explain it. Everything fits together."

" But suppose it were so, we are still as far as ever from unravelling the mystery of his death. Indeed, it becomes not simpler, but stranger."

" Perhaps," said Holmes, thoughtfully ; " perhaps." He relapsed into a silent reverie, which lasted until the slow train drew up at last in Woolwich Station. There he called a cab and drew Mycroft's paper from his pocket.

" We have quite a little round of afternoon calls to make," said he. " I think that Sir James Walter claims our first attention."

The house of the famous official was a fine villa with green lawns stretching down to the Thames. As we reached it the fog was lifting, and a thin, watery sunshine was breaking through. A butler answered our ring.

" Sir James, sir ! " said he, with solemn face. " Sir James died this morning."

" Good heavens ! " cried Holmes, in amazement. " How did he die ? "

" Perhaps you would care to step in, sir, and see his brother, Colonel Valentine ? "   **23**

" Yes, we had best do so."

We were ushered into a dim-lit drawing-room, where an instant later we were joined by a very tall, handsome, light-bearded man of fifty, the younger brother of the dead scientist. His wild eyes, stained cheeks, and unkempt hair all spoke of the sudden blow which had fallen upon the household. He was hardly articulate as he spoke of it.

" It was this horrible scandal," said he. " My brother, Sir James, was a man of very sensitive honour, and he could not survive such an affair. It broke his heart. He was always so proud of the efficiency of his department, and this was a crushing blow."

" We had hoped that he might have given us some indications which would have helped us to clear the matter up."

" I assure you that it was all a mystery to him as it is to you and to all of us. He had already put all his knowledge at the disposal of the police. Naturally, he had no doubt that Cadogan West was guilty. But all the rest was inconceivable."

" You cannot throw any new light upon the affair ? "

" I know nothing myself save what I have read or heard. I have no desire to be discourteous, but you can understand, Mr. Holmes, that we are much disturbed at present, and I must ask you to hasten this interview to an end."

" This is indeed an unexpected development," said my friend when we had regained the cab. " I wonder if the death was natural, or whether the poor old fellow killed himself ! If the latter, may it be taken as some sign of self-reproach for duty neglected ? We must leave that question to the future. Now we shall turn to the Cadogan Wests."

A small but well-kept house in the outskirts of the town sheltered the bereaved mother. The old lady was too dazed with grief to be of any use to us, but at her side was a white-faced young lady, who introduced herself as Miss Violet Westbury, the fiancée of the dead man, and the last to see him upon that fatal night.

" I cannot explain it, Mr. Holmes," she said. " I have not shut an eye since the tragedy, thinking, thinking, thinking, night and day, what the true meaning of it can be. Arthur was the most single-minded, chivalrous, patriotic man upon earth. He would have cut his right hand off before he would sell a State secret confided to his keeping. It is absurd, impossible, preposterous to anyone who knew him."

" But the facts, Miss Westbury ? "

" Yes, yes ; I admit I cannot explain them."

" Was he in any want of money ? "

" No ; his needs were very simple and his salary ample. He had saved a few hundreds, and we were to marry at the New Year."

" No signs of any mental excitement ? Come, Miss

23 *his brother, Colonel Valentine?"* "Does—or did—a well-trained British butler refer to his employer's brother by his first name—Colonel Valentine?" Dr. Felix Morley asked in "The Bruce-Partington Keys."

Westbury, be absolutely frank with us."

The quick eye of my companion had noted some change in her manner. She coloured and hesitated.

" Yes," she said, at last. " I had a feeling that there was something on his mind."

" For long ? "

" Only for the last week or so. He was thoughtful and worried. Once I pressed him about it. He admitted that there was something, and that it was concerned with his official life. ' It is too serious for me to speak about, even to you,' said he. I could get nothing more."

Holmes looked grave.

" Go on, Miss Westbury. Even if it seems to tell against him, go on. We cannot say what it may lead to."

" Indeed I have nothing more to tell. Once or twice it seemed to me that he was on the point of telling me something. He spoke one evening of the importance of the secret, and I have some recollection that he said that no doubt foreign spies would pay a great deal to have it."

My friend's face grew graver still.

" Anything else ? "

" He said that we were slack about such matters—that it would be easy for a traitor to get the plans."

" Was it only recently that he made such remarks ? "

" Yes, quite recently."

" Now tell us of that last evening."

" We were to go to the theatre. The fog was so thick that a cab was useless. We walked, and our way took us close to the office. Suddenly he darted away into the fog."

" Without a word ? "

" He gave an exclamation ; that was all. I waited but he never returned. Then I walked home. Next morning, after the office opened, they came to inquire. About twelve o'clock we heard the terrible news. Oh, Mr. Holmes, if you could only, only save his honour ! It was so much to him."

Holmes shook his head sadly.

" Come, Watson," said he, " our ways lie elsewhere. Our next station must be the office from which the papers were taken."

" It was black enough before against this young man, but our inquiries make it blacker," he remarked, as the cab lumbered off. " His coming marriage gives a motive for the crime. He naturally wanted money. The idea was in his head, since he spoke about it. He nearly made the girl an accomplice in the treason by telling her his plans. It is all very bad."

" But surely, Holmes, character goes for something ? Then, again, why should he leave the girl in the street and dart away to commit a felony ? "

" Exactly ! There are certainly objections. But it is a formidable case which they have to meet."

Mr. Sidney Johnson, the senior clerk, met us at the office, and received us with that respect which my companion's card always commanded. He was a thin, gruff, bespectacled man of middle age, his cheeks haggard, and his hands twitching from the nervous strain to which he had been subjected.

" It is bad, Mr. Holmes, very bad !   Have you heard of the death of the Chief ? "

" We have just come from his house."

" The place is disorganized.   The Chief dead, Cadogan West dead, our papers stolen.   And yet, when we closed our door on Monday evening we were as efficient an office as any in the Government service.   Good God, it's dreadful to think of !   That West, of all men, should have done such a thing ! "

" You are sure of his guilt, then ? "

" I can see no other way out of it.   And yet I would have trusted him as I trust myself."

" At what hour was the office closed on Monday ? "

" At five."

" Did you close it ? "

" I am always the last man out."

" Where were the plans ? "

" In that safe.   I put them there myself."

" Is there no watchman to the building ? "

" There is ; but he has other departments to look after as well.   He is an old soldier and a most trustworthy man. He saw nothing that evening.   Of course, the fog was very thick."

" Suppose that Cadogan West wished to make his way into the building after hours ; he would need three keys, would he not, before he could reach the papers ? "

" Yes, he would.   The key of the outer door, the key of the office, and the key of the safe."

" Only Sir James Walter and you had those keys ? "

" I had no keys of the doors—only of the safe."

" Was Sir James a man who was orderly in his habits ? "

" Yes, I think he was.   I know that so far as those three keys are concerned he kept them on the same ring.   I have often seen them there."

" And that ring went with him to London ? "

" He said so."

" And your key never left your possession ? "

" Never."

24

" Then West, if he is the culprit, must have had a duplicate.   And yet none was found upon his body.   One other point : if a clerk in this office desired to sell the plans, would it not be simpler to copy the plans for himself than to take the originals, as was actually done ? "

" It would take considerable technical knowledge to copy the plans in an effective way."

" But I suppose either Sir James, or you, or West had that technical knowledge ? "

" No doubt we had, but I beg you won't try to drag me into the matter, Mr. Holmes.   What is the use of our speculating in this way when the original plans were actually found on West ? "

" Well, it is certainly singular that he should run the risk of taking originals, if he could safely have taken copies, which would have equally served his turn."

" Singular, no doubt—and yet he did so."

" Every inquiry in this case reveals something inexplicable.   Now there are three papers still missing.   They are, as I understand, the vital ones."

" Yes, that is so."

24 *"Never."* Wrote the editors of the *Sherlock Holmes Journal* in their issue of December, 1954: "[Reuben] Kelf-Cohen, a senior Civil Servant, recently discovered that the keys mentioned [in "The Adventure of the Bruce-Partington Plans"] just didn't add up. He thereupon wrote to Paul Gore-Booth, now H. M. Ambassador at Rangoon, for an explanation. Their letters . . . are given below. . . .

R. Kelf-Cohen to Paul Gore-Booth: "The safe in which the Plans were kept had two keys, one kept by Sir James Walter and the other by Mr. Sidney Johnson, the Senior Clerk at Woolwich—a typical Civil Servant. Sir James had three keys on his ring—the key of the outer door, the key of the office and the key of the safe. Mr. Sidney Johnson, *according to his own statement*, had only the key of the safe. Yet, according to the story told by Mycroft, 'Sir James left for London about three o'clock, taking his keys with him.' Mr. Johnson, on the other hand, informed Sherlock Holmes that the office closed on Monday at five o'clock and that he was, as always, 'the last man out.' How could Mr. Johnson let himself out without a complete set of keys? Why did he conceal the fact that he had such a set? You will agree that it is normal Civil Service practice for Sidney Johnson, the Senior Clerk, to be responsible for closing the office and making everything secure. Would the Head of Chancery leave it to the Ambassador to secure everything in the Chancery at the end of the day? And yet this is what Mycroft suggested and Sherlock Holmes swallowed."

Paul Gore-Booth to R. Kelf-Cohen: " 'All my instincts are against this explanation,' as a better man than I am said in the same context. We clearly cannot infer that Mr. Johnson was lying. Civil Servants do not—but need I say more. We must therefore seek the solution elsewhere. Two possibilities suggest themselves. 1. The offices had spring locks. I do not know whether spring locks had been invented in 1895, but there is a pretty little problem to examine. 2. The offices, as opposed to the safe, were closed with keys on one of those clumsy bits of wood which, in my day when I was 'twenty-seven years of age, unmarried and a clerk,' were handed in at some central point and were not taken home. 1. is the obvious first resort, but I don't like it much. Supposing the door blew shut in office hours and Mr. Johnson had gone out for natural purposes, could he only get in by summoning Sir James to open the door? Nothing is impossible—only that doesn't seem likely. The advantage of 2. is that it is good Civil Servant practice, or was, anyway. The Head of the Department probably would have his private keys of the doors but there was no good reason to make a lot of spares, if there was some way of getting at the Departmental set. Perhaps they were left with the 'old soldier and . . . most trustworthy man.' The weakness of 2. is that, if it is correct, it was all taken for granted in rather a surprising way. But what seems to me much more surprising was the way Colonel Valentine Walter was allowed to go messing about the place within reach of the documents; no wonder Sir J. found it all a crushing blow."

25 *after he had left the lady about 7.30.* "This was doubly not true," Mr. Roger Clapp wrote in "The Curious Problem of the Railway Time-tables," "since there was no 8.15 train and there were two earlier trains at 7.44 and 8.04."

"DO YOU MEAN TO SAY THAT ANYONE HOLDING THESE THREE PAPERS . . . COULD CONSTRUCT A BRUCE-PARTINGTON SUBMARINE?"

Illustration by Arthur Twidle for the *Strand Magazine,* December, 1908.

"Do you mean to say that anyone holding these three papers, and without the seven others, could construct a Bruce-Partington submarine?"

"I reported to that effect to the Admiralty. But to-day I have been over the drawings again, and I am not so sure of it. The double valves with the automatic self-adjusting slots are drawn in one of the papers which have been returned. Until the foreigners had invented that for themselves they could not make the boat. Of course, they might soon get over the difficulty."

"But the three missing drawings are the most important?"

"Undoubtedly."

"I think, with your permission, I will now take a stroll round the premises. I do not recall any other question which I desired to ask."

He examined the lock of the safe, the door of the room, and finally the iron shutters of the window. It was only when we were on the lawn outside that his interest was strongly excited. There was a laurel bush outside the window, and several of the branches bore signs of having been twisted or snapped. He examined them carefully with his lens, and then some dim and vague marks upon the earth beneath. Finally he asked the chief clerk to close the iron shutters, and he pointed out to me that they hardly met in the centre, and that it would be possible for anyone outside to see what was going on within the room.

"The indications are ruined by the three days' delay. They may mean something or nothing. Well, Watson, I do not think that Woolwich can help us further. It is a small crop which we have gathered. Let us see if we can do better in London."

Yet we added one more sheaf to our harvest before we left Woolwich Station. The clerk in the ticket office was able to say with confidence that he saw Cadogan West— whom he knew well by sight—upon the Monday night, and that he went to London by the 8.15 to London Bridge. He was alone, and took a single third-class ticket. The clerk was struck at the time by his excited and nervous manner. So shaky was he that he could hardly pick up his change, and the clerk had helped him with it. A reference to the time-table showed that the 8.15 was the first train which it was possible for West to take after he had **25** left the lady about 7.30.

"Let us reconstruct, Watson," said Holmes, after half an hour of silence. "I am not aware that in all our joint researches we have ever had a case which was more difficult to get at. Every fresh advance which we make only reveals a fresh ridge beyond. And yet we have surely made some appreciable progress.

"The effect of our inquiries at Woolwich has in the main been against young Cadogan West; but the indications at the window would lend themselves to a more favourable hypothesis. Let us suppose, for example, that he had been approached by some foreign agent. It might have been done under such pledges as would have prevented him from speaking of it, and yet would have affected his thoughts in the direction indicated by his remarks to his fiancée. Very good. We will now suppose that as he went to the theatre with the young lady he suddenly, in the fog, caught a glimpse of this same agent going in the direction of the office. He was an impetuous man, quick in his decisions. Everything gave way to his duty. He followed the man, reached the window, saw the abstraction of the documents, and pursued the thief. In this way we get over the objection that no one would take originals when he could make copies. This outsider had to take originals. So far it holds together."

"What is the next step?"

"Then we come into difficulties. One would imagine that under such circumstances the first act of young Cadogan West would be to seize the villain and raise the alarm. Why did he not do so? Could it have been an official superior who took the papers? That would explain West's conduct. Or could the Chief have given West the slip in the fog, and West started at once to London to head him off from his own rooms, presuming that he knew where the rooms were? The call must have been very pressing, since he left his girl standing in the fog, and made no effort to communicate with her. Our scent runs cold here, and there is a vast gap between either hypothesis and the laying of West's body, with seven papers in his pocket, on the roof of a Metropolitan train. My instinct now is to work from the other end. If Mycroft has given us the list of addresses we may be able to pick our man, and follow two tracks instead of one."

Surely enough, a note awaited us at Baker Street. A Government messenger had brought it post-haste. Holmes glanced at it and threw it over to me.

"There are numerous small fry, but few who would handle so big an affair. The only men worth considering are Adolph Meyer, of 13 Great George Street, West- **26** minster; Louis La Rothière, of Campden Mansions, Notting Hill; and Hugo Oberstein, 13 Caulfield Gardens, Kensington. The latter was known to be in town **27** on Monday, and is now reported as having left. Glad to hear you have seen some light. The Cabinet awaits your final report with the utmost anxiety. Urgent representations have arrived from the very highest quarter. The whole force of the State is at your back if you should need it.—MYCROFT."

"I'm afraid," said Holmes, smiling, "that all the Queen's horses and all the Queen's men cannot avail in this matter." He had spread out his big map of London, and leaned eagerly over it. "Well, well," said he presently, with an exclamation of satisfaction, "things are turning a little in our direction at last. Why, Watson, I do honestly believe that we are going to pull it off after all." He slapped me on the shoulder with a sudden burst of hilarity. "I am going out now. It is only a reconnaissance. I will do nothing serious without my trusted comrade and biographer at my elbow. Do you stay here, and the odds are that you will see me again in an hour or two. If time hangs heavy get foolscap and a pen, and

26 *13 Great George Street.* Great George Street runs from the corner of Birdcage Walk and Prince Street to the corner of Parliament Square. "Talk about squatting on the enemy's doorstep!" Mr. Michael Harrison wrote (*In the Footsteps of Sherlock Holmes*). "Mr. Meyer had almost taken up his quarters in the enemy's office!"

27 *13 Caulfield Gardens.* The late Christopher Morley thought that "Caulfield Gardens" was probably "Courtfield Road or Courtfield Gardens." But Mr. Michael Harrison suggests that "Caulfield Gardens" should be read "Cornwall Gardens." Oberstein's house, he writes, must have lain "at the southern side of the western half . . . , for here the back of the houses overlook a vast, open cutting in which the District and Metropolitan lines are joined."

begin your narrative of how we saved the State."

I felt some reflection of his elation in my own mind, for I knew well that he would not depart so far from his usual austerity of demeanour unless there was good cause for exultation. All the long November evening I waited, filled with impatience for his return. At last, shortly after nine o'clock there arrived a messenger with a note:

" Am dining at Goldini's Restaurant, Gloucester Road, Kensington. Please come at once and join me there. Bring with you a jemmy, a dark lantern, a chisel, and a revolver.—S.H."

It was a nice equipment for a respectable citizen to carry through the dim, fog-draped streets. I stowed them all discreetly away in my overcoat, and drove straight to the address given. There sat my friend at a little round table near the door of the garish Italian restaurant.

" Have you had something to eat ? Then join me in a coffee and curaçao. Try one of the proprietor's cigars. They are less poisonous than one would expect. Have you the tools ? "

" They are here, in my overcoat."

" Excellent. Let me give you a short sketch of what I have done, with some indication of what we are about to do. Now it must be evident to you, Watson, that this young man's body was *placed* on the roof of the train. That was clear from the instant that I determined the fact that it was from the roof, and not from a carriage, that he had fallen."

" Could it not have been dropped from a bridge ? "

" I should say it was impossible. If you examine the roofs you will find that they are slightly rounded, and there is no railing round them. Therefore, we can say for certain that young Cadogan West was placed on it."

" How could he be placed there ? "

" That was the question which we had to answer. There is only one possible way. You are aware that the Underground runs clear of tunnels at some points in the West End. I had a vague memory that as I have travelled by it I have occasionally seen windows just above my head. Now, suppose that a train halted under such a window, would there be any difficulty in laying a body upon the roof ? "

" It seems most improbable."

" We must fall back upon the old axiom that when all other contingencies fail, whatever remains, however improbable, must be the truth. Here all other contingencies *have* failed. When I found that the leading international agent, who had just left London, lived in a row of houses which abutted upon the Underground, I was so pleased that you were a little astonished at my sudden frivolity."

" Oh, that was it, was it ? "

" Yes, that was it. Mr. Hugo Oberstein, of 13 Caulfield Gardens, had become my objective. I began my operations at Gloucester Road Station, where a very helpful official walked with me along the track, and allowed me to satisfy myself, not only that the back-stair windows of

Caulfield Gardens open on the line, but the even more essential fact that, owing to the intersection of one of the larger railways, the Underground trains are frequently held motionless for some minutes at that very spot."

" Splendid, Holmes ! You have got it ! "

" So far—so far, Watson. We advance, but the goal is afar. Well, having seen the back of Caulfield Gardens, I visited the front and satisfied myself that the bird was indeed flown. It is a considerable house, unfurnished, so far as I could judge, in the upper rooms. Oberstein lived there with a single valet, who was probably a confederate entirely in his confidence. We must bear in mind that Oberstein has gone to the Continent to dispose of his booty, but not with any idea of flight ; for he had no reason to fear a warrant, and the idea of an amateur domiciliary visit would certainly never occur to him. Yet that is precisely what we are about to make."

" Could we not get a warrant and legalize it ? "

" Hardly on the evidence."   **28**

" What can we hope to do ? "

" We cannot tell what correspondence may be there."

" I don't like it, Holmes."

" My dear fellow, you shall keep watch in the street. I'll do the criminal part. It's not a time to stick at trifles. Think of Mycroft's note, of the Admiralty, the Cabinet, the exalted person who waits for news. We are bound to go."

My answer was to rise from the table.

" You are right, Holmes. We are bound to go."

He sprang up and shook me by the hand.

" I knew you would not shrink at the last," said he, and for a moment I saw something in his eyes which was nearer to tenderness than I had ever seen. The next instant he was his masterful, practical self once more.

" It is nearly half a mile, but there is no hurry. Let us walk," said he. " Don't drop the instruments, I beg. Your arrest as a suspicious character would be a most unfortunate complication."   **29**

Caulfield Gardens was one of those lines of flat-faced, pillared, and porticoed houses which are so prominent a product of the middle Victorian epoch in the West End of London. Next door there appeared to be a children's party, for the merry buzz of young voices and the clatter of a piano resounded through the night. The fog still hung about and screened us with its friendly shade. Holmes had lit his lantern and flashed it upon the massive door.

" This is a serious proposition," said he. " It is certainly bolted as well as locked. We would do better in the area. There is an excellent archway down yonder in case a too zealous policeman should intrude. Give me a hand, Watson, and I'll do the same for you."

A minute later we were both in the area. Hardly had we reached the dark shadows before the step of the policeman was heard in the fog above. As its soft rhythm died away, Holmes set to work upon the lower door. I saw him stoop and strain until with a sharp crash it flew open. We sprang through into the dark passage, closing the area

28 *"Hardly on the evidence."* Again "the reader gets a chance to see the detective's legal mind at work," Mr. Albert P. Blaustein wrote in "Sherlock Holmes As a Lawyer."

29 *a most unfortunate complication."* Again "Holmes' knowledge of the British law [is] in evidence, for he was well aware that it is a serious offense to be caught in possession of housebreaking tools by night," Mr. Doyle W. Beckemeyer commented in "The Irregular Holmes."

30 *His little fan of yellow light shone upon a low window.* "It should be pointed out that the expression . . . 'His little fan of yellow light' is not merely a phrase to catch the fancy," Mr. Melvin Cross wrote in "The Lantern of Sherlock Holmes." "With many lanterns, an inverted, more or less indistinct image of the flame is actually projected, let us say, upon the wall; it is roughly triangular, with the base of the triangle at the top. So Dr. Watson's metaphor 'fan' is quite precise. To the general reader this will not be considered a technical detail drawn to a nicety." Mr. Cross pointed out in this same article that the most satisfactory illuminant for a dark lantern is signal oil; this, undoubtedly, was what Holmes used: "It gives a rather yellow light."

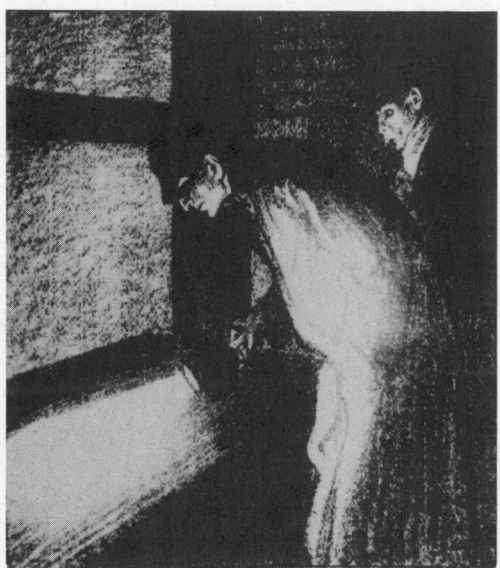

HOLMES SWEPT HIS LIGHT ALONG THE WINDOW-SILL.

The same scene as depicted by two different artists: *Above*, by Frederic Dorr Steele for *Collier's Magazine*, December 18, 1908; *Below*, by Arthur Twidle for the *Strand Magazine*, December, 1908.

door behind us. Holmes led the way up the curving, uncarpeted stair. His little fan of yellow light shone **30** upon a low window.

"Here we are, Watson—this must be the one." He threw it open, and as he did so there was a low, harsh murmur, growing steadily into a loud roar as a train dashed past us in the darkness. Holmes swept his light along the window-sill. It was thickly coated with soot from the passing engines, but the black surface was blurred and rubbed in places.

"You can see where they rested the body. Halloa, Watson ! what is this ? There can be no doubt that it is a blood mark." He was pointing to faint discolorations along the woodwork of the window. " Here it is on the stone of the stair also. The demonstration is complete. Let us stay here until a train stops."

We had not long to wait. The very next train roared from the tunnel as before, but slowed in the open, and then, with a creaking of brakes, pulled up immediately beneath us. It was not four feet from the window-ledge to the roof of the carriages. Holmes softly closed the window.

"So far we are justified," said he. "What do you think of it, Watson ? "

"A masterpiece. You have never risen to a greater height."

"I cannot agree with you there. From the moment that I conceived the idea of the body being upon the roof, which surely was not a very abstruse one, all the rest was inevitable. If it were not for the grave interests involved the affair up to this point would be insignificant. Our difficulties are still before us. But perhaps we may find something here which may help us."

We had ascended the kitchen stair and entered the suite of rooms upon the first floor. One was a dining-room, severely furnished and containing nothing of interest. A second was a bedroom, which also drew blank. The remaining room appeared more promising, and my companion settled down to a systematic examination. It was littered with books and papers, and was evidently used as a study. Swiftly and methodically Holmes turned over the contents of drawer after drawer and cupboard after cupboard, but no gleam of success came to brighten his austere face. At the end of an hour he was no further than when he started.

"The cunning dog has covered his tracks," said he. " He has left nothing to incriminate him. His dangerous correspondence has been destroyed or removed. This is our last chance."

It was a small tin cash-box which stood upon the writing-desk. Holmes prised it open with his chisel. Several rolls of paper were within, covered with figures and calculations, without any note to show to what they referred. The recurring words, " Water pressure," and " Pressure to the square inch " suggested some possible relation to a submarine. Holmes tossed them all impatiently aside. There only remained an envelope with some small newspaper slips inside it. He shook them out on the table, and at once I saw by his eager face that his hopes had been raised.

" What's this, Watson ? Eh ? What's this ? Record of a series of messages in the advertisements of a paper. *Daily Telegraph* agony column by the print and paper. Right-hand top corner of a page. No dates—but messages arrange themselves. This must be the first :

" ' Hoped to hear sooner. Terms agreed to. Write fully to address given on card.—Pierrot.'

" Next comes : ' Too complex for description. Must have full report. Stuff awaits you when goods delivered. —Pierrot.'

" Then comes : ' Matter presses. Must withdraw offer unless contract completed. Make appointment by letter. Will confirm by advertisement.—Pierrot.'

" Finally : ' Monday night after nine. Two taps. Only ourselves. Do not be so suspicious. Payment in hard cash when goods delivered.—Pierrot.'

" A fairly complete record, Watson ! If we could only get at the man at the other end ! " He sat lost in thought, tapping his fingers on the table. Finally he sprang to his feet.

" Well, perhaps it won't be so difficult after all. There is nothing more to be done here, Watson. I think we might drive round to the offices of the *Daily Telegraph*, and so bring a good day's work to a conclusion."

Mycroft Holmes and Lestrade had come round by appointment after breakfast next day and Sherlock Holmes had recounted to them our proceedings of the day before. The professional shook his head over our confessed burglary. **31**

" We can't do these things in the force, Mr. Holmes," said he. " No wonder you get results that are beyond us. But some of these days you'll go too far, and you'll find yourself and your friend in trouble."

" For England, home and beauty—eh, Watson ? Mar-**32** tyrs on the altar of our country. But what do you think of it, Mycroft ? "

" Excellent, Sherlock ! Admirable ! But what use will you make of it ? "

Holmes picked up the *Daily Telegraph* which lay upon the table.

" Have you seen Pierrot's advertisement to-day ? "

" What ! Another one ? "

" Yes, here it is : ' To-night. Same hour. Same place. Two taps. Most vitally important. Your own safety at stake.—Pierrot.' "

" By George ! " cried Lestrade. " If he answers that we've got him ! "

" That was my idea when I put it in. I think if you could both make it convenient to come with us about eight o'clock to Caulfield Gardens we might possibly get a little nearer to a solution."

One of the most remarkable characteristics of Sherlock Holmes was his power of throwing his brain out of action and switching all his thoughts on to lighter things whenever he had convinced himself that he could no longer work to advantage. I remember that during the whole of that memorable day he lost himself in a monograph which he had undertaken upon the Polyphonic Motets of Lassus. **33**

31 *our confessed burglary.* But Magistrate S. Tupper Bigelow has shown ("Sherlock Holmes Was No Burglar") that, under the letter of British law, Holmes and Watson were guilty of neither burglary nor unlawful entry.

32 *"For England, home and beauty.* A traditional toast in the British Navy.

33 *the Polyphonic Motets of Lassus.* "Briefly, [a motet] is a musical composition not very different from an anthem," Mr. Richard Wait wrote in "The Case of the Neophyte and the Motet." "Its words generally have a biblical origin and are in continuous or prose form (although there are motets which are metrical and rhymed) and it is usually founded upon Gregorian tones. Originally it was sung between the *credo* and the *sanctus* in the mass. The words of the motets which Holmes fancied were Latin but some may be found in the vulgar tongue. The motet is polyphonic when composed for several voices."

Orlando or Orlande or Orlandus (or Roland or Robert) Lassus or di Lasso or de Lattre was born at Mons in 1532 and died at Munich, June 14, 1594. If not the greatest composer of the sixteenth century he was undoubtedly one of the greatest influences in sixteenth-century music. His first book of motets, dedicated to Antoine Perrenet, Bishop of Arras, was published at Antwerp in 1556. On December 7, 1570, at the Diet of Spires, the Emperor Maximilian ennobled Lassus and his posterity, and gave the eminent musician a grant of arms. Two years earlier, in 1568, Lassus had published two comprehensive collections of motets at Nuremberg.

"Musicians have often wondered why Holmes evinced special interest in the motets and seemingly paid no attention to the approximately 2,500 other liturgical and secular works with which this master enriched our musical heritage," Mr. Benjamin Grosbayne wrote in "Sherlock Holmes— Musician." "Perhaps Holmes returned to Lassus on his bee farm and wrote other monographs on the masses, the madrigals, the villanelles, the chansons, and especially, on the Psalmi Davidis poenitentiales."

In any case, only a Watson could have described a monograph on Lassus as one of the "lighter things," fit only for one who "could no longer work," as the late Harvey Officer pointed out in "Sherlock Holmes and Music." "The motets of di Lasso number five hundred and ten, filling eleven volumes of the great Breitkopf and Härtel edition. They are written for voices ranging in number from two to twelve. One cannot hear these motets today anywhere in the world. One cannot play them, for they are meant for voices only, and would be meaningless if played on instruments. One can only do what Sherlock Holmes must have been able to do, i.e., read them, and then with the ear of the mind hear their complicated web of sounds."

For my own part I had none of this power of detachment, and the day, in consequence, appeared to be interminable. The great national importance of the issue, the suspense in high quarters, the direct nature of the experiment which we were trying—all combined to work upon my nerve. It was a relief to me when at last, after a light dinner, we set out upon our expedition. Lestrade and Mycroft met us by appointment at the outside of Gloucester Road Station. The area door of Oberstein's house had been left open the night before, and it was necessary for me, as Mycroft Holmes absolutely and indignantly declined to climb the railings, to pass in and open the hall door. By nine o'clock we were all seated in the study, waiting patiently for our man.

An hour passed and yet another. When eleven struck, **34** the measured beat of the great church clock seemed to sound the dirge of our hopes. Lestrade and Mycroft were fidgeting in their seats and looking twice a minute at their watches. Holmes sat silent and composed, his eyelids half shut, but every sense on the alert. He raised his head with a sudden jerk.

" He is coming," said he.

There had been a furtive step past the door. Now it returned. We heard a shuffling sound outside, and then two sharp taps with the knocker. Holmes rose, motioning to us to remain seated. The gas in the hall was a mere point of light. He opened the outer door, and then as a dark figure slipped past him he closed and fastened it. " This way ! " we heard him say, and a moment later our man stood before us. Holmes had followed him closely, and as the man turned with a cry of surprise and alarm he caught him by the collar and threw him back into the room. Before our prisoner had recovered his balance the door was shut and Holmes standing with his back against it. The man glared round him, staggered, and fell senseless upon the floor. With the shock, his broad-brimmed hat flew from his head, his cravat slipped down from his lips, and there was the long light beard and the soft, handsome delicate features of Colonel Valentine Walter.

Holmes gave a whistle of surprise.

" You can write me down an ass this time, Watson," **35** said he. " This was not the bird that I was looking for."

" Who is he ? " asked Mycroft eagerly.

" The younger brother of the late Sir James Walter, the head of the Submarine Department. Yes, yes ; I see the fall of the cards. He is coming to. I think that you had best leave his examination to me."

We had carried the prostrate body to the sofa. Now our prisoner sat up, looked round him with a horror-stricken face, and passed his hand over his forehead, like one who cannot believe his own senses.

" What is this ? " he asked. " I came here to visit Mr. Oberstein."

" Everything is known, Colonel Walter," said Holmes. " How an English gentleman could behave in such a manner is beyond my comprehension. But your whole correspondence and relations with Oberstein are within our knowledge. So also are the circumstances connected with the death of young Cadogan West. Let me advise you to gain at least the small credit for repentance and confession,

BEFORE OUR PRISONER HAD RECOVERED HIS BALANCE THE DOOR WAS SHUT AND HOLMES STANDING WITH HIS BACK AGAINST IT.

Illustration by Arthur Twidle for the *Strand Magazine,* December, 1908.

34 *the great church clock.* Probably St. Stephen's Church on Gloucester Road.

35 *"This was not the bird that I was looking for."* ". . . who, if not Walter, was the 'bird' Holmes was expecting?" Mr. Nathan L. Bengis has asked. "There can be little doubt that the man Holmes had in mind was Sidney Johnson, the senior clerk. Logically, indeed, he was the ideal suspect, as all indications point to him, whereas few if any point to Colonel Walter: Johnson had locked up the plans for the night, he was always the last man out, and he was known to have a key to the safe."

since there are still some details which we can only learn from your lips."

The man groaned and sank his face in his hands. We waited, but he was silent.

" I can assure you," said Holmes, " that every essential is already known. We know that you were pressed for money ; that you took an impress of the keys which your brother held ; and that you entered into a correspondence with Oberstein, who answered your letters through the advertisement columns of the *Daily Telegraph*. We are aware that you went down to the office in the fog on Monday night, but that you were seen and followed by young Cadogan West, who had probably some previous reason to suspect you. He saw your theft, but could not give the alarm, as it was just possible that you were taking the papers to your brother in London. Leaving all his private concerns, like the good citizen that he was, he followed you closely in the fog, and kept at your heels until you reached this very house. There he intervened, and then it was, Colonel Walter, that to treason you added the more terrible crime of murder."

" I did not ! I did not ! Before God I swear that I did not ! " cried our wretched prisoner.

" Tell us, then, how Cadogan West met his end before you laid him upon the roof of a railway carriage."

" I will. I swear to you that I will. I did the rest. I confess it. It was just as you say. A Stock Exchange debt had to be paid. I needed the money badly. Oberstein offered me five thousand. It was to save myself from ruin. But as to murder, I am as innocent as you."

" What happened then ? "

" He had his suspicions before, and he followed me as you describe. I never knew it until I was at the very door. It was thick fog, and one could not see three yards. I had given two taps and Oberstein had come to the door. The young man rushed up and demanded to know what we were about to do with the papers. Oberstein had a short life-preserver. He always carried it with him. As West forced his way after us into the house Oberstein struck him on the head. The blow was a fatal one. He was dead within five minutes. There he lay in the hall, and we were at our wits' end what to do. Then Oberstein had this idea about the trains which halted under his back window. But first he examined the papers which I had brought. He said that three of them were essential, and that he must keep them. ' You cannot keep them,' said I. ' There will be a dreadful row at Woolwich if they are not returned.' ' I must keep them,' said he, ' for they are so technical that it is impossible in the time to make copies.' ' Then they must all go back together to-night,' said I. He thought for a little, and then he cried out that he had it. ' Three I will keep,' said he. ' The others we will stuff into the pocket of this young man. When he is found the whole business will assuredly be put to his account.' I could see no other way out of it, so we did as he suggested. We waited half an hour at the window before a train stopped. It was so thick that nothing could be seen, and we had no difficulty in lowering West's body on to the train. That was the end of the matter so far as I was concerned."

36

"THAT WAS THE END OF THE MATTER"

Illustration by Arthur Twidle for the *Strand Magazine*, December, 1908.

36 *That was the end of the matter so far as I was concerned*." But the question remains: did Cadogan West's body travel from Gloucester Road to Aldgate on the "inner rail" (that is, via Victoria), or on the "outer rail" (that is, via Baker Street)? In October, 1951, the late Norman Crump went over the same ground as Sherlock Holmes and concluded that "the inner rail is the most probable, in all respects save one. This is the absence of any windows overlooking it between High Street and Gloucester Road. Therefore it looks like the outer rail [although] this postulates [six] extreme improbabilities . . ."

On the other hand, Mr. Cornelis Helling, referring to *The Railways of Britain, Past and Present*, by O. S. Nock (London: B. T. Batsford, Ltd., Second Edition, 1949) has written that "an Inner Circle train was concerned, and at that time, of course, it would have been steam hauled, by one of those supremely ugly, yet most efficient Beyer-Peacock tank engines. Had the train chanced instead to be one on the Outer Circle service, the body, far from remaining on the roof all the way from Gloucester Road till the sharp curve at Minories Junction, might have rolled off at the very first start with [that] one particular engine. The 'Outer Circle' was not really a circle at all, but merely a horseshoe as it consisted of a shuttle service between Broad Street and Mansion House, by way of Hampstead Heath, Willesden and Earl's Court. It was operated by the London and North Western Railway, utilizing running powers over the Underground line from Earl's Court to Mansion House."

37 *was safely engulfed for fifteen years in a British prison.* "What were the extenuating circumstances whereby Oberstein got only fifteen years for as cold-blooded and indefensible a murder as can be found?" Dr. Felix Morley asked in "The Bruce-Partington Keys."

" And your brother ? "

" He said nothing, but he had caught me once with his keys, and I think that he suspected. I read in his eyes that he suspected. As you know, he never held up his head again."

There was silence in the room. It was broken by Mycroft Holmes.

" Can you not make reparation ? It would ease your conscience, and possibly your punishment."

" What reparation can I make ? "

" Where is Oberstein with the papers ? "

" I do not know."

" Did he give you no address ? "

" He said that letters to the Hôtel du Louvre, Paris, would eventually reach him."

" Then reparation is still within your power," said Sherlock Holmes.

" I will do anything I can. I owe this fellow no particular goodwill. He has been my ruin and my downfall."

" Here are paper and pen. Sit at this desk and write to my dictation. Direct the envelope to the address given. That is right. Now the letter : ' Dear Sir,—With regard to our transaction, you will no doubt have observed by now that one essential detail is missing. I have a tracing which will make it complete. This has involved me in extra trouble, however, and I must ask you for a further advance of five hundred pounds. I will not trust it to the post, nor will I take anything but gold or notes. I would come to you abroad, but it would excite remark if I left the country at present. Therefore I shall expect to meet you in the smoking-room of the Charing Cross Hotel at noon on Saturday. Remember that only English notes, or gold, will be taken.' That will do very well. I shall be very much surprised if it does not fetch our man."

And it did ! It is a matter of history—that secret history of a nation which is often so much more intimate and interesting than its public chronicles—that Oberstein, eager to complete the coup of his lifetime, came to the lure and **37** was safely engulfed for fifteen years in a British prison. In his trunk were found the invaluable Bruce-Partington plans, which he had put up for auction in all the naval centres of Europe.

Colonel Walter died in prison towards the end of the second year of his sentence. As to Holmes, he returned refreshed to his monograph upon the Polyphonic Motets of Lassus, which has since been printed for private circulation, and is said by experts to be the last word upon the subject. Some weeks afterwards I learned incidentally that my friend spent a day at Windsor, whence he returned with a remarkably fine emerald tie-pin. When I asked him if he had bought it, he answered that it was a present from a certain gracious lady in whose interests he had once been fortunate enough to carry out a small commission. He said no more ; but I fancy that I could guess at that lady's august name, and I have little doubt that the emerald pin will for ever recall to my friend's memory the adventure of the Bruce-Partington plans.

56

THE ADVENTURE OF THE VEILED LODGER

[October, 1896; one day]

WHEN one considers that Mr. Sherlock Holmes was in active practice for twenty-three years, and that during seventeen of these I was allowed to co-operate with him and to keep notes of his doings, it will be clear that I have a mass of material at my command. The problem has always been, not to find, but to choose. There is the long row of year-books which fill a shelf, and there are the dispatch-cases filled with documents, a perfect quarry for the student, not only of crime, but of the social and official scandals of the late Victorian era. Concerning these latter, I may say that the writers of agonized letters, who beg that the honour of their families or the reputation of famous forbears may not be touched, have nothing to fear. The discretion and high sense of professional honour which have always distinguished my friend are still at work in the choice of these memoirs, and no confidence will be abused. I deprecate, however, in the strongest way the attempts which have been made lately to get at and to destroy these papers. The source of these outrages is known, and if they are repeated I have Mr. Holmes' authority for saying that the whole story concerning the politician, the lighthouse and the trained cormorant will **1** be given to the public. There is at least one reader who will understand.

It is not reasonable to suppose that every one of these cases gave Holmes the opportunity of showing those curious gifts of instinct and observation which I have endeavoured to set forth in these memoirs. Sometimes he had with much effort to pick the fruit, sometimes it fell easily into his lap. But the most terrible human tragedies were often involved in these cases which brought him the fewest personal opportunities, and it is one of these which I now desire to record. In telling it, I have made a slight change of name and place, but otherwise the facts are as stated.

One forenoon—it was late in 1896—I received a hur- **2** ried note from Holmes asking for my attendance. When I arrived, I found him seated in a smoke-laden atmosphere, with an elderly, motherly woman of the buxom landlady type in the corresponding chair in front of him.

1 *the politician, the lighthouse and the trained cormorant.* "The training of cormorants is not widely practiced in Britain," Mr. Paul H. Gore-Booth wrote in "The Journeys of Sherlock Holmes." "But it is a well-known Far Eastern custom to train cormorants to catch fish in such a way that they are not swallowed, but are brought back to the owner (of the cormorant), and this suggests that there may have been a Chinese or Japanese involved in the case. A lighthouse suggests a shipwreck, and the significance of the title must suddenly dawn on us when we remember that the first Japanese (Nippon Yusen Kaisha) steamship came to Europe in 1895. There we have the whole scene; Japan emerging as a modern power (she had just defeated China in the war of 1894 and the era of the Russo-Japanese War and the Anglo-Japanese Alliance was fast approaching); a prominent Japanese politician embarks secretly on one of the new Japanese ships for England; there is a mishap in a storm or a fog; the ship and the politician disappear within hail of the lighthouse, and all that is left as material for Mr. Holmes is the trained cormorant. A fascinating case."

It has fascinated, among others, Mr. Ralph A. Ashton, whose pastiche, "The Adventure of the Pius Missal," appeared in the *Baker Street Journal*, Vol. VII, No. 3, New Series, July, 1957, pp. 149–52; and Mr. Howard Collins, whose pastiche, "The Affair of the Politician, the Lighthouse, and the Trained Cormorant," appeared in the *Baker Street Journal*, Vol. II, No. 2, Old Series, April, 1947, pp. 195–204.

2 *it was late in 1896.* Mrs. Ronder had been a lodger at Mrs. Merrilow's "for seven years," before which she had suffered "for many a weary month" as a result of the Abbas Parva tragedy. Watson had no recollection of that case, although Holmes had been brought into it by young Edmunds of the Berkshire Constabulary and Watson was with Holmes at the time. The Abbas Parva tragedy would seem to have taken place early in 1889 or late in 1888, and Watson, as we have seen, was with Holmes all through the year 1888 and the first four months of 1889. Watson's date of 1896 for "The Adventure of the Veiled Lodger" would seem to be substantiated.

" This is Mrs. Merrilow, of South Brixton," said my friend, with a wave of the hand. " Mrs. Merrilow does not object to tobacco, Watson, if you wish to indulge your filthy habits. Mrs. Merrilow has an interesting story to tell which may well lead to further developments in which your presence may be useful."

" Anything I can do——"

" You will understand, Mrs. Merrilow, that if I come to Mrs. Ronder I should prefer to have a witness. You will make her understand that before we arrive."

" Lord bless you, Mr. Holmes," said our visitor ; " she is that anxious to see you that you might bring the whole parish at your heels ! "

" Then we shall come early in the afternoon. Let us see that we have our facts correct before we start. If we go over them it will help Dr. Watson to understand the situation. You say that Mrs. Ronder has been your lodger for seven years and that you have only once seen her face."

" And I wish to God I had not ! " said Mrs. Merrilow.

" It was, I understand, terribly mutilated."

" Well, Mr. Holmes, you would hardly say it was a face at all. That's how it looked. Our milkman got a glimpse of her once peeping out of the upper window, and he dropped his tin and the milk all over the front garden. That is the kind of face it is. When I saw her—I happened on her unawares—she covered up quick, and then she said, ' Now, Mrs. Merrilow, you know at last why it is that I never raise my veil.' "

" Do you know anything about her history ? "

" Nothing at all."

" Did she give references when she came ? "

" No, sir, but she gave hard cash, and plenty of it. A quarter's rent right down on the table in advance and no arguing about terms. In these times a poor woman like me can't afford to turn down a chance like that."

" Did she give any reason for choosing your house ? "

" Mine stands well back from the road and is more private than most. Then, again, I only take the one, and I have no family of my own. I reckon she had tried others and found that mine suited her best. It's privacy she is after, and she is ready to pay for it."

" You say that she never showed her face from first to last save on the one accidental occasion. Well, it is a very remarkable story, most remarkable, and I don't wonder that you want it examined."

" I don't, Mr. Holmes. I am quite satisfied so long as I get my rent. You could not have a quieter lodger or one who gives less trouble."

" Then what has brought matters to a head ? "

" Her health, Mr. Holmes. She seems to be wasting away. And there's something terrible on her mind. ' Murder ! ' she cries. ' Murder ! ' And once I heard her, ' You cruel beast ! You monster ! ' she cried. It was in the night, and it fair rang through the house and sent the shivers through me. So I went to her in the morning. ' Mrs. Ronder,' I says, ' if you have anything that is troubling your soul, there's the clergy,' I says, ' and there's the police. Between them you should get some help.' ' For God's sake, not the police ! ' says she, ' and the clergy can't change what is past. And yet,' she says, ' it would ease my mind if someone knew the truth before I died.' ' Well,' says I, ' if you won't have the regulars, there is this detective man what we read about '—beggin' your pardon, Mr. Holmes. And she, she fair jumped at it. ' That's the man,' says she. ' I wonder I never thought of it before. Bring him here, Mrs. Merrilow, and if he won't come, tell him I am the wife of Ronder's wild beast show. Say that, and give him the name Abbas Parva. Here it is as she wrote it, Abbas Parva. ' That will bring him, if he's the man I think he is.' ' "

" And it will, too," remarked Holmes. " Very good, Mrs. Merrilow. I should like to have a little chat with Dr. Watson. That will carry us till lunch-time. About three o'clock you may expect to see us at your house in Brixton."

Our visitor had no sooner waddled out of the room —no other verb can describe Mrs. Merrilow's method of progression—than Sherlock Holmes threw himself with fierce energy upon the pile of commonplace books in the corner. For a few minutes there was a constant swish of the leaves, and then with a grunt of satisfaction he came upon what he sought. So excited was he that he did not rise, but sat upon the floor like some strange Buddha, with crossed legs, the huge books all round him, and one open upon his knees.

" The case worried me at the time, Watson. Here are my marginal notes to prove it. I confess that I could make nothing of it. And yet I was convinced that the coroner was wrong. Have you no recollection of the Abbas Parva tragedy ? "

" None, Holmes."

" And yet you were with me then. But certainly my own impression was very superficial, for there was nothing to go by, and none of the parties had engaged my services. Perhaps you would care to read the papers ? "

" Could you not give me the points ? "

" That is very easily done. It will probably come back to your memory as I talk. Ronder, of course, was a household word. He was the rival of Wombwell, and of Sanger, one of the greatest showmen of his day. **3** There is evidence, however, that he took to drink, and that both he and his show were on the down grade at the time of the great tragedy. The caravan had halted for the night at Abbas Parva, which is a small village in Berkshire, when this horror occurred. They were on their way to Wimbledon, travelling by road, and they were simply camping, and not exhibiting, as the place is so small a one that it would not have paid them to open.

" They had among their exhibits a very fine North African lion. Sahara King was its name, and it was the habit, both of Ronder and his wife, to give exhibitions inside its cage. Here, you see, is a photograph of the performance, by which you will perceive that Ronder was a huge porcine person and that his wife was a very magnificent woman. It was deposed at the inquest that there had been some signs that the lion was danger-ous, but, as usual, familiarity begat contempt, and no

. . . HE DID NOT RISE, BUT SAT UPON THE FLOOR
LIKE SOME STRANGE BUDDHA . . .

Illustration by Frank Wiles for the *Strand Maga-zine*, February, 1927.

"SAHARA KING WAS ITS NAME . . ."

Illustration by Frederic Dorr Steele for *Liberty Magazine*, January 22, 1927.

3 *the rival of Wombwell, and of Sanger.* Womb-well's Traveling Menagerie and the circus of "Lord" George Sanger were two of the best-known shows of the day.

notice was taken of the fact.

" It was usual for either Ronder or his wife to feed the lion at night. Sometimes one went, sometimes both, but they never allowed anyone else to do it, for they believed that so long as they were the food-carriers he would regard them as benefactors, and would never molest them. On this particular night, seven years ago, they both went, and a very terrible happening followed, the details of which have never been made clear.

" It seems that the whole camp was roused near midnight by the roars of the animal and the screams of the woman. The different grooms and *employés* rushed from their tents, carrying lanterns, and by their light an awful sight was revealed. Ronder lay, with the back of his head crushed in and deep claw-marks across his scalp, some ten yards from the cage, which was open. Close to the door of the cage lay Mrs. Ronder, upon her back, with the creature squatting and snarling above her. It had torn her face in such a fashion that it was never thought that she could live. Several of the circus men, headed by Leonardo, the strong man, and Griggs, the clown, drove the creature off with poles, upon which it sprang back into the cage, and was at once locked in. How it had got loose was a mystery. It was conjectured that the pair intended to enter the cage, but that when the door was loosed the creature bounded out upon them. There was no other point of interest in the evidence, save that the woman in a delirium of agony kept screaming, ' Coward ! Coward ! ' as she was carried back to the van in which they lived. It was six months before she was fit to give evidence, but the inquest was duly held, with the obvious verdict of death from misadventure."

" What alternative could be conceived ? " said I.

" You may well say so. And yet there were one or two points which worried young Edmunds, of the Berkshire Constabulary. A smart lad that ! He was sent later to Allahabad. That was how I came into the matter, for he dropped in and smoked a pipe or two over it."

" A thin, yellow-haired man ? "

" Exactly. I was sure you would pick up the trail presently."

" But what worried him ? "

" Well, we were both worried. It was so deucedly difficult to reconstruct the affair. Look at it from the lion's point of view. He is liberated. What does he do ? He takes half a dozen bounds forward, which brings him to Ronder. Ronder turns to fly—the claw-marks were on the back of his head—but the lion strikes him down. Then, instead of bounding on and escaping, he returns to the woman, who was close to the cage, and he knocks her over and chews her face up. Then, again, those cries of hers would seem to imply that her husband had in some way failed her. What could the poor devil have done to help her ? You see the difficulty ? "

" Quite."

" And then there was another thing. It comes back

to me now as I think it over.   There was some evidence that, just at the time the lion roared and the woman screamed, a man began shouting in terror."

" This man Ronder, no doubt."

" Well, if his skull was smashed in you would hardly expect to hear from him again.   There were at least two witnesses who spoke of the cries of a man being mingled with those of a woman."

" I should think the whole camp was crying out by then.   As to the other points, I think I could suggest a solution."

" I should be glad to consider it."

" The two were together, ten yards from the cage, when the lion got loose.   The man turned and was struck down.   The woman conceived the idea of getting into the cage and shutting the door.   It was her only refuge.   She made for it, and just as she reached it the beast bounded after her and knocked her over. She was angry with her husband for having encouraged the beast's rage by turning.   If they had faced it, they might have cowed it.   Hence her cries of ' Coward ! ' "

" Brilliant, Watson !   Only one flaw in your diamond."

" What is the flaw, Holmes ? "

" If they were both ten paces from the cage, how came the beast to get loose ? "

" Is it possible that they had some enemy who loosed it ? "

" And why should it attack them savagely when it was in the habit of playing with them, and doing tricks with them inside the cage ? "

" Possibly the same enemy had done something to enrage it."

Holmes looked thoughtful and remained in silence for some moments.

" Well, Watson, there is this to be said for your theory. Ronder was a man of many enemies.   Edmunds told me that in his cups he was horrible.   A huge bully of a man, he cursed and slashed at everyone who came in his way.   I expect those cries about a monster, of which our visitor has spoken, were nocturnal reminiscences of the dear departed.   However, our speculations are futile until we have all the facts.   There is a cold partridge on the sideboard, Watson, and a bottle of Montrachet. **4** Let us renew our energies before we make a fresh call upon them."

When our hansom deposited us at the house of Mrs. Merrilow, we found that plump lady blocking up the open door of her humble but retired abode.   It was very clear that her chief preoccupation was lest she should lose a valuable lodger, and she implored us, before showing us up, to say and do nothing which could lead to so undesirable an end.   Then, having reassured her, we followed her up the straight, badly-carpeted staircase and were shown into the room of the mysterious lodger.

It was a close, musty, ill-ventilated place, as might be expected, since its inmate seldom left it.   From keeping beasts in a cage, the woman seemed, by some retribution of Fate, to have become herself a beast in a

4 *a bottle of Montrachet.* "Why a white Burgundy could be found here is still an unsolved problem," Mr. Jorgen Cold wrote in "What Did Sherlock Holmes Drink?" "Holmes may have bought it before he sent for Watson in order to take it with the cold partridge which was there also."

cage. She sat now in a broken arm-chair in the shadowy corner of the room.   Long years of inaction had coarsened the lines of her figure, but at some period it must have been beautiful, and was still full and voluptuous. A thick dark veil covered her face, but it was cut off close at her upper lip, and disclosed a perfectly-shaped mouth and a delicately-rounded chin. I could well conceive that she had indeed been a very remarkable woman. Her voice, too, was well-modulated and pleasing.

" My name is not unfamiliar to you, Mr. Holmes," said she. " I thought that it would bring you."

" That is so, madam, though I do not know how you are aware that I was interested in your case."

" I learned it when I had recovered my health and was examined by Mr. Edmunds, the County detective. I fear I lied to him. Perhaps it would have been wiser had I told the truth."

" It is usually wiser to tell the truth. But why did you lie to him ? "

" Because the fate of someone else depended upon it. I know that he was a very worthless being, and yet I would not have his destruction upon my conscience. We had been so close—so close ! "

" But has this impediment been removed ? "

" Yes, sir. The person that I allude to is dead."

" Then why should you not now tell the police anything you know ? "

" Because there is another person to be considered. That other person is myself. I could not stand the scandal and publicity which would come from a police examination. I have not long to live, but I wish to die undisturbed. And yet I wanted to find one man of judgment to whom I could tell my terrible story, so that when I am gone all might be understood."

" You compliment me, madam. At the same time, I am a responsible person. I do not promise you that when you have spoken I may not myself think it my duty to refer the case to the police."

" I think not, Mr. Holmes. I know your character and methods too well, for I have followed your work for some years. Reading is the only pleasure which Fate has left me, and I miss little which passes in the world. But in any case, I will take my chance of the use which you may make of my tragedy. It will ease my mind to tell it."

" My friend and I would be glad to hear it."

The woman rose and took from a drawer the photograph of a man. He was clearly a professional acrobat, a man of magnificent physique, taken with his huge arms folded across his swollen chest and a smile breaking from under his heavy moustache—the self-satisfied smile of the man of many conquests.

" That is Leonardo," she said.

" Leonardo, the strong man, who gave evidence ? "

" The same. And this—this is my husband."

It was a dreadful face—a human pig, or rather a human wild boar, for it was formidable in its bestiality. One could imagine that vile mouth champing and foaming in its rage, and one could conceive those small, vicious eyes darting pure malignancy as they looked forth

"THAT IS LEONARDO," SHE SAID.

Illustration by Frederic Dorr Steele for *Liberty Magazine*, January 22, 1927.

upon the world.   Ruffian, bully, beast—it was all written on that heavy-jowled face.

"Those two pictures will help you, gentlemen, to understand the story.   I was a poor circus girl brought up on the sawdust, and doing springs through the hoop before I was ten.   When I became a woman this man loved me, if such lust as his can be called love, and in an evil moment I became his wife.   From that day I was in hell, and he the devil who tormented me.   There was no one in the show who did not know of his treatment. He deserted me for others.   He tied me down and lashed me with his riding-whip when I complained. They all pitied me and they all loathed him, but what could they do ?   They feared him, one and all.   For he was terrible at all times, and murderous when he was drunk.   Again and again he was had for assault, and for cruelty to the beasts, but he had plenty of money and the fines were nothing to him.   The best men all left us and the show began to go downhill.   It was only Leonardo and I who kept it up—with little Jimmy Griggs, the clown.   Poor devil, he had not much to be funny about, but he did what he could to hold things together.

"Then Leonardo came more and more into my life. You see what he was like.   I know now the poor spirit that was hidden in that splendid body, but compared to my husband he seemed like the Angel Gabriel.   He pitied me and helped me, till at last our intimacy turned to love—deep, deep, passionate love, such love as I had dreamed of but never hoped to feel.   My husband suspected it, but I think that he was a coward as well as a bully, and that Leonardo was the one man that he was afraid of.   He took revenge in his own way by torturing me more than ever.   One night my cries brought Leonardo to the door of our van.   We were near tragedy that night, and soon my lover and I understood that it could not be avoided.   My husband was not fit to live.   We planned that he should die.

"Leonardo had a clever, scheming brain.   It was he who planned it.   I do not say that to blame him, for I was ready to go with him every inch of the way.   But I should never have had the wit to think of such a plan. We made a club—Leonardo made it—and in the leaden head he fastened five long steel nails, the points outwards, with just such a spread as the lion's paw.   This was to give my husband his death-blow, and yet to leave the evidence that it was the lion which we would loose who had done the deed.

"It was a pitch-dark night when my husband and I went down, as was our custom, to feed the beast.   We carried with us the raw meat in a zinc pail.   Leonardo was waiting at the corner of the big van which we should have to pass before we reached the cage.   He was too slow, and we walked past him before he could strike, but he followed us on tiptoe and I heard the crash as the club smashed my husband's skull.   My heart leaped with joy at the sound.   I sprang forward, and I undid the catch which held the door of the great lion's cage.

"And then the terrible thing happened.   You may have heard how quick these creatures are to scent human

"AS I SLIPPED THE BARS IT BOUNDED OUT,
AND WAS ON ME IN AN INSTANT."

Illustration by Frank Wiles for the *Strand Magazine*, February, 1927.

blood, and how it excites them. Some strange instinct had told the creature in one instant that a human being had been slain. As I slipped the bars it bounded out, and was on me in an instant. Leonardo could have saved me. If he had rushed forward and struck the beast with his club he might have cowed it. But the man lost his nerve. I heard him shout in his terror, and then I saw him turn and fly. At the same instant the teeth of the lion met in my face. Its hot, filthy breath had already poisoned me and I was hardly conscious of pain. With the palms of my hands I tried to push the great steaming, blood-stained jaws away from me, and I screamed for help. I was conscious that the camp was stirring, and then dimly I remember a group of men, Leonardo, Griggs and others, dragging me from under the creature's paws. That was my last memory, Mr. Holmes, for many a weary month. When I came to myself, and saw myself in the mirror, I cursed that lion—oh, how I cursed him!—not because he had torn away my beauty, but because he had not torn away my life. I had but one desire, Mr. Holmes, and I had enough money to gratify it. It was that I should cover myself so that my poor face should be seen by none, and that I should dwell where none whom I had ever known should find me. That was all that was left to me to do—and that is what I have done. A poor wounded beast that has crawled into its hole to die—that is the end of Eugenia Ronder."

We sat in silence for some time after the unhappy woman had told her story. Then Holmes stretched out his long arm and patted her hand with such a show of sympathy as I had seldom known him to exhibit.

"Poor girl!" he said. "Poor girl! The ways of Fate are indeed hard to understand. If there is not some compensation hereafter, then the world is a cruel jest. But what of this man Leonardo?"

"I never saw him or heard from him again. Perhaps I have been wrong to feel so bitterly against him. He might as soon have loved one of the freaks whom we carried round the country as the thing which the lion had left. But a woman's love is not so easily set aside. He had left me under the beast's claws, he had deserted me in my need, and yet I could not bring myself to give him to the gallows. For myself, I cared nothing what became of me. What could be more dreadful than my actual life? But I stood between Leonardo and his fate."

"And he is dead?"

"He was drowned last month when bathing near 5 Margate. I saw his death in the paper."

"And what did he do with this five-clawed club, which is the most singular and ingenious part of all your story?"

"I cannot tell, Mr. Holmes. There is a chalk-pit by the camp, with a deep green pool at the base of it. Perhaps in the depths of that pool——"

"Well, well, it is of little consequence now. The case is closed."

"Yes," said the woman, "the case is closed."

We had risen to go, but there was something in the

5 *when bathing near Margate*. Even a strong man would hardly have gone bathing at Margate after September; our month would seem to be October. The day was probably not a Friday ("Two days later," when Watson called on Holmes, he found that a small blue bottle had come by post, presumably on the day of his call), but there does not seem to be any other evidence by which one can determine the day of the month.

woman's voice which arrested Holmes' attention. He turned swiftly upon her.

" Your life is not your own," he said. " Keep your hands off it."

" What use is it to anyone ? "

" How can you tell ? The example of patient suffering is in itself the most precious of all lessons to an impatient world."

The woman's answer was a terrible one. She raised her veil and stepped forward into the light.

" I wonder if you would bear it," she said.

It was horrible. No words can describe the framework of a face when the face itself is gone. Two living and beautiful brown eyes looking sadly out from that grisly ruin did but make the view more awful. Holmes held up his hand in a gesture of pity and protest, and together we left the room.

Two days later, when I called upon my friend, he pointed with some pride to a small blue bottle upon his mantelpiece. I picked it up. There was on it a red poison label. A pleasant almondy odour rose when I opened it.

" Prussic acid ? " said I.

" Exactly. It came by post. ' I send you my temptation. I will follow your advice.' That was the message. I think, Watson, we can guess the name of the brave woman who sent it."

On the Canonicity of "The Adventure of the Veiled Lodger": Commentators have questioned the "Canonicity" of some of the adventures supposedly narrated by Watson in *The Case-Book of Sherlock Holmes*. But Mr. D. Martin Dakin has written of this adventure ("The Problem of the Case-Book") that it is "in all probability genuine. Holmes' own part in it is so unsensational that there would be no reason for inventing it. His advice to Mrs. Ronder to keep her hands off her life shows him at his best as a good man as well as a good detective (compare his treatment of Ryder at the end of 'The Adventure of the Blue Carbuncle'), and his comment 'The ways of Fate are indeed hard to understand. If there is not some compensation hereafter, then the world is a cruel jest'—is parallel to his philosophic collections on the same theme in 'The Boscombe Valley Mystery' and 'The Cardboard Box.' Indeed his whole conversation reads like the authentic Holmes. But above all we have the unmistakable mark of Watsonian authorship in the passage at the beginning with the dark hints of the unpublished cases, particularly that most tantalising of them all, the 'story concerning the politician, the lighthouse and the trained cormorant' . . ."

. . . THERE WAS SOMETHING IN THE WOMAN'S VOICE WHICH ARRESTED HOLMES' ATTENTION.

Illustration by Frank Wiles for the *Strand Magazine*, February, 1927.

57

THE ADVENTURE OF THE SUSSEX VAMPIRE

[Thursday, November 19, to Saturday, November 21, 1896]

1 *Old Jewry.* Old Jewry, in the City, on the north side of Cheapside, was the street where the original synagogue of the Jews was erected, and was their headquarters till their expulsion in 1291.

2 *Mincing Lane.* Named from houses which belonged to the Minchuns or nuns of St. Helen's.

3 *"It was a ship.* And a real ship, identified by Mr. Richard W. Clarke ("On the Nomenclature of Watson's Ships") as having been owned by the Oriental Trading Company of Shanghai. " I fear she came to her end in the East," the late Christopher Morley wrote, "for my grand old Findlay's *Sailing Directory of the Indian Archipelago and China and Japan* (1878 edition, the one used by Conrad) lists on p. 679 as a hazard of Batavia Bay the Matilda Rock. According to the custom of marine geographers, a reef or shoal is named for the vessel that first ran upon it, or surveyed it." And the late Edgar W. Smith once noted that the ill-fated *Mary Celeste,* found abandoned for no known reason, in a high running sea between the Azores and Portugal in the year 1872, "was commanded . . . by Captain Benjamin Spooner Briggs—and aboard her when she sailed from New York—in addition to a first and second mate, a cook, and four seamen—were the captain's wife and his two-year-old daughter. The wife's name was Sarah Elizabeth Briggs. The daughter's name . . . was Sophia Matilda Briggs."

4 *the giant rat of Sumatra. Rhizomys sumatrensis,* the great Sumatran bamboo rat, which may attain a length of nineteen inches excluding the tail. The world's largest rats, however, are three-foot-long animals from the Caroline Islands in the Pacific. They weigh twenty pounds and have black and yellow stomachs. Their teeth are yellow in front, white behind, and are shaped like tusks, 1½ inches long. The animals have sealed throats which permit them to eat under water without strangling.

HOLMES had read carefully a note which the last post had brought him. Then, with the dry chuckle which was his nearest approach to a laugh, he tossed it over to me.

" For a mixture of the modern and the mediæval, of the practical and of the wildly fanciful, I think this is surely the limit," said he. " What do you make of it, Watson ? "

I read as follows :

1   46 OLD JEWRY,
Nov. 19th.

Re Vampires.

SIR,—

Our client, Mr. Robert Ferguson, of Ferguson &
2 Muirhead, tea brokers, of Mincing Lane, has made some inquiry from us in a communication of even date concerning vampires. As our firm specializes entirely upon the assessment of machinery the matter hardly comes within our purview, and we have therefore recommended Mr. Ferguson to call upon you and lay the matter before you. We have not forgotten your successful action in the case of Matilda Briggs.

We are, Sir, faithfully yours,
MORRISON, MORRISON, AND DODD.
per E. J. C.

" Matilda Briggs was not the name of a young woman, Watson," said Holmes, in a reminiscent voice. " It
3 was a ship which is associated with the giant rat of
4 Sumatra, a story for which the world is not yet prepared. But what do we know about vampires ? Does it come within our purview either ? Anything is better than stagnation, but really we seem to have been switched on to a Grimm's fairy tale. Make a long arm, Watson, and see what V has to say."

I leaned back and took down the great index volume to which he referred. Holmes balanced it on his knee and his eyes moved slowly and lovingly over the record of old cases, mixed with the accumulated information of a lifetime.

" Voyage of the *Gloria Scott*," he read. " That was a bad business. I have some recollection that you made

a record of it, Watson, though I was unable to con- **5**
gratulate you upon the result.   Victor Lynch, the forger. **6-7**
Venomous lizard or gila. Remarkable case, that ! **8**
Vittoria, the circus belle. Vanderbilt and the Yeggman.
Vipers. Vigor, the Hammersmith wonder. Hullo !
Hullo ! Good old index. You can't beat it. Listen to
this, Watson. Vampirism in Hungary. And again,
Vampires in Transylvania." He turned over the pages **9**
with eagerness, but after a short intent perusal he threw
down the great book with a snarl of disappointment.

" Rubbish, Watson, rubbish ! What have we to do
with walking corpses who can only be held in their grave
by stakes driven through their hearts ?   It's pure lunacy."

" But surely," said I, " the vampire was not necessarily
a dead man ? A living person might have the habit.
I have read, for example, of the old sucking the blood
of the young in order to retain their youth."

" You are right, Watson. It mentions the legend
in one of these references. But are we to give serious
attention to such things ? This Agency stands flat-
footed upon the ground, and there it must remain. **10**
The world is big enough for us. No ghosts need apply.
I fear that we cannot take Mr. Robert Ferguson very
seriously. Possibly this note may be from him, and
may throw some light upon what is worrying him."

He took up a second letter which had lain unnoticed
upon the table whilst he had been absorbed with the
first. This he began to read with a smile of amusement
upon his face which gradually faded away into an expression of intense interest and concentration. When he had
finished he sat for some little time lost in thought with
the letter dangling from his fingers. Finally, with a
start, he aroused himself from his reverie.

" Cheeseman's, Lamberley. Where is Lamberley,
Watson ? "

" It is in Sussex, south of Horsham."

" Not very far, eh ? And Cheeseman's ? "

" I know that country, Holmes. It is full of old
houses which are named after the men who built them
centuries ago. You get Odley's and Harvey's and
Carriton's—the folk are forgotten but their names live
in their houses."

" Precisely," said Holmes coldly. It was one of
the peculiarities of his proud, self-contained nature
that, though he docketed any fresh information very
quickly and accurately in his brain, he seldom made any
acknowledgment to the giver. " I rather fancy we shall
know a good deal more about Cheeseman's, Lamberley,
before we are through. The letter is, as I had hoped,
from Robert Ferguson. By the way, he claims acquaintance with you."

" With me ! "

" You had better read it."

He handed the letter across. It was headed with
the address quoted.

DEAR MR. HOLMES, (it said)—I have been recommended
to you by my lawyers, but indeed the matter is so extraordinarily delicate that it is most difficult to discuss.

5 *I have some recollection that you made a record
of it, Watson.* "The Adventure of the Sussex Vampire" cannot be earlier than November, 1894, or
later than November, 1899: 1) Holmes speaks of
Watson's "record" of the voyage of the *Gloria
Scott,* published in April, 1893. 2) Watson, as we
shall see, played rugby for Blackheath when Ferguson was three-quarter for Richmond. Thus the
two men were much of an age. Since Watson took
his medical degree in 1878, 1852 is a probable year
for his birth. Ferguson was twice married; he had
a fifteen-year-old son by his first wife and had
married his second wife "some five years ago."
He cannot have been less than forty at the time
of "The Sussex Vampire," and he was most probably some years older than that. 3) Billy the page
was on duty at Baker Street from October, 1900,
on ("The Problem of Thor Bridge"). But there
is no page boy at Baker Street at the time of "The
Sussex Vampire"; Holmes, having written a telegram, says to Watson, "Take a wire down, like a
good fellow." The year was not 1894: "The Sussex Vampire" is not mentioned in the list of important cases for that year given in "The Adventure of the Golden Pince-Nez"; also, it would
have come too soon after that case for Holmes to
say to Ferguson: "There is a lull at present." The
year was not 1895: in that year Holmes spent the
three days November 18th–20th in his rooms, as
we know from "The Adventure of the Bruce-
Partington Plans." The year was not 1897: Holmes
wrote his reply to Morrison, Morrison, and Dodd's
letter of the 19th on the 21st; he would not have
written a business communication on a Sunday.
The year was not 1898 nor 1899: the letter from
Morrison, Morrison, and Dodd, dated the 19th,
arrived by "the last post" and was therefore dispatched that day. November 19th is therefore not
a Sunday and almost certainly not a Saturday. As
the late H. W. Bell wrote: "If [the letter] had
been dispatched before one o'clock it would have
been delivered earlier in the day." We therefore
date the adventure *Thursday, November 19, to
Saturday, November 21, 1896.*

6 *I was unable to congratulate you upon the result.* ". . . one would not expect [Holmes] to . . .
tell Watson he could not congratulate him on his
record of a case which (as we know) consists almost entirely of narrative by Holmes himself,"
Mr. D. Martin Dakin commented in "Second
Thoughts on the Case-Book."

7 *Victor Lynch, the forger.* "Sherlock Holmes'
method of indexing 'Victor Lynch' under 'V' has
aroused nasty sniggers and smiles among the up-
to-date experts in cataloguing," Mr. Humfrey
Michell wrote. "But I perceive from indexes of
various volumes of the *Strand* that this method,
if not standard, was at least quite common. E.g.,
Vol. 6: 'Charles Kean, an unpublished letter of'
is included under 'C.' 'Martin Hewitt, Investigator'
is put under 'M.' So Sherlock Holmes was follow-

ing a sound tradition when in 'the good old index' Victor Lynch went into 'V.'"

"Holmes had no time to waste on the nice gradation of alphabetic initials," "A Penang Lawyer" wrote in "The Name's the Same." "He just stuck a case under the letter which first occurred to his curiously ill-balanced mind, and relied on his remarkable memory of association of ideas when he needed to refer to the subject again."

8 *Venomous lizard or gila.* "The Gila, or *Heloderma suspectum* . . . is of course a native of Arizona and New Mexico," Mr. Paul H. Gore-Booth wrote in "The Journeys of Sherlock Holmes." "Unfortunately, this does not enable us to deduce a visit to one of these states, since it appears that the creature thrives in captivity . . . and the specimen in question may well have been a captive brought to Britain for some sinister purpose by a countryman of Killer Evans or Jefferson Hope. But what a loss this case is! 'It is well,' says a leading authority (Raymond L. Ditmars, *Reptiles of the World*, Pitman, 1910, p. 164), 'to rate this species as among the reptiles highly dangerous to man.' And there, alas, our knowledge ends."

9 *Vampires in Transylvania.*" Under "Vampirism in London" Holmes' scrapbooks would surely have contained cuttings which appeared in the *Daily-graph* of August 5, 1890, the *Pall Mall Gazette* of September 18, 1890, and the *Westminster Gazette* of September 25, 1890, all describing the outrages perpetrated by Count Voivode Dracula (of Bram Stoker's *Dracula*, 1879). Whether Holmes—disguised, perhaps, as the mysterious Dr. Adolph Von Helsing, ostensibly of Amsterdam—actually participated in the hunt for the monster is a point debated by scholars, as is the theory that Count Dracula and Professor James Moriarty were one and the same man. The most convincing elucidation of this interesting theory is to be found in Mr. William Leonard's "Re: Vampires."

10 *This Agency stands flatfooted upon the ground.* "The most interesting feature of 'The Adventure of the Sussex Vampire' is Holmes' reference on two separate occasions to his 'Agency,' the word being spelt each time with a capital 'A,'" the late Gavin Brend wrote in *My Dear Holmes*. "Search where we will there is no mention of the Agency elsewhere, and it must be something more than a coincidence that the only two references to it should both occur in the same case. Can the explanation have something to do with the missing year 1896?"

It concerns a friend for whom I am acting. This gentleman married some five years ago a Peruvian lady, the daughter of a Peruvian merchant, whom he had met in connection with the importation of nitrates. The lady was very beautiful, but the fact of her foreign birth and of her alien religion always caused a separation of interests and of feelings between husband and wife, so that after a time his love may have cooled towards her and he may have come to regard their union as a mistake. He felt there were sides of her character which he could never explore or understand. This was the more painful as she was as loving a wife as a man could have—to all appearance absolutely devoted.

Now for the point which I will make more plain when we meet. Indeed, this note is merely to give you a general idea of the situation and to ascertain whether you would care to interest yourself in the matter. The lady began to show some curious traits, quite alien to her ordinarily sweet and gentle disposition. The gentleman had been married twice and he had one son by the first wife. This boy was now fifteen, a very charming and affectionate youth, though unhappily injured through an accident in childhood. Twice the wife was caught in the act of assaulting this poor lad in the most unprovoked way. Once she struck him with a stick and left a great weal on his arm.

This was a small matter, however, compared with her conduct to her own child, a dear boy just under one year of age. On one occasion about a month ago this child had been left by its nurse for a few minutes. A loud cry from the baby, as of pain, called the nurse back. As she ran into the room she saw her employer, the lady, leaning over the baby and apparently biting his neck. There was a small wound in the neck, from which a stream of blood had escaped. The nurse was so horrified that she wished to call the husband, but the lady implored her not to do so, and actually gave her five pounds as a price for her silence. No explanation was ever given, and for the moment the matter was passed over.

It left, however, a terrible impression upon the nurse's mind, and from that time she began to watch her mistress closely, and to keep a closer guard upon the baby, whom she tenderly loved. It seemed to her that even as she watched the mother, so the mother watched her, and that every time she was compelled to leave the baby alone the mother was waiting to get at it. Day and night the nurse covered the child, and day and night the silent, watchful mother seemed to be lying in wait as a wolf waits for a lamb. It must read most incredible to you, and yet I beg you to take it seriously, for a child's life and a man's sanity may depend upon it.

At last there came one dreadful day when the facts could no longer be concealed from the husband. The nurse's nerve had given way; she could stand the strain no longer, and she made a clean breast of it all to the man. To him it seemed as wild a tale as it may now seem to you. He knew his wife to be a loving wife, and, save for the assaults upon her stepson, a loving mother. Why, then, should she wound her own dear little baby? He told the nurse that she was dreaming, that her suspicions were those of a lunatic, and that such libels upon her mistress were not to be tolerated. Whilst they were talking, a sudden cry of pain was heard. Nurse and master rushed together to the nursery. Imagine his feelings, Mr. Holmes, as he saw his wife rise from a kneeling position beside the cot, and saw blood upon the child's exposed neck and upon the sheet. With a cry of horror, he turned his wife's face to the light and saw blood all round her lips. It was she—she beyond all question—who had drunk the poor baby's blood.

So the matter stands. She is now confined to her room. There has been no explanation. The husband is half demented. He knows, and I know, little of Vampirism beyond the name. We had thought it was some wild tale of foreign parts. And yet here in the very heart of the English Sussex—well, all this can be discussed with you in the morning. Will you see me? Will you use your great powers in aiding a distracted man? If so, kindly wire to Ferguson, Cheeseman's, Lamberley, and I will be at your rooms by ten o'clock.

Yours faithfully,
ROBERT FERGUSON.

PS.—I believe your friend Watson played Rugby for Blackheath when I was three-quarter for Richmond. It is the only personal introduction which I can **11** give.

"Of course I remember him," said I, as I laid down the letter. "Big Bob Ferguson, the finest three-quarter Richmond ever had. He was always a good-natured chap. It's like him to be so concerned over a friend's case."

Holmes looked at me thoughtfully and shook his head.

"I never get your limits, Watson," said he. "There are unexplored possibilities about you. Take a wire down, like a good fellow. 'Will examine your case with pleasure.'"

"*Your* case!"

"We must not let him think that this Agency is a home for the weak-minded. Of course it is his case. Send him that wire and let the matter rest till morning."

Promptly at ten o'clock next morning Ferguson strode into our room. I had remembered him as a long, slab-sided man with loose limbs and a fine turn of speed, which had carried him round many an opposing back. There is surely nothing in life more painful than to meet the wreck of a fine athlete whom one has known in his prime. His great frame had fallen in, his flaxen hair was scanty, and his shoulders were bowed. I fear that I roused corresponding emotions in him.

"Hullo, Watson," said he, and his voice was still deep and hearty. "You don't look quite the man you did when I threw you over the ropes into the crowd at the Old Deer Park. I expect I have changed a bit also. **12** But it's this last day or two that has aged me. I see by

11 *three-quarter for Richmond.* Football, played at an earlier period as a rough country game without any fixed rules, had fallen into disrepute by 1801. Then the public schools revived it on their playing fields. Rugger came into existence at Rugby, where, in 1823, William Webb Ellis first took the ball into his arms and ran with it. Blackheath, for which Watson played, was an amateur Rugby club which in 1871 was one of the founders of the Rugby Football Union; Richmond was another club in the same Union. "Watson had to be a forward," Mr. Frederick Byran-Brown wrote in "Sherlockian Schools and Schoolmasters"; "he was a man of action and common sense but his best friends would hardly call him a schemer. In those days the game was less complex and law-bound and would have suited his qualities well: Watson was probably captain and certainly leader of the pack. After his five years with the Barts' XV he established himself in the leading London Club side, perhaps with international hopes, which were to be foiled by his Army service abroad."

"NURSE AND MASTER RUSHED TOGETHER
TO THE NURSERY."

Illustration by W. T. Benda for *Hearst's International*, January, 1924.

12 *the Old Deer Park.* At Richmond. It contains the Kew Observatory built by Sir William Chambers in 1769, the Mid-Surrey Golf Course, and a large public recreation ground fronting the Great Chertsey Road. Here George II set up a court of his own when he was Prince of Wales.

"FOR GOD'S SAKE, GIVE ME SOME ADVICE, FOR I AM AT MY WITS' END."

Illustration by Howard K. Elcock for the *Strand Magazine*, January, 1924.

your telegram, Mr. Holmes, that it is no use my pretending to be anyone's deputy."

"It is simpler to deal direct," said Holmes.

"Of course it is. But you can imagine how difficult it is when you are speaking of the one woman whom you are bound to protect and help. What can I do? How am I to go to the police with such a story? And yet the kiddies have got to be protected. Is it madness, Mr. Holmes? Is it something in the blood? Have you any similar case in your experience? For God's sake, give me some advice, for I am at my wits' end."

"Very naturally, Mr. Ferguson. Now sit here and pull yourself together and give me a few clear answers. I can assure you that I am very far from being at my wits' end, and that I am confident we shall find some solution. First of all, tell me what steps you have taken. Is your wife still near the children?"

"We had a dreadful scene. She is a most loving woman, Mr. Holmes. If ever a woman loved a man with all her heart and soul, she loves me. She was cut to the heart that I should have discovered this horrible, this incredible, secret. She would not even speak. She gave no answer to my reproaches, save to gaze at me with a sort of wild, despairing look in her eyes. Then she rushed to her room and locked herself in. Since then she has refused to see me. She has a maid who was with her before her marriage, Dolores by name—a friend rather than a servant. She takes her food to her."

"Then the child is in no immediate danger?"

"Mrs. Mason, the nurse, has sworn that she will not leave it night or day. I can absolutely trust her. I am more uneasy about poor little Jack, for, as I told you in my note, he has twice been assaulted by her."

"But never wounded?"

"No; she struck him savagely. It is the more terrible as he is a poor little inoffensive cripple." Ferguson's gaunt features softened as he spoke of his boy. "You would think that the dear lad's condition would soften anyone's heart. A fall in childhood and a twisted spine, Mr. Holmes. But the dearest, most loving heart within."

Holmes had picked up the letter of yesterday and was reading it over. "What other inmates are there in your house, Mr. Ferguson?"

"Two servants who have not been long with us. One stable-hand, Michael, who sleeps in the house. My wife, myself, my boy Jack, baby, Dolores, and Mrs. Mason. That is all."

"I gather that you did not know your wife well at the time of your marriage?"

"I had only known her a few weeks."

"How long had this maid Dolores been with her?"

"Some years."

"Then your wife's character would really be better known by Dolores than by you?"

"Yes, you may say so."

Holmes made a note.

"I fancy," said he, "that I may be of more use at Lamberley than here.   It is eminently a case for personal investigation.   If the lady remains in her room, our presence could not annoy or inconvenience her.   Of course, we would stay at the inn."

Ferguson gave a gesture of relief.

"It is what I hoped, Mr. Holmes. There is an excellent train at two from Victoria, if you could come." **13**

"Of course we could come.   There is a lull at present. I can give you my undivided energies.   Watson, of course, comes with us.   But there are one or two points upon which I wish to be very sure before I start.   This unhappy lady, as I understand it, has appeared to assault both the children, her own baby and your little son ? "

"That is so."

"But the assaults take different forms, do they not ? She has beaten your son."

"Once with a stick and once very savagely with her hands."

"Did she give no explanation why she struck him ? "

"None, save that she hated him.   Again and again she said so."

"Well, that is not unknown among stepmothers.   A posthumous jealousy, we will say.   Is the lady jealous by nature ? "

"Yes, she is very jealous—jealous with all the strength of her fiery tropical love."

"But the boy—he is fifteen, I understand, and probably very developed in mind, since his body has been circumscribed in action.   Did he give you no explanation of these assaults ? "

"No ; he declared there was no reason."

"Were they good friends at other times ? "

"No ; there was never any love between them."

"Yet you say he is affectionate ? "

"Never in the world could there be so devoted a son. My life is his life. He is absorbed in what I say or do."

Once again Holmes made a note.   For some time he sat lost in thought.

"No doubt you and the boy were great comrades before this second marriage. You were thrown very close together, were you not ? "

"Very much so."

"And the boy, having so affectionate a nature, was devoted, no doubt, to the memory of his mother ? "

"Most devoted."

"He would certainly seem to be a most interesting lad. There is one other point about these assaults. Were the strange attacks upon the baby and the assaults upon your son at the same period ? "

"In the first case it was so.   It was as if some frenzy had seized her, and she had vented her rage upon both. In the second case it was only Jack who suffered.   Mrs. Mason had no complaint to make about the baby."

"That certainly complicates matters."

"I don't quite follow you, Mr. Holmes."

"Possibly not. One forms provisional theories and

13 *There is an excellent train at two from Victoria.* There was no 2:00 o'clock train from Victoria to Lamberley, but a train to Horsham left Victoria at 1:45.

waits for time or fuller knowledge to explode them. A bad habit, Mr. Ferguson ; but human nature is weak. I fear that your old friend here has given an exaggerated view of my scientific methods. However, I will only say at the present stage that your problem does not appear to me to be insoluble, and that you may expect to find us at Victoria at two o'clock."

It was evening of a dull, foggy November day when, having left our bags at the " Chequers," Lamberley, we drove through the Sussex clay of a long winding lane, and finally reached the isolated and ancient farm-house in which Ferguson dwelt. It was a large, straggling building, very old in the centre, very new at the wings, with towering Tudor chimneys and a lichen-spotted, high-pitched roof of Horsham slabs. The doorsteps were worn into curves, and the ancient tiles which lined the porch were marked with the rebus of a cheese and a man, after the original builder. Within, the ceilings were corrugated with heavy oaken beams, and the uneven floors sagged into sharp curves. An odour of age and decay pervaded the whole crumbling building.

There was one very large central room, into which Ferguson led us. Here, in a huge old-fashioned fire-place with an iron screen behind it dated 1670, there blazed and spluttered a splendid log fire.

The room, as I gazed round, was a most singular mixture of dates and of places. The half-panelled walls may well have belonged to the original yeoman farmer of the seventeenth century. They were ornamented, however, on the lower part by a line of well-chosen modern water-colours ; while above, where yellow plaster took the place of oak, there was hung a fine collection of South American utensils and weapons, which had been brought, no doubt, by the Peruvian lady upstairs. Holmes rose, with that quick curiosity which sprang from his eager mind, and examined them with some care. He returned with his eyes full of thought.

" Hullo ! " he cried. " Hullo ! "

A spaniel had lain in a basket in the corner. It came slowly forward towards its master, walking with difficulty. Its hind-legs moved irregularly and its tail was on the
14 ground. It licked Ferguson's hand.

" What is it, Mr. Holmes ? "

" The dog. What's the matter with it ? "

" That's what puzzled the vet. A sort of paralysis. Spinal meningitis, he thought. But it is passing. He'll be all right soon—won't you, Carlo ? "

A shiver of assent passed through the drooping tail. The dog's mournful eyes passed from one of us to the other. He knew that we were discussing his case.

" Did it come on suddenly ? "

" In a single night."

" How long ago ? "

" It may have been four months ago."

" Very remarkable. Very suggestive."

" What do you see in it, Mr. Holmes ? "

" A confirmation of what I had already thought."

" For God's sake, what *do* you think, Mr. Holmes ?

HOLMES ROSE, WITH THAT QUICK CURIOSITY WHICH SPRANG FROM HIS EAGER MIND, AND EXAMINED THEM WITH SOME CARE.

Illustration by W. T. Benda for *Hearst's International*, January, 1924.

14 *and its tail was on the ground.* "Since spaniels of all types have tails shortened very early in life to approximately two or three inches, the position assumed by this unhappy spaniel must have been an extremely odd one," Mr. Stuart Palmer commented in "Notes on Certain Evidences of Caniphobia in Mr. Sherlock Holmes and His Associates."

It may be a mere intellectual puzzle to you, but it is life and death to me! My wife a would-be murderer —my child in constant danger! Don't play with me, Mr. Holmes. It is too terribly serious."

The big Rugby three-quarter was trembling all over. Holmes put his hand soothingly upon his arm.

" I fear that there is pain for you, Mr. Ferguson, whatever the solution may be," said he. " I would spare you all I can. I cannot say more for the instant, but before I leave this house I hope I may have something definite."

" Please God you may! If you will excuse me, gentlemen, I will go up to my wife's room and see if there has been any change."

He was away some minutes, during which Holmes resumed his examination of the curiosities upon the wall. When our host returned it was clear from his downcast face that he had made no progress. He brought with him a tall, slim, brown-faced girl.

" The tea is ready, Dolores," said Ferguson. " See that your mistress has everything she can wish."

" She verra ill," cried the girl, looking with indignant eyes at her master. " She no ask for food. She verra ill. She need doctor. I frightened stay alone with her without doctor."

Ferguson looked at me with a question in his eyes.

" I should be so glad if I could be of use."

" Would your mistress see Dr. Watson ? "

" I take him. I no ask leave. She needs doctor."

" Then I'll come with you at once."

I followed the girl, who was quivering with strong emotion, up the staircase and down an ancient corridor. At the end was an iron-clamped and massive door. It struck me as I looked at it that if Ferguson tried to force his way to his wife he would find it no easy matter. The girl drew a key from her pocket, and the heavy oaken planks creaked upon their old hinges. I passed in and she swiftly followed, fastening the door behind her.

On the bed a woman was lying who was clearly in a high fever. She was only half conscious, but as I entered she raised a pair of frightened but beautiful eyes and glared at me in apprehension. Seeing a stranger, she appeared to be relieved, and sank back with a sigh upon the pillow. I stepped up to her with a few reassuring words, and she lay still while I took her pulse and temperature. Both were high, and yet my impression was that the condition was rather that of mental and nervous excitement than of any actual seizure.

" She lie like that one day, two day. I 'fraid she die," said the girl.

The woman turned her flushed and handsome face towards me.

" Where is my husband ? "

" He is below, and would wish to see you."

" I will not see him. I will not see him." Then she seemed to wander off into delirium. " A fiend ! A fiend ! Oh, what shall I do with this devil ? "

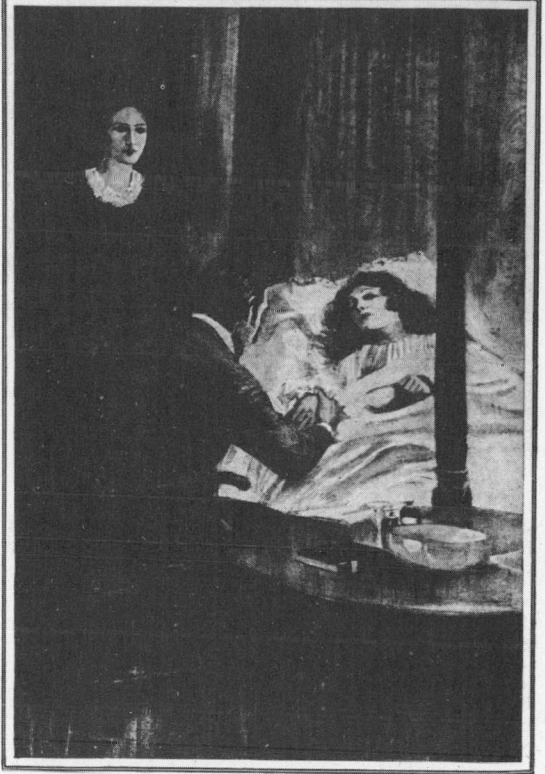

THE WOMAN TURNED HER FLUSHED AND HANDSOME
FACE TOWARDS ME.

Illustration by Howard K. Elcock for the *Strand Magazine*, January, 1924.

"Can I help you in any way?"

"No. No one can help. It is finished. All is destroyed. Do what I will, all is destroyed."

The woman must have some strange delusion. I could not see honest Bob Ferguson in the character of fiend or devil.

"Madame," I said, "your husband loves you dearly. He is deeply grieved at this happening."

Again she turned on me those glorious eyes.

"He loves me. Yes. But do I not love him? Do I not love him even to sacrifice myself rather than break his dear heart. That is how I love him. And yet he could think of me—he could speak of me so."

"He is full of grief, but he cannot understand."

"No, he cannot understand. But he should trust."

"Will you not see him?" I suggested.

"No, no; I cannot forget those terrible words nor the look upon his face. I will not see him. Go now. You can do nothing for me. Tell him only one thing. I want my child. I have a right to my child. That is the only message I can send him." She turned her face to the wall and would say no more.

I returned to the room downstairs, where Ferguson and Holmes still sat by the fire. Ferguson listened moodily to my account of the interview.

"How can I send her the child?" he said. "How do I know what strange impulse might come upon her? How can I ever forget how she rose from beside it with its blood upon her lips?" He shuddered at the recollection. "The child is safe with Mrs. Mason, and there he must remain."

A smart maid, the only modern thing which we had seen in the house, had brought in some tea. As she was serving it the door opened and a youth entered the room. He was a remarkable lad, pale-faced and fair-haired, with excitable light blue eyes which blazed into a sudden flame of emotion and joy as they rested upon his father. He rushed forward and threw his arms round his neck with the abandon of a loving girl.

"Oh, daddy," he cried, "I did not know that you were due yet. I should have been here to meet you. Oh, I am so glad to see you!"

Ferguson gently disengaged himself from the embrace with some little show of embarrassment.

"Dear old chap," said he, patting the flaxen head with a very tender hand. "I came early because my friends, Mr. Holmes and Dr. Watson, have been persuaded to come down and spend an evening with us."

"Is that Mr. Holmes, the detective?"

"Yes."

The youth looked at us with a very penetrating and, as it seemed to me, unfriendly gaze.

"What about your other child, Mr. Ferguson?" asked Holmes. "Might we make the acquaintance of the baby?"

"Ask Mrs. Mason to bring baby down," said Ferguson. The boy went off with a curious, shambling gait which told my surgical eyes that he was suffering **15** from a weak spine. Presently he returned, and behind

---

15 *which told my surgical eyes that he was suffering from a weak spine.* "Watson is always careful not to use expressions which may puzzle the layman," Miss Helen Simpson wrote in "Medical Career and Capacities of Dr. J. H. Watson," "but these simplifications make interpretation difficult for the commentator. Had he used the words 'ataxic gait,' we might have known that the boy suffered from some congenital syphilitic affliction; but had he spoken of a 'spastic gait,' we should have pictured some trouble as that which afflicted Byron. A gait showing signs of paralysis of one or more muscles is probably what he meant, but he is evidently mistaken in suggesting spinal injury as the cause. Any injury sufficient to affect the walk would certainly not permit the boy to 'rush,' and would be far more likely to involve complete paralysis below the waist."

him came a tall, gaunt woman bearing in her arms a very beautiful child, dark-eyed, golden-haired, a wonderful mixture of the Saxon and the Latin. Ferguson was evidently devoted to it, for he took it into his arms and fondled it most tenderly.

" Fancy anyone having the heart to hurt him," he muttered, as he glanced down at the small, angry red pucker upon the cherub throat.

It was at this moment that I chanced to glance at Holmes, and saw a most singular intentness in his expression. His face was as set as if it had been carved out of old ivory, and his eyes, which had glanced for a moment at father and child, were now fixed with eager curiosity upon something at the other side of the room. Following his gaze I could only guess that he was looking out through the window at the melancholy, dripping garden. It is true that a shutter had half closed outside and obstructed the view, but none the less it was certainly at the window that Holmes was fixing his concentrated attention. Then he smiled, and his eyes came back to the baby. On its chubby neck there was this small puckered mark. Without speaking, Holmes examined it with care. Finally he shook one of the dimpled fists which waved in front of him.

" Good-bye, little man. You have made a strange start in life. Nurse, I should wish to have a word with you in private."

He took her aside and spoke earnestly for a few minutes. I only heard the last words, which were : " Your anxiety will soon, I hope, be set at rest." The woman, who seemed to be a sour, silent kind of creature, withdrew with the child.

" What is Mrs. Mason like ? " asked Holmes.

" Not very prepossessing externally, as you can see, but a heart of gold, and devoted to the child."

IT WAS AT THIS MOMENT THAT I CHANCED TO GLANCE
AT HOLMES . . .

Illustration by Howard K. Elcock for the *Strand Magazine*, January, 1924.

"FANCY ANYONE HAVING THE HEART TO HURT HIM,"
HE MUTTERED . . .

(*Above*) Illustration by Howard K. Elcock for the Louisville *Courier-Journal*, March 8, 1925. (*Below*) W. T. Benda illustrated the same scene for *Hearst's International*, January, 1924.

" Do you like her, Jack ? " Holmes turned suddenly upon the boy. His expressive mobile face shadowed over, and he shook his head.

" Jacky has very strong likes and dislikes," said Ferguson, putting his arm round the boy. " Luckily I am one of his likes."

The boy cooed and nestled his head upon his father's breast. Ferguson gently disengaged him.

" Run away, little Jacky," said he, and he watched his son with loving eyes until he disappeared. " Now, Mr. Holmes," he continued, when the boy was gone, " I really feel that I have brought you on a fool's errand, for what can you possibly do, save give me your sympathy ? It must be an exceedingly delicate and complex affair from your point of view."

" It is certainly delicate," said my friend, with an amused smile, " but I have not been struck up to now with its complexity. It has been a case for intellectual deduction, but when this original intellectual deduction is confirmed point by point by quite a number of independent incidents, then the subjective becomes objective and we can say confidently that we have reached our goal. I had, in fact, reached it before we left Baker Street, and the rest has merely been observation and confirmation."

Ferguson put his big hand to his furrowed forehead.

" For Heaven's sake, Holmes," he said hoarsely, " if you can see the truth in this matter, do not keep me in suspense. How do I stand ? What shall I do ? I care nothing as to how you have found your facts so long as you have really got them."

" Certainly I owe you an explanation, and you shall have it. But you will permit me to handle the matter in my own way ? Is the lady capable of seeing us, Watson ? "

" She is ill, but she is quite rational."

" Very good. It is only in her presence that we can clear the matter up. Let us go up to her."

" She will not see me," cried Ferguson.

" Oh, yes, she will," said Holmes. He scribbled a few lines upon a sheet of paper. " You at least have the *entrée*, Watson. Will you have the goodness to give the lady this note ? "

I ascended again and handed the note to Dolores, who cautiously opened the door. A minute later I heard a cry from within, a cry in which joy and surprise seemed to be blended. Dolores looked out.

" She will see them. She will leesten," said she.

At my summons Ferguson and Holmes came up. As we entered the room Ferguson took a step or two towards his wife, who had raised herself in the bed, but she held out her hand to repulse him. He sank into an arm-chair, while Holmes seated himself beside him, after bowing to the lady, who looked at him with wide-eyed amazement.

" I think we can dispense with Dolores," said Holmes. " Oh, very well, madame, if you would rather she stayed I can see no objection. Now, Mr. Ferguson, I am a busy man with many calls, and my methods have to be short and direct. The swiftest surgery is the least painful. Let me first say what will ease your mind. Your wife is a very good, a very loving, and a very ill-used woman."

Ferguson sat up with a cry of joy.

"Prove that, Mr. Holmes, and I am your debtor for ever."

"I will do so, but in doing so I must wound you deeply in another direction."

"I care nothing so long as you clear my wife. Everything on earth is insignificant compared to that."

"Let me tell you, then, the train of reasoning which passed through my mind in Baker Street. The idea of a vampire was to me absurd. Such things do not happen in criminal practice in England. And yet your observation was precise. You had seen the lady rise from beside the child's cot with the blood upon her lips."

"I did."

"Did it not occur to you that a bleeding wound may be sucked for some other purpose than to draw the blood from it? Was there not a Queen in English history who sucked such a wound to draw poison from it?" **16**

"Poison!"

"A South American household. My instinct felt the presence of those weapons upon the wall before my eyes ever saw them. It might have been other poison, but that was what occurred to me. When I saw that little empty quiver beside the small bird-bow, it was just what I expected to see. If the child were pricked with one of those arrows dipped in curare or some other devilish drug, it would mean death if the venom were not sucked out.

"And the dog! If one were to use such a poison, would one not try it first in order to see that it had not lost its power? I did not foresee the dog, but at least I understood him and he fitted into my reconstruction. **17**

"Now do you understand? Your wife feared such an attack. She saw it made and saved the child's life, and yet she shrank from telling you all the truth, for she knew how you loved the boy and feared lest it break your heart."

"Jacky!"

"I watched him as you fondled the child just now. His face was clearly reflected in the glass of the window where the shutter formed a background. I saw such jealousy, such cruel hatred, as I have seldom seen in a human face."

"My Jacky!"

"You have to face it, Mr. Ferguson. It is the more painful because it is a distorted love, a maniacal exaggerated love for you, and possibly for his dead mother, which has prompted his action. His very soul is consumed with hatred for this splendid child, whose health and beauty are a contrast to his own weakness."

"Good God! It is incredible!"

"Have I spoken the truth, madame?"

The lady was sobbing, with her face buried in the pillows. Now she turned to her husband.

"How could I tell you, Bob? I felt the blow it

16 *who sucked such a wound to draw poison from it?"* Holmes refers to Eleanor of Castile, Queen of England, 1272–1290. But in his *Popular Fallacies*, Alfred S. E. Ackermann denies that "the Queen Eleanor, Consort of Edward I, sucked poison from the arm of her husband while he was on his Palestine expedition."

17 *he fitted into my reconstruction.* Curare works by paralyzing the thorax and chest muscles, not the legs, and it kills within minutes or has no effect at all.

"The spaniel Carlo should have died at once, when pierced by a poison dart, for, if 'it would mean death if the venom were not sucked out' for the baby, it would certainly mean the same for the dog, which did not weigh as much," Mrs. Eleanor S. Cole wrote in "Holmes, Watson and the K'9's." "It is safe to surmise that the demonic little Jackie, filled with unusual remorse, sucked some of the poison from the dog's wound, yet not enough to leave him completely unimpaired."

And F. A. Allen, M.P.S., has written in "Devilish Drugs": "The persistence of the paralytic effect . . . must be taken as traumatic or infective. This was strangely localized in the hind quarters of [the] dog, following the would-be murderer's preliminary experiment on the animal—a clumsy job in the back, near the cord, with a dirty half-scraped arrow-tip."

To this, Dr. George B. Koelle has added ("The Poisons of the Canon"): ". . . the effects of a non-fatal dose of [curare] should wear off in a day. Consequently, the protracted lameness which the dog Carlo developed was probably due to spinal meningitis . . . or to mechanical injury or secondary infection of the sciatic nerve, as a result of the arrow-puncture. Curare is very poorly absorbed when taken by mouth; hence Mrs. Ferguson actually did not expose herself to serious risk when she immediately sucked the wound inflicted on her child."

A Note on the "Canonicity" of "The Adventure of the Sussex Vampire": Mr. D. Martin Dakin, who rejects from the Canon many of the stories in *The Case-Book of Sherlock Holmes*, accepts "The Sussex Vampire" as genuine. "The trivial details about the Doctor's early life are not such as would occur to a pseudo-Watson," he writes, "and Holmes' contemptuous dismissal of the vampire superstitions is thoroughly characteristic. 'I never get your limits, Watson . . . There are unexplored possibilities about you. . . . We must not let him think that this Agency is a home for the weakminded.' This is Holmes in his genuinely satirical vein. It is true that some have seen a suspicious similarity between the lame spaniel and the famous sheep in the paddock [in "Silver Blaze"], but we need not assume that there were never any similar features in Holmes' cases, and perhaps Jack Ferguson had even been reading 'Silver Blaze' himself? It is true that many critics have raised their eyebrows at Holmes' indexing system, but it is possible that we have here another instance of Watson's faulty memory . . ."

would be to you. It was better that I should wait and that it should come from some other lips than mine. When this gentleman, who seems to have powers of magic, wrote that he knew all, I was glad."

" I think a year at sea would be my prescription for Master Jacky," said Holmes, rising from his chair. " Only one thing is still clouded, madame. We can quite understand your attacks upon Master Jacky. There is a limit to a mother's patience. But how did you dare to leave the child these last two days ? "

" I had told Mrs. Mason. She knew."

" Exactly. So I imagined."

Ferguson was standing by the bed, choking, his hands outstretched and quivering.

" This, I fancy, is the time for our exit, Watson," said Holmes in a whisper. " If you will take one elbow of the too faithful Dolores, I will take the other. There, now," he added, as he closed the door behind him. " I think we may leave them to settle the rest among themselves."

I have only one further note of this case. It is the letter which Holmes wrote in final answer to that with which the narrative begins. It ran thus :

BAKER STREET,
Nov. 21st.

Re Vampires.

SIR,—

Referring to your letter of the 19th, I beg to state that I have looked into the inquiry of your client, Mr. Robert Ferguson, of Ferguson & Muirhead, tea brokers, of Mincing Lane, and that the matter has been brought to a satisfactory conclusion. With thanks for your recommendation,

I am, Sir,
Faithfully yours,
SHERLOCK HOLMES.

58

THE ADVENTURE OF THE MISSING THREE-QUARTER

[Tuesday, December 8, to Thursday, December 10, 1896]

WE were fairly accustomed to receive weird telegrams at Baker Street, but I have a particular recollection of one which reached us on a gloomy February morning some seven or eight years ago, and gave Mr. Sherlock Holmes a puzzled **1** quarter of an hour. It was addressed to him, and ran thus :

"Please await me. Terrible misfortune. Right wing three-quarter missing ; indispensable to-morrow.—OVER-TON."

2

"Strand postmark, and despatched ten thirty-six," said Holmes, reading it over and over. "Mr. Overton was evidently considerably excited when he sent it, and somewhat incoherent in consequence. Well, well, he will be here, I dare say, by the time I have looked through *The Times*, and then we shall know all about it. Even the most insignificant problem would be welcome in these stagnant days."

Things had indeed been very slow with us, and I had learned to dread such periods of inaction, for I knew by experience that my companion's brain was so abnormally active that it was dangerous to leave it without material upon which to work. For years I had gradually weaned him from that drug mania which had threatened once to check his remarkable career. Now I knew that under ordinary conditions he no longer craved for this artificial stimulus ; but I was well aware that the fiend was not dead, but sleeping ; and I have known that the sleep was a light one and the waking near when in periods of idleness I have seen the drawn look upon Holmes' ascetic face, and the brooding of his deep-set and inscrutable eyes. Therefore I blessed this Mr. Overton, whoever he might be, since he had come with his enigmatic message to break that dangerous calm which brought more peril to my friend than all the storms of his tempestuous life.

As we expected, the telegram was soon followed by its sender, and the card of Mr. Cyril Overton, of Trinity College, Cambridge, announced the arrival of an enormous young man, sixteen stone of solid bone and muscle, who spanned the doorway with his broad shoulders and looked

1 *a gloomy February morning some seven or eight years ago.* The year was not earlier than 1894: Holmes later says of Dr. Leslie Armstrong, "I have not seen a man . . . more calculated to fill the gap left by the illustrious Moriarty." Nor was it later than mid-1897: while we cannot say with any degree of certainty when the case was *chronicled*, it was certainly *published* in August, 1904, and Watson tells us that it began "some seven or eight years ago." But Watson's "February" is clearly an error. As the late Professor Jay Finley Christ wrote, the game of Rugby employs the three-quarter line, as Association football, or soccer, does not. The game of importance in this adventure is Rugby, then—and in the nineties, the Cambridge-Oxford Rugby matches were always played at the Queen's Club in December, on a Wednesday, usually the second Wednesday in the month. The month, therefore, is December, and the year is 1894, 1895, or 1896; we shall shortly determine which.

2 OVERTON." ". . . if Watson were the old rugger player that he claimed to be [in "The Adventure of the Sussex Vampire"]—big-time rugger, at that —the name of Cyril Overton would hardly have been unknown to him; nor would there have been anything enigmatic about Overton's telegram to Holmes," the late Elmer Davis commented in his introduction to *The Return of Sherlock Holmes*. "Accordingly J. P. Mallalieu, M.P.—himself an old Oxford rugger Blue—has argued (in the London *Tribune*) that Watson's story of his own football prowess was not merely sheer invention, but invention in an alcoholic haze. Watson, says Mallalieu, was a dipsomaniac, at least between his marriages. This accounts for his lapses of memory —dates and details jotted down in his notebook while he was drunk; accounts for his not knowing the name of so celebrated a medical man as Dr. Leslie Armstrong; and probably explains the quarrel with Holmes which . . . occasioned his leaving Baker Street in 1896."

3 *a comely face which was haggard with anxiety.* As we have seen, Mr. Rolfe Boswell has suggested that *this* was the adventure to which Watson alluded, in "The Naval Treaty," as "The Adventure of the Tired Captain."

4 *or dribbling.* "Is there dribbling in *rugby* football?" the late Christopher Morley asked. "It is an expertise in soccer, of course. I know nothing of rugger, but I am wondering whether it is possible, in any exact sense, to dribble the oval ball?"

5 *Henry Staunton, whom I helped to hang.* Historically, there was also Louis Staunton, who starved his half-witted wife to death in the gray dreariness of Penge.

"WHY, MR. HOLMES, I THOUGHT YOU KNEW THINGS,"
SAID HE.

Illustration by Sidney Paget for the *Strand Magazine,* August, 1904.

from one of us to the other with a comely face which was **3** haggard with anxiety.

"Mr. Sherlock Holmes ? "

My companion bowed.

" I've been down to Scotland Yard, Mr. Holmes. I saw Inspector Stanley Hopkins. He advised me to come to you. He said the case, so far as he could see, was more in your line than in that of the regular police."

" Pray sit down and tell me what is the matter."

" It's awful, Mr. Holmes, simply awful ! I wonder my hair isn't grey. Godfrey Staunton—you've heard of him, of course ? He's simply the hinge that the whole team turns on. I'd rather spare two from the pack and have Godfrey for my three-quarter line. Whether it's passing, **4** or tackling, or dribbling, there's no one to touch him ; and then, he's got the head and can hold us all together. What am I to do ? That's what I ask you, Mr. Holmes. There's Moorhouse, first reserve, but he is trained as a half, and he always edges right in on to the scrum instead of keeping out on the touch-line. He's a fine place-kick, it's true, but, then, he has no judgment, and he can't sprint for nuts. Why, Morton or Johnson, the Oxford fliers, could romp round him. Stevenson is fast enough, but he couldn't drop from the twenty-five line, and a three-quarter who can't either punt or drop isn't worth a place for pace alone. No, Mr. Holmes, we are done unless you can help me to find Godfrey Staunton."

My friend had listened with amused surprise to this long speech, which was poured forth with extraordinary vigour and earnestness, every point being driven home by the slapping of a brawny hand upon the speaker's knee. When our visitor was silent Holmes stretched out his hand and took down letter " S " of his commonplace book. For once he dug in vain into that mine of varied information.

" There is Arthur H. Staunton, the rising young forger;" said he, " and there was Henry Staunton, whom **5** I helped to hang, but Godfrey Staunton is a new name to me."

It was our visitor's turn to look surprised.

" Why, Mr. Holmes, I thought you knew things," said he. " I suppose, then, if you have never heard of Godfrey Staunton you don't know Cyril Overton either ? "

Holmes shook his head good-humouredly.

" Great Scott ! " cried the athlete. " Why, I was first reserve for England against Wales, and I've skippered the 'Varsity all this year. But that's nothing. I didn't think there was a soul in England who didn't know Godfrey Staunton, the crack three-quarter, Cambridge, Blackheath, and five Internationals. Good Lord ! Mr. Holmes, where *have* you lived ? "

Holmes laughed at the young giant's naïve astonishment.

" You live in a different world to me, Mr. Overton, a sweeter and healthier one. My ramifications stretch out into many sections of society, but never, I am happy to say, into amateur sport, which is the best and soundest thing in England. However, your unexpected visit this morning shows me that even in that world of fresh air and fair play there may be work for me to do ; so now, my good sir, I beg you to sit down and to tell me slowly and quietly exactly what it is that has occurred, and how you desire that I should help you."

Young Overton's face assumed the bothered look of the man who is more accustomed to using his muscles than his wits ; but by degrees, with many repetitions and obscurities which I may omit from his narrative, he laid his strange story before us.

" It's this way, Mr. Holmes.   As I have said, I am the skipper of the Rugger team of Cambridge 'Varsity, and Godfrey Staunton is my best man.   To-morrow we play Oxford.   Yesterday we all came up and we settled at Bentley's private hotel.   At ten o'clock I went round and saw that all the fellows had gone to roost, for I believe in strict training and plenty of sleep to keep a team fit.   I had a word or two with Godfrey before he turned in. He seemed to me to be pale and bothered.   I asked him what was the matter.   He said he was all right—just a touch of headache.   I bade him good night and left him. Half an hour later the porter tells me that a rough-looking man with a beard called with a note for Godfrey.   He had not gone to bed, and the note was taken to his room. Godfrey read it and fell back in a chair as if he had been pole-axed.   The porter was so scared that he was going to fetch me, but Godfrey stopped him, had a drink of water, and pulled himself together.   Then he went downstairs, said a few words to the man who was waiting in the hall, and the two of them went off together.   The last that the porter saw of them, they were almost running down the street in the direction of the Strand. This morning Godfrey's room was empty, his bed had never been slept in, and his things were all just as I had seen them the night before.   He had gone off at a moment's notice with this stranger, and no word has come from him since.   I don't believe he will ever come back. He was a sportsman, was Godfrey, down to his marrow, and he wouldn't have stopped his training and let in his skipper if it were not for some cause that was too strong for him.   No ; I feel as if he were gone for good and we should never see him again."

Sherlock Holmes listened with the deepest attention to this singular narrative.

" What did you do ? " he asked.

" I wired to Cambridge to learn if anything had been heard of him there.   I have had an answer.   No one has seen him."

" Could he have got back to Cambridge ? "

" Yes, there is a late train—quarter-past eleven."   **6**

" But, so far as you can ascertain, he did not take it ? "

" No, he has not been seen."

" What did you do next ? "

" I wired to Lord Mount-James."

" Why to the Lord Mount-James ? "

" Godfrey is an orphan, and Lord Mount-James is his nearest relative—his uncle, I believe."

" Indeed.   This throws new light upon the matter.

6 *"Yes, there is a late train—quarter-past eleven."* The fact that Holmes did not know whether or not there was a late train to Cambridge has been scored as a point against his having himself attended that great University. "It may be, however, in this particular case, that the difficulty can be removed by assuming that this late train was not in existence in Holmes' time but was put on at some later date," the late Gavin Brend wrote in *My Dear Holmes*.

In any case, however, as the late Christopher Morley pointed out, there never *was* an 11:15 train to Cambridge either from King's Cross or from Liverpool Station. "There would be no point, and no passengers, for such a train. The whole purpose of the late trains (10:02 from Liverpool Station, and 10:25 from King's Cross, per Bradshaw, July, 1894) was, and still is, to get students back to the university before midnight, by order of the Vice Chancellor and Proctors."

Lord Mount-James is one of the richest men in England."

" So I've heard Godfrey say."

" And your friend was closely related ? "

" Yes, he was his heir, and the old boy is nearly eighty —cram full of gout, too. They say he could chalk his billiard-cue with his knuckles. He never allowed Godfrey a shilling in his life, for he is an absolute miser, but it will all come to him right enough."

" Have you heard from Lord Mount-James ? "

" No."

" What motive could your friend have in going to Lord Mount-James ? "

" Well, something was worrying him the night before, and if it was to do with money it is possible that he would make for his nearest relative who had so much of it, though from all I have heard he would not have much chance of getting it. Godfrey was not fond of the old man. He would not go if he could help it."

" Well, we can soon determine that. If your friend was going to his relative Lord Mount-James, you have then to explain the visit of this rough-looking fellow at so late an hour, and the agitation that was caused by his coming."

Cyril Overton pressed his hands to his head. " I can make nothing of it ! " said he.

" Well, well, I have a clear day, and I shall be happy to look into the matter," said Holmes. " I should strongly recommend you to make your preparations for your match without reference to this young gentleman. It must, as you say, have been an overpowering necessity which tore him away in such a fashion, and the same necessity is likely to hold him away. Let us step round together to this hotel, and see if the porter can throw any fresh light upon the matter."

Sherlock Holmes was a past master in the art of putting a humble witness at his ease, and very soon, in the privacy of Godfrey Staunton's abandoned room, he had extracted all that the porter had to tell. The visitor of the night before was not a gentleman, neither was he a working man. He was simply what the porter described as a " medium-looking chap " ; a man of fifty, beard grizzled, pale face, quietly dressed. He seemed himself to be agitated. The porter had observed his hand trembling when he had held out the note. Godfrey Staunton had crammed the note into his pocket. Staunton had not shaken hands with the man in the hall. They had exchanged a few sentences, of which the porter had only distinguished the one word " time." Then they had hurried off in the manner described. It was just half-past ten by the hall clock.

" Let me see," said Holmes, seating himself on Staunton's bed. " You are the day porter, are you not ? "

" Yes, sir ; I go off duty at eleven."

" The night porter saw nothing, I suppose ? "

" No, sir ; one theatre party came in late. No one else."

" Were you on duty all day yesterday ? "

" Yes, sir."

" Did you take any message to Mr. Staunton ? "

" Yes, sir ; one telegram."

"DID YOU TAKE ANY MESSAGE TO MR. STAUNTON?"

Illustration by Sidney Paget for the *Strand Magazine*, August, 1904.

" Ah ! that is interesting. What o'clock was this ? "

" About six."

" Where was Mr. Staunton when he received it ? "

" Here in his room."

" Were you present when he opened it ? "

" Yes, sir ; I waited to see if there was an answer."

" Well, was there ? "

" Yes, sir. He wrote an answer."

" Did you take it ? "

" No ; he took it himself."

" But he wrote it in your presence ? "

" Yes, sir. I was standing by the door, and he with his back turned at that table. When he had written it he said, ' All right, porter, I will take this myself.' "

" What did he write it with ? "

" A pen, sir."

" Was the telegraphic form one of these on the table ? "

" Yes, sir ; it was the top one."

Holmes rose. Taking the forms, he carried them over to the window and carefully examined that which was uppermost.

" It is a pity he did not write in pencil," said he, throwing them down again with a shrug of disappointment. " As you have no doubt frequently observed, Watson, the impression usually goes through—a fact which has dissolved many a happy marriage. However, I can find no trace here. I rejoice, however, to perceive that he wrote with a broad-pointed quill pen, and I can hardly doubt that we will find some impression upon this blotting-pad. Ah, yes, surely this is the very thing ! "

He tore off a strip of the blotting-paper and turned towards us the following hieroglyphic :

Cyril Overton was much excited. " Hold it to the glass," he cried.

" That is unnecessary," said Holmes. " The paper is thin, and the reverse will give the message. Here it is." He turned it over, and we read :

" So that is the tail end of the telegram which Godfrey Staunton despatched within a few hours of his disappearance. There are at least six words of the message which have escaped us ; but what remains—' Stand by us for God's sake ! '—proves that this young man saw a formidable danger which approached him, and from which someone else could protect him. ' *Us*,' mark you ! Another person was involved. Who should it be but the pale-faced, bearded man who seemed himself in so nervous a state ? What, then, is the connection between Godfrey Staunton and the bearded man ? And what is the third source from which each of them sought for help against pressing danger ? Our inquiry has already narrowed down to that."

7 *He has been laid up with a hack.* Laid up with a *back* in some editions. Overton means, not a hacking cough, but a gash on the shin.

8 *Bayswater.* The name given to a district between the north side of Hyde Park and Notting Hill Gate. Bayswater has always been a favorite abode of foreigners of every nationality; today many of its shops are owned by foreigners, and its restaurants are amongst the best in London.

"ONE MOMENT, ONE MOMENT!" CRIED A QUERULOUS VOICE . . .

Illustration by Frederic Dorr Steele for *Collier's Magazine*, November 26, 1904. Sidney Paget illustrated the same scene for the *Strand Magazine*, August, 1904.

"We have only to find to whom that telegram is addressed," I suggested.

"Exactly, my dear Watson. Your reflection, though profound, had already crossed my mind. But I dare say it may have come to your notice that if you walk into a post-office and demand to see the counterfoil of another man's message there may be some disinclination on the part of the officials to oblige you. There is so much red tape in these matters ! However, I have no doubt that with a little delicacy and finesse the end may be attained. Meanwhile, I should like in your presence, Mr. Overton, to go through these papers which have been left upon the table."

There were a number of letters, bills, and notebooks, which Holmes turned over and examined with quick, nervous fingers and darting, penetrating eyes. "Nothing here," he said at last. "By the way, I suppose your friend was a healthy young fellow—nothing amiss with him ? "

"Sound as a bell."

"Have you ever known him ill ? "

7 "Not a day. He has been laid up with a hack, and once he slipped his knee-cap, but that was nothing."

"Perhaps he was not so strong as you suppose. I should think he may have had some secret trouble. With your assent I will put one or two of these papers in my pocket, in case they should bear upon our future inquiry."

"One moment, one moment ! " cried a querulous voice, and we looked up to find a queer little old man jerking and twitching in the doorway. He was dressed in rusty black, with a very broad-brimmed top-hat and a loose white necktie—the whole effect being that of a very rustic parson or of an undertaker's mute. Yet, in spite of his shabby and even absurd appearance, his voice had a sharp crackle, and his manner a quick intensity which commanded attention.

"Who are you, sir, and by what right do you touch this gentleman's papers ? " he asked.

"I am a private detective, and I am endeavouring to explain his disappearance."

"Oh, you are, are you ? And who instructed you, eh ? "

"This gentleman, Mr. Staunton's friend, was referred to me by Scotland Yard."

"Who are you, sir ? "

"I am Cyril Overton."

"Then it is you who sent me a telegram. My name is Lord Mount-James. I came round as quickly as the **8** Bayswater bus would bring me. So you have instructed a detective ? "

"Yes, sir."

"And are you prepared to meet the cost ? "

"I have no doubt, sir, that my friend Godfrey, when we find him, will be prepared to do that."

"But if he is never found, eh ? Answer me that ? "

"In that case no doubt his family——"

"Nothing of the sort, sir ! " screamed the little man. "Don't look to me for a penny—not a penny ! You understand that, Mr. Detective! I am all the family that this young man has got, and I tell you that I am not responsible. If he has any expectations it is due to the fact that I have never wasted money, and I do not propose to begin to do so now. As to those papers with which you are making so free, I may tell you that in case there should be anything of any value among them you will be held strictly to account for what you do with them."

" Very good, sir," said Sherlock Holmes. " May I ask in the meanwhile whether you have yourself any theory to account for this young man's disappearance ? "

" No, sir, I have not. He is big enough and old enough to look after himself, and if he is so foolish as to lose himself I entirely refuse to accept the responsibility of hunting for him."

" I quite understand your position," said Holmes, with a mischievous twinkle in his eyes. " Perhaps you don't quite understand mine. Godfrey Staunton appears to have been a poor man. If he has been kidnapped it could not have been for anything which he himself possesses. The fame of your wealth has gone abroad, Lord Mount-James, and it is entirely possible that a gang of thieves has secured your nephew in order to gain from him some information as to your house, your habits, and your treasure."

The face of our unpleasant little visitor turned as white as his neckcloth.

" Heavens, sir, what an idea ! I never thought of such villainy ! What inhuman rogues there are in the world ! But Godfrey is a fine lad—a staunch lad. Nothing would induce him to give his old uncle away. I'll have the plate moved over to the bank this evening. In the meantime spare no pains, Mr. Detective. I beg you to leave no stone unturned to bring him safely back. As to money, well, so far as a fiver, or even a tenner, goes, you can always look to me."

Even in his chastened frame of mind the noble miser could give us no information which could help us, for he knew little of the private life of his nephew. Our only clue lay in the truncated telegram, and with a copy of this in his hand Holmes set forth to find a second link for his chain. We had shaken off Lord Mount-James, and Overton had gone to consult with the other members of his team over the misfortune which had befallen them.

There was a telegraph office at a short distance from the hotel. We halted outside it.

" It's worth trying, Watson," said Holmes. " Of course, with a warrant we could demand to see the counterfoils, but we have not reached that stage yet. I don't suppose they remember faces in so busy a place. Let us venture it."

" I am sorry to trouble you," said he in his blandest manner to the young woman behind the grating ; " there is some small mistake about a telegram I sent yesterday. I have had no answer, and I very much fear that I must have omitted to put my name at the end. Could you tell me if this was so ? "

The young lady turned over a sheaf of counterfoils.

9 *I had seven different schemes for getting a glimpse of that telegram.* Mr. Colin Prestige has noted that "It was reported in the *Daily Telegraph* of June 2, 1955, that a Post Office telegraphist . . . residing at Hove, Sussex . . . was, on the previous day, fined £5 with costs for disclosing the contents of a telegram. . . . The above news item, and particularly the penalty imposed, are of obvious interest since Dr. Watson recorded a similar instance of telegram disclosure in 'The Adventure of the Missing Three-Quarter.' . . . Presumably the persuasive charm ('bland,' as Watson puts it) of Mr. Holmes was in itself sufficient to overcome any question of scruple or conscience or fear of dismissal on the part of the young lady concerned."

10 *"King's Cross Station," said he.* In fact, a quicker and more direct route to Cambridge would have been from Liverpool Street Station.

11 *I think we must run down to Cambridge.* It has been said (by Sir Sydney Roberts) that this statement is another indication that Holmes was an Oxford, never a Cambridge, man. "You talk about going up to Cambridge," said Sir Sydney in a newspaper interview (Cambridge *Daily News*, March 23, 1962).

12 *Gray's Inn Road.* One of the principal thoroughfares leading north from High Holborn, so called because it contains on the west side Gray's Inn, one of the four great Inns of Court, originally founded for the education and lodging of law students. Gray's Inn Road from Holborn to Theobald's Road was considerably widened in Holmes' and Watson's day; before then it was called Gray's Inn Lane.

13 *it might be worth someone's while to get at a player.* "Worth someone's while, eh?" Mr. "Red" Smith commented in "The Game's Afoot." "Almost from the outset, Holmes was aware that Dr. Armstrong . . . held the key to the puzzle. Yet when he questioned Armstrong he allowed himself to be put off with windy bluff, learning nothing. Shadowing Armstrong to locate the missing man's hideout, he managed to lose sight of a carriage in a Cambridgeshire landscape 'as flat and clean as the palm of your hand.' Finally when Watson wanted to grab a bike and chase the doctor's carriage to the place of concealment, Holmes flatly forbade it. Why? Well, the match hadn't been played yet [and Holmes knew that Cambridge would stand no chance against Oxford without Staunton. He] was busy in Cambridge sending and receiving telegrams. Not until word was received of Oxford's victory . . . did the great detective strike upon an elementary device that should have occurred to anybody hours earlier . . .'"

"What o'clock was it?" she asked.

"A little after six."

"Whom was it to?"

Holmes put his finger to his lips and glanced at me. "The last words in it were ' for God's sake,' " he whispered confidentially ; " I am very anxious at getting no answer."

The young woman separated one of the forms..

"This is it. There is no name," said she, smoothing it out upon the counter.

"Then that, of course, accounts for my getting no answer," said Holmes. "Dear me, how very stupid of me, to be sure ! Good morning, miss, and many thanks for having relieved my mind." He chuckled and rubbed his hands when we found ourselves in the street once more.

"Well?" I asked.

"We progress, my dear Watson, we progress. I had **9** seven different schemes for getting a glimpse of that telegram, but I could hardly hope to succeed the very first time."

"And what have you gained?"

"A starting-point for our investigation." He hailed **10** a cab. "King's Cross Station," said he.

"We have a journey, then?"

11 "Yes, I think we must run down to Cambridge together. All the indications seem to point in that direction."

12 "Tell me," I asked as we rattled up Gray's Inn Road, "have you any suspicion yet as to the cause of the disappearance ? I don't think that among all our cases I have known one where the motives were more obscure. Surely you don't really imagine that he may be kidnapped in order to give information against his wealthy uncle ?"

"I confess, my dear Watson, that that does not appeal to me as a very probable explanation. It struck me, however, as being the one which was most likely to interest that exceedingly unpleasant old person."

"It certainly did that. But what are your alternatives ?"

"I could mention several. You must admit that it is curious and suggestive that this incident should occur on the eve of this important match, and should involve the only man whose presence seems essential to the success of the side. It may, of course, be coincidence, but it is interesting. Amateur sport is free from betting, but a good deal of outside betting goes on among the public, and it is possible that it might be worth someone's while **13** to get at a player as the ruffians of the Turf get at a racehorse. There is one explanation. A second very obvious one is that this young man really is the heir of a great property, however modest his means may be at present, and it is not impossible that a plot to hold him for ransom might be concocted."

"These theories take no account of the telegram."

"Quite true, Watson. The telegram still remains the only solid thing with which we have to deal, and we must not permit our attention to wander away from it. It is to gain light upon the purpose of this telegram that we are now upon our way to Cambridge. The path of our investigation is at present obscure, but I shall be very much surprised if before evening we have not cleared it up or made a considerable advance along it."

It was already dark when we reached the old University city. Holmes took a cab at the station, and ordered the man to drive to the house of Dr. Leslie Armstrong. A few minutes later we had stopped at a large mansion in the busiest thoroughfare. We were shown in, and after a long wait were admitted into the consulting-room, where we found the doctor seated behind his table.

It argues the degree in which I had lost touch with my profession that the name of Leslie Armstrong was unknown to me. Now I am aware that he is not only one of the heads of the medical school of the University, but a thinker of European reputation in more than one branch of science. Yet even without knowing his brilliant record one could not fail to be impressed by a mere glance at the man—the square, massive face, the brooding eyes under the thatched brows, and the granite moulding of the inflexible jaw. A man of deep character, a man with an alert mind, grim, ascetic, self-contained, formidable—so I read Dr. Leslie Armstrong. He held my friend's card in his hand, and he looked up with no very pleased expression upon his dour features.

" I have heard your name, Mr. Sherlock Holmes, and I am aware of your profession, one of which I by no means approve."

" In that, doctor, you will find yourself in agreement with every criminal in the country," said my friend quietly.

" So far as your efforts are directed towards the suppression of crime, sir, they must have the support of every reasonable member of the community, though I cannot doubt that the official machinery is amply sufficient for the purpose. Where your calling is more open to criticism is when you pry into the secrets of private individuals, when you rake up family matters which are better hidden, and when you incidentally waste the time of men who are more busy than yourself. At the present moment, for example, I should be writing a treatise instead of conversing with you."

" No doubt, doctor ; and yet the conversation may prove more important than the treatise. Incidentally I may tell you that we are doing the reverse of what you very justly blame, and that we are endeavouring to prevent anything like public exposure of private matters which must necessarily follow when once the case is fairly in the hands of the official police. You may look upon me simply as an irregular pioneer who goes in front of the regular force of the country. I have come to ask you about Mr. Godfrey Staunton."

" What about him ? "

" You know him, do you not ? "

" He is an intimate friend of mine."

" You are aware that he has disappeared ? "

" Ah, indeed ! " There was no change of expression in the rugged features of the doctor.

. . . HE LOOKED UP WITH NO VERY PLEASED EXPRESSION UPON HIS DOUR FEATURES.

Illustration by Sidney Paget for the *Strand Magazine*, August, 1904.

" He left his hotel last night.   He has not been heard of."

" No doubt he will return."

" To-morrow is the 'Varsity football match."

" I have no sympathy with these childish games.   The young man's fate interests me deeply, since I know him and like him.   The football match does not come within my horizon at all."

" I claim your sympathy, then, in my investigation of Mr. Staunton's fate.   Do you know where he is ? "

" Certainly not."

" You have not seen him since yesterday ? "

" No, I have not."

" Was Mr. Staunton a healthy man ? "

" Absolutely."

" Did you ever know him ill ? "

" Never."

Holmes popped a sheet of paper before the doctor's eyes.   " Then perhaps you will explain this receipted bill for thirteen guineas, paid by Mr. Godfrey Staunton last month to Dr. Leslie Armstrong, of Cambridge.   I picked it out from among the papers upon his desk."

The doctor flushed with anger.

" I do not feel that there is any reason why I should render an explanation to you, Mr. Holmes."

Holmes replaced the bill in his notebook.

" If you prefer a public explanation it must come sooner or later," said he.   " I have already told you that I can hush up that which others will be bound to publish, and you would really be wiser to take me into your complete confidence."

" I know nothing about it."

" Did you hear from Mr. Staunton in London ? "

" Certainly not."

" Dear me, dear me !—the post office again ! " Holmes sighed wearily.   " A most urgent telegram was despatched to you from London by Godfrey Staunton at six-fifteen yesterday evening—a telegram which is undoubtedly associated with his disappearance—and yet you have not had it.   It is most culpable.   I shall certainly go down to the office here and register a complaint."

Dr. Leslie Armstrong sprang up from behind his desk, and his dark face was crimson with fury.

" I'll trouble you to walk out of my house, sir," said he. " You can tell your employer, Lord Mount-James, that I do not wish to have anything to do either with him or with his agents.   No, sir, not another word ! "   He rang the bell furiously.   " John, show these gentlemen out." A pompous butler ushered us severely to the door, and we found ourselves in the street.   Holmes burst out laughing.

" Dr. Leslie Armstrong is certainly a man of energy and character," said he.   " I have not seen a man who, if he turned his talents that way, was more calculated to fill the gap left by the illustrious Moriarty.   And now, my poor Watson, here we are, stranded and friendless, in this **14** inhospitable town, which we cannot leave without abandoning our case.   This little inn just opposite

14 *this inhospitable town.* Why does Holmes call Cambridge an "inhospitable town"? Perhaps, as a student, he had considerable trouble finding lodgings after he had given up living in college there.

Armstrong's house is singularly adapted to our needs. If you would engage a front room and purchase the necessaries for the night, I may have time to make a few inquiries."

These few inquiries proved, however, to be a more lengthy proceeding than Holmes had imagined, for he did not return to the inn until nearly nine o'clock. He was pale and dejected, stained with dust, and exhausted with hunger and fatigue. A cold supper was ready upon the table, and when his needs were satisfied and his pipe alight he was ready to take that half-comic and wholly philosophic view which was natural to him when his affairs were going awry. The sound of carriage wheels caused him to rise and glance out of the window. A brougham and pair of greys under the glare of a gas-lamp stood before the doctor's door.

"It's been out three hours," said Holmes ; "started at half-past six, and here it is back again. That gives a radius of ten or twelve miles, and he does it once, or sometimes twice, a day."

"No unusual thing for a doctor in practice."

"But Armstrong is not really a doctor in practice. He is a lecturer and a consultant, but he does not care for general practice, which distracts him from his literary work. Why, then, does he make these long journeys, which must be exceedingly irksome to him, and who is it that he visits ? "

"His coachman——"

"My dear Watson, can you doubt that it was to him that I first applied ? I do not know whether it came from his own innate depravity or from the promptings of his master, but he was rude enough to set a dog at me. Neither dog nor man liked the look of my stick, however, and the matter fell through. Relations were strained after that, and further inquiries out of the question. All that I have learned I got from a friendly native in the yard of our own inn. It was he who told me of the doctor's habits and of his daily journey. At that instant, to give point to his words, the carriage came round to the door."

"Could you not follow it ? "

"Excellent, Watson ! You are scintillating this evening. The idea did cross my mind. There is, as you may have observed, a bicycle shop next to our inn. Into this I rushed, engaged a bicycle, and was able to get started before the carriage was quite out of sight. I rapidly overtook it, and then, keeping at a discreet distance of a hundred yards or so, I followed its lights until we were clear of the town. He had got well out on the country road when a somewhat mortifying incident occurred. The carriage stopped, the doctor alighted, walked swiftly back to where I had also halted, and told me in an excellent sardonic fashion that he feared the road was narrow, and that he hoped his carriage did not impede the passage of my bicycle. Nothing could have been more admirable than his way of putting it. I at once rode past the carriage, and, keeping to the main road, I went on for a few miles, and then halted in a convenient place to see if the carriage passed. There was no sign of it,

15 *You are not familiar with Cambridgeshire scenery, are you?* Holmes implies that he, Holmes, *is* familiar with Cambridgeshire scenery. "But in that case," the late Gavin Brend wrote in *My Dear Holmes*, "why does Holmes even undertake a pursuit which was foredoomed to failure? The answer would appear to be that having never been in Cambridge before he was in the same state of lamentable ignorance as to the distinctive peculiarities of Cambridgeshire scenery. We now see the significance of Watson's remark that it was after dark when they first arrived in Cambridge. Had they arrived by daylight, Holmes would have seen the difficulties from the window of his train, but as it was, they only became apparent after he had actually started out."

The fact of the matter is, however, that Holmes would have been familiar with the Fens scenery whether or not he was ever a student at Cambridge: in the 1870's he would almost certainly have had to travel to Donnithorpe ("The *Gloria Scott*") via Cambridge to get there, as the University town was on the main line from London (Liverpool Street Station) to Ely, Norwich, Yarmouth and Cromer.

There is a further point here of interest to students: if Watson was not familiar with Cambridgeshire scenery, as Holmes implies, then (it has been said) the University of "The Three Students," where Watson had previously spent "some weeks," must be Oxford. But Dr. W. S. Bristowe has answered this as follows: "Cambridge is a town full of interesting things to do and see and I, for one, would not have recommended Watson to foresake its hospitality in April for a country walk. If he had expressed a desire to go for a walk I would have directed him to the Gogamog Hills which would not have taught him of the flatness of the countryside in other directions of which he appears to be ignorant a few years later."

however, and so it became evident that it had turned down one of several side-roads which I had observed. I rode back, but again saw nothing of the carriage, and now, as you perceive, it has returned after me. Of course, I had at the outset no particular reason to connect these journeys with the disappearance of Godfrey Staunton, and was only inclined to investigate them on the general grounds that everything which concerns Dr. Armstrong is at present of interest to us ; but, now that I find he keeps so keen a lookout upon anyone who may follow him on these excursions, the affair appears more important, and I shall not be satisfied until I have made the matter clear."

" We can follow him to-morrow."

" Can we ? It is not so easy as you seem to think. **15** You are not familiar with Cambridgeshire scenery, are you ? It does not lend itself to concealment. All this country that I passed over to-night is as flat and clean as the palm of your hand, and the man we are following is no fool, as he very clearly showed to-night. I have wired to Overton to let us know any fresh London developments at this address, and in the meantime we can only concentrate our attention upon Dr. Armstrong, whose name the obliging young lady at the office allowed me to read upon the counterfoil of Staunton's urgent message. He knows where that young man is—to that I'll swear—and if he knows, then it must be our own fault if we cannot manage to know also. At present it must be admitted that the odd trick is in his possession, and, as you are aware, Watson, it is not my habit to leave the game in that condition."

And yet the next day brought us no nearer to the solution of the mystery. A note was handed in after breakfast, which Holmes passed across to me with a smile.

SIR [it ran],—I can assure you that you are wasting your time in dogging my movements. I have, as you discovered last night, a window at the back of my brougham, and if you desire a twenty-mile ride which will lead you to the spot from which you started, you have only to follow me. Meanwhile, I can inform you that no spying upon me can in any way help Mr. Godfrey Staunton, and I am convinced that the best service you can do to that gentleman is to return at once to London and to report to your employer that you are unable to trace him. Your time in Cambridge will certainly be wasted.—Yours faithfully,

" LESLIE ARMSTRONG."

" An outspoken, honest antagonist is the doctor," said Holmes. " Well, well, he excites my curiosity, and I must really know more before I leave him."

" His carriage is at his door now," said I. " There he is stepping into it. I saw him glance up at our window as he did so. Suppose I try my luck upon the bicycle ? "

" No, no, my dear Watson ! With all respect for your natural acumen, I do not think that you are quite a match for the worthy doctor. I think that possibly I can attain our end by some independent explorations of my own. I am afraid that I must leave you to your own devices, as the appearance of *two* inquiring strangers upon a sleepy country-side might excite more gossip than I care for. No doubt you will find some sights to amuse you in this venerable city, and I hope to bring back a more favourable report to you before evening."

Once more, however, my friend was destined to be disappointed. He came back at night weary and unsuccessful.

"I have had a blank day, Watson. Having got the doctor's general direction, I spent the day in visiting all the villages upon that side of Cambridge, and comparing notes with publicans and other local news agencies. I have covered some ground : Chesterton, Histon, Waterbeach, and Oakington have each been explored, and have each proved disappointing. The daily appearance of a brougham and pair could hardly have been overlooked in such Sleepy Hollows. The doctor has scored once more. Is there a telegram for me ? "

"Yes ; I opened it. Here it is : ' Ask for Pompey from Jeremy Dixon, Trinity College.' I don't understand it."

"Oh, it is clear enough. It is from our friend Overton, and is in answer to a question from me. I'll just send round a note to Mr. Jeremy Dixon, and then I have no doubt that our luck will turn. By the way, is there any news of the match ? "

"Yes, the local evening paper has an excellent account in its last edition. Oxford won by a goal and two tries. **16** The last sentences of the description say : ' The defeat of the Light Blues may be entirely attributed to the unfortunate absence of the crack International, Godfrey Staunton, whose want was felt at every instant of the game. The lack of combination in the three-quarter line and their weakness both in attack and defence more than neutralized the efforts of a heavy and hard-working pack.' "

"Then our friend Overton's forebodings have been justified," said Holmes. "Personally I am in agreement with Dr. Armstrong, and football does not come within my horizon. Early to bed to-night, Watson, for I foresee that to-morrow may be an eventful day."

I was horrified by my first glimpse of Holmes next morning, for he sat by the fire holding his tiny hypodermic syringe. I associated that with the single weakness of his nature, and I feared the worst when I saw it glittering in his hand. He laughed at my expression of dismay, and laid it upon the table.

"No, no, my dear fellow, there is no cause for alarm. It is not upon this occasion the instrument of evil, but it will rather prove to be the key which will unlock our mystery. On this syringe I base all my hopes. I have just returned from a small scouting expedition, and everything is favourable. Eat a good breakfast, Watson, for I propose to get upon Dr. Armstrong's trail to-day, and once on it I will not stop for rest or food until I run him to his burrow."

"In that case," said I, "we had best carry our breakfast with us, for he is making an early start. His car-

16 *Oxford won by a goal and two tries.* The year of "The Adventure of the Missing Three-Quarter," as we have seen, was 1894, 1895, or 1896. In 1894, the Cambridge-Oxford Rugby match was *drawn;* this is clearly not the year. In 1895, *Cambridge* won the match—again, this cannot be the year. In 1896, on the other hand, Oxford won— with a score of two goals to Cambridge's score of a goal and a try. In other words, as the late Dr. Ernest Bloomfield Zeisler so shrewdly observed, Oxford *won* by a goal, as Watson says it did. The Cambridge-Oxford game of 1896 was played on December 9th. The case, as we have seen, began on the preceding day, *Tuesday, December 8, 1896.* It closed on the day following the game—*Thursday, December 10, 1896.*

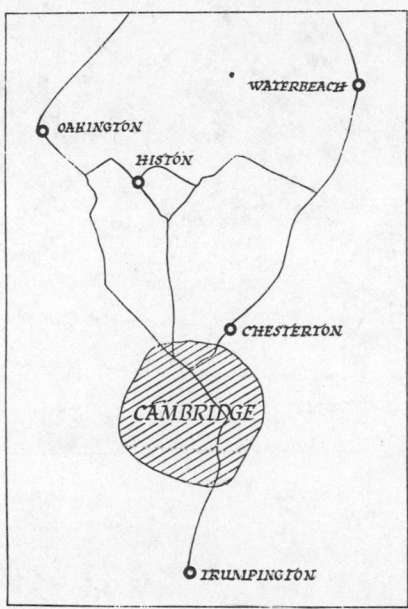

"I HAVE COVERED SOME GROUND: CHESTERTON, HISTON, WATERBEACH, AND OAKINGTON . . ."

Our map is from *My Dear Holmes*, by the late Gavin Brend. "Note the order," Mr. Brend wrote, "for it is a rather peculiar one. Presumably [Holmes] visited them in the order in which he names them, particularly in view of the certainty that in any circumstances Chesterton would obviously come first. But consider the position of the other three. From Cambridge or from Chesterton, Histon lies to the northwest, Oakington is still further northwest, but Waterbeach is to the northeast. So that if he went to Waterbeach after Histon he would probably come back again through Histon in order to get to Oakington. The obvious route which anyone familiar with the neighbourhood would take would be Chesterton, Waterbeach, Histon, Oakington, and the route actually taken reveals the Oxonian in a hurry who has not yet had time to procure a map."

17 *loose-box.* An enclosure in a stable in which a horse is kept unhaltered.

18 *no very great flier.* "Flier," as Mrs. Eleanor S. Cole noted in "Holmes, Watson and the K-9's," is "a word in common parlance today among dog fanciers to denote one which flies through to his champion title."

19 *John o' Groats.* John o' Groat, a Dutchman, was said to have settled in the north of Scotland in the year 1489. His house was near Dunscansby Head, the northernmost point of the British Isles.

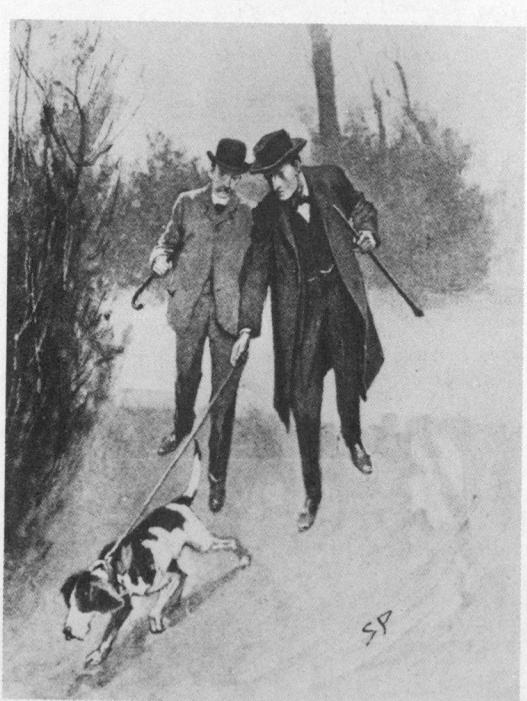

riage is at the door."

"Never mind. Let him go. He will be clever if he can drive where I cannot follow him. When you have finished come downstairs with me, and I will introduce you to a detective who is a very eminent specialist in the work that lies before us."

17 When we descended I followed Holmes into the stable-yard, where he opened the door of a loose-box and led out a squat, lop-eared, white-and-tan dog, something between a beagle and a foxhound.

"Let me introduce you to Pompey," said he. "Pompey is the pride of the local draghounds, no very great **18** flier, as his build will show, but a staunch hound on a scent. Well, Pompey, you may not be fast, but I expect you will be too fast for a couple of middle-aged London gentlemen, so I will take the liberty of fastening this leather leash to your collar. Now, boy, come along, and show what you can do." He led him across to the doctor's door. The dog sniffed round for an instant, and then with a shrill whine of excitement started off down the street, tugging at his leash in his efforts to go faster. In half an hour we were clear of the town and hastening down a country road.

"What have you done, Holmes?" I asked.

"A threadbare and venerable device, but useful upon occasion. I walked into the doctor's yard this morning and shot my syringe full of aniseed over the hind wheel. A draghound will follow aniseed from here to John o' **19** Groats, and our friend Armstrong would have to drive through the Cam before he would shake Pompey off his trail. Oh, the cunning rascal! This is how he gave me the slip the other night."

The dog had suddenly turned out of the main road into a grass-grown lane. Half a mile farther this opened into another broad road, and the trail turned hard to the right in the direction of the town, which we had just quitted. The road took a sweep to the south of the town and continued in the opposite direction to that in which we started.

"This detour has been entirely for our benefit, then?" said Holmes. "No wonder that my inquiries among those villages led to nothing. The doctor has certainly played the game for all it is worth, and one would like to know the reason for such elaborate deception. This **20** should be the village of Trumpington to the right of us. And, by Jove! here is the brougham coming round the corner! Quick, Watson, quick, or we are done!"

He sprang through a gate into a field, dragging the reluctant Pompey after him. We had hardly got under

THE DOG SNIFFED ROUND FOR AN INSTANT, AND THEN WITH A SHRILL WHINE OF EXCITEMENT STARTED OFF DOWN THE STREET . . .

(*Above*) Cover illustration by Frederic Dorr Steele for *Collier's Magazine*, November 26, 1904.

(*Below*) Illustration by Sidney Paget for the *Strand Magazine*, August, 1904.

the shelter of the hedge when the carriage rattled past. I caught a glimpse of Dr. Armstrong within, his shoulders bowed, his head sunk on his hands, the very image of distress. I could tell by my companion's graver face that he also had seen.

"I fear there is some dark ending to our quest," said he. "It cannot be long before we know it. Come, Pompey! Ah, it is the cottage in the field."

There could be no doubt that we had reached the end of our journey. Pompey ran about and whined eagerly outside the gate, where the marks of the brougham's wheels were still to be seen. A footpath led across to the lonely cottage. Holmes tied the dog to the hedge, and we hastened onwards. My friend knocked at the little rustic door, and knocked again without response. And yet the cottage was not deserted, for a low sound came to our ears—a kind of drone of misery and despair, which was indescribably melancholy. Holmes paused irresolute, and then he glanced back at the road which we had just traversed. A brougham was coming down it, and there could be no mistaking those grey horses.

"By Jove, the doctor is coming back!" cried Holmes. "That settles it. We are bound to see what it means before he comes."

He opened the door, and we stepped into the hall. The droning sound swelled louder upon our ears, until it became one long, deep wail of distress. It came from upstairs. Holmes darted up, and I followed him. He pushed open a half-closed door, and we both stood appalled at the sight before us.

A woman, young and beautiful, was lying dead upon the bed. Her calm, pale face, with dim, wide-opened blue eyes, looked upwards from amid a great tangle of golden hair. At the foot of the bed, half sitting, half kneeling, his face buried in the clothes, was a young man, whose frame was racked by his sobs. So absorbed was he by his bitter grief that he never looked up until Holmes' hand was on his shoulder.

"Are you Mr. Godfrey Staunton?"

"Yes, yes; I am—but you are too late. She is dead."

The man was so dazed that he could not be made to understand that we were anything but doctors who had been sent to his assistance. Holmes was endeavouring to utter a few words of consolation, and to explain the alarm which had been caused to his friends by his sudden disappearance, when there was a step upon the stairs, and there was the heavy, stern, questioning face of Dr. Armstrong at the door.

"So, gentlemen," said he, "you have attained your end, and have certainly chosen a particularly delicate moment for your intrusion. I would not brawl in the presence of death, but I can assure you that if I were a younger man your monstrous conduct would not pass with impunity."

"Excuse me, Dr. Armstrong, I think we are a little at cross purposes," said my friend with dignity. "If you could step downstairs with us we may each be able to give some light to the other upon this miserable affair."

20 *This should be the village of Trumpington.* Holmes, the late Gavin Brend wrote, "could hardly have been at Cambridge without visiting a place so near. The Cantab would certainly say 'This *is* Trumpington.' The 'should be' is the mark of the Oxonian. So too we suggest is the expression 'the village of Trumpington' as opposed to mere 'Trumpington.' The former suggests the stranger, the latter the neighbour."

I CAUGHT A GLIMPSE OF DR. ARMSTRONG WITHIN . . .

Illustration by Sidney Paget for the *Strand Magazine*, August, 1904. Charles Raymond Macauley illustrated the same scene for *The Return of Sherlock Holmes*, New York: McClure, Phillips & Co., 1905.

. . . HE NEVER LOOKED UP UNTIL HOLMES' HAND WAS ON HIS SHOULDER.

Illustration by Sidney Paget for the *Strand Magazine*, August, 1904.

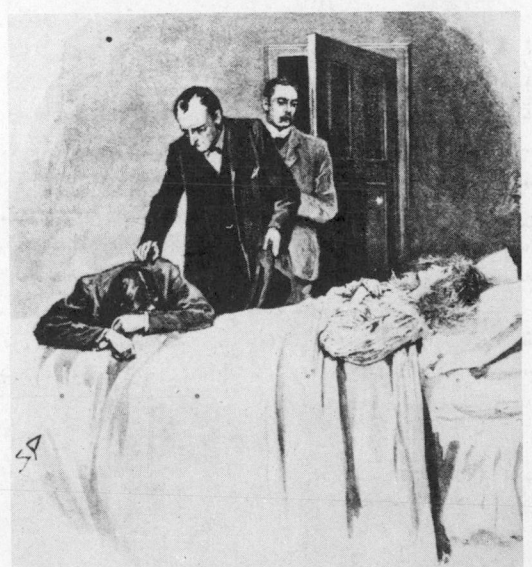

Bibliographical Note: The original manuscript of "The Adventure of the Missing Three-Quarter," about 8,000 words in 25 folio pages, white vellum by Spealls, was auctioned in New York City on January 30, 1923, bringing $130. It was listed in Scribner's Sherlock Holmes Catalogue at $450. At one time owned by Mr. Vincent Starrett of Chicago, it became the first Conan Doyle manuscript to become vested in the British people when it was presented in 1959 to the British Museum by the Sherlock Holmes Society of London, aided by generous donations from the Friends of the National Libraries and five American donors, J. Bliss Austin, Lew David Feldman, E. T. Guymon, Jr., Rollin V. N. Hadley, Jr., and the late Edgar W. Smith. The purchase price was $1,000.

The Adventure of the Missing Three Quarters.

We were fairly accustomed to receive weird telegrams at Baker Street but I have a particular recollection of one which reached us on a gloomy February morning some seven or eight years ago and gave Mr. Sherlock Holmes a puzzled quarter of an hour. It was addressed to him and ran thus

"Please await me, Terrible misfortune, Right wing three quarter indispensable missing indispensable tomorrow. Overton"

"Strand post mark and dispatched 9 36" said Holmes, reading it over and over. "Mr. Overton was evidently considerably excited when he sent it and somewhat incoherent in consequence. Well, well, he will be here I dare say by the time I have looked through the Times that the table is cleared and then we shall know all about it. Even the most insignificant problem would be welcome in these stagnant times."

Things had indeed been very slow with us, and I had learned to dread such periods of inaction for I knew by experience that my companion's brain was so abnormally active that it was dangerous to leave it without material upon which to work. For years I had gradually weaned him from that drug mania which had threatened once to check his remarkable career. Now I knew that under ordinary conditions he no longer craved for this artificial stimulus but I was well aware that the fiend was not dead but sleeping, and I have known that the sleep was a light one and the waking near when in periods of idleness I have seen the drawn look upon Holmes' ascetic face, and the brooding of his deep set and inscrutable eyes. Therefore I blessed Mr. Overton, whoever he might be, since he had come with his enigmatic message to break that dangerous calm which brought more danger to my friend than all the storms of his tempestuous life.

A minute later the grim doctor and ourselves were in the sitting-room below.

" Well, sir ? " said he.

" I wish you to understand, in the first place, that I am not employed by Lord Mount-James, and that my sympathies in this matter are entirely against that nobleman. When a man is lost it is my duty to ascertain his fate, but having done so the matter ends so far as I am concerned ; and so long as there is nothing criminal, I am much more anxious to hush up private scandals than to give them publicity. If, as I imagine, there is no breach of the law in this matter, you can absolutely depend upon my discretion and my co-operation in keeping the facts out of the papers ! "

Dr. Armstrong took a quick step forward and wrung Holmes by the hand.

" You are a good fellow," said he. " I had misjudged you. I thank Heaven that my compunction at leaving poor Staunton all alone in this plight caused me to turn my carriage back, and so to make your acquaintance. Knowing as much as you do, the situation is very easily explained. A year ago Godfrey Staunton lodged in London for a time, and became passionately attached to his landlady's daughter, whom he married. She was as good as she was beautiful, and as intelligent as she was good. No man need be ashamed of such a wife. But Godfrey was the heir to this crabbed old nobleman, and it was quite certain that the news of his marriage would have been the end of his inheritance. I knew the lad well, and I loved him for his many excellent qualities. I did all I could to help him to keep things straight. We did our very best to keep the thing from everyone, for when once such a whisper gets about it is not long before everyone has heard it. Thanks to this lonely cottage and his own discretion, Godfrey has up to now succeeded. Their secret was known to no one save to me and to one excellent servant who has at present gone for assistance to Trumpington. But at last there came a terrible blow in the shape of dangerous illness to his wife. It was consumption of the most virulent kind. The poor boy was half crazed with grief, and yet he had to go to London to play this match, for he could not get out of it without explanations which would expose the secret. I tried to cheer him up by a wire, and he sent me one in reply imploring me to do all I could. This was the telegram which you appear in some inexplicable way to have seen. I did not tell him how urgent the danger was, for I knew that he could do no good here, but I sent the truth to the girl's father, and he very injudiciously communicated to Godfrey. The result was that he came straight away in a state bordering on frenzy, and has remained in the same state, kneeling at the end of her bed, until this morning death put an end to her sufferings. That is all, Mr. Holmes, and I am sure that I can rely upon your discretion and that of your friend."

Holmes grasped the doctor's hand.

" Come, Watson," said he, and we passed from that house of grief into the pale sunlight of the winter day.

59

THE ADVENTURE OF THE ABBEY GRANGE

[Saturday, January 23, 1897]

IT was on a bitterly cold and frosty morning during the winter of '97 that I was wakened by a tugging at my shoulder. It was Holmes. The candle in his hand shone upon his eager, stooping face, and told me at a glance that something was amiss.

" Come, Watson, come ! " he cried. " The game is afoot. Not a word ! Into your clothes and come ! "

Ten minutes later we were both in a cab and rattling through the silent streets on our way to Charing Cross Station. The first faint winter's dawn was beginning to appear, and we could dimly see the occasional figure of an early workman as he passed us, blurred and indistinct in the opalescent London reek. Holmes nestled in silence into his heavy coat, and I was glad to do the same, for the air was most bitter, and neither of us had broken our fast. It was not until we had consumed some hot tea at the station, and taken our places in the Kentish train, that we were sufficiently thawed, he to speak and I to listen. Holmes drew a note from his pocket and read it aloud :

" ABBEY GRANGE, MARSHAM, KENT, 3.30 a.m.

" MY DEAR MR. HOLMES,—I should be very glad of your immediate assistance in what promises to be a most remarkable case. It is something quite in your line. Except for releasing the lady I will see that everything is kept exactly as I have found it, but I beg you not to lose an instant, as it is difficult to leave Sir Eustace there.—Yours faithfully,

" STANLEY HOPKINS.

" Hopkins has called me in seven times, and on each **1** occasion his summons has been entirely justified," said Holmes. " I fancy that every one of his cases has found its way into your collection, and I must admit, Watson, that you have some power of selection which atones for much which I deplore in your narratives. Your fatal habit of looking at everything from the point of view of a story instead of as a scientific exercise has ruined what might have been an instructive and even classical series of demonstrations. You slur over work of the utmost finesse and delicacy in order to dwell upon sensational details which may excite but cannot possibly instruct the reader."

1 *"Hopkins has called me in seven times.* Holmes helped Hopkins in "The Adventure of the Golden Pince-Nez," "The Adventure of Black Peter" and "The Adventure of the Missing Three-Quarter" prior to the time he made this statement. But what were the other four cases?

"COME, WATSON, COME!" HE CRIED.
"THE GAME IS AFOOT."

Holmes quotes Shakespeare: *The First Part of Henry the Fourth*, Act I, Scene 3, line 276: "Before the game's afoot . . ." and *The Life of Henry the Fifth*, Act III, Scene 1, line 32: "The game's afoot!" His words epitomize the whole Saga. With the possible exception of the obnoxious—and wholly apocryphal—"Quick, Watson, the needle!"—they are no doubt more often quoted than any other Holmes-Watson expression. The illustration by Sidney Paget was drawn for the *Strand Magazine*, September, 1904.

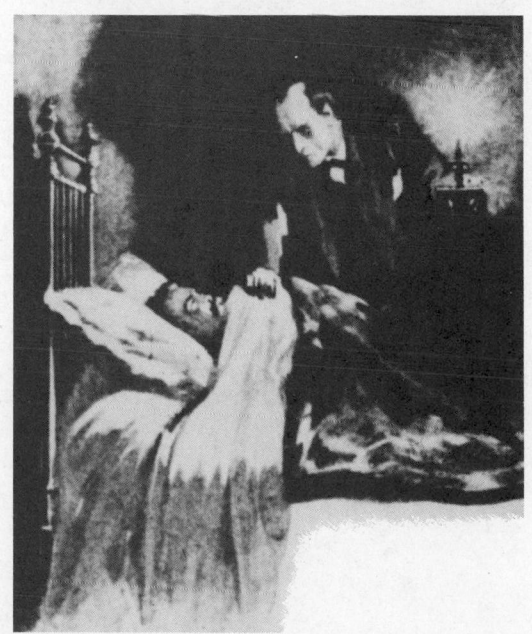

2 *"I will, my dear Watson, I will.* And he did, at the age of 72, in 1926, with the appearance of "The Adventure of the Blanched Soldier" and "The Adventure of the Lion's Mane."

3 *brought us to a park gate.* Mr. Michael Harrison believes that "Marsham, Kent" may reasonably be identified with St. Mary Cray. In *In the Footsteps of Sherlock Holmes* he wrote: "Most of the old houses in this once most select of all London's suburbs remain: turned . . . into golf-clubs, or hospitals or schools or lunatic asylums . . . if 'Abbey Grange' . . . still survives, it will no longer be in private occupation."

4 *the fashion of Palladio.* Andrea Palladio, 1518–1580, was an Italian architect of the Renaissance, known for formal, grandiose designs based on the Roman style. The Palladian style, characterized by arches supported by minor columns and framed between larger columns, was followed by architects of the Georgian period.

" Why do you not write them yourself ? " I said, with some bitterness.

2   " I will, my dear Watson, I will. At present I am, as you know, fairly busy, but I propose to devote my declining years to the composition of a textbook which shall focus the whole art of detection into one volume. Our present research appears to be a case of murder."

" You think this Sir Eustace is dead, then ? "

" I should say so. Hopkins' writing shows considerable agitation, and he is not an emotional man. Yes, I gather there has been violence, and that the body is left for our inspection. A mere suicide would not have caused him to send for me. As to the release of the lady, it would appear that she has been locked in her room during the tragedy. We are moving in high life. Watson—crackling paper, 'E.B.' monogram, coat-of-arms, picturesque address. I think that friend Hopkins will live up to his reputation, and that we shall have an interesting morning. The crime was committed before twelve last night."

" How can you possibly tell ? "

" By an inspection of the trains and by reckoning the time. The local police had to be called in, they had to communicate with Scotland Yard, Hopkins had to go out, and he in turn had to send for me. All that makes a fair night's work. Well, here we are at Chislehurst Station, and we shall soon set our doubts at rest."

A drive of a couple of miles through narrow country

3 lanes brought us to a park gate, which was opened for us by an old lodge-keeper, whose haggard face bore the reflection of some great disaster. The avenue ran through a noble park, between lines of ancient elms, and ended in a low, widespread house, pillared in front after the

4 fashion of Palladio. The central part was evidently of a great age and shrouded in ivy, but the large windows showed that modern changes had been carried out, and one wing of the house appeared to be entirely new. The youthful figure and alert, eager face of Inspector Stanley Hopkins confronted us in the open doorway.

" I'm very glad you have come, Mr. Holmes. And you, too, Dr. Watson ! But, indeed, if I had my time over again I should not have troubled you, for since the lady has come to herself she has given so clear an account of the affair that there is not much left for us to do. You remember that Lewisham gang of burglars ? "

" What, the three Randalls ? "

" Exactly ; the father and two sons. It's their work. I have not a doubt of it. They did a job at Sydenham a fortnight ago, and were seen and described. Rather cool to do another so soon and so near ; but it is they, beyond all doubt. It's a hanging matter this time."

" Sir Eustace is dead, then ? "

" Yes ; his head was knocked in with his own poker."

" Sir Eustace Brackenstall, the driver tells me."

" Exactly—one of the richest men in Kent. Lady Brackenstall is in the morning-room. Poor lady, she has had a most dreadful experience. She seemed half dead when I saw her first. I think you had best see her and hear her account of the facts. Then we will examine the dining-room together."

Lady Brackenstall was no ordinary person. Seldom have I seen so graceful a figure, so womanly a presence, and so beautiful a face. She was a blonde, golden-haired, blue-eyed, and would, no doubt, have had the perfect complexion which goes with such colouring had not her recent experience left her drawn and haggard. Her sufferings were physical as well as mental, for over one eye rose a hideous, plum-coloured swelling, which her maid, a tall, austere woman, was bathing assiduously with vinegar and water. The lady lay back exhausted upon a couch, but her quick, observant gaze as we entered the room, and the alert expression of her beautiful features, showed that neither her wits nor her courage had been shaken by her terrible experience. She was enveloped in a loose dressing-gown of blue and silver, but a black sequin-covered dinner-dress was hung upon the couch beside her.

" I have told you all that happened, Mr. Hopkins," she said wearily ; " could you not repeat it for me ? Well, if you think it necessary, I will tell these gentlemen what occurred. Have they been in the dining-room yet ? "

" I thought they had better hear your ladyship's story first."

" I shall be glad when you can arrange matters. It is horrible to me to think of him still lying there." She shuddered and buried her face for a moment in her hands. As she did so the loose gown fell back from her fore-arm. Holmes uttered an exclamation.

" You have other injuries, madam ! What is this ? " Two vivid red spots stood out on one of the white, round limbs. She hastily covered it.

" It is nothing. It has no connection with the hideous business of last night. If you and your friend will sit down I will tell you all I can.

" I am the wife of Sir Eustace Brackenstall. I have been married about a year. I suppose that it is no use **5** my attempting to conceal that our marriage has not been a happy one. I fear that all our neighbours would tell you that, even if I were to attempt to deny it. Perhaps the fault may be partly mine. I was brought up in the freer, less conventional atmosphere of South Australia, and this English life, with its proprieties and its primness, is not congenial to me. But the main reason lies in the one fact which is notorious to everyone, and that is that Sir Eustace was a confirmed drunkard. To be with such a man for an hour is unpleasant. Can you imagine what it means for a sensitive and high-spirited woman to be tied to him for day and night ? It is a sacrilege, a crime, a villainy to hold that such a marriage is binding. I say that these monstrous laws of yours will bring a curse upon the land—Heaven will not let such wickedness endure." For an instant she sat up, her cheeks flushed, and her eyes blazing from under the terrible mark upon her brow. Then the strong, soothing hand of the austere maid drew her head down on to the cushion, and the wild anger died away into passionate sobbing. At last she continued :

" I will tell you about last night. You are aware, perhaps, that in this house all servants sleep in the modern

THE LADY LAY BACK EXHAUSTED UPON A COUCH . . .

Illustration by Frederic Dorr Steele for *Collier's Magazine*, December 31, 1904. Sidney Paget portrayed the same scene for the *Strand Magazine*, September, 1904.

5 *I have been married about a year.* Watson's dating of this adventure—"the winter of '97"—could mean that it took place in the January, February, or December of that year. The correct month, as we shall see, is *January:* the manager of the steamer line later told Holmes that the *Rock of Gibralter,* on which Miss Mary Fraser (later Lady Brackenstall) sailed to England, docked at a home port in "June of '95." Miss Fraser had "only just arrived in London," according to Theresa Wright, when she met Sir Eustace Brackenstall. This was "only eighteen months ago." "They first left Australia eighteen months ago," Stanley Hopkins later tells Holmes, and Theresa Wright adds: "We arrived in June, and it was July [when Miss Fraser and Sir Eustace met]. They were married in January of last year." "I have been married about a year," Lady Brackenstall says here. It is clear that Miss Fraser and Theresa Wright arrived in England in June, 1895; in July, Miss Fraser and Sir Eustace met; in January, 1896, they were married, bringing us to a date eighteen months after July, 1895, twelve months after January, 1896: to *January, 1897.*

wing. This central block is made up of the dwelling-rooms, with the kitchen behind and our bedroom above. My maid Theresa sleeps above my room. There is no one else, and no sound could alarm those who are in the farther wing. This must have been well known to the robbers, or they would not have acted as they did.

" Sir Eustace retired about half-past ten. The servants had already gone to their quarters. Only my maid was up, and she had remained in her room at the top of the house until I needed her services. I sat until after eleven in this room, absorbed in a book. Then I walked round to see that all was right before I went upstairs. It was my custom to do this myself, for, as I have explained, Sir Eustace was not always to be trusted. I went into the kitchen, the butler's pantry, the gun-room, the billiard-room, the drawing-room, and finally the dining-room. As I approached the window, which is covered with thick curtains, I suddenly felt the wind blow upon my face, and realized that it was open. I flung the curtain aside, and found myself face to face with a broad-shouldered, elderly man who had just stepped into the room. The window is a long French one, which really forms a door leading to the lawn. I held my bedroom candle lit in my hand, and, by its light, behind the first man I saw two others, who were in the act of entering. I stepped back, but the fellow was on me in an instant. He caught me first by the wrist and then by the throat. I opened my mouth to scream, but he struck me a savage blow with his fist over the eye, and felled me to the ground. I must have been unconscious for a few minutes, for when I came to myself I found that they had torn down the bell-rope and had secured me tightly to the oaken chair which stands at the head of the dining-room table. I was so firmly bound that I could not move, and a handkerchief round my mouth prevented me from uttering any sound. It was at this instant that my unfortunate husband entered the room. He had evidently heard some suspicious sounds, and he came prepared for such a scene as he found. He was dressed in his shirt and trousers, with his favourite blackthorn cudgel in his hand. He rushed at one of the burglars, but another—it was the elderly man—stooped, picked the poker out of the grate, and struck him a terrible blow as he passed. He fell without a groan, and never moved again. I fainted once more, but again it could only have been a very few minutes during which I was insensible. When I opened my eyes I found that they had collected the silver from the sideboard, and they had drawn a bottle of wine which stood there. Each of them had a glass in his hand. I have already told you, have I not, that one was elderly, with a beard, and the others young, hairless lads. They might have been a father with his two sons. They talked together in whispers. Then they came over and made sure that I was still securely bound. Finally they withdrew, closing the window after them. It was quite a quarter of an hour before I got my mouth free. When I did so my screams brought the maid to my assistance. The other servants were soon alarmed, and we sent for the local police, who instantly communicated with

London. That is really all I can tell you, gentlemen, and I trust that it will not be necessary for me to go over so painful a story again."

" Any questions, Mr. Holmes ? " asked Hopkins.

" I will not impose any further tax upon Lady Brackenstall's patience and time," said Holmes. " Before I go into the dining-room I should be glad to hear your experience." He looked at the maid.

" I saw the men before ever they came into the house," said she. " As I sat by my bedroom window I saw three men in the moonlight down by the lodge gate yonder, **6** but I thought nothing of it at the time. It was more than an hour after that I heard my mistress scream, and down I ran, to find her, poor lamb, just as she says, and him on the floor with his blood and brains over the room. It was enough to drive a woman out of her wits, tied there, and her very dress spotted with him ; but she never wanted courage, did Miss Mary Fraser of Adelaide, and Lady Brackenstall of Abbey Grange hasn't learned new ways. You've questioned her long enough, you gentlemen, and now she is coming to her own room, just with her old Theresa, to get the rest that she badly needs."

With a motherly tenderness the gaunt woman put her arm round her mistress and led her from the room.

" She has been with her all her life," said Hopkins. " Nursed her as a baby, and came with her to England when they first left Australia eighteen months ago. Theresa Wright is her name, and the kind of maid you don't pick up nowadays. This way, Mr. Holmes, if you please ! "

The keen interest had passed out of Holmes' expressive face, and I knew that with the mystery all the charm of the case had departed. There still remained an arrest to be effected, but what were these commonplace rogues that he should soil his hands with them ? An abstruse and learned specialist who finds that he has been called in for a case of measles would experience something of the annoyance which I read in my friend's eyes. Yet the scene in the dining-room of the Abbey Grange was sufficiently strange to arrest his attention and to recall his waning interest.

It was a very large and high chamber, with carved oak ceiling, oaken panelling, and a fine array of deers' heads and ancient weapons around the walls. At the farther end from the door was the high French window of which we had heard. Three smaller windows on the right-hand side filled the apartment with cold winter sunshine. On the left was a large, deep fireplace, with a massive overhanging oak mantelpiece. Beside the fireplace was a heavy oaken chair with arms and cross-bars at the bottom. In and out through the open woodwork was woven a crimson cord, which was secured at each side to the crosspiece below. In releasing the lady the cord had been slipped off her, but the knots with which it had been secured still remained. These details only struck our attention afterwards, for our thoughts were entirely absorbed by the terrible object which lay spread upon the tiger-skin hearthrug in front of the fire.

6 *in the moonlight.* The maid, as we shall learn, lied about the three men but she would not have lied about something on which Holmes, Watson, and even Hopkins could at once have caught her out. The moon must therefore have been shining at about 11:00 P.M. on the night of the murder. As the late Dr. Ernest Bloomfield Zeisler wrote (*Baker Street Chronology*): "In January of 1897 the moon had set before 11:00 P.M. on the 1st to the 8th and did not rise until after 11:00 P.M. on the 24th to the 31st. Hence the murder must have been on one of the 9th to the 23rd, inclusive." To this the late Professor Jay Finley Christ added (*An Irregular Chronology*): "January, 1897, was nearly 100 per cent cloudy until the 22nd. The moon probably was not visible until midnight on the 21st, at the earliest." The murder must therefore have taken place on the night of the 22nd (a Friday) or the 23rd (a Saturday); Holmes solved it the next day (a Saturday or a Sunday). But the day was not a Sunday: at dawn, Holmes and Watson "could dimly see an occasional figure of an early workman as he passed us . . . in the opalescent London reek." We can now say with some confidence that Holmes' investigation of the Abbey Grange affair took place on *Saturday, January 23, 1897.*

IT WAS THE BODY OF A TALL, WELL-MADE MAN,
ABOUT FORTY YEARS OF AGE.

Illustration by Sidney Paget for the *Strand Magazine*, September, 1904.

"WHAT ARE YOU LOOKING AT NOW?"

Cover illustration by Frederic Dorr Steele for *Collier's Magazine*, December 31, 1904.

It was the body of a tall, well-made man, about forty years of age. He lay upon his back, his face upturned, with his white teeth grinning through his short, black beard. His two clenched hands were raised above his head, and a heavy blackthorn stick lay across them. His dark, handsome, aquiline features were convulsed into a spasm of vindictive hatred, which had set his dead face in a terribly fiendish expression. He had evidently been in his bed when the alarm had broken out, for he wore a foppish, embroidered night-shirt, and his bare feet projected from his trousers. His head was horribly injured, and the whole room bore witness to the savage ferocity of the blow which had struck him down. Beside him lay the heavy poker, bent into a curve by the concussion. Holmes examined both it and the indescribable wreck which it had wrought.

"He must be a powerful man, this elder Randall," he remarked.

"Yes," said Hopkins. "I have some record of the fellow, and he is a rough customer."

"You should have no difficulty in getting him."

"Not the slightest. We have been on the look-out for him, and there was some idea that he had got away to America. Now that we know the gang are here I don't see how they can escape. We have the news at every seaport already, and a reward will be offered before evening. What beats me is how they could have done so mad a thing, knowing that the lady would describe them, and that we could not fail to recognize the description."

"Exactly. One would have expected that they would have silenced Lady Brackenstall as well."

"They may not have realized," I suggested, "that she had recovered from her faint."

"That is likely enough. If she seemed to be senseless they would not take her life. What about this poor fellow, Hopkins? I seem to have heard some queer stories about him."

"He was a good-hearted man when he was sober, but a perfect fiend when he was drunk, or rather when he was half drunk, for he seldom really went the whole way. The devil seemed to be in him at such times, and he was capable of anything. From what I hear, in spite of all his wealth and his title, he very nearly came our way once or twice. There was a scandal about his drenching a dog with petroleum and setting it on fire—her ladyship's dog, to make the matter worse—and that was only hushed up with difficulty. Then he threw a decanter at that maid Theresa Wright; there was trouble about that. On the whole, and between ourselves, it will be a brighter house without him. What are you looking at now?"

Holmes was down on his knees examining with great attention the knots upon the red cord with which the lady had been secured. Then he carefully scrutinized the broken and frayed end where it had snapped off when the burglar had dragged it down.

"When this was pulled down the bell in the kitchen must have rung loudly," he remarked.

"No one could hear it. The kitchen stands right at the back of the house."

"How did the burglar know no one would hear it? How dare he pull at a bell-rope in that reckless fashion?"

"Exactly, Mr. Holmes, exactly. You put the very question which I have asked myself again and again. There can be no doubt that this fellow must have known the house and its habits. He must have perfectly understood that the servants would all be in bed at that comparatively early hour, and that no one could possibly hear a bell ring in the kitchen. Therefore he must have been in close league with one of the servants. Surely that is evident. But there are eight servants, and all of good character."

"Other things being equal," said Holmes, "one would suspect the one at whose head the master threw a decanter. And yet that would involve treachery towards the mistress to whom this woman seems devoted. Well, well, the point is a minor one, and when you have Randall you will probably find no difficulty in securing his accomplices. The lady's story certainly seems to be corroborated, if it needed corroboration, by every detail which we see before us." He walked to the French window and threw it open. "There are no signs here, but the ground is iron hard, and one would not expect them. I see that these candles on the mantelpiece have been lighted."

"Yes, it was by their light and that of the lady's bed-room candle that the burglars saw their way about."

"And what did they take?"

"Well, they did not take much—only half a dozen articles of plate off the sideboard. Lady Brackenstall thinks that they were themselves so disturbed by the death of Sir Eustace that they did not ransack the house as they would otherwise have done."

"No doubt that is true. And yet they drank some wine, I understand."

"To steady their own nerves."

"Exactly. These three glasses upon the sideboard have been untouched, I suppose?"

"Yes; and the bottle stands as they left it."

"Let us look at it. Halloa, halloa! what is this?"

The three glasses were grouped together, all of them tinged with wine, and one of them containing some dregs of beeswing. The bottle stood near them, two-thirds **7** full, and beside it lay a long, deeply stained cork. Its appearance and the dust upon the bottle showed that it was no common vintage which the murderers had enjoyed.

A change had come over Holmes' manner. He had lost his listless expression, and again I saw an alert light of interest in his keen deep-set eyes. He raised the cork and examined it minutely.

"How did they draw it?" he asked.

Hopkins pointed to a half-opened drawer. In it lay some table linen and a large corkscrew.

"Did Lady Brackenstall say that screw was used?"

"No; you remember that she was senseless at the moment when the bottle was opened."

"THESE THREE GLASSES UPON THE SIDEBOARD HAVE BEEN UNTOUCHED, I SUPPOSE?"

Illustration by Charles Raymond Macauley for *The Return of Sherlock Holmes*, New York: McClure, Phillips & Co., 1905.

7 *beeswing*. "This word may occasion a trifle of difficulty among Americans, in its syllabic division," Mr. Cyrus Durgin noted in "The Speckled Band." "It is not bee-swing . . . but 'bee's-wing,' or 'bees'-wing,' depending upon how much sediment is in the bottle. Scant, fine sediment would take the singular possessive, large, plentiful sediment the plural."

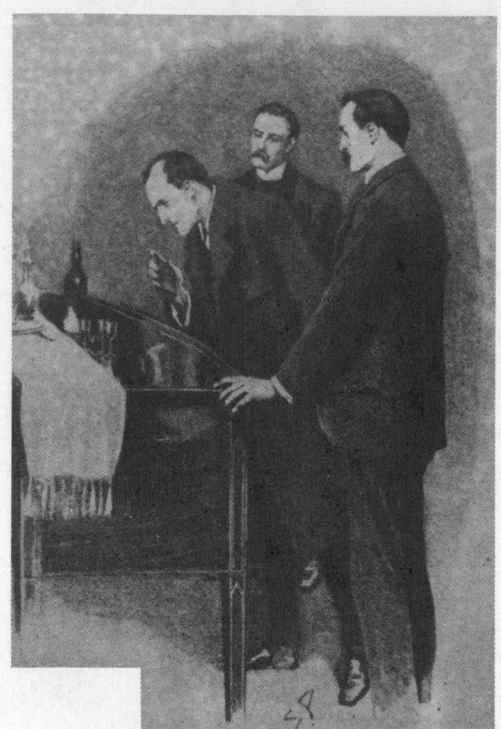

"HALLOA, HALLOA! WHAT IS THIS?"

Illustration by Sidney Paget for the *Strand Magazine*, September, 1904.

"BUT THESE GLASSES DO PUZZLE ME, I CONFESS."

Illustration by Frederic Dorr Steele for *Collier's Magazine*, December 31, 1904.

8 de novo. Latin: new; afresh.

" Quite so. As a matter of fact, that screw was *not* used. This bottle was opened by a pocket-screw, probably contained in a knife, and not more than an inch and a half long. If you examine the top of the cork you will observe that the screw was driven in three times before the cork was extracted. It has never been transfixed. This long screw would have transfixed it and drawn it with a single pull. When you catch this fellow you will find that he has one of these multiplex knives in his possession."

" Excellent ! " said Hopkins.

" But these glasses do puzzle me, I confess. Lady Brackenstall actually *saw* the three men drinking, did she not ? "

" Yes ; she was clear about that."

" Then there is an end of it. What more is to be said ? And yet you must admit that the three glasses are very remarkable, Hopkins. What, you see nothing remarkable ! Well, well, let it pass. Perhaps when a man has special knowledge and special powers like my own it rather encourages him to seek a complex explanation when a simpler one is at hand. Of course, it must be a mere chance about the glasses. Well, good morning, Hopkins. I don't see that I can be of any use to you, and you appear to have your case very clear. You will let me know when Randall is arrested, and any further developments which may occur. I trust that I shall soon have to congratulate you upon a successful conclusion. Come, Watson, I fancy that we may employ ourselves more profitably at home."

During our return journey I could see by Holmes' face that he was much puzzled by something which he had observed. Every now and then, by an effort, he would throw off the impression and talk as if the matter were clear, but then his doubts would settle down upon him again, and his knitted brows and abstracted eyes would show that his thoughts had gone back once more to the great dining-room of the Abbey Grange in which this midnight tragedy had been enacted. At last, by a sudden impulse, just as our train was crawling out of a suburban station, he sprang on to the platform and pulled me out after him.

" Excuse me, my dear fellow," said he, as we watched the rear carriages of our train disappearing round a curve ; " I am sorry to make you the victim of what may seem a mere whim, but on my life, Watson, I simply *can't* leave that case in this condition. Every instinct that I possess cries out against it. It's wrong—it's all wrong—I'll swear that it's wrong. And yet the lady's story was complete, the maid's corroboration was sufficient, the detail was fairly exact. What have I to put against that ? Three wine-glasses, that is all. But if I had not taken things for granted, if I had examined everything with the care which I would have shown had **8** we approached the case *de novo* and had no cut-and-dried story to warp my mind, would I not then have found something more definite to go upon ? Of course I should. Sit down on this bench, Watson, until a train for Chislehurst arrives, and allow me to lay the evidence before you, imploring you in the first instance to dismiss from your mind the idea that anything which the maid or mistress may have said must necessarily be true. The lady's charming personality must not be permitted to warp our judgment.

" Surely there are details in her story which, if we look at it in cold blood, would excite our suspicion. These burglars made a considerable haul at Sydenham a fort-night ago. Some account of them and their appearance was in the papers, and would naturally occur to anyone who wished to invent a story in which imaginary robbers should play a part. As a matter of fact, burglars who have done a good stroke of business are, as a rule, only too glad to enjoy the proceeds in peace and quiet without embarking on another perilous undertaking. Again, it is unusual for burglars to operate at so early an hour ; it is unusual for burglars to strike a lady to prevent her screaming, since one would imagine that was the sure way to make her scream ; it is unusual for them to commit murder when their numbers are sufficient to overpower one man ; it is unusual for them to be content with a limited plunder when there is much more within their reach ; and, finally, I should say that it was very unusual for such men to leave a bottle half empty. How do all these unusuals strike you, Watson ? "

" Their cumulative effect is certainly considerable, and yet each of them is quite possible in itself. The most unusual thing of all, as it seems to me, is that the lady should be tied to the chair."

" Well, I am not so sure about that, Watson, for it is evident that they must either kill her or else secure her in such a way that she could not give immediate notice of their escape. But at any rate I have shown, have I not, that there is a certain element of improbability about the lady's story ? And now on the top of this comes the incident of the wine-glasses."

" What about the wine-glasses ? "

" Can you see them in your mind's eye ? "

" I see them clearly."

" We are told that three men drank from them. Does that strike you as likely ? "

" Why not ? There was wine in each glass."

" Exactly ; but there was beeswing only in one glass. You must have noticed that fact. What does that suggest to your mind ? "

" The last glass filled would be most likely to contain beeswing."

" Not at all. The bottle was full of it, and it is incon-ceivable that the first two glasses were clear and the third heavily charged with it. There are two possible explana-tions, and only two. One is that after the second glass was filled the bottle was violently agitated, and so the third glass received the beeswing. That does not appear prob-able. No, no ; I am sure that I am right."

" What, then, do you suppose ? "

" That only two glasses were used, and that the dregs of both were poured into a third glass, so as to give the false impression that three people had been there. In that way all the beeswing would be in the last glass, would it

DURING OUR RETURN JOURNEY I COULD SEE BY HOLMES'
FACE THAT HE WAS MUCH PUZZLED . . .

Illustration by Sidney Paget for the *Strand Maga-zine*, September, 1904.

not ? Yes, I am convinced that this is so. But if I
have hit upon the true explanation of this one small
phenomenon, then in an instant the case rises from the
commonplace to the exceedingly remarkable, for it can
only mean that Lady Brackenstall and her maid have
deliberately lied to us, that not one word of their story
is to be believed, that they have some very strong reason
for covering the real criminal, and that we must construct
our case for ourselves without any help from them. That
is the mission which now lies before us, and here, Watson,
is the Chislehurst train."

The household of the Abbey Grange were much surprised at our return, but Sherlock Holmes, finding that
Stanley Hopkins had gone off to report to headquarters,
took possession of the dining-room, locked the door upon
the inside and devoted himself for two hours to one of
those minute and laborious investigations which formed
the solid basis on which his brilliant edifices of deduction
were reared. Seated in a corner like an interested student
who observes the demonstration of his professor, I followed every step of that remarkable research. The window, the curtains, the carpet, the chair, the rope—each
in turn was minutely examined and duly pondered. The
body of the unfortunate baronet had been removed, but
all else remained as we had seen it in the morning. Then,
to my astonishment, Holmes climbed up on to the massive
mantelpiece. Far above his head hung the few inches of
red cord which were still attached to the wire. For a
long time he gazed upwards at it, and then in an attempt
to get nearer to it he rested his knee upon a wooden
bracket on the wall. This brought his hand within a
few inches of the broken end of the rope ; but it was not
this so much as the bracket itself which seemed to engage
his attention. Finally he sprang down with an ejaculation of satisfaction.

" It's all right, Watson," said he. " We have got our
case—one of the most remarkable in our collection. But,
dear me, how slow-witted I have been, and how nearly I
have committed the blunder of my lifetime ! Now, I
think that with a few missing links my chain is almost
complete."

" You have got your men ? "

" Man, Watson, man. Only one, but a very formidable
person. Strong as a lion—witness the blow which bent
that poker. Six foot three in height, active as a squirrel,
dexterous with his fingers ; finally, remarkably quick-
witted, for this whole ingenious story is of his concoction.
Yes, Watson, we have come upon the handiwork of a very
remarkable individual. And yet in that bell-rope he has
given us a clue which should not have left us a doubt."

" Where was the clue ? "

" Well, if you were to pull down a bell-rope, Watson,
where would you expect it to break ? Surely at the spot
where it is attached to the wire. Why should it break
three inches from the top as this one has done ? "

" Because it is frayed there ? "

" Exactly. This end, which we can examine, is frayed.
He was cunning enough to do that with his knife. But the
other end is not frayed. You could not observe that

from here, but if you were on the mantelpiece you would see that it is cut clean off without any mark of fraying whatever. You can reconstruct what occurred. The man needed the rope. He would not tear it down for fear of giving the alarm by ringing the bell. What did he do? He sprang up on the mantelpiece, could not quite reach it, put his knee on the bracket—you will see the impression in the dust—and got his knife to bear upon the cord. I could not reach the place by at least three inches, from which I infer that he is at least three inches a bigger man than I. Look at that mark upon the seat of the oaken chair! What is it?"

" Blood."

" Undoubtedly it is blood. This alone puts the lady's story out of court. If she were seated on the chair when the crime was done, how comes that mark? No, no; she was placed in the chair *after* the death of her husband. I'll wager that the black dress shows a corresponding mark to this. We have not yet met our Waterloo, Watson, but this is our Marengo, for it begins in defeat **9** and ends in victory. I should like now to have a few words with the nurse Theresa. We must be wary for a while, if we are to get the information which we want."

She was an interesting person, this stern Australian nurse. Taciturn, suspicious, ungracious, it took some time before Holmes' pleasant manner and frank acceptance of all that she said thawed her into a corresponding amiability. She did not attempt to conceal her hatred for her late employer.

" Yes, sir, it is true that he threw the decanter at me. I heard him call my mistress a name, and I told him that he would not dare to speak so if her brother had been there. Then it was that he threw it at me. He might have thrown a dozen if he had but left my bonny bird alone. He was for ever ill-treating her, and she was too proud to complain. She will not even tell me all that he has done to her. She never told me of those marks on her arm that you saw this morning, but I know very well that they come from a stab with a hat-pin. The sly fiend—Heaven forgive me that I should speak of him so, now that he is dead, but a fiend he was if ever one walked the earth. He was all honey when first we met him, only eighteen months ago, and we both feel as if it were eighteen years. She had only just arrived in London. Yes, it was her first voyage—she had never been from home before. He won her with his title and his money and his false London ways. If she made a mistake she has paid for it, if ever a woman did. What month did we meet him? Well, I tell you it was just after we arrived. We arrived in June, and it was July. They were married in January of last year. Yes, she is down in the morning-room again, and I have no doubt she will see you, but you must not ask too much of her, for she has gone through all that flesh and blood will stand."

Lady Brackenstall was reclining on the same couch, but looked brighter than before. The maid had entered with us, and began once more to foment the bruise upon her mistress's brow.

9 *We have not yet met our Waterloo, Watson, but this is our Marengo.* "The reference . . . is very apt," Mr. T. S. Blakeney wrote in *Sherlock Holmes: Fact or Fiction?*, "and Holmes must surely have devoted some attention to Napoleonic history, for the remark is not one to occur to anybody."

"LOOK AT THAT MARK UPON THE SEAT OF THE OAKEN CHAIR!"

Illustration by Sidney Paget for the *Strand Magazine*, September, 1904.

IT WAS FROZEN OVER, BUT A SINGLE HOLE WAS LEFT
FOR THE CONVENIENCE OF A SOLITARY SWAN.

The day, Watson has already told us, was "bitterly
cold and frosty." In January, 1897, the temperature
was below freezing every day from the 15th to the
29th—corroboration that we have correctly assigned the date of this adventure to Saturday, the
23rd. The illustration, by Sidney Paget, is from the
Strand Magazine, September, 1904.

10 *which stands at the end of Pall Mall.* The
main Australian shipping line of the day was the
Orient Line, with offices "at the end of Pall Mall"
at 16 Cockspur Street.

11 *their new ship, the* Bass Rock. In "Some Diggings Down Under," Mrs. Jennifer Chorley has
pointed out that the "new ship" of the Orient
Line was "the glorious *Ophir*, known as the Queen
of the Indian Ocean, the first twin-screw liner
on the Australian run, built in 1891. Electric lighting and hot and cold baths were part of the luxuries offered." Apart from the *Ophir*, the "largest
and best boat" of the Orient Line was the *Orizaba*,
which we may take to have been the *Rock of
Gibraltar*. Watson's ships sailed from Southampton, but the Orient Line used Tilbury (a village
and docks in Essex, north of the Thames, and
within the Port of London), as did all the larger
ships bound for Australia at the time.

"I hope," said the lady, "that you have not come to
cross-examine me again?"

"No," Holmes answered, in his gentlest voice, "I
will not cause you any unnecessary trouble, Lady Brackenstall, and my whole desire is to make things easy for you,
for I am convinced that you are a much-tried woman.
If you will treat me as a friend and trust me, you may
find that I will justify your trust."

"What do you want me to do?"

"To tell me the truth."

"Mr. Holmes!"

"No, no, Lady Brackenstall, it is no use. You may
have heard of any little reputation which I possess. I
will stake it all on the fact that your story is an absolute
fabrication."

Mistress and maid were both staring at Holmes with
pale faces and frightened eyes.

"You are an impudent fellow!" cried Theresa. "Do
you mean to say that my mistress has told a lie?"

Holmes rose from his chair.

"Have you nothing to tell me?"

"I have told you everything."

"Think once more, Lady Brackenstall. Would it
not be better to be frank?"

For an instant there was hesitation in her beautiful face.
Then some new strong thought caused it to set like a
mask.

"I have told you all I know."

Holmes took his hat and shrugged his shoulders. "I
am sorry," he said, and without another word we left
the room and the house. There was a pond in the park,
and to this my friend led the way. It was frozen over,
but a single hole was left for the convenience of a solitary
swan. Holmes gazed at it, and then passed on to the
lodge gate. There he scribbled a short note for Stanley
Hopkins, and left it with the lodge-keeper.

"It may be a hit, or it may be a miss, but we are bound
to do something for friend Hopkins, just to justify this
second visit," said he. "I will not quite take him into
my confidence yet. I think our next scene of operations
must be the shipping office of the Adelaide-Southampton
10 line, which stands at the end of Pall Mall, if I remember
right. There is a second line of steamers which connect
South Australia with England, but we will draw the larger
cover first."

Holmes' card sent in to the manager ensured instant
attention, and he was not long in acquiring all the information which he needed. In June of '95 only one of their
line had reached a home port. It was the *Rock of
Gibraltar*, their largest and best boat. A reference to the
passenger list showed that Miss Fraser of Adelaide, with
her maid, had made the voyage in her. The boat was
now on her way to Australia, somewhere to the south of
the Suez Canal. Her officers were the same as in '95,
with one exception. The first officer, Mr. Jack Croker,
had been made a captain, and was to take charge of their
11 new ship, the *Bass Rock*, sailing in two days' time from
Southampton. He lived at Sydenham, but he was likely
to be in that morning for instructions, if we cared to
wait for him.

No ; Mr. Holmes had no desire to see him, but would be glad to know more about his record and character.

His record was magnificent. There was not an officer in the fleet to touch him. As to his character, he was reliable on duty, but a wild, desperate fellow off the deck of his ship, hot-headed, excitable, but loyal, honest, and kind-hearted. That was the pith of the information with which Holmes left the office of the Adelaide-Southampton Company. Thence he drove to Scotland Yard, but instead of entering he sat in his cab, with his brows drawn down, lost in profound thought. Finally he drove round to the Charing Cross telegraph office, sent off a message, and then, at last, we made for Baker Street once more.

" No, I couldn't do it, Watson," said he, as we re-entered our room. " Once that warrant was made out nothing on earth would save him. Once or twice in my career I feel that I have done more real harm by my discovery of the criminal than ever he had done by his crime. I have learned caution now, and I had rather play tricks with the law of England than with my own conscience. Let us know a little more before we act."

Before evening we had a visit from Inspector Stanley Hopkins. Things were not going very well with him.

" I believe that you are a wizard, Mr. Holmes. I really do sometimes think that you have powers that are not human. Now, how on earth could you know that the stolen silver was at the bottom of that pond ? "

" I didn't know it."

" But you told me to examine it."

" You got it then ? "

" Yes, I got it."

" I am very glad if I have helped you."

" But you haven't helped me. You have made the affair far more difficult. What sort of burglars are they who steal silver and then throw it into the nearest pond ? "

" It was certainly rather eccentric behaviour. I was merely going on the idea that if the silver had been taken by persons who did not want it, who merely took it for a blind, as it were, then they would naturally be anxious to get rid of it."

" But why should such an idea cross your mind ? "

" Well, I thought it was possible. When they came out through the French window there was the pond, with one tempting little hole in the ice right in front of their noses. Could there be a better hiding-place ? "

" Ah, a hiding-place—that is better ! " cried Stanley Hopkins. " Yes, yes, I see it all now ! It was early, there were folk upon the roads, they were afraid of being seen with the silver, so they sank it in the pond, intending to return for it when the coast was clear. Excellent, Mr. Holmes—that is better than your idea of a blind."

" Quite so ; you have got an admirable theory. I have no doubt that my own ideas were quite wild, but you must admit that they have ended in discovering the silver."

" Yes, sir ; yes. It was all your doing. But I have had a bad set-back."

" A set-back ? "

" Yes, Mr. Holmes. The Randall gang were arrested

in New York this morning."

" Dear me, Hopkins. That is certainly rather against your theory that they committed a murder in Kent last night."

" It is fatal, Mr. Holmes, absolutely fatal. Still, there are other gangs of three besides the Randalls, or it may be some new gang of which the police have never heard."

" Quite so ; it is perfectly possible. What, are you off ? "

" Yes, Mr. Holmes ; there is no rest for me until I have got to the bottom of the business. I suppose you have no hint to give me ? "

" I have given you one."

" Which ? "

" Well, I suggested a blind."

" But why, Mr. Holmes, why ! "

" Ah, that's the question, of course. But I commend the idea to your mind. You might possibly find that there was something in it. You won't stop for dinner ? Well, good-bye, and let us know how you get on."

Dinner was over and the table cleared before Holmes alluded to the matter again. He had lit his pipe, and held his slippered feet to the cheerful blaze of the fire. Suddenly he looked at his watch.

" I expect developments, Watson."

" When ? "

" Now—within a few minutes. I dare say you thought I acted rather badly to Stanley Hopkins just now ? "

" I trust your judgment."

" A very sensible reply, Watson. You must look at it this way : what I know is unofficial ; what he knows is official. I have the right to private judgment, but he has none. He must disclose all, or he is a traitor to his service. In a doubtful case I would not put him in so painful a position, and so I reserve my information until my own mind is clear upon the matter."

" But when will that be ? "

" The time has come. You will now be present at the last scene of a remarkable little drama."

There was a sound upon the stairs, and our door was opened to admit as fine a specimen of manhood as ever passed through it. He was a very tall young man, golden-moustached, blue-eyed, with a skin which had been burned by tropical suns, and a springy step which showed that the huge frame was as active as it was strong. He closed the door behind him, and then he stood with clenched hands and heaving breast, choking down some overmastering emotion.

" Sit down, Captain Croker. You got my telegram ? "

Our visitor sank into an arm-chair and looked from one to the other of us with questioning eyes.

" I got your telegram, and I came at the hour you said. I heard that you had been down to the office. There was no getting away from you. Let's hear the worst. What are you going to do with me ? Arrest me ? Speak out, man ! You can't sit there and play with me like a cat with a mouse."

" Give him a cigar," said Holmes. " Bite on that, Captain Croker, and don't let your nerves run away with you. I should not sit here smoking with you if I thought

... HE STOOD WITH CLENCHED HANDS AND HEAVING BREAST ...

Illustration by Frederic Dorr Steele for *Collier's Magazine*, December 31, 1904. Note the copy of *Punch*. The cover illustration indicated here—used on every issue of *Punch* for many years—was drawn by Richard Doyle, artist, man-about-town —and Conan Doyle's uncle. Again, Sidney Paget chose to illustrate this same scene for the *Strand Magazine*, September, 1904.

that you were a common criminal, you may be sure of that. Be frank with me, and we may do some good. Play tricks with me, and I'll crush you."

" What do you wish me to do ? "

" To give me a true account of all that happened at the Abbey Grange last night—a *true* account, mind you, with nothing added and nothing taken off. I know so much already that if you go one inch off the straight I'll blow this police whistle from my window and the affair goes out of my hands for ever."

The sailor thought for a little. Then he struck his leg with his great sunburnt hand.

" I'll chance it," he cried. " I believe you are a man of your word, and a white man, and I'll tell you the whole story. But one thing I will say first. So far as I am concerned, I regret nothing and I fear nothing, and I would do it all again and be proud of the job. Curse the beast—if he had as many lives as a cat he would owe them all to me ! But it's the lady, Mary—Mary Fraser—for never will I call her by that accursed name. When I think of getting her into trouble, I who would give my life just to bring one smile to her dear face, it's that that turns my soul into water. And yet—and yet—what less could I do ? I'll tell you my story, gentlemen, and then I'll ask you as man to man what less could I do.

" I must go back a bit. You seem to know everything, so I expect that you know that I met her when she was a passenger and I was first officer of the *Rock of Gibraltar*. From the first day I met her she was the only woman to me. Every day of that voyage I loved her more, and many a time since have I kneeled down in the darkness of the night watch and kissed the deck of that ship because I knew her dear feet had trod it. She was never engaged to me. She treated me as fairly as ever a woman treated a man. I have no complaint to make. It was all love on my side, and all good comradeship and friendship on hers. When we parted she was a free woman, but I could never again be a free man.

" Next time I came back from sea I heard of her marriage. Well, why shouldn't she marry whom she liked ? Title and money—who could carry them better than she ? She was born for all that is beautiful and dainty. I didn't grieve over her marriage. I was not such a selfish hound as that. I just rejoiced that good luck had come her way, and that she had not thrown herself away on a penniless sailor. That's how I loved Mary Fraser.

" Well, I never thought to see her again ; but last voyage I was promoted, and the new boat was not yet launched, so I had to wait for a couple of months with my people at Sydenham. One day out in a country lane I met Theresa Wright, her old maid. She told me about her, about him, about everything. I tell you, gentlemen, it nearly drove me mad. This drunken hound, that he should dare to raise his hand to her whose boots he was not worthy to lick ! I met Theresa again. Then I met Mary herself—and met her again. Then she would meet me no more. But the other day I had a notice that I was to start on my voyage within a week, and I determined that I would see her once before I left. Theresa was always my friend, for she loved Mary and hated this villain almost as much as I did. From her I learned the ways of the house. Mary used to sit up reading in her own little room downstairs. I crept round there last night and scratched at the window. At first she would not open to me, but in her heart I know that now she loves me, and she could not leave me in the frosty night. She whispered to me to come round to the big front window, and I found it open before me so as to let me into the dining-room. Again I heard from her own lips things that made my blood boil, and again I cursed this brute who mishandled the woman that I loved. Well, gentlemen, I was standing with her just inside the window, in all innocence, as Heaven is my judge, when he rushed like a madman into the room, called her the vilest name that a man could use to a woman, and welted her across the face with the stick he had in his hand. I had sprung for the poker, and it was a fair fight between us. See here on my arm where his first blow fell. Then it was my turn, and I went through him as if he had been a rotten pumpkin. Do you think I was sorry? Not I! It was his life or mine; but far more than that—it was his life or hers, for how could I leave her in the power of this madman? That was how I killed him. Was I wrong? Well, then, what would either of you gentlemen have done if you had been in my position?

"She had screamed when he struck her, and that brought old Theresa down from the room above. There was a bottle of wine on the sideboard, and I opened it and poured a little between Mary's lips, for she was half dead with the shock. Then I took a drop myself. Theresa was as cool as ice, and it was her plot as much as mine. We must make it appear that burglars had done the thing. Theresa kept on repeating our story to her mistress, while I swarmed up and cut the rope of the bell. Then I lashed her in her chair, and frayed out the end of the rope to make it look natural, else they would wonder how in the world a burglar could have got up there to cut it. Then I gathered up a few plates and pots of silver, to carry out the idea of a robbery, and there I left them, with orders to give the alarm when I had a quarter of an hour's start. I dropped the silver into the pond and made off for Sydenham, feeling that for once in my life I had done a real good night's work. And that's the truth and the whole truth, Mr. Holmes, if it costs me my neck."

Holmes smoked for some time in silence. Then he crossed the room and shook our visitor by the hand.

"That's what I think," said he. "I know that every word is true, for you have hardly said a word which I did not know. No one but an acrobat or a sailor could have got up to that bell-rope from the bracket, and no one but a sailor could have made the knots with which the cord was fastened to the chair. Only once had this lady been brought into contact with sailors, and that was on her voyage, and it was someone of her own class of life, since she was trying hard to shield him and so showing that she loved him. You see how easy it was for me to lay my hands upon you when once I had started upon the right trail."

" I thought the police never could have seen through our dodge."

" And the police haven't ; nor will they, to the best of my belief. Now, look here, Captain Croker, this is a very serious matter, though I am willing to admit that you acted under the most extreme provocation to which any man could be subjected. I am not sure that in defence of your own life your action will not be pronounced legitimate. However, that is for a British jury to decide. Meanwhile I have so much sympathy for you that if you choose to disappear in the next twenty-four hours I will promise you that no one will hinder you."

" And then it will all come out ? "

" Certainly it will come out."

The sailor flushed with anger.

" What sort of proposal is that to make to a man ? I know enough of law to understand that Mary would be had as accomplice. Do you think I would leave her alone to face the music while I slunk away ? No, sir ; let them do their worst upon me, but for Heaven's sake, Mr. Holmes, find some way of keeping my poor Mary out of the courts."

Holmes for the second time held out his hand to the sailor.

" I was only testing you, and you ring true every time. Well, it is a great responsibility that I take upon myself, but I have given Hopkins an excellent hint, and if he can't avail himself of it I can do no more. See here, Captain Croker, we'll do this in due form of law. You are the prisoner. Watson, you are a British jury, and I never met a man who was more eminently fitted to represent one. I am the judge. Now, gentlemen of the jury, you have heard the evidence. Do you find the prisoner guilty or not guilty ? "

" Not guilty, my lord," said I.

" *Vox populi, vox Dei.* You are acquitted, Captain **12** Croker. So long as the law does not find some other victim, you are safe from me. Come back to this lady in a year, and may her future and yours justify us in the judgment which we have pronounced this night."

12 "Vox populi, vox Dei. "The voice of the people is the voice of God"—a phrase first used by the English scholar, educator and ecclesiastical reformer Albinus Flaccus, called Alcuin or Alchuine, 735–804, in his Epistle to his friend Charlemagne.

Bibliographical Note: The original manuscript of "The Adventure of the Abbey Grange," consisting of 26 folio leaves, was auctioned in New York City on February 13, 1923, bringing $105. Once owned by the late James Montgomery of Philadelphia, it is now the property of Mr. Rollin V. Hadley, Jr., of Corning, New York.

60

THE ADVENTURE OF THE DEVIL'S FOOT

[Tuedsay, March 16, to Saturday, March 20, 1897]

1 *in the spring of the year 1897.* The month was "March," by three mentions. It has been objected that March is not "spring" in the astronomical sense, but we know that there were other occasions on which both Holmes and Watson spoke of the seasons in other than the astronomical sense. To cite only two: Holmes used "autumn" in the popular sense in "The *Gloria Scott*"; November was "winter" to Watson in "The Adventure of the Golden Pince-Nez." It has also been said that the month must be later than March because Holmes expressed surprise at finding that there had been a fire in the Tregennis grate "on a spring evening." But the March of 1897 must have been an exceptionally mild one in Cornwall—Watson speaks of "the glorious sunshine," and he says the Tregennis garden was "*already* well-filled with spring flowers." These evidences of unusually fine weather make Holmes' surprise as apropos in March as it would have been, say, in April. (Despite the fineness of the days, it would grow chilly at night. The Tregennis family lit a fire because, as Mortimer explains, "the night was cold and damp." A cold, damp night is of course more likely to occur in March than in April.)

IN recording from time to time some of the curious experiences and interesting recollections which I associate with my long and intimate friendship with Mr. Sherlock Holmes, I have continually been faced by difficulties caused by his own aversion to publicity. To his sombre and cynical spirit all popular applause was always abhorrent, and nothing amused him more at the end of a successful case than to hand over the actual exposure to some orthodox official, and to listen with a mocking smile to the general chorus of misplaced congratulation. It was indeed, this attitude upon the part of my friend, and certainly not any lack of interesting material which has caused me of late years to lay very few of my records before the public. My participation in some of his adventures was always a privilege which entailed discretion and reticence upon me.

It was, then, with considerable surprise that I received a telegram from Holmes last Tuesday—he has never been known to write where a telegram would serve—in the following terms : " Why not tell them of the Cornish horror—strangest case I have handled." I have no idea what backward sweep of memory had brought the matter fresh to his mind, or what freak had caused him to desire that I should recount it ; but I hasten, before another cancelling telegram may arrive, to hunt out the notes which give me the exact details of the case, and to lay the narrative before my readers.

1 It was, then, in the spring of the year 1897 that Holmes' iron constitution showed some symptoms of giving way in the face of constant hard work of a most exacting kind, aggravated, perhaps, by occasional indiscretions of his own. In March of that year Dr. Moore Agar, of Harley Street, whose dramatic introduction to Holmes I may some day recount, gave positive injunctions that the famous private agent would lay aside all his cases and surrender himself to complete rest if he wished to avert an absolute break-down. The state of his health was not a matter in which he himself took the faintest interest, for his mental detachment was absolute, but he was induced at last, on the threat of being permanently disqualified from work, to give himself a complete change of scene and air. Thus it was that in the early spring of that year we found ourselves together in a small cottage near Poldhu Bay, at the further extremity of the Cornish peninsula.

It was a singular spot, and one peculiarly well suited to the grim humour of my patient. From the windows of our little whitewashed house, which stood high upon a grassy headland, we looked down upon the whole sinister semicircle of Mounts Bay, that old death trap of sailing vessels, with its fringe of black cliffs and surge-swept reefs on which innumerable seamen have met their end. With a northerly breeze it lies placid and sheltered, inviting the storm-tossed craft to tack into it for rest and protection.

Then comes the sudden swirl round of the wind, the blustering gale from the south-west, the dragging anchor, the lee shore, and the last battle in the creaming breakers. The wise mariner stands far out from that evil place.

On the land side our surroundings were as sombre as on the sea. It was a country of rolling moors, lonely and dun-coloured, with an occasional church tower to mark the site of some old-world village. In every direction upon these moors there were traces of some vanished race which had passed utterly away, and left as its sole record strange monuments of stone, irregular mounds which contained the burned ashes of the dead, and curious earthworks which hinted at prehistoric strife. The glamour and mystery of the place, with its sinister atmosphere of forgotten nations, appealed to the imagination of my friend, and he spent much of his time in long walks and solitary meditations upon the moor. The ancient Cornish language had also arrested his attention, and he had, I remember, conceived the idea that it was akin to the Chaldean, and had been largely derived from the Phœnician traders in tin. He had received a consignment of books upon philology and was settling down to develop this **2** thesis, when suddenly, to my sorrow and to his unfeigned delight, we found ourselves, even in that land of dreams, plunged into a problem at our very doors which was more intense, more engrossing, and infinitely more mysterious than any of those which had driven us from London. Our simple life and peaceful, healthy routine were violently interrupted, and we were precipitated into the midst of a series of events which caused the utmost excitement not only in Cornwall, but throughout the whole West of England. Many of my readers may retain some recollection of what was called at the time " The Cornish Horror," though a most imperfect account of the matter reached the London Press. Now, after thirteen years, I will give the **3** true details of this inconceivable affair to the public.

I have said that scattered towers marked the villages which dotted this part of Cornwall. The nearest of these was the hamlet of Tredannick Wollas, where the cottages **4** of a couple of hundred inhabitants clustered round an ancient, moss-grown church. The vicar of the parish, Mr. Roundhay, was something of an archæologist, and as such Holmes had made his acquaintance. He was a middle-aged man, portly and affable, with a considerable fund of local lore. At his invitation we had taken tea at the vicarage, and had come to know, also, Mr. Mortimer Tregennis, an independent gentleman, who increased the clergyman's scanty resources by taking rooms in his large straggling house. The vicar, being a bachelor, was glad to come to such an arrangement, though he had little in

. . . HE SPENT MUCH OF HIS TIME IN LONG WALKS . . .

Illustration by Gilbert Holiday for the *Strand Magazine*, December, 1910.

2 *a consignment of books upon philology.* "Among them," Miss Madeleine B. Stern wrote in "Sherlock Holmes: Rare Book Collector," "was surely to be found a copy of Lhuyd's *Archaeologica Britannica* of 1707, a work containing a grammar of the language. There also must have been included . . . Edward Norris' *Ancient Cornish Drama* printed in Penzance in 1859, to which a 'Sketch of Cornish Grammar' is added as an appendix. Nor could the collection have been complete without Jago's *Dialect of Cornwall* printed at Truro in 1882, Williams' *Lexicon Cornu-Britannicum* (Landovery, 1865), Bannister's *Glossary of Cornish Names* (Truro, 1871) and the Courtney and Couch *Glossary of Words in Use in Cornwall* (Penzance, 1880)."

3 *Now, after thirteen years.* "The Adventure of the Devil's Foot" was published in December, 1910—confirming Watson's "1897" as the year of the adventure.

4 *the hamlet of Tredannick Wollas.* There is a hamlet called Predannack Wollas near Poldhu Bay in Cornwall, and the nearby village of Cwry answers closely to Watson's description of "Tredannick Wollas."

5 *Tuesday, March the 16th.* And the 16th of March, 1897, *did*, curiously enough, fall on a Tuesday.

"THE MOST EXTRAORDINARY AND TRAGIC AFFAIR HAS OCCURRED DURING THE NIGHT."

Illustration by Gilbert Holiday for the *Strand Magazine*, December, 1910.

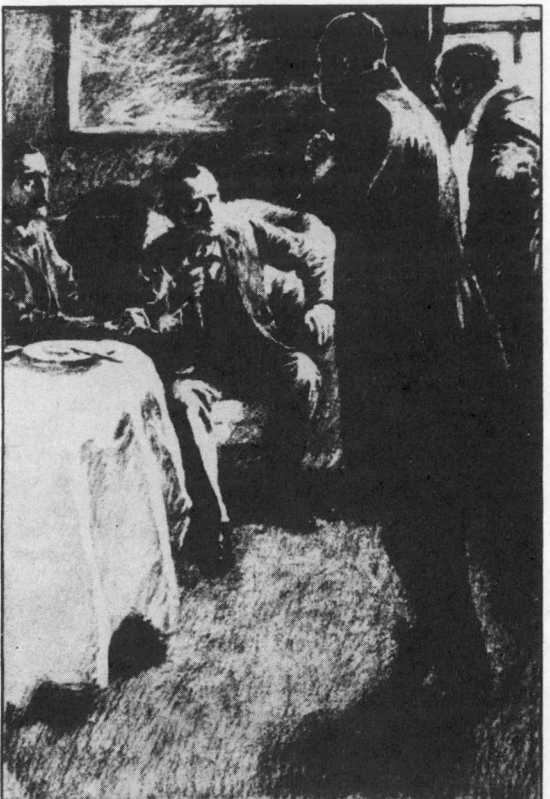

common with his lodger, who was a thin, dark, spectacled man, with a stoop which gave the impression of actual physical deformity. I remember that during our short visit we found the vicar garrulous, but his lodger strangely reticent, a sad-faced, introspective man, sitting with averted eyes, brooding apparently upon his own affairs.

These were the two men who entered abruptly into our **5** little sitting-room on Tuesday, March the 16th, shortly after our breakfast hour, as we were smoking together, preparatory to our daily excursion upon the moors.

"Mr. Holmes," said the vicar, in an agitated voice, "the most extraordinary and tragic affair has occurred during the night. It is the most unheard-of business. We can only regard it as a special Providence that you should chance to be here at the time, for in all England you are the one man we need."

I glared at the intrusive vicar with no very friendly eyes; but Holmes took his pipe from his lips and sat up in his chair like an old hound who hears the view-holloa. He waved his hand to the sofa, and our palpitating visitor with his agitated companion sat side by side upon it. Mr. Mortimer Tregennis was more self-contained than the clergyman, but the twitching of his thin hands and the brightness of his dark eyes showed that they shared a common emotion.

"Shall I speak or you?" he asked of the vicar.

"Well, as you seem to have made the discovery, whatever it may be, and the vicar to have had it second-hand, perhaps you had better do the speaking," said Holmes.

I glanced at the hastily-clad clergyman, with the formally-dressed lodger seated beside him, and was amused at the surprise which Holmes' simple deduction had brought to their faces.

"Perhaps I had best say a few words first," said the vicar, "and then you can judge if you will listen to the details from Mr. Tregennis, or whether we should not hasten at once to the scene of this mysterious affair. I may explain, then, that our friend here spent last evening in the company of his two brothers, Owen and George, and of his sister Brenda, at their house of Tredannick Wartha, which is near the old stone cross upon the moor. He left them shortly after ten o'clock, playing cards round the dining-room table, in excellent health and spirits. This morning, being an early riser, he walked in that direction before breakfast, and was overtaken by the carriage of Dr. Richards, who explained that he had just been sent for on a most urgent call to Tredannick Wartha. Mr. Mortimer Tregennis naturally went with him. When he arrived at Tredannick Wartha he found an extraordinary state of things. His two brothers and his sister were seated round the table exactly as he had left them, the cards still spread in front of them and the candles burned down to their sockets. The sister lay back stone-dead in her chair, while the two brothers sat on each side of her laughing, shouting, and singing, the senses stricken clean out of them. All three of them, the dead woman and the two demented men, retained upon their faces an expression of the utmost horror—a convulsion of terror which was dreadful to look upon. There was no sign of the presence of anyone in the house, except Mrs. Porter, the old cook and housekeeper, who declared that she had slept deeply and heard no sound during the night. Nothing had been stolen or disarranged, and there is absolutely no explanation of what the horror can be which has frightened a woman to death and two strong men out of their senses. There is the situation, Mr. Holmes, in a nutshell and if you can help us to clear it up you will have done a great work."

I had hoped that in some way I could coax my companion back into the quiet which had been the object of our journey ; but one glance at his intense face and contracted eyebrows told me how vain was now the expectation. He sat for some little time in silence, absorbed in the strange drama which had broken in upon our peace.

" I will look into this matter," he said at last. " On the face of it, it would appear to be a case of a very excep tional nature. Have you been there yourself, Mr. Round-hay ? "

" No, Mr. Holmes. Mr. Tregennis brought back the account to the vicarage, and I at once hurried over with him to consult you."

" How far is it to the house where this singular tragedy occurred ? "

" About a mile inland."

" Then we shall walk over together. But, before we start, I must ask you a few questions, Mr. Mortimer Tregennis."

The other had been silent all this time, but I had observed that his more controlled excitement was even greater than the obtrusive emotion of the clergyman. He sat with a pale, drawn face, his anxious gaze fixed upon Holmes, and his thin hands clasped convulsively together. His pale lips quivered as he listened to the dreadful experience which had befallen his family, and his dark eyes seemed to reflect something of the horror of the scene.

" Ask what you like, Mr. Holmes," said he eagerly. " It is a bad thing to speak of, but I will answer you the truth."

" Tell me about last night."

" Well, Mr. Holmes, I supped there, as the vicar has said, and my elder brother George proposed a game of whist afterwards. We sat down about nine o'clock. It was a quarter-past ten when I moved to go. I left them all round the table, as merry as could be."

" Who let you out ? "

" Mrs. Porter had gone to bed, so I let myself out. I shut the hall door behind me. The window of the room in which they sat was closed, but the blind was not drawn down. There was no change in door or window this morning, nor any reason to think that any stranger had been to the house. Yet there they sat, driven clean mad with terror, and Brenda lying dead of fright, with her head hanging over the arm of the chair. I'll never get the sight of that room out of my mind so long as I live."

" The facts, as you state them, are certainly most remarkable," said Holmes. " I take it that you have no theory yourself which can in any way account for them ? "

" It's devilish, Mr. Holmes ; devilish ! " cried Mortimer Tregennis. " It is not of this world. Something has come into that room which has dashed the light of reason from their minds. What human contrivance could do that ? "

" I fear," said Holmes, " that if the matter is beyond humanity it is certainly beyond me. Yet we must exhaust all natural explanations before we fall back upon such a theory as this. As to yourself, Mr. Tregennis, I take it you were divided in some way from your family, since they lived together and you had rooms apart ? "

" That is so, Mr. Holmes, though the matter is past and done with. We were a family of tin-miners at Redruth, but we sold out our venture to a company, and so retired with enough to keep us. I won't deny that there was some feeling about the division of the money and it stood between us for a time, but it was all forgiven and forgotten, and we were the best of friends together."

" Looking back at the evening which you spent together, does anything stand out in your memory as throwing any possible light upon the tragedy ? Think carefully, Mr. Tregennis, for any clue which can help me."

" There is nothing at all, sir."

" Your people were in their usual spirits ? "

" Never better."

" Were they nervous people ? Did they ever show any apprehension of coming danger ? "

" Nothing of the kind."

" You have nothing to add then, which could assist me ? "

Mortimer Tregennis considered earnestly for a moment.

" There is one thing occurs to me," said he at last. " As we sat at the table my back was to the window, and my brother George, he being my partner at cards, was facing it. I saw him once look hard over my shoulder, so I turned round and looked also. The blind was up and the window shut, but I could just make out the bushes on the lawn, and it seemed to me for a moment that I saw something moving among them. I couldn't even say if it were man or animal, but I just thought there was something there. When I asked him what he was looking at, he told me that he had the same feeling. That is all that I can say."

" Did you not investigate ? "

" No ; the matter passed as unimportant."

" You left them, then, without any premonition of evil ? "

" None at all."

" I am not clear how you came to hear the news so early this morning."

" I am an early riser, and generally take a walk before breakfast. This morning I had hardly started when the doctor in his carriage overtook me. He told me that old Mrs. Porter had sent a boy down with an urgent message. I sprang in beside him and we drove on. When we got there we looked into that dreadful room. The candles and the fire must have burned out hours before, and they had been sitting there in the dark until dawn had broken. The doctor said Brenda must have been dead at least six hours. There were no signs of violence. She just lay across the arm of the chair with that look on her face. George and Owen were singing snatches of songs and gibbering like two great apes. Oh, it was awful to see! I couldn't stand it, and the doctor was as white as a sheet. Indeed, he fell into a chair in a sort of faint, and we nearly had him on our hands as well."

"Remarkable—most remarkable!" said Holmes, rising and taking his hat. "I think, perhaps, we had better go down to Tredannick Wartha without further delay. I confess that I have seldom known a case which at first sight presented a more singular problem."

Our proceedings of that first morning did little to advance the investigation. It was marked, however, at the outset by an incident which left the most sinister impression upon my mind. The approach to the spot at which the tragedy occurred is down a narrow winding country lane. While we made our way along it we heard the rattle of a carriage coming towards us, and stood aside to let it pass. As it drove by us I caught a glimpse through the closed window of a horribly contorted, grinning face glaring out at us. Those staring eyes and gnashing teeth flashed past us like a dreadful vision.

"My brothers!" cried Mortimer Tregennis, white to his lips. "They are taking them to Helston."

We looked with horror after the black carriage, lumbering upon its way. Then we turned our steps towards this ill-omened house in which they had met their strange fate.

It was a large and bright dwelling, rather a villa than a cottage, with a considerable garden which was already, in that Cornish air, well filled with spring flowers. Towards this garden the window of the sitting-room fronted, and from it, according to Mortimer Tregennis, must have come that thing of evil which had by sheer horror in a single instant blasted their minds. Holmes walked slowly and thoughtfully among the flower-pots and along the path before we entered the porch. So absorbed was he in his thoughts, I remember, that he stumbled over the watering-pot, upset its contents, and deluged both our feet and the garden path. Inside the house we were met by the elderly Cornish housekeeper, Mrs. Porter, who, with the aid of a young girl, looked after the wants of the family. She readily answered all Holmes' questions. She had heard nothing in the night. Her employers had all been in excellent spirits lately, and she had never known them more cheerful and prosperous. She had fainted with horror upon entering the room in the morning and seeing that dreadful company round the table. She had, when she recovered, thrown open the window to let the morning air in, and had run down to the lane, whence she sent a farm-lad for the doctor. The lady was on her bed upstairs, if we cared to see her. It took four strong men to get the brothers into the asylum carriage. She would not herself stay in the house another day, and was starting that very afternoon to rejoin her family at St. Ives.

We ascended the stairs and viewed the body. Miss Brenda Tregennis had been a very beautiful girl, though now verging upon middle age. Her dark, clear-cut face was handsome, even in death, but there still lingered upon it something of that convulsion of horror which had been

THOSE STARING EYES AND GNASHING TEETH FLASHED PAST US LIKE A DREADFUL VISION.

Illustration by Gilbert Holiday for the *Strand Magazine*, December, 1910.

WE ASCENDED THE STAIRS AND VIEWED THE BODY.

Illustration by Gilbert Holiday for the *Strand Magazine*, December, 1910.

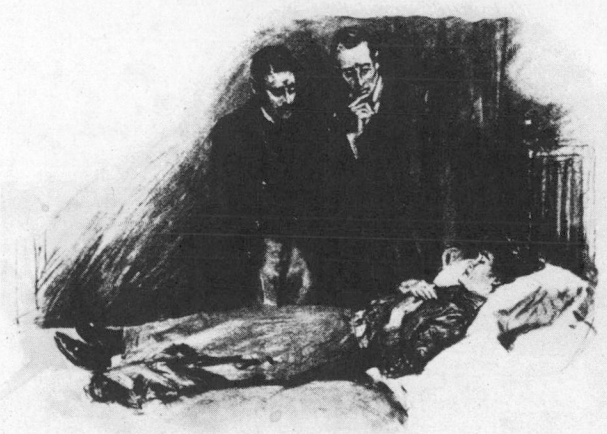

her last human emotion. From her bedroom we descended to the sitting-room where this strange tragedy had actually occurred. The charred ashes of the overnight fire lay in the grate. On the table were the four guttered and burned-out candles, with the cards scattered over its surface. The chairs had been moved back against the walls, but all else was as it had been the night before. Holmes paced with light, swift steps about the room; he sat in the various chairs, drawing them up and reconstructing their positions. He tested how much of the garden was visible; he examined the floor, the ceiling, and the fireplace; but never once did I see that sudden brightening of his eyes and tightening of his lips which would have told me that he saw some gleam of light in this utter darkness.

"Why a fire?" he asked once.   Had they always a fire in this small room on a spring evening?"

Mortimer Tregennis explained that the night was cold and damp. For that reason, after his arrival, the fire was lit. "What are you going to do now, Mr. Holmes?" he asked.

My friend smiled and laid his hand upon my arm. "I think, Watson, that I shall resume that course of tobacco-poisoning which you have so often and so justly condemned," said he. "With your permission, gentlemen, we will now return to our cottage, for I am not aware that any new factor is likely to come to our notice here. I will turn the facts over in my mind, Mr. Tregennis, and should anything occur to me I will certainly communicate with you and the vicar. In the meantime I wish you both good morning."

It was not until long after we were back in Poldhu Cottage that Holmes broke his complete and absorbed silence. He sat coiled in his arm-chair, his haggard and ascetic face hardly visible amid the blue swirl of his tobacco smoke, his black brows drawn down, his forehead contracted, his eyes vacant and far away. Finally, he laid down his pipe and sprang to his feet.

"It won't do, Watson!" said he, with a laugh. "Let us walk along the cliffs together and search for flint arrows. We are more likely to find them than clues to this problem. To let the brain work without sufficient material is like racing an engine. It racks itself to pieces. The sea air, sunshine, and patience, Watson—all else will come.

"Now, let us calmly define our position, Watson," he continued, as we skirted the cliffs together. "Let us get a firm grip of the very little which we *do* know, so that when fresh facts arise we may be ready to fit them into their places. I take it, in the first place, that neither of us is prepared to admit diabolical intrusions into the affairs of men. Let us begin by ruling that entirely out of our minds. Very good. There remain three persons who have been grievously stricken by some conscious or unconscious human agency. That is firm ground. Now, when did this occur? Evidently, assuming his narrative to be true, it was immediately after Mr. Mortimer Tregennis had left the room. That is a very important point. The presumption is that it was within a few minutes afterwards. The cards still lay upon the table. It was already past their usual hour for bed.   Yet they had not changed their position or pushed back their chairs.   I repeat, then, that the occurrence was immediately after his departure, and not later than eleven o'clock last night.

" Our next obvious step is to check, so far as we can, the movements of Mortimer Tregennis after he left the room.   In this there is no difficulty, and they seem to be above suspicion.   Knowing my methods as you do, you were, of course, conscious of the somewhat clumsy water-pot expedient by which I obtained a clearer impress of his foot than might otherwise have been possible.   The wet sandy path took it admirably.   Last night was also wet, you will remember, and it was not difficult—having obtained a sample print—to pick out his track among others and to follow his movements.   He appears to have walked away swiftly in the direction of the vicarage.

" If, then, Mortimer Tregennis disappeared from the scene, and yet some outside person affected the card-players, how can we reconstruct that person, and how was such an impression of horror conveyed ? Mrs. Porter may be eliminated.   She is evidently harmless.   Is there any evidence that someone crept up to the garden window and in some manner produced so terrific an effect that he drove those who saw it out of their senses ?   The only suggestion in this direction comes from Mortimer Tregennis himself, who says that his brother spoke about some movement in the garden.   That is certainly remarkable, as the night was rainy, cloudy, and dark.   Anyone who had the design to alarm these people would be compelled to place his very face against the glass before he could be seen.   There is a three-foot flower-border outside this window, but no indication of a footmark.   It is difficult to imagine, then, how an outsider could have made so terrible an impression upon the company, nor have we found any possible motive for so strange and elaborate an attempt.   You perceive our difficulties, Watson ? "

" They are only too clear," I answered, with conviction.

" And yet, with a little more material, we may prove that they are not insurmountable," said Holmes.   " I fancy that among your extensive archives, Watson, you may find some which were nearly as obscure.   Meanwhile, we shall put the case aside until more accurate data are available, and devote the rest of our morning to the pursuit of neolithic man."

I may have commented upon my friend's power of mental detachment, but never have I wondered at it more than upon that spring morning in Cornwall when for two hours he discoursed upon celts, arrowheads, and shards, as lightly as if no sinister mystery was waiting for his solution.   It was not until we had returned in the afternoon to our cottage that we found a visitor awaiting us, who soon brought our minds back to the matter in hand. Neither of us needed to be told who that visitor was.   The huge body, the craggy and deeply-seamed face with the fierce eyes and hawk-like nose, the grizzled hair which nearly brushed our cottage ceiling, the beard—golden at the fringes and white near the lips, save for the nicotine stain from his perpetual cigar—all these were as well known in London as in Africa, and could only be associated with the tremendous personality of Dr. Leon Sterndale, the great lion-hunter and explorer.

We had heard of his presence in the district, and had once or twice caught sight of his tall figure upon the moorland paths. He made no advances to us, however, nor would we have dreamed of doing so to him, as it was well known that it was his love of seclusion which caused him to spend the greater part of the intervals between his journeys in a small bungalow buried in the lonely wood of Beauchamp Arriance. Here, amid his books and his maps, he lived an absolutely lonely life, attending to his own simple wants, and paying little apparent heed to the affairs of his neighbours. It was a surprise to me, therefore. to hear him asking Holmes in an eager voice, whether he had made any advance in his reconstruction of this mysterious episode. "The county police are utterly at fault," said he ; "but perhaps your wider experience has suggested some conceivable explanation. My only claim to being taken into your confidence is that during my many residences here I have come to know this family of Tregennis very well—indeed, upon my Cornish mother's side I could call them cousins—and their strange fate has naturally been a great shock to me. I may tell you that I had got as far as Plymouth upon my way to Africa, but the news reached me this morning, and I came straight back again to help in the inquiry."

Holmes raised his eyebrows.

"Did you lose your boat through it ? "

"I will take the next."

"Dear me ! that is friendship indeed."

"I tell you they were relatives."

"Quite so—cousins of your mother. Was your baggage aboard the ship ? "

"Some of it, but the main part at the hotel.'

"I see. But surely this event could not have found its way into the Plymouth morning papers ? "

"No, sir ; I had a telegram."

"Might I ask from whom ? "

A shadow passed over the gaunt face of the explorer.

"You are very inquisitive, Mr. Holmes."

"It is my business."

With an effort, Dr. Sterndale recovered his ruffled composure.

"I have no objection to telling you," he said. "It was Mr. Roundhay, the vicar, who sent me the telegram which recalled me."

"Thank you," said Holmes. "I may say in answer to your original question, that I have not cleared my mind entirely on the subject of this case, but that I have every hope of reaching some conclusion. It would be premature to say more."

"Perhaps you would not mind telling me if your suspicions point in any particular direction ? "

"No, I can hardly answer that."

"Then I have wasted my time, and need not prolong my visit." The famous doctor strode out of our cottage in considerable ill-humour, and within five minutes Holmes had followed him. I saw him no more until the evening, when he returned with a slow step and haggard face which assured me that he had made no great progress with his investigation. He glanced at a telegram which awaited him, and threw it into the grate.

" From the Plymouth hotel, Watson," he said. " I learned the name of it from the vicar, and I wired to make certain that Dr. Leon Sterndale's account was true. It appears that he did indeed spend last night there, and that he has actually allowed some of his baggage to go on to Africa, while he returned to be present at this investigation. What do you make of that, Watson ? "

" He is deeply interested."

" Deeply interested—yes. There is a thread here which we have not yet grasped, and which might lead us through the tangle. Cheer up, Watson, for I am very sure that our material has not yet all come to hand. When it does, we may soon leave our difficulties behind us."

Little did I think how soon the words of Holmes would be realized, or how strange and sinister would be that new development which opened up an entirely fresh line of investigation. I was shaving at my window in the morning when I heard the rattle of hoofs, and, looking up, saw a dog-cart coming at a gallop down the road. It pulled up at our door, and our friend the vicar sprang from it and rushed up our garden path. Holmes was already dressed, and we hastened down to meet him.

Our visitor was so excited that he could hardly articulate, but at last in gasps and bursts his tragic story came out of him.

" We are devil-ridden, Mr. Holmes ! My poor parish is devil-ridden ! " he cried. " Satan himself is loose in it ! We are given over into his hands ! " He danced about in his agitation, a ludicrous object if it were not for his ashy face and startled eyes. Finally he shot out his terrible news.

" Mr. Mortimer Tregennis died during the night, and with exactly the same symptoms as the rest of his family."

Holmes sprang to his feet, all energy in an instant.

" Can you fit us both into your dog-cart ? "

" Yes, I can."

" Then, Watson, we will postpone our breakfast. Mr. Roundhay, we are entirely at your disposal. Hurry— hurry, before things get disarranged."

The lodger occupied two rooms at the vicarage, which were in an angle by themselves, the one above the other. Below was a large sitting-room ; above, his bedroom. They looked out upon a croquet lawn which came up to the windows. We had arrived before the doctor or the police, so that everything was absolutely undisturbed. Let me describe exactly the scene as we saw it upon that misty March morning. It has left an impression which can never be effaced from my mind.

The atmosphere of the room was of a horrible and depressing stuffiness. The servant who had first entered had thrown up the window, or it would have been even more intolerable. This might partly be due to the fact that a lamp stood flaring and smoking on the centre table. Beside it sat the dead man, leaning back in his chair, his thin beard projecting, his spectacles pushed up on to his forehead, and his lean, dark face turned towards the window and twisted into the same distortion of terror which had marked the features of his dead sister. His

BESIDE IT SAT THE DEAD MAN, LEANING BACK
IN HIS CHAIR . . .

Illustration by Gilbert Holiday for the *Strand Magazine*, U.S. edition only, February, 1911. The late James Montgomery wrote (*A Study in Pictures*) that "This is the only instance on record where the *Strand* reproduced two different pictures to portray the same episode, and undoubtedly came about through the necessity of providing a full page frontispiece for the second part when the story was split into two installments in America." (The original illustration, in the London *Strand*, was a half-page sketch of the body.)

limbs were convulsed and his fingers contorted as though he had died in a very paroxysm of fear. He was fully clothed, though there were signs that his dressing had been done in a hurry. We had already learned that his bed had been slept in, and that the tragic end had come to him in the early morning.

One realized the red-hot energy which underlay Holmes' phlegmatic exterior when one saw the sudden change which came over him from the moment that he entered the fatal apartment. In an instant he was tense and alert, his eyes shining, his face set, his limbs quivering with eager activity. He was out on the lawn, in through the window, round the room, and up into the bedroom, for all the world like a dashing foxhound drawing a cover. In the bedroom he made a rapid cast around, and ended by throwing open the window, which appeared to give him some fresh cause for excitement, for he leaned out of it with loud ejaculations of interest and delight. Then he rushed down the stair, out through the open window, threw himself upon his face on the lawn, sprang up and into the room once more, all with the energy of the hunter who is at the very heels of his quarry. The lamp, which was an ordinary standard, he examined with minute care, making certain measurements upon its bowl. He carefully scrutinized with his lens the talc shield which covered the top of the chimney, and scraped off some ashes which adhered to its upper surface, putting some of them into an envelope, which he placed in his pocket-book. Finally, just as the doctor and the official police put in an appearance, he beckoned to the vicar and we all three went out upon the lawn.

"I am glad to say that my investigation has not been entirely barren," he remarked. "I cannot remain to discuss the matter with the police, but I should be exceedingly obliged, Mr. Roundhay, if you would give the inspector my compliments and direct his attention to the bedroom window and to the sitting-room lamp. Each is suggestive, and together they are almost conclusive. If the police would desire further information I shall be happy to see any of them at the cottage. And now, Watson, I think that, perhaps, we shall be better employed elsewhere."

It may be that the police resented the intrusion of an amateur, or that they imagined themselves to be upon some hopeful line of investigation ; but it is certain that we **6** heard nothing from them for the next two days. During this time Holmes spent some of his time smoking and dreaming in the cottage ; but a greater portion in country walks which he undertook alone, returning after many hours without remark as to where he had been. One experiment served to show me the line of his investigation. He had bought a lamp which was the duplicate of the one which had burned in the room of Mortimer Tregennis on the morning of the tragedy. This he filled with the same oil as that used at the vicarage, and he carefully timed the period which it would take to be exhausted. Another experiment which he made was of a more unpleasant nature, and one which I am not likely ever to forget.

"You will remember, Watson," he remarked one after-

6 *the next two days.* It is probable, but not certain, that this adventure ended on *Saturday, March 20th.* The "two days" of which Watson speaks would be the Thursday and Friday following Wednesday the 17th; it was "one afternoon" after Friday the 19th that Holmes made the experiment that solved the case.

noon, " that there is a single common point of resemblance in the varying reports which have reached us.   This concerns the effect of the atmosphere of the room in each case upon those who had first entered it.   You will recollect that Mortimer Tregennis, in describing the episode of his last visit to his brothers' house, remarked that the doctor on entering the room fell into a chair ?   You had forgotten ?   Well, I can answer for it that it was so.   Now, you will remember also that Mrs. Porter, the housekeeper, told us that she herself fainted upon entering the room and had afterwards opened the window.   In the second case—that of Mortimer Tregennis himself—you cannot have forgotten the horrible stuffiness of the room when we arrived, though the servant had thrown open the window. That servant, I found upon inquiry, was so ill that she had gone to her bed.   You will admit, Watson, that these facts are very suggestive.   In each case there is evidence of a poisonous atmosphere.   In each case, also, there is combustion going on in the room—in the one case a fire, in the other a lamp.   The fire was needed, but the lamp was lit—as a comparison of the oil consumed will show—long after it was broad daylight.   Why ?   Surely because there is some connection between three things—the burning, the stuffy atmosphere, and, finally, the madness or death of those unfortunate people.   That is clear, is it not ? "

" It would appear so."

" At least we may accept it as a working hypothesis. We will suppose, then, that something was burned in each case which produced an atmosphere causing strange toxic effects.   Very good.   In the first instance—that of the Tregennis family—this substance was placed in the fire. Now the window was shut, but the fire would naturally carry fumes to some extent up the chimney.   Hence one would expect the effects of the poison to be less than in the second case, where there was less escape for the vapour. The result seems to indicate that it was so, since in the first case only the woman, who had presumably the more sensitive organism, was killed, the others exhibiting that temporary or permanent lunacy which is evidently the first effect of the drug.   In the second case the result was complete.   The facts, therefore, seem to bear out the theory of a poison which worked by combustion.   **7**

" With this train of reasoning in my head I naturally looked about in Mortimer Tregennis' room to find some remains of this substance.   The obvious place to look was the talc shield or smoke-guard of the lamp.   There, sure enough, I perceived a number of flaky ashes, and round the edges a fringe of brownish powder, which had not yet been consumed.   Half of this I took, as you saw, and I placed it in an envelope."

" Why half, Holmes ? "

" It is not for me, my dear Watson, to stand in the way of the official police force.   I leave them all the evidence which I found.   The poison still remained upon the talc, had they the wit to find it.   Now, Watson, we will light our lamp ; we will, however, take the precaution to open our window to avoid the premature decease of two deserving members of society, and you will seat yourself near

7 *a poison which worked by combustion.* In "Tregennis and Poe," Mr. Stephen Saxe has suggested that the murderer in this adventure must have derived his idea for the murder from reading Edgar Allan Poe's story, "The Imp of the Perverse," just as the murderer in Poe's story got the idea from reading some French memoirs.

that open window in an arm-chair, unless, like a sensible man, you determine to have nothing to do with the affair. Oh, you will see it out, will you ? I thought I knew my Watson. This chair I will place opposite yours, so that we may be the same distance from the poison, and face to face. The door we will leave ajar. Each is now in a position to watch the other and to bring the experiment to an end should the symptoms seem alarming. Is that all clear ? Well, then, I take our powder—or what remains of it—from the envelope, and I lay it above the burning lamp. So ! Now, Watson, let us sit down and await developments."

They were not long in coming. I had hardly settled in my chair before I was conscious of a thick, musky odour, subtle and nauseous. At the very first whiff of it my brain and my imagination were beyond all control. A thick, black cloud swirled before my eyes, and my mind told me that in this cloud, unseen as yet, but about to spring out upon my appalled senses, lurked all that was vaguely horrible, all that was monstrous and inconceivably wicked in the universe. Vague shapes swirled and swam amid the dark cloud-bank, each a menace and a warning of something coming, the advent of some unspeakable dweller upon the threshold, whose very shadow would blast my soul. A freezing horror took possession of me. I felt that my hair was rising, that my eyes were protruding, that my mouth was opened, and my tongue like leather. The turmoil within my brain was such that something must surely snap. I tried to scream, and was vaguely aware of some hoarse croak which was my own voice, but distant and detached from myself. At the same moment, in some effort of escape, I broke through that cloud of despair, and had a glimpse of Holmes' face, white, rigid, and drawn with horror—the very look which I had seen upon the features of the dead. It was that vision which gave me an instant of sanity and of strength. I dashed from my chair, threw my arms round Holmes, and together we lurched through the door, and an instant afterwards had thrown ourselves down upon the grass plot and were lying side by side, conscious only of the glorious sunshine which was bursting its way through the hellish cloud of terror which had girt us in. Slowly it rose from our souls like the mists from a landscape, until peace and reason had returned, and we were sitting upon the grass, wiping our clammy foreheads, and looking with apprehension at each other to mark the last traces of that terrific experience which we had undergone.

"Upon my word, Watson !" said Holmes at last, with an unsteady voice ; "I owe you both my thanks and an apology. It was an unjustifiable experiment even for oneself, and doubly so for a friend. I am really very sorry."

"You know," I answered, with some emotion, for I had never seen so much of Holmes' heart before, "that it is my greatest joy and privilege to help you."

He relapsed at once into the half-humorous, half-cynical vein which was his habitual attitude to those about him. "It would be superfluous to drive us mad, my dear Watson," said he. "A candid observer would certainly

. . . TOGETHER WE LURCHED THROUGH THE DOOR . . .

Illustration by Gilbert Holiday for the *Strand Magazine*, December, 1910.

declare that we were so already before we embarked upon so wild an experiment. I confess that I never imagined that the effect could be so sudden and so severe." He dashed into the cottage, and reappearing with the burning lamp held at full arm's length, he threw it among a bank of brambles. " We must give the room a little time to clear. I take it, Watson, that you have no longer a shadow of a doubt as to how these tragedies were produced ? "

" None whatever."

" But the cause remains as obscure as before. Come into the arbour here, and let us discuss it together. That villainous stuff seems still to linger round my throat. I think we must admit that all the evidence points to this man, Mortimer Tregennis, having been the criminal in the first tragedy, though he was the victim in the second one. We must remember, in the first place, that there is some story of a family quarrel, followed by a reconciliation. How bitter that quarrel may have been, or how hollow the reconciliation we cannot tell. When I think of Mortimer Tregennis, with the foxy face and the small shrewd, beady eyes behind the spectacles, he is not a man whom I should judge to be of a particularly forgiving disposition. Well, in the next place, you will remember that this idea of someone moving in the garden, which took our attention for a moment from the real cause of the tragedy, emanated from him. He had a motive in misleading us. Finally, if he did not throw this substance into the fire at the moment of leaving the room, who did do so ? The affair happened immediately after his departure. Had anyone else come in, the family would certainly have risen from the table. Besides, in peaceful Cornwall, visitors do not arrive after ten o'clock at night. We may take it, then, that all the evidence points to Mortimer Tregennis as the culprit."

" Then his own death was suicide ! "

" Well, Watson, it is on the face of it a not impossible supposition. The man who had the guilt upon his soul of having brought such a fate upon his own family might well be driven by remorse to inflict it upon himself. There are, however, some cogent reasons against it. Fortunately, there is one man in England who knows all about it, and I have made arrangements by which we shall hear the facts this afternoon from his own lips. Ah ! he is a little before his time. Perhaps you would kindly step this way, Dr. Leon Sterndale. We have been conducting a chemical experiment indoors which has left our little room hardly fit for the reception of so distinguished a visitor."

I had heard the click of the garden gate, and now the majestic figure of the great African explorer appeared upon the path. He turned in some surprise towards the rustic arbour in which we sat.

" You sent for me, Mr. Holmes. I had your note about an hour ago, and I have come, though I really do not know why I should obey your summons."

" Perhaps we can clear the point up before we separate," said Holmes. " Meanwhile, I am much obliged to you for your courteous acquiescence. You will excuse this informal reception in the open air, but my friend Watson and I have nearly furnished an additional chapter to what the papers call the ' Cornish Horror,' and we prefer a clear atmosphere for the present. Perhaps, since the matters which we have to discuss will affect you personally in a very intimate fashion, it is as well that we should talk where there can be no eavesdropping."

The explorer took his cigar from his lips and gazed sternly at my companion.

" I am at a loss to know, sir," he said, " what you can have to speak about which affects me personally in a very intimate fashion."

" The killing of Mortimer Tregennis," said Holmes.

For a moment I wished that I were armed. Sterndale's fierce face turned to a dusky red, his eyes glared, and the knotted, passionate veins started out in his forehead, while he sprang forward with clenched hands towards my companion. Then he stopped, and with a violent effort he resumed a cold, rigid calmness which was, perhaps, more suggestive of danger than his hot-headed outburst.

" I have lived so long among savages and beyond the law," said he, " that I have got into the way of being a law to myself. You would do well, Mr. Holmes, not to forget it, for I have no desire to do you an injury."

" Nor have I any desire to do you an injury, Dr. Sterndale. Surely the clearest proof of it is that, knowing what I know, I have sent for you and not for the police."

Sterndale sat down with a gasp, overawed for, perhaps, the first time in his adventurous life. There was a calm assurance of power in Holmes' manner which could not be withstood. Our visitor stammered for a moment, his great hands opening and shutting in his agitation.

" What do you mean ? " he asked, at last. " If this is bluff upon your part, Mr. Holmes, you have chosen a bad man for your experiment. Let us have no more beating about the bush. What *do* you mean ? "

" I will tell you," said Holmes, " and the reason why I tell you is that I hope frankness may beget frankness. What my next step may be will depend entirely upon the nature of your own defence."

" My defence ? "

" Yes, sir."

" My defence against what ? "

" Against the charge of killing Mortimer Tregennis."

Sterndale mopped his forehead with his handkerchief. " Upon my word, you are getting on," said he. " Do all your successes depend upon this prodigious power of bluff ? "

" The bluff," said Holmes, sternly, " is upon your side, Dr. Leon Sterndale, and not upon mine. As a proof I will tell you some of the facts upon which my conclusions are based. Of your return from Plymouth, allowing much of your property to go on to Africa, I will say nothing save that it first informed me that you were one of the factors which had to be taken into account in reconstructing this drama——"

" I came back——"

" I have heard your reasons and regard them as unconvincing and inadequate. We will pass that. You came down here to ask me whom I suspected. I refused to

. . . HE SPRANG FORWARD WITH CLENCHED HANDS
TOWARDS MY COMPANION.

Illustration by Gilbert Holiday for the *Strand Magazine*, December, 1910.

answer you.   You then went to the vicarage, waited outside it for some time, and finally returned to your cottage."

"How do you know that ? "

" I followed you."

" I saw no one."

"That is what you may expect to see when I follow
you.   You spent a restless night at your cottage, and you
formed certain plans, which in the early morning you proceeded to put into execution.   Leaving your door just as
day was breaking, you filled your pocket with some reddish
gravel that was lying heaped beside your gate."

Sterndale gave a violent start and looked at Holmes in
amazement.

" You then walked swiftly for the mile which separated
you from the vicarage.   You were wearing, I may remark,
the same pair of ribbed tennis shoes which are at the present
moment upon your feet.   At the vicarage you passed
through the orchard and the side hedge, coming out under
the window of the lodger Tregennis.   It was now daylight,
but the household was not yet stirring.   You drew some
of the gravel from your pocket, and you threw it up at the
window above you."

Sterndale sprang to his feet.

" I believe that you are the devil himself ! " he cried.

Holmes smiled at the compliment.   " It took two, or
possibly three, handfuls before the lodger came to the
window.   You beckoned him to come down.   He dressed
hurriedly and descended to his sitting-room.   You entered
by the window.   There was an interview—a short one—
during which you walked up and down the room.   Then
you passed out and closed the window, standing on the
lawn outside smoking a cigar and watching what occurred.
Finally, after the death of Tregennis, you withdrew as you
had come.   Now, Dr. Sterndale, how do you justify such
conduct, and what were the motives for your actions ?   If
you prevaricate or trifle with me, I give you my assurance
that the matter will pass out of my hands for ever."

Our visitor's face had turned ashen grey as he listened
to the words of his accuser.   Now he sat for some time
in thought with his face sunk in his hands.   Then with a
sudden impulsive gesture he plucked a photograph from
his breast-pocket and threw it on the rustic table before us.

" That is why I have done it," said he.

It showed the bust and face of a very beautiful woman.
Holmes stooped over it.

" Brenda Tregennis," said he.

" Yes, Brenda Tregennis," repeated our visitor.   " For
years I have loved her.   For years she has loved me.
There is the secret of that Cornish seclusion which people
have marvelled at.   It has brought me close to the one
thing on earth that was dear to me.   I could not marry
her, for I have a wife who has left me for years and yet
whom, by the deplorable laws of England, I could not
divorce.   For years Brenda waited.   For years I waited.
And this is what we have waited for."   A terrible sob
shook his great frame, and he clutched his throat under his
brindled beard.   Then with an effort he mastered himself
and spoke on.

" The vicar knew.   He was in our confidence.   He
would tell you that she was an angel upon earth.   That

8 *or into the literature of toxicology.* Dr. George B. Koelle has commented ("The Poisons in the Canon"): "The situation has not changed since Dr. Leon Sterndale stated, over a half century ago, that [*radix pedis diaboli*] is not to be found in any pharmacopeia; in fact, it is not yet known to modern science. Until recently, skeptics might have questioned the possible existence of a drug which could produce such bizarre effects. . . . Recent discoveries have shed new light on the matter. A few days ago two Swiss chemists, Stoll and Hoffmann, synthesized a remarkable compound known as lysergic acid diethylamide, or LSD-25. . . . In doses of less than one-thousandth of a grain, it causes strange hallucinations, visions and fantasies, not unlike those presumably experienced by the ill-fated members of the Tregennis family. . . . The compound used in the synthesis of LSD-25 is lysergic acid, which is prepared from a natural alkaloid. Thus it is not difficult to conceive of the presence of a compound similar to or more potent than LSD-25 itself in some unidentified root. Time alone can establish the validity of this hypothesis."

On the other hand, F. A. Allen, M.P.S., has written in "Devilish Drugs" that while "the poison in . . . 'The Adventure of the Devil's Foot,' is, on a first impression virtually unknown to science . . . rauwolfia species, suitably trimmed, suggest themselves. There are the recent reports of acute depression following large doses of reserpine. In fact, [authorities] explicitly list *nightmares* among its undesirable possible side-effects. *Rauwolfia serpentina* is an Asiatic plant; *radix pedis diaboli* was obtained 'in curious circumstances,' from the Ubangi district of the Congo where, as an ordeal poison, it could well be a secret and nightmare-enhanced African species."

was why he telegraphed to me and I returned. What was my baggage or Africa to me when I learned that such a fate had come upon my darling? There you have the missing clue to my action, Mr. Holmes."

"Proceed," said my friend.

Dr. Sterndale drew from his pocket a paper packet and laid it upon the table. On the outside was written, "*Radix pedis diaboli*" with a red poison label beneath it. He pushed it towards me. "I understand that you are a doctor, sir. Have you ever heard of this preparation?"

"Devil's-foot root! No, I have never heard of it."

"It is no reflection upon your professional knowledge," said he, "for I believe that, save for one sample in a laboratory at Buda, there is no other specimen in Europe. It has not yet found its way either into the pharmacopœia **8** or into the literature of toxicology. The root is shaped like a foot, half human, half goat-like; hence the fanciful name given by a botanical missionary. It is used as an ordeal poison by the medicine-men in certain districts of West Africa, and is kept as a secret among them. This particular specimen I obtained under very extraordinary circumstances in the Ubanghi country." He opened the paper as he spoke, and disclosed a heap of reddish-brown, snuff-like powder.

"Well, sir?" asked Holmes sternly.

"I am about to tell you, Mr. Holmes, all that actually occurred, for you already know so much that it is clearly to my interest that you should know all. I have already explained the relationship in which I stood to the Tregennis family. For the sake of the sister I was friendly with the brothers. There was a family quarrel about money which estranged this man Mortimer, but it was supposed to be made up, and I afterwards met him as I did the others. He was a sly, subtle, scheming man, and several things arose which gave me a suspicion of him, but I had no cause for any positive quarrel.

"One day, only a couple of weeks ago, he came down to my cottage and I showed him some of my African curiosities. Among other things I exhibited this powder, and I told him of its strange properties, how it stimulates those brain centres which control the emotion of fear, and how either madness or death is the fate of the unhappy native who is subjected to the ordeal by the priest of his tribe. I told him also how powerless European science would be to detect it. How he took it I cannot say, for I never left the room, but there is no doubt that it was then, while I was opening cabinets and stooping to boxes, that he managed to abstract some of the devil's-foot root. I well remember how he plied me with questions as to the amount and the time that was needed for its effect, but I little dreamed that he could have a personal reason for asking.

"I thought no more of the matter until the vicar's telegram reached me at Plymouth. This villain had thought that I would be at sea before the news could reach me, and that I should be lost for years in Africa. But I returned at once. Of course, I could not listen to the details without feeling assured that my poison had been used. I came round to see you on the chance that some other explanation had suggested itself to you.   But there could be none. I was convinced that Mortimer Tregennis was the murderer ; that for the sake of money, and with the idea, perhaps, that if the other members of his family were all insane he would be the sole guardian of their joint property, he had used the devil's-foot powder upon them, driven two of them out of their senses, and killed his sister Brenda, the one human being whom I have ever loved or who has ever loved me.   There was his crime ; what was to be his punishment ?

" Should I appeal to the law ?   Where were my proofs ? I knew that the facts were true, but could I help to make a jury of countrymen believe so fantastic a story ?   I might or I might not.   But I could not afford to fail.   My soul cried out for revenge.   I have said to you once before, Mr. Holmes, that I have spent much of my life outside the law, and that I have come at last to be a law to myself. So it was now.   I determined that the fate which he had given to others should be shared by himself.   Either that or I would do justice upon him with my own hand.   In all England there can be no man who sets less value upon his own life than I do at the present moment.

" Now I have told you all.   You have yourself supplied the rest.   I did, as you say, after a restless night, set off early from my cottage.   I foresaw the difficulty of arousing him, so I gathered some gravel from the pile which you have mentioned, and I used it to throw up to his window. He came down and admitted me through the window of the sitting-room.   I laid his offence before him.   I told him that I had come both as judge and executioner.   The wretch sank into a chair paralysed at the sight of my revolver.   I lit the lamp, put the powder above it, and stood outside the window, ready to carry out my threat to shoot him should he try to leave the room.   In five minutes he died.   My God ! how he died ! But my heart was flint, for he endured nothing which my innocent darling had not felt before him.   There is my story, Mr. Holmes.   Perhaps, if you loved a woman, you would have done as much yourself.   At any rate, I am in your hands. You can take what steps you like.   As I have already said, there is no man living who can fear death less than I do."

Holmes sat for some little time in silence.

" What were your plans ? " he asked, at last.

" I had intended to bury myself in Central Africa.   My work there is but half finished."

" Go and do the other half," said Holmes.   " I, at least, am not prepared to prevent you."

Dr. Sterndale raised his giant figure, bowed gravely, and walked from the arbour.   Holmes lit his pipe and handed me his pouch.

" Some fumes which are not poisonous would be a welcome change," said he.   " I think you must agree, Watson, that it is not a case in which we are called upon to interfere.   Our investigation has been independent, and our action shall be so also.   You would not denounce the man ? "

" Certainly not," I answered.

" I have never loved, Watson, but if I did and if the

Auctorial and Bibliographical Note: Conan Doyle ranked "The Adventure of the Devil's Foot" No. 9 on his list of the "twelve best" Sherlock Holmes short stories, excluding those in *The Case-Book.* The original manuscript, 58 4to pages written in two exercise books, white vellum, is owned by the New York Public Library, the gift of Lucius Wilmerding.

woman I loved had met such an end, I might act even as our lawless lion-hunter has done. Who knows? Well, Watson, I will not offend your intelligence by explaining what is obvious. The gravel upon the window-sill was, of course, the starting-point of my research. It was unlike anything in the vicarage garden. Only when my attention had been drawn to Dr. Sterndale and his cottage did I find its counterpart. The lamp shining in broad daylight and the remains of powder upon the shield were successive links in a fairly obvious chain. And now, my dear Watson, I think we may dismiss the matter from our mind, and go back with a clear conscience to the study of those Chaldean roots which are surely to be traced in the Cornish branch of the great Celtic speech."

THE ROAD TO "TREDANNICK WOLLAS"

The photograph is by Mr. C. O. Merriman of the Sherlock Holmes Society of London, who adds this informative note: "A hamlet of Tredannick Wartha exists. I think the name given of Tredannick Wartha to the house where the Cornish Horror took place probably is that of Predannack Manor Farm which is one of the major farms in the hamlet of Predannack Wartha. The origin of the Wollas and Wartha is that at one time Predannack consisted of fourteen small holdings which formed two hamlets, High Predannack (Wartha) and Lower Predannack (Wollas). The larger farms took over the smaller but the names remained."

61

THE ADVENTURE OF THE DANCING MEN

[*Wednesday, July 27, to Wednesday, August 10, and Saturday, August 13, 1898*]

HOLMES had been seated for some hours in silence, with his long, thin back curved over a chemical vessel in which he was brewing a particularly malodorous product. His head was sunk upon his breast, and he looked from my point of view like a strange, lank bird, with dull grey plumage and a black top-knot.

" So, Watson," said he suddenly, " you do not propose to invest in South African securities ? " **1**

I gave a start of astonishment. Accustomed as I was to Holmes' curious faculties, this sudden intrusion into my most intimate thoughts was utterly inexplicable.

" How on earth do you know that ? " I asked.

He wheeled round upon his stool, with a steaming **test-tube** in his hand and a gleam of amusement in his deep-set eyes.

" Now, Watson, confess yourself utterly taken aback," said he.

" I am."

" I ought to make you sign a paper to that effect."

" Why ? "

" Because in five minutes you will say that it is all so absurdly simple."

" I am sure that I shall say nothing of the kind."

" You see, my dear Watson "—he propped his test-tube in the rack and began to lecture with the air of a professor addressing his class—" it is not really difficult to construct a series of inferences, each dependent upon its predecessor and each simple in itself. If, after doing so, one simply knocks out all the central inferences and presents one's audience with the starting-point and the conclusion, one may produce a startling, though possibly a meretricious, effect. Now, it was not really difficult, by an inspection of the groove between your left fore-finger and thumb, to feel sure that you did *not* propose to invest your small capital in the goldfields."

" I see no connection."

" Very likely not ; but I can quickly show you a close connection. Here are the missing links of the very simple chain : 1. You had chalk between your left finger and thumb when you returned from the club last night. 2. You put chalk there when you play **2**

1 *"you do not propose to invest in South African securities?"* Dr. Felix Morley has suggested ("The Significance of the Second Stain") that here is an indication that Dr. Watson's isolationist attitude (noted in "The Adventure of the Bruce-Partington Plans") continued: ". . . the doctor, although possessed of a strong gambling instinct, refused pointblank to take an inside tip for investment in South African gold fields. Had Watson taken advantage of [this] advice . . . the speculation would by this time have richly retrieved the shattered fortunes of the family. But it was a foreign commitment with political implications, and the doctor would have none of it."

2 *when you returned from the club last night.* "It is hard to believe," the late Edgar W. Smith commented, "that a man with medical training . . . could so far depart from the elementary principles of hygiene as to forget to wash his hands."

"YOU NEVER PLAY BILLIARDS EXCEPT WITH THURSTON."

Thurston is a famous name in the world of billiards. John Thurston of 78 Margaret Street, Cavendish Square, started making "superior" billiard tables sometime prior to 1814. A few years later he moved to 14 Catherine Street, The Strand. In 1869, Messrs. Thurston & Coy, still on Catherine Street, were one of the chief table-makers in England. As Mr. Ralph Hodgson once wrote to the late Christopher Morley: "Dr. Watson *may* have had a friend of the name, who though a billiards player was not a member of the illustrious family. He *may* have had. There *were* other Thurstons." "Playing with Thurston would not have been outrageously expensive," Mr. Michael Harrison noted (*In the Footsteps of Sherlock Holmes*): "The standard charge for billiards in the 1880's was 1s [25¢] an hour by the day, or 1s 6d [about 37¢] an hour by gas-light."

3 *Your cheque-book is locked in my drawer.* "It is evident . . . that Holmes kept the watchful eye of an elder brother upon Watson's gambling propensities," Mr. S. C. Roberts commented in *Doctor Watson.*

4 *Ridling Thorpe Manor. Riding Thorp* or plain *Ridling* in other editions. "If you will open your Batholomew survey map of Norfolk, and study the neighborhood of North Walsham," the late Christopher Morley wrote, "you will see that it was only a short drive from there to the house of Hilton Cubitt, Esq. He lived either at *Edingthorp* or at *Ridlington*, which accounts for the confusion of the . . . texts."

billiards to steady the cue. 3. You never play billiards except with Thurston. 4. You told me four weeks ago that Thurston had an option on some South African property which would expire in a month, and which he desired you to share with him. 5. Your **3** cheque-book is locked in my drawer, and you have not asked for the key. 6. You do not propose to invest your money in this manner."

"How absurdly simple!" I cried.

"Quite so!" said he, a little nettled. "Every problem becomes very childish when once it is explained to you. Here is an unexplained one. See what you can make of that, friend Watson." He tossed a sheet of paper upon the table, and turned once more to his chemical analysis.

I looked with amazement at the absurd hieroglyphics upon the paper.

"Why, Holmes, it is a child's drawing!" I cried.

"Oh, that's your idea!"

"What else should it be?"

"That is what Mr. Hilton Cubitt, of Ridling Thorpe **4** Manor, Norfolk, is very anxious to know. This little conundrum came by the first post, and he was to follow by the next train. There's a ring at the bell, Watson. I should not be very much surprised if this were he."

A heavy step was heard upon the stairs, and an instant later there entered a tall, ruddy, clean-shaven gentleman, whose clear eyes and florid cheeks told of a life led far from the fogs of Baker Street. He seemed to bring a whiff of his strong, fresh, bracing, east-coast air with him as he entered. Having shaken hands with each of us, he was about to sit down, when his eye rested upon the paper with the curious markings, which I had just examined and left upon the table.

"Well, Mr. Holmes, what do you make of these?" he cried. "They told me that you were fond of queer mysteries, and I don't think you can find a queerer one than that. I sent the paper on ahead so that you might have time to study it before I came."

"It is certainly rather a curious production," said Holmes. "At first sight it would appear to be some childish prank. It consists of a number of absurd little figures dancing across the paper upon which they are drawn. Why should you attribute any importance to so grotesque an object?"

"I never should, Mr. Holmes. But my wife does. It is frightening her to death. She says nothing, but I can see terror in her eyes. That's why I want to sift the matter to the bottom."

Holmes held up the paper so that the sunlight shone full upon it. It was a page torn from a notebook. The markings were done in pencil, and ran in this way:

🕺🕺🕺🕺🕺🕺🕺🕺🕺🕺🕺🕺🕺🕺🕺

Holmes examined it for some time, and then, folding it carefully up, he placed it in his pocket-book.

"This promises to be a most interesting and unusual case," said he. "You gave me a few particulars in your letter, Mr. Hilton Cubitt, but I should be very much obliged if you would kindly go over it all again for the benefit of my friend, Dr. Watson."

"I'm not much of a story-teller," said our visitor, nervously clasping and unclasping his great, strong hands. "You'll just ask me anything that I don't make clear. I'll begin at the time of my marriage last year; but I want to say first of all that, though I'm not a rich man, my people have been at Ridling Thorpe for a matter of five centuries, and there is no better-known family in the county of Norfolk. Last year I came up to London for the Jubilee, and I stopped at a boarding-house in **5** Russell Square, because Parker, the vicar of our parish, **6** was staying in it. There was an American young lady there—Patrick was the name—Elsie Patrick. In some way we became friends, until before my month was up I was as much in love as a man could be. We were quietly married at a registry office, and we returned to Norfolk a wedded couple. You'll think it very mad, Mr. Holmes, that a man of a good old family should marry a wife in this fashion, knowing nothing of her past or of her people; but if you saw her and knew her it would help you to understand.

"She was very straight about it, was Elsie. I can't say that she did not give me every chance of getting out of it if I wished to do so. 'I have had some very disagreeable associations in my life,' said she; 'I wish to forget all about them. I would rather never allude to the past, for it is very painful to me. If you take me, Hilton, you will take a woman who has nothing that she need be personally ashamed of; but you will have to be content with my word for it, and to allow me to be silent as to all that passed up to the time when I became yours. If these conditions are too hard, then go back to Norfolk and leave me to the lonely life in which you found me.' It was only the day before our wedding that she said those very words to me. I told her that I was content to take her on her own terms, and I have been as good as my word.

"Well, we have been married now for a year, and very happy we have been. But about a month ago, at the end of June, I saw for the first time signs of trouble. One day my wife received a letter from America. I saw the American stamp. She turned deadly white, read the letter, and threw it into the fire. She made no allusion to it afterwards, and I made none, for a promise is a

HOLMES HELD UP THE PAPER SO THAT THE SUNLIGHT SHONE FULL UPON IT.

Illustration by Sidney Paget for the *Strand Magazine*, December, 1903.

5 *Last year I came up to London for the Jubilee.* The year is therefore 1888, the year after the Golden Jubilee of 1887, or 1898, the year after the Diamond Jubilee of 1897.

6 *Russell Square.* ". . . a name which will recall to many minds the homes of the Selbys and Osbornes in Thackeray's *Vanity Fair,*" Augustus J. C. Hare wrote in *Walks in London,* Vol. II. "On its north side is a seated statue of Francis Russell, Duke of Bedford, by Westmacott. It was in No. 21 that Sir Samuel Romilly died by his own hand in 1818. In No. 66, Sir Thomas Lawrence, who had lived and painted in that house for twenty-five years, died January 7, 1830. Cossacks 'mounted on their small white horses, with their long spears grounded,' stood sentinels at its door while he was painting their general, Platoff."

". . . THERE IS NO BETTER-KNOWN FAMILY IN THE COUNTY OF NORFOLK."

"There is only one Cubitt listed in Robson's *British Heraldry,* published in 1830," Dr. Julian Wolff wrote in his *Practical Guide to Sherlockian Heraldry.* "The arms are: 'ermine a lion's head erased azure.'"

7 *it was the Tuesday of last week*—. Since Tuesday was not "a week ago" but "about a week ago," the day of Hilton Cubitt's visit to Holmes must have been a Monday or a Wednesday. But Holmes deduced that Watson had been playing billiards with Thurston at his club the night before the day of Cubitt's visit. That day was therefore not a Sunday and the day of Cubitt's visit not a Monday. We are at the end of July or early in August: the Wednesdays in that period in 1888 and 1898 are Wednesday, July 25, 1888; Wednesday, August 1, 1888; Wednesday, July 27, 1898; and Wednesday, August 3, 1898.

promise; but she has never known an easy hour from that moment. There is always a look of fear upon her face —a look as if she were waiting and expecting. She would do better to trust me. She would find that I was her best friend. But until she speaks I can say nothing. Mind you, she is a truthful woman, Mr. Holmes, and whatever trouble there may have been in her past life, it has been no fault of hers. I am only a simple Norfolk squire, but there is not a man in England who ranks his family honour more highly than I do. She knows it well, and she knew it well before she married me. She would never bring any stain upon it—of that I am sure.

"Well, now I come to the queer part of my story.

7 About a week ago—it was the Tuesday of last week—I found on one of the window-sills a number of absurd little dancing figures, like these upon the paper. They were scrawled with chalk. I thought that it was the stable-boy who had drawn them, but the lad swore he knew nothing about it. Anyhow, they had come there during the night. I had them washed out, and I only mentioned the matter to my wife afterwards. To my surprise she took it very seriously, and begged me if any more came to let her see them. None did come for a week, and then yesterday morning I found this paper lying on the sun-dial in the garden. I showed it to Elsie, and down she dropped in a dead faint. Since then she has looked like a woman in a dream, half dazed, and with terror always lurking in her eyes. It was then that I wrote and sent the paper to you, Mr. Holmes. It was not a thing that I could take to the police, for they would have laughed at me, but you will tell me what to do. I am not a rich man; but if there is any danger threatening my little woman, I would spend my last copper to shield her."

He was a fine creature, this man of the old English soil, simple, straight, and gentle, with his great, earnest blue eyes and broad, comely face. His love for his wife and his trust in her shone in his features. Holmes had listened to his story with the utmost attention, and now he sat for some time in silent thought.

"Don't you think, Mr. Cubitt," said he at last, "that your best plan would be to make a direct appeal to your wife, and to ask her to share her secret with you?"

Hilton Cubitt shook his massive head.

"A promise is a promise, Mr. Holmes. If Elsie wished to tell me, she would. If not, it is not for me to force her confidence. But I am justified in taking my own line —and I will."

"Then I will help you with all my heart. In the first place, have you heard of any strangers being seen in your neighbourhood?"

"No."

"I presume that it is a very quiet place. Any fresh face would cause comment?"

"In the immediate neighbourhood, yes. But we have several small watering-places not very far away. And the farmers take in lodgers."

"These hieroglyphics have evidently a meaning. If it is a purely arbitrary one, it may be impossible for us to solve it. If, on the other hand, it is systematic, I have no doubt that we shall get to the bottom of it. But this particular sample is so short that I can do nothing, and the facts which you have brought me are so indefinite that we have no basis for an investigation. I would suggest that you return to Norfolk, that you keep a keen look-out, and that you take an exact copy of any fresh dancing men which may appear. It is a thousand pities that we have not a reproduction of those which were done in chalk upon the window-sill. Make a discreet inquiry, also, as to any strangers in the neighbourhood. When you have collected some fresh evidence, come to me again. That is the best advice which I can give you, Mr. Hilton Cubitt. If there are any pressing fresh developments, I shall be always ready to run down and see you in your Norfolk home."

The interview left Sherlock Holmes very thoughtful, and several times in the next few days I saw him take his slip of paper from his notebook and look long and earnestly at the curious figures inscribed upon it. He made no allusion to the affair, however, until one afternoon a fortnight or so later. I was going out, when he called me back.

"You had better stay here, Watson."

"Why ? "

"Because I had a wire from Hilton Cubitt this morning—you remember Hilton Cubitt, of the dancing men ? He was to reach Liverpool Street at one-twenty. He may be here at any moment. I gather from his wire that there have been some new incidents of importance."

We had not long to wait, for our Norfolk squire came straight from the station as fast as a hansom could bring him. He was looking worried and depressed, with tired eyes and a lined forehead.

"It's getting on my nerves, this business, Mr. Holmes," said he, as he sank, like a wearied man, into an arm-chair. "It's bad enough to feel that you are surrounded by unseen, unknown folk, who have some kind of design upon you ; but when, in addition to that, you know that it is just killing your wife by inches, then it becomes as much as flesh and blood can endure. She's wearing away under it—just wearing away before my eyes."

"Has she said anything yet ? "

"No, Mr. Holmes, she has not. And yet there have been times when the poor girl has wanted to speak, and yet could not quite bring herself to take the plunge. I have tried to help her ; but I dare say I did it clumsily, and scared her off from it. She has spoken about my old family, and our reputation in the county, and our pride in our unsullied honour, and I always felt it was leading to the point ; but somehow it turned off before we got there."

"But you have found out something for yourself ? "

"A good deal, Mr. Holmes. I have several fresh dancing men pictures for you to examine, and, what is more important, I have seen the fellow."

"What—the man who draws them ? "

"Yes, I saw him at his work. But I will tell you everything in order. When I got back after my visit to you, the

8 *I saw her white face grow whiter yet in the moonlight.* On Cubitt's second visit to Holmes—"a fortnight or so" after his first visit—he says the first thing he saw on the morning of the day after his return to Norfolk—a Thursday morning, then—was another row of dancing men. "Two mornings later"—a Saturday—a fresh inscription appeared. "Three days later"—a Tuesday—a message on paper was placed upon the sundial. That night Cubitt lay in wait; "about two o'clock in the morning"—a Wednesday morning—all was dark "save for the moonlight outside" and Cubitt saw his wife's "white face grow whiter yet in the moonlight." Of the four Wednesdays under consideration, only one will serve—the morning of Wednesday, August 3, 1898: there was a full moon on the night of the 2nd–3rd, and it did not set until 4:38 A.M. The day of Cubitt's first visit to Holmes was therefore Wednesday, July 27, 1898; his second visit was on Wednesday, August 10, or a few days thereafter; "two days of impatience followed"; "on the evening of the second there came a letter from Hilton Cubitt"; Holmes went to Ridling Thorpe Manor the next morning—Saturday, August 13th, or a few days thereafter (but not on Sunday, August 14th—on the journey from town he "turned over the morning papers with anxious attention").

"... MY WIFE THREW HER ARMS ROUND ME ..."

Illustration by Sidney Paget for the *Strand Magazine*, December, 1903.

very first thing I saw next morning was a fresh crop of dancing men. They had been drawn in chalk upon the black wooden door of the tool-house, which stands beside the lawn in full view of the front windows. I took an exact copy, and here it is." He unfolded a paper and laid it upon the table. Here is a copy of the hieroglyphics :

" Excellent ! " said Holmes. " Excellent ! Pray continue."

" When I had taken the copy I rubbed out the marks ; but two mornings later a fresh inscription had appeared. I have a copy of it here " :

Holmes rubbed his hands and chuckled with delight. " Our material is rapidly accumulating," said he.

" Three days later a message was left scrawled upon paper, and placed under a pebble upon the sundial. Here it is. The characters are, as you see, exactly the same as the last one. After that I determined to lie in wait ; so I got out my revolver and I sat up in my study, which overlooks the lawn and garden. About two in the morning I was seated by the window, all being dark save for the moonlight outside, when I heard steps behind me, and there was my wife in her dressing-gown. She implored me to come to bed. I told her frankly that I wished to see who it was who played such absurd tricks upon us. She answered that it was some senseless practical joke, and that I should not take any notice of it.

" ' If it really annoys you, Hilton, we might go and travel, you and I, and so avoid this nuisance.'

" ' What, be driven out of our own house by a practical joker ? ' said I. ' Why, we should have the whole county laughing at us ! '

" ' Well, come to bed,' said she, ' and we can discuss it in the morning.'

" Suddenly, as she spoke, I saw her white face grow
8 whiter yet in the moonlight, and her hand tightened upon my shoulder. Something was moving in the shadow of the tool-house. I saw a dark, creeping figure which crawled round the corner and squatted in front of the door. Seizing my pistol I was rushing out, when my wife threw her arms round me and held me with convulsive strength. I tried to throw her off, but she clung to me most desperately. At last I got clear, but by the time I had opened the door and reached the house the creature was gone. He had left a trace of his presence, however, for there on the door was the very same arrangement of dancing men which had already twice appeared, and which I have copied on that paper. There was no other sign of the fellow anywhere, though I ran all over the grounds. And yet the amazing thing is that

he must have been there all the time, for when I examined the door again in the morning he had scrawled some more of his pictures under the line which I had already seen."

" Have you that fresh drawing ? "

" Yes ; it is very short, but I made a copy of it, and here it is."

Again he produced a paper. The new dance was in this form :

" Tell me," said Holmes—and I could see by his eyes that he was much excited—" was this a mere addition to the first, or did it appear to be entirely separate ? "

" It was on a different panel of the door."

" Excellent ! This is far the most important of all for our purpose. It fills me with hopes. Now, Mr. Hilton Cubitt, please continue your most interesting statement."

" I have nothing more to say, Mr. Holmes, except that I was angry with my wife that night for having held me back when I might have caught the skulking rascal. She said that she feared that I might come to harm. For an instant it had crossed my mind that perhaps what she really feared was that *he* might come to harm, for I could not doubt that she knew who this man was and what he meant by these strange signals. But there is a tone in my wife's voice, Mr. Holmes, and a look in her eyes which forbid doubt, and I am sure that it was indeed my own safety that was in her mind. There's the whole case, and now I want your advice as to what I ought to do. My own inclination is to put half a dozen of my farm lads in the shrubbery, and when this fellow comes again to give him such a hiding that he will leave us in peace for the future."

" I fear it is too deep a case for such simple remedies," said Holmes. " How long can you stop in London ? "

" I must go back to-day. I would not leave my wife alone at night for anything. She is very nervous and begged me to come back."

" I dare say you are right. But if you could have stopped I might possibly have been able to return with you in a day or two. Meanwhile, you will leave me these papers, and I think that it is very likely that I shall be able to pay you a visit shortly and to throw some light upon your case."

Sherlock Holmes preserved his calm professional manner until our visitor had left us, although it was easy for me, who knew him so well, to see that he was profoundly excited. The moment that Hilton Cubitt's broad back had disappeared through the door my comrade rushed to the table, laid out all the slips of paper containing dancing men in front of him, and threw himself into an intricate and elaborate calculation.

For two hours I watched him as he covered sheet after sheet of paper with figures and letters, so completely absorbed in his task that he had evidently forgotten my presence. Sometimes he was making progress, and whistled and sang at his work; sometimes he was puzzled and would sit for a long spell with a furrowed brow and a vacant eye. Finally he sprang from his chair with a cry of satisfaction, and walked up and down the room rubbing his hands together. Then he wrote a long telegram upon a cable form. "If my answer to this is as I hope, you will have a very pretty case to add to your collection, Watson," said he. "I expect that we shall be able to go down to Norfolk to-morrow, and to take our friend some very definite news as to the secret of his annoyance."

I confess that I was filled with curiosity, but I was aware that Holmes liked to make his disclosures at his own time and in his own way; so I waited until it should suit him to take me into his confidence.

But there was a delay in that answering telegram, and two days of impatience followed, during which Holmes pricked up his ears at every ring of the bell. On the evening of the second there came a letter from Hilton Cubitt. All was quiet with him, save that a long inscription had appeared that morning upon the pedestal of the sundial. He enclosed a copy of it, which is here reproduced:

Holmes bent over this grotesque frieze for some minutes and then suddenly sprang to his feet with an exclamation of surprise and dismay. His face was haggard with anxiety.

"We have let this affair go far enough," said he. "Is there a train to North Walsham to-night?"

I turned up the time-table. The last had just gone.

"Then we shall breakfast early and take the very first in the morning," said Holmes. "Our presence is most urgently needed. Ah, here is our expected cablegram. One moment, Mrs. Hudson—there may be an answer. No, that is quite as I expected. This message makes it even more essential that we should not lose an hour in letting Hilton Cubitt know how matters stand, for it is a singular and dangerous web in which our simple Norfolk squire is entangled."

So, indeed, it proved, and as I come to the dark conclusion of a story which had seemed to me to be only childish and bizarre, I experience once again the dismay and horror with which I was filled. Would that I had some brighter ending to communicate to my readers; but these are the chronicles of facts, and I must follow to their dark crisis the strange chain of events which for some days made Ridling Thorpe Manor a household word through the length and breadth of England.

We had hardly alighted at North Walsham, and mentioned the name of our destination, when the station-master hurried towards us. "I suppose that you are the detectives from London?" said he.

A look of annoyance passed over Holmes' face.

"What makes you think such a thing?"

"Because Inspector Martin from Norwich has just

"I SUPPOSE THAT YOU ARE THE DETECTIVES FROM LONDON?" SAID HE.

Illustration by Sidney Paget for the *Strand Magazine*, December, 1903.

passed through.   But maybe you are the surgeons.   She's not dead—or wasn't by last accounts.   You may be in time to save her yet—though it be for the gallows."

Holmes' brow was dark with anxiety.

" We are going to Ridling Thorpe Manor," said he, " but we have heard nothing of what has passed there."

" It's a terrible business," said the station-master. " They are shot, both Mr. Hilton Cubitt and his wife. She shot him and then herself—so the servants say. He's dead, and her life is despaired of.   Dear, dear ! one of the oldest families in the county of Norfolk, and one of the most honoured."

Without a word Holmes hurried to a carriage, and during the long seven-miles drive he never opened his mouth.   Seldom have I seen him so utterly despondent. He had been uneasy during all our journey from town, and I had observed that he had turned over the morning papers with anxious attention ; but now this sudden realization of his worst fears left him in a blank melancholy.   He leaned back in his seat, lost in gloomy speculation.   Yet there was much around us to interest us, for we were passing through as singular a countryside as any in England, where a few scattered cottages **9** represented the population of to-day, while on every hand enormous square-towered churches bristled up from the flat, green landscape and told of the glory and prosperity of old East Anglia.   At last the violet rim of the German Ocean appeared over the green edge of the Norfolk coast, and the driver pointed with his whip to two old brick-and-timber gables which projected from a grove of trees. " That's Ridling Thorpe Manor," said he.

As we drove up to the porticoed front door I observed in front of it, beside the tennis lawn, the black toolhouse and the pedestalled sundial with which we had such strange associations.   A dapper little man, with a quick, alert manner and a waxed moustache, had just descended from a high dog-cart.   He introduced himself as Inspector Martin, of the Norfolk Constabulary, and he was considerably astonished when he heard the name of my companion.

" Why, Mr. Holmes, the crime was only committed at three this morning !   How could you hear of it in London and get to the spot as soon as I ? "

" I anticipated it.   I came in the hope of preventing it."

" Then you must have important evidence of which we are ignorant, for they were said to be a most united couple."

" I have only the evidence of the dancing men," said Holmes. " I will explain the matter to you later.   Meanwhile, since it is too late to prevent this tragedy, I am very anxious that I should use the knowledge which I possess in order to ensure that justice be done.   Will you associate me in your investigation, or will you prefer that I should act independently ? "

" I should be proud to feel that we were acting together, Mr. Holmes," said the Inspector earnestly.

" In that case I should be glad to hear the evidence and to examine the premises without an instant of unnecessary delay."

9 *as singular a countryside as any in England.* Watson's description remains true today with the square-towered churches prominent on the horizon and with Norfolk farms reputed to be among the most prosperous in Great Britain. The term "German Ocean" was—before the first World War—an alternative name for the North Sea. On maps of this period "the North Sea or German Ocean" was always given.

"THAT'S RIDLING THORPE MANOR," SAID HE.

"Walcott is a small village near the North Sea and lies approximately seven miles from North Walsham, on the road to Happisburgh," Miss Shirley Sanderson wrote in "Another Case of Identity." "If Holmes and Watson approached Walcott via Keswick, 'the violet rim of the German Ocean' would be very apparent. Two or three miles south of Walcott lies East Ruston, where the villain, Mr. Abe Slaney, lived at Elrige's Farm (as yet unidentified by us). The main house in the village is Walcott House, owned by a Miss Wenn . . ."

Inspector Martin had the good sense to allow my friend to do things in his own fashion, and contented himself with carefully noting the results. The local surgeon, an old, white-haired man, had just come down from Mrs. Hilton Cubitt's room, and he reported that her injuries were serious, but not necessarily fatal. The bullet had passed through the front of her brain, and it would probably be some time before she could regain consciousness. On the question of whether she had been shot or had shot herself he would not venture to express any decided opinion. Certainly the bullet had been discharged at very close quarters. There was only the one pistol found in the room, two barrels of which had been emptied. Mr. Hilton Cubitt had been shot through the heart. It was equally conceivable that he had shot her and then himself, or that she had been the criminal, for the revolver lay upon the floor midway between them.

" Has he been moved ? " asked Holmes.

" We have moved nothing except the lady. We could not leave her lying wounded upon the floor."

" How long have you been here, doctor ? "

" Since four o'clock."

" Anyone else ? "

" Yes, the constable here."

" And you have touched nothing ? "

" Nothing."

" You have acted with great discretion. Who sent for you ? "

" The housemaid, Saunders."

" Was it she who gave the alarm ? "

" She and Mrs. King, the cook."

" Where are they now ? "

" In the kitchen, I believe."

" Then I think we had better hear their story at once."

The old hall, oak-panelled and high-windowed, had been turned into a court of investigation. Holmes sat in a great, old-fashioned chair, his inexorable eyes gleaming out of his haggard face. I could read in them a set purpose to devote his life to this quest until the client whom he had failed to save should at last be avenged. The trim Inspector Martin, the old grey-bearded country doctor, myself, and a stolid village policeman made up the rest of that strange company.

The two women told their story clearly enough. They had been aroused from their sleep by the sound of an explosion, which had been followed a minute later by a second one. They slept in adjoining rooms, and Mrs. King had rushed in to Saunders. Together they had descended the stairs. The door of the study was open and a candle was burning upon the table. Their master lay upon his face in the centre of the room. He was quite dead. Near the window his wife was crouching, her head leaning against the wall. She was horribly wounded, and the side of the face was red with blood. She breathed heavily, but was incapable of saying anything. The passage, as well as the room, was full of smoke and the smell of powder. The window was certainly shut and fastened upon the inside. Both women were positive upon the point. They had at once sent for the doctor and for the constable. Then, with the aid of the groom and the stable-boy, they had conveyed their injured mistress to her room. Both she and her husband had occupied the bed. She was clad in her dress—he in his dressing-gown, over his night-clothes. Nothing had been moved in the study. So far as they knew, there had never been any quarrel between husband and wife. They had always looked upon them as a very united couple.

These were the main points of the servants' evidence. In answer to Inspector Martin they were clear that every door was fastened upon the inside and that no one could have escaped from the house. In answer to Holmes, they both remembered that they were conscious of the smell of powder from the moment that they ran out of their rooms upon the top floor. " I commend that fact very carefully to your attention," said Holmes to his professional colleague. " And now I think that we are in a position to undertake a thorough examination of the room."

The study proved to be a small chamber, lined on three sides with books, and with a writing-table facing an ordinary window, which looked out upon the garden. Our first attention was given to the body of the unfortunate squire, whose huge frame lay stretched across the room. His disordered dress showed that he had been hastily aroused from sleep. The bullet had been fired at him from the front, and had remained in his body after penetrating the heart. His death had certainly been instantaneous and painless. There was no powder-marking either upon his dressing-gown or on his hands. According to the country surgeon, the lady had stains upon her face, but none upon her hand.

" The absence of the latter means nothing, though its presence may mean everything," said Holmes. " Unless the powder from a badly fitting cartridge happens to spurt backwards, one may fire many shots without leaving a sign. I would suggest that Mr. Cubitt's body may now be removed. I suppose, doctor, you have not recovered the bullet which wounded the lady ? "

" A serious operation will be necessary before that can be done. But there are still four cartridges in the revolver. Two have been fired and two wounds inflicted, so that each bullet can be accounted for."

" So it would seem," said Holmes. " Perhaps you can account also for the bullet which has so obviously struck the edge of the window ? "

He had turned suddenly, and his long, thin finger was pointing to a hole which had been drilled right through the lower window-sash about an inch above the bottom.

" By George ! " cried the Inspector. " How ever did you see that ? "

" Because I looked for it."

" Wonderful ! " said the country doctor. " You are certainly right, sir. Then a third shot has been fired, and therefore a third person must have been present. But who could that have been, and how could he have got away ? "

. . . THEY BOTH REMEMBERED THAT THEY WERE
CONSCIOUS OF THE SMELL OF POWDER . . .

Illustration by Sidney Paget for the *Strand Magazine*, December, 1903.

OUR FIRST ATTENTION WAS GIVEN TO THE BODY OF THE
UNFORTUNATE SQUIRE . . .

Illustration by Frederic Dorr Steele for *Collier's Magazine*, December 5, 1903.

"That is the problem which we are now about to solve," said Sherlock Holmes. "You remember, Inspector Martin, when the servants said that on leaving their room they were at once conscious of a smell of powder, I remarked that the point was an extremely important one?"

"Yes, sir; but I confess I did not quite follow you."

"It suggested that at the time of the firing the window as well as the door of the room had been open. Otherwise the fumes of powder could not have been blown so rapidly through the house. A draught in the room was necessary for that. Both door and window were only open for a short time, however."

"How do you prove that?"

"Because the candle has not gutted."

"Capital!" cried the Inspector. "Capital!"

"Feeling sure that the window had been open at the time of the tragedy, I conceived that there might have been a third person in the affair, who stood outside this opening and fired through it. Any shot directed at this person might hit the sash. I looked, and there, sure enough, was the bullet mark!"

"But how came the window to be shut and fastened?"

"The woman's first instinct would be to shut and fasten the window. But, halloa! what is this?"

It was a lady's hand-bag which stood upon the study table—a trim little hand-bag of crocodile-skin and silver. Holmes opened it and turned the contents out. There were twenty fifty-pound notes of the Bank of England, held together by an india-rubber band—nothing else.

"This must be preserved, for it will figure in the trial," said Holmes, as he handed the bag with its contents to the Inspector. "It is now necessary that we should try to throw some light upon this third bullet, which has clearly, from the splintering of the wood, been fired from inside the room. I should like to see Mrs. King, the cook, again. . . . You said, Mrs. King, that you were awakened by a *loud* explosion. When you said that, did you mean that it seemed to you to be louder than the second one?"

"Well, sir, it wakened me from my sleep, and so it is hard to judge. But it did seem very loud."

"You don't think that it might have been two shots fired almost at the same instant?"

"I am sure I couldn't say, sir."

"I believe that it was undoubtedly so. I rather think, Inspector Martin, that we have now exhausted all that this room can teach us. If you will kindly step round with me we shall see what fresh evidence the garden has to offer."

A flower-bed extended up to the study window, and we all broke into an exclamation as we approached it. The flowers were trampled down, and the soft soil was imprinted all over with footmarks. Large, masculine feet they were, with peculiarly long, sharp toes. Holmes hunted about among the grass and leaves like a retriever after a wounded bird. Then, with a cry of satisfaction, bent forward and picked up a little brazen cylinder.

. . . HE BENT FORWARD AND PICKED UP A LITTLE BRAZEN CYLINDER.

Illustration by Sidney Paget for the *Strand Magazine*, December, 1903.

" I thought so," said he; " the revolver had an ejector, and here is the third cartridge. I really think, Inspector Martin, that our case is almost complete."

The country inspector's face had shown his intense amazement at the rapid and masterful progress of Holmes' investigations. At first he had shown some disposition to assert his own position; but now he was overcome with admiration, and ready to follow without question wherever Holmes led.

" Whom do you suspect? " he asked.

" I'll go into that later. There are several points in this problem which I have not been able to explain to you yet. Now that I have got so far I had best proceed on my own lines, and then clear the whole matter up once and for all."

" Just as you wish, Mr. Holmes, so long as we get our man."

" I have no desire to make mysteries, but it is impossible at the moment of action to enter into long and complex explanations. I have the threads of this affair all in my hand. Even if this lady should never recover consciousness we can still reconstruct the events of last night and ensure that justice be done. First of all I wish to know whether there is any inn in this neighbourhood known as ' Elrige's ' ? "

The servants were cross-questioned, but none of them had heard of such a place. The stable-boy threw a light upon the matter by remembering that a farmer of that name lived miles off in the direction of East Rust

" Is it a lonely farm? "

" Very lonely, sir."

" Perhaps they have not heard yet of all that happened here during the night? "

" Maybe not, sir."

Holmes thought for a little, and then a curious smile played over his face.

" Saddle a horse, my lad," said he. " I shall wish you to take a note to Elrige's Farm."

He took from his pocket the various slips of the dancing men. With these in front of him he worked for some time at the study table. Finally he handed a note to the boy, with directions to put it into the hands of the person to whom it was addressed, and especially to answer no questions of any sort which might be put to him. I saw the outside of the note, addressed in straggling, irregular characters, very unlike Holmes' usual precise hand. It was consigned to Mr. Abe Slaney, Elrige's Farm, East Ruston, Norfolk.

" I think, Inspector," Holmes remarked, " that you would do well to telegraph for an escort, as, if my calculations prove to be correct, you may have a particularly dangerous prisoner to convey to the county gaol. The boy who takes this note could no doubt forward your telegram. If there is an afternoon train to town, Watson, I think we should do well to take it, as I have a chemical analysis of some interest to finish, and this investigation draws rapidly to a close."

When the youth had been despatched with the note, Sherlock Holmes gave his instructions to the servants.

10 *a trifling monograph upon the subject.*
Holmes' "little collection on ciphers and secret writings . . . undoubtedly included two fine seventeenth-century works: Falconer's *Cryptomenysis Patefacta* (London, 1685), on such pertinent subjects as deciphering secret writings, Bacon's cipher and the systems used by the Turks, as well as that ingenious volume on cryptography, John Wilkins' *Mercury* (London, 1694)," Miss Madeleine B. Stern wrote in "Sherlock Holmes: Rare Book Collector." "Eighteenth-century researches in the field were represented among the Holmes sources by John Lockington's edition of Bowle's *New and Complete Book of Cyphers* (1795), illustrated with plates of ciphers. Holmes' shelf undoubtedly also contained the study of Thomas Young, who deciphered the Rosetta Stone: *An Account of some Recent Discoveries in Hieroglyphical Literature* (London, 1823) as well as Champollion's *Précis du Système Hiéroglyphique des Anciens Égyptiens* (Paris, 1828), with its useful plates of hieroglyphic alphabets."

11 *I confess that this is entirely new to me.*
Holmes of course meant that the symbols of the Dancing Men were new to him, not the cipher system itself, which is simple substitution.

"The fact that a code of such transparent simplicity baffled the Master for a time has long been a matter of wonder," Mr. Ed S. Woodhead wrote in "In Defense of Dr. Watson." "Is it not obvious that he suppressed the true code as too abstruse, substituting a type which would baffle the reader of his day but would not require a treatise to explain it?"

The late Fletcher Pratt was in complete agreement with this view: "We are driven almost irresistibly to the conclusion that the cipher in the printed account was no more the one actually used than Upper Swandam Lane was actually named Upper Swandam Lane," he wrote in "The Secret Message of the Dancing Men." "The internal evidence points to the same conclusion. If the cipher of the dancing men is far too simple for practical use, with its single unvarying character for each letter, it is also far too complex for simple substitution cipher. It offers too many opportunities for variation of which no advantage has been taken. Let us consider the little mannikins in detail. . . . When we combine the various leg possibilities with the various arm possibilities the result is represented by the multiplication of the possible arm and leg types and we obtain the astonishing figure of 784 possible little dancing men to be made with the elements shown in those few messages. But this is not all: D, G and T show the little figures standing on their heads, and T is simply an E in reverse. Obviously the meaning of any one of the 784 characters can be changed by turning it upside down, which doubles the total, giving 1,568 characters. . . . The discovered messages in the Great Cipher [compiled by Rossignol in the reign of Louis XIV] show a total of 587

If any visitor were to call asking for Mrs. Hilton Cubitt no information should be given as to her condition, but he was to be shown at once into the drawing-room. He impressed these points upon them with the utmost earnestness. Finally he led the way into the drawing-room, with the remark that the business was now out of our hands, and that we must while away the time as best we might until we could see what was in store for us. The doctor had departed to his patients, and only the Inspector and myself remained.

"I think I can help you to pass an hour in an interesting and profitable manner," said Holmes, drawing his chair up to the table and spreading out in front of him the various papers upon which were recorded the antics of the dancing men. "As to you, friend Watson, I owe you every atonement for having allowed your natural curiosity to remain so long unsatisfied. To you, Inspector, the whole incident may appeal as a remarkable professional study. I must tell you first of all the interesting circumstances connected with the previous consultations which Mr. Hilton Cubitt has had with me in Baker Street." He then shortly recapitulated the facts which have already been recorded.

"I have here in front of me these singular productions, at which one might smile had they not proved themselves to be the forerunners of so terrible a tragedy. I am fairly familiar with all forms of secret writings, and am myself
10 the author of a trifling monograph upon the subject, in which I analyse one hundred and sixty separate ciphers;
11 but I confess that this is entirely new to me. The object of those who invented the system has apparently been to conceal that these characters convey a message, and to give the idea that they are the mere random sketches of children.

"Having once recognized, however, that the symbols stood for letters, and having applied the rules which guide us in all forms of secret writings, the solution was easy enough. The first message submitted to me was so short that it was impossible for me to do more than to say with some confidence that the symbol   stood for E. As you are aware, E is the most   common letter in the English alphabet and it   predominates to so marked an extent that even in a short sentence one would expect to find it most often. Out of fifteen symbols in the first message four were the same, so it was reasonable to set this down as E. It is true that in some cases the figure was bearing a flag, and in some cases not, but it was probable from the way in which the flags were distributed that they were used to break the sentence up into words. I accepted this as an hypothesis, and noted that E was represented by
"But now came the real difficulty of the inquiry. The order of the English letters after E is by no means well-marked, and any preponderance which may be shown in an average of a printed sheet may be reversed in a single short sentence. Speaking roughly, T, A, O, I, N, S, H, R, D, and L are the numerical
12 order in which letters occur; but T, A, O, and I are very nearly abreast of each other, and it would be an endless task to try each combination until a meaning was

arrived at. I, therefore, waited for fresh material. In my second interview with Mr. Hilton Cubitt he was able to give me two other short sentences and one message, which appeared—since there was no flag—to be a single word. Here are the symbols. Now, in the single word I have already got the two E's coming second and fourth in a word of five letters. It might be 'sever,' or 'lever,' or 'never.' There can be no question that the latter as a **13** reply to an appeal is far the most probable, and the circumstances pointed to its being a reply written by the lady. Accepting it as correct, we are now able to say that the symbols   stand respectively for N, V, and R.   **14**

"Even now I was in considerable difficulty, but a happy thought put me in possession of several other letters. It occurred to me that if these appeals came, as I expected, from someone who had been intimate with the lady in her early life, a combination which contained two E's with three letters between might very well stand for the name 'ELSIE.' On examination I found that such a combination formed the termination of the message which was three times repeated. It was certainly some appeal to 'Elsie.' In this way I had got my L, S, and I. But what appeal could it be? There were only four letters in the word which preceded 'Elsie,' and it ended in E. Surely the word must be 'COME.' I tried all other four letters ending in E, but could find none to fit the case. So now I was in possession of C, O, and M, and I was in a position to attack the first message once more, dividing it into words and putting dots for each symbol which was still unknown. So treated it worked out in this fashion :

.M .ERE ..E SL.NE .

"Now, the first letter can only be A, which is a most useful discovery, since it occurs no fewer than three times in this short sentence, and the H is also apparent in the second word. Now it becomes :

AM HERE A.E SLANE.

Or, filling in the obvious vacancies in the name :

AM HERE ABE SLANEY.

I had so many letters now that I could proceed with considerable confidence to the second message, which worked out in this fashion :

A.ELRI.ES.

Here I could only make sense by putting T and G for the missing letters, and supposing that the name was that of some house or inn at which the writer was staying."

Inspector Martin and I had listened with the utmost interest to the full and clear account of how my friend had produced results which had led to so complete a command over our difficulties.

"What did you do then, sir?" asked the Inspector.

"I had every reason to suppose that this Abe Slaney was an American, since Abe is an American contraction, and since a letter from America had been the starting-

different characters; but not all the possible characters are used, and when the permutations and combinations were studied by Bazéries he reported that the possible total of characters was exactly *1,568.* The long arm of coincidence would have to stretch itself right out of joint to cover such a set of figures if it were accidental. We have good reason to believe that it was not accidental; that with the connivance of Holmes, Watson deliberately eliminated from the record the cipher used by Abe Slaney (probably . . . a root cipher or a variant on the Vigenère tableau) and inserted in its place this other."

12 *Speaking roughly, T, A, O, I, N, S, H, R, D, and L are the numerical order in which letters occur.* The order of frequency of single letters in English is given as follows by Mr. Laurence Dwight Smith in his fascinating little book *Cryptography: The Science of Secret Writing,* New York: Dover Publications, Inc., 1955: E T O A N I : R S H : D L : C W U M : F Y G P B : V K : X Q J Z. The table of frequency in normal *literary* text and in normal *telegraphic* text appears as follows in Miss Eugenia Williams' *An Invitation to Cryptograms;* New York: Simon and Schuster, 1959:

Literary: E T A O I N S R H L D C U M F W G Y P B V K X J Q Z

Telegraphic: E O A N I R S T D L H U C M P Y F G W B V K X J Q Z

13 *It might be 'sever,' or 'lever,' or 'never.'* "This dictum implies that the five-letter word *must* be one of these alternatives," Mr. Colin Prestige wrote in "Agents of Evil." "Never! A simple mental exercise reveals more than 30 alternatives, some possible and some improbable."

14 *stand respectively for N, V, and R.* But the symbol used for V in message No. IV is the same as that used for P in message No. V in all the texts which your editor has examined, including the original publication in the *Strand Magazine.* In some texts, in addition, the symbol used for C in message No. VI is the same as that used for M throughout, and different from that used for C in Message No. III. We may note here that a number of Sherlockian scholars have amused themselves by devising complete alphabets in the "Dancing Men" cipher.

15 *the New York Police Bureau.* "This was Watson's error; it was even then the New York Police *Department*," the late Fletcher Pratt wrote in "The Secret Message of the Dancing Men."

point of all the trouble. I had also every cause to think that there was some criminal secret in the matter. The lady's allusions to her past and her refusal to take her husband into her confidence both pointed in that direction. I therefore cabled to my friend, Wilson Hargreave, of the New York Police Bureau, who has more than once made use of my knowledge of London crime. I asked him whether the name of Abe Slaney was known to him. Here is his reply: ' The most dangerous crook in Chicago.' On the very evening upon which I had his answer Hilton Cubitt sent me the last message from Slaney. Working with known letters it took this form:

ELSIE . RE . ARE TO MEET THY GO .

The addition of a P and a D completed a message which showed me that the rascal was proceeding from persuasion to threats, and my knowledge of the crooks of Chicago prepared me to find that he might very rapidly put his words into action. I at once came to Norfolk with my friend and colleague, Dr. Watson, but, unhappily, only in time to find that the worst had already occurred."

" It is a privilege to be associated with you in the handling of a case," said the Inspector warmly. " You will excuse me, however, if I speak frankly to you. You are only answerable to yourself, but I have to answer to my superiors. If this Abe Slaney, living at Elrige's, is indeed the murderer, and if he has made his escape while I am seated here, I should certainly get into serious trouble."

" You need not be uneasy. He will not try to escape."

" How do you know ? "

" To fly would be a confession of guilt."

" Then let us go to arrest him."

" I expect him here every instant."

" But why should he come ? "

" Because I have written and asked him."

" But this is incredible, Mr. Holmes ! Why should he come because you have asked him ? Would not such a request rather rouse his suspicions and cause him to fly ? "

" I think I have known how to frame the letter," said Sherlock Holmes. " In fact, if I am not very much mistaken, here is the gentleman himself coming up the drive."

A man was striding up the path which led to the door. He was a tall, handsome, swarthy fellow, clad in a suit of grey flannel, with a Panama hat, a bristling black beard, and a great, aggressive, hooked nose, and flourishing a cane as he walked. He swaggered up the path as if the place belonged to him, and we heard his loud, confident peal at the bell.

" I think, gentlemen," said Holmes quietly, " that we had best take up our position behind the door. Every precaution is necessary when dealing with such a fellow. You will need your handcuffs, Inspector. You can leave the talking to me."

We waited in silence for a minute—one of those minutes which one can never forget. Then the door opened, and the man stepped in. In an instant Holmes clapped a pistol to his head, and Martin slipped the handcuffs over his wrists. It was all done so swiftly and deftly that the fellow was helpless before he knew that he was attacked.

IN AN INSTANT HOLMES CLAPPED A PISTOL
TO HIS HEAD . . .

Illustration by Sidney Paget for the *Strand Magazine*, December, 1903.

He glared from one to the other of us with a pair of blazing black eyes. Then he burst into a bitter laugh.

"Well, gentlemen, you have the drop on me this time. I seem to have knocked up against something hard. But I came here in answer to a letter from Mrs. Hilton Cubitt. Don't tell me that she is in this? Don't tell me that she helped to set a trap for me?"

"Mrs. Hilton Cubitt was seriously injured, and is at death's door."

The man gave a hoarse cry of grief which rang through the house.

"You're crazy!" he cried fiercely. "It was he that was hurt, not she. Who would have hurt little Elsie? I may have threatened her, God forgive me, but I would not have touched a hair of her pretty head. Take it back—you! Say that she is not hurt!"

"She was found badly wounded by the side of her dead husband."

He sank with a deep groan on to the settee, and buried his face in his manacled hands. For five minutes he was silent. Then he raised his face once more, and spoke with the cold composure of despair.

"I have nothing to hide from you, gentlemen," said he. "If I shot the man he had his shot at me, and there's no murder in that. But if you think I could have hurt that woman, then you don't know either me or her. I tell you there was never a man in this world loved a woman more than I loved her. I had a right to her. She was pledged to me years ago. Who was this Englishman that he should come between us? I tell you that I had the first right to her, and that I was only claiming my own."

"She broke away from your influence when she found the man that you are," said Holmes sternly. "She fled from America to avoid you, and she married an honourable gentleman in England. You dogged her and followed her, and made her life a misery to her in order to induce her to abandon the husband whom she loved and respected in order to fly with you, whom she feared and hated. You have ended by bringing about the death of a noble man and driving his wife to suicide. That is your record in this business, Mr. Abe Slaney, and you will answer for it to the law."

"If Elsie dies I care nothing what becomes of me," said the American. He opened one of his hands and looked at a note crumpled up in his palm. "See here, mister," he cried, with a gleam of suspicion in his eyes, "you're not trying to scare me over this, are you? If the lady is hurt as bad as you say, who was it that wrote this note?" He tossed it forward on to the table.

"I wrote it to bring you here."

"You wrote it? There was no one on earth outside the Joint who knew the secret of the dancing men. How came you to write it?"

"What one man can invent another can discover," said Holmes. "There is a cab coming to convey you to Norwich, Mr. Slaney. But, meanwhile, you have time to make some small reparation for the injury you have wrought. Are you aware that Mrs. Hilton Cubitt has herself lain under grave suspicion of the murder of her

HE SANK WITH A DEEP GROAN ON TO THE SETTEE, AND BURIED HIS FACE IN HIS MANACLED HANDS.

Illustration by Sidney Paget for the *Strand Magazine*, December, 1903.

16 *It was he who invented that writing.* In the year 1903, Sir Arthur Conan Doyle stayed briefly at Hill House Hotel at Happisburgh, near Norwich. Asked to sign an autograph book, he saw in it a signature and address written in "dancing men" by G. J. Cubitt, the proprietor's son, then about seven. Conan Doyle then and there set to work upon "The Adventure of the Dancing Men," using not only the cipher but the name Cubitt for the central character in his tale. Neither Mr. Cubitt nor Sir Arthur ever claimed to have *invented* the cipher, and it is certainly possible, as some commentators have claimed, that it originated with the "Restless Imps" which appeared in *St. Nicholas Magazine* for June, 1874. On the other hand, the late Professor Jay Finley Christ demonstrated ("The Dancing Men") that "there is only one instance in which even approximately similar characters are used in the two alphabets." A cipher very similar to *St. Nicholas'* "Restless Imps" is also said to have appeared in the *Boy's Own Paper* in 1881 as "The Restless Fays." It is interesting to note that Conan Doyle contributed at least two stories to the *Boy's Own Paper:* "The Fate of the *Evangeline*" appeared in the Christmas number for 1885 and "The Stone of Boxman's Drift" somewhat later on. The late William Swift Dalliba found still another possible source of the "dancing men" in the book *Secret Missions of the Civil War*, by Philip Van Doren Stern, New York: Bonanza Books, 1959: "Major Alfred J. Meyer, Signal Corps of the Union Army . . . wrote a book, *A Manual of Signals*, in 1864. In this second edition, 1866, he described various methods of transferring letters of the alphabet into signals that can be sent by flags, etc. Then in order to show that practically anything can be used to convey a secret message, he printed a pictograph based on what he calls 'ludicrous sketches of little figures of men.' A similar device was used by Conan Doyle in his Sherlock Holmes story 'The Adventure of the Dancing Men'; Doyle is said to have gotten the idea for his grotesque cipher from the Carbonari, an early nineteenth-century Italian secret society, but he may very well have seen Meyer's book." To add to the confusion, Professor Christ also noted similarities between the Dancing Men cipher and a tree alphabet and "Alphabet of Hermes" illustrated in Albert Mackey's *Encyclopedia of Freemasonry* (1874).

husband, and that it was only my presence here and the knowledge which I happened to possess which has saved her from the accusation ? The least that you owe her is to make it clear to the whole world that she was in no way directly or indirectly responsible for his tragic end."

" I ask nothing better," said the American. " I guess the very best case I can make for myself is the absolute naked truth."

" It is my duty to warn you that it will be used against you," cried the Inspector, with the magnificent fair-play of the British criminal law.

Slaney shrugged his shoulders.

" I'll chance that," said he. " First of all, I want you gentlemen to understand that I have known this lady since she was a child. There were seven of us in a gang in Chicago, and Elsie's father was the boss of the Joint. He was a clever man, was old Patrick. It was he who **16** invented that writing, which would pass as a child's scrawl unless you just happened to have the key to it. Well, Elsie learned some of our ways ; but she couldn't stand the business, and she had a bit of honest money of her own, so she gave us all the slip and got away to London. She had been engaged to me, and she would have married me, I believe, if I had taken over another profession ; but she would have nothing to do with anything on the cross. It was only after her marriage to this Englishman that I was able to find out where she was. I wrote to her, but got no answer. After that I came over, and, as letters were of no use, I put my messages where she could read them.

" Well, I have been here a month now. I lived in that farm, where I had a room down below, and could get in and out every night, and no one the wiser. I tried all I could to coax Elsie away. I knew that she read the messages, for once she wrote an answer under one of them. Then my temper got the better of me, and I began to threaten her. She sent me a letter then, imploring me to go away, and saying that it would break her heart if any scandal should come upon her husband. She said that she would come down when her husband was asleep at three in the morning, and speak with me through the end window, if I would go away afterwards and leave her in peace. She came down and brought money with her, trying to bribe me to go. This made me mad, and I caught her arm and tried to pull her through the window. At that moment in rushed the husband with his revolver in his hand. Elsie had sunk down upon the floor, and we were face to face. I was heeled also, and I held up my gun to scare him off and let me get away. He fired and missed me. I pulled off almost at the same instant, and down he dropped. I made away across the garden, and as I went I heard the window shut behind me. That's God's truth, gentlemen, every word of it, and I heard no more about it until that lad came riding up with a note which made me walk in here, like a jay, and give myself into your hands."

A cab had driven up whilst the American had been talking. Two uniformed policemen sat inside. Inspector Martin rose and touched his prisoner on the shoulder.

" It is time for us to go."

" Can I see her first ? "

" No, she is not conscious. Mr. Sherlock Holmes, I only hope that if ever again I have an important case I shall have the good fortune to have you by my side."

We stood at the window and watched the cab drive away. As I turned back my eye caught the pellet of paper which the prisoner had tossed upon the table. It was the note with which Holmes had decoyed him.

" See if you can read it, Watson," said he, with a smile.

It contained no word, but this little line of dancing men :

" If you use the code which I have explained," said Holmes, " you will find that it simply means ' Come here at once.' I was convinced that it was an invitation which he would not refuse, since he could never imagine that it could come from anyone but the lady. And so, my dear Watson, we have ended by turning the dancing men to good when they have so often been the agents of evil, and I think that I have fulfilled my promise of giving you something unusual for your notebook. Three-forty is our train, and I fancy we should be back in **17** Baker Street for dinner."

Only one word of epilogue.

The American, Abe Slaney, was condemned to death at the winter assizes at Norwich ; but his penalty was changed to penal servitude in consideration of mitigating circumstances, and the certainty that Hilton Cubitt had fired the first shot.

Of Mrs. Hilton Cubitt I only know that I have heard she recovered entirely, and that she still remains a widow, devoting her whole life to the care of the poor and to the administration of her husband's estate.

17 *Three-forty is our train.* There unhappily was no such train—nor was there the earlier "one-twenty" to Liverpool Street.

Auctorial and Bibliographical Note: Conan Doyle placed "The Adventure of the Dancing Men" high on his "twelve best" list—he rated it No. 3. The original manuscript, donated by Sir Arthur to a Red Cross Charity Sale, was auctioned in London on April 22, 1918, bringing £10 10s. It was auctioned again in New York City on February 13, 1923, bringing $105, and again in London on January 28, 1925, where it was sold in one lot with "The Adventure of the Priory School" and "The Adventure of the Solitary Cyclist" for £66. Its present location is unknown.

62

THE ADVENTURE OF THE RETIRED COLOURMAN

[Thursday, July 28, to Saturday, July 30, 1898]

1 *Or worse than a shadow—misery.*" "These depressing reflections are not typical of Holmes, although the tragic might move him to philosophic melancholy, as we see in the Boscombe Valley case, and over the wretched story of Browner in 'The Cardboard Box,'" Mr. T. S. Blakeney wrote in *Sherlock Holmes: Fact or Fiction?*

2 *Lewisham.* An extensive metropolitan borough of London, now the third largest borough in area of the County of London. A century ago it was an attractive village, with a branch of the River Ravensbourne running alongside its main street. With the land rising gently on either side of the stream, it was then a very pleasant rural district.

3 *And yet within two years.* The year of the adventure, then, is 1898.

SHERLOCK HOLMES was in a melancholy and philosophic mood that morning. His alert practical nature was subject to such reactions.

" Did you see him ? " he asked.

" You mean the old fellow who has just gone out ? "

" Precisely."

" Yes, I met him at the door."

" What did you think of him ? "

" A pathetic, futile, broken creature."

" Exactly, Watson. Pathetic and futile. But is not all life pathetic and futile ? Is not his story a microcosm of the whole ? We reach. We grasp. And what is left in our hands at the end ? A shadow. Or worse than a **1** shadow—misery."

" Is he one of your clients ? "

" Well, I suppose I may call him so. He has been sent on by the Yard. Just as medical men occasionally send their incurables to a quack. They argue that they can do nothing more, and that whatever happens the patient can be no worse than he is."

" What is the matter ? "

Holmes took a rather soiled card from the table. " Josiah Amberley. He says he was junior partner of Brickfall & Amberley, who are manufacturers of artistic materials. You will see their names upon paint-boxes. He made his little pile, retired from business at the age **2** of sixty-one, bought a house at Lewisham, and settled down to rest after a life of ceaseless grind. One would think his future was tolerably assured."

" Yes, indeed."

Holmes glanced over some notes which he had scribbled upon the back of an envelope.

" Retired in 1896, Watson. Early in 1897 he married a woman twenty years younger than himself—a good-looking woman, too, if the photograph does not flatter. A competence, a wife, leisure—it seemed a straight road **3** which lay before him. And yet within two years he is, as you have seen, as broken and miserable a creature as crawls beneath the sun."

" But what has happened ? "

" The old story, Watson. A treacherous friend and a fickle wife. It would appear that Amberley has one hobby in life, and it is chess. Not far from him at Lewisham there lives a young doctor who is also a chess-player. I have noted his name as Dr. Ray Ernest. Ernest was frequently in the house, and an intimacy between him and Mrs. Amberley was a natural sequence, for you must admit that our unfortunate client has few outward graces, whatever his inner virtues may be. The couple went off together last week—destination untraced. What is more, the faithless spouse carried off the old man's deed-box as her personal luggage with a good part of his life's savings within. Can we find the lady? Can we save the money? A commonplace problem so far as it has developed, and yet a vital one for Josiah Amberley."

"What will you do about it?"

"Well, the immediate question, my dear Watson, happens to be, What will *you* do?—if you will be good enough to understudy me. You know that I am pre-occupied with this case of the two Coptic Patriarchs, **4** which should come to a head to-day. I really have not time to go out to Lewisham, and yet evidence taken on the spot has a special value. The old fellow was quite insistent that I should go, but I explained my difficulty. He is prepared to meet a representative."

"By all means," I answered. "I confess I don't see that I can be of much service, but I am willing to do my best." And so it was that on a summer afternoon I set forth to Lewisham, little dreaming that within a week the affair in which I was engaging would be the eager debate of all England.

It was late that evening before I returned to Baker Street and gave an account of my mission. Holmes lay with his gaunt figure stretched in his deep chair, his pipe curling forth slow wreaths of acrid tobacco, while his eyelids drooped over his eyes so lazily that he might almost have been asleep were it not that at any halt or questionable passage of my narrative they half lifted, and two grey eyes, as bright and keen as rapiers, transfixed me with their searching glance.

"The Haven is the name of Mr. Josiah Amberley's house," I explained. "I think it would interest you, Holmes. It is like some penurious patrician who has sunk into the company of his inferiors. You know that particular quarter, the monotonous brick streets, the weary suburban highways. Right in the middle of them, a little island of ancient culture and comfort, lies this old home, surrounded by a high sun-baked wall mottled with lichens and topped with moss, the sort of wall——"

"Cut out the poetry, Watson," said Holmes severely. "I note that it was a high brick wall."

"Exactly. I should not have known which was The Haven had I not asked a lounger who was smoking in the street. I have a reason for mentioning him. He was a tall, dark, heavily-moustached, rather military-looking man. He nodded in answer to my inquiry and gave me a curiously questioning glance, which came back to my memory a little later.

"I had hardly entered the gateway before I saw Mr. Amberley coming down the drive. I only had a glimpse

4 *this case of the two Coptic Patriarchs*. "Patriarchs of the Coptic Church must by rule and tradition be plain, hard-working monks, chosen from the desert monasteries," Mr. John A. Wilson noted in a pastiche stemming from this reference of Holmes' ("The Case of the Two Coptic Patriarchs," The *Baker Street Journal*, Vol. IV, No. 1, Old Series, January, 1949, pp. 74–85).

"CUT OUT THE POETRY, WATSON,"
SAID HOLMES SEVERELY.

Illustration by Frank Wiles for the *Strand Magazine*, January, 1927.

5 *the Haymarket Theatre.* Opened December, 1720, the Haymarket Theatre stood on the right of the Haymarket, the street so called from the market for hay and straw which was held there in the reign of Elizabeth I, and was not finally abolished until 1830. Addison lived in the Haymarket, and wrote his *Campaign* there; certainly Holmes' records of crime would have included an account of the murder, at the foot of the Haymarket, of Thomas Thynne of Longleat on Sunday, February 12, 1681; the villain in the case was Count Königsmarck, who hoped, when Thynne was out of the way, to ingratiate himself with his affianced bride, the rich, young Lady Elizabeth Percy, already, in her sixteenth year, the widow of Lord Ogle.

The late H. W. Bell noted that the Haymarket Theatre, in the summer of 1898, was playing Sir James M. Barrie's *The Little Minister. But the play closed on Friday, July 22nd.* The "sun-baked wall" around Amberley's house, the "garden . . . all running to seed" point to late July; almost certainly, Amberley must have purchased his seats for a night in the closing week of the play, Monday, July 18th, to Friday, July 22nd. Mrs. Amberley and her lover "disappeared" on the night for which the tickets were purchased—and Holmes tells us that "The couple went off together last week." The case began, then, on a day in the week of Monday, July 25, to Saturday, July 30, 1898. It occupied three days—none of which would seem to have been a Sunday: 1) On the evening of the first day, Holmes invited Watson to hear Carina sing at the Albert Hall—an event which would not have taken place on a Sunday in the 1890's. 2) On the second day, Watson and Amberley paid a call on Vicar Elman, something Holmes would not have suggested their doing on a Sunday. 3) On the third day, Watson asked Amberley to "take Baker Street as we pass . . . Mr. Holmes may have fresh instructions." Watson would not have made such a suggestion on a Sunday. The three-day period under consideration is therefore: Monday-Wednesday; Tuesday-Thursday; Wednesday-Friday; Thursday-Saturday. Monday-Wednesday is extremely unlikely: this would place both the taking of Amberley and Holmes' interview with Hilton Cubitt ("The Adventure of the Dancing Men") on Wednesday, July 27th. Tuesday-Thursday is quite impossible: the interview with Cubitt could not have taken place on the second day of "The Adventure of the Retired Colourman," when Watson did not see Holmes until three o'clock in the afternoon, and then proceeded to pay his call on Vicar Elman with Amberley, not returning to Baker Street until the following morning. We may also eliminate Wednesday-Friday: the by-weekly North Surrey *Observer* reported the solution of the case "a couple of days" after the concluding day; on whatever day the *Observer* was published, it was certainly not Sunday. In short, our vote is cast for *Thursday, July 28– Saturday, July 30, 1898.*

of him this morning, and he certainly gave me the impression of a strange creature, but when I saw him in full light his appearance was even more abnormal."

" I have, of course, studied it, and yet I should be interested to have your impression," said Holmes.

" He seemed to me like a man who was literally bowed down by care. His back was curved as though he carried a heavy burden. Yet he was not the weakling that I had at first imagined, for his shoulders and chest have the framework of a giant, though his figure tapers away into a pair of spindled legs."

" Left shoe wrinkled, right one smooth."

" I did not observe that."

" No, you wouldn't. I spotted his artificial limb. But proceed."

" I was struck by the snaky locks of grizzled hair which curled from under his old straw hat, and his face with its fierce, eager expression and the deeply-lined features."

" Very good, Watson. What did he say ? "

" He began pouring out the story of his grievances. We walked down the drive together, and of course I took a good look round. I have never seen a worse-kept place. The garden was all running to seed, giving me an impression of wild neglect in which the plants had been allowed to find the way of nature rather than of art. How any decent woman could have tolerated such a state of things, I don't know. The house, too, was slatternly to the last degree, but the poor man seemed himself to be aware of it and to be trying to remedy it, for a great pot of green paint stood in the centre of the hall and he was carrying a thick brush in his left hand. He had been working on the woodwork.

" He took me into his dingy sanctum, and we had a long chat. Of course, he was disappointed that you had not come yourself. ' I hardly expected,' he said, ' that so humble an individual as myself, especially after my heavy financial loss, could obtain the complete attention of so famous a man as Mr. Sherlock Holmes.'

" I assured him that the financial question did not arise. ' No, of course, it is art for art's sake with him,' said he ; ' but even on the artistic side of crime he might have found something here to study. And human nature, Dr. Watson—the black ingratitude of it all ! When did I ever refuse one of her requests ? Was ever a woman so pampered ? And that young man—he might have been my own son. He had the run of my house. And yet see how they have treated me ! Oh, Dr. Watson, it is a dreadful, dreadful world ! '

" That was the burden of his song for an hour or more. He had, it seems, no suspicion of an intrigue. They lived alone save for a woman who comes in by the day and leaves every evening at six. On that particular evening old Amberley, wishing to give his wife a treat, had taken two upper circle seats at the Haymarket **5** Theatre. At the last moment she had complained of a headache and had refused to go. He had gone alone. There seemed to be no doubt about the fact, for he produced the unused ticket which he had taken for his wife."

" That is remarkable—most remarkable," said Holmes,

whose interest in the case seemed to be rising. "Pray continue, Watson. I find your narrative most arresting. Did you personally examine this ticket? You did not, perchance, take the number?"

"It so happens that I did," I answered with some pride. "It chanced to be my old school number, thirty-one, and so it stuck in my head."

"Excellent, Watson! His seat, then, was either thirty or thirty-two."

"Quite so," I answered, with some mystification. "And on B row."

"That is most satisfactory. What else did he tell you?"

"He showed me his strong-room, as he called it. It really is a strong-room—like a bank—with iron door and shutter—burglar-proof, as he claimed. However, the woman seems to have had a duplicate key, and between them they had carried off some seven thousand pounds' worth of cash and securities."

"Securities! How could they dispose of those?"

"He said that he had given the police a list and that he hoped they would be unsaleable. He had got back from the theatre about midnight, and found the place plundered, the door and window open and the fugitives gone. There was no letter or message, nor has he heard a word since. He at once gave the alarm to the police."

Holmes brooded for some minutes.

"You say he was painting. What was he painting?"

"Well, he was painting the passage. But he had already painted the door and woodwork of this room I spoke of."

"Does it not strike you as a strange occupation in the circumstances?"

"'One must do something to ease an aching heart.' That was his own explanation. It was eccentric, no doubt, but he is clearly an eccentric man. He tore up one of his wife's photographs in my presence—tore it up furiously in a tempest of passion. 'I never wish to see her damned face again,' he shrieked."

"Anything more, Watson?"

"Yes, one thing which struck me more than anything else. I had driven to the Blackheath Station and had caught my train there, when just as it was starting I saw a man dart into the carriage next to my own. You know that I have a quick eye for faces, Holmes. It was undoubtedly the tall, dark man whom I had addressed in the street. I saw him once more at London Bridge, and then I lost him in the crowd. But I am convinced that he was following me."

"No doubt! No doubt!" said Holmes. "A tall, dark, heavily-moustached man, you say, with grey-tinted sun-glasses?"

"Holmes, you are a wizard. I did not say so, but he *had* grey-tinted sun-glasses."

"And a Masonic tie-pin?"

"Holmes!"

"Quite simple, my dear Watson. But let us get down to what is practical. I must admit to you that the case, which seemed to me to be so absurdly simple as to be hardly worth my notice, is rapidly assuming a very

"HE TORE UP ONE OF HIS WIFE'S PHOTOGRAPHS
IN MY PRESENCE . . ."

Illustration by Frank Wiles for the *Strand Magazine*, January, 1927. Frederic Dorr Steele illustrated the same scene for *Liberty Magazine*, December 18, 1926.

"... YOUNG DR. ERNEST ... PLAYED CHESS
WITH AMBERLEY ..."

Mr. Nathan L. Bengis, in his fascinating article, "Smothered Mate," has expressed his conviction that the Amberley tragedy was foreshadowed in two chess games played between Amberley and Dr. Ernest a month previous to Holmes' investigation. In them, Dr. Ernest won Amberley's queen (that is, his wife) and in retaliation Amberley sacrificed his queen (that is, his wife) to inflict death by suffocation (that is, smothered mate) on both her and her king (that is, Dr. Ernest). The end-positions of the two games are shown here.

6 *Thanks to the telephone.* Here is the telephone in Baker Street at last. And once installed, it was evidently there to stay: in "The Adventure of the Three Garridebs," in 1902, Watson writes: "the telephone directory lay on the table beside me . . ." "Just ring him up, Watson," says Sherlock Holmes. In "The Adventure of the Illustrious Client," also in 1902, Holmes says that "the General 'phoned that all was ready" and adds "but, in case of emergency, there is a private telephone call, XX.31."

7 *Carina sings to-night at the Albert Hall.* The Albert Hall, a vast elliptical building of brick, with terra-cotta decorations, was commenced in 1867. "This huge pile has no beauty, except in the

different aspect. It is true that though in your mission you have missed everything of importance, yet even those things which have obtruded themselves upon your notice give rise to serious thought."

"What have I missed?"

"Don't be hurt, my dear fellow. You know that I am quite impersonal. No one else would have done better. Some possibly not so well. But clearly you have missed some vital points. What is the opinion of the neighbours about this man Amberley and his wife? That surely is of importance. What of Dr. Ernest? Was he the gay Lothario one would expect? With your natural advantages, Watson, every lady is your helper and accomplice. What about the girl at the post office, or the wife of the greengrocer? I can picture you whispering soft nothings with the young lady at the ' Blue Anchor,' and receiving hard somethings in exchange. All this you have left undone."

"It can still be done."

6 "It has been done. Thanks to the telephone and the help of the Yard, I can usually get my essentials without leaving this room. As a matter of fact, my information confirms the man's story. He has the local repute of being a miser as well as a harsh and exacting husband. That he had a large sum of money in that strong-room of his is certain. So also is it that young Dr. Ernest, an unmarried man, played chess with Amberley, and probably played the fool with his wife. All this seems plain sailing, and one would think that there was no more to be said—and yet!—and yet!"

"Where lies the difficulty?"

"In my imagination, perhaps. Well, leave it there, Watson. Let us escape from this weary workaday world by the side door of music. Carina sings to-night at the **7** Albert Hall, and we still have time to dress, dine and enjoy."

In the morning I was up betimes, but some toast crumbs and two empty egg-shells told me that my companion was earlier still. I found a scribbled note upon the table.

DEAR WATSON,—

There are one or two points of contact which I should wish to establish with Mr. Josiah Amberley. When I have done so we can dismiss the case—or not. I would only ask you to be on hand about three o'clock, as I conceive it possible that I may want you.

S. H.

I saw nothing of Holmes all day, but at the hour named he returned, grave, preoccupied and aloof. At such times it was wiser to leave him to himself.

"Has Amberley been here yet?"

"No."

"Ah! I am expecting him."

He was not disappointed, for presently the old fellow arrived with a very worried and puzzled expression upon his austere face.

"I've had a telegram, Mr. Holmes. I can make

nothing of it." He handed it over, and Holmes read it aloud.

"Come at once without fail. Can give you information as to your recent loss.—ELMAN. The Vicarage."

"Dispatched at two-ten from Little Purlington," said Holmes. "Little Purlington is in Essex, I believe, not far from Frinton. Well, of course you will start at once. This is evidently from a responsible person, the vicar of the place. Where is my Crockford? Yes, here we have **8** him. J. C. Elman, M.A., Living of Mossmoor-cum-Little Purlington. Look up the trains, Watson."

"There is one at five-twenty from Liverpool Street." **9**

"Excellent. You had best go with him, Watson. He may need help or advice. Clearly we have come to a crisis in this affair."

But our client seemed by no means eager to start.

"It's perfectly absurd, Mr. Holmes," he said. "What can this man possibly know of what has occurred? It is waste of time and money."

"He would not have telegraphed to you if he did not know something. Wire at once that you are coming."

"I don't think I shall go."

Holmes assumed his sternest aspect.

"It would make the worst possible impression both on the police and upon myself, Mr. Amberley, if when so obvious a clue arose you should refuse to follow it up. We should feel that you were not really in earnest in this investigation."

Our client seemed horrified at the suggestion.

"Why, of course I shall go if you look at it in that way," said he. "On the face of it, it seems absurd to suppose that this parson knows anything, but if you think——"

"I *do* think," said Holmes, with emphasis, and so we were launched upon our journey. Holmes took me aside before we left the room and gave me one word of counsel which showed that he considered the matter to be of importance. "Whatever you do, see that he really *does* go," said he. "Should he break away or return, get to the nearest telephone exchange and send the single word ' Bolted.' I will arrange here that it shall reach me wherever I am."

Little Purlington is not an easy place to reach, for it is on a branch line. My remembrance of the journey is not a pleasant one, for the weather was hot, the train slow, and my companion sullen and silent, hardly talking at all, save to make an occasional sardonic remark as to the futility of our proceedings. When we at last reached the little station it was a two-mile drive before we came to the Vicarage, where a big, solemn, rather pompous clergyman received us in his study. Our telegram lay before him.

"Well, gentlemen," he asked, "what can I do for you?"

"We came," I explained, "in answer to your wire."

"My wire! I sent no wire."

"I mean the wire which you sent to Mr. Josiah Amberley about his wife and his money."

porches, which are exceedingly grandiose in form and effective in shadow and colour," Augustus J. C. Hare wrote in his *Walks in London*, Vol. II.

As for Carina—all scholars to date have unanimously failed to identify any singer of the period with that name. Mr. Guy Warrack's attempt (*Sherlock Holmes and Music*) to identify her with Annie Louise Cary is, as he says, "tempting" but inconclusive. However, Mr. Anthony Boucher has written ("The Records of Baker Street"): "Observe three things—1) that every other musician referred to in the Canon is of great historical eminence; 2) that all research has thus far failed to unearth a singer named Carina; 3) that *carina* is a common enough Italian term of endearment, roughly equivalent to *darling*. Who this *carina* of Holmes' was can never be ascertained certainly." But may we surmise again that Watson was wrong in calling *the* woman "the late" Irene Adler?

8 *Where is my Crockford?* "Crockford's *Clerical Directory* was on Holmes' shelf by 1898, when he took the name of J. C. Elman from it in connection with 'The Adventure of the Retired Colourman,'" Miss Madeleine B. Stern noted in "Sherlock Holmes: Rare Book Collector."

9 *"There is one at five-twenty from Liverpool Street."* Watson's Bradshaw is playing him false again: there was no 5:20 train from Liverpool Street to Little Purlington—perhaps because there was no Little Purlington.

"IF THIS IS A JOKE, SIR, IT IS A VERY QUESTIONABLE ONE," SAID THE VICAR ANGRILY.

Illustration by Frank Wiles for the *Strand Magazine*, January, 1927.

"If this is a joke, sir, it is a very questionable one," said the vicar angrily. "I have never heard of the gentleman you name, and I have not sent a wire to anyone."

Our client and I looked at each other in amazement.

"Perhaps there is some mistake," said I; "are there perhaps two vicarages? Here is the wire itself, signed Elman, and dated from the Vicarage."

"There is only one vicarage, sir, and only one vicar, and this wire is a scandalous forgery, the origin of which shall certainly be investigated by the police. Meanwhile, I can see no possible object in prolonging this interview."

So Mr. Amberley and I found ourselves on the roadside in what seemed to me to be the most primitive village in England. We made for the telegraph office, but it was already closed. There was a telephone, however, at the little 'Railway Arms,' and by it I got into touch with Holmes, who shared in our amazement at the result of our journey.

"Most singular!" said the distant voice. "Most remarkable! I much fear, my dear Watson, that there is no return train to-night. I have unwittingly condemned you to the horrors of a country inn. However, there is always Nature, Watson—Nature and Josiah Amberley—you can be in close commune with both." I heard his dry chuckle as he turned away.

It was soon apparent to me that my companion's reputation as a miser was not undeserved. He had grumbled at the expense of the journey, had insisted upon travelling third-class, and was now clamorous in his objections to the hotel bill. Next morning, when we did at last arrive in London, it was hard to say which of us was in the worse humour.

"You had best take Baker Street as we pass," said I. "Mr. Holmes may have some fresh instructions."

"If they are not worth more than the last ones they are not of much use," said Amberley, with a malevolent scowl. None the less, he kept me company. I had already warned Holmes by telegram of the hour of our arrival, but we found a message waiting that he was at Lewisham, and would expect us there. That was a surprise, but an even greater one was to find that he was not alone in the sitting-room of our client. A stern-looking, impassive man sat beside him, a dark man with grey-tinted glasses and a large Masonic pin projecting from his tie.

"This is my friend Mr. Barker," said Holmes. "He has been interesting himself also in your business, Mr. Josiah Amberley, though we have been working independently. But we both have the same question to ask you!"

Mr. Amberley sat down heavily. He sensed impending danger. I read it in his straining eyes and his twitching features.

"What is the question, Mr. Holmes?"

"Only this: What did you do with the bodies?"

The man sprang to his feet with a hoarse scream. He

10 *We made for the telegraph office.* "We get the impression that [the telephone] is like a new toy to the Master. It is not so with Watson, however," Colonel E. Ennalls Berl wrote in "Sherlock Holmes and the Telephone."

11 *I had already warned Holmes by telegram.* Again, Watson's ingrained instinct leads him to the Post Office to handle the matter by telegram rather than by resorting once more to the telephone at the little Railway Arms.

clawed into the air with his bony hands. His mouth was open, and for the instant he looked like some horrible bird of prey. In a flash we got a glimpse of the real Josiah Amberley, a misshapen demon with a soul as distorted as his body. As he fell back into his chair he clapped his hand to his lips as if to stifle a cough. Holmes sprang at his throat like a tiger, and twisted his face towards the ground. A white pellet fell from between his gasping lips. **12**

"No short cuts, Josiah Amberley. Things must be done decently and in order. What about it, Barker?" **13**

"I have a cab at the door," said our taciturn companion.

"It is only a few hundred yards to the station. We will go together. You can stay here, Watson. I shall be back within half an hour."

The old colourman had the strength of a lion in that great trunk of his, but he was helpless in the hands of the two experienced man-handlers. Wriggling and twisting he was dragged to the waiting cab, and I was left to my solitary vigil in the ill-omened house. In less time than he had named, however, Holmes was back, in company with a smart young police inspector.

"I've left Barker to look after the formalities," said Holmes. "You had not met Barker, Watson. He is my hated rival upon the Surrey shore. When you said a tall, dark man it was not difficult for me to complete the picture. He has several good cases to his credit, has he not, Inspector?"

"He has certainly interfered several times," the Inspector answered with reserve.

"His methods are irregular, no doubt, like my own. The irregulars are useful sometimes, you know. You, for example, with your compulsory warning about whatever he said being used against him, could never have bluffed this rascal into what is virtually a confession." **14**

"Perhaps not. But we get there all the same, Mr. Holmes. Don't imagine that we had not formed our own views of this case, and that we would not have laid our

HOLMES SPRANG AT HIS THROAT LIKE A TIGER . . .

Illustration by Frederic Dorr Steele for *Liberty Magazine*, December 18, 1926.

THE MAN SPRANG TO HIS FEET WITH A HOARSE SCREAM.

Illustration by Frank Wiles for the *Strand Magazine*, January, 1927.

12 *A white pellet fell from between his gasping lips.* "Cyanide of potassium is believed to be the intended suicide vehicle of Josiah Amberley," Dr. J. W. Sovine wrote in "The Toxicanon." "His poison was contained in a white pellet. Only an extremely rapid deadly poison effective in small dose would suffice for Josiah's purpose. Cyanide of potassium qualifies. In addition, as a colourman, Mr. Amberley would have had access to potassium cyanide or to potassium ferrocyanide, from which the cyanide can be easily prepared."

13 *Things must be done decently and in order.* "Let all things be done decently and in order."— I Corinthians 14.40.

14 *could never have bluffed this rascal into what is virtually a confession.* "In England," Mr. Doyle W. Beckemeyer wrote in "The Irregular Holmes," "private detectives are . . . without [the] official status they have in the United States, because they are not licensed as they are here. Thus, they are not bound by Judges' Rules, nor by the laws of the land. . . . The English Police [on the other hand] operate under conditions designed to be so scrupulously fair to the suspect that one wonders how they ever get their man at all. In Holmes' day they often didn't; but they were wise enough to condone the irregular methods employed by Sherlock Holmes . . ."

15 *this man's mentality.* "It should be noted that Watson's account of the case was written long after the event," the late H. W. Bell noted in *Sherlock Holmes and Dr. Watson: The Chronology of Their Adventures.* "He puts into Holmes' mouth the neologism 'this man's mentality,' which could not possibly have been uttered in 1898." And Mr. D. Martin Dakin has added ("The Problem of the Case-Book"): "Mr. Bell has . . . pointed out that in 1895–9 Holmes could never have referred to 'this man's mentality,' and I have confirmed this from the Oxford Dictionary."

16 *one mark, Watson, of a scheming mind.*" We have noted that most students do not believe that Holmes was himself a player, although he studded his talk with chess terms and expressions. However, a very different view is held by Mr. Harold Schonberg, the music critic of *The New York Times.* Mr. Schonberg has shown ("Yet Another Case of Identity") that Holmes had good reasons for not wanting anyone to think that he knew the game: it was in 1895, Mr. Schonberg has pointed out, that the Brooklyn Chess Club sent young Harry Nelson Pillsbury to England to participate in the great tournament at Hastings. To everybody's amazement, Pillsbury took first prize. He never again won a major tournament, dying in 1906. "Nobody can understand this sudden flash of greatness. . . . A twenty-two-year-old unknown licked the cream of Europe's experts, trouncing such formidable masters as Lasker, Tarrasch, Tchigorin, Gunsberg and Mieses." The mystery is easily solved, Mr. Schonberg explained, if we suppose that it was not Pillsbury but "the finest analytical mind in Europe, the mind of one who had genius, infinite capacity for concentration, and a brilliant insight into chess. Suppose that it was Sherlock Holmes, the master of disguise, who impersonated Pillsbury [whom Holmes somewhat resembled] at Hastings, letting Pillsbury, on his own after that, sink to his normal level."

hands on our man. You will excuse us for feeling sore when you jump in with methods which we cannot use, and so rob us of the credit."

"There shall be no such robbery, MacKinnon. I assure you that I efface myself from now onwards, and as to Barker, he has done nothing save what I told him."

The Inspector seemed considerably relieved.

"That is very handsome of you, Mr. Holmes. Praise or blame can matter little to you, but it is very different to us when the newspapers begin to ask questions."

"Quite so. But they are pretty sure to ask questions anyhow, so it would be as well to have answers. What will you say, for example, when the intelligent and enterprising reporter asks you what the exact points were which aroused your suspicion, and finally gave you a certain conviction as to the real facts?"

The Inspector looked puzzled.

"We don't seem to have got any real facts yet, Mr. Holmes. You say that the prisoner, in the presence of three witnesses, practically confessed, by trying to commit suicide, that he had murdered his wife and her lover. What other facts have you?"

"Have you arranged for a search?"

"There are three constables on their way."

"Then you will soon get the clearest fact of all. The bodies cannot be far away. Try the cellars and the garden. It should not take long to dig up the likely places. This house is older than the water-pipes. There must be a disused well somewhere. Try your luck there."

"But how did you know of it, and how was it done?"

"I'll show you first how it was done, and then I will give the explanation which is due to you, and even more to my long-suffering friend here, who has been invaluable throughout. But, first, I would give you an **15** insight into this man's mentality. It is a very unusual one—so much so that I think his destination is more likely to be Broadmoor than the scaffold. He has, to a high degree, the sort of mind which one associates with the mediæval Italian nature rather than with the modern Briton. He was a miserable miser who made his wife so wretched by his niggardly ways that she was a ready prey for any adventurer. Such a one came upon the scene in the person of this chess-playing doctor. Amberley excelled at chess—one mark, Watson, of a scheming **16** mind. Like all misers, he was a jealous man, and his jealousy became a frantic mania. Rightly or wrongly, he suspected an intrigue. He determined to have his revenge, and he planned it with diabolical cleverness. Come here!"

Holmes led us along the passage with as much certainty as if he had lived in the house, and halted at the open door of the strong-room.

"Pooh! What an awful smell of paint!" cried the Inspector.

"That was our first clue," said Holmes. "You can thank Dr. Watson's observation for that, though he failed to draw the inference. It set my foot upon the trail. Why should this man at such a time be filling his house with strong odours? Obviously, to cover some other smell which he wished to conceal—some guilty smell which would suggest suspicions. Then came the idea of a room such as you see here with iron door and shutter —a hermetically sealed room. Put those two facts together, and whither do they lead? I could only determine that by examining the house myself. I was already certain that the case was serious, for I had examined the box-office chart at the Haymarket Theatre—another of Dr. Watson's bull's-eyes—and ascertained that neither B thirty nor thirty-two of the upper circle had been occupied that night. Therefore, Amberley had not been to the theatre, and his alibi fell to the ground. He made a bad slip when he allowed my astute friend to notice the number of the seat taken for his wife. The question now arose how I might be able to examine the house. I sent an agent to the most impossible village I could think of, and summoned my man to it at such an hour that he could not possibly get back. To prevent any miscarriage, Dr. Watson accompanied him. The good vicar's name I took, of course, out of my Crockford. Do I make it all clear to you?"

"It is masterly," said the Inspector, in an awed voice.

"There being no fear of interruption I proceeded to burgle the house. Burglary has always been an alter- **17** native profession, had I cared to adopt it, and I have little doubt that I should have come to the front. Observe what I found. You see the gas-pipe along the skirting here. Very good. It rises in the angle of the wall, and there is a tap here in the corner. The pipe runs out into the strong-room, as you can see, and ends in that plaster rose in the centre of the ceiling, where it is concealed by the ornamentation. That end is wide open. At any moment by turning the outside tap the room could be flooded with gas. With door and shutter closed and the tap full on I would not give two minutes of conscious sensation to anyone shut up in that little chamber. By what devilish device he decoyed them there I do not know, but once inside the door they were at his mercy."

17 *I proceeded to burgle the house.* But again Magistrate S. Tupper Bigelow has shown ("Sherlock Holmes Was No Burglar") that under the letter of the British law Holmes was guilty of neither burglary nor unlawful entry.

"... I HAD EXAMINED THE BOX-OFFICE CHART
AT THE HAYMARKET THEATRE ..."

There is no seat numbered 31 (30 is the last number) in B row of the upper circle at the Haymarket Theatre—in spite of the fact that Watson told Holmes he had seen Josiah Amberley's unused ticket for that very seat. The diagram is from *The Combined Atlas and Guide of London*, H. Grube, Ltd., *c.* 1900.

"... I FELT A HAND INSIDE MY COLLAR ..."

Illustration by Frank Wiles for the *Strand Magazine*, January, 1927.

18 *If you find an indelible pencil on the body—"*
But how could the indelible pencil have found "a place on the *body* of the deceased Dr. Ray, as he himself could not be in a position to place it there as he gave up the ghost even before writing *four letters*," Mr. T. V. Ramamurthy has asked. "The chances of Amberley picking it up and placing the same on the body of Dr. Ray is most preposterous and unbelievable, as it will not do credit to the scheming brain of Amberley who has dared to consult not only the police but even Sherlock Holmes." We may add that the offending words "on the body" were wisely deleted by the editors of *Liberty Magazine* when "The Adventure of the Retired Colourman" appeared in that periodical.

The Inspector examined the pipe with interest. " One of our officers mentioned the smell of gas," said he, " but, of course, the window and door were open then, and the paint—or some of it—was already about. He had begun the work of painting the day before, according to his story. But what next, Mr. Holmes ? "

" Well, then came an incident which was rather unexpected to myself. I was slipping through the pantry window in the early dawn when I felt a hand inside my collar, and a voice said : ' Now, you rascal, what are you doing in there ? ' When I could twist my head round I looked into the tinted spectacles of my friend and rival, Mr. Barker. It was a curious forgathering, and set us both smiling. It seems that he had been engaged by Dr. Ray Ernest's family to make some investigations, and had come to the same conclusion as to foul play. He had watched the house for some days, and had spotted Dr. Watson as one of the obviously suspicious characters who had called there. He could hardly arrest Watson, but when he saw a man actually climbing out of the pantry window there came a limit to his restraint. Of course, I told him how matters stood and we continued the case together."

" Why him ? Why not us ? "

" Because it was in my mind to put that little test which answered so admirably. I fear you would not have gone so far."

The Inspector smiled.

" Well, maybe not. I understand that I have your word, Mr. Holmes, that you step right out of the case now and that you turn all your results over to us."

" Certainly, that is always my custom."

" Well, in the name of the Force I thank you. It seems a clear case, as you put it, and there can't be much difficulty over the bodies."

" I'll show you a grim little bit of evidence," said Holmes, " and I am sure Amberley himself never observed it. You'll get results, Inspector, by always putting yourself in the other fellow's place, and thinking what you would do yourself. It takes some imagination, but it pays. Now, we will suppose that you were shut up in this little room, had not two minutes to live, but wanted to get even with the fiend who was probably mocking at you from the other side of the door. What would you do ? "

" Write a message."

" Exactly. You would like to tell people how you died. No use writing on paper. That would be seen. If you wrote on the wall some eye might rest upon it. Now, look here ! Just above the skirting is scribbled with a purple indelible pencil : ' We we——' That's all."

" What do you make of that ? "

" Well, it's only a foot above the ground. The poor devil was on the floor and dying when he wrote it. He lost his senses before he could finish."

" He was writing, ' We were murdered.' "

" That's how I read it. If you find an indelible pencil **18** on the body——"

" We'll look out for it, you may be sure. But those securities ? Clearly there was no robbery at all. And yet he *did* possess those bonds. We verified that."

" You may be sure he has them hidden in a safe place. When the whole elopement had passed into history he would suddenly discover them, and announce that the guilty couple had relented and sent back the plunder or had dropped it on the way."

" You certainly seem to have met every difficulty," said the Inspector. " Of course, he was bound to call us in, but why he should have gone to you I can't understand."

" Pure swank ! " Holmes answered. " He felt so clever and so sure of himself that he imagined no one could touch him. He could say to any suspicious neighbour, ' Look at the steps I have taken. I have consulted not only the police, but even Sherlock Holmes.' "

The Inspector laughed.

" We must forgive you your ' even,' Mr. Holmes," said he ; " it's as workmanlike a job as I can remember."

A couple of days later my friend tossed across to me a copy of the bi-weekly *North Surrey Observer*. Under a series of flaming headlines, which began with " The Haven Horror " and ended with " Brilliant Police Investigation," there was a packed column of print which gave the first consecutive account of the affair. The concluding paragraph is typical of the whole. It ran thus :

" The remarkable acumen by which Inspector Mac-Kinnon deduced from the smell of paint that some other smell, that of gas, for example, might be concealed ; the bold deduction that the strong-room might also be the death-chamber, and the subsequent inquiry which led to the discovery of the bodies in a disused well, cleverly concealed by a dog-kennel, should live in the history of crime as a standing example of the intelligence of our professional detectives."

" Well, well, MacKinnon is a good fellow," said Holmes, with a tolerant smile. " You can file it in our archives, Watson. Some day the true story may be **19** told."

19 *"You can file it in our archives, Watson.* Mr. D. Martin Dakin has questioned the "Canonicity" of this adventure "partly as it is a rather loosely constructed, inconsequential story and partly owing to the ambiguous part played by Barker—it is never quite clear whether he was an agent of Holmes' or a rival practitioner."

Bibliographical Note: The manuscript of "The Adventure of the Retired Colourman" was lent by Jean Conan Doyle to the Abbey House Sherlock Holmes Exhibition in 1951; it is presumably still in the possession of the Doyle Estate.

THE ADVENTURE OF CHARLES AUGUSTUS MILVERTON

[Thursday, January 5, to Saturday, January 14, 1899]

1 *by which he might trace the actual occurrence.*
Watson has to a great extent succeeded: there are few adventures about which chronologists are in greater disagreement (their suggested dates range from 1882 to 1899). "The Adventure of Charles Augustus Milverton" is thought by some to be one of the earliest adventures shared by Holmes and Watson; as many hold, and for good reasons, that it was one of the latest adventures.

Watson in this paragraph tells us that "It is years since the incidents of which I speak took place . . ." Since his account of the case was first published in *Collier's Magazine* for March 26, 1904, this statement, taken by itself, would seem to indicate that the adventure took place before or very soon after the Return.

Watson says he alludes to the incidents "with diffidence"—and Lawyer Irving M. Fenton has shown ("An Analysis of the Crimes and Near-Crimes at Appledore Towers in the Light of the English Criminal Law") that his phrase is well chosen: "In the light of the present English criminal law, we are presented [in this case] with what might be paradoxically termed a miniature omnibus of crime. All the principals are involved in one way or another."

Watson tells us that the principal person concerned "is beyond the reach of human law." It has usually been taken to mean that this implied the recent death of Milverton's executor, but Mr. L. W. Bailey has pointed out ("The Dark Lady of Appledore Towers") that "Watson's words could bear a more subtle explanation. The story was first published in April, 1904 [Mr. Bailey is speaking of its first *English* appearance—in the *Strand Magazine*]. Allowing for customary publication delays, therefore, it is likely Watson started to write it early in 1903. On the 26th of June, 1902, Edward VII had been crowned King of England, and had thus become technically above the law and so 'beyond its reach.' Is it not possible that by his choice of words Watson was hinting at a truth he dare not reveal, and into which even now it would be indelicate to probe any further?"

IT is years since the incidents of which I speak took place, and yet it is with diffidence that I allude to them. For a long time, even with the utmost discretion and reticence, it would have been impossible to make the facts public ; but now the principal person concerned is beyond the reach of human law, and with due suppression the story may be told in such fashion as to injure no one. It records an absolutely unique experience in the career both of Mr. Sherlock Holmes and of myself. The reader will excuse me if I conceal the date or any other fact by which he might trace the actual **1** occurrence.

We had been out for one of our evening rambles, Holmes and I, and had returned about six o'clock on a cold, frosty winter's evening. As Holmes turned up the lamp the light fell upon a card on the table. He glanced at it, and then, with an ejaculation of disgust, threw it on the floor. I picked it up and read :

CHARLES AUGUSTUS MILVERTON,
APPLEDORE TOWERS,
HAMPSTEAD.

Agent.

"Who is he ? " I asked.

" The worst man in London," Holmes answered, as he sat down and stretched his legs before the fire. " Is anything on the back of the card ? "

I turned it over.

" Will call at 6.30.—C. A. M.," I read.

" Hum ! He's about due. Do you feel a creeping, shrinking sensation, Watson, when you stand before the **2** serpents in the Zoo and see the slithery, gliding, venomous creatures, with their deadly eyes and wicked, flattened faces ? Well, that's how Milverton impresses me. I've **3** had to do with fifty murderers in my career, but the worst of them never gave me the repulsion which I have for this fellow. And yet I can't get out of doing business with him—indeed, he is here at my invitation."

" But who is he ? "

" I'll tell you, Watson. He is the king of all the black-mailers. Heaven help the man, and still more the woman, whose secret and reputation come into the power

"THE WORST MAN IN LONDON . . ."

Two portraits of Charles Augustus Milverton: the first, by Sidney Paget, for the *Strand Magazine*, April, 1904; the second, by Frederic Dorr Steele, for *Collier's Magazine*, March 26, 1904. We may note, in addition, that Holmes in "The Adventure of the Empty House" (April, 1894) remarked to Watson that his collection of M's was a fine one. He named Moriarty and Moran, Morgan, Merridew and Mathews. If "The Adventure of Charles Augustus Milverton" took place *before* that time, it is curious that Holmes made no mention of "the worst man in London" as well as "the second most dangerous man in London."

of Milverton. With a smiling face and a heart of marble he will squeeze and squeeze until he has drained them dry. The fellow is a genius in his way, and would have made his mark in some more savoury trade. His method is as follows : He allows it to be known that he is prepared to pay very high sums for letters which compromise people of wealth or position. He receives these wares not only from treacherous valets or maids, but frequently from genteel ruffians who have gained the confidence and affection of trusting women. He deals with no niggard hand. I happen to know that he paid seven hundred pounds to a footman for a note two lines in length, and that the ruin of a noble family was the result. Everything which is in the market goes to Milverton, and there are hundreds in this great city who turn white at his name. No one knows where his grip may fall, for he is far too rich and far too cunning to work from hand to mouth. He will hold a card back for years in order to play it at the moment when the stake is best worth winning. I have said that he is the worst man in London, and I would ask you how could one compare the ruffian who in hot blood bludgeons his mate with this man, who methodically and at his leisure tortures the soul and wrings the nerves in order to add to his already swollen money-bags ? "

I had seldom heard my friend speak with such intensity of feeling.

" But surely," said I, " the fellow must be within the grasp of the law ? "

" Technically, no doubt, but practically not. What would it profit a woman, for example, to get him a few months' imprisonment if her own ruin must immediately follow ? His victims dare not hit back. If ever he blackmailed an innocent person, then, indeed, we should have him ; but he is as cunning as the Evil One. No, no ; we must find other ways to fight him."

" And why is he here ? "

" Because an illustrious client has placed her piteous case in my hands. It is the Lady Eva Brackwell, the most beautiful *débutante* of last season. She is to be married

2 *the Zoo*. Holmes refers to the wonderful Zoological Gardens on the northeast side of Regent's Park, founded in 1826. Admission in his day was 1s (6d on Mondays and holidays). The Gardens comprise thirty-four acres and have one of the largest and finest exhibits in the world; today they are visited annually by about two million people. It is unfortunate that the Zoo, in Holmes' day, did not have a panda on display, for it seems likely that Holmes would have encountered the animal during his Tibetan expedition, and would have been happy to renew its acquaintance.

3 *I've had to do with fifty murderers in my career*. Since Holmes had dealt with five hundred cases of capital importance by the autumn of 1888 (*The Hound of the Baskervilles*) and over a thousand cases by the spring of 1891 ("The Final Problem"), this case would seem to have taken place very soon after he and Watson began to share the rooms at 221B Baker Street. We take Holmes' statement here to be a red herring, deliberately inserted into the text by Watson to confuse the chronology of "Charles Augustus Milverton."

in a fortnight to the Earl of Dovercourt. This fiend has several imprudent letters—imprudent, Watson, nothing worse—which were written to an impecunious young squire in the country. They would suffice to break off the match. Milverton will send the letters to the earl unless a large sum of money is paid him. I have been commissioned to meet him, and—to make the best terms I can."

At that instant there was a clatter and a rattle in the street below. Looking down I saw a stately carriage and pair, the brilliant lamps gleaming on the glossy haunches of the noble chestnuts. A footman opened the door, and a small, stout man in a shaggy astrachan overcoat descended. A minute later he was in the room.

Charles Augustus Milverton was a man of fifty, with a large, intellectual head, a round, plump, hairless face, a perpetual frozen smile, and two keen grey eyes, which gleamed brightly from behind broad, golden-rimmed glasses. There was something of Mr. Pickwick's benevolence in his appearance, marred only by the insincerity of the fixed smile and by the hard glitter of those restless and penetrating eyes. His voice was as smooth and suave as his countenance, as he advanced with a plump little hand extended, murmuring his regret for having missed us at his first visit.

Holmes disregarded the outstretched hand and looked at him with a face of granite. Milverton's smile broadened ; he shrugged his shoulders, removed his overcoat, folded it with great deliberation over the back of a chair, and then took a seat.

" This gentleman," said he, with a wave in my direction. " Is it discreet ? Is it right ? "

" Dr. Watson is my friend and partner."

" Very good, Mr. Holmes. It is only in your client's interests that I protested. The matter is so very delicate——"

" Dr. Watson has already heard of it."

" Then we can proceed to business. You say that you are acting for Lady Eva. Has she empowered you to accept my terms ? "

" What are your terms ? "

4   " Seven thousand pounds."

" And the alternative ? "

" My dear sir, it is painful to me to discuss it ; but if the money is not paid on the 14th there certainly will be no

5   marriage on the 18th." His insufferable smile was more complacent than ever. Holmes thought for a little.

" You appear to me," he said at last, " to be taking matters too much for granted. I am, of course, familiar with the contents of these letters. My client will certainly do what I may advise. I shall counsel her to tell her future husband the whole story and to trust to his generosity."

Milverton chuckled.

" You evidently do not know the earl," said he.

From the baffled look upon Holmes' face I could clearly see that he did.

" What harm is there in the letters ? " he asked.

" They are sprightly—very sprightly," Milverton

4 *"Seven thousand pounds."* "Milverton's insistence on £7,000 'or there will be no marriage on the 18th' falls into [the category of attempted extortion]. 'Attempt' is, of course, a crime per se," Lawyer Fenton noted.

5 *no marriage on the 18th."* Watson has told us that the season was "winter." Milverton now tells us that Lady Eva Brackwell was to be married "on the 18th." That the month was December or March is possible but unlikely: December 18th would fall in Advent, March 18th in Lent, seasons in which marriages are frowned upon by the Church. Nevertheless, in the interest of complete accuracy, we will consider December and March with January and February in attempting to date this case. We have also seen (in "The Adventure of the Golden Pince-Nez") that Watson at least once spoke of November as a "winter" month. We must therefore take November, as well as December and March, into our calculations.

Since the marriage was to take place on the 18th, that day was not a Sunday. This eliminates December, 1898; February, 1900; March, 1900; and January, 1903.

answered. "The lady was a charming correspondent. But I can assure you that the Earl of Dovercourt would fail to appreciate them. However, since you think otherwise, we will let it rest at that. It is purely a matter of business. If you think that it is in the best interests of your client that these letters should be placed in the hands of the earl, then you would indeed be foolish to pay so large a sum of money to regain them." He rose and seized his astrachan coat.

Holmes was grey with anger and mortification.

"Wait a little," he said. "You go too fast. We would certainly make every effort to avoid scandal in so delicate a matter."

Milverton relapsed into his chair.

"I was sure that you would see it in that light," he purred.

"At the same time," Holmes continued, "Lady Eva is not a wealthy woman. I assure you that two thousand pounds would be a drain upon her resources, and that the sum you name is utterly beyond her power. I beg, therefore, that you will moderate your demands, and that you will return the letters at the price I indicate, which is, I assure you, the highest that you can get."

Milverton's smile broadened and his eyes twinkled humorously.

"I am aware that what you say is true about the lady's resources," said he. "At the same time, you must admit that the occasion of a lady's marriage is a very suitable time for her friends and relatives to make some little effort upon her behalf. They may hesitate as to an acceptable wedding present. Let me assure them that this little bundle of letters would give more joy than all the candelabra and butter-dishes in London."

"It is impossible," said Holmes.

"Dear me, dear me, how unfortunate!" cried Milverton, taking out a bulky pocket-book. "I cannot help thinking that ladies are ill-advised in not making an effort. Look at this!" He held up a little note with a coat-of-arms upon the envelope. "That belongs to—well, **6** perhaps it is hardly fair to tell the name until to-morrow morning. But at that time it will be in the hands of the lady's husband. And all because she will not find a beggarly sum which she could get in an hour by turning her diamonds into paste. It *is* such a pity. Now, you remember the sudden end of the engagement between the Honourable Miss Miles and Colonel Dorking? Only two days before the wedding there was a paragraph in the *Morning Post* to say that it was all off. And why? It is almost incredible, but the absurd sum of twelve hundred pounds would have settled the whole question. Is it not pitiful? And there I find you, a man of sense, boggling about terms when your client's future and honour are at stake. You surprise me, Mr. Holmes."

"What I say is true," Holmes answered. "The money cannot be found. Surely it is better for you to take the substantial sum which I offer than to ruin this woman's career, which can profit you in no way?"

"There you make a mistake, Mr. Holmes. An exposure would profit me indirectly to a considerable

6 *with a coat-of-arms upon the envelope.* Mr. Russell L. Merritt has suggested ("Re: The Adventure of the Worst Man in London") that it well may be that Holmes immediately recognized the coat-of-arms, and that his future course in this adventure was dictated by his knowledge of the bearer, the bearer's wife, and what that lady was capable of.

7 *I have eight or ten similar cases maturing.* "Contemporary philanderers whose first principle is never to commit anything to writing may find this *penchant* for exchanging passionate *billets-doux* incomprehensible, but two points should be considered," Mr. L. W. Bailey wrote in "The Dark Lady of Appledore Towers." "As there were no private telephones the only means of communication and of making appointments between two people living in separate establishments was the written word, and as letters could not be safely posted and dropped naked on the matrimonial mat, they had to be entrusted for personal delivery to a valet or lady's maid. These servants, alas, were perpetually tempted by scoundrels like Milverton with large sums of money, and too often, as in other fields of human activity, avarice proved stronger than loyalty. The second point is that what seems to us a perfectly innocent message could at that time be construed as a confession of guilt. Lax though the standards of actual behaviour were, the outward appearance had to be rigidly correct, and an appointment between a man and a woman (especially if one or both were married to someone else) to meet alone was considered sufficient evidence of a 'guilty' accusation."

"MR. HOLMES, MR. HOLMES!" HE SAID, TURNING THE FRONT OF HIS COAT AND EXHIBITING THE BUTT OF A LARGE REVOLVER . . .

Illustration by Sidney Paget for the *Strand Magazine*, April, 1904.

7 extent. I have eight or ten similar cases maturing. If it was circulated among them that I had made a severe example of the Lady Eva I should find all of them much more open to reason. You see my point?"

Holmes sprang from his chair.

"Get behind him, Watson. Don't let him out!
8 Now, sir, let us see the contents of that notebook."

Milverton had glided as quick as a rat to the side of the room, and stood with his back against the wall.

"Mr. Holmes, Mr. Holmes!" he said, turning the front of his coat and exhibiting the butt of a large revolver, which projected from the inside pocket. "I have been expecting you to do something original. This has been done so often, and what good has ever come from it? I assure you that I am armed to the teeth, and I am perfectly prepared to use my weapon, knowing that the law will support me. Besides, your supposition that I would bring the letters here in a notebook is entirely mistaken. I would do nothing so foolish. And now, gentlemen, I have one or two little interviews this evening, and it is a long drive to Hampstead." He stepped forward, took up his coat, laid his hand on his revolver, and turned to the door. I picked up a chair, but Holmes shook his head, and I laid it down again. With a bow, a smile, and a twinkle Milverton was out of the room, and a few moments after we heard the slam of the carriage door and the rattle of the wheels as he drove away.

Holmes sat motionless by the fire, his hands buried deep in his trouser pockets, his chin sunk upon his breast, his eyes fixed upon the glowing embers. For half an hour he was silent and still. Then, with the gesture of a man who has taken his decision, he sprang to his feet and passed into his bedroom. A little later a rakish young workman with a goatee beard and a swagger lit his clay pipe at the lamp before descending into the street. "I'll be back some time, Watson," said he, and vanished into the night. I understood that he had opened his campaign against Charles Augustus Milverton; but I little dreamed the strange shape which that campaign was destined to take.

For some days Holmes came and went at all hours in this attire, but beyond a remark that his time was spent at Hampstead, and that it was not wasted, I knew nothing of what he was doing. At last, however, on a wild, tempestuous evening, when the wind screamed and rattled against the windows, he returned from his last expedition, and, having removed his disguise, he sat before the fire and laughed heartily in his silent, inward fashion.

"You would not call me a marrying man, Watson?"

"No, indeed!"

"You will be interested to hear that I am engaged."

"My dear fellow! I congrat——"

"To Milverton's housemaid."

"Good heavens, Holmes!"

9 "I wanted information, Watson."

"Surely you have gone too far?"

"It was a most necessary step. I am a plumber with

a rising business, Escott by name. I have walked out with her each evening, and I have talked with her. Good heavens, those talks! However, I have got all I **10** wanted. I know Milverton's house as I know the palm of my hand."

" But the girl, Holmes ? "

He shrugged his shoulders.

" You can't help it, my dear Watson. You must play your cards as best you can when such a stake is on the table. However, I rejoice to say that I have a hated rival who will certainly cut me out the instant that my back is turned. What a splendid night it is ! "

" You like this weather ? "

" It suits my purpose. Watson, I mean to burgle Milverton's house to-night."

I had a catching of the breath, and my skin went cold at the words, which were slowly uttered in a tone of concentrated resolution. As a flash of lightning in the night shows up in an instant every detail of a wide landscape, so at one glance I seemed to see every possible result of such an action—the detection, the capture, the honoured career ending in irreparable failure and disgrace, my friend himself lying at the mercy of the odious Milverton.

" For Heaven's sake, Holmes, think what you are doing ! " I cried. **11**

" My dear fellow, I have given it every consideration. I am never precipitate in my actions, nor would I adopt so energetic and indeed so dangerous a course if any other were possible. Let us look at the matter clearly and fairly. I suppose that you will admit that the action is morally justifiable, though technically criminal. To burgle his house is no more than to forcibly take his pocket-book—an action in which you were prepared to aid me."

I turned it over in my mind.

" Yes," I said ; " it is morally justifiable so long as our object is to take no articles save those which are used for an illegal purpose."

" Exactly. Since it is morally justifiable, I have only to consider the question of personal risk. Surely a gentleman should not lay much stress upon this when a lady is in most desperate need of his help ? "

" You will be in such a false position."

" Well, that is part of the risk. There is no other possible way of regaining these letters. The unfortunate lady has not the money, and there are none of her people in whom she could confide. To-morrow is the last day of grace, and unless we can get the letters to-night this villain will be as good as his word, and will bring about her ruin. I must, therefore, abandon my client to her fate, or I must play this last card. Between ourselves, Watson, it's a sporting duel between this fellow Milverton and me. He had, as you saw, the best of the first exchanges ; but my self-respect and my reputation are concerned to fight it to a finish."

" Well, I don't like it ; but I suppose it must be," said I. " When do we start ? "

" You are not coming."

" Then you are not going," said I. " I give you my

8 *Now, sir, let us see the contents of that notebook.*" Lawyer Fenton: "Holmes' counter-offer of £2,000 made for the purpose of disentangling Lady Eva Brackwell from the slimy Milverton's meshes does not make him a *particeps criminis*, for his purpose is not criminal—but he is treading on thin ice. When, however, he tries to detain Milverton in order to take away his notebook he is guilty of attempted 'unlawful detention,' a crime in itself, and 'taking and carrying away'—larceny, in fact. 'Taking' includes possession by intimidation. . . . 'Carrying away' presupposes the permanent removal of anything from the place it occupies. It is indisputable that Holmes and Watson had no intention of returning the notebook to Milverton. Nor could Holmes and Watson plead as a valid defense that the blackmailer intended to use the documents it contained for improper purposes. It would still be a technical larceny."

9 *"Surely you have gone too far?"* Lawyer Fenton: "Holmes is guilty here of no more than the commission of a tort. The Larceny Act of 1916, codifying the criminal law, provides that 'every person who by any false pretence, with intent to defraud, obtains from any other person, any chattel, money or valuable security . . . shall be guilty . . .' Holmes had no intention of depriving Agatha of money or valuable security, neither of which she appears to have had to offer. The common law generally afforded little protection against fraud, holding it no crime for a man to make a fool of another man (or woman either, for that matter). This would not have prevented the maid of Hampstead, however, from suing for breach of promise in what is strangely referred to as a civil action."

10 *Good heavens, those talks!* "Is it not a tribute to Holmes' versatility," Dr. Richard Asher wrote in "Holmes and the Fair Sex," "that he, a man accustomed to discourse upon the Chaldean roots of the ancient Cornish language and the Polyphonic Motets of Lassus, should be equally capable of love talk with a housemaid? Is it not remarkable that a man accustomed to the company of khalifas, dukes, headmasters and llamas should be such a success with a servant?"

11 *"For Heaven's sake, Holmes, think what you are doing!"* Compare Watson's reaction to Holmes' suggestion that they spend the night in Stoke Moran without the sinister Dr. Roylott's permission or knowledge in "The Adventure of the Speckled Band," which we know took place in 1883: "I have really some scruples as to taking you tonight. There is a distinct element of danger." "Can I be of assistance?" "Your presence might be invaluable." "Then I shall certainly come." As the late Gavin Brend noted, it is curious that Watson should react so violently to Holmes' suggestion in this adventure *unless it were their first experience in lawbreaking together.* In so doing, he provided a powerful argument for placing the adventure earlier rather than later. But Mr. Brend himself provided an alternative explanation: that Watson, at the time of this adventure, had recently suffered a shocking experience which had left him shaken and totally unnerved for any form of housebreaking. In Mr. Brend's view, this experience was Watson's recent encounter on the moor with that dreadful apparition, the Hound of the Baskervilles.

12 *we have shared the same room for some years.* Holmes *could* have made this statment as early as 1883 (although he would have been more likely to say "two years" in that year). Taken by itself, however, the statment indicates a later rather than an earlier year for this adventure.

13 *I would have made a highly efficient criminal.* Lawyer Fenton: "Freudians may make what they will of Holmes' often-expressed desire to become a highly efficient criminal, a burglar by choice. The casual reader detects a note of yearning, but a closer examination discloses a substantial fulfillment."

14 *"I have rubber-soled tennis shoes."* If Watson's presumptive leg wound was bothering him so little at this period that he was able to enjoy a game of tennis, "The Adventure of Charles Augustus Milverton" must be 1) prior to the time that he supposedly sustained his leg wound; or 2) very late in his career. It is otherwise difficult to see what use he could have made of tennis shoes—they are not worn ordinarily for comfort, certainly.

15 *we shall drive as far as Church Row.* This beautiful road of old houses in Hampstead has hardly changed through the years and, apart from the cars that now line its pavements, Holmes and Watson would find little difference in the street if they visited Church Row today.

16 *so that we might appear to be two theatregoers homeward bound.* The money was to be paid "on the 14th." On the preceding night—"Tomorrow is the last day of grace"—"Holmes and I put on our dress-clothes, so that we might appear to be two theatre-goers homeward bound." The 13th was therefore not a Sunday. This eliminates January, 1895; December, 1896; February, 1898; March, 1898; January, 1901; December, 1903; and March, 1904.

17 *In Oxford Street we picked up a hansom.* But "why did Holmes and Watson [go] into Oxford Street on a bitterly cold night in order to pick up a hansom to take them to Hampstead?" Mr. James Edward Holroyd has asked. "They would be walking *away* from their destination no matter in which part of Baker Street 221B lay."

To this, Mr. Humphrey Morton has replied ("A Long Drive to Hampstead"): "Obviously, one presumes, with Holmes' customary thoroughness and attention to detail he desired to make the entire

word of honour—and I never broke it in my life—that I will take a cab straight to the police-station and give you away unless you let me share this adventure with you."

"You can't help me."

"How do you know that? You can't tell what may happen. Anyway, my resolution is taken. Other people besides you have self-respect and even reputations."

Holmes had looked annoyed, but his brow cleared, and he clapped me on the shoulder.

"Well, well, my dear fellow, be it so. We have shared **12** the same room for some years, and it would be amusing if we ended by sharing the same cell. You know, Watson, I don't mind confessing to you that I have always had an **13** idea that I would have made a highly efficient criminal. This is the chance of my lifetime in that direction. See here!" He took a neat little leather case out of a drawer, and opening it he exhibited a number of shining instruments. "This is a first-class, up-to-date burgling kit, with nickel-plated jemmy, diamond-tipped glass cutter, adaptable keys, and every modern improvement which the march of civilization demands. Here, too, is my dark lantern. Everything is in order. Have you a pair of silent shoes?"

14 "I have rubber-soled tennis shoes."

"Excellent. And a mask?"

"I can make a couple out of black silk."

"I can see that you have a strong natural turn for this sort of thing. Very good; do you make the masks. We shall have some cold supper before we start. It is now nine-thirty. At eleven we shall drive as far as Church **15** Row. It is a quarter of an hour's walk from there to Appledore Towers. We shall be at work before midnight. Milverton is a heavy sleeper, and retires punctually at ten-thirty. With any luck we should be back here by two, with the Lady Eva's letters in my pocket."

Holmes and I put on our dress-clothes, so that we might **16** appear to be two theatre-goers homeward bound. In **17** Oxford Street we picked up a hansom and drove to an address in Hampstead. Here we paid off our cab, and with our greatcoats buttoned up—for it was bitterly cold, and the wind seemed to blow through us—we walked along the edge of the Heath.

"It's a business that needs delicate treatment," said Holmes. "These documents are contained in a safe in the fellow's study, and the study is the ante-room of his bedchamber. On the other hand, like all these stout, little men who do themselves well, he is a plethoric sleeper. Agatha—that's my fiancée—says it is a joke in the servants' hall that it's impossible to wake the master. He has a secretary who is devoted to his interests, and never budges from the study all day. That's why we are going at night. Then he has a beast of a dog which roams the garden. I met Agatha late the last two evenings, and she locks the brute up so as to give me a clear run. This is the house, this big one in its own grounds. Through the gate—now to the right among the laurels. We might put on our masks here, I think. You see, there is not a glimmer of light in any of the windows, and everything is working splendidly."

With our black silk face-coverings, which turned us into two of the most truculent figures in London, we stole up to the silent, gloomy house. A sort of tiled veranda extended along one side of it, lined by several windows and two doors.

"That's his bedroom," Holmes whispered. "This door opens straight into the study. It would suit us best, but it is bolted as well as locked, and we should make too much noise getting in. Come round here. There's a greenhouse which opens into the drawing-room."

The place was locked, but Holmes removed a circle of glass and turned the key from the inside. An instant **18** afterwards he had closed the door behind us, and we had become felons in the eyes of the law. The thick warm air of the conservatory and the rich, choking fragrance of exotic plants took us by the throat. He seized my hand in the darkness and led me swiftly past banks of shrubs which brushed against our faces. Holmes had remarkable powers, carefully cultivated, of seeing in the dark. Still holding my hand in one of his, he opened a door, and I was vaguely conscious that we had entered a large room in which a cigar had been smoked not long before. He felt his way among the furniture, opened another door, and closed it behind us. Putting out my hand I felt several coats hanging from the wall, and I understood that I was in a passage. We passed along it, and Holmes very gently opened a door upon the right-hand side. Something rushed out at us, and my heart sprang into my mouth, but I could have laughed when I realized that it was the cat. A fire was burning in this new room, and again the air was heavy with tobacco smoke. Holmes entered on tiptoe, waited for me to follow, and then very gently closed the door. We were in Milverton's study, and a *portière* at the farther side showed the entrance to his bedroom.

It was a good fire, and the room was illuminated by it. Near the door I saw the gleam of an electric switch, but **19** it was unnecessary, even if it had been safe, to turn it on. At one side of the fireplace was a heavy curtain, which covered the bay window we had seen from outside. On the other side was the door which communicated with the veranda. A desk stood in the centre, with a turning chair of shining red leather. Opposite was a large bookcase, with a marble bust of Athene on the top. In the corner between the bookcase and the wall there stood a tall green safe, the firelight flashing back from the polished brass knobs upon its face. Holmes stole across and looked at it. Then he crept to the door of the bedroom, and stood with slanting head listening intently. No sound came from within. Meanwhile it had struck me that it would be wise to secure our retreat through the outer door, so I examined it. To my amazement it was neither locked nor bolted! I touched Holmes on the arm, and he turned his masked face in that direction. I saw him start, and he was evidently as surprised as I.

"I don't like it," he whispered, putting his lips to my very ear. "I can't quite make it out. Anyhow, we have no time to lose."

"THIS IS THE HOUSE, THIS BIG ONE IN ITS OWN GROUNDS."

"There are varied theories as to which house is Appledore Towers," Mr. Humphrey Morton wrote in "'A Long Drive to Hampstead!'" "Mr. Ivor Brown thinks there is a case for citing the big house on the corner of Spaniards Road and North End Road, but to reach that from Church Row does not entail walking along the edge of the heath. The direct route to this house would be to walk straight up Heath Street, where Holmes and Watson were now near, and the house would have been facing them with the heath upon *either* side, and with Jack Straw's Castle on the left. One is inclined to assume, therefore, that they did indeed walk up Heath Street, and then to the right down East Heath Road (along the edge of the heath) and so to the 'silent, gloomy house,' let us say, at the corner of Well Road."

Elsewhere (in "A Milvertonian Identification"), Mr. Morton identified "Appledore Towers" as the house now known as "The Logs." At the east end of Well Walk, he wrote, East Heath Road is reached. At the corner of Well Road stands The Logs. "The house was designed by J. S. Nightingale and built in 1868. There appears to be no record of its first owner, but it was occupied by Edward Gotto from 1873 until 1896. Following this lengthy occupation there is a mysterious gap of two years, from 1896 to 1898, during which period it is said that the house was 'apparently empty.' . . . Cannot we assume . . . that Milverton moved to The Logs in 1896, changed its name to Appledore Towers and was in residence until his timely and unlamented death a year or two later?"

journey to Hampstead appear convincing from the start. There might be a chance of suspicion falling on them had they hailed a cab outside 221B. C. A. M. might have had Holmes' movements watched. Theatre-goers. Right. Now in Oxford Street in the '80s and '90s the nearest theatre to Baker Street was the old Princess's, which stood upon the north side of Oxford Street between what is now Upper Regent Street and Tottenham Court Road. Suppose that they hailed their hansom outside the Princess's Theatre, which route to Hampstead would they take? Either via Tottenham Court Road, through Hampstead Road, Camden Town and thus, on to Haverstock Hill, Rosslyn Hill and Hampstead High Street *or* via Portland Place, the Outer Circle of Regent's Park, Avenue Road and so up to Fitzjohn's Avenue to Church Row. One is inclined to accept the former theory, and surely it would have been superfluous to return westward along Oxford Street and into Baker Street once more and north from there."

18 *Holmes removed a circle of glass and turned the key from the inside.* Lawyer Fenton: "At this point 'breaking and entering are complete. Burglary has, in fact, been committed. Section 25 of the Larceny Act states, 'Every person who breaks and enters the dwelling house of another with intent to commit a felony therein . . . shall be guilty of burglary.' It has been held that the insertion of any part of the intruder's body, even a finger or part of a finger, will suffice for 'entry.' Burglary here is limited to dwelling houses and only is committed between the hours of 9 P.M. and 6 A.M. The crime is triable at assizes and quarter-sessions and is punishable by imprisonment for life. Housebreaking, not essentially a nocturnal activity, carries a maximum penalty of 14 years."

19 *Near the door I saw the gleam of an electric switch.* This is the first of many references to electricity in Appledore Towers, and it raises, chronologically, a most interesting point. Appledore Towers, it will be remembered, was in Hampstead. Your editor is indebted to the late Gavin Brend for the following information, communicated to him in a letter from Mr. Brend dated June 27, 1954: "The position as regards electricity in England at that time was briefly as follows. It would have been theoretically possible at any time after 1880 but in practice it was most unlikely, for the original legislation was most restrictive and the first supply companies found it practically impossible to function. Only later in the eighties

THEN HE CREPT TO THE DOOR OF THE BEDROOM, AND STOOD WITH SLANTING HEAD LISTENING INTENTLY.

Illustration by Sidney Paget for the *Strand Magazine*, April, 1904.

" Can I do anything ? "

" Yes ; stand by the door. If you hear anyone come, bolt it on the inside, and we can get away as we came. If they come the other way, we can get through the door if our job is done, or hide behind these window curtains if it is not. Do you understand ? "

I nodded and stood by the door. My first feeling of fear had passed away, and I thrilled now with a keener zest than I had ever enjoyed when we were the defenders of the law instead of its defiers. The high object of our mission, the consciousness that it was unselfish and chivalrous, the villainous character of our opponent, all added to the sporting interest of the adventure. Far from feeling guilty, I rejoiced and exulted in our dangers. With a glow of admiration I watched Holmes unrolling his case of instruments and choosing his tool with the calm, scientific accuracy of a surgeon who performs a delicate operation. I knew that the opening of safes was a particular hobby with him, and I understood the joy which it gave him to be confronted with this green and gold monster, the dragon which held in its maw the reputations of many fair ladies. Turning up the cuffs of his dress-coat—he had placed his overcoat on a chair—Holmes laid out two drills, a jemmy, and several skeleton keys. I stood at the centre door with my eyes glancing at each of the others, ready for any emergency ; though, indeed, my plans were somewhat vague as to what I should do if we were interrupted. For half an hour Holmes worked with concentrated energy, laying down one tool, picking up another, handling each with the strength and delicacy of the trained mechanic. Finally I heard a click, the broad green door swung open, and inside I had a glimpse of a number of paper packets, each tied, sealed, and inscribed. Holmes picked one out, but it was hard to read by the flickering fire, and he drew out his little dark lantern, for it was too dangerous, with

Milverton in the next room, to switch on the electric light. Suddenly I saw him halt, listen intently, and then in an instant he had swung the door of the safe to, picked up his coat, stuffed his tools into the pockets, and darted behind the window curtain, motioning me to do the same.

It was only when I had joined him there that I heard what had alarmed his quicker senses. There was a noise somewhere within the house. A door slammed in the distance. Then a confused, dull murmur broke itself into the measured thud of heavy footsteps rapidly approaching. They were in the passage outside the room. They paused at the door. The door opened. There was a sharp snick as the electric light was turned on. The door closed once more, and the pungent reek of a strong cigar was borne to our nostrils. Then the footsteps continued backwards and forwards, backwards and forwards, within a few yards of us. Finally, there was a creak from a chair, and the footsteps ceased. Then a key clicked in a lock, and I heard the rustle of papers. So far I had not dared to look out, but now I gently parted the division of the curtains in front of me and peeped through. From the pressure of Holmes' shoulder against mine I knew that he was sharing my observations. Right in front of us, and almost within our reach, was the broad, rounded back of Milverton. It was evident that we had entirely miscalculated his movements, that he had never been to his bedroom, but that he had been sitting up in some smoking- or billiard-room in the farther wing of the house, the windows of which we had not seen. His broad, grizzled head, with its shining patch of baldness, was in the immediate foreground of our vision. He was leaning far back in the red leather chair, his legs outstretched, a long black cigar projecting at an angle from his mouth. He wore a semi-military smoking-jacket, claret-coloured, with a black velvet collar. In his hand he held a long legal document, which he was reading in an indolent fashion, blowing rings of tobacco smoke from his lips as he did so. There was no promise of a speedy departure in his composed bearing and his comfortable attitude.

I felt Holmes' hand steal into mine and give me a reassuring shake, as if to say that the situation was within his powers, and that he was easy in his mind. I was not sure whether he had seen what was only too obvious from my position—that the door of the safe was imperfectly closed, and that Milverton might at any moment observe it. In my own mind I had determined that if I were sure, from the rigidity of his gaze, that it had caught his eye, I would at once spring out, throw my greatcoat over his head, pinion him, and leave the rest to Holmes. But Milverton never looked up. He was languidly interested by the papers in his hand, and page after page was turned as he followed the argument of the lawyer. At least, I thought, when he has finished the document and the cigar he will go to his room ; but before he had reached the end of either there came a remarkable development which turned our thoughts into quite another channel.

were the restrictions removed. For some time I left it at that. After all, Milverton was a blackmailer. Perhaps he had jumped the queue, although obviously this would take a bit of doing. But finally I decided I ought to look further into it. It so happens that I too live in Hampstead. When paying my electricity bill I asked the authority The London Electricity Board (North Western Sub-Area), when electricity was first installed in Hampstead. *The reply was in 1894.*"

This seemed to Mr. Brend, and to your editor, to prove conclusively that "The Adventure of Charles Augustus Milverton" belongs to the period after the Return. Still, a Sherlockian whose opinion is always to be highly respected, Mr. Elliot Kimball, has written that: "The fact that public electrical supply did not become available at Hampstead until 1894 does not apply with exclusive force. Milverton was a sybarite, and would be precisely the sort of an individual who would avail himself of a Swan System, providing himself with electric light by means of a privately-operated plant. Such apparatus might have been installed as early as 1880. No necessity arises to assign the Milverton adventure to a period after the Return."

In rebuttal, your editor would submit the following statement from Mr. William E. Plimental: "This . . . accessory [the electric switch, which we are later told operated with "a sharp snick"] is very much more recent that the date usually given to Milverton's crimes. The two accessories in use at the time accepted by most authorities were the little square attached to a table lamp, and the push-button in the wall for a chandelier, neither of which gave what might be called a 'snick.' If I am correct, the date for ["The Adventure of Charles Augustus Milverton"] would be around 1900 or 1901."

"YOU COULDN'T COME ANY OTHER TIME—EH?"

Illustration by Frederic Dorr Steele for *Collier's Magazine*, March 26, 1904. Sidney Paget illustrated the same scene for the *Strand Magazine*, April, 1904.

20 *and a straight, thin-lipped mouth set in a dangerous smile.* "It is surprising," Mr. L. W. Bailey wrote in "The Dark Lady of Appledore Towers," "that Watson should so stress the facial contours of one whose identity he is anxious to hide, but unless he is deliberately misleading us, we must accept his description and surmise that the lady was probably a member of one of the wealthy Jewish titled families of the period. These were quite a recent phenomena. Until the rise of the Rothschilds, Jews had not been accepted into aristocratic circles, and in 1869 Queen Victoria had refused to grant a peerage to Baron Lionel Rothschild, saying, 'To make a Jew a peer is a step the Queen could not assent to.' By the eighteen-eighties, however, the picture had changed radically. A Jew —D'Israeli—had been Prime Minister and the intimate confidant of the Queen herself, and was eventually ennobled as Lord Beaconsfield. In 1885 the Queen conferred a peerage on Nathaniel Rothschild, and against much opposition from the landed aristocracy the Prince of Wales had become intimate with the Rothschild family and admitted them into his circle. If the lady was of Jewish extraction it is quite clear that her husband was not, since he had a 'time-honoured title.' One may surmise therefore that he had married into one of the Jewish families he had met through the Prince of Wales . . ."

Several times I had observed that Milverton looked at his watch, and once he had risen and sat down again, with a gesture of impatience. The idea, however, that he might have an appointment at so strange an hour never occurred to me until a faint sound reached my ears from the veranda outside. Milverton dropped his papers and sat rigid in his chair. The sound was repeated, and then there came a gentle tap at the door. Milverton rose and opened it.

"Well," said he curtly, "you are nearly half an hour late."

So this was the explanation of the unlocked door and of the nocturnal vigil of Milverton. There was the gentle rustle of a woman's dress. I had closed the slit between the curtains as Milverton's face turned in our direction, but now I ventured very carefully to open it once more. He had resumed his seat, the cigar still projecting at an insolent angle from the corner of his mouth. In front of him, in the full glare of the electric light, there stood a tall, slim, dark woman, a veil over her face, a mantle drawn round her chin. Her breath came quick and fast, and every inch of the lithe figure was quivering with strong emotion.

"Well," said Milverton, "you've made me lose a good night's rest, my dear. I hope you'll prove worth it. You couldn't come any other time—eh?"

The woman shook her head.

"Well, if you couldn't you couldn't. If the countess is a hard mistress you have your chance to get level with her now. Bless the girl, what are you shivering about? That's right! Pull yourself together! Now, let us get down to business." He took a note from the drawer of his desk. "You say that you have five letters which compromise the Countess d'Albert. You want to sell them. I want to buy them. So far so good. It only remains to fix a price. I should want to inspect the letters, of course. If they are really good specimens—— Great heavens, is it you?"

The woman without a word had raised her veil and dropped the mantle from her chin. It was a dark, handsome, clear-cut face which confronted Milverton, a face with a curved nose, strong, dark eyebrows, shading hard, glittering eyes, and a straight, thin-lipped mouth set **20** in a dangerous smile.

"It is I," she said—"the woman whose life you have ruined."

Milverton laughed, but fear vibrated in his voice. "You were so very obstinate," said he. "Why did you drive me to such extremities? I assure you I wouldn't hurt a fly of my own accord, but every man has his business, and what was I to do? I put the price well within your means. You would not pay."

"So you sent the letters to my husband, and he—the noblest gentleman that ever lived, a man whose boots I was never worthy to lace—he broke his gallant heart and died. You remember that last night when I came through that door I begged and prayed you for mercy, and you laughed in my face as you are trying to laugh now, only your coward heart cannot keep your lips from twitching?

Yes ; you never thought to see me here again, but it was that night which taught me how I could meet you face to face, and alone. Well, Charles Milverton, what have you to say ? ''

" Don't imagine that you can bully me," said he, rising to his feet. " I have only to raise my voice, and I could call my servants and have you arrested. But I will make allowance for your natural anger. Leave the room at once as you came, and I will say no more."

The woman stood with her hand buried in her bosom, and the same deadly smile on her thin lips.

" You will ruin no more lives as you ruined mine. You will wring no more hearts as you wrung mine. I will free the world of a poisonous thing. Take that, you hound, and that !—and that !—and that !—and that ! ''

She had drawn a little gleaming revolver, and emptied barrel after barrel into Milverton's body, the muzzle **21** within two feet of his shirt-front. He shrank away, and then fell forward upon the table, coughing furiously and clawing among the papers. Then he staggered to his feet, received another shot, and rolled upon the floor. " You've done me," he cried, and lay still. The woman looked at him intently and ground her heel into his upturned face. She looked again, but there was no sound or movement. I heard a sharp rustle, the night air blew into the heated room, and the avenger was gone.

No interference upon our part could have saved the man from his fate ; but as the woman poured bullet after bullet into Milverton's shrinking body, I was about to spring out, when I felt Holmes' cold, strong grasp upon my wrist. I understood the whole argument of that firm, restraining grip—that it was no affair of ours ; that justice had overtaken a villain ; that we had our own duties and our own objects which were not to be lost sight of. But hardly had the woman rushed from the room when Holmes, with swift, silent steps, was over at the other door. He turned the key in the lock. At the same instant we heard voices in the house and the sound of hurrying feet. The revolver shots had roused the household. With perfect coolness Holmes slipped across to the safe, filled his two arms with bundles of letters, and poured them all into the fire. Again and again he did it, until the safe was empty. **22** Someone turned the handle and beat upon the outside of the door. Holmes looked swiftly round. The letter which had been the messenger of death for Milverton lay, all mottled with his blood, upon the table. Holmes tossed it in among the blazing papers. Then he drew the key from the outer door, passed through after me, and locked it on the outside. " This way, Watson," said he ; " we can scale the garden wall in this direction."

I could not have believed that an alarm could have spread so swiftly. Looking back, the huge house was one blaze of light. The front door was open, and figures were rushing down the drive. The whole garden was alive with people, and one fellow raised a view-halloa as we emerged from the veranda and followed hard at our heels. Holmes seemed to know the ground perfectly, and he threaded his way swiftly among a plantation of small trees, I close at his heels, and our foremost pursuer

21 *emptied barrel after barrel into Milverton's body*. Surely Watson meant "chamber after chamber" instead of "barrel after barrel"? Still, there was, as Professor Remsen Ten Eyck Schenck once pointed out, "a type of revolver, now obsolete, called . . . a 'pepperbox'; the antique was no more than an elongated cylinder revolving before the hammer, and may be variously considered to have either no barrel or a separate barrel for each chamber, however you choose to regard it." But this was a gun of great weight and could hardly have been called "a little gleaming revolver."

22 *Again and again he did it*. Lawyer Fenton: "A fairly clear case of malicious damage, and actionable at law."

But there is (perhaps) more to Holmes' action than this. As Dr. Richard Asher wrote, in "Holmes and the Fair Sex," "Was he doing this purely for his client Lady Eva Brackwell whose sprightly, very sprightly, letters to an impecunious country squire were endangering her impending marriage with the Earl of Dovercourt? Surely Lady Eva was quite safe once Milverton was dead. The letters could only have come into the hands of the police. Was it possible that among the papers in the safe there were some sprightly, very sprightly, letters from Holmes himself—perhaps to the woman who poisoned children for their insurance money [*The Sign of the Four*]. Perhaps to Milverton's housemaid, but in any case letters which had they reached Scotland Yard might have caused Holmes as much embarrassment as he usually gave to them?"

. . . RECEIVED ANOTHER SHOT, AND ROLLED UPON THE FLOOR.

Illustration by Sidney Paget for the *Strand Magazine*, April, 1904.

23 *but I kicked myself free*. Lawyer Fenton: "Watson kicks himself free from the arresting under-gardener and flees safely, terminating an incredibly felonious night by committing a technical battery on a citizen and violating the Persons Act of 1861 which brands as a crime 'an assault upon any constable in the execution of his duty or upon any person acting in aid of such a constable; an assault with intent to prevent the lawful apprehension either of the assailant himself or of any other person.' Lestrade, that odd mixture of obstinacy and futility, had of course placed a constable there, for he [later] tells Holmes, 'We have had our eyes on this Mr. Milverton for some time.'"

24 *We had run two miles, I suppose*. The late H. W. Bell was perhaps the first to say that this feat alone should indicate that this adventure took place some years before the duel at the Reichenbach Falls, when Holmes and Watson were both young men. But many other commentators have doubted that the two-mile run ever took place. "For," as the late Gavin Brend wrote, "apparently [Holmes and Watson] were not pursued out of the garden and although a man might run for a quarter of a mile before he realized that he was not being followed, a two-mile run in these circumstances would be fantastic." Indeed, as Mr. Michael Harrison pointed out (*In the Footsteps of Sherlock Holmes*) *it is not possible* "to run for two miles across the Heath; not even by loosely calling Parliament Hill and Ken Wood part of Hampstead Heath. The overall breadth of the Heath is just about one mile, only; while the maximum width across the open area comprising Hampstead Heath, Parliament Hill and Ken Wood is only about one and a half miles."

panting behind us. It was a six-foot wall which barred our path, but he sprang to the top and over. As I did the same I felt the hand of the man behind me grab at my **23** ankle ; but I kicked myself free, and scrambled over a glass-strewn coping. I fell upon my face among some bushes ; but Holmes had me on my feet in an instant, and together we dashed away across the huge expanse of **24** Hampstead Heath. We had run two miles, I suppose, before Holmes at last halted and listened intently. All was absolutely silence behind us. We had shaken off our pursuers, and were safe.

We had breakfasted and were smoking our morning pipe, on the day after the remarkable experience which I have recorded, when Mr. Lestrade, of Scotland Yard, very solemn and impressive, was ushered into our modest sitting-room.

" Good morning, Mr. Holmes," said he—" good morning. May I ask if you are very busy just now ? "

" Not too busy to listen to you."

" I thought that, perhaps, if you had nothing particular on hand, you might care to assist us in a most remarkable case which occurred only last night at Hampstead."

" Dear me ! " said Holmes. " What was that ? "

" A murder—a most dramatic and remarkable murder. I know how keen you are upon these things, and I would take it as a great favour if you would step down to Appledore Towers and give us the benefit of your advice. It is no ordinary crime. We have had our eyes upon this Mr. Milverton for some time, and, between ourselves, he was a bit of a villain. He is known to have held papers which he used for blackmailing purposes. These papers have all been burned by the murderers. No article of value was taken, as it is probable that the criminals were men of good position, whose sole object was to prevent social exposure."

" Criminals ! " exclaimed Holmes. " Plural ! "

" Yes, there were two of them. They were, as nearly as possible, captured red-handed. We have their footmarks, we have their description ; it's ten to one that we trace them. The first fellow was a bit too active, but the second was caught by the under-gardener, and only got away after a struggle. He was a middle-sized, strongly built man—square jaw, thick neck, moustache, a mask over his eyes."

" That's rather vague," said Sherlock Holmes. " Why, it might be a description of Watson ! "

" It's true," said the Inspector, with much amusement. " It might be a description of Watson."

" Well, I am afraid I can't help you, Lestrade," said Holmes. " The fact is that I knew this fellow Milverton, that I considered him one of the most dangerous men in London, and that I think there are certain crimes which the law cannot touch, and which therefore, to some extent, justify private revenge. No, it's no use arguing. I have made up my mind. My sympathies are with the criminals rather than with the victim, and I will not handle this case."

Holmes had not said one word to me about the tragedy

which we had witnessed, but I observed all the morning that he was in the most thoughtful mood, and he gave me the impression, from his vacant eyes and his abstracted manner, of a man who is striving to recall something to his memory. We were in the middle of our lunch, when he suddenly sprang to his feet. " By Jove, Watson ! I've got it ! " he cried. " Take your hat ! Come with me ! " He hurried at his top speed down Baker Street and along Oxford Street, until we had almost reached Regent Circus. Here on the left hand there stands a shop window filled with photographs of the **25** celebrities and beauties of the day. Holmes' eyes fixed themselves upon one of them, and following his gaze I saw the picture of a regal and stately lady in Court dress, with a high diamond tiara upon her noble head. I looked at that delicately curved nose, at the marked eyebrows, at the straight mouth, and the strong little chin beneath it. Then I caught my breath as I read the time-honoured title of the great nobleman and statesman whose wife she had been. My eyes met those of Holmes, and he put his finger to his lips as we turned away from the window.

. . . I SAW THE PICTURE OF A REGAL AND
STATELY LADY . . .

Illustration by Sidney Paget for the *Strand Magazine*, April, 1904.

25 *a shop window filled with photographs.* This day, if we can believe Watson, was the 14th of the month—and no shop window, in the eighties, would be unshuttered on the Sabbath. Since the 14th of the month in question was not a Sunday, this eliminates February, 1897; March, 1897; January, 1900; December, 1902; and February, 1904— and we must now ask the thorny question: in what month of what year did "The Adventure of Charles Augustus Milverton" take place? Watson has told us that the evening of the 13th was "a wild, tempestuous evening, when the wind screamed and rattled against the windows"; "it was bitterly cold, and the wind seemed to blow through us." Milverton, we know, called on Holmes "on a cold, frosty winter's evening"; on that evening, Holmes said: "She [Lady Eva] is to be married in a fortnight." As the late Dr. Ernest Bloomfield Zeisler wrote, Holmes may not have meant a fortnight to the day, but Milverton's call on Holmes must certainly have been within a day or two at the most of the 4th of the month in question. A careful examination of the meteorological records of all the months remaining to us has dictated your editor's choice of *January, 1899*. In that month, the temperature fell to 31.3° on the 5th (a Thursday). On the 13th (a Friday) the wind achieved a pressure of 15.9 pounds to the inch. The minimum temperature was 39.6°—not, perhaps, as bitter as we would like to have it, but uncomfortable enough in such a gale, and within eight degrees of freezing. The fact that Holmes and Watson burgled Appledore Towers on the night of *Friday the 13th* leads us to wonder if the date itself could have been the cause of Watson's uneasiness. Was the good doctor by any chance exceptionally superstitious?

Bibliographical Note: The original manuscript of this chronicle, titled "The Adventure of the Worst Man in London," about 6,800 words in 21 folio pages, vellum by Spealls, was auctioned in New York City on January 30, 1923, bringing $70. It was listed in Scribner's Sherlock Holmes Catalogue at $450. Its owner, at one time, was the late Edgar W. Smith. It was sold, on Mr. Smith's death, to Mr. Carl Anderson of Philadelphia as part of Mr. Smith's Sherlockian estate.

64

THE ADVENTURE OF THE SIX NAPOLEONS

[Friday, June 8, to Sunday, June 10, 1900]

IT was no very unusual thing for Mr. Lestrade, of Scotland Yard, to look in upon us of an evening, and his visits were welcome to Sherlock Holmes, for they enabled him to keep in touch with all that was going on at the police headquarters. In return for the news which Lestrade would bring, Holmes was always ready to listen with attention to the details of any case upon which the detective was engaged, and was able occasionally, without any active interference, to give some hint or suggestion drawn from his own vast knowledge and experience.

On this particular evening Lestrade had spoken of the weather and the newspapers. Then he had fallen silent, puffing thoughtfully at his cigar. Holmes looked keenly at him.

" Anything remarkable on hand ? " he asked.

" Oh, no, Mr. Holmes, nothing very particular."

" Then tell me all about it."

Lestrade laughed.

" Well, Mr. Holmes, there is no use denying that there *is* something on my mind. And yet it is such an absurd business that I hesitated to bother you about it. On the other hand, although it is trivial, it is undoubtedly queer, and I know that you have a taste for all that is out of the common. But in my opinion it comes more in Dr. Watson's line than ours."

" Disease ? " said I.

" Madness, anyhow. And a queer madness too ! You wouldn't think there was anyone living at this time of day who had such a hatred of Napoleon the First that he would break any image of him that he could see."

Holmes sank back in his chair.

" That's no business of mine," said he.

" Exactly. That's what I said. But then, when the man commits burglary in order to break images which are not his own, that brings it away from the doctor and on to the policeman."

Holmes sat up again.

" Burglary ! This is more interesting. Let me hear the details."

Lestrade took out his official notebook and refreshed his memory from its pages.

" The first case reported was four days ago," said he. " It was at the shop of Morse Hudson, who has a place **1** for the sale of pictures and statues in the Kennington Road. The assistant had left the front shop for an instant, when he heard a crash, and, hurrying in, found a plaster bust of Napoleon, which stood with several other works of art upon the counter, lying shivered into fragments. He rushed out into the road, but, although several passers-by declared that they had noticed a man run out of the shop, he could neither see anyone nor could he find any means of identifying the rascal. It seemed to be one of those senseless acts of hooliganism which occur from time to time, and it was reported to the constable on the beat as such. The plaster cast was not worth more than a few shillings, and the whole affair appeared to be too childish for any particular investigation.

" The second case, however, was more serious and also more singular. It occurred only last night.

" In Kennington Road, and within a few hundred yards of Morse Hudson's shop, there lives a well-known medical practitioner, named Dr. Barnicot, who has one of the largest practices upon the south side of the Thames. His residence and principal consulting-room is at Kennington Road, but he has a branch surgery and dispensary at Lower Brixton Road, two miles away. This Dr. Barnicot is an enthusiastic admirer of Napoleon, and his house is full of books, pictures, and relics of the French Emperor. Some little time ago he purchased from Morse Hudson two duplicate plaster casts of the famous head of Napoleon by the French sculptor Devine. One of these he placed in his hall in the house at Kennington Road, and the other on the mantelpiece of the surgery at Lower Brixton. Well, when Dr. Barnicot came down this morning he was astonished to find that his house had been burgled during the night, but that nothing had been taken save the plaster head from the hall. It had been carried out, and had been dashed savagely against the garden wall, under which its splintered fragments were discovered."

Holmes rubbed his hands.

" This is certainly very novel," said he.

" I thought it would please you. But I have not got to the end yet. Dr. Barnicot was due at his surgery at twelve o'clock, and you can imagine his amazement when, on arriving there, he found that the window had been opened in the night, and that the broken pieces of his second bust were strewn all over the room. It had been smashed to atoms where it stood. In neither case were there any signs which could give us a clue as to the criminal or lunatic who had done the mischief. Now, Mr. Holmes, you have got the facts."

" They are singular, not to say grotesque," said Holmes. " May I ask whether the two busts smashed in Dr. Barnicot's rooms were the exact duplicates of the one which was destroyed in Morse Hudson's shop ? "

" They were taken from the same mould."

" Such a fact must tell against the theory that the man

1 *Morse Hudson.* As we have previously noted, Mr. Manly Wade Wellman, in "The Great Man's Great Son," has identified Morse Hudson both as the Hudson who blackmailed Squire Trevor ("The *Gloria Scott*") and the estranged husband of Holmes' landlady, Mrs. Hudson.

who breaks them is influenced by any general hatred of Napoleon. Considering how many hundreds of statues of the great Emperor must exist in London, it is too much to suppose such a coincidence as that a promiscuous iconoclast should chance to begin upon three specimens of the same bust."

"Well, I thought as you do," said Lestrade. "On the other hand, this Morse Hudson is the purveyor of busts in that part of London, and these three were the only ones which had been in his shop for years. So although, as you say, there are many hundreds of statues in London, it is very probable that these three were the only ones in that district. Therefore a local fanatic would begin with them. What do you think, Dr. Watson ? "

"There are no limits to the possibilities of monomania," I answered. "There is the condition which the modern French psychologists have called the ' *idée fixe*,' which may be trifling in character, and accompanied by complete sanity in every other way. A man who had read deeply about Napoleon, or who had possibly received some hereditary family injury through the great war, might conceivably form such an ' *idée fixe*,' and under its influence be capable of any fantastic outrage."

"That won't do, my dear Watson," said Holmes, shaking his head ; " for no amount of ' *idée fixe* ' would enable your interesting monomaniac to find out where these busts were situated."

"Well, how do *you* explain it ? "

" I don't attempt to do so. I would only observe that there is a certain method in the gentleman's eccentric proceedings. For example, in Dr. Barnicot's hall where a sound might arouse the family, the bust was taken outside before being broken, whereas in the surgery, where there was less danger of an alarm, it was smashed where it stood. The affair seems absurdly trifling, and yet I dare call nothing trivial when I reflect that some of my most classic cases have had the least promising commencement. You will remember, Watson, how the dreadful business of the Abernetty family was first brought to my notice by the depth which the parsley had **2** sunk into the butter upon a hot day. I can't afford, therefore, to smile at your three broken busts, Lestrade, and I shall be very much obliged to you if you will let me hear of any fresh developments of so singular a chain of events."

The development for which my friend had asked came in a quicker and an infinitely more tragic form than he could have imagined. I was still dressing in my bedroom next morning, when there was a tap at the door, and Holmes entered, a telegram in his hand. He read it aloud :

"Come instantly, 131 Pitt Street, Kensington.— LESTRADE."

"What is it, then ? " I asked.
"Don't know—may be anything. But I suspect it is the sequel of the story of the statues. In that case our friend the image-breaker has begun operations in another

2 *by the depth which the parsley had sunk into the butter upon a hot day.* "We may compare a somewhat similar example in the career of Sergt. Cuff—see Wilkie Collins, *The Moonstone*, chap. xii," Mr. T. S. Blakeney commented. For a pastiche by Mr. Richard W. Clarke stemming from this reference of Holmes', see "The Dreadful Business of the Abernetty Family" in the *Baker Street Journal*, Vol. XI, No. 1, New Series, January, 1961, pp. 13–26.

quarter of London. There's coffee on the table, Watson, and I have a cab at the door."

In half an hour we had reached Pitt Street, a quiet little backwater just beside one of the briskest currents of London life. No. 131 was one of a row, all flat-chested, **3** respectable, and most unromantic dwellings. As we drove up we found the railings in front of the house lined by a curious crowd. Holmes whistled.

" By George ! it's attempted murder at the least. Nothing less will hold the London message boy. There's a deed of violence indicated in that fellow's round shoulders and outstretched neck. What's this, Watson ? The top step swilled down and the other ones dry. Footsteps enough, anyhow ! Well, well, there's Lestrade at the front window, and we shall soon know all about it."

The official received us with a very grave face and showed us into a sitting-room, where an exceedingly unkempt and agitated elderly man, clad in a flannel dressing-gown, was pacing up and down. He was introduced to us as the owner of the house—Mr. Horace Harker, of the Central Press Syndicate. **4**

" It's the Napoleon bust business again," said Lestrade. " You seemed interested last night, Mr. Holmes, so I thought perhaps you would be glad to be present now that the affair has taken a very much graver turn."

" What has it turned to, then ? "

" To murder. Mr. Harker, will you tell these gentlemen exactly what has occurred ? "

The man in the dressing-gown turned upon us with a most melancholy face.

" It's an extraordinary thing," said he, " that all my life I have been collecting other people's news, and now that a real piece of news has come my own way I am so confused and bothered that I can't put two words together. If I had come in here as a journalist I should have interviewed myself and had two columns in every evening paper. **5** As it is, I am giving away valuable copy by telling my story over and over to a string of different people, and I can make no use of it myself. However, I've heard your name, Mr. Sherlock Holmes, and if you'll only explain this queer business I shall be paid for my trouble in telling you the story."

Holmes sat down and listened.

" It all seems to centre round that bust of Napoleon which I bought for this very room about four months ago. I picked it up cheap from Harding Brothers, two doors from the High Street Station. A great deal of my journalistic work is done at night, and I often write until the early morning. So it was to-day. I was sitting in my den, which is at the back of the top of the house, about three o'clock, when I was convinced that I heard some sounds downstairs. I listened, but they were not repeated, and I concluded that they came from outside. Then suddenly, about five minutes later, there came a most horrible yell—the most dreadful sound, Mr. Holmes, that ever I heard. It will ring in my ears as long as I live. I sat frozen with horror for a minute or two. Then I seized the poker and went downstairs. When I entered this room I found the window wide open, and I at once observed that the bust was gone from the mantel-

3 *No. 131 was one of a row.* "There are not many houses [in Pitt Street]," the late H. W. Bell wrote in "Three Identifications," "—they are numbered 1–13, and 2–18—and most of them have bow-windows and a low balustraded front; but a group of five (Nos. 10–18) corresponds in every way to Watson's account. . . . The number as reported is a disguise. Perhaps it stands for No. 14."

4 *the Central Press Syndicate.* In fact, the Central News Agency. It was to the Central News Agency that Jack the Ripper mailed two horribly jocund notes in late September and early October, 1888. In "A Challenge from Baker Street," Mr. Charles Fisher has set forth the interesting hypothesis that Mr. Horace Harker was himself Jack the Ripper.

5 *in every evening paper.* "How was Mr. Harker going to do this?" John Hyslop asked in "Sherlock Holmes and the Press." "Two columns amounted to about 2,000 words, and even with 'his pen travelling shrilly over the foolscap' that would have taken Mr. Harker two hours to write. He would then have to get it across London to Fleet Street, and it would have to be duplicated and delivered to . . . six or seven newspaper offices. Nevertheless, he did succeed in getting something into the evening papers, including a few sly paragraphs suggested by Holmes . . ."

HE WAS INTRODUCED TO US AS THE OWNER
OF THE HOUSE . . .

Illustration by Sidney Paget for the *Strand Magazine*, May, 1904.

piece. Why any burglar should take such a thing passes my understanding, for it was only a plaster cast, and of no real value whatever.

"You can see for yourself that anyone going out through that open window could reach the front doorstep by taking a long stride. This was clearly what the burglar had done, so I went round and opened the door. Stepping out into the dark I nearly fell over a dead man who was lying there. I ran back for a light, and there was the poor fellow, a great gash in his throat and the whole place swimming in blood. He lay on his back, his knees drawn up, and his mouth horribly open. I shall see him in my dreams. I had just time to blow on my police whistle, and then I must have fainted, for I knew nothing more until I found the policeman standing over me in the hall."

"Well, who was the murdered man?" asked Holmes.

"There's nothing to show who he was," said Lestrade. "You shall see the body at the mortuary, but we have made nothing of it up to now. He is a tall man, sunburnt, very powerful, not more than thirty. He is poorly dressed, and yet does not appear to be a labourer. A horn-handled clasp-knife was lying in a pool of blood beside him. Whether it was the weapon which did the deed, or whether it belonged to the dead man, I do not know. There was no name on his clothing, and nothing in his pockets save an apple, some string, a shilling map of London, and a photograph. Here it is."

It was evidently taken by a snap-shot from a small camera. It represented an alert, sharp-featured simian man with thick eyebrows, and a very peculiar projection of the lower part of the face like the muzzle of a baboon.

"And what became of the bust?" asked Holmes, after a careful study of this picture.

"We had news of it just before you came. It has been found in the front garden of an empty house in Campden **6** House Road. It was broken into fragments. I am going round now to see it. Will you come?"

"Certainly. I must just take one look round." He examined the carpet and the window. "The fellow had either very long legs or was a most active man," said he. "With an area beneath it was no mean feat to reach that window-ledge and open that window. Getting back was comparatively simple. Are you coming with us to see the remains of your bust, Mr. Harker?"

The disconsolate journalist had seated himself at a writing-table.

"I must try and make something of it," said he, "though I have no doubt that the first editions of the evening papers are out already with full details. It's like my luck! You remember when the stand fell at **7** Doncaster! Well, I was the only journalist in the stand, and my journal the only one that had no account of it, for I was too shaken to write it. And now I'll be too late with a murder done on my own doorstep."

As we left the room we heard his pen travelling shrilly over the foolscap.

The spot where the fragments of the bust had been found was only a few hundred yards away. For the first

6 *Campden House Road.* "There is no Campden *House* Road," Mr. Bell wrote in "Three Identifications." "Watson certainly meant to write Campden Hill Road, but his eye was caught by the word 'house' immediately before, in the same sentence. In this long street only two houses (Nos. 49 and 51) within a reasonable distance of Pitt Street possess front grass-plots; the others are separated from the pavement by narrow sunken areas. On the pavement before one of them, No. 51, is a lamppost, as required by the narrative. It is less than 400 yards from the group of five houses in Pitt Street."

7 *You remember when the stand fell at Doncaster!* The late Professor Jay Finley Christ believed that the news current at the time he was writing had a considerable effect on Watson. "The Adventure of the Six Napoleons" was first published in the spring of 1904, and "In Whitaker for 1903, one finds that a stand had fallen in April, 1902, at Glasgow, killing some 21 persons."

time our eyes rested upon this presentment of the great Emperor, which seemed to raise such frantic and destructive hatred in the mind of the unknown. It lay scattered in splintered shards upon the grass. Holmes picked up several of them and examined them carefully. I was convinced from his intent face and his purposeful manner that at last he was upon a clue.

" Well ? " asked Lestrade.

Holmes shrugged his shoulders.

" We have a long way to go yet," said he. " And yet —and yet—well, we have some suggestive facts to act upon. The possession of this trifling bust was worth more in the eyes of this strange criminal than a human life. That is one point. Then there is the singular fact that he did not break it in the house, or immediately outside the house, if to break it was his sole object."

" He was rattled and bustled by meeting this other fellow. He hardly knew what he was doing."

" Well, that's likely enough. But I wish to call your attention very particularly to the position of this house in the garden of which the bust was destroyed."

Lestrade looked about him.

" It was an empty house, and so he knew that he would not be disturbed in the garden."

" Yes, but there is another empty house farther up the street which he must have passed before he came to this one. Why did he not break it there, since it is evident that every yard that he carried it increased the risk of someone meeting him ? "

" I give it up," said Lestrade.

Holmes pointed to the street lamp above our heads.

" He could see what he was doing here, and he could not there. That was the reason."

" By Jove ! that's true," said the detective. " Now that I come to think of it, Mr. Barnicot's bust was broken not far from his red lamp. Well, Mr. Holmes, what are we to do with that fact ? "

" To remember it—to docket it. We may come on something later which will bear upon it. What steps do you propose to take now, Lestrade ? "

" The most practical way of getting at it, in my opinion, is to identify the dead man. There should be no difficulty about that. When we have found who he is and who his associates are, we should have a good start in learning what he was doing in Pitt Street last night, and who it was who met him and killed him on the doorstep of Mr. Horace Harker. Don't you think so ? "

" No doubt ; and yet it is not quite the way in which I should approach the case."

" What would you do then ? "

" Oh, you must not let me influence you in any way. I suggest that you go on your line and I on mine. We can compare notes afterwards, and each will supplement the other."

" Very good," said Lestrade.

" If you are going back to Pitt Street you might see Mr. Horace Harker. Tell him from me that I have quite made up my mind, and that it is certain that a dangerous homicidal lunatic with Napoleonic delusions was in his

HOLMES POINTED TO THE STREET LAMP
ABOVE OUR HEADS.

Illustration by Sidney Paget for the *Strand Magazine*, May, 1904.

8 *Until then I should like to keep this photograph.* ". . . how frightfully irregular of Holmes to ask to keep the photograph found in the dead man's pocket and of Lestrade to allow him to do!" Mr. James Edward Holroyd commented. "One feels that if the Commissioner of the time had heard of this misdemeanour he would have 'snapped at it like a hungry wolf.'"

9 *Stepney.* Stepney is "the Stibbenhidde or Stebenheth of early deeds: the affix indicating the *hid* or Haeredium of a Saxon freeman," wrote Augustus J. C. Hare in *Walks in London,* Vol. I. One of the largest of the metropolitan boroughs, it extends from the City boundary to Poplar from west to east and from the Thames to Bethnal Green from south to north.

house last night. It will be useful for his article."

Lestrade stared.

" You don't seriously believe that ? "

Holmes smiled.

" Don't I ? Well, perhaps I don't. But I am sure that it will interest Mr. Horace Harker and the subscribers of the Central Press Syndicate. Now, Watson, I think that we shall find that we have a long and rather complex day's work before us. I should be glad, Lestrade, if you could make it convenient to meet us at Baker Street at six o'clock this evening. Until then I should like to keep **8** this photograph found in the dead man's pocket. It is possible that I may have to ask your company and assistance upon a small expedition which will have to be undertaken to-night, if my chain of reasoning should prove to be correct. Until then, good-bye, and good luck."

Sherlock Holmes and I walked together to the High Street, where he stopped at the shop of Harding Brothers, whence the bust had been purchased. A young assistant informed us that Mr. Harding would be absent until afternoon, and that he was himself a new-comer, who could give us no information. Holmes' face showed his disappointment and annoyance.

" Well, well, we can't expect to have it all our own way, Watson," he said at last. " We must come back in the afternoon, if Mr. Harding will not be here until then. I am, as you have no doubt surmised, endeavouring to trace these busts to their source, in order to find if there is not something peculiar which may account for their remarkable fate. Let us make for Mr. Morse Hudson, of the Kennington Road, and see if he can throw any light upon the problem."

A drive of an hour brought us to the picture-dealer's establishment. He was a small, stout man with a red face and a peppery manner.

" Yes, sir. On my very counter, sir," said he. " What we pay rates and taxes for I don't know, when any ruffian can come in and break one's goods. Yes, sir, it was I who sold Dr. Barnicot his two statues. Disgraceful, sir ! A Nihilist plot, that's what I make it. No one but an Anarchist would go about breaking statues. Red republicans, that's what I call 'em. Who did I get the statues from ? I don't see what that has to do with it. Well, if you really want to know, I got them from Gelder & Co., **9** in Church Street, Stepney. They are a well-known house in the trade, and have been this twenty years. How many had I ? Three—two and one are three— two of Dr. Barnicot's and one smashed in broad daylight on my own counter. Do I know that photograph ? No, I don't. Yes, I do, though. Why, it's Beppo ! He was a kind of Italian piecework man, who made himself useful in the shop. He could carve a bit, and gild a frame, and do odd jobs. The fellow left me last week, and I've heard nothing of him since. No, I don't know where he came from nor where he went to. I have nothing against him while he was here. He was gone two days before the bust was smashed."

" Well, that's all we could reasonably expect to get

from Morse Hudson," said Holmes, as we emerged from the shop. "We have this Beppo as a common factor, both in Kennington and in Kensington, so that is worth a ten-mile drive. Now, Watson, let us make for Gelder & Co., of Stepney, the source and origin of busts. I shall be surprised if we don't get some help down there."

In rapid succession we passed through the fringe of fashionable London, hotel London, theartical London, literary London, commercial London, and, finally, maritime London, till we came to a river-side city of a hundred **10** thousand souls, where the tenement houses swelter and reek with the outcasts of Europe. Here, in a broad thoroughfare, once the abode of wealthy city merchants, we found the sculptor works for which we searched. Outside was a considerable yard full of monumental masonry. Inside was a large room in which fifty workers were carving or moulding. The manager, a big blond German, received us civilly, and gave a clear answer to all Holmes' questions. A reference to his books showed that hundreds of casts had been taken from a marble copy of Devine's head of Napoleon, but that the three which had been sent to Morse Hudson a year or so before had been half of a batch of six, the other three being sent to Harding Brothers, of Kensington. There was no reason why those six should be different to any of the other casts. He could suggest no possible cause why anyone should wish to destroy them—in fact, he laughed at the idea. Their wholesale price was six shillings, but the retailer would get twelve or more. The cast was taken in two moulds from each side of the face, and then these two profiles of plaster of Paris were joined together to make the complete bust. The work was usually done by Italians in the room we were in. When finished the busts were put on a table in the passage to dry, and afterwards stored. That was all he could tell us.

But the production of the photograph had a remarkable effect upon the manager. His face flushed with anger, and his brows knotted over his blue Teutonic eyes.

"Ah, the rascal!" he cried. "Yes, indeed, I know him very well. This has always been a respectable establishment, and the only time that we have ever had the police in it was over this very fellow. It was more than a year ago now. He knifed another Italian in the street, and then he came to the works with the police on his heels, and he was taken here. Beppo was his name—his second name I never knew. Serve me right for engaging a man with such a face. But he was a good workman—one of the best."

"What did he get?"

"The man lived, and he got off with a year. I have no doubt he is out now; but he has not dared to show his nose here. We have a cousin of his here, and I dare say he could tell you where he is."

"No, no," cried Holmes, "not a word to the cousin —not a word, I beg you. The matter is very important, and the farther I go with it the more important it seems to grow. When you referred in your ledger to the sale of

10 *and, finally, maritime London.* "How, in driving from Kennington to Stepney, would you pass successively through fashionable London, hotel London, theatrical London and literary London?" Mr. James Edward Holroyd has asked. "All these quarters are on the north side of the river, whereas the map suggests that the shorter and more obvious way would have been to continue on the south side, crossing at London Bridge."

"AH, THE RASCAL!" HE CRIED.

Illustration by Sidney Paget for the *Strand Magazine*, May, 1904.

11 *"Yes," he continued, after some turning over of pages.* ". . . although the manager of Gelder & Co. . . . had never known Beppo's second name, he was able to spot him immediately in the firm's paylist," Mr. Holroyd continued. "I should like to have seen the index to that pay-list. How do you enter the name of a man who has no surname? As Beppo 'X'? Or was the index conducted on the simple Holmesian principle of first names first as in Victor Lynch, the forger?"

12 *May 20."* Since May 20th was a payday, it must have been a Saturday; May 20th fell on a Saturday in 1882, 1893, and 1899; "The Adventure of the Six Napoleons" took place somewhat "more than a year" later, so the year in which the case took place is 1883, 1894, or 1900. It was not 1883, for two reasons: 1) Holmes later says to Watson: "If ever I permit you to chronicle any more of my little problems . . ." Watson evidently did not begin to chronicle Holmes' problems until 1887 ("A Scandal in Bohemia"). 2) Lestrade later says to Holmes: "I've seen you handle a good many cases, Mr. Holmes, but I don't know that I ever knew a more workmanlike one than that. We're not jealous of you at Scotland Yard. No sir, we are very proud of you, and if you come down to-morrow there is not a man, from the oldest inspector to the youngest constable, who wouldn't be glad to shake you by the hand." It was not until 1888–1889, as we have seen (*The Hound of the Baskervilles*), that Lestrade and other Scotland Yarders began to adopt a "reverential" attitude toward Holmes. Nor is the year 1894: the famous black pearl of the Borgias (we later learn) disappeared "exactly two days before the arrest of Beppo," and this, as we have seen, was "roughly" around "May 20." The disappearance created a sensation and Holmes says "I was myself consulted upon the case." But in late May, 1893, Holmes was believed dead beneath the Reichenbach. The year, then, was 1900. To determine the month of the adventure we must start with the date of Beppo's arrest—shortly after Saturday, May 20, 1889. It was not Sunday, May 21—his arrest "took place in the factory . . . at the very moment when [the] busts were being made"— and it was before Saturday, May 26th, since he was *not* paid on that day. His arrest was therefore on one of the five days Monday, May 22nd to Friday, May 26th, inclusive. We are justified in assuming that Beppo was sentenced very soon after his arrest, for the police only wished to determine whether or not his victim would live. The date of Beppo's sentencing cannot be much earlier than Thursday, May 25th, or much later than Monday, May 29th. Beppo got a year; he was therefore released from prison between May 25th and May 29, 1900. Certainly he would lose no time in looking up his cousin and obtaining employment at Morse Hudson's shop, and we know he worked for Hudson during the week preceding the week in which the adventure began: "The

those casts I observed that the date was June 3 of last year. Could you give me the date when Beppo was arrested ? "

" I could tell you roughly by the pay-list," the manager answered. "Yes," he continued, after some turning **11-12** over of pages, " he was paid last on May 20."

"Thank you," said Holmes. " I don't think that I need intrude upon your time and patience any more." With a last word of caution that he should say nothing as to our researches we turned our faces westward once more.

The afternoon was far advanced before we were able to snatch a hasty luncheon at a restaurant. A news-bill at the entrance announced " Kensington Outrage. Murder by a Madman," and the contents of the paper showed that Mr. Horace Harker had got his account into print after all. Two columns were occupied with a highly sensational and flowery rendering of the whole incident. Holmes propped it against the cruet-stand and read it while he ate. Once or twice he chuckled.

" This is all right, Watson," said he. " Listen to this : ' It is satisfactory to know that there can be no difference of opinion upon this case, since Mr. Lestrade, one of the most experienced members of the official force, and Mr. Sherlock Holmes, the well-known consulting expert, have each come to the conclusion that the grotesque series of incidents, which have ended in so tragic a fashion, arise from lunacy rather than from deliberate crime. No explanation save mental aberration can cover the facts.' The Press, Watson, is a most valuable institution, if you only know how to use it. And now, if you have quite finished, we will hark back to Kensington, and see what the manager of Harding Brothers has to say to the matter."

The founder of that great emporium proved to be a brisk, crisp little person, very dapper and quick, with a clear head and a ready tongue.

" Yes, sir, I have already read the account in the evening papers. Mr. Horace Harker is a customer of ours. We supplied him with the busts some months ago. We ordered three busts of that sort from Gelder & Co., of Stepney. They are all sold now. To whom ? Oh, I dare say by consulting our sales book we could very easily tell you. Yes, we have the entries here. One to Mr. Harker, you see, and one to Mr. Josiah Brown, of Laburnum Lodge, Laburnum Vale, Chiswick, and one to Mr. Sandeford, of Lower Grove Road, Reading. No, I have never seen this face which you show me in the photograph. You would hardly forget it—would you, sir ?—for I've seldom seen an uglier. Have we any Italians on the staff ? Yes, sir, we have several among our workpeople and cleaners. I dare say they might get a peep at that sales book if they wanted to. There is no particular reason for keeping a watch upon that book. Well, well, it's a very strange business, and I hope that you'll let me know if anything comes of your inquiries."

Holmes had taken several notes during Mr. Harding's evidence, and I could see that he was thoroughly satisfied by the turn which affairs were taking. He made no remark, however, save that, unless we hurried, we should be late for our appointment with Lestrade. Sure enough, when we reached Baker Street the detective was already there, and we found him pacing up and down in a fever of impatience. His look of importance showed that his day's work had not been in vain.

" Well ? " he asked. " What luck, Mr. Holmes ? "

" We have had a very busy day, and not entirely a wasted one," my friend explained. " We have seen both the retailers and also the wholesale manufacturers. I can trace each of the busts now from the beginning."

" The busts ! " cried Lestrade. " Well, well, you have your own methods, Mr. Sherlock Holmes, and it is not for me to say a word against them, but I think I have done a better day's work than you. I have identified the dead man."

" You don't say so ! "

" And found a cause for the crime."

" Splendid ! "

" We have an inspector who makes a speciality of Saffron Hill and the Italian quarter. Well, this dead **13** man had some Catholic emblem round his neck, and that, along with his colour, made me think he was from the South. Inspector Hill knew him the moment he caught sight of him. His name is Pietro Venucci, from Naples, and he is one of the greatest cut-throats in London. He is connected with the Mafia, which, as you know, is a secret political society, enforcing its decrees by murder. Now you see how the affair begins to clear up. The other fellow is probably an Italian also, and a member of the Mafia. He has broken the rules in some fashion. Pietro is set upon his track. Probably the photograph we found in his pocket is the man himself, so that he may not knife the wrong person. He dogs the fellow, he sees him enter a house, he waits outside for him, and in the scuffle he receives his own death-wound. How is that, Mr. Sherlock Holmes ? "

Holmes clapped his hands approvingly.

" Excellent, Lestrade, excellent ! " he cried. " But I didn't quite follow your explanation of the destruction of the busts."

" The busts ! You never can get those busts out of your head. After all, that is nothing ; petty larceny, six months at the most. It is the murder that we are really investigating, and I tell you that I am gathering all the threads into my hands."

" And the next stage ? "

" Is a very simple one. I shall go down with Hill to the Italian quarter, find the man whose photograph we have got, and arrest him on the charge of murder. Will you come with us ? "

" I think not. I fancy we can attain our end in a simpler way. I can't say for certain, because it all depends—well, it all depends upon a factor which is completely outside our control. But I have great hopes— in fact, the betting is exactly two to one—that if you will come with us to-night I shall be able to help you to lay him by the heels."

" In the Italian quarter ? "

fellow left me last week. . . . He was gone two days when the bust was smashed." It is extremely unlikely that Beppo left Hudson without collecting his pay for a week's work—to do so would be to arouse suspicion and perhaps investigation of his activities, the last thing he would want. We deduce that he worked for Hudson from Monday, May 28th, to Saturday, June 2nd, collected his pay on the Saturday and left. (To suppose that Beppo worked for Hudson from Monday, June 4th, to Saturday, June 9th, leaves much too long a gap between his release from prison and his obtaining employment at Hudson's shop.) It is not clear from Mr. Hudson's account whether the first bust was smashed on the second or third day after Beppo's departure; in either case, the day must be Monday, June 4th, or Tuesday, June 5th. On the first day of the case, Lestrade told Holmes that the first instance of bust-smashing was reported "four days ago." The case must therefore open on Friday, June 8th, or Saturday, June 9th. We know that the first day was not Saturday, June 9th, since on the *second* day evening newspapers were published; the shop of Harding Brothers was open, as was Morse Hudson's, as was Gelder & Co. Furthermore, as we learn later, Mr. Sandeford of Reading sold his bust of Napoleon to Holmes on the third day of the case. "Not a very rich man," he could hardly have afforded to take time from work to journey from Reading to Baker Street. Almost certainly, he would have called on Holmes on a Sunday—and this is substantiated by his remark that "the trains were awkward"; they would hardly have been so on a weekday. We conclude that the case began on *Friday, June 8,* and ended on *Sunday, June 10, 1900.*

13 *Saffron Hill.* So called because saffron once grew in the garden of Ely House, the old palace of the Bishops of Ely, built in 1388 by Bishop Arundel.

... HE CARRIED SOMETHING WHITE UNDER HIS ARM.

Illustration by Charles Raymond Macauley for *The Return of Sherlock Holmes,* New York: McClure, Phillips & Co., 1905.

WITH THE BOUND OF A TIGER HOLMES WAS ON HIS BACK . . .

Illustration by Sidney Paget for the *Strand Magazine,* May, 1904.

" No ; I fancy Chiswick is an address which is more likely to find him. If you will come with me to Chiswick to-night, Lestrade, I'll promise to go to the Italian quarter with you to-morrow, and no harm will be done by the delay. And now I think that a few hours' sleep would do us all good, for I do not propose to leave before eleven o'clock, and it is unlikely that we shall be back before morning. You'll dine with us, Lestrade, and then you are welcome to the sofa until it is time for us to start. In the meantime, Watson, I should be glad if you would ring for an express messenger, for I have a letter to send, and it is important that it should go at once."

Holmes spent the evening in rummaging among the files of the old daily papers with which one of our lumber-rooms was packed. When at last he descended it was with triumph in his eyes, but he said nothing to either of us as to the result of his researches. For my own part, I had followed step by step the methods by which he had traced the various windings of this complex case, and, though I could not yet perceive the goal which we would reach, I understood clearly that Holmes expected this grotesque criminal to make an attempt upon the two remaining busts, one of which, I remember, was at Chiswick. No doubt the object of our journey was to catch him in the very act, and I could not but admire the cunning with which my friend had inserted a wrong clue in the evening paper so as to give the fellow the idea that he could continue his scheme with impunity. I was not surprised when Holmes suggested that I should take my revolver with me. He had himself picked up the loaded hunting-crop which was his favourite weapon.

A four-wheeler was at the door at eleven, and in it we drove to a spot at the other side of Hammersmith Bridge. Here the cabman was directed to wait. A short walk brought us to a secluded road fringed with pleasant houses, each standing in its own grounds. In the light of a street lamp we read " Laburnum Villa " upon the gate-post of one of them. The occupants had evidently retired to rest, for all was dark save for a fanlight over the hall door, which shed a single blurred circle on to the garden path. The wooden fence which separated the grounds from the road threw a dense black shadow upon the inner side, and here it was that we crouched.

" I fear that you'll have a long time to wait," Holmes whispered. " We may thank our stars that it is not raining. I don't think we can even venture to smoke to pass the time. However, it's a two to one chance that we get something to pay us for our trouble."

It proved, however, that our vigil was not to be so long as Holmes had led us to fear, and it ended in a very sudden and singular fashion. In an instant, without the least sound to warn us of his coming, the garden gate swung open, and a lithe, dark figure, as swift and active as an ape, rushed up the garden path. We saw it whisk past the light thrown from over the door and disappear against the black shadow of the house. There was a long pause, during which we held our breath, and then a very gentle creaking sound came to our ears. The window was being opened. The noise ceased, and again there was a long silence. The fellow was making his way into the house. We saw the sudden flash of a dark lantern inside the room. What he sought was evidently not there, for again we saw the flash through another blind, and then through another.

"Let us get to the open window. We will nab him as he climbs out," Lestrade whispered.

But before we could move the man had emerged again. As he came out into the glimmering patch of light we saw that he carried something white under his arm. He looked stealthily all round him. The silence of the deserted street reassured him. Turning his back upon us, he laid down his burden, and the next instant there was the sound of a sharp tap, followed by a clatter and rattle. The man was so intent upon what he was doing that he never heard our steps as we stole across the grass plot. With the bound of a tiger Holmes was on his back, and an instant later Lestrade and I had him by either wrist, and the handcuffs had been fastened. As we turned him over I saw a hideous, sallow face, with writhing, furious features glaring up at us, and I knew that it was indeed the man of the photograph whom we had secured.

But it was not our prisoner to whom Holmes was giving his attention. Squatted on the doorstep, he was engaged in most carefully examining that which the man had brought from the house. It was a bust of Napoleon like the one which we had seen that morning, and it had been broken into similar fragments. Carefully Holmes held each separate shard to the light, but in no way did it differ from any other shattered piece of plaster. He had just completed his examination, when the hall lights flew up, the door opened, and the owner of the house, a jovial, rotund figure in shirt and trousers, presented himself.

"Mr. Josiah Brown, I suppose?" said Holmes.

"Yes, sir; and you no doubt are Mr. Sherlock Holmes? I had the note which you sent by the express messenger, and I did exactly what you told me. We locked every door on the inside and awaited developments. Well, I'm very glad to see that you have got the rascal. I hope, gentlemen, that you will come in and have some refreshment."

However, Lestrade was anxious to get his man into safe quarters, so within a few minutes our cab had been summoned and we were all four upon our way to London. Not a word would our captive say; but he glared at us from the shadow of his matted hair, and once, when my hand seemed within his reach, he snapped at it like a hungry wolf. We stayed long enough at the police-station to learn that a search of his clothing revealed nothing save a few shillings and a long sheath knife, the handle of which bore copious traces of recent blood.

"That's all right," said Lestrade, as we parted. "Hill knows all these gentry, and he will give a name to him. You'll find that my theory of the Mafia will work out all right. But I'm sure I am exceedingly obliged to you, Mr. Holmes, for the workmanlike way in which you laid hands upon him. I don't quite understand it all yet."

HE HAD JUST COMPLETED HIS EXAMINATION, WHEN THE HALL LIGHTS FLEW UP . . .

Illustration by Frederic Dorr Steele for *Collier's Magazine*, April 30, 1904.

. . . THE DOOR OPENED, AND THE OWNER OF THE HOUSE . . . PRESENTED HIMSELF.

Illustration by Sidney Paget for the *Strand Magazine*, May, 1904.

" I fear it is rather too late an hour for explanations," said Holmes. " Besides, there are one or two details which are not finished off, and it is one of those cases which are worth working out to the very end. If you will come round once more to my rooms at six o'clock to-morrow I think I shall be able to show you that even now you have not grasped the entire meaning of this business, which presents some features which make it absolutely original in the history of crime. If ever I permit you to chronicle any more of my little problems, Watson, I foresee that you will enliven your pages by an account of the singular adventure of the Napoleonic busts."

When we met again next evening, Lestrade was furnished with much information concerning our prisoner. His name, it appeared, was Beppo, second name unknown. He was a well-known ne'er-do-well among the Italian colony. He had once been a skilful sculptor and had earned an honest living, but he had taken to evil courses, and had twice already been in gaol—once for a petty theft and once, as we had already heard, for stabbing a fellow-countryman. He could talk English perfectly well. His reasons for destroying the busts were still unknown, and he refused to answer any questions upon the subject ; but the police had discovered that these same busts might very well have been made by his own hands, since he was engaged in this class of work at the establishment of Gelder & Co. To all this information, much of which we already knew, Holmes listened with polite attention ; but I, who knew him so well, could clearly see that his thoughts were elsewhere, and I detected a mixture of mingled uneasiness and expectation beneath that mask which he was wont to assume. At last he started in his chair and his eyes brightened. There had been a ring at the bell. A minute later we heard steps upon the stairs, and an elderly, red-faced man with grizzled side-whiskers was ushered in. In his right hand he carried an old-fashioned carpet-bag, which he placed upon the table.

" Is Mr. Sherlock Holmes here ? "

My friend bowed and smiled. " Mr. Sandeford, of Reading, I suppose ? " said he.

" Yes, sir. I fear that I am a little late ; but the trains were awkward. You wrote to me about a bust that is in my possession."

" Exactly."

" I have your letter here. You said, ' I desire to possess a copy of Devine's Napoleon, and am prepared to pay you ten pounds for the one which is in your possession.' Is that right ? "

" Certainly."

" I was very much surprised at your letter, for I could not imagine how you knew that I owned such a thing."

" Of course you must have been surprised, but the explanation is very simple. Mr. Harding, of Harding Brothers, said that they had sold you their last copy, and he gave me your address."

" Oh, that was it, was it ? Did he tell you what I paid for it ? "

" No, he did not."

" Well, I am an honest man, though not a very rich one. I only gave fifteen shillings for the bust, and I think you ought to know that before I take ten pounds from you."

" I am sure the scruple does you honour, Mr. Sandeford. But I have named that price, so I intend to stick to it."

" Well, it is very handsome of you, Mr. Holmes. I brought the bust up with me, as you asked me to do. Here it is ! "

He opened his bag, and at last we saw placed upon our table a complete specimen of that bust which we had already seen more than once in fragments.

Holmes took a paper from his pocket and laid a ten-pound note upon the table.

" You will kindly sign that paper, Mr. Sandeford, in the presence of these witnesses. It is simply to say that you transfer every possible right that you ever had in the bust to me. I am a methodical man, you see, and you never know what turn events might take afterwards. Thank you, Mr. Sandeford ; here is your money, and I wish you a very good evening."

When our visitor had disappeared Sherlock Holmes' movements were such as to rivet our attention. He began by taking a clean white cloth from a drawer and laying it over the table. Then he placed his newly acquired bust in the centre of the cloth. Finally he picked up his hunting-crop and struck Napoleon a sharp blow on the top of the head. The figure broke into fragments, and Holmes bent eagerly over the shattered remains. Next instant, with a loud shout of triumph, he held up one splinter, in which a round, dark object was fixed like a plum in a pudding.

" Gentlemen," he cried, " let me introduce you to the famous black pearl of the Borgias ! "

Lestrade and I sat silent for a moment, and then, with a spontaneous impulse, we both broke out clapping as at the well-wrought crisis of a play. A flush of colour sprang to Holmes' pale cheeks, and he bowed to us like the master dramatist who receives the homage of his audience. It was at such moments that for an instant he ceased to be a reasoning machine, and betrayed his human love for admiration and applause. The same singularly proud and reserved nature which turned away with disdain from popular notoriety was capable of being moved to its depths by spontaneous wonder and praise from a friend.

" Yes, gentlemen," said he, " it is the most famous pearl now existing in the world, and it has been my good fortune by a connected chain of inductive reasoning, to trace it from the Prince of Colonna's bedroom at the Dacre Hotel, where it was lost, to the interior of this, the last of the six busts of Napoleon which were manufactured by Gelder & Co., of Stepney. You will remember, Lestrade, the sensation caused by the disappearance of this valuable jewel, and the vain efforts of the London police to recover it. I was myself consulted upon the case ; but I was unable to throw any light upon it. Suspicion fell upon the maid of the Princess, who was an Italian, and it was proved that she had a brother in London, but

"I BROUGHT THE BUST UP WITH ME,
AS YOU ASKED ME TO DO."

Illustration by Sidney Paget for the *Strand Magazine*, May, 1904.

we failed to trace any connection between them. The maid's name was Lucretia Venucci, and there is no doubt in my mind that this Pietro who was murdered two nights ago was the brother. I have been looking up the dates in the old files of the paper, and I find that the disappearance of the pearl was exactly two days before the arrest of Beppo for some crime of violence—an event which took place in the factory of Gelder & Co., at the very moment when these busts were being made. Now you clearly see the sequence of events, though you see them, of course, in the inverse order to the way in which they presented themselves to me. Beppo had the pearl in his possession. He may have stolen it from Pietro, he may have been Pietro's confederate, he may have been the go-between of Pietro and his sister. It is of no consequence to us which is the correct solution.

"The main fact is that he *had* the pearl, and at that moment, when it was on his person, he was pursued by the police. He made for the factory in which he worked, and he knew that he had only a few minutes in which to conceal this enormously valuable prize, which would otherwise be found on him when he was searched. Six plaster casts of Napoleon were drying in the passage. One of them was still soft. In an instant Beppo, a skilful workman, made a small hole in the wet plaster, dropped in the pearl, and with a few touches covered over the aperture once more. It was an admirable hiding-place. No one could possibly find it. But Beppo was condemned to a year's imprisonment, and in the meanwhile his six busts were scattered over London. He could not tell which contained his treasure. Only by breaking them could he see. Even shaking would tell him nothing for as the plaster was wet it was probable that the pearl would adhere to it—as, in fact, it has done. Beppo did not despair, and he conducted his search with considerable ingenuity and perseverance. Through a cousin who works with Gelder he found out the retail firms who had bought the busts. He managed to find employment with Morse Hudson, and in that way tracked down three of them. The pearl was not there. Then with the help of some Italian employé, he succeeded in finding out where the other three busts had gone. The first was at Harker's. There he was dogged by his confederate, who held Beppo responsible for the loss of the pearl, and he stabbed him in the scuffle which followed."

" If he was his confederate, why should he carry his photograph ? " I asked.

" As a means of tracing him if he wished to inquire about him from any third person. That was the obvious reason. Well, after the murder I calculated that Beppo would probably hurry rather than delay his movements. He would fear that the police would read his secret, and so he hastened on before they should get ahead of him. Of course, I could not say that he had not found the pearl in Harker's bust. I had not even concluded for certain that it was the pearl ; but it was evident to me that he was looking for something, since he carried the bust past the other houses in order to break it in the garden which had a lamp overlooking it. Since Harker's bust was one in three, the chances were exactly as I told you—two to one against the pearl being inside it. There remained two busts, and it was obvious that he would go for the London one first. I warned the inmates of the house, so as to avoid a second tragedy, and we went down, with the happiest results. By that time, of course, I knew for certain that it was the Borgia pearl that we were after. The name of the murdered man linked the one event with the other. There only remained a single bust —the Reading one—and the pearl must be there. I bought it in your presence from the owner—and there it lies.”

We sat in silence for a moment.

“ Well,” said Lestrade, “ I’ve seen you handle a good many cases, Mr. Holmes, but I don’t know that I ever knew a more workmanlike one than that. We’re not jealous of you at Scotland Yard. No, sir, we are very proud of you, and if you come down to-morrow there’s not a man, from the oldest inspector to the youngest constable, who wouldn’t be glad to shake you by the hand.”

“ Thank you ! ” said Holmes. “ Thank you ! ” and as he turned away it seemed to me that he was more nearly moved by the softer human emotions than I had ever seen him. A moment later he was the cold and practical thinker once more. “ Put the pearl in the safe, Watson,” said he, “ and get out the papers of the **14** Conk-Singleton forgery case. Good-bye, Lestrade. If **15** any little problem comes your way I shall be happy, if I can, to give you a hint or two as to its solution.”

14 *“Put the pearl in the safe, Watson.”* “The pearl after all had been stolen,” Mr. S. T. L. Harbottle wrote in “Sherlock Holmes and the Law.” “The thief had no right to it and could give no one else any right to it. Sandeford was not the owner, and, as against the Prince of Colonna who was, Holmes had no title to the pearl at all. He was in fact a receiver of stolen goods. There was no suggestion of returning the pearl to the Prince —far from it. ‘Put the pearl in the safe, Watson,’ said Holmes quite unblushingly.”

15 *the papers of the Conk-Singleton forgery case.* A version of this unreported case, in the form of a playlet, was enacted in 1948 at the Mystery Writers of America Edgar Award Dinner, with the following cast: Clayton Rawson as Sherlock Holmes, Lawrence G. Blochman as Dr. Watson, John Dickson Carr as The Visitor. The playlet— as “by Dr. John H. Watson”—was published in the *Unicorn Mystery Book Club News*, Vol. I, No. 9, pp. 8–9, 16. Of interest here also is the late Gavin Brend’s “Prooimion” to this case, as published in the *Sherlock Holmes Journal*, Vol. I, No. 4, December, 1953, pp. 2–4.

65

THE PROBLEM OF THOR BRIDGE

[*Thursday, October 4, to Friday, October 5, 1900*]

1 *tin dispatch-box with my name.* To the never-ending regret of all Sherlockians, the Charing Cross banking firm of Cox & Co. was wiped out in the World War II bombings that so badly damaged that section of London.

2 *Late Indian Army.* If Watson's service with the Berkshires and the Northumberland Fusiliers was all the army service he had, he was never in the Indian Army (as we have previously noted), for those two regiments are part of the regular establishment of the British Army and were merely ordered to India, while the Indian Army, as an organization, is an entirely separate thing.

3 *was never more seen in this world.* A pastiche of this adventure by the late Edgar W. Smith has appeared in *A Baker Street Four-Wheeler;* a second, titled "Sunshine, Sunshine," by Mr. Benjamin S. Clark, has appeared in the *Baker Street Journal Christmas Annual* for 1960; and a third, titled "The Adventure of the Highgate Miracle," by Adrian M. Conan Doyle and John Dickson Carr has appeared in *The Exploits of Sherlock Holmes.*

4 *nor was anything further ever heard of herself and her crew.* Watson's reference here reminded both Mr. T. S. Blakeney and the late Edgar W. Smith of the mystery of the *Mary Celeste:* "Perhaps Holmes' failure over the cutter *Alicia* decided him not to add to the number of would-be solvers of the mystery of the *Mary Celeste*" (Blakeney); "The fate of the *Alicia* reminds us, somehow, of what befell the brigantine *Mary Celeste . . .* which was found abandoned, for no known reason, in a high-running sea between the Azores and Portugal in the year 1872" (Smith). In addition, Mr. Richard W. Clarke has speculated that "the cutter *Alicia* was so named by Watson for a Miss Alicia Cutter of New York City, whom Watson met in Lausanne during the search for Lady Frances Carfax, and whom he later married ("On the Nomenclature of Watson's Ships").

1 2 3 SOMEWHERE in the vaults of the bank of Cox & Co., at Charing Cross, there is a travel-worn and battered tin dispatch-box with my name, John H. Watson, M.D., Late Indian Army, painted upon the lid. It is crammed with papers, nearly all of which are records of cases to illustrate the curious problems which Mr. Sherlock Holmes had at various times to examine. Some, and not the least interesting, were complete failures, and as such will hardly bear narrating, since no final explanation is forthcoming. A problem without a solution may interest the student, but can hardly fail to annoy the casual reader. Among these unfinished tales is that of Mr. James Phillimore, who, stepping back into his own house to get his umbrella, was never more seen in this world. No less remarkable is that of the cutter *Alicia*, which sailed one spring morning into a small patch of mist from where she never again emerged, nor was anything further ever heard **4** of herself and her crew. A third case worthy of note is that of Isadora Persano, the well-known journalist and duellist, who was found stark staring mad with a match-box in front of him which contained a remarkable worm, **5** said to be unknown to science. Apart from these unfathomed cases, there are some which involve the secrets of private families to an extent which would mean consternation in many exalted quarters if it were thought possible that they might find their way into print. I need not say that such a breach of confidence is unthinkable, and that these records will be separated and destroyed now that my friend has time to turn his energies to the matter. There remain a considerable residue of cases of greater or less interest which I might have edited before had I not feared to give the public a surfeit which might react upon the reputation of the man whom above all others I revere. In some I was myself concerned and can speak as an eye-witness, while in others I was either not present or played so small a part that they **6** could only be told as by a third person. The following narrative is drawn from my own experience.

It was a wild morning in October, and I observed as I was dressing how the last remaining leaves were being **7** whirled from the solitary plane tree which graces the yard behind our house. I descended to breakfast prepared to find my companion in depressed spirits, for, like all great artists, he was easily impressed by his surroundings. On the contrary, I found that he had nearly finished his meal, and that his mood was particularly bright and joyous, with that somewhat sinister cheerfulness which was characteristic of his lighter moments.

" You have a case, Holmes ? " I remarked.

" The faculty of deduction is certainly contagious, Watson," he answered. " It has enabled you to probe my secret. Yes, I have a case. After a month of trivialities and stagnation the wheels move once more."

" Might I share it ? "

" There is little to share, but we may discuss it when you have consumed the two hard-boiled eggs with which our new cook has favoured us. Their condition may not be unconnected with the copy of the *Family Herald* which I observed yesterday upon the hall-table. Even so trivial a matter as cooking an egg demands an attention which is conscious of the passage of time, and incompatible with the love romance in that excellent periodical."

A quarter of an hour later the table had been cleared and we were face to face. He had drawn a letter from his pocket.

" You have heard of Neil Gibson, the Gold King ? " he said.

" You mean the American Senator ? "

" Well, he was once Senator for some Western State, but is better known as the greatest gold-mining magnate in the world."

" Yes, I know of him. He has surely lived in England for some time. His name is very familiar."

" Yes ; he bought a considerable estate in Hampshire some five years ago. Possibly you have already heard of the tragic end of his wife ? "

" Of course. I remember it now. That is why the name is familiar. But I really know nothing of the details."

Holmes waved his hand towards some papers on a chair. " I had no idea that the case was coming my way or I should have had my extracts ready," said he. " The fact is that the problem, though exceedingly sensational, appeared to present no difficulty. The interesting personality of the accused does not obscure the clearness of the evidence. That was the view taken by the coroner's jury and also in the police-court proceedings. It is now referred to the Assizes at Winchester. I fear it is a thankless business. I can discover facts, Watson, but I cannot change them. Unless some entirely new and unexpected ones come to light I do not see what my client can hope for."

" Your client ? '

" Ah, I forgot I had not told you. I am getting into your involved habit, Watson, of telling a story backwards. You had best read this first."

The letter which he handed to me, written in a bold, masterful hand, ran as follows :

CLARIDGE'S HOTEL, *October 3rd.*   **8**
DEAR MR. SHERLOCK HOLMES,—

5 *said to be unknown to science.* "One optical illusion used in the German *Gestalt-Psycholgie* is a spiral, a line beginning with a central dot and forming a whirling curve until the whole is approximately an inch in diameter," Mr. Rolfe Boswell once wrote. "Intense concentration upon this optical cynosure induces self-hypnosis. Prolonged concentration might cause madness. The same effect might be caused by prolonged gazing at a tightly coiled watch spring. The *Shorter Oxford English Dictionary* gives this definition of worm: III. g. A spring or strip of metal of spiral shape 1724. Presumably, if you gaze at such a *worm* long enough, you'll be *Persano non grata*, if not 'stark staring mad.' "

"In a work entitled *A Voyage of Discovery, made under the Orders of the Admiralty, in His Majesty's Ships Isabella and Alexander, for the Purpose of Exploring Baffin's Bay and Enquiring into the Probability of a North West Passage,* written by Sir John Ross in 1819, one finds the statement: '. . . it fell bearly calm for a short time and we sounded with the deepsea clamms, which brought up a quantity of mud, in which were *five worms of a species that had not been seen before,'*" Mr. R. P. Graham wrote. "Who of Ross's crew . . . preserved these Baffin Bay worms, and who put one of their descendants into a match-box to help drive poor Isadora Persano 'stark staring mad'?"

And Mr. James Edward Holroyd has added that: "Isadora Persano was not the first journalist to be confronted with a remarkable worm said to be unknown to science. I find that a correspondent wrote to Dr. Johnson in No. 82 of *The Rambler,* December 29, 1750: 'I have three species of earthworms not known to the naturalists . . .'"

We should also note here that Mr. Stuart Palmer has written a pastiche stemming from this reference of Dr. Watson's which Ellery Queen has called "utterly delightful and satisfying"; see *The Misadventures of Sherlock Holmes.*

6 *they could only be told as by a third person.* Of the sixty Canonical Tales, two—"The Adventure of the Mazarin Stone" and "His Last Bow" —are told in the third person. There has been much controversy as to the authorship of these two adventures. Some students have advanced the theory that they were written by Mycroft Holmes; others have maintained that their authoress was the second, or third, Mrs. Watson; still others have claimed that they were written by Sir Arthur Conan Doyle. In the view of other commentators Watson's statement here, properly interpreted, can point to only one conclusion: both cases were recorded by none other than Watson.

7 *the solitary plane tree.* Americans would call the plane tree a sycamore.

8 CLARIDGE'S HOTEL. On Brook Street, at the south corner of Davies Street, stands the world-famous Claridge's Hotel. This hotel, formerly Mivart's, was opened in 1808 by M. Mivart, a Frenchman, at a time when sumptuous accommodation was very much lacking in the metropolis. So well did M. Mivart prosper that he added four adjoining houses to the one originally leased before he sold the business to Mr. and Mrs. Claridge in the middle of the last century. In 1895, after the death of Mr. Claridge, the old premises were pulled down and the present magnificent hotel erected.

9 *I'll come at eleven to-morrow.* J. Neil Gibson therefore called on Holmes on October 4th. On this day Holmes complained that the breakfast eggs were hard-boiled; the new cook had been reading the love romance in her copy of the *Family Herald*, which Holmes had "observed yesterday upon the hall-table." The late H. W. Bell long ago demonstrated that the *Family Herald*, a weekly publication, was published on *Wednesdays*. The case therefore opened on Thursday, October 4th—but in what year? The case is obviously a late one: 1) Watson calls Holmes "my famous friend." And, as Mr. Bell wrote, "Judging from Senator Gibson's letter, in which he writes: 'If ever in your life you showed your powers, put them now into this case,' Holmes must have been in practice for years and have acquired an immense reputation." 2) Holmes speaks of Watson's "annals," and says that he, Holmes, is "getting into your involved habit, Watson, of telling a story backwards." 3) Holmes says he has been threatened often. 4) To these evidences of "lateness," add the fact that Billy the page opened the door to Mr. Marlow Bates. This cannot be the Billy of *The Valley of Fear*; it must therefore be the Billy of "The Adventure of the Mazarin Stone," which took place, as we shall see, in the summer of 1903. A subtle point, provided by the late Gavin Brend, furnishes further evidence that the case began in fact on *Thursday, October 4, 1900*. (It ended the next day.) "1901," Mr. Brend wrote (a year suggested by some commentators), "can be deleted on account of Holmes' grandiloquent remark to Neil Gibson, 'My professional charges are upon a fixed scale. I do not vary them save when I remit them altogether.' In the case of 'The Priory School' which . . . occurred in May, 1901, Holmes received for his services the sum of £6,000, which was paid to him by the Duke of Holdernesse. . . . It is true that the initiative came from the Duke, but even so, [Holmes] would hardly be justified in making the above remark in the month of October after pocketing the Duke's cheque in the month of May. Accordingly we are left with October, 1900, as the only possible date for 'Thor Bridge.'"

I can't see the best woman God ever made go to her death without doing all that is possible to save her. I can't explain things—I can't even try to explain them, but I know beyond all doubt that Miss Dunbar is innocent. You know the facts—who doesn't ? It has been the gossip of the country. And never a voice raised for her ! It's the damned injustice of it all that makes me crazy. That woman has a heart that wouldn't let her **9** kill a fly. Well, I'll come at eleven to-morrow and see if you can get some ray of light in the dark. Maybe I have a clue and don't know it. Anyhow, all I know and all I have and all I am are for your use if only you can save her. If ever in your life you showed your powers, put them now into this case.

Yours faithfully,

J. NEIL GIBSON.

" There you have it," said Sherlock Holmes, knocking out the ashes of his after-breakfast pipe and slowly refilling it. " That is the gentleman I await. As to the story, you have hardly time to master all these papers, so I must give it to you in a nutshell if you are to take an intelligent interest in the proceedings. This man is the greatest financial power in the world, and a man, as I understand, of most violent and formidable character. He married a wife, the victim of this tragedy, of whom I know nothing save that she was past her prime, which was the more unfortunate as a very attractive governess superintended the education of two young children. These are the three people concerned, and the scene is a grand old manor-house, the centre of an historical English estate. Then as to the tragedy. The wife was found in the grounds nearly half a mile from the house, late at night, clad in her dinner dress, with a shawl over her shoulders and a revolver bullet through her brain. No weapon was found near her and there was no local clue as to the murder. No weapon near her, Watson— mark that ! The crime seems to have been committed late in the evening, and the body was found by a gamekeeper about eleven o'clock, when it was examined by the police and by a doctor before being carried up to the house. Is this too condensed, or can you follow it clearly ? "

" It is all very clear. But why suspect the governess ? "

" Well, in the first place there is some very direct evidence. A revolver with one discharged chamber and a calibre which corresponded with the bullet was found on the floor of her wardrobe." His eyes fixed and he repeated in broken words, " On—the—floor— of—her—wardrobe." Then he sank into silence, and I saw that some train of thought had been set moving which I should be foolish to interrupt. Suddenly with a start he emerged into brisk life once more. " Yes, Watson, it was found. Pretty damning, eh ? So the two juries thought. Then the dead woman had a note upon her making an appointment at that very place and signed by the governess. How's that ? Finally, there is the motive. Senator Gibson is an attractive person. If his wife dies, who more likely to succeed her than the young lady who had already by all accounts received

pressing attentions from her employer. Love, fortune,
power, all depending upon one middle-aged life. Ugly,
Watson—very ugly ! "

" Yes, indeed, Holmes."

" Nor could she prove an alibi. On the contrary,
she had to admit that she was down near Thor Bridge
—that was the scene of the tragedy—about that hour.
She couldn't deny it, for some passing villager had
seen her there."

" That really seems final."

" And yet, Watson—and yet ! This bridge—a single
broad span of stone with balustraded sides—carries the
drive over the narrowest part of a long, deep, reed-girt
sheet of water. Thor Mere it is called. In the mouth
of the bridge lay the dead woman. Such are the main
facts. But here, if I mistake not, is our client, considerably before his time."

Billy had opened the door, but the name which he
announced was an unexpected one. Mr. Marlow Bates
was a stranger to both of us. He was a thin, nervous wisp
of a man with frightened eyes, and a twitching, hesitating
manner—a man whom my own professional eye would
judge to be on the brink of an absolute nervous break-
down.

" You seem agitated, Mr. Bates," said Holmes.
" Pray sit down. I fear I can only give you a short
time, for I have an appointment at eleven."

" I know you have," our visitor gasped, shooting
out short sentences like a man who is out of breath.
" Mr. Gibson is coming. Mr. Gibson is my employer.
I am manager of his estate. Mr. Holmes, he is a villain
—an infernal villain."

" Strong language, Mr. Bates."

" I have to be emphatic, Mr. Holmes, for the time
is so limited. I would not have him find me here for the
world. He is almost due now. But I was so situated
that I could not come earlier. His secretary, Mr.
Ferguson, only told me this morning of his appointment
with you."

" And you are his manager ? "

" I have given him notice. In a couple of weeks I
shall have shaken off his accursed slavery. A hard man,
Mr. Holmes, hard to all about him. Those public
charities are a screen to cover his private iniquities. But
his wife was his chief victim. He was brutal to her—yes,
sir, brutal ! How she came by her death I do not know,
but I am sure that he had made her life a misery to her.
She was a creature of the Tropics, a Brazilian by birth,
as no doubt you know ? "

" No ; it had escaped me."

" Tropical by birth and tropical by nature. A child
of the sun and of passion. She had loved him as such
women can love, but when her own physical charms had
faded—I am told that they once were great—there was
nothing to hold him. We all liked her and felt for her
and hated him for the way that he treated her. But he is
plausible and cunning. That is all I have to say to you.
Don't take him at his face value. There is more behind.
Now I'll go. No, no, don't detain me ! He is almost due."

With a frightened look at the clock our strange visitor

"THE WIFE WAS FOUND IN THE GROUNDS NEARLY
HALF A MILE FROM THE HOUSE, LATE AT NIGHT . . ."

Illustration by A. Gilbert for the *Strand Magazine*,
February, 1922. G. Patrick Nelson illustrated the
same scene for *Hearst's International*, February,
1922.

literally ran to the door and disappeared.

" Well ! Well ! " said Holmes, after an interval of silence. " Mr. Gibson seems to have a nice loyal household. But the warning is a useful one, and now we can only wait till the man himself appears."

Sharp at the hour we heard a heavy step upon the stairs and the famous millionaire was shown into the room. As I looked upon him I understood not only the fears and dislike of his manager, but also the execrations which so many business rivals have heaped upon his head. If I were a sculptor and desired to idealize the successful man of affairs, iron of nerve and leathery of conscience, I should choose Mr. Neil Gibson as my model. His tall, gaunt craggy figure had a suggestion of hunger and rapacity. An Abraham Lincoln keyed to base uses instead of high ones would give some idea of the man. His face might have been chiselled in granite, hard-set, craggy, remorseless, with deep lines upon it, the scars of many a crisis. Cold grey eyes, looking shrewdly out from under bristling brows, surveyed us each in turn. He bowed in perfunctory fashion as Holmes mentioned my name, and then with a masterful air of possession he drew a chair up to my companion and seated himself with his bony knees almost touching him.

" Let me say right here, Mr. Holmes," he began, " that money is nothing to me in this case. You can burn it if it's any use in lighting you to the truth. This woman is innocent and this woman has to be cleared, and it's up to you to do it. Name your figure ! "

10 " My professional charges are upon a fixed scale," said Holmes coldly. " I do not vary them, save when I remit them altogether."

" Well, if dollars make no difference to you, think of the reputation. If you pull this off every paper in England and America will be booming you. You'll be the talk of two continents."

" Thank you, Mr. Gibson, I do not think that I am in need of booming. It may surprise you to know that I prefer to work anonymously, and that it is the problem itself which attracts me. But we are wasting time. Let us get down to the facts."

" I think that you will find all the main ones in the Press reports. I don't know that I can add anything which will help you. But if there is anything you would wish more light upon—well, I am here to give it."

" Well, there is just one point."

" What is it ? "

" What were the exact relations between you and Miss Dunbar ? "

The Gold King gave a violent start, and half rose from his chair. Then his massive calm came back to him.

" I suppose you are within your rights—and maybe doing your duty—in asking such a question, Mr. Holmes."

" We will agree to suppose so," said Holmes.

" Then I can assure you that our relations were entirely and always those of an employer towards a young lady whom he never conversed with, or ever saw, save when

10 *"My professional charges are upon a fixed scale."* "On what was [this "fixed scale"] to be based?" Mr. S. T. L. Harbottle asked in " 'My Charges Are Upon a Fixed Scale—' ". "On the value of property recovered? But few would care to put a price on the Naval Treaty or the ancient crown of England, to take but two examples. On the time taken by the investigation? But are we to equate, for instance, the 4½ hours in the train on the way to Boscombe Valley with the 4½ hours spent in vigil at Stoke Moran? The only thing clear about this scale is that it cannot have been fixed."

she was in the company of his children."

Holmes rose from his chair.

" I am a rather busy man, Mr. Gibson," said he, " and I have no time or taste for aimless conversations. I wish you good morning."

Our visitor had risen also and his great loose figure towered above Holmes.   There was an angry gleam from under those bristling brows and a tinge of colour in the sallow cheeks.

" What the devil do you mean by this, Mr. Holmes ? Do you dismiss my case ? "

" Well, Mr. Gibson, at least I dismiss you.   I should have thought my words were plain."

" Plain enough, but what's at the back of it ?   Raising the price on me, or afraid to tackle it, or what ?   I've a right to a plain answer."

" Well, perhaps you have," said Holmes.   " I'll give you one.   This case is quite sufficiently complicated to start with, without the further difficulty of false information."

" Meaning that I lie."

" Well, I was trying to express it as delicately as I could, but if you insist upon the word I will not contradict you."

I sprang to my feet, for the expression upon the millionaire's face was fiendish in its intensity, and he had raised his great knotted fist.   Holmes smiled languidly, and reached his hand out for his pipe.

" Don't be noisy, Mr. Gibson.   I find that after breakfast even the smallest argument is unsettling.   I suggest that a stroll in the morning air and a little quiet thought will be greatly to your advantage."

With an effort the Gold King mastered his fury.   I could not but admire him, for by a supreme self-command he had turned in a minute from a hot flame of anger to a frigid and contemptuous indifference.

" Well, it's your choice.   I guess you know how to run your own business.   I can't make you touch the case against your will.   You've done yourself no good this morning, Mr. Holmes, for I have broken stronger men than you.   No man ever crossed me and was the better for it."

" So many have said so, and yet here I am," said Holmes, smiling.   " Well, good morning, Mr. Gibson. You have a good deal yet to learn."

Our visitor made a noisy exit, but Holmes smoked in imperturbable silence with dreamy eyes fixed upon the ceiling.

" Any views, Watson ? " he asked at last.

" Well, Holmes, I must confess that when I consider that this is a man who would certainly brush any obstacle from his path, and when I remember that his wife may have been an obstacle and an object of dislike, as that man Bates plainly told us, it seems to me——"

" Exactly.   And to me also."

" But what were his relations with the governess, and how did you discover them ? "

" Bluff, Watson, bluff !   When I considered the passionate, unconventional, unbusiness-like tone of his letter, and contrasted it with his self-contained manner

I SPRANG TO MY FEET, FOR THE EXPRESSION UPON THE MILLIONAIRE'S FACE WAS FIENDISH IN ITS INTENSITY . . .

How two artists depicted the same scene: *above,* G. Patrick Nelson for *Hearst's International,* February, 1922; *below,* A. Gilbert for the *Strand Magazine,* February, 1922.

and appearance, it was pretty clear that there was some deep emotion which centred upon the accused woman rather than upon the victim. We've got to understand the exact relations of those three people if we are to reach the truth. You saw the frontal attack which I made upon him and how imperturbably he received it. Then I bluffed him by giving him the impression that I was absolutely certain, when in reality I was only extremely suspicious."

" Perhaps he will come back ? "

" He is sure to come back. He *must* come back. He can't leave it where it is   Ha ! isn't that a ring ? Yes, there is his footstep. Well, Mr. Gibson, I was just saying to Dr. Watson that you were somewhat overdue."

The Gold King had re-entered the room in a more chastened mood than he had left it. His wounded pride still showed in his resentful eyes, but his common sense had shown him that he must yield if he would attain his end.

" I've been thinking it over, Mr. Holmes, and I feel that I have been hasty in taking your remarks amiss. You are justified in getting down to the facts, whatever they may be, and I think the more of you for it. I can assure you, however, that the relations between Miss Dunbar and me don't really touch this case."

" That is for me to decide, is it not ? "

" Yes, I guess that is so. You're like a surgeon who wants every symptom before he can give his diagnosis."

" Exactly. That expresses it. And it is only a patient who has an object in deceiving his surgeon who would conceal the facts of his case."

" That may be so, but you will admit, Mr. Holmes, that most men would shy off a bit when they are asked point-blank what their relations with a woman may be —if there is really some serious feeling in the case. I guess most men have a little private reserve of their own in some corner of their souls where they don't welcome intruders. And you burst suddenly into it. But the object excuses you, since it was to try and save her. Well, the stakes are down and the reserve open and you can explore where you will. What is it you want ? "

" The truth."

The Gold King paused for a moment, as one who marshals his thoughts. His grim, deep-lined face had become even sadder and more grave.

" I can give it to you in a very few words, Mr. Holmes," said he at last. " There are some things that are painful as well as difficult to say, so I won't go deeper than is needful. I met my wife when I was gold-hunting in Brazil. Maria Pinto was the daughter of a Government official at Manaos, and she was very beautiful. I was young and ardent in those days, but even now, as I look back with colder blood and a more critical eye, I can see that she was rare and wonderful in her beauty. It was a deep rich nature, too, passionate, wholehearted, tropical, ill-balanced, very different from the American women whom I had known. Well, to make a long story short, I loved her and I married her. It was only when the romance had passed—and it lingered for years —that I realized that we had nothing—absolutely nothing—in common. My love faded. If hers had faded also it might have been easier. But you know the wonderful way of women! Do what I might nothing could turn her from me. If I have been harsh to her, even brutal as some have said, it has been because I knew that if I could kill her love, or if it turned to hate, it would be easier for both of us. But nothing changed her. She adored me in those English woods as she had adored me twenty years ago on the banks of the Amazon. Do what I might, she was as devoted as ever.

"Then came Miss Grace Dunbar. She answered our advertisement and became governess to our two children. Perhaps you have seen her portrait in the papers. The whole world has proclaimed that she also is a very beautiful woman. Now, I make no pretence to be more moral than my neighbours, and I will admit to you that I could not live under the same roof with such a woman and in daily contact with her without feeling a passionate regard for her. Do you blame me, Mr. Holmes?"

"I do not blame you for feeling it. I should blame you if you expressed it, since this young lady was in a sense under your protection."

"Well, maybe so," said the millionaire, though for a moment the reproof had brought the old angry gleam into his eyes. "I'm not pretending to be any better than I am. I guess all my life I've been a man that reached out his hand for what he wanted, and I never wanted anything more than the love and possession of that woman. I told her so."

"Oh, you did, did you?"

Holmes could look very formidable when he was moved.

"I said to her that if I could marry her I would, but that it was out of my power. I said that money was no object and that all I could do to make her happy and comfortable would be done."

"Very generous, I am sure," said Holmes, with a sneer.

"See here, Mr. Holmes. I came to you on a question of evidence, not on a question of morals. I'm not asking for your criticism."

"It is only for the young lady's sake that I touch your case at all," said Holmes sternly. "I don't know that anything she is accused of is really worse than what you have yourself admitted, that you have tried to ruin a defenceless girl who was under your roof. Some of you rich men have to be taught that all the world cannot be bribed into condoning your offences."

To my surprise the Gold King took the reproof with equanimity.

"That's how I feel myself about it now. I thank God that my plans did not work out as I intended. She would have none of it, and she wanted to leave the house instantly."

"Why did she not?"

"Well, in the first place, others were dependent upon her, and it was no light matter for her to let them all down by sacrificing her living. When I had sworn —as I did—that she should never be molested again, she consented to remain. But there was another reason. She knew the influence she had over me, and that it was stronger than any other influence in the world. She wanted to use it for good."

" How ? "

" Well, she knew something of my affairs. They are large, Mr. Holmes—large beyond the belief of an ordinary man. I can make or break—and it is usually break. It wasn't individuals only. It was communities, cities, even nations. Business is a hard game, and the weak go to the wall. I played the game for all it was worth. I never squealed myself and I never cared if the other fellow squealed. But she saw it different. I guess she was right. She believed and said that a fortune for one man that was more than he needed should not be built on ten thousand ruined men who were left without the means of life. That was how she saw it, and I guess she could see past the dollars to something that was more lasting. She found that I listened to what she said, and she believed she was serving the world by influencing my actions. So she stayed—and then this came along."

" Can you throw any light upon that ? "

The Gold King paused for a minute or more, his head sunk in his hands, lost in deep thought.

" It's very black against her. I can't deny that. And women lead an inward life and may do things beyond the judgment of a man. At first I was so rattled and taken aback that I was ready to think she had been led away in some extraordinary fashion that was clean against her usual nature. One explanation came into my head. I give it to you, Mr. Holmes, for what it is worth. There is no doubt that my wife was bitterly jealous. There is a soul-jealousy that can be as frantic as any body-jealousy, and though my wife had no cause —and I think she understood this—for the latter, she was aware that this English girl exerted an influence upon my mind and my acts that she herself never had. It was an influence for good, but that did not mend the matter. She was crazy with hatred, and the heat of the Amazon was always in her blood. She might have planned to murder Miss Dunbar—or we will say to threaten her with a gun and so frighten her into leaving us. Then there might have been a scuffle and the gun gone off and shot the woman who held it."

" That possibility had already occurred to me," said Holmes. " Indeed, it is the only obvious alternative to deliberate murder."

" But she utterly denies it."

" Well, that is not final—is it ? One can understand that a woman placed in so awful a position might hurry home still in her bewilderment holding the revolver. She might even throw it down among her clothes, hardly knowing what she was doing, and when it was found she might try to lie her way out by a total denial, since all explanation was impossible. What is against such a supposition ? "

" Miss Dunbar herself."

" Well, perhaps."

Holmes looked at his watch. " I have no doubt we can get the necessary permits this morning and reach Winchester by the evening train.   When I have seen this young lady, it is very possible that I may be of more use to you in the matter, though I cannot promise that my conclusions will necessarily be such as you desire."

There was some delay in the official pass, and instead of reaching Winchester that day we went down to Thor Place, the Hampshire estate of Mr. Neil Gibson.   He did not accompany us himself, but we had the address of Sergeant Coventry, of the local police, who had first examined into the affair.   He was a tall, thin, cadaverous man, with a secretive and mysterious manner, which conveyed the idea that he knew or suspected a very great deal more than he dared say.   He had a trick, too, of suddenly sinking his voice to a whisper as if he had come upon something of vital importance, though the information was usually commonplace enough.   Behind these tricks of manner he soon showed himself to be a decent, honest fellow who was not too proud to admit that he was out of his depth and would welcome any help.

" Anyhow, I'd rather have you than Scotland Yard, Mr. Holmes," said he.   " If the Yard gets called into a case, then the local loses all credit for success and may be blamed for failure.   Now, you play straight, so I've heard."

" I need not appear in the matter at all," said Holmes, to the evident relief of our melancholy acquaintance. " If I can clear it up I don't ask to have my name mentioned."

" Well, it's very handsome of you, I am sure.   And your friend, Dr. Watson, can be trusted, I know.   Now, Mr. Holmes, as we walk down to the place there is one question I should like to ask you.   I'd breathe it to no soul but you."   He looked round as though he hardly dare utter the words.   " Don't you think there might be a case against Mr. Neil Gibson himself ? "

" I have been considering that."

" You've not seen Miss Dunbar.   She is a wonderfully fine woman in every way.   He may well have wished his wife out of the road.   And these Americans are readier with pistols than our folk are.   It was *his* pistol, you know."

" Was that clearly made out ? "

" Yes, sir.   It was one of a pair that he had."

" One of a pair ?   Where is the other ? "

" Well, the gentleman has a lot of fire-arms of one sort and another.   We never quite matched that particular pistol—but the box was made for two."

" If it was one of a pair you should surely be able to match it."

" Well, we have them all laid out at the house if you would care to look them over."

" Later, perhaps.   I think we will walk down together and have a look at the scene of the tragedy."

This conversation had taken place in the little front room of Sergeant Coventry's humble cottage which served as the local police-station.   A walk of half a mile or so

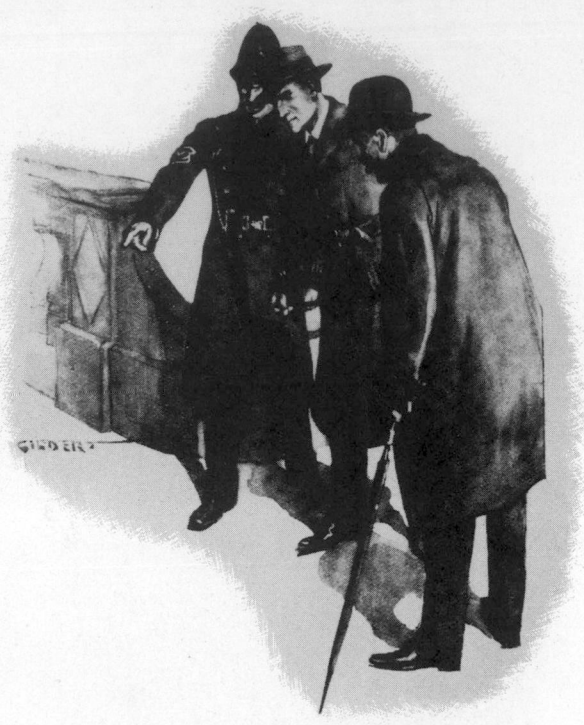

OUR GUIDE PAUSED AT THE MOUTH OF THIS BRIDGE,
AND HE POINTED TO THE GROUND.

Illustration by A. Gilbert for the *Strand Magazine*,
February, 1922.

across a wind-swept heath, all gold and bronze with the fading ferns, brought us to a side-gate opening into the grounds of the Thor Place estate. A path led us through the pheasant preserves, and then from a clearing we saw the widespread, half-timbered house, half Tudor and half Georgian, upon the crest of the hill. Beside us there was a long, reedy pool, constricted in the centre where the main carriage drive passed over a stone bridge, but swelling into small lakes on either side. Our guide paused at the mouth of this bridge, and he pointed to the ground.

" That was where Mrs. Gibson's body lay. I marked it by that stone."

" I understand that you were there before it was moved ? "

" Yes ; they sent for me at once."

" Who did ? "

" Mr. Gibson himself. The moment the alarm was given and he had rushed down with others from the house, he insisted that nothing should be moved until the police should arrive."

" That was sensible. I gathered from the newspaper report that the shot was fired from close quarters."

" Yes, sir, very close."

" Near the right temple ? "

" Just behind it, sir."

" How did the body lie ? "

" On the back, sir. No trace of a struggle. No marks. No weapon. The short note from Miss Dunbar was clutched in her left hand."

" Clutched, you say ? "

" Yes, sir ; we could hardly open the fingers."

" That is of great importance. It excludes the idea that anyone could have placed the note there after death in order to furnish a false clue. Dear me ! The note, as I remember, was quite short. ' I will be at Thor Bridge at nine o'clock.—G. Dunbar.' Was that not so ? "

" Yes, sir."

" Did Miss Dunbar admit writing it ? "

" Yes, sir."

" What was her explanation ? "

" Her defence was reserved for the Assizes. She would say nothing."

" The problem is certainly a very interesting one. The point of the letter is very obscure, is it not ? "

" Well, sir," said the guide, " it seemed, if I may be so bold as to say so, the only really clear point in the whole case."

Holmes shook his head.

" Granting that the letter is genuine and was really written, it was certainly received some time before—say one hour or two. Why, then, was this lady still clasping it in her left hand ? Why should she carry it so carefully ? She did not need to refer to it in the interview. Does it not seem remarkable ? "

" Well, sir, as you put it, perhaps it does."

" I think I should like to sit quietly for a few minutes and think it out." He seated himself upon the stone ledge of the bridge, and I could see his quick grey eyes darting their questioning glances in every direction.

Suddenly he sprang up again and ran across to the opposite parapet, whipped his lens from his pocket, and began to examine the stonework.

"This is curious," said he.

"Yes, sir; we saw the chip on the ledge. I expect it's been done by some passer-by."

The stonework was grey, but at this one point it showed white for a space not larger than a sixpence. When examined closely one could see that the surface was chipped as by a sharp blow.

"It took some violence to do that," said Holmes thoughtfully. With his cane he struck the ledge several times without leaving a mark. "Yes, it was a hard knock. In a curious place, too. It was not from above but from below, for you see that it is on the *lower* edge of the parapet."

"But it is at least fifteen feet from the body."

"Yes, it is fifteen feet from the body. It may have nothing to do with the matter, but it is a point worth noting. I do not think that we have anything more to learn here. There were no footsteps, you say?"

"The ground was iron hard, sir. There were no traces at all."

"Then we can go. We will go up to the house first and look over these weapons of which you speak. Then we shall get on to Winchester, for I should desire to see Miss Dunbar before we go farther."

Mr. Neil Gibson had not returned from town, but we saw in the house the neurotic Mr. Bates who had called upon us in the morning. He showed us with a sinister relish the formidable array of fire-arms of various shapes and sizes which his employer had accumulated in the course of an adventurous life.

Mr. Gibson has his enemies, as anyone would expect who knew him and his methods," said he. "He sleeps with a loaded revolver in the drawer beside his bed. He is a man of violence, sir, and there are times when all of us are afraid of him. I am sure that the poor lady who has passed was often terrified."

"Did you ever witness physical violence towards her?"

"No, I cannot say that. But I have heard words which were nearly as bad—words of cold, cutting contempt, even before the servants."

"Our millionaire does not seem to shine in private life," remarked Holmes, as we made our way to the station. "Well, Watson, we have come on a good many facts, some of them new ones, and yet I seem some way from my conclusion. In spite of the very evident dislike which Mr. Bates has to his employer, I gather from him that when the alarm came he was undoubtedly in his library. Dinner was over at eight-thirty and all was normal up to then. It is true that the alarm was somewhat late in the evening, but the tragedy certainly occurred about the hour named in the note. There is no evidence at all that Mr. Gibson had been out of doors since his return from town at five o'clock. On the other hand, Miss Dunbar, as I understand it, admits that she had made an appointment to meet Mrs. Gibson at the bridge. Beyond this she would say nothing, as her

WITH HIS CANE HE STRUCK THE LEDGE SEVERAL TIMES WITHOUT LEAVING A MARK.

Illustration by A. Gilbert for the *Strand Magazine*, February, 1922.

lawyer had advised her to reserve her defence. We have several very vital questions to ask that young lady, and my mind will not be easy until we have seen her. I must confess that the case would seem to me to be very black against her if it were not for one thing."

" And what is that, Holmes ? "

" The finding of the pistol in her wardrobe."

" Dear me, Holmes ! " I cried, " that seemed to me to be the most damning incident of all."

" Not so, Watson. It had struck me even at my first perfunctory reading as very strange, and now that I am in closer touch with the case it is my only firm ground for hope. We must look for consistency. Where there is a want of it we must suspect deception."

" I hardly follow you."

" Well now, Watson, suppose for a moment that we visualize you in the character of a woman who, in a cold, premeditated fashion, is about to get rid of a rival. You have planned it. A note has been written. The victim has come. You have your weapon. The crime is done. It has been workmanlike and complete. Do you tell me that after carrying out so crafty a crime you would now ruin your reputation as a criminal by forgetting to fling your weapon into those adjacent reed-beds which would forever cover it, but you must needs carry it carefully home and put it in your own wardrobe, the very first place that would be searched ? Your best friends would hardly call you a schemer, Watson, and yet I could not picture you doing anything so crude as that."

" In the excitement of the moment——"

" No, no, Watson, I will not admit that it is possible. Where a crime is coolly premeditated, then the means of covering it are coolly premeditated also. I hope, therefore, that we are in the presence of a serious misconception."

" But there is so much to explain."

" Well, we shall set about explaining it. When once your point of view is changed, the very thing which was so damning becomes a clue to the truth. For example, there is this revolver. Miss Dunbar disclaims all knowledge of it. On our new theory she is speaking truth when she says so. Therefore, it was placed in her wardrobe. Who placed it there ? Someone who wished to incriminate her. Was not that person the actual criminal ? You see how we come at once upon a most fruitful line of inquiry."

We were compelled to spend the night at Winchester, as the formalities had not yet been completed, but next morning, in the company of Mr. Joyce Cummings, the rising barrister who was entrusted with the defence, we were allowed to see the young lady in her cell. I had expected from all that we had heard to see a beautiful woman, but I can never forget the effect which Miss Dunbar produced upon me. It was no wonder that even the masterful millionaire had found in her something more powerful than himself—something which could control and guide him. One felt, too, as one looked at that strong, clear-cut, and yet sensitive face, that even should she be capable of some impetuous deed, none the less there was an innate nobility of character which would make her influence always for the good. She was a brunette, tall, with a noble figure and commanding presence, but her dark eyes had in them the appealing, helpless expression of the hunted creature who feels the nets around it, but can see no way out from the toils. Now, as she realized the presence and the help of my famous friend, there came a touch of colour in her wan cheeks and a light of hope began to glimmer in the glance which she turned upon us.

"Perhaps Mr. Neil Gibson has told you something of what occurred between us?" she asked, in a low, agitated voice.

"Yes," Holmes answered; "you need not pain yourself by entering into that part of the story. After seeing you, I am prepared to accept Mr. Gibson's statement both **11** as to the influence which you had over him and as to the innocence of your relations with him. But why was the whole situation not brought out in court?"

"It seemed to me incredible that such a charge could be sustained. I thought that if we waited the whole thing must clear itself up without our being compelled to enter into painful details of the inner life of the family. But I understand that far from clearing it has become even more serious."

"My dear young lady," cried Holmes earnestly, "I beg you to have no illusions upon the point. Mr. Cummings here would assure you that all the cards are at present against us, and that we must do everything that is possible if we are to win clear. It would be a cruel deception to pretend that you are not in very great danger. Give me all the help you can, then, to get at the truth."

"I will conceal nothing."

"Tell us, then, of your true relations with Mr. Gibson's wife."

"She hated me, Mr. Holmes. She hated me with all the fervour of her tropical nature. She was a woman who would do nothing by halves, and the measure of her love for her husband was the measure also of her hatred for me. It is probable that she misunderstood our relations. I would not wish to wrong her, but she loved so vividly in a physical sense that she could hardly understand the mental, and even spiritual, tie which held her husband to me, or imagine that it was only my desire to influence his power to good ends which kept me under his roof. I can see now that I was wrong. Nothing could justify me in remaining where I was a cause of unhappiness, and yet it is certain that the unhappiness would have remained even if I had left the house."

"Now, Miss Dunbar," said Holmes, "I beg you to tell us exactly what occurred that evening."

"I can tell you the truth so far as I know it, Mr. Holmes, but I am in a position to prove nothing, and there are points—the most vital points—which I can neither explain nor can I imagine any explanation."

"If you will find the facts, perhaps others may find the explanation."

"With regard, then, to my presence at Thor Bridge

11 *After seeing you, I am prepared to accept Mr. Gibson's statement.* "We all know that Holmes often cautioned Watson against being unduly impressed by the appearance of a client," Mr. Nathan L. Bengis wrote in "Sherlock Stays After School." "It is more than slightly remarkable that the same Holmes who failed to see the naive sweetness of Mary Morstan should be able to tell from one look at Grace Dunbar that her relations with Neil Gibson had been completely innocent. Is this the same man who boasted of never making exceptions?"

that night, I received a note from Mrs. Gibson in the morning. It lay on the table of the schoolroom, and it may have been left there by her own hand. It implored me to see her there after dinner, said she had something important to say to me, and asked me to leave an answer on the sundial in the garden, as she desired no one to be in our confidence. I saw no reason for such secrecy, but I did as she asked, accepting the appointment. She asked me to destroy her note and I burned it in the schoolroom grate. She was very much afraid of her husband, who treated her with a harshness for which I frequently reproached him, and I could only imagine that she acted in this way because she did not wish him to know of our interview."

" Yet she kept your reply very carefully ? "

" Yes. I was surprised to hear that she had it in her hand when she died."

" Well, what happened then ? "

" I went down as I had promised. When I reached the bridge she was waiting for me. Never did I realize till that moment how this poor creature hated me. She was like a mad woman—indeed, I think she *was* a mad woman, subtly mad with the deep power of deception which insane people may have. How else could she have met me with unconcern every day and yet had so raging a hatred of me in her heart ? I will not say what she said. She poured her whole wild fury out in burning and horrible words. I did not even answer—I could not. It was dreadful to see her. I put my hands to my ears and rushed away. When I left her she was standing still shrieking out her curses at me, in the mouth of the bridge."

" Where she was afterwards found ? "

" Within a few yards from the spot."

" And yet, presuming that she met her death shortly after you left her, you heard no shot ? "

" No, I heard nothing. But, indeed, Mr. Holmes, I was so agitated and horrified by this terrible outbreak that I rushed to get back to the peace of my own room, and I was incapable of noticing anything which happened."

" You say that you returned to your room. Did you leave it again before next morning ? "

" Yes ; when the alarm came that the poor creature had met her death I ran out with the others."

" Did you see Mr. Gibson ? "

" Yes ; he had just returned from the bridge when I saw him. He had sent for the doctor and the police."

" Did he seem to you much perturbed ? "

" Mr. Gibson is a very strong, self-contained man. I do not think that he would ever show his emotions on the surface. But I, who knew him so well, could see that he was deeply concerned."

" Then we come to the all-important point. This pistol that was found in your room. Had you ever seen it before ? "

" Never, I swear it."

" When was it found ? "

" Next morning, when the police made their search."

" Among your clothes ? "

" Yes ; on the floor of my wardrobe under my dresses."

"SHE POURED HER WHOLE WILD FURY OUT
IN BURNING AND HORRIBLE WORDS."

Illustration by A. Gilbert for the *Strand Magazine*, March, 1922. G. Patrick Nelson illustrated the same scene for *Hearst's International*, February, 1922.

"You could not guess how long it had been there ? "

"It had not been there the morning before."

"How do you know ? "

"Because I tidied out the wardrobe."

"That is final. Then someone came into your room and placed the pistol there in order to inculpate you."

"It must have been so."

"And when ? "

"It could only have been at meal-time, or else at the hours when I would be in the schoolroom with the children."

"As you were when you got the note ? "

"Yes ; from that time onwards for the whole morning."

"Thank you, Miss Dunbar. Is there any other point which could help me in the investigation ? "

"I can think of none."

"There was some sign of violence on the stonework of the bridge—a perfectly fresh chip just opposite the body. Could you suggest any possible explanation of that ? "

"Surely it must be a mere coincidence."

"Curious, Miss Dunbar, very curious. Why should it appear at the very time of the tragedy and why at the very place ? "

"But what could have caused it ? Only great violence could have such an effect."

Holmes did not answer. His pale, eager face had suddenly assumed that tense, far-away expression which I had learned to associate with the supreme manifestations of his genius. So evident was the crisis in his mind that none of us dared to speak, and we sat, barrister, prisoner, and myself, watching him in a concentrated and absorbed silence. Suddenly he sprang from his chair, vibrating with nervous energy and the pressing need for action.

"Come, Watson, come ! " he cried.

"What is it, Mr. Holmes ? "

"Never mind, my dear lady. You will hear from me, Mr. Cummings. With the help of the God of justice I will give you a case which will make England ring. You will get news by to-morrow, Miss Dunbar, and meanwhile take my assurance that the clouds are lifting and that I have every hope that the light of truth is breaking through."

It was not a long journey from Winchester to Thor Place, but it was long to me in my impatience, while for Holmes it was evident that it seemed endless ; for, in his nervous restlessness, he could not sit still, but paced the carriage or drummed with his long, sensitive fingers upon the cushions beside him. Suddenly, however, as we neared our destination he seated himself opposite to me—we had a first-class carriage to ourselves—and laying a hand upon each of my knees he looked into my eyes with the peculiarly mischievous gaze which was characteristic of his more imp-like moods.

"Watson," said he, " I have some recollection that you go armed upon these excursions of ours."

It was as well for him that I did so, for he took little care for his own safety when his mind was once absorbed by a problem, so that more than once my revolver had

SUDDENLY HE SPRANG FROM HIS CHAIR . . .

Illustration by A. Gilbert for the *Strand Magazine*, March, 1922.

12 *a short, handy, but very serviceable little weapon.* The description, thought the editors of the Catalogue of the Sherlock Holmes Exhibition, "can only refer to the Webley hammerless .320, which is not common today. It had six chambers whereas most .32 revolvers have only five; and it had a stirrup catch without the familiar thumb lever, and a shot-gun type 'safety catch.' "

been a good friend in need. I reminded him of the fact.

" Yes, yes, I am a little absent-minded in such matters. But have you your revolver on you ? "

I produced it from my hip-pocket, a short, handy, **12** but very serviceable little weapon. He undid the catch, shook out the cartridges, and examined it with care.

" It's heavy—remarkably heavy," said he.

" Yes, it is a solid bit of work."

He mused over it for a minute.

" Do you know, Watson," said he, " I believe your revolver is going to have a very intimate connection with the mystery which we are investigating."

" My dear Holmes, you are joking."

" No, Watson, I am very serious. There is a test before us. If the test comes off, all will be clear. And the test will depend upon the conduct of this little weapon. One cartridge out. Now we will replace the other five and put on the safety-catch. So ! That increases the weight and makes it a better reproduction."

I had no glimmer of what was in his mind nor did he enlighten me, but sat lost in thought until we pulled up in the little Hampshire station. We secured a ramshackle trap and in a quarter of an hour were at the house of our confidential friend, the sergeant.

" A clue, Mr. Holmes ? What is it ? "

" It all depends upon the behaviour of Dr. Watson's revolver," said my friend. " Here it is. Now, officer, can you give me ten yards of string ? "

The village shop provided a ball of stout twine.

" I think that this is all we will need," said Holmes. " Now, if you please, we will get off on what I hope is the last stage of our journey."

The sun was setting and turning the rolling Hampshire moor into a wonderful autumnal panorama. The sergeant, with many critical and incredulous glances, which showed his deep doubts of the sanity of my companion, lurched along beside us. As we approached the scene of the crime I could see that my friend under all his habitual coolness was in truth deeply agitated.

" Yes," he said, in answer to my remark, " you have seen me miss my mark before, Watson. I have an instinct for such things, and yet it has sometimes played me false. It seemed a certainty when first it flashed across my mind in the cell at Winchester, but one drawback of an active mind is that one can always conceive alternative explanations which would make our scent a false one. And yet—and yet—— Well, Watson, we can but try."

As he walked he had firmly tied one end of the string to the handle of the revolver. We had now reached the scene of the tragedy. With great care he marked out under the guidance of the policeman the exact spot where the body had been stretched. He then hunted among the heather and the ferns until he found a considerable stone. This he secured to the other end of his line of string, and he hung it over the parapet of the bridge so that it swung clear above the water. He then stood on the fatal spot, some distance from the edge of the bridge, with my revolver in his hand, the string being taut between the weapon and the heavy stone on the farther side.

" Now for it ! " he cried.

At the words he raised the pistol to his head, and then let go his grip. In an instant it had been whisked away by the weight of the stone, had struck with a sharp crack against the parapet and had vanished over the side into the water. It had hardly gone before Holmes was kneeling beside the stonework, and a joyous cry showed that he had found what he expected.

" Was there ever a more exact demonstration ? " he cried. " See, Watson, your revolver has solved the problem ! " As he spoke he pointed to a second chip of the exact size and shape of the first which had appeared on the under edge of the stone balustrade.

" We'll stay at the inn to-night," he continued, as he rose and faced the astonished sergeant. " You will, of course, get a grappling-hook and you will easily restore my friend's revolver. You will also find beside it the revolver, string and weight with which this vindictive woman attempted to disguise her own crime and to fasten a charge of murder upon an innocent victim. You **13** can let Mr. Gibson know that I will see him in the morning, when steps can be taken for Miss Dunbar's vindication."

Late that evening, as we sat together smoking our pipes in the village inn, Holmes gave me a brief review of what had passed.

" I fear, Watson," said he, " that you will not improve any reputation which I may have acquired by adding the Case of the Thor Bridge Mystery to your annals. I have been sluggish in mind and wanting in that mixture of imagination and reality which is the basis of my art. I confess that the chip in the stonework was a sufficient clue to suggest the true solution, and that I blame myself for not having attained it sooner.

" It must be admitted that the workings of this unhappy woman's mind were deep and subtle, so that it was no very simple matter to unravel her plot. I do not think that in our adventures we have ever come across a stranger example of what perverted love can bring about. Whether Miss Dunbar was her rival in a physical or in a merely mental sense seems to have been equally unforgivable in her eyes. No doubt she blamed this innocent lady for all those harsh dealings and unkind words with which her husband tried to repel her too demonstrative affection. Her first resolution was to end her own life. Her second was to do it in such a way as to involve her victim in a fate which was worse far than any sudden death could be.

" We can follow the various steps quite clearly, and they show a remarkable subtlety of mind. A note was extracted very cleverly from Miss Dunbar which would make it appear that she had chosen the scene of the crime. In her anxiety that it should be discovered she somewhat overdid it, by holding it in her hand to the last. This alone should have excited my suspicions earlier than it did.

" Then she took one of her husband's revolvers—there

IT HAD HARDLY GONE BEFORE HOLMES WAS KNEELING BESIDE THE STONEWORK . . .

Two artists depict the same scene: *above*, G. Patrick Nelson for *Hearst's International*, March, 1922; *below*, A. Gilbert for the *Strand Magazine*, March, 1922.

13 *to fasten a charge of murder upon an innocent victim.* There seems little doubt that Conan Doyle's inspiration for this adventure came from Dr. Hans Gross, Professor of Criminology at the University of Prague, whose great work on criminal investigation, *System der Kriminalistik*, was published in 1893.

14 *A similar one she concealed that morning.* At the Sherlock Holmes Exhibition, a matched pair of small revolvers, lent by Major Hugh Pollard, was exhibited, with the comment, in the Catalogue: "These ivory-handled Whitneyville armoury revolvers are more powerful than the saloon pistol as they take the standard .22 rimfire short case; at close range they are fatal. First developed by Smith and Wesson in 1856 these little .22 revolvers were made in many types and patterns by both English and American makers. They were almost invariably 'seven-shooters,' as are the specimens shown. These represent an improved model which was made with little variation from about 1875 to the close of the century, and are of American origin."

A Note on the "Canonicity" of "The Problem of Thor Bridge": Mr. D. Martin Dakin, who has decisively rejected from the Canon many of the adventures that appear in *The Case-Book of Sherlock Holmes,* has written that "there are others in the collection that bear just as clearly the stamp of authenticity. 'Thor Bridge' is one. The plot and style are excellent, and it shows in every line the marks of a genuine Watson reminiscence. Holmes dealing with Mr. Neil Gibson, the Gold King, is Holmes at his best. . . ."

Bibliographical Note: The manuscript of "The Problem of Thor Bridge" is owned by Mr. Adrian M. Conan Doyle.

was, as you saw, an arsenal in the house—and kept it for her own use. A similar one she concealed that morning in Miss Dunbar's wardrobe after discharging one barrel, which she could easily do in the woods without attracting attention. She then went down to the bridge where she had contrived this exceedingly ingenious method for getting rid of her weapon. When Miss Dunbar appeared she used her last breath in pouring out her hatred, and then, when she was out of hearing, carried out her terrible purpose. Every link is now in its place and the chain is complete. The papers may ask why the mere was not dragged in the first instance, but it is easy to be wise after the event, and in any case the expanse of a reed-filled lake is no easy matter to drag unless you have a clear perception of what you are looking for, and where. Well, Watson, we have helped a remarkable woman, and also a formidable man. Should they in the future join their forces, as seems not unlikely, the financial world may find that Mr. Neil Gibson has learned something in that schoolroom of Sorrow where our earthly lessons are taught."

·   ·   ·

THE HEAVY WHITE FACE WAS SEAMED WITH LINES OF TROUBLE . . .

Illustration by Sidney Paget for the *Strand Magazine*, February, 1904.

66

THE ADVENTURE OF THE PRIORY SCHOOL

[Thursday, May 16, to Saturday, May 18, 1901]

WE have had some dramatic entrances and exits upon our small stage at Baker Street, but I cannot recollect anything more sudden and startling than the first appearance of Dr. Thorneycroft Huxtable, M.A., Ph.D., etc. His card, which **1** seemed too small to carry the weight of his academic distinctions, preceded him by a few seconds, and then he entered himself—so large, so pompous, and so dignified that he was the very embodiment of self-possession and solidity. And yet his first action when the door had closed behind him was to stagger against the table, whence he slipped down upon the floor, and there was that majestic figure prostrate and insensible upon our bearskin hearthrug.

We had sprung to our feet, and for a few moments we stared in silent amazement at this ponderous piece of wreckage, which told of some sudden and fatal storm far out on the ocean of life. Then Holmes hurried with a cushion for his head, and I with brandy for his lips. The heavy white face was seamed with lines of trouble, the hanging pouches under the closed eyes were leaden in colour, the loose mouth drooped dolorously at the corners, the rolling chins were unshaven. Collar and shirt bore the grime of a long journey, and the hair bristled unkempt from the well-shaped head. It was a sorely stricken man who lay before us.

" What is it, Watson ? " asked Holmes.

" Absolute exhaustion—possibly mere hunger and fatigue," said I, with my finger on the thready pulse, where the stream of life trickled thin and small.

" Return ticket from Mackleton, in the North of England," said Holmes, drawing it from the watch-pocket. **2** " It is not twelve o'clock yet. He has certainly been an early starter."

The puckered eyelids had begun to quiver, and now a pair of vacant grey eyes looked up at us. An instant later the man had scrambled on to his feet, his face crimson with shame.

" Forgive this weakness, Mr. Holmes ; I have been a little overwrought. Thank you, if I might have a glass of milk and a biscuit I have no doubt that I should be better. I came personally, Mr. Holmes, in order to ensure that you would return with me. I feared that no telegram would convince you of the absolute urgency of the case."

1 *M.A., Ph.D., etc.* "Except apparently at the Court of Siam," Mr. Frederick Bryan-Brown wrote in "Sherlockian Schools and Schoolmasters," " 'etc.' is not a word well thought of in educational circles, being normally interpreted as 'I don't know any more' or 'I can't be bothered to put any more.' . . . Also the Dr. in front, when the Ph.D. is behind, is somewhat redundant and merely to impress credulous parents. True Classical scholars from the major universities go for Doctor of Letters or nothing, and one suspects Huxtable of travelling to Europe in the summer vacation to buy his Doctorate . . ."

2 *Mackleton, in the North of England.* ". . . we must identify 'Mackleton' with the well known Derbyshire spa of Matlock, some ten miles from Chesterfield," Mr. Michael Harrison wrote (*In the Footsteps of Sherlock Holmes*). "It was at Chesterfield, by the way, that Neville St. Clair, the Man with the Twisted Lip, was at school. The nearby town of Alfreton, distant 11 miles from Chesterfield, 9 miles from Matlock, will explain the construction of 'Mackleton': Ma(tlo)ck—(A)l(fr)eton." But the problem remains: why did Holmes call Derbyshire, the epitome of the Midlands, the "North of England"?

3 *this case of the Ferrers Documents.* For a pastiche stemming from this reference of Holmes', see "The Adventure of the Dark Angels," by Adrian M. Conan Doyle in *The Exploits of Sherlock Holmes.*

4 *the Abergavenny murder.* "The Abergavenny murder presumably took place at Abergavenny," Mr. Paul H. Gore-Booth wrote in "The Journeys of Sherlock Holmes," "(it does not seem to have been the murder of Lord or Mr. Abergavenny, as far as we can tell) so that implies a visit to Monmouthshire."

5 *K.G., P.C.'* "The K.G., of course, stands for Knight of the Garter, while the P.C. is presumably for Privy Councillor, rather than Police Constable, for which it is used elsewhere in the Sacred Writings," the late A. Carson Simpson wrote in *Numismatics in the Canon*, Part III. "This Order, originally known as the Society (or Fraternity) of St. George, is generally said to date back to 1349; probably it began between 1346 and 1348. . . . As originally constituted, the Order of the Garter consisted of the sovereign (Edward III) and 25 Knights (including the Prince of Wales). Later, important foreign rulers were admitted, then lineal descendants of George I; certain clerical and heraldic officials were attached for administrative purposes. Until after the Napoleonic Wars, all members were nobles, generally of no less degree than an earl, but later a few distinguished commoners (e.g., Austin Chamberlain) were admitted to what came to be known as the Most Noble Order of the Garter. The original

"I CANNOT IMAGINE HOW I CAME TO BE SO WEAK."

Illustration by Frederic Dorr Steele for *Collier's Magazine*, January 30, 1904.

"When you are quite restored——"

"I am quite well again.   I cannot imagine how I came to be so weak.   I wish you, Mr. Holmes, to come to Mackleton with me by the next train."

My friend shook his head.

"My colleague, Dr. Watson, could tell you that we are very busy at present.   I am retained in this case of the **3-4** Ferrers Documents, and the Abergavenny murder is coming up for trial.   Only a very important issue could call me from London at present."

"Important!"   Our visitor threw up his hands. "Have you heard nothing of the abduction of the only son of the Duke of Holdernesse?"

"What!   the late Cabinet Minister?"

"Exactly.   We had tried to keep it out of the papers, but there was some rumour in the *Globe* last night.   I thought it might have reached your ears."

Holmes shot out his long, thin arm and picked out Volume "H" in his encyclopædia of reference.

5   "'Holdernesse, sixth Duke, K.G., P.C.'—half the alphabet!   'Baron Beverley, Earl of Carston'—dear me, what a list!   'Lord-Lieutenant of Hallamshire since 1900.   Married Edith, daughter of Sir Charles Appledore, 1888.   Heir and only child, Lord Saltire.   Owns about two hundred and fifty thousand acres.   Minerals in Lancashire and Wales.   Address: Carlton House Terrace; Holdernesse Hall, Hallamshire; Carston Castle, **6** Bangor, Wales.   Lord of the Admiralty, 1872; Chief Secretary of State for——'   Well, well, this man is **7** certainly one of the greatest subjects of the Crown!"

"The greatest and perhaps the wealthiest.   I am aware, Mr. Holmes, that you take a very high line in professional matters, and that you are prepared to work for the work's

"'LORD-LIEUTENANT OF HALLAMSHIRE SINCE 1900.'"

Hallamshire, though not a county of England, is a well-known district—as Mr. T. H. B. Symons has pointed out in "Some Notes on the Sixth Duke of Holdernesse": "Watson's Hallamshire, like Hardy's Wessex and Trollope's Barsetshire, may be identified fairly readily. The ancient lordship of Hallamshire embraced parts of Yorkshire and Derbyshire, and this historic place name is preserved in the community of West Hallam which still remains in Derbyshire." By law (sec. 3 [1] of the Criminal Justice Administration Act), Hallamshire "is to include Sheffield, Doncaster, Barnsley and Rotherham," Magistrate S. Tupper Bigelow wrote in "Hallamshire Revisited."

sake. I may tell you, however, that his Grace has already intimated that a cheque for five thousand pounds will be handed over to the person who can tell him where his son is, and another thousand to him who can name the man, or men, who have taken him."

" It is a princely offer," said Holmes. " Watson, I think that we shall accompany Dr. Huxtable back to the North of England. And now, Dr. Huxtable, when you have consumed that milk you will kindly tell me what has happened, when it happened, how it happened, and, finally, what Dr. Thorneycroft Huxtable, of the Priory School, near Mackleton, has to do with the matter, and why he comes three days after an event—the state of your chin gives the date—to ask for my humble services."

Our visitor had consumed his milk and biscuits. The light had come back to his eyes and the colour to his cheeks as he set himself with great vigour and lucidity to explain the situation.

" I must inform you, gentlemen, that the Priory is a preparatory school, of which I am the founder and principal. *Huxtable's Sidelights on Horace* may possibly **8** recall my name to your memories. The Priory is, without exception, the best and most select preparatory school in England. Lord Leverstoke, the Earl of Blackwater, Sir Cathcart Soames—they all have entrusted their sons to me. But I felt that my school had reached its zenith when, three weeks ago, the Duke of Holdernesse sent Mr. James Wilder, his secretary, with the intimation that young Lord Saltire, ten years old, his only son and heir, was about to be committed to my charge. Little did I think that this would be the prelude to the most crushing misfortune of my life.

" On May 1 the boy arrived, that being the beginning of the summer term. He was a charming youth, and he soon fell into our ways. I may tell you—I trust that I am not indiscreet ; half-confidences are absurd in such a case—that he was not entirely happy at home. It is an open secret that the duke's married life had not been a peaceful one, and the matter had ended in a separation by mutual consent, the duchess taking up her residence in the South of France. This had occurred very shortly before, and the boy's sympathies are known to have been strongly with his mother. He moped after her departure from Holdernesse Hall, and it was for this reason that the duke desired to send him to my establishment. In a fortnight the boy was quite at home with us, and was apparently absolutely happy.

" He was last seen on the night of May 13—that is, the night of last Monday. His room was on the second floor, and was approached through another larger room in which two boys were sleeping. These boys saw and heard nothing, so that it is certain that young Saltire did not pass out that way. His window was open, and there is a stout ivy plant leading to the ground. We could trace no footmarks below, but it is sure that this is the only possible exit.

" His absence was discovered at seven o'clock on Tuesday morning. His bed had been slept in. He had dressed himself fully before going off in his usual school suit of black Eton jacket and dark grey trousers. There

insigne of the Order was the blue silk buckled Garter with the motto HONI SOIT QUI MAL Y PENSE embroidered on it with gold thread. About 1503 the Collar was added, consisting of 24 Tudor roses enamelled red and white, each surrounded by a buckled Garter with motto; these are linked together by 'lover's knots' of heavy gold wire. From this hung the 'Great George,' a gold and enamel equestrian figure of the Order's patron saint killing the dragon. The Collar is today generally worn only on occasions of great moment, such as coronations, etc. Instead, the 'Lesser George'—a smaller copy of the 'Great George,' but enclosed in an enamel Garter—is worn attached to a wide deep-blue ribbon slung over the left shoulder. The Knights also wear the Garter Star on their robes. It is an enamelled radiate St. George's Cross within a Garter with motto, all surrounded by silver rays. A curious feature of the Order of the Garter is that all the insignia must be returned on the death of a member. The Garter and the Collar (including the Great George) must be turned in to the Central Chancery of the Orders of Knighthood, while the heir of the Knight must deliver the Star and Badge (the Lesser George) direct to the Sovereign. These articles are later reissued to subsequently-created Knights, hence they may pass through many hands over the centuries. Only the shoulder-ribbon, apparently, remains with the family."

6 *Carlton House Terrace.* The two handsome blocks of houses, known as Carlton House Terrace, adorn the north side of the Mall. They were completed about 1831, and occupy the site of Carlton House and its grounds, the residence of George IV when Prince Regent. Among the Duke of Holdernesse's onetime neighbors were Lord Goderich, who paid £25,000 for his house, and the Count de Salis, who gave £10,000 for his. At Number 13, and afterwards Number 11, Mr. W. E. Gladstone resided for many years. Carlton House Terrace was badly damaged in the blitz but its houses have been repaired and repainted.

7 *Well, well, this man is certainly one of the greatest subjects of the Crown!"* In a thoughtful and persuasive paper delivered to the Society of Baker Street Squires of Toronto, Mr. Gordon Macpherson has suggested that it was the Sixth Duke of Northumberland who figures in "The Adventure of the Priory School."

On the other hand, Dr. Julian Wolff, in his *Practical Handbook of Sherlockian Heraldry*, has written that "In view of the fact that his son was called Lord Saltire, it would seem likely that the Duke of Holdernesse belonged to the great family of Neville, since a saltire [a diagonal cross] is prominent in their arms. However, none of them can be fitted into the frame provided and one more coruscation is necessary. Careful study of the problem suggests . . . the 8th Duke of Devonshire . . ."

Dr. Wolff's identification has received the

wholehearted support of Mr. T. H. B. Symons, who wrote, in "Some Notes on the Sixth Duke of Holdernesse," "a number of considerations suggest that the person disguised as the sixth Duke of Holdernesse by Watson was in fact the Eighth Duke of Devonshire. [He] was in fact the Lord-Lieutenant [of Derbyshire], and in this shire were his ancestral estates. Such a location of Holdernesse Hall, in Hallamshire, in Derbyshire, would seem to fit in with a number of other geographic facts noted in 'The Adventure of the Priory School.' Like Holdernesse Hall, the Devonshire estates are set in the Peak country. . . . Nearby is Chesterfield . . . and close by in other directions is Macclesfield, which may be the Mackleton near which the Priory School was located. . . . There is strong heraldic support for [this] view. . . . Hardwick Hall [one of the two famous Devonshire estates owned by the Duke of Devonshire] is enriched at many points, in panel, fireplace and lock, with the arms of [Bess of Hardwick, who married William Cavendish, whose son was the first Earl of Devonshire]: 'a saltire engrailed azure; on a chief of the second three cinquefoils of the field,' set in a lozenge-shaped shield and bearing the coronet. The supporters are two 'stags proper, each gorged with a chaplet of roses, argent, between two bars azure.' . . . It is not surprising that Dr. Watson, who was we know impressed by the entrance to the Hall should be struck at once by these fine emblazonments and that they should suggest to him the idea of disguising the heir to the estate under the title of Lord Saltire. . . . The Duke of Devonshire was very much 'the late Cabinet Minister' at the time of 'The Adventure of the Priory School,' having resigned from Balfour's Cabinet a few months before as the result of a celebrated row with Joseph Chamberlain over the comparative merits of free trade and imperial preference. His earlier political career was one of great distinction which matched very closely that of the Duke of Holdernesse."

It is equally understandable that Watson should have disguised his great northern magnate under the title of *Holdernesse*. As Mr. Symons has also pointed out: "In bygone centuries, the great northern family of d'Arcy held the earldom of Holderness. From a medieval house, the d'Arcy's had developed into one of the powerful landowning Whig families. Their Yorkshire estates drew praise from Arthur Young when he wrote of his northern town in 1768. Robert d'Arcy, the Fourth Earl, was Lord-Lieutenant of the North Riding of Yorkshire, and Secretary for the North in Pitt's administration. On his death, predeceased by his two sons, the ancient barony of d'Arcy and the earldom of Holderness became extinct. But the d'Arcy pride and the family's tradition of participation in public affairs had become a legend, and the title of Holderness had been at times almost synonymous with the north of England. When the direct male line, and with it the title of Holderness, disappeared, there remained many remind-

were no signs that anyone had entered the room, and it is quite certain that anything in the nature of cries or a struggle would have been heard, since Caunter, the elder boy in the inner room, is a very light sleeper.

" When Lord Saltire's disappearance was discovered I at once called a roll of the whole establishment—boys, masters, and servants. It was then that we ascertained that Lord Saltire had not been alone in his flight. Heidegger, the German master, was missing. His room was on the second floor, at the farther end of the building, facing the same way as Lord Saltire's. His bed had also been slept in ; but he had apparently gone away partly dressed, since his shirt and socks were lying on the floor. He had undoubtedly let himself down by the ivy, for we could see the marks of his feet where he had landed on the lawn. His bicycle was kept in a small shed beside this lawn, and it also was gone.

" He had been with me for two years, and came with the best references ; but he was a silent, morose man, not very popular either with masters or boys. No trace could be found of the fugitives, and now on Thursday morning we are as ignorant as we were on Tuesday. Inquiry was, of course, made at once at Holdernesse Hall. It is only a few miles away, and we imagined that in some sudden attack of home-sickness he had gone back to his father ; but nothing had been heard of him. The duke is greatly agitated—and as to me, you have seen yourselves the state of nervous prostration to which the suspense and the responsibility have reduced me. Mr. Holmes, if ever you put forward your full powers, I implore you to do so now, for never in your life could you have a case which is more worthy of them."

Sherlock Holmes had listened with the utmost intentness to the statement of the unhappy schoolmaster. His drawn brows and the deep furrow between them showed that he needed no exhortation to concentrate all his attention upon a problem which, apart from the tremendous interests involved, must appeal so directly to his love of the complex and the unusual. He now drew out his notebook and jotted down one or two memoranda.

" You have been very remiss in not coming to me sooner," said he severely. " You start me on my investigation with a very serious handicap. It is inconceivable, for example, that this ivy and this lawn would have yielded nothing to an expert observer."

" I am not to blame, Mr. Holmes. His Grace was extremely desirous to avoid all public scandal. He was afraid of his family unhappiness being dragged before the world. He has a deep horror of anything of the kind."

" But there has been some official investigation ? "

" Yes, sir, and it has proved most disappointing. An apparent clue was at once obtained, since a boy and a young man were reported to have been seen leaving a neighbouring station by an early train. Only last night we had news that the couple had been hunted down in Liverpool, and they prove to have no connection whatever with the matter in hand. Then it was that in my despair and disappointment, after a sleepless night, I came straight to you by the early train."

" I suppose the local investigation was relaxed while this false clue was being followed up ? "

" It was entirely dropped."

" So that three days have been wasted. The affair has been most deplorably handled."

" I feel it, and admit it."

" And yet the problem should be capable of ultimate solution. I shall be very happy to look into it. Have you been able to trace any connection between the missing boy and this German master ? "

" None at all."

" Was he in the master's class ? "

" No ; he never exchanged a word with him, so far as I know."

" That is certainly very singular. Had the boy a bicycle ? "

" No."

" Was any other bicycle missing ? "

" No."

" Is that certain ? "

" Quite."

" Well, now, you do not mean to seriously suggest that this German rode off upon a bicycle in the dead of the night bearing the boy in his arms ? "

" Certainly not."

" Then what is the theory in your mind ? "

" The bicycle may have been a blind. It may have been hidden somewhere, and the pair gone off on foot."

" Quite so ; but it seems rather an absurd blind, does it not ? Were there other bicycles in this shed ? "

" Several."

" Would he not have hidden a *couple* had he desired to give the idea that they had gone off upon them ? "

" I suppose he would."

" Of course he would. The blind theory won't do. But the incident is an admirable starting-point for an investigation. After all, a bicycle is not an easy thing to conceal or to destroy. One other question. Did any-one call to see the boy on the day before he disappeared ? "

" No."

" Did he get any letters ? "

" Yes ; one letter."

" From whom ? "

" From his father."

" Do you open the boys' letters ? "

" No."

" How do you know it was from the father ? "

" The coat-of-arms was on the envelope, and it was addressed in the duke's peculiar stiff hand. Besides, the duke remembers having written."

" When had he a letter before that ? "

" Not for several days."

" Had he ever one from France ? "

" No ; never."

" You see the point of my questions, of course. Either the boy was carried off by force or he went of his own free will. In the latter case you would expect that some prompting from outside would be needed to make so young a lad do such a thing. If he has had no visitors, that prompting must have come in letters. Hence I

ers and historical echoes from the activities of this famous house. Its honours and line are examined in the *Official Baronage of England*, published in 1888. This magnificent classic of genealogy was the product of thirteen years of scholarly endeavour by James Doyle, the uncle of . . . Arthur Conan Doyle."

8 Huxtable's Sidelights on Horace . "So elusive is this rarest of all Horatiana that many a scholar would be willing to part with his Aldine in exchange," Mr. Morris Rosenblum wrote in "Hafiz and Horace, Huxtable and Holmes."

9 *and now on Thursday morning*. The case began, according to Dr. Thorneycroft Huxtable's statement, on Thursday, May 16. Young Lord Saltire "was last seen on the night of May 13— that is, the night of last Monday." "His absence was discovered at seven o'clock on Tuesday morning." "And now on Thursday we are as ignorant as we were on Tuesday." It has been suggested that the year was 1900, but we very much doubt it: Holmes' encyclopedia of reference read: "Holdernesse, sixth Duke . . . Lord-Lieutenant of Hallamshire since 1900." Were this account written in the year 1900, it is hardly likely that the word "since" would have been included. On the other hand, the case cannot have taken place long after 1900: the Duke of Holdernesse had married in 1888; Lord Saltire was ten years old; "the duke's married life had not been a peaceful one"—Lord Saltire's birth must have come earlier rather than later in the duke's married life. Indeed, the latest possible date for the case is May, 1903: "The Adventure of the Priory School" was published in *Collier's Magazine* for January 30, 1904, the *Strand Magazine* for February, 1904. In 1901, the earliest year for the case if we discard 1900, the 16th of May *was* a Thursday. We accordingly date the case *Thursday, May 16, to Saturday, May 18, 1901.*

"THEN WHAT IS THE THEORY IN YOUR MIND?"

Illustration by Sidney Paget for the *Strand Magazine*, February, 1904.

10 *it is time that we were leaving for Euston.*"

"... no mean feat as the Derbyshire Peak District, where the Priory School was obviously situated, can only be reached from St. Pancras and that part of the country is still the preserve of the old Midland Railway," Mr. E. P. Greenwood commented in "Some Random Thoughts on Railway Journeys by Holmes and Watson."

BESIDE HIM STOOD A VERY YOUNG MAN . . .

Illustration by Sidney Paget for the *Strand Magazine*, February, 1904. Frederic Dorr Steele illustrated the same scene for *Collier's Magazine*, January 30, 1904.

try to find out who were his correspondents."

" I fear I cannot help you much.   His only correspondent, so far as I know, was his own father."

" Who wrote to him on the very day of his disappearance.   Were the relations between father and son very friendly ? "

" His Grace is never very friendly with anyone.   He is completely immersed in large public questions, and is rather inaccessible to all ordinary emotions.   But he was always kind to the boy in his own way."

" But the sympathies of the latter were with the mother ? "

" Yes."

" Did he say so ? "

" No."

" The duke, then ? "

" Good heavens, no ! "

" Then how could you know ? "

" I have had some confidential talk with Mr. James Wilder, his Grace's secretary.   It was he who gave me the information about Lord Saltire's feelings."

" I see.   By the way, that last letter of the duke's— was it found in the boy's room after he was gone ? "

" No ; he had taken it with him.   I think, Mr. Holmes, **10** it is time that we were leaving for Euston."

" I will order a four-wheeler.   In a quarter of an hour we shall be at your service.   If you are telegraphing home, Mr. Huxtable, it would be well to allow the people in your neighbourhood to imagine that the inquiry is still going on in Liverpool, or wherever else that red herring led your pack.   In the meantime, I will do a little quiet work at your own doors, and perhaps the scent is not so cold but that two old hounds like Watson and myself may get a sniff of it."

That evening found us in the cold, bracing atmosphere of the Peak country, in which Dr. Huxtable's famous school is situated.   It was already dark when we reached it.   A card was lying on the hall table, and the butler whispered something to his master, who turned to us with agitation in every heavy feature.

" The duke is here," said he.   " The duke and Mr. Wilder are in the study.   Come, gentlemen, and I will introduce you."

I was, of course, familiar with the pictures of the famous statesman, but the man himself was very different from his representation.   He was a tall and stately person, scrupulously dressed, with a drawn, thin face, and a nose which was grotesquely curved and long.   His complexion was of a dead pallor, which was more startling by contrast with a long, dwindling beard of vivid red, which flowed down over his white waistcoat, with his watch-chain gleaming through its fringe.   Such was the stately presence who looked stonily at us from the centre of Dr. Huxtable's hearthrug.   Beside him stood a very young man, whom I understood to be Wilder, the private secretary.   He was small, nervous, alert, with intelligent, light blue eyes and mobile features.   It was he who at once, in an incisive and positive tone, opened the conversation.

" I called this morning, Dr. Huxtable, too late to prevent you from starting for London. I learned that your object was to invite Mr. Sherlock Holmes to undertake the conduct of this case. His Grace is surprised, Dr. Huxtable, that you should have taken such a step without consulting him."

" When I learned the police had failed——"

" His Grace is by no means convinced that the police have failed."

" But surely, Mr. Wilder——"

" You are well aware, Dr. Huxtable, that his Grace is particularly anxious to avoid all public scandal. He prefers to take as few people as possible into his confidence."

" The matter can be easily remedied," said the browbeaten doctor. " Mr. Sherlock Holmes can return to London by the morning train."

" Hardly that, doctor, hardly that," said Holmes, in his blandest voice. " This northern air is invigorating and pleasant, so I propose to spend a few days upon your moors, and to occupy my mind as best I may. Whether I have the shelter of your roof or of the village inn is, of course, for you to decide."

I could see that the unfortunate doctor was in the last stage of indecision, from which he was rescued by the deep, sonorous voice of the red-bearded duke, which boomed out like a dinner-gong.

" I agree with Mr. Wilder, Dr. Huxtable, that you would have done wisely to consult me. But since Mr. Holmes has already been taken into your confidence, it would indeed be absurd that we should not avail ourselves of his services. Far from going to the inn, Mr. Holmes, I should be pleased if you would come and stay with me at Holdernesse Hall ? "

" I thank your Grace. For the purposes of my investigation I think that it would be wiser for me to remain at the scene of the mystery."

" Just as you like, Mr. Holmes. Any information which Mr. Wilder or I can give you is, of course, at your disposal."

" It will probably be necessary for me to see you at the Hall," said Holmes. " I would only ask you now, sir, whether you have formed any explanation in your own mind as to the mysterious disappearance of your son ? "

" No, sir, I have not."

" Excuse me if I allude to that which is painful to you, but I have no alternative. Do you think that the duchess had anything to do with the matter ? "

The great minister showed perceptible hesitation.

" I do not think so," he said at last.

" The other most obvious explanation is that the child had been kidnapped for the purpose of levying ransom. You have not had any demand of the sort ? "

" No, sir."

" One more question, your Grace. I understand that you wrote to your son upon the day when this incident occurred."

" No ; I wrote upon the day before."

" Exactly. But he received it on that day ? "

" Yes."

" Was there anything in your letter which might have unbalanced him or induced him to take such a step ? "

" No, sir, certainly not."

" Did you post that letter yourself ? "

The nobleman's reply was interrupted by his secretary, who broke in with some heat.

" His Grace is not in the habit of posting letters himself," said he. " This letter was laid with others upon the study table, and I myself put them in the post-bag."

" You are sure this one was among them ? "

" Yes ; I observed it."

" How many letters did your Grace write that day ? "

" Twenty or thirty. I have a large correspondence. But surely this is somewhat irrelevant ? "

" Not entirely," said Holmes.

" For my own part," the duke continued, " I have advised the police to turn their attention to the South of France. I have already said that I do not believe that the duchess would encourage so monstrous an action, but the lad had the most wrong-headed opinions, and it is possible that he may have fled to her, aided and abetted by this German. I think, Dr. Huxtable, that we will now return to the Hall."

I could see that there were other questions which Holmes would have wished to put ; but the nobleman's abrupt manner showed that the interview was at an end. It was evident that to his intensely aristocratic nature this discussion of his intimate family affairs with a stranger was most abhorrent, and that he feared lest every fresh question would throw a fiercer light into the discreetly shadowed corners of his ducal history.

When the nobleman and his secretary had left, my friend flung himself at once with characteristic eagerness into the investigation.

The boy's chamber was carefully examined, and yielded nothing save the absolute conviction that it was only through the window that he could have escaped. The German master's room and effects gave no further clue. In his case a trailer of ivy had given way under his weight, and we saw by the light of a lantern the mark on the lawn where his heels had come down. That one dent in the short green grass was the only material witness left of this inexplicable nocturnal flight.

Sherlock Holmes left the house alone, and only returned after eleven. He had obtained a large ordnance map of the neighbourhood, and this he brought into my room, where he laid it out on the bed, and, having balanced the lamp in the middle of it, he began to smoke over it, and occasionally to point out objects of interest with the reeking amber of his pipe.

" This case grows upon me, Watson," said he. " There are decidedly some points of interest in connection with it. In this early stage I want you to realize these geographical features, which may have a good deal to do with our investigation.

" Look at this map. This dark square is the Priory School. I'll put a pin in it. Now, this line is the main road. You see that it runs east and west past the school, and you see also there is no side-road for a mile either way. If these two folk passed away by road it was *this* road."

" Exactly."

" By a singular and happy chance we are able to some extent to check what passed along this road during the night in question. At this point, where my pipe is now resting, a country constable was on duty from twelve to six. It is, as you perceive, the first cross-road on the east side. This man declares that he was not absent from his post for an instant, and he is positive that neither boy nor man could have gone that way unseen. I have

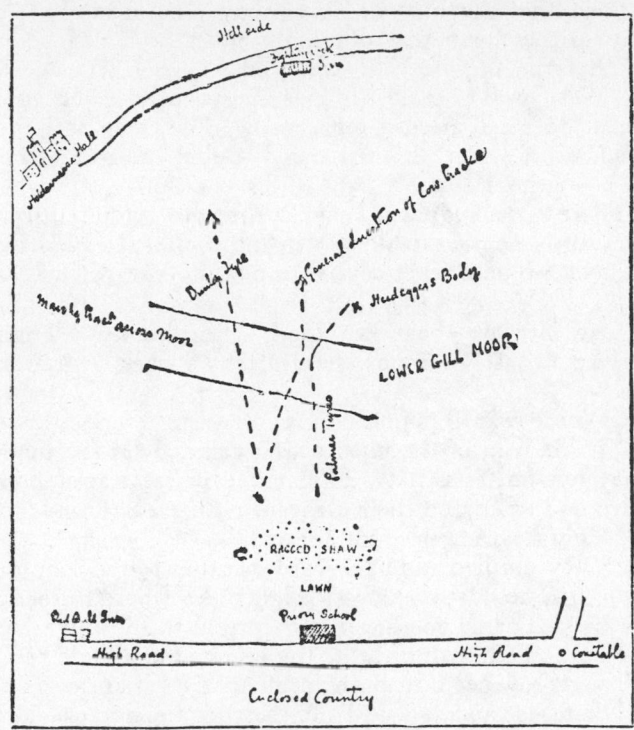

SKETCH MAP SHOWING THE LOCALITY.

spoken with this policeman to-night, and he appears to me to be a perfectly reliable person. That blocks this end. We have now to deal with the other. There is an inn here, the ' Red Bull,' the landlady of which was ill. She had sent to Mackleton for a doctor, but he did not arrive until morning, being absent at another case. The people at the inn were alert all night, awaiting his coming, and one or other of them seems to have continually had an eye upon the road. They declare that no one passed. If their evidence is good, then we are fortunate enough to be able to block the west, and also to be able to say that the fugitives did *not* use the road at all."

" But the bicycle ? " I objected.

" Quite so. We will come to the bicycle presently. To continue our reasoning : if these people did not go by the road, they must have traversed the country to the north of the house or to the south of the house. That is certain. Let us weigh the one against the other. On the south of the house is, as you perceive, a large district of arable land, cut up into small fields, with stone walls between them. There, I admit that a bicycle is impossible. We can dismiss the idea. We turn to the country on the north. Here there lies a grove of trees, marked as the ' Ragged Shaw,' and on the farther side

11 *the moon was at the full*. There is one objection to 1901 as the year of the case: Holmes said the moon was at the full "on the night the boy disappeared," and the moon was *not* at the full on the night of Monday, May 13, 1901; it was ten days past the full. This led the late Dr. Ernest Bloomfield Zeisler to conclude that the case must have taken place in May, 1900.

12 *in this dry weather*. Unhappily, this is of little help to us in dating the adventure: before the 16th of the month, it rained on only four days in *both* the May of 1900 and the May of 1901. In the entire month of May, 1900, it rained on nine days for a total fall of 1.32 inch, 0.68 inch below the 1841–1890 average; in the entire month of May, 1901, it rained on five days for a total fall of 1.79 inch, 0.18 inch below the 1841–1890 average.

stretches a great rolling moor, Lower Gill Moor, extending for ten miles, and sloping gradually upwards. Here, at one side of this wilderness, is Holdernesse Hall, ten miles by road, but only six across the moor. It is a peculiarly desolate plain. A few moor farmers have small holdings, where they rear sheep and cattle. Except these, the plover and the curlew are the only inhabitants until you come to the Chesterfield high road. There is a church there, you see, a few cottages, and an inn. Beyond that the hills become precipitous. Surely it is here to the north that our quest must lie."

"But the bicycle?" I persisted.

"Well, well!" said Holmes impatiently. "A good cyclist does not need a high road. The moor is inter-
11 sected with paths, and the moon was at the full. Halloa! What is this?"

There was an agitated knock at the door, and an instant afterwards Dr. Huxtable was in the room. In his hand he held a blue cricket-cap, with a white chevron on the peak.

"At last we have a clue!" he cried. "Thank Heaven, at last we are on the dear boy's track! It is his cap."

"Where was it found?"

"In the van of the gipsies who camped on the moor. They left on Tuesday. To-day the police traced them down and examined their caravan. This was found."

"How do they account for it?"

"They shuffled and lied—said that they found it on the moor on Tuesday morning. They know where he is, the rascals! Thank goodness, they are all safe under lock and key. Either the fear of the law or the duke's purse will certainly get out of them all that they know."

"So far, so good," said Holmes, when the doctor had at last left the room. "It at least bears out the theory that it is on the side of the Lower Gill Moor that we must hope for results. The police have really done nothing locally, save the arrest of these gipsies. Look here, Watson! There is a watercourse across the moor. You see it marked here in the map. In some parts it widens into a morass. This is particularly so in the region between Holdernesse Hall and the school. It is vain to look else-
12 where for tracks in this dry weather; but at *that* point there is certainly a chance of some record being left. I will call you early to-morrow morning, and you and I will try if we can throw some light upon the mystery."

The day was just breaking when I woke to find the long, thin form of Holmes by my bedside. He was fully dressed, and had apparently already been out.

"I have done the lawn and the bicycle shed," said he. "I have also had a ramble through the Ragged Shaw. Now, Watson, there is cocoa ready in the next room. I must beg you to hurry, for we have a great day before us."

His eyes shone, and his cheek was flushed with the exhilaration of the master workman who sees his work lies ready before him. A very different Holmes, this active, alert man, from the introspective and pallid dreamer of Baker Street. I felt, as I looked upon that supple figure, alive with nervous energy, that it was indeed a strenuous day that awaited us.

And yet it opened in the blackest disappointment. With high hopes we struck across the peaty, russet moor, intersected with a thousand sheep-paths, until we came to the broad light green-belt which marked the morass between us and Holdernesse. Certainly, if the lad had gone homewards, he must have passed this, and he would not pass it without leaving his trace. But no sign of him or the German could be seen. With a darkening face my friend strode along the margin, eagerly observant of every muddy stain upon the mossy surface. Sheep-marks there were in profusion, and at one place, some miles down, cows had left their tracks. Nothing more.

"Check number one," said Holmes, looking gloomily over the rolling expanse of the moor. "There is another morass down yonder, and a narrow neck between. Halloa! halloa! halloa! What have we here?"

We had come on a small black ribbon of pathway. In the middle of it, clearly marked on the sodden soil, was the track of a bicycle.

"Hurrah!" I cried. "We have it."

But Holmes was shaking his head, and his face was puzzled and expectant rather than joyous.

"A bicycle certainly, but not *the* bicycle," said he. "I am familiar with forty-two different impressions left by tyres. This, as you perceive, is a Dunlop, with a patch **13** upon the outer cover. Heidegger's tyres were Palmer's, leaving longitudinal stripes. Aveling, the mathematical master, was sure upon the point. Therefore it is not Heidegger's track."

"The boy's, then?"

"Possibly, if we could prove a bicycle to have been in his possession. But this we have utterly failed to do. This track, as you perceive, was made by a rider who was going from the direction of the school."

"Or towards it?"

"No, no, my dear Watson. The more deeply sunk impression is, of course, the hind wheel, upon which the weight rests. You perceive several places where it has passed across and obliterated the more shallow mark of the front one. It was undoubtedly heading away from the school. It may or may not be connected **14** with our inquiry, but we will follow it backwards before we go any farther."

We did so, and at the end of a few hundred yards lost the tracks as we emerged from the boggy portion of the moor. Following the path backwards, we picked out another spot, where a spring trickled across it. Here, once again, was the mark of the bicycle, though nearly obliterated by the hoofs of cows. After that there was no sign, but the path ran right on into Ragged Shaw, the wood which backed on to the school. From this wood the cycle must have emerged. Holmes sat down on a boulder and rested his chin in his hands. I had smoked two cigarettes before he moved.

"Well, well," said he at last. "It is, of course, possible that a cunning man might change the tyre of his bicycle in order to leave unfamiliar tracks. A criminal

13 *a Dunlop.* Named for its developer, John Boyd Dunlop, 1840–1921.

14 *It was undoubtedly heading away from the school.* Much, perhaps too much, has been written about these tire tracks. Holmes' deduction has been challenged by Mr. A. D. Galbraith ("The Real Moriarty") and Mr. Stuart C. Rand ("What Sherlock Didn't Know"), among others; defended by Mr. T. S. Blakeney (*Sherlock Holmes: Fact or Fiction?*) and Mr. George K. Gardner ("What Sherlock Did Know"), among others. "But it is clear that the tracks would look the same both ways, unless the tread had some lack of symmetry, or other peculiarity, and the manner of mounting it on the wheel were known," Mr. Galbraith wrote. ". . . the depth of the mark of the rear wheel, when the bicycle was going uphill, would indicate the direction of travel, for on the down slope it is markedly less," Mr. Blakeney wrote. "In any case, Holmes probably had a dozen other small indications to guide him; though he might mention only one factor, he usually had others in reserve as evidenced by the twenty-three additional points of difference in the joint letter of the Cunninghams ["The Reigate Squires"]."

"CHECK NUMBER ONE," SAID HOLMES, LOOKING GLOOMILY OVER THE ROLLING EXPANSE OF THE MOOR.

Cover illustration by Frederic Dorr Steele for *Collier's Magazine*, January 30, 1904.

AN IMPRESSION LIKE A FINE BUNDLE OF TELEGRAPH
WIRES RAN DOWN THE CENTRE OF IT.

Illustration by Sidney Paget for the *Strand Magazine*, February, 1904.

WE RAN ROUND, AND THERE LAY THE
UNFORTUNATE RIDER.

Illustration by Sidney Paget for the *Strand Magazine*, February, 1904.

who was capable of such a thought is a man whom I should be proud to do business with. We will leave this question undecided and hark back to our morass again, for we have left a good deal unexplored."

We continued our systematic survey of the edge of the sodden portion of the moor, and soon our perseverance was gloriously rewarded.

Right across the lower part of the bog lay a miry path. Holmes gave a cry of delight as he approached it. An impression like a fine bundle of telegraph wires ran down the centre of it. It was the Palmer tyre.

"Here is Herr Heidegger, sure enough!" cried Holmes exultantly. "My reasoning seems to have been pretty sound, Watson."

"I congratulate you."

"But we have a long way still to go. Kindly walk clear of the path. Now let us follow the trail. I fear that it will not lead very far."

We found, however, as we advanced, that this portion of the moor is intersected with soft patches, and, though we frequently lost sight of the track, we always succeeded in picking it up once more.

"Do you observe," said Holmes, "that the rider is now undoubtedly forcing the pace? There can be no doubt of it. Look at this impression, where you get both tyres clear. The one is as deep as the other. That can only mean that the rider is throwing his weight on to the handle-bar as a man does when he is sprinting. By Jove! he has had a fall."

There was a broad, irregular smudge covering some yards of the track. Then there were a few footmarks, and the tyre reappeared once more.

"A side-slip," I suggested.

Holmes held up a crumpled branch of flowering gorse. To my horror I perceived that the yellow blossoms were all dabbled with crimson. On the path, too, and among the heather were dark stains of clotted blood.

"Bad!" said Holmes. "Bad! Stand clear, Watson! Not an unnecessary footstep! What do I read here? He fell wounded, he stood up, he remounted, he proceeded. But there is no other track. Cattle on this side-path. He was surely not gored by a bull? Impossible! But I see no traces of anyone else. We must push on, Watson. Surely, with stains as well as the track to guide us, he cannot escape us now."

Our search was not a very long one. The tracks of the tyre began to curve fantastically upon the wet and shining path. Suddenly, as I looked ahead, the gleam of metal caught my eye from amid the thick gorse bushes. Out of them we dragged a bicycle, Palmer-tyred, one pedal bent, and the whole front of it horribly smeared and slobbered with blood. On the other side of the bushes a shoe was projecting. We ran round, and there lay the unfortunate rider. He was a tall man, full bearded, with spectacles, one glass of which had been knocked out. The cause of his death was a frightful blow upon the head, which had crushed in part of his skull. That he could have gone on after receiving such an injury said much for the vitality and courage of the man. He wore shoes, but no socks, and his open coat disclosed a night-shirt beneath it. It was undoubtedly the German master.

Holmes turned the body over reverently, and examined it with great attention. He then sat in deep thought for a time, and I could see by his ruffled brow that this grim discovery had not, in his opinion, advanced us much in our inquiry.

" It is a little difficult to know what to do, Watson," said he, at last. " My own inclinations are to push this inquiry on, for we have already lost so much time that we cannot afford to waste another hour. On the other hand, we are bound to inform the police of this discovery, and to see that this poor fellow's body is looked after."

" I could take a note back."

" But I need your company and assistance. Wait a bit ! There is a fellow cutting peat up yonder. Bring him over here, and he will guide the police."

I brought the peasant across, and Holmes despatched the frightened man with a note to Dr. Huxtable.

" Now, Watson," said he, " we have picked up two clues this morning. One is the bicycle with the Palmer tyre, and we see what that has led to. The other is the bicycle with the patched Dunlop. Before we start to investigate that, let us try to realize what we *do* know, so as to make the most of it, and to separate the essential from the accidental.

" First of all, I wish to impress upon you that the boy certainly left of his own free will. He got down from his window and he went off, either alone or with someone. That is sure."

I assented.

" Well, now, let us turn to this unfortunate German master. The boy was fully dressed when he fled. Therefore he foresaw what he would do. But the German went without his socks. He certainly acted on very short notice."

" Undoubtedly."

" Why did he go ? Because, from his bedroom window, he saw the flight of the boy. Because he wished to overtake him and bring him back. He seized his bicycle, pursued the lad, and in pursuing him met his death."

" So it would seem."

" Now I come to the critical part of my argument. The natural action of a man in pursuing a little boy would be to run after him. He would know that he could overtake him. But the German does not do so. He turns to his bicycle. I am told that he was an excellent cyclist. He would not do this if he did not see that the boy had some swift means of escape."

" The other bicycle."

" Let us continue our reconstruction. He meets his death five miles from the school—not by a bullet, mark you, which even a lad might conceivably discharge, but by a savage blow dealt by a vigorous arm. The lad, then, *had* a companion in his flight. And the flight was a swift one, since it took five miles before an expert cyclist could overtake them. Yet we survey the ground round the scene of the tragedy. What do we find ? A few cattle tracks, nothing more. I took a wide sweep round,

... THE FORBIDDING AND SQUALID INN, WITH THE SIGN
OF A GAMECOCK ABOVE THE DOOR ...

To Mr. Charles O. Merriman of the Sherlock
Holmes Society of London goes the credit for
identifying what must have been the Fighting Cock
Inn. He found it at the proper location, in Old
Whittington, on the high road, four miles from
Chesterfield, and it bears a plaque which reads:
A.D. 1688 / IN A ROOM WHICH FORMERLY /
EXISTED AT THE END OF THIS / COT-
TAGE (WHAT IS LEFT OF THE / OLD
COCK & PYNOT) THE EARL / OF DANBY
THE EARL OF DEVONSHIRE / AND MR.
JOHN D'ARCY (ELDEST SON / OF THE
EARL OF HOLDERNESS) MET / SOME-
TIME IN 1688 TO CONCERT / MEASURES
WHICH RESULTED IN THE / REVOLU-
TION OF THAT YEAR.

and there is no path within fifty yards. Another cyclist
could have had nothing to do with the actual murder.
Nor were there any human footmarks."

" Holmes," I cried, " this is impossible."

" Admirable ! " he said. " A most illuminating remark. It *is* impossible as I state it, and therefore I must
in some respect have stated it wrong. Yet you saw for
yourself. Can you suggest any fallacy ? "

" He could not have fractured his skull in a fall ? "

" In a morass, Watson ? "

" I am at my wits' end."

" Tut, tut ; we have solved some worse problems. At
least we have plenty of material, if we can only use it.
Come, then, and, having exhausted the Palmer, let us see
what the Dunlop with the patched cover has to offer us."

We picked up the track and followed it onwards for
some distance ; but soon the moor rose into a long,
heather-tufted curve, and we left the watercourse behind
us. No further help from tracks could be hoped for.
At the spot where we saw the last of the Dunlop tyre it
might equally have led to Holdernesse Hall, the stately
towers of which rose some miles to our left, or to a low,
grey village which lay in front of us, and marked the
position of the Chesterfield high-road.

As we approached the forbidding and squalid inn, with
the sign of a game-cock above the door, Holmes gave a
sudden groan and clutched me by the shoulder to save
himself from falling. He had had one of those violent
strains of the ankle which leave a man helpless. With
difficulty he limped up to the door, where a squat, dark,
elderly man was smoking a black clay pipe.

" How are you, Mr. Reuben Hayes ? " said Holmes.

" Who are you, and how do you get my name so pat ? "
the countryman answered, with a suspicious flash of a
pair of cunning eyes.

" Well, it's printed on the board above your head. It's
easy to see a man who is master of his own house. I
suppose you haven't such a thing as a carriage in your
stables ? "

" No ; I have not."

" I can hardly put my foot to the ground."

" Don't put it to the ground."

" But I can't walk."

" Well, then, hop."

Mr. Reuben Hayes' manner was far from gracious,
but Holmes took it with admirable good humour.

" Look here, my man," said he. " This is really
rather an awkward fix for me. I don't mind how I get
on."

" Neither do I," said the morose landlord.

" The matter is very important. I would offer you a
sovereign for the use of a bicycle."

The landlord pricked up his ears.

" Where do you want to go ? "

" To Holdernesse Hall."

" Pals of the dook, I suppose ? " said the landlord,
surveying our mud-stained garments with ironical eyes.

Holmes laughed good-naturedly.

" He'll be glad to see us, anyhow."

" Why ? "

" Because we bring him news of his lost son."

The landlord gave a very visible start.

" What, you're on his track ? "

" He has been heard of in Liverpool. They expect to get him every hour."

Again a swift change passed over the heavy, unshaven face. His manner was suddenly genial.

" I've less reason to wish the dook well than most men," said he, " for I was his head coachman once, and cruel bad he treated me. It was him that sacked me without a character on the word of a lying corn-chandler. But I'm glad to hear that the young lord was heard of in Liverpool, and I'll help you to take the news to the Hall."

" Thank you," said Holmes. " We'll have some food first. Then you can bring round the bicycle."

" I haven't got a bicycle."

Holmes held up a sovereign.

" I tell you, man, that I haven't got one. I'll let you have two horses as far as the Hall."

" Well, well," said Holmes, " we'll talk about it when we've had something to eat."

When we were left alone in the stone-flagged kitchen it was astonishing how rapidly that sprained ankle recovered. It was nearly nightfall, and we had eaten nothing since early morning, so that we spent some time over our meal. Holmes was lost in thought, and once or twice he walked over to the window and stared earnestly out. It opened on to a squalid courtyard. In the far corner was a smithy, where a grimy lad was at work. On the other side were the stables. Holmes had sat down again after one of these excursions, when he suddenly sprang out of his chair with a loud exclamation.

" By Heaven, Watson, I believe that I've got it ! " he cried. " Yes, yes, it must be so. Watson, do you remember seeing any cow-tracks to-day ? "

" Yes, several."

" Where ? "

" Well, everywhere. They were at the morass, and again on the path, and again near where poor Heidegger met his death."

" Exactly. Well, now, Watson, how many cows did you see on the moor ? "

" I don't remember seeing any."

" Strange, Watson, that we should see tracks all along our line, but never a cow on the whole moor ; very strange, Watson, eh ? "

" Yes, it is strange."

" Now, Watson, make an effort ; throw your mind back ! Can you see those tracks upon the path ? "

" Yes, I can."

" Can you recall that the tracks were sometimes like that, Watson "—he arranged a number of breadcrumbs in this fashion—: : : :—" and sometimes like this "—: · · · : · · ·—" and occasionally like this—. · · · ·

" Can you remember that ? "   **15**

" No, I cannot."

" But I can. I could swear to it. However, we will go back at our leisure and verify it. What a blind beetle I have been not to draw my conclusion ? "

WITH DIFFICULTY HE LIMPED UP TO THE DOOR . . .

Illustration by Sidney Paget for the *Strand Magazine*, February, 1904.

15 *"Can you remember that?"* In his searching and prize-winning study of "The Hoof-Marks in 'The Priory School,'" Magistrate S. Tupper Bigelow has shown that the walk of a horse is more correctly depicted in dots as:

: :   : :   : :   : :

the canter as

· ·   · ·

and the gallop more or less as Holmes has it in our text and in most, but not all, other editions.

"And what is your conclusion?"

"Only that it is a remarkable cow which walks, canters, and gallops. By George, Watson, it was no brain of a country publican that thought out such a blind as that! The coast seems to be clear, save for that lad in the smithy. Let us slip out and see what we can see."

There were two rough-haired, unkempt horses in the tumble-down stable. Holmes raised the hind-leg of one of them and laughed aloud.

"Old shoes, but newly shod—old shoes, but new nails. This case deserves to be a classic. Let us go across to the smithy."

The lad continued his work without regarding us. I saw Holmes' eye darting to right and left among the litter of iron and wood, which was scattered about the floor. Suddenly, however, we heard a step behind us, and there was the landlord, his heavy eyebrows drawn down over his savage eyes, his swarthy features convulsed with passion.

He held a short metal-headed stick in his hand, and he advanced in so menacing a fashion that I was right glad to feel the revolver in my pocket.

"You infernal spies!" the man cried. "What are you doing there?"

"Why, Mr. Reuben Hayes," said Holmes coolly, "one might think that you were afraid of our finding something out."

The man mastered himself with a violent effort, and his grim mouth loosened into a false laugh, which was more menacing than his frown.

"You're welcome to all you can find out in my smithy," said he. "But look here, mister, I don't care for folk poking about my place without my leave, so the sooner you pay your score and get out of this the better I shall be pleased."

"All right, Mr. Hayes—no harm meant," said Holmes. "We have been having a look at your horses; but I think I'll walk after all. It's not far, I believe."

"Not more than two miles to the Hall gates. That's the road to the left." He watched us with sullen eyes until we had left his premises.

We did not go very far along the road, for Holmes stopped the instant that the curve hid us from the landlord's view.

"We were warm, as the children say, at that inn," said he. "I seem to grow colder every step that I take away from it. No, no; I can't possibly leave it."

"I am convinced," said I, "that this Reuben Hayes knows all about it. A more self-evident villain I never saw."

"Oh! he impressed you in that way, did he? There are the horses, there is the smithy. Yes, it is an interesting place, this 'Fighting Cock.' I think we shall have another look at it in an unobtrusive way."

A long, sloping hill-side, dotted with grey limestone boulders, stretched behind us. We had turned off the road, and were making our way up the hill, when, looking in the direction of Holdernesse Hall, I saw a cyclist coming swiftly along.

WE HAD HARDLY SUNK FROM VIEW WHEN THE MAN FLEW PAST US ON THE ROAD.

Illustration by Sidney Paget for the *Strand Magazine*, February, 1904.

" Get down, Watson ! " cried Holmes, with a heavy hand upon my shoulder. We had hardly sunk from view when the man flew past us on the road. Amid a rolling cloud of dust I caught a glimpse of a pale, agitated face—a face with horror in every lineament, the mouth open, the eyes staring wildly in front. It was like some strange caricature of the dapper James Wilder whom we had seen the night before.

" The duke's secretary ! " cried Holmes. " Come, Watson, let us see what he does."

We scrambled from rock to rock until in a few moments we had made our way to a point from which we could see the front door of the inn. Wilder's bicycle was leaning against the wall beside it. No one was moving about the house, nor could we catch a glimpse of any faces at the windows. Slowly the twilight crept down as the sun sank behind the high towers of Holdernesse Hall. Then in the gloom we saw the two side-lamps of a trap light up in the stable-yard of the inn, and shortly afterwards heard the rattle of hoofs, as it wheeled out into the road and tore off at a furious pace in the direction of Chesterfield.

" What do you make of that, Watson ? " Holmes whispered.

" It looks like a flight."

" A single man in a dog-cart, so far as I could see. Well, it certainly was not Mr. James Wilder, for there he is at the door."

A red square of light had sprung out of the darkness. In the middle of it was the black figure of the secretary, his head advanced, peering out into the night. It was evident that he was expecting some one. Then at last there were steps in the road, a second figure was visible for an instant against the light, the door shut, and all was black once more. Five minutes later a lamp was lit in a room upon the first floor.

" It seems to be a curious class of custom that is done by the ' Fighting Cock,' " said Holmes.

" The bar is on the other side."

" Quite so. These are what one may call the private guests. Now, what in the world is Mr. James Wilder doing in that den at this hour of night, and who is the companion who comes to meet him there ? Come, Watson, we must really take a risk and try to investigate this a little more closely."

Together we stole down to the road and crept across to the door of the inn. The bicycle still leaned against the wall. Holmes struck a match and held it to the back wheel, and I heard him chuckle as the light fell upon a patched Dunlop tyre. Up above us was the lighted window.

" I must have a peep through that, Watson. If you bend your back and support yourself upon the wall, I think that I can manage."

An instant later his feet were on my shoulders. But he was hardly up before he was down again.

" Come, my friend," said he, " our day's work has been quite long enough. I think that we have gathered all that we can. It's a long walk to the school, and the sooner we get started the better."

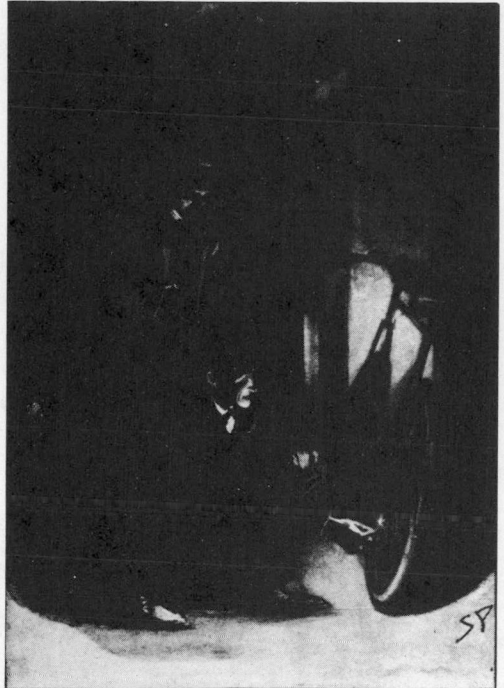

. . . I HEARD HIM CHUCKLE AS THE LIGHT FELL
UPON A PATCHED DUNLOP TYRE.

Illustration by Sidney Paget for the *Strand Magazine*, February, 1904.

AN INSTANT LATER HIS FEET WERE ON MY SHOULDERS.

Illustration by Charles Raymond Macauley for *The Return of Sherlock Holmes*, New York: McClure, Phillips & Co., 1905.

He hardly opened his lips during that weary trudge across the moor, nor would he enter the school when he reached it, but went on to Mackleton Station, whence he could send some telegrams.   Late at night I heard him consoling Dr. Huxtable, prostrated by the tragedy of his master's death, and later still he entered my room as alert and vigorous as he had been when he started in the morning.   " All goes well, my friend," said he.   " I promise that before to-morrow evening we shall have reached the solution of the mystery."

At eleven o'clock next morning my friend and I were walking up the famous yew avenue of Holdernesse Hall. We were ushered through the magnificent Elizabethan doorway and into his Grace's study.   There we found Mr. James Wilder, demure and courtly, but with some trace of that wild terror of the night before still lurking in his furtive eyes and in his twitching features.

" You have come to see his Grace ?   I am sorry ; but the fact is that the duke is far from well.   He has been very much upset by the tragic news.   We received a telegram from Dr. Huxtable yesterday afternoon, which told us of your discovery."

" I must see the duke, Mr. Wilder."

" But he is in his room."

" Then I must go to his room."

" I believe he is in his bed."

" I will see him there."

Holmes' cold and inexorable manner showed the secretary that it was useless to argue with him.

" Very good, Mr. Holmes ; I will tell him that you are here."

After half an hour's delay the great nobleman appeared. His face was more cadaverous than ever, his shoulders had rounded, and he seemed to me to be an altogether older man than he had been the morning before.   He greeted us with a stately courtesy, and seated himself at his desk, his red beard streaming down on to the table.

" Well, Mr. Holmes ? " said he.

But my friend's eyes were fixed upon the secretary, who stood by his master's chair.

" I think, your Grace, that I could speak more freely in Mr. Wilder's absence."

The man turned a shade paler and cast a malignant glance at Holmes.

" If your Grace wishes——"

" Yes, yes ; you had better go.   Now, Mr. Holmes, what have you to say ? "

My friend waited until the door had closed behind the retreating secretary.

" The fact is, your Grace," said he, " that my colleague, Dr. Watson, and myself had an assurance from Dr. Huxtable that a reward had been offered in this case.   I should like to have this confirmed from your own lips."

" Certainly, Mr. Holmes."

" It amounted, if I am correctly informed, to five thousand pounds to anyone who will tell you where your son is ? "

" Exactly."

" And another thousand to the man who will name

the person or persons who keep him in custody?"

"Exactly."

"Under the latter heading is included, no doubt, not only those who may have taken him away, but also those who conspire to keep him in his present position?"

"Yes, yes," cried the duke impatiently. "If you do your work well, Mr. Sherlock Holmes, you will have no reason to complain of niggardly treatment."

My friend rubbed his thin hands together with an appearance of avidity which was a surprise to me, who knew his frugal tastes.

"I fancy that I see your Grace's cheque-book upon the table," said he. "I should be glad if you would make me out a cheque for six thousand pounds. It would be as well, perhaps, for you to cross it. The Capital and **16** Counties Bank, Oxford Street branch, are my agents." **17**

His Grace sat very stern and upright in his chair, and looked stonily at my friend.

"Is this a joke, Mr. Holmes? It is hardly a subject for pleasantry."

"Not at all, your Grace. I was never more earnest in my life."

"What do you mean, then?"

"I mean that I have earned the reward. I know where your son is, and I know some, at least, of those who are holding him."

The duke's beard had turned more aggressively red than ever against his ghastly white face.

"Where is he?" he gasped.

"He is, or was last night, at the Fighting Cock Inn, about two miles from your park gate."

The duke fell back in his chair.

"And whom do you accuse?"

Sherlock Holmes' answer was an astounding one. He stepped swiftly forward and touched the duke upon the shoulder.

"I accuse *you*," said he. "And now, your Grace, I'll trouble you for that cheque."

Never shall I forget the duke's appearance as he sprang up and clawed with his hand like one who is sinking into an abyss. Then, with an extraordinary effort of aristocratic self-command, he sat down and sank his face in his hands. It was some minutes before he spoke.

"How much do you know?" he asked at last, without raising his head.

"I saw you together last night."

"Does anyone else besides your friend know?"

"I have spoken to no one."

The duke took a pen in his quivering fingers and opened his cheque-book.

"I shall be as good as my word, Mr. Holmes. I am about to write your cheque, however unwelcome the information which you have gained may be to me. When the offer was first made I little thought the turn which events would take. But you and your friend are men of discretion, Mr. Holmes?"

"I hardly understand your Grace."

"I must put it plainly, Mr. Holmes. If only you two know of the incident, there is no reason why it should go any farther. I think twelve thousand pounds is the sum **18**

16 *to cross it.* To write something, such as the name of a bank, across the face of the check, requiring its deposit in the bank by the payee before collection.

17 *The Capital and Counties Bank, Oxford Street branch.* In Holmes' day, the Oxford Street branch of the Capital and Counties Bank was located at No. 125.

18 *twelve thousand pounds.* "The Duke, when it came to paying, spoke of £12,000 being the sum owed, presumably intending to give the promised reward of £6,000 to Watson as well, unless, indeed, he was hoping to purchase Holmes' silence by doubling the amount due to him," Mr. T. S. Blakeney commented in *Sherlock Holmes: Fact or Fiction?*

that I owe you, is it not ? "

But Holmes smiled, and shook his head.

" I fear, your Grace, that matters can hardly be arranged so easily. There is the death of this school-master to be accounted for."

" But James knew nothing of that. You cannot hold him responsible for that. It was the work of this brutal ruffian whom he had the misfortune to employ."

" I must take the view, your Grace, that when a man embarks upon a crime he is morally guilty of any other crime which may spring from it."

" Morally, Mr. Holmes. No doubt you are right. But surely not in the eyes of the law. A man cannot be con-demned for a murder at which he was not present, and which he loathes and abhors as much as you do. The instant that he heard of it he made a complete confession to me, so filled was he with horror and remorse. He lost not an hour in breaking entirely with the murderer. Oh, Mr. Holmes, you must save him—you must save him ! I tell you that you must save him ! " The duke had dropped the last attempt at self-command, and was pacing the room with a convulsed face and with his clenched hands raving in the air. At last he mastered himself and sat down once more at his desk. " I appre-ciate your conduct in coming here before you spoke to anyone else," said he. " At least we may take counsel how far we can minimize this hideous scandal."

" Exactly," said Holmes. " I think, your Grace, that this can only be done by absolute and complete frankness between us. I am disposed to help your Grace to the best of my ability ; but in order to do so I must under-stand to the last detail how the matter stands. I realize that your words applied to Mr. James Wilder, and that he is not the murderer."

" No ; the murderer has escaped."

Sherlock Holmes smiled demurely.

" Your Grace can hardly have heard of any small reputation which I possess, or you would not imagine that it is so easy to escape me. Mr. Reuben Hayes was arrested at Chesterfield on my information at eleven o'clock last night. I had a telegram from the head of the local police before I left the school this morning."

The duke leaned back in his chair and stared with amazement at my friend.

" You seem to have powers that are hardly human," said he. " So Reuben Hayes is taken ? I am right glad to hear it, if it will not react upon the fate of James."

" Your secretary ? "

" No, sir ; my son."

It was Holmes' turn to look astonished.

" I confess that this is entirely new to me, your Grace. I must beg of you to be more explicit."

" I will conceal nothing from you. I agree with you that complete frankness, however painful it may be to me, is the best policy in this desperate situation to which James' folly and jealousy have reduced us. When I was a young man, Mr. Holmes, I loved with such a love as comes only once in a lifetime. I offered the lady mar-riage, but she refused it on the grounds that such a match might mar my career. Had she lived I would certainly

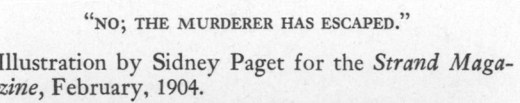

"NO; THE MURDERER HAS ESCAPED."

Illustration by Sidney Paget for the *Strand Maga-zine*, February, 1904.

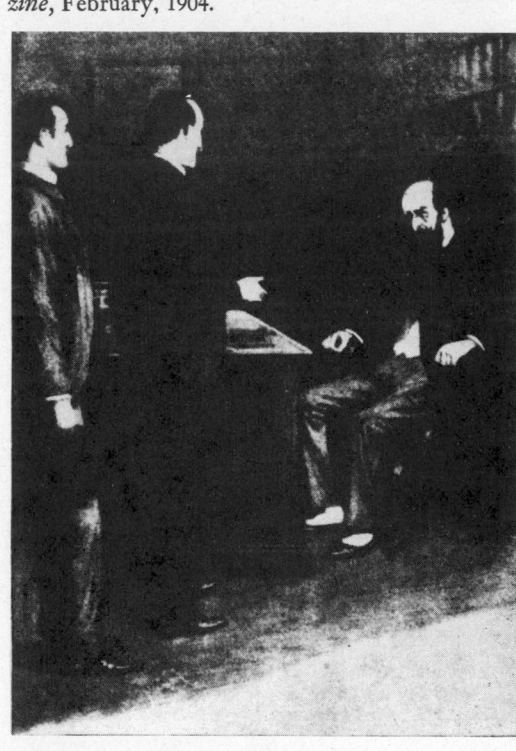

never have married anyone else. She died, and left this
one child, whom for her sake I have cherished and cared
for. I could not acknowledge the paternity to the world ;
but I gave him the best of educations, and since he came
to manhood I have kept him near my person. He
surprised my secret, and has presumed ever since upon
the claim which he has upon me and upon his power of
provoking a scandal, which would be abhorrent to me.
His presence had something to do with the unhappy issue
of my marriage.   Above all, he hated my young legitimate
heir from the first with a persistent hatred. You may
well ask me why, under these circumstances, I still kept
James under my roof. I answer that it was because I
could see his mother's face in his, and that for her dear
sake there was no end to my long-suffering. All her
pretty ways, too—there was not one of them which he
could not suggest and bring back to my memory. I
could not send him away. But I feared so lest he should
do Arthur—that is, Lord Saltire—a mischief that I despatched him for safety to Dr. Huxtable's school.

" James came into contact with this fellow Hayes
because the man was a tenant of mine, and James acted as
agent.   The fellow was a rascal from the beginning ; but
in some extraordinary way James became intimate with
him. He had always a taste for low company. When
James determined to kidnap Lord Saltire it was of this
man's service that he availed himself. You remember
that I wrote to Arthur upon that last day. Well, James
opened the letter and inserted a note asking Arthur to
meet him in a little wood called the Ragged Shaw which
is near to the school. He used the duchess' name, and
in that way got the boy to come. That evening James
cycled over—I am telling you what he has himself confessed to me—and he told Arthur, whom he met in the
wood, that his mother longed to see him, that she was
awaiting him on the moor, and that if he would come
back into the wood at midnight he would find a man with
a horse, who would take him to her. Poor Arthur fell
into the trap. He came to the appointment, and found
this fellow Hayes with a led pony. Arthur mounted,
and they set off together. It appears—though this
James only heard yesterday—that they were pursued, that
Hayes struck the pursuer with his stick, and that the man
died of his injuries. Hayes brought Arthur to his public-
house, the ' Fighting Cock,' where he was confined in an
upper room, under the care of Mrs. Hayes, who is a
kindly woman, but entirely under the control of her
brutal husband.

" Well, Mr. Holmes, that was the state of affairs when I
first saw you two days ago. I had no more idea of the
truth than you. You will ask me what was James'
motive in doing such a deed. I answer that there was a
great deal which was unreasoning and fanatical in the hatred
which he bore my heir. In his view he should himself
have been heir of all my estates, and he deeply resented
those social laws which made it impossible. At the same
time, he had a definite motive also. He was eager that I
should break the entail, and he was of opinion that it lay
in my power to do so. He intended to make a bargain
with me—to restore Arthur if I would break the entail,

and so make it possible for the estate to be left to him by will. He knew well that I should never willingly invoke the aid of the police against him. I say that he would have proposed such a bargain to me, but he did not actually do so, for events moved too quickly for him, and he had not time to put his plans into practice.

" What brought all his wicked scheme to wreck was your discovery of this man Heidegger's dead body. James was seized with horror at the news. It came to us yesterday as we sat together in this study. Dr. Huxtable had sent a telegram. James was so overwhelmed with grief and agitation that my suspicions, which had never been entirely absent, rose instantly to a certainty, and I taxed him with the deed. He made a complete voluntary confession. Then he implored me to keep his secret for three days longer, so as to give his wretched accomplice a chance of saving his guilty life. I yielded—as I have always yielded—to his prayers, and instantly James hurried off to the ' Fighting Cock ' to warn Hayes and give him the means of flight. I could not go there by daylight without provoking comment, but as soon as night fell I hurried off to see my dear Arthur. I found him safe and well, but horrified beyond expression by the dreadful deed he had witnessed. In deference to my promise, and much against my will, I consented to leave him there for three days under the charge of Mrs. Hayes, since it was evident that it was impossible to inform the police where he was without telling them also who was the murderer, and I could not see how that murderer could be punished without ruin to my unfortunate James. You asked for frankness, Mr. Holmes, and I have taken you at your word, for I have now told you everything without an attempt at circumlocution or concealment. Do you in your turn be as frank with me."

" I will," said Holmes. " In the first place, your Grace, I am bound to tell you that you have placed yourself in a most serious position in the eyes of the law. You have condoned a felony, and you have aided the escape of a murderer ; for I cannot doubt that any money which was taken by James Wilder to aid his accomplice in his flight came from your Grace's purse."

The duke bowed his assent.

" This is indeed a most serious matter. Even more culpable, in my opinion, your Grace, is your attitude towards your younger son. You leave him in this den for three days."

" Under solemn promises——"

" What are promises to such people as these ? You have no guarantee that he will not be spirited away again. To humour your guilty elder son you have exposed your innocent younger son to imminent and unnecessary danger. It was a most unjustifiable action."

The proud lord of Holdernesse was not accustomed to be so rated in his own ducal hall. The blood flushed into his high forehead, but his conscience held him dumb.

" I will help you, but on one condition only. It is that you ring for the footman and let me give such orders as I like."

Without a word the duke pressed the electric button. A servant entered.

" You will be glad to hear," said Holmes, " that your young master is found. It is the duke's desire that the carriage shall go at once to the Fighting Cock Inn to bring Lord Saltire home."

" Now," said Holmes, when the rejoicing lackey had disappeared, " having secured the future we can afford to be more lenient with the past. I am not in an official position, and there is no reason, so long as the ends of justice are served, why I should disclose all that I know. As to Hayes I say nothing. The gallows awaits him, and I would do nothing to save him from it. What he will divulge I cannot tell, but I have no doubt that your Grace could make him understand that it is to his interest to be silent. From the police point of view he will **19** have kidnapped the boy for the purpose of ransom. If they do not themselves find it out I see no reason why I should prompt them to take a broader view. I would warn your Grace, however, that the continued presence of Mr. James Wilder in your household can only lead to misfortune."

" I understand that, Mr. Holmes, and it is already settled that he shall leave me for ever and go to seek his fortune in Australia."

" In that case, your Grace, since you have yourself stated that any unhappiness in your married life was caused by his presence, I would suggest that you make such amends as you can to the duchess, and that you try to resume those relations which have been so unhappily interrupted."

" That also I have arranged, Mr. Holmes. I wrote to the duchess this morning."

" In that case," said Holmes, rising, " I think that my friend and I can congratulate ourselves upon several most happy results from our little visit to the North. There is one other small point upon which I desire some light. This fellow Hayes had shod his horses with shoes which counterfeited the tracks of cows. Was it from Mr. Wilder that he learned so extraordinary a device ? "

The duke stood in thought for a moment, with a look of intense surprise on his face. Then he opened a door and showed us into a large room furnished as a museum. He led the way to a glass case in a corner, and pointed to the inscription.

" These shoes," it ran, " were dug up in the moat of Holdernesse Hall. They are for the use of horses ; but they are shaped below with a cloven foot of iron, so as to **20** throw pursuers off the track. They are supposed to have belonged to some of the marauding Barons of Holdernesse in the Middle Ages."

Holmes opened the case, and, moistening his finger, he passed it along the shoe. A thin film of recent mud was left upon his skin.

" Thank you," said he, as he replaced the glass. " It is the second most interesting object that I have seen in the North."

" And the first ? "

Holmes folded up his cheque, and placed it carefully **21** in his notebook. " I am a poor man," said he, as he patted it affectionately, and thrust it into the depths of his inner pocket.

19 *it is to his interest to be silent.* "Whether Reuben Hayes was able to see that it would serve his interest to keep his tongue quiet appears a little questionable," Mr. T. S. Blakeney wrote in *Sherlock Holmes: Fact or Fiction?* "One would have thought that, with the scaffold in prospect, he might consider it worth while to do all the harm he could to others, for though it would not help him, it would at least hurt them, and particularly the Duke, for whom he had a strong dislike. It is true he would have to make his damaging statements at the trial, or they were not likely to be made public at all, and to do this would involve admitting his guilt. We presume that the Crown so presented their case as to leave out all possible mention of the Duke, though one hardly sees how they could avoid bringing in Mr. Wilder's complicity in the abduction of Lord Saltire. If not, Mr. Wilder probably found himself unable to leave for Australia."

20 *a cloven foot of iron.* "The Adventure of the Priory School" first appeared in the *Strand Magazine* in February, 1904. Nine months before—in its May, 1903, number—the *Strand* had carried a brief paragraph in a letter from a correspondent, reproducing a photograph of two ancient horseshoes recently found in the moat at Birtsmorton Court, near Tewkesbury. One was so contrived as to make the imprint of a child's foot; the other counterfeited the mark of a cloven hoof. It seems reasonable to suppose that the *Strand* paragraph provided in part at least Conan Doyle's inspiration for the plot of "The Priory School."

21 *Holmes folded up his cheque.* This is one of the few Canonical occasions on which Holmes accepted payment for his services. He perhaps had good reason to: as the late Gavin Brend pointed out in *My Dear Holmes*, the British Government, in 1901, raised the rate of income tax from one shilling to one and two-pence on the pound. "When we recall that 'The Priory School,' being in the month of May, would come just after the Budget, we realize the significance of Holmes' comment, 'I am a poor man.' "

Auctorial and Bibliographical Note: Conan Doyle ranked "The Adventure of the Priory School" No. 10 on his list of the "twelve best" Sherlock Holmes short stories. The original manuscript, about 13,500 words in 71 4to pages with corrections and cancellations in the author's hand, vellum, was auctioned in New York City on January 26, 1922, bringing $155. It was auctioned again in London on January 28, 1925, when it was sold in one lot with "The Adventure of the Dancing Men" and "The Adventure of the Solitary Cyclist" for £66. In October, 1946, it was owned by Mr. Leigh Block of Chicago.

67

THE ADVENTURE OF SHOSCOMBE OLD PLACE

[*Tuesday, May 6, to Wednesday, May 7, 1902*]

1 *Those brown blobs in the centre are undoubtedly glue.*" "Glue it may well have been, but neither Holmes nor anyone else ever made the identification in such a manner," Professor Remsen Ten Eyck Schenck wrote in "Baker Street Fables." "Glue, which is an amorphous, impure form of gelatin, can exist in particles of any size and shape and could be positively identified only by chemical means. Microscopically it would be quite indistinguishable from rosin, shellac or any one of dozens of physically similar substances."

2 *St. Pancras.* This metropolitan borough, which extends from Islington to Marylebone east to west, and from Holborn to Hampstead and Hornsey south to north, derives its name from a youthful nobleman of Phrygia who suffered martyrdom at Rome by order of Diocletian. Until about two hundred years ago St. Pancras was a spa containing mineral springs which attracted many visitors. Not only were digestive troubles alleged to be removed by a cure at St. Pancras, but even leprosy, scurvy, and cancer. The site of St. Pancras Wells is now occupied by British Railways, Midland Region.

3 *by the zinc and copper filings in the seam of his cuff.* Zinc and copper filings "could be unequivocally identified even in minute amounts by a chemical analysis, [but] visual examination would reveal no more than that they were probably (but not certainly) metallic," Professor Schenck wrote. "No slightest clue as to the metal of which they were composed could be hoped for."

To this, Mr. Leon S. Holstein has replied ("'7. Knowledge of Chemistry—Profound'"): "I personally have seen and recognized as such, zinc and copper filings under a microscope—and if an amateur can do so today, surely the outstanding professional of all time should have had no trouble in doing so . . ."

SHERLOCK HOLMES had been bending for a long time over a low-power microscope. Now he straightened himself up and looked round at me in triumph.

" It is glue, Watson," said he. " Unquestionably it is glue. Have a look at these scattered objects in the field ! "

I stooped to the eyepiece and focused for my vision.

" Those hairs are threads from a tweed coat. The irregular grey masses are dust. There are epithelial scales on the left. Those brown blobs in the centre are **1** undoubtedly glue."

" Well," I said, laughing, " I am prepared to take your word for it. Does anything depend upon it ? "

" It is a very fine demonstration," he answered. " In **2** the St. Pancras case you may remember that a cap was found beside the dead policeman. The accused man denies that it is his. But he is a picture-frame maker who habitually handles glue."

" Is it one of your cases ? "

" No ; my friend, Merivale of the Yard, asked me to look into the case. Since I ran down that coiner **3** by the zinc and copper filings in the seam of his cuff they have begun to realize the importance of the microscope." He looked impatiently at his watch. " I had a new client calling, but he is overdue. By the way, Watson, you know something of racing ? "

" I ought to. I pay for it with about half my wound pension."

4 " Then I'll make you my ' Handy Guide to the Turf.' What about Sir Robert Norberton ? Does the name recall anything ? "

" Well, I should say so. He lives at Shoscombe Old Place, and I know it well, for my summer quarters were down there once. Norberton nearly came within your province once."

" How was that ? "

" It was when he horsewhipped Sam Brewer, the well-**5** known Curzon Street moneylender, on Newmarket Heath. He nearly killed the man."

" Ah, he sounds interesting ! Does he often indulge in that way ? "

SHERLOCK HOLMES HAD BEEN BENDING FOR A LONG TIME OVER A LOW-POWER MICROSCOPE.

Illustration by Frederic Dorr Steele for *Liberty Magazine*, March 5, 1927.

"IT IS GLUE, WATSON," SAID HE.

Illustration by Frank Wiles for the *Strand Magazine*, April, 1927.

"Well, he has the name of being a dangerous man. He is about the most daredevil rider in England—second in the Grand National a few years back. He is one of those men who have overshot their true generation. He should have been a buck in the days of the Regency —a boxer, an athlete, a plunger on the Turf, a lover of fair ladies, and, by all account, so far down Queer Street that he may never find his way back again."

"Capital, Watson! A thumb-nail sketch. I seem to know the man. Now, can you give me some idea of Shoscombe Old Place?"

"Only that it is in the centre of Shoscombe Park, and that the famous Shoscombe stud and training quarters are to be found there."

"And the head trainer," said Holmes, "is John Mason. You need not look surprised at my knowledge, Watson, for this is a letter from him which I am unfolding. But let us have some more about Shoscombe. I seem to have struck a rich vein."

"There are the Shoscombe spaniels," said I. "You hear of them at every dog show. The most exclusive breed in England. They are the special pride of the **6** lady of Shoscombe Old Place."

"Sir Robert Norberton's wife, I presume!"

"Sir Robert has never married. Just as well, I think, considering his prospects. He lives with his widowed sister, Lady Beatrice Falder."

"You mean that she lives with him?"

"No, no. The place belonged to her late husband, Sir James. Norberton has no claim on it at all. It is only a life interest and reverts to her husband's brother. Meantime, she draws the rents every year."

"And brother Robert, I suppose, spends the said rents?"

"That is about the size of it. He is a devil of a fellow and must lead her a most uneasy life. Yet I have heard that she is devoted to him. But what is amiss at Shoscombe?"

"Ah, that is just what I want to know. And here, I expect, is the man who can tell us."

The door had opened and the page had shown in a tall, clean-shaven man with the firm, austere expression which is only seen upon those who have to control horses or boys. Mr. John Mason had many of both under his sway, and he looked equal to the task. He bowed with cold self-possession and seated himself upon the chair to which Holmes had waved him.

4 my 'Handy Guide to the Turf.'" Holmes, once so knowledgeable about racing matters ("Silver Blaze") now seems to have lost all interest in the Sport of Kings. This is perhaps balanced by Watson: although the doctor showed an almost complete ignorance of racing in 1890, at the time of the Wessex Cup (or Plate), he now reveals himself as a slave to the turf. On the other hand, Mr. R. M. McLaren has expressed considerable doubt that Watson in fact paid for racing with about half of his wound pension. In "Doctor Watson— Punter or Speculator?", he wrote: "[Watson] spent half his wound pension on gambling—not on the Turf but on the Stock Exchange. In sharp contrast to his fumbling approach to the Turf is his interest, and to some extent his informed interest, about the Stock Exchange. On this subject he wrote with a much surer and more certain hand. He was clearly familiar with the circumstances under which Coxon and Woodhouse failed through the Venezuelan loan ["The Stockbroker's Clerk"]. In reporting 'A Case of Identity' the exact investment of Miss Mary Sutherland's inheritance from her Uncle Ned had no bearing on Holmes' investigation, but Watson duly recorded that it was in New Zealand 4½ per cent. He remembered exactly the prices of three of the securities quoted by Hall Pycroft in reply to the questions of Mr. Arthur Pinner. It appears probable, though he does not claim it, that it was he who suggested to Holmes that Cornelius to whom Jonas Oldacre was making large payments was a broker ["The Adventure of the Norwood Builder"]. He was immensely impressed by Sir Charles Baskerville having made ¾ million pounds in South African speculation."

5 *Curzon Street*. Named for George Augustus Curzon, third Viscount Howe, Curzon Street, Augustus J. C. Hare tells us in *Walks in London*, Vol. II, was "associated in the recollection of so many living persons with the charming parties of the sisters Mary and Agnes Berry, who died in 1852 equally honoured and beloved. They lived at No. 8, where Murrell, their servant, used to set up a lamp over their door, as a sign when they had 'too many women' at their parties: a few habitues of the male sex, however, knew that they could still come in, whether the lamp was lighted or not. 'The day may be distant,' says Lord Houghton, 'before social tradition forgets the house in Curzon Street where dwelt the Berrys.' . . . Chantrey lived in an attic of No. 24, Curzon Street, and modelled several of his busts there."

6 *The most exclusive breed in England*. "Of course [Watson] means *strain*," Mrs. Eleanor S. Cole wrote in "Holmes, Watson and the K-9's," "for the breed is spaniel, although he neglects to tell us which kind. We may safely assume they were English cocker spaniels, although they could have been Brittany, Clumber, English springer, field, Irish water, Sussex, or Welsh springer spaniels."

7 *"The best in England, Mr. Holmes*. The late Gavin Brend wrote:

"I'm Shoscombe Prince and I'd have you know
That I won the Derby long ago.
So I can't understand this ridiculous craze
For that fatuous animal, Silver Blaze.
Isonomy's son is so stuck up
Yet all he has won is the Wessex Cup.
(The Wessex Cup, or, as some relate,
A piffling affair called the Wessex Plate.)
But *I* came first in a classic race
And saved Sir Robert from dire disgrace.
I repeat that I can't understand this craze
For that ludicrous quadruped, Silver Blaze."

"You had my note, Mr. Holmes?"

"Yes, but it explained nothing."

"It was too delicate a thing for me to put the details on paper. And too complicated. It was only face to face I could do it."

"Well, we are at your disposal."

"First of all, Mr. Holmes, I think that my employer, Sir Robert, has gone mad."

Holmes raised his eyebrows. "This is Baker Street, not Harley Street," said he. "But why do you say so?"

"Well, sir, when a man does one queer thing, or two queer things, there may be a meaning to it, but when everything he does is queer, then you begin to wonder. I believe Shoscombe Prince and the Derby have turned his brain."

"That is a colt you are running?"

7   "The best in England, Mr. Holmes. I should know, if anyone does. Now, I'll be plain with you, for I know you are gentlemen of honour and that it won't go beyond the room. Sir Robert has got to win this Derby. He's up to the neck, and it's his last chance. Everything he could raise or borrow is on the horse—and at fine odds, too! You can get forties now, but it was nearer the hundred when he began to back him."

"But how is that, if the horse is so good?"

"The public don't know how good he is. Sir Robert has been too clever for the touts. He has the Prince's half-brother out for spins. You can't tell 'em apart. But there are two lengths in a furlong between them when it comes to a gallop. He thinks of nothing but the horse and the race. His whole life is on it. He's holding off the Jews till then. If the Prince fails him, he is done."

"It seems a rather desperate gamble, but where does the madness come in?"

"Well, first of all, you have only to look at him. I don't believe he sleeps at night. He is down at the stables at all hours. His eyes are wild. It has all been too much for his nerves. Then there is his conduct to Lady Beatrice!"

"Ah! what is that?"

"They have always been the best of friends. They had the same tastes, the two of them, and she loved the horses as much as he did. Every day at the same hour she would drive down to see them—and, above all, she loved the Prince. He would prick up his ears when he heard the wheels on the gravel, and he would trot out each morning to the carriage to get his lump of sugar. But that's all over now."

"Why?"

"Well, she seems to have lost all interest in the horses. For a week now she has driven past the stables with never so much as 'good morning'!"

"You think there has been a quarrel?"

"And a bitter, savage, spiteful quarrel at that. Why else would he give away her pet spaniel that she loved as if he were her child? He gave it a few days ago to old Barnes, what keeps the 'Green Dragon,' three miles off, at Crendall."

" That certainly did seem strange."

" Of course, with her weak heart and dropsy one couldn't expect that she could get about with him, but he spent two hours every evening in her room. He might well do what he could, for she has been a rare good friend to him. But that's all over, too. He never goes near her. And she takes it to heart. She is brooding and sulky and drinking, Mr. Holmes—drinking like a fish."

" Did she drink before this estrangement ? "

" Well, she took her glass, but now it is often a whole bottle of an evening. So Stephens, the butler, told me. It's all changed, Mr. Holmes, and there is something damned rotten about it. But then, again, what is master doing down at the old church crypt at night ? And who is the man that meets him there ? "

Holmes rubbed his hands.

" Go on, Mr. Mason. You get more and more interesting."

" It was the butler who saw him go. Twelve o'clock at night and raining hard. So next night I was up at the house and, sure enough, master was off again. Stephens and I went after him, but it was jumpy work, for it would have been a bad job if he had seen us. He's a terrible man with his fists if he gets started, and no respecter of persons. So we were shy of getting too near, but we marked him down all right. It was the haunted crypt that he was making for, and there was a man waiting for him there."

" What is this haunted crypt ? "

" Well, sir, there is an old ruined chapel in the park. It is so old that nobody could fix its date. And under it there's a crypt which has a bad name among us. It's a dark, damp, lonely place by day, but there are few in that county that would have the nerve to go near it at night. But master's not afraid. He never feared anything in his life. But what is he doing there in the night-time ? "

" Wait a bit ! " said Holmes. " You say there is another man there. It must be one of your own stablemen, or someone from the house ! Surely you have only to spot who it is and question him ? "

" It's no one I know."

" How can you say that ? "

" Because I have seen him, Mr. Holmes. It was on that second night. Sir Robert turned and passed us— me and Stephens, quaking in the bushes like two bunny-rabbits, for there was a bit of moon that night. But we could hear the other moving about behind. We were not afraid of him. So we up when Sir Robert was gone and pretended we were just having a walk like in the moon-light, and so we came right on him as casual and innocent as you please. ' Hullo, mate ! who may you be ? ' says I. I guess he had not heard us coming, so he looked over his shoulder with a face as if he had seen the Devil coming out of Hell. He let out a yell, and away he went as hard as he could lick it in the darkness. He could run !—I'll give him that. In a minute he was out of sight and hearing, and who he was, or what he was, we never found."

" But you saw him clearly in the moonlight ? "

" Yes, I would swear to his yellow face—a mean dog,

"I GUESS HE HAD NOT HEARD US COMING . . ."

Illustration by Frank Wiles for the *Strand Magazine*, April, 1927.

I should say. What could he have in common with Sir Robert ? ”

Holmes sat for some time lost in thought.

“ Who keeps Lady Beatrice Falder company ? ” he asked at last.

“ There is her maid, Carrie Evans. She has been with her this five years.”

“ And is, no doubt, devoted ? ”

Mr. Mason shuffled uncomfortably.

“ She's devoted enough,” he answered at last. “ But I won't say to whom.”

“ Ah ! ” said Holmes.

“ I can't tell tales out of school.”

“ I quite understand, Mr. Mason. Of course, the situation is clear enough.   From Dr. Watson's description of Sir Robert I can realize that no woman is safe from him. Don't you think the quarrel between brother and sister may lie there ? ”

“ Well, the scandal has been pretty clear for a long time.”

“ But she may not have seen it before. Let us suppose that she has suddenly found it out. She wants to get rid of the woman. Her brother will not permit it. The invalid, with her weak heart and inability to get about, has no means of enforcing her will. The hated maid is still tied to her. The lady refuses to speak, sulks, takes to drink. Sir Robert in his anger takes her pet spaniel away from her. Does not all this hang together ? ”

“ Well, it might do—so far as it goes.”

“ Exactly ! As far as it goes. How would all that bear upon the visits by night to the old crypt ? We can't fit that into our plot.”

“ No, sir, and there is something more that I can't fit in. Why should Sir Robert want to dig up a dead body ? ”

Holmes sat up abruptly.

“ We only found it out yesterday—after I had written to you. Yesterday Sir Robert had gone to London, so Stephens and I went down to the crypt. It was all in order, sir, except that in one corner was a bit of a human body.”

“ You informed the police, I suppose ? ”

Our visitor smiled grimly.

“ Well, sir, I think it would hardly interest them. It was just the head and a few bones of a mummy. It may have been a thousand years old. But it wasn't there before. That I'll swear, and so will Stephens. It had been stowed away in a corner and covered over with a board, but that corner had always been empty before.”

“ What did you do with it ? ”

“ Well, we just left it there.”

“ That was wise. You say Sir Robert was away yesterday. Has he returned ? ”

“ We expect him back to-day.”

“ When did Sir Robert give away his sister's dog ? ”

“ It was just a week ago to-day. The creature was howling outside the old well-house, and Sir Robert was in one of his tantrums that morning. He caught it up and I thought he would have killed it. Then he gave it to Sandy Bain, the jockey, and told him to take the dog to old Barnes at the ' Green Dragon,' for he never wished to see it again."

Holmes sat for some time in silent thought. He had lit the oldest and foulest of his pipes.   **8**

" I am not clear yet what you want me to do in this matter, Mr. Mason," he said at last. " Can't you make it more definite ? "

" Perhaps this will make it more definite, Mr. Holmes," said our visitor.

He took a paper from his pocket and, unwrapping it carefully, he exposed a charred fragment of bone.

Holmes examined it with interest.

" Where did you get it ? "

" There is a central heating furnace in the cellar under Lady Beatrice's room. It's been off for some time, but Sir Robert complained of cold and had it on again. Harvey runs it—he's one of my lads. This very morning he came to me with this which he found raking out the cinders. He didn't like the look of it."

" Nor do I," said Holmes. " What do you make of it, Watson ? "

It was burned to a black cinder, but there could be no question as to its anatomical significance.

" It's the upper condyle of a human femur," said I. **9**

" Exactly ! " Holmes had become very serious. " When does this lad attend to the furnace ? "

" He makes it up every evening and then leaves it."

" Then anyone could visit it during the night ? "

" Yes, sir."

" Can you enter it from outside ? "

" There is one door from outside. There is another which leads up by a stair to the passage in which Lady Beatrice's room is situated."

" These are deep waters, Mr. Mason ; deep and rather dirty. You say that Sir Robert was not at home last night ?"

" No, sir."

" Then, whoever was burning bones, it was not he."

" That's true, sir."

" What is the name of that inn you spoke of ? "

" The ' Green Dragon.' "

" Is there good fishing in that part of Berkshire ? "

The honest trainer showed very clearly upon his face that he was convinced that yet another lunatic had come into his harassed life.

" Well, sir, I've heard there are trout in the mill-stream and pike in the Hall lake."

" That's good enough. Watson and I are famous fishermen—are we not, Watson ? You may address us in future at the ' Green Dragon.' We should reach it to-night. I need not say that we don't want to see you, Mr. Mason, but a note will reach us, and no doubt I could find you if I want you. When we have gone a little further into the matter I will let you have a considered opinion."

Thus it was that on a bright May evening Holmes and I found ourselves alone in a first-class carriage and bound for the little " halt-on-demand " station of Shoscombe. The rack above us was covered with a for-

8 *the oldest and foulest of his pipes.* "One can hardly doubt that when . . . Holmes lit 'the oldest and foulest of his pipes,' he was lighting the 'old briar pipe' of 'The Man with the Twisted Lip'— a pipe mellowed by years of devoted attention," Mr. John L. Hicks wrote in "No Fire Without Some Smoke."

9 *the upper condyle of a human femur.*" Watson's "anatomy was rusty . . . in point of fact there is no such part," Dr. Samuel R. Meaker wrote in "Watson Medicus."

midable litter of rods, reels and baskets. On reaching our destination a short drive took us to an old-fashioned tavern, where a sporting host, Josiah Barnes, entered eagerly into our plans for the extirpation of the fish of the neighbourhood.

"What about the Hall lake and the chance of a pike?" said Holmes.

The face of the innkeeper clouded.

"That wouldn't do, sir. You might chance to find yourself in the lake before you were through."

"How's that, then?"

"It's Sir Robert, sir. He's terrible jealous of touts. If you two strangers were as near his training quarters as that he'd be after you as sure as fate. He ain't taking no chances, Sir Robert ain't."

"I've heard he has a horse entered for the Derby."

"Yes, and a good colt, too. He carries all our money for the race, and all Sir Robert's into the bargain. By the way"—he looked at us with thoughtful eyes—"I suppose you ain't on the Turf yourselves?"

"No, indeed. Just two weary Londoners who badly need some good Berkshire air."

"Well, you are in the right place for that. There is a deal of it lying about. But mind what I have told you about Sir Robert. He's the sort that strikes first and speaks afterwards. Keep clear of the park."

"Surely, Mr. Barnes! We certainly shall. By the way, that was a most beautiful spaniel that was whining in the hall."

"I should say it was. That was the real Shoscombe breed. There ain't a better in England."

"I am a dog-fancier myself," said Holmes. "Now, if it is a fair question, what would a prize dog like that cost?"

"More than I could pay, sir. It was Sir Robert himself who gave me this one. That's why I have to keep it on a lead. It would be off to the Hall in a jiffy if I gave it its head."

"We are getting some cards in our hand, Watson," said Holmes, when the landlord had left us. "It's not an easy one to play, but we may see our way in a day or two. By the way, Sir Robert is still in London, I hear. We might, perhaps, enter the sacred domain to-night without fear of bodily assault. There are one or two points on which I should like reassurance."

"Have you any theory, Holmes?"

"Only this, Watson, that something happened a week or so ago which has cut deep into the life of the Shoscombe household. What is that something? We can only guess at it from its effects. They seem to be of a curiously mixed character. But that should surely help us. It is only the colourless, uneventful case which is hopeless."

"Let us consider our data. The brother no longer visits the beloved invalid sister. He gives away her favourite dog. Her dog, Watson! Does that suggest nothing to you?"

"Nothing but the brother's spite."

"Well, it might be so. Or—well, there is an alternative. Now to continue our review of the situation from the time that the quarrel, if there is a quarrel, began. The lady keeps her room, alters her habits, is not seen save when she drives out with her maid, refuses to stop at the stables to greet her favourite horse, and apparently takes to drink. That covers the case, does it not ? "

" Save for the business in the crypt."

" That is another line of thought. There are two, and I beg you will not tangle them. Line A, which concerns Lady Beatrice, has a vaguely sinister flavour, has it not ? "

" I can make nothing of it."

" Well, now, let us take up line B, which concerns Sir Robert. He is mad keen upon winning the Derby. He is in the hands of the Jews, and may at any moment be sold up and his racing stables seized by his creditors. He is a daring and desperate man. He derives his income from his sister. His sister's maid is his willing tool. So far we seem to be on fairly safe ground, do we not ? "

" But the crypt ? "

" Ah, yes, the crypt ! Let us suppose, Watson—it is merely a scandalous supposition, a hypothesis put forward for argument's sake—that Sir Robert has done away with his sister."

" My dear Holmes, it is out of the question."

" Very possibly, Watson. Sir Robert is a man of an honourable stock. But you do occasionally find a carrion crow among the eagles. Let us for a moment argue upon this supposition. He could not fly the country until he had realized his fortune, and that fortune could only be realized by bringing off this coup with Shoscombe Prince. Therefore, he has still to stand his ground. To do this he would have to dispose of the body of his victim, and he would also have to find a substitute who would impersonate her. With the maid as his confidante that would not be impossible. The woman's body might be conveyed to the crypt, which is a place so seldom visited, and it might be secretly destroyed at night in the furnace, leaving behind it such evidence as we have already seen. What say you to that, Watson ? "

" Well, it is all possible if you grant the original monstrous supposition."

" I think that there is a small experiment which we may try to-morrow, Watson, in order to throw some light on the matter. Meanwhile, if we mean to keep up our characters, I suggest that we have our host in for a glass of his own wine and hold some high converse upon eels and dace, which seems to be the straight road to his affections. We may chance to come upon some useful local gossip in the process."

In the morning Holmes discovered that we had come without our spoon-bait for jack, which absolved us from fishing for the day. About eleven o'clock we started for a walk, and he obtained leave to take the black spaniel with us.

" This is the place," said he, as we came to two high park gates with heraldic griffins towering above them. " About midday, Mr. Barnes informs me, the old lady

. . . WITH HERALDIC GRIFFINS TOWERING ABOVE THEM.

"At the outset it must be acknowledged that it has not been possible to find any Berkshire family that fulfills all the requirements of the Canon," Dr. Julian Wolff wrote in his *Practical Handbook of Sherlockian Heraldry*. "But some interesting information presents itself when the base of operations is slightly shifted to the adjacent county of Hampshire. Burke's *Visitation of Seats and Arms* has an extensive description of Highclere in Hampshire, the estate of the old and honoured Herbert family. . . . 'The Herbert griffin' [Burke wrote] 'holding in its mouth the bloody hand appears beautifully carved in stone in every variety of attitude.' . . . After all this talk of griffins, by both Watson and Burke, it comes as a shock to learn that the creature of the family crest is not a griffin at all, but is actually a wyvern—but vert, and so accounting for the Green Dragon Inn at Crendall (or is it really Kendall?) three miles off. But this mistake is not a fatal one, and certainly Watson may be excused when the Great Burke himself made the same error. The arms are: Per pale, azure and gules three lions rampant argent. Crest—a wyvern, wings elevated, vert, holding in the mouth a sinister hand couped at the wrist, gules.' . . . The Norberton arms have not been found and it is not discreet to enquire too deeply in view of Sir Robert's escapades. The matter must rest here and readers will have to be content with the arms of the Falders alone—the dexter half of the lady's lozenge [reproduced above]."

10 *barouche.* A four-wheeled carriage with a seat in front for the driver, two double seats inside, one facing back and the other front and facing each other, with a folding top over the back seat which may be raised to cover the occupants, but not the driver.

11 *Dogs don't make mistakes.*" No dog, particularly a spaniel, would be fooled into thinking that it *saw* his or her mistress. Or so Mr. Stuart Palmer claimed in "Notes on Certain Evidences of Caniphobia in Mr. Sherlock Holmes and His Associates": "Anyone who has had even a passing acquaintance with dogs knows that their eyesight is extremely poor (except for the greyhound) and that most dogs rely almost entirely on their senses of smell and hearing. No dog, for instance, ever paid any attention to his image in a mirror. The image has no smell or sound; therefore it isn't there. We must reluctantly conclude that the spaniel fell into a rage about something else, or was troubled by worms."

AT THE SAME MOMENT HOLMES STEPPED OUT AND
RELEASED THE SPANIEL.

Illustration by Frank Wiles for the *Strand Magazine*, April, 1927.

takes a drive, and the carriage must slow down while the gates are opened. When it comes through, and before it gathers speed, I want you, Watson, to stop the coachman with some question. Never mind me. I shall stand behind this holly-bush and see what I can see."

It was not a long vigil. Within a quarter of an hour **10** we saw the big open yellow barouche coming down the long avenue, with two splendid, high-stepping grey carriage horses in the shafts. Holmes crouched behind his bush with the dog. I stood unconcernedly swinging a cane in the roadway. A keeper ran out and the gates swung open.

The carriage had slowed to a walk and I was able to get a good look at the occupants. A highly-coloured young woman with flaxen hair and impudent eyes sat on the left. At her right was an elderly person with rounded back and a huddle of shawls about her face and shoulders which proclaimed the invalid. When the horses reached the high road I held up my hand with an authoritative gesture, and as the coachman pulled up I inquired if Sir Robert was at Shoscombe Old Place.

At the same moment Holmes stepped out and released the spaniel. With a joyous cry it dashed forward to the carriage and sprang upon the step. Then in a moment its eager greeting changed to furious rage, and it snapped at the black skirt above it.

" Drive on ! Drive on ! " shrieked a harsh voice. The coachman lashed the horses, and we were left standing in the roadway.

" Well, Watson, that's done it," said Holmes, as he fastened the lead to the neck of the excited spaniel. " He thought it was his mistress and he found it was a **11** stranger. Dogs don't make mistakes."

" But it was the voice of a man ! " I cried.

" Exactly ! We have added one card to our hand, Watson, but it needs careful playing, all the same."

My companion seemed to have no further plans for the day, and we did actually use our fishing tackle in the mill-stream, with the result that we had a dish of trout for our supper. It was only after that meal that Holmes showed signs of renewed activity. Once more we found ourselves upon the same road as in the morning, which led us to the park gates. A tall, dark figure was awaiting us there, who proved to be our London acquaintance, Mr. John Mason, the trainer.

" Good evening, gentlemen," said he. " I got your note, Mr. Holmes. Sir Robert has not returned yet, but I hear that he is expected to-night."

" How far is this crypt from the house ? " asked Holmes.

" A good quarter of a mile."

" Then I think we can disregard him altogether."

" I can't afford to do that, Mr. Holmes. The moment he arrives he will want to see me to get the last news of Shoscombe Prince."

" I see ! In that case we must work without you, Mr. Mason. You can show us the crypt and then leave us."

It was pitch-dark and without a moon, but Mason led us over the grass-lands until a dark mass loomed up in front of us which proved to be the ancient chapel.

We entered the broken gap which was once the porch, and our guide, stumbling among heaps of loose masonry, picked his way to the corner of the building, where a steep stair led down into the crypt. Striking a match, he illuminated the melancholy place—dismal and evil-smelling, with ancient crumbling walls of rough-hewn stone, and piles of coffins, some of lead and some of stone, extending upon one side right up to the arched and groined roof which lost itself in the shadows above our heads. Holmes had lit his lantern, which shot a tiny tunnel of vivid yellow light upon the mournful scene. Its rays were reflected back from the coffin-plates, many of them adorned with the griffin and coronet of this old family which carried its honours even to the gate of Death.

"You spoke of some bones, Mr. Mason. Could you show them before you go?"

"They are here in this corner." The trainer strode across and then stood in silent surprise as our light was turned upon the place. "They are gone," said he.

"So I expected," said Holmes, chuckling. "I fancy the ashes of them might even now be found in that oven which had already consumed a part."

"But why in the world would anyone want to burn the bones of a man who has been dead a thousand years?" asked John Mason.

"That is what we are here to find out," said Holmes. "It may mean a long search, and we need not detain you. I fancy that we shall get our solution before morning."

When John Mason had left us, Holmes set to work making a very careful examination of the graves, ranging from a very ancient one, which appeared to be Saxon, in the centre, through a long line of Norman Hugos and Odos, until we reached the Sir William and Sir Denis Falder of the eighteenth century. It was an hour or more before Holmes came to a leaden coffin standing on end before the entrance to the vault. I heard his little cry of satisfaction, and was aware from his hurried but purposeful movements that he had reached a goal. With his lens he was eagerly examining the edges of the heavy lid. Then he drew from his pocket a short jemmy, a box-opener, which he thrust into a chink, levering back the whole front, which seemed to be secured by only a couple of clamps. There was a rending, tearing sound as it gave way, but it had hardly hinged back and partly revealed the contents before we had an unforeseen interruption.

Someone was walking in the chapel above. It was the firm, rapid step of one who came with a definite purpose and knew well the ground upon which he walked. A light streamed down the stairs, and an instant later the man who bore it was framed in the Gothic archway. He was a terrible figure, huge in stature and fierce in manner. A large stable-lantern which he held in front of him shone upwards upon a strong, heavily-moustached face and angry eyes, which glared round him into every recess of the vault, finally fixing themselves with a deadly stare upon my companion and myself.

HOLMES HAD LIT HIS LANTERN . . .

Illustration by Frank Wiles for the *Strand Magazine*, April, 1927.

"WHO THE DEVIL ARE YOU?" HE THUNDERED.
"AND WHAT ARE YOU DOING UPON
MY PROPERTY?"

Illustration by Frederic Dorr Steele for *Liberty Magazine*, March 5, 1927.

"I ALSO HAVE A QUESTION TO ASK YOU, SIR ROBERT,"
HE SAID IN HIS STERNEST TONE.

Illustration by Frank Wiles for the *Strand Magazine*, April, 1927.

" Who the devil are you ? " he thundered. " And what are you doing upon my property ? " Then, as Holmes returned no answer, he took a couple of steps forward and raised a heavy stick which he carried. " Do you hear me ? " he cried. " Who are you ? What are you doing here ? " His cudgel quivered in the air.

But instead of shrinking, Holmes advanced to meet him.

" I also have a question to ask you, Sir Robert," he said in his sternest tone. " Who is this ? And what is it doing here ? "

He turned and tore open the coffin-lid behind him. In the glare of the lantern I saw a body swathed in a sheet from head to foot, with dreadful, witch-like features, all nose and chin, projecting at one end, the dim, glazed eyes staring from a discoloured and crumbling face.

The Baronet had staggered back with a cry and supported himself against a stone sarcophagus.

" How came you to know of this ? " he cried. And then, with some return of his truculent manner : " What business is it of yours ? "

" My name is Sherlock Holmes," said my companion. " Possibly it is familiar to you. In any case, my business is that of every other good citizen—to uphold the law. It seems to me that you have much to answer for."

Sir Robert glared for a moment, but Holmes' quiet voice and cool, assured manner had their effect.

" 'Fore God, Mr. Holmes, it's all right," said he. " Appearances are against me, I'll admit, but I could act no otherwise."

" I should be happy to think so, but I fear your explanations must be for the police."

Sir Robert shrugged his broad shoulders.

" Well, if it must be, it must. Come up to the house and you can judge for yourself how the matter stands."

Quarter of an hour later we found ourselves in what I judge, from the lines of polished barrels behind glass covers, to be the gun-room of the old house. It was comfortably furnished, and here Sir Robert left us for a few moments. When he returned he had two companions with him ; the one, the florid young woman whom we had seen in the carriage ; the other, a small rat-faced man with a disagreeably furtive manner. These two wore an appearance of utter bewilderment, which showed that the Baronet had not yet had time to explain to them the turn events had taken.

" There," said Sir Robert, with a wave of his hand, " are Mr. and Mrs. Norlett. Mrs. Norlett, under her maiden name of Evans, has for some years been my sister's confidential maid. I have brought them here because I feel that my best course is to explain the true position to you, and they are the two people upon earth who can substantiate what I say."

" Is this necessary, Sir Robert ? Have you thought what you are doing ? " cried the woman.

" As to me, I entirely disclaim all responsibility," said her husband.

Sir Robert gave him a glance of contempt. " I will take all responsibility," said he. " Now, Mr. Holmes, listen to a plain statement of the facts.

" You have clearly gone pretty deeply into my affairs or I should not have found you where I did. Therefore, you know already, in all probability, that I am running a dark horse for the Derby and that everything depends upon my success. If I win, all is easy. If I lose—well, I dare not think of that ! "

" I understand the position," said Holmes.

" I am dependent upon my sister, Lady Beatrice, for everything. But it is well known that her interest in the estate is for her own life only. For myself, I am deeply in the hands of the Jews. I have always known that if my sister were to die my creditors would be on to my estate like a flock of vultures. Everything would be seized ; my stables, my horses—everything. Well, Mr. Holmes, my sister *did* die just a week ago."

" And you told no one ! "

" What could I do ? Absolute ruin faced me. If I could stave things off for three weeks all would be well. **12** Her maid's husband—this man here—is an actor. It came into our heads—it came into my head—that he could for that short period personate my sister. It was but a case of appearing daily in the carriage, for no one need enter her room save the maid. It was not difficult to arrange. My sister died of the dropsy which had long afflicted her."

" That will be for a coroner to decide."

" Her doctor would certify that for months her symptoms have threatened such an end."

" Well, what did you do ? "

" The body could not remain there. On the first night Norlett and I carried it out to the old well-house, which is now never used. We were followed, however, by her pet spaniel, which yapped continually at the door, so I felt some safer place was needed. I got rid of the spaniel and we carried the body to the crypt of the church. There was no indignity or irreverence, Mr. Holmes. I do not feel that I have wronged the dead."

" Your conduct seems to me inexcusable, Sir Robert."

The Baronet shook his head impatiently. " It is easy to preach," said he. " Perhaps you would have felt differently if you had been in my position. One cannot see all one's hopes and all one's plans shattered at the last moment and make no effort to save them. It seemed to me that it would be no unworthy resting-place if we put her for the time in one of the coffins of her husband's ancestors lying in what is still consecrated ground. We opened such a coffin, removed the contents, and placed her as you have seen her. As to the old relics which we took out, we could not leave them on the floor of the crypt. Norlett and I removed them, and he descended at night and burned them in the central furnace. There is my story, Mr. Holmes, though how you forced my hand so that I have to tell it is more than I can say."

Holmes sat for some time lost in thought.

" There is one flaw in your narrative, Sir Robert,"

12 *If I could stave things off for three weeks.* The month we know was May—but what was the year? It must have been after Holmes' Return: Watson, so ignorant of racing matters in 1890 is now Holmes' "Handy Guide to the Turf." On the other hand, the year cannot be long before Holmes' retirement: 1) Holmes on the opening day was using a microscope, and says that Scotland Yard is beginning to appreciate its importance. In none of the other chronicles is a microscope mentioned, as it almost certainly would have been if it had come into general use in detection shortly after Holmes' Return. 2) "The page had shown in a tall, clean-shaven man . . ." This page must have been none other than the later Billy, introduced to us as a member of the Baker Street staff in "Thor Bridge," which, as we have seen, took place in October, 1900. The year was not 1903, however: Watson was married again in the last quarter of 1902, and he is clearly living at Baker Street at the time of this adventure. Derby Day was three weeks away. If the year were 1900, then, when Derby Day fell on June 6th, the concluding night must have been May 29th. But this would make the opening day of the case as chronicled by Watson the *thirteenth* day, counting the day of Lady Beatrice's death as the first day, and this is impossible by *either* Mason's or Sir Robert's statements. If the year were 1901, when Derby Day fell on May 29th, the concluding night must have been May 18th, and the opening day of the case was the *tenth* day. This comes very close to the situation *according to Mason,* and it would mean that Sir Robert was speaking approximately rather than literally when he said that Derby Day was "three weeks" after his sister's death. If the year were 1902, when Derby Day fell on May 21st, the concluding night must have been May 7th, and the opening day of the case the *seventh* day. This is *precisely* the situation *according to Sir Robert,* and—as the late Dr. Ernest Bloomfield Zeisler wrote—"There was one thing about which [Sir Robert] would be quite certain not to be mistaken, and that was the date of the coming Derby." In addition, we know that Holmes and Watson, from Thursday, May 16, to Saturday, May 18, 1901, were engaged in "The Adventure of the Priory School." The adventure of Shoscombe Old Place therefore began on *Tuesday, May 6,* and ended on *Wednesday, May 7, 1902.*

13 *this singular episode.* Mr. D. Martin Dakin, writing on the "Canonicity" of "The Adventure of Shoscombe Old Place," inclined to accept it as genuine, "as there seems to be no particular reason for doubting it, in spite of its distressing revelations as to some of the sources of Watson's income."

14 *eighty thousand pounds.* About $400,000.

Bibliographical Note: The manuscript of "The Adventure of Shoscombe Old Place," the property of Mr. Adrian M. Conan Doyle, reveals that Conan Doyle originally intended to call the tale "The Adventure of Shoscombe *Abbey*." The change was perhaps made to avoid confusion with "The Adventure of the Abbey Grange." Something of the same thought seems to have occurred to the editors of the *Strand Magazine:* they announced the story as "The Adventure of the Black Spaniel."

he said at last. " Your bets on the race, and therefore your hopes for the future, would hold good even if your creditors seized your estate."

" The horse would be part of the estate. What do they care for my bets ? As likely as not they would not run him at all. My chief creditor is, unhappily, my most bitter enemy—a rascally fellow, Sam Brewer, whom I was once compelled to horsewhip on Newmarket Heath. Do you suppose that he would try to save me ? "

" Well, Sir Robert," said Holmes, rising, " this matter must, of course, be referred to the police. It was my duty to bring the facts to light and there I must leave it. As to the morality or decency of your own conduct, it is not for me to express an opinion. It is nearly midnight, Watson, and I think we may make our way back to our humble abode."

13   It is generally known now that this singular episode ended upon a happier note than Sir Robert's actions deserved. Shoscombe Prince did win the Derby, the **14** sporting owner did net eighty thousand pounds in bets, and the creditors did hold their hand until the race was over, when they were paid in full, and enough was left to re-establish Sir Robert in a fair position in life. Both police and coroner took a lenient view of the transaction, and beyond a mild censure for the delay in registering the lady's decease, the lucky owner got away scatheless from this strange incident in a career which has now outlived its shadows and promises to end in an honoured old age.

68

THE ADVENTURE OF THE THREE GARRIDEBS

[Thursday, June 26, to Friday, June 27, 1902]

IT may have been a comedy, or it may have been a tragedy. It cost one man his reason, it cost me a blood-letting, and it cost yet another man the penalties of the law. Yet there was certainly an element of comedy. Well, you shall judge for yourselves.

I remember the date very well, for it was in the same month that Holmes refused a knighthood for services **1** which may perhaps some day be described. I only refer to the matter in passing, for in my position of partner and confidant I am obliged to be particularly careful to avoid any indiscretion. I repeat, however, that this enables me to fix the date, which was the latter end of June, 1902, shortly after the conclusion of the South African War. Holmes had spent several days in bed, as was his habit from time to time, but he emerged that morning with a long foolscap document in his hand and a twinkle of amusement in his austere grey eyes.

"There is a chance for you to make some money, friend Watson," said he. "Have you ever heard the name of Garrideb?"

I admitted that I had not.

"Well, if you can lay your hand upon a Garrideb, there's money in it."

"Why?"

"Ah, that's a long story—rather a whimsical one, too. I don't think in all our explorations of human complexities we have ever come upon anything more singular. The fellow will be here presently for cross-examination, so I won't open the matter up till he comes. But meanwhile, that's the name we want."

The telephone directory lay on the table beside me, and I turned over the pages in a rather hopeless quest. But to my amazement there was this strange name in its due place. I gave a cry of triumph.

"Here you are, Holmes! Here it is!"

Holmes took the book from my hand.

"'Garrideb, N.,'" he read, "'136 Little Ryder Street, W.' Sorry to disappoint you, my dear Watson, but this is the man himself. That is the address upon his letter. We want another to match him."

1 *the same month that Holmes refused a knighthood.* Miss Marcella Holmes, in "Sherlock Holmes and the Prime Ministers," has noted that "Lord Salisbury's resignation [as Prime Minister of Britain] occurred in early July [1902], and as retiring Prime Ministers often recommend well-deserving friends and supporters for honours before relinquishing office, was this a belated acknowledgment of Holmes' invaluable work in 'The Second Stain'? . . . For what else would knighthood have been given but for Holmes' work in his most important international case?"

But why was it that Holmes declined a knighthood or even mention in the Honours List, though he accepted the Legion of Honour from France and a remarkably fine emerald tie-pin from a certain gracious lady? We must remember that Edward VII was on the throne at this time, Queen Victoria having died on January 22, 1901. If Edward VII was that Prince of Wales who once masqueraded as "the King of Bohemia," we have, perhaps, the reason why Holmes declined to accept a knighthood from him.

The late A. Carson Simpson pointed out that it was nevertheless *Sir* Sherlock, for even members of the lowest grade of the Legion of Honour were known as "Chevaliers," anglicized "Knights." Chevalier Holmes, therefore, in France, is Sir Sherlock Holmes in England.

Moorville, Kansas, U.S.A." "In Kansas there is no Moorville. There are no moors," Mr. Willis B. Wood wrote in "Sherlock in Kansas."

"WHY DID HE EVER DRAG YOU INTO IT AT ALL?"
ASKED OUR VISITOR . . .

Illustration by Howard K. Elcock for the *Strand Magazine*, January, 1925.

Mrs. Hudson had come in with a card upon a tray. I took it up and glanced at it.

"Why, here it is!" I cried in amazement. "This is a different initial. John Garrideb, Counsellor at Law, 2 Moorville, Kansas, U.S.A."

Holmes smiled as he looked at the card. "I am afraid you must make yet another effort, Watson," said he. "This gentleman is also in the plot already, though I certainly did not expect to see him this morning. However, he is in a position to tell us a good deal which I want to know."

A moment later he was in the room. Mr. John Garrideb, Counsellor at Law, was a short, powerful man with the round, fresh, clean-shaven face characteristic of so many American men of affairs. The general effect was chubby and rather childlike, so that one received the impression of quite a young man with a broad set smile upon his face. His eyes, however, were arresting. Seldom in any human head have I seen a pair which bespoke a more intense inward life, so bright were they, so alert, so responsive to every change of thought. His accent was American, but was not accompanied by any eccentricity of speech.

"Mr. Holmes?" he asked, glancing from one to the other. "Ah, yes! Your pictures are not unlike you, sir, if I may say so. I believe you have had a letter from my namesake, Mr. Nathan Garrideb, have you not?"

"Pray sit down," said Sherlock Holmes. "We shall, I fancy, have a good deal to discuss." He took up his sheets of foolscap. "You are, of course, the Mr. John Garrideb mentioned in this document. But surely you have been in England some time?"

"Why do you say that, Mr. Holmes?" I seemed to read sudden suspicion in those expressive eyes.

"Your whole outfit is English."

Mr. Garrideb forced a laugh. "I've read of your tricks, Mr. Holmes, but I never thought I would be the subject of them. Where do you read that?"

"The shoulder cut of your coat, the toes of your boots—could anyone doubt it?"

"Well, well, I had no idea I was so obvious a Britisher. But business brought me over here some time ago, and so, as you say, my outfit is nearly all London. However, I guess your time is of value, and we did not meet to talk about the cut of my socks. What about getting down to that paper you hold in your hand?"

Holmes had in some way ruffled our visitor, whose chubby face had assumed a far less amiable expression.

"Patience! Patience, Mr. Garrideb!" said my friend in a soothing voice. "Dr. Watson would tell you that these little digressions of mine sometimes prove in the end to have some bearing on the matter. But why did Mr. Nathan Garrideb not come with you?"

"Why did he ever drag you into it at all?" asked our visitor, with a sudden outflame of anger. "What in thunder had you to do with it? Here was a bit of professional business between two gentlemen, and one of them must needs call in a detective! I saw him this morning, and he told me this fool-trick he had played me, and that's why I am here.   But I feel bad about it, all the same."

" There was no reflection upon you, Mr. Garrideb. It was simply zeal upon his part to gain your end—an end which is, I understand, equally vital for both of you. He knew that I had means of getting information, and, therefore, it was very natural that he should apply to me."

Our visitor's angry face gradually cleared.

" Well, that puts it different," said he.   " When I went to see him this morning and he told me he had sent to a detective, I just asked for your address and came right away.   I don't want police butting into a private matter.   But if you are content just to help us find the man, there can be no harm in that."

" Well, that is just how it stands," said Holmes.   " And now, sir, since you are here, we had best have a clear account from your own lips.   My friend here knows nothing of the details."

Mr. Garrideb surveyed me with not too friendly a gaze.

" Need he know ? " he asked.

" We usually work together."

" Well, there's no reason it should be kept a secret. I'll give you the facts as short as I can make them.   If you came from Kansas I would not need to explain to you who Alexander Hamilton Garrideb was.   He made his money in real estate, and afterwards in the wheat pit at Chicago, but he spent it in buying up as much land as would make one of your counties, lying along the Arkansas River, west of Fort Dodge.   It's grazing-land and lumber-land and arable-land and mineralized-land, and just every sort of land that brings dollars to the man that owns it.

" He had no kith nor kin—or, if he had, I never heard of it.   But he took a kind of pride in the queerness of his name.   That was what brought us together.   I was in the law at Topeka, and one day I had a visit from the old man, and he was tickled to death to meet another man with his own name.   It was his pet fad, and he was dead set to find out if there were any more Garridebs in the world.   'Find me another !' said he.   I told him I was a busy man and could not spend my life hiking round the world in search of Garridebs.   'None the less,' said he, 'that is just what you will do if things pan out as I planned them.'   I thought he was joking, but there was a powerful lot of meaning in the words, as I was soon to discover.

" For he died within a year of saying them, and he left a will behind him.   It was the queerest will that has ever been filed in the State of Kansas.   His property was divided into three parts, and I was to have one on condition that I found two Garridebs who would share the remainder.   It's five million dollars for each if it is a cent, but we can't lay a finger on it until we all three stand in a row.

" It was so big a chance that I just let my legal practice slide and I set forth looking for Garridebs.   There is

3 *old Dr. Lysander Starr.* Holmes, groping for a fictitious name, comes up with a minor variant on Lysander Stark, the alias of the elusive counterfeiter in "The Adventure of the Engineer's Thumb." For the sake of the record, as Mr. Bliss Austin noted in "Thumbing His Way to Fame," the Mayor of Topeka in 1890 was the Honorable Roswell F. Cofran.

"WELL, WE SHALL BE ROUND ABOUT SIX."

Illustration by Howard K. Elcock for the *Strand Magazine*, January, 1925.

not one in the United States. I went through it, sir, with a fine-toothed comb and never a Garrideb could I catch. Then I tried the old country. Sure enough there was the name in the London Telephone Directory. I went after him two days ago and explained the whole matter to him. But he is a lone man, like myself, with some women relations, but no men. It says three adult men in the will. So you see we still have a vacancy, and if you can help to fill it we will be very ready to pay your charges."

" Well, Watson," said Holmes, with a smile, " I said it was rather whimsical, did I not ? I should have thought, sir, that your obvious way was to advertise in the agony columns of the papers."

" I have done that, Mr. Holmes. No replies."

" Dear me ! Well, it is certainly a most curious little problem. I may take a glance at it in my leisure. By the way, it is curious that you should have come from Topeka. I used to have a correspondent—he is **3** dead now—old Dr. Lysander Starr, who was Mayor in 1890."

" Good old Dr. Starr ! " said our visitor. " His name is still honoured. Well, Mr. Holmes, I suppose all we can do is to report to you and let you know how we progress. I reckon you will hear within a day or two." With this assurance our American bowed and departed.

Holmes had lit his pipe, and he sat for some time with a curious smile upon his face.

" Well ? " I asked at last.

" I am wondering, Watson—just wondering ! "

" At what ? "

Holmes took his pipe from his lips.

" I was wondering, Watson, what on earth could be the object of this man in telling us such a rigmarole of lies. I nearly asked him so—for there are times when a brutal frontal attack is the best policy—but I judged it better to let him think he had fooled us. Here is a man with an English coat frayed at the elbow and trousers bagged at the knee with a year's wear, and yet by this document and by his own account he is a provincial American lately landed in London. There have been no advertisements in the agony columns. You know that I miss nothing there. They are my favourite covert for putting up a bird, and I would never have overlooked such a cock pheasant as that. I never knew a Dr. Lysander Starr of Topeka. Touch him where you would he was false. I think the fellow is really an American, but he has worn his accent smooth with years of London. What is his game, then, and what motive lies behind this preposterous search for Garridebs ? It's worth our attention, for, granting that the man is a rascal, he is certainly a complex and ingenious one. We must now find out if our other correspondent is a fraud also. Just ring him up, Watson."

I did so, and heard a thin, quavering voice at the other end of the line.

" Yes, yes, I am Mr. Nathan Garrideb. Is Mr. Holmes there ? I should very much like to have a word with Mr. Holmes."

My friend took the instrument and I heard the usual syncopated dialogue.

" Yes, he has been here. I understand that you don't know him. . . . How long ? . . . Only two days ! . . . Yes, yes, of course, it is a most captivating prospect. Will you be at home this evening ? I suppose your namesake will not be there ? . . . Very good, we will come then, for I would rather have a chat without him. . . . Dr. Watson will come with me. . . . I understood from your note that you did not go out often. . . . Well, we shall be round about six. You need not mention it to the American lawyer. . . . Very good. Good-bye ! "

It was twilight of a lovely spring evening, and even Little Ryder Street, one of the smaller offshoots from the Edgware Road, within a stone-cast of old Tyburn Tree of evil memory, looked golden and wonderful **4** in the slanting rays of the setting sun. The particular house to which we were directed was a large, old-fashioned, Early Georgian edifice with a flat brick face broken only by two deep bay windows on the ground floor. It was on this ground floor that our client lived, and, indeed, the low windows proved to be the front of the huge room in which he spent his waking hours. Holmes pointed as we passed to the small brass plate which bore the curious name.

" Up some years, Watson," he remarked, indicating its discoloured surface. " It's *his* real name, anyhow, and that is something to note."

The house had a common stair, and there were a number of names painted in the hall, some indicating offices and some private chambers. It was not a collection of residential flats, but rather the abode of Bohemian bachelors. Our client opened the door for us himself and apologized by saying that the woman in charge left at four o'clock. Mr. Nathan Garrideb proved to be a very tall, loose-jointed, round-backed person, gaunt and bald, some sixty-odd years of age. He had a cadaverous face, with the dull dead skin of a man to whom exercise was unknown. Large round spectacles and a small projecting goat's beard combined with his stooping attitude to give him an expression of peering curiosity. The general effect, however, was amiable, though eccentric.

The room was as curious as its occupant. It looked like a small museum. It was both broad and deep, with cupboards and cabinets all round, crowded with specimens, geological and anatomical. Cases of butterflies and moths flanked each side of the entrance. A large table in the centre was littered with all sorts of debris, while the tall brass tube of a powerful microscope bristled up amongst them. As I glanced round I was surprised at the universality of the man's interests. Here was a case of ancient coins. There was a cabinet of flint instruments. Behind his central table was a large cupboard of fossil bones. Above was a line of plaster skulls with such names as " Neanderthal," " Heidelberg," " Cromagnon " printed beneath them. It was clear that he was a student of many subjects. As he stood in front of us now, he held a piece of chamois leather in his right hand with which he was polishing a coin. **5**

" Syracusan—of the best period," he explained, holding it up. " They degenerated greatly towards the end.

4 *old Tyburn Tree of evil memory.* "At [the] corner of Hyde Park, where the angle of Connaught Place now stands, was the famous 'Tyburn Tree,' sometimes called the 'Three-Legged Mare,' being a triangle on three legs, where the public executions took place till they were transferred to Newgate in 1783," Augustus J. C. Hare wrote in *Walks in London*, Vol. II. "The manor of Tyburn took its name from the Tye Bourne or brook, which rose under Primrose Hill, and the place was originally chosen for executions because, though on the highroad to Oxford, it was remote from London. The condemned were brought hither in a cart from Newgate—'thief and parson in a Tyburn cart' [Dryden, 1684]—the prisoner usually carrying the immense nosegay which, by old custom, was presented to him on the steps of St. Sepulchre's Church, and having been refreshed with a bowl of ale at St. Gile's. The cart was driven underneath the gallows, and, after the noose was adjusted, was driven quickly away by Jack Ketch, the hangman, so that the prisoner was left suspended. (The scene is depicted in Hogarth's 'Idle Apprentice Executed at Tyburn.') Death by this method was much slower and more uncertain than it has been since the drop was invented, and there have been several cases in which animation has been restored after the prisoner was cut down. Around the place of execution were raised galleries which were let to spectators; they were destroyed by the disappointed mob who had engaged them when Dr. Henesey was reprieved in 1758. One Mammy Douglas, who kept the key of the boxes, bore the name of the 'Tyburn Pewopener.' The bodies of Cromwell, Ireton, and Bradshaw were buried under the tyburn tree after hanging there for a day. Some bones discovered in 1840, on removing the pavement close to Arklow House, at the southwest angle of the Edgware Road, are supposed to have been theirs. On the corner of Upper Bryanston Street and the Edgware Road the iron balconies remained till 1785, whence the sheriffs used to watch the executions . . ." Jonathan Wild, whom Holmes mentioned in *The Valley of Fear*, was hanged from Tyburn Tree on May 24, 1725; at his execution he "picked the parson's pocket of his corkscrew, which he carried out of the world in his hand."

5 *he was polishing a coin.* The late Professor Jay Finley Christ, in his article, "Glittering Golden Guineas," doubted Nathan's right to be called a "numismatist," as distinct from a collector of coins. "His misgivings are due to the strong feeling of a large group of numismatists—especially in England —that coins should never be cleaned," the late A. Carson Simpson wrote in *Numismatics in the Canon*, Part II. "An equally large group takes the view that such cleaning as will bring out the design clearly is desirable; careful polishing, so long as it does not scratch the coin or impair its 'tone,' would be acceptable to them. We should give Nathan the benefit of the doubt and assume he was proceeding with due care."

6 *the Alexandrian school.* "Nathan's high esteem for the coins of Syracuse is generally shared by numismatists," Mr. Simpson continued, "even those whose activities do not fall in the ancient field. They were, of course, Greek coins, and the period 400–336 B.C. is generally accepted as that in which the numismatic art reached the highest point of excellence it ever attained. Thereafter, although portraiture on coins became more lifelike and individual, the general level of artistic treatment declined. . . . Garrideb's remark that 'some prefer the Alexandrian school' is perhaps not as clear as it seems to be. Taken literally, it would refer to the 'school of Alexandria,' that is to say, to coins struck in that city. There were, of course, several Alexandrians, but the coinages of the smaller ones are not of especial numismatic importance. The greater city of Alexandria, Egypt, produced coins chiefly notable for their number and variety, rather than for their artistry."

7 *Sotheby's or Christie's.* Two of London's great sales rooms celebrated for their picture and china sales.

8 *the Hans Sloane of my age."* Sir Hans Sloane, 1660–1753, naturalist, physician, collector, and benefactor. The late A. Carson Simpson noted that Nathan Garrideb's ambition recalls another connection between Holmes and Montpellier, for Sir Hans Sloane studied there also. Like Holmes, he was interested in poisons, and witnessed the opening of the body of the tragedian, Barton Booth, who had died of excessive doses of mercury. Again, among his numerous "trifling monographs" published in the *Transactions of the Royal Philosophical Society* was one on "Poisoning from the Ingestion of Henbane Seeds." In his medical practice he was accustomed to prescribe viper's fat for all sorts of ailments, and he was a Governor of Bart's Hospital. Like the Master, he too was interested in America, for he helped General Oglethorpe to promote the settlement of Captain James Calhoun's destination ("The Five Orange Pips") and was made a Commissioner of the Colony of Georgia.

9 *He called last Tuesday."* It was on a day in "the latter end of June, 1902" that "John Garrideb, Counsellor at Law," called upon Sherlock Holmes. He said to Holmes: "I went after [Mr. Nathan Garrideb] two days ago and explained the whole matter to him." On the evening of that day, Holmes said to Nathan Garrideb: "I understand that up to this week you were unaware of [John Garrideb's] existence." "That is so," Nathan replied. "He called last Tuesday." The case opened, then, on a Thursday that can only be *Thursday, June 26, 1902.* It ended the next day.

At their best I hold them supreme, though some prefer **6** the Alexandrian school. You will find a chair here, Mr. Holmes. Pray allow me to clear these bones. And you, sir—ah, yes, Dr. Watson—if you would have the goodness to put the Japanese vase to one side. You see round me my little interests in life. My doctor lectures me about never going out, but why should I go out when I have so much to hold me here? I can assure you that the adequate cataloguing of one of those cabinets would take me three good months."

Holmes looked round him with curiosity.

"But do you tell me that you *never* go out?" he said.

7 "Now and again I drive down to Sotheby's or Christie's. Otherwise I very seldom leave my room. I am not too strong, and my researches are very absorbing. But you can imagine, Mr. Holmes, what a terrific shock—pleasant but terrific—it was for me when I heard of this unparalleled good fortune. It only needs one more Garrideb to complete the matter, and surely we can find one. I had a brother, but he is dead, and female relatives are disqualified. But there must surely be others in the world. I had heard that you handled strange cases, and that was why I sent to you. Of course, this American gentleman is quite right, and I should have taken his advice first, but I acted for the best."

"I think you acted very wisely indeed," said Holmes. "But are you really anxious to acquire an estate in America?"

"Certainly not, sir. Nothing would induce me to leave my collection. But this gentleman has assured me that he will buy me out as soon as we have established our claim. Five million dollars was the sum named. There are a dozen specimens in the market at the present moment which fill gaps in my collection, and which I am unable to purchase for want of a few hundred pounds. Just think what I could do with five million dollars. Why, I have the nucleus of a national collection. I shall **8** be the Hans Sloane of my age."

His eyes gleamed behind his great spectacles. It was very clear that no pains would be spared by Mr. Nathan Garrideb in finding a namesake.

"I merely called to make your acquaintance, and there is no reason why I should interrupt your studies," said Holmes. "I prefer to establish personal touch with those with whom I do business. There are few questions I need ask, for I have your very clear narrative in my pocket, and I filled up the blanks when this American gentleman called. I understand that up to this week you were unaware of his existence."

9 "That is so. He called last Tuesday."

"Did he tell you of our interview to-day?"

"Yes, he came straight back to me. He had been very angry."

"Why should he be angry?"

"He seemed to think it was some reflection on his honour. But he was quite cheerful again when he returned."

"Did he suggest any course of action?"

" No, sir, he did not."

" Has he had, or asked for, any money from you ? "

" No, sir, never ! "

" You see no possible object he has in view ? "

" None, except what he states."

" Did you tell him of our telephone appointment ? "

" Yes, sir, I did."

Holmes was lost in thought. I could see that he was puzzled.

" Have you any articles of great value in your collection ? "

" No, sir. I am not a rich man. It is a good collection, but not a very valuable one."

" You have no fear of burglars ? "

" Not the least."

" How long have you been in these rooms ? "

" Nearly five years."

Holmes' cross-examination was interrupted by an imperative knocking at the door. No sooner had our client unlatched it than the American lawyer burst excitedly into the room.

" Here you are ! " he cried, waving a paper over his head. " I thought I should be in time to get you. Mr. Nathan Garrideb, my congratulations ! You are a rich man, sir. Our business is happily finished and all is well. As to you, Mr. Holmes, we can only say we are sorry if we have given you any useless trouble."

He handed over the paper to our client, who stood staring at a marked advertisement. Holmes and I leaned forward and read it over his shoulder. This is how it ran :

"HERE YOU ARE!" HE CRIED, WAVING A PAPER
OVER HIS HEAD.

Illustration by Howard K. Elcock for the *Strand Magazine*, January, 1925.

HOWARD GARRIDEB.

Constructor of Agricultural Machinery.

Binders, reapers' steam and hand plows, drills, harrows, farmers' carts, buckboards, and all other appliances.

Estimates for Artesian Wells.

Apply Grosvenor Buildings, Aston.

" Glorious ! " gasped our host. " That makes our third man."

" I had opened up inquiries in Birmingham," said the American, " and my agent there has sent me this advertisement from a local paper. We must hustle and put the thing through. I have written to this man and told him that you will see him in his office to-morrow afternoon at four o'clock."

" You want *me* to see him ? "

" What do you say, Mr. Holmes ? Don't you think it would be wiser ? Here am I, a wandering American with a wonderful tale. Why should he believe what I tell him ? But you are a Britisher with solid references, and he is bound to take notice of what you say. I would go with you if you wished, but I have a very busy day to-morrow, and I could always follow you if you are in any trouble."

" Well, I have not made such a journey for years."

" It is nothing, Mr. Garrideb. I have figured out your connections. You leave at twelve and should be there soon after two. Then you can be back the same night. All you have to do is to see this man, explain the matter, and get an affidavit of his existence. By the Lord ! " he added hotly, " considering I've come all the way from the centre of America, it is surely little enough if you go a hundred miles in order to put this matter through."

" Quite so," said Holmes. " I think what this gentleman says is very true."

Mr. Nathan Garrideb shrugged his shoulders with a disconsolate air. " Well, if you insist I shall go," said he. " It is certainly hard for me to refuse you anything, considering the glory of hope that you have brought into my life."

" Then that is agreed," said Holmes, " and no doubt you will let me have a report as soon as you can."

" I'll see to that," said the American. " Well," he added, looking at his watch, " I'll have to get on. I'll call to-morrow, Mr. Nathan, and see you off to Birmingham. Coming my way, Mr. Holmes ? Well, then, good-bye, and we may have good news for you to-morrow night."

I noticed that my friend's face cleared when the American left the room, and the look of thoughtful perplexity had vanished.

" I wish I could look over your collection, Mr. Garrideb," said he. " In my profession all sorts of odd knowledge comes useful, and this room of yours is a storehouse of it."

Our client shone with pleasure and his eyes gleamed from behind his big glasses.

" I had always heard, sir, that you were a very intelligent man," said he. " I could take you round now, if you have the time."

" Unfortunately, I have not. But these specimens are so well labelled and classified that they hardly need your personal explanation. If I should be able to look in to-morrow, I presume that there would be no objection to my glancing over them ? "

" None at all. You are most welcome. The place will, of course, be shut up, but Mrs. Saunders is in the basement up to four o'clock and would let you in with her key."

" Well, I happen to be clear to-morrow afternoon. If you would say a word to Mrs. Saunders it would be quite in order. By the way, who is your house-agent ? "

Our client was amazed at the sudden question.

" Holloway and Steele, in the Edgware Road. But why ? "

" I am a bit of an archæologist myself when it comes to houses," said Holmes, laughing. " I was wondering if this was Queen Anne or Georgian."

" Georgian, beyond doubt."

" Really. I should have thought a little earlier. However, it is easily ascertained. Well, good-bye, Mr. Garrideb, and may you have every success in your Birmingham journey."

The house-agent's was close by, but we found that it was closed for the day, so we made our way back to Baker Street. It was not till after dinner that Holmes reverted to the subject.

" Our little problem draws to a close," said he. " No doubt you have outlined the solution in your own mind."

" I can make neither head nor tail of it."

" The head is surely clear enough and the tail we should see to-morrow. Did you notice nothing curious about that advertisement ? "

" I saw that the word ' plough ' was mis-spelt."

" Oh, you did notice that, did you ? Come, Watson, you improve all the time. Yes, it was bad English but good American. The printer had set it up as received. Then the buckboards. That is American also. And artesian wells are commoner with them than with us. It was a typical American advertisement, but purporting to be from an English firm. What do you make of that ? "

" I can only suppose that this American lawyer put it in himself. What his object was I fail to understand."

" Well, there are alternative explanations. Anyhow, he wanted to get this good old fossil up to Birmingham. That is very clear. I might have told him that he was clearly going on a wild-goose chase, but, on second thoughts, it seemed better to clear the stage by letting him go. To-morrow, Watson—well, to-morrow will speak for itself."

Holmes was up and out early. When he returned at lunch-time I noticed that his face was very grave.

" This is a more serious matter than I had expected, Watson," said he. " It is fair to tell you so, though I know it will only be an additional reason to you for running your head into danger. I should know my Watson by now. But there *is* danger, and you should know it."

" Well, it is not the first we have shared, Holmes. I hope it may not be the last. What is the particular danger this time ? "

" We are up against a very hard case. I have identified Mr. John Garrideb, Counsellor at Law. He is none other than ' Killer ' Evans, of sinister and murderous reputation."

" I fear I am none the wiser."

" Ah, it is not part of your profession to carry about a portable Newgate Calendar in your memory. I have been down to see friend Lestrade at the Yard. There **10** may be an occasional want of imaginative intuition down there, but they lead the world for thoroughness and method. I had an idea that we might get on the track of our American friend in their records. Sure enough, I found his chubby face smiling up at me from the Rogues' Portrait Gallery. James Winter, *alias* Morecroft, *alias* Killer Evans, was the inscription below." Holmes drew an envelope from his pocket. " I scribbled down a few points from his dossier. Aged forty-four. Native of Chicago. Known to have shot three men in the States. Escaped from penitentiary through political influence. Came to London in 1893. Shot a man

10 *I have been down to see friend Lestrade at the Yard.* "After twenty years of more-or-less congenial association between [Holmes and Lestrade], during which time Lestrade repeatedly went out of his way to let Holmes 'in' on strange and bizarre problems, Holmes deliberately by-passes Lestrade, even after the Scotland Yarder has kindly supplied Sherlock with a complete biography of 'Killer' Evans," the late Clifton R. Andrew wrote in "That Scotland Yarder, Gregson—What a Help (?) He Was." "Holmes, apparently, gave Lestrade no inkling of what he [Holmes] was up to. Instead, with the information that the Scotland Yard Inspector gave them, Holmes and Watson slipped out themselves to apprehend the vicious criminal without asking Lestrade to assist them in the potential 'pinch.' A little unappreciative, I call it—and it doesn't seem as if Lestrade merited a 'go-by' such as that."

11 *"I have my old favourite.* Mr. Robert Keith Leavitt has assumed that the weapon to which Holmes refers here is still the impractical little Webley of his early days. But, as the late H. T. Webster wrote in "Observations on Sherlock Holmes as an Athlete and Sportsman," "such a weapon would make a very inefficient bludgeon [as Holmes later in this case had to make use of it]. What, then, is more probable that Sir Henry Baskerville or some other grateful transatlantic client had presented Holmes with a Colt Frontier Model .45, or some other well-designed American arm which would have been a practical substitute for either a rifle or a loaded hunting crop?"

12 *a certain devilish ingenuity.* "There is something very curious about this affair," the late Gavin Brend wrote in *My Dear Holmes* "The crime is a work of art, but the criminal seems to fall far below the level of the crime. Could Killer Evans, who appears to be rather a humdrum personality, have invented this very ingenious scheme? It certainly looks as if it were a one-man job, but it may be that the Killer sought out one of his associates, explained his difficulties and asked for advice. The advice was given, the adviser taking care to keep well in the background, so that when the Killer was arrested he escaped. There exists a theory that most criminals repeat certain details every time they commit a crime, so that they may be said to write their signatures across it. If this be so then the signature on 'The Adventure of the Three Garridebs' can easily be read. It is one that we have met before . . . in the matter of 'The Red-Headed League.' It is the signature of the most interesting of all Holmes' opponents, our old acquaintance, John Clay, once of Eton and Oxford, the grandson of a Royal Duke."

over cards in a night club in the Waterloo Road in January, 1895. Man died, but he was shown to have been the aggressor in the row. Dead man was identified as Rodger Prescott, famous as forger and coiner in Chicago. Killer Evans released in 1901. Has been under police supervision since, but so far as known has led an honest life. Very dangerous man, usually carries arms and is prepared to use them. That is our bird, Watson— a sporting bird, as you must admit."

" But what is his game ? "

" Well, it begins to define itself. I have been to the house-agents. Our client, as he told us, has been there five years. It was unlet for a year before then. The previous tenant was a gentleman at large named Waldron. Waldron's appearance was well remembered at the office. He had suddenly vanished and nothing more been heard of him. He was a tall, bearded man with very dark features. Now, Prescott, the man whom Killer Evans had shot, was, according to Scotland Yard, a tall, dark man with a beard. As a working hypothesis, I think we may take it that Prescott, the American criminal, used to live in the very room which our innocent friend now devotes to his museum. So at last we get a link, you see."

" And the next link ? "

" Well, we must go now and look for that."

He took a revolver from the drawer and handed it to me.

11 " I have my old favourite with me. If our Wild West friend tries to live up to his nickname, we must be ready for him. I'll give you an hour for a siesta, Watson, and then I think it will be time for our Ryder Street adventure."

It was just four o'clock when we reached the curious apartment of Nathan Garrideb. Mrs. Saunders, the caretaker, was about to leave, but she had no hesitation in admitting us, for the door shut with a spring lock and Holmes promised to see that all was safe before we left. Shortly afterwards the outer door closed, her bonnet passed the bow window, and we knew that we were alone in the lower floor of the house. Holmes made a rapid examination of the premises. There was one cupboard in a dark corner which stood out a little from the wall. It was behind this that we eventually crouched, while Holmes in a whisper outlined his intentions.

" He wanted to get our amiable friend out of his room —that is very clear, and, as the collector never went out, it took some planning to do it. The whole of this Garrideb invention was apparently for no other end. I **12** must say, Watson, that there is a certain devilish ingenuity about it even if the queer name of the tenant did give him an opening which he could hardly have expected. He wove his plot with remarkable cunning."

" But what did he want ? "

" Well, that is what we are here to find out. It has nothing whatever to do with our client, so far as I can read the situation. It is something connected with the man he murdered—the man who may have been his confederate in crime. There is some guilty secret in the room. That is how I read it. At first I thought our friend might have something in his collection more valuable than he knew—something worth the attention of a big criminal. But the fact that Rodger Prescott of evil memory inhabited these rooms points to some deeper reason. Well, Watson, we can but possess our souls in patience and see what the hour may bring."

That hour was not long in striking. We crouched closer in the shadow as we heard the outer door open and shut. Then came the sharp, metallic snap of a key, and the American was in the room. He closed the door softly behind him, took a sharp glance around him to see that all was safe, threw off his overcoat, and walked up to the central table with the brisk manner of one who knows exactly what he has to do and how to do it. He pushed the table to one side, tore up the square of carpet on which it rested, rolled it completely back, and then, drawing a jemmy from his inside pocket, he knelt down and worked vigorously upon the floor. Presently we heard the sound of sliding boards, and an instant later a square had opened in the planks. Killer Evans struck a match, lit a stump of candle, and vanished from our view.

Clearly our moment had come. Holmes touched my wrist as a signal, and together we stole across to the open trap-door. Gently as we moved, however, the old floor must have creaked under our feet, for the head of our American, peering anxiously round, emerged suddenly from the open space. His face turned upon us with a glare of baffled rage, which gradually softened into a rather shamefaced grin as he realized that two pistols were pointed at his head.

"Well, well!" said he, coolly, as he scrambled to the surface. "I guess you have been one too many for me, Mr. Holmes. Saw through my game, I suppose, and played me for a sucker from the first. Well, sir, I hand it to you; you have me beat and——"

In an instant he had whisked out a revolver from his breast and had fired two shots. I felt a sudden hot sear as if a red-hot iron had been pressed to my thigh. There was a crash as Holmes' pistol came down on the man's head. I had a vision of him sprawling upon the floor with blood running down his face while Holmes rummaged him for weapons. Then my friend's wiry arms were round me and he was leading me to a chair.

"You're not hurt, Watson? For God's sake, say that you are not hurt!"

It was worth a wound—it was worth many wounds—to know the depth of loyalty and love which lay behind that cold mask. The clear, hard eyes were dimmed for a moment, and the firm lips were shaking. For the one and only time I caught a glimpse of a great heart as well as of a great brain. All my years of humble but **13** single-minded service culminated in that moment of revelation.

"It's nothing, Holmes. It's a mere scratch."

He had ripped up my trousers with his pocket-knife.

"You are right," he cried, with an immense sigh of

HIS FACE TURNED UPON US WITH A GLARE
OF BAFFLED RAGE . . .

Illustration by Howard K. Elcock for the *Strand Magazine*, January, 1925.

13 *a great heart as well as of a great brain.* Mr. T. S. Blakeney has made an apt comparison between Holmes and the Iron Duke of Wellington: "In both, despite an outwardly cold aspect, we are vouchsafed glimpses of an emotional (not sentimental) nature kept in strong control, repressed, perhaps, from a sense that any display was a sign of weakness. Both were keen musicians, and music is the most emotional of all the arts; both could be delightful with children, who instinctively know real from feigned affability. The Iron Duke broke down seldom, but those breaks were very complete; the other side of Holmes' nature peeps through even less thoroughly, but not less certainly."

THERE WAS A CRASH AS HOLMES' PISTOL CAME DOWN
ON THE MAN'S HEAD.

Illustration by Howard K. Elcock for the *Strand
Magazine*, January, 1925. "Holmes' return shot was
as curious an incident as that of the dog in the
nighttime," Mr. Robert Keith Leavitt wrote in
"Annie Oakley in Baker Street." "There *was* no
return shot from Holmes. That was the curious incident. Instead, the great detective, confronted
with a life-and-death emergency, at the muzzle of
an armed opponent going full blast, *hit that opponent over the head*. . . . Effective though such a
crack could be—and was—nothing could more
completely reveal Holmes' distrust of his own
markmanship with the pistol."

relief. "It is quite superficial." His face set like flint
as he glared at our prisoner, who was sitting up with a
dazed face. "By the Lord, it is as well for you. If
you had killed Watson, you would not have got out of
this room alive. Now, sir, what have you to say for
yourself ? "

He had nothing to say for himself. He only lay
and scowled. I leaned on Holmes' arm, and together
we looked down into the small cellar which had been
disclosed by the secret flap. It was still illuminated
by the candle which Evans had taken down with him.
Our eyes fell upon a mass of rusted machinery, great
rolls of paper, a litter of bottles, and, neatly arranged
upon a small table, a number of neat little bundles.

"A printing press—a counterfeiter's outfit," said
Holmes.

"Yes, sir," said our prisoner, staggering slowly to
his feet and then sinking into the chair. "The greatest counterfeiter London ever saw. That's Prescott's
machine, and those bundles on the table are two thousand
of Prescott's notes worth a hundred each and fit to pass
anywhere. Help yourselves, gentlemen. Call it a deal
and let me beat it."

Holmes laughed.

"We don't do things like that, Mr. Evans. There
is no bolt-hole for you in this country. You shot this
man Prescott, did you not ? "

"Yes, sir, and got five years for it, though it was
he who pulled on me. Five years—when I should
have had a medal the size of a soup plate. No living
man could tell a Prescott from a Bank of England, and
if I hadn't put him out he would have flooded London
with them. I was the only one in the world who knew
where he made them. Can you wonder that I wanted to
get to the place ? And can you wonder that when I
found this crazy boob of a bug-hunter with the queer
name squatting right on the top of it, and never quitting
his room, I had to do the best I could to shift him ?
Maybe I would have been wiser if I had put him away.
It would have been easy enough, but I'm a soft-hearted
guy that can't begin shooting unless the other man has a
gun also. But say, Mr. Holmes, what have I done
wrong, anyhow ? I've not used this plant. I've not
hurt this old stiff. Where do you get me ? "

"Only attempted murder, so far as I can see," said
Holmes. "But that's not our job. They take that at the
next stage. What we wanted at present was just your
sweet self. Please give the Yard a call, Watson. It
won't be entirely unexpected."

So those were the facts about Killer Evans and his
remarkable invention of the three Garridebs. We heard
later that our poor old friend never got over the shock
of his dissipated dreams. When his castle in the air fell
down, it buried him beneath the ruins. He was last
heard of at a nursing-home in Brixton. It was a glad
day at the Yard when the Prescott outfit was discovered,
for, though they knew that it existed, they had never
been able, after the death of the man, to find out where

it was. Evans had indeed done great service and caused several worthy C.I.D. men to sleep the sounder, for the counterfeiter stands in a class by himself as a public danger. They would willingly have subscribed to that soup-plate medal of which the criminal had spoken, but an unappreciative Bench took a less favourable view, and the Killer returned to those shades from which he had just emerged.

"A PRINTING PRESS—A COUNTERFEITER'S OUTFIT,"
SAID HOLMES.

Illustration by John Richard Flanagan for *Collier's Magazine*, October 25, 1924.

A Note on the "Canonicity" of "The Adventure of the Three Garridebs": Mr. Russell McLauchlin feels that it is time "to call into serious question the Canonicity of [this adventure]. . . . I suggest that it was the work of a well-known hand. We are aware that the literary agent, who served Dr. Watson effectively for many years, was himself a writer of some repute in other fields. It is by no means improbable that, after long association with the doctor, he was tempted to compose a pastiche."

On the other hand, Mr. D. Martin Dakin, who rejects from the Canon many of the adventures in *The Case-Book*, accepts "The Adventure of the Three Garridebs" as genuine. "[It] is a story told in Watson's best manner," he wrote in "The Problem of the Case-Book." "There can be few Baker Street enthusiasts who would sacrifice the account of the supreme moment in the Doctor's life when Killer Evans' bullet-wound was the means of revealing to him the depth of Holmes' devotion to him." Later, in "Second Thoughts on the Case-Book," Mr. Dakin wrote: "I must add that it is a little startling to learn that, if Evans had killed Watson, Holmes proposed to take the law into his own hands and murder him in retaliation. Still we should probably not take too seriously a remark that escaped him in the heat of his indignation for his friend."

Bibliographical Note: The manuscript of "The Adventure of the Three Garridebs" is the property of Mr. Adrian M. Conan Doyle.

69

THE DISAPPEARANCE OF LADY FRANCES CARFAX

[Tuesday, July 1, to Friday, July 18, 1902]

1 *I have been feeling rheumatic and old.* Your editor, while acknowledging that this case is a chronologist's nightmare, has nevertheless dated it more or less to his own satisfaction as having taking place between Tuesday, July 1st, and Friday, July 18th, in the year 1902. It is clearly a late case: 1) Certainly it was after 1889, because Holy Peters' ear "was badly bitten in a saloon-fight in Adelaide" in that year. 2) Watson's account of the adventure was not published until December, 1911. 3) Watson has just said that he was feeling "rheumatic and old." 4) Holmes introduces Watson as his "old friend and associate." 5) Watson says: "But neither the official police nor Holmes' own small, but every efficient organization sufficed to clear away the mystery." Except for Holmes' references to his "Agency" in "The Adventure of the Sussex Vampire" this is the first we have heard of an organization supporting Holmes, apart from the Baker Street Irregulars. Did the case take place in 1890? Surely not: 1) Holmes would have said that Peters' ear had been bitten "last year" instead of "in '89." 2) Watson was married to Mary Morstan in 1890; it is unthinkable that Holmes under those conditions would twit Watson about riding in a hansom cab with a lady. 3) Finally, "in the year 1890 there were only three cases of which [Watson retained] any record"—and these, as we have seen, were "The Adventure of Wisteria Lodge," "Silver Blaze," and "The Adventure of the Beryl Coronet." The Great Hiatus makes 1891, 1892, and 1893 quite impossible. Watson did not mention the case in "The Adventure of the Golden Pince-Nez" as one of the important cases of 1894—we must discard this year also. "The Adventure of Black Peter" beginning on Wednesday, July 3, 1895, makes that year dubious but not impossible. For the present, let us say only that the years between 1896 and Holmes' retirement in late 1904 provide the *probable* period—and add the fact that Watson having been shot in the thigh on Friday, June 27, 1902 ("The Adventure of the Three Garridebs") may have accounted in part for his feeling "rheumatic and old."

"BUT why Turkish ? " asked Mr. Sherlock Holmes, gazing fixedly at my boots. I was reclining in a cane-backed chair at the moment, and my protruded feet had attracted his ever-active attention.

" English," I answered, in some surprise. " I got them at Latimer's, in Oxford Street."

Holmes smiled with an expression of weary patience.

" The bath ! " he said ; " the bath ! Why the relaxing and expensive Turkish rather than the invigorating home-made article ? "

1 " Because for the last few days I have been feeling rheumatic and old. A Turkish bath is what we call an alterative in medicine—a fresh starting-point, a cleanser of the system.

" By the way, Holmes," I added, " I have no doubt the connection between my boots and a Turkish bath is a perfectly self-evident one to a logical mind, and yet I should be obliged to you if you would indicate it."

" The train of reasoning is not very obscure, Watson," said Holmes, with a mischievous twinkle. " It belongs to the same elementary class of deduction which I should illustrate if I were to ask you who shared your cab in your drive this morning."

" I don't admit that a fresh illustration is an explanation," said I, with some asperity.

" Bravo, Watson ! A very dignified and logical remonstrance. Let me see, what were the points ? Take the last one first—the cab. You observe that you have some splashes on the left sleeve and shoulder of your coat. Had you sat in the centre of a hansom you would probably have had no splashes, and if you had they would certainly have been symmetrical. Therefore it is clear that you sat at the side. Therefore it is equally clear that you had a **2** companion."

" That is very evident."

" Absurdly commonplace, is it not ? "

" But the boots and the bath ? "

" Equally childish. You are in the habit of doing up your boots in a certain way. I see them on this occasion fastened with an elaborate double bow, which is not your usual method of tying them. You have, therefore, had them off. Who has tied them ? A bootmaker—or the boy at the bath. It is unlikely that it is the bootmaker, since your boots are nearly new. Well, what remains ? The bath. Absurd, is it not ? But, for all that, the Turkish bath has served a purpose."

" What is that ? "

" You say that you have had it because you need a change. Let me suggest that you take one. How would Lausanne do, my dear Watson—first-class tickets and all expenses paid on a princely scale ? "

" Splendid ! But why ? "

Holmes leaned back in his arm-chair and took his note-book from his pocket.

" One of the most dangerous classes in the world," said he, " is the drifting and friendless woman. She is the most harmless, and often the most useful of mortals, but she is the inevitable inciter of crime in others. She is **3** helpless. She is migratory. She has sufficient means to take her from country to country and from hotel to hotel. She is lost, as often as not, in a maze of obscure *pensions* and boarding-houses. She is a stray chicken in a world of foxes. When she is gobbled up she is hardly missed. I much fear that some evil has come to the Lady Frances Carfax." **4**

I was relieved at this sudden descent from the general to the particular. Holmes consulted his notes.

" Lady Frances," he continued, " is the sole survivor of the direct family of the late Earl of Rufton. The estates went, as you may remember, in the male line. She was left with limited means, but with some very remarkable old Spanish jewellery of silver and curiously-cut diamonds to which she was fondly attached—too attached, for she refused to leave them with her banker and always carried them about with her. A rather pathetic figure, the Lady Frances, a beautiful woman, still in fresh middle age, and yet, by a strange chance, the last derelict of what only twenty years ago was a goodly fleet."

" What has happened to her, then ? "

" Ah, what has happened to the Lady Frances ? Is she alive or dead ? There is our problem. She is a lady of precise habits, and for four years it has been her invariable custom to write every second week to Miss Dobney, her old governess, who has long retired, and lives in Camber-well. It is this Miss Dobney who has consulted me. Nearly five weeks have passed without a word. The last letter was from the Hôtel National at Lausanne. Lady **5** Frances seems to have left there and given no address. The family are anxious, and, as they are exceedingly wealthy, no sum will be spared if we can clear the matter up."

" Is Miss Dobney the only source of information ? Surely she had other correspondents ? "

" There is one correspondent who is a sure draw, Watson. That is the bank. Single ladies must live, and their pass-books are compressed diaries. She banks at Silvester's. I have glanced over her account. The last cheque but one paid her bill at Lausanne, but it was a large one and probably left her with cash in hand. Only one cheque has been drawn since."

2 *you had a companion.*" The late H. W. Bell pointed out that Watson would have sat upon the left side of the cab if his companion had been a lady, and saw in this incident "an unmistakable hint [that Watson is] preparing his readers for a change in his circumstances." We later learn that Watson married for a third time in the last quarter of 1902; it seems logical to think that he might well be sharing his cab with his bride-to-be a few months before the marriage took place.

3 *the inevitable inciter of crime in others.* "Holmes' experience of women was, of course, limited, and perhaps if he had had experience of life in a London boarding-house he might have altered somewhat the first half of his sentence," Mr. T. S. Blakeney commented in *Sherlock Holmes: Fact or Fiction?*

4 *the lady Frances Carfax.*" "In . . . 'The Disappearance of Lady Frances Carfax' [Watson] is guilty of calling her, and of making Holmes call her, at least once, *the* Lady Frances Carfax; which is wrong," Dr. William Braid White wrote in "Dr. Watson and the Peerage." "She could have been *the* Lady Frances Carfax, but actually she was not. She was Lady Frances Carfax. I shall leave it to another scholar to supply the reason for this subtle distinction."

Another scholar, Mr. Humfrey Michell, was quick to disagree with Dr. White: "The lady in question was the sole survivor of the late Earl of Rufton, 'the last derelict of what only twenty years ago was a goodly fleet.' As the daughter of an earl she ranked with her father, and since the prefix 'the' is the equivalent of 'Right Honourable' she was entitled to be called 'the Lady Frances Carfax,' as Holmes correctly calls her when first speaking of her to Watson. In all, the right appellation is used nine times during the story and the incorrect 'Lady Frances Carfax' twelve times."

On the postulation that Holmes instructed Watson to conceal the Lady Frances Carfax's real identity, and that he personally selected the pseudonym for this unfortunate lady, Lord Donegall has insisted that Holmes identifies himself irrevocably as an Oxford man. No Cantabrigian, he asserts, would ever have thought of this appellation which attaches to the main square in the town of Oxford.

5 *the Hôtel National at Lausanne.* Mr. Michael Kaser has pointed out in a paper on the dating of this case that the Hôtel National at Lausanne was open between 1886 and 1951 and that it did possess "luxurious rooms overlooking the lake" as Watson later described the Lady Frances' suite. "Slight evidence for a later [rather than an earlier] dating may be found in the absence of the Hôtel from the 1896 edition of Baedeker's *Switzerland*," he wrote, "whereas it was listed in the 1902 edition. One could surmise that the Lady Frances, of wealthy and noble family, would have selected for her season's stay a hotel of confirmed international standing, and that so far as Baedeker (then virtually the only reliable guide) went, that standing was not ratified until 1902."

There is every reason to believe that the Lady Frances intended to remain for the season in her luxurious rooms; since the Continental "season" is from May 1st to October 1st, and the Lady Frances had not been heard from for "nearly five weeks," it seems logical to surmise that the case opened no earlier than June 30th, no later than July 7th. Watson's bullet wound on Friday, June 27, 1902, coupled with his phrase "the last few days," added to the fact that the closing day of the case was neither a Sunday nor a Monday, lead us to *Tuesday, July 1, 1902,* as the opening day of the case; it ended, we think, on *Friday, July 18, 1902.*

6 *at so extravagant a rate as twopence a word.* Mr. Kaser has noted that: "The telegram rate to France of twopence a word was introduced in 1889 and continued until 1920, when it changed to twopence halfpenny; the rate to Switzerland at the time was threepence a word (it dropped to twopence halfpenny in 1909 but reverted to threepence in 1926). Leaving aside the query why Holmes should have referred to the rate to France and not to Switzerland, which was Watson's immediate destination (one could suppose intuition on Holmes' part that the trail would lead out of Switzerland into France; Holmes did not in fact send any telegram to Watson in Switzerland— only to Baden and Montpellier), it is clear that any dating beyond 1889 would satisfy the evidence of the telegram charge."

7 *11 Rue de Trajan.* "No 'Rue de Trajan' is to be found on the maps of Montpellier in the 1897 edition of Baedeker's guide to that region of France, but the street, patently a minor one, was of insufficient importance for depiction on such a map," Mr. Kaser wrote.

" To whom, and where ? "

" To Miss Marie Devine. There is nothing to show where the cheque was drawn. It was cashed at the Crédit Lyonnais at Montpelier less than three weeks ago. The sum was fifty pounds."

" And who is Miss Marie Devine ? "

" That also I have been able to discover. Miss Marie Devine was the maid of Lady Frances Carfax. Why she should have paid her this cheque we have not yet determined. I have no doubt, however, that your researches will soon clear the matter up."

" *My* researches ! "

" Hence the health-giving expedition to Lausanne. You know that I cannot possibly leave London while old Abrahams is in such mortal terror of his life. Besides, on general principles it is best that I should not leave the country. Scotland Yard feels lonely without me, and it causes an unhealthy excitement among the criminal classes. Go, then, my dear Watson, and if my humble counsel can **6** ever be valued at so extravagant a rate as twopence a word, it waits your disposal night and day at the end of the Continental wire."

Two days later found me at the National Hotel at Lausanne, where I received every courtesy at the hands of M. Moser, the well-known manager. Lady Frances, as he informed me, had stayed there for several weeks. She had been much liked by all who met her. Her age was not more than forty. She was still handsome, and bore every sign of having in her youth been a very lovely woman. M. Moser knew nothing of any valuable jewellery, but it had been remarked by the servants that the heavy trunk in the lady's bedroom was always scrupulously locked. Marie Devine, the maid, was as popular as her mistress. She was actually engaged to one of the head waiters in the hotel, and there was no difficulty in **7** getting her address. It was 11 Rue de Trajan, Montpelier. All this I jotted down, and felt that Holmes himself could not have been more adroit in collecting his facts.

Only one corner still remained in the shadow. No light which I possessed could clear up the cause for the lady's sudden departure. She was very happy at Lausanne. There was every reason to believe that she intended to remain for the season in her luxurious rooms overlooking the lake. And yet she had left at a single day's notice, which involved her in the useless payment of a week's rent. Only Jules Vibart, the lover of the maid, had any suggestion to offer. He connected the sudden departure with the visit to the hotel a day or two before of a tall, dark, bearded man. " *Un sauvage—un véritable sauvage !* " cried Jules Vibart. The man had rooms somewhere in the town. He had been seen talking earnestly to madame on the promenade by the lake. Then he had called. She had refused to see him. He was English, but of his name there was no record. Madame had left the place immediately afterwards. Jules Vibart, and, what was of more importance, Jules Vibart's sweetheart, thought that this call and this departure were cause and effect. Only one thing Jules could not discuss. That was the reason why Marie had left her mistress. Of that he could or would say nothing. If I wished to know, I must go to Montpelier and ask her.

So ended the first chapter of my inquiry. The second was devoted to the place which Lady Frances Carfax had sought when she left Lausanne. Concerning this there had been some secrecy, which confirmed the idea that she had gone with the intention of throwing someone off her track. Otherwise why should not her luggage have been openly labelled for Baden ? Both she and it reached the Rhenish spa by some circuitous route. Thus much I gathered from the manager of Cook's local office. So to **8** Baden I went, after dispatching to Holmes an account of all my proceedings, and receiving in reply a telegram of half-humorous commendation.

At Baden the track was not difficult to follow. Lady Frances had stayed at the Englischer Hof for a fortnight. **9** Whilst there she had made the acquaintance of a Dr. Shlessinger and his wife, a missionary from South America. Like most lonely ladies, Lady Frances found her comfort and occupation in religion. Dr. Shlessinger's remarkable personality, his whole-hearted devotion, and the fact that he was recovering from a disease contracted in the exercise of his apostolic duties, affected her deeply. She had helped Mrs. Shlessinger in the nursing of the convalescent saint. He spent his day, as the manager described it to me, upon a lounge-chair on the verandah, with an attendant lady upon either side of him. He was preparing a map of the Holy Land, with special reference to the kingdom of the Midianites, upon which he was writing a monograph. Finally, having improved much in health, he and his wife had returned to London, and Lady Frances had started thither in their company. This was just three weeks before, and the manager had heard nothing since. As to the maid, Marie, she had gone off some days beforehand in floods of tears, after informing the other maids that she was leaving service for ever. Dr. Shlessinger had paid the bill of the whole party before his departure.

" By the way," said the landlord, in conclusion, " you are not the only friend of Lady Frances Carfax who is inquiring after her just now. Only a week or so ago we had a man here upon the same errand."

" Did he give a name ? " I asked.

" None ; but he was an Englishman, though of an unusual type."

" A savage ? " said I, linking my facts after the fashion of my illustrious friend.

" Exactly. That describes him very well. He is a bulky, bearded, sunburned fellow, who looks as if he would be more at home in a farmers' inn than in a fashionable hotel. A hard, fierce man, I should think, and one whom I should be sorry to offend."

Already the mystery began to define itself, as figures grow clearer with the lifting of a fog. Here was this good and pious lady pursued from place to place by a sinister and unrelenting figure. She feared him, or she would not have fled from Lausanne. He had still followed. Sooner or later he would overtake her. Had he already overtaken her ? Was *that* the secret of her continued silence ?

8 *Cook's local office*. "Thomas Cook's office in Lausanne was opened April, 1891, at No. 1 Rue Pépinet; consequently any date beyond 1891 is satisfactory," Mr. Kaser wrote.

9 *the Englischer Hof*. "The Englischer Hof in Baden . . . is listed in both the 1893 and 1902 edition's of Baedeker's *Southern Germany*," Mr. Kaser wrote, adding in a footnote: "The Hotel changed its name during the First World War for obvious reasons."

HE SPENT HIS DAY . . . UPON A LOUNGE-CHAIR
ON THE VERANDAH . . .

Illustration by Alec Ball for the *Strand Magazine*, December, 1911. Here is additional evidence that Watson's trip to the Continent was made in the early summer.

10 *To Holmes I wrote.* "It would appear that [Watson's information] was fairly vital," Mr. Benjamin Clark, Jr., wrote in "Holmes on the Range," "and yet, although he had been advised before leaving to call on Holmes' aid if needed via the Continental wire (at twopence a word), Watson nevertheless saw fit to report his findings by letter. If, however, one feels that Watson was dilatory in this action, how about Holmes? Might he not himself, before sending Watson abroad ('First class tickets and all expenses paid on a princely scale') have tried to get a little information via this same Continental wire? As it turned out, Watson's information could have been produced by telegrams in half the time, and at a fraction of the expense."

11 *my senses were nearly gone.* "This is an unusual incident and Watson must have been unprepared, for in a rough-and-tumble fight he could take care of himself in fast company," Dr. Edward J. Van Liere wrote in "Sherlock Holmes and Doctor Watson, Perennial Athletes." "He had the courage and tenacity of an English bulldog, and, what is more important, knew how to use his strength."

THE FELLOW GAVE A BELLOW OF ANGER AND SPRANG UPON ME LIKE A TIGER.

Illustration by Alec Ball for the *Strand Magazine*, December, 1911.

Could the good people who were her companions not screen her from his violence or his blackmail? What horrible purpose, what deep design, lay behind this long pursuit? There was the problem which I had to solve.

10   To Holmes I wrote showing how rapidly and surely I had got down to the roots of the matter. In reply I had a telegram asking for a description of Dr. Shlessinger's left ear. Holmes' ideas of humour are strange and occasionally offensive, so I took no notice of his ill-timed jest—indeed, I had already reached Montpelier in my pursuit of the maid, Marie, before his message came.

I had no difficulty in finding the ex-servant and in learning all that she could tell me. She was a devoted creature, who had only left her mistress because she was sure that she was in good hands, and because her own approaching marriage made a separation inevitable in any case. Her mistress had, as she confessed with distress, shown some irritability of temper towards her during their stay in Baden, and had even questioned her once as if she had suspicions of her honesty, and this had made the parting easier than it would otherwise have been. Lady Frances had given her fifty pounds as a wedding-present. Like me, Marie viewed with deep distrust the stranger who had driven her mistress from Lausanne. With her own eyes she had seen him seize the lady's wrist with great violence on the public promenade by the lake. He was a fierce and terrible man. She believed that it was out of dread of him that Lady Frances had accepted the escort of the Shlessingers to London. She had never spoken to Marie about it, but many little signs had convinced the maid that her mistress lived in a state of continual nervous apprehension. So far she had got in her narrative, when suddenly she sprang from her chair and her face was convulsed with surprise and fear. "See!" she cried. "The miscreant follows still! There is the very man of whom I speak."

Through the open sitting-room window I saw a huge, swarthy man with a bristling black beard walking slowly down the centre of the street and staring eagerly at the numbers of the houses. It was clear that, like myself, he was on the track of the maid. Acting upon the impulse of the moment, I rushed out and accosted him.

"You are an Englishman," I said.

"What if I am?" he asked, with a most villainous scowl.

"May I ask what your name is?"

"No, you may not," said he, with decision.

The situation was awkward, but the most direct way is often the best.

"Where is the Lady Frances Carfax?" I asked.

He stared at me in amazement.

"What have you done with her? Why have you pursued her? I insist upon an answer!" said I.

The fellow gave a bellow of anger and sprang upon me like a tiger. I have held my own in many a struggle, but the man had a grip of iron and the fury of a fiend. His **11** hand was on my throat and my senses were nearly gone **12** before an unshaven French *ouvrier*, in a blue blouse, darted out from a *cabaret* opposite, with a cudgel in his hand, and struck my assailant a sharp crack over the forearm, which made him leave go his hold. He stood for an instant fuming with rage and uncertain whether he should not renew his attack. Then, with a snarl of anger, he left me and entered the cottage from which I had just come. I turned to thank my preserver, who stood beside me in the roadway.

" Well, Watson," said he, " a very pretty hash you have made of it ! I rather think you had better come back with **13** me to London by the night express."

An hour afterwards Sherlock Holmes, in his usual garb and style, was seated in my private room at the hotel. His explanation of his sudden and opportune appearance was simplicity itself, for, finding that he could get away from **14** London, he determined to head me off at the next obvious point of my travels. In the disguise of a working-man he had sat in the *cabaret* waiting for my appearance.

" And a singularly consistent investigation you have made, my dear Watson," said he. " I cannot at the moment recall any possible blunder which you have omitted. The total effect of your proceedings has been to give the alarm everywhere and yet to discover nothing."

" Perhaps you would have done no better," I answered, **15** bitterly.

" There is no ' perhaps ' about it. I *have* done better. Here is the Hon. Philip Green, who is a fellow-lodger with you in this hotel, and we may find in him the starting-point for a more successful investigation."

A card had come up on a salver, and it was followed by the same bearded ruffian who had attacked me in the street. He started when he saw me.

" What is this, Mr. Holmes ? " he asked. " I had your note and I have come. But what has this man to do with the matter ? "

" This is my old friend and associate, Dr. Watson, who is helping us in this affair."

The stranger held out a huge, sunburned hand, with a few words of apology.

" I hope I didn't harm you. When you accused me of hurting her I lost my grip of myself. Indeed, I'm not responsible in these days. My nerves are like live wires. But this situation is beyond me. What I want to know, in the first place, Mr. Holmes, is, how in the world you came to hear of my existence at all."

" I am in touch with Miss Dobney, Lady Frances' governess."

" Old Susan Dobney with the mob cap ! I remember her well."

" And she remembers you. It was in the days before— before you found it better to go to South Africa."

" Ah, I see you know my whole story. I need hide nothing from you. I swear to you, Mr. Holmes, that there never was in this world a man who loved a woman with a more whole-hearted love than I had for Frances. I was a wild youngster, I know—not worse than others of my class. But her mind was pure as snow. She could not bear a shadow of coarseness. So, when she came to hear of things that I had done, she would have no more to

12 ouvrier. French: workman.

13 *"a very pretty hash you have made of it!* "If Holmes' conduct of the case up to now has been illogical," Mr. Benjamin Clark, Jr., wrote, "it assumes aspects from here on that are both illogical and bizarre. So far as the detective knows, the Lady Frances Carfax was last seen headed for London in the company of, as Holmes strongly suspects . . . one Holy Peters—that is, the Rev. Shlessinger. Under these circumstances, why should Holmes take such pains to conceal his identity in Montpellier? Surely there was no reason for believing that Peters was anywhere near that city, and yet the detective chose this moment to indulge his craving for fancy dress by disguising himself as a French workman. Was his only purpose in doing so to have the pleasure of startling Watson? Certainly one can think of no other plausible reason."

14 *was simplicity itself.* "Of Holmes' next move," Mr. Clark continued, "we can only say, like Alice, 'curiouser and curiouser,' for certainly it is an extraordinary *non sequitur* for the detective, having just received information from Watson placing the Lady Frances in London with the Shlessingers, to up and *leave* London."

15 *"Perhaps you would have done no better.* "Now the facts of the matter are" (we are still quoting Mr. Benjamin Clark, Jr.) "that if poor Watson had not been so in awe of the detective he could have availed himself of an unparalleled opportunity to indulge in one of his rare flashes of . . . 'pawky humour,' instead of his feeble 'perhaps you would have done no better.' What Watson could have said would have been something along the following lines: 'Holmes, your accusations are so easily refuted that it is ridiculous. In the first place, I have picked up the Lady Frances' trail. I have found out in whose company she left Baden for London. What is more, if what I have discovered is true, I have given no alarm, because the criminals left the Continent over three weeks ago. You, on the other hand, for some obscure reason of your own, have seen fit to completely disregard my information placing the Lady Frances in London, and you now appear in Montpellier unaccountably disguised as a French *ouvrier*. You must have good reasons for acting in this strange fashion, but at the moment they escape me.'"

16 *Barberton.* A gold-mining town in the Transvaal, South Africa.

say to me. And yet she loved me—that is the wonder of it !—loved me well enough to remain single all her sainted days just for my sake alone. When the years had passed

16 and I had made my money at Barberton I thought perhaps I could seek her out and soften her. I had heard that she was still unmarried. I found her at Lausanne, and tried all I knew. She weakened, I think, but her will was strong, and when next I called she had left the town. I traced her to Baden, and then after a time heard that her maid was here. I'm a rough fellow, fresh from a rough life, and when Dr. Watson spoke to me as he did I lost hold of myself for a moment. But for God's sake tell me what has become of the Lady Frances."

" That is for us to find out," said Sherlock Holmes, with peculiar gravity. " What is your London address, Mr. Green ? "

" The Langham Hotel will find me."

" Then may I recommend that you return there and be on hand in case I should want you ? I have no desire to encourage false hopes, but you may rest assured that all that can be done will be done for the safety of Lady Frances. I can say no more for the instant. I will leave you this card so that you may be able to keep in touch with us. Now, Watson, if you will pack your bag I will cable to Mrs. Hudson to make one of her best efforts for two hungry travellers at seven-thirty to-morrow."

A telegram was awaiting us when we reached our Baker Street rooms, which Holmes read with an exclamation of interest and threw across to me. " Jagged or torn," was the message, and the place of origin Baden.

" What is this ? " I asked.

" It is everything," Holmes answered. " You may remember my seemingly irrelevant question as to this clerical gentleman's left ear. You did not answer it."

" I had left Baden, and could not inquire."

" Exactly. For this reason I sent a duplicate to the manager of the Englischer Hof, whose answer lies here."

" What does it show ? "

" It shows, my dear Watson, that we are dealing with an exceptionally astute and dangerous man. The Rev. Dr. Shlessinger, missionary from South America, is none other than Holy Peters, one of the most unscrupulous rascals that Australia has ever evolved—and for a young country it has turned out some very finished types. His particular speciality is the beguiling of lonely ladies by playing upon their religious feelings, and his so-called wife, an Englishwoman named Fraser, is a worthy helpmate. The nature of his tactics suggested his identity to me, and this physical peculiarity—he was badly bitten in a saloon-fight at Adelaide in '89—confirmed my suspicion. This poor lady is in the hands of a most infernal couple, who will stick at nothing, Watson. That she is already dead is a very likely supposition. If not, she is undoubtedly in some sort of confinement, and unable to write to Miss Dobney or her other friends. It is always possible that she never reached London, or that she has passed through it, but the former is improbable, as, with their system of registration, it is not easy for foreigners to play tricks with the Continental police ; and the latter is also unlikely, as these rogues could not hope to find any other place where it would be as easy to keep a person under restraint.   All my instincts tell me that she is in London, but, as we have at present no possible means of telling where, we can only take the obvious steps, eat our dinner, and possess our souls in patience.   Later in the evening I will stroll down and have a word with friend Lestrade at Scotland Yard.''

But neither the official police nor Holmes' own small, but very efficient, organization sufficed to clear away the mystery.   Amid the crowded millions of London the three persons we sought were as completely obliterated as if they had never lived.   Advertisements were tried, and failed. Clues were followed, and led to nothing.   Every criminal resort which Shlessinger might frequent was drawn in vain.   His old associates were watched, but they kept clear of him.   And then suddenly, after a week of helpless suspense, there came a flash of light.   A silver-and-brilliant pendant of old Spanish design had been pawned at Bevington's, in Westminster Road.   The pawner was a large, clean-shaven man of clerical appearance.   His name and address were demonstrably false.   The ear had escaped notice, but the description was surely that of Shlessinger.

Three times had our bearded friend from the Langham called for news—the third time within an hour of this fresh development.   His clothes were getting looser on his great body.   He seemed to be wilting away in his anxiety. '' If you will only give me something to do ! '' was his constant wail.   At last Holmes could oblige him.

'' He has begun to pawn the jewels.   We should get him now.''

'' But does this mean that any harm has befallen the Lady Frances ? ''

Holmes shook his head very gravely.

'' Supposing that they have held her prisoner up to now, it is clear that they cannot let her loose without their own destruction.   We must prepare for the worst.''

'' What can I do ? ''

'' These people do not know you by sight ? ''

'' No.''

'' It is possible that he will go to some other pawnbroker in the future.   In that case, we must begin again.   On the other hand, he has had a fair price and no questions asked, so if he is in need of ready money he will probably come back to Bevington's.   I will give you a note to them, and they will let you wait in the shop.   If the fellow comes you will follow him home.   But no indiscretion, and, **17** above all, no violence.   I put you on your honour that you will take no step without my knowledge and consent.''

For two days the Hon. Philip Green (he was, I may mention, the son of the famous admiral of that name who commanded the Sea of Azof fleet in the Crimean War) brought us no news.   On the evening of the third he rushed into our sitting-room, pale, trembling, with every muscle of his powerful frame quivering with excitement.

'' We have him !   We have him ! '' he cried.

He was incoherent in his agitation.   Holmes soothed him with a few words, and thrust him into an arm-chair.

17 *you will follow him home.* "One might query this use of the Honourable Philip Green to detect Holy Peters on his expected second visit to the pawnshop, inasmuch as, of all concerned in the case, he, it would appear, was the most likely to have been seen by the Shlessingers on the Continent," Mr. Benjamin Clark, Jr., wrote. "The selection of Green must have been quite a slap in the face to Scotland Yard, whose men Holmes apparently did not consider good enough for the job, and may possibly explain the unconscionable delay shortly after in the procuring of a search warrant—a delay which . . . came close to costing the Lady Frances her life."

"WE HAVE HIM! WE HAVE HIM!" HE CRIED.

Illustration by Alec Ball for the *Strand Magazine*, December, 1911.

" Come, now, give us the order of events," said he.

" She came only an hour ago. It was the wife, this time, but the pendant she brought was the fellow of the other. She is a tall, pale woman, with ferret eyes."

" That is the lady," said Holmes.

" She left the office and I followed her. She walked up the Kennington Road, and I kept behind her. Presently she went into a shop. Mr. Holmes, it was an undertaker's."

My companion started. " Well ? " he asked, in that vibrant voice which told of the fiery soul behind the cold, grey face.

" She was talking to the woman behind the counter. I entered as well. ' It is late,' I heard her say, or words to that effect. The woman was excusing herself. ' It should be there before now,' she answered. ' It took longer, being out of the ordinary.' They both stopped and looked at me, so I asked some question and then left the shop."

" You did excellently well. What happened next ? "

" The woman came out, but I had hid myself in a doorway. Her suspicions had been aroused, I think, for she looked round her. Then she called a cab and got in. I was lucky enough to get another and so to follow her. She got down at last at No. 36 Poultney Square, Brixton. I drove past, left my cab at the corner of the square, and watched the house."

" Did you see anyone ? "

" The windows were all in darkness save one on the lower floor. The blind was down, and I could not see in. I was standing there, wondering what I should do next, when a covered van drove up with two men in it. They descended, took something out of the van, and carried it up the steps to the hall door. Mr. Holmes, it was a coffin."

" Ah ! "

" For an instant I was on the point of rushing in. The door had been opened to admit the men and their burden. It was the woman who had opened it. But as I stood there she caught a glimpse of me, and I think that she recognized me. I saw her start, and she hastily closed the door. I remembered my promise to you, and here I am."

" You have done excellent work," said Holmes, scribbling a few words upon a half-sheet of paper. " We can do nothing legal without a warrant, and you can serve the cause best by taking this note down to the authorities and getting one. There may be some difficulty, but I should think that the sale of the jewellery should be sufficient. Lestrade will see to all details."

" But they may murder her in the meanwhile. What could the coffin mean, and for whom could it be but for her ? "

" We will do all that can be done, Mr. Green. Not a moment will be lost. Leave it in our hands. Now, Watson," he added, as our client hurried away, " he will set the regular forces on the move. We are, as usual, the irregulars, and we must take our own line of action. The situation strikes me as so desperate that the most extreme measures are justified. Not a moment is to be lost in **18** getting to Poultney Square."

18 *Not a moment is to be lost in getting to Poultney Square.*" Noting that "Holmes did not use the telephone in order to alert someone who could have reached Poultney Square more promptly than they could," Dr. Theodore Gibson of the University of Virginia, in a letter to Mr. Michael Kaser, pointed out that he was not inclined to date "The Disappearance of Lady Frances Carfax" subsequent to July, 1898 ("The Adventure of the Retired Colourman"), by which time, as we know, a telephone had been installed at 221B Baker Street. Dr. Gibson has certainly put his finger on an important clue, and one which has led Mr. Kaser to date "The Disappearance of Lady Frances Carfax" to the early summer of 1897.

" Let us try to reconstruct the situation," said he, as we drove swiftly past the Houses of Parliament and over Westminster Bridge. " These villains have coaxed this unhappy lady to London, after first alienating her from her faithful maid. If she has written any letters they have been intercepted. Through some confederate they have engaged a furnished house. Once inside it, they have made her a prisoner, and they have become possessed of the valuable jewellery which has been their object from the first. Already they have begun to sell part of it, which seems safe enough to them, since they have no reason to think that anyone is interested in the lady's fate. When **19** she is released she will, of course, denounce them. Therefore, she must not be released. But they cannot keep her under lock and key for ever. So murder is their only solution."

" That seems very clear."

" Now we will take another line of reasoning. When you follow two separate chains of thought, Watson, you will find some point of intersection which should approximate to the truth. We will start now, not from the lady, but from the coffin, and argue backwards. That incident proves, I fear, beyond all doubt that the lady is dead. It points also to an orthodox burial with proper accompaniment of medical certificate and official sanction. Had the lady been obviously murdered, they would have buried her in a hole in the back garden. But here all is open and regular. What does that mean ? Surely that they have done her to death in some way which has deceived the doctor, and simulated a natural end—poisoning, perhaps. And yet how strange that they should ever let a doctor approach her unless he were a confederate, which is hardly a credible proposition."

" Could they have forged a medical certificate ? "

" Dangerous, Watson, very dangerous. No, I hardly see them doing that. Pull up, cabby ! This is evidently the undertaker's, for we have just passed the pawnbroker's. Would you go in, Watson ? Your appearance inspires confidence. Ask what hour the Poultney Square funeral takes place to-morrow."

The woman in the shop answered me without hesitation that it was to be at eight o'clock in the morning.

" You see, Watson, no mystery ; everything aboveboard ! In some way the legal forms have undoubtedly been complied with, and they think that they have little to fear. Well, there's nothing for it now but a direct frontal attack. Are you armed ? "

" My stick ! "

" Well, well, we shall be strong enough. 'Thrice is he armed who hath his quarrel just.' We simply can't afford **20** to wait for the police, or to keep within the four corners of the law. You can drive off, cabby. Now, Watson, we'll just take our luck together, as we have occasionally done in the past."

He had rung loudly at the door of a great dark house in the centre of Poultney Square. It was opened immediately, and the figure of a tall woman was outlined against the dim-lit hall.

" Well, what do you want ? " she asked, sharply, peering at us through the darkness.

19 *they have no reason to think that anyone is interested in the lady's fate.* "No reason to think anyone is interested in the lady's fate!" Mr. Benjamin Clark, Jr., wrote. "Why, for a week, Holmes, with what he describes as his own small but very efficient organization, together with Scotland Yard, has been investigating, advertising, combing Shlessinger's haunt, watching his old associates, and heaven knows what else. . . . No! If Peters failed to be alarmed under the above-described conditions, he certainly does not deserve the title of astute. Nor was it astute to pawn the two pendants, and separately at that, thereby running a double risk which in the end was his undoing. As a matter of fact, if Peters had not outbungled Holmes, the Lady Frances would have long since been buried before the detective ever reached the scene."

20 '*Thrice is he armed who hath his quarrel just.*' Holmes quotes from *King Henry VI*, Act III, Scene 2, line 233.

"THERE IS SURELY SOME MISTAKE HERE, GENTLEMEN,"
HE SAID . . .

Illustration by Frederic Dorr Steele for the *American Magazine*, December, 1911.

HOLMES HALF DREW A REVOLVER FROM HIS POCKET

Illustration by Alec Ball for the *Strand Magazine*, December, 1911.

" I want to speak to Dr. Shlessinger," said Holmes.

" There is no such person here," she answered, and tried to close the door, but Holmes had jammed it with his foot.

" Well, I want to see the man who lives here, whatever he may call himself," said Holmes, firmly.

She hesitated. Then she threw open the door. " Well, come in ! " said she. " My husband is not afraid to face any man in the world." She closed the door behind us, and showed us into a sitting-room on the right side of the hall, turning up the gas as she left us. " Mr. Peters will be with you in an instant," she said.

Her words were literally true, for we had hardly time to look round the dusty and moth-eaten apartment in which we found ourselves before the door opened and a big, clean-shaven, bald-headed man stepped lightly into the room. He had a large red face, with pendulous cheeks, and a general air of superficial benevolence which was marred by a cruel, vicious mouth.

" There is surely some mistake here, gentlemen," he said, in an unctuous, make-everything-easy voice. " I fancy that you have been misdirected. Possibly if you tried farther down the street——"

" That will do ; we have no time to waste," said my companion, firmly. " You are Henry Peters, of Adelaide, late the Rev. Dr. Shlessinger, of Baden and SouthAmerica. I am as sure of that as that my own name is Sherlock Holmes."

Peters, as I will now call him, started and stared hard at his formidable pursuer. " I guess your name does not frighten me, Mr. Holmes," said he, coolly. " When a man's conscience is easy you can't rattle him. What is your business in my house ? "

" I want to know what you have done with the Lady Frances Carfax, whom you brought away with you from Baden."

" I'd be very glad if you could tell me where that lady may be," Peters answered, coolly. " I've a bill against her for nearly a hundred pounds, and nothing to show for it but a couple of trumpery pendants that the dealer would hardly look at. She attached herself to Mrs. Peters and me at Baden (it is a fact that I was using another name at the time), and she stuck on to us until we came to London. I paid her bill and her ticket. Once in London, she gave us the slip, and, as I say, left these out-of-date jewels to pay her bills. You find her, Mr. Holmes, and I'm your debtor."

" *I mean* to find her," said Sherlock Holmes. " I'm going through this house till I do find her."

" Where is your warrant ? "

Holmes half drew a revolver from his pocket. " This will have to serve till a better one comes."

" Why, you are a common burglar."

" So you might describe me," said Holmes, cheerfully. " My companion is also a dangerous ruffian. And together we are going through your house."

Our opponent opened the door.

" Fetch a policeman, Annie ! " said he. There was a

whisk of feminine skirts down the passage, and the hall door was opened and shut.

" Our time is limited, Watson," said Holmes. " If you try to stop us, Peters, you will most certainly get hurt. Where is that coffin which was brought into your house ? "

" What do you want with the coffin ? It is in use. There is a body in it."

" I must see that body."

" Never with my consent."

" Then without it." With a quick movement Holmes pushed the fellow to one side and passed into the hall. A door half-open stood immediately before us. We entered. It was the dining-room. On the table, under a half-lit chandelier, the coffin was lying. Holmes turned up the gas and raised the lid. Deep down in the recesses of the coffin lay an emaciated figure. The glare from the lights above beat down upon an aged and withered face. By no possible process of cruelty, starvation, or disease could this worn-out wreck be the still beautiful Lady Frances. Holmes' face showed his amazement, and also his relief.

" Thank God ! " he muttered. " It's someone else."

" Ah, you've blundered badly for once, Mr. Sherlock Holmes," said Peters, who had followed us into the room.

" Who is this dead woman ? "

" Well, if you really must know, she is an old nurse of my wife's, Rose Spender her name, whom we found in the Brixton Workhouse Infirmary. We brought her round here, called in Dr. Horsom, of 13 Firbank Villas— mind you take the address, Mr. Holmes—and had her carefully tended, as Christian folk should. On the third day she died—certificate says senile decay—but that's only the doctor's opinion, and, of course, you know better. We ordered her funeral to be carried out by Stimson & Co., of the Kennington Road, who will bury her at eight o'clock to-morrow morning. Can you pick any hole in that, Mr. Holmes ? You've made a silly blunder, and you may as well own up to it. I'd give something for a photograph of your gaping, staring face when you pulled aside that lid expecting to see the Lady Frances Carfax, and only found a poor old woman of ninety."

Holmes' expression was as impassive as ever under the jeers of his antagonist, but his clenched hands betrayed his acute annoyance.

" I am going through your house," said he.

" Are you, though ! " cried Peters, as a woman's voice and heavy steps sounded in the passage. " We'll soon see about that. This way, officers, if you please. These men have forced their way into my house, and I cannot get rid of them. Help me to put them out."

A sergeant and a constable stood in the doorway. Holmes drew his card from his case.

" This is my name and address. This is my friend, Dr. Watson."

" Bless you, sir, we know you very well," said the sergeant, " but you can't stay here without a warrant."

" Of course not. I quite understand that."

" Arrest him ! " cried Peters.

" We know where to lay our hands on this gentleman if he is wanted," said the sergeant, majestically ; " but you'll have to go, Mr. Holmes."

" Yes, Watson, we shall have to go."

A minute later we were in the street once more. Holmes was as cool as ever, but I was hot with anger and humiliation. The sergeant had followed us.

" Sorry, Mr. Holmes, but that's the law."

" Exactly, sergeant ; you could not do otherwise."

" I expect there was good reason for your presence there. If there is anything I can do——"

" It's a missing lady, sergeant, and we think she is in that house. I expect a warrant presently."

" Then I'll keep my eye on the parties, Mr. Holmes. If anything comes along, I will surely let you know."

It was only nine o'clock, and we were off full cry upon the trail at once. First we drove to Brixton Workhouse Infirmary, where we found that it was indeed the truth that a charitable couple had called some days before, that they had claimed an imbecile old woman as a former servant, and that they had obtained permission to take her away with them. No surprise was expressed at the news that she had since died.

The doctor was our next goal. He had been called in, had found the woman dying of pure senility, had actually seen her pass away, and had signed the certificate in due form. " I assure you that everything was perfectly normal and there was no room for foul play in the matter," said he. Nothing in the house had struck him as suspicious, save that for people of their class it was remarkable that they should have no servant. So far and no farther went the doctor.

Finally, we found our way to Scotland Yard. There had been difficulties of procedure in regard to the warrant. Some delay was inevitable. The magistrate's signature might not be obtained until next morning. If Holmes would call about nine he could go down with Lestrade and see it acted upon. So ended the day, save that near midnight our friend, the sergeant, called to say that he had seen flickering lights here and there in the windows of the great dark house, but that no one had left it and none had entered. We could but pray for patience, and wait for the morrow.

Sherlock Holmes was too irritable for conversation and too restless for sleep. I left him smoking hard, with his heavy, dark brows knotted together, and his long, nervous fingers tapping upon the arms of his chair, as he turned over in his mind every possible solution of the mystery. Several times in the course of the night I heard him prowling about the house. Finally, just after I had been called in the morning, he rushed into my room. He was in his dressing-gown, but his pale, hollow-eyed face told me that his night had been a sleepless one.

" What time was the funeral ? Eight, was it not ? " he asked, eagerly. " Well, it is seven-twenty now. Good heavens, Watson, what has become of any brains that God has given me ? Quick, man, quick ! It's life or death—a hundred chances on death to one on life. I'll never forgive myself, never, if we are too late ! "

Five minutes had not passed before we were flying in a hansom down Baker Street. But even so it was twenty-five to eight as we passed Big Ben, and eight struck as we tore down the Brixton Road. But others were late as well as we. Ten minutes after the hour the hearse was still standing at the door of the house, and even as our foaming horse came to a halt the coffin, supported by three men, appeared on the threshold. Holmes darted forward and barred their way.

" Take it back ! " he cried, laying his hand on the breast of the foremost. " Take it back this instant ! "

" What the devil do you mean ? Once again I ask you, where is your warrant ? " shouted the furious Peters, his big red face glaring over the farther end of the coffin.

" The warrant is on its way. This coffin shall remain in the house until it comes."

The authority in Holmes' voice had its effect upon the bearers. Peters had suddenly vanished into the house, and they obeyed these new orders. " Quick, Watson, quick ! Here is a screw-driver ! " he shouted, as the coffin was replaced upon the table. " Here's one for you, my man : a sovereign if the lid comes off in a minute ! Ask no questions—work away ! That's good ! Another ! And another ! Now pull all together ! It's giving ! It's giving ! Ah, that does it at last ! "

With a united effort we tore off the coffin-lid. As we did so there came from the inside a stupefying and over-powering smell of chloroform. A body lay within, its head all wreathed in cotton-wool, which had been soaked in the narcotic. Holmes plucked it off and disclosed the statuesque face of a handsome and spiritual woman of middle age. In an instant he had passed his arm round the figure and raised her to a sitting position.

" Is she gone, Watson ? Is there a spark left ? Surely we are not too late ! "

For half an hour it seemed that we were. What with actual suffocation, and what with the poisonous fumes of the chloroform, the Lady Frances seemed to have passed the last point of recall. And then, at last, with artificial respiration, with injected ether, with every device that **21** science could suggest, some flutter of life, some quiver of the eyelids, some dimming of a mirror, spoke of the slowly returning life. A cab had driven up, and Holmes, parting the blind, looked out at it. " Here is Lestrade with his warrant," said he. " He will find that his birds have flown. And here," he added, as a heavy step hurried along the passage, " is someone who has a better right to nurse this lady than we have. Good morning, Mr. Green ; I think that the sooner we can move the Lady Frances the better. Meanwhile, the funeral may proceed, and the poor old woman who still lies in that coffin may go to her last resting-place alone."

" Should you care to add the case to your annals, my dear Watson," said Holmes that evening, " it can only be as an example of that temporary eclipse to which even the best-balanced mind may be exposed. Such slips are com-mon to all mortals, and the greatest is he who can recog-nize and repair them. To this modified credit I may, per-haps, make some claim. My night was haunted by the thought that somewhere a clue, a strange sentence, a

21 *with injected ether.* "This . . . was rather startling treatment for a patient already over-dosed with chloroform," Dr. Samuel R. Meaker noted in "Watson Medicus."

HOLMES DARTED FORWARD AND BARRED THEIR WAY.

Illustration by Alec Ball for the *Strand Magazine*, December, 1911.

22 *A clever device, Watson.* "'Unusual' might have been a better adjective," Mr. Benjamin Clark, Jr., wrote. "Surely it was a device with truly extraordinary risks. In the first place, the extraction from the workhouse had to be done in an innocent and plausible manner. Then it was important that the Shlessingers pick an inmate who had to be, one might say, 'just right'—not yet dead, but *awful close;* and yet not so close but what she could be moved. A very 'nice' calculation, all things considered." Mr. Clark was forced to conclude that Holmes in this adventure was still feeling the effect of the deadly fumes of *radix pedis diaboli* ("The Adventure of the Devil's Foot")—another vote, it would seem, for dating "The Disappearance of Lady Frances Carfax" in the early summer of 1897.

Bibliographical Note: The original manuscript of this adventure, about 7,500 words in 28 pages, 4to, white vellum, was auctioned in New York City on February 5, 1929, bringing $285. Its present location is unknown.

curious observation, had come under my notice and had been too easily dismissed. Then, suddenly, in the grey of the morning, the words came back to me. It was the remark of the undertaker's wife, as reported by Philip Green. She had said, ' It should be there before now. It took longer, being out of the ordinary.' It was the coffin of which she spoke. It had been out of the ordinary. That could only mean that it had been made to some special measurement. But why ? Why ? Then in an instant I remembered the deep sides, and the little wasted figure at the bottom. Why so large a coffin for so small a body ? To leave room for another body. Both would be buried under the one certificate. It had all been so clear, if only my own sight had not been dimmed. At eight the Lady Frances would be buried. Our one chance was to stop the coffin before it left the house.

" It was a desperate chance that we might find her alive, but it *was* a chance, as the result showed. These people had never, to my knowledge, done a murder. They might shrink from actual violence at the last. They could bury her with no sign of how she met her end, and even if she were exhumed there was a chance for them. I hoped that such considerations might prevail with them. You can reconstruct the scene well enough. You saw the horrible den upstairs, where the poor lady had been kept so long. They rushed in and overpowered her with their chloroform, carried her down, poured more into the coffin to ensure against her waking, and then screwed down the **22** lid. A clever device, Watson. It is new to me in the annals of crime. If our ex-missionary friends escape the clutches of Lestrade, I shall expect to hear of some brilliant incidents in their future career."

. . .

. . . FOR ANSWER HE HAD SHOT HIS LONG, THIN, NERVOUS ARM OUT OF THE SHEETS . . .

Illustration by Howard K. Elcock for the *Strand Magazine*, February, 1925.

70

THE ADVENTURE OF THE ILLUSTRIOUS CLIENT

[*Wednesday, September 3, to Tuesday, September 16, 1902*]

"IT can't hurt now," was Mr. Sherlock Holmes' comment when, for the tenth time in as many years, I asked his leave to reveal the following **1** narrative. So it was that at last I obtained permission to put on record what was, in some ways, the supreme moment of my friend's career. **2**

Both Holmes and I had a weakness for the Turkish Bath. It was over a smoke in the pleasant lassitude of the drying-room that I have found him less reticent and more human than anywhere else. On the upper floor of the Northumberland Avenue establishment there is an **3** isolated corner where two couches lie side by side, and it was on these that we lay upon September 3, 1902, the **4** day when my narrative begins. I had asked him whether anything was stirring, and for answer he had shot his long, thin, nervous arm out of the sheets which enveloped him and had drawn an envelope from the inside pocket of the coat which hung beside him.

" It may be some fussy, self-important fool, it may be a matter of life or death," said he, as he handed me the note. " I know no more than this message tells me."

It was from the Carlton Club, and dated the evening before. This is what I read :

" Sir James Damery presents his compliments to Mr. Sherlock Holmes, and will call upon him at 4.30 to-morrow. Sir James begs to say that the matter upon which he desires to consult Mr. Holmes is very delicate, and also very important. He trusts, therefore, that Mr. Holmes will make every effort to grant this interview, and that he will confirm it over the telephone to the Carlton Club."

" I need not say that I have confirmed it, Watson," said Holmes, as I returned the paper. " Do you know anything of this man Damery ? "

" Only that his name is a household word in Society."

" Well, I can tell you a little more than that. He has rather a reputation for arranging delicate matters which are to be kept out of the papers. You may remember his negotiations with Sir George Lewis over the Hammerford Will case. He is a man of the world with a natural

1 *for the tenth time in as many years.* Watson presumably chronicled "The Adventure of the Illustrious Client" in 1912, although it was not published until twelve years after that.

2 *the supreme moment of my friend's career.* Watson exaggerates when he calls this adventure the supreme moment of Holmes' career. As Mr. T. S. Blakeney wrote in *Sherlock Holmes: Fact or Fiction?*: "Baron Gruner had achieved a European reputation, it is true, but the successful breaking off of his engagement with Miss de Merville can hardly be considered as of prime importance save to the small circle of individuals concerned. If, as Watson is probably implying, it was the exalted standing of the Illustrious Client that gave the case its significance, there could only be one person in England whose position would suit the requirements, and seeing that that person's interests were only involved as a matter of friendly concern, we cannot surely rate this case above the services rendered by Holmes to the nation in 'The Naval Treaty,' 'The Second Stain,' or 'The Bruce-Partington Plans,' or to the royal houses of Holland, Scandinavia and Bohemia. Indeed, from what we learn of Baron Gruner, he was not in the same class as Professor Moriarty or even Colonel Moran, nor did he give Holmes so good a run for his money as did Stapleton."

3 *the Northumberland Avenue establishment.* Identified by Mr. Michael Harrison (*In the Footsteps of Sherlock Holmes*) as Nevill's, at the corner of Craven Passage. Before 7 P.M. Holmes and Watson would have paid 3s 6d. (about 87½¢) each; after, the charge would have been reduced to 2s (50¢).

4 *September 3, 1902.* A Wednesday.

THE BIG, MASTERFUL ARISTOCRAT DOMINATED
THE LITTLE ROOM.

"The go-between used by the illustrious client was
an arranger of delicate matters, and as such, may
have been descended from Sir Amery of Pavia, the
Lombard, who also tried to arrange a very delicate
matter—the betrayal of Calais to the French in
1348," Dr. Julian Wolff wrote in his *Practical
Handbook of Sherlockian Heraldry*. "His story
appears in both Conan Doyle's *Sir Nigel* and in
Froissart's *Chronycles*. . . . It seems more worthy
of belief, however, that Sir James was descended
from an honourable man, Sir Thomas Dammery,
who was knighted by the Duke of Lancaster in the
Spanish war, as related by Froissart. His arms were
blazoned: Barry wavy argent and gules, a bend
or."

COLONEL DAMERY THREW UP HIS KID-GLOVED HANDS
WITH A LAUGH.

Illustration by Howard K. Elcock for the *Strand
Magazine*, February, 1925.

turn for diplomacy. I am bound, therefore, to hope
that it is not a false scent and that he has some real
need for our assistance."

" Our ? "

" Well, if you will be so good, Watson."

" I shall be honoured."

" Then you have the hour—four-thirty. Until then
we can put the matter out of our heads."

5   I was living in my own rooms in Queen Anne Street
at the time, but I was round at Baker Street before the
time named. Sharp to the half-hour, Colonel Sir James
Damery was announced. It is hardly necessary to describe him, for many will remember that large, bluff,
honest personality, that broad, clean-shaven face, above
all, that pleasant, mellow voice. Frankness shone from
his grey Irish eyes, and good humour played round his
mobile, smiling lips. His lucent top-hat, his dark frock-
coat, indeed, every detail, from the pearl pin in the black
satin cravat to the lavender spats over the varnished shoes,
spoke of the meticulous care in dress for which he was
famous. The big, masterful aristocrat dominated the
little room.

" Of course, I was prepared to find Dr. Watson," he
remarked, with a courteous bow. " His collaboration
may be very necessary, for we are dealing on this occasion, Mr. Holmes, with a man to whom violence is familiar and who will, literally, stick at nothing. I should
say that there is no more dangerous man in Europe."

" I have had several opponents to whom that flattering term has been applied," said Holmes, with a smile.
" Don't you smoke ? Then you will excuse me if I
6 light my pipe. If your man is more dangerous than
the late Professor Moriarty, or than the living Colonel
7 Sebastian Moran, then he is indeed worth meeting.
May I ask his name ? "

" Have you ever heard of Baron Gruner ? "

" You mean the Austrian murderer ? "

Colonel Damery threw up his kid-gloved hands with
a laugh. " There is no getting past you, Mr. Holmes !
Wonderful ! So you have already sized him up as a
murderer ? "

" It is my business to follow the details of Continental
crime. Who could possibly have read what happened
at Prague and have any doubts as to the man's guilt ! It
was a purely technical legal point and the suspicious
death of a witness that saved him ! I am as sure that
he killed his wife when the so-called ' accident ' happened
8 in the Splügen Pass as if I had seen him do it. I knew,
also, that he had come to England, and had a presentiment that sooner or later he would find me some work to
do. Well, what has Baron Gruner been up to ? I presume it is not this old tragedy which has come up again ? "

" No, it is more serious than that. To revenge crime
is important, but to prevent it is more so. It is a terrible
thing, Mr. Holmes, to see a dreadful event, an atrocious
situation, preparing itself before your eyes, to clearly
understand whither it will lead and yet to be utterly
unable to avert it. Can a human being be placed in a
more trying position ? "

"Perhaps not."

"Then you will sympathize with the client in whose interests I am acting."

"I did not understand that you were merely an intermediary. Who is the principal?"

"Mr. Holmes, I must beg you not to press that question. It is important that I should be able to assure him that his honoured name has been in no way dragged into the matter. His motives are, to the last degree, honourable and chivalrous, but he prefers to remain unknown. I need not say that your fees will be assured and that you will be given a perfectly free hand. Surely the actual name of your client is immaterial?"

"I am sorry," said Holmes. "I am accustomed to have mystery at one end of my cases, but to have it at both ends is too confusing. I fear, Sir James, that I must decline to act."

Our visitor was greatly disturbed. His large, sensitive face was darkened with emotion and disappointment.

"You hardly realize the effect of your own action, Mr. Holmes," said he. "You place me in a most serious dilemma, for I am perfectly certain that you would be proud to take over the case if I could give you the facts, and yet a promise forbids me from revealing them all. May I, at least, lay all that I can before you?"

"By all means, so long as it is understood that I commit myself to nothing."

"That is understood. In the first place, you have no doubt heard of General de Merville?"

"De Merville of Khyber fame? Yes, I have heard of him."

"He has a daughter, Violet de Merville, young, rich, beautiful, accomplished, a wonder-woman in every way. It is this daughter, this lovely, innocent girl, whom we are endeavouring to save from the clutches of a fiend."

"Baron Gruner has some hold over her, then?"

"The strongest of all holds where a woman is concerned—the hold of love. The fellow is, as you may have heard, extraordinarily handsome, with a most fascinating manner, a gentle voice, and that air of romance and mystery which means so much to a woman. He is said to have the whole sex at his mercy and to have made ample use of the fact."

"But how came such a man to meet a lady of the standing of Miss Violet de Merville?"

"DE MERVILLE OF KHYBER FAME?"

"Indian and Afghan wars in the nineteenth century produced many great English soldiers," Dr. Julian Wolff wrote in his *Practical Handbook of Sherlockian Heraldry*. "The entry under the name of one of the Goughs in a standard work of reference possibly indicates he whom Dr. Watson had in mind when he wrote of General de Merville: K.C.B., C.B.; entered the Bengal cavalry as cornet in 1848; colonel in 1875; Punjab campaign; battle of Chilian Wallah; Indian mutiny, capture at Delhi and Lucknow; commanded a brigade at Jugdullak Pass during Afghan War, V.C.; brigadier-general, 1881. The slight discrepancy between Jugdullak Pass and Khyber Pass, mentioned by Holmes, is just sufficient to give the identification the proper Canonical touch . . . The arms: a lion passant on a fess between three boars' heads couped. The tinctures differ for each branch of the family."

5 *my own rooms in Queen Anne Street*. Another sure indication that Watson is preparing the reader to hear of another marriage. The new address, Queen Anne Street, with Weymouth Street and Portland Place, are suburbs of Harley Street, the highest *geographical qualification* for a doctor in London. "That very citadel of medicine," Dr. Vernon Pennell calls the area in his "Resumé of the Medical Life of John H. Watson, M.D., Late of the Army Medical Department"; he adds that even today "the ability to pay rent for the occasional use of a room and a half, and part salary of a receptionist in Harley Street or Queen Anne Street is considered by many of the lay public to be the highest qualification that medicine or surgery has to offer."

6 *Then you will excuse me if I light my pipe.* "This case provides one of the best examples of Holmes' subtle wit, directed, in this instance, at Colonel James Damery, though ineffectively, as it turned out, because of that worthy's impenetrable stuffiness," Mr. Bliss Austin wrote in "Three Footnotes to 'The Adventure of the Illustrious Client.'" "The appearance of this fop must have been enough to tempt any man of Holmes' sensitivity. Thus, it is recorded that he wore a lucent top-hat, a dark frock coat, a black satin cravat complete with pearl pin and—believe it or not—lavender spats over varnished shoes. But what of his manners? Judge for yourself. It is stated that on meeting Holmes and Watson, he made a courteous bow —nothing more. Later, after a bit of conversation, we learn that 'Colonel Damery threw up his kid-gloved hands with a laugh.' Imagine it! The elegant lout had not yet removed his gloves, from which one infers that he did not altogether approve of the general state of cleanliness at 221B, Baker Street; also, that he had not shaken hands with Holmes. One would hardly expect Sherlock to overlook these nuances and he did not, for one finds him baiting the Colonel. 'Don't you smoke?' he asks slyly. The trap was not obvious but it was there. Unless the Colonel refused altogether, he must either remove his gloves or treat Holmes to the delicious sight of a man in lavender spats smoking with kid gloves on. But refuse he did, so Holmes continued: 'Then you will excuse me if I light my pipe.' And one can be certain that he smiled as he said it."

7 *the living Colonel Sebastian Moran.* Mr. O. F. Grazebrook, writing in "Royalty," states his conviction that Watson's phrase "the supreme moment of my friend's career" dates "The Adventure of the Illustrious Client" *before* "The Adventure of the Bruce-Partington Plans" (November, 1895), and that Holmes' phrase "the living Sebastian Moran" dates the adventure *shortly after* "The Adventure of the Empty House" (April, 1894). Watson's reference to "September 3, 1902, the day when my narrative begins" indicates to Mr. Grazebrook only that that was the day of the Turkish bath shared by Holmes and Watson.

8 *the so-called 'accident' happened in the Splügen Pass.* Mr. Bliss Austin ("Three Footnotes to 'The Adventure of the Illustrious Client'") and Mr. Michael Kayser ("Sherlock Holmes on the Continent") both have a fault to find with Holmes' statement. "Holmes refers to Baron Gruner's trial in Prague for the alleged murder of his wife at the Splügen Pass," Mr. Kaser wrote. "But why, the reader asks, should a Prague court have had jurisdiction in a crime committed on the Swiss-Trentino (then, of course, Austrian) frontier?"

9 *Kingston.* The Royal Borough of Kingston, including the district of Norbiton. Kingston-on-Thames was already in existence a thousand years ago, and King Edward the Elder was crowned there in 900.

10 *Hurlingham.* The grounds used by the Polo Club have since been acquired by the London County Council, partly for a housing estate and partly for a park.

11 *Wainwright was no mean artist.* Holmes refers to Thomas Griffiths Wainwright, who poisoned George Edward Griffiths and others (including, for esthetic reasons, a girl whose ankles he found too thick). The reader is recommended to "Pen, Pencil, and Poison," by Oscar Wilde (in *The Pocket Book of True Crime Stories*, edited by Anthony Boucher) for an excellent account of this poisoner and "no mean artist."

12 *he became a valuable assistant.* Shinwell Johnson was obviously a part of that "small, but very efficient" organization to which Watson referred in "The Disappearance of Lady Frances Carfax." We learn now that this organization was formed "During the first years of the century"—a point in favor of dating "The Disappearance of Lady Frances Carfax" (as we have) in 1902.

13 *looking down at the rushing stream of life in the Strand.* "The description no longer applies," as Mr. Michael Harrison noted (*In the Footsteps of Sherlock Holmes*): "there are no front windows at Simpson's now—through which the customers can look—as well as be looked at. The rebuilding was completed in 1904."

"It was on a Mediterranean yachting voyage. The company, though select, paid their own passages. No doubt the promoters hardly realized the Baron's true character until it was too late. The villain attached himself to the lady, and with such effect that he has completely and absolutely won her heart. To say that she loves him hardly expresses it. She dotes upon him, she is obsessed by him. Outside of him there is nothing on earth. She will not hear one word against him. Everything has been done to cure her of her madness, but in vain. To sum up, she proposes to marry him next month. As she is of age and has a will of iron, it is hard to know how to prevent her."

"Does she know about the Austrian episode?"

"The cunning devil has told her every unsavoury public scandal of his past life, but always in such a way as to make himself out to be an innocent martyr. She absolutely accepts his version and will listen to no other."

"Dear me! But surely you have inadvertently let out the name of your client? It is no doubt General de Merville."

Our visitor fidgeted in his chair.

"I could deceive you by saying so, Mr. Holmes, but it would not be true. De Merville is a broken man. The strong soldier has been utterly demoralized by this incident. He has lost the nerve which never failed him on the battlefield and has become a weak, doddering old man, utterly incapable of contending with a brilliant, forceful rascal like this Austrian. My client, however, is an old friend, one who has known the General intimately for many years and taken a paternal interest in this young girl since she wore short frocks. He cannot see this tragedy consummated without some attempt to stop it. There is nothing in which Scotland Yard can act. It was his own suggestion that you should be called in, but it was, as I have said, on the express stipulation that he should not be personally involved in the matter. I have no doubt, Mr. Holmes, with your great powers you could easily trace my client back through me, but I must ask you, as a point of honour, to refrain from doing so, and not to break in upon his incognito."

Holmes gave a whimsical smile.

"I think I may safely promise that," said he. "I may add that your problem interests me, and that I shall be prepared to look into it. How shall I keep in touch with you?"

"The Carlton Club will find me. But, in case of emergency, there is a private telephone call, 'XX.31.'"

Holmes noted it down and sat, still smiling, with the open memorandum-book upon his knee.

"The Baron's present address, please?"

9   "Vernon Lodge, near Kingston. It is a large house. He has been fortunate in some rather shady speculations and is a rich man, which, naturally, makes him a more dangerous antagonist."

"Is he at home at present?"

"Yes."

"Apart from what you have told me, can you give

me any further information about the man?"

"He has expensive tastes. He is a horse fancier. For a short time he played polo at Hurlingham, but then this **10** Prague affair got noised about and he had to leave. He collects books and pictures. He is a man with a considerable artistic side to his nature. He is, I believe, a recognized authority upon Chinese pottery, and has written a book upon the subject."

"A complex mind," said Holmes. "All great criminals have that. My old friend Charlie Peace was a violin virtuoso. Wainwright was no mean artist. I **11** could quote many more. Well, Sir James, you will inform your client that I am turning my mind upon Baron Gruner. I can say no more. I have some sources of information of my own, and I dare say we may find some means of opening the matter up."

When our visitor had left us, Holmes sat so long in deep thought that it seemed to me that he had forgotten my presence. At last, however, he came briskly back to earth.

"Well, Watson, any views?" he asked.

"I should think you had better see the young lady herself."

"My dear Watson, if her poor old broken father cannot move her, how shall I, a stranger, prevail? And yet there is something in the suggestion if all else fails. But I think we must begin from a different angle. I rather fancy that Shinwell Johnson might be a help."

I have not had occasion to mention Shinwell Johnson in these memoirs because I have seldom drawn my cases from the latter phases of my friend's career. During the first years of the century he became a valuable assistant. Johnson, I grieve to say, made his name first as **12** a very dangerous villain and served two terms at Parkhurst. Finally, he repented and allied himself to Holmes, acting as his agent in the huge criminal underworld of London, and obtaining information which often proved to be of vital importance. Had Johnson been a "nark" of the police he would soon have been exposed, but as he dealt with cases which never came directly into the courts, his activities were never realized by his companions. With the glamour of his two convictions upon him, he had the *entrée* of every night-club, doss-house, and gambling-den in the town, and his quick observation and active brain made him an ideal agent for gaining information. It was to him that Sherlock Holmes now proposed to turn.

It was not possible for me to follow the immediate steps taken by my friend, for I had some pressing professional business of my own, but I met him by appointment that evening at Simpson's, where, sitting at a small table in the front window, and looking down at the rushing stream of life in the Strand, he told me some- **13** thing of what had passed.

"Johnson is on the prowl," said he. "He may pick up some garbage in the darker recesses of the underworld, for it is down there, amid the black roots of crime, that we must hunt for this man's secrets."

"MY OLD FRIEND CHARLIE PEACE ..."

Mr. Vernon Rendall ("The Limitations of Sherlock Holmes"), the late Clifton R. Andrew ("My Old Friend Charlie Peace") and Mr. Irving Fenton ("On Friendship") have all given us illuminating comments on Holmes' statement.

"Charles Peace—burglar, murderer, liar, wife-beater, braggart, actor, inventor, violin virtuoso and old friend of Sherlock Holmes—was born in Sheffield, England, on May 14, 1832, of respectable parents," Mr. Fenton wrote. "He received no formal education, but was endowed with intelligence, a mechanical bent, and an inventive genius. One of his early accomplishments was to fashion the tools of his trade, a burglar's kit. In prison at Dartmoor he suggested some improvements in the machinery then in use which Dartmoor and some other English prisons adopted. . . . While engaged in a burglary in a suburb of Manchester, Peace shot and killed Constable Cook, whose sense of duty outweighed his discretion when he closed in, unarmed, on this dangerous jailbird. He committed his second murder when he shot Arthur Dyson, who resented Peace's attentions to Dyson's wife. . . . He got safely away with both murders, but had to keep constantly on the move. Yet, about this time, he patented an invention for raising sunken vessels and worked on a smoke helmet for firemen. . . . Peace was finally captured during a burglary in Blackheath in 1878 and recognized as the murderer of Arthur Dyson. After a sensational trial during which he almost succeeded in escaping, he was sentenced to death (the jury was out ten minutes), and on February 25, 1879, the law ended his terrestrial friendship, at least, with Sherlock Holmes."

Mr. Andrew added that Peace was "minus the forefinger of his left hand, and after he left Sheffield on 29th November, 1876, his description was posted at every police station in the country. So he made himself [a false arm] which he placed in his sleeve, hanging his violin on the hook . . . and screwing in a fork in the place of the hook for use at meals. For something like two years, the irrepressible Peace walked this earth short of a hand, while the police were looking for a man short of a finger."

Mr. Rendall inclined to the belief that Holmes had no personal acquaintance with Peace, and referred to him as his "old friend" only because Holmes was familiar with all the famous trials of the century.

The illustration is from *The Fifty Most Amazing Crimes of the Last 100 Years*, edited by J. M. Parrish and John R. Crossland, London: Odhams Press, Ltd., 1936.

" But, if the lady will not accept what is already known, why should any fresh discovery of yours turn her from her purpose ? "

" Who knows, Watson ? Woman's heart and mind are insoluble puzzles to the male. Murder might be condoned or explained, and yet some smaller offence might rankle. Baron Gruner remarked to me——"

" He remarked to you ! "

" Oh, to be sure, I had not told you of my plans ! Well, Watson, I love to come to close grips with my man. I like to meet him eye to eye and read for myself the stuff that he is made of. When I had given Johnson his instructions, I took a cab out to Kingston and found the Baron in a most affable mood."

" Did he recognize you ? "

" There was no difficulty about that, for I simply sent in my card. He is an excellent antagonist, cool as ice, silky voiced and soothing as one of your fashionable consultants and poisonous as a cobra. He has breed in him, a real aristocrat of crime, with a superficial suggestion of afternoon tea and all the cruelty of the grave behind it. Yes, I am glad to have had my attention called to Baron Adelbert Gruner."

" You say he was affable ? "

" A purring cat who thinks he sees prospective mice. Some people's affability is more deadly than the violence of coarser souls. His greeting was characteristic. ' I rather thought I should see you sooner or later, Mr. Holmes,' said he. ' You have been engaged, no doubt, by General de Merville to endeavour to stop my marriage with his daughter, Violet. That is so, is it not ? '

" I acquiesced.

" ' My dear man,' said he, ' you will only ruin your own well-deserved reputation. It is not a case in which you can possibly succeed. You will have barren work, to say nothing of incurring some danger. Let me very strongly advise you to draw off at once.'

" ' It is curious,' I answered, ' but that was the very advice which I had intended to give you. I have a respect for your brains, Baron, and the little which I have seen of your personality has not lessened it. Let me put it to you as man to man. No one wants to rake up your past and make you unduly uncomfortable. It is over, and you are now in smooth waters, but if you persist in this marriage you will raise up a swarm of powerful enemies who will never leave you alone until they have made England too hot to hold you. Is the game worth it ? Surely you would be wiser if you left the lady alone. It would not be pleasant for you if these facts of your past were brought to her notice.'

" The Baron has little waxed tips of hair under his nose, like the short antennæ of an insect. These quivered with amusement as he listened, and he finally broke into a gentle chuckle.

" ' Excuse my amusement, Mr. Holmes,' said he, ' but it is really funny to see you trying to play a hand with no cards in it. I don't think anyone could do it better, but it is rather pathetic, all the same. Not a colour card there, Mr. Holmes, nothing but the smallest of the small.'

" ' So you think.'

" ' So I know. Let me make the thing clear to you, for my own hand is so strong that I can afford to show it. I have been fortunate enough to win the entire affection of this lady. This was given to me in spite of the fact that I told her very clearly of all the unhappy incidents in my past life. I also told her that certain wicked and designing persons—I hope you recognize yourself—would come to her and tell her these things, and I warned her how to treat them. You have heard of post-hypnotic suggestion, Mr. Holmes ? Well, you will see how it works, for a man of personality can use hypnotism without any vulgar passes or tomfoolery. So she is ready for you and, I have no doubt, would give you an appointment, for she is quite amenable to her father's will—save only in the one little matter.'

" Well, Watson, there seemed to be no more to say, so I took my leave with as much cold dignity as I could summon, but, as I had my hand on the door-handle, he stopped me.

" ' By the way, Mr. Holmes,' said he, ' did you know Le Brun, the French agent ? '

" ' Yes,' said I.

" ' Do you know what befell him ? '

" ' I heard that he was beaten by some Apaches in the Montmartre district and crippled for life.'

" ' Quite true, Mr. Holmes. By a curious coincidence he had been inquiring into my affairs only a week before. Don't do it, Mr. Holmes ; it's not a lucky thing to do. Several have found that out. My last word to you is, go your own way and let me go mine. Good-bye ! '

" So there you are, Watson. You are up to date now."

" The fellow seems dangerous."

" Mighty dangerous. I disregard the blusterer, but this is the sort of man who says rather less than he means."

" Must you interfere ? Does it really matter if he marries the girl ? "

" Considering that he undoubtedly murdered his last wife, I should say it mattered very much. Besides, the client ! Well, well, we need not discuss that. When you have finished your coffee you had best come home with me, for the blithe Shinwell will be there with his report."

We found him sure enough, a huge, coarse, red-faced, scorbutic man, with a pair of vivid black eyes which were the only external sign of the very cunning mind within. It seems that he had dived down into what was peculiarly his kingdom, and beside him on the settee was a brand which he had brought up in the shape of a slim, flame-like young woman with a pale, intense face, youthful, and yet so worn with sin and sorrow that one read the terrible years which had left their leprous mark upon her.

" This is Miss Kitty Winter," said Shinwell Johnson, waving his fat hand as an introduction. " What she don't know—well, there, she'll speak for herself. Put

AS I HAD MY HAND ON THE DOOR HANDLE,
HE STOPPED ME.

Illustration by Howard K. Elcock for the *Strand Magazine*, February, 1925.

my hand right on her, Mr. Holmes, within an hour of your message."

" I'm easy to find," said the young woman. " Hell, London, gets me every time. Same address for Porky Shinwell. We're old mates, Porky, you and I. But, by Cripes ! there is another who ought to be down in a lower hell than we if there was any justice in the world ! That is the man you are after, Mr. Holmes."

Holmes smiled. " I gather we have your good wishes, Miss Winter."

" If I can help to put him where he belongs, I'm yours to the rattle," said our visitor, with fierce energy. There was an intensity of hatred in her white, set face and her blazing eyes such as woman seldom and man never can attain. " You needn't go into my past, Mr. Holmes. That's neither here nor there. But what I am Adelbert Gruner made me. If I could pull him down !" She clutched frantically with her hands into the air. " Oh, if I could only pull him into the pit where he has pushed so many !"

" You know how the matter stands ? "

" Porky Shinwell has been telling me. He's after some other poor fool and wants to marry her this time. You want to stop it. Well, you surely know enough about this devil to prevent any decent girl in her senses wanting to be in the same parish with him."

" She is not in her senses. She is madly in love. She has been told all about him. She cares nothing."

" Told about the murder ? "

" Yes."

" My Lord, she must have a nerve ! "

" She puts them all down as slanders."

" Couldn't you lay proofs before her silly eyes ? "

" Well, can you help us do so ? "

" Ain't I a proof myself ? If I stood before her and told her how he used me——"

" Would you do this ? "

" Would I ? Would I not ! "

" Well, it might be worth trying. But he has told her most of his sins and had pardon from her, and I understand she will not reopen the question."

" I'll lay he didn't tell her all," said Miss Winter. " I caught a glimpse of one or two murders besides the one that made such a fuss. He would speak of someone in his velvet way and then look at me with a steady eye and say : ' He died within a month.' It wasn't hot air, either. But I took little notice—you see, I loved him myself at that time. Whatever he did went with me, same as with this poor fool ! There was just one thing that shook me. Yes, by Cripes ! if it had not been for his poisonous, lying tongue that explains and soothes, I'd have left him that very night. It's a book he has— a brown leather book with a lock, and his arms in gold on the outside. I think he was a bit drunk that night, or he would not have shown it to me."

" What was it, then ? "

" I tell you, Mr. Holmes, this man collects women, and takes a pride in his collection, as some men collect moths or butterflies. He had it all in that book. Snap-shot photographs, names, details, everything about them. It was a beastly book—a book no man, even if he had come from the gutter, could have put together. But it was Adelbert Gruner's book all the same. ' Souls I have ruined.' He could have put that on the outside if he had been so minded. However, that's neither here nor there, for the book would not serve you, and, if it would, you can't get it."

" Where is it ? "

" How can I tell you where it is now ? It's more than a year since I left him. I know where he kept it then. He's a precise, tidy cat of a man in many of his ways, so maybe it is still in the pigeon-hole of the old bureau in the inner study. Do you know his house ? "

" I've been in the study," said Holmes.

" Have you, though ? You haven't been slow on the job if you only started this morning. Maybe dear Adelbert has met his match this time. The outer study is the one with the Chinese crockery in it—big glass cupboard between the windows. Then behind his desk is the door that leads to the inner study—a small room where he keeps papers and things."

" Is he not afraid of burglars ? "

" Adelbert is no coward. His worst enemy couldn't say that of him. He can look after himself. There's a burglar alarm at night. Besides, what is there for a burglar—unless they got away with all this fancy crockery ? "

" No good," said Shinwell Johnson, with the decided voice of the expert. " No fence wants stuff of that sort that you can neither melt nor sell."

" Quite so," said Holmes. " Well, now, Miss Winter, if you would call here to-morrow evening at five, I would consider in the meanwhile whether your suggestion of seeing this lady personally may not be arranged. I am exceedingly obliged to you for your co-operation. I need not say that my clients will consider liberally——"

" None of that, Mr. Holmes," cried the young woman. " I am not out for money. Let me see this man in the mud, and I've got all I worked for—in the mud with my foot on his cursed face. That's my price. I'm with you to-morrow or any other day so long as you are on his track. Porky here can tell you always where to find me."

I did not see Holmes again until the following evening, when we dined once more at our Strand restaurant. He shrugged his shoulders when I asked him what luck he had had in his interview. Then he told the story, which I would repeat in this way. His hard, dry statement needs some little editing to soften it into the terms of real life.

" There was no difficulty at all about the appointment," said Holmes, " for the girl glories in showing abject filial obedience in all secondary things in an attempt to atone for her flagrant breach of it in her engagement. The General 'phoned that all was ready and the fiery Miss W. turned up according to schedule, so that at half-past five a cab deposited us outside 104 Berkeley Square, where the old soldier resides—one of those awful grey London castles which would make a

14 *the cave-man to the angel.* Dr. Richard Asher has deduced from Holmes' remarks on this occasion ("Holmes and the Fair Sex") that it "seems highly probable that Holmes the scholar and aesthete had suffered the mortifying experience of being attracted to one who was intellectually and socially below him. His antagonism to sentiment and his support of pure reasoning against emotional thinking no doubt sprang from his youthful suffering (a type of suffering so brilliantly portrayed by Mr. Somerset Maugham in *Of Human Bondage* and again in *His Excellency*), and his immediate success with Milverton's housemaid no doubt reflects his previous experience in that field."

church seem frivolous. A footman showed us into a great yellow-curtained drawing-room, and there was the lady awaiting us, demure, pale, self-contained, as inflexible and remote as a snow image on a mountain.

"I don't quite know how to make her clear to you, Watson. Perhaps you may meet her before we are through, and you can use your own gift of words. She is beautiful, but with the ethereal other-world beauty of some fanatic whose thoughts are set on high. I have seen such faces in the pictures of the old masters of the Middle Ages. How a beast-man could have laid his vile paws upon such a being of the beyond I cannot imagine. You may have noticed how extremes call to each other, the spiritual to the animal, the cave-man to the **14** angel. You never saw a worse case than this.

"She knew what we had come for, of course—that villain had lost no time in poisoning her mind against us. Miss Winter's advent rather amazed her, I think, but she waved us into our respective chairs like a reverend abbess receiving two rather leprous mendicants. If your head is inclined to swell, my dear Watson, take a course of Miss Violet de Merville.

"'Well, sir,' said she, in a voice like the wind from an iceberg, 'your name is familiar to me. You have called, as I understand, to malign my fiancé, Baron Gruner. It is only by my father's request that I see you at all, and I warn you in advance that anything you can say could not possibly have the slightest effect upon my mind.'

"I was sorry for her, Watson. I thought of her for the moment as I would have thought of a daughter of my own. I am not often eloquent. I use my head, not my heart. But I really did plead with her with all the warmth of words that I could find in my nature. I pictured to her the awful position of the woman who only wakes to a man's character after she is his wife—a woman who has to submit to be caressed by bloody hands and lecherous lips. I spared her nothing—the shame, the fear, the agony, the hopelessness of it all. All my hot words could not bring one tinge of colour to those ivory cheeks or one gleam of emotion to those abstracted eyes. I thought of what the rascal had said about a post-hypnotic influence. One could really believe that she was living above the earth in some ecstatic dream. Yet there was nothing indefinite in her replies.

"'I have listened to you with patience, Mr. Holmes,' said she. 'The effect upon my mind is exactly as predicted. I am aware that Adelbert, that my fiancé, has had a stormy life in which he has incurred bitter hatreds and most unjust aspersions. You are only the last of a series who have brought their slanders before me. Possibly you mean well, though I learn that you are a paid agent who would have been equally willing to act for the Baron as against him. But in any case I wish you to understand once for all that I love him and that he loves me, and that the opinion of all the world is no more to me than the twitter of those birds outside the window. If his noble nature has ever for an instant fallen, it may be that I have been specially sent to raise it to its true and lofty level. I am not clear,' here she turned her eyes upon my companion, 'who this young lady may be.'

" I was about to answer when the girl broke in like a whirlwind. If ever you saw flame and ice face to face, it was those two women.

" ' I'll tell you who I am,' she cried, springing out of her chair, her mouth all twisted with passion—' I am his last mistress. I am one of a hundred that he has tempted and used and ruined and thrown into the refuse heap, as he will you also. *Your* refuse heap is more likely to be a grave, and maybe that's the best. I tell you, you foolish woman, if you marry this man he'll be the death of you. It may be a broken heart or it may be a broken neck, but he'll have you one way or the other. It's not out of love for you I'm speaking. I don't care a tinker's curse whether you live or die. It's out of hate for him and to spite him and to get back on him for what he did to me. But it's all the same, and you needn't look at me like that, my fine lady, for you may be lower than I am before you are through with it.'

" ' I should prefer not to discuss such matters,' said Miss de Merville coldly. ' Let me say once for all that I am aware of three passages in my fiancé's life in which he became entangled with designing women, and that I am assured of his hearty repentance for any evil that he may have done.'

" ' Three passages ! ' screamed my companion. ' You fool ! You unutterable fool ! '

" ' Mr. Holmes, I beg that you will bring this interview to an end,' said the icy voice. ' I have obeyed my father's wish in seeing you, but I am not compelled to listen to the ravings of this person.'

" With an oath Miss Winter darted forward, and if I had not caught her wrist she would have clutched this maddening woman by the hair. I dragged her towards the door, and was lucky to get her back into the cab without a public scene, for she was beside herself with rage. In a cold way I felt pretty furious myself, Watson, for there was something indescribably annoying in the calm aloofness and supreme self-complaisance of the woman whom we were trying to save. So now once again you know exactly how we stand, and it is clear that I must plan some fresh opening move, for this gambit won't work. I'll keep in touch with you, Watson, for it is more than likely that you will have your part to play, though it is just possible that the next move may lie with them rather than with us."

" 'MR. HOLMES, I BEG THAT YOU WILL BRING THIS INTERVIEW TO AN END,' SAID THE ICY VOICE."

Illustration by Howard K. Elcock for the *Strand Magazine*, February, 1925.

15 *the Grand Hotel.* In Trafalgar Square; it has now been converted into business premises.

MURDEROUS ATTACK UPON SHERLOCK HOLMES.

Illustration by Howard K. Elcock for the *Strand Magazine*, February, 1925.

"... OUTSIDE THE CAFÉ ROYAL."

The illustration shows the Regent Street entrance to the Café Royal, London. The Café lies only a hundred yards from the Criterion Restaurant, across the width of Piccadilly Circus. Mr. Michael Harrison has called it "the nearest thing London has ever had to the artist-patronized restaurants and cafés of the better class with which Paris is still well-provided. . . . The original Café Royal was opened by a Frenchman, Monsieur Nicol, in 1865, in Glasshouse Street. . . . When M. Nicol died, in 1907, the Café Royal was established as the most popular restaurant-café with the artist and writer of London."

And it did. Their blow fell—or his blow rather, for never could I believe that the lady was privy to it. I think I could show you the very paving-stone upon which I stood when my eyes fell upon the placard, and a pang of horror passed through my very soul. It was between **15** the Grand Hotel and Charing Cross Station, where a one-legged newsvendor displayed his evening papers. The date was just two days after the last conversation. There, black upon yellow, was the terrible news-sheet:

> MURDEROUS
> ATTACK
> UPON
> SHERLOCK
> HOLMES.

I think I stood stunned for some moments. Then I have a confused recollection of snatching at a paper, of the remonstrance of the man, whom I had not paid, and, finally, of standing in the doorway of a chemist's shop while I turned up the fateful paragraph. This was how it ran:

" We learn with regret that Mr. Sherlock Holmes, the well-known private detective, was the victim this morning of a murderous assault which has left him in a precarious position. There are no exact details to hand, but the event seems to have occurred about twelve o'clock in Regent Street, outside the Café Royal. The attack was made by two men armed with sticks, and Mr. Holmes was beaten about the head and body, receiving injuries which the doctors describe as most serious. He was carried to Charing Cross Hospital, and afterwards insisted upon being taken to his rooms in Baker Street. The miscreants who attacked him appear to have

been respectably dressed men, who escaped from the bystanders by passing through the Café Royal and out into Glasshouse Street behind it. No doubt they belonged to that criminal fraternity which has so often had occasion to bewail the activity and ingenuity of the injured man."

I need not say that my eyes had hardly glanced over the paragraph before I had sprung into a hansom and was on my way to Baker Street. I found Sir Leslie Oakshott, the famous surgeon, in the hall and his brougham waiting at the kerb.

"No immediate danger," was his report. "Two lacerated scalp wounds and some considerable bruises. Several stitches have been necessary. Morphine has been injected and quiet is essential, but an interview of a few minutes would not be absolutely forbidden."

With this permission I stole into the darkened room. The sufferer was wide awake, and I heard my name in a hoarse whisper. The blind was three-quarters down, but one ray of sunlight slanted through and struck the bandaged head of the injured man. A crimson patch had soaked through the white linen compress. I sat **16** beside him and bent my head.

"All right, Watson. Don't look so scared," he muttered in a very weak voice. "It's not as bad as it seems."

"Thank God for that!"

"I'm a bit of a single-stick expert, as you know. I took most of them on my guard. It was the second man that was too much for me."

"What can I do, Holmes? Of course, it was that damned fellow who set them on. I'll go and thrash the hide off him if you give the word."

"Good old Watson! No, we can do nothing there unless the police lay their hands on the men. But their get-away had been well prepared. We may be sure of that. Wait a little. I have my plans. The first thing is to exaggerate my injuries. They'll come to you for news. Put it on thick, Watson. Lucky if I live the week out—concussion—delirium—what you like! You can't overdo it."

"But Sir Leslie Oakshott?"

"Oh, he's all right. He shall see the worst side of me. I'll look after that."

"Anything else?"

"Yes. Tell Shinwell Johnson to get that girl out of the way. Those beauties will be after her now. They know, of course, that she was with me in the case. If they dared to do me in it is not likely they will neglect her. That is urgent. Do it to-night."

"I'll go now. Anything more?"

"Put my pipe on the table—and the tobacco-slipper. Right! Come in each morning and we will plan our campaign."

I arranged with Johnson that evening to take Miss Winter to a quiet suburb and see that she lay low until the danger was past.

For six days the public were under the impression that Holmes was at the door of death. The bulletins were very grave and there were sinister paragraphs in the papers. My continual visits assured me that it was

"THE ATTACK WAS MADE BY TWO MEN ARMED WITH STICKS . . ."

Illustration by Howard K. Elcock for the *Strand Magazine*, March, 1925.

16 *A crimson patch had soaked through the white linen compress.* "It would seem that [Sir Leslie Oakshott, the famous surgeon] did a pretty poor job of suturing, for the dressing was blood-soaked almost before he got out of the house, and an even worse job of after-care, for eight days later Holmes' head was still girt with bloody bandages," Dr. Samuel R. Meaker commented in "Watson Medicus."

17 *"Friday!" he cried. "Only three clear days.* Something is clearly wrong here, and there would seem to be two alternatives: 1) Holmes and Kitty Winter saw Violet de Merville on Thursday, September 4; Holmes and Watson dined that night; Holmes was attacked on the following Monday, September 8th, just *four—not two—*days "after the last conversation." 2) Holmes and Kitty Winter saw Violet de Merville on Saturday, September 6th; Holmes and Watson dined that night —the following *Saturday* evening, *not* "the following evening"; Holmes was attacked on the following Monday, September 8th. We believe the second alternative to be the correct one. Had Holmes and Kitty Winter seen Violet de Merville on Thursday, Baron Adelbert Gruner would hardly have waited until the following Monday morning to launch his attack on Holmes. In brief, we believe that Watson is once again up to his literary trick of telescoping a time period to create a more dramatic effect. We have seen that he did just this in *A Study in Scarlet*. We shall see that he will do it again in "The Adventure of the Creeping Man." Clearly, Holmes spent *several days* considering whether or not it would be wise to arrange an appointment between Miss de Merville and Miss Winter: "I would consider in the meanwhile whether your suggestion of seeing this lady personally may not be arranged." When Holmes decided, *on the Saturday*, that the suggestion was a good one, "There was no difficulty at all about the appointment." It was on the evening of Monday, September 15th, then—*not* the evening of Saturday, September 13th—that Holmes said: "Friday! Only three clear days."

18 *St. James's Square.* St. James's Square dates from the time of Charles II, when the adjoining King Street and Charles Street were named in honor of the Duke of York. Formerly consisting mostly of aristocratic private residences, this square now contains several large office buildings and several of the leading West End clubs.

not so bad as that. His wiry constitution and his determined will were working wonders. He was recovering fast, and I had suspicions at times that he was really finding himself faster than he pretended, even to me. There was a curious secretive streak in the man which led to many dramatic effects, but left even his closest friend guessing as to what his exact plans might be. He pushed to an extreme the axiom that the only safe plotter was he who plotted alone. I was nearer him than anyone else, and yet I was always conscious of the gap between.

On the seventh day the stitches were taken out, in spite of which there was a report of erysipelas in the evening papers. The same evening papers had an announcement which I was bound, sick or well, to carry to my friend. It was simply that among the passengers on the Cunard boat *Ruritania*, starting from Liverpool on Friday, was the Baron Adelbert Gruner, who had some important financial business to settle in the States before his impending wedding to Miss Violet de Merville, only daughter of, etc., etc. Holmes listened to the news with a cold, concentrated look upon his pale face, which told me that it hit him hard.

17 " Friday ! " he cried. " Only three clear days. I believe the rascal wants to put himself out of danger's way. But he won't, Watson ! By the Lord Harry, he won't ! Now, Watson, I want you to do something for me."

" I am here to be used, Holmes."

" Well, then, spend the next twenty-four hours in an intensive study of Chinese pottery."

He gave no explanations and I asked for none. By long experience I had learned the wisdom of obedience. But when I had left his room I walked down Baker Street, revolving in my head how on earth I was to carry out so strange an order. Finally I drove to the London

18 Library in St. James' Square, put the matter to my friend Lomax, the sub-librarian, and departed to my rooms with a goodly volume under my arm.

It is said that the barrister who crams up a case with such care that he can examine an expert witness upon the Monday has forgotten all his forced knowledge before the Saturday. Certainly I should not like now to pose as an authority upon ceramics. And yet all that evening, and all that night with a short interval for rest, and all next morning I was sucking in knowledge and committing names to memory. There I learned of the hall-marks of the great artist-decorators, of the mystery of cyclical dates, the marks of the Hung-wu and the beauties of the Yung-lo, the writings of Tang-ying, and the glories of the primitive period of the Sung and the Yuan. I was charged with all this information when I called upon Holmes next evening. He was out of bed now, though you would not have guessed it from the published reports, and he sat with his much-bandaged head resting upon his hand in the depth of his favourite arm-chair.

" Why, Holmes," I said, " if one believed the papers you are dying."

" That," said he, " is the very impression which I

intended to convey. And now, Watson, have you learned your lessons ? "

" At least I have tried to."

" Good. You could keep up an intelligent conversation on the subject ? "

" I believe I could."

" Then hand me that little box from the mantelpiece."

He opened the lid and took out a small object most carefully wrapped in some fine Eastern silk. This he unfolded, and disclosed a delicate little saucer of the most beautiful deep-blue colour.

" It needs careful handling, Watson. This is the real egg-shell pottery of the Ming dynasty. No finer piece **19** ever passed through Christie's. A complete set of this would be worth a king's ransom—in fact, it is doubtful if there is a complete set outside the Imperial palace of Peking. The sight of this would drive a real connoisseur wild."

" What am I to do with it ? "

Holmes handed me a card upon which was printed : " Dr. Hill Barton, 369 Half Moon Street." **20**

" That is your name for the evening, Watson. You will call upon Baron Gruner. I know something of his habits, and at half-past eight he would probably be disengaged. A note will tell him in advance that you are about to call, and you will say that you are bringing him a specimen of an absolutely unique set of Ming china. You may as well be a medical man, since that is a part which you can play without duplicity. You are a collector, this set has come your way, you have heard of the Baron's interest in the subject, and you are not averse to selling at a price."

" What price ? "

" Well asked, Watson. You would certainly fall down badly if you did not know the value of your own wares. This saucer was got for me by Sir James, and comes, I understand, from the collection of his client. You will not exaggerate if you say that it could hardly be matched in the world."

" I could perhaps suggest that the set should be valued by an expert."

" Excellent, Watson ! You scintillate to-day. Suggest Christie or Sotheby. Your delicacy prevents your putting a price for yourself."

" But if he won't see me ? "

" Oh, yes, he will see you. He has the collection mania in its most acute form—and especially on this subject, on which he is an acknowledged authority. Sit down, Watson, and I will dictate the letter. No answer needed. You will merely say that you are coming, and why."

It was an admirable document, short, courteous, and stimulating to the curiosity of the connoisseur. A district messenger was duly dispatched with it. On the same evening, with the precious saucer in my hand and the card of Dr. Hill Barton in my pocket, I set off on my own adventure.

The beautiful house and grounds indicated that Baron

"IT NEEDS CAREFUL HANDLING, WATSON."

Illustration by John Richard Flanagan for *Collier's Magazine*, November 8, 1924.

19 *This is the real egg-shell pottery of the Ming dynasty.* In his autobiography, *Those Days* (London, 1940), Mr. E. C. Bentley tells of an early dinner of the original Sherlock Holmes Society at which Sir Eric MacLaglan, the Director of the Victoria and Albert Museum, declared that there *is no* Ming pottery of a "deep-blue colour."

20 *Half Moon Street*." So called from a tavern located there. Half Moon Street leads into Curzon Street.

Gruner was, as Sir James had said, a man of considerable wealth. A long winding drive, with banks of rare shrubs on either side, opened out into a great gravelled square adorned with statues. The place had been built by a South African gold king in the days of the great boom, and the long, low house with the turrets at the corners, though an architectural nightmare, was imposing in its size and solidity. A butler who would have adorned a bench of bishops showed me in, and handed me over to a plush-clad footman, who ushered me into the Baron's presence.

He was standing at the open front of a great case which stood between the windows, and which contained part of his Chinese collection. He turned as I entered, with a small brown vase in his hand.

"Pray sit down, doctor," said he. "I was looking over my own treasures and wondering whether I could really afford to add to them. This little Tang specimen, which dates from the seventh century, would probably interest you. I am sure you never saw finer workmanship or a richer glaze. Have you the Ming saucer with you of which you spoke?"

I carefully unpacked it and handed it to him. He seated himself at his desk, pulled over the lamp, for it was growing dark, and set himself to examine it. As he did so the yellow light beat upon his own features, and I was able to study them at my ease.

He was certainly a remarkably handsome man. His European reputation for beauty was fully deserved. In figure he was not more than of middle size, but was built upon graceful and active lines. His face was swarthy, almost Oriental, with large, dark, languorous eyes which might easily hold an irresistible fascination for women. His hair and moustache were raven black: the latter short, pointed, and carefully waxed. His features were regular and pleasing, save only his straight, thin-lipped mouth. If ever I saw a murderer's mouth it was there—a cruel, hard gash in the face, compressed, inexorable, and terrible. He was ill-advised to train his moustache away from it, for it was Nature's danger-signal, set as a warning to his victims. His voice was engaging and his manners perfect. In age I should have put him at little over thirty, though his record afterwards showed that he was forty-two.

"Very fine—very fine indeed!" he said at last. "And you say you have a set of six to correspond. What puzzles me is that I should not have heard of such magnificent specimens. I only know of one in England to match this, and it is certainly not likely to be in the market. Would it be indiscreet if I were to ask you, Dr. Hill Barton, how you obtained this?"

"Does it really matter?" I asked, with as careless an air as I could muster. "You can see that the piece is genuine, and, as to the value, I am content to take an expert's valuation."

"Very mysterious," said he, with a quick, suspicious flash of his dark eyes. "In dealing with objects of such value, one naturally wishes to know all about the transaction. That the piece is genuine is certain. I have no

"VERY FINE—VERY FINE INDEED!" HE SAID AT LAST.

Illustration by Howard K. Elcock for the *Strand Magazine*, March, 1925.

doubts at all about that. But suppose—I am bound to take every possibility into account—that it should prove afterwards that you had no right to sell ? "

" I would guarantee you against any claim of the sort."

" That, of course, would open up the question as to what your guarantee was worth."

" My bankers would answer that."

" Quite so. And yet the whole transaction strikes me as rather unusual."

" You can do business or not," said I, with indifference. " I have given you the first offer, as I understood that you were a connoisseur, but I shall have no difficulty in other quarters."

" Who told you I was a connoisseur ? "

" I was aware that you had written a book upon the subject."

" Have you read the book ? "

" No."

" Dear me, this becomes more and more difficult for me to understand ! You are a connoisseur and collector with a very valuable piece in your collection, and yet you have never troubled to consult the one book which would have told you of the real meaning and value of what you held. How do you explain that ? "

" I am a very busy man. I am a doctor in practice."

" That is no answer. If a man has a hobby he follows it up, whatever his other pursuits may be. You said in your note that you were a connoisseur."

" So I am."

" Might I ask you a few questions to test you ? I am obliged to tell you, doctor—if you are indeed a doctor—that the incident becomes more and more suspicious. I would ask you what do you know of the Emperor Shomu and how do you associate him with the Shoso-in near Nara ? Dear me, does that puzzle you ? Tell me a little about the Northern Wei dynasty and its place in the history of ceramics."

I sprang from my chair in simulated anger.

" This is intolerable, sir," said I. " I came here to do you a favour, and not to be examined as if I were a schoolboy. My knowledge on these subjects may be second only to your own, but I certainly shall not answer questions which have been put in so offensive a way."

He looked at me steadily. The languor had gone from his eyes. They suddenly glared. There was a gleam of teeth from between those cruel lips.

" What is the game ? You are here as a spy. You are an emissary of Holmes. This is a trick that you are playing upon me. The fellow is dying, I hear, so he sends his tools to keep watch upon me. You've made your way in here without leave, and, by God ! you may find it harder to get out than to get in."

He had sprung to his feet, and I stepped back, bracing myself for an attack, for the man was beside himself with rage. He may have suspected me from the first ; certainly this cross-examination had shown him the truth ; but it was clear that I could not hope to deceive him. He dived his hand into a side-drawer and rummaged

"AH!" HE CRIED. "AH!" AND DASHED INTO THE ROOM
BEHIND HIM.

Illustration by Howard K. Elcock for the *Strand
Magazine*, March, 1925.

21 *a hypodermic of morphia.* "Perfectly reasonable treatment at that time but where, oh, where
did Dr. Hill Barton, Watson's alias and disguise,
carry his oil, wadding and morphia?" Dr. Vernon
Pennell asked in his "Resume of the Medical Life
of John H. Watson, M.D., Late of the Army
Medical Department." "Why on earth should he
take these with him on an expedition to one with
whom he only expected a discussion on ceramics?"

furiously. Then something struck upon his ear, for he
stood listening intently.

"Ah!" he cried. "Ah!" and dashed into the room
behind him.

Two steps took me to the open door, and my mind
will ever carry a clear picture of the scene within. The
window leading out to the garden was wide open. Beside
it, looking like some terrible ghost, his head girt with
bloody bandages, his face drawn and white, stood Sherlock Holmes. The next instant he was through the
gap, and I heard the crash of his body among the laurel
bushes outside. With a howl of rage the master of the
house rushed after him to the open window.

And then! It was done in an instant, and yet I
clearly saw it. An arm—a woman's arm—shot out
from among the leaves. At the same instant the Baron
uttered a horrible cry—a yell which will always ring
in my memory. He clapped his two hands to his face
and rushed round the room, beating his head horribly
against the walls. Then he fell upon the carpet, rolling
and writhing, while scream after scream resounded
through the house.

"Water! For God's sake, water!" was his cry.

I seized a carafe from a side-table and rushed to his
aid. At the same moment the butler and several footmen ran in from the hall. I remember that one of them
fainted as I knelt by the injured man and turned that
awful face to the light of the lamp. The vitriol was
eating into it everywhere and dripping from the ears and
the chin. One eye was already white and glazed. The
other was red and inflamed. The features which I had
admired a few minutes before were now like some beautiful painting over which the artist has passed a wet and
foul sponge. They were blurred, discoloured, inhuman,
terrible.

In a few words I explained exactly what had occurred,
so far as the vitriol attack was concerned. Some had
climbed through the window and others had rushed out
on to the lawn, but it was dark and it had begun to rain.
Between his screams the victim raged and raved against
the avenger. "It was that hell-cat, Kitty Winter!"
he cried. "Oh, the she-devil! She shall pay for it!
She shall pay! Oh, God in heaven, this pain is more
than I can bear!"

I bathed his face in oil, put cotton wadding on the
21 raw surfaces, and administered a hypodermic of morphia.
All suspicion of me had passed from his mind in the
presence of this shock, and he clung to my hands as
if I might have the power even yet to clear those dead-
fish eyes which gazed up at me. I could have wept over
the ruin had I not remembered very clearly the vile life
which had led up to so hideous a change. It was loathsome to feel the pawing of his burning hands, and I
was relieved when his family surgeon, closely followed
by a specialist, came to relieve me of my charge. An
inspector of police had also arrived, and to him I handed
my real card. It would have been useless as well as
foolish to do otherwise, for I was nearly as well known by
sight at the Yard as Holmes himself. Then I left that

house of gloom and terror. Within an hour I was at Baker Street.

Holmes was seated in his familiar chair, looking very pale and exhausted. Apart from his injuries, even his iron nerves had been shocked by the events of the evening, and he listened with horror to my account of the Baron's transformation.

" The wages of sin, Watson—the wages of sin ! " said **22** he. " Sooner or later it will always come. God knows, there was sin enough," he added, taking up a brown volume from the table. " Here is the book the woman talked of. If this will not break off the marriage, nothing ever could. But it will, Watson. It must. No self-respecting woman could stand it."

" It is his love diary ? "

" Or his lust diary. Call it what you will. The moment the woman told us of it I realized what a tremendous weapon was there, if we could but lay our hands on it. I said nothing at the time to indicate my thoughts, for this woman might have given it away. But I brooded over it. Then this assault upon me gave me the chance of letting the Baron think that no precautions need be taken against me. That was all to the good. I would have waited a little longer, but his visit to America forced my hand. He would never have left so compromising a document behind him. Therefore we had to act at once. Burglary at night is impossible. He takes precautions. But there was a chance in the evening if I could only be sure that his attention was engaged. That was where you and your blue saucer came in. But I had to be sure of the position of the book, and I knew I had only a few minutes in which to act, for my time was limited by your knowledge of Chinese pottery. Therefore I gathered the girl up at the last moment. How could I guess what the little packet was that she carried so carefully under her cloak ? I thought she had come altogether on my business, but it seems she had some of her own."

" He guessed I came from you."

" I feared he would. But you held him in play just long enough for me to get the book, though not long enough for an unobserved escape. Ah, Sir James, I am very glad you have come ! "

Our courtly friend had appeared in answer to a previous summons. He listened with the deepest attention to Holmes' account of what had occurred.

" You have done wonders—wonders ! " he cried, when he had heard the narrative. " But if these injuries are as terrible as Dr. Watson describes, then surely our purpose of thwarting the marriage is sufficiently gained without the use of this horrible book."

Holmes shook his head.

" Women of the de Merville type do not act like that. She would love him the more as a disfigured martyr. No, no. It is his moral side, not his physical, which we have to destroy. That book will bring her back to earth—and I know nothing else that could. It is in his own writing. She cannot get past it."

Sir James carried away both it and the precious saucer. As I was myself overdue, I went down with him into **23**

22 *"The wages of sin, Watson—the wages of sin!"* Holmes draws upon Romans, 6.23.

23 *As I was myself overdue.* "Overdue where?" the late Elmer Davis asked in his essay, "On the Emotional Geology of Baker Street." "Not at the bedside of a patient; since Holmes' distant cousin Dr. Verner had bought up his practice, eight years earlier, he had not returned to his profession. Overdue, obviously, (in view of his marriage soon after) in the drawing-room of a fiancée who did not take his involvement in Holmes' affairs as lightly as did Mary Morstan Watson."

24 *a loyal friend and a chivalrous gentleman.*"
We see that King Edward VII continued to give
evidence of his faith in Holmes' powers. We see
also that Holmes, since his refusal to accept a
knighthood, has mellowed somewhat in his personal attitude toward King Edward.

25 *the lowest that was possible for such an
offence.* "Of all the persons involved in this sordid affair," Mr. Bliss Austin wrote in "Three
Footnotes to 'The Adventure of the Illustrious
Client,' " "the one who makes the greatest claim
to our sympathies is Kitty Winter, the lass who
went to see Baron Gruner's etchings and then repaid him by etching his face with acid. Was she
English and descended from that branch of the
family which lost a pair of brothers in Guy Fawkes'
plot? Perhaps, but her experience with the Baron
suggests that her origin was Central European. It
is possible that she was a relative of Zigmund
Winter, the great Czech novelist, whose historical
fiction is described by the *Encyclopædia Britannica* as possessing artistic force and delicacy of
treatment. Since the gentleman was born in 1846,
Kitty might even have been his daughter. It is
difficult to prove this, however, because of the
lack of data about her. For, in spite of Watson's
statement that her first police-court trial was reported by the papers, a search through the dailies
of the day fails to reveal anything of the kind.
Apparently the patronage of the Illustrious Client
carried great weight with the press."

*A Note on the "Canonicity" of "The Adventure
of the Illustrious Client":* Mr. D. Martin Dakin
writes: "Of 'The Illustrious Client' it is . . . difficult to speak with confidence. Mr. Blakeney has
seen in Holmes' remarks to Sir James Damery
("I am accustomed to have mystery at one end of
my cases, but to have it at both ends is too confusing')—an echo of what he said in 'The Second
Stain,' and felt it was unlike him to yield so easily
and not insist on the complete confidence of his
client as he did to Lord Bellinger and Mr. Trelawney Hope. Yet the story is well-written.
Holmes' account of his impression of Miss Violet
de Merville is admirable, and the description of
the vitriol-throwing, horrible as it is, shows Watson at his most powerful as a word-painter. I am
inclined to think that the story as a whole is by
Watson, but that the editor of the series has added
paragraphs at the beginning and end—possibly the
title also—to exaggerate its importance. It is absurd to describe it as 'the supreme moment of my

the street. A brougham was waiting for him. He
sprang in, gave a hurried order to the cockaded coachman, and drove swiftly away. He flung his overcoat
half out of the window to cover the armorial bearings
upon the panel, but I had seen them in the glare of
our fanlight none the less. I gasped with surprise. Then
I turned back and ascended the stair to Holmes' room.

" I have found out who our client is," I cried, bursting
with my great news. " Why, Holmes, it is——"

24 " It is a loyal friend and a chivalrous gentleman," said
Holmes, holding up a restraining hand. " Let that now
and for ever be enough for us."

I do not know how the incriminating book was used.
Sir James may have managed it. Or it is more probable
that so delicate a task was entrusted to the young lady's
father. The effect, at any rate, was all that could be
desired. Three days later appeared a paragraph in the
Morning Post to say that the marriage between Baron Adelbert Gruner and Miss Violet de Merville would not
take place. The same paper had the first police-court
hearing of the proceedings against Miss Kitty Winter
on the grave charge of vitriol-throwing. Such extenuating circumstances came out in the trial that the sentence, as will be remembered, was the lowest that was
25 possible for such an offence. Sherlock Holmes was
threatened with a prosecution for burglary, but when an
object is good and a client is sufficiently illustrious, even
the rigid British law becomes human and elastic. My
friend has not yet stood in the dock.

friend's career,' for even if we assume the Client
to have been Edward VII, Holmes had already
rendered services to the reigning families of Holland and Scandinavia, not to speak of the Pope,
and possessed an amethyst-and-gold snuff-box from
the King of Bohemia and an emerald tie-pin from
Queen Victoria herself for his services in the
matter of the Bruce-Partington plans, while the
issues at stake, however charming Miss de Merville may have been, must be counted trivial indeed compared with those in, say, 'The Second
Stain.' "

We may add that Conan Doyle's own opinion
of "The Adventure of the Illustrious Client" was
a high one: ". . . not remarkable for plot," he
wrote in the *Strand Magazine*, March, 1927, "but
it has a certain quality and moves adequately in
lofty circles . . ." And in a letter to John Gore
(1926), Conan Doyle wrote: "If I were to choose
the six best Holmes stories I should certainly include 'The Illustrious Client.' "

71

THE ADVENTURE OF THE RED CIRCLE

[*Wednesday, September 24, to Thursday, September 25, 1902*]

I

"WELL, Mrs. Warren, I cannot see that you have any particular cause for uneasiness, nor do I understand why I, whose time is of some value, should interfere in the matter. I really have other things to engage me." So spoke Sherlock Holmes, and turned back to the great scrap-book in which he was arranging and indexing some of his recent material.

But the landlady had the pertinacity, and also the cunning, of her sex. She held her ground firmly.

"You arranged an affair for a lodger of mine last year," she said—"Mr. Fairdale Hobbs."

"Ah, yes—a simple matter."

"But he would never cease talking of it—your kindness, sir, and the way in which you brought light into the darkness. I remembered his words when I was in doubt and darkness myself. I know you could if you only would."

Holmes was accessible upon the side of flattery, and also, to do him justice, upon the side of kindliness. The two forces made him lay down his gum-brush with a sigh of resignation and push back his chair.

"Well, well, Mrs. Warren, let us hear about it, then. You don't object to tobacco, I take it? Thank you, Watson—the matches! You are uneasy, as I understand, because your new lodger remains in his rooms and you cannot see him. Why, bless you, Mrs. Warren, if I were your lodger you often would not see me for weeks on end."

"No doubt, sir; but this is different. It frightens me, Mr. Holmes. I can't sleep for fright. To hear his quick step moving here and moving there from early morning to late at night, and yet never to catch so much as a glimpse of him—it's more than I can stand. My husband is as nervous over it as I am, but he is out at his work all day, while I get no rest from it. What is he hiding for? What has he done? Except for the girl, I am all alone in the house with him, and it's more than my nerves can stand."

Holmes leaned forward and laid his long, thin fingers upon the woman's shoulder. He had an almost hypnotic power of soothing when he wished. The scared look faded from her eyes, and her agitated features smoothed into their usual commonplace. She sat down in the chair which he had indicated.

1 *fifty shillings a week.* About $12.50 U.S. at the time.

2 *five pounds a week.* About $25.

"DEAR ME, WATSON," SAID HOLMES, STARING WITH GREAT CURIOSITY AT THE SLIPS OF FOOLSCAP . . .

Illustration by Joseph Simpson for the *Strand Magazine*, March, 1911.

" If I take it up I must understand every detail," said he. " Take time to consider. The smallest point may be the most essential. You say that the man came ten days ago, and paid you for a fortnight's board and lodging ? "

1 " He asked my terms, sir. I said fifty shillings a week. There is a small sitting-room and bedroom, and all complete, at the top of the house."

" Well ? "

2 " He said, ' I'll pay you five pounds a week if I can have it on my own terms.' I'm a poor woman, sir, and Mr. Warren earns little, and the money meant much to me. He took out a ten-pound note, and he held it out to me then and there. ' You can have the same every fortnight for a long time to come if you keep the terms,' he said. ' If not, I'll have no more to do with you.' "

" What were the terms ? "

" Well, sir, they were that he was to have a key of the house. That was all right. Lodgers often have them. Also, that he was to be left entirely to himself, and never, upon any excuse, to be disturbed."

" Nothing wonderful in that, surely ? "

" Not in reason, sir. But this is out of all reason. He has been there for ten days, and neither Mr. Warren, nor I, nor the girl has once set eyes upon him. We can hear that quick step of his pacing up and down, up and down, night, morning, and noon ; but except on that first night he has never once gone out of the house."

" Oh, he went out the first night, did he ? "

" Yes, sir, and returned very late—after we were all in bed. He told me after he had taken the rooms that he would do so, and asked me not to bar the door. I heard him come up the stair after midnight."

" But his meals ? "

" It was his particular direction that we should always, when he rang, leave his meal upon a chair, outside his door. Then he rings again when he has finished, and we take it down from the same chair. If he wants anything else he prints it on a slip of paper and leaves it."

" Prints it ? "

" Yes, sir ; prints it in pencil. Just the word, nothing more. Here's one I brought to show you—SOAP. Here's another—MATCH. This is one he left the first morning—DAILY GAZETTE. I leave that paper with his breakfast every morning."

" Dear me, Watson," said Holmes, staring with great curiosity at the slips of foolscap which the landlady had handed to him, " this is certainly a little unusual. Seclusion I can understand ; but why print ? Printing is a clumsy process. Why not write ? What would it suggest, Watson ? "

" That he desired to conceal his handwriting."

" But why ? What can it matter to him that his landlady should have a word of his writing ? Still, it may be as you say. Then, again, why such laconic messages ? "

" I cannot imagine."

" It opens a pleasing field for intelligent speculation. The words are written with a broad-pointed, violet-tinted pencil of a not unusual pattern. You will observe that the paper is torn away at the side here after the printing was done, so that the ' S ' of ' SOAP ' is partly gone. Suggestive, Watson, is it not ? ''

" Of caution ? "

" Exactly. There was evidently some mark, some thumb-print, something which might give a clue to the person's identity. Now, Mrs. Warren, you say that the **3** man was of middle size, dark, and bearded. What age would he be ? "

" Youngish, sir—not over thirty."

" Well, can you give me no further indications ? "

" He spoke good English, sir, and yet I thought he was a foreigner by his accent."

" And he was well dressed ? "

" Very smartly dressed, sir—quite the gentleman. Dark clothes—nothing you would note."

" He gave no name ? "

" No, sir."

" And has had no letters or callers ? "

" None."

" But surely you or the girl enter his room of a morning ? "

" No, sir ; he looks after himself entirely."

" Dear me ! that is certainly remarkable. What about his luggage ? "

" He had one big brown bag with him—nothing else."

" Well, we don't seem to have much material to help us. Do you say nothing has come out of that room—absolutely nothing ? "

The landlady drew an envelope from her bag ; from it she shook out two burnt matches and a cigarette-end upon the table.

" They were on his tray this morning. I brought them because I had heard that you can read great things out of small ones."

Holmes shrugged his shoulders.

" There is nothing here," said he. " The matches have, of course, been used to light cigarettes. That is obvious from the shortness of the burnt end. Half the match is consumed in lighting a pipe or cigar. But, dear me ! this cigarette stub is certainly remarkable. The gentleman was bearded and moustached, you say ? "

" Yes, sir."

" I don't understand that. I should say that only a clean-shaven man could have smoked this. Why, Watson, even your modest moustache would have been singed."

" A holder ? " I suggested.

" No, no ; the end is matted. I suppose there could not be two people in your rooms, Mrs. Warren ? "

" No, sir. He eats so little that I often wonder it can keep life in one."

" Well, I think we must wait for a little more material. After all, you have nothing to complain of. You have received your rent, and he is not a troublesome lodger, though he is certainly an unusual one. He pays you well, and if he chooses to lie concealed it is no direct business of yours. We have no excuse for an intrusion upon his privacy until we have some reason to think that there

3 *some thumb-print, something which might give a clue to the person's identity.* Mr. Rolfe Boswell, in his article, "Squaring the Red Circle," provides chronologists with a valuable clue to the proper dating of this adventure: "It was Sir Francis Galton (b. 1822, Birmingham; d. 1911, London) famous British anthropologist, who worked out the foundations of the Galton-Henry system of fingerprint classification. Final touches were added by Sir Edward Richard Henry, the knight with no last name, who later became police commissioner for the metropolitan district of London. This system was adopted by Scotland Yard in 1901. . . . The point here is that few criminals were aware of the evidential utility of fingerprints before the turn of this century. Certainly non-criminals . . . would not have known earlier about such police methods for establishing identities. Therefore, the [mysterious lodger] in 'The Adventure of the Red Circle' case tore off the corner of [the] notepaper because, during 1901, or thereafter, [that lodger] had read magazine or newspaper articles about Scotland Yard's fingerprint system, newly-introduced." The year, then, was not before 1901.

is a guilty reason for it. I've taken up the matter, and I won't lose sight of it. Report to me if anything fresh occurs, and rely upon my assistance if it should be needed."

" There are certainly some points of interest in this case, Watson," he remarked, when the landlady had left us. " It may, of course, be trivial—individual eccentricity ; or it may be very much deeper than appears on the surface. The first thing that strikes one is the obvious possibility that the person now in the rooms may be entirely different from the one who engaged them."

" Why should you think so ? "

" Well, apart from this cigarette-end, was it not suggestive that the only time the lodger went out was immediately after his taking the rooms ? He came back—or someone came back—when all witnesses were out of the way. We have no proof that the person who came back was the person who went out. Then, again, the man who took the rooms spoke English well. This other, however, prints 'match' when it should have been 'matches.' I can imagine that the word was taken out of a dictionary, which would give the noun but not the plural. The laconic style may be to conceal the absence of knowledge of English. Yes, Watson, there are good reasons to suspect that there has been a substitution of lodgers."

" But for what possible end ? "

" Ah ! there lies our problem. There is one rather obvious line of investigation." He took down the great book in which, day by day, he filed the agony columns of the various London journals. " Dear me ! " said he, turning over the pages, " what a chorus of groans, cries, and bleatings ! What a rag-bag of singular happenings ! But surely the most valuable hunting-ground that ever was given to a student of the unusual ! This person is alone, and cannot be approached by letter without a breach of that absolute secrecy which is desired. How is any news or any message to reach him from without ? Obviously by advertisement through a newspaper. There seems no other way, and fortunately we need concern ourselves with the one paper only. Here are the *Daily Gazette* extracts of the last fortnight. ' Lady with a black boa at Prince's Skating Club '—that we may pass. ' Surely Jimmy will not break his mother's heart '—that appears to be irrelevant. ' If the lady who fainted in the Brixton bus '—she does not interest me. ' Every day my heart longs——' Bleat, Watson—unmitigated bleat ! Ah ! this is a little more possible. Listen to this : ' Be patient. Will find some sure means of communication. Meanwhile, this column.—G.' That is two days after Mrs. Warren's lodger arrived. It sounds plausible, does it not ? The mysterious one could understand English, even if he could not print it. Let us see if we can pick up the trace again. Yes, here we are—three days later. ' Am making successful arrangements. Patience and prudence. The clouds will pass.—G.' Nothing for a week after that. Then comes something much more definite : ' The path is clearing. If I find chance signal message remember code agreed—one A, two B, and so on. You will hear soon.— G.' That was in yesterday's paper, and there is nothing **4** in to-day's. It's all very appropriate to Mrs. Warren's

---

4 *nothing in to-day's.* It should be noted that there is a discrepancy between Mrs. Warren's statement regarding the length of time her lodger had occupied the "small sitting-room and bedroom, and all complete" ("He has been there for ten days"), and Holmes' comments while searching the file of the *Daily Gazette.* The schedule is clearly as follows: First day—lodger arrives. Third day—first advertisement appears ("two days after Mrs. Warren's lodger arrived"). Sixth day—second advertisement appears ("three days later"). "Nothing for a week after that." Fourteenth day—third advertisement appears ("yesterday's paper"). Fifteenth day—"nothing in to-day's." By the days on which the newspapers were published, we see that "to-day" was not Sunday, Monday, Tuesday, or Friday; it follows that it must be Wednesday, Thursday, or Saturday. But it was not Saturday: on the *second* day Holmes picked up the morning newspaper from the table; Mr. Warren was on his way to work at Morton & Waylight's when he was assaulted. The second day was certainly not a Sunday. The case opened, then, on a Wednesday or a Thursday.

lodger. If we wait a little, Watson, I don't doubt that the affair will grow more intelligible."

So it proved ; for in the morning I found my friend standing on the hearthrug with his back to the fire, and a **5** smile of complete satisfaction upon his face.

" How's this, Watson ? " he cried, picking up the paper from the table. " ' High red house with white stone facings. Third floor. Second window left. After dusk. —G.' That is definite enough. I think after breakfast we must make a little reconnaissance of Mrs. Warren's neighbourhood. Ah, Mrs. Warren ! what news do you bring us this morning ? "

Our client had suddenly burst into the room with an explosive energy which told of some new and momentous development.

" It's a police matter, Mr. Holmes ! " she cried. " I'll have no more of it ! He shall pack out of that with his baggage. I would have gone straight up and told him so, only I thought it was but fair to you to take your opinion first. But I'm at the end of my patience, and when it comes to knocking my old man about——"

" Knocking Mr. Warren about ? "

" Using him roughly, anyway."

" But who used him roughly ? "

" Ah ! that's what we want to know ! It was this morning, sir. Mr. Warren is a timekeeper at Morton & Waylight's, in Tottenham Court Road. He has to be out of the house before seven. Well, this morning he had not got ten paces down the road when two men came up behind him, threw a coat over his head, and bundled him into a cab that was beside the kerb. They drove him an hour, and then opened the door and shot him out. He lay in the roadway so shaken in his wits that he never saw what became of the cab. When he picked himself up he found he was on Hampstead Heath ; so he took a bus home, and there he lies now on the sofa, while I came straight round to tell you what had happened."

" Most interesting," said Holmes. " Did he observe the appearance of these men—did he hear them talk ? "

" No ; he is clean dazed. He just knows that he was lifted up as if by magic and dropped as if by magic. Two at least were in it, and maybe three."

" And you connect this attack with your lodger ? "

" Well, we've lived there fifteen years and no such happenings ever came before. I've had enough of him. Money's not everything. I'll have him out of my house before the day is done."

" Wait a bit, Mrs. Warren. Do nothing rash. I begin to think that this affair may be very much more important than appeared at first sight. It is clear now that some danger is threatening your lodger. It is equally clear that his enemies, lying in wait for him near your door, mistook your husband for him in the foggy morning light. On discovering their mistake they released him. What they would have done had it not been a mistake, we can only conjecture."

" Well, what am I to do, Mr. Holmes ? "

" I have a great fancy to see this lodger of yours, Mrs. Warren."

5 *I found my friend standing on the hearthrug.* As the late Professor Jay Finley Christ was one of the first to point out, "It is uncertain whether or not Watson was living at Baker Street [at this time]. On the second morning he 'found Holmes waiting,' and Holmes made reference to 'our quarters.' These things are not conclusive; they might have been said in either case." We shall see that "The Adventure of the Red Circle" was subsequent to "The Adventure of the Illustrious Client"; Watson was therefore in his rooms in Queen Anne Street at this time.

" . . . TWO MEN CAME UP BEHIND HIM, THREW A COAT OVER HIS HEAD, AND BUNDLED HIM INTO A CAB . . ."

Illustration by H. M. Brock for the *Strand Magazine*, March, 1911.

6 *Howe Street.* "Watson's 'Great Orme Street . . . at the northeast side of the British Museum' identifies itself so readily with Great Ormond Street, which ends a very few blocks to the northeast of the Museum, that it is disappointing to find no Howe Street running into it, or any street with a name in any way suggesting Howe," Mr. S. F. Blake wrote in "Sherlock Holmes and the Italian Cipher." "In fact, no Howe Street or Place is listed for the entire London area in the City Council's 'List of streets and places within the administrative county of London' (1901)."

. . . I CAUGHT A GLIMPSE OF A DARK, BEAUTIFUL, HORRIFIED FACE . . .

Illustration by H. M. Brock for the *Strand Magazine*, March, 1911.

" I don't see how that is to be managed, unless you break in the door.   I always hear him unlock it as I go down the stair after I leave the tray."

" He has to take the tray in.   Surely we could conceal ourselves and see him do it."

The landlady thought for a moment.

" Well, sir, there's the box-room opposite.   I could arrange a looking-glass, maybe, and if you were behind the door——"

" Excellent ! " said Holmes.   " When does he lunch ? "

" About one, sir."

" Then Dr. Watson and I will come round in time. For the present, Mrs. Warren, good-bye."

At half-past twelve we found ourselves upon the steps of Mrs. Warren's house—a high, thin, yellow-brick edifice in Great Orme Street, a narrow thoroughfare at the northeast side of the British Museum.   Standing as it does near the corner of the street, it commands a view down Howe **6** Street, with its more pretentious houses.   Holmes pointed with a chuckle to one of these, a row of residential flats, which projected so that they could not fail to catch the eye.

" See, Watson ! " said he.   " ' High red house with stone facings.'   There is the signal station all right.   We know the place, and we know the code ; so surely our task should be simple.   There's a ' To Let ' card in that window.   It is evidently an empty flat to which the confederate has access.   Well, Mrs. Warren, what now ? "

" I have it all ready for you.   If you will both come up and leave your boots below on the landing, I'll put you there now."

It was an excellent hiding-place which she had arranged. The mirror was so placed that, seated in the dark, we could very plainly see the door opposite.   We had hardly settled down in it, and Mrs. Warren left us, when a distant tinkle announced that our mysterious neighbour had rung. Presently the landlady appeared with the tray, laid it down upon a chair beside the closed door, and then, treading heavily, departed.   Crouching together in the angle of the door, we kept our eyes fixed upon the mirror.   Suddenly, as the landlady's footsteps died away, there was the creak of a turning key, the handle revolved, and two thin hands darted out and lifted the tray from the chair.   An instant later it was hurriedly replaced, and I caught a glimpse of a dark, beautiful, horrified face glaring at the narrow opening of the box-room.   Then the door crashed to, the key turned once more, and all was silence.   Holmes twitched my sleeve, and together we stole down the stair.

" I will call again in the evening," said he to the expectant landlady.   " I think, Watson, we can discuss this business better in our own quarters."

" My surmise, as you saw, proved to be correct," said he, speaking from the depths of his easy-chair.   " There has been a substitution of lodgers.   What I did not foresee is that we should find a woman, and no ordinary woman, Watson."

" She saw us."

" Well, she saw something to alarm her.   That is certain.   The general sequence of events is pretty clear, is it not ? A couple seek refuge in London from a very terrible and instant danger. The measure of that danger is the rigour of their precautions. The man, who has some work which he must do, desires to leave the woman in absolute safety while he does it. It is not an easy problem, but he solved it in an original fashion, and so effectively that her presence was not even known to the landlady who supplies her with food. The printed messages, as is now evident, were to prevent her sex being discovered by her writing. The man cannot come near the woman, or he will guide their enemies to her. Since he cannot communicate with her direct, he has recourse to the agony column of a paper. So far all is clear."

" But what is at the root of it ? "

" Ah, yes, Watson—severely practical, as usual ! What is at the root of it all ? Mrs. Warren's whimsical problem enlarges somewhat and assumes a more sinister aspect as we proceed. This much we can say : that it is no ordinary love escapade. You saw the woman's face at the sign of danger. We have heard, too, of the attack upon the landlord, which was undoubtedly meant for the lodger. These alarms, and the desperate need for secrecy, argue that the matter is one of life or death. The attack upon Mr. Warren further shows that the enemy, whoever they are, are themselves not aware of the substitution of the female lodger for the male. It is very curious and complex, Watson."

" Why should you go further in it ? What have you to gain from it ? "

" What, indeed ? It is Art for Art's sake, Watson. I suppose when you doctored you found yourself studying cases without thought of a fee ? "

" For my education, Holmes."

" Education never ends, Watson. It is a series of lessons, with the greatest for the last. This is an instructive case. There is neither money nor credit in it, and yet one would wish to tidy it up. When dusk comes we should find ourselves one stage advanced in our investigation."

When we returned to Mrs. Warren's rooms, the gloom of a London winter evening had thickened into one grey curtain, a dead monotone of colour, broken only by the sharp yellow squares of the windows and the blurred haloes of the gas-lamps. As we peered from the darkened sitting-room of the lodging-house, one more dim light glimmered high up through the obscurity.

" Someone is moving in that room," said Holmes in a whisper, his gaunt and eager face thrust forward to the window-pane. " Yes, I can see his shadow. There he is again ! He has a candle in his hand. Now he is peering across. He wants to be sure that she is on the look-out. Now he begins to flash. Take the message also, Watson, that we may check each other. A single flash—that is ' A,' surely. Now, then. How many did you make it ? Twenty. So did I. That should mean ' T.' A T— **7** that's intelligible enough ! Another ' T.' Surely this is the beginning of a second word. Now, then—TENTA. Dead stop. That can't be all, Watson ? ' ATTENTA ' gives no sense. Nor is it any better as three words—

7 *Twenty*. The manuscript of "The Adventure of the Red Circle" reads here: *Nineteen*.

8 *'PERI.'* Almost half a century after the event, the late Professor Louis E. Lord of the Classics Department at Oberlin College pointed out that the Italian alphabet contains no K (and, he might have added, no W, X, or Y, and precious little of J). His argument, as reported by Mr. Vincent Starrett in his "Explanation" (Introduction) to *221B: Studies in Sherlock Holmes,* was as follows: "The language used is Italian, we are informed, although Holmes and Watson, who are intercepting the message, do not at first suspect it. The first letter of the message is a single flash, A, and the next is twenty flashes—'T' says Holmes. But, alas, the Italian alphabet has no letter K. . . . and so its twentieth letter is U. The full message as read by Holmes is 'Attenta, pericolo.' Yet the omission of K must have misplaced every letter below it, and Holmes should have read, not 'Attenta pericolo,' but 'Assemsa, oeqicnkn.' Or, if Signor Lucca, sending his warning, had—for the convenience of Holmes and Watson—used the English alphabet, his wife, who knew little English and was expecting the message in Italian, would have read 'Auueoua, qesicpmp.' Well, it is a sufficiently startling message, either way; and it is no slight testimony to the ability of Sherlock Holmes that he brought off the case with honors."

To this, Mr. S. F. Blake has responded that ". . . it is unfortunately necessary for me to point out [an error] which Prof. Lord himself committed. He says that Holmes should have read the message "Assemsa, oeqicnkn.' Since Holmes counted the first three series of flashes as 1, 20, 20, and then translated them A, T, T, we have to infer that he counted the other flashes in this word as 5, 14, 20, 1 in order to translate it as 'attenta.' But 1, 20, 20, 5, 14, 20, 1 flashes do not spell out 'assemsa' in any language known to me, certainly not in English or Italian, the only two in question here. They spell 'attenta' in the English alphabet and 'auueoua' in the Italian. In the English alphabet, 'assemsa' would call for 1, 19, 19, 5, 13, 19, 1 flashes, and in Italian, 1, 18, 18, 5, 12, 18, 1. A similar situation holds, obviously, with regard to the word 'pericolo' (or oeqicnkn). It is clearly *lèse majesté,* or something approaching it, to accuse the keen-eyed Holmes of being unable to count up to 20."

We have noted above that the manuscript of the adventure *does* read *Nineteen* for *Twenty* (enabling Holmes to spell out "assemsa" *in English,* and Mr. Donald A. Yates has expressed his view that the code agreed upon must have been *to spell Italian in the English alphabet* ("A Final Illumination of the Lucca Code'). But this still leaves an element of mystery in the situation: Holmes did not know that the message was in Italian when he was counting to 19; he realized that later. Thus neither a *Nineteen* or a *Twenty* will fully resolve the problem. We may conclude this note by adding that Mr. Blake's own experiments in flashing messages by means of a lighted candle have convinced him that it would have taken at least 477 waves of the candle, occupying about 4¾ minutes, to deliver the message.

' AT. TEN. TA,' unless ' T.A.' are a person's initials. There it goes again ! What's that ? ATTE—why, it is the same message over again. Curious, Watson, very curious ! Now he is off once more ! AT—why, he is repeating it for the third time. ' ATTENTA ' three times ! How often will he repeat it ? No, that seems to be the finish. He has withdrawn from the window. What do you make of it, Watson ? "

" A cipher message, Holmes."

My companion gave a sudden chuckle of comprehension. " And not a very obscure cipher, Watson," said he. " Why, of course, it is Italian ! The ' A ' means that it is addressed to a woman. ' Beware ! Beware ! Beware !' How's that, Watson ? "

" I believe you have hit it."

" Not a doubt of it. It is a very urgent message, thrice repeated to make it more so. But beware of what ? Wait a bit ; he is coming to the window once more."

Again we saw the dim silhouette of a crouching man and the whisk of the small flame across the window, as the signals were renewed. They came more rapidly than before—so rapid that it was hard to follow them.

" ' PERICOLO '—' Pericolo '—Eh, what's that, Watson ? Danger, isn't it ? Yes, by Jove ! it's a danger signal. **8** There he goes again !' PERI.' Halloa, what on earth——"

The light had suddenly gone out, the glimmering square of window had disappeared, and the third floor formed a dark band round the lofty building, with its tiers of shining casements. That last warning cry had been suddenly cut short. How, and by whom ? The same thought occurred on the instant to us both. Holmes sprang up from where he crouched by the window.

" This is serious, Watson," he cried. " There is some devilry going forward ! Why should such a message stop in such a way ? I should put Scotland Yard in touch with this business—and yet, it is too pressing for us to leave."

" Shall I go for the police ? "

" We must define the situation a little more clearly. It may bear some more innocent interpretation. Come, Watson, let us go across ourselves and see what we can make of it."

II

As we walked rapidly down Howe Street I glanced back at the building which we had left. There, dimly outlined at the top window, I could see the shadow of a head, a woman's head, gazing tensely, rigidly, out into the night, waiting with breathless suspense for the renewal of that interrupted message. At the doorway of the Howe Street flats a man, muffled in a cravat and greatcoat, was leaning against the railing. He started as the hall-light fell upon our faces.

" Holmes !" he cried.

9 " Why, Gregson !" said my companion, as he shook hands with the Scotland Yard detective. " Journeys end **10** with lovers' meetings. What brings you here ? "

" The same reasons that bring you, I expect," said Gregson. " How you got on to it I can't imagine."

" Different threads, but leading up to the same tangle.

I've been taking the signals."

" Signals ? "

" Yes, from that window. They broke off in the middle. We came over to see the reason. But since it is safe in your hands I see no object in continuing the business."

" Wait a bit ! " cried Gregson, eagerly. " I'll do you this justice, Mr. Holmes, that I was never in a case yet that I didn't feel stronger for having you on my side. There's only the one exit to these flats, so we have him safe."

" Who is he ? "

" Well, well, we score over you for once, Mr. Holmes. You must give us best this time." He struck his stick sharply upon the ground, on which a cabman, his whip in his hand, sauntered over from a four-wheeler which stood on the far side of the street. " May I introduce you to Mr. Sherlock Holmes ? " he said to the cabman. " This is Mr. Leverton, of Pinkerton's American Agency."

" The hero of the Long Island Cave mystery ? " said **11** Holmes. " Sir, I am pleased to meet you."

The American, a quiet, business-like young man, with a clean-shaven, hatchet face, flushed up at the words of commendation. " I am on the trail of my life now, Mr. Holmes," said he. " If I can get Gorgiano——"

" What ! Gorgiano of the Red Circle ? "

" Oh, he has a European fame, has he ? Well, we've learned all about him in America. We *know* he is at the bottom of fifty murders, and yet we have nothing positive we can take him on. I tracked him over from New York, and I've been close to him for a week in London, waiting some excuse to get my hand on his collar. Mr. Gregson and I ran him to ground in that big tenement house, and there's only the one door, so he can't slip us. There's three folk come out since he went in, but I'll swear he wasn't one of them."

" Mr. Holmes talks of signals," said Gregson. " I expect, as usual, he knows a good deal that we don't."

In a few clear words Holmes explained the situation as it had appeared to us. The American struck his hands together with vexation.

" He's on to us ! " he cried.

" Why do you think so ? "

" Well, it figures out that way, does it not ? Here he is, sending out messages to an accomplice—there are several of his gang in London. Then suddenly, just as by your own account he was telling them that there was danger, he broke short off. What could it mean except that from the window he had suddenly either caught sight of us in the street, or in some way come to understand how close the danger was, and that he must act right away, if he was to avoid it ? What do you suggest, Mr. Holmes ? "

" That we go up at once and see for ourselves."

" But we have no warrant for his arrest."

" He is in unoccupied premises under suspicious circumstances," said Gregson. " That is good enough for the moment. When we have him by the heels we can see if New York can't help us to keep him. I'll take the responsibility of arresting him now."

9 *"Why, Gregson!"* Mr. T. S. Blakeney has noted that we "so seldom see [Inspector Gregson] in late years that an early date may be assumed for most of his cases." "The Adventure of the Red Circle" must therefore be taken as an indication that Inspector Gregson's tenure at Scotland Yard (like Inspector Lestrade's) was a lengthy one.

10 *"Journeys end with lovers' meetings.* For the second time, Holmes slightly misquotes *Twelfth Night*, Act II, Scene 3, line 46.

11 *"The hero of the Long Island Cave mystery?"* "The mystery, on true Sherlockian principles, is that there are no caves on Long Island," the late Christopher Morley wrote in "Was Sherlock Holmes an American?"

"BY GEORGE! IT'S BLACK GORGIANO HIMSELF!" CRIED
THE AMERICAN DETECTIVE.

Illustration by H. M. Brock for the *Strand Magazine*, April, 1911.

HOLMES . . . WAS PASSING IT BACKWARDS AND
FORWARDS ACROSS THE WINDOW-PANES.

Illustration by H. M. Brock for the *Strand Magazine*, April, 1911.

Our official detectives may blunder in the matter of intelligence, but never in that of courage. Gregson climbed the stair to arrest this desperate murderer with the same absolutely quiet and business-like bearing with which he would have ascended the official staircase of Scotland Yard. The Pinkerton man had tried to push past him, but Gregson had firmly elbowed him back. London dangers were the privilege of the London force.

The door of the left-hand flat upon the third landing was standing ajar. Gregson pushed it open. Within all was absolute silence and darkness. I struck a match, and lit the detective's lantern. As I did so, and as the flicker steadied into a flame, we all gave a gasp of surprise. On the deal boards of the carpetless floor there was outlined a fresh track of blood. The red steps pointed towards us, and led away from an inner room, the door of which was closed. Gregson flung it open and held his light full blaze in front of him, whilst we all peered eagerly over his shoulders.

In the middle of the floor of the empty room was huddled the figure of an enormous man, his clean-shaven, swarthy face grotesquely horrible in its contortion, and his head encircled by a ghastly crimson halo of blood, lying in a broad wet circle upon the white woodwork. His knees were drawn up, his hands thrown out in agony, and from the centre of his broad, brown, upturned throat there projected the white haft of a knife driven blade-deep into his body. Giant as he was, the man must have gone down like a pole-axed ox before that terrific blow. Beside his right hand a most formidable horn-handled, two-edged dagger lay upon the floor, and near it a black kid glove.

"By George! it's Black Gorgiano himself!" cried the American detective. "Someone has got ahead of us this time."

"Here is the candle in the window, Mr. Holmes," said Gregson. "Why, whatever are you doing?"

Holmes had stepped across, had lit the candle, and was passing it backwards and forwards across the window-panes. Then he peered into the darkness, blew the candle out, and threw it on the floor.

"I rather think that will be helpful," said he. He came over and stood in deep thought while the two professionals were examining the body. "You say that three people came out from the flat while you were waiting downstairs," said he, at last. "Did you observe them closely?"

"Yes, I did."

"Was there a fellow about thirty, black-bearded, dark, of middle size?"

"Yes; he was the last to pass me."

"That is your man, I fancy. I can give you his description, and we have a very excellent outline of his footmark. That should be enough for you."

"Not much, Mr. Holmes, among the millions of London."

"Perhaps not. That is why I thought it best to summon this lady to your aid."

We all turned round at the words. There, framed in the doorway, was a tall and beautiful woman—the mysterious lodger of Bloomsbury.   Slowly she advanced, her face pale and drawn with a frightful apprehension, her eyes fixed and staring, her terrified gaze riveted upon the dark figure on the floor.

"You have killed him!" she muttered. "Oh, *Dio mio*, you have killed him!" Then I heard a sudden sharp intake of her breath, and she sprang into the air with a cry of joy.   Round and round the room she danced, her hands clapping, her dark eyes gleaming with delighted wonder, and a thousand pretty Italian exclamations pouring from her lips.   It was terrible and amazing to see such a woman so convulsed with joy at such a sight.   Suddenly she stopped and gazed at us all with a questioning stare.

"But you! You are police, are you not? You have killed Giuseppe Gorgiano. Is it not so?"

"We are police, madam."

She looked round into the shadows of the room.

"But where, then, is Gennaro?" she asked.   "He is my husband, Gennaro Lucca.   I am Emilia Lucca, and we are both from New York.   Where is Gennaro?   He called me this moment from this window, and I ran with all my speed."

"It was I who called," said Holmes.

"You! How could you call?"

"Your cipher was not difficult, madam.   Your presence here was desirable.   I knew that I had only to flash 'Vieni' and you would surely come."

The beautiful Italian looked with awe at my companion.

"I do not understand how you know these things," she said. "Giuseppe Gorgiano—how did he——" She paused, and then suddenly her face lit up with pride and delight. "Now I see it! My Gennaro! My splendid, beautiful Gennaro, who has guarded me safe from all harm, he did it, with his own strong hand he killed the monster! Oh, Gennaro, how wonderful you are! What woman could ever be worthy of such a man?"

"Well, Mrs. Lucca," said the prosaic Gregson, laying his hand upon the lady's sleeve with as little sentiment as if she were a Notting Hill hooligan, "I am not very clear yet who you are or what you are; but you've said enough to make it very clear that we shall want you at the Yard."

"One moment, Gregson," said Holmes. "I rather fancy that this lady may be as anxious to give us information as we can be to get it.   You understand, madam, that your husband will be arrested and tried for the death of the man who lies before us?   What you say may be used in evidence.   But if you think that he has acted from **12** motives which are not criminal, and which he would wish to have known, then you cannot serve him better than by telling us the whole story."

"Now that Gorgiano is dead we fear nothing," said the lady.   "He was a devil and a monster, and there can be no judge in the world who would punish my husband for having killed him."

"In that case," said Holmes, "my suggestion is that we lock this door, leave things as we found them, go with this lady to her room, and form our opinion after we have heard what it is that she has to say to us."

SLOWLY SHE ADVANCED, HER FACE PALE AND DRAWN
WITH A FRIGHTFUL APPREHENSION . . .

Illustration by H. M. Brock for the *Strand Magazine*, April, 1911.

12 *What you say may be used in evidence.* We note that Holmes here uses the correct formula—not the "used in evidence against you" favored by some writers of fictional detective stories.

Half an hour later we were seated, all four, in the small sitting-room of Signora Lucca, listening to her remarkable narrative of those sinister events, the ending of which we had chanced to witness. She spoke in rapid and fluent but very unconventional English, which, for the sake of clearness, I will make grammatical.

" I was born in Posilippo, near Naples," said she, " and was the daughter of Augusto Barelli, who was the chief lawyer and once the deputy of that part. Gennaro was in my father's employment, and I came to love him, as any woman must. He had neither money nor position—nothing but his beauty and strength and energy—so my father forbade the match. We fled together, were married at Bari, and sold my jewels to gain the money which would take us to America. This was four years ago, and we have been in New York ever since.

" Fortune was very good to us at first. Gennaro was able to do a service to an Italian gentleman—he saved him from some ruffians in the place called the Bowery, and so made a powerful friend. His name was Tito Castalotte, and he was the senior partner of the great firm of Castalotte & Zamba, who are the chief fruit importers of New York. Signor Zamba is an invalid, and our new friend Castalotte has all power within the firm, which employs more than three hundred men. He took my husband into his employment, made him head of a department, and showed his goodwill towards him in every way. Signor Castalotte was a bachelor, and I believe that he felt as if Gennaro was his son, and both my husband and I loved him as if he were our father. We had taken and furnished a little house in Brooklyn, and our whole future seemed assured, when that black cloud appeared which was soon to overspread our sky.

" One night, when Gennaro returned from his work, he brought a fellow-countryman back with him. His name was Gorgiano, and he had come also from Posilippo. He was a huge man, as you can testify, for you have looked upon his corpse. Not only was his body that of a giant, but everything about him was grotesque, gigantic, and terrifying. His voice was like thunder in our little house. There was scarce room for the whirl of his great arms as he talked. His thoughts, his emotions, his passions, all were exaggerated and monstrous. He talked, or rather roared, with such energy that others could but sit and listen, cowed with the mighty stream of words. His eyes blazed at you and held you at his mercy. He was a terrible and wonderful man. I thank God that he is dead !

" He came again and again. Yet I was aware that Gennaro was no more happy than I was in his presence. My poor husband would sit pale and listless, listening to the endless raving upon politics and upon social questions which made up our visitor's conversation. Gennaro said nothing, but I who knew him so well could read in his face some emotion which I had never seen there before. At first I thought that it was dislike. And then, gradually, I understood that it was more than dislike. It was fear—a deep, secret, shrinking fear. That night—the night that I read his terror—I put my arms round him and I implored him by his love for me and by all that he held dear to hold nothing from me, and to tell me why this huge man overshadowed him so.

"He told me, and my own heart grew cold as ice as I listened. My poor Gennaro, in his wild and fiery days, when all the world seemed against him and his mind was driven half mad by the injustices of life, had joined a Neapolitan society, the Red Circle, which was allied to the old Carbonari. The oaths and secrets of this brotherhood **13** were frightful ; but once within its rule no escape was possible. When we had fled to America Gennaro thought that he had cast it all off for ever. What was his horror one evening to meet in the streets the very man who had initiated him in Naples, the giant Gorgiano, a man who had earned the name of ' Death ' in the South of Italy, for he was red to the elbow in murder ! He had come to New York to avoid the Italian police, and he had already planted a branch of this dreadful society in his new home. All this Gennaro told me, and showed me a summons which he had received that very day, a Red Circle drawn upon the head of it, telling him that a lodge would be held upon a certain date, and that his presence at it was required and ordered.

"That was bad enough, but worse was to come. I had noticed for some time that when Gorgiano came to us, as he constantly did, in the evening, he spoke much to me ; and even when his words were to my husband those terrible, glaring, wild-beast eyes of his were always turned upon me. One night his secret came out. I had awakened what he called ' love ' within him—the love of a brute—a savage. Gennaro had not yet returned when he came. He pushed his way in, seized me in his mighty arms, hugged me in his bear's embrace, covered me with kisses, and implored me to come away with him. I was struggling and screaming when Gennaro entered and attacked him. He struck Gennaro senseless and fled from the house which he was never more to enter. It was a deadly enemy that we made that night.

"A few days later came the meeting. Gennaro returned from it with a face which told me that something dreadful had occurred. It was worse than we could have imagined possible. The funds of the society were raised by blackmailing rich Italians and threatening them with violence should they refuse the money. It seems that Castalotte, our dear friend and benefactor, had been approached. He had refused to yield to threats, and he had handed the notices to the police. It was resolved now that such an example should be made of him as would prevent any other victim from rebelling. At the meeting it was arranged that he and his house should be blown up with dynamite. There was a drawing of lots as to who should carry out the deed. Gennaro saw our enemy's cruel face smiling at him as he dipped his hand in the bag. No doubt it had been prearranged in some fashion, for it was the fatal disc with the Red Circle upon it, the mandate for murder, which lay upon his palm. He was to kill his best friend, or he was to expose himself and me to the vengeance of his comrades. It was part of their fiendish system to punish those whom they feared or hated by injuring not only their own persons, but those whom they

13 *the old Carbonari.* The manuscript reads here *the famous Camorra.*

14 *a Wagner night at Covent Garden!* Again, Mr. Rolfe Boswell, an eminent musicologist, has proved himself invaluable in dating "The Adventure of the Red Circle." His essay on the case continues: "There were no winter performances of opera at Covent Garden in those times: there was, in 1901, only a summer season. In 1902 an autumnal series was added, and there were several Wagner nights, the last of which was on Thursday, 25 September, when Philip Brozel and Blanch Marchesi were starred in *Tristan and Isolda* with Marie Alexander as Brängane. Bearing in mind that London's equinoctial gales, as Watson remarked in 'The Five Orange Pips,' often are 'very long and very severe,' he can be excused for believing, nearly a decade later ["The Adventure of the Red Circle" was published in March–April, 1911], when he wrote up the case, that he became an Imperfect Wagnerite in 'the gloom of a London winter evening.'" We have said that the case opened on a Wednesday or a Thursday. Since Holmes' Wagner night at Covent Garden was the night of the second day, and Mr. Boswell's Wagner night at Covent Garden was Thursday, September 25, 1902, we hold that the case opened on *Wednesday, September 24, 1902.*

Bibliographical Note: As the opening page of the manuscript of this adventure attests, Conan Doyle's first thought was to call it "The Adventure of the Bloomsbury Lodger." The manuscript consists of 23 pages, folio, white vellum; it was listed in Scribner's Sherlock Holmes Catalogue at $450; in October, 1946, it was owned by Mr. Vincent Starrett of Chicago; in April, 1947, it was listed for sale by the House of El Dieff at $600; it is presently owned by Mr. J. Bliss Austin of Philadelphia.

The Adventure of the ~~Bloomsbury Lodger~~ Red Circle

" Well, Mrs. Warren, I cannot see that you have any particular cause for uneasiness, nor do I understand why I, whose time is of some value, should interfere in the matter. I really have other things to engage me". So spoke Sherlock Holmes, and turned back to the great scrap book in which he was arranging and indexing some of his recent material.

But the landlady had the pertinacity, and also the cunning of her sex. She held her ground firmly.

" You arranged an affair for a lodger of mine last year" she said " Mr. Fairdale Hobbs "

" Ah yes — a simple matter "

" But he would never cease talking of it — your

loved, and it was the knowledge of this which hung as a terror over my poor Gennaro's head and drove him nearly crazy with apprehension.

" All that night we sat together, our arms round each other, each strengthening each for the troubles that lay before us. The very next evening had been fixed for the attempt. By midday my husband and I were on our way to London, but not before he had given our benefactor full warning of his danger, and had also left such information for the police as would safeguard his life for the future.

" The rest, gentlemen, you know for yourselves. We were sure that our enemies would be behind us like our own shadows. Gorgiano had his private reasons for vengeance, but in any case we knew how ruthless, cunning, and untiring he could be. Both Italy and America are full of stories of his dreadful powers. If ever they were exerted it would be now. My darling made use of the few clear days which our start had given us in arranging for a refuge for me in such a fashion that no possible danger could reach me. For his own part, he wished to be free that he might communicate both with the American and with the Italian police. I do not myself know where he lived, or how. All that I learned was through the columns of a newspaper. But once, as I looked through my window, I saw two Italians watching the house, and I understood that in some way Gorgiano had found out our retreat. Finally Gennaro told me, through the paper, that he would signal to me from a certain window, but when the signals came they were nothing but warnings, which were suddenly interrupted. It is very clear to me now that he knew Gorgiano to be close upon him, and that, thank God! he was ready for him when he came. And now, gentlemen, I would ask you whether we have anything to fear from the Law, or whether any judge upon earth would condemn my Gennaro for what he has done ? "

" Well, Mr. Gregson," said the American, looking across at the official, " I don't know what your British point of view may be, but I guess that in New York this lady's husband will receive a pretty general vote of thanks."

" She will have to come with me and see the Chief," Gregson answered. " If what she says is corroborated, I do not think she or her husband has much to fear. But what I can't make head or tail of, Mr. Holmes, is how on earth *you* got yourself mixed up in the matter."

" Education, Gregson, education. Still seeking knowledge at the old university. Well, Watson, you have one more specimen of the tragic and grotesque to add to your collection. By the way, it is not eight o'clock, and a **14** Wagner night at Covent Garden ! If we hurry, we might be in time for the second act."

VIII. THE PARTNERSHIP
COMES TO A CLOSE

[January to October, 1903]

The good Watson had at that time deserted me for a wife.
—Sherlock Holmes,
"The Adventure of the Blanched Soldier"

The relations between us in those latter days were peculiar.
—John H. Watson, M.D.,
"The Adventure of the Creeping Man"

72

THE ADVENTURE OF THE BLANCHED SOLDIER

[Wednesday, January 7, to Monday, January 12, 1903]

THE ideas of my friend Watson, though limited, are exceedingly pertinacious. For a long time he has worried me to write an experience of my own. Perhaps I have rather invited this persecu- **1** tion, since I have often had occasion to point out to him how superficial are his own accounts and to accuse him of pandering to popular taste instead of confining himself rigidly to facts and figures. " Try it yourself, Holmes ! " he has retorted, and I am compelled to admit that, having taken my pen in my hand, I do begin to realize that the matter must be presented in such a way as may interest the reader. The following case can hardly fail to do so, as it is among the strangest happenings in my collection, though it chanced that Watson had no note of it in his collection. Speaking of my old friend and biographer, I would take this opportunity to remark that if I burden myself with a companion in my various little inquiries it is not done out of sentiment or caprice, but it is that Watson has some remarkable characteristics of his own, to which in his modesty he has given small attention amid his exaggerated estimates of my own performances. A confederate who foresees your conclusions and course of action is always dangerous, but one to whom each development comes as a perpetual surprise, and to whom the future is always a closed book, is, indeed, an ideal helpmate.

I find from my notebook that it was in January, 1903, just after the conclusion of the Boer War, that I had my visit from Mr. James M. Dodd, a big, fresh, sunburned, upstanding Briton. The good Watson had at that time deserted me for a wife, the only selfish action which I can recall in our association. I was alone.

It is my habit to sit with my back to the window and to place my visitors in the opposite chair, where the light falls full upon them. Mr. James M. Dodd seemed somewhat at a loss how to begin the interview. I did not attempt to help him, for his silence gave me more time for observation. I have found it wise to impress clients with a sense of power, and so I gave him some of my conclusions.

" From South Africa, sir, I perceive."

" Yes, sir," he answered, with some surprise.

1 *to write an experience of my own.* "The Adventure of the Blanched Soldier" and a later adventure, "The Lion's Mane," are both ostensibly from the pen of Holmes, not Watson. But critics have found reason to doubt that he really wrote them.

"It seems very unlikely that he would start to record his cases at this stage in his career," the late Gavin Brend commented in *My Dear Holmes*. "Moreover, if he were the author the style would surely be quite different. The probability is that Watson was the author of both ["The Adventure of the Blanched Soldier" and "The Adventure of the Lion's Mane," as well as the "third-person narrative, "The Adventure of the Mazarin Stone."]"

And D. Martin Dakin has written ("The Problem of the Case-Book"): "After [Holmes'] caustic comments on Watson's attempt at popular stories, is it credible that he would have tried to write in the same vein himself? (The excuses for doing so prefaced to 'The Adventure of the Blanched Soldier' are singularly unconvincing.) Would he not rather have reserved his analytical comments on his own cases for that monumental work on the *Whole Art of Detection* which his admirers are still eagerly awaiting and which presumably is still in the hands of his literary executors? Even if he did decide to try his hand at a popular account, could he have found nothing better, even among the cases unknown to Watson, than these two rather undistinguished adventures, which do not even display his powers to any marked advantage? The narrative and style are not such as we would expect from Holmes' keen incisive mind: and if it be argued that we have no other means of telling what Holmes was like as a writer, I reply that we have. In 'The *Gloria Scott*' and 'The Musgrave Ritual' we have what are, in effect, two cases of Holmes as related by himself (not to speak of shorter accounts of past exploits given to Watson in such stories as 'The Final Problem' and 'The Adventure of the Empty House'), and they show Holmes as an excellent story-teller—lucid, powerful and clear in every detail. 'The

Adventure of the Blanched Soldier' and 'The Adventure of the Lion's Mane' come poorly out of the comparison. We conclude that these two are pseudonymous stories, possibly written up from facts supplied by Holmes to the author (whoever he may have been), but more likely pure inventions."

2 *Throgmorton Street*. This street, which lies just behind the Bank of England, is the "home" of London's stockbrokers. Its name recalls Sir Nicholas Throgmorton, a Tudor statesman who was instrumental in bringing Lady Jane Grey to the throne, and was the father-in-law of Sir Walter Raleigh. Sir Nicholas was the Ambassador to France in the reign of Queen Elizabeth I, and was said to have been poisoned by the Earl of Leicester.

3 *the Crimean V.C.* "The medal," the late A. Carson Simpson wrote in *Numismatics in the Canon*, Part III, "is an attractive one, with the diademed young head of Queen Victoria left, the legend VICTORIA REGINA and the date 1854. The reverse shows a Roman soldier with short sword and round shield; he is being crowned with a laurel-wreath by a smaller winged figure of Victory; the word CRIMEA appears on the left. The medal is suspended by a light blue ribbon, with narrow yellow edges, from a pin on a top bar of leaf design."

I LIT MY PIPE AND LEANED BACK IN MY CHAIR.

Illustration by Howard K. Elcock for the *Strand Magazine*, November, 1926.

"Imperial Yeomanry, I fancy."

"Exactly."

"Middlesex Corps, no doubt."

"That is so. Mr. Holmes, you are a wizard."

I smiled at his bewildered expression.

"When a gentleman of virile appearance enters my room with such tan upon his face as an English sun could never give, and with his handkerchief in his sleeve instead of in his pocket, it is not difficult to place him. You wear a short beard, which shows that you were not a regular. You have the cut of a riding-man. As to Middlesex, your card has already shown me that you are **2** a stockbroker from Throgmorton Street. What other regiment would you join?"

"You see everything."

"I see no more than you, but I have trained myself to notice what I see. However, Mr. Dodd, it was not to discuss the science of observation that you called upon me this morning. What has been happening at Tuxbury Old Park?"

"Mr. Holmes——!"

"My dear sir, there is no mystery. Your letter came with that heading, and as you fixed this appointment in very pressing terms it was clear that something sudden and important had occurred."

"Yes, indeed. But the letter was written in the afternoon, and a good deal has happened since then. If Colonel Emsworth had not kicked me out——"

"Kicked you out!"

"Well, that was what it amounted to. He is a hard nail, is Colonel Emsworth. The greatest martinet in the Army in his day, and it was a day of rough language, too. I couldn't have stuck the Colonel if it had not been for Godfrey's sake."

I lit my pipe and leaned back in my chair.

"Perhaps you will explain what you are talking about."

My client grinned mischievously.

"I had got into the way of supposing that you knew everything without being told," said he. "But I will give you the facts, and I hope to God that you will be able to tell me what they mean. I've been awake all night puzzling my brain, and the more I think the more incredible does it become.

"When I joined up in January, 1901—just two years ago—young Godfrey Emsworth had joined the same squadron. He was Colonel Emsworth's only son— **3** Emsworth, the Crimean V.C.—and he had the fighting blood in him, so it is no wonder he volunteered. There was not a finer lad in the regiment. We formed a friendship—the sort of friendship which can only be made when one lives the same life and shares the same joys and sorrows. He was my mate—and that means a good deal in the Army. We took the rough and the smooth together for a year of hard fighting. Then he was hit with a bullet from an elephant gun in the action near Diamond Hill outside Pretoria. I got one letter from the hospital at Cape Town and one from Southampton. Since then not a word—not one word, Mr. Holmes, for six months and more, and he my closest pal.

" Well, when the war was over, and we all got back, I wrote to his father and asked where Godfrey was. No answer.   I waited a bit and then I wrote again.   This time I had a reply, short and gruff.   Godfrey had gone on a voyage round the world, and it was not likely that he would be back for a year.   That was all.

" I wasn't satisfied, Mr. Holmes.   The whole thing seemed to me so damned unnatural.   He was a good lad and he would not drop a pal like that.   It was not like him.   Then, again, I happened to know that he was heir to a lot of money, and also that his father and he did not always hit it off too well.   The old man was sometimes a bully, and young Godfrey had too much spirit to stand it.   No, I wasn't satisfied, and I determined that I would get to the root of the matter.   It happened, however, that my own affairs needed a lot of straightening out, after two years' absence, and so it is only this week that I have been able to take up Godfrey's case again.   But since I have taken it up I mean to drop everything in order to see it through."

Mr. James M. Dodd appeared to be the sort of person whom it would be better to have as a friend than as an enemy.   His blue eyes were stern and his square jaw had set hard as he spoke.

" Well, what have you done ? " I asked.

" My first move was to get down to his home, Tuxbury Old Park, near Bedford, and to see for myself how **4** the ground lay.   I wrote to the mother, therefore—I had had quite enough of the curmudgeon of a father—and I made a clean frontal attack : Godfrey was my chum, I had a great deal of interest which I might tell her of our common experiences, I should be in the neighbourhood, would there be any objection, et cetera ?   In reply I had quite an amiable answer from her and an offer to put me up for the night.   That was what took me down on Monday.

" Tuxbury Old Hall is inaccessible—five miles from anywhere.   There was no trap at the station, so I had to walk, carrying my suit-case, and it was nearly dark before I arrived.   It is a great wandering house, standing in a considerable park.   I should judge it was of all sorts of ages and styles, starting on a half-timbered Elizabethan foundation and ending in a Victorian portico. Inside it was all panelling and tapestry and half-effaced old pictures, a house of shadows and mystery.   There was a butler, old Ralph, who seemed about the same age as the house, and there was his wife, who might have been older.   She had been Godfrey's nurse, and I had heard him speak of her as second only to his mother in his affections, so I was drawn to her in spite of her queer appearance.   The mother I liked also—a gentle little white mouse of a woman.   It was only the Colonel himself whom I barred.

" We had a bit of a barney right away, and I should have walked back to the station if I had not felt that it might be playing his game for me to do so.   I was shown straight into his study, and there I found him, a huge, bow-backed man with a smoky skin and a straggling grey beard, seated behind his littered desk.   A red-veined nose jutted out like a vulture's beak, and two fierce grey

4 *Bedford*. A market center on the Ouse River in Bedfordshire in south central England. John Bunyan preached there, and it is the location of one of England's largest public schools.

eyes glared at me from under tufted brows. I could understand now why Godfrey seldom spoke of his father.

" ' Well, sir,' said he in a rasping voice. ' I should be interested to know the real reasons for this visit.'

" I answered that I had explained them in my letter to his wife.

" ' Yes, yes ; you said that you had known Godfrey in Africa. We have, of course, only your word for that.'

" ' I have his letters to me in my pocket.'

" ' Kindly let me see them.'

" He glanced at the two which I handed him, and then he tossed them back.

" ' Well, what then ? ' he asked.

" ' I was fond of your son Godfrey, sir. Many ties and memories united us. Is it not natural that I should wonder at his sudden silence and should wish to know what has become of him ? '

" ' I have some recollection, sir, that I had already corresponded with you and had told you what had become of him. He has gone upon a voyage round the world. His health was in a poor way after his African experiences, and both his mother and I were of opinion that complete rest and change were needed. Kindly pass that explanation on to any other friends who may be interested in the matter.'

" ' Certainly,' I answered. ' But perhaps you would have the goodness to let me have the name of the steamer and of the line by which he sailed, together with the date. I have no doubt that I should be able to get a letter through to him.'

" My request seemed both to puzzle and to irritate my host. His great eyebrows came down over his eyes and he tapped his fingers impatiently on the table. He looked up at last with the expression of one who has seen his adversary make a dangerous move at chess, and has decided how to meet it.

" ' Many people, Mr. Dodd,' said he, ' would take offence at your infernal pertinacity and would think that this insistence had reached the point of damned impertinence.'

" ' You must put it down, sir, to my real love for your son.'

" ' Exactly. I have already made every allowance upon that score. I must ask you, however, to drop these inquiries. Every family has its own inner knowledge and its own motives, which cannot always be made clear to outsiders, however well-intentioned. My wife is anxious to hear something of Godfrey's past which you are in a position to tell her, but I would ask you to let the present and the future alone. Such inquiries serve no useful purpose, sir, and place us in a delicate and difficult position.'

" So I came to a dead end, Mr. Holmes. There was no getting past it. I could only pretend to accept the situation and register a vow inwardly that I would never rest until my friend's fate had been cleared up. It was a dull evening. We dined quietly, the three of us in a gloomy, faded old room. The lady questioned me eagerly about her son, but the old man seemed morose and depressed. I was so bored by the whole proceeding that I made an excuse as soon as I decently could and retired to my bedroom. It was a large, bare room on the ground floor, as gloomy as the rest of the house, but after a year of sleeping upon the veldt, Mr. Holmes, one is not too particular about one's quarters. I opened the curtains and looked out into the garden, remarking that it was a fine night with a bright half-moon. Then I sat down by the roaring fire with the lamp on a table beside me, and endeavoured to distract my mind with a novel. I was interrupted, however, by Ralph, the old butler, who came in with a fresh supply of coals.

" ' I thought you might run short in the night-time, sir. It is bitter weather and these rooms are cold.'

" He hesitated before leaving the room, and when I looked round he was standing facing me with a wistful look upon his wrinkled face.

" ' Beg your pardon, sir, but I could not help hearing what you said of young Master Godfrey at dinner. You know, sir, that my wife nursed him, and so I may say I am his foster-father. It's natural we should take an interest. And you say he carried himself well, sir ? '

" ' There was no braver man in the regiment. He pulled me out once from under the rifles of the Boers, or maybe I should not be here.'

" The old butler rubbed his skinny hands.

" ' Yes, sir, yes, that is Master Godfrey all over. He was always courageous. There's not a tree in the park, sir, that he has not climbed. Nothing would stop him. He was a fine boy—and oh, sir, he was a fine man.'

" I sprang to my feet.

" ' Look here ! ' I cried. ' You say he *was*. You speak as if he were dead. What is all this mystery ? What has become of Godfrey Emsworth ? '

" I gripped the old man by the shoulder, but he shrank away.

" ' I don't know what you mean, sir. Ask the master about Master Godfrey. He knows. It is not for me to interfere.'

" He was leaving the room, but I held his arm.

" ' Listen,' I said. ' You are going to answer one question before you leave if I have to hold you all night. Is Godfrey dead ? '

" He could not face my eyes. He was like a man hypnotized. The answer was dragged from his lips. It was a terrible and unexpected one.

" ' I wish to God he was ! ' he cried, and, tearing himself free, he dashed from the room.

" You will think, Mr. Holmes, that I returned to my chair in no very happy state of mind. The old man's words seemed to me to bear only one interpretation. Clearly my poor friend had become involved in some criminal, or, at the least, disreputable, transaction which touched the family honour. That stern old man had sent his son away and hidden him from the world lest some scandal should come to light. Godfrey was a reckless fellow. He was easily influenced by those around him. No doubt he had fallen into bad hands and

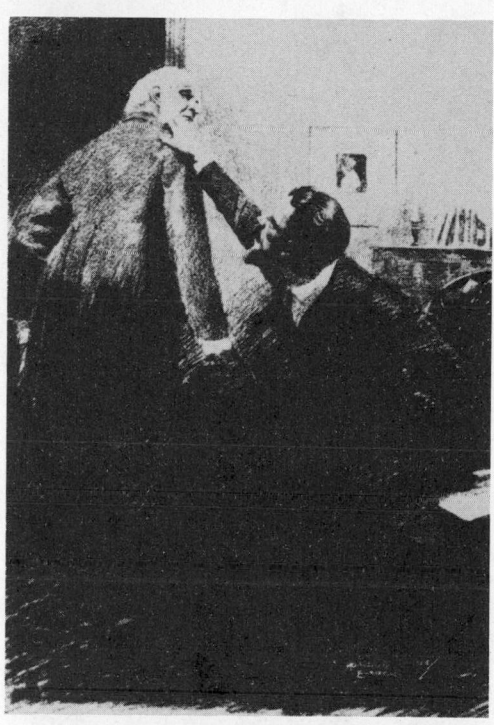

"I GRIPPED THE OLD MAN BY THE SHOULDER, BUT HE SHRANK AWAY."

Illustration by Howard K. Elcock for the *Strand Magazine*, November, 1926.

"... IT WAS HIS FACE WHICH HELD MY GAZE."

Illustration by Frederic Dorr Steele for *Liberty Magazine*, October 16, 1926.

"HE SPRANG BACK WHEN HE SAW THAT I WAS LOOKING AT HIM ..."

Illustration by Howard K. Elcock for the *Strand Magazine*, November, 1926.

been misled to his ruin. It was a piteous business, if it was indeed so, but even now it was my duty to hunt him out and see if I could aid him. I was anxiously pondering the matter when I looked up, and there was Godfrey Emsworth standing before me."

My client had paused as one in deep emotion.

"Pray continue," I said. "Your problem presents some very unusual features."

"He was outside the window, Mr. Holmes, with his face pressed against the glass. I have told you that I looked out at the night. When I did so, I left the curtains partly open. His figure was framed in this gap. The window came down to the ground and I could see the whole length of it, but it was his face which held my gaze. He was deadly pale—never have I seen a man so white. I reckon ghosts may look like that ; but his eyes met mine, and they were the eyes of a living man. He sprang back when he saw that I was looking at him, and he vanished into the darkness.

"There was something shocking about the man, Mr. Holmes. It wasn't merely that ghastly face glimmering as white as cheese in the darkness. It was more subtle than that—something slinking, something furtive, something guilty—something very unlike the frank, manly lad that I had known. It left a feeling of horror in my mind.

"But when a man has been soldiering for a year or two with brother Boer as a playmate, he keeps his nerve and acts quickly. Godfrey had hardly vanished before I was at the window. There was an awkward catch, and I was some little time before I could throw it up. Then I nipped through and ran down the garden path in the direction that I thought he might have taken.

"It was a long path and the light was not very good, but it seemed to me something was moving ahead of me. I ran on and called his name, but it was no use. When I got to the end of the path there were several others branching in different directions to various outhouses. I stood hesitating, and as I did so I heard distinctly the sound of a closing door. It was not behind me in the house, but ahead of me, somewhere in the darkness. That was enough, Mr. Holmes, to assure me that what I had seen was not a vision. Godfrey had run away from me and he had shut a door behind him. Of that I was certain.

"There was nothing more I could do, and I spent an uneasy night turning the matter over in my mind and trying to find some theory which would cover the facts. Next day I found the Colonel rather more conciliatory, and as his wife remarked that there were some places of interest in the neighbourhood, it gave me an opening to ask whether my presence for one more night would incommode them. A somewhat grudging acquiescence from the old man gave me a clear day in which to make my observations. I was already perfectly convinced that Godfrey was in hiding somewhere near, but where and why remained to be solved.

" The house was so large and so rambling that a regiment might be hid away in it and no one the wiser. If the secret lay there, it was difficult for me to penetrate it. But the door which I had heard close was certainly not in the house. I must explore the garden and see what I could find. There was no difficulty in the way, for the old people were busy in their own fashion and left me to my own devices.

" There were several small outhouses, but at the end of the garden there was a detached building of some size—large enough for a gardener's or a game-keeper's residence. Could this be the place whence the sound of that shutting door had come ? I approached it in a careless fashion, as though I were strolling aimlessly round the grounds. As I did so, a small, brisk, bearded man in a black coat and bowler hat—not at all the gardener type—came out of the door. To my surprise, he locked it after him and put the key in his pocket. Then he looked at me with some surprise on his face.

" ' Are you a visitor here ? ' he asked.

" I explained that I was and that I was a friend of Godfrey's.

" ' What a pity that he should be away on his travels, for he would have so liked to see me,' I continued.

" ' Quite so. Exactly,' said he, with a rather guilty air. ' No doubt you will renew your visit at some more propitious time.' He passed on, but when I turned I observed that he was standing watching me, half-concealed by the laurels at the far end of the garden.

" I had a good look at the little house as I passed it, but the windows were heavily curtained, and, so far as one could see, it was empty. I might spoil my own game, and even be ordered off the premises, if I were too audacious, for I was still conscious that I was being watched. Therefore, I strolled back to the house and waited for night before I went on with my inquiry. When all was dark and quiet, I slipped out of my window and made my way as silently as possible to the mysterious lodge.

" I have said that it was heavily curtained, but now I found that the windows were shuttered as well. Some light, however, was breaking through one of them, so I concentrated my attention upon this. I was in luck, for the curtain had not been quite closed, and there was a crack in the shutter so that I could see the inside of the room. It was a cheery place enough, a bright lamp and a blazing fire. Opposite to me was seated the little man whom I had seen in the morning. He was smoking a pipe and reading a paper——"

" What paper ? " I asked.

My client seemed annoyed at the interruption of his narrative.

" Can it matter ? " he asked.

" It is most essential."

" I really took no notice."

" Possibly you observed whether it was a broad-leafed paper or of that smaller type which one associates with weeklies."

" Now that you mention it, it was not large. It might have been the *Spectator*. However, I had little thought to spare upon such details, for a second man was seated with his back to the window, and I could swear that this second man was Godfrey. I could not see his face, but I knew the familiar slope of his shoulders. He was leaning upon his elbow in an attitude of great melancholy, his body turned towards the fire. I was hesitating as to what I should do when there was a sharp tap on my shoulder, and there was Colonel Emsworth beside me.

" ' This way, sir ! ' said he in a low voice. He walked in silence to the house and I followed him into my own bedroom. He had picked up a time-table in the hall.

" ' There is a train to London at eight-thirty,' said he. ' The trap will be at the door at eight.'

" He was white with rage, and, indeed, I felt myself in so difficult a position that I could only stammer out a few incoherent apologies, in which I tried to excuse myself by urging my anxiety for my friend.

" ' The matter will not bear discussion,' said he abruptly. ' You have made a most damnable intrusion into the privacy of our family. You were here as a guest and you have become a spy. I have nothing more to say, sir, save that I have no wish ever to see you again.'

" At this I lost my temper, Mr. Holmes, and I spoke with some warmth.

" ' I have seen your son, and I am convinced that for some reason of your own you are concealing him from the world. I have no idea what your motives are in cutting him off in this fashion, but I am sure that he is no longer a free agent. I warn you, Colonel Emsworth, that until I am assured as to the safety and well-being of my friend I shall never desist in my efforts to get to the bottom of the mystery, and I shall certainly not allow myself to be intimidated by anything which you may say or do.'

" The old fellow looked diabolical, and I really thought he was about to attack me. I have said that he was a gaunt, fierce old giant, and though I am no weakling I might have been hard put to it to hold my own against him. However, after a long glare of rage he turned upon his heel and walked out of the room. For my part, I took the appointed train in the morning, with the **5** full intention of coming straight to you and asking for your advice and assistance at the appointment for which I had already written."

Such was the problem which my visitor laid before me. It presented, as the astute reader will have already perceived, few difficulties in its solution, for a very limited choice of alternatives must get to the root of the matter. Still, elementary as it was, there were points of interest and novelty about it which may excuse my placing it upon record. I now proceeded, using my familiar method of logical analysis, to narrow down the possible solutions.

" The servants," I asked ; " how many were in the house ? "

" To the best of my belief there were only the old

5 *with the full intention of coming straight to you.* Mr. James M. Dodd journeyed to Tuxbury Old Park "on Monday." "Next day" Colonel Emsworth ordered him to leave. He took the train "in the morning"—and therefore on Wednesday morning—and came straight around to ask the advice of Holmes. Mr. Dodd further states that on the Monday night he retired after dinner "as soon as I decently could" and, looking out into the garden, saw that it was "a fine night with a bright half-moon." In 1903, there were half-moons on Monday, January 5th, and Monday, January 19th, but on the 19th the moon did not rise until close to midnight; Mr. Dodd therefore called on Holmes on the morning of *Wednesday, January 7th;* Holmes cleared up the case on a day at the "beginning of the next week"—probably Monday, January 12th, but possibly Tuesday, January 13th.

butler and his wife.   They seemed to live in the simplest fashion."

" There was no servant, then, in the detached house ? "

" None, unless the little man with the beard acted as such.   He seemed, however, to be quite a superior person."

" That seems very suggestive.   Had you any indication that food was conveyed from the one house to the other ? "

" Now that you mention it, I did see old Ralph carrying a basket down the garden walk and going in the direction of this house.   The idea of food did not occur to me at the moment."

" Did you make any local inquiries ? "

" Yes, I did.   I spoke to the station-master and also to the innkeeper in the village.   I simply asked if they knew anything of my old comrade, Godfrey Emsworth. Both of them assured me that he had gone for a voyage round the world.   He had come home and then had almost at once started off again.   The story was evidently universally accepted."

" You said nothing of your suspicions ? "

" Nothing."

" That was very wise.   The matter should certainly be inquired into.   I will go back with you to Tuxbury Old Park."

" To-day ? "

It happened that at the moment I was clearing up the case which my friend Watson has described as that of the Abbey School, in which the Duke of Greyminster was so deeply involved.   I had also a commission from **6** the Sultan of Turkey which called for immediate action, **7** as political consequences of the gravest kind might arise from its neglect.   Therefore it was not until the beginning of the next week, as my diary records, that I was able to start forth on my mission to Bedfordshire in company with Mr. James M. Dodd.   As we drove to Euston we **8** picked up a grave and taciturn gentleman of iron-grey aspect, with whom I had made the necessary arrangements.

" This is an old friend," said I to Dodd.   " It is possible that his presence may be entirely unnecessary, and, on the other hand, it may be essential.   It is not necessary at the present stage to go further into the matter."

The narratives of Watson have accustomed the reader, no doubt, to the fact that I do not waste words or disclose my thoughts while a case is actually under consideration.   Dodd seemed surprised, but nothing more was said and the three of us continued our journey together. In the train I asked Dodd one more question which I wished our companion to hear.

" You say that you saw your friend's face quite clearly at the window, so clearly that you are sure of his identity ? "

" I have no doubt about it whatever.   His nose was pressed against the glass.   The lamplight shone full upon him."

" It could not have been someone resembling him ? "

" No, no ; it was he."

" But you say he was changed ? "

6 *in which the Duke of Greyminster was so deeply involved.* Holmes is clearly giving the correct name of "the Priory school," although he, like Watson, is presumably using another alias for "the Duke of Holdernesse." Since "The Adventure of the Priory School" took place in May, 1901, and Holmes says he was clearing up the case in January, 1903, it seems that the Duke of Holdernesse-Greyminster had not heard the last of his wayward illegitimate son, and again called on Holmes' services. (We recall Holmes' remark in "The Adventure of the Priory School": "I would warn your Grace, however, that the continued presence of Mr. James Wilder in your household can only lead to misfortune." Presumably Wilder did *not* "leave . . . forever and go to seek his fortune in Australia"). We see, again, that His Holiness the Pope was not the only client who twice, by Canonical record, called in Holmes.

7 *the Sultan of Turkey.* Abdul-Hamid II, "Abdul the Damned," as some put it; Lord, as he liked to put it, of Two Continents and Two Oceans. "To F. Yeats-Brown, the old Bengal Lancer," the late Alexander Woollcott wrote in his article on "The Baker Street Irregulars," "we are all indebted for some knowledge of how . . . Abdul-Hamid spent his last night as Caliph of Islam. . . . If he must somehow while away the time until dawn, he would need a . . . special anodyne. Happily this was provided by the linguists at the Press Bureau, for in the nick of time there came dawdling into Constantinople from London a recent issue of the *Strand Magazine.* . . . I suspect it was the issue distinguished in the minds of collectors by the first publication of the magnificent story called 'The Bruce-Partington Plans.' Thus it befell that the Great Assassin spent his last night as Sultan sitting with a shawl pulled over his knees while his Chamberlain deferentially read aloud to him the newest story about Sherlock Holmes."

8 *As we drove to Euston.* As the late Christopher Morley long ago pointed out, "You can't go to Bedfordshire via Euston. It was Midland Ry, from St. Pancras, as every traveler knows."

"Only in colour. His face was—how shall I describe it ?—it was of a fish-belly whiteness. It was bleached."

"Was it equally pale all over ? "

"I think not. It was his brow which I saw so clearly as it was pressed against the window."

"Did you call to him ? "

"I was too startled and horrified for the moment. Then I pursued him, as I have told you, but without result."

My case was practically complete, and there was only one small incident needed to round it off. When, after a considerable drive, we arrived at the strange old rambling house which my client had described, it was Ralph, the elderly butler, who opened the door. I had requisitioned the carriage for the day and had asked my elderly friend to remain within it unless we should summon him. Ralph, a little wrinkled old fellow, was in the conventional costume of black coat and pepper-and-salt trousers, with only one curious variant. He wore brown leather gloves, which at sight of us he instantly shuffled off, laying them down on the hall-table as we passed in. I have, as my friend Watson may have remarked, an abnormally acute set of senses, and a faint but incisive scent was apparent. It seemed to centre on the hall-table. I turned, placed my hat there, knocked it off, stooped to pick it up, and contrived to bring my nose within a foot of the gloves. Yes, it was undoubtedly from them that the curious tarry odour was oozing. I passed on into the study with my case complete. Alas, that I should have to show my hand so when I tell my own story ! It was by concealing such links in the chain that Watson was enabled to produce his meretricious finales.

Colonel Emsworth was not in his room, but he came quickly enough on receipt of Ralph's message. We heard his quick, heavy step in the passage. The door was flung open and he rushed in with bristling beard and twisted features, as terrible an old man as ever I have seen. He held our cards in his hand, and he tore them up and stamped on the fragments.

"Have I not told you, you infernal busybody, that you are warned off the premises ? Never dare to show your damned face here again. If you enter again without my leave I shall be within my rights if I use violence. I'll shoot you, sir ! By God, I will ! As to you, sir," turning upon me, "I extend the same warning to you. I am familiar with your ignoble profession, but you must take your reputed talents to some other field. There is no opening for them here."

"I cannot leave here," said my client firmly, "until I hear from Godfrey's own lips that he is under no restraint."

Our involuntary host rang the bell.

"Ralph," he said, "telephone down to the county police and ask the inspector to send up two constables. Tell him there are burglars in the house."

"One moment," said I. "You must be aware, Mr. Dodd, that Colonel Emsworth is within his rights and that we have no legal status within his house. On the other hand, he should recognize that your action is prompted entirely by solicitude for his son. I venture to

THE DOOR WAS FLUNG OPEN . . .

Illustration by Howard K. Elcock for the *Strand Magazine*, November, 1926.

. . . "I EXTEND THE SAME WARNING TO YOU."

Illustration by Frederic Dorr Steele for *Liberty Magazine*, October 16, 1926.

hope that, if I were allowed to have five minutes' conversation with Colonel Emsworth, I could certainly alter his view of the matter."

"I am not so easily altered," said the old soldier. "Ralph, do what I have told you. What the devil are you waiting for ? Ring up the police !"

"Nothing of the sort," I said, putting my back to the door. "Any police interference would bring about the very catastrophe which you dread." I took out my notebook and scribbled one word upon a loose sheet. "That," said I, as I handed it to Colonel Emsworth, "is what has brought us here."

He stared at the writing with a face from which every expression save amazement had vanished.

"How do you know ? " he gasped, sitting down heavily in his chair.

"It is my business to know things. That is my trade."

He sat in deep thought, his gaunt hand tugging at his straggling beard. Then he made a gesture of resignation.

"Well, if you wish to see Godfrey, you shall. It is no doing of mine, but you have forced my hand. Ralph, tell Mr. Godfrey and Mr. Kent that in five minutes we shall be with them."

At the end of that time we passed down the garden path and found ourselves in front of the mystery house at the end. A small bearded man stood at the door with a look of considerable astonishment upon his face.

"This is very sudden, Colonel Emsworth," said he. "This will disarrange all our plans."

"I can't help it, Mr. Kent. Our hands have been forced. Can Mr. Godfrey see us ? "

"Yes ; he is waiting inside." He turned and led us into a large, plainly furnished front room. A man was standing with his back to the fire, and at the sight of him my client sprang forward with outstretched hand.

"Why, Godfrey, old man, this is fine ! "

But the other waved him back.

"Don't touch me, Jimmie. Keep your distance. Yes, you may well stare ! I don't quite look the smart Lance-Corporal Emsworth, of B Squadron, do I ? "

His appearance was certainly extraordinary. One could see that he had indeed been a handsome man with clear-cut features sunburned by an African sun, but mottled in patches over this darker surface were curious whitish patches which had bleached his skin.

"That's why I don't court visitors," said he. "I don't mind you, Jimmie, but I could have done without your friend. I suppose there is some good reason for it, but you have me at a disadvantage."

"I wanted to be sure that all was well with you, Godfrey. I saw you that night when you looked into my window, and I could not let the matter rest till I had cleared things up."

"Old Ralph told me you were there, and I couldn't help taking a peep at you. I hoped you would not have seen me, and I had to run to my burrow when I heard the window go up."

"But what in Heaven's name is the matter ? "

9 *on the Eastern railway line?* The Imperial Yeomanry, a real regiment, was in action near Diamond Hill outside of Pretoria. Conan Doyle, in *The Great Boer War*, has described the fight at Bronkhorst Spruit ("Buffelsspruit") and his map shows the Delagoa Bay Railway line, which did run east of the city to the ocean.

10 *stoep*. South African Dutch for a covered platform or veranda at the door of a house.

" Well, it's not a long story to tell," said he, lighting a cigarette. " You remember that morning fight at Buffelsspruit, outside Pretoria, on the Eastern railway **9** line ? You heard I was hit ? "

" Yes, I heard that, but I never got particulars."

" Three of us got separated from the others. It was very broken country, you may remember. There was Simpson—the fellow we called Baldy Simpson— and Anderson, and I. We were clearing brother Boer, but he lay low and got the three of us. The other two were killed. I got an elephant bullet through my shoulder. I stuck on to my horse, however, and he galloped several miles before I fainted and rolled off the saddle.

" When I came to myself it was nightfall, and I raised myself up, feeling very weak and ill. To my surprise there was a house close beside me, a fairly large house **10** with a broad stoep and many windows. It was deadly cold. You remember the kind of numb cold which used to come at evening, a deadly, sickening sort of cold, very different from a crisp healthy frost. Well, I was chilled to the bone, and my only hope seemed to lie in reaching that house. I staggered to my feet and dragged myself along, hardly conscious of what I did. I have a dim memory of slowly ascending the steps, entering a wide-opened door, passing into a large room which contained several beds, and throwing myself down with a gasp of satisfaction upon one of them. It was unmade, but that troubled me not at all. I drew the clothes over my shivering body and in a moment I was in a deep sleep.

" It was morning when I wakened, and it seemed to me that instead of coming out into a world of sanity I had emerged into some extraordinary nightmare. The African sun flooded through the big, curtainless windows, and every detail of the great, bare, white-washed dormitory stood out hard and clear. In front of me was standing a small, dwarf-like man with a huge bulbous head, who was jabbering excitedly in Dutch, waving two horrible hands which looked to me like brown sponges. Behind him stood a group of people who seemed to be intensely amused by the situation, but a chill came over me as I looked at them. Not one of them was a normal human being. Every one was twisted or swollen or disfigured in some strange way. The laughter of these strange monstrosities was a dreadful thing to hear.

" It seemed that none of them could speak English, but the situation wanted clearing up, for the creature with the big head was growing furiously angry and, uttering wild-beast cries, he had laid his deformed hands upon me and was dragging me out of bed, regardless of the fresh flow of blood from my wound. The little monster was as strong as a bull, and I don't know what he might have done to me had not an elderly man who was clearly in authority been attracted to the room by the hubbub. He said a few stern words in Dutch, and my persecutor shrank away. Then he turned upon me, gazing at me in the utmost amazement.

" ' How in the world did you come here ? ' he asked, in amazement. ' Wait a bit ! I see that you are tired out and that wounded shoulder of yours wants looking after. I am a doctor, and I'll soon have you tied up. But, man alive ! you are in far greater danger here than ever you were on the battlefield. You are in the Leper Hospital, and you have slept in a leper's bed.'

" Need I tell you more, Jimmie ? It seems that in view of the approaching battle all these poor creatures had been evacuated the day before. Then, as the British advanced, they had been brought back by this, their medical superintendent, who assured me that, though he believed he was immune to the disease, he would none the less never have dared to do what I had done. He put me in a private room, treated me kindly, and within a week or so I was removed to the general hospital at Pretoria.

" So there you have my tragedy. I hoped against hope, but it was not until I had reached home that the terrible signs which you see upon my face told me that I had not escaped. What was I to do ? I was in this lonely house. We had two servants whom we could utterly trust. There was a house where I could live. Under pledge of secrecy, Mr. Kent, who is a surgeon, was prepared to stay with me. It seemed simple enough on those lines. The alternative was a dreadful one—segregation for life among strangers with never a hope of release. But absolute secrecy was necessary, or even in this quiet country-side there would have been an outcry, and I should have been dragged to my horrible doom. Even you, Jimmie—even you had to be kept in the dark. Why my father has relented I cannot imagine."

Colonel Emsworth pointed to me.

" This is the gentleman who forced my hand." He unfolded the scrap of paper on which I had written the word " Leprosy." " It seemed to me that if he knew so much as that it was safer that he should know all."

" And so it was," said I. " Who knows but good may come of it ? I understand that only Mr. Kent has seen the patient. May I ask, sir, if you are an authority on such complaints, which are, I understand, tropical or semi-tropical in their nature ? "

" I have the ordinary knowledge of the educated medical man," he observed, with some stiffness.

" I have no doubt, sir, that you are fully competent, but I am sure that you will agree that in such a case a second opinion is valuable. You have avoided this, I understand, for fear that pressure should be put upon you to segregate the patient."

" That is so," said Colonel Emsworth.

" I foresaw this situation," I explained, " and I have brought with me a friend whose discretion may absolutely be trusted. I was able once to do him a professional service, and he is ready to advise as a friend rather than as a specialist. His name is Sir James Saunders."

The prospect of an interview with Lord Roberts would not have excited greater wonder and pleasure in a raw

"THIS IS THE GENTLEMAN WHO FORCED MY HAND."

Illustration by Howard K. Elcock for the *Strand Magazine*, November, 1926.

subaltern than was now reflected upon the face of Mr. Kent.

" I shall indeed be proud," he murmured.

" Then I will ask Sir James to step this way. He is at present in the carriage outside the door. Meanwhile, Colonel Emsworth, we may perhaps assemble in your study, where I could give the necessary explanations."

And here it is that I miss my Watson. By cunning questions and ejaculations of wonder he could elevate my simple art, which is but systematized common sense, into a prodigy. When I tell my own story I have no such aid. And yet I will give my process of thought even as I gave it to my small audience, which included Godfrey's mother, in the study of Colonel Emsworth.

" That process," said I, " starts upon the supposition that when you have eliminated all which is impossible, then whatever remains, however improbable, must be the truth. It may well be that several explanations remain, in which case one tries test after test until one or other of them has a convincing amount of support. We will now apply this principle to the case in point. As it was first presented to me, there were three possible explanations of the seclusion or incarceration of this gentleman in an outhouse of his father's mansion. There was the explanation that he was in hiding for a crime, or that he was mad and that they wished to avoid an asylum, or that he had some disease which caused his segregation. I could think of no other adequate solutions. These, then, had to be sifted and balanced against each other.

" The criminal solution would not bear inspection. No unsolved crime had been reported from that district. I was sure of that. If it were some crime not yet discovered, then clearly it would be to the interest of the family to get rid of the delinquent and send him abroad rather than keep him concealed at home. I could see no explanation for such a line of conduct.

" Insanity was more plausible. The presence of the second person in the outhouse suggested a keeper. The fact that he locked the door when he came out strengthened the supposition and gave the idea of constraint. On the other hand, this constraint could not be severe or the young man could not have got loose and come down to have a look at his friend. You will remember, Mr. Dodd, that I felt round for points, asking you, for example, about the paper which Mr. Kent was reading. Had it been the *Lancet* or the *British Medical Journal* it would have helped me. It is not illegal, however, to keep a lunatic upon private premises so long as there is a qualified person in attendance and that the authorities have been duly notified. Why, then, all this desperate desire for secrecy? Once again I could not get the theory to fit the facts.

" There remained the third possibility, into which, rare and unlikely as it was, everything seemed to fit. Leprosy is not uncommon in South Africa. By some extraordinary chance this youth might have contracted it. His people would be placed in a very dreadful position, since they would desire to save him from segregation. Great secrecy would be needed to prevent rumours from getting about and subsequent interference by the authorities. A devoted medical man, if sufficiently paid, would easily be found to take charge of the sufferer. There would be no reason why the latter should not be allowed freedom after dark. Bleaching of the skin is a common result of the disease. The case was a strong one—so strong that I determined to act as if it were actually proved. When on arriving here I noticed that Ralph, who carries out the meals, had gloves which are impregnated with disinfectants, my last doubts were removed. A single word showed you, sir, that your secret was discovered, and if I wrote rather than said it, it was to prove to you that my discretion was to be trusted."

I was finishing this little analysis of the case when the door was opened and the austere figure of the great dermatologist was ushered in. But for once his sphinx-like features had relaxed and there was a warm humanity in his eyes. He strode up to Colonel Emsworth and shook him by the hand.

" It is often my lot to bring ill-tidings, and seldom good," said he. " This occasion is the more welcome. It is not leprosy."

" What ? "

" A well-marked case of pseudo-leprosy or ichthyosis, a scale-like affection of the skin, unsightly, obstinate, but possibly curable, and certainly non-infective. Yes, Mr. Holmes, the coincidence is a remarkable one. But is it coincidence ? Are there not subtle forces at work of which we know little ? Are we assured that the apprehension, from which this young man has no doubt suffered terribly since his exposure to its contagion, may not produce a physical effect which simulates that which it fears ? At any rate, I pledge my professional reputation—— But the lady has fainted ! I think that Mr. Kent had better be with her until she recovers from this joyous shock." **11**

11 *recovers from this joyous shock.*" "The incredibility of the denouement whereby Godfrey turns out not to have leprosy at all, must have struck every reader," Mr. D. Martin Dakin wrote in "The Problem of the Case-Book." "Watson was never guilty of forcing such 'happy endings' to please his readers—witness 'The Adventure of the Dancing Men' or 'The Greek Interpreter.' "

Bibliographical Note: The manuscript of "The Adventure of the Blanched Soldier," 26 pages, 4to vellum, was auctioned in New York City in January, 1944, bringing $310. It is presently owned by the New York Public Library.

73

THE ADVENTURE OF THE THREE GABLES

[Tuesday, May 26, to Wednesday, May 27, 1903]

"SEE HERE, MASSER HOLMES, YOU KEEP YOUR HANDS OUT OF OTHER FOLKS' BUSINESS."

Illustration by Frederic Dorr Steele for *Liberty Magazine*, September 18, 1926. Howard K. Elcock illustrated the same scene for the *Strand Magazine*, October, 1926.

I DON'T think that any of my adventures with Mr. Sherlock Holmes opened quite so abruptly, or so dramatically, as that which I associate with The Three Gables. I had not seen Holmes for some days, and had no idea of the new channel into which his activities had been directed. He was in a chatty mood that morning, however, and had just settled me into the well-worn low arm-chair on one side of the fire, while he had curled down with his pipe in his mouth upon the opposite chair, when our visitor arrived. If I had said that a mad bull had arrived, it would give a clearer impression of what occurred.

The door had flown open and a huge negro had burst into the room. He would have been a comic figure if he had not been terrific, for he was dressed in a very loud grey check suit with a flowing salmon-coloured tie. His broad face and flattened nose were thrust forward, as his sullen dark eyes, with a smouldering gleam of malice in them, turned from one of us to the other.

"Which of you genelmen is Masser Holmes?" he asked.

Holmes raised his pipe with a languid smile.

"Oh! it's you, is it?" said our visitor, coming with an unpleasant, stealthy step round the angle of the table. "See here, Masser Holmes, you keep your hands out of other folks' business. Leave folks to manage their own affairs. Got that, Masser Holmes?"

"Keep on talking," said Holmes. "It's fine."

"Oh! it's fine, is it?" growled the savage. "It won't be so damn fine if I have to trim you up a bit. I've handled your kind before now, and they didn't look fine when I was through with them. Look at that, Masser Holmes!"

He swung a huge knotted lump of a fist under my friend's nose. Holmes examined it closely with an air of great interest. "Were you born so?" he asked. "Or did it come by degrees?"

It may have been the icy coolness of my friend, or it may have been the slight clatter which I made as I picked up the poker. In any case, our visitor's manner became less flamboyant.

" Well, I've given you fair warnin'," said he. " I've a friend that's interested out Harrow way—you know what I'm meaning—and he don't intend to have no buttin' in by you. Got that ? You ain't the law, and I ain't the law either, and if you come in I'll be on hand also. Don't you forget it."

" I've wanted to meet you for some time," said Holmes. " I won't ask you to sit down, for I don't like the smell of you, but aren't you Steve Dixie, the bruiser ? "

" That's my name, Masser Holmes, and you'll get put through it for sure if you give me any lip."

" It is certainly the last thing you need," said Holmes, staring at our visitor's hideous mouth. " But it was the killing of young Perkins outside the Holborn Bar—— **1** What ! you're not going ? "

The negro had sprung back, and his face was leaden. " I won't listen to no such talk," said he. " What have I to do with this 'ere Perkins, Masser Holmes ? I was trainin' at the Bull Ring in Birmingham when this boy done gone get into trouble."

" Yes, you'll tell the magistrate about it, Steve," said Holmes. " I've been watching you and Barney Stockdale——"

" So help me the Lord ! Masser Holmes——"

" That's enough. Get out of it. I'll pick you up when I want you."

" Good mornin', Masser Holmes. I hope there ain't no hard feelin's about this 'ere visit ? "

" There will be unless you tell me who sent you."

" Why, there ain't no secret about that, Masser Holmes. It was that same genelman that you have just done gone mention."

" And who set him on to it ? "

" S'elp me. I don't know, Masser Holmes. He just say, ' Steve, you go see Mr. Holmes, and tell him his life ain't safe if he go down Harrow way.' That's the whole truth."

Without waiting for any further questioning, our visitor bolted out of the room almost as precipitately as he had entered. Holmes knocked out the ashes of his pipe with a quiet chuckle.

" I am glad you were not forced to break his woolly head, Watson. I observed your manœuvres with the poker. But he is really rather a harmless fellow, a great muscular, foolish, blustering baby, and easily cowed, as you have seen. He is one of the Spencer John gang and has taken part in some dirty work of late which I may clear up when I have time. His immediate principal, Barney, is a more astute person. They specialize in assaults, intimidation, and the like. What I want to know is, who is at the back of them on this particular occasion ? "

" But why do they want to intimidate you ? "

" It is this Harrow Weald case. It decides me to look into the matter, for if it is worth anyone's while to take so much trouble, there must be something in it."

" But what is it ? "

" I was going to tell you when we had this comic interlude. Here is Mrs. Maberley's note. If you care to come with me we will wire her and go out at once."

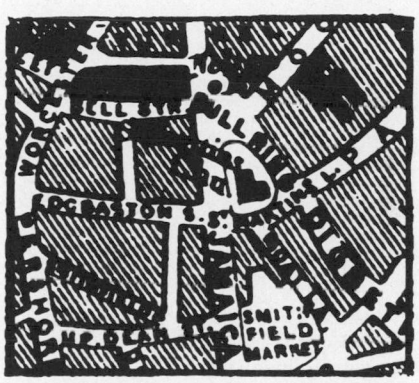

". . . AT THE BULL RING IN BIRMINGHAM . . ."

"The plan of the town is irregular," says the *Encyclopædia Britannica*, 1894 edition, under "Birmingham," "and the streets are mostly winding, and many of them somewhat narrow. In the centre, however, is a large open space, known as the Bull Ring . . ."

1 *the killing of young Perkins outside the Holborn Bar——*. "I have always felt," the late Clifton R. Andrew wrote in "Sherlock Holmes on the Turf," "that the 'killing of young Perkins outside the Holborn Bar,' which Holmes seemed to know so much about, was the tragic outcome of some race-betting embroilment. It has all the earmarks of such. Bars are not above being rendezvous for the fraternity of the race-track, of higher or lower estate, depending upon the class of the bar . . ."

2 *and a shorter drive.* Mr. Michael Harrison has noted (*In the Footsteps of Sherlock Holmes*) that Holmes and Watson, calling on Mrs. Maberley, would have passed "Grim's Dyke," Sir W. S. Gilbert's famous Norman Shaw mansion at Harrow Weald.

. . . A BRICK AND TIMBER VILLA, STANDING IN ITS OWN ACRE OF UNDEVELOPED GRASSLAND.

This is Fairmead, a mansion typical of the larger houses of Harrow Weald at the time when Holmes and Watson were involved in the mysterious affair of "The Three Gables." The illustration is from Mr. Michael Harrison's *In the Footsteps of Sherlock Holmes*.

DEAR MR. SHERLOCK HOLMES, (I read)—

I have had a succession of strange incidents occur to me in connection with this house, and I should much value your advice. You would find me at home any time to-morrow. The house is within a short walk of the Weald Station. I believe that my late husband, Mortimer Maberley, was one of your early clients.

Yours faithfully,

MARY MABERLEY.

The address was " The Three Gables, Harrow Weald."

" So that's that ! " said Holmes. " And now, if you can spare the time, Watson, we will get upon our way."

2   A short railway journey, and a shorter drive, brought us to the house, a brick and timber villa, standing in its own acre of undeveloped grassland. Three small projections above the upper windows made a feeble attempt to justify its name. Behind was a grove of melancholy, half-grown pines, and the whole aspect of the place was poor and depressing. None the less, we found the house to be well furnished, and the lady who received us was a most engaging elderly person, who bore every mark of refinement and culture.

" I remember your husband well, madam," said Holmes, " though it is some years since he used my services in some trifling matter."

" Probably you would be more familiar with the name of my son Douglas."

Holmes looked at her with great interest.

" Dear me ! Are you the mother of Douglas Maberley ? I knew him slightly. But, of course, all London knew him. What a magnificent creature he was ! Where is he now ? "

" Dead, Mr. Holmes, dead ! He was Attaché at Rome, and he died there of pneumonia last month."

"I am sorry. One could not connect death with such a man. I have never known anyone so vitally alive. He lived intensely—every fibre of him!"

"Too intensely, Mr. Holmes. That was the ruin of him. You remember him as he was—debonair and splendid. You did not see the moody, morose, brooding creature into which he developed. His heart was broken. In a single month I seemed to see my gallant boy turn into a worn-out cynical man."

"A love-affair—a woman?"

"Or a fiend. Well, it was not to talk of my poor lad that I asked you to come, Mr. Holmes."

"Dr. Watson and I are at your service."

"There have been some very strange happenings. I have been in this house more than a year now, and as I wished to lead a retired life I have seen little of my neighbours. Three days ago I had a call from a man who said that he was a house agent. He said that this house would exactly suit a client of his and that if I would part with it money would be no object. It seemed to me very strange, as there are several empty houses on the market which appear to be equally eligible, but naturally I was interested in what he said. I therefore named a price which was five hundred pounds more than I gave. He at once closed with the offer, but added that his client desired to buy the furniture as well and would I put a price upon it. Some of this furniture is from my old home, and it is, as you see, very good, so that I named a good round sum. To this also he at once agreed. I had always wanted to travel, and the bargain was so good a one that it really seemed that I should be my own mistress for the rest of my life.

"Yesterday the man arrived with the agreement all drawn out. Luckily I showed it to Mr. Sutro, my lawyer, who lives in Harrow. He said to me, 'This is a very strange document. Are you aware that if you sign it you could not legally take *anything* out of the house—not even your own private possessions?' When the man came again in the evening I pointed this out, and I said that I meant only to sell the furniture.

"'No, no; everything,' said he.

"'But my clothes? My jewels?'

"'Well, well, some concession might be made for your personal effects. But nothing shall go out of the house unchecked. My client is a very liberal man, but he has his fads and his own way of doing things. It is everything or nothing with him.'

"'Then it must be nothing,' said I. And there the matter was left, but the whole thing seemed to me to be so unusual that I thought——"

Here we had a very extraordinary interruption.

Holmes raised his hand for silence. Then he strode across the room, flung open the door, and dragged in a great gaunt woman whom he had seized by the shoulder. She entered with ungainly struggles, like some huge awkward chicken, torn squawking out of its coop.

"Leave me alone! What are you a-doin' of?" she screeched.

"Why, Susan, what is this?"

THEN HE STRODE ACROSS THE ROOM, FLUNG OPEN THE DOOR . . .

Illustration by Howard K. Elcock for the *Strand Magazine*, October, 1926.

"Well, ma'am, I was comin' in to ask if the visitors was stayin' for lunch when this man jumped out at me."

"I have been listening to her for the last five minutes, but did not wish to interrupt your most interesting narrative. Just a little wheezy, Susan, are you not? You breathe too heavily for that kind of work."

Susan turned a sulky but amazed face upon her captor. "Who be you, anyhow, and what right have you a-pullin' me about like this?"

"It was merely that I wished to ask a question in your presence. Did you, Mrs. Maberley, mention to anyone that you were going to write to me and consult me?"

"No, Mr. Holmes, I did not."

"Who posted your letter?"

"Susan did."

"Exactly. Now, Susan, to whom was it that you wrote or sent a message to say that your mistress was asking advice from me?"

"It's a lie. I sent no message."

"Now, Susan, wheezy people may not live long, you know. It's a wicked thing to tell fibs. Whom did you tell?"

"Susan!" cried her mistress, "I believe you are a bad, treacherous woman. I remember now that I saw you speaking to someone over the hedge."

"That was my own business," said the woman sullenly.

"Suppose I tell you that it was Barney Stockdale to whom you spoke?" said Holmes.

"Well, if you know, what do you want to ask for?"

"I was not sure, but I know now. Well now, Susan, it will be worth ten pounds to you if you will tell me who is at the back of Barney."

"Someone that could lay down a thousand pounds for every ten you have in the world."

"So, a rich man? No; you smiled—a rich woman. Now we have got so far, you may as well give the name and earn the tenner."

"I'll see you in hell first."

"Oh, Susan! Language!"

"I am clearing out of here. I've had enough of you all. I'll send for my box to-morrow." She flounced for the door.

"Good-bye, Susan. Paregoric is the stuff. . . . Now," he continued, turning suddenly from lively to severe when the door had closed behind the flushed and angry woman, "this gang means business. Look how close they play the game. Your letter to me had the 10 p.m. postmark. And yet Susan passes the word to Barney. Barney has time to go to his employer and get instructions; he or she—I incline to the latter from Susan's grin when she thought I had blundered—forms a plan. Black Steve is called in, and I am warned off by eleven o'clock next morning. That's quick work, you **3** know."

"But what do they want?"

"Yes, that's the question. Who had the house before you?"

3 *That's quick work, you know.*" The opening day was not Sunday: Mrs. Maberley's note, which "had the 10 P.M. postmark" and was written the night before ("You would find me at home any time to-morrow") could not have been delivered on that day. Nor was the opening day Wednesday: "Three days ago I had a call from a man who said he was a house agent." Such a call would of course not have been made on a Sunday. Nor was the opening day Monday: "Yesterday the man arrived with the agreement all drawn out." Nor was the opening day Saturday: Susan said, "I'll send for my box to-morrow," as she flounced off. Douglas Maberley's effects had been delivered to Mrs. Maberley "last week." We may be sure that Susan immediately informed her husband ("This gang means business. Look how close they play the game. . . . That's quick work, you know.") We are justified in assuming that the "house agent" would have called on the very day the effects were delivered. Since this was "three weeks ago," and the effects were delivered "last week," the opening day could not have been Thursday or Friday. The case opened, then, on a *Tuesday.*

" A retired sea captain, called Ferguson."

" Anything remarkable about him ? "

" Not that ever I heard of."

" I was wondering whether he could have buried something. Of course, when people bury treasure nowadays they do it in the Post Office bank. But there are always some lunatics about. It would be a dull world without them. At first I thought of some buried valuable. But why, in that case, should they want your furniture ? You don't happen to have a Raphael or a First Folio **4** Shakespeare without knowing it ? "

" No, I don't think I have anything rarer than a Crown Derby tea-set."

" That would hardly justify all this mystery. Besides, why should they not openly state what they want ? If they covet your tea-set, they can surely offer a price for it without buying you out, lock, stock, and barrel. No, as I read it, there is something which you do not know that you have, and which you would not give up if you did know."

" That is how I read it," said I.

" Dr. Watson agrees, so that settles it."

" Well, Mr. Holmes, what can it be ? "

" Let us see whether by this purely mental analysis we can get it to a finer point. You have been in this house a year."

" Nearly two."

" All the better. During this long period no one wants anything from you. Now suddenly within three or four days you have urgent demands. What would you gather from that ? "

" It can only mean," said I, " that the object, whatever it may be, has only just come into the house."

" Settled once again," said Holmes. " Now, Mrs. Maberley, has any object just arrived ? "

" No ; I have bought nothing new this year."

" Indeed ! That is very remarkable. Well, I think we had best let matters develop a little further until we have clearer data. Is that lawyer of yours a capable man ? "

" Mr. Sutro is most capable."

" Have you another maid, or was the fair Susan, who has just banged your front door, alone ? "

" I have a young girl."

" Try and get Sutro to spend a night or two in the house. You might possibly want protection."

" Against whom ? "

" Who knows ? The matter is certainly obscure. If I can't find what they are after, I must approach the matter from the other end, and try to get at the principal. Did this house-agent man give any address ? "

" Simply his card and occupation. Haines-Johnson, Auctioneer and Valuer."

" I don't think we shall find him in the Directory. Honest business men don't conceal their place of business. Well, you will let me know any fresh development. I have taken up your case, and you may rely upon it that I shall see it through."

As we passed through the hall Holmes' eyes, which missed nothing, lighted upon several trunks and cases

4 *a Raphael.* Raffaello Santi or Raffaello Sanzio, 1483–1520, Italian painter, one of the great artists of the Renaissance.

5 *These are from Italy*." "These are the stations at which baggage from Rome to London via the St. Gotthard route would normally have been transferred," Mr. Michael C. Kaser wrote in "Sherlock Holmes on the Continent." "However, while baggage from Rome would correctly have had its immediate destination marked in Italian, that is, 'Milano,' how could the Italian authorities have inscribed the next transfer point in French? They would certainly have used either Italian ('Lucerna') or German ('Luzern'), for Lucerne is German-speaking. It can only be concluded that between Milan and Lucerne the pieces so labeled had passed through a French-speaking intermediate transfer point and the relevant label had been deliberately removed. The reason is not far to seek. Mrs. Klein's agents had succeeded in having the baggage directed to a locality in France where —perhaps by corruption of the railway staff—they were able to examine the trunks. France, and not French-speaking Switzerland, is indicated, since at that time . . . the only direct connection between Milan and Switzerland lay through Lucerne. Either they were unable to open all the trunks or they had selected the wrong pieces for diversion. In either case, the thieves would have had to return the bags to their original route (hence the addressing to Lucerne in French) to preclude suspicion and await delivery at Harrow, where the keys of the cases which they had been unable to inspect would be available for felony. It is impossible that Sherlock Holmes should have missed this obvious clue that the trunks had been tampered with en route, and it was this which must have led him to direct that they be examined and guarded."

. . . THERE WAS THE NEGRO PRIZE-FIGHTER STANDING IN THE SHADOW.

Illustration by Howard K. Elcock for the *Strand Magazine*, October, 1926.

which were piled in the corner. The labels shone out upon them.

5 "' Milano.' ' Lucerne.' These are from Italy."

"They are poor Douglas' things."

"You have not unpacked them ? How long have you had them ? "

"They arrived last week."

"But you said—why, surely this might be the missing link. How do we know that there is not something of value there ? "

"There could not possibly be, Mr. Holmes. Poor Douglas had only his pay and a small annuity. What could he have of value ? "

Holmes was lost in thought.

"Delay no longer, Mrs. Maberley," he said at last. "Have these things taken upstairs to your bedroom. Examine them as soon as possible and see what they contain. I will come to-morrow and hear your report."

It was quite evident that The Three Gables was under very close surveillance, for as we came round the high hedge at the end of the lane there was the negro prize-fighter standing in the shadow. We came on him quite suddenly, and a grim and menacing figure he looked in that lonely place. Holmes clapped his hand to his pocket.

"Lookin' for your gun, Masser Holmes ? "

"No ; for my scent-bottle, Steve."

"You are funny, Masser Holmes, ain't you ? "

"It won't be funny for you, Steve, if I get after you. I gave you fair warning this morning."

"Well, Masser Holmes, I done gone think over what you said, and I don't want no more talk about that affair of Masser Perkins. S'pose I can help you, Masser Holmes, I will."

"Well, then, tell me who is behind you on this job ? "

"So help me the Lord ! Masser Holmes, I told you the truth before. I don't know. My boss Barney gives me orders and that's all."

"Well, just bear in mind, Steve, that the lady in that house, and everything under that roof, is under my protection. Don't you forget it."

"All right, Masser Holmes. I'll remember."

"I've got him thoroughly frightened for his own skin, Watson," Holmes remarked as we walked on. "I think he would double-cross his employer if he knew who he was. It was lucky I had some knowledge of the Spencer John crowd, and that Steve was one of them. Now, **6** Watson, this is a case for Langdale Pike, and I am going to see him now. When I get back I may be clearer in the matter."

I saw no more of Holmes during the day, but I could well imagine how he spent it, for Langdale Pike was his human book of reference upon all matters of social scandal. This strange, languid creature spent his waking hours in the bow window of a St. James' Street **7** club, and was the receiving-station, as well as the transmitter, for all the gossip of the Metropolis. He made, it was said, a four-figure income by the paragraphs which he contributed every week to the garbage papers which cater for an inquisitive public. If ever, far down in the turbid depths of London life, there was some strange swirl or eddy, it was marked with automatic exactness by this human dial upon the surface. Holmes discreetly helped Langdale to knowledge, and on occasion was helped in turn.

When I met my friend in his room early next morning, I was conscious from his bearing that all was well, but none the less a most unpleasant surprise was awaiting us. It took the shape of the following telegram :

" Please come out at once. Client's house burgled in the night. Police in possession.

" SUTRO."

Holmes whistled. " The drama has come to a crisis, and quicker than I had expected. There is a great driving-power at the back of this business, Watson, which does not surprise me after what I have heard. This Sutro, of course, is her lawyer. I made a mistake, I fear, in not asking you to spend the night on guard. This fellow has clearly proved a broken reed. Well, **8** there is nothing for it but another journey to Harrow Weald."

We found The Three Gables a very different establishment to the orderly household of the previous day. A small group of idlers had assembled at the garden gate, while a couple of constables were examining the windows and the geranium beds. Within we met a grey **9** old gentleman, who introduced himself as the lawyer, together with a bustling, rubicund Inspector, who greeted Holmes as an old friend.

" Well, Mr. Holmes, no chance for you in this case, I'm afraid. Just a common, ordinary burglary, and well within the capacity of the poor old police. No experts need apply."

" I am sure the case is in very good hands," said Holmes. " Merely a common burglary, you say ? "

" Quite so. We know pretty well who the men are and where to find them. It is that gang of Barney Stockdale, with the big nigger in it—they've been seen about here."

" Excellent ! What did they get ? "

" Well, they don't seem to have got much. Mrs. Maberley was chloroformed and the house was—— Ah ! here is the lady herself."

Our friend of yesterday, looking very pale and ill, had entered the room, leaning upon a little maid-servant.

" You gave me good advice, Mr. Holmes," said she, smiling ruefully. " Alas, I did not take it ! I did not wish to trouble Mr. Sutro, and so I was unprotected."

" I only heard of it this morning," the lawyer explained.

" Mr. Holmes advised me to have some friend in the house. I neglected his advice, and I have paid for it."

" You look wretchedly ill," said Holmes. " Perhaps you are hardly equal to telling me what occurred."

" It is all here," said the Inspector, tapping a bulky notebook.

6 *Langdale Pike.* In fact, the Landale Pikes are two hills in Westmoreland overlooking Wordsworth's Grasmere.

7 *a St. James Street club.* Perhaps the Conservative Club (the second Tory club) built by Smirke and Basevi, 1845, and occupying partly the site of the old Thatched House Tavern, celebrated for its literary meetings, and partly that of the house in which Edward Gibbon, the historian of the Roman Empire, died on January 16, 1794. Perhaps Brooks' Club (Whig) built by Holland, 1778. Perhaps the New University Club at No. 57. Or No. 28, Boodle's, the country gentleman's club —"Every Sir John belongs to Boodle's." Perhaps White's at Nos. 37–38 (Tory) built by Wyatt.

8 *This fellow has clearly proved a broken reed.* "Thou trustest in the staff of this broken reed." —Isaiah, 36.6.

9 *the geranium beds.* "The reference to 'geranium beds' around Mrs. Maberley's house is important," the late H. W. Bell wrote, "for geraniums are not bedded out even in the south of England until the second half of May, in case of spring frosts." The deduction is borne out by the fact that Douglas Maberley died of pneumonia—especially prevalant in the spring.

10 *the chance of finger-marks or something.*" It was in 1901, as we saw in "The Adventure of the Red Circle," that the fingerprint system was introduced to Scotland Yard. "The Adventure of the Three Gables," then, is not before that time. Watson "had not seen Holmes for some days, and had no idea of the new channel into which his activities had been directed." Watson met his friend "in his room early next morning." Since Watson is not living at Baker Street, and has not seen Holmes "for some days," the case must fall between September, 1902 ("The Adventure of the Illustrious Client," "The Adventure of the Red Circle") and the summer of 1903 ("The Adventure of the Mazarin Stone").

" Still, if the lady is not too exhausted——"

" There is really so little to tell. I have no doubt that wicked Susan had planned an entrance for them. They must have known the house to an inch. I was conscious for a moment of the chloroform rag which was thrust over my mouth, but I have no notion how long I may have been senseless. When I woke, one man was at the bedside and another was rising with a bundle in his hand from among my son's baggage, which was partially opened and littered over the floor. Before he could get away I sprang up and seized him."

" You took a big risk," said the Inspector.

" I clung to him, but he shook me off, and the other may have struck me, for I can remember no more. Mary the maid heard the noise and began screaming out of the window. That brought the police, but the rascals had got away."

" What did they take ? "

" Well, I don't think there is anything of value missing. I am sure there was nothing in my son's trunks."

" Did the men leave no clue ? "

" There was one sheet of paper which I may have torn from the man that I grasped. It was lying all crumpled on the floor. It is in my son's handwriting."

" Which means that it is not of much use," said the Inspector. " Now if it had been in the burglar's——"

" Exactly," said Holmes. " What rugged common sense ! None the less, I should be curious to see it."

The Inspector drew a folded sheet of foolscap from his pocket-book.

" I never pass anything, however trifling," said he, with some pomposity. " That is my advice to you, Mr. Holmes. In twenty-five years' experience I have learned my lesson. There is always the chance of finger-marks **10** or something."

Holmes inspected the sheet of paper.

" What do you make of it, Inspector ? "

" Seems to be the end of some queer novel, so far as I can see."

" It may certainly prove to be the end of a queer tale," said Holmes. " You have noticed the number on the top of the page. It is two hundred and forty-five. Where are the odd two hundred and forty-four pages ? "

" Well, I suppose the burglars got those. Much good may it do them ! "

" It seems a queer thing to break into a house in order to steal such papers as that. Does it suggest anything to you, Inspector ? "

" Yes, sir ; it suggests that in their hurry the rascals just grabbed at what came first to hand. I wish them joy of what they got."

" Why should they go to my son's things ? " asked Mrs. Maberley.

" Well, they found nothing valuable downstairs, so they tried their luck upstairs. That is how I read it. What do you make of it, Mr. Holmes ? "

" I must think it over, Inspector. Come to the window, Watson." Then, as we stood together, he read over the fragment of paper. It began in the middle of a sentence and ran like this:

" . . . face bled considerably from the cuts and blows, but it was nothing to the bleeding of his heart as he saw that lovely face, the face for which he had been prepared to sacrifice his very life, looking out at his agony and humiliation. She smiled—yes, by Heaven! she smiled, like the heartless fiend she was, as he looked up at her. It was at that moment that love died and hate was born. Man must live for something. If it is not for your embrace, my lady, then it shall surely be for your undoing and my complete revenge."

" Queer grammar!" said Holmes, with a smile, as he handed the paper back to the Inspector. " Did you notice how the ' he ' suddenly changed to ' my.' The writer was so carried away by his own story that he imagined himself at the supreme moment to be the hero."

" It seemed mighty poor stuff," said the Inspector, as he replaced it in his book. " What! are you off, Mr. Holmes ? "

" I don't think there is anything more for me to do now that the case is in such capable hands. By the way, Mrs. Maberley, did you say you wished to travel ? "

" It has always been my dream, Mr. Holmes."

" Where would you like to go—Cairo, Madeira, the Riviera ? "

" Oh! if I had the money I would go round the world."

" Quite so. Round the world. Well, good morning. I may drop you a line in the evening." As we passed the window I caught a glimpse of the Inspector's smile and shake of the head. " These clever fellows have always a touch of madness." That was what I read in the Inspector's smile.

" Now, Watson, we are at the last lap of our little journey," said Holmes, when we were back in the roar of Central London once more. " I think we had best clear the matter up at once, and it would be well that you should come with me, for it is safer to have a witness when you are dealing with such a lady as Isadora Klein."

We had taken a cab and were speeding to some address in Grosvenor Square. Holmes had been sunk in thought, but he roused himself suddenly.

" By the way, Watson, I suppose you see it all clearly ? "

" No, I can't say that I do. I only gather that we are going to see the lady who is behind all this mischief."

" Exactly! But does the name Isadora Klein convey nothing to you ? She was, of course, *the* celebrated beauty. There was never a woman to touch her. She is pure Spanish, the real blood of the masterful Conquistadors, and her people have been leaders in Pernambuco for generations. She married the aged German sugar king, Klein, and presently found herself the richest as well as the most lovely widow upon earth. Then there was an interval of adventure when she pleased her own tastes. She had several lovers, and Douglas Maberley,

11 *the 'belle dame sans merci.'* "Did Holmes borrow the epithet [from Keats or] directly from the 15th-century poet Alain Chartier?" Mr. Leslie Cross asked in "Sherlock Holmes, Writer: An Unsolved Case."

12 *she is about to marry the young Duke of Lomond.* The second half of May corresponds well, as the late H. W. Bell noted, with the fact that Frau Klein had not yet left her house in Grosvenor Square for the country. It corresponds also, as the late Dr. Ernest Bloomfield Zeisler noted, with the fact that the beautiful widow is "about to marry the young Duke of Lomond": this "suggests that the impending marriage is only a few days off, for similar words in 'A Scandal in Bohemia' meant this; and the marriage was most likely planned for a date near June 1st." The case opened, then, on a Tuesday in late May in the year 1903—*Tuesday, May 26, 1903,* beyond a doubt; it closed the next day.

"STOP! WHERE ARE YOU GOING?"

Illustration by Howard K. Elcock for the *Strand Magazine*, October, 1926.

one of the most striking men in London, was one of them.

"It was by all accounts more than an adventure with him.   He was not a Society butterfly, but a strong, proud man who gave and expected all.   But she is the '*belle dame* **11** *sans merci*' of fiction.   When her caprice is satisfied, the matter is ended, and if the other party in the matter can't take her word for it, she knows how to bring it home to him."

"Then that was his own story——"

"Ah! you are piecing it together now.   I hear that **12** she is about to marry the young Duke of Lomond, who might almost be her son.   His Grace's ma might overlook the age, but a big scandal would be a different matter, so it is imperative—— Ah! here we are."

It was one of the finest corner-houses of the West End.   A machine-like footman took up our cards and returned with word that the lady was not at home. "Then we shall wait until she is," said Holmes cheerfully.

The machine broke down.

"Not at home means not at home to *you*," said the footman.

"Good," Holmes answered.   "That means that we shall not have to wait.   Kindly give this note to your mistress."

He scribbled three or four words upon a sheet of his notebook, folded it, and handed it to the man.

"What did you say, Holmes?" I asked.

"I simply wrote 'Shall it be the police, then?' I think that should pass us in."

It did—with amazing celerity.   A minute later we were in an Arabian Nights' drawing-room, vast and wonderful, in a half gloom, picked out with an occasional pink electric light.   The lady had come, I felt, to that time of life when even the proudest beauty finds the half-light more welcome.   She rose from a settee as we entered: tall, queenly, a perfect figure, a lovely mask-like face, with two wonderful Spanish eyes which looked murder at us both.

"What is this intrusion—and this insulting message?" she asked, holding up the slip of paper.

"I need not explain, madame.   I have too much respect for your intelligence to do so—though I confess that intelligence has been surprisingly at fault of late."

"How so, sir?"

"By supposing that your hired bullies could frighten me from my work.   Surely no man would take up my profession if it were not that danger attracts him.   It was you, then, who forced me to examine the case of young Maberley."

"I have no idea what you are talking about.   What have I to do with hired bullies?"

Holmes turned away wearily.

"Yes, I have underrated your intelligence.   Well, good afternoon!"

"Stop! Where are you going?"

"To Scotland Yard."

We had not got half-way to the door before she had overtaken us and was holding his arm.   She had turned in a moment from steel to velvet.

" Come and sit down, gentlemen. Let us talk this matter over. I feel that I may be frank with you, Mr. Holmes. You have the feelings of a gentleman. How quick a woman's instinct is to find it out. I will treat you as a friend."

" I cannot promise to reciprocate, madame. I am not the law, but I represent justice so far as my feeble powers go. I am ready to listen, and then I will tell you how I will act."

" No doubt it was foolish of me to threaten a brave man like yourself."

" What was really foolish, madame, is that you have placed yourself in the power of a band of rascals who may blackmail or give you away."

" No, no ! I am not so simple. Since I have promised to be frank, I may say that no one, save Barney Stockdale and Susan, his wife, have the least idea who their employer is. As to them, well, it is not the first——" She smiled and nodded, with a charming coquettish intimacy.

" I see. You've tested them before."

" They are good hounds who run silent."

" Such hounds have a way sooner or later of biting the hand that feeds them. They will be arrested for this burglary. The police are already after them."

" They will take what comes to them. That is what they are paid for. I shall not appear in the matter."

" Unless I bring you into it."

" No, no ; you would not. You are a gentleman. It is a woman's secret."

" In the first place you must give back this manuscript."

She broke into a ripple of laughter, and walked to the fire-place. There was a calcined mass which she broke up with the poker. " Shall I give this back ? " she asked. So roguish and exquisite did she look as she stood before us with a challenging smile that I felt of all Holmes' criminals this was the one whom he would find it hardest to face. However, he was immune from sentiment.

" That seals your fate," he said coldly. " You are very prompt in your actions, madame, but you have overdone it on this occasion."

She threw the poker down with a clatter.

" How hard you are ! " she cried. " May I tell you the whole story ? "

" I fancy I could tell it to you."

" But you must look at it with my eyes, Mr. Holmes. You must realize it from the point of view of a woman who sees all her life's ambition about to be ruined at the last moment. Is such a woman to be blamed if she protects herself ? "

" The original sin was yours."

" Yes, yes ! I admit it. He was a dear boy, Douglas, but it so chanced that he could not fit into my plans. He wanted marriage—marriage, Mr. Holmes—with a penniless commoner. Nothing less would serve him. Then he became pertinacious. Because I had given he seemed to think that I still must give, and to him only. It was intolerable. At last I had to make him realize it."

13 *to compound a felony as usual.* Magistrate S. Tupper Bigelow has pointed out ("Sherlock Holmes and the Misprision of Felony") that *Russell on Crime* (5th edition, 1877; 6th edition, 1896; 7th edition, 1909; 8th edition, 1923) says: "Compounding a felony is committed where the party robbed not only knows the felon but also takes his goods again, or other amends, upon agreement not to prosecute." In the Canon, Magistrate Bigelow maintains, compounding a felony is confused with *misprision of felony,* an offense which "Holmes committed . . . no less than seventeen times in twelve cases." Russell says of misprision of felony: it "closely resembles the offence of being accessory after the fact to felony. It consists of concealing or procuring the concealment of a felony by the common law or by statute. . . . It is the duty of a man to discover the felony of another to a magistrate. . . . The law does not allow private persons the right to forego a prosecution. . . . There must be knowledge without assent, for any assent or participation will make the man a principal or an accessory. . . . Misprision of felony is distinct from compounding a felony."

A Note on the "Canonicity" of "The Adventure of the Three Gables": This is another of the adventures recounted in *The Case-Book of Sherlock Holmes* which Mr. D. Martin Dakin would reject from the Canon as spurious: "Although it bears Watson's name, I cannot believe that he wrote it. The plot is fantastic and improbable, and is it likely that any man would bear the name Langdale Pike? But the chief argument against the case is the poor figure Holmes cuts in it. Never has a feebler story insulted the memory of the great detective. In the final scene, after telling the fair Isadora Klein coldly that her fate is sealed, he gives in to her in the end and lets her off with a contribution of £5,000. The roguish badinage of his exchanges with Susan ('Oh, Susan! Language!' . . . 'Good-bye, Susan. Paregoric is the stuff . . .') —is even more embarrassing than his remarks to Count Sylvius [in "The Adventure of the Mazarin Stone"], and strongly suggests the same author (who seems to have been determined to show us Holmes as a funny man.) But the falsest note of all is struck in his cheap jeers at Steve Dixie. No admirer of Holmes can read this scene without a blush. For Holmes was a gentleman. And one thing no gentleman does is to taunt another man for his racial characteristics. . . . We must definitely reject [this story]."

" By hiring ruffians to beat him under your own window."

" You do indeed seem to know everything. Well, it is true. Barney and the boys drove him away, and were, I admit, a little rough in doing so. But what did he do then ? Could I have believed that a gentleman would do such an act ? He wrote a book in which he described his own story. I, of course, was the wolf ; he the lamb. It was all there, under different names, of course ; but who in all London would have failed to recognize it ? What do you say to that, Mr. Holmes ? "

" Well, he was within his rights."

" It was as if the air of Italy had got into his blood and brought with it the old cruel Italian spirit. He wrote to me and sent me a copy of his book that I might have the torture of anticipation. There were two copies, he said—one for me, one for his publisher."

" How did you know the publisher's had not reached him ? "

" I knew who his publisher was. It is not his only novel, you know. I found out that he had not heard from Italy. Then came Douglas' sudden death. So long as that other manuscript was in the world there was no safety for me. Of course, it must be among his effects, and these would be returned to his mother. I set the gang at work. One of them got into the house as servant. I wanted to do the thing honestly. I really and truly did. I was ready to buy the house and everything in it. I offered any price she cared to ask. I only tried the other way when everything else had failed. Now, Mr. Holmes, granting that I was too hard on Douglas —and, God knows, I am sorry for it !—what else could I do with my whole future at stake ? "

Sherlock Holmes shrugged his shoulders.

" Well, well," said he, " I suppose I shall have to **13** compound a felony as usual. How much does it cost to go round the world in first-class style ? "

The lady stared in amazement.

" Could it be done on five thousand pounds ? "

" Well, I should think so, indeed ! "

" Very good. I think you will sign me a cheque for that, and I will see that it comes to Mrs. Maberley. You owe her a little change of air. Meantime, lady " —he wagged a cautionary forefinger—" have a care ! Have a care ! You can't play with edged tools for ever without cutting those dainty hands."

74

THE ADVENTURE OF THE MAZARIN STONE

[Summer, 1903; one day]

IT was pleasant to Dr. Watson to find himself once more in the untidy room of the first floor in Baker Street which had been the starting-point of so many remarkable adventures. He looked round him at the scientific charts upon the wall, the acid-charred bench of chemicals, the violin-case leaning in the corner, the coal-scuttle, which contained of old the pipes and tobacco. Finally, his eyes came round to the fresh and smiling face of Billy, the young but very wise and tactful page, who had helped a little to fill up the gap of loneliness and isolation which surrounded the saturnine figure of the great detective.

" It all seems very unchanged, Billy. You don't change, either. I hope the same can be said of him ? "

Billy glanced, with some solicitude, at the closed door of the bedroom.

" I think he's in bed and asleep," he said.

It was seven in the evening of a lovely summer's day, **1** but Dr. Watson was sufficiently familiar with the irregularity of his old friend's hours to feel no surprise at the idea.

" That means a case, I suppose ? "

" Yes, sir ; he is very hard at it just now. I'm frightened for his health. He gets paler and thinner, and he eats nothing. ' When will you be pleased to dine, Mr. Holmes ? ' Mrs. Hudson asked. ' Seven-thirty, the day after to-morrow,' said he. You know his way when he is keen on a case."

" Yes, Billy, I know."

" He's following someone. Yesterday he was out as a workman looking for a job. To-day he was an old woman. Fairly took me in, he did, and I ought to know his ways by now." Billy pointed with a grin to a very baggy parasol which leaned against the sofa. " That's part of the old woman's outfit," he said.

" But what is it all about, Billy ? "

Billy sank his voice, as one who discusses great secrets of State. " I don't mind telling you, sir, but it should go no farther. It's this case of the Crown diamond."

" What—the hundred-thousand-pound burglary ? "

" Yes, sir. They must get it back, sir. Why, we had

1 *It was seven in the evening of a lovely summer's day.* Watson is not living at Baker Street in this case; more, he is again in practice, and his practice is a successful one; Holmes later says to him: "You bear every mark of the busy medical man, with calls on him every hour." "The Adventure of the Mazarin Stone" is certainly after Holmes' Return (Watson, seeing "the facsimile of his old friend . . . in an arm-chair," says, "We used something of the sort once before," and this is clearly a reference to "The Adventure of the Empty House" in 1894. So Dr. Watson's current practice cannot be the successful practice of his second marriage; far less can it be the unsuccessful practice of Marriage I. Nor can the page boy, Billy, be the Billy of *The Valley of Fear* (1888). *This* Billy is described as "young but very wise and tactful," and "The Adventure of the Empty House" was "before [his] time." Can this be the summer of 1894, in the period between Holmes' Return to London and Watson's return to Baker Street, before he sold his Kensington practice to Dr. Verner? It hardly seems that it can: 1) "The Adventure of the Mazarin Stone" is not included in the list of important cases of 1894 given in "The Adventure of the Golden Pince-Nez." 2) If Billy the page was hired shortly after "The Adventure of the Empty House" his tenure at Baker Street was indeed a short one; he is not mentioned in any case we have assigned to the period immediately following the Return. But it is apparent that Billy has been with Holmes for some time: "I ought to know [Holmes'] ways by now," he says. 3) Watson was evidently sharing the Baker Street rooms at a time when *this* Billy was the page there: "You don't change, either," Watson says to him. 4) Watson, in "The Adventure of the Mazarin Stone," has been away from Baker Street for some months, and has not seen Holmes in some time: Billy had "helped a little to fill up the gap of loneliness and isolation which surrounded the saturnine figure of the great detective"; "You have not learned . . . to despise my pipe and my lamentable tobacco?" Holmes asks Watson. That the case is a very late one is further evidenced by the fact that it is "Youghal of the C.I.D."—not Gregson or Lestrade or Hopkins—that Holmes calls in. The contemporary reader would know that Holmes had retired by December, 1904 ("The Second Stain") but he would be hard put to determine between 1903 and 1904. The modern student has the advantage of knowing that Holmes had in fact retired shortly after September, 1903, and he would have no hesitation in dating "The Adventure of the Mazarin Stone" in the summer of that year. Holmes says it was a "chilly" day "for the time of the year," but this statement can be taken as part of his joke on Lord Cantlemere; the anonymous writer called it a "lovely" evening. There does not seem to be any other evidence from which one might determine either the month or the day.

2 *the Prime Minister and the Home Secretary*. Arthur James Balfour, 1848–1930, Prime Minister, 1902–1905, and A. Akers-Douglas.

"THEN THERE IS LORD CANTLEMERE ——"

"This crusty old peer . . . has been given a name that does not appear in heraldic records," Dr. Julian Wolff wrote in his *Practical Handbook of Sherlockian Heraldry*. "It is evident that one of Watson's weak attempts at concealment has been made for it seems that the Cantilupe family is involved. The following is from *The Siege of Carlaverock:* "And William de Cantilupe . . . had on a red shield a fess vair, with three fleurs de lis of bright gold issuing from leopards' heads.'"

2 the Prime Minister and the Home Secretary both sitting on that very sofa. Mr. Holmes was very nice to them. He soon put them at their ease and promised he would do all he could. Then there is Lord Cantlemere——"
   "Ah !"
   "Yes, sir; you know what that means. He's a stiff 'un, sir, if I may say so. I can get along with the Prime Minister, and I've nothing against the Home Secretary, who seemed a civil, obliging sort of man, but I can't stand his lordship. Neither can Mr. Holmes, sir. You see, he don't believe in Mr. Holmes and he was against employing him. He'd *rather* he failed."
   "And Mr. Holmes knows it ?"
   "Mr. Holmes always knows whatever there is to know."
   "Well, we'll hope he won't fail and that Lord Cantlemere will be confounded. But I say, Billy, what is that curtain for across the window ?"
   "Mr. Holmes had it put up there three days ago. We've got something funny behind it."
   Billy advanced and drew away the drapery which screened the alcove of the bow window.
   Dr. Watson could not restrain a cry of amazement. There was a facsimile of his old friend, dressing-gown and all, the face turned three-quarters towards the window and downwards, as though reading an invisible book, while the body was sunk deep in an arm-chair. Billy detached the head and held it in the air.
   "We put it at different angles, so that it may seem more life-like. I wouldn't dare touch it if the blind were not down. But when it's up you can see this from across the way."
   "We used something of the sort once before."
   "Before my time," said Billy. He drew the window curtains apart and looked out into the street. "There are folk who watch us from over yonder. I can see a fellow now at the window. Have a look for yourself."
   Watson had taken a step forward when the bedroom door opened, and the long, thin form of Holmes emerged, his face pale and drawn, but his step and bearing as active as ever. With a single spring he was at the window, and had drawn the blind once more.
   "That will do, Billy," said he. "You were in danger of your life then, my boy, and I can't do without you just yet. Well, Watson, it is good to see you in your old quarters once again. You come at a critical moment."
   "So I gather."
   "You can go, Billy. That boy is a problem, Watson. How far am I justified in allowing him to be in danger ?"
   "Danger of what, Holmes ?"
   "Of sudden death. I'm expecting something this evening."
   "Expecting what ?"
   "To be murdered, Watson."
   "No, no; you are joking, Holmes !"
   "Even my limited sense of humour could evolve a better joke than that. But we may be comfortable in the meantime, may we not ? Is alcohol permitted ?

The gasogene and cigars are in the old place. Let me see you once more in the customary arm-chair. You have not, I hope, learned to despise my pipe and my lamentable tobacco? It has to take the place of food these days."

" But why not eat? "

" Because the faculties become refined when you starve them. Why, surely, as a doctor, my dear Watson, you must admit that what your digestion gains in the way of blood supply is so much lost to the brain. I am a brain, Watson. The rest of me is a mere appendix. **3** Therefore, it is the brain I must consider."

" But this danger, Holmes? "

" Ah, yes; in case it should come off, it would perhaps be as well that you should burden your memory with the name and address of the murderer. You can give it to Scotland Yard, with my love and a parting blessing. Sylvius is the name—Count Negretto Sylvius. Write it down, man, write it down! 136 Moorside Gardens, N.W. Got it? "

Watson's honest face was twitching with anxiety. He knew only too well the immense risks taken by Holmes, and was well aware that what he said was more likely to be under-statement than exaggeration. Watson was always the man of action, and he rose to the occasion.

" Count me in, Holmes. I have nothing to do for a day or two."

" Your morals don't improve, Watson. You have added fibbing to your other vices. You bear every sign of the busy medical man, with calls on him every hour."

" Not such important ones. But can't you have this fellow arrested? "

" Yes, Watson, I could. That's what worries him so."

" But why don't you? "

" Because I don't know where the diamond is."

" Ah! Billy told me—the missing Crown jewel! "

" Yes, the great yellow Mazarin stone. I've cast **4** my net and I have my fish. But I have not got the stone. What is the use of taking *them*? We can make the world a better place by laying them by the heels. But that is not what I am out for. It's the stone I want."

" And is this Count Sylvius one of your fish? "

" Yes, and he's a shark. He bites. The other is Sam Merton, the boxer. Not a bad fellow, Sam, but the Count has used him. Sam's not a shark. He is a great big silly bull-headed gudgeon. But he is flopping about in my net all the same."

" Where is this Count Sylvius? "

" I've been at his very elbow all the morning. You've seen me as an old lady, Watson. I was never more convincing. He actually picked up my parasol for me once. ' By your leave, madame,' said he—half-Italian, you know, and with the Southern graces of manner when in the mood, but a devil incarnate in the other

BILLY ADVANCED AND DREW AWAY THE DRAPERY . . .

Illustration by A. Gilbert for the *Strand Magazine*, October, 1921.

3 *The rest of me is a mere appendix.* "But independent observation would [not] confirm that statement . . . ; not so long as we are constantly encountering appetizing references in the stories to 'oysters and a brace of grouse, with something a little choice in white wines' (the prelude to the wild chase down the Thames in the steam-launch *Aurora*) and 'a couple of brace of cold woodcock, a pheasant, a *pâté de fois gras* pie with a group of ancient and cobwebby bottles' ["The Noble Bachelor"]. . . . Epicure that [Holmes] was he . . . minded his belly very studiously," Mr. Richard D. Altick wrote in "Mr. Sherlock Holmes and Dr. Samuel Johnson."

4 *the great yellow Mazarin stone.* The gem was named for Cardinal Jules Mazarin, 1602–1661.

5 *the Minories.* The street in the City called the Minories takes its name from the community of the "Sorores Minores," which was established just outside the walls of the City in 1293. It belonged to the second Order of St. Francis and consisted of "the Abbess and Sisters Minoresses of the Order of St. Clare." The name Minories seems to have been given to the street at the end of the sixteenth or the beginning of the seventeenth century.

6 *Grasp the nettle, Watson!* From verses written by Aaron Hill (1685–1750):

> Tender-handed stroke a nettle,
>   And it stings you for your pains;
> Grasp it like a man of mettle
>   And it soft as silk remains.

7 *a shooter of big game.* As we have previously noted, the villain in Conan Doyle's original version of "The Adventure of the Mazarin Stone"—the one-act play called *The Crown Diamond: An Evening with Sherlock Holmes*—was, not Count Negretto Sylvius, but our old friend Colonel Sebastian Moran.

8 *the waiting-room, sir,"* It is possible that 221 Baker Street may, at this time, have boasted a "waiting-room," but all reliable commentators have warned that we must be very careful about taking "The Adventure of the Mazarin Stone" as our authority for any details concerning the home of Holmes.

9 *This second exit is exceedingly useful.* See Note 8 above.

mood. Life is full of whimsical happenings, Watson."

" It might have been tragedy."

" Well, perhaps it might. I followed him to old **5** Straubenzee's workshop in the Minories. Straubenzee made the air-gun—a very pretty bit of work, as I understand, and I rather fancy it is in the opposite window at the present moment. Have you seen the dummy? Of course, Billy showed it to you. Well, it may get a bullet through its beautiful head at any moment. Ah, Billy, what is it?"

The boy had reappeared in the room with a card upon a tray. Holmes glanced at it with raised eyebrows and an amused smile.

" The man himself. I had hardly expected this. **6** Grasp the nettle, Watson! A man of nerve. Possibly **7** you have heard of his reputation as a shooter of big game. It would indeed be a triumphant ending to his excellent sporting record if he added me to his bag. This is a proof that he feels my toe very close behind his heel."

" Send for the police."

" I probably shall. But not just yet. Would you glance carefully out of the window, Watson, and see if anyone is hanging about in the street? "

Watson looked warily round the edge of the curtain.

" Yes, there is one rough fellow near the door."

" That will be Sam Merton—the faithful but rather fatuous Sam. Where is this gentleman, Billy? "

8   " In the waiting-room, sir."

" Show him up when I ring."

" Yes, sir."

" If I am not in the room, show him in all the same."

" Yes, sir."

Watson waited until the door was closed, and then he turned earnestly to his companion.

" Look here, Holmes, this is simply impossible. This is a desperate man, who sticks at nothing. He may have come to murder you."

" I should not be surprised."

" I insist upon staying with you."

" You would be horribly in the way."

" In *his* way? "

" No, my dear fellow—in my way."

" Well, I can't possibly leave you."

" Yes, you can, Watson. And you will, for you have never failed to play the game. I am sure you will play it to the end. This man has come for his own purpose, but he may stay for mine." Holmes took out his notebook and scribbled a few lines. " Take a cab to Scotland Yard and give this to Youghal of the C.I.D. Come back with the police. The fellow's arrest will follow."

" I'll do that with joy."

" Before you return I may have just time enough to find out where the stone is." He touched the bell. " I think we will go out through the bedroom. This **9** second exit is exceedingly useful. I rather want to see my shark without his seeing me, and I have, as you will remember, my own way of doing it."

It was, therefore, an empty room into which Billy, a minute later, ushered Count Sylvius. The famous game-shot, sportsman, and man-about-town was a big, swarthy fellow, with a formidable dark moustache, shading a cruel, thin-lipped mouth, and surmounted by a long, curved nose, like the beak of an eagle. He was well dressed, but his brilliant necktie, shining pin, and glittering rings were flamboyant in their effect. As the door closed behind him he looked round him with fierce, startled eyes, like one who suspects a trap at every turn. Then he gave a violent start as he saw the impassive head and the collar of the dressing-gown which projected above the arm-chair in the window. At first his expression was one of pure amazement. Then the light of a horrible hope gleamed in his dark, murderous eyes. He took one more glance round to see that there were no witnesses, and then, on tiptoe, his thick stick half raised, he approached the silent figure. He was crouching for his final spring and blow when a cool, sardonic voice greeted him from the open bedroom door :

" Don't break it, Count ! Don't break it ! "

The assassin staggered back, amazement in his convulsed face. For an instant he half raised his loaded cane once more, as if he would turn his violence from the effigy to the original ; but there was something in that steady grey eye and mocking smile which caused his hand to sink to his side.

" It's a pretty little thing," said Holmes, advancing towards the image. " Tavernier, the French modeller, made it. He is as good at wax-works as your friend Straubenzee is at air-guns."

" Air-guns, sir ! What do you mean ? "

" Put your hat and stick on the side-table. Thank you ! Pray take a seat. Would you care to put your revolver out also ? Oh, very good, if you prefer to sit upon it. Your visit is really most opportune, for I wanted badly to have a few minutes' chat with you."

The Count scowled, with heavy, threatening eyebrows.

" I, too, wished to have some words with you, Holmes. That is why I am here. I won't deny that I intended to assault you just now."

Holmes swung his leg on the edge of the table.

" I rather gathered that you had some idea of the sort in your head," said he. " But why these personal attentions ? "

" Because you have gone out of your way to annoy me. Because you have put your creatures upon my track."

" My creatures ! I assure you no ! "

" Nonsense ! I have had them followed. Two can play at that game, Holmes."

" It is a small point, Count Sylvius, but perhaps you would kindly give me my prefix when you address me. You can understand that, with my routine of work, I should find myself on familiar terms with half the rogues' gallery, and you will agree that exceptions are invidious."

" Well, *Mr.* Holmes, then."

" Excellent ! But I assure you you are mistaken about my alleged agents."

Count Sylvius laughed contemptuously.

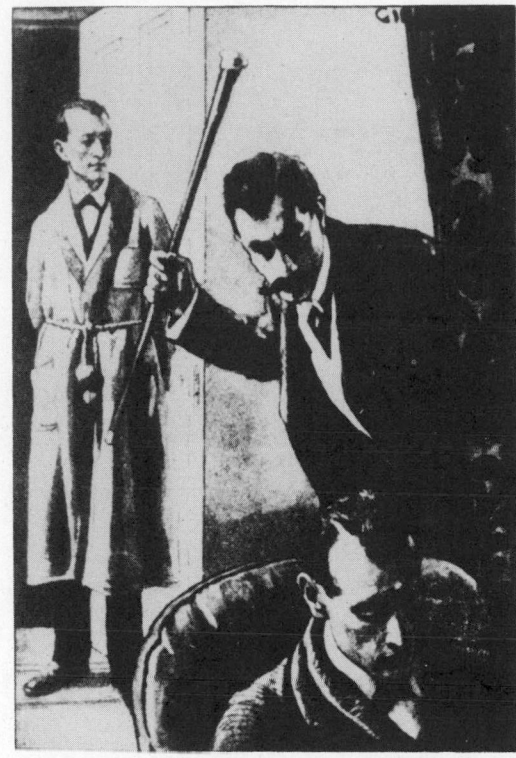

"DON'T BREAK IT, COUNT! DON'T BREAK IT!"

Illustration by A. Gilbert for the *Strand Magazine*, October, 1921. Frederic Dorr Steele illustrated the same scene for *Hearst's International*, November, 1921.

" Other people can observe as well as you. Yesterday there was an old sporting man. To-day it was an elderly woman. They held me in view all day."

" Really, sir, you compliment me. Old Baron Dowson said the night before he was hanged that in my case what the law had gained the stage had lost. And now you give my little impersonations your kindly praise ! "

" It was you—you yourself ? "

Holmes shrugged his shoulders. " You can see in the corner the parasol which you so politely handed to me in the Minories before you began to suspect."

" If I had known, you might never——"

" Have seen this humble home again. I was well aware of it. We all have neglected opportunities to deplore. As it happens, you did not know, so here we are ! "

The Count's knotted brows gathered more heavily over his menacing eyes. " What you say only makes the matter worse. It was not your agents, but your play-acting, busybody self ! You admit that you have dogged me. Why ? "

" Come now, Count. You used to shoot lions in Algeria."

" Well ? "

" But why ? "

" Why ? The sport—the excitement—the danger ! "

" And, no doubt, to free the country from a pest ? "

" Exactly ! "

" My reasons in a nutshell ! "

The Count sprang to his feet, and his hand involuntarily moved back to his hip-pocket.

" Sit down, sir, sit down ! There was another, more practical, reason. I want that yellow diamond ! "

Count Sylvius lay back in his chair with an evil smile.

" Upon my word ! " said he.

" You knew that I was after you for that. The real reason why you are here to-night is to find out how much I know about the matter and how far my removal is absolutely essential. Well, I should say that, from your point of view, it *is* absolutely essential, for I know all about it, save only one thing, which you are about to tell me."

" Oh, indeed ! And, pray, what is this missing fact ? "

" Where the Crown diamond now is."

The Count looked sharply at his companion. " Oh, you want to know that, do you ? How the devil should I be able to tell you where it is ? "

" You can, and you will."

" Indeed ! "

" You can't bluff me, Count Sylvius." Holmes' eyes, as he gazed at him, contracted and lightened until they were like two menacing points of steel. " You are absolute plate-glass. I see to the very back of your mind."

" Then, of course, you see where the diamond is ! "

Holmes clapped his hands with amusement, and then pointed a derisive finger. " Then you do know. You have admitted it ! "

" I admit nothing."

" Now, Count, if you will be reasonable we can do business. If not, you will get hurt."

Count Sylvius threw up his eyes to the ceiling. " And you talk about bluff ! " said he.

Holmes looked at him thoughtfully, like a master chess-player who meditates his crowning move. Then he threw open the table drawer and drew out a squat notebook.

" Do you know what I keep in this book ? "

" No, sir, I do not ! "

" You ! "

" Me ? "

" Yes, sir, *you* ! You are all here—every action of your vile and dangerous life."

" Damn you, Holmes ! " cried the Count, with blazing eyes. " There are limits to my patience ! "

" It's all here, Count. The real facts as to the death of old Mrs. Harold, who left you the Blymer estate, which you so rapidly gambled away."

" You are dreaming ! "

" And the complete life history of Miss Minnie War-render."

" Tut ! You will make nothing of that ! "

" Plenty more here, Count. Here is the robbery in the train-de-luxe to the Riviera on February 13, 1892. Here is the forged cheque in the same year on the Crédit Lyonnais."

" No ; you're wrong there."

" Then I am right on the others ! Now, Count, you are a card-player. When the other fellow has all the trumps, it saves time to throw down your hand."

" What has all this talk to do with the jewel of which you spoke ? "

" Gently, Count. Restrain that eager mind ! Let me get to the points in my own humdrum fashion. I have all this against you ; but, above all, I have a clear case against both you and your fighting bully in the case of the Crown diamond."

" Indeed ! "

" I have the cabman who took you to Whitehall and the cabman who brought you away. I have the Commissionaire who saw you near the case. I have Ikey Sanders, who refused to cut it up for you. Ikey has peached, and the game is up."

The veins stood out on the Count's forehead. His dark, hairy hands were clenched in a convulsion of restrained emotion. He tried to speak, but the words would not shape themselves.

" That's the hand I play from," said Holmes. " I put it all upon the table. But one card is missing. It's the King of Diamonds. I don't know where the stone is."

" You never shall know."

" No ? Now, be reasonable, Count. Consider the situation. You are going to be locked up for twenty years. So is Sam Merton. What good are you going to get out of your diamond ? None in the world. But if you hand it over—well, I'll compound a felony. We **10** don't want you or Sam. We want the stone. Give that up, and so far as I am concerned you can go free so long as you behave yourself in the future. If you make

10 *I'll compound a felony.* See "The Adventure of the Three Gables," Note 13.

11 *the unrestrained enjoyment of the present?"* In "The Adventure of the Norwood Builder," Holmes tells Watson, "We must use what time we have." In *The Hound of the Baskervilles*, Holmes asserts, "The past and the present are within the field of my inquiry, but what a man may do in the future is a hard question to answer." In "The Adventure of the Veiled Lodger," he reflects, "The ways of fate are indeed hard to understand." "These are but a few of the echoes," Mr. Morris Rosenblum wrote in "The Horation Spirit in Holmes," "of lines in the poems of Horace.

Carpe diem, quam minimum credula postero.
Odes, Book 1, 11.

'Make the most of today; put as little trust as possible in the future.' "

another slip—well, it will be the last. But this time my commission is to get the stone, not you."

" But if I refuse ? "

" Why, then—alas !—it must be you and not the stone."

Billy had appeared in answer to a ring.

" I think, Count, that it would be as well to have your friend Sam at this conference. After all, his interests should be represented. Billy, you will see a large and ugly gentleman outside the front door. Ask him to come up."

" If he won't come, sir ? "

" No violence, Billy. Don't be rough with him. If you tell him that Count Sylvius wants him he will certainly come."

" What are you going to do now ? " asked the Count, as Billy disappeared.

" My friend Watson was with me just now. I told him that I had a shark and a gudgeon in my net ; now I am drawing the net and up they come together."

The Count had risen from his chair, and his hand was behind his back. Holmes held something half protruding from the pocket of his dressing-gown.

" You won't die in your bed, Holmes."

" I have often had the same idea. Does it matter very much ? After all, Count, your own exit is more likely to be perpendicular than horizontal. But these anticipations of the future are morbid. Why not give **11** ourselves up to the unrestrained enjoyment of the present?"

A sudden wild-beast light sprang up in the dark, menacing eyes of the master criminal. Holmes' figure seemed to grow taller as he grew tense and ready.

" It is no use your fingering your revolver, my friend," he said, in a quiet voice. " You know perfectly well that you dare not use it, even if I gave you time to draw it. Nasty, noisy things, revolvers, Count. Better stick to air-guns. Ah ! I think I hear the fairy footstep of your estimable partner. Good day, Mr. Merton. Rather dull in the street, is it not ? "

The prize-fighter, a heavily built young man with a stupid, obstinate, slab-sided face, stood awkwardly at the door, looking about him with a puzzled expression. Holmes' debonair manner was a new experience, and though he vaguely felt that it was hostile, he did not know how to counter it. He turned to his more astute comrade for help.

" What's the game now, Count ? What's this fellow want ? What's up ? " His voice was deep and raucous.

The Count shrugged his shoulders and it was Holmes who answered.

" If I may put it in a nutshell, Mr. Merton, I should say it was *all* up."

The boxer still addressed his remarks to his associate.

" Is this cove trying to be funny, or what ? I'm not in the funny mood myself."

" No, I expect not," said Holmes. " I think I can promise you that you will feel even less humorous as the evening advances. Now, look here, Count Sylvius. I'm a busy man and I can't waste time. I'm going into that bedroom. Pray make yourselves quite at home in my absence. You can explain to your friend how the matter lies without the restraint of my presence. I shall try over the Hoffmann Barcarolle upon my violin. In five minutes I shall return for your final answer. You quite grasp the alternative, do you not? Shall we take you, or shall we have the stone?"

Holmes withdrew, picking up his violin from the corner as he passed. A few moments later the long-drawn, wailing notes of that most haunting of tunes came faintly **12** through the closed door of the bedroom.

"What is it, then?" asked Merton anxiously, as his companion turned to him. "Does he know about the stone?"

"He knows a damned sight too much about it. I'm not sure that he doesn't know all about it."

"Good Lord!" The boxer's sallow face turned a shade whiter.

"Ikey Sanders has split on us."

"He has, has he? I'll do him down a thick 'un for that if I swing for it."

"That won't help us much. We've got to make up our minds what to do."

"Half a mo'," said the boxer, looking suspiciously at the bedroom door. "He's a leary cove that wants watching. I suppose he's not listening?"

"How can he be listening with that music going?"

"That's right. Maybe somebody's behind a curtain. Too many curtains in this room." As he looked round he suddenly saw for the first time the effigy in the window, and stood staring and pointing, too amazed for words.

"Tut! it's only a dummy," said the Count.

"A fake, is it? Well, strike me! Madame Tussaud ain't in it. It's the living spit of him, gown and all. But them curtains, Count!"

"Oh, confound the curtains! We are wasting our time, and there is none too much. He can lag us over this stone."

"The deuce he can!"

"But he'll let us slip if we only tell him where the swag is."

"I'M GOING INTO THAT BEDROOM."

Illustration by A. Gilbert for the *Strand Magazine*, October, 1921.

12 *the long-drawn, wailing notes of that most haunting of tunes.* "It would hardly be possible to apply less idoneous adjectives to [the Barcarolle from Offenbach's *The Tales of Hoffmann*] than ... 'wailing' and 'haunting,'" Mr. Benjamin Grosbayne wrote in "Sherlock Holmes—Musician." "Moreover, the use of the word 'tune' is particularly inept as applied to this limpid and translucent melody."

"MADAME TUSSAUD AIN'T IN IT."

The home of the famous waxworks in the Marylebone Road, after the move from Baker Street. This building was burnt down; the "Buffalo's Head" and the old houses on the left were demolished to make way for the new Baker Street Metropolitan Railway just before the first World War. The illustration is from *In the Footsteps of Sherlock Holmes*, by Michael Harrison.

13 *Lime Street.* So called from the lime-burners; the neighboring Coleman Street and Seacoal Lane have the same origin. Lime Street, on the south side of Leadenhall Street, was until the close of the eighteenth century inhabited by wealthy City merchants. Today it is the home of the magnificent new headquarters of Lloyd's.

" What ! Give it up ? Give up a hundred thousand quid ? "

" It's one or the other."

Merton scratched his short-cropped pate.

" He's alone in there. Let's do him in. If his light were out we should have nothing to fear."

The Count shook his head.

" He is armed and ready. If we shot him we could hardly get away in a place like this. Besides, it's likely enough that the police know whatever evidence he has got. Hallo ! What was that ? "

There was a vague sound which seemed to come from the window. Both men sprang round, but all was quiet. Save for the one strange figure seated in the chair, the room was certainly empty.

" Something in the street," said Merton. " Now look here, guv'nor, you've got the brains. Surely you can think a way out of it. If slugging is no use then it's up to you."

" I've fooled better men than he," the Count answered. " The stone is here in my secret pocket. I take no chances leaving it about. It can be out of England to-night and cut into four pieces in Amsterdam before Sunday. He knows nothing of Van Seddar."

" I thought Van Seddar was going next week."

" He *was*. But now he must get off by the next boat. One or other of us must slip round with the stone to **13** Lime Street and tell him."

" But the false bottom ain't ready."

" Well, he must take it as it is and chance it. There's not a moment to lose." Again, with the sense of danger which becomes an instinct with the sportsman, he paused and looked hard at the window. Yes, it was surely from the street that the faint sound had come.

" As to Holmes," he continued, " we can fool him easily enough. You see, the damned fool won't arrest us if he can get the stone. Well, we'll promise him the stone. We'll put him on the wrong track about it, and before he finds that it *is* the wrong track it will be in Holland and we out of the country."

" That sounds good to me ! " cried Sam Merton, with a grin.

" You go on and tell the Dutchman to get a move on him. I'll see this sucker and fill him up with a bogus confession. I'll tell him that the stone is in Liverpool. Confound that whining music ; it gets on my nerves ! By the time he finds it isn't in Liverpool it will be in quarters and we on the blue water. Come back here, out of a line with that keyhole. Here is the stone."

" I wonder you dare carry it."

" Where could I have it safer ? If we could take it out of Whitehall someone else could surely take it out of my lodgings."

" Let's have a look at it."

Count Sylvius cast a somewhat unflattering glance at his associate, and disregarded the unwashed hand which was extended towards him.

" What—d'ye think I'm going to snatch it off you ? See here, mister, I'm getting a bit tired of your ways."

" Well, well ; no offence, Sam. We can't afford to quarrel. Come over to the window if you want to see the beauty properly. Now hold it to the light ! Here ! "

" Thank you ! "

With a single spring Holmes had leaped from the dummy's chair and had grasped the precious jewel. He held it now in one hand, while his other pointed a revolver at the Count's head. The two villains staggered back in utter amazement. Before they had recovered Holmes had pressed the electric bell.

" No violence, gentlemen—no violence, I beg of you ! Consider the furniture ! It must be very clear to you that your position is an impossible one. The police are waiting below."

The Count's bewilderment overmastered his rage and fear.

" But how the deuce—— ? " he gasped.

" Your surprise is very natural. You are not aware that a second door from my bedroom leads behind that curtain. I fancied that you must have heard me when **14** I displaced the figure, but luck was on my side. It gave me a chance of listening to your racy conversation which would have been painfully constrained had you been aware of my presence."

The Count gave a gesture of resignation.

" We give you best, Holmes. I believe you are the devil himself."

" Not far from him, at any rate," Holmes answered, with a polite smile.

Sam Merton's slow intellect had only gradually appreciated the situation. Now, as the sound of heavy steps came from the stairs outside, he broke silence at last.

" A fair cop ! " said he. " But, I say, what about that bloomin' fiddle ! I hear it yet."

" Tut, tut ! " Holmes answered. " You are perfectly right. Let it play ! These modern gramophones are a remarkable invention." **15**

There was an inrush of police, the handcuffs clicked and the criminals were led to the waiting cab. Watson lingered with Holmes, congratulating him upon this fresh leaf added to his laurels. Once more their conversation was interrupted by the imperturbable Billy with his card-tray.

" Lord Cantlemere, sir."

" Show him up, Billy. This is the eminent peer who represents the very highest interests," said Holmes. " He is an excellent and loyal person, but rather of the old regime. Shall we make him unbend ? Dare we venture upon a slight liberty ? He knows, we may conjecture, nothing of what has occurred."

The door opened to admit a thin, austere figure with a hatchet face and drooping mid-Victorian whiskers of a glossy blackness which hardly corresponded with the rounded shoulders and feeble gait. Holmes advanced affably, and shook an unresponsive hand.

" How-do-you-do, Lord Cantlemere ? It is chilly, for the time of year, but rather warm indoors. May I take your overcoat ? "

" No, I thank you ; I will not take it off."

14 *a second door from my bedroom behind that curtain.* See Note 8.

15 *These modern gramophones are a remarkable invention.* "Let us stress here the fact that it was a *gramophone*," Mr. Anthony Boucher wrote in "The Records of Baker Street." "To most modern readers, *gramophone* and *phonograph* are interchangeable words, respectively British and American, like *lift* and *elevator*. . . . But in England in 1903, *gramophone* distinctly meant the Berliner-Gramophone & Typewriter *disc* machine, while cyclinder machines were known as *phonographs* or *graphophones*."

Elsewhere (in "Prolegomena to a Holmesian Discography"), Mr. Boucher has written: "It was almost certainly a single 12″ [disc]. Single, from the date of the events . . . ; 12″ because it was still playing after at least three and a half minutes of dialogue. . . . But the most curious factor concerning the record is that it must . . . have been a performance of the Hoffmann Barcarolle by *unaccompanied* violin. Such a transcription is so unlikely a choice for commercial recording that one is led to consider . . . that this was a private recording made by Holmes himself."

Holmes laid his hand insistently upon the sleeve.

" Pray allow me ! My friend Dr. Watson would assure you that these changes of temperature are most insidious."

His lordship shook himself free with some impatience.

" I am quite comfortable, sir. I have no need to stay. I have simply looked in to know how your self-appointed task was progressing."

" It is difficult—very difficult."

" I feared that you would find it so."

There was a distinct sneer in the old courtier's words and manner.

" Every man finds his limitations, Mr. Holmes, but at least it cures us of the weakness of self-satisfaction."

" Yes, sir, I have been much perplexed."

" No doubt."

" Especially upon one point. Possibly you could help me upon it ? "

" You apply for my advice rather late in the day. I thought that you had your own all-sufficient methods. Still, I am ready to help you."

" You see, Lord Cantlemere, we can no doubt frame a case against the actual thieves."

" When you have caught them."

" Exactly. But the question is—how shall we proceed against the receiver ? "

" Is this not rather premature ? "

" It is as well to have our plans ready. Now, what would you regard as final evidence against the receiver ? "

" The actual possession of the stone."

" You would arrest him upon that ? "

" Most undoubtedly."

Holmes seldom laughed, but he got as near it as his old friend Watson could remember.

" In that case, my dear sir, I shall be under the painful necessity of advising your arrest."

Lord Cantlemere was very angry. Some of the ancient fires flickered up into his sallow cheeks.

" You take a great liberty, Mr. Holmes. In fifty years of official life I cannot recall such a case. I am a busy man, sir, engaged upon important affairs, and I have no time or taste for foolish jokes. I may tell you frankly, sir, that I have never been a believer in your powers, and that I have always been of the opinion that the matter was far safer in the hands of the regular police force. Your conduct confirms all my conclusions. I have the honour, sir, to wish you good evening."

Holmes had swiftly changed his position and was between the peer and the door.

" One moment, sir," said he. " To actually go off with the Mazarin stone would be a more serious offence than to be found in temporary possession of it."

" Sir, this is intolerable ! Let me pass."

" Put your hand in the right-hand pocket of your overcoat."

" What do you mean, sir ? "

" Come—come ; do what I ask."

An instant later the amazed peer was standing, blinking and stammering, with the great yellow stone on his shaking palm.

" What ! What ! How is this, Mr. Holmes ? "

" Too bad, Lord Cantlemere, too bad ! " cried Holmes. " My old friend here will tell you that I have an impish habit of practical joking. Also that I can never resist a dramatic situation. I took the liberty—the very great liberty, I admit—of putting the stone into your pocket at the beginning of our interview."

The old peer stared from the stone to the smiling face before him.

" Sir, I am bewildered. But—yes—it is indeed the Mazarin stone. We are greatly your debtors, Mr. Holmes. Your sense of humour may, as you admit, be somewhat perverted, and its exhibition remarkably untimely, but at least I withdraw any reflection I have made upon your amazing professional powers. But how——"

" The case is but half finished ; the details can wait. No doubt, Lord Cantlemere, your pleasure in telling of this successful result in the exalted circle to which you return will be some small atonement for my practical joke. Billy, you will show his lordship out, and tell Mrs. Hudson that I should be glad if she would send up dinner for two as soon as possible."

75

"... IT IS UNDOUBTEDLY QUEER ..."

[Sherlock Holmes to John H. Watson, M.D., "The Adventure of the Six Napoleons"]

"Of all the stories in the Canon which have moved scholars to discussion and argument, none has aroused more controversial opinion than 'The Adventure of the Mazarin Stone,'" the late James Montgomery wrote in "Speculation in Diamonds."

Mr. Anthony Boucher has found the story "dubious" and labeled it a "farrago."

Mr. D. Martin Dakin is less harsh than Mr. Boucher, but he too has concluded that the adventure is "spurious": "It . . . bristles with improbabilities. Yet the scene at the end with Lord Cantlemere has a lifelike ring about it and agrees with Holmes' 'impish habit of practical joking' and love of a dramatic situation as shown in 'The Naval Treaty' and 'The Adventure of the Six Napoleons.' Indeed it is scarcely a coincidence that the best parts of the story are those at both ends in which Watson personally appears. It almost looks as if the author, having come across some notes by Watson which he had discarded as only providing half a story, decided to fill in the gap from his imagination. It bear every mark of such an origin. How could anyone know the initial detail of the conversation between Count Sylvius and Sam Merton, unless indeed Holmes had his ear to the keyhole from the moment he put the record on? Holmes had a delicate vein of sarcasm and was not above twitting an adversary, as witness his interview with Col. Sebastian Moran; but the forced facetiousness of his conversation with the Count . . . reads like a violent caricature of this and must grate on the ears of all Holmesians. Finally, is it conceivable that so astute a planner as Holmes would rely for his success on the off chance that the two criminals would not be looking in his direction when he displaced the dummy, or would not notice the sound he made?"

Mr. S. C. Roberts has agreed that the tale presents many difficulties, and he has argued that since Watson was a busy practitioner at the time, it might be a compilation from the doctor's notes edited by the Mrs. Watson of 1902, who would "naturally take a proud interest in her husband's part in the adventure."

The late Gavin Brend also admitted a 1902 Mrs. Watson, but held that her attitude toward her husband's participation in Sherlock Holmes' cases and his written accounts of the same were the exact opposite of the stand taken by Mary Morstan Watson: whereas Mary had always been extremely sympathetic toward Watson's association with Holmes, and had constantly encouraged him to go running all over England on little or no notice whenever the game was afoot, her successor took a dim view of these diversions and insisted on an undivided attention to her and to his practice. Mr. Brend theorized that because of the later Mrs. Watson's attitude, Watson tried the experiment of deceiving her by writing "The Adventure of the Mazarin Stone" in the third person, but almost immediately realized that the result was too negative, and the whole idea an unsatisfactory subterfuge at best.

Mr. Guy Warrack has sided with Messrs. Boucher, Dakin, and Roberts in pronouncing the story unreliable on points of detail, and he also believes that Mrs. Watson had a hand in it, even to the invention of the gramophone incident.

The late Christopher Morley also agreed that Mrs. Watson wrote the story ("her first and last attempt") but insisted that there was never more than one Mrs. Watson— therefore the author would of necessity have been Mary. This theory has also been accepted by Mr. Russell McLauchlin, who calls the adventure "an amateurish effort which a shrewd guess ascribes to Mary Watson."

The late H. W. Bell felt that both "His Last Bow" and "The Adventure of the Mazarin Stone" were probably written by one and the same person, and although he did not presume to name the author he speculated that if Mr. Roberts' theory of Mrs. Watson's authorship was correct she may have been connected with the stage; he based this on the theatrical flavor of the bow window (a shrewd guess, as we shall see).

Mr. T. S. Blakeney has also refrained from naming the author, but has said that a third hand has written up Watson's notes, not only in "The Adventure of the Mazarin Stone" but also in *all* the adventures in *The Case-Book*, and in so doing has clumsily endeavored to imitate Watson's style.

The late Page Heldenbrand, on the other hand, agreed with Mr. Brend that the story was written by Watson himself, basing his viewpoint on a quotation from "The Problem of Thor Bridge" in which Watson says: "In some [cases] I was myself concerned and can speak as an eye-witness, while in others I was either not present or played so small a part that they could only *be told as by a third person.*" Mr. Heldenbrand held that in "The Adventure of the Mazarin Stone" Watson deemed his part sufficiently unimportant to warrant adoption of the third person form of narrative as a simple matter of literary expediency. This same point of view has been effectively stated by Mr. Cornelis Helling in his brief essay, "The Third Person."

Mr. O. F. Grazebrook, however, has speculated that the entire *Case-Book*, which of course includes "The Adventure of the Mazarin Stone," was written by young Dr. Verner, that distant relative of Holmes who bought, with Holmes' money, Watson's small practice in Kensington.

DENNIS NEILSON-TERRY AS SHERLOCK HOLMES IN "THE CROWN DIAMOND: AN EVENING WITH SHERLOCK HOLMES."

Mr. S. T. L. Harbottle, in "The Case-Book Cipher Unveiled," has attributed the authorship of "The Adventure of the Mazarin Stone"—and perhaps the rest of the *Case-Book* as well—to Inspector G. Lestrade, and Mr. G. B. Newton has put forward the interesting suggestion that the author of "The Adventure of the Mazarin Stone" was none other than Billy the page.

Still another point of view was expressed by the late Edgar W. Smith, who boldly declared that the story's true creator was Sir Arthur Conan Doyle: "Surely it is a measure both of Dr. Doyle's loyalty to his friend [Watson], and of his rank below him in the scale of literary achievement, that it should have been he—as it must have been he—who wrote 'The Adventure of the Mazarin Stone.' " Mr. Smith's view was later buttressed by Mr. Nathan L. Bengis, who pointed out in his "Thanks to Dr. Watson: A Study in Conanical Plagiarism" that "further proof, if any were needed, that ["The Adventure of the Mazarin Stone"] is apocryphal and was almost certainly written by [Conan Doyle himself] is provided by Professor John Robert Moore in 'Sherlock Holmes Borrows a Plot' in the *Modern Language Quarterly*, Vol. VIII, No. 1, March, 1947. Professor Moore . . . cites an example of where Conan Doyle 'reworked an incident from one of his earlier stories,' viz. the gramophone which is mistaken for a human voice in 'The Japanned Box' [see *The Conan Doyle Stories*] becomes the gramophone which substitutes for the violin of Holmes in 'The Adventure of the Mazarin Stone.' "

The late James Montgomery, who had the first word on this subject, should also have the last: "Just how right Mr. [Edgar W.] Smith is finds ample proof in a series of events that had their inception in 1947," Montgomery wrote in "Speculation in Diamonds." "On July 11th of that year press dispatches reported the discovery by Conan Doyle's sons and daughters of an old cardboard hatbox in the vaults of an English country bank at Crowborough, Sussex. The box contained, among other interesting memorabilia, the manuscript of a one-act play called *The Crown Diamond: An Evening with Sherlock Holmes*. . . . Although never published.**1** [the play] was actually produced by Stanley Bell at the Coliseum in London in 1921, opening on Monday, May 16th, and running for one week with Dennis Neilson-Terry in the role of Holmes. It also had a return date for an additional week commencing August 29th. . . . My reading of the manuscript does indeed confirm definitely the fact that the plots of *The Crown Diamond* and 'The Adventure of the Mazarin Stone' are identical. . . . All evidence indicates that . . . the story was written *after*, not before the play. Anthony Boucher proves himself to be a critic of startling clairvoyance when he speculates in 'The Records of Baker Street' . . . that the story represents an effort on the part of [Conan Doyle] to salvage an unsuccessful dramatic work of his own. Mr. Boucher further enhances his reputation for discernment by declaring that 'a careful examination of the structure of this much-disputed story will disclose that it is essentially a one-act play, seen from a fourth-wall viewpoint.' "

1 In point of fact, the playlet was published by the Baskerette Press in 1958 in an edition of 59 copies. No copies of this beautiful little hardcover volume were ever placed on sale, but one was given to each member of The Baker Street Irregulars, Inc., who subscribed to a "Sustentation Fund" used to meet the expenses of financing the *Baker Street Journal*.

76

THE ADVENTURE OF THE CREEPING MAN

[Sunday, September 6; Monday, September 14; Tuesday, September 22, 1903]

MR. SHERLOCK HOLMES was always of opinion that I should publish the singular facts connected with Professor Presbury, if only to dispel once for all the ugly rumours which some twenty years ago agitated the University and were echoed in the learned societies of London. There were, however, certain obstacles in the way, and the true history of this curious case remained entombed in the tin box which contains so many records of my friend's adventures. Now we have at last obtained permission to ventilate the facts which formed one of the very last cases handled by Holmes before his retirement from practice. Even now a certain reticence and discretion have to be observed in laying the matter before the public.

It was one Sunday evening early in September of the year 1903 that I received one of Holmes' laconic messages: " Come at once if convenient—if inconvenient come all the same.—S. H." The relations between us in those latter days were peculiar. He was a man of habits, narrow and concentrated habits, and I had become one of them. As an institution I was like the violin, the shag tobacco, the old black pipe, the index books, and others perhaps less excusable. When it was a case of active work and a comrade was needed upon whose nerve he could place some reliance, my rôle was obvious. But apart from this I had uses. I was a whetstone for his mind. I stimulated him. He liked to think aloud in my presence. His remarks could hardly be said to be made to me—many of them would have been as appropriately addressed to his bedstead—but none the less, having formed the habit, it had become in some way helpful that I should register and interject. If I irritated him by a certain methodical slowness in my mentality, that irritation served only to make his own flame-like intuitions and impressions flash up the more vividly and swiftly. Such was my humble rôle in our alliance. **1**
When I arrived at Baker Street I found him huddled

1 *Such was my humble rôle in our alliance.* It is interesting here to compare Holmes' remarks on his relationship with Watson, at the beginning of "The Adventure of the Blanched Soldier": "Speaking of my old friend and biographer . . ."

up in his arm-chair with updrawn knees, his pipe in his mouth and his brow furrowed with thought. It was clear that he was in the throes of some vexatious problem. With a wave of his hand he indicated my old arm-chair, but otherwise for half an hour he gave no sign that he was aware of my presence. Then with a start he seemed to come from his reverie, and, with his usual whimsical smile, he greeted me back to what had once been my home.

" You will excuse a certain abstraction of mind, my dear Watson," said he. " Some curious facts have been submitted to me within the last twenty-four hours, and they in turn have given rise to some speculations of a more general character. I have serious thoughts of writing a small monograph upon the uses of dogs in the work of the detective."

" But surely, Holmes, this has been explored," said I. " Bloodhounds—sleuth-hounds——"

" No, no, Watson ; that side of the matter is, of course, obvious. But there is another which is far more subtle. You may recollect that in the case which you, in your sensational way, coupled with the Copper Beeches, I was able, by watching the mind of the child, to form a deduction as to the criminal habits of the very smug and respectable father."

" Yes, I remember it well."

" My line of thoughts about dogs is analogous. A dog reflects the family life. Whoever saw a frisky dog in a gloomy family, or a sad dog in a happy one ? Snarling people have snarling dogs, dangerous people have dangerous ones. And their passing moods may reflect the passing moods of others."

I shook my head. " Surely, Holmes, this is a little far-fetched," said I.

He had refilled his pipe and resumed his seat, taking no notice of my comment.

" The practical application of what I have said is very close to the problem which I am investigating. **2** It is a tangled skein, you understand, and I am looking for a loose end. One possible loose end lies in the question : Why does Professor Presbury's faithful wolf-hound, Roy, endeavour to bite him ? "

I sank back in my chair in some disappointment. Was it for so trivial a question as this that I had been summoned from my work ? Holmes glanced across at me.

" The same old Watson ! " said he. " You never learn that the gravest issues may depend upon the smallest things. But is it not on the face of it strange that a staid, elderly philosopher—you've heard of Presbury, of course, the famous Camford physiologist ?—that such a man, whose friend has been his devoted wolf-hound, should now have been twice attacked by his own dog ? What do you make of it ? "

" The dog is ill."

" Well, that has to be considered. But he attacks no one else, nor does he apparently molest his master, save on very special occasions. Curious, Watson— very curious. But young Mr. Bennett is before his time, if that is his ring. I had hoped to have a longer chat with you before he came."

2 *a tangled skein.* We recall that this was Conan Doyle's original title for *A Study in Scarlet.*

There was a quick step on the stairs, a sharp tap at the door, and a moment later the new client presented himself. He was a tall, handsome youth about thirty, well dressed and elegant, but with something in his bearing which suggested the shyness of the student rather than the self-possession of the man of the world. He shook hands with Holmes, and then looked with some surprise at me.

" This matter is very delicate, Mr. Holmes," he said. " Consider the relation in which I stand to Professor Presbury, both privately and publicly. I really can hardly justify myself if I speak before any third person."

" Have no fear, Mr. Bennett. Dr. Watson is the very soul of discretion, and I can assure you that this is a matter in which I am very likely to need an assistant."

" As you like, Mr. Holmes. You will, I am sure, understand my having some reserves in the matter."

" You will appreciate it, Watson, when I tell you that this gentleman, Mr. Trevor Bennett, is professional assistant to the great scientist, lives under his roof, and is engaged to his only daughter. Certainly we must agree that the Professor has every claim upon his loyalty and devotion. But it may best be shown by taking the necessary steps to clear up this strange mystery."

" I hope so, Mr. Holmes. That is my one object. Does Dr. Watson know the situation ? "

" I have not had time to explain it."

" Then perhaps I had better go over the ground again before explaining some fresh developments."

" I will do so myself," said Holmes, " in order to show that I have the events in their due order. The Professor, Watson, is a man of European reputation. His life has been academic. There has never been a breath of scandal. He is a widower with one daughter, Edith. He is, I gather, a man of very virile and positive, one might almost say combative, character. So the matter stood until a very few months ago.

" Then the current of his life was broken. He is sixty-one years of age, but he became engaged to the daughter of Professor Morphy, his colleague in the chair of Comparative Anatomy. It was not, as I understand, **3** the reasoned courting of an elderly man, but rather the passionate frenzy of youth, for no one could have shown himself a more devoted lover. The lady, Alice Morphy, was a very perfect girl both in mind and body, so that there was every excuse for the Professor's infatuation. None the less, it did not meet with full approval in his own family."

" We thought it rather excessive," said our visitor.

" Exactly. Excessive and a little violent and unnatural. Professor Presbury was rich, however, and there was no objection upon the part of the father. The daughter, however, had other views, and there were already several candidates for her hand, who, if they were less eligible from a worldly point of view, were at least more of an age. The girl seemed to like the Professor in spite of his eccentricities. It was only age which stood in the way.

THERE WAS A QUICK STEP ON THE STAIRS, A SHARP RAP AT THE DOOR, AND A MOMENT LATER THE NEW CLIENT PRESENTED HIMSELF.

Illustration by Howard K. Elcock for the *Strand Magazine*, March, 1923.

3 *the chair of Comparative Anatomy.* One of the problems that this adventure poses for the student is that of determining whether "Camford" is *Cambridge* or *Oxford*. In this connection, Mr. N. P. Metcalfe has written ("Oxford or Cambridge or Both?") that "The Historical Registers of both Oxford and Cambridge for the years up to 1910 show that there was a Chair of Physiology [Professor Presbury's post] at both. . . . There was no Chair of Comparative Anatomy as such at Cambridge, but one of Zoology and Comparative Anatomy was founded in 1866. . . . At Oxford, on the other hand, in 1903 there was a Chair of Comparative Anatomy, held since 1899 by W. F. R. Weldon, M.A., of Merton, sometime fellow of St. John's, Cambridge. . . . Despite Watson's discretion, this points . . . to Oxford as the location of 'The Adventure of the Creeping Man.'"

" About this time a little mystery suddenly clouded the normal routine of the Professor's life. He did what he had never done before. He left home and gave no indication where he was going. He was away a fortnight, and returned looking rather travel-worn. He made no allusion to where he had been, although he was usually the frankest of men. It chanced, however, that our client here, Mr. Bennett, received a letter from a fellow-student in Prague, who said that he was glad to have seen Professor Presbury there, although he had not been able to talk to him. Only in this way did his own household learn where he had been.

" Now comes the point. From that time onwards a curious change came over the Professor. He became furtive and sly. Those around him had always the feeling that he was not the man that they had known, but that he was under some shadow which had darkened his higher qualities. His intellect was not affected. His lectures were as brilliant as ever. But always there was something new, something sinister and unexpected. His daughter, who was devoted to him, tried again and again to resume the old relations and to penetrate this mask which her father seemed to have put on. You, sir, as I understand, did the same—but all was in vain. And now, Mr. Bennett, tell in your own words the incident of the letters."

" You must understand, Dr. Watson, that the Professor had no secrets from me. If I were his son or his younger brother, I could not have more completely enjoyed his confidence. As his secretary I handled every paper which came to him, and I opened and subdivided his letters. Shortly after his return all this was changed. He told me that certain letters might come to him from London which would be marked by a cross under the stamp. These were to be set aside for his own eyes only. I may say that several of these did pass through my hands, that they had the E.C. mark, and were in an illiterate handwriting. If he answered them at all the answers did not pass through my hands nor into the letter-basket in which our correspondence was collected."

" And the box," said Holmes.

" Ah, yes, the box. The Professor brought back a little wooden box from his travels. It was the one thing which suggested a Continental tour, for it was one of those quaint carved things which one associates with Germany. This he placed in his instrument cupboard.

4 One day, in looking for a cannula, I took up the box. To my surprise he was very angry, and reproved me in words which were quite savage for my curiosity. It was the first time such a thing had happened, and I was deeply hurt. I endeavoured to explain that it was a mere accident that I had touched the box, but all the evening I was conscious that he looked at me harshly and that the incident was rankling in his mind." Mr. Bennett drew a little diary book from his pocket. " That was on July 2," said he.

" You are certainly an admirable witness," said Holmes. " I may need some of these dates which you have noted."

" I learned method among other things from my great teacher. From the time that I observed abnormality

4 *a cannula.* A tube to be inserted into a cavity, through which pus may be drained or medicine introduced.

in his behaviour I felt that it was my duty to study his case. Thus I have it here that it was on that very day, July 2, that Roy attacked the Professor, as he came from his study into the hall. Again on July 11, there was a scene of the same sort and then I have a note of yet another upon July 20. After that we had to banish Roy to the stables. He was a dear, affectionate animal—but I fear I weary you."

Mr. Bennett spoke in a tone of reproach, for it was very clear that Holmes was not listening. His face was rigid and his eyes gazed abstractedly at the ceiling. With an effort he recovered himself.

"Singular! Most singular!" he murmured. "These details were new to me, Mr. Bennett. I think we have now fairly gone over the old ground, have we not? But you spoke of some fresh developments."

The pleasant, open face of our visitor clouded over, shadowed by some grim remembrance. "What I speak of occurred the night before last," said he. "I was lying awake about two in the morning, when I was aware of a dull muffled sound coming from the passage. I opened my door and peeped out. I should explain that the Professor sleeps at the end of the passage——"

"The date being——?" asked Holmes.

Our visitor was clearly annoyed at so irrelevant an interruption.

"I have said, sir, that it was the night before last—that is, September 4." **5**

Holmes nodded and smiled.

"Pray continue," said he.

"He sleeps at the end of the passage, and would have to pass my door in order to reach the staircase. It was a really terrifying experience, Mr. Holmes. I think that I am as strong-nerved as my neighbours, but I was shaken by what I saw. The passage was dark save that one window half-way along it threw a patch of light. I could see that something was coming along the passage, something dark and crouching. Then suddenly it emerged into the light, and I saw that it was he. He was crawling, Mr. Holmes—crawling! He was not quite on his hands and knees. I should rather say on his hands and feet, with his face sunk between his hands. Yet he seemed to move with ease. I was so paralysed by the sight that it was not until he had reached my door that I was able to step forward and ask if I could assist him. His answer was extraordinary. He sprang up, spat out some atrocious word at me, and hurried on past me, and down the staircase. I waited about for an hour, but he did not come back. It must have been daylight before he regained his room."

"Well, Watson, what make you of that?" asked Holmes, with the air of the pathologist who presents a rare specimen.

"Lumbago, possibly. I have known a severe attack make a man walk in just such a way, and nothing would be more trying to the temper."

"Good, Watson! You always keep us flat-footed on the ground. But we can hardly accept lumbago, since he was able to stand erect in a moment."

"He was never better in health," said Bennett. "In

"I COULD SEE THAT SOMETHING WAS COMING ALONG THE PASSAGE . . ."

Illustration by Frederic Dorr Steele for *Hearst's International*, March, 1923.

"HE SPRANG UP, SPAT OUT SOME ATROCIOUS WORD AT ME . . ."

Illustration by Howard K. Elcock for the *Strand Magazine*, March, 1923.

6 *Oh, Jack.* Mr. D. Martin Dakin has noted ("Second Thoughts on the Case-Book") the surprising change of Mr. Bennett's name from Trevor to Jack. He cites "Watson's notorious carelessness about Christian names," and adds: "Or had Miss Presbury a pet name for her man, as certain authorities consider Mrs. [Mary Morstan] Watson had?"

fact, he is stronger than I have known him for years. But there are the facts, Mr. Holmes. It is not a case in which we can consult the police, and yet we are utterly at our wits' end as to what to do, and we feel in some strange way that we are drifting towards disaster. Edith —Miss Presbury—feels as I do, that we cannot wait passively any longer."

" It is certainly a very curious and suggestive case. What do you think, Watson ? "

" Speaking as a medical man," said I, " it appears to be a case for an alienist. The old gentleman's cerebral processes were disturbed by the love affair. He made a journey abroad in the hope of breaking himself of the passion. His letters and the box may be connected with some other private transaction—a loan, perhaps, or share certificates, which are in the box."

" And the wolf-hound no doubt disapproved of the financial bargain. No, no, Watson, there is more in it than this. Now, I can only suggest——"

What Sherlock Holmes was about to suggest will never be known, for at this moment the door opened and a young lady was shown into the room. As she appeared Mr. Bennett sprang up with a cry and ran forward with his hands out to meet those which she had herself outstretched.

" Edith, dear ! Nothing the matter, I hope ? "

6 " I felt I must follow you. Oh, Jack, I have been so dreadfully frightened ! It is awful to be there alone."

" Mr. Holmes, this is the young lady I spoke of. This is my fiancée."

" We were gradually coming to that conclusion, were we not, Watson ? " Holmes answered, with a smile. " I take it, Miss Presbury, that there is some fresh development in the case, and that you thought we should know ? "

Our new visitor, a bright, handsome girl of a conventional English type, smiled back at Holmes as she seated herself beside Mr. Bennett.

" When I found Mr. Bennett had left his hotel I thought I should probably find him here. Of course, he had told me that he would consult you. But, oh, Mr. Holmes, can you do nothing for my poor father ? "

" I have hopes, Miss Presbury, but the case is still obscure. Perhaps what you have to say may throw some fresh light upon it."

" It was last night, Mr. Holmes. He had been very strange all day. I am sure that there are times when he has no recollection of what he does. He lives as in a strange dream. Yesterday was such a day. It was not my father with whom I lived. His outward shell was there, but it was not really he."

" Tell me what happened."

" I was awakened in the night by the dog barking most furiously. Poor Roy, he is chained now near the stable. I may say that I always sleep with my door locked ; for, as Jack—as Mr. Bennett—will tell you, we all have a feeling of impending danger. My room is on the second floor. It happened that the blind was up in my window, and there was bright moonlight outside. As I lay with my eyes fixed upon the square of light, listening to the frenzied barkings of the dog, I was amazed to see my father's face looking in at me. Mr. Holmes, I nearly died of surprise and horror. There it was pressed against the window-pane, and one hand seemed to be raised as if to push up the window. If that window had opened, I think I should have gone mad. It was no delusion, Mr. Holmes. Don't deceive yourself by thinking so. I dare say it was twenty seconds or so that I lay paralysed and watched the face. Then it vanished, but I could not—I could not spring out of bed and look out after it. I lay cold and shivering till morning. At breakfast he was sharp and fierce in manner, and made no allusion to the adventure of the night. Neither did I, but I gave an excuse for coming to town —and here I am."

Holmes looked thoroughly surprised at Miss Presbury's narrative.

"My dear young lady, you say that your room is on the second floor. Is there a long ladder in the garden?"

"No, Mr. Holmes; that is the amazing part of it. There is no possible way of reaching the window—and yet he was there."

"The date being September 5," said Holmes. "That certainly complicates matters."

It was the young lady's turn to look surprised. "This is the second time that you have alluded to the date, Mr. Holmes," said Bennett. "Is it possible that it has any bearing upon the case?"

"It is possible—very possible—and yet I have not my full material at present."

"Possibly you are thinking of the connection between insanity and phases of the moon?"

"No, I assure you. It was quite a different line of thought. Possibly you can leave your notebook with me and I will check the dates. Now I think, Watson, that our line of action is perfectly clear. This young lady has informed us—and I have the greatest confidence in her intuition—that her father remembers little or nothing which occurs upon certain dates. We will therefore call upon him as if he had given us an appointment upon such a date. He will put it down to his own lack of memory. Thus we will open our campaign by having a good close view of him."

"That is excellent," said Mr. Bennett. "I warn you, however, that the Professor is irascible and violent at times."

Holmes smiled. "There are reasons why we should come at once—very cogent reasons if my theories hold good. To-morrow, Mr. Bennett, will certainly see us in Camford. There is, if I remember right, an inn called the 'Chequers' where the port used to be above mediocrity, and the linen was above reproach. I think, **7** Watson, that our lot for the next few days might lie in less pleasant places."

Monday morning found us on our way to the famous University town—an easy effort on the part of Holmes,

"... I WAS AMAZED TO SEE MY FATHER'S FACE
LOOKING IN AT ME."

Illustration by Frederic Dorr Steele for *Hearst's International*, March, 1923. Howard K. Elcock illustrated the same scene for the *Strand Magazine*, March, 1923.

7 *and the linen was above reproach.*" No Chequers Inn exists, or, as far as I can ascertain, has ever existed at either [Oxford or Cambridge]," Mr. Metcalfe wrote, "but I am inclined to credit the Mitre at Oxford as the subject of Holmes' recommendation. (A chequer is a pattern like a chessboard, and is not a mitre a bishop?)."

The Reverend Stephen Adams, who holds that Holmes was a student at neither Oxford nor Cambridge, but at the University of London, writes of this statement ("Holmes: A Student of London?"): "The crucial word is 'linen'; obviously Holmes had *stayed* there. Oxford and Cambridge graduates are familiar enough with their pubs, but how often have they stayed at them? A bed in college or with friends is surely the normal thing. The fact that [Holmes] had stayed there strongly suggests that his previous visit(s) had been for the purpose of tracking down other misguided dons."

8 *We can but try—the motto of the firm.* Mr. Rolfe Boswell, who holds that Holmes substituted his own coat-of-arms for that of the Noble Bachelor in the adventure of that name, has added "We can but try" as a motto to his achievement. He has also added as a crest "a sinister hand proper encrusted with icicles grasping a banner gules, thereon a golden bee and the watchword EXCELSIOR in silver letters."

9 *a row of ancient colleges.* "Whilst at a pinch this might be King's Parade or Trinity Street in Cambridge, colleges in rows, on the whole, suggest Oxford," the late Gavin Brend wrote in *My Dear Holmes.* And Mr. N. P. Metcalfe has added that "The drive past a row of ancient colleges suggests either the 'High' at Oxford, or 'K. P.' and Trinity Street at Cambridge. If a Cambridge man, one would expect the Professor to live in the Grange Road area; if Oxford, then the Woodstock Road or Boar's Hill."

who had no roots to pull up, but one which involved frantic planning and hurrying on my part, as my practice was by this time not inconsiderable. Holmes made no allusion to the case until after we had deposited our suit-cases at the ancient hostel of which he had spoken.

" I think, Watson, that we can catch the Professor just before lunch. He lectures at eleven, and should have an interval at home."

" What possible excuse have we for calling ? "

Holmes glanced at his notebook.

" There was a period of excitement upon August 26. We will assume that he is a little hazy as to what he does at such times. If we insist that we are there by appointment I think he will hardly venture to contradict us. Have you the effrontery necessary to put it through ? "

" We can but try."

" Excellent, Watson ! Compound of the Busy Bee **8** and Excelsior. We can but try—the motto of the firm. A friendly native will surely guide us."

Such a one on the back of a smart hansom swept **9** us past a row of ancient colleges, and finally turning into a tree-lined drive pulled up at the door of a charming house, girt round with lawns and covered with purple wistaria. Professor Presbury was certainly surrounded with every sign not only of comfort but of luxury. Even as we pulled up a grizzled head appeared at the front window, and we were aware of a pair of keen eyes from under shaggy brows which surveyed us through large horn glasses. A moment later we were actually in his sanctum, and the mysterious scientist, whose vagaries had brought us from London, was standing before us. There was certainly no sign of eccentricity either in his manner or appearance, for he was a portly, large-featured man, grave, tall, and frock-coated, with the dignity of bearing which a lecturer needs. His eyes were his most remarkable feature, keen, observant, and clever to the verge of cunning.

He looked at our cards. " Pray sit down, gentlemen. What can I do for you ? "

Mr. Holmes smiled amiably.

" It was the question which I was about to put to you, Professor."

" To me, sir ! "

" Possibly there is some mistake. I heard through a second person that Professor Presbury of Camford had need of my services."

" Oh, indeed ! " It seemed to me that there was a malicious sparkle in the intense grey eyes. " You heard that, did you ? May I ask the name of your informant ? "

" I am sorry, Professor, but the matter was rather confidential. If I have made a mistake there is no harm done. I can only express my regret."

" Not at all. I should wish to go further into this matter. It interests me. Have you any scrap of writing, any letter or telegram, to bear out your assertion ? "

" No, I have not."

" I presume that you do not go so far as to assert that I summoned you ? "

" I would rather answer no questions," said Holmes.

" No, I dare say not," said the Professor, with asperity. " However, that particular one can be answered very easily without your aid."

He walked across the room to the bell. Our London friend, Mr. Bennett, answered the call.

" Come in, Mr. Bennett. These two gentlemen have come from London under the impression that they have been summoned. You handle all my correspondence. Have you a note of anything going to a person named Holmes ? "

" No, sir," Bennett answered, with a flush.

" That is conclusive," said the Professor, glaring angrily at my companion. " Now, sir "—he leaned forward with his two hands upon the table—" it seems to me that your position is a very questionable one."

Holmes shrugged his shoulders.

" I can only repeat that I am sorry that we have made a needless intrusion."

" Hardly enough, Mr. Holmes ! " the old man cried, in a high screaming voice, with extraordinary malignancy upon his face. He got between us and the door as he spoke, and he shook his two hands at us with furious passion. " You can hardly get out of it so easily as that." His face was convulsed and he grinned and gibbered at us in his senseless rage. I am convinced that we should have had to fight our way out of the room if Mr. Bennett had not intervened.

" My dear Professor," he cried, " consider your position ! Consider the scandal at the University ! Mr. Holmes is a well-known man. You cannot possibly treat him with such discourtesy."

Sulkily our host—if I may call him so—cleared the path to the door. We were glad to find ourselves outside the house, and in the quiet of the tree-lined drive. Holmes seemed greatly amused by the episode.

" Our learned friend's nerves are somewhat out of order," said he. " Perhaps our intrusion was a little crude, and yet we have gained that personal contact which I desired. But, dear me, Watson, he is surely at our heels. The villain still pursues us."

There were the sounds of running feet behind, but it was, to my relief, not the formidable Professor but his assistant who appeared round the curve of the drive. He came panting up to us.

" I am so sorry, Mr. Holmes. I wished to apologize."

" My dear sir, there is no need. It is all in the way of professional experience."

" I have never seen him in a more dangerous mood. But he grows more sinister. You can understand now why his daughter and I are alarmed. And yet his mind is perfectly clear."

" Too clear ! " said Holmes. " That was my miscalculation. It is evident that his memory is much more reliable than I had thought. By the way, can we, before we go, see the window of Miss Presbury's room ? "

Mr. Bennett pushed his way through some shrubs and

HIS FACE WAS CONVULSED AND HE GRINNED AND GIBBERED AT US IN HIS SENSELESS RAGE.

Illustration by Howard K. Elcock for the *Strand Magazine*, March, 1923.

we had a view of the side of the house.

" It is there. The second on the left."

" Dear me, it seems hardly accessible. And yet you will observe that there is a creeper below and a water-pipe above which give some foothold."

" I could not climb it myself," said Mr. Bennett.

" Very likely. It would certainly be a dangerous exploit for any normal man."

" There was one other thing I wished to tell you, Mr. Holmes. I have the address of the man in London to whom the Professor writes. He seems to have written this morning and I got it from his blotting-paper. It is an ignoble position for a trusted secretary, but what else can I do ? "

Holmes glanced at the paper and put it into his pocket.

" Dorak—a curious name. Slavonic, I imagine. Well, it is an important link in the chain. We return to London this afternoon, Mr. Bennett. I see no good purpose to be served by our remaining. We cannot arrest the Professor, because he has done no crime, nor can we place him under constraint, for he cannot be proved to be mad. No action is as yet possible."

" Then what on earth are we to do ? "

" A little patience, Mr. Bennett. Things will soon develop. Unless I am mistaken next Tuesday may mark a crisis. Certainly we shall be in Camford on that day. Meanwhile, the general position is undeniably unpleasant, and if Miss Presbury can prolong her visit— "

" That is easy."

" Then let her stay till we can assure her that all danger is past. Meanwhile, let him have his way and do not cross him. So long as he is in a good humour all is well."

" There he is ! " said Bennett, in a startled whisper. Looking between the branches we saw the tall, erect figure emerge from the hall door and look around him. He stood leaning forward, his hands swinging straight before him, his head turning from side to side. The secretary with a last wave slipped off among the trees, and we saw him presently rejoin his employer, the two entering the house together in what seemed to be animated and even excited conversation.

" I expect the old gentleman has been putting two and two together," said Holmes, as we walked hotelwards. " He struck me as having a particularly clear and logical brain, from the little I saw of him. Explosive, no doubt, but then from his point of view he has something to explode about if detectives are put on his track and he suspects his own household of doing it. I rather fancy that friend Bennett is in for an uncomfortable time."

Holmes stopped at a post office and sent off a telegram on our way. The answer reached us in the evening, and he tossed it across to me. " Have visited the Commercial Road and seen Dorak. Suave person, Bohemian, elderly. Keeps large general store.—Mercer."

" Mercer is since your time," said Holmes. " He is my general utility man who looks up routine business. It was important to know something of the man with

10 *the Commercial Road.* Commercial Road traverses the densely populated quarters of Lime-house and St.-George's-in-the-East, a broad thoroughfare constructed in 1800 near Whitechapel in order to provide direct access from the City to the newly constructed West India Docks. It was cut across what was previously known as Stepney Fields, which became rapidly built over as a result of the formation of these new docks. In 1802 it was extended to the East India Docks, and in May, 1870, it was extended from Church Lane to Leman Street.

11 *"Mercer is since your time," said Holmes.* Obviously, Mercer is a part of that "small, but very efficient, organization" which Holmes was building up in the early years of this century.

whom our Professor was so secretly corresponding. His nationality connects up with the Prague visit."

" Thank goodness that something connects with something," said I. " At present we seem to be faced by a long series of inexplicable incidents with no bearing upon each other. For example, what possible connection can there be between an angry wolf-hound and a visit to Bohemia, or either of them with a man crawling down a passage at night ? As to your dates, that is the biggest mystification of all."

Holmes smiled and rubbed his hands. We were, I may say, seated in the old sitting-room of the ancient hotel, with a bottle of the famous vintage of which **12** Holmes had spoken on the table between us.

" Well, now, let us take the dates first," said he, his finger-tips together and his manner as if he were addressing a class. " This excellent young man's diary shows that there was trouble upon July 2, and from then onwards it seems to have been at nine-day intervals, with, so far as I remember, only one exception. Thus the last outbreak upon Friday was on September 3, which also falls into the series, as did August 26, which preceded it. The thing is beyond coincidence." **13**

I was forced to agree.

" Let us, then, form the provisional theory that every nine days the Professor takes some strong drug which has a passing but highly poisonous effect. His naturally violent nature is intensified by it. He learned to take this drug while he was in Prague, and is now supplied with it by a Bohemian intermediary in London. This all hangs together, Watson ! "

" But the dog, the face at the window, the creeping man in the passage ? "

" Well, well, we have made a beginning. I should not expect any fresh developments until next Tuesday. In the meantime we can only keep in touch with friend Bennett and enjoy the amenities of this charming town." **14**

In the morning Mr. Bennett slipped round to bring us the latest report. As Holmes had imagined, times had not been easy with him. Without exactly accusing him of being responsible for our presence, the Professor had been very rough and rude in his speech, and evidently felt some strong grievance. This morning he was quite himself again, however, and had delivered his usual brilliant lecture to a crowded class. " Apart from his queer fits," said Bennett, " he has actually more energy and vitality than I can ever remember, nor was his brain ever clearer. But it's not he—it's never the man whom we have known."

" I don't think you have anything to fear now for a week at least," Holmes answered. " I am a busy man, and Dr. Watson has his patients to attend to. Let us agree that we meet here at this hour next Tuesday, and I shall be surprised if before we leave you again we are not able to explain, even if we cannot perhaps put an end to, your troubles. Meanwhile, keep us posted in what occurs."

12 *a bottle of the famous vintage.* "There is not much doubt," Mr. Jørgen Cold wrote in "What Did Sherlock Holmes Drink?", "that the old firm, C. N. Kopke & Co., Ltd., Oporto and London, was the purveyor of that vintage, and most certainly the brand Quinta Noval."

13 *The thing is beyond coincidence.*" Watson has told us that the case began "one Sunday evening in September of the year 1903." Let us check his "Sunday," his "September," and his "1903." 1) Watson says his purpose in publishing an account of the case is to "dispel once for all the ugly rumours which some twenty years ago agitated the University . . ." Since "The Adventure of the Creeping Man" was published in March, 1923, Watson's "1903" would seem to be corroborated. 2) "I have said, sir, that it was the night before last—that is, September 4," Mr. Bennett told Holmes and Watson. Here is a corroboration of Watson's "September." Since "September 4" was two nights before the case opened, and September 6, 1903 (as we have seen) was indeed a Sunday, here also is a confirmation of Watson's day and a further confirmation of the year. 3) Miss Presbury said: "Yesterday was such a day." "The date being September 5," Holmes noted. Here again is a corroboration that the case did indeed begin on Sunday, September 6, 1903. 4) Miss Presbury has said that at the time of the attack (2:00 A.M. of the 5th) "there was bright moonlight outside." The moon was two days before the full on the night of September 4th–5th; it rose at 5:49 P.M. on the afternoon of the 4th and set at 3:37 A.M. on the morning of the 5th. 5) Holmes said: "The last outbreak upon Friday was on September 3." Holmes is speaking of the outbreak on the night of Friday, September 4th, to Saturday, September 5th; the "Friday" is clearly correct, but the "3" must be a typographical error. Professor Presbury's first attack had come on July 2nd, according to Mr. Bennett. "It was on that very day, July 2, that Roy attacked the Professor. . . . Again on July 11 there was a scene of the same sort and then I have a note of yet another upon July 20." Later Holmes says: "There was a period of excitement upon August 26"— and Holmes notes at once that the attacks in the period July 2nd to September 4th have come at nine-day intervals, with "only one exception." He is quite correct: it is 37 days from July 20th to August 26th, so one of the intervals between the attacks that took place during this period must have been of *ten* rather than nine days. So far all seems clear. It is with the events that took place after Sunday, September 6th, that the difficulties arise.

14 *this charming town.*" Here at last is proof positive that "Camford" is *Oxford*. In "The Adventure of the Missing Three-Quarter," the University of the adventure was identified as Cambridge, which Holmes called "this inhospitable town."

15 *we shall have the Professor at his worst to-night.*" "It was nearly midnight" on the Tuesday when the crisis came, and this crisis clearly followed the nine-day pattern: Holmes said, on the concluding day, "If the cycle of nine days holds good, then we shall have the Professor at his worst to-night" (which they did) and, "He takes [the drug] under definite directions which regulate this ninth-day system." Nine days after the attack on the night of September 4th–5th brings us to the night of September 13th–14th. But September 13, 1903, was not a Tuesday but a *Sunday*. Commentators have generally agreed that Holmes' *three* references to Tuesday must be dismissed, but your editor does not feel that we can dismiss so lightly three such direct quotations fom the Master. We believe that Watson was here guilty of a literary license—of trifling with time in his account of this case for the sake of making the account slightly more dramatic—just as he did in *A Study in Scarlet* and again in "The Adventure of the Illustrious Client." In your editor's opinion, some exceedingly pressing business prevented Holmes from journeying to "Camford" on Monday, September 7th, and observing the Professor's outbreak on Sunday, September 13th. *It was on Monday, September 14th, that Holmes and Watson first journeyed to Camford; the outbreak they observed was that of Tuesday, September 22nd—just nine days after the outbreak of Sunday, September 13th.* It may be objected that Holmes in his references on Monday, September 14th, to "next Tuesday" would seem to be indicating Tuesday, September 15th rather than Tuesday, September 22nd. By that time, however, the significance of the nine-day cycle was understood by everyone—Holmes' Tuesday references meant *Tuesday* week, as is plainly shown by his "I don't think we have anything to fear now for a week at least." It is true that our explanation plays hob with Watson's "half-moon" on the night of the climax, but Watson, as we have seen, has been careless about his moons on many other occasions. We vastly prefer to make sense of the Master's remarks on Monday—Monday, September 14th.

I saw nothing of my friend for the next few days, but on the following Monday evening I had a short note asking me to meet him next day at the train. From what he told me as we travelled up to Camford all was well, the peace of the Professor's house had been unruffled, and his own conduct perfectly normal. This also was the report which was given us by Mr. Bennett himself when he called upon us that evening at our old quarters in the "Chequers." "He heard from his London correspondent to-day. There was a letter and there was a small packet, each with the cross under the stamp which warned me not to touch them. There has been nothing else."

"That may prove quite enough," said Holmes grimly. "Now, Mr. Bennett, we shall, I think, come to some conclusion to-night. If my deductions are correct we should have an opportunity of bringing matters to a head. In order to do so it is necessary to hold the Professor under observation. I would suggest, therefore, that you remain awake and on the look-out. Should you hear him pass your door do not interrupt him, but follow him as discreetly as you can. Dr. Watson and I will not be far off. By the way, where is the key of that little box of which you spoke?"

"Upon his watch-chain."

"I fancy our researches must lie in that direction. At the worst the lock should not be very formidable. Have you any other able-bodied man on the premises?"

"There is the coachman, Macphail."

"Where does he sleep?"

"Over the stables."

"We might possibly want him. Well, we can do no more until we see how things develop. Good-bye—but I expect that we shall see you before morning."

It was nearly midnight before we took our station among some bushes immediately opposite the hall door of the Professor. It was a fine night, but chilly, and we were glad of our warm overcoats. There was a breeze, and clouds were scudding across the sky, obscuring from time to time the half-moon. It would have been a dismal vigil were it not for the expectation and excitement which carried us along, and the assurance of my comrade that we had probably reached the end of the strange sequence of events which had engaged our attention.

"If the cycle of nine days holds good, then we shall **15** have the Professor at his worst to-night," said Holmes. "The fact that these strange symptoms began after his visit to Prague, that he is in secret correspondence with a Bohemian dealer in London, who presumably represents someone in Prague, and that he received a packet from him this very day, all point in one direction. What he takes and why he takes it are still beyond our ken, but that it emanates in some way from Prague is clear enough. He takes it under definite directions which regulate this ninth-day system, which was the first point which attracted my attention. But his symptoms are most remarkable. Did you observe his knuckles?"

I had to confess that I did not.

"Thick and horny in a way which is quite new in my experience. Always look at the hands first, Watson.

Then cuffs, trouser-knees, and boots. Very curious knuckles which can only be explained by the mode of progression observed by——" Holmes paused, and suddenly clapped his hand to his forehead. " Oh, Watson, Watson, what a fool I have been ! It seems incredible, and yet it must be true. All points in one direction. How could I miss seeing the connection of ideas ? Those knuckles—how could I have passed those knuckles ? And the dog ! And the ivy ! It's surely time that I disappeared into that little farm of my dreams. Look out, Watson ! Here he is ! We shall **16** have the chance of seeing for ourselves."

The hall door had slowly opened, and against the lamp-lit background we saw the tall figure of Professor Presbury. He was clad in his dressing-gown. As he stood outlined in the doorway he was erect but leaning forward with dangling arms, as when we saw him last.

Now he stepped forward into the drive, and an extraordinary change came over him. He sank down into a crouching position, and moved along upon his hands and feet, skipping every now and then as if he were overflowing with energy and vitality. He moved along the face of the house and then round the corner. As he disappeared Bennett slipped through the hall door and softly followed him.

" Come, Watson, come ! " cried Holmes, and we stole as softly as we could through the bushes until we had gained a spot whence we could see the other side of the house, which was bathed in the light of the half-moon. The Professor was clearly visible crouching at the foot of the ivy-covered wall. As we watched him he suddenly began with incredible agility to ascend it. From branch to branch he sprang, sure of foot and firm of grasp, climbing apparently in mere joy at his own powers, with no definite object in view. With his dressing-gown flapping on each side of him he looked like some huge bat glued against the side of his own house, a great square dark patch upon the moonlit wall. Presently he tired of this amusement, and, dropping from branch to branch, he squatted down into the old attitude and moved towards the stables, creeping along in the same strange way as before. The wolf-hound was out now, barking furiously, and more excited than ever when it actually caught sight of its master. It was straining on its chain, and quivering with eagerness and rage. The Professor squatted down very deliberately just out of reach of the hound, and began to provoke it in every possible way. He took handfuls of pebbles from the drive and threw them in the dog's face, prodded him with a stick which he had picked up, flicked his hands about only a few inches from the gaping mouth, and endeavoured in every way to increase the animal's fury, which was already beyond all control. In all our adventures I do not know that I have ever seen a more strange sight than this impassive and still dignified figure crouching frog-like upon the ground and goading to a wilder exhibition of passion the maddened hound, which ramped and raged in front of him, by all manner of ingenious and calculated cruelty.

And then in a moment it happened ! It was not the

16 *It's surely time that I disappeared into that little farm of my dreams.* It must have been a consolation to Holmes, as he contemplated retirement, that another great expert in scientific crime detection had by that time established himself in London. Dr. John Evelyn Thorndyke had commenced his practice as a consulting detective in King's Bench Walk in 1897, or perhaps in 1896. In 1901 he had dealings with Scotland Yard in at least twenty cases. In 1902 he solved the Blackmore problem. In November of that year, when he first came in contact with the Bellingham case, he was obviously a recognized expert. In July, 1903, he investigated the famous Hardcastle murder, committed the month before. All this was prior to Holmes' retirement. See Francis M. Currier, "Holmes and Thorndyke: A Real Friendship."

chain that broke, but it was the collar that slipped, for it had been made for a thick-necked Newfoundland. We heard the rattle of falling metal, and the next instant dog and man were rolling on the ground together, the one roaring in rage, the other screaming in a strange shrill falsetto of terror. It was a very narrow thing for the Professor's life. The savage creature had him fairly by the throat, its fangs had bitten deep, and he was senseless before we could reach them and drag the two apart. It might have been a dangerous task for us, but Bennett's voice and presence brought the great wolf-hound instantly to reason. The uproar had brought the sleepy and astonished coachman from his room above the stables. " I'm not surprised," said he, shaking his head. " I've seen him at it before. I knew the dog would get him sooner or later."

The hound was secured, and together we carried the Professor up to his room, where Bennett, who had a medical degree, helped me to dress his torn throat. The sharp teeth had passed dangerously near the carotid artery, and the hæmorrhage was serious. In half an hour the danger was past, I had given the patient an injection of morphia, and he had sunk into deep sleep. Then, and only then, were we able to look at each other and to take stock of the situation.

" I think a first-class surgeon should see him," said I.

" For God's sake, no ! " cried Bennett. " At present the scandal is confined to our own household. It is safe with us. If it gets beyond these walls it will never stop. Consider his position at the University, his European reputation, the feelings of his daughter."

" Quite so," said Holmes. " I think it may be quite possible to keep the matter to ourselves, and also to prevent its recurrence now that we have a free hand. The key from the watch-chain, Mr. Bennett. Macphail will guard the patient and let us know if there is any change. Let us see what we can find in the Professor's mysterious box."

There was not much, but there was enough—an empty phial, another nearly full, a hypodermic syringe, several letters in a crabbed, foreign hand. The marks on the envelopes showed that they were those which had disturbed the routine of the secretary, and each was dated from the Commercial Road and signed " A. Dorak." They were mere invoices to say that a fresh bottle was being sent to Professor Presbury, or receipts to acknowledge money. There was one other envelope, however, in a more educated hand and bearing the Austrian stamp with the postmark of Prague. " Here we have our material ! " cried Holmes, as he tore out the enclosure.

" HONOURED COLLEAGUE," it ran. " Since your esteemed visit I have thought much of your case, and though in your circumstances there are some special reasons for the treatment, I would none the less enjoin caution, as my results have shown that it is not without danger of a kind.

" It is possible that the Serum of Anthropoid would have been better. I have, as I explained to you, used

. . . DOG AND MAN WERE ROLLING ON THE
GROUND TOGETHER . . .

Illustration by Howard K. Elcock for the *Strand Magazine*, March, 1923.

black-faced Langur because a specimen was accessible. Langur is, of course, a crawler and climber, while Anthropoid walks erect, and is in all ways nearer.

" I beg you to take every possible precaution that there be no premature revelation of the process. I have one other client in England, and Dorak is my agent for both. **17**

" Weekly reports will oblige.
                    " Yours with high esteem,
                        " H. LOWENSTEIN."

Lowenstein ! The name brought back to me the memory of some snippet from a newspaper which spoke of an obscure scientist who was striving in some unknown way for the secret of rejuvenescence and the elixir of life. Lowenstein of Prague ! Lowenstein with the wondrous strength-giving serum, tabooed by the profession because he refused to reveal its source. In a few words I said what I remembered. Bennett had taken a manual of Zoology from the shelves. ' Langur,' " he read, " ' the great black-faced monkey of the Himalayan slopes, biggest and most human of climbing monkeys.' Many details are added. Well, thanks to you, Mr. Holmes, it is very clear that we have traced the evil to its source."

" The real source," said Holmes, " lies, of course, in that untimely love affair which gave our impetuous Professor the idea that he could only gain his wish by turning himself into a younger man. When one tries to rise above Nature one is liable to fall below it. The highest type of man may revert to the animal if he leaves the straight road of destiny." He sat musing for a little with the phial in his hand, looking at the clear liquid within. " When I have written to this man and told him that I hold him criminally responsible for the poisons which he circulates, we will have no more trouble. But it may recur. Others may find a better way. There is danger there—a very real danger to humanity. Consider, Watson, that the material, the sensual, the worldly would all prolong their worthless lives. The spiritual would not avoid the call to something higher. It would be the survival of the least fit. What sort of cesspool may not our poor world become ? " Suddenly the dreamer disappeared, and Holmes, the man of action, sprang from his chair. " I think there is nothing more to be said, Mr. Bennett. The various incidents will now fit themselves easily into the general scheme. The dog, of course, was aware of the change far more quickly than you. His smell would ensure that. It was the **18** monkey, not the Professor, whom Roy attacked, just as it was the monkey who teased Roy. Climbing was a joy to the creature, and it was a mere chance, I take it, that the pastime brought him to the young lady's window. There is an early train to town, Watson, but I think we shall just have time for a cup of tea at the ' Chequers ' before we catch it."

17 *Dorak is my agent for both.* The wording suggests that there were also clients in other countries. "In fact," Mr. Arthur L. Levine writes, "the whole picture of the Creeping Man smacks so of the picture of the Abominable Snowman that there is a strong probability that they are of the same origin—that Lowenstein's other creeper [and his descendants are the creature known as] the Abominable Snowman of the Himalayas!" ("Lowenstein's Other Creeper").

18 *His smell would ensure that.* Dr. Samuel R. Meaker, in "Watson Medicus," has pointed out that while Holmes "rightly deduced that [Professor Presbury] was taking something powerful in the endocrine line . . . he was wrong in assuming that treatment with monkey-serum could make a human being behave or smell like a monkey. The venerable physiologist was evidently a victim of simple autosuggestion or self-hypnosis; and as to the wolfhound, it only reacted as any sensitive dog might do to a weird and apparently hostile change in its master's conduct. This time Watson saw clearer than Holmes for, after a tentative diagnosis of lumbago to explain the professor's creeping style of locomotion, he concluded 'Speaking as a medical man, it appears to be a case for an alienist.' "

A Note on the "Canonicity" of "The Adventure of the Creeping Man": This is another of the *Case-Book* adventures which Mr. D. Martin Dakin finds some reason to doubt: "The story is fantastic and more reminiscent of Dr. Jekyll or the Werewolf than a Sherlock Holmes case. The transparent device of referring to 'Camford' University is a trick of the second-rate writer; and there was the less need to practice such mystification, as Watson has already recorded a visit to Cambridge in 'The Missing Three-Quarter' and to a University easily recognizable as Oxford in 'The Three Students.' Indeed, the interview with Professor Presbury reads like a rather feeble imitation of that with the redoubtable Leslie Armstrong in Cambridge from which Holmes and Watson were, more excusably, ejected. Yet Watson's characteristically prosaic remark, attributing the Professor's peculiarities to lumbago, causes me, I confess, to hesitate in my judgment."

Dr. George B. Koelle is another who questions the authenticity of this adventure: "In *The Valley of Fear* [Holmes] comments on the unexpected vein of pawky humor which Watson is developing. May not the latter have been indulging this humor when, during a period lacking in authentic case material to record, he allowed his fancy to dictate this account? Its acceptance by a gullible publisher served merely to consolidate the joke. Certainly, the good doctor would never have expected anyone to take it seriously."

A Sherlock Holmes Competition

Set by A. CONAN DOYLE

£100 Cash Prize and 100 Autographed Copies of " Memories and Adventures "

In the following article Sir A. Conan Doyle makes the interesting announcement that from the forty-four Sherlock Holmes stories already published in book form in four volumes he has selected the twelve stories which he considers the best, and he now invites readers to do likewise. A sealed copy of this list is in the Editor's possession, and a prize of £100 and an autographed copy of Sir A. Conan Doyle's "Memories and Adventures" is offered to the sender of the coupon which coincides most nearly with this list. In the event of ties the prize of £100 will be divided. The actual order of the stories will not be regarded. Autographed copies of "Memories and Adventures" will also be awarded to 100 readers submitting the next nearly correct coupons.

An illustration from each of the stories is here given. Each illustration being numbered, competitors need only state on the coupon (which will be found on page 68 of the advertisement section) the numbers of the stories selected.

The four volumes of stories, "The Adventures of Sherlock Holmes," "The Memoirs of Sherlock Holmes," "The Return of Sherlock Holmes," and "His Last Bow," are published by Messrs. John Murray in two-shilling editions and may be obtained from all booksellers.

MR. SHERLOCK HOLMES TO HIS READERS

By A. CONAN DOYLE

I FEAR that Mr. Sherlock Holmes may become like one of those popular tenors who, having outlived their time, are still tempted to make repeated farewell bows to their indulgent audiences. This must cease and he must go the way of all flesh, material or imaginary. One likes to think that there is some fantastic limbo for the children of imagination, some strange, impossible place where the beaux of Fielding may still make love to the belles of Richardson, where Scott's heroes still may strut, Dickens's delightful Cockneys still raise a laugh, and Thackeray's worldlings continue to carry on their reprehensible careers. Perhaps in some humble corner of such a Valhalla, Sherlock and his Watson may for a time find a place, while some more astute sleuth with some even less astute comrade may fill the stage which they have vacated.

His career has been a long one— though it is possible to exaggerate it.

1.—A SCANDAL IN BOHEMIA.

2.—THE RED-HEADED LEAGUE.

"A SHERLOCK HOLMES COMPETITION"

In the March, 1927, issue of the *Strand Magazine*, Sir Arthur Conan Doyle announced that he had selected the twelve Sherlock Holmes stories which he considered the best, and invited readers to do likewise for a cash prize of £100 and one hundred autographed copies of his autobiography, *Memories and Adventures*. His own list was published when the winners had been judged.

IX. SHERLOCK HOLMES
IN RETIREMENT
[1909]

"It's surely time that I disappeared into that little farm of my dreams."
—Sherlock Holmes, "The Adventure of the Creeping Man"

Some Personalia About Mr. Sherlock Holmes.

By
A. CONAN DOYLE.

T the request of the Editor I have spent some days in looking over an old letter-box in which from time to time I have placed letters referring directly or indirectly to the notorious Mr. Holmes. I wish now that I had been more careful in preserving the references to this gentleman and his little problems. A great many have been lost or mislaid. His biographer has been fortunate enough to find readers in many lands, and the reading has elicited the same sort of response, though in many cases that response has been in a tongue difficult to comprehend. Very often my distant correspondent could neither spell my own name nor that of my imaginary hero, as in a recent instance which I here append. Many such letters have been from Russians. Where the Russian letters have been in the vernacular I have been compelled, I am afraid, to take them as read, but when they have been in English they have been among the most curious in my collection. There was one young lady who began all her epistles with the words "Good Lord." Another had a large amount of guile underlying her simplicity. Writing from Warsaw she stated that she had been bedridden for two years, and that my novels had been her only, etc., etc. So touched was I by this flattering statement that I at once prepared an autographed parcel of them to complete the fair invalid's collection. By good luck, however, I met a brother author upon the same day to whom I recounted the touching incident. With a cynical smile he drew an identical letter out of his pocket. His novels also had been for two years her only, etc., etc. I do not know how many more the lady had written to, but if, as I imagine, her correspondence had extended to several countries, she must have amassed a rather interesting library.

The young Russian's habit of addressing me as "Good Lord" had an even stranger parallel at home, which links it up with the subject of this article. Shortly after I received a knighthood I had a bill from a tradesman which was quite correct and businesslike in every detail save that it was made out to Sir Sherlock Holmes. I hope that I can stand a joke as well as my neighbours, but this particular piece of humour seemed rather misapplied, and I wrote sharply upon the subject. In response to my letter

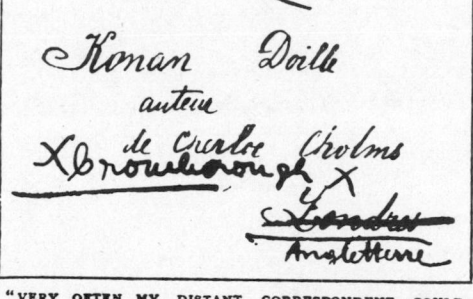

"VERY OFTEN MY DISTANT CORRESPONDENT COULD NEITHER SPELL MY OWN NAME NOR THAT OF MY IMAGINARY HERO."

"SOME PERSONALIA ..."

Conan Doyle writes of his friends, Mr. Sherlock Holmes and Dr. John H. Watson, for the pages of the *Strand*, issue of December, 1917.

77

THE FRIENDS OF MR. SHERLOCK HOLMES WILL BE GLAD TO LEARN THAT HE IS STILL ALIVE AND WELL . . .

[John H. Watson, M.D. Preface to "His Last Bow"]

Since "The Second Stain," in which Watson, for the first time in print, referred to Holmes' retirement from active practice, was published in October, 1904, it is clear that Holmes had retired by that time.

"Precisely how long before October [1904] Holmes had given over his practice it is only possible to guess," Mr. Vincent Starrett wrote in *The Private Life of Sherlock Holmes*, "but one ventures to think that it must have been a number of months, at least, in view of Watson's reference to his friend's objections—obviously over a period of recent time—to the 'continued publication' of his experiences."

In point of fact, however, we have been told (in "The Adventure of the Creeping Man," which took place in September, 1903) that this was "one of the very last cases handled by Holmes before his retirement from practice," and Holmes confirms this: "It's surely time that I disappeared into that little farm of my dreams."

"We may conjecture, therefore," Mr. T. S. Blakeney wrote in *Sherlock Holmes: Fact or Fiction?*, "that by the end of the year [1903] the great detective had laid aside his calling, and it is pleasing to know that many offers were made to settle him on the South Downs with his bees, and even to recommend a suitable housekeeper. (See the *Strand Magazine*, December, 1917.)"

"It is fair to assume that [Holmes'] withdrawal to private life occurred during the autumn of the year 1903," the late H. W. Bell wrote in *Sherlock Holmes and Dr. Watson: The Chronology of Their Adventures*.

"Inasmuch as the Master's tremendous repute precluded his being long without a case, ["The Adventure of the Creeping Man"] must have been very shortly before his retirement," the late Dr. Ernest Bloomfield Zeisler wrote in *Baker Street Chronology*. "We may recall in 'The Adventure of the Solitary Cyclist' Watson says that in the eight years from 1894 to 1901 the Master was consulted in every public case of any difficulty and in hundreds of private cases. Hence the Master retired from practice several months before the end of 1903."

Watson himself, in his Preface to "His Last Bow," published in 1917, has told us that Holmes chose as his retirement retreat "a small farm upon the Downs, five miles from Eastbourne . . ."

In 1953 the late Christopher Morley, on a visit to England, announced to the press that he had searched for Holmes' downland cottage—and found it. The cottage, he declared, was "about one-and-a-half miles from salt water and about the same distance from the Seven Sisters, near a plantation of pine trees only a quarter of a mile from a No. 12 bus stop on the Eastbourne to Brighton road." Alluding to "The Adventure of the Lion's Mane," Morley added: "The cottage is stated to be at the top of the cliffs. I keep bees myself at home in Long Island, and I know that's nonsense. It was a red herring to put Moriarty's men off the scent. You can't keep bees on a cliff-top—they need a more sheltered spot."

"An Eastbourne resident," Mr. W. H. Chenhall later wrote ("The Retirement of Sherlock Holmes"), "has suggested that the cottage Morley found is one that nestles on a wooded slope above the road running southward from the village of East Dean, on the No. 12 bus route, to the coast at Birling Gap. This would be roughly the right distance from Eastbourne, but not one-and-a-half miles from the sea. It may be only half as far, but it would need to be even nearer to the sea to square with 'The Adventure of the Lion's Mane.'

"Almost every sentence in Holmes' description of the place throws up a snag," Mr. Chenhall continued, ". . . except at Birling Gap, where the descent to the beach is relatively short and by means of steps cut in the chalk; the cliffs stretching in either direction are high and precipitous. If a path did exist it must have been dangerous, and it is a wonder, as Vincent Starrett remarked, that Holmes did not break his neck. . . . It seems unlikely that there would be . . . a beach [consisting of a hundred yards of pebble and shingle] hereabout, where the danger of falling from the top of the cliffs is matched by the risk of being entrapped by the tides below. The next difficulty is 'the little cove and village of Fulworth,' breaking the long line of beach. The only approximation to a village on the five mile stretch from Beachy Head in the east to Cuckmere Haven in the west is Birling itself and this could hardly be said to be in a cove.

ON THE SUSSEX DOWNS

The photograph, by Will F. Taylor of Reigate, is from *Sussex,* by Esther Meynell, London: Robert Hale, Ltd., 1947.

That this line of coast faces roughly south-west is a further obstacle, if [other] statements by Holmes are considered. . . . The implication in each case is of cliffs facing east or possibly south-east, but certainly not south-west. It so happens, however, that there is a section of coast facing south-east at each end of the five-mile limit. At the western end, across the Cuckmere River, the coast runs in this direction for about half a mile before bending round to face south-west again. At the eastern end there is a longer stretch from the top of Beachy Head (near the lighthouse) to the final downward slope of the Downs just outside Eastbourne. The cliffs here are different. Though high, they are not so sheer and are terraced, with green slopes and levels. A cottage here could have the required view of the Channel and also shelter for the bees. There is access to the beach at Cow's Gap by means of steps, as at Birling Gap. An objection to this region is that it is much less than five miles from Eastbourne, just as the Cuckmere area is much more."

Despite the obstacles cited by Mr. Chenhall, Mr. Charles O. Merriman, at this writing the Chairman of the Sherlock Holmes Society of London, is convinced that he has located Holmes' farm. "Inland, running east to west from Eastbourne to Birling Gap across the Downs escarpment, are only four farms," Mr. Merriman wrote in "The Game Is Afoot." "In order they are Black Robin Farm, Bullock Down Farm, Cornish Farm and Birling Manor Farm. Birling Manor Farm is sheltered in a woodland dell in the Downs about three-quarters of a mile from Birling Gap, but gives a view of the Channel from an adjoining field. The land attached to the farm rises to an eminence eastwards known as Michel Dean, which gives a commanding view of the Channel. When I was informed in the course of conversation with some of the downsfolk that Cornish Farm produced acres of white clover each year and that the bees from Birling Manor Farm, the only farm of the four which keeps bees by reason of its sheltered position, feasted on the white clover after an earlier-in-the-season diet of wild raspberry, which is prevalent on the Downs in this area, I felt my researches had at last borne fruit. I have not pursued the matter further but I should imagine that Mr. Stackhurst's school, The Gables, must lie at East Dean or Friston or its environs up to a mile north of Birling Manor Farm."

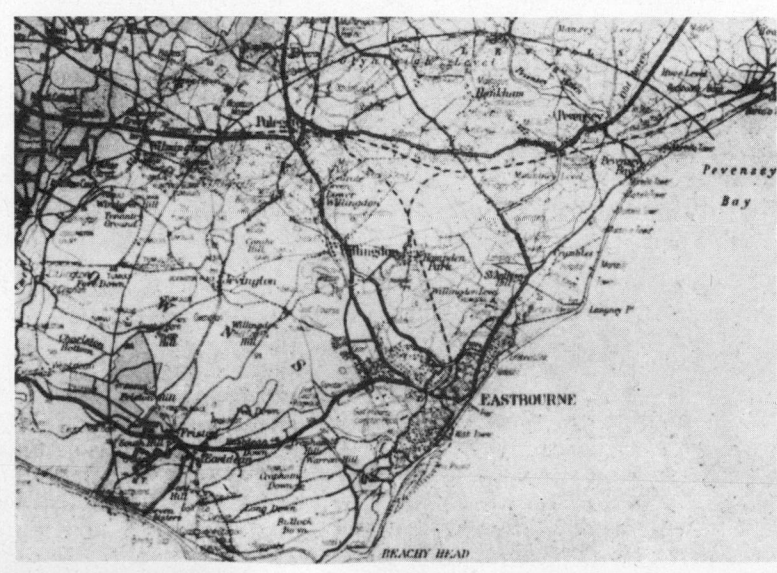

TO FIND MR. HOLMES' BEE FARM

Put a ruler through the final "E" of Eastbourne and the capital "S" of "Sisters" in Seven Sisters (on the coast almost due west of Beachy Head). Birling Farm should appear above your ruler, just east of West Hill.

Watson tells us—again in his Preface to "His Last Bow"—that Holmes in retirement divided his time "between philosophy and agriculture," and in "The Second Stain" he has pinpointed Holmes' interest in agriculture, or a large part of his interest: specifically, Holmes became a bee-farmer.

"What prompted the Master to take up bee-keeping in Sussex during his retirement?" Mr. James Edward Holroyd once asked. And continued: "I have recently acquired a copy of *The British Bee-Keeper's Guide Book*, first published by T. W. Cowan, of Compton Lea, Horsham, in 1881, the opening year of the great partnership. The book went into as many editions as some of Watson's own writings and it is quite possible that Holmes ran into the author during one of his Sussex inquiries. How appropriate was the hobby to a man of Holmes' training may be judged by this quotation from the Introduction: 'Although anyone may possess bees, it is not everyone who can become a proficient bee-master. Only energy and perseverance, *together with aptness for investigation*, can ensure real success.'"

On the other hand, Mr. Pope R. Hill, Sr., has written that Holmes owed his interest in bees to France, not Sussex ("Sherlock Holmes Meets Jean Henri Fabre"): Holmes first became interested in entomology, Mr. Hill wrote, when he spent "several months at Montpellier, in the south of France ['The Adventure of the Empty House']. [Jean Henri] Fabre's home was in the village of Serignan at the foot of Mount Ventoux, an outlying summit of the Alps, and situated in the South of France less than 75 miles from Montpellier. . . . Holmes . . . would surely have arranged to visit him there at the time. . . . The slightest contact would instantly have aroused Holmes' deepest interest and enthusiasm, for Fabre was an observor and reasoner after Holmes' own heart—as Holmes was after his."

The writing of Holmes' *Practical Handbook of Bee Culture with Some Observations upon the Segregation of the Queen* ("His Last Bow") must have occupied much of Holmes' time between 1904 and 1912, and during this period "he must have acquired a remarkably fine apiarian collection," Miss Madeleine B. Stern wrote in "Sherlock Holmes: Rare Book Collector." "Holmes' shelf on bee culture boasted undoubtedly a copy of Charles Butler's *The Feminin' Monarchi' Or The Histori of Bee's* (Oxford, 1634), a volume of interest not only for its useful advice on the subject, but for its introduction of the use of phonetics in English. Close by this curious treatise stood Bazin's lengthy dialogue entitled *Histoire Naturelle des Abeilles* (Paris, 1744) with its finely engraved folding plates. Réaumur's *Natural History of Bees* (London, 1744), together with Rucellai's poem on bees, *Le Api* (Parma, 1797) with its observations made by means of a magnifying mirror, were surely included in the Holmes collection. Only two copies of Rucellai's work were printed on silk, and it is quite possible, though not definite, that the Holmes copy was one of them. Thacher's *Practical Treatise on the Management of Bees* (Boston, 1829) probably completed the small but select apiarian collection enhanced by a Holmes provenance."

"It is impossible to do more than venture a guess at the books that may have facilitated those [philosophical] studies of Holmes' later years," Miss Stern continued. "In philosophy, he probably dipped into his first editions of Hume and Kant, Leibnitz and Locke, Spinoza, Hobbes and Berkeley. For agricultural entertainment, he may have turned to his 1560 edition of Tatti's compendium, *Della Agricultura*, or to such works as Blith's *English Improver, or a New Survey of Husbandry* (1649)."

We may be sure, too, that Holmes' interest in chemical research continued during his years of "retirement." Mr. R. P. Graham, for example, has pointed to Holmes' statement in "The Final Problem" that his recent investigations had left him "in such a position that I could continue to live in the quiet fashion which is most congenial to me, and to concentrate my attention upon my chemical researches." In "Sherlock Holmes in Retirement," Mr. Graham has noted that when Mr. P. M. Stone visited Holmes in Sussex (see "Sussex Interview" in *221B: Studies in Sherlock Holmes*), the retired detective had a laboratory with chemical apparatus and equipment.

Messrs. J. H. and Humfrey Michell have concurred with Mr. Graham. In "Sherlock Holmes the Chemist," they hold that Holmes' specific interest in chemical research was again the coal tar derivatives. "The last picture we have of [Holmes] in retirement, so charmingly portrayed by Mr. P. M. Stone, shows him still interested in the coal tar derivatives. A glance into the laboratory revealed a 'brick-coated blast furnace.' But Mr. Stone is not an expert in these matters, and what he saw was in reality a coking still, inclosed in a 'setting' of insulating brick. Such a still is used for the isolation of some of the rare and unique hydrocarbons to be found in coal tar. The tar is distilled off in small fractions, some at high temperatures, leaving a residue of coke, and thus Holmes was perhaps in process of isolating some new hydrocarbons of strange properties and values."

Still, with all this research, a question remains: *Why* did Sherlock Holmes retire from active practice when, according to the consensus of expert opinion, he was not yet fifty years of age?

"It was no accident," Professor John B. Wolf wrote in "Another Incubus in the Saddle," "that Holmes 'retired' in 1903. Everyone knows that after 1903 the heretofore reasonably friendly relations between England and Germany deteriorated rapidly. By 1907 the Triple Entente and the Triple Alliance faced each other in an uneasy truce while the naval race between England and Germany (after 1905) grew to monstrous proportions. Crises in 1908 (Bosnia), 1909 (Morocco), 1911 (Morocco), 1912 (Lybia), and 1913 (Balkan Wars) pointed to the catastrophe of 1914. Is it conceivable that Holmes was merely keeping bees while this mortal danger threatened England? Of course not. How can anyone doubt that Holmes was concealing his reasons for having a villa so near the sea? It must be clear to everyone that the Master had more important business than solving the problem of poor Fitzroy McPherson's death ["The Adventure of the Lion's Mane"] and keeping bees. Undoubtedly, beekeeping was a blind, as von Bork discovered ["His Last Bow"], for Holmes' counterespionage activities. It is hard to understand why either Watson or Holmes himself failed to

1 During World War I, Sir Arthur Conan Doyle, on a tour of the Allied front, was asked by the French General Humbert: "What rank does Sherlock Holmes hold in the English army, *monsieur?*" Sir Arthur, staggered, replied in halting French that Holmes was unhappily "too old for active service."

give us the details of those exciting years. It could be that Dr. Watson feared that publicity would limit the Master's usefulness, but it could also have been argued that publicity would have convinced the German government that it would be futile to send spies to England while Holmes was on guard."

Mr. T. S. Blakeney has also written that "no student of Sherlock Holmes can doubt that the years of 1914–18 found him hard at work in the nation's interests**1**—doubtless the perspicacity of the genial but anonymous head of the Secret Service (Sir Samuel Hoare, *The Fourth Seal*, p. 28 *seq.*) secured the willing assistance of the one who stood head and shoulders above the common order of men. Whether Holmes could stand the Secret Service for long is, of course, arguable; it is difficult to see him suffering very gladly the strange medley of affairs outlined, for example, in Mr. Compton Mackenzie's *First Athenian Memories*."

Mr. Arthur L. Levine is another who believes that Holmes was indeed active during the years just before World War I. In "A Man of 'Formidable Resourcefulness,' " he has written that it was due to Holmes' efforts that the famous Zimmermann note (proposing an alliance between Germany, Mexico, and Japan against the United States, if the United States did not remain neutral) was discovered. "It was turned over to the United States Government on February 24, 1917. On March 1st it was made public. On April 6th, the United States declared war on Germany. The tide was turned. Britain was saved. Holmes could return to his bees."

But he probably did not remain with them for long: "At Constantinople, during 1920—according to the London *Times* —the Turks were certain that the great English detective was at work behind the scenes," Mr. Vincent Starrett wrote in his introduction to *221B: Studies in Sherlock Holmes*.

"From about 1920 to the beginning of the second World War," Mr. Norman V. Ballou has written, Holmes lived continuously in northern India. Here he succeeded in at least partially discovering the secret of life and the indefinite extension of man's allotted span by developing an elixir prepared from young queens of the Oriental Hive Bee (*Apis indica*), the largest of the honeybees, which occurs throughout India, Ceylon, and Malasia. "Throughout his sojourn in northern India, Sherlock Holmes is known to have dominated the planning and espionage activities for two great governments while continuing his chemical research. During this period, he is reported to have made several trips to Tibet to consult Buddhist scholars reputed to be engaged in study of the life principle. . . . Shortly after the beginning of World War II, Holmes made his way to Lhasa, where he resided, until very recently, possibly as the secret guest of the Dalai Lama. Again, during nearly two decades in Tibet, Holmes continued to control espionage activities of the governments he served. . . . The activities and whereabouts of Sherlock Holmes go far toward explaining the Chinese Communist Government's recent activities and the flight of the Dalai Lama. Whether Holmes . . . has made good his escape from Tibet or whether he is hiding at some isolated monastery I do not know."

On the other hand, Mrs. Crighton Sellars has written ("A Visit with Sherlock Holmes") that she has no doubts that Holmes was "the famous British scientist whose name and peronality were for so long guarded with such secrecy. If I am not mistaken [he] even had the temerity to land in Normandy with our troops on D-Day. I know the person concerned was given another name than [Holmes], but I can very well see that was because [he] did not want our enemies to know [he was] actually engaged against them."

While it is true that Watson has lamentably failed to fill in the record of Holmes' later cases, we have, at least, some tantalizing references to them. See, for example, the Introduction to *The Hound of the Baskervilles* written, in 1926, for the Doubleday, Page & Company edition. Here the late Professor Frank Condie Baxter has revealed that Holmes in 1904 conducted an investigation (no doubt of supreme importance) for the British Admiralty in Shantung—that he was presented with a diamond sword by King Albert of Belgium for his masterly work in clearing up The Affair of the Winking Light in the winter of 1916—and that the Congress of the United States once struck off a Holmes Medal in gratitude for the master detective's services in The Adventure of the American Ambassador and the Thermite Bullet.

It is also suggested that the student of Holmes' later years will find much to interest him in "The Man Who Was Not Dead" by Manly Wade Wellman and "The Adventure of the Illustrious Imposter" by Anthony Boucher (both in *The Misadventures of Sherlock Holmes*), as well as "The Singular Affair of Mr. Phillip Phot," by the Greek Interpreters of East Lansing, Michigan, compiled by the late Page Heldenbrand (in the *Baker Street Journal*, Vol. II, No. 1, Old Series, January, 1947, pp. 67–84).

78

THE ADVENTURE OF THE LION'S MANE

[Tuesday, July 27, to Thursday, August 3, 1909]

IT is a most singular thing that a problem which was certainly as abstruse and unusual as any which I have faced in my long professional career should have come to me after my retirement ; and be brought, as it were, to my very door. It occurred after my withdrawal to my little Sussex home, when I had given myself up entirely to that soothing life of Nature for which I had so often yearned during the long years spent amid the gloom of London. At this period of my life the good Watson had passed almost beyond my ken. An occasional week-end visit was the most that I ever saw of him. Thus I must act as my own chronicler. Ah ! had he but been with me, how much he might have made of so wonderful a happening and of my eventual triumph against every difficulty ! As it is, however, I must needs tell my tale in my own plain way, showing by my words each step upon the difficult road which lay before me as I searched for the mystery of the Lion's Mane.

My villa is situated upon the southern slope of the Downs, commanding a great view of the Channel. At this point the coast-line is entirely of chalk cliffs, which can only be descended by a single, long, tortuous path, which is steep and slippery. At the bottom of the path lie a hundred yards of pebbles and shingle, even when the tide is at full. Here and there, however, there are curves and hollows which make splendid swimming-pools filled afresh with each flow. This admirable beach extends for some miles in each direction, save only at one point where the little cove and village of Fulworth break the line.

My house is lonely. I, my old housekeeper, and my bees have the estate all to ourselves. Half a mile off, however, is Harold Stackhurst's well-known coaching establishment, The Gables, quite a large place, which contains some score of young fellows preparing for various professions, with a staff of several masters. Stackhurst himself was a well-known rowing Blue in his day, and an excellent all-round scholar. He and I were always friendly from the day I came to the coast, and he was the one man who was on such terms with me that we could drop in on each other in the evenings without an invitation.

---

1 *my old housekeeper*. Her first name, as we learn in "His Last Bow," was Martha. Commentators have generally assumed that Holmes' housekeeper in retirement was Mrs. Hudson.

Towards the end of July, 1907, there was a severe gale, the wind blowing up-Channel, heaping the seas to the base of the cliffs, and leaving a lagoon at the turn of the **2** tide. On the morning of which I speak the wind had abated, and all Nature was newly washed and fresh. It was impossible to work upon so delightful a day, and I strolled out before breakfast to enjoy the exquisite air. I walked along the cliff path which led to the steep descent to the beach. As I walked I heard a shout behind me, and there was Harold Stackhurst waving his hand in cheery greeting.

"What a morning, Mr. Holmes! I thought I should see you out."

"Going for a swim, I see."

"At your old tricks again," he laughed, patting his bulging pocket. "Yes. McPherson started early, and I expect I may find him there."

Fitzroy McPherson was the science master, a fine upstanding young fellow whose life had been crippled by heart trouble following rheumatic fever. He was a natural athlete, however, and excelled in every game which did not throw too great a strain upon him. Summer and winter he went for his swim, and, as I am a swimmer myself, I have often joined him.

At this moment we saw the man himself. His head showed above the edge of the cliff where the path ends. Then his whole figure appeared at the top, staggering like a drunken man. The next instant he threw up his hands, and, with a terrible cry, fell upon his face. Stackhurst and I rushed forward—it may have been fifty yards—and turned him on his back. He was obviously dying. Those glazed sunken eyes and dreadful livid cheeks could mean nothing else. One glimmer of life came into his face for an instant, and he uttered two or three words with an eager air of warning. They were slurred and indistinct, but to my ear the last of them, which burst in a shriek from his lips, were "the lion's mane." It was utterly irrelevant and unintelligible, and yet I could twist the sound into no other sense. Then he half raised himself from the ground, threw his arms into the air and fell forward on his side. He was dead.

My companion was paralysed by the sudden horror of it, but I, as may well be imagined, had every sense on the alert. And I had need, for it was speedily evident that we were in the presence of an extraordinary case. The man was dressed only in his Burberry overcoat, his trousers, and an unlaced pair of canvas shoes. As he fell over, his Burberry, which had been simply thrown round his shoulders, slipped off, exposing his trunk. We stared at it in amazement. His back was covered with dark red lines as though he had been terribly flogged by a thin wire scourge. The instrument with which this punishment had been inflicted was clearly flexible, for the long, angry weals curved round his shoulders and ribs. There was blood dripping down his chin, for he had bitten through his lower lip in the paroxysm of his agony. His drawn and distorted face told how terrible that agony had been.

I was kneeling and Stackhurst standing by the body

2 *heaping the seas to the base of the cliffs.* There was in fact no such gale in July, 1907, and this led the late Professor Jay Finley Christ to date the case in the June of that year, when there was a substantial Channel wind on the 25th. The late Dr. Ernest Bloomfield Zeisler, on the other hand, has shown that "There were high winds and rough sea in the Channel and off the Sussex coast on three successive days, from Saturday, July 24th through Monday, July 26th" in the year 1909. We are later told that the case opened on a Tuesday ("Tuesday was to-day . . ."). Since June 25, 1907, the day of Professor Christ's storm, was a Tuesday, and Holmes tells us that "the wind had abated" on the morning of the opening day, we believe that the evidence is in favor of Dr. Zeisler's date; the "1907" must be a typographical error. The case opened, then, on *Tuesday, July 27, 1909;* Holmes says that "a week passed," so it closed on *Tuesday, August 3rd,* or, perhaps, a day or two later.

THE NEXT INSTANT HE THREW UP HIS HANDS, AND, WITH A TERRIBLE CRY, FELL UPON HIS FACE.

Illustration by Howard K. Elcock for the *Strand Magazine*, December, 1926.

3 *some high, abstract region of surds and conic sections.* "Now these words were written by Holmes himself," Mr. A. S. Galbraith wrote in "The Real Moriarty," "and if he thought of 'surds' as typifying the sort of thing a mathematician would have uppermost in his mind, obviously he knew little of [mathematics]."

when a shadow fell across us, and we found that Ian Murdoch was by our side. Murdoch was the mathematical coach at the establishment, a tall, dark, thin man, so taciturn and aloof that none can be said to have been his friend. He seemed to live in some high, abstract **3** region of surds and conic sections with little to connect him with ordinary life. He was looked upon as an oddity by the students, and would have been their butt, but there was some strange outlandish blood in the man, which showed itself not only in his coal-black eyes and swarthy face, but also in occasional outbreaks of temper which could only be described as ferocious. On one occasion, being plagued by a little dog belonging to McPherson, he had caught the creature up and hurled it through the plate-glass window, an action for which Stackhurst would certainly have given him his dismissal had he not been a very valuable teacher. Such was the strange, complex man who now appeared beside us. He seemed to be honestly shocked at the sight before him, though the incident of the dog may show that there was no great sympathy between the dead man and himself.

"Poor fellow! Poor fellow! What can I do? How can I help?"

"Were you with him? Can you tell us what has happened?"

"No, no, I was late this morning. I was not on the beach at all. I have come straight from The Gables. What can I do?"

"You can hurry to the police-station at Fulworth. Report the matter at once."

Without a word he made off at top speed, and I proceeded to take the matter in hand, while Stackhurst, dazed at this tragedy, remained by the body. My first task naturally was to note who was on the beach. From the top of the path I could see the whole sweep of it, and it was absolutely deserted save that two or three dark figures could be seen far away moving towards the village of Fulworth. Having satisfied myself upon this point, I walked slowly down the path. There was clay or soft marl mixed with the chalk, and every here and there I saw the same footstep, both ascending and descending. No one else had gone down to the beach by this track that morning. At one place I observed the print of an open hand with the fingers towards the incline. This could only mean that poor McPherson had fallen as he ascended. There were rounded depressions, too, which suggested that he had come down upon his knees more than once. At the bottom of the path was the considerable lagoon left by the retreating tide. At the side of it McPherson had undressed, for there lay his towel on a rock. It was folded and dry, so that it would seem that after all he had never entered the water. Once or twice as I hunted round amid the hard shingle I came on little patches of sand where the print of his canvas shoe, and also of his naked foot, could be seen. The latter fact proved that he had made all ready to bathe, though the towel indicated that he had not actually done so.

And here was the problem clearly defined—as strange a one as had ever confronted me. The man had not been on the beach more than a quarter of an hour at the most. Stackhurst had followed him from The Gables, so there could be no doubt about that. He had gone to bathe and had stripped, as the naked footsteps showed. Then he had suddenly huddled on his clothes again—they were all dishevelled and unfastened—and he had returned without bathing, or at any rate without drying himself. And the reason for his change of purpose had been that he had been scourged in some savage, inhuman fashion, tortured until he bit his lip through in his agony, and was left with only strength enough to crawl away and to die. Who had done this barbarous deed? There were, it is true, small grottos and caves in the base of the cliffs, but the low sun shone directly into them, and there was no place for concealment. Then, again, there were those distant figures on the beach. They seemed too far away to have been connected with the crime, and the broad lagoon in which McPherson had intended to bathe lay between him and them, lapping up to the rocks. On the sea two or three fishing-boats were at no great distance. Their occupants might be examined at our leisure. There were several roads for inquiry, but none which led to any very obvious goal.

When I at last returned to the body I found that a little group of wandering folk had gathered round it. Stackhurst was, of course, still there, and Ian Murdoch had just arrived with Anderson, the village constable, a big, ginger-moustached man of the slow, solid Sussex breed—a breed which covers much good sense under a heavy, silent exterior. He listened to everything, took note of all we said, and finally drew me aside.

" I'd be glad of your advice, Mr. Holmes. This is a big thing for me to handle, and I'll hear of it from Lewes **4** if I go wrong."

I advised him to send for his immediate superior, and for a doctor; also to allow nothing to be moved, and as few fresh footmarks as possible to be made, until they came. In the meantime I searched the dead man's pockets. There were his handkerchief, a large knife, and a small folding card-case. From this projected a slip of paper, which I unfolded and handed to the constable. There was written on it in a scrawling, feminine hand : " I will be there, you may be sure.—Maudie." It read like a love affair, an assignation, though when and where were a blank. The constable replaced it in the card-case and returned it with the other things to the pockets of the Burberry. Then, as nothing more suggested itself, I walked back to my house for breakfast, having first arranged that the base of the cliffs should be thoroughly searched.

Stackhurst was round in an hour or two to tell me that the body had been removed to The Gables, where the inquest would be held. He brought with him some serious and definite news. As I expected, nothing had been found in the small caves below the cliff, but he had examined the papers in McPherson's desk, and there were several which showed an intimate correspondence with a certain Miss Maud Bellamy, of Fulworth. We had then

4 *Lewes.* Municipal borough of Sussex East, on the Ouse River.

5 *some algebraic demonstration before breakfast.*
This "shows [Murdoch] sadistic or mad," Mr.
Galbraith wrote. "In the writer's moderately wide
experience in mathematical circles, [it is] unheard
of."

established the identity of the writer of the note.

" The police have the letters," he explained. " I
could not bring them.   But there is no doubt that it was a
serious love affair.   I see no reason, however, to connect
it with that horrible happening save, indeed, that the
lady had made an appointment with him."

" But hardly at a bathing-pool which all of you were
in the habit of using," I remarked.

" It is mere chance," said he, " that several of the
students were not with McPherson."

" *Was* it mere chance ? "

Stackhurst knit his brows in thought.

" Ian Murdoch held them back," said he ; " he would
insist upon some algebraic demonstration before break-
5 fast.   Poor chap, he is dreadfully cut up about it
all."

" And yet I gather that they were not friends."

" At one time they were not.   But for a year or more
Murdoch has been as near to McPherson as he ever could
be to anyone.   He is not of a very sympathetic disposition
by nature."

" So I understand.   I seem to remember your telling
me once about a quarrel over the ill-usage of a dog."

" That blew over all right."

" But left some vindictive feeling, perhaps."

" No, no ; I am sure they were real friends."

" Well, then, we must explore the matter of the girl.
Do you know her ? "

" Everyone knows her.   She is the beauty of the neighbourhood—a real beauty, Holmes, who would draw
attention everywhere.   I knew that McPherson was
attracted by her, but I had no notion that it had gone so
far as these letters would seem to indicate."

" But who is she ? "

" She is the daughter of old Tom Bellamy, who
owns all the boats and bathing-cots at Fulworth.   He
was a fisherman to start with, but is now a man of some
substance.   He and his son William run the business."

" Shall we walk into Fulworth and see them ? "

" On what pretext ? "

" Oh, we can easily find a pretext.   After all, this
poor man did not ill-use himself in this outrageous way.
Some human hand was on the handle of that scourge, if
indeed it was a scourge which inflicted the injuries.   His
circle of acquaintances in this lonely place was surely
limited.   Let us follow it up in every direction and we
can hardly fail to come upon the motive, which in turn
should lead us to the criminal."

It would have been a pleasant walk across the thyme-
scented Downs had our minds not been poisoned by the
tragedy we had witnessed.   The village of Fulworth lies
in a hollow curving in a semicircle round the bay.   Behind the old-fashioned hamlet several modern houses
have been built upon the rising ground.   It was to one
of these that Stackhurst guided me.

" That's The Haven, as Bellamy called it.   The one
with the corner tower and slate roof.   Not bad for a
man who started with nothing but—— By Jove, look
at that ! "

The garden gate of The Haven had opened and a man had emerged. There was no mistaking that tall, angular, straggling figure. It was Ian Murdoch, the mathematician. A moment later we confronted him upon the road.

"Hullo!" said Stackhurst. The man nodded, gave us a sideways glance from his curious dark eyes, and would have passed us, but his principal pulled him up.

"What were you doing there?" he asked.

Murdoch's face flushed with anger. "I am your subordinate, sir, under your roof. I am not aware that I owe you any account of my private actions."

Stackhurst's nerves were near the surface after all he had endured. Otherwise, perhaps, he would have waited. Now he lost his temper completely.

"In the circumstances your answer is pure impertinence, Mr. Murdoch."

"Your own question might perhaps come under the same heading."

"This is not the first time that I have had to overlook your insubordinate ways. It will certainly be the last. You will kindly make fresh arrangements for your future as speedily as you can."

"I had intended to do so. I have lost to-day the only person who made The Gables habitable."

He strode off upon his way, while Stackhurst, with angry eyes, stood glaring after him. "Is he not an impossible, intolerable man?" he cried.

The one thing that impressed itself forcibly upon my mind was that Mr. Ian Murdoch was taking the first chance to open a path of escape from the scene of the crime. Suspicion, vague and nebulous, was now beginning to take outline in my mind. Perhaps the visit to the Bellamys might throw some further light upon the matter. Stackhurst pulled himself together and we went forward to the house.

Mr. Bellamy proved to be a middle-aged man with a flaming red beard. He seemed to be in a very angry mood, and his face was soon as florid as his hair.

"No, sir, I do not desire any particulars. My son here"—indicating a powerful young man, with a heavy, sullen face, in the corner of the sitting-room—"is of one mind with me that Mr. McPherson's attentions to Maud were insulting. Yes, sir, the word 'marriage' was never mentioned, and yet there were letters and meetings, and a great deal more of which neither of us could approve. She has no mother, and we are her only guardians. We are determined——"

But the words were taken from his mouth by the appearance of the lady herself. There was no gainsaying that she would have graced any assembly in the world. Who could have imagined that so rare a flower would grow from such a root and in such an atmosphere? Women have seldom been an attraction to me, for my brain has always governed my heart, but I could not look upon her perfect clear-cut face, with all the soft freshness of the Downlands in her delicate colouring, without realizing that no young man would cross her path unscathed. Such was the girl who had pushed open the door and stood now, wide-eyed and intense, in front of Harold Stackhurst.

" I know already that Fitzroy is dead," she said. " Do not be afraid to tell me the particulars."

" This other gentleman of yours let us know the news," explained the father.

" There is no reason why my sister should be brought into the matter," growled the younger man.

The sister turned a sharp, fierce look upon him. " This is my business, William. Kindly leave me to manage it in my own way. By all accounts there has been a crime committed. If I can help to show who did it, it is the least I can do for him who is gone."

She listened to a short account from my companion, with a composed concentration which showed me that she possessed strong character as well as great beauty. Maud Bellamy will always remain in my memory as a most complete and remarkable woman. It seems that she already knew me by sight, for she turned to me at the end.

" Bring them to justice, Mr. Holmes. You have my sympathy and my help, whoever they may be." It seemed to me that she glanced defiantly at her father and brother as she spoke.

" Thank you," said I. " I value a woman's instinct in such matters. You use the word ' they.' You think that more than one was concerned ? "

" I knew Mr. McPherson well enough to be aware that he was a brave and a strong man. No single person could ever have inflicted such an outrage upon him."

" Might I have one word with you alone ? "

" I tell you, Maud, not to mix yourself up in the matter," cried her father angrily.

She looked at me helplessly. " What can I do ? "

" The whole world will know the facts presently, so there can be no harm if I discuss them here," said I. " I should have preferred privacy, but if your father will not allow it, he must share the deliberations." Then I spoke of the note which had been found in the dead man's pocket. " It is sure to be produced at the inquest. May I ask you to throw any light upon it that you can ? "

" I see no reason for mystery," she answered. " We were engaged to be married, and we only kept it secret because Fitzroy's uncle, who is very old and said to be dying, might have disinherited him if he had married against his wish. There was no other reason."

" You could have told us," growled Mr. Bellamy.

" So I would, father, if you had ever shown sympathy."

" I object to my girl picking up with men outside her own station."

" It was your prejudice against him which prevented us from telling you. As to this appointment "—she fumbled in her dress and produced a crumpled note— " it was in answer to this."

" DEAREST," ran the message : " The old place on the beach just after sunset on Tuesday. It is the only time I can get away.—F. M."

"THE WHOLE WORLD WILL KNOW THE FACTS PRESENTLY . . ."

Illustration by Frederic Dorr Steele for *Liberty Magazine*, November 27, 1926.

" Tuesday was to-day, and I had meant to meet him to-night."

I turned over the paper. " This never came by post. How did you get it ? "

" I would rather not answer that question. It has really nothing to do with the matter which you are investigating. But anything which bears upon that I will most freely answer."

She was as good as her word, but there was nothing which was helpful in our investigation. She had no reason to think that her fiancé had any hidden enemy, but she admitted that she had had several warm admirers.

" May I ask if Mr. Ian Murdoch was one of them ? "
She blushed and seemed confused.

" There was a time when I thought he was. But that was all changed when he understood the relations between Fitzroy and myself."

Again the shadow round this strange man seemed to me to be taking more definite shape. His record must be examined. His rooms must be privately searched. Stackhurst was a willing collaborator, for in his mind also suspicions were forming. We returned from our visit to The Haven with the hope that one free end of this tangled skein was already in our hands.

A week passed. The inquest had thrown no light upon the matter and had been adjourned for further evidence. Stackhurst had made discreet inquiry about his subordinate, and there had been a superficial search of his room, but without result. Personally, I had gone over the whole ground again, both physically and mentally, but with no new conclusions. In all my chronicles the reader will find no case which brought me so completely to the limit of my powers. Even my imagination could conceive no solution to the mystery. And then there came the incident of the dog.

It was my old housekeeper who heard of it first by that strange wireless by which such people collect the news of the country-side.

" Sad story this, sir, about Mr. McPherson's dog," said she one evening.

I do not encourage such conversations, but the words arrested my attention.

" What of Mr. McPherson's dog ? "

" Dead, sir. Died of grief for its master."

" Who told you this ? "

" Why, sir, everyone is talking of it. It took on terrible, and has eaten nothing for a week. Then to-day two of the young gentlemen from The Gables found it dead—down on the beach, sir, at the very place where its master met his end."

" At the very place." The words stood out clear in my memory. Some dim perception that the matter was vital rose in my mind. That the dog should die was after the beautiful, faithful nature of dogs. But ' in the very place ' ! Why should this lonely beach be fatal to it ? Was it possible that it also, had been sacrificed to some revengeful feud ? Was it possible—— ? Yes, the perception was dim, but already something was building up in my mind. In a few minutes I was on my way to

I TURNED OVER THE PAPER. "THIS NEVER CAME BY POST. HOW DID YOU GET IT?"

Illustration by Howard K. Elcock for the *Strand Magazine*, December, 1926.

6 *an Airedale terrier.* "Anyone who knows anything about terriers knows that Airedales are large," Mrs. Eleanor S. Cole wrote in "Holmes, Watson and the K-9's." "The breed standard (*The Complete Dog Book*, The American Kennel Club, New York City) lists the males as standing 23 inches at the wither (shoulder) and therefore weighing upwards of sixty pounds. To have picked up and hurled a dog of this size and weight through a plate-glass window would have required the thrower to be a veritable giant. Nowhere in the story is Ian Murdoch described as such. Therefore, the dog must have been a Welsh terrier, which to the uninitiate, strongly resembles an Airedale in miniature."

7 *My mind is like a crowded box-room.* Holmes' observation here is of course in direct contradiction to what he told Watson of his mental habits in *A Study in Scarlet*.

The Gables, where I found Stackhurst in his study. At my request he sent for Sudbury and Blount, the two students who had found the dog.

" Yes, it lay on the very edge of the pool," said one of them. " It must have followed the trail of its dead master."

6   I saw the faithful little creature, an Airedale terrier, laid out upon the mat in the hall. The body was stiff and rigid, the eyes projecting, and the limbs contorted. There was agony in every line of it.

From The Gables I walked down to the bathing-pool. The sun had sunk and the shadow of the great cliff lay black across the water, which glimmered dully like a sheet of lead. The place was deserted and there was no sign of life save for two sea-birds circling and screaming overhead. In the fading light I could dimly make out the little dog's spoor upon the sand round the very rock on which his master's towel had been laid. For a long time I stood in deep meditation while the shadows grew darker around me. My mind was filled with racing thoughts. You have known what it was to be in a nightmare in which you feel that there is some all-important thing for which you search and which you know is there, though it remains for ever just beyond your reach. That was how I felt that evening as I stood alone by that place of death. Then at last I turned and walked slowly homewards.

I had just reached the top of the path when it came to me. Like a flash, I remembered the thing for which I had so eagerly and vainly grasped. You will know, or Watson has written in vain, that I hold a vast store of out-of-the-way knowledge, without scientific system, but very available for the needs of my work. My mind is

7 like a crowded box-room with packets of all sorts stowed away therein—so many that I may well have but a vague perception of what was there. I had known that there was something which might bear upon this matter. It was still vague, but at least I knew how I could make it clear. It was monstrous, incredible, and yet it was always a possibility. I would test it to the full.

There is a great garret in my little house which is stuffed with books. It was into this that I plunged and rummaged for an hour. At the end of that time I emerged with a little chocolate and silver volume. Eagerly I turned up the chapter of which I had a dim remembrance. Yes, it was indeed a far-fetched and unlikely proposition, and yet I could not be at rest until I had made sure if it might, indeed, be so. It was late when I retired, with my mind eagerly awaiting the work of the morrow.

But that work met with an annoying interruption. I had hardly swallowed my early cup of tea and was starting for the beach when I had a call from Inspector Bardle of the Sussex Constabulary—a steady, solid, bovine man with thoughtful eyes, which looked at me now with a very troubled expression.

" I know your immense experience, sir," said he. " This is quite unofficial, of course, and need go no further. But I am fairly up against it in this McPherson case. The question is, shall I make an arrest, or shall I not ? "

" Meaning Mr. Ian Murdoch ? "

" Yes, sir. There is really no one else when you come to think of it. That's the advantage of this solitude. We narrow it down to a very small compass. If he did not do it, then who did ? "

" What have you against him ? "

He had gleaned along the same furrows as I had. There was Murdoch's character and the mystery which seemed to hang round the man. His furious bursts of temper, as shown in the incident of the dog. The fact that he had quarrelled with McPherson in the past, and that there was some reason to think that he might have resented his attentions to Miss Bellamy. He had all my points, but no fresh ones, save that Murdoch seemed to be making every preparation for departure.

" What would my position be if I let him slip away with all this evidence against him ? " The burly, phlegmatic man was sorely troubled in his mind.

" Consider," I said, " all the essential gaps in your case. On the morning of the crime he can surely prove an alibi. He had been with his scholars till the last moment, and within a few minutes of McPherson's appearance he came upon us from behind. Then bear in mind the absolute impossibility that he could single-handed have inflicted this outrage upon a man quite as strong as himself. Finally, there is this question of the instrument with which these injuries were inflicted."

" What could it be but a scourge or flexible whip of some sort ? "

" Have you examined the marks ? " I asked.

" I have seen them. So has the doctor."

" But I have examined them very carefully with a lens. They have peculiarities."

" What are they, Mr. Holmes ? "

I stepped to my bureau and brought out an enlarged photograph. " This is my method in such cases," I explained.

" You certainly do things thoroughly, Mr. Holmes."

" I should hardly be what I am if I did not. Now let us consider this weal which extends round the right shoulder. Do you observe nothing remarkable ? "

" I can't say I do."

" Surely it is evident that it is unequal in its intensity. There is a dot of extravasated blood here, and another there. There are similar indications in this other weal down here. What can that mean ? "

" I have no idea. Have you ? "

" Perhaps I have. Perhaps I haven't. I may be able to say more soon. Anything which will define what made that mark will bring us a long way towards the criminal."

" It is, of course, an absurd idea," said the policeman, " but if a red-hot net of wire had been laid across the back, then these better-marked points would represent where the meshes crossed each other."

" A most ingenious comparison. Or shall we say a very stiff cat-o'-nine-tails with small hard knots upon it ? "

" By Jove, Mr. Holmes, I think you have hit it."

MY OUTER DOOR WAS FLUNG OPEN . . .

Illustration by Howard K. Elcock for the *Strand Magazine*, December, 1926.

" Or there may be some very different cause, Mr. Bardle. But your case is far too weak for an arrest. Besides, we have those last words—' Lion's Mane.' "

" I have wondered whether Ian——"

" Yes, I have considered that. If the second word had borne any resemblance to Murdoch—but it did not. He gave it almost in a shriek. I am sure that it was ' Mane.' "

" Have you no alternative, Mr. Holmes ? "

" Perhaps I have. But I do not care to discuss it until there is something more solid to discuss."

" And when will that be ? "

" In an hour—possibly less."

The Inspector rubbed his chin and looked at me with dubious eyes.

" I wish I could see what was in your mind, Mr. Holmes. Perhaps it's those fishing-boats."

" No, no ; they were too far out."

" Well, then, is it Bellamy and that big son of his ? They were not too sweet upon Mr. McPherson. Could they have done him a mischief ? "

" No, no ; you won't draw me until I am ready," said I with a smile. " Now, Inspector, we each have our own work to do. Perhaps if you were to meet me here at midday—— ? "

So far we had got when there came the tremendous interruption which was the beginning of the end.

My outer door was flung open, there were blundering footsteps in the passage, and Ian Murdoch staggered into the room, pallid, dishevelled, his clothes in wild disorder, clawing with his bony hands at the furniture to hold himself erect. " Brandy ! Brandy ! " he gasped, and fell groaning upon the sofa.

He was not alone. Behind him came Stackhurst, hatless and panting, almost as *distrait* as his companion.

" Yes, yes, brandy ! " he cried. " The man is at his last gasp. It was all I could do to bring him here. He fainted twice upon the way."

Half a tumbler of the raw spirit brought about a wondrous change. He pushed himself up on one arm and swung his coat from off his shoulders. " For God's sake ! oil, opium, morphia ! " he cried. " Anything to ease this infernal agony ! "

The Inspector and I cried out at the sight. There, criss-crossed upon the man's naked shoulder, was the same strange reticulated pattern of red, inflamed lines which had been the death-mark of Fitzroy McPherson.

The pain was evidently terrible and was more than local, for the sufferer's breathing would stop for a time, his face would turn black, and then with loud gasps he would clap his hand to his heart, while his brow dropped beads of sweat. At any moment he might die. More and more brandy was poured down his throat, each fresh dose bringing him back to life. Pads of cotton-wool soaked in salad-oil seemed to take the agony from the strange wounds. At last his head fell heavily upon the cushion. Exhausted Nature had taken refuge in its last storehouse of vitality. It was half a sleep and half a faint, but at least it was ease from pain.

To question him had been impossible, but the moment

we were assured of his condition Stackhurst turned upon me.

"My God !" he cried, "what is it, Holmes ? What is it ?"

"Where did you find him ?"

"Down on the beach. Exactly where poor McPherson met his end. If this man's heart had been weak as McPherson's was, he would not be here now. More than once I thought he was gone as I brought him up. It was too far to The Gables, so I made for you."

"Did you see him on the beach ?"

"I was walking on the cliff when I heard his cry. He was at the edge of the water, reeling about like a drunken man. I ran down, threw some clothes about him, and brought him up. For Heaven's sake, Holmes, use all the powers you have and spare no pains to lift the curse from this place, for life is becoming unendurable. Can you, with all your world-wide reputation, do nothing for us ?"

"I think I can, Stackhurst. Come with me now ! And you, Inspector, come along ! We will see if we cannot deliver this murderer into your hands."

Leaving the unconscious man in the charge of my housekeeper, we all three went down to the deadly lagoon. On the shingle there was piled a little heap of towels and clothes, left by the stricken man. Slowly I walked round the edge of the water, my comrades in Indian file behind me. Most of the pool was quite shallow, but under the cliff where the beach was hollowed out it was four or five feet deep. It was to this part that a swimmer would naturally go, for it formed a beautiful pellucid green pool as clear as crystal. A line of rocks lay above it at the base of the cliff, and along this I led the way, peering eagerly into the depths beneath me. I had reached the deepest and stillest pool when my eyes caught that for which they were searching, and I burst into a shout of triumph.

"Cyanea !" I cried. "Cyanea ! Behold the Lion's **8** Mane !"

The strange object at which I pointed did indeed look like a tangled mass torn from the mane of a lion. It lay upon a rocky shelf some three feet under the water, a curious waving, vibrating, hairy creature with streaks of silver among its yellow tresses. It pulsated with a slow, heavy dilation and contraction.

"It has done mischief enough. Its day is over !" I cried. "Help me, Stackhurst ! Let us end the murderer for ever."

There was a big boulder just above the ledge, and we pushed it until it fell with a tremendous splash into the water. When the ripples had cleared we saw that it had settled upon the ledge below. One flapping edge of yellow membrane showed that our victim was beneath it. A thick oily scum oozed out from below the stone and stained the water round, rising slowly to the surface.

"Well, this gets me !" cried the Inspector. "What was it, Mr. Holmes ? I'm born and bred in these parts, but I never saw such a thing. It don't belong to Sussex."

"Just as well for Sussex," I remarked. "It may have been the south-west gale that brought it up. Come

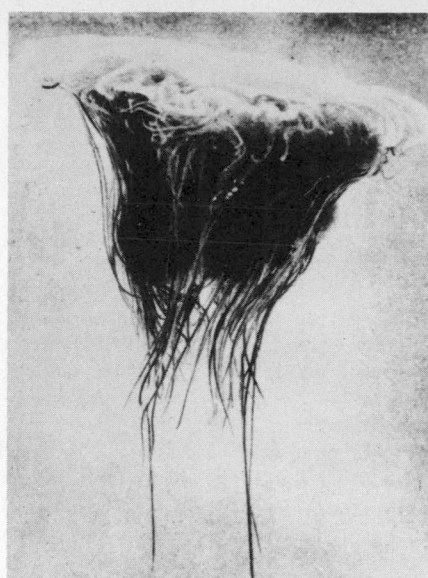

"BEHOLD THE LION'S MANE !"

A specimen of *Cyanea capillata*, or the lion's mane jellyfish. One was found to have tentacles of over 120 feet in length. The photograph is the copyright of Robert C. Hermes, and appeared in the Winter, 1963, issue of *The Sherlock Holmes Journal*.

8 "*Cyanea!*" *I cried.* "The acraspedote tetramerous medusan *Cyanea capillata*, popularly known by such names as 'hairy stinger,' 'sea nettle,' or 'lion's mane,' " Mr. Joel W. Hedgpeth wrote in his "Re-Examination of 'The Adventure of the Lion's Mane.' " "For those unfamiliar with the esoteric jargon of zoology it should be explained that 'acraspedote tetramerous medusan' means a simple bellshaped medusa (i.e., without a velum) whose principal organs are divided in fours. The medusa is actually the adult or sexual phase of a complicated life cycle and is produced from a sedentary hydra-like form by asexual budding. . . . Since the days of Edward Forbes, who called it 'the terror of tender skinned bathers' in his famous *Monograph of the Naked-Eyed Medusas* (published by the Ray Society in 1848) *Cyanea capillata* has been characterized as one of the more formidable creatures of the temperate seas. . . . The medical history of jellyfish stings, however, while recording some rather severe cases, is nevertheless more encouraging for those who may have misgivings about swimming in English and North Atlantic waters in general, for there is no recorded fatality that can be attributed solely to jellyfish poisoning in temperate waters." Mr. Hedgpeth added that "jellyfish do not usually sit on rocks" (see below—"It lay upon a rocky shelf") and that "another curious discrepancy is the discharge of oil, which can be explained at this late date only by the suggestion that the jellyfish was eating some oily fish, possibly a small shark, and the oil actually came from the shark."

But the editors of the Catalogue of the Sherlock Holmes Exhibition have cast some doubt on whether the jellyfish of "The Adventure of the Lion's Mane" was, in fact, *Cyanea capillata*. They suggest that it was the Portugese Man-of-War,

Physalia: "This complex creature is actually a colony—an aggregate of organisms acting in some ways as an individual; it is not a very close relative of the ordinary jellyfishes of which *Cyanea* is representative. It is, however, a far more formidable object to the bather. The tentacles of [a] relatively small specimen . . . might, when fully extended, reach to perhaps 50 feet from the float; and much larger specimens—such as the remarkable Atlantic form described by Haeckel under the name *Caravella*—are on record. It is typically an inhabitant of warmer waters, though, as Holmes suggested, it might well be driven on to the Sussex coast by a south-west gale; it is occasionally recorded off our southern shores. There seems little doubt, moreover, that a large specimen could kill even a healthy man; a specimen of no more than average size has been seen to kill and ingest a full-grown mackerel. . . ."

9 *the famous observer J. G. Wood.* The Reverend John George Wood, 1827–1889, was the author of nearly sixty books and of many popular articles, many of them for children. His great service was that he popularized the study of natural history. *Out of Doors: A Selection of Original Articles on Practical Natural History*, was published in London by Longmans, Green and Co. in 1874 and appeared in new editions in 1882 and 1890. "Undoubtedly [Wood] was particularly sensitive to the sting of the jellyfish," Mr. Hedgpeth noted, "for his account is by all odds the most harrowing in the literature of marine natural history." "It is quite likely that Holmes' obligation to [Wood] is even greater than has been acknowledged," Dr. Julian Wolff added in "Remember the Mane?", "since he was also the author of *Bees, Their Habits and Management*, published in 1853 by G. Routledge & Company of London."

10 *"And incidentally exonerates me," remarked Ian Murdoch.* "The possibility never seemed to have occurred to Holmes that this disarming young man . . . had secured a *Cyanea* in some manner and placed it in the tidepool with diabolical malice aforethought," Mr. Hedgpeth wrote. "Beyond all doubt this dark, brooding, 'ferocious tempered' young man, disappointed in love and capable of throwing innocent dogs through windows, had conceived a most ingenious crime and to allay suspicion had caressed his own monstrous pet. . . . It is most unlikely than an Airedale terrier would have succumbed to the sting of a jellyfish—its hair alone would protect it—and it seems evident that Murdoch poisoned the dog, for he was a man who did not like dogs, and placed its body in the pool where McPherson had met disaster, as a red herring."

back to my house, both of you, and I will give you the terrible experience of one who has good reason to remember his own meeting with the same peril of the seas."

When we reached my study, we found that Murdoch was so far recovered that he could sit up. He was dazed in mind, and every now and then was shaken by a paroxysm of pain. In broken words he explained that he had no notion what had occurred to him, save that terrific pangs had suddenly shot through him, and that it had taken all his fortitude to reach the bank.

"Here is a book," I said, taking up the little volume, "which first brought light into what might have been for ever dark. It is *Out of Doors*, by the famous observer **9** J. G. Wood. Wood himself very nearly perished from contact with this vile creature, so he wrote with a very full knowledge. *Cyanea Capillata* is the miscreant's full name, and he can be as dangerous to life as, and far more painful than, the bite of the cobra. Let me briefly give this extract.

" ' If the bather should see a loose roundish mass of tawny membranes and fibres, something like very large handfuls of lion's mane and silver paper, let him beware, for this is the fearful stinger, *Cyanea Capillata*.' Could our sinister acquaintance be more clearly described?

" He goes on to tell his own encounter with one when swimming off the coast of Kent. He found that the creature radiated almost invisible filaments to the distance of fifty feet, and that anyone within that circumference from the deadly centre was in danger of death. Even at a distance the effect upon Wood was almost fatal. ' The multitudinous threads caused light scarlet lines upon the skin which on closer examination resolved into minute dots or pustules, each dot charged as it were with a red-hot needle making its way through the nerves.'

" The local pain was, as he explains, the least part of the exquisite torment. ' Pangs shot through the chest, causing me to fall as if struck by a bullet. The pulsation would cease, and then the heart would give six or seven leaps as if it would force its way through the chest.'

" It nearly killed him, although he had only been exposed to it in the disturbed ocean and not in the narrow calm waters of a bathing-pool. He says that he could hardly recognize himself afterwards, so white, wrinkled and shrivelled was his face. He gulped down brandy, a whole bottleful, and it seems to have saved his life. There is the book, Inspector. I leave it with you, and you cannot doubt that it contains a full explanation of the tragedy of poor McPherson."

" And incidentally exonerates me," remarked Ian Mur**10** doch with a wry smile. " I do not blame you, Inspector, nor you, Mr. Holmes, for your suspicions were natural. I feel that on the very eve of my arrest I have only cleared myself by sharing the fate of my poor friend."

" No, Mr. Murdoch. I was already upon the track, and had I been out as early as I intended I might well have saved you from this terrific experience."

" But how did you know, Mr. Holmes?"

" I am an omnivorous reader with a strangely retentive memory for trifles. That phrase ' Lion's Mane ' haunted my mind. I knew that I had seen it somewhere in an unexpected context. You have seen that it does describe the creature. I have no doubt that it was floating on the water when McPherson saw it, and that this phrase was the only one by which he could convey to us a warning as to the creature which had been his death."

" Then I, at least, am cleared," said Murdoch, rising slowly to his feet. " There are one or two words of explanation which I should give, for I know the direction in which your inquiries have run. It is true that I loved this lady, but from the day when she chose my friend McPherson my one desire was to help her to happiness. I was well content to stand aside and act as their go-between. Often I carried their messages, and it was because I was in their confidence and because she was so dear to me that I hastened to tell her of my friend's death, lest someone should forestall me in a more sudden and heartless manner. She would not tell you, sir, of our relations lest you should disapprove and I might suffer. But with your leave I must try to get back to The Gables, for my bed will be very welcome."

Stackhurst held out his hand. " Our nerves have all been at concert-pitch," said he. " Forgive what is past, Murdoch. We shall understand each other better in the future." They passed out together with their arms linked in friendly fashion. The Inspector remained, staring at me in silence with his ox-like eyes.

" Well, you've done it ! " he cried at last. " I had read of you, but I never believed it. It's wonderful ! "

I was forced to shake my head. To accept such praise was to lower one's own standards.

" I was slow at the outset—culpably slow. Had **11** the body been found in the water I could hardly have missed it. It was the towel which misled me. The poor fellow had never thought to dry himself, and so I in turn was led to believe that he had never been in the water. Why, then, should the attack of any water creature suggest itself to me ? That was where I went astray. Well, well, Inspector, I often ventured to chaff you gentlemen of the police force, but *Cyanea Capillata* very nearly avenged Scotland Yard."

11 *"I was slow at the outset—culpably slow.* "Fi, fi, Sherlock!" Mr. Nathan L. Bengis wrote in "Sherlock Stays After School." "Even the 'gentlemen of the police force' should have seen through that one. You were more than 'culpably slow'— you were downright befuddled. . . . You should have known from the very first that McPherson had been in the water, and could not have been out of it by more than a very few minutes. How? By the very simplest of deductions. McPherson's body must still have been wet when you examined it. The lining of his Burberry overcoat must have been moist, as would also his hair. His canvas shoes, unlaced because he had not had time in his mortal agony to lace them, would certainly have shown a trace of moisture. That you should have failed to notice all these obvious signs that McPherson had just emerged from the water, and merely from the dryness of his towel should have jumped to the conclusion that he had not gone in, almost passes belief. What is quite incredible and unpardonable is your sorry attempt to exonerate yourself. Surely at least in retrospect the flimsiness of your excuse should have been apparent to you, and you should have been too ashamed of your performance to make a permanent record of it for future generations."

Auctorial Note: Conan Doyle barred all stories in the *Case-Book* from consideration when he compiled his "twelve best list" (these stories had not yet appeared in book form). He nonetheless is on record as having thought highly of "The Adventure of the Lion's Mane." In an early number of the *Sussex County Magazine* he was quoted as saying: "I have done three new Sherlock Holmes stories for the *Strand*. I don't think they show any falling off. In fact, one of them 'The Lion's Mane,' I should put in the front row. But that is for the public to judge." Later (in the *Strand Magazine* for March, 1927) Conan Doyle wrote: "The [story] is hampered by being told by Holmes himself, a method which . . . certainly cramps the narrative. On the other hand, the actual plot is among the very best of the whole series."

THE OFFICES OF THE STRAND MAGAZINE

Said the *Strand* in a description of its own offices: "Its fine, broad front, wherein the architect has with a just hand distributed the red brick and white stone in the parts above the stone ground floor, stretches through four numbers on the right-hand side [of Southampton Street], and the building is carried, in depth, through to Exeter Street . . . A handsome, triple entrance stands between large plate-glass windows. . . ."

X. AN EPILOGUE OF SHERLOCK HOLMES

"But you had retired, Holmes. We heard of you as living the life of a hermit among your bees and your books in a small farm upon the South Downs."

—John H Watson, M.D., "His Last Bow."

79

HIS LAST BOW

[Sunday, August 2, 1914]

1 *the second of August.* The year was of course 1914: "Well, I chose August for the word, and 1914 for the figures, and here we are," Von Bork says later. August 2, 1914, fell on a Sunday. "His Last Bow" is the second of the two Sherlock Holmes adventures recounted by "a third person," although "it is difficult," as Mr. S. C. Roberts wrote in *Doctor Watson,* "to believe that the opening passage is not taken verbatim from Watson's notes." The late A. Carson Simpson has held that Holmes himself was the author, but the late Edgar W. Smith argued ("The Adventure of the Veiled Author") that only Mycroft Holmes could have transcribed the tale.

2 *had perched himself four years before* ". . . there is evidence, I think, that the seaside gabled house which was the headquarters of Von Bork . . . was on the South Coast," Mr. Gordon Sewell wrote in "Holmes and Watson in the South Country." "Watson writes of it being perched on a cliff. Dover, perhaps? Too conspicuous, surely. Cornwall? Too remote. Von Bork was interested in naval matters, and he would have chosen a residence somewhere within easy distance of both Portland and Portsmouth. . . . What more likely place than Studland, a discreet hideout for the master spy?"

1 IT was nine o'clock at night upon the second of August —the most terrible August in the history of the world. One might have thought already that God's curse hung heavy over a degenerate world, for there was an awesome hush and a feeling of vague expectancy in the sultry and stagnant air. The sun had long set, but one blood-red gash like an open wound lay low in the distant west. Above, the stars were shining brightly ; and below, the lights of the shipping glimmered in the bay. The two famous Germans stood beside the stone parapet of the garden walk, with the long, low, heavily gabled house behind them, and they looked down upon the broad sweep of the beach at the foot of the great chalk cliff on which Von Bork, like some wandering eagle, had perched himself **2** four years before. They stood with their heads close together, talking in low, confidential tones. From below the two glowing ends of their cigars might have been the smouldering eyes of some malignant fiend looking down in the darkness.

A remarkable man this Von Bork—a man who could hardly be matched among all the devoted agents of the Kaiser. It was his talents which had first recommended him for the English mission, the most important mission of all, but since he had taken it over, those talents had become more and more manifest to the half-dozen people in the world who were really in touch with the truth. One of these was his present companion, Baron Von Herling, the chief secretary of the legation, whose huge 100-horse-power Benz car was blocking the country lane as it waited to waft its owner back to London.

" So far as I can judge the trend of events, you will probably be back in Berlin within the week," the secretary was saying. " When you get there, my dear Von Bork, I think you will be surprised at the welcome you will receive. I happen to know what is thought in the highest quarters of your work in this country." He was a huge man, the secretary, deep, broad, and tall, with a slow, heavy fashion of speech which had been his main asset in his political career.

Von Bork laughed.

" They are not very hard to deceive," he remarked.

"A more docile, simple folk could not be imagined."

"I don't know about that," said the other thoughtfully. "They have strange limits and one must learn to observe them. It is that surface simplicity of theirs which makes a trap for the stranger. One's first impression is that they are entirely soft. Then one comes suddenly upon something very hard and you know that you have reached the limit, and must adapt yourself to the fact. They have, for example, their insular conventions which simply *must* be observed."

"Meaning, 'good form' and that sort of thing?" Von Bork sighed, as one who had suffered much.

"Meaning British prejudice in all its queer manifestations. As an example I may quote one of my own worst blunders—I can afford to talk of my blunders, for you know my work well enough to be aware of my successes. It was on my first arrival. I was invited to a week-end gathering at the country house of a Cabinet Minister. The conversation was amazingly indiscreet."

Von Bork nodded. "I've been there," said he dryly.

"Exactly. Well, I naturally sent a résumé of the information to Berlin. Unfortunately our good Chancellor is a little heavy-handed in these matters, and he transmitted a remark which showed that he was aware of what had been said. This, of course, took the trail straight up to me. You've no idea the harm that it did me. There was nothing soft about our British hosts on that occasion, I can assure you. I was two years living it down. Now you, with this sporting pose of yours."

"No, no, don't call it a pose. A pose is an artificial thing. This is quite natural. I am a born sportsman. I enjoy it."

"Well, that makes it the more effective. You yacht against them, you hunt with them, you play polo, you match them in every game, your four-in-hand takes the **3** prize at Olympia. I have even heard that you go the **4** length of boxing with the young officers. What is the result? Nobody takes you seriously. You are a 'good old sport,' 'quite a decent fellow for a German,' a hard-drinking, night-club, knock-about-town, devil-may-care young fellow. And all the time this quiet country house of yours is the centre of half the mischief in England, and the sporting squire the most astute Secret Service man in Europe. Genius, my dear Von Bork—genius!"

"You flatter me, Baron. But certainly I may claim that my four years in this country have not been unproductive. I've never shown you my little store. Would you mind stepping in for a moment?"

The door of the study opened straight on to the terrace. Von Bork pushed it back, and, leading the way, he clicked the switch of the electric light. He then closed the door behind the bulky form which followed him, and carefully adjusted the heavy curtain over the latticed window. Only when all these precautions had been taken and tested did he turn his sunburned aquiline face to his guest.

"Some of my papers have gone," said he; "when my wife and the household left yesterday for Flushing they took the less important with them. I must, of course, claim the protection of the Embassy for the others."

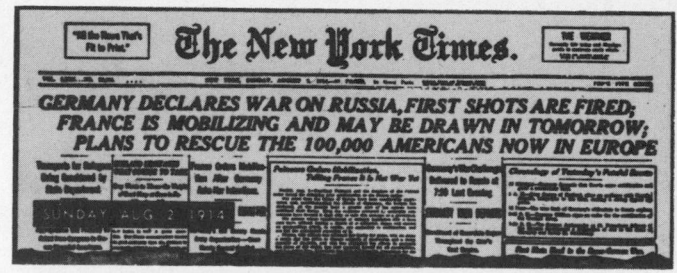

. . . THE MOST TERRIBLE AUGUST IN THE HISTORY OF THE WORLD.

Headlines from the New York *Times* on Sunday, August 2, 1914—the day of Holmes' last recorded adventure.

3 *your four-in-hand*. A four-horse team driven by one person.

4 *Olympia*. Olympia, which is situated on the north side of the Hammersmith Road, adjoining the West London Railway, was erected in 1886 by the National Agricultural Hall Company. The original buildings had an area of four acres. The grand hall, two and a half acres in extent, is one of the largest in the kingdom, and is covered by one span of iron and glass 450 feet long by 250 feet wide. The Horse Show was indeed held at the Olympia.

"Your name has already been filed as one of the personal suite. There will be no difficulties for you or your baggage. Of course, it is just possible that we may not have to go. England may leave France to her fate. We are sure that there is no binding treaty between them."

"And Belgium?"

"Yes, and Belgium, too."

Von Bork shook his head. "I don't see how that could be. There is a definite treaty there. She could never recover from such a humiliation."

"She would at least have peace for the moment."

"But her honour?"

"Tut, my dear sir, we live in a utilitarian age. Honour is a mediæval conception. Besides England is not ready. It is an inconceivable thing, but even our special war tax of fifty millions, which one would think made our purpose as clear as if we had advertised it on the front page of *The Times*, has not roused these people from their slumbers. Here and there one hears a question. It is my business to find an answer. Here and there also there is an irritation. It is my business to soothe it. But I can assure you that so far as the essentials go—the storage of munitions, the preparation for submarine attack, the arrangements for making high explosives—nothing is prepared. How then can England come in, especially when we have stirred her up such a devil's brew of Irish civil war, window-breaking Furies, and God knows what to keep her thoughts at home?"

"She must think of her future."

"Ah, that is another matter. I fancy that in the future, we have our own very definite plans about England, and that your information will be very vital to us. It is to-day or to-morrow with Mr. John Bull. If he prefers to-day we are perfectly ready. If it is to-morrow we shall be more ready still. I should think they would be wiser to fight with allies than without them, but that is their own affair. This week is their week of destiny. But you were speaking of your papers." He sat in the arm-chair with the light shining upon his broad bald head, while he puffed sedately at his cigar.

The large oak-panelled book-lined room had a curtain hung in the further corner. When this was drawn it disclosed a large brass-bound safe. Von Bork detached a small key from his watch-chain, and after some considerable manipulation of the lock he swung open the heavy door.

"Look!" said he, standing clear, with a wave of his hand.

The light shone vividly into the opened safe, and the secretary of the Embassy gazed with an absorbed interest at the rows of stuffed pigeon-holes with which it was furnished. Each pigeon-hole had its label, and his eyes as he glanced along them read a long series of such titles as "Fords," "Harbour-defences," "Aeroplanes," "Ireland," "Egypt," "Portsmouth forts," "The Channel," "Rosyth," and a score of others. Each compartment was bristling with papers and plans.

"Colossal!" said the secretary. Putting down his cigar he softly clapped his fat hands.

5 *This week is their week of destiny.* Headlines from *The New York Times:* (Monday, August 3) RUSSIA INVADES GERMANY; GERMANY INVADES FRANCE, BUT DOES NOT DECLARE WAR; ENGLAND'S DECISION TO-DAY; BELGIUM MENACED, LUXEMBURG AND SWITZERLAND INVADED; GERMAN MARKSMEN SHOOT DOWN A FRENCH AEROPLANE. (Tuesday, August 4) ENGLAND WILL PROTECT FRENCH COAST AND DEFEND BELGIUM; GERMANY RECALLS ENVOY; HESITATES AT FRENCH FRONTIER; HER ARMY SEIZES RUSSIAN TOWNS, NAVY WINS A VICTORY; GERMAN LINER SLIPS OUT OF NEW YORK IN WAR PAINT. (Wednesday, August 5) ENGLAND DECLARES WAR ON GERMANY; BRITISH SHIP SUNK; FRENCH SHIPS DEFEAT GERMAN, BELGIUM ATTACKED; 17,000,000 MEN ENGAGED IN GREAT WAR OF EIGHT NATIONS; GREAT ENGLISH AND GERMAN ARMIES ABOUT TO GRAPPLE; RIVAL WARSHIPS OFF THIS PORT AS LUSITANIA SAILS. (Thursday, August 6) BELGIANS DEFEAT GERMANS, KILL OR WOUND 3,500 MEN; BRITISH THIRD FLOTILLA HAS A BATTLE IN THE NORTH SEA; RUSSIANS DRIVE OUT THE GERMANS AND ENTER PRUSSIA; GERMANY SAID TO HAVE SENT AN ULTIMATUM TO ITALY. (Friday, August 7) GERMAN FLEET SWEPT DOWN NORTH SEA TO DUTCH COAST IN GREAT GENERAL ENGAGEMENT, WON BY THE ENGLISH; BRITISH CRUISER AMPHION IS SUNK BY A MINE, 131 LOST; GERMANS TAKE 2 FORTS AT LIEGE; FRENCH ARMY COMING.

" And all in four years, Baron.   Not such a bad show for the hard-drinking, hard-riding country squire.   But the gem of my collection is coming and there is the setting all ready for it."   He pointed to a space over which " Naval Signals " was printed.

" But you have a good dossier there already."

" Out of date and waste paper.   The Admiralty in some way got the alarm and every code has been changed.   It was a blow, Baron—the worst set-back in my whole campaign.   But thanks to my cheque-book and the good Altamont all will be well to-night."

The Baron looked at his watch, and gave a guttural exclamation of disappointment.

" Well, I really can wait no longer.   You can imagine that things are moving at present in Carlton Terrace and **6** that we have all to be at our posts.   I had hoped to be able to bring news of your great coup.   Did Altamont name no hour ? "

Von Bork pushed over a telegram.

" Will come without fail to-night and bring new sparking plugs.—ALTAMONT."

" Sparking plugs, eh ? "

" You see he poses as a motor expert and I keep a full garage.   In our code everything likely to come up is named after some spare part.   If he talks of a radiator it is a battleship, of an oil-pump a cruiser, and so on.   Sparking plugs are naval signals."

" From Portsmouth at midday," said the secretary, examining the superscription.   " By the way, what do you give him ? "

" Five hundred pounds for this particular job.   Of course he has a salary as well."

" The greedy rogue.   They are useful, these traitors, but I grudge them their blood-money."

" I grudge Altamont nothing.   He is a wonderful worker.   If I pay him well, at least he delivers the goods, to use his own phrase.   Besides he is not a traitor.   I assure you that our most pan-Germanic Junker is a sucking dove in his feelings towards England as compared with a real bitter Irish-American."

" Oh, an Irish-American ? "

" If you heard him talk you would not doubt it.   Sometimes I assure you I can hardly understand him.   He seems to have declared war on the King's English as well as on the English King.   Must you really go ?   He may be here any moment."

" No.   I'm sorry, but I have already overstayed my time.   We shall expect you early to-morrow, and when you get that signal-book through the little door on the Duke of York's steps you can put a triumphant Finis to **7** your record in England.   What !   Tokay ! "   He indicated a heavily sealed dust-covered bottle which stood with two high glasses upon a salver.

" May I offer you a glass before your journey ? "

" No, thanks.   But it looks like revelry."

" Altamont has a nice taste in wines, and he took a fancy to my Tokay.   He is a touchy fellow, and needs

6 *Carlton Terrace*. Then the site of the German Embassy and Consulate, located in the house adjoining, on the west, the Duke of York's steps.

7 *the Duke of York's steps*. The steps made of granite, quarried in the Island of Herm, near Guernsey, which form the base of the Duke of York's Column. This column was erected by public subscription to the memory of Frederick, Duke of York, second son of George III, at a cost of £25,000. The column is 124 feet high and is surmounted by a bronze statue fourteen feet high. It contains a gallery which at one time was open to the public during the summer months.

8 *Harwich*. A seaport in Essex, England.

9 *Zeppelin*. Ferdinand A. A. H., Count Von Zeppelin, 1838–1917, inventor and builder of the dirigible airship—essentially a controllable balloon —capable of long-range flights and used by the Germans in World War I for the bombing of Britain.

humouring in small things.   I have to study him, I assure you."   They had strolled out on to the terrace again, and along it to the further end where at a touch from the Baron's chauffeur the great car shivered and chuckled.   " Those

8 are the lights of Harwich, I suppose," said the secretary, pulling on his dust coat.   " How still and peaceful it all seems.   There may be other lights within the week, and the English coast a less tranquil place !   The heavens, too,

9 may not be quite so peaceful if all that the good Zeppelin promises us comes true.   By the way, who is that ? "

Only one window showed a light behind them ; in it there stood a lamp, and beside it, seated at a table, was a dear old ruddy-faced woman in a country cap.   She was bending over her knitting and stopping occasionally to stroke a large black cat upon a stool beside her.

" That is Martha, the only servant I have left."

The secretary chuckled.

" She might almost personify Britannia," said he, " with her complete self-absorption and general air of comfortable somnolence.   Well, au revoir, Von Bork ! "—with a final wave of his hand he sprang into the car, and a moment later the two golden cones from the headlights shot forward through the darkness.   The secretary lay back in the cushions of the luxurious limousine, with his thoughts so full of the impending European tragedy that he hardly observed that as his car swung round the village street it nearly passed over a little Ford coming in the opposite direction.

Von Bork walked slowly back to the study when the last gleams of the motor lamps had faded into the distance. As he passed he observed that his old housekeeper had put out her lamp and retired.   It was a new experience to him, the silence and darkness of his widespread house, for his family and household had been a large one.   It was a relief to him, however, to think that they were all in safety and that, but for that one old woman who had lingered in the kitchen, he had the whole place to himself.   There was a good deal of tidying up to do inside his study and he set himself to do it, until his keen, handsome face was flushed with the heat of the burning papers.   A leather valise stood beside his table, and into this he began to pack very neatly and systematically the precious contents of his safe.   He had hardly got started with the work, however, when his quick ears caught the sound of a distant car. Instantly he gave an exclamation of satisfaction, strapped up the valise, shut the safe, locked it, and hurried out on to the terrace.   He was just in time to see the lights of a small car come to a halt at the gate.   A passenger sprang out and advanced swiftly towards him, while the chauffeur, a heavily built, elderly man, with a grey moustache, settled down, like one who resigns himself to a long vigil.

" Well ? " asked Von Bork eagerly, running forward to meet his visitor.

For answer the man waved a small brown-paper parcel triumphantly above his head.

" You can give me the glad hand to-night, Mister," he cried.   " I'm bringing home the bacon at last."

" The signals ? "

" Same as I said in my cable.   Every last one of them,

semaphore, lamp code, Marconi—a copy, mind you, not
the original. That was too dangerous. But it's the real
goods, and you can lay to that." He slapped the German
upon the shoulder with a rough familiarity from which the
other winced.

"Come in," he said. "I'm all alone in the house. I
was only waiting for this. Of course a copy is better than
the original. If an original were missing they would
change the whole thing. You think it's all safe about the
copy ? "

The Irish-American had entered the study and stretched
his long limbs from the arm-chair. He was a tall, gaunt
man of sixty, with clear-cut features and a small goatee
beard which gave him a general resemblance to the carica-
tures of Uncle Sam. A half-smoked, sodden cigar hung
from the corner of his mouth, and as he sat down he struck
a match and relit it. "Making ready for a move ? " he
remarked as he looked round him. "Say, Mister," he
added, as his eyes fell upon the safe from which the curtain
was now removed, "you don't tell me you keep your
papers in that ? "

"Why not ? "

"Gosh, in a wide-open contraption like that ! And
they reckon you to be some spy. Why a Yankee crook
would be into that with a can-opener. If I'd known that
any letter of mine was goin' to lie loose in a thing like that
I'd have been a mug to write to you at all."

"It would puzzle any crook to force that safe," Von
Bork answered. "You won't cut that metal with any
tool."

"But the lock ? "

"No, it's a double combination lock. You know what
that is ? "

"Search me," said the American.

"Well, you need a word as well as a set of figures before
you can get the lock to work." He rose and showed a
double-radiating disc round the keyhole. "This outer
one is for the letters, the inner one for the figures."

"Well, well, that's fine."

"So it's not quite as simple as you thought. It was
four years ago that I had it made, and what do you think I
chose for the word and figures ? "

"It's beyond me."

"Well, I chose August for the word, and 1914 for the
figures, and here we are."

The American's face showed his surprise and admiration.

"My, but that was smart ! You had it down to a fine
thing."

"Yes, a few of us even then could have guessed the
date. Here it is, and I'm shutting down to-morrow
morning."

"Well, I guess you'll have to fix me up also. I'm not
staying in this goldarned country all on my lonesome.
In a week or less from what I see, John Bull will be on his
hind legs and fair ramping. I'd rather watch him from
over the water."

"But you're an American citizen ? "

"Well, so was Jack James an American citizen, but he's

HE WAS A TALL, GAUNT MAN OF SIXTY, WITH CLEAR-
CUT FEATURES AND A SMALL GOATEE BEARD . . .

Cover illustration by Frederic Dorr Steele for
Collier's Magazine, September 22, 1917.

10 *Portland*. In the stone quarries of the Isle of Portland, in Dorsetshire.

10 doing time in Portland all the same. It cuts no ice with a British copper to tell him you're an American citizen. ' It's British law and order over here,' says he. By the way, Mister, talking of Jack James, it seems to me you don't do much to cover your men."

" What do you mean ? " Von Bork asked sharply.

" Well, you are their employer, ain't you ? It's up to you to see that they don't fall down. But they do fall down, and when did you ever pick them up ? There's James——"

" It was James' own fault. You know that yourself. He was too self-willed for the job."

" James was a bonehead—I give you that. Then there was Hollis."

" The man was mad."

" Well, he went a bit woozy towards the end. It's enough to make a man bughouse when he has to play a part from morning to night with a hundred guys all ready to set the coppers wise to him. But now there is Steiner ——"

Von Bork started violently, and his ruddy face turned a shade paler.

" What about Steiner ? "

" Well, they've got him, that's all. They raided his store last night, and he and his papers are all in Portsmouth gaol. You'll go off and he, poor devil, will have to stand the racket, and lucky if he gets off with his life. That's why I want to get over the water as soon as you do."

Von Bork was a strong, self-contained man, but it was easy to see that the news had shaken him.

" How could they have got on to Steiner ? " he muttered. " That's the worst blow yet."

" Well, you nearly had a worse one, for I believe they are not far off me."

" You don't mean that ! "

" Sure thing. My landlady down Fratton way had some inquiries, and when I heard of it I guessed it was time for me to hustle. But what I want to know, Mister, is how the coppers know these things ? Steiner is the fifth man you've lost since I signed on with you, and I know the name of the sixth if I don't get a move on. How do you explain it, and ain't you ashamed to see your men go down like this ? "

Von Bork flushed crimson.

" How dare you speak in such a way ! "

" If I didn't dare things, Mister, I wouldn't be in your service. But I'll tell you straight what is in my mind. I've heard that with you German politicians when an agent has done his work you are not sorry to see him put away."

Von Bork sprang to his feet.

" Do you dare to suggest that I have given away my own agents ! "

" I don't stand for that, Mister, but there's a stool pigeon or a cross somewhere, and it's up to you to find out where it is. Anyhow I am taking no more chances. It's me for little Holland, and the sooner the better."

Von Bork had mastered his anger.

" We have been allies too long to quarrel now at the very hour of victory," he said. " You've done splendid work and taken risks and I can't forget it. By all means go to

"IF I DIDN'T DARE THINGS, MISTER, I WOULDN'T BE IN YOUR SERVICE."

Illustration by Frederic Dorr Steele for *Collier's Magazine*, September 22, 1917.

Holland, and you can get a boat from Rotterdam to New York. No other line will be safe a week from now. I'll take that book and pack it with the rest."

The American held the small parcel in his hand, but made no motion to give it up.

" What about the dough ? " he asked.

" The what ? "

" The boodle. The reward. The £500. The gunner turned damned nasty at the last, and I had to square him with an extra hundred dollars or it would have been nitsky for you and me. ' Nothin' doin' ! ' says he, and he meant it too, but the last hundred did it. It's cost me two hundred pound from first to last, so it isn't likely I'd give it up without gettin' my wad."

Von Bork smiled with some bitterness. " You don't seem to have a very high opinion of my honour," said he, " you want the money before you give up the book."

" Well, Mister, it is a business proposition."

" All right. Have your way." He sat down at the table and scribbled a cheque, which he tore from the book, but he refrained from handing it to his companion. " After all, since we are to be on such terms, Mr. Altamont," said he, " I don't see why I should trust you any more than you trust me. Do you understand ? " he added, looking back over his shoulder at the American. " There's the cheque upon the table. I claim the right to examine that parcel before you pick the money up."

The American passed it over without a word. Von Bork undid a winding of string and two wrappers of paper. Then he sat gazing for a moment in silent amazement at a small blue book which lay before him. Across the cover was printed in golden letters *Practical Handbook of Bee Culture*. Only for one instant did the master spy glare at this strangely irrelevant inscription. The next he was gripped at the back of his neck by a grasp of iron, and a chloroformed sponge was held in front of his writhing face.

" Another glass, Watson ! " said Mr. Sherlock Holmes, **11** as he extended the bottle of Imperial Tokay.

The thick-set chauffeur, who had seated himself by the table, pushed forward his glass with some eagerness.

" It is a good wine, Holmes."

" A remarkable wine, Watson. Our friend upon the sofa has assured me that it is from Franz Joseph's special cellar at the Schoenbrunn Palace. Might I trouble you to open the window, for chloroform vapour does not help the palate."

The safe was ajar, and Holmes standing in front of it was removing dossier after dossier, swiftly examining each, and then packing it neatly in Von Bork's valise. The German lay upon the sofa sleeping stertorously with a strap round his upper arms and another round his legs.

" We need not hurry ourselves, Watson. We are safe from interruption. Would you mind touching the bell. There is no one in the house except old Martha, who has played her part to admiration. I got her the situation here when first I took the matter up. Ah, Martha, you will be glad to hear that all is well."

The pleasant old lady had appeared in the doorway. She curtseyed with a smile to Mr. Holmes, but glanced

11 *"Another glass, Watson!"* ". . . it might be thought," the late Edgar W. Smith wrote in "On the Forms of Address," that "as the years wore on and the laxities of the approaching Edwardian age impinged upon the inhibiting Victorian strictures, [Holmes and Watson might address each other as] 'John' and 'Sherlock.' . . . But no—in 1914, when they had shared each others' lives for a full thirty-five years, we find them still ingrained in their old habit."

Elsewhere (in "Dr. Watson and the Great Censorship") Mr. Smith wrote: "It is interesting to speculate . . . that even as Watson was sitting . . . in Von Bork's parlor on that fateful August 2nd, with the war-clouds looming heavy in the east, he may have had in his breast-pocket at that very moment, ready for mailing, the manuscript of *The Valley of Fear*—for that long novel out of the past began to run in the *Strand* just a month later."

And Mr. Anthony Boucher, in his introduction to *The Final Adventures of Sherlock Holmes, Vol. 1 (The Valley of Fear)* has written: "In the very year in which *The Valley of Fear* was published [1914], Holmes was completing a case in which he precisely adopted the methods of Birdy Edwards. In order to learn the secrets of a nefarious organization, he changed his name, cut himself loose from all ties, . . . seemed one of the most dangerous and active men in the organization, while slyly seeing to it that all its plans went awry, and finally upset the whole apple-cart immediately after discussing with the top man the terrible possibility that 'there's a stool-pigeon or a cross somewhere.'"

. . . HE WAS GRIPPED AT THE BACK OF HIS NECK BY A GRASP OF IRON . . .

Illustration by A. Gilbert for the *Strand Magazine*, September, 1917.

12 *His car passed ours.*" In the *Strand Magazine* version of "His Last Bow," Holmes says here: "I know. His car passed ours. But for your excellent driving, Watson, we should have been the very type of Europe under the Prussian Juggernaut."

13 *the Solent.* A strait, varying from two to five miles wide, between the Isle of Wight and Hampshire.

14 *You look the same blithe boy as ever.*" "A remarkable tribute," Mr. S. C. Roberts wrote in *Doctor Watson*, "to an old campaigner of sixty-two."

with some apprehension at the figure upon the sofa.

" It is all right, Martha.   He has not been hurt at all."

" I am glad of that, Mr. Holmes.   According to his lights he has been a kind master.   He wanted me to go with his wife to Germany yesterday, but that would hardly have suited your plans, would it, sir ? "

" No, indeed, Martha.   So long as you were here I was easy in my mind.   We waited some time for your signal to-night."

" It was the secretary, sir."

12   " I know.   His car passed ours."

" I thought he would never go.   I knew that it would not suit your plans, sir, to find him here."

" No, indeed.   Well, it only meant that we waited half an hour or so until I saw your lamp go out and knew that the coast was clear.   You can report to me to-morrow in London, Martha, at Claridge's Hotel."

" Very good, sir."

" I suppose you have everything ready to leave."

" Yes, sir.   He posted seven letters to-day.   I have the addresses as usual."

" Very good, Martha.   I will look into them to-morrow. Good night.   These papers," he continued, as the old lady vanished, " are not of very great importance, for, of course, the information which they represent has been sent off long ago to the German Government.   These are the originals which could not safely be got out of the country."

" Then they are of no use."

" I should not go so far as to say that, Watson.   They will at least show our people what is known and what is not.   I may say that a good many of these papers have come through me, and I need not add are thoroughly untrustworthy.   It would brighten my declining years to

13 see a German cruiser navigating the Solent according to the minefield plans which I have furnished.   But you, Watson," he stopped his work and took his old friend by the shoulders ; " I've hardly seen you in the light yet. How have the years used you ?   You look the same blithe

14 boy as ever."

" I feel twenty years younger, Holmes.   I have seldom felt so happy as when I got your wire asking me to meet you at Harwich with the car.   But you, Holmes—you have changed very little—save for that horrible goatee."

" These are the sacrifices one makes for one's country, Watson," said Holmes, pulling at his little tuft.   " To-morrow it will be but a dreadful memory.   With my hair cut and a few other superficial changes I shall no doubt reappear at Claridge's to-morrow as I was before this American stunt—I beg your pardon, Watson, my well of English seems to be permanently defiled—before this American job came my way."

" But you had retired, Holmes.   We heard of you as living the life of a hermit among your bees and your books in a small farm upon the South Downs."

" Exactly, Watson.   Here is the fruit of my leisured ease, the *magnum opus* of my latter years ! "   He picked up the volume from the table and read out the whole title, *Practical Handbook of Bee Culture, with some Observations upon the Segregation of the Queen.*   Alone I did it.   Behold the fruit of pensive nights and laborious days, when I watched the little working gangs as once I watched the criminal world of London."

" But how did you get to work again ? "

" Ah, I have often marvelled at it myself. The Foreign Minister alone I could have withstood, but when the Premier also deigned to visit my humble roof——! The **15** fact is, Watson, that this gentleman upon the sofa was a bit too good for our people. He was in a class by himself. Things were going wrong, and no one could understand why they were going wrong. Agents were suspected or even caught, but there was evidence of some strong and secret central force. It was absolutely necessary to expose it. Strong pressure was brought upon me to look into the matter. It has cost me two years, Watson, but they have not been devoid of excitement. When I say that I started my pilgrimage at Chicago, graduated in an Irish secret society at Buffalo, gave serious trouble to the constabulary at Skibbareen and so eventually caught the eye of a subordinate agent of Von Bork, who recommended me as a **16** likely man, you will realize that the matter was complex. Since then I have been honoured by his confidence, which has not prevented most of his plans going subtly wrong and five of his best agents being in prison. I watched them, Watson, and I picked them as they ripened. Well, sir, I hope that you are none the worse ! "

The last remark was addressed to Von Bork himself, who after much gasping and blinking had lain quietly listening to Holmes' statement. He broke out now into a furious stream of German invective, his face convulsed with passion. Holmes continued his swift investigation of documents while his prisoner cursed and swore.

" Though unmusical, German is the most expressive of all languages," he observed, when Von Bork had stopped from pure exhaustion. " Hullo ! Hullo ! " he added, as he looked hard at the corner of a tracing before putting it in the box. " This should put another bird in the cage. I had no idea that the paymaster was such a rascal, though I have long had an eye upon him. Mister Von Bork, you have a great deal to answer for."

The prisoner had raised himself with some difficulty upon the sofa and was staring with a strange mixture of amazement and hatred at his captor.

" I shall get level with you, Altamont," he said, speaking with slow deliberation, " if it takes me all my life I shall get level with you ! "

" The old sweet song," said Holmes. " How often have I heard it in days gone by. It was a favourite ditty of the late lamented Professor Moriarty. Colonel Sebastian Moran has also been known to warble it. And yet I live and keep bees upon the South Downs."

" Curse you, you double traitor ! " cried the German, straining against his bonds and glaring murder from his furious eyes.

" No, no, it is not so bad as that," said Holmes, smiling. " As my speech surely shows you, Mr. Altamont of Chicago had no existence in fact. I used him and he is gone."

" Then who are you ? "

" It is really immaterial who I am, but since the matter seems to interest you, Mr. Von Bork, I may say that this is not my first acquaintance with the members of your

15 *the Premier also deigned to visit my humble roof——!* Holmes allowed Prime Minister Herbert Henry Asquith, Earl of Oxford and Asquith, 1852–1928, Prime Minister of England, 1908–1916, to persuade him to forsake his bees, though he might have withstood Sir Edward Grey, Viscount Grey of Fallodon, 1862–1933, Foreign Minister, 1905–1916.

16 *and so eventually caught the eye of a subordinate agent of Von Bork.* Mr. Donald Hayne has written: ". . . obviously [Holmes] would need some time to prepare himself for the pilgrimage properly so-called, in some quiet place where, with some plausible excuse for staying there, he could unobtrusively acquire an American accent and an American wardrobe while waiting for the propitious moment to appear among the crooks of Chicago. The Foreign Office would of course arrange for his secret debarkation at a Canadian port, to avoid the American ships news reporters, and in 1912, I imagine, he could easily have been spirited into New York State. The investigator of Chaldean roots in the ancient Cornish dialect was certainly philologist enough to know that the standard American accent is derived from the New England hill accent which passes across central New York to the Middle West. Sigerson, the explorer, would find both interest and ostensible purpose in studying the ancient and significant geological formations in the Helderberg Mountains near Albany. Mr. Holmes would want to be near a city the size

"CURSE YOU, YOU DOUBLE TRAITOR!" CRIED THE GERMAN . . .

Illustration by A. Gilbert for the *Strand Magazine,* September, 1917. Frederic Dorr Steele illustrated the same scene for *Collier's Magazine,* September 22, 1917.

of Albany, to shop for his wardrobe, etc., but would prefer actually residing in a much smaller place, where he could, for his linguistic and sociological purposes, mingle more familiarly with all types and strata of people. A middle class summer resort (he came, presumably, in July, 1912) where strangers were coming and going every week, would be ideal. All this adds up—elementarily—to the town of *Altamont*, New York; and was it not a gracious gesture on the Master's part, and a sign that he enjoyed that summer's peace before starting on his arduous pilgrimage in the service of the Empire, that he took as his own the name of the village and bore it for two years . . . ?"

On the other hand, Mr. Willis B. Wood has suggested (in "Sherlock in Kansas") that Holmes took his alias in memory of a station on the Frisco Railroad between Joplin, Missouri, and Wichita, Kansas. He reminds us that Mr. Christopher Morley suggested 1876 as a year when Holmes journeyed to America, and he further suggests that Holmes ventured into the American West at that time.

It is also worth noting—as did Mrs. Crighton Sellars (in verse) in "Altamont," that both Thackeray and Scott chose "Altamont" as the name for their villains (Thackeray in *Pendennis*, Scott in *The Pirate*)—"so the idea appealed to our Sherlock at once."

To these fascinating speculations should be added the fact that the full name of Conan Doyle's father was Charles *Altamont* Doyle.

17 *still bound hand and foot.* "Gentlemen," Mr. John V. L. Hogan has asked, "if you will explain to me how a man 'bound hand and foot' can be 'walked' anywhere, I shall be duly grateful."

FINALLY, HOLDING EITHER ARM, THE TWO FRIENDS WALKED HIM VERY SLOWLY DOWN THE GARDEN WALK . . .

Illustration by A. Gilbert for the *Strand Magazine*, September, 1917.

family. I have done a good deal of business in Germany in the past, and my name is probably familiar to you."

" I would wish to know it," said the Prussian grimly.

" It was I who brought about the separation between Irene Adler and the late King of Bohemia when your cousin Heinrich was the Imperial Envoy. It was I also who saved from murder, by the Nihilist Klopman, Count Von und Zu Grafenstein, who was your mother's elder brother. It was I——"

Von Bork sat up in amazement.

" There is only one man," he cried.

" Exactly," said Holmes.

Von Bork groaned and sank back on the sofa. " And most of that information came through you," he cried. " What is it worth ? What have I done ? It is my ruin for ever ! "

" It is certainly a little untrustworthy," said Holmes. " It will require some checking, and you have little time to check it. Your admiral may find the new guns rather larger than he expects, and the cruisers perhaps a trifle faster."

Von Bork clutched at his own throat in despair.

" There are a good many other points of detail which will, no doubt, come to light in good time. But you have one quality which is very rare in a German, Mr. Von Bork, you are a sportsman and you will bear me no ill-will when you realize that you, who have outwitted so many other people, have at last been outwitted yourself. After all, you have done your best for your country, and I have done my best for mine, and what could be more natural ? Besides," he added, not unkindly, as he laid his hand upon the shoulder of the prostrate man, " it is better than to fall before some more ignoble foe. These papers are now ready, Watson. If you will help me with our prisoner, I think that we may get started for London at once."

It was no easy task to move Von Bork, for he was a strong and a desperate man. Finally, holding either arm, the two friends walked him very slowly down the garden walk which he had trod with such proud confidence when he received the congratulations of the famous diplomatist only a few hours before. After a short, final struggle he

17 was hoisted, still bound hand and foot, into the spare seat of the little car. His precious valise was wedged in beside him.

" I trust that you are as comfortable as circumstances permit," said Holmes, when the final arrangements were made. " Should I be guilty of a liberty if I lit a cigar and placed it between your lips ? "

But all amenities were wasted upon the angry German.

" I suppose you realize, Mr. Sherlock Holmes," said he, " that if your Government bears you out in this treatment it becomes an act of war."

" What about your Government and all this treatment ? " said Holmes, tapping the valise.

" You are a private individual. You have no warrant for my arrest. The whole proceeding is absolutely illegal and outrageous."

" Absolutely," said Holmes.

" Kidnapping a German subject."

" And stealing his private papers."

" Well, you realize your position, you and your accomplice here.   If I were to shout for help as we pass through the village——"

" My dear sir, if you did anything so foolish you would probably enlarge the too limited titles of our village inns by giving us ' The Dangling Prussian ' as a sign-post. The Englishman is a patient creature, but at present his temper is a little inflamed and it would be as well not to try him too far.   No, Mr. Von Bork, you will go with us in a quiet, sensible fashion to Scotland Yard, whence you can send for your friend Baron Von Herling and see if even now you may not fill that place which he has reserved for you in the ambassadorial suite.   As to you, Watson, **18** you are joining us with your old service, as I understand, **19** so London won't be out of your way.   Stand with me here upon the terrace, for it may be the last quiet talk that we shall ever have."

The two friends chatted in intimate converse for a few minutes, recalling once again the days of the past whilst their prisoner vainly wriggled to undo the bonds that held him.   As they turned to the car, Holmes pointed back to the moonlit sea, and shook a thoughtful head.

" There's an east wind coming, Watson."

" I think not, Holmes.   It is very warm."

" Good old Watson !   You are the one fixed point in a changing age.   There's an east wind coming all the same, such a wind as never blew on England yet.   It will be cold and bitter, Watson, and a good many of us may wither before its blast.   But it's God's own wind none the less, and a cleaner, better, stronger land will lie in the sunshine when the storm has cleared.   Start her up, Watson, for it's time that we were on our way.   I have a cheque for five hundred pounds which should be cashed early, for the drawer is quite capable of stopping it, if he can."

18 *that place which he has reserved for you in the ambassadorial suite.* "Can any suggestion by Holmes be less likely?" Mr. Ronald S. Bonn wrote in "The Problem of the Postulated Doctor." "Von Herline would never be permitted to see Von Bork at ten leagues' distance with [the information Von Bork had gathered] in the balance. No wonder Watson chose to recount this operation in the third person, relying, no doubt, on the detective's arthritic isolation on the South Downs to keep it from him. There is only one possible reason for the ridiculous hint that Von Bork was permitted to go home in the ambassadorial train. For the secret *did* get back to Germany, and it was desperately necessary that the actual betrayer suggest a fictional channel. Perhaps no German cruiser navigated the Solent, but in the very week of Von Bork's arrest, the Grand Fleet was forced to open fire on a submarine *inside the defences of Scapa Flow*. And there is certainly no evidence that, at Jutland, Tirpitz was under any delusions about the calibre of Jellicoe's guns."

19 *you are joining us with your old service, as I understand.* "What further part Watson took in the war remains unknown," Mr. S. C. Roberts wrote in *Doctor Watson*. "It is doubtful whether he was permitted, at [his] age, to proceed on foreign service, but we may be confident that in some capacity, possibly on the staff of a military hospital, he was at the post of duty."

There is, however, at least an indication that Watson was on *active* duty in a charming anecdote related by Mr. Vincent Starrett: during World War I, an English medical officer named *Dr. John Watson*, captured by the enemy at the battle of Mons, was helped to escape by a bespectacled, bewhiskered officer of the German general staff. In a discreet moment, the German whispered to the Englishman: "Steady, Watson, steady, and don't start! Comfortable, thank you, but I miss my shag. Meet you ten days from now in the Baker Street digs."

Bibliographical Note: The manuscript of "His Last Bow" is owned by Mr. Adrian M. Conan Doyle.

Appendix I

L'ENVOI

"... they still live for all that love them well ..."
—Vincent Starrett, *The Private Life of Sherlock Holmes*

"One likes to think"—Sir Arthur Conan Doyle wrote in his Preface to the final volume of Sherlock Holmes short stories, *The Case-Book of Sherlock Holmes*—"that there is some fantastic limbo for the children of imagination, some strange, impossible place where the beaux of Fielding may still make love to the belles of Richardson, where Scott's heroes may still strut, Dickens's delightful Cockneys still raise a laugh, and Thackeray's worldlings continue to carry on their reprehensible careers. Perhaps in some humble corner of such a Valhalla, Sherlock and his Watson may for a time find a place, while some more astute sleuth with some even less astute comrade may fill the stage which they have vacated."

And so at last we come to say farewell to an immortal three—to the Detective and the Doctor and the man who created them both.

And yet—as Vincent Starrett has so truly put into words the thoughts that many of us feel:

> ... they still live for all that love them well:
> in a romantic chamber of the heart: in a nostal-
> gic country of the mind: where it is always 1895.

Ave atque vale, Sherlock!
Ave atque vale, John!
Ave atque vale, Sir Arthur!

Appendix II

"I HAVE SOME FEW REFERENCES TO MAKE"

—Sherlock Holmes, *The Sign of the Four*

For the sake of uniformity, we have adopted one set of standards for style and punctuation (although we have not Americanized British spellings); the quoted material otherwise appears here exactly as the numerous authors wrote it. For the benefit of the younger student, we have taken the liberty of translating the French, Latin, and German words and phrases with which Holmes so liberally sprinkled his conversation. For the benefit of the American student who knows not his England, we have been generous with notes on the counties, cities, towns, and villages referred to in the Canon—as we have also with notes on the streets and landmarks of Victorian London. Here our principle source has been the works of Augustus J. C. Hare, whose *Walks in London* was published in two volumes by George Routledge and Sons. No date of publication appears in our copy, but the preface to Volume I indicates that Hare's essays began to appear in British periodicals some ten years before John H. Watson, M.D., published his early reminiscences as *A Study in Scarlet*. The antiquarian Hare was therefore a contemporary of the master detective and the good doctor, and we can see through his eyes the bustling, fog-enshrouded city in which Holmes and Watson walked, talked, and adventured. In a few instances, we have given full information about our sources in the text of the notes and picture captions; for the most part, however, we have reserved this information for this list of "References," alphabetically arranged by author (collections of essays by various authors are also listed by title). A book of this kind manifestly relies heavily on the writings of others; while the editor has made every effort to give credit where credit is due, he begs the forgiveness of any commentator he may have overlooked, however inadvertently.

The editor deeply regrets that while the first volume of THE ANNOTATED SHERLOCK HOLMES was still on the press, two distinguished Sherlockians broke from the ranks. The text should properly read, now, "the late Sir Sydney Roberts" and "the late Robert Keith Leavitt."

INDEX OF TITLES

Alphabetical Listing of Novels and Short Stories in Volumes I and II

The novels are indicated by an asterisk; the rest are short stories.

SOME OF "THE WRITINGS ABOUT THE WRITINGS"

A. E. P.
"The End of Sherlock Holmes"; *The Manchester Guardian*, July 7, 1927; *The Living Age*, August 15, 1927; *The Misadventures of Sherlock Holmes*, pp. 256–60.

ADAMS, ROBERT WINTHROP
"John H. Watson, M.D., Characterologist"; *The Baker Street Journal*, Vol. IV, No. 2, New Series, April, 1954, pp. 81–92.

ADAMS, *The Reverend* STEPHEN
"Holmes: A Student of London?"; *The Sherlock Holmes Journal*, Vol. II, No. 4, Winter, 1955, pp. 17–8.

AKERS, ARTHUR K.
"Who Was Mrs. Watson's First Husband?"; *The Baker Street Journal*, Vol. X, No. 1, New Series, January, 1960, pp. 45–6.

ALLEN, F. A., *M.P.S.*
"Devilish Drugs," Part One; *May and Baker Pharmaceutical Bulletin*, December, 1956; *The Sherlock Holmes Journal*, Vol. III, No. 3, Autumn, 1957, pp. 12–4.

ALTICK, RICHARD D.
"Mr. Sherlock Holmes and Dr. Samuel Johnson"; *221B*, pp. 109–28.

ANDERSON, KAREN
"On the Difference Between a 'Cup' and a 'Plate' "; *The Baker Street Journal*, Vol. XII, No. 3, New Series, September, 1962, p. 176.

(with POUL ANDERSON) "The Peculiar Behavior of the Ritual in the Daytime"; *The Baker Street Journal Christmas Annual*, 1960, pp. 304–11.

ANDERSON, POUL
"Art in the Blood"; *The Baker Street Journal*, Vol. VI, No. 3, New Series, July, 1956, pp. 133–7.

(with KAREN ANDERSON) "The Peculiar Behavior of the Ritual in the Daytime"; *The Baker Street Journal Christmas Annual*, 1960, pp. 304–11.

"A Treatise on the Binomial Theorem"; *The Baker Street Journal*, Vol. V, No. 1, New Series, January, 1955, pp. 13–8.

ANDREW, CLIFTON R.
"A Difficulty in *A Study in Scarlet*"; *The Baker Street Journal*, Vol. III, No. 1, Old Series, January, 1948, pp. 13–4.

"Don't Sell Holmes' Memory Short"; *The Baker Street Journal*, Vol. IV, No. 4, New Series, October, 1954, pp. 219–22.

"Memorials to Sherlock Holmes"; *The Baker Street Journal*, Vol. VII, No. 4, New Series, October, 1957, pp. 240–2.

"My Old Friend Charlie Peace"; *The Sherlock Holmes Journal*, Vol. IV, No. 4, Spring, 1960, pp. 118–9.

"On the Dating of *The Sign of the Four*"; *The Baker Street Journal*, Vol. I, No. 2, New Series, April, 1951, pp. 66–9.

"A Rejoinder to Professor Hill"; *The Baker Street Journal*, Vol. V, No. 3, New Series, July, 1955, pp. 154–6.

"Sherlock Holmes on the Turf"; *A Baker Street Four-Wheeler*, pp. 38–42.

"That Scotland Yarder, Gregson—What a Help (?) He Was"; *Client's Second Case-Book*, pp. 35–9.

"Was It July or September in *The Sign of the Four?*"; *Client's Third Case-Book*, pp. 141–9.

"What Happened to Watson's Married Life After June 14, 1889?"; *The Baker Street Journal Christmas Annual*, 1958, pp. 42–4.

"What Kind of Shenanigans Went On at St. Monica's?"; *The Baker Street Journal Christmas Annual*, 1956, pp. 42–5.

"Who Is Who, and When in 'The Gloria Scott' "; *Client's Case-Book*, pp. 30–2.

ARENFALK, POUL
"The Mormon Mystery and Other Mysteries in *A Study in Scarlet*"; *The Sherlock Holmes Journal*, Vol. IV, No. 4, Spring, 1960, pp. 128–32.

ARMSTRONG, WALTER P., JR.
"The Truth About Sherlock Holmes"; *The Baker Street Journal*, Vol. I, No. 4, Old Series, October, 1946, pp. 391–401.

ASHER, *Dr.* RICHARD
"Holmes and the Fair Sex"; *The Sherlock Holmes Journal*, Vol. II, No. 3, Summer, 1955, pp. 15–22.

ASHTON, RALPH A.
"Colonel Moran's Infamous Air Rifle"; *The Baker Street Journal*, Vol. X, No. 3, July, 1960, pp. 155–9.

"Forget St. Monica's . . . What Happened at Briony Lodge?"; *The Baker Street Journal*, Vol. VIII, No. 3, New Series, July, 1958, pp. 163–8.

"The Fourth Occupant, or The Room with the Twisted Tongue"; *The Baker Street Journal*, Vol. XI, No. 1, New Series, March, 1961, pp. 38–40.

"The Secret Weapons of 221B Baker Street"; *The Baker Street Journal*, Vol. IX, No. 2, New Series, April, 1959, pp. 99–102.

AUSTIN, J. BLISS
A Baker Street Christmas Stocking for 1955; Westfield, New Jersey: The Hydraulic Press.

A Baker Street Christmas Stocking for 1962; Westfield, New Jersey: The Hydraulic Press.

"Dartmoor Revisited, or Discoveries in Devonshire"; Pittsburgh: The Hydraulic Press, 1964.

"Furor Teutonicus"; *The Baker Street Journal*, Vol. V, No. 1, New Series, January, 1955, pp. 19–24.

"Shakespeare and Watson"; *The Sherlock Holmes Journal*, Vol. I, No. 4, December, 1953, p. 42.

"Three Footnotes to 'The Adventure of the Illustrious Client' "; *Client's Third Case-Book*, pp. 89–92.

"Thumbing His Way to Fame"; *The Baker Street Journal*, Vol. I, No. 4, Old Series, October, 1946, pp. 424–32.

"Two Bibliographical Footnotes"; *The Baker Street Journal*, Vol. IV, No. 1, New Series, January, 1954, pp. 41–3.

"What Son Was Watson?: A Case of Identity"; *A Baker Street Four-Wheeler*, pp. 43–53.

BAILEY, L. W.
"The Dark Lady of Appledore Towers"; *The Sherlock Holmes Journal*, Vol. IV, No. 4, Spring, 1960, pp. 43–5.

A Baker Street Four-Wheeler, edited by Edgar W. Smith; Maplewood, New Jersey: The Pamphlet House, 1944.

Baker Street Studies, edited by H. W. Bell; London: Constable & Co., 1934; reissued in paperbound format by the Baker Street Irregulars, Inc., 1955.

BALL, JOHN, JR.
"The Case of the Elderly Actor"; *The Baker Street Journal*, Vol. IX, No. 4, New Series, pp. 209–22.

807

"Early Days in Baker Street"; *The Baker Street Journal*, Vol. V, No. 4, New Series, October, 1955, pp. 211–9.

"The Jezail Bullet"; *Leaves from the Copper Beeches*, pp. 121–6.

"Practical Art of Baritsu: The Japanese Wrestling System with Some Observations on Its Use by Mr. Sherlock Holmes"; *The Baker Street Journal*, Vol. XIV, No. 1, New Series, March, 1964, pp. 31–6.

"The Second Collaboration"; *The Baker Street Journal*, Vol. IV, No. 2, New Series, April, 1954, pp. 69–74.

"The Twenty-Three Deductions"; *The Baker Street Journal*, Vol. VIII, No. 4, New Series, October, 1958, pp. 234–7.

BALLOU, NORMAN V.
"Top Secret"; *The Third Cab*, pp. 48–51.

BARING-GOULD, *The Reverend* SABINE
A Book of Dartmoor; London: Methuen & Co., Ltd., 1900.

BARING-GOULD, WILLIAM S.
(Editor) *The Adventure of the Speckled Band and Other Stories of Sherlock Holmes*, by Sir Arthur Conan Doyle; New York: The New American Library, Inc., 1965.

The Chronological Holmes; New York: Privately printed, 1955.

"Dr. Watson Has Gone to Widecombe"; *The Baker Street Journal*, Vol. XV, No. 1, New Series, March, 1965, pp. 8–14.

" 'He Is the Napoleon of Crime, Watson' "; *Show*, March, 1965.

"The London of Holmes and Watson"; *The Baker Street Journal*, Vol. IX, No. 3, New Series, July, 1959, pp. 165–8.

"A New Chronology of Holmes and Watson"; Part I, *The Baker Street Journal*, Vol. III, No. 1, Old Series, January, 1948, pp. 107–25; Part II, *The Baker Street Journal*, Vol. III, No. 2, Old Series, April, 1948, pp. 238–51.

"The Problem of No. 221"; *The Baker Street Journal*, Vol. VIII, No. 2, New Series, April, 1958, pp. 69–77.

"Re: The Baker Street Irregulars"; *The American Book Collector*, May, 1959, pp. 20–1.

Sherlock Holmes of Baker Street: A Life of the World's First Consulting Detective; New York: Clarkson N. Potter, Inc., 1962; as *Sherlock Holmes: A Biography*, London: Rupert Hart-Davis, Ltd., 1962; as *Moi, Sherlock Holmes*, Paris: Editions Buchet/Chastel, 1965; as *Er, Sherlock Holmes*, Hamburg: Nannen, 1965.

"Sherlock Holmes, Sportsman"; *Sports Illustrated*, May 27, 1963.

" 'You Would Have Made an Actor and a Rare One' "; Program of the "musical adventure," *Baker Street*, 1965.

BARNES, W. J.
"Saxe-Coburg Square–A New Identification"; *The Sherlock Holmes Journal*, Vol. II, No. 3, Summer, 1955, pp. 31–4.

BARZUN, *Professor* JACQUES
"How Holmes Came to Play the Violin"; *The Baker Street Journal*, Vol. I, No. 3, New Series, July, 1951, pp. 108–12.

"Sherlock Holmes' Will—A Forgery"; *The Baker Street Journal*, Vol. VI, No. 2, New Series, April, 1956, pp. 75–9.

BAXTER, *Professor* FRANK CONDIE
Introduction to *The Hound of the Baskervilles*; Garden City, New York: Doubleday, Page & Company, 1926; reprinted in *The Baker Street Journal*, Vol. XII, No. 2, New Series, June, 1962, pp. 106–12.

BECKEMEYER, DOYLE W.
"The Irregular Holmes"; *The Baker Street Journal*, Vol. II, No. 1, New Series, January, 1952, pp. 18–20.

"Valuable Sherlockian Hunting-Ground"; *Client's Third Case-Book*, pp. 135–40.

BEIERLE, JOHN D.
"The Curious Incident of the Drive Through Middlesex and Surrey"; *The Baker Street Journal*, Vol. VII, No. 4, New Series, October, 1957, pp. 216–9.

BELL, H. W.
"The Date of *The Sign of the Four*"; *Baker Street Studies*, pp. 203–19.

"Note on Dr. Watson's Wound"; *Baker Street Studies*, pp. 220–3.

Sherlock Holmes and Dr. Watson: The Chronology of Their Adventures; London: Constable & Co., Ltd., 1932; re-issued in paperbound format by the Baker Street Irregulars, Inc., 1953.

"Three Identifications: Lauriston Gardens, Upper Swandam Lane, Saxe-Coburg Square"; *221B*, pp. 59–67.

"Three Identifications: Two Localities in 'The Six Napoleons,' The Drive to Thaddeus Sholto's House, Birlstone Manor"; *Profile by Gaslight*, pp. 283–9.

BELL, JOSEPH
"Mr. Sherlock Holmes"; *The Bookman*, London; *A Study in Scarlet*, London: Ward, Lock & Bowden, 1893; *The Baker Street Journal*, Vol. II, No. 1, Old Series, January, 1947, pp. 45–9.

BELL, WHITFIELD J., JR.
"Holmes and History"; *The Baker Street Journal*, Vol. II, No. 4, Old Series, October, 1947, pp. 447–56.

BENGIS, NATHAN L.
"Conan Doyle and T. S. Eliot"; *The Times Literary Supplement*, London, September 25, 1951.

"The Graft I Refused to Take"; *The Baker Street Gasogene*, Vol. I, No. 1, 1961, pp. 5–9.

"A Scandal in Baker Street"; Part I, *The Baker Street Journal*, Vol. II, No. 2, Old Series, April, 1947, pp. 145–57; Part II, *The Baker Street Journal*, Vol. II, No. 3, Old Series, July, 1947, pp. 311–21.

"Sherlock Holmes' Will"; *The London Mystery Magazine*, June, 1955; reprinted in *The Baker Street Journal*, Vol. VI, No. 2, New Series, April, 1956, pp. 80–1.

"Sherlock Stays After School"; *Client's Second Case-Book*, pp. 72–8.

"Sherlock Stays After School: An Addendum"; *Client's Third Case-Book*, p. 15.

"Sidney Johnson—Suspect"; *The Sherlock Holmes Journal*, Vol. II, No. 3, Summer, 1955, p. 24.

The "Signs" of Our Times; New York: Privately printed, 1956.

"Smothered Mate"; *The Baker Street Journal*, Vol. X, No. 4, New Series, October, 1960, pp. 213–20.

"Take a Bow, Dr. Watson"; *The Baker Street Journal*, Vol. VIII, No. 4, New Series, October, 1958, pp. 218–29.

"What Was the Month?"; *The Baker Street Journal*, Vol. VII, No. 4, New Series, October, 1957, pp. 204-14.

"Where on Earth . . ."; *The Sherlock Holmes Journal*, Vol. II, No. 2, December, 1954, p. 43.

"Where There's a Will, There's a Pay"; *The Baker Street Journal*, Vol. VI, No. 4, New Series, October, 1956, pp. 226–32.

"Whose Was It? An Examination into the Crowning Lapse of Sherlockian Scholarship"; *The Baker Street Journal*, Vol. III, No. 2, New Series, April, 1953, pp. 69–76.

BERG, EMMANUEL
"For It's Greatly to Their Credit"; *The Baker Street Journal*, Vol. IX, No. 2, New Series, April, 1959, pp. 90–8.

BERL, *Colonel* E. ENNALLS
"Sherlock Holmes and the Telephone"; *The Baker Street Journal*, Vol. III, No. 4, New Series, October, 1953, pp. 197–210.

BERMAN, RUTH
"On Docketing a Hebrew Rabbi"; *The Baker Street Journal*, Vol. X, No. 2, New Series, April, 1960, pp. 80–2.

"On Holmium"; *The Baker Street Journal*, Vol. X, No. 4, New Series, October, 1960, p. 250.

The Best of the Pips; sponsored by Richard W. Clarke; New York: The Five Orange Pips of Westchester County, 1955.

BETT, WINGATE H.
"Watson's Second Marriage"; *The Sherlock Holmes Journal*, Vol. III, No. 1, Summer, 1956, pp. 21–2.

BIGELOW, *Magistrate* S. TUPPER
"Barred-Tail Geese"; *The Sherlock Holmes Journal*, Vol. VI, No. 4, Spring, 1964, pp. 108–9.

"The Blue Enigma"; *The Baker Street Journal*, Vol. XI, No. 4, New Series, December, 1961, pp. 203–14.

"Hallamshire Revisited"; *The Baker Street Journal*, Vol. XIII, No. 2, New Series, June, 1963, pp. 87–90.

"The Hoof-Marks in 'The Priory School'"; *The Baker Street Journal*, Vol. XII, No. 3, New Series, September, 1962, pp. 169–74.

"In Defense of Joseph Bell"; *The Baker Street Journal*, Vol. X, No. 4, New Series, October, 1960, pp. 207–12.

An Irregular Anglo-American Glossary of More or Less Unfamiliar Words, Terms and Phrases in the Sherlock Holmes Saga; Toronto: Castalotte & Zamba, 1959.

"Misprision of Felony and Sherlock Holmes"; *The Sherlock Holmes Journal*, Vol. V, No. 3, Winter, 1961, pp. 68–70.

"No Colour-Bull"; *The Sherlock Holmes Journal*, Vol. V, No. 2, Spring, 1961, p. 62.

"Sherlock Holmes and the Misprision of Felony"; *The Baker Street Journal*, Vol. VIII, No. 3, New Series, July, 1958, pp. 139–46.

"Sherlock Holmes Was No Burglar"; *The Baker Street Journal Christmas Annual*, 1958, pp. 26–37.

"The Singular Case of Fletcher Robinson"; *The Baker Street Gasogene*, Vol. I, No. 2, 1961, pp. 19–21.

"Those Five Volumes"; *The Baker Street Journal*, Vol. XI, No. 1, New Series, March, 1961, pp. 31–7.

"Two Canonical Problems Solved"; *The Baker Street Journal Christmas Annual*, 1959, pp. 261–71.

"Was It Attempted Murder?"; *The Baker Street Journal*, Vol. XIV, No. 2, New Series, June, 1964, pp. 99–107.

BLACKER, *Lieutenant Colonel* L. V. S.
"Dr. Watson's Wound(s)"; *The Sherlock Holmes Journal*, Vol. I, No. 1, May, 1952, pp. 31–2.

BLAKE, S. F.
"Sherlock Holmes and the Italian Cipher"; *The Baker Street Journal*, Vol. IX, No. 1, New Series, January, 1959, pp. 14–20.

"Sherlock Holmes' Dressing Gown(s)"; *The Baker Street Journal*, Vol. X, No. 2, New Series, April, 1960, pp. 86–9.

BLAKENEY, T. S.
"The Apocryphal Ancestry of Dr. Watson"; *The Baker Street Journal*, Vol. VII, No. 2, New Series, April, 1957, pp. 69–73.

"A Case for Identification—in Bohemia"; *The Sherlock Holmes Journal*, Vol. III, No. 2, Winter, 1956, pp. 15–6.

"The Location of 'The Three Students'"; *The Sherlock Holmes Journal*, Vol. IV, No. 1, Winter, 1958, p. 14; reprinted in *Leaves from the Copper Beeches*, pp. 9–10.

"More Disjecta Membra"; *The Sherlock Holmes Journal*, Vol. V, No. 2, Spring, 1961, pp. 55–6.

"On Watson's Pension"; *The Baker Street Journal*, Vol. VII, No. 4, New Series, October, 1957, pp. 249–50.

Sherlock Holmes: Fact or Fiction?; London: John Murray, 1932; reissued in paperbound format by the Baker Street Irregulars, Inc., 1954.

"Some Disjecta Membra"; *The Sherlock Holmes Journal*, Vol. IV, No. 3, Winter, 1959, pp. 101–3.

"Thoughts on *The Sign of the Four*"; *The Sherlock Holmes Journal*, Vol. III, No. 4, Summer, 1958, pp. 6–8.

BLANK, E. W.
"Holmes the Chemist"; *The Baker Street Journal*, Vol. III, No. 2, Old Series, April, 1948, pp. 226–7.

"Is Professor Moriarty Afoot?"; *The Baker Street Journal*, Vol. I, No. 2, Old Series, April, 1946, pp. 209–10.

BLAUSTEIN, ALBERT P.
"Sherlock Holmes As a Lawyer"; *The Baker Street Journal*, Vol. III, No. 3, Old Series, July, 1948, pp. 306–8.

BLEGEN, *Dean* THEODORE C.
"These Were Hidden Fires, Indeed!"; *Exploring Sherlock Holmes*, pp. 9–26.

BLOCH, ROBERT
"The Dynamics of an Asteriod"; *The Baker Street Journal*, Vol. III, No. 4, New Series, October, 1953, pp. 225–33.

BONN, RONALD S.
"The Problem of the Postulated Doctor; *The Baker Street Journal*, Vol. XIV, No. 1, New Series, March, 1964, pp. 14–21.

BOSWELL, ROLFE
"A Connecticut Yankee in Support of Sir Arthur"; *The Baker Street Journal*, Vol. II, No. 2, Old Series, April, 1947, pp. 119–27.

"Dr. Roylott's Wily Fillip"; *The Baker Street Journal*, Vol. I, No. 3, Old Series, July, 1946, pp. 307–11.

"'In Uffish Thought'"; *The Baker Street Journal*, Vol. I, No. 1, Old Series, January, 1946, pp. 21–4.

"On 'The Adventure of the Tired Captain'"; *The Baker Street Journal*, Vol. II, No. 2, Old Series, April, 1947, pp. 160–2.

"On the Aluminium Crutch (or Crotch)"; *The Baker Street Journal*, Vol. I, No. 2, Old Series, April, 1946, pp. 190–2.

"On the Remarkable Worm"; *The Baker Street Journal*, Vol. II, No. 2, Old Series, April, 1947, pp. 161–2.

"On the Trepoff Murder"; *The Baker Street Journal*, Vol. I, No. 1, New Series, January, 1951, p. 40.

"Quick, Watson, the Fiddle!"; *The Baker Street Journal*, Vol. III, No. 4, Old Series, October, 1948, pp. 435–40.

"A Rare Day in June"; *The Baker Street Journal*, Vol. VII, No. 1, New Series, January, 1957, pp. 13–7.

"Sarasate, Sherlock and Shaw"; *The Baker Street Journal*, Vol. II, No. 1, New Series, January, 1952, pp. 13–7.

"Squaring 'The Red Circle'"; *The Baker Street Journal*, Vol. I, No. 3, New Series, July, 1951, pp. 113–4.

BOUCHER, ANTHONY
Introduction to *The Final Adventures of Sherlock Holmes, Vol. I (The Valley of Fear);* New York: The Limited Editions Club, 1932; reprinted in *Introducing Mr. Sherlock Holmes.*

"On a Certain Foreign Potentate"; *The Baker Street Journal*, Vol. II, No. 1, Old Series, January, 1947, pp. 60–1.

"On 'The Second Stains' As One Adventure"; *The Baker Street Journal*, Vol. II, No. 1, Old Series, January, 1947, pp. 60–1.

"Prolegomena to a Holmesian Discography"; *The Baker Street Journal*, Vol. I, No. 2, Old Series, April, 1946, pp. 229–31.

"The Records of Baker Street"; *The*

Baker Street Journal, Vol. IV, No. 1, Old Series, January, 1949, pp. 97–104.

"Was the Later Holmes an Imposter?"; *Profile by Gaslight*, pp. 60–70.

BOYD, *Dr.* ANDREW

"Dr. Watson's Dupe"; *Encounter*, Vol. XIV, No. 3, March, 1960; reprinted in *The Sherlock Holmes Journal*, Vol. V, No. 2, Spring, 1961, pp. 42–4.

BREND, GAVIN

"The Black Boy's Visit to Hurlstone"; *The Baker Street Journal*, Vol. III, No. 4, New Series, October, 1953, pp. 217–24.

"Charles Augustus Milverton: The Date"; *The Sherlock Holmes Journal*, Vol. VI, No. 3, Winter, 1963, pp. 74-6.

"The Five Orange Pips"; *The Sherlock Holmes Journal*, Vol. II, No. 3, Summer, 1955, p. 2.

"From the Horse's Mouth"; *The Sherlock Holmes Journal*, Vol. I, No. 4, December, 1953, pp. 39–40.

"From Maiwand to Marylebone"; *The Sherlock Holmes Journal*, Vol. I, No. 3, June, 1953, pp. 40–4.

"A Hint to the Next Chronologist"; *The Baker Street Journal*, Vol. VIII, No. 2, New Series, April, 1958, pp. 123–5.

"A Horse! A Horse!"; *The Sherlock Holmes Journal*, Vol. II, No. 2, December, 1954, p. 20.

"Jabez Muses"; *The Baker Street Journal*, Vol. III, No. 3, New Series, July, 1953, p. 169.

"The Man from the Yard"; *The Sherlock Holmes Journal*, Vol. I, No. 1, May, 1952, p. 14.

My Dear Holmes; London: George Allen & Unwin, Ltd., 1951.

"Our Future Centenaries"; *The Sherlock Holmes Journal*, Vol. III, No. 4, Summer, 1958, pp. 4–5.

"The Route of the Blue Carbuncle"; *The Sherlock Holmes Journal*, Vol. II, No. 4, Winter, 1955, pp. 2–6.

"A Sherlock Holmes Anniversary"; *The Sherlock Holmes Journal*, Vol. I, No. 1, May, 1952, pp. 30–1.

"Was Sherlock Holmes at Westminster?"; *The Trifler*, July, 1953; reprinted in the *Sherlock Holmes Journal*, Vol. II, No. 1, July, 1954, pp. 39–41.

BRISTOWE, *Dr.* W. S.

"The Mystery of the Third Continent, or, Was Dr. John H. Watson a Philanderer?"; *The Sherlock Holmes Journal*, Vol. II, No. 2, December, 1954, pp. 27–39.

"A Note on the Watson-Doyle Partnership"; *The Sherlock Holmes Journal*, Vol. III, No. 3, Autumn, 1957, pp. 4–5.

"Oxford or Cambridge?"; *The Sherlock Holmes Journal*, Vol. IV, No. 2, Spring, 1959, pp. 75–6.

" 'The Three Students' in Limelight, Electric Light and Daylight"; *The Sherlock Holmes Journal*, Vol. III, No. 2, Winter, 1956, pp. 2–5.

" 'What a Terrible Criminal He Would Have Made' "; *The Sherlock Holmes Journal*, Vol. V, No. 1, Winter, 1960, pp. 6–14.

BROOK, GEOFFREY

"Sherlock Holmes' Pipe"; *The Baker Street Journal*, Vol. X, No. 3, New Series, July, 1960, pp. 152–4.

"The Bruce-Partington Keys: Correspondence between R. Kelf-Cohen and Paul Gore-Booth, with Comment by Felix Morley"; *The Sherlock Holmes Journal*, Vol. II, No. 2, December, 1954, pp. 14–5.

"The Bruce-Partington Night"; *The Sherlock Holmes Journal*, Vol. III, No. 1, Summer, 1956, pp. 17–8.

BRYAN-BROWN, FREDERICK

"Sherlockian Schools and Schoolmasters"; *The Sherlock Holmes Journal*, Vol. III, No. 1, Summer, 1956, pp. 2–7.

BUCHHOLTZ, JAMES

"A Tremor at the Edge of the Web"; *The Baker Street Journal*, Vol. VIII, No. 1, New Series, January, 1958, pp. 5–9.

BURNHAM, ERNEST C., JR.

"The Tattooed Fish in 'The Red-Headed League' "; *The Baker Street Journal*, Vol. XII, No. 4, New Series, October, 1942, pp. 219–22.

BUSH, ARTHUR

Portrait of London; London: Frederick Muller, Ltd., 1950.

BUXTON, EDWARD T.

"He Solved the Case and Won the Race"; *The Third Cab*, pp. 39–41.

CAMERON, MARY S.

"Joseph Aloysius Hansom and His 'Patent Safety Cab' "; *The Baker Street Gasogene*, Vol. I, No. 4, 1962, pp. 51–4.

"Mr. and Mrs. Beeton's Christmas Annual"; *The Baker Street Journal Christmas Annual*, 1957, pp. 5–8.

CAMPBELL, *Dr.* MAURICE

"The First Sherlockian Critic—1902"; *The Sherlock Holmes Journal*, Vol. I, No. 2, September, 1952, pp. 3–5, 24.

Sherlock Holmes and Dr. Watson: A Medical Digression; London: Ash & Co., Ltd., 1935.

CAREY, *Dr.* EUGENE F.

"Holmes, Watson and Cocaine"; *The Baker Street Journal*, Vol. XIII, No. 3, New Series, September, 1963, pp. 176–81, 195.

CARR, JOHN DICKSON

(with ADRIAN M. CONAN DOYLE) *The Exploits of Sherlock Holmes*; New York: Random House, 1954.

The Life of Sir Arthur Conan Doyle; New York: Harper & Brothers, 1949.

Catalogue of an Exhibition on Sherlock Holmes Held at Abbey House, Baker Street, London N. W. 1, May–September, 1951.

Catalogue of the Collection in the Bars and Grill Room and in the Reconstruction of the Living Room at 221B Baker Street [in] *The Sherlock Holmes* [*Tavern*]; with Introductory Essays by A. Lloyd-Taylor and John Dickson Carr, and a Critical Miscellany edited by H. Douglas Thomson; London: Whitbread & Co., Ltd., n.d.

CHENHALL, W. H.

"The Retirement of Sherlock Holmes"; *The Sherlock Holmes Journal*, Vol. V, No. 1, Winter, 1960, pp. 19–22.

CHIECO, LORENZO J.

"The Signature of Sherlock Holmes"; *The Baker Street Journal*, Vol. III, No. 3, New Series, July, 1953, pp. 157–9.

CHORLEY, *Mrs.* JENNIFER

" 'Briarbrae' Revisited"; *The Sherlock Holmes Journal*, Vol. VI, No. 2, Spring, 1963, pp. 56–7.

"1896–1964, 'The Wheel Has Come Full Circle' "; *The Sherlock Holmes Journal*, Vol. VI, No. 3, Winter, 1963, pp. 89–90.

"Some Diggings Down Under"; *The Sherlock Holmes Journal*, Vol. VI, No. 2, Spring, 1963, pp. 49–51.

CHRIST, *Professor* JAY FINLEY

"An Adventure in the Lower Criticism"; Part I: "Doctor Watson and the Calendar"; *The Baker Street Gasogene*, Vol. I, No. 3, 1961, pp. 28–35; Part II: "Dr. Watson and the Moon"; *The Baker Street Gasogene*, Vol. I, No. 4, 1962, pp. 13–9.

The Chicago *Tribune* Sketches:
Flashes by Fanlight (1946).
Gleanings by Gaslight (1947).
Soundings in the Saga (1948).
Sherlock's Anniversaries (1961).
Finch's Final Fling (1963).

"Commuting a Felony"; *The Baker Street Journal*, Vol. II, No. 2, Old Series, April, 1947, pp. 211–2.

"The Dancing Men"; *The Sherlock*

Holmes Journal, Vol. I, No. 4, December, 1953, pp. 24–5.

"Glittering Golden Guineas"; *The Numismatist,* October, 1951.

"The House in Baker Street"; *The Baker Street Journal,* Vol. II, No. 1, Old Series, January, 1947, pp. 91–2.

An Irregular Chronology of Sherlock Holmes of Baker Street; Ann Arbor, Michigan: The Fanlight House, 1947.

An Irregular Guide to Sherlock Holmes of Baker Street; New York: The Pamphlet House and Argus Books, 1947.

"James Boswell and the Island of Uffa"; *The Baker Street Journal,* Vol. I, No. 1, Old Series, January, 1946, pp. 24–7.

"The Later Holmes an Imposter: A Sequel"; *The Baker Street Gasogene,* Vol. I, No. 1, 1962, pp. 21–33.

"'The Missing Three-Quarter'"; *The Baker Street Journal,* Vol. I, No. 2, Old Series, April, 1946, pp. 208–9.

"'The Missing Three-Quarter' Again"; *The Baker Street Journal,* Vol. I, No. 3, Old Series, July, 1946, pp. 363–4.

"Musgrave Mathematics"; *Client's Second Case-Book,* pp. 14–9.

"The Mystery of the One-Way Dunlops"; *The Baker Street Journal,* Vol. II, No. 4, Old Series. October, 1947, p. 474.

"The Pipe and the Cap"; *The Baker Street Journal,* Vol. IX, No. 1, New Series, January, 1959, pp. 43–5.

"Problems in 'A Scandal in Bohemia'"; *The Baker Street Gasogene,* Vol. I, No. 2, 1961, pp. 5–13.

"Sherlock and the Canons"; *The Baker Street Journal,* Vol. III, No. 1, New Series, January, 1953, pp. 5–12.

"Sherlock Backs a Turkey"; *Sherlockian Studies,* p. 23.

"Silver Blaze: An Identification (as of 1893 A.D.)"; *The Baker Street Journal,* Vol. IV, No. 1, Old Series, January, 1949, pp. 12–5.

"Thumbs Up: Thumbs Down?"; *The Sherlock Holmes Journal,* Vol. II, No. 1, July, 1954, pp. 41–2.

"A Very Large-Scale Map"; *The Sherlock Holmes Journal,* Vol. VI, No. 3, Winter, 1963, pp. 72–4.

CHRISTIE, *Mrs.* WINIFRED M.
"On the Remarkable Explorations of Sigerson"; *The Sherlock Holmes Journal,* Vol. I, No. 2, September, 1952, pp. 39–44.

"Sherlock Holmes and Graphology"; *The Sherlock Holmes Journal,* Vol. II, No. 4, Winter, 1955, pp. 28–31.

"Some Reflections on That Little Thing of Chopin's"; *Leaves from the Copper Beeches,* pp. 81–9.

CHUJOY, ANATOLE
"The Only Second Stain"; *The Baker Street Journal,* Vol. IV, No. 3, New Series, July, 1954, pp. 165–8.

CLAPP, ROGER T.
"The Curious Problem of the Railway Timetables"; *The Second Cab,* pp. 34–8.

CLARK, BENJAMIN
"Dr. Mortimer Before the Bar"; *The Baker Street Journal,* Vol. III, No. 3, Old Series, July, 1948, pp. 269–77; *The Best of the Pips,* pp. 97–106.

"The Horsham Fiasco"; *The Baker Street Journal,* Vol. I, No. 1, New Series, January, 1951, pp. 4–8.

"On the Stock Prices Quoted in 'The Stockbroker's Clerk'"; *The Baker Street Journal,* Vol. XII, No. 4, New Series, December, 1962, p. 245.

CLARK, BENJAMIN, JR.
"Holmes on the Range"; *The Baker Street Journal,* Vol. III, No. 2, New Series, April, 1953, pp. 91–7.

CLARK, EDWARD F., JR.
"Study of an Untold Tale"; *The Baker Street Journal,* Vol. XIII, No. 4, New Series, December, 1963, pp. 217–28.

CLARK, *Dr.* JOHN D.
"A Chemist's View of Canonical Chemistry"; *The Baker Street Journal,* Vol. XIV, No. 3, New Series, September, 1964, pp. 153–5.

"Some Notes Relating to a Preliminary Investigation into the Paternity of Nero Wolfe"; *The Baker Street Journal,* Vol. VI, No. 1, New Series, January, 1956, pp. 5–11.

CLARKE, RICHARD W.
"Certain Ladies of Baker Street"; *The Baker Street Journal,* Vol. II, No. 1, New Series, January, 1952, pp. 34–8; *The Best of the Pips,* pp. 9–13.

"On 'The Five Orange Pips'"; *The Best of the Pips,* pp. 3–6.

"On the Nomenclature of Watson's Ships"; *The Baker Street Journal,* Vol. I, No. 2, Old Series, April, 1946, pp. 119–21; *The Best of the Pips,* pp. 6–9.

CLARKSON, PAUL S.
"'In the Beginning . . .'"; *The Baker Street Journal,* Vol. VIII, No. 4, New Series, October, 1958, pp. 197–209.

CLAYTON, J. K.
"The Hat Trick"; *The Sherlock Holmes Journal,* Vol. II, No. 1, July, 1954, pp. 19–21.

Client's Case-Book, edited by Jerry Neal Williamson; Indianapolis: The Illustrious Clients, 1947.

Client's Second Case-Book, edited by Jerry Neal Williamson; Indianapolis: The Illustrious Clients, 1951.

Client's Third Case-Book, edited by Jerry Neal Williamson and H. B. Williams; Indianapolis: The Illustrious Clients, 1953.

CLUM, FLORENCE
"So He Boxed Their Ears"; *The Baker Street Journal,* Vol. II, No. 4, New Series, October, 1958, pp. 210–3.

CLUNN, HAROLD P.
The Face of London; New Edition, Revised by E. R. Wethersett, London; Spring Books, n.d.

CLYNE, ROBERT
"On the Footprints of a Gigantic Hound"; *The Baker Street Journal,* Vol. III, No. 1, New Series, January, 1953, pp. 60, 62.

COLBORNE, R. S.
"Orphans of the Storm?"; *The Sherlock Holmes Journal,* Vol. II, No. 3, Summer, 1955, pp. 24–5.

COLD, JØRGEN
"What Did Sherlock Holmes Drink?"; *Client's Third Case-Book,* pp. 110–18.

COLE, *Mrs.* ELEANOR S.
"Holmes, Watson and the K-9's"; *The Baker Street Journal,* Vol. I, No. 1, New Series, January, 1951, pp. 25–9.

COLLINS, HOWARD
"Ex Libris Sherlock Holmes"; *Profile by Gaslight,* pp. 26–39.

COOPER, ANTHONY G.
"Browsings in Birmingham"; *The Sherlock Holmes Journal,* Vol. IV, No. 4, Spring, 1960, p. 140.

"Holmesian Humour"; *The Sherlock Holmes Journal,* Vol. VI, No. 4, Spring, 1964, pp. 109–13.

CORRINGTON, *Dr.* J. D.
"Baker Street Weather"; *The Saint Detective Magazine,* Vol. VIII, No. 5, November, 1957, pp. 33–53.

COX, J. RANDOLPH
"Mycroft Holmes: Private Detective"; *The Baker Street Journal,* Vol. VI, No. 4, New Series, October, 1956, pp. 197–200.

CRAWFORD, BRYCE, JR.
(with R. C. MOORE) "The Final Problem—Where?"; *Exploring Sherlock Holmes,* pp. 82–7.

CROCKER, *Professor* STEPHEN F.
"The Barometric Dr. Watson: A Study of *The Sign of the Four*"; *The Quarterly of Phi Beta Pi,* November, 1946;

The Baker Street Journal, Vol. III, No. 2, April, 1948, pp. 196–201.

"Louder, Holmes! and Stop Muttering!, or, The Route to Thaddeus Sholto's"; *The Sherlock Holmes Journal*, Vol. I, No. 2, September, 1952, pp. 14–21.

"Pseudepigraphical Matter in the Holmesian Canon"; *The Baker Street Journal*, Vol. II, No. 3, New Series, July, 1952, pp. 158–64.

"Sherlock Holmes Recommends Winwood Reade"; *The Baker Street Journal*, Vol. XIV, No. 3, New Series, September, 1964, pp. 142–4.

"Watson Doctors the Venerable Bede"; *The Baker Street Journal*, Vol. IX, No. 3, New Series, July, 1959, pp. 157–64.

CROSS, LESLIE
"Sherlock Holmes, Writer: An Unsolved Case"; *The Baker Street Journal*, Vol. XIV, No. 1, New Series, March, 1964, pp. 39–42.

CROSS, MELVIN
"The Lantern of Sherlock Holmes"; *The Baker Street Journal*, Vol. I, No. 4, Old Series, October, 1946, pp. 433–42.

CRUIKSHANK, R. J.
Roaring Century; London: Hamish Hamilton, 1946.

CRUMP, NORMAN
"Inner or Outer Rail?"; *The Sherlock Holmes Journal*, Vol. I, No. 1, May, 1952, pp. 16–23.

CUMINGS, THAYER
"Concerning Mr. Holmes' Fees"; *The Baker Street Journal*, Vol. VIII, No. 4, New Series, October, 1958, pp. 210–3.

"Don't Write—Telegraph!"; *The Best of the Pips*, pp. 87–95.

CURRIER, FRANCIS M.
"Holmes and Thorndyke: A Real Friendship"; *The Baker Street Journal*, Vol. III, No. 2, Old Series, April, 1948, pp. 176–82.

CUTTER, ROBERT A.
"The Underground"; *Client's Second Case-Book*, pp. 83–7.

DAISH, W. G.
"Pondering on Pitfalls"; *The Sherlock Holmes Journal*, Vol. IV, No. 4, Spring, 1962, pp. 118–9.

DAKIN, D. MARTIN
"The Problem of the *Case-Book*"; *The Sherlock Holmes Journal*, Vol. I, No. 3, June, 1953, pp. 29–34.

"Second Thoughts on the *Case-Book*"; *The Sherlock Holmes Journal*, Vol. III, No. 1, Summer, 1956, pp. 8–9.

DALLIBA, WILLIAM SWIFT
"The Manuscripts of the Sherlock Holmes Stories"; *The Baker Street Journal*, Vol. X, No. 3, New Series, July, 1960, pp. 164–6.

DARDESS, *Dr.* JOHN
"The Maiwand-Criterion Hiatus"; *The Baker Street Journal*, Vol. IV, No. 1, Old Series, October, 1949, pp. 115–7.

"On the Dating of *The Valley of Fear*"; *The Baker Street Journal*, Vol. III, No. 4, Old Series, October, 1948, pp. 481–2.

DAVIES, BERNARD
"The Back Yards of Baker Street"; *The Sherlock Holmes Journal*, Vol. III, No. 4, Winter, 1959, pp. 83–8.

"Canonical Connections"; *The Sherlock Holmes Journal*, Vol. V, No. 2, Spring, 1961, pp. 37–41.

"Doctor Boyd's Bleat"; *The Sherlock Holmes Journal*, Vol. V, No. 3, Winter, 1961, pp. 88–9.

"The Mews of Marylebone"; *The Sherlock Holmes Journal*, Vol. VI, No. 1, Winter, 1962, pp. 6–10.

"Was Holmes a Londoner?"; *The Sherlock Holmes Journal*, Vol. IV, No. 2, Spring, 1959, pp. 42–7.

DAVIS, ELMER
Introduction to *The Later Adventures of Sherlock Holmes, Vol. I (The Return of Sherlock Holmes)*; New York: The Limited Editions Club, 1952; *Introducing Mr. Sherlock Holmes*.

"On the Emotional Geology of Baker Street"; *221B*, pp. 37–45.

"The Real Sherlock Holmes"; *The Saturday Review of Literature*, December 3, 1933; *The Baker Street Journal*, Vol. I, No. 4, 1962, pp. 65–73.

DE GROAT, RAYMOND A.
"The Guilty Pawnbroker, or The Lost Summer of 1890"; *The Baker Street Journal*, Vol. XIV, No. 1, New Series, March, 1964, pp. 27–30.

DE WITT, OMAR L.
"On the Mystery of Baritsu"; *The Baker Street Journal*, Vol. VI, No. 2, New Series, April, 1956, p. 121.

DICKENS, CHARLES
Dickens' Dictionary of the Thames from Its Source to the Nore: An Unconventional Handbook; London: Charles Dickens & Evans, 1892.

DICKENSHEET, DEAN W.
"Sherlock Holmes — Linguist"; *The Baker Street Journal*, Vol. X, No. 3, New Series, July, 1960, pp. 133–42.

DONEGALL, LORD
"Lunatic Banker's Royal Client—Dr. Watson Tries Semi-Fiction"; *The Sherlock Holmes Journal*, Vol. VI, No. 2, Spring, 1963, pp. 46–9.

"Watson and Bradshaw"; *The Sherlock Holmes Journal*, Vol. V, No. 2, Spring, 1961, p. 36.

"Who Painted Hugo Baskerville?"; *The Sherlock Holmes Journal*, Vol. III, No. 3, Autumn, 1957, pp. 23, 24.

DORIAN, N. CURRIER
"'A Bad Lot'"; *The Baker Street Journal*, Vol. VI, No. 1, New Series, January, 1956, pp. 51–7.

DOUGLASS, *Mrs.* RUTH
"The Camberwell Poisoner"; *Ellery Queen's Mystery Magazine*, February, 1947.

DOYLE, ADRIAN M. CONAN
"Deep Waters"; *The Sherlock Holmes Journal*, Vol. VI, No. 3, Winter, 1963, p. 96.

(with JOHN DICKSON CARR) *The Exploits of Sherlock Holmes*; New York: Random House, 1954.

Introduction to *A Treasury of Sherlock Holmes*; Garden City, New York: Hanover House, 1955.

"On Conan Doyle and the Vernets"; *The Sherlock Holmes Journal*, Vol. VI, No. 2, Spring, 1963, p. 38.

"Some Family Facts"; *The Baker Street Journal*, Vol. XII, No. 3, New Series, September, 1962, pp. 139–41.

The True Conan Doyle; London: John Murray, 1945; New York: Coward-McCann, 1946.

DOYLE, *Dr.*, later *Sir* ARTHUR CONAN
Memories and Adventures: The Autobiography of Sir Arthur Conan Doyle; London: Hodder & Stoughton, 1924; Boston: Little, Brown and Company, 1924.

Preface to *The Complete Sherlock Holmes Long Stories*; London: John Murray, 1929.

"A Sherlock Holmes Competition"; *The Strand Magazine*, March, 1927.

"Some Personalia About Mr. Sherlock Holmes"; *The Strand Magazine*, December, 1917.

Through the Magic Door; London: Smith, Elder, 1907.

"To an Undiscerning Critic"; *Some Piquant People* (Lincoln Springfield); London: T. Fisher Unwin, 1924; Private edition by Edwin B. Hill, Ysleta, Texas, October, 1937; *Profile by Gaslight*.

"The Truth About Sherlock Holmes"; *Collier's Magazine*, December 29, 1931.

DURGIN, CYRUS
"The Speckled Band"; *The Third Cab*, pp. 12–6.

E. J. C.
"An Opinion from British Counsel on 'Commuting a Felony'"; *The Baker Street Journal*, Vol. III, No. 3, Old Series, July, 1948, pp. 309–13.

ELIE, RUDOLPH
"The Battle of Charing Cross"; *The Third Cab*, pp. 17–25.

ERICKSON, CARL T.
"Royal Blood and Feet of Clay"; *The Baker Street Journal*, Vol. IV, No. 2, New Series, April, 1954, pp. 98–9.

EVANS, WEBSTER
"Sherlock Holmes and Sport"; *The Sherlock Holmes Journal*, Vol. II, No. 3, Summer, 1955, pp. 35–42.

Exploring Sherlock Holmes, edited by E. W. McDiarmid and Theodore C. Blegen; La Crosse, Wisconsin: The Sumac Press, 1957.

FELDMAN, LEW DAVID
"Hitherto Unrecorded First Separate Editions"; *The Baker Street Gasogene*, Vol. I, No. 1, 1961, pp. 17–20.

FENTON, IRVING
"An Analysis of the Crimes and Near-Crimes at Appledore Towers in the Light of the English Criminal Law"; *The Baker Street Journal*, Vol. VI, No. 2, New Series, April, 1956, pp. 69–74.

"Holmes and the Law"; *The Baker Street Journal*, Vol. VII, No. 2, New Series, April, 1957, pp. 79–83.

"On Friendship"; *The Baker Street Journal*, Vol. IX, No. 1, January, 1959, pp. 23–5.

FITZ, *Dr.* REGINALD
"A Belated Eulogy: To John H. Watson, M.D."; *Profile by Gaslight*, pp. 141–53.

FOLSOM, *The Reverend* HENRY T.
"Seventeen Out of Twenty-Three"; *The Baker Street Journal*, Vol. XIV, No. 1, New Series, March, 1964, pp. 24–6.

Through the Years at Baker Street: A Chronology of Sherlock Holmes, Revised Edition; Washington, New Jersey: Privately printed, 1964.

FREDMAN, L. E.
"A Note on Watson's Youth"; *The Sherlock Holmes Journal*, Vol. V, No. 3, Winter, 1961, p. 87.

FRISBIE, OWEN P.
"On the Origin of the Hound of the Baskervilles"; *The Best of the Pips*, pp. 51–5.

GALBRAITH, A. D.
"The Real Moriarty"; *The Baker Street Journal Christmas Annual*, 1957, pp. 55–62.

GARDNER, GEORGE K.
"What Sherlock Did Know"; *The Baker Street Journal*, Vol. I, No. 3, New Series, July, 1951, pp. 89–90.

GEORGE, ISAAC S.
"Violet the Hunter"; *The Baker Street Journal*, Vol. IV, No. 1, Old Series, January, 1949, pp. 29–37.

GIBSON, THEODORE W.
"The Birlstone Masquerade"; *The Baker Street Journal*, Vol. VI, No. 3, New Series, July, 1956, pp. 168–9.

"On the 'Silver Blaze' Formula"; *The Baker Street Journal*, Vol. XIV, No. 2, New Series, June, 1964, p. 123.

GILL, WILLIAM H.
"Always on Sunday, Watson!"; *The Sherlock Holmes Journal*, Vol. V, No. 2, Spring, 1961, pp. 62, 64.

"Some Notable Sherlockian Buildings"; *The Sherlock Holmes Journal*, Vol. IV, No. 4, Spring, 1960, pp. 124–6.

GODFREY, ARTHUR
"On the Alternative Use of the Long and Short S"; *The Baker Street Journal*, Vol. XI, No. 4, New Series, December, 1961, pp. 246–7.

GOODMAN, CHARLES, *D.D.S.*
"The Dental Holmes"; *Profile by Gaslight*, pp. 85–96.

GORDON, *Dr.* HAROLD
"Some Recollections of Sir Arthur Conan Doyle"; *The Baker Street Journal*, Vol. XII, No. 3, New Series, July, 1962, pp. 137–8.

GORE-BOOTH, *Sir* PAUL
"The Journeys of Sherlock Holmes: A Topographical Monograph"; *The Baker Street Journal*, Vol. III, No. 2, Old Series, April, 1948, pp. 159–68.

GRAHAM, R. P.
"Dr. Watson, I Presume?"; *Client's Third Case-Book*, pp. 72–3.

"Sherlock Holmes in Retirement"; *The Baker Street Journal*, Vol. I, No. 4, Old Series, October, 1946, pp. 469–72.

"The Unknown Worm"; *The Baker Street Journal*, Vol. II, No. 2, Old Series, April, 1947, p. 212.

GRASSE, MARVIN
"Who Killed Holmes?"; *The Atlantic Monthly*, June, 1955.

GRAZEBROOK, O. F.
Studies in Sherlock Holmes; London: Privately printed, n.d. [*c.* 1949]:
    I. Oxford or Cambridge.
    II. Politics and Premiers.
    III. Royalty.
    IV. Dr. Watson and Rudyard Kipling.
    V. The Author of the *Case-Book*.
    VI. Something of Dr. Watson.
(Study III, Royalty, has been reprinted in *Client's Third Case-Book*, p. 27–59.)

GREEN, ROGER LANCELYN
"Dr. Watson's First Critic"; *The Sherlock Holmes Journal*, Vol. III, No. 4, Summer, 1958, pp. 8–9.

"Sherlock Holmes at Oxford"; *The Sherlock Holmes Journal*, Vol. IV, No. 1, Winter, 1958, p. 24.

GREENWOOD, E. P.
"Some Random Thoughts on Railway Journeys by Holmes and Watson"; *The Sherlock Holmes Journal*, Vol. I, No. 3, June, 1953, pp. 19–21.

GRIFFITH, A. N.
"Some Observations on Sherlock Holmes and Dr. Watson at Bart's"; *St. Bartholomew's Hospital Journal*, Vol. LV, No. 12, pp. 273–4.

GROSBAYNE, BENJAMIN
"Sherlock Holmes — Musician"; *The Baker Street Journal*, Vol. III, No. 1, Old Series, January, 1948, pp. 47–57.

HALL, WILLIAM S.
"Don't Blame Watson"; *The Baker Street Journal*, Vol. III, No. 2, New Series, April, 1953, pp. 84–6.

"The True and Proper Coat of Arms of Mr. Sherlock Holmes; With Also the Coats of Arms of John H. Watson, M.D., and James Moriarty, Sc.D."; *Profile by Gaslight*, pp. 114–24.

HAMMOND, *Dr.* ROLAND
"The Attempted Mayhem of 'Silver Blaze'"; *The Baker Street Journal*, Vol. I, No. 2, Old Series, April, 1946, pp. 157–61.

"The Surgeon Probes Doctor Watson's Wound"; *The Second Cab*, pp. 28–31.

HAND, HERBERT T., JR.
"Where Did You Get That Hat . . . Band?"; *The Baker Street Journal*, Vol. IV, No. 1, Old Series, January, 1949, pp. 18–23.

HARBOTTLE, S. T. L.
"'My Charges Are Upon a Fixed Scale—'"; *The Sherlock Holmes Journal*, Vol. II, No. 1, July, 1954, pp. 22–5.

"Sherlock Holmes and the Law"; *The Sherlock Holmes Journal*, Vol. I, No. 3, June, 1953, pp. 7–10.

HARDWICK, MICHAEL and MOLLIE
The Man Who Was Sherlock Holmes; London: John Murray, 1964; Garden City, New York: Doubleday & Company, 1964.

The Sherlock Holmes Companion; London; John Murray, 1962.

HARRIS, ROBERT G.
"It's Not Always 1957"; *The Baker Street Journal,* Vol. VIII, No. 1, New Series, January, 1958, pp. 29–32.

HARRISON, MICHAEL
"The Blue Blood of the Holmes"; *The Baker Street Journal,* Vol. XIV, No. 2, New Series, June, 1964, pp. 81–3.

"Found: Pope's Court"; *The Sherlock Holmes Journal,* Vol. IV, No. 2, Spring, 1959, p. 80.

In the Footsteps of Sherlock Holmes; London: Cassell & Co., Ltd., 1958; New York: Frederick Fell, Inc., 1960.

London by Gaslight; London: Peter Davies, 1963.

"Why '221B'?"; *The Baker Street Journal,* Vol. XIV, No. 4, New Series, December, 1964, pp. 219–22.

HART, ARCHIBALD
"The Effects of Trades Upon Hands"; *The Baker Street Journal,* Vol. III, No. 4, Old Series, October, 1948, pp. 418–20.

HAYCRAFT, HOWARD
Murder for Pleasure: The Life and Times of the Detective Story; New York and London: D. Appleton-Century Company, Inc., 1941.

HAYNE, DONALD
"On Holmes' Visit to the United States in 1912"; *The Baker Street Journal,* Vol. I, No. 2, Old Series, April, 1946, pp. 189–90.

HAYNES, GEORGE
"The Last Mrs. Watson"; *The Sherlock Holmes Journal,* Vol. VI, No. 2, Spring, 1963, pp. 53–4.

HEDGPETH, JOEL W.
"Re-Examination of 'The Adventure of the Lion's Mane' "; *Scientific Monthly,* March, 1945; *The Baker Street Journal,* Vol. III, No. 3, Old Series, July, 1948, pp. 285–94.

HELDENBRAND, PAGE
"The Adventures of the Dead Detective"; *Leaves from the Copper Beeches,* pp. 33–4.

"Another Bohemian Scandal"; *The Baker Street Journal,* Vol. IV, No. 1, Old Series, January, 1949, pp. 72–3.

"A Ghostly Watson?"; *The Baker Street Journal,* Vol. III, No. 4, Old Series, October, 1948, pp. 482–3.

"On the Island of Uffa"; *Heldenbrand's Christmas Perennial,* New York: Appledore Towers Letter Press, 1954.

"On an Obscure Nervous Page"; *The Baker Street Journal,* Vol. IV, No. 3,

New Series, July, 1954, pp. 154–5.

"Sherlock Holmes in Disguise"; *The Baker Street Journal,* Vol. I, No. 3, Old Series, July, 1946, pp. 318–22.

HELLING, CORNELIS
"The Third Person"; *The Baker Street Journal,* Vol. VI, No. 4, New Series, October, 1956, p. 203.

"The True Story of the Dancing Men"; *The Baker Street Journal,* Vol. IV, No. 3, New Series, July, 1954, pp. 160–3.

HENDRICKSON, J. RAYMOND
"De Re Pharmaca"; *Leaves from the Copper Beeches,* pp. 11–4.

HENDRIKSEN, A. D.
"On the Year of Sherlock Holmes' Birth"; *The Sherlock Holmes Journal,* Vol. I, No. 1, May, 1952, pp. 39–40.

HICKS, JOHN L.
"No Fire Without Some Smoke"; *The Baker Street Journal,* Vol. V, No. 1, New Series, January, 1955, pp. 27–33.

HILL, *Professor* POPE R., SR.
"The Final Problem: An Exemplification of the Substructure Theory"; *The Baker Street Journal,* Vol. V, No. 3, New Series, July, 1955, pp. 149–53.

"Sherlock Holmes Meets Jean Henri Fabre"; *The Baker Street Journal,* Vol. II, No. 1, Old Series, January, 1947, pp. 63–6.

HINRICH, D.
"Munsters v. Mallows"; *The Sherlock Holmes Journal,* Vol. VI, No. 4, Spring, 1964, p. 131.

"The Royal Mallows, 1854–1888"; *The Sherlock Holmes Journal,* Vol. VI, No. 1, Winter, 1962, pp. 20–2.

HITCHINGS, J. L.
"Sherlock Holmes the Logician"; *The Baker Street Journal,* Vol. I, No. 2, Old Series, April, 1946, pp. 113–7.

HOFF, *Dr.* EBBE CURTIS
"The Adventure of John and Mary"; *The Baker Street Journal,* Vol. IX, No. 3, New Series, July, 1959, pp. 136–52.

(with PHOEBE M. HOFF) "The Affair at St. Monica's"; *The Baker Street Journal,* Vol. XIII, No. 1, New Series, March, 1963, pp. 5–15.

HOFFECKER, DOUGLAS M.
"Forgive Us, Oh Lord!"; *The Baker Street Journal,* Vol. V, No. 1, New Series, January, 1955, pp. 40–2.

HOGAN, JOHN V. L.
"An Unsolved Puzzle in the Writings"; *The Baker Street Journal,* Vol. III, No. 3, New Series, July, 1953, pp. 173–4.

HOLMES, MARCELLA
"Sherlock Holmes and the Prime Min-

isters"; *The Baker Street Journal,* Vol. V, No. 1, New Series, January, 1955, pp. 34–9.

HOLROYD, JAMES EDWARD
Baker Street Byways; London: George Allen & Unwin, Ltd., 1959.

"Dr. Watson at the Criterion"; *The Sherlock Holmes Journal,* Vol. II, No. 2, December, 1954, p. 26.

"On the Cab-Rank in Baker Street"; *The Sherlock Holmes Journal,* Vol. II, No. 4, Winter, 1955, p. 27.

"On the Cheetah as Watch-Dog"; *The Sherlock Holmes Journal,* Vol. II, No. 3, Summer, 1955, p. 14.

"On the Evening Papers of London"; *The Sherlock Holmes Journal,* Vol. II, No. 4, Winter, 1955, pp. 26–7.

"On the Grassing of Mr. Joseph Harrison"; *The Sherlock Holmes Journal,* Vol. I, No. 2, September, 1952, p. 32.

"On the Holborn Restaurant"; *The Sherlock Holmes Journal,* Vol. II, No. 1, July, 1954, p. 19.

"On Holmes as Bee-Keeper"; *The Sherlock Holmes Journal,* Vol. II, No. 3, Summer, 1955, pp. 12–3.

"On Holmes Being Fully Dressed in 'The Speckled Band' "; *The Sherlock Holmes Journal,* Vol. II, No. 3, Summer, 1955, p. 13.

"On the Manuscript of *The Valley of Fear*"; *The Sherlock Holmes Journal,* Vol. III, No. 2, Winter, 1956, p. 20.

"On the Picture of General Gordon"; *The Sherlock Holmes Journal,* Vol. I, No. 1, May, 1952, p. 26.

"On the Rooms in Montague Street"; *The Sherlock Holmes Journal,* Vol. II, No. 3, Summer, 1955, p. 12.

"On the Route to Appledore Towers"; *The Sherlock Holmes Journal,* Vol. II, No. 1, July, 1954, p. 17.

"On the Westwardness of 221 Baker Street"; *The Sherlock Holmes Journal,* Vol. I, No. 1, May, 1952, p. 24.

"Some Problems in 'The Six Napoleons' "; *The Sherlock Holmes Journal,* Vol. I, No. 4, December, 1953, pp. 22–3.

HOLSTEIN, L. S.
"Bull Pups and Literary Agents"; *The Baker Street Journal Christmas Annual,* 1958, pp. 54–7.

"Inspector G. Lestrade"; *The Baker Street Journal,* Vol. VIII, No. 2, New Series, April, 1958, pp. 78–84.

"A Scandal in St. Monica"; *The Baker Street Journal,* Vol. XI, No. 1, New Series, January, 1952, pp. 49–52.

" '7. Knowledge of Chemistry–Profound' "; *The Baker Street Journal*, Vol. IV, No. 1, New Series, January, 1954, pp. 44–9.

HOOK, D. MARCUS
"More on the Railway Journeys"; *The Baker Street Journal*, Vol. III, No. 2, Old Series, April, 1948, pp. 228–9.

HOWARD, ALAN
"A New Year for the Hound"; *The Sherlock Holmes Journal*, Vol. II, No. 3, Summer, 1955, pp. 3–6.

HOWARD, SAMUEL F.
"More About Maiwand"; *The Baker Street Journal*, Vol. II, No. 1, New Series, January, 1957, pp. 20–5.

HOWLETT, ANTHONY D.
(with HUMPHREY MORTON) "The Ethereal Hound"; *The Sherlock Holmes Journal*, Vol. IV, No. 1, Winter, 1956, pp. 15–6.
"The Horror Hound"; *The Sherlock Holmes Journal*, Vol. IV, No. 1, Winter, 1958, pp. 16–7.
"*The Hound of the Baskervilles* on the Screen"; *The Sherlock Holmes Journal*, Vol. I, No. 1, May, 1952, pp. 33–5.
"*The Hound of the Baskervilles*: Vintage 1939"; *The Sherlock Holmes Journal*, Vol. IV, No. 4, Spring, 1960, pp. 134–5.
"Mr. Arthur Wontner"; *The Sherlock Holmes Journal*, Vol. I, No. 2, September, 1952, pp. 12, 13.
"Mr. Carleton Hobbs"; *The Sherlock Holmes Journal*, Vol. VI, No. 4, September, 1964, pp. 118–20.
"Shinwell-Johnsoniana"; *The Sherlock Holmes Journal*, Vol. IV, No. 4, September, 1960, pp. 135, 140.
"The Whimpering Hound"; *The Sherlock Holmes Journal*, Vol. IV, No. 2, September, 1959, pp. 71–2.

HUNT, T. B.
(With *Professor* H. W. STARR) "What Happened to Mary Morstan"; *The Baker Street Journal*, Vol. II, No. 3, Old Series, July, 1947, pp. 237–46.

HYSLOP, JAMES T.
"The Master Adds a Postcript"; *The Baker Street Journal*, Vol. II, No. 2, Old Series, April, 1947, pp. 113–8.

HYSLOP, JOHN
"Sherlock Holmes and the Press"; *The Sherlock Holmes Journal*, Vol. IV, No. 1, Winter, 1958, pp. 4–8.
The Incunabular Holmes, edited by Edgar W. Smith; Morristown, New Jersey: The Baker Street Irregulars, Inc., 1958.
Introducing Mr. Sherlock Holmes, edited by Edgar W. Smith; Morristown, New Jersey: The Baker Street Irregulars, Inc., 1959.

IRALDI, JAMES C.
"That Extraordinary Man"; *The Baker Street Journal*, Vol. III, No. 1, New Series, January, 1953, pp. 13–7.
"The Other Geese"; *The Baker Street Journal*, Vol. III, No. 1, July, 1954, pp. 156–9.
"The Victorian Gondola"; *The Baker Street Journal*, Vol. I, No. 3, New Series, July, 1951, pp. 99–103.

JACOBS, LEONARD
"Baker Street"; *The Baker Street Journal*, Vol. VI, No. 2, New Series, April, 1956, pp. 101–5.

JENKINS, WILLIAM D.
"A Peculiar Persecution"; *The Baker Street Journal*, Vol. XIV, No. 1, New Series, March, 1964, pp. 45–53.

JONES, *The Reverend* G. BASIL
"The Dog and the Date"; *The Sherlock Holmes Journal*, Vol. II, No. 2, December, 1954, pp. 11–3.

JUDSON, RALPH
"The Mystery of Baritsu: A Sidelight Upon Sherlock Holmes' Accomplishments"; *The Baker Street Journal Christmas Annual*, 1958, pp. 10–6.

KASER, MICHAEL C.
"The Dating of 'Lady Frances Carfax' "; *The Baker Street Journal*, Vol. VII, No. 2, New Series, April, 1957, pp. 87–91.
"Sherlock Holmes on the Continent"; *The Baker Street Journal*, Vol. VI, No. 1, New Series, January, 1956, pp. 19–24.
"A Solution to 'Lady Frances Carfax' "; *The Baker Street Journal*, Vol. IX, No. 2, New Series, April, 1959, pp. 85–7.

KASSON, PHILIP
"The True Blue: A Case of Identification"; *The Baker Street Journal*, Vol. XI, No. 4, New Series, December, 1961, pp. 200–2.

KEDDIE, JAMES, SR.
"Gasogene, Coal Box, Persian Slipper"; *The Saturday Review of Literature*, June 27, 1936; *The Second Cab*, pp. 15–7.
"The Mystery of the Second Wound"; *Profile by Gaslight*, pp. 173–7.

KEEN, SHERRY
"Ship's or 'ship's'?"; *The Baker Street Journal*, Vol. III, No. 4, New Series, October, 1953, pp. 234–5.

KENT, WILLIAM
An Encyclopaedia of London; New York: The Macmillan Company, 1951.

KIERMAN, RAY
" 'It Is a Curious Little Problem' "; *The Baker Street Journal Christmas Annual*, 1957, pp. 26–30.
"A Shocking Affair"; *The Baker Street Journal*, Vol. II, No. 2, New Series, April, 1952, pp. 103–7.

KIMBALL, ELLIOT
"The Admirable Murray"; *Watsoniana: First Series*; Clinton, Connecticut: The Toille Press, 1962.
"Chronology of 'The Blue Carbuncle' "; *The Baker Street Journal*, Vol. XI, No. 4, New Series, December, 1961, pp. 215–7.
Dr. Watson at Netley; Clinton, Connecticut: The Toille Press, 1962.
"The First Man Who Beat Holmes"; *The Baker Street Gasogene*, Vol. I, No. 4, 1962, pp. 47–50.
"The Milverton Mess"; *The Sherlock Holmes Journal*, Vol. V, No. 4, Spring, 1962, pp. 100–2.
"The Missing Year"; *Watsoniana: First Series*.
"Origin and Evolution of G. Lestrade: 1 — Onomatological Considerations"; *The Sherlock Holmes Journal*, Vol. VI, No. 1, Winter, 1962, pp. 4–5; "2—A Matter of Mancinism"; *The Sherlock Holmes Journal*, Vol. VI, No. 2, Spring, 1963, pp. 43–5.
"The Stature of John H. Watson"; *The Baker Street Gasogene*, Vol. I, No. 3, 1961, pp. 5–10.
"Watson's Neurosis"; *Watsoniana: First Series*.
"The Watsons of Northumberland"; *Watsoniana: First Series*.

KLAUBER, LAURENCE M.
"The Truth About the Speckled Band"; *The Baker Street Journal*, Vol. III, No. 2, Old Series, April, 1948, pp. 149–57.

KLINEFELTER, WALTER
Sherlock Holmes in Portrait and Profile; Syracuse, New York: Syracuse University Press, 1963.
"The Writings of Mr. Sherlock Holmes"; *The Baker Street Journal*, Vol. I, No. 4, Old Series, October, 1946, pp. 409–16.

KNOX, *Monsignor* RONALD A.
"The Mystery of Mycroft"; *Baker Street Studies*, pp. 131–58.
"Studies in the Literature of Sherlock Holmes"; *The Blue Book*, 1912; *Essays in Satire*, London: Sheed & Ward, Ltd., 1928; *The Incunabular Holmes*.

KOELLE, *Dr.* GEORGE B.
"The Poisons of the Canon"; *Leaves from the Copper Beeches*, pp. 91–6.

LAUTERBACH, CHARLES E. and EDWARD S.
"The Man Who Seldom Laughed"; *The Baker Street Journal Christmas Annual*, 1960, pp. 265–71.

LAWSON, DOUGLAS
"The Speckled Band—What Is It?"; *The Baker Street Journal*, Vol. IV, No. 1, New Series, January, 1954, pp. 12–20.

Leaves from the Copper Beeches, edited by H. W. Starr, Thomas Hart, Ames Johnston, and Henry Shalet; Narbeth, Pennsylvania: The Livingston Publishing Company for the Sons of the Copper Beeches, 1958.

LEAVITT, ROBERT KEITH
"Annie Oakley in Baker Street"; *Profile by Gaslight,* pp. 230–42.

"Nummi in Arca or The Fiscal Holmes"; *221B,* pp. 16–36.

"The Origin of 221B Worship, Part I: The Chaldean Roots"; *The Baker Street Journal*, Vol. XI, No. 3, New Series, September, 1961, pp. 135–49; "Part II: Our Own Dear Little Girlie Becomes a) Legitimate, b) the Subject of Unmitigated Bleat"; *The Baker Street Journal*, Vol. XI, No. 4, New Series, December, 1961, pp. 225–34.

"The Preposterously Paired Performances of the Preacher's Portrait"; *The Baker Street Journal*, Vol. III, No. 4, Old Series, October, 1948, pp. 404–17.

"Who Was Cecil Forrester?"; *The Baker Street Journal*, Vol. I, No. 2, Old Series, April, 1946, pp. 201–4.

LEONARD, WILLIAM
"Re: Vampires"; *The Baker Street Journal Christmas Annual,* 1957, pp. 20–5.

LESH, *Professor* RICHARD D.
"Watson, Come Here; I Want You: in Afghanistan"; *The Baker Street Journal,* Vol. XIV, No. 3, New Series, September, 1964, pp. 136–8.

LESLIE, IAN M.
"Dr. Watson's Christmas Party of 1889"; *The Sherlock Holmes Journal*, Vol. I, No. 1, May, 1952, pp. 29–30.

L'ETANG, HUGH
"Some Observations on the Black Formosa Corruption and Tapanuli Fever"; *The Sherlock Holmes Journal*, Vol. IV, No. 2, Spring, 1959, pp. 58–60.

LEVERTON, JEFFERY SPRY
"On Watson's Having Taken his M.D. Degree"; *The Baker Street Journal,* Vol. III, No. 2, New Series, April, 1953, p. 117.

LEVINE, ARTHUR L.
"Lowenstein's Other Creeper"; *The Baker Street Journal*, Vol. VI, No. 1, New Series, January, 1956, pp. 30–3.

"A Man of 'Formidable Resourcefulness' "; *The Baker Street Journal*, Vol. IV, No. 3, New Series, July, 1954, pp. 169–73.

LIEB, POUL IB
"Sherlock's Delights"; *The Baker Street Journal*, Vol. VIII, No. 2, New Series, April, 1958, pp. 104–6.

LONGFELLOW, ESTHER
"The Distaff Side of Baker Street"; *The Baker Street Journal*, Vol. I, No. 1, Old Series, January, 1946, pp. 9–13.

MACCARTHY, *Sir* DESMOND
"Dr. Watson"; *The Listener,* December 11, 1929.

MACDONELL, A. G.
"The Truth About Moriarty"; *The New Statesman,* October 5, 1929; as "Mr. Moriarty"; *Baker Street Studies,* pp. 159–75; *The Baker Street Journal,* Vol. II, No. 2, Old Series, April, 1947, pp, 164–71.

MACDOUGLAD, DUNCAN, JR.
"Some Onomatological Notes on 'Sherlock Holmes' and Other Names in the Sacred Writings"; *The Baker Street Journal*, Vol. XII, No. 4, New Series, October, 1962, pp. 213–8.

MACGOWAN, KENNETH, *Editor*
Sleuths: Twenty-Three Great Detectives of Fiction and Their Best Stories; New York: Harcourt, Brace and Company, 1931.

MACKAY, IAN
" 'Knowledge of Politics—Feeble'?"; *The Sherlock Holmes Journal,* Vol. I, No. 2, September, 1952, pp. 25–30.

MACKENZIE, ARMINE D.
"The Case of the Illustrious Predecessor"; *Wilson Library Bulletin,* Vol. XIX, December, 1944, pp. 278–9; *The Baker Street Gasogene,* Vol. I, No. 2, 1961, pp. 29–31.

MACKENZIE, J. B.
"Sherlock Holmes' Plots and Strategy"; *The Green Bag,* The Boston Book Company, September, 1902; *The Baker Street Journal Christmas Annual,* 1956, pp. 56–61.

MACKENZIE, STANLEY
"The Engineer's Thumb"; *The Sherlock Holmes Journal,* Vol. II, No. 4, Winter, 1955, pp. 32–3.

MAURICE, ARTHUR BARTLETT
"More Sherlock Holmes Theories"; *The Bookman,* New York, May, 1902; *The Incunabular Sherlock Holmes.*

"Some Inconsistencies of Sherlock Holmes"; *The Bookman,* New York, January, 1902; *The Incunabular Sherlock Holmes.*

MAY, R. F.
"*The Hound of the Baskervilles:* A Botanical Enquiry"; *The Sherlock Holmes Journal,* Vol. VI, No. 1, Winter, 1962, p. 26.

McCLEARY, *Dr.* GEORGE F.
"Was Sherlock Holmes a Drug Addict?" *Profile by Gaslight,* pp. 40–5.

"When Did Watson Meet His First Wife?"; *The Baker Street Journal,* Vol. II, No. 1, Old Series, January, 1947, pp. 50–3.

McCOMAS, STANLEY
"Love at Lhasa"; *The Baker Street Journal,* Vol. I, No. 2, New Series, April, 1951, pp. 43–51.

McDADE, THOMAS M.
"Heads and Holmes"; *The Baker Street Journal,* Vol. XI, No. 3, New Series, September, 1961, pp. 162–6.

McDIARMID, E. W.
"Professor Sherlock Holmes, Ph.D."; *Exploring Sherlock Holmes,* pp. 27–41.

"Reichenbach and Beyond"; *The Baker Street Journal Christmas Annual,* 1957, pp. 34–43.

McGAW, LISA
"Some Trifling Notes on Sherlock Holmes and Ornithology"; *The Baker Street Journal,* Vol. X, No. 4, October, 1960, pp. 231–4.

McKEE, WILBUR K.
"The Son of a Certain Gracious Lady"; *The Baker Street Journal,* Vol. VIII, No. 3, New Series, July, 1958, pp. 133–8.

McLAREN, R. M.
"Doctor Watson—Punter or Speculator?"; *The Sherlock Holmes Journal,* Vol. I, No. 1, May, 1952, pp. 8–10.

McLAUCHLIN, RUSSELL
"Ballade on a Daring Theme"; *The Baker Street Journal,* Vol. II, No. 1, Old Series, January, 1947, pp. 16–7.

"On the Dating of the Master's Birth"; *The Baker Street Journal,* Vol. VI, No. 3, New Series, July, 1956, pp. 138–42.

"What Price Baker Street?"; *The Baker Street Journal,* Vol. II, No. 2, New Series, April, 1952, pp. 65–70.

McNEIL, IAN
"An Engineer's Thoughts on 'The Engineer's Thumb' "; *The Sherlock Holmes Journal,* Vol. V, No. 4, Spring, 1962, pp. 108–10.

McPHARLIN, PAUL
"221B Baker Street: Certain Physical Details"; *The Baker Street Journal,* Vol. II, No. 2, Old Series, April, 1947, pp, 180–94.

MEAKER, Dr. SAMUEL R.
"Watson Medicus"; *The Third Cab*, pp. 27–37.

MERRIMAN, CHARLES O.
"Birthplace of Holmes"; *The Sherlock Holmes Journal*, Vol. III, No. 1, Summer, 1956, pp. 22–3.

"A Case of Identity—No. 2"; *The Sherlock Holmes Journal*, Vol. V, No. 3, Winter, 1961, pp. 83–6.

"The Game Is Afoot"; *The Sherlock Holmes Journal*, Vol. V, No. 4, Spring, 1962, pp. 105–6.

"On the Fighting Cock Inn"; *The Baker Street Journal*, Vol. XII, No. 4, New Series, December, 1962, p. 245.

"Tar Derivatives Not Wanted"; *The Sherlock Holmes Journal*, Vol. VI, No. 1, Winter, 1962, p. 33.

"Unfair to Mycroft"; *The Sherlock Holmes Journal*, Vol. I, No. 4, December, 1953, pp. 41–2.

MERRITT, RUSSELL L.
"Re: The Adventure of the Worst Man in London"; *The Baker Street Journal Christmas Annual*, 1959, pp. 296–301.

METCALFE, N. P.
"The Date of the *Study in Scarlet*"; *The Sherlock Holmes Journal*, Vol. IV, No. 2, Spring, 1959, pp. 37–40.

"Holmes and Politics—A Retrospection"; *The Sherlock Holmes Journal*, Vol. I, No. 4, December, 1953; pp. 11–9.

"Oxford or Cambridge or Both?" *The Baker Street Journal Christmas Annual*, 1956, pp. 7–14.

MICHELL, HUMFREY
"Lady Frances Carfax Reappears"; *The Baker Street Journal*, Vol. II, No. 4, Old Series, October, 1947, p. 472.

"On the Bankruptcy of Dawson and Neligan"; *The Baker Street Journal*, Vol. III, No. 2, Old Series, April, 1948, pp. 230–1.

"On Sherlock Holmes' Method of Indexing"; *The Baker Street Journal*, Vol. IV, No. 3, New Series, July, 1954, pp. 187–8.

"On *the* Lady Frances Carfax"; *The Baker Street Journal*, Vol. II, No. 4, Old Series, October, 1947, p. 472.

"On Watson As a Writer"; *The Baker Street Journal*, Vol. II, No. 1, New Series, January, 1952, pp. 55–6.

"The Palace Clock"; *The Baker Street Journal*, Vol. I, No. 1, Old Series, January, 1946, p. 89.

"The Sartorial Sherlock Holmes"; *A Baker Street Four-Wheeler*, pp. 31–6.

(With J. H. MICHELL) "Sherlock Holmes the Chemist"; *The Baker Street Journal*, Vol. I, No. 3, Old Series, July, 1946, pp. 245–52.

"That 'Tenacious Black Clay' "; *The Sherlock Holmes Journal*, Vol. II, No. 1, July, 1954, p. 36.

"The Wonderful Wedding"; *The Baker Street Journal*, Vol. IV, No. 1, New Series, January, 1954, pp. 22–3.

MINGEY, EDWARD J., JR.
"The Bull Pup's Disappearance; or, Who Paid Watson's Rent?"; *The Baker Street Journal*, Vol. VII, No. 3, New Series, July, 1957, pp. 141–6.

The Misadventures of Sherlock Holmes, edited by Ellery Queen; Boston: Little, Brown & Co., 1944.

MONTGOMERY, JAMES
Art in the Blood and What Is This Thing Called Music (or Body and Soul); Philadelphia: Privately printed, 1950.

A Case of Identity; Philadelphia: International Printing Company, 1955.

Shots from the Canon; Philadelphia: Privately printed, 1953.

Sidelights on Sherlock; Philadelphia: Privately printed, 1951.

"Speculation in Diamonds"; *The Sherlock Holmes Journal*, Vol. I, No. 4, December, 1953, pp. 30–6.

A Study in Pictures: Being a "Trifling Monograph" on the Iconography of Sherlock Holmes; Philadelphia: International Printing Company, 1954.

MOORE, R. C.
(with BRYCE CRAWFORD, JR.) "The Final Problem—Where?"; *Exploring Sherlock Holmes*, pp. 82–7.

MORGAN, ROBERT S.
"The Puzzle of the Bull Pup"; *The Baker Street Journal Christmas Annual*, 1956, pp. 35–40.

Spotlight on a Simple Case, or Wiggins, Who Was That Horse I Saw With You Last Night; Wilmington, Delaware: The Cedar Tree Press, n.d. (1959).

MORIARTY, DANIEL L.
"The Woman Who Beat Sherlock Holmes"; *The Baker Street Journal*, Vol. IX, No. 2, New Series, April, 1959, pp. 69–82.

MORLEY, CHRISTOPHER
"The Blue Carbuncle, or, the Season of Forgiveness"; *The Adventure of the Blue Carbuncle*, New York: The Baker Street Irregulars, Inc., 1948.

"Dr. Watson's Secret"; *221B*, pp. 46–53.

Introduction and Notes to *Sherlock Holmes and Dr. Watson: A Textbook of Friendship*; New York: Harcourt, Brace & Co., 1944.

Introduction to *The Complete Sherlock Holmes*; Garden City, New York: Doubleday, Doran and Company, Inc., 1930.

"On the 'B' in 221B"; *The Baker Street Journal*, Vol. II, No. 3, Old Series, July, 1947, p. 270.

"On Baker Street"; *The Baker Street Journal*, Vol. I, No. 3, Old Series, July, 1946, p. 303.

"On the Baker Street Irregulars"; *The Baker Street Journal*, Vol. I, No. 3, July, 1946, pp. 286–91; reprinted, *The Baker Street Journal*, Vol. XIII, No. 1, New Series, March, 1963, pp. 17–22.

"On the Chamber As Opposed to the Barrel in Small Arms"; *The Baker Street Journal*, Vol. II, No. 2, Old Series, April, 1947, pp, 142–3.

"On Clark Russell"; *Profile by Gaslight*, pp. 54–5; *The Baker Street Journal*, Vol. III, No. 4, Old Series, October, 1948, p. 444.

"On the Day of Watson's First Meeting with Holmes"; *The Baker Street Journal Christmas Annual*, 1960, p. 281.

"On the Derivation of 'Ridling Thorpe' "; *The Baker Street Journal*, Vol. I, No. 2, New Series, April, 1951, p. 55.

"On Dribbling in Rugby Football"; *The Baker Street Journal*, Vol. III, No. 2, Old Series, April, 1948, p. 171.

"On the Dutch Steamship *Friesland*"; *Profile by Gaslight*, p. 57.

"On the Fate of the *Matilda Briggs*"; *The Baker Street Journal*, Vol. I, No. 4, Old Series, October, 1946, p. 408.

"On Holmes' Birthplace at Holmes Mall in the North Riding of Yorkshire"; *The Baker Street Journal Christmas Annual*, 1960, pp. 284–5.

"On the Island of Uffa"; *The Baker Street Journal*, Vol. I, No. 2, New Series, April, 1951, p. 57.

"On John Hector McFarlane's Inability to Get Back from Lower Norwood"; *The Baker Street Journal*, Vol. III, No. 1, Old Series, January, 1948, pp. 41–2.

"On Lady Frances Carfax as Watson's Third Wife"; *The Baker Street Journal*, Vol. II, No. 2, Old Series, April, 1947, p. 141.

"On the Late Train to Cambridge"; *The Baker Street Journal*, Vol. III, No. 2, Old Series, April, 1948, p. 171.

"On 'Long Vacation' as a Cambridge Term"; *The Baker Street Journal*, Vol. III, No. 2, Old Series, April, 1948, p. 172.

"On the Name 'Mycroft'"; *Profile by Gaslight*, p. 58.

"On Peterhouse as Holmes' Cambridge College"; *The Baker Street Journal*, Vol. III, No. 3, Old Series, July, 1948, p. 296.

"On Putting One's Boots on Backwards"; *The Baker Street Journal*, Vol. II, No. 2, Old Series, April, 1947, p. 142.

"On Raffles Holmes as a Brother of Sherlock's"; *The Baker Street Journal*, Vol. II. No. 2, Old Series, April, 1947, p. 140.

"On Sherlock Holmes' Full Name"; *The Baker Street Journal*, Vol. I, No. 2, Old Series, April, 1946, pp. 127–8.

"On the Stop at Swindon"; *The Baker Street Journal*, Vol. II, No. 3, Old Series, July, 1947, pp. 270–1.

"On Thomas Carlyle"; *Profile by Gaslight*, pp. 52–3.

"On Thurston the Billiard Player"; *The Baker Street Journal*, Vol. I, No. 4, Old Series, October, 1946, pp. 404–6.

"On the Tide-Waiter"; *Profile by Gaslight*, pp. 55–6.

"On Watson's Landing at Troopship Jetty"; *Profile by Gaslight*, p. 56.

"On Watson's Removal from the Northumberlands"; *The Baker Street Journal*, Vol. I, No. 2, New Series, April, 1951, p. 56.

"On Yorkshire as Holmes' Native County"; *The Baker Street Journal*, Vol. IV, No. 1, Old Series, January, 1949, p. 42.

"Was Sherlock Holmes an American?"; *221B*, pp. 5–15.

"Watson a la Mode"; *The Baker Street Journal*, Vol. I, No. 1, Old Series, January, 1946, pp. 15–20.

MORLEY, Dr. FELIX

"As Felix Morley Wrote to William S. Baring-Gould: An Addendum to 'Dr. Watson Has Gone to Widecombe'"; *The Baker Street Journal*, Vol. XV, No. 1, New Series, March, 1965, pp. 16–7.

"How the Child Got Into the Chimney"; *The Baker Street Journal Christmas Annual*, 1958, pp. 7–9.

"The Significance of the Second Stain"; *Profile by Gaslight*, pp. 243–59.

MORLEY, FRANK V.

"I Am Puzzled About Saxe-Coburg Square"; *The Baker Street Journal*, Vol. V, No. 3, New Series, July, 1955, pp. 139–41.

MORROW, L. A.

"A Diplomatic Secret"; *The Sherlock Holmes Journal*, Vol. II, No. 4, Winter, 1955, pp. 21–5.

"The Game Is . . ."; *The Baker Street Journal*, Vol. VII, No. 1, New Series, January, 1957, pp. 32–8.

MORTON, HUMPHREY

(with ANTHONY D. HOWLETT) "The Ether-eal Hound"; *The Sherlock Holmes Journal*, Vol. IV, No. 1, Winter, 1956, pp. 15–6.

"'A Long Drive to Hampstead'"; *The Sherlock Holmes Journal*, Vol. V, No. 1, Winter, 1960, pp. 22–3.

"A Milvertonian Identification"; *The Sherlock Holmes Journal*, Vol. VI, No. 1, Winter, 1962, pp. 14–5.

MURCH, A. E.

The Development of the Detective Novel; London: Peter Owen Limited, 1958.

NAGANUMA, Dr. KOHKI

"Sherlock Holmes and Cocaine"; *The Baker Street Journal*, Vol. XIII, No. 3, New Series, September, 1963, pp. 170–5.

NEITZKE, GORDON

"Sherlock Holmes and Jack the Ripper"; *Client's Third Case-Book*, pp. 80–3.

NELSON, JAMES

"Sherlock and the Sherpas"; *The Baker Street Journal*, Vol. VII, No. 3, New Series, July, 1957, pp. 161–4.

NEWTON, G. B.

"Billy the Page"; *The Sherlock Holmes Journal*, Vol. II, No. 3, September, 1955, pp. 7–10.

"Concerning the Authorship of 'The Mazarin Stone'"; *The Sherlock Holmes Journal*, Vol. IV, No. 2, Spring, 1959, pp. 52–4.

"The Date of *The Valley of Fear*"; *The Sherlock Holmes Journal*, Vol. II, No. 4, Winter, 1955, pp. 38–42.

"This Desirable Residence"; *The Sherlock Holmes Journal*, Vol. III, No. 2, Winter, 1956, pp. 12–4.

NIEMINSKI, JOHN

"On Watson's Possessing a Pair of Tennis Shoes"; *The Baker Street Journal*, Vol. V, No. 3, New Series, July, 1955, pp. 182–3.

OFFICER, HARVEY

"Sherlock Holmes and Music"; *221B*, pp. 71–3.

OFFORD, LENORE GLEN

"The Brief Adventure of Mr. Turner"; *The Baker Street Journal*, Vol. I, No. 3, Old Series, July, 1946, pp. 253–9.

OLNEY, Professor CLARKE

"The Literacy of Sherlock Holmes"; *The Sherlock Holmes Journal*, Vol. II, No. 4, Winter, 1955, pp. 9–15.

OURSLER, WILL

"His French Cousin"; *The Baker Street Journal Christmas Annual*, 1956, pp. 32–4.

PAGET, WINIFRED

"Full Circle"; *The Sherlock Holmes Journal*, Vol. I, No. 1, May, 1952, pp. 27–8.

PALMER, STUART

"The Adventure of the Marked Man"; *Ellery Queen's Mystery Magazine*, July, 1944.

"Notes on Certain Evidences of Caniphobia in Mr. Sherlock Holmes and His Associates"; *The Baker Street Journal*, Vol. V, No. 4, New Series, October, 1955, pp. 197–204.

PARK, ORLANDO

Sherlock Holmes, Esq., and John H. Watson, M.D.: An Encyclopaedia of Their Affairs; Evanston, Illinois: Northwestern University Press, 1962.

PARKER, HYMAN

"Birdy Edwards and the Scowrers Reconsidered"; *The Baker Street Journal*, Vol. IV, No. 1, New Series, March, 1964, pp. 3–7.

PATTRICK, ROBERT R.

"The Case of the Superfluous Landlady"; *The Baker Street Journal*, Vol. III, No. 4, New Series, October, 1953, pp. 241–3.

"Moriarty Was There"; *The Baker Street Journal Christmas Annual*, 1958, pp. 45–53.

"The Oasis in the Howling Desert"; *The Sherlock Holmes Journal*, Vol. IV, No. 4, Spring, 1960, pp. 126–8.

"October 9, 1890"; *The Sherlock Holmes Journal*, Vol. III, No. 1, Summer, 1956, pp. 126–8.

"On the Number of Henry Bakers in the London of the Eighties"; *The Baker Street Journal*, Vol. III, No. 2, New Series, April, 1953, pp. 125–6.

"A Sherlock Holmes Chronology"; *The Baker Street Journal*, Vol. XIII, No. 1, New Series, March, 1963, p. 62.

"A Study in Crypto-Choreography"; *The Baker Street Journal*, Vol. V, No. 4, New Series, October, 1955, pp. 205–9.

"Watson Writes from Baskerville Hall"; *The Baker Street Journal Christmas Annual*, 1960, pp. 293–8.

PEARSON, EDMUND

"Sherlock Holmes Among the Illustrators"; *The Bookman*, New York, August, 1932.

"PENANG LAWYER, A"

"The Name's the Same"; *The Sherlock Holmes Journal*, Vol. II, No. 1, p. 11.

PENNELL, *Dr.* VERNON
"A Resumé of the Medical Life of John H. Watson, M.D., Late of the Army Medical Department, with an Appendix of the London University Regulations for Medical Degrees for the Year 1875"; *The Sherlock Holmes Journal*, Vol. III, No. 2, Winter, 1956, pp. 6–11.

PERCIVAL, WILLIAM
"Sherlock Holmes and Air-Guns"; *The Sherlock Holmes Journal*, Vol. VI, No. 1, Winter, 1962, pp. 15–6.

PETERSEN, SVEND
A Sherlock Holmes Almanac; Washington, D.C.: Privately printed, 1956.
"When the Game Was Not Afoot"; *The Baker Street Journal*, Vol. IV, No. 1, Old Series, January, 1949, pp. 59–71.

PICKARD, CHARLES M.
"The Reticence of Dr. Mortimer"; *The Baker Street Journal*, Vol. VII, No. 3, New Series, July, 1957, pp. 153–5.

PITTS, ZASU
"Mrs. Hudson Speaks"; a recording made for the meeting of the Amateur Mendicants Society of Detroit on March 14, 1947, and reported in the *Baker Street Journal*, Vol. II, No. 3, Old Series, July, 1947, pp. 328–31.

PLAYFAIR, GILES
"John and James"; *The Baker Street Journal*, Vol. I, No. 3, Old Series, July, 1946, pp. 271–6.

PLIMENTEL, WILLIAM E.
"On the Electric Switch at Appledore Towers"; *The Baker Street Journal*, Vol. V, No. 2, New Series, April, 1955, p. 121.

PORTUGAL, EUSTACE
"The Holmes-Moriarty Duel"; *The Bookman*, London, May, 1934.

PRATT, FLETCHER
"The Gastronomic Holmes"; *The Baker Street Journal*, Vol. II, No. 2, New Series, April, 1952, pp. 94–9.
"Holmes and the Royal Navy"; *The Second Cab*, pp. 65–9.
"The Secret Message of the Dancing Men"; *Profile by Gaslight*, pp. 274–82.
"Very Little Murder"; *The Baker Street Journal*, Vol. V, No. 2, New Series, April, 1955, pp. 69–76.

PRESTIGE, COLIN
"Agents of Evil"; *The Baker Street Journal*, Vol. V, No. 2, New Series, July, 1955, pp. 144–7.
"The Criterion Plaque"; *The Sherlock Holmes Journal*, Vol. I, No. 3, June, 1953, pp. 10–1.

"For a World Now Prepared"; *The Sherlock Holmes Journal*, Vol. IV, No. 2, Spring, 1959, pp. 61–2.
"Problem of Pope's Court"; *The Sherlock Holmes Journal*, Vol. I, No. 3, June, 1953, pp. 27–8.
"South London Adventures"; *The Sherlock Holmes Journal*, Vol. III, No. 3, Autumn, 1957, pp. 5–8.

PRICE, EDMUND T.
"The Singular Adventures of the Grice Patersons in the Island of Uffa and the Loss of the British Barque *Sophy Anderson*"; *The Baker Street Journal Christmas Annual*, 1959, pp. 302–10.

PRINCE, MARION
"Sherlock and Son"; *A Baker Street Four-Wheeler*, pp. 27–9.
Profile by Gaslight: An Irregular Reader about the Private Life of Sherlock Holmes, edited by Edgar W. Smith; New York: Simon & Schuster, 1944.

PULLING, CHRISTOPHER
"Sherlock Holmes and Scotland Yard"; *The Sherlock Holmes Journal*, Vol. I, No. 3, June, 1953, pp. 12–7.

QUAYLE, EDWARD
"Suffer the Little Children . . ."; *The Baker Street Journal*, Vol. III, No. 4, Old Series, October, 1948, pp. 463–70

QUEEN, ELLERY
In the Queen's Parlor; New York: Simon & Schuster, 1957.
Introduction to *Client's Second Case-Book.*
Introduction to *The Memoirs of Solar Pons*, by August Derleth; Sauk City: Wisconsin: Mycroft & Moran, 1951.
Introduction and Notes to *The Misadventures of Sherlock Holmes.*
"Sherlock Holmes First Editions: A New and Revised Catalogue of the Queen Collection"; *Ellery Queen's Mystery Magazine*, February, 1954.

RAMAMURTHY, T. V.
"The Case of the Awkward Pencil"; *The Sherlock Holmes Journal*, Vol. I, No. 4, December, 1953, pp. 40–1.

RAND, STUART C.
"What Sherlock Didn't Know"; *The Atlantic Monthly*, November, 1945; *The Baker Street Journal*, Vol. I, No. 3, New Series, July, 1951, pp. 83–8.

RANDALL, *Professor* DAVID A.
"The Adventure of the Notorious Forger"; *The Baker Street Journal*, Vol. I, No. 3, Old Series, July, 1946, pp. 371–7.
"A Census of the Known Existing Orig-

inal Manuscripts of the Sacred Writings: Their Auction Records, Present Locations, etc., Chronologically Arranged"; *The Baker Street Journal*, Vol. I, No. 4, Old Series, October, 1946, pp. 504–8.
"On the First Book Publication of 'The Red-Headed League' and 'The Boscombe Valley Mystery'"; *The Baker Street Journal*, Vol. II, No. 4, Old Series, October, 1947, pp. 491–6.
"On the Manuscript of *The Sign of the Four*"; *The Baker Street Journal*, Vol. I, No. 4, Old Series, October, 1946, pp. 504–8.
"*The Valley of Fear* Bibliographically Considered"; *The Baker Street Journal*, Vol. I, No. 2, Old Series, April, 1946, pp. 232–7.
"'The Red-Headed League' Reviewed"; *The Sherlock Holmes Journal*, Vol. II, No. 1, July, 1954, pp. 29–34.

REDMOND, D. A.
"Some Chemical Problems in the Canon"; *The Baker Street Journal*, Vol. XIV, No. 3, New Series, September, 1964, pp. 145–52.

RENDALL, VERNON
"Belsize As a Commentator: Sherlock Holmes"; *The London Nights of Belsize;* London: John Lane, 1917; *The Incunabular Holmes.*
"The Limitations of Sherlock Holmes"; *Baker Street Studies*, pp. 63–84.

RICE, *The Reverend* OTIS R.
"Clergymen in the Canon"; *The Baker Street Journal*, Vol. IV, No. 3, New Series, July, 1954, pp. 133–43.

RICHARD, PETER
"Completing the Canon," Part I; *The Sherlock Holmes Journal*, Vol. VI, No. 1, Winter, 1962, pp. 10–4; Part II, *The Sherlock Holmes Journal*, Vol. VI, No. 3, Winter, 1963, pp. 76–81.
"A Postscript to 'Completing the Canon'"; *The Sherlock Holmes Journal*, Vol. VI, No. 4, Spring, 1964, pp. 114–5.

ROBERTS, S. C., *later Sir* SYDNEY
Doctor Watson: Prolegomena to the Study of a Biographical Problem; London, Faber & Faber, Ltd., 1931; *The Incunabular Holmes.*
Holmes and Watson: A Miscellany; London: Oxford University Press, 1953.
"The Music of Baker Street"; *The Oxford Magazine*, May 1, 1947; *The Baker Street Journal*, Vol. II, No. 4, Old Series, October, 1947, pp. 429–32.
"A Note on the Watson Problem"; Cambridge, England: The University Press, 1929; *The Baker Street Journal*,

Vol. I, No. 1, Old Series, January, 1946, pp. 29–32.

"The Personality of Sherlock Holmes," Part I; *The Sherlock Holmes Journal*, Vol. I, No. 1, May, 1952, pp. 2–7; Part II, *The Sherlock Holmes Journal*, Vol. I, No. 3, June, 1953, pp. 3–6, 18.

"Sherlock Holmes and the Fair Sex"; *Baker Street Studies*, pp. 177–9.

ROBERTSHAW, WILFRID
"Bradshaw: The Story of a Time-Table"; *The Baker Street Journal*, Vol. XII, No. 2, New Series, June, 1962, pp. 102–5.

RODELL, MARIE F.
"Living on Baker Street"; *The Baker Street Journal*, Vol. II, No. 1, Old Series, January, 1947, pp. 35–7.

ROOSEVELT, FRANKLIN DELANO
A Baker Street Folio, edited by Edgar W. Smith; Morristown, New Jersey: The Baker Street Irregulars, Inc., 1945.

"Sherlock Holmes in the White House"; *The Baker Street Journal*, Vol. V, No. 2, New Series, April, 1955, pp. 78–9.

ROSENBERGER, EDGAR S.
"On the Railway Journeys of Sherlock Holmes"; *The Baker Street Journal*, Vol. II, No. 2, Old Series, April, 1947, pp. 175–9.

"The Religious Sherlock Holmes"; *The Baker Street Journal*, Vol. III, No. 2, Old Series, April, 1948, pp. 138–47.

ROSENBLUM, MORRIS
"Foreign Language Quotations in the Canon"; *The Baker Street Journal*, Vol. III, No. 4, Old Series, October, 1948, pp. 425–34.

"Hafiz and Horace, Huxtable and Holmes"; *The Baker Street Journal*, Vol. I, No. 3, Old Series, July, 1946, pp. 261–9.

"The Horatian Spirit in Holmes"; *Client's Third Case-Book*, pp. 119–26.

"On Holmes' Use of the Word 'Vaseline' in 'The Adventure of the Dying Detective'"; *The Baker Street Journal*, Vol. X, No. 4, New Series, October, 1960, p. 250.

"On the *Pâté-de-Fois-Gras* Pie"; *The Baker Street Journal*, Vol. II, No. 4, Old Series, October, 1947, pp. 438–9.

"Some Latin Byways in the Canon"; *The Baker Street Journal*, Vol. III, No. 1, Old Series, January, 1948, pp. 15–20.

RUBER, PETER A.
"On a Defense of H. W. Bell"; *The Baker Street Gasogene*, Vol. III, No. 3, 1961, pp. 15–7.

"Sir Arthur Conan Doyle and Fletcher Robinson: An Epitaph"; *The Baker Street Gasogene*, Vol. I, No. 2, 1961, pp. 22–8.

SANDERSON, SHIRLEY
"Another Case of Identity"; *The Sherlock Holmes Journal*, Vol. VI, No. 3, Winter, 1963, pp. 86–7.

SAXE, STEPHEN
"Tregennis and Poe"; *The Baker Street Journal*, Vol. I, No. 1, Old Series, January, 1946; pp. 90–1.

SAYERS, DOROTHY L.
"The Dates in 'The Red-Headed League'"; *The Colophon*, Part 17, 1934; *The Baker Street Journal*, Vol. II, No. 3, Old Series, July, 1947, pp. 279–90; *Unpopular Opinions*; London: Victor Gollancz, 1946.

"Dr. Watson, Widower"; *Unpopular Opinions*; *The Incunabular Sherlock Holmes*.

"Dr. Watson's Christian Name"; *Profile by Gaslight*, pp. 180–6; *Unpopular Opinions*.

"Holmes' College Career"; *Baker Street Studies*, pp. 1–34; *Unpopular Opinions*.

Introduction to *Great Short Stories of Detection, Mystery and Horror*; London: Victor Gollancz, 1928; as *The Omnibus of Crime*, New York: Payson & Clarke Limited, 1929.

SCHENCK, *Professor* REMSEN TEN EYCK
"Baker Street Fables"; *The Baker Street Journal*, Vol. II, No. 2, New Series, April, 1952, pp. 85–92.

"The Effect of Trades Upon the Body"; *The Baker Street Journal*, Vol. III, No. 1, New Series, January, 1953, pp. 31–6.

"Holmes, Cryptanalysis and the Dancing Men"; *The Baker Street Journal*, Vol. V, No. 2, New Series, April, 1955, pp. 80–91.

"On the Footprints of a Gigantic Hound"; *The Baker Street Journal*, Vol. II, No. 4, New Series, October, 1952, pp. 232–3.

"On the Gun That Killed Charles Augustus Milverton"; *The Baker Street Journal*, Vol. IV, No. 1, Old Series, January, 1949, pp. 95–6.

SCHONBERG, HAROLD
"Yet Another Case of Identity"; *The Sherlock Holmes Journal*, Vol. VI, No. 4, Spring, 1964, pp. 115–8.

SCHORIN, HOWARD R.
"Cryptography in the Canon"; *The Baker Street Journal*, Vol. XIII, No. 4, December, 1963, pp. 214–6.

SCHULMAN, DAVID
"Sherlock Holmes: Cryptanalyst"; *The*

Baker Street Journal, Vol. III, No. 2, Old Series, April, 1948, pp. 233–7.

SCHULTZ, ROBERT S.
"The Ballistics of the Empty House"; *The Baker Street Journal*, Vol. II, No. 4, Old Series, October, 1947, pp. 373–9.

SCHUTZ, ROBERT H.
"Half-Sister; No Mystery"; *The Baker Street Gasogene*, Vol. I, No. 2, 1961, pp. 14–5.

"Some Problems in 'The Yellow Face'"; *The Baker Street Journal*, Vol. XII, No. 1, March, 1962, p. 31

SCHWARTZ, RICHARD S.
"Three Students in Search of a Scholar"; *The Baker Street Journal Christmas Annual*, 1957, pp. 45–9.

The Science Fictional Sherlock Holmes, edited by Norman Metcalf; Lowry Air Force Base, Colorado: The Council of Four, 1960.

The Second Cab; edited by James Keddie, Jr.; Boston: Stoke Moran, 1947.

SELLARS, *Mrs.* CRIGHTON
"Altamont"; *The Baker Street Journal*, Vol. III, No. 1, Old Series, January, 1948, p. 59.

"Dr. Watson and the British Army"; *The Baker Street Journal*, Vol. II, No. 3, Old Series, July, 1947, pp. 332–41.

"On Greuze's *Jeune Fille à l'Agneau*"; *The Baker Street Journal*, Vol. I, No. 4, Old Series, October, 1946, p. 468.

"On Woolwich as an Army Arsenal"; *The Baker Street Journal*, Vol. IV, No. 1, Old Series, January, 1949, pp. 54–6.

"Uffa Again"; *The Baker Street Journal*, Vol. I, No. 3, Old Series, July, 1946, p. 362.

"A Visit to Sherlock Holmes"; *The Baker Street Journal*, Vol. II, No. 1, New Series, January, 1952, pp. 5–17.

SEWELL, GORDON
"Holmes and Watson in the South Country"; *The Southern Daily Echo*, October 2, 1957; *The Sherlock Holmes Journal*, Vol. III, No. 3, Autumn, 1957, pp. 10–2.

SHEARER, JAMES, II
"'This Forty-Grain Weight of Crystallized Charcoal'"; *The Loupe*, July–August, 1952; quoted in the *Baker Street Journal*, Vol. III, No. 1, New Series, January, 1953, p. 63.

SHEARN, A. L.
"The Street and the Detective"; *The Baker Street Journal Christmas Annual*, 1957, pp. 50–4.

SHERBROOKE-WALKER, *Colonel* RONALD D.
"Clothes Canonical"; *The Sherlock*

Holmes Journal, Vol. VI, No. 4, Spring, 1964, pp. 104–8.

"Holmes, Watson and Tobacco"; *The Sherlock Holmes Journal,* Vol. I, No. 2, September, 1952, pp. 7–12.

Sherlockian Studies: Seven Pieces of Sherlockiana, edited by Robert A. Cutter; Jackson Heights, New York: Privately printed, 1947.

SHORT, ERNEST H.
"On No. 109 as No. 221 Baker Street"; *The Baker Street Journal,* Vol. I, No. 4, October, 1946, pp. 51–2.

SIDGWICK, FRANK
"The Hound of the Baskervilles At Fault (An Open Letter to Dr. Watson)"; *The Cambridge Review,* January 23, 1902; *The Incunabular Sherlock Holmes.*

SIMMONS, GEORGE
"Sherlock Holmes—The Inner Man"; *The Baker Street Journal,* Vol. II, No. 2, Old Series, April, 1947, pp. 129–35.

SIMPSON, A. CARSON
"A Chronometric Excogitation"; *The Baker Street Journal Christmas Annual,* 1959, pp. 273–9.

"The Curious Incident of the Missing Corpse"; *The Baker Street Journal,* Vol. IV, No. 1, New Series, January, 1954, pp. 24–34.

"It Must Have Been Two Other Fellows"; *Leaves from the Copper Beeches,* pp. 41–53.

"On Oxford as the University of 'The Three Students'; *The Baker Street Journal,* Vol. V, No. 3, New Series, July, 1955, p. 187.

Simpson's Sherlockian Studies; Philadelphia: International Printing Company:

Vol. I. *Sherlock Holmes' Wanderjahre: Fanget An!* (1953).

Vol. II. *Sherlock Holmes' Wanderjahre: Post Huc Nec Ergo Propter Huc Gabetque* (1954).

Vol. III. *Sherlock Holmes' Wanderjahre: In Fernen Land, Unnahbar Ruren, Schritten (1955).*

Vol. IV. *Sherlock Holmes' Wanderjahre: Auf Der Erde Rücken Ruhrt' Ich Mich Viel (1956).*

Vol. V. *Numismatics in the Canon: Full Thirty Thousand Marks of English Coin (1957).*

Vol. VI. *Numismatics in the Canon: A Very Treasury of Divers Realms* (1958).

Vol. VII. *Numismatics in the Canon: Small Titles and Orders* (1959).

Vol. VIII. *I'm Off for Philadelphia in the Morning* (1960).

"Whose Was It? Conjectures on a Coronet"; *The Baker Street Journal Christmas Annual,* 1957, pp. 9–17.

SIMPSON, HELEN
"Medical Career and Capacities of Dr. J. H. Watson"; *Baker Street Studies,* pp. 35–61.

SMITH, EDGAR W.
"The Adventure of the Veiled Author"; *The Baker Street Journal,* Vol. I, No. 2, Old Series, April, 1946, pp. 129–35.

"Appointment in Baker Street"; *221B,* pp. 142–243.

Baker Street and Beyond: A Sherlockian Gazetteer, with Five Detailed and Illustrated Maps by Julian Wolff, M.D.; New York: The Pamphlet House, 1940.

Baker Street Inventory; Summit, New Jersey: The Pamphlet House, 1945.

"The Baker Street Irregulars"; *The Courier,* London, January, 1954; *The Baker Street Journal,* Vol. XII, No. 3, New Series, September, 1962, pp. 151–6.

"A Bibliographical Note"; *The Baker Street Journal,* Vol. IX, No. 1, New Series, January, 1959, pp. 3–4.

"Dr. Watson and the Great Censorship"; *The Baker Street Journal,* Vol. II, No. 3, New Series, January, 1947, pp. 138–51.

Introduction to *Baker Street Studies,* 1955.

Introduction to *The Return of Solar Pons,* by August Derleth; Sauk City, Wisconsin: Mycroft & Moran, 1958.

Introduction to *Sherlock Holmes and Dr. Watson: The Chronology of Their Adventures,* by H. W. Bell, 1955.

"The Long Road from Maiwand"; *Profile by Gaslight,* pp. 195–201.

"The Old Shikari"; *The Best of the Pips,* pp. 25–34.

"On the Forms of Address"; *The Baker Street Journal,* Vol. IX, No. 3, New Series, July, 1959, pp. 131–2.

"On the *Mary Celeste* and the *Matilda Briggs";* *The Baker Street Journal,* Vol. II, No. 2, New Series, April, 1952, pp. 115–6.

"Prolegomena to a Memoir of Professor Moriarty"; *The Second Cab,* pp. 57–64; as *The Napoleon of Crime,* Summit: New Jersey, The Pamphlet House, 1953.

"A Scandal in Identity"; *Profile by Gaslight,* pp. 262–73.

"Sherlock Holmes and the Great Hiatus"; *The Baker Street Journal,* Vol. I, No. 3, Old Series, July, 1946.

Sherlock Holmes: The Writings of

John H. Watson, M.D.; Morristown, New Jersey: The Baker Street Irregulars, Inc., 1962.

"A Textual Aberration in *The Hound of the Baskervilles";* *The Baker Street Journal,* Vol. V, No. 4, New Series, October, 1955, pp. 243–4.

"Up from the Needle"; *The Baker Street Journal,* Vol. II, No. 1, Old Series, January, 1957, pp. 85–8.

SMITH, "RED" (WALTER W.)
"The Game's Afoot"; *Views of Sport,* New York: Alfred A. Knopf, 1954.

"The Nefarious Holmes"; *Views of Sport.*

SMITH, WILLIAM
"That Little Thing of Chopin's: The Laying of the Ghost"; *The Baker Street Journal,* Vol. XIII, No. 1, New Series, March, 1963, pp. 24–30.

" 'You Have Been in Gettysburg, I Perceive' "; *The Baker Street Journal,* Vol. XIII, No. 2, New Series, June, 1963, pp. 77–85.

SOVINE, *Dr.* J. W.
"The Singular Bullet"; *The Baker Street Journal,* Vol. IX, No. 1, New Series, January, 1959, pp. 28–32.

"The Toxicanon"; *The Baker Street Journal,* Vol. VIII, No. 2, New Series, April, 1958, pp. 107–12.

STARR, *Professor* H. W.
"Singleton Singlestick"; *The Sherlock Holmes Journal,* Vol. II, No. 4, Winter, 1955, p. 34.

"Some New Light on Watson"; *The Baker Street Journal,* Vol. I, No. 1, Old Series, January, 1946, pp. 55–63.

"A Submersible Subterfuge or Proof Impositive"; *Leaves from the Copper Beeches,* pp. 97–108.

(with T. B. HUNT) "What Happened to Mary Morstan"; *The Baker Street Journal,* Vol. II, No. 3, Old Series, July, 1947, pp. 237–46.

STARRETT, VINCENT
"Before Sherlock Holmes"; *The Baker Street Journal,* Vol. II, No. 1, Old Series, January, 1947, pp. 5–11.

Introduction to *The Adventures of Sherlock Holmes, Vol. I;* New York: The Limited Editions Club, 1950.

Introduction to *The Adventures of Solar Pons,* by August Derleth; Sauk City, Wisconsin: Mycroft & Moran, 1945.

Introduction to *Baker Street Chronology,* by Dr. Ernest Bloomfield Zeisler, 1953.

"On the Three Moriarty Brothers Named James"; Footnote to *Appoint-*

ment in Baker Street, by Edgar W. Smith.

"A Note on Baker Street," in *Baker Street and Beyond*, by Edgar W. Smith.

"A Note on Mr. Sherlock Holmes"; *Esquire*, May, 1934.

The Private Life of Sherlock Holmes; New York: The Macmillan Company, 1933; London: Nicholson & Watson, 1934; revised and enlarged edition published by the University of Chicago Press, 1960; London: Allen & Unwin, 1961.

"The Singular Adventures of Martha Hudson"; *Baker Street Studies*, pp. 85–130; *Profile by Gaslight*, pp. 202–29; *Bookman's Holiday*, New York: Random House, 1942, pp. 47–81.

STEELE, FREDERIC DORR
"Sherlock Holmes in Pictures"; *221B*, pp. 129–37.

STEPHENS, CHARLES B.
"The Birlstone Hoax"; *The Baker Street Journal*, Vol. IV, No. 1, Old Series, January, 1949, pp. 5–11.

"Holmes' Longest Shot?"; *The Baker Street Journal*, Vol. III, No. 1, Old Series, January, 1948, pp. 44–6.

"Silas Brown, or, Who Shot Desborough's Bolt?"; *The Baker Street Journal*, Vol. II, No. 3, Old Series, July, 1947, pp. 357–61.

STERN, MADELEINE B.
"Sherlock Holmes: Rare Book Collector"; *Papers of the Bibliographical Society of America*, Second Quarter, 1953; *The Baker Street Journal*, Vol. III, No. 3, New Series, July, 1953, pp. 133–55; New York: Schulte Publishing Company.

STIX, THOMAS L.
"Casual Comments on 'The Crooked Man'"; *The Baker Street Journal*, Vol. XII, No. 2, New Series, June, 1962, pp. 99–100.

"Concerning 'The Red-Headed League'"; *The Baker Street Journal*, Vol. IV, No. 2, New Series, April, 1954, pp. 93–6.

"A Few Irreverent Remarks on 'The Second Stain'"; *The Sherlock Holmes Journal*, Vol. VI, No. 1, Winter, 1962, pp. 19–20.

"A Little Dirt on 'The Empty House'"; *The Baker Street Journal*, Vol. XIV, No. 2, New Series, June, 1964, pp. 93–5.

"The Reigate Puzzler"; *The Baker Street Journal*, Vol. XIII, No. 2, New Series, June, 1963, pp. 93–5.

"Un-Christmaslike Thoughts on 'The Blue Carbuncle'"; *The Baker Street*

Journal, Vol. XI, No. 4, New Series, December, 1961, pp. 218–20.

"Who's Afraid of the Big Bad Moriarty?"; *The Baker Street Journal*, Vol. XII, No. 4, December, 1962, pp. 200, 243.

STONE, P. M.
"The Other Friendship: A Speculation"; *Profile by Gaslight*, pp. 97–103.

"Sussex Interview"; *221B*, pp. 74–87.

William Hooker Gillette; a pamphlet issued as a supplement to *The Baker Street Journal*, Vol. III, No. 3, New Series, July, 1953.

STOUT, REX
"Watson Was a Woman"; *The Saturday Review of Literature*, March 1, 1941; *The Pocket Mystery Reader*, 1941; *Profile by Gaslight*, 1944; *Ellery Queen's Mystery Magazine*, April, 1946; *The Art of the Mystery Story: A Collection of Critical Essays*, edited by Howard Haycraft; New York: Simon & Schuster, 1946.

STROUT, Professor ALAN LANG
"On the *Norah Creina*"; *The Saturday Review of Literature*, April 8, 1939; quoted in the *Baker Street Journal*, Vol. I, No. 4, Old Series, October, 1946, p. 408.

SWANSON, MARTIN J.
"Graphologists in the Canon"; *The Baker Street Journal*, Vol. XII, No. 2, New Series, June, 1962, pp. 73–80.

"On the Chinese Coin in 'The Red-Headed League'"; *The Baker Street Journal*, Vol. XIII, No. 1, New Series, March, 1963, p. 54.

SYMONS, T. H. B.
"Some Notes on the Sixth Duke of Holdernesse"; *The Baker Street Journal*, Vol. IX, No. 1, January, 1959, pp. 6–9.

THIMAN, ERIC. H., *Mus. D.*
"Tra-la-la-la-lira-lira-lay"; *The Sherlock Holmes Journal*, Vol. IV, No. 3, Winter, 1959, p. 105.

The Third Cab: A Collection of Sherlockiana from the Files of the Speckled Band; Boston: Privately printed at Stoke Moran, 1960.

THOMSON, H. DOUGLAS
Masters of Mystery, London: Collins, 1931.

THROCKMORTON, JANE
"'H.' Stands for —?"; *Client's Case-Book*, pp. 7–8.

TOWNSEND, C. E. C.
"The Bar of Gold"; *The Sherlock Holmes Journal*, Vol. II, No. 1, July, 1954, pp. 25–8.

TREVELYAN, G. M.
Illustrated English Social History; London and New York: Longmans, Green & Co., Ltd., 1942 and 1944.

TUCKER, *Dr.* RUFUS S.
"Genealogical Notes on Holmes"; *Profile by Gaslight*, pp. 125–34.

221B: Studies in Sherlock Holmes, edited by Vincent Starrett; New York: The Macmillan Company, 1940; reissued in paperbound format by the Baker Street Irregulars, Inc., 1956.

VAILL, C. B. H.
"Quick, Watson, the Needle!"; *The Baker Street Journal*, Vol. I, No. 4, Old Series, October, 1946, pp. 445–8.

"A Study in Intellects"; *The Baker Street Journal*, Vol. III, No. 3, Old Series, July, 1948, pp. 278–82.

VAN GELDER, LARRY
"On the Suggested Suicide of Jefferson Hope"; *The Baker Street Journal*, Vol. I, No. 4, New Series, October, 1951, p. 160.

VAN LIERE, *Dr.* EDWARD J.
A Doctor Enjoys Sherlock Holmes; New York: The Vantage Press, 1960.

"Dr. Watson and Nervous Maladies"; *The Baker Street Journal*, Vol. IV, No. 2, New Series, April, 1954, pp. 100–8.

"Dr. Watson's Universal Specific"; *The Baker Street Journal*, Vol. II, No. 4, New Series, October, 1952, pp. 215–20.

"Sherlock Holmes and Doctor Watson, Perennial Athletes"; *The Baker Street Journal*, Vol. VI, No. 3, New Series, July, 1956, pp. 155–64.

VISIAK, E. H.
"New Light on Holmes"; *The Sherlock Holmes Journal*, Vol. VI, No. 4, Spring, 1964, pp. 122–3.

WAIT, RICHARD
"The Case of the Neophyte and the Motet"; *The Second Cab*, pp. 70–2.

WALBRIDGE, EARLE F.
"Care and Feeding of Sherlock Holmes"; *221B*, pp. 54–8.

"Jabez Wilson Reports"; *The Sherlock Holmes Journal*, Vol. I, No. 3, Old Series, July, 1946, p. 361.

WALLACE, IRVING
The Fabulous Originals; New York: Alfred A. Knopf, 1955.

WARRACK, GUY
"Passed to You, Admiralty Intelligence"; *The Sherlock Holmes Journal*, Vol. IV, No. 2, Spring, 1959, pp. 79–80.

Sherlock Holmes and Music; London: Faber & Faber, Ltd., 1957.

WATERS, FRANK A.
" 'Holmes or Watson Here' "; *The Sherlock Holmes Journal*, Vol. III, No. 2, Winter, 1956, p. 21.

"The Rooms in Baker Street"; *The Best of the Pips*, pp. 15–20.

"Upon the Probable Number of Cases of Mr. Sherlock Holmes"; *The Baker Street Journal*, Vol. III, No. 1, New Series, January, 1953, pp. 25–8; *The Best of the Pips*, pp. 21–4.

WATERS, FRED
"Re-Dating the Reichenbach Incident"; *The Baker Street Journal*, Vol. VIII, No. 4, New Series, October, 1958, pp. 280–3.

WEATHERBEE, *Dr.* WINTHROP
"The Third Continent: Further Light on Watson"; *The Baker Street Journal*, Vol. II, No. 3, New Series, July, 1952, pp. 125–34.

WEAVER, RONALD R.
"Bow Window in Baker Street"; *The Baker Street Journal*, Vol. V, No. 2, New Series, April, 1955, pp. 93–5.

WEBSTER, H. T.
"Observations on Sherlock Holmes as an Athlete and Sportsman"; *The Baker Street Journal*, Vol. III, No. 1, Old Series, January, 1948, pp. 24–31.

WEIL-NORDEN, P.
Introduction to *Sir Arthur Conan Doyle*, Centenary Edition; London: John Murray, 1959; Garden City, New York: Doubleday & Company, Inc. 1959.

WEISS, JAY, *D.M.D.*
"Holmes as a Patient"; *The Baker Street Journal*, Vol. XIII, No. 2, New Series, June, 1963, pp. 96–8.

WELCH, GEORGE B.
" 'No Mention of That Local Hunt, Watson' "; *The Sherlock Holmes Journal*, Vol. V, No. 3, Winter, 1961, pp. 82–3.

"The 'Silver Blaze' Formula"; *The Sherlock Holmes Journal*, Vol. III, No. 1, Summer, 1956, p. 19.

"A Study in Moonlight"; *The Baker Street Gasogene*, Vol. I, No. 3, 1961, pp. 18–25.

"The Terai Planter"; *The Baker Street Journal*, Vol. VI, No. 1, New Series, January, 1956, pp. 35–9.

"Which University?"; *The Sherlock Holmes Journal*, Vol. V, No. 3, Winter, 1961, pp. 94, 96.

WELLMAN, MANLY WADE
"The Great Man's Great Son"; *The Baker Street Journal*, Vol. I, No. 3, Old Series, July, 1946, pp. 326–36.

"A New Scandal in Bohemia"; *The Baker Street Journal*, Vol. II, No. 1, Old Series, January, 1947, p. 90.

"Scoundrels in Bohemia"; *The Baker Street Journal*, Vol. IV, No. 4, New Series, October, 1954, pp. 232–8.

"Two Southern Exposures of Sherlock Holmes"; *The Baker Street Journal*, Vol. II, No. 4, Old Series, October, 1947, pp. 422–6.

WHITE, PAUL
"The Case of the Men Named James"; *The Baker Street Journal*, Vol. VI, No. 1, New Series, January, 1956, pp. 46–50.

WHITE, WILLIAM BRAID, *Mus. Doc.*
"Dr. Watson and the Peerage"; *The Baker Street Journal*, Vol. II, No. 1, Old Series, January, 1947, pp. 18–23.

"Sherlock Holmes and the Equal Temperament"; *The Baker Street Journal*, Vol. I, No. 1, Old Series, January, 1946, pp. 39–43.

WIGGLESWORTH, BELDEN
"The Coat of Arms of Sherlock Holmes"; *Profile by Gaslight*, pp. 104–13.

"The French Background of Sherlock Holmes: Aspects and Possibilities"; *The Second Cab*, pp. 39–45.

" 'Many Nations and Three Separate Continents' "; *The Baker Street Journal*, Vol. II, No. 3, Old Series, July, 1947, pp. 273–8.

WILDE, PERCIVAL
"The Bust in the Window"; *The Baker Street Journal*, Vol. III, No. 3, Old Series, July, 1948, pp. 300–5.

WILLIAMS, H. B.
"Curses Canonical"; *Client's Second Case-Book*, pp. 50–4.

"Half-Sister; Half Mystery"; *The Baker Street Journal*, Vol. VIII, No. 2, New Series, April, 1958, pp. 100–3.

"Light Blue Black Clay"; *The Sherlock Holmes Journal*, Vol. II, No. 3, Summer, 1955, p. 23.

"A Non-Canonical Clue"; *Client's Third Case-Book*, pp. 94–9.

"Pleasure in Pictures"; *The Baker Street Journal*, Vol. XIII, No. 4, New Series, December, 1963, pp. 232–5.

"Then Falls Thy Shadow"; *Client's Case-Book*, pp. 50–3.

"The Unknown Watson"; *The Baker Street Journal*, Vol. XIII, No. 1, New Series, March, 1963, pp. 43–5.

WILLIAMS, VALENTINE
"Gaboriau: Father of Detective Novels"; *The National Review*, December, 1923.

WILLIAMSON, JERRY NEAL
" 'And Especially Your Eyes' "; *The Sherlock Holmes Journal*, Vol. III, No. 3, Autumn, 1957, pp. 17–9.

"Dr. Mortimer-Moriarty"; *The Baker Street Journal*, Vol. IV, No. 1, Old Series, January, 1949, p. 95.

"In Defense of Scotland Yard: A Communication from Inspector Athelney Jones"; *Client's Case-Book*, pp. 28–9.

"The Latest Treatise Upon Pathology"; *The Baker Street Journal*, Vol. VI, No. 4, New Series, October, 1956, pp. 208–14.

"The Sad Case of Young Stamford"; *The Baker Street Journal*, Vol. III, No. 4, Old Series, October, 1948, pp. 449–51.

"A Scandal in 'A Scandal in Bohemia' "; *The Baker Street Journal*, Vol. I, No. 4, New Series, October, 1951, pp. 141–3.

"Sherlock's Murder Bag"; *Client's Third Case-Book*, pp. 84–8.

" 'There Was Something Very Strange' "; *The Baker Street Journal*, Vol. XII, No. 4, New Series, December, 1962, pp. 201–9.

WILSON, ALAN
"Where Was the 'Bar of Gold'?"; *The Sherlock Holmes Journal*, Vol. VI, No. 3, Winter, 1963, pp. 84–5.

" 'You Crossed My Path' "; *The Sherlock Holmes Journal*, Vol. IV, No. 3, Winter, 1959, pp. 89–90.

WIMBUSH, J. C.
"Watson's Tobacconist"; *The Sherlock Holmes Journal*, Vol. I, No. 2, September, 1952, pp. 35–6.

WOLF, BEN
"Zero Wolf Meets Sherlock Holmes"; *The Baker Street Journal*, Vol. XIV, No. 2, New Series, June, 1964, pp. 108–17.

WOLF, *Professor* JOHN B.
"Another Incubus in the Saddle"; *Exploring Sherlock Holmes*, pp. 66–81.

WOLFF, *Dr.* JULIAN
"The Adventuress of Sherlock Holmes: Some Observations Upon the Identification of Irene"; *The Baker Street Journal*, Vol. VII, No. 1, New Series, January, 1957, pp. 29–31.

"The Dynamics of the Binomial Theorem"; *The Baker Street Journal*, Vol. XIII, No. 4, New Series, December, 1963, pp. 199–200.

"I Have My Eye on a Suite in Baker Street"; *The Baker Street Journal*, Vol. I, No. 3, Old Series, July, 1946, pp. 296–9.

"Just What Was That Little Thing of Chopin's?"; *The Baker Street Journal*,

Vol. XIII, No. 1, New Series, March, 1963, pp. 3–4.

"A Narcotic Monograph"; *The Baker Street Journal*, Vol. XIII, No. 3, New Series, 1963, pp. 182–3.

Practical Handbook of Sherlockian Heraldry; New York: Privately printed, 1955.

"Re: Greuze"; *The Baker Street Journal*, Vol. XII, No. 4, New Series, December, 1962, pp. 195–7.

"Remember the Mane?"; *The Baker Street Journal*, Vol. III, No. 4, Old Series, October, 1948, pp. 471–3.

The Sherlockian Atlas; New York: Privately printed, 1952.

"That Was No Lady; with Some Observations Upon the Nature of Dr. Watson's Wound"; *Profile by Gaslight*, pp. 166–72.

WOOD, WILLIS B.
"Sherlock in Kansas"; *The Second Cab*, pp. 78–81.

WOODHEAD, ED S.
"In Defense of Dr. Watson"; *The Baker Street Journal*, Vol. I, No. 4, Old Series, October, 1946, pp. 417–22.

WOOLLCOTT, ALEXANDER
"The Baker Street Irregulars; *Long, Long Ago,* New York: The Viking Press, Inc., 1943; *Profile by Gaslight*, pp. 294–7.

YATES, DONALD A.
"A Final Illumination of the Lucca Code"; *The Baker Street Journal*, Vol. VI, No. 3, New Series, July, 1956, pp. 146–51.

YOUNG, FRANCIS ALBERT
"Upon the Identification of Cardinal Tosca"; *The Baker Street Journal*, Vol. IV, No. 2, New Series, June, 1964, p. 80.

ZEISLER, *Dr.* ERNEST BLOOMFIELD
Baker Street Chronology: Commentaries on the Sacred Writings of Dr. John H. Watson; Chicago: Alexander J. Isaacs, 1953.

"A Chronological *Study in Scarlet*"; *The Baker Street Journal*, Vol. VIII, No. 3, New Series, July, 1957, pp. 133–40.

"Concerning *The Valley of Fear*"; *The Baker Street Journal*, Vol. IV, No. 3, New Series, July, 1954, pp. 144–7.

"A Final Word About Maiwand"; *The Baker Street Journal*, Vol. IX, No. 2, New Series, April, 1959, pp. 103–10.

"A Pigment of the Imagination"; *The Sherlock Holmes Journal*, Vol. V, No. 2, Spring, 1961, pp. 50–2.

"The Road from Maiwand"; *The Baker Street Journal*, Vol. V, No. 4, New Series, October, 1955, pp. 220–5.

"Some Observations Upon 'Silver Blaze' "; *The Baker Street Journal*, Vol. XI, No. 4, New Series, December, 1961, pp. 238–40.

"Some Points Concerning *The Sign of the Four*"; *The Sherlock Holmes Journal*, Vol. IV, No. 2, Spring, 1959, pp. 70–1.

"Tra-la-la-lira-lira-lay"; *The Sherlock Holmes Journal*, Vol. IV, No. 1, Winter, 1958, pp. 11–2.

ZIEBARTH, E. W.
"The Master and Mass Media"; *Exploring Sherlock Holmes,* pp. 42–65.